Tellers of Tales

Tellers of Tales

100 SHORT STORIES FROM THE UNITED STATES, ENGLAND, FRANCE, RUSSIA AND GERMANY

SELECTED AND WITH AN INTRODUCTION BY

W. Somerset Maugham

Doubleday, Doran & Company, Inc.

NEW YORK   1939

PRINTED AT THE *Country Life Press*, GARDEN CITY, N. Y., U. S. A.

Acknowledgments

THANKS are due to the following publishers, agents and authors, for permission to use the material indicated:

Bermann-Fischer Verlag, Vienna—for "Cavalry Patrol," by Hugo von Hofmannsthal.

Jacques Bernard—for "The Tragedy of Goupil," by Louis Pergaud.

Hans Friedrich Blunck—for "On the Farm."

Elizabeth Bowen—for "Reduced."

Brandt & Brandt—for "A. V. Laider," from *Seven Men,* by Max Beerbohm, copyright, 1920, published by Alfred A. Knopf, New York, and William Heinemann, Ltd., London.

Brandus'sche Verlagschandlung, Berlin—for "Youth," by Karl Emil Franzos.

Curtis Brown, Ltd.—for "The Desert Islander," from *Collected Short Stories of Stella Benson.*

Jonathan Cape, Ltd.—for "Counterparts," from *Dubliners,* by James Joyce; "The Station," from *Cut and Come Again,* by H. E. Bates, with special permission from the author.

Denyse Clairouin—for "The Doll," by Joseph Kessel.

W. Collins Sons & Co., Ltd.—for "The Happy Prince," by Oscar Wilde, with special permission from Vyvyan Holland.

J. M. Dent & Sons, Ltd.—for "La Grande Bretèche," by Honoré de Balzac, from *Tales from Balzac.*

Dodd, Mead & Company—for "The Procurator of Judaea," from *Mother of Pearl,* by Anatole France, published in England by John Lane the Bodley Head Limited.

Doubleday, Doran & Company, Inc.—for "The Typhoon," by Joseph Conrad, copyright, 1902, 1932, published in England by William Heinemann, Ltd.; "The Whirligig of Life," from *Whirligigs,* by O. Henry, copyright, 1903, 1931.

E. P. Dutton & Co., Inc.—for "The Child," from *Short Stories Out of Soviet Russia*, compiled and translated by John Cournos, copyrighted; published in England by J. M. Dent & Sons, Ltd.

Farrar & Rinehart, Inc.—for "A Start in Life," from *Iowa Interiors*, by Ruth Sukow, copyright, 1926.

William Faulkner—for "Turn About."

Edna Ferber—for "Old Man Minick," from *Gigolo*, copyright, 1922, by Doubleday, Doran & Company, Inc., published in England by William Heinemann, Ltd.

E. M. Forster—for "Mr. and Mrs. Abbey's Difficulties," from *Abinger Harvest*, published in New York by Harcourt, Brace & Company, in London by E. Arnold, Ltd.

Bruno Frank—for "The Golden Beetle."

Ernst Glaeser—for "The Cherry Feast."

Stephen Graham—for "Twenty-Six and One," by Maxim Gorky; "Sunstroke," by Ivan Bunin; "Without Cherry Blossom," by Panteleimon Romanof.

Harcourt, Brace and Company, Inc.—for "María Concepción," from *Flowering Judas and Other Stories*, by Katherine Anne Porter, copyright, 1935; published in England by Jonathan Cape, Ltd.; "Convalescence," from *The White Horses of Vienna*, by Kay Boyle, copyright, 1936, with special permission from the author and Faber & Faber, Ltd., English publishers.

Houghton Mifflin Company—for "The Gray Champion," by Nathaniel Hawthorne; "The Outcasts of Poker Flat," by Bret Harte; "Papago Wedding," by Mary Austin.

Violet Hunt—for "The Coach."

Aldous Huxley—for "Nuns at Luncheon," from *Mortal Coils*, published by Doubleday, Doran & Co., Inc., New York, and Chatto & Windus, London.

Christopher Isherwood—for "The Nowaks."

Alfred A. Knopf, Inc.—for "The Crimson Curtain," by Jules Barbey d'Aurevilly, from *The Diaboliques*, translated by Ernest Boyd; "A Simple Heart," from *Three Tales*, by Gustave Flaubert, translated by Arthur McDowall, published in England by Chatto & Windus; "Olympe and Henriette," by V. de l'Isle Adam, from *Sardonic Tales*, translated by Hamish Miles; "The Legacy," "The Necklace," from *The Collected Works of Guy de Maupassant*, translated by Ernest Boyd, published in England by Cassell & Co., Ltd.; "An Experiment in Misery," from *Men, Women and Boats*, by Stephen Crane, copyright, 1898, 1902, 1926; "The Toupee Artist," by Nicolai Lyeskov, published in England by John Lane the Bodley Head Limited; "Early Sorrow," by Thomas Mann, published in England by Secker & Warburg, Ltd.; "The Stranger," from *The Garden Party*, by Katherine Mansfield, published in London by Middleton Murry & Constable & Co., Ltd.

John Lane the Bodley Head Limited—for "In the Last Coach," by Leonhard Frank.

Albert Langen-Georg Muller, Munich—for "Uncle Franz," by Ludwig Thoma.

Mrs. Frieda Lawrence, for "Odour of Chrysanthemums," by D. H. Lawrence, published by Viking Press, Inc., New York, and William Heinemann, Ltd., London.

The Macmillan Company, New York—for "The Jolly Corner," from *The Altar of the Dead,* by Henry James.

Macmillan & Co., Ltd.—for "The Three Strangers," from *Wessex Tales,* by Thomas Hardy, published by Harper & Brothers, New York; "The Jolly Corner," from *The Altar of the Dead,* by Henry James.

Heinrich Mann—for "Pippo Spano," translated by Basil Creighton.

Aylmer Maude—for his translation of "The Death of Iván Ilých," by Leo Tolstoy, published by Oxford University Press.

Methuen & Co., Ltd.—for "Without Visible Means," from *Tales of Mean Street,* by Arthur Morrison, with special permission from the author.

J. Middleton Murry, for the translation of "Captain Ribnikoff," by Alexander Kuprin.

Louis Paul—for "No More Trouble for Jedwick."

James B. Pinker & Son—for "The Monkey's Paw," from *The Lady of the Barge,* by William Wymark Jacobs, with special permission from the author; "If You Can't Be Good, Be Cautious," from *You Must Break Out Sometimes,* by T. O. Beachcroft, published by Boriswood, Ltd., London.

G. P. Putnam's Sons—for "Rip Van Winkle" and "The Stout Gentleman," from *Bracebridge Hall,* by Washington Irving.

John Rodker—for "In the Town of Berdichev," by Vassili Grossman; "Romance," by Vera Inber.

H. Schmidt & C. Günther—for "Krambambuli," by Marie von Ebner-Eschenbach, translated by Basil Creighton.

Charles Scribner's Sons—for "Markheim," from *The Merry Men and Other Tales,* by Robert Louis Stevenson, copyright, 1905, 1922, 1925, published in England by Chatto & Windus; "Haircut" and "Champion" from *Roundup: The Stories of Ring Lardner;* "Silent Snow, Secret Snow," by Conrad Aiken; "The Killers," from *Men Without Women,* by Ernest Hemingway, copyright, 1927; "The Rich Boy," by F. Scott Fitzgerald; "Oklahoma Race Riot," by Frances W. Prentice, from *Life in the United States.*

Mrs. Eliza London Shepard—for "To Build a Fire," by Jack London.

Simon and Schuster, Inc.—for "The Fate of the Baron," from *Little Novels,* by Arthur Schnitzler, translated by Eric Sutton, copyright, 1929, with special permission from the author; "Old Rogaum and His Theresa," from *Free and Other Stories,* by Theodore Dreiser.

Société des Gens de Lettres de France—for "The Crimson Curtain," by

Jules Barbey d'Aurevilly; "Olympe and Henriette," by V. de l'Isle Adam; "The Procurator of Judaea," by Anatole France; "Useless Mouths," by Octave Mirbeau; "The Stricken Doe," by Pierre Mille; "The Last Visit," by Tristan Bernard; "The Chink," by Alexandre Arnoux; "The Catalan Night," by Paul Morand; "The Lovely Day," by Jacques de Lacretelle; "The Ball," by Irène Nemirovsky.

L. A. G. Strong—for "The Imposition."

Gleb Struve—for his translation of "The Customer," by G. Peskov.

The Viking Press, Inc.—for "Tobermory," from *The Short Stories of Saki* (H. H. Munro), copyright, 1930, published in England by John Lane the Bodley Head Limited; "Seeds" and "The Other Woman," from *The Triumph of the Egg*, by Sherwood Anderson, copyright, 1921; "The Invisible Collection," from *Kaleidoscope*, by Stefan Zweig, copyright, 1934, published by Cassell & Company, Ltd., London; "The House of Mourning," from *Twilight of a World*, by Franz Werfel, copyright, 1937; "Big Blonde," from *Laments for the Living*, by Dorothy Parker, copyright, 1930; "Kneel to the Rising Sun," from *Kneel to the Rising Sun*, by Erskine Caldwell, copyright, 1935, published in London by Martin Secker and Warburg, Ltd.

Dr. Albert Wassermann and Marta Wassermann-Karlweis—for "The Amulet," by Jacob Wassermann.

A. P. Watt & Son—for "The Bruce Partington Plans," from *His Last Bow*, by A. Conan Doyle, copyright, 1917, by Doubleday, Doran & Company, Inc.; "The Man Who Would Be King," from *Under the Deodars*, by Rudyard Kipling, copyright, 1895, 1897, 1899, 1923; "Without Benefit of Clergy," copyright, 1891, with special permission from Mrs. Kipling.

H. G. Wells—for "The Door in the Wall," from *The Short Stories of H. G. Wells*, copyright, 1911, 1939, published by Doubleday, Doran & Co., Inc.

Thyra Samter Winslow—for "Orphant Annie."

P. G. Wodehouse—for "Uncle Fred Flits By," from *Young Men in Spats*, copyright, 1931, 1936, published by Doubleday, Doran & Co., Inc., New York, and Herbert Jenkins, Ltd., London.

Arnold Zweig—for "A Balaam."

Contents

ix

CONTENTS

CONTENTS

Introduction

i

Fɪʀsᴛ ᴏғ ᴀʟʟ I should like to tender my thanks to the various persons who have helped me to make this collection of short stories. They are Jacques de Lacretelle, of the French Academy, and Paul Morand; Dr Carl Stransky, Bruno Frank and Stefan Zweig; Baroness Budberg, Graham Greene and Nella Henney. I must also declare my indebtedness to Fred Lewis Pattee whose book, *The Development of the American Short Story,* is invaluable to the student of this form of fiction.

ii

When I set about gathering material for this anthology it was with the ambitious aim of showing how the short story had developed since the beginning of the nineteenth century. My notion was to trace its evolution as the evolution of the horse may be traced from the tiny creature with five toes that ran about the forests of the Neocene period to the noble beast that, notwithstanding the mechanization of the age, still provides a decent living for bookmakers and tipsters. It is natural for men to tell tales, and I suppose the short story began in the night of time when the hunter, to beguile the leisure of his fellows when they had eaten and drunk their fill, narrated by the cavern fire some marvellous incident of which he had heard. In cities of the East you can to this day see the storyteller sitting in the market place, surrounded by a circle of eager listeners, and hear him tell the tales that he has inherited from an immemorial past. But I chose to start with the nineteenth century because it was then that the short story acquired a character and a currency that it had not had before. Of course short stories had been written: there were the religious stories of Greek origin, there were the edifying narratives popular in the Middle Ages, and there were the immortal stories of *The Thousand and One Nights;* throughout the Renaissance, in Italy and Spain, in France and England, there was a great vogue for brief narrative. The *Decameron* of Boccaccio and the *Exemplary Tales* of Cervantes are its unperished monuments. But with the rise of the novel the vogue dwindled. The booksellers would no longer pay good money for a collection of short tales, and the authors soon came to look askance on a form of fiction that brought them neither profit nor renown. When from time to time, conceiving a theme that they could adequately treat in a little space, they wrote a short story, they did not quite know what to do with it; and so, unwilling to waste it, they inserted it, sometimes, one must admit, very clumsily, into the body of their novels.

But at the beginning of the nineteenth century a new form of publication was put before the reading public which very soon acquired an immense popularity. The result shows that the authors welcomed with delight the chance thus offered to them for disposing to advantage of the brief pieces which for one reason or another they had occasion to write. This was the annual. It seems to have started in Germany. It was a miscellany of prose and verse; and in its native land offered its readers substantial fare, for we are told that Schiller's *Maid of Orleans* and Goethe's *Hermann and Dorothea* first appeared in periodicals of this character. But when their success led English publishers to imitate them they relied chiefly on short stories to attract a sufficiency of readers. The annual soon found its way to America and gave American authors an opportunity they had long been looking for.

iii

Now I must interrupt myself to tell the reader something about literary composition of which, so far as I know, the critics, whose duty it is doubtless to guide and instruct him, have neglected to apprise him. The writer has in him the desire to create, but he has also the desire to place before readers the result of his labour and the desire (a harmless one with which the reader is not concerned) to earn his bread and butter. On the whole he finds it possible to direct his creative gifts into the channels that will enable him to satisfy these desires. At the risk of shocking the reader who thinks the writer's inspiration should be uninfluenced by practical considerations, I must further tell him that writers quite naturally find themselves impelled to write the sort of things for which there is a demand. When plays in verse might bring an author fame and fortune it would probably have been difficult to find a young man of literary bent who had not among his papers a tragedy in five acts. I think it would occur to few young men to write one now. Today they write plays in prose, novels and short stories. The possibility of publication, the exigencies of editors, that is to say their notion of what their readers want, have a great influence on the kind of work that at a particular time is produced. So, when magazines flourish which have room for stories of considerable length, stories of that length are written; when on the other hand newspapers publish fiction, but can give it no more than a small space, stories to fill that space are supplied. There is nothing disgraceful in this. The competent author can write a story in a couple of thousand words as easily as he can write one in ten thousand. But he chooses a different story or treats it in a different way. Guy de Maupassant wrote one of his most celebrated tales, *The Legacy,* twice over, once in a few hundred words for a newspaper and the second time in several thousand for a magazine; both are published in the collected edition of his works, and I think no one can read the two versions without admitting that in the first there is not a word too little and in the second not a word too much. The point I want to make is this: the nature of the vehicle whereby the writer approaches his public is one of the conventions he has to accept, and on the whole he finds that he can do this without any violence to his own inclinations.

Now at the beginning of the nineteenth century the annuals and keep-sakes offered writers a means of introducing themselves to the public by way of the short story, and so short stories, serving a better purpose than merely to give a fillip to the reader's interest in the course of a long novel, began to be written in greater numbers than ever before. More especially was this the case in America where the lack of a copyright law made it difficult for American authors to find a publisher to publish their novels. English novels were pirated and the competition was too severe for the American author to meet; he was almost forced to write short stories, and fortunately for him, the public, which was content to read of foreign people and foreign scenes in novels, insisted in briefer narratives on native themes and native authors. Many hard things have been said of the annual and the lady's book, and harder things still of the magazine which succeeded them in the public favour; but it can scarcely be denied that the rich abundance of short stories that were produced in the nineteenth century was directly occasioned by the opportunity which these periodicals afforded. In America they gave rise to a school of writers so brilliant and so fertile that some persons, unacquainted with the history of literature, have claimed that the short story is an American invention. That is not so; but it may very well be admitted that in none of the countries of Europe has this form of fiction been so assiduously cultivated as it has been in the United States; nor have its methods, technique and possibilities been else-where more attentively studied. The *North American Review* in 1829 looked upon the brief narrative as a literary toy and encouraged it only because it would prepare American authors 'for nobler and greater exer-tions.' But the event has proved that it could be an end in itself. Many writers have found in it so adequate a means of expression that they have been content to write nothing else. Nor need it be forgotten that the American short story has on more than one occasion profoundly influenced the practice of short-story writers in other countries.

It did not seem unreasonable then, when I set out to show the development of the short story, to start with the nineteenth century. The first piece I chose was Sir Walter Scott's *The Two Drovers,* because it began my anthology with a great name and it had several qualities that I thought a good story should possess. But when I embarked upon the serious reading that my aim involved I made a most inconvenient discovery. I began with Washington Irving, whose tales I had not read since I was a boy. He wrote them in a style which is now old-fashioned, and he had the mannerisms of his period; he did not attach importance, as have later authors, to the dramatic value of his theme, and he was inclined to talk, though very pleasantly, about his characters, rather than let them by dialogue and action disclose themselves; but when you have made allowances for all that, when you take them as stories apart from the telling, you can hardly fail to see how modern they really are. Of course Chekhov, if he had written *Rip Van Winkle,* would have written it very differently, but it is a story he might quite well have penned. The most astonishing thing in it is that the hero's strange experience has so little effect either on him or on the people of the village to which after his long sleep he returns. The incident is queer and affords a topic for the village gossip, but that is all. I think the truth and humour of this would have greatly pleased the Russian writer. And *The Stout Gentleman,* the second of Irving's tales that I have chosen for this collection, is as modern as it can be. Katherine Mansfield might easily have written it. I could not escape the conclusion that the short story which was written at the beginning of my period was as finished, well constructed, sophisticated and accomplished as any that were written during the last ten years.

When the nineteenth century was young, men had fewer ways of amusing their leisure than they have now and were not displeased if their fiction moved at a deliberate pace; they accepted without reluctance a dilatory exposition and a sauntering digressiveness. Writers still under the influence of the prose of Queen Anne wrote with greater elaboration than is now esteemed. Now everyone reads newspapers every day, one or more, and the reading public has grown to demand succinctness and a graphic way of putting things; the authors of short stories, newspaper readers themselves and often writers for the newspapers, have adopted the style that is in the air; and the elegant period of Washington Irving, the stately phrase of Hawthorne, are time-worn. But idiom changes; fashions come and go. The modern short story with its lack of ornament may well seem bare to a succeeding generation, and the colloquial manner which is the mode of the day may easily give way to a more formal style. The more I read the more was it forced upon my notice that in essentials the short story has changed little; what was a good story at the beginning of the nineteenth century is a good story today. I could not in face of this continue with the instructive intention with which I had started. I was obliged to relinquish my aim of showing the same sort of development in the brief narration as the biologist can show you in the development of the horse. It has been a disappointment to me. Notwithstanding, in the course of reading a vast number of stories written during the last century I have learnt a good deal about the form. It is this, and no more, that I can impart to the reader if he will have the patience to follow me through the remainder of this introduction.

v

I have had to abandon some of the notions I held before. The first of these concerns the nature of the short story. Now I should warn the reader at once that a writer treating of the art he pursues is biassed. He very naturally thinks his own practice best. He writes as he can, and as he must, because he is a certain sort of man; he has his own parts, and his own idiosyncrasy, so that he sees things in a manner peculiar to himself, and he gives his vision the form that is forced upon him by his nature. He requires a singular vigour of mind to sympathize with work that is antagonistic to all his instincts. One should be on one's guard when one reads a novelist's criticisms of other people's novels. He is apt to find that excellent which he is aiming at himself and he is likely to see little merit in qualities that he does not himself possess. One of the best books on the novel that has been published in recent years is by an admirable writer who has never in his life been able to devise a plausible story. I was not surprised to find that he held in small esteem the novelists whose great gift is that they can lend a thrilling verisimilitude to the events they relate. I do not blame him for this. Tolerance is a very good quality in a man: if it were commoner, the world of today would be a more agreeable place to live in than it is; but I am not so sure that it is so good in a writer. For what in the long run has the writer to give you? Himself. It is well that he should have breadth of vision, for life in all its extent is his province; but he must see it not only with his own eyes, he must apprehend it with his own nerves, his own heart and his own bowels; his knowledge is partial, of course, but it is distinct, because he is himself and not somebody else. His attitude is definite and characteristic. If he really feels that any other point of view is as valid as his own, he will hardly hold his own with energy and is unlikely to present it with force. It is commendable that a man should see that there are two sides to a question; but the writer face to face with the art he practises (and his view of life is of course part of his art) can only attain this standpoint by an effort of ratiocination: in his blood and his bones he feels that it is not six of one and half a dozen of the other, but twelve on his side and on the other zero. This unreasonableness would be most unfortunate if writers were few, or if the influence of one were so great as to compel the rest to conformity; but there are thousands of us. Each one of us has his little communication to make, a restricted one, and from all these communications the readers can choose, according to their own inclinations and their own experience of life, what suits them.

I have said all this to clear the ground. I like best the sort of story I can myself write. This is the sort of story that many people have written well, but no one more admirably than Maupassant, so I cannot do better, to show exactly what its nature is, than to discuss one of his most famous productions, *The Necklace*, which the reader will find in this volume. One thing you will notice about it is that you could tell it over the dinner table or in a ship's smoking room and hold the attention of your listeners. At the base of it is an anecdote. It relates an incident which is curious, striking and original. But of course it is much more than an anecdote, for when you know this you can read the story with as much interest as before. The scene is set before you with brevity, as the medium requires, but with clearness; and the persons concerned, the kind of life they lead and their deterioration, are shown you with just the amount of detail that is needed to make the circumstances of the case plain. You are told everything that you should know about them. From this appears the second excellence of this sort of story; when you have read it to find out what happens you can read it again for the cleverness of the telling. *The Necklace* is not from its own standpoint perfect, for this kind of narrative should have a beginning, a middle and an end; and when the end is reached the whole story should have been told and you should neither wish nor need to ask a further question. Your crossword is filled up. But in this case Maupassant satisfied himself with an end that was ironic and effective. The practical reader can hardly fail to ask himself, what next? It is true that the unfortunate couple had lost their youth and most of what makes life pleasant in the dreary years they had passed saving money to pay for the lost necklace; but when they discovered that it was worthless they might very well have claimed the real one with which they had replaced it and then found themselves in possession of a small fortune. In the aridity of spirit to which their sacrifices had brought them, it might very well have seemed a satisfactory compensation. It is a tribute to Maupassant's skill that few readers remain so self-possessed that the objection occurs to them. This brings me to the third characteristic of this kind of story. The author does not copy life; he arranges it in order the better to interest, excite and surprise. He demands from you a willing suspension of disbelief.

This has caused the sort of narrative with which I am now dealing to fall of late years into some discredit. People say that in real life things do not happen with this neatness; real life is an affair of broken threads and loose ends: to arrange them into a pattern falsifies. Such an author as Maupassant does not mind; he is not aiming at a transcription of life, but at a dramatization of it. He is willing to sacrifice plausibility to effect, and the test is whether he can get away with it: if he has so shaped the incidents he describes and the persons concerned in them that you are conscious of the violence he has put on them, he has failed. But that he sometimes fails is no argument against the method. I am disposed to think that the desire to tell stories and to listen to them is inherent in the human race. At some periods readers exact a close adherence to the facts of life as they know them—it is then that realism is in fashion; at others, indifferent to this, they ask for the strange, the unusual, the marvellous—these are periods that historians of literature call romantic; and then, so long as they are held, readers are willing to accept pretty well anything. They are willing to accept *Sindbad the Sailor* and *Monsieur Beaucaire*. In fiction probability changes with the inclinations of the time; it is what you can get your readers to swallow. No one has stated the canons of the kind of story which I am now discussing with more precision than Edgar Allan Poe. But for its length I would quote in full his review of Hawthorne's *Twice-Told Tales;* it says everything that is to be said on the matter. It is, however, so well known that I can content myself with a short extract.

A skilful literary artist has constructed a tale. If wise, he has not fashioned his thoughts to accommodate his incidents: but having conceived, with deliberate care, a certain unique or single effect to be brought out, he then invents such incidents—he then combines such effects as may best aid him in establishing this preconceived effect. If his very initial sentence tend not to the outbringing of this effect, then he has failed in his first step. In the whole composition there should be no word written, of which the tendency, direct or indirect, is not to the pre-established design. And by such means, with such care and skill, a picture is at length painted which leaves in the mind of him who contemplates it with a kindred art, a sense of the fullest satisfaction. The idea of the tale has been presented unblemished, because undisturbed. . . . .

With this declaration to help one I think it is possible to frame a definition of what Poe meant by a good short story: it is a piece of fiction, dealing with a single incident, material or spiritual, that can be read at a sitting; it is original, it must sparkle, excite or impress; and it must have unity of effect or impression. It should move in an even line from its exposition to its close.

vi

But as I continued to read, I could not but grow conscious of the fact that there are a great many excellent stories which by these canons would have to be condemned. Now the critic does not prescribe laws for the artist; he takes note of his common practice and from this deduces rules; but when an original talent breaks them, the critic, though he may jib like the devil, in the end is forced to change his rules to accommodate the novelty. It is evident that there are other ways than Poe's of writing a good story.

People grow tired even of good things. They want change. To take an example from another art: domestic architecture during the Georgian Era reached a rare perfection; the houses that were built then were good to look at and comfortable to live in. The rooms were spacious, airy and well proportioned. You would have thought people would be content with such houses for ever. But no. The romantic era approached; they wanted the quaint, the fanciful and the picturesque; and the architects, not unwilling, built them what they wanted. It is hard to invent such a story as Poe wrote and, as we know, even he, in his small output, more than once repeated himself. There is a good deal of trickiness in a narrative of this kind, and when, with the appearance and immediate popularity of the monthly magazine, the demand for such narratives became great, authors were not slow to learn the tricks. Craftsmen rather than artists, in order to make their stories effective they forced upon them a conventional design and presently deviated so far from plausibility in their delineation of life that their readers rebelled. They grew weary of stories written to a pattern they knew only too well. They demanded greater realism. Now to copy life has never been the artist's business. If you look at the painting and sculpture of the past you cannot but be surprised to see how little the great artists have occupied themselves with an exact rendering of what they saw before them. We are apt to think that the distortions the plastic artists have imposed upon their materials, best illustrated in the cubists of yesterday, are an invention of our own times. That is not so. From the beginnings of Western painting artists have sacrificed verisimilitude to the effects they sought. If El Greco gave an extravagant length to the figures he painted, it was surely not because he thought human beings, even though saintly, looked like that, but because he wanted to get on canvas an idea in his mind's eye. It is the same with fiction. Not to go far back, take Poe; it is incredible that he should have thought human beings spoke in the way he made his characters speak: if he put into their mouths dialogue that seems to us so unreal, it must be because he thought it suited the kind of story he was telling and helped him to achieve the deliberate purpose which we know he had in view. Artists have only affected naturalism when it was borne in upon them that they had gone so far from life that a return was necessary, and then they have set themselves to copy it as exactly as they could, not as an end in itself, but as a salutary discipline.

In the short story naturalism in the nineteenth century came into fashion in reaction to a romanticism that had become tedious. One after the other writers attempted to portray life with unflinching veracity. 'I have never truckled,' said Frank Norris, 'I never took off the hat to fashion and held it out for pennies. By God! I told them the Truth. They liked it or they didn't like it. What had that to do with me? I told them the Truth, I knew it for the Truth then, and I know it for the Truth now.' (These are brave words. But it is hard to tell what the truth is; it is not necessarily the opposite of what you know to be a lie.) Writers of this school looked upon life with less partial eyes than those of the generation that had preceded them; they were less sugary and less optimistic, more violent and more direct; their dialogue was more natural and they chose their characters from a world that since the days of Defoe writers of fiction had somewhat neglected; but they made no innovations in technique. So far as the essentials of the short story are concerned they were content with the old models. The effects they pursued were still those that had been pursued by Poe; they used the formula he had laid down. Their merit proves its value; their artificiality exposes its weakness.

But there was a country in which the formula had little prevailed. In Russia they had been writing for a couple of generations stories of quite another order; and when the fact forced itself upon the attention both of readers and of authors that the kind of story that had so long found favour was grown tediously mechanical, it was discovered that in that country there was a body of writers who had made of the short story something new and vital. I would not offer it as a dogmatic statement but merely as a suggestion that the inventor of the Russian story as we know it was Tolstoy. In *The Death of Iván Ilých*, which the reader will find in this volume, is a great deal more than the germ of all the Russian stories that have been written since. It comprehends all the merits and all the defects of the Russian story.

It is singular that it took so long for this variety of the brief narrative, not to reach the Western world, for the stories of Turgenev were read in French translations when the Goncourts were writing their Journal, but to have any effect on it. About 1905 I was in Paris, where Arnold Bennett was then living. He was widely read in modern literature and was always alert for anything new within the field of his interests. He knew the work of Tolstoy and Turgenev, and his admiration for it, though discriminating, was great; but I do not think that he found in it anything that was personally important to him as a writer. It was another matter when he read Chekhov; in him he found something that very definitely affected him. A writer of short stories himself, he saw in the Russian's impressive achievement new life for an exhausted form. Since then the prestige of the Russian writers in general, and of Chekhov in particular, has been immense. It has to a large extent transformed the composition and the appreciation of short stories. Critical readers turn away with indifference from the story which is technically known as well made, and the writers who produce it still, for the delectation of the great mass of the public, are little considered. The stories that Maupassant wrote in France, Rudyard Kipling in England and Bret Harte in America have come to be regarded with some disdain. Today most young writers of ambition model themselves on Chekhov, and magazines are issued, for even stories of this kind are dependent on magazines, to present their productions to the public.

But when I come to the consideration of Chekhov's stories (and it is best to consider them because it is they that have chiefly influenced contemporary authors), in order to put into precise words in what exactly their characteristic merits lie, I find myself in a strait. One must put aside first of all the taking novelty of the setting and the strangeness of the life that is represented. This has nothing to do with the intrinsic quality of the stories. It gives them, of course, a romantic complexion which doubtless has contributed not a little to their success with Western readers. In the same way the life of California, with its fantastic personages, captivated the Eastern seaboard and England when first the stories Bret Harte were given to the world. The storyteller from the beginning of time has used this means of holding the attention. Distance and novelty have always appealed. It has caused me not a little surprise to notice that the critics lay little stress on the variety of invention shown by the great short-story writers. They seem to see nothing remarkable in the fact that they should be able to think of so many themes and create so great a throng of characters. The short-story writer cannot describe the persons he has need of as fully as the novelist can, but he must know them just as well, and he must call into being a great many. The number that Maupassant created and clearly put before the reader is vast. Chekhov had no such capacity. His characters are few. He makes use of the same types over and over again. I have a notion, indeed, that he was insufficiently interested in the individual to see him with great distinctness. Nor are his stories, using the word for the moment to mean a succession of coherent incidents, of great note. He seldom hit upon an anecdote that was in itself very interesting. He had no talent for telling the sort of story that you can repeat over the dinner table, and we know that he did not want to. But for all that his best stories linger in the memory longer than do many with a thrilling plot and sharply individualized characters. Why? I am not sure. I can only tell the reader what is the effect they have on me, asking him once more to remember that I do not pretend to be a critic; I can only judge them from my own standpoint of a writer who writes stories of a different kind.

I find that the impression they make on me is powerful but indeterminate; they leave me with a feeling that all is futility, all is frustration; that men are weak, foolish and at the mercy of every untoward circumstance, often brutal and cruel; but that nothing matters very much. This is indeed life, but something in me of vital energy protests that it is not the whole of it. I think Chekhov's delineation would be intolerable if you could feel very strongly about the persons who take part in the incidents he describes. They are real enough, and true enough, but you do not see them face to face; you see them as it were through a veil of their common flesh, their individualities slightly blurred, and so your sympathies are imperfectly engaged. I have a notion, however, that it is just to this limitation, to the fact that he could not give the creatures of his fancy that last happy flick of idiosyncrasy which brings a character to separate life, that he owes his great and special quality. His people are shadowy; but because they have not the clean-cut outline of a silhouette, because they are like vapours that rise towards evening from the surface of a lake and lose themselves in the enveloping dusk, though lacking the fine distinction of personality they have a common humanity. I despair of making myself clear when I say that they strike me less as persons than as human beings. Each one is as it were a part of everyone else, and the hurt that one does to another is bearable because in a way it is a hurt that he does to himself. And because they are shadowy they remain secret. We understand them as little as we understand ourselves. And so Chekhov gets the effect which is perhaps the most impressive that the writer of fiction can achieve: he fills you with an overpowering sense of the mystery of life. That is the sense, terrifying and yet imposing, that lies at the bottom of all our activities, that lurks at the back of all our thoughts, the most trivial as well as the most subtle; and to my mind it is by his power to do this that Chekhov is unique. It is this power that gives a point to stories that otherwise seem pointless and significance to characters and incidents that are on the surface of no great moment.

vii

To write a story in accordance with the principles laid down by Edgar Allan Poe is not so easy as some think. It requires intelligence, not perhaps of a very high order, but of a special kind; it requires a sense of form and no small power of invention. But it is plain that this manner of story no longer carries conviction. The modern story fulfills a spiritual need in the modern reader which the old story cannot satisfy. The technique and the outlook of the writers of today differ a good deal from those of the masters of the nineteenth century; but before I go into this I must mention a circumstance that has forced itself upon my attention and that has caused me a certain perplexity; this is that so many of these stories might have been written by the same hand. It looks as though there were something in the method of the modern short story that submerges the personality of the author. The stories of Henry James, of Maupassant and of Chekhov could only have been written by themselves. You may not like the personality of these authors, but there it is, manifest to the grossest sense, in their every page. For my part I have always thought that just this, the personality of the creator, was what gave a work of art its lasting interest; it does not matter if it is a slightly absurd one, as with Henry James, a somewhat vulgar one, as with Maupassant, or a grey, melancholic one, as with Chekhov: so long as he can present it, distinct and idiosyncratic, his work has life. The short-story writers of our time seem to lack this curious power. Violent though they often are, hard, ruthless and devoid of sentimentality, they seldom manage to impress their special individuality upon their work. They are communal writers. They remind one of the decorative painters in the eighteenth century who painted flower pieces to put over doors or let into panels above the chimneypiece; it is a pleasant art, but its merit owes more to a period than to a personal gift.

When Chekhov's stories come off they give you a sense of reality which Maupassant's, even at their best, hardly do, for the pattern he has forced upon them prevents your complete surrender; somewhere in your subconscious the recollection lingers that what you are reading is after all only a fiction. And in the best of the modern short stories you do get a feeling of real life that I think has not often before been so closely attained; this, you say, is how things do happen, I believe in these people, I know the look of the streets they walk in and I recognize the smell of their houses. But in fiction, as in life, you can seldom get one thing except at the cost of another; and I have a notion that these writers, in order to get the particular effect they do, have had to sacrifice what is often thought the greatest resource of the storyteller, the eagerness he excites in you to know how things will turn out. They often interest, they may even give you cause for reflection, but they do not thrill; your blood runs no faster as you read and you do not feverishly turn the pages to discover what will happen next. Modern writers lay little emphasis on plot and for this reason are at their best when they are brief, for as soon as stories lengthen they need the support that a plot gives them in order to maintain coherence. They omit a good deal which at the beginning of his narrative the writer, in order to explain the circumstances, was accustomed to tell. They are apt at the end to leave things in the air so that the reader must answer for himself any questions he has to ask. They fight shy of the dramatic and the unexpected. Chekhov in one of his letters, defending his own practice, says that people do not go to the North Pole and fall off icebergs; they go to offices, quarrel with their wives and eat cabbage soup. Of course it is untrue that people do not do adventurous things, but even if it were, it would be no argument against writing stories about people who did. Man has always been excited by the marvellous and has listened with pleasure to tales of it. After all, one of the best and most moving stories in the world is the story in the Book of Genesis of Joseph and his Brethren.

The writers of the present time, unless I am mistaken, are more interested in social circumstances, in the injustice of modern conditions, in the relation of persons to their environment, in short, than in their relations to one another. The result of this is that they are likely to suffer from a certain shortage of material. If you know all about a sawmill, for instance, if you have yourself worked in one, you can probably write a very good story about it, even two or three; but you cannot go on writing stories about sawmills indefinitely; presently you will have said all you can on the subject, and then you are obliged to look for some other environment. You are lucky if you can find one about which you can learn to write with first-hand knowledge. It is a grave handicap that these specialist writers, of which there are so many nowadays, labour under; they exhaust their subjects, and, as we know, either go on writing the same old story to the weariness of their readers, or lapse into silence. The only subject that is inexhaustible is man. You can go on writing all your life and touch no more than the fringe of it. The difficulty of the writer who eschews a plot—and a plot, I should add, is no more than the pattern that is imposed upon the conduct of the various persons with whom you are dealing—in favour of a narration of the circumstances offered by a certain environment is that, getting nearer and nearer to life as we know it is lived, avoiding surprise, thrill, unexpected yet logical accident, which are the essential characteristics of the formal story, he has nothing to offer the reader that the narrator of actual facts cannot give him with greater force. He has ceased to be a writer of fiction; he has become a reporter. To prove this point I have printed at the end of this anthology a piece from a collection of true accounts of events written by the persons who took part in them. They are so good, so complete, so vivid that the candid reader can hardly fail to admit that they are as well worth reading as many short stories. And the fact that he knows they are true gives them an added point.

It is the death of the short story if it can be beaten at its own game by the naked truth. If the short story is to be a work of art it must be more than that. It will not do to say that the storyteller selects. The writers of this volume of true stories (it is called *Life in the United States* and is published by Scribners) have also selected: from the mass of their experience they have taken occasions that seemed to them significant and their attitude towards life has influenced their choice. They too have had an emotional reaction to the circumstances they describe. It happens to be a different one from those that chiefly affect modern writers, but I cannot bring myself to think it less admirable. It is fortitude. Modern writers are mostly moved by pity and anger; indeed pity is the fashionable literary emotion of our day. It is that for which a novelist is most praised. Critics have even found it in Chekhov, though the readers of his own time often complained that his objectivity was such that you could not tell from his stories where his sympathies lay. Now everyone knows that the world is in a bad way, liberty is dead or dying, poverty, relentless exploitation of labour, cruelty, injustice are everywhere. There is good cause for anger and pity; but they are unprofitable emotions unless they lead you to some effort. They are despicable when, satisfied that you have the generosity to feel them, you will not get busy to change the conditions that have aroused them. It is not for nothing that the tender Spinoza called pity womanish. In our small contemporary world of writers and readers it is too often a balm we apply to our wounded souls in order that we may spare ourselves the inconvenience of action. The writer's business is not to pity, nor to rage, but to understand.

At the beginning of this introduction I called the reader's attention to the fact that writers are more likely to write stories when they can get a public for them. The great flowering of the art during the nineteenth century is due to the popularity of the magazines. As we know, they began to prosper round about the forties and their success finally killed the decaying annuals and keepsakes which at an earlier period had given writers their only opportunity. I suppose that this success reached its culmination during the first third of the present century. Never was there a greater demand for short stories, never were higher prices paid for them, and never was there a larger number of writers to write them. But the vogue of the magazine, I suspect, is waning. People spend an increasing part of their leisure in athletic exercises, they golf, play tennis, motor and swim; they have the cinema to go to and the gramophone to listen to; they have the radio. Cheaper and cheaper books, of a size convenient for the pocket, offer reading matter that more satisfactorily supplies present needs. One can hardly suppose that the magazines will be displaced by some other form of periodical as the magazines displaced the annuals that once flourished so luxuriantly, but it is at least not unlikely that the magazines will change their character and so cease to offer an outlet to the writer of short stories. Already editors, disturbed by their falling circulations and thinking that in the distressed condition of the world their readers demand more solid fare than fiction, are giving more space to articles of an informative character. But I cannot believe that people will lose their desire to listen to stories. As I said before, that seems to me a desire inherent in the human race. It is not my business to prophesy, the world is sufficiently full of prophets, mostly, I am afraid, of evil; but it is at least not absurd to suggest that this need may well be satisfied by the radio. It may be that listeners will take the place of readers and that those who want the entertainment of the short story will be content to hear it over the air. Then the art will have gone full circle. The short story started with the tale told by the hunter round the fire in the cave which was the dwelling of primitive man, and, having run its long course, will then return to its origins. The teller of tales, sitting before his microphone, will narrate his story to an immense crowd of unseen listeners.

But if this happens it is hard to believe that he will have an attentive audience if he tells stories that depend on atmosphere, if he tells stories that are sketchy or digressive, stories of implication, or stories whose meaning is obscure. One can but suppose that his stories will have to be direct, gripping, surprising and dramatic. They will have to move swiftly in one unbroken line from the beginning that arouses interest to the end that satisfies the curiosity that has been excited. They will in a word have to resemble more closely the stories of Maupassant than the stories of Chekhov. But that is not yet. Tolstoy, Chekhov and many another writer either influenced by them or, like Sherwood Anderson, arriving at a similar form by native idiosyncrasy, have enriched literature with a number of pieces the merit of which is great; and if these compositions will not fit into the definition of a short story which may be deduced from the formula so well stated by Poe, then the definition must be changed to include them. I would now offer a very simple one. I should define a short story as a piece of fiction that has unity of impression and that can be read at a single sitting. I should be inclined to say that the only test of its excellence is that it interests. It is with this principle in mind that I have chosen the stories in this volume.

ix

But before I go on to consider more particularly the stories which I am inviting the reader to read, I should like to point out to him that no one is under an obligation to read fiction. To read some of the books on the subject that are written for the edification of the young, you would imagine that it was a duty that a man owed, not only to himself, but to society, to read certain novels. From the seriousness with which the authors of these handbooks treat the psychological, political, sociological characteristics of the novels they discuss, you would think that the main object of a work of fiction is to impart knowledge. I imagine that these persons adopt this attitude because it adds dignity to studies which they fear may seem a trifle frivolous. They wish to offer a contribution to science no less important than that provided by the biologists who study rats, newts and guinea pigs. It is an attitude which has much gratified the vanity of authors. They have always had an uneasy feeling that there was something not quite serious in the writing of fiction, and it has been pleasant for them to look upon themselves as scientific workers; and of no small importance either, for the field they cultivated was after all nothing less than human nature. When they were told that the novel had taken the place of the pulpit, and that it offered the most convenient means at the present day for the propagation of ideas, they were quite ready to assume the position thus thrust upon them. They were very willing to look upon themselves as philosophers, teachers, reformers and politicians. Education during the last forty years has become general, and these authors found a vast public that was conscious of its ignorance and anxious to assimilate knowledge at no great expense of mental effort. Readers were glad to read an interesting story, and if they could convince themselves that, far from wasting their time—for such is the frowardness of human nature we have all at the back of our minds the sensation that pleasure is a trifle reprehensible—they were getting useful information, they were very naturally delighted. And even when the stories were not very interesting they were prepared to read on because they were improving their minds.

Unfortunately knowledge is not come by so easily. There is only one way to acquire it and that is by work. On all such matters as science deals with, the knowledge which the novelist gives you is valueless; even in psychology, which he is apt to look upon as something of which he can speak with authority, his statements must be received with caution. For the writer of fiction is concerned with the particular rather than with the general. He chooses his instances. He directs your interest to suit his purpose. By emphasis, by throwing a high light here or leaving in shadow there, he inevitably falsifies; and, however honest he would be, his very nature forces him to load the dice. If the novelist is an acute observer he can sometimes provide material that the scientist can make use of; but at best he is only the field naturalist, whose merit is accuracy and receptiveness, and who, if he is wise, leaves theoretical conclusions to the specialist. It would be all to the good if the novelist were a scientist and a philosopher, for the more he knows the richer his books will be, but even though he were, when he wrote he would cease to be either; he would be an artist. The artist's truth is a different truth from the philosopher's and the scientist's; for truth, we all know now, is not one and indivisible, truth is relative to needs. Their aim is knowledge, but his is liberation. The artist has a natural facility for creation, and to exercise his gifts is a delight to him; he creates in order to disembarrass his soul of a burden that oppressed it and thus gain release. But this is no concern of the layman who reads his poems or looks at his pictures: to the layman art offers solace and relaxation and an escape from the reality of life; and sometimes it enlarges his soul, presents new ideas to his spirit and heartens him to cope with the difficult business of living. If it can do this its power is so great that the artist need not disparage himself because he cannot provide the knowledge that is found in textbooks. But only the greatest art has such power. It is when the artist thus moves you that you are justified in ascribing genius to him. Genius is rare. No artist need be ashamed if he can do no more than offer entertainment. That too has its value.

There is a certain amount of fiction that it becomes every well-bred man to have read; it belongs to the culture of the world, and so far as culture is a part of knowledge it must be regarded as essential to everyone's education. But there is not much of it. I think a bookcase that held twenty books would be large enough to contain all the works of fiction that it would leave a man spiritually poorer not to have read. This bookcase would contain *Don Quixote, Wilhelm Meister, Pride and Prejudice, Le Rogue et le Noir, Le Père Goriot, Madame Bovary, War and Peace, David Copperfield, The Brothers Karamazov* and *À la Recherche du Temps Perdu;* but I am not sure that it would contain any short stories. For the short story is a minor art, and it must content itself with moving, exciting and amusing the reader. There are a hundred stories in this book, and I do not think there is a single one that will fail to do at least one of these things, but also I do not think that there is any that will give the reader that thrill, that rapture, that fruitful energy which great art can produce. The most important short-story writers of the nineteenth century were not men who had it in them to achieve such effects. They had talent and they were artists; but Maupassant had some commonness in his nature, and Henry James, who took his calling with such an admirable seriousness, was defeated by a peculiar triviality of soul; Chekhov was neither trivial nor common, but, as is evident when on occasion he indulges in general reflection, his mental capacity was mediocre. None of these writers impresses you by the power and fullness of his personality as you are impressed when you read Balzac or Tolstoy.

It is wise then to read short stories for the extertainment they provide. It is unreasonable to ask of them more than they can give you. But it would be foolish to despise them on that account. In those treatises on the art of fiction of which I spoke before, I have noticed with surprise that though the authors discourse at length on the technique, moral attitude and I know not what of the novels with which they are dealing, they make no mention of their value as entertainment. This seems to me wrongheaded. The first demand the reader should make of a novel is that it should entertain him; if it does not do this, whatever its other merits, it is a poor novel. I think that in a number of stories in this volume the reader will find something besides entertainment: he will find curiosities of construction, should this interest him, excellence of style, an insight into the multiplicity of human nature, and here and there food for reflection. But unless chief of all he finds entertainment, I have chosen badly. Let no one think that entertainment is a cheap and shoddy thing, let him leave such a belief to the most snobbish and vulgar of the highbrows; entertainment is a form of pleasure and pleasure is in itself good. There is no need for pleasure to be unintelligent. One of the signs of culture is that you are able to extract pleasure from objects or events to which the ignorant are indifferent. A culture is meagre that cannot get fun out of push pin as well as out of poetry.

But entertainment is a personal thing. Just as there is no obligation to read fiction there is no obligation to like it. The critics often try to browbeat us plain men by telling us that we ought to like this, that and the other, and they call us hard names if we will not do as they bid. There is no ought in the matter. The critic can point out the excellences he sees, and since they may have escaped your attention, in this he does you a service; but when he condemns you because you do not care for the work he admires he is foolish. The history of criticism shows that critics are often mistaken. The only thing that really matters to you is what a work of art says to you. Even if the consensus of educated opinion is against you, you should be unperturbed. However great a work is commonly agreed to be, if it bores you, to read it is futile; it must entertain *you,* or so far as you are concerned it is valueless.

It is on this principle that I have chosen the stories in this volume. I have been influenced neither by the reputation nor by the common opinion that ascribed them merit. These stories are stories I like. I cannot hope that all readers will like them all. To do so they would have had to have my particular experience of life and to share my prejudices and my interests. I do not claim that they are the best stories that have been written during the last century; they are the stories amongst all those that I have read that have interested me most.

When my reading forced me to broaden my definition of a short story so that it included almost anything approaching fiction that was not of excessive length, I was able to insert a number of pieces that, if I had adhered to Poe's canon, I should have felt bound to omit. I was able to put in Flaubert's *A Simple Heart,* which he himself called a short story, but which is really a short novel. Such unity of impression as it has depends only on the fact that the interest is concentrated on a single person. But it is only as short as it is and no longer, because in comparatively few pages Flaubert was able to say all there was to say about the straightforward, limited character he set out to describe. It is a moving tale, and it is somewhat important in the history of fiction because it has given rise to numberless studies, sometimes in the form of the short story, sometimes in that of the novel, of women of the servant class. It is besides a story which, I think, no one can read without gaining a sympathetic understanding of the French nature, with its great virtues and pardonable failings; for all France is there. This looseness of definition has also made it possible for me to put in Joseph Conrad's excellent *Typhoon* rather than one of his briefer pieces. Conrad rarely wrote anything but short stories, though, being a writer of an exuberant verbosity, he often made them as long as most novels. He needed sea-room. He had little sense of concision. A theme with him was like the stem of a cauliflower; it grew and grew under his active pen until, all its branches headed with succulent flowers, it became a very fine but somewhat monstrous plant. *Typhoon* shows all his power and none of his weakness. It is a tale of the sea, which he knew better than he knew the land, and it is concerned with men, whom he knew better than he knew women. These sailor chaps are a little simpler than most of us now think human beings really are, but they live. *Typhoon* narrates an incident, which was a thing Conrad could do with mastery, and the subject gives him opportunity for his wonderful and vivid descriptions of the phenomena of nature. My final definition has even allowed me to adorn my pages with

E. M. Forster's *Mr and Mrs Abbey's Difficulties,* which is a little bit of literary history written in the guise of fiction; it has a surprise ending that would have delighted the mind of O. Henry. It is a moving and exquisite piece, written in such admirable English that it might well find a place in any manual for teaching the language.

When I abandoned my ambitious project of showing the development of the short story from the beginning of the nineteenth century, I was able to do something that caused me a considerable measure of relief. I was able, to wit, to omit a number of stories that under my original scheme I should have had to insert. There are few works of art that preserve their vitality from age to age. Even they have their ups and downs. For long periods they lie comatose like hibernating animals, and then, as a new generation finds something in them to satisfy its new wants, they take on a new lease of life. Thus, the archaic sculpture of Greece, the paintings of the school of Siena, after being neglected for a long period, in our own day, with its relish for the primitive, its taste for suggestion rather than for downright statement, have been found to possess a troubling beauty that corresponds to our high-strung needs as does neither the resolute achievement of Phidias nor the opulent splendour of Titian. And in literature, when romanticism, fired by the discovery of the Middle Ages, rejected the measure and reason of the eighteenth century, when the sensitiveness of the human soul first recoiled from the mechanization of life, writers found inspiration and readers refreshment in books like Malory's *Morte d'Arthur* and Froissart's *Chronicles.*

But there are many works of art that live their lives and die. They have had something to say to the generation that saw their birth, but with the passing of that generation lose their import. They may still have an interest for the student or the historian, but they are no longer works of art. They can no longer give its specific thrill. They have had a long and honourable career, and there is no cause for their authors to turn uneasily in their graves; they have fulfilled their purpose and may now rest in peace. But I have not wished any of the stories in this collection to be looked upon as museum pieces. I have inserted nothing that does not seem to me to have a living interest. That is why I have chosen mostly stories that are contemporary, or almost so. I dare say that in fifty years many of them will seem as old-fashioned as the stories of fifty years ago that I have discarded. That is not my affair. Now they have the merit of actuality. It is this merit that enables us to compete with the great authors of the past. Otherwise who would read us? The bad, the mediocre, have long since been forgotten and only the best has remained. Who would bother to read a modern novel if *Roxana, Tom Jones* and *Middlemarch* had just that appeal that we can give to our works because we can dress our characters in the clothes of today and make them speak the language of our time?

I hesitated a good deal when I considered the tales of Nathaniel Hawthorne. He was a distinguished and important writer of short stories, and he had a considerable influence both on his contemporaries and on his successors. I read him and reread him. It seemed to me that his stories had lost the life they once assuredly had. In order to find an interest in them now, one has to bethink oneself of the circumstances of his life, the period he lived in and the effect on him of the romantic revival which at the time swept Europe like a tidal wave. Historians of literature claim that *Rappucini's Daughter* is a masterpiece. To me it seems stuff and nonsense. I am only too willing to suspend my disbelief, but that is a mouthful that I really cannot swallow. I think the story of Hawthorne's that has most life in it today is *The Artist of the Beautiful,* for that is the story of every creator in relation to his creation and to the world without; it is universal, but alas, so diffuse and so repetitive that its power is sadly diminished. To my mind Hawthorne's best story is the story of his own life, and that you may read in that enchanting book, *The Flowering of New England,* by Van Wyck Brooks. It is on account of this that I could not bring myself to omit Hawthorne from this anthology, and so I have chosen *The Gray Champion.* It has thrill and is informed with a noble patriotism which you will have to hunt far and wide to find represented in the short story. Now that liberty in so many quarters of the world is immured and fettered, it is more than ever necessary to cherish an expression of its beauty.

I had no such hesitations when I came to read the stories that depended for their interest on local colour and dialect. Their vogue started in the seventies and lasted for many years. The manner reached its greatest excellence in the work of Mary Wilkins Freeman. She had grace, feeling and sincerity. I am sure her stories were very good in their day, but their day is past; the sun has faded their delicate tints and they are now somewhat namby-pamby. It is the namby-pamby which till quite recently has been the bane of the English short story. This failing has made it difficult for me to find any stories written in the last third of the century in England that seemed to me to have merit. The writers of that period were gentle, urbane and sentimental. They closed their eyes to such aspects of life as they did not wish to see. English writers on the whole have not taken kindly to the art of the short story. They have felt the novel more congenial to their idiosyncrasy, for the English, though in conversation often tongue-tied, when they take a pen in their hands are inclined to prolixity. They have no natural instinct for succinctness, which is indispensable to the short story, nor a sense of form, which is essential to its significance. So the diffuseness of the national temper has found its most satisfactory literary expression in the long, unwieldy, shapeless novels of the Victorian Era which still remain the country's outstanding contribution to the world's fiction. English writers find it difficult to be brief without being trivial, and for the most part they have looked upon the short story as a thing of no great matter to be thrown off in their spare time in order to earn a few useful guineas without much expenditure of effort. I know only two English writers who have taken the short story as seriously as it must be taken if excellence is to be achieved, Rudyard Kipling, namely, and Katherine Mansfield. Miss Mansfield had a small, derivative, but exquisite talent; and her shorter pieces—for she had insufficient power to deal with a theme that demanded a solid gift of construction—are admirable. Rudyard Kipling stands in a different category. He alone among English writers of the short story can bear comparison with the masters of France and Russia.

Though Rudyard Kipling captured the attention of the public when first he began to write, and has retained a firm hold on it ever since, there was a time when educated opinion was somewhat disdainful of him. He was identified with an imperialism which events made obnoxious to many sensible persons. Certain characteristics of his style, which at first had seemed fresh and amusing, became irksome to readers of fastidious taste. But that time is past. I think there would be few now to deny that he was a wonderful, varied and original teller of tales. He had a fertile invention, and to a supreme degree the gift of narrating incident in a surprising and dramatic fashion. His influence for a while was great on his fellow-writers, but perhaps greater on his fellow-men, who led in one way or another the sort of life he dealt with. When one travelled in the East it was astonishing how often one came across men who had modelled themselves on the creatures of his fancy. They always say that Balzac's characters were more true of the generation that followed him than of that which he purported to describe; I know from my own experience that twenty years after Kipling wrote his first important stories there were men scattered about the outlying parts of the world who would never have been just what they were if he had not written them. He not only created characters, he created men. Rudyard Kipling is generally supposed to have rendered the British people conscious of their Empire, but that is a political achievement with which I have not here to deal; what is significant to my present standpoint is that in his discovery of the exotic story he opened a new and fruitful field to writers. This is the story, the scene of which is set in some country little known to the majority of readers, and which deals with the reactions upon the white man of his sojourn in an alien land and the effect which contact with peoples of another race has upon him. Subsequent writers have treated this subject in their different ways, but Rudyard Kipling was the first to blaze the trail through this new-found country, and no one has invested it with a more romantic glamour, no one has made it more exciting and no one has presented it so vividly and with such a wealth of colour. He wrote many stories of other kinds, but none in my opinion which surpassed these. He had, like every writer that ever lived, his shortcomings, but remains notwithstanding the best short-story writer that England can boast of.

Now I wish to speak of Henry James. Greatness is a quality which is loosely ascribed to writers, and it is well to be cautious in one's use of the word, but I think no one will quarrel with me when I say that Henry James is the most distinguished literary figure that America has produced. He was a voluminous writer of short stories. Though he lived so long in England, and indeed in the end was naturalized, he remained an American to the last. I cannot feel that he ever knew the English as an Englishman instinctively knows them, and for that reason I have chosen for this book an American, rather than an English, story. The characters ring more true to life; his English people are more Jamesian than English.

It is impossible, I imagine, for anyone who knew Henry James in the flesh to read his stories dispassionately. He got the sound of his voice into every line he wrote, and you accept the convoluted style of his later work, his long-windedness and his mannerisms, because they are part and parcel of the charm, benignity and amusing pomposity of the man you remember. He was, if not a great, a remarkable man, so the reader will perhaps forgive me if in what follows I do not confine myself precisely to the consideration of his stories, which in this introduction is my only concern. The number of persons who knew him is growing smaller year by year, and such recollections of him as they have must be worth preservation. I do not foresee that I shall ever have a more suitable occasion than this to put my own on record. I knew Henry James for many years, but I was never more than an acquaintance of his. I am not sure that he was fortunate in his friends. They were disposed to be possessive, and they regarded one another's claim to be in the inner circle of his confidence with no conspicuous amiability. Like a dog with a bone, each was inclined to growl when another showed an inclination to dispute his exclusive right to the precious object of his admiration. The reverence with which they treated him was of no great service to him. They seemed to me, indeed, sometimes a trifle silly: they whispered to one another with delighted giggles that Henry James privately stated that the article in *The Ambassador* the nature of which he had left in polite obscurity and on whose manufacture the fortune of the widow Newsome was founded, was in fact a chamber pot. I did not find this so amusing as they did. But I must admit I was often doubtful of the quality of Henry James's humour. When someone transplants himself from his own country to another he is more likely to assimilate the defects of its inhabitants than their virtues. The England in which Henry James lived was excessively class-conscious, and I think it is to this that must be ascribed the somewhat disconcerting attitude that he adopted in his writings to those who were so unfortunate as to be of humble origin. Unless he were an artist, by choice a writer, it seemed to him more than a little ridiculous that anyone should be under the necessity of earning his living. The death of a member of the lower classes could be trusted to give him a good chuckle. I think this attitude was emphasized by the fact that, himself of exalted lineage, he could not have dwelt long in England without becoming aware that to the English one American was very like another. He saw compatriots, on the strength of a fortune acquired in Michigan or Ohio, received with as great cordiality as though they belonged to the eminent families of Boston and New York; and in self-defence somewhat exaggerated his native fastidiousness in social relations. I think it should be added that perhaps in England his more intimate associations were with persons who were not, to use the vulgar phrase, out of the top drawer; but out of a drawer just below. Their own position was not so secure that they could ignore it.

Two of my meetings with Henry James stand out in my memory. One was in London at a performance of a Russian play by the Stage Society. I think it must have been *The Cherry Orchard*, but after so many years I cannot be certain. It was very badly acted. I found myself sitting with Henry James and Mrs Clifford, the widow of a celebrated mathematician and herself a well-known novelist; and we could none of us make head or tail of it. The intervals were long, and there was ample opportunity for conversation. The play disconcerted Henry James, and he set out to explain to us how antagonistic to his French sympathies was this Russian incoherence. Lumbering through his tortuous phrases, he hesitated now and again in search of the exact word to express his dismay; but Mrs Clifford had a quick and agile mind, she knew the word he was looking for and every time he paused immediately supplied it. But this was the last thing he wanted. He was too well mannered to protest, but an almost imperceptible expression on his face betrayed his irritation, and obstinately refusing the word she offered, he laboriously sought another. The climax came when they began to discuss the actress who was playing the leading part. Henry James wanted to know to what class she belonged, and both Mrs Clifford and I knew exactly what in plain terms he wished to say. But that, he thought, would be tasteless, and so he wrapped up his meaning in an increasingly embarrassed flow of circumlocution till at last Mrs Clifford could bear it no longer and blurted out: 'Do you mean, is she a lady?' A look of real suffering crossed his face. Put so, the question had a vulgarity that outraged him. He pretended not to hear. He made a little gesture of desperation and said: 'Is she, *enfin,* what you'd call, if you were asked point-blank, if you were put with your back to the wall, is she a *femme du monde?*'

The second occasion I remember is when Henry James, his brother William having recently died, was staying at Cambridge, Massachusetts, with his sister-in-law. I happened to be in Boston, and Mrs James asked me to dinner. There were but the three of us; I can remember nothing of the conversation at table, but it seemed to me that Henry James was troubled in spirit; after dinner the widow left us alone in the dining room, and he told me that he had promised his brother to stay at Cambridge for, I think, six months after his death, so that if he found himself able to make a communication from beyond the grave there would be two sympathetic witnesses on the spot ready to receive it. I could not but reflect that Henry James was in such a state of nervousness that it would be difficult to place implicit confidence in any report he might make. His sensibility was so exasperated that he was capable of imagining anything. But hitherto no message had come, and the six months were drawing to their end.

When it was time for me to go, Henry James insisted on accompanying me to the corner where I could take the streetcar back to Boston. I protested that I was perfectly capable of getting there by myself, but he would not hear of it; this not only on account of the kindness and the great courtesy that were natural to him, but also because America seemed to him a strange and terrifying labyrinth in which without his guidance I was bound to get hopelessly lost. When we were on the way, by ourselves, he told me what his good manners had prevented him from saying before Mrs James, that he was counting the days that must elapse before, having fulfilled his promise, he could sail for the blessed shores of England. He yearned for it. There in Cambridge he felt himself forlorn. He was determined never again to set foot on the bewildering and unknown country that America was to him. It was then that he uttered the phrase which seemed to me so fantastic that I have always remembered it. 'I wander about those great empty streets of Boston,' he said, 'and I never see a living creature. I could not be more alone in the Sahara.' The streetcar hove in sight and Henry James was seized with agitation. He began waving frantically when it was still a quarter of a mile away. He was afraid it wouldn't stop, and he besought me to jump on with the greatest agility of which I was capable, for it would not pause for more than an instant, and if I were not very careful I might be dragged along, and if not killed, at least mangled and dismembered. I assured him that I was quite accustomed to getting on streetcars. Not American streetcars, he told me; they were of a savagery, an inhumanity, a ruthlessness beyond any conception. I was so infected by his anxiety that when the car pulled up and I leapt on, I had almost the sensation that I had had a miraculous escape from a fearful death. I saw him standing on his short legs in the middle of the road, looking after the car, and I felt that he was trembling still at my narrow shave.

When for this book I read, yet once again, the short stories of Henry James, I was troubled by the contrast offered by the triviality of so many of his themes and the elaboration of his treatment. He seems to have had no inkling that his subject might be too slight to justify so intricate a method. This is a fault that lessens one's enjoyment of some of his most famous tales. A world that has gone through the great war, that has lived through the troubled years that have followed it, can hardly fail to be impatient with events, persons and subtleties that seem so remote from life. Henry James had discernment, a generous heart and artistic integrity; but he applied his gifts to matters of no great import. He was like a man who should provide himself with all the impedimenta necessary to ascend Mount Everest in order to climb Primrose Hill. Let us not forget that here was a novelist who had to his hand one of the most stupendous subjects that any writer ever had the chance of dealing with, the rise of the United States from the small, provincial country that he knew in his youth to the vast and powerful commonwealth that it has become; and he turned his back on it to write about tea parties in Mayfair and country-house visits in the home shires. The great novelists, even in seclusion, have lived life passionately; Henry James was content to observe it from a window. But you cannot describe life unless you have partaken of it; nor, should your object be different, can you fantasticate upon it (as Balzac and Dickens did) unless you know it first. Something escapes you unless you have been an actor in the tragicomedy. Henry James was shy of the elementals of human nature. His heart was an organ subject to no serious agitation, and his interests were confined to persons of his own class. He failed of being a very great writer because his experience was inadequate and his sympathies were imperfect.

xiii

Now I have little more to say. I have limited myself in this anthology to five countries, France, Germany, Russia, England and the United States. Scandinavia, Denmark especially, has produced stories of uncommon merit, and Italy, too, has several writers who should find a place in any anthology; but if I had inserted them, there seemed no reason why I should leave out Spain, Hungary and half a dozen more. It would have made this book unwieldy. None of these countries, moreover, has produced the immense body of work that has been produced in the five countries from which I have chosen; nor has any of them (with the exception of Denmark with Hans Andersen) produced anything that could not be paralleled in them. At one time I used to buy modern pictures, and Rosenberg, the dealer, said to me: don't bother with any but the *chefs d'école;* their followers may have merits, but in the long run it is only the leaders that count. So far as short stories are concerned the *chefs d'école* are to be found in the countries whose works are represented in this volume.

The reader who glances at the table of contents will notice that I have chosen more stories from England and America than from France and Russia and Germany. This is not because I think they are better, but because the book is designed for American and English readers, and to them stories of their own writers will, I imagine, prove more interesting. Besides, however well a story is translated, it loses something in the process; it can never have the flavour it had and so is not quite so good as it was in its own language. I have arranged the stories roughly in chronological order, but not so strictly as to prevent me from putting them in the order in which I thought they could be most agreeably read. I have sought to balance matter and manner, the serious and the gay, the short and the long, so that the reader should be led from story to story without tedium. I have mixed up the various countries in such a manner as I have thought would help me in this. The exception I have made is in the case of Russia. Russian stories are so singular, they have on the whole so slender a connection with occidental culture, that I feel they must be taken by themselves. One has to get oneself into a peculiar frame of mind to read them to advantage, and one has to shift one's outlook on life, one's feelings on all manner of things, on to another plane, as it were, in order to get into a suitable relation with their authors. I am afraid that few of the contemporary ones, judged by even the most tolerant standard, can be described as good stories, but I do not think in this case it much matters. Their interest is documentary rather than artistic. I have chosen those printed in this volume because there was in them at least some glimmering of form; but more particularly because they give a picture of an experiment in civilization to which none of us who have to live for some little time yet on this earth can be indifferent. Their authors are Soviet authors, now living in Russia; the lack of skill shown by most of them gives their stories a convincing character which, if they had known their business, might not have been so apparent. To my mind they show very strikingly how men and women have been living together in Russia in the recent past and how the conditions of existence have affected their attitude towards the elemental things of life and love and death which are the essential materials not only of poetry but of fiction. I should like to point out that in the humorous story called *The Knives,* the reader will find one that might have been written in any country in the world. It is foolish to generalize on a single instance, but this suggests to me that humour has a universal quality, so that it is at least possible that if it were more generally exercised among the nations there is a chance that the differences dividing us, and the discords that afflict us, might be in some measure mitigated.

Now I have but one more thing to say. I have left out stories by certain living writers who hold an honourable position in the world of letters. I have done so because I do not myself happen to like them. Their authors, should they chance to glance over this book, would be wrong to be offended with me. We can none of us expect to be liked by everybody, and when we realize that somebody has no fancy for us, we may be curious to know why but we have no right to be angry. There are doubtless excellent stories by writers of perhaps considerable talent that do not chance to please me. That does not in the least affect their merit. I would never claim that my taste is perfect; all I can claim is that in making such a selection as this the anthologist's taste is the only standard.

W. S. M.

Tellers of Tales

THE TWO DROVERS

Sir Walter Scott

(1771–1832)

It was the day after Doune Fair when my story commences. It had been a brisk market; several dealers had attended from the northern and midland counties in England, and English money had flown so merrily about as to gladden the hearts of the Highland farmers. Many large droves were about to set off for England, under the protection of their owners, or of the tops-men whom they employed in the tedious, laborious, and responsible office of driving the cattle for many hundred miles, from the market where they had been purchased, to the fields or farm-yards where they were to be fattened for the shambles.

The Highlanders, in particular, are masters of this difficult trade of driving, which seems to suit them as well as the trade of war. It affords exercise for all their habits of patient endurance and active exertion. They are required to know perfectly the drove-roads, which lie over the wildest tracks of the country, and to avoid as much as possible the highways, which distress the feet of the bullocks, and the turnpikes, which annoy the spirit of the drover; whereas on the broad green or gray track, which leads across the pathless moor, the herd not only move at ease and without taxation, but, if they mind their business, may pick up a mouthful of food by the way. At night, the drovers usually sleep along with their cattle, let the weather be what it will; and many of these hardy men do not once rest under a roof during a journey on foot from Lochaber to Lincolnshire. They are paid very highly, for the trust reposed is of the last importance, as it depends on their prudence, vigilance, and honesty, whether the cattle reach the final market in good order, and afford a profit to the grazier. But as they maintain themselves at their own expense, they are especially economical in that particular. At the period we speak of, a Highland drover was victualled for his long and toilsome journey with a few handfuls of oatmeal, and two or three onions, renewed from time to time, and a ram's horn filled with whiskey, which he used regularly but sparingly, every night and morning. His dirk, or *skene-dhu* (*i.e.*, black-knife), so worn as to be concealed beneath the arm, or by the folds of the plaid, was his only weapon, excepting the cudgel with which he directed the movements of the cattle. A Highlander was never so happy as on these occasions. There was a variety in the whole journey, which exercised the Celt's natural curiosity and love of motion; there were the constant change of place and scene, the petty adventures incidental to the traffic, and the intercourse with the various farmers, graziers, and traders, intermingled with occasional merrymakings, not the less acceptable to Donald that they were void of expense;—and there was the consciousness of superior skill; for the Highlander, a child amongst flocks, is a prince amongst herds, and his natural habits induce him to disdain the shepherd's slothful life, so that he feels himself nowhere more at home than when following a gallant drove of his country cattle in the character of their guardian.

Of the number who left Doune in the morning, and with the purpose we described, not a *Glunamie* of them all cocked his bonnet more briskly, or gartered his tartan hose under knee over a pair of more promising *spiogs* (legs), than did Robin Oig, that is, Young, or the Lesser, Robin. Though small of stature, as the epithet Oig implies, and not very strongly limbed, he was light and alert as one of the deer of the mountains. He had an elasticity of step, which, in the course of a long march, made many a stout fellow envy him; and the manner in which he busked his plaid and adjusted his bonnet, argued a consciousness that so smart a John Highlandman as himself would not pass unnoticed among the Lowland lasses. The ruddy cheek, red lips, and white teeth, set off a countenance which had gained by exposure to the weather a healthful and hardy rather than a rugged hue. If Robin Oig did not laugh, or even smile frequently, as indeed is not the practice among his countrymen, his bright eyes usually gleamed from under his bonnet with an expression of cheerfulness ready to be turned into mirth.

The departure of Robin Oig was an incident in the little town, in and near which he had many friends, male and female.

He was a topping person in his way, transacted considerable business on his own behalf, and was intrusted by the best farmers in the Highlands, in preference to any other drover in that district. He might have increased his business to any extent had he condescended to manage it by deputy; but except a lad or two, sister's sons of his own, Robin rejected the idea of assistance, conscious, perhaps, how much his reputation depended upon his attending in person to the practical discharge of his duty in every instance. He remained, therefore, contented with the highest premium given to persons of his description, and comforted himself with the hopes that a few journeys to England might enable him to conduct business on his own account, in a manner becoming his birth. For Robin Oig's father, Lachlan M'Combich (or *son of my friend,* his actual clan-surname being M'Gregor), had been so called by the celebrated Rob Roy, because of the particular friendship which had subsisted between the grandsire of Robin and that renowned cateran. Some people even say, that Robin Oig derived his Christian name from one as renowned in the wilds of Loch-

lomond as ever was his namesake Robin Hood in the precincts of merry
Sherwood. "Of such ancestry," as James Boswell says, "who would not be
proud?" Robin Oig was proud accordingly; but his frequent visits to
England and to the Lowlands had given him tact enough to know that pretensions, which still gave him a little right to distinction in his own lonely
glen, might be both obnoxious and ridiculous if preferred elsewhere. The
pride of birth, therefore, was like the miser's treasure, the secret subject of
his contemplation, but never exhibited to strangers as a subject of boasting.

Many were the words of gratulation and good luck which were bestowed
on Robin Oig. The judges commended his drove, especially Robin's own
property, which were the best of them. Some thrust out their snuff-mulls for
the parting pinch—other tendered the *doch-an-dorrach,* or parting cup. All
cried—"Good-luck travel out with you and come home with you.—Give you
luck in the Saxon market—brave notes in the *leabhardhu*" (black pocket-
book), "and plenty of English gold in the *sporran*" (pouch of goat-skin).

The bonny lasses made their adieus more modestly, and more than one,
it was said, would have given her best brooch to be certain that it was
upon her that his eye last rested as he turned towards the road.

Robin Oig had just given the preliminary *"Hoo-hoo!"* to urge forward
the loiterers of the drove, when there was a cry behind him.

"Stay, Robin—bide a blink. Here is Janet of Tomahourich—auld Janet,
your father's sister."

"Plague on her, for an auld Highland witch and spaewife," said a farmer
from the carse of Stirling; "she'll cast some of her cantrips on the cattle."

"She canna do that," said another sapient of the same profession—
"Robin Oig is no the lad to leave any of them without tying Saint Mungo's
knot on their tails, and that will put to her speed the best witch that ever
flew over Dimayet upon a broomstick."

It may not be indifferent to the reader to know, that the Highland
cattle are peculiarly liable to be *taken,* or infected, by spells and witchcraft;
which judicious people guard against, by knitting knots of peculiar com-
plexity on the tuft of hair which terminates the animal's tail.

But the old woman who was the object of the farmer's suspicion, seemed
only busied about the drover, without paying any attention to the drove.
Robin, on the contrary, appeared rather impatient of her presence.

"What auld-world fancy," he said, "has brought you so early from the
ingle-side this morning, Muhme? I am sure I bid you good-even, and had
your God-speed, last night."

"And left me more siller than the useless old woman will use till you
come back again, bird of my bosom," said the sibyl. "But it is little that I
would care for the food that nourishes me, or the fire that warms me, or
for God's blessed sun itseif, if aught but weel should happen to the grandson of my father. So let me walk the *deasil* round you, that you may go
safe out into the foreign land, and come safe home."

Robin Oig stopped, half embarrassed, half laughing, and signing to those near that he only complied with the old woman to soothe her humour. In the mean time, she traced around him, with wavering steps, the propitiation, which some have thought has been derived from the Druidical mythology. It consists, as is well known, in the person who makes the *deasil* walking three times round the person who is the object of the ceremony, taking care to move according to the course of the sun. At once, however, she stopped short, and exclaimed, in a voice of alarm and horror, "Grandson of my father, there is blood on your hand."

"Hush, for God's sake, aunt," said Robin Oig; "you will bring more trouble on yourself with this Taishataragh" (second sight) "than you will be able to get out of for many a day."

The old woman only repeated with a ghastly look, "There is blood on your hand, and it is English blood. The blood of the Gael is richer and redder. Let us see—let us——"

Ere Robin Oig could prevent her, which, indeed, could only have been done by positive violence, so hasty and peremptory were her proceedings, she had drawn from his side the dirk which lodged in the folds of his plaid, and held it up, exclaiming, although the weapon gleamed clear and bright in the sun, "Blood, blood—Saxon blood again. Robin Oig M'Combich, go not this day to England!"

"Prutt trutt," answered Robin Oig, "that will never do neither—it would be next thing to running the country. For shame, Muhme—give me the dirk. You cannot tell by the color the difference betwixt the blood of a black bullock and a white one, and you speak of knowing Saxon from Gaelic blood. All men have their blood from Adam, Muhme. Give me my skene-dhu, and let me go on my road. I should have been half-way to Stirling Brig by this time.—Give me my dirk, and let me go."

"Never will I give it to you," said the old woman—"Never will I quit my hold on your plaid, unless you promise me not to wear that unhappy weapon."

The women around him urged him also, saying few of his aunt's words fell to the ground; and as the Lowland farmers continued to look moodily on the scene, Robin Oig determined to close it at any sacrifice.

"Well, then," said the young drover, giving the scabbard of the weapon to Hugh Morrison, "you Lowlanders care nothing for these freats. Keep my dirk for me. I cannot give it to you, because it was my father's; but your drove follows ours, and I am content it should be in your keeping, not in mine.—Will this do, Muhme?"

"It must," said the old woman,—"that is, if the Lowlander is mad enough to carry the knife."

The strong westlandman laughed aloud.

"Goodwife," said he, "I am Hugh Morrison from Glenae, come of the Manly Morrisons of auld langsyne, that never took short weapon against a man in their lives. And neither needed they. They had their broad-swords, and I have this bit supple," showing a formidable cudgel—"for dirking ower the board, I leave that to John Highlandman—Ye needa snort, none of you Highlanders, and you in especial, Robin. I'll keep the bit knife, if you are feared for the auld spaewife's tale, and give it back to you whenever you want it."

Robin was not particularly pleased with some part of Hugh Morrison's speech; but he had learned in his travels more patience than belonged to his Highland constitution originally and he accepted the service of the descendant of the Manly Morrisons without finding fault with the rather depreciating manner in which it was offered.

"If he had not had his morning in his head, and been but a Dumfriesshire hog into the boot, he would have spoken more like a gentleman. But you cannot have more of a sow than a grumph. It's shame my father's knife should ever slash a haggis for the like of him."

Thus saying (but saying it in Gaelic), Robin drove on his cattle, and waved farewell to all behind him. He was in the greater haste, because he expected to join at Falkirk a comrade and brother in profession, with whom he proposed to travel in company.

Robin Oig's chosen friend was a young Englishman, Harry Wakefield by name, well known at every northern market, and in his way as much famed and honored as our Highland driver of bullocks. He was nearly six feet high, gallantly formed to keep the rounds at Smithfield, or maintain the ring at a wrestling match; and although he might have been over-matched perhaps, among the regular professors of the Fancy, yet, as a yokel, or rustic, or a chance customer, he was able to give a bellyful to any amateur of the pugilistic art. Doncaster races saw him in his glory, betting his guinea, and generally successfully; nor was there a main fought in Yorkshire, the feeders being persons of celebrity, at which he was not to be seen, if business permitted. But though a *sprack* lad, and fond of pleasure and its haunts, Harry Wakefield was steady, and not the cautious Robin Oig M'Combich himself was more attentive to the main chance. His holidays were holidays indeed; but his days of work were dedicated to steady and persevering labor. In countenance and temper, Wakefield was the model of old England's merry yeomen, whose clothyard shafts, in so many hundred battles, asserted her superiority over the nations, and whose good sabres, in our own time, are her cheapest and most assured defence. His mirth was readily excited; for, strong in limb and constitution, and fortunate in circumstances, he was disposed to be pleased with everything about him; and such difficulties as he might occasionally encounter, were, to a man of his energy, rather matter of amusement than serious annoy-ance. With all the merits of a sanguine temper, our young English drover was not without his defects. He was irascible, sometimes to the verge of being quarrelsome; and perhaps not the less inclined to bring his disputes to a pugilistic decision, because he found few antagonists able to stand up to him in the boxing ring.

It is difficult to say how Harry Wakefield and Robin Oig first became intimates; but it is certain a close acquaintance had taken place betwixt them, although they had apparently few common subjects of conversation or of interest, so soon as their talk ceased to be of bullocks. Robin Oig, indeed, spoke the English language rather imperfectly upon any other topics but stots and kyloes, and Harry Wakefield could never bring his broad Yorkshire tongue to utter a single word of Gaelic. It was in vain Robin spent a whole morning, during a walk over Minch Moor, in attempting to teach his companion to utter, with true precision, the shibboleth *Llhu*, which is the Gaelic for a calf. From Traquair to Murder-cairn, the hill rang with the discordant attempts of the Saxon upon the unmanageable monosyllable, and the heartfelt laugh which followed at every failure. They had, however, better modes of awakening the echoes; for Wakefield could sing many a ditty to the praise of Moll, Susan, and Cicely, and Robin Oig had a particular gift at whistling interminable pibrochs through all their involutions, and what was more agreeable to his companion's southern ear, knew many of the northern airs, both lively and pathetic, to which Wakefield learned to pipe a bass. Thus, though Robin could hardly have comprehended his companion's stories about horse-racing, and cock-fighting, or fox-hunting, and although his own legends of clan-fights and *creaghs,* varied with talk of Highland goblins and fairy folk, would have been caviare to his companion, they contrived nevertheless to find a degree of pleasure in each other's company, which had for three years back induced them to join company and travel together, when the direction of their journey permitted. Each, indeed, found his advantage in this companionship; for where could the Englishman have found a guide through the Western Highlands like Robin Oig M'Combich? and when they were on what Harry called the *right* side of the border, his patronage, which was extensive, and his purse, which was heavy, were at all times at the service of his Highland friend, and on many occasions his liberality did him genuine yeoman's service.

II

> Were ever two such loving friends!—
> How could they disagree?
> Oh, thus it was, he loved him dear,
> And thought how to requite him,
> And having no friend left but he,
> He did resolve to fight him.
>
> DUKE UPON DUKE

THE PAIR OF FRIENDS had traversed with their usual cordiality the grassy wilds of Liddesdale, and crossed the opposite part of Cumberland, emphatically called The Waste. In these solitary regions, the cattle under the charge of our drovers derived their subsistence chiefly by picking their food as they went along the drove road, or sometimes by the tempting opportunity of a *start and owerloup,* or invasion of the neighboring pasture, where an occasion presented itself. But now the scene changed before them; they were descending towards a fertile and enclosed country, where no such liberties could be taken with impunity, or without a previous arrangement and bargain with the possessors of the ground. This was more especially the case, as a great northern fair was upon the eve of taking place, where both the Scotch and English drover expected to dispose of a part of their cattle, which it was desirable to produce in the market rested and in good order. Fields were therefore difficult to be obtained, and only upon high terms. This necessity occasioned a temporary separation betwixt the two friends, who went to bargain, each as he could, for the separate accommodation of his herd. Unhappily it chanced that both of them, unknown to each other, thought of bargaining for the ground they wanted on the property of a country gentleman of some fortune, whose estate lay in the neighborhood. The English drover applied to the bailiff on the property, who was known to him. It chanced that the Cumbrian Squire, who had entertained some suspicions of his manager's honesty, was taking occasional measures to ascertain how far they were well founded, and had desired that any inquiries about his enclosures, with a view to occupy them for a temporary purpose, should be referred to himself. As, however, Mr. Ireby had gone the day before upon a journey of some miles' distance to the northward, the bailiff chose to consider the check upon his full powers as for the time removed, and concluded that he should best consult his master's interest, and perhaps his own, in making an agreement with Harry Wakefield. Meanwhile, ignorant of what his comrade was doing, Robin Oig, on his side, chanced to be overtaken by a good-looking smart little man upon a pony, most knowingly bogged and cropped, as was then the fashion, the rider wearing tight leather breeches, and long-necked bright spurs. This cavalier asked one or two pertinent questions about markets and the price of stock. So Robin, seeing him a well-judging civil gentleman, took the freedom to ask him whether he could let him know if there was any grass land to be let in that neighborhood, for the temporary accommodation of his drove. He could not have put the question to more willing ears. The gentleman of the buckskin was the proprietor, with whose bailiff Harry Wakefield had dealt, or was in the act of dealing.

"Thou art in good luck, my canny Scot," said Mr. Ireby, "to have spoken to me, for I see thy cattle have done their day's work, and I have at my disposal the only field within three miles that is to be let in these parts."

"The drove can pe gang two, three, four miles very pratty weel indeed," said the cautious Highlander; "put what would his honor be axing for the peasts pe the head, if she was to tak the park for two or three days?"

"We don't differ, Sawney, if you let me have six stots for winterers, in the way of reason."

"And which peasts wad your honor pe for having?"

"Why—let me see—the two black—the dun one—yon doddy—him with the twisted horn—the brocket—— How much by the head?"

"Ah," said Robin, "your honor is a shudge—a real shudge—I couldna have set off the pest six peasts better mysell, me that ken them as if they were my pairns, puir things."

"Well, how much per head, Sawney?" continued Mr. Ireby.

"It was high markets at Doune and Falkirk," answered Robin.

And thus the conversation proceeded, until they had agreed on the *prix juste* for the bullocks, the Squire throwing in the temporary accommodation of the enclosure for the cattle into the boot, and Robin making, as he thought, a very good bargain, provided the grass was but tolerable. The Squire walked his pony alongside of the drove, partly to show him the way, and see him put into possession of the field, and partly to learn the latest news of the northern markets.

They arrived at the field, and the pasture seemed excellent. But what was their surprise when they saw the bailiff quietly inducting the cattle of Harry Wakefield into the grassy Goshen which had just been assigned to those of Robin Oig M'Combich by the proprietor himself! Squire Ireby set spurs to his horse, dashed up to his servant, and learning what had passed between the parties, briefly informed the English drover that his bailiff had let the ground without his authority, and that he might seek grass for his cattle wherever he would, since he was to get none there. At the same time he rebuked his servant severely for having transgressed his commands, and ordered him instantly to assist in ejecting the hungry and weary cattle of Harry Wakefield, which were just beginning to enjoy a meal of unusual plenty, and to introduce those of his comrade, whom the English drover now began to consider as a rival.

The feelings which arose in Wakefield's mind would have induced him to resist Mr. Ireby's decision; but every Englishman has a tolerably accurate sense of law and justice, and John Fleecebumpkin, the bailiff, having acknowledged that he had exceeded his commission, Wakefield saw nothing else for it than to collect his hungry and disappointed charges, and drive them on to seek quarters elsewhere. Robin Oig saw what had happened with regret, and hastened to offer to his English friend to share with him the disputed possession. But Wakefield's pride was severely hurt, and he answered disdainfully, "Take it all, man—take it all—never make two bites of a cherry—thou canst talk over the gentry, and blear a plain man's eye—Out upon you, man—I would not kiss any man's dirty latchets for leave to bake in his oven."

Robin Oig, sorry but not surprised at his comrade's displeasure, hastened to entreat his friend to wait but an hour till he had gone to the Squire's house to receive payment for the cattle he had sold, and he would come back and help him to drive the cattle into some convenient place of rest, and explain to him the whole mistake they had both of them fallen into. But the Englishman continued indignant: "Thou hast been selling, hast thou? Ay, ay—thou is a cunning lad for kenning the hours of bargaining. Go to the devil with thyself, for I will ne'er see thy fause loon's visage again—thou should be ashamed to look me in the face."

"I am ashamed to look no man in the face," said Robin Oig, something moved; "and, moreover, I will look you in the face this blessed day, if you will bide at the clachan down yonder."

"Mayhap you had as well keep away," said his comrade; and, turning his back on his former friend, he collected his unwilling associates, assisted by the bailiff, who took some real and affected interest in seeing Wakefield accommodated.

After spending some time in negotiating with more than one of the neighboring farmers, who could not, or would not, afford the accommodation desired, Harry Wakefield at last, and in his necessity, accomplished his point by means of the landlord of the alehouse at which Robin Oig and he had agreed to pass the night, when they first separated from each other. Mine host was content to let him turn his cattle on a piece of barren moor, at a price little less than the bailiff had asked for the disputed enclosure; and the wretchedness of the pasture, as well as the price paid for it, were set down as exaggerations of the breach of faith and friendship of his Scottish crony. This turn of Wakefield's passions was encouraged by the bailiff (who had his own reasons for being offended against poor Robin, as having been the unwitting cause of his falling into disgrace with his master), as well as by the innkeeper, and two or three chance guests, who stimulated the drover in his resentment against his quondam associate—some from the ancient grudge against the Scots, which, when it exists anywhere, is to be found lurking in the Border counties, and some from the general love of mischief, which characterizes mankind in all ranks of life, to the honor of Adam's children be it spoken. Good John Barleycorn also, who always heightens and exaggerates the prevailing passions, be they angry or kindly, was not wanting in his offices on this occasion; and confusion to false friends and hard masters was pledged in more than one tankard.

In the meanwhile Mr. Ireby found some amusement in detaining the northern drover at his ancient hall. He caused a cold round of beef to be placed before the Scot in the butler's pantry, together with a foaming tankard of home-brewed, and took pleasure in seeing the hearty appetite with which these unwonted edibles were discussed by Robin Oig M'Combich. The Squire himself, lighting his pipe, compounded between his patrician dignity and his love of agricultural gossip, by walking up and down while he conversed with his guest.

"I passed another drove," said the Squire, "with one of your country-men behind them—they were something less beasts than your drove, doddies most of them—a big man was with them—none of your kilts though, but a decent pair of breeches—D'ye know who he may be?"

"Hout ay—that might, could, and would be Hughie Morrison—I didna think he could hae peen sae weel up. He has made a day on us; but his Argyleshires will have wearied shanks. How far was he pehind?"

"I think about six or seven miles," answered the Squire, "for I passed them at the Christenbury Crag, and I overtook you at the Hollan Bush. If his beasts be leg-weary, he may be selling bargains."

"Na, na, Hughie Morrison is no the man for pargains—ye maun come to some Highland body like Robin Oig hersell for the like of these—put I maun pe wishing you goot-night, and twenty of them let alane ane, and I maun down to the clachan to see if the lad Harry Waakfelt is out of his humdudgeons yet."

The party at the alehouse were still in full talk, and the treachery of Robin Oig still the theme of conversation, when the supposed culprit entered the apartment. His arrival, as usually happens in such a case, put an instant stop to the discussion of which he had furnished the subject, and he was received by the company assembled with that chilling silence, which, more than a thousand exclamations, tells an intruder that he is unwelcome. Surprised and offended, but not appalled by the reception which he experienced, Robin entered with an undaunted and even a haughty air, attempted no greeting, as he saw he was received with none, and placed himself by the side of the fire, a little apart from a table at which Harry Wakefield, the bailiff, and two or three other persons, were seated. The ample Cumbrian kitchen would have afforded plenty of room even for a larger separation.

Robin, thus, seated, proceeded to light his pipe, and call for a pint of twopenny.

"We have no twopence ale," answered Robert Heskett, the landlord; "but as thou find'st thy own tobacco, it's like thou may'st find thy own liquor too—it's the wont of thy country, I wot."

"Shame, goodman," said the landlady, a blithe bustling housewife, hasting herself to supply the guest with liquor—"Thou knowest well enow what the strange man wants, and it's thy trade to be civil, man. Thou shouldst know, that if the Scot likes a small pot, he pays a sure penny."

Without taking any notice of this nuptial dialogue, the Highlander took the flagon in his hand, and addressing the company generally, drank the interesting toast of "Good Markets," to the party assembled.

"The better, that the wind blew fewer dealers from the north," said one of the farmers, "and fewer Highland runts to eat up the English meadows."

"Saul of my pody, put you are wrang there, my friend," answered Robin, with composure; "it is your fat Englishmen that eat up our Scots cattle, puir things."

"I wish there was a summat to eat up their drovers," said another; "a plain Englishman canna make bread within a kenning of them."

"Or an honest servant keep his master's favor, but they will come sliding in between him and the sunshine," said the bailiff.

"If these pe jokes," said Oig, with the same composure, "there is ower mony jokes upon one man."

"It is no joke, but downright earnest," said the bailiff. "Harkye, Mr. Robin Ogg, or whatever is your name, it's right we should tell you that we are all of one opinion, and that is, that you, Mr. Robin Ogg, have behaved to our friend, Mr. Harry Wakefield here, like a raff and a blackguard."

"Nae doubt, nae doubt," answered Robin with great composure; "and you are a set of very pretty judges, for whose prains or pehavior I wad not give a pinch of sneeshing. If Mr. Harry Waakfelt kens where he is wranged, he kens where he may be righted."

"He speaks truth," said Wakefield, who had listened to what passed, divided between the offence which he had taken at Robin's late behavior, and the revival of his habitual feelings of regard.

He now arose, and went towards Robin, who got up from his seat as he approached, and held out his hand.

"That's right, Harry—go it—serve him out," resounded on all sides— "tip him the nailer—show him the mill."

"Hold your peace all of you, and be ——," said Wakefield; and then addressing his comrade, he took him by the extended hand, with something alike of respect and defiance. "Robin," he said, "thou hast used me ill enough this day; but if you mean, like a frank fellow, to shake hands, and make a tussel for love on the sod, why I'll forgie thee, man, and we shall be better friends than ever."

"And would it not pe petter to pe cood friends without more of the matter?" said Robin; "we will be much petter friendships with our panes hale than proken."

Harry Wakefield dropped the hand of his friend, or rather threw it from him.

"I did not think I had been keeping company for three years with a coward.*

"Coward pelongs to none of my name," said Robin, whose eyes began to kindle, but keeping the command of his temper. "It was no coward's legs or hands, Harry Waakfelt, that drew you out of the fords of Frew, when you was drifting ower the plack rock, and every eel in the river expected his share of you."

"And that is true enough, too," said the Englishman, struck by the appeal.

"Adzooks!" exclaimed the bailiff—"sure Harry Wakefield, the nattiest lad at Whitson Tryste, Wooler Fair, Carlisle Sands, or Stagshaw Bank, is not going to show white feather? Ah, this comes of living so long with kilts and bonnets—men forget the use of their daddles."

"I may teach you, Master Fleecebumpkin, that I have not lost the use of mine," said Wakefield, and then went on. "This will never do, Robin. We must have a turn-up, or we shall be the talk of the country-side. I'll be d——d if I hurt thee—I'll put on the gloves gin thou like. Come, stand forward like a man."

"To pe peaten like a dog," said Robin; "is there any reason in that? If you think I have done you wrong, I'll go before your shudge, though I neither know his law nor his language."

A general cry of "No, no—no law, no lawyer! a bellyful and be friends," was echoed by the bystanders.

"But," continued Robin, "if I am to fight, I've no skill to fight like a jackanapes, with hands and nails."

"How would you fight then?" said his antagonist; "though I am thinking it would be hard to bring you to the scratch any how."

"I would fight with proadswords, and sink points on the first plood drawn—like a gentlemans."

A loud shout of laughter followed the proposal, which indeed had rather escaped from poor Robin's swelling heart, than been the dictate of his sober judgment.

"Gentleman, quotha!" was echoed on all sides, with a shout of un-extinguishable laughter; "a very pretty gentleman, God wot—Canst get two swords for the gentlemen to fight with, Ralph Heskett?"

"No, but I can send to the armory at Carlisle, and lend them two forks, to be making shift with in the mean time."

"Tush, man," said another, "the bonny Scots come into the world with the blue bonnet on their heads, and dirk and pistol at their belt."

"Best send post," said Mr. Fleecebumpkin, "to the Squire of Corby Castle, to come and stand second to the *gentleman.*"

In the midst of this torrent of general ridicule, the Highlander instinctively gripped beneath the folds of his plaid.

"But it's better not," he said in his own language. "A hundred curses on the swine-eaters, who know neither decency nor civility!"

"Make room, the pack of you," he said, advancing to the door.

But his former friend interposed his sturdy bulk, and opposed his leaving the house; and when Robin Oig attempted to make his way by force, he hit him down on the floor, with as much ease as a boy bowls down a nine-pin.

"A ring, a ring!" was now shouted until the dark rafters, and the hams that hung on them, trembled again, and the very platters on the *bink* clattered against each other. "Well done, Harry,"—"Give it him home, Harry,"—"take care of him now,—he sees his own blood!"

Such were the exclamations, while the Highlander, starting from the ground, all his coldness and caution lost in frantic rage, sprung at his antagonist with the fury, the activity, and the vindictive purpose, of an incensed tiger-cat. But when could rage encounter science and temper? Robin Oig again went down in the unequal contest; and as the blow was a severe one, he lay motionless on the floor of the kitchen. The landlady ran to offer some aid, but Mr. Fleecebumpkin would not permit her to approach.

"Let him alone," he said, "he will come to within time, and come up to the scratch again. He has not got half his broth yet."

"He has got all I mean to give him, though," said his antagonist, whose heart began to relent towards his old associate; "and I would rather by half give the rest to yourself, Mr. Fleecebumpkin, for you pretend to know a thing or two, and Robin had not art enough even to peel before setting to, but fought with his plaid dangling about him—Stand up, Robin, my man! all friends now; and let me hear the man that will speak a word against you or your country for your sake."

Robin Oig was still under the dominion of his passion, and eager to renew the onset; but being withheld on the one side by the peacemaking Dame Heskett, and on the other, aware that Wakefield no longer meant to renew the combat, his fury sunk into gloomy sullenness.

"Come, come, never grudge so much at it, man," said the brave-spirited Englishman, with the placability of his country; "shake hands, and we will be better friends than ever."

"Friends!" exclaimed Robin Oig, with strong emphasis—"friends!— Never. Look to yourself, Harry Waakfelt."

"Then the curse of Cromwell on your proud Scots stomach, as the man says in the play, and you may do your worst, and be d——d! for one man can say nothing more to another after a tussle, than that he is sorry for it."

On these terms the friends parted; Robin Oig drew out, in silence, a piece of money, threw it on the table, and then left the alehouse. But turning at the door, he shook his hand at Wakefield, pointing with his forefinger upwards, in a manner which might imply either a threat or a caution. He then disappeared in the moonlight.

Some words passed after his departure, between the bailiff, who piqued himself on being a little of a bully, and Harry Wakefield, who, with generous inconsistency, was now not indisposed to begin a new combat in defence of Robin Oig's reputation, "although he could not use his daddles like an Englishman, as it did not come natural to him." But Dame Heskett prevented his second quarrel from coming to a head by her peremptory interference. "There should be no more fighting in her house," she said; "there had been too much already.—And you, Mr. Wakefield, may live to

learn," she added, "what it is to make a deadly enemy out of a good
friend."

"Pshaw, dame! Robin Oig is an honest fellow, and will never keep
malice."

"Do not trust to that—you do not know the dour temper of the Scots,
though you have dealt with them so often. I have a right to know them, my
mother being a Scot."

"And so is well seen on her daughter," said Ralph Heskett.

This nuptial sarcasm gave the discourse another turn; fresh customers
entered the tap-room or kitchen, and others left it. The conversation turned
on the expected markets, and the report of prices from different parts both
of Scotland and England—treaties were commenced, and Harry Wakefield was lucky enough to find a chap for a part of his drove, and at a very
considerable profit; an event of consequence more than sufficient to blot
out all remembrances of the unpleasant scuffle in the earlier part of the
day. But there remained one party from whose mind that recollection
could not have been wiped away by the possession of every head of
cattle betwixt Esk and Eden.

This was Robin Oig M'Combich—"That I should have had no weapon,"
he said, "and for the first time in my life!—Blighted be the tongue that
bids the Highlander part with the dirk—the dirk—ha! the English blood!
—My Muhme's word—when did her word fall to the ground?"

The recollection of the fatal prophecy confirmed the deadly intention
which instantly sprung up in his mind.

"Ha! Morrison cannot be many miles behind; and if it were a hundred,
what then?"

His impetuous spirit had now a fixed purpose and motive of action,
and he turned the light foot of his country towards the wilds, through
which he knew, by Mr. Ireby's report, that Morrison was advancing. His
mind was wholly engrossed by the sense of injury—injury sustained from a
friend; and by the desire of vengeance on one whom he now accounted
his most bitter enemy. The treasured ideas of self-importance and self-
opinion—of ideal birth and quality, had become more precious to him, like
the hoard to the miser, because he could only enjoy them in secret. But
that hoard was pillaged, the idols which he had secretly worshipped had
been desecrated and profaned. Insulted, abused, and beaten, he was no
longer worthy, in his own opinion, of the name he bore, or the lineage
which he belonged to—nothing was left to him—nothing but revenge; and,
as the reflection added a galling spur to every step, he determined it should
be as sudden and signal as the offence.

When Robin Oig left the door of the alehouse, seven or eight English
miles at least lay betwixt Morrison and him. The advance of the former
was slow, limited by the sluggish pace of his cattle; the last left behind
him stubble-field and hedgerow, crag and dark heath, all glittering with

frost-rime in the broad November moonlight, at the rate of six miles an hour. And now the distant lowing of Morrison's cattle is heard; and now they are seen creeping like moles in size and slowness of motion on the broad face of the moor; and now he meets them—passes them, and stops their conductor.

"May good betide us," said the Southlander—"Is this you, Robin M'Combich, or your wraith?"

"It is Robin Oig M'Combich," answered the Highlander, "and it is not. —But never mind that, put pe giving me the skene-dhu."

"What! you are for back to the Highlands—The devil!—Have you selt all off before the fair? This beats all for quick markets!"

"I have not sold—I am not going north—May pe I will never go north again.—Give me pack my dirk, Hugh Morrison, or there will pe words petween us."

"Indeed, Robin, I'll be better advised before I gie it back to you—it is a wanchancy weapon in a Highlandman's hand, and I am thinking you will be about some barn's-breaking."

"Prutt, trutt! let me have my weapon," said Robin Oig, impatiently.

"Hooly and fairly," said his well-meaning friend. "I'll tell you what will do better than these dirking doings—Ye ken Highlander, and Lowlander, and Border-men, are a' ae man's bairns when you are over the Scots dyke. See, the Eskdale callants, and fighting Charlie of Liddesdale, and the Lockerby lads, and the four Dandies of Lustruther, and a wheen mair gray plaids, are coming up behind, and if you are wranged, there is the hand of a Manly Morrison, we'll see you righted, if Carlisle and Stanwix baith took up the feud."

"To tell you the truth," said Robin Oig, desirous of eluding the suspicions of his friend, "I have enlisted with a party of the Black Watch, and must march off to-morrow morning."

"Enlisted! Were you mad or drunk?—You must buy yourself off— I can lend you twenty notes, and twenty to that, if the drove sell."

"I thank you—thank ye, Hughie; but I go with good will the gate that I am going,—so the dirk—the dirk!"

"There it is for you then, since less wunna serve. But think on what I was saying.—Waes me, it will be sair news in the Braes of Balquidder, that Robin Oig M'Combich should have run an ill gate, and ta'en on."

"Ill news in Balquidder, indeed!" echoed poor Robin. "But Cot speed you, Hughie, and send you good marcats. Ye winna meet with Robin Oig again, either at tryste or fair."

So saying, he shook hastily the hand of his acquaintance, and set out in the direction from which he had advanced, with the spirit of his former pace.

"There is something wrang with the lad," muttered the Morrison to himself; "but we'll maybe see better into it the morn's morning."

But long ere the morning dawned, the catastrophe of our tale had taken place. It was two or three hours after the affray had happened, and it was totally forgotten by almost every one, when Robin Oig returned to Heskett's inn. The place was filled at once by various sorts of men, and with noises corresponding to their character. There were the grave low sounds of men engaged in busy traffic, with the laugh, the song, and the riotous jest of those who had nothing to do but to enjoy themselves. Among the last was Harry Wakefield, who, amidst a grinning group of smock-frocks, hobnailed shoes, and jolly English physiognomies, was trolling forth the old ditty,

> "What though my name be Roger,
> Who drives the plough and cart"—

when he was interrupted by a well-known voice saying in a high and stern tone, marked by the sharp Highland accent, "Harry Waakfelt—if you be a man, stand up!"

"What is the matter?—what is it?" the guests demanded of each other.

"It is only a d——d Scotsman," said Fleecebumpkin, who was by this time very drunk, "whom Harry Wakefield helped to his broth the day, who is now come to have *his cauld kail* het again."

"Harry Waakfelt," repeated the same ominous summons, "stand up, if you be a man!"

There is something in the tone of deep and concentrated passion, which attracts attention and imposes awe, even by the very sound. The guests shrunk back on every side, and gazed at the Highlander as he stood in the middle of them, his brows bent and his features rigid with resolution.

"I will stand up with all my heart, Robin, my boy, but it shall be to shake hands with you, and drink down all unkindness. It is not the fault of your heart, man, that you don't know how to clench your hands."

By this time he stood opposite to his antagonist; his open and unsuspecting look strangely contrasted with the stern purpose, which gleamed wild, dark, and vindictive in the eyes of the Highlander.

" 'T is not thy fault, man, that, not having the luck to be an Englishman, thou canst not fight more than a school-girl."

"I *can* fight," answered Robin Oig sternly, but calmly, "and you shall know it. You, Harry Waakfelt, showed me to-day how the Saxon churls fight—I show you now how the Highland Dunniè-wassel fights."

He seconded the word with the action, and plunged the dagger, which he suddenly displayed, into the broad breast of the English yeoman, with such fatal certainty and force, that the hilt made a hollow sound against the breast-bone, and the double-edged point split the very heart of his victim. Harry Wakefield fell and expired with a single groan. His assassin next seized the bailiff by the collar, and offered the bloody poniard to his throat, whilst dread and surprise rendered the man incapable of defence.

"It were very just to lay you beside him," he said, "but the blood of a base pick-thank shall never mix on my father's dirk with that of a brave man."

As he spoke, he cast the man from him with so much force that he fell on the floor, while Robin, with his other hand, threw the fatal weapon into the blazing turf-fire.

"There," he said, "take me who likes—and let fire cleanse blood if it can."

The pause of astonishment still continuing, Robin Oig asked for a peace-officer, and a constable having stepped out, he surrendered himself to his custody.

"A bloody night's work you have made of it," said the constable.

"Your own fault," said the Highlander. "Had you kept his hands off me twa hours since he would have been now as well and merry as he was twa minutes since."

"It must be sorely answered," said the peace-officer.

"Never you mind that—death pays all debts; it will pay that too."

The horror of the bystanders began now to give way to indignation; and the sight of a favorite companion murdered in the midst of them, the provocation being, in their opinion, so utterly inadequate to the excess of vengeance, might have induced them to kill the perpetrator of the deed even upon the very spot. The constable, however, did his duty on this occasion, and, with the assistance of some of the more reasonable persons present, procured horses to guard the prisoner to Carlisle, to abide his doom at the next assizes. While the escort was preparing, the prisoner neither expressed the least interest nor attempted the slightest reply. Only before he was carried from the fatal apartment, he desired to look at the dead body, which, raised from the floor, had been deposited upon the large table (at the head of which Harry Wakefield had presided but a few minutes before, full of life, vigor, and animation) until the surgeons should examine the mortal wound. The face of the corpse was decently covered with a napkin. To the surprise and horror of the bystanders, which displayed itself in a general *Ah!* drawn through clenched teeth and half-shut lips, Robin Oig removed the cloth, and gazed with a mournful but steady eye on the lifeless visage, which had been so lately animated, that the smile of good-humored confidence in his own strength, of conciliation at once, and contempt towards his enemy, still curled his lip. While those present expected that the wound, which had so lately flooded the apartment with gore, would send forth fresh streams at the touch of the homicide, Robin Oig replaced the covering, with the brief exclamation, "He was a pretty man!"

My story is nearly ended. The unfortunate Highlander stood his trial at Carlisle. I was myself present, and as a young Scottish lawyer, or barrister at least, and reputed a man of some quality, the politeness of the Sheriff of Cumberland offered me a place on the bench. The facts of the case were proved in the manner I have related them; and whatever might be at first the prejudice of the audience against a crime so un-English as that of assassination from revenge, yet when the rooted national prejudices of the prisoner had been explained, which made him consider himself as stained with indelible dishonor, when subjected to personal violence; when his previous patience, moderation, and endurance, were considered, the generosity of the English audience was inclined to regard his crime as the wayward aberration of a false idea of honor rather than as flowing from a heart naturally savage, or perverted by habitual vice. I shall never forget the charge of the venerable Judge to the jury, although not at that time liable to be much affected either by that which was eloquent or pathetic.

"We have had," he said, "in the previous part of our duty" (alluding to some former trials), "to discuss crimes which infer disgust and abhorrence, while they call down the well-merited vengeance of the law. It is now our still more melancholy task to apply its salutary though severe enactments to a case of a very singular character, in which the crime (for a crime it is, and a deep one) arose less out of the malevolence of the heart, than the error of the understanding—less from any idea of committing wrong, than from an unhappily perverted notion of that which is right. Here we have two men, highly esteemed, it has been stated, in their rank of life, and attached, it seems, to each other as friends, one of whose lives has been already sacrificed to a punctilio, and the other is about to prove the vengeance of the offended laws; and yet both may claim our commiseration at least, as men acting in ignorance of each other's national prejudices, and unhappily misguided rather than voluntarily erring from the path of right conduct.

"In the original cause of the misunderstanding, we must in justice give the right to the prisoner at the bar. He had acquired possession of the enclosure, which was the object of competition, by a legal contract with the proprietor, Mr. Ireby; and yet, when accosted with reproaches undeserved in themselves, and galling doubtless to a temper at least sufficiently susceptible of passion, he offered notwithstanding to yield up half his acquisition, for the sake of peace and good neighborhood, and his amicable proposal was rejected with scorn. Then follows the scene at Mr. Heskett the publican's, and you will observe how the stranger was treated by the deceased, and, I am sorry to observe, by those around, who seem to have urged him in a manner which was aggravating in the highest degree. While he asked for peace and for composition, and offered submission to a magistrate, or to a mutual arbiter, the prisoner was insulted by a whole company, who seem on this occasion to have forgotten the national maxim of 'fair play'; and while attempting to escape from the place in peace, he was intercepted, struck down, and beaten to the effusion of his blood.

"Gentlemen of the Jury, it was with some impatience that I heard my learned brother, who opened the case for the crown, give an unfavorable turn to the prisoner's conduct on this occasion. He said the prisoner was afraid to encounter his antagonist in fair fight, or to submit to the laws of the ring; and that, therefore, like a cowardly Italian, he had recourse to his fatal stiletto, to murder the man whom he dared not meet in manly encounter. I observed the prisoner shrink from this part of the accusation with the abhorrence natural to a brave man; and as I would wish to make my words impressive, when I point his real crime, I must secure his opinion of my impartiality, by rebutting everything that seems to me a false accusation. There can be no doubt that the prisoner is a man of resolution—too much resolution—I wish to Heaven that he had less, or rather that he had had a better education to regulate it.

"Gentlemen, as to the laws my brother talks of, they may be known in the Bull-ring, or the Bear-garden, or the Cockpit, but they are not known here. Or, if they should be so far admitted as furnishing a species of proof that no malice was intended in this sort of combat, from which fatal accidents do sometimes arise, it can only be so admitted when both parties are *in pari casu,* equally acquainted with, and equally willing to refer themselves to, that species of arbitrament. But will it be contended that a man of superior rank and education is to be subjected, or is obliged to subject himself, to this coarse and brutal strife, perhaps in opposition to a younger, stronger, or more skilful opponent? Certainly even the pugilistic code, if founded upon the fair play of Merry Old England, as my brother alleges it to be, can contain nothing so preposterous. And, gentlemen of the jury, if the laws would support an English gentleman, wearing, we will suppose, his sword, in defending himself by force against a violent personal aggression of the nature offered to this prisoner, they will not less protect a foreigner and a stranger, involved in the same unpleasing circumstances. If, therefore, gentlemen of the jury, when thus pressed by a *vis major,* the object of obloquy to a whole company, and of direct violence from one at least, and, as he might reasonably apprehend, from more, the panel had produced the weapon which his countrymen, as we are informed generally carry about their persons, and the same unhappy circumstances had ensued which you have heard detailed in evidence, I could not in my conscience have asked from you a verdict of murder. The prisoner's personal defence might, indeed, even in that case, have gone more or less beyond the *Moderamen inculpatæ tutelæ,* spoken of by lawyers, but the punishment incurred would have been that of manslaughter, not of murder. I beg leave to add, that I should have thought this milder species of charge was demanded in the case supposed, notwithstanding the statute of James I. cap. 8, which takes the case of slaughter by stabbing with a short weapon, even without malice prepense, out of the benefit of clergy. For this statute of stabbing, as it is termed, arose out of a temporary cause; and as the real guilt is the same, whether the slaughter be committed by the dagger, or by sword or pistol, the benignity of the modern law places them all on the same, or nearly the same footing.

"But, gentlemen of the jury, the pinch of the case lies in the interval of two hours interposed betwixt the reception of the injury and the fatal retaliation. In the heat of affray and *chaude mêlée,* law, compassionating the infirmities of humanity, makes allowance for the passions which rule such a stormy moment, . . . for the sense of present pain, for the apprehension of farther injury, for the difficulty of ascertaining with due accuracy the precise degree of violence which is necessary to protect the person of the individual, without annoying or injuring the assailant more than is absolutely requisite. But the time necessary to walk twelve miles, however speedily performed, was sufficient for the prisoner to have recollected himself; and the violence with which he carried his purpose into effect, with so many circumstances of deliberate determination, could neither be induced by the passion of anger, nor that of fear. It was the purpose and the act of predetermined revenge, for which law neither can, will, nor ought, to have sympathy or allowance.

"It is true, we may repeat to ourselves, in alleviation of this poor man's unhappy action, that his case is a very peculiar one. The country which he inhabits was, in the days of many now alive, inaccessible to the laws, not only of England, which have not even yet penetrated thither, but to those to which our neighbors of Scotland are subjected, and which must be supposed to be, and no doubt actually are, founded upon the general principles of justice and equity which pervade every civilized country. Amongst their mountains, as among the North American Indians, the various tribes were wont to make war upon each other, so that each man was obliged to go armed for his own protection. These men, from the ideas which they entertained of their own descent and of their own consequence, regarded themselves as so many cavaliers or men-at-arms, rather than as the peasantry of a peaceful country. Those laws of the ring, as my brother terms them, were unknown to the race of warlike mountaineers; that decision of quarrels by no other weapons than those which nature has given every man, must to them have seemed as vulgar and as preposterous as to the Noblesse of France. Revenge, on the other hand, must have been as familiar to their habits of society as to those of the Cherokees or Mohawks. It is indeed, as described by Bacon, at bottom, a kind of wild untutored justice; for the fear of retaliation must withhold the hands of the oppressor where there is no regular law to check daring violence. But though all this may be granted, and though we may allow that, such having been the case of the Highlands in the days of the prisoner's fathers, many of the opinions and sentiments must still continue to influence the present generation, it cannot, and ought not, even in this most painful case, to alter the administration of the law, either in your hands, gentlemen of the jury, or in mine. The first object of civilization is to place the general protection of the law, equally administered, in the room of that wild justice, which every man cut and carved for himself, according to the length of his sword and the strength of his arm. The law says to the subjects, with a voice only inferior to that of the Deity, 'Vengeance is mine.' The instant that there is time for passion to cool, and reason to interpose, an injured party must become aware, that the law assumes the exclusive cognizance of the right and wrong betwixt the parties, and opposes her inviolable buckler to every attempt of the private party to right himself. I repeat, that this unhappy man ought personally to be the object rather of our pity than our abhorrence, for he failed in his ignorance, and from mistaken notions of honor. But his crime is not the less that of murder, gentlemen, and in your high and important office, it is your duty so to find. Englishmen have their angry passions as well as Scots; and should this man's action remain unpunished you may unsheath, under various pretences, a thousand daggers betwixt the Land's-end and the Orkneys."

The venerable Judge thus ended what, to judge by his apparent emotion, and by the tears which filled his eyes, was really a painful task. The jury, according to his instructions, brought in a verdict of Guilty; and Robin Oig M'Combich, *alias* M'Gregor, was sentenced to death, and left for execution, which took place accordingly. He met his fate with great firmness, and acknowledged the justice of his sentence. But he repelled indignantly the observations of those who accused him of attacking an unarmed man. "I give a life for the life I took," he said, "and what can I do more?"

RIP VAN WINKLE

Washington Irving

(1783–1859)

THE FOLLOWING TALE was found among the papers of the late Diedrich Knickerbocker, an old gentleman of New York, who was very curious in the Dutch history of the province, and the manners of the descendants from its primitive settlers. His historical researches, however, did not lie so much among books as among men; for the former are lamentably scanty on his favorite topics, whereas he found the old burghers, and still more their wives, rich in that legendary lore so invaluable to true history. Whenever, therefore, he happened upon a genuine Dutch family, snugly shut up in its low-roofed farm-house, under a spreading sycamore, he looked upon it as a little clasped volume of black letter, and studied it with the zeal of a book-worm.

The result of all these researches was a history of the province during the reign of the Dutch governors, which he published some years since. There have been various opinions as to the literary character of his work, and, to tell the truth, it is not a whit better than it should be. Its chief merit is its scrupulous accuracy, which indeed was a little questioned on its first appearance, but has since been completely established; and it is now admitted into all historical collections as a book of unquestionable authority.

The old gentleman died shortly after the publication of his work, and now that he is dead and gone, it cannot do much harm to his memory to say, that his time might have been much better employed in weightier labors. He, however, was apt to ride his hobby his own way; and though it did now and then kick up the dust a little in the eyes of his neighbors, and grieve the spirit of some friends, for whom he felt the truest deference and affection; yet his errors and follies are remembered "more in sorrow than in anger," and it begins to be suspected that he never intended to injure or offend. But however his memory may be appreciated by critics, it is still held dear by many folk whose good opinion is well worth having, particularly by certain biscuit-bakers, who have gone so far as to imprint his likeness on their new-year cakes, and have thus given him a chance for immortality, almost equal to the being stamped on a Waterloo medal or a Queen Anne's farthing.

> By Woden, God of Saxons,
> From whence comes Wensday, that is Wodensday.
> Truth is a thing that ever I will keep
> Unto thylke day in which I creep into
> My sepulchre—
>
> CARTWRIGHT

WHOEVER has made a voyage up the Hudson must remember the Kaatskill mountains. They are a dismembered branch of the great Appalachian family, and are seen away to the west of the river, swelling up to a noble height, and lording it over the surrounding country. Every change of season, every change of weather, indeed, every hour of the day, produces some change in the magical hues and shapes of these mountains, and they are regarded by all the good wives, far and near, as perfect barometers. When the weather is fair and settled, they are clothed in blue and purple, and print their bold outlines on the clear evening sky; but sometimes, when the rest of the landscape is cloudless, they will gather a hood of gray vapors about their summits, which, in the last rays of the setting sun, will glow and light up like a crown of glory.

At the foot of these fairy mountains, the voyager may have descried the light smoke curling up from a village, whose shingle-roofs gleam among the trees, just where the blue tints of the upland melt away into the fresh green of the nearer landscape. It is a little village, of great antiquity, having been founded by some of the Dutch colonists, in the early times of the province, just about the beginning of the government of the good Peter Stuyvesant (may he rest in peace!) and there were some of the houses of the original settlers standing within a few years, built of small yellow bricks brought from Holland, having latticed windows and gable fronts, surmounted with weathercocks.

In that same village and in one of these very houses (which, to tell the precise truth, was sadly time-worn and weather-beaten), there lived many years since, while the country was yet a province of Great Britain, a simple good-natured fellow, of the name of Rip Van Winkle. He was a descendant of the Van Winkles who figured so gallantly in the chivalrous days of Peter Stuyvesant, and accompanied him to the siege of Fort Christina. He inherited, however, but little of the martial character of his ancestors. I have observed that he was a simple good-natured man; he was, moreover, a kind neighbor, and an obedient hen-pecked husband. Indeed, to the latter circumstance might be owing that meekness of spirit which gained him such universal popularity; for those men are most apt to be obsequious and conciliating abroad, who are under the discipline of shrews at home. Their tempers, doubtless, are rendered pliant and malleable in the fiery furnace of domestic tribulation, and a curtain lecture is worth all the sermons in the world for teaching the virtues of patience and long-suffering. A termagant wife may, therefore, in some respects, be considered a tolerable blessing; and if so, Rip Van Winkle was thrice blessed.

Certain it is that he was a great favorite among all the good wives of the village, who, as usual with the amiable sex, took his part in all family squabbles; and never failed, whenever they talked those matters over in their evening gossipings, to lay all the blame on Dame Van Winkle. The children of the village, too, would shout with joy whenever he approached. He assisted at their sports, made their playthings, taught them to fly kites and shoot marbles, and told them long stories of ghosts, witches, and Indians. Whenever he went dodging about the village, he was surrounded by a troop of them hanging on his skirts, clambering on his back, and playing a thousand tricks on him with impunity; and not a dog would bark at him throughout the neighborhood.

The great error in Rip's composition was an insuperable aversion to all kinds of profitable labor. It could not be from the want of assiduity or perseverance; for he would sit on a wet rock, with a rod as long and heavy as a Tartar's lance, and fish all day without a murmur, even though he should not be encouraged by a single nibble. He would carry a fowling-piece on his shoulder for hours together, trudging through woods and swamps, and up hill and down dale, to shoot a few squirrels or wild pigeons. He would never refuse to assist a neighbor even in the roughest toil, and was a foremost man at all country frolics for husking Indian corn, or building stone fences; the women of the village, too, used to employ him to run their errands, and to do such little odd jobs as their less obliging husbands would not do for them. In a word, Rip was ready to attend to anybody's business but his own; but as to doing family duty, and keeping his farm in order, he found it impossible.

In fact, he declared it was of no use to work on his farm; it was the most pestilent little piece of ground in the whole country; everything about it went wrong, and would go wrong, in spite of him. His fences were continually falling to pieces; his cow would either go astray, or get among the cabbages; weeds were sure to grow quicker in his fields than anywhere else; the rain always made a point of setting in just as he had some outdoor work to do; so that though his patrimonial estate had dwindled away under his management, acre by acre, until there was little more left than a mere patch of Indian corn and potatoes, yet it was the worst conditioned farm in the neighborhood.

His children, too, were as ragged and wild as if they belonged to nobody. His son Rip, an urchin begotten in his own likeness, promised to inherit the habits, with the old clothes, of his father. He was generally seen trooping like a colt at his mother's heels, equipped in a pair of his father's cast-off galligaskins which he had much ado to hold up with one hand, as a fine lady does her train in bad weather.

Rip Van Winkle, however, was one of those happy mortals, of foolish, well-oiled dispositions, who take the world easy, eat white bread or brown, whichever can be got with least thought or trouble, and would rather starve on a penny than work for a pound. If left to himself, he would have whistled life away in perfect contentment; but his wife kept continually dinning in his ears about his idleness, his carelessness, and the ruin he was bringing on his family. Morning, noon, and night, her tongue was incessantly going, and everything he said or did was sure to produce a torrent of household eloquence. Rip had but one way of replying to all lectures of the kind, and that, by frequent use, had grown into a habit. He shrugged his shoulders, shook his head, cast up his eyes, but said nothing. This, however, always provoked a fresh volley from his wife; so that he was fain to draw off his forces, and take to the outside of the house—the only side which, in truth, belongs to a hen-pecked husband.

Rip's sole domestic adherent was his dog Wolf, who was as much henpecked as his master; for Dame Van Winkle regarded them as companions in idleness, and even looked upon Wolf with an evil eye, as the cause of his master's going so often astray. True it is, in all points of spirit, befitting an honorable dog, he was as courageous an animal as ever scoured the woods —but what courage can withstand the ever-during and all-besetting terrors of a woman's tongue? The moment Wolf entered the house, his crest fell, his tail drooped to the ground, or curled between his legs, he sneaked about with a gallows air, casting many a side-long glance at Dame Van Winkle, and at the least flourish of a broomstick or ladle, he would fly to the door with yelping precipitation.

Times grew worse and worse with Rip Van Winkle as years of matrimony rolled on; a tart temper never mellows with age, and a sharp tongue is the only edged tool that grows keener with constant use. For a long while he used to console himself, when driven from home, by frequenting a kind of perpetual club of the sages, philosophers, and other idle personages of the village; which held its sessions on a bench before a small inn, designated by a rubicund portrait of His Majesty George the Third. Here they used to sit in the shade through a long lazy summer's day, talking listlessly over village gossip, or telling endless sleepy stories about nothing. But it would have been worth any statesman's money to have heard the profound discussions that sometimes took place, when by chance an old newspaper fell into their hands from some passing traveller. How solemnly they would listen to the contents, as drawled out by Derrick Van Bummel, the schoolmaster, a dapper learned little man, who was not to be daunted by the most gigantic word in the dictionary; and how sagely they would deliberate upon public events some months after they had taken place.

The opinions of this junto were completely controlled by Nicholas Vedder, a patriarch of the village, and landlord of the inn, at the door of which he took his seat from morning till night, just moving sufficiently to avoid the sun and keep in the shade of a large tree; so that the neighbors could tell the hour by his movements as accurately as by a sundial. It is true he was rarely heard to speak, but smoked his pipe incessantly. His adherents, however (for every great man has his adherents), perfectly understood him, and knew how to gather his opinions. When anything that was read or related displeased him, he was observed to smoke his pipe vehemently, and to send forth short, frequent, and angry puffs, but when pleased he would inhale the smoke slowly and tranquilly, and emit it in light and placid clouds; and sometimes, taking the pipe from his mouth, and letting the fragrant vapor curl about his nose, would gravely nod his head in token of perfect approbation.

From even this stronghold the unlucky Rip was at length routed by his termagant wife, who would suddenly break in upon the tranquillity of the assemblage and call the members all to naught; nor was that august personage, Nicholas Vedder himself, sacred from the daring tongue of this terrible virago, who charged him outright with encouraging her husband in habits of idleness.

Poor Rip was at last reduced almost to despair; and his only alternative, to escape from the labor of the farm and clamor of his wife, was to take gun in hand and stroll away into the woods. Here he would sometimes seat himself at the foot of a tree, and share the contents of his wallet with Wolf, with whom he sympathized as a fellow-sufferer in persecution. "Poor Wolf," he would say, "thy mistress leads thee a dog's life of it; but never mind, my lad, whilst I live thou shalt never want a friend to stand by thee!" Wolf would wag his tail, look wistfully in his master's face, and if dogs can feel pity, I verily believe he reciprocated the sentiment with all his heart.

In a long ramble of the kind on a fine autumnal day, Rip had unconsciously scrambled to one of the highest parts of the Kaatskill mountains. He was after his favorite sport of squirrel-shooting, and the still solitudes had echoed and re-echoed with the reports of his gun. Panting and fatigued, he threw himself, late in the afternoon, on a green knoll, covered with mountain herbage, that crowned the brow of a precipice. From an opening between the trees he could overlook all the lower country for many a mile of rich woodland. He saw at a distance the lordly Hudson, far, far below him, moving on its silent but majestic course, with the reflection of a purple cloud, or the sail of a lagging bark, here and there sleeping on its glassy bosom, and at last losing itself in the blue highlands.

On the other side he looked down into a deep mountain glen, wild, lonely, and shagged, the bottom filled with fragments from the impending cliffs, and scarcely lighted by the reflected rays of the setting sun. For some time Rip lay musing on this scene; evening was gradually advancing; the mountains began to throw their long blue shadows over the valleys; he saw that it would be dark long before he could reach the village, and he heaved a heavy sigh when he thought of encountering the terrors of Dame Van Winkle.

As he was about to descend, he heard a voice from a distance, hallooing, "Rip Van Winkle! Rip Van Winkle!" He looked round, but could see nothing but a crow winging its solitary flight across the mountain. He thought his fancy must have deceived him, and turned again to descend, when he heard the same cry ring through the still evening air: "Rip Van Winkle! Rip Van Winkle!"—at the same time Wolf bristled up his back, and, giving a loud growl, skulked to his master's side, looking fearfully down into the glen. Rip now felt a vague apprehension stealing over him; he looked anxiously in the same direction, and perceived a strange figure slowly toiling up the rocks, and bending under the weight of something he carried on his back. He was surprised to see any human being in this lonely and unfrequented place; but supposing it to be some one of the neighborhood in need of his assistance, he hastened down to yield it.

On nearer approach he was still more surprised at the singularity of the stranger's appearance. He was a short, square-built old fellow, with thick bushy hair and a grizzled beard. His dress was of the antique Dutch fashion —a cloth jerkin, strapped round the waist—several pair of breeches, the outer one of ample volume, decorated with rows of buttons down the sides, and bunches at the knees. He bore on his shoulder a stout keg, that seemed full of liquor, and made signs for Rip to approach and assist him with the load. Though rather shy and distrustful of this new acquaintance, Rip complied with his usual alacrity; and mutually relieving each other, they clambered up a narrow gully, apparently the dry bed of a mountain torrent. As they ascended, Rip every now and then heard long rolling peals, like distant thunder, that seemed to issue out of a deep ravine, or rather cleft, between lofty rocks, towards which their rugged path conducted. He paused for an instant, but supposing it to be the muttering of one of those transient thunder-showers which often take place in mountain heights, he proceeded. Passing through the ravine, they came to a hollow, like a small amphitheatre, surrounded by perpendicular precipices, over the brinks of which impending trees shot their branches, so that you only caught glimpses of the azure sky and the bright evening cloud. During the whole time Rip and his companion had labored on in silence, for though the former marvelled greatly what could be the object of carrying a keg of liquor up this wild mountain; yet there was something strange and incomprehensible about the unknown, that inspired awe and checked familiarity.

On entering the amphitheatre, new objects of wonder presented themselves. On a level spot in the center was a company of odd-looking personages playing at nine-pins. They were dressed in a quaint outlandish fashion; some wore short doublets, others jerkins, with long knives in their belts, and most of them had enormous breeches, of similar style with that of the guide's. Their visages, too, were peculiar; one had a large head, broad face, and small piggish eyes; the face of another seemed to consist entirely of nose, and was surmounted by a white sugar-loaf hat, set off with a little red cock's tail. They all had beards, of various shapes and colors. There was one who seemed to be the commander. He was a stout old gentleman, with a weather-beaten countenance; he wore a laced doublet, broad belt and hanger, high-crowned hat and feather, red stockings, and high-heeled shoes, with roses in them. The whole group reminded Rip of the figures in an old Flemish painting, in the parlor of Dominie Van Shaick, the village parson, and which had been brought over from Holland at the time of the settlement.

What seemed particularly odd to Rip was, that though these folks were evidently amusing themselves, yet they maintained the gravest faces, the most mysterious silence, and were, withal, the most melancholy party of pleasure he had ever witnessed. Nothing interrupted the stillness of the scene but the noise of the balls, which, whenever they were rolled, echoed along the mountains like rumbling peals of thunder.

As Rip and his companion approached them, they suddenly desisted from their play, and stared at him with such fixed, statue-like gaze, and such strange, uncouth, lack-luster countenances, that his heart turned within him, and his knees smote together. His companion now emptied the contents of the keg into large flagons, and made signs to him to wait upon the company.

He obeyed with fear and trembling; they quaffed the liquor in profound silence, and then returned to their game.

By degrees Rip's awe and apprehension subsided. He even ventured, when no eye was fixed upon him, to taste the beverage, which he found had much of the flavor of excellent Hollands. He was naturally a thirsty soul, and was soon tempted to repeat the draught. One taste provoked another; and he reiterated his visits to the flagon so often, that at length his senses were overpowered, his eyes swam in his head, his head gradually declined, and he fell into a deep sleep.

On waking, he found himself on the green knoll whence he had first seen the old man of the glen. He rubbed his eyes—it was a bright sunny morning. The birds were hopping and twittering among the bushes, and the eagle was wheeling aloft, and breasting the pure mountain breeze. "Surely," thought Rip, "I have not slept here all night." He recalled the occurrences before he fell asleep. The strange man with a keg of liquor—the mountain ravine—the wild retreat among the rocks—the woebegone party at nine-pins —the flagon—"Oh! that flagon! that wicked flagon!" thought Rip; "what excuse shall I make to Dame Van Winkle?"

He looked round for his gun, but in place of the clean well-oiled fowling-piece, he found an old firelock lying by him, the barrel incrusted with rust, the lock falling off, and the stock worm-eaten. He now suspected that the grave roysters of the mountain had put a trick upon him, and, having dosed him with liquor, had robbed him of his gun. Wolf, too, had disappeared, but he might have strayed away after a squirrel or partridge. He whistled after him, and shouted his name, but all in vain; the echoes repeated his whistle and shout, but no dog was to be seen.

He determined to revisit the scene of the last evening's gambol, and, if he met with any of the party, to demand his dog and gun. As he rose to walk he found himself stiff in the joints, and wanting in his usual activity. "These mountain beds do not agree with me," thought Rip; "and if this frolic should lay me up with a fit of the rheumatism, I shall have a blessed time with Dame Van Winkle." With some difficulty he got down into the glen: he found the gully up which he and his companion had ascended the preceding evening; but, to his astonishment, a mountain stream was now foaming down it—leaping from rock to rock, and filling the glen with babbling murmurs. He, however, made shift to scramble up its sides, working his toilsome way through thickets of birch, sassafras, and witch-hazel, and sometimes tripped up or entangled by the wild grape-vines that twisted their coils or tendrils from tree to tree, and spread a kind of network in his path.

At length he reached to where the ravine had opened through the cliffs to the amphitheatre; but no traces of such opening remained. The rocks presented a high impenetrable wall, over which the torrent came tumbling in a sheet of feathery foam, and fell into a broad, deep basin, black from the shadows of the surrounding forest. Here, then, poor Rip was brought to a stand. He again called and whistled after his dog; he was only answered by the cawing of a flock of idle crows, sporting high in air about a dry tree that overhung a sunny precipice; and who, secure in their elevation, seemed to look down and scoff at the poor man's perplexities. What was to be done?—the morning was passing away, and Rip felt famished for want of his breakfast. He grieved to give up his dog and his gun; he dreaded to meet his wife; but it would not do to starve among the mountains. He shook his head, shouldered the rusty firelock, and, with a heart full of trouble and anxiety, turned his steps homeward.

As he approached the village he met a number of people, but none whom he knew, which somewhat surprised him, for he had thought himself acquainted with everyone in the country round. Their dress, too, was of a different fashion from that to which he was accustomed. They all stared at him with equal marks of surprise, and, whenever they cast their eyes upon him, invariably stroked their chins. The constant recurrence of this gesture induced Rip, involuntarily, to do the same—when, to his astonishment, he found his beard had grown a foot long!

He had now entered the skirts of the village. A troop of strange children ran at his heels, hooting after him, and pointing at his gray beard. The dogs, too, not one of which he recognized for an old acquaintance, barked at him as he passed. The very village was altered; it was larger and more populous. There were rows of houses which he had never seen before, and those which had been his familiar haunts had disappeared. Strange names were over the doors—strange faces at the windows—everything was strange. His mind now misgave him; he began to doubt whether both he and the world around him were not bewitched. Surely this was his native village, which he had left but the day before. There stood the Kaatskill mountains —there ran the silver Hudson at a distance—there was every hill and dale precisely as it had always been. Rip was sorely perplexed. "That flagon last night," thought he, "has addled my poor head sadly!"

It was with some difficulty that he found the way to his own house, which he approached with silent awe, expecting every moment to hear the shrill voice of Dame Van Winkle. He found the house gone to decay—the roof fallen in, the windows shattered, and the doors off the hinges. A half-starved dog that looked like Wolf, was skulking about it. Rip called him by name, but the cur snarled, showed his teeth, and passed on. This was an unkind cut indeed—"My very dog," sighed poor Rip, "has forgotten me!"

He entered the house, which, to tell the truth, Dame Van Winkle had always kept in neat order. It was empty, forlorn, and apparently abandoned. The desolateness overcame all his connubial fears—he called loudly for his wife and children—the lonely chambers rang for a moment with his voice, and then all again was silence.

He now hurried forth, and hastened to his old resort, the village inn—but it too was gone. A large, rickety, wooden building stood in its place, with great gaping windows, some of them broken and mended with old hats and petticoats, and over the door was painted, "The Union Hotel, by Jonathan Doolittle." Instead of the great tree that used to shelter the quiet little Dutch inn of yore, there was now reared a tall naked pole, with something on the top that loked like a red nightcap, and from it was fluttering a flag, on which was a singular assemblage of stars and stripes—all this was strange and incomprehensible. He recognized on the sign, however, the ruby face of King George, under which he had smoked so many a peaceful pipe; but even this was singularly metamorphosed. The red coat was changed for one of blue and buff, a sword was held in the hand instead of a scepter, the head was decorated with a cocked hat, and underneath was painted in large characters, GENERAL WASHINGTON.

There was, as usual, a crowd of folks about the door, but none that Rip recollected. The very character of the people seemed changed. There was a busy, bustling, disputatious tone about it, instead of the accustomed phlegm and drowsy tranquillity. He looked in vain for the sage Nicholas Vedder, with his broad face, double chin, and fair long pipe, uttering clouds of tobacco-smoke instead of idle speeches; or Van Bummel, the schoolmaster, doling forth the contents of an ancient newspaper. In place of these, a lean, bilious-looking fellow, with his pockets full of handbills, was haranguing vehemently about rights of citizens—elections—members of Congress—liberty—Bunker's Hill—heroes of seventy-six—and other words, which were a perfect Babylonish jargon to the bewildered Van Winkle.

The appearance of Rip, with his long grizzled beard, his rusty fowling-piece, his uncouth dress, and an army of women and children at his heels, soon attracted the attention of the tavern politicians. They crowded round him, eyeing him from head to foot with great curiosity. The orator bustled up to him, and, drawing him partly aside, inquired "on which side he voted?" Rip stared in vacant stupidity. Another short but busy little fellow pulled him by the arm, and, rising on tiptoe, inquired in his ear, "Whether he was Federal or Democrat?" Rip was equally at a loss to comprehend the question; when a knowing, self-important old gentleman, in a sharp cocked hat, made his way through the crowd, putting them to the right and left with his elbows as he passed, and planting himself before Van Winkle, with one arm akimbo, the other resting on his cane, his keen eyes and sharp hat penetrating, as it were, into his very soul, demanded in an austere tone, "What brought him to the election with a gun on his shoulder, and a mob at his heels, and whether he meant to breed a riot in the village?"—"Alas! gentlemen," cried Rip, somewhat dismayed, "I am a poor quiet man, a native of the place, and a loyal subject of the king, God bless him!"

Here a general shout burst from the bystanders—"A tory! a tory! a spy! a refugee! hustle him! away with him!" It was with great difficulty that the self-important man in the cocked hat restored order; and, having assumed a tenfold austerity of brow, demanded again of the unknown culprit, what he came there for, and whom he was seeking? The poor man humbly assured him that he meant no harm, but merely came there in search of some of his neighbors, who used to keep about the tavern.

"Well—who are they?—name them."

Rip bethought himself a moment, and inquired, "Where's Nicholas Vedder?"

There was a silence for a little while, when an old man replied in a thin piping voice, "Nicholas Vedder why, he is dead and gone these eighteen years! There was a wooden tombstone in the churchyard that used to tell all about him, but that's rotten and gone too."

"Where's Brom Dutcher?"

"Oh, he went off to the army in the beginning of the war; some say he was killed at the storming of Stony Point—others say he was drowned in a squall at the foot of Antony's Nose. I don't know—he never came back again."

"Where's Van Bummel, the schoolmaster?"

"He went off to the wars too, was a great militia general, and is now in Congress."

Rip's heart died away at hearing of these sad changes in his home and friends, and finding himself thus alone in the world. Every answer puzzled him too, by treating of such enormous lapses of time, and of matters which he could not understand; war—Congress—Stony Point—he had no courage to ask after any more friends, but cried out in despair, "Does nobody here know Rip Van Winkle?"

"Oh, Rip Van Winkle!" exclaimed two or three. "Oh, to be sure! that's Rip Van Winkle yonder, leaning against the tree."

Rip looked, and beheld a precise counterpart of himself, as he went up the mountain: apparently as lazy, and certainly as ragged. The poor fellow was now completely confounded. He doubted his own identity, and whether he was himself or another man. In the midst of his bewilderment, the man in the cocked hat demanded who he was, and what was his name?

"God knows," exclaimed he, at his wit's end; "I'm not myself—I'm somebody else—that's me yonder—no—that's somebody else got into my shoes—I was myself last night, but I fell asleep on the mountain, and they've changed my gun, and everything's changed, and I'm changed, and I can't tell what's my name, or who I am!"

The bystanders began now to look at each other, nod, wink significantly, and tap their fingers against their foreheads. There was a whisper, also, about securing the gun, and keeping the old fellow from doing mischief, at the very suggestion of which the self-important man in the cocked hat retired with some precipitation. At this critical moment a fresh comely woman pressed through the throng to get a peep at the gray-bearded man. She had a chubby child in her arms, which, frightened at his looks, began to cry.

"Hush, Rip," cried she, "hush, you little fool; the old man won't hurt you." The name of the child, the air of the mother, the tone of her voice, all awakened a train of recollections in his mind.

"What is your name, my good woman?" asked he.

"Judith Gardenier."

"And your father's name?"

"Ah, poor man, Rip Van Winkle was his name, but it's twenty years since he went away from home with his gun, and never has been heard of since—his dog came home without him; but whether he shot himself, or was carried away by the Indians, nobody can tell. I was then but a little girl."

Rip had but one question more to ask; but he put it with a faltering voice,—

"Where's your mother?"

"Oh, she too had died but a short time since; she broke a blood-vessel in a fit of passion at a New-England pedlar."

There was a drop of comfort, at least, in this intelligence. The honest man could contain himself no longer. He caught his daughter and her child in his arms. "I am your father!" cried he—"Young Rip Van Winkle once—old Rip Van Winkle now!—Does nobody know poor Rip Van Winkle?"

All stood amazed, until an old woman, tottering out from among the crowd, put her hand to her brow, and peering under it in his face for a moment, exclaimed, "Sure enough! it is Rip Van Winkle—it is himself! Welcome home again, old neighbor—Why, where have you been these twenty long years?"

Rip's story was soon told, for the whole twenty years had been to him but as one night. The neighbors stared when they heard it; some were seen to wink at each other, and put their tongues in their cheeks: and the self-important man in the cocked hat, who, when the alarm was over, had returned to the field, screwed down the corners of his mouth, and shook his head—upon which there was a general shaking of the head throughout the assemblage.

It was determined, however, to take the opinion of old Peter Vanderdonk, who was seen slowly advancing up the road. He was a descendant of the historian of that name, who wrote one of the earliest accounts of the province. Peter was the most ancient inhabitant of the village, and well versed in all the wonderful events and traditions of the neighborhood. He recollected Rip at once, and corroborated his story in the most satisfactory manner. He assured the company that it was a fact, handed down from his ancestor the historian, that the Kaatskill mountains had always been haunted by strange beings. That it was affirmed that the great Hendrik Hudson, the first discoverer of the river and country, kept a kind of vigil there every twenty years, with his crew of the *Halfmoon;* being permitted in this way to revisit the scenes of his enterprise, and keep a guardian eye upon the river, and the great city called by his name. That his father had once seen them in their old Dutch dresses playing at nine-pins in a hollow of the mountain; and that he himself had heard, one summer afternoon, the sound of their balls, like distant peals of thunder.

To make a long story short, the company broke up, and returned to the more important concerns of the election. Rip's daughter took him home to live with her; she had a snug, well-furnished house, and a stout cheery farmer for her husband, whom Rip recollected for one of the urchins that used to climb upon his back. As to Rip's son and heir, who was the ditto of himself, seen leaning against the tree, he was employed to work on the farm; but evinced an hereditary disposition to attend to anything else but his business.

Rip now resumed his old walks and habits; he soon found many of his former cronies, though all rather the worse for the wear and tear of time; and preferred making friends among the rising generation, with whom he soon grew into great favor.

Having nothing to do at home, and being arrived at that happy age when a man can be idle with impunity, he took his place once more on the bench at the inn door, and was reverenced as one of the patriarchs of the village, and a chronicle of the old times "before the war." It was some time before he could get into the regular track of gossip, or could be made to comprehend the strange events that had taken place during his torpor. How that there had been a revolutionary war—that the country had thrown off the yoke of Old England—and that, instead of being a subject of His Majesty George the Third, he was now a free citizen of the United States. Rip, in fact, was no politician; the changes of states and empires made but little impression on him; but there was one species of despotism under which he had long groaned, and that was—petticoat government. Happily that was at an end; he had got his neck out of the yoke of matrimony, and could go in and out whenever he pleased without dreading the tyranny of Dame Van Winkle. Whenever her name was mentioned, however, he shook his head, shrugged his shoulders, and cast up his eyes; which might pass either for an expression of resignation to his fate, or joy at his deliverance.

He used to tell his story to every stranger that arrived at Mr. Doolittle's hotel. He was observed at first to vary on some points every time he told it, which was, doubtless, owing to his having so recently awaked. It at last settled down precisely to the tale I have related, and not a man, woman, or child in the neighborhood but knew it by heart. Some always pretended to doubt the reality of it, and insisted that Rip had been out of his head, and that this was one point on which he always remained flighty. The old Dutch inhabitants, however, almost universally gave it full credit. Even to this day they never hear a thunder-storm of a summer afternoon about the Kaatskill, but they say Hendrick Hudson and his crew are at their game of nine-pins; and it is a common wish of all hen-pecked husbands in the neighborhood, when life hangs heavy on their hands, that they might have a quieting draught out of Rip Van Winkle's flagon.

NOTE: The foregoing tale, one would suspect, had been suggested to Mr. Knicker-bocker by a little German superstition about the Emperor Frederick *der Roth-bart,* and the Kypphaüser mountain; the subjoined note, however, which he had appended to the tale, shows that it is an absolute fact, narrated with his usual fidelity:—

The story of Rip Van Winkle may seem incredible to many, but nevertheless I give it my full belief, for I know the vicinity of our old Dutch settlements to have been very subject to marvellous events and appearances. Indeed, I have heard many stranger stories than this in the villages along the Hudson, all of which were too well authenticated to admit of a doubt. I have even talked with Rip Van Winkle myself, who, when I last saw him, was a very venerable old man, and so perfectly rational and consistent on every other point, that I think no conscientious person could refuse to take this into the bargain; nay, I have seen a certificate on the subject, taken before a country justice, and signed with a cross, in the justice's own handwriting. The story, therefore, is beyond the possibility of doubt.

D. K.

POSTSCRIPT

THE FOLLOWING ARE TRAVELING NOTES FROM A MEMORANDUM-BOOK OF MR. KNICKERBOCKER

THE KAATSBERG, or Catskill Mountains, have always been a region full of fable. The Indians considered them the abode of spirits, who influenced the weather, spreading sunshine or clouds over the landscape, and sending good or bad hunting seasons. They were ruled by an old squaw spirit, said to be their mother. She dwelt on the highest peak of the Catskills, and had charge of the doors of day and night, to open and shut them at the proper hour. She hung up the new moons in the skies, and cut up the old ones into stars. In times of drought, if properly propitiated, she would spin light summer clouds out of cobwebs and morning dew, and send them off from the crest of the mountain, flake after flake, like flakes of carded cotton, to float in the air, until, dissolved by the heat of the sun, they would fall in gentle showers, causing the grass to spring, the fruits to ripen, and the corn to grow an inch an hour. If displeased, however, she would brew up clouds black as ink, sitting in the midst of them like a bottle-bellied spider in the midst of its web; and when these clouds broke, woe betide the valleys!

In old times, say the Indian traditions, there was a kind of Manitou or Spirit, who kept about the wildest recesses of the Catskill Mountains, and took a mischievous pleasure in wreaking all kinds of evils and vexations upon the red men. Sometimes he would assume the form of a bear, a panther, or a deer, lead the bewildered hunter a weary chase through tangled forests and among ragged rocks, and then spring off with a loud ho! ho! leaving him aghast on the brink of a beetling precipice or raging torrent.

The favorite abode of this Manitou is still shown. It is a great rock or cliff on the loneliest part of the mountains, and, from the flowering vines which clamber about it, and the wild flowers which abound in its neighborhood, is known by the name of the Garden Rock. Near the foot of it is a small lake, the haunt of the solitary bittern, with water-snakes basking in the sun on the leaves of the pond-lilies which lie on the surface. This place was held in great awe by the Indians, insomuch that the boldest hunter would not pursue his game within its precincts. Once upon a time, however, a hunter who had lost his way penetrated to the Garden Rock, where he beheld a number of gourds placed in the crotches of trees. One of these he seized and made off with, but in the hurry of his retreat he let it fall among the rocks, when a great stream gushed forth, which washed him away and swept him down precipices, where he was dashed to pieces, and the stream made its way to the Hudson, and continues to flow to the present-day, being the identical stream known by the name of the Kaaters-kill.

THE STOUT GENTLEMAN

A STAGE-COACH ROMANCE

Washington Irving

(1783–1859)

I'll cross it though it blast me!

HAMLET

IT WAS A RAINY SUNDAY in the gloomy month of November. I had been detained, in the course of a journey, by a slight indisposition, from which I was recovering; but was still feverish, and obliged to keep within doors all day, in an inn of the small town of Derby. A wet Sunday in a country inn!—whoever has had the luck to experience one can alone judge of my situation. The rain pattered against the casements; the bells tolled for church with a melancholy sound. I went to the windows in quest of something to amuse the eye; but it seemed as if I had been placed completely out of the reach of all amusement. The windows of my bedroom looked out among tiled roofs and stacks of chimneys, while those of my sitting-room commanded a full view of the stable-yard. I know of nothing more calculated to make a man sick of this world than a stable-yard on a rainy day. The place was littered with wet straw that had been kicked about by

travellers and stable-boys. In one corner was a stagnant pool of water, surrounding an island of muck; there were several half-drowned fowls crowded
together under a cart, among which was a miserable, crest-fallen cock,
drenched out of all life and spirit, his drooping tail matted, as it were, into
a single feather, along which the water trickled from his back; near the cart
was a half-dozing cow, chewing the cud, and standing patiently to be rained
on, with wreaths of vapor rising from her reeking hide; a wall-eyed horse,
tired of the loneliness of the stable, was poking his spectral head out of a
window, with the rain dripping on it from the eaves; an unhappy cur,
chained to a doghouse hard by, uttered something, every now and then,
between a bark and a yelp; a drab of a kitchen-wench tramped backward
and forward through the yard in pattens, looking as sulky as the weather
itself; everything, in short, was comfortless and forlorn, excepting a crew of
hardened ducks, assembled like boon companions round a puddle, and
making a riotous noise over their liquor.

I was lonely and listless, and wanted amusement. My room soon become
insupportable, I abandoned it, and sought what is technically called the
travellers' room. This is a public room set apart at most inns for the accommodation of a class of wayfarers called travellers, or riders; a kind of
commercial knights-errant, who are incessantly scouring the kingdom in
gigs, on horseback, or by coach. They are the only successors that I know
of at the present day to the knights-errant of yore. They lead the same kind
of roving, adventurous life, only changing the lance for a driving-whip, the
buckler for a pattern-card, and the coat of mail for an upper Benjamin.
Instead of vindicating the charms of peerless beauty, they rove about,
spreading the fame and standing of some substantial tradesman, or manufacturer, and are ready at any time to bargain in his name; it being the
fashion nowadays to trade, instead of fight, with one another. As the room
of the hostel, in the good old fighting-times, would be hung round at night
with the armor of wayworn warriors, such as coats of mail, falchions, and
yawning helmets, so the travellers' room is garnished with the harnessing of
their successors, with box-coats, whips of all kinds, spurs, gaiters, and oil-
cloth covered hats.

I was in hopes of finding some of these worthies to talk with, but was
disappointed. There were, indeed, two or three in the room; but I could
make nothing of them. One was just finishing his breakfast, quarrelling with
his bread and butter, and huffing the waiter; another buttoned on a pair
of gaiters, with many execrations at Boots for not having cleaned his shoes
well; a third sat drumming on the table with his fingers and looking at the
rain as it streamed down the window-glass; they all appeared infected by
the weather, and disappeared, one after the other, without exchanging a
word.

I sauntered to the window, and stood gazing at the people, picking their
way to church, with petticoats hoisted midleg high, and dripping umbrellas.

The bell ceased to toll, and the streets became silent. I then amused myself with watching the daughters of a tradesman opposite; who, being confined to the house for fear of wetting their Sunday finery, played off their charms at the front windows, to fascinate the chance tenants of the inn. They at length were summoned away by a vigilant, vinegar-faced mother, and I had nothing further from without to amuse me.

What was I to do to pass away the long-lived day? I was sadly nervous and lonely; and everything about an inn seems calculated to make a dull day ten times duller. Old newspapers, smelling of beer and tobacco-smoke, and which I had already read half a dozen times. Good-for-nothing books, that were worse than rainy weather. I bored myself to death with an old volume of the *Lady's Magazine*. I read all the commonplace names of ambitious travellers scrawled on the panes of glass; the eternal families of the Smiths, and the Browns, and the Jacksons, and the Johnsons, and all the other sons; and I deciphered several scraps of fatiguing inn-window poetry which I have met with in all parts of the world.

The day continued lowering and gloomy; the slovenly, ragged, spongy cloud drifted heavily along; there was no variety even in the rain: it was one dull, continued, monotonous patter—patter—patter, excepting that now and then I was enlivened by the idea of a brisk shower, from the rattling of the drops upon a passing umbrella.

It was quite *refreshing* (if I may be allowed a hackneyed phrase of the day) when, in the course of the morning, a horn blew, and a stage-coach whirled through the street, with outside passengers stuck all over it, cowering under cotton umbrellas, and seethed together, and reeking with the steams of wet box-coats and upper Benjamins.

The sound brought out from their lurking-places a crew of vagabond boys, and vagabond dogs, and the carroty-headed hostler, and that nondescript animal ycleped Boots, and all the other vagabond race that infest the purlieus of an inn; but the bustle was transient; the coach again whirled on its way; and boy and dog, and hostler and Boots, all slunk back again to their holes; the street again became silent, and the rain continued to rain on. In fact, there was no hope of its clearing up; the barometer pointed to rainy weather; mine hostess's tortoise-shell cat sat by the fire washing her face, and rubbing her paws over her ears; and, on referring to the Almanac, I found a direful prediction stretching from the top of the page to the bottom through the whole month, "expect—much—rain—about—this—time!"

I was dreadfully hipped. The hours seemed as if they would never creep by. The very ticking of the clock became irksome. At length the stillness of the house was interrupted by the ringing of a bell. Shortly after I heard the voice of a waiter at the bar: "The stout gentleman in No. 13 wants his breakfast. Tea and bread and butter, with ham and eggs; the eggs not to be too much done."

In such a situation as mine, every incident is of importance. Here was a subject of speculation presented to my mind, and ample exercise for my imagination. I am prone to paint pictures to myself, and on this occasion I had some materials to work upon. Had the guest upstairs been mentioned as Mr. Smith, or Mr. Brown, or Mr. Jackson, or Mr. Johnson, or merely as "the gentleman in No. 13," it would have been a perfect blank to me. I should have thought nothing of it; but "The stout gentleman!"—the very name had something in it of the picturesque. It at once gave the size; it embodied the personage to my mind's eye, and my fancy did the rest.

He was stout, or, as some term it, lusty; in all probability, therefore, he was advanced in life, some people expanding as they grow old. By his breakfasting rather late, and in his own room, he must be a man accustomed to live at his ease, and above the necessity of early rising; no doubt, a round, rosy, lusty old gentleman.

There was another violent ringing. The stout gentleman was impatient for his breakfast. He was evidently a man of importance; "well to do in the world"; accustomed to be promptly waited upon; of a keen appetite, and a little cross when hungry; "perhaps," thought I, "he may be some London Alderman; or who knows but he may be a Member of Parliament?"

The breakfast was sent up, and there was a short interval of silence; he was, doubtless, making the tea. Presently there was a violent ringing; and before it could be answered, another ringing still more violent. "Bless me! what a choleric old gentleman!" The waiter came down in a huff. The butter was rancid, the eggs were overdone, the ham was too salt; the stout gentleman was evidently nice in his eating; one of those who eat and growl, and keep the waiter on the trot, and live in a state militant with the household.

The hostess got into a fume. I should observe that she was a brisk, coquettish woman; a little of a shrew, and something of a slammerkin, but very pretty withal; with a nincompoop for a husband, as shrews are apt to have. She rated the servants roundly for their negligence in sending up so bad a breakfast, but said not a word against the stout gentleman; by which I clearly perceived that he must be a man of consequence, entitled to make a noise and to give trouble at a country inn. Other eggs, and ham, and bread and butter were sent up. They appeared to be more graciously received; at least there was no further complaint.

I had not made many turns about the travellers' room, when there was another ringing. Shortly afterward there was a stir and an inquest about the house. The stout gentleman wanted the *Times* or the *Chronicle* newspaper. I set him down, therefore, for a Whig; or, rather, from his being so absolute and lordly where he had a chance, I suspected him of being a Radical. Hunt, I had heard, was a large man; "who knows," thought I, "but it is Hunt himself!"

My curiosity began to be awakened. I inquired of the waiter who was this stout gentleman that was making all this stir; but I could get no information: nobody seemed to know his name. The landlords of bustling inns seldom trouble their heads about the names or occupations of their transient guests. The color of a coat, the shape or size of the person, is enough to suggest a travelling name. It is either the tall gentleman, or the short gentleman, or the gentleman in black, or the gentleman in snuff-color; or, as in the present instance, the stout gentleman. A designation of the kind once hit on, answers every purpose, and saves all further inquiry.

Rain—rain—rain! pitiless, ceaseless rain! No such thing as putting a foot out of doors, and no occupation nor amusement within. By and by I heard someone walking overhead. It was in the stout gentleman's room. He evidently was a large man by the heaviness of his tread; and an old man from his wearing such creaking soles. "He is doubtless," thought I, "some rich old square-toes of regular habits, and is now taking exercise after breakfast."

I now read all the advertisements of coaches and hotels that were stuck about the mantelpiece. The *Lady's Magazine* had become an abomination to me; it was as tedious as the day itself. I wandered out, not knowing what to do, and ascended again to my room. I had not been there long, when there was a squall from a neighboring bedroom. A door opened and slammed violently; a chambermaid, that I had remarked for having a ruddy, good-humored face, went downstairs in a violent flurry. The stout gentleman had been rude to her!

This sent a whole host of my deductions to the deuce in a moment. This unknown personage could not be an old gentleman; for old gentlemen are not apt to be so obstreperous to chambermaids. He could not be a young gentleman; for young gentlemen are not apt to inspire such indignation. He must be a middle-aged man, and confounded ugly into the bargain, or the girl would not have taken the matter in such terrible dudgeon. I confess I was sorely puzzled.

In a few minutes I heard the voice of my landlady. I caught a glance of her as she came tramping upstairs—her face glowing, her cap flaring, her tongue wagging the whole way. "She'd have no such doings in her house, she'd warrant. If gentlemen did spend money freely, it was no rule. She'd have no servant-maids of hers treated in that way, when they were about their work, that's what she wouldn't."

As I hate squabbles, particularly with women, and above all with pretty women, I slunk back into my room, and partly closed the door; but my curiosity was too much excited not to listen. The landlady marched intrepidly to the enemy's citadel, and entered it with a storm: the door closed after her. I heard her voice in high windy clamor for a moment or two. Then it gradually subsided, like a gust of wind in a garret; then there was a laugh; then I heard nothing more.

After a little while my landlady came out with an odd smile on her face.

adjusting her cap, which was a little on one side. As she went downstairs, I heard the landlord ask her what was the matter; she said, "Nothing at all, only the girl's a fool." I was more than ever perplexed what to make of this unaccountable personage, who could put a good-natured chambermaid in a passion, and send away a termagant landlady in smiles. He could not be so old, nor cross, nor ugly either.

I had to go to work at his picture again, and to paint him entirely different. I now set him down for one of those stout gentlemen that are frequently met with swaggering about the doors of country inns. Moist, merry fellows, in Belcher handkerchiefs, whose bulk is a little assisted by malt-liquors. Men who have seen the world, and been sworn at Highgate; who are used to tavern-life; up to all the tricks of tapsters, and knowing in the ways of sinful publicans. Free-livers on a small scale; who are prodigal within the compass of a guinea; who call all the waiters by name, tousle the maids, gossip with the landlady at the bar, and prose over a pint of port, or a glass of negus, after dinner.

The morning wore away in forming these and similar surmises. As fast as I wove one system of belief, some movement of the unknown would completely overturn it, and throw all my thoughts again into confusion. Such are the solitary operations of a feverish mind. I was, as I have said, extremely nervous; and the continual meditation in the concerns of this invisible personage began to have its effect—I was getting a fit of the fidgets.

Dinner-time came. I hoped the stout gentleman might dine in the travellers' room, and that I might at length get a view of his person; but no—he had dinner served in his own room. What could be the meaning of this solitude and mystery? He could not be a radical; there was something too aristocratical in thus keeping himself apart from the rest of the world, and condemning himself to his own dull company throughout a rainy day. And then, too, he lived too well for a discontented politician. He seemed to expatiate on a variety of dishes, and to sit over his wine like a jolly friend of good living. Indeed, my doubts on this head were soon at an end; for he could not have finished his first bottle before I could faintly hear him humming a tune; and on listening I found it to be "God Save the King." 'Twas plain, then, he was no radical, but a faithful subject; one who grew loyal over his bottle, and was ready to stand by king and constitution, when he could stand by nothing else. But who could he be? My conjectures began to run wild. Was he not some personage of distinction travelling incog.? "God knows!" said I, at my wit's end; "it may be one of the royal family for aught I know, for they are all stout gentlemen!"

The weather continued rainy. The mysterious unknown kept his room, and, as far as I could judge, his chair, for I did not hear him move. In the meantime, as the day advanced, the travellers' room began to be frequented. Some, who had just arrived, came in buttoned up in box-coats; others came home who had been dispersed about the town; some took their dinners, and some their tea. Had I been in a different mood, I should have found entertainment in studying this peculiar class of men. There were two especially who were regular wags of the road, and up to all the standing jokes of travellers. They had a thousand sly things to say to the waiting-maid, whom they called Louisa, and Ethelinda, and a dozen other fine names, changing the name every time, and chuckling amazingly at their own waggery. My mind, however, had been completely engrossed by the stout gentleman. He had kept my fancy in chase during a long day, and it was not now to be diverted from the scent.

The evening gradually wore away. The travellers read the papers two or three times over. Some drew round the fire and told long stories about their horses, about their adventures, their overturns, and breaking-down. They discussed the credit of different merchants and different inns; and the two wags told several choice anecdotes of pretty chambermaids and kind landladies. All this passed as they were quietly taking what they called their night-caps, that is to say, strong glasses of brandy and water and sugar, or some other mixture of the kind; after which they one after another rang for "Boots" and the chambermaid, and walked off to bed in old shoes cut down into marvellously uncomfortable slippers.

There was now only one man left: a short-legged, long-bodied, plethoric fellow, with a very large, sandy head. He sat by himself, with a glass of port-wine negus, and a spoon; sipping and stirring, and meditating and sipping, until nothing was left but the spoon. He gradually fell asleep bolt upright in his chair, with the empty glass standing before him; and the candle seemed to fall asleep, too, for the wick grew long, and black, and cabbaged at the end, and dimmed the little light that remained in the chamber. The gloom that now prevailed was contagious. Around hung the shapeless, and almost spectral, box-coats of departed travellers, long since buried in deep sleep. I only heard the ticking of the clock, with the deep-drawn breathings of the sleeping topers, and the drippings of the rain, drop —drop—drop, from the eaves of the house. The church-bells chimed mid-night. All at once the stout gentleman began to walk overhead, pacing slowly backward and forward. There was something extremely awful in all this, especially to one in my state of nerves. These ghastly great-coats, these guttural breathings, and the creaking footsteps of this mysterious being. His steps grew fainter and fainter, and at length died away. I could bear it no longer. I was wound up to the desperation of a hero of romance. "Be he who or what he may," said I to myself, "I'll have a sight of him!" I seized a chamber-candle, and hurried up to No. 13. The door stood ajar. I hesitated —I entered: the room was deserted. There stood a large, broad-bottomed elbow-chair at a table, on which was an empty tumbler, and a *Times* news-paper, and the room smelt powerfully of Stilton cheese.

The mysterious stranger had evidently but just retired. I turned off, sorely disappointed, to my room, which had been changed to the front of the house. As I went along the corridor, I saw a large pair of boots, with dirty, waxed tops, standing at the door of a bedchamber. They doubtless belonged to the unknown: but it would not do to disturb so redoubtable a personage in his den: he might discharge a pistol, or something worse, at my head. I went to bed, therefore, and lay awake half the night in a terribly nervous state; and even when I fell asleep, I was still haunted in my dreams by the idea of the stout gentleman and his wax-topped boots.

I slept rather late the next morning, and was awakened by some stir and bustle in the house, which I could not at first comprehend; until getting more awake, I found there was a mail-coach starting from the door. Suddenly there was a cry from below, "The gentleman has forgotten his umbrella! Look for the gentleman's umbrella in No. 13!" I heard an immediate scampering of a chambermaid along the passage, and a shrill reply as she ran, "Here it is! here's the gentleman's umbrella!"

The mysterious stranger then was on the point of setting off. This was the only chance I should ever have of knowing him. I sprang out of bed, scrambled to the window, snatched aside the curtains, and just caught a glimpse of the rear of a person getting in at the coach-door. The skirts of a brown coat parted behind, and gave me a full view of the broad disk of a pair of drab breeches. The door closed—"all right!" was the word—the coach whirled off; and that was all I ever saw of the stout gentleman!

LA GRANDE BRETÊCHE

Honoré de Balzac

(1799–1850)

TRANSLATED BY CLARA BELL

"Ah! MADAME," replied the doctor, "I have some appalling stories in my collection. But each one has its proper hour in a conversation—you know the pretty jest recorded by Chamfort, and said to the Duc de Fronsac: 'Between your sally and the present moment lie ten bottles of champagne.'"

"But it is two in the morning, and the story of Rosina has prepared us," said the mistress of the house.

"Tell us, Monsieur Bianchon!" was the cry on every side.

The obliging doctor bowed, and silence reigned.

"At about a hundred paces from Vendôme, on the banks of the Loire," said he, "stands an old brown house, crowned with very high roofs, and so

completely isolated that there is nothing near it, not even a fetid tannery or
a squalid tavern, such as are commonly seen outside small towns. In front
of this house is a garden down to the river, where the box shrubs, formerly
clipped close to edge the walks, now straggle at their own will. A few
willows, rooted in the stream, have grown up quickly like an enclosing
fence, and half hide the house. The wild plants we call weeds have clothed
the bank with their beautiful luxuriance. The fruit-trees, neglected for these
ten years past, no longer bear a crop, and their suckers have formed a
thicket. The espaliers are like a copse. The paths, once gravelled, are overgrown with purslane; but, to be accurate, there is no trace of a path.

"Looking down from the hill-top, to which cling the ruins of the old
castle of the Dukes of Vendôme, the only spot whence the eye can see into
this enclosure, we think that at a time, difficult now to determine, this spot
of earth must have been the joy of some country gentleman devoted to roses
and tulips, in a word, to horticulture, but above all a lover of choice fruit.
An arbour is visible, or rather the wreck of an arbour, and under it a table
still stands not entirely destroyed by time. At the aspect of this garden that
is no more, the negative joys of the peaceful life of the provinces may be
divined as we divine the history of a worthy tradesman when we read the
epitaph on his tomb. To complete the mournful and tender impressions
which seize the soul, on one of the walls there is a sundial graced with this
homely Christian motto, '*Ultimam cogita.*'

"The roof of this house is dreadfully dilapidated; the outside shutters are
always closed; the balconies are hung with swallows' nests; the doors are
for ever shut. Straggling grasses have outlined the flagstones of the steps
with green; the ironwork is rusty. Moon and sun, winter, summer, and
snow have eaten into the wood, warped the boards, peeled off the paint.
The dreary silence is broken only by birds and cats, pole-cats, rats, and mice,
free to scamper round, and fight, and eat each other. An invisible hand has
written over it all: 'Mystery.'

"If, prompted by curiosity, you go to look at this house from the street,
you will see a large gate, with a round-arched top; the children have made
many holes in it. I learned later that this door had been blocked for ten
years. Through these irregular breaches you will see that the side towards
the courtyard is in perfect harmony with the side towards the garden. The
same ruin prevails. Tufts of weeds outline the paving stones; the walls are
scored by enormous cracks, and the blackened coping is laced with a thousand festoons of pellitory. The stone steps are disjointed; the bell-cord is
rotten; the gutter-spouts broken. What fire from heaven can have fallen
there? By what decree has salt been sown on this dwelling? Has God been
mocked here? Or was France betrayed? These are the questions we ask
ourselves. Reptiles crawl over it, but give no reply. This empty and deserted
house is a vast enigma of which the answer is known to none.

"It was formerly a little domain, held in fief, and is known as La Grande

Bretêche. During my stay at Vendôme, where Despleins had left me in charge of a rich patient, the sight of this strange dwelling became one of my keenest pleasures. Was it not far better than a ruin? Certain memories of indisputable authenticity attach themselves to a ruin; but this house, still standing, though being slowly destroyed by an avenging hand, contained a secret, an unrevealed thought. At the very least it testified to a caprice. More than once in the evening I attacked the hedge, run wild, which surrounded the enclosure. I braved scratches, I got into this ownerless garden, this plot which was no longer public or private; I lingered there for hours gazing at the disorder. I would not, as the price of the story to which this strange scene no doubt was due, have asked a single question of any gossiping native. On that spot I wove delightful romances, and abandoned myself to little debauches of melancholy which enchanted me. If I had known the reason—perhaps quite commonplace—of this neglect, I should have lost the unwritten poetry which intoxicated me. To me this refuge represented the most various phases of human life, shadowed by misfortune; sometimes the calm of a cloister without the monks; sometimes the peace of the graveyard without the dead, who speak in the language of epitaphs; one day I saw in it the home of lepers; another, the house of the Atridæ; but above all, I found there provincial life, with its contemplative ideas, its hour-glass existence. I often wept there, I never laughed.

"More than once I felt involuntary terrors as I heard overhead the dull hum of the wings of some hurrying wood-pigeon. The earth is dank; you must be on the watch for lizards, vipers, and frogs, wandering about with the wild freedom of nature; above all, you must have no fear of cold, for in a few minutes you feel an icy cloak settle on your shoulders, like the Commendatore's hand on Don Giovanni's neck.

"One evening I felt a shudder; the wind had turned an old rusty weather-cock, and the creaking sounded like a cry from the house, at the very moment when I was finishing a gloomy drama to account for this monumental embodiment of woe. I returned to my inn, lost in gloomy thoughts. When I had supped, the hostess came in to my room with an air of mystery, and said, 'Monsieur, here is Monsieur Regnault.'

" 'Who is Monsieur Regnault?'

" 'What, sir, do not you know Monsieur Regnault?—Well, that's odd,' said she, leaving the room.

"On a sudden I saw a man appear, tall, slim, dressed in black, hat in hand, who came in like a ram ready to butt his opponent, showing a receding forehead, a small pointed head, and a colourless face of the hue of a glass of dirty water. You would have taken him for an usher. The stranger wore an old coat, much worn at the seams; but he had a diamond in his shirt frill, and gold rings in his ears.

" 'Monsieur,' said I, 'whom have I the honour of addressing?'—He took a chair, placed himself in front of my fire, put his hat on my table, and answered while he rubbed his hands: 'Dear me, it is very cold.—Monsieur, I am Monsieur Regnault.'

"I was encouraging myself by saying to myself, '*Il bondo cani!* Seek!'

"'I am,' he went on, 'notary at Vendôme.'

"'I am delighted to hear it, Monsieur,' I exclaimed. 'But I am not in a position to make a will for reasons best known to myself.'

"'One moment!' said he, holding up his hand as though to gain silence. 'Allow me, Monsieur, allow me! I am informed that you sometimes go to walk in the garden of la Grande Bretêche.'

"'Yes, Monsieur.'

"'One moment!' said he, repeating his gesture. 'That constitutes a misdemeanour. Monsieur, as executor under the will of the late Comtesse de Merret, I come in her name to beg you to discontinue the practice. One moment! I am not a Turk, and do not wish to make a crime of it. And besides, you are free to be ignorant of the circumstances which compel me to leave the finest mansion in Vendôme to fall into ruin. Nevertheless, Monsieur, you must be a man of education, and you should know that the laws forbid, under heavy penalties, any trespass on enclosed property. A hedge is the same as a wall. But, the state in which the place is left may be an excuse for your curiosity. For my part, I should be quite content to make you free to come and go in the house; but being bound to respect the will of the testatrix, I have the honour, Monsieur, to beg that you will go into the garden no more. I myself, Monsieur, since the will was read, have never set foot in the house, which, as I had the honour of informing you, is part of the estate of the late Madame de Merret. We have done nothing there but verify the number of doors and windows to assess the taxes I have to pay annually out of the funds left for that purpose by the late Madame de Merret. Ah! my dear sir, her will made a great commotion in the town.'

"The good man paused to blow his nose. I respected his volubility, perfectly understanding that the administration of Madame de Merret's estate had been the most important event of his life, his reputation, his glory, his Restoration. As I was forced to bid farewell to my beautiful reveries and romances, I was to reject learning the truth on official authority.

"'Monsieur,' said I, 'would it be indiscreet if I were to ask you the reasons for such eccentricity?'

"At these words an expression, which revealed all the pleasure which men feel who are accustomed to ride a hobby, overspread the lawyer's countenance. He pulled up the collar of his shirt with an air, took out his snuff-box, opened it, and offered me a pinch; on my refusing, he took a large one. He was happy! A man who has no hobby does not know all the good to be got out of life. A hobby is the happy medium between a passion and a monomania. At this moment I understood the whole bearing of Sterne's charming passion, and had a perfect idea of the delight with which my uncle Toby, encouraged by Trim, bestrode his hobby-horse.

" 'Monsieur,' said Monsieur Regnault, 'I was head clerk in Monsieur Roguin's office, in Paris. A first-rate house, which you may have heard mentioned? No! An unfortunate bankruptcy made it famous.—Not having money enough to purchase a practice in Paris at the price to which they were run up in 1816, I came here and bought my predecessor's business. I had relations in Vendôme; among others, a wealthy aunt, who allowed me to marry her daughter.—Monsieur,' he went on after a little pause, 'three months after being licensed by the Keeper of the Seals, one evening, as I was going to bed—it was before my marriage—I was sent for by Madame la Comtesse de Merret, to her Château of Merret. Her maid, a good girl, who is now a servant in this inn, was waiting at my door with the Countess's own carriage. Ah! one moment! I ought to tell you that Monsieur le Comte de Merret had gone to Paris to die two months before I came here. He come to a miserable end, flinging himself into every kind of dissipation. You understand?

" 'On the day when he left, Madame la Comtesse had quitted la Grande Bretêche, having dismantled it. Some people even say that she had burnt all the furniture, the hangings—in short, all the chattels and furniture whatever used in furnishing the premises now let by the said M.—(Dear! what am I saying? I beg your pardon, I thought I was dictating a lease.)—In short, that she burnt everything in the meadow at Merret. Have you been to Merret, Monsieur?—No,' said he, answering himself. 'Ah, it is a very fine place.'

" 'For about three months previously,' he went on, with a jerk of his head, 'the Count and Countess had lived in a very eccentric way; they admitted no visitors; Madame lived on the ground floor, and Monsieur on the first floor. When the Countess was left alone, she was never seen excepting at church. Subsequently, at home, at the château, she refused to see the friends, whether gentlemen or ladies, who went to call on her. She was already very much altered when she left la Grande Bretêche to go to Merret. That dear lady—I say dear lady, for it was she who gave me this diamond, but indeed I saw her but once—that kind lady was very ill; she had, no doubt, given up all hope, for she died without choosing to send for a doctor; indeed, many of our ladies fancied she was not quite right in her head. Well, sir, my curiosity was strangely excited by hearing that Madame de Merret had need of my services. Nor was I the only person who took an interest in the affair. That very night, though it was already late, all the town knew that I was going to Merret.

" 'The waiting-woman replied but vaguely to the questions I asked her on the way; nevertheless, she told me that her mistress had received the Sacrament in the course of the day at the hands of the Curé of Merret, and seemed unlikely to live through the night. It was about eleven when I reached the château. I went up the great staircase. After crossing some large, lofty, dark rooms, diabolically cold and damp, I reached the state bedroom where the Countess lay. From the rumours that were current concerning this lady (Monsieur, I should never end if I were to repeat all the tales that were told about her), I had imagined her a coquette. Imagine, then, that I had great difficulty in seeing her in the great bed where she was lying. To be sure, to light this enormous room, with old-fashioned heavy cornices, and so thick with dust that merely to see it was enough to make you sneeze, she had only an old Argand lamp. Ah! but you have not been to Merret. Well, the bed is one of those old-world beds, with a high tester hung with flowered chintz. A small table stood by the bed, on which I saw an "Imitation of Christ," which, by the way, I bought for my wife, as well as the lamp. There were also a deep armchair for her confidential maid, and two small chairs. There was no fire. That was all the furniture; not enough to fill ten lines in an inventory.

" 'My dear sir, if you had seen, as I then saw, that vast room, papered and hung with brown, you would have felt yourself transported into a scene of romance. It was icy, nay more, funereal,' and he lifted his hand with a theatrical gesture and paused.

" 'By dint of seeking, as I approached the bed, at last I saw Madame de Merret, under the glimmer of the lamp, which fell on the pillows. Her face was as yellow as wax, and as narrow as two folded hands. The Countess had a lace cap showing abundant hair, but as white as linen thread. She was sitting up in bed, and seemed to keep upright with great difficulty. Her large black eyes, dimmed by fever, no doubt, and half-dead already, hardly moved under the bony arch of her eyebrows.—There,' he added, pointing to his own brow. 'Her forehead was clammy; her fleshless hands were like bones covered with soft skin; the veins and muscles were perfectly visible. She must have been very handsome; but at this moment I was startled into an indescribable emotion at the sight. Never, said those who wrapped her in her shroud, had any living creature been so emaciated and lived. In short, it was awful to behold! Sickness had so consumed that woman, that she was no more than a phantom. Her lips, which were pale violet, seemed to me not to move when she spoke to me.

" 'Though my profession has familiarized me with such spectacles, by calling me not unfrequently to the bedside of the dying to record their last wishes, I confess that families in tears and the agonies I have seen were as nothing in comparison with this lonely and silent woman in her vast château. I heard not the least sound, I did not perceive the movement which the sufferer's breathing ought to have given to the sheets that covered her, and I stood motionless, absorbed in looking at her in a sort of stupor. In fancy I am there still.—At last her large eyes moved; she tried to raise her right hand, but it fell back on the bed, and she uttered these words, which came like a breath, for her voice was no longer a voice: "I have waited for you with the greatest impatience." A bright flush rose to her cheeks. It was a great effort to her to speak.

" 'Madame,' I began. She signed to me to be silent. At that moment the old housekeeper rose and said in my ear, "Do not speak; Madame la Comtesse is not in a state to bear the slightest noise, and what you would say might agitate her."

" 'I sat down. A few instants after, Madame de Merret collected all her remaining strength to move her right hand, and slipped it, not without infinite difficulty, under the bolster; she then paused a moment. With a last effort she withdrew her hand; and when she brought out a sealed paper, drops of perspiration rolled from her brow. "I place my will in your hands —Oh! God! Oh!" and that was all. She clutched a crucifix that lay on the bed, lifted it hastily to her lips, and died.

" 'The expression of her eyes still makes me shudder as I think of it. She must have suffered much! There was joy in her last glance, and it remained stamped on her dead eyes.

" 'I brought away the will, and when it was opened I found that Madame de Merret had appointed me her executor. She left the whole of her property to the hospital of Vendôme excepting a few legacies. But these were her instructions as relating to la Grande Bretêche: She ordered me to leave the place, for fifty years counting from the day of her death, in the state in which it might be at the time of her decease, forbidding anyone, whoever he might be, to enter the apartments, prohibiting any repairs whatever, and even settling a salary to pay watchmen if it were needful to secure the absolute fulfilment of her intentions. At the expiration of that term, if the will of the testatrix has been duly carried out, the house is to become the property of my heirs, for, as you know, a notary cannot take a bequest. Otherwise la Grande Bretêche reverts to the heirs-at-law, but on condition of fulfilling certain conditions set forth in a codicil to the will, which is not to be opened till the expiration of the said term of fifty years. The will has not been disputed, so——' And without finishing his sentence, the lanky notary looked at me with an air of triumph; I made him quite happy by offering him my congratulations.

" 'Monsieur,' I said in conclusion, 'you have so vividly impressed me that I fancy I see the dying woman whiter than her sheets; her glittering eyes frighten me; I shall dream of her to-night.—But you must have formed some idea as to the instructions contained in that extraordinary will.'

" 'Monsieur,' said he, with comical reticence, 'I never allow myself to criticize the conduct of a person who honours me with the gift of a diamond.'

" "However, I soon loosened the tongue of the discreet notary of Vendôme, who communicated to me, not without long digressions, the opinions of the deep politicians of both sexes whose judgments are law in Vendôme. But these opinions were so contradictory, so diffuse, that I was near falling asleep in spite of the interest I felt in this authentic history. The notary's ponderous voice and monotonous accent, accustomed no doubt to listen to himself and to make himself listened to by his clients or fellow-townsmen, were too much for my curiosity. Happily, he soon went away.

"'Ah, ha, Monsieur,' said he on the stairs, 'a good many persons would be glad to live five-and-forty years longer; but—one moment!' and he laid the first finger of his right hand to his nostril with a cunning look, as much as to say, 'Mark my words!—To last as long as that—as long as that,' said he, 'you must not be past sixty now.'

"I closed my door, having been roused from my apathy by this last speech, which the notary thought very funny; then I sat down in my armchair, with my feet on the fire-dogs. I had lost myself in a romance *à la* Radcliffe, constructed on the juridical base given me by Monsieur Regnault, when the door, opened by a woman's cautious hand, turned on the hinges. I saw my landlady come in, a buxom, florid dame, always good-humoured, who had missed her calling in life. She was a Fleming, who ought to have seen the light in a picture by Teniers.

"'Well, Monsieur,' said she, 'Monsieur Regnault has no doubt been giving you his history of la Grande Bretêche?'

"'Yes, Madame Lepas.'

"'And what did he tell you?'

"I repeated in a few words the creepy and sinister story of Madame de Merret. At each sentence my hostess put her head forward, looking at me with an innkeeper's keen scrutiny, a happy compromise between the instinct of a police constable, the astuteness of a spy, and the cunning of a dealer.

"'My good Madame Lepas,' said I as I ended, 'you seem to know more about it. Heh? If not, why have you come up to me?'

"'On my word, as an honest woman——'

"'Do not swear; your eyes are big with a secret. You knew Monsieur de Merret; what sort of man was he?'

"'Monsieur de Merret—well, you see he was a man you never could see the top of, he was so tall! A very good gentleman, from Picardy, and who had, as we say, his head close to his cap. He paid for everything down, so as never to have difficulties with anyone. He was hot-tempered, you see! All our ladies liked him very much.'

"'Because he was hot-tempered?' I asked her.

"'Well, may be,' said she; 'and you may suppose, sir, that a man had to have something to show for a figure-head before he could marry Madame de Merret, who, without any reflection on others, was the handsomest and richest heiress in our parts. She had about twenty thousand francs a year. All the town was at the wedding; the bride was pretty and sweet-looking, quite a gem of a woman. Oh, they were a handsome couple in their day!'

"'And were they happy together?'

"'Hm, hm! so-so—so far as can be guessed, for, as you may suppose, we of the common sort were not hail-fellow-well-met with them.—Madame de Merret was a kind woman and very pleasant, who had no doubt sometimes to put up with her husband's tantrums. But though he was rather haughty, we were fond of him. After all, it was his place to behave so. When a man is a born nobleman, you see——'

" 'Still, there must have been some catastrophe for Monsieur and Madame de Merret to part so violently?'

" 'I did not say there was any catastrophe, sir. I know nothing about it.'

" 'Indeed. Well, now, I am sure you know everything.'

" 'Well, sir, I will tell you the whole story.—When I saw Monsieur Regnault go up to see you, it struck me that he would speak to you about Madame de Merret as having to do with la Grande Bretêche. That put it into my head to ask your advice, sir, seeming to me that you are a man of good judgment and incapable of playing a poor woman like me false—for I never did anyone a wrong, and yet I am tormented by my conscience. Up to now I have never dared to say a word to the people of these parts; they are all chatter-mags, with tongues like knives. And never till now, sir, have I had any traveller here who stayed so long in the inn as you have, and to whom I could tell the history of the fifteen thousand francs——'

" 'My dear Madame Lepas, if there is anything in your story of a nature to compromise me,' I said, interrupting the flow of her words, 'I would not hear it for all the world.'

" 'You need have no fears,' said she; 'you will see.'

"Her eagerness made me suspect that I was not the only person to whom my worthy landlady had communicated the secret of which I was to be sole possessor, but I listened.

" 'Monsieur,' said she, 'when the Emperor sent the Spaniards here, prisoners of war and others, I was required to lodge at the charge of the Government a young Spaniard sent to Vendôme on parole. Notwithstanding his parole, he had to show himself every day to the sub-prefect. He was a Spanish grandee—neither more nor less. He had a name in os and dia, something like Bagos de Férédia. I wrote his name down in my books, and you may see it if you like. Ah! he was a handsome young fellow for a Spaniard, who are all ugly they say. He was not more than five feet two or three in height, but so well made; and he had little hands that he kept so beautifully! Ah! you should have seen them. He had as many brushes for his hands as a woman has for her toilet. He had thick, black hair, a flame in his eye, a somewhat coppery complexion, but which I admired all the same. He wore the finest linen I have ever seen, though I have had princesses to lodge here, and, among others, General Bertrand, the Duc and Duchesse d'Abrantès, Monsieur Descazes, and the King of Spain. He did not eat much, but he had such polite and amiable ways that it was impossible to owe him a grudge for that. Oh! I was very fond of him, though he did not say four words to me in a day, and it was impossible to have the least bit of talk with him; if he was spoken to, he did not answer; it is a way, a mania they all have, it would seem.

" 'He read his breviary like a priest, and went to Mass and all the services quite regularly. And where did he post himself?—we found this out later. —Within two yards of Madame de Merret's chapel. As he took that place the very first time he entered the church, no one imagined that there was any purpose in it. Besides, he never raised his nose above his book, poor young man! And then, Monsieur, of an evening he went for a walk on the hill among the ruins of the old castle. It was his only amusement, poor man; it reminded him of his native land. They say that Spain is all hills!

" 'One evening, a few days after he was sent here, he was out very late. I was rather uneasy when he did not come in till just on the stroke of midnight; but we all got used to his whims; he took the key of the door, and we never sat up for him. He lived in a house belonging to us in the Rue des Casernes. Well, then, one of our stable-boys told us one evening that, going down to wash the horses in the river, he fancied he had seen the Spanish grandee swimming some little way off, just like a fish. When he came in, I told him to be careful of the weeds, and he seemed put out at having been seen in the water.

" 'At last, Monsieur, one day, or rather one morning, we did not find him in his room; he had not come back. By hunting through his things, I found a written paper in the drawer of his table, with fifty pieces of Spanish gold of the kind they call doubloons, worth about five thousand francs; and in a little sealed box ten thousand francs' worth of diamonds. The paper said that in case he should not return, he left us this money and these diamonds in trust to found Masses to thank God for his escape and for his salvation.

" 'At that time I still had my husband, who ran off in search of him. And this is the queer part of the story: he brought back the Spaniard's clothes, which he had found under a big stone on a sort of breakwater along the river bank, nearly opposite la Grande Bretêche. My husband went so early that no one saw him. After reading the letter, he burnt the clothes, and, in obedience to Count Férédia's wish, we announced that he had escaped.

" 'The sub-prefect set all the constabulary at his heels; but, pshaw! he was never caught. Lepas believed that the Spaniard had drowned himself. I, sir, have never thought so; I believe, on the contrary, that he had something to do with the business about Madame de Merret, seeing that Rosalie told me that the crucifix her mistress was so fond of that she had it buried with her, was made of ebony and silver; now in the early days of his stay here, Monsieur Férédia had one of ebony and silver which I never saw later.— And now, Monsieur, do not you say that I need have no remorse about the Spaniard's fifteen thousand francs? Are they not really and truly mine?'

" 'Certainly.—But have you never tried to question Rosalie?' said I.

" 'Oh, to be sure I have, sir. But what is to be done? That girl is like a wall. She knows something, but it is impossible to make her talk.'

"After chatting with me for a few minutes, my hostess left me a prey to vague and sinister thoughts, to romantic curiosity, and a religious dread, not unlike the deep emotion which comes upon us when we go into a dark church at night and discern a feeble light glimmering under a lofty vault— a dim figure glides across—the sweep of a gown or of a priest's cassock is audible—and we shiver! La Grande Bretêche, with its rank grasses, its shuttered windows, its rusty ironwork, its locked doors, its deserted rooms, suddenly rose before me in fantastic vividness. I tried to get into the mysterious dwelling to search out the heart of this solemn story, this drama which had killed three persons.

"Rosalie became in my eyes the most interesting being in Vendôme. As I studied her, I detected signs of an inmost thought, in spite of the blooming health that glowed in her dimpled face. There was in her soul some element of ruth or of hope; her manner suggested a secret, like the expression of devout souls who pray in excess, or of a girl who has killed her child and for ever hears its last cry. Nevertheless, she was simple and clumsy in her ways; her vacant smile had nothing criminal in it, and you would have pronounced her innocent only from seeing the large red and blue checked kerchief that covered her stalwart bust, tucked into the tight-laced square bodice of a lilac- and white-striped gown. 'No,' said I to myself, 'I will not quit Vendôme without knowing the whole history of la Grande Bretêche. To achieve this end, I will make love to Rosalie if it proves necessary.'

"'Rosalie!' said I one evening.

"'Your servant, sir?'

"'You are not married?' She started a little.

"'Oh! there is no lack of men if ever I take a fancy to be miserable!' she replied, laughing. She got over her agitation at once; for every woman, from the highest lady to the inn-servant inclusive, has a native presence of mind.

"'Yes; you are fresh and good-looking enough never to lack lovers! But tell me, Rosalie, why did you become an inn-servant on leaving Madame de Merret? Did she not leave you some little annuity?'

"'Oh yes, sir. But my place here is the best in all the town of Vendôme.'

"This reply was such a one as judges and attorneys call evasive. Rosalie, as it seemed to me, held in this romantic affair the place of a middle square of the chess-board; she was at the very centre of the interest and of the truth; she appeared to me to be tied into the knot of it. It was not a case for ordinary love-making; this girl contained the last chapter of a romance, and from that moment all my attentions were devoted to Rosalie. By dint of studying the girl, I observed in her, as in every woman whom we make our ruling thought, a variety of good qualities; she was clean and neat; she was handsome, I need not say; she soon was possessed of every charm that desire can lend to a woman in whatever rank of life. A fortnight after the notary's visit, one evening, or rather one morning, in the small hours, I said to Rosalie:

"'Come, tell me all you know about Madame de Merret.'

" 'Oh!' she cried in terror, 'do not ask me that, Monsieur Horace!'

"Her handsome features clouded over, her bright colouring grew pale, and her eyes lost their artless, liquid brightness.

" 'Well,' she said, 'I will tell you; but keep the secret carefully.'

" 'All right, my child; I will keep all your secrets with a thief's honour, which is the most loyal known.'

" 'If it is all the same to you,' said she, 'I would rather it should be with your own.'

"Thereupon she set her head-kerchief straight, and settled herself to tell the tale; for there is no doubt a particular attitude of confidence and security is necessary to the telling of a narrative. The best tales are told at a certain hour—just as we are all here at table. No one ever told a story well standing up, or fasting.

"If I were to reproduce exactly Rosalie's diffuse eloquence, a whole volume would scarcely contain it. Now, as the event of which she gave me a confused account stands exactly midway between the notary's gossip and that of Madame Lepas, as precisely as the middle term of a rule-of-three sum stands between the first and third, I have only to relate it in as few words as may be. I shall therefore be brief.

"The room at la Grande Bretêche in which Madame de Merret slept was on the ground floor; a little cupboard in the wall, about four feet deep, served her to hang her dresses in. Three months before the evening of which I have to relate the events, Madame de Merret had been seriously ailing, so much so that her husband had left her to herself, and had his own bed-room on the first floor. By one of those accidents which it is impossible to foresee, he came in that evening two hours later than usual from the club, where he went to read the papers and talk politics with the residents in the neighbourhood. His wife supposed him to have come in, to be in bed and asleep. But the invasion of France had been the subject of a very animated discussion; the game of billiards had waxed vehement; he had lost forty francs, an enormous sum at Vendôme, where everybody is thrifty, and where social habits are restrained within the bounds of a simplicity worthy of all praise, and the foundation perhaps of a form of true happiness which no Parisian would care for.

"For some time past Monsieur de Merret had been satisfied to ask Rosalie whether his wife was in bed; on the girl's replying always in the affirmative, he at once went to his own room, with the good faith that comes of habit and confidence. But this evening, on coming in, he took it into his head to go to see Madame de Merret, to tell her of his ill-luck, and perhaps to find consolation. During dinner he had observed that his wife was very becomingly dressed; he reflected as he came home from the club that his wife was certainly much better, that convalescence had improved her beauty, discovering it, as husbands discover everything, a little too late. Instead of calling Rosalie, who was in the kitchen at the moment watching the cook and the coachman playing a puzzling hand at cards, Monsieur de Merret made his way to his wife's room by the light of his lantern, which he set down on the lowest step of the stairs. His step, easy to recognize, rang under the vaulted passage.

"At the instant when the gentleman turned the key to enter his wife's room, he fancied he heard the door shut of the closet of which I have spoken; but when he went in, Madame de Merret was alone, standing in front of the fireplace. The unsuspecting husband fancied that Rosalie was in the cupboard; nevertheless, a doubt, ringing in his ears like a peal of bells, put him on his guard; he looked at his wife, and read in her eyes an indescribably anxious and haunted expression.

"'You are very late,' said she.—Her voice, usually so clear and sweet, struck him as being slightly husky.

"Monsieur de Merret made no reply, for at this moment Rosalie came in. This was like a thunderclap. He walked up and down the room, going from one window to another at a regular pace, his arms folded.

"'Have you had bad news, or are you ill?' his wife asked him timidly, while Rosalie helped her to undress. He made no reply.

"'You can go, Rosalie,' said Madame de Merret to her maid; 'I can put in my curl-papers myself.'—She scented disaster at the mere aspect of her husband's face, and wished to be alone with him. As soon as Rosalie was gone, or supposed to be gone, for she lingered a few minutes in the passage, Monsieur de Merret came and stood facing his wife, and said coldly, 'Madame, there is someone in your cupboard!' She looked at her husband calmly, and replied quite simply, 'No, Monsieur.'

"This 'No' wrung Monsieur de Merret's heart; he did not believe it; and yet his wife had never appeared purer or more saintly than she seemed to be at this moment. He rose to go and open the closet door. Madame de Merret took his hand, stopped him, looked at him sadly, and said in a voice of strange emotion, 'Remember, if you should find no one there, everything must be at an end between you and me.'

"The extraordinary dignity of his wife's attitude filled him with deep esteem for her, and inspired him with one of those resolves which need only a grander stage to become immortal.

"'No, Josephine,' he said, 'I will not open it. In either event we should be parted for ever. Listen; I know all the purity of your soul, I know you lead a saintly life, and would not commit a deadly sin to save your life.'—At these words Madame de Merret looked at her husband with a haggard stare —'See, her is your crucifix,' he went on. 'Swear to me before God that there is no one in there; I will believe you—I will never open that door.'

"Madame de Merret took up the crucifix and said, 'I swear it.'

"'Louder,' said her husband; 'and repeat: "I swear before God that there is nobody in that closet."' She repeated the words without flinching.

"'That will do,' said Monsieur de Merret coldly. After a moment's silence: 'You have there a fine piece of work which I never saw before,' said he, examining the crucifix of ebony and silver, very artistically wrought.

"'I found it at Duvivier's; last year when that troop of Spanish prisoners came through Vendôme, he bought it of a Spanish monk.'

"'Indeed,' said Monsieur de Merret, hanging the crucifix on its nail; and he rang the bell.

"He had not to wait for Rosalie. Monsieur de Merret went forward quickly to meet her, led her into the bay of the window that looked on to the garden, and said to her in an undertone:

"'I know that Gorenflot wants to marry you, that poverty alone prevents your setting up house, and that you told him you would not be his wife till he found means to become a master mason.—Well, go and fetch him; tell him to come here with his trowel and tools. Contrive to wake no one in his house but himself. His reward will be beyond your wishes. Above all, go out without saying a word—or else!' and he frowned.

"Rosalie was going, and he called her back. 'Here, take my latch-key,' said he.

"'Jean!' Monsieur de Merret called in a voice of thunder down the passage. Jean, who was both coachman and confidential servant, left his cards and came.

"'Go to bed, all of you,' said his master, beckoning him to come close; and the gentleman added in a whisper, 'When they are all asleep—mind, *asleep*—you understand?—come down and tell me.'

"Monsieur de Merret, who had never lost sight of his wife while giving his orders, quietly came back to her at the fireside, and began to tell her the details of the game of billiards and the discussion at the club. When Rosalie returned she found Monsieur and Madame de Merret conversing amiably.

"Not long before this Monsieur de Merret had had new ceilings made to all the reception-rooms on the ground floor. Plaster is very scarce at Vendôme; the price is enhanced by the cost of carriage; the gentleman had therefore had a considerable quantity delivered to him, knowing that he could always find purchasers for what might be left. It was this circumstance which suggested the plan he carried out.

"'Gorenflot is here, sir,' said Rosalie in a whisper.

"'Tell him to come in,' said her master aloud.

"Madame de Merret turned paler when she saw the mason.

"'Gorenflot,' said her husband, 'go and fetch some bricks from the coach-house; bring enough to wall up the door of this cupboard; you can use the plaster that is left for cement.' Then, dragging Rosalie and the workman close to him—'Listen, Gorenflot,' said he, in a low voice, 'you are to sleep here to-night; but to-morrow morning you shall have a passport to take you abroad to a place I will tell you of. I will give you six thousand francs

for your journey. You must live in that town for ten years; if you find you
do not like it, you may settle in another, but it must be in the same country. Go through Paris and wait there till I join you. I will there give you
an agreement for six thousand francs more, to be paid to you on your return, provided you have carried out the conditions of the bargain. For that
price you are to keep perfect silence as to what you have to do this night.
To you, Rosalie, I will secure ten thousand francs, which will not be paid
to you till your wedding day, and on condition of your marrying Gorenflot; but, to get married, you must hold your tongue. If not, no wedding
gift!'

"'Rosalie,' said Madame de Merret, 'come and brush my hair.'

"Her husband quietly walked up and down the room, keeping an eye
on the door, on the mason, and on his wife, but without any insulting display of suspicion. Gorenflot could not help making some noise. Madame
de Merret seized a moment when he was unloading some bricks, and when
her husband was at the other end of the room, to say to Rosalie: 'My dear
child, I will give you a thousand francs a year if only you will tell Gorenflot to leave a crack at the bottom.' Then she added aloud quite coolly:
'You had better help him.'

"Monsieur and Madame de Merret were silent all the time while Gorenflot was walling up the door. This silence was intentional on the husband's
part; he did not wish to give his wife the opportunity of saying anything
with a double meaning. On Madame de Merret's side it was pride or prudence. When the wall was half built up the cunning mason took advantage
of his master's back being turned to break one of the two panes in the top of
the door with a blow of his pick. By this Madame de Merret understood
that Rosalie had spoken to Gorenflot. They all three then saw the face of
a dark, gloomy-looking man, with black hair and flaming eyes.

"Before her husband turned round again the poor woman had nodded to
the stranger, to whom the signal was meant to convey, 'Hope.'

"At four o'clock, as day was dawning, for it was the month of September, the work was done. The mason was placed in charge of Jean, and
Monsieur de Merret slept in his wife's room.

"Next morning when he got up he said with apparent carelessness, 'Oh,
by the way, I must go to the Mairie for the passport.' He put on his hat,
took two or three steps towards the door, paused, and took the crucifix.
His wife was trembling with joy.

"'He will go to Duvivier's,' thought she.

"As soon as he had left, Madame de Merret rang for Rosalie, and then in
a terrible voice she cried: 'The pick! Bring the pick! and set to work. I saw
how Gorenflot did it yesterday; we shall have time to make a gap and
build it up again.'

"In an instant Rosalie had brought her mistress a sort of cleaver; she, with
a vehemence of which no words can give an idea, set to work to demolish

the wall. She had already got out a few bricks, when, turning to deal a stronger blow than before, she saw behind her Monsieur de Merret. She fainted away.

" 'Lay Madame on her bed,' said he coldly.

"Foreseeing what would certainly happen in his absence, he had laid this trap for his wife; he had merely written to the Maire and sent for Duvivier. The jeweller arrived just as the disorder in the room had been repaired.

" 'Duvivier,' asked Monsieur de Merret, 'did not you buy some crucifixes of the Spaniards who passed through the town?'

" 'No, Monsieur.'

" 'Very good; thank you,' said he, flashing a tiger's glare at his wife. 'Jean,' he added, turning to his confidential valet, 'you can serve my meals here in Madame de Merret's room. She is ill, and I shall not leave her till she recovers.'

"The cruel man remained in his wife's room for twenty days. During the earlier time, when there was some little noise in the closet, and Josephine wanted to intercede for the dying man, he said, without allowing her to utter a word, 'You swore on the Cross that there was no one there.' "

After this story all the ladies rose from table, and thus the spell under which Bianchon had held them was broken. But there were some among them who had almost shivered at the last words.

THE GRAY CHAMPION

Nathaniel Hawthorne

(1804–1864)

THERE WAS ONCE A TIME when New England groaned under the actual pressure of heavier wrongs than those threatened ones which brought on the Revolution. James II, the bigoted successor of Charles the Voluptuous, had annulled the charters of all the colonies, and sent a harsh and unprincipled soldier to take away our liberties and endanger our religion. The administration of Sir Edmund Andros lacked scarcely a single characteristic of tyranny: a Governor and Council, holding office from the King, and wholly independent of the country; laws made and taxes levied without concurrence of the people immediate or by their representatives; the rights of private citizens violated, and the titles of all landed property declared void; the voice of complaint stifled by restrictions on the press; and, finally, disaffection overawed by the first band of mercenary troops that ever marched on our free soil. For two years our ancestors were kept in sullen submission by that filial love which had invariably secured their allegiance to the mother country, whether its head chanced to be a Parliament, Protector, or Popish Monarch. Till these evil times, however, such allegiance had been merely nominal, and the colonists had ruled themselves, enjoying far more freedom than is even yet the privilege of the native subjects of Great Britain.

At length a rumor reached our shores that the Prince of Orange had ventured on an enterprise, the success of which would be the triumph of civil and religious rights and the salvation of New England. It was but a doubtful whisper; it might be false, or the attempt might fail; and, in either case, the man that stirred against King James would lose his head. Still the intelligence produced a marked effect. The people smiled mysteriously in the streets, and threw bold glances at their oppressors; while far and wide there was a subdued and silent agitation, as if the slightest signal would rouse the whole land from its sluggish despondency. Aware of their danger, the rulers resolved to avert it by an imposing display of strength, and perhaps to confirm their despotism by yet harsher measures. One afternoon in April, 1689, Sir Edmund Andros and his favorite councillors, being warm with wine, assembled the red-coats of the Governor's Guard, and made their appearance in the streets of Boston. The sun was near setting when the march commenced.

The roll of the drum at that unquiet crisis seemed to go through the streets, less as the martial music of the soldiers, than as a muster-call to the inhabitants themselves. A multitude, by various avenues, assembled in King Street, which was destined to be the scene, nearly a century afterwards, of another encounter between the troops of Britain, and a people struggling against her tyranny. Though more than sixty years had elapsed since the pilgrims came, this crowd of their descendants still showed the strong and sombre features of their character perhaps more strikingly in such a stern emergency than on happier occasions. There were the sober garb, the general severity of mien, the gloomy but undismayed expression, the scriptural forms of speech, and the confidence in Heaven's blessing on a righteous cause, which would have marked a band of the original Puritans, when threatened by some peril of the wilderness. Indeed, it was not yet time for the old spirit to be extinct; since there were men in the street that day who had worshipped there beneath the trees, before a house was reared to the God for whom they had become exiles. Old soldiers of the Parliament were here, too, smiling grimly at the thought that their aged arms might strike another blow against the house of Stuart. Here, also, were the veterans of King Philip's war, who had burned villages and slaughtered young and old, with pious fierceness, while the godly souls throughout the land were helping them with prayer. Several ministers were scattered among the crowd, which, unlike all other mobs, regarded them with such reverence, as if there were sanctity in their very garments. These holy men exerted their influence to quiet the people, but not to disperse them. Meantime, the purpose of the Governor, in disturbing the peace of the town at a period when the slightest commotion might throw the country into a ferment, was almost the universal subject of inquiry, and variously explained.

"Satan will strike his master-stroke presently," cried some, "because he knoweth that his time is short. All our godly pastors are to be dragged to prison! We shall see them at a Smithfield fire in King Street!"

Hereupon the people of each parish gathered closer round their minister, who looked calmly upwards and assumed a more apostolic dignity, as well befitted a candidate for the highest honor of his profession, the crown of martyrdom. It was actually fancied, at that period, that New England might have a John Rogers of her own to take the place of that worthy in the Primer.

"The Pope of Rome has given orders for a new St. Bartholomew!" cried others. "We are to be massacred, man and male child!"

Neither was this rumor wholly discredited, although the wiser class believed the Governor's object somewhat less atrocious. His predecessor under the old charter, Bradstreet, a venerable companion of the first settlers, was known to be in town. There were grounds for conjecturing, that Sir Edmund Andros intended at once to strike terror by a parade of military force, and to confound the opposite faction by possessing himself of their chief.

"Stand firm for the old charter, Governor!" shouted the crowd, seizing upon the idea. "The good old Governor Bradstreet!"

While this cry was at the loudest, the people were surprised by the well-known figure of Governor Bradstreet himself, a patriarch of nearly ninety, who appeared on the elevated steps of a door, and, with characteristic mildness, besought them to submit to the constituted authorities.

"My children," concluded this venerable person, "do nothing rashly. Cry not aloud, but pray for the welfare of New England, and expect patiently what the Lord will do in this matter!"

The event was soon to be decided. All this time, the roll of the drum had been approaching through Cornhill, louder and deeper, till with reverberations from house to house, and the regular tramp of martial footsteps, it burst into the street. A double rank of soldiers made their appearance, occupying the whole breadth of the passage, with shouldered matchlocks, and matches burning, so as to present a row of fires in the dusk. Their steady march was like the progress of a machine, that would roll irresistibly over everything in its way. Next, moving slowly, with a confused clatter of hoofs on the pavement, rode a party of mounted gentlemen, the central figure being Sir Edmund Andros, elderly, but erect and soldier-like. Those around him were his favorite councillors, and the bitterest foes of New England. At his right hand rode Edward Randolph, our arch-enemy, that "blasted wretch," as Cotton Mather calls him, who achieved the downfall of our ancient government, and was followed with a sensible curse, through life and to his grave. On the other side was Bullivant, scattering jests and mockery as he rode along. Dudley came behind, with a downcast look, dreading, as well he might, to meet the indignant gaze of the people, who beheld him, their only countryman by birth, among the oppressors of his native land. The captain of a frigate in the harbor, and two or three civil officers under the Crown, were also there. But the figure which most attracted the public eye, and stirred up the deepest feeling, was the Episcopal clergyman of King's Chapel, riding haughtily among the magistrates in his priestly vestments, the fitting representative of prelacy and persecution, the union of church and state, and all those abominations which had driven the Puritans to the wilderness. Another guard of soldiers, in double rank, brought up the rear.

The whole scene was a picture of the condition of New England, and its moral, the deformity of any government that does not grow out of the nature of things and the character of the people. On one side the religious multitude, with their sad visages and dark attire, and on the other, the group of despotic rulers, with the high churchman in the midst, and here and there a crucifix at their bosoms, all magnificently clad, flushed with wine, proud of unjust authority, and scoffing at the universal groan. And the mercenary soldiers, waiting but the word to deluge the street with blood, showed the only means by which obedience could be secured.

"O Lord of Hosts," cried a voice among the crowd, "provide a Champion for thy people!"

This ejaculation was loudly uttered, and served as a herald's cry, to introduce a remarkable personage. The crowd had rolled back, and were now huddled together nearly at the extremity of the street, while the soldiers had advanced no more than a third of its length. The intervening space was empty—a paved solitude, between lofty edifices, which threw almost a twilight shadow over it. Suddenly, there was seen the figure of an ancient man, who seemed to have emerged from among the people, and was walking by himself along the centre of the street, to confront the armed band. He wore the old Puritan dress, a dark cloak and a steeple-crowned hat, in the fashion of at least fifty years before, with a heavy sword upon his thigh, but a staff in his hand to assist the tremulous gait of age.

When at some distance from the multitude, the old man turned slowly round, displaying a face of antique majesty, rendered doubly venerable by the hoary beard that descended on his breast. He made a gesture at once of encouragement and warning, then turned again, and resumed his way.

"Who is this gray patriarch?" asked the young men of their sires.

"Who is this venerable brother?" asked the old men among themselves.

But none could make reply. The fathers of the people, those of fourscore years and upwards, were disturbed, deeming it strange that they should forget one of such evident authority, whom they must have known in their early days, the associate of Winthrop, and all the old councillors, giving laws, and making prayers, and leading them against the savage. The elderly men ought to have remembered him, too, with locks as gray in their youth, as their own were now. And the young! How could he have passed so utterly from their memories—that hoary sire, the relic of long-departed times, whose awful benediction had surely been bestowed on their uncovered heads, in childhood?

"Whence did he come? What is his purpose? Who can this old man be?" whispered the wondering crowd.

Meanwhile, the venerable stranger, staff in hand, was pursuing his solitary walk along the centre of the street. As he drew near the advancing soldiers, and as the roll of their drum came full upon his ear, the old man raised himself to a loftier mien, while the decrepitude of age seemed to fall from his shoulders, leaving him in gray but unbroken dignity. Now, he marched onward with a warrior's step, keeping time to the military music. Thus the aged form advanced on one side, and the whole parade of soldiers and magistrates on the other, till, when scarcely twenty yards remained between, the old man grasped his staff by the middle, and held it before him like a leader's truncheon.

"Stand!" cried he.

The eye, the face, and attitude of command; the solemn, yet warlike peal of that voice, fit either to rule a host in the battle-field or be raised to God in prayer, were irresistible. At the old man's word and outstretched arm, the roll of the drum was hushed at once, and the advancing line stood still. A tremulous enthusiasm seized upon the multitude. That stately form, combining the leader and the saint, so gray, so dimly seen, in such an ancient garb, could only belong to some old champion of the righteous cause, whom the oppressor's drum had summoned from his grave. They raised a shout of awe and exultation, and looked for the deliverance of New England.

The Governor, and the gentlemen of his party, perceiving themselves brought to an unexpected stand, rode hastily forward, as if they would have pressed their snorting and affrighted horses right against the hoary apparition. He, however, blenched not a step, but glancing his severe eye round the group, which half encompassed him, at last bent it sternly on Sir Edmund Andros. One would have thought that the dark old man was chief ruler there, and that the Governor and Council, with soldiers at their back, representing the whole power and authority of the Crown, had no alternative but obedience.

"What does this old fellow here?" cried Edward Randolph, fiercely. "On, Sir Edmund! Bid the soldiers forward, and give the dotard the same choice that you give all his countrymen—to stand aside or be trampled on!"

"Nay, nay, let us show respect to the good grand-sire," said Bullivant, laughing. "See you not, he is some old round-headed dignitary, who hath lain asleep these thirty years, and knows nothing of the change of times? Doubtless, he thinks to put us down with a proclamation in Old Noll's name!"

"Are you mad, old man?" demanded Sir Edmund Andros, in loud and harsh tones. "How dare you stay the march of King James's Governor?"

"I have stayed the march of a King himself, ere now," replied the gray figure, with stern composure. "I am here, Sir Governor, because the cry of an oppressed people hath disturbed me in my secret place; and beseeching this favor earnestly of the Lord, it was vouchsafed me to appear once again on earth, in the good old cause of his saints. And what speak ye of James? There is no longer a Popish tyrant on the throne of England, and by to-morrow noon, his name shall be a byword in this very street, where ye would make it a word of terror. Back, thou that wast a Governor, back! With this night thy power is ended—to-morrow, the prison!—back, lest I foretell the scaffold!"

The people had been drawing nearer and nearer and drinking in the words of their champion, who spoke in accents long disused, like one un-accustomed to converse, except with the dead of many years ago. But his voice stirred their souls. They confronted the soldiers, not wholly without arms, and ready to convert the very stones of the street into deadly weapons. Sir Edmund Andros looked at the old man; then he cast his hard and cruel eye over the multitude, and beheld them burning with that lurid wrath, so difficult to kindle or to quench; and again he fixed his gaze on the aged form, which stood obscurely in an open space, where neither friend nor foe had thrust himself. What were his thoughts, he uttered no word which might discover. But whether the oppressor were overawed by the Gray Champion's look, or perceived his peril in the threatening attitude of the people, it is certain that he gave back, and ordered his soldiers to com-mence a slow and guarded retreat. Before another sunset, the Governor, and all that rode so proudly with him, were prisoners, and long ere it was known that James had abdicated, King William was proclaimed throughout New England.

But where was the Gray Champion? Some reported that, when the troops had gone from King Street, and the people were thronging tumultuously in their rear, Bradstreet, the aged Governor, was seen to embrace a form more aged than his own. Others soberly affirmed, that while they marvelled at the venerable grandeur of his aspect, the old man had faded from their eyes, melting slowly into the hues of twilight, till, where he stood, there was an empty space. But all agreed that the hoary shape was gone. The men of that generation watched for his reappearance, in sunshine and in twilight, but never saw him more, nor knew when his funeral passed, nor where his gravestone was.

And who was the Gray Champion? Perhaps his name might be found in the records of that stern Court of Justice, which passed a sentence, too mighty for the age, but glorious in all after-times, for its humbling lesson to the monarch and its high example to the subject. I have heard, that whenever the descendants of the Puritans are to show the spirit of their sires, the old man appears again. When eighty years had passed, he walked once more in King Street. Five years later, in the twilight of an April morning, he stood on the green, beside the meeting-house, at Lexington, where now the obelisk of granite, with a slab of slate inlaid, commemorates the first fallen of the Revolution. And when our fathers were toiling at the breastwork on Bunker's Hill, all through that night the old warrior walked his rounds. Long, long may it be, ere he comes again! His hour is one of darkness, and adversity, and peril. But should domestic tyranny oppress us, or the invader's step pollute our soil, still may the Gray Champion come, for he is the type of New England's hereditary spirit; and his shadowy march, on the eve of danger, must ever be the pledge, that New England's sons will vindicate their ancestry.

THE CRIMSON CURTAIN

Jules Barbey d'Aurevilly

(1808–1889)

TRANSLATED BY ERNEST BOYD

A CONSIDERABLE NUMBER of years ago I went to shoot waterfowl in the western marshes, and, as there was no railway then, I took the diligence, which passed the cross-roads near the Château de Rueil, and which at that precise moment contained only one passenger inside. This person, a very remarkable man in every respect, and whom I knew by having often met him in society, I will ask your permission to introduce as the Vicomte de Brassard. The precaution is probably useless! The few hundred people who constitute Parisian society are, no doubt, able to supply the real name. It was about five o'clock in the evening. The sun shed its slanting rays on a dusty road, edged with poplar-trees and fields, through which we rattled, drawn by four stout horses, whose strong flanks rolled heavily at each crack of the postilion's whip—a postilion always reminds me of life, there is a great deal too much whip-cracking at the outset.

Vicomte de Brassard was at that time of life when he was no longer disposed to crack his whip. But he was one of those men worthy of being an Englishman (he was educated in England), who, if he had been mortally wounded, would have died declaring he was alive. In the world, and even in books, we are used to laugh at the pretensions to youth of those who have passed the happy age of inexperience and foolishness—and the custom is not a bad one when the pretensions take a ridiculous form; but when they do not, but on the contrary assume a pride that will not confess defeat, I do not say they are not senseless, for they are useless, but they deserve respect, like many other senseless things. If it was heroic of the Guards at Waterloo to die and not surrender, it is the same when we are face to face with old age, which is not so romantic as bayonets. Some heads are built in a military manner, never to surrender, and that is the whole question, as it was at Waterloo.

Vicomte de Brassard, who has not surrendered—he is still alive, and I will tell you about him later, for it is worth knowing—Vicomte de Brassard was then, at the time when I travelled with him in the diligence, what the world, which is as spiteful as an old woman, rudely calls "an old beau." For those who care little for words or figures, and who deem that in the matter of age a man is only as old as he appears to be, Vicomte de Brassard might have passed for a "beau" without any qualification. At least, at that very time the Marquise de V . . . —who was an expert judge of young men, and who had shaved a dozen men as clean as Delilah shaved Samson—wore, with much pride in an enamelled gold bracelet, one of the ends of the Vicomte's moustache, of which time, or the devil, had not changed the colour. Only, whether old or not, do not attach to the expression "beau," as the world has done, an idea of someone frivolous, lean, and cadaverous, for you would not have a proper idea of Vicomte de Brassard, in whom everything—intellect, manners, physiognomy—was large, opulent, redolent of patrician calmness, as befitted the most magnificent dandy I have ever known—I, who have seen Brummell go mad, and d'Orsay die.

For he was really a true dandy. If he had been less so, he would certainly have become Marshal of France. He had been in his youth one of the most brilliant officers of the latter days of the First Empire. I have heard it said many times by his regimental comrades that he was distinguished by the bravery of Murat added to that of Marmont, and that as he was cool and level-headed when the drums were not beating, he might in a short time have attained to the highest rank of the military hierarchy if it had not been for dandyism. If you combine dandyism with the qualities which go to make up an officer—discipline, regularity, etc.—you will see how much of the officer will remain in the combination, and whether he does not blow up like a powder-magazine. If the Vicomte de Brassard had never exploded, it was because, like all dandies, he was happy. Mazarin would have employed him—and so would Mazarin's nieces, but for another reason. He was superb.

He had had that beauty which is necessary to a soldier more than to any-one else, for there is no youth without beauty, and the army is the youth of France! It was that beauty, moreover, which not only seduces women; but circumstances themselves—the rascals—had not been the only protection spread over the head of Captain de Brassard. He was, I believe, of Norman family, of the race of William the Conqueror, and he had, it is said, con-quered a good deal himself. After the abdication of the Emperor, he had naturally gone over to the Bourbons, and, during the Hundred Days, had remained supernaturally faithful to them. So, when the Bourbons came back for the second time, the Vicomte was made a Chevalier of Saint-Louis and decorated by Charles X (then Monsieur) with his own royal hand. During the whole time of the Restoration, the handsome de Brassard never once mounted Guard at the Tuileries without the Duchesse of Angoulême addressing a few gracious words to him as she passed. She in whom mis-fortune had slain graciousness, managed to find some for him. The Minister, seeing this favour, would have done all he could to advance the man whom Madame thus singled out; but, with the best will in the world, what could be done for this terrible dandy who, at a review, had drawn his sword on the inspecting general for having made some remarks about his military duties? It was quite enough to save him from a court martial. This careless disdain of discipline always distinguished Vicomte de Brassard.

Except when on a campaign, when he was a thorough officer, he was never amenable to discipline. Many times he had been known—at the risk of being imprisoned for an indefinite period—to have secretly left a garrison, to go and amuse himself in some neighbouring town, and only to return when there was a review or a parade—warned by one of the soldiers, who loved him, for if his superiors scarcely cared to have under their orders a man to whom were repugnant all routine and discipline, the soldiers, on the other hand, adored him. To them he was an excellent officer. He only required that they should be brave, punctilious, and careful in their persons and dress, and thus realize the old type of the French soldier, as he is depicted in *La Permission de dix heures,* and in two or three old songs which are masterpieces in their way. He was, perhaps, too fond of making them fight duels, but he asserted that it was the best means he knew to develop the military spirit. "I am not the government," he said, "and I have no medals to give them when they fight bravely amongst themselves, but the Orders of which I am the grandmaster (he had a considerable private fortune) are gloves, spare cross-belts, and whatever may spruce them up—so far as the regulations will allow."

So the company which he commanded eclipsed, in the matter of equip-ment, all the other companies of the Grenadiers of the Guard, brilliant as they were. Thus he flattered to excess the soldiers, who in France are always prone to fatuity and coquetry, two permanent provocations, the one because of its tone, the other because of the envy it excites. It will easily be understood, after this, that all the other companies were jealous of his. The men would fight to get into it, and then had to fight not to get out of it.

Such had been, during the Restoration, the exceptional position of Captain Vicomte de Brassard. And as he had not then every day, as he had during the Empire, the resource of doing brave deeds which would have caused all to be forgiven, no one could have foreseen or guessed how long this insubordination which astonished his comrades, would have lasted, but the Revolution of 1830 happened just in time to prevent him from being cashiered. He was badly wounded during the Three Days, and disdained to take service under the new dynasty of the Orleans, for whom he had contempt. When the Revolution of July made them masters of a country they did not know how to keep, it found the Captain in bed, laid up with an injury to his foot which he had received in dancing—as he would have charged—at the last ball of the Duchesse de Berry.

But at the first roll of the drum he, nevertheless, rose and joined his company, and as he would not put on his boots on account of his wound, he went to the rioting as he would have gone to a ball, in varnished shoes and silk socks, and it was thus he led his grenadiers to the Place de la Bastille, with instructions to clear the whole length of the Boulevards.

Paris, in which no barricades had yet been erected, had a gloomy and terrible appearance. It was deserted. The sun glared down, and seemed a fiery rain, soon to be followed by another, when from behind the closed shutters of every window there should pour a deadly storm.

Captain de Brassard drew up his men in two lines, as close as possible to each row of houses so that each file of soldiers was exposed only to the fire from the houses opposite, whilst he, more dandified than ever, walked down the middle of the road. Aimed at from both sides by thousands of guns, pistols, and carbines, all the way from the Bastille to the Rue de Richelieu, he was not hit, in spite of the breadth of his chest, of which he was perhaps a little too proud—for Captain de Brassard swelled out his chest in a fight, as a pretty woman who wants to show off her charms does at a ball—when, just as he arrived in front of Frascati's, at the corner of the Rue de Richelieu, and at the moment when he commanded the troops to mass together in order to carry the first barricade which he had found on his road, he received a ball in his magnificent chest, which was doubly tempting, both on account of its size and the long silver braid which went from one shoulder to the other, and he had also his arm broken by a stone—which did not prevent him from carrying the barricade, and proceeding as far as the Madeleine at the head of his excited soldiers.

There, two ladies in a carriage, who were fleeing from the insurrection in Paris, seeing an officer of the Guards wounded, covered with blood, and lying on the blocks of stone which at that time surrounded the Madeleine, which was still in course of construction, placed their carriage at his disposal, and he was taken by them to Gros Caillou, where the Marshal de

Raguse was, to whom he said, in military fashion: "Marshal, I have not, perhaps, more than two hours to live, but during those two hours put me wherever you like."

Only he was wrong. He was good for more than two hours. The ball which passed through his body did not kill him. It was more than fifteen years later when I knew him, and he declared then that in defiance of all the doctors, who had expressly forbidden him to drink as long as the fever caused by his wound continued, he had been saved from a certain death only by Bordeaux wine.

And how he did drink!—for, dandy as he was, he drank as he did every-thing else—he drank like a trooper. He had made for him a splendid goblet of Bohemian glass, which held a whole bottle of Bordeaux, by God, and he would drain it off at a draught. He would say, after he had drunk it, that he always drank like that—and it was true. But in these days, when strength of every kind is continually diminishing and is no longer thought much of, it may seem that this feat is nothing to boast about. He was like Bassom-pierre, and could take his wine as he did. I have seen him toss off his Bohemian glass a dozen times without seeming any the worse for it. I have often seen him also on those occasions which respectable people call "orgies," and never, after even the most inordinate bouts, did he appear to be more than what he called a "little tight." I—who wish to make you understand what sort of man he was, in order that you may follow my story —may as well tell you that I have known him to keep seven mistresses at the same time. He entitled them, poetically, "the seven strings of his lyre"— and I must say that I disapprove of his speaking in this jesting and musical way of his immorality. But what would you have? If Captain Vicomte de Brassard had not been all that I have had the honour to tell you, my story would have been less sensational, and probably I should not have thought it worth while to relate it to you.

It is quite certain that I did not expect to find him there when I got into the diligence at the Château de Rueil cross-roads. It was a long time since I had seen him, and I took much pleasure in the prospect of spending several hours in the company of a man who belonged to our time, and yet differed so much from the men of our day.

The Vicomte de Brassard, who could have worn the armour of Francis I as easily as he did the officer's tunic of the Royal Guards, resembled neither in his proportions nor his appearance the young men of the present time. This setting sun, so grand and radiant, made the rising crescent moons look very pale and poor. He had the beauty of the Emperor Nicholas, whom he resembled in body, but his face was less ideal and Greek, and he wore a short beard, which, like his hair, had remained black in some mysterious way, and this beard grew high on his cheeks which had a manly ruddy tinge. His forehead was high, projecting, unwrinkled, and as white as a woman's arm, and beneath it were two dark-blue eyes, sparkling like cut emeralds. Those eyes never glanced; they penetrated.

We shook hands, and talked. Captain de Brassard spoke slowly, with a resonant voice that was capable of filling the Champ de Mars when he gave the word of command. Having been brought up from infancy in England, as I have already said, perhaps he thought in English, but this slowness, which was devoid of embarrassment by the way, gave a distinction to what he said, even when he joked, for the Captain loved to joke, and his jokes were sometimes rather broad. Captain de Brassard always went *too far,* as the Comtesse de F . . . used to say, that pretty widow who since her husband's death had worn only three colours—black, violet, and white. He must have been very good company, or people would have thought him impossible, and when that is the case, you know that much will be forgiven in the Faubourg Saint-Germain.

One of the advantages of talking in a carriage is that you can leave off when you have nothing more to say, without troubling anybody. In a drawing-room that liberty does not exist. Politeness compels you to talk, and this innocent hypocrisy is often punished by the hollowness and boredom of the conversation, in which the fools, even those born silent (and there are such), do their best to say something and be very amiable. In a public conveyance you are as much at home as anyone else is—and you may without rudeness lapse into the silence and reverie which follows a conversation. Unfortunately, the chances are against you in this life, and formerly (for there is a "formerly" already) you rode twenty times in a public conveyance—as you may now twenty times in a railway carriage—without meeting a man whose conversation was animated and interesting.

Vicomte de Brassard and I talked, at first, about the journey, the landscape, and old memories of the fashionable world which cropped up in the course of conversation—then the sun declined, and we both fell into the twilight silence. Night, which in autumn seems to fall from the sky at once, it comes so quickly, chilled us, and we rolled ourselves in our cloaks, resting our heads against the hard corner which is the traveller's pillow.

I do not know whether my companion slept in his corner, but I was wide awake in mine: I was so well acquainted with the route we were travelling, which I had gone over often, that I hardly noticed the external objects which disappeared as the diligence rolled on, and which seemed travelling through the night in an opposite direction to us. We passed through several small towns dotted here and there along the long road. The night became as black as an extinguished stove; and, in this obscurity, the unknown towns through which we passed took on a strange appearance, and made us think we were at the world's end. In most of these little towns gaslamps were rare, and there was less light than on the country roads behind us. In the country the sky was broader and there was a kind of dim light, but it was blotted out in the narrow streets of the towns, and only a star or two was to be seen between the roofs, adding to the mysterious air of these sleepy towns, where the only person we saw was the ostler with his lantern, at the door of some inn, as he brought out the fresh horses and buckled the straps of the harness, whistling meanwhile, or swearing at some obstinate or skittish horse.

Except for that, and the eternal question, always the same, of some traveller awakened from sleep, who lowered the window and cried in a voice which the silence of the night rendered louder: "Where are we now, postilion?" no sign of life was heard. Nothing was seen but the carriage full of sleeping people, in a sleeping town; though perhaps some dreamer like myself would try to discern through the window the fronts of the houses, or fix his attention and thoughts on some casement still lighted up at this late hour, even in those towns where early and regular hours are the rule, and the night is specially devoted to sleep. A human being watching— even if it be a sentinel—when all others are plunged in that rest which comes from physical fatigue, is always an affecting sight. But ignorance as to who is watching behind the curtains of a window, where the light gleaming betokens life and thought, adds poetry—the poetry of reality—to the dream. At least, for my part, I can never see a window lighted up in the night, in a sleeping town through which I am passing, without attaching a whole crowd of fancies to that light; without imagining behind those curtains all kinds of domestic affairs or dramas. Even now, after all these years, I can still think of those windows with their eternal and melancholy light, and I often say to myself, fancying I see them again in my dreams:

"What can there be behind those curtains?"

Well, one of those which has remained longest in my memory (you will know the reason presently) was a window in one of the streets of the town of ——, which we passed that night. It was in the third house—you see how exact my memory is—beyond the inn at which we changed horses; but this window I had leisure to examine for longer than a mere change of horses would have necessitated. An accident had happened to one of the wheels of our coach, and they had to send and wake up the wheelwright. Now to wake up a wheelwright in a sleeping town, and get him to come and tighten up a nut on a diligence, when there is no competition on that line, is not a trifling affair of a few minutes.

In the first place, if the wheelwright was as fast asleep as everybody in our coach, it could not have been easy to wake him. I could hear, through the partition, the snores of the inside passengers, and not one of the outside passengers, who, as you know, have a mania for getting down whenever the coach stops, probably—for vanity is found everywhere in France, even on the outside of coaches—in order to show their agility in getting up again, had descended from his seat.

It is true that the inn at which we were, was shut up. We did not sup there. We had supped at the last stage. The inn was sleeping like the rest of us. Nothing betrayed a sign of life. Not a sound disturbed the profound silence—unless it was the wearisome, monotonous sound of a broom wielded by someone (man or woman—we knew not, and it was too dark to ascertain) who was sweeping out the court-yard of this silent inn, the yard-gates of which were usually open. Even the broom dragged as though the sweeper were asleep, or were devilishly anxious to be. The front of the inn was as black as the other houses in the street, where indeed there was only a light at one window—precisely that window which is still fixed in my memory. The house, in which you could not actually say that this light shone, for it was screened by a double crimson curtain, through whose thicknesses the light filtered mysteriously, was a large building with only one upper story, but that placed very high.

"It is very singular," said Vicomte de Brassard, as though he were talking to himself; "one would think it was still the same curtain!"

I turned towards him to look at him, but the lamp which was by the coachman's box, and which is intended to show the horses the road, had just gone out. I thought he was asleep, but he was not, and he had been struck, like me, by the appearance of the window; but he knew more than I, because he knew why it was lighted up.

But the tone in which he had said that—though it was a simple remark—was so unlike the voice of the worldly Vicomte de Brassard, and astonished me so much, that I was overcome by curiosity to see his face, and I struck a match, as though I had wanted to light a cigar. The blue flame of the match lit up the gloom.

He was pale—not pale as a dead man, but as pale as Death itself.

Why should he turn pale? This window, with its peculiar appearance, the remark, and the pallor of a man who very rarely turned pale, for he was full-blooded, and emotion, when he was moved, made him turn scarlet up to the crown of his head, the shiver that I felt run down the muscles of his powerful biceps, which, as we were sitting close together, was against my arm—all gave me the impression that there was something hidden that I, the seeker after stories, might perhaps learn with a little pains.

"You were looking then at that window, Captain, and even seemed to recognize it," I said in that tone which does not seem to court a reply, and is the hypocrisy of curiosity.

"*Parbleu!* I do recognize it," he replied in his rich, deep voice, seeming to dwell on every word.

Calmness had again resumed its sway over this dandy, the most stolid and majestic of all dandies, who—as you know—scorn all emotions as being beneath them, and do not believe, like that idiot Goethe, that astonishment can ever be a proper feeling for the human mind.

"I do not come by here often," continued the Vicomte de Brassard quietly; "I even avoid passing by here. But there are some things one never forgets. There are not many, but there are some. I know of three: the first uniform one puts on, the first battle one was in, the first woman one ever slept with. Well, for me that window is the fourth thing I cannot forget."

He stopped and lowered the window which was in front of him. Was it that he might the better see the window of which we spoke?

The conductor had gone for the wheelwright, and had not returned. The fresh horses were late, and had not yet come. Those which had brought us were motionless from fatigue, worn out, and not unharnessed, and, with their heads between their legs, they did not even stamp on the silent pavement with impatience to return to their stable. Our sleepy diligence resembled an enchanted coach, fixed by some fairy's wand in some open glade in the forest of the Sleeping Beauty.

"The fact is," I said, "that for any man with imagination, that window possesses a certain character."

"I don't know what it has for you," replied Vicomte de Brassard, "but I know what it has for me. That is the window of the room in which I lived when I was first in garrison. Confound it! that is fully thirty-five years ago!

"Behind that curtain—which does not seem to have changed in all those years—and which is now lighted as it was when——"

He stopped and left his thought unexpressed, but I was determined to make him speak out.

"When you were studying tactics, Captain, in those early days when you were a second lieutenant."

"You give me more than my due," he replied. "I was, it is true, a second lieutenant at that time, but I did not spend my nights in studying tactics, and if my light was burning at unaccustomed hours, as respectable people say, it was not to read Marshal Saxe."

"But," I said—quick as a ball from a racket—"it was perhaps to imitate him."

He returned the ball as promptly.

"Oh," he said, "it was not then that I imitated Marshal Saxe in the way you mean. That was not till much later. Then I was merely a brat of a second lieutenant, very stiff and prim in my uniform, but very awkward and timid with women, though they would never believe it—probably on account of my confounded face. I never got the full benefit of my timidity from them. Moreover, I was but seventeen in those happy days. I had just left the military college. We left in those days at the age at which you enter nowadays, for if the Emperor, that terrible consumer of men, had lasted longer, he would have ended by having soldiers twelve years of age, as some of the Asiatic sultans have concubines nine years of age."

"If he goes on talking about the Emperor and concubines," I thought to myself, "I shall not learn what I want to know."

"Yet, Vicomte," I replied, "I would wager that you would never have preserved the memory of that window which is shining there unless there had been a woman behind the curtain."

"And you would have won your bet, sir," he said, gravely.

"Ah, *parbleu!*" I replied. "I was sure of it. For a man like you, in a little provincial town that you have not perhaps passed through ten times since you were first in garrison there, it must be some siege you have sustained, or some woman you took by storm, that could make you remember so vividly the window of a house that is now lighted up amidst the general gloom."

"Yet I did not, however, sustain any siege—at least in the military sense," he replied, still gravely, but gravity was sometimes his way of joking; "and, on the other hand, when one surrenders so quickly, can it be called a siege? But as to taking a woman, by storm or otherwise, I have told you that in those days I was quite incapable of it. So it was not a woman who was taken here—it was I."

I bowed; did he see it in the dark carriage?

"Berg op Zoom was taken," I said.

"And subalterns of seventeen," he replied, "are not generally Berg op Zooms of impregnable wisdom and chastity."

"So," I said gaily, "it was some Madame or Mademoiselle Potiphar."

"It was a demoiselle," he interrupted with a frankness that was almost comic.

"To add to the sum of all the others, Captain. Only in this case the Joseph was a soldier—a Joseph not likely to run away."

"But who certainly did run away, on the contrary," he replied with the greatest coolness; "although too late, and very much afraid!!! With a fright which made me understand the expression used by Marshal Ney, which I heard with my own ears, and which, coming from such a man, I must own somewhat comforted me, I should like to see the b——[only he gave the words in full] who has never been afraid!"

"The story of how *you* came to feel that sensation must be interesting, Captain."

"*Pardieu!*" he said quickly; "I can, if you are curious, tell you the story of an event which bit into my life as acid bites into steel, and which has left a dark stain on the page of my libertine pleasures.—Ah, it is not always profitable to be a rake," he added in a melancholy voice, which struck me as rather strange coming from one I had always regarded as a regular hardened rogue.

He pulled up the glass he had lowered, as though he feared the sound of his voice might be heard outside, though there was no one near the coach, which was motionless as though deserted—or else he thought the regular beat of the broom would interrupt his story. I listened attentively to his voice—to the slightest expression of his voice—for I could not see his face in the dark—and with my eyes fixed more than ever on the window with the crimson curtain, behind which the light still burned with such fascinating power, and about which he was ready to speak.

"I was then seventeen," he continued, "and had just left the military college. I had been appointed ensign in a regiment of the line, which was then impatiently awaiting orders to leave for Germany, where the Emperor was conducting that campaign which history has named the campaign of 1813. I had just time to kiss my old father before joining, in this town, the battalion of which I formed part—for in this little town of some few thousands of inhabitants at most, the garrison consisted of only our two first battalions. The two other battalions were in some neighbouring town.

"You, who have probably seen this town only when you were travelling towards the West, cannot imagine what it is—or at least what it was thirty years ago—when you are obliged, as I was then, to live in it. It was certainly the worst garrison to which chance—which I believe to be the devil, at that time represented by the Minister of War—could have sent me as a starting-place for my military career. What an infernally dull hole it was! I do not remember ever having been in a more wearisome place. But, at my age, and in the first intoxication of the uniform—a feeling you do not know, but which all who have worn it have experienced—I scarcely suffered from what at a later time would have seemed insupportable.

"After all, how could this dull provincial town affect me? I lived in it much less than I did in my uniform—a masterpiece of sartorial art which delighted me. My uniform, of which I was madly fond, hid or adorned everything, and it was—though this may appear an exaggeration, but it is the truth—the uniform which was, strictly speaking, my garrison. When I was too much bored by this uninteresting and lifeless town, I put on full uniform, and boredom fled. I was like those women who give extra attention to their *toilette* when they are alone and expect no one. I dressed myself *for* myself. I enjoyed in solitude my epaulets and the clank of my sabre, as I promenaded the lonely streets in the afternoons, and I felt as puffed up with pride as I have done since in Paris when I have heard people say behind me: 'There is a really fine-looking officer.'

"In the town, which was not a rich one, and had no commerce or activity of any kind, there were only a few old and almost ruined families who grumbled at the Emperor, because he had not, as they said, made the robbers of the Revolution yield up their booty, and who for that reason paid no great heed to the officers. Therefore there were no parties, or balls, or soirées, or dances. At the best there was but the Promenade, where on Sunday, after church, the mothers came to show off their daughters until two o'clock in the afternoon—and when the first bell rang for Vespers all the petticoats disappeared, and the Promenade was deserted.

"This midday Mass, to which we never go, became, by the way, a military Mass during the Restoration, and all the officers were obliged to attend it, and that was quite an event in this dead-alive town. For young fellows like us, who were at a time of life when we care greatly for love or women, this military Mass was quite a pleasure. All the officers, except those on duty, were scattered about the nave of the church. We nearly always contrived to sit behind the prettiest women who came to Mass, because they were sure to be looked at, and whom we delighted by talking between ourselves, loud enough for them to hear, about their charms or appearance. Ah, that military Mass, what romances have I seen begin there! I have seen many love-letters slipped into the muffs which the girls left on their chairs when they knelt by the side of their mothers—letters to which they brought the reply on the following Sunday, also in their muffs.

"But in the days of the Emperor there was no military Mass, and consequently no means of approaching the 'respectable' girls of the little town. Nor were there any compensations. Those establishments which are never mentioned in good society were simply horrible. The cafés, in which so much home-sickness is drowned during the long idleness of garrison life, it was impossible for anyone who respected his epaulets to enter.

"Luxury is now found here, as elsewhere, but there was not then a single hotel where the officers could dine together without being horribly swindled, so we were forced to give up all ideas of a mess-table, and we were scattered about various boarding-houses, amongst households that were not over-rich —people who let their apartments as dearly as they could, and so added a little to their skimpy revenues.

"I lived in lodgings. One of my comrades lived at the *Poste aux Chevaux,* which was in this street at that time—there! a few houses behind us, and if it were daylight you could see on the house an old golden sun emerging from a cherry-coloured cloud, with the inscription, 'The Rising Sun.' This comrade found an apartment for me close to his own—where that window is perched up there, and which seems to me this evening to belong to me still, as it did then. I let him find my lodgings for me. He was older than I was, had been longer in the regiment, and he liked to give advice to one who was inexperienced and careless.

"I have already said that except for the uniform—a point on which I lay stress, because that is a feeling of which your generation, with your Peace Congresses, and philosophical and humanitarian clowning, will soon have no idea—and the hope of hearing the cannon in my first battle, in which I was to lose my military maidenhead—excuse the expression—it was all much alike to me. I lived only in those two ideas—in the second especially, for it was a hope, and we always care more for what we have not than for that which we have.

"This is how I spent my life. Except during meal-times—and I took my meals with the people of the house, and about whom I will tell you presently —and the time devoted daily to military duties, I lived nearly always in my own room, lying on a huge dark-blue sofa, which was so cool that it seemed to me like a cold bath after the hot parade-ground, and I scarcely ever left this sofa except to take a fencing-lesson, or have a game of cards with my neighbour opposite, Louis de Meung, who was not so lazy as I was, for he had picked up, amongst the *grisettes* of the town, a rather pretty girl, whom he had taken for his mistress and who served, as he said, to kill time.

"But what I knew of women did not tempt me to imitate my friend Louis. What little I knew of them I had picked up where the cadets of Saint-Cyr acquire that information when they are out on leave. Besides, some phases of character are late in developing. Did you know Saint-Rémy, one of the greatest rakes of his day, and who was called by the other libertines 'the Minotaur'; not because of his horns, although he wore them, for he had killed his wife's lover, but because of the number of virgins he had destroyed?"

"Yes, I knew him," I replied, "but when he was old and incorrigible, and becoming more of a debauchee each year that passed over his head; of course I knew that *rompu,* as Brantôme would have called him."

"He was, in fact, like one of Brantôme's men," replied the Vicomte. "But, at any rate, Saint-Rémy, when he was twenty-seven, had never touched a glass or a petticoat. He will tell you the same thing if you ask him. At twenty-seven years of age, he was, in the matter of women, as innocent as a new-born babe, and though his nurse no longer suckled him, he had never drunk anything but milk or water."

"He made up well for lost time," I remarked.

"Yes," said the Vicomte, "and so did I. But I had less lost time to make up. My first period of prudence hardly exceeded the time that I spent in this town, and although I was not so absolutely chaste as Saint-Rémy, I lived like a Knight of Malta—and indeed I was one, by birth.—Did you know that? I should even have succeeded one of my uncles as a 'Master' if the Revolution had not abolished the Order, the ribbon of which—though the Order is abolished—I sometimes wear—foolishly perhaps.—As to the people who had let me their apartment," continued Vicomte de Brassard, "they were, as you may imagine, thoroughly bourgeois. They were only two —husband and wife; both old, and well-behaved. In their relations with me, they even displayed that politeness you never find in these days—especially in their class—and which is like the scent of a bygone period. I was not of an age to observe, and they interested me so little that I never cared to penetrate the past of these two old people, into whose life I entered only in the most superficial way, two hours a day—noon and evening—when I dined or supped with them. Nothing concerning this past transpired in their conversation before me, for this conversation generally turned on persons or matters relating to the town, of which they informed me—the husband in a spirit of humorous backbiting, and his wife, who was very pious, with more reserve, but certainly with no less pleasure.

"I think, however, I have heard it said that the husband travelled in his youth, but for whom or what I know not, and that when he returned, he married—the girl having waited for him. They were good, honest people, calm and quiet. The wife spent her time in knitting socks for her husband,

and he, being music-mad, scraped old airs on his violin in a garret over my room. Perhaps they had once been better off. Perhaps some loss of fortune (which they concealed) had obliged them to take a lodger; but, except for that, they showed no sign of poverty. Everything in the house breathed an air of comfort, as is the case in old-fashioned houses, which abound with linen that smells fresh and good, heavy silver plate, and movables which seem to be immovable, they are so seldom renewed. I was very comfortable there. The table was good, and I had full permission to quit it as soon as I had 'wiped my beard'—as old Olive, the servant who waited on us, called it, though she did me too much honour in dignifying by the name of a beard the cat's whiskers which constituted the moustache of an ensign who was still a growing lad.

"I had been there about six months, living as quietly as my hosts, and I had never heard a single word of the existence of the person I was about to meet at their house, when one day, in going down to dinner at the accustomed hour, I saw, in a corner of the dining-room, a tall young woman standing on tiptoe and hanging her hat by its ribbons on a hat-rack, like a woman who feels herself quite at home, and has just come in from a walk. Her body was stretched to reach the peg, which was placed high, and she displayed a figure as graceful as an opera-dancer. She was dressed in a tight-fitting bodice and a narrow skirt, which revealed the shape of her hips.

"With the arms still raised, she turned her head when she heard me enter, and thus I was enabled to see her face; but she finished what she was about as though I had not been there, and looked to see whether the ribbons of her bonnet had not crumpled in hanging it up, and she did all this slowly, carefully, and almost impertinently—for, after all, I was standing waiting to bow to her—before she took any notice of me, and did me the honour to regard me with two very cold, black eyes, to which her hair, which was done in wavy curls massed on the forehead, gave that deep expression which is peculiar to that kind of *coiffure*.

"I could not imagine who she could be at that hour, and in that place. No one ever came to dine with my hosts—yet she had certainly come to dine, for the table was prepared, and four covers were laid. But my astonishment to see her there was greatly surpassed by my astonishment to learn who she was; as I did when my hosts entered the room and presented her to me as their daughter, who had just left boarding-school, and who was going in future to live with them.

"Their daughter! It was impossible for anyone to be more unlike the daughter of people like them! Not but what the prettiest girls are the daughters of all sorts of people. I have known many such, and you also, no doubt. Physiologically speaking, the ugliest being may produce the most beautiful. But there was the chasm of a whole race between her and them! Moreover, physiologically, if I may employ that pedantic word, which belongs to your days and not to mine, one could not help remarking her air, which was very singular in a girl as young as she was, for it was a kind of impassive air very difficult to describe. If she had not had it, one would have said: 'That is a pretty girl,' without thinking any more of her than of all the pretty girls one meets by chance, and about whom one has said that and never thought any more about it. But this air—which distinguished her not only from her parents, but from everyone else, amazed you and petrified you; for she appeared to have neither passions nor feelings. 'The Infanta with the Spaniel,' by Velasquez, may, if you know the picture, give you an idea of that air, which was neither proud, nor scornful, nor disdainful, but simply impassive; for a proud, scornful, or contemptuous air informs people that they do exist, since one takes the trouble to despise or contemn them, whilst this air said coolly: 'For me, you do not even exist.'

"I own that her appearance made me put to myself on that first day and many others, a question which is still unsolved: how that tall, slim girl could be the offspring of the little, stout man in a greenish-yellow coat and a white waistcoat, who had a complexion the colour of his wife's jam, and a wen on the back of his fat neck, and stuttered in his speech. And if the husband did not trouble me much, for the husband may be eliminated from questions of this sort—the wife appeared quite impossible to explain. Mademoiselle Albertine (that was the name of this archduchess who had fallen from heaven into this bourgeois family, as though heaven had tried to play a joke upon them) was called Alberte by her parents, because her name was too long. The name suited her face and figure, but she did not appear to be the daughter of either of her parents.

"At this first dinner, and those which followed, she appeared to me to be a young girl very well brought up, with no affectation, and habitually silent, but who, when she did speak, said clearly and sensibly what she had to say, and never exceeded those limits. Besides, if she had had more wit than I knew of, she would hardly have found an opportunity to show it at the dinner-table. The presence of their daughter necessarily had some effect on the gossip of the two old people. All the little scandals about the townsfolk were suppressed. As a matter of course, we never talked about anything more interesting than the weather. There was only the impassive air of Mademoiselle Albertine or Alberte, which had so much struck me at first, and I soon wearied of that. If I had met her in that society for which I was intended, her impassiveness would have aroused my curiosity. But to me she was not a girl to whom I could make love—even with the eyes. My position in respect to her—as I was living with her parents—was delicate, and a mere trifle might have made it much worse. She was neither sufficiently near nor sufficiently remote to be anything in my life, and I soon fell naturally, and quite unintentionally, into the most complete indifference to her impassiveness.

"Nor was this disturbed either on her part or on mine. There was nothing between us but the merest politeness, and the most indifferent speeches. To me she was just a figure that I scarcely saw—and what was I to her? At table—we never met elsewhere—she looked more at the stopper of the decanter or the sugar-basin than she did at me. All that she said was correct, and very well expressed, but signified little or nothing, and gave me no clue to her character. Besides, what did that matter to me? I should have passed my whole life without dreaming of even looking at that quiet and insolent girl, had it not been for a circumstance about which I will tell you, and which struck me like a thunderbolt—a bolt from the blue, indeed.

"One evening, nearly a month after Mademoiselle Alberte had come home, we were sitting down to supper. She was seated next to me, and I really paid so little attention to her that I had never noticed that she had changed her place, and was next to me instead of sitting between her father and mother as usual. I was unfolding my napkin on my knees when—I shall never be able to express my feeling of astonishment—I felt a hand boldly press mine under the table. I thought I was dreaming—or, rather, I could think of nothing at all. I could only feel the touch of that hand, boldly seeking mine under the napkin. It was so extraordinary and unexpected. All my blood, set aglow by that touch, rushed from my heart to my hand, as though attracted by her, and then returned violently as though driven by a pump to my heart. Everything swam before my eyes—my ears tingled. I must have turned deadly pale. I thought I was going to faint—that I should melt away in the inexpressible pleasure caused by the pressure of that hand,—which was rather large and strong, like that of a boy—when it closed upon mine.

"When you are young, you know, pleasure always brings with it a sense of shame, and I tried to withdraw my hand, but hers seemed aware of the pleasure it had caused me, and compelled mine to remain by a deliciously warm squeeze. . . . That is thirty-five years ago, and, as you may believe, I have touched many a woman's hand since, but I still feel, when I think of it, the sensation of that hand pressing mine with despotic passion.

"The thousand tremors which that hand caused to shoot through my whole body made me fear to betray what I felt to the father and mother whose daughter, before their eyes, dared to . . . Ashamed, however, to prove myself less of a man than this bold girl who risked her reputation, and whose incredible coolness concealed her follies, I bit my lips till they bled, in a superhuman effort to stop the tremors of desire which might have told these poor people so much, and then my eyes sought her other hand, which I had not yet looked at, and which at this dangerous moment was calmly turning up the wick of a lamp which had just been placed on the table, for the evening was beginning to grow dark. I looked at it. It was the fellow of the hand whose touch was thrilling me, and sending long tongues of fire as from a furnace through my veins! The hand was rather thick, but the fingers were long and well-shaped, and looked transparently rosy in the light which fell full upon them, but they never trembled, and performed the little operation on which they were engaged with firmness, ease, and an incomparable, graceful languor.

"We could not stop like that for ever! We needed our hands to eat with. Mademoiselle Alberte's hand dropped mine, but at the same moment her foot, which was quite as expressive as her hand, placed itself on mine in the same despotic manner during all this too brief dinner, and reminded me of one of those baths which are insufferably hot to begin with, but to which you get accustomed, and end by thinking so comfortable that you willingly believe that the damned in their cauldron must be as cool and as much at home as fish in water.

"You may fancy whether I dined that day, or if I took much part in the chatter of my worthy hosts, who were far from suspecting the mysterious and terrible drama which was going on under the table. They saw nothing, but they easily might have seen, and really I was more disturbed on their account than I was for myself, or for her. I had all the frankness and sympathy of seventeen. I said to myself: 'Is she quite shameless? Is she mad?' And I looked out of the corner of my eye at her, but she did not lose for a single second, during the whole of the dinner, her air of a princess at a state ceremony, and her face remained as calm as ever, though her foot was saying and doing all the foolish things which a foot can say or do—to mine. I must confess that I was more surprised at her coolness than at her imprudence. I had read a good deal of light literature, in which women were not spared. I had been educated at a military school. I considered myself quite a Lovelace, like every lad who has kissed his mother's chambermaid behind the door or on the staircase. But my experience as a Lovelace of seventeen was upset. This appeared to me worse than anything I had ever heard or read about the deceit of women, and how they could conceal their deepest or most violent emotions. Only fancy! she was but eighteen! Was she even as much? She had just left a school which I had no reason to suspect, considering the morality and the piety of her mother, who had selected it for her daughter. This absence of all constraint, or, to speak plainly, this absolute want of modesty, this perfect control over herself whilst doing the most imprudent things that could be done by a young girl who had never by a sign or a glance forewarned the man to whom she made such an advance—all this rose clearly to my mind, despite my confusion.

"But neither then nor later did I stop to philosophize about it. I had no sham horror for the conduct of this girl who had shown such terribly precocious depravity. Besides, at the age I was then, or even much later, you do not consider a girl depraved because she throws herself into your arms. On the contrary, you are almost inclined to regard it as a matter of course, and if you say 'Poor girl,' it is more out of modesty than pity. But though I was shy, I did not want to be taken for a ninny—the good old French reason for doing a bad deed without any remorse. I knew without doubt that it was not love the girl felt for me. Love does not act in that shameless, impudent way; and I also knew well enough that what she had caused me to feel was not love either. But, love or not—whatever it was, I wanted it. When I rose from the table, my mind was made up. Alberte's hand, of which I had not thought for a moment before it seized mine, had stirred in my soul a desire to embrace her whole body as her hand had embraced mine!

"I went up to my room like a madman, and when I was a little bit calmed by reflection, I asked myself what I should do to clinch this 'intrigue'—as they call it in the country—with a girl who was so devilishly tempting. I knew pretty well—like one who has never tried to know more —that she never left her mother, and that the two worked side by side all day in the window-seat of the dining-room, which also served as their drawing-room; that she had no lady-friend who came to see her, and that she hardly ever went out except to Mass or Vespers on Sunday, with her parents.

"That was not very encouraging, was it? I began to regret that I had not seen more of these worthy people; for though I had not held aloof from them, I had treated them with that distant or somewhat listless politeness you show to people in whom you take only a remote interest; but I reflected that I could not very well change my attitude towards them without exposing myself to the chance of revealing to them, or making them suspect, that which I wished to conceal.

"The only opportunities I had to speak to Mademoiselle Alberte in secret were meetings on the staircase, as I went up or came down from my room—but on the staircase we might be seen and heard. The best resource open to me—in that small and well-regulated house where everybody was close to everybody else's elbow—was to write; and since the hand of that brazen hussy knew so well how to find mine under the table, it would perhaps not make much ado about taking a note that was slipped into it; and so I wrote.

"It was a letter suited to the circumstances—supplicatory, commanding, and delirious—of a man who has drunk his first draught of happiness and asks for a second.

"Only, in order to give it to her, I must wait till dinner-time the next day, and that seemed a long time; but at last dinner-time came! The incentive hand, whose touch I had felt for twenty-four hours, did not fail to seek mine under the table as on the previous evening. Mademoiselle Alberte felt my letter, and took it, as I foresaw. But what I did not foresee was, that with that Infanta-like air of sublime indifference, she should slip it into her breast, under the pretence of arranging a bit of lace that was doubled down, and perform the act so naturally and so quickly that her mother, who was engaged in serving the soup, saw nothing; and whilst her old idiot of a father, who was always humming something, and thinking of his violin when he was not playing, was gazing into the fire."

"Oh, that is done every day, Captain," I interrupted gaily, for his story appeared to me to be likely to turn soon into a mere history of a garrison love-affair—for I did not suspect what was to follow. "Why, only a few days ago there was at the opera, in the box next to mine, a lady of probably the same sort as your Mademoiselle Alberte. She was more than eighteen, certainly; but, I give you my word of honour, I have rarely seen more majestic modesty in any woman. During the whole performance she sat as motionless as though she had been on a granite pedestal. She did not turn once, either to the right or left, but no doubt she saw with her shoulders, which were very bare and very beautiful, for there was in the same box with me, and consequently behind us both, a young man who appeared quite as indifferent as she was to everything but the opera that was being sung. I can certify that this young man had not made one of those grimaces which men make to women in public places, and which you may call declarations from a distance. Only, when the piece was over, and amid the general confusion as the boxes emptied, the lady rose and buttoned her cloak, and I heard her say to her husband in a clear and conjugally imperious voice, 'Henri, pick up my hood!' and then over his back, as he was stooping down, she extended her hand and arm, and took a note the young man handed her, just as though she had been taking her fan or her bouquet from her husband's hand. He rose up, poor man! holding the hood—a scarlet satin hood, but not so scarlet as his face, for which he had, at the risk of apoplexy, dived under the seats as he best could. Upon my word, when I saw that, I went away thinking that, instead of giving it to his wife, he ought to have kept that hood to hide his own head in, for the horns were about to sprout."

"Your story is a good one," said Vicomte de Brassard calmly, "and at another time I should have enjoyed it more—but allow me to finish my tale. I confess that with a girl of that sort I was not for a moment doubtful of the fate of my letter. She might be tied to her mother's apron-strings, but she would find means to read my letter and reply to it. I even expected a long correspondence, carried on under the table as we had begun, and when the next day I entered the dining-room, firmly convinced in my own mind that I was about to have a reply to my letter of the previous evening, I thought my eyes must have played me a trick when I saw that the covers had been changed, and that Mademoiselle Alberte was placed, where she always ought to have been, between her father and mother.

"What was the meaning of this change? Did her father and mother suspect anything? Mademoiselle Alberte was opposite to me, and I looked at her with that fixed expression which demands an answer. There were twenty-five notes of interrogation in my eyes; but hers were as calm, as silent, as indifferent as usual. They looked at me as though they did not see me. I have never seen a look more annoying than that long calm gaze, which fell on you as though you were an inanimate object. I boiled with curiosity, vexation, impatience, and many other emotions—and I could not understand how it was that this girl, who was so sure of herself, did not dare to give me a sign which would warn me, or make me guess, or tell me, that we understood each other, and that we were conniving or conspiring together in the same mystery, whether it was love or something else.

"I asked myself if it could be really the same girl who had touched my hand and foot under the table; who had received the letter the previous evening and had slipped it so cleverly into her breast, before her parents, as she would have placed a flower there. She had done so much already that she need not have been embarrassed to give me a glance. But no! I had nothing. The dinner passed without that glance for which I was watching and waiting. 'She must have found some means to reply to me,' I said to myself as I left the table and went up to my room, not believing that such a woman would retreat after such an incredible advance—not admitting that fear or prudence could stand between her and her fancies, and *parbleu!* frankly refusing to acknowledge that she had not a fancy for me.

"'If her parents have no suspicion,' I said to myself, 'if it is by chance that she has changed her place at the table, to-morrow I shall find her by my side again.'—But on the morrow, and on the following days, I was not seated near Mademoiselle Alberte, who continued to wear the same incomprehensible look, and to say the same ordinary phrases in the same impassive way.

"You may well imagine that I observed her with much interest. She appeared as undisturbed as possible, whilst I was horribly annoyed, even to anger—an anger that I was forced to conceal! This air, which she never lost, made me seem farther away from her than ever. I was so exasperated that in the end I did not fear to compromise her by looking at her, and fixing on her impenetrable eyes the earnest, burning gaze of mine. Was it a clever manœuvre on her part? Was it coquetry? Was it but one caprice following another—or simply stupidity? 'If one knew the right moment!' as Ninon used to say. Had the right moment already passed?

"However, I still waited—for what?—a word, a sign—so easily given as we pushed the chairs back when we rose from dinner—and as that did not come, all the most foolish and absurd ideas began to fill my head. I imagined that because of the difficulties which surrounded us in the house, she would write to me by post—she was quite cunning enough to slip a letter into the box when she was out with her mother—and impressed by that idea, my blood boiled twice a day, an hour before the postman passed. Ten times a day did I ask the old servant, in a voice choked with emotion: 'Are there any letters for me, Olive?' to which she replied imperturbably: 'No, sir, there are not.'

"Finally the anxiety grew too intense. Desire deceived turned to hate. I began to hate Alberte, and to explain to myself her conduct towards me by motives which would cause me to despise her, for hate needs scorn. 'Cowardly little wretch, she is afraid to write,' I said to myself. I endeavoured not to think of her, and I heaped abuse upon her when I spoke of her to Louis de Meung—for I did tell him about her, for she had extinguished all my sense of chivalry, and I related the whole adventure to my friend, who twisted his long fair moustache whilst he listened to me, and who frankly replied—for we were not moralists in the 27th:

" 'Do as I do. One nail drives out another. Take one of the little sempstresses of the town for a mistress, and think no more about the young devil.'

"But I did not follow his advice. I had too much at stake. If I had taken a mistress, and she had known of it, I might have aroused her vanity or her jealousy. But she would not know it. How should she? If I had brought home some woman to my lodgings, as Louis did, I should have embroiled myself with the worthy people of the house, who would at once have requested me to look out for other apartments, and I was not willing to give up the chance of again meeting the hand or the foot of that confounded Alberte, who, after all she had dared to do, still remained 'Mademoiselle Impassible.'

" 'Call her, rather, impossible,' said Louis, who made fun of me.

"A whole month passed, and in spite of my resolutions to forget Alberte, and to seem as indifferent as she was—to oppose marble to marble, and coldness to coldness—my whole life was passed on the watch—which I detest, even when I am shooting. Yes, sir, my days were spent on the watch. I was on the watch when I went down to dinner, and hoped to find her alone in the dining-room as on the first occasion. On the watch during dinner, when she met my eyes with a calm cold gaze which did not avoid mine, or reply to it either. On the watch after dinner, when I remained a little time to see the two women resume their work in the window-seat; hoping that she would drop something—her thimble, or scissors, or a bit of work—that I could pick up, and in restoring touch her hand—that hand which burned into my brain! On the watch when I had regained my own room, and thought I heard in the corridor the foot which had pressed on mine so firmly. On the watch on the staircase, where I hoped I might meet her, and where old Olive discovered me one day, to my great confusion. On the watch at my window—the window you see—where I planted myself when she was going out with her mother, and from which I did not budge until she returned; but which was as useless as all the rest. When she went out—wearing a shawl with red and white stripes, printed with black and yellow flowers—she never once turned; and when she returned, still by her mother's side, she never raised her head or her eyes to the window where I was awaiting her.

"Such were the miserable practices to which she had condemned me.

Of course I know that women make lackeys of us—but not to that extent. Ah, I no longer took pleasure in my uniform! When the duties of the day were over—after the drill or the parade—I returned home quickly, but not to read a pile of memoirs or novels, my sole reading at that time. I never went to see Louis de Meung. I never touched the foils. I had not even the resource of tobacco which deadens the nerves, and which you young men of the present day use. We did not smoke then in the 27th, or only the privates did in the guard-room, when they played cards on the head of the drum. The only exercise I took was to tramp up and down the six feet of clear space in my room, like a caged lioness that smells raw meat.

"And if it were so in the day, it was also the same for a great part of the night. I went to bed late. I did not sleep. That infernal Alberte kept me awake. She had kindled a fire in my veins, and then gone away— like an incendiary who does not even turn his head to see the flames burst forth behind him. In the evening, I lowered, as it is now"—here the Vicomte passed his glove over the coach-window, to wipe away the moisture—"the same crimson curtain in front of the same window, and which was better than shutters to prevent inquisitive neighbours from seeing into the room.

"The room was furnished in the style of the period—the Empire—with a parquetry floor, no carpet, and a bed all bronze and cherry-wood, with a sphinx at each corner, and lion's paws for the feet. There was also on each drawer of the writing-table a lion's head with a ring in its mouth, by which ring you pulled the drawer open. A square table, also in cherrywood, but of a rather pinker shade than the rest of the furniture, and having a grey marble top and copper ornaments, stood opposite the bed against the wall, between the window and the door of a dressing-room; and opposite the fire-place was the large blue morocco sofa of which I have already spoken. High up in each corner stood a bracket of imitation lacquer, and upon one of them was a statuette of Niobe—rather an astonishing ornament to find in a bourgeois family. But wasn't this incomprehensible Alberte even more astonishing? The walls were painted a whitish yellow, and were devoid of pictures and engravings. I hung up my arms, suspended on gilt copper hooks. When I hired this great calabash of an apartment—as Louis de Meung, who was not poetical, elegantly called it— I had placed in the centre a large round table, which I covered with military maps, books, and papers. It was my bureau, at which I wrote—whenever I did write.

"Well, one evening, or rather one night, I had wheeled the sofa up to this large table, and I was drawing by the light of the lamp—not to distract my mind from the sole thought which had occupied it for a month, but rather the reverse, for it was the head of that perplexing Alberte which I was sketching—it was the face of that she-devil, who worried me as a devotee is worried by the other devil.

"It was late. The street—through which passed two diligences every night, one each way (as now), one at a quarter to one in the morning, and the other at half past two, and both of which stopped to change horses at the Hotel de la Poste—the street was as silent as the grave. I could have heard a fly, and if by chance there was one in my room, it must have been asleep in a corner of the window-pane, or in one of the pleats of the curtain, which was of heavy stuff, and hung stiff and motionless before the window. The only noise was that which I myself made with my pencil and stump.

"Yes, it was her face I was drawing; God knows with what care and attention! Suddenly, without any sound from the lock to forewarn me, my door opened a little way, giving that squeaky sound which doors make when the hinges are dry, and remained ajar, as though it were frightened by the sound it had made. I raised my eyes, thinking that I could not have closed the door properly that it should have opened in this unexpected way with a plaintive squeak that might frighten all those who were awake, and wake those who were asleep. I rose from the table in order to close it, but the half-opened door opened still wider, and still very gently, but with a repetition of that shrill sound which echoed like a groan through the silent house, and I saw, when it had opened to its full extent—Alberte!

"Alberte, who in spite of all her precautions, and the deadly fear in which she was, could not prevent that cursed door from crying out.

"Ah, *tonnerre de Dieu!* they may talk about visions—but not the most supernatural vision would have surprised me, or made my heart bound as it did when I saw coming towards me Alberte, frightened at the noise the door had made in opening, and which it would repeat when she closed it. Remember that I was but eighteen! Perhaps she saw my terror, and her own, and repressed by a quick sign the cry of surprise which might have escaped me—and certainly would have escaped but for this gesture—then she closed the door; not slowly but rapidly, to prevent the hinges from squeaking. It did not prevent them, and they gave one short shrill cry. The door being closed, she listened with her ear against it, if another sound more terrible might not reply to that of the door. . . . I thought I saw her totter. I sprang towards her, and she was soon in my arms."

"She seems to be getting along very nicely, your Miss Alberte," I said to the Captain.

"You think, perhaps," he continued, as though he had not heard my jesting remark, "that when she fell into my arms she had lost her head through fright, or love—like a girl who is pursued, or may be pursued; who does not know what she is doing when she does the most stupid things, but abandons herself to that devil which is in every woman (they say) and which would always be her master, were it not that she has two others also in her—Cowardice and Shame—to interfere with the first one. Well, no, it was not like that! If you think so, you are wrong. She had no vulgar and shamefaced fears. It was rather she who took me to her arms than I who took her to mine. . . . . Her first movement had been to throw her head on my breast, but she raised it again, and looked at me with her great eyes—those wonderful eyes—as if to see if it were really I she held in her arms.

"She was horribly pale—more pale than I had ever seen her—but she had not lost that look of a princess. Her features were still as hard and unimpressionable as a medal. Only on the slightly pouting lips there hovered an expression of I know not what, unless it was passion satisfied, or soon to be satisfied! Yet there was something so sad about this, that, in order not to see it, I impressed on her beautiful pink and pouting lips the kiss of triumphant desire! The mouth was half open, but the dark eyes, whose long lashes almost touched mine, did not close—or even wink—but behind them, as upon her mouth, I saw the same expression of madness.

"As she clung to me in a burning kiss, I carried her to the blue morocco sofa—which had been St. Laurence's grill to me during the month that I had rolled upon it thinking of her—and it creaked voluptuously under her bare back, for she was half naked. She had come from her bed and— would you believe it?—had been obliged to pass through the chamber where her father and mother slept! She had crept groping, with her hands in front of her, in order not to knock against some piece of furniture, and so make a noise which would wake them up."

"Ah!" I said, "one is not braver than that in the trenches. She was worthy to be a soldier's mistress."

"And that she was, the first night," replied the Vicomte.

"She was as violent as I was, and I can swear that I was bad enough. But, in spite of that, there was a drawback. Neither she nor I could forget, in our most delicious transports, the dreadful situation in which we both were. In the midst of the happiness which she came to offer me, she was as though stupefied by the act which she had accomplished with such a firm will and such stubborn obstinacy. I was not astonished at it. I, for my part, was also stupefied. I had—though I did not tell her, or show it—a most terrible anxiety in my heart, whilst she pressed me closely to her own. I listened through her sighs and kisses, and through the terrifying silence which lay on that sleeping and trusting household, for something terrible —for the mother who did not awake, for the father who did not get out of bed! And I looked over her shoulder to see if the door—of which she had not taken out the key for fear of the noise it might make—would not open again, and show me the Medusa heads, pale and indignant, of the two old people whom we were deceiving so boldly and so shamefully —spectres of violated hospitality and justice.

"Even the creaking of the blue sofa, though it sounded the reveille of Love, made me tremble dreadfully. My heart beat against hers, which seemed to re-echo the beatings. It was simultaneously intoxicating and sobering; but it was terrible. Afterwards I did not so much mind. By dint of repeating this incredible imprudence, it ceased to disturb me. I grew accustomed to the danger of being surprised. I did not think of it. I thought only of being happy. At this first critical meeting she decided that she would come to me every other night—since I could not go to her, her room having only one door which led to the room of her parents—and she came every second night, but she never got rid of the sensation—the stupor —of the first night! Time did not produce on her the effect that it did on me. She was never inured to the risk she ran each time. She always lay on my breast, hardly speaking—for, as you may suppose, she was not a great talker—and when later on I grew calmer, seeing the danger always avoided, and spoke to her, as a man speaks to his mistress, of what had already passed between us—of that strange insane coldness which had followed her bold step; when I asked her all those endless questions put by a lover, and which are, after all, nothing but curiosity, her only reply was a long embrace. Her sad mouth was dumb—in all but kisses.

"There are women who tell you: 'I have ruined myself for you'; and there are others who say: 'How you must despise me!' They are different ways of expressing the fatality of love—but she, no! She said nothing! A strange thing! A still stranger personality! She gave me the idea of a thick, hard marble slab which had a fire burning beneath it. I believed there would come a moment when the marble would be cracked by the heat, but the marble continued to be as solid as ever. Night after night saw no change in her, and, if I may be permitted an ecclesiastical expression, she was always as 'difficult to confess' as she had been the first night. I could get nothing out of her. At the most a syllable wrung from those beautiful lips, which I doted on the more because I had seen them cold and indifferent during the day, and this syllable did not give me much insight into the character of a girl who appeared to be more of a sphinx than all the others which adorned the Empire furniture."

"But, Captain," I interrupted, "there must, however, have been an end to all this. You are a sensible man, and the sphinxes are fabulous animals. Devil take it! you must at last have found out what idea had got into the girl's mind."

"An end! Yes, there was an end," said Vicomte de Brassard, suddenly lowering the coach-window, as though the breath had failed in his broad chest, and he needed air before he could finish what he had to say. "But the idea, as you call it, of this singular girl was not discovered, after all. Our love, our relations, our intrigue—call it what you will—gave us, or rather gave me, sensations which I do not think I have ever experienced since with women I loved more than Alberte, who, perhaps, did not love me, and whom, perhaps, I did not love! I never fully understood what I was to her, and what she was to me—and this lasted more than six months. During these six months, all that I understood was a kind of happiness of which you have not an idea when you are young. I understood the happiness of those who have something to hide. I understood the enjoyment of complicity in mystery, which, even without the hope of success, is the delight of conspirators. Alberte, at her parents' table and elsewhere, was still always the 'Infanta' who had made such an impression on me the first time I saw her. Her Nero face, beneath the hard curls of the blue-black hair which touched her eyebrows, told nothing of the guilty nights, showed no blush.

"I tried to be as impenetrable as she was, but I am sure I must have betrayed myself ten times if I had been well observed. I flattered myself proudly, and almost sensually, at the bottom of my heart, that all this superb indifference was for me, and that she felt for me all the baseness of passion—if passion can ever be base. No one but ourselves knew that; the thought was delicious. No one—not even my friend, Louis de Meung, with whom I had been discreet since I had become happy! He had guessed all, no doubt, but then he was as discreet as I was. He did not question me. I had, without any effort, resumed my friendly habits with him, the walks on the Promenade, in full uniform or undress, cards, fencing, and punch! *Pardieu!* when you know that happiness will come in the shape of a pretty girl, whose senses are aflame, and visit you regularly every other night at the same hour, that simplifies your existence wonderfully!"

"But the parents of Alberte must have slept like the Seven Sleepers!" I said jokingly, cutting short the reflection of the old dandy by a jest, in order not to appear too much interested in his story, though it did interest me; for with dandies a joke is the only way of making yourself respected.

"You imagine, then, I am romancing, and exaggerating the effects?" said the Viscomte. "But I am not a novelist. Sometimes Alberte did not come. The door—the hinges of which were oiled now and went as soft as wool—sometimes did not open all night—because her mother had heard her, and cried out, or her father had seen her creeping on tiptoe across the room. But Alberte, having a head like iron, had always a pretext ready. She was ill. She was seeking the sugar-basin, and without a light, in order not to awake anyone."

"Those heads of iron are not so rare as you seem to think, Captain," I interrupted again. "Your Alberte, after all, was no cleverer than the girl who received every night, in her grandmother's room—whilst the old lady was asleep behind the curtains—a lover, who came in through the window, and, as they had no blue sofa, they calmly lay down on the carpet. You know the story as well as I do. One night, a sigh louder than usual woke the grandmother, who cried from behind the curtains: 'What is the matter, little one?' and the girl nearly fainted on her lover's breast, but nevertheless recovered herself, and replied: 'The busk of my stays hurt me whilst I was looking for a needle which has fallen on the floor, and which I cannot find.'"

"Yes, I know the story," replied the Vicomte. "The young girl of whom you speak was, if I remember rightly, one of the Guises. She acted up to her name, but you do not mention that after that night she never opened her window again to her lover, who was, I think, M. de Noirmoutier; whereas Alberte came to me the day after one of these terrible shocks, and exposed herself again to danger just as though nothing had occurred. I was then only an ensign, and not very strong in mathematics, with which I did not trouble myself; but it must have been evident to one who could calculate chances that some day—or night—there would be a *dénouement*."

"Ah, yes," I remarked, remembering what he had said before he began his story, "the *dénouement* which made you acquainted with the sensation of fear, Captain."

"Precisely," he replied, in a voice so grave that it contrasted strongly with the flippant tone I had assumed. "You have seen, have you not? that from the time she seized my hand under the table, to the moment when she appeared like a ghost framed in my open doorway, Alberte had made me suffer all kinds of emotion. She had caused to pass through me more than one kind of shudder, more than one kind of terror; but they had been merely like the bullets which whistle round you—like the cannon-balls of which you feel only the wind: you shudder, but you go on. Well! it was not that. It was fear—thorough and complete fear, and no longer for Alberte, but for myself; for myself alone. What I felt was that sensation which makes the heart as pale as the face—that panic fear which makes whole regiments take to flight. I have seen the whole Chamboran regiment take to its heels, carrying with it its colonel and all the officers. But at that time I had seen nothing of the kind, and I learned—that which I believed to be impossible. . . .

"Listen! It was one night. In the life we were leading, it was bound to be at night—a long winter's night. I will not say it was one of our calmest nights. Our nights were all calm. We were so happy that they became so. We slept over a powder-magazine. We were not disturbed at the thought of making love on a sword-blade over an abyss, like the bridge which leads to the Turkish hell. Alberte had come earlier than usual, in order to stay longer. When she thus came, my first caress, my first attention, was for her feet—those pretty feet, not now encased in green or blue slippers, but bare in order to make no sound—for they were icy from the cold bricks over which she walked the length of the corridor which led from her parents' room to mine, which was at the other side of the house.

"I warmed those icy feet, which for my sake had come out of a warm bed, fearing that she might catch some terrible disease of the lungs. I knew how to warm them, and bring back the pink or red tint to those pale, cold feet; but that night my method failed. My mouth was powerless to bring back the flush of blood.

"Alberte was that night more silently loving than ever.

"Her embraces had that languor and that force which were to me like a language, and a language so expressive that, if I had told her all my mad intoxication of joy, I should have needed no other answer. I understood those embraces.

"But suddenly I felt them no longer. Her arms ceased to press me to her heart. I thought it was one of those swoons such as she often had, though generally in these swoons her embrace never relaxed.—I need not be prudish to you. We are both men, and we can speak as men.

"I had had some experience of the voluptuous spasms of Alberte, and when they seized her, they did not interrupt my embraces.

"I remained as I was, on her breast, waiting till she should return to consciousness, and proud in the certainty she would recover her senses under my embraces, and that the blow which had struck her, by striking again, would revive her.

"But this was the exception to the rule. I gazed at her as she lay close to me on the blue sofa, awaiting the moment when her eyes, now hidden under the long lids, should again reveal to me those splendid orbs of black velvet and flame; when those teeth which clenched almost tight enough to break the enamel at the least kiss on her neck or shoulders, should reopen and allow her breath to pass. But the eyes did not reopen, and the teeth did not unclench.

"The icy chill rose from her feet, and mounted even to her lips. When I felt that horrible cold, I sat up, in order to look at her the better; with a bound I tore myself from her arms, one of which fell back on her body, and the other dropped to the ground by the side of the sofa on which she lay. Frightened, but having still my senses about me, I put my hand on her heart. . . . No sign of life! No sign in the pulse, in the temples, no sign in the carotid arteries, no sign anywhere.—Death with its terrible rigidity was everywhere!

"I was sure of her death—and yet I could not believe it.

"The human brain sometimes makes those stupid resolutions even in the face of clear evidence and destiny. Alberte was dead. Of what? I did not know; I was not a doctor. But she was dead, and though I saw as clearly as the sun at noonday that all I could do would be useless, yet I did everything that I knew would be absurdly useless. In my absolute ignorance of all knowledge, and want of all instruments and resources, I emptied over her face all the bottles on my dressing-table. I beat her hand, in spite of the noise it made in a house where the least sound made us tremble. I had heard one of my uncles, a captain in the 4th Dragoons, say that he had once saved one of his friends from apoplexy by bleeding him with a fleam, such as is used for bleeding horses. I had plenty of weapons in my room. I picked up a dagger, and cut Alberte's arm deeply, but no blood flowed.

"At the most a few drops coagulated. Neither kisses nor bites could galvanize into life that stiff corpse—which had become a corpse beneath my lips. Not knowing what more to do, I ended by extending myself on her body—the means employed (according to the old legends) by all the miracle-workers of the past when they resuscitated dead bodies—not hoping to restore her to life, but acting as though I did so hope. And it was whilst I was lying on this cold body that a thought, which had not before been able to form itself in the mental chaos in which the frightfully sudden death of Alberte had thrown me, appeared clearly, and I was afraid.

"Yes, I was seized by a dread—a terrible dread. Alberte had died in my room, and her death would reveal everything. What would become of me? What should I do?

"At the thought, I seemed to feel a terrible physical dread, and my hair stood on end. My backbone turned to ice, and I tried to struggle—but in vain—against the unmanly feeling. I told myself I must be calm; that I was a man—a soldier. I took my head in my hands, and whilst my brain reeled, I compelled myself to think of the terrible situation in which I was, and consider all the ideas which whipped my brain as though it were a top—and all these ideas centred in the inanimate body of Alberte, and how her mother would find her in the morning in 'the officer's room'— dead and dishonoured!

"The thought of the mother whose daughter I had dishonoured and perhaps killed, weighed more on my mind than even the corpse of Alberte. The death could not be concealed—but was there no means of concealing the dishonour proved by the discovery of the body in my room? That was the question I asked myself; the point on which I fixed all my attention.

"The difficulty increased the more I studied it, until it assumed the proportions of an absolute impossibility. Frightful hallucination! Sometimes the corpse of Alberte seemed to fill the whole room. Ah, if her bedroom had not been placed behind that of her parents, I would have carried her back, at all risks, to her own bed.

"But how could I, with a dead body in my arms, pass through a room with which I was unacquainted, and which I had never entered, and where the father and mother of the unfortunate girl slumbered in the light sleep of old people?

"Yet such was my state of mind, and my fear of the morrow and of the dead body found in my room galloped so madly through my brain, that this bold madness of carrying Alberte to her own room possessed me as the only means of saving the honour of the poor girl, and sparing me the shame of the reproaches of the father and mother. Would you believe it?— I can hardly believe it myself when I think of it!—I had the strength to take Alberte's dead body, raising it by the arms, and place it on my shoulders. Horrible burden! heavier by far than that of the damned in Dante's hell. You must have carried, as I did, that fardel of flesh which but

an hour before had made my blood boil with desire, and which now terrified me! You must have carried it yourself ere you can know what I felt
and suffered.

"Thus laden, I opened the door, and, like her, with bare feet that I
might make no noise, I entered the corridor which led to her parents'
room, the door of which was at the end of the passage, and, stopping at
each step, whilst my legs almost gave way under me, I listened for the
least sound, and could hear nothing but the beating of my own heart.
The moments seemed terribly long. Nothing moved. One step succeeded
another. But when I arrived in front of that fatal door which I must enter,
and which she had not quite closed, that she might find it still open on
her return—and when I heard the long, quiet breathing of those two poor
old people who were sleeping in such peace and confidence, I dared go no
farther. I dared not pass that doorway, looking so black and threatening
in the darkness.

"I drew back; I almost fled with my burden. I returned to my room
more and more terror-struck. I replaced the body of Alberte on the sofa,
and, on my knees beside her, I repeated those supplicating questions.
What is to be done? What will be the end? So perturbed was I, that the
senseless and atrocious idea occurred to me to throw the body of this
beautiful girl, who had been my mistress six months, out of the window.
Despise me if you will! I opened the window—I drew aside the curtain
you see there, and I looked into the black hole at the bottom of which
was the street, for it was very dark that night. I could not see the pavement. 'They will believe it is a suicide,' I said to myself—and I once more
raised Alberte's body. But then a ray of common sense shot across my
madness. 'How was she killed? From whence could she have fallen if she
is found under my window?'

"I fully realized the impossibility of what I had been about to do. I
closed the window, the fastening of which creaked dismally. I drew the curtain again, feeling more dead than alive at each sound I made. Besides,
either through the window—on the staircase—in the corridor—wherever
I might leave or throw the body, it would be an eternal accuser—the
profanation would be useless. An examination of the corpse would reveal
everything, and a mother's eyes would see all that the doctor or the judge
tried to conceal from her.

"What I suffered was insupportable, and I had a good mind to finish
it all with a pistol-shot and in the 'demoralized' (an expression of the
Emperor's that I learned to understand later) condition in which I was, I
looked at the weapons shining on the walls. But there! I will be frank. I
was seventeen, and I loved—my sword. Both by inclination and race, I was
a soldier. I had never been under fire, and I wished to be. I had military
ambitions. In the regiment we joked about Werther—regarded as a hero
at that time—but whom we officers pitied. The thought which prevented

me from getting rid, by killing myself, of the ignoble fear which oppressed me, led to another which appeared to be salvation in the strait in
which I was.

"If I went and saw the Colonel! I said to myself. The Colonel is the
father of the regiment—and I dressed myself as though the call to arms
were beating for a surprise attack. I took my pistols as a precaution. Who
knew what might happen? I embraced for the last time, with all the affection of seventeen—one is always sentimental at seventeen—the dumb
mouth of the poor dead Alberte, which during the last six months had
showered upon me such delights. I descended the stair on tiptoe. Breathless as one who is fleeing for his life, I took an hour (it seemed to me an
hour) to unbolt the street-door and turn the big key in the enormous
lock; and, after having closed the door again with all the precautions of a
thief, I ran like one fleeing for his life to the Colonel's house.

"I rang as though the house had been on fire. I shouted as though the
enemy had been about to capture the flag of the regiment. I knocked
everything over, including the orderly who tried to prevent me from entering his master's room, and when once the Colonel was awake, I told him
everything. I made a complete confession rapidly and boldly, for time
pressed, and I begged of him to save me.

"The Colonel was a man of action. He saw at a glance in what a horrible gulf I was struggling. He had pity on the youngest of his children, as
he called us, and indeed I was in a condition to be pitied. He told me—
accentuating the statement with a round oath—that I must begin by clearing out of the town, immediately, and that he would undertake the rest;
that he would see the parents as soon as I had gone, but that I must go at
once, and take the diligence which would stop in ten minutes' time at the
Hotel de la Poste, and go to a town which he named, where he would
write. He gave me some money, for I had omitted to put any in my pocket,
pressed his old grey moustache to my cheeks, and ten minutes after this
interview I had climbed on the roof—it was the only place left—of the
diligence which was making the same journey as we are now, and I passed
at a gallop under the window (you may guess how I looked at it) of
the funeral chamber where I had left Alberte dead, and which was lighted
up as it is to-night."

Vicomte de Brassard stopped, his voice quite broken.

I no longer felt inclined to joke. The silence did not last long.

"And after?" I said.

"Well," he replied, "there was no after. For a long time I was tortured
by curiosity. I followed faithfully the Colonel's instructions. I impatiently
awaited a letter that would inform me of what had happened after my departure. I waited about a month; but at the end of the month it was not a
letter from the Colonel I received, for he scarcely ever wrote, except with
a sabre on the bodies of his enemies, but an order to join in twenty-

four hours the 33rd Regiment, to which I had been appointed. A campaign, and that my first, distracted my thoughts. The battles in which I took part, the hardships, and also some adventures with women, caused me to neglect to write to the Colonel, and turned my thoughts from the sad memory of Alberte, without, however, effacing it. I preserved it still, like a bullet that cannot be extracted. I said to myself that I should some day meet the Colonel, who would inform me of that which I wished to know, but the Colonel was killed at the head of his regiment at Leipsic. Louis de Meung also had been killed about a month before.

"It is shameful, no doubt," added the Captain, "but memories end by dying. The devouring curiosity to know what had happened after my departure no longer disturbed me. I might have come back in after years to this little town—and, changed as I was, I should never have been recognized—and learned what had been the end of my tragic adventure. But something, which was certainly not respect for public opinion, which I have all my life despised, but rather a disinclination to face a second time that which had given me such a deadly fear, always restrained me."

This dandy, who had related without any dandyism such a grim and true story, was silent. I was thinking over his story, and I understood that this fine flower of dandyism had other sides to his character than those which appeared to his acquaintances. I remembered that he had said at the beginning that there was a black blot which had all his life destroyed his pleasures as a libertine—when suddenly he astonished me still more by seizing my arm roughly.

"Look!" he said. "Look at the curtain!"

The slim shadow of a woman was plainly delineated on the curtain.

"The ghost of Alberte!" said the Captain. "Fortune is mocking us to-night," he added bitterly.

The shadow passed, and the red bright square was again empty. But the wheelwright, who, whilst the Captain was speaking, had been busy with his screw, had finished his task. The fresh horses were ready, and were pawing the ground, striking out sparks with their iron shoes.

The driver, his astrakhan cap over his ears, and the way-bill between his teeth, took the reins and climbed to the box, and, when once he was in his seat, cried in a loud clear voice:

"Go on!"

And we went on, and had soon passed the mysterious window with its red curtain—but I still continue to see it in my dreams.

THE GOLD–BUG

Edgar Allan Poe
(1809–1849)

What ho! what ho! this fellow is dancing mad!
He hath been bitten by the Tarantula.

—ALL IN THE WRONG

MANY YEARS AGO, I contracted an intimacy with a Mr. William Legrand. He was of an ancient Huguenot family, and had once been wealthy; but a series of misfortunes had reduced him to want. To avoid the mortification consequent upon his disasters, he left New Orleans, the city of his fore-fathers, and took up his residence at Sullivan's Island, near Charleston, South Carolina.

This Island is a very singular one. It consists of little else than the sea sand, and is about three miles long. Its breadth at no point exceeds a quarter of a mile. It is separated from the mainland by a scarcely per-ceptible creek, oozing its way through a wilderness of reeds and slime, a favorite resort of the marsh-hen. The vegetation, as might be supposed, is scant, or at least dwarfish. No trees of any magnitude are to be seen. Near the western extremity, where Fort Moultrie stands, and where are some miserable frame buildings, tenanted, during the summer, by the fugitives from Charleston dust and fever, may be found, indeed, the bristly pal-metto; but the whole island, with the exception of this western point, and a line of hard, white beach on the seacoast, is covered with a dense under-growth of the sweet myrtle, so much prized by the horticulturists of Eng-land. The shrub here often attains the height of fifteen or twenty feet, and forms an almost impenetrable coppice, burthening the air with its fra-grance.

In the inmost recesses of this coppice, not far from the eastern or more remote end of the island, Legrand had built himself a small hut, which he occupied when I first, by mere accident, made his acquaintance. This soon ripened into friendship—for there was much in the recluse to excite interest and esteem. I found him well educated, with unusual powers of mind, but infected with misanthropy, and subject to perverse moods of alternate enthusiasm and melancholy. He had with him many books, but rarely employed them. His chief amusements were gunning and fishing, or sauntering along the beach and through the myrtles, in quest of shells or

entomological specimens;—his collection of the latter might have been
envied by a Swammerdamm. In these excursions he was usually accompanied by an old negro, called Jupiter, who had been manumitted before
the reverses of the family, but who could be induced, neither by threats
nor by promises, to abandon what he considered his right of attendance
upon the footsteps of his young "Massa Will." It is not improbable that
the relatives of Legrand, conceiving him to be somewhat unsettled in intellect, had contrived to instil this obstinacy into Jupiter, with a view to
the supervision and guardianship of the wanderer.

The winters in the latitude of Sullivan's Island are seldom very severe,
and in the fall of the year it is a rare event indeed when a fire is considered
necessary. About the middle of October, 18—, there occurred, however, a
day of remarkable chilliness. Just before sunset I scrambled my way
through the evergreens to the hut of my friend, whom I had not visited
for several weeks—my residence being, at that time, in Charleston, a distance of nine miles from the Island, while the facilities of passage and re-
passage were very far behind those of the present day. Upon reaching the
hut I rapped, as was my custom, and getting no reply, sought for the key
where I knew it was secreted, unlocked the door and went in. A fine fire
was blazing upon the hearth. It was a novelty, and by no means an ungrateful one. I threw off an overcoat, took an arm-chair by the crackling logs,
and awaited patiently the arrival of my hosts.

Soon after dark they arrived, and gave me a most cordial welcome.
Jupiter, grinning from ear to ear, bustled about to prepare some marsh-
hens for supper. Legrand was in one of his fits—how else shall I term
them?—of enthusiasm. He had found an unknown bivalve, forming a new
genus, and, more than this, he had hunted down and secured, with
Jupiter's assistance, a *scarabæus* which he believed to be totally new, but in
respect to which he wished to have my opinion on the morrow.

"And why not to-night?" I asked, rubbing my hands over the blaze, and
wishing the whole tribe of *scarabæi* at the devil.

"Ah, if I had only known you were here!" said Legrand, "but it's so
long since I saw you; and how could I foresee that you would pay me a
visit this very night of all others? As I was coming home I met Lieutenant G——, from the fort, and, very foolishly, I lent him the bug; so it
will be impossible for you to see it until morning. Stay here to-night, and I
will send Jup down for it at sunrise. It is the loveliest thing in creation!"

"What?—sunrise?"

"Nonsense! no!—the bug. It is of a brilliant gold color—about the size
of a large hickory-nut—with two jet-black spots near one extremity of the
back, and another, somewhat longer, at the other. The *antennæ* are——"

"Dey ain't *no* tin in him, Massa Will, I keep a tellin on you," here interrupted Jupiter; "de bug is a goole bug, solid, ebery bit of him, inside and
all, sep him wing—neber feel half so hebby a bug in my life."

"Well, suppose it is, Jup," replied Legrand, somewhat more earnestly, it seemed to me, than the case demanded, "is that any reason for your letting the birds burn? The color"—here he turned to me—"is really almost enough to warrant Jupiter's idea. You never saw a more brilliant metallic lustre than the scales emit—but of this you cannot judge till to-morrow. In the mean time I can give you some idea of the shape." Saying this, he seated himself at a small table, on which were a pen and ink, but no paper. He looked for some in a drawer, but found none.

"Never mind," said he at length, "this will answer"; and he drew from his waistcoat pocket a scrap of what I took to be very dirty foolscap, and made upon it a rough drawing with the pen. While he did this, I retained my seat by the fire, for I was still chilly. When the design was complete, he handed it to me without rising. As I received it, a loud growl was heard, succeeded by a scratching at the door. Jupiter opened it, and a large Newfoundland, belonging to Legrand, rushed in, leaped upon my shoulders, and loaded me with caresses; for I had shown him much attention during previous visits. When his gambols were over, I looked at the paper, and, to speak the truth, found myself not a little puzzled at what my friend had depicted.

"Well!" I said, after contemplating it for some minutes, "this *is* a strange *scarabæus*, I must confess: new to me: never saw anything like it before —unless it was a skull, or a death's-head—which it more nearly resembles than anything else that has come under *my* observation."

"A death's-head!" echoed Legrand—"Oh—yes—well, it has something of that appearance upon paper, no doubt. The two upper black spots look like eyes, eh? and the longer one at the bottom like a mouth—and then the shape of the whole is oval."

"Perhaps so," said I; "but, Legrand, I fear you are no artist. I must wait until I see the beetle itself, if I am to form any idea of its personal appearance."

"Well, I don't know," said he, a little nettled, "I draw tolerably—*should* do it at least—have had good masters, and flatter myself that I am not quite a blockhead."

"But, my dear fellow, you are joking then," said I, "this is a very passable *skull*—indeed, I may say that it is a very excellent skull, according to the vulgar notions about such specimens of physiology—and your *scarabæus* must be the queerest *scarabæus* in the world if it resembles it. Why, we may get up a very thrilling bit of superstition upon this hint. I presume you will call the bug *scarabæus caput hominis,* or something of that kind —there are many similar titles in the Natural Histories. But where are the *antennæ* you spoke of?"

"The *antennæ!*" said Legrand, who seemed to be getting unaccountably warm upon the subject; "I am sure you must see the *antennæ*. I made them as distinct as they are in the original insect, and I presume that is sufficient."

"Well, well," I said, "perhaps you have—still I don't see them;" and I handed him the paper without additional remark, not wishing to ruffle his temper; but I was much surprised at the turn affairs had taken; his ill humor puzzled me—and, as for the drawing of the beetle, there were positively *no antennæ* visible, and the whole *did* bear a very close resemblance to the ordinary cuts of a death's-head.

He received the paper very peevishly, and was about to crumple it, apparently to throw it in the fire, when a casual glance at the design seemed suddenly to rivet his attention. In an instant his face grew violently red—in another as excessively pale. For some minutes he continued to scrutinize the drawing minutely where he sat. At length he arose, took a candle from the table, and proceeded to seat himself upon a sea-chest in the farthest corner of the room. Here again he made an anxious examination of the paper; turning it in all directions. He said nothing, however, and his conduct greatly astonished me; yet I thought it prudent not to exacerbate the growing moodiness of his temper by any comment. Presently he took from his coat pocket a wallet, placed the paper carefully in it, and deposited both in a writing-desk, which he locked. He now grew more composed in his demeanor; but his original air of enthusiasm had quite disappeared. Yet he seemed not so much sulky as abstracted. As the evening wore away he became more and more absorbed in reverie, from which no sallies of mine could arouse him. It had been my intention to pass the night at the hut, as I had frequently done before, but, seeing my host in this mood, I deemed it proper to take leave. He did not press me to remain, but, as I departed, he shook my hand with even more than his usual cordiality.

It was about a month after this (and during the interval I had seen nothing of Legrand) when I received a visit, at Charleston, from his man, Jupiter. I had never seen the good old negro look so dispirited, and I feared that some serious disaster had befallen my friend.

"Well, Jup," said I, "what is the matter now?—how is your master?"

"Why, to speak de troof, massa, him not so berry well as mought be."

"Not well! I am truly sorry to hear it. What does he complain of?"

"Dar! dat's it!—him neber plain of notin—but him berry sick for all dat."

"*Very* sick, Jupiter!—why didn't you say so at once? Is he confined to bed?"

"No, dat he ain't!—he ain't find nowhar—dat's just whar de shoe pinch—my mind is got to be berry hebby bout poor Massa Will."

"Jupiter, I should like to understand what it is you are talking about. You say your master is sick. Hasn't he told you what ails him?"

"Why, massa, tain't worf while for to git mad bout de matter—Massa Will say noffin at all ain't de matter wid him—but den what make him go about looking dis here way, wid he head down and he soldiers up, and as white as a gose? And den he keep a syphon all de time——"

"Keeps a what, Jupiter?"

"Keeps a syphon wid de figgurs on de slate—de queerest figgurs I ebber did see. I'se gittin be skeered, I tell you. Hab for to keep mighty tight eye pon him noovers. Todder day he gib me slip fore de sun up and was gone de whole ob de blessed day. I had a big stick ready cut for to gib him d—d good beating when he did come—but I'se sich a fool dat I had-n't de heart arter all—he look so berry poorly."

"Eh?—what? ah yes!—upon the whole I think you had better not be too severe with the poor fellow—don't flog him, Jupiter—he can't very well stand it—but can you form no idea of what has occasioned this illness, or rather this change of conduct? Has anything unpleasant happened since I saw you?"

"No, massa, dey ain't bin noffin onpleasant *since* den—'twas *fore* den I'm feared—'twas de berry day you was dare."

"How? what do you mean?"

"Why, massa, I mean de bug—dare now."

"The what?"

"De bug—I'm berry sartain dat Massa Will bin bit somewhere bout de head by dat goole-bug."

"And what cause have you, Jupiter, for such a supposition?"

"Claws enuff, massa, and mouff too. I nebber did see sich a d—d bug—he kick and he bite ebery ting what cum near him. Massa Will cotch him fuss, but had for to let him go gin mighty quick, I tell you—den was de time he must ha got de bite. I didn't like de look ob de bug mouff, myself, no how, so I wouldn't take hold ob him wid my finger, but I cotch him wid a piece ob paper dat I found. I rap him up in de paper and stuff piece ob it in he mouff—dat was de way."

"And you think, then, that your master was really bitten by the beetle, and that the bite made him sick?"

"I don't tink noffin about it—I nose it. What make him dream bout de goole so much, if tain't cause he bit by de goole-bug? I'se heerd bout dem goole-bugs fore dis."

"But how do you know he dreams about gold?"

"How I know? why cause he talk about it in he sleep—dat's how I nose."

"Well, Jup, perhaps you are right; but to what fortunate circumstance am I to attribute the honor of a visit from you to-day?"

"What de matter, massa?"

"Did you bring any message from Mr. Legrand?"

"No, massa, I bring dis here pissel"; and here Jupiter handed me a note which ran thus:

MY DEAR—

Why have I not seen you for so long a time? I hope you have not been so foolish as to take offence at any little *brusquerie* of mine; but no, that is im-probable.

Since I saw you I have had great cause for anxiety. I have something to tell you, yet scarcely know how to tell it, or whether I should tell it at all.

I have not been quite well for some days past, and poor old Jup annoys me, almost beyond endurance, by his well-meant attentions. Would you believe it?— he had prepared a huge stick, the other day, with which to chastise me for giving him the slip, and spending the day, *solus,* among the hills on the main land. I verily believe that my ill looks alone saved me a flogging.

I have made no addition to my cabinet since we met.

If you can, in any way, make it convenient, come over with Jupiter. *Do* come. I wish to see you *to-night,* upon business of importance. I assure you that it is of the *highest* importance.

Ever yours,
WILLIAM LEGRAND

There was something in the tone of this note which gave me great uneasiness. Its whole style differed materially from that of Legrand. What could be be dreaming of? What new crotchet possessed his excitable brain? What "business of the highest importance" could *he* possibly have to transact? Jupiter's account of him boded no good. I dreaded lest the continued pressure of misfortune had, at length, fairly unsettled the reason of my friend. Without a moment's hesitation, therefore, I prepared to accompany the negro.

Upon reaching the wharf, I noticed a scythe and three spades, all apparently new, lying in the bottom of the boat in which we were to embark.

"What is the meaning of all this, Jup?" I inquired.

"Him syfe, massa, and spade."

"Very true; but what are they doing here?"

"Him de syfe and de spade what Massa Will sis pon my buying for him in de town, and de debbil's own lot of money I had to gib for 'em."

"But what, in the name of all that is mysterious, is your 'Massa Will' going to do with scythes and spades?"

"Dat's more dan *I* know, and debbil take me if I don't believe 'tis more dan he know, too. But it's all cum ob de bug."

Finding that no satisfaction was to be obtained of Jupiter, whose whole intellect seemed to be absorbed by "de bug," I now stepped into the boat and made sail. With a fair and strong breeze we soon ran into the little cove to the northward of Fort Moultrie, and a walk of some two miles brought us to the hut. It was about three in the afternoon when we arrived. Legrand had been awaiting us in eager expectation. He grasped my hand with a nervous *empressement* which alarmed me and strengthened the suspicions already entertained. His countenance was pale even to ghastliness, and his deep-set eyes glared with unnatural lustre. After some inquiries respecting his health, I asked him, not knowing what better to say, if he had yet obtained the *scarabæus* from Lieutenant G——.

"Oh, yes," he replied, coloring violently, "I got it from him the next morning. Nothing should tempt me to part with that *scarabæus*. Do you know that Jupiter is quite right about it?"

"In what way?" I asked, with a sad foreboding at heart.

"In supposing it to be a bug of *real gold*." He said this with an air of profound seriousness, and I felt inexpressibly shocked.

"This bug is to make my fortune," he continued, with a triumphant smile, "to reinstate me in my family possessions. Is it any wonder, then, that I prize it? Since Fortune has thought fit to bestow it upon me, I have only to use it properly and I shall arrive at the gold of which it is the index. Jupiter, bring me that *scarabæus!*"

"What! de bug, massa? I'd rudder not go fer trubble dat bug—you mus git him for your own self." Hereupon Legrand arose, with a grave and stately air, and brought me the beetle from a glass case in which it was enclosed. It was a beautiful *scarabæus,* and, at that time, unknown to naturalists—of course a great prize in a scientific point of view. There were two round, black spots near one extremity of the back, and a long one near the other. The scales were exceedingly hard and glossy, with all the appearance of burnished gold. The weight of the insect was very remarkable, and, taking all things into consideration, I could hardly blame Jupiter for his opinion respecting it; but what to make of Legrand's agreement with that opinion, I could not, for the life of me, tell.

"I sent for you," said he, in a grandiloquent tone, when I had completed my examination of the beetle, "I sent for you, that I might have your counsel and assistance in furthering the views of Fate and of the bug——"

"My dear Legrand," I cried, interrupting him, "you are certainly unwell, and had better use some little precautions. You shall go to bed, and I will remain with you a few days, until you get over this. You are feverish and——"

"Feel my pulse," said he.

I felt it, and, to say the truth, found not the slightest indication of fever.

"But you may be ill and yet have no fever. Allow me this once to prescribe for you. In the first place, go to bed. In the next——"

"You are mistaken," he interposed, "I am as well as I can expect to be under the excitement which I suffer. If you really wish me well, you will relieve this excitement."

"And how is this to be done?"

"Very easily. Jupiter and myself are going upon an expedition into the hills, upon the main land, and, in this expedition, we shall need the aid of some person in whom we can confide. You are the only one we can trust. Whether we succeed or fail, the excitement which you now perceive in me will be equally allayed."

"I am anxious to oblige you in any way," I replied; "but do you mean

to say that this infernal beetle has any connection with your expedition
into the hills?"

"It has."

"Then, Legrand, I can become a party to no such absurd proceeding."

"I am sorry—very sorry—for we shall have to try it by ourselves."

"Try it by yourselves! The man is surely mad!—but stay!—how long
do you propose to be absent?"

"Probably all night. We shall start immediately, and be back, at all events,
by sunrise."

"And will you promise me, upon your honor, that when this freak of
yours is over, and the bug business (good God!) settled to your satisfaction, you will then return home and follow my advice implicitly, as that
of your physician?"

"Yes; I promise; and now let us be off, for we have no time to lose."

With a heavy heart I accompanied my friend. We started about four
o'clock—Legrand, Jupiter, the dog, and myself. Jupiter had with him the
scythe and spades—the whole of which he insisted upon carrying—more
through fear, it seemed to me, of trusting either of the implements within
reach of his master, than from any excess of industry or complaisance. His
demeanor was dogged in the extreme, and "dat d—d bug" were the sole
words which escaped his lips during the journey. For my own part, I had
charge of a couple of dark lanterns, while Legrand contented himself with
the *scarabæus,* which he carried attached to the end of a bit of whip-cord;
twirling it to and fro, with the air of a conjuror, as he went. When I
observed this last, plain evidence of my friend's aberration of mind, I could
scarcely refrain from tears. I thought it best, however, to humor his fancy,
at least for the present, or until I could adopt some more energetic measures
with a chance of success. In the mean time I endeavored, but all in vain,
to sound him in regard to the object of the expedition. Having succeeded in
inducing me to accompany him, he seemed unwilling to hold conversation
upon any topic of minor importance, and to all my questions vouchsafed no
other reply than "we shall see!"

We crossed the creek at the head of the island by means of a skiff, and,
ascending the high grounds on the shore of the main land, proceeded in a
northwesterly direction, through a tract of country excessively wild and
desolate, where no trace of a human footstep was to be seen. Legrand led
the way with decision; pausing only for an instant, here and there, to consult what appeared to be certain landmarks of his own contrivance upon a
former occasion.

In this manner we journeyed for about two hours, and the sun was just
setting when we entered a region infinitely more dreary than any yet seen.
It was a species of table land, near the summit of an almost inaccessible
hill, densely wooded from base to pinnacle, and interspersed with huge
crags that appeared to lie loosely upon the soil, and in many cases were

prevented from precipitating themselves into the valleys below, merely by the support of the trees against which they reclined. Deep ravines, in various directions, gave an air of still sterner solemnity to the scene.

The natural platform to which we had clambered was thickly overgrown with brambles, through which we soon discovered that it would have been impossible to force our way but for the scythe; and Jupiter, by direction of his master, proceeded to clear for us a path to the foot of an enormously tall tulip-tree, which stood, with some eight or ten oaks, upon the level, and far surpassed them all, and all other trees which I had then ever seen, in the beauty of its foliage and form, in the wide spread of its branches, and in the general majesty of its appearance. When we reached this tree, Legrand turned to Jupiter, and asked him if he thought he could climb it. The old man seemed a little staggered by the question, and for some moments made no reply. At length he approached the huge trunk, walked slowly around it, and examined it with minute attention. When he had completed his scrutiny, he merely said,

"Yes, massa, Jup climb any tree he ebber see in he life."

"Then up with you as soon as possible, for it will soon be too dark to see what we are about."

"How far mus go up, massa?" inquired Jupiter.

"Get up the main trunk first, and then I will tell you which way to go—and here—stop! take this beetle with you."

"De bug, Massa Will!—de goole bug!" cried the negro, drawing back in dismay—"what for mus tote de bug way up de tree?—d—n if I do!"

"If you are afraid, Jup, a great big negro like you, to take hold of a harmless little dead beetle, why you can carry it up by this string—but, if you do not take it up with you in some way, I shall be under the necessity of breaking your head with this shovel."

"What de matter now, massa?" said Jup, evidently shamed into compliance; "always want for to raise fuss wid old nigger. Was only funnin any how. *Me* feered de bug! what I keer for de bug?" Here he took cautiously hold of the extreme end of the string, and, maintaining the insect as far from his person as circumstances would permit, prepared to ascend the tree.

In youth, the tulip-tree, or *Liriodendron Tulipiferum,* the most magnificent of American foresters, has a trunk peculiarly smooth, and often rises to a great height without lateral branches; but, in its riper age, the bark becomes gnarled and uneven, while many short limbs make their appearance on the stem. Thus the difficulty of ascension, in the present case, lay more in semblance than in reality. Embracing the huge cylinder, as closely as possible, with his arms and knees, seizing with his hands some projections, and resting his naked toes upon others, Jupiter, after one or two narrow escapes from falling, at length wriggled himself into the first great fork, and seemed to consider the whole business as virtually accomplished.

The *risk* of the achievement was, in fact, now over, although the climber was some sixty or seventy feet from the ground.

"Which way mus go now, Massa Will?" he asked.

"Keep up the largest branch—the one on this side," said Legrand. The negro obeyed him promptly, and apparently with but little trouble; ascending higher and higher, until no glimpse of his squat figure could be obtained through the dense foliage which enveloped it. Presently his voice was heard in a sort of halloo.

"How much fudder is got for go?"

"How high up are you?" asked Legrand.

"Ebber so fur," replied the negro; "can see de sky fru de top ob de tree."

"Never mind the sky, but attend to what I say. Look down the trunk and count the limbs below you on this side. How many limbs have you passed?"

"One, two, tree, four, fibe—I done pass fibe big limb, massa, pon dis side."

"Then go one limb higher."

In a few minutes the voice was heard again, announcing that the seventh limb was attained.

"Now, Jup," cried Legrand, evidently much excited, "I want you to work your way out upon that limb as far as you can. If you see anything strange, let me know."

By this time what little doubt I might have entertained of my poor friend's insanity, was put finally at rest. I had no alternative but to conclude him stricken with lunacy, and I became seriously anxious about getting him home. While I was pondering upon what was best to be done, Jupiter's voice was again heard.

"Mos feered for to ventur pon dis limb berry far—'tis dead limb putty much all de way."

"Did you say it was a *dead* limb, Jupiter?" cried Legrand in a quavering voice.

"Yes, massa, him dead as de door-nail—done up for sartain—done departed dis here life."

"What in the name of heaven shall I do?" asked Legrand, seemingly in the greatest distress.

"Do!" said I, glad of an opportunity to interpose a word, "why come home and go to bed. Come now!—that's a fine fellow. It's getting late, and, besides, you remember your promise."

"Jupiter," cried he, without heeding me in the least, "do you hear me?"

"Yes, Massa Will, hear you ebber so plain."

"Try the wood well, then, with your knife, and see if you think it *very* rotten."

"Him rotten, massa, sure nuff," replied the negro in a few moments, "but not so berry rotten as mought be. Mought ventur out leetle way pon de limb by myself, dat's true."

"By yourself!—what do you mean?"

"Why I mean de bug. 'Tis *berry* hebby bug. Spose I drop him down fuss, and den de limb won't break wid just de weight ob one nigger."

"You infernal scoundrel!" cried Legrand, apparently much relieved, "what do you mean by telling me such nonsense as that? As sure as you let that beetle fall!—I'll break your neck. Look here, Jupiter! do you hear me?"

"Yes, massa, needn't hollo at poor nigger dat style."

"Well! now listen!—if you will venture out on the limb as far as you think safe, and not let go the beetle, I'll make you a present of a silver dollar as soon as you get down."

"I'm gwine, Massa Will—deed I is," replied the negro very promptly—"mos out to the eend now."

"*Out to the end!*" here fairly screamed Legrand, "do you say you are out to the end of that limb?"

"Soon be to de eend, massa,—o-o-o-o-oh! Lor-gol-a-marcy! what *is* dis here pon de tree?"

"Well!" cried Legrand, highly delighted, "what is it?"

"Why tain't noffin but a skull—somebody bin lef him head up de tree, and de crows done gobble ebery bit ob de meat off."

"A skull, you say!—very well!—how is it fastened to the limb?—what holds it on?"

"Sure nuff, massa; mus look. Why dis berry curous sarcumstance, pon my word—dare's a great big nail in de skull, what fastens ob it on to de tree."

"Well now, Jupiter, do exactly as I tell you—do you hear?"

"Yes, massa."

"Pay attention, then!—find the left eye of the skull."

"Hum! hoo! dat's good! why dar ain't no eye lef at all."

"Curse your stupidity! do you know your right hand from your left?"

"Yes, I nose dat—nose all bout dat—'tis my left hand what I chops de wood wid."

"To be sure! you are left-handed; and your left eye is on the same side as your left hand. Now, I suppose, you can find the left eye of the skull, or the place where the left eye has been. Have you found it?"

Here was a long pause. At length the negro asked,

"Is de lef eye of de skull pon de same side as de lef hand of de skull, too?—cause de skull ain't got not a bit ob a hand at all—nebber mind! I got de lef eye now—here the lef eye! what mus do wid it?"

"Let the beetle drop through it, as far as the string will reach—but be careful and not let go your hold of the string."

"All dat done, Massa Will; mighty easy ting for to put de bug fru de hole—look out for him dar below!"

During this colloquy no portion of Jupiter's person could be seen; but the beetle, which he had suffered to descend, was now visible at the end of the string, and glistened, like a globe of burnished gold, in the last rays of the setting sun, some of which still faintly illumined the eminence upon which we stood. The *scarabæus* hung quite clear of any branches, and, if allowed to fall, would have fallen at our feet. Legrand immediately took the scythe, and cleared with it a circular space, three or four yards in diameter, just beneath the insect, and, having accomplished this, ordered Jupiter to let go the string and come down from the tree.

Driving a peg, with great nicety, into the ground, at the precise spot where the beetle fell, my friend now produced from his pocket a tape-measure. Fastening one end of this at that point of the trunk of the tree which was nearest the peg, he unrolled it till it reached the peg, and thence farther unrolled it, in the direction already established by the two points of the tree and the peg, for the distance of fifty feet—Jupiter clearing away the brambles with the scythe. At the spot thus attained a second peg was driven, and about this, as a centre, a rude circle, about four feet in diameter, described. Taking now a spade himself, and giving one to Jupiter and one to me, Legrand begged us to set about digging as quickly as possible.

To speak the truth, I had no especial relish for such amusement at any time, and, at that particular moment, would most willingly have declined it; for the night was coming on, and I felt much fatigued with the exercise already taken; but I saw no mode of escape, and was fearful of disturbing my poor friend's equanimity by a refusal. Could I have depended, indeed, upon Jupiter's aid, I would have had no hesitation in attempting to get the lunatic home by force; but I was too well assured of the old negro's disposition, to hope that he would assist me, under any circumstances, in a personal contest with his master. I made no doubt that the latter had been infected with some of the innumerable Southern superstitions about money buried, and that his phantasy had received confirmation by the finding of the *scarabæus,* or, perhaps, by Jupiter's obstinacy in maintaining it to be "a bug of real gold." A mind disposed to lunacy would readily be led away by such suggestions—especially if chiming in with favorite preconceived ideas—and then I called to mind the poor fellow's speech about the beetle's being "the index of his fortune." Upon the whole, I was sadly vexed and puzzled, but, at length, I concluded to make a virtue of necessity—to dig with a good will, and thus the sooner to convince the visionary, by ocular demonstration, of the fallacy of the opinions he entertained.

The lanterns having been lit, we all fell to work with a zeal worthy a more rational cause; and, as the glare fell upon our persons and implements, I could not help thinking how picturesque a group we composed, and how strange and suspicious our labors must have appeared to any interloper who, by chance, might have stumbled upon our whereabouts.

We dug very steadily for two hours. Little was said; and our chief embarrassment lay in the yelpings of the dog, who took exceeding interest in our proceedings. He, at length, became so obstreperous that we grew fearful of his giving the alarm to some stragglers in the vicinity;—or, rather, this was the apprehension of Legrand;—for myself, I should have rejoiced at any interruption which might have enabled me to get the wanderer home. The noise was, at length, very effectually silenced by Jupiter, who, getting out of the hole with a dogged air of deliberation, tied the brute's mouth up with one of his suspenders, and then returned, with a grave chuckle, to his task.

When the time mentioned had expired, we had reached a depth of five feet, and yet no signs of any treasure became manifest. A general pause ensued, and I began to hope that the farce was at an end. Legrand, however, although evidently much disconcerted, wiped his brow thoughtfully and recommenced. We had excavated the entire circle of four feet diameter, and now we slightly enlarged the limit, and went to the farther depth of two feet. Still nothing appeared. The gold-seeker, whom I sincerely pitied, at length clambered from the pit, with the bitterest disappointment imprinted upon every feature, and proceeded, slowly and reluctantly, to put on his coat, which he had thrown off at the beginning of his labor. In the mean time I made no remark. Jupiter, at a signal from his master, began to gather up his tools. This done, and the dog having been unmuzzled, we turned in profound silence towards home.

We had taken, perhaps, a dozen steps in this direction, when, with a loud oath, Legrand strode up to Jupiter, and seized him by the collar. The astonished negro opened his eyes and mouth to the fullest extent, let fall the spades, and fell upon his knees.

"You scoundrel," said Legrand, hissing out the syllables from between his clenched teeth—"you infernal black villain!—speak, I tell you!—answer me this instant, without prevarication!—which—which is your left eye?"

"Oh, my golly, Massa Will! ain't dis here my lef eye for sartin?" roared the terrified Jupiter, placing his hand upon his *right* organ of vision, and holding it there with a desperate pertinacity, as if in immediate dread of his master's attempt at a gouge.

"I thought so!—I knew it!—hurrah!" vociferated Legrand, letting the negro go, and executing a series of curvets and caracols, much to the astonishment of his valet, who, arising from his knees, looked, mutely, from his master to myself, and then from myself to his master.

"Come! we must go back," said the latter, "the game's not up yet"; and he again led the way to the tulip-tree.

"Jupiter," said he, when we reached its foot, "come here! was the skull nailed to the limb with the face outward or with the face to the limb?"

"De face was out, massa, so dat de crows could get at de eyes good, widout any trouble."

"Well, then, was it this eye or that through which you let the beetle fall?"
—here Legrand touched each of Jupiter's eyes.

"'Twas dis eye, massa—de lef eye—jis as you tell me," and here it was his right eye that the negro indicated.

"That will do—we must try again."

Here my friend, about whose madness I now saw, or fancied that I saw, certain indications of method, removed the peg which marked the spot where the beetle fell, to a spot about three inches to the west-ward of its former position. Taking, now, the tape-measure from the nearest point of the trunk to the peg, as before, and continuing the extension in a straight line to the distance of fifty feet, a spot was indicated, removed, by several yards, from the point at which we had been digging.

Around the new position a circle, somewhat larger than in the former instance, was now described, and we again set to work with the spades. I was dreadfully weary, but, scarcely understanding what had occasioned the change in my thoughts, I felt no longer any great aversion from the labor imposed. I had become most unaccountably interested—nay, even excited. Perhaps there was something, amid all the extravagant demeanor of Legrand—some air of forethought, or of deliberation, which impressed me. I dug eagerly, and now and then caught myself actually looking, with something that very much resembled expectation, for the fancied treasure, the vision of which had demented my unfortunate companion. At a period when such vagaries of thought most fully possessed me, and when we had been at work perhaps an hour and a half, we were again interrupted by the violent howlings of the dog. His uneasiness, in the first instance, had been, evidently, but the result of playfulness or caprice, but he now assumed a bitter and serious tone. Upon Jupiter's again attempting to muzzle him, he made furious resistance, and, leaping into the hole, tore up the mould frantically with his claws. In a few seconds he had uncovered a mass of human bones, forming two complete skeletons, intermingled with several buttons of metal, and what appeared to be the dust of decayed woollen. One or two strokes of a spade upturned the blade of a large Spanish knife, and, as we dug farther, three or four loose pieces of gold and silver coin came to light.

At sight of these the joy of Jupiter could scarcely be restrained, but the countenance of his master wore an air of extreme disappointment. He urged us, however, to continue our exertions, and the words were hardly uttered when I stumbled and fell forward, having caught the toe of my boot in a large ring of iron that lay half buried in the loose earth.

We now worked in earnest, and never did I pass ten minutes of more intense excitement. During this interval we had fairly unearthed an oblong chest of wood, which, from its perfect preservation, and wonderful hardness, had plainly been subjected to some mineralizing process—perhaps that of the Bi-chloride of Mercury. This box was three feet and a half long, three feet broad, and two and a half feet deep. It was firmly secured by bands of wrought iron, riveted, and forming a kind of trellis-work over the whole. On each side of the chest, near the top, were three rings of iron—six in all— by means of which a firm hold could be obtained by six persons. Our utmost united endeavors served only to disturb the coffer very slightly in its bed.

We at once saw the impossibility of removing so great a weight. Luckily, the sole fastenings of the lid consisted of two sliding bolts. These we drew back—trembling and panting with anxiety. In an instant, a treasure of incalculable value lay gleaming before us. As the rays of the lanterns fell within the pit, there flashed upwards, from a confused heap of gold and of jewels, a glow and a glare that absolutely dazzled our eyes.

I shall not pretend to describe the feelings with which I gazed. Amazement was, of course, predominant. Legrand appeared exhausted with excitement, and spoke very few words. Jupiter's countenance wore, for some minutes, as deadly a pallor as it is possible, in the nature of things, for any negro's visage to assume. He seemed stupefied—thunderstricken. Presently he fell upon his knees in the pit, and, burying his naked arms up to the elbows in gold, let them there remain, as if enjoying the luxury of a bath. At length, with a deep sigh, he exclaimed, as if in a soliloquy,

"And dis all cum ob de goole-bug! de putty goole-bug! de poor little goole-bug, what I boosed in dat sabage kind ob style! Ain't you shamed ob yourself, nigger?—answer me dat!"

It became necessary, at last, that I should arouse both master and valet to the expediency of removing the treasure. It was growing late, and it behooved us to make exertion, that we might get every thing housed before daylight. It was difficult to say what should be done; and much time was spent in deliberation—so confused were the ideas of all. We, finally, lightened the box by removing two thirds of its contents, when we were enabled, with some trouble, to raise it from the hole. The articles taken out were deposited among the brambles, and the dog left to guard them, with strict orders from Jupiter neither, upon any pretence, to stir from the spot, nor to open his mouth until our return. We then hurriedly made for home with the chest; reaching the hut in safety, but after excessive toil, at one o'clock in the morning. Worn out as we were, it was not in human nature to do more just then. We rested until two, and had supper; starting for the hills immediately afterwards, armed with three stout sacks, which, by good luck, were upon the premises. A little before four we arrived at the pit, divided the remainder of the booty, as equally as might be, among us, and, leaving the holes unfilled, again set out for the hut, at which, for the second time, we deposited our golden burthens, just as the first streaks of the dawn gleamed from over the tree-tops in the East.

We were now thoroughly broken down; but the intense excitement of the time denied us repose. After an unquiet slumber of some three or four hours' duration, we arose, as if by preconcert, to make examination of our treasure.

The chest had been full to the brim, and we spent the whole day, and the greater part of the next night, in a scrutiny of its contents. There had been nothing like order or arrangement. Everything had been heaped in promiscuously. Having assorted all with care, we found ourselves possessed of even

vaster wealth than we had at first supposed. In coin there was rather more
than four hundred and fifty thousand dollars—estimating the value of the
pieces, as accurately as we could, by the tables of the period. There was not
a particle of silver. All was gold of antique date and of great variety—
French, Spanish, and German money, with a few English guineas, and some
counters, of which we had never seen specimens before. There were several
very large and heavy coins, so worn that we could make nothing of their
inscriptions. There was no American money. The value of the jewels we
found more difficulty in estimating. There were diamonds—some of them
exceedingly large and fine—a hundred and ten in all, and not one of them
small; eighteen rubies of remarkable brilliancy;—three hundred and ten
emeralds, all very beautiful; and twenty-one sapphires, with an opal. These
stones had all been broken from their settings and thrown loose in the
chest. The settings themselves, which we picked out from among the other
gold, appeared to have been beaten up with hammers, as if to prevent identification. Besides all this, there was a vast quantity of solid gold ornaments;
—nearly two hundred massive finger and ear rings;—rich chains—thirty of
these, if I remember;—eighty-three very large and heavy crucifixes;—five
gold censers of great value;—a prodigious golden punch-bowl, ornamented
with richly chased vine-leaves and Bacchanalian figures; with two sword-
handles exquisitely embossed, and many other smaller articles which I cannot recollect. The weight of these valuables exceeded three hundred and
fifty pounds avoirdupois; and in this estimate I have not included one
hundred and ninety-seven superb gold watches; three of the number being
worth each five hundred dollars, if one. Many of them were very old, and as
time keepers valueless; the works having suffered, more or less, from cor-
rosion—but all were richly jewelled and in cases of great worth. We estimated the entire contents of the chest, that night, at a million and a half of
dollars; and, upon the subsequent disposal of the trinkets and jewels (a few
being retained for our own use), it was found that we had greatly under-
valued the treasure.

When, at length, we had concluded our examination, and the intense
excitement of the time had, in some measure, subsided, Legrand, who saw
that I was dying with impatience for a solution of this most extraordinary
riddle, entered into a full detail of all the circumstances connected with it.

"You remember," said he, "the night when I handed you the rough sketch
I had made of the *scarabæus*. You recollect also, that I became quite vexed
at you for insisting that my drawing resembled a death's-head. When you
first made this assertion I thought you were jesting; but afterwards I called
to mind the peculiar spots on the back of the insect, and admitted to myself
that your remark had some little foundation in fact. Still, the sneer at my
graphic powers irritated me—for I am considered a good artist—and, therefore, when you handed me the scrap of parchment, I was about to crumble
it up and throw it angrily into the fire."

"The scrap of paper, you mean," said I.

"No; it had much of the appearance of paper, and at first I supposed it to be such, but when I came to draw upon it, I discovered it, at once, to be a piece of very thin parchment. It was quite dirty, you remember. Well, as I was in the very act of crumpling it up, my glance fell upon the sketch at which you had been looking, and you may imagine my astonishment when I perceived, in fact, the figure of a death's-head just where, it seemed to me, I had made the drawing of the beetle. For a moment I was too much amazed to think with accuracy. I knew that my design was very different in detail from this—although there was a certain similarity in general outline. Presently I took a candle, and seating myself at the other end of the room, proceeded to scrutinize the parchment more closely. Upon turning it over, I saw my own sketch upon the reverse, just as I had made it. My first idea, now, was mere surprise at the really remarkable similarity of outline—at the singular coincidence involved in the fact, that unknown to me, there should have been a skull upon the other side of the parchment, immediately beneath my figure of the *scarabæus,* and that this skull, not only in outline, but in size, should so closely resemble my drawing. I say the singularity of this coincidence absolutely stupefied me for a time. This is the usual effect of such coincidences. The mind struggles to establish a connection—a sequence of cause and effect—and, being unable to do so, suffers a species of temporary paralysis. But, when I recovered from this stupor, there dawned upon me gradually a conviction which startled me even far more than the coincidence. I began distinctly, positively, to remember that there had been *no* drawing on the parchment when I made my sketch of the *scarabæus.* I became perfectly certain of this; for I recollected turning up first one side and then the other, in search of the cleanest spot. Had the skull been then there, of course I could not have failed to notice it. Here was indeed a mystery which I felt it impossible to explain; but, even at that early moment, there seemed to glimmer, faintly, within the most remote and secret chambers of my intellect, a glowworm-like conception of that truth which last night's adventure brought to so magnificent a demonstration. I arose at once, and putting the parchment securely away, dismissed all farther reflection until I should be alone.

"When you had gone, and when Jupiter was fast asleep, I betook myself to a more methodical investigation of the affair. In the first place I considered the manner in which the parchment had come into my possession. The spot where we discovered the *scarabæus* was on the coast of the main land, about a mile eastward of the island, and but a short distance above high water mark. Upon my taking hold of it, it gave me a sharp bite, which caused me to let it drop. Jupiter, with his accustomed caution, before seizing the insect, which had flown towards him, looked about him for a leaf, or something of that nature, by which to take hold of it. It was at this moment that his eyes, and mine also, fell upon the scrap of parchment, which I then supposed to be paper. It was lying half buried in the sand, a corner sticking up. Near the spot where we found it, I observed the remnants of the hull of what appeared to have been a ship's long boat. The wreck seemed to have been there for a very great while; for the resemblance to boat timbers could scarcely be traced.

"Well, Jupiter picked up the parchment, wrapped the beetle in it, and gave it to me. Soon afterwards we turned to go home, and on the way met Lieutenant G——. I showed him the insect, and he begged me to let him take it to the fort. On my consenting, he thrust it forthwith into his waist-coat pocket, without the parchment in which it had been wrapped, and which I had continued to hold in my hand during his inspection. Perhaps he dreaded my changing my mind, and thought it best to make sure of the prize at once—you know how enthusiastic he is on all subjects connected with Natural History. At the same time, without being conscious of it, I must have deposited the parchment in my own pocket.

"You remember that when I went to the table, for the purpose of making a sketch of the beetle, I found no paper where it was usually kept. I looked in the drawer, and found none there. I searched my pockets, hoping to find an old letter—and then my hand fell upon the parchment. I thus detail the precise mode in which it came into my possession; for the circumstances impressed me with peculiar force.

"No doubt you will think me fanciful—but I had already established a kind of *connection*. I had put together two links of a great chain. There was a boat lying on a sea-coast, and not far from the boat was a parchment—*not a paper*—with a skull depicted on it. You will, of course, ask 'where is the connection?' I reply that the skull, or death's-head, is the well-known emblem of the pirate. The flag of the death's-head is hoisted in all engagements.

"I have said that the scrap was parchment, and not paper. Parchment is durable—almost imperishable. Matters of little moment are rarely consigned to parchment; since, for the mere ordinary purposes of drawing or writing, it is not nearly so well adapted as paper. This reflection suggested some meaning—some relevancy—in the death's-head. I did not fail to observe, also, the *form* of the parchment. Although one of its corners had been, by some accident, destroyed, it could be seen that the original form was oblong. It was just such a slip, indeed, as might have been chosen for a memoran-dum—for a record of something to be long remembered and carefully pre-served."

"But," I interposed, "you say that the skull was *not* upon the parchment when you made the drawing of the beetle. How then do you trace any connection between the boat and the skull—since this latter, according to your own admission, must have been designed (God only knows how or by whom) at some period subsequent to your sketching the *scarabæus?*"

"Ah, hereupon turns the whole mystery; although the secret, at this point,

I had comparatively little difficulty in solving. My steps were sure, and could afford but a single result. I reasoned, for example, thus: When I drew the *scarabæus,* there was no skull apparent on the parchment. When I had completed the drawing, I gave it to you, and observed you narrowly until you returned it. *You,* therefore, did not design the skull, and no one else was present to do it. Then it was not done by human agency. And nevertheless it was done.

"At this stage of my reflections I endeavored to remember, and *did* remember, with entire distinctness, every incident which occurred about the period in question. The weather was chilly (oh rare and happy accident!), and a fire was blazing on the hearth. I was heated with exercise and sat near the table. You, however, had drawn a chair close to the chimney. Just as I placed the parchment in your hand, and as you were in the act of inspecting it, Wolf, the Newfoundland, entered, and leaped upon your shoulders. With your left hand you caressed him and kept him off, while your right, holding the parchment, was permitted to fall listlessly between your knees, and in close proximity to the fire. At one moment I thought the blaze had caught it, and was about to caution you, but, before I could speak, you had withdrawn it, and were engaged in its examination. When I considered all these particulars, I doubted not for a moment that *heat* had been the agent in bringing to light, on the parchment, the skull which I saw designed on it. You are well aware that chemical preparations exist, and have existed time out of mind, by means of which it is possible to write on either paper or vellum, so that the characters shall become visible only when subjected to the action of fire. Zaffre, digested in *aqua regia,* and diluted with four times its weight of water, is sometimes employed; a green tint results. The regulus of cobalt, dissolved in spirit of nitre, gives a red. These colors disappear at longer or shorter intervals after the material written on cools, but again become apparent upon the reapplication of heat.

"I now scrutinized the death's-head with care. Its outer edges—the edges of the drawing nearest the edge of the vellum—were far more *distinct* than the others. It was clear that the action of the caloric had been imperfect or unequal. I immediately kindled a fire, and subjected every portion of the parchment to a glowing heat. At first, the only effect was the strengthening of the faint lines in the skull; but, on persevering in the experiment, there became visible, at the corner of the slip, diagonally opposite to the spot in which the death's-head was delineated, the figure of what I at first supposed to be a goat. A closer scrutiny, however, satisfied me that it was intended for a kid."

"Ha! ha!" said I, "to be sure I have no right to laugh at you—a million and a half of money is too serious a matter for mirth—but you are not about to establish a third link in your chain—you will not find any especial connexion between your pirates and a goat—pirates, you know, have nothing to do with goats; they appertain to the farming interest."

"But I have just said that the figure was *not* that of a goat."

"Well, a kid then—pretty much the same thing."

"Pretty much, but not altogether," said Legrand. "You may have heard of one *Captain* Kidd. I at once looked on the figure of the animal as a kind of punning or hieroglyphical signature. I say signature; because its position on the vellum suggested this idea. The death's-head at the corner diagonally opposite, had, in the same manner, the air of a stamp, or seal. But I was sorely put out by the absence of all else—of the body to my imagined instrument—of the text for my context."

"I presume you expected to find a letter between the stamp and the signature."

"Something of that kind. The fact is, I felt irresistibly impressed with a presentiment of some vast good fortune impending. I can scarcely say why. Perhaps, after all, it was rather a desire than an actual belief;—but do you know that Jupiter's silly words, about the bug being of solid gold, had a remarkable effect on my fancy? And then the series of accidents and co-incidences—these were so *very* extraordinary. Do you observe how mere an accident it was that these events should have occurred on the *sole* day of all the year in which it has been, or may be, sufficiently cool for fire, and that without the fire, or without the intervention of the dog at the precise moment in which he appeared, I should never have become aware of the death's-head, and so never the possessor of the treasure?"

"But proceed—I am all impatience."

"Well; you have heard, of course, the many stories current—the thousand vague rumors afloat about money buried somewhere on the Atlantic coast, by Kidd and his associates. These rumors must have had some foundation in fact. And that the rumors have existed so long and so continuously could have resulted, it appeared to me, only from the circumstance of the buried treasure still *remaining* entombed. Had Kidd concealed his plunder for a time, and afterwards reclaimed it, the rumors would scarcely have reached us in their present unvarying form. You will observe that the stories told are all about money-seekers, not about money-finders. Had the pirate recovered his money, there the affair would have dropped. It seemed to me that some accident—say the loss of a memorandum indicating its locality—had deprived him of the means of recovering it, and that this accident had become known to his followers, who otherwise might never have heard that treasure had been concealed at all, and who, busying themselves in vain, because unguided attempts, to regain it, had given first birth, and then universal currency, to the reports which are now so common. Have you ever heard of any important treasure being unearthed along the coast?"

"Never."

"But that Kidd's accumulations were immense, is well known. I took it for granted, therefore, that the earth still held them; and you will scarcely be surprised when I tell you that I felt a hope, nearly amounting to certainty, that the parchment so strangely found, involved a lost record of the place of deposit."

"But how did you proceed?"

"I held the vellum again to the fire, after increasing the heat; but nothing appeared. I now thought it possible that the coating of dirt might have something to do with the failure; so I carefully rinsed the parchment by pouring warm water over it, and, having done this, I placed it in a tin pan, with the skull downwards, and put the pan upon a furnace of lighted charcoal. In a few minutes, the pan having become thoroughly heated, I removed the slip, and, to my inexpressible joy, found it spotted, in several places, with what appeared to be figures arranged in lines. Again I placed it in the pan, and suffered it to remain another minute. On taking it off, the whole was just as you see it now."

Here Legrand, having re-heated the parchment, submitted it to my inspection. The following characters were rudely traced, in a red tint, between the death's-head and the goat:

53‡‡†305))6*;4826)4‡.)4‡);806*;48†8¶60))85;]3*;:‡*8†83(88)5*†;46(;88*96*
?;8)*‡(;485);5*†2:*‡(;4956*2(5*—4) 8¶8*;4069285);)6†8)4‡‡;1 (‡9;48081;8:8‡
1;48†85;4)485†528806*81 (‡9;48;(88;4 (‡?34;48)4‡;161;:188;‡?;

"But," said I, returning him the slip, "I am as much in the dark as ever. Were all the jewels of Golconda awaiting me on my solution of this enigma, I am quite sure that I should be unable to earn them."

"And yet," said Legrand, "the solution is by no means so difficult as you might be led to imagine from the first hasty inspection of the characters. These characters, as any one might readily guess, form a cipher—that is to say, they convey a meaning; but then, from what is known of Kidd, I could not suppose him capable of constructing any of the more abstruse cryptographs. I made up my mind, at once, that this was of a simple species—such, however, as would appear, to the crude intellect of the sailor, absolutely insoluble without the key."

"And you really solved it?"

"Readily; I have solved others of an abstruseness ten thousand times greater. Circumstances, and a certain bias of mind, have led me to take interest in such riddles, and it may well be doubted whether human ingenuity can construct an enigma of the kind which human ingenuity may not, by proper application, resolve. In fact, having once established connected and legible characters, I scarcely gave a thought to the mere difficulty of developing their import.

"In the present case—indeed in all cases of secret writing—the first question regards the *language* of the cipher; for the principles of solution, so far, especially, as the more simple ciphers are concerned, depend on, and are varied by, the genius of the particular idiom. In general, there is no alternative but experiment (directed by probabilities) of every tongue known to him who attempts the solution, until the true one be attained. But, with the cipher now before us, all difficulty is removed by the signature. The pun on the word 'Kidd' is appreciable in no other language than the English. But for this consideration I should have begun my attempts with the Spanish and French, as the tongues in which a secret of this kind would most naturally have been written by a pirate of the Spanish main. As it was, I assumed the cryptograph to be English.

"You observe there are no divisions between the words. Had there been divisions, the task would have been comparatively easy. In such case I should have commenced with a collation and analysis of the shorter words, and, had a word of a single letter occurred as is most likely, (*a* or *I,* for example,) I should have considered the solution as assured. But, there being no division, my first step was to ascertain the predominant letters, as well as the least frequent. Counting all, I constructed a table, thus:

Of the character 8 there are		33.
;	"	26.
4	"	19.
‡)	"	16.
*	"	13.
5	"	12.
6	"	11.
† 1	"	8.
0	"	6.
9 2	"	5.
: 3	"	4.
?	"	3.
¶	"	2.
—.	"	1.

"Now, in English, the letter which most frequently occurs is *e.* Afterwards, the succession runs thus: *a o i d h n r s t u y c f g l m w b k p q x z.* E however predominates so remarkably that an individual sentence of any length is rarely seen, in which it is not the prevailing character.

"Here, then, we have, in the very beginning, the ground-work for something more than a mere guess. The general use which may be made of the table is obvious—but, in this particular cipher, we shall only very partially require its aid. As our predominant character is 8, we will commence by assuming it as the *e* of the natural alphabet. To verify the supposition, let us observe if the 8 be seen often in couples—for *e* is doubled with great frequency in English—in such words, for example, as 'meet,' 'fleet,' 'speed,' 'seen,' 'been,' 'agree,' &c. In the present instance we see it doubled no less than five times, although the cryptograph is brief.

"Let us assume 8, then, as *e.* Now, of all *words* in the language, 'the' is most usual; let us see, therefore, whether there are not repetitions of any three characters, in the same order of collocation, the last of them being 8. If we discover repetitions of such letters, so arranged, they will most probably represent the word 'the.' On inspection we find no less than seven such arrangements, the characters being ;48. We may, therefore, assume that the semicolon represents *t,* that 4 represents *h,* and that 8 represents *e*—the last being now well confirmed. Thus a great step has been taken.

"But, having established a single word, we are enabled to establish a vastly important point; that is to say, several commencements and terminations of other words. Let us refer, for example, to the last instance but one, in which the combination ;48 occurs—not far from the end of the cipher. We know that the semicolon immediately ensuing is the commencement of a word, and, of the six characters succeeding this 'the,' we are cognizant of no less than five. Let us set these characters down, thus, by the letters we know them to represent, leaving a space for the unknown—

t eeth.

"Here we are enabled, at once, to discard the '*th,*' as forming no portion of the word commencing with the first *t;* since, by experiment of the entire alphabet for a letter adapted to the vacancy we perceive that no word can be formed of which this *th* can be a part. We are thus narrowed into

t ee,

and, going through the alphabet, if necessary, as before, we arrive at the word 'tree,' as the sole possible reading. We thus gain another letter, *r,* represented by (, with the words 'the tree' in juxtaposition.

"Looking beyond these words, for a short distance, we again see the combination of ;48, and employ it by way of *termination* to what immediately precedes. We have thus this arrangement:

the tree;4 (‡?34 the,

or, substituting the natural letters, where known, it reads thus:

the tree thr ‡?3h the.

"Now, if, in place of the unknown characters, we leave blank spaces, or substitute dots, we read thus:

the tree thr . . . h the,

when the word '*through*' makes itself evident at once. But this discovery gives us three new letters, *o, u* and *g,* represented by ‡? and 3.

"Looking now, narrowly, through the cipher for combinations of known characters, we find, not very far from the beginning, this arrangement,

83(88, or egree,

which, plainly, is the conclusion of the word 'degree,' and gives us another letter, *d,* represented by †.

"Four letters beyond the word 'degree,' we perceive the combination

;46(;88*.

"Translating the known characters, and representing the unknown by dots, as before, we read thus:

th .rtee.

an arrangement immediately suggestive of the word 'thirteen,' and again furnishing us with two new characters, i and n, represented by 6 and *.

"Referring, now, to the beginning of the cryptograph, we find the combination,

53‡‡†.

"Translating, as before, we obtain

.good,

which assures us that the first letter is A, and that the first two words are 'A good.'

"To avoid confusion, it is now time that we arrange our key, as far as discovered, in a tabular form. It will stand thus:

5	represents	a
†	"	d
8	"	e
3	"	g
4	"	h
6	"	i
*	"	n
‡	"	o
(	"	r
;	"	t

"We have, therefore, no less than ten of the most important letters represented, and it will be unnecessary to proceed with the details of the solution. I have said enough to convince you that ciphers of this nature are readily soluble, and to give you some insight into the *rationale* of their development. But be assured that the specimen before us appertains to the very simplest species of cryptograph. It now only remains to give you the full translation of the characters upon the parchment, as unriddled. Here it is:

"*'A good glass in the bishop's hostel in the devil's seat twenty-one degrees and thirteen minutes northeast and by north main branch seventh limb east side shoot from the left eye of the death's-head a bee line from the tree through the shot fifty feet out.'*"

"But," said I, "the enigma seems still in as bad a condition as ever. How is it possible to extort a meaning from all this jargon about 'devil's seats,' 'death's-heads,' and 'bishop's hotels?'"

"I confess," replied Legrand, "that the matter still wears a serious aspect, when regarded with a casual glance. My first endeavor was to divide the sentence into the natural division intended by the cryptographist."

"You mean, to punctuate it?"

"Something of that kind."

"But how was it possible to effect this?"

"I reflected that it had been a *point* with the writer to run his words together without division, so as to increase the difficulty of solution. Now, a not over-acute man, in pursuing such an object, would be nearly certain to overdo the matter. When, in the course of his composition, he arrived at a break in his subject which would naturally require a pause, or a point, he would be exceedingly apt to run his characters, at this place, more than usually close together. If you will observe the MS., in the present instance, you will easily detect five such cases of unusual crowding. Acting on this hint, I made the division thus:

"'A good glass in the Bishop's hostel in the Devil's seat—twenty-one degrees and thirteen minutes—northeast and by north—main branch seventh limb east side—shoot from the left eye of the death's-head—a bee line from the tree through the shot fifty feet out.'"

"Even this division," said I, "leaves me still in the dark."

"It left me also in the dark," replied Legrand, "for a few days; during which I made diligent inquiry, in the neighborhood of Sullivan's Island, for any building which went by the name of the 'Bishop's Hotel'; for, of course, I dropped the obsolete word 'hostel.' Gaining no information on the subject, I was on the point of extending my sphere of search, and proceeding in a more systematic manner, when, one morning, it entered into my head, quite suddenly, that this 'Bishop's Hostel' might have some reference to an old family, of the name of Bessop, which, time out of mind, had held possession of an ancient manor-house, about four miles to the northward of the Island. I accordingly went over to the plantation, and re-instituted my inquiries among the older negroes of the place. At length one of the most aged of the women said that she had heard of such a place as Bessop's Castle, and thought that she could guide me to it, but that it was not a castle, nor a tavern, but a high rock.

"I offered to pay her well for her trouble, and, after some demur, she consented to accompany me to the spot. We found it without much difficulty, when, dismissing her, I proceeded to examine the place. The 'castle' consisted of an irregular assemblage of cliffs and rocks—one of the latter being quite remarkable for its height as well as for its insulated and artificial appearance. I clambered to its apex, and then felt much at a loss as to what should be next done.

"While I was busied in reflection, my eyes fell upon a narrow ledge in the eastern face of the rock, perhaps a yard below the summit on which I stood. This ledge projected about eighteen inches, and was not more than a foot wide, while a niche in the cliff just above it, gave it a rude resemblance to one of the hollow-backed chairs used by our ancestors. I made no doubt that here was the 'devil's-seat' alluded to in the MS., and now I seemed to grasp the full secret of the riddle.

"The 'good glass,' I knew, could have reference to nothing but a telescope; for the word 'glass' is rarely employed in any other sense by seamen. Now here, I at once saw, was a telescope to be used, and a definite point of view, *admitting no variation,* from which to use it. Nor did I hesitate to believe that the phrases, 'twenty-one degrees and thirteen minutes,' and 'northeast and by north,' were intended as directions for the levelling of the glass. Greatly excited by these discoveries, I hurried home, procured a telescope, and returned to the rock.

"I let myself down to the ledge, and found that it was impossible to retain a seat on it unless in one particular position. This fact confirmed my preconceived idea. I proceeded to use the glass. Of course, the 'twenty-one degrees and thirteen minutes' could allude to nothing but elevation above the visible horizon, since the horizontal direction was clearly indicated by the words, 'northeast and by north.' This latter direction I at once established by means of a pocket-compass; then, pointing the glass as nearly at an angle of twenty-one degrees of elevation as I could do it by guess, I moved it cautiously up or down, until my attention was arrested by a circular rift or opening in the foliage of a large tree that overtopped its fellows in the distance. In the centre of this rift I perceived a white spot, but could not, at first, distinguish what it was. Adjusting the focus of the telescope, I again looked, and now made it out to be a human skull.

"On this discovery I was so sanguine as to consider the enigma solved for the phrase 'main branch, seventh limb, east side,' could refer only to the position of the skull on the tree, while 'shoot from the left eye of the death's-head' admitted, also, of but one interpretation, in regard to a search for buried treasure. I perceived that the design was to drop a bullet from the left eye of the skull, and that a bee line, or, in other words, a straight line, drawn from the nearest point of the trunk through 'the shot,' (or the spot where the bullet fell,) and thence extended to a distance of fifty feet, would indicate a definite point—and beneath this point I thought it at least possible that a deposit of value lay concealed."

"All this," I said, "is exceedingly clear, and, although ingenious, still simple and explicit. When you left the Bishop's Hotel, what then?"

"Why, having carefully taken the bearings of the tree, I turned homewards. The instant that I left 'the devil's seat,' however, the circular rift vanished; nor could I get a glimpse of it afterwards, turn as I would. What seems to me the chief ingenuity in this whole business, is the fact (for repeated experiment has convinced me it *is* a fact) that the circular opening in question is visible from no other attainable point of view than that afforded by the narrow ledge on the face of the rock.

"In this expedition to the 'Bishop's Hotel' I had been attended by Jupiter, who had, no doubt, observed, for some weeks past, the abstraction of my demeanor, and took especial care not to leave me alone. But, on the next day, getting up very early, I contrived to give him the slip, and went into the hills in search of the tree. After much toil I found it. When I came home at night my valet proposed to give me a flogging. With the rest of the adventure I believe you are as well acquainted as myself."

"I suppose," said I, "you missed the spot, in the first attempt at digging, through Jupiter's stupidity in letting the bug fall through the right instead of through the left eye of the skull."

"Precisely. This mistake made a difference of about two inches and a half in the 'shot'—that is to say, in the position of the peg nearest the tree; and had the treasure been *beneath* the 'shot,' the error would have been of little moment; but 'the shot,' together with the nearest point of the tree, were merely two points for the establishment of a line of direction; of course the error, however trivial in the beginning, increased as we proceeded with the line, and by the time we had gone fifty feet, threw us quite off the scent. But for my deep-seated convictions that treasure was here somewhere actually buried, we might have had all our labor in vain."

"I presume the fancy of *the skull,* of letting fall a bullet through the skull's eye—was suggested to Kidd by the piratical flag. No doubt he felt a kind of poetical consistency in recovering his money through this ominous insignium."

"Perhaps so; still I cannot help thinking that common-sense had quite as much to do with the matter as poetical consistency. To be visible from the devil's-seat, it was necessary that the object, if small, should be white; and there is nothing like your human skull for retaining and even increasing its whiteness under exposure to all vicissitudes of weather."

"But your grandiloquence, and your conduct in swinging the beetle—how excessively odd! I was sure you were mad. And why did you insist on letting fall the bug, instead of a bullet, from the skull?"

"Why, to be frank, I felt somewhat annoyed by your evident suspicions touching my sanity, and so resolved to punish you quietly, in my own way, by a little bit of sober mystification. For this reason I swung the beetle, and for this reason I let it fall from the tree. An observation of yours about its great weight suggested the latter idea."

"Yes, I perceive; and now there is only one point which puzzles me. What are we to make of the skeletons found in the hole?"

"That is a question I am no more able to answer than yourself. There seems, however, only one plausible way of accounting for them—and yet it is dreadful to believe in such atrocity as my suggestion would imply. It is clear that Kidd—if Kidd indeed secreted this treasure, which I doubt not—it is clear that he must have had assistance in the labor. But, the worst of this labor concluded, he may have thought it expedient to remove all participants in his secret. Perhaps a couple of blows with a mattock were sufficient, while his coadjutors were busy in the pit; perhaps it required a dozen—who shall tell?"

First published in the Philadelphia *Dollar Newspaper*, June 21–28, 1843. Text: Edition of 1845 with Lorimer Graham corrections.

A SIMPLE HEART

Gustave Flaubert

(1821–1880)

TRANSLATED BY ARTHUR McDOWALL

Madame aubain's servant Félicité was the envy of the ladies of Pont-l'Évêque for half a century.

She received four pounds a year. For that she was cook and general servant, and did the sewing, washing, and ironing; she could bridle a horse, fatten poultry, and churn butter—and she remained faithful to her mistress, unamiable as the latter was.

Mme. Aubain had married a gay bachelor without money who died at the beginning of 1809, leaving her with two small children and a quantity of debts. She then sold all her property except the farms of Toucques and Geffosses, which brought in two hundred pounds a year at most, and left her house in Saint-Melaine for a less expensive one that had belonged to her family and was situated behind the market.

This house had a slate roof and stood between an alley and a lane that went down to the river. There was an unevenness in the levels of the rooms which made you stumble. A narrow hall divided the kitchen from the "parlour" where Mme. Aubain spent her day, sitting in a wicker easy chair by the window. Against the panels, which were painted white, was a row of eight mahogany chairs. On an old piano under the barometer a heap of wooden and cardboard boxes rose like a pyramid. A stuffed armchair stood on either side of the Louise-Quinze chimney-piece, which was in yellow marble with a clock in the middle of it modelled like a temple of Vesta. The whole room was a little musty, as the floor was lower than the garden.

The first floor began with "Madame's" room: very large, with a pale-flowered wall-paper and a portrait of "Monsieur" as a dandy of the period. It led to a smaller room, where there were two children's cots without mattresses. Next came the drawing-room, which was always shut up and full of furniture covered with sheets. Then there was a corridor leading to a study. The shelves of a large bookcase were respectably lined with books and papers, and its three wings surrounded a broad writing-table in dark-wood. The two panels at the end of the room were covered with pen-drawings, water-colour landscapes, and engravings by Audran, all relics of better days and vanished splendour. Félicité's room on the top floor got its light from a dormer-window, which looked over the meadows.

She rose at daybreak to be in time for Mass, and worked till evening without stopping. Then, when dinner was over, the plates and dishes in order, and the door shut fast, she thrust the log under the ashes and went to sleep in front of the hearth with her rosary in her hand. Félicité was the stubbornest of all bargainers; and as for cleanness, the polish on her sauce-pans was the despair of other servants. Thrifty in all things, she ate slowly, gathering off the table in her fingers the crumbs of her loaf—a twelve-pound loaf expressly baked for her, which lasted for three weeks.

At all times of year she wore a print handkerchief fastened with a pin behind, a bonnet that covered her hair, grey stockings, a red skirt, and a bibbed apron—such as hospital nurses wear—over her jacket.

Her face was thin and her voice sharp. At twenty-five she looked like forty. From fifty onwards she seemed of no particular age; and with her silence, straight figure, and precise movements she was like a woman made of wood, and going by clockwork.

II

She had had her love-story like another.

Her father, a mason, had been killed by falling off some scaffolding. Then her mother died, her sisters scattered, and a farmer took her in and employed her, while she was still quite little, to herd the cows at pasture. She shivered in rags and would lie flat on the ground to drink water from the ponds; she was beaten for nothing, and finally turned out for the theft of a shilling which she did not steal. She went to another farm, where she became dairy-maid; and as she was liked by her employers her companions were jealous of her.

One evening in August (she was then eighteen) they took her to the assembly at Colleville. She was dazed and stupefied in an instant by the noise of the fiddlers, the lights in the trees, the gay medley of dresses, the lace, the gold crosses, and the throng of people jigging all together. While she kept shyly apart a young man with a well-to-do air, who was leaning on the shaft of a cart and smoking his pipe, came up to ask her to dance. He treated her to cider, coffee, and cake, and bought her a silk handker-chief; and then, imagining she had guessed his meaning, offered to see her home. At the edge of a field of oats he pushed her roughly down. She was frightened and began to cry out; and he went off.

One evening later she was on the Beaumont road. A big hay-wagon was moving slowly along; she wanted to get in front of it, and as she brushed past the wheels she recognized Theodore. He greeted her quite calmly, saying she must excuse it all because it was "the fault of the drink." She could not think of any answer and wanted to run away.

He began at once to talk about the harvest and the worthies of the commune, for his father had left Colleville for the farm at Les Écots, so that now he and she were neighbours. "Ah!" she said. He added that they thought of settling him in life. Well, he was in no hurry; he was waiting for a wife to his fancy. She dropped her head; and then he asked her if she thought of marrying. She answered with a smile that it was mean to make fun of her.

"But I am not, I swear!"—and he passed his left hand round her waist. She walked in the support of his embrace; their steps grew slower. The wind was soft, the stars glittered, the huge wagon-load of hay swayed in front of them, and dust rose from the dragging steps of the four horses. Then, without a word of command, they turned to the right. He clasped her once more in his arms, and she disappeared into the shadow.

The week after Theodore secured some assignations with her.

They met at the end of farmyards, behind a wall, or under a solitary tree. She was not innocent as young ladies are—she had learned knowledge from the animals—but her reason and the instinct of her honour would not let her fall. Her resistance exasperated Theodore's passion; so much so that to satisfy it—or perhaps quite artlessly—he made her an offer of marriage. She was in doubt whether to trust him, but he swore great oaths of fidelity.

Soon he confessed to something troublesome; the year before his parents had bought him a substitute for the army, but any day he might be taken again, and the idea of serving was a terror to him. Félicité took this cowardice of his as a sign of affection, and it redoubled hers. She stole away at night to see him, and when she reached their meeting-place Theodore racked her with his anxieties and urgings.

At last he declared that he would go himself to the prefecture for information, and would tell her the result on the following Sunday, between eleven and midnight.

When the moment came she sped towards her lover. Instead of him she found one of his friends.

He told her that she would not see Theodore any more. To ensure himself against conscription he had married an old woman, Madame Lehoussais, of Toucques, who was very rich.

There was an uncontrollable burst of grief. She threw herself on the ground, screamed, called to the God of mercy, and moaned by herself in the fields till daylight came. Then she came back to the farm and announced that she was going to leave; and at the end of the month she received her wages, tied all her small belongings with a handkerchief, and went to Pont-l'Évêque.

In front of the inn there she made inquiries of a woman in a widow's cap, who, as it happened, was just looking for a cook. The girl did not know much, but her willingness seemed so great and her demands so small that Mme. Aubain ended by saying:

"Very well, then, I will take you."

A quarter of an hour afterwards Félicité was installed in her house.

She lived there at first in a tremble, as it were, at "the style of the house" and the memory of "Monsieur" floating over it all. Paul and Virginie, the first aged seven and the other hardly four, seemed to her beings of a precious substance; she carried them on her back like a horse; it was a sorrow to her that Mme. Aubain would not let her kiss them every minute. And yet she was happy there. Her grief had melted in the pleasantness of things all round.

Every Thursday regular visitors came in for a game of boston, and Félicité got the cards and foot-warmers ready beforehand. They arrived punctually at eight and left before the stroke of eleven.

On Monday mornings the dealer who lodged in the covered passage spread out all his old iron on the ground. Then a hum of voices began to fill the town, mingled with the neighing of horses, bleating of lambs, grunting of pigs, and the sharp rattle of carts along the street. About noon, when the market was at its height, you might see a tall, hook-nosed old countryman with his cap pushed back making his appearance at the door. It was Robelin, the farmer of Geffosses. A little later came Liébard, the farmer from Toucques—short, red, and corpulent—in a grey jacket and gaiters shod with spurs.

Both had poultry or cheese to offer their landlord. Félicité was invariably a match for their cunning and they went away filled with respect for her.

At vague intervals Mme. Aubain had a visit from the Marquis de Gremanville, one of her uncles, who had ruined himself by debauchery and now lived at Falaise on his last remaining morsel of land. He invariably came at the luncheon hour, with a dreadful poodle whose paws left all the furniture in a mess. In spite of efforts to show his breeding, which he carried to the point of raising his hat every time he mentioned "my late father," habit was too strong for him; he poured himself out glass after glass and fired off improper remarks. Félicité edged him politely out of the house—"You have had enough, Monsieur de Gremanville! Another time!"—and she shut the door on him.

She opened it with pleasure to M. Bourais, who had been a lawyer. His boldness, his white stock, frilled shirt, and roomy brown coat, his way of rounding the arm as he took snuff—his whole person, in fact, created that disturbance of mind which overtakes us at the sight of extraordinary men.

As he looked after the property of "Madame" he remained shut up with her for hours in "Monsieur's" study, though all the time he was afraid of compromising himself. He respected the magistracy immensely, and had some pretensions to Latin.

To combine instruction and amusement he gave the children a geography book made up of a series of prints. They represented scenes in different parts of the world: cannibals with feathers on their heads, a monkey carrying off a young lady, Bedouins in the desert, the harpooning of a whale, and so on. Paul explained these engravings to Félicité; and that, in fact, was the whole of her literary education. The children's education was undertaken by Guyot, a poor creature employed at the town hall, who was famous for his beautiful hand and sharpened his penknife on his boots.

When the weather was bright the household set off early for a day at Geffosses Farm.

Its courtyard is on a slope, with the farmhouse in the middle, and the sea looks like a grey streak in the distance.

Félicité brought slices of cold meat out of her basket, and they breakfasted in a room adjoining the dairy. It was the only surviving fragment of a country house which was now no more. The wall-paper hung in tatters, and quivered in the draughts. Mme. Aubain sat with bowed head, overcome by her memories; the children became afraid to speak. "Why don't you play, then?" she would say, and off they went.

Paul climbed into the barn, caught birds, played at ducks and drakes over the pond, or hammered with his stick on the big casks which boomed like drums. Virginie fed the rabbits or dashed off to pick cornflowers, her quick legs showing their embroidered little drawers.

One autumn evening they went home by the fields. The moon was in its first quarter, lighting part of the sky; and mist floated like a scarf over the windings of the Toucques. Cattle, lying out in the middle of the grass, looked quietly at the four people as they passed. In the third meadow some of them got up and made a half-circle in front of the walkers. "There's nothing to be afraid of," said Félicité, as she stroked the nearest on the back with a kind of crooning song; he wheeled round and the others did the same. But when they crossed the next pasture there was a formidable bellow. It was a bull, hidden by the mist. Mme. Aubain was about to run. "No! no! don't go so fast!" They mended their pace, however, and heard a loud breathing behind them which came nearer. His hoofs thudded on the meadow grass like hammers; why, he was galloping now! Félicité turned round, and tore up clods of earth with both hands and threw them in his eyes. He lowered his muzzle, waved his horns, and quivered with fury, bellowing terribly. Mme. Aubain, now at the end of the pasture with her two little ones, was looking wildly for a place to get over the high bank. Félicité was retreating, still with her face to the bull, keeping up a shower of clods which blinded him, and crying all the time, "Be quick! be quick!"

Mme. Aubain went down into the ditch, pushed Virginie first and then Paul, fell several times as she tried to climb the bank, and managed it at last by dint of courage.

The bull had driven Félicité to bay against a rail-fence; his slaver was streaming into her face; another second, and he would have gored her. She had just time to slip between two of the rails, and the big animal stopped short in amazement.

This adventure was talked of at Pont-l'Évêque for many a year. Félicité did not pride herself on it in the least, not having the barest suspicion that she had done anything heroic.

Virginie was the sole object of her thoughts, for the child developed a nervous complaint as a result of her fright, and M. Poupart, the doctor, advised sea-bathing at Trouville. It was not a frequented place then. Mme. Aubain collected information, consulted Bourais, and made preparations as though for a long journey.

Her luggage started a day in advance, in Liébard's cart. The next day he brought round two horses, one of which had a lady's saddle with a velvet back to it, while a cloak was rolled up to make a kind of seat on the crupper of the other. Mme. Aubain rode on that, behind the farmer. Félicité took charge of Virginie, and Paul mounted M. Lechaptois' donkey, lent on condition that great care was taken of it.

The road was so bad that its five miles took two hours. The horses sank in the mud up to their pasterns, and their haunches jerked abruptly in the effort to get out; or else they stumbled in the ruts, and at other moments had to jump. In some places Liébard's mare came suddenly to a halt. He waited patiently until she went on again, talking about the people who had properties along the road, and adding moral reflections to their history. So it was that as they were in the middle of Toucques, and passed under some windows bowered with nasturtiums, he shrugged his shoulders and said: "There's a Mme. Lehoussais lives there; instead of taking a young man she . . ." Félicité did not hear the rest; the horses were trotting and the donkey galloping. They all turned down a bypath; a gate swung open and two boys appeared; and the party dismounted in front of a manure-heap at the very threshold of the farmhouse door.

When Mme. Liébard saw her mistress she gave lavish signs of joy. She served her a luncheon with a sirloin of beef, tripe, black-pudding, a fricassee of chicken, sparkling cider, a fruit tart, and brandied plums; seasoning it all with compliments to Madame, who seemed in better health; Mademoiselle, who was "splendid" now; and Monsieur Paul, who had "filled out" wonderfully. Nor did she forget their deceased grandparents, whom the Liébards had known, as they had been in the service of the family for several generations. The farm, like them, had the stamp of antiquity. The beams on the ceiling were worm-eaten, the walls blackened with smoke, and the window-panes grey with dust. There was an oak dresser laden with every sort of useful article—jugs, plates, pewter bowls, wolf-traps, and sheep-shears; and a huge syringe made the children laugh. There was not a tree in the three courtyards without mushrooms growing at the bottom of it or a tuft of mistletoe on its boughs. Several of them had been thrown down by the wind. They had taken root again at the middle; and all were bending under their wealth of apples. The thatched roofs, like brown velvet and of varying thickness, withstood the heaviest squalls. The cart-shed, however, was falling into ruin. Mme. Aubain said she would see about it, and ordered the animals to be saddled again.

It was another half-hour before they reached Trouville. The little caravan dismounted to pass Écores—it was an overhanging cliff with boats below it—and three minutes later they were at the end of the quay and entered the courtyard of the Golden Lamb, kept by good Mme. David.

From the first days of their stay Virginie began to feel less weak, thanks to the change of air and the effect of the sea-baths. These, for want of a bathing-dress, she took in her chemise; and her nurse dressed her afterwards in a coastguard's cabin which was used by the bathers.

In the afternoons they took the donkey and went off beyond the Black Rocks, in the direction of Hennequeville. The path climbed at first through ground with dells in it like the green sward of a park, and then reached a plateau where grass fields and arable lay side by side. Hollies rose stiffly out of the briary tangle at the edge of the road; and here and there a great withered tree made zigzags in the blue air with its branches.

They nearly always rested in a meadow, with Deauville on their left, Havre on their right, and the open sea in front. It glittered in the sunshine, smooth as a mirror and so quiet that its murmur was scarcely to be heard; sparrows chirped in hiding and the immense sky arched over it all. Mme. Aubain sat doing her needlework; Virginie plaited rushes by her side; Félicité pulled up lavender, and Paul was bored and anxious to start home.

Other days they crossed the Toucques in a boat and looked for shells. When the tide went out sea-urchins, starfish, and jelly-fish were left exposed; and the children ran in pursuit of the foam-flakes which scudded in the wind. The sleepy waves broke on the sand and unrolled all along the beach; it stretched away out of sight, bounded on the land-side by the dunes which parted it from the Marsh, a wide meadow shaped like an arena. As they came home that way, Trouville, on the hill-slope in the background, grew bigger at every step, and its miscellaneous throng of houses seemed to break into a gay disorder.

On days when it was too hot they did not leave their room. From the dazzling brilliance outside light fell in streaks between the laths of the blinds. There were no sounds in the village; and on the pavement below not a soul. This silence round them deepened the quietness of things. In the distance, where men were caulking, there was a tap of hammers as they plugged the hulls, and a sluggish breeze wafted up the smell of tar.

The chief amusement was the return of the fishing-boats. They began to tack as soon as they had passed the buoys. The sails came down on two of the three masts; and they drew on with the foresail swelling like a balloon, glided through the splash of the waves, and when they had reached the middle of the harbour suddenly dropped anchor. Then the boats drew up against the quay. The sailors threw quivering fish over the side; a row of carts was waiting, and women in cotton bonnets darted out to take the baskets and give their men a kiss.

One of them came up to Félicité one day, and she entered the lodgings a little later in a state of delight. She had found a sister again—and then Nastasie Barette, "wife of Leroux," appeared, holding an infant at her breast and another child with her right hand, while on her left was a little cabin boy with his hands on his hips and a cap over his ear.

After a quarter of an hour Mme. Aubain sent them off; but they were always to be found hanging about the kitchen, or encountered in the course of a walk. The husband never appeared.

Félicité was seized with affection for them. She bought them a blanket, some shirts, and a stove; it was clear that they were making a good thing out of her. Mme. Aubain was annoyed by this weakness of hers, and she did not like the liberties taken by the nephew, who said "thee" and "thou" to Paul. So as Virginie was coughing and the fine weather gone, she returned to Pont-l'Évêque.

There M. Bourais enlightened her on the choice of a boys' school. The one at Caen was reputed to be the best, and Paul was sent to it. He said his good-byes bravely, content enough at going to live in a house where he would have companions.

Mme. Aubain resigned herself to her son's absence as a thing that had to be. Virginie thought about it less and less. Félicité missed the noise he made. But she found an occupation to distract her; from Christmas onward she took the little girl to catechism every day.

III

After making a genuflexion at the door she walked up between the double row of chairs under the lofty nave, opened Mme. Aubain's pew, sat down, and began to look about her. The choir stalls were filled with the boys on the right and the girls on the left, and the curé stood by the lectern. On a painted window in the apse the Holy Ghost looked down upon the Virgin. Another window showed her on her knees before the child Jesus, and a group carved in wood behind the altar-shrine represented St. Michael overthrowing the dragon.

The priest began with a sketch of sacred history. The Garden, the Flood, the Tower of Babel, cities in flames, dying nations, and overturned idols passed like a dream before her eyes; and the dizzying vision left her with reverence for the Most High and fear of his wrath. Then she wept at the story of the Passion. Why had they crucified Him, when He loved the children, fed the multitudes, healed the blind, and had willed, in His meekness, to be born among the poor, on the dung-heap of a stable? The

sowings, harvests, wine-presses, all the familiar things the Gospel speaks of,
were a part of her life. They had been made holy by God's passing; and
she loved the lambs more tenderly for her love of the Lamb, and the doves
because of the Holy Ghost.

She found it hard to imagine Him in person, for He was not merely a
bird, but a flame as well, and a breath at other times. It may be His light,
she thought, which flits at night about the edge of the marshes, His
breathing which drives on the clouds, His voice which gives harmony to
the bells; and she would sit rapt in adoration, enjoying the cool walls and
the quiet of the church.

Of doctrines she understood nothing—did not even try to understand.
The curé discoursed, the children repeated their lesson, and finally she
went to sleep, waking up with a start when their wooden shoes clattered
on the flagstones as they went away.

It was thus that Félicité, whose religious education had been neglected in
her youth, learned the catechism by dint of hearing it; and from that time
she copied all Virginie's observances, fasting as she did and confessing
with her. On Corpus Christi Day they made a festal altar together.

The first communion loomed distractingly ahead. She fussed over the
shoes, the rosary, the book and gloves; and how she trembled as she helped
Virginie's mother to dress her!

All through the mass she was racked with anxiety. She could not see one
side of the choir because of M. Bourais; but straight in front of her was
the flock of maidens, with white crowns above their hanging veils, making the impression of a field of snow; and she knew her dear child at a
distance by her dainty neck and thoughtful air. The bell tinkled. The
heads bowed, and there was silence. As the organ pealed, singers and
congregation took up the "Agnus Dei"; then the procession of the boys began, and after them the girls rose. Step by step, with their hands joined in
prayer, they went towards the lighted altar, knelt on the first step, received
the sacrament in turn, and came back in the same order to their places.
When Virginie's turn came Félicité leaned forward to see her; and with the
imaginativeness of deep and tender feeling it seemed to her that she
actually was the child; Virginie's face became hers, she was dressed in her
clothes, it was her heart beating in her breast. As the moment came to
open her mouth she closed her eyes and nearly fainted.

She appeared early in the sacristy next morning for Monsieur the curé to
give her the communion. She took it with devotion, but it did not give her
the same exquisite delight.

Mme. Aubain wanted to make her daughter into an accomplished person; and as Guyot could not teach her music or English she decided to
place her in the Ursuline Convent at Honfleur as a boarder. The child made
no objection. Félicité sighed and thought that Madame lacked feeling.

Then she reflected that her mistress might be right; matters of this kind were beyond her.

So one day an old spring-van drew up at the door, and out of it stepped a nun to fetch the young lady. Félicité hoisted the luggage on to the top, admonished the driver, and put six pots of preserves, a dozen pears, and a bunch of violets under the seat.

At the last moment Virginie broke into a fit of sobbing; she threw her arms round her mother, who kissed her on the forehead, saying over and over "Come, be brave! be brave!" The step was raised, and the carriage drove off.

Then Mme. Aubain's strength gave way; and in the evening all her friends—the Lormeau family, Mme. Lechaptois, the Rochefeuille ladies, M. de Houppeville, and Bourais—came in to console her.

To be without her daughter was very painful for her at first. But she heard from Virginie three times a week, wrote to her on the other days, walked in the garden, and so filled up the empty hours.

From sheer habit Félicité went into Virginie's room in the mornings and gazed at the walls. It was boredom to her not to have to comb the child's hair now, lace up her boots, tuck her into bed—and not to see her charming face perpetually and hold her hand when they went out together. In this idle condition she tried making lace. But her fingers were too heavy and broke the threads; she could not attend to anything, she had lost her sleep, and was, in her own words, "destroyed."

To "divert herself" she asked leave to have visits from her nephew Victor.

He arrived on Sundays after mass, rosy-cheeked, bare-chested, with the scent of the country he had walked through still about him. She laid her table promptly and they had lunch, sitting opposite each other. She ate as little as possible herself to save expense, but stuffed him with food so generously that at last he went to sleep. At the first stroke of vespers she woke him up, brushed his trousers, fastened his tie, and went to church, leaning on his arm with maternal pride.

Victor was always instructed by his parents to get something out of her —a packet of moist sugar, it might be, a cake of soap, spirits, or even money at times. He brought his things for her to mend and she took over the task, only too glad to have a reason for making him come back.

In August his father took him off on a coasting voyage. It was holiday time, and she was consoled by the arrival of the children. Paul, however, was getting selfish, and Virginie was too old to be called "thou" any longer; this put a constraint and barrier between them.

Victor went to Morlaix, Dunkirk, and Brighton in succession and made Félicité a present on his return from each voyage. It was a box made of shells the first time, a coffee cup the next, and on the third occasion a large gingerbread man. Victor was growing handsome. He was well made, had a hint of a moustache, good honest eyes, and a small leather hat pushed backwards like a pilot's. He entertained her by telling stories embroidered with nautical terms.

On a Monday, July 14, 1819 (she never forgot the date), he told her that he had signed on for the big voyage and next night but one he would take the Honfleur boat and join his schooner, which was to weigh anchor from Havre before long. Perhaps he would be gone two years.

The prospect of this long absence threw Félicité into deep distress; one more good-bye she must have, and on the Wednesday evening, when Madame's dinner was finished, she put on her clogs and made short work of the twelve miles between Pont-l'Évêque and Honfleur.

When she arrived in front of the Calvary she took the turn to the right instead of the left, got lost in the timber-yards, and retraced her steps; some people to whom she spoke advised her to be quick. She went all round the harbour basin, full of ships, and knocked against hawsers; then the ground fell away, lights flashed across each other, and she thought her wits had left her, for she saw horses up in the sky.

Others were neighing by the quay-side, frightened at the sea. They were lifted by a tackle and deposited in a boat, where passengers jostled each other among cider casks, cheese baskets, and sacks of grain; fowls could be heard clucking, the captain swore; and a cabin-boy stood leaning over the bows, indifferent to it all. Félicité, who had not recognized him, called "Victor!" and he raised his head; all at once, as she was darting forwards, the gangway was drawn back.

The Honfleur packet, women singing as they hauled it, passed out of harbour. Its framework creaked and the heavy waves whipped its bows. The canvas had swung round, no one could be seen on board now; and on the moon-silvered sea the boat made a black speck which paled gradually, dipped, and vanished.

As Félicité passed by the Calvary she had a wish to commend to God what she cherished most, and she stood there praying a long time with her face bathed in tears and her eyes towards the clouds. The town was asleep, coastguards were walking to and fro; and water poured without cessation through the holes in the sluice, with the noise of a torrent. The clocks struck two.

The convent parlour would not be open before day. If Félicité were late Madame would most certainly be annoyed; and in spite of her desire to kiss the other child she turned home. The maids at the inn were waking up as she came in to Pont-l'Évêque.

So the poor slip of a boy was going to toss for months and months at sea! She had not been frightened by his previous voyages. From England or Brittany you came back safe enough; but America, the colonies, the islands—these were lost in a dim region at the other end of the world.

Félicité's thoughts from that moment ran entirely on her nephew. On sunny days she was harassed by the idea of thirst; when there was a storm she was afraid of the lightning on his account. As she listened to the wind growling in the chimney or carrying off the slates she pictured him lashed by that same tempest, at the top of a shattered mast, with his body thrown backwards under a sheet of foam; or else (with a reminiscence of the illustrated geography) he was being eaten by savages, captured in a wood by monkeys, or dying on a desert shore. And never did she mention her anxieties.

Mme. Aubain had anxieties of her own, about her daughter. The good sisters found her an affectionate but delicate child. The slightest emotion unnerved her. She had to give up the piano.

Her mother stipulated for regular letters from the convent. She lost patience one morning when the postman did not come, and walked to and fro in the parlour from her arm-chair to the window. It was really amazing; not a word for four days!

To console Mme. Aubain by her own example Félicité remarked:

"As for me, Madame, it's six months since I heard . . ."

"From whom, pray?"

"Why . . . from my nephew," the servant answered gently.

"Oh! your nephew!" And Mme. Aubain resumed her walk with a shrug of the shoulders, as much as to say: "I was not thinking of him! And what is more, it's absurd! A scamp of a cabin-boy—what does he matter? . . . whereas my daughter . . . why, just think!"

Félicité, though she had been brought up on harshness, felt indignant with Madame—and then forgot. It seemed the simplest thing in the world to her to lose one's head over the little girl. For her the two children were equally important; a bond in her heart made them one, and their destinies must be the same.

She heard from the chemist that Victor's ship had arrived at Havana. He had read this piece of news in a gazette.

Cigars—they made her imagine Havana as a place where no one does anything but smoke, and there was Victor moving among the negroes in a cloud of tobacco. Could you, she wondered, "in case you needed," return by land? What was the distance from Pont-l'Évêque? She questioned M. Bourais to find out.

He reached for his atlas and began explaining the longitudes; Félicité's consternation provoked a fine pedantic smile. Finally he marked with his pencil a black, imperceptible point in the indentations of an oval spot, and said as he did so, "Here it is." She bent over the map; the maze of coloured lines wearied her eyes without conveying anything; and on an invitation from Bourais to tell him her difficulty she begged him to show her the house where Victor was living. Bourais threw up his arms, sneezed, and laughed immensely: a simplicity like hers was a positive joy. And

Félicité did not understand the reason; how could she when she expected, very likely, to see the actual image of her nephew—so stunted was her mind!

A fortnight afterwards Liébard came into the kitchen at market-time as usual and handed her a letter from her brother-in-law. As neither of them could read she took it to her mistress.

Mme. Aubain, who was counting the stitches in her knitting, put the work down by her side, broke the seal of the letter, started, and said in a low voice, with a look of meaning:

"It is bad news . . . that they have to tell you. Your nephew . . ."

He was dead. The letter said no more.

Félicité fell on to a chair, leaning her head against the wainscot; and she closed her eyelids, which suddenly flushed pink. Then with bent forehead, hands hanging, and fixed eyes, she said at intervals:

"Poor little lad! poor little lad!"

Liébard watched her and heaved sighs. Mme. Aubain trembled a little.

She suggested that Félicité should go to see her sister at Trouville. Félicité answered by a gesture that she had no need.

There was a silence. The worthy Liébard thought it was time for them to withdraw.

Then Félicité said:

"They don't care, not they!"

Her head dropped again; and she took up mechanically, from time to time, the long needles on her work-table.

Women passed in the yard with a barrow of dripping linen.

As she saw them through the window-panes she remembered her washing; she had put it to soak the day before, to-day she must wring it out; and she left the room.

Her plank and tub were at the edge of the Toucques. She threw a pile of linen on the bank, rolled up her sleeves, and taking her wooden beater dealt lusty blows whose sound carried to the neighbouring gardens. The meadows were empty, the river stirred in the wind; and down below long grasses wavered, like the hair of corpses floating in the water. She kept her grief down and was very brave until the evening; but once in her room she surrendered to it utterly, lying stretched on the mattress with her face in the pillow and her hands clenched against her temples.

Much later she heard, from the captain himself, the circumstances of Victor's end. They had bled him too much at the hospital for yellow fever. Four doctors held him at once. He had died instantly, and the chief had said:

"Bah! there goes another!"

His parents had always been brutal to him. She preferred not to see them again; and they made no advances, either because they forgot her or from the callousness of the wretchedly poor.

Virginie began to grow weaker.

Tightness in her chest, coughing, continual fever, and veinings on her cheek-bones betrayed some deep-seated complaint. M. Poupart had advised a stay in Provence. Mme. Aubain determined on it, and would have brought her daughter home at once but for the climate of Pont-l'Évêque.

She made an arrangement with a job-master, and he drove her to the convent every Tuesday. There is a terrace in the garden, with a view over the Seine. Virginie took walks there over the fallen vine-leaves, on her mother's arm. A shaft of sunlight through the clouds made her blink sometimes, as she gazed at the sails in the distance and the whole horizon from the castle of Tancarville to the lighthouses at Havre. Afterwards they rested in the arbour. Her mother had secured a little cask of excellent Malaga; and Virginie, laughing at the idea of getting tipsy, drank a thimbleful of it, no more.

Her strength came back visibly. The autumn glided gently away. Félicité reassured Mme. Aubain. But one evening, when she had been out on a commission in the neighbourhood, she found M. Poupart's gig at the door. He was in the hall, and Mme. Aubain was tying her bonnet.

"Give me my foot-warmer, purse, gloves! Quicker, come!"

Virginie had inflammation of the lungs; perhaps it was hopeless.

"Not yet!" said the doctor, and they both got into the carriage under whirling flakes of snow. Night was coming on and it was very cold.

Félicité rushed into the church to light a taper. Then she ran after the gig, came up with it in an hour, and jumped lightly in behind. As she hung on by the fringes a thought came into her mind: "The courtyard has not been shut up; supposing burglars got in!" And she jumped down.

At dawn next day she presented herself at the doctor's. He had come in and started for the country again. Then she waited in the inn, thinking that a letter would come by some hand or other. Finally, when it was twilight, she took the Lisieux coach.

The convent was at the end of a steep lane. When she was about half-way up it she heard strange sounds—a death-bell tolling. "It is for someone else," thought Félicité, and she pulled the knocker violently.

After some minutes there was a sound of trailing slippers, the door opened ajar, and a nun appeared.

The good sister, with an air of compunction, said that "she had just passed away." On the instant the bell of St. Leonard's tolled twice as fast.

Félicité went up to the second floor.

From the doorway she saw Virginie stretched on her back, with her hands joined, her mouth open, and head thrown back under a black crucifix that leaned towards her, between curtains that hung stiffly, less pale than was her face. Mme. Aubain, at the foot of the bed which she clasped with her arms, was choking with sobs of agony. The mother superior stood on the right. Three candlesticks on the chest of drawers made spots of red, and the mist came whitely through the windows. Nuns came and took Mme. Aubain away.

For two nights Félicité never left the dead child. She repeated the same prayers, sprinkled holy water over the sheets, came and sat down again, and watched her. At the end of the first vigil she noticed that the face had grown yellow, the lips turned blue, the nose was sharper, and the eyes sunk in. She kissed them several times, and would not have been immensely surprised if Virginie had opened them again; to minds like hers the supernatural is quite simple. She made the girl's toilette, wrapped her in her shroud, lifted her down into her bier, put a garland on her head, and spread out her hair. It was fair, and extraordinarily long for her age. Félicité cut off a big lock and slipped half of it into her bosom, determined that she should never part with it.

The body was brought back to Pont-l'Évêque, as Mme. Aubain intended; she followed the hearse in a closed carriage.

It took another three-quarters of an hour after the mass to reach the cemetery. Paul walked in front, sobbing. M. Bourais was behind, and then came the chief residents, the women shrouded in black mantles, and Félicité. She thought of her nephew; and because she had not been able to pay these honours to him her grief was doubled, as though the one were being buried with the other.

Mme. Aubain's despair was boundless. It was against God that she first rebelled, thinking it unjust of Him to have taken her daughter from her—she had never done evil and her conscience was so clear! Ah, no!—she ought to have taken Virginie off to the south. Other doctors would have saved her. She accused herself now, wanted to join her child, and broke into cries of distress in the middle of her dreams. One dream haunted her above all. Her husband, dressed as a sailor, was returning from a long voyage, and shedding tears he told her that he had been ordered to take Virginie away. Then they consulted how to hide her somewhere.

She came in once from the garden quite upset. A moment ago—and she pointed out the place—the father and daughter had appeared to her, standing side by side, and they did nothing, but they looked at her.

For several months after this she stayed inertly in her room. Félicité lectured her gently; she must live for her son's sake, and for the other, in remembrance of "her."

"Her," answered Mme. Aubain, as though she were just waking up. "Ah, yes! . . . yes! . . . You do not forget her!" This was an allusion to the cemetery, where she was strictly forbidden to go.

Félicité went there every day.

Precisely at four she skirted the houses, climbed the hill, opened the gate, and came to Virginie's grave. It was a little column of pink marble with a stone underneath and a garden plot enclosed by chains. The beds were hidden under a coverlet of flowers. She watered their leaves, freshened the gravel, and knelt down to break up the earth better. When Mme. Aubain was able to come there she felt a relief and a sort of consolation.

Then years slipped away, one like another, and their only episodes were the great festivals as they recurred—Easter, the Assumption, All Saints' Day. Household occurrences marked dates that were referred to afterwards. In 1825, for instance, two glaziers whitewashed the hall; in 1827 a piece of the roof fell into the courtyard and nearly killed a man. In the summer of 1828 it was Madame's turn to offer the consecrated bread; Bourais, about this time, mysteriously absented himself; and one by one the old acquaintances passed away: Guyot, Liébard, Mme. Lechaptois, Robelin, and Uncle Gremanville, who had been paralysed for a long time.

One night the driver of the mail-coach announced the Revolution of July in Pont-l'Évêque. A new sub-prefect was appointed a few days later —Baron de Larsonnière, who had been consul in America, and brought with him, besides his wife, a sister-in-law and three young ladies, already growing up. They were to be seen about on their lawn, in loose blouses, and they had a negro and a parrot. They paid a call on Mme. Aubain which she did not fail to return. The moment they were seen in the distance Félicité ran to let her mistress know. But only one thing could really move her feelings—the letters from her son.

He was swallowed up in a tavern life and could follow no career. She paid his debts, he made new ones; and the sighs that Mme. Aubain uttered as she sat knitting by the window reached Félicité at her spinning-wheel in the kitchen.

They took walks together along the espaliered wall, always talking of Virginie and wondering if such and such a thing would have pleased her and what, on some occasion, she would have been likely to say.

All her small belongings filled a cupboard in the two-bedded room. Mme. Aubain inspected them as seldom as she could. One summer day she made up her mind to it—and some moths flew out of the wardrobe.

Virginie's dresses were in a row underneath a shelf, on which there were three dolls, some hoops, a set of toy pots and pans, and the basin that she used. They took out her petticoats as well, and the stockings and handkerchiefs, and laid them out on the two beds before folding them up again. The sunshine lit up these poor things, bringing out their stains and the creases made by the body's movements. The air was warm and blue, a blackbird warbled, life seemed bathed in a deep sweetness. They found a little plush hat with thick, chestnut-coloured pile; but it was eaten all over by moth. Félicité begged it for her own. Their eyes met fixedly and filled with tears; at last the mistress opened her arms, the servant threw herself into them, and they embraced each other, satisfying their grief in a kiss that made them equal.

It was the first time in their lives, Mme. Aubain's nature not being expansive. Félicité was as grateful as though she had received a favour, and cherished her mistress from that moment with the devotion of an animal and a religious worship.

The kindness of her heart unfolded.

When she heard the drums of a marching regiment in the street she posted herself at the door with a pitcher of cider and asked the soldiers to drink. She nursed cholera patients and protected the Polish refugees; one of these even declared that he wished to marry her. They quarrelled, however; for when she came back from the Angelus one morning she found that he had got into her kitchen and made himself a vinegar salad which he was quietly eating.

After the Poles came father Colmiche, an old man who was supposed to have committed atrocities in '93. He lived by the side of the river in the ruins of a pigsty. The little boys watched him through the cracks in the wall, and threw pebbles at him which fell on the pallet where he lay constantly shaken by a catarrh; his hair was very long, his eyes inflamed, and there was a tumour on his arm bigger than his head. She got him some linen and tried to clean up his miserable hole; her dream was to establish him in the bakehouse, without letting him annoy Madame. When the tumour burst she dressed it every day; sometimes she brought him cake, and would put him in the sunshine on a truss of straw. The poor old man, slobbering and trembling, thanked her in his worn-out voice, was terrified that he might lose her, and stretched out his hands when he saw her go away. He died; and she had a mass said for the repose of his soul.

That very day a great happiness befell her; just at dinner-time appeared Mme. de Larsonnière's negro, carrying the parrot in its cage, with perch, chain, and padlock. A note from the baroness informed Mme. Aubain that her husband had been raised to a prefecture and they were starting that evening; she begged her to accept the bird as a memento and mark of her regard.

For a long time he had absorbed Félicité's imagination, because he came from America; and that name reminded her of Victor, so much so that she made inquiries of the negro. She had once gone so far as to say "How Madame would enjoy having him!"

The negro repeated the remark to his mistress; and as she could not take the bird away with her she chose this way of getting rid of him.

IV

His name was Loulou. His body was green and the tips of his wings rose-pink; his forehead was blue and his throat golden.

But he had the tiresome habits of biting his perch, tearing out his feathers, sprinkling his dirt about, and spattering the water of his tub. He annoyed Mme. Aubain, and she gave him to Félicité for good.

She endeavoured to train him; soon he could repeat "Nice boy! Your servant, sir! Good morning, Marie!" He was placed by the side of the door, and astonished several people by not answering to the name Jacquot, for all parrots are called Jacquot. People compared him to a turkey and a log of wood, and stabbed Félicité to the heart each time. Strange obstinacy on Loulou's part!—directly you looked at him he refused to speak.

None the less he was eager for society; for on Sundays, while the Roche-feuille ladies, M. de Houppeville, and new familiars—Onfroy the apothe-cary, Monsieur Varin, and Captain Mathieu—were playing their game of cards, he beat the windows with his wings and threw himself about so frantically that they could not hear each other speak.

Bourais' face, undoubtedly, struck him as extremely droll. Directly he saw it he began to laugh—and laugh with all his might. His peals rang through the courtyard and were repeated by the echo; the neighbours came to their windows and laughed too; while M. Bourais, gliding along under the wall to escape the parrot's eye, and hiding his profile with his hat, got to the river and then entered by the garden gate. There was a lack of ten-derness in the looks which he darted at the bird.

Loulou had been slapped by the butcher-boy for making so free as to plunge his head into his basket; and since then he was always trying to nip him through his shirt. Fabu threatened to wring his neck, although he was not cruel, for all his tattooed arms and large whiskers. Far from it; he really rather liked the parrot, and in a jovial humour even wanted to teach him to swear. Félicité, who was alarmed by such proceedings, put the bird in the kitchen. His little chain was taken off and he roamed about the house.

His way of going downstairs was to lean on each step with the curve of his beak, raise the right foot, and then the left; and Félicité was afraid that these gymnastics brought on fits of giddiness. He fell ill and could not talk or eat any longer. There was a growth under his tongue, such as fowls have sometimes. She cured him by tearing the pellicle off with her finger-nails. Mr. Paul was thoughtless enough one day to blow some cigar smoke into his nostrils, and another time when Mme. Lormeau was teasing him with the end of her umbrella he snapped at the ferrule. Finally he got lost.

Félicité had put him on the grass to refresh him, and gone away for a minute, and when she came back—no sign of the parrot! She began by look-ing for him in the shrubs, by the waterside, and over the roofs, without listening to her mistress's cries of "Take care, do! You are out of your wits!" Then she investigated all the gardens in Pont-l'Évêque, and stopped the passers-by. "You don't ever happen to have seen my parrot, by any chance, do you?" And she gave a description of the parrot to those who did not know him. Suddenly, behind the mills at the foot of the hill she thought she could make out something green that fluttered. But on the top of the hill there was nothing. A hawker assured her that he had come across the parrot just before, at Saint-Melaine, in Mère Simon's shop. She rushed there; they had no idea of what she meant. At last she came home exhausted, with her slippers in shreds and despair in her soul; and as she was sitting in the middle of the garden-seat at Madame's side, telling the whole story of her efforts, a light weight dropped on to her shoulder—it was Loulou! What on earth had he been doing? Taking a walk in the neighbourhood, perhaps!

She had some trouble in recovering from this, or rather never did recover. As the result of a chill she had an attack of quinsy, and soon afterwards an earache. Three years later she was deaf; and she spoke very loud, even in church. Though Félicité's sins might have been published in every corner of the diocese without dishonour to her or scandal to anybody, his Reverence the priest thought it right now to hear her confession in the sacristy only.

Imaginary noises in the head completed her upset. Her mistress often said to her, "Heavens! how stupid you are!" "Yes, Madame," she replied, and looked about for something.

Her little circle of ideas grew still narrower; the peal of church-bells and the lowing of cattle ceased to exist for her. All living beings moved as silently as ghosts. One sound only reached her ears now—the parrot's voice.

Loulou, as though to amuse her, reproduced the click-clack of the turn-spit, the shrill call of a man selling fish, and the noise of the saw in the joiner's house opposite; when the bell rang he imitated Mme. Aubain's "Félicité! the door! the door!"

They carried on conversations, he endlessly reciting the three phrases in his repertory, to which she replied with words that were just as discon-nected but uttered what was in her heart. Loulou was almost a son and a lover to her in her isolated state. He climbed up her fingers, nibbled at her lips, and clung to her kerchief; and when she bent her forehead and shook her head gently to and fro, as nurses do, the great wings of her bonnet and the bird's wings quivered together.

When the clouds massed and the thunder rumbled Loulou broke into cries, perhaps remembering the downpours in his native forests. The streaming rain made him absolutely mad; he fluttered wildly about, dashed up to the ceiling, upset everything, and went out through the window to dabble in the garden; but he was back quickly to perch on one of the fire-dogs and hopped about to dry himself, exhibiting his tail and his beak in turn.

One morning in the terrible winter of 1837 she had put him in front of the fireplace because of the cold. She found him dead, in the middle of his cage: head downwards, with his claws in the wires. He had died from con-gestion, no doubt. But Félicité thought he had been poisoned with parsley, and though there was no proof of any kind her suspicions inclined to Fabu.

She wept so piteously that her mistress said to her, "Well, then, have him stuffed!"

She asked advice from the chemist, who had always been kind to the parrot. He wrote to Havre, and a person called Fallacher undertook the business. But as parcels sometimes got lost in the coach she decided to take the parrot as far as Honfleur herself.

Along the sides of the road were leafless apple-trees, one after the other. Ice covered the ditches. Dogs barked about the farms; and Félicité, with her hands under her cloak, her little black sabots and her basket, walked briskly in the middle of the road.

She crossed the forest, passed High Oak, and reached St. Gatien.

A cloud of dust rose behind her, and in it a mail-coach, carried away by the steep hill, rushed down at full gallop like a hurricane. Seeing this woman who would not get out of the way, the driver stood up in front and the postilion shouted too. He could not hold in his four horses, which increased their pace, and the two leaders were grazing her when he threw them to one side with a jerk of the reins. But he was wild with rage, and lifting his arm as he passed at full speed, gave her such a lash from waist to neck with his big whip that she fell on her back.

Her first act, when she recovered consciousness, was to open her basket. Loulou was happily none the worse. She felt a burn in her right cheek, and when she put her hands against it they were red; the blood was flowing.

She sat down on a heap of stones and bound up her face with her handkerchief. Then she ate a crust of bread which she had put in the basket as a precaution, and found a consolation for her wound in gazing at the bird.

When she reached the crest of Ecquemauville she saw the Honfleur lights sparkling in the night sky like a company of stars; beyond, the sea stretched dimly. Then a faintness overtook her and she stopped; her wretched childhood, the disillusion of her first love, her nephew's going away, and Virginie's death all came back to her at once like the waves of an oncoming tide, rose to her throat, and choked her.

Afterwards, at the boat, she made a point of speaking to the captain, begging him to take care of the parcel, though she did not tell him what was in it.

Fellacher kept the parrot a long time. He was always promising it for the following week. After six months he announced that a packing-case had started, and then nothing more was heard of it. It really seemed as though Loulou was never coming back. "Ah, they have stolen him!" she thought.

He arrived at last, and looked superb. There he was, erect upon a branch which screwed into a mahogany socket, with a foot in the air and his head on one side, biting a nut which the bird-stuffer—with a taste for impressiveness—had gilded.

Félicité shut him up in her room. It was a place to which few people were admitted, and held so many religious objects and miscellaneous things that it looked like a chapel and bazaar in one.

A big cupboard impeded you as you opened the door. Opposite the window commanding the garden a little round one looked into the court; there was a table by the folding-bed with a water-jug, two combs, and a cube of blue soap in a chipped plate. On the walls hung rosaries, medals, several benign Virgins, and a holy water vessel made out of cocoa-nut; on the chest of drawers, which was covered with a cloth like an altar, was the shell box that Victor had given her, and after that a watering-can, a toy-balloon, exercise-books, the illustrated geography, and a pair of young lady's boots; and, fastened by its ribbons to the nail of the looking-glass, hung the little plush hat! Félicité carried observances of this kind so far as to keep one of Monsieur's frock-coats. All the old rubbish which Mme. Aubain did not want any longer she laid hands on for her room. That was why there were artificial flowers along the edge of the chest of drawers and a portrait of the Comte d'Artois in the little window recess.

With the aid of a bracket Loulou was established over the chimney, which jutted into the room. Every morning when she woke up she saw him there in the dawning light, and recalled old days and the smallest details of insignificant acts in a deep quietness which knew no pain.

Holding, as she did, no communication with anyone, Félicité lived as insensibly as if she were walking in her sleep. The Corpus Christi processions roused her to life again. Then she went round begging mats and candlesticks from the neighbours to decorate the altar they put up in the street.

In church she was always gazing at the Holy Ghost in the window, and observed that there was something of the parrot in him. The likeness was still clearer, she thought, on a crude colour-print representing the baptism of Our Lord. With his purple wings and emerald body he was the very image of Loulou.

She bought him, and hung him up instead of the Comte d'Artois, so that she could see them both together in one glance. They were linked in her thoughts; and the parrot was consecrated by his association with the Holy Ghost, which became more vivid to her eye and more intelligible. The Father could not have chosen to express Himself through a dove, for such creatures cannot speak; it must have been one of Loulou's ancestors, surely. And though Félicité looked at the picture while she said her prayers she swerved a little from time to time towards the parrot.

She wanted to join the Ladies of the Virgin, but Mme. Aubain dissuaded her.

And then a great event loomed up before them—Paul's marriage.

He had been a solicitor's clerk to begin with, and then tried business, the Customs, the Inland Revenue, and made efforts, even, to get into the Rivers and Forests. By an inspiration from heaven he had suddenly, at thirty-six, discovered his real line—the Registrar's Office. And there he showed such marked capacity that an inspector had offered him his daughter's hand and promised him his influence.

So Paul, grown serious, brought the lady to see his mother.

She sniffed at the ways of Pont-l'Évêque, gave herself great airs, and wounded Félicité's feelings. Mme. Aubain was relieved at her departure.

The week after came news of M. Bourais' death in an inn in Lower Brittany. The rumour of suicide was confirmed, and doubts arose as to his honesty. Mme. Aubain studied his accounts, and soon found out the whole tale of his misdoings—embezzled arrears, secret sales of wood, forged receipts, etc. Besides that he had an illegitimate child, and "relations with a person at Dozulé."

These shameful facts distressed her greatly. In March 1853 she was seized with a pain in the chest; her tongue seemed to be covered with film, and leeches did not ease the difficult breathing. On the ninth evening of her illness she died, just at seventy-two.

She passed as being younger, owing to the bands of brown hair which framed her pale, pock-marked face. There were few friends to regret her, for she had a stiffness of manner which kept people at a distance.

But Félicité mourned for her as one seldom mourns for a master. It upset her ideas and seemed contrary to the order of things, impossible and monstrous, that Madame should die before her.

Ten days afterwards, which was the time it took to hurry there from Besançon, the heirs arrived. The daughter-in-law ransacked the drawers, chose some furniture, and sold the rest; and then they went back to their registering.

Madame's armchair, her small round table, her foot-warmer, and the eight chairs were gone! Yellow patches in the middle of the panels showed where the engravings had hung. They had carried off the two little beds and the mattresses, and all Virginie's belongings had disappeared from the cupboard. Félicité went from floor to floor dazed with sorrow.

The next day there was a notice on the door, and the apothecary shouted in her ear that the house was for sale.

She tottered, and was obliged to sit down. What distressed her most of all was to give up her room, so suitable as it was for poor Loulou. She enveloped him with a look of anguish when she was imploring the Holy Ghost, and formed the idolatrous habit of kneeling in front of the parrot to say her prayers. Sometimes the sun shone in at the attic window and caught his glass eye, and a great luminous ray shot out of it and put her in an ecstasy.

She had a pension of fifteen pounds a year which her mistress had left her. The garden gave her a supply of vegetables. As for clothes, she had enough to last her to the end of her days, and she economized in candles by going to bed at dusk.

She hardly ever went out, as she did not like passing the dealer's shop, where some of the old furniture was exposed for sale. Since her fit of giddiness she dragged one leg; and as her strength was failing Mère Simon, whose grocery business had collapsed, came every morning to split the wood and pump water for her.

Her eyes grew feeble. The shutters ceased to be thrown open. Years and years passed, and the house was neither let nor sold.

Félicité never asked for repairs because she was afraid of being sent away. The boards on the roof rotted; her bolster was wet for a whole winter. After Easter she spat blood.

Then Mère Simon called in a doctor. Félicité wanted to know what was the matter with her. But she was too deaf to hear, and the only word which reached her was "pneumonia." It was a word she knew, and she answered softly "Ah! like Madame," thinking it natural that she should follow her mistress.

The time for the festal shrines was coming near. The first one was always at the bottom of the hill, the second in front of the post-office, and the third towards the middle of the street. There was some rivalry in the matter of this one, and the women of the parish ended by choosing Mme. Aubain's courtyard.

The hard breathing and fever increased. Félicité was vexed at doing nothing for the altar. If only she could at least have put something there! Then she thought of the parrot. The neighbours objected that it would not be decent. But the priest gave her permission, which so intensely delighted her that she begged him to accept Loulou, her sole possession, when she died.

From Tuesday to Saturday, the eve of the festival, she coughed more often. By the evening her face had shrivelled, her lips stuck to her gums, and she had vomitings; and at twilight next morning, feeling herself very low, she sent for a priest.

Three kindly women were round her during the extreme unction. Then she announced that she must speak to Fabu. He arrived in his Sunday clothes, by no means at his ease in the funereal atmosphere.

"Forgive me," she said, with an effort to stretch out her arm: "I thought it was you who had killed him."

What did she mean by such stories? She suspected him of murder—a man like him! He waxed indignant, and was on the point of making a row.

"There," said the women, "she is no longer in her senses, you can see it well enough!"

Félicité spoke to shadows of her own from time to time. The women went away, and Mère Simon had breakfast. A little later she took Loulou and brought him close to Félicité with the words:

"Come, now, say good-bye to him!"

Loulou was not a corpse, but the worms devoured him; one of his wings was broken, and the tow was coming out of his stomach. But she was blind now; she kissed him on the forehead and kept him close against her cheek. Mère Simon took him back from her to put him on the altar.

v

Summer scents came up from the meadows; flies buzzed; the sun made the river glitter and heated the slates. Mère Simon came back into the room and fell softly asleep.

She woke at the noise of bells; the people were coming out from vespers. Félicité's delirium subsided. She thought of the procession and saw it as if she had been there.

All the school children, the church-singers, and the firemen walked on the pavement, while in the middle of the road the verger armed with his hallebard and the beadle with a large cross advanced in front. Then came the schoolmaster, with an eye on the boys, and the sister, anxious about her little girls; three of the daintiest, with angelic curls, scattered rose-petals in the air; the deacon controlled the band with outstretched arms; and two censer-bearers turned back at every step towards the Holy Sacrament, which was borne by Monsieur the curé, wearing his beautiful chasuble, under a canopy of dark-red velvet held up by four churchwardens. A crowd of people pressed behind, between the white cloths covering the house walls, and they reached the bottom of the hill.

A cold sweat moistened Félicité's temples. Mère Simon sponged her with a piece of linen, saying to herself that one day she would have to go that way.

The hum of the crowd increased, was very loud for an instant, and then went further away.

A fusillade shook the window-panes. It was the postilions saluting the monstrance. Félicité rolled her eyes and said as audibly as she could: "Does he look well?" The parrot was weighing on her mind.

Her agony began. A death-rattle that grew more and more convulsed made her sides heave. Bubbles of froth came at the corners of her mouth and her whole body trembled.

Soon the booming of the ophicleides, the high voices of the children, and the deep voices of the men were distinguishable. At intervals all was silent, and the tread of feet, deadened by the flowers they walked on, sounded like a flock pattering on grass.

The clergy appeared in the courtyard. Mère Simon clambered on to a chair to reach the attic window, and so looked down straight upon the shrine. Green garlands hung over the altar, which was decked with a flounce of English lace. In the middle was a small frame with relics in it; there were two orange-trees at the corners, and all along stood silver candle-

sticks and china vases, with sunflowers, lilies, peonies, foxgloves, and tufts
of hortensia. This heap of blazing colour slanted from the level of the
altar to the carpet which went on over the pavement; and some rare objects caught the eye. There was a silver-gilt sugar-basin with a crown of
violets; pendants of Alençon stone glittered on the moss, and two Chinese
screens displayed their landscapes. Loulou was hidden under roses, and
showed nothing but his blue forehead, like a plaque of lapis lazuli.

The churchwardens, singers, and children took their places round the
three sides of the court. The priest went slowly up the steps, and placed
his great, radiant golden sun upon the lace. Everyone knelt down. There
was a deep silence; and the censers glided to and fro on the full swing
of their chains.

An azure vapour rose up into Félicité's room. Her nostrils met it; she
inhaled it sensuously, mystically; and then closed her eyes. Her lips smiled.
The beats of her heart lessened one by one, vaguer each time and softer,
as a fountain sinks, an echo disappears; and when she sighed her last
breath she thought she saw an opening in the heavens, and a gigantic parrot hovering above her head.

KRAMBAMBULI

Marie von Ebner-Eschenbach

(1830–1916)

TRANSLATED BY BASIL CREIGHTON

A MAN MAY FEEL a liking for all kinds of things, but real, undying love
comes but once, if ever. That at least was the opinion of Hopp, the gamekeeper. He had had any number of dogs and liked them all, but only
Krambambuli inspired a love he could not forget. He bought him at the
Lion at Wischau from a vagabond woodman, or rather swapped him.
At the very first sight of the dog he took a fancy to him that was to last
till his dying day. The dog's master was sitting at the table with an
empty glass in front of him, abusing the innkeeper because he would not
let him have a second without payment. He was a little fellow, with a
rascally look, and though still a young man he was as sallow as a withered
tree, with yellow hair and a sparse yellow beard. The coat he wore suggested the faded glories of his last settled job, and it bore the marks of a

night spent in a damp ditch. Although Hopp was not fond of keeping low company he sat down beside the man and began talking to him at once. It soon came out that the ne'er-do-well had already pledged his gun and cartridge-bag for drink and now wanted to pledge his dog too; but the innkeeper, the dirty skinflint, would have nothing to do with a pledge that needed feeding.

Hopp said nothing at first about having taken a fancy to the dog, but he ordered a bottle of the good Dantzig cherry brandy, which the Lion stocked at that time, and poured out a glass for the woodman—and, to cut a long story short, in an hour it was all settled. The gamekeeper offered twelve bottles of the same brand and the deal was done—the vagrant gave up his dog, much against his will, to his honour be it said. His hands trembled so violently as he tied the cord round the dog's neck that it seemed he would never get it done. Hopp waited patiently, admiring the animal in silence, for he was a wonderful dog in spite of the poor condition he was in. He looked two years old at most and in colour he resembled the scoundrel who was handing him over, though a shade or two darker. He had a white mark on his forehead, which branched into two thin lines like the needles on a fir twig. His eyes were large, black and lustrous and rimmed with light yellow as clear as dew; his long ears were set high and perfect in shape. Everything about him was perfect from his claws to his keenly scenting nose and his strong agile frame; his legs and feet were beyond all praise, four living pillars which might have carried a stag, and no thicker than a hare's. By St. Hubert, the animal must have had a pedigree as old and untarnished as that of a knight of a German order.

The gamekeeper's heart rejoiced within him at the fine bargain he had made. He stood up and took hold of the cord which the woodman had at last succeeded in knotting. "What's his name?" he asked.

"His name is the same as what you gave for him—Krambambuli," was the answer.

"Right. Come along, Krambambuli."

It was no good calling, whistling and tugging—the dog would not obey him but turned his head to the man he still took to be his master, yelping when he was told to go, and though he got a kick into the bargain, even then he struggled hard to get loose. It took Hopp all his time to get hold of the dog. At last he had to put him in a sack and carry him on his back to his gamekeeper's cottage, which was some hours' walk away.

Two whole months passed before Krambambuli, half beaten to death and kept on a chain with a spiked collar after every attempt to escape, at last understood to whom he now belonged. But, once his submission was complete, what a dog he was! No tongue can describe the heights he attained to, not only in the exercise of his profession, but as zealous servant, good friend and protector. It is often said of intelligent dogs that

they can do everything but speak. Krambambuli did not lack even this.
His master at least had long talks with him. The gamekeeper's wife was
thoroughly jealous of Buli, as she contemptuously called him, and
often reproached her husband. She spent the whole day knitting in silence
when she was not tidying up, washing or cooking. At night after supper
when she started on her knitting again she would have liked to have someone to speak to for once.

"You've plenty to say to Buli, but you've nothing to say to me. You talk
so much to animals you've forgotten how to talk to human beings." The
gamekeeper admitted there was some truth in this but he did not know
what to do about it. What was there they could talk about? They had
never had children, they were not allowed to keep a cow, and chickens were
of no interest to a gamekeeper in their living state and of not much more
when roasted. On the other hand his wife took no interest in pheasant
rearing or shooting stories. Hopp at last found a way out of his dilemma;
instead of talking to Krambambuli he talked about Krambambuli, about
the glories he reflected on him on every hand, about the envy he excited,
about the fantastic sums he was offered for him and which he scornfully
rejected.

When two years had gone by the Countess, the wife of his employer, paid
a visit one day to the keeper's cottage. He knew at once what the object
of it was and as soon as the amiable and beautiful lady began: "Good
morning, Hopp, it is the Count's birthday——" he quietly concluded her
sentence for her with a smile: "And so your ladyship would like to give
the Count a present and you don't know of anything that would please
him so much as Krambambuli."

"Yes, Hopp——" and the Countess flushed with pleasure at his friendly
way of meeting the suggestion, said how grateful she was and asked him
to name what price he liked for the dog.

The old fox of a gamekeeper chuckled and then, putting on an air of
resignation, he came out with it: "Your ladyship, if the dog stays at the castle and doesn't bite through every cord and break every chain, or if he
doesn't strangle himself in trying, then you can keep him for nothing, for
in that case he is no more good to me."

The trial was made, but it did not get as far as strangling, for before
that the Count lost all interest in the obstinate animal. In vain they tried
to win him over first by kindness and then with harshness. He bit everyone who approached him, refused to eat and—for a keeper's dog has little
flesh to lose—began to pine away. After a few weeks Hopp was told he
could come and fetch his cur. He lost no time and when he went to find
the dog in his kennel there was a scene of the wildest delight. Krambambuli barked in a frenzy of joy, jumped up at his master and with his
forefeet on his chest licked away the tears of joy which ran down
the old man's cheeks.

On the evening of this happy day they went to the inn together. The keeper played Taroc with the doctor and the solicitor while Krambambuli lay in a corner behind his master, who often glanced round at him, and then the dog, however fast asleep he seemed to be, began to beat the floor with his tail, as though to say: "Here I am." And when Hopp absent-mindedly started singing his little triumphal song: "What's my Krambambuli doing?" the dog rose with respectful dignity and his bright eyes answered: "I'm all right."

About this time there was a gang of poachers at work, not only in the Count's forests but throughout the whole neighbourhood. They were reckless fellows and the leader of them was said to be a thorough bad lot. The woodmen, who sometimes came across him drinking brandy in disreputable alehouses, called him the Yellow-skin; so did the keepers, who had got on his track now and again but had never been able to catch him, and so did his own spies of whom he had many among the roughs in every village.

He was the most impudent customer that ever an honest keeper had to deal with and he must at one time have been a keeper or a woodman himself, otherwise he would not have known so well where game was to be found nor been able to elude so skilfully every trap that was set for him.

Such depredations had never been known before and keepers and foresters were roused to revengeful fury. In consequence insignificant trespasses were too often visited with harsher punishment than was either customary or justifiable. There was great indignation over this in all the villages. The head forester, who was the first to incur hatred, was given a number of well-meant warnings. It was going round that the poachers had sworn to take a stern revenge on him at the first opportunity. He was a headstrong and fearless man and instead of paying the least attention he let it be known far and wide that he had instructed his underlings to treat all trespassers with the utmost severity and that he took full responsibility for the consequences. He was always telling Hopp to keep his eyes open and sometimes accused him of being slow, at which the old man only smiled. But Krambambuli, whom the keeper was wont to look down at on such occasions, yawned loudly and contemptuously. Neither he nor his master took it amiss of the head forester. Hopp never forgot that it was the forester's father who had taught him the noble art of venery and Hopp in turn had taught the son the rudiments of it when he was a little boy. The trouble he had spent on him once upon a time was still a pleasure to look back on; he was proud of his one-time pupil and loved him in spite of the rough treatment that he as well as everybody else had to take at his hands.

One morning in June he came across him again when he was after some trespassers.

It was in the circular group of lime trees at the bottom of the park where it bordered on the "Count's Wood" and not far from the tree nursery, which the head forester would dearly have liked to protect with gunpowder mines. The limes were just in full bloom and a gang of small boys had come stealing the blossom. They were climbing like squirrels along the branches of the fine trees, breaking off all the sprays they could reach and throwing them down to the ground. Two women were hastily collecting them and stuffing them into baskets, which were already more than half full of the fragrant plunder. The head forester came striding up in ungovernable rage. He told his men to shake the children from the trees, never mind from what height they fell. While they crawled at his feet whimpering and crying, one with a torn face, another with his arm out of joint, a third with a broken leg, he thrashed the two women with his own hands. Hopp did not feel very happy about it when he recognised one of them as the wanton who was rumoured to be the Yellow-skin's sweetheart. And when, after the baskets and shawls of the women and the hats of the boys had been impounded, Hopp was instructed to bring the culprits to justice, he could not help a dark foreboding.

The head forester, raging like the devil in hell and like him surrounded by wailing and suffering sinners, shouted the order after him and these were the last words the keeper ever heard him speak. A week later he came across him again among the lime trees—dead. The state in which the body was found showed that it had been dragged over marshy as well as stony ground in order to be laid out on that particular spot. The head forester lay on a bier of branches; round his head was a thick wreath of lime blossom and another was wound about his chest as a bandolier. His hat was beside him, full of lime blossom. The murderer had left him his cartridge-bag, only he had taken out the cartridges and put in lime blossom instead. His fine breech-loader was missing and replaced by a wretched old blunderbuss. When later the bullet was extracted from his chest, it was found to fit exactly in the barrel of the blunderbuss which had been mockingly laid over his shoulder. At the sight of the corpse Hopp came to a stop, motionless with horror. He could not have raised a finger, and even his brain seemed paralysed; he only stared and stared and at first thought of nothing at all. It was only after some moments that he came to his senses and mutely asked himself the question: What's the matter with the dog?

Krambambuli was sniffing at the dead man and then running round about him as though bereft of his senses, his nose always to the ground. Once he gave a whimper, once he uttered a shrill bark of joy, ran forward a few steps, barked again and behaved exactly as though the memory of something long forgotten had come back to him.

"Come to heel," Hopp called, "come here!" and Krambambuli obeyed but looked up at his master in the wildest excitement and—as the keeper used to say—said to him: "I implore you by all that's holy, don't you see anything? Don't you smell anything? . . . Dear mother, just look, just smell! Master, do come! Come here!" and after nozzling at his knee, he crept back to the corpse, looking round, as though to ask: "Are you following me?" and started lifting and pushing the heavy gun and taking it in his jaws with the obvious intention of bringing it along with him.

A shudder ran down the keeper's spine and a dim conjecture formed in his mind. But conjecture was no concern of his and also it was none of his business to teach the authorities their business, but rather to leave his ghastly find just as he had found it and go his way, which in this case was straight to the police. So he did simply what he thought it his business to do.

When he had done it, and all the formalities which the law prescribes in such catastrophes had been completed and the whole day and part of the night spent over them, Hopp, before going to sleep took counsel once more with his dog.

"Krambambuli," he said, "the police are afoot now and there'll be an everlasting coming and going. Are we going to leave it to others to finish off the scoundrel who shot our head forester? My dog knows the dirty loafer, he knows him all right. But nobody need know that. I have never said a word . . . I . . . I'll bring my dog into this story . . . that's an idea!" He bent over Krambambuli, who was sitting between his knees, pressed his cheek to the dog's head and was gratefully caressed in return. Meanwhile he murmured: "What's my Krambambuli doing?" until sleep overcame him.

Psychologists have tried to explain the strange impulse that often takes a criminal back again and again to the scene of his crime. Hopp knew nothing of these learned investigations, but all the same he and his dog were never long away from the circle of lime trees. On the tenth day after the murder he had been thinking for the first time for some hours on end of something else than his revenge and was busied in the "Count's Wood" marking the trees which were next to be felled.

When he had done he slung his gun over his shoulder again and made a bee-line through the wood for the pheasant coops near the limes. Just as he was about to emerge on to the footpath which ran along the beech hedge he thought he heard a rustle among the leaves. But next moment there was utter silence. He might have thought he had been mistaken if the dog's attention had not been so strangely roused. He stood with his coat bristling, his neck stretched out, his tail erect, gazing at a particular spot in the hedge. Ha, ha! Hopp thought. You wait, my lad, if that's you. He then stepped behind a tree and cocked his gun. His heart pounded and, as he was always a bit short-winded, he was scarcely able to breathe. Then suddenly the Yellow-skin stepped out of the hedge on to the footpath. Two leverets hung out of his side pockets and over his shoulder, by the leather strap Hopp knew so well, hung the head forester's breech-loader.

Now was the moment to shoot the blackguard from a safe ambush.

But Hopp was not the man to shoot at even the worst of scoundrels without giving him warning. In one stride he left the shelter of the tree and shouted from the footpath: "Hands up, you skunk!" Then as the poacher's only answer was to snatch the breech-loader from his shoulder, the keeper fired . . . by all the saints in heaven, a fine shot. The only report was a click. He had left his gun too long against a tree, with the cap exposed and there was a misfire.

Goodnight, that's what dying means—went through the old man's head and at the same moment his hat flew into the grass . . . The other's luck was out too, the swine. He had wasted the only shot he had in the breech and there was an interval while he felt in his pocket for another cartridge . . .

"Go for him!" Hopp shouted hoarsely to his dog, "go for him!"

"Come here to me, here, Krambambuli," the dog heard from over there in a caressing voice he had once known and loved so well.

Krambambuli recognised his old master and ran half way towards him. Then Hopp whistled and he turned round. The Yellow-skin whistled and he turned round again, and kept on revolving on one spot midway between the keeper and the poacher, torn both ways . . .

At last the poor animal gave up and made an end of his agonising doubts, though not of the agonies they caused him. Whimpering and whining, with his belly to the ground, wriggling his body along, head in air as though calling heaven to witness his agony of mind, he crawled—to his first master.

Hopp saw red at the sight. His fingers trembled as he put a fresh cap beneath the hammer and deliberately took his aim. The Yellow-skin too put his rifle to his shoulder. This time there would be no mistake. Both knew that, as they drew a bead on each other and, come what might, aimed as quietly as if they were marksmen in a painted picture.

Two bullets flew. The keeper's found its mark, the poacher's—missed. At the very moment he pressed the trigger the dog jumped up at him in a frenzy of joy to lick his face and jerked his aim. "You beast," he hissed and then fell backwards and moved no more.

The man who had killed him came slowly up. You've done for yourself, he thought, you're not worth powder and shot. Nevertheless he put the stock to the ground and loaded again. The dog sat upright on his haunches, his tongue out, his breath coming in short pants, looking at him. And when the keeper had done loading and picked up his gun they had a talk of which no third person would have understood a word even though he had been alive instead of dead.

"Do you know who this bullet's for?"

"I can make a guess."

"Deserter, traitor——"

"Yes, master, I know."

"You were my joy. Now it's over. I shall never have joy in you again."

"I quite understand, master," and Krambambuli laid his head on his paws and looked at the gamekeeper.

Yes, if only the cursed brute had not looked at him! Then he would have put an end to him on the spot and saved himself and the dog much misery. But you cannot shoot a creature that looks at you like that. Hopp muttered a few curses through his teeth, one blasphemy after another, shouldered his gun, took the poacher's leverets from him and went away.

The dog followed him with his eyes until he was lost to sight among the trees and then he got up and his long-drawn, piercing howl rang through the wood. He turned round in circles once or twice and then sat down on his haunches again beside the dead man. He was still there when the police, and Hopp with them, came back at nightfall to view the poacher's body and remove it. Krambambuli retreated a little way as the men came up. "That's your dog, isn't it?" one of them remarked to the keeper. "I left him there on guard," Hopp replied, for he was ashamed to confess the truth. But what was the use? It all came out when the corpse was put in the cart and driven away and Krambambuli trotted behind it with his head down and his tail between his legs. Next day the court usher saw him hanging about the mortuary, where the body of the Yellow-skin had been laid out. He gave him a kick and told him to go home. Krambambuli showed his teeth and ran away in the direction of the keeper's cottage, the man said. But he never got there. He led a wretched vagabond life.

He slunk about the outskirts of the village, where the poorer cottagers lived, in a half wild state until he was reduced to skin and bone. One day he rushed out at a child outside a cottage on the extreme edge of the village and greedily snatched from his hand the piece of bread he was eating. The child was transfixed with fright, but a little Pomeranian ran out of the cottage and barked at the thief, who let his plunder drop and ran away.

That night Hopp was standing at the window before going to bed and looking out into the starlit summer night. He thought he saw his dog sitting at the edge of the wood across the meadow, gazing fixedly and yearningly at the scene of his past happiness—the truest of the true, homeless and masterless.

The keeper shut the window and went to bed. But after a time he got up and went back to the window—the dog was no longer there. He lay down and tried to sleep and again could find no rest.

He could stand it no longer. Let bygones be bygones—he could stand it no longer without his dog. I'll fetch him home, he thought, and as soon as he came to this decision he felt a new man. He put on his clothes at daybreak, told his wife not to wait dinner for him and hurried out. But as he opened the door his journey was ended. His foot kicked against a body on the doorstep. It was Krambambuli, dead, with his head pressed to the threshold he had not dared to cross again.

The gamekeeper never got over his grief. His happiest moments were those in which he forgot that he had lost him. Then sunk in happy memories he hummed his famous "What's my Krambambuli . . ." But stopping in the middle, he shook his head and said with a deep sigh: "Pity about that dog."

THE OUTCASTS OF POKER FLAT

Francis Bret Harte
(1839–1902)

As Mr. JOHN OAKHURST, gambler, stepped into the main street of Poker Flat on the morning of the twenty-third of November, 1850, he was conscious of a change in its moral atmosphere since the preceding night. Two or three men, conversing earnestly together, ceased as he approached, and exchanged significant glances. There was a Sabbath lull in the air, which, in a settlement unused to Sabbath influences, looked ominous.

Mr. Oakhurst's calm, handsome face betrayed small concern of these indications. Whether he was conscious of any predisposing cause, was another question. "I reckon they're after somebody," he reflected; "likely it's me." He returned to his pocket the handkerchief with which he had been whipping away the red dust of Poker Flat from his neat boots, and quietly discharged his mind of any further conjecture.

In point of fact, Poker Flat was "after somebody." It had lately suffered the loss of several thousand dollars, two valuable horses, and a prominent citizen. It was experiencing a spasm of virtuous reaction, quite as lawless and ungovernable as any of the acts that had provoked it. A secret committee had determined to rid the town of all improper persons. This was done permanently in regard to two men who were then hanging from the boughs of a sycamore in the gulch, and temporarily in the banishment of certain other objectionable characters. I regret to say that some of these were ladies. It is but due to the sex, however, to state that their impropriety was professional, and it was only in such easily established standards of evil that Poker Flat ventured to sit in judgment.

Mr. Oakhurst was right in supposing that he was included in this category. A few of the committee had urged hanging him as a possible example, and a sure method of reimbursing themselves from his pockets of the sums he had won from them. "It's agin justice," said Jim Wheeler, "to let this yer young man from Roaring Camp—an entire stranger—carry away our money." But a crude sentiment of equality residing in the breasts of those who had been fortunate enough to win from Mr. Oakhurst overruled this narrower local prejudice.

Mr. Oakhurst received his sentence with philosophic calmness, none the less coolly that he was aware of the hesitation of his judges. He was too much of a gambler not to accept Fate. With him life was at best an uncertain game, and he recognized the usual percentage in favor of the dealer.

A body of armed men accompanied the deported wickedness of Poker Flat to the outskirts of the settlement. Besides Mr. Oakhurst, who was known to be a coolly desperate man, and for whose intimidation the armed escort was intended, the expatriated party consisted of a young woman familiarly known as "The Duchess"; another, who had gained the infelicitous title of "Mother Shipton"; and "Uncle Billy," a suspected sluice-robber and confirmed drunkard. The cavalcade provoked no comments from the spectators, nor was any word uttered by the escort. Only, when the gulch which marked the uttermost limit of Poker Flat was reached, the leader spoke briefly and to the point. The exiles were forbidden to return at the peril of their lives.

As the escort disappeared, their pent-up feelings found vent in a few hysterical tears from the Duchess, some bad language from Mother Shipton, and a Parthian volley of expletives from Uncle Billy. The philosophic Oakhurst alone remained still. He listened calmly to Mother Shipton's desire to cut somebody's heart out, to the repeated statements of the Duchess that she would die on the road, and to the alarming oaths that seemed to be bumped out of Uncle Billy as he rode forward. With the easy good humor characteristic of his class, he insisted upon exchanging his own riding-horse, Five Spot, for the sorry mule which the Duchess rode. But even this act did not draw the party into any closer sympathy. The young woman readjusted her somewhat draggled plumes with a feeble, faded coquetry; Mother Shipton eyed the possessor of Five Spot with malevolence, and Uncle Billy included the whole party in one sweeping anathema.

The road to Sandy Bar—a camp that, not having as yet experienced the regenerating influences of Poker Flat, consequently seemed to offer some invitation to the emigrants—lay over a steep mountain range. It was distant a day's severe journey. In that advanced season, the party soon passed out of the moist, temperate regions of the foothills into the dry, cold bracing air of the Sierras. The trail was narrow and difficult. At noon the Duchess, rolling out of her saddle upon the ground, declared her intention of going no farther, and the party halted.

The spot was singularly wild and impressive. A wooded amphitheater, surrounded on three sides by precipitous cliffs of naked granite, sloped gently toward the crest of another precipice that overlooked the valley. It was undoubtedly the most suitable spot for a camp, had camping been advisable. But Mr. Oakhurst knew that scarcely half the journey to Sandy

Bar was accomplished, and the party were not equipped or provisioned for delay. This fact he pointed out to his companions curtly, with a philosophic commentary on the folly of "throwing up their hand before the game was played out." But they were furnished with liquor, which in this emergency stood them in place of food, fuel, rest, and prescience. In spite of his remonstrances, it was not long before they were more or less under its influence. Uncle Billy passed rapidly from a bellicose state into one of stupor, the Duchess became maudlin, and Mother Shipton snored. Mr. Oakhurst alone remained erect, leaning against a rock, calmly surveying them.

Mr. Oakhurst did not drink. It interfered with a profession which required coolness, impassiveness, and presence of mind, and, in his own language, he "couldn't afford it." As he gazed at his recumbent fellow-exiles, the loneliness begotten of his pariah-trade, his habits of life, his very vices, for the first time seriously oppressed him. He bestirred himself in dusting his black clothes, washing his hands and face, and other acts characteristic of his studiously neat habits, and for a moment forgot his annoyance. The thought of deserting his weaker and more pitiable companions never perhaps occurred to him. Yet he could not help feeling the want of that excitement which, singularly enough, was most conducive to that calm equanimity for which he was notorious. He looked at the gloomy walls that rose a thousand feet sheer above the circling pines around him; at the sky, ominously clouded; at the valley below, already deepening into shadow. And, doing so, suddenly he heard his own name called.

A horseman slowly ascended the trail. In the fresh, open face of the newcomer Mr. Oakhurst recognized Tom Simson, otherwise known as "The Innocent" of Sandy Bar. He had met him some months before over a "little game," and had, with perfect equanimity, won the entire fortune—amounting to some forty dollars—of that guileless youth. After the game was finished, Mr. Oakhurst drew the youthful speculator behind the door and thus addressed him: "Tommy, you're a good little man, but you can't gamble worth a cent. Don't try it over again." He then handed him his money back, pushed him gently from the room, and so made a devoted slave of Tom Simson.

There was a remembrance of this in his boyish and enthusiastic greeting of Mr. Oakhurst. He had started, he said, to go to Poker Flat to seek his fortune. "Alone?" No, not exactly alone; in fact—a giggle—he had run away with Piney Woods. Didn't Mr. Oakhurst remember Piney? She that used to wait on the table at the Temperance House? They had been engaged a long time, but old Jake Woods had objected, and so they had run away, and were going to Poker Flat to be married, and here they were. And they were tired out, and how lucky it was they had found a place to camp and company. All this the Innocent delivered rapidly, while Piney —a stout, comely damsel of fifteen—emerged from behind the pine tree, where she had been blushing unseen, and rode to the side of her lover.

Mr. Oakhurst seldom troubled himself with sentiment, still less with propriety; but he had a vague idea that the situation was not felicitous. He retained, however, his presence of mind sufficiently to kick Uncle Billy, who was about to say something, and Uncle Billy was sober enough to recognize in Mr. Oakhurst's kick a superior power that would not bear trifling. He then endeavored to dissuade Tom Simson from delaying further, but in vain. He even pointed out the fact that there was no provision, nor means of making a camp. But, unluckily, the Innocent met this objection by assuring the party that he was provided with an extra mule loaded with provisions, and by the discovery of a rude attempt at a log-house near the trail. "Piney can stay with Mrs. Oakhurst," said the Innocent, pointing to the Duchess, "and I can shift for myself."

Nothing but Mr. Oakhurst's admonishing foot saved Uncle Billy from bursting into a roar of laughter. As it was, he felt compelled to retire up the canyon until he could recover his gravity. There he confided the joke to the tall pine trees, with many slaps of his leg, contortions of his face, and the usual profanity. But when he returned to the party, he found them seated by a fire—for the air had grown strangely chill and the sky overcast—in apparently amicable conversation. Piney was actually talking in an impulsive, girlish fashion to the Duchess, who was listening with an interest and animation she had not shown for many days. The Innocent was holding forth, apparently with equal effect, to Mr. Oakhurst and Mother Shipton, who was actually relaxing into amiability. "Is this yer a d—d picnic?" said Uncle Billy, with inward scorn, as he surveyed the sylvan group, the glancing fire-light, and the tethered animals in the foreground. Suddenly an idea mingled with the alcoholic fumes that disturbed his brain. It was apparently of a jocular nature, for he felt impelled to slap his leg again and cram his fist into his mouth.

As the shadows crept slowly up the mountain, a slight breeze rocked the tops of the pine trees, and moaned through their long and gloomy aisles. The ruined cabin, patched and covered with pine boughs, was set apart for the ladies. As the lovers parted, they unaffectedly exchanged a kiss, so honest and sincere that it might have been heard above the swaying pines. The frail Duchess and the malevolent Mother Shipton were probably too stunned to remark upon this last evidence of simplicity, and so turned without a word to the hut. The fire was replenished, the men lay down before the door, and in a few minutes were asleep.

Mr. Oakhurst was a light sleeper. Toward morning he awoke benumbed and cold. As he stirred the dying fire, the wind, which was now blowing strongly, brought to his cheek that which caused the blood to leave it— snow!

He started to his feet with the intention of awakening the sleepers, for there was no time to lose. But turning to where Uncle Billy had been lying, he found him gone. A suspicion leaped to his brain and a curse to his lips.

He ran to the spot where the mules had been tethered; they were no longer there. The tracks were already rapidly disappearing in the snow.

The momentary excitement brought Mr. Oakhurst back to the fire with his usual calm. He did not waken the sleepers. The Innocent slumbered peacefully, with a smile on his good-humored, freckled face; the virgin Piney slept beside her frailer sisters as sweetly as though attended by celestial guardians, and Mr. Oakhurst, drawing his blanket over his shoulders, stroked his mustachios and waited for the dawn. It came slowly in the whirling mist of snowflakes, that dazzled and confused the eye. What could be seen of the landscape appeared magically changed. He looked over the valley, and summed up the present and future in two words—"Snowed in!"

A careful inventory of the provisions, which, fortunately for the party, had been stored within the hut, and so escaped the felonious fingers of Uncle Billy, disclosed the fact that with care and prudence they might last ten days longer. "That is," said Mr. Oakhurst, *sotto voce* to the Innocent, "if you're willing to board us. If you ain't—and perhaps you'd better not—you can wait till Uncle Billy gets back with provisions." For some occult reason, Mr. Oakhurst could not bring himself to disclose Uncle Billy's rascality, and so offered the hypothesis that he had wandered from the camp and had accidentally stampeded the animals. He dropped a warning to the Duchess and Mother Shipton, who of course knew the facts of their associate's defection. "They'll find out the truth about us *all*, when they find out anything," he added, significantly, "and there's no good frightening them now."

Tom Simson not only put all his worldly store at the disposal of Mr. Oakhurst, but seemed to enjoy the prospect of their enforced seclusion. "We'll have a good camp for a week, and then the snow'll melt, and we'll all go back together." The cheerful gayety of the young man and Mr. Oakhurst's calm infected the others. The Innocent, with the aid of pine boughs, extemporized a thatch for the roofless cabin, and the Duchess directed Piney in the rearrangement of the interior with a taste and tact that opened the blue eyes of that provincial maiden to their fullest extent.

"I reckon now you're used to fine things at Poker Flat," said Piney. The Duchess turned away sharply to conceal something that reddened her cheek through its professional tint, and Mother Shipton requested Piney not to "chatter." But when Mr. Oakhurst returned from a weary search for the trail, he heard the sound of happy laughter echoed from the rocks. He stopped in some alarm, and his thoughts first naturally reverted to the whisky, which he had prudently *cached*. "And yet it don't somehow sound like whisky," said the gambler. It was not until he caught sight of the blazing fire through the still blinding storm, and the group around it, that he settled to the conviction that it was "square fun."

Whether Mr. Oakhurst had *cached* his cards with the whisky as some-

thing debarred the free access of the community, I cannot say. It was
certain that, in Mother Shipton's words, he "didn't say cards once" during
the evening. Haply the time was beguiled by an accordion produced somewhat ostentatiously by Tom Simson, from his pack. Notwithstanding some
difficulties attending the manipulation of this instrument, Piney Woods
managed to pluck several reluctant melodies from its keys, to an accompaniment by the Innocent on a pair of bone castinets. But the crowning
festivity of the evening was reached in a rude camp-meeting hymn, which
the lovers, joining hands, sang with great earnestness and vociferation. I
fear that a certain defiant tone and Covenanter's swing to its chorus, rather
than any devotional quality, caused it speedily to infect the others, who at
last joined in the refrain:

> I'm proud to live in the service of the Lord,
> And I'm bound to die in His army.

The pines rocked, the storm eddied and whirled above the miserable
group, and the flames of their altar leaped heavenward, as if in token of
the vow.

At midnight the storm abated, the rolling clouds parted, and the stars
glittered keenly above the sleeping camp. Mr. Oakhurst, whose professional
habits had enabled him to live on the smallest possible amount of sleep, in
dividing the watch with Tom Simson, somehow managed to take upon himself the greater part of that duty. He excused himself to the Innocent, by saying that he had "often been a week without sleep." "Doing what?" asked
Tom. "Poker!" replied Oakhurst, sententiously, "when a man gets a streak of
luck—nigger-luck—he don't get tired. The luck gives in first. Luck," continued the gambler, reflectively, "is a mighty queer thing. All you know
about it for certain is that it's bound to change. And it's finding out when
it's going to change that makes you. We've had a streak of bad luck since
we left Poker Flat—you come along, and slap you get into it, too. If you
can hold your cards right along you're all right. For," added the gambler,
with cheerful irrelevance,

> "I'm proud to live in the service of the Lord,
> And I'm bound to die in His army."

The third day came, and the sun, looking through the white-curtained
valley, saw the outcasts divide their slowly decreasing store of provisions
for the morning meal. It was one of the peculiarities of that mountain
climate that its rays diffused a kindly warmth over the wintry landscape,
as if in regretful commiseration of the past. But it revealed drift on drift of
snow piled high around the hut; a hopeless, uncharted, trackless sea of
white lying below the rocky shores to which the castaways still clung.
Through the marvelously clear air, the smoke of the pastoral village of
Poker Flat rose miles away. Mother Shipton saw it, and from a remote

pinnacle of her rocky fastness, hurled in that direction a final malediction. It was her last vituperative attempt, and perhaps for that reason was invested with a certain degree of sublimity. It did her good, she privately informed the Duchess, "Just to go out there and cuss, and see." She then set herself to the task of amusing "the child," as she and the Duchess were pleased to call Piney. Piney was no chicken, but it was a soothing and ingenious theory of the pair thus to account for the fact that she didn't swear and wasn't improper.

When night crept up again through the gorges, the reedy notes of the accordion rose and fell in fitful spasms and long-drawn gasps by the flickering camp-fire. But music failed to fill entirely the aching void left by insufficient food, and a new diversion was proposed by Piney—storytelling. Neither Mr. Oakhurst nor his female companions caring to relate their personal experiences, this plan would have failed, too, but for the Innocent. Some months before he had chanced upon a stray copy of Mr. Pope's ingenious translation of the Iliad. He now proposed to narrate the principal incidents of that poem—having thoroughly mastered the argument and fairly forgotten the words—in the current vernacular of Sandy Bar. And so for the rest of that night the Homeric demigods again walked the earth. Trojan bully and wily Greek wrestled in the winds, and the great pines in the canyon seemed to bow to the wrath of the son of Peleus. Mr. Oakhurst listened with quiet satisfaction. Most especially was he interested in the fate of "Ash-heels," as the Innocent persisted in denominating the "swift-footed Achilles."

So with small food and much of Homer and the accordion, a week passed over the heads of the outcasts. The sun again forsook them, and again from leaden skies the snowflakes were sifted over the land. Day by day closer around them drew the snowy circle, until at last they looked from their prison over drifted walls of dazzling white, that towered twenty feet above their heads. It became more and more difficult to replenish their fires, even from the fallen trees beside them, now half-hidden in the drifts. And yet no one complained. The lovers turned from the dreary prospect and looked into each other's eyes, and were happy. Mr. Oakhurst settled himself coolly to the losing game before him. The Duchess, more cheerful than she had been, assumed the care of Piney. Only Mother Shipton—once the strongest of the party—seemed to sicken and fade. At midnight on the tenth day she called Oakhurst to her side. "I'm going," she said, in a voice of querulous weakness, "but don't say anything about it. Don't waken the kids. Take the bundle from under my head and open it." Mr. Oakhurst did so. It contained Mother Shipton's rations for the last week, untouched. "Give 'em to the child," she said, pointing to the sleeping Piney. "You've starved yourself," said the gambler. "That's what they call it," said the woman, querulously, as she lay down again, and, turning her face to the wall, passed quietly away.

The accordion and the bones were put aside that day, and Homer was forgotten. When the body of Mother Shipton had been committed to the snow, Mr. Oakhurst took the Innocent aside, and showed him a pair of snowshoes, which he had fashioned from the old pack-saddle. "There's one chance in a hundred to save her yet," he said, pointing to Piney; "but it's there," he added, pointing toward Poker Flat. "If you can reach there in two days she's safe." "And you?" asked Tom Simson. "I'll stay here," was the curt reply.

The lovers parted with a long embrace. "You are not going, too?" said the Duchess, as she saw Mr. Oakhurst apparently waiting to accompany him. "As far as the canyon," he replied. He turned suddenly, and kissed the Duchess, leaving her pallid face aflame, and her trembling limbs rigid with amazement.

Night came, but not Mr. Oakhurst. It brought the storm again and the whirling snow. Then the Duchess, feeding the fire, found that some one had quietly piled beside the hut enough fuel to last a few days longer. The tears rose to her eyes, but she hid them from Piney.

The women slept but little. In the morning, looking into each other's faces, they read their fate. Neither spoke; but Piney, accepting the position of the stronger, drew near and placed her arm around the Duchess's waist. They kept this attitude for the rest of the day. That night the storm reached its greatest fury, and, rending asunder the protecting pines, invaded the very hut.

Toward morning they found themselves unable to feed the fire, which gradually died away. As the embers slowly blackened, the Duchess crept closer to Piney, and broke the silence of many hours: "Piney, can you pray?" "No, dear," said Piney, simply. The Duchess without knowing exactly why, felt relieved, and, putting her head upon Piney's shoulder, spoke no more. And so reclining, the younger and purer pillowing the head of her soiled sister upon her virgin breast, they fell asleep.

The wind lulled as if it feared to waken them. Feathery drifts of snow, shaken from the long pine boughs, flew like white-winged birds, and settled about them as they slept. The moon through the rifted clouds looked down upon what had been the camp. But all human stain, all trace of earthly travail, was hidden beneath the spotless mantle mercifully flung from above.

They slept all that day and the next, nor did they waken when voices and footsteps broke the silence of the camp. And when pitying fingers brushed the snow from their wan faces, you could scarcely have told from the equal peace that dwelt upon them, which was she that had sinned. Even the Law of Poker Flat recognized this, and turned away, leaving them still locked in each other's arms.

But at the head of the gulch, on one of the largest pine trees, they found the deuce of clubs pinned to the bark with a bowie knife. It bore the following, written in pencil, in a firm hand:

✝

BENEATH THIS TREE

LIES THE BODY

OF

JOHN OAKHURST,

WHO STRUCK A STREAK OF BAD LUCK

ON THE 23D OF NOVEMBER, 1850,

AND

HANDED IN HIS CHECKS

ON THE 7TH OF DECEMBER, 1850.

✝

And pulseless and cold, with a Derringer by his side and a bullet in his heart, though still calm as in life, beneath the snow lay he who was at once the strongest and yet the weakest of the outcasts of Poker Flat.

OLYMPE AND HENRIETTE

Villiers de l'Isle Adam

(1838–1889)

TRANSLATED BY HAMISH MILES

[TO M. THÉODORE DE BANVILLE]

"Light, light!"
Last words of GOETHE

PASCAL TELLS US that, so far as actions are concerned, good and evil are a question of "latitude." One human action, in fact, is called a crime in one place, but somewhere else a good deed; and so inversely.

In Europe, for instance, one generally cherishes one's aged parents; but among certain tribes of America one persuades them to climb up into a tree—and then shakes the tree. If they fall, then it is the sacred duty of every good son, as among the Messenians of old, to despatch them forthwith with a determined tomahawk and spare them the cares of decrepitude. But if they muster the strength to cling on to a branch, why, then they are still fit for the chase or for fishing, and their immolation is accordingly postponed. Again, the northern peoples are fond of drinking wine, that gleaming stream wherein the cherished sunlight lies asleep, and our national religion even advises us that "good wine makes glad the heart of man." But southwards, among our Mahometan neighbours, the act is viewed as a grave misdeed. In Sparta, thieving was both practised and honoured; it was an hieratic institution, an indispensable piece of every sound Lacedæmonian's education—whence, no doubt, the Greeks. In Lapland, the father of a family holds it a point of honour that his daughter should receive all the affectionate favours which could be bestowed by the traveller who is enjoying his hospitality. In Bessarabia likewise. In the northern parts of Persia, and among the peoples of Cabul who have their habitation in ancient tombs, you may receive, in some comfortable sepulchre, a hospitable and cordial welcome, but if at the end of twenty-four hours you are not on the very best of terms with every one of your host's offspring, be he fire-worshipper, Parsee, or Wahabite, there is every reason to expect that quite as a matter of course your head will be taken off—the punishment favoured in these climes.

Actions, then, as regards their physical nature, are matters of indifference: it is the conscience of each one of us, and conscience alone, that makes them good or evil. The mysterious seed from which this immense misunderstanding is sprung, is the inborn need which Man feels of creating for himself distinctions and scruples, of forbidding himself such and such an action rather than some other one. One might imagine, in fact, that there exists some great Law, lost and mysterious, forgotten by the whole mass of Mankind, a law after which, in their efforts to recall it, men are blindly groping.

Some years ago there flourished a certain café, spacious, luminous, the pride of our boulevards. It was situated almost directly opposite one of our important theatres, the pediment of which recalls that of a pagan temple. It was a daily meeting-place for the choice spirits among the youth, who since then have become distinguished, whether for their work as artists, for their incapacity, or for their attitude during the troubled times through which we have passed.

Among the latter, some have even stood at the helm of the ship of state. And, looking back, they were no small beer, the frequenters of this Arabian Nights café. Respectable citizens of Paris bated their breath whenever they mentioned it. Many a time, the *préfet* of the city used to fling down there, with a careless air, as one might a visiting-card, a choice nosegay, an unexpected bouquet of police sergeants, who then, with that air of smiling absent-mindedness which is peculiarly their own, proceeded in an effortless way to lay about them with their loaded batons on mischievous and rebellious heads; an attention which, for all its delicacy, was none the less noticeable. On the following day he was not to be seen there any more.

Out on the terrace, between the row of hackney-cabs and the window

front, was a paddock of women, a flowering of chignons plucked from the
pencil of Guys. Bedecked with the utmost extremes of fashion, they were
ensconced in the chairs beside the round wrought-iron tables painted in
bright green. On these tables drinks were set. Their eyes had something of
the falcon, something of poultry. Some would hold large bouquets upon
their laps, others little dogs, others nothing. You would have said they were
waiting for someone.

Amongst these young women two were marked out by their constant
attendance. By the regular frequenters of the famous room they were
named Olympe and Henriette—just that. These two used to arrive about
dusk; they installed themselves in a well-lighted corner, ordered a glass of
vespétro or a *mazagran*, as an excuse rather than from any real need, and
then surveyed the passer-by with meticulous scrutiny.

And these were the daughters of Bienfilâtre!

Their parents, honest folk, hard-schooled in misfortune, had not had the
means of letting them taste the joys of apprenticeship, the vocation of this
austere couple consisting mainly of continually hanging, in attitudes of
despair, upon that long spiral rope which communicates with the lock of a
carriage gateway. A hard life! And to pick up, occasionally and just barely,
a few scattered pence! No turn of luck ever came their way. And Bienfilâtre grumbled away as he made his morning caramel for himself.

As dutiful daughters, Olympe and Henriette understood early in life
that some intervention was necessary. Sisters in the gay life from their
tenderest childhood, they consecrated the price of their vigils and their toils
to maintaining a degree of comfort in the home, modest, it is true, but
honourable. "May God send His blessing on our efforts!" they used to say
from time to time, for they had been imbued with good principles, and
sooner or later the earliest teachings, based on solid principles, will bear
fruit. When anyone was concerned to know if their labours, sometimes
excessive, did not affect their health, they would answer evasively, with the
gentle and embarrassed air of modesty, and lowering their eyes: "There
are consolations. . . ."

The daughters of Bienfilâtre were among those work-women who, as
they say, "go to their day's work at night." They accomplished with as
much dignity as possible (considering certain prejudices people have) a
thankless and often painful task. They were not amongst those idle women
who proscribe, as degrading, the hand made horny and sacred by work, and
they never blushed for it. Several fine anecdotes were told of them which
would have stirred the ashes of Monthyon in his noble cenotaph. One
evening, for instance, they had vied in emulation of each other and had
surpassed even themselves, in order to meet the expense of burying an aged
uncle, who in any case had left them nothing but the memory of sundry
cuffs on the ear, distributed long ago in the days of their childhood. Moreover, they were favourably looked upon by all the frequenters of this

worthy resort, amongst whom were some who were not the kind to make allowances. A glance or smile of theirs always found the response of a friendly signal, a waved "Good evening." Never had reproach or complaint been levelled against them by anyone. Their commerce was recognized by all as kindly and affable. In short, they owed no man anything, they honoured all their engagements, and in consequence they could hold up their heads without fear. They were exemplary: did they not put something aside against the unforeseen, something "for a rainy day," so as one day to retire honourably from business? They were orthodox: did they not close on Sundays? And as "good young girls," they never lent an ear to the blandishments of young sparks fit only to turn maidens aside from the straight path of work and duty. They considered that nowadays the only gratuitous thing in love is the moon. Their motto was: "Celerity, Security, Discretion." And on their professional cards they added "Specialties."

One day, Olympe, the younger sister, broke down. Up to then irreproachable, this unhappy child yielded to temptations to which, more than other people (who will perhaps be too prompt in blaming her), she was inevitably exposed by the surroundings of her life. In short, she took a false step: she *loved*.

It was her first error. But who, after all, has ever fathomed the abyss to which a first error can lead us? A young student, frank, handsome, gifted with an impassioned artist's soul (but poor as Job himself), a youth named Maxime, whose family name we suppress, beguiled her with pretty words, and led her astray.

He inspired a heavenly passion in this poor girl who, considering her situation, had no more right to experience this than Eve had to taste of the divine fruit of the Tree of Life. From that day onwards all her duties were forgotten. Everything fell into disorder and confusion. When a girl has her head filled with love—the game is up!

And as for her sister—alas! the noble Henriette was now bending, as it were, beneath the burden! Sometimes she used to clasp her head between her hands, with grave doubts of everything, of the family, of principles, of society even! "They're nothing but words!" she exclaimed. One day she had met Olympe clothed in a little black dress, bare-headed, with a small tin milk-basin in her hand. As she passed, Henriette had said to her, without any appearance of recognizing her: "Sister, your conduct is unpardonable. You might at least have some respect for appearances!"

By these words she perhaps hoped for a return to propriety.

All was in vain. Henriette felt that Olympe was lost. She blushed, and passed on.

The fact is that there had been gossiping in the celebrated room. When she arrived alone in the evening, Henriette's welcome was no longer the same. She noticed differences, and humiliating ones. She was remarked to be colder since the news of Olympe's downfall. Proudly she smiled, like the young Spartan with the fox gnawing at his vitals, but, deep within that sensitive and upright heart, all these blows told. To the truly delicate, a trifle will often hurt more keenly than a gross outrage, and in this respect Henriette had the most sensitive of feelings. How she must have suffered!

And the evenings too, at the family supper! The father and mother, with bowed heads, ate in silence. Not even one word passed of the absent one. With the dessert, when the moment for the liqueur came, Henriette and her mother would exchange a quick, secret glance, wipe away each a tear, and clasp hands silently under the table. And the old door-keeper, completely upset, then tugged unbidden at the cord, to conceal a tear. Sometimes, turning away his head, he abruptly put his hand up to his buttonhole as if to tear away some vague decorations.

On one occasion the porter even made an attempt to reclaim his daughter. Gloomily he took it upon himself to mount the several flights of stairs where the young man lodged. Arrived there, he sobbed: "My poor child, I want her!"

"Sir," answered Maxime, "I love her, and I beg you to grant me her hand."

"Wretch!" exclaimed Bienfilâtre as he hurried off, revolted by this "cynicism."

Henriette had drained the cup to the dregs. One last attempt was necessary, and so she resigned herself to risking everything, even scandal. Learning one evening that the deplorable Olympe was to go to the café to settle some small debt remaining from the old days, she warned the family, and a procession was made towards the illuminated café.

Like Mallonia dishonoured by Tiberius, and presenting herself before the Roman senate to lay accusation against her violator before stabbing herself in despair, Henriette entered the room of the austere. The father and mother, from a sense of dignity, remained by the door. Coffee was being drunk. At the sight of Henriette faces lengthened gravely and with a certain severity, but when it was seen that she wanted to speak, the long panels of the newspapers were lowered on to the marble tables, and there fell a religious silence: there was question of a judgment.

In a corner, ashamed and making herself almost invisible, Olympe and her little black dress could be distinguished at a small isolated table.

Henriette spoke. During her speech one could catch glimpses of the Bienfilâtres, uneasy, watching without hearing. At last the father could bear it no longer. He pushed the door ajar, and leaning forward with attentive ear, one hand on the door-handle, he listened.

And shreds of phrases reached him whenever Henriette raised her voice a little: One should keep to one's own sort. . . . Such conduct . . . it was putting all respectable folk against one. . . . A silly boy who doesn't give a brass farthing . . . ! A good-for-nothing . . . ! The weight of ostracism on her. . . . Throwing off her responsibilities. . . . A girl who has flung away her reputation . . . who stares like a stupid . . . and only a little while ago . . . could keep her end up with anyone. . . . She hoped that the words of these gentlemen, which had more authority than hers, that the counsels of their enlightened experience . . . would bring her back to saner ideas, more practical. . . . One isn't in this world for one's amusement. . . . She implored them to intervene. . . . She had appealed to memories of childhood . . . ! To the call of the blood! All in vain! Not one answering chord could be struck in her. A lost girl! And what an aberration . . . ! Alas! Alas!

At that moment, bowed down, the father entered the distinguished gathering-place. At this spectacle of unmerited woe, everyone rose. There are some sorrows before which one does not try to proffer consolation. Silently everyone came up to shake the hand of the deserving old man, to give discreet evidence of their sharing his misfortune.

Olympe withdrew, pale and shamefaced. For an instant, with the sense of guilt in her heart, she had hesitated, on the point of throwing herself into the arms of the family and of friendship, ever open to repentance. But passion had carried her away. A first love throws down into the heart deep-spreading roots which will stifle earlier sentiments, even to their smallest germs.

All the same, the shock of the scandal had dealt a shattering blow to Olympe's personality. Her tortured conscience rose in revolt, and next day a fever seized her. She took to her bed. Quite literally she *died of shame*. The physical was slain by the moral. The sheath was worn out by the blade.

Lying in her tiny room, and feeling that the hour of her passing was at hand, she called out. Some good souls among the neighbours brought her a heavenly minister. One of them let fall the remark that Olympe was very weak, and ought to be *fortified*. Whereupon a maid-of-all-work brought up some soup for her.

The priest appeared.

The old ecclesiastic strove to calm her with words of peace, forgetfulness, and forgiveness.

"I have had a lover . . ." murmured Olympe, using these words to accuse herself of her disgrace.

She omitted all the peccadilloes, the complainings, the impatience of her life. That, and that only, came to her mind. It obsessed her. "A lover! For pleasure! Without a penny of gain!" *There* lay the crime.

She was not concerned to whittle away her transgression by telling of her former life, always up till then pure and full of self-denial. In all that, she felt certain, she was beyond reproach. But to have succumbed to this shame, to have faithfully cherished a love for a youth who had no position and, in the truthful and avenging words of her sister, never gave her so much as a brass farthing! Henriette, who had never yielded, appeared to her as crowned with a halo. She felt herself condemned, and dreaded already the thunder-bolts of the All-powerful Judge, face to face with whom she might now at any moment be standing.

The priest, used to all the woes of humanity, attributed to delirium certain points in Olympe's confessions which seemed to him to be inexplicable, diffuse even. There was in this perhaps a *quid pro quo*, certain of the poor girl's expressions having once or twice left the abbé wondering. But as repentance, remorse, was his sole concern, the detail of the sin mattered little; the good-will of the penitent and her sincere grief—these were enough. And at the very moment when he was about to raise his hand to grant the absolution, the door burst noisily open: it was Maxime, glowing, with a joyful, beaming air, with a handful of a few silver crowns and three or four gold pieces which he was tossing and jingling triumphantly. His family had raised the money on the occasion of his examinations: it was for his entrance. . . .

At first Olympe did not notice this significant and extenuating circumstance. She threw out her arms towards him, with horror.

Maxime had stopped short, stupefied at what he saw before him.

"Courage, my daughter!" murmured the priest, who read in this gesture of Olympe's a final farewell to her partner in guilty and immodest joys.

In reality it was only the young man's *crime* that she was thrusting from her—and the crime was that of not being "serious."

But on the instant when the august pardon was descending upon her, a heavenly smile lit up her innocent features: the priest imagined that she felt herself saved, that through the mortal shadows of these last moments there shone for her some dim seraphic vision. —— But in reality Olympe had just caught sight, vaguely, of the pieces of the sacred metal gleaming between the transfigured fingers of Maxime. Then, and only then, did she experience the life-giving effects of the supreme forgiveness! A veil was rent asunder. A miracle! By this manifest sign she saw herself pardoned from on high, and ransomed.

Dazzled, with conscience set at rest, she closed her eyelids as if to gather strength before spreading her wings towards the everlasting blue. Then her lips were parted, and like the perfume of a lily her last breath issued forth, murmuring the words of hope—"It has grown light!"

THE THREE STRANGERS

Thomas Hardy

(1840–1928)

AMONG THE FEW FEATURES of agricultural England which retain an appearance but little modified by the lapse of centuries, may be reckoned the high, grassy and furzy downs, coombs, or ewe-leases, as they are indifferently called, that fill a large area of certain counties in the south and southwest. If any mark of human occupation is met with hereon, it usually takes the form of the solitary cottage of some shepherd.

Fifty years ago such a lonely cottage stood on such a down, and may possibly be standing there now. In spite of its loneliness, however, the spot, by actual measurement, was not more than five miles from a county-town. Yet that affected it little. Five miles of irregular upland, during the long inimical seasons, with their sleets, snows, rains, and mists, afford withdrawing space enough to isolate a Timon or a Nebuchadnezzar; much less, in fair weather, to please that less repellent tribe, the poets, philosophers, artists, and others who "conceive and meditate of pleasant things."

Some old earthen camp or barrow, some clump of trees, at least some starved fragment of ancient hedge is usually taken advantage of in the erection of these forlorn dwellings. But, in the present case, such a kind of shelter had been disregarded. Higher Crowstairs, as the house was called, stood quite detached and undefended. The only reason for its precise situation seemed to be the crossing of two footpaths at right angles hard by, which may have crossed there and thus for a good five hundred years. Hence the house was exposed to the elements on all sides. But, though the wind up here blew unmistakably when it did blow, and the rain hit hard whenever it fell, the various weathers of the winter season were not quite so formidable on the coomb as they were imagined to be by dwellers on low ground. The raw rimes were not so pernicious as in the hollows, and the frosts were scarcely so severe. When the shepherd and his family who tenanted the house were pitied for their sufferings from the exposure, they said that upon the whole they were less inconvenienced by "wuzzes and flames" (hoarses and phlegms) than when they had lived by the stream of a snug neighboring valley.

The night of March 28, 182–, was precisely one of the nights that were wont to call forth these expressions of commiseration. The level rainstorm smote walls, slopes, and hedges like the clothyard shafts of Senlac and Crecy. Such sheep and outdoor animals as had no shelter stood with their buttocks to the winds; while the tails of little birds trying to roost on some scraggy thorn were blown inside-out like umbrellas. The gable-end of the cottage was stained with wet, and the eavesdroppings flapped against the wall. Yet never was commiseration for the shepherd more misplaced. For that cheerful rustic was entertaining a large party in glorification of the christening of his second girl.

The guests had arrived before the rain began to fall, and they were all now assembled in the chief or living room of the dwelling. A glance into the apartment at eight o'clock on this evening would have resulted in the opinion that it was as cozy and comfortable a nook as could be wished for in boisterous weather. The calling of its inhabitant was proclaimed by a number of highly-polished sheep-crooks without stems that were hung ornamentally over the fireplace, the curl of each shining crook varying from the antiquated type engraved in the patriarchal pictures of old family Bibles to the most approved fashion of the last local sheep-fair. The room was lighted by half-a-dozen candles, having wicks only a trifle smaller than the grease which enveloped them, in candlesticks that were never used but at high-days, holy-days, and family feasts. The lights were scattered about the room, two of them standing on the chimney-piece. This position of candles was in itself magnificent. Candles on the chimney-piece always meant a party.

On the hearth, in front of a back-brand to give substance, blazed a fire of thorns, that crackled "like the laughter of the fool."

Nineteen persons were gathered there. Of these, five women, wearing gowns of various bright hues, sat in chairs along the wall; girls shy and not shy filled the window-bench; four men, including Charley Jake the hedge-carpenter, Elijah New the parish-clerk, and John Pitcher, a neighboring dairyman, the shepherd's father-in-law, lolled in the settle; a young man and maid, who were blushing over tentative *pourparlers* on a life-companionship, sat beneath the corner-cupboard; and an elderly engaged man of fifty or upward moved restlessly about from spots where his betrothed was not to the spot where she was. Enjoyment was pretty general, and so much the more prevailed in being unhampered by conventional restrictions. Absolute confidence in each other's good opinion begat perfect ease, while the finishing stroke of manner, amounting to a truly princely serenity, was lent to the majority by the absence of any expression or trait denoting that they wished to get on in the world, enlarge their minds, or do any eclipsing thing whatever—which nowadays so generally nips the bloom and *bonhomie* of all except the two extremes of the social scale.

Shepherd Fennel had married well, his wife being a dairyman's daughter from a vale at a distance, who brought fifty guineas in her pocket—and

kept them there, till they should be required for ministering to the needs
of a coming family. This frugal woman had been somewhat exercised as to
the character that should be given to the gathering. A sit-still party had its
advantages; but an undisturbed position of ease in chairs and settles was
apt to lead on the men to such an unconscionable deal of toping that they
would sometimes fairly drink the house dry. A dancing-party was the
alternative; but this, while avoiding the foregoing objection on the score
of good drink, had a counterbalancing disadvantage in the matter of good
victuals, the ravenous appetites engendered by the exercise causing immense havoc in the buttery. Shepherdess Fennel fell back upon the intermediate plan of mingling short dances with short periods of talk and
singing, so as to hinder any ungovernable rage in either. But this scheme
was entirely confined to her own gentle mind: the shepherd himself was
in the mood to exhibit the most reckless phases of hospitality.

The fiddler was a boy of those parts, about twelve years of age, who had
a wonderful dexterity in jigs and reels, though his fingers were so small
and short as to necessitate a constant shifting for the high notes, from
which he scrambled back to the first position with sounds not of unmixed
purity of tone. At seven the shrill tweedle-dee of this youngster had begun,
accompanied by a booming ground-bass from Elijah New, the parish-clerk,
who had thoughtfully brought with him his favorite musical instrument,
the serpent. Dancing was instantaneous, Mrs. Fennel privately enjoining
the players on no account to let the dance exceed the length of a quarter
of an hour.

But Elijah and the boy, in the excitement of their position, quite forgot
the injunction. Moreover, Oliver Giles, a man of seventeen, one of the
dancers, who was enamored of his partner, a fair girl of thirty-three rolling
years, had recklessly handed a new crown-piece to the musicians, as a bribe
to keep going as long as they had muscle and wind. Mrs. Fennel, seeing the
steam begin to generate on the countenances of her guests, crossed over
and touched the fiddler's elbow and put her hand on the serpent's mouth.
But they took no notice, and fearing she might lose her character of genial
hostess if she were to interfere too markedly, she retired and sat down
helpless. And so the dance whizzed on with cumulative fury, the per-
formers moving in their planet-like courses, direct and retrograde, from
apogee to perigee, till the hand of the well-kicked clock at the bottom of
the room had travelled over the circumference of an hour.

While these cheerful events were in course of enactment within Fennel's
pastoral dwelling, an incident having considerable bearing on the party
had occurred in the gloomy night without. Mrs. Fennel's concern about
the growing fierceness of the dance corresponded in point of time with
the ascent of a human figure to the solitary hill of Higher Crowstairs from
the direction of the distant town. This personage strode on through the

rain without a pause, following the little-worn path which, further on in its course, skirted the shepherd's cottage.

It was nearly the time of full moon, and on this account, though the sky was lined with a uniform sheet of dripping cloud, ordinary objects out of doors were readily visible. The sad wan light revealed the lonely pedestrian to be a man of supple frame; his gait suggested that he had somewhat passed the period of perfect and instinctive agility, though not so far as to be otherwise than rapid of motion when occasion required. At a rough guess, he might have been about forty years of age. He appeared tall, but a recruiting sergeant, or other person accustomed to the judging of men's heights by the eye, would have discerned that this was chiefly owing to his gauntness, and that he was not more than five-feet-eight or nine.

Notwithstanding the regularity of his tread, there was caution in it, as in that of one who mentally feels his way; and despite the fact that it was not a black coat nor a dark garment of any sort that he wore, there was something about him which suggested that he naturally belonged to the black-coated tribes of men. His clothes were of fustian, and his boots hobnailed, yet in his progress he showed not the mud-accustomed bearing of hobnailed and fustianed peasantry.

By the time that he had arrived abreast of the shepherd's premises the rain came down, or rather came along, with yet more determined violence. The outskirts of the little settlement partially broke the force of wind and rain, and this induced him to stand still. The most salient of the shepherd's domestic erections was an empty sty at the forward corner of his hedgeless garden, for in these latitudes the principle of masking the homelier features of your establishment by a conventional frontage was unknown. The traveler's eye was attracted to this small building by the pallid shine of the wet slates that covered it. He turned aside, and, finding it empty, stood under the pent-roof for shelter.

While he stood, the boom of the serpent within the adjacent house, and the lesser strains of the fiddler, reached the spot as an accompaniment to the surging hiss of the flying rain on the sod, its louder beating on the cabbage-leaves of the garden, on the eight or ten beehives just discernible by the path, and its dripping from the eaves into a row of buckets and pans that had been placed under the walls of the cottage. For at Higher Crow-stairs, as at all such elevated domiciles, the grand difficulty of housekeeping was an insufficiency of water; and a casual rainfall was utilized by turning out, as catchers, every utensil that the house contained. Some queer stories might be told of the contrivances for economy in suds and dish-waters that are absolutely necessitated in upland habitations during the droughts of summer. But at this season there were no such exigencies; a mere acceptance of what the skies bestowed was sufficient for an abundant store.

At last the notes of the serpent ceased and the house was silent. This cessation of activity aroused the solitary pedestrian from the reverie into which he had lapsed, and, emerging from the shed, with an apparently new intention, he walked up the path to the house-door. Arrived here, his first act was to kneel down on a large stone beside the row of vessels, and to drink a copious draught from one of them. Having quenched his thirst he rose and lifted his hand to knock, but paused with his eye upon the panel. Since the dark surface of the wood revealed absolutely nothing, it was evident that he must be mentally looking through the door, as if he wished to measure thereby all the possibilities that a house of this sort might include, and how they might bear upon the question of his entry.

In his indecision he turned and surveyed the scene around. Not a soul was anywhere visible. The garden-path stretched downward from his feet, gleaming like the track of a snail; the roof of the little well (mostly dry), the well-cover, the top rail of the garden-gate, were varnished with the same dull liquid glaze; while, far away in the vale, a faint whiteness of more than usual extent showed that the rivers were high in the meads. Beyond all this winked a few bleared lamplights through the beating drops —lights that denoted the situation of the county-town from which he had appeared to come. The absence of all notes of life in that direction seemed to clinch his intentions, and he knocked at the door.

Within, a desultory chat had taken the place of movement and musical sound. The hedge-carpenter was suggesting a song to the company, which nobody just then was inclined to undertake, so that the knock afforded a not unwelcome diversion.

"Walk in!" said the shepherd promptly.

The latch clicked upward, and out of the night our pedestrian appeared upon the door-mat. The shepherd arose, snuffed two of the nearest candles, and turned to look at him.

Their light disclosed that the stranger was dark in complexion and not unprepossessing as to feature. His hat, which for a moment he did not remove, hung low over his eyes, without concealing that they were large, open, and determined, moving with a flash rather than a glance round the room. He seemed pleased with his survey, and, baring his shaggy head, said, in a rich deep voice, "The rain is so heavy, friends, that I ask leave to come in and rest awhile."

"To be sure, stranger," said the shepherd. "And faith, you've been lucky in choosing your time, for we are having a bit of a fling for a glad cause— though, to be sure, a man could hardly wish that glad cause to happen more than once a year."

"Nor less," spoke up a woman. "For 'tis best to get your family over and done with, as soon as you can, so as to be all the earlier out of the fag o't."

"And what may be this glad cause?" asked the stranger.

"A birth and christening," said the shepherd.

The stranger hoped his host might not be made unhappy either by too many or too few of such episodes, and being invited by a gesture to a pull at the mug, he readily acquiesced. His manner, which, before entering, had been so dubious, was now altogether that of a careless and candid man.

"Late to be traipsing athwart this coomb—hey?" said the engaged man of fifty.

"Late it is, master, as you say.—I'll take a seat in the chimney-corner, if you have nothing to urge against it, ma'am; for I am a little moist on the side that was next the rain."

Mrs. Shepherd Fennel assented, and made room for the self-invited comer, who, having got completely inside the chimney-corner, stretched out his legs and his arms with the expansiveness of a person quite at home.

"Yes, I am rather cracked in the vamp," he said freely, seeing that the eyes of the shepherd's wife fell upon his boots, "and I am not well fitted either. I have had some rough times lately, and have been forced to pick up what I can get in the way of wearing, but I must find a suit better fit for working-days when I reach home."

"One of hereabouts?" she inquired.

"Not quite that—further up the county."

"I thought so. And so be I; and by your tongue you come from my neighborhood."

"But you would hardly have heard of me," he said quickly. "My time would be long before yours, ma'am, you see."

This testimony to the youthfulness of his hostess had the effect of stopping her cross-examination.

"There is only one thing more wanted to make me happy," continued the new-comer. "And that is a little baccy, which I am sorry to say I am out of."

"I'll fill your pipe," said the shepherd.

"I must ask you to lend me a pipe likewise."

"A smoker, and no pipe about 'ee?"

"I have dropped it somewhere on the road."

The shepherd filled and handed him a new clay pipe, saying, as he did so, "Hand me your baccy-box—I'll fill that too, now I am about it."

The man went through the movement of searching his pockets.

"Lost that too?" said his entertainer, with some surprise.

"I am afraid so," said the man with some confusion. "Give it to me in a screw of paper." Lighting his pipe at the candle with a suction that drew the whole flame into the bowl, he resettled himself in the corner and bent his looks upon the faint steam from his damp legs, as if he wished to say no more.

Meanwhile the general body of guests had been taking little notice of this visitor by reason of an absorbing discussion in which they were engaged with the band about a tune for the next dance. The matter being settled, they were about to stand up when an interruption came in the shape of another knock at the door.

At sound of the same the man in the chimney-corner took up the poker and began stirring the brands as if doing it thoroughly were the one aim of his existence; and a second time the shepherd said, "Walk in!" In a moment another man stood upon the straw-woven door-mat. He too was a stranger.

This individual was one of a type radically different from the first. There was more of the commonplace in his manner, and a certain jovial cosmopolitanism sat upon his features. He was several years older than the first arrival, his hair being slightly frosted, his eyebrows bristly, and his whiskers cut back from his cheeks. His face was rather full and flabby, and yet it was not altogether a face without power. A few grog-blossoms marked the neighborhood of his nose. He flung back his long drab greatcoat, revealing that beneath it he wore a suit of cinder-gray shade throughout, large heavy seals, of some metal or other that would take a polish, dangling from his fob as his only personal ornament. Shaking the water-drops from his low-crowned glazed hat, he said, "I must ask for a few minutes' shelter, comrades, or I shall be wetted to my skin before I get to Casterbridge."

"Make yourself at home, master," said the shepherd, perhaps a trifle less heartily than on the first occasion. Not that Fennel had the least tinge of niggardliness in his composition; but the room was far from large, spare chairs were not numerous, and damp companions were not altogether desirable at close quarters for the women and girls in their bright-colored gowns.

However, the second comer, after taking off his greatcoat, and hanging his hat on a nail in one of the ceiling-beams as if he had been specially invited to put it there, advanced and sat down at the table. This had been pushed so closely into the chimney-corner, to give all available room to the dancers, that its inner edge grazed the elbow of the man who had ensconced himself by the fire; and thus the two strangers were brought into close companionship. They nodded to each other by way of breaking the ice of unacquaintance, and the first stranger handed his neighbor the family mug—a huge vessel of brown ware, having its upper edge worn away like a threshold by the rub of whole generations of thirsty lips that had gone the way of all flesh, and bearing the following inscription burnt upon its rotund side in yellow letters:—

THERE IS NO FUN
UNTILL i CUM.

The other man, nothing loath, raised the mug to his lips, and drank on, and on, and on—till a curious blueness overspread the countenance of the shepherd's wife, who had regarded with no little surprise the first stranger's free offer to the second of what did not belong to him to dispense.

"I knew it!" said the toper to the shepherd with much satisfaction. "When I walked up your garden before coming in, and saw the hives all of a row, I said to myself, 'Where there's bees there's honey, and where there's honey there's mead.' But mead of such a truly comfortable sort as this I really didn't expect to meet in my older days." He took yet another pull at the mug, till it assumed an ominous elevation.

"Glad you enjoy it!" said the shepherd warmly.

"It is goodish mead," assented Mrs. Fennel, with an absence of enthusiasm which seemed to say that it was possible to buy praise for one's cellar at too heavy a price. "It is trouble enough to make—and really I hardly think we shall make any more. For honey sells well, and we ourselves can make shift with a drop o' small mead and metheglin for common use from the comb-washings."

"Oh, but you'll never have the heart!" reproachfully cried the stranger in cinder-gray, after taking up the mug a third time and setting it down empty. "I love mead, when 'tis old like this, as I love to go to church o' Sundays, or to relieve the needy any day of the week."

"Ha, ha, ha!" said the man in the chimney-corner, who in spite of the taciturnity induced by the pipe of tobacco, could not or would not refrain from this slight testimony to his comrade's humor.

Now the old mead of those days, brewed of the purest first-year or maiden honey, four pounds to the gallon—with its due complement of white of eggs, cinnamon, ginger, cloves, mace, rosemary, yeast, and processes of working, bottling, and cellaring—tasted remarkably strong; but it did not taste so strong as it actually was. Hence, presently, the stranger in cinder-gray at the table, moved by its creeping influence, unbuttoned his waistcoat, threw himself back in his chair, spread his legs, and made his presence felt in various ways.

"Well, well, as I say," he resumed, "I am going to Casterbridge, and to Casterbridge I must go. I should have been almost there by this time; but the rain drove me into your dwelling, and I'm not sorry for it."

"You don't live in Casterbridge?" said the shepherd.

"Not as yet; though I shortly mean to move there."

"Going to set up in trade, perhaps?"

"No, no," said the shepherd's wife. "It is easy to see that the gentleman is rich, and don't want to work at anything."

The cinder-gray stranger paused, as if to consider whether he would accept that definition of himself. He presently rejected it by answering, "Rich is not quite the word for me, dame. I do work, and I must work. And even if I only get to Casterbridge by midnight I must begin work there at eight tomorrow morning. Yes, het or wet, blow or snow, famine or sword, my day's work tomorrow must be done."

"Poor man! Then, in spite o' seeming, you be worse off than we?" replied the shepherd's wife.

"'Tis the nature of my trade, men and maidens. 'Tis the nature of my trade more than my poverty. . . . But really and truly I must up and off, or I shan't get a lodging in the town." However, the speaker did not move, and directly added, "There's time for one more draught of friendship before I go; and I'd perform it at once if the mug were not dry."

"Here's a mug o' small," said Mrs. Fennel. "Small, we call it, though to be sure 'tis only the first wash o' the combs."

"No," said the stranger disdainfully. "I won't spoil your first kindness by partaking o' your second."

"Certainly not," broke in Fennel. "We don't increase and multiply every day, and I'll fill the mug again." He went away to the dark place under the stairs where the barrel stood. The shepherdess followed him.

"Why should you do this?" she said reproachfully, as soon as they were alone. "He's emptied it once, though it held enough for ten people; and now he's not contented wi' the small, but must needs call for more o' the strong! And a stranger unbeknown to any of us. For my part, I don't like the look o' the man at all."

"But he's in the house, my honey; and 'tis a wet night, and a christening. Daze it, what's a cup of mead more or less? There'll be plenty more next bee-burning."

"Very well—this time, then," she answered, looking wistfully at the barrel. "But what is the man's calling, and where is he one of, that he should come in and join us like this?"

"I don't know. I'll ask him again."

The catastrophe of having the mug drained dry at one pull by the stranger in cinder-gray was effectually guarded against this time by Mrs. Fennel. She poured out his allowance in a small cup, keeping the large one at a discreet distance from him. When he had tossed off his portion the shepherd renewed his inquiry about the stranger's occupation.

The latter did not immediately reply, and the man in the chimney-corner, with sudden demonstrativeness, said, "Anybody may know my trade—I'm a wheelwright."

"A very good trade for these parts," said the shepherd.

"And anybody may know mine—if they've the sense to find it out," said the stranger in cinder-gray.

"You may generally tell what a man is by his claws," observed the hedge-carpenter, looking at his own hands. "My fingers be as full of thorns as an old pin-cushion is of pins."

The hands of the man in the chimney-corner instinctively sought the shade, and he gazed into the fire as he resumed his pipe. The man at the table took up the hedge-carpenter's remark, and added smartly, "True; but the oddity of my trade is that, instead of setting a mark upon me, it sets a mark upon my customers."

No observation being offered by anybody in elucidation of this enigma, the shepherd's wife once more called for a song. The same obstacles presented themselves as at the former time—one had no voice, another had forgotten the first verse. The stranger at the table, whose soul had now risen to a good working temperature, relieved the difficulty by exclaiming that, to start the company, he would sing himself. Thrusting one thumb into the arm-hole of his waistcoat, he waved the other hand in the air, and, with an extemporizing gaze at the shining sheep-crooks above the mantel-piece, began:—

> "O my trade it is the rarest one,
>   Simple shepherds all—
> My trade is a sight to see;
>   For my customers I tie, and take them up on high,
> And waft 'em to a far countree!"

The room was silent when he had finished the verse—with one exception, that of the man in the chimney-corner, who, at the singer's word, "Chorus!" joined him in a deep bass voice of musical relish—

> "And waft 'em to a far countree!"

Oliver Giles, John Pitcher the dairyman, the parish-clerk, the engaged man of fifty, the row of young women against the wall, seemed lost in thought not of the gayest kind. The shepherd looked meditatively on the ground, the shepherdess gazed keenly at the singer, and with some suspicion; she was doubting whether this stranger were merely singing an old song from recollection, or was composing one there and then for the occasion. All were as perplexed at the obscure revelation as the guests at Belshazzar's Feast, except the man in the chimney-corner, who quietly said, "Second verse, stranger," and smoked on.

The singer thoroughly moistened himself from his lips inwards, and went on with the next stanza as requested:—

> "My tools are but common ones,
>   Simple shepherds all—
> My tools are no sight to see:
>   A little hempen string, and a post whereon to swing,
> Are implements enough for me!"

Shepherd Fennel glanced round. There was no longer any doubt that the stranger was answering his question rhythmically. The guests one and all started back with suppressed exclamations. The young woman engaged to the man of fifty fainted half-way, and would have proceeded, but finding him wanting in alacrity for catching her she sat down trembling.

"Oh, he's the—!" whispered the people in the background, mentioning the name of an ominous public officer. "He's come to do it! 'Tis to be at Casterbridge jail tomorrow—the man for sheep-stealing—the poor clock-maker we heard of, who used to live away at Shottsford and had no work

to do—Timothy Summers, whose family were a-starving, and so he went
out of Shottsford by the high road, and took a sheep in open daylight
defying the farmer and the farmer's wife and the farmer's lad, and every
man jack among 'em. He" (and they nodded towards the stranger of the
deadly trade) "is come from up the country to do it because there's not
enough to do in his own county-town, and he's got the place here now our
own county man's dead; he's going to live in the same cottage under the
prison wall."

The stranger in cinder-gray took no notice of this whispered string of
observations, but again wetted his lips. Seeing that his friend in the
chimney-corner was the only one who reciprocated his joviality in any way,
he held out his cup towards that appreciative comrade, who also held out
his own. They clinked together, the eyes of the rest of the room hanging
upon the singer's actions. He parted his lips for the third verse; but at that
moment another knock was audible upon the door. This time the knock
was faint and hesitating.

The company seemed scared; the shepherd looked with consternation
towards the entrance, and it was with some effort that he resisted his
alarmed wife's deprecatory glance, and uttered for the third time the wel-
coming words "Walk in!"

The door was gently opened, and another man stood upon the mat. He,
like those who had preceded him, was a stranger. This time it was a short,
small personage, of fair complexion, and dressed in a decent suit of dark
clothes.

"Can you tell me the way to ——" he began: when, gazing round the
room to observe the nature of the company amongst whom he had fallen,
his eyes lighted on the stranger in cinder-gray. It was just at the instant
when the latter, who had thrown his mind into his song with such a will
that he scarcely heeded the interruption, silenced all whispers and inquiries
by bursting into his third verse:—

> "Tomorrow is my working day,
>   Simple shepherds all—
> Tomorrow is a working day for me:
> For the farmer's sheep is slain, and the lad who did it ta'en,
>   And on his soul may God ha' merc-y!"

The stranger in the chimney-corner, waving cups with the singer so
heartily that his mead splashed over on the hearth, repeated in his bass
voice as before:—

> "And on his soul may God ha' merc-y!"

All this time the third stranger had been standing in the doorway. Finding now that he did not come forward or go on speaking, the guests particularly regarded him. They noticed to their surprise that he stood before

them the picture of abject terror—his knees trembling, his hand shaking so violently that the door-latch by which he supported himself rattled audibly: his white lips were parted, and his eyes fixed on the merry officer of justice in the middle of the room. A moment more and he had turned, closed the door, and fled.

"What a man can it be?" said the shepherd.

The rest, between the awfulness of their late discovery and the odd conduct of this third visitor, looked as if they knew not what to think, and said nothing. Instinctively they withdrew further and further from the grim gentleman in their midst, whom some of them seemed to take for the Prince of Darkness himself, till they formed a remote circle, an empty space of floor being left between them and him—

". . . circulus, cujus centrum diabolus."

The room was so silent—though there were more than twenty people in it —that nothing could be heard but the patter of the rain against the window-shutters, accompanied by the occasional hiss of a stray drop that fell down the chimney into the fire, and the steady puffing of the man in the corner, who had now resumed his long pipe of clay.

The stillness was unexpectedly broken. The distant sound of a gun reverberated through the air—apparently from the direction of the county-town.

"Be jiggered!" cried the stranger who had sung the song, jumping up.

"What does that mean?" asked several.

"A prisoner escaped from the jail—that's what it means."

All listened. The sound was repeated, and none of them spoke but the man in the chimney-corner, who said quietly, "I've often been told that in this county they fire a gun at such times; but I never heard it till now."

"I wonder if it is *my* man?" murmured the personage in cinder-gray.

"Surely it is!" said the shepherd involuntarily. "And surely we've zeed him! That little man who looked in at the door by now, and quivered like a leaf when he zeed ye and heard your song!"

"His teeth chattered, and the breath went out of his body," said the dairy-man.

"And his heart seemed to sink within him like a stone," said Oliver Giles.

"And he bolted as if he'd been shot at," said the hedge-carpenter.

"True—his teeth chattered, and his heart seemed to sink; and he bolted as if he'd been shot at," slowly summed up the man in the chimney-corner.

"I didn't notice it," remarked the hangman.

"We were all a-wondering what made him run off in such a fright," faltered one of the women against the wall, "and now 'tis explained!"

The firing of the alarm-gun went on at intervals, low and sullenly, and their suspicions became a certainty. The sinister gentleman in cinder-gray roused himself. "Is there a constable here?" he asked, in thick tones. "If so, let him step forward."

The engaged man of fifty stepped quavering out from the wall, his betrothed beginning to sob on the back of the chair.

"You are a sworn constable?"

"I be, sir."

"Then pursue the criminal at once, with assistance, and bring him back here. He can't have gone far."

"I will, sir, I will—when I've got my staff. I'll go home and get it, and come sharp here, and start in a body."

"Staff!—never mind your staff; the man'll be gone!"

"But I can't do nothing without my staff—can I, William, and John, and Charles Jake? No; for there's the king's royal crown a painted on en in yaller and gold, and the lion and the unicorn, so as when I raise en up and hit my prisoner, 'tis made a lawful blow thereby. I wouldn't 'tempt to take up a man without my staff—no, not I. If I hadn't the law to gie me courage, why, instead o' my taking up him he might take up me!"

"Now, I'm a king's man myself, and can give you authority enough for this," said the formidable officer in gray. "Now then, all of ye, be ready. Have ye any lanterns?"

"Yes—have ye any lanterns?—I demand it!" said the constable.

"And the rest of you able-bodied——"

"Able-bodied men—yes—the rest of ye!" said the constable.

"Have you some good stout staves and pitchforks——"

"Staves and pitchforks—in the name o' the law! And take 'em in yer hands and go in quest, and do as we in authority tell ye!"

Thus aroused, the men prepared to give chase. The evidence was, indeed, though circumstantial, so convincing, that but little argument was needed to show the shepherd's guests that after what they had seen it would look very much like connivance if they did not instantly pursue the unhappy third stranger, who could not as yet have gone more than a few hundred yards over such uneven country.

A shepherd is always well provided with lanterns; and, lighting these hastily, and with hurdle-staves in their hands, they poured out of the door, taking a direction along the crest of the hill, away from the town, the rain having fortunately a little abated.

Disturbed by the noise, or possibly by unpleasant dreams of her baptism, the child who had been christened began to cry heart-brokenly in the room overhead. These notes of grief came down through the chinks of the floor to the ears of the women below, who jumped up one by one, and seemed glad of the excuse to ascend and comfort the baby, for the incidents of the last half-hour greatly oppressed them. Thus in the space of two or three minutes the room on the ground-floor was deserted quite.

But it was not for long. Hardly had the sound of footsteps died away

when a man returned round the corner of the house from the direction
the pursuers had taken. Peeping in at the door, and seeing nobody there,
he entered leisurely. It was the stranger of the chimney-corner, who had
gone out with the rest. The motive of his return was shown by his helping
himself to a cut piece of skimmer-cake that lay on a ledge beside where
he had sat, and which he had apparently forgotten to take with him. He
also poured out half a cup more mead from the quantity that remained,
ravenously eating and drinking these as he stood. He had not finished
when another figure came in just as quietly—his friend in cinder-gray.

"Oh—you here?" said the latter, smiling. "I thought you had gone to
help in the capture." And this speaker also revealed the object of his return by looking solicitously round for the fascinating mug of old mead.

"And I thought you had gone," said the other, continuing his skimmer-
cake with some effort.

"Well, on second thoughts, I felt there were enough without me," said
the first confidentially, "and such a night as it is, too. Besides, 'tis the business o' the Government to take care of its criminals—not mine."

"True; so it is. And I felt as you did, that there were enough without
me."

"I don't want to break my limbs running over the humps and hollows of
this wild country."

"Nor I neither, between you and me."

"These shepherd-people are used to it—simple-minded souls, you know,
stirred up to anything in a moment. They'll have him ready for me before
the morning, and no trouble to me at all."

"They'll have him, and we shall have saved ourselves all labor in the
matter."

"True, true. Well, my way is to Casterbridge; and 'tis as much as my
legs will do to take me that far. Going the same way?"

"No, I am sorry to say! I have to get home over there" (he nodded indefinitely to the right), "and I feel as you do, that it is quite enough for my
legs to do before bedtime."

The other had by this time finished the mead in the mug, after which,
shaking hands heartily at the door, and wishing each other well, they went
their several ways.

In the meantime the company of pursuers had reached the end of the
hog's-back elevation which dominated this part of the down. They had decided on no particular plan of action; and, finding that the man of the
baleful trade was no longer in their company, they seemed quite unable to
form any such plan now. They descended in all directions down the hill,
and straightway several of the party fell into the snare set by Nature for all
misguided midnight ramblers over this part of the cretaceous formation.
The "lanchets," or flint slopes, which belted the escarpment at intervals of
a dozen yards, took the less cautious ones unawares, and losing their foot-

ing on the rubbly steep they slid sharply downwards, the lanterns rolling from their hands to the bottom, and there lying on their sides till the horn was scorched through.

When they had again gathered themselves together, the shepherd, as the man who knew the country best, took the lead, and guided them round these treacherous inclines. The lanterns, which seemed rather to dazzle their eyes and warn the fugitive than to assist them in the exploration, were extinguished, due silence was observed; and in this more rational order they plunged into the vale. It was grassy, briery, moist defile, affording some shelter to any person who had sought it; but the party perambulated it in vain, and ascended on the other side. Here they wandered apart, and after an interval closed together again to report progress. At the second time of closing in they found themselves near a lonely ash, the single tree on this part of the coomb, probably sown there by a passing bird some fifty years before. And here, standing a little to one side of the trunk, as motionless as the trunk itself, appeared the man they were in quest of, his outline being well defined against the sky beyond. The band noiselessly drew up and faced him.

"Your money or your life!" said the constable sternly to the still figure. "No, no," whispered John Pitcher. "'Tisn't our side ought to say that. That's the doctrine of vagabonds like him, and we be on the side of the law."

"Well, well," replied the constable impatiently; "I must say something, mustn't I? and if you had all the weight o' this undertaking upon your mind, perhaps you'd say the wrong thing too!—Prisoner at the bar, surrender, in the name of the Father—the Crown, I mane!"

The man under the tree seemed now to notice them for the first time, and, giving them no opportunity whatever for exhibiting their courage, he strolled slowly towards them. He was, indeed, the little man, the third stranger; but his trepidation had in a great measure gone.

"Well, travelers," he said, "did I hear ye speak to me?"

"You did: you've got to come and be our prisoner at once!" said the constable. "We arrest 'ee on the charge of not biding in Casterbridge jail in a decent proper manner to be hung tomorrow morning. Neighbors, do your duty, and seize the culpet!"

On hearing the charge, the man seemed enlightened, and, saying not another word, resigned himself with preternatural civility to the search-party, who, with their staves in their hands, surrounded him on all sides, and marched him back towards the shepherd's cottage.

It was eleven o'clock by the time they arrived. The light shining from the open door, a sound of men's voices within, proclaimed to them as they approached the house that some new events had arisen in their absence. On entering they discovered the shepherd's living room to be invaded by two officers from Casterbridge jail, and a well-known magistrate who lived at the nearest country-seat, intelligence of the escape having become generally circulated.

"Gentlemen," said the constable, "I have brought back your man—not without risk and danger; but every one must do his duty! He is inside this circle of able-bodied persons, who have lent me useful aid, considering their ignorance of Crown work. Men, bring forward your prisoner!" And the third stranger was led to the light.

"Who is this?" said one of the officials.

"The man," said the constable.

"Certainly not," said the turnkey; and the first corroborated his statement.

"But how can it be otherwise?" asked the constable. "Or why was he so terrified at sight o' the singing instrument of the law who sat there?" Here he related the strange behavior of the third stranger on entering the house during the hangman's song.

"Can't understand it," said the officer coolly. "All I know is that it is not the condemned man. He's quite a different character from this one; a gauntish fellow, with dark hair and eyes, rather good-looking, and with a musical bass voice that if you heard it once you'd never mistake as long as you lived."

"Why, souls—'twas the man in the chimney-corner!"

"Hey—what?" said the magistrate, coming forward after inquiring particulars from the shepherd in the background. "Haven't you got the man after all?"

"Well, sir," said the constable, "he's the man we were in search of, that's true; and yet he's not the man we were in search of. For the man we were in search of was not the man we wanted, sir, if you understand my everyday way; for 'twas the man in the chimney-corner!"

"A pretty kettle of fish altogether!" said the magistrate. "You had better start for the other man at once."

The prisoner now spoke for the first time. The mention of the man in the chimney-corner seemed to have moved him as nothing else could do. "Sir," he said, stepping forward to the magistrate, "take no more trouble about me. The time is come when I may as well speak. I have done nothing; my crime is that the condemned man is my brother. Early this afternoon I left home at Shottsford to tramp it all the way to Casterbridge jail to bid him farewell. I was benighted, and called here to rest and ask the way. When I opened the door I saw before me the very man, my brother, that I thought to see in the condemned cell at Casterbridge. He was in this chimney-corner; and jammed close to him, so that he could not have got out if he had tried, was the executioner who'd come to take his life, singing a song about it and not knowing that it was his victim who was close by, joining in to save appearances. My brother looked a glance of agony at me, and I knew he meant, 'Don't reveal what you see; my life depends on it.' I was so terror-struck that I could hardly stand, and, not knowing what I did, I turned and hurried away."

The narrator's manner and tone had the stamp of truth, and his story made a great impression on all around. "And do you know where your brother is at the present time?" asked the magistrate.

"I do not. I have never seen him since I closed this door."

"I can testify to that, for we've been between ye ever since," said the constable.

"Where does he think to fly to?—what is his occupation?"

"He's a watch-and-clock-maker, sir."

"'A said 'a was a wheelwright—a wicked rogue," said the constable.

"The wheels of clocks and watches he meant, no doubt," said Shepherd Fennel. "I thought his hands were palish for's trade."

"Well, it appears to me that nothing can be gained by retaining this poor man in custody," said the magistrate; "your business lies with the other, unquestionably."

And so the little man was released off-hand; but he looked nothing the less sad on that account, it being beyond the power of magistrate or constable to raze out the written troubles in his brain, for they concerned another whom he regarded with more solicitude than himself. When this was done, and the man had gone his way, the night was found to be so far advanced that it was deemed useless to renew the search before the next morning.

Next day, accordingly, the quest for the clever sheep-stealer became general and keen, to all appearance at least. But the intended punishment was cruelly disproportioned to the transgression, and the sympathy of a great many country-folk in that district was strongly on the side of the fugitive. Moreover, his marvelous coolness and daring in hob-and-nobbing with the hangman, under the unprecedented circumstances of the shepherd's party, won their admiration. So that it may be questioned if all those who ostensibly made themselves so busy in exploring woods and fields and lanes were quite so thorough when it came to the private examination of their own lofts and outhouses. Stories were afloat of a mysterious figure being occasionally seen in some old overgrown trackway or other, remote from turnpike roads; but when a search was instituted in any of these suspected quarters nobody was found. Thus the days and weeks passed without tidings.

In brief, the bass-voiced man of the chimney-corner was never recaptured. Some said that he went across the sea, others that he did not, but buried himself in the depths of a populous city. At any rate, the gentleman in cinder-gray never did his morning's work at Casterbridge, nor met anywhere at all, for business purposes, the genial comrade with whom he had passed an hour of relaxation in the lonely house on the coomb.

The grass has long been green on the graves of Shepherd Fennel and

his frugal wife; the guests who made up the christening party have mainly
followed their entertainers to the tomb; the baby in whose honor they all
had met is a matron in the sere and yellow leaf. But the arrival of the three
strangers at the shepherd's that night, and the details connected therewith,
is a story as well known as ever in the country about Higher Crowstairs.

THE JOLLY CORNER

Henry James

(1843–1916)

Every one asks me what I 'think' of everything," said Spencer Brydon;
"and I make answer as I can—begging or dodging the question, putting
them off with any nonsense. It wouldn't matter to any of them really," he
went on, "for, even were it possible to meet in that stand-and-deliver way
so silly a demand on so big a subject, my 'thoughts' would still be almost
altogether about something that concerns only myself." He was talking to
Miss Staverton, with whom for a couple of months now he had availed
himself of every possible occasion to talk; this disposition and this resource, this comfort and support, as the situation in fact presented itself,
having promptly enough taken the first place in the considerable array of
rather unattenuated surprises attending his so strangely belated return to
America. Everything was somehow a surprise; and that might be natural
when one had so long and so consistently neglected everything, taken
pains to give surprises so much margin for play. He had given them more
than thirty years—thirty-three, to be exact; and they now seemed to him
to have organised their performance quite on the scale of that licence. He
had been twenty-three on leaving New York—he was fifty-six to-day: unless indeed he were to reckon as he had sometimes, since his repatriation,
found himself feeling; in which case he would have lived longer than is
often allotted to man. It would have taken a century, he repeatedly said
to himself, and said also to Alice Staverton, it would have taken a longer
absence and a more averted mind than those even of which he had been
guilty, to pile up the differences, the newnesses, the queernesses, above
all the bignesses, for the better or the worse, that at present assaulted his
vision wherever he looked.

The great fact all the while however had been the incalculability; since he *had* supposed himself, from decade to decade, to be allowing, and in the most liberal and intelligent manner, for brilliancy of change. He actually saw that he had allowed for nothing; he missed what he would have been sure of finding, he found what he would never have imagined. Proportions and values were upside-down; the ugly things he had expected, the ugly things of his far-away youth, when he had too promptly waked up to a sense of the ugly—these uncanny phenomena placed him rather, as it happened, under the charm; whereas the "swagger" things, the modern, the monstrous, the famous things, those he had more particularly, like thousands of ingenuous inquirers every year, come over to see, were exactly his sources of dismay. They were as so many set traps for displeasure, above all for reaction, of which his restless tread was constantly pressing the spring. It was interesting, doubtless, the whole show, but it would have been too disconcerting hadn't a certain finer truth saved the situation. He had distinctly not, in this steadier light, come over *all* for the monstrosities; he had come, not only in the last analysis but quite on the face of the act, under an impulse with which they had nothing to do. He had come— putting the thing pompously—to look at his "property," which he had thus for a third of a century not been within four thousand miles of; or, expressing it less sordidly, he had yielded to the humour of seeing again his house on the jolly corner, as he usually, and quite fondly, described it—the one in which he had first seen the light, in which various members of his family had lived and had died, in which the holidays of his overschooled boyhood had been passed and the few social flowers of his chilled adolescence gathered, and which, alienated then for so long a period, had, through the successive deaths of his two brothers and the termination of old arrangements, come wholly into his hands. He was the owner of another, not quite so "good"—the jolly corner having been, from far back, superlatively extended and consecrated; and the value of the pair represented his main capital, with an income consisting, in these later years, of their respective rents which (thanks precisely to their original excellent type) had never been depressingly low. He could live in "Europe," as he had been in the habit of living, on the product of these flourishing New York leases, and all the better since, that of the second structure, the mere number in its long row, having within a twelvemonth fallen in, renovation at a high advance had proved beautifully possible.

These were items of property indeed, but he had found himself since his arrival distinguishing more than ever between them. The house within the street, two bristling blocks westward, was already in course of reconstruction as a tall mass of flats; he had acceded, some time before, to overtures for this conversion—in which, now that it was going forward, it had been not the least of his astonishments to find himself able, on the spot, and thought without a previous ounce of such experience, to participate with a certain intelligence, almost with a certain authority. He had lived his life with his back so turned to such concerns and his face addressed to those of so different an order that he scarce knew what to make of this lively stir, in a compartment of his mind never yet penetrated, of a capacity for business and a sense for construction. These virtues, so common all round him now, had been dormant in his own organism—where it might be said of them perhaps that they had slept the sleep of the just. At present, in the splendid autumn weather—the autumn at least was a pure boon in the terrible place—he loafed about his "work" undeterred, secretly agitated; not in the least "minding" that the whole proposition, as they said, was vulgar and sordid, and ready to climb ladders, to walk the plank, to handle materials and look wise about them, to ask questions, in fine, and challenge explanations and really "go into" figures.

It amused, it verily quite charmed him; and, by the same stroke, it amused, and even more, Alice Staverton, though perhaps charming her perceptibly less. She wasn't however going to be better-off for it, as *he* was —and so astonishingly much: nothing was now likely, he knew, ever to make her better-off than she found herself, in the afternoon of life, as the delicately frugal possessor and tenant of the small house in Irving Place to which she had subtly managed to cling through her almost unbroken New York career. If he knew the way to it now better than to any other address among the dreadful multiplied numberings which seemed to him to reduce the whole place to some vast ledger-page, overgrown, fantastic, of ruled and criss-crossed lines and figures—if he had formed, for his consolation, that habit, it was really not a little because of the charm of his having encountered and recognised, in the vast wilderness of the wholesale, breaking through the mere gross generalisation of wealth and force and success, a small still scene where items and shades, all delicate things, kept the sharpness of the notes of a high voice perfectly trained, and where economy hung about like the scent of a garden. His old friend lived with one maid and herself dusted her relics and trimmed her lamps and polished her silver; she stood off, in the awful modern crush, when she could, but she sallied forth and did battle when the challenge was really to "spirit," the spirit she after all confessed to, proudly and a little shyly, as to that of the better time, that of *their* common, their quite far-away and antediluvian social period and order. She made use of the street-cars when need be, the terrible things that people scrambled for as the panic-stricken at sea scramble for the boats; she affronted, inscrutably, under stress, all the public concussions and ordeals; and yet, with that slim mystifying grace of her appearance, which defied you to say if she were a fair young woman who looked older through trouble, or a fine smooth older one who looked young through successful indifference; with her precious reference, above all, to memories and histories into which he could enter, she was as exquisite for him as some pale pressed flower (a rarity to begin with), and, failing other sweetnesses, she was a sufficient reward of his effort.

They had communities of knowledge, "their" knowledge (this discriminating possessive was always on her lips) of presences of the other age,
presences all overlaid, in his case, by the experience of a man and the freedom of a wanderer, overlaid by pleasure, by infidelity, by passages of life
that were strange and dim to her, just by "Europe" in short, but still un-
obscured, still exposed and cherished, under that pious visitation of the
spirit from which she had never been diverted.

She had come with him one day to see how his "apartment-house" was
rising; he had helped her over gaps and explained to her plans, and while
they were there had happened to have, before her, a brief but lively discussion with the man in charge, the representative of the building-firm that
had undertaken his work. He had found himself quite "standing-up" to
this personage over a failure on the latter's part to observe some detail of
one of their noted conditions, and had so lucidly argued his case that,
besides ever so prettily flushing, at the time, for sympathy in his triumph,
she had afterwards said to him (though to a slightly greater effect of irony)
that he had clearly for too many years neglected a real gift. If he had
but stayed at home he would have anticipated the inventor of the sky-
scraper. If he had but stayed at home he would have discovered his genius
in time really to start some new variety of awful architectural hare and run
it till it burrowed in a gold-mine. He was to remember these words, while
the weeks elapsed, for the small silver ring they had sounded over the
queerest and deepest of his own lately most disguised and most muffled
vibrations.

It had begun to be present to him after the first fortnight, it had broken
out with the oddest abruptness, this particular wanton wonderment: it met
him there—and this was the image under which he himself judged the matter, or at least, not a little, thrilled and flushed with it—very much as he
might have been met by some strange figure, some unexpected occupant,
at a turn of one of the dim passages of an empty house. The quaint
analogy quite hauntingly remained with him, when he didn't indeed
rather improve it by a still intenser form: that of his opening a door behind
which he would have made sure of finding nothing, a door into a room
shuttered and void, and yet so coming, with a great suppressed start, on
some quite erect confronting presence, something planted in the middle of
the place and facing him through the dusk. After that visit to the house in
construction he walked with his companion to see the other and always
so much the better one, which in the eastward direction formed one of the
corners, the "jolly" one precisely, of the street now so generally dishonoured and disfigured in its westward reaches, and of the comparatively conservative Avenue. The Avenue still had pretensions, as Miss
Staverton said, to decency; the old people had mostly gone, the old names
were unknown, and here and there an old association seemed to stray,
all vaguely, like some very aged person, out too late, whom you might

meet and feel the impulse to watch or follow, in kindness, for safe restoration to shelter.

They went in together, our friends; he admitted himself with his key, as he kept no one there, he explained, preferring, for his reasons, to leave the place empty, under a simple arrangement with a good woman living in the neighbourhood and who came for a daily hour to open windows and dust and sweep. Spencer Brydon had his reasons and was growingly aware of them; they seemed to him better each time he was there, though he didn't name them all to his companion, any more than he told her as yet how often, how quite absurdly often, he himself came. He only let her see for the present, while they walked through the great blank rooms, that absolute vacancy reigned and that, from top to bottom, there was nothing but Mrs. Muldoon's broomstick, in a corner, to tempt the burglar. Mrs. Muldoon was then on the premises, and she loquaciously attended the visitors, preceding them from room to room and pushing back shutters and throwing up sashes—all to show them, as she remarked, how little there was to see. There was little indeed to see in the great gaunt shell where the main dispositions and the general apportionment of space, the style of an age of ampler allowances, had nevertheless for its master their honest pleading message, affecting him as some good old servant's, some lifelong retainer's appeal for a character, or even for a retiring-pension; yet it was also a remark of Mrs. Muldoon's that, glad as she was to oblige him by her noonday round, there was a request she greatly hoped he would never make of her. If he should wish her for any reason to come in after dark she would just tell him, if he "plased," that he must ask it of somebody else.

The fact that there was nothing to see didn't militate for the worthy woman against what one *might* see, and she put it frankly to Miss Staverton that no lady could be expected to like, could she? "craping up to thim top storeys in the ayvil hours." The gas and the electric light were off the house, and she fairly evoked a gruesome vision of her march through the great grey rooms—so many of them as there were too!—with her glimmering taper. Miss Staverton met her honest glare with a smile and the profession that she herself certainly would recoil from such an adventure. Spencer Brydon meanwhile held his peace—for the moment; the question of the "evil" hours in his old home had already become too grave for him. He had begun some time since to "crape," and he knew just why a packet of candles addressed to that pursuit had been stowed by his own hand, three weeks before, at the back of a drawer of the fine old sideboard that occupied, as a "fixture," the deep recess in the dining-room. Just now he laughed at his companions—quickly however changing the subject; for the reason that, in the first place, his laugh struck him even at that moment as starting the odd echo, the conscious human resonance (he scarce knew how to qualify it) that sounds made while he was there alone sent back to

his ear or his fancy; and that, in the second, he imagined Alice Staverton
for the instant on the point of asking him, with a divination, if he ever so
prowled. There were divinations he was unprepared for, and he had at all
events averted inquiry by the time Mrs. Muldoon had left them, passing on
to other parts.

There was happily enough to say, on so consecrated a spot, that could be
said freely and fairly; so that a whole train of declarations was precipitated
by his friend's having herself broken out, after a yearning look round: "But
I hope you don't mean they want you to pull *this* to pieces!" His answer
came, promptly, with his reawakened wrath: it was of course exactly what
they wanted, and what they were "at" him for, daily, with the iteration of
people who couldn't for their life understand a man's liability to decent
feelings. He had found the place, just as it stood and beyond what he could
express, an interest and a joy. There were values other than the beastly rent-
values, and in short, in short——! But it was thus Miss Staverton took him
up. "In short you're to make so good a thing of your sky-scraper that, living
in luxury on *those* ill-gotten gains, you can afford for a while to be sentimental here!" Her smile had for him, with the words, the particular mild
irony with which he found half her talk suffused; an irony without bitterness and that came, exactly, from her having so much imagination—not,
like the cheap sarcasms with which one heard most people, about the world
of "society," bid for the reputation of cleverness, from nobody's really having
any. It was agreeable to him at this very moment to be sure that when he
had answered, after a brief demur, "Well yes: so, precisely, you may put it!"
her imagination would still do him justice. He explained that even if never
a dollar were to come to him from the other house he would nevertheless
cherish this one; and he dwelt, further, while they lingered and wandered,
on the fact of the stupefaction he was already exciting, the positive mystification he felt himself create.

He spoke of the value of all he read into it, into the mere sight of the
walls, mere shapes of the rooms, mere sound of the floors, mere feel, in his
hand, of the old silver-plated knobs of the several mahogany doors, which
suggested the pressure of the palms of the dead; the seventy years of the
past in fine that these things represented, the annals of nearly three generations, counting his grandfather's, the one that had ended there, and the im-
palpable ashes of his long-extinct youth, afloat in the very air like microscopic
motes. She listened to everything; she was a woman who answered intimately but who utterly didn't chatter. She scattered abroad therefore no
cloud of words; she could assent, she could agree, above all she could
encourage, without doing that. Only at the last she went a little further than
he had done himself. "And then how do you know? You may still, after all,
want to live here." It rather indeed pulled him up, for it wasn't what he had
been thinking, at least in her sense of the words. "You mean I may decide
to stay on for the sake of it?"

"Well, *with* such a home——!" But, quite beautifully, she had too much tact to dot so monstrous an *i,* and it was precisely an illustration of the way she didn't rattle. How could any one—of any wit—insist on any one else's "wanting" to live in New York?

"Oh," he said, "I *might* have lived here (since I had my opportunity early in life); I might have put in here all these years. Then everything would have been different enough—and, I daresay, 'funny' enough. But that's another matter. And then the beauty of it—I mean of my perversity, of my refusal to agree to a 'deal'—is just in the total absence of a reason. Don't you see that if I had a reason about the matter at all it would *have* to be the other way, and would then be inevitably a reason of dollars? There are no reasons here *but* of dollars. Let us therefore have none whatever—not the ghost of one."

They were back in the hall then for departure, but from where they stood the vista was large, through an open door, into the great square main saloon, with its almost antique felicity of brave spaces between windows. Her eyes came back from that reach and met his own a moment. "Are you very sure the 'ghost' of one doesn't, much rather, serve——?"

He had a positive sense of turning pale. But it was as near as they were then to come. For he made answer, he believed, between a glare and a grin: "Oh ghosts—of course the place must swarm with them! I should be ashamed of it if it didn't. Poor Mrs. Muldoon's right, and it's why I haven't asked her to do more than look in."

Miss Staverton's gaze lost itself, and things she didn't utter, it was clear, came and went in her mind. She might even for the minute, off there in the fine room, have imagined some element dimly gathering. Simplified like the death-mask of a handsome face, it perhaps produced for her just then an effect akin to the stir of an expression in the "set" commemorative plaster. Yet whatever her impression may have been she produced instead a vague platitude. "Well, if it were only furnished and lived in——!"

She appeared to imply that in case of its being still furnished he might have been a little less opposed to the idea of a return. But she passed straight into the vestibule, as if to leave her words behind her, and the next moment he had opened the house-door and was standing with her on the steps. He closed the door and, while he re-pocketed his key, looking up and down, they took in the comparatively harsh actuality of the Avenue, which reminded him of the assault of the outer light of the Desert on the traveller emerging from an Egyptian tomb. But he risked before they stepped into the street his gathered answer to her speech. "For me it *is* lived in. For me it *is* furnished." At which it was easy for her to sigh "Ah yes——!" all vaguely and discreetly; since his parents and his favourite sister, to say nothing of other kin, in numbers, had run their course and met their end there. That represented, within the walls, ineffaceable life.

It was a few days after this that, during an hour passed with her again, he had expressed his impatience of the too flattering curiosity—among the people he met—about his appreciation of New York. He had arrived at none at all that was socially producible, and as for that matter of his "thinking" (thinking the better or the worse of anything there) he has wholly taken up with one subject of thought. It was mere vain egoism, and it was moreover, if she liked, a morbid obsession. He found all things come back to the question of what he personally might have been, how he might have led his life and "turned out," if he had not so, at the outset, given it up. And confessing for the first time to the intensity within him of his absurd speculation—which but proved also, no doubt, the habit of too selfishly thinking—he affirmed the impotence there of any other source of interest, any other native appeal. "What would it have made of me, what would it have made of me? I keep for ever wondering, all idiotically; as if I could possibly know! I see what it has made of dozens of others, those I meet, and it positively aches within me, to the point of exasperation, that it would have made something of me as well. Only I can't make out *what,* and the worry of it, the small rage of curiosity never to be satisfied, brings back what I remember to have felt, once or twice, after judging best, for reasons, to burn some important letter unopened. I've been sorry, I've hated it—I've never known what was in the letter. You may of course say it's a trifle——!"

"I don't say it's a trifle," Miss Staverton gravely interrupted.

She was seated by her fire, and before her, on his feet and restless, he turned to and fro between this intensity of his idea and a fitful and unseeing inspection, through his single eye-glass, of the dear little old objects on her chimney-piece. Her interruption made him for an instant look at her harder. "I shouldn't care if you did!" he laughed, however; "and it's only a figure, at any rate, for the way I now feel. *Not* to have followed my perverse young course—and almost in the teeth of my father's curse, as I may say; not to have kept it up, so, 'over there,' from that day to this, without a doubt or a pang; not, above all, to have liked it, to have loved it, so much, loved it, no doubt, with such an abysmal conceit of my own preference: some variation from *that,* I say, must have produced some different effect for my life and for my 'form.' I should have stuck here—if it had been possible; and I was too young, at twenty-three, to judge, *pour deux sous,* whether it *were* possible. If I had waited I might have seen it was, and then I might have been, by staying here, something nearer to one of these types who have been hammered so hard and made so keen by their conditions. It isn't that I admire them so much—the question of any charm in them, or of any charm, beyond that of the rank money-passion, exerted by their conditions *for* them, has nothing to do with the matter: it's only a question of what fantastic, yet perfectly possible, development of my own nature I mayn't have missed. It comes over me that I had then a strange *alter ego* deep down somewhere within me, as the full-grown flower is in the small tight bud, and that I just took the course, I just transferred him to the climate, that blighted him for once and for ever."

"And you wonder about the flower," Miss Staverton said. "So do I, if you want to know; and so I've been wondering these several weeks. I believe in the flower," she continued, "I feel it would have been quite splendid, quite huge and monstrous."

"Monstrous above all!" her visitor echoed; "and I imagine, by the same stroke, quite hideous and offensive."

"You don't believe that," she returned; "if you did you wouldn't wonder. You'd know, and that would be enough for you. What you feel—and what I feel *for* you—is that you'd have had power."

"You'd have liked me that way?" he asked.

She barely hung fire. "How should I not have liked you?"

"I see. You'd have liked me, have preferred me, a billionaire!"

"How should I not have liked you?" she simply again asked.

He stood before her still—her question kept him motionless. He took it in, so much there was of it; and indeed his not otherwise meeting it testified to that. "I know at least what I am," he simply went on; "the other side of the medal's clear enough. I've not been edifying—I believe I'm thought in a hundred quarters to have been barely decent. I've followed strange paths and worshipped strange gods; it must have come to you again and again—in fact you've admitted to me as much—that I was leading, at any time these thirty years, a selfish frivolous scandalous life. And you see what it has made of me."

She just waited, smiling at him. "You see what it has made of *me.*"

"Oh you're a person whom nothing can have altered. You were born to be what you are, anywhere, anyway: you've the perfection nothing else could have blighted. And don't you see how, without my exile, I shouldn't have been waiting till now——?" But he pulled up for the strange pang.

"The great thing to see," she presently said, "seems to me to be that it has spoiled nothing. It hasn't spoiled your being here at last. It hasn't spoiled this. It hasn't spoiled your speaking——" She also however faltered.

He wondered at everything her controlled emotion might mean. "Do you believe then—too dreadfully!—that I *am* as good as I might ever have been?"

"Oh no! Far from it!" With which she got up from her chair and was nearer to him. "But I don't care," she smiled.

"You mean I'm good enough?"

She considered a little. "Will you believe it if I say so? I mean will you let that settle your question for you?" And then as if making out in his face that he drew back from this, that he had some idea which, however absurd, he couldn't yet bargain away: "Oh you don't care either—but very differently: you don't care for anything but yourself."

Spencer Brydon recognised it—it was in fact what he had absolutely professed. Yet he importantly qualified. "*He* isn't myself. He's the just so totally other person. But I do want to see him," he added. "And I can. And I shall."

Their eyes met for a minute while he guessed from something in hers that she divined his strange sense. But neither of them otherwise expressed it, and her apparent understanding, with no protesting shock, no easy derision, touched him more deeply than anything yet, constituting for his stifled perversity, on the spot, an element that was like breatheable air. What she said however was unexpected. "Well, *I've* seen him."

"You——?"

"I've seen him in a dream."

"Oh a 'dream'——!" It let him down.

"But twice over," she continued. "I saw him as I see you now."

"You've dreamed the same dream——?"

"Twice over," she repeated. "The very same."

This did somehow a little speak to him, as it also gratified him. "You dream about me at that rate?"

"Ah about *him!*" she smiled.

His eyes again sounded her. "Then you know all about him." And as she said nothing more: "What's the wretch like?"

She hesitated, and it was as if he were pressing her so hard that, resisting for reasons of her own, she had to turn away. "I'll tell you some other time!"

II

It was after this that there was most of a virtue for him, most of a cultivated charm, most of a preposterous secret thrill, in the particular form of surrender to his obsession and of address to what he more and more believed to be his privilege. It was what in these weeks he was living for—since he really felt life to begin but after Mrs. Muldoon had retired from the scene and, visiting the ample house from attic to cellar, making sure he was alone, he knew himself in safe possession and, as he tacitly expressed it, let himself go. He sometimes came twice in the twenty-four hours; the moments he liked best were those of gathering dusk, of the short autumn twilight; this was the time of which, again and again, he found himself hoping most. Then he could, as seemed to him, most intimately wander and wait, linger and listen, feel his fine attention, never in his life before so fine, on the pulse of the great vague place: he preferred the lampless hour and only wished he might have prolonged each day the deep crepuscular spell. Later—rarely much before midnight, but then for a considerable vigil—he watched with his glimmering light; moving slowly, holding it high, playing it far, rejoicing above all, as much as he might, in open vistas, reaches of communication between rooms and by passages; the long straight chance or show, as he would have called it, for the revelation he pretended to invite. It was a practice he found he could perfectly "work" without exciting remark; no one was in the least the wiser for it; even Alice Staverton, who was moreover a well of discretion, didn't quite fully imagine.

He let himself in and let himself out with the assurance of calm proprietorship; and accident so far favoured him that, if a fat Avenue "officer" had happened on occasion to see him entering at eleven-thirty, he had never yet, to the best of his belief, been noticed as emerging at two. He walked there on the crisp November nights, arrived regularly at the evening's end; it was as easy to do this after dining out as to take his way to a club or to his hotel. When he left his club, if he hadn't been dining out, it was ostensibly to go to his hotel; and when he left his hotel, if he had spent a part of the evening there, it was ostensibly to go to his club. Everything was easy in fine; everything conspired and promoted: there was truly even in the strain of his experience something that glossed over, something that salved and simplified, all the rest of consciousness. He circulated, talked, renewed, loosely and pleasantly, old relations—met indeed, so far as he could, new expectations and seemed to make out on the whole that in spite of the career, of such different contacts, which he had spoken of to Miss Staverton as ministering so little, for those who might have watched it, to edification, he was positively rather liked than not. He was a dim secondary social success—and all with people who had truly not an idea of him. It was all mere surface sound, this murmur of their welcome, this popping of their corks— just as his gestures of response were the extravagant shadows, emphatic in proportion as they meant little, of some game of *ombres chinoises*. He projected himself all day, in thought, straight over the bristling line of hard unconscious heads and into the other, the real, the waiting life; the life that, as soon as he had heard behind him the click of his great house-door, began for him, on the jolly corner, as beguiling as the slow opening bars of some rich music follows the tap of the conductor's wand.

He always caught the first effect of the steel point of his stick on the old marble of the hall pavement, large black-and-white squares that he remembered as the admiration of his childhood and that had then made in him, as he now saw, for the growth of an early conception of style. This effect was the dim reverberating tinkle as of some far-off bell hung who should say where?—in the depths of the house, of the past, of that mystical other world that might have flourished for him had he not, for weal or woe, abandoned it. On this impression he did ever the same thing; he put his stick noiselessly away in a corner—feeling the place once more in the likeness of some great glass bowl, all precious concave crystal, set delicately humming by the play of a moist finger round its edge. The concave crystal held, as it were, this mystical other world, and the indescribably fine murmur of its rim was the sigh there, the scarce audible pathetic wail to his strained ear, of all the old baffled forsworn possibilities. What he did therefore by this appeal of his hushed presence was to wake them into such measure of ghostly life as they might still enjoy. They were shy, all but unappeasably shy, but they weren't really sinister; at least they weren't as he had hitherto felt them—before they had taken the Form he so yearned to make them take, the Form he at moments saw himself in the light of fairly hunting on tiptoe, the points of his evening-shoes, from room to room and from storey to storey.

That was the essence of his vision—which was all rank folly, if one would, while he was out of the house and otherwise occupied, but which took on the last verisimilitude as soon as he was placed and posted. He knew what he meant and what he wanted; it was as clear as the figure on a cheque presented in demand for cash. His *alter ego* "walked"—that was the note of his image of him, while his image of his motive for his own odd pastime was the desire to waylay him and meet him. He roamed, slowly, warily, but all restlessly, he himself did—Mrs. Muldoon had been right, absolutely, with her figure of their "craping"; and the presence he watched for would roam restlessly too. But it would be as cautious and as shifty; the conviction of its probable, in fact its already quite sensible, quite audible evasion of pursuit grew for him from night to night, laying on him finally a rigour to which nothing in his life had been comparable. It had been the theory of many superficially-judging persons, he knew, that he was wasting that life in a surrender to sensations, but he had tasted of no pleasure so fine as his actual tension, had been introduced to no sport that demanded at once the patience and the nerve of this stalking of a creature more subtle, yet at bay perhaps more formidable, than any beast of the forest. The terms, the comparisons, the very practices of the chase positively came again into play; there were even moments when passages of his occasional experience as a sportsman, stirred memories, from his younger time, of moor and mountain and desert, revived for him—and to the increase of his keenness—by the tremendous force of analogy. He found himself at moments—once he had placed his single light on some mantel-shelf or in some recess—stepping back into shelter or shade, effacing himself behind a door or in an embrasure, as he had sought of old the vantage of rock and tree; he found himself holding his breath and living in the joy of the instant, the supreme suspense created by big game alone.

He wasn't afraid (though putting himself the question as he believed gentlemen on Bengal tiger-shoots or in close quarters with the great bear of the Rockies had been known to confess to having put it); and this indeed —since here at least he might be frank!—because of the impression, so intimate and so strange, that he himself produced as yet a dread, produced certainly a strain, beyond the liveliest he was likely to feel. They fell for him into categories, they fairly became familiar, the signs, for his own perception, of the alarm his presence and his vigilance created; though leaving him always to remark, portentously, on his probably having formed a relation, his probably enjoying a consciousness, unique in the experience of man.

People enough, first and last, had been in terror of apparitions, but who had ever before so turned the tables and become himself, in the apparitional world, an incalculable terror? He might have found this sublime had he quite dared to think of it; but he didn't too much insist, truly, on that side of his privilege. With habit and repetition he gained to an extraordinary degree the power to penetrate the dusk of distances and the darkness of corners, to resolve back into their innocence the treacheries of uncertain light, the evil-looking forms taken in the gloom by mere shadows, by accidents of the air, by shifting effects of perspective; putting down his dim luminary he could still wander on without it, pass into other rooms and, only knowing it was there behind him in case of need, see his way about, visually project for his purpose a comparative clearness. It made him feel, this acquired faculty, like some monstrous stealthy cat; he wondered if he would have glared at these moments with large shining yellow eyes, and what it mightn't verily be, for the poor hard-pressed *alter ego,* to be confronted with such a type.

He liked however the open shutters; he opened everywhere those Mrs. Muldoon had closed, closing them as carefully afterwards, so that she shouldn't notice: he liked—oh this he did like, and above all in the upper rooms!—the sense of the hard silver of the autumn stars through the window-panes, and scarcely less the flare of the street-lamps below, the white electric lustre which it would have taken curtains to keep out. This was human actual social; this was of the world he had lived in, and he was more at his ease certainly for the countenance, coldly general and impersonal, that all the while and in spite of his detachment it seemed to give him. He had support of course mostly in the rooms at the wide front and the prolonged side; it failed him considerably in the central shades and the parts at the back. But if he sometimes, on his rounds, was glad of his optical reach, so none the less often the rear of the house affected him as the very jungle of his prey. The place was there more subdivided; a large "extension" in particular, where small rooms for servants had been multiplied, abounded in nooks and corners, in closets and passages, in the ramifications especially of an ample back staircase over which he leaned, many a time, to look far down—not deterred from his gravity even while aware that he might, for a spectator, have figured some solemn simpleton playing at hide-and-seek. Outside in fact he might himself make that ironic *rapprochement;* but within the walls, and in spite of the clear windows, his consistency was proof against the cynical light of New York.

It had belonged to that idea of the exasperated consciousness of his victim to become a real test for him; since he had quite put it to himself from the first that, oh distinctly! he could "cultivate" his whole perception. He had felt it as above all open to cultivation—which indeed was but another name for his manner of spending his time. He was bringing it on, bringing it to perfection, by practice; in consequence of which it had grown so fine that he was now aware of impressions, attestations of his general postulate, that couldn't have broken upon him at once. This was the case more specifically with a phenomenon at last quite frequent for him in the upper rooms, the recognition—absolutely unmistakable, and by a turn dating from a particular hour, his resumption of his campaign after a diplomatic drop, a calculated absence of three nights—of his being definitely followed, tracked at a distance carefully taken and to the express end that he should the less confidently, less arrogantly, appear to himself merely to pursue. It worried, it finally broke him up, for it proved, of all the conceivable impressions, the one least suited to his book. He was kept in sight while remaining himself—as regards the essence of his position—sightless, and his only recourse then was in abrupt turns, rapid recoveries of ground. He wheeled about, retracing his steps, as if he might so catch in his face at least the stirred air of some other quick revolution. It was indeed true that his fully dislocalised thought of these manœuvres recalled to him Pantaloon, at the Christmas farce, buffeted and tricked from behind by ubiquitous Harlequin; but it left intact the influence of the conditions themselves each time he was re-exposed to them, so that in fact this association, had he suffered it to become constant, would on a certain side have but ministered to his intenser gravity. He had made, as I have said, to create on the premises the baseless sense of a reprieve, his three absences; and the result of the third was to confirm the after-effect of the second.

On his return, that night—the night succeeding his last intermission—he stood in the hall and looked up the staircase with a certainty more intimate than any he had yet known. "He's *there,* at the top, and waiting—not, as in general, falling back for disappearance. He's holding his ground, and it's the first time—which is a proof, isn't it? that something has happened for him." So Brydon argued with his hand on the banister and his foot on the lowest stair; in which position he felt as never before the air chilled by his logic. He himself turned cold in it, for he seemed of a sudden to know what now was involved. "Harder pressed?—yes, he takes it in, with its thus making clear to him that I've come, as they say, 'to stay.' He finally doesn't like and can't bear it, in the sense, I mean, that his wrath, his menaced interest, now balances with his dread. I've hunted him till he has 'turned': that, up there, is what has happened—he's the fanged or the antlered animal brought at last to bay." There came to him, as I say—but determined by an influence beyond my notation!—the acuteness of this certainty; under which, however, the next moment he had broken into a sweat that he would as little have consented to attribute to fear as he would have dared immediately to act upon it for enterprise. It marked none the less a prodigious thrill, a thrill that represented sudden dismay, no doubt, but also represented, and with the selfsame throb, the strangest, the most joyous, possibly the next minute almost the proudest, duplication of consciousness.

"He has been dodging, retreating, hiding, but now, worked up to anger, he'll fight!"—this intense impression made a single mouthful, as it were, of terror and applause. But what was wondrous was that the applause, for the felt fact, was so eager, since, if it was his other self he was running to earth, this ineffable identity was thus in the last resort not unworthy of him. It bristled there—somewhere near at hand, however unseen still—as the hunted thing, even as the trodden worm of the adage *must* at last bristle; and Brydon at this instant tasted probably of a sensation more complex than had ever before found itself consistent with sanity. It was as if it would have shamed him that a character so associated with his own should triumphantly succeed in just skulking, should to the end not risk the open; so that the drop of this danger was, on the spot, a great lift of the whole situation. Yet with another rare shift of the same subtlety he was already trying to measure by how much more he himself might now be in peril of fear; so rejoicing that he could, in another form, actively inspire that fear, and simultaneously quaking for the form in which he might passively know it.

The apprehension of knowing it must after a little have grown in him, and the strangest moment of his adventure perhaps, the most memorable or really most interesting, afterwards, of his crisis, was the lapse of certain instants of concentrated conscious *combat,* the sense of a need to hold on to something, even after the manner of a man slipping and slipping on some awful incline; the vivid impulse, above all, to move, to act, to charge, some-how and upon something—to show himself, in a word, that he wasn't afraid. The state of "holding-on" was thus the state to which he was momentarily reduced; if there had been anything, in the great vacancy, to seize, he would presently have been aware of having clutched it as he might under a shock at home have clutched the nearest chair-back. He had been surprised at any rate—of this he *was* aware—into something unprecedented since his original appropriation of the place; he had closed his eyes, held them tight, for a long minute, as with that instinct of dismay and that terror of vision. When he opened them the room, the other contiguous rooms, extraordinarily, seemed lighter—so light, almost, that at first he took the change for day. He stood firm, however that might be, just where he had paused; his resistance had helped him—it was as if there were something he had tided over. He knew after a little what this was—it had been in the imminent danger of flight. He had stiffened his will against going; without this he would have made for the stairs, and it seemed to him that, still with his eyes closed, he would have descended them, would have known how, straight and swiftly, to the bottom.

Well, as he had held out, here he was—still at the top, among the more intricate upper rooms and with the gauntlet of the others, of all the rest of the house, still to run when it should be his time to go. He would go at his time—only at his time: didn't he go every night very much at the same hour? He took out his watch—there was light for that: it was scarcely a quarter past one, and he had never withdrawn so soon. He reached his

lodgings for the most part at two—with his walk of a quarter of an hour.
He would wait for the last quarter—he wouldn't stir till then; and he kept
his watch there with his eyes on it, reflecting while he held it that this
deliberate wait, a wait with an effort, which he recognised, would serve perfectly for the attestation he desired to make. It would prove his courage—
unless indeed the latter might most be proved by his budging at last from
his place. What he mainly felt now was that, since he hadn't originally
scuttled, he had his dignities—which had never in his life seemed so many—
all to preserve and to carry aloft. This was before him in truth as a physical
image, an image almost worthy of an age of greater romance. That remark
indeed glimmered for him only to glow the next instant with a finer light;
since what age of romance, after all, could have matched either the state of
his mind or, "objectively," as they said, the wonder of his situation? The
only difference would have been that, brandishing his dignities over his head
as in a parchment scroll, he might then—that is in the heroic time—have
proceeded downstairs with a drawn sword in his other grasp.

At present, really, the light he had set down on the mantel of the next
room would have to figure his sword; which utensil, in the course of a
minute, he had taken the requisite number of steps to possess himself of.
The door between the rooms was open, and from the second another door
opened to a third. These rooms, as he remembered, gave all three upon a
common corridor as well, but there was a fourth, beyond them, without
issue save through the preceding. To have moved, to have heard his step
again, was appreciably a help; though even in recognising this he lingered
once more a little by the chimney-piece on which his light had rested. When
he next moved, just hesitating where to turn, he found himself considering
a circumstance that, after his first and comparatively vague apprehension of
it, produced in him the start that often attends some pang of recollection,
the violent shock of having ceased happily to forget. He had come into
sight of the door in which the brief chain of communication ended and
which he now surveyed from the nearer threshold, the one not directly
facing it. Placed at some distance to the left of this point, it would have
admitted him to the last room of the four, the room without other approach
or egress, had it not, to his intimate conviction, been closed *since* his former
visitation, the matter probably of a quarter of an hour before. He stared with
all his eyes at the wonder of the fact, arrested again where he stood and
again holding his breath while he sounded its sense. Surely it had been
subsequently closed—that is it had been on his previous passage indubitably
open!

He took it full in the face that something had happened between—that
he couldn't not have noticed before (by which he meant on his original tour
of all the rooms that evening) that such a barrier had exceptionally presented itself. He had indeed since that moment undergone an agitation so
extraordinary that it might have muddled for him any earlier view; and he

tried to convince himself that he might perhaps then have gone into the room and, inadvertently, automatically, on coming out, have drawn the door after him. The difficulty was that this exactly was what he never did; it was against his whole policy, as he might have said, the essence of which was to keep vistas clear. He had them from the first, as he was well aware, quite on the brain: the strange apparition, at the far end of one of them, of his baffled "prey" (which had become by so sharp an irony so little the term now to apply!) was the form of success his imagination had most cherished, projecting into it always a refinement of beauty. He had known fifty times the start of perception that had afterwards dropped; had fifty times gasped to himself "There!" under some fond brief hallucination. The house, as the case stood, admirably lent itself; he might wonder at the taste, the native architecture of the particular time, which could rejoice so in the multiplication of doors—the opposite extreme to the modern, the actual almost complete proscription of them; but it had fairly contributed to provoke this obsession of the presence encountered telescopically, as he might say, focussed and studied in diminishing perspective and as by a rest for the elbow.

It was with these considerations that his present attention was charged—they perfectly availed to make what he saw portentous. He *couldn't,* by any lapse, have blocked that aperture; and if he hadn't, if it was unthinkable, why what else was clear but that there had been another agent? Another agent?—he had been catching, as he felt, a moment back, the very breath of him; but when he had been so close as in this simple, this logical, this completely personal act? It was so logical, that is, that one might have *taken* it for personal; yet for what did Brydon take it, he asked himself, while, softly panting, he felt his eyes almost leave their sockets. Ah this time at last they *were,* the two, the opposed projections of him, in presence; and this time, as much as one would, the question of danger loomed. With it rose, as not before, the question of courage—for what he knew the blank face of the door to say to him was "Show us how much you have!" It stared, it glared back at him with that challenge; it put to him the two alternatives: should he just push it open or not? Oh to have this consciousness was to *think*—and to think, Brydon knew, as he stood there, was, with the lapsing moments, not to have acted! Not to have acted—that was the misery and the pang—was even still not to act; was in fact *all* to feel the thing in another, in a new and terrible way. How long did he pause and how long did he debate? There was presently nothing to measure it; for his vibration had already changed—as just by the effect of its intensity. Shut up there, at bay, defiant, and with the prodigy of the thing palpably, proving *done,* thus giving notice like some stark signboard—under that accession of accent the situation itself had turned; and Brydon at last remarkably made up his mind on what it had turned to.

It had turned altogether to a different admonition; to a supreme hint, for him, of the value of Discretion! This slowly dawned, no doubt—for it could take its time; so perfectly, on his threshold, had he been stayed, so little as yet had he either advanced or retreated. It was the strangest of all things that now when, by his taking ten steps and applying his hand to a latch, or even his shoulder and his knee, if necessary, to a panel, all the hunger of his prime need might have been met, his high curiosity crowned, his unrest assuaged—it was amazing, but it was also exquisite and rare, that insistence should have, at a touch, quite dropped from him. Discretion—he jumped at that; and yet not, verily, at such a pitch, because it saved his nerves or his skin, but because, much more valuably, it saved the situation. When I say he "jumped" at it I feel the consonance of this term with the fact that—at the end indeed of I know not how long—he did move again, he crossed straight to the door. He wouldn't touch it—it seemed now that he might *if* he would: he would only just wait there a little, to show, to prove, that he wouldn't. He had thus another station, close to the thin partition by which revelation was denied him; but with his eyes bent and his hands held off in a mere intensity of stillness. He listened as if there had been something to hear, but this attitude, while it lasted, was his own communication. "If you won't then—good: I spare you and I give up. You affect me as by the appeal positively for pity: you convince me that for reasons rigid and sublime—what do I know?—we both of us should have suffered. I respect them then, and, though moved and privileged as, I believe, it has never been given to man, I retire, I renounce—never, on my honour, to try again. So rest for ever—and let *me*!"

That, for Brydon was the deep sense of this last demonstration—solemn, measured, directed, as he felt it to be. He brought it to a close, he turned away; and now verily he knew how deeply he had been stirred. He retraced his steps, taking up his candle, burnt, he observed, well-nigh to the socket, and marking again, lighten it as he would, the distinctness of his footfall; after which, in a moment, he knew himself at the other side of the house. He did here what he had not yet done at these hours—he opened half a casement, one of those in the front, and let in the air of the night; a thing he would have taken at any time previous for a sharp rupture of his spell. His spell was broken now, and it didn't matter—broken by his concession and his surrender, which made it idle henceforth that he should ever come back. The empty street—its other life so marked even by the great lamplit vacancy—was within call, within touch; he stayed there as to be in it again, high above it though he was still perched; he watched as for some comforting common fact, some vulgar human note, the passage of a scavenger or a thief, some night-bird however base. He would have blessed that sign of life; he would have welcomed positively the slow approach of his friend the policeman, whom he had hitherto only sought to avoid, and was not sure that if the patrol had come into sight he mightn't have felt the impulse to get into relation with it, to hail it, on some pretext, from his fourth floor.

The pretext that wouldn't have been too silly or too compromising, the explanation that would have saved his dignity and kept his name, in such a case, out of the papers, was not definite to him: he was so occupied with the thought of recording his Discretion—as an effect of the vow he had just uttered to his intimate adversary—that the importance of this loomed large and something had overtaken all ironically his sense of proportion. If there had been a ladder applied to the front of the house, even one of the vertiginous perpendiculars employed by painters and roofers and sometimes left standing overnight, he would have managed somehow, astride of the window-sill, to compass by outstretched leg and arm that mode of descent. If there had been some such uncanny thing as he had found in his room at hotels, a workable fire-escape in the form of notched cable or a canvas shoot, he would have availed himself of it as a proof—well, of his present delicacy. He nursed that sentiment, as the question stood, a little in vain, and even—at the end of he scarce knew, once more, how long—found it, as by the action on his mind of the failure of response of the outer world, sinking back to vague anguish. It seemed to him he had waited an age for some stir of the great grim hush; the life of the town was itself under a spell—so unnaturally, up and down the whole prospect of known and rather ugly objects, the blankness and the silence lasted. Had they ever, he asked himself, the hard-faced houses, which had begun to look livid in the dim dawn, had they ever spoken so little to any need of his spirit? Great builded voids, great crowded stillnesses put on, often, in the heart of cities, for the small hours, a sort of sinister mask, and it was of this large collective negation that Brydon presently became conscious—all the more that the break of day was, almost incredibly, now at hand, proving to him what a night he had made of it.

He looked again at his watch, saw what had become of his time-values (he had taken hours for minutes—not, as in other tense situations, minutes for hours) and the strange air of the streets was but the weak, the sullen flush of a dawn in which everything was still locked up. His choked appeal from his own open window had been the sole note of life, and he could but break off at last as for a worse despair. Yet while so deeply demoralised he was capable again of an impulse denoting—at least by his present measure—extraordinary resolution; of retracing his steps to the spot where he had turned cold with the extinction of his last pulse of doubt as to there being in the place another presence than his own. This required an effort strong enough to sicken him; but he had his reason, which overmastered for the moment everything else. There was the whole of the rest of the house to traverse, and how should he screw himself to that if the door he had seen closed were at present open? He could hold to the idea that the closing had practically been for him an act of mercy, a chance offered him to descend, depart, get off the ground and never again profane it. This conception held together, it worked; but what it meant for him depended now clearly on the amount of forbearance his recent action, or rather his recent inaction, had engendered. The image of the "presence," whatever it was, waiting there for him to go—this image had not yet been so concrete for his nerves as when he stopped short of the point at which certainty would have come to him. For, with all his resolution, or more exactly with all his dread, he did stop short—he hung back from really seeing. The risk was too great and his fear too definite: it took at this moment an awful specific form.

He knew—yes, as he had never known anything—that, *should* he see the door open, it would all too abjectly be the end of him. It would mean that the agent of his shame—for his shame was the deep abjection—was once more at large and in general possession; and what glared him thus in the face was the act that this would determine for him. It would send him straight about to the window he had left open, and by that window, be long ladder and dangling rope as absent as they would, he saw himself uncontrollably insanely fatally take his way to the street. The hideous chance of this he at least could avert; but he could only avert it by recoiling in time from assurance. He had the whole house to deal with, this fact was still there; only he now knew that uncertainty alone could start him. He stole back from where he had checked himself—merely to do so was suddenly like safety—and, making blindly for the greater staircase, left gaping rooms and sounding passages behind. Here was the top of the stairs, with a fine large dim descent and three spacious landings to mark off. His instinct was all for mildness, but his feet were harsh on the floors, and, strangely, when he had in a couple of minutes become aware of this, it counted somehow for help. He couldn't have spoken, the tone of his voice would have scared him, and the common conceit or resource of "whistling in the dark" (whether literally or figuratively) have appeared basely vulgar; yet he liked none the less to hear himself go, and when he had reached his first landing —taking it all with no rush, but quite steadily—that stage of success drew from him a gasp of relief.

The house, withal, seemed immense, the scale of space again inordinate; the open rooms, to no one of which his eyes deflected, gloomed in their shuttered state like mouths of caverns; only the high skylight that formed the crown of the deep well created for him a medium in which he could advance, but which might have been, for queerness of colour, some watery under-world. He tried to think of something noble, as that his property was really grand, a splendid possession; but this nobleness took the form too of the clear delight with which he was finally to sacrifice it. They might come in now, the builders, the destroyers—they might come as soon as they would. At the end of two flights he had dropped to another zone, and from the middle of the third, with only one more left, he recognised the influence of the lower windows, of half-drawn blinds, of the occasional gleam of street-lamps, of the glazed spaces of the vestibule. This was the bottom of the sea, which showed an illumination of its own and which he even saw paved

—when at a given moment he drew up to sink a long look over the banis-
ters—with the marble squares of his childhood. By that time indubitably he
felt, as he might have said in a commoner cause, better; it had allowed him
to stop and draw breath, and the ease increased with the sight of the old
black-and-white slabs. But what he most felt was that now surely, with the
element of impunity pulling him as by hard firm hands, the case was settled
for what he might have seen above had he dared that last look. The closed
door, blessedly remote now, was still closed—and he had only in short to
reach that of the house.

   He came down further, he crossed the passage forming the access to the
last flight; and if here again he stopped an instant it was almost for the
sharpness of the thrill of assured escape. It made him shut his eyes—which
opened again to the straight slope of the remainder of the stairs. Here was
impunity still, but impunity almost excessive; inasmuch as the sidelights
and the high fan-tracery of the entrance were glimmering straight into the
hall; an appearance produced, he the next instant saw, by the fact that the
vestibule gaped wide, that the hinged halves of the inner door had been
thrown far back. Out of that again the *question* sprang at him, making his
eyes, as he felt, half-start from his head, as they had done, at the top of
the house, before the sign of the other door. If he had left that one open,
hadn't he left this one closed, and wasn't he now in *most* immediate presence of some inconceivable occult activity? It was as sharp, the question, as
a knife in his side, but the answer hung fire still and seemed to lose itself in
the vague darkness to which the thin admitted dawn, glimmering archwise
over the whole outer door, made a semicircular margin, a cold silvery
nimbus that seemed to play a little as he looked—to shift and expand and
contract.

   It was as if there had been something within it, protected by indistinctness and corresponding in extent with the opaque surface behind, the
painted panels of the last barrier to his escape, of which the key was in his
pocket. The indistinctness mocked him even while he stared, affected him
as somehow shrouding or challenging certitude, so that after faltering an
instant on his step he let himself go with the sense that here *was* at last
something to meet, to touch, to take, to know—something all unnatural and
dreadful, but to advance upon which was the condition for him either of
liberation or of supreme defeat. The penumbra, dense and dark, was the
virtual screen of a figure which stood in it as still as some image erect in a
niche or as some black-vizored sentinel guarding a treasure. Brydon was
to know afterwards, was to recall and make out, the particular thing he had
believed during the rest of his descent. He saw, in its great grey glimmering
margin, the central vagueness diminish, and he felt it to be taking the very
form toward which, for so many days, the passion of his curiosity had
yearned. It gloomed, it loomed, it was something, it was somebody, the
prodigy of a personal presence.

Rigid and conscious, spectral yet human, a man of his own substance and stature waited there to measure himself with his power to dismay. This only could it be—this only till he recognised, with his advance, that what made the face dim was the pair of raised hands that covered it and in which, so far from being offered in defiance, it was buried as for dark deprecation. So Brydon, before him, took him in; with every fact of him now, in the higher light, hard and acute—his planted stillness, his vivid truth, his grizzled bent head and white masking hands, his queer actuality of evening-dress, of dangling double eye-glass, of gleaming silk lappet and white linen, of pearl button and gold watch-guard and polished shoe. No portrait by a great modern master could have presented him with more intensity, thrust him out of his frame with more art, as if there had been "treatment," of the consummate sort, in his every shade and salience. The revulsion, for our friend, had become, before he knew it, immense—this drop, in the act of apprehension, to the sense of his adversary's inscrutable manœuvre. That meaning at least, while he gaped, it offered him; for he could but gape at his other self in this other anguish, gape as a proof that *he,* standing there for the achieved, the enjoyed, the triumphant life, couldn't be faced in his triumph. Wasn't the proof in the splendid covering hands, strong and completely spread?—so spread and so intentional that, in spite of a special verity that surpassed every other, the fact that one of these hands had lost two fingers, which were reduced to stumps, as if accidentally shot away, the face was effectually guarded and saved.

"Saved," though, *would* it be?—Brydon breathed his wonder till the very impunity of his attitude and the very insistence of his eyes produced, as he felt, a sudden stir which showed the next instant as a deeper portent, while the head raised itself, the betrayal of a braver purpose. The hands, as he looked, began to move to open; then, as if deciding in a flash, dropped from the face and left it uncovered and presented. Horror, with the sight, had leaped into Brydon's throat, gasping there in a sound he couldn't utter; for the bared identity was too hideous as *his,* and his glare was the passion of his protest. The face, *that* face. Spencer Brydon's?—he searched it still, but looking away from it in dismay and denial, falling straight from his height of sublimity. It was unknown, inconceivable, awful, disconnected from any possibility——! He had been "sold," he inwardly moaned, stalking such game as this: the presence before him was a presence, the horror within him a horror, but the waste of his nights had been only grotesque and the success of his adventure an irony. Such an identity fitted his at *no* point, made its alternative monstrous. A thousand times yes, as it came upon him nearer now—the face was the face of a stranger. It came upon him nearer now, quite as one of those expanding fantastic images projected by the magic lantern of childhood; for the stranger, whoever he might be, evil, odious, blatant, vulgar, had advanced as for aggression, and he knew himself give ground. Then harder pressed still, sick with the force of his shock, and fall-

ing back as under the hot breath and the roused passion of a life larger than
his own, a rage of personality before which his own collapsed, he felt the
whole vision turn to darkness and his very feet give way. His head went
round; he was going; he had gone.

III

What had next brought him back, clearly—though after how long?—was
Mrs. Muldoon's voice, coming to him from quite near, from so near that he
seemed presently to see her as kneeling on the ground before him while he
lay looking up at her; himself not wholly on the ground, but half-raised and
upheld—conscious, yes, of tenderness of support and, more particularly, of
a head pillowed in extraordinary softness and fainly refreshing fragrance.
He considered, he wondered, his wit but half at his service; then another
face intervened, bending more directly over him, and he finally knew that
Alice Staverton had made her lap an ample and perfect cushion to him, and
that she had to this end seated herself on the lowest degree of the staircase,
the rest of his long person remaining stretched on his old black-and-white
slabs. They were cold, these marble squares of his youth; but *he* somehow
was not, in this rich return of consciousness—the most wonderful hour,
little by little, that he had ever known, leaving him, as it did, so gratefully,
so abysmally passive, and yet as with a treasure of intelligence waiting all
round him for quiet appropriation; dissolved, he might call it, in the air of
the place and producing the golden glow of a late autumn afternoon. He
had come back, yes—come back from further away than any man but himself had ever travelled; but it was strange how with this sense what he had
come back *to* seemed really the great thing, and as if his prodigious journey
had been all for the sake of it. Slowly but surely his consciousness grew, his
vision of his state thus completing itself: he had been miraculously *carried*
back—lifted and carefully borne as from where he had been picked up, the
uttermost end of an interminable grey passage. Even with this he was
suffered to rest, and what had now brought him to knowledge was the
break in the long mild motion.

It had brought him to knowledge, to knowledge—yes, this was the
beauty of his state; which came to resemble more and more that of a man
who has gone to sleep on some news of a great inheritance, and then, after
dreaming it away, after profaning it with matters strange to it, has waked
up again to serenity of certitude and has only to lie and watch it grow.
This was the drift of his patience—that he had only to let it shine on him.
He must moreover, with intermissions, still have been lifted and borne;
since why and how else should he have known himself, later on, with the
afternoon glow intenser, no longer at the foot of his stairs—situated as these
now seemed at that dark other end of his tunnel—but on a deep window-
bench of his high saloon, over which had been spread, couch-fashion, a

mantle of soft stuff lined with grey fur that was familiar to his eyes and that one of his hands kept fondly feeling as for its pledge of truth. Mrs. Muldoon's face had gone, but the other, the second he had recognised, hung over him in a way that showed how he was still propped and pillowed. He took it all in, and the more he took it the more it seemed to suffice: he was as much at peace as if he had had food and drink. It was the two women who had found him, on Mrs. Muldoon's having plied, at her usual hour, her latch-key—and on her having above all arrived while Miss Staverton still lingered near the house. She had been turning away, all anxiety, from worrying the vain bell-handle—her calculation having been of the hour of the good woman's visit; but the latter, blessedly, had come up while she was still there, and they had entered together. He had then lain, beyond the vestibule, very much as he was lying now—quite, that is, as he appeared to have fallen, but all so wondrously without bruise or gash; only in a depth of stupor. What he most took in, however, at present, with the steadier clearance, was that Alice Staverton had for a long unspeakable moment not doubted he was dead.

"It must have been that I *was*." He made it out as she held him. "Yes—I can only have died. You brought me literally to life. Only," he wondered, his eyes rising to her, "only, in the name of all the benedictions, how?"

It took her but an instant to bend her face and kiss him, and something in the manner of it, and in the way her hands clasped and locked his head while he felt the cool charity and virtue of her lips, something in all this beatitude somehow answered everything. "And now I keep you," she said.

"Oh keep me, keep me!" he pleaded while her face still hung over him: in response to which it dropped again and stayed close, clingingly close. It was the seal of their situation—of which he tasted the impress for a long blissful moment in silence. But he came back. "Yet how did you know——?"

"I was uneasy. You were to have come, you remember—and you had sent no word."

"Yes, I remember—I was to have gone to you at one to-day." It caught on to their "old" life and relation—which were so near and so far. "I was still out there in my strange darkness—where was it, what was it? I must have stayed there so long." He could but wonder at the depth and the duration of his swoon.

"Since last night?" she asked with a shade of fear for her possible indiscretion.

"Since this morning—it must have been: the cold dim dawn of to-day. Where have I been," he vaguely wailed, "where have I been?" He felt her hold him close, and it was as if this helped him now to make in all security his mild moan. "What a long dark day!"

All in her tenderness she had waited a moment. "In the cold dim dawn?" she quavered.

But he had already gone on piecing together the parts of the whole prodigy. "As I didn't turn up you came straight——?"

She barely cast about. "I went first to your hotel—where they told me of your absence. You had dined out last evening and hadn't been back since. But they appeared to know you had been at your club."

"So you had the idea of *this*——?"

"Of what?" she asked in a moment.

"Well—of what has happened."

"I believed at least you'd have been here. I've known, all along," she said, "that you've been coming."

"'Known' it——?"

"Well, I've believed it. I said nothing to you after that talk we had a month ago—but I felt sure. I knew you *would,*" she declared.

"That I'd persist, you mean?"

"That you'd see him."

"Ah but I didn't!" cried Brydon with his long wail. "There's somebody— an awful beast; whom I brought, too horribly, to bay. But it's not me."

At this she bent over him again, and her eyes were in his eyes. "No—it's not you." And it was as if, while her face hovered, he might have made out in it, hadn't it been so near, some particular meaning blurred by a smile. "No, thank heaven," she repeated—"it's not you! Of course it wasn't to have been."

"Ah but it *was,*" he gently insisted. And he stared before him now as he had been staring for so many weeks. "I was to have known myself."

"You couldn't!" she returned consolingly. And then reverting, and as if to account further for what she had herself done, "But it wasn't only *that,* that you hadn't been at home," she went on. "I waited till the hour at which we had found Mrs. Muldoon that day of my going with you; and she arrived, as I've told you, while, failing to bring any one to the door, I lingered in my despair on the steps. After a little, if she hadn't come, by such a mercy, I should have found means to hunt her up. But it wasn't," said Alice Staverton, as if once more with her fine intention—"it wasn't only that."

His eyes, as he lay, turned back to her. "What more then?"

She met it, the wonder she had stirred. "In the cold dim dawn, you say? Well, in the cold dim dawn of this morning I too saw you."

"Saw *me*——?"

"Saw *him,*" said Alice Staverton. "It must have been at the same moment."

He lay an instant taking it in—as if he wished to be quite reasonable. "At the same moment?"

"Yes—in my dream again, the same one I've named to you. He came back to me. Then I knew it for a sign. He had come to you."

At this Brydon raised himself; he had to see her better. She helped him when she understood his movement, and he sat up, steadying himself beside her there on the window-bench and with his right hand grasping her left. "*He* didn't come to me."

"You came to yourself," she beautifully smiled.

"Ah I've come to myself now—thanks to you, dearest. But this brute, with his awful face—this brute's a black stranger. He's none of *me*, even as I *might* have been," Brydon sturdily declared.

But she kept the clearness that was like the breath of infallibility. "Isn't the whole point that you'd have been different?"

He almost scowled for it. "As different as *that*——?"

Her look again was more beautiful to him than the things of this world. "Haven't you exactly wanted to know *how* different? So this morning," she said, "you appeared to me."

"Like *him*?"

"A black stranger!"

"Then how did you know it was I?"

"Because, as I told you weeks ago, my mind, my imagination, had worked so over what you might, what you mightn't have been—to show you, you see, how I've thought of you. In the midst of that you came to me—that my wonder might be answered. So I knew," she went on; "and believed that, since the question held you too so fast, as you told me that day, you too would see for yourself. And when this morning I again saw I knew it would be because you had—and also then, from the first moment, because you somehow wanted me. *He* seemed to tell me of that. So why," she strangely smiled, "shouldn't I like him?"

It brought Spencer Brydon to his feet. "You 'like' that horror——?"

"I *could* have liked him. And to me," she said, "he was no horror. I had accepted him."

" 'Accepted'——?" Brydon oddly sounded.

"Before, for the interest of his difference—yes. And as *I* didn't disown him, as *I* knew him—which you at last, confronted with him in his difference, so cruelly didn't, my dear—well, he must have been, you see, less dreadful to me. And it may have pleased him that I pitied him."

She was beside him on her feet, but still holding his hand—still with her arm supporting him. But though it all brought for him thus a dim light, "You 'pitied' him?" he grudgingly, resentfully asked.

"He has been unhappy, he has been ravaged," she said.

"And haven't I been unhappy? Am not I—you've only to look at me!—ravaged?"

"Ah I don't say I like him *better*," she granted after a thought. "But he's grim, he's worn—and things have happened to him. He doesn't make shift, for sight, with your charming monocle."

"No"—it struck Brydon: "I couldn't have sported mine 'downtown.' They'd have guyed me there."

"His great convex pince-nez—I saw it, I recognised the kind—is for his poor ruined sight. And his poor right hand——!"

"Ah!" Brydon winced—whether for his proved identity or for his lost fingers. Then, "He has a million a year," he lucidly added. "But he hasn't you."

"And he isn't—no, he isn't—*you!*" she murmured as he drew her to his breast.

THE PROCURATOR OF JUDÆA

Anatole France

(1844–1924)

TRANSLATED BY FREDERICK CHAPMAN

L. AELIUS LAMIA, born in Italy of illustrious parents, had not yet discarded the *toga prætexta* when he set out for the schools of Athens to study philosophy. Subsequently he took up his residence at Rome, and in his house on the Esquiline, amid a circle of youthful wastrels, abandoned himself to licentious courses. But being accused of engaging in criminal relations with Lepida, the wife of Sulpicius Quirinus, a man of consular rank, and being found guilty, he was exiled by Tiberius Cæsar. At that time he was just entering his twenty-fourth year. During the eighteen years that his exile lasted he traversed Syria, Palestine, Cappadocia, and Armenia, and made prolonged visits to Antioch, Cæsarea, and Jerusalem. When, after the death of Tiberius, Caius was raised to the purple, Lamia obtained permission to return to Rome. He even regained a portion of his possessions. Adversity had taught him wisdom.

He avoided all intercourse with the wives and daughters of Roman citizens, made no efforts towards obtaining office, held aloof from public honours, and lived a secluded life in his house on the Esquiline. Occupying himself with the task of recording all the remarkable things he had seen during his distant travels, he turned, as he said, the vicissitudes of his years of expiation into a diversion for his hours of rest. In the midst of these calm employments, alternating with assiduous study of the works of Epicurus, he recognized with a mixture of surprise and vexation that age was stealing upon him. In his sixty-second year, being afflicted with an illness which proved in no slight degree troublesome, he decided to have recourse to the waters at Baiæ. The coast at that point, once frequented by the halcyon, was at this date the resort of the wealthy Roman, greedy of pleasure. For a week Lamia lived alone, without a friend in the brilliant crowd. Then one day, after dinner, an inclination to which he yielded urged him to ascend the incline, which, covered with vines that resembled bacchantes, looked out upon the waves.

Having reached the summit he seated himself by the side of a path beneath a terebinth, and let his glances wander over the lovely landscape. To his left, livid and bare, the Phlegræan plain stretched out towards the ruins of Cumæ. On his right, Cape Misenum plunged its abrupt spur beneath the Tyrrhenian sea. Beneath his feet luxurious Baiæ, following the graceful outline of the coast, displayed its gardens, its villas thronged with statues, its porticos, its marble terraces along the shores of the blue ocean where the dolphins sported. Before him, on the other side of the bay, on the Campanian coast, gilded by the already sinking sun, gleamed the temples which far away rose above the laurels of Posilippo, whilst on the extreme horizon Vesuvius looked forth smiling.

Lamia drew from a fold of his toga a scroll containing the *Treatise upon Nature,* extended himself upon the ground, and began to read. But the warning cries of a slave necessitated his rising to allow of the passage of a litter which was being carried along the narrow pathway through the vineyards. The litter being uncurtained, permitted Lamia to see stretched upon the cushions as it was borne nearer to him the figure of an elderly man of immense bulk, who, supporting his head on his hand, gazed out with a gloomy and disdainful expression. His nose, which was aquiline, and his chin, which was prominent, seemed desirous of meeting across his lips, and his jaws were powerful.

From the first moment Lamia was convinced that the face was familiar to him. He hesitated a moment before the name came to him. Then suddenly hastening towards the litter with a display of surprise and delight—

"Pontius Pilate!" he cried. "The gods be praised who have permitted me to see you once again!"

The old man gave a signal to the slaves to stop, and cast a keen glance upon the stranger who had addressed him.

"Pontius, my dear host," resumed the latter, "have twenty years so far whitened my hair and hollowed my cheeks that you no longer recognize your friend Ælius Lamia?"

At this time Pontius Pilate dismounted from the litter as actively as the weight of his years and the heaviness of his gait permitted him, and embraced Ælius Lamia again and again.

"Gods! what a treat it is to me to see you once more! But, alas, you call up memories of those long-vanished days when I was Procurator of Judæa in the province of Syria. Why, it must be thirty years ago that I first met

you. It was at Cæsarea, whither you came to drag out your weary term of
exile. I was fortunate enough to alleviate it a little, and out of friendship,
Lamia, you followed me to that depressing place Jerusalem, where the Jews
filled me with bitterness and disgust. You remained for more than ten
years my guest and my companion, and in converse about Rome and things
Roman we both of us managed to find consolation—you for your misfortunes, and I for my burdens of State."

Lamia embraced him afresh.

"You forget two things, Pontius; you are overlooking the facts that you
used your influence on my behalf with Herod Antipas, and that your purse
was freely open to me."

"Let us not talk of that," replied Pontius, "since after your return to
Rome you sent me by one of your freedmen a sum of money which repaid
me with usury."

"Pontius, I could never consider myself out of your debt by the mere
payment of money. But tell me, have the gods fulfilled your desires? Are
you in the enjoyment of all the happiness you deserve? Tell me about your
family, your fortunes, your health."

"I have withdrawn to Sicily, where I possess estates, and where I cultivate wheat for the market. My eldest daughter, my best-beloved Pontia,
who has been left a widow, lives with me, and directs my household. The
gods be praised, I have preserved my mental vigour; my memory is not in
the least degree enfeebled. But old age always brings in its train a long
procession of griefs and infirmities. I am cruelly tormented with gout. And
at this very moment you find me on my way to the Phlegræan plain in
search of a remedy for my sufferings. From that burning soil, whence at
night flames burst forth, proceed acrid exhalations of sulphur, which, so
they say, ease the pains and restore suppleness to the joints. At least, the
physicians assure me that it is so."

"May you find it so in your case, Pontius! But, despite the gout and its
burning torments, you scarcely look as old as myself, although in reality
you must be my senior by ten years. Unmistakably you have retained a
greater degree of vigour than I ever possessed, and I am overjoyed to find
you looking so hale. Why, dear friend, did you retire from the public
service before the customary age? Why, on resigning your governorship in
Judæa, did you withdraw to a voluntary exile on your Sicilian estates? Give
me an account of your doings from the moment that I ceased to be a witness of them. You were preparing to suppress a Samaritan rising when I set
out for Cappadocia, where I hoped to draw some profit from the breeding
of horses and mules. I have not seen you since then. How did that expedition succeed? Pray tell me. Everything interests me that concerns you in
any way."

Pontius Pilate sadly shook his head.

"My natural disposition," he said, "as well as a sense of duty, impelled me

to fulfill my public responsibilities, not merely with diligence, but even with
ardour. But I was pursued by unrelenting hatred. Intrigues and calumnies
cut short my career in its prime, and the fruit it should have looked to bear
has withered away. You ask me about the Samaritan insurrection. Let us
sit down on this hillock. I shall be able to give you an answer in a few
words. Those occurrences are as vividly present to me as if they had happened yesterday.

  "A man of the people, of persuasive speech—there are many such to be
met with in Syria—induced the Samaritans to gather together in arms on
Mount Gerizim (which in that country is looked upon as a holy place)
under the promise that he would disclose to their sight the sacred vessels
which in the ancient days of Evander and our father, Æneas, had been
hidden away by an eponymous hero, or rather a tribal deity, named Moses.
Upon this assurance the Samaritans rose in rebellion; but having been
warned in time to forestall them, I dispatched detachments of infantry to
occupy the mountain, and stationed cavalry to keep the approaches to it
under observation.

  "These measures of prudence were urgent. The rebels were already laying siege to the town of Tyrathaba, situated at the foot of Mount Gerizim.
I easily dispersed them, and stifled the as yet scarcely organized revolt.
Then, in order to give a forcible example with as few victims as possible, I
handed over to execution the leaders of the rebellion. But you are aware,
Lamia, in what strait dependence I was kept by the proconsul Vitellius,
who governed Syria not in, but against the interests of Rome, and looked
upon the provinces of the empire as territories which could be farmed out
to tetrarchs. The head-men among the Samaritans, in their resentment
against me, came and fell at his feet lamenting. To listen to them, nothing
had been further from their thoughts than to disobey Cæsar. It was I who
had provoked the rising, and it was purely in order to withstand my
violence that they had gathered together round Tyrathaba. Vitellius listened
to their complaints, and handing over the affairs of Judæa to his friend
Marcellus, commanded me to go and justify my proceedings before the
Emperor himself. With a heart overflowing with grief and resentment I
took ship. Just as I approached the shores of Italy, Tiberius, worn out with
age and the cares of empire, died suddenly on the selfsame Cape Misenum,
whose peak we see from this very spot magnified in the mists of evening.
I demanded justice of Caius, his successor, whose perception was naturally
acute, and who was acquainted with Syrian affairs. But marvel with me,
Lamia, at the maliciousness of fortune, resolved on my discomfiture. Caius
then had in his suite at Rome the Jew Agrippa, his companion, the friend
of his childhood, whom he cherished as his own eyes. Now Agrippa
favoured Vitellius, inasmuch as Vitellius was the enemy of Antipas, whom
Agrippa pursued with his hatred. The Emperor adopted the prejudices of
his beloved Asiatic, and refused even to listen to me. There was nothing for

me to do but bow beneath the stroke of unmerited misfortune. With tears for my meat and gall for my portion, I withdrew to my estates in Sicily, where I should have died of grief if my sweet Pontia had not come to console her father. I have cultivated wheat, and succeeded in producing the fullest ears in the whole province. But now my life is ended; the future will judge between Vitellius and me."

"Pontius," replied Lamia, "I am persuaded that you acted towards the Samaritans according to the rectitude of your character, and solely in the interests of Rome. But were you not perchance on that occasion a trifle too much influenced by that impetuous courage which has always swayed you? You will remember that in Judæa it often happened that I who, younger than you, should naturally have been more impetuous than you, was obliged to urge you to clemency and suavity."

"Suavity towards the Jews!" cried Pontius Pilate. "Although you have lived amongst them, it seems clear that you ill understand those enemies of the human race. Haughty and at the same time base, combining an invincible obstinacy with a despicably mean spirit, they weary alike your love and your hatred. My character, Lamia, was formed upon the maxims of the divine Augustus. When I was appointed Procurator of Judæa, the world was already penetrated with the majestic ideal of the *pax romana*. No longer, as in the days of our internecine strife, were we witnesses to the sack of a province for the aggrandisement of a proconsul. I knew where my duty lay. I was careful that my actions should be governed by prudence and moderation. The gods are my witnesses that I was resolved upon mildness, and upon mildness only. Yet what did my benevolent intentions avail me? You were at my side, Lamia, when, at the outset of my career as ruler, the first rebellion came to a head. Is there any need for me to recall the details to you? The garrison had been transferred from Cæsarea to take up its winter quarters at Jerusalem. Upon the ensigns of the legionaries appeared the presentment of Cæsar. The inhabitants of Jerusalem, who did not recognize the indwelling divinity of the Emperor, were scandalized at this, as though, when obedience is compulsory, it were not less abject to obey a god than a man. The priests of their nation appeared before my tribunal imploring me with supercilious humility to have the ensigns removed from within the holy city. Out of reverence for the divine nature of Cæsar and the majesty of the empire, I refused to comply. Then the rabble made common cause with the priests, and all around the pretorium portentous cries of supplication arose. I ordered the soldiers to stack their spears in front of the tower of Antonia, and to proceed, armed only with sticks like lictors, to disperse the insolent crowd. But, heedless of blows, the Jews continued their entreaties, and the more obstinate amongst them threw themselves on the ground and, exposing their throats to the rods, deliberately courted death. You were a witness of my humiliation on that occasion, Lamia. By the order of Vitellius I was forced to send the insignia back to Cæsarea. That disgrace I had certainly not merited. Before the immortal gods I swear that never once during my term of office did I flout justice and the laws. But I am grown old. My enemies and detractors are dead. I shall die unavenged. Who will now retrieve my character?"

He moaned and lapsed into silence. Lamia replied—

"That man is prudent who neither hopes nor fears anything from the uncertain events of the future. Does it matter in the least what estimate men may form of us hereafter? We ourselves are after all our own witnesses, and our own judges. You must rely, Pontius Pilate, on the testimony you yourself bear to your own rectitude. Be content with your own personal respect and that of your friends. For the rest, we know that mildness by itself will not suffice for the work of government. There is but little room in the actions of public men for that indulgence of human frailty which the philosophers recommend."

"We'll say no more at present," said Pontius. "The sulphureous fumes which rise from the Phlegræan plain are more powerful when the ground which exhales them is still warm beneath the sun's rays. I must hasten on. Adieu! But now that I have rediscovered a friend, I should wish to take advantage of my good fortune. Do me the favour, Ælius Lamia, to give me your company at supper at my house to-morrow. My house stands on the seashore, at the extreme end of the town in the direction of Misenum. You will easily recognize it by the porch which bears a painting representing Orpheus surrounded by tigers and lions, whom he is charming with the strains from his lyre.

"Till to-morrow, Lamia," he repeated, as he climbed once more into his litter. "To-morrow we will talk about Judæa."

The following day at the supper hour Lamia presented himself at the house of Pontius Pilate. Two couches only were in readiness for occupants. Creditably but simply equipped, the table held a silver service in which were set out beccaficos in honey, thrushes, oysters from the Lucrine lake, and lampreys from Sicily. As they proceeded with their repast, Pontius and Lamia interchanged inquiries with one another about their ailments, the symptoms of which they described at considerable length, mutually emulous of communicating the various remedies which had been recommended to them. Then, congratulating themselves on being thrown together once more at Baiæ, they vied with one another in praise of the beauty of that enchanting coast and the mildness of the climate they enjoyed. Lamia was enthusiastic about the charms of the courtesans who frequented the seashore laden with golden ornaments and trailing draperies of barbaric broidery. But the aged Procurator deplored the ostentation with which by means of trumpery jewels and filmy garments foreigners and even enemies of the empire beguiled the Romans of their gold. After a time they turned to the subject of the great engineering feats that had been accomplished in the country; the prodigious bridge constructed by Caius between Puteoli and Baiæ, and the canals which Augustus excavated to convey the waters of the ocean to Lake Avernus and the Lucrine lake.

"I also," said Pontius, with a sigh, "I also wished to set afoot public works of great utility. When, for my sins, I was appointed Governor of Judæa, I conceived the idea of furnishing Jerusalem with an abundant supply of pure water by means of an aqueduct. The elevation of the levels, the proportionate capacity of the various parts, the gradient for the brazen reservoirs to which the distribution pipes were to be fixed—I had gone into every detail, and decided everything for myself with the assistance of mechanical experts. I had drawn up regulations for the superintendents so as to prevent individuals from making unauthorized depredations. The architects and the workmen had their instructions. I gave orders for the commencement of operations. But far from viewing with satisfaction the construction of that conduit, which was intended to carry to their town upon its massive arches not only water but health, the inhabitants of Jerusalem gave vent to lamentable outcries. They gathered tumultuously together, exclaiming against the sacrilege and impiousness, and, hurling themselves upon the workmen, scattered the foundation stones. Can you picture to yourself, Lamia, a filthier set of barbarians? Nevertheless, Vitellius decided in their favour, and I received orders to put a stop to the work."

"It is a knotty point," said Lamia, "how far one is justified in devising things for the commonweal against the will of the populace."

Pontius Pilate continued as though he had not heard this interruption. "Refuse an aqueduct! What madness! But whatever is of Roman origin is distasteful to the Jews. In their eyes we are an unclean race, and our very presence appears a profanation to them. You will remember that they would never venture to enter the pretorium for fear of defiling themselves, and that I was consequently obliged to discharge my magisterial functions in an open-air tribunal on that marble pavement your feet so often trod.

"They fear us and they despise us. Yet is not Rome the mother and warden of all those peoples who nestle smiling upon her venerable bosom? With her eagles in the van, peace and liberty have been carried to the very confines of the universe. Those whom we have subdued we look on as our friends, and we leave those conquered races, nay, we secure to them the permanence of their customs and their laws. Did Syria, aforetime rent asunder by its rabble of petty kings, ever even begin to taste of peace and prosperity until it submitted to the armies of Pompey? And when Rome might have reaped a golden harvest as the price of her goodwill, did she lay hands on the hoards that swell the treasuries of barbaric temples? Did she despoil the shrine of Cybele at Pessinus, or the Morimene and Cilician sanctuaries of Jupiter, or the temple of the Jewish god at Jerusalem? Antioch, Palmyra, and Apamea, secure despite their wealth, and no longer in dread of the wandering Arab of the desert, have erected temples to the

genius of Rome and the divine Cæsar. The Jews alone hate and withstand
us. They withhold their tribute till it is wrested from them, and obstinately
rebel against military service."

"The Jews," replied Lamia, "are profoundly attached to their ancient
customs. They suspected you, unreasonably I admit, of a desire to abolish
their laws and change their usages. Do not resent it, Pontius, if I say that
you did not always act in such a way as to disperse their unfortunate
illusion. It gratified you, despite your habitual self-restraint, to play upon
their fears, and more than once have I seen you betray in their presence
the contempt with which their beliefs and religious ceremonies inspired
you. You irritated them particularly by giving instructions for the sacerdotal
garments and ornaments of their high priest to be kept in ward by your
legionaries in the Antonine tower. One must admit that though they have
never risen like us to an appreciation of things divine, the Jews celebrate
rites which their very antiquity renders venerable."

Pontius Pilate shrugged his shoulders.

"They have very little exact knowledge of the nature of the gods," he
said. "They worship Jupiter, yet they abstain from naming him or erecting
a statue of him. They do not even adore him under the semblance of a rude
stone, as certain of the Asiatic peoples are wont to do. They know nothing
of Apollo, of Neptune, of Mars, nor of Pluto, nor of any goddess. At the
same time, I am convinced that in days gone by they worshipped Venus.
For even to this day their women bring doves to the altar as victims; and
you know as well as I that the dealers who trade beneath the arcades of
their temple supply those birds in couples for sacrifice. I have even been
told that on one occasion some madman proceeded to overturn the stalls
bearing these offerings, and their owners with them. The priests raised an
outcry about it, and looked on it as a case of sacrilege. I am of opinion that
their custom of sacrificing turtle-doves was instituted in honour of Venus.
Why are you laughing, Lamia?"

"I was laughing," said Lamia, "at an amusing idea which, I hardly know
how, just occurred to me. I was thinking that perchance some day the
Jupiter of the Jews might come to Rome and vent his fury upon you. Why
should he not? Asia and Africa have already enriched us with a considerable number of gods. We have seen temples in honour of Isis and the dog-
faced Anubis erected in Rome. In the public squares, and even on the race-
courses, you may run across the Bona Dea of the Syrians mounted on an
ass. And did you never hear how, in the reign of Tiberius, a young patrician
passed himself off as the horned Jupiter of the Egyptians, Jupiter Ammon,
and in this disguise procured the favours of an illustrious lady who was too
virtuous to deny anything to a god? Beware, Pontius, lest the invisible
Jupiter of the Jews disembark some day on the quay at Ostia!"

At the idea of a god coming out of Judæa, a fleeting smile played over the
severe countenance of the Procurator. Then he replied gravely—

"How would the Jews manage to impose their sacred law on outside peoples when they are in a perpetual state of tumult amongst themselves as to the interpretation of that law? You have seen them yourselves, Lamia, in the public squares, split up into twenty rival parties, with staves in their hands, abusing each other and clutching one another by the beard. You have seen them on the steps of the temple, tearing their filthy garments as a symbol of lamentation, with some wretched creature in a frenzy of prophetic exaltation in their midst. They have never realized that it is possible to discuss peacefully and with an even mind those matters concerning the divine which yet are hidden from the profane and wrapped in uncertainty. For the nature of the immortal gods remains hidden from us, and we cannot arrive at a knowledge of it. Though I am of opinion, none the less, that it is a prudent thing to believe in the providence of the gods. But the Jews are devoid of philosophy, and cannot tolerate any diversity of opinions. On the contrary, they judge worthy of the extreme penalty all those who on divine subjects profess opinions opposed to their law. And as, since the genius of Rome has towered over them, capital sentences pronounced by their own tribunals can only be carried out with the sanction of the proconsul or the procurator, they harry the Roman magistrate at any hour to procure his signature to their baleful decrees, they besiege the pretorium with their cries of 'Death!' A hundred times, at least, have I known them, mustered, rich and poor together, all united under their priests, make a furious onslaught on my ivory chair, seizing me by the skirts of my robe, by the thongs of my sandals, and all to demand of me—nay, to exact from me—the death sentence on some unfortunate whose guilt I failed to perceive, and as to whom I could only pronounce that he was as mad as his accusers. A hundred times, do I say! Not a hundred, but every day and all day. Yet it was my duty to execute their law as if it were ours, since I was appointed by Rome not for the destruction, but for the upholding of their customs, and over them I had the power of the rod and the axe. At the outset of my term of office I endeavoured to persuade them to hear reason; I attempted to snatch their miserable victims from death. But this show of mildness only irritated them the more; they demanded their prey, fighting around me like a horde of vultures with wing and beak. Their priests reported to Cæsar that I was violating their law, and their appeals, supported by Vitellius, drew down upon me a severe reprimand. How many times did I long, as the Greeks used to say, to dispatch accusers and accused in one convoy to the crows!"

"Do not imagine, Lamia, that I nourish the rancour of the discomfited, the wrath of the superannuated, against a people which in my person has prevailed against both Rome and tranquillity. But I foresee the extremity to which sooner or later they will reduce us. Since we cannot govern them, we shall be driven to destroy them. Never doubt it. Always in a state of insubordination, brewing rebellion in their inflammatory minds, they will one day burst forth upon us with a fury beside which the wrath of the Numidians and the mutterings of the Parthians are mere child's play. They are secretly nourishing preposterous hopes, and madly premeditating our ruin. How can it be otherwise, when, on the strength of an oracle, they are living in expectation of the coming of a prince of their own blood whose kingdom shall extend over the whole earth? There are no half measures with such a people. They must be exterminated. Jerusalem must be laid waste to the very foundation. Perchance, old as I am, it may be granted me to behold the day when her walls shall fall and the flames shall envelop her houses, when her inhabitants shall pass under the edge of the sword, when salt shall be strown on the place where once the temple stood. And in that day I shall at length be justified."

Lamia exerted himself to lead the conversation back to a less acrimonious note.

"Pontius," he said, "it is not difficult for me to understand both your long-standing resentment and your sinister forebodings. Truly, what you have experienced of the character of the Jews is nothing to their advantage. But I lived in Jerusalem as an interested onlooker, and mingled freely with the people, and I succeeded in detecting certain obscure virtues in these rude folk which were altogether hidden from you. I have met Jews who were all mildness, whose simple manners and faithfulness of heart recalled to me what our poets have related concerning the Spartan lawgiver. And you yourself, Pontius, have seen perish beneath the cudgels of your legionaries simple-minded men who have died for a cause they believed to be just without revealing their names. Such men do not deserve our contempt. I am saying this because it is desirable in all things to preserve moderation and an even mind. But I own that I never experienced any lively sympathy for the Jews. The Jewesses, on the contrary, I found extremely pleasing. I was young then, and the Syrian women stirred all my senses to response. Their ruddy lips, their liquid eyes that shone in the shade, their sleepy gaze pierced me to the very marrow. Painted and stained, smelling of nard and myrrh, steeped in odours, their physical attractions are both rare and delightful."

Pontius listened impatiently to these praises.

"I was not the kind of man to fall into the snares of the Jewish women," he said; "and since you have opened the subject yourself, Lamia, I was never able to approve of your laxity. If I did not express with sufficient emphasis formerly how culpable I held you for having intrigued at Rome with the wife of a man of consular rank, it was because you were then enduring heavy penance for your misdoings. Marriage from the patrician point of view is a sacred tie; it is one of the institutions which are the support of Rome. As to foreign women and slaves, such relations as one may enter into with them would be of little account were it not that they habituate the body to a humiliating effeminacy. Let me tell you that you have been too liberal in your offerings to the Venus of the Market-place; and what, above all, I blame in you is that you have not married in compliance with the law and given children to the Republic, as every good citizen is bound to do."

But the man who had suffered exile under Tiberius was no longer listening to the venerable magistrate. Having tossed off his cup of Falernian, he was smiling at some image visible to his eye alone.

After a moment's silence he resumed in a very deep voice, which rose in pitch by little and little—

"With what languorous grace they dance, those Syrian women! I knew a Jewess at Jerusalem who used to dance in a poky little room, on a threadbare carpet, by the light of one smoky little lamp, waving her arms as she clanged her cymbals. Her loins arched, her head thrown back, and, as it were, dragged down by the weight of her heavy red hair, her eyes swimming with voluptuousness, eager, languishing, compliant, she would have made Cleopatra herself grow pale with envy. I was in love with her barbaric dances, her voice—a little raucous and yet so sweet—her atmosphere of incense, the semi-somnolescent state in which she seemed to live. I followed her everywhere. I mixed with the vile rabble of soldiers, conjurers, and extortioners with which she was surrounded. One day, however, she disappeared, and I saw her no more. Long did I seek her in disreputable alleys and taverns. It was more difficult to learn to do without her than to lose the taste for Greek wine. Some months after I lost sight of her, I learned by chance that she had attached herself to a small company of men and women who were followers of a young Galilean thaumaturgist. His name was Jesus; he came from Nazareth, and he was crucified for some crime, I don't quite know what. Pontius, do you remember anything about the man?"

Pontius Pilate contracted his brows, and his hand rose to his forehead in the attitude of one who probes the deeps of memory. Then after a silence of some seconds—

"Jesus?" he murmured, "Jesus—of Nazareth? I cannot call him to mind."

YOUTH

Karl Emil Franzos

(1848–1904)

TRANSLATED BY BASIL CREIGHTON

Early one may morning the scent of lilacs and roses in the gardens at Hilmteich was mingled with the odour of strong tobacco, beer, herrings and hot sausages—a phenomenon that usually occurred only towards evening. The "Germans" of Graz were giving their seniors and themselves a "cat's breakfast" there. There was every excuse for it, for the carousal of the night before, in celebration of the Club's thirtieth anniversary, had gone with such a swing that it only broke up at dawn; whereupon the whole company, including all the freshmen, had reeled out of the Puntigam Beer Tavern in a high state of elation and made their way straight to Hilmteich as the town was just waking up.

The breakfast too was a glorious affair. There were hard on a couple of hundred red Cerevises, or club caps, adorned with an elaborately embroidered G, on fair heads and dark heads, grey heads and bald heads. The company was now reinforced by a score of seniors, old gentlemen who were not as a rule much pleased to be reminded that they too had once been members of the "dangerous" club, whose first proceeding in the year 1876 had been to send a telegram of greetings to Bismarck. And manfully they played their part, even though the weakness of the flesh could not always keep pace with the ardour of the spirit. When towards midday the chorus: "Oh, glorious college days" rose above the din, they joined heartily in the tune though the words escaped them:

> One drafts reports with sombre frown,
> A foe to witticisms,
> Another drones in cap and gown,
> A third scrawl criticisms.

—and the fingers the old boys wagged at one another trembled more than they intended.

Yet not one of them made a move to go. They had to keep it up as long as his Excellency remained seated. It was out of the question for anyone to leave until he gave the signal. He was only a shop-keeper's son, who had

taken to the law and within twenty years had risen to be a baron and a
minister; he was now one of the highest officials of the state and once the
breeze over the Czechs died down he was bound to have his chance again.
Today he sat in the place of honour next the "spokesman" of the club, a
sturdy young Carinthian with fearsomely gashed cheeks; and he sat as
blithe and erect as he had during the festivities of the night before, after
arriving by the evening express from Vienna, carrying it off, as he always
did, by his power to captivate all about him.

Nature herself had cast him for the part. He had a slender, well-
proportioned figure and there was grace as well as strength in every
movement he made. His head, set on a magnificent neck, was the despair of the black-and-white artists of the Vienna newspapers, for it was
impossible to caricature without removing all trace of a likeness. His open,
rounded brow was framed in light, curly hair, his nose was bold and well-
cut, with sensitive nostrils, and his chin set like a wedge and yet not
obstinate. Profiles such as his might be found among the poachers of his
native Tauern, but not a mouth of so soft a charm as his. Last but not least
there were his eyes, radiantly blue eyes in which for all their keenness there
was always an engaging expression. You had only to look at him to see that
he could hit fortune on the wing and had never failed to bag any game
that caught his fancy.

Very different game from the artless company he was now set on winning
back to him. The Germania Club had been not only astonished but indignant when the telegram arrived the day before announcing his intention of
attending the celebrations; he, the vile apostate, who a few years before had
instructed the public prosecutor to take severe measures against treasonable speeches at German nationalist celebrations. A man like that daring to
show his nose! They decided to give him a rough-house, and the freshmen
even brought whistles with them for that laudable purpose. But as soon as
he came in, wearing the black, red and gold ribbon adorned with the signs
of the zodiac across his chest, the Cerevis on his blond head and a sunny
smile on his lips, they were silent and confounded. They could not believe
that this handsome, affable man, who would never be credited with more
than three-fourths of his forty-five years, could be the morose, unbending
minister they had taken him for. You had only to shake hands with him to
be won over at once; there was a warmth and cordiality in the grasp of his
hand that seemed to say: "I'm nothing out of the common, a fellow like
you could get as far. Let's be friends!"

But in the course of the evening the reconciliation was wrought up to
the pitch of enthusiasm by a single gesture. Of course at the conclusion of
"Deutschland, Deutschland über alles!" the "spokesman" made an uncompromising speech about "our hopes," and of course there was present a
particularly officious superintendent of police, Herr Franz Nawratil, representing His Majesty, the King and Emperor, who first pricked up his ears

and then sharpened his pencil and finally cut the speaker short, and of course an angry "pereat" thereupon went the round of the whole assembly. But, in spite of the excitement which ensued, not an eye missed what next occurred at the seniors' table: the ex-minister leapt impulsively to his feet as though urged by an irresistible force; he drew himself up to his full height, a deep flush overspread his intrepid face, which was almost contorted by the violence of his feelings, and with right arm extended he stood there and stared at the Czech, the officer of the Dual Monarchy, until the man went pale and collapsed. The manly rage of a German had flared out and shown that patience was at last exhausted.

But, as ever, he had his wits about him. He did not forget that others had as long a memory as he, or that the instructions Herr Nawratil had just carried out had been signed by himself! For that reason his hand instantly fell limply to his side; the colour left his face as it clouded over, and he sank dismayed into his chair. But after a moment his face cleared again; he stretched his hand out across the broad tavern table to his vis-à-vis, a long-haired Grammar-School master, who had recently been reprimanded for a thin volume of political verse. "From now on we fight shoulder to shoulder!" The words remained unspoken but everyone read them in his look. The schoolmaster's eyes filled as he grasped the proffered hand and the company was proud to witness the historic moment which restored its great son to the German people of Austria. The reporters, who were able to telegraph their accounts of the sensational episode to the Vienna newspapers that very night, were the most delighted of all. And now, while he was being feasted at Hilmteich, the whole of Austria rang with his name and his reputation shone with all its old lustre. All this without a word's having been uttered which could be brought up against him.

Nevertheless, he was no lover of ceremonious speeches. They were not in keeping with a man of his clubbable, cordial disposition. The night before he had forbidden the reprimanded poet to propose his health and now, the morning after, he put a veto on any such mark of homage. "For God's sake, boys, don't be so tactless! At a 'cat's breakfast' too. And if anyone calls me Excellency again I'll bring my tankard down on his head!" And so the familiar "thou" was bandied to and fro. The subservient kept it up just because he was an Excellency and the out-and-outers because after all he was such a thorough-going nationalist. When the talk—Lord knows how, for no one noticed how cunningly he steered it in that direction—turned on the forthcoming elections to complete the Council of the Empire, the long-haired schoolmaster suddenly shouted enthusiastically: "We'll have you brought in for Leibnitz! Say the word, brother, and you're elected." Whereupon the great man blushed in his modesty—and he did really blush —and could only stammer his thanks. When he was urged on all hands to accept nomination he was deeply moved. "If I can and, above all, if you can find no one better. You must think twice and twice again." And he stuck to it, say what they liked; their only consolation was that he was obviously disposed to accept the kind offer.

One man alone held aloof. He had scarcely spoken a word throughout the whole carousal. He was a small, thin man between forty and fifty; his face had a gentle expression and a look of ill-health and the short beard that framed his face was already quite grey. He had followed the discussion with a quiet smile on his lips and now he nodded to himself as though something he had puzzled over in vain was suddenly clear to him. He was sitting opposite his Excellency, at his Excellency's wish, not his own. By rights he had no claim to so exalted a place. Every finger had pointed at him when the allusion to critics came in the song shortly before. It was Franz Hubmann, dramatic critic on a Graz newspaper, a position he had held for the last twenty-five years.

Then a faint chime came wafted faintly on the warm spring air. It was the clock of the ancient little Leechkirche striking one. "Good Lord, I must run if I want to catch the Vienna train."

At this signal chairs were pushed back and the company rose, some more, some less heavily, to their feet; and lastly the stalwart "spokesman" said: "Must your Ex——", but that was against the rules of the club. "You off?" he corrected himself, but that was lacking in respect. Then he found the way out. "Has the time to go really come?" The question was repeated in the same tone on all sides. Only two of the seniors jumped up simultaneously and shouted as though with one voice: "I'll see you off, Hans!" No wonder, for one was a district judge who wanted to be elevated to the Supreme Court, the other was a prison doctor who had long been asking for a rise. The way they shouted it out in unison was extraordinarily comic, but nobody paid any attention. Nor did his Excellency hear them apparently.

"Come with me, Hubmann," he said, and when the critic demurred he added insistently: "Do, Franz."

At this Hubmann got up and followed him, but the guest of honour had many hands still to shake and many effusive speeches to listen to before they were outside in the road. Cheers pursued them as they walked on.

As soon as they were out of earshot the object of this acclamation stopped, stretched as though a load had fallen from his shoulders and heaved a sigh. "Well, well, how jolly it all was, so hearty—really delightful. But we should have left a bit sooner."

Hubmann looked him straight in the face. "No," he said, "not a minute sooner . . ." But when his companion looked questioningly at him, he replied only with his quiet smile and said no more.

The handsome face frowned but next moment broke into a hearty laugh.

"You haven't changed, Franz! . . . The wily fellow had his axe to grind . . . And what Machiavellian trick am I up to with you?"

"I could tell you that too," Hubmann replied.

"You could? You make me really inquisitive now———"

"It can't be put in one word," the critic replied. "Or if it could it would sound—unkind . . . Now, Hans," he resumed, "there's not a great deal of time if you're going to catch that train." And he pointed to the horse-tram, which was just going to start.

"That contraption!" Hans laughed. "God forbid! I'm going by the night train, of course. Travelling by day at my time of life! The day is for enjoyment and a railway carriage is only meant for sleeping in . . . This way, Franz, if you're game, by Hilmgasse and up on to the Rosenberg and then down into the town by our old path. You haven't forgotten it?"

"How could I?" was the reply. "I've loved the old path all my days."

Once more a shadow clouded that fearless face, and again it was laughed away. "Pin-pricks don't draw blood . . . but all the same you shouldn't indulge in them," he went on in a cordial tone, putting his arm round his friend's shoulder. "Don't let us spoil this happy occasion. I've been looking forward to it all the time we've been celebrating. You'll go the same old walk with your old Franz, I kept telling myself, and have a heart-to-heart talk and it will all be good again, as it was in the good old days . . ."

He stopped and looked full in his eyes.

"And now, Franz, what are you angry with me for?"

The writer returned the look without flinching.

"Must you?" he asked gravely. "There's hardly a thing we can say to one another we don't know already. And is there any sense at our time of life in probing to the bottom of things? I knew at once that that was your aim, and the one, not very kind word I kept back a moment ago was 'rehabilitation'." And when he was answered by a gesture of protest: "Or however you choose to put it. You want to explain yourself to me, to prove that you could not have behaved otherwise than as you have behaved. Put it how you like. You see, I know you better perhaps than anyone else in the world does and since I know that the leopard cannot change his spots I am not angry with you, but———"

He stopped and shut his lips tight as though to prevent a word escaping against his will.

"But sad," the minister put in. "You admit I must go my own way until the devil claims me, but in my youth I might still have been an honest fellow." He said it without scorn or bitterness, though in a tone of raillery, and then went on earnestly: "But I, your closest friend in those old days, have got to be pleased when I see what has become of you, you the most talented of us all, the man we dreamed would be a second Lessing or at least a second Vischer . . . Tell me, Franz, if anyone were to look at us now, which of us would seem the more incomprehensible—you or I?"

"It would depend," the other replied with deliberation, "what sort of man it was and whether he set more store by a great career or a good

conscience . . . No, no," he said abruptly, cutting himself short, "not another word about it. It's bad enough when two people, who have been as
fond of one another as we two, fall apart—why should they quarrel on the
top of it? And besides, it would be so pointless. Word of honour, Hans,
why is it you want to talk me over? Isn't it because any person you cannot
captivate is a thorn in your side? It is not purely vanity: it is a characteristic
that goes to the very roots of your nature, and it has its good side. You play
to win, but always in a friendly spirit! You like to push obstacles gently
from your path. And you live up to it; you don't often clear a path for
yourself by a punch in the ribs and I know well that you would never use a
poisoned dagger. A decent fellow, in fact, and why should anyone be
churlish with a fellow like that? It seems to you incredible and—it under-
mines your self-confidence. I agree you wouldn't take it so hardly if I were
someone else; it's our old friendship, I know. But I can't help it. What
drives us apart is, after all, a conflict of principles . . ."

"You're wrong there!" Hans exclaimed. "Principles? I'm every bit as
principled a person as you are. It's the contrast of temperament, of age.
Yes, of age. Don't look at me with such astonishment. I know you're a few
months younger than I am. But that does not alter the fact that you belong
to the old brigade and I to the young. You were an old man at eighteen
and I shall be a boy at eighty! That's the trouble."

The critic shrugged his shoulders. "Possibly," he said. "If it's any comfort
to you . . . and there's a grain of truth in it, I agree . . ."

"No, the whole truth! Young people like me take advantage of the day,
the passing hour; they know instinctively without needing to bother their
heads over it that life is not a preordained whole but made up of days and
hours. Enjoy the day and the day's work; the next day brings other work
and let's hope other joys. In this way we keep responsive, alive, self-reliant,
adventurous. And egoistic, you are saying to yourself, I know. Well, is that
a crime? Not unless one employs poisoned daggers—and you have acquitted me of that. Think first of yourself, that too is part of the gospel of
youth. You throw my career in my teeth—but what right have you? I owe
it to my hard work, my gifts, my personality. As a student I was an ultra-
nationalist. Was I not to be a judge on that account? Is one a better German
if one despairs of Austria or maintains it to be a part of Germany? And
when I became a Minister was I not to carry out my duty? Certainly in
view of today's doings I say good-bye to the hope——"

"—of being a Minister again very soon," Hubmann put in. "However, you
have at last seen to the bottom of the fundamental law of the Imperial and
Royal, Austro-Hungarian pedagogy: The birch for good children and cake
for the naughty ones. That is why you are pleased we are beginning to get
naughty and why you join us. Perhaps that may get you on faster; but once
you are a Minister again you'll soon help make us good again . . ." Hans
was about to flare up in indignation, but Franz went on: "Sorry, but that is

what I think. And it is possible, nay, probable, that you will achieve your aim. I looked in at the office before driving out to Hilmteich. There was a pile of telegrams. All the Vienna morning papers are discussing your presence at yesterday's club meeting and the scene with the superintendent."

The politician had clearly quite got over his annoyance. "In what tone?" he asked hastily.

"Exactly in the tone you meant them to. If even a man like you loses patience, and so on. We can come back by Stempfergasse, where our printing works are, and I'll get you a galley-proof . . . But enough of that, or at least of you. If you must stick to your theme at any cost, you can prove to me that I was always as old as you say. Or I'll do it for you. Certainly I have never been self-assured or adventurous, nor, I think, more egoistic than everyone is bound to be, and if it belongs only to age to see life as a whole and to look to the end in all one does, in a word, to be conscientious, then I agree that I have always been an old man."

"Yes, an old man!" Hans exclaimed. "But it's a thousand pities. There was no need for it and there is still time to alter it. I admit your book on the drama can never now be more than a torso—it is too late now for that. But you could still have a sphere of work worthy of your talents. It's a scandal that you are still the Lessing of Graz, at a farthing a line—why, even as a student you were too good for that. I know that time and time again you need only have said the word to be on a Vienna paper, and each time you refused. But I could never make head or tail of your reasons. 'They want witty causeries in Vienna,' you used to say. 'And I can't do that kind of thing.' Devil take it, if they had only wanted that, they would not have offered you the job. But to come to the point, Franz, you had one genuine reason, though you never mention it, and it is because this no longer stands in your way that I am bringing the matter up again, as I should not otherwise have done. You know I have influence with the Vienna press. Say yes and within six months at longest you're there."

"Thank you, it's very good of you. But it's too late for that too . . . What is the genuine reason you allude to?"

"Well of course—your scruples about your wife. You have been a widower for some months now."

The critic came to a stop and a faint flush tinged his pallid cheeks.

"Yes," he said, looking straight at his friend, "it was that above all. Here she felt fairly happy. At least she had her sister. In Vienna she would have been utterly alone. And also I could not have kept an eye on my two boys in the capital as well as I can here. But, to be honest, it was not merely my scruples on her account and the children's. Here, people by degrees have stopped asking why my wife was never to be seen anywhere, why we had no social life. Everybody knew. And in Vienna all the gossip would start afresh . . . It is not that I have any reason for shame. I can look any man in the face. But all the same it gets on your nerves when you know that the most intimate matters of your life are the subject of ceaseless tittle-tattle . . . But," he added, breathing more freely, "you must not think that I regret having made the poor girl my wife on that account. You were wrong there—you haven't forgotten our talk about it?"

"I should think not! It was twenty-two years ago and on this very spot. But much later in the year, early in August—and in September the wedding took place! How could I fail to remember it? All that a man could do to keep you from it I did . . . ."

"Yes. But fortunately you did not succeed."

"Fortunately?" Hans exclaimed. "You say that still—today? And after confessing a moment ago that it was actually nothing but your marriage that kept you here in a provincial town with no scope for your talents and sunk in petty cares? . . . Pardon me, Franz. Honestly I don't want to hurt you, but it's past my understanding."

"In spite of knowing me so well?" the writer asked. "It is just because I was an 'old man' even in those days and because I found strength to do my duty and because I stuck to it and shall stick to it that I can never regret my decision. On the contrary, if I had followed your advice how miserable I should have been for the rest of my life."

"You mean that she would have destroyed herself? Do you really believe that today? She was not a light girl, I know. But she was a seamstress, her sister was a waitress, her mother a cook and therefore she had the moral outlook of her station on life. She did not kill herself when her first lover, the shoemaker, left her in the lurch and still less would she have done so on your account."

"It was not that I meant. But she was with child by me. And what would have become of my child? That is why I did it. No doubt it would have been better for me if I had never known her. But once it happened I had to pay—thank God, I prevailed on myself to do so. She was a good wife to me; it was fortunate too that she had only boys. They were easier to bring up. But however it had turned out it was lucky for me that I did my duty. Now I have the consolation of being able to say: I have no one on my conscience, no one——"

"Except yourself!"

"Better myself than another."

"Yes, if that were really the question. But it is not! It is not," the politician repeated almost passionately. "If you want to call that sort of thing a sin, where does the sin lie? It lies with Youth. And therefore it is not right that we should atone as grown men with our whole lives. These affairs are best ended in the spirit in which they are begun—the spirit of Youth. What would come of most young people otherwise? Few would ever arrive at having educated wives, and think of all the well-brought-up girls of good family who would never find suitable husbands at all."

"There is a grain of truth in that too," the other replied. "Except that everyone is the keeper of his own conscience. You got away with it and I did not."

"I?" Hans asked with a smile. "So far as I remember I have never spoken to you on the subject. But I don't deny, of course, that I have had troubles of the sort. And once I was very, very near the edge of the precipice."

"I got that impression at the very time we are speaking of," Hubmann said. "Friendship's all very well, but you spoke then with a heart that's only inspired when the cause is one's own! You must have been through it just before?"

"At that very time," Hans replied.

For some moments they said no more. They climbed in silence to the top of the Rosenberg. What in their young days had been a narrow, stony path was now a well-kept road, with pretty villas on either side, but the same beeches and pines still rose from the steep hillside, and over their tops the same lovely and luxuriant landscape still met the eye. The old grey town with its medley of tall gables and towers, from which rose the massive tower-crowned fortress of the Schlossberg, was at their feet, its crag circled by the broad green ribbon of the swift Mur; but stretching far beyond it on every side as far as the eye could see, bathed in a sea of light, were the white villas of the modern town, their gardens veiled in green and bluish haze and, like a wreath flung around them, the gold of the ripening fields of corn. There are many landscapes of more striking and compelling beauty, but few that have such a gentle and soothing charm.

They surveyed the scene in silence and when they came to an old and spreading oak, past which a path wound its way to the bottom, they stopped by common consent and sat on the tree's mossy roots.

"It was here," Hans said. "Our friendship's oak—you remember, how they used to tease us about it. But all the same we chose the loveliest spot." His eyes lit up as they swept the horizon. "How lovely it is . . ."

Hubmann nodded sadly. "Lovely as on the first of days," he quoted. "And the sight gives one strength too. How often have I climbed up to this spot in bitterness of heart and then taken the path back into my life, my grief assuaged . . ."

He looked out across the country. On the far side of the Mur a black serpent slowly wound its way from a group of white, shimmering masonry and then sped ever faster through the deep green of the meadows, until it was lost to sight behind the sunlit rocks of Gösting. "That," he said pointing, "didn't make it any easier for me." And he smiled sadly.

"The train to Vienna?" Hans cried out. "It shan't worry us today! Later, some other time, not today. Come on! We're having a holiday . . . today we're young again."

Hubmann glanced at his friend. He saw his handsome, vivacious face, his sparkling eyes and slim, athletic figure. "You have never been anything else," he said with a smile, and in his glance there flickered a gleam of the tenderness which used once to light his face as he looked at this magnificent young fellow who was his dearest friend. "Inside and out."

"Outside because inside," the politician said smiling. "Franz, old boy, if only you would take a leaf from my book even now. You've no idea how jolly and how sensible it is to be young, and how beautiful. Yes, beautiful, Franz. That should count for something with you. You who are an aesthete by profession." And when Franz looked questioningly at him, he added: "I'm thinking of the story we touched on just now."

"I don't know it, you see," Hubmann answered. "But was the end beautiful too?"

"Perhaps! Only you must see the end in the right perspective and look back on it from today. From that point of view it is even instructive as well. But I don't tell you the story for that reason, but because old times come back so clearly to me today. I'd like to talk of them . . ."

And he began:

"Well, it was at the very time when you were plumbing the depths of joy and sorrow with Kathi. That winter, my seventh term, I had more than my fill of work and pleasure, though, as you know, I was always a glutton for both. I was president of the Students' Society, 'spokesman' of the 'Germania,' tutor in Baron Walchberg's family, in demand at every ball, not to mention five lectures daily and the—Cornaro. You haven't forgotten her? Therese Cornaro, née Schlögelmaier, from Munich, second lady at the Thalia Theatre. You always hauled her over the coals unmercifully. She was a charming girl all the same and a decent girl too in her way —for what could I, a poor student, offer her? It was just as well for both of us when she got an engagement at Prague for Easter, and when that was fixed up I made a clean sweep of everything else that could get in my way. I slipped all bonds, onerous and honourable, gave up my job with Walchberg, came down on my uncle, the inn-keeper at Dollach, for a loan of two hundred florins and made up my mind to swot, till I couldn't see, from the spring until the autumn. For I had the second civil service examination to take in August, the third in October and both with honours; that too was essential. I knew very well it wasn't of great importance to my future career—Good Lord, what did I care? If I had played a leading part in University life and was looked on as a promising fellow, it had precious little to do with the examinations I had passed! But it was, so to say, part of my programme and so it had to be . . ."

Hubmann smiled. "So this was the young fellow who lived only for the day," he said with kindly raillery. "But I know what you would say in reply to that—forgive my interruption. And so you moved into that garden pavilion in the Heinrichstrasse and buried yourself in your books. I remember. It was nothing but a cabin, but its bulging sides were wreathed in ivy, and all round there was a large, half-derelict garden. It was quite poetical . . ."

"It was. But that was not why I chose it, but because it gave me exactly what I wanted—silence and seclusion. The gardener had once inhabited it, but now the old couple in the big house let their grounds run wild; meanwhile they were glad enough of the few coppers of rent. I dug myself in there and for some weeks I didn't see a soul except the old woman who tidied up my den for me in the mornings. It was a bit dreary when it rained, I grant, but all the more beautiful when the sun shone again. Through all the windows the limes besieged me with their blossoming branches and I sat embowered in light and scent and the songs of birds; if I chose to go out there was beauty at every turn—everywhere trees were in blossom and the neglected flowers pushed up their blooms through rank grass and bushes. In spite of the staid law book in my hand, which I memorised aloud, I often felt I was the victim of enchantment in that luxuriant wilderness, stretching on apparently without end. For though a low hedge bounded my domain at no great distance from my cabin, another garden began on the other side which also seemed to be in a state of dereliction—a pathless tangle of trees and weeds with a pile of tree trunks here and there. And now and then I heard the grating sounds of plane and saw. A carpenter's shop, apparently; but naturally I did not think twice about it."

Hubmann's features came to life.

"A carpenter's shop?" he muttered and then nodded to himself as his habit was when anything became clear to him. And he listened more attentively than before.

Hans did not notice anything.

"But that was not for long," he went on. "I soon became very inquisitive about my neighbours. Between my cabin and the hedge there was a tall rose bush in full bloom. One day, when I came back from my midday meal, I noticed at once that a whole lot of roses had only just been picked, and the tall grass was freshly trodden in a track leading to the hedge. I followed it and found a piece of white cotton with blue spots caught on one of the thorn bushes. 'Serves you right, you little thief!' I thought, laughing to myself. Next day the bush was plundered once more—and a long, silken, auburn hair glistened in the sunshine on one of the bluish green branches. I carefully released it, wound it round my finger and put the little curly ring of hair between the pages of a book. That ought to have been the end of it and yet, naturally, it was not, for I thought more about the hair than I did about my law books. And next day as I sat over my meal I was suddenly seized by the longing to catch the marauder red-handed. I hastened home hot foot and then cautiously approached my cabin under cover of the ditch. I had a suspicion, an inkling, that she couldn't help being young and pretty.

"And—how pretty she was! A lovely, slender girl of eighteen or so. Her white cotton dress with the blue spots proudly revealed the ripened charms of her buxom figure, her face was soft and merry, her lips full and her clear, grey eyes drooped as though the crown of auburn hair rested too heavily upon them. I could see her clearly, for she was standing at the open window, intent on turning the pages of my photograph album, which she had taken from the table close by. I was about ten paces from her and my aim now was to creep silently round the building so as to get between her and the hedge and cut off her retreat. But I trod on a twig and the sound betrayed me. She looked up, flushed as crimson as the bunch of roses she had laid down beside her and in a trice she was over the hedge. I was close on her heels. Her foot caught in the creepers twining in the hedge and the next moment I had my arms around her and, lifting her face to mine, I kissed her soft lips. She lay pale and helpless in my arms, making no resistance, and then uttered a low cry and ran away.

"I pursued her, but after a little while I stopped and finally turned round. No, it was scarcely suitable for a student of law to run after the carpenter's daughter and perhaps end by running into the arms of the carpenter's apprentices. So I contented myself with the spoil which this time too had been left on the field of battle—a shoe caught in the creepers. It was not so very small and it was made of stout leather and yet it seemed to me one of the prettiest shoes I had ever seen. But after I had gazed at it for full five minutes I lectured myself sternly for another five and then sat down to my books.

"It was not till evening that I inspected the shoe again. 'Anyway, you'll have to give it back to her,' I told myself hypocritically and I jumped over into the neighbouring garden. I wound my way through a maze of weeds and vegetable plots, of bushes, tree trunks and open sheds, in which hardwood for cabinet-making was stored, and slowly approached the house. It was a long, low building and the space in front was obviously used as a workshop: there were benches and saws and great stacks of planks. The day's work was done, no one was to be seen—what was I to do now? Next I heard a brief and muttered mumble from a window and then the clatter of spoons on plates. The old boy had just said grace and now they were busy with their soup. It was odd that a man who came with such honest intent should find his heart beating so hard, and now—I crept silently round the house. There too was a joiner's yard, enclosed by a wooden railing with a massive gate in the middle, opening on a road which so far had no other houses in it. There was a sign board over the gate, but perhaps I ought not to mention the name——"

Hubmann made as though to speak, but then went on listening in silence.

"I stood in the road for a time looking at the house from the front as well. The shoe was all the while in my breast pocket, and by degrees it dawned on me what a fool I was making of myself. I quickly walked away as the door of the house opened and some of the carpenters with pipes or cigars in their mouths emerged on to the space in front of it. I had never been along that road before, but Heinrichstrasse, where I lived, was close by and so I never doubted that I would soon find out where I was, in spite of the pitch darkness. But the road got narrower and rougher until it dwindled to a narrow path between hedges and ended at a garden gate. So there I was in the pitch-black night and the deathly silence. There was nothing for it but to return to the carpenter's house: it was bound to have some other approach. But now when I began retracing my steps I saw for the first time that the path forked; I took the broader of the two but soon found my way barred once more by a locked gate. This game was played on me several times before I finally arrived at the house again.

"As I approached it three shadowy figures came walking slowly along the road, two women and a man; I heard their voices long before I could see them. 'Yes, yes, Fräulein Mariechen,' I heard an oily voice say in Saxon dialect, 'there's more education among us at home, believe me. More civilised. That's what it is. In Chemnitz, Saxony, my native place, this lane would long since have been lighted by gas.' In reply a girlish voice giggled: 'Then what d'you stay here for, Herr Gottfried, if everything there's so much more nicer?' 'Now, Mizzerl,' said a deep woman's voice in protest. 'How can you talk like that? You're very pleased, very pleased indeed that Herr Gottfried is here.' There was no reply and then the Saxon's voice: 'Certainly she's pleased, Frau——' (the name he called her by was not the name on the sign board) 'You can't believe all a girl says! We'll talk about that tomorrow!' He laughed smugly. 'If the ladies have no objection'—and he lit the stump of his cigar. By the light of the match I saw what I had already guessed—it was my blonde arm in arm with a stout elderly woman and a tall, black-bearded fellow . . . You can imagine how I dressed myself down when at last, quite tired out, I got back to my room. But next morning . . ."

Hubmann raised his hand. "It's really more candid to tell you, Hans. The Saxon called the girl's aunt Frau Maschinger. And the name on the sign board was Hans Gassner . . ."

"Oh, do you know the people?" Hans said with indifference. "That's not very surprising. And it's of no consequence. Your discretion can be relied upon by all concerned. But you don't know what followed?"

"No."

"Well," Hans resumed, "next morning my feelings about the situation altered once more, owing to a conversation I had with my old servant. I had hidden the shoe in a drawer, but the fading bunch of roses was still on the window ledge and the old woman at once asked whether it was Mizzi who had left it there. I shrugged my shoulders and said I didn't know, and who was Mizzi? Oh, she said, she was the carpenter's daughter from over there, a regular tomboy, but a sweet dear girl and a favourite with everybody; and the lady of the house had given her permission to pick as many flowers in the garden as she liked. 'But fancy,' the old lady went on, 'the poor dear's having any heart for such things now!' For in spite of all she could say or do she had to marry her father's foreman, Herr Kretschmar. 'A horrible Prussian, a Lutheran, a scarecrow, who's never done droning on in that outlandish jargon of his.' Her father would have it. He was quite in love with the 'nasty fellow,' though no one could understand it, and her mother, who would have stuck up for her child, had died long since and her aunt, Frau Maschinger, took the suitor's part. So the poor creature had at last given in and today or next day would see the betrothal. When I heard this, pity crowded out all other feelings. And what business was it of mine, quite apart from having my hands full with the examination ahead of me . . . . Before going out to my midday meal I hung the shoe on the hedge with a fresh bunch of roses beside it and a note: 'I am never in between twelve and two.' That day I purposely stayed out even longer.

"In the meantime she recovered her property. And when, to make up for lost time, I was sitting that night over my books, I heard cheering and singing through the still night air: they were celebrating the betrothal. I shut the windows. 'That's the end of that,' I thought and sat down again at my desk. But of course it was only the beginning. Next morning my old lady began telling me all about the betrothal as soon as she entered the room. She had been there and so had all the neighbours. The bride-to-be, she said, had been very quiet, but all the same not so down-hearted as they had expected her to be. 'The little feather-brain,' she went on with her account, 'she little knows what it is to be married!' Only, when 'the Prussian' made tender advances, she always put him off. 'But, trust me, sir,' the old lady assured me artlessly, 'a bride can only do that when others are by.'

"But then she shook her finger threateningly at me and said I was a soapy Sam. Why had I pretended yesterday that I didn't know who Mizzi was and now she had a message of thanks to give me from her. 'What for?' I asked. Because I had let her know when I went out; for the garden, she had said, was the only joy left her now, and yet she did not want to disturb me. And then Mizzi had gone on to ask a question, but I didn't deserve to hear what it was. What was it, I asked. Oh, whether all the pretty girls in my album were old sweethearts of mine. And whether I had one at present. The old lady had come to my defence and said that I lived like a hermit and thought of nothing but my books.

"You can imagine the effect all this had on me. It's true I went out on the stroke of twelve, but I gathered a bunch of roses and tied a note to it, on which I wrote: 'Congratulations,' and put it on the window sill. I found the answer when I came in. 'Thank you'—written on a page torn from my notebook. But there were two others lying torn up in front of the window and I picked them up and pieced them together. First she had written: 'Why do you make fun of me?' and then: 'I thank you, but only for the flowers,' before at last she decided on her final, harmless reply. Poor girl— I felt so sorry for her . . ."

"And she was so pretty," Hubmann interposed, "and had such kissable lips."

"True—there was that too, or, if you like, that above all. And for that reason my reading next day took a back seat. Naturally she had to have her roses and her note that day as well, but what was my message to be? I wasted half the pages of my notebook, but I could not hit on anything that seemed to me to meet the case. But when midday came, it occurred to me: why write when I can deliver my message by word of mouth? I went to the window that looked out on to the hedge and peeped across. I had not long to wait. It had hardly gone twelve when her golden head emerged from the thickets. She wore a green dress that day and it made her lovely face seem doubly lovely. My heart pounded and when she sprang over the hedge and showed her ankle the blood rushed into my face. For a moment she stood listening and then walked up to the window, peered in and then —her eyes met mine. She started back and tried to escape, but I was already outside and grasping her by the hand. 'Dear Fräulein Mizzi,' I implored, 'you can't treat me like that. And I promise to be as good as gold.' At that she grew calmer and I kept my promise, too. We went to pick her roses together and talked of nothing but the roses and other harmless things; not a word of her engagement. If only there had not been those long pauses, when embarrassment made us silent while we stole glances at one another. At last, we laughed outright and the spell was broken. We talked about the loss of her shoe. 'Oh, how terrified I was,' she told me. 'And then that night—I was just helping out the soup—and there I saw you outside. And then afterwards, when you passed us in the dark—Jesus Maria, I said to myself, if he gives me back my shoe in front of my aunt I'll sink through the ground . . . You must never do that again,' she concluded. 'What?'—'Come across or go past our house.'—'I promise that and very gladly,' I said, 'if you will come here every day!'—'But you wrote . . .'— 'Well then, I'll be out as I said.' She burst out laughing. 'We shall see!' and still laughing she gave me her hand.

"So you see, Franz, that was not so very compromising and during the following days too not a word passed between us which Herr Gottfried Kretschmar need have been pained to hear, though I won't say the same for the looks we exchanged. We only mentioned him once or twice and I could tell that the man was really repulsive to her, if only because everything about him was strange and chilling—his religion, his way of speaking, his boasted 'civilisation,' his arrogant nature. She told me that, since he had taken up his quarters with them a year and a half before, he had greatly increased the turnover of the business; he had started a furniture store and set the firm on to copying old furniture and for this reason her father had given in to him when he threatened to go elsewhere unless he married into the firm. And her aunt Anna, her father's sister, was on his side because she had a stake in the business. 'What could I do?' she sobbed. 'I am only one against them all.' I said nothing to this, for I was resolved not to utter a word of consolation that might have raised hopes which could never be fulfilled. But even apart from that I can take credit for having kept a tight rein on myself, bitter as it was to me, for she was so lovely and I could see how blindly and passionately in love with me she was. Yet I never touched her lips again and scarcely even her hand. I admit I ought to have torn myself away and left my retreat, but that was beyond me. The times when I looked into her face and listened to her merry prattle were very dear to me. They were the poetry of days otherwise barren of enjoyment and given up to hard work. She had little education and was not even particularly intelligent, but 'such a sweet dear girl'—I can find no more apt description of her than those words of my old servant's: she was a perfect specimen of our race, innocent and pleasure-loving, merry and good. And—young, so young, young as I was. She did not ask what was to come of it; and how could I be so cruel as to snatch from her the only pleasure she had in all her sorrow? All I had to do was to see that she did not pay bitterly in the end for this transient happiness and I thought I could answer for that. Did I ask too much of myself? Even today I think not. It went on for two weeks at least. But they got on our tracks and separated us and then, when we got together again——"

He stopped and breathed more heavily.

"The old story," Hubmann said. "And yet—was it not their duty to separate you? . . . Her aunt no doubt interfered?"

"No, the bridegroom himself. One day he spied on us from behind the hedge. He did not overhear anything so very bad. She was seated on the window sill, hearing me from my notebooks and playing all sorts of harmless pranks in between. All the same he naturally didn't like it. 'Enough of that, Marie!' he suddenly shouted, trembling with rage. 'You can come along with me now.' She gave a terrible start and I started too. 'Don't shout at the young lady like that,' I told him when I had recovered myself. The lean fellow clenched his fists and started to clamber over the hedge and come for me. Then he controlled himself. 'She is my bride, Herr Studiosus,' he said, 'if you really do not know that already. Now then, are you coming?' he said to her. She followed him. And for several days I heard and saw nothing more of her—hideous days of vacancy which made me realise for the first time how dear she was to me. The old lady, when I asked her, could only tell me that a strict watch was kept on her. 'God knows what for,' she added to tease me. And next morning—it was the last week of May—my landlord called to ask whether I would have the kindness to leave immediately. His neighbour Gassner was complaining that I was running after his daughter. 'That is not true.' The old gentleman gave me a searching look. 'When term is up at the end of July you will have to leave in any case. I've promised him not to renew your tenancy. But it depends on your answer to one question whether you go at once. You are a man of honour and I—can hold my tongue. Can you give me your word that nothing serious has happened between the girl and you?'

"'I give you my word.'

"'Then you can stay on till the end of July.'

"That very night it would have been too late to give him this assurance. In spite of the time of year it was a sultry evening. I came home at about ten and lit my lamp, meaning to work. But I could not. The heaviness in the air made me restless and I couldn't get the girl out of my head. I went out into the garden and walked up and down. But this only increased my restlessness. The fragrance of the flowers, the fresh pungent scent of new-mown hay from the fields near by and the smell of the spring earth made my pulses beat and my nerves tingle. And all the while there was only one vision before my eyes—I saw her walking to and fro in her dark bedroom just as I was doing there in the garden, leaning out and listening to the darkness and longing for me as I longed for her . . .

"I resisted for a moment more and then I could resist no longer. An irresistible force drew me to her. I did not want to. I had to.

"I sprang over the hedge and crept softly on in the darkness, cautiously step by step. Even so, I collided with a shed one moment and bumped my head against a branch the next. At intervals I stopped to listen. Every breath of wind in the leaves, all the soft mysterious voices of the night, indistinguishable and yet so distinctly heard, made me tremble. It was not coward-ice, but my blood and my nerves obeyed me no longer; they had their own way with me. And not once but a dozen times, as I stood still and listened, I thought I heard soft footsteps coming to meet me. It was an illusion—but now—not now. I bent forward and peered and listened with all my senses taut . . . there was a light footfall on the grass and then again—a sigh, audible, unmistakable—someone was coming towards me, not straight for me but nearer and nearer in my direction. And now I heard her voice: 'Hans!' . . . Next moment we lay in each other's arms, our mouths pressed together as if we must melt in one another and could not be released as long as there was breath in our bodies . . . She had got out of the window of her room at the very moment when I vaulted the hedge . . .'

He stopped and turning away his face sighed deeply and resumed only after a long silence.

"What else is there to say? That was our life for weeks after. They kept watch over her by day and as soon as they were asleep she came to me . . . That spring must have been for both of us the wildest, sweetest time of our lives. And for her it was that and nothing else; she asked no questions, knew no dread, made no resistance—not a thought for the morrow dimmed the happiness of the passing days. I know it because not a corner of her soul was hidden from me. And if you choose to call it debauch, it would merely be a quibble, for even debauch like that is happiness . . .

"But for me, at least at moments, it was an agonising time as well. A man cannot drown his cares in bliss as a woman can, and besides I was not an innocent child as she was. I knew something of life . . . But still I will not make myself out better than I am; even I felt such scruples rarely. I lived as she did—from one moment of joy to the next. Let the future bring what it liked—the passing moment was beautiful. For I was young, so young, never younger than in those days of spring . . .

"It was not until the middle of July that anxiety and remorse descended in an avalanche and threatened to overwhelm me. I learnt at one blow that the marriage was to take place in August and also that she was with child by me. And as soon as she knew this she asked—her very heart cried aloud: 'What now? What now?'

"For me too, Franz, it was a frightful time. Even you have not suffered a pang of conflict and agony that I too have not suffered. And perhaps in spite of the difference of age—to return to that—my suffering might have come down as heavily on my head. Might have—for my case turned out otherwise than yours.

"Well, in spite of all I came to a different decision. I could not pay with my whole life. Even my love and my pity for the girl could not persuade me to do so. She herself made no supplications, no reproaches. She loved me too much for that. 'After all, you made me no promises,' she said over and over again. And it was a mercy for us both that she did love me so much. I shall never forget our last night, the night of the 30th of July, 1876. She told me that she was going to kill herself and was only dissuaded when I swore that I would follow her to the grave the very hour I heard of her fate. This induced her to live and be the wife of Gottfried Kretschmar. By a strange coincidence the wedding took place on the very day when I took my examination. And in fact with honours . . .

"Well, that is my story, Franz. And now let us go."

They walked on along the summit of the Rosenberg. Hubmann was very grave. He walked slowly with head bent, as though a load weighed him down. He stopped at the point where Charlottendorfgasse turns to the left to lead down to the town.

"You have something else to ask?" the politician said. "You want to know why even today I feel I did the right thing?"

"No! . . . What is the use of talking any more about it now?"

"Of course. Because the answer is obvious. Suppose that I, twenty-three years old and still a student, had married Mizzi Gassner, what would I be today? At best, at the very best, a district judge at Knittelfeld or Marau. Even that is unlikely. It is much more likely that a man who had had a child a few months after his marriage would have been advised to take to some other career than that of a judge. That would have meant sheer poverty, for I am as unsuited to be a solicitor as any man could be—in all that I can and cannot do. Don't you agree?"

Franz shrugged his shoulders. "Possibly! How do I know?"

"But suppose I had become a district judge at Marau. Could you imagine a more appalling fate for a man whose strongest motive is ambition? And how could I in my misery have made my wife happy when it would have been for her sake that I had submitted to that frightful fate? She would have been made doubly unhappy on that very account whenever she said to herself: 'What might not the man you love have been—but for you?' That is the point. My decision has given me a happy life and she has at least been no unhappier than she would have been as my wife. Certainly no unhappier, and just because she loved me and whatever her fate as Kretschmar's wife has been. But I have no reason to believe that her fate has been a hard one. He was—no doubt he still is—a man of her station in life and he owes his prosperity to her. That counts for a lot."

Hubmann sighed deeply. "There is a great deal to be said on the other side," he said slowly, as though each word cost him an effort. "But not another syllable . . . You did the right thing according to your lights and you can even see a good example for others in your story. You even see beauty in it all, even in the end . . ."

"Certainly," the politician put in. "When one looks back on it today. I tell you it was the wildest, sweetest time of my life. How could it fail to have beauty when I look back on it? And as for the end, in spite of all conflicts and tortures, is it not more beautiful than if we had lived as two slaves shackled by the same chain, toiling and panting on our dusty way? And what I say of myself is true word for word of her——"

Hubmann had gone pale; the hand he raised in deprecation trembled. "Don't speak of her," he said in a dull and menacing tone.

"Why not?" Hans asked, though he too blanched for a moment.

"Because you know nothing about her," was the answer. "And you shall learn nothing from me."

"I don't know what you mean," Hans said. "Is it to spare me? I am not so weak as that. However bad it is I would rather hear it from a friend than from strangers. If you won't tell me I will find out from someone else, today even. It is my duty. Perhaps I could be of some help."

"No," Hubmann said. "Help has come to her."

"Is she dead?"

The critic nodded. "Seventeen years ago. After my marriage I lived in the house next door. Körblergasse, that lane is called now. That is how I came to know her and her story. Only in outline, of course; not the details. I never dreamt you had played any part in it. She never mentioned your name."

The politician was deeply moved. His eyes filled with tears. "Dead—so long ago!" he said. "Dead—so young—that lovely radiant creature . . . But"—a stab of anguish made his voice quiver and he seized his friend's arm—"you should not have thought of keeping it from me. What did she die of?"

"Consumption was entered on the death certificate . . . But her death was due to the cruelties inflicted by her husband. Naturally he soon discovered, even before the boy was born, that she had deceived him. As long as old Gassner and Frau Maschinger were alive he choked back his rancour and treated the woman fairly well. But when the old people died, one soon after the other, he took his revenge. He was a brutal, spiteful fellow, but one must remember what rankled in him. Moreover, the boy was the only child. The thought of this boy being the heir to the fruits of all his labours turned him into a drunkard and a spendthrift. Shortly after his wife's death he had to sell the business and he died in poverty. We must not forget that he was once a capable man, who was ruined by this affair, although nothing could excuse the way he treated her. It was horrible— as I can testify. Don't ask me, Hans—it was horrible . . . One bitter winter night when he was drunk he threw her out of the house. She took refuge with us, but she had caught her death of cold . . . And well it was for her! A few weeks later she was dead . . ."

The politician sank on to a bench by the roadside. His head hung low and he was white to the lips. "And I let her be murdered . . ." he muttered. "But I did not know—how could I ever have imagined—— In the early days I made enquiries about her, cautiously and at third hand, and the news was always good. Then I heard that it was a fine strong boy and that they had called him Hans; the name struck me, but it was his grandfather's name too. That was the last I heard; true, I have made no enquiries since . . . I feel bitter remorse now, but I am not so terribly to blame . . . Or am I, Franz?"

Hubmann turned away. He made no reply.

"But consider it," the other said in self-defence. "I was far away in a life of my own . . . I lived in Vienna and was married by that time . . . besides, in spite of all precautions, enquiries were dangerous . . . But, my God!" He broke off suddenly and jumped up. "If the mother is dead, what has become of the boy?"

At this Hubmann turned round again and his eyes blazed with pain and anger.

"At last!" he groaned hoarsely. "At last you ask that . . . And that was the first, the very first thought you should have had . . . That question would have come in well even in the middle of your instructive tale, when I told you I knew the people. Or, at the very least, after you had pointed out to me what a beautiful story it was . . . Your marriage has been childless."

The politician stood before the indignant man as a broken sinner. "I have no children," he murmured. "Not from any other love affair either . . . You are right. Hans Kretschmar . . ."

"Is your only child. And so you have not troubled about him all these years and now you ask about him casually as an afterthought!"

Hans wiped the sweat of agony from his brow. "You are right . . ." he said again. "But now have pity and tell me: is he alive?"

"Yes."

"Here in Graz?"

"Yes."

"And has he grown up to be a useful member of society?"

"No."

Hans swayed. "Not a criminal?"

"No."

"What is wrong with him then?"

Hubmann fought hard with himself; abruptly, for the second time that day, he opened his lips and shut them tight.

At last he made up his mind.

"That you shall never know from me," he said. "If you could mitigate his lot I would tell you. But neither you nor anyone else can do that. So why should I tell you? I am not your judge, Hans. Your judge is your conscience —Nemesis. I know her. I have heard her voice all my life and he who knows and fears her dare not presume to usurp her office. For that reason I did not mean to tell you anything at all, not even about the mother. You got that much out of me, but about your son I keep silence. Come!"

Hans looked at him and said no more. He knew that this time it was useless to question him further.

In silence they descended Charlottengasse; it was a new road, which Hans had not seen before. Nor had he seen the next one on the right, into which Franz now turned. He saw "Körblergasse" on the corner house and stopped. That was the road then. "Is the house no longer standing?"

Franz was by this time ten paces ahead of him. When Hans called to him and repeated his question he only said:

"Come along! This is the way into the town."

Hans looked round about him and then across at the Schlossberg and soon got his bearings. "No," he said in surprise. "We must turn left down Körblergasse."

Franz stopped, hesitated for a moment and then turned round.

"Where were you off to?" Hans asked him in astonishment when he came up, but a look in his face made the words die on his lips . . . He shuddered: his heart began to beat wildly in agonised apprehension.

Slowly without a word, without a glance at one another, they walked along the dusty road, while Hans looked about him to right and left.

At last he found what he was seeking.

"Here——" he muttered and stood still. "It was here . . . But the house is new . . ."

They came to a stop in front of a three-storeyed workshop separated from the road by a large yard; smoke rose from the chimney of the machine shed. On the sign board over the gateway was to be seen:

Mathias Nabenlecher & Company,
late Hans Gassner & Kretschmar.
Furniture Manufacturers.

"It has all changed," Hans said, "even the caretaker's cottage is new."

He made one step towards the entrance. Involuntarily Hubmann put out his hand to hold him back. Then he let it fall. Fool that I am, he thought. She will have her way when her moment has come. No one can gainsay her.

Hans by this time was in the yard close to the caretaker's cottage. A large watch-dog lying on the ground before his kennel raised his head, growled and barked. At the same moment his bark was repeated by a human throat. A cripple tottered out of the door of the cottage. He was a wretched, hideous and deformed creature—obviously an idiot, a loony—with a pipe in his mouth.

"Bow-wow!" he said to the intruder and then grinned in a friendly way and held out his hand.

"Give us a copper or two for tobacco——"

Hans looked away in disgust as he took out his purse. But the wretched youth had now caught sight of Hubmann and staggered gleefully up to him.

"Uncle Franz!" he stuttered. "You'll give me something for tobacco . . . Hans has been a good boy, Uncle Franz."

"Begging again?" the old white-bearded caretaker called out from the cottage door. But then he caught sight of Hans and hurried towards him. "Jesus! Is the gentleman bad?" And he laid his hand on the arm of the tottering man, whose face was as white as chalk and contorted as though by a frightful access of pain.

It was some minutes before the cab, which the obliging caretaker had sent for, arrived.

"To the Elephant Hotel," Franz told the driver, but Hans said, "No! Through the suburbs! Where you like, but in the open. I should suffocate in a room," he said to Franz.

When the cab started he clasped his friend's hand.

"Good God," he said, "it was a healthy child . . . Did Kretschmar hit him on the head?"

"He threw him downstairs," was the reply. "The child was three years old then. But now pull yourself together, Hans. You must not give way. There's nothing to be done now. . . ."

"Very little," the politician admitted with trembling lips. "Naturally, I'll have him put into an asylum where he can be properly fed and clothed."

"As you think best," Franz replied. "I don't advise it. Here he has the sur-

roundings he likes and is used to. Those people, too, are kind to him.
Otherwise, why should they have kept him when the factory passed into
other hands . . . One hears various accounts of asylums. Not always good.
Anyway, you can think that over."

These were the last words that passed between them for a long time.
The cab trundled through the suburbs to the town, taking the direction of
Stiftungsthal. Thus they passed Hilmgasse once more, where two hours
before they had begun their talk. Then Hans grasped his friend's hand.

"You were right—I envy you."

Franz silently pressed his hand.

They now made a wide circle out of Stiftungsthal and round towards the
town. By the time they passed the town park, which was crowded with
people taking a walk, Hans had recovered sufficiently to sit upright and to
acknowledge all the salutations with his characteristic affability. He might
just as well have held his hat in his hand the whole time. Many who did
not know him personally greeted the man whose name that day was on all
lips.

As they drove along Herrengasse he called out to the coachman to go by
Stempfergasse. "You were going to get those galleys for me," he said. . . .

MARKHEIM

Robert Louis Stevenson
(1850–1894)

Y ES," SAID THE DEALER, "our windfalls are of various kinds. Some customers
are ignorant, and then I touch a dividend of my superior knowledge. Some
are dishonest," and here he held up the candle, so that the light fell strongly
on his visitor, "and in that case," he continued, "I profit by my virtue."

Markheim had but just entered from the daylight streets, and his eyes
had not yet grown familiar with the mingled shine and darkness in the
shop. At these pointed words, and before the near presence of the flame, he
blinked painfully and looked aside.

The dealer chuckled. "You come to me on Christmas Day," he resumed,
"when you know that I am alone in my house, put up my shutters, and
make a point of refusing business. Well, you will have to pay for that; you
will have to pay for my loss of time, when I should be balancing my books;
you will have to pay, for a kind of manner that I remark in you to-day very

strongly. I am the essence of discretion, and ask no awkward questions; but when a customer cannot look me in the eye, he has to pay for it." The dealer once more chuckled; and then, changing to his usual business voice, though still with a note of irony, "You can give, as usual, a clear account of how you came into the possession of the object?" he continued. "Still your uncle's cabinet? A remarkable collector, sir!"

And the little pale, round-shouldered dealer stood almost on tiptoe, looking over the top of his gold spectacles, and nodding his head with every mark of disbelief. Markheim returned his gaze with one of infinite pity, and a touch of horror.

"This time," said he, "you are in error. I have not come to sell, but to buy. I have no curios to dispose of; my uncle's cabinet is bare to the wainscot; even were it still intact, I have done well on the Stock Exchange, and should more likely add to it than otherwise, and my errand to-day is simplicity itself. I seek a Christmas present for a lady," he continued, waxing more fluent as he struck into the speech he had prepared; "and certainly I owe you every excuse for thus disturbing you upon so small a matter. But the thing was neglected yesterday; I must produce my little compliment at dinner; and, as you very well know, a rich marriage is not a thing to be neglected."

There followed a pause, during which the dealer seemed to weigh this statement incredulously. The ticking of many clocks among the curious lumber of the shop, and the faint rushing of the cabs in a rear thoroughfare, filled up the interval of silence.

"Well, sir," said the dealer, "be it so. You are an old customer after all; and if, as you say, you have the chance of a good marriage, far be it from me to be an obstacle.—Here is a nice thing for a lady now," he went on, "this hand glass—fifteenth century, warranted; comes from a good collection, too; but I reserve the name, in the interests of my customer, who was just like yourself, my dear sir, the nephew and sole heir of a remarkable collector."

The dealer, while he thus ran on in his dry and biting voice, had stooped to take the object from its place; and, as he had done so, a shock had passed through Markheim, a start both of hand and foot, a sudden leap of many tumultuous passions to the face. It passed as swiftly as it came, and left no trace beyond a certain trembling of the hand that now received the glass.

"A glass," he said hoarsely, and then paused, and repeated it more clearly. "A glass? For Christmas? Surely not?"

"And why not?" cried the dealer. "Why not a glass?"

Markheim was looking upon him with an indefinable expression. "You ask me why not?" he said. "Why, look here—look in it—look at yourself! Do you like to see it? No! nor I—nor any man."

The little man had jumped back when Markheim had so suddenly confronted him with the mirror; but now, perceiving there was nothing worse on hand, he chuckled. "Your future lady, sir, must be pretty hard-favoured," said he.

"I ask you," said Markheim, "for a Christmas present, and you give me this—this damned reminder of years, and sins and follies—this hand-conscience! Did you mean it? Had you a thought in your mind? Tell me. It will be better for you if you do. Come, tell me about yourself. I hazard a guess now, that you are in secret a very charitable man?"

The dealer looked closely at his companion. It was very odd, Markheim did not appear to be laughing; there was something in his face like an eager sparkle of hope, but nothing of mirth.

"What are you driving at?" the dealer asked.

"Not charitable?" returned the other, gloomily. "Not charitable; not pious; not scrupulous; unloving, unbeloved; a hand to get money, a safe to keep it. Is that all? Dear God, man, is that all?"

"I will tell you what it is," began the dealer, with some sharpness, and then broke off again into a chuckle. "But I see this is a love-match of yours, and you have been drinking the lady's health."

"Ah!" cried Markheim, with a strange curiosity. "Ah, have you been in love? Tell me about that."

"I," cried the dealer. "I in love! I never had the time, nor have I the time to-day for all this nonsense. Will you take the glass?"

"Where is the hurry?" returned Markheim. "It is very pleasant to stand here talking; and life is so short and insecure that I would not hurry away from any pleasure—no, not even from so mild a one as this. We should rather cling, cling to what little we can get, like a man at a cliff's edge. Every second is a cliff, if you think about it—a cliff a mile high—high enough, if we fall, to dash us out of every feature of humanity. Hence it is best to talk pleasantly. Let us talk of each other; why should we wear this mask? Let us be confidential. Who knows we might become friends?"

"I have just one word to say to you," said the dealer. "Either make your purchase, or walk out of my shop."

"True, true," said Markheim. "Enough fooling. To business. Show me something else."

The dealer stooped once more, this time to replace the glass upon the shelf, his thin blond hair falling over his eyes as he did so. Markheim moved a little nearer, with one hand in the pocket of his great-coat; he drew himself up and filled his lungs; at the same time many different emotions were depicted together on his face—terror, horror, and resolve, fascination and a physical repulsion; and through a haggard lift of his upper lip, his teeth looked out.

"This, perhaps, may suit," observed the dealer; and then, as he began to re-arise, Markheim bounded from behind upon his victim. The long, skewer-like dagger flashed and fell. The dealer struggled like a hen, striking his temple on the shelf, and then tumbled on the floor in a heap.

Time had some score of small voices in that shop, some stately and slow as was becoming to their great age; others garrulous and hurried. All these told out the seconds in an intricate chorus of tickings. Then the passage of a lad's feet, heavily running on the pavement, broke in upon these smaller voices and startled Markheim into the consciousness of his surroundings. He looked about him awfully. The candle stood on the counter, its flame solemnly wagging in a draught; and by that inconsiderable movement, the whole room was filled with noiseless bustle and kept heaving like a sea: the tall shadows nodding, the gross blots of darkness swelling and dwindling as with respiration, the faces of the portraits and the china gods changing and wavering like images in water. The inner door stood ajar, and peered into that leaguer of shadows with a long slit of daylight like a pointing finger.

From these fear-stricken rovings, Markheim's eyes returned to the body of his victim, where it lay both humped and sprawling, incredibly small and strangely meaner than in life. In these poor, miserly clothes, in that ungainly attitude, the dealer lay like so much sawdust. Markheim had feared to see it, and, lo! it was nothing. And yet, as he gazed, this bundle of old clothes and pool of blood began to find eloquent voices. There it must lie; there was none to work the cunning hinges or direct the miracle of locomotion—there it must lie till it was found. Found! ay, and then? Then would this dead flesh lift up a cry that would ring over England, and fill the world with the echoes of pursuit. Ay, dead or not, this was the enemy. "Time was that when the brains were out," he thought; and the first word struck into his mind. Time, now that the deed was accomplished —time, which had closed for the victim, had become instant, and momentous for the slayer.

The thought was yet in his mind, when, first one and then another, with every variety of pace and voice—one deep as the bell from a cathedral turret, another ringing on its treble notes the prelude of a waltz—the clocks began to strike the hour of three in the afternoon.

The sudden outbreak of so many tongues in that dumb chamber staggered him. He began to bestir himself, going to and fro with the candle, beleaguered by moving shadows, and startled to the soul by chance reflections. In many rich mirrors, some of home designs, some from Venice or Amsterdam, he saw his face repeated and repeated, as it were an army of spies; his own eyes met and detected him; and the sound of his own steps, lightly as they fell, vexed the surrounding quiet. And still as he continued to fill his pockets, his mind accused him, with a sickening iteration, of the thousand faults of his design. He should have chosen a more quiet hour; he should have prepared an alibi; he should not have used a knife; he should have been more cautious, and only bound and gagged the dealer, and not killed him; he should have been more bold, and killed the servant also; he should have done all things otherwise; poignant regrets, weary, incessant toiling of the mind to change what was unchangeable, to plan what was now useless, to be the architect of the irrevocable past. Meanwhile, and behind all this activity, brute terrors, like the scurrying of rats in a deserted attic, filled the more remote chambers of his brain with riot; the hand of the constable would fall heavy on his shoulder, and his nerves would jerk like a hooked fish; or he beheld, in galloping defile, the dock, the prison, the gallows, and the black coffin.

Terror of the people in the street sat down before his mind like a besieging army. It was impossible, he thought, but that some rumour of the struggle must have reached their ears and set on edge their curiosity; and now, in all the neighbouring houses, he divined them sitting motionless and with uplifted ear—solitary people, condemned to spend Christmas dwelling alone on memories of the past, and now startlingly recalled from that tender exercise; happy family parties, struck into silence round the table, the mother still with raised finger: every degree and age and humour, but all, by their own hearts, prying and hearkening and weaving the rope that was to hang him. Sometimes it seemed to him he could not move too softly; the clink of the tall Bohemian goblets rang out loudly like a bell; and alarmed by the bigness of the ticking, he was tempted to stop the clocks. And then, again, with a swift transition of his terrors, the very silence of the place appeared a source of peril, and a thing to strike and freeze the passer-by; and he would step more boldly, and bustle aloud among the contents of the shop, and imitate, with elaborate bravado, the movements of a busy man at ease in his own house.

But he was now so pulled about by different alarms that, while one portion of his mind was still alert and cunning, another trembled on the brink of lunacy. One hallucination in particular took a strong hold on his credulity. The neighbour hearkening with white face beside his window, the passer-by arrested by a horrible surmise on the pavement—these could at worst suspect, they could not know; through the brick walls and shuttered windows only sounds could penetrate. But here, within the house, was he alone? He knew he was; he had watched the servant set forth sweethearting, in her poor best, "out for the day" written in every ribbon and smile. Yes, he was alone, of course; and yet, in the bulk of empty house above him, he could surely hear a stir of delicate footing—he was surely conscious, inexplicably conscious of some presence. Ay, surely; to every room and corner of the house his imagination followed it; and now it was a faceless thing, and yet had eyes to see with; and again it was a shadow of himself; and yet again beheld the image of the dead dealer, reinspired with cunning and hatred.

At times, with a strong effort, he would glance at the open door which still seemed to repel his eyes. The house was tall, the skylight small and dirty, the day blind with fog; and the light that filtered down to the ground story was exceedingly faint, and showed dimly on the threshold of the shop.

And yet, in that strip of doubtful brightness, did there not hang wavering a shadow?

Suddenly, from the street outside, a very jovial gentleman began to beat with a staff on the shop-door, accompanying his blows with shouts and railleries in which the dealer was continually called upon by name. Markheim, smitten into ice, glanced at the dead man. But no! he lay quite still; he was fled away far beyond ear-shot of these blows and shoutings; he was sunk beneath seas of silence; and his name, which would once have caught his notice above the howling of a storm, had become an empty sound. And presently the jovial gentleman desisted from his knocking and departed.

Here was a broad hint to hurry what remained to be done, to get forth from this accusing neighbourhood, to plunge into a bath of London multitudes, and to reach, on the other side of day, that haven of safety and apparent innocence—his bed. One visitor had come: at any moment another might follow and be more obstinate. To have done the deed, and yet not to reap the profit would be too abhorrent a failure. The money, that was now Markheim's concern; and as a means to that, the keys.

He glanced over his shoulder at the open door, where the shadow was still lingering and shivering; and with no conscious repugnance of the mind, yet with a tremor of the belly, he drew near the body of his victim. The human character had quite departed. Like a suit half stuffed with bran, the limbs lay scattered, the trunk doubled, on the floor; and yet the thing repelled him. Although so dingy and inconsiderable to the eye, he feared it might have more significance to the touch. He took the body by the shoulders, and turned it on its back. It was strangely light and supple, and the limbs, as if they had been broken, fell into the oddest postures. The face was robbed of all expression; but it was as pale as wax, and shockingly smeared with blood about one temple. That was, for Markheim, the one displeasing circumstance. It carried him back, upon the instant, to a certain fair day in a fishers' village: a grey day, a piping wind, a crowd upon the street, the blare of brasses, the booming of drums, the nasal voice of a ballad-singer; and a boy going to and fro, buried over head in the crowd and divided between interest and fear, until coming out upon the chief place of concourse, he beheld a booth and a great screen with pictures, dismally designed, garishly coloured: Brownrigg with her apprentice; the Mannings with their murdered guest; Weare in the death-grip of Thurtell; and a score besides of famous crimes. The thing was as clear as an illusion; he was once again that little boy; he was looking once again, and with the same sense of physical revolt, at these vile pictures; he was still stunned by the thumping of the drums. A bar of that day's music returned upon his memory; and at that, for the first time, a qualm came over him, a breath of nausea, a sudden weakness of the joints, which he must instantly resist and conquer.

He judged it more prudent to confront than to flee from these considerations; looking the more hardily in the dead face, bending his mind to realise the nature and greatness of his crime. So little a while ago that face had moved with every change of sentiment, that pale mouth had spoken, that body had been all on fire with governable energies; and now, and by his act, that piece of life had been arrested, as the horologist, with inter-jected finger, arrests the beating of the clock. So he reasoned in vain; he could rise to no more remorseful consciousness; the same heart which had shuddered before the painted effigies of crime looked on its reality un-moved. At best, he left a gleam of pity for one who had been endowed in vain with all those faculties that can make the world a garden of enchant-ment, one who had never lived and who was now dead. But of penitence, no, not a tremor.

With that, shaking himself clear of these considerations, he found the keys and advanced towards the open door of the shop. Outside, it had begun to rain smartly; and the sound of the shower upon the roof had banished silence. Like some dripping cavern, the chambers of the house were haunted by an incessant echoing, which filled the ear and mingled with the ticking of the clocks. And, as Markheim approached the door, he seemed to hear, in answer to his own cautious tread, the steps of another foot withdrawing up the stair. The shadow still palpitated loosely on the threshold. He threw a ton's weight of resolve upon his muscles, and drew back the door.

The faint, foggy daylight glimmered dimly on the bare floor and stairs; on the bright suit of armour posted, halbert in hand, upon the landing; and on the dark wood-carvings and framed pictures that hung against the yellow panels of the wainscot. So loud was the beating of the rain through all the house that, in Markheim's ears, it began to be distinguished into many different sounds. Footsteps and sighs, the tread of regiments march-ing in the distance, the chink of money in the counting, and the creak-ing of doors held stealthily ajar, appeared to mingle with the patter of the drops upon the cupola and the gushing of the water in the pipes. The sense that he was not alone grew upon him to the verge of madness. On every side he was haunted and begirt by presences. He heard them mov-ing in the upper chambers; from the shop, he heard the dead man getting to his legs; and as he began with a great effort to mount the stairs, feet fled quietly before him and followed stealthily behind. If he were but deaf, he thought, how tranquilly he would possess his soul! And then again, and hearkening with ever fresh attention, he blessed himself for that un-resting sense which held the outposts and stood a trusty sentinel upon his life. His head turned continually on his neck; his eyes, which seemed start-ing from their orbits, scouted on every side, and on every side were half rewarded as with the tail of something nameless vanishing. The four-and-twenty steps to the first floor were four-and-twenty agonies.

On that first story, the doors stood ajar, three of them like three ambushes, shaking his nerves like the throats of cannon. He could never again, he felt, be sufficiently immured and fortified from men's observing eyes; he longed to be home, girt in by walls, buried among bed-clothes, and invisible to all but God. And at that thought he wondered a little, recollecting tales of other murderers and the fear they were said to entertain of heavenly avengers. It was not so, at least, with him. He feared the laws of nature, lest, in their callous and immutable procedure, they should preserve some damning evidence of his crime. He feared tenfold more, with a slavish, superstitious terror, some scission in the continuity of man's experience, some wilful illegality of nature. He played a game of skill, depending on the rules, calculating consequence from cause; and what if nature, as the defeated tyrant overthrew the chess-board, should break the mould of their succession? The like had befallen Napoleon (so writers said) when the winter changed the time of its appearance. The like might befall Markheim: the solid walls might become transparent and reveal his doings like those of bees in a glass hive; the stout planks might yield under his foot like quicksands and detain him in their clutch; ay, and there were soberer accidents that might destroy him: if, for instance, the house should fall and imprison him beside the body of his victim; or the house next door should fly on fire, and the firemen invade him from all sides. These things he feared; and, in a sense, these things might be called the hands of God reached forth against sin. But about God himself he was at ease; his act was doubtless exceptional, but so were his excuses, which God knew; it was there, and not among men, that he felt sure of justice.

When he had got safe into the drawing-room, and shut the door behind him, he was aware of a respite from alarms. The room was quite dismantled, uncarpeted besides, and strewn with packing-cases and incongruous furniture; several great pier-glasses, in which he beheld himself at various angles, like an actor on a stage; many pictures, framed and unframed, standing, with their faces to the wall; a fine Sheraton sideboard, a cabinet of marquetry, and a great old bed, with tapestry hangings. The windows opened to the floor; but by great good-fortune the lower part of the shutters had been closed, and this concealed him from the neighbours. Here, then, Markheim drew in a packing-case before the cabinet, and began to search among the keys. It was a long business, for there were many; and it was irksome, besides; for, after all, there might be nothing in the cabinet, and time was on the wing. But the closeness of the occupation sobered him. With the tail of his eye he saw the door—even glanced at it from time to time directly, like a besieged commander pleased to verify the good estate of his defences. But in truth he was at peace. The rain falling in the street sounded natural and pleasant. Presently, on the other side, the notes of a piano were wakened to the music of a hymn, and the voices of many children took up the air and words. How stately, how comfortable was the melody! How fresh the youthful voices! Markheim gave ear to it smilingly, as he sorted out the keys; and his mind was thronged with answerable ideas and images; church-going children and the pealing of the high organ; children afield, bathers by the brookside, ramblers on the brambly common, kite-fliers in the windy and cloud-navigated sky; and then, at another cadence of the hymn, back again to church, and the somnolence of summer Sundays, and the high genteel voice of the parson (which he smiled a little to recall) and the painted Jacobean tombs, and the dim lettering of the Ten Commandments in the chancel.

And as he sat thus, at once busy and absent, he was startled to his feet. A flash of ice, a flash of fire, a bursting gush of blood, went over him, and then he stood transfixed and thrilling. A step mounted the stair slowly and steadily, and presently a hand was laid upon the knob, and the lock clicked, and the door opened.

Fear held Markheim in a vice. What to expect he knew not, whether the dead man walking, or the official ministers of human justice, or some chance witness blindly stumbling in to consign him to the gallows. But when a face was thrust into the aperture, glanced round the room, looked at him, nodded and smiled as if in friendly recognition, and then withdrew again, and the door closed behind it, his fear broke loose from his control in a hoarse cry. At the sound of this the visitant returned.

"Did you call me?" he asked, pleasantly and with that he entered the room and closed the door behind him.

Markheim stood and gazed at him with all his eyes. Perhaps there was a film upon his sight, but the outlines of the new-comer seemed to change and waver like those of the idols in the wavering candle-light of the shop; and at times he thought he knew him; and at times he thought he bore a likeness to himself; and always, like a lump of living terror, there lay in his bosom the conviction that this thing was not of the earth and not of God.

And yet the creature had a strange air of the commonplace, as he stood looking on Markheim with a smile; and when he added: "You are looking for the money, I believe?" it was in the tones of every-day politeness.

Markheim made no answer.

"I should warn you," resumed the other, "that the maid has left her sweetheart earlier than usual and will soon be here. If Mr. Markheim be found in this house, I need not describe to him the consequences."

"You know me?" cried the murderer.

The visitor smiled. "You have long been a favourite of mine," he said; "and I have long observed and often sought to help you."

"What are you?" cried Markheim: "the devil?"

"What I may be," returned the other, "cannot affect the service I propose to render you."

"It can," cried Markheim; "it does! Be helped by you? No, never; not by you! You do not know me yet; thank God, you do not know me!"

"I know you," replied the visitant, with a sort of kind severity or rather firmness. "I know you to the soul."

"Know me!" cried Markheim. "Who can do so? My life is but a travesty and slander on myself. I have lived to belie my nature. All men do; all men are better than this disguise that grows about and stifles them. You see each dragged away by life, like one whom bravos have seized and muffled in a cloak. If they had their own control—if you could see their faces, they would be altogether different, they would shine out for heroes and saints! I am worse than most; my self is more overlaid; my excuse is known to me and God. But, had I the time, I could disclose myself."

"To me?" inquired the visitant.

"To you before all," returned the murderer. "I supposed you were intelligent. I thought—since you exist—you would prove a reader of the heart. And yet you would propose to judge me by my acts! Think of it; my acts! I was born and I have lived in a land of giants; giants have dragged me by the wrists since I was born out of my mother—the giants of circumstance. And you would judge me by my acts! But can you not look within? Can you not understand that evil is hateful to me? Can you not see within me the clear writing of conscience, never blurred by any wilful sophistry, although too often disregarded? Can you not read me for a thing that surely must be common as humanity—the unwilling sinner?"

"All this is very feelingly expressed," was the reply, "but it regards me not. These points of consistency are beyond my province, and I care not in the least by what compulsion you may have been dragged away, so as you are but carried in the right direction. But time flies; the servant delays, looking in the faces of the crowd and at the pictures on the hoardings, but still she keeps moving nearer; and remember, it is as if the gallows itself was striding towards you through the Christmas streets! Shall I help you; I, who know all? Shall I tell you where to find the money?"

"For what price?" asked Markheim.

"I offer you the service for a Christmas gift," returned the other.

Markheim could not refrain from smiling with a kind of bitter triumph. "No," said he, "I will take nothing at your hands; if I were dying of thirst, and it was your hand that put the pitcher to my lips, I should find the courage to refuse. It may be credulous, but I will do nothing to commit myself to evil."

"I have no objection to a death-bed repentance," observed the visitant.

"Because you disbelieve their efficacy!" Markheim cried.

"I do not say so," returned the other; "but I look on these things from a different side, and when the life is done my interest falls. The man has lived to serve me, to spread black looks under colour of religion, or to sow tares in the wheat-field, as you do, in a course of weak compliance with desire. Now that he draws so near to his deliverance, he can add but one act of service—to repent, to die smiling, and thus to build up in confidence and hope the more timorous of my surviving followers. I am not so hard a master. Try me. Accept my help. Please yourself in life as you have done hitherto; please yourself more amply, spread your elbows at the board; and when the night begins to fall and the curtains to be drawn, I tell you, for your greater comfort, that you will find it even easy to compound your quarrel with your conscience, and to make a truckling peace with God. I came but now from such a death-bed, and the room was full of sincere mourners, listening to the man's last words: and when I looked into that face, which had been set as a flint against mercy, I found it smiling with hope."

"And do you, then, suppose me such a creature?" asked Markheim. "Do you think I have no more generous aspirations than to sin, and sin, and sin, and, at last, sneak into heaven? My heart rises at the thought. Is this, then, your experience of mankind? or is it because you find me with red hands that you presume such baseness? and is this crime of murder indeed so impious as to dry up the very springs of good?"

"Murder is to me no special category," replied the other. "All sins are murder, even as all life is war. I behold your race, like starving mariners on a raft, plucking crusts out of the hands of famine and feeding on each other's lives. I follow sins beyond the moment of their acting; I find in all that the last consequence is death; and to my eyes, the pretty maid who thwarts her mother with such taking graces on a question of a ball, drips no less visibly with human gore than such a murderer as yourself. Do I say that I follow sins? I follow virtues also; they differ not by the thickness of a nail, they are both scythes for the reaping angel of Death. Evil, for which I live, consists not in action but in character. The bad man is dear to me; not the bad act, whose fruits, if we could follow them far enough down the hurtling cataract of the ages, might yet be found more blessed than those of the rarest virtues. And it is not because you have killed a dealer, but because you are Markheim, that I offered to forward your escape."

"I will lay my heart open to you," answered Markheim. "This crime on which you find me is my last. On my way to it I have learned many lessons; itself is a lesson, a momentous lesson. Hitherto I have been driven with revolt to what I would not; I was a bond-slave to poverty, driven and scourged. There are robust virtues that can stand in these temptations; mine was not so: I had a thirst of pleasure. But to-day, and out of this deed, I pluck both warning and riches—both the power and a fresh resolve to be myself. I become in all things a free actor in the world; I begin to see myself all changed, these hands the agents of good, this heart at peace. Something comes over me out of the past; something of what I have dreamed on Sabbath evenings to the sound of the church organ, of what I forecast when I shed tears over noble books, or talked, an innocent child, with my mother. There lies my life; I have wandered a few years, but now I see once more my city of destination."

"You are to use this money on the Stock Exchange, I think?" remarked the visitor; "and there, if I mistake not, you have already lost some thousands?"

"Ah," said Markheim, "but this time I have a sure thing."

"This time, again, you will lose," replied the visitor quietly.

"Ah, but I keep back the half!" cried Markheim.

"That also you will lose," said the other.

The sweat started upon Markheim's brow. "Well, then, what matter?" he exclaimed. "Say it be lost, say I am plunged again in poverty, shall one part of me, and that the worst, continue until the end to override the better? Evil and good run strong in me, haling me both ways. I do not love the one thing, I love all. I can conceive great deeds, renunciations, martyrdoms; and though I be fallen to such a crime as murder, pity is no stranger to my thoughts. I pity the poor; who knows their trials better than myself? I pity and help them; I prize love, I love honest laughter; there is no good thing nor true thing on earth but I love it from my heart. And are my vices only to direct my life, and my virtues to lie without effect, like some passive lumber of the mind? Not so; good, also, is a spring of acts."

But the visitant raised his finger. "For six-and-thirty years that you have been in this world," said he, "through many changes of fortune and varie-ties of humour, I have watched you steadily fall. Fifteen years ago you would have started at a theft. Three years back you would have blenched at the name of murder. Is there any crime, is there any cruelty of mean-ness, from which you still recoil?—five years from now I shall detect you in the fact! Downward, downward, lies your way; nor can anything but death avail to stop you."

"It is true," Markheim said huskily, "I have in some degree complied with evil. But it is so with all: the very saints, in the mere exercise of living, grow less dainty and take on the tone of their surroundings."

"I will propound to you one simple question," said the other; "and as you answer, I shall read to you your moral horoscope. You have grown in many things more lax; possibly you do right to be so; and at any account, it is the same with all men. But granting that, are you in any one particular, however trifling, more difficult to please with your own conduct, or do you go in all things with a looser rein?"

"In any one?" repeated Markheim, with an anguish of consideration. "No," he added, with despair, "in none! I have gone down in all."

"Then," said the visitor, "content yourself with what you are, for you will never change; and the words of your part on this stage are irrevocably written down."

Markheim stood for a long while silent, and indeed it was the visitor who first broke the silence. "That being so," he said, "shall I show you the money?"

"And grace?" cried Markheim.

"Have you not tried it?" returned the other. "Two or three years ago, did I not see you on the platform of revival meetings, and was not your voice the loudest in the hymn?"

"It is true," said Markheim; "and I see clearly what remains for me by way of duty. I thank you for these lessons from my soul; my eyes are opened, and I behold myself at last for what I am."

At this moment, the sharp note of the door-bell rang through the house; and the visitant, as though this were some concerted signal for which he had been waiting, changed at once in his demeanour. "The maid!" he cried. "She has returned, as I forewarned you, and there is now before you one more difficult passage. Her master, you must say, is ill; you must let her in, with an assured but rather serious countenance—no smiles, no over-acting, and I promise you success! Once the girl within, and the door closed, the same dexterity that has already rid you of the dealer will relieve you of this last danger in your path. Thenceforward you have the whole evening —the whole night, if needful—to ransack the treasures of the house and to make good your safety. This is help that comes to you with the mask of danger. Up!" he cried: "up, friend; your life hangs trembling in the scales: up, and act!"

Markheim steadily regarded his counsellor. "If I be condemned to evil acts," he said, "there is still one door of freedom open—I can cease from action. If my life be an ill thing, I can lay it down. Though I be, as you say truly, at the beck of every small temptation, I can yet, by one decisive gesture, place myself beyond the reach of all. My love of good is damned to barrenness; it may, and let it be! But I have still my hatred of evil; and from that, to your galling disappointment, you shall see that I can draw both energy and courage."

The features of the visitor began to undergo a wonderful and lovely change: they brightened and softened with a tender triumph; and, even as they brightened, faded and dislimned. But Markheim did not pause to watch or understand the transformation. He opened the door and went down-stairs very slowly, thinking to himself. His past went soberly before him; he beheld it as it was, ugly and strenuous like a dream, random as chance-medley—a scene of defeat. Life, as he thus reviewed it, tempted him no longer; but on the further side he perceived a quiet haven for his bark. He paused in the passage, and looked into the shop, where the candle still burned by the dead body. It was strangely silent. Thoughts of the dealer swarmed into his mind, as he stood gazing. And then the bell once more broke out into impatient clamour.

He confronted the maid upon the threshold with something like a smile. "You had better go for the police," said he: "I have killed your master."

THE NECKLACE

Guy de Maupassant

(1850–1893)

TRANSLATED BY ERNEST BOYD

She was one of those pretty and charming girls born, as though fate had blundered over her, into a family of artisans. She had no marriage portion, no expectations, no means of getting known, understood, loved, and wedded by a man of wealth and distinction; and she let herself be married off to a little clerk in the Ministry of Education.

Her tastes were simple because she had never been able to afford any other, but she was as unhappy as though she had married beneath her; for women have no caste or class, their beauty, grace, and charm serving them for birth or family. Their natural delicacy, their instinctive elegance, their nimbleness of wit, are their only mark of rank, and put the slum girl on a level with the highest lady in the land.

She suffered endlessly, feeling herself born for every delicacy and luxury. She suffered from the poorness of her house, from its mean walls, worn chairs, and ugly curtains. All these things, of which other women of her class would not even have been aware, tormented and insulted her. The sight of the little Breton girl who came to do the work in her little house aroused heart-broken regrets and hopeless dreams in her mind. She imagined silent antechambers, heavy with Oriental tapestries, lit by torches in lofty bronze sockets, with two tall footmen in knee-breeches sleeping in large arm-chairs, overcome by the heavy warmth of the stove. She imagined vast saloons hung with antique silks, exquisite pieces of furniture supporting priceless ornaments, and small, charming, perfumed rooms, created just for little parties of intimate friends, men who were famous and sought after, whose homage roused every other woman's envious longings.

When she sat down for dinner at the round table covered with a three-days-old cloth, opposite her husband, who took the cover off the soup tureen, exclaimed delightedly: "Aha! Scotch broth! There's nothing better," she imagined delicate meals, gleaming silver, tapestries peopling the walls with folk of a past age and strange birds in faery forests; she imagined delicate food served in marvellous dishes, murmured gallantries, listened to with an inscrutable smile as one trifled with the rosy flesh of trout or wings of asparagus chicken.

She had no clothes, no jewels, nothing. And these were the only things she loved; she felt that she was made for them. She had longed so eagerly to charm, to be desired, to be wildly attractive and sought after.

She had a rich friend, an old school friend whom she refused to visit, because she suffered so keenly when she returned home. She would weep whole days, with grief, regret, despair, and misery.

One evening her husband came home with an exultant air, holding a large envelope in his hand.

"Here's something for you," he said.

Swiftly she tore the paper and drew out a printed card on which were these words:

"The Minister of Education and Madame Ramponneau request the pleasure of the company of Monsieur and Madame Loisel at the Ministry on the evening of Monday, January the 18th."

Instead of being delighted, as her husband hoped, she flung the invitation petulantly across the table, murmuring:

"What do you want me to do with this?"

"Why, darling, I thought you'd be pleased. You never go out, and this is a great occasion. I had tremendous trouble to get it. Everyone wants one; it's very select, and very few go to the clerks. You'll see all the really big people there."

She looked at him out of furious eyes, and said impatiently:

"And what do you suppose I am to wear at such an affair?"

He had not thought about it; he stammered:

"Why, the dress you go to the theatre in. It looks very nice, to me. . . ."

He stopped, stupefied and utterly at a loss when he saw that his wife was beginning to cry. Two large tears ran slowly down from the corners of her eyes towards the corners of her mouth.

"What's the matter with you? What's the matter with you?" he faltered.

But with a violent effort she overcame her grief and replied in a calm voice, wiping her wet cheeks:

"Nothing. Only I haven't a dress and so I can't go to this party. Give your invitation to some friend of yours whose wife will be turned out better than I shall."

He was heart-broken.

"Look here, Mathilde," he persisted. "What would be the cost of a suitable dress, which you could use on other occasions as well, something very simple?"

She thought for several seconds, reckoning up prices and also wondering for how large a sum she could ask without bringing upon herself an immediate refusal and an exclamation of horror from the careful-minded clerk.

At last she replied with some hesitation:

"I don't know exactly, but I think I could do it on four hundred francs."

He grew slightly pale, for this was exactly the amount he had been saving for a gun, intending to get a little shooting next summer on the plain of Nanterre with some friends who went lark-shooting there on Sundays.

Nevertheless he said: "Very well. I'll give you four hundred francs. But try and get a really nice dress with the money."

The day of the party drew near, and Madame Loisel seemed sad, uneasy and anxious. Her dress was ready, however. One evening her husband said to her:

"What's the matter with you? You've been very odd for the last three days."

"I'm utterly miserable at not having any jewels, not a single stone, to wear," she replied. "I shall look absolutely no one. I would almost rather not go to the party."

"Wear flowers," he said. "They're very smart at this time of year. For ten francs you could get two or three gorgeous roses."

She was not convinced.

"No . . . there's nothing so humiliating as looking poor in the middle of a lot of rich women."

"How stupid you are!" exclaimed her husband. "Go and see Madame Forestier and ask her to lend you some jewels. You know her quite well enough for that."

She uttered a cry of delight.

"That's true. I never thought of it."

Next day she went to see her friend and told her her trouble.

Madame Forestier went to her dressing-table, took up a large box, brought it to Madame Loisel, opened it, and said:

"Choose, my dear."

First she saw some bracelets, then a pearl necklace, then a Venetian cross in gold and gems, of exquisite workmanship. She tried the effect of the jewels before the mirror, hesitating, unable to make up her mind to leave them, to give them up. She kept on asking:

"Haven't you anything else?"

"Yes. Look for yourself. I don't know what you would like best."

Suddenly she discovered, in a black satin case, a superb diamond necklace; her heart began to beat covetously. Her hands trembled as she lifted it. She fastened it round her neck, upon her high dress, and remained in ecstasy at sight of herself.

Then, with hesitation, she asked in anguish:

"Could you lend me this, just this alone?"

"Yes, of course."

She flung herself on her friend's breast, embraced her frenziedly, and went away with her treasure.

The day of the party arrived. Madame Loisel was a success. She was the prettiest woman present, elegant, graceful, smiling, and quite above herself with happiness. All the men stared at her, inquired her name, and asked to be introduced to her. All the under-secretaries of state were eager to waltz with her. The Minister noticed her.

She danced madly, ecstatically, drunk with pleasure, with no thought for anything, in the triumph of her beauty, in the pride of her success, in a cloud of happiness made up of this universal homage and admiration, of the desires she had aroused, of the completeness of a victory so dear to her feminine heart.

She left about four o'clock in the morning. Since midnight her husband had been dozing in a deserted little room, in company with three other men whose wives were having a good time.

He threw over her shoulders the garments he had brought for them to go home in, modest everyday clothes, whose poorness clashed with the beauty of the ball dress. She was conscious of this and was anxious to hurry away, so that she would not be noticed by the other women putting on their costly furs.

Loisel restrained her.

"Wait a little. You'll catch cold in the open. I'm going to fetch a cab."

But she did not listen to him and rapidly descended the staircase. When they were out in the street they could not find a cab; they began to look for one, shouting at the drivers whom they saw passing in the distance.

They walked down towards the Seine, desperate and shivering. At last they found on the quay one of those old night-prowling carriages which are only to be seen in Paris after dark, as though they were ashamed of their shabbiness in the daylight.

It brought them to their door in the Rue des Martyrs, and sadly they walked up to their own apartment. It was the end, for her. As for him, he was thinking that he must be at the office at ten.

She took off the garments in which she had wrapped her shoulders, so as to see herself in all her glory before the mirror. But suddenly she uttered a cry. The necklace was no longer round her neck!

"What's the matter with you?" asked her husband, already half undressed.

She turned towards him in the utmost distress.

"I . . . I . . . I've no longer got Madame Forestier's necklace. . . ."

He started with astonishment.

"What! . . . Impossible!"

They searched in the folds of her dress, in the folds of the coat, in the pockets, everywhere. They could not find it.

"Are you sure that you still had it on when you came away from the ball?" he asked.

"Yes, I touched it in the hall at the Ministry."

"But if you had lost it in the street, we should have heard it fall."

"Yes. Probably we should. Did you take the number of the cab?"

"No. You didn't notice it, did you?"

"No."

They stared at one another, dumbfounded. At last Loisel put on his clothes again.

"I'll go over all the ground we walked," he said, "and see if I can't find it."

And he went out. She remained in her evening clothes, lacking strength to get into bed, huddled on a chair, without volition or power of thought.

Her husband returned about seven. He had found nothing.

He went to the police station, to the newspapers, to offer a reward, to the cab companies, everywhere that a ray of hope impelled him.

She waited all day long, in the same state of bewilderment at this fearful catastrophe.

Loisel came home at night, his face lined and pale; he had discovered nothing.

"You must write to your friend," he said, "and tell her that you've broken the clasp of her necklace and are getting it mended. That will give us time to look about us."

She wrote at his dictation.

By the end of a week they had lost all hope.

Loisel, who had aged five years, declared:

"We must see about replacing the diamonds."

Next day they took the box which had held the necklace and went to the jewellers whose name was inside. He consulted his books.

"It was not I who sold this necklace, madame; I must have merely supplied the clasp."

Then they went from jeweller to jeweller, searching for another necklace like the first, consulting their memories, both ill with remorse and anguish of mind.

In a shop at the Palais-Royal they found a string of diamonds which seemed to them exactly like the one they were looking for. It was worth forty thousand francs. They were allowed to have it for thirty-six thousand.

They begged the jeweller not to sell it for three days. And they arranged matters on the understanding that it would be taken back for thirty-four thousand francs, if the first one were found before the end of February.

Loisel possessed eighteen thousand francs left to him by his father. He intended to borrow the rest.

He did borrow it, getting a thousand from one man, five hundred from another, five louis here, three louis there. He gave notes of hand, entered into ruinous agreements, did business with usurers and the whole race of money-lenders. He mortgaged the whole remaining years of his existence, risked his signature without even knowing if he could honour it, and, appalled at the agonising face of the future, at the black misery about to fall upon him, at the prospect of every possible physical privation and moral torture, he went to get the new necklace and put down upon the jeweller's counter thirty-six thousand francs.

When Madame Loisel took back the necklace to Madame Forestier, the latter said to her in a chilly voice:

"You ought to have brought it back sooner; I might have needed it."

She did not, as her friend had feared, open the case. If she had noticed the substitution, what would she have thought? What would she have said? Would she not have taken her for a thief?

Madame Loisel came to know the ghastly life of abject poverty. Right from the start she played her part heroically. This fearful debt must be paid off. She would pay it. The servant was dismissed. They changed their apartment; they took a garret under the roof.

She came to know the heavy work of the house, the hateful duties of the kitchen. She washed the plates, wearing out her pink nails on the coarse pottery and the bottoms of pans. She washed the dirty linen, the shirts and dish-cloths, and hung them out to dry on a string; every morning she took the dustbin down into the street and carried up the water, stopping on each landing to get her breath. And, clad like a poor woman, she went to the fruiterer, to the grocer, to the butcher, a basket on her arm, haggling, insulted, fighting for every wretched halfpenny of her money.

Every month notes had to be paid off, others to be renewed, time to be gained.

Her husband worked in the evenings at putting straight a merchant's accounts, and often at night he did copying at twopence halfpenny a page.

And this life lasted ten years.

At the end of ten years everything was paid off, everything, the usurer's charges and the accumulation of superimposed interest.

Madame Loisel looked old now. She had become like all the other strong, hard, coarse women of poor households. Her hair was badly done, her skirts were awry, her hands were red. She spoke in a shrill voice, and the water slopped all over the floor when she scrubbed it. But sometimes, when her husband was at the office, she sat down by the window and thought of that evening long ago, of the ball at which she had been so beautiful and so much admired.

What would have happened if she had never lost those jewels? Who knows? Who knows? How strange life is, how fickle! How little is needed to ruin or to save!

One Sunday, as she had gone for a walk along the Champs-Élysées to freshen herself after the labours of the week, she caught sight suddenly of a woman who was taking a child out for a walk. It was Madame Forestier, still young, still beautiful, still attractive.

Madame Loisel was conscious of some emotion. Should she speak to her? Yes, certainly. And now that she had paid, she would tell her all. Why not?

She went up to her.

"Good morning, Jeanne."

The other did not recognise her, and was surprised at being thus familiarly addressed by a poor woman.

"But . . . madame . . ." she stammered. "I don't know . . . you must be making a mistake."

"No . . . I am Mathilde Loisel."

Her friend uttered a cry.

"Oh! . . . my poor Mathilde, how you have changed! . . ."

"Yes, I've had some hard times since I saw you last; and many sorrows . . . and all on your account."

"On my account! . . . How was that?"

"You remember the diamond necklace you lent me for the ball at the Ministry?"

"Yes. Well?"

"Well, I lost it."

"How could you? Why, you brought it back."

"I brought you another one just like it. And for the last ten years we have been paying for it. You realise it wasn't easy for us; we had no money . . . Well, it's paid for at last, and I'm mighty glad."

Madame Forestier had halted.

"You say you bought a diamond necklace to replace mine?"

"Yes. You hadn't noticed it? They were very much alike."

And she smiled in proud and innocent happiness.

Madame Forestier, deeply moved, took her two hands.

"Oh, my poor Mathilde! But mine was imitation. It was worth at the very most only five hundred francs! . . ."

THE LEGACY

Guy de Maupassant

(1850–1893)

TRANSLATED BY ERNEST BOYD

Aₗₜₕₒᵤgₕ it was not yet ten o'clock, the employees were pouring in like waves through the great doorway of the Ministry of Marine, having come in haste from every corner of Paris, for the first of the year was approaching, the time for renewed zeal—and for promotions. A noise of hurrying footsteps filled the vast building, which was as tortuous as a labyrinth, and honeycombed with inextricable passages, pierced by innumerable doors opening into the various offices.

Each one entered his particular room, pressed the hands of his colleagues who had already arrived, threw off his coat, put on his office jacket, and seated himself before the table, where a pile of papers awaited him. Then they went for news into the neighbouring offices. They asked whether their chief had arrived, if he was in an agreeable humour, and if the day's mail was a heavy one.

The clerk in charge of "general matter," M. César Cachelin, an old non-commissioned officer of the marine infantry, who had become chief-clerk by priority of office, registered in a big book all the documents as they were brought in by the messenger. Opposite him the copy-clerk, old father Savon, a stupid old fellow, celebrated throughout the whole ministry for his conjugal misfortunes, copied in a slow hand a dispatch from the chief, sitting with his body held sidewise and his eyes askew, in the stiff attitude of the careful copyist.

M. Cachelin, a big man, whose short, white hair stood up like a brush on his head, talked all the time while performing his daily work: "Thirty-two dispatches from Toulon. That port gives us as much as any four others put together."

Then he asked the old man Savon the question he put to him every morning:

"Well, father Savon, how is Madame?"

The old man, without stopping his work, replied: "You know very well, Monsieur Cachelin, that subject is a most painful one to me."

Then the chief clerk laughed as he laughed every day at hearing the same phrase.

The door opened and M. Maze entered. He was a handsome, dark young fellow dressed with an exaggerated elegance, who thought his position beneath his dignity, and his person and manners above his position. He wore large rings, a heavy gold watch chain, a monocle (which he discarded while at work), and he made a frequent movement of his wrists in order to bring into view his cuffs ornamented with great shining buttons.

At the door he asked: "Much work to-day?" M. Cachelin replied: "It is always Toulon which keeps sending in. One can easily see that the first of the year is at hand, from the way they are hustling down there."

But another employee, a great joker, always in high spirits, appeared in his turn and said laughing:

"We are not hustling at all, are we?" Then taking out his watch he added: "Seven minutes to ten and every man at his post! By George, what do you think of that? and I'll wager anything that his Dignity M. Lesable arrived at nine o'clock—at the same hour as our illustrious chief."

The chief clerk ceased writing, put his pen behind his ear, and leaning his elbow on the desk said: "Oh! there is a man for you! If he does not succeed, it will not be for want of trying."

M. Pitolet, seating himself on the corner of the table and swinging his leg, replied:

"But he will succeed, papa Cachelin; he will succeed, you may be sure. I will bet you twenty francs to a sou that he will be chief within ten years."

M. Maze, who rolled a cigarette while warming his calves before the fire, said:

"Pshaw! for my part I would rather remain all my life on a salary of twenty-four hundred francs than wear myself to a skeleton the way he is doing."

Pitolet turned on his heels and said in a bantering tone: "But that does not prevent you, my dear fellow, from being here on this twentieth of December before ten o'clock."

The other shrugged his shoulders with an air of indifference. "Hang it all! I do not want everybody to walk over my head, either! Since you come here to see the sun rise, I am going to do it, too, however much I may deplore your officiousness. From doing that to calling the chief 'dear master,' as Lesable does, and staying until half past six and then carrying work home with you is a long way. Besides, I am in society and I have other demands upon my time."

M. Cachelin had ceased his registering and begun to dream, his eyes fixed on vacancy. At last he asked: "Do you believe that he will get an increase again this year?"

Pitolet cried: "I will bet you ten to one he gets it. He is not wearing himself out for nothing."

And so they talked of the eternal question of promotion which for a month had excited the whole hive of clerks from the ground floor to the roof.

They calculated chances, computed figures, compared their various claims to promotion, and waxed indignant over former injustices. These discussions lasted from morning until evening, and the next day were begun all over again, with the same reasons, the same arguments, the same words.

A new clerk entered, a little, pale, sick-looking man, M. Boissel, who lived as in a romance of Alexandre Dumas, *père*. Everything with him was an extraordinary adventure, and he recounted every morning to his friend Pitolet his strange encounters of the previous evening, imaginary scenes enacted in his house, strange cries uttered in the street which caused him to open his window at half past three in the morning. Every day he had separated combatants, stopped runaway horses, rescued women from danger; and although of a deplorably weak constitution he talked unceasingly, in a slow and satisfied tone, of exploits accomplished by his strong arm.

As soon as he understood that they were talking of Lesable he declared: "Some day I will give that little pup his deserts; and if he ever walks over my head, I'll give him something that will prevent him from trying again."

Maze, continuing to smoke, sneered: "You would do well, then, to begin at once, for I hear on good authority that you are to be set aside this year for Lesable."

Boissel raised his hand. "I swear that if——"

The door opened once more, and a dapper little man wearing the side-whiskers of an officer of marine or lawyer, and a high, stiff collar, who spoke his words rapidly as though he could not take the time to finish what he had to say, entered quickly with a preoccupied manner. He shook hands all around with the air of a man who had no leisure for dallying, and approaching the chief clerk said: "My dear Cachelin, will you give me the Chapelou papers, rope yarn, Toulon A. T. V., 1875?"

The clerk rose, reached for a portfolio above his head, took out a package of sealed documents wrapped in blue linen, and presenting them said: "There, M. Lesable; you remember the chief took three dispatches from their package yesterday."

"Yes, I have them. Thanks," and the young man went out hurriedly.

Hardly had he gone when Maze ejaculated:

"Well, what an air! One would swear he was already chief."

And Pitolet replied: "Patience, patience; he will be before any of us."

M. Cachelin had not resumed his writing. A fixed thought seemed to have taken possession of him. At last he said: "He has a fine future, that boy!"

But Maze murmured in a disdainful tone: "For those who think the ministry is a career—yes. For the others it is a little——"

Pitolet interrupted him: "Perhaps you intend to become ambassador?"

The other made an impatient gesture. "It is not a question of me. I can take care of myself. That has nothing to do with the fact that the position of the head of a department will never be anything very much."

Father Savon, the copyist, had never ceased his work. But for some little time he had been dipping his pen in the inkstand, then wiping it vigorously on the sponge which stood in a little glass of water on his desk, without being able to trace a letter. The black liquid slipped along the point of the metal and fell in round spots on the paper. The good man, driven to despair as sheet after sheet of paper was thus spoiled, said in a deep and sorrowful voice:

"Here is more adulterated ink!"

A shout of laughter came from every mouth. Cachelin shook the table with his stomach. Maze bent double, as though he were going up the chimney backward. Pitolet stamped and roared and waved his hands in the air, and even Boissel was almost suffocated, although he generally looked at these things on the tragic rather than the comic side.

But father Savon, wiping his pen on the tail of his overcoat, said: "There is nothing to laugh at. I have to go over my whole work two or three times."

He took from his box another sheet of paper, laid his wax sheet over it, and commenced again at the beginning: "Monsieur le Ministre and dear Colleague——" The pen now held the ink and traced the letters neatly. The old man settled down into his oblique posture and continued his copy.

The others had not stopped laughing. They were fairly choking. For six months they had played the same game on the poor old fellow, who had never detected it. It consisted in pouring several drops of oil on the damp sponge used for wiping pens. The metal, thus becoming coated with liquid grease, would not take the ink, and the perplexed copying-clerk would pass hours in using boxes of pens and bottles of ink, and finally declare that the supplies of the department were becoming perfectly worthless.

Then the jokers would torment the old man in other ways. They put gunpowder in his tobacco, poured drugs into his drinking water, and made him believe that, since the Commune, the majority of articles for general use had been adulterated by the socialists, to put the government in the wrong and bring about a revolution. He had conceived a terrible hatred against the anarchists, whom he believed to be concealed everywhere, and had a mysterious fear of an unknown woman—veiled and formidable.

A sharp ring of the bell sounded in the corridor. They well knew the emphatic ring of their chief, M. Torchebeuf, and each one sprang toward the door that he might regain his own compartment.

Cachelin returned to his work. Then he laid down his pen again, and took his head in his hands and began to think.

He turned over in his mind an idea which had tormented him for some time. An old non-commissioned officer of the marine infantry, retired after receiving three wounds, one at Senegal and two at Cochin China, who had been given a position in the ministry as an exceptional favour, he had had to endure many miseries, many hardships, and many griefs in his long career as an insignificant subordinate. He considered authority, official authority, as the finest thing in the world. The head of a Department seemed to him an exceptional being, living in a higher sphere; and the employee of whom he heard it said: "He is a sharp one; he will get there yet," appeared to him of another race, another nature, than himself.

He had therefore for his colleague Lesable a high respect which approached veneration, and he cherished the secret desire, which was never absent from his mind, to have him marry his daughter.

She would be rich one day, very rich. This was known throughout the entire ministry, for his sister, Mlle. Cachelin, possessed a million, a clear, cool million, acquired through love, they said, but purified by belated piety.

This ancient spinster, who had led a gay life in her youth, had retired with five hundred thousand francs, which she had more than doubled in eighteen years, thanks to her ferocious economy and more than frugal habits. She had lived for a long time with her brother, who was a widower with one daughter, Coralie; but she did not contribute in the slightest degree to the expenses of the house, guarding and accumulating her gold, and always repeating to Cachelin: "It makes no difference, since it is all for your daughter; but marry her quickly, for I want to see my little nephews around me. It is she who will give me the joy of embracing a child of our blood."

This was well understood at the office, and suitors were not lacking for Coralie's hand. It was said that Maze himself, the handsome Maze, the lion of the bureau, hovered around father Cachelin with a palpable intent. But the former sergeant, who had roamed through all latitudes, wanted a young man with a future, a young man who would be chief, and who would be able to make some return to him, the old clerk. Lesable suited him to a nicety, and he cast about in his mind for a means of attaching him to himself.

All of a sudden he sat upright, striking his hands together. He had found it. He well understood the weakness of each one of his colleagues. Lesable could be approached only through his vanity, his professional vanity. He would go to him and demand his protection as one goes to a senator or a deputy—as one goes to a high personage.

Not having had any promotion for five years, Cachelin considered himself as certain to obtain one this year. He would make it appear then that he owed it to Lesable, and would invite him to dinner as a means of thanking him.

As soon as his project was conceived he began to put it into execution. He took off his office jacket, put on his coat, and, gathering up all the registered papers which concerned the services of his colleague, he betook himself to the office which Lesable occupied all alone, by special favour, because of his zeal and the importance of his functions.

The young man was writing at a great table, covered with bundles of documents and loose papers numbered with red or blue figures.

As soon as he saw the chief clerk enter, he said in a familiar tone, which also betokened consideration: "Well, my dear fellow, do you bring me a lot of business?"

"Yes, a good deal. And then I want to speak to you."

"Sit down, my friend; I am listening."

Cachelin seated himself, coughed, put on a troubled look, and finally said in a despondent tone:

"This is what brings me here, Monsieur Lesable. I will not beat about the bush. I will be frank like an old soldier. I have come to demand a service of you."

"What is it?"

"In a few words, I wish very much to be promoted this year. I have nobody to help me, and I have thought of you."

Lesable reddened somewhat. He was surprised, flattered, and filled with a pleased confusion. However, he replied:

"But I am nobody here, my friend. I am much less than you, who are going to be principal clerk. I can do nothing. Believe me that if——"

Cachelin cut him short with respectful brusqueness: "Oh, nonsense. You have the ear of the chief, and if you speak a word for me I shall get it. Remember that in eighteen months I shall have the right to retire, and I shall be just five hundred francs to the bad if I obtain nothing on the first of January. I know very well that they say: 'Cachelin is all right; his sister has a million.' It is true enough that my sister has a million, but she doesn't give any of it away. It is also true that her fortune is for my daughter, but my daughter and I are two different persons. I shall be in a nice fix if, when my daughter and my son-in-law are rolling in their carriage, I have nothing to eat. You see my position, do you not?"

Lesable agreed. "It is true—what you say is very true. Your son-in-law may not be well disposed toward you. Besides, one is always more at ease when owing nothing to anybody. Well, I promise you I shall do my best; I shall speak to the chief, place the case before him, and shall insist if it be necessary. Count on me!"

Cachelin rose, took the hands of his colleague, and pressing them hard while he shook them in military fashion, stammered: "Thank you, thank you; believe me, if ever I have the opportunity—if I can ever——" He stopped, not being able to finish what he had begun, and went away making the corridor resound with the rhythmical tread of an old trooper.

But he heard from afar the sharp ring of a bell and he began to run. He knew that ring. It was the chief, M. Torchebeuf, who wanted him.

Eight days later Cachelin found one morning on his desk a sealed letter, which contained the following:

My DEAR COLLEAGUE: I am happy to announce to you that the minister, at the instance of our director and our chief, yesterday signed your nomination to the position of principal clerk. You will receive to-morrow your official notification. Until then you know nothing, you understand?

Yours ever,
LESABLE.

César ran at once to the office of his young colleague, thanked him, excused himself, offered his everlasting devotion, overwhelmed him with his gratitude.

It was known on the morrow that MM. Lesable and Cachelin had each been promoted. The other employees must wait another year, receiving by way of compensation a gratuity which varied from one hundred and fifty to three hundred francs.

M. Boissel declared that he would lie in wait for Lesable at the corner of the street at midnight some night and give him a drubbing which would leave its mark. The other clerks kept silent.

The following Monday, on his arrival, Cachelin went to the office of his protector, entered with solemnity, and in a ceremonious tone said: "I hope that you will do me the honour to dine with us during the New Year holidays. You may choose the day yourself."

The young man, somewhat surprised, raised his head and looked his colleague full in the face. Then he replied without removing his eyes, that he might read the thoughts of the other: "But, my dear fellow, you see—all my evenings are promised here for some time to come."

Cachelin insisted in a good-humoured tone: "Oh, but, I say, you will not disappoint us by refusing, after the service that you have rendered me. I beg you in the name of my family and in mine."

Lesable hesitated, perplexed. He had understood well enough, but he did not know what to reply, not having had time to reflect and to weigh the pros and the cons. At last he thought: "I commit myself to nothing by going to dinner," and he accepted with a satisfied air, choosing the Saturday following. He added, smiling: "So that I shall not have to get up too soon the next morning."

II

M. Cachelin lived in a small apartment on the fifth floor of a house at the upper end of the Rue Rochechouart. There was a balcony from which one could see all Paris, and three rooms, one for his sister, one for his daughter, and one for himself. The dining-room served also for a parlour.

He occupied himself during the whole week in preparing for this dinner.

The menu was discussed at great length, in order that they might have a repast which should be at the same time home-like and elegant. The following was finally decided upon: A consommé with eggs, shrimps and sausage for hors d'œuvre, a lobster, a fine chicken, preserved peas, a *pâté de foie gras,* a salad, an ice, and dessert.

The *foie gras* was ordered from a neighbouring pork butcher with the injunction to furnish the best quality. The pot alone cost three francs and a half.

For the wine, Cachelin applied to the wine merchant at the corner who supplied him with the red beverage with which he ordinarily quenched his thirst. He did not want to go to a big dealer reasoning thus: "The small dealers find few occasions to sell their best brands. On this account they keep them a long time in their cellars, and they are therefore better."

He came home at the earliest possible hour on Saturday to assure himself that all was ready. The maid who opened the door for him was red as a tomato, for she had lighted her fire at midday through fear of not being ready in time, and had roasted her face at it all day. Emotion also excited her. He entered the dining-room to inspect everything. In the middle of the little room the round table made a great white spot under the bright light of a lamp covered with a green shade.

The four plates were almost concealed by napkins folded in the form of an archbishop's miter by Mlle. Cachelin, the aunt, and were flanked by knives and forks of white metal. In front of each stood two glasses, one large and one small. César found this insufficient at a glance, and he called: "Charlotte!"

The door at the left opened and a little old woman appeared. Older than her brother by ten years, she had a narrow face framed with white ringlets. She did these up in papers every night.

Her thin voice seemed too weak for her little bent body, and she moved with a slightly dragging step and tired gestures.

They had said of her when she was young: "What a dear little creature!" She was now a shrivelled up old woman, very clean because of her early training, headstrong, spoiled, narrow-minded, fastidious, and easily irritated. Having become very devout, she seemed to have totally forgotten the adventures of her past.

She asked: "What do you want?"

He replied: "I find that two glasses do not make much of a show. If we could have champagne—it would not cost me more than three or four francs; we have the glasses already, and it would entirely change the aspect of the table."

Mlle. Charlotte replied: "I do not see the use of going to that expense. But you are paying; it does not concern me."

He hesitated, seeking to convince himself:

"I assure you it would be much better. And then, with the cake it would make things more lively." This decided him. He took his hat and went downstairs, returning in five minutes with a bottle under his arm which bore on a large white label, ornamented with an enormous coat of arms, the words: "Grand vin mousseux de Champagne du Comte de Chatel-Rénovau."

Cachelin declared: "It cost only three francs, and the man says it is delicious."

He took the champagne glasses from the cupboard and placed them before each place.

The door at the right opened. His daughter entered. She was a tall girl with firm, rosy flesh—a handsome daughter of a strong race. She had chestnut hair and blue eyes. A simple gown outlined her round and supple figure; her voice was strong, almost the voice of a man, with those deep notes which make the nerves vibrate. She cried: "Heavens! Champagne! What luck!" clapping her hands like a child.

Her father said to her: "I wish you to be particularly nice to this gentleman; he has done such a lot for me."

She began to laugh—a sonorous laugh, which said: "I know."

The bell in the vestibule rang. The doors opened and closed and Lesable appeared.

He wore a black coat, a white cravat, and white gloves. He created a stir. Cachelin sprang forward, embarrassed and delighted: "But, my dear fellow, this is among ourselves. See me—I am in ordinary dress."

The young man replied: "I know, you told me so; but I never go out in the evening without my dress-coat." He saluted, his opera-hat under his arm, a flower in his buttonhole. César presented him: "My sister, Mlle. Charlotte; my daughter Coralie, whom at home we call Cora."

Everybody bowed. Cachelin continued: "We have no salon. It is rather troublesome, but one gets used to it."

Lesable replied: "It is charming."

Then he was relieved of his hat, which he wished to hang up, and he began immediately to draw off his gloves.

They sat down and looked at one another across the table, and no one said anything more until Cachelin asked: "Did the chief remain late tonight? I left very early to help the ladies."

Lesable replied in a careless tone: "No, we went away together, because we were obliged to discuss the matter of the payment for the canvasses at Brest. It is a very complicated affair, which will give us a great deal of trouble."

Cachelin believed he ought to bring his sister into the conversation, and turning to her said: "It is M. Lesable who decides all the difficult questions at the office. One might say that he was the deputy chief."

The old spinster bowed politely, saying: "Oh, I know that Monsieur has great capabilities."

The maid entered, pushing open the door with her knee, and holding aloft with both hands a great soup tureen. Then the master of the house cried: "Come—dinner! Sit there, M. Lesable, between my sister and my daughter. I hope you are not afraid of the ladies," and the dinner began.

Lesable made himself agreeable, with a little air of self-sufficiency, almost of condescension, and he glanced now and then at the young girl, astonished at her freshness, at her beautiful, appetising health. Mlle. Charlotte showed her best side, knowing the intentions of her brother, and she took part in the conversation so long as it was confined to commonplace topics. Cachelin was radiant; he talked and joked in a loud voice while he poured out the wine bought an hour previous at the store on the corner: "A glass of this little Burgundy, M. Lesable. I do not say that it is anything remarkable, but it is good; it is from the cellar and it is pure—I can say that much. We get it from some friends down there."

The young girl said nothing; a little red, a little shy, she was awed by the presence of this man, whose thoughts she suspected.

When the lobster appeared, César declared: "Here comes a personage whose acquaintance I shall be glad to make."

Lesable, smiling, told a story of a writer who had called the lobster "the cardinal of the seas," not knowing that before being cooked the animal was a dark greenish black. Cachelin laughed with all his might, repeating: "Ha, ha, ha! that is first rate!" But Mlle. Charlotte, becoming serious, said sharply:

"I do not see anything amusing in that. That gentleman was an improper person. I understand all kinds of pleasantries, but I am opposed to anything which casts ridicule on the clergy in my presence."

The young man, who wished to please the old maid, profited by this occasion to make a profession of the Catholic faith. He spoke of the bad taste of those who treated great truths with lightness. And in conclusion he said: "For myself I respect and venerate the religion of my fathers; I have been brought up in it, and I will remain in it till my death."

Cachelin laughed no longer. He rolled little crumbs of bread between his finger and thumb while he murmured: "That's right, that's right." Then he changed the conversation, and, with an impulse natural to those who follow the same routine every day, he said: "Our handsome Maze—must have been furious at not having been promoted?"

Lesable smiled. "Well, why not? To everyone according to his deserts." And they continued talking about the ministry, which interested everybody, for the two women knew the employees almost as well as Cachelin himself, through hearing them spoken of every day.

Mlle. Charlotte was particularly pleased to hear about Boissel, on account of his romantic spirit, and the adventures he was always telling about, while Cora was secretly interested in the handsome Maze. They had never seen either of the men, however.

Lesable talked about them with a superior air, as a minister might have done in speaking of his staff.

"Maze is not lacking in a certain kind of merit, but when one wishes to accomplish anything it is necessary to work harder than he does. He is fond of society and of pleasure. All that distracts the mind; he will never advance much on this account. He will be an Assistant Secretary, perhaps, thanks to the influence he commands, but nothing more. As for Pitolet, he is a good clerk, I must say. He has a superficial elegance which cannot be gainsaid, but nothing deep. There is a young man whom one could never put at the head of an important bureau, but who can always be utilised by an intelligent chief who would lay out his work for him."

"And M. Boissel?" asked Mlle. Charlotte.

Lesable shrugged his shoulders: "A poor chap, a poor chap. He can see nothing in its proper proportions, and is continually imagining wonderful stories while half asleep. To us he is of no earthly use."

Cachelin began to laugh. "But the best of all," he declared, "is old father Savon."

Then everybody laughed.

After that they talked of the theatres and the different plays of the year. Lesable judged the dramatic literature of the day with the same authority, concisely classifying the authors, determining the strength and weakness of each, with the assurance of a man who believes himself to be infallible and universal.

They had finished the roast. César now uncovered the pot of *foie gras* with the most delicate precautions, which made one imagine the contents to be something wonderful. He said: "I do not know if this one will be a success, but generally they are perfect. We get them from a cousin who lives in Strasburg."

With respectful deliberation each one ate the butcher's *pâté* in its little yellow pot.

But disaster came with the ice. It was a sauce, a soup, a clear liquid which floated in the dish. The little maid had begged the pastry cook's boy, who brought the ice at seven o'clock, to take it out of the mold himself, fearing that she would not know how.

Cachelin, in despair, wished to make her carry it back again; then he calmed himself at the thought of the Twelfth Night cake, which he divided with great mystery as though it contained a prime secret. All fixed their gaze on the symbolic cake, then Mlle. Charlotte directed that each one close his eyes while taking a piece.

Who would be the king? A childish, expectant smile was on the lips of everyone. M. Lesable uttered a little "ah" of astonishment, and showed between his thumb and forefinger a great white bean still covered with pastry. Cachelin began to applaud, then cried: "Choose the queen! choose the queen!"

The king hesitated an instant only. Would it not be a politic act to choose Mlle. Charlotte? She would be flattered, brought over, his friend ever after! Then he reflected that it was really Mlle. Cora for whom he had been invited, and that he would seem like a ninny in choosing the aunt. He turned toward his youthful neighbour, and handing her the royal bean said: "Mademoiselle, will you permit me to offer it to you?" And they looked one another in the face for the first time.

She replied: "Thank you, Monsieur," and received the gage of sovereignty.

He thought: "She is enormously pretty, this girl. Her eyes are superb. She is gay, too, if I am not mistaken!"

A sharp detonation made the two women jump. Cachelin had just opened the champagne, which escaped from the bottle and ran over the table-cloth. Then the glasses were filled with the frothy stuff and the host declared: "It is of good quality, one can see that." But as Lesable was about to drink to prevent his glass from running over, César cried: "The king drinks! the king drinks! the king drinks!" And Mlle. Charlotte, also excited, squeaked in her thin voice: "The king drinks! the king drinks!"

Lesable emptied his glass with composure, and replacing it on the table said: "You see I am not lacking in assurance." Then turning toward Mlle. Cora he said: "It is yours, Mademoiselle!"

She wished to drink, but everybody having cried: "The queen drinks! the queen drinks!" she blushed, began to laugh, and put the glass down again.

The end of the dinner was full of gaiety; the king showed himself most attentive and gallant toward the queen. Then when they had finished the liqueurs, Cachelin announced:

"We will have the table cleared away now to give us more room. If it is not raining, we can go to the balcony for a few minutes." He wanted Lesable to see the view, although it was night.

The glass door was thrown open. A moist, warm breeze entered. It was mild outdoors as in the month of April. They all mounted the step which separated the dining-room from the large balcony. They could see nothing but a vague glimmer hovering over the great city, like the gilt halos which they put on the heads of the saints. In some spots this light seemed more brilliant, and Cachelin began to explain:

"See, that is the Eden blazing down there. Look at the line of the boulevards. Isn't it wonderful, how you can distinguish them! In the daytime it is splendid, this view. You would have to travel a long way before you saw anything finer!"

Lesable was leaning on the iron balustrade, by the side of Cora, who gazed into the void, silent, distraught, seized of a sudden with one of those melancholy languors which sometimes oppress the soul. Mlle. Charlotte returned to the room, fearing the damp. Cachelin continued to speak, his outstretched hand indicating the places where they would find the Invalides, the Trocadéro, the Arc de Triomphe.

Lesable in a low voice asked: "And you, Mlle. Cora, do you like to look at Paris from this height?"

She gave a little shiver, as though she had been dreaming and answered: "I? Yes, especially at night. I think of all the things which are happening there in front of us. How many happy people and how many who are unhappy in all these houses! If one could see everything, how many things one might learn!"

He came a little nearer, until their elbows and their shoulders touched:

"By moonlight this should be like fairyland."

She murmured: "Ah, yes, indeed. One would say it was an engraving by Gustave Doré. What a pleasure it would be to take a long walk on these roofs."

Then he questioned her regarding her tastes, her dreams, her pleasures. And she replied without embarrassment, after the manner of an intelligent, sensible girl—one who was not more imaginative than was necessary.

He found her full of good sense, and he said to himself that it would be wonderfully sweet to put his arm about that firm, round figure, and to press a score of little slow kisses, as one drinks in little sips of excellent brandy, on that fresh cheek, near the ear, just where a ray from the lamp fell upon it. He felt himself attracted, moved by the sensation of the proximity of a beautiful woman, by the thirst for her ripe and virginal flesh and by that delicate seductive influence a young girl possesses. It seemed to him he could remain there for hours, nights, weeks, forever, leaning towards her, feeling her near to him, thrilled by the charm of that contact. And something like a poetic sentiment stirred his heart in the face of that great Paris, spread out before him, brilliant in her nocturnal life, her life of pleasure and debauchery. It seemed to him that he dominated the enormous city, that he hovered over it; and he thought how delicious it would be to recline every evening on such a balcony beside a woman, to love her and be loved by her, to press her to his breast, far above the vast city, and all the earthly loves it contained, above all the vulgar satisfactions and common desires, near to the stars.

There are nights when even the least exalted souls begin to dream, and Lesable felt as though he were spreading his wings for the first time. Perhaps he was a little tipsy.

Cachelin went inside to get his pipe, and came back lighting it. "I know," he said, "that you do not smoke or I would offer you a cigarette. There is nothing more delightful than to smoke here. If I had to live on the ground floor I should die. We could do it if we wanted to, for the house belongs to my sister, as well as the two neighbouring ones—the one on the right and the one on the left. She has a nice little revenue from these alone. They did not cost a great deal, either, when she bought them." And turning toward the window he cried: "How much did you pay for the ground here, Charlotte?"

Then the thin voice of the old spinster was heard speaking. Lesable could only hear broken fragments of the sentences: "In eighteen hundred and sixty-three—thirty-five francs—built afterward—the three houses—a banker —sold for at least five hundred thousand francs——"

She talked of her fortune with the complacency of an old soldier who reels off stories of his campaigns. She enumerated her purchases, the high offers she had since had, the rise in values, etc.

Lesable, immediately interested, turned about, resting now his back against the balustrade of the balcony. But as he still caught only tantalizing scraps of what the old woman said, he brusquely left his young companion and went within where he might hear everything; and seating himself beside Mademoiselle Charlotte conversed with her for a long time on the probable increase in rents and what income should accrue from money well placed in stocks and bonds. He left toward midnight, promising to return.

A month later there was nothing talked about in the whole office but the marriage of Jacques Léopold Lesable with Mademoiselle Céleste Coralie Cachelin.

III

The young people began housekeeping on the same floor with Cachelin and Mlle. Charlotte, in an apartment similar to theirs from which the tenant was expelled.

A certain uneasiness, however, disturbed the mind of Lesable: the aunt had not wished to assure her heritage to Cora by any definitive act. She had, however, consented to swear "before God" that her will was made and deposited with Maître Belhomme, the notary. She had promised, moreover, that her entire fortune should revert to her niece on one sole condition. Being pressed to reveal this condition she refused to explain herself, but averred with a little amiable smile that it was very easy of fulfillment.

Notwithstanding these explanations and the stubbornness of the pious old woman, Lesable thought he ought to have further assurance; but, as the young woman pleased him greatly, his desire triumphed over his incertitude, and he yielded to the determined efforts of Cachelin.

Now he was happy, notwithstanding that he was always tormented by a doubt, and he loved his wife, who had in nowise disappointed his expectations. His life flowed along, tranquil and monotonous. He became, in several weeks, perfectly inured to his new position of married man, and he continued to be the same faithful and accomplished employee as formerly.

A year rolled away. The first of the year came round again. He did not receive, to his great surprise, the promotion on which he had counted. Maze and Pitolet alone passed to the grade above, and Boissel declared confidentially to Cachelin that he had promised himself to give his two fellow-

clerks a good thrashing at the main entrance before everybody. But he did
nothing.

For a whole week Lesable did not sleep a wink because of the anguish he
felt at not having been promoted, despite his zeal. He had been working
like a dog; he had filled the place of the assistant-chief, M. Rabot, who had
been in the hospital of Val-de-Grâce for nine months; he had been coming
to the office at half past eight every morning, remaining until half past six
in the evening. What more could they ask? If they could not appreciate
such faithful service he would do like the others, that was all. To everyone
according to his deserts. How could M. Torchebeuf, who had always treated
him like a son, have sacrificed him thus? He wanted to get at the bottom
of the thing. He would go to the chief and have an explanation with him.

On Monday morning, therefore, before the arrival of his comrades, he
knocked at the door of that potentate.

A sharp voice cried: "Come in!" He entered.

Seated before a great table strewn with papers, his little body bent over a
writing-pad which his big head almost touched, M. Torchebeuf was busily
writing. On seeing his favourite employee he said cheerfully: "Good morning, Lesable; you are well?"

The young man replied: "Good morning, dear master, I am very well;
and you?"

The chief ceased writing and turned about in his revolving chair. His
frail, slender body, clad in a black surtout of severe cut, seemed ridiculously
disproportioned to the great leather-covered chair. The brilliant rosette of
an officer of the Legion of Honour, a hundred times too large for the small
body which it decorated, burned like a live coal upon his narrow chest. His
skull was of considerable size, as though the entire development of the individual had been at the top, after the manner of mushrooms.

His chin was pointed, his cheeks hollow, his eyes protruding, and his
great bulging forehead was surmounted with white hair which he wore
thrown backward.

M. Torchebeuf said: "Sit down, my friend, and tell me what brings you
here."

Toward all the other clerks he displayed a military brusqueness, considering himself to be their captain, for the ministry was to him as a great vessel,
the flag-ship of all the French fleet.

Lesable, somewhat moved, a little pale, stammered: "Dear master, I come
to ask you if I have been lacking in any way."

"Certainly not, my dear fellow; why do you ask me such a question?"

"Because I was a little surprised at not receiving my promotion this year,
as in former years. Allow me to finish my explanation, dear master, and
pardon my audacity. I know that I have obtained from you exceptional
favours and unlooked-for advantages. I know that promotions are only
made, as a general thing, every two or three years; but permit me to remind

you that I furnish the bureau with nearly four times the amount of work of an ordinary employee, and at least twice as much time. If, then, you put in the balance the result of labour and the remuneration, you will certainly find the one far outweighs the other."

He had carefully prepared this speech, which he judged to be excellent.

M. Torchebeuf, surprised, hesitated before replying. At length he said in a rather cool tone: "Although it is not admissible, on principle, that these subjects should be discussed between chief and employee, I am willing to reply for this once to your question regarding your very meritorious services.

"I proposed your name for promotion as in preceding years. The chief, however, crossed out your name on the ground that by your marriage your fortune was assured. You are to come into an inheritance such as your modest colleagues can never hope to possess. Is it not, therefore, just to take into consideration the condition of each one? You will be rich, very rich. Three hundred francs more per year will be as nothing to you, whereas this little increase will count for a great deal in the pockets of the others. There, my friend, you have the reason why you remain stationary this year."

Lesable, irritated and covered with confusion, retired.

That evening at dinner he was disagreeable to his wife. She, however, was gay and pleasant as usual. Although she was of an even temper, she was headstrong, and when she desired anything greatly she never yielded her point. She possessed no longer for him the sensual charm of the early days, and although he still looked upon her with the eye of desire, for she was fresh and charming, he experienced at times that disillusion so near to estrangement which soon comes to two beings who live a common life. The thousand trivial or grotesque details of existence, the loose toilettes of the morning, the common linen *robe-de-chambre,* the faded *peignoir,* for they were not rich, and all the necessary home duties which are seen too near at hand in a poor household—all these things took the glamour from marriage and withered the flower of poetry which, from a distance, is so attractive to lovers.

Aunt Charlotte also rendered herself as disagreeable as possible. She never went out, but stayed indoors and busied herself in everything which concerned the two young people. She wished everything conducted in accordance with her notions, made observations on everything, and as they had a horrible fear of offending her, they bore it all with resignation, but also with a suppressed and ever-increasing exasperation.

She went through their apartment with her slow, dragging step, constantly saying in her sharp, nasal voice: "You ought to do this; you certainly ought to do that."

When the husband and wife found themselves alone together, Lesable, who was a perfect bundle of nerves, would cry out: "Your aunt is growing intolerable. I won't stand her here any longer, do you hear? I won't stand it!" And Cora would reply tranquilly: "What do you want me to do?"

Then flying into a passion he would say: "It is dreadful to have such a family!"

And she, still calm, would reply: "Yes, the family is dreadful, but the inheritance is good, isn't it? Now don't be an imbecile. You have as much interest as I in managing Aunt Charlotte."

Then he would be silent, not knowing what to say.

The aunt now harried them unceasingly on the subject of a child. She pushed Lesable into corners and hissed in his face: "My nephew, I intend that you shall be a father before I die. I want to see my little heir. You cannot make me believe that Cora was not made to be a mother. It is only necessary to look at her. When one gets married, my nephew, it is to have a family—to send out little branches. Our holy mother, the Church, forbids sterile marriages. I know very well that you are not rich, and that a child causes extra expense. But after me you will want for nothing. I want a little Lesable, do you understand? I want him."

When, after fifteen months of marriage, her desire was not yet realized, she began to have doubts and became very urgent; and she gave Cora in private advice—practical advice, that of a woman who has known many things in her time, and who has still the recollection of them on occasion.

But one morning she was not able to rise from her bed, feeling very unwell. As she had never been ill before, Cachelin ran in great agitation to the door of his son-in-law: "Run quickly for Dr. Barbette," he said, "and you will tell the chief, won't you, that I shall not be at the office to-day."

Lesable passed an agonizing day, incapable of working himself, or of giving directions to the other clerks. M. Torchebeuf, surprised, remarked: "You are somewhat distraught to-day, M. Lesable." And Lesable answered nervously: "I am greatly fatigued, dear master; I have passed the entire night at the bedside of our aunt, whose condition is very serious."

The chief replied coldly: "As M. Cachelin is with her I think that should suffice. I cannot allow my bureau to be disorganized for the personal reasons of my employees."

Lesable had placed his watch on the table before him, and he waited for five o'clock with feverish impatience. As soon as the big clock in the grand court struck he hurried away, quitting the office, for the first time, at the regular hour.

He even took a cab to return home, so great was his anxiety, and he mounted the staircase at a run. The nurse opened the door; he stammered: "How is she?"

"The doctor says that she is very low."

His heart began to beat rapidly. He was greatly agitated. "Ah, indeed!"

Could she, by any chance, be going to die?

He did not dare to go into the sick woman's chamber now, and he asked that Cachelin, who was watching by her side, be called.

His father-in-law appeared immediately, opening the door with precaution. He had on his dressing-gown and skullcap, as on the pleasant evenings which he passed in the corner by the fire; and he murmured in a low voice: "It's very bad, very bad. She has been unconscious since four o'clock. She even received the viaticum this afternoon."

Then Lesable felt a weakness descending into his legs, and he sat down.

"Where is my wife?"

"She is at the bedside."

"What is it the doctor says? Tell me exactly."

"He says it is a stroke. She may come out of it, but she may also die to-night."

"Do you need me? If not, I would rather not go in. It would be very painful to me to see her in this state."

"No, go to your own apartment. If there is anything new I will call you at once."

Lesable went to his own quarters. The apartment seemed to him changed —it was larger, clearer. But, as he could not keep still, he went out onto the balcony.

They were then in the last days of July, and the great sun, on the point of disappearing behind the two towers of the Trocadéro, rained fire on the immense conglomeration of roofs.

The sky, a brilliant shining red at the horizon, took on, higher up, tints of pale gold, then of yellow, then of green—a delicate green flecked with light; then it became blue—a pure and fresh blue overhead.

The swallows passed like flashes, scarcely visible, painting against the vermilion sky the curved and flying profile of their wings. And above the infinite number of houses, above the far-off country, floated a rose-tinted cloud, a vapour of fire toward which ascended, as in an apotheosis, the points of the church-steeples and all the slender pinnacles of the monuments. The Arc de Triomphe appeared enormous and black against the conflagration on the horizon, and the dome of the Invalides seemed another sun fallen from the firmament upon the roof of a building.

Lesable held with his two hands to the iron railing, drinking in the air as one drinks of wine, feeling a desire to leap, to cry out, to make violent gestures, so completely was he given over to a profound and triumphant joy. Life seemed to him radiant, the future full of richness! What would he do? And he began to dream.

A noise behind him made him tremble. It was his wife. Her eyes were red, her cheeks slightly swollen: she looked tired. She bent down her forehead for him to kiss; then she said: "We are going to dine with Papa so that we may be near her. The nurse will not leave her while we are eating."

He followed her into the next apartment.

Cachelin was already at table awaiting his daughter and his son-in-law. A cold chicken, a potato salad, and a *compote* of strawberries were on the buffet, and the soup was smoking in the plates.

They sat down at table. Cachelin said: "These are days that I wouldn't like to see often. They are not gay." He said this with a tone of indifference and a sort of satisfaction in his face. He set himself to eat with the appetite of a hungry man, finding the chicken excellent and the potato salad most refreshing.

But Lesable felt his stomach oppressed and his mind ill at ease. He hardly ate at all, keeping his ear strained toward the next room, which was as still as though no one was within it. Nor was Cora hungry, but silent and tearful she wiped her eyes from time to time with the corner of her napkin. Cachelin asked: "What did the chief say?" and Lesable gave the details, which his father-in-law insisted on having to the last particular, making him repeat everything as though he had been absent from the ministry for a year.

"It must have made a sensation there when it became known that she was sick." And he began to dream of his glorious re-entry when she should be dead, at the head of all the other clerks. He said, however, as though in reply to a secret remorse: "It is not that I desire any evil to the dear woman. God knows I would have her preserved for many years yet, but it will have that effect all the same. Father Savon will even forget the Commune on account of it."

They were commencing to eat their strawberries, when the door of the sick-room opened. The commotion among the diners was such that with a common impulse all three of them sprang to their feet, terrified. The little nurse appeared, still preserving her calm, stupid manner, and said tranquilly:

"She has stopped breathing."

Cachelin, throwing his napkin among the dishes, sprang forward like a madman; Cora followed him, her heart beating; but Lesable remained standing near the door, spying from a distance the white spot of the bed, scarcely visible by the light of the dying day. He saw the back of his father-in-law as he stooped over the couch, examining but disturbing nothing; and suddenly he heard his voice, which seemed to him to come from afar—from very far off—the other end of the world, one of those voices which pass through our dreams and which tell us astonishing things. Cachelin said: "It is all over. She is dead." He saw his wife fall upon her knees and bury her face in the bedclothes, sobbing. Then he decided to go in, and, as Cachelin straightened himself up, the young man saw on the whiteness of the pillow the face of Aunt Charlotte, so hollow, so rigid, so pale, that with its closed eyes it looked like the face of a waxen figure.

He asked in a tone of anguish: "Is it over?"

Cachelin, who was gazing at his sister, too, turned towards Lesable, and the two men looked at each other.

"Yes," replied the elder, wishing to force his face into an expression of sorrow, but the two understood one another at a glance, and without knowing why, instinctively, they shook hands, as though each would thank the other for a service rendered.

Then, without losing any time, they quickly occupied themselves with the offices required by the dead.

Lesable undertook to fetch the doctor, and to discharge as quickly as possible the most urgent errands.

He took his hat and ran down the staircase, in haste to be in the street, to be alone, to breathe, to think, to rejoice in solitude over his good fortune.

When he had attended to his errands, instead of returning he went across to the boulevard, possessed with a desire to see the crowds, to mingle in the movement of the happy life of the evening. He felt like crying out to the passers-by: "I have fifty thousand francs a year," and he walked along, his hands in his pockets, stopping before the show-windows, examining the rich stuffs, the jewels, the artistic furniture, with this joyous thought: "I can buy these for myself now."

Suddenly he stopped in front of a mourning store and the startling thought came into his mind: "What if she is not dead? What if they are mistaken?"

And he quickly turned homeward with this doubt troubling his mind. On entering he demanded: "Has the doctor come?"

Cachelin replied: "Yes, he has confirmed the death, and is now writing the certificate."

They re-entered the death-chamber. Cora was still weeping, seated in an armchair. She wept very gently, without noise, almost without grief now, with that facility for tears which women have.

As soon as they were all three alone in the room Cachelin said in a low voice: "Now that the nurse has gone to bed, we might look around to see if anything is concealed in the furniture."

The two men set about the work. They emptied the drawers, rummaged through the pockets, unfolded every scrap of paper. By midnight they had found nothing of interest. Cora had fallen asleep, and she snored a little, in a regular fashion. César said: "Are we going to stay here until daybreak?" Lesable, perplexed, thought it was the proper thing. Then the father-in-law said: "In that case let us bring in armchairs"; and they went out to get the two big, soft easy-chairs which furnished the room of the young married couple.

An hour later the three relatives slept, with uneven snorings, before the corpse, icy in its eternal immobility.

They awakened when, at daybreak, the little nurse entered the chamber. Cachelin immediately said, rubbing his eyes: "I have been a little drowsy for the last half hour."

Lesable, who was now sitting very upright, declared: "Yes, I noticed it very plainly. As for me, I have not lost consciousness for a second! I just closed my eyes to rest them."

Cora went to her own room.

Then Lesable asked with apparent indifference:

"When do you think we should go to the notary's to find out about the will?"

"Why—this morning if you wish."

"Is it necessary that Cora should accompany us?"

"That would be better, perhaps, since she is in fact the heir."

"In that case I shall go and tell her to get ready."

Lesable went out with a quick step. The office of Maître Belhomme was just opening its doors when Cachelin, Lesable and his wife presented themselves in deep mourning, with faces full of woe.

The notary at once appeared and, greeting them, bade them sit down. Cachelin spoke up: "Monsieur, you remember me: I am the brother of Mlle. Charlotte Cachelin. These are my daughter and my son-in-law. My poor sister died yesterday; we will bury her to-morrow. As you are the depositary of her will we come to ask you if she has not formulated some request relative to her inhumation, or if you have not some communication to make to us."

The notary opened a drawer, took out an envelope from which he drew a paper, and said:

"Here, Monsieur, is a duplicate of the will, the contents of which I will make you acquainted with immediately. The other document, exactly similar to this, is to remain in my hands." And he read:

"I, the undersigned, Victorine-Charlotte Cachelin, here express my last wishes:

"I leave my entire fortune, amounting to about one million one hundred and twenty thousand francs, to the children who will be born of the marriage of my niece Céleste-Coralie Cachelin, the possession of the income to go to the parents until the majority of the eldest of their descendants.

"The provisions which follow regulate the share which shall fall to each child, and the share remaining to the parents until their death.

"In the event of my death before my niece has an heir, all my fortune is to remain in the hands of my notary, for the term of three years, for my wish above expressed to be complied with if a child is born during that time.

"But in the case of Coralie's not obtaining from Heaven a descendant during the three years following my death, my fortune is to be distributed, by the hands of my notary, among the poor and the benevolent institutions contained in the following list."

There followed an interminable series of names of communities, of societies, of orders, and of instructions.

Then Maître Belhomme politely placed the paper in the hands of Cachelin, who stood speechless with astonishment.

The notary thought he ought to add something by way of explanation to his visitors.

"Mlle. Cachelin," said he, "when she did me the honour to speak to me for the first time of her project of making her will according to this plan, expressed to me the great desire which she had to see an heir of her race. She replied to all my reasoning by a more and more positive expression of her wishes, which were based, moreover, on a religious sentiment, she holding every sterile union to be the sign of divine malediction. I have not been able to modify her intentions in the least. Believe me, I regret this fact exceedingly." Then he added, smiling at Coralie: "But I do not doubt that the *desideratum* of the deceased will be quickly realized."

And the three relatives went away, too bewildered to think of anything. Side by side they walked home, without speaking, ashamed and furious, as though they had robbed each other. All of Cora's grief, even, had suddenly disappeared, the ingratitude of her aunt driving away all disposition to weep.

At last Lesable, whose pale lips were drawn with rage, said to his father-in-law:

"Pass me that paper, that I may read it with my own eyes." Cachelin handed him the document and the young man began to read. He had stopped on the footpath and, jostled by the passers-by, he stood there scanning the words with his piercing and practical eye. The two others waited a few steps in front, still silent.

Then he handed back the paper, saying:

"There is nothing to be done. She has tricked us beautifully."

Cachelin, who was irritated by the failure of his hopes, replied:

"It was for you to have a child, damn it! You knew well enough that she wanted it long ago."

Lesable shrugged his shoulders without answering.

On entering they found a crowd of people awaiting them, those whose calling brings them where a corpse is. Lesable went to his room, not wishing to be bothered, and César spoke roughly to all of them, crying out to them to leave him in peace, demanding that they get through with it as quickly as possible, thinking that they were very long in relieving him of the dead.

Cora, shut up in her room, made no sound, but after an hour Cachelin came and rapped on the door of his son-in-law.

"I come, my dear Léopold," said he, "to submit some reflections to you, for it is necessary to come to some understanding. My opinion is that we should give her a befitting funeral in order to give no hint at the Ministry of what has happened. We will arrange about the expense. Besides, nothing is lost. You have not been married very long, and it would be too great a misfortune if you had no children. You must set about it, that's all. And now to business. Will you drop in at the Ministry after a while? I am going to address the envelopes for the death announcements."

Lesable grudgingly agreed that his father-in-law was right, and they sat down face to face, each at an end of a long table, to fill in the black-bordered cards.

Then they lunched. Cora reappeared, indifferent as though nothing of what had passed concerned her, and she ate a good deal, having fasted the evening before.

As soon as the meal was finished she returned to her room. Lesable left to go to the Ministry, and Cachelin installed himself on the balcony, his chair tilted back, in order to enjoy a pipe.

The broad sun of a summer day fell perpendicularly upon the multitude of roofs, some of which were pierced with windows which blazed as with fire and threw back the dazzling rays which the sight could not sustain.

And Cachelin, in his shirt-sleeves, looked, with his eyes blinking under this stream of light, upon the green hillocks far, far away beyond the great city, beyond the dusty suburbs. He thought of how the Seine flowed there, broad, calm, and fresh, at the foot of hills which had trees on their slopes, and how much better it would be to be lying on one's stomach in that greenery on the bank of the river, gazing into the water, than to be sitting on the burning lead of his balcony. And an uneasiness oppressed him, the tormenting thought, the grievous sensation of their disaster, of that unfortunate, unexpected thing, so much more bitter and brutal because the hope had been so ardent and so long-lived; and he said aloud, as people do in time of great trouble of mind, in the uprooting of a fixed idea: "Damned old witch!"

Behind him in the bedroom he heard the movements of those who were busying themselves with the preparations for the funeral, and the continuous noise of the hammer which nailed up the coffin. He had not looked at his sister since his visit to the lawyer.

But little by little the warmth, the gaiety, the clear charm of this beautiful day penetrated to his mind and his soul, and he thought that things were not so desperate. Why should his daughter not have a child? She had not been married two years yet! His son-in-law appeared vigorous, well built, and in good health, although small. They would have a child, and then besides, by Jupiter, they had to!

Lesable furtively entered the Ministry and slunk to his room. He found on the table a paper bearing these words: "The chief wants you." He made a gesture of impatience. He felt a revolt against this yoke which had again fallen on his back; then a sudden and violent desire to succeed seized him. He would be chief in his turn, and soon; he would then go higher still. Without removing his frock-coat he went at once to M. Torchebeuf. He presented himself with one of those solemn faces which one assumes on sad occasions. But there was something more—an expression of sincere and profound sorrow, that involuntary dejection which a deep disappointment leaves upon the features.

The head of the chief was bent over his papers. He raised it suddenly, and said in a sharp tone: "I have needed you all morning. Why have you not come?"

Lesable replied: "Dear master, we have had the misfortune to lose my aunt, Mademoiselle Cachelin, and I have just come to ask you to attend the funeral, which will take place to-morrow."

The frown on the brow of M. Torchebeuf immediately disappeared, and he replied with a touch of consideration: "That alters the case, my dear friend. I thank you and give you the day, for you must have a great deal to attend to."

But Lesable, desiring to show his zeal, said: "Thanks, dear master, everything is finished, and I expected to remain here until the regular hour for closing."

And he returned to his desk.

The news soon spread, and his fellows came from all the departments to bring him their congratulation rather than their condolences, and also to see how he bore himself. He endured their speeches and their looks with the resigned appearance of an actor, and also with a tact which astonished them.

"He conducts himself very well," said some.

"Well he may," added others; "he ought to be content—lucky dog!"

Maze, more audacious than any of them, asked with the careless air of a man of the world: "Do you know exactly the amount of the fortune?"

Lesable replied in a perfectly disinterested tone: "No, not precisely. The will says about twelve hundred thousand francs. I know that, as the notary was obliged to make us acquainted immediately with certain clauses relative to the funeral."

It was the general opinion that Lesable would not remain in the Ministry. With an income of sixty thousand francs one does not remain a quill-driver. One is somebody and can be something according to one's inclination.

Some thought that he was aiming at the Cabinet; others believed that he thought of the Chamber of Deputies. The chief was expecting to receive his resignation to transmit to the head of the department.

The entire Ministry came to the funeral, which was thought to be very meagre. But the word was around: "It is Mlle. Cachelin herself who wished it so. It was in the will."

On the very next day Cachelin was at his post, and Lesable, after a week of indisposition, also returned, a little pale but assiduous and zealous as formerly. One would have said that nothing unlooked-for had happened to them. It was only remarked that they ostentatiously smoked very large cigars, that they talked of consols, railways, of stocks and shares, like men who have scrip in their pockets, and it became known, in a short time, that they had rented a country-house in the neighbourhood of Paris, in which to spend the summer season.

"They are miserly like the old woman," they said. "It runs in the family. Birds of a feather flock together. But it doesn't look well to retain a clerk-ship with such a fortune."

In a short time the matter was forgotten. They were rated and judged.

IV

After the burial of Aunt Charlotte, Lesable thought again of the million, and, tormented by a rage all the more violent because it must be kept secret, he hated all the world on account of his deplorable ill-luck. "Why, having been married two years, have I not had a child?" he asked himself, and the fear of seeing his household remain sterile made his heart sink. Then, as an urchin who sees from afar the shining prize at the end of the goal, and swears to himself to attain it, and exerts all the vigour and tenacity necessary to reach it, so Lesable took the desperate resolution to become a parent. So many others had, why might not he also? Perhaps he had been negligent, careless, ignorant of something, the consequence of complete indifference. Never having felt a violent desire for an heir, he had never directed all his energies to obtaining this result. He determined to concentrate all his efforts; he would neglect nothing, and he must succeed because he so much desired to. But when he returned home, he felt ill enough to take to his bed. The disappointment had been too bitter and he bowed himself to the blow.

This nervous strain brought him to such a state that the physician judged his condition serious enough to prescribe absolute rest as well as an inter-minable course of treatment. They feared brain fever. In eight days, how-ever, he was about again and resumed his work at the office. But he dare not yet, he believed, approach the conjugal bed. He hesitated and trembled as a general who is going to give battle, a battle on which depends his future. Each evening he awaited the next day, hoping for an access of virility and energy, a happy moment in which he might accomplish his desire. He felt his pulse every minute, and if it was too feeble or too rapid, he took a tonic, ate raw meat, and strengthened himself in every possible way. As his im-provement was not very rapid, Lesable determined to pass the hot months in the country. He persuaded himself that the country air would be a sovereign balm for his weakness, and he assured himself of the accomplish-ment of the hoped-for success. He said to his father-in-law, in a confidential tone: "When we are once in the country my health will improve, and all will go well." That one word "country" seemed to carry for him a mysterious significance.

They rented a small house in the village of Bezons, and the whole family took up their residence there. The two men started out on foot every morning for the station of Colombes, returning in the evening.

Cora, enchanted at living thus on the banks of the peaceful river, would seat herself on the sward, gather flowers, and bring home great bunches of delicate, trembling ferns.

Every evening they all three walked along the river as far as the tollgate of Morue, and, entering, drank a bottle of beer at the Restaurant des Til-leuls. The river, retarded by the long file of stakes, poured between them and leaped, bubbled, and foamed for the distance of a hundred feet. The roaring of the falls made the ground tremble, while a fine mist of vapour floated in the air, rising from the cascade like a light smoke, throwing on the surroundings a delightful odour of spray and a savour of wet earth. As night fell, a great light below and in front indicated Paris, and Cachelin exclaimed every evening: "What a city, after all!"

From time to time, a train, passing on the iron bridge which crossed the end of the island, made a rolling as of thunder and suddenly disappeared, sometimes to the left, sometimes to the right, toward Paris or toward the sea. They returned home slowly, seating themselves on the bank, watching the moon rise and pour on the river her soft and yellow light, which seemed to fuse with the water, and the wrinkles of the current moved like waves of fire. The toads uttered their short and metallic cries. The calls of the night birds rang out on the air, and sometimes a large, mute shadow glided on the river, troubling her calm and luminous course. It was a band of free-booters who, throwing in suddenly their net, drew it back without noise into their boat, dragging in its vast and sombre mesh a shoal of shining and trembling gudgeons, like a treasure drawn from the bottom of the sea, a living treasure of silver fish.

Cora, deeply moved, leaned tenderly upon the arm of her husband, whose design she suspected, although nothing of it had been spoken between them. It was for them like a new betrothal, a second expectation of the kiss of love. Sometimes he would bestow a furtive caress behind her ear, on that charming spot of tender flesh where curls the first hair. She responded by a pressure of the hand, and they attracted while refusing each other, incited and held back by a will more energetic, by the phantom of the million. Cachelin, appeased by the hope which he felt around him, was happy. He drank deeply and ate much, feeling born in him at twilight, the hour of poetry, that foolish tenderness which comes to the dullest persons in certain aspects of nature: a rain of light through the branches, a sunset behind the distant hills, with purple reflections on the water. He declared: "As for me, in the presence of such things I believe in God. It touches me here," and he indicated the pit of his stomach. "I feel myself turned upside down. I feel queer. It seems to me I have been steeped in a bath which makes me want to cry."

As for Lesable, his health rapidly improved. He was seized with sudden ardours, which he did not understand, and he felt a desire to run like a young colt, to roll in the grass and neigh with delight.

He thought the favoured time was approaching. It was a true wedding night. Then they had a new honeymoon full of caresses and hopes. Later they perceived that their experiments were fruitless and their confidence was in vain.

But in the midst of despair Lesable did not lose courage; he continued to make the most superhuman efforts. His wife, moved by the same desire and trembling with the same fear, more robust too than he, encouraged him in his attempts and stimulated his flagging ardour. They returned to Paris in the early days of October.

Life became hard for them again. Unkind words fell from their lips, and Cachelin, who scented the situation, harassed them with the coarse and venomous epigrams of an old trooper.

And one incessant thought pursued them, tortured them, and sharpened their mutual rancour—that of the unattainable legacy. Cora now carried a sharp tongue, and lashed her husband. She treated him like a little boy, a mere brat, a man of no importance. Cachelin at every meal repeated: "If I were rich, I should have children in plenty; when one is poor it is necessary to be reasonable." Then turning to his daughter he added: "You must be like me; but there——" and he looked at his son-in-law significantly, accompanying the look with a movement of the shoulders full of contempt.

Lesable made no reply. He felt himself to be a superior man allied to a family of boors.

At the Ministry they noticed the alteration in his manner, and even the chief one day asked him: "Are you not ill? You appear to me to be somewhat changed."

Lesable replied: "Not at all, my dear sir. I am a little tired, perhaps, having worked very constantly, as you may have seen."

He counted very surely on his promotion at the end of the year, and he had resumed, in this hope, the laborious life of a model employee. But among the meagre bonuses that were distributed Lesable's was the smallest of all, and Cachelin received nothing. Struck to the heart, Lesable sought the chief, whom, for the first time, he addressed as "Monsieur."

"Of what use is it, Monsieur, to work as I do, if I do not reap any reward?"

The head of Monsieur Torchebœuf appeared to bristle.

"I have already told you, Monsieur Lesable, that I will admit of no discussion of this nature between us. I repeat to you again that your claim is unreasonable, your actual fortune being so great as compared to the poverty of your colleagues——"

Lesable could not contain himself. "But I have nothing, Monsieur. Our aunt has left her fortune to the first child which shall be born of our marriage. We live, my father-in-law and I, on our salaries."

The chief was greatly surprised. "If you have no fortune to-day, you will be rich, in any case, at some future day. It amounts to the same thing."

Lesable withdrew, more cast down by his failure than by the uncertainty of Aunt Charlotte's million.

As Cachelin came to his desk some days later the handsome Maze entered with a smile on his lips; next Pitolet appeared, his eyes shining; then Boissel opened the door, and advanced with an excited air, tittering and exchanging meaning looks with the others. Old Savon continued his copying, his clay pipe in the corner of his mouth, seated on his high chair, his feet twisted about the rounds after the fashion of little boys. Nobody spoke. They seemed to be waiting for something, and Cachelin continued to register his papers, announcing in a loud voice according to his custom: "Toulon: Furniture for the officers of the Richelieu. Lorient: Diving apparatus for the Desaix. Brest: Samples of sails of English manufacture."

Lesable entered. He came now every morning for information in regard to the affairs which concerned him, his father-in-law no longer taking the trouble to send him instructions by the office boy.

While he was looking amongst the papers spread out on the table of the chief-clerk, Maze watched him from his corner, rubbing his hands, and Pitolet, who was rolling a cigarette, seemed full of mirth he could not control. He turned toward the copying-clerk:

"Say now, papa Savon, you have learned many things in your time, haven't you?"

The old man, knowing they meant to tease him and to speak to him of his wife, did not reply.

Pitolet began: "You must have discovered the secret of begetting children, since you have had several."

The old clerk raised his head. "You know, M. Pitolet, that I do not like any joking on this subject. I have had the misfortune to marry an unworthy woman, and when I became convinced of her faithlessness I separated from her."

Maze asked in an indifferent tone: "You have had several proofs of her infidelity, have you not?"

And the old man gravely replied: "I have."

Pitolet put in again: "That has not prevented you from becoming the father of three or four children, I am told."

The poor old man, growing very red, stammered: "You are trying to wound me, Monsieur Pitolet; but you will not succeed. My wife has had, in fact, three children. I have reason to believe that the first born is mine, but I deny the two others."

Pitolet continued: "Everybody says, in truth, that the first one is yours. That is sufficient. It is very gratifying to have a child, very gratifying and very delightful. I wager Lesable there would be enchanted to have one— only one, like you."

Cachelin had stopped writing. He did not laugh, although old Savon was his butt ordinarily, and he had poured out his stock of cruel jokes on the subject of the old clerk's conjugal sorrows.

Lesable had collected his papers; but feeling himself attacked he wished to remain, held back by pride, confused and irritated, and wishing to know who had betrayed his secret.

Then the recollection of the confidence he had made to his chief came back to him, and he at once understood it was necessary to express his indignation if he did not wish to become the butt of the whole Ministry.

Boissel marched up and down the room, all the time tittering. He imitated the hoarse voices of the street criers, and bellowed: "The secret of begetting children, for ten centimes—two sous! Buy the secret of begetting children—revealed by Monsieur Savon, with many horrible details." Everybody began to laugh except Lesable and his father-in-law, and Pitolet, turning toward the order-clerk, said: "What is the matter with you, Cachelin? You seem to have lost your habitual gaiety. One would think that you do not find it amusing to believe that old Savon could have had a child by his wife. I think it very funny. Everybody cannot do as much."

Lesable pretended to be deeply absorbed in his papers and to hear nothing of what was going on about him, but he was as white as a ghost.

Boissel took up the strain in the same mocking voice: "The utility of heirs for getting an inheritance, ten centimes, two sous; who will buy?"

Then Maze, who thought this was very poor sort of wit, and who personally was enraged at Lesable having robbed him of the hope of a fortune which he had secretly cherished, said pointedly: "What is the matter with you, Lesable? You are very pale."

Lesable raised his head and looked his colleague full in the face. He hesitated a second, while his lip trembled as he tried to formulate a bitter reply, but, unable to find the phrase he sought, he responded: "There is nothing the matter with me. I am only astonished that you display so much delicacy."

Maze, who stood with his back to the fire and his hands under his coattails, replied, laughing: "One does the best one can, old man. We are like you, we do not always succeed——"

An explosion of laughter interrupted his words. Old Savon, who now vaguely comprehended that the clerks no longer addressed their railleries to him, looked around with his mouth gaping and his pen suspended in the air. And Cachelin waited, ready to come to blows with the first person who came in his way.

Lesable stammered: "I do not understand. In what have I not succeeded?"

The handsome Maze dropped the tails of his coat, and began to stroke his mustache. "I know that you ordinarily succeed in all that you undertake. I have done wrong to speak of you. Besides, we were speaking of old Savon's children, and not of yours, as you haven't any. Now since you succeed in all your enterprises, it is evident that, if you do not have children, it is because you do not want them."

"What business is it of yours?" demanded Lesable sharply.

At this provoking tone Maze in his turn raised his voice: "Hold on! what do you take me for? Try to be polite, or I'll settle you!"

Lesable trembled with anger, and losing all self-control, replied: "Monsieur Maze, I am not, like you, a great booby, or a great coxcomb. And I forbid you ever to speak to me again. I care neither for you nor your kind." And he threw a look of defiance at Pitolet and Boissel.

Maze suddenly understood that true force is in calmness and irony, but wounded in his most vulnerable part—his vanity—he wished to strike his enemy to the very heart, and replied in the protecting tone of a benevolent well-wisher, but with rage in his eyes: "My dear Lesable, you pass all bounds. But I understand your vexation. It is pitiful to lose a fortune, and to lose it for so little, for a thing so easy, so simple. If you wish, I will do you this service myself, for nothing, out of pure friendship. It is only an affair of five minutes——"

He was still speaking when Lesable hurled the inkstand of old Savon full at his head.

A flood of ink covered his face and metamorphosed him into a negro with surprising rapidity. He sprang forward, rolling the whites of his eyes, with his hands raised ready to strike. But Cachelin covered his son-in-law, and grasping Maze by the arms pushed him aside, and, after pounding him well, dashed him against the wall. Maze disengaged himself with a violent effort, and rushed through the door, crying to the two men: "You shall soon hear from me!" Pitolet and Boissel followed him.

Boissel explained his moderation by declaring he should have killed some one if he had taken part in the struggle.

As soon as he entered his room Maze endeavoured to remove the stain, but without success. The ink was violet, and was indelible and ineffaceable. He stood before his glass furious and disconsolate, rubbing savagely at his face with a napkin rolled in a knot. He obtained only a richer black, mixed with red, the blood coming to the surface with the friction.

Boissel and Pitolet strove to advise and console him. One suggested the application of pure olive oil, the other prescribed a bath of ammonia. The office boy was sent to ask the advice of a chemist. He brought back a yellow liquid and pumice stone, which was used with no result.

Maze, disheartened, sank into a chair and declared: "Now it only remains to settle the question of honour. Will you act as seconds for me, and demand of Monsieur Lesable a sufficient apology, or the reparation by arms?"

They both at once consented, and began to discuss the steps to be taken. They had no idea about affairs of this kind, but not wishing to betray their ignorance, and desiring to appear correct, their advice was timorous and

conflicting. It was finally decided that they should consult a sea captain
who was attached to the Ministry to look after the coal distribution. But he
was as ignorant as they were. After some moments of reflection, however,
he advised them to go and see Lesable and ask to be put in touch with two
of his friends.

As they proceeded to the office of their colleague, Boissel suddenly
stopped. "Is it not imperative that we should have gloves?" he asked.

Pitolet hesitated an instant. "Perhaps it is," he replied seriously. But in
order to procure the gloves it would have been necessary to go out, and the
chief was rather severe.

They sent the office boy to bring an assortment from the nearest glove-
store.

To decide upon the colour was a question of time. Boissel preferred
black. Pitolet thought that shade out of place in the circumstances. At last
they chose violet.

Seeing the two men enter gloved and solemn, Lesable raised his head and
brusquely demanded: "What do you want?"

Pitolet replied: "Monsieur, we are charged by our friend, Monsieur Maze,
to ask of you an apology, or a reparation by arms for the insult you have
inflicted on him."

Lesable, still greatly exasperated, cried: "What, he insults me, and sends
you to provoke me? Tell him that I despise him—that I despise all he can
say or do."

Boissel advanced with a tragic air. "You will force us, Monsieur, to publish in the papers an official report, which will be very disagreeable to you."

Pitolet maliciously added: "And which will gravely injure your honour,
and your future advancement."

Lesable, overwhelmed, looked at them. What should he do? He sought
to gain time. "Will you wait a moment in the office of Monsieur Pitolet?
You shall have my answer in ten minutes."

When at last alone he looked around him, seeking for some counsel, some
protection.

A duel! He was going to fight a duel!

He sat terrified, with a beating heart. He, a peaceful man, who had never
dreamed of such a possibility, who was not prepared for the risk, whose
courage was not equal to such a formidable event. He rose from his chair
and sat down again, his heart wildly beating, his legs sinking under him.
His anger and his strength had totally deserted him.

But the thought of the opinion of the Ministry, the gossip the story would
make among his acquaintances, aroused his failing pride, and, not knowing
what to decide, he sought his chief to ask his advice. M. Torchebeuf was
surprised and perplexed. An armed encounter seemed to him unnecessary,
and he thought a duel would demoralise the service. He replied: "I can give
you no advice. It is a question of honour, which does not concern me. Do

you wish that I should give you a note to Commandant Bouc? He is a competent man in such matters, and will be able to advise you."

Lesable accepted the offer, and saw the commandant, who even consented to be his second; he took an under-chief for another.

Boissel and Pitolet waited with their gloves on. They had borrowed two chairs from another office, in order to have four seats.

They saluted gravely and took their places, while Pitolet explained the situation. The commandant, having listened attentively, replied: "The case is serious, but it does not appear to me to be irreparable. Everything depends on the intention." He was a sly old sailor, who was enjoying himself.

A long discussion began regarding the reciprocal apologies the principals should make. M. Maze acknowledging not to have had the intention to offend, M. Lesable should hasten to avow himself in the wrong in throwing the inkstand at the head of M. Maze, and pray to be excused for his inconsiderate violence.

The four proxies returned to their clients.

Maze, seated before his table, was agitated by the dread of the possible duel, although expecting to see his adversary retreat, and regarded his face attentively in one of those little, round tin mirrors which the employees concealed in a drawer for the purpose of adjusting their hair and ties before leaving in the evening. He read the letter of apology which had been prepared by the seconds of both parties, and declared with evident satisfaction: "That appears to me to be very honourable; I am willing to sign it."

Lesable, for his part, accepted without discussion the arrangement of his seconds, and declared: "As this is the result of your mutual consultation, I can but acquiesce."

The four plenipotentiaries assembled. The letters were exchanged, they saluted gravely, and so the affair terminated. An extraordinary excitement reigned in the Ministry. The employees, carrying the news, passed from one door to the other, and lingered to gossip about in the lobbies. When they heard how the affair had ended, there was general disappointment. Some one said: "Still, that will not get Lesable a baby." And the saying took. One employee made a rhyme upon it.

But at the moment when everything seemed adjusted, a difficulty suggested itself to Boissel: "What would be the attitude of the two adversaries when they found themselves face to face? Would they speak, or would they ignore each other?" It was decided that they should meet, as if by chance, in the office of the chief, and exchange, in the presence of M. Torchebeuf, some words of politeness.

This ceremony was accordingly accomplished, and Maze, having sent for a carriage, returned home, to try to remove the stain from his face.

Lesable and Cachelin drove home together without speaking, mutually exasperated, each blaming the other for the disgraceful affair.

The moment he entered the house, Lesable threw his hat violently on the table and cried to his wife: "I have had enough of it! I have a duel on your account now!" She looked at him in angry surprise.

"A duel? How is that?"

"Because Maze has insulted me on your account."

She approached him. "On my account? How?"

He threw himself passionately into an armchair and exclaimed: "He has insulted me—no need to say any more about it."

But she would know. "You must repeat to me the words he used about me."

Lesable blushed, and then stammered: "He told me—he told me—it was in regard to your sterility."

She gave a start; then recoiling in fury, the paternal rudeness showing through the woman's nature, she burst out:

"I! I am sterile, am I? What does that clown know about it? Sterile with you, yes; because you are not a man. But if I had married another, no matter who, do you hear? I should have had children. Ah, you had better talk! It has cost me dear to have married a softy like you! And what did you reply to this good-for-nothing?"

Lesable, frightened before this storm, stuttered: "I—I slapped his face."

She looked at him in astonishment.

"And what did he do?"

"He sent me a challenge; that was all."

She was instantly interested, attracted, like all women, by the dramatic element, and she asked, immediately softened, and suddenly seized with a sort of esteem for this man who was going to risk his life for her sake:

"When are you going to fight him?"

He replied tranquilly: "We are not going to fight: the matter has been arranged by our seconds. Maze has sent me an apology."

Transported with rage, she boxed his ears. "Ah, he insults me in your presence, and you permit it, and refuse to fight him! It needed but this to make you a coward."

Enraged at this he cried: "I command you to hold your tongue. I know better than you do how to protect my honour. To convince you, here is the letter of M. Maze; take it and read it, and see for yourself."

She took the letter, ran her eye over it, and divining the whole truth, sneered: "You wrote him a letter also? You are afraid of each other. What cowards men are! If we were in your place, we women—after all, it is I who have been insulted, your wife, and you are willing to let it pass. That need not astonish me, for you are not man enough to beget a child. That explains everything. You are as impotent before women as you are cowardly among men. Ah, I have married a nice worm!"

She had suddenly assumed the voice and gestures of her father, the coarse and vulgar manners of an old trooper, and the intonations of a man.

Standing before him, her hands on her hips, tall, strong, vigorous, her chest protruding, her cheeks flushed, her voice deep and vibrant, she looked at this little man seated in front of her, a trifle bald, clean shaven except for the short side-whiskers of the lawyer, and she felt a desire to crush, to strangle him.

She continued: "You are capable of nothing—of nothing whatever! You allow everybody at the Ministry, even, to be promoted over your head!"

The door opened, and Cachelin entered, attracted by the sound of their voices, and demanded to know what was the matter. "I told the truth to that worm!" answered Cora.

Lesable raised his eyes, and for the first time noticed the resemblance between father and daughter. It seemed to him that a veil was lifted and the pair were revealed in their true colours—the same coarse nature was common to both; and he, a ruined man, was condemned to live between the two forever.

Cachelin exclaimed: "If you only could get a divorce! It is not very satisfactory to have married a capon."

At that word, trembling and blazing with fury, Lesable sprang up with a bound. He rushed at his father-in-law shouting: "Get out of here! Begone! You are in my house—do you understand?—and I order you to leave it." He seized from the table a bottle of sedative water and brandished it like a club.

Cachelin, intimidated, backed out of the room, muttering: "What will he do next, I wonder?"

But Lesable was too angry to be easily appeased. He turned upon his wife, who regarded this outburst in astonishment, and placing the bottle on the table cried: "As for you—as for you——" But as words failed him to express his rage, he was choked into silence, and stood glaring at her with a distorted visage.

She began to laugh.

This mocking laughter put him beside himself, and springing upon her he seized her by the throat with his left hand, while he boxed her ears furiously with the right. She recoiled, terrified and suffocating, and fell backward on the bed, while he continued to strike her. Suddenly he raised himself, out of breath, exhausted and heartily ashamed of his brutality; he stammered: "There—there—there—that will do!"

But she did not move; it seemed as if he had killed her. She lay on her back, on the side of the bed, her face concealed by her hands.

He approached her in alarm, wondering what had happened, and expecting her to uncover her face and look at him. She made no sign, and suspense becoming intolerable he murmured: "Cora, Cora, speak!" But she did not move or reply.

What was the matter with her? What was she going to do?

His rage had passed—fallen as suddenly as it had been aroused. He felt that his conduct was odious, almost criminal. He had beaten his wife, his

own wife—he who was circumspect, cold, and courteous. And in the softness his remorse awakened, he would ask her forgiveness. He threw himself
on his knees at her side and covered with kisses the cheek he had just
smitten. He softly touched the end of a finger of the hand that covered her
face. She seemed to feel nothing. He coaxed her, caressing her as one caresses
a beaten dog. She took no notice of him. "Cora, listen: I have done wrong!
Cora, hear me!" She seemed as one dead. Then he tried to take her hand
from her face. It obeyed his effort passively, and he saw an open eye, which
stared at him with a fixed and alarming gaze.

He continued: "Listen, Cora, I was transported with fury. It was your
father who drove me to do this shameful thing. A man cannot take such an
insult as that." She made no reply, as if she heard nothing. He did not
know what to say, or what to do. He kissed her under the ear, and raising
himself he saw a tear in the corner of her eye, a great tear which rolled
slowly down her cheek, and her eyelids fluttered and closed convulsively.
He was seized with shame, deeply moved, and opening his arms he threw
himself on his wife; he removed the other hand from her face and covered
it with kisses, crying: "My poor Cora, forgive me! forgive me!"

Still she wept, without a sound, without a sob, as one weeps from the
deepest grief. He held her pressed closely against him, caressing her and
whispering in her ear all the tender words he could command. But she remained insensible. However, she ceased to weep. They continued thus a
long time locked in each other's arms.

The night fell, folding in its sombre shadow the little room; and when
it was entirely dark he was emboldened to solicit her pardon in a manner
that was calculated to revive their hopes.

When they had risen he resumed his ordinary voice and manner, as if
nothing had happened. She appeared, on the contrary, softened, and spoke
in a gentler tone than usual, regarding her husband with submissive, almost
caressing eyes, as if this unexpected correction had relaxed her nerves and
softened her heart.

Lesable said quietly: "Your father must be tired of being alone so long.
It will soon be dinner-time; go and fetch him."

She obeyed him.

It was seven o'clock indeed, and the little maid announced dinner, as
Cachelin, serene and smiling, appeared with his daughter. They seated
themselves at table and talked on this evening with more cordiality than
they had done for a long time, as if something agreeable had happened to
everybody.

V

But their hopes, always sustained, always renewed, ended in nothing.
From month to month their expectations declined, in spite of the persistence of Lesable and the co-operation of his wife. They were consumed

with anxiety. Each without ceasing reproached the other for their want of success, and the husband in despair, emaciated, fatigued, had to suffer all the vulgarity of Cachelin, who in their domestic warfare called him "M. Lecoq," in remembrance, no doubt, of the day that he missed receiving a bottle in his face for having called his son-in-law a capon.

He and his daughter, whose interests were in league, enraged by the constant thought of this great fortune so near, and yet impossible to seize, racked their invention to humiliate and torture this impotent man, who was the cause of all their misfortune.

As they sat at table, Cora repeated each day: "There is very little for dinner. If we were rich, it would be otherwise. It is not my fault."

When Lesable set out for his office, she called from her room: "Do not forget your umbrella or you will come back as muddy as an omnibus wheel. It's not my fault that you are still obliged to follow the trade of a quill-driver."

When she went out herself, she never failed to cry: "If I had married another man, I should have a carriage of my own."

Every hour and on every occasion she harped on this subject. She pricked her husband with reproaches, lashed him with insult, held him alone guilty, and made him responsible for the loss of the fortune that should have been hers.

At last, one evening, losing all patience, Lesable exclaimed: "In the dog's name, can't you hold your tongue? From first to last it is your fault, and yours alone, do you hear, if we have not a child, because I have already had one."

He lied, preferring anything to this eternal reproach, to this shame of appearing impotent. She looked at him, astonished at first, seeking the truth in his eyes; at last comprehending, and full of disdain, she cried: "You have a child, have you?"

He replied with effrontery: "Yes, an illegitimate child, that I am bringing up at Asniéres."

She answered quietly: "We will go and see it to-morrow, so that I may find out how what he is like."

He only blushed to the ears and stammered: "Just as you please."

She rose the next morning at seven o'clock, very much to her husband's astonishment.

"Are we not going to see your child? You promised me yesterday evening. Perhaps you haven't got it any more to-day."

He sprang from the bed hastily. "It is not my child we are going to see, but a physician, who will give us his opinion on your case."

She replied in the tone of a woman who was sure of herself: "I shall ask nothing better."

Cachelin was instructed to inform the chief that his son-in-law was ill, and Lesable and his wife, advised by a neighbouring chemist, rang at one o'clock exactly the office-bell of Dr. Lefilleul, author of several works on the hygiene of generation.

They were shown into a salon decorated in white and gold, but scantily furnished in spite of the number of chairs and sofas. They seated themselves and waited. Lesable was excited, trembling, and also ashamed. Their turn came at last, and they were shown into a sort of office, where they were received by a short, stout man of dignified and ceremonious demeanour.

He waited till they should explain their case, but Lesable had not courage to utter a word, and blushed up to the roots of his hair. It therefore devolved on his wife to speak, and with a resolute manner and in a tranquil voice, she made known their errand.

"Monsieur, we have come to discover the reason why we cannot have children. A large fortune depends upon this for us."

The consultation was long, minute, and painful. Cora alone seemed unembarrassed, and submitted to the critical examination of the medical expert, sustained by the great interest she had at stake.

After having studied for nearly two hours the constitutions of the married pair, the practitioner said: "I discover nothing either abnormal or special. Your case is by no means an uncommon one. There is as much divergence in constitutions as in characters. When we see so many households out of joint through incompatibility of temper, it is not astonishing to see others sterile through incompatibility of physique. Madame appears to be particularly well fitted for the offices of motherhood. Monsieur, on his side, although presenting no conformation outside of the general rule, seems to me enfeebled, perhaps the consequence of his ardent desire to become a parent. Will you permit me to make an auscultation?"

Lesable, greatly disturbed, removed his waistcoat, and the doctor glued his ear to the thorax, and then to the back of his patient, tapping him continuously from the throat to the stomach, and from the loins to the nape of his neck. He discovered a slight irregularity in the action of the heart, and even a menace to the right lung. "—It is necessary for you to be very careful, Monsieur, very careful. This is anæmia, and comes from exhaustion —nothing else. These conditions, although now insignificant, may in a short time become incurable."

Lesable turned pale with anguish and begged for a prescription.

The doctor ordered a complicated régime consisting of iron, raw meat, and soup, combined with exercise, rest, and a sojourn in the country during the hot weather. He indicated, moreover, the symptoms that proclaimed the desired fecundity, and initiated them into the secrets which were usually practised with success in such cases.

The consultation cost forty francs.

When they were in the street, Cora burst out full of wrath:

"I have discovered what my fate is to be!"

Lesable made no reply. He was tormented by anxiety, he was recalling and weighing each word of the physician. Had the doctor made a mistake, or had he judged truly? He thought no more of the inheritance now, or the desired offspring; it was a question of life or death. He seemed to hear a whistling in his lungs, and his heart sounded as though it were beating in his ears. In crossing the garden of the Tuileries he was overcome with faintness and had to sit down to recover himself. His wife, as though to humiliate him by her superior strength, remained standing in front of him, regarding him from head to foot with pitying contempt. He breathed heavily, exaggerating the effort by his fears, and with the fingers of his left hand on his right wrist he counted the pulsations of the artery.

Cora, who was stamping with impatience, cried: "When will you be ready? It's time to stop this nonsense!" He arose with the air of a martyr, and went on his way without uttering a word.

When Cachelin was informed of the result of the consultation, his fury knew no bounds. He bawled out: "We know now whose fault it is to a certainty. Ah, well!" And he looked at his son-in-law with his ferocious eyes as though he would devour him.

Lesable neither listened nor heard, being totally absorbed in thoughts of his health and the menace to his existence. Father and daughter might say what they pleased. They were not in his skin, and as for him he meant to preserve his skin at all hazards. He had the various prescriptions of the physician filled, and at each meal he produced an array of bottles with the contents of which he dosed himself regardless of the sneers of his wife and her father. He looked at himself in the glass every instant, placed his hand on his heart each moment to study its action, and removed his bed to a dark room which was used as a clothes closet to put himself beyond the reach of carnal temptation.

He conceived for his wife a hatred mingled with contempt and disgust. All women, moreover, appeared to him to be monsters, dangerous beasts, whose mission it was to destroy men; and he thought no more of the will of Aunt Charlotte, except as one recalls a past accident which might have been fatal.

Some months passed. There remained but one year before the fatal term.

Cachelin had suspended in the dining-room an enormous calendar, from which he effaced a day each morning, raging at the impotence of his son-in-law, who was allowing this great fortune to escape week by week. And the thought that he would have to drudge at the office all his life, and limit his expenses to the pitiful sum of two thousand francs a year, filled him with a passion of anger that found vent in the most violent abuse. He could not look at Lesable without shaking with rage, with a brutal desire to beat, to crush, to trample on him. He hated him with an inordinate hatred. Every time he saw him open the door and enter the room, it seemed to him that a robber had broken into the house and robbed him of a sacred inheritance.

He hated him more than his most mortal enemy, and he despised him at the same time for his weakness, and above all for the baseness which caused him to sacrifice their common hope of posterity to the fear of his health. Lesable, in fact, lived as completely apart from his wife as if no tie united them. He never approached or touched her; he avoided even looking at her, as much through shame as through fear.

Cachelin, every morning asked his daughter: "Well, how about your husband? Has he made up his mind?"

And she would reply: "No, papa."

Each evening saw the most painful scenes take place at table. Cachelin continually reiterated: "When a man is not a man, he had better get out and yield his place to another."

And Cora added: "The fact is, there are some men who are both useless and wearisome. I do not know why they are permitted to live only to become a burden to everyone."

Lesable dosed himself and made no reply. At last one day his father-in-law cried: "Say, you, if you do not change your manners now that your health is improving, do you know what my daughter means to do?"

The son-in-law raised his eyes, foreseeing a new outrage. Cachelin continued: "She will take somebody else, confound you! You may consider yourself lucky if she hasn't done so already. When a girl has married a weakling like you, she is entitled to do anything."

Lesable, turning livid with wrath, replied: "It is not I who prevents her from following your good counsel."

Cora lowered her eyes, and Cachelin, knowing that he had said an outrageous thing, remained silent and confused.

VI

At the office the two men seemed to live on good enough terms. A sort of tacit pact was entered into between them to conceal from their colleagues their internal warfare. They addressed each other as "my dear Cachelin," "my dear Lesable"; they even feigned to laugh and talk together as men who were satisfied and happy in their domestic relations.

Lesable and Maze, for their part, comported themselves in the presence of each other with the ceremonious politeness of adversaries who had met in battle.

The duel they had escaped, but whose shadow had chilled them, exacted of them an exaggerated courtesy, a more marked consideration, and perhaps a secret desire for reconciliation, born of the vague fear of a new complication. Their attitude was recognised and approved as that of men of the world, who had had an affair of honour. They saluted each other from a distance with severe gravity, and with a flourish of hats that was graceful and dignified. They did not speak, their pride preventing either from making the first advances. But one day, Lesable, whom the Chief demanded to see immediately, to show his zeal, started with a great rush through the lobby and ran right into the stomach of an employee. It was Maze. They recoiled before each other, and Lesable exclaimed with eager politeness: "I hope I have not hurt you, Monsieur?"

Maze responded: "Not at all, sir."

From this moment they thought it expedient to exchange some phrases when they met. Then, in the interchange of courtesies, there were little attentions they paid each other from which arose in a short time certain familiarities, then an intimacy tempered with reserve and restrained by a certain hesitation; then on the strength of their increasing goodwill and visits made to the room of each other, a comradeship was established. They often gossiped together now of the news that found its way into the bureau. Lesable laid aside his air of superiority, and Maze no longer paraded his social successes. Cachelin often joined in the conversation and watched with interest their growing friendship. Sometimes as the handsome Maze left the apartment with head erect and square shoulders, he turned to his son-in-law and hissed: "There goes a fine man!" One morning when they were all four together, for old Savon never left his copying, the chair of the old clerk, having been tampered with no doubt by some practical joker, collapsed under him, and the good man rolled on the floor uttering cries of affright. The three others flew to his assistance. The order-clerk attributed this machination to the communists, and Maze earnestly desired to see the wounded part. Cachelin and he even essayed to take off the poor old fellow's clothes to dress the injury, they said, but he resisted desperately, crying that he was not hurt.

When the fun was over, Cachelin suddenly exclaimed: "I say, M. Maze, now that we are all together, can you not do us the honour of dining with us next Sunday? It will give pleasure to all three of us, myself, my son-in-law, and my daughter, who has often heard your name when we speak of the office. Shall it be yes?"

Lesable added his entreaty, but more coldly than his father-in-law: "Pray come," he said; "it will give us great pleasure."

Maze hesitated, embarrassed and smiling at the remembrance of past events.

Cachelin urged him: "Come, say we may expect you!"

"Very well, then, I accept."

Cachelin said on entering the house: "Cora, do you know that M. Maze is coming here to dinner next Sunday?"

Cora, surprised at first, stammered: "M. Maze? Really!" She blushed up to her hair without knowing why. She had so often heard him spoken of, his manners, his successes, for he was looked upon at the office as a man who was irresistible with women, that she had long felt a desire to know him.

Cachelin continued, rubbing his hands: "You will see that he is a real man, and a fine fellow. He is as tall as a carbineer; he does not resemble your husband there."

She did not reply, confused as if they had divined her dreams of him.

They prepared this dinner with as much solicitude as the one to which Lesable had been formerly invited. Cachelin discussed the dishes, wishing to have everything served in perfection; and as though a confidence unavowed and still undetermined had risen up in his heart, he seemed more gay, tranquilised by some secret and sure prevision.

Through all that Sunday he watched the preparations with the utmost solicitude, while Lesable was doing some urgent work, brought the evening before from the office.

It was the first week of November, and the new year was at hand.

At seven o'clock Maze arrived, in high good humour. He entered as though he felt very much at home, with a compliment and a great bouquet of roses for Cora. He added, as he presented them, in the familiar tone of a man of the world: "It seems to me, Madame, I know you already, and that I have known you from your childhood, for many years your father has spoken to me of you."

Cachelin, seeing the flowers, cried: "Ah, they are charming!" and his daughter recalled that Lesable had not brought her a bouquet the day he was introduced. The handsome clerk seemed enchanted, laughing and bestowing on Cora the most delicate flatteries, which brought the colour to her cheeks.

He found her very attractive. She thought him charming and seductive. When he had gone, Cachelin exclaimed: "Isn't he a fine fellow? What havoc he creates! They say he can wheedle any woman!"

Cora, less demonstrative, avowed, however, that she thought him very agreeable, and not so much of a *poseur* as she had believed.

Lesable, who seemed less sad and weary than usual, acknowledged that he had underrated Maze on his first acquaintance.

Maze returned at intervals, which gradually grew shorter. He delighted everybody. They petted and coddled him. Cora prepared for him the dishes he liked, and the intimacy of the three men soon became so great that they were seldom seen apart.

The new friend took the whole family to the theatre in boxes procured through the press. They returned on foot, through the streets thronged with people, to the door of Lesable's apartments, Maze and Cora walking before, keeping step, hip to hip, swinging with the same movement, the same rhythm, like two beings created to walk side by side through life. They spoke to each other in a low tone, laughing softly together, and seemed to understand each other instinctively: sometimes the young woman would turn her head and throw behind her a glance at her husband and father.

Cachelin followed them with a look of benevolent regard, and often, forgetting that he spoke to his son-in-law, he declared: "They have the same physique exactly. It is a pleasure to see them together."

Lesable replied quietly: "Yes, they are about the same figure." He was happy now in the consciousness that his heart was beating more vigorously, that his lungs acted more freely, and that his health had improved in every respect; his rancour against his father-in-law, whose cruel taunts had now entirely ceased, vanished little by little.

The first day of January he was promoted to the chief clerkship. His joy was so excessive over his happy event that on returning home he embraced his wife for the first time in six months. She appeared embarrassed, as if he had done something improper, and she looked at Maze, who had called to present to her his devotion and respect on the first day of the year. He also had an embarrassed air, and turned toward the window like a man who does not wish to see.

But Cachelin very soon resumed his brutalities, and began to harass his son-in-law with his coarse jests.

Sometimes he even attacked Maze, as though he blamed him also for the catastrophe suspended over them—the inevitable date of which approached nearer every minute.

Cora alone appeared composed, entirely happy and radiant. She had forgotten, it seemed, the threatening nearness of the term.

March had come. All hope seemed lost, for it would be three years on the twentieth of July since Aunt Charlotte's death.

An early spring had advanced the vegetation, and Maze proposed to his friends one Sunday to make an excursion to the banks of the Seine, to gather the violets in the shady places. They set out by a morning train and got off at Maisons-Laffitte. A breath of winter still lingered among the bare branches, but the turf was green and lustrous, flecked with flowers of white and blue, and the fruit-trees on the hillsides seemed garlanded with roses as their bare branches showed through the clustering blossoms. The Seine, thick and muddy from the late rains, flowed slowly between its banks gnawed by the frosts of winter; and all the country, steeped in vapour, exhaled a savour of sweet humidity under the warmth of the first days of spring.

They wandered in the park. Cachelin, more glum than usual, tapped his cane on the gravelled walk, thinking bitterly of their misfortune, so soon to be irremediable. Lesable, morose also, feared to wet his feet in the grass, while his wife and Maze were gathering flowers to make a bouquet. Cora for several days had seemed suffering, and looked weary and pale. She was soon tired and wished to return for luncheon. They came upon a little restaurant near an old ruined mill, and the traditional repast of a Parisian picnic party was soon served under a green arbour, on a little table covered with two napkins, and quite near the banks of the river. They had fried gudgeons, roast beef cooked with potatoes, and they had come to the salad of fresh green lettuce, when Cora rose brusquely and ran toward the river, pressing her napkin with both hands to her mouth.

Lesable, uneasy, wondered what could be the matter. Maze, disconcerted, blushed, and stammered, "I do not know—she was well a moment since."

Cachelin appeared frightened, and remained seated, with his fork in the air, a leaf of salad suspended at the end. Then he rose, trying to see his daughter. Bending forward, he perceived her leaning against a tree and seeming very ill. A swift suspicion flashed through his mind, and he fell back into his seat and regarded with an embarrassed air the two men, both of whom seemed now equally confused. He looked at them with anxious eyes, no longer daring to speak, wild with anguish and hope.

A quarter of an hour passed in utter silence. Then Cora reappeared, a little pale and walking slowly. No one questioned her; each seemed to divine a happy event, difficult to speak of. They burned to know, but feared also to hear, the truth. Cachelin alone had the courage to ask: "You are better now?" And she replied: "Yes, thank you; there is not much the matter; but we will return early, as I have a slight headache." When they set out she took the arm of her husband as if to signify something mysterious she had not yet dared to avow.

They separated at the station of Saint-Lazare. Maze, making a pretext of some business affair which he had just remembered, bade them adieu, after having shaken hands with all of them. As soon as Cachelin was alone with his daughter and his son-in-law, he asked: "What was the matter with you at luncheon?"

But Cora did not reply at first; after hesitating for a moment she said: "It was nothing much; a little sickness of the stomach was all." She walked with a languid step, but with a smile on her lips.

Lesable was ill at ease, his mind distracted; haunted with confused and contradictory ideas, angry, feeling an unavowable shame, cherishing a cowardly jealousy, he was like those sleepers who close their eyes in the morning that they may not see the ray of light which glides between the curtains and strikes the bed like a brilliant shaft.

As soon as he entered the house, he shut himself in his own room, pretending to be occupied with some unfinished work. Then Cachelin, placing his hands on his daughter's shoulders, exclaimed: "You are pregnant, aren't you?"

She stammered: "Yes, I think so. Two months."

Before she had finished speaking, he bounded with joy, then began to dance the *cancan* around her, an old recollection of his garrison days. He lifted his leg and leaped like a young kid in spite of his great paunch, and made the whole apartment shake with his gambols. The furniture jostled, the glasses on the buffet rattled, and the chandelier oscillated like the lamp of a ship.

He took his beloved daughter in his arms and embraced her frantically.

Then tapping her lightly on the shoulder he cried: "Ah, it is done, then, at last! Have you told your husband?"

She murmured, suddenly intimidated: "No,—not yet—I—I—was waiting——"

But Cachelin exclaimed: "Good, very good. You find it awkward. I will run and tell him myself." And he rushed to the apartment of his son-in-law. On seeing him enter, Lesable, who was doing nothing, rose and looked inquiringly at Cachelin, who left him no time for conjecture, but cried: "Do you know your wife is in the family way?"

The husband was stricken speechless, his countenance changed, and the blood surged to the roots of his hair: "What? How? Cora? you say——" he faltered when he recovered his voice.

"I say that she is pregnant; do you understand? Now is our chance!"

In his joy he took Lesable's hands and pressed and shook them, as if to felicitate him, to thank him, and cried: "Ah, at last it is true, it is true! it is true! Think of the fortune we shall have!" and unable to contain himself longer, he caught his son-in-law in his arms and embraced him, crying: "More than a million! Think of it! more than a million!" and he began to dance more violently than ever.

"But come, she is waiting for you, come and embrace her, at least," and taking him by the shoulders he pushed Lesable before him, and threw him like a ball into the apartment where Cora stood anxiously waiting and listening.

The moment she saw her husband, she recoiled, stifled with a sudden emotion. He stood before her, pale and severe. He had the air of a judge, and she of a culprit. At last he said: "It seems that you are pregnant."

She stammered in a trembling voice: "Yes, that seems to be the case."

But Cachelin seized each of them by the neck, and, bringing them face to face, cried: "Now kiss each other, by George! It is a fitting occasion."

And after releasing them, he capered about like a schoolboy, shouting: "Victory, victory, we have won our case! I say, Léopold, we must purchase a country house; there, at least, you will certainly recover your health." At this idea Lesable trembled. His father-in-law continued: "We will invite M. Torchebeuf and his wife to visit us, and as the under-chief is at the end of his term you may take his place. That is the way to bring it about."

Lesable was now beginning to regard things from Cachelin's standpoint, and he saw himself receiving his chief at a beautiful country place on the banks of the river, dressed in coat of white twill, with a Panama hat on his head.

Something sweet entered into his heart with this hope, something warm and good seemed to melt within him, rendering him light of heart and healthier in feeling. He smiled, still without speaking.

Cachelin, intoxicated with joy, transported at the thought of his fine prospects, continued:

"Who knows, we may gain some political influence. Perhaps you will be deputy. At all events, we can see the society of the neighbourhood, and enjoy some luxuries. And you shall have a little pony to convey you every morning to the station."

These images of luxury, of elegance and prosperity aroused the drooping spirits of Lesable. The thought that he could be driven in his own carriage, like the rich people he had so often envied, filled him with satisfaction, and he could not refrain from exclaiming: "Ah, that will be delightful indeed."

Cora, seeing him won over, smiled tenderly and gratefully, and Cachelin, who saw no obstacles now in the way of indulgence, declared: "We will dine at the restaurant, to celebrate the happy event."

When they reached home, the two men were a little tipsy, and Lesable, who saw double and whose ideas were all topsy-turvy, could not find his bedroom. He made his way by mistake, or forgetfulness, into the long vacant bed of his wife. And all night long it seemed to him that the bed oscillated like a boat, rolling and pitching as though it would upset. He was even a little seasick.

He was surprised on awaking to find Cora in his arms. She opened her eyes with a smile and kissed him with a sudden effusion of gratitude and affection. Then she said to him, in that caressing voice which women employ in their cajoleries: "If you wish to be very nice, you will not go to your office to-day. There is no need to be so punctual now that we are going to be rich, and we will make a little visit to the country, all by ourselves."

Lesable was content to remain quiet, with the feeling for self-indulgence which follows an evening of excess, and the warmth of the bed was grateful. He felt the drowsy wish to lie a long time, to do nothing more but to live in tranquil idleness. An unusual sloth paralyzed his soul and subdued his body, and one vague, happy, and continuous thought never left him— "He was going to be rich, independent."

But suddenly a fear seized him, and he whispered softly, as if he thought the walls might hear him: "Are you very sure you are pregnant, after all?"

She reassured him at once. "Oh, yes! I am certain of it. I could not be mistaken."

And, as if still doubting, he traced the outline of her figure with his hand, and feeling convinced declared: "Yes, it is true—but you will not be brought to bed before the date. They will contest our right on that account, perhaps."

At this supposition she grew angry.

"Oh, no indeed, they are not going to trick us now after so much misery, so much trouble, and so many efforts. Oh, no, indeed!" She was overwhelmed with indignation. "Let us go at once to the notary," she said.

But his advice was to get a physician's certificate first, and they presented themselves again to Dr. Lefilleul.

He recognized them immediately, and exclaimed: "Ah well, have you succeeded?"

They both blushed up to their ears, and Cora a little shamefacedly stammered: "I believe we have, Doctor."

The doctor rubbed his hands, crying: "I expected it, I expected it. The means I recommended to you never fail; at least, only from some radical incapacity of one of the parties."

When he had made an examination of the young wife, he declared: "It is true, bravo!" and he wrote on a sheet of paper:

"I, the undersigned, doctor of medicine, of the Faculty of Paris, certify that Madame Léopold Lesable, née Cachelin, presents all the symptoms of pregnancy, dating from over three months."

Then, turning toward Lesable: "And you," he said, "how is that chest and that heart?" and having made an auscultation, he declared that the patient was entirely cured. They set out happy and joyous, arm in arm, with elastic steps. But on the route Léopold had an idea. "We had better go home before we see the lawyer, and rearrange your dress; you'll put two or three towels under your belt it will draw attention to it and that will be better; he will not believe then that we are trying to gain time."

They returned home, and he himself undressed his wife in order to adjust the deception. Ten consecutive times Lesable changed the position of the towels, and stepped back some paces to get the proper effect, wishing to obtain an absolutely perfect resemblance. Satisfied with the result at last, they set out again, and walked proudly through the streets, Lesable carrying himself with the air of one whose virility was established and patent to all the world.

The notary received them kindly. Then he listened to their explanation, ran his eye over the certificate, and, as Lesable insisted, "For the rest, Monsieur, it is only necessary to glance for a second," he threw a convinced look on the tell-tale figure of the young woman.

There was a moment of anxious suspense, when the man of law declared: "Assuredly, whether the infant is born or to be born, it exists, it lives; so we will suspend the exception of the testament till the confinement of Madame."

After leaving the office of the notary, they embraced each other on the stairway, so exuberant was their joy.

VII

From the moment of this happy discovery, the three relatives lived in the most perfect accord. They were good-humoured, reasonable, and kind. Cachelin had recovered all his old gaiety, and Cora loaded her husband with attentions. Lesable also seemed like another man, and more gay than he had ever been in his life. Maze came less often, and seemed ill at ease in the family circle; they received him kindly, but with less warmth than formerly, for happiness is egotistical and excludes strangers.

Cachelin himself seemed to feel a certain secret hostility against the handsome clerk whom some months before he had introduced so eagerly into his household. It was he who announced to this friend the pregnancy of Cora. He said to him brusquely: "You know my daughter is pregnant!"

Maze, feigning surprise, replied: "Ah, indeed! you ought to be very happy."

Cachelin responded with a "Humph!" for he perceived that his colleague, on the contrary, did not appear to be delighted. Men care but little to see in this state (whether or not the cause lies with them) women in whom they are interested.

Every Sunday, however, Maze continued to dine with the family, but it was no longer pleasant to spend the evening with them, albeit no serious difference had arisen; and this strange embarrassment increased from week to week. One evening, just after Maze had gone, Cachelin cried with an air of annoyance: "That fellow is beginning to weary me to death!"

Lesable replied: "The fact is, he does not improve on acquaintance." Cora lowered her eyes. She did not give her opinion. She always seemed embarrassed in the presence of the handsome Maze, who, on his side, appeared almost ashamed when he found himself near her. He no longer smiled on looking at her as formerly, no longer asked her and her husband to accompany him to the theatre, and the intimacy, which till lately had been so cordial, seemed to have become but an irksome burden.

One Thursday, when her husband came home to dinner, Cora kissed him with more coquetry than usual and whispered in his ear:

"Perhaps you are going to scold me now?"

"Why should I?" he inquired.

"Well, because—M. Maze came to see me a little while ago, and, as I do not wish to be gossiped about on his account, I begged him never to come when you were not at home. He seemed a little hurt."

Lesable, very much surprised, demanded:

"Very well, what did he say to that?"

"Oh! he did not say much, but it did not please me all the same, and then I asked him to cease his visits entirely. You know very well that it is you and Papa who brought him here—I was not consulted at all about it— and I feared you would be displeased because I had dismissed him."

A grateful joy beamed from the face of her husband.

"You did right, perfectly right, and I even thank you for it."

She went on, in order to establish the understanding between the two men, which she had arranged in advance: "At the office you must conduct yourself as though nothing had happened, and speak to him as you have been in the habit of doing; but he is not to come here any more."

Taking his wife tenderly in his arms, Lesable impressed long kisses on her eyelids and on her cheeks. "You are an angel! You are an angel!" he repeated, and he felt pressing against his stomach the already lusty child.

VIII

Nothing of importance happened up to the date of Cora's confinement, which occurred on the last day of September. The child, being a daughter, was called Désirée. As they wished to make the christening an imposing event, it was decided to postpone the ceremony until they were settled in the new country house which they were going to buy.

They chose a beautiful estate at Asnières, on the hills that overlook the Seine. Great changes had taken place during the winter. As soon as the legacy was secured, Cachelin asked for his pension, which was granted, and he left the office. He employed his leisure moments in cutting, with the aid of a little scroll-saw, the covers of cigar-boxes. He made clocks, caskets, *jardinières,* and all sorts of odd little pieces of furniture. He had a passion for this work, the taste for which had come to him on seeing a peripatetic merchant working thus with sheets of wood on the Avenue de l'Opéra; and each day he obliged everybody to admire some new design both complicated and puerile. He was amazed at his own work, and kept on saying: "It is astonishing what one can accomplish!"

The assistant-chief, M. Rabot, being dead at last, Lesable fulfilled the duties of his place, although he did not receive the title, for sufficient time had not elapsed since his last promotion.

Cora had become a wholly different woman, more refined, more elegant, instinctively divining all the transformations that wealth imposes. On New Year's Day she made a visit to the wife of her husband's chief, a commonplace person, who remained a provincial, notwithstanding a residence of thirty-five years in Paris, and she put so much grace and seductiveness into her prayer that Mme. Torchebeuf should stand godmother to her child that the good woman consented. Grandpapa Cachelin was the godfather.

The ceremony took place on a brilliant Sunday in June. All the employees of the office were invited to witness it, except the handsome Maze, who was seen no more in the Cachelin circle.

At nine o'clock Lesable waited at the railway station for the train from Paris, while a groom, in livery covered with great gilt buttons, held by the bridle a plump pony hitched to a brand-new phaeton.

The engine whistled, then appeared, dragging its train of cars, which soon discharged their freight of passengers.

M. Torchebeuf descended from a first-class carriage with his wife, in a magnificent toilette, while Pitolet and Boissel got out of a second-class carriage. They had not dared to invite old Savon, but it was understood that they were to meet him by chance in the afternoon and bring him to dinner with the consent of the chief.

Lesable hurried to meet his superior, who advanced slowly, the lapel of his frock-coat ornamented with a decoration that resembled a full-blown red rose. His enormous head, surmounted by a large hat that seemed to crush his small body, gave him the appearance of a phenomenon, and his wife, if she had stood on tiptoe, could have looked over his head without any trouble.

Léopold, radiant, bowed and thanked his guests. He seated them in the phaeton, then running toward his two colleagues, who were walking modestly behind, he pressed their hands, regretting that his phaeton was too small to accommodate them also. "Follow the quay," he directed, "and you will reach my door—'Villa Désirée,' the fourth one after the turn. Make haste!"

And mounting the phaeton, he took the reins and drove off, while the groom leaped lightly to the little seat behind.

The ceremony was very brilliant, and afterwards they returned for luncheon. Each one found under his napkin a present proportioned to his station. The godmother received a bracelet of solid gold, her husband a scarf-pin of rubies, Boissel a pocket book of Russian leather, and Pitolet a superb meerschaum pipe. "It was Désirée," they said, "who offered these presents to her new friends."

Mme. Torchebeuf, blushing with confusion and pleasure, placed on her fat arm the brilliant circle, and, as the chief wore a narrow black cravat, which would not receive the pin, he stuck the jewel in the lapel of his frock-coat, under the Legion of Honour, as if it had been another decoration of an inferior order.

Outside the window the shining band of the river was seen, curving toward Suresnes, its banks shaded with trees. The sun fell in a rain on the water, making it seem a river of fire. The beginning of the repast was rather solemn, being made formal by the presence of M. and Mme. Torchebeuf. After a while, however, things began to go better. Cachelin threw out some heavy jokes, which he felt would be permitted him since he was rich, and everyone laughed at them. If Pitolet or Boissel had uttered them, the guests would certainly have been shocked.

At dessert, the infant was brought in and received a kiss from each of the company. Smothered in a cloud of snowy lace, the baby looked at the guests with its blue eyes void of intelligence or expression, and rolled its bald head from side to side with an air of newly awakened interest.

Pitolet, amid the confusion of voices, whispered in the ear of Boissel: "It looks like a little Mazette."

The joke went round the Ministry next day.

At two o'clock the health of the newly christened baby was drunk, and Cachelin proposed to show his guests over the property, and then to take them for a walk on the banks of the Seine.

They moved in a slow procession from room to room, from the cellar to the garret; then they examined the garden tree by tree, plant by plant; after which, separating into two parties, they set out for a walk.

Cachelin, who did not feel at home in the company of ladies, drew Boissel and Pitolet into a café on the bank of the river, while Mesdames Torchebeuf and Lesable, with their husbands, walked in the opposite direction, these refined ladies not being able to mingle with the common Sunday herd.

They walked slowly along the path, followed by the two men, who talked gravely of the affairs of the office. On the river the boats were continually passing, propelled by long strokes of the oars in the hands of jolly fellows, the muscles of whose bare arms rolled under the sunburned skin. Women, reclining on black or white fur rugs, managed the tillers, drowsing under the hot sun, holding open over their heads, like enormous flowers floating on the surface of the water, umbrellas of red, yellow, and blue silk. Cries from one boat to the other, calls, and shouts, and a remote murmur of human voices lower down, confused and continuous, indicated where the swarming crowds were enjoying a holiday.

Long files of fishermen stood motionless all along the river, while the swimmers, almost naked, standing in heavy fishing boats, plunged in head-foremost, climbed back upon the boats and leaped into the water again.

Mme. Torchebeuf looked on in surprise.

Cora said to her: "It is like this every Sunday; it spoils this charming country for me."

A canoe moved softly by. Two women rowed, while two men were stretched in the bottom of the boat. One of the women, turning her head towards the shore, cried:

"Hello! hello! you respectable women! I have a man for sale, very cheap! Do you want him?"

Cora turned away contemptuously and taking the arm of her companion said: "We cannot remain here; let us go. What infamous creatures!"

They moved away as M. Torchebeuf was saying to Lesable: "It is settled for the first of January. The head of the Department has positively promised me."

"I don't know how to thank you, dear master," Lesable replied.

When they reached home they found Cachelin, Pitolet, and Boissel laughing immoderately and almost carrying old Savon, whom they jokingly declared they had found on the beach in the company of a girl.

The frightened old man was crying: "It is not true, no, it is not true. It is not right to say that, M. Cachelin, it is not kind."

And Cachelin, choking with laughter, cried: "Ah, you old rogue, did you not call her your 'sweet goose quill'? We caught you, you rascal!"

Then the ladies, too, began to laugh at the dismay of the poor old man.

Cachelin continued: "With M. Torchebeuf's permission, we will keep him prisoner as a punishment and make him dine with us."

The chief good-humouredly consented, and they continued to laugh about the lady abandoned by the old man, who protested all the time, annoyed at this mischievous farce.

The subject was the occasion of inexhaustible wit throughout the evening, which sometimes even bordered on the obscene.

Cora and Mme. Torchebeuf, seated under a tent on the lawn, watched the reflections of the setting sun, which threw upon the leaves a purple glow.

Not a breath stirred the branches, a serene and infinite peace fell from the calm and flaming heavens.

Some boats still passed, more slowly, drifting with the tide.

Cora remarked: "It appears that poor M. Savon married a bad woman."

Mme. Torchebeuf, who was familiar with everything of the office, replied:

"Yes, she was an orphan, very much too young for him, and deceived him with a worthless fellow, and she ended in running away with him."

Then the fat lady added: "I say he was a worthless fellow, but I know nothing about it. It is reported that they loved one another very much. In any case, old Savon is not very seductive."

Mme. Lesable replied gravely:

"That is no excuse; the poor man is much to be pitied. Our next-door neighbour, M. Barbou, has had the same experience. His wife fell in love with a sort of painter who passed his summers here, and she has gone abroad with him. I do not understand how women can fall so low. To my mind it seems a special chastisement should be meted out to those wicked creatures who bring shame upon their families."

At the end of the alley the nurse appeared, carrying the little Désirée wrapped in her laces. The child, all rosy in the red gold of the evening light, was coming towards the two women. She stared at the fiery sky with the same pale and astonished eyes with which she regarded their faces.

All the men who were talking at a distance drew near, and Cachelin, seizing his little granddaughter, tossed her aloft in his arms as if he would carry her to the skies. Her figure was outlined against the brilliant line of the horizon, while her long white robe almost touched the ground; and the grandfather cried: "Look! isn't this the best thing in the world, after all, father Savon?"

But the old man made no reply, having nothing to say, or perhaps thinking too many things.

A servant opened the door and announced: "Madame is served!"

USELESS MOUTHS

Octave Mirbeau

(1850–1917)

TRANSLATED BY VYVYAN HOLLAND

ON THE DAY upon which it became quite certain that old François could no longer work, his wife, who was much younger than he was and very active, with two bright miserly little eyes, said to him:

"What can you expect, man? It's no good fretting your heart out about it. Everything in this world has to come to an end. You're as old as the hills. You're nearly eighty, and you're twisted like an old elm stump. You must be reasonable. And you'd better rest now."

And that evening she gave him nothing to eat.

When he saw that there was no bread and no coffee on the table as there usually was, old François' heart went cold, and in a meek, trembling, beseeching voice he said:

"I'm hungry, wife. I want a piece of bread."

And she replied, calmly:

"You're hungry? You're hungry, are you? That's a pity, my poor old man. I can't do anything about it. When one doesn't work one has no right to eat. One must earn the bread one eats. Isn't that true? A man who doesn't work is no longer a man. He's nothing at all. He's less use than a stone in a garden. He's worse than a dead fruit-tree against a wall."

"But if I can't work? There! You know quite well," protested the old man, "that I want to work. But I can't: my arms and legs won't let me."

"I'm not reproaching you. But it isn't my fault, is it? One must always be fair. I'm always fair. When you worked you ate. Now that you don't work any more you can't eat any more. That's what it comes to. There's no answer to that. It's as plain as the nose on your face. Would you keep an old screw in your stable with a full hay-rack and corn in the manger, when he could no longer stand up to his work? Would you?"

"No, of course not!" loyally replied old François, clearly overwhelmed by the pitiless logic of this comparison.

"There, then! You see how it is. You must be reasonable!"

And she added, chaffingly:

"If you're hungry, eat your fist . . . And keep the other for tomorrow!"

The woman bustled about the poorly furnished but scrupulously clean room, getting everything ready for the next day's work—for in future she would have to do the work of two people—and, so as not to waste time, she gnawed hastily at a piece of brown bread and an unripe apple which she had picked up under one of the trees in the courtyard.

The old man watched her gloomily with his small screwed-up eyes into which, possibly for the first time in his life, tears were starting. And over him, over his poor stiff bones, a great load of misery came in a wave, for he knew that no argument and no plea could move that heart which was as hard and cold as steel. He knew, too, that she would stoically have accepted for herself the ruthless law which she was applying to him, because she was uncompromising, simple and loyal as death itself. And yet he suggested timidly and without any conviction, with a half-hearted little grin on his lips:

"I've got some savings . . ."

The woman quickly protested:

"Savings? Savings, indeed! Thank you for nothing! You must be out of your mind. If we began touching our savings what would happen to me, tell me that? And our son, for whom we made them, what would he say? No, no! Work and you'll get some bread. Don't work and you won't get any. That's fair. That's how it should be."

"All right," said old François.

And he relapsed into silence, his eyes fixed hungrily on the bare table, which thenceforth would always be bare for him. He felt that it was hard but in the main he felt that it was just, for his primitive soul had never been able to rise from the savage depths of Nature to the luminous concert of Human Egoism and Love.

He rose painfully, muttering, with little groans of pain: "Oh! my back! Oh! my back!" And he passed into the bedroom whose door opened before him like the dark entrance to a tomb.

.   .

This terrible moment had to come to him as it had formerly come to his father and his mother whom he himself had refused to feed during their last workless days, deeming them to be nothing but impotent arms and useless mouths. He had seen this moment approaching for a long while. As his strength diminished, so the parsimoniously dealt-out helpings at meal-times had decreased. At first they had cut down his meat on Sundays and Thursdays, then the vegetables on other days. And now the time had come when his bread was to be taken away. He did not complain and got ready to die in silence, without a sound, like a worn-out plant whose dried-up stem and rotten roots can no longer suck up the rich juices of the earth.

He who had never had a dream in his life dreamed that night of his last goat. It was a very old, very gentle goat, white all over, with little black horns and a long beard like those of the stone devils which disported themselves over the church porch. After having for years produced pretty little kids and good milk, her womb had become sterile and her udders ran dry. She cost nothing to feed or for bedding and did no one any harm. Tied to a stake all day, a few yards away from the house she browsed on the gorse bushes on the common land and moved about at the end of her rope, bleating joyously at the people passing along the distant lane. He might have let her die too. But he had cut her throat one morning, because everything which does not produce something, whether it be milk, seed or work, must disappear and die. And he remembered the goat's eyes, her mildly astonished eyes, her soft eyes full of affectionate and dying reproach when, holding her gripped between his thighs, he had probed with his knife in her bleeding throat. When he woke, with his mind still full of his dream, old François murmured:

"That's fair. A man is a man, just as a goat is a goat. I've nothing to say. It's quite fair."

Old François never once complained or rebelled. He no longer left the bedroom; he no longer left the bed. Lying on his back with his legs straight out and pressed close together, his arms glued to his sides, his mouth open and his eyes closed, he remained as motionless as though he were dead. In this corpse-like attitude his back no longer ached and he no longer thought of anything, gradually falling into a gentle stupor, a sort of perpetual somnolence which wafted him far from the earth, far from the ambience of his pallet bed, in a sort of large, pale, endless wave through which little red flashes shot and which was dotted with tiny sparks of fire. And a stench rose from his bed as from a dung-hill.

When she went out to work next morning, his wife treble-locked the door of the bedroom. When she came back in the evening she said nothing to him, did not even glance at him and lay down near the bed on a straw mattress, on which she fell into a heavy sleep uninterrupted by any dream or waking. And at dawn the following morning she went about her ordinary work with the same care for order and cleanliness as usual.

She spent the Sunday in collecting the old man's rags and mending them. Then she folded them up and put them carefully away in a corner of the cupboard. In the evening she went and fetched the priest to administer the last sacraments to her man, as she felt that his end was near.

"What's the matter with old François?" asked the priest.

"He's got old age," replied the woman in a peremptory voice. "He's got death. It's his turn, poor chap."

The priest anointed the old man's limbs with the holy oils and said a few prayers.

"He thought he was further off it than that," the priest observed, as he left.

"It's his turn," repeated the woman stolidly.

And when she went into the room on the following day she could no longer hear the vague low rattle, the gurgling sound which issued from the old man's nose as from an emptying bottle. She felt his forehead, his chest and his hands, and found that they were cold.

"He's gone," she said gravely and respectfully, but without any emotion.

Old François' eyelids had opened at the moment of his last agony and had uncovered his dull, sightless eyes. She drew them down quickly with her thumbs, then she looked dreamily at the corpse for a few seconds and thought:

"He was a good man, thrifty and brave. He behaved well all his life. He worked well. I'll put a new shirt on him and his wedding suit and a white shroud and then, if the son will allow it, we might buy a grave for ten years, in a cemetery, like a rich man's."

THE HAPPY PRINCE

Oscar Wilde
(1856–1900)

HIGH ABOVE THE CITY, on a tall column, stood the statue of the Happy Prince. He was gilded all over with thin leaves of fine gold, for eyes he had two bright sapphires, and a large red ruby glowed on his sword-hilt.

He was very much admired indeed. "He is as beautiful as a weathercock," remarked one of the Town Councillors who wished to gain a reputation for having artistic tastes; "only not quite so useful," he added, fearing lest people should think him unpractical, which he really was not.

"Why can't you be like the Happy Prince?" asked a sensible mother of her little boy who was crying for the moon. "The Happy Prince never dreams of crying for anything."

"I am glad there is some one in the world who is quite happy," muttered a disappointed man as he gazed at the wonderful statue.

"He looks just like an angel," said the Charity Children as they came out of the cathedral in their bright scarlet cloaks, and their clean white pinafores.

"How do you know?" said the Mathematical Master, "you have never seen one."

"Ah! but we have, in our dreams," answered the children; and the Mathematical Master frowned and looked very severe, for he did not approve of children dreaming.

One night there flew over the city a little Swallow. His friends had gone away to Egypt six weeks before, but he had stayed behind, for he was in love with the most beautiful Reed. He had met her early in the spring as he was flying down the river after a big yellow moth, and had been so attracted by her slender waist that he had stopped to talk to her.

"Shall I love you?" said the Swallow, who liked to come to the point at once, and the Reed made him a low bow. So he flew round and round her, touching the water with his wings, and making silver ripples. This was his courtship, and it lasted all through the summer.

"It is a ridiculous attachment," twittered the other Swallows, "she has no money, and far too many relations;" and indeed the river was quite full of Reeds. Then, when the autumn came, they all flew away.

After they had gone he felt lonely, and began to tire of his lady-love. "She has no conversation," he said, "and I am afraid that she is a coquette, for she is always flirting with the wind." And certainly, whenever the wind blew, the Reed made the most graceful curtsies. "I admit that she is domestic," he continued, "but I love travelling, and my wife, consequently, should love travelling also."

"Will you come away with me?" he said finally to her; but the Reed shook her head, she was so attached to her home.

"You have been trifling with me," he cried. "I am off to the Pyramids. Good-bye!" and he flew away.

All day long he flew, and at nighttime he arrived at the city. "Where shall I put up?" he said; "I hope the town has made preparations."

Then he saw the statue on the tall column. "I will put up there," he cried; "it is a fine position with plenty of fresh air." So he alighted just between the feet of the Happy Prince.

"I have a golden bedroom," he said softly to himself as he looked round, and he prepared to go to sleep; but just as he was putting his head under his wing a large drop of water fell on him. "What a curious thing!" he cried, "there is not a single cloud in the sky, the stars are quite clear and bright, and yet it is raining. The climate in the north of Europe is really dreadful. The Reed used to like the rain, but that was merely her selfishness."

Then another drop fell.

"What is the use of a statue if it cannot keep the rain off?" he said; "I must look for a good chimney-pot," and he determined to fly away.

But before he had opened his wings, a third drop fell, and he looked up, and saw—Ah! what did he see?

The eyes of the Happy Prince were filled with tears, and tears were running down his golden cheeks. His face was so beautiful in the moonlight that the little Swallow was filled with pity.

"Who are you?" he said.

"I am the Happy Prince."

"Why are you weeping then?" asked the Swallow; "you have quite drenched me."

"When I was alive and had a human heart," answered the statue, "I did not know what tears were, for I lived in the Palace of Sans Souci, where sorrow is not allowed to enter. In the day time I played with my companions in the garden, and in the evening I led the dance in the Great Hall. Round the garden ran a very lofty wall, but I never cared to ask what lay beyond it, everything about me was so beautiful. My courtiers called me the Happy Prince, and happy indeed I was, if pleasure be happiness. So I lived, and so I died. And now that I am dead they have set me up here so high that I can see all the ugliness and all the misery of my city, and though my heart is made of lead yet I cannot choose but weep."

"What, is he not solid gold?" said the Swallow to himself. He was too polite to make any personal remarks out loud.

"Far away," continued the statue in a low musical voice, "far away in a little street there is a poor house. One of the windows is open, and through it I can see a woman seated at a table. Her face is thin and worn, and she has coarse red hands, all pricked by the needle, for she is a seamstress. She is embroidering passion-flowers on a satin gown for the loveliest of the Queen's maids-of-honour to wear at the next Court-ball. In a bed in the corner of the room her little boy is lying ill. He has a fever, and is asking for oranges. His mother has nothing to give him but river water, so he is crying. Swallow, Swallow, little Swallow, will you not bring her the ruby out of my sword-hilt? My feet are fastened to this pedestal and I cannot move."

"I am waited for in Egypt," said the Swallow. "My friends are flying up and down the Nile, and talking to the large lotus-flowers. Soon they will be going to sleep in the tomb of the great King. The King is there himself in his painted coffin. He is wrapped in yellow linen, and embalmed with spices. Round his neck is a chain of pale green jade, and his hands are like withered leaves."

"Swallow, Swallow, little Swallow," said the Prince, "will you not stay with me for one night, and be my messenger? The boy is so thirsty, and the mother so sad."

"I don't think I like boys," answered the Swallow. "Last summer, when I was staying on the river, there were two rude boys, the miller's sons, who were always throwing stones at me. They never hit me, of course; we swallows fly far too well for that, and besides, I come of a family famous for its agility; but still, it was a mark of disrespect."

But the Happy Prince looked so sad that the little Swallow was sorry. "It is very cold here," he said; "but I will stay with you for one night, and be your messenger."

"Thank you, little Swallow," said the Prince.

So the Swallow picked out the great ruby from the Prince's sword, and flew away with it in his beak over the roofs of the town.

He passed by the cathedral tower, where the white marble angels were sculptured. He passed by the palace and heard the sound of dancing. A beautiful girl came out on the balcony with her lover. "How wonderful the stars are," he said to her, "and how wonderful is the power of love!" "I hope my dress will be ready in time for the State-ball," she answered; "I have ordered passion-flowers to be embroidered on it; but the seamstresses are so lazy."

He passed over the river, and saw the lanterns hanging to the masts of the ships. He passed over the Ghetto, and saw the old Jews bargaining with each other, and weighing out money in copper scales. At last he came to the poor house and looked in. The boy was tossing feverishly on his bed, and the mother had fallen asleep, she was so tired. In he hopped, and laid the great ruby on the table beside the woman's thimble. Then he flew gently round the bed, fanning the boy's forehead with his wings. "How cool I feel," said the boy, "I must be getting better;" and he sank into a delicious slumber.

Then the Swallow flew back to the Happy Prince, and told him what he had done. "It is curious," he remarked, "but I feel quite warm now, although it is so cold."

"That is because you have done a good action," said the Prince. And the little Swallow began to think, and then he fell asleep. Thinking always made him sleepy.

When day broke he flew down to the river and had a bath. "What a remarkable phenomenon," said the Professor of Ornithology as he was passing over the bridge. "A swallow in winter!" And he wrote a long letter about it to the local newspaper. Every one quoted it, it was full of so many words that they could not understand.

"To-night I go to Egypt," said the Swallow, and he was in high spirits at the prospect. He visited all the public monuments, and sat a long time on top of the church steeple. Wherever he went the Sparrows chirruped, and said to each other, "What a distinguished stranger!" so he enjoyed himself very much.

When the moon rose he flew back to the Happy Prince. "Have you any commissions for Egypt?" he cried. "I am just starting."

"Swallow, Swallow, little Swallow," said the Prince, "will you not stay with me one night longer?"

"I am waited for in Egypt," answered the Swallow. "To-morrow my friends will fly up to the Second Cataract. The river-horse couches there among the bulrushes, and on a great granite throne sits the God Memnon. All night long he watches the stars, and when the morning star shines he utters one cry of joy, and then he is silent. At noon the yellow lions come down to the water's edge to drink. They have eyes like green beryls, and their roar is louder than the roar of the cataract."

"Swallow, Swallow, little Swallow," said the Prince, "far away across the city I see a young man in a garret. He is leaning over a desk covered with papers, and in a tumbler by his side there is a bunch of withered violets. His hair is brown and crisp, and his lips are red as a pomegranate, and he has large and dreamy eyes. He is trying to finish a play for the Director of the Theatre, but he is too cold to write any more. There is no fire in the grate, and hunger has made him faint."

"I will wait with you one night longer," said the Swallow, who really had a good heart. "Shall I take him another ruby?"

"Alas! I have no ruby now," said the Prince; "my eyes are all that I have left. They are made of rare sapphires, which were brought out of India a thousand years ago. Pluck out one of them and take it to him. He will sell it to the jeweller, and buy food and firewood, and finish his play."

"Dear Prince," said the Swallow, "I cannot do that;" and he began to weep.

"Swallow, Swallow, little Swallow," said the Prince, "do as I command you."

So the Swallow plucked out the Prince's eye, and flew away to the student's garret. It was easy enough to get in, as there was a hole in the roof. Through this he darted, and came into the room. The young man had his head buried in his hands, so he did not hear the flutter of the bird's wings, and when he looked up he found the beautiful sapphire lying on the withered violets.

"I am beginning to be appreciated," he cried; "this is from some great admirer. Now I can finish my play," and he looked quite happy.

The next day the Swallow flew down to the harbour. He sat on the mast of a large vessel and watched the sailors hauling big chests out of the hold with ropes. "Heave a-hoy!" they shouted as each chest came up. "I am going to Egypt!" cried the Swallow, but nobody minded, and when the moon rose he flew back to the Happy Prince.

"I am come to bid you good-bye," he cried.

"Swallow, Swallow, little Swallow," said the Prince, "will you not stay with me one night longer?"

"It is winter," answered the Swallow, "and the chill snow will soon be here. In Egypt the sun is warm on the green palm-trees, and the crocodiles lie in the mud and look lazily about them. My companions are building a nest in the Temple of Baalbec, and the pink and white doves are watching them, and cooing to each other. Dear Prince, I must leave you, but I will never forget you, and next spring I will bring you back two beautiful jewels in place of those you have given away. The ruby shall be redder than a red rose, and the sapphire shall be as blue as the great sea."

"In the square below," said the Happy Prince, "there stands a little match-girl. She has let her matches fall in the gutter, and they are all spoiled. Her father will beat her if she does not bring home some money, and she is crying. She has no shoes or stockings, and her little head is bare. Pluck out my other eye, and give it to her, and her father will not beat her."

"I will stay with you one night longer," said the Swallow, "but I cannot pluck out your eye. You would be quite blind then."

"Swallow, Swallow, little Swallow," said the Prince, "do as I command you."

So he plucked out the Prince's other eye, and darted down with it. He swooped past the match-girl, and slipped the jewel into the palm of her hand. "What a lovely bit of glass," cried the little girl; and she ran home, laughing.

Then the Swallow came back to the Prince. "You are blind now," he said, "so I will stay with you always."

"No, little Swallow," said the poor Prince, "you must go away to Egypt."

"I will stay with you always," said the Swallow, and he slept at the Prince's feet.

All the next day he sat on the Prince's shoulder, and told him stories of what he had seen in strange lands. He told him of the red ibises, who stand in long rows on the banks of the Nile, and catch gold fish in their beaks; of the Sphinx, who is as old as the world itself, and lives in the desert, and knows everything; of the merchants, who walk slowly by the side of their camels, and carry amber beads in their hands; of the King of the Mountains of the Moon, who is as black as ebony, and worships a large crystal; of the great green snake that sleeps in a palm-tree, and has twenty priests to feed it with honey-cakes; and of the pygmies who sail over a big lake on large flat leaves, and are always at war with the butterflies.

"Dear little Swallow," said the Prince, "you tell me of marvellous things, but more marvellous than anything is the suffering of men and of women. There is no Mystery so great as Misery. Fly over my city, little Swallow, and tell me what you see there."

So the Swallow flew over the great city, and saw the rich making merry in their beautiful houses, while the beggars were sitting at the gates. He flew into dark lanes, and saw the white faces of starving children looking out listlessly at the black streets. Under the archway of a bridge two little boys were lying in one another's arms to try and keep themselves warm. "How hungry we are!" they said. "You must not lie here," shouted the Watchman, and they wandered out into the rain.

Then he flew back and told the Prince what he had seen.

"I am covered with fine gold," said the Prince, "you must take it off, leaf by leaf, and give it to my poor; the living always think that gold can make them happy."

Leaf after leaf of the fine gold the Swallow picked off, till the Happy Prince looked quite dull and grey. Leaf after leaf of the fine gold he brought to the poor, and the children's faces grew rosier, and they laughed and played games in the street. "We have bread now!" they cried.

Then the snow came, and after the snow came the frost. The streets looked as if they were made of silver, they were so bright and glistening; long icicles like crystal daggers hung down from the eaves of the houses, everybody went about in furs, and the little boys wore scarlet caps and skated on the ice.

The poor little Swallow grew colder and colder, but he would not leave the Prince, he loved him too well. He picked up crumbs outside the baker's door when the baker was not looking, and tried to keep himself warm by flapping his wings.

But at last he knew that he was going to die. He had just strength to fly up to the Prince's shoulder once more. "Good-bye, dear Prince!" he murmured, "will you let me kiss your hand?"

"I am glad that you are going to Egypt at last, little Swallow," said the Prince, "you have stayed too long here; but you must kiss me on the lips, for I love you."

"It is not to Egypt that I am going," said the Swallow. "I am going to the House of Death. Death is the brother of Sleep, is he not?"

And he kissed the Happy Prince on the lips, and fell down dead at his feet.

At that moment a curious crack sounded inside the statue, as if something had broken. The fact is that the leaden heart had snapped right in two. It certainly was a dreadfully hard frost.

Early the next morning the Mayor was walking in the square below in company with the Town Councillors. As they passed the column he looked up at the statue: "Dear me! how shabby the Happy Prince looks!" he said.

"How shabby indeed!" cried the Town Councillors, who always agreed with the Mayor, and they went up to look at it.

"The ruby has fallen out of his sword, his eyes are gone, and he is golden no longer," said the Mayor; "in fact, he is little better than a beggar!"

"Little better than a beggar," said the Town Councillors.

"And here is actually a dead bird at his feet!" continued the Mayor. "We must really issue a proclamation that birds are not to be allowed to die here." And the Town Clerk made a note of the suggestion.

So they pulled down the statue of the Happy Prince. "As he is no longer beautiful he is no longer useful," said the Art Professor at the University.

Then they melted the statue in a furnace, and the Mayor held a meeting of the Corporation to decide what was to be done with the metal. "We must have another statue, of course," he said, "and it shall be a statue of myself."

"Of myself," said each of the Town Councillors, and they quarrelled. When I last heard of them they were quarrelling still.

"What a strange thing," said the overseer of the workmen at the foundry. "This broken lead heart will not melt in the furnace. We must throw it away." So they threw it on a dust heap where the dead Swallow was also lying.

"Bring me the two most precious things in the city," said God to one of His Angels; and the Angel brought Him the leaden heart and the dead bird.

"You have rightly chosen," said God, "for in my garden of Paradise this little bird shall sing for evermore, and in my city of gold the Happy Prince shall praise me."

THE ADVENTURE OF THE BRUCE–PARTINGTON PLANS

A. Conan Doyle
(1859–1930)

I N THE THIRD WEEK OF NOVEMBER, in the year 1895, a dense yellow fog settled down upon London. From the Monday to the Thursday I doubt whether it was ever possible from our windows in Baker Street to see the loom of the opposite houses. The first day Holmes had spent in cross-indexing his huge book of references. The second and third had been patiently occupied upon a subject which he had recently made his hobby—the music of the Middle Ages. But when, for the fourth time, after pushing back our chairs from breakfast we saw the greasy, heavy brown swirl still drifting past us and condensing in oily drops upon the window-panes, my comrade's impatient and active nature could endure this drab existence no longer. He paced restlessly about our sitting-room in a fever of suppressed energy, biting his nails, tapping the furniture, and chafing against inaction.

"Nothing of interest in the paper, Watson?" he said.

I was aware that by anything of interest, Holmes meant anything of criminal interest. There was the news of a revolution, of a possible war, and of an impending change of government; but these did not come within the horizon of my companion. I could see nothing recorded in the shape of crime which was not commonplace and futile. Holmes groaned and resumed his restless meanderings.

"The London criminal is certainly a dull fellow," said he in the querulous voice of the sportsman whose game has failed him. "Look out of this window, Watson. See how the figures loom up, are dimly seen, and then blend once more into the cloud-bank. The thief or the murderer could roam London on such a day as the tiger does the jungle, unseen until he pounces, and then evident only to his victim."

"There have," said I, "been numerous petty thefts."

Holmes snorted his contempt.

"This great and sombre stage is set for something more worthy than that," said he. "It is fortunate for this community that I am not a criminal."

"It is, indeed!" said I heartily.

"Suppose that I were Brooks or Woodhouse, or any of the fifty men who have good reason for taking my life, how long could I survive against my own pursuit? A summons, a bogus appointment, and all would be over. It is well they don't have days of fog in the Latin countries—the countries of assassination. By Jove! here comes something at last to break our dead monotony."

It was the maid with a telegram. Holmes tore it open and burst out laughing.

"Well, well! What next?" said he. "Brother Mycroft is coming round."

"Why not?" I asked.

"Why not? It is as if you met a tram-car coming down a country lane. Mycroft has his rails and he runs on them. His Pall Mall lodgings, the Diogenes Club, Whitehall—that is his cycle. Once, and only once, he has been here. What upheaval can possibly have derailed him?"

"Does he not explain?"

Holmes handed me his brother's telegram.

Must see you over Cadogan West. Coming at once.

MYCROFT

"Cadogan West? I have heard the name."

"It recalls nothing to my mind. But that Mycroft should break out in this erratic fashion! A planet might as well leave its orbit. By the way, do you know what Mycroft is?"

I had some vague recollection of an explanation at the time of the Adventure of the Greek Interpreter.

"You told me that he had some small office under the British government."

Holmes chuckled.

"I did not know you quite so well in those days. One has to be discreet when one talks of high matters of state. You are right in thinking that he is under the British government. You would also be right in a sense if you said that occasionally he *is* the British government."

"My dear Holmes!"

"I thought I might surprise you. Mycroft draws four hundred and fifty pounds a year, remains a subordinate, has no ambitions of any kind, will receive neither honour nor title, but remains the most indispensable man in the country."

"But how?"

"Well, his position is unique. He has made it for himself. There has never been anything like it before, nor will be again. He has the tidiest and most orderly brain, with the greatest capacity for storing facts, of any man living. The same great powers which I have turned to the detection of crime he has used for this particular business. The conclusions of every department are passed to him, and he is the central exchange, the clearing-house, which makes out the balance. All other men are specialists, but his specialism is omniscience. We will suppose that a minister needs information as to a point which involves the Navy, India, Canada and the bimetallic question; he could get his separate advices from various departments upon each, but only Mycroft can focus them all, and say offhand how each factor would affect the other. They began by using him as a short-cut, a convenience; now he has made himself an essential. In that great brain of his everything is pigeon-holed and can be handed out in an instant. Again and again his word has decided the national policy. He lives in it. He thinks of nothing else save when, as an intellectual exercise, he unbends if I call upon him and ask him to advise me on one of my little problems. But Jupiter is descending to-day. What on earth can it mean? Who is Cadogan West, and what is he to Mycroft?"

"I have it," I cried, and plunged among the litter of papers upon the sofa. "Yes, yes, here he is, sure enough! Cadogan West was the young man who was found dead on the Underground on Tuesday morning."

Holmes sat up at attention, his pipe halfway to his lips.

"This must be serious, Watson. A death which has caused my brother to alter his habits can be no ordinary one. What in the world can he have to do with it? The case was featureless as I remember it. The young man had apparently fallen out of the train and killed himself. He had not been robbed, and there was no particular reason to suspect violence. Is that not so?"

"There has been an inquest," said I, "and a good many fresh facts have come out. Looked at more closely, I should certainly say that it was a curious case."

"Judging by its effect upon my brother, I should think it must be a most extraordinary one." He snuggled down in his armchair. "Now, Watson, let us have the facts."

"The man's name was Arthur Cadogan West. He was twenty-seven years of age, unmarried, and a clerk at Woolwich Arsenal."

"Government employ. Behold the link with brother Mycroft!"

"He left Woolwich suddenly on Monday night. Was last seen by his fiancée, Miss Violet Westbury, whom he left abruptly in the fog about 7:30 that evening. There was no quarrel between them and she can give no motive for his action. The next thing heard of him was when his dead body was discovered by a plate-layer named Mason, just outside Aldgate Station on the Underground system in London."

"When?"

"The body was found at six on the Tuesday morning. It was lying wide of the metals upon the left hand of the track as one goes eastward, at a point close to the station, where the line emerges from the tunnel in which it runs. The head was badly crushed—an injury which might well have been caused by a fall from the train. The body could only have come on the line in that way. Had it been carried down from any neighbouring street, it must have passed the station barriers, where a collector is always standing. This point seems absolutely certain."

"Very good. The case is definite enough. The man, dead or alive, either fell or was precipitated from a train. So much is clear to me. Continue."

"The trains which traverse the lines of rail beside which the body was found are those which run from west to east, some being purely Metropolitan, and some from Willesden and outlying junctions. It can be stated for certain that this young man, when he met his death, was travelling in this direction at some late hour of the night, but at what point he entered the train it is impossible to state."

"His ticket, of course, would show that."

"There was no ticket in his pockets."

"No ticket! Dear me, Watson, this is really very singular. According to my experience it is not possible to reach the platform of a Metropolitan train without exhibiting one's ticket. Presumably, then, the young man had one. Was it taken from him in order to conceal the station from which he came? It is possible. Or did he drop it in the carriage? That also is possible. But the point is of curious interest. I understand that there was no sign of robbery?"

"Apparently not. There is a list here of his possessions. His purse contained two pounds fifteen. He had also a check-book on the Woolwich branch of the Capital and Counties Bank. Through this his identity was established. There were also two dress-circle tickets for the Woolwich Theatre, dated for that very evening. Also a small packet of technical papers."

Holmes gave an exclamation of satisfaction.

"There we have it at last, Watson! British government—Woolwich. Arsenal—technical papers—Brother Mycroft, the chain is complete. But here he comes, if I am not mistaken, to speak for himself."

A moment later the tall and portly form of Mycroft Holmes was ushered into the room. Heavily built and massive, there was a suggestion of uncouth physical inertia in the figure, but above this unwieldy frame there was perched a head so masterful in its brow, so alert in its steel-grey, deep-set eyes, so firm in its lips, and so subtle in its play of expression, that after the first glance one forgot the gross body and remembered only the dominant mind.

At his heels came our old friend Lestrade, of Scotland Yard—thin and austere. The gravity of both their faces foretold some weighty quest. The detective shook hands without a word. Mycroft Holmes struggled out of his overcoat and subsided into an armchair.

"A most annoying business, Sherlock," said he. "I extremely dislike altering my habits, but the powers that be would take no denial. In the present state of Siam it is most awkward that I should be away from the office. But it is a real crisis. I have never seen the Prime Minister so upset. As to the Admiralty—it is buzzing like an overturned bee-hive. Have you read up the case?"

"We have just done so. What were the technical papers?"

"Ah, there's the point! Fortunately, it has not come out. The press would be furious if it did. The papers which this wretched youth had in his pocket were the plans of the Bruce-Partington submarine."

Mycroft Holmes spoke with a solemnity which showed his sense of the importance of the subject. His brother and I sat expectant.

"Surely you have heard of it? I thought everyone had heard of it."

"Only as a name."

"Its importance can hardly be exaggerated. It has been the most jealously guarded of all government secrets. You may take it from me that naval warfare becomes impossible within the radius of a Bruce-Partington's operation. Two years ago a very large sum was smuggled through the Estimates and was expended in acquiring a monopoly of the invention. Every effort has been made to keep the secret. The plans, which are exceedingly intricate, comprising some thirty separate patents, each essential to the working of the whole, are kept in an elaborate safe in a confidential office adjoining the arsenal, with burglar-proof doors and windows. Under no conceivable circumstances were the plans to be taken from the office. If the chief constructor of the Navy desired to consult them, even he was forced to go to the Woolwich office for the purpose. And yet here we find them in the pockets of a dead junior clerk in the heart of London. From an official point of view it's simply awful."

"But you have recovered them?"

"No, Sherlock, no! That's the pinch. We have not. Ten papers were taken from Woolwich. There were seven in the pockets of Cadogan West. The three most essential are gone—stolen, vanished. You must drop everything, Sherlock. Never mind your usual petty puzzles of the police-court. It's a vital international problem that you have to solve. Why did Cadogan West take the papers, where are the missing ones, how did he die, how came his body where it was found, how can the evil be set right? Find an answer to all these questions, and you will have done good service for your country."

"Why do you not solve it yourself, Mycroft? You can see as far as I."

"Possibly, Sherlock. But it is a question of getting details. Give me your details, and from an armchair I will return you an excellent expert opinion. But to run here and run there, to cross-question railway guards, and lie on my face with a lens to my eye—it is not my *métier*. No, you are the one man who can clear the matter up. If you have a fancy to see your name in the next honours list——"

My friend smiled and shook his head.

"I play the game for the game's own sake," said he. "But the problem certainly presents some points of interest, and I shall be very pleased to look into it. Some more facts, please."

"I have jotted down the more essential ones upon this sheet of paper, together with a few addresses which you will find of service. The actual official guardian of the papers is the famous government expert, Sir James Walter, whose decorations and sub-titles fill two lines of a book of reference. He has grown grey in the service, is a gentleman, a favoured guest in the most exalted houses, and, above all, a man whose patriotism is beyond suspicion. He is one of two who have a key of the safe. I may add that the papers were undoubtedly in the office during working hours on Monday, and that Sir James left for London about three o'clock taking his key with him. He was at the house of Admiral Sinclair at Barclay Square during the whole of the evening when this incident occurred."

"Has the fact been verified?"

"Yes; his brother, Colonel Valentine Walter, has testified to his departure from Woolwich, and Admiral Sinclair to his arrival in London; so Sir James is no longer a direct factor in the problem."

"Who was the other man with a key?"

"The senior clerk and draughtsman, Mr. Sidney Johnson. He is a man of forty, married, with five children. He is a silent, morose man, but he has, on the whole, an excellent record in the public service. He is unpopular with his colleagues, but a hard worker. According to his own account, corroborated only by the word of his wife, he was at home the whole of Monday evening after office hours, and his key has never left the watch-chain upon which it hangs."

"Tell us about Cadogan West."

"He has been ten years in the service and has done good work. He has the reputation of being hot-headed and impetuous, but a straight, honest man. We have nothing against him. He was next Sidney Johnson in the office. His duties brought him into daily, personal contact with the plans. No one else had the handling of them."

"Who locked the plans up that night?"

"Mr. Sidney Johnson, the senior clerk."

"Well, it is surely perfectly clear who took them away. They are actually found upon the person of this junior clerk, Cadogan West. That seems final, does it not?"

"It does, Sherlock, and yet it leaves so much unexplained. In the first place, why did he take them?"

"I presume they were of value?"

"He could have got several thousands for them very easily."

"Can you suggest any possible motive for taking the papers to London except to sell them?"

"No, I cannot."

"Then we must take that as our working hypothesis. Young West took the papers. Now this could only be done by having a false key——"

"Several false keys. He had to open the building and the room."

"He had, then, several false keys. He took the papers to London to sell the secret, intending, no doubt, to have the plans themselves back in the safe next morning before they were missed. While in London on this treasonable mission he met his end."

"How?"

"We will suppose that he was travelling back to Woolwich when he was killed and thrown out of the compartment."

"Aldgate, where the body was found, is considerably past the station for London Bridge, which would be his route to Woolwich."

"Many circumstances could be imagined under which he would pass London Bridge. There was someone in the carriage, for example, with whom he was having an absorbing interview. This interview led to a violent scene in which he lost his life. Possibly he tried to leave the carriage, fell out on the line, and so met his end. The other closed the door. There was a thick fog, and nothing could be seen."

"No better explanation can be given with our present knowledge; and yet consider, Sherlock, how much you leave untouched. We will suppose, for argument's sake, that young Cadogan West *had* determined to convey these papers to London. He would naturally have made an appointment with the foreign agent and kept his evening clear. Instead of that he took two tickets for the theatre, escorted his fiancée halfway there, and then suddenly disappeared."

"A blind," said Lestrade, who had sat listening with some impatience to the conversation.

"A very singular one. That is objection No. 1. Objection No. 2: We will suppose that he reaches London and sees the foreign agent. He must bring back the papers before morning or the loss will be discovered. He took away ten. Only seven were in his pocket. What had become of the other three? He certainly would not leave them of his own free will. Then, again, where is the price of his treason? One would have expected to find a large sum of money in his pocket."

"It seems to me perfectly clear," said Lestrade. "I have no doubt at all as to what occurred. He took the papers to sell them. He saw the agent. They could not agree as to price. He started home again, but the agent went with him. In the train the agent murdered him, took the more essential papers, and threw his body from the carriage. That would account for everything, would it not?"

"Why had he no ticket?"

"The ticket would have shown which station was nearest the agent's house. Therefore he took it from the murdered man's pocket."

"Good, Lestrade, very good," said Holmes. "Your theory holds together. But if this is true, then the case is at an end. On the one hand, the traitor is dead. On the other, the plans of the Bruce-Partington submarine are presumably already on the Continent. What is there for us to do?"

"To act, Sherlock—to act!" cried Mycroft, springing to his feet. "All my instincts are against this explanation. Use your powers! Go to the scene of the crime! See the people concerned! Leave no stone unturned! In all your career you have never had so great a chance of serving your country."

"Well, well!" said Holmes, shrugging his shoulders. "Come, Watson! And you, Lestrade, could you favour us with your company for an hour or two? We will begin our investigation by a visit to Aldgate Station. Good-bye, Mycroft. I shall let you have a report before evening, but I warn you in advance that you have little to expect."

An hour later Holmes, Lestrade and I stood upon the Underground railroad at the point where it emerges from the tunnel immediately before Aldgate Station. A courteous red-faced old gentleman represented the railway company.

"This is where the young man's body lay," said he, indicating a spot about three feet from the metals. "It could not have fallen from above, for these, as you see, are all blank walls. Therefore, it could only have come from a train, and that train, so far as we can trace it, must have passed about midnight on Monday."

"Have the carriages been examined for any sign of violence?"

"There are no such signs, and no ticket has been found."

"No record of a door being found open?"

"None."

"We have had some fresh evidence this morning," said Lestrade. "A passenger who passed Aldgate in an ordinary Metropolitan train about 11:40 on Monday night declares that he heard a heavy thud, as of a body striking the line, just before the train reached the station. There was dense fog, however, and nothing could be seen. He made no report of it at the time. Why, whatever is the matter with Mr. Holmes?"

My friend was standing with an expression of strained intensity upon his face, staring at the railway metals where they curved out of the tunnel. Aldgate is a junction, and there was a network of points. On these his eager, questioning eyes were fixed, and I saw on his keen, alert face that tightening of the lips, that quiver of the nostrils, and concentration of the heavy, tufted brows which I knew so well.

"Points," he muttered; "the points."

"What of it? What do you mean?"

"I suppose there are no great number of points on a system such as this?"

"No; there are very few."

"And a curve, too. Points, and a curve. By Jove! if it were only so."

"What is it, Mr. Holmes? Have you a clue?"

"An idea—an indication, no more. But the case certainly grows in interest. Unique, perfectly unique, and yet why not? I do not see any indications of bleeding on the line."

"There were hardly any."

"But I understand that there was a considerable wound."

"The bone was crushed, but there was no great external injury."

"And yet one would have expected some bleeding. Would it be possible for me to inspect the train which contained the passenger who heard the thud of a fall in the fog?"

"I fear not, Mr. Holmes. The train has been broken up before now, and the carriages redistributed."

"I can assure you, Mr. Holmes," said Lestrade, "that every carriage has been carefully examined. I saw to it myself."

It was one of my friend's most obvious weaknesses that he was impatient with less alert intelligences than his own.

"Very likely," said he, turning away. "As it happens, it was not the carriages which I desired to examine. Watson, we have done all we can here. We need not trouble you any further, Mr. Lestrade. I think our investigations must now carry us to Woolwich."

At London Bridge, Holmes wrote a telegram to his brother, which he handed to me before dispatching it. It ran thus:

See some light in the darkness, but it may possibly flicker out. Meanwhile, please send by messenger, to await return at Baker Street, a complete list of all foreign spies or international agents known to be in England, with full address.

SHERLOCK

"That should be helpful, Watson," he remarked as we took our seats in the Woolwich train. "We certainly owe brother Mycroft a debt for having introduced us to what promises to be a really very remarkable case."

His eager face still wore that expression of intense and high-strung energy, which showed me that some novel and suggestive circumstance had opened up a stimulating line of thought. See the foxhound with hanging ears and drooping tail as it lolls about the kennels, and compare it with the same hound as, with gleaming eyes and straining muscles, it runs upon a breast-high scent—such was the change in Holmes since the morning. He was a different man from the limp and lounging figure in the mouse-coloured dressing-gown who had prowled so restlessly only a few hours before round the fog-girt room.

"There is material here. There is scope," said he. "I am dull indeed not to have understood its possibilities."

"Even now they are dark to me."

"The end is dark to me also, but I have hold of one idea which may lead us far. The man met his death elsewhere, and his body was on the *roof* of a carriage."

"On the roof!"

"Remarkable, is it not? But consider the facts. Is it a coincidence that it is found at the very point where the train pitches and sways as it comes round on the points? Is not that the place where an object upon the roof might be expected to fall off? The points would affect no object inside the train. Either the body fell from the roof, or a very curious coincidence has occurred. But now consider the question of the blood. Of course, there was no bleeding on the line if the body had bled elsewhere. Each fact is suggestive in itself. Together they have a cumulative force."

"And the ticket, too!" I cried.

"Exactly. We could not explain the absence of a ticket. This would explain it. Everything fits together."

"But suppose it were so, we are still as far as ever from unravelling the mystery of his death. Indeed, it becomes not simpler but stranger."

"Perhaps," said Holmes thoughtfully, "perhaps." He relapsed into a silent reverie, which lasted until the slow train drew up at last in Woolwich Station. There he called a cab and drew Mycroft's paper from his pocket.

"We have quite a little round of afternoon calls to make," said he. "I think that Sir James Walter claims our first attention."

The house of the famous official was a fine villa with green lawns stretching down to the Thames. As we reached it the fog was lifting, and a thin, watery sunshine was breaking through. A butler answered our ring.

"Sir James, sir?" said he with solemn face. "Sir James died this morning."

"Good heavens!" cried Holmes in amazement. "How did he die?"

"Perhaps you would care to step in, sir, and see his brother, Colonel Valentine?"

"Yes, we had best do so."

We were ushered into a dim-lit drawing-room, where an instant later we were joined by a very tall, handsome, light-bearded man of fifty, the younger brother of the dead scientist. His wild eyes, stained cheeks, and unkempt hair all spoke of the sudden blow which had fallen upon the household. He was hardly articulate as he spoke of it.

"It was this horrible scandal," said he. "My brother, Sir James, was a man of very sensitive honour, and he could not survive such an affair. It broke his heart. He was always so proud of the efficiency of his department, and this was a crushing blow."

"We had hoped that he might have given us some indications which would have helped us to clear the matter up."

"I assure you that it was all a mystery to him as it is to you and to all of us. He had already put all his knowledge at the disposal of the police. Naturally he had no doubt that Cadogan West was guilty. But all the rest was inconceivable."

"You cannot throw any new light upon the affair?"

"I know nothing myself save what I have read or heard. I have no desire to be discourteous, but you can understand, Mr. Holmes, that we are much disturbed at present, and I must ask you to hasten this interview to an end."

"This is indeed an unexpected development," said my friend when we had regained the cab. "I wonder if the death was natural, or whether the poor old fellow killed himself! If the latter, may it be taken as some sign of self-reproach for duty neglected? We must leave that question to the future. Now we shall turn to the Cadogan Wests."

A small but well-kept house in the outskirts of the town sheltered the bereaved mother. The old lady was too dazed with grief to be of any use to us, but at her side was a white-faced young lady, who introduced herself as Miss Violet Westbury, the fiancée of the dead man, and the last to see him upon that fatal night.

"I cannot explain it, Mr. Holmes," she said. "I have not shut an eye since the tragedy, thinking, thinking, thinking, night and day, what the true meaning of it can be. Arthur was the most single-minded, chivalrous, patriotic man upon earth. He would have cut his right hand off before he would sell a State secret confided to his keeping. It is absurd, impossible, preposterous to anyone who knew him."

"But the facts, Miss Westbury?"

"Yes, yes; I admit I cannot explain them."

"Was he in any want of money?"

"No; his needs were very simple and his salary ample. He had saved a few hundreds, and we were to marry at the New Year."

"No signs of any mental excitement? Come, Miss Westbury, be absolutely frank with us."

The quick eye of my companion had noted some change in her manner. She coloured and hesitated.

"Yes," she said at last, "I had a feeling that there was something on his mind."

"For long?"

"Only for the last week or so. He was thoughtful and worried. Once I pressed him about it. He admitted that there was something, and that it was concerned with his official life. 'It is too serious for me to speak about, even to you,' said he. I could get nothing more."

Holmes looked grave.

"Go on, Miss Westbury. Even if it seems to tell against him, go on. We cannot say what it may lead to."

"Indeed, I have nothing more to tell. Once or twice it seemed to me that he was on the point of telling me something. He spoke one evening of the importance of the secret, and I have some recollection that he said that no doubt foreign spies would pay a great deal to have it."

My friend's face grew graver still.

"Anything else?"

"He said that we were slack about such matters—that it would be easy for a traitor to get the plans."

"Was it only recently that he made such remarks?"

"Yes, quite recently."

"Now tell us of that last evening."

"We were to go to the theatre. The fog was so thick that a cab was useless. We walked, and our way took us close to the office. Suddenly he darted away into the fog."

"Without a word?"

"He gave an exclamation; that was all. I waited but he never returned. Then I walked home. Next morning, after the office opened, they came to inquire. About twelve o'clock we heard the terrible news. Oh, Mr. Holmes, if you could only, only save his honour! It was so much to him."

Holmes shook his head sadly.

"Come, Watson," said he, "our ways lie elsewhere. Our next station must be the office from which the papers were taken.

"It was black enough before against this young man, but our inquiries make it blacker," he remarked as the cab lumbered off. "His coming marriage gives a motive for the crime. He naturally wanted money. The idea was in his head, since he spoke about it. He nearly made the girl an accomplice in the treason by telling her his plans. It is all very bad."

"But surely, Holmes, character goes for something? Then, again, why should he leave the girl in the street and dart away to commit a felony?"

"Exactly! There are certainly objections. But it is a formidable case which they have to meet."

Mr. Sidney Johnson, the senior clerk, met us at the office and received us with that respect which my companion's card always commanded. He was a thin, gruff, bespectacled man of middle age, his cheeks haggard, and his hands twitching from the nervous strain to which he had been subjected.

"It is bad, Mr. Holmes, very bad! Have you heard of the death of the chief?"

"We have just come from his house."

"The place is disorganized. The chief dead, Cadogan West dead, our papers stolen. And yet, when we closed our door on Monday evening, we were as efficient an office as any in the government service. Good God, it's dreadful to think of! That West, of all men, should have done such a thing!"

"You are sure of his guilt, then?"

"I can see no other way out of it. And yet I would have trusted him as I trust myself."

"At what hour was the office closed on Monday?"

"At five."

"Did you close it?"

"I am always the last man out."

"Where were the plans?"

"In that safe. I put them there myself."

"Is there no watchman to the building?"

"There is, but he has other departments to look after as well. He is an old soldier and a most trustworthy man. He saw nothing that evening. Of course the fog was very thick."

"Suppose that Cadogan West wished to make his way into the building after hours; he would need three keys, would he not, before he could reach the papers?"

"Yes, he would. The key of the outer door, the key of the office, and the key of the safe."

"Only Sir James Walter and you had those keys?"

"I had no keys of the doors—only of the safe."

"Was Sir James a man who was orderly in his habits?"

"Yes, I think he was. I know that so far as those three keys are concerned he kept them on the same ring. I have often seen them there."

"And that ring went with him to London?"

"He said so."

"And your key never left your possession?"

"Never."

"Then West, if he is the culprit, must have had a duplicate. And yet none was found upon his body. One other point: if a clerk in this office desired to sell the plans, would it not be simpler to copy the plans for himself than to take the originals, as was actually done?"

"It would take considerable technical knowledge to copy the plans in an effective way."

"But I suppose either Sir James, or you, or West had that technical knowledge?"

"No doubt we had, but I beg you won't try to drag me into the matter, Mr. Holmes. What is the use of our speculating in this way when the original plans were actually found on West?"

"Well, it is certainly singular that he should run the risk of taking originals if he could safely have taken copies, which would have equally served his turn."

"Singular, no doubt—and yet he did so."

"Every inquiry in this case reveals something inexplicable. Now there are three papers still missing. They are, as I understand, the vital ones."

"Yes, that is so."

"Do you mean to say that anyone holding these three papers, and without the seven others, could construct a Bruce-Partington submarine?"

"I reported to that effect to the Admiralty. But to-day I have been over the drawings again, and I am not so sure of it. The double valves with the automatic self-adjusting slots are drawn in one of the papers which have been returned. Until the foreigners had invented that for themselves they could not make the boat. Of course they might soon get over the difficulty."

"But the three missing drawings are the most important?"

"Undoubtedly."

"I think, with your permission, I will now take a stroll round the premises. I do not recall any other question which I desired to ask."

He examined the lock of the safe, the door of the room, and finally the iron shutters of the window. It was only when we were on the lawn outside that his interest was strongly excited. There was a laurel bush outside the window, and several of the branches bore signs of having been twisted or snapped. He examined them carefully with his lens, and then some dim and vague marks upon the earth beneath. Finally he asked the chief clerk to close the iron shutters, and he pointed out to me that they hardly met in the centre, and that it would be possible for anyone outside to see what was going on within the room.

"The indications are ruined by the three days' delay. They may mean something or nothing. Well, Watson, I do not think that Woolwich can help us further. It is a small crop which we have gathered. Let us see if we can do better in London."

Yet we added one more sheaf to our harvest before we left Woolwich Station. The clerk in the ticket office was able to say with confidence that he saw Cadogan West—whom he knew well by sight—upon the Monday night, and that he went to London by the 8:15 to London Bridge. He was alone and took a single third-class ticket. The clerk was struck at the time by his excited and nervous manner. So shaky was he that he could hardly pick up his change, and the clerk had helped him with it. A reference to the timetable showed that the 8:15 was the first train which it was possible for West to take after he had left the lady about 7:30.

"Let us reconstruct, Watson," said Holmes after half an hour of silence. "I am not aware that in all our joint researches we have ever had a case which was more difficult to get at. Every fresh advance which we make only reveals a fresh ridge beyond. And yet we have surely made some appreciable progress.

"The effect of our inquiries at Woolwich has in the main been against young Cadogan West; but the indications at the window would lend themselves to a more favourable hypothesis. Let us suppose, for example, that he had been approached by some foreign agent. It might have been done under such pledges as would have prevented him from speaking of it, and yet would have affected his thoughts in the direction indicated by his remarks to his fiancée. Very good. We will now suppose that as he went to the theatre with the young lady he suddenly, in the fog, caught a glimpse of this same agent going in the direction of the office. He was an impetuous man, quick in his decisions. Everything gave way to his duty. He followed the man, reached the window, saw the abstraction of the documents, and pursued the thief. In this way we get over the objection that no one would take originals when he could make copies. This outsider had to take originals. So far it holds together."

"What is the next step?"

"Then we come into difficulties. One would imagine that under such circumstances the first act of young Cadogan West would be to seize the villain and raise the alarm. Why did he not do so? Could it have been an official superior who took the papers? That would explain West's conduct. Or could the chief have given West the slip in the fog, and West started at once to London to head him off from his own rooms, presuming that he knew where the rooms were? The call must have been very pressing, since he left his girl standing in the fog, and made no effort to communicate with her. Our scent runs cold here, and there is a vast gap between either hypothesis and the laying of West's body, with seven papers in his pocket, on the roof of a Metropolitan train. My instinct now is to work from the other end. If Mycroft has given us the list of addresses we may be able to pick our man and follow two tracks instead of one."

Surely enough, a note awaited us at Baker Street. A government messenger had brought it post-haste. Holmes glanced at it and threw it over to me.

There are numerous small fry, but few who would handle so big an affair. The only men worth considering are Adolph Meyer, of 13 Great George Street, Westminster; Louis La Rothière, of Campden Mansions, Notting Hill; and Hugo Oberstein, 13 Caulfield Gardens, Kensington. The latter was known to be in town on Monday and is now reported as having left. Glad to hear you have seen some light. The Cabinet awaits your final report with the utmost anxiety. Urgent representations have arrived from the very highest quarter. The whole force of the State is at your back if you should need it.

MYCROFT

"I'm afraid," said Holmes, smiling, "that all the queen's horses and all the queen's men cannot avail in this matter." He had spread out his big map of London and leaned eagerly over it. "Well, well," said he presently with an exclamation of satisfaction, "things are turning a little in our direction at last. Why, Watson, I do honestly believe that we are going to pull it off, after all." He slapped me on the shoulder with a sudden burst of hilarity.

"I am going out now. It is only a reconnaissance. I will do nothing serious without my trusted comrade and biographer at my elbow. Do you stay here, and the odds are that you will see me again in an hour or two. If time hangs heavy get foolscap and a pen, and begin your narrative of how we saved the State."

I felt some reflection of his elation in my own mind, for I knew well that he would not depart so far from his usual austerity of demeanour unless there was good cause for exultation. All the long November evening I waited, filled with impatience for his return. At last, shortly after nine o'clock, there arrived a messenger with a note:

Am dining at Goldini's Restaurant, Gloucester Road, Kensington. Please come at once and join me there. Bring with you a jemmy, a dark lantern, a chisel, and a revolver.

S. H.

It was a nice equipment for a respectable citizen to carry through the dim, fog-draped streets. I stowed them all discreetly away in my overcoat and drove straight to the address given. There sat my friend at a little round table near the door of the garish Italian restaurant.

"Have you had something to eat? Then join me in a coffee and curaçao. Try one of the proprietor's cigars. They are less poisonous than one would expect. Have you the tools?"

"They are here, in my overcoat."

"Excellent. Let me give you a short sketch of what I have done, with some indication of what we are about to do. Now it must be evident to you, Watson, that this young man's body was *placed* on the roof of the train. That was clear from the instant that I determined the fact that it was from the roof, and not from a carriage, that he had fallen."

"Could it not have been dropped from a bridge?"

"I should say it was impossible. If you examine the roofs you will find that they are slightly rounded, and there is no railing round them. Therefore, we can say for certain that young Cadogan West was placed on it."

"How could he be placed there?"

"That was the question which we had to answer. There is only one possible way. You are aware that the Underground runs clear of tunnels at some points in the West End. I had a vague memory that as I have travelled by it I have occasionally seen windows just above my head. Now, suppose that a train halted under such a window, would there be any difficulty in laying a body upon the roof?"

"It seems most improbable."

"We must fall back upon the old axiom that when all other contingencies fail, whatever remains, however improbable, must be the truth. Here all other contingencies *have* failed. When I found that the leading international agent, who had just left London, lived in a row of houses which abutted upon the Underground. I was so pleased that you were a little astonished at my sudden frivolity."

"Oh, that was it, was it?"

"Yes, that was it. Mr. Hugo Oberstein, of 13 Caulfield Gardens, had become my objective. I began my operations at Gloucester Road Station, where a very helpful official walked with me along the track and allowed me to satisfy myself not only that the back-stair windows of Caulfield Gardens open on the line but the even more essential fact that, owing to the intersection of one of the larger railways, the Underground trains are frequently held motionless for some minutes at that very spot."

"Splendid, Holmes! You have got it!"

"So far—so far, Watson. We advance, but the goal is afar. Well, having seen the back of Caulfield Gardens, I visited the front and satisfied myself that the bird was indeed flown. It is a considerable house, unfurnished, so far as I could judge, in the upper rooms. Oberstein lived there with a single valet, who was probably a confederate entirely in his confidence. We must bear in mind that Oberstein has gone to the Continent to dispose of his booty, but not with any idea of flight; for he had no reason to fear a warrant, and the idea of an amateur domiciliary visit would certainly never occur to him. Yet that is precisely what we are about to make."

"Could we not get a warrant and legalize it?"

"Hardly on the evidence."

"What can we hope to do?"

"We cannot tell what correspondence may be there."

"I don't like it, Holmes."

"My dear fellow, you shall keep watch in the street. I'll do the criminal part. It's not a time to stick at trifles. Think of Mycroft's note, of the Admiralty, the Cabinet, the exalted person who waits for news. We are bound to go."

My answer was to rise from the table.

"You are right, Holmes. We are bound to go."

He sprang up and shook me by the hand.

"I knew you would not shrink at the last," said he, and for a moment I saw something in his eyes which was nearer to tenderness than I had ever seen. The next instant he was his masterful, practical self once more.

"It is nearly half a mile, but there is no hurry. Let us walk," said he. "Don't drop the instruments, I beg. Your arrest as a suspicious character would be a most unfortunate complication."

Caulfield Gardens was one of those lines of flat-faced, pillared and porticoed houses which are so prominent a product of the middle Victorian epoch in the West End of London. Next door there appeared to be a children's party, for the merry buzz of young voices and the clatter of a piano resounded through the night. The fog still hung about and screened us with its friendly shade. Holmes had lit his lantern and flashed it upon the massive door.

"This is a serious proposition," said he. "It is certainly bolted as well as locked. We would do better in the area. There is an excellent archway down yonder in case a too zealous policeman should intrude. Give me a hand, Watson, and I'll do the same for you."

A minute later we were both in the area. Hardly had we reached the dark shadows before the step of the policeman was heard in the fog above. As its soft rhythm died away, Holmes set to work upon the lower door. I saw him stoop and strain until with a sharp crash it flew open. We sprang through into the dark passage, closing the area door behind us. Holmes led the way up the curving, uncarpeted stair. His little fan of yellow light shone upon a low window.

"Here we are, Watson—this must be the one." He threw it open, and as he did so there was a low, harsh murmur, growing steadily into a loud roar as a train dashed past us in the darkness. Holmes swept his light along the window-sill. It was thickly coated with soot from the passing engines, but the black surface was blurred and rubbed in places.

"You can see where they rested the body. Halloa, Watson! what is this? There can be no doubt that it is a blood mark." He was pointing to faint discolourations along the woodwork of the window. "Here it is on the stone of the stair also. The demonstration is complete. Let us stay here until a train stops."

We had not long to wait. The very next train roared from the tunnel as before, but slowed in the open, and then, with a creaking of brakes, pulled up immediately beneath us. It was not four feet from the window-ledge to the roof of the carriages. Holmes softly closed the window.

"So far we are justified," said he. "What do you think of it, Watson?"

"A masterpiece. You have never risen to a greater height."

"I cannot agree with you there. From the moment that I conceived the idea of the body being upon the roof, which surely was not a very abstruse one, all the rest was inevitable. If it were not for the grave interests involved the affair up to this point would be insignificant. Our difficulties are still before us. But perhaps we may find something here which may help us."

We had ascended the kitchen stair and entered the suite of rooms upon the first floor. One was a dining-room, severely furnished and containing nothing of interest. A second was a bedroom, which also drew blank. The remaining room appeared more promising, and my companion settled down to a systematic examination. It was littered with books and papers, and was evidently used as a study. Swiftly and methodically Holmes turned over the contents of drawer after drawer and cupboard after cupboard, but no gleam of success came to brighten his austere face. At the end of an hour he was no further than when he started.

"The cunning dog has covered his tracks," said he. "He has left nothing to incriminate him. His dangerous correspondence has been destroyed or removed. This is our last chance."

It was a small tin cash-box which stood upon the writing-desk. Holmes pried it open with his chisel. Several rolls of paper were within, covered with figures and calculations, without any note to show to what they referred. The recurring words, "water pressure" and "pressure to the square inch" suggested some possible relation to a submarine. Holmes tossed them all impatiently aside. There only remained an envelope with some small newspaper slips inside it. He shook them out on the table, and at once I saw by his eager face that his hopes had been raised.

"What's this, Watson? Eh? What's this? Record of a series of messages in the advertisements of a paper. *Daily Telegraph* agony column by the print and paper. Right-hand top corner of a page. No dates—but messages arrange themselves. This must be the first:

"Hoped to hear sooner. Terms agreed to. Write fully to address given on card.
"PIERROT

"Next comes:

"Too complex for description. Must have full report. Stuff awaits you when goods delivered.
"PIERROT

"Then comes:

"Matter presses. Must withdraw offer unless contract completed. Make appointment by letter. Will confirm by advertisement.
"PIERROT

"Finally:

"Monday night after nine. Two taps. Only ourselves. Do not be so suspicious. payment in hard cash when goods delivered.
"PIERROT

"A fairly complete record, Watson! If we could only get at the man at the other end!" He sat lost in thought, tapping his fingers on the table. Finally he sprang to his feet.

"Well, perhaps it won't be so difficult, after all. There is nothing more to be done here, Watson. I think we might drive round to the offices of the *Daily Telegraph,* and so bring a good day's work to a conclusion."

Mycroft Holmes and Lestrade had come round by appointment after breakfast next day and Sherlock Holmes had recounted to them our proceedings of the day before. The professional shook his head over our confessed burglary.

"We can't do these things in the force, Mr. Holmes," said he. "No wonder you get results that are beyond us. But some of these days you'll go too far, and you'll find yourself and your friend in trouble."

"For England, home and beauty—eh, Watson? Martyrs on the altar of our country. But what do you think of it, Mycroft?"

"Excellent, Sherlock! Admirable! But what use will you make of it?"

Holmes picked up the *Daily Telegraph* which lay upon the table. "Have you seen Pierrot's advertisement to-day?"

"What? Another one?"

"Yes, here it is:

"To-night. Same hour. Same place. Two taps. Most vitally important. Your own safety at stake.

"PIERROT."

"By George!" cried Lestrade. "If he answers that we've got him!"

"That was my idea when I put it in. I think if you could both make it convenient to come with us about eight o'clock to Caulfield Gardens we might possibly get a little nearer to a solution."

One of the most remarkable characteristics of Sherlock Holmes was his power of throwing his brain out of action and switching all his thoughts on to lighter things whenever he had convinced himself that he could no longer work to advantage. I remember that during the whole of that memorable day he lost himself in a monograph which he had undertaken upon the Polyphonic Motets of Lassus. For my own part I had none of this power of detachment, and the day, in consequence, appeared to be interminable. The great national importance of the issue, the suspense in high quarters, the direct nature of the experiment which we were trying—all combined to work upon my nerve. It was a relief to me when at last, after a light dinner, we set out upon our expedition. Lestrade and Mycroft met us by appointment at the outside of Gloucester Road Station. The area door of Oberstein's house had been left open the night before, and it was necessary for me, as Mycroft Holmes absolutely and indignantly declined to climb the railings, to pass in and open the hall door. By nine o'clock we were all seated in the study, waiting patiently for our man.

An hour passed and yet another. When eleven struck, the measured beat of the great church clock seemed to sound the dirge of our hopes. Lestrade and Mycroft were fidgeting in their seats and looking twice a minute at their watches. Holmes sat silent and composed, his eyelids half shut, but every sense on the alert. He raised his head with a sudden jerk.

"He is coming," said he.

There had been a furtive step past the door. Now it returned. We heard a shuffling sound outside, and then two sharp taps with the knocker. Holmes rose, motioning to us to remain seated. The gas in the hall was a mere point of light. He opened the outer door, and then as a dark figure slipped past him he closed and fastened it. "This way!" we heard him say, and a moment later our man stood before us. Holmes had followed him closely, and as the man turned with a cry of surprise and alarm he caught him by the collar and threw him back into the room. Before our prisoner had recovered his balance the door was shut and Holmes standing with his back against it. The man glared round him, staggered, and fell senseless upon the floor. With the shock, his broad-brimmed hat flew from his head, his cravat slipped down from his lips, and there were the long light beard and the soft, handsome delicate features of Colonel Valentine Walter.

Holmes gave a whistle of surprise.

"You can write me down an ass this time, Watson," said he. "This was not the bird that I was looking for."

"Who is he?" asked Mycroft eagerly.

"The younger brother of the late Sir James Walter, the head of the Submarine Department. Yes, yes; I see the fall of the cards. He is coming to. I think that you had best leave his examination to me."

We had carried the prostrate body to the sofa. Now our prisoner sat up, looked round him with a horror-stricken face, and passed his hand over his forehead, like one who cannot believe his own senses.

"What is this?" he asked. "I came here to visit Mr. Oberstein."

"Everything is known, Colonel Walter," said Holmes. "How an English gentleman could behave in such a manner is beyond my comprehension. But your whole correspondence and relations with Oberstein are within our knowledge. So also are the circumstances connected with the death of young Cadogan West. Let me advise you to gain at least the small credit for repentance and confession, since there are still some details which we can only learn from your lips."

The man groaned and sank his face in his hands. We waited, but he was silent.

"I can assure you," said Holmes, "that every essential is already known. We know that you were pressed for money; that you took an impress of the keys which your brother held; and that you entered into a correspondence with Oberstein, who answered your letters through the advertisement columns of the *Daily Telegraph*. We are aware that you went down to the office in the fog on Monday night, but that you were seen and followed by young Cadogan West, who had probably some previous reason to suspect you. He saw your theft, but could not give the alarm, as it was just possible that you were taking the papers to your brother in London. Leaving all his private concerns like the good citizen that he was, he followed you closely in the fog and kept at your heels until you reached this very house. There he intervened, and then it was, Colonel Walter, that to treason you added the more terrible crime of murder."

"I did not! I did not! Before God I swear that I did not!" cried our wretched prisoner.

"Tell us, then, how Cadogan West met his end before you laid him upon the roof of a railway carriage."

"I will. I swear to you that I will. I did the rest. I confess it. It was just as you say. A Stock Exchange debt had to be paid. I needed the money badly. Oberstein offered me five thousand. It was to save myself from ruin. But as to murder, I am as innocent as you."

"What happened, then?"

"He had his suspicions before, and he followed me as you describe. I never knew it until I was at the very door. It was thick fog, and one could not see three yards. I had given two taps and Oberstein had come to the door. The young man rushed up and demanded to know what we were about to do with the papers. Oberstein had a short life-preserver. He always carried it with him. As West forced his way after us into the house Oberstein struck him on the head. The blow was a fatal one. He was dead within five minutes. There he lay in the hall, and we were at our wit's end what to do. Then Oberstein had this idea about the trains which halted under his back window. But first he examined the papers which I had brought. He said that three of them were essential, and that he must keep them. 'You cannot keep them,' said I. 'There will be a dreadful row at Woolwich if they are not returned.' 'I must keep them,' said he, 'for they are so technical that it is impossible in the time to make copies.' 'Then they must all go back together to-night,' said I. He thought for a little, and then he cried out that he had it. 'Three I will keep,' said he. 'The others we will stuff into the pocket of this young man. When he is found the whole business will assuredly be put to his account. I could see no other way out of it, so we did as he suggested. We waited half an hour at the window before a train stopped. It was so thick that nothing could be seen, and we had no difficulty in lowering West's body on to the train. That was the end of the matter so far as I was concerned."

"And your brother?"

"He said nothing, but he had caught me once with his keys, and I think that he suspected. I read in his eyes that he suspected. As you know, he never held up his head again."

There was silence in the room. It was broken by Mycroft Holmes.

"Can you not make reparation? It would ease your conscience, and possibly your punishment."

"What reparation can I make?"

"Where is Oberstein with the papers?"

"I do not know."

"Did he give you no address?"

"He said that letters to the Hôtel du Louvre, Paris, would eventually reach him."

"Then reparation is still within your power," said Sherlock Holmes.

"I will do anything I can. I owe this fellow no particular good-will. He has been my ruin and my downfall."

"Here are paper and pen. Sit at this desk and write to my dictation. Direct the envelope to the address given. That is right. Now the letter:

"DEAR SIR:

"With regard to our transaction, you will no doubt have observed by now that one essential detail is missing. I have a tracing which will make it complete. This has involved me in extra trouble, however, and I must ask you for a further advance of five hundred pounds. I will not trust it to the post, nor will I take anything but gold or notes. I would come to you abroad, but it would excite remark if I left the country at present. Therefore I shall expect to meet you in the smoking-room of the Charing Cross Hotel at noon on Saturday. Remember that only English notes, or gold, will be taken.

That will do very well. I shall be very much surprised if it does not fetch our man."

And it did! It is a matter of history—that secret history of a nation which is often so much more intimate and interesting than its public chronicles—that Oberstein, eager to complete the coup of his lifetime, came to the lure and was safely engulfed for fifteen years in a British prison. In his trunk were found the invaluable Bruce-Partington plans, which he had put up for auction in all the naval centres of Europe.

Colonel Walter died in prison towards the end of the second year of his sentence. As to Holmes, he returned refreshed to his monograph upon the Polyphonic Motets of Lassus, which has since been printed for private circulation, and is said by experts to be the last word upon the subject. Some weeks afterwards I learned incidentally that my friend spent a day at Windsor, whence he returned with a remarkably fine emerald tie-pin. When I asked him if he had bought it, he answered that it was a present from a certain gracious lady in whose interests he had once been fortunate enough to carry out a small commission. He said no more; but I fancy that I could guess at that lady's august name, and I have little doubt that the emerald pin will forever recall to my friend's memory the adventure of the Bruce-Partington plans.

TYPHOON

Joseph Conrad
(1857–1924)

CAPTAIN MACWHIRR, of the steamer *Nan-Shan*, had a physiognomy that, in the order of material appearances, was the exact counterpart of his mind:

it presented no marked characteristics of firmness or stupidity; it had no pronounced characteristics whatever; it was simply ordinary, irresponsive, and unruffled.

The only thing his aspect might have been said to suggest, at times, was bashfulness; because he would sit, in business offices ashore, sunburnt and smiling faintly, with downcast eyes. When he raised them, they were perceived to be direct in their glance and of blue colour. His hair was fair and extremely fine, clasping from temple to temple the bald dome of his skull in a clamp as of fluffy silk. The hair of his face, on the contrary, carroty and flaming, resembled a growth of copper wire clipped short to the line of the lip; while, no matter how close he shaved, fiery metallic gleams passed, when he moved his head, over the surface of his cheeks. He was rather below the medium height, a bit round-shouldered, and so sturdy of limb that his clothes always looked a shade too tight for his arms and legs. As if unable to grasp what is due to the difference of latitudes, he wore a brown bowler hat, a complete suit of a brownish hue, and clumsy black boots. These harbour togs gave to his thick figure an air of stiff and uncouth smartness. A thin silver watch-chain looped his waistcoat, and he never left his ship for the shore without clutching in his powerful, hairy fist an elegant umbrella of the very best quality, but generally unrolled. Young Jukes, the chief mate, attending his commander to the gangway, would sometimes venture to say, with the greatest gentleness, "Allow me, sir"— and possessing himself of the umbrella deferentially, would elevate the ferule, shake the folds, twirl a neat furl in a jiffy, and hand it back; going through the performance with a face of such portentous gravity, that Mr. Solomon Rout, the chief engineer, smoking his morning cigar over the skylight, would turn away his head in order to hide a smile. "Oh! aye! The blessed gamp. . . . Thank 'ee, Jukes, thank 'ee," would mutter Captain MacWhirr, heartily, without looking up.

Having just enough imagination to carry him through each successive day, and no more, he was tranquilly sure of himself; and from the very same cause he was not in the least conceited. It is your imaginative superior who is touchy, overbearing, and difficult to please; but every ship Captain MacWhirr commanded was the floating abode of harmony and peace. It was, in truth, as impossible for him to take a flight of fancy as it would be for a watchmaker to put together a chronometer with nothing except a two-pound hammer and a whip-saw in the way of tools. Yet the uninteresting lives of men so entirely given to the actuality of the bare existence have their mysterious side. It was impossible in Captain MacWhirr's case, for instance, to understand what under heaven could have induced that perfectly satisfactory son of a petty grocer in Belfast to run away to sea. And yet he had done that very thing at the age of fifteen. It was enough, when you thought it over, to give you the idea of an immense, potent, and invisible hand thrust into the ant-heap of the earth, laying hold of shoulders, knocking heads together, and setting the unconscious faces of the multitude towards inconceivable goals and in undreamt-of directions.

His father never really forgave him for this undutiful stupidity. "We could have got on without him," he used to say later on, "but there's the business. And he an only son, too!" His mother wept very much after his disappearance. As it had never occurred to him to leave word behind, he was mourned over for dead till, after eight months, his first letter arrived from Talcahuano. It was short, and contained the statement: "We had very fine weather on our passage out." But evidently, in the writer's mind, the only important intelligence was to the effect that his captain had, on the very day of writing, entered him regularly on the ship's articles as Ordinary Seaman. "Because I can do the work," he explained. The mother again wept copiously, while the remark, "Tom's an ass," expressed the emotions of the father. He was a corpulent man, with a gift for sly chaffing, which to the end of his life he exercised in his intercourse with his son, a little pityingly, as if upon a half-witted person.

MacWhirr's visits to his home were necessarily rare, and in the course of years he despatched other letters to his parents, informing them of his successive promotions and of his movements upon the vast earth. In these missives could be found sentences like this: "The heat here is very great." Or: "On Christmas day at 4 P.M. we fell in with some icebergs." The old people ultimately became acquainted with a good many names of ships, and with the names of the skippers who commanded them—with the names of Scots and English shipowners—with the names of seas, oceans, straits, promontories—with outlandish names of lumber-ports, of rice-ports, of cotton-ports—with the names of islands—with the name of their son's young woman. She was called Lucy. It did not suggest itself to him to mention whether he thought the name pretty. And then they died.

The great day of MacWhirr's marriage came in due course, following shortly upon the great day when he got his first command.

All these events had taken place many years before the morning when, in the chart-room of the steamer *Nan-Shan,* he stood confronted by the fall of a barometer he had no reason to distrust. The fall—taking into account the excellence of the instrument, the time of the year, and the ship's position on the terrestrial globe—was of a nature ominously prophetic; but the red face of the man betrayed no sort of inward disturbance. Omens were as nothing to him, and he was unable to discover the message of a prophecy till the fulfilment had brought it home to his very door. "That's a fall, and no mistake," he thought. "There must be some uncommonly dirty weather knocking about."

The *Nan-Shan* was on her way from the southward to the treaty port of Fu-chau, with some cargo in her lower holds, and two hundred Chinese coolies returning to their village homes in the province of Fo-kien, after a few years of work in various tropical colonies. The morning was fine, the

oily sea heaved without a sparkle, and there was a queer white misty patch
in the sky like a halo of the sun. The fore-deck, packed with Chinamen,
was full of sombre clothing, yellow faces, and pigtails, sprinkled over with
a good many naked shoulders, for there was no wind, and the heat was
close. The coolies lounged, talked, smoked, or stared over the rail; some,
drawing water over the side, sluiced each other; a few slept on hatches,
while several small parties of six sat on their heels surrounding iron trays
with plates of rice and tiny teacups; and every single Celestial of them was
carrying with him all he had in the world—a wooden chest with a ringing
lock and brass on the corners, containing the savings of his labours: some
clothes of ceremony, sticks of incense, a little opium maybe, bits of nameless rubbish of conventional value, and a small hoard of silver dollars, toiled
for in coal lighters, won in gambling-houses or in petty trading, grubbed
out of earth, sweated out in mines, on railway lines, in deadly jungle, under
heavy burdens—amassed patiently, guarded with care, cherished fiercely.

A cross swell had set in from the direction of Formosa Channel about ten
o'clock, without disturbing these passengers much, because the *Nan-Shan,*
with her flat bottom rolling chocks on bilges, and great breadth of beam,
had the reputation of an exceptionally steady ship in a sea-way. Mr. Jukes,
in moments of expansion on shore, would proclaim loudly that the "old
girl was as good as she was pretty." It would never have occurred to Captain MacWhirr to express his favourable opinion so loud or in terms so
fanciful.

She was a good ship, undoubtedly, and not old either. She had been
built in Dumbarton less than three years before, to the order of a firm of
merchants in Siam—Messrs. Sigg and Son. When she lay afloat, finished in
every detail and ready to take up the work of her life, the builders contemplated her with pride.

"Sigg has asked us for a reliable skipper to take her out," remarked one
of the partners; and the other, after reflecting for a while, said: "I think
MacWhirr is ashore just at present." "Is he? Then wire him at once. He's
the very man," declared the senior, without a moment's hesitation.

Next morning MacWhirr stood before them unperturbed, having
travelled from London by the midnight express after a sudden but un-
demonstrative parting with his wife. She was the daughter of a superior
couple who had seen better days.

"We had better be going together over the ship, Captain," said the senior
partner; and the three men started to view the perfections of the *Nan-Shan*
from stem to stern, and from her keelson to the trucks of her two stumpy
pole-masts.

Captain MacWhirr had begun by taking off his coat, which he hung on
the end of a steam windlass embodying all the latest improvements.

"My uncle wrote of you favourably by yesterday's mail to our good
friends—Messrs. Sigg, you know—and doubtless they'll continue you out

there in command," said the junior partner. "You'll be able to boast of being in charge of the handiest boat of her size on the coast of China, Captain," he added.

"Have you? Thank 'ee," mumbled vaguely MacWhirr, to whom the view of a distant eventuality could appeal no more than the beauty of a wide landscape to a purblind tourist; and his eyes happening at the moment to be at rest upon the lock of the cabin door, he walked up to it, full of purpose, and began to rattle the handle vigorously, while he observed, in his low, earnest voice, "You can't trust the workmen nowadays. A brand-new lock, and it won't act at all. Stuck fast. See? See?"

As soon as they found themselves alone in their office across the yard: "You praised that fellow up to Sigg. What is it you see in him?" asked the nephew, with faint contempt.

"I admit he has nothing of your fancy skipper about him, if that's what you mean," said the elder man, curtly. "Is the foreman of the joiners on the *Nan-Shan* outside? . . . Come in, Bates. How is it that you let Tait's people put us off with a defective lock on the cabin door? The Captain could see directly he set eye on it. Have it replaced at once. The little straws, Bates . . . the little straws. . . ."

The lock was replaced accordingly, and a few days afterwards the *Nan-Shan* steamed out to the East, without MacWhirr having offered any further remark as to her fittings, or having been heard to utter a single word hinting at pride in his ship, gratitude for his appointment, or satisfaction at his prospects.

With a temperament neither loquacious nor taciturn he found very little occasion to talk. There were matters of duty, of course—directions, orders, and so on; but the past being to his mind done with, and the future not there yet, the more general actualities of the day required no comment—because facts can speak for themselves with overwhelming precision.

Old Mr. Sigg liked a man of few words, and one that "you could be sure would not try to improve upon his instructions." MacWhirr satisfying these requirements, was continued in command of the *Nan-Shan,* and applied himself to the careful navigation of his ship in the China seas. She had come out on a British register, but after some time Messrs. Sigg judged it expedient to transfer her to the Siamese flag.

At the news of the contemplated transfer Jukes grew restless, as if under a sense of personal affront. He went about grumbling to himself, and uttering short scornful laughs. "Fancy having a ridiculous Noah's Ark elephant in the ensign of one's ship," he said once at the engine-room door. "Dash me if I can stand it: I'll throw up the billet. Don't it make *you* sick, Mr. Rout?" The chief engineer only cleared his throat with the air of a man who knows the value of a good billet.

The first morning the new flag floated over the stern of the *Nan-Shan* Jukes stood looking at it bitterly from the bridge. He struggled with his feelings for a while, and then remarked, "Queer flag for a man to sail under, sir."

"What's the matter with the flag?" inquired Captain MacWhirr. "Seems all right to me." And he walked across to the end of the bridge to have a good look.

"Well, it looks queer to me," burst out Jukes, greatly exasperated, and flung off the bridge.

Captain MacWhirr was amazed at these manners. After a while he stepped quietly into the chart-room, and opened his International Signal Code-book at the plate where the flags of all the nations are correctly figured in gaudy rows. He ran his finger over them, and when he came to Siam he contemplated with great attention the red field and the white elephant. Nothing could be more simple; but to make sure he brought the book out on the bridge for the purpose of comparing the coloured drawing with the real thing at the flag-staff astern. When next Jukes, who was carrying on the duty that day with a sort of suppressed fierceness, happened on the bridge, his commander observed:

"There's nothing amiss with that flag."

"Isn't there?" mumbled Jukes, falling on his knees before a deck-locker and jerking therefrom viciously a spare lead-line.

"No. I looked up the book. Length twice the breadth and the elephant exactly in the middle. I thought the people ashore would know how to make the local flag. Stands to reason. You were wrong, Jukes. . . ."

"Well, sir," began Jukes, getting up excitedly, "all I can say——" He fumbled for the end of the coil of line with trembling hands.

"That's all right." Captain MacWhirr soothed him, sitting heavily on a little canvas folding-stool he greatly affected. "All you have to do is to take care they don't hoist the elephant upside-down before they get quite used to it."

Jukes flung the new lead-line over on the fore-deck with a loud "Here you are, bo'ss'en—don't forget to wet it thoroughly," and turned with immense resolution towards his commander; but Captain MacWhirr spread his elbows on the bridge-rail comfortably.

"Because it would be, I suppose, understood as a signal of distress," he went on. "What do you think? That elephant there, I take it, stands for something in the nature of the Union Jack in the flag. . . ."

"Does it!" yelled Jukes, so that every head on the Nan-Shan's decks looked towards the bridge. Then he sighed, and with sudden resignation: "It would certainly be a dam' distressful sight," he said, meekly.

Later in the day he accosted the chief engineer with a confidential, "Here, let me tell you the old man's latest."

Mr. Solomon Rout (frequently alluded to as Long Sol, Old Sol, or Father Rout), from finding himself almost invariably the tallest man on board every ship he joined, had acquired the habit of a stooping, leisurely condescension. His hair was scant and sandy, his flat cheeks were pale, his bony wrists and long scholarly hands were pale, too, as though he had lived all his life in the shade.

He smiled from on high at Jukes, and went on smoking and glancing about quietly, in the manner of a kind uncle lending an ear to the tale of an excited schoolboy. Then, greatly amused but impassive, he asked:

"And did you throw up the billet?"

"No," cried Jukes, raising a weary, discouraged voice above the harsh buzz of the *Nan-Shan's* friction winches. All of them were hard at work, snatching slings of cargo, high up, to the end of long derricks, only, as it seemed, to let them rip down recklessly by the run. The cargo chains groaned in the gins, clinked on coamings, rattled over the side; and the whole ship quivered, with her long gray flanks smoking in wreaths of steam. "No," cried Jukes, "I didn't. What's the good? I might just as well fling my resignation at this bulkhead. I don't believe you can make a man like that understand anything. He simply knocks me over."

At that moment Captain MacWhirr, back from the shore, crossed the deck, umbrella in hand, escorted by a mournful, self-possessed Chinaman, walking behind in paper-soled silk shoes, and who also carried an umbrella.

The master of the *Nan-Shan,* speaking just audibly and gazing at his boots as his manner was, remarked that it would be necessary to call at Fu-chau this trip, and desired Mr. Rout to have steam up to-morrow afternoon at one o'clock sharp. He pushed back his hat to wipe his forehead, observing at the same time that he hated going ashore anyhow; while overtopping him Mr. Rout, without deigning a word, smoked austerely, nursing his right elbow in the palm of his left hand. Then Jukes was directed in the same subdued voice to keep the forward 'tween-deck clear of cargo. Two hundred coolies were going to be put down there. The Bun Hin Company were sending that lot home. Twenty-five bags of rice would be coming off in a sampan directly, for stores. All seven-years'-men they were, said Captain MacWhirr, with a camphor-wood chest to every man. The carpenter should be set to work nailing three-inch battens along the deck below, fore and aft, to keep these boxes from shifting in a sea-way. Jukes had better look to it at once. "D'ye hear, Jukes?" This Chinaman here was coming with the ship as far as Fu-chau—a sort of interpreter he would be. Bun Hin's clerk he was, and wanted to have a look at the space. Jukes had better take him forward. "D'ye hear, Jukes?"

Jukes took care to punctuate these instructions in proper places with the obligatory "Yes, sir," ejaculated without enthusiasm. His brusque "Come along, John; make look see" set the Chinaman in motion at his heels.

"Wanchee look see, all same look see can do," said Jukes, who having no talent for foreign languages mangled the very pidgin-English cruelly. He pointed at the open hatch. "Catchee number one piecie place to sleep in. Eh?"

He was gruff, as became his racial superiority, but not unfriendly. The Chinaman, gazing sad and speechless into the darkness of the hatchway, seemed to stand at the head of a yawning grave.

"No catchee rain down there—savee?" pointed out Jukes. "Suppose all'ee same fine weather, one piecie coolieman come topside," he pursued, warming up imaginatively. "Make so—Phooooo!" He expanded his chest and blew out his cheeks. "Savee, John? Breathe—fresh air. Good. Eh? Washee him piecie pants, chow-chow top-side—see, John?"

With his mouth and hands he made exuberant motions of eating rice and washing clothes; and the Chinaman, who concealed his distrust of this pantomime under a collected demeanour tinged by a gentle and refined melancholy, glanced out of his almond eyes from Jukes to the hatch and back again. "Velly good," he murmured, in a disconsolate undertone, and hastened smoothly along the decks, dodging obstacles in his course. He disappeared, ducking low under a sling of ten dirty gunny-bags full of some costly merchandise and exhaling a repulsive smell.

Captain MacWhirr meantime had gone on the bridge, and into the chart-room, where a letter, commenced two days before, awaited termination. These long letters began with the words, "My darling wife," and the steward, between the scrubbing of the floors and the dusting of chronometer-boxes, snatched at every opportunity to read them. They interested him much more than they possibly could the woman for whose eye they were intended; and this for the reason that they related in minute detail each successive trip of the *Nan-Shan*.

Her master, faithful to facts, which alone his consciousness reflected, would set them down with painstaking care upon many pages. The house in a northern suburb to which these pages were addressed had a bit of garden before the bow-windows, a deep porch of good appearance, coloured glass with imitation lead frame in the front door. He paid five-and-forty pounds a year for it, and did not think the rent too high, because Mrs. MacWhirr (a pretentious person with a scraggy neck and a disdainful manner) was admittedly ladylike, and in the neighbourhood considered as "quite superior." The only secret of her life was her abject terror of the time when her husband would come home to stay for good. Under the same roof there dwelt also a daughter called Lydia and a son, Tom. These two were but slightly acquainted with their father. Mainly, they knew him as a rare but privileged visitor, who of an evening smoked his pipe in the dining-room and slept in the house. The lanky girl, upon the whole, was rather ashamed of him; the boy was frankly and utterly indifferent in a straightforward, delightful, unaffected way manly boys have.

And Captain MacWhirr wrote home from the coast of China twelve times every year, desiring quaintly to be "remembered to the children," and subscribing himself "your loving husband," as calmly as if the words so long used by so many men were, apart from their shape, wornout things, and of a faded meaning.

The China seas north and south are narrow seas. They are seas full of every-day, eloquent facts, such as islands, sand-banks, reefs, swift and changeable currents—tangled facts that nevertheless speak to a seaman in clear and definite language. Their speech appealed to Captain MacWhirr's sense of realities so forcibly that he had given up his state-room below and practically lived all his days on the bridge of his ship, often having his meals sent up, and sleeping at night in the chart-room. And he indited there his home letters. Each of them, without exception, contained the phrase, "The weather has been very fine this trip," or some other form of a statement to that effect. And this statement, too, in its wonderful persistence, was of the same perfect accuracy as all the others they contained.

- Mr. Rout likewise wrote letters; only no one on board knew how chatty he could be pen in hand, because the chief engineer had enough imagination to keep his desk locked. His wife relished his style greatly. They were a childless couple, and Mrs. Rout, a big high-bosomed, jolly woman of forty, shared with Mr. Rout's toothless and venerable mother a little cottage near Teddington. She would run over her correspondence, at breakfast, with lively eyes, and scream out interesting passages in a joyous voice at the deaf old lady, prefacing each extract by the warning shout, "Solomon says!" She had the trick of firing off Solomon's utterances also upon strangers, astonishing them easily by the unfamiliar text and the unexpectedly jocular vein of these quotations. On the day the new curate called for the first time at the cottage, she found occasion to remark, "As Solomon says: 'the engineers that go down to the sea in ships behold the wonders of sailor nature';" when a change in the visitor's countenance made her stop and stare.

"Solomon. . . . Oh! . . . . Mrs. Rout," stuttered the young man, very red in the face, "I must say . . . I don't. . . ."

"He's my husband," she announced in a great shout, throwing herself back in the chair. Perceiving the joke, she laughed immoderately with a handkerchief to her eyes, while he sat wearing a forced smile, and, from his inexperience of jolly women, fully persuaded that she must be deplorably insane. They were excellent friends afterwards; for, absolving her from irreverent intention, he came to think she was a very worthy person indeed; and he learned in time to receive without flinching other scraps of Solomon's wisdom.

"For my part," Solomon was reported by his wife to have said once, "give me the dullest ass for a skipper before a rogue. There is a way to take a fool; but a rogue is smart and slippery." This was an airy generalization drawn from the particular case of Captain MacWhirr's honesty, which, in itself, had the heavy obviousness of a lump of clay. On the other hand, Mr. Jukes, unable to generalize, unmarried, and unengaged, was in the habit of opening his heart after another fashion to an old chum and former ship-mate, actually serving as second officer on board an Atlantic liner.

First of all he would insist upon the advantages of the Eastern trade, hinting at its superiority to the Western ocean service. He extolled the sky, the seas, the ships, and the easy life of the Far East. The *Nan-Shan,* he affirmed, was second to none as a sea-boat.

"We have no brass-bound uniforms, but then we are like brothers here," he wrote. "We all mess together and live like fighting-cocks. . . . All the chaps of the black-squad are as decent as they make that kind, and old Sol, the Chief, is a dry stick. We are good friends. As to our old man, you could not find a quieter skipper. Sometimes you would think he hadn't sense enough to see anything wrong. And yet it isn't that. Can't be. He has been in command for a good few years now. He doesn't do anything actually foolish, and gets his ship along all right without worrying anybody. I be-lieve he hasn't brains enough to enjoy kicking up a row. I don't take ad-vantage of him. I would scorn it. Outside the routine of duty he doesn't seem to understand more than half of what you tell him. We get a laugh out of this at times; but it is dull, too, to be with a man like this—in the long-run. Old Sol says he hasn't much conversation. Conversation! O Lord! He never talks. The other day I had been yarning under the bridge with one of the engineers, and he must have heard us. When I came up to take my watch, he steps out of the chart-room and has a good look all round, peeps over at the sidelights, glances at the compass, squints upwards at the stars. That's his regular performance. By-and-by he says: 'Was that you talking just now in the port alleyway?' 'Yes, sir.' 'With the third engineer?' 'Yes, sir.' He walks off to starboard, and sits under the dodger on a little camp-stool of his, and for half an hour perhaps he makes no sound, except that I heard him sneeze once. Then after a while I hear him getting up over there, and he strolls across to port, where I was. 'I can't understand what you can find to talk about,' says he. 'Two solid hours. I am not blaming you. I see people ashore at it all day long, and then in the evening they sit down and keep at it over the drinks. Must be saying the same things over and over again. I can't understand.'

"Did you ever hear anything like that? And he was so patient about it. It made me quite sorry for him. But he is exasperating, too, sometimes. Of course one would not do anything to vex him even if it were worth while. But it isn't. He's so jolly innocent that if you were to put your thumb to your nose and wave your fingers at him he would only wonder gravely to himself what got into you. He told me once quite simply that he found it very difficult to make out what made people always act so queerly. He's too dense to trouble about, and that's the truth."

Thus wrote Mr. Jukes to his chum in the Western ocean trade, out of the fulness of his heart and the liveliness of his fancy.

He had expressed his honest opinion. It was not worth while trying to im-

press a man of that sort. If the world had been full of such men, life
would have probably appeared to Jukes an unentertaining and unprofitable
business. He was not alone in his opinion. The sea itself, as if sharing Mr.
Jukes' good-natured forbearance, had never put itself out to startle the silent
man, who seldom looked up, and wandered innocently over the waters
with the only visible purpose of getting food, raiment, and house-room for
three people ashore. Dirty weather he had known, of course. He had been
made wet, uncomfortable, tired in the usual way, felt at the time and
presently forgotten. So that upon the whole he had been justified in reporting fine weather at home. But he had never been given a glimpse of
immeasurable strength and of immoderate wrath, the wrath that passes exhausted but never appeased—the wrath and fury of the passionate sea. He
knew it existed, as we know that crime and abomination exist; he had
heard of it as a peaceable citizen in a town hears of battles, famines, and
floods, and yet knows nothing of what these things mean—though, indeed,
he may have been mixed up in a street row, have gone without his dinner
once, or been soaked to the skin in a shower. Captain MacWhirr had sailed
over the surface of the oceans as some men go skimming over the years
of existence to sink gently into a placid grave, ignorant of life to the last,
without ever having been made to see all it may contain of perfidy, of
violence, and of terror. There are on sea and land such men thus fortunate
—or thus disdained by destiny or by the sea.

II

Observing the steady fall of the barometer, Captain MacWhirr thought,
"There's some dirty weather knocking about." This is precisely what he
thought. He had had an experience of moderately dirty weather—the term
dirty as applied to the weather implying only moderate discomfort to the
seaman. Had he been informed by an indisputable authority that the end
of the world was to be finally accomplished by a catastrophic disturbance
of the atmosphere, he would have assimilated the information under the
simple idea of dirty weather, and no other, because he had no experience of
cataclysms, and belief does not necessarily imply comprehension. The wisdom of his county had pronounced by means of an Act of Parliament that
before he could be considered as fit to take charge of a ship he should be
able to answer certain simple questions on the subject of circular storms
such as hurricanes, cyclones, typhoons; and apparently he had answered
them, since he was now in command of the *Nan-Shan* in the China seas
during the season of typhoons. But if he had answered he remembered
nothing of it. He was, however, conscious of being made uncomfortable by
the clammy heat. He came out on the bridge, and found no relief to this
oppression. The air seemed thick. He gasped like a fish, and began to believe himself greatly out of sorts.

The *Nan-Shan* was ploughing a vanishing furrow upon the circle of the sea that had the surface and the shimmer of an undulating piece of gray silk. The sun, pale and without rays, poured down leaden heat in a strangely indecisive light, and the Chinamen were lying prostrate about the decks. Their bloodless, pinched, yellow faces were like the faces of bilious invalids. Captain MacWhirr noticed two of them especially, stretched out on their backs below the bridge. As soon as they had closed their eyes they seemed dead. Three others, however, were quarrelling barbarously away forward; and one big fellow, half naked, with herculean shoulders, was hanging limply over a winch; another, sitting on the deck, his knees up and his head drooping sideways in a girlish attitude, was plaiting his pig-tail with infinite languor depicted in his whole person and in the very movement of his fingers. The smoke struggled with difficulty out of the funnel, and instead of streaming away spread itself out like an infernal sort of cloud, smelling of sulphur and raining soot all over the decks.

"What the devil are you doing there, Mr. Jukes?" asked Captain Mac-Whirr.

This unusual form of address, though mumbled rather than spoken, caused the body of Mr. Jukes to start as though it had been prodded under the fifth rib. He had had a low bench brought on the bridge, and sitting on it, with a length of rope curled about his feet and a piece of canvas stretched over his knees, was pushing a sail-needle vigorously. He looked up, and his surprise gave to his eyes an expression of innocence and candour.

"I am only roping some of that new set of bags we made last trip for whipping up coals," he remonstrated, gently. "We shall want them for the next coaling, sir."

"What became of the others?"

"Why, worn out of course, sir."

Captain MacWhirr, after glaring down irresolutely at his chief mate, disclosed the gloomy and cynical conviction that more than half of them had been lost overboard, "if only the truth was known," and retired to the other end of the bridge. Jukes, exasperated by this unprovoked attack, broke the needle at the second stitch, and dropping his work got up and cursed the heat in a violent undertone.

The propeller thumped, the three Chinamen forward had given up squabbling very suddenly, and the one who had been plaiting his tail clasped his legs and stared dejectedly over his knees. The lurid sunshine cast faint and sickly shadows. The swell ran higher and swifter every moment, and the ship lurched heavily in the smooth, deep hollows of the sea.

"I wonder where that beastly swell comes from," said Jukes aloud, recovering himself after a stagger.

"North-east," grunted the literal MacWhirr, from his side of the bridge.

"There's some dirty weather knocking about. Go and look at the glass."

When Jukes came out of the chart-room, the cast of his countenance had changed to thoughtfulness and concern. He caught hold of the bridge-rail and stared ahead.

The temperature in the engine-room had gone up to a hundred and seventeen degrees. Irritated voices were ascending through the skylight and through the fiddle of the stokehold in a harsh and resonant uproar, mingled with angry clangs and scrapes of metal, as if men with limbs of iron and throats of bronze had been quarrelling down there. The second engineer was falling foul of the stokers for letting the steam go down. He was a man with arms like a blacksmith, and generally feared; but that afternoon the stokers were answering him back recklessly, and slammed the furnace doors with the fury of despair. Then the noise ceased suddenly, and the second engineer appeared, emerging out of the stokehold streaked with grime and soaking wet like a chimney-sweep coming out of a well. As soon as his head was clear of the fiddle he began to scold Jukes for not trimming properly the stokehold ventilators; and in answer Jukes made with his hands deprecatory soothing signs meaning: "No wind—can't be helped —you can see for yourself." But the other wouldn't hear reason. His teeth flashed angrily in his dirty face. He didn't mind, he said, the trouble of punching their blanked heads down there, blank his soul, but did the condemned sailors think you could keep steam up in the God-forsaken boilers simply by knocking the blanked stokers about? No, by George! You had to get some draught, too—may he be everlastingly blanked for a swab-headed deck-hand if you didn't! And the chief, too, rampaging before the steam-gauge and carrying on like a lunatic up and down the engine-room ever since noon. What did Jukes think he was stuck up there for, if he couldn't get one of his decayed, good-for-nothing deck-cripples to turn the ventilators to the wind?

The relations of the "engine-room" and the "deck" of the Nan-Shan were, as is known, of a brotherly nature; therefore Jukes leaned over and begged the other in a restrained tone not to make a disgusting ass of himself; the skipper was on the other side of the bridge. But the second declared mutinously that he didn't care a rap who was on the other side of the bridge, and Jukes, passing in a flash from lofty disapproval into a state of exaltation, invited him in unflattering terms to come up and twist the beastly things to please himself, and catch such wind as a donkey of his sort could find. The second rushed up to the fray. He flung himself at the port ventilator as though he meant to tear it out bodily and toss it overboard. All he did was to move the cowl round a few inches, with an enormous expenditure of force, and seemed spent in the effort. He leaned against the back of the wheel-house, and Jukes walked up to him.

"Oh, Heavens!" ejaculated the engineer in a feeble voice. He lifted his eyes to the sky, and then let his glassy stare descend to meet the horizon that, tilting up to an angle of forty degrees, seemed to hang on a slant for a while and settled down slowly. "Heavens! Phew! What's up, anyhow?"

Jukes, straddling his long legs like a pair of compasses, put on an air of superiority. "We're going to catch it this time," he said. "The barometer is tumbling down like anything, Harry. And you trying to kick up that silly row. . . ."

The word "barometer" seemed to revive the second engineer's mad animosity. Collecting afresh all his energies, he directed Jukes in a low and brutal tone to shove the unmentionable instrument down his gory throat. Who cared for his crimson barometer? It was the steam—the steam—that was going down; and what between the firemen going faint and the chief going silly, it was worse than a dog's life for him; he didn't care a tinker's curse how soon the whole show was blown out of the water. He seemed on the point of having a cry, but after regaining his breath he muttered darkly, "I'll faint them," and dashed off. He stopped upon the fiddle long enough to shake his fist at the unnatural daylight, and dropped into the dark hole with a whoop.

When Jukes turned, his eyes fell upon the rounded back and the big red ears of Captain MacWhirr, who had come across. He did not look at his chief officer, but said at once, "That's a very violent man, that second engineer."

"Jolly good second, anyhow," grunted Jukes. "They can't keep up steam," he added, rapidly, and made a grab at the rail against the coming lurch.

Captain MacWhirr, unprepared, took a run and brought himself up with a jerk by an awning stanchion.

"A profane man," he said, obstinately. "If this goes on, I'll have to get rid of him the first chance."

"It's the heat," said Jukes. "The weather's awful. It would make a saint swear. Even up here I feel exactly as if I had my head tied up in a woollen blanket."

Captain MacWhirr looked up. "D'ye mean to say, Mr. Jukes, you ever had your head tied up in a blanket? What was that for?"

"It's a manner of speaking, sir," said Jukes, stolidly.

"Some of you fellows do go on! What's that about saints swearing? I wish you wouldn't talk so wild. What sort of saint would that be that would swear? No more saint than yourself, I expect. And what's a blanket got to do with it—or the weather either. . . . The heat does not make me swear—does it? It's filthy bad temper. That's what it is. And what's the good of your talking like this?"

Thus Captain MacWhirr expostulated against the use of images in speech, and at the end electrified Jukes by a contemptuous snort, followed by words of passion and resentment: "Damme! I'll fire him out of the ship if he don't look out."

And Jukes, incorrigible, thought: "Goodness me! Somebody's put a new inside to my old man. Here's temper, if you like. Of course it's the weather; what else? It would make an angel quarrelsome—let alone a saint."

All the Chinamen on deck appeared at their last gasp.

At its setting the sun had a diminished diameter and an expiring brown, rayless glow, as if millions of centuries elapsing since the morning had brought it near its end. A dense bank of cloud became visible to the northward; it had a sinister dark olive tint, and lay low and motionless upon the sea, resembling a solid obstacle in the path of the ship. She went floundering towards it like an exhausted creature driven to its death. The coppery twilight retired slowly, and the darkness brought out overhead a swarm of unsteady, big stars, that, as if blown upon, flickered exceedingly and seemed to hang very near the earth. At eight o'clock Jukes went into the chart-room to write up the ship's log.

He copied neatly out of the rough-book the number of miles, the course of the ship, and in the column for "wind" scrawled the word "calm" from top to bottom of the eight hours since noon. He was exasperated by the continuous, monotonous rolling of the ship. The heavy inkstand would slide away in a manner that suggested perverse intelligence in dodging the pen. Having written in the large space under the head of "Remarks" "Heat very oppressive," he stuck the end of the penholder in his teeth, pipe fashion, and mopped his face carefully.

"Ship rolling heavily in a high cross swell," he began again, and commented to himself, "Heavily is no word for it." Then he wrote: "Sunset threatening, with a low bank of clouds to N. and E. Sky clear overhead."

Sprawling over the table with arrested pen, he glanced out of the door, and in that frame of his vision he saw all the stars flying upwards between the teakwood jambs on a black sky. The whole lot took flight together and disappeared, leaving only a blackness flecked with white flashes, for the sea was as black as the sky and speckled with foam afar. The stars that had flown to the roll came back on the return swing of the ship, rushing downwards in their glittering multitude, not of fiery points, but enlarged to tiny discs brilliant with a clear wet sheen.

Jukes watched the flying big stars for a moment, and then wrote: "8 P.M. Swell increasing. Ship labouring and taking water on her decks. Battened down the coolies for the night. Barometer still falling." He paused, and thought to himself, "Perhaps nothing whatever'll come of it." And then he closed resolutely his entries: "Every appearance of a typhoon coming on."

On going out he had to stand aside, and Captain MacWhirr strode over the doorstep without saying a word or making a sign.

"Shut the door, Mr. Jukes, will you?" he cried from within.

Jukes turned back to do so, muttering ironically: "Afraid to catch cold, I suppose." It was his watch below, but he yearned for communion with his kind; and he remarked cheerily to the second mate: "Doesn't look so bad, after all—does it?"

The second mate was marching to and fro on the bridge, tripping down with small steps one moment, and the next climbing with difficulty the shifting slope of the deck. At the sound of Jukes' voice he stood still, facing forward, but made no reply.

"Hallo! That's a heavy one," said Jukes, swaying to meet the long roll till his lowered hand touched the planks. This time the second mate made in his throat a noise of an unfriendly nature.

He was an oldish, shabby little fellow, with bad teeth and no hair on his face. He had been shipped in a hurry in Shanghai, that trip when the second officer brought from home had delayed the ship three hours in port by contriving (in some manner Captain MacWhirr could never understand) to fall overboard into an empty coal-lighter lying alongside, and had to be sent ashore to the hospital with concussion of the brain and a broken limb or two.

Jukes was not discouraged by the unsympathetic sound. "The Chinamen must be having a lovely time of it down there," he said. "It's lucky for them the old girl has the easiest roll of any ship I've ever been in. There now! This one wasn't so bad."

"You wait," snarled the second mate.

With his sharp nose, red at the tip, and his thin pinched lips, he always looked as though he were raging inwardly; and he was concise in his speech to the point of rudeness. All his time off duty he spent in his cabin with the door shut, keeping so still in there that he was supposed to fall asleep as soon as he had disappeared; but the man who came in to wake him for his watch on deck would invariably find him with his eyes wide open, flat on his back in the bunk, and glaring irritably from a soiled pillow. He never wrote any letters, did not seem to hope for news from anywhere; and though he had been heard once to mention West Hartlepool, it was with extreme bitterness, and only in connection with the extortionate charges of a boarding-house. He was one of those men who are picked up at need in the ports of the world. They are competent enough, appear hopelessly hard up, show no evidence of any sort of vice, and carry about them all the signs of manifest failure. They come aboard on an emergency, care for no ship afloat, live in their own atmosphere of casual connection amongst their shipmates who know nothing of them, and make up their minds to leave at inconvenient times. They clear out with no words of leave-taking in some God-forsaken port other men would fear to be stranded in, and go ashore in company of a shabby sea-chest, corded like a treasure-box, and with an air of shaking the ship's dust off their feet.

"You wait," he repeated, balanced in great swings with his back to Jukes, motionless and implacable.

"Do you mean to say we are going to catch it hot?" asked Jukes with boyish interest.

"Say? . . . I say nothing. You don't catch me," snapped the little second mate, with a mixture of pride, scorn, and cunning, as if Jukes' question had been a trap cleverly detected. "Oh, no! None of you here shall make a fool of me if I know it," he mumbled to himself.

Jukes reflected rapidly that this second mate was a mean little beast, and in his heart he wished poor Jack Allen had never smashed himself up in the coal-lighter. The far-off blackness ahead of the ship was like another night seen through the starry night of the earth—the starless night of the immensities beyond the created universe, revealed in its appalling stillness through a low fissure in the glittering sphere of which the earth is the kernel.

"Whatever there might be about," said Jukes, "we are steaming straight into it."

"*You've* said it," caught up the second mate, always with his back to Jukes. "You've said it, mind—not I."

"Oh, go to Jericho!" said Jukes, frankly; and the other emitted a triumphant little chuckle.

"You've said it," he repeated.

"And what of that?"

"I've known some real good men get into trouble with their skippers for saying a dam' sight less," answered the second mate feverishly. "Oh, no! You don't catch me."

"You seem deucedly anxious not to give yourself away," said Jukes, completely soured by such absurdity. "I wouldn't be afraid to say what I think."

"Aye, to me! That's no great trick. I am nobody, and well I know it."

The ship, after a pause of comparative steadiness, started upon a series of rolls, one worse than the other, and for a time Jukes, preserving his equilibrium, was too busy to open his mouth. As soon as the violent swinging had quieted down somewhat, he said: "This is a bit too much of a good thing. Whether anything is coming or not I think she ought to be put head on to that swell. The old man is just gone in to lie down. Hang me if I don't speak to him."

But when he opened the door of the chart-room he saw his captain reading a book. Captain MacWhirr was not lying down: he was standing up with one hand grasping the edge of the bookshelf and the other holding open before his face a thick volume. The lamp wriggled in the gimbals, the loosened books toppled from side to side on the shelf, the long barometer swung in jerky circles, the table altered its slant every moment. In the midst of all this stir and movement Captain MacWhirr, holding on, showed his eyes above the upper edge, and asked, "What's the matter?"

"Swell getting worse, sir."

"Noticed that in here," muttered Captain MacWhirr. "Anything wrong?"

Jukes, inwardly disconcerted by the seriousness of the eyes looking at him over the top of the book, produced an embarrassed grin.

"Rolling like old boots," he said, sheepishly.

"Aye! Very heavy—very heavy. What do you want?"

At this Jukes lost his footing and began to flounder.

"I was thinking of our passengers," he said, in the manner of a man clutching at a straw.

"Passengers?" wondered the Captain, gravely. "What passengers?"

"Why, the Chinamen, sir," explained Jukes, very sick of this conversation.

"The Chinamen! Why don't you speak plainly? Couldn't tell what you meant. Never heard a lot of coolies spoken of as passengers before. Passengers, indeed! What's come to you?"

Captain MacWhirr, closing the book on his forefinger, lowered his arm and looked completely mystified. "Why are you thinking of the Chinamen, Mr. Jukes?" he inquired.

Jukes took a plunge, like a man driven to it. "She's rolling her decks full of water, sir. Thought you might put her head on perhaps—for a while. Till this goes down a bit—very soon, I dare say. Head to the eastward. I never knew a ship roll like this."

He held on in the doorway, and Captain MacWhirr, feeling his grip on the shelf inadequate, made up his mind to let go in a hurry, and fell heavily on the couch.

"Head to the eastward?" he said, struggling to sit up. "That's more than four points off her course."

"Yes, sir. Fifty degrees. . . . Would just bring her head far enough round to meet this. . . ."

Captain MacWhirr was now sitting up. He had not dropped the book, and he had not lost his place.

"To the eastward?" he repeated, with dawning astonishment. "To the . . . Where do you think we are bound to? You want me to haul a full-powered steamship four points off her course to make the Chinamen comfortable! Now, I've heard more than enough of mad things done in the world—but this. . . . If I didn't know you, Jukes, I would think you were in liquor. Steer four points off. . . . And what afterwards? Steer four points over the other way, I suppose, to make the course good. What put it into your head that I would start to tack a steamer as if she were a sailing-ship?"

"Jolly good thing she isn't," threw in Jukes, with bitter readiness. "She would have rolled every blessed stick out of her this afternoon."

"Aye! And you just would have had to stand and see them go," said Captain MacWhirr, showing a certain animation. "It's a dead calm, isn't it?"

"It is, sir. But there's something out of the common coming, for sure."

"Maybe. I suppose you have a notion I should be getting out of the way of that dirt," said Captain MacWhirr, speaking with the utmost simplicity of manner and tone, and fixing the oilcloth on the floor with a heavy stare. Thus he noticed neither Jukes' discomfiture nor the mixture of vexation and astonished respect on his face.

"Now, here's this book," he continued with deliberation, slapping his thigh with the closed volume. "I've been reading the chapter on the storms there."

This was true. He had been reading the chapter on the storms. When he had entered the chart-room, it was with no intention of taking the book down. Some influence in the air—the same influence, probably, that caused the steward to bring without orders the Captain's sea-boots and oilskin coat up to the chart-room—had as it were guided his hand to the shelf; and without taking the time to sit down he had waded with a conscious effort into the terminology of the subject. He lost himself amongst advancing semi-circles, left- and right-hand quadrants, the curves of the tracks, the probable bearing of the centre, the shifts of wind and the readings of barometer. He tried to bring all these things into a definite relation to himself, and ended by becoming contemptuously angry with such a lot of words and with so much advice, all head-work and supposition, without a glimmer of certitude.

"It's the damnedest thing, Jukes," he said. "If a fellow was to believe all that's in there, he would be running most of his time all over the sea trying to get behind the weather."

Again he slapped his leg with the book; and Jukes opened his mouth, but said nothing.

"Running to get behind the weather! Do you understand that, Mr. Jukes? It's the maddest thing!" ejaculated Captain MacWhirr, with pauses, gazing at the floor profoundly. "You would think an old woman had been writing this. It passes me. If that thing means anything useful, then it means that I should at once alter the course away, away to the devil somewhere, and come booming down on Fu-chau from the northward at the tail of this dirty weather that's supposed to be knocking about in our way. From the north! Do you understand, Mr. Jukes? Three hundred extra miles to the distance, and a pretty coal bill to show. I couldn't bring myself to do that if every word in there was gospel truth, Mr. Jukes. Don't you expect me. . . ."

And Jukes, silent, marvelled at this display of feeling and loquacity.

"But the truth is that you don't know if the fellow is right, anyhow. How can you tell what a gale is made of till you get it? He isn't aboard here, is he? Very well. Here he says that the centre of them things bears eight points off the wind; but we haven't got any wind, for all the barometer falling. Where's his centre now?"

"We will get the wind presently," mumbled Jukes.

"Let it come, then," said Captain MacWhirr, with dignified indignation. "It's only to let you see, Mr. Jukes, that you don't find everything in books. All these rules for dodging breezes and circumventing the winds of heaven, Mr. Jukes, seem to me the maddest thing, when you come to look at it sensibly."

He raised his eyes, saw Jukes gazing at him dubiously, and tried to illustrate his meaning.

"About as queer as your extraordinary notion of dodging the ship head to sea, for I don't know how long, to make the Chinamen comfortable; whereas all we've got to do is to take them to Fu-chau, being timed to get there before noon on Friday. If the weather delays me—very well. There's your log-book to talk straight about the weather. But suppose I went swinging off my course and came in two days late, and they asked me: 'Where have you been all that time, Captain?' What could I say to that? 'Went around to dodge the bad weather,' I would say. 'It must've been dam' bad,' they would say. 'Don't know,' I would have to say; 'I've dodged clear of it.' See that, Jukes? I have been thinking it all out this afternoon."

He looked up again in his unseeing, unimaginative way. No one had ever heard him say so much at one time. Jukes, with his arms open in the doorway, was like a man invited to behold a miracle. Unbounded wonder was the intellectual meaning of his eye, while incredulity was seated in his whole countenance.

"A gale is a gale, Mr. Jukes," resumed the Captain, "and a full-powered steam-ship has got to face it. There's just so much dirty weather knocking about the world, and the proper thing is to go through it with none of what old Captain Wilson of the *Melita* calls 'storm strategy.' The other day ashore I heard him hold forth about it to a lot of shipmasters who came in and sat at a table next to mine. It seemed to me the greatest nonsense. He was telling them how he out-manœuvred, I think he said, a terrific gale, so that it never came nearer than fifty miles to him. A neat piece of head-work he called it. How he knew there was a terrific gale fifty miles off beats me altogether. It was like listening to a crazy man. I would have thought Captain Wilson was old enough to know better."

Captain MacWhirr ceased for a moment, then said, "It's your watch below, Mr. Jukes?"

Jukes came to himself with a start. "Yes, sir."

"Leave orders to call me at the slightest change," said the Captain. He reached up to put the book away, and tucked his legs upon the couch. "Shut the door so that it don't fly open, will you? I can't stand a door banging. They've put a lot of rubbishy locks into this ship, I must say."

Captain MacWhirr closed his eyes.

He did so to rest himself. He was tired, and he experienced that state of mental vacuity which comes at the end of an exhaustive discussion that has liberated some belief matured in the course of meditative years. He had indeed been making his confession of faith, had he only known it; and its effect was to make Jukes, on the other side of the door, stand scratching his head for a good while.

Captain MacWhirr opened his eyes.

He thought he must have been asleep. What was that loud noise? Wind? Why had he not been called? The lamp wriggled in its gimbals, the barometer swung in circles, the table altered its slant every moment; a pair of limp sea-boots with collapsed tops went sliding past the couch. He put out his hand instantly, and captured one.

Jukes' face appeared in a crack of the door: only his face, very red, with staring eyes. The flame of the lamp leaped, a piece of paper flew up, a rush of air enveloped Captain MacWhirr. Beginning to draw on the boot, he directed an expectant gaze at Jukes' swollen, excited features.

"Came on like this," shouted Jukes, "five minutes ago . . . all of a sudden."

The head disappeared with a bang, and a heavy splash and patter of drops swept past the closed door as if a pailful of melted lead had been flung against the house. A whistling could be heard now upon the deep vibrating noise outside. The stuffy chart-room seemed as full of draughts as a shed. Captain MacWhirr collared the other sea-boot on its violent passage along the floor. He was not flustered, but he could not find at once the opening for inserting his foot. The shoes he had flung off were scurrying from end to end of the cabin, gambolling playfully over each other like puppies. As soon as he stood up he kicked at them viciously, but without effect.

He threw himself into the attitude of a lunging fencer, to reach after his oilskin coat; and afterwards he staggered all over the confined space while he jerked himself into it. Very grave, straddling his legs far apart, and stretching his neck, he started to tie deliberately the strings of his sou-wester under his chin, with thick fingers that trembled slightly. He went through all the movements of a woman putting on her bonnet before a glass, with a strained, listening attention, as though he had expected every moment to hear the shout of his name in the confused clamour that had suddenly beset his ship. Its increase filled his ears while he was getting ready to go out and confront whatever it might mean. It was tumultuous and very loud— made up of the rush of the wind, the crashes of the sea, with that prolonged deep vibration of the air, like the roll of an immense and remote drum beating the charge of the gale.

He stood for a moment in the light of the lamp, thick, clumsy, shapeless in his panoply of combat, vigilant and red-faced.

"There's a lot of weight in this," he muttered.

As soon as he attempted to open the door the wind caught it. Clinging to the handle, he was dragged out over the doorstep, and at once found himself engaged with the wind in a sort of personal scuffle whose object was the shutting of that door. At the last moment a tongue of air scurried in and licked out the flame of the lamp.

Ahead of the ship he perceived a great darkness lying upon a multitude of white flashes; on the starboard beam a few amazing stars drooped, dim and fitful, above an immense waste of broken seas, as if seen through a mad drift of smoke.

On the bridge a knot of men, indistinct and toiling, were making great efforts in the light of the wheelhouse windows that shone mistily on their heads and backs. Suddenly darkness closed upon one pane, then on another. The voices of the lost group reached him after the manner of men's voices in a gale, in shreds and fragments of forlorn shouting snatched past the ear. All at once Jukes appeared at his side, yelling, with his head down.

"Watch—put in—wheelhouse shutters—glass—afraid—blow in."

Jukes heard his commander upbraiding.

"This—come—anything—warning—call me."

He tried to explain, with the uproar pressing on his lips.

"Light air—remained—bridge—sudden—north-east—could turn—thought —you—sure—hear."

They had gained the shelter of the weather-cloth, and could converse with raised voices, as people quarrel.

"I got the hands along to cover up all the ventilators. Good job I had remained on deck. I didn't think you would be asleep, and so . . . What did you say, sir? What?"

"Nothing," cried Captain MacWhirr. "I said—all right."

"By all the powers! We've got it this time," observed Jukes in a howl.

"You haven't altered her course?" inquired Captain MacWhirr, straining his voice.

"No, sir. Certainly not. Wind came out right head. And here comes the head sea."

A plunge of the ship ended in a shock as if she had landed her forefoot upon something solid. After a moment of stillness a lofty flight of sprays drove hard with the wind upon their faces.

"Keep her at it as long as we can," shouted Captain MacWhirr.

Before Jukes had squeezed the salt water out of his eyes all the stars had disappeared.

III

Jukes was as ready a man as any half-dozen young mates that may be caught by casting a net upon the waters; and though he had been somewhat taken aback by the startling viciousness of the first squall, he had pulled himself together on the instant, had called out the hands and had rushed them along to secure such openings about the deck as had not been already battened down earlier in the evening. Shouting in his fresh, sten-torian voice, "Jump, boys, and bear a hand!" he led in the work, telling him-self the while that he had "just expected this."

But at the same time he was growing aware that this was rather more than he had expected. From the first stir of the air felt on his cheek the gale seemed to take upon itself the accumulated impetus of an avalanche. Heavy sprays enveloped the *Nan-Shan* from stem to stern, and instantly in the midst of her regular rolling she began to jerk and plunge as though she had gone mad with fright.

Jukes thought, "This is no joke." While he was exchanging explanatory yells with his captain, a sudden lowering of the darkness came upon the night, falling before their vision like something palpable. It was as if the masked lights of the world had been turned down. Jukes was uncritically glad to have his captain at hand. It relieved him as though that man had, by simply coming on deck, taken most of the gale's weight upon his shoulders. Such is the prestige, the privilege, and the burden of com-mand.

Captain MacWhirr could expect no relief of that sort from any one on earth. Such is the loneliness of command. He was trying to see, with that watchful manner of a seaman who stares into the wind's eye as if into the eye of an adversary, to penetrate the hidden intention and guess the aim and force of the thrust. The strong wind swept at him out of a vast obscurity; he felt under his feet the uneasiness of his ship, and he could not even discern the shadow of her shape. He wished it were not so; and very still he waited, feeling stricken by a blind man's helplessness.

To be silent was natural to him, dark or shine. Jukes, at his elbow, made himself heard yelling cheerily in the gusts, "We must have got the worst of it at once, sir." A faint burst of lightning quivered all round, as if flashed into a cavern—into a black and secret chamber of the sea, with a floor of foaming crests.

It unveiled for a sinister, fluttering moment a ragged mass of clouds hang-ing low, the lurch of the long outlines of the ship, the black figures of men caught on the bridge, heads forward, as if petrified in the act of butting. The darkness palpitated down upon all this, and then the real thing came at last.

It was something formidable and swift, like the sudden smashing of a vial of wrath. It seemed to explode all round the ship with an overpowering concussion and a rush of great waters, as if an immense dam had been blown up to windward. In an instant the men lost touch of each other. This is the disintegrating power of a great wind: it isolates one from one's kind. An earthquake, a landslip, an avalanche, overtake a man incidentally, as it were—without passion. A furious gale attacks him like a personal enemy, tries to grasp his limbs, fastens upon his mind, seeks to rout his very spirit out of him.

Jukes was driven away from his commander. He fancied himself whirled
a great distance through the air. Everything disappeared—even, for a
moment, his power of thinking; but his hand had found one of the rail-
stanchions. His distress was by no means alleviated by an inclination to
disbelieve the reality of this experience. Though young, he had seen some
bad weather, and had never doubted his ability to imagine the worst; but
this was so much beyond his powers of fancy that it appeared incom-
patible with the existence of any ship whatever. He would have been incredulous about himself in the same way, perhaps, had he not been so
harassed by the necessity of exerting a wrestling effort against a force trying
to tear him away from his hold. Moreover, the conviction of not being
utterly destroyed returned to him through the sensations of being half-
drowned, bestially shaken, and partly choked.

It seemed to him he remained there precariously alone with the stanchion,
for a long, long time. The rain poured on him, flowed, drove in sheets. He
breathed in gasps; and sometimes the water he swallowed was fresh and
sometimes it was salt. For the most part he kept his eyes shut tight, as if
suspecting his sight might be destroyed in the immense flurry of the
elements. When he ventured to blink hastily, he derived some moral support from the green gleam of the starboard light shining feebly upon the
flight of rain and sprays. He was actually looking at it when its ray fell upon
the uprearing sea which put it out. He saw the head of the wave topple
over, adding the mite of its crash to the tremendous uproar raging around
him, and almost at the same instant the stanchion was wrenched away
from his embracing arms. After a crushing thump on his back he found
himself suddenly afloat and borne upwards. His first irresistible notion was
that the whole China Sea had climbed on the bridge. Then, more sanely, he
concluded himself gone overboard. All the time he was being tossed, flung,
and rolled in great volumes of water, he kept on repeating mentally, with
the utmost precipitation, the words: "My God! My God! My God! My
God!"

All at once, in a revolt of misery and despair, he formed the crazy resolution to get out of that. And he began to thresh about with his arms and
legs. But as soon as he commenced his wretched struggles he discovered
that he had become somehow mixed up with a face, an oil-skin coat, somebody's boots. He clawed ferociously all these things in turn, lost them,
found them again, lost them once more, and finally was himself caught in
the firm clasp of a pair of stout arms. He returned the embrace closely
round a thick solid body. He had found his captain.

They tumbled over and over, tightening their hug. Suddenly the water let
them down with a brutal bang; and, stranded against the side of the wheelhouse, out of breath and bruised, they were left to stagger up in the
wind and hold on where they could.

Jukes came out of it rather horrified, as though he had escaped some un-

paralleled outrage directed at his feelings. It weakened his faith in himself. He started shouting aimlessly to the man he could feel near him
in that fiendish blackness, "Is it you, sir? Is it you, sir?" till his temples
seemed ready to burst. And he heard in answer a voice, as if crying far
away, as if screaming to him fretfully from a very great distance, the one
word "Yes!" Other seas swept again over the bridge. He received them
defencelessly right over his bare head, with both his hands engaged in
holding.

The motion of the ship was extravagant. Her lurches had an appalling
helplessness: she pitched as if taking a header into a void, and seemed to
find a wall to hit every time. When she rolled she fell on her side headlong,
and she would be righted back by such a demolishing blow that Jukes
felt her reeling as a clubbed man reels before he collapses. The gale howled
and scuffled about gigantically in the darkness, as though the entire world
were one black gully. At certain moments the air streamed against the ship
as if sucked through a tunnel with a concentrated solid force of impact
that seemed to lift her clean out of the water and keep her up for an instant with only a quiver running through her from end to end. And then
she would begin her tumbling again as if dropped back into a boiling
cauldron. Jukes tried hard to compose his mind and judge things coolly.

The sea, flattened down in the heavier gusts, would uprise and overwhelm both ends of the *Nan-Shan* in snowy rushes of foam, expanding
wide, beyond both rails, into the night. And on this dazzling sheet, spread
under the blackness of the clouds and emitting a bluish glow, Captain
MacWhirr could catch a desolate glimpse of a few tiny specks black as
ebony, the tops of the hatches, the battened companions, the heads of the
covered winches, the foot of a mast. This was all he could see of his ship.
Her middle structure, covered by the bridge which bore him, his mate,
the closed wheelhouse where a man was steering shut up with the fear of
being swept overboard together with the whole thing in one great crash—
her middle structure was like a half-tide rock awash upon a coast. It was
like an outlying rock with the water boiling up, streaming over, pouring
off, beating round—like a rock in the surf to which shipwrecked people
cling before they let go—only it rose, it sank, it rolled continuously, without respite and rest, like a rock that should have miraculously struck adrift
from a coast and gone wallowing upon the sea.

The *Nan-Shan* was being looted by the storm with a senseless, destructive fury: trysails torn out of the extra gaskets, double-lashed awnings
blown away, bridge swept clean, weather-cloths burst, rails twisted, light-
screens smashed—and two of the boats had gone already. They had gone
unheard and unseen, melting, as it were, in the shock and smother of the
wave. It was only later, when upon the white flash of another high sea
hurling itself amidships, Jukes had a vision of two pairs of davits leaping
black and empty out of the solid blackness, with one overhauled fall flying

and an iron-bound block capering in the air, that he became aware of what had happened within about three yards of his back.

He poked his head forward, groping for the ear of his commander. His lips touched it—big, fleshy, very wet. He cried in an agitated tone, "Our boats are going now, sir."

And again he heard that voice, forced and ringing feebly, but with a penetrating effect of quietness in the enormous discord of noises, as if sent out from some remote spot of peace beyond the black wastes of the gale; again he heard a man's voice—the frail and indomitable sound that can be made to carry an infinity of thought, resolution and purpose, that shall be pronouncing confident words on the last day, when heavens fall, and justice is done—again he heard it, and it was crying to him, as if from very, very far—"All right."

He thought he had not managed to make himself understood. "Our boats—I say boats—the boats, sir! Two gone!"

The same voice, within a foot of him and yet so remote, yelled sensibly, "Can't be helped."

Captain MacWhirr had never turned his face, but Jukes caught some more words on the wind.

"What can—expect—when hammering through—such—— Bound to leave—something behind—stands to reason."

Watchfully Jukes listened for more. No more came. This was all Captain MacWhirr had to say; and Jukes could picture to himself rather than see the broad squat back before him. An impenetrable obscurity pressed down upon the ghostly glimmers of the sea. A dull conviction seized upon Jukes that there was nothing to be done.

If the steering-gear did not give way, if the immense volumes of water did not burst the deck in or smash one of the hatches, if the engines did not give up, if way could be kept on the ship against this terrific wind, and she did not bury herself in one of these awful seas, of whose white crests alone, topping high above her bows, he could now and then get a sickening glimpse—then there was a chance of her coming out of it. Something within him seemed to turn over, bringing uppermost the feeling that the *Nan-Shan* was lost.

"She's done for," he said to himself, with a surprising mental agitation, as though he had discovered an unexpected meaning in this thought. One of these things was bound to happen. Nothing could be prevented now, and nothing could be remedied. The men on board did not count, and the ship could not last. This weather was too impossible.

Jukes felt an arm thrown heavily over his shoulders; and to this overture he responded with great intelligence by catching hold of his captain round the waist.

They stood clasped thus in the blind night, bracing each other against the wind, cheek to cheek and lip to ear, in the manner of two hulks lashed stem to stern together.

And Jukes heard the voice of his commander hardly any louder than before, but nearer, as though, starting to march athwart the prodigious rush of the hurricane, it had approached him, bearing that strange effect of quietness like the serene glow of a halo.

"D'ye know where the hands got to?" it asked, vigorous and evanescent at the same time, overcoming the strength of the wind, and swept away from Jukes instantly.

Jukes didn't know. They were all on the bridge when the real force of the hurricane struck the ship. He had no idea where they had crawled to. Under the circumstances they were nowhere, for all the use that could be made of them. Somehow the Captain's wish to know distressed Jukes.

"Want the hands, sir?" he cried, apprehensively.

"Ought to know," asserted Captain MacWhirr. "Hold hard."

They held hard. An outburst of unchained fury, a vicious rush of the wind absolutely steadied the ship; she rocked only, quick and light like a child's cradle, for a terrific moment of suspense, while the whole atmosphere, as it seemed, streamed furiously past her, roaring away from the tenebrous earth.

It suffocated them, and with eyes shut they tightened their grasp. What from the magnitude of the shock might have been a column of water running upright in the dark, butted against the ship, broke short, and fell on her bridge, crushingly, from on high, with a dead burying weight.

A flying fragment of that collapse, a mere splash, enveloped them in one swirl from their feet over their heads, filling violently their ears, mouths and nostrils with salt water. It knocked out their legs, wrenched in haste at their arms, seethed away swiftly under their chins; and opening their eyes, they saw the piled-up masses of foam dashing to and fro amongst what looked like the fragments of a ship. She had given way as if driven straight in. Their panting hearts yielded, too, before the tremendous blow; and all at once she sprang up again to her desperate plunging, as if trying to scramble out from under the ruins.

The seas in the dark seemed to rush from all sides to keep her back where she might perish. There was hate in the way she was handled, and ferocity in the blows that fell. She was like a living creature thrown to the rage of a mob: hustled terribly, struck at, borne up, flung down, leaped upon. Captain MacWhirr and Jukes kept hold of each other, deafened by the noise, gagged by the wind; and the great physical tumult beating about their bodies, brought, like an unbridled display of passion, a profound trouble to their souls. One of those wild and appalling shrieks that are heard at times passing mysteriously overhead in the steady roar of a hurricane, swooped, as if borne on wings, upon the ship, and Jukes tried to out-scream it.

"Will she live through this?"

The cry was wrenched out of his breast. It was as unintentional as the birth of a thought in the head, and he heard nothing of it himself. It all became extinct at once—thought, intention, effort—and of his cry the inaudible vibration added to the tempest waves of the air.

He expected nothing from it. Nothing at all. For indeed what answer could be made? But after a while he heard with amazement the frail and resisting voice in his ear, the dwarf sound, unconquered in the giant tumult.

"She may!"

It was a dull yell, more difficult to seize than a whisper. And presently the voice returned again, half submerged in the vast crashes, like a ship battling against the waves of an ocean.

"Let's hope so!" it cried—small, lonely and unmoved, a stranger to the visions of hope or fear; and it flickered into disconnected words: "Ship. . . . This. . . . Never—Anyhow . . . for the best." Jukes gave it up.

Then, as if it had come suddenly upon the one thing fit to withstand the power of a storm, it seemed to gain force and firmness for the last broken shouts:

"Keep on hammering . . . builders . . . good men. . . . And chance it . . . engines. . . . Rout . . . good man."

Captain MacWhirr removed his arm from Jukes' shoulders, and thereby ceased to exist for his mate, so dark it was; Jukes, after a tense stiffening of every muscle, would let himself go limp all over. The gnawing of profound discomfort existed side by side with an incredible disposition to somnolence, as though he had been buffeted and worried into drowsiness. The wind would get hold of his head and try to shake it off his shoulders; his clothes, full of water, were as heavy as lead, cold and dripping like an armour of melting ice: he shivered—it lasted a long time; and with his hands closed hard on his hold, he was letting himself sink slowly into the depths of bodily misery. His mind became concentrated upon himself in an aimless, idle way, and when something pushed lightly at the back of his knees he nearly, as the saying is, jumped out of his skin.

In the start forward he bumped the back of Captain MacWhirr, who didn't move; and then a hand gripped his thigh. A lull had come, a menacing lull of the wind, the holding of a stormy breath—and he felt himself pawed all over. It was the boatswain. Jukes recognized these hands, so thick and enormous that they seemed to belong to some new species of man.

The boatswain had arrived on the bridge, crawling on all fours against the wind, and had found the chief mate's legs with the top of his head. Immediately he crouched and began to explore Jukes' person upwards with prudent, apologetic touches, as became an inferior.

He was an ill-favoured, undersized, gruff sailor of fifty, coarsely hairy, short-legged, long-armed, resembling an elderly ape. His strength was immense; and in his great lumpy paws, bulging like brown boxing-gloves on the end of furry forearms, the heaviest objects were handled like playthings. Apart from the grizzled pelt on his chest, the menacing demeanour and the hoarse voice, he had none of the classical attributes of his rating. His good nature almost amounted to imbecility: the men did what they liked with him, and he had not an ounce of initiative in his character, which was easy-going and talkative. For these reasons Jukes disliked him; but Captain MacWhirr, to Jukes' scornful disgust, seemed to regard him as a first-rate petty officer.

He pulled himself up by Jukes' coat, taking that liberty with the greatest moderation, and only so far as it was forced upon him by the hurricane.

"What is it, boss'n, what is it?" yelled Jukes, impatiently. What could that fraud of a boss'n want on the bridge? The typhoon had got on Jukes' nerves. The husky bellowings of the other, though unintelligible, seemed to suggest a state of lively satisfaction. There could be no mistake. The old fool was pleased with something.

The boatswain's other hand had found some other body, for in a changed tone he began to inquire: "Is it you, sir? Is it you, sir?" The wind strangled his howls.

"Yes!" cried Captain MacWhirr.

IV

All that the boatswain, out of a superabundance of yells, could make clear to Captain MacWhirr was the bizarre intelligence that "All them Chinamen in the fore 'tween deck have fetched away, sir."

Jukes to leeward could hear these two shouting within six inches of his face, as you may hear on a still night half a mile away two men conversing across a field. He heard Captain MacWhirr's exasperated "What? What?" and the strained pitch of the other's hoarseness. "In a lump . . . seen them myself. . . . Awful sight, sir . . . thought . . . tell you."

Jukes remained indifferent, as if rendered irresponsible by the force of the hurricane, which made the very thought of action utterly vain. Besides, being very young, he had found the occupation of keeping his heart completely steeled against the worst so engrossing that he had come to feel an over-powering dislike towards any other form of activity whatever. He was not scared; he knew this because, firmly believing he would never see another sunrise, he remained calm in that belief.

These are the moments of do-nothing heroics to which even good men surrender at times. Many officers of ships can no doubt recall a case in their experience when just such a trance of confounded stoicism would come all at once over a whole ship's company. Jukes, however, had no wide experi-ence of men or storms. He conceived himself to be calm—inexorably calm; but as a matter of fact he was daunted; not abjectly, but only so far as a decent man may, without becoming loathsome to himself.

It was rather like a forced-on numbness of spirit. The long, long stress of a gale does it; the suspense of the interminably culminating catastrophe; and there is a bodily fatigue in the mere holding on to existence within the excessive tumult; a searching and insidious fatigue that penetrates deep into a man's breast to cast down and sadden his heart, which is incorrigible, and of all the gifts of the earth—even before life itself—aspires to peace.

Jukes was benumbed much more than he supposed. He held on—very wet, very cold, stiff in every limb; and in a momentary hallucination of swift visions (it is said that a drowning man thus reviews all his life) he beheld all sorts of memories altogether unconnected with his present situation. He remembered his father, for instance: a worthy business man, who at an unfortunate crisis in his affairs went quietly to bed and died forthwith in a state of resignation. Jukes did not recall these circumstances, of course, but remaining otherwise unconcerned he seemed to see distinctly the poor man's face; a certain game of nap played when quite a boy in Table Bay on board a ship, since lost with all hands; the thick eyebrows of his first skipper; and without any emotion, as he might years ago have walked listlessly into her room and found her sitting there with a book, he remembered his mother—dead, too, now—the resolute woman, left badly off, who had been very firm in his bringing up.

It could not have lasted more than a second, perhaps not so much. A heavy arm had fallen about his shoulders; Captain MacWhirr's voice was speaking his name into his ear.

"Jukes! Jukes!"

He detected the tone of deep concern. The wind had thrown its weight on the ship, trying to pin her down amongst the seas. They made a clean breach over her, as over a deep-swimming log; and the gathered weight of crashes menaced monstrously from afar. The breakers flung out of the night with a ghostly light on their crests—the light of sea-foam that in a ferocious, boiling-up pale flash showed upon the slender body of the ship the toppling rush, the downfall, and the seething mad scurry of each wave. Never for a moment could she shake herself clear of the water; Jukes, rigid, perceived in her motion the ominous sign of haphazard floundering. She was no longer struggling intelligently. It was the beginning of the end; and the note of busy concern in Captain MacWhirr's voice sickened him like an exhibition of blind and pernicious folly.

The spell of the storm had fallen upon Jukes. He was penetrated by it, absorbed by it; he was rooted in it with a rigour of dumb attention. Captain MacWhirr persisted in his cries, but the wind got between them like a solid wedge. He hung round Jukes' neck as heavy as a mill-stone, and suddenly the sides of their heads knocked together.

"Jukes! Mr. Jukes, I say!"

He had to answer that voice that would not be silenced. He answered in the customary manner: ". . . Yes, sir."

And directly, his heart, corrupted by the storm that breeds a craving for peace, rebelled against the tyranny of training and command.

Captain MacWhirr had his mate's head fixed firm in the crook of his elbow, and pressed it to his yelling lips mysteriously. Sometimes Jukes would break in, admonishing hastily: "Look out, sir!" or Captain MacWhirr would bawl an earnest exhortation to "Hold hard, there!" and the whole black universe seemed to reel together with the ship. They paused. She floated yet. And Captain MacWhirr would resume his shouts. ". . . . Says . . . whole lot . . . fetched away. . . . Ought to see . . . what's the matter."

Directly the full force of the hurricane had struck the ship, every part of her deck became untenable; and the sailors, dazed and dismayed, took shelter in the port alleyway under the bridge. It had a door aft, which they shut; it was very black, cold, and dismal. At each heavy fling of the ship they would groan all together in the dark, and tons of water could be heard scuttling about as if trying to get at them from above. The boatswain had been keeping up a gruff talk, but a more unreasonable lot of men, he said afterwards, he had never been with. They were snug enough there, out of harm's way, and not wanted to do anything, either; and yet they did nothing but grumble and complain peevishly like so many sick lads. Finally, one of them said that if there had been at least some light to see each other's noses by, it wouldn't be so bad. It was making him crazy, he declared, to lie there in the dark waiting for the blamed hooker to sink.

"Why don't you step outside, then, and be done with it at once?" the boatswain turned on him.

This called up a shout of execration. The boatswain found himself overwhelmed with reproaches of all sorts. They seemed to take it ill that a lamp was not instantly created for them out of nothing. They would whine after a light to get drowned by—anyhow! And though the unreason of their revilings was patent—since no one could hope to reach the lamp-room, which was forward—he became greatly distressed. He did not think it was decent of them to be nagging at him like this. He told them so, and was met by general contumely. He sought refuge, therefore, in an embittered silence. At the same time their grumbling and sighing and muttering worried him greatly, but by-and-by it occurred to him that there were six globe lamps hung in the 'tween-deck, and that there could be no harm in depriving the coolies of one of them.

The *Nan-Shan* had an athwartship coal-bunker, which, being at times used as cargo space, communicated by an iron door with the fore 'tween-deck. It was empty then, and its manhole was the foremost one in the alleyway. The boatswain could get in, therefore, without coming out on deck at all; but to his great surprise he found he could induce no one to help him in taking off the manhole cover. He groped for it all the same, but one of the crew lying in his way refused to budge.

"Why, I only want to get you that blamed light you are crying for," he expostulated, almost pitifully.

Somebody told him to go and put his head in a bag. He regretted he could not recognize the voice, and that it was too dark to see, otherwise, as he said, he would have put a head on *that* son of a sea-cook, anyway, sink or swim. Nevertheless, he had made up his mind to show them he could get a light, if he were to die for it.

Through the violence of the ship's rolling, every movement was dangerous. To be lying down seemed labour enough. He nearly broke his neck dropping into the bunker. He fell on his back, and was sent shooting helplessly from side to side in the dangerous company of a heavy iron bar—a coal-trimmer's slice probably—left down there by somebody. This thing made him as nervous as though it had been a wild beast. He could not see it, the inside of the bunker coated with coal-dust being perfectly and impenetrably black; but he heard it sliding and clattering, and striking here and there, always in the neighbourhood of his head. It seemed to make an extraordinary noise, too—to give heavy thumps as though it had been as big as a bridge girder. This was remarkable enough for him to notice while he was flung from port to starboard and back again, and clawing desperately the smooth sides of the bunker in the endeavour to stop himself. The door into the 'tween-deck not fitting quite true, he saw a thread of dim light at the bottom.

Being a sailor, and a still active man, he did not want much of a chance to regain his feet; and as luck would have it, in scrambling up he put his hand on the iron slice, picking it up as he rose. Otherwise he would have been afraid of the thing breaking his legs, or at least knocking him down again. At first he stood still. He felt unsafe in this darkness that seemed to make the ship's motion unfamiliar, unforeseen, and difficult to counteract. He felt so much shaken for a moment that he dared not move for fear of "taking charge again." He had no mind to get battered to pieces in that bunker.

He had struck his head twice; he was dazed a little. He seemed to hear yet so plainly the clatter and bangs of the iron slice flying about his ears that he tightened his grip to prove to himself he had it there safely in his hand. He was vaguely amazed at the plainness with which down there he could hear the gale raging. Its howls and shrieks seemed to take on, in the emptiness of the bunker, something of the human character, of human rage and pain—being not vast but infinitely poignant. And there were, with every roll, thumps, too—profound, ponderous thumps, as if a bulky object of five-ton weight or so had got play in the hold. But there was no such thing in the cargo. Something on deck? Impossible. Or alongside? Couldn't be.

He thought all this quickly, clearly, competently, like a seaman, and in the end remained puzzled. This noise, though, came deadened from outside, together with the washing and pouring of water on deck above his head.

Was it the wind? Must be. It made down there a row like the shouting of a big lot of crazed men. And he discovered in himself a desire for a light, too—if only to get drowned by—and a nervous anxiety to get out of that bunker as quickly as posible.

He pulled back the bolt: the heavy iron plate turned on its hinges; and it was as though he had opened the door to the sounds of the tempest. A gust of hoarse yelling met him: the air was still; and the rushing of water overhead was covered by a tumult of strangled, throaty shrieks that produced an effect of desperate confusion. He straddled his legs the whole width of the doorway and stretched his neck. And at first he perceived only what he had come to seek: six small yellow flames swinging violently on the great body of the dusk.

It was stayed like the gallery of a mine, with a row of stanchions in the middle, and cross-beams overhead, penetrating into the gloom ahead—indefinitely. And to port there loomed, like the caving in of one of the sides, a bulky mass with a slanting outline. The whole place, with the shadows and the shapes, moved all the time. The boatswain glared: the ship lurched to starboard, and a great howl came from that mass that had the slant of fallen earth.

Pieces of wood whizzed past. Planks, he thought, inexpressibly startled, and flinging back his head. At his feet a man went sliding over, open-eyed, on his back, straining with uplifted arms for nothing: and another came bounding like a detached stone with his head between his legs and his hands clenched. His pigtail whipped in the air; he made a grab at the boatswain's legs, and from his opened hand a bright white disc rolled against the boatswain's foot. He recognized a silver dollar, and yelled at it with astonishment. With a precipitated sound of trampling and shuffling of bare feet, and with guttural cries, the mound of writhing bodies piled up to port detached itself from the ship's side and sliding, inert and struggling, shifted to starboard, with a dull, brutal thump. The cries ceased. The boatswain heard a long moan through the roar and whistling of the wind; he saw an inextricable confusion of heads and shoulders, naked soles kicking upwards, fists raised, tumbling backs, legs, pigtails, faces.

"Good Lord!" he cried, horrified, and banged-to the iron door upon this vision.

This was what he had come on the bridge to tell. He could not keep it to himself; and on board ship there is only one man to whom it is worth while to unburden yourself. On his passage back the hands in the alleyways swore at him for a fool. Why didn't he bring that lamp? What the devil did the coolies matter to anybody? And when he came out, the extremity of the ship made what went on inside of her appear of little moment.

At first he thought he had left the alleyway in the very moment of her sinking. The bridge ladders had been washed away, but an enormous sea filling the after-deck floated him up. After that he had to lie on his stomach for some time, holding to a ring-bolt, getting his breath now and then, and swallowing salt water. He struggled farther on his hands and knees, too frightened and distracted to turn back. In this way he reached the afterpart of the wheelhouse. In that comparatively sheltered spot he found the second mate. The boatswain was pleasantly surprised—his impression being that everybody on deck must have been washed away a long time ago. He asked eagerly where the Captain was.

The second mate was lying low, like a malignant little animal under a hedge.

"Captain? Gone overboard, after getting us into this mess." The mate, too, for all he knew or cared. Another fool. Didn't matter. Everybody was going by-and-by.

The boatswain crawled out again into the strength of the wind; not because he much expected to find anybody, he said, but just to get away from "that man." He crawled out as outcasts go to face an inclement world. Hence his great joy at finding Jukes and the Captain. But what was going on in the 'tween-deck was to him a minor matter by that time. Besides, it was difficult to make yourself heard. But he managed to convey the idea that the Chinamen had broken adrift together with their boxes, and that he had come up on purpose to report this. As to the hands, they were all right. Then, appeased, he subsided on the deck in a sitting posture, hugging with his arms and legs the stand of the engine-room telegraph—an iron casting as thick as a post. When that went, why, he expected he would go, too. He gave no more thought to the coolies.

Captain MacWhirr had made Jukes understand that he wanted him to go down below—to see.

"What am I to do then, sir?" And the trembling of his whole wet body caused Jukes' voice to sound like bleating.

"See first . . . Boss'n . . . says . . . adrift."

"That boss'n is a confounded fool," howled Jukes, shakily.

The absurdity of the demand made upon him revolted Jukes. He was as unwilling to go as if the moment he had left the deck the ship were sure to sink.

"I must know . . . can't leave. . . ."

"Fight . . . boss'n says they fight. . . . Why? Can't have . . . fighting . . . board ship. . . . Much rather keep you here . . . case . . . I should . . . washed overboard myself. . . . Stop it . . . some way. You see and tell me . . . through engine-room tube. Don't want you . . . come up here . . . too often. Dangerous . . . moving about . . . deck."

Jukes, held with his head in chancery, had to listen to what seemed horrible suggestions.

"Don't want . . . you get lost . . . so long . . . ship isn't. . . . Rout . . .

Good man . . . Ship . . . may . . . through this . . . all right yet."

All at once Jukes understood he would have to go.

"Do you think she may?" he screamed.

But the wind devoured the reply, out of which Jukes heard only the one word, pronounced with great energy " . . . Always. . . ."

Captain MacWhirr released Jukes, and bending over the boatswain, yelled, "Get back with the mate." Jukes only knew that the arm was gone off his shoulders. He was dismissed with his orders—to do what? He was exasperated into letting go his hold carelessly, and on the instant was blown away. It seemed to him that nothing could stop him from being blown right over the stern. He flung himself down hastily, and the boatswain, who was following, fell on him.

"Don't you get up yet, sir," cried the boatswain. "No hurry!"

A sea swept over. Jukes understood the boatswain to splutter that the bridge ladders were gone. "I'll lower you down, sir, by your hands," he screamed. He shouted also something about the smoke-stack being as likely to go overboard as not. Jukes thought it very possible, and imagined the fires out, the ship helpless. . . . The boatswain by his side kept on yelling. "What? What is it?" Jukes cried distressfully; and the other repeated, "What would my old woman say if she saw me now?"

In the alleyway, where a lot of water had got in and splashed in the dark, the men were still as death, till Jukes stumbled against one of them and cursed him savagely for being in the way. Two or three voices then asked, eager and weak, "Any chance for us, sir?"

"What's the matter with you fools?" he said brutally. He felt as though he could throw himself down amongst them and never move any more. But they seemed cheered; and in the midst of obsequious warnings, "Look out! Mind that manhole lid, sir," they lowered him into the bunker. The boatswain tumbled down after him, and as soon as he had picked himself up he remarked, "She would say, 'Serve you right, you old fool, for going to sea.'"

The boatswain had some means, and made a point of alluding to them frequently. His wife—a fat woman—and two grown-up daughters kept a greengrocer's shop in the East-end of London.

In the dark, Jukes, unsteady on his legs, listened to a faint thunderous patter. A deadened screaming went on steadily at his elbow, as it were; and from above the louder tumult of the storm descended upon these near sounds. His head swam. To him, too, in that bunker, the motion of the ship seemed novel and menacing, sapping his resolution as though he had never been afloat before.

He had half a mind to scramble out again; but the remembrance of Captain MacWhirr's voice made this impossible. His orders were to go and see. What was the good of it, he wanted to know. Enraged, he told himself he would see—of course. But the boatswain, staggering clumsily, warned him to be careful how he opened that door; there was a blamed fight going on. And Jukes, as if in great bodily pain, desired irritably to know what the devil they were fighting for.

"Dollars! Dollars, sir. All their rotten chests got burst open. Blamed money skipping all over the place, and they are tumbling after it head over heels—tearing and biting like anything. A regular little hell in there."

Jukes convulsively opened the door. The short boatswain peered under his arm.

One of the lamps had gone out, broken perhaps. Rancorous, guttural cries burst out loudly on their ears, and a strange panting sound, the working of all these straining breasts. A hard blow hit the side of the ship: water fell above with a stunning shock, and in the forefront of the gloom, where the air was reddish and thick, Jukes saw a head bang the deck violently, two thick calves waving on high, muscular arms twined round a naked body, a yellow-face, open-mouthed and with a set wild stare, look up and slide away. An empty chest clattered turning over; a man fell head first with a jump, as if lifted by a kick; and farther off, indistinct, others streamed like a mass of rolling stones down a bank, thumping the deck with their feet and flourishing their arms wildly. The hatchway ladder was loaded with coolies swarming on it like bees on a branch. They hung on the steps in a crawling, stirring cluster, beating madly with their fists the underside of the battened hatch, and the headlong rush of the water above was heard in the intervals of their yelling. The ship heeled over more, and they began to drop off: first one, then two, then all the rest went away together, falling straight off with a great cry.

Jukes was confounded. The boatswain, with gruff anxiety, begged him, "Don't you go in there, sir."

The whole place seemed to twist upon itself, jumping incessantly the while; and when the ship rose to a sea Jukes fancied that all these men would be shot upon him in a body. He backed out, swung the door to, and with trembling hands pushed at the bolt. . . .

As soon as his mate had gone Captain MacWhirr, left alone on the bridge, sidled and staggered as far as the wheelhouse. Its door being hinged forward, he had to fight the gale for admittance, and when at last he managed to enter, it was with an instantaneous clatter and a bang, as though he had been fired through the wood. He stood within, holding on to the handle.

The steering-gear leaked steam, and in the confined space the glass of the binnacle made a shiny oval of light in a thin white fog. The wind howled, hummed, whistled, with sudden booming gusts that rattled the doors and shutters in the vicious patter of sprays. Two coils of lead-line and a small canvas bag hung on a long lanyard, swung wide off, and came back clinging to the bulkheads. The gratings underfoot were nearly afloat; with every sweeping blow of a sea, water squirted violently through the cracks all round the door, and the man at the helm had flung down his cap, his coat, and stood propped against the gear-casing in a striped cotton shirt open on his breast. The little brass wheel in his hands had the appearance of a bright and fragile toy. The cords of his neck stood hard and lean, a dark patch lay in the hollow of his throat, and his face was still and sunken as in death.

Captain MacWhirr wiped his eyes. The sea that had nearly taken him overboard had, to his great annoyance, washed his sou'-wester hat off his bald head. The fluffy, fair hair, soaked and darkened, resembled a mean skein of cotton threads festooned round his bare skull. His face, glistening with sea-water, had been made crimson with the wind, with the sting of sprays. He looked as though he had come off sweating from before a furnace.

"You here?" he muttered, heavily.

The second mate had found his way into the wheelhouse some time before. He had fixed himself in a corner with his knees up, a fist pressed against each temple; and this attitude suggested rage, sorrow, resignation, surrender, with a sort of concentrated unforgiveness. He said mournfully and defiantly, "Well, it's my watch below now: ain't it?"

The steam gear clattered, stopped, clattered again; and the helmsman's eyeballs seemed to project out of a hungry face as if the compass card behind the binnacle glass had been meat. God knows how long he had been left there to steer, as if forgotten by all his shipmates. The bells had not been struck; there had been no reliefs; the ship's routine had gone down wind; but he was trying to keep her head north-north-east. The rudder might have been gone for all he knew, the fires out, the engines broken down, the ship ready to roll over like a corpse. He was anxious not to get muddled and lose control of her head, because the compass-card swung far both ways, wriggling on the pivot, and sometimes seemed to whirl right round. He suffered from mental stress. He was horribly afraid, also, of the wheelhouse going. Mountains of water kept on tumbling against it. When the ship took one of her desperate dives the corners of his lips twitched.

Captain MacWhirr looked up at the wheelhouse clock. Screwed to the bulk-head, it had a white face on which the black hands appeared to stand quite still. It was half-past one in the morning.

"Another day," he muttered to himself.

The second mate heard him, and lifting his head as one grieving amongst ruins, "You won't see it break," he exclaimed. His wrists and his knees could be seen to shake violently. "No, by God! You won't. . . ."

He took his face again between his fists.

The body of the helmsman had moved slightly, but his head didn't budge on his neck,—like a stone head fixed to look one way from a column. During a roll that all but took his booted legs from under him, and in the very stagger to save himself, Captain MacWhirr said austerely, "Don't you pay any attention to what that man says." And then, with an indefinable change of tone, very grave, he added, "He isn't on duty."

The sailor said nothing.

The hurricane boomed, shaking the little place, which seemed air-tight; and the light of the binnacle flickered all the time.

"You haven't been relieved," Captain MacWhirr went on, looking down. "I want you to stick to the helm, though, as long as you can. You've got the hang of her. Another man coming here might make a mess of it Wouldn't do. No child's play. And the hands are probably busy with a job down below. . . . Think you can?"

The steering-gear leaped into an abrupt short clatter, stopped smouldering like an ember; and the still man, with a motionless gaze, burst out, as if all the passion in him had gone into his lips: "By Heavens, sir! I can steer for ever if nobody talks to me."

"Oh! aye! All right. . . ." The Captain lifted his eyes for the first time to the man, ". . . Hackett."

And he seemed to dismiss this matter from his mind. He stooped to the engine-room speaking-tube, blew in, and bent his head. Mr. Rout below answered, and at once Captain MacWhirr put his lips to the mouthpiece.

With the uproar of the gale around him he applied alternately his lips and his ear, and the engineer's voice mounted to him, harsh and as if out of the heat of an engagement. One of the stokers was disabled, the others had given in, the second engineer and the donkey-man were firing-up. The third engineer was standing by the steam-valve. The engines were being tended by hand. How was it above?

"Bad enough. It mostly rests with you," said Captain MacWhirr. Was the mate down there yet? No? Well, he would be presently. Would Mr. Rout let him talk through the speaking-tube?—through the deck speaking-tube, because he—the Captain—was going out again on the bridge directly. There was some trouble amongst the Chinamen. They were fighting, it seemed. Couldn't allow fighting anyhow. . . .

Mr. Rout had gone away, and Captain MacWhirr could feel against his ear the pulsation of the engines, like the beat of the ship's heart. Mr. Rout's voice down there shouted something distantly. The ship pitched headlong, the pulsation leaped with a hissing tumult, and stopped dead. Captain Mac-Whirr's face was impassive, and his eyes were fixed aimlessly on the crouching shape of the second mate. Again Mr. Rout's voice cried out in the depths, and the pulsating beats recommenced, with slow strokes—growing swifter.

Mr. Rout had returned to the tube. "It don't matter much what they do," he said, hastily; and then, with irritation, "She takes these dives as if she never meant to come up again."

"Awful sea," said the Captain's voice from above.

"Don't let me drive her under," barked Solomon Rout up the pipe.

"Dark and rain. Can't see what's coming," uttered the voice. "Must—keep

—her—moving—enough to steer—and chance it," it went on to state distinctly.

"I am doing as much as I dare."

"We are—getting—smashed up—a good deal up here," proceeded the voice mildly. "Doing—fairly well—though. Of course, if the wheelhouse should go. . . ."

Mr. Rout, bending an attentive ear, muttered peevishly something under his breath.

But the deliberate voice up there became animated to ask: "Jukes turned up yet?" Then, after a short wait, "I wish he would bear a hand. I want him to be done and come up here in case of anything. To look after the ship. I am all alone. The second mate's lost. . . ."

"What?" shouted Mr. Rout into the engine-room, taking his head away. Then up the tube he cried, "Gone overboard?" and clapped his ear to.

"Lost his nerve," the voice from above continued in a matter-of-fact tone. "Damned awkward circumstance."

Mr. Rout, listening with bowed neck, opened his eyes wide at this. However, he heard something like the sounds of a scuffle and broken exclamations coming down to him. He strained his hearing; and all the time Beale, the third engineer, with his arms uplifted, held between the palms of his hands the rim of a little black wheel projecting at the side of a big copper pipe. He seemed to be poising it above his head, as though it were a correct attitude in some sort of game.

To steady himself, he pressed his shoulder against the white bulkhead, one knee bent, and a sweat-rag tucked in his belt hanging on his hip. His smooth cheek was begrimed and flushed, and the coal dust on his eyelids, like the black pencilling of a make-up, enhanced the liquid brilliance of the whites, giving to his youthful face something of a feminine, exotic and fascinating aspect. When the ship pitched he would with hasty movements of his hands screw hard at the little wheel.

"Gone crazy," began the Captain's voice suddenly in the tube. "Rushed at me. . . . Just now. Had to knock him down. . . . This minute. You heard, Mr. Rout?"

"The devil!" muttered Mr. Rout. "Look out, Beale!"

His shout rang out like the blast of a warning trumpet, between the iron walls of the engine-room. Painted white, they rose high into the dusk of the skylight, sloping like a roof; and the whole lofty space resembled the interior of a monument, divided by floors of iron grating, with lights flickering at different levels, and a mass of gloom lingering in the middle, within the columnar stir of machinery under the motionless swelling of the cylinders. A loud and wild resonance, made up of all the noises of the hurricane, dwelt in the still warmth of the air. There was in it the smell of hot metal, of oil, and a slight mist of steam. The blows of the sea seemed to traverse it in an unringing, stunning shock, from side to side.

Gleams, like pale long flames, trembled upon the polish of metal; from the flooring below the enormous crank-heads emerged in their turns with a flash of brass and steel—going over; while the connecting-rods, big-jointed, like skeleton limbs, seemed to thrust them down and pull them up again with an irresistible precision. And deep in the half-light other rods dodged deliberately to and fro, crossheads nodded, discs of metal rubbed smoothly against each other, slow and gentle, in a commingling of shadows and gleams.

Sometimes all those powerful and unerring movements would slow down simultaneously, as if they had been the functions of a living organism, stricken suddenly by the blight of languor; and Mr. Rout's eyes would blaze darker in his long sallow face. He was fighting this fight in a pair of carpet slippers. A short shiny jacket barely covered his loins, and his white wrists protruded far out of the tight sleeves, as though the emergency had added to his stature, had lengthened his limbs, augmented his pallor, hollowed his eyes.

He moved, climbing high up, disappearing low down, with a restless, purposeful industry, and when he stood still, holding the guard-rail in front of the starting-gear, he would keep glancing to the right at the steam-gauge, at the water-gauge, fixed upon the white wall in the light of a swaying lamp. The mouths of two speaking-tubes gaped stupidly at his elbow, and the dial of the engine-room telegraph resembled a clock of large diameter, bearing on its face curt words instead of figures. The grouped letters stood out heavily black, around the pivot-head of the indicator, emphatically symbolic of loud exclamations: AHEAD, ASTERN, SLOW, HALF, STAND BY; and the fat black hand pointed downwards to the word FULL, which, thus singled out, captured the eye as a sharp cry secures attention.

The wood-encased bulk of the low-pressure cylinder, frowning portly from above, emitted a faint wheeze at every thrust, and except for that low hiss the engines worked their steel limbs headlong or slow with a silent, determined smoothness. And all this, the white walls, the moving steel, the floor plates under Solomon Rout's feet, the floors of iron grating above his head, the dusk and the gleams, uprose and sank continuously, with one accord, upon the harsh wash of the waves against the ship's side. The whole loftiness of the place, booming hollow to the great voice of the wind, swayed at the top like a tree, would go over bodily, as if borne down this way and that by the tremendous blasts.

"You've got to hurry up," shouted Mr. Rout, as soon as he saw Jukes appear in the stokehold doorway.

Jukes' glance was wandering and tipsy; his red face was puffy, as though he had overslept himself. He had had an arduous road, and had travelled over it with immense vivacity, the agitation of his mind corresponding to the exertions of his body. He had rushed up out of the bunker, stumbling in the dark alleyway amongst a lot of bewildered men who, trod upon, asked

"What's up, sir?" in awed mutters all round him;—down the stokehold
ladder, missing many iron rungs in his hurry, down into a place deep as a
well, black as Tophet, tipping over back and forth like a see-saw. The water
in the bilges thundered at each roll, and lumps of coal skipped to and fro,
from end to end, rattling like an avalanche of pebbles on a slope of iron.

Somebody in there moaned with pain, and somebody else could be seen
crouching over what seemed the prone body of a dead man; a lusty voice
blasphemed; and the glow under each fire-door was like a pool of flaming
blood radiating quietly in a velvety blackness.

A gust of wind struck upon the nape of Jukes' neck and next moment he
felt it streaming about his wet ankles. The stokehold ventilators hummed:
in front of the six fire-doors two wild figures, stripped to the waist, staggered and stooped, wrestling with two shovels.

"Hallo! Plenty of draught now," yelled the second engineer at once, as
though he had been all the time looking out for Jukes. The donkeyman, a
dapper little chap with a dazzling fair skin and a tiny, gingery moustache,
worked in a sort of mute transport. They were keeping a full head of steam,
and a profound rumbling, as of an empty furniture van trotting over a
bridge, made a sustained bass to all the other noises of the place.

"Blowing off all the time," went on yelling the second. With a sound as
of a hundred scoured saucepans, the orifice of a ventilator spat upon his
shoulder a sudden gush of salt water, and he volleyed a stream of curses
upon all things on earth including his own soul, ripping and raving, and all
the time attending to his business. With a sharp clash of metal the ardent
pale glare of the fire opened upon his bullet head, showing his spluttering
lips, his insolent face, and with another clang closed like the white-hot wink
of an iron eye.

"Where's the blooming ship? Can you tell me? blast my eyes! Under
water—or what? It's coming down here in tons. Are the condemned cowls
gone to Hades? Hey? Don't you know anything—you jolly sailor-man
you . . . ?"

Jukes, after a bewildered moment, had been helped by a roll to dart
through; and as soon as his eyes took in the comparative vastness, peace and
brilliance of the engine-room, the ship, setting her stern heavily in the
water, sent him charging head down upon Mr. Rout.

The chief's arm, long like a tentacle, and straightening as if worked by a
spring, went out to meet him, and deflected his rush into a spin towards the
speaking-tubes. At the same time Mr. Rout repeated earnestly:

"You've got to hurry up, whatever it is."

Jukes yelled "Are you there, sir?" and listened. Nothing. Suddenly the
roar of the wind fell straight into his ear, but presently a small voice shoved
aside the shouting hurricane quietly.

"You, Jukes?—Well?"

Jukes was ready to talk: it was only time that seemed to be wanting. It was easy enough to account for everything. He could perfectly imagine the coolies battened down in the reeking 'tween-deck, lying sick and scared between the rows of chests. Then one of these chests—or perhaps several at once—breaking loose open, and all these clumsy Chinamen rising up in a body to save their property. Afterwards every fling of the ship would hurl that tramping, yelling mob here and there, from side to side, in a whirl of smashed wood, torn clothing, rolling dollars. A struggle once started, they would be unable to stop themselves. Nothing could stop them now except main force. It was a disaster. He had seen it, and that was all he could say. Some of them must be dead, he believed. The rest would go on fighting. . . .

He sent up his words, tripping over each other, crowding the narrow tube. They mounted as if into a silence of an enlightened comprehension dwelling alone up there with a storm. And Jukes wanted to be dismissed from the face of that odious trouble intruding on the great need of the ship.

v

He waited. Before his eyes the engines turned with slow labour, that in the moment of going off into a mad fling would stop dead at Mr. Rout's shout, "Look out, Beale!" They paused in an intelligent immobility, stilled in midstroke, a heavy crank arrested on the cant, as if conscious of danger and the passage of time. Then, with a "Now, then!" from the chief, and the sound of a breath expelled through clenched teeth, they would accomplish the interrupted revolution and begin another.

There was the prudent sagacity of wisdom and the deliberation of enormous strength in their movements. This was their work—this patient coaxing of a distracted ship over the fury of the waves and into the very eye of the wind. At times Mr. Rout's chin would sink on his breast, and he watched them with knitted eyebrows as if lost in thought.

The voice that kept the hurricane out of Jukes' ear began: "Take the hands with you . . . ," and left off unexpectedly.

"What could I do with them, sir?"

A harsh, abrupt, imperious clang exploded suddenly. The three pairs of eyes flew up to the telegraph dial to see the hand jump from FULL to STOP, as if snatched by a devil. And then these three men in the engine-room had the intimate sensation of a check upon the ship, of a strange shrinking, as if she had gathered herself for a desperate leap.

"Stop her!" bellowed Mr. Rout.

Nobody—not even Captain MacWhirr, who alone on deck had caught sight of a white line of foam coming on at such a height that he couldn't believe his eyes—nobody was to know the steepness of that sea and the awful depth of the hollow the hurricane had scooped out behind the running wall of water.

It raced to meet the ship, and, with a pause, as of girding the loins, the *Nan-Shan* lifted her bows and leaped. The flames in all the lamps sank, darkening the engine-room. One went out. With a tearing crash and a swirling, raving tumult, tons of water fell upon the deck, as though the ship had darted under the foot of a cataract.

Down there they looked at each other, stunned.

"Swept from end to end, by God!" bawled Jukes.

She dipped into the hollow straight down, as if going over the edge of the world. The engine-room toppled forward menacingly, like the inside of a tower nodding in an earthquake. An awful racket, of iron things falling, came from the stokehold. She hung on this appalling slant long enough for Beale to drop on his hands and knees and begin to crawl as if he meant to fly on all fours out of the engine-room, and for Mr. Rout to turn his head slowly, rigid, cavernous, with the lower jaw dropping. Jukes had shut his eyes, and his face in a moment became hopelessly blank and gentle, like the face of a blind man.

At last she rose slowly, staggering, as if she had to lift a mountain with her bows.

Mr. Rout shut his mouth; Jukes blinked; and little Beale stood up hastily. "Another one like this, and that's the last of her," cried the chief.

He and Jukes looked at each other, and the same thought came into their heads. The Captain! Everything must have been swept away. Steering-gear gone—ship like a log. All over directly.

"Rush!" ejaculated Mr. Rout thickly, glaring with enlarged, doubtful eyes at Jukes, who answered him by an irresolute glance.

The clang of the telegraph gong soothed them instantly. The black hand dropped in a flash from STOP to FULL.

"Now then, Beale!" cried Mr. Rout.

The steam hissed low. The piston-rods slid in and out. Jukes put his ear to the tube. The voice was ready for him. It said: "Pick up all the money. Bear a hand now. I'll want you up here." And that was all.

"Sir?" called up Jukes. There was no answer.

He staggered away like a defeated man from the field of battle. He had got, in some way or other, a cut above his left eyebrow—a cut to the bone. He was not aware of it in the least: quantities of the China Sea, large enough to break his neck for him, had gone over his head, had cleaned, washed, and salted that wound. It did not bleed, but only gaped red; and this gash over the eye, his dishevelled hair, the disorder of his clothes, gave him the aspect of a man worsted in a fight with fists.

"Got to pick up the dollars." He appealed to Mr. Rout, smiling pitifully at random.

"What's that?" asked Mr. Rout, wildly. "Pick up . . . ? I don't care. . . ." Then, quivering in every muscle, but with an exaggeration of paternal tone, "Go away now, for God's sake. You deck people'll drive me silly. There's that second mate been going for the old man. Don't you know? You fellows are going wrong for want of something to do. . . ."

At these words Jukes discovered in himself the beginnings of anger. Want of something to do—indeed. . . . Full of hot scorn against the chief, he turned to go the way he had come. In the stokehold the plump donkeyman toiled with his shovel mutely, as if his tongue had been cut out; but the second was carrying on like a noisy, undaunted maniac, who had preserved his skill in the art of stoking under a marine boiler.

"Hallo, you wandering officer! Hey! Can't you get some of your slush-slingers to wind up a few of them ashes? I am getting choked with them here. Curse it! Hallo! Hey! Remember the articles: *Sailors and firemen to assist each other*. Hey! D'ye hear?"

Jukes was climbing out frantically, and the other, lifting up his face after him, howled, "Can't you speak? What are you poking about here for? What's your game, anyhow?"

A frenzy possessed Jukes. By the time he was back amongst the men in the darkness of the alleyway, he felt ready to wring all their necks at the slightest sign of hanging back. The very thought of it exasperated him. *He* couldn't hang back. They shouldn't.

The impetuosity with which he came amongst them carried them along. They had already been excited and startled at all his comings and goings— by the fierceness and rapidity of his movements; and more felt than seen in his rushes, he appeared formidable—busied with matters of life and death that brooked no delay. At his first word he heard them drop into the bunker one after another obediently, with heavy thumps.

They were not clear as to what would have to be done. "What is it? What is it?" they were asking each other. The boatswain tried to explain; the sounds of a great scuffle surprised them: and the mighty shocks, rever-berating awfully in the black bunker, kept them in mind of their danger. When the boatswain threw open the door it seemed that an eddy of the hurricane, stealing through the iron sides of the ship, had set all these bodies whirling like dust: there came to them a confused uproar, a tem-pestuous tumult, a fierce mutter, gusts of screams dying away, and the tramping of feet mingling with the blows of the sea.

For a moment they glared amazed, blocking the doorway. Jukes pushed through them brutally. He said nothing, and simply darted in. Another lot of coolies on the ladder, struggling suicidally to break through the battened hatch to a swamped deck, fell off as before, and he disappeared under them like a man overtaken by a landslide.

The boatswain yelled excitedly: "Come along. Get the mate out. He'll be trampled to death. Come on."

They charged in, stamping on breasts, on fingers, on faces, catching their feet in heaps of clothing, kicking broken wood; but before they could get hold of him, Jukes emerged waist deep in a multitude of clawing hands. In the instant he had been lost to view, all the buttons of his jacket had gone, its back had got split up to the collar, his waistcoat had been torn open. The central struggling mass of Chinamen went over to the roll, dark, indistinct, helpless, with a wild gleam of many eyes in the dim light of the lamps.

"Leave me alone—damn you. I am all right," screeched Jukes. "Drive them forward. Watch your chance when she pitches. Forward with 'em. Drive them against the bulkhead. Jam 'em up."

The rush of the sailors into the seething 'tween-deck was like a splash of cold water into a boiling cauldron. The commotion sank for a moment.

The bulk of Chinamen were locked in such a compact scrimmage that, linking their arms and aided by an appalling dive of the ship, the seamen sent it forward in one great shove, like a solid block. Behind their backs small clusters and loose bodies tumbled from side to side.

The boatswain performed prodigious feats of strength. With his long arms open, and each great paw clutching at a stanchion, he stopped the rush of seven entwined Chinamen rolling like a boulder. His joints cracked; he said, "Ha!" and they flew apart. But the carpenter showed the greater intelligence. Without saying a word to anybody he went back into the alleyway, to fetch several coils of cargo gear he had seen there—chain and rope. With these life-lines were rigged.

There was really no resistance. The struggle, however it began, had turned into a scramble of blind panic. If the coolies had started up after their scattered dollars they were by that time fighting only for their footing. They took each other by the throat merely to save themselves from being hurled about. Whoever got a hold anywhere would kick at the others who caught at his legs and hung on, till a roll sent them flying together across the deck.

The coming of the white devils was a terror. Had they come to kill? The individuals torn out of the ruck became very limp in the seamen's hands: some, dragged aside by the heels, were passive, like dead bodies, with open, fixed eyes. Here and there a coolie would fall on his knees as if begging for mercy; several, whom the excess of fear made unruly, were hit with hard fists between the eyes, and cowered; while those who were hurt submitted to rough handling, blinking rapidly without a plaint. Faces streamed with blood; there were raw places on the shaven heads, scratches, bruises, torn wounds, gashes. The broken porcelain out of the chests was mostly responsible for the latter. Here and there a Chinaman, wild-eyed, with his tail unplaited, nursed a bleeding sole.

They had been ranged closely, after having been shaken into submission, cuffed a little to allay excitement, addressed in gruff words of encouragement that sounded like promises of evil. They sat on the deck in ghastly, drooping rows, and at the end the carpenter, with two hands to help him, moved busily from place to place, setting taut and hitching the life-lines. The boatswain, with one leg and one arm embracing a stanchion, struggled with a lamp pressed to his breast, trying to get a light, and growling all the time like an industrious gorilla. The figures of seamen stooped repeatedly, with the movements of gleaners, and everything was being flung into the bunker: clothing, smashed wood, broken china, and the dollars, too, gathered up in men's jackets. Now and then a sailor would stagger towards the doorway with his arms full of rubbish; and dolorous, slanting eyes followed his movements.

With every roll of the ship the long rows of sitting Celestials would sway forward brokenly, and her headlong dives knocked together the line of shaven polls from end to end. When the wash of water rolling on the deck died away for a moment, it seemed to Jukes, yet quivering from his exertions, that in his mad struggle down there he had overcome the wind somehow: that a silence had fallen upon the ship, a silence in which the sea struck thunderously at her sides.

Everything had been cleared out of the 'tween-deck—all the wreckage, as the men said. They stood erect and tottering above the level of heads and drooping shoulders. Here and there a coolie sobbed for his breath. Where the high light fell, Jukes could see the salient ribs of one, the yellow, wistful face of another; bowed necks; or would meet a dull stare directed at his face. He was amazed that there had been no corpses; but the lot of them seemed at their last gasp, and they appeared to him more pitiful than if they had been all dead.

Suddenly one of the coolies began to speak. The light came and went on his lean, straining face; he threw his head up like a baying hound. From the bunker came the sounds of knocking and the tinkle of some dollars rolling loose; he stretched out his arm, his mouth yawned black, and the incomprehensible guttural hooting sounds, that did not seem to belong to a human language, penetrated Jukes with a strange emotion as if a brute had tried to be eloquent.

Two more started mouthing what seemed to Jukes fierce denunciations; the others stirred with grunts and growls. Jukes ordered the hands out of the 'tween-decks hurriedly. He left last himself, backing through the door, while the grunts rose to a loud murmur and hands were extended after him as after a malefactor. The boatswain shot the bolt, and remarked uneasily, "Seems as if the wind had dropped, sir."

The seamen were glad to get back into the alleyway. Secretly each of them thought that at the last moment he could rush out on deck—and that was a comfort. There is something horribly repugnant in the idea of being drowned under a deck. Now they had done with the Chinamen, they again became conscious of the ship's position.

Jukes on coming out of the alleyway found himself up to the neck in the noisy water. He gained the bridge, and discovered he could detect obscure shapes as if his sight had become preternaturally acute. He saw faint outlines. They recalled not the familiar aspect of the *Nan-Shan,* but something remembered—an old dismantled steamer he had seen years ago rotting on a mudbank. She recalled that wreck.

There was no wind, not a breath, except the faint currents created by the lurches of the ship. The smoke tossed out of the funnel was settling down upon her deck. He breathed it as he passed forward. He felt the deliberate throb of the engines, and heard small sounds that seemed to have survived the great uproar: the knocking of broken fittings, the rapid tumbling of some piece of wreckage on the bridge. He perceived dimly the squat shape of his captain holding on to a twisted bridge-rail, motionless and swaying as if rooted to the planks. The unexpected stillness of the air oppressed Jukes.

"We have done it, sir," he gasped.

"Thought you would," said Captain MacWhirr.

"Did you?" murmured Jukes to himself.

"Wind fell all at once," went on the Captain.

Jukes burst out: "If you think it was an easy job——"

But his captain, clinging to the rail, paid no attention. "According to the books the worst is not over yet."

"If most of them hadn't been half dead with seasickness and fright, not one of us would come out of that 'tween-deck alive," said Jukes.

"Had to do what's fair by them," mumbled MacWhirr, stolidly. "You don't find everything in books."

"Why, I believe they would have risen on us if I hadn't ordered the hands out of that pretty quick," continued Jukes with warmth.

After the whisper of their shouts, their ordinary tones, so distinct, rang out very loud to their ears in the amazing stillness of the air. It seemed to them they were talking in a dark and echoing vault.

Through a jagged aperture in the dome of clouds the light of a few stars fell upon the black sea, rising and falling confusedly. Sometimes the head of a watery cone would topple on board and mingle with the rolling flurry of foam on the swamped deck; and the *Nan-Shan* wallowed heavily at the bottom of a circular cistern of clouds. This ring of dense vapours, gyrating madly round the calm of the centre, encompassed the ship like a motionless and unbroken wall of an aspect inconceivably sinister. Within, the sea, as if agitated by an internal commotion, leaped in peaked mounds that jostled each other, slapping heavily against her sides; and a low moaning sound, the infinite plaint of the storm's fury, came from beyond the limits of the menacing calm. Captain MacWhirr remained silent, and Jukes' ready ear caught suddenly the faint, long-drawn roar of some immense wave rushing unseen under that thick blackness, which made the appalling boundary of his vision.

"Of course," he started resentfully, "they thought we had caught at the chance to plunder them. Of course! You said—pick up the money. Easier said than done. They couldn't tell what was in our heads. We came in, smash—right into the middle of them. Had to do it by a rush."

"As long as it's done . . . ," mumbled the Captain, without attempting to look at Jukes. "Had to do what's fair."

"We shall find yet there's the devil to pay when this is over," said Jukes, feeling very sore. "Let them only recover a bit, and you'll see. They will fly at our throats, sir. Don't forget, sir, she isn't a British ship now. These brutes know it well, too. The damned Siamese flag."

"We are on board, all the same," remarked Captain MacWhirr.

"The trouble's not over yet," insisted Jukes, prophetically, reeling and catching on. "She's a wreck," he added, faintly.

"The trouble's not over yet," assented Captain MacWhirr, half aloud. . . . "Look out for her a minute."

"Are you going off the deck, sir?" asked Jukes, hurriedly, as if the storm were sure to pounce upon him as soon as he had been left alone with the ship.

He watched her, battered and solitary, labouring heavily in a wild scene of mountainous black waters lit by the gleams of distant worlds. She moved slowly, breathing into the still core of the hurricane the excess of her strength in a white cloud of steam—and the deep-toned vibration of the escape was like the defiant trumpeting of a living creature of the sea impatient for the renewal of the contest. It ceased suddenly. The still air moaned. Above Jukes' head a few stars shone into a pit of black vapours. The inky edge of the cloud-disc frowned upon the ship under the patch of glittering sky. The stars, too, seemed to look at her intently, as if for the last time, and the cluster of their splendour sat like a diadem on a lowering brow.

Captain MacWhirr had gone into the chart-room. There was no light there; but he could feel the disorder of that place where he used to live tidily. His armchair was upset. The books had tumbled out on the floor: he scrunched a piece of glass under his boot. He groped for the matches, and found a box on a shelf with a deep ledge. He struck one, and puckering the corners of his eyes, held out the little flame towards the barometer whose glittering top of glass and metals nodded at him continuously.

It stood very low—incredibly low, so low that Captain MacWhirr grunted. The match went out, and hurriedly he extracted another, with thick, stiff fingers.

Again a little flame flared up before the nodding glass and metal of the top. His eyes looked at it, narrowed with attention, as if expecting an imperceptible sign. With his grave face he resembled a booted and misshapen pagan burning incense before the oracle of a Joss. There was no mistake. It was the lowest reading he had ever seen in his life.

Captain MacWhirr emitted a low whistle. He forgot himself till the flame diminished to a blue spark, burnt his fingers and vanished. Perhaps something had gone wrong with the thing!

There was an aneroid glass screwed above the couch. He turned that way, struck another match, and discovered the white face of the other instrument looking at him from the bulkhead, meaningly, not to be gainsaid, as though the wisdom of men were made unerring by the indifference of matter. There was no room for doubt now. Captain MacWhirr pshawed at it, and threw the match down.

The worst was to come, then—and if the books were right this worst would be very bad. The experience of the last six hours had enlarged his conception of what heavy weather could be like. "It'll be terrific," he pronounced, mentally. He had not consciously looked at anything by the light of the matches except at the barometer; and yet somehow he had seen that his water-bottle and the two tumblers had been flung out of their stand. It seemed to give him a more intimate knowledge of the tossing the ship had gone through. "I wouldn't have believed it," he thought. And his table had been cleared, too; his rulers, his pencils, the inkstand—all the things that had their safe appointed places—they were gone, as if a mischievous hand had plucked them out one by one and flung them on the wet floor. The hurricane had broken in upon the orderly arrangements of his privacy. This had never happened before, and the feeling of dismay reached the very seat of his composure. And the worst was to come yet! He was glad the trouble in the 'tween-deck had been discovered in time. If the ship had to go after all, then, at least, she wouldn't be going to the bottom with a lot of people in her fighting teeth and claw. That would have been odious. And in that feeling there was a humane intention and a vague sense of the fitness of things.

These instantaneous thoughts were yet in their essence heavy and slow, partaking of the nature of the man. He extended his hand to put back the matchbox in its corner of the shelf. There were always matches there—by his order. The steward had his instructions impressed upon him long before. "A box . . . just there, see? Not so very full . . . where I can put my hand on it, steward. Might want a light in a hurry. Can't tell on board ship *what* you might want in a hurry. Mind, now."

And of course on his side he would be careful to put it back in its place scrupulously. He did so now, but before he removed his hand it occurred to him that perhaps he would never have occasion to use that box any more. The vividness of the thought checked him and for an infinitesimal fraction of a second his fingers closed again on the small object as though it had been the symbol of all these little habits that chain us to the weary round of life. He released it at last, and letting himself fall on the settee, listened for the first sounds of returning wind.

Not yet. He heard only the wash of water, the heavy splashes, the dull shocks of the confused seas boarding his ship from all sides. She would never have a chance to clear her decks.

But the quietude of the air was startlingly tense and unsafe, like a slender hair holding a sword suspended over his head. By this awful pause the storm penetrated the defences of the man and unsealed his lips. He spoke out in the solitude and the pitch darkness of the cabin, as if addressing another being awakened within his breast.

"I shouldn't like to lose her," he said half aloud.

He sat unseen, apart from the sea, from his ship, isolated, as if withdrawn from the very current of his own existence, where such freaks as talking to himself surely had no place. His palms reposed on his knees, he bowed his short neck and puffed heavily, surrendering to a strange sensation of weariness he was not enlightened enough to recognize for the fatigue of mental stress.

From where he sat he could reach the door of a washstand locker. There should have been a towel there. There was. Good. . . . He took it out, wiped his face, and afterwards went on rubbing his wet head. He towelled himself with energy in the dark, and then remained motionless with the towel on his knees. A moment passed, of a stillness so profound that no one could have guessed there was a man sitting in that cabin. Then a murmur arose.

"She may come out of it yet."

When Captain MacWhirr came out on deck, which he did brusquely, as though he had suddenly become conscious of having stayed away too long, the calm had lasted already more than fifteen minutes—long enough to make itself intolerable even to his imagination. Jukes, motionless on the forepart of the bridge, began to speak at once. His voice, blank and forced as though he were talking through hard-set teeth, seemed to flow away on all sides into the darkness, deepening again upon the sea.

"I had the wheel relieved. Hackett began to sing out that he was done. He's lying in there alongside the steering-gear with a face like death. At first I couldn't get anybody to crawl out and relieve the poor devil. That boss'en's worse than no good, I always said. Thought I would have had to go myself and haul out one of them by the neck."

"Ah, well," muttered the Captain. He stood watchful by Jukes' side.

"The second mate's in there, too, holding his head. Is he hurt, sir?"

"No—crazy," said Captain MacWhirr, curtly.

"Looks as if he had a tumble, though."

"I had to give him a push," explained the Captain.

Jukes gave an impatient sigh.

"It will come very sudden," said Captain MacWhirr, "and from over there, I fancy. God only knows though. These books are only good to muddle your head and make you jumpy. It will be bad, and there's an end. If we only can steam her round in time to meet it. . . ."

A minute passed. Some of the stars winked rapidly and vanished.

"You left them pretty safe?" began the Captain abruptly, as though the silence were unbearable.

"Are you thinking of the coolies, sir? I rigged life-lines all ways across that 'tween-deck."

"Did you? Good idea, Mr. Jukes."

"I didn't . . . think you cared to . . . know," said Jukes—the lurching of the ship cut his speech as though somebody had been jerking him around while he talked—"how I got on with . . . that infernal job. We did it. And it may not matter in the end."

"Had to do what's fair, for all—they are only Chinamen. Give them the same chance with ourselves—hang it all. She isn't lost yet. Bad enough to be shut up below in a gale——"

"That's what I thought when you gave me the job, sir," interjected Jukes, moodily.

"——without being battered to pieces," pursued Captain MacWhirr with rising vehemence. "Couldn't let that go on in my ship, if I knew she hadn't five minutes to live. Couldn't bear it, Mr. Jukes."

A hollow echoing noise, like that of a shout rolling in a rocky chasm, approached the ship and went away again. The last star, blurred, enlarged, as if returning to the fiery mist of its beginning, struggled with the colossal depth of blackness hanging over the ship—and went out.

"Now for it!" muttered Captain MacWhirr. "Mr. Jukes."

"Here, sir."

The two men were growing indistinct to each other.

"We must trust her to go through it and come out on the other side. That's plain and straight. There's no room for Captain Wilson's storm-strategy here."

"No, sir."

"She will be smothered and swept again for hours," mumbled the Captain. "There's not much left by this time above deck for the sea to take away—unless you or me."

"Both, sir," whispered Jukes, breathlessly.

"You are always meeting trouble half way, Jukes," Captain MacWhirr remonstrated quaintly. "Though it's a fact that the second mate is no good. D'ye hear, Mr. Jukes? You would be left alone if. . . ."

Captain MacWhirr interrupted himself, and Jukes, glancing on all sides, remained silent.

"Don't you be put out by anything," the Captain continued, mumbling rather fast. "Keep her facing it. They may say what they like, but the heaviest seas run with the wind. Facing it—always facing it—that's the way to get through. You are a young sailor. Face it. That's enough for any man. Keep a cool head."

"Yes, sir," said Jukes, with a flutter of the heart.

In the next few seconds the Captain spoke to the engine-room and got an answer.

For some reason Jukes experienced an access of confidence, a sensation that came from outside like a warm breath, and made him feel equal to every demand. The distant muttering of the darkness stole into his ears. He noted it unmoved, out of that sudden belief in himself, as a man safe in a shirt of mail would watch a point.

The ship laboured without intermission amongst the black hills of water, paying with this hard tumbling the price of her life. She rumbled in her depths, shaking a white plummet of steam into the night, and Jukes' thought skimmed like a bird through the engine-room, where Mr. Rout—good man—was ready. When the rumbling ceased it seemed to him that there was a pause of every sound, a dead pause in which Captain Mac-Whirr's voice rang out startlingly.

"What's that? A puff of wind?"—it spoke much louder than Jukes had ever heard it before—"On the bow. That's right. She may come out of it yet."

The mutter of the winds drew near apace. In the forefront could be distinguished a drowsy waking plaint passing on, and far off the growth of a multiple clamour, marching and expanding. There was the throb as of many drums in it, a vicious rushing note, and like the chant of a tramping multitude.

Jukes could no longer see his captain distinctly. The darkness was absolutely piling itself upon the ship. At most he made out movements, a hint of elbows spread out, a head thrown up.

Captain MacWhirr was trying to do up the top button of his oilskin coat with unwonted haste. The hurricane, with its power to madden the seas, to sink ships, to uproot trees, to overturn strong walls and dash the very birds of the air to the ground, had found this taciturn man in its path, and, doing its utmost, had managed to wring out a few words. Before the renewed wrath of winds swooped on his ship, Captain MacWhirr was moved to declare, in a tone of vexation, as it were: "I wouldn't like to lose her."

He was spared that annoyance.

VI

On a bright sunshiny day, with the breeze chasing her smoke far ahead, the *Nan-Shan* came into Fu-chau. Her arrival was at once noticed on shore, and the seamen in harbour said: "Look! Look at that steamer. What's that? Siamese—isn't she? Just look at her!"

She seemed, indeed, to have been used as a running target for the secondary batteries of a cruiser. A hail of minor shells could not have given her upper works a more broken, torn, and devastated aspect: and she had about her the worn, weary air of ships coming from the far ends of the world—and indeed with truth, for in her short passage she had been very far; sighting, verily, even the coast of the Great Beyond, whence no ship ever returns to give up her crew to the dust of the earth. She was incrusted and gray with salt to the trucks of her masts and to the top of her funnel; as though (as some facetious seaman said) "the crowd on board had fished her out somewhere from the bottom of the sea and brought her in here for salvage." And further, excited by the felicity of his own wit, he offered to give five pounds for her—"as she stands."

Before she had been quite an hour at rest, a meagre little man, with a red-tipped nose and a face cast in an angry mould, landed from a sampan on the quay of the Foreign Concession, and incontinently turned to shake his fist at her.

A tall individual, with legs much too thin for a rotund stomach, and with watery eyes, strolled up and remarked, "Just left her—eh? Quick work."

He wore a soiled suit of blue flannel with a pair of dirty cricketing shoes; a dingy gray moustache drooped from his lip, and daylight could be seen in two places between the rim and the crown of his hat.

"Hallo! what are you doing here?" asked the ex-second-mate of the *Nan-Shan,* shaking hands hurriedly.

"Standing by for a job—chance worth taking—got a quiet hint," explained the man with the broken hat, in jerky, apathetic wheezes.

The second shook his fist again at the *Nan-Shan.* "There's a fellow there that ain't fit to have the command of a scow," he declared, quivering with passion, while the other looked about listlessly.

"Is there?"

But he caught sight on the quay of a heavy seaman's chest, painted brown under a fringed sailcloth cover, and lashed with new manila line. He eyed it with awakened interest.

"I would talk and raise trouble if it wasn't for that damned Siamese flag. Nobody to go to—or I would make it hot for him. The fraud! Told his chief engineer—that's another fraud for you—I had lost my nerve. The greatest lot of ignorant fools that ever sailed the seas. No! You can't think . . ."

"Got your money all right?" inquired his seedy acquaintance suddenly.

"Yes. Paid me off on board," raged the second mate. " 'Get your break-fast on shore,' says he."

"Mean skunk!" commented the tall man, vaguely, and passed his tongue on his lips. "What about having a drink of some sort?"

"He struck me," hissed the second mate.

"No! Struck! You don't say?" The man in blue began to bustle about sympathetically. "Can't possibly talk here. I want to know all about it. Struck—eh? Let's get a fellow to carry your chest. I know a quiet place where they have some bottled beer. . . ."

Mr. Jukes, who had been scanning the shore through a pair of glasses, informed the chief engineer afterwards that "our late second mate hasn't been long in finding a friend. A chap looking uncommonly like a bummer. I saw them walk away together from the quay."

The hammering and banging of the needful repairs did not disturb Captain MacWhirr. The steward found in the letter he wrote, in a tidy chart-room, passages of such absorbing interest that twice he was nearly caught in the act. But Mrs. MacWhirr, in the drawing-room of the forty-pound house, stifled a yawn—perhaps out of self-respect—for she was alone.

She reclined in a plush-bottomed and gilt hammock-chair near a tiled fire-place, with Japanese fans on the mantel and a glow of coals in the grate. Lifting her hands, she glanced wearily here and there into the many pages. It was not her fault they were so prosy, so completely uninteresting—from "My darling wife" at the beginning, to "Your loving husband" at the end. She couldn't be really expected to understand all these ship affairs. She was glad, of course, to hear from him, but she had never asked herself why, precisely.

". . . They are called typhoons . . . The mate did not seem to like it . . . Not in books . . . Couldn't think of letting it go on. . . ."

The paper rustled sharply. ". . . A calm that lasted more than twenty minutes," she read perfunctorily; and the next words her thoughtless eyes caught, on the top of another page, were: "see you and the children again. . . ." She had a movement of impatience. He was always thinking of coming home. He had never had such a good salary before. What was the matter now?

It did not occur to her to turn back overleaf to look. She would have found it recorded there that between 4 and 6 A.M. on December 25th, Captain MacWhirr did actually think that his ship could not possibly live another hour in such a sea, and that he would never see his wife and children again. Nobody was to know this (his letters got mislaid so quickly)—nobody whatever but the steward, who had been greatly impressed by that disclosure. So much so, that he tried to give the cook some idea of the "narrow squeak we all had" by saying solemnly, "The old man himself had a dam' poor opinion of our chance."

"How do you know?" asked, contemptuously, the cook, an old soldier. "He hasn't told you, maybe?"

"Well, he did give me a hint to that effect," the steward brazened it out.

"Get along with you! He will be coming to tell me next," jeered the old cook, over his shoulder.

Mrs. MacWhirr glanced farther, on the alert. ". . . Do what's fair. . . . Miserable objects . . . Only three, with a broken leg each, and one . . . Thought had better keep the matter quiet . . . hope to have done the fair thing. . . ."

She let fall her hands. No: there was nothing more about coming home.

Must have been merely expressing a pious wish. Mrs. MacWhirr's mind was set at ease, and a black marble clock, priced by the local jeweller at £3 18s. 6d., had a discreet stealthy tick.

The door flew open, and a girl in the long-legged, short-frocked period of existence, flung into the room. A lot of colourless, rather lanky hair was scattered over her shoulders. Seeing her mother, she stood still, and directed her pale prying eyes upon the letter.

"From father," murmured Mrs. MacWhirr. "What have you done with your ribbon?"

The girl put her hands up to her head and pouted.

"He's well," continued Mrs. MacWhirr, languidly. "At least I think so. He never says." She had a little laugh. The girl's face expressed a wandering indifference, and Mrs. MacWhirr surveyed her with fond pride.

"Go and get your hat," she said after a while. "I am going out to do some shopping. There is a sale at Linom's."

"Oh, how jolly!" uttered the child, impressively, in unexpectedly grave vibrating tones, and bounded out of the room.

It was a fine afternoon, with a gray sky and dry sidewalks. Outside the draper's Mrs. MacWhirr smiled upon a woman in a black mantle of generous proportions armoured in jet and crowned with flowers blooming falsely above a bilious matronly countenance. They broke into a swift little babble of greetings and exclamations both together, very hurried, as if the street were ready to yawn open and swallow all that pleasure before it could be expressed.

Behind them the high glass doors were kept on the swing. People couldn't pass, men stood aside waiting patiently, and Lydia was absorbed in poking the end of her parasol between the stone flags. Mrs. MacWhirr talked rapidly.

"Thank you very much. He's not coming home yet. Of course it's very sad to have him away, but it's such a comfort to know he keeps so well." Mrs. MacWhirr drew breath. "The climate there agrees with him," she added, beamingly, as if poor MacWhirr had been away touring in China for the sake of his health.

Neither was the chief engineer coming home yet. Mr. Rout knew too well the value of a good billet.

"Solomon says wonders will never cease," cried Mrs. Rout joyously at the old lady in her armchair by the fire. Mr. Rout's mother moved slightly, her withered hands lying in black half-mittens on her lap.

The eyes of the engineer's wife fairly danced on the paper. "That captain of the ship he is in—a rather simple man, you remember, mother?—has done something rather clever, Solomon says."

"Yes, my dear," said the old woman meekly, sitting with bowed silvery head, and that air of inward stillness characteristic of very old people who seem lost in watching the last flickers of life. "I think I remember."

Solomon Rout, Old Sol, Father Sol, the Chief, "Rout, good man"—Mr. Rout, the condescending and paternal friend of youth, had been the baby of her many children—all dead by this time. And she remembered him best as a boy of ten—long before he went away to serve his apprenticeship in some great engineering works in the North. She had seen so little of him since, she had gone through so many years, that she had now to retrace her steps very far back to recognize him plainly in the mist of time. Sometimes it seemed that her daughter-in-law was talking of some strange man.

Mrs. Rout junior was disappointed. "H'm. H'm." She turned the page. "How provoking! He doesn't say what it is. Says I couldn't understand how much there was in it. Fancy! What could it be so very clever? What a wretched man not to tell us!"

She read on without further remark soberly, and at last sat looking into the fire. The chief wrote just a word or two of the typhoon; but something had moved him to express an increased longing for the companionship of the jolly woman. "If it hadn't been that mother must be looked after, I would send you your passage-money to-day. You could set up a small house out here. I would have a chance to see you sometimes then. We are not growing younger. . . ."

"He's well, mother," sighed Mrs. Rout, rousing herself.

"He always was a strong healthy boy," said the old woman, placidly.

But Mr. Jukes' account was really animated and very full. His friend in the Western Ocean trade imparted it freely to the other officers of his liner. "A chap I know writes to me about an extraordinary affair that happened on board his ship in that typhoon—you know—that we read of in the papers two months ago. It's the funniest thing! Just see for yourself what he says. I'll show you his letter."

There were phrases in it calculated to give the impression of light-hearted, indomitable resolution. Jukes had written them in good faith, for he felt thus when he wrote. He described with lurid effect the scenes in the 'tween-deck. ". . . It struck me in a flash that those confounded Chinamen couldn't tell we weren't a desperate kind of robbers. 'Tisn't good to part the China-man from his money if he is the stronger party. We need have been desperate indeed to go thieving in such weather, but what could these beggars know of us? So, without thinking of it twice, I got the hands away in a jiffy. Our work was done—that the old man had set his heart on. We cleared out without staying to inquire how they felt. I am convinced that if they had not been so unmercifully shaken, and afraid—each individual one of them—to stand up, we would have been torn to pieces. Oh! It was pretty complete, I can tell you; and you may run to and fro across the Pond to the end of time before you find yourself with such a job on your hands."

After this he alluded professionally to the damage done to the ship, and went on thus:

"It was when the weather quieted down that the situation became confoundedly delicate. It wasn't made any better by us having been lately transferred to the Siamese flag; though the skipper can't see that it makes any difference—'as long as *we* are on board'—he says. There are feelings that this man simply hasn't got—and there's an end of it. You might just as well try to make a bedpost understand. But apart from this it is an infernally lonely state for a ship to be going about the China seas with no proper consuls, not even a gunboat of her own anywhere, nor a body to go to in case of some trouble.

"My notion was to keep these Johnnies under hatches for another fifteen hours or so; as we weren't much farther than that from Fu-chau. We would find there, most likely, some sort of a man-of-war, and once under her guns we were safe enough; for surely any skipper of a man-of-war—English, French or Dutch—would see white men through as far as row on board goes. We could get rid of them and their money afterwards by delivering them to their Mandarin or Taotai, or whatever they call these chaps in goggles you see being carried about in sedan-chairs through their stinking streets.

"The old man wouldn't see it somehow. He wanted to keep the matter quiet. He got that notion into his head, and a steam windlass couldn't drag it out of him. He wanted as little fuss made as possible, for the sake of the ship's name and for the sake of the owners—'for the sake of all concerned,' says he, looking at me very hard. It made me angry hot. Of course you couldn't keep a thing like that quiet; but the chests had been secured in the usual manner and were safe enough for any earthly gale, while this had been an altogether fiendish business I couldn't give you even an idea of.

"Meantime, I could hardly keep on my feet. None of us had a spell of any sort for nearly thirty hours, and there the old man sat rubbing his chin, rubbing the top of his head, and so bothered he didn't even think of pulling his long boots off.

"'I hope, sir,' says I, 'you won't be letting them out on deck before we make ready for them in some shape or other.' Not, mind you, that I felt very sanguine about controlling these beggars if they meant to take charge. A trouble with a cargo of Chinamen is no child's play. I was dam' tired, too. 'I wish,' said I, 'you would let us throw the whole lot of these dollars down to them and leave them to fight it out amongst themselves, while we get a rest.'

"'Now you talk wild, Jukes,' says he, looking up in his slow way that makes you ache all over, somehow. 'We must plan out something that would be fair to all parties.'

"I had no end of work on hand, as you may imagine, so I set the hands going, and then I thought I would turn in a bit. I hadn't been asleep in my bunk ten minutes when in rushes the steward and begins to pull at my leg.

"'For God's sake, Mr. Jukes, come out! Come on deck quick, sir. Oh, do come out!'

"The fellow scared all the sense out of me. I didn't know what had happened: another hurricane—or what. Could hear no wind.

"'The Captain's letting them out. Oh, he is letting them out! Jump on deck, sir, and save us. The chief engineer has just run below for his revolver.'

"That's what I understood the fool to say. However, Father Rout swears he went in there only to get a clean pocket-handkerchief. Anyhow, I made one jump into my trousers and flew on deck aft. There was certainly a good deal of noise going on forward of the bridge. Four of the hands with the boss'en were at work aft. I passed up to them some of the rifles all the ships on the China coast carry in the cabin, and led them on the bridge. On the way I ran against Old Sol, looking startled and sucking at an unlighted cigar.

"'Come along,' I shouted to him.

"We charged, the seven of us, up to the chart-room. All was over. There stood the old man with his sea-boots still drawn up to the hips and in shirt-sleeves—got warm thinking it out, I suppose. Bun Hin's dandy clerk at his elbow, as dirty as a sweep, was still green in the face. I could see directly I was in for something.

"'What the devil are these monkey tricks, Mr. Jukes?' asks the old man, as angry as ever he could be. I tell you frankly it made me lose my tongue. 'For God's sake, Mr. Jukes,' says he, 'do take away these rifles from the men. Somebody's sure to get hurt before long if you don't. Damme, if this ship isn't worse than Bedlam! Look sharp now. I want you up here to help me and Bun Hin's Chinaman to count that money. You wouldn't mind lending a hand, too, Mr. Rout, now you are here. The more of us the better.'

"He had settled it all in his mind while I was having a snooze. Had we been an English ship, or only going to land our cargo of coolies in an English part, like Hong-Kong, for instance, there would have been no end of inquiries and bother, claims for damages and so on. But these Chinamen know their officials better than we do.

"The hatches had been taken off already, and they were all on deck after a night and a day down below. It made you feel queer to see so many gaunt, wild faces together. The beggars stared about at the sky, at the sea, at the ship, as though they had expected the whole thing to have been blown to pieces. And no wonder! They had had a doing that would have shaken the soul out of a white man. But then they say a Chinaman has no soul. He has, though, something about him that is deuced tough. There was a fellow (amongst others of the badly hurt) who had had his eye all but knocked out. It stood out of his head the size of half a hen's egg. This would have laid out a white man on his back for a month: and yet there was that chap elbowing here and there in the crowd and talking to the others as if nothing had been the matter. They made a great hubbub amongst themselves, and whenever the old man showed his bald head on the fore-side of the bridge, they would all leave off jawing and look at him from below.

"It seems that after he had done his thinking he made that Bun Hin's fellow go down and explain to them the only way they could get their money back. He told me afterwards that, all the coolies having worked in the same place and for the same length of time, he reckoned he would be doing the fair thing by them as near as possible if he shared all the cash we had picked up equally among the lot. You couldn't tell one man's dollars from another's, he said, and if you asked each man how much money he brought on board he was afraid they would lie, and he would find himself a long way short. I think he was right there. As to giving up the money to any Chinese official he could scare up in Fu-chau, he said he might just as well put the lot in his own pocket at once for all the good it would be to them. I suppose they thought so, too.

"We finished the distribution before dark. It was rather a sight: the sea running high, the ship a wreck to look at, these Chinamen staggering up on the bridge one by one for their share, and the old man still booted, and in his shirt-sleeves, busy paying out at the chart-room door, perspiring like anything, and now and then coming down sharp on myself or Father Rout about one thing or another not quite to his mind. He took the share of those who were disabled himself to them on the No. 2 hatch. There were three dollars left over, and these went to the three most damaged coolies, one to each. We turned-to afterwards, and shovelled out on deck heaps of wet rags, all sorts of fragments of things without shape, and that you couldn't give a name to, and let them settle the ownership themselves.

"This certainly is coming as near as can be to keeping the thing quiet for the benefit of all concerned. What's your opinion, you pampered mail-boat swell? The old chief says that this was plainly the only thing that could be done. The skipper remarked to me the other day, 'There are things you find nothing about in books.' I think that he got out of it very well for such a stupid man."

THE FATE OF THE BARON

Arthur Schnitzler

(1862–1931)

TRANSLATED BY ERIC SUTTON

I⟨T WAS ON A MILD EVENING⟩ in May that Kläre Hell made her first reappearance as Queen of the Night. The circumstances that had kept the singer away from the stage for nearly two months were well known. On March 15th the Prince Richard Bedenbruck had been thrown from his horse, and after lingering for a few hours, during which Kläre had not stirred from his side, had died in her arms. Kläre's despair had been so terrible that her friends feared first for her life, then for her reason, and, until lately, for her voice. The last anxiety proved as unfounded as the first two. When she appeared on the stage she was greeted with friendly curiosity, but after the first great aria it was clear that her intimate friends could safely accept the congratulations of her more distant acquaintances. In the gallery the childish face of little Fräulein Fanny Ringeiser could be seen glowing with delight, and the regular opera-goers in the upper tiers smiled knowingly at their little friend. They all knew that Fanny, although she was only the daughter of a shop assistant on the Mariahilferstrasse, belonged to the beloved singer's inner circle, had often been invited to parties at her house and had been secretly in love with the dead Prince. In the interval, Fanny explained to her many male and female friends that Baron von Leisenbohg had suggested to Kläre the idea of choosing the Queen of the Night for her first part—thinking that the dark costume would be most in harmony with her state of mind.

The Baron himself took his usual stall, the corner seat on the gangway in the first row, and acknowledged the greetings of his acquaintances with a cordial, but almost melancholy, smile. Her mind was full of many memories that evening. He had first met Kläre ten years ago. At that time he was making himself responsible for the artistic training of a slim young lady with red hair, and had looked in one evening for a performance at the Eisenstein School of Singing, in which his protégée was making her first public performance as Mignon. On that same evening he saw and heard Kläre who was singing Philine in the same scene. He was then twenty-five years old, independent, and impulsive. He took no further interest in

Mignon, made Frau Natalie Eisenstein introduce him to Philine after the performance and told her that his heart, his fortune, and his influence with the management of the Opera were all at her disposal. At that time Kläre was living with her mother, the widow of a higher official in the Post Office, and was in love with a young medical student, with whom she often went to tea in his room out in the Alser district. She rejected the Baron's impetuous proposals, but Leisenbohg's homage inclined her to a more complaisant attitude of mind, and she became the medical student's mistress. She made no secret of this to the Baron, who returned to his red-haired protégée, but pursued his acquaintance with Kläre. On all festivals that gave him any sort of excuse, he sent her presents of flowers and sweets, and from time to time he paid a formal call at the house of the postal official's widow.

In the autumn of that year, Kläre got her first engagement at Detmold. Baron von Leisenbohg, who at that time still had a post under the Government, took advantage of his first Christmas leave to pay Kläre a visit in her new abode. He knew that the medical student had become a doctor and had married in September, and he was tempted to hope once more. But Kläre, with her usual straightforwardness, told the Baron immediately he arrived that she had established tender relations with the tenor at the Court Theatre: thus it befell therefore, that the only memories Leisenbohg could carry away from Detmold were of a platonic stroll in the little public park, and a supper at the theatre restaurant with a few fellow artists of both sexes. In spite of this, he made several more journeys to Detmold, took great pleasure in Kläre's devotion to her art and the unmistakable progress that she made, and, moreover, hoped for better luck next season, for which the tenor was under contract to sing in Hamburg. But that year, too, he was disappointed, as Kläre felt obliged to yield to the solicitations of a Dutch merchant in a large way of business, by the name of Louis Verhajen.

When Kläre, in her third season, was offered an engagement at the Dresden Court Theatre, in spite of his youth the Baron gave up a very promising official career and migrated to Dresden. He spent every evening with Kläre and her mother, who had always known how to maintain the most admirable detachment in all her relations with her daughter, and began to hope again. Unfortunately the Dutchman had the unpleasant habit whenever he wrote of announcing his arrival for the following day, and informing his beloved that she was surrounded by an army of spies, and threatening her with every variety of painful death, if she was not faithful to him. As he never came, and Kläre was gradually getting into an extremely nervous state, Leisenbohg decided to end the business at any cost, and went to Detmold to try to see the man personally. To his amazement, the Dutchman explained that he had sent these passionate and threatening missives purely from a sense of chivalry, and that he would really be exceedingly relieved to be freed from any further responsibility. In high satisfaction

Leisenbohg took the train back to Dresden, and informed Kläre of the agreeable outcome of the interview. She thanked him warmly, but avoided the Baron's attempts at tender advances in so decided a manner that he was quite taken aback. After a few brief and searching questions she finally admitted that during his absence no less a person than Prince Kajetan had conceived a violent passion for her and had sworn to do himself an injury if she did not take pity on him. So, of course, she had had at last to give way, to avoid plunging the ruling family and the nation into the most unspeakable grief.

With a heart that showed signs of breaking, Leisenbohg left the city and went back to Vienna. Here he began to pull wires, and it was not a little due to his persistent efforts that Kläre received an offer from the Vienna Opera for the very next year. After a successful tour, she took up her engagement in October, and the Baron's magnificent basket of flowers, that she found on the evening when she first entered her dressing-room, seemed like the expression of an entreaty and a hope. But her generous admirer had once again to endure the experience of having come too late. The fair-haired gentleman who played for her while she had been practising during the last few weeks—he was pretty well known as a song composer—had acquired rights over her which she was bound in honour to respect. Since then seven years had passed. The accompanist had been succeeded by Herr Klemens von Rhodoewyl, the dashing gentleman-jockey; Herr von Rhodoewyl was followed by Vincenz Klaudi, the conductor, who often sang the music of the operas he was conducting, so loudly that the singers could not be heard; after him came the Count von Alban-Rattony, who had gambled away his Hungarian estates at cards, but had made up for it by winning a castle in Lower Austria; the next was Herr Edgar Wilhelm, who wrote ballet librettos (for which highly paid composers wrote the music), tragedies produced at his own expense at the Jansch theatre, and poems printed in elegant type in the stupidest kind of Court journal. Herr Wilhelm was succeeded by a gentleman named Amandus Meier, who had nothing to recommend him but his age, which was nineteen, and his appearance, which was charming, and whose sole possession was a fox-terrier that could stand on its head; after Herr Meier came the best dressed man in the kingdom—Prince Richard Bedenbruck.

Kläre had never made any secret of these affairs. Hers was, and continued to be, a simple bourgeois household in which the master changed from time to time. Her public popularity was extraordinary. In higher circles she was looked on with not a little favour for going to Mass every Sunday, confessing twice a month, wearing on her bosom as an amulet a picture of the Madonna blessed by the Pope, and never going to bed without saying her prayers. There were few bazaars at which she was not in charge of a stall, and ladies of the aristocracy, as well as those of Jewish financial circles, were delighted to be able to offer their wares under the same marquee as Kläre.

She bestowed fascinating smiles on youthful enthusiasts of both sexes who waited for her by the stage door. She distributed her bouquets among the patient crowd, and once, when she had left the flowers behind her in her dressing-room, she said in that refreshing Viennese of hers that seemed to suit her looks so well: "Oh God, I've left the stuff up in my room; come to-morrow afternoon, my dears, if you still want any." Then she jumped into her carriage, put her head out of the window, and cried as she drove off: "You'll get some coffee, too!"

Fanny Ringeiser had been one of the few who had had the nerve to accept this invitation. Kläre fell into a chaffing conversation with her, enquired about her family with all the affability of an archduchess, and found the ingenuous and adoring girl's chatter so much to her liking that she asked her to come again soon. Fanny did so, and it came about that she soon achieved a position of importance in the singer's household; and she managed to keep it, mainly because, though Kläre was very ready with her confidences, Fanny never fully confided in her in return. In the course of years, Fanny had received a succession of proposals, mostly from the young sons of the Mariahilferstrasse shopkeepers with whom she used to go to dances. But she rejected them all, owing to the fact that she fell, with irrevocable regularity, in love with Kläre's admirer for the time being.

Kläre had in fact loved Prince Bedenbruck just as faithfully but much more passionately than his predecessors, and Leisenbohg, who in spite of his innumerable disappointments had never given up hope, had begun to be seriously afraid that the happiness he had yearned for these ten long years would never blossom now. Whenever he saw anyone falling out of her favour, he had always discharged his mistress so as to be ready for all contingencies, and at any moment. And he did so after Prince Richard's sudden death; but, for the first time, more from habit than conviction. For Kläre's grief seemed so boundless that everyone could not help believing that she had finished for ever with the delights of love. She drove out to the cemetery every day and laid flowers on the grave of the departed. She flung away all her gay clothes and locked up her jewelry in the innermost drawers of her writing-table. Much serious expostulation was needed to dissuade her from leaving the stage for ever.

After her first reappearance, which had gone off so brilliantly, her life, outwardly at any rate, resumed its wonted course. Her original circle of less intimate acquaintances gathered round once more. The music critic, Bernhard Feuerstein, appeared, his coat stained with spinach or tomato, in accordance with what he might have had for lunch, and, to Kläre's unconcealed delight, abused her fellow artists of both sexes, including the Director himself. She allowed Prince Richard's two cousins, Lucius and Christian, Bedenbrucks of the other line, to make love to her in their usual light-hearted but respectful way; a gentleman from the French Embassy and a young Czech pianist were brought to see her, and on June 10th she drove to the races again for the first time. But, as Prince Lucius, who had a touch of poetry about him, expressed it, only her soul was awake, her heart was still sunk in slumber. It was true that if one of her younger or older friends ventured the slightest suggestion that there were such things as love and passion in the world, every trace of a smile vanished from her face, she stared darkly in front of her, and from time to time raised her hand in a strange gesture of repulsion which seemed intended to apply to all men, and for ever.

In the latter half of the month of June it so happened that a singer from the north, named Sigurd Ölse, sang Tristan at the Opera. His voice was clear and powerful, though it was not really first-rate; he was almost a giant in stature, though inclining towards stoutness, and, in repose, his face was lacking in individual expression; but as soon as he began to sing, his steel-grey eyes flashed with a sort of secret inner light, and his voice and look seemed to reduce everybody, more especially women, to a state of ecstatic admiration.

Kläre sat in the theatre-box with some of her fellow artists who were not singing that night. She alone seemed to remain unmoved. Next morning Sigurd Ölse was introduced to her in the manager's office. She spoke kindly, but quite coldly about his performance on the previous evening. The same afternoon he called upon her, though she had not invited him to do so. Leisenbohg and Fanny Ringeiser were present and Sigurd drank tea with them. He spoke of his parents who were fisher-folk living in a little Norwegian village, of the marvellous discovery of his talent as a singer by a passing Englishman who had landed from a white yacht in that far-distant fjord; of his wife, an Italian, who had died on the Atlantic Ocean during their honeymoon and who had been buried at sea. After he had taken his departure the others stayed for some time in silence. Fanny stared gravely into her empty tea cup, Kläre sat down at the piano with her elbows on the closed keyboard, while the Baron sank into a silent and anxious meditation as to why, during the account of Sigurd's honeymoon, Kläre had omitted that strange gesture by which, since the Prince's death, she indicated that any suggestion of passion or affection could have no place whatever in her future life.

The next parts that Sigurd Ölse sang were Siegfried and Lohengrin. On each occasion Kläre sat in her box and made no sign. But the singer, whose only other acquaintance was the Norwegian Ambassador, appeared at Kläre's house every afternoon; Fräulein Fanny Ringeiser was usually there, and the Baron von Leisenbohg always.

On June 27th he sang Tristan for the last time. Kläre sat in the theatre-box and made no sign. The next day she drove with Fanny to the cemetery and laid a gigantic cross on the Prince's grave; and in the evening she gave a party in honour of the singer who was to leave Vienna on the morrow.

Her circle of friends was present in full strength. The passion that Sigurd had conceived for Kläre was obvious to everyone; as his custom was, he was voluble and excited. He mentioned incidentally that while on the ship crossing to the Continent an Arabian lady, married to a Russian Grand Duke, had read his hand and prophesied that the immediate future would be the most fateful period in his life. He believed firmly in this prophecy, and, indeed, superstition seemed to him something more than a means of exciting interest. He also said it was generally known that last year, on landing in New York, where he had gone to fulfill an engagement, that every day—that every hour in fact—notwithstanding the enormous fine involved, he boarded a ship for Europe simply because a black cat had walked between his legs on the gangway. He had certainly every reason to believe in the secret connections between such inexplicable omens and the fates of men. One evening at the Covent Garden Theatre in London, before going on the stage he had omitted to repeat a certain magic formula he had received from his grandmother, and his voice had suddenly failed him. One night a winged genius in pink tights had appeared to him in a dream and predicted the death of his favourite barber, and sure enough the unfortunate man was found hanged the next morning. Moreover, he always carried about with him a short but highly significant missive which had been handed to him at a spiritualist séance in Brussels by the spirit of the dead singer, Cornelia Lujan, and contained a prophecy, in fluent Portuguese, that he was destined to become the greatest singer in the Old and New Worlds.

All these experiences he related that evening; and when the spirit letter (written on rose-coloured paper manufactured by Glienwood & Co.) was passed from hand to hand, the effect on the company was profound and universal. Kläre did not move a muscle, but merely nodded indifferently once or twice. In spite of this Leisenbohg's anxiety grew more and more acute. To his penetrating eyes the signs of threatening danger grew ever more ominous. Worst of all, Sigurd, like all Kläre's previous lovers, conceived an extraordinary liking for him during supper, invited him to his house on the Molde-Fjord, and ended by addressing him as "du." Moreover, Fanny trembled all over when Sigurd spoke a word to her, her colour came and went when he looked at her with his great steel-grey eyes, and when he spoke of his approaching departure she burst openly into tears. But Kläre remained perfectly quiet and serious. She barely returned Sigurd's burning glances, she spoke to him no more eagerly than to the rest, and when he at last kissed her hand and then looked up at her with eyes that seemed full of prayers and promises and desperation, her own remained veiled and her expression unmoved. Leisenbohg observed all this with suspicion and anxiety. But when the party came to an end and all the guests departed, something unexpected happened that took the Baron completely by surprise. He was the last of all to take Kläre's hand in farewell, and hurried to depart; but she held his hand fast and whispered: "Come back again." He thought he could not have heard her rightly. But she pressed his hand again, and, with her lips quite close to his ear, repeated, "Come back again; I shall expect you in an hour."

In a state bordering on ecstasy he went out with the rest. He and Fanny accompanied Sigurd to his hotel, and as though from a far distance he heard the tenor raving about Kläre. Then he took Fanny Ringeiser back through the silent streets, in soft cool night air, to Mariahilferstrasse, and he saw, as though through a mist, her girlish cheeks wet with foolish tears. Then he got into a cab and drove up to Kläre's door. He saw the light glimmering through the curtains of her bedroom, he saw her shadow glide past, her head appeared in the gap between the curtain and the window, and she nodded to him. He had not been dreaming: she was waiting for him.

Next morning Baron von Leisenbohg went for a ride in the Prater. He felt young and happy. In the late fulfillment of his passion there seemed to be some deeper meaning. His experience of the past night had been the most marvellous surprise—and yet, again, it was nothing but the climax and the inevitable conclusion of his relations with Kläre hitherto. He now felt that it could not have happened otherwise, and fell to making plans for the immediate and more distant future. "How long will she stay on the stage?" he wondered . . . "Perhaps for a few years. Then, but not until then, we will get married. We will live together somewhere in the country not far from Vienna, perhaps in St. Veit or in Lainz. I will buy a small house there, or build one to her liking. We shall live a rather retired life, but often take long trips abroad . . . to Spain, Egypt or India . . ." Thus he dreamed, as he let his horse canter across the meadows towards the hay-stall. Then he trotted back into the main avenue and got into his carriage at the cross-roads. He told his coachman to stop at Fossatti's and sent Kläre a bouquet of beautiful dark roses. He breakfasted at home alone, as his custom was, in his house on the Schwarzenbergplatz, and when he had finished he lay down on the divan. He was filled with the most fervent longing for Kläre. What meaning had all the other women had for him? . . . They had served to pass the time, nothing more. And he felt a day would come when Kläre too would say to him: "What were all the others to me? You are the first and only one I ever loved. . . ." And while he lay on the divan with closed eyes, he let the whole succession of them glide past his inner vision. He was sure she had loved none of them before him—perhaps she had loved him always, and in each and all of them! . . .

The Baron then dressed himself and walked slowly through the familiar streets towards her house, as though to savour their first reunion for a few more seconds. There were a good many people about on the Ring, but still it was observable that the season was coming to an end. And Leisenbohg was glad that summer was there, that he could travel with Kläre and they could see the sea and the mountains together—indeed he had very nearly shouted aloud in his delight.

He stood before her house and looked up at her windows. The light of the afternoon sun was reflected from them and almost blinded him. He walked up the two flights of stairs to her door and rang. No one opened. He rang again. No one opened. Then Leisenbohg noticed that the door was padlocked. What did it mean? Had he made a mistake? . . . As a matter of fact there was no plate on her door, but opposite was the one he knew so well: "Lt.-Colonel von Jeleskowitz." . . . There could be no doubt: this was her flat and it was shut up. He hurried down the stairs and flung open the door of the porter's lodge. The porter's wife was sitting in the half-darkness on a bed, one child was peering up at the street through the small underground window, the other was blowing an unrecognisable tune on a comb.

"Is Fräulein Hell not at home?" asked the Baron.

The woman stood up. "No, Herr Baron, Fräulein Hell has gone away."

"What!" cried the Baron. . . . "Oh, yes, of course," he added quickly. "She went about three o'clock, didn't she?"

"No, Herr Baron, about eight o'clock this morning."

"Where did she go? . . . I mean did she go straight . . ." he was talking at random . . . "did she go straight to Dresden?"

"No, Herr Baron; she left no address. She said she would write and say where she was."

"Ah . . . yes—yes . . . of course. Thank you very much."

He hurried away and went out into the street: unconsciously he looked back at the house. The evening sunlight shining in those windows looked very different now! And the sultry summer evening lay like a pall of oppression over the city. Kläre had gone? . . . Why? . . . Had she fled from him? What did it mean? . . . His first thought was to go to the Opera House. But it occurred to him that the vacation began the day after tomorrow, and that Kläre was not singing the last two days. Then he went to 76 Mariahilferstrasse where the Ringeisers lived. An elderly cook opened the door to him and looked at the well-dressed visitor with a certain mistrust. He asked her to call Frau Ringeiser.

"Is Fräulein Fanny at home?" he asked in a tone of excitement that he could no longer control.

"I beg your pardon?" said Frau Ringeiser sharply.

He introduced himself.

"Ah, of course," said Frau Ringeiser. "Please come in, Herr Baron."

He remained standing in the hall and asked once more:

"Is Fräulein Fanny not at home?"

"But the Herr Baron must come in." Leisenbohg had to follow her, and found himself in a dark low-ceilinged room with furniture covered in blue velvet and rep window curtains of the same colour. "No," said Frau Ringeiser, "Fanny is not at home. Fräulein Hell has taken her away for a holiday trip."

"Where?" asked the Baron, and stared at a photograph of Kläre that stood on the piano in a gold frame.

"I don't know where," said Frau Ringeiser. "Fräulein Hell was here at eight o'clock this morning and begged me to let Fanny go with her. . . . And she begged so nicely that I could not say No."

"But where have they gone—where have they gone?" persisted Leisenbohg.

"That I can't tell you. Fanny is going to telegraph as soon as Fräulein Hell has made up her mind where she is going to stay. Perhaps to-morrow or the day after."

"Ah," said Leisenbohg, and dropped on to a kind of cane stool in front of the piano. He was silent for a few moments, then he suddenly stood up, shook hands with Frau Ringeiser, asked her to excuse him for having disturbed her, and went slowly down the dark staircase of the old house.

He shook his head. She had indeed been careful . . . more careful than was necessary. . . . She might have known that he would not come where he was not wanted.

"Where to now, Herr Baron?" asked the coachman, and Leisenbohg realised that he had been sitting in the open carriage, staring in front of him, for some minutes. And, following a sudden instinct, he answered: "Hotel Bristol."

Sigurd Ölse had not yet gone. He invited the Baron up to his rooms, greeted him eagerly and asked him to spend the last evening in Vienna in his company. Leisenbohg was much struck by the fact that Sigurd Ölse was still actually in Vienna, and the singer's friendliness positively stirred him to tears. Sigurd began at once to talk about Kläre. He asked Leisenbohg to tell him all he knew about her—he knew that the Baron was her oldest and most faithful friend. So Leisenbohg sat down on one of his host's trunks and began to speak of Kläre. It did him good to be able to talk about her. He told the singer almost everything, except such matters as he felt bound in honour not to mention. Sigurd listened and appeared enraptured.

At supper the singer invited his friend to leave Vienna with him that very evening, and go with him to his estate near Molde. The Baron felt wonderfully comforted. He excused himself for the time being, but promised Ölse to visit him in the course of the summer.

They drove to the station together. "You will take me for a simpleton," said Sigurd, "but I want to pass her window once again."

Leisenbohg threw a sidelong glance at him. Was this perhaps an attempt to make a fool of him, or was it a final proof of the singer's honesty? . . . As they went by Kläre's house, Sigurd flung a kiss at the closed windows. Then he said: "Say good-bye for me once more."

Leisenbohg nodded. "I will give her your message when she comes back."

Sigurd looked at him in amazement.

"As a matter of fact she has gone away," Leisenbohg continued. "She went off early this morning—without a word to anyone. It is a habit of hers," he added, untruthfully.

"Gone away?" repeated Sigurd, and sank into thought.

Then they were both silent.

Before the departure of the train they embraced like old friends.

That night the Baron wept as he lay in bed, more bitterly than he had done since his childhood. The hour of delight that he had spent with Kläre seemed to him beset by gloom and terror. There had been, he thought, a gleam of madness in her eyes last night. Now he understood. He had obeyed her summons too soon. The shadow of Prince Bedenbruck still had power over her, and Leisenbohg felt that he had possessed Kläre only to lose her for ever.

He wandered about Vienna for a few days without knowing what to do with his days and nights: everything that used to occupy his time—the newspapers, bridge and riding, had become completely indifferent to him. He realised that the meaning of his whole existence depended on Kläre, and even that his relations with other women had their being only as reflections of his passion for her. An eternal grey mist seemed to hang over the city; the people to whom he spoke had hushed voices and stared at him in a strange, almost treacherous way. One evening he drove to the station and almost mechanically took a ticket to Ischl. There he met acquaintances who asked him unsuspectingly for news of Kläre; he answered in an irritable and offensive tone, and had to fight a duel with one man who did not interest him in the least. He went nonchalantly into the field, heard the bullet whistle past his ear, fired in the air and left Ischl half an hour afterwards. He travelled to Tyrol, the Engadine and the Bernese Oberland, and to Lake Geneva, swam, crossed mountain passes, climbed mountains, and remembered nothing from one day to the next.

One day he received a telegram that had been sent on from Vienna. He opened it with feverish fingers. In it were these words: "If you are my friend, keep your word and come to me quickly, for I need a friend. Sigurd Ölse." Leisenbohg did not doubt for a moment that the contents of this telegram must have some sort of connection with Kläre. He packed as quickly as possible and left Aix, where he then happened to be, at the earliest opportunity. He travelled straight through to Hamburg via Munich, and took the boat via Stavanger to Molde, where he arrived on a fine summer evening. The journey had seemed interminable, and the beauties of the scenery had left him quite unmoved. Moreover, latterly he had not been able to remember Kläre's voice when she sang, or even her features. It seemed like a year, ten years, since he had left Vienna. But when he saw Sigurd standing on the shore in a white flannel suit and white cap, he felt as though he had seen him only the evening before. And, dishevelled as he

was, he smilingly returned Sigurd's greeting from where he was standing
on the deck, and walked cheerfully down the gangway.

"I thank you a thousand times for coming so promptly," said Sigurd;
and then he added simply: "I'm done for."

The Baron eyed him. Sigurd looked very pale and the hair on his temples
had grown astonishingly grey. Over his arm he was carrying a green rug of
dimly iridescent material.

"What is it? What has happened?" asked Leisenbohg with a fixed smile.

"I will tell you the whole story," said Sigurd Ölse. It struck the Baron
that Sigurd's voice was less resonant than it had been. They drove in a small
carriage along the lovely avenue along the shore of the blue sea. Both were
silent. Leisenbohg did not dare to ask a question. He stared vacantly at the
water which was almost motionless. The strange and (as it proved) impossible idea of counting the ripples came into his mind; then he looked up
into the sky and it seemed as though the stars were dropping slowly down
to earth. At last it also occurred to him that a singer, by name Kläre Hell,
was wandering somewhere about in the wide world—a fact which did not
matter much. Then the carriage stopped with a jerk before a simple white
house entirely surrounded by trees and foliage. In the evening they dined
upon a verandah that looked out upon the sea. A servant with a stern, and,
as he poured out the wine, almost a menacing expression, waited on them.
The distant horizon slept under the clear northern light.

"Well?" asked Leisenbohg, in a sudden burst of impatience.

"I am a lost man," said Sigurd Ölse, and stared in front of him.

"What do you mean by that?" asked Leisenbohg in a toneless voice, "and
what can I do for you?" he added mechanically.

"Not much. I don't know yet," and he looked beyond the tablecloth, the
balustrade, the garden and the garden fence, the road, and the sea into the
far distance.

Leisenbohg felt numb within him . . . all manner of notions flashed
across his mind . . . what was going to happen? . . . was Kläre dead? . . .
had Sigurd murdered her? . . . thrown her into the sea? . . . Or was
Sigurd dead? . . . No, that was impossible—there he was sitting opposite.
. . . But why didn't he speak? . . . and suddenly, in an access of terror,
Leisenbohg burst out, "Where is Kläre?"

The singer turned slowly towards him. His rather fleshy face began to
light up with a sort of inner glow and seemed to smile, unless it was the
moonlight playing over it. In any case, at that moment, it seemed to
Leisenbohg that the man sitting near him leaning back in his chair with his
hands in his pockets and his legs outstretched under the table, and gazing
at him with veiled eyes, looked exactly like a Pierrot. The green shawl hung
down over the balustrade of the verandah and at that moment seemed to
the Baron so like an old acquaintance. . . . But what on earth had this

ridiculous old shawl to do with him? Was he dreaming perhaps? . . .
he was in Molde; it was all very strange; if he had been sensible he ought
really to have telegraphed to the singer from Aix: "What is the matter?
What do you want me to do for you, Pierrot?" And he suddenly repeated
his earlier question only in a much politer and calmer tone: "Where is
Kläre?"

The singer nodded several times. "Yes," he said, "it is something to do
with her, of course. Are you a friend of mine?"

Leisenbohg nodded, he felt slightly chilly; a light wind was blowing in
from the sea. "I am your friend. What do you want of me?"

"Do you remember the evening I left Vienna, Baron, when we had supper
together at the Bristol, and you went with me to the station?"

Leisenbohg nodded once more.

"You had no idea, of course, that Kläre Hell was leaving Vienna in that
same train?"

Leisenbohg let his head sink heavily on his chest. . . .

"Nor had I," went on Sigurd. "I saw Kläre for the first time next morning
at the station where we stopped for breakfast. She was sitting with Fanny
Ringeiser in the dining-room drinking coffee. Her demeanour led me to
suppose that this meeting was a fortunate accident. It was not an accident
at all."

"Go on," said the Baron, looking at the green shawl which was moving
slightly.

"Later on, of course, she confessed that it was not an accident. From that
morning we all stayed together, Kläre, Fanny and I. We settled down by
one of your enchanting little Austrian lakes, in a charming house between
the shore and the forest, quite by ourselves. We were very happy."

He spoke so slowly that Leisenbohg thought he was going mad.

"Why did he send for me?" he thought. "What does he want of me? Had
she confessed? What's the matter with him? Why is he staring at me like
that? . . . Why am I sitting here at Molde on a verandah with a Pierrot?
Can it be all a dream after all? Perhaps I am still asleep in Kläre's arms.
Perhaps that night of ours has not yet ended after all." . . . And he unconsciously opened his eyes wide.

"Will you avenge me?" said Sigurd, suddenly.

"Avenge you? Whatever for? What has happened?" asked the Baron, and
his words sounded as if they came from a distance.

"Because she has destroyed me, and I am a lost man."

"Tell me all about it," said Leisenbohg in a hard, dry voice.

"Fanny Ringeiser was with us," Sigurd went on. "She is a good girl, isn't
she?"

"Yes, she is a good girl," answered Leisenbohg, and all at once he saw a
dim room with furniture covered in blue velvet and rep curtains where,
several hundred years before, he had spoken to Fanny's mother.

"She is rather a stupid girl, is she not?"

"I believe she is," answered the Baron.

"I am sure of it," answered Sigurd. "She did not realise how happy we were." And he was silent for some while.

"Go on," said Leisenbohg, and waited.

"One morning Kläre was still asleep," began Sigurd afresh. "She always slept late into the morning. But I had gone for a walk into the forest. Suddenly Fanny came running up behind me: 'Fly, Herr Ölse, before it is too late; leave this place, for you are in dreadful danger!' Strangely enough, to begin with she absolutely refused to say any more. But I persisted and at last found out what kind of danger it was that she believed to be threatening me. You see, she believed that I could still be saved or she would certainly have told me nothing!"

The green shawl on the balustrade bellied out like a sail, and the lamp flickered a little on the table.

"What did Fanny tell you?" asked Leisenbohg in a rasping tone.

"Do you remember the evening," asked Sigurd, "when we were all at Kläre's house? On the next day Kläre drove out with Fanny to the cemetery, and on the Prince's grave she confided the dreadful secret to her friend."

"The dreadful secret . . . ?" stammered the Baron.

"Yes. You know how the Prince died? He was thrown from his horse and lingered for an hour."

"I know."

"Nobody was with him but Kläre."

"That also I know."

"He would see no one but her, and on his deathbed he uttered a curse."

"A curse?"

"A curse. 'Kläre,' said the Prince, 'do not forget me. I shall have no peace in the grave if you forget me.'—'I will never forget you,' replied Kläre.— 'Do you swear you will never forget me?'—'I swear it.'—'Kläre, I love you and I must die!'"

"Who is it speaking?" cried the Baron.

"I am," said Sigurd; "I am telling you what Fanny said; Fanny told me what Kläre said, and Kläre told her what the Prince said. Don't you understand?"

Leisenbohg listened with strained attention: it seemed as though he could hear the voice of the dead Prince ringing out from the triply-sealed coffin into the night.

"'Kläre, I love you, and I must die! You are so young, and I must die. . . . And after me another man will come. . . . I know it will be so, another man will hold you in his arms and be happy with you . . . he must not be—he shall not be—I lay my curse on him, do you hear, Kläre? I curse him!—The first man that kisses those lips and holds that body in his arms when I am gone shall go down to hell! Kläre, Heaven hears the curses of dying men. Beware—and let him beware; he shall go down to hell in madness, misery and death! Woe be to that man—woe!'"

Sigurd, from whose mouth the dead man's voice thundered out, had got up from his chair and stood, a tall heavy figure in his white flannel suit, staring into the clear night. The green shawl slipped down from the balustrade into the garden. An icy chill came over the Baron; he felt as though his whole body was growing stiff; he would gladly have cried out, but though he opened his mouth wide no sound came . . . in a flash he was back again in Frau Eisenstein, the singing teacher's, little room where he had seen Kläre for the first time. On the stage stood a Pierrot, and shouted out: 'With this curse on his lips Prince Bedenbruck died, and the unhappy man in whose arms she lay, the wretch upon whom the curse must be fulfilled, is I—I!' "

Then the stage collapsed with a loud crash and sank before Leisenbohg's eyes into the sea. But he, without a word, fell backwards with his chair, like a marionette.

Sigurd leapt up and shouted for help. Two servants came, picked up the unconscious man and laid him out in an armchair that stood beside the table; one of them went for a doctor, and the other brought some water and vinegar. Sigurd rubbed the Baron's forehead and temples, but he did not stir. Then the doctor came and began his examination. It did not last long. When he had finished he said: "This gentleman is dead."

Sigurd Ölse was much upset, asked the doctor to make the necessary arrangements and left the verandah. He walked through the drawing-room, went upstairs, entered his bedroom, lit a lamp and hurriedly wrote the following words: "Kläre! I found your telegram waiting for me in Molde where I had fled without stopping on the way. I will confess that I did not believe you; I thought that you were trying to set my mind at rest by a lie. Forgive me; I no longer doubt you. Baron von Leisenbohg has been here. I asked him to come, but I did not question him because as an honourable man he would have had to lie. I had an ingenious idea. I told him about the dead Prince's curse. The effect was amazing. The Baron fell backwards as he sat, and died on the spot."

Sigurd paused for a moment, looked very serious and seemed to be reflecting. Then he took up his stand in the middle of the room and began to sing. At first his voice sounded timid and subdued, but gradually it grew clearer and rang out strong and splendid into the night—so powerfully at last that it seemed full of the thunder of the sea. A satisfied smile spread over Sigurd's features and he breathed a deep sigh of relief. Once more he sat down at the writing-table, and added the following words to his letter:

"Darling Kläre! Forgive me—all is well again. I shall be with you in three days. . . ."

THE WHIRLIGIG OF LIFE

O. Henry

(1862–1910)

Justice-of-the-peace Benaja Widdup sat in the door of his office smoking his elder-stem pipe. Halfway to the zenith the Cumberland range rose blue-gray in the afternoon haze. A speckled hen swaggered down the main street of the "settlement," cackling foolishly.

Up the road came a sound of creaking axles, and then a slow cloud of dust, and then a bull-cart bearing Ransie Bilbro and his wife. The cart stopped at the Justice's door, and the two climbed down. Ransie was a narrow six feet of sallow brown skin and yellow hair. The imperturbability of the mountains hung upon him like a suit of armor. The woman was calicoed, angled, snuff-brushed, and weary with unknown desires. Through it all gleamed a faint protest of cheated youth unconscious of its loss.

The Justice of the Peace slipped his feet into his shoes, for the sake of dignity, and moved to let them enter.

"We-all," said the woman, in a voice like the wind blowing through pine boughs, "wants a divo'ce." She looked at Ransie to see if he noted any flaw or ambiguity or evasion or partiality or self-partisanship in her statement of their business.

"A divo'ce," repeated Ransie, with a solemn nod. "We-all can't git along together nohow. It's lonesome enough fur to live in the mount'ins when a man and a woman keers fur one another. But when she's a-spittin' like a wildcat or a-sullenin' like a hoot-owl in the cabin, a man ain't got no call to live with her."

"When he's a no-'count varmint," said the woman, without any especial warmth, "a-traipsin' along of scalawags and moonshiners and a-layin' on his back pizen 'ith co'n whiskey, and a-pesterin' folks with a pack o' hungry, triflin' houn's to feed!"

"When she keeps a-throwin' skillet lids," came Ransie's antiphony, "and slings b'ilin' water on the best coon-dog in the Cumberlands, and sets herself agin' cookin' a man's victuals, and keeps him awake o' nights accusin' him of a sight of doin's!"

"When he's al'ays a-fightin' the revenues, and gits a hard name in the mount'ins fur a mean man, who's gwine to be able fur to sleep o' nights?"

The Justice of the Peace stirred deliberately to his duties. He placed his one chair and a wooden stool for his petitioners. He opened his book of statutes on the table and scanned the index. Presently he wiped his spectacles and shifted his inkstand.

"The law and the statutes," said he, "air silent on the subjeck of divo'ce as fur as the jurisdiction of this co't air concerned. But, accordin' to equity and the Constitution and the golden rule, it's a bad barg'in that can't run both ways. If a justice of the peace can marry a couple, it's plain that he is bound to be able to divo'ce 'em. This here office will issue a decree of divo'ce and abide by the decision of the Supreme Co't to hold it good."

Ransie Bilbro drew a small tobacco-bag from his trousers pocket. Out of this he shook upon the table a five-dollar note. "Sold a b'arskin and two foxes fur that," he remarked. "It's all the money we got."

"The regular price of a divo'ce in this co't," said the Justice, "air five dollars." He stuffed the bill into the pocket of his homespun vest with a deceptive air of indifference. With much bodily toil and mental travail he wrote the decree upon half a sheet of foolscap, and then copied it upon the other. Ransie Bilbro and his wife listened to his reading of the document that was to give them freedom:

"Know all men by these presents that Ransie Bilbro and his wife, Ariela Bilbro, this day personally appeared before me and promises that hereinafter they will neither love, honor, nor obey each other, neither for better nor worse, being of sound mind and body, and accept summons for divorce according to the peace and dignity of the State. Herein fail not, so help you God. Benaja Widdup, justice of the peace in and for the county of Piedmont, State of Tennessee."

The Justice was about to hand one of the documents to Ransie. The voice of Ariela delayed the transfer. Both men looked at her. Their dull masculinity was confronted by something sudden and unexpected in the woman.

"Judge, don't you give him that air paper yit. 'Tain't all settled, nohow. I got to have my rights first. I got to have my ali-money. 'Tain't no kind of a way to do fur a man to divo'ce his wife 'thout her havin' a cent fur to do with. I'm a-layin' off to be a-goin' up to brother Ed's up on Hogback Mount'in. I'm bound fur to hev a pa'r of shoes and some snuff and things besides. Ef Rance kin affo'd a divo'ce, let him pay me ali-money."

Ransie Bilbro was stricken to dumb perplexity. There had been no previous hint of alimony. Women were always bringing up startling and unlooked-for issues.

Justice Benaja Widdup felt that the point demanded judicial decision. The authorities were also silent on the subject of alimony. But the woman's feet were bare. The trail to Hogback Mountain was steep and flinty.

"Ariela Bilbro," he asked, in official tones, "how much did you 'low would be good and sufficient ali-money in the case befo' the co't."

"I 'lowed," she answered, "fur the shoes and all, to say five dollars. That ain't much fur ali-money, but I reckon that'll git me up to brother Ed's."

"The amount," said the Justice, "air not onreasonable. Ransie Bilbro, you air ordered by the co't to pay the plaintiff the sum of five dollars befo' the decree of divo'ce air issued."

"I hain't no mo' money," breathed Ransie, heavily. "I done paid you all I had."

"Otherwise," said the Justice, looking severely over his spectacles, "you air in contempt of co't."

"I reckon if you gimme till to-morrow," pleaded the husband, "I mout be able to rake or scrape it up somewhars. I never looked for to be a-payin' no ali-money."

"The case air adjourned," said Benaja Widdup, "till to-morrow, when you-all will present yo'selves and obey the order of the co't. Followin' of which the decrees of divo'ce will be delivered." He sat down in the door and began to loosen a shoestring.

"We mout as well go down to Uncle Ziah's," decided Ransie, "and spend the night." He climbed into the cart on one side, and Ariela climbed in on the other. Obeying the flap of his rope, the little red bull slowly came around on a tack, and the cart crawled away in the nimbus arising from its wheels.

Justice-of-the-peace Benaja Widdup smoked his elder-stem pipe. Late in the afternoon he got his weekly paper, and read it until the twilight dimmed its lines. Then he lit the tallow candle on his table, and read until the moon rose, marking the time for supper. He lived in the double log cabin on the slope near the girdled poplar. Going home to supper he crossed a little branch darkened by a laurel thicket. The dark figure of a man stepped from the laurels and pointed a rifle at his breast. His hat was pulled down low, and something covered most of his face.

"I want yo' money," said the figure, "'thout any talk. I'm gettin' nervous, and my finger's a-wabblin' on this here trigger."

"I've only got f-f-five dollars," said the Justice, producing it from his vest pocket.

"Roll it up," came the order, "and stick it in the end of this here gun-bar'l."

The bill was crisp and new. Even fingers that were clumsy and trembling found little difficulty in making a spill of it and inserting it (this with less ease) into the muzzle of the rifle.

"Now I reckon you kin be goin' along," said the robber.

The Justice lingered not on his way.

The next day came the little red bull, drawing the cart to the office door. Justice Benaja Widdup had his shoes on, for he was expecting the visit. In his presence Ransie Bilbro handed to his wife a five-dollar bill. The official's eye sharply viewed it. It seemed to curl up as though it had been rolled and

inserted into the end of a gun-barrel. But the Justice refrained from comment. It is true that other bills might be inclined to curl. He handed each
one a decree of divorce. Each stood awkwardly silent, slowly folding the
guarantee of freedom. The woman cast a shy glance full of constraint at
Ransie.

"I reckon you'll be goin' back up to the cabin," she said, "along 'ith the
bull-cart. There's bread in the tin box settin' on the shelf. I put the bacon in
the b'ilin'-pot to keep the hounds from gittin' it. Don't forget to wind the
clock to-night."

"You air a-goin' to your brother Ed's?" asked Ransie, with fine unconcern.

"I was 'lowin' to get along up thar afore night. I ain't sayin' as they'll
pester theyselves any to make me welcome, but I hain't nowhar else fur to
go. It's a right smart ways, and I reckon I better be goin'. I'll be a-sayin'
good-bye, Ranse—that is, if you keer fur to say so."

"I don't know as anybody's a hound dog," said Ransie, in a martyr's
voice, "fur to not want to say good-bye—'less you air so anxious to git away
that you don't want me to say it."

Ariela was silent. She folded the five-dollar bill and her decree carefully,
and placed them in the bosom of her dress. Benaja Widdup watched the
money disappear with mournful eyes behind his spectacles.

And then with his next words he achieved rank (as his thoughts ran)
with either the great crowd of the world's sympathizers or the little crowd
of its great financiers.

"Be kind o' lonesome in the old cabin to-night, Ranse," he said.

Ransie Bilbro stared out at the Cumberlands, clear blue now in the sunlight. He did not look at Ariela.

"I 'low it might be lonesome," he said; "but when folks gits mad and
wants a divo'ce, you can't make folks stay."

"There's others wanted a divo'ce," said Ariela, speaking to the wooden
stool. "Besides, nobody don't want nobody to stay."

"Nobody never said they didn't."

"Nobody never said they did. I reckon I better start on now to brother
Ed's."

"Nobody can't wind that old clock."

"Want me to go back along 'ith you in the cart and wind it fur you,
Ranse?"

The mountaineer's countenance was proof against emotion. But he
reached out a big hand and enclosed Ariela's thin brown one. Her soul
peeped out once through her impassive face, hallowing it.

"Them hounds shan't pester you no more," said Ransie. "I reckon I been
mean and low down. You wind that clock, Ariela."

"My heart hit's in that cabin, Ranse," she whispered, "along 'ith you. I ain't a-goin' to git mad no more. Le's be startin', Ranse, so's we kin git home by sundown."

Justice-of-the-peace Benaja Widdup interposed as they started for the door, forgetting his presence.

"In the name of the State of Tennessee," he said, "I forbid you-all to be a-defyin' of its laws and statutes. This co't is mo' than willin' and full of joy to see the clouds of discord and misunderstandin' rollin' away from two lovin' hearts, but it air the duty of the co't to p'eserve the morals and integrity of the State. The co't reminds you that you air no longer man and wife, but air divo'ced by regular decree, and as such air not entitled to the benefits and 'purtenances of the mattermonal estate."

Ariela caught Ransie's arm. Did those words mean that she must lose him now when they had just learned the lesson of life?

"But the co't air prepared," went on the Justice, "fur to remove the disabilities set up by the decree of divo'ce. The co't air on hand to perform the solemn ceremony of marri'ge, thus fixin' things up and enablin' the parties in the case to resume the honor'ble and elevatin' state of mattermony which they desires. The fee fur performin' said ceremony will be, in this case, to wit, five dollars."

Ariela caught the gleam of promise in his words. Swiftly her hand went to her bosom. Freely as an alighting dove the bill fluttered to the Justice's table. Her sallow cheek colored as she stood hand in hand with Ransie and listened to the reuniting words.

Ransie helped her into the cart, and climbed in beside her. The little red bull turned once more, and they set out, hand-clasped, for the mountains.

Justice-of-the-peace Benaja Widdup sat in his door and took off his shoes. Once again he fingered the bill tucked down in his vest pocket. Once again he smoked his elder-stem pipe. Once again the speckled hen swaggered down the main street of the "settlement," cackling foolishly.

WITHOUT VISIBLE MEANS

Arthur Morrison

(1863–)

ALL EAST LONDON IDLED, or walked in a procession, or waylaid and bashed, or cried in an empty kitchen: for it was the autumn of the Great Strikes. One army of men, having been prepared, was ordered to strike—and struck.

Other smaller armies of men, with no preparation, were ordered to strike to express sympathy—and struck. Other armies still were ordered to strike because it was the fashion—and struck. Then many hands were discharged because the strikes in other trades left them no work. Many others came from other parts in regiments to work, but remained to loaf in gangs; taught by the example of earlier regiments, which, the situation being explained (an expression devised to include mobbings and kickings and flingings into docks), had returned whence they came. So that East London was very noisy and largely hungry; and the rest of the world looked on with intense interest, making earnest suggestions, and comprehending nothing. Lots of strikers, having no strike pay and finding little nourishment in processions, started off to walk to Manchester, Birmingham, Liverpool or Newcastle, where work might be got. Along the Great North Road such men might be seen in silent companies of a dozen or twenty, now and again singly or in couples.

At the tail of one such gang, which gathered in the Burdett Road and found its way into the Enfield Road by way of Victoria Park, Clapton, and Stamford Hill, walked a little group of three: a voluble young man of thirty, a stolid workman rather older, and a pale, anxious little fellow, with a nasty spasmic cough and a canvas bag of tools.

The little crowd straggled over the footpath and the road, few of its members speaking, most of them keeping to their places and themselves. As yet there was nothing of the tramp in the aspect of these mechanics. With their washed faces and well-mended clothes they might have been taken for a jury coming from a local inquest. As the streets became broken and detached, with patches of field between, the men began to look about them. One young fellow in front (with no family to think of), who looked upon the enterprise as an amusing sort of tour, and had even brought an accordion, began to rebel against the general depression, and attempted a joke about going to the Alexandra Palace. But in the rear, the little man with the canvas bag, putting his hand abstractedly into his pocket, suddenly stared and stopped. He drew out the hand, and saw in it three shillings.

"S'elp me," he said, "the missis is done that—shoved it in unbeknown when I come away! An' she's on'y got a bob for 'erself an' the kids." He broke into a sweat of uneasiness. "I'll 'ave to send it back at the next post-office, that's all."

"Send it back? not you!" Thus with deep scorn the voluble young man at his side. "She'll be all right, you lay your life. A woman allus knows 'ow to look after 'erself. You'll bleed'n' soon want it, an' bad. You do as I tell you, Joey; stick to it. That's right, Dave, ain't it?"

"Matter o' fancy," replied the stolid man. "My missis cleared my pockets out 'fore I got away. Shouldn't wonder at bein' sent after for leavin' 'er chargeable if I don't soon send some more. Women's different."

The march continued, and grew dustier. The cheerful pilgrim in front produced his accordion. At Palmer's Green four went straight ahead to try for work at the Enfield Arms Factory. The others knowing the thing hopeless turned off to the left for Potter's Bar.

After a long silence, "Which'll be nearest, Dave," asked little Joey Clayton, "Newcastle or Middlesbrough?"

"Middlesbrough," said Dave; "I done it afore."

"Trampin' ain't so rough on a man, is it, after all?" asked Joey wistfully. "*You* done all right, didn't you?"

"Got through. All depends, though it's rough enough. Matter o' luck. I 'ad the bad weather."

"If I don't get a good easy job where we're goin'," remarked the voluble young man, "I'll 'ave a strike there too."

"'Ave a strike there?" exclaimed Joey. "'Ow? Who'd call 'em out?"

"Wy, I would. I think I'm equal to doin' it, ain't I? An' when workin' men stand idle an' 'ungry in the midst o' the wealth an' the lukshry an' the igstravagance they've produced with the sweat of their brow, why, then, feller-workmen, it's time to act. It's time to bring the nigger-drivin' bloated capitalists to their knees."

"'Ear, 'ear," applauded Joey Clayton; tamely, perhaps, for the words were not new. "Good on yer, Newman!" Newman had a habit of practising this sort of thing in snatches whenever he saw the chance. He had learned the trick in a debating society; and Joey Clayton was always an applausive audience. There was a pause, the accordion started another tune, and Newman tried a different passage of his harangue.

"In the shop they call me Skulky Newman. Why? 'Cos I skulk, o' course" ("'Ear, 'ear," dreamily—from Dave this time). "I ain't ashamed of it, my friends. I'm a miker out an' out, an' I 'ope I shall always remain a miker. The less a worker does the more 'as to be imployed, don't they? An' the more the toilers wrings out o' the capitalists, don't they? Very well, then, I mike, an' I do it as a sacred dooty."

"You'll 'ave all the mikin' you want for a week or two," said Dave Burge placidly. "Stow it."

At Potter's Bar the party halted and sat under a hedge to eat hunks of bread and cheese (or hunks of bread and nothing else) and to drink cold tea out of cans. Skulky Newman, who had brought nothing, stood in with his two friends. As they started anew and turned into the Great North Road he said, stretching himself and looking slyly at Joey Clayton, "If I'd got a bob or two I'd stand you two blokes a pint apiece."

Joey looked troubled. "Well, as you ain't, I suppose I ought to," he said uneasily, turning toward the little inn hard by. "Dave," he cried to Burge, who was walking on, "won't you 'ave a drink?" And, "Well, if you *are* goin' to do the toff, I ain't proud," was the slow reply.

Afterward, Joey was inclined to stop at the post-office to send away at least two shillings. But Newman wouldn't. He enlarged on the improvidence of putting out of reach that which might be required on an emergency, he repeated his axiom as to a woman's knack of keeping alive in spite of all things: and Joey determined not to send—for a day or so at any rate.

The road got looser and dustier; the symptoms of the tramp came out stronger and stronger on the gang. The accordion struck up from time to time but ceased toward the end of the afternoon. The player wearied, and some of the older men, soon tired of walking, were worried by the noise. Joey Clayton, whose cough was aggravated by the dust, was especially tortured, after every fit, to hear the thing drawling and whooping the tune it had drawled and whooped a dozen times before; but he said nothing, scarce knowing what annoyed him.

At Hatfield Station two of the foremost picked up a few coppers by helping with a heavy trapload of luggage. Up Digswell Hill the party trailed out lengthily, and Newman, who had been letting off a set speech, was fain to save his wind. The night came, clear to see and sweet to smell. Between Welwyn and Codicote the company broke up to roost in such barns as they might possess: all but the master of the accordion, who had stayed at a little public-house at Welwyn, with the notion of earning a pot of beer and a stable-corner (or better) by a tune in the tap-room. Dave Burge lighted on a lone shed of thatched hurdles with loose hay in it and Newman straightway curled in the snuggest corner on most of the hay. Dave Burge pulled some from under him, and, having helped Joey Clayton to build a nest in the best place left, was soon snoring. But Joey lay awake all night, and sat up and coughed and turned restlessly, being unused to the circumstances and apprehensive of those months in jail, which (it is well known) are rancorously dealt forth among all them that sleep in barns.

Luck provided a breakfast next morning at Codicote: for three bicyclists, going north, stood cold beef and bread round at The Anchor. The man with the accordion caught up. He had made his lodging and breakfast and eightpence: this had determined him to stay at Hitchin, and work it for, at least, a day, and then to diverge into the towns and let the rest go their way. So beyond Hitchin there was no music.

Joey Clayton soon fell slow. Newman had his idea; and the three were left behind, and Joey staggered after his mates with difficulty. He lacked sleep, and he lacked stamina. Dave Burge took the canvas bag, and there were many rests: when Newman, expressing a resolve to stick by his fellow-man through thick and thin, hinted at drinks. Dave Burge made twopence at Henlow level crossing by holding an unsteady horse while a train passed. Joey saw little of the rest of the day; the road was yellow and dazzling, his cough tore him, and things were red sometimes and sometimes blue. He walked without knowing it, now helped, now lurching on alone. The others of the party were far ahead and forgotten. There was talk of a windmill!

ahead, where there would be rest; and the three men camped in an old boat-house by the river just outside Biddleswade. Joey, sleeping as he tottered, fell in a heap and lay without moving from sunset to broad morning.

When he woke Dave Burge was sitting at the door, but Newman was gone. Also, there was no sign of the canvas bag.

"No use lookin'," said Dave; " 'e's done it."

"Eh?"

"Skulky's 'opped the twig an' sneaked your tools. Gawd knows where 'e is by now."

"No—" the little man gasped, sitting up in a pale sweat. . . . "Not sneaked 'em . . . is 'e? . . . S'elp me, there's a set o' callipers worth fifteen bob in that bag . . . 'e ain't gawn . . . ?"

Dave Burge nodded inexorably.

"Best feel in your pockets," he said, "p'raps e's bin there."

He had. The little man broke down. "I was a-goin' to send 'ome that two bob—s'elp me, I was . . . An' what can I do without my tools? If I'd got no job I could 'a pawned 'em—an' then I'd 'a sent 'ome the money—s'elp me I would . . . O, it's crool!"

The walking, with the long sleep after it, had left him sore and stiff, and Dave had work to put him on the road again. He had forgotten yesterday afternoon and asked at first for the others. They tramped in silence for a few miles: when Joey suddenly flung himself upon a tussock by the way-side.

"Why won't nobody let me live?" he snivelled. "I'm a 'armless bloke enough. I worked at Ritterson's, man and boy, very nigh twenty year. When they come an' ordered us out, I come out with the others, peaceful enough; I didn't want to chuck it up, Gawd knows, but I come out promp' when they told me. And when I found another job on the island, four big blokes set about me an' 'arf killed me. I didn't know the place was blocked. And when two o' the blokes was took up, they said I'd get strike pay again if I didn't identify 'em; so I didn't. But they never give me no strike pay—they laughed an' chucked me out. An' now I'm a-starvin' on the 'igh road. An' Skulky . . . blimy . . . 'e's done me too!"

There were days wherein Joey learned to eat a swede pulled from behind a wagon, and to feel thankful for an early turnip; might have learned, too, just what tramping means in many ways to a man unskilled both in begging and in theft, but was never equal to it. He coughed—and worse: holding to posts and gates, and often spitting blood. He had little to say, but trudged mechanically, taking note of nothing.

Once, as though aroused from a reverie, he asked, "Wasn't there some others?"

"Others?" said Dave, for a moment taken aback. "Oh, yes, there was some others. They're gone on ahead, y'know."

Joey tramped for half-a-mile in silence. Then he said, "Expect they're 'avin' a rough time too."

"Ah—very like," said Dave.

For a space Joey was silent, save for the cough. Then he went on: "Comes o' not bringing 'cordions with 'em. Everyone ought to take a 'cordion what goes trampin'. I knew a man once that went trampin', an' 'e took a 'cordion. He done all right. It ain't so rough for them as plays on the 'cordion." And Dave Burge rubbed his cap about his head and stared; but answered nothing.

It was a bad day. Crusts were begged at cottages. Every rise and every turn, the eternal yellow road lay stretch on stretch before them, flouting their unrest. Joey, now unimpressionable, endured more placidly than even Dave Burge. Late in the afternoon, "No," he said, "it ain't so rough for them as plays the 'cordion. They 'as the best of it . . . S'elp me," he added suddenly, "*we're* all 'cordions!" He sniggered thoughtfully, and then burst into a cough that left him panting. "We're nothin' but a bloomin' lot o' 'cordions ourselves," he went on, having got his breath, "an' they play any toon they like on us; and that's 'ow they make their livin'. S'elp me, Dave, we're all 'cordions." And he laughed.

"Um—yus," the other man grunted. And he looked curiously at his mate; for he had never heard that sort of laugh before.

But Joey fondled the conceit, and returned to it from time to time; now aloud, now to himself. "All 'cordions: playin' any toon as is ordered, blimy . . . *Are* we 'cordious? I don't believe we're as much as that . . . no, s'elp me. We're on'y the footlin' little keys; shoved about to soot the toon . . . Little tin keys, blimy . . . footlin' little keys . . . I've bin played on plenty, I 'ave. . . ."

Dave Burge listened with alarm, and tried to talk of other things. But Joey rarely heard him. "I've bin played on plenty, I 'ave," he persisted. "I was played on once by a pal: an' my spring broke."

At nightfall there was more bad luck. They were driven from a likely barn by a leather-gaitered man with a dog, and for some distance no dormitory could be found. Then it was a cut haystack, with a nest near the top and steps to reach it.

In the night Burge was awakened by a clammy hand upon his face. There was a thick mist.

"It's you, Dave ain't it?" Clayton was saying. "Good Gawd, I thought I'd lawst you. What's all this 'ere—not the water is it?—not the dock? I'm soppin' wet."

Burge himself was wet to the skin. He made Joey lie down, and told him to sleep; but a coughing fit prevented that. "It was them 'cordions woke me," he explained when it was over.

So the night put on the shuddering grey of the fore-dawn. And the two tramps left their perch, and betook them, shivering and stamping, to the road.

That morning Joey had short fits of dizziness and faintness. "It's my spring broke," he would say after such an attack. "Bloomin' little tin key put out o' toon." And once he added, "I'm up to one toon, though, now: this 'ere bloomin' Dead March."

Just at the outskirts of the town, where he stopped to cough over a gate, a stout old lady, walking out with a shaggy little dog, gave him a shilling. Dave Burge picked it up as it dropped from his incapable hand, and "Joey, 'ere's a bob," he said, "a lady give it you. You come an' git a drop o' beer."

They carried a twopenny loaf into the tap-room of a small tavern, and Dave had mild ale himself, but saw that Joey was served with stout with a penn'orth of gin in it. Soon the gin and stout reached Joey's head, and drew it to the table. And he slept, leaving the rest of the shilling where it lay.

Dave arose, and stuffed the last of the twopenny loaf into his pocket. He took a piece of chalk from the bagatelle board in the corner, and wrote this on the table:—"*dr. sir, for god sake take him to the work house.*"

Then he gathered up the coppers where they lay and stepped quietly into the street.

THE STRICKEN DOE

Pierre Mille

(1864–   )

TRANSLATED BY VYVYAN HOLLAND

Aᴼᴛᴇʀ ᴅɪɴɪɴɢ ᴀᴛ ʙʀᴀɴᴛᴇs, at the Deux Couronnes, the three men made ready to get into their motor-car. Suddenly a little servant-girl appeared: Béville had left his camera behind in the dining-room: she handed it to him without a word and went back into the hotel.

"She's not very talkative!" he observed.

"Oh!" said the garage attendant, "that's the Breton girl. She only arrived here from Brittany two days ago and she doesn't know a word of French yet."

"The Breton girl?" echoed Béville.

"Why, doesn't Monsieur know?" asked the fellow with a snigger. "In hotels like this, small-town hotels, they always get hold of a Breton girl. For the travellers, in case . . ."

The three laughed. The car started, and a few moments later they were in the open country.

"Do you notice the smell of the air; isn't it delightful?" Béville asked the man next to him.

"Yes," replied Bottiaux. "That's because it's been raining and the earth is still warm and the car is going very fast, so that the air is full of fragrance."

Béville spread himself out, half asleep, a little intoxicated from the champagne he had drunk at dinner and intoxicated, too, by the brisk, warm night air which bathed him, buffeted him, impregnated his body and gave him a feeling of lazy, languid voluptuousness. He was no longer on earth, but floated above it, and from time to time he stretched out his arms as though trying to seize some delectable object of his thoughts.

"Pity there are no women, eh, Jalin?"

But Jalin, the owner of the car, who was driving, did not even turn his head. He had quite enough to do to steer the formidable machine over the road along which they sped, whitened by the light of the huge headlights, and on either side of which the straight lines of the trees formed, as it were, two solid walls, so fast were they travelling.

He merely growled:

"Women? Certainly not!"

All his virility, all his vigour, all his strength as a male and as an intelligent athlete were now concentrated in his brain and in his hands. But, like the others, he spread his nostrils to inhale the perfumes of the summer night, those of the limes, of the mountain-ash and of thousands of little herbs, whose names no one knows, which have been fertilized by the sun-lit hours and during the night enjoy the raptures of that contact within their closed petals. That was enough for him. He merely murmured:

"It's lovely, isn't it?"

Rabbits, roused by the roar of the car, blinded by the headlights and crazy with fear, ran out of the ditches beside the road and sped like black bullets across their path. But suddenly the road was plunged into darkness and the branches above their heads were interspersed with patches of sky. One second before, this machine, this meteor, this furious rushing object seemed to be the sole source of light in the world; and now it was nothing but the centre of a world of darkness, while other objects sprang into life again in the gloom. It was staggeringly sudden and unexpected. Jalin exclaimed:

"Good Heavens, the lights have gone out!"

"Light them again, then," said Bottiaux.

Jalin shrugged his shoulders.

"I'm afraid they're short-circuited. I can't do anything about it."

"Well then, drive by the side-lights."

"Yes, but they're really only parking lights!" replied Jalin.

"They're quite enough for the police. Anyway, drive on! We must get to Paris. I want to sleep in Paris."

Jalin nodded his head. An eighty horse-power car is no more capable of travelling slowly than a race-horse on a track or a destroyer on the seas. However much one tries to hold it back it leaps forward and takes matters into its own hands. Jalin knew the folly of travelling blindly at sixty miles an hour when in two seconds one is upon an object which one first sees sixty yards away. Yet he consented. Like the other two he was feeling too happy, too impetuous, too much lifted out of himself, and too much carried away by the movement of which he thought himself master. It is the same in a cavalry charge: one goes straight to one's death and one cannot prevent oneself from doing so.

The gloom above them and on each side of the road became more intense. They were travelling through a wood, a dark confused mass of serried trees whose trunks and branches seemed to be intertwined. It was dark, so dark that it almost hurt their eyes, and made them want to shade them with their hands, as though to protect them from a sudden shock. And at that very moment, when this alarming condition seemed at its worst, Jalin thought he could distinguish something in front of him, a shadow even darker than the prevailing gloom, a living, terrified shadow. He wrenched his steering-wheel and jammed on the brakes. Anyone who knows about the modern machine has experienced the physical consequences of that sudden stopping, that abrupt deviation of a projectile meant to travel in a straight line; the whole of one's inside seems to displace itself, and one has a sort of bitter forecast of the agony of death. But the car was wide and low-sprung, so it did not turn over but obeyed as best it could, mounted a heap of stones and came shudderingly to a standstill.

"What's the matter?" asked Béville, who had gone quite grey.

Bottiaux jumped out and joined Jalin who was mopping his forehead and kneeling before a pathetic object which still quivered as it lay stretched on the ground, dimly lit by one of the side-lights of the car.

"What a bit of luck," observed Béville who had also got out of the car. "It's only a doe!"

The three men sighed deeply and their voices echoed among the trees as they expressed their relief. With their heavy overcoats, caps and goggles they were strangely alike: fine-looking men, all three bearded, and with an air of wealth, vigour and strength.

"What a bit of luck!" repeated Jalin.

But his laughter, which mingled with that of the others, suddenly ceased. He had just noticed the doe's eyes: they were so soft, so sad and so frightened, full of the puzzled terror of not knowing why it was there and of what had struck it in the night. Poor pretty little thing! Poor little woodland beast, so wild and innocent! They had all killed many others

when they were out hunting with horses and hounds and beaters. But not
like that. It lay mangled, wounded and dying, and quivering so painfully,
with that despairing look still in its suffering eyes.

"We'll have to go back to Brantes," said Jalin. "I can't go on without my
headlights. We can sleep at the hotel where we dined."

He turned the car and they returned to Brantes as slowly as they could.

Gradually the memory of the slaughtered animal was obliterated from
their minds. It might have been a human being, they might themselves
have been killed, indeed they had for a moment been faced by the fear of
death. But they were alive, their blood coursed healthily through their
veins and the world would still be theirs for years and years to come. The
future stretched before them like a colonnade which one can follow endlessly with one's eyes, in an atmosphere of pure happiness.

The door of the Hôtel des Deux Couronnes was shut. Everyone was
asleep. They knocked for a long time before a light appeared. Even then
they had to wait a little longer, because in small towns people have to be
cautious: they want to know with whom they are dealing.

"Look," said Bottiaux, when the door opened at last, "it's the Breton
girl."

In her hand she held one of those tiny lamps, the wicks of which are
protected by small globes, and which for the past twenty years have taken
the place of night-lights. This feeble light gave a pink tinge to one side
of her soft, childish, homely face, and everything else, her dressing-jacket
hurriedly thrown over her rough night-dress, her linen petticoat, her bare
slippered feet were lost in shadow. All that was visible was her sensitive
little face, suspended in the air like a disembodied soul.

"Room?" she asked in rather a husky voice, in the way people do when
they speak a foreign language.

"Yes, sleep; beds, eh? Good beds!" explained Bottiaux.

She lit candles for them, smiled, showed them to their rooms and retired.

But when Béville got to bed he found that he was unable to sleep. He was
feeling too shattered, and still too excited by the fragrance of the night, by
the speed of the car and by that strong feeling of gratitude towards life
which infects everyone who has just escaped a great danger. Then he remembered the words of the garage attendant: "The Breton girl? That's
what she's there for!" and he left his room, bare-footed, and crept noiselessly along the passage.

Béville had noticed where the Breton girl slept; in a kind of lean-to, a
cupboard fixed up on the staircase, between the ground floor and the first
floor. He went straight there, shading his candle with his hand. Yes, that
was the right place: she was sleeping on a common iron bedstead, her hair
loose about her shoulders and one hand beneath her head to raise it as she
had no pillow. All that could be seen of her body was a rounded neck and
the delicate swell of a very young breast. Béville put his hand on her

shoulder and kissed her. He had blown out the candle. The girl woke with a start and put her hands out in an instinctive gesture of self-protection:

"Ma Doué," she said.

But Béville already had her in his arms and she felt his mouth upon hers again. Yes, it was true, she was the Breton girl, she was employed for that, paid for that, thirty francs a month in addition to presents from the guests. And besides, this man was a gentleman. Centuries of domination, almost of slavery, had taught her race that one must always obey "gentlemen," the leaders, the masters; their men followed them to war, their women to bed. So she must submit. Her poor little servile soul dared not protest. Only her body recoiled in horror, because it was still pure. Every virgin defends herself, every virgin is afraid. No doubt this is an instinct which nature has given her so that she must need courage to give herself and that thus she should only give herself from choice and, as it were, as a sacrifice to the man she loves. The Breton girl, humble savage, sold as in ancient days, but even more basely, experienced a feeling of terror. She implored him to let her go, in confused hurried words, in her obscure language, the language spoken on the shores of western seas, the only one she knew; but Béville did not understand.

He never knew why the girl did not return the kisses he gave her before possessing her. Neither did he understand when, a satisfied and yet sadly disappointed male—for such is the punishment of careless, brutal males that his only thought was to leave an offering and to get away—he never understood why a mouth had brushed, not his lips, she would not have dared, but his cheek and his forehead: the caress of a timid child who wanted so much, yes, so much, to be able to imagine the memory of the shadow of true tenderness after the horror of her ravishment. But there was nothing. He just went away and that was all.

Next day at dawn Jalin came and woke his two friends. When Béville came down he had almost forgotten. Happy men have, as it were, no memories. They live in advance and discount their future pleasures daily. If he had thought at all about the events of the night he would merely have felt that he had been rather unkind and, as he knew this, he took care to divert his thoughts into other channels. Moreover, Jalin had already got everything ready for their departure. The bill was paid and the engine of the car was running. He threw his two companions their coats and caps.

"Off we go!"

He backed into the hotel courtyard to enable him to turn before the front door. And at that moment there appeared in the doorway the mis-used slave who had let them in the previous night. She had just come out of her room where she had no doubt lain awake for hours, alone and defiled. She was wearing the same clothes, humble to the point of abject-ness, a rough chemise and a shapeless jacket. She had not done her hair, she was not pretty, even her youth seemed to have become tarnished, and she stared at the three men hopelessly, her eyes full of misery. For the appalling thing that had happened to her and had perhaps left a living result within her, had taken place in inky darkness and she could not tell *which* of the three men it had been. Nor would she ever know.

The motor-car turned, well under control, and shot off. Bottiaux remarked musingly:

"That Breton girl's eyes. . . . What did they remind me of? Oh! yes, they were just like those of that doe last night. Did you see them?"

"No," replied Béville, "I didn't notice."

THE MONKEY'S PAW

W. W. Jacobs
(1863–   )

Without, the night was cold and wet, but in the small parlor of Lakesnam Villa the blinds were drawn and the fire burned brightly. Father and son were at chess, the former, who possessed ideas about the game involving radical changes, putting his king into such sharp and unnecessary perils that it even provoked comment from the white-haired old lady knitting placidly by the fire.

"Hark at the wind," said Mr. White, who, having seen a fatal mistake after it was too late, was amiably desirous of preventing his son from seeing it.

"I'm listening," said the latter, grimly surveying the board as he stretched out his hand. "Check."

"I should hardly think that he'd come tonight," said his father, with his hand poised over the board.

"Mate," replied the son.

"That's the worst of living so far out," bawled Mr. White, with sudden and unlooked-for violence; "of all the beastly, slushy, out-of-the-way places to live in, this is the worst. Pathway's a bog, and the road's a torrent. I don't know what people are thinking about. I suppose because only two houses on the road are let, they think it doesn't matter."

"Never mind, dear," said his wife soothingly; "perhaps you'll win the next one."

Mr. White looked up sharply, just in time to intercept a knowing glance between mother and son. The words died away on his lips, and he hid a guilty grin in his thin gray beard.

"There he is," said Herbert White, as the gate banged to loudly and heavy footsteps came toward the door.

The old man rose with hospitable haste, and opening the door, was heard condoling with the new arrival. The new arrival also condoled with himself, so that Mrs. White said, "Tut, tut!" and coughed gently as her husband entered the room, followed by a tall burly man, beady of eye and rubicund of visage.

"Sergeant-Major Morris," he said, introducing him.

The sergeant-major shook hands, and taking the proffered seat by the fire, watched contentedly while his host got out whisky and tumblers and stood a small copper kettle on the fire.

At the third glass his eyes got brighter, and he began to talk, the little family circle regarding with eager interest this visitor from distant parts, as he squared his broad shoulders in the chair and spoke of strange scenes and doughty deeds, of wars and plagues and strange peoples.

"Twenty-one years of it," said Mr. White, nodding at his wife and son. "When he went away he was a slip of a youth in the warehouse. Now look at him."

"He don't look to have taken much harm," said Mrs. White politely.

"I'd like to go to India myself," said the old man, "just to look round a bit, you know."

"Better where you are," said the sergeant-major, shaking his head. He put down the empty glass and, sighing softly, shook it again.

"I should like to see those old temples and fakirs and jugglers," said the old man. "What was that you started telling me the other day about a monkey's paw or something, Morris?"

"Nothing," said the soldier hastily. "Leastways, nothing worth hearing."

"Monkey's paw?" said Mrs. White curiously.

"Well, it's just a bit of what you might call magic, perhaps," said the sergeant-major off-handedly.

His three listeners leaned forward eagerly. The visitor absent-mindedly put his empty glass to his lips and then set it down again. His host filled it for him.

"To look at," said the sergeant-major, fumbling in his pocket, "it's just an ordinary little paw, dried to a mummy."

He took something out of his pocket and proffered it. Mrs. White drew back with a grimace, but her son, taking it, examined it curiously.

"And what is there special about it?" inquired Mr. White, as he took it from his son and, having examined it, placed it upon the table.

"It had a spell put on it by an old fakir," said the sergeant-major, "a very holy man. He wanted to show that fate ruled people's lives, and that those who interfered with it did so to their sorrow. He put a spell on it so that three separate men could each have three wishes from it."

His manner was so impressive that his hearers were conscious that their light laughter jarred somewhat.

"Well, why don't you have three, sir?" said Herbert White cleverly.

The soldier regarded him in the way that middle age is wont to regard presumptuous youth. "I have," he said quietly, and his blotchy face whitened.

"And did you really have the three wishes granted?" asked Mrs. White.

"I did," said the sergeant-major, and his glass tapped against his strong teeth.

"And has anybody else wished?" inquired the old lady.

"The first man had his three wishes, yes," was the reply. "I don't know what the first two were, but the third was for death. That's how I got the paw."

His tones were so grave that a hush fell upon the group.

"If you've had your three wishes, it's no good to you now, then, Morris," said the old man at last. "What do you keep it for?"

The soldier shook his head. "Fancy, I suppose," he said slowly. "I did have some idea of selling it, but I don't think I will. It has caused enough mischief already. Besides, people won't buy. They think it's a fairy tale, some of them, and those who do think anything of it want to try it first and pay me afterward."

"If you could have another three wishes," said the old man, eyeing him keenly, "would you have them?"

"I don't know," said the other. "I don't know."

He took the paw, and dangling it between his front finger and thumb, suddenly threw it upon the fire. White, with a slight cry, stooped down and snatched it off.

"Better let it burn," said the soldier solemnly.

"If you don't want it, Morris," said the old man, "give it to me."

"I won't," said his friend doggedly. "I threw it on the fire. If you keep it, don't blame me for what happens. Pitch it on the fire again, like a sensible man."

The other shook his head and examined his new possession closely. "How do you do it?" he inquired.

"Hold it up in your right hand and wish aloud," said the sergeant-major, "but I warn you of the consequences."

"Sounds like the *Arabian Nights*," said Mrs. White, as she rose and began to set the supper. "Don't you think you might wish for four pairs of hands for me?"

Her husband drew the talisman from his pocket and then all three burst into laughter as the sergeant-major, with a look of alarm on his face, caught him by the arm.

"If you must wish," he said gruffly, "wish for something sensible."

Mr. White dropped it back into his pocket, and placing chairs, motioned his friend to the table. In the business of supper the talisman was partly forgotten, and afterward the three sat listening in an enthralled fashion to a second installment of the soldier's adventures in India.

"If the tale about the monkey paw is not more truthful than those he has been telling us," said Herbert, as the door closed behind their guest, just in time for him to catch the last train, "we shan't make much out of it."

"Did you give him anything for it, father?" inquired Mrs. White, regarding her husband closely.

"A trifle," said he, coloring slightly. "He didn't want it, but I made him take it. And he pressed me again to throw it away."

"Likely," said Herbert, with pretended horror. "Why, we're going to be rich, and famous, and happy. Wish to be an emperor, father, to begin with; then you can't be henpecked."

He darted round the table, pursued by the maligned Mrs. White armed with an antimacassar.

Mr. White took the paw from his pocket and eyed it dubiously. "I don't know what to wish for, and that's a fact," he said slowly. "It seems to me I've got all I want."

"If you only cleared the house, you'd be quite happy, wouldn't you?" said Herbert, with his hand on his shoulder. "Well, wish for two hundred pounds, then; that'll just do it."

His father, smiling shamefacedly at his own credulity, held up the talisman, as his son, with a solemn face somewhat marred by a wink at his mother, sat down at the piano and struck a few impressive chords.

"I wish for two hundred pounds," said the old man distinctly.

A fine crash from the piano greeted the words, interrupted by a shuddering cry from the old man. His wife and son ran toward him.

"It moved," he cried, with a glance of disgust at the object as it lay on the floor. "As I wished it twisted in my hands like a snake."

"Well, I don't see the money," said his son, as he picked it up and placed it on the table, "and I bet I never shall."

"It must have been your fancy, father," said his wife, regarding him anxiously.

He shook his head. "Never mind, though; there's no harm done, but it gave me a shock all the same."

They sat down by the fire again while the two men finished their pipes. Outside, the wind was higher than ever, and the old man started nervously at the sound of a door banging upstairs. A silence unusual and depressing settled upon all three, which lasted until the old couple rose to retire for the night.

"I expect you'll find the cash tied up in a big bag in the middle of your bed," said Herbert, as he bade them good night, "and something horrible squatting up on top of the wardrobe watching you as you pocket your ill-gotten gains."

In the brightness of the wintry sun next morning as it streamed over the breakfast table Herbert laughed at his fears. There was an air of prosaic wholesomeness about the room which it had lacked on the previous night, and the dirty, shriveled little paw was pitched on the sideboard with a carelessness which betokened no great belief in its virtues.

"I suppose all old soldiers are the same," said Mrs. White. "The idea of our listening to such nonsense! How could wishes be granted in these days? And if they could, how could two hundred pounds hurt you, father?"

"Might drop on his head from the sky," said the frivolous Herbert.

"Morris said the things happened so naturally," said his father, "that you might if you so wished attribute it to coincidence."

"Well, don't break into the money before I come back," said Herbert, as he rose from the table. "I'm afraid it'll turn you into a mean, avaricious man, and we shall have to disown you."

His mother laughed, and following him to the door, watched him down the road, and returning to the breakfast table, was very happy at the expense of her husband's credulity. All of which did not prevent her from scurrying to the door at the postman's knock, nor prevent her from referring somewhat shortly to retired sergeant-majors of bibulous habits when she found that the post brought a tailor's bill.

"Herbert will have some more of his funny remarks, I expect, when he comes home," she said, as they sat at dinner.

"I dare say," said Mr. White, pouring himself out some beer; "but for all that, the thing moved in my hand; that I'll swear to."

"You thought it did," said the old lady soothingly.

"I say it did," replied the other. "There was no thought about it; I had just— What's the matter?"

His wife made no reply. She was watching the mysterious movements of a man outside, who, peering in an undecided fashion at the house, appeared to be trying to make up his mind to enter. In mental connection with the two hundred pounds, she noticed that the stranger was well dressed and wore a silk hat of glossy newness. Three times he paused at the gate, and then walked on again. The fourth time he stood with his hand upon it, and then with sudden resolution flung it open and walked up the path. Mrs. White at the same moment placed her hands behind her, and hurriedly unfastening the strings of her apron, put that useful article of apparel beneath the cushion of her chair.

She brought the stranger, who seemed ill at ease, into the room. He gazed furtively at Mrs. White, and listened in a preoccupied fashion as the old lady apologized for the appearance of the room, and her husband's coat, a garment which he usually reserved for the garden. She then waited as patiently as her sex would permit for him to broach his business, but he was at first strangely silent.

"I—was asked to call," he said at last, and stooped and picked a piece of cotton from his trousers. "I come from Maw and Meggins."

The old lady started. "Is anything the matter?" she asked breathlessly. "Has anything happened to Herbert? What is it? What is it?"

Her husband interposed. "There, there, mother," he said hastily. "Sit down, and don't jump to conclusions. You've not brought bad news, I'm sure, sir," and he eyed the other wistfully.

"I'm sorry——" began the visitor.

"Is he hurt?" demanded the mother.

The visitor bowed in assent. "Badly hurt," he said quietly, "but he is not in any pain."

"Oh, thank God!" said the old woman, clasping her hands. "Thank God for that! Thank——"

She broke off suddenly as the sinister meaning of the assurance dawned upon her and she saw the awful confirmation of her fears in the other's averted face. She caught her breath, and turning to her slower-witted husband, laid her trembling old hand upon his. There was a long silence.

"He was caught in the machinery," said the visitor at length, in a low voice.

"Caught in the machinery," repeated Mr. White, in a dazed fashion, "yes."

He sat staring blankly out at the window, and taking his wife's hand between his own, pressed it as he had been wont to do in their old courting days nearly forty years before.

"He was the only one left to us," he said, turning gently to the visitor. "It is hard."

The other coughed, and rising, walked slowly to the window. "The firm wished me to convey their sincere sympathy with you in your great loss," he said, without looking round. "I beg that you will understand I am only their servant and merely obeying orders."

There was no reply; the old woman's face was white, her eyes staring, and her breath inaudible; on the husband's face was a look such as his friend the sergeant might have carried into his first action.

"I was to say that Maw and Meggins disclaim all responsibility," continued the other. "They admit no liability at all, but in consideration of your son's services they wish to present you with a certain sum as compensation."

Mr. White dropped his wife's hand, and rising to his feet, gazed with a look of horror at his visitor. His dry lips shaped the words, "How much?"

"Two hundred pounds," was the answer.

Unconscious of his wife's shriek, the old man smiled faintly, put out his hands like a sightless man, and dropped, a senseless heap, to the floor.

III

In the huge new cemetery, some two miles distant, the old people buried their dead, and came back to a house steeped in shadow and silence. It was all over so quickly that at first they could hardly realize it, and remained in a state of expectation as though of something else to happen—something else which was to lighten this load, too heavy for old hearts to bear. But the days passed, and expectation gave place to resignation—the hopeless resignation of the old, sometimes miscalled apathy. Sometimes they hardly exchanged a word, for now they had nothing to talk about, and their days were long to weariness.

It was about a week after that that the old man, waking suddenly in the night, stretched out his hand and found himself alone. The room was in darkness, and the sound of subdued weeping came from the window. He raised himself in bed and listened.

"Come back," he said tenderly. "You will be cold."

"It is colder for my son," said the old woman, and wept afresh.

The sound of her sobs died away on his ears. The bed was warm, and his eyes heavy with sleep. He dozed fitfully, and then slept until a sudden wild cry from his wife awoke him with a start.

"The monkey's paw!" she cried wildly. "The monkey's paw!"

He started up in alarm. "Where? Where is it? What's the matter?"

She came stumbling across the room toward him. "I want it," she said quietly. "You've not destroyed it?"

"It's in the parlor, on the bracket," he replied, marveling. "Why?"

She cried and laughed together, and bending over, kissed his cheek.

"I only just thought of it," she said hysterically. "Why didn't I think of it before? Why didn't you think of it?"

"Think of what?" he questioned.

"The other two wishes," she replied rapidly. "We've only had one."

"Was not that enough?" he demanded fiercely.

"No," she cried triumphantly; "we'll have one more. Go down and get it quickly, and wish our boy alive again."

The man sat up in bed and flung the bedclothes from his quaking limbs. "Good God, you are mad!" he cried, aghast.

"Get it," she panted; "get it quickly, and wish— Oh, my boy, my boy!"

Her husband struck a match and lit the candle. "Get back to bed," he said unsteadily. "You don't know what you are saying."

"We had the first wish granted," said the old woman feverishly; "why not the second?"

"A coincidence," stammered the old man.

"Go and get it and wish," cried the old woman, and dragged him toward the door.

He went down in the darkness, and felt his way to the parlor, and then to the mantelpiece. The talisman was in its place, and a horrible fear that the unspoken wish might bring his mutilated son before him ere he could escape from the room seized upon him, and he caught his breath as he found that he had lost the direction of the door. His brow cold with sweat, he felt his way round the table, and groped along the wall until he found himself in the small passage with the unwholesome thing in his hand.

Even his wife's face seemed changed as he entered the room. It was white and expectant, and to his fears seemed to have an unnatural look upon it. He was afraid of her.

"Wish!" she cried, in a strong voice.

"It is foolish and wicked," he faltered.

"Wish!" repeated his wife.

He raised his hand. "I wish my son alive again."

The talisman fell to the floor, and he regarded it shudderingly. Then he sank trembling into a chair as the old woman, with burning eyes, walked to the window and raised the blind.

He sat until he was chilled with the cold, glancing occasionally at the figure of the old woman peering through the window. The candle end, which had burnt below the rim of the china candlestick, was throwing pulsating shadows on the ceiling and walls, until, with a flicker larger than the rest, it expired. The old man, with an unspeakable sense of relief at the failure of the talisman, crept back to his bed, and a minute or two afterward the old woman came silently and apathetically beside him.

Neither spoke, but both lay silently listening to the ticking of the clock. A stair creaked, and a squeaky mouse scurried noisily through the wall. The darkness was oppressive, and after lying for some time screwing up his courage, the husband took the box of matches, and striking one, went downstairs for a candle.

At the foot of the stairs the match went out, and he paused to strike another, and at the same moment a knock, so quiet and stealthy as to be scarcely audible, sounded on the front door.

The matches fell from his hand. He stood motionless, his breath suspended until the knock was repeated. Then he turned and fled swiftly back to his room, and closed the door behind him. A third knock sounded through the house.

"*What's that?*" cried the old woman, starting up.

"A rat," said the old man, in shaking tones—"a rat. It passed me on the stairs."

His wife sat up in bed listening. A loud knock resounded through the house.

"It's Herbert!" she screamed. "It's Herbert!"

She ran to the door, but her husband was before her, and catching her by the arm, held her tightly.

"What are you going to do?" he whispered hoarsely.

"It's my boy; it's Herbert!" she cried, struggling mechanically. "I forgot it was two miles away. What are you holding me for? Let go. I must open the door."

"For God's sake don't let it in," cried the old man, trembling.

"You're afraid of your own son," she cried, struggling. "Let me go. I'm coming, Herbert; I'm coming."

There was another knock, and another. The old woman with a sudden wrench broke free and ran from the room. Her husband followed to the landing, and called after her appealingly as she hurried downstairs. He heard the chain rattle back and the bottom bolt drawn slowly and stiffly from the socket. Then the old woman's voice, strained and panting.

"The bolt," she cried loudly. "Come down. I can't reach it."

But her husband was on his hands and knees groping wildly on the floor in search of the paw. If he could only find it before the thing outside got in. A perfect fusillade of knocks reverberated through the house, and he heard the scraping of a chair as his wife put it down in the passage against the door. He heard the creaking of the bolt as it came slowly back, and at the same moment he found the monkey's paw, and frantically breathed his third and last wish.

The knocking ceased suddenly, although the echoes of it were still in the house. He heard the chair drawn back and the door opened. A cold wind rushed up the staircase, and a long loud wail of disappointment and misery from his wife gave him courage to run down to her side, and then to the gate beyond. The street lamp flickering opposite shone on a quiet and deserted road.

THE COACH

Violet Hunt

(1866–   )

IT was in a part of the country so far north that the summer nights are pale and light and scant of shade, and even when there is no moon, it is not dark. This night for hours the flat, depreciating earth had lain prone under a storm of wind and rain, its patient surface drenched, blanched, smitten into blindness. The tumbled waters of the Firth that splashed on the edges of the plain were daunted by the wind-driven showers; gloomy drops tapped them into sullen acquiescence. Half a mile inland the road to the north was laid and ran with never a house or homestead to break

it, viscous with clay here, shining with quartz there, exact, uncompromising, hedgeless, between its borders of short scant grass. Very seldom
the undeviating line of it passed through a coppice or little clump of
gnarled, ill-conditioned, nameless trees that seemed to lean forward vin-
dictively on either side, snapping their horny fingers at each other, waving
their cantankerous branches as the gusts took them, broke them, and
whirled the fragments of their ruin far away and out of ken, as a kite that a
child has allowed to pass beyond his control. Nor was the white surface of
the road blotted for a single moment, swept and cleared by the play of the
air-currents, surging backwards and forwards, blind, stupid and swelled
with pride of power. Completely out of hand, intriguing but ineffectual
giants, these forces of the sky staggered hither and thither, buffeting all
impartially, instigating the hapless branches at their mercy to wild lashings
of each other, to useless accesses of the spirit of self-destruction. Bending
slavishly under the heavy gusts, each shabby blade of grass by the roadside
rose again and was on the *qui vive* after the rustling tyrants had passed.

It was then, in the succeeding moments of comparative peace, when the
directors of the passionate aërial revolt had managed to call their panting
rabble off for the time, that great perpendicular sheets of rain, like stage
films, slung evenly from the pillars that upbore the heavens, descended and
began moving continuously sideways, like a wall, across the level track. A
sheet of whole water blotted out the tangled border of herbage; the heaps
of stones set at intervals ready for breaking. When the slab of rain had
moved on again, the road, shining out sturdily with its embedded quartz
and milky kneaded clay, lay clear once more. Calm, ordered and tranquil
in the midst of tumult and discord, it pursued its appointed course, edging
off from its sloping, evenly bevelled sides the noisy moorland streams, that
had come jostling each other in their haste to reach it, only to be relegated,
noisily complaining by the unrecognisable camber of the gutter.

At a certain point on the line of way, a tall, spare, respectable-looking
man in a well-fitting grey frock coat stood like a weary, foredone clerk
waiting at the corner of the city street for the omnibus that was to carry
him home to his slippered comfort and sober pipe of peace. The rain
dripped peaceably off the rim of his top hat and ran down his coat collar.
He wore no muffler, but then it was summer—St. John's Eve. He leaned
on an ivory-headed ebony stick of which he seemed fond, and peered, not
very eagerly, along the road, which now—for there was a lull in the storm
—lay in dazzling rain-washed clarity under the struggling moon. He had no
luggage, no umbrella, yet his grey coat looked neat, and his hat shiny.

Far in the distance, from the south, a dark, clumsy object appeared,
labouring slowly along—a coach, of heavy and antique pattern. As soon as
he had sighted it, the passenger's faint interest seemed diminished. With
a bored air of fulfilment, he dropped his eyes and looked down disapprovingly at the clayey mud at his feet, although, indeed, the sticky substance

did not appear to have marred the exquisite polish of his shoes. His palm rested composedly on the ivory knob of his trusty stick, as it were the hand of an old friend.

With some signs of difficult going, but no noise of straining or grinding, the coach drew up in front of the expectant passenger. He looked up quietly, and recognised it as the vehicle wherein it was appointed that he should travel for a stage, or two, maybe. All was correct, the coachman, grave, business-like, headless as of usage, the horses long-tailed, black, conventional. . . .

The door opened noiselessly, and the step was let down. Nodding at the coachman, he delicately put his foot on to it; he observed for the benefit of the persons inside:

"I see old Joe on the box in his official trim. Rather unnecessary, all this ceremony, I venture to think! A few yokels and old women to impress, if indeed, anyone not positively obliged, is abroad on a night like this! For form's sake, I suppose!"

He took his seat next the window. The four occupants of the coach nodded, some stiffly, but not unkindly. He returned their salutations in a way that showed him unacquainted with any of them.

Sitting next to him was a woman evidently of fashion. Her heavy and valuable furs were cast on one side, to show a wide breast covered with jewels. She wore two enamelled and jewel-encrusted watches pinned to her bosom as a mark for thieves to covet. It was foolish of her, the man in the grey frock coat thought. Her yellow wig was much awry. Her eyes were weak, stained, and fearful, and she aided their vision with a diamond-beset pince-nez. Now and again she glanced over her left shoulder as if in alarm, and at such times grasped her gold-net reticule feverishly. She was obviously a rich woman, a first-class, train-de-luxe, passenger.

The woman opposite her belonged, he considered, to the people, hard-featured, worn with a life of sordid toil and calculation, but withal stout and motherly, a figure to inspire the fullest confidence. She wore a black bonnet with strings, and black silk gloves heavily darned. Round her sunken white collar, a golden gleam of watch-chain was now and then discernible.

At the other end of the coach, squeezed up into the corner where the vacillating light of the lamp hung from the roof least penetrated, a neat, sharp-featured man nestled or hid. His forehead retreated, and his bowler hat was set far back, lending him an air of folly and congenital weakness which his long, cold, clever nose set in a face white as old enamel, could not dissipate.

But the man whom the gentleman in the frock coat took to among his casual fellow-travellers was the one directly opposite him, a rough, hearty creature. Alone of all the taciturn coachful he seemed disposed to enter into conversation which might enliven the dreariness entailed by this old-fashioned mode of travelling. Gay talk might help to drown the dashing of the waters of the Firth lying close on the right hand of the road they were even now traversing, and the ugly roar of the wind and rain against the windows. This—by comparison—cheerful fellow was dressed in a shabby suit of corduroys. He wore no collar; a twisted red cotton handkerchief was wound tightly round his thick squat neck. His little mean eyes swinish, but twinkling good-humouredly, stared enviously at the gentleman's stiff collar and the delicate grey tones of his suiting. Crossing and uncrossing his creasy legs, in the unusual effort of conviviality, the man in corduroys addressed the man in the frock coat:

"Well, mate! They've chosen a rare rough night to shift us on! Orders from headquarters, I suppose? I've been here nigh on a year and never set eyes on my boss!"

"We used to call him God the Father," said the elder man rather coldly. . . . "But there is no earthly sense in questioning the arrangements of Him who orders our ways down here; we can only fall in with them. Perhaps you do not as yet conceive fully of the silent impelling force that sways us. It is the same in the world we have left, only that there we were only concerned with the titles and standing of our 'boss,' as you call Him, and obeyed His laws not a whit. I must say I consider this system of yearly soul transference that we have to submit to, very unsettling and productive of restlessness among us—a mere survival of superstition—tiresome and affected to my mind. But one merit it has; one sees something of the under world travelling about as we do, and meeting chance, perhaps kindred spirits on the road. One realises, too, that Hades is not quite as grey, shall I say, as it is painted! I fear," he added, with a slight touch of class hauteur, "you do not quite follow me?"

"Oh, yes, master, I do," eagerly replied the fellow-traveller to whom he chose to address his monologue. "Since I've been dead, I have learned the meaning of many things. I turn up my nose at nothing these days. I always neglected my schooling, but now I tell you I try to make up for lost time. From a rough sort of fellow that I was, with not an idea in my head beyond my beer and my prog, I have come to take my part in the whole of knowledge. It was all mine before, so to speak, but I didn't trouble to put my hand out for it. Didn't care, didn't listen to Miss that taught me, or to Parson, either. Parson had some good ideas too, as I've come to know, though his Vice isn't exactly our Vice now, in a manner of speaking. If God Almighty made us, why did He make us, even in parts, bad? That's what I want to know, and I'll know that when I've been dead a bit longer. Why did He give me rotten teeth so that I couldn't chew properly and didn't care for my food and liked drink better? It's dirt and digestion makes drinking and devilry, I say."

The smart woman interrupted him with a kind of languid eagerness, exclaiming:

"I must say I agree with you. Since the pestle fell on my shoulder in that lonely villa at Monte, I have realised what the dreadful gambling fever may lead to. It had turned those two who wanted my guilty gains into wild beasts! To tell the truth, I ought never to have accepted their invitation to luncheon, never tempted them with my display of jewels! . . . And alas! I was tarred with the same stick: I gambled too——"

She rummaged in her reticule and fished out a ticket for the Rooms at Monte Carlo.

"I always call that the ticket for my execution. I had earned it. And although my executioners were rather brutal, they will attain unto this place more easily than I did, and will have hardly any pain, I am told. The arm of the law is gentle, compared with that of Sir——"

The man in the grey frock coat raised his finger warningly. "No names, I beg. One of our little conventions. . . . !"

"Have a drop?" said the calm motherly woman to the excited fine lady. "Your wound is recent, isn't it? Yours was a very severe case! A bloody murder, I call it, if ever there was one, and clumsy at that! And you only passive, which is always so much harder, they say! I can't tell, for I was what you may call an active party. They don't seem to mind mixing, them that looks after us here! Lump us all together—in travelling, at any rate! Though when I think of what I was actually turned off for, well—the way I look at it, what I did was a positive benefit to Society, and some sections of Society knew it, too, and would have liked to preserve my life."

"But what, Madam, if I may ask, was your little difficulty?"

"It is called, I believe, baby farming," she replied off-handedly, receiving her flask back from the smart woman and stowing it away in a capacious pocket. A shudder like a ripple on a rain-swept stream came over her hearers, with the exception of the thin man in the far corner, who preserved his calm. Raising his sunken chin, he observed the lady with some interest. But the gentleman in grey apologised.

"Excuse us, Madam. A remnant of old-world squeamishness, uncontrollable by us for the moment. Though, if you would, perhaps you could somewhat dissipate our preconceived notions of your profession, by explaining clearly your ancient point of view."

"Delighted, I'm sure," she answered. "Funny, though, how seriously you all take it, even here! The feeling against my profession seems as absurdly strong below as it was above. I was hooted as I left the court, I recollect. It annoyed me then considerably. I thought them that hooted had more need to be grateful to me if all was known and paid for. I saved their pockets for them and their lovely honour too. They knew they had to thank me for that, and for the rest, Lord! what did they care? They went on, bless 'em, raising up seed for me to mow down as soon as its head came above ground, and welcome! Sly dogs, no thanks from them! But those shivering, shrinking women that came to me, some of them hardly out of their teens, some of them so delicate they had no right to have a baby at all! Ah, if only I hadn't let myself take their money it would have been a work of what they call philanthropy. But I had to live, then. Now that one is relieved of that duty one has time to think it out. But Lord!—Society, to cry shame on me! They might as well hang any other useful public servant, like dustmen, rat-catchers, and such-like ridders of pests. Good old Herod, that I used to hear about at school, knew what he was doing when he cleared off all those useless Innocents! He was the first baby farmer, I guess."

"You take large ground, Madam," said the man in the frock coat.

"And I have the right," said she, her determined chin pointing from its rolls of fat, in her eagerness. "You men ought to know it, and you do well enough, when you're honest with yourselves. I was only the 'scape-goat,' and took on me the little sins of the race. It's an easy job enough, what I did, but there's few have the stomach for it. Not that you need call it dirty work neither! Just stand by and leave 'em alone—to girn and bleat and squinny and die."

"No blood, eh?" the man in the corner said suddenly. "I like blood."

"What a fine night it has turned!" said the man in the grey frock coat, raising the window and putting his head out of it. . . . "Something rather uncanny, eh, about that man?" he remarked half to himself, half to his friend in corduroys.

"Take your head in," said the latter, almost affectionately, "or you'll be catching cold, and you've a nasty scar on your neck that I could see as you leaned forward, and which you oughtn't to go getting the cold into."

"Oh, that!" said the other with complacence, sitting down again, but averting his gaze carefully from the man in the corner, for whom he seemed to feel a repulsion as marked as was his preference for his cheerful *vis-à-vis*. "That! That's actually the scar of the blow that killed me. A fearful gash! He was a powerful man that dealt it. He got me, of course, from behind. I never even saw him. I was drafted off here *at once,* his hand had been so sure." He felt nervously in his pockets. "I have a foulard somewhere, but I am apt to mislay it. . . ."

"You should do like me, have a good strong handkercher and knot it round your neck firm. I've got a mark of sorts on my neck too, but it isn't an open wound—never was," the bluff man sniggered. "It is sheer vanity with me, but I don't care to have it seen. It goes well all round, mine does—done by a rope, eh!"

He paused and nodded slyly. "For killing a toff. Nice old gentleman he seemed, too, but I hadn't much time to look at him. Had to get to work——"

He was rudely interrupted by a cry of pleasure from the baby farmer.

"Lord!" she cried, "do I see another conveyance coming on this lonely road? I do 'ope so. I'm one for seeing plenty of people. I always like a crowd, and I must tell you, this sort of humdrum jogging along was beginning to get on my nerves."

They all, except the man in the corner, jerked themselves round, and peered through the glass panes behind them.

A dark object, plainly outlined in the clear moonlight which now lit up the heavens, where heavy masses of cloud had until now obscured its effulgence, was plainly visible. It blotted the ribbon of white that lay in front of them. . . . Nearer and nearer it came. All heads were craned at the windows of the coach. . . . Now it was seen to be a high-hung dog-cart, of the most modern pattern, drawn by a little mettled pony, and containing two slight young girls. . . . The one that drove held the ribbons in hands that were covered with white doe-skin gloves, and which looked immense in the pallid moonshine. . . .

"What an excitement!" said the stout woman. "We shall pass them. Some member of one of the country families about here, I suppose."

"I hope—for all things considering, I'm not a blood-thirsty man"—the man in corduroys murmured, "that we're not a-going to give them a shock! Bound to, when we meet them plumb like this! 'Orses mostly can't abide the sight of the likes of us, no more than they could those nasty motors when they first came in. And we're worse than motors—they seem to smell us out at once for what we are!"

"If you do really think that pony is likely to swerve," said the man in the grey suit, anxiously, "would it be of any use our asking old Diggory to drive more slowly and humour them?"

"Couldn't go no slower than we are!" replied the man in corduroys. "Besides, it's not the pace that kills! I'll bet you that pony's all of a sweat already!"

The dog-cart approached. The faces of the two young women were discernible—white—blanched with fear. It may have been the effect of the strong moonlight, but there was no doubt that they were disturbed, and that the girl who was driving fully realised the necessity of controlling the pony, whose nostrils were quivering, and on whose sides foam appeared in white swathes. . . .

"It won't pass us!" said the man in the corner, speaking suddenly. He rubbed his hands slowly one over the other. "There will be blood!"

"For goodness' sake stop gloating like that!" said the stout woman. "It turns my stomach to hear you. Wherever can you have come from, I wonder? 'Tisn't manners . . . I say, can't we hail them?" she inquired of the man in grey. "All at once give one big shout!"

"They wouldn't be able to hear us," he replied, shaking his head sadly. "You must not forget that we are ghosts. We are not really here."

"Ay, and that's what the beasts know!" cried the man in corduroys. He jumped about on his seat. "The 'oss won't be able to stand it. That kid'll not be able to hold him in. . . ."

"They're on us!" screamed the smart woman. "Oh, my God! Do we have to sit still and see it?" She covered her eyes with her hands.

"Yes, Missus, I reckon you have, and what's more, run away after like any shoffer that's killed his man and left him lying in the roadside. Old Diggory's got his orders."

The snorting of the pony was now audible. The coachful of ghosts distinctly saw the lather of foam dropping from its jaws. They were able, some of them, to realise the agonised tension of one girl's hands, pulling for all she was worth, and the scared sideways twist of her forcedly inactive companion. Alone the disc of the yellow carriage-lamp glared, immovable. . . .

Then it flew down, and was extinguished. There was a crash—a convulsion—and the great road to the north lay clear again.

The Coach of Death rolled on remorselessly past a black heap that filled the ditch on one side. It lay quite still, after that first almost human leap and heave. . . .

The smart woman fainted, or appeared to do so. The baby farmer sat quivering in her fat.

"But it's iniquitous!" exclaimed the man in grey, turning round from the window, his eyes wet—"to leave them behind like that—without a word of inquiry, when it's our conveyance has done all the mischief!"

His friend in corduroys tried to soothe him. "We ain't to blame, sir, don't you think it!" he repeated. "As you said to the lady, we aren't really here!"

"That is small consolation to a man of honour," the old man said sadly. "Still, as you say, we are but tools——"

He devoted himself to the smart woman, who revived a little under his civil ministrations.

"After all," she said, "aren't we somehow or other all in the same boat? I shouldn't be surprised if those two nice girls didn't join us at the next stage? If they do, we'll make them tell us how they felt when they first saw the coachful of ghosts coming down on them. They're certainly dead, for they were both pitched into the ditch with the cart and horse on top of them. Did anybody see what became of the horse? No. . . . Well, we must settle down to dullness again, I am afraid, or, suppose, to while away the time we all started to tell each other the story of how we came to be here? A lively tale might cheer us all up, after the accident."

"Agreed, Madam, heartily for my part," said the man in grey, "though my own story is very humdrum, and not in the least amusing. You want, of course, an account of the particular accident that sent me here. Very well! But, ladies first! Will you not begin, Madam?"

She tossed her head with an affected air.

"My story, perhaps," she insinuated with modesty, "might not be very new to you. It was in all the papers so recently."

"That will not affect me," he answered, "for if, as I presume, it was a murder case, I never read them."

"I read yours then, Missus, I expect," said the man in corduroys. "I generally get the wife to read them out to me—anything spicy."

"And yet the people that did it are not hanged yet, if, indeed, they ever are, poor souls! I am quite anxious," said the smart woman, "to see how it goes. If the pair are really sent here, I suppose I shall be running up against them some night or other on one of these transference parties. It will be very interesting. But"—she leaned across to the baby farmer—"could we not persuade you to give us some of your—nursery experiences, Madam?"

"There's not much story about the drowning of a litter of squalling puppies or whining kittens," said that lady shortly, "we want something livelier —more personal, if I may say so. From a remark that gentleman in the corner let drop a little while ago, I fancy his reminiscences would be quite worth hearing, as good as a shilling shocker."

"My story," replied the individual thus pointedly addressed, "is impossible, frankly impossible."

"Indecent, do you mean?" The smart woman's eyes shone. "Oh, let us have it. You can veil it, can't you?"

"Have you ever heard of mental degenerates?" he asked her compassionately. "I was one. I was called mad—a simple way of expressing it. I was a chemist. I dissected neatly enough, too, like a regular butcher. They did quite right to destroy me."

His head dropped, and he seemed disinclined to say more, but the smart woman persisted:

"But the details——?"

"Are purely medical, Ma'am. Not without a pathological interest, I may say. Interesting at least to men of science. The"—he named a daily paper much in vogue at that time—"made a good deal of the strong sense of artistry—of contrast—the morbid warp inherent in the executant——"

His head sank again on his chest.

"I do believe," said the baby farmer, nudging the smart woman, "that we shall find he's the man who killed his sweetheart and then carefully tied her poor inside all into true lover's knots with sky-blue ribbon. Artist, indeed! They're common enough colours—blue and red——"

"Disgusting!" The delicate lady from Monte Carlo shuddered, and turning coldly away, joined in the petition proffered by the other ghosts to the breezy man in corduroys to relate his experiences.

"Oh, I'll tell you how I came to join you and welcome!" he said, rolling his huge neck about in its setting of red cotton. "Well, to begin with, I was drunk. Equally, of course, I was hard up. My missus—she's married again, by the way, blast her!—was always nagging me to do something for her and the kids. I did. Nation's taking care of them now, along of what I did. Work, she meant, but that was only by the way. I did choose to take on a job, though, on a rich man's estate, building some kind of Folly, lots of glass and that, working away day and night by naphtha flares, you know. He was one of those men, you know the sort, that has more money than a man can properly spend, and feels quite sick about it, and says so, in interviews and so on, in the papers a working man reads. That's the mischief. He was always giving away chunks of money to charities and libraries and that sort of useless lumber, but none of it ever seemed to come the way of those that were in real need of it. They said the money had got on his nerves, and would not let him sleep o' nights, and that he was afraid by day and went about with a loaded stick and I don't know what all. And he was looked after by detectives, at one time, so the papers said—again the papers, putting things in people's heads, as it's their way! So one blessed evening I was very low—funds and all, and my missus and the kids hollering and complaining as they always do when luck's bad. Lord bless them, they never thought as they were 'citing their man to murder. Women never do think. And going out with their snivelling in my ears, I passed the station where he landed every evening after his day in town, and I happened to see him come out of the train and send away his motor that was awaiting for him all regular, and start out to walk 'ome alone by a short cut across a little plantation there was, very thick and dark, just the place for a murder. Well—I told you I was half drunk—I raced home and got something to do it with—our meat chopper——"

The old man opposite put his hand nervously to the back of his neck.

"Ay, Mister, it takes you just there, does it? You look a regular bundle of nerves, you do. Well, as I was saying, I went round by a short cut that I happened to know of, and got in front of him and hid in the hedge. Ten mortal minutes I waited for my man to come by. Lord, how my hand did tremble! I'd have knocked off for twopence. I was nervous as a cat, but all the same it didn't prevent me from striking out for wife and children with a will when my chance came. I caught him behind with my chopper, and he fell like a log. Never lifted a hand to defend himself—hadn't got any gumph. Ladies dear, I don't suppose I hurt him much, for he never even cried out when I struck or groaned when it was done. Then I looked him over, turned out his pockets and collared his watch and season ticket and seals and money. Money—hah!—I had been fairly done over that. Would you believe it of a rich fellow like him, he hadn't got more than the change of a sovereign on him?"

"Shame!" ejaculated the taciturn man in the corner.

"I admit it was hard on you," the man in grey observed kindly. "Very hard, for I believe the retribution came all too quickly. You foolishly left your family chopper about to identify you, and were apprehended at once by our excellent rural police. Yet the law is so dilatory that you lay in gaol a whole year before you were free to join your victim here?"

"Right you are, mate. Yes, I swung for it, sure enough. Short and sweet it was once I stood on the drop, but it still makes my poor old throat ache to think of it. . . ."

He wriggled and twisted his neck in its ruddy cincture. . . .

"Now, governor, I'm done, and if you've no objection we'd all like to hear how you came by that ugly gash of yours? It wasn't no rope did that. Common or garden murder, I'll be bound."

"Certainly, my man, it was a murder—a murder most *apropos.* The circumstances were peculiar. I have often longed to get the ear of the jury who tried a man for relieving me of my light purse and intolerably heavy life, and tell them—the whole hard-working, conscientious twelve of them, trying their best to avenge my wrongs—my own proper feelings, surely no negligible factor in the case! They could not guess, these ignorant living men, whose eyes had not yet been opened by death to a due sense of the proportions of things—that I bore the poor creature no malice, but instead was actually grateful for his skilful surgery that had severed the life-cord that wearied me, so neatly and completely."

"It isn't everyone would take it like that!" remarked the smart woman. "Yet that is, more or less, how I feel about these things myself. Only in my case it is impossible to speak of skilful surgery! I was so disgracefully cut up, I couldn't possibly have worn a low dress again!"

"Have you ever heard," said the man in grey thoughtfully, "of the Greek story of the Gold of Rhampsinitos, and the cellar he built to store it in? According to the modern system, *my* gold was hoarded in my brain, where fat assets and sordid securities bred and bred all day long. The laws that govern wealth are hard. You must give it, devise it, you must not allow it to be taken. But for my part I would have welcomed the two sons of the master builder who broke into the Greek King's Treasure House. In the strong-room of my brain it lodged. With one careless calculation, one stroke of a pen, I could make money breed money there to madden me. I was lonely, too. I had no wife to divide my responsibilities. I dared approach no woman in the way of love—I did not choose to be loved for my cheque-signing powers. I was not loved at all. I was hated. Unrighteous things were done in my name, by the greedy husbandmen of my load of money. Then I was told that I went in danger of my life, and I condescended to take care of that—for a time—only for a time!

"One dark winter evening—I forget what had happened during the day, what fresh instance of turpitude or greed had come before me—I was so revolted that I kicked away all the puling safeguards by which my agents guarded their best asset of all, and gave the rein to my instinct. I disregarded precautions of every sort—with the exception of my faithful loaded stick, and the carrying of that had come to be a mere matter of habit with me—and I walked home from the station alone, up to my big house and good dinner which I hoped—nay, I almost knew—that I should not be alive to eat. And indeed, as luck would have it, on that night of all nights the trap was set for me, the death-dealer was waiting—he took me on at once. I got my desire—kind, speedy, merciful, violent Death. I never even saw the face of my deliverer."

"By George!" softly swore the man in corduroys. "This beats all. Are you sure you aren't kidding us?"

"No indeed, that is exactly how I felt about it, and if I had known of knowledge, as I knew of instinct, what was going to happen I would have thought to realize some of my wealth before setting out to walk through that wood, and made it more worth the honest fellow's while. But as you are aware, a millionaire does not carry portable gold about with him, and my cheque-book which I had on me would, of course, be of no use to him. Alas, all the poor devil got for his pains was exactly nineteen shillings and eleven pence. I had changed a sovereign at the bookstall to buy a paper, and out of habit, had waited for the change."

The man in corduroys had rent the red handkerchief fiercely from his neck, and now made as if to tear it across his knee.

"Why, governor," he exclaimed passionately, "do you mean to say it was through you that I got this here"—he put both hands behind his head and interlocked them—"in return for giving you that there cut at the back of your neck? Well, how things do come about, to be sure!"

"Gently, my man!" the elder soothed him. "Don't be so melodramatic about a very ordinary coincidence. See, the ladies are quite upset. It doesn't do to allow oneself to get excited here—it's not in the rules. If I had made the little discovery you have done, I don't think—no, I really don't think I would have made it public. This undue exhibition of emotion of yours strikes me as belonging to the vulgar world we have all left. But since you have allowed it to come out, and everyone is now aware of the peculiar relation in which we stand to each other, you must let me tender you my best thanks, as to a most skilful and firm operator, and believe me to be truly grateful to you for your services in the past."

"Quite the old school!" said the smart woman.

"I must say, sir, I consider you the real gentleman," said the baby farmer.

"I *am* a gentleman."

"And a fairly accommodating one!" said the rough man, wiping his brow where, however, no sweat was. "It isn't every man as would give thanks for being scragged!"

"Every man isn't a millionaire," said his victim calmly.

The smart woman, leaning forward, tapped the old gentleman amiably with her jewelled pince-nez.

"We belong to the same world, I perceive," she said, "and I am quite able to understand your refined feeling. It is as I said in my own case. Indeed if those two good people, who shall be nameless, had only dealt with me a little more gently, I don't know that I should not forgive them absolutely. I shall at any rate be perfectly civil when I do meet them—only perhaps a *little* distant. But that Monte Carlo existence I was leading when they interrupted it, was really becoming intolerable! Glare, noise, glitter, fever—that heartless, blue, laughing sea they talk of in the railway advertisements——"

The baby farmer, left out in this elegant discussion, obviously took no pleasure in it, but staring straight before her, muttered sulkily:

"Cote d'Azur and Pentonville! There's some little difference, isn't there, between one life and the other? Yet I enjoyed my life I did, and as for gratitude, I can't say as I see all those blessed infants a-coming up to me, and slobbering me for what I did for 'em. I may meet them one of these days, but they'll not notice me. 'Tisn't in human nature. Their mothers thanked me before-hand, in cash, for what I was a-going to do. Lord, what's a rickety baby more or less? I say, we're slowing up! Going to stop perhaps, and a good thing too!"

"Yes," continued the man in the grey frock coat, "I cordially thank the man who rid me with one clean blow of my wretched life. A skilled workman is worthy of his hire."

"Mercy," muttered the baby farmer. "Is he never going to stop? If it was for nothing else he ought to have got scragged for being a bore!"

But being fully wound up, though in the excitement of arriving at the depot no one was attending, the man in grey continued, "Suicide I had thought of, but abhorred, though on my soul I had nearly come to that, and then it was merely a question of courage—you spoke truly, sir. Mine was a thin, pusillanimous nature, as you said. You came by, a kind Samaritan, and sacrificed your own good life freely to rid me of my wretched one. I think I told you that when you were being tried, I followed urgently all the details of the trial, and made interest with the authorities here to allow me to appear to the judge—or the foreman of the jury—in their sleep, say— and instil some inkling of the true state of my feeling towards you. I do not know, however, if you would have thanked me, for life may have been no sweeter to you than it was to me—you spoke of an uncongenial helpmate, I think? Still one never knows. I might have been the means of procuring you some good years yet in the full exercise of your vigour and remarkable decision of character. But it was not to be. You followed me here after an interval, and now we have met, face to face. The introduction on that dark night was worth nothing. I like your face. We shall probably never meet again—I, or you, may be on a different round next year, so I am the more glad of this opportunity of opening my mind to you on a delicate subject, perhaps, but one that has always been very near my heart. By the way"—he lifted his stick with its shining ivory crown—"did you notice this? You read the papers, you said, and they told you it was heavily weighted and that I carried it always as a precaution. Well, on that night perhaps you were too hurried to notice?—I never used it. Accept it now, will you, as a memento? . . . I think, from these truly unearthly bumpings, that we have come to our journey's end? Yes, I am right, the coachman has got down from his perch and taken his head under his arm. . . . We part.

Mesdames, I salute you. Again, sir"—he addressed himself very particularly to the shamefaced man in corduroys—"farewell. Very pleased to have met you!"

The coach had drawn up in the semblance of an inn yard, and one by one the passengers faded away into the distance. The old man was the last to get out carefully, when a pale, proud woman's face, shining up from where she stood by the step, fixed his weary eyes. She was an intending passenger, and she was alone. She wore white doe-skin gloves, but no hat. Unusual, he fancied, in a woman of her class. On looking closer, he saw that she had a hat, but that it hung over her shoulder by an elastic, and was much battered and destroyed. He decided to speak to her:

"You are the lady we killed, I think?" he asked gently.

She acknowledged with a bow that it was so.

"We could none of us do anything," he apologised, "or—I hope you will believe——"

"Certainly, sir, it was no fault of yours, or indeed of the company's, I am sure. The accident was inevitable!" so she assured him, smiling faintly. He looked at her kindly. There was blood on her hair; his eyes were good, he was able to convince himself. . . . "But Rory—our pony—never can pass things, at the best of times, and the look of your conveyance was certainly rather unusual. And at that time of night we rarely meet anything on the Great North Road. We chose that time on purpose, my sister and I—we had been staying away for a week with friends, and we were going home. When we saw you coming, Lucy said, half in jest—she is older than I—'Suppose that thing in front were the Coach of Death the foolish country people talk about? They say it travels this way once a year, with its cargo of souls, on St. John's Eve.' I bade her not be superstitious, but I confess I thought the vehicle looked odd myself, and I did wonder how Rory would stand it. When it came near I saw distinctly that the coachman was headless, and I laughingly told my sister so. She bade me not disturb her, for death coach or live coach, she meant to do her best to get Rory past it. She failed——"

The man in grey looked nervously around. He was alone with the young lady in the dull inn yard. The headless coachman was preparing to ascend to the box seat again. . . .

"Where is your sister now?" he inquired.

"She lies at the bottom of the ditch. Rory has galloped home. She fell on her head, but she is still alive. When they find her in the morning, she will be dead, I know that. For now I know all things. I am at peace. You need have no care for me. . . ."

"Let me at least put you into the coach," he begged. "And you will prefer the corner seat?" . . .

She took it; he went on:

"It looks, however, as if you were going to have all the accommodation to yourself, for this stage at all events."

He raised his hat; she bowed.

"I am grieved that I cannot have the pleasure—that I cannot offer to accompany you, but I have my marching orders. . . ."

He raised his hat again. . . . The coach moved on out of the yard. Soon it was lost in the mists. . . . The summer dawn was just breaking.

Invergordon, September, 1906.

THE LAST VISIT

Tristan Bernard

(1866–   )

TRANSLATED BY VYVYAN HOLLAND

You MAY LEAVE my petticoat for the moment, Madame Léon. You can finish it tomorrow. I want you to work on my husband's overcoat today; we are going out this evening and there'll be no end of a fuss if the lining of the sleeve is still torn. I'll give you some satinette which I've been saving up for a skirt for myself. But what's the matter, Madame Léon? You look as if you had been crying."

"It's nothing, madame."

"Come! Tell me what the matter is."

"I'd rather not talk about it, madame. It's four years ago today that my poor son . . ."

"You lost your boy?"

"Yes, and in what a dreadful way!"

"I'm not asking you . . ."

"You've no doubt heard of Hucheux? That's my real name, madame. It doesn't matter much in Paris, because it all took place in the Provinces, in my native town. I must tell you that I was married at the age of twenty to a man a year younger than myself."

"You loved each other?"

"No, madame. We were cousins. We just got married; the idea struck us one day because we knew each other so well; we liked each other as cousins. We would never have thought of getting married otherwise. He was a nice, rather plump boy, who never talked very much. When we had been married for six weeks he died of a chill. I was pregnant at the time and bore a child eight months afterwards.

"My husband caught pneumonia at the funeral of his aunt, who had a draper's shop in the town in which we lived. So I took the shop on in order to have some sort of position, being a woman alone, rather than go out and sew for people. And I set about bringing up my child myself, without marrying again, which I could have done easily. There were three fellows after me, telling me I was pretty and asking me to marry them. One, indeed, was a quarter-master sergeant in the Army Postal Service, who made an extra forty francs a month doing clerical work for a butcher.

"My boy grew up sturdily. I sent him to school. He had beautiful manners and was clever, madame, always being first in arithmetic and hand-writing. Up to the age of eighteen he never gave me a moment's worry. He never went out and was always reading. I thought that this was a good thing and would keep him on the right path. Also, it appeared that so far as affairs with women were concerned, he took after his father, a rather quiet man who knew no more than I did when we were married. And then suddenly, madame, he met a lady at the house of one of his friends. She was the wife of a local tradesman.

"One day he came to me and said: 'Mother, I simply must have four thousand francs.' He knew I had a little money put by. Naturally I asked him what he wanted it for. He wouldn't tell me at first, but in the end he told me the whole story, namely that he was having an affair with this lady and that her husband was about to go bankrupt and that he wanted to avoid this. Naturally, I refused. Whereupon he made a terrible scene. But what was I to do? I didn't want to give him such a large sum of money. I was keeping it for him. Besides, how was I to know where it would all end? And you can't give money away like that.

"'If that's it,' he said, 'I'll go and ask my god-father for it.'

"His god-father lived outside the town in the last house in the suburbs. He was a retired barrel-manufacturer, nearly eighty years of age.

"'I know your god-father,' I told him. 'He won't lend you a penny, my son. You'll only put him against you, which might be awkward.'

"Well, he went all the same. It was just after dinner. I waited up for him until eleven that night. Then I went to bed.

"I was a little anxious. But he had slept out on two or three previous occasions. Next morning came, and still no Henri. It was market day and I went to the market-square with my basket. And there I heard two old country-women talking, two market-gardeners.

"'Yes,' said one, 'he can't have put up much of a fight. An old man like him, over a hundred years of age. He hit him on the head with a brass candlestick.'

"'It was probably some tramp who thought the old barrel-maker must have some money hidden away somewhere.'

"When I heard this, madame, I don't know how I managed to keep on my legs. My limbs shook all over. I no longer realised where I was. I could hear the ceaseless din made by the fowls and the women. Then I heard some other people talking about it. They said that a soldier on furlough had committed the crime and that he was already under lock and key. Then I felt happy, happier than I had ever felt before. The market noises became sweet music in my ears. The smell of butter and chickens was delicious to me.

"I couldn't even make up my mind whether to buy a cabbage or some carrots. Then I heard other people discussing the same story and this time a girl, the servant at the chemist's shop, said that no one knew who had committed the crime. So I interrupted with:

" 'It was a soldier on furlough.'

" 'Oh, no!' replied the girl. 'They certainly arrested a soldier. But they released him almost at once. He was able to explain his movements at the time the crime was committed!'

"I returned home without buying anything. My mind was a blank. My legs were like water and I felt sick and giddy. But I didn't know whether I was unhappy or calm. And when I went into my boy's room, madame, what did I see? Henri washing his overcoat in a basin of water placed on the floor. I began to cry and to scream like a lunatic. He cried, too, and told me to be quiet.

" 'What have you done, Henri?'

"And I went on crying: I cried as I am crying now."

"And weren't you at all afraid of him? Weren't you rather repelled?"

"Of my own child, madame? Oh, how unhappy I felt! He stood there quietly, without thinking of saving himself from the police. It was I who told him to go away. But he couldn't go by train. He was a good cyclist, but he had sold his bicycle for that woman, so I gave him some money to buy another and enough for him to live on for some time. He kissed me and left me to hide his clothes. They were not stained but they were wet and people might have asked why he had used soap and water for things which are usually sent to the cleaners. That night I buried them in the garden.

"I saw no one until the next day, when two men from the police-station came to enquire about my son. The superintendent came too and he searched everywhere but he didn't find anything. I told them that my son had left several days before. And you should have seen how calm I was! I should never have believed that I, who am so shy of talking to people, should have been capable of lying so brazenly to these gentlemen. But since I had to, I did so.

"I thought that everything would be all right. There was not really much evidence against Henri, and he would not be back for some time. He could easily have got right away and hidden himself. But what do you think happened? He came back two days later, because he couldn't keep away from that woman. He had always been a nice lad, very gentle and very modest. But since she had got him into her clutches he had ceased to be afraid of anything. He came back just to catch a glimpse of her. He hung about her house in the Rue des Chaumières. There an urchin saw him and told another one, who knew that he was wanted, and told Chevalet, the policeman. And Chevalet, with one of his comrades, only had to come and pick him up at the corner of the street, as easy as picking a bird out of a nest.

"All the people I knew were very kind to me. They went out of their way to be nice. I felt that they rather enjoyed the thought that they were being tolerant, and they infuriated me by telling me over and over again that it was not my fault if I had brought an unnatural creature into the world. They said that he must be a hardened criminal and a frightful monster, because the victim's skull had been completely crushed in by repeated blows from the candlestick. But I believed it had all happened in a moment of brain-storm and that when he delivered all those savage blows he was not aware of what he was doing. I said this over and over again to his lawyer, Maître René Ginard. But he never mentioned it in Court. Indeed, he never listened to anything I said to him. I'm afraid I was wrong in choosing this man to defend my son. He was a young man who was always bustling about, organising meetings of young lawyers, but without much practice of his own. He was tall and dark and very conscious of his fine curly beard. How furious I was with him at the Assizes! It was so obvious that he was only thinking of showing off and flattering the Judge and the Prosecuting Counsel. He didn't care a rap for our own misfortunes.

"The worst moment was when the jury retired and we had to wait in Court. The Court usher returned before the jury. He had been taking lights to them. He said something to the lawyers and they all looked at me.

"When they brought Henri back to pass sentence on him he listened attentively. Then he looked round him as though he were looking for me, but he didn't see me. He turned towards the policeman and touched his cap politely to him as he passed him. And he left the Court as though nothing had happened.

"I hadn't said anything to the lawyer about Fanny, the woman, because Henri had made me swear not to. You can well understand that I didn't like this lady, if only for all the trouble she had brought upon us. Besides, she hadn't given a sign of life since my child had been in prison. She hadn't even sent a message. This was understandable, as she had to consider her position and her husband and her children. When Henri spoke to me of her and seemed miserable at not seeing her, I ought to have told him that she had a good excuse. But, all the same, I couldn't do it. I felt so jealous because I meant less to him than this Fanny. It was all very well my telling myself that children are like that; it still hurt me terribly.

"Maître René Ginard went to Paris to try to get a reprieve and lots of people thought it was very nice of him to put himself out to go and see the President of the Republic. But I knew that he only went for the pleasure of making his application and of having the privilege of seeing the head of the State . . . Anyway the journey was a fruitless one."

"It must have been a terrible time for you!"

"I am afraid of recalling it, madame. And yet at certain moments I ceased to suffer any more or to think about anything. People used to come in in the evening and talk about the trial and about other things. I used to mull some wine. Sometimes it seemed to me as though I were dreaming and that nothing had happened.

"And then one night I suddenly told myself that the hour was drawing near, and I began to shiver in my bed. And I decided that from then onwards I must try to find out when it was to take place. When I did find out I should pass a terrible night but until that moment at least I should not have the haunting fear each evening on going to bed that I should be told something on waking up the next morning. So after that I used to go at dusk and hang round the exit of the station when the Paris train was due. And one evening I saw the man arrive with his two assistants. They wore grey overcoats and bowler hats. And they had their gear, which was swathed in cloths, put on a barrow.

"It was about seven in the evening. I had seen Henri on the morning of the day before, and I was to see him again two days later. But I could not let him go without saying good-bye to him.

"I knew quite well that no one could enter the prison except during visiting hours. But I knew Monsieur Bellot, the Chief Warder, and I told myself that he might perhaps give me leave. When I entered his dining room—it's silly what small details one remembers—I noticed that the salad-bowl on the table was full of potatoes. He was dining with his wife and children. I stood there crying, unable to utter a word. He must have known what was going to happen next morning, for he did not ask me why I was crying.

"'Monsieur Bellot,' I said, 'I want to see him again!'

"'It's quite impossible, madame,' he replied. 'I should be dismissed for certain.'

"But seeing me so unhappy he had pity and told me I could come with him on his rounds and that I could say good-bye to my son for a moment as we passed. So we went along the prison galleries. It was a very old building and was very dark at night. One could hardly even see the lamps at each end of the galleries. Monsieur Bellot carried a lantern which shone a dim light on the floor.

"We went up two flights of steps and stopped before a cell door.

" 'This is it,' he said. 'You can kiss him through the grating. Hucheux,' he whispered, 'someone wants to talk to you.'

"Then I guessed rather than saw that he was at the grating and I heard him say in a low voice:

" 'It's you, Fanny!'

"And at the same time he pressed his face against mine and kissed me as no one had ever kissed me before."

"Poor woman! It must have made you terribly miserable that he was thinking of the other?"

"Me miserable, madame? Oh! I wasn't thinking of that. He was so happy! So very happy! I felt it in his kiss. And my only fear was that he would realise his mistake. So I was glad when Monsieur Bellot led me away. And on that last night which I had dreaded so much and through which I had not thought I should have been able to live, on that night I slept until it was broad daylight. When I first awoke I felt a sudden wave of faintness when I realised that it was all over. Then I remembered that he had died happy, and I spent the day in silence, knitting a wide-meshed jumper which I had scarcely begun and which I finished that evening."

THE MAN WHO WOULD BE KING

Rudyard Kipling
(1865–1936)

Brother to a Prince and fellow to a beggar if he be found worthy.

THE LAW, as quoted, lays down a fair conduct of life, and one not easy to follow. I have been fellow to a beggar again and again under circumstances which prevented either of us finding out whether the other was worthy. I have still to be brother to a Prince, though I once came near to kinship with what might have been a veritable King and was promised the reversion of a Kingdom—army, law-courts, revenue and policy all complete. But, to-day, I greatly fear that my King is dead, and if I want a crown I must go hunt it for myself.

The beginning of everything was in a railway train upon the road to Mhow from Ajmir. There had been a Deficit in the Budget, which necessitated travelling, not Second-class, which is only half as dear as First-class, but by Intermediate, which is very awful indeed. There are no cushions in the Intermediate class, and the population are either Intermediate, which is Eurasian, or native, which for a long night journey is nasty, or Loafer, which is amusing though intoxicated. Intermediates do not buy from refreshment-rooms. They carry their food in bundles and pots, and buy sweets from the native sweetmeat-sellers, and drink the roadside water. That is why in hot weather Intermediates are taken out of the carriages dead, and in all weathers are most properly looked down upon.

My particular Intermediate happened to be empty till I reached Nasira-bad, when a big black-browed gentleman in shirt-sleeves entered, and, following the custom of Intermediates, passed the time of day. He was a wanderer and a vagabond like myself, but with an educated taste for whiskey. He told tales of things he had seen and done, of out-of-the-way corners of the Empire into which he had penetrated, and of adventures in which he risked his life for a few days' food.

"If India was filled with men like you and me, not knowing more than the crows where they'd get their next day's rations, it isn't seventy millions of revenue the land would be paying—it's seven hundred millions," said he; and as I looked at his mouth and chin I was disposed to agree with him.

We talked politics—the politics of Loaferdom that sees things from the underside where the lath and plaster is not smoothed off—and we talked postal arrangements because my friend wanted to send a telegram back from the next station to Ajmir, the turning-off place from the Bombay to the Mhow line as you travel westward. My friend had no money beyond eight annas which he wanted for dinner, and I had no money at all, owing to the hitch in the Budget before mentioned. Further, I was going into a wilderness where, though I should resume touch with the Treasury, there were no telegraph offices. I was, therefore, unable to help him in any way.

"We might threaten a Station-master, and make him send a wire on tick," said my friend, "but that'd mean enquiries for you and for me, and I've got my hands full these days. Did you say you were travelling back along this line, within any days?"

"Within ten," I said.

"Can't you make it eight?" said he. "Mine is rather urgent business."

"I can send your telegram within ten days if that will serve you," I said.

"I couldn't trust the wire to fetch him now I think of it, It's this way. He leaves Delhi on the 23rd for Bombay. That means he'll be running through Ajmir about the night of the 23rd."

"But I'm going into the Indian Desert," I explained.

"Well *and* good," said he. "You'll be changing at Marwar Junction to get into Jodhpore territory—you must do that—and he'll be coming through Marwar Junction in the early morning of the 24th by the Bombay Mail. Can you be at Marwar Junction on that time? 'Twon't be inconveniencing you because I know that there's precious few pickings to be got out of these Central India States—even though you pretend to be correspondent of the *Backwoodsman*."

"Have you ever tried that trick?" I asked.

"Again and again, but the Residents find you out, and then you get escorted to the Border before you've time to get your knife into them. But about my friend here. I *must* give him a word o' mouth to tell him what's come to me or else he won't know where to go. I would take it more than kind of you if you was to come out of Central India in time to catch him at Marwar Junction, and say to him: 'He has gone South for the week.' He'll know what that means. He's a big man with a red beard, and a great swell he is. You'll find him sleeping like a gentleman with all his luggage round him in a Second-class apartment. But don't you be afraid. Slip down the window and say: 'He has gone South for the week,' and he'll tumble. It's only cutting your time of stay in those parts by two days. I ask you as a stranger—going to the West," he said with emphasis.

"Where have *you* come from?" said I.

"From the East," said he, "and I am hoping that you will give him the message on the Square—for the sake of my Mother as well as your own."

Englishmen are not usually softened by appeals to the memory of their mothers; but for certain reasons, which will be fully apparent, I saw fit to agree.

"It's more than a little matter," said he, "and that's why I asked you to do it—and now I know that I can depend on you doing it. A Second-class carriage at Marwar Junction, and a red-haired man asleep in it. You'll be sure to remember. I get out at the next station, and I must hold on there till he comes or sends me what I want."

"I'll give the message if I catch him," I said, "and for the sake of your Mother as well as mine I'll give you a word of advice. Don't try to run the Central India States just now as the correspondent of the *Backwoodsman*. There's a real one knocking about here, and it might lead to trouble."

"Thank you," said he simply, "and when will the swine be gone? I can't starve because he's ruining my work. I wanted to get hold of the Degumber Rajah down here about his father's widow, and give him a jump."

"What did he do to his father's widow, then?"

"Filled her up with red pepper and slippered her to death as she hung from a beam. I found that out myself and I'm the only man that would dare going into the State to get hush-money for it. They'll try to poison me, same as they did in Chortumna when I went on the loot there. But you'll give the man at Marwar Junction my message?"

He got out at a little roadside station, and I reflected, I had heard, more than once, of men personating correspondents of newspapers and bleeding small Native States with threats of exposure, but I had never met any of the caste before. They lead a hard life, and generally die with great suddenness. The Native States have a wholesome horror of English newspapers, which may throw light on their peculiar methods of government, and do their best to choke correspondents with champagne, or drive them out of their mind with four-in-hand barouches. They do not understand that nobody cares a straw for the internal administration of Native States so long as oppression and crime are kept within decent limits, and the ruler is not drugged, drunk, or diseased from one end of the year to the other. They are the dark places of the earth, full of unimaginable cruelty, touching the Railway and the Telegraph on one side, and, on the other, the days of Harun-al-Raschid. When I left the train I did business with divers Kings, and in eight days passed through many changes of life. Sometimes I wore dress-clothes and consorted with Princes and Politicals, drinking from crystal and eating from silver. Sometimes I lay out upon the ground and devoured what I could get, from a plate made of leaves, and drank the running water, and slept under the same rug as my servant. It was all in the day's work.

Then I headed for the Great Indian Desert upon the proper date, as I had promised, and the night Mail set me down at Marwar Junction, where a funny little, happy-go-lucky, native-managed railway runs to Jodhpore. The Bombay Mail from Delhi makes a short halt at Marwar. She arrived as I got in, and I had just time to hurry to her platform and go down the carriages. There was only one Second-class on the train. I slipped the window and looked down upon a flaming red beard, half covered by a railway rug. That was my man, fast asleep, and I dug him gently in the ribs. He woke with a grunt and I saw his face in the light of the lamps. It was a great and shining face.

"Tickets again?" said he.

"No," said I. "I am to tell you that he is gone South for the week. He has gone South for the week!"

The train had begun to move out. The red man rubbed his eyes. "He has gone South for the week," he repeated. "Now that's just like his impidence. Did he say that I was to give you anything? 'Cause I won't."

"He didn't," I said and dropped away, and watched the red lights die out in the dark. It was horribly cold because the wind was blowing off the sands. I climbed into my own train—not an Intermediate carriage this time —and went to sleep.

If the man with the beard had given me a rupee I should have kept it as a memento of a rather curious affair. But the consciousness of having done my duty was my only reward.

Later on I reflected that two gentlemen like my friends could not do any good if they foregathered and personated correspondents of newspapers, and might, if they black-mailed one of the little rat-trap states of Central India or Southern Rajputana, get themselves into serious difficulties. I therefore took some trouble to describe them as accurately as I could re-

member to people who would be interested in deporting them: and succeeded, so I was later informed, in having them headed back from the
Degumber borders.

Then I became respectable, and returned to an Office where there were
no Kings and no incidents outside the daily manufacture of a newspaper.
A newspaper office seems to attract every conceivable sort of person, to the
prejudice of discipline. Zenana-mission ladies arrive, and beg that the
Editor will instantly abandon all his duties to describe a Christian prize-
giving in a back-slum of a perfectly inaccessible village; Colonels who have
been overpassed for command sit down and sketch the outline of a series of
ten, twelve, or twenty-four leading articles on Seniority *versus* Selection;
missionaries wish to know why they have not been permitted to escape
from their regular vehicles of abuse and swear at a brother-missionary under
special patronage of the editorial We; stranded theatrical companies troop
up to explain that they cannot pay for their advertisements, but on their return from New Zealand or Tahiti will do so with interest; inventors of
patent punkah-pulling machines, carriage couplings and unbreakable
swords and axle-trees call with specifications in their pockets and hours at
their disposal; tea-companies enter and elaborate their prospectuses with
the office pens; secretaries of ball-committees clamour to have the glories of
their last dance more fully described; strange ladies rustle in and say: "I
want a hundred lady's cards printed *at once,* please," which is manifestly
part of an Editor's duty; and every dissolute ruffian that ever tramped the
Grand Trunk Road makes it his business to ask for employment as a proof-
reader. And, all the time, the telephone-bell is ringing madly, and Kings
are being killed on the Continent, and Empires are saying—"You're another," and Mister Gladstone is calling down brimstone upon the British
Dominions, and the little black copy-boys are whining, "*kaa-pi chay-ha-yeh*"
(copy wanted) like tired bees, and most of the paper is as blank as Modred's
shield.

But that is the amusing part of the year. There are six other months
when none ever come to call, and the thermometer walks inch by inch up
to the top of the glass, and the office is darkened to just above reading-light,
and the press-machines are red-hot to touch, and nobody writes anything
but accounts of amusements in the Hill-stations or obituary notices. Then
the telephone becomes a tinkling terror, because it tells you of the sudden
deaths of men and women that you knew intimately, and the prickly heat
covers you with a garment, and you sit down and write: "A slight increase
of sickness is reported from the Khuda Janta Khan District. The outbreak is
purely sporadic in its nature, and, thanks to the energetic efforts of the
District authorities, is now almost at an end. It is, however, with deep regret
we record the death," etc.

Then the sickness really breaks out, and the less recording and reporting
the better for the peace of the subscribers. But the Empires and the Kings

continue to divert themselves as selfishly as before, and the Foreman thinks that a daily paper really ought to come out once in twenty-four hours, and all the people at the Hill-stations in the middle of their amusements say: "Good gracious! Why can't the paper be sparkling? I'm sure there's plenty going on up here."

That is the dark half of the moon, and, as the advertisements say, "must be experienced to be appreciated."

It was in that season, and a remarkably evil season, that the paper began running the last issue of the week on Saturday night, which is to say Sunday morning, after the custom of a London paper. This was a great convenience, for immediately after the paper was put to bed, the dawn would lower the thermometer from 96° to almost 84° for half an hour, and in that chill—you have no idea how cold is 84° on the grass until you begin to pray for it—a very tired man could get off to sleep ere the heat roused him.

One Saturday night it was my pleasant duty to put the paper to bed alone. A King or courtier or a courtesan or a Community was going to die or get a new Constitution, or do something that was important on the other side of the world, and the paper was to be held open till the latest possible minute in order to catch the telegram.

It was a pitchy black night, as stifling as a June night can be, and the *loo*, the red-hot wind from the westward, was booming among the tinder-dry trees and pretending that the rain was on its heels. Now and again a spot of almost boiling water would fall on the dust with the flop of a frog, but all our weary world knew that was only pretence. It was a shade cooler in the press-room than the office, so I sat there, while the type ticked and clicked, and the night-jars hooted at the windows, and the all but naked compositors wiped the sweat from their foreheads, and called for water. The thing that was keeping us back, whatever it was, would not come off, though the *loo* dropped and the last type was set, and the whole round earth stood still in the choking heat, with its finger on its lip, to wait the event. I drowsed, and wondered whether the telegraph was a blessing, and whether this dying man, or struggling people, might be aware of the inconvenience the delay was causing. There was no special reason beyond the heat and worry to make tension, but, as the clock-hands crept up to three o'clock and the machines spun their fly-wheels two and three times to see that all was in order, before I said the word that would set them off, I could have shrieked aloud.

Then the roar and rattle of the wheels shivered the quiet into little bits. I rose to go away, but two men in white clothes stood in front of me. The first one said: "It's him!" The second said: "So it is!" And they both laughed almost as loudly as the machinery roared, and mopped their foreheads. "We seed there was a light burning across the road and we were sleeping in that ditch there for coolness, and I said to my friend here, The office is open. Let's come along and speak to him as turned us back from the Degumber State," said the smaller of the two. He was the man I had met in the Mhow train, and his fellow was the red-bearded man of Marwar Junction. There was no mistaking the eyebrows of the one or the beard of the other.

I was not pleased, because I wished to go to sleep, not to squabble with loafers. "What do you want?" I asked.

"Half an hour's talk with you, cool and comfortable, in the office," said the red-bearded man. "We'd *like* some drink—the Contrack doesn't begin yet, Peachey, so you needn't look—but what we really want is advice. We don't want money. We ask you as a favour, because we found out you did us a bad turn about Degumber State."

I led from the press-room to the stifling office with the maps on the walls, and the red-haired man rubbed his hands. "That's something like," said he. "This was the proper shop to come to. Now, Sir, let me introduce to you Brother Peachey Carnehan, that's him, and Brother Daniel Dravot, that is *me*, and the less said about our professions the better, for we have been most things in our time. Soldier, sailor, compositor, photographer, proof-reader, street-preacher, and correspondents of the *Backwoodsman* when we thought the paper wanted one. Carnehan is sober, and so am I. Look at us first, and see that's sure. It will save you cutting into my talk. We'll take one of your cigars apiece, and you shall see us light up."

I watched the test. The men were absolutely sober, so I gave them each a tepid whiskey and soda.

"Well *and* good," said Carnehan of the eyebrows, wiping the froth from his moustache. "Let me talk now, Dan. We have been all over India, mostly on foot. We have been boiler-fitters, engine-drivers, petty contractors, and all that, and we have decided that India isn't big enough for such as us."

They certainly were too big for the office. Dravot's beard seemed to fill half the room and Carnehan's shoulders the other half, as they sat on the big table. Carnehan continued: "The country isn't half worked out because they that governs it won't let you touch it. They spend all their blessed time in governing it, and you can't lift a spade, nor chip a rock, nor look for oil, nor anything like that without all the Government saying—'Leave it alone, and let us govern.' Therefore, such *as* it is, we will let it alone, and go away to some other place where a man isn't crowded and can come to his own. We are not little men, and there is nothing that we are afraid of except Drink, and we have signed a Contrack on that. *Therefore*, we are going away to be Kings."

"Kings in our own right," muttered Dravot.

"Yes, of course," I said. "You've been tramping in the sun, and it's a very warm night, and hadn't you better sleep over the notion? Come to-morrow."

"Neither drunk nor sunstruck," said Dravot. "We have slept over the no-tion half a year, and require to see Books and Atlases, and we have decided that there is only one place now in the world that two strong men can Sar-a-*whack*. They call it Kafiristan. By my reckoning it's the top right-hand corner of Afghanistan, not more than three hundred miles from Peshawar. They have two-and-thirty heathen idols there, and we'll be the thirty-third and fourth. It's a mountaineous country, and the women of those parts are very beautiful."

"But that is provided against in the Contrack," said Carnehan. "Neither Woman nor Liqu-or, Daniel."

"And that's all we know, except that no one has gone there, and they fight, and in any place where they fight a man who knows how to drill men can always be a King. We shall go to those parts and say to any King we find—'D'you want to vanquish your foes?' and we will show him how to drill men; for that we know better than anything else. Then we will sub-vert that King and seize his Throne and establish a Dy-nasty."

"You'll be cut to pieces before you're fifty miles across the Border," I said. "You have to travel through Afghanistan to get to that country. It's one mass of mountains and peaks and glaciers, and no Englishman has been through it. The people are utter brutes, and even if you reached them you couldn't do anything."

"That's more like," said Carnehan. "If you could think us a little more mad we would be more pleased. We have come to you to know about this country, to read a book about it, and to be shown maps. We want you to tell us that we are fools and to show us your books." He turned to the book-cases.

"Are you at all in earnest?" I said.

"A little," said Dravot sweetly. "As big a map as you have got, even if it's all blank where Kafiristan is, and any books you've got. We can read, though we aren't very educated."

I uncased the big thirty-two-miles-to-the-inch map of India, and two smaller Frontier maps, hauled down volume INF-KAN of the *Encyclopædia Britannica,* and the men consulted them.

"See here!" said Dravot, his thumb on the map. "Up to Jagdallak, Peachey and me know the road. We was there with Roberts' Army. We'll have to turn off to the right at Jagdallak through Laghmann territory. Then we get among the hills—fourteen thousand feet—fifteen thousand—it will be cold work there, but it don't look very far on the map."

I handed him Wood on the *Sources of the Oxus.* Carnehan was deep in the *Encyclopædia.*

"They're a mixed lot," said Dravot reflectively; "and it won't help us to know the names of their tribes. The more tribes the more they'll fight, and the better for us. From Jagdallak to Ashang. H'mm!"

"But all the information about the country is as sketchy and inaccurate as

can be," I protested. "No one knows anything about it really. Here's the
file of the *United Services' Institute*. Read what Bellew says."

"Blow Bellew!" said Carnehan. "Dan, they're a stinkin' lot of heathens,
but this book here says they think they're related to us English."

I smoked while the men pored over *Raverty, Wood,* the maps, and the
Encyclopædia.

"There is no use your waiting," said Dravot politely. "It's about four
o'clock now. We'll go before six o'clock if you want to sleep, and we won't
steal any of the papers. Don't you sit up. We're two harmless lunatics, and
if you come to-morrow evening down to the Serai we'll say good-bye to
you."

"You *are* two fools," I answered. "You'll be turned back at the Frontier or
cut up the minute you set foot in Afghanistan. Do you want any money
or a recommendation down-country? I can help you to the chance of work
next week."

"Next week we shall be hard at work ourselves, thank you," said Dravot.
"It isn't so easy being a King as it looks. When we've got our Kingdom in
going order we'll let you know, and you can come up and help us to govern it."

"Would two lunatics make a Contrack like that?" said Carnehan, with
subdued pride, showing me a greasy half-sheet of notepaper on which was
written the following. I copied it, then and there, as a curiosity—

This Contract between me and you persuing witnesseth in the name of God—
Amen and so forth.

(One)   That me and you will settle this matter together; i.e., to be Kings
   of Kafiristan.

(Two)   That you and me will not, while this matter is being settled, look
   at any Liquor, nor any Woman black, white, or brown, so as to
   get mixed up with one or the other harmful.

(Three)   That we conduct ourselves with Dignity and Discretion, and if one
   of us gets into trouble the other will stay by him.

   Signed by you and me this day.
   Peachey Taliaferro Carnehan.
   Daniel Dravot.
   Both Gentlemen at Large.

"There was no need for the last article," said Carnehan, blushing modestly; "but it looks regular. Now you know the sort of men that loafers are
—we *are* loafers, Dan, until we get out of India—and *do* you think that we
would sign a Contrack like that unless we was in earnest? We have kept
away from the two things that make life worth having."

"You won't enjoy your lives much longer if you are going to try this
idiotic adventure. Don't set the office on fire," I said, "and go away before
nine o'clock."

I left them still poring over the maps and making notes on the back of the "Contrack." "Be sure to come down to the Serai to-morrow," were their parting words.

The Kumharsen Serai is the great four-square sink of humanity where the strings of camels and horses from the North load and unload. All the nationalities of Central Asia may be found there, and most of the folk of India proper. Balkh and Bokhara there meet Bengal and Bombay, and try to draw eye-teeth. You can buy ponies, turquoises, Persian pussy-cats, saddle-bags, fat-tailed sheep and musk in the Kumharsen Serai, and get many strange things for nothing. In the afternoon I went down to see whether my friends intended to keep their word or were lying there drunk.

A priest attired in fragments of ribbons and rags stalked up to me, gravely twisting a child's paper whirligig. Behind him was his servant bending under the load of a crate of mud toys. The two were loading up two camels, and the inhabitants of the Serai watched them with shrieks of laughter.

"The priest is mad," said a horse-dealer to me. "He is going up to Kabul to sell toys to the Amir. He will either be raised to honour or have his head cut off. He came in here this morning and has been behaving madly ever since."

"The witless are under the protection of God," stammered a flat-cheeked Usbeg in broken Hindi. "They foretell future events."

"Would they could have foretold that my caravan would have been cut up by the Shinwaris almost within shadow of the Pass!" grunted the Eusufzai agent of a Rajputana trading-house whose goods had been diverted into the hands of other robbers just across the Border, and whose misfortunes were the laughing-stock of the bazar. "Ohé, priest, whence come you and whither do you go?"

"From Roum have I come," shouted the priest, waving his whirligig; "from Roum, blown by the breath of a hundred devils across the sea! O thieves, robbers, liars, the blessing of Pir Khan on pigs, dogs, and perjurers! Who will take the Protected of God to the North to sell charms that are never still to the Amir? The camels shall not gall, the sons shall not fall sick, and the wives shall remain faithful while they are away, of the men who give me place in their caravan. Who will assist me to slipper the King of the Roos with a golden slipper with a silver heel? The protection of Pir Khan be upon his labours!" He spread out the skirts of his gaberdine and pirouetted between the lines of tethered horses.

"There starts a caravan from Peshawar to Kabul in twenty days, *Huzrut,*" said the Eusufzai trader. "My camels go therewith. Do thou also go and bring us good-luck."

"I will go even now!" shouted the priest. "I will depart upon my winged camels, and be at Peshawar in a day! Ho! Hazar Mir Khan," he yelled to his servant, "drive out the camels, but let me first mount my own."

He leaped on the back of his beast as it knelt, and, turning round to me, cried: "Come thou also, Sahib, a little along the road, and I will sell thee a charm—an amulet that shall make thee King of Kafiristan."

Then the light broke upon me, and I followed the two camels out of the Serai till we reached open road and the priest halted.

"What d'you think o' that?" said he in English. "Carnehan can't talk their patter, so I've made him my servant. He makes a handsome servant. 'Tisn't for nothing that I've been knocking about the country for fourteen years. Didn't I do that talk neat? We'll hitch on to a caravan at Peshawar till we get to Jagdallak, and then we'll see if we can get donkeys for our camels, and strike into Kafiristan. Whirligigs for the Amir, O Lor! Put your hand under the camel-bags and tell me what you feel."

I felt the butt of a Martini, and another and another.

"Twenty of 'em," said Dravot placidly. "Twenty of 'em and ammunition to correspond, under the whirligigs and the mud dolls."

"Heaven help you if you are caught with those things!" I said. "A Martini is worth her weight in silver among the Pathans."

"Fifteen hundred rupees of capital—every rupee we could beg, borrow, or steal—are invested on these two camels," said Dravot. "We won't get caught. We're going through the Khaiber with a regular caravan. Who'd touch a poor mad priest?"

"Have you got everything you want?" I asked, overcome with astonishment.

"Not yet, but we shall soon. Give us a memento of your kindness, *Brother*. you did me a service, yesterday, and that time in Marwar. Half my Kingdom shall you have as the saying is." I slipped a small charm compass from my watch chain and handed it up to the priest.

"Good-bye," said Dravot, giving me hand cautiously. "It's the last time we'll shake hands with an Englishman these many days. Shake hands with him, Carnehan," he cried, as the second camel passed me.

Carnehan leaned down and shook hands. Then the camels passed away along the dusty road, and I was left alone to wonder. My eye could detect no failure in the disguises. The scene in the Serai proved that they were complete to the native mind. There was just the chance, therefore, that Carnehan and Dravot would be able to wander through Afghanistan without detection. But, beyond, they would find death—certain and awful death.

Ten days later a native correspondent giving me the news of the day from Peshawar, wound up his letter with: "There has been much laughter here on account of a certain mad priest who is going in his estimation to sell petty gauds and insignificant trinkets which he ascribes as great charms to H.H. the Amir of Bokhara. He passed through Peshawar and associated himself to the Second Summer caravan that goes to Kabul. The merchants are pleased because through superstition they imagine that such mad fellows bring good-fortune."

The two, then, were beyond the Border. I would have prayed for them, but, that night, a real King died in Europe, and demanded an obituary notice.

The wheel of the world swings through the same phases again and again. Summer passed and winter thereafter, and came and passed again. The daily paper continued and I with it, and upon the third summer there fell a hot night, a night-issue, and a strained waiting for something to be telegraphed from the other side of the world, exactly as had happened before. A few great men had died in the past two years, the machines worked with more clatter, and some of the trees in the Office garden were a few feet taller. But that was all the difference.

I passed over to the press-room, and went through just such a scene as I have already described. The nervous tension was stronger than it had been two years before, and I felt the heat more acutely. At three o'clock I cried, "Print off," and turned to go, when there crept to my chair what was left of a man. He was bent into a circle, his head was sunk between his shoulders, and he moved his feet one over the other like a bear. I could hardly see whether he walked or crawled—this rag-wrapped, whining cripple who addressed me by name, crying that he was come back. "Can you give me a drink?" he whimpered. "For the Lord's sake, give me a drink!"

I went back to the office, the man following with groans of pain, and I turned up the lamp.

"Don't you know me?" he gasped, dropping into a chair, and he turned his drawn face, surmounted by a shock of gray hair, to the light.

I looked at him intently. Once before had I seen eyebrows that met over the nose in an inch-broad black band, but for the life of me I could not tell where.

"I don't know you," I said, handing him the whiskey. "What can I do for you?"

He took a gulp of the spirit raw, and shivered in spite of the suffocating heat.

"I've come back," he repeated; "and I was the King of Kafiristan—me and Dravot—crowned Kings we was! In this office we settled it—you setting there and giving us the books. I am Peachey—Peachey Taliaferro Carnehan, and you've been setting here ever since—O Lord!"

I was more than a little astonished, and expressed my feelings accordingly.

"It's true," said Carnehan, with a dry cackle, nursing his feet, which were wrapped in rags. "True as gospel. Kings we were, with crowns upon our heads—me and Dravot—poor Dan—oh, poor, poor Dan, that would never take advice, not though I begged of him!"

"Take the whiskey," I said, "and take your own time. Tell me all you can recollect of everything from beginning to end. You got across the border on your camels, Dravot dressed as a mad priest and you his servant. Do you remember that?"

"I ain't mad—yet, but I shall be that way soon. Of course I remember. Keep looking at me, or maybe my words will go all to pieces. Keep looking at me in my eyes and don't say anything."

I leaned forward and looked into his face as steadily as I could. He dropped one hand upon the table and I grasped it by the wrist. It was twisted like a bird's claw, and upon the back was a ragged, red diamond-shaped scar.

"No, don't look there. Look at *me*," said Carnehan. "That comes afterwards, but for the Lord's sake don't distrack me. We left with that caravan, me and Dravot playing all sorts of antics to amuse the people we were with. Dravot used to make us laugh in the evenings when all the people was cooking their dinners—cooking their dinners, and . . . what did they do then? They lit little fires with sparks that went into Dravot's beard, and we all laughed—fit to die. Little red fires they was, going into Dravot's big red beard—so funny." His eyes left mine and he smiled foolishly.

"You went as far as Jagdallak with that caravan," I said at a venture, "after you had lit those fires. To Jagdallak, where you turned off to try to get into Kafiristan."

"No, we didn't neither. What are you talking about? We turned off before Jagdallak, because we heard the roads was good. But they wasn't good enough for our two camels—mine and Dravot's. When we left the caravan, Dravot took off all his clothes and mine too, and said we would be heathen, because the Kafirs didn't allow Mohammedans to talk to them. So we dressed betwixt and between, and such a sight as Daniel Dravot I never saw yet nor expect to see again. He burned half his beard, and slung a sheep-skin over his shoulder, and shaved his head into patterns. He shaved mine, too, and made me wear outrageous things to look like a heathen. That was in a most mountaineous country, and our camels couldn't go along any more because of the mountains. They were tall and black, and coming home I saw them fight like wild goats—there are lots of goats in Kafiristan. And these mountains, they never keep still, no more than the goats. Always fighting they are, and don't let you sleep at night."

"Take some more whiskey," I said very slowly. "What did you and Daniel Dravot do when the camels could go no further because of the rough roads that led into Kafiristan?"

"What did which do? There was a party called Peachey Taliaferro Carnehan that was with Dravot. Shall I tell you about him? He died out there in the cold. Slap from the bridge fell old Peachey, turning and twisting in the air like a penny whirligig that you can sell to the Amir.—No; they was two for three ha'pence, those whirligigs, or I am much mistaken and woeful sore. . . . And then these camels were no use, and Peachey said to Dravot—'For the Lord's sake let's get out of this before our heads are chopped off,' and with that they killed the camels all among the mountains, not having anything in particular to eat, but first they took off the boxes with the guns and the ammunition, till two men came along driving four mules. Dravot up and dances in front of them, singing—'Sell me four mules.' Says the first man—'If you are rich enough to buy, you are rich enough to rob;' but before ever he could put his hand to his knife, Dravot breaks his neck over his knee, and the other party runs away. So Carnehan loaded the mules with the rifles that was taken off the camels, and together we starts forward into those bitter cold mountaineous parts, and never a road broader than the back of your hand."

He paused for a moment, while I asked him if he could remember the nature of the country through which he had journeyed.

"I am telling you as straight as I can, but my head isn't as good as it might be. They drove nails through it to make me hear better how Dravot died. The country was mountaineous and the mules were most contrary, and the inhabitants were dispersed and solitary. They went up and up, and down and down, and that other party, Carnehan, was imploring of Dravot not to sing and whistle so loud, for fear of bringing down the tremenjus avalanches. But Dravot says that if a King couldn't sing it wasn't worth being King, and whacked the mules over the rump, and never took no heed for ten cold days. We came to a big level valley all among the mountains, and the mules were near dead, so we killed them, not having anything in special for them or us to eat. We sat upon the boxes, and played odd and even with the cartridges that was jolted out.

"Then ten men with bows and arrows ran down that valley, chasing twenty men with bows and arrows, and the row was tremenjus. They was fair men—fairer than you or me—with yellow hair and remarkable well built. Says Dravot, unpacking the guns—'This is the beginning of the business. We'll fight for the ten men,' and with that he fires two rifles at the twenty men, and drops one of them at two hundred yards from the rock where he was sitting. The other men began to run, but Carnehan and Dravot sits on the boxes picking them off at all ranges, up and down the valley. Then we goes up to the ten men that had run across the snow too, and they fires a footy little arrow at us. Dravot he shoots above their heads and they all falls down flat. Then he walks over them and kicks them, and then he lifts them up and shakes hands all round to make them friendly like. He calls them and gives them the boxes to carry, and waves his hand for all the world as though he was King already. They takes the boxes and him across the valley and up the hill into a pine wood on the top, where there was half a dozen big stone idols. Dravot he goes to the biggest—a fellow they call Imbra—and lays a rifle and a cartridge at his feet, rubbing his nose respectful with his own nose, patting him on the head, and saluting in front of it. He turns round to the men and nods his head, and says— 'That's all right. I'm in the know, too, and all these old jim-jams are my friends.' Then he opens his mouth and points down it, and when the first man brings him food, he says—'No;' and when the second man brings him food he says—'No;' but when one of the old priests and the boss of the village brings him food, he says—'Yes;' very haughty, and eats it slow. That was how we came to our first village, without any trouble, just as though we had tumbled from the skies. But we tumbled from one of those damned rope-bridges, you see and—you couldn't expect a man to laugh much after that?"

"Take some more whiskey and go on," I said. "That was the first village you came into. How did you get to be King?"

"I wasn't King," said Carnehan. "Dravot he was the King, and a handsome man he looked with the gold crown on his head and all. Him and the other party stayed in that village, and every morning Dravot sat by the side of old Imbra, and the people came and worshipped. That was Dravot's order. Then a lot of men came into the valley, and Carnehan Dravot picks them off with the rifles before they knew where they was, and runs down into the valley and up again the other side and finds another village, same as the first one, and the people all falls down flat on their faces, and Dravot says—'Now what is the trouble between you two villages?' and the people points to a woman, as fair as you or me, that was carried off, and Dravot takes her back to the first village and counts up the dead—eight there was. For each dead man Dravot pours a little milk on the ground and waves his arms like a whirligig and 'That's all right,' says he. Then he and Carnehan takes the big boss of each village by the arm and walks them down into the valley, and shows them how to scratch a line with a spear right down the valley, and gives each a sod of turf from both sides of the line. Then all the people comes down and shouts like the devil and all, and Dravot says— 'Go and dig the land, and be fruitful and multiply,' which they did, though they didn't understand. Then we asks the names of things in their lingo— bread and water and fire and idols and such, and Dravot leads the priest of each village up to the idol, and says he must sit there and judge the people, and if anything goes wrong he is to be shot.

"Next week they was all turning up the land in the valley as quiet as bees and much prettier, and the priests heard all the complaints and told Dravot in dumb show what it was about. 'That's just the beginning,' says Dravot. 'They think we're Gods.' He and Carnehan picks out twenty good men and shows them how to click off a rifle, and form fours, and advance in line, and they was very pleased to do so, and clever to see the hang of it. Then he takes out his pipe and his baccy-pouch and leaves one at one village, and one at the other, and off we two goes to see what was to be done in the next valley. That was all rock, and there was a little village there, and Carnehan says— 'Send 'em to the old valley to plant,' and takes 'em there and gives 'em some land that wasn't took before. They were a poor lot, and we blooded 'em with a kid before letting 'em into the new Kingdom. That was to impress the people, and then they settled down quiet, and Carnehan went back to Dravot who had got into another valley, all snow and ice and most mountaineous. There was no people there and the Army got afraid, so Dravot shoots one of them, and goes on till he finds some people in a village, and the Army explains that unless the people wants to be killed they had better not shoot their little matchlocks; for they had matchlocks. We makes friends with the priest and I stays there alone with two of the Army, teaching the men how to drill, and a thundering big Chief comes across the snow with kettle-drums and horns twanging, because he heard there was a new God kicking about. Carnehan sights for the brown of the men half a mile across the snow and wings one of them. Then he sends a message to the Chief that, unless he wished to be killed, he must come and shake hands with me and leave his arms behind. The Chief comes alone first, and Carnehan shakes hands with him and whirls his arms about, same as Dravot used, and very much surprised that Chief was, and strokes my eyebrows. Then Carnehan goes alone to the Chief, and asks him in dumb show if he had an enemy he hated. 'I have,' says the Chief. So Carnehan weeds out the pick of the men, and sets the two of the Army to show them drill and at the end of two weeks the men can manœuvre about as well as Volunteers. So he marches with the Chief to a great big plain on the top of a mountain, and the Chief's men rushes into a village and takes it; we three Martinis firing into the brown of the enemy. So we took that village too, and I gives the Chief a rag from my coat and says 'Occupy till I come;' which was scriptural. By way of a reminder, when me and the Army was eighteen hundred yards away, I drops a bullet near him standing on the snow, and all the people falls flat on their faces. Then I sends a letter to Dravot wherever he be by land or by sea."

At the risk of throwing the creature out of train I interrupted—"How could you write a letter up yonder?"

"The letter?—Oh!—The letter! Keep looking at me between the eyes, please. It was a string-talk letter, that we'd learned the way of it from a blind beggar in the Punjab."

I remember that there had once come to the office a blind man with a knotted twig and a piece of string which he wound round the twig according to some cipher of his own. He could, after the lapse of days or hours, repeat the sentence which he had reeled up. He had reduced the alphabet to eleven primitive sounds; and tried to teach me his method, but I could not understand.

"I sent that letter to Dravot," said Carnehan; "and told him to come back because this Kingdom was growing too big for me to handle, and then I struck for the first valley, to see how the priests were working. They called the village we took along with the Chief, Bashkai, and the first village we took, Er-Heb. The priests at Er-Heb was doing all right, but they had a lot of pending cases about land to show me, and some men from another village had been firing arrows at night. I went out and looked for that village, and fired four rounds at it from a thousand yards. That used all the cartridges I cared to spend, and I waited for Dravot, who had been away two or three months, and I kept my people quiet.

"One morning I heard the devil's own noise of drums and horns, and Dan Dravot marches down the hill with his Army and a tail of hundreds of men, and, which was the most amazing, a great gold crown on his head. 'My Gord, Carnehan,' says Daniel, 'this is a tremenjus business, and we've got the whole country as far as it's worth having. I am the son of Alexander by Queen Semiramis, and you're my younger brother and a God too! It's the biggest thing we've ever seen. I've been marching and fighting for six weeks with the Army, and every footy little village for fifty miles has come in rejoiceful; and more than that, I've got the key of the whole show, as you'll see, and I've got a crown for you! I told 'em to make two of 'em at a place called Shu, where the gold lies in the rock like suet in mutton. Gold I've seen, and turquoise I've kicked out of the cliffs, and there's garnets in the sands of the river, and here's a chunk of amber that a man brought me. Call up all the priests and, here, take your crown.'

"One of the men opens a black hair bag, and I slips the crown on. It was too small and too heavy, but I wore it for the glory. Hammered gold it was —five pound weight, like a hoop of a barrel.

" 'Peachey,' says Dravot, 'we don't want to fight no more. The Craft's the trick so help me!' and he brings forward that same Chief that I left at Bashkai—Billy Fish we called him afterwards, because he was so like Billy Fish that drove the big tank-engine at Mach on the Bolan in the old days. 'Shake hands with him,' says Dravot, and I shook hands and nearly dropped, for Billy Fish gave me the Grip. I said nothing, but tried him with the Fellow Craft Grip. He answers, all right, and I tried the Master's Grip, but that was a slip. 'A Fellow Craft he is;' I says to Dan. 'Does he know the word?'—'He does,' says Dan, 'and all the priests know. It's a miracle. The Chiefs and the priests can work a Fellow Craft Lodge in a way that's very like ours, and they've cut the marks on the rocks, but they don't know the Third Degree, and they've come to find out. It's Gord's Truth. I've known these long years that the Afghans knew up to the Fellow Craft Degree, but this is a miracle. A God and a Grand-Master of the Craft am I, and a Lodge in the Third Degree I will open, and we'll raise the head priests and the Chiefs of the villages.'

" 'It's against all the law,' I says, 'holding a Lodge without warrant from any one; and you know we never held office in any Lodge.'

" 'It's a master-stroke o' policy,' says Dravot. 'It means running the country as easy as a four-wheeled bogie on a down grade. We can't stop to enquire now, or they'll turn against us. I've forty Chiefs at my heel, and passed and raised according to their merit they shall be. Billet these men on his villages, and see that we run up a Lodge of some kind. The temple of Imbra will do for the Lodge-room. The women must make aprons as you show them. I'll hold a levee of Chiefs to-night and Lodge to-morrow.'

"I was fair run off my legs, but I wasn't such a fool as not to see what a pull this Craft business gave us. I showed the priests' families how to make aprons of the degrees, but for Dravot's apron the blue border and marks was made of turquoise lumps on white hide, not cloth. We took a great square stone in the temple for the Master's chair, and little stones for the officers' chairs, and painted the black pavement with white squares, and did what we could to make things regular.

"At the levee which was held that night on the hillside with big bonfires, Dravot gives out that him and me were Gods and sons of Alexander, and Past Grand Masters in the Craft, and was come to make Kafiristan a country where every man should eat in peace and drink in quiet, and specially obey us. Then the Chiefs come round to shake hands, and they were so hairy and white and fair it was just shaking hands with old friends. We gave them names according as they was like men we had known in India—Billy Fish, Holly Dilworth, Pikky Kergan, that was Bazar-master when I was at Mhow, and so on, and so on.

"*The* most amazing miracles was at Lodge next night. One of the old priests was watching us continuous, and I felt uneasy, for I knew we'd have to fudge the Ritual, and I didn't know what the men knew. The old priest was a stranger come in from beyond the village of Bashkai. The minute Dravot puts on the Master's apron that the girls had made for him, the priest fetches a whoop and a howl, and tries to overturn the stone that Dravot was sitting on. 'It's all up now,' I says. 'That comes of meddling with the Craft without warrant!' Dravot never winked an eye, not when ten priests took and tilted over the Grand-Master's chair—which was to say the stone of Imbra. The priest begins rubbing the bottom end of it to clear away the black dirt, and presently he shows all the other priests the Master's Mark, same as was on Dravot's apron, cut into the stone. Not even the priests of the temple of Imbra knew it was there. The old chap falls flat on his face at Dravot's feet and kisses 'em. 'Luck again,' says Dravot, across the Lodge to me, 'they say it's the missing Mark that no one could understand the why of. We're more than safe now.' Then he bangs the butt of his gun for a gavel and says: 'By virtue of the authority vested in me by my own right hand and the help of Peachey, I declare myself Grand-Master of all Freemasonry in Kafiristan in this the Mother Lodge o' the country, and King of Kafiristan equally with Peachey!' At that he puts on his crown and I puts on mine—I was doing Senior Warden—and we opens the Lodge in most ample form. It was a amazing miracle! The priests moved in Lodge through the first two degrees almost without telling, as if the memory was coming back to them. After that, Peachey and Dravot raised such as was worthy—high priests and Chiefs of far-off villages. Billy Fish was the first, and I can tell you we scared the soul out of him. It was not in any way according to Ritual, but it served our turn. We didn't raise more than ten of the biggest men, because we didn't want to make the Degree common. And they was clamouring to be raised.

"'In another six months,' says Dravot, 'we'll hold another Communication, and see how you are working.' Then he asks them about their villages, and learns that they was fighting one against the other, and were sick and tired of it. And when they wasn't doing that they was fighting with the Mohammedans. 'You can fight those when they come into our country,' says Dravot. 'Tell off every tenth man of your tribes for a Frontier guard, and send two hundred at a time to this valley to be drilled. Nobody is going to be shot or speared any more so long as he does well, and I know that you won't cheat me, because you're white people—sons of Alexander—and not like common, black Mohammedans. You are *my* people, and by God,' says he, running off into English at the end—'I'll make a damned fine Nation of you, or I'll die in the making!'

"I can't tell all we did for the next six months, because Dravot did a lot I couldn't see the hang of, and he learned their lingo in a way I never could. My work was to help the people plough, and now and again go out with some of the Army and see what the other villages were doing, and make 'em throw rope-bridges across the ravines which cut up the country horrid. Dravot was very kind to me, but when he walked up and down in the pine wood pulling that bloody red beard of his with both fists I knew he was thinking plans I could not advise about, and I just waited for orders.

"But Dravot never showed me disrespect before the people. They were afraid of me and the Army, but they loved Dan. He was the best of friends with the priests and the Chiefs; but any one could come across the hills with a complaint, and Dravot would hear him out fair, and call four priests together and say what was to be done. He used to call in Billy Fish from Bashkai, and Pikky Kergan from Shu, and an old Chief we called Kafuzelum —it was like enough to his real name—and hold councils with 'em when there was any fighting to be done in small villages. That was his Council of War, and the four priests of Bashkai, Shu, Khawak, and Madora was his Privy Council. Between the lot of 'em they sent me, with forty men and twenty rifles, and sixty men carrying turquoises, into the Ghorband country to buy those hand-made Martini rifles, that come out of the Amir's workshops at Kabul, from one of the Amir's Herati regiments that would have sold the very teeth out of their mouths for turquoises.

"I stayed in Ghorband a month, and gave the Governor there the pick of my baskets for hush-money, and bribed the Colonel of the regiment some more, and, between the two and the tribes-people, we got more than a hundred hand-made Martinis, a hundred good Kohat Jezails that'll throw to six hundred yards, and forty manloads of very bad ammunition for the rifles. I came back with what I had, and distributed 'em among the men that the Chiefs sent in to me to drill. Dravot was too busy to attend to those things, but the old Army that we first made helped me, and we turned out five hundred men that could drill, and two hundred that knew how to hold arms pretty straight. Even those cork-screwed, hand-made guns was a miracle to them. Dravot talked big about powder-shops and factories, walking up and down in the pine wood when the winter was coming on.

"'I won't make a Nation,' says he. 'I'll make an Empire! These men aren't niggers; they're English! Look at their eyes—look at their mouths. Look at the way they stand up. They sit on chairs in their own houses. They're the Lost Tribes, or something like it, and they've grown to be English. I'll take a census in the spring if the priests don't get frightened. There must be a fair two million of 'em in these hills. The villages are full o' little children. Two million people—two hundred and fifty thousand fighting men—and all English! They only want the rifles and a little drilling. Two hundred and fifty thousand men, ready to cut in on Russia's right flank when she tries for India! Peachey, man,' he says, chewing his beard in great hunks, 'we shall be Emperors—Emperors of the Earth! Rajah Brooke will be a suckling to us. I'll treat with the Viceroy on equal terms. I'll ask him to send me twelve picked English—twelve that I know of—to help us govern a bit. There's Mackray, Sergeant-pensioner at Segowli—many's the good dinner he's given me, and his wife a pair of trousers. There's Donkin, the Warder of Tounghoo Jail; there's hundreds that I could lay my hand on if I was in India. The Viceroy shall do it for me, I'll send a man through in the spring for those men, and I'll write for a dispensation from the Grand Lodge for what I've done as Grand-Master. That—and all the Sniders that'll be thrown out when the native troops in India take up the Martini. They'll be worn smooth, but they'll do for fighting in these hills. Twelve English, a hundred thousand Sniders run through the Amir's country in driblets—I'd be content with twenty thousand in one year—and we'd be an Empire. When everything was shipshape, I'd hand over the crown—this crown I'm wearing now—to Queen Victoria on my knees, and she'd say: "Rise up, Sir Daniel Dravot." Oh, it's big! It's big, I tell you! But there's so much to be done in every place—Bashkai, Khawak, Shu, and everywhere else.'

"'What is it?' I says. 'There are no more men coming in to be drilled this autumn. Look at those fat, black clouds. They're bringing the snow.'

"'It isn't that,' says Daniel, putting his hand very hard on my shoulder; 'and I don't wish to say anything that's against you, for no other living man would have followed me and made me what I am as you have done. You're a first-class Commander-in-Chief, and the people know you; but—it's a big country, and somehow you can't help me, Peachey, in the way I want to be helped.'

"'Go to your blasted priests, then!' I said, and I was sorry when I made that remark, but it did hurt me sore to find Daniel talking so superior when I'd drilled all the men, and done all he told me.

"'Don't let's quarrel, Peachey,' says Daniel without cursing. 'You're a King too, and the half of this Kingdom is yours; but can't you see, Peachey, we want cleverer men than us now—three or four of 'em, that we can scatter about for our Deputies. It's a hugeous great State, and I can't always tell the right thing to do, and I haven't time for all I want to do, and here's the winter coming on and all.' He put half his beard into his mouth, all red like the gold of his crown.

"'I'm sorry, Daniel,' says I. 'I've done all I could. I've drilled the men and shown the people how to stack their oats better; and I've brought in those tin-ware rifles from Ghorband—but I know what you're driving at. I take it Kings always feel oppressed that way.'

"'There's another thing too,' says Dravot, walking up and down. 'The winter's coming and these people won't be giving much trouble, and if they do we can't move about. I want a wife.'

"'For Gord's sake leave the women alone!' I says. 'We've both got all the work we can, though I am a fool. Remember the Contrack, and keep clear o' women.'

"'The Contrack only lasted till such time as we was Kings; and Kings we have been these months past,' says Dravot, weighing his crown in his hand. 'You go get a wife too, Peachey—a nice, strappin', plump girl that'll keep you warm in the winter. They're prettier than English girls, and we can take the pick of 'em. Boil 'em once or twice in hot water, and they'll come out like chicken and ham.'

"'Don't tempt me!' I says. 'I will not have any dealings with a woman not till we are a dam' side more settled than we are now. I've been doing the work o' two men, and you've been doing the work o' three. Let's lie off a bit, and see if we can get some better tobacco from Afghan country and run in some good liquor; but no women.'

"'Who's talking o' women?' says Dravot. 'I said wife—a queen to breed a King's son for the King. A Queen out of the strongest tribe, that'll make them your blood-brothers, and that'll lie by your side and tell you all the people thinks about you and their own affairs. That's what I want.'

"'Do you remember that Bengali woman I kept at Mogul Serai when I was a plate-layer?' says I. 'A fat lot o' good she was to me. She taught me the lingo and one or two other things; but what happened? She ran away with the Station Master's servant and half my month's pay. Then she turned up at Dadur Junction in tow of a half-caste, and had the impidence to say I was her husband—all among the drivers in the running-shed too!'

"'We've done with that,' says Dravot, 'these women are whiter than you or me, and a Queen I will have for the winter months.'

"'For the last time o' asking, Dan, do not,' I says. 'It'll only bring us harm. The Bible says that Kings ain't to waste their strength on women, 'specially when they've got a new raw Kingdom to work over.'

"'For the last time of answering I will,' said Dravot, and he went away through the pine-trees looking like a big red devil, the sun being on his crown and beard and all.

"But getting a wife was not as easy as Dan thought. He put it before the Council, and there was no answer till Billy Fish said he'd better ask the girls. Dravot damned them all round. 'What's wrong with me?' he shouts, standing by the idol Imbra. 'Am I a dog or am I not enough of a man for your wenches? Haven't I put the shadow of my hand over this country? Who stopped the last Afghan raid?' It was me really, but Dravot was too angry to remember. 'Who bought your guns? Who repaired the bridges? Who's the Grand-Master of the sign cut in the stone?' says he, and he thumped his hand on the block that he used to sit on in Lodge, and at Council, which opened like Lodge always. Billy Fish said nothing and no more did the others. 'Keep your hair on, Dan,' said I; 'and ask the girls. That's how it's done at Home, and these people are quite English.'

"'The marriage of the King is a matter of State,' says Dan, in a white-hot rage, for he could feel, I hope, that he was going against his better mind. He walked out of the Council-room, and the others sat still, looking at the ground.

"'Billy Fish,' says I to the Chief of Bashkai, 'what's the difficulty here? A straight answer to a true friend.'

"'You know,' says Billy Fish. 'How should a man tell you who knows everything? How can daughters of men marry Gods or Devils? It's not proper.'

"I remembered something like that in the Bible; but if, after seeing us as long as they had, they still believed we were Gods, it wasn't for me to undeceive them.

"'A God can do anything,' says I. 'If the King is fond of a girl he'll not let her die.'—'She'll have to,' said Billy Fish. 'There are all sorts of Gods and Devils in these mountains, and now and again a girl marries one of them and isn't seen any more. Besides, you two know the Mark cut in the stone. Only the Gods know that. We thought you were men till you showed the sign of the Master.'

"I wished then that we had explained about the loss of the genuine secrets of a Master-Mason at the first go-off; but I said nothing. All that night there was a blowing of horns in a little dark temple half-way down the hill, and I heard a girl crying fit to die. One of the priests told us that she was being prepared to marry the King.

"'I'll have no nonsense of that kind,' says Dan. 'I don't want to interfere with your customs, but I'll take my own wife.'—'The girl's a little bit afraid,' says the priest. 'She thinks she's going to die, and they are a-heartening of her up down in the temple.'

"'Hearten her very tender, then,' says Dravot, 'or I'll hearten you with the butt of a gun so you'll never want to be heartened again.' He licked his lips, did Dan, and stayed up walking about more than half the night, thinking of the wife that he was going to get in the morning. I wasn't by any means comfortable, for I knew that dealings with a woman in foreign parts, though you was a crowned King twenty times over, could not but be risky. I got up very early in the morning while Dravot was asleep, and I saw the priests talking together in whispers, and the Chiefs talking together too, and they looked at me out of the corners of their eyes.

"'What is up, Fish?' I say to the Bashkai man, who was wrapped up in his furs and looking splendid to behold.

"'I can't rightly say,' says he; 'but if you can make the King drop all this nonsense about marriage, you'll be doing him and me and yourself a great service.'

"'That I do believe,' says I. 'But sure, you know, Billy, as well as me, having fought against and for us, that the King and me are nothing more than two of the finest men that God Almighty ever made. Nothing more, I do assure you.'

"'That may be,' says Billy Fish, 'and yet I should be sorry if it was.' He sinks his head upon his great fur cloak for a minute and thinks. 'King,' says he, 'be you man or God or Devil, I'll stick by you to-day. I have twenty of my men with me, and they will follow me. We'll go to Bashkai until the storm blows over.'

"A little snow had fallen in the night, and everything was white except the greasy fat clouds that blew down and down from the north. Dravot came out with his crown on his head, swinging his arms and stamping his feet, and looking more pleased than Punch.

"'For the last time, drop it, Dan,' says I in a whisper, 'Billy Fish here says that there will be a row.'

"'A row among my people!' says Dravot. 'Not much. Peachey, you're a fool not to get a wife too. Where's the girl?' says he with a voice as loud as the braying of a jackass. 'Call up all the Chiefs and priests, and let the Emperor see if his wife suits him.'

"There was no need to call any one. They were all there leaning on their guns and spears round the clearing in the centre of the pine wood. A lot of priests went down to the little temple to bring up the girl, and the horns blew fit to wake the dead. Billy Fish saunters round and gets as close to Daniel as he could, and behind him stood his twenty men with matchlocks. Not a man of them under six feet. I was next to Dravot, and behind me was twenty men of the regular Army. Up comes the girl, and a strapping wench she was, covered with silver and turquoises but white as death, and looking back every minute at the priests.

"'She'll do,' said Dan, looking her over. 'What's to be afraid of, lass? Come and kiss me.' He puts his arm round her. She shuts her eyes, gives a bit of a squeak, and down goes her face in the side of Dan's flaming red beard.

"'The slut's bitten me!' says he, clapping his hand to his neck, and, sure enough, his hand was red with blood. Billy Fish and two of his matchlock-men catches hold of Dan by the shoulders and drags him into the Bashkai lot, while the priests howls in their lingo,—'Neither God nor Devil but a man!' I was all taken aback, for a priest cut at me in front, and the Army began firing into the Bashkai men.

"'God A'mighty!' says Dan. 'What is the meaning o' this?'

"'Come back! Come away!' says Billy Fish. 'Ruin and Mutiny is the matter. We'll break for Bashkai if we can.'

"I tried to give some sort of orders to my men—the men o' the regular Army—but it was no use, so I fired into the brown of 'em with an English Martini and drilled three beggars in a line. The valley was full of shouting, howling creatures, and every soul was shrieking, 'Not a God nor a Devil but only a man!' The Bashkai troops stuck to Billy Fish all they were worth, but their matchlocks wasn't half as good as the Kabul breech-loaders, and four of them dropped. Dan was bellowing like a bull, for he was very wrathy; and Billy Fish had a hard job to prevent him running out at the crowd.

"'We can't stand,' says Billy Fish. 'Make a run for it down the valley! The whole place is against us.' The matchlock-men ran, and we went down the valley in spite of Dravot. He was swearing horrible and crying out he was a King. The priests rolled great stones on us, and the regular Army fired hard, and there wasn't more than six men, not counting Dan, Billy Fish, and Me, that came down to the bottom of the valley alive.

"Then they stopped firing and the horns in the temple blew again. 'Come away—for Gord's sake come away!' says Billy Fish. 'They'll send runners out to all the villages before ever we get to Bashkai. I can protect you there, but I can't do anything now.'

"My own notion is that Dan began to go mad in his head from that hour. He stared up and down like a stuck pig. Then he was all for walking back alone and killing the priests with his bare hands; which he could have done. 'An Emperor am I,' says Daniel, 'and next year I shall be a Knight of the Queen.'

"'All right, Dan,' says I; 'but come along now while there's time.'

"'It's your fault,' says he, 'for not looking after your Army better. There was mutiny in the midst, and you didn't know—you damned engine-driving, plate-laying, missionary's-pass-hunting hound!' He sat upon a rock and called me every foul name he could lay tongue to. I was too heart-sick to care, though it was all his foolishness that brought the smash.

"'I'm sorry, Dan,' says I, 'but there's no accounting for natives. This business is our Fifty-seven. Maybe we'll make something out of it yet, when we've got to Bashkai.'

"'Let's get to Bashkai, then,' says Dan, 'and, by God, when I come back here again I'll sweep the valley so there isn't a bug in a blanket left!'

"We walked all that day, and all that night Dan was stumping up and down on the snow, chewing his beard and muttering to himself.

"'There's no hope o' getting clear,' said Billy Fish. 'The priests will have sent runners to the villages to say that you are only men. Why didn't you stick on as Gods till things was more settled? I'm a dead man,' says Billy Fish, and he throws himself down on the snow and begins to pray to his Gods.

"Next morning we was in a cruel bad country—all up and down, no level ground at all, and no food either. The six Bashkai men looked at Billy Fish hungry-way as if they wanted to ask something, but they said never a word. At noon we came to the top of a flat mountain all covered with snow, and when we climbed up into it, behold, there was an Army in position waiting in the middle!

"'The runners have been very quick,' says Billy Fish, with a little bit of a laugh. 'They are waiting for us.'

"Three or four men began to fire from the enemy's side, and a chance shot took Daniel in the calf of the leg. That brought him to his senses. He looks across the snow at the Army, and sees the rifles that we had brought into the country.

"'We're done for,' says he. 'They are Englishmen, these people,—and it's my blasted nonsense that has brought you to this. Get back, Billy Fish, and take your men away; you've done what you could, and now cut for it. Carnehan,' says he, 'shake hands with me and go along with Billy. Maybe they won't kill you. I'll go and meet 'em alone. It's me that did it. Me, the King!'

"'Go!' says I. 'Go to Hell, Dan. I'm with you here. Billy Fish, you clear out, and we two will meet those folk.'

"'I'm a Chief,' says Billy Fish, quite quiet. 'I stay with you. My men can go.'

"The Bashkai fellows didn't wait for a second word but ran off, and Dan and Me and Billy Fish walked across to where the drums were drumming and the horns were horning. It was cold—awful cold. I've got that cold in the back of my head now. There's a lump of it there."

The punkah-coolies had gone to sleep. Two kerosene lamps were blazing in the office, and the perspiration poured down my face and splashed on the blotter as I leaned forward. Carnehan was shivering, and I feared that his mind might go. I wiped my face, took a fresh grip of the piteously mangled hands, and said, "What happened after that?"

The momentary shift of my eyes had broken the clear current.

"What was you pleased to say?" whined Carnehan. "They took them without any sound. Not a little whisper all along the snow, not though the King knocked down the first man that set hand on him—not though old Peachey fired his last cartridge into the brown of 'em. Not a single solitary sound did those swines make. They just closed up tight, and I tell you their furs stunk. There was a man called Billy Fish, a good friend of us all, and they cut his throat, Sir, then and there, like a pig; and the King kicks up the bloody snow and says: 'We've had a dashed fine run for our money.

What's coming next?' But Peachey, Peachey Taliaferro, I tell you, Sir, in confidence as betwixt two friends, he lost his head, Sir. No, he didn't neither The King lost his head, so he did, all along o' one of those cunning rope bridges. Kindly let me have the paper-cutter, Sir. It tilted this way. They marched him a mile across that snow to a rope-bridge over a ravine with a river at the bottom. You may have seen such. They prodded him behind like an ox. 'Damn your eyes!' says the King. 'D'you suppose I can't die like a gentleman?' He turns to Peachey—Peachey that was crying like a child. 'I've brought you to this, Peachey,' says he. 'Brought you out of your happy life to be killed in Kafiristan where you was late Commander-in-Chief of the Emperor's forces. Say you forgive me, Peachey.'—'I do,' says Peachey. 'Fully and freely do I forgive you, Dan.'—'Shake hands, Peachey,' says he. 'I'm going now.' Out he goes, looking neither right nor left, and when he was plumb in the middle of those dizzy dancing ropes,—'Cut, you beggars,' he shouts; and they cut, and old Dan fell, turning round and round and round, twenty thousand miles, for he took half an hour to fall till he struck the water, and I could see his body caught on a rock with the gold crown close beside.

"But do you know what they did to Peachey between two pine-trees? They crucified him, Sir, as Peachey's hands will show. They used wooden pegs for his hands and his feet; and he didn't die. He hung there and screamed, and they took him down next day, and said it was a miracle that he wasn't dead. They took him down—poor old Peachey that hadn't done them any harm—that hadn't done them any——"

He rocked to and fro and wept bitterly, wiping his eyes with the back of his scarred hands and moaning like a child for some ten minutes.

"They was cruel enough to feed him up in the temple, because they said he was more of a God than old Daniel that was a man. Then they turned him out on the snow, and told him to go home, and Peachey came home in about a year, begging along the roads quite safe; for Daniel Dravot he walked before and said: 'Come along, Peachey. It's a big thing we're doing.' The mountains they danced at night, and the mountains they tried to fall on Peachey's head, but Dan he held up his hand, and Peachey came along bent double. He never let go of Dan's hand, and he never let go of Dan's head. They gave it to him as a present in the temple, to remind him not to come again, and though the crown was pure gold, and Peachey was starving, never would Peachey sell the same. You knew Dravot, Sir! You knew Right Worshipful Brother Dravot! Look at him now!"

He fumbled in the mass of rags round his bent waist; brought out a black horsehair bag embroidered with silver thread; and shook therefrom on to my table—the dried, withered head of Daniel Dravot! The morning sun that had long been paling the lamps struck the red beard and blind sunken eyes; struck, too, a heavy circlet of gold studded with raw turquoises, that Carnehan placed tenderly on the battered temples.

"You be'old now," said Carnehan, "the Emperor in his 'abit as he lived—the King of Kafiristan with his crown upon his head. Poor old Daniel that was a monarch once!"

I shuddered, for, in spite of defacements manifold, I recognized the head of the man of Marwar Junction. Carnehan rose to go. I attempted to stop him. He was not fit to walk abroad. "Let me take away the whiskey, and give me a little money," he gasped. "I was a King once. I'll go to the Deputy Commissioner and ask to set in the Poorhouse till I get my health. No, thank you, I can't wait till you get a carriage for me. I've urgent private affairs—in the south—at Marwar."

He shambled out of the office and departed in the direction of the Deputy Commissioner's house. That day at noon I had occasion to go down the blinding hot Mall, and I saw a crooked man crawling along the white dust of the roadside, his hat in his hand, quavering dolorously after the fashion of street-singers at Home. There was not a soul in sight, and he was out of all possible earshot of the houses. And he sang through his nose, turning his head from right to left:—

> "The Son of Man goes forth to war,
>   A golden crown to gain;
>   His blood-red banner streams afar—
>   Who follows in his train?"

I waited to hear no more, but put the poor wretch into my carriage and drove him off to the nearest missionary for eventual transfer to the Asylum. He repeated the hymn twice while he was with me whom he did not in the least recognize, and I left him singing it to the missionary.

Two days later I enquired after his welfare of the Superintendent of the Asylum.

"He was admitted suffering from sun-stroke. He died early yesterday morning," said the Superintendent. "Is it true that he was half an hour bareheaded in the sun at midday?"

"Yes," said I, "but do you happen to know if he had anything upon him by any chance when he died?"

"Not to my knowledge," said the Superintendent.

And there the matter rests.

WITHOUT BENEFIT OF CLERGY

Rudyard Kipling

(1865-1936)

Before my Spring I garnered Autumn's gain,
Out of her time my field was white with grain,
The year gave up her secrets to my woe.
Forced and deflowered each sick season lay,
In mystery of increase and decay;
I saw the sunset ere men saw the day,
Who am too wise in that I should not know.
—BITTER WATERS

BUT IF IT BE A GIRL?"

"Lord of my life, it cannot be. I have prayed for so many nights, and sent gifts to Sheikh Badl's shrine so often, that I know God will give us a son— a man-child that shall grow into a man. Think of this and be glad. My mother shall be his mother till I can take him again, and the mullah of the Pattan mosque shall cast his nativity—God send he be born in an auspicious hour!—and then, and then thou wilt never weary of me, thy slave."

"Since when hast thou been a slave, my queen?"

"Since the beginning—till this mercy came to me. How could I be sure of thy love when I knew that I had been bought with silver?"

"Nay, that was the dowry. I paid it to thy mother."

"And she has buried it, and sits upon it all day long like a hen. What talk is yours of dower! I was bought as though I had been a Lucknow dancing-girl instead of a child."

"Art thou sorry for the sale?"

"I have sorrowed; but to-day I am glad. Thou wilt never cease to love me now?—answer, my king."

"Never—never. No."

"Not even though the *mem-log*—the white women of thy own blood— love thee? And remember, I have watched them driving in the evening; they are very fair."

"I have seen fire-balloons by the hundred. I have seen the moon, and— then I saw no more fire-balloons."

Ameera clapped her hands and laughed. "Very good talk," she said. Then with an assumption of great stateliness, "It is enough. Thou hast my permission to depart,—if thou wilt."

The man did not move. He was sitting on a low red-lacquered couch in a room furnished only with a blue and white floor-cloth, some rugs, and a very complete collection of native cushions. At his feet sat a woman of sixteen, and she was all but all the world in his eyes. By every rule and law she should have been otherwise, for he was an Englishman, and she a Mussulman's daughter bought two years before from her mother, who, being left without money, would have sold Ameera shrieking to the Prince of Darkness if the price had been sufficient.

It was a contract entered into with a light heart; but even before the girl had reached her bloom she came to fill the greater portion of John Holden's life. For her, and the withered hag her mother, he had taken a little house overlooking the great red-walled city, and found,—when the marigolds had sprung up by the well in the courtyard and Ameera had established herself according to her own ideas of comfort, and her mother had ceased grumbling at the inadequacy of the cooking-places, the distance from the daily market, and at matters of house-keeping in general,—that the house was to him his home. Anyone could enter his bachelor's bungalow by day or night, and the life that he led there was an unlovely one. In the house in the city his feet only could pass beyond the outer courtyard to the women's rooms; and when the big wooden gate was bolted behind him he was king in his own territory, with Ameera for queen. And there was going to be added to this kingdom a third person whose arrival Holden felt inclined to resent. It interfered with his perfect happiness. It disarranged the orderly peace of the house that was his own. But Ameera was wild with delight at the thought of it, and her mother not less so. The love of a man, and particularly a white man, was at the best an inconstant affair, but it might, both women argued, be held fast by a baby's hands. "And then," Ameera would always say, "then he will never care for the white *mem-log*. I hate them all—I hate them all."

"He will go back to his own people in time," said the mother; "but by the blessing of God that time is yet afar off."

Holden sat silent on the couch thinking of the future, and his thoughts were not pleasant. The drawbacks of a double life are manifold. The Government, with singular care, had ordered him out of the station for a fortnight on special duty in the place of a man who was watching by the bedside of a sick wife. The verbal notification of the transfer had been edged by a cheerful remark that Holden ought to think himself lucky in being a bachelor and a free man. He came to break the news to Ameera.

"It is not good," she said slowly, "but it is not all bad. There is my mother here, and no harm will come to me—unless indeed I die of pure joy. Go thou to thy work and think no troublesome thoughts. When the days are done I believe . . . nay, I am sure. And—and then I shall lay *him* in thy arms, and thou wilt love me for ever. The train goes to-night, at midnight is it not? Go now, and do not let thy heart be heavy by cause of me. But thou wilt not delay in returning? Thou wilt not stay on the road to talk to the bold white *mem-log*. Come back to me swiftly, my life."

As he left the courtyard to reach his horse that was tethered to the gate-post, Holden spoke to the white-haired old watchman who guarded the house, and bade him under certain contingencies despatch the filled-up telegraph-form that Holden gave him. It was all that could be done, and with the sensations of a man who has attended his own funeral Holden went away by the night mail to his exile. Every hour of the day he dreaded the arrival of the telegram, and every hour of the night he pictured to himself the death of Ameera. In consequence his work for the State was not of first-rate quality, nor was his temper towards his colleagues of the most amiable. The fortnight ended without a sign from his home, and, torn to pieces by his anxieties, Holden returned to be swallowed up for two precious hours by a dinner at the club, wherein he heard, as a man hears in a swoon, voices telling him how execrably he had performed the other man's duties, and how he had endeared himself to all his associates. Then he fled on horseback through the night with his heart in his mouth. There was no answer at first to his blows on the gate, and he had just wheeled his horse round to kick it in when Pir Khan appeared with a lantern and held his stirrup.

"Has aught occurred?" said Holden.

"The news does not come from my mouth, Protector of the Poor, but——" He held out his shaking hand as befitted the bearer of good news who is entitled to a reward.

Holden hurried through the courtyard. A light burned in the upper room. His horse neighed in the gateway, and he heard a shrill little wail that sent all the blood into the apple of his throat. It was a new voice, but it did not prove that Ameera was alive.

"Who is there?" he called up the narrow brick staircase.

There was a cry of delight from Ameera, and then the voice of the mother, tremulous with old age and pride—"We be two women and—the—man—thy—son."

On the threshold of the room Holden stepped on a naked dagger, that was laid there to avert ill-luck, and it broke at the hilt under his impatient heel.

"God is great!" cooed Ameera in the half-light. "Thou hast taken his misfortunes on thy head."

"Ay, but how is it with thee, life of my life? Old woman, how is it with her?"

"She has forgotten her sufferings for joy that the child is born. There is no harm; but speak softly," said the mother.

"It only needed thy presence to make me all well," said Ameera. "My king, thou hast been very long away. What gifts hast thou for me? Ah, ah!

It is I that bring gifts this time. Look, my life, look. Was there ever such a babe? Nay, I am too weak even to clear my arm from him."

"Rest then, and do not talk. I am here, *bachari* [little woman]."

"Well said, for there is a bond and a heel-rope [*peecharee*] between us now that nothing can break. Look—canst thou see in this light? He is without spot or blemish. Never was such a man-child. *Ya illah!* he shall be a pundit—no, a trooper of the Queen. And, my life, dost thou love me as well as ever, though I am faint and sick and worn? Answer truly."

"Yea. I love as I have loved, with all my soul. Lie still, pearl, and rest."

"Then do not go. Sit by my side here—so. Mother, the lord of this house needs a cushion. Bring it." There was an almost imperceptible movement on the part of the new life that lay in the hollow of Ameera's arm. "Aho!" she said, her voice breaking with love. "The babe is a champion from his birth. He is kicking me in the side with mighty kicks. Was there ever such a babe! And he is ours to us—thine and mine. Put thy hand on his head, but carefully, for he is very young, and men are unskilled in such matters."

Very cautiously Holden touched with the tips of his fingers the downy head.

"He is of the faith," said Ameera; "for lying here in the night-watches I whispered the call to prayer and the profession of faith into his ears. And it is most marvellous that he was born upon a Friday, as I was born. Be careful of him, my life; but he can almost grip with his hands."

Holden found one helpless little hand that closed feebly on his finger. And the clutch ran through his body till it settled about his heart. Till then his sole thought had been for Ameera. He began to realize that there was some one else in the world, but he could not feel that it was a veritable son with a soul. He sat down to think, and Ameera dozed lightly.

"Get hence, *sahib,*" said her mother under her breath. "It is not good that she should find you here on waking. She must be still."

"I go," said Holden submissively. "Here be rupees. See that my *baba* gets fat and finds all that he needs."

The clink of the silver roused Ameera. "I am his mother, and no hireling," she said weakly. "Shall I look to him more or less for the sake of money? Mother, give it back. I have borne my lord a son."

The deep sleep of weakness came upon her almost before the sentence was completed. Holden went down to the courtyard very softly with his heart at ease. Pir Khan, the old watchman, was chuckling with delight. "This house is now complete," he said, and without further comment thrust into Holden's hands the hilt of a sabre worn many years ago when he, Pir Khan, served the Queen in the police. The bleat of a tethered goat came from the well-kerb.

"There be two," said Pir Khan, "two goats of the best. I bought them, and they cost much money; and since there is no birth-party assembled their flesh will be all mine. Strike craftily, *sahib!* 'Tis an ill-balanced sabre at the best. Wait till they raise their heads from cropping the marigolds."

"And why?" said Holden, bewildered.

"For the birth-sacrifice. What else? Otherwise the child being unguarded from fate may die. The Protector of the Poor knows the fitting words to be said."

Holden had learned them once with little thought that he would ever speak them in earnest. The touch of the cold sabre-hilt in his palm turned suddenly to the clinging grip of the child upstairs—the child that was his own son—and a dread of loss filled him.

"Strike!" said Pir Khan. "Never life came into the world but life was paid for it. See, the goats have raised their heads. Now! With a drawing cut!"

Hardly knowing what he did Holden cut twice as he muttered the Mahomedan prayer that runs: "Almighty! In place of this my son I offer life for life, blood for blood, head for head, bone for bone, hair for hair, skin for skin." The waiting horse snorted and bounded in his pickets at the smell of the raw blood that spirted over Holden's riding-boots.

"Well smitten!" said Pir Khan, wiping the sabre. "A swordsman was lost in thee. Go with a light heart, Heaven-born. I am thy servant, and the servant of thy son. May the Presence live a thousand years and . . . the flesh of the goats is all mine?" Pir Khan drew back richer by a month's pay. Holden swung himself into the saddle and rode off through the low-hanging wood-smoke of the evening. He was full of riotous exultation, alternating with a vast vague tenderness directed towards no particular object, that made him choke as he bent over the neck of his uneasy horse. "I never felt like this in my life," he thought. "I'll go to the club and pull myself together."

A game of pool was beginning, and the room was full of men. Holden entered, eager to get to the light and the company of his fellows, singing at the top of his voice—

> In Baltimore a-walking, a lady I did meet!

"Did you?" said the club-secretary from his corner. "Did she happen to tell you that your boots were wringing wet? Great goodness, man, it's blood!"

"Bosh!" said Holden, picking his cue from the rack. "May I cut in? It's dew. I've been riding through high crops. My faith! my boots are in a mess though!

> "And if it be a girl she shall wear a wedding-ring,
>   And if it be a boy he shall fight for his king,
>   With his dirk, and his cap, and his little jacket blue,
>   He shall walk the quarter-deck—"

"Yellow on blue—green next player," said the marker monotonously.

"*He shall walk the quarter-deck,—*Am I green, marker? *He shall walk the quarter-deck,—*eh! that's a bad shot,—*As his daddy used to do!*"

"I don't see that you have anything to crow about," said a zealous junior civilian acidly. "The Government is not exactly pleased with your work when you relieved Sanders."

"Does that mean a wigging from headquarters?" said Holden with an abstracted smile. "I think I can stand it."

The talk beat up round the ever-fresh subject of each man's work, and steadied Holden till it was time to go to his dark empty bungalow, where his butler received him as one who knew all his affairs. Holden remained awake for the greater part of the night, and his dreams were pleasant ones.

II

"How old is he now?"

"*Ya illah!* What a man's question! He is all but six weeks old; and on this night I go up to the housetop with thee, my life, to count the stars. For that is auspicious. And he was born on a Friday under the sign of the Sun, and it has been told to me that he will outlive us both and get wealth. Can we wish for aught better, beloved?"

"There is nothing better. Let us go up to the roof, and thou shalt count the stars—but a few only for the sky is heavy with cloud."

"The winter rains are late, and maybe they come out of season. Come, before all the stars are hid. I have put on my richest jewels."

"Thou hast forgotten the best of all."

"*Ai!* Ours. He comes also. He has never yet seen the skies."

Ameera climbed the narrow staircase that led to the flat roof. The child, placid and unwinking, lay in the hollow of her right arm, gorgeous in silver-fringed muslin with a small skull-cap on his head. Ameera wore all that she valued most. The diamond nose-stud that takes the place of the Western patch in drawing attention to the curve of the nostril, the gold ornament in the centre of the forehead studded with tallow-drop emeralds and flawed rubies, the heavy circlet of beaten gold that was fastened round her neck by the softness of the pure metal, and the chinking curb-patterned silver anklets hanging low over the rosy ankle-bone. She was dressed in jade-green muslin as befitted a daughter of the Faith, and from shoulder to elbow and elbow to wrist ran bracelets of silver tied with floss silk, frail glass bangles slipped over the wrist in proof of the slenderness of the hand, and certain heavy gold bracelets that had no part in her country's ornaments but, since they were Holden's gift and fastened with a cunning European snap, delighted her immensely.

They sat down by the low white parapet of the roof, overlooking the city and its lights.

"They are happy down there," said Ameera. "But I do not think that they are as happy as we. Nor do I think the white *mem-log* are as happy. And thou?"

"I know they are not."

"How dost thou know?"

"They give their children over to the nurses."

"I have never seen that," said Ameera with a sigh, "nor do I wish to see. *Ahi!*"—she dropped her head on Holden's shoulder,—"I have counted forty stars, and I am tired. Look at the child, love of my life, he is counting too."

The baby was staring with round eyes at the dark of the heavens. Ameera placed him in Holden's arms, and he lay there without a cry.

"What shall we call him among ourselves?" she said. "Look! Art thou ever tired of looking? He carries thy very eyes. But the mouth——"

"Is thine, most dear. Who should know better than I?"

" 'Tis such a feeble mouth. Oh, so small! And yet it holds my heart between its lips. Give him to me now. He has been too long away."

"Nay, let him lie; he has not yet begun to cry."

"When he cries thou wilt give him back—eh? What a man of mankind thou art! If he cried he were only the dearer to me. But, my life, what little name shall we give him?"

The small body lay close to Holden's heart. It was utterly helpless and very soft. He scarcely dared to breathe for fear of crushing it. The caged green parrot that is regarded as a sort of guardian-spirit in most native households moved on its perch and fluttered a drowsy wing.

"There is the answer," said Holden. "Mian Mittu has spoken. He shall be the parrot. When he is ready he will talk mightily and run about. Mian Mittu is the parrot in thy—in the Mussulman tongue, is it not?"

"Why put me so far off?" said Ameera fretfully. "Let it be like unto some English name—but not wholly. For he is mine."

"Then call him Tota, for that is likest English."

"Ay, Tota, and that is still the parrot. Forgive me, my lord, for a minute ago, but in truth he is too little to wear all the weight of Mian Mittu for name. He shall be Tota—our Tota to us. Hearest thou, O small one? Littlest, thou art Tota." She touched the child's cheek, and he waking wailed, and it was necessary to return him to his mother, who soothed him with the wonderful rhyme of *Aré koko, Jaré koko!* which says:

> Oh crow! Go crow! Baby's sleeping sound,
> And the wild plums grow in the jungle, only a penny a pound.
> Only a penny a pound, *baba,* only a penny a pound.

Reassured many times as to the price of those plums, Tota cuddled himself down to sleep. The two sleek, white well-bullocks in the courtyard were steadily chewing the cud of their evening meal; old Pir Khan squatted at the head of Holden's horse, his police sabre across his knees, pulling drowsily at a big water-pipe that croaked like a bull-frog in a pond. Ameera's mother sat spitting in the lower verandah, and the wooden gate was shut and barred. The music of a marriage-procession came to the roof above the gentle hum of the city, and a string of flying-foxes crossed the face of the low moon.

"I have prayed," said Ameera after a long pause, "I have prayed for two things. First, that I may die in thy stead if thy death is demanded, and in the second that I may die in the place of the child. I have prayed to the Prophet and to Beebee Miriam [the Virgin Mary]. Thinkest thou either will hear?"

"From thy lips who would not hear the lightest word?"

"I asked for straight talk, and thou hast given me sweet talk. Will my prayers be heard?"

"How can I say? God is very good."

"Of that I am not sure. Listen now. When I die, or the child dies, what is thy fate? Living, thou wilt return to the bold white *mem-log*, for kind calls to kind."

"Not always."

"With a woman, no; with a man it is otherwise. Thou wilt in this life, later on, go back to thine own folk. That I could almost endure, for I should be dead. But in thy very death thou wilt be taken away to a strange place and a paradise that I do not know."

"Will it be paradise?"

"Surely, for who would harm thee? But we two—I and the child—shall be elsewhere, and we cannot come to thee, nor canst thou come to us. In the old days, before the child was born, I did not think of these things; but now I think of them always. It is very hard talk."

"It will fall as it will fall. To-morrow we do not know, but to-day and love we know well. Surely we are happy now."

"So happy that it were well to make our happiness assured. And thy Beebee Miriam should listen to me; for she is also a woman. But then she would envy me! It is not seemly for men to worship a woman."

Holden laughed aloud at Ameera's little spasm of jealousy.

"Is it not seemly? Why didst thou not turn me from worship of thee, then?"

"Thou a worshipper! And of me? My king, for all thy sweet words, well I know that I am thy servant and thy slave, and the dust under thy feet. And I would not have it otherwise. See!"

Before Holden could prevent her she stooped forward and touched his feet; recovering herself with a little laugh she hugged Tota closer to her bosom. Then almost savagely—

"Is it true that the bold white *mem-log* live for three times the length of my life? Is it true that they make their marriages not before they are old women?"

"They marry as do others—when they are women."

"That I know, but they wed when they are twenty-five. Is that true?"

"That is true."

"*Ya illah!* At twenty-five! Who would of his own will take a wife even of eighteen? She is a woman—aging every hour. Twenty-five! I shall be an old woman at that age, and—— Those *mem-log* remain young for ever. How I hate them!"

"What have they to do with us?"

"I cannot tell. I know only that there may now be alive on this earth a woman ten years older than I who may come to thee and take thy love ten years after I am an old woman, gray-headed, and the nurse of Tota's son. That is unjust and evil. They should die too."

"Now, for all thy years thou art a child, and shalt be picked up and carried down the staircase."

"Tota! Have a care for Tota, my lord! Thou at least art as foolish as any babe!" Ameera tucked Tota out of harm's way in the hollow of her neck, and was carried downstairs laughing in Holden's arms, while Tota opened his eyes and smiled after the manner of the lesser angels.

He was a silent infant, and, almost before Holden could realize that he was in the world, developed into a small gold-coloured little god and unquestioned despot of the house overlooking the city. Those were months of absolute happiness to Holden and Ameera—happiness withdrawn from the world, shut in behind the wooden gate that Pir Khan guarded. By day Holden did his work with an immense pity for such as were not so fortunate as himself, and a sympathy for small children that amazed and amused many mothers at the little station-gatherings. At nightfall he returned to Ameera,—Ameera, full of the wondrous doings of Tota; how he had been seen to clap his hands together and move his fingers with intention and purpose—which was manifestly a miracle—how later, he had of his own initiative crawled out of his low bedstead on to the floor and swayed on both feet for the space of three breaths.

"And they were long breaths, for my heart stood still with delight," said Ameera.

Then Tota took the beasts into his councils—the well-bullocks, the little gray squirrels, the mongoose that lived in a hole near the well, and especially Mian Mittu, the parrot, whose tail he grievously pulled, and Mian Mittu screamed till Ameera and Holden arrived.

"O villain! Child of strength! This to thy brother on the house-top! *Tobah, tobah!* Fie! Fie! But I know a charm to make him wise as Suleiman and Aflatoun [Solomon and Plato]. Now look," said Ameera. She drew from an embroidered bag a handful of almonds. "See! we count seven. In the name of God!"

She placed Mian Mittu, very angry and rumpled, on the top of his cage, and seating herself between the babe and the bird she cracked and peeled an almond less white than her teeth. "This is a true charm, my life, and do not laugh. See! I give the parrot one half and Tota the other." Mian Mittu with careful beak took his share from between Ameera's lips, and she kissed the other half into the mouth of the child, who ate it slowly with wondering eyes. "This I will do each day of seven, and without doubt he who is ours will be a bold speaker and wise. Eh, Tota, what wilt thou be when thou art a man and I am gray-headed?" Tota tucked his fat legs into adorable creases. He could crawl, but he was not going to waste the spring of his youth in idle speech. He wanted Mian Mittu's tail to tweak.

When he was advanced to the dignity of a silver belt—which, with a magic square engraved on silver and hung round his neck, made up the greater part of his clothing—he staggered on a perilous journey down the garden to Pir Khan and proffered him all his jewels in exchange for one little ride on Holden's horse, having seen his mother's mother chaffering with pedlars in the verandah. Pir Khan wept and set the untried feet on his own gray head in sign of fealty, and brought the bold adventurer to his mother's arms, vowing that Tota would be a leader of men ere his beard was grown.

One hot evening, while he sat on the roof between his father and mother watching the never-ending warfare of the kites that the city boys flew, he demanded a kite of his own with Pir Khan to fly it, because he had a fear of dealing with anything larger than himself, and when Holden called him a "spark," he rose to his feet and answered slowly in defence of his new-found individuality, "Hum'park nahin hai. Hum admi hai [I am no spark, but a man]."

The protest made Holden choke and devote himself very seriously to a consideration of Tota's future. He need hardly have taken the trouble. The delight of that life was too perfect to endure. Therefore it was taken away as many things are taken away in India—suddenly and without warning. The little lord of the house, as Pir Khan called him, grew sorrowful and complained of pains who had never known the meaning of pain. Ameera, wild with terror, watched him through the night, and in the dawning of the second day the life was shaken out of him by fever—the seasonal autumn fever. It seemed altogether impossible that he could die, and neither Ameera nor Holden at first believed the evidence of the little body on the bedstead. Then Ameera beat her head against the wall and would have flung herself down the well in the garden had Holden not restrained her by main force.

One mercy only was granted to Holden. He rode to his office in broad daylight and found waiting him an unusually heavy mail that demanded concentrated attention and hard work. He was not, however, alive to this kindness of the gods.

III

The first shock of a bullet is no more than a brisk pinch. The wrecked body does not send in its protest to the soul till ten or fifteen seconds later. Holden realized his pain slowly, exactly as he had realized his happiness, and with the same imperious necessity for hiding all trace of it. In the beginning he only felt that there had been a loss, and that Ameera needed comforting, where she sat with her head on her knees shivering as Mian Mittu from the house-top called, *Tota! Tota! Tota!* Later all his world and the daily life of it rose up to hurt him. It was an outrage that any one of the children at the band-stand in the evening should be alive and clamorous, when his own child lay dead. It was more than mere pain when one of them touched him, and stories told by over-fond fathers of their children's latest performances cut him to the quick. He could not declare his pain. He had neither help, comfort, nor sympathy; and Ameera at the end of each weary day would lead him through the hell of self-questioning reproach which is reserved for those who have lost a child and believe that with a little—just a little—more care it might have been saved.

"Perhaps," Ameera would say, "I did not take sufficient heed. Did I, or did I not? The sun on the roof that day when he played so long alone and I was—*ahi!* braiding my hair—it may be that the sun then bred the fever. If I had warned him from the sun he might have lived. But, oh my life, say that I am guiltless! Thou knowest that I loved him as I love thee. Say that there is no blame on me, or I shall die—I shall die!"

"There is no blame,—before God, none. It was written and how could we do aught to save? What has been, has been. Let it go, beloved."

"He was all my heart to me. How can I let the thought go when my arm tells me every night that he is not here? *Ahi! Ahi!* O Tota, come back to me—come back again, and let us be all together as it was before!"

"Peace, peace! For thine own sake, and for mine also, if thou lovest me—rest."

"By this I know thou dost not care; and how shouldst thou? The white men have hearts of stone and souls of iron. Oh, that I had married a man of mine own people—though he beat me—and had never eaten the bread of an alien!"

"Am I an alien—mother of my son?"

"What else—*Sahib?* . . . Oh, forgive me—forgive! The death has driven me mad. Thou art the life of my heart, and the light of my eyes, and the breath of my life, and—and I have put thee from me, though it was but for a moment. If thou goest away, to whom shall I look for help? Do not be angry. Indeed, it was the pain that spoke and not thy slave."

"I know, I know. We be two who were three. The greater need therefore that we should be one."

They were sitting on the roof as of custom. The night was a warm one in early spring, and sheet-lightning was dancing on the horizon to a broken tune played by far-off thunder. Ameera settled herself in Holden's arms.

"The dry earth is lowing like a cow for the rain, and I—I am afraid. It was hot like this when we counted the stars. But thou lovest me as much as before, though a bond is taken away? Answer!"

"I love more because a new bond has come out of the sorrow that we have eaten together, and that thou knowest."

"Yea, I knew," said Ameera in a very small whisper. "But it is good to hear thee say so, my life, who art so strong to help. I will be a child no more, but a woman and an aid to thee. Listen! Give me my *sitar* and I will sing bravely."

She took the light silver-studded *sitar* and began a song of the great hero Rajah Rasalu. The hand failed on the strings, the tune halted, checked, and at a low note turned off to the poor little nursery-rhyme about the wicked crow—

And the wild plums grow in the jungle, only a penny a pound.
Only a penny a pound, *baba*—only . . .

Then came the tears, and the piteous rebellion against fate till she slept, moaning a little in her sleep, with the right arm thrown clear of the body as though it protected something that was not there. It was after this night that life became a little easier for Holden. The ever-present pain of loss drove him into his work, and the work repaid him by filling up his mind for nine or ten hours a day. Ameera sat alone in the house and brooded, but grew happier when she understood that Holden was more at ease, according to the custom of women. They touched happiness again, but this time with caution.

"It was because we loved Tota that he died. The jealousy of God was upon us," said Ameera. "I have hung up a large black jar before our window to turn the evil eye from us, and we must make no protestations of delight, but go softly underneath the stars, lest God find us out. Is that not good talk, worthless one?"

She had shifted the accent on the word that means "beloved," in proof of the sincerity of her purpose. But the kiss that followed the new christening was a thing that any deity might have envied. They went about henceforward saying, "It is naught, it is naught;" and hoping that all the Powers heard.

The Powers were busy on other things. They had allowed thirty million people four years of plenty wherein men fed well and the crops were certain, and the birthrate rose year by year; the districts reported a purely agricultural population varying from nine hundred to two thousand to the square mile of the overburdened earth; and the Member for Lower Tooting, wandering about India in pot-hat and frock-coat, talked largely of the benefits of British rule and suggested as the one thing needful the establishment of a duly qualified electoral system and a general bestowal of the franchise. His long-suffering hosts smiled and made him welcome, and when he paused to admire, with pretty picked words, the blossom of the blood-red *dhak*-tree that had flowered untimely for a sign of what was coming, they smiled more than ever.

It was the Deputy Commissioner of Kot-Kumharsen, staying at the club for a day, who lightly told a tale that made Holden's blood run cold as he overheard the end.

"He won't bother any one any more. Never saw a man so astonished in my life. By Jove, I thought he meant to ask a question in the House about it. Fellow passenger in his ship—dined next him—bowled over by cholera and died in eighteen hours. You needn't laugh, you fellows. The Member for Lower Tooting is awfully angry about it; but he's more scared. I think he's going to take his enlightened self out of India."

"I'd give a good deal if he were knocked over. It might keep a few vestry-men of his kidney to their own parish. But what's this about cholera? It's full early for anything of that kind," said the warden of an unprofitable salt-lick.

"Don't know," said the Deputy Commissioner reflectively. "We've got locusts with us. There's sporadic cholera all along the north—at least we're calling it sporadic for decency's sake. The spring crops are short in five districts, and nobody seems to know where the rains are. It's nearly March now. I don't want to scare anybody, but it seems to me that Nature's going to audit her accounts with a big red pencil this summer."

"Just when I wanted to take leave, too!" said a voice across the room.

"There won't be much leave this year, but there ought to be a great deal of promotion. I've come in to persuade the Government to put my pet canal on the list of famine-relief works. It's an ill-wind that blows no good. I shall get that canal finished at last."

"Is it the old programme then," said Holden; "famine, fever, and cholera?"

"Oh, no. Only local scarcity and an unusual prevalence of seasonal sickness. You'll find it all in the reports if you live till next year. You're a lucky chap. *You* haven't got a wife to send out of harm's way. The hill-stations ought to be full of women this year."

"I think you're inclined to exaggerate the talk in the *bazars*," said a young civilian in the Secretariat. "Now I have observed——"

"I daresay you have," said the Deputy Commissioner, "but you've a great deal more to observe, my son. In the meantime, I wish to observe to you ——" and he drew him aside to discuss the construction of the canal that was so dear to his heart. Holden went to his bungalow and began to understand that he was not alone in the world, and also that he was afraid for the sake of another,—which is the most soul-satisfying fear known to man.

Two months later, as the Deputy had foretold, Nature began to audit her accounts with a red pencil. On the heels of the spring-reapings came a cry for bread, and the Government, which had decreed that no man should die of want, sent wheat. Then came the cholera from all four quarters of the compass. It struck a pilgrim-gathering of half a million at a sacred shrine. Many died at the feet of their god; the others broke and ran over the face of the land carrying the pestilence with them. It smote a walled city and killed two hundred a day. The people crowded the trains, hanging on to the footboards and squatting on the roofs of the carriages, and the cholera followed them, for at each station they dragged out the dead and the dying. They died by the roadside, and the horses of the Englishmen shied at the corpses in the grass. The rains did not come, and the earth turned to iron lest man should escape death by hiding in her. The English sent their wives away to the hills and went about their work, coming forward as they were bidden to fill the gaps in the fighting-line. Holden, sick with fear of losing his chiefest treasure on earth, had done his best to persuade Ameera to go away with her mother to the Himalayas.

"Why should I go?" said she one evening on the roof.

"There is sickness, and people are dying, and all the white *mem-log* have gone."

"All of them?"

"All—unless perhaps there remain some old scald-head who vexes her husband's heart by running risk of death."

"Nay; who stays is my sister, and thou must not abuse her, for I will be a scald-head too. I am glad all the bold *mem-log* are gone."

"Do I speak to a woman or a babe? Go to the hills and I will see to it that thou goest like a queen's daughter. Think, child. In a red-lacquered bullock-cart, veiled and curtained, with brass peacocks upon the pole and red cloth hangings. I will send two orderlies for guard, and——"

"Peace! Thou art the babe in speaking thus. What use are those toys to me? *He* would have patted the bullocks and played with the housings. For his sake, perhaps,—thou hast made me very English—I might have gone. Now, I will not. Let the *mem-log* run."

"Their husbands are sending them, beloved."

"Very good talk. Since when hast thou been my husband to tell me what to do? I have but borne thee a son. Thou art only all the desire of my soul to me. How shall I depart when I know that if evil befall thee by the breadth of so much as my littlest finger-nail—is that not small?—I should be aware of it though I were in paradise. And here, this summer thou mayest die—*ai, janee,* die! and in dying they might call to tend thee a white woman, and she would rob me in the last of thy love!"

"But love is not born in a moment or on a death-bed!"

"What dost thou know of love, stoneheart? She would take thy thanks at least and, by God and the Prophet and Beebee Miriam the mother of thy Prophet, that I will never endure. My lord and my love, let there be no more foolish talk of going away. Where thou art, I am. It is enough." She put an arm round his neck and a hand on his mouth.

There are not many happinesses so complete as those that are snatched under the shadow of the sword. They sat together and laughed, calling each other openly by every pet name that could move the wrath of the gods. The city below them was locked up in its own torments. Sulphur fires blazed in the streets; the conches in the Hindu temples screamed and bellowed, for the gods were inattentive in those days. There was a service in the great Mahomedan shrine, and the call to prayer from the minarets was almost unceasing. They heard the wailing in the houses of the dead, and once the shriek of a mother who had lost a child and was calling for its return. In the gray dawn they saw the dead borne out through the city gates, each litter with its own little knot of mourners. Wherefore they kissed each other and shivered.

It was a red and heavy audit, for the land was very sick and needed a little breathing-space ere the torrent of cheap life should flood it anew. The children of immature fathers and undeveloped mothers made no resistance. They were cowed and sat still, waiting till the sword should be sheathed in November if it were so willed. There were gaps among the English, but the gaps were filled. The work of superintending famine-relief, cholera-sheds, medicine-distribution, and what little sanitation was possible, went forward because it was so ordered.

Holden had been told to keep himself in readiness to move to replace the next man who should fall. There were twelve hours in each day when he could not see Ameera, and she might die in three. He was considering what his pain would be if he could not see her for three months, or if she died out of his sight. He was absolutely certain that her death would be demanded—so certain that when he looked up from the telegram and saw Pir Khan breathless in the doorway, he laughed aloud. "And?" said he,——

"When there is a cry in the night and the spirit flutters into the throat, who has a charm that will restore? Come swiftly, Heaven-born! It is the black cholera."

Holden galloped to his home. The sky was heavy with clouds, for the long-deferred rains were near and the heat was stifling. Ameera's mother met him in the courtyard, whimpering, "She is dying. She is nursing herself into death. She is all but dead. What shall I do, *sahib?*"

Ameera was lying in the room in which Tota had been born. She made no sign when Holden entered, because the human soul is a very lonely thing and, when it is getting ready to go away, hides itself in a misty borderland where the living may not follow. The black cholera does its work quietly and without explanation. Ameera was being thrust out of life as though the Angel of Death had himself put his hand upon her. The quick breathing seemed to show that she was either afraid or in pain, but neither eyes nor mouth gave any answer to Holden's kisses. There was nothing to be said or done, Holden could only wait and suffer. The first drops of the rain began to fall on the roof, and he could hear shouts of joy in the parched city.

The soul came back a little and the lips moved. Holden bent down to listen. "Keep nothing of mine," said Ameera. "Take no hair from my head.

She would make thee burn it later on. That flame I should feel. Lower! Stoop lower! Remember only that I was thine and bore thee a son. Though thou wed a white woman to-morrow, the pleasure of receiving in thy arms thy first son is taken from thee for ever. Remember me when thy son is born—the one that shall carry thy name before all men. His misfortunes be on my head. I bear witness—I bear witness"—the lips were forming the words on his ear—"that there is no God but—thee, beloved!"

Then she died. Holden sat still, and all thought was taken from him,—till he heard Ameera's mother lift the curtain.

"Is she dead, *sahib?*"

"She is dead."

"Then I will mourn, and afterwards take an inventory of the furniture in this house. For that will be mine. The *sahib* does not mean to resume it? It is so little, so very little, *sahib,* and I am an old woman. I would like to lie softly."

"For the mercy of God be silent a while. Go out and mourn where I cannot hear."

"*Sahib,* she will be buried in four hours."

"I know the custom. I shall go ere she is taken away. That matter is in thy hands. Look to it, that the bed on which—on which she lies——"

"Aha! That beautiful red-lacquered bed. I have long desired——"

"That the bed is left here untouched for my disposal. All else in the house is thine. Hire a cart, take everything, go hence, and before sunrise let there be nothing in this house but that which I have ordered thee to respect."

"I am an old woman. I would stay at least for the days of mourning, and the rains have just broken. Whither shall I go?"

"What is that to me? My order is that there is a going. The house-gear is worth a thousand rupees and my orderly shall bring thee a hundred rupees to-night."

"That is very little. Think of the cart-hire."

"It shall be nothing unless thou goest, and with speed. O woman, get hence and leave me with my dead!"

The mother shuffled down the staircase, and in her anxiety to take stock of the house-fittings forgot to mourn. Holden stayed by Ameera's side and the rain roared on the roof. He could not think connectedly by reason of the noise, though he made many attempts to do so. Then four sheeted ghosts glided dripping into the room and stared at him through their veils. They were the washers of the dead. Holden left the room and went out to his horse. He had come in a dead, stifling calm through ankle-deep dust. He found the courtyard a rain-lashed pond alive with frogs; a torrent of yellow water ran under the gate, and a roaring wind drove the bolts of the rain like buckshot against the mud-walls. Pir Khan was shivering in his little hut by the gate, and the horse was stamping uneasily in the water.

"I have been told the *sahib's* order," said Pir Khan. "It is well. This house is now desolate. I go also, for my monkey-face would be a reminder of that which has been. Concerning the bed, I will bring that to thy house yonder in the morning; but remember, *sahib,* it will be to thee a knife turning in a green wound. I go upon a pilgrimage, and I will take no money. I have grown fat in the protection of the Presence whose sorrow is my sorrow. For the last time I hold his stirrup."

He touched Holden's foot with both hands and the horse sprang out into the road, where the creaking bamboos were whipping the sky and all the frogs were chuckling. Holden could not see for the rain in his face. He put his hands before his eyes and muttered—

"Oh you brute! You utter brute!"

The news of his trouble was already in his bungalow. He read the knowledge in his butler's eyes when Ahmed Khan brought in food, and for the first and last time in his life laid a hand upon his master's shoulder, saying, "Eat, *sahib,* eat. Meat is good against sorrow. I also have known. Moreover the shadows come and go, *sahib;* the shadows come and go. These be curried eggs."

Holden could neither eat nor sleep. The heavens sent down eight inches of rain in that night and washed the earth clean. The waters tore down walls, broke roads, and scoured open the shallow graves on the Mahomedan burying-ground. All next day it rained, and Holden sat still in his house considering his sorrow. On the morning of the third day he received a telegram which said only, "Ricketts, Myndonie. Dying. Holden relieve. Immediate." Then he thought that before he departed he would look at the house wherein he had been master and lord. There was a break in the weather, and the rank earth steamed with vapour.

He found that the rains had torn down the mud pillars of the gateway, and the heavy wooden gate that had guarded his life hung lazily from one hinge. There was grass three inches high in the courtyard; Pir Khan's lodge was empty, and the sodden thatch sagged between the beams. A gray squirrel was in possession of the verandah, as if the house had been untenanted for thirty years instead of three days. Ameera's mother had removed everything except some mildewed matting. The *tick-tick* of the little scorpions as they hurried across the floor was the only sound in the house. Ameera's room and the other one where Tota had lived were heavy with mildew; and the narrow staircase leading to the roof was streaked and stained with rain-borne mud. Holden saw all these things, and came out again to meet in the road Durga Dass, his landlord,—portly, affable, clothed in white muslin, and driving a Cee-spring buggy. He was overlooking his property to see how the roofs stood the stress of the first rains.

"I have heard," said he, "you will not take this place any more, *sahib?*"

"What are you going to do with it?"

"Perhaps I shall let it again."

"Then I will keep it on while I am away."

Durga Dass was silent for some time. "You shall not take it on, *sahib*," he said. "When I was a young man I also——, but to-day I am a member of the Municipality. Ho! Ho! No. When the birds have gone what need to keep the nest? I will have it pulled down—the timber will sell for something always. It shall be pulled down, and the Municipality shall make a road across, as they desire, from the burning-ghat to the city wall, so that no man may say where this house stood."

PAPAGO WEDDING

Mary Austin

(1868–1934)

THERE WAS a Papago woman out of Panták who had a marriage paper from a white man after she had borne him five children, and the man himself was in love with another woman. This Shuler was the first to raise cotton for selling in the Gila Valley—but the Pimas and Papagoes had raised it long before that—and the girl went with him willingly. As to the writing of marriage, it was not then understood that the white man is not master of his heart, but is mastered by it, so that if it is not fixed in writing it becomes unstable like water and is puddled in the lowest place. The Sisters at San Xavier del Bac had taught her to clean and cook. Shuler called her Susie, which was nearest to her Papago name, and was fond of the children. He sent them to school as they came along, and had carpets in the house.

In all things Susie was a good wife to him, though she had no writing of marriage and she never wore a hat. This was a mistake which she learned from the sisters. They, being holy women, had no notion of the *brujeria* which is worked in the heart of the white man by a hat. Into the presence of their God also, without that which passes for a hat, they do not go. Even after her children were old enough to notice it, Susie went about the country with a handkerchief tied over her hair, which was long and smooth on either side of her face, like the shut wings of a raven.

By the time Susie's children were as tall as their mother, there were many white ranchers in the Gila country, with their white wives, who are like Papago women in this, that if they see a man upstanding and prosperous, they think only that he might make some woman happy, and if they have a cousin or a friend, that she should be the woman. Also the white ones think it so shameful for a man to take a woman to his house without a writing that they have no scruple to take him away from her. At Rinconada there was a woman with large breasts, surpassing well looking, and with many hats. She had no husband and was new to the country, and when Shuler drove her about to look at it, she wore each time a different hat.

This the Papagoes observed, and, not having visited Susie when she was happy with her man, they went now in numbers, and by this Susie understood that it was in their hearts that she might have need of them. For it was well known that the white woman had told Shuler that it was a shame for him to have his children going about with a Papago woman who had only a handkerchief to cover her head. She said it was keeping Shuler back from being the principal man among the cotton growers of Gila Valley, to have in his house a woman who would come there without a writing. And when the other white women heard that she had said that, they said the same thing. Shuler said, "My God, this is the truth, I know it," and the woman said that she would go to Susie and tell her that she ought to go back to her own people and not be a shame to her children and Shuler. There was a man from Panták on the road, who saw them go, and turned in his tracks and went back, in case Susie should need him, for the Papagoes, when it is their kin against whom there is *brujeria* made, have in-knowing hearts. Susie sat in the best room with the woman and was polite. "If you want Shuler," she said, "you can have him, but I stay with my children." The white woman grew red in the face and went out to Shuler in the field where he was pretending to look after something, and they went away together.

After that Shuler would not go to the ranch except of necessity. He went around talking to his white friends. "My God," he kept saying, "what can I do, with my children in the hands of that Papago?" Then he sent a lawyer to Susie to say that if she would go away and not shame his children with a mother who had no marriage writing and no hat, he would give her money, so much every month. But the children all came in the room and stood by her, and Susie said, "What I want with money when I got my children and this good ranch?" Then Shuler said "My God!" again, and "What can I do?"

The lawyer said he could tell the Judge that Susie was not a proper person to have care of his children, and the Judge would take them away from Susie and give them to Shuler. But when the day came for Susie to come into court, it was seen that though she had a handkerchief on her hair, her dress was good, and the fringe of her shawl was long and fine. All the five children came also, with new clothes, well looking. "My God!" said Shuler, "I must get those kids away from that Papago and into the hands of a white woman." But the white people who had come to see the children taken away saw that although the five looked like Shuler, they had their mouths shut like Papagoes; so they waited to see how things turned out.

Shuler's lawyer makes a long speech about how Shuler loves his children, and how sorry he is in his heart to see them growing up like Papagoes, and water is coming out of Shuler's eyes. Then the Judge asks Susie if she has anything to say why her children shall not be taken away.

"You want to take these children away and giff them to Shuler?" Susie asks him. "What for you giff them to Shuler?" says Susie, and the white people are listening. She says, "Shuler's not the father of them. Thees children all got different fathers," says Susie. "Shuler——"

Then she makes a sign with her hand. I tell you if a woman makes that sign to a Papago he could laugh himself dead but he would not laugh off that. Some of the white people who have been in the country a long time know that sign and they begin to laugh.

Shuler's lawyer jumps up. . . . "Your Honour, I object——"

The Judge waves his hand. "I warn you the Court cannot go behind the testimony of the mother in such a case. . . ."

By this time everybody is laughing, so that they do not hear what the lawyer says. Shuler is trying to get out of the side door, and the Judge is shaking hands with Susie.

"You tell Shuler," she says, "if he wants people to think hees the father of thees children he better giff me a writing. Then maybe I think so myself."

"I *will*," said the Judge, and maybe two, three days after that he takes Shuler out to the ranch and makes the marriage writing. Then all the children come around Susie and say, "Now, Mother, you will have to wear a hat." Susie, she says, "Go, children, and ask your father." But it is not known to the Papagoes what happened after that.

UNCLE FRANZ

Ludwig Thoma

(1867–1921)

TRANSLATED BY BASIL CREIGHTON

A<small>ND THEN</small> one day Mother had a letter from Uncle Franz, who was a retired major. And she said she was very glad, because uncle wrote that he would make a proper man of me and it would be eighty marks a month. So I had to go to the town where uncle lived. It was very dreary. Four floors up and nothing but tall houses all round and no garden.

I was never allowed to play and generally there was nobody there.

Only Uncle Franz and Aunt Anna, who went round and round all day taking care that nothing happened. And uncle was very strict and said whenever he saw me: "Just wait, you little scamp, I'll catch you out one of these days."

You could spit out of the window into the street and it made a frightful splash when it missed. But when it hit people they were wild and looked up and were very abusive. That made me laugh, but there was nothing to laugh about as a rule.

My form-master could not bear me, because he said I had brought a very bad character with me. But it wasn't true, for the only bad mark against me was because I'd put fizzy powder in the headmaster's wife's chamber pot.

And that was a long time ago and the master needn't have taken it so hard. Uncle Franz knew him well and often went to pay him a visit.

Then they put their heads together to see how they could catch me out.

As soon as I got home from school I had to sit down again at once and do my homework.

Uncle kept on looking at me all the time and said: "Making a hash of it as usual, I suppose! Just wait, you scamp—I'll be after you one of these days."

Once I had some arithmetic to do. It wouldn't come right and so I asked uncle, because he had told Mother he would help me. And my aunt had said too that my uncle was so clever and that I could learn a lot from him.

And so I asked him to help me and he looked at the question and said: "Can't you even do that, you good-for-nothing scamp? Why, that's simple."

And then he sat down and tried it. But he did not get on very fast. He was working it out all afternoon and when I asked him whether he had done it yet, he got into a frightful temper and shouted at me. It was supper time before he brought me the sum and said: "Now you can make a fair copy. It was perfectly simple, but I had something else to do—you blockhead."

I made a fair copy and showed it up to the master. Our papers were given back on Thursday, and I made sure I should get full marks. But I only got four again as usual and the whole page was covered with red ink and the master said: "Nobody but a donkey would do a sum like that."

"It was my uncle who did it," I said. "I only copied it out."

The whole class laughed, but the master went red in the face.

"You are nothing but a liar," he said, "and you'll end by going to prison."

Then he gave me two hours detention. My uncle was waiting for me, for he always gave me a hiding when I was kept in. But I shouted out at once that it was his fault, because he had done the sum wrong and the master had said it took a donkey to do it like that.

He gave me the worst hiding I'd ever had and then he went out.

Greither Heinrich, my friend, saw him walking along the street with the master, and every now and then they stood still and my uncle talked very loud.

Next day the master called me up and said: "I have looked at your sum again. It is quite right, but it is done in an old-fashioned way that is no longer used, but it will do you no harm to have been kept in. You deserve it every day by rights and, besides that, you made some mistakes in copying it out."

That's how they arranged it between them, for as soon as I got home my uncle said: "I have spoken to your form-master. There was nothing wrong with the sum, but you didn't even take the trouble to copy it out correctly."

I copied it out quite right, but he had done it all wrong.

But Mother wrote and said my uncle had written to say he could not give me any more help, because I could not copy out the simplest sums and this put him in a false position.

That's the low sort of man he is.

THE DOOR IN THE WALL

H. G. Wells

(1866–)

O NE CONFIDENTIAL EVENING, not three months ago, Lionel Wallace told me this story of the Door in the Wall. And at the time I thought that so far as he was concerned it was a true story.

He told it me with such a direct simplicity of conviction that I could not do otherwise than believe in him. But in the morning, in my own flat, I woke to a different atmosphere; and as I lay in bed and recalled the things he had told me, stripped of the glamour of his earnest slow voice, denuded of the focussed, shaded table light, the shadowy atmosphere that wrapped about him and me, and the pleasant bright things, the dessert and glasses and napery of the dinner we had shared, making them for the time a bright little world quite cut off from everyday realities, I saw it all as frankly incredible. "He was mystifying!" I said, and then: "How well he did it! . . . It isn't quite the thing I should have expected him, of all people, to do well."

Afterwards as I sat up in bed and sipped my morning tea, I found myself trying to account for the flavour of reality that perplexed me in his impossible reminiscences, by supposing they did in some way suggest, present, convey—I hardly know which word to use—experiences it was otherwise impossible to tell.

Well, I don't resort to that explanation now. I have got over my intervening doubts. I believe now, as I believed at the moment of telling, that Wallace did to the very best of his ability strip the truth of his secret for me. But whether he himself saw, or only thought he saw, whether he himself was the possessor of an inestimable privilege or the victim of a fantastic dream, I cannot pretend to guess. Even the facts of his death, which ended my doubts for ever, throw no light on that.

That much the reader must judge for himself.

I forget now what chance comment or criticism of mine moved so reticent a man to confide in me. He was, I think, defending himself against an imputation of slackness and unreliability I had made in relation to a great public movement, in which he had disappointed me. But he plunged suddenly. "I have," he said, "a preoccupation——

"I know," he went on, after a pause, "I have been negligent. The fact is— it isn't a case of ghosts or apparitions—but—it's an odd thing to tell of, Redmond—I am haunted. I am haunted by something—that rather takes the light out of things, that fills me with longings. . . ."

He paused, checked by that English shyness that so often overcomes us when we would speak of moving or grave or beautiful things. "You were at Saint Athelstan's all through," he said, and for a moment that seemed to me quite irrelevant. "Well"—and he paused. Then very haltingly at first, but afterwards more easily, he began to tell of the thing that was hidden in his life, the haunting memory of a beauty and a happiness that filled his heart with insatiable longings, that made all the interests and spectacle of worldly life seem dull and tedious and vain to him.

Now that I have the clue to it, the thing seems written visibly in his face. I have a photograph in which that look of detachment has been caught and intensified. It reminds me of what a woman once said of him—a woman who had loved him greatly. "Suddenly," she said, "the interest goes out of him. He forgets you. He doesn't care a rap for you—under his very nose . . ."

Yet the interest was not always out of him, and when he was holding his attention to a thing Wallace could contrive to be an extremely successful man. His career, indeed, is set with successes. He left me behind him long ago; he soared up over my head, and cut a figure in the world that I couldn't cut—anyhow. He was still a year short of forty, and they say now that he would have been in office and very probably in the new Cabinet if he had lived. At school he always beat me without effort—as it were by nature. We were at school together at Saint Athelstan's College in West Kensington for almost all our school-time. He came into the school as my co-equal, but he left far above me, in a blaze of scholarships and brilliant performance. Yet I think I made a fair average running. And it was at school I heard first of the "Door in the Wall"—that I was to hear of a second time only a month before his death.

To him at least the Door in the Wall was a real door, leading through a real wall to immortal realities. Of that I am now quite assured.

And it came into his life quite early, when he was a little fellow between five and six. I remember how, as he sat making his confession to me with a slow gravity, he reasoned and reckoned the date of it. "There was," he said, "a crimson Virginia creeper in it—all one bright uniform crimson, in a clear amber sunshine against a white wall. That came into the impression somehow, though I don't clearly remember how, and there were horse-chestnut leaves upon the clean pavement outside the green door. They were blotched yellow and green, you know, not brown nor dirty, so that they must have been new fallen. I take it that means October. I look out for horse-chestnut leaves every year and I ought to know.

"If I'm right in that, I was about five years and four months old."

He was, he said, rather a precocious little boy—he learned to talk at an abnormally early age, and he was so sane and "old-fashioned," as people say, that he was permitted an amount of initiative that most children scarcely attain by seven or eight. His mother died when he was two, and he was under the less vigilant and authoritative care of a nursery governess. His father was a stern, preoccupied lawyer, who gave him little attention and expected great things of him. For all his brightness he found life grey and dull, I think. And one day he wandered.

He could not recall the particular neglect that enabled him to get away, nor the course he took among the West Kensington roads. All that had faded among the incurable blurs of memory. But the white wall and the green door stood out quite distinctly.

As his memory of that childish experience ran, he did at the very first sight of that door experience a peculiar emotion, an attraction, a desire to get to the door and open it and walk in. And at the same time he had the clearest conviction that either it was unwise or it was wrong of him—he could not tell which—to yield to this attraction. He insisted upon it, as a curious thing that he knew from the very beginning—unless memory has played him the queerest trick—that the door was unfastened, and that he could go in as he chose.

I seem to see the figure of that little boy, drawn and repelled. And it was very clear in his mind, too, though why it should be so was never explained, that his father would be very angry if he went in through that door.

Wallace described all these moments of hesitation to me with the utmost particularity. He went right past the door, and then, with his hands in his pockets and making an infantile attempt to whistle, strolled right along beyond the end of the wall. There he recalls a number of mean dirty shops, and particularly that of a plumber and decorator with a dusty disorder of earthenware pipes, sheet lead, ball taps, pattern books of wall paper, and tins of enamel. He stood pretending to examine these things, and *coveting,* passionately desiring, the green door.

Then, he said, he had a gust of emotion. He made a run for it, lest hesitation should grip him again; he went plumb with outstretched hand through the green door and let it slam behind him. And so, in a trice, he came into the garden that has haunted all his life.

It was very difficult for Wallace to give me his full sense of that garden into which he came.

There was something in the very air of it that exhilarated, that gave one a sense of lightness and good happening and well-being; there was something in the sight of it that made all its colour clean and perfect and subtly luminous. In the instant of coming into it one was exquisitely glad—as only in rare moments, and when one is young and joyful one can be glad in this world. And everything was beautiful there. . . .

Wallace mused before he went on telling me. "You see," he said, with the doubtful inflection of a man who pauses at incredible things, "there were two great panthers there. . . . Yes, spotted panthers. And I was not afraid. There was a long wide path with marble-edged flower borders on either side, and these two huge velvety beasts were playing there with a ball. One looked up and came towards me, a little curious as it seemed. It came right up to me, rubbed its soft round ear very gently against the small hand I held out, and purred. It was, I tell you, an enchanted garden. I know. And the size? Oh! it stretched far and wide, this way and that. I believe there were hills far away. Heaven knows where West Kensington had suddenly got to. And somehow it was just like coming home.

"You know, in the very moment the door swung to behind me, I forgot the road with its fallen chestnut leaves, its cabs and tradesmen's carts, I forgot the sort of gravitational pull back to the discipline and obedience of home, I forgot all hesitations and fear, forgot discretion, forgot all the intimate realities of this life. I became in a moment a very glad and wonder-happy little boy—in another world. It was a world with a different quality, a warmer, more penetrating and mellower light, with a faint clear gladness in its air, and wisps of sun-touched cloud in the blueness of its sky. And before me ran this long wide path, invitingly, with weedless beds on either side, rich with untended flowers, and these two great panthers. I put my little hands fearlessly on their soft fur, and caressed their round ears and the sensitive corners under their ears, and played with them, and it was as though they welcomed me home. There was a keen sense of home-coming in my mind, and when presently a tall, fair girl appeared in the pathway and came to meet me, smiling, and said 'Well?' to me, and lifted me and kissed me, and put me down and led me by the hand, there was no amazement, but only an impression of delightful rightness, of being reminded of happy things that had in some strange way been overlooked. There were broad red steps, I remember, that came into view between spikes of delphinium, and up these we went to a great avenue between very old and shady dark trees. All down this avenue, you know, between the red chapped stems, were marble seats of honour and statuary, and very tame and friendly white doves. . . .

"Along this cool avenue my girl-friend led me, looking down—I recall the pleasant lines, the finely-modelled chin of her sweet kind face—asking me questions in a soft, agreeable voice, and telling me things, pleasant things I know, though what they were I was never able to recall. . . . Presently a Capuchin monkey, very clean, with a fur of ruddy brown and kindly hazel eyes, came down a tree to us and ran beside me, looking up at me and grinning, and presently leaped to my shoulder. So we two went on our way in great happiness."

He paused.

"Go on," I said.

"I remember little things. We passed an old man musing among laurels, I remember, and a place gay with paroquets, and came through a broad shaded colonnade to a spacious cool palace, full of pleasant fountains, full of beautiful things, full of the quality and promise of heart's desire. And there were many things and many people, some that still seem to stand out clearly and some that are vaguer; but all these people were beautiful and kind. In some way—I don't know how—it was conveyed to me that they all were kind to me, glad to have me there, and filling me with gladness by their gestures, by the touch of their hands, by the welcome and love in their eyes. Yes——"

He mused for a while. "Playmates I found there. That was very much to me, because I was a lonely little boy. They played delightful games in a grass-covered court where there was a sun-dial set about with flowers. And as one played one loved. . . .

"But—it's odd—there's a gap in my memory. I don't remember the games we played. I never remembered. Afterwards, as a child, I spent long hours trying, even with tears, to recall the form of that happiness. I wanted to play it all over again—in my nursery—by myself. No! All I remember is the happiness and two dear playfellows who were most with me. . . . Then presently came a sombre dark woman, with a grave, pale face and dreamy eyes, a sombre woman, wearing a soft long robe of pale purple, who carried a book, and beckoned and took me aside with her into a gallery above a hall —though my playmates were loth to have me go, and ceased their game and stood watching as I was carried away. 'Come back to us!' they cried, 'Come back to us soon!' I looked up at her face, but she heeded them not at all. Her face was very gentle and grave. She took me to a seat in the gallery, and I stood beside her, ready to look at her book as she opened it upon her knee. The pages fell open. She pointed, and I looked, marvelling, for in the living pages of that book I saw myself; it was a story about myself, and in it were all the things that had happened to me since ever I was born. . . .

"It was wonderful to me, because the pages of that book were not pictures, you understand, but realities."

Wallace paused gravely—looked at me doubtfully.

"Go on," I said. "I understand."

"They were realities—yes, they must have been; people moved and things came and went in them; my dear mother, whom I had near forgotten; then my father, stern and upright, the servants, the nursery, all the familiar things of home. Then the front door and the busy streets, with traffic to and fro. I looked and marvelled, and looked half doubtfully again into the woman's face and turned the pages over, skipping this and that, to see more of this book and more, and so at last I came to myself hovering and hesitating outside the green door in the long white wall, and felt again the conflict and the fear.

" 'And next?' I cried, and would have turned on, but the cool hand of the grave woman delayed me.

" 'Next?' I insisted, and struggled gently with her hand, pulling up her fingers with all my childish strength, and as she yielded and the page came over she bent down upon me like a shadow and kissed my brow.

"But the page did not show the enchanted garden, nor the panthers, nor the girl who had led me by the hand, nor the playfellows who had been so loth to let me go. It showed a long grey street in West Kensington, in that chill hour of afternoon before the lamps are lit; and I was there, a wretched little figure, weeping aloud, for all that I could do to restrain myself, and I was weeping because I could not return to my dear playfellows who had called after me, 'Come back to us! Come back to us soon!' I was there. This was no page in a book but harsh reality; that enchanted place and the restraining hand of the grave mother at whose knee I stood had gone—whither had they gone?"

He halted again, and remained for a time staring into the fire.

"Oh! the woefulness of that return!" he murmured.

"Well?" I said, after a minute or so.

"Poor little wretch I was!—brought back to this grey world again! As I realized the fulness of what had happened to me, I gave way to quite ungovernable grief. And the shame and humiliation of that public weeping and my disgraceful home-coming remain with me still. I see again the benevolent-looking old gentleman in gold spectacles who stopped and spoke to me—prodding me first with his umbrella. 'Poor little chap,' said he; 'and are you lost then?'—and me a London boy of five and more! And he must needs bring in a kindly young policeman and make a crowd of me, and so march me home. Sobbing, conspicuous, and frightened, I came back from the enchanted garden to the steps of my father's house.

"That is as well as I can remember my vision of that garden—the garden that haunts me still. Of course, I can convey nothing of that indescribable quality of translucent unreality, that *difference* from the common things of experience that hung about it all; but that—that is what happened. If it was a dream, I am sure it was a day-time and altogether extraordinary dream. . . . H'm!—naturally there followed a terrible questioning, by my aunt, my father, the nurse, the governess—everyone. . . .

"I tried to tell them, and my father gave me my first thrashing for telling lies. When afterwards I tried to tell my aunt, she punished me again for my wicked persistence. Then, as I said, everyone was forbidden to listen to me, to hear a word about it. Even my fairy-tale books were taken away from me for a time—because I was too 'imaginative.' Eh? Yes, they did that! My father belonged to the old school. . . . And my story was driven back upon myself. I whispered it to my pillow—my pillow that was often damp and salt to my whispering lips with childish tears. And I added always to my official and less fervent prayers this one heartfelt request: 'Please God I may dream of the garden. Oh! take me back to my garden!' Take me back to my garden! I dreamt often of the garden. I may have added to it, I may have changed it! I do not know. . . . All this, you understand, is an attempt to reconstruct from fragmentary memories a very early experience. Between that and the other consecutive memories of my boyhood there is a gulf. A time came when it seemed impossible I should ever speak of that wonder glimpse again."

I asked an obvious question.

"No," he said. "I don't remember that I ever attempted to find my way back to the garden in those early years. This seems odd to me now, but I think that very probably a closer watch was kept on my movements after this misadventure to prevent my going astray. No, it wasn't till you knew me that I tried for the garden again. And I believe there was a period— incredible as it seems now—when I forgot the garden altogether—when I was about eight or nine it may have been. Do you remember me as a kid at Saint Althelstan's?"

"Rather!"

"I didn't show any signs, did I, in those days of having a secret dream?"

II

He looked up with a sudden smile.

"Did you ever play North-West Passage with me? . . . No, of course you didn't come my way!"

"It was the sort of game," he went on, "that every imaginative child plays all day. The idea was the discovery of a North-West Passage to school. The way to school was plain enough; the game consisted in finding some way that wasn't plain, starting off ten minutes early in some almost hopeless direction, and working my way round through unaccustomed streets to my goal. And one day I got entangled among some rather low-class streets on the other side of Campden Hill, and I began to think that for once the game would be against me and that I should get to school late. I tried rather desperately a street that seemed a *cul-de-sac,* and found a passage at the end. I hurried through that with renewed hope. 'I shall do it yet,' I said, and passed a row of frowsy little shops that were inexplicably familiar to me, and behold! there was my long white wall and the green door that led to the enchanted garden!

"The thing whacked upon me suddenly. Then, after all, that garden, that wonderful garden, wasn't a dream!"

He paused.

"I suppose my second experience with the green door marks the world of difference there is between the busy life of a schoolboy and the infinite leisure of a child. Anyhow, this second time I didn't for a moment think of going in straight away. You see——. For one thing, my mind was full of the idea of getting to school in time—set on not breaking my record for punctuality. I must surely have felt *some* little desire at least to try the door —yes. I must have felt that. . . . But I seem to remember the attraction of the door mainly as another obstacle to my overmastering determination to get to school. I was immensely interested by this discovery I had made, of course—I went on with my mind full of it—but I went on. It didn't check me. I ran past, tugging out my watch, found I had ten minutes still to spare, and then I was going downhill into familiar surroundings. I got to school, breathless, it is true, and wet with perspiration, but in time. I can remember hanging up my coat and hat. . . . Went right by it and left it behind me. Odd, eh?"

He looked at me thoughtfully. "Of course I didn't know then that it wouldn't always be there. Schoolboys have limited imaginations. I suppose I thought it was an awfully jolly thing to have it there, to know my way back to it; but there was the school tugging at me. I expect I was a good deal distraught and inattentive that morning, recalling what I could of the beautiful strange people I should presently see again. Oddly enough I had no doubt in my mind that they would be glad to see me. . . . Yes, I must have thought of the garden that morning just as a jolly sort of place to which one might resort in the interludes of a strenuous scholastic career.

"I didn't go that day at all. The next day was a half-holiday, and that may have weighed with me. Perhaps, too, my state of inattention brought down impositions upon me, and docked the margin of time necessary for the *détour.* I don't know. What I do know is that in the meantime the enchanted garden was so much upon my mind that I could not keep it to myself.

"I told—what was his name?—a ferrety-looking youngster we used to call 'Squiff.'"

"Young Hopkins," said I.

"Hopkins it was. I did not like telling him. I had a feeling that in some way it was against the rules to tell him, but I did. He was walking part of the way home with me; he was talkative, and if we had not talked about the enchanted garden we should have talked of something else, and it was intolerable to me to think about any other subject. So I blabbed.

"Well, he told my secret. The next day in the play interval I found myself surrounded by half-a-dozen bigger boys, half teasing, and wholly curious to hear more of the enchanted garden. There was that big Fawcett—you remember him?—and Carnaby and Morley Reynolds. You weren't there by any chance? No, I think I should have remembered if you were. . . .

"A boy is a creature of odd feelings. I was, I really believe, in spite of my secret self-disgust, a little flattered to have the attention of these big fellows. I remember particularly a moment of pleasure caused by the praise of Crawshaw—you remember Crawshaw major, the son of Crawshaw the composer?—who said it was the best lie he had ever heard. But at the same time there was a really painful undertow of shame at telling what I felt was indeed a sacred secret. That beast Fawcett made a joke about the girl in green——"

Wallace's voice sank with the keen memory of that shame. "I pretended not to hear," he said. "Well, then Carnaby suddenly called me a young liar, and disputed with me when I said the thing was true. I said I knew where to find the green door, could lead them all there in ten minutes. Carnaby became outrageously virtuous, and said I'd have to—and bear out my words or suffer. Did you ever have Carnaby twist your arm? Then perhaps you'll understand how it went with me. I swore my story was true. There was nobody in the school then to save a chap from Carnaby, though Crawshaw put in a word or so. Carnaby had got his game. I grew excited and red-eared, and a little frightened. I behaved altogether like a silly little chap, and the outcome of it all was that instead of starting alone for my enchanted garden, I led the way presently—cheeks flushed, ears hot, eyes smarting, and my soul one burning misery and shame—for a party of six mocking, curious, and threatening schoolfellows.

"We never found the white wall and the green door. . . ."

"You mean——?"

"I mean I couldn't find it. I would have found it if I could.

"And afterwards when I could go alone I couldn't find it. I never found it. I seem now to have been always looking for it through my school-boy days, but I never came upon it—never."

"Did the fellows—make it disagreeable?"

"Beastly. . . . Carnaby held a council over me for wanton lying. I remember how I sneaked home and upstairs to hide the marks of my blubbering. But when I cried myself to sleep at last it wasn't for Carnaby, but for the garden, for the beautiful afternoon I had hoped for, for the sweet friendly women and the waiting playfellows, and the game I had hoped to learn again, that beautiful forgotten game. . . .

"I believed firmly that if I had not told—— . . . I had bad times after that—crying at night and wool-gathering by day. For two terms I slacked and had bad reports. Do you remember? Of course you would! It was *you* —your beating me in mathematics that brought me back to the grind again."

III

For a time my friend stared silently into the red heart of the fire. Then he said: "I never saw it again until I was seventeen.

"It leaped upon me for the third time—as I was driving to Paddington on my way to Oxford and a scholarship. I had just one momentary glimpse. I was leaning over the apron of my hansom smoking a cigarette, and no doubt thinking myself no end of a man of the world, and suddenly there was the door, the wall, the dear sense of unforgettable and still attainable things.

"We clattered by—I too taken by surprise to stop my cab until we were well past and round a corner. Then I had a queer moment, a double and divergent movement of my will: I tapped the little door in the roof of the cab, and brought my arm down to pull out my watch. 'Yes, sir!' said the cab-man, smartly. 'Er—well—it's nothing,' I cried. '*My* mistake! We haven't much time! Go on!' And he went on. . . .

"I got my scholarship. And the night after I was told of that I sat over my fire in my little upper room, my study, in my father's house, with his praise —his rare praise—and his sound counsels ringing in my ears, and I smoked my favourite pipe—the formidable bulldog of adolescence—and thought of that door in the long white wall. 'If I had stopped,' I thought, 'I should have missed my scholarship, I should have missed Oxford—muddled all the fine career before me! I begin to see things better!' I fell musing deeply, but I did not doubt then this career of mine was a thing that merited sacrifice.

"Those dear friends and that clear atmosphere seemed very sweet to me, very fine but remote. My grip was fixing now upon the world. I saw another door opening—the door of my career."

He stared again into the fire. Its red light picked out a stubborn strength in his face for just one flickering moment, and then it vanished again.

"Well," he said, and sighed, "I have served that career. I have done—much work, much hard work. But I have dreamt of the enchanted garden a thousand dreams, and seen its door, or at least glimpsed its door, four times since then. Yes—four times. For a while this world was so bright and inter-esting, seemed so full of meaning and opportunity, that the half-effaced charm of the garden was by comparison gentle and remote. Who wants to pat panthers on the way to dinner with pretty women and distinguished men? I came down to London from Oxford, a man of bold promise that I have done something to redeem. Something—and yet there have been dis-appointments. . . .

"Twice I have been in love—I will not dwell on that—but once, as I went to someone who, I knew, doubted whether I dared to come, I took a short cut at a venture through an unfrequented road near Earl's Court, and so happened on a white wall and a familiar green door. 'Odd!' said I to myself, 'but I thought this place was on Campden Hill. It's the place I never could find somehow—like counting Stonehenge—the place of that queer daydream of mine.' And I went by it intent upon my purpose. It had no appeal to me that afternoon.

"I had just a moment's impulse to try the door, three steps aside were needed at the most—though I was sure enough in my heart that it would open to me—and then I thought that doing so might delay me on the way to that appointment in which my honour was involved. Afterwards I was sorry for my punctuality—I might at least have peeped in and waved a hand to those panthers, but I knew enough by this time not to seek again belatedly that which is not found by seeking. Yes, that time made me very sorry. . . .

"Years of hard work after that, and never a sight of the door. It's only recently it has come back to me. With it there has come a sense as though some thin tarnish had spread itself over my world. I began to think of it as a sorrowful and bitter thing that I should never see that door again. Perhaps I was suffering a little from overwork—perhaps it was what I've heard spoken of as the feeling of forty. I don't know. But certainly the keen brightness that makes effort easy has gone out of things recently, and that just at a time—with all these new political developments—when I ought to be working. Odd, isn't it? But I do begin to find life toilsome, its rewards, as I come near them, cheap. I began a little while ago to want the garden quite badly. Yes—and I've seen it three times."

"The garden?"

"No—the door! And I haven't gone in!"

He leaned over the table to me, with an enormous sorrow in his voice as he spoke. "Thrice I have had my chance—*thrice!* If ever that door offers itself to me again, I swore, I will go in, out of this dust and heat, out of this dry glitter of vanity, out of these toilsome futilities. I will go and never return. This time I will stay. . . . I swore it, and when the time came—*I didn't go.*

"Three times in one year have I passed that door and failed to enter. Three times in the last year.

"The first time was on the night of the snatch division on the Tenants' Redemption Bill, on which the Government was saved by a majority of three. You remember? No one on our side—perhaps very few on the opposite side—expected the end that night. Then the debate collapsed like eggshells. I and Hotchkiss were dining with his cousin at Brentford; we were both unpaired, and we were called up by telephone, and set off at once in his cousin's motor. We got in barely in time, and on the way we passed my wall and door—livid in the moonlight, blotched with hot yellow as the glare of our lamps lit it, but unmistakable. 'My God!' cried I. 'What?' said Hotchkiss. 'Nothing!' I answered, and the moment passed.

" 'I've made a great sacrifice,' I told the whip as I got in. 'They all have,' he said, and hurried by.

"I do not see how I could have done otherwise then. And the next occasion was as I rushed to my father's bedside to bid that stern old man farewell. Then, too, the claims of life were imperative. But the third time was different; it happened a week ago. It fills me with hot remorse to recall it. I was with Gurker and Ralphs—it's no secret now, you know, that I've had my talk with Gurker. We had been dining at Frobisher's, and the talk had become intimate between us. The question of my place in the reconstructed Ministry lay always just over the boundary of the discussion. Yes—yes. That's all settled. It needn't be talked about yet, but there's no reason to keep it secret from you. . . . Yes—thanks! thanks! But let me tell you my story.

"Then, on that night things were very much in the air. My position was a very delicate one. I was keenly anxious to get some definite word from Gurker, but was hampered by Ralphs' presence. I was using the best power of my brain to keep that light and careless talk not too obviously directed to the point that concerned me. I had to. Ralphs' behaviour since has more than justified my caution. . . . Ralphs, I knew, would leave us beyond the Kensington High Street, and then I could surprise Gurker by a sudden frankness. One has sometimes to resort to these little devices. . . . And then it was that in the margin of my field of vision I became aware once more of the white wall, the green door before us down the road.

"We passed it talking. I passed it. I can still see the shadow of Gurker's marked profile, his opera hat tilted forward over his prominent nose, the many folds of his neck wrap going before my shadow and Ralphs' as we sauntered past.

"I passed within twenty inches of the door. 'If I say good-night to them, and go in,' I asked myself, 'what will happen?' And I was all a-tingle for that word with Gurker.

"I could not answer that question in the tangle of my other problems. 'They will think me mad,' I thought. 'And suppose I vanish now!—Amazing disappearance of a prominent politician!' That weighed with me. A thousand inconceivably petty worldlinesses weighed with me in that crisis."

Then he turned on me with a sorrowful smile, and, speaking slowly, "Here I am!" he said.

"Here I am!" he repeated, "and my chance has gone from me. Three times in one year the door has been offered me—the door that goes into peace, into delight, into a beauty beyond dreaming, a kindness no man on earth can know. And I have rejected it, Redmond, and it has gone——"

"How do you know?"

"I know. I know. I am left now to work it out, to stick to the tasks that held me so strongly when my moments came. You say I have success—this vulgar, tawdry, irksome, envied thing. I have it." He had a walnut in his big hand. "If that was my success," he said, and crushed it, and held it out for me to see.

"Let me tell you something, Redmond. This loss is destroying me. For two months, for ten weeks nearly now, I have done no work at all, except the most necessary and urgent duties. My soul is full of inappeasable regrets. At nights—when it is less likely I shall be recognised—I go out. I wander. Yes. I wonder what people would think of that if they knew. A Cabinet Minister, the responsible head of that most vital of all departments, wandering alone—grieving—sometimes near audibly lamenting—for a door, for a garden!"

IV

I can see now his rather pallid face, and the unfamiliar sombre fire that had come into his eyes. I see him very vividly to-night. I sit recalling his words, his tones, and last evening's *Westminster Gazette* still lies on my sofa, containing the notice of his death. At lunch to-day the club was busy with his death. We talked of nothing else.

They found his body very early yesterday morning in a deep excavation near East Kensington Station. It is one of two shafts that have been made in connection with an extension of the railway southward. It is protected from the intrusion of the public by a hoarding upon the high-road, in which a small doorway has been cut for the convenience of some of the workmen who live in that direction. The doorway was left unfastened through a misunderstanding between two gangers, and through it he made his way.

My mind is darkened with questions and riddles.

It would seem he walked all the way from the House that night—he has frequently walked home during the past Session—and so it is I figure his dark form coming along the late and empty streets, wrapped up, intent. And then did the pale electric lights near the station cheat the rough planking into a semblance of white? Did that fatal unfastened door awaken some memory?

Was there, after all, ever any green door in the wall at all?

I do not know. I have told his story as he told it to me. There are times when I believe that Wallace was no more than the victim of the coincidence between a rare but not unprecedented type of hallucination and a careless trap, but that indeed is not my profoundest belief. You may think me superstitious, if you will, and foolish; but, indeed, I am more than half convinced that he had, in truth, an abnormal gift, and a sense, something—I know not what—that in the guise of wall and door offered him an outlet, a secret and peculiar passage of escape into another and altogether more beautiful world. At any rate, you will say, it betrayed him in the end. But did it betray him? There you touch the inmost mystery of these dreamers, these men of vision and the imagination. We see our world fair and common, the hoarding and the pit. By our daylight standard he walked out of security into darkness, danger, and death.

But did he see like that?

AN EXPERIMENT IN MISERY

Stephen Crane

(1871–1900)

I<small>T WAS LATE AT NIGHT</small>, and a fine rain was swirling softly down, causing the pavements to glisten with hue of steel and blue and yellow in the rays of the innumerable lights. A youth was trudging slowly, without enthusiasm, with his hands buried deep in his trousers' pockets, toward the downtown places where beds can be hired for coppers. He was clothed in an aged and tattered suit, and his derby was a marvel of dust-covered crown and torn rim. He was going forth to eat as the wanderer may eat, and sleep as the homeless sleep. By the time he had reached City Hall Park he was so completely plastered with yells of "bum" and "hobo," and with various unholy epithets that small boys had applied to him at intervals, that he was in a state of the most profound dejection. The sifting rain saturated the old velvet collar of his overcoat, and as the wet cloth pressed against his neck, he felt that there no longer could be pleasure in life. He looked about him searching for an outcast of highest degree that they too might share miseries, but the lights threw a quivering glare over rows and circles of deserted benches that glistened damply, showing patches of wet sod behind them. It seemed that their usual freights had fled on this night to better things. There were only squads of well-dressed Brooklyn people who swarmed towards the bridge.

The young man loitered about for a time and then went shuffling off down Park Row. In the sudden descent in style of the dress of the crowd he felt relief, and as if he were at last in his own country. He began to see tatters that matched his tatters. In Chatham Square there were aimless men strewn in front of saloons and lodging-houses, standing sadly, patiently, reminding one vaguely of the attitudes of chickens in a storm. He aligned himself with these men, and turned slowly to occupy himself with the flowing life of the great street.

Through the mists of the cold and storming night, the cable cars went in silent procession, great affairs shining with red and brass, moving with formidable power, calm and irresistible, dangerful and gloomy, breaking silence only by the loud fierce cry of the gong. Two rivers of people swarmed along the sidewalks, spattered with black mud, which made each shoe leave a scarlike impression. Overhead elevated trains with a shrill grinding of the wheels stopped at the station, which upon its leglike pillars seemed to resemble some monstrous kind of crab squatting over the street. The quick fat puffings of the engines could be heard. Down an alley there were somber curtains of purple and black, on which street lamps dully glittered like embroidered flowers.

A saloon stood with a voracious air on a corner. A sign leaning against the front of the door-post announced "Free hot soup to-night!" The swing doors, snapping to and fro like ravenous lips, made gratified smacks as the saloon gorged itself with plump men, eating with astounding and endless appetite, smiling in some indescribable manner as the men came from all directions like sacrifices to a heathenish superstition.

Caught by the delectable sign the young man allowed himself to be swallowed. A bartender placed a schooner of dark and portentous beer on the bar. Its monumental form upreared until the froth a-top was above the crown of the young man's brown derby.

"Soup over there, gents," said the bartender affably. A little yellow man in rags and the youth grasped their schooners and went with speed toward a lunch counter, where a man with oily but imposing whiskers ladled genially from a kettle until he had furnished his two mendicants with a soup that was steaming hot, and in which there were little floating suggestions of chicken. The young man, sipping his broth, felt the cordiality expressed by the warmth of the mixture, and he beamed at the man with oily but imposing whiskers, who was presiding like a priest behind an altar. "Have some more, gents?" he inquired of the two sorry figures before him. The little yellow man accepted with a swift gesture, but the youth shook his head and went out, following a man whose wondrous seediness promised that he would have a knowledge of cheap lodging-houses.

On the sidewalk he accosted the seedy man. "Say, do you know a cheap place to sleep?"

The other hesitated for a time, gazing sideways. Finally he nodded in the direction of the street, "I sleep up there," he said, "when I've got the price."

"How much?"

"Ten cents."

The young man shook his head dolefully. "That's too rich for me."

At that moment there approached the two a reeling man in strange garments. His head was a fuddle of bushy hair and whiskers, from which his eyes peered with a guilty slant. In a close scrutiny it was possible to distinguish the cruel lines of a mouth which looked as if its lips had just closed with satisfaction over some tender and piteous morsel. He appeared like an assassin steeped in crimes performed awkwardly.

But at this time his voice was tuned to the coaxing key of an affectionate puppy. He looked at the men with wheedling eyes, and began to sing a little melody for charity.

"Say, gents, can't yeh give a poor feller a couple of cents t' git a bed? I got five, and I gits anudder two I gits me a bed. Now, on th' square, gents, can't yeh jest gimme two cents t' git a bed? Now, yeh know how a respecter'ble gentlem'n feels when he's down on his luck, an' I——"

The seedy man, staring with imperturbable countenance at a train which clattered overhead, interrupted in an expressionless voice—"Ah, go t' h——!"

But the youth spoke to the prayerful assassin in tones of astonishment and inquiry. "Say, you must be crazy! Why don't yeh strike somebody that looks as if they had money?"

The assassin, tottering about on his uncertain legs, and at intervals brushing imaginary obstacles from before his nose, entered into a long explanation of the psychology of the situation. It was so profound that it was unintelligible.

When he had exhausted the subject, the young man said to him: "Let's see th' five cents."

The assassin wore an expression of drunken woe at this sentence, filled with suspicion of him. With a deeply pained air he began to fumble in his clothing, his red hands trembling. Presently he announced in a voice of bitter grief, as if he had been betrayed—"There's on'y four."

"Four," said the young man thoughtfully. "Well, look here, I'm a stranger here, an' if ye'll steer me to your cheap joint I'll find the other three."

The assassin's countenance became instantly radiant with joy. His whiskers quivered with the wealth of his alleged emotions. He seized the young man's hand in a transport of delight and friendliness.

"B' Gawd," he cried, "if ye'll do that, b' Gawd, I'd say yeh was a damned good fellow, I would, an' I'd remember yeh all m' life, I would, b' Gawd, an' if I ever got a chance I'd return the compliment"—he spoke with drunken dignity—"b' Gawd, I'd treat yeh white, I would, an' I'd allus remember yeh."

The young man drew back, looking at the assassin coldly. "Oh, that's all right," he said. "You show me th' joint—that's all you've got t' do."

The assassin, gesticulating gratitude, led the young man along a dark street. Finally he stopped before a little dusty door. He raised his hand impressively. "Look-a-here," he said, and there was a thrill of deep and ancient wisdom upon his face, "I've brought yeh here, an' that's my part, ain't it? If th' place don't suit yeh, yeh needn't git mad at me, need yeh? There won't be no bad feelin', will there?"

"No," said the young man.

The assassin waved his arm tragically, and led the march up the steep stairway. On the way the young man furnished the assassin with three pennies. At the top a man with benevolent spectacles looked at them through a hole in a board. He collected their money, wrote some names on a register, and speedily was leading the two men along a gloom-shrouded corridor.

Shortly after the beginning of this journey the young man felt his liver turn white, for from the dark and secret places of the building there suddenly came to his nostrils strange and unspeakable odors, that assailed him like malignant diseases with wings. They seemed to be from human bodies closely packed in dens; the exhalations from a hundred pairs of reeking lips; the fumes from a thousand bygone debauches; the expression of a thousand present miseries.

A man, naked save for a little snuff-colored undershirt, was parading sleepily along the corridor. He rubbed his eyes, and, giving vent to a prodigious yawn, demanded to be told the time.

"Half-past one."

The man yawned again. He opened a door, and for a moment his form was outlined against a black, opaque interior. To this door came the three men, and as it was again opened the unholy odors rushed out like fiends, so that the young man was obliged to struggle as against an overpowering wind.

It was some time before the youth's eyes were good in the intense gloom within, but the man with benevolent spectacles led him skillfully, pausing but a moment to deposit the limp assassin upon a cot. He took the youth to a cot that lay tranquilly by the window, and showing him a tall locker for clothes that stood near the head with the ominous air of a tombstone, left him.

The youth sat on his cot and peered about him. There was a gas-jet in a distant part of the room, that burned a small flickering orange-hued flame. It caused vast masses of tumbled shadows in all parts of the place, save where, immediately about it, there was a little grey haze. As the young man's eyes became used to the darkness, he could see upon the cots that thickly littered the floor the forms of men sprawled out, lying in deathlike silence, or heaving and snoring with tremendous effort, like stabbed fish.

The youth locked his derby and his shoes in the mummy case near him, and then lay down with an old and familiar coat around his shoulders. A blanket he handed gingerly, drawing it over part of the coat. The cot was covered with leather, and as cold as melting snow. The youth was obliged to shiver for some time on this affair, which was like a slab. Presently, however, his chill gave him peace, and during this period of leisure from it he turned his head to stare at his friend the assassin, whom he could dimly discern where he lay sprawled on a cot in the abandon of a man filled with drink. He was snoring with incredible vigor. His wet hair and beard dimly glistened, and his inflamed nose shone with subdued lustre like a red light in a fog.

Within reach of the youth's hand was one who lay with yellow breast and shoulders bare to the cold drafts. One arm hung over the side of the cot, and the fingers lay full length upon the wet cement floor of the room. Beneath the inky brows could be seen the eyes of the man exposed by the partly opened lids. To the youth it seemed that he and this corpse-like being were exchanging a prolonged stare, and that the other threatened with his eyes. He drew back, watching his neighbor from the shadows of his blanket edge. The man did not move once through the night, but lay in this stillness as of death like a body stretched out expectant of the surgeon's knife.

And all through the room could be seen the tawny hues of naked flesh, limbs thrust into the darkness, projecting beyond the cots; upreared knees, arms hanging long and thin over the cot edges. For the most part they were statuesque, carven, dead. With the curious lockers standing all about like tombstones, there was a strange effect of a graveyard where bodies were merely flung.

Yet occasionally could be seen limbs wildly tossing in fantastic nightmare gestures, accompanied by guttural cries, grunts, oaths. And there was one fellow off in a gloomy corner, who in his dreams was oppressed by some frightful calamity, for of a sudden he began to utter long wails that went almost like yells from a hound, echoing wailfully and weird through this chill place of tombstones where men lay like the dead.

The sound in its high piercing beginnings, that dwindled to final melancholy moans, expressed a red and grim tragedy of the unfathomable possibilities of the man's dreams. But to the youth these were not merely the shrieks of a vision-pierced man: they were an utterance of the meaning of the room and its occupants. It was to him the protest of the wretch who feels the touch of the imperturbable granite wheels, and who then cries with an impersonal eloquence, with a strength not from him, giving voice to the wail of a whole section, a class, a people. This, weaving into the young man's brain, and mingling with his views of the vast and sombre shadows that, like mighty black fingers, curled around the naked bodies, made the young man so that he did not sleep, but lay carving the biographies for these men from his meagre experience. At times the fellow in the corner howled in a writhing agony of his imaginations.

Finally a long lance-point of grey light shot through the dusty panes of the window. Without, the young man could see roofs drearily white in the dawning. The point of light yellowed and grew brighter, until the golden rays of the morning sun came in bravely and strong. They touched with radiant color the form of a small fat man, who snored in stuttering fashion. His round and shiny bald head glowed suddenly with the valor of a decoration. He sat up, blinked at the sun, swore fretfully, and pulled his blanket over the ornamental splendors of his head.

The youth contentedly watched this rout of the shadows before the bright spears of the sun, and presently he slumbered. When he awoke he heard the voice of the assassin raised in valiant curses. Putting up his head, he perceived his comrade seated on the side of the cot engaged in scratching his neck with long finger-nails that rasped like files.

"Hully Jee, dis is a new breed. They've got can-openers on their feet." He continued in a violent tirade.

The young man hastily unlocked his closet and took out his shoes and hat. As he sat on the side of the cot lacing his shoes, he glanced about and saw that daylight had made the room comparatively commonplace and uninteresting. The men, whose faces seemed stolid, serene or absent, were engaged in dressing, while a great crackle of bantering conversation arose.

A few were parading in unconcerned nakedness. Here and there were men of brawn, whose skins shone clear and ruddy. They took splendid poses, standing massively like chiefs. When they had dressed in their ungainly garments there was an extraordinary change. They then showed bumps and deficiencies of all kinds.

There were others who exhibited many deformities. Shoulders were slanting, humped, pulled this way and pulled that way. And notable among these latter men was the little fat man who had refused to allow his head to be glorified. His pudgy form, builded like a pear, bustled to and fro, while he swore in fishwife fashion. It appeared that some article of his apparel had vanished.

The young man attired speedily, and went to his friend the assassin. At first the latter looked dazed at the sight of the youth. This face seemed to be appealing to him through the cloud wastes of his memory. He scratched his neck and reflected. At last he grinned, a broad smile gradually spreading until his countenance was a round illumination. "Hello, Willie," he cried cheerily.

"Hello," said the young man. "Are yeh ready t' fly?"

"Sure." The assassin tied his shoe carefully with some twine and came ambling.

When he reached the street the young man experienced no sudden relief from unholy atmospheres. He had forgotten all about them, and had been breathing naturally, and with no sensation of discomfort or distress.

He was thinking of these things as he walked along the street, when he was suddenly startled by feeling the assassin's hand, trembling with excitement, clutching his arm, and when the assassin spoke, his voice went into quavers from a supreme agitation.

"I'll be hully, bloomin' blowed if there wasn't a feller with a nightshirt on up there in that joint."

The youth was bewildered for a moment, but presently he turned to smile indulgently at the assassin's humor.

"Oh, you're a d——d liar," he merely said.

Whereupon the assassin began to gesture extravagantly, and take oath by strange gods. He frantically placed himself at the mercy of remarkable fates if his tale were not true.

"Yes, he did! I cross m' heart thousan' times!" he protested, and at the moment his eyes were large with amazement, his mouth wrinkled in un- natural glee.

"Yessir! A nightshirt! A hully white nightshirt!"

"You lie!"

"No, sir! I hope ter die b'fore I kin git anudder ball if there wasn't a jay wid a hully, bloomin' white nightshirt!"

His face was filled with the infinite wonder of it. "A hully white night- shirt," he continually repeated.

The young man saw the dark entrance to a basement restaurant. There was a sign which read "No mystery about our hash!" and there were other age-stained and world-battered legends which told him that the place was within his means. He stopped before it and spoke to the assassin. "I guess I'll git somethin' t' eat."

At this the assassin, for some reason, appeared to be quite embarrassed. He gazed at the seductive front of the eating place for a moment. Then he started slowly up the street. "Well, good-bye, Willie," he said bravely.

For an instant the youth studied the departing figure. Then he called out, "Hol' on a minnet." As they came together he spoke in a certain fierce way, as if he feared that the other would think him to be charitable. "Look-a- here, if yeh wanta git some breakfas' I'll lend yeh three cents t' do it with. But say, look-a-here, you've gota git out an' hustle. I ain't goin' t' support yeh, or I'll go broke b'fore night. I ain't no millionaire."

"I take me oath, Willie," said the assassin earnestly, "th' on'y thing I really needs is a ball. Me t'roat feels like a fryin'-pan. But as I can't get a ball, why, th' next bes' thing is breakfast, an' if yeh do that for me, b' Gawd, I say yeh was th' whitest lad I ever see."

They spent a few moments in dexterous exchanges of phrases, in which they each protested that the other was, as the assassin had originally said, "a respecter'ble gentlem'n." And they concluded with mutual assurances that they were the souls of intelligence and virtue. Then they went into the restaurant.

There was a long counter, dimly lighted from hidden sources. Two or three men in soiled white aprons rushed here and there.

The youth bought a bowl of coffee for two cents and a roll for one cent. The assassin purchased the same. The bowls were webbed with brown seams, and the tin spoons wore an air of having emerged from the first pyramid. Upon them were black mosslike encrustations of age, and they were bent and scarred from the attacks of long-forgotten teeth. But over their repast the wanderers waxed warm and mellow. The assassin grew affable as the hot mixture went soothingly down his parched throat, and the young man felt courage flow in his veins.

Memories began to throng in on the assassin, and he brought forth long tales, intricate, incoherent, delivered with a chattering swiftness as from an old woman. "——great job out'n Orange. Boss keep yeh hustlin' though all time. I was there three days, and then I went an' ask 'im t' lend me a dollar. 'G-g-go ter the devil,' he ses, an' I lose me job."

"South no good. Damn niggers work for twenty-five an' thirty cents a day. Run white man out. Good grub, though. Easy livin'."

"Yas; useter work little in Toledo, raftin' logs. Make two or three dollars er day in the spring. Lived high. Cold as ice, though, in the winter."

"I was raised in northern N'York. O-a-ah, yeh jest oughto live there. No beer ner whisky, though, way off in the woods. But all th' good hot grub yeh can eat. B'Gawd, I hung around there long as I could till th' ol' man fired me. 'Git t' hell outa here, yeh wuthless skunk, git t' hell outa here, an' go die,' he ses. 'You're a hell of a father,' I ses, 'you are,' an' I quit 'im."

As they were passing from the dim eating place, they encountered an old man who was trying to steal forth with a tiny package of food, but a tall man with an indomitable moustache stood dragon fashion, barring the way of escape. They heard the old man raise a plaintive protest. "Ah, you always want to know what I take out, and you never see that I usually bring a package in here from my place of business."

As the wanderers trudged slowly along Park Row, the assassin began to expand and grow blithe. "B'Gawd, we've been livin' like kings," he said, smacking appreciative lips.

"Look out, or we'll have t' pay fer it t'night," said the youth with gloomy warning.

But the assassin refused to turn his gaze toward the future. He went with a limping step, into which he injected a suggestion of lamblike gambols. His mouth was wreathed in a red grin.

In the City Hall Park the two wanderers sat down in the little circle of benches sanctified by traditions of their class. They huddled in their old garments, slumbrously conscious of the march of the hours which for them had no meaning.

The people of the street hurrying hither and thither made a blend of black figures changing yet frieze-like. They walked in their good clothes as upon important missions, giving no gaze to the two wanderers seated upon the benches. They expressed to the young man his infinite distance from all that he valued. Social position, comfort, the pleasures of living, were unconquerable kingdoms. He felt a sudden awe.

And in the background a multitude of buildings, of pitiless hues and sternly high, were to him emblematic of a nation forcing its regal head into the clouds, throwing no downward glances; in the sublimity of its aspirations ignoring the wretches who may flounder at its feet. The roar of the city in his ear was to him the confusion of strange tongues, babbling heedlessly; it was the clink of coin, the voice of the city's hopes which were to him no hopes.

He confessed himself an outcast, and his eyes from under the lowered rim of his hat began to glance guiltily, wearing the criminal expression that comes with certain convictions.

TOBERMORY

Saki

(1870–1916)

It was a chill, rain-washed afternoon of a late August day, that indefinite season when partridges are still in security or cold storage, and there is nothing to hunt—unless one is bounded on the north by the Bristol Channel, in which case one may lawfully gallop after fat red stags. Lady Blemley's house-party was not bounded on the north by the Bristol Channel, hence there was a full gathering of her guests round the tea-table on this particular afternoon. And, in spite of the blankness of the season and the triteness of the occasion, there was no trace in the company of that fatigued restlessness which means a dread of the pianola and a subdued hankering for auction bridge. The undisguised open-mouthed attention of the entire party was fixed on the homely negative personality of Mr. Cornelius Appin. Of all her guests, he was the one who had come to Lady Blemley with the vaguest reputation. Some one had said he was "clever," and he had got his invitation in the moderate expectation, on the part of his hostess, that some portion at least of his cleverness would be contributed to the general entertainment. Until tea-time that day she had been unable to discover in what direction, if any, his cleverness lay. He was neither a wit nor a croquet champion, a hypnotic force nor a begetter of amateur theatricals. Neither did his exterior suggest the sort of man in whom women are willing to pardon a generous measure of mental deficiency. He had subsided into mere Mr. Appin, and the Cornelius seemed a piece of transparent baptismal bluff. And now he was claiming to have launched on the world a discovery beside which the invention of gunpowder, of the printing-press, and of steam locomotion were inconsiderable trifles. Science had made bewildering strides in many directions during recent decades, but this thing seemed to belong to the domain of miracle rather than to scientific achievement.

"And do you really ask us to believe," Sir Wilfrid was saying, "that you have discovered a means for instructing animals in the art of human speech, and that dear old Tobermory has proved your first successful pupil?"

"It is a problem at which I have worked for the last seventeen years," said Mr. Appin, "but only during the last eight or nine months have I been rewarded with glimmerings of success. Of course I have experimented with thousands of animals, but latterly only with cats, those wonderful creatures which have assimilated themselves so marvellously with our civilization while retaining all their highly developed feral instincts. Here and there among cats one comes across an outstanding superior intellect, just as one does among the ruck of human beings, and when I made the acquaintance of Tobermory a week ago I saw at once that I was in contact with a 'Beyond-cat' of extraordinary intelligence. I had gone far along the road to success in recent experiments; with Tobermory, as you call him, I have reached the goal."

Mr. Appin concluded his remarkable statement in a voice which he strove to divest of a triumphant inflection. No one said "Rats," though Clovis's lips moved in a monosyllabic contortion which probably invoked those rodents of disbelief.

"And do you mean to say," asked Miss Resker, after a slight pause, "that you have taught Tobermory to say and understand easy sentences of one syllable?"

"My dear Miss Resker," said the wonder-worker patiently, "one teaches little children and savages and backward adults in that piecemeal fashion; when one has once solved the problem of making a beginning with an animal of highly developed intelligence one has no need for those halting methods. Tobermory can speak our language with perfect correctness."

This time Clovis very distinctly said, "Beyond-rats!" Sir Wilfrid was more polite, but equally sceptical.

"Hadn't we better have the cat in and judge for ourselves?" suggested Lady Blemley.

Sir Wilfrid went in search of the animal, and the company settled themselves down to the languid expectation of witnessing some more or less adroit drawing-room ventriloquism.

In a minute Sir Wilfrid was back in the room, his face white beneath its tan and his eyes dilated with excitement.

"By Gad, it's true!"

His agitation was unmistakably genuine, and his hearers started forward in a thrill of awakened interest.

Collapsing into an armchair he continued breathlessly: "I found him dozing in the smoking-room, and called out to him to come for his tea. He blinked at me in his usual way, and I said, 'Come on, Toby; don't keep us waiting'; and, by Gad! he drawled out in a most horribly natural voice that he'd come when he dashed well pleased! I nearly jumped out of my skin!"

Appin had preached to absolutely incredulous hearers; Sir Wilfrid's statement carried instant conviction. A Babel-like chorus of startled exclamation arose, amid which the scientist sat mutely enjoying the first fruit of his stupendous discovery.

In the midst of the clamour Tobermory entered the room and made his way with velvet tread and studied unconcern across to the group seated round the tea-table.

A sudden hush of awkwardness and constraint fell on the company. Somehow there seemed an element of embarrassment in addressing on equal terms a domestic cat of acknowledged dental ability.

"Will you have some milk, Tobermory?" asked Lady Blemley in a rather strained voice.

"I don't mind if I do," was the response, couched in a tone of even indifference. A shiver of suppressed excitement went through the listeners, and Lady Blemley might be excused for pouring out the saucerful of milk rather unsteadily.

"I'm afraid I've spilt a good deal of it," she said apologetically.

"After all, it's not my Axminster," was Tobermory's rejoinder.

Another silence fell on the group, and then Miss Resker, in her best district-visitor manner, asked if the human language had been difficult to learn. Tobermory looked squarely at her for a moment and then fixed his gaze serenely on the middle distance. It was obvious that boring questions lay outside his scheme of life.

"What do you think of human intelligence?" asked Mavis Pellington lamely.

"Of whose intelligence in particular?" asked Tobermory coldly.

"Oh, well, mine for instance," said Mavis, with a feeble laugh.

"You put me in an embarrassing position," said Tobermory, whose tone and attitude certainly did not suggest a shred of embarrassment. "When your inclusion in this house-party was suggested Sir Wilfrid protested that you were the most brainless woman of his acquaintance, and that there was a wide distinction between hospitality and the care of the feeble-minded. Lady Blemley replied that your lack of brain-power was the precise quality which had earned you your invitation, as you were the only person she could think of who might be idiotic enough to buy their old car. You know, the one they call 'The Envy of Sisyphus,' because it goes quite nicely up-hill if you push it."

Lady Blemley's protestations would have had greater effect if she had not casually suggested to Mavis only that morning that the car in question would be just the thing for her down at her Devonshire home.

Major Barfield plunged in heavily to effect a diversion.

"How about your carryings-on with the tortoise-shell puss up at the stables, eh?"

The moment he had said it every one realized the blunder.

"One does not usually discuss these matters in public," said Tobermory frigidly. "From a slight observation of your ways since you've been in this house I should imagine you'd find it inconvenient if I were to shift the conversation on to your own little affairs."

The panic which ensued was not confined to the Major.

"Would you like to go and see if cook has got your dinner ready?" suggested Lady Blemley hurriedly, affecting to ignore the fact that it wanted at least two hours to Tobermory's dinner-time.

"Thanks," said Tobermory, "not quite so soon after my tea. I don't want to die of indigestion."

"Cats have nine lives, you know," said Sir Wilfrid heartily.

"Possibly," answered Tobermory; "but only one liver."

"Adelaide!" said Mrs. Cornett, "do you mean to encourage that cat to go out and gossip about us in the servants' hall?"

The panic had indeed become general. A narrow ornamental balustrade ran in front of most of the bedroom windows at the Towers, and it was recalled with dismay that this had formed a favourite promenade for Tobermory at all hours, whence he could watch the pigeons—and heaven knew what else besides. If he intended to become reminiscent in his present outspoken strain the effect would be something more than disconcerting. Mrs. Cornett, who spent much time at her toilet table, and whose complexion was reputed to be of a nomadic though punctual disposition, looked as ill at ease as the Major. Miss Scrawen, who wrote fiercely sensuous poetry and led a blameless life, merely displayed irritation; if you are methodical and virtuous in private you don't necessarily want every one to know it. Bertie van Tahn, who was so depraved at seventeen that he had long ago given up trying to be any worse, turned a dull shade of gardenia white, but he did not commit the error of dashing out of the room like Odo Finsberry, a young gentleman who was understood to be reading for the Church and who was possibly disturbed at the thought of scandals he might hear concerning other people. Clovis had the presence of mind to maintain a composed exterior; privately he was calculating how long it would take to procure a box of fancy mice through the agency of the *Exchange and Mart* as a species of hush-money.

Even in a delicate situation like the present, Agnes Resker could not endure to remain too long in the background.

"Why did I ever come down here?" she asked dramatically.

Tobermory immediately accepted the opening.

"Judging by what you said to Mrs. Cornett on the croquet-lawn yesterday, you were out for food. You described the Blemleys as the dullest people to stay with that you knew, but said they were clever enough to employ a first-rate cook; otherwise they'd find it difficult to get any one to come down a second time."

"There's not a word of truth in it! I appeal to Mrs. Cornett——" exclaimed the discomfited Agnes.

"Mrs. Cornett repeated your remark afterwards to Bertie van Tahn," continued Tobermory, "and said, 'That woman is a regular Hunger Marcher; she'd go anywhere for four square meals a day,' and Bertie van Tahn said——"

At this point the chronicle mercifully ceased. Tobermory had caught a glimpse of the big yellow Tom from the Rectory working his way through the shrubbery towards the stable wing. In a flash he had vanished through the open French window.

With the disappearance of his too brilliant pupil Cornelius Appin found himself beset by a hurricane of bitter upbraiding, anxious inquiry, and frightened entreaty. The responsibility for the situation lay with him, and he must prevent matters from becoming worse. Could Tobermory impart his dangerous gift to other cats? was the first question he had to answer. It was possible, he replied, that he might have initiated his intimate friend the stable puss into his new accomplishment, but it was unlikely that his teaching could have taken a wider range as yet.

"Then," said Mrs. Cornett, "Tobermory may be a valuable cat and a great pet; but I'm sure you'll agree, Adelaide, that both he and the stable cat must be done away with without delay."

"You don't suppose I've enjoyed the last quarter of an hour, do you?" said Lady Blemley bitterly. "My husband and I are very fond of Tobermory—at least, we were before this horrible accomplishment was infused into him; but now, of course, the only thing is to have him destroyed as soon as possible."

"We can put some strychnine in the scraps he always gets at dinner-time," said Sir Wilfrid, "and I will go and drown the stable cat myself. The coachman will be very sore at losing his pet, but I'll say a very catching form of mange has broken out in both cats and we're afraid of it spreading to the kennels."

"But my great discovery!" expostulated Mr. Appin; "after all my years of research and experiment——"

"You can go and experiment on the short-horns at the farm, who are under proper control," said Mrs. Cornett, "or the elephants at the Zoological Gardens. They're said to be highly intelligent, and they have this recommendation, that they don't come creeping about our bedrooms and under chairs, and so forth."

An archangel ecstatically proclaiming the Millennium, and then finding that it clashed unpardonably with Henley and would have to be indefinitely postponed, could hardly have felt more crestfallen than Cornelius Appin at the reception of his wonderful achievement. Public opinion, however, was against him—in fact, had the general voice been consulted on the subject it is probable that a strong minority vote would have been in favour of including him in the strychnine diet.

Defective train arrangements and a nervous desire to see matters brought to a finish prevented an immediate dispersal of the party, but dinner that evening was not a social success. Sir Wilfrid had had rather a trying time with the stable cat and subsequently with the coachman. Agnes Resker ostentatiously limited her repast to a morsel of dry toast, which she bit as though it were a personal enemy; while Mavis Pellington maintained a vindictive silence throughout the meal. Lady Blemley kept up a flow of what she hoped was conversation, but her attention was fixed on the doorway. A plateful of carefully dosed fish scraps was in readiness on the sideboard, but sweets and savoury and dessert went their way, and no Tobermory appeared either in the dining-room or kitchen.

The sepulchral dinner was cheerful compared with the subsequent vigil in the smoking-room. Eating and drinking had at least supplied a distraction and cloak to the prevailing embarrassment. Bridge was out of the question in the general tension of nerves and tempers, and after Odo Finsberry had given a lugubrious rendering of "Mélisande in the Wood" to a frigid audience, music was tacitly avoided. At eleven the servants went to bed, announcing that the small window in the pantry had been left open as usual for Tobermory's private use. The guests read steadily through the current batch of magazines, and fell back gradually on the "Badminton Library" and bound volumes of *Punch*. Lady Blemley made periodic visits to the pantry, returning each time with an expression of listless depression which forestalled questioning.

At two o'clock Clovis broke the dominating silence.

"He won't turn up tonight. He's probably in the local newspaper office at the present moment, dictating the first instalment of his reminiscences. Lady What's-her-name's book won't be in it. It will be the event of the day."

Having made this contribution to the general cheerfulness, Clovis went to bed. At long intervals the various members of the house-party followed his example.

The servants taking round the early tea made a uniform announcement in reply to a uniform question. Tobermory had not returned.

Breakfast was, if anything, a more unpleasant function than dinner had been, but before its conclusion the situation was relieved. Tobermory's corpse was brought in from the shrubbery, where a gardener had just discovered it. From the bites on his throat and the yellow fur which coated his claws it was evident that he had fallen in unequal combat with the big Tom from the Rectory.

By midday most of the guests had quitted the Towers, and after lunch
Lady Blemley had sufficiently recovered her spirits to write an extremely
nasty letter to the Rectory about the loss of her valuable pet.

Tobermory had been Appin's one successful pupil, and he was destined
to have no successor. A few weeks later an elephant in the Dresden Zoological Garden, which had shown no previous signs of irritability, broke loose
and killed an Englishman who had apparently been teasing it. The victim's
name was variously reported in the papers as Oppin and Eppelin, but his
front name was faithfully rendered Cornelius.

"If he was trying German irregular verbs on the poor beast," said Clovis,
"he deserved all he got."

TO BUILD A FIRE

Jack London

(1876–1916)

DAY HAD BROKEN cold and grey, exceedingly cold and grey, when the man
turned aside from the main Yukon trail and climbed the high earth-bank,
where a dim and little-travelled trail led eastward through the fat spruce
timberland. It was a steep bank, and he paused for breath at the top, excusing the act to himself by looking at his watch. It was nine o'clock. There was
no sun nor hint of sun, though there was not a cloud in the sky. It was a
clear day, and yet there seemed an intangible pall over the face of things, a
subtle gloom that made the day dark, and that was due to the absence of
sun. This fact did not worry the man. He was used to the lack of sun. It
had been days since he had seen the sun, and he knew that a few more days
must pass before that cheerful orb, due south, would just peep above the
sky-line and dip immediately from view.

The man flung a look back along the way he had come. The Yukon lay
a mile wide and hidden under three feet of ice. On top of this ice were as
many feet of snow. It was all pure white, rolling in gentle undulations where
the ice-jams of the freeze-up had formed. North and south, as far as his eye
could see, it was unbroken white, save for a dark hair-line that curved and
twisted from around the spruce-covered island to the south, and that curved
and twisted away into the north, where it disappeared behind another
spruce-covered island. This dark hair-line was the trail—the main trail—

that led south five hundred miles to the Chilcoot Pass, Dyea, and salt water; and that led north seventy miles to Dawson, and still on to the north a thousand miles to Nulato, and finally to St. Michael on Bering Sea, a thousand miles and half a thousand more.

But all this—the mysterious, far-reaching hair-line trail, the absence of sun from the sky, the tremendous cold, and the strangeness and weirdness of it all—made no impression on the man. It was not because he was long used to it. He was a newcomer in the land, a *chechaquo,* and this was his first winter. The trouble with him was that he was without imagination. He was quick and alert in the things of life, but only in the things, and not in the significances. Fifty degrees below zero meant eighty-odd degrees of frost. Such fact impressed him as being cold and uncomfortable, and that was all. It did not lead him to meditate upon his frailty as a creature of temperature, and upon man's frailty in general, able only to live within certain narrow limits of heat and cold; and from there on it did not lead him to the conjectural field of immortality and man's place in the universe. Fifty degrees below zero stood for a bite of frost that hurt and that must be guarded against by the use of mittens, ear-flaps, warm moccasins, and thick socks. Fifty degrees below zero was to him just precisely fifty degrees below zero. That there should be anything more to it than that was a thought that never entered his head.

As he turned to go on, he spat speculatively. There was a sharp, explosive crackle that startled him. He spat again. And again, in the air, before it could fall to the snow, the spittle crackled. He knew that at fifty below spittle crackled on the snow, but this spittle had crackled in the air. Undoubtedly it was colder than fifty below—how much colder he did not know. But the temperature did not matter. He was bound for the old claim on the left fork of Henderson Creek, where the boys were already. They had come over across the divide from the Indian Creek country, while he had come the roundabout way to take a look at the possibilities of getting out logs in the spring from the islands in the Yukon. He would be in to camp by six o'clock; a bit after dark, it was true, but the boys would be there, a fire would be going, and a hot supper would be ready. As for lunch, he pressed his hand against the protruding bundle under his jacket. It was also under his shirt, wrapped up in a handkerchief and lying against the naked skin. It was the only way to keep the biscuits from freezing. He smiled agreeably to himself as he thought of those biscuits, each cut open and sopped in bacon grease, and each enclosing a generous slice of fried bacon.

He plunged in among the big spruce trees. The trail was faint. A foot of snow had fallen since the last sled had passed over, and he was glad he was without a sled, travelling light. In fact, he carried nothing but the lunch wrapped in the handkerchief. He was surprised, however, at the cold. It certainly was cold, he concluded, as he rubbed his numb nose and cheek-

bones with his mittened hand. He was a warm-whiskered man, but the hair
on his face did not protect the high cheek-bones and the eager nose that
thrust itself aggressively into the frosty air.

At the man's heels trotted a dog, a big native husky, the proper wolf-dog,
grey-coated and without any visible or temperamental difference from its
brother, the wild wolf. The animal was depressed by the tremendous cold.
It knew that it was no time for travelling. Its instinct told it a truer tale than
was told to the man by the man's judgment. In reality, it was not merely
colder than fifty below zero; it was colder than sixty below, than seventy
below. It was seventy-five below zero. Since the freezing-point is thirty-two
above zero, it meant that one hundred and seven degrees of frost obtained.
The dog did not know anything about thermometers. Possibly in its brain
there was no sharp consciousness of a condition of very cold such as was in
the man's brain. But the brute had its instinct. It experienced a vague but
menacing apprehension that subdued it and made it slink along at the man's
heels, and that made it question eagerly every unwonted movement of the
man as if expecting him to go into camp or to seek shelter somewhere and
build a fire. The dog had learned fire, and it wanted fire, or else to burrow
under the snow and cuddle its warmth away from the air.

The frozen moisture of its breathing had settled on its fur in a fine
powder of frost, and especially were its jowls, muzzle, and eyelashes
whitened by its crystalled breath. The man's red beard and mustache were
likewise frosted, but more solidly, the deposit taking the form of ice and
increasing with every warm, moist breath he exhaled. Also, the man was
chewing tobacco, and the muzzle of ice held his lips so rigidly that he was
unable to clear his chin when he expelled the juice. The result was that a
crystal beard of the color and solidity of amber was increasing its length
on his chin. If he fell down it would shatter itself, like glass, into brittle
fragments. But he did not mind the appendage. It was the penalty all
tobacco-chewers paid in that country, and he had been out before in two
cold snaps. They had not been so cold as this, he knew, but by the spirit
thermometer at Sixty Mile he knew they had been registered at fifty below
and at fifty-five.

He held on through the level stretch of woods for several miles, crossed
a wide flat of nigger-heads, and dropped down a bank to the frozen bed of
a small stream. This was Henderson Creek, and he knew he was ten miles
from the forks. He looked at his watch. It was ten o'clock. He was making
four miles an hour, and he calculated that he would arrive at the forks at
half-past twelve. He decided to celebrate that event by eating his lunch
there.

The dog dropped in again at his heels, with a tail drooping discouragement, as the man swung along the creek-bed. The furrow of the old sled-
trail was plainly visible, but a dozen inches of snow covered the marks of
the last runners. In a month no man had come up or down that silent creek.

The man held steadily on. He was not much given to thinking, and just then particularly he had nothing to think about save that he would eat lunch at the forks and that at six o'clock he would be in camp with the boys. There was nobody to talk to; and, had there been, speech would have been impossible because of the ice-muzzle on his mouth. So he continued monotonously to chew tobacco and to increase the length of his amber beard.

Once in a while the thought reiterated itself that it was very cold and that he had never experienced such cold. As he walked along he rubbed his cheek-bones and nose with the back of his mittened hand. He did this automatically, now and again changing hands. But rub as he would, the instant he stopped his cheek-bones went numb, and the following instant the end of his nose went numb. He was sure to frost his cheeks; he knew that, and experienced a pang of regret that he had not devised a nose-strap of the sort Bud wore in cold snaps. Such a strap passed across the cheeks, as well, and saved them. But it didn't matter much, after all. What were frosted cheeks? A bit painful, that was all; they were never serious.

Empty as the man's mind was of thoughts, he was keenly observant, and he noticed the changes in the creek, the curves and bends and timber-jams, and always he sharply noted where he placed his feet. Once, coming around a bend, he shied abruptly, like a startled horse, curved away from the place where he had been walking, and retreated several paces back along the trail. The creek he knew was frozen clear to the bottom,—no creek could contain water in that arctic winter,—but he knew also that there were springs that bubbled out from the hillsides and ran along under the snow and on top the ice of the creek. He knew that the coldest snaps never froze these springs, and he knew likewise their danger. They were traps. They hid pools of water under the snow that might be three inches deep, or three feet. Sometimes a skin of ice half an inch thick covered them, and in turn was covered by the snow. Sometimes there were alternate layers of water and ice-skin, so that when one broke through he kept on breaking through for a while, sometimes wetting himself to the waist.

That was why he had shied in such panic. He had felt the give under his feet and heard the crackle of a snow-hidden ice-skin. And to get his feet wet in such a temperature meant trouble and danger. At the very least it meant delay, for he would be forced to stop and build a fire, and under its protection to bare his feet while he dried his socks and moccasins. He stood and studied the creek-bed and its banks, and decided that the flow of water came from the right. He reflected awhile, rubbing his nose and cheeks, then skirted to the left, stepping gingerly and testing the footing for each step. Once clear of the danger, he took a fresh chew of tobacco and swung along at his four-mile gait.

In the course of the next two hours he came upon several similar traps. Usually the snow above the hidden pools had a sunken, candied appearance that advertised the danger. Once again, however, he had a close call; and once, suspecting danger, he compelled the dog to go on in front. The dog did not want to go. It hung back until the man shoved it forward, and then it went quickly across the white, unbroken surface. Suddenly it broke through, floundered to one side, and got away to firmer footing. It had wet its forefeet and legs, and almost immediately the water that clung to it turned to ice. It made quick efforts to lick the ice off its legs, then dropped down in the snow and began to bite out the ice that had formed between the toes. This was a matter of instinct. To permit the ice to remain would mean sore feet. It did not know this. It merely obeyed the mysterious prompting that arose from the deep crypts of its being. But the man knew, having achieved a judgment on the subject, and he removed the mitten from his right hand and helped tear out the ice-particles. He did not expose his fingers more than a minute, and was astonished at the swift numbness that smote them. It certainly was cold. He pulled on the mitten hastily, and beat the hand savagely across his chest.

At twelve o'clock the day was at its brightest. Yet the sun was too far south on its winter journey to clear the horizon. The bulge of the earth intervened between it and Henderson Creek, where the man walked under a clear sky at noon and cast no shadow. At half-past twelve, to the minute, he arrived at the forks of the creek. He was pleased at the speed he had made. If he kept it up, he would certainly be with the boys by six. He un-buttoned his jacket and shirt and drew forth his lunch. The action consumed no more than a quarter of a minute, yet in that brief moment the numbness laid hold of the exposed fingers. He did not put the mitten on, but, instead, struck the fingers a dozen sharp smashes against his leg. Then he sat down on a snow-covered log to eat. The sting that followed upon the striking of his fingers against his leg ceased so quickly that he was startled. He had had no chance to take a bite of biscuit. He struck the fingers repeatedly and returned them to the mitten, baring the other hand for the purpose of eating. He tried to take a mouthful, but the ice-muzzle prevented. He had forgotten to build a fire and thaw out. He chuckled at his foolishness, and as he chuckled he noted the numbness creeping into the exposed fingers. Also, he noted that the stinging which had first come to his toes when he sat down was already passing away. He wondered whether the toes were warm or numb. He moved them inside the moccasins and decided that they were numb.

He pulled the mitten on hurriedly and stood up. He was a bit frightened. He stamped up and down until the stinging returned into the feet. It certainly was cold, was his thought. That man from Sulphur Creek had spoken the truth when telling how cold it sometimes got in the country. And he had laughed at him at the time! That showed one must not be too sure of things. There was no mistake about it, it *was* cold. He strode up and down, stamping his feet and threshing his arms, until reassured by the returning warmth. Then he got out matches and proceeded to make a fire. From the undergrowth, where high water of the previous spring had lodged a supply of seasoned twigs, he got his fire-wood. Working carefully from a small beginning, he soon had a roaring fire, over which he thawed the ice from his face and in the protection of which he ate his biscuits. For the moment the cold of space was outwitted. The dog took satisfaction in the fire, stretching out close enough for warmth and far enough away to escape being singed.

When the man had finished, he filled his pipe and took his comfortable time over a smoke. Then he pulled on his mittens, settled the earflaps of his cap firmly about his ears, and took the creek trail up the left fork. The dog was disappointed and yearned back toward the fire. This man did not know cold. Possibly all the generations of his ancestry had been ignorant of cold, of real cold, of cold one hundred and seven degrees below freezing-point. But the dog knew; all its ancestry knew, and it had inherited the knowledge. And it knew that it was not good to walk abroad in such fearful cold. It was the time to lie snug in a hole in the snow and wait for a curtain of cloud to be drawn across the face of outer space whence this cold came. On the other hand, there was no keen intimacy between the dog and the man. The one was the toil-slave of the other, and the only caresses it had ever received were the caresses of the whip-lash and of harsh and menacing throat-sounds that threatened the whip-lash. So the dog made no effort to communicate its apprehension to the man. It was not concerned in the welfare of the man; it was for its own sake that it yearned back toward the fire. But the man whistled, and spoke to it with the sound of whip-lashes, and the dog swung in at the man's heels and followed after.

The man took a chew of tobacco and proceeded to start a new amber beard. Also, his moist breath quickly powdered with white his mustache, eyebrows, and lashes. There did not seem to be so many springs on the left fork of the Henderson, and for half an hour the man saw no signs of any. And then it happened. At a place where there were no signs, where the soft, unbroken snow seemed to advertise solidity beneath, the man broke through. It was not deep. He wet himself halfway to the knees before he floundered out to the firm crust.

He was angry, and cursed his luck aloud. He had hoped to get into camp with the boys at six o'clock, and this would delay him an hour, for he would have to build a fire and dry out his foot-gear. This was imperative at that low temperature—he knew that much; and he turned aside to the bank, which he climbed. On top, tangled in the underbrush about the trunks of several small spruce trees, was a high-water deposit of dry fire-wood—sticks and twigs, principally, but also larger portions of seasoned branches and fine, dry, last-year's grasses. He threw down several large pieces on top of the snow. This served for a foundation and prevented the young flame from drowning itself in the snow it otherwise would melt. The flame he got by touching a match to a small shred of birch-bark that he took from his pocket. This burned even more readily than paper. Placing it on the foundation, he fed the young flame with wisps of dry grass and with the tiniest dry twigs.

He worked slowly and carefully, keenly aware of his danger. Gradually, as the flame grew stronger, he increased the size of the twigs with which he fed it. He squatted in the snow, pulling the twigs out from their entanglement in the brush and feeding directly to the flame. He knew there must be no failure. When it is seventy-five below zero, a man must not fail in his first attempt to build a fire—that is, if his feet are wet. If his feet are dry, and he fails, he can run along the trail for half a mile and restore his circulation. But the circulation of wet and freezing feet cannot be restored by running when it is seventy-five below. No matter how fast he runs, the wet feet will freeze the harder.

All this the man knew. The old-timer on Sulphur Creek had told him about it the previous fall, and now he was appreciating the advice. Already all sensation had gone out of his feet. To build the fire he had been forced to remove his mittens, and the fingers had quickly gone numb. His pace of four miles an hour had kept his heart pumping blood to the surface of his body and to all the extremities. But the instant he stopped, the action of the pump eased down. The cold of space smote the unprotected tip of the planet, and he, being on that unprotected tip, received the full force of the blow. The blood of his body recoiled before it. The blood was alive, like the dog, and like the dog it wanted to hide away and cover itself up from the fearful cold. So long as he walked four miles an hour, he pumped that blood, willy-nilly, to the surface; but now it ebbed away and sank down into the recesses of his body. The extremities were the first to feel its absence. His wet feet froze the faster, and his exposed fingers numbed the faster, though they had not yet begun to freeze. Nose and cheeks were already freezing, while the skin of all his body chilled as it lost its blood.

But he was safe. Toes and nose and cheeks would be only touched by the frost, for the fire was beginning to burn with strength. He was feeding it with twigs the size of his finger. In another minute he would be able to feed it with branches the size of his wrist, and then he could remove his wet foot-gear, and, while it dried, he could keep his naked feet warm by the fire, rubbing them at first, of course, with snow. The fire was a success. He was safe. He remembered the advice of the old-timer on Sulphur Creek, and smiled. The old-timer had been very serious in laying down the law that no man must travel alone in the Klondike after fifty below. Well, here he was; he had had the accident; he was alone; and he had saved himself. Those old-timers were rather womanish, some of them, he thought. All a man had to do was to keep his head, and he was all right. Any man who was a man could travel alone. But it was surprising, the rapidity with which his cheeks and nose were freezing. And he had not thought his fingers could go lifeless in so short a time. Lifeless they were, for he could scarcely make them move together to grip a twig, and they seemed remote from his body and from him. When he touched a twig, he had to look and see whether or not he had hold of it. The wires were pretty well down between him and his finger-ends.

All of which counted for little. There was the fire, snapping and crackling and promising life with every dancing flame. He started to untie his moccasins. They were coated with ice; the thick German socks were like sheaths of iron halfway to the knees; and the moccasin strings were like rods of steel all twisted and knotted as by some conflagration. For a moment he tugged with his numb fingers, then, realizing the folly of it, he drew his sheath-knife.

But before he could cut the strings, it happened. It was his own fault or, rather, his mistake. He should not have built the fire under the spruce tree. He should have built it in the open. But it had been easier to pull the twigs from the brush and drop them directly on the fire. Now the tree under which he had done this carried a weight of snow on its boughs. No wind had blown for weeks, and each bough was fully freighted. Each time he had pulled a twig he had communicated a slight agitation to the tree—an imperceptible agitation, so far as he was concerned, but an agitation sufficient to bring about the disaster. High up in the tree one bough capsized its load of snow. This fell on the boughs beneath, capsizing them. This process continued, spreading out and involving the whole tree. It grew like an avalanche, and it descended without warning upon the man and the fire, and the fire was blotted out! Where it had burned was a mantle of fresh and disordered snow.

The man was shocked. It was as though he had just heard his own sentence of death. For a moment he sat and stared at the spot where the fire had been. Then he grew very calm. Perhaps the old-timer on Sulphur Creek was right. If he had only had a trail-mate he would have been in no danger now. The trail-mate could have built the fire. Well, it was up to him to build the fire over again, and this second time there must be no failure. Even if he succeeded, he would most likely lose some toes. His feet must be badly frozen by now, and there would be some time before the second fire was ready.

Such were his thoughts, but he did not sit and think them. He was busy all the time they were passing through his mind. He made a new foundation for a fire, this time in the open, where no treacherous tree could blot it out. Next, he gathered dry grasses and tiny twigs from the high-water flotsam. He could not bring his fingers together to pull them out, but he was able to gather them by the handful. In this way he got many rotten twigs and bits of green moss that were undesirable, but it was the best he could do. He worked methodically, even collecting an armful of the larger branches to be used later when the fire gathered strength. And all the while the dog sat and watched him, a certain yearning wistfulness in its eyes, for it looked upon him as the fire-provider, and the fire was slow in coming.

When all was ready, the man reached in his pocket for a second piece of birch-bark. He knew the bark was there, and, though he could not feel it with his fingers, he could hear its crisp rustling as he fumbled for it. Try as he would, he could not clutch hold of it. And all the time, in his consciousness, was the knowledge that each instant his feet were freezing. This thought tended to put him in a panic, but he fought against it and kept calm. He pulled on his mittens with his teeth, and threshed his arms back and forth, beating his hands with all his might against his sides. He did this sitting down, and he stood up to do it; and all the while the dog sat in the snow, its wolf-brush of a tail curled around warmly over its forefeet, its sharp wolf-ears pricked forward intently as it watched the man. And the man, as he beat and threshed with his arms and hands, felt a great surge of envy as he regarded the creature that was warm and secure in its natural covering.

After a time he was aware of the first far-away signals of sensation in his beaten fingers. The faint tingling grew stronger till it evolved into a stinging ache that was excruciating, but which the man hailed with satisfaction. He stripped the mitten from his right hand and fetched forth the birch-bark. The exposed fingers were quickly going numb again. Next he brought out his bunch of sulphur matches. But the tremendous cold had already driven the life out of his fingers. In his effort to separate one match from the others, the whole bunch fell in the snow. He tried to pick it out of the snow, but failed. The dead fingers could neither touch nor clutch. He was very careful. He drove the thought of his freezing feet, and nose, and cheeks, out of his mind, devoting his whole soul to the matches. He watched, using the sense of vision in place of that of touch, and when he saw his fingers on each side the bunch, he closed them—that is, he willed to close them, for the wires were down, and the fingers did not obey. He pulled the mitten on the right hand, and beat it fiercely against his knee. Then, with both mittened hands, he scooped the bunch of matches, along with much snow, into his lap. Yet he was no better off.

After some manipulation he managed to get the bunch between the heels of his mittened hands. In this fashion he carried it to his mouth. The ice crackled and snapped when by a violent effort he opened his mouth. He drew the lower jaw in, curled the upper lip out of the way, and scraped the bunch with his upper teeth in order to separate a match. He succeeded in getting one, which he dropped on his lap. He was no better off. He could not pick it up. Then he devised a way. He picked it up in his teeth and scratched it on his leg. Twenty times he scratched before he succeeded in lighting it. As it flamed he held it with his teeth to the birch-bark. But the burning brimstone went up his nostrils and into his lungs, causing him to cough spasmodically. The match fell into the snow and went out.

The old-timer on Sulphur Creek was right, he thought in the moment of controlled despair that ensued: after fifty below, a man should travel with a partner. He beat his hands, but failed in exciting any sensation. Suddenly he bared both hands, removing the mittens with his teeth. He caught the whole bunch between the heels of his hands. His arm-muscles not being frozen enabled him to press the hand-heels tightly against the matches. Then he scratched the bunch along his leg. It flared into flame, seventy sulphur matches at once! There was no wind to blow them out. He kept his head to one side to escape the strangling fumes, and held the blazing bunch to the birch-bark. As he so held it, he became aware of sensation in his hand. His flesh was burning. He could smell it. Deep down below the surface he could feel it. The sensation developed into pain that grew acute. And still he endured it, holding the flame of the matches clumsily to the bark that would not light readily because his own burning hands were in the way, absorbing most of the flame.

At last, when he could endure no more, he jerked his hands apart. The blazing matches fell sizzling into the snow, but the birch-bark was alight. He began laying dry grasses and the tiniest twigs on the flame. He could not pick and choose, for he had to lift the fuel between the heels of his hands. Small pieces of rotten wood and green moss clung to the twigs, and he bit them off as well as he could with his teeth. He cherished the flame carefully and awkwardly. It meant life, and it must not perish. The withdrawal of blood from the surface of his body now made him begin to shiver, and he grew more awkward. A large piece of green moss fell squarely on the little fire. He tried to poke it out with his fingers, but his shivering frame made him poke too far, and he disrupted the nucleus of the little fire, the burning grasses and tiny twigs separating and scattering. He tried to poke them together again, but in spite of the tenseness of the effort, his shivering got away with him, and the twigs were hopelessly scattered. Each twig gushed a puff of smoke and went out. The fire-provider had failed. As he looked apathetically about him, his eyes chanced on the dog, sitting across the ruins of the fire from him, in the snow, making restless, hunching movements, slightly lifting one forefoot and then the other, shifting its weight back and forth on them with wistful eagerness.

The sight of the dog put a wild idea into his head. He remembered the tale of the man, caught in a blizzard, who killed a steer and crawled inside the carcass, and so was saved. He would kill the dog and bury his hands in the warm body until the numbness went out of them. Then he could build another fire. He spoke to the dog, calling it to him; but in his voice was a strange note of fear that frightened the animal, who had never known the man to speak in such way before. Something was the matter, and its suspicious nature sensed danger—it knew not what danger, but somewhere, somehow, in its brain arose an apprehension of the man. It flattened its ears down at the sound of the man's voice, and its restless, hunching movements and the liftings and shiftings of its forefeet became more pronounced; but it would not come to the man. He got on his hands and knees and crawled toward the dog. This unusual posture again excited suspicion, and the animal sidled mincingly away.

The man sat up in the snow for a moment and struggled for calmness. Then he pulled on his mittens, by means of his teeth, and got upon his feet. He glanced down at first in order to assure himself that he was really standing up, for the absence of sensation in his feet left him unrelated to the earth. His erect position in itself started to drive the webs of suspicion from the dog's mind; and when he spoke peremptorily, with the sound of whip-lashes in his voice, the dog rendered its customary allegiance and came to him. As it came within reaching distance, the man lost his control. His arms flashed out to the dog, and he experienced genuine surprise when he discovered that his hands could not clutch, that there was neither bend nor feeling in the fingers. He had forgotten for the moment that they were frozen and that they were freezing more and more. All this happened quickly, and before the animal could get away, he encircled its body with his arms. He sat down in the snow, and in this fashion held the dog, while it snarled and whined and struggled.

But it was all he could do, hold its body encircled in his arms and sit there. He realized that he could not kill the dog. There was no way to do it. With his helpless hands he could neither draw nor hold his sheath-knife nor throttle the animal. He released it, and it plunged wildly away, with tail between its legs, and still snarling. It halted forty feet away and surveyed him curiously, with ears sharply pricked forward. The man looked down at his hands in order to locate them, and found them hanging on the ends of his arms. It struck him as curious that one should have to use his eyes in order to find out where his hands were. He began threshing his arms back and forth, beating the mittened hands against his sides. He did this for five minutes, violently, and his heart pumped enough blood up to the surface to put a stop to his shivering. But no sensation was aroused in the hands. He had an impression that they hung like weights on the ends of his arms, but when he tried to run the impression down, he could not find it.

A certain fear of death, dull and oppressive, came to him. This fear quickly became poignant as he realized that it was no longer a mere matter of freezing his fingers and toes, or of losing his hands and feet, but that it was a matter of life and death with the chances against him. This threw him into a panic, and he turned and ran up the creek-bed along the old, dim trail. The dog joined in behind and kept up with him. He ran blindly, without intention, in fear such as he had never known in his life. Slowly, as he ploughed and floundered through the snow, he began to see things again,—the banks of the creek, the old timber-jams, the leafless aspens, and the sky. The running made him feel better. He did not shiver. Maybe, if he ran on, his feet would thaw out; and, anyway, if he ran far enough, he would reach camp and the boys. Without doubt he would lose some fingers and toes and some of his face; but the boys would take care of him, and save the rest of him when he got there. And at the same time there was another thought in his mind that said he would never get to the camp and the boys; that it was too many miles away, that the freezing had too great a start on him, and that he would soon be stiff and dead. This thought he kept in the background and refused to consider. Sometimes it pushed itself forward and demanded to be heard, but he thrust it back and strove to think of other things.

It struck him as curious that he could run at all on feet so frozen that he could not feel them when they struck the earth and took the weight of his body. He seemed to himself to skim along above the surface, and to have no connection with the earth. Somewhere he had once seen a winged Mercury, and he wondered if Mercury felt as he felt when skimming over the earth.

His theory of running until he reached camp and the boys had one flaw in it: he lacked the endurance. Several times he stumbled, and finally he tottered, crumpled up, and fell. When he tried to rise, he failed. He must sit and rest, he decided, and next time he would merely walk and keep on going. As he sat and regained his breath, he noted that he was feeling quite warm and comfortable. He was not shivering, and it even seemed that a warm glow had come to his chest and trunk. And yet, when he touched his nose or cheeks, there was no sensation. Running would not thaw them out. Nor would it thaw out his hands and feet. Then the thought came to him that the frozen portions of his body must be extending. He tried to keep this thought down, to forget it, to think of something else; he was aware of the panicky feeling that it caused, and he was afraid of the panic. But the thought asserted itself, and persisted, until it produced a vision of his body totally frozen. This was too much, and he made another wild run along the trail. Once he slowed down to a walk, but the thought of the freezing extending itself made him run again.

And all the time the dog ran with him, at his heels. When he fell down a second time, it curled its tail over its forefeet and sat in front of him, facing him, curiously eager and intent. The warmth and security of the animal angered him, and he cursed it till it flattened down its ears appeasingly. This time the shivering came more quickly upon the man. He was losing in his battle with the frost. It was creeping into his body from all sides. The thought of it drove him on, but he ran no more than a hundred feet, when he staggered and pitched headlong. It was his last panic. When he had recovered his breath and control, he sat up and entertained in his mind the conception of meeting death with dignity. However, the conception did not come to him in such terms. His idea of it was that he had been making a fool of himself, running around like a chicken with its head cut off—such was the simile that occurred to him. Well, he was bound to freeze anyway, and he might as well take it decently. With this new-found peace of mind came the first glimmerings of drowsiness. A good idea, he thought, to sleep off to death. It was like taking an anæsthetic. Freezing was not so bad as people thought. There were lots worse ways to die.

He pictured the boys finding his body next day. Suddenly he found himself with them, coming along the trail and looking for himself. And, still with them, he came around a turn in the trail and found himself lying in the snow. He did not belong with himself any more, for even then he was out of himself, standing with the boys and looking at himself in the snow. It certainly was cold, was his thought. When he got back to the States he could tell the folks what real cold was. He drifted on from this to a vision of the old-timer on Sulphur Creek. He could see him quite clearly, warm and comfortable, and smoking a pipe.

"You were right, old hoss; you were right," the man mumbled to the old-timer of Sulphur Creek.

Then the man drowsed off into what seemed to him the most comfortable and satisfying sleep he had ever known. The dog sat facing him and waiting. The brief day drew to a close in a long, slow twilight. There were no signs of a fire to be made, and, besides, never in the dog's experience had it known a man to sit like that in the snow and make no fire. As the twilight drew on, its eager yearning for the fire mastered it, and with a great lifting and shifting of forefeet, it whined softly, then flattened its ears down in anticipation of being chidden by the man. But the man remained silent. Later, the dog whined loudly. And still later it crept close to the man and caught the scent of death. This made the animal bristle and back away. A little longer it delayed, howling under the stars that leaped and danced and shone brightly in the cold sky. Then it turned and trotted up the trail in the direction of the camp it knew, where were the other food-providers and fire-providers.

THE DEATH OF IVÁN ILÝCH

Leo Tolstoy

THE NEXT SIXTEEN STORIES *are by Russian authors. I have placed them together for the reason stated in the introduction, and I have put them just here because on the whole the stories that precede them seem in no way to have been affected by a foreign influence, whereas the stories that follow them have been to a greater or a less extent, directly or indirectly, conditioned by the theory and practice of the Russians. It may be that some of the authors of our own day have never read a single Russian story, but have been notwithstanding responsive to the feeling in the air and would not have written in quite the same way if neither Tolstoy nor Chekhov had lived. But my division is rough and ready. Some of the earlier stories have such a modern air that one can hardly believe that their authors were born so long ago, while among the later ones the reader will find several (and very good they are too in their way) which show no signs that their authors are aware of any change in outlook on the short story since the middle of the nineteenth century. But it is no new thing that artists will not fit themselves into the patterns that are convenient to the critic; and if a man who was born in 1840 insists on writing as though he were contemporary with Christopher Isherwood, or, contrariwise, if a man who was born at the end of the nineteen hundreds constructs a story in the manner of Guy de Maupassant, the anthologist can do nothing but make the best of it. The moral is that a lot of theorizing about artistic products is moonshine.*

W. S. M.

THE DEATH OF IVÁN ILÝCH

Leo Tolstoy

(1828–1910)

TRANSLATED BY AYLMER MAUDE

D<small>URING AN INTERVAL</small> in the Melvínski trial in the large building of the Law
Courts the members and public prosecutor met in Iván Egórovich Shébek's
private room, where the conversation turned on the celebrated Krasóvski
case. Fëdor Vasílievich warmly maintained that it was not subject to their
jurisdiction, Iván Egórovich maintained the contrary, while Peter Ivánovich,
not having entered into the discussion at the start, took no part in it but
looked through the *Gazette* which had just been handed in.

'Gentlemen,' he said, 'Iván Ilých has died!'

'You don't say so!'

'Here, read it yourself,' replied Peter Ivánovich, handing Fëdor Vasílievich
the paper still damp from the press. Surrounded by a black border were the
words: 'Praskóvya Fëdorovna Goloviná, with profound sorrow, informs
relatives and friends of the demise of her beloved husband Iván Ilých
Golovín, Member of the Court of Justice, which occurred on February the
4th of this year 1882. The funeral will take place on Friday at one o'clock in
the afternoon.'

Iván Ilých had been a colleague of the gentlemen present and was liked
by them all. He had been ill for some weeks with an illness said to be incurable. His post had been kept open for him, but there had been conjectures
that in case of his death Alexéev might receive his appointment, and that
either Vínnikov or Shtábel would succeed Alexéev. So on receiving the
news of Iván Ilých's death the first thought of each of the gentlemen in that
private room was of the changes and promotions it might occasion among
themselves or their acquaintances.

'I shall be sure to get Shtábel's place or Vínnikov's,' thought Fëdor
Vasílievich. 'I was promised that long ago, and the promotion means an
extra eight hundred rubles a year for me besides the allowance.'

'Now I must apply for my brother-in-law's transfer from Kalúga,' thought
Peter Ivánovich. 'My wife will be very glad, and then she won't be able to
say that I never do anything for her relations.'

'I thought he would never leave his bed again,' said Peter Ivánovich aloud. 'It's very sad.'

'But what really was the matter with him?'

'The doctors couldn't say—at least they could, but each of them said something different. When last I saw him I thought he was getting better.'

'And I haven't been to see him since the holidays. I always meant to go.'

'Had he any property?'

'I think his wife had a little—but something quite trifling.'

'We shall have to go to see her, but they live so terribly far away.'

'Far away from you, you mean. Everything's far away from your place.'

'You see, he never can forgive my living on the other side of the river,' said Peter Ivánovich, smiling at Shébek. Then, still talking of the distances between different parts of the city, they returned to the Court.

Besides considerations as to the possible transfers and promotions likely to result from Iván Ilých's death, the mere fact of the death of a near acquaintance aroused, as usual, in all who heard of it the complacent feeling that, 'it is he who is dead and not I.'

Each one thought or felt, 'Well, he's dead but I'm alive!' But the more intimate of Iván Ilých's acquaintances, his so-called friends, could not help thinking also that they would now have to fulfil the very tiresome demands of propriety by attending the funeral service and paying a visit of condolence to the widow.

Fëdor Vasílievich and Peter Ivánovich had been his nearest acquaintances. Peter Ivánovich had studied law with Iván Ilých and had considered himself to be under obligations to him.

Having told his wife at dinner-time of Iván Ilých's death, and of his conjecture that it might be possible to get her brother transferred to their circuit, Peter Ivánovich sacrificed his usual nap, put on his evening clothes, and drove to Iván Ilých's house.

At the entrance stood a carriage and two cabs. Leaning against the wall in the hall downstairs near the cloak-stand was a coffin-lid covered with cloth of gold, ornamented with gold cord and tassels, that had been polished up with metal powder. Two ladies in black were taking off their fur cloaks. Peter Ivánovich recognized one of them as Iván Ilých's sister, but the other was a stranger to him. His colleague Schwartz was just coming downstairs, but on seeing Peter Ivánovich enter he stopped and winked at him, as if to say: 'Iván Ilých has made a mess of things—not like you and me.'

Schwartz's face with his Piccadilly whiskers, and his slim figure in evening dress, had as usual an air of elegant solemnity which contrasted with the playfulness of his character and had a special piquancy here, or so it seemed to Peter Ivánovich.

Peter Ivánovich allowed the ladies to precede him and slowly followed them upstairs. Schwartz did not come down but remained where he was, and Peter Ivánovich understood that he wanted to arrange where they should play bridge that evening. The ladies went upstairs to the widow's room, and Schwartz with seriously compressed lips but a playful look in his eyes, indicated by a twist of his eyebrows the room to the right where the body lay.

Peter Ivánovich, like everyone else on such occasions, entered feeling uncertain what he would have to do. All he knew was that at such times it is always safe to cross oneself. But he was not quite sure whether one should make obeisances while doing so. He therefore adopted a middle course. On entering the room he began crossing himself and made a slight movement resembling a bow. At the same time, as far as the motion of his head and arm allowed, he surveyed the room. Two young men—apparently nephews, one of whom was a high-school pupil—were leaving the room, crossing themselves as they did so. An old woman was standing motionless, and a lady with strangely arched eyebrows was saying something to her in a whisper. A vigorous, resolute Church Reader, in a frock-coat, was reading something in a loud voice with an expression that precluded any contradiction. The butler's assistant, Gerásim, stepping lightly in front of Peter Ivánovich, was strewing something on the floor. Noticing this, Peter Ivánovich was immediately aware of a faint odour of a decomposing body.

The last time he had called on Iván Ilých, Peter Ivánovich had seen Gerásim in the study. Iván Ilých had been particularly fond of him and he was performing the duty of a sick nurse.

Peter Ivánovich continued to make the sign of the cross slightly inclining his head in an intermediate direction between the coffin, the Reader, and the icons on the table in a corner of the room. Afterwards, when it seemed to him that this movement of his arm in crossing himself had gone on too long, he stopped and began to look at the corpse.

The dead man lay, as dead men always lie, in a specially heavy way, his rigid limbs sunk in the soft cushions of the coffin, with the head forever bowed on the pillow. His yellow waxen brow with bald patches over his sunken temples was thrust up in the way peculiar to the dead, the protruding nose seeming to press on the upper lip. He was much changed and had grown even thinner since Peter Ivánovich had last seen him, but, as is always the case with the dead, his face was handsomer and above all more dignified than when he was alive. The expression on the face said that what was necessary had been accomplished, and accomplished rightly. Besides this there was in that expression a reproach and a warning to the living. This warning seemed to Peter Ivánovich out of place, or at least not applicable to him. He felt a certain discomfort and so he hurriedly crossed himself once more and turned and went out of the door—too hurriedly and too regardless of propriety, as he himself was aware.

Schwartz was waiting for him in the adjoining room with legs spread wide apart and both hands toying with his top-hat behind his back. The mere sight of that playful, well-groomed, and elegant figure refreshed Peter

Ivánovich. He felt that Schwartz was above all these happenings and would not surrender to any depressing influences. His very look said that this incident of a church service for Iván Ilých could not be a sufficient reason for infringing the order of the session—in other words, that it would certainly not prevent his unwrapping a new pack of cards and shuffling them that evening while a footman placed four fresh candles on the table: in fact, there was no reason for supposing that this incident would hinder their spending the evening agreeably. Indeed he said this in a whisper as Peter Ivánovich passed him, proposing that they should meet for a game at Fëdor Vasílievich's. But apparently Peter Ivánovich was not destined to play bridge that evening. Praskóvya Fëdorovna (a short, fat woman who despite all efforts to the contrary had continued to broaden steadily from her shoulders downwards and who had the same extraordinarily arched eyebrows as the lady who had been standing by the coffin), dressed all in black, her head covered with lace, came out of her own room with some other ladies, conducted them to the room where the dead body lay, and said: 'The service will begin immediately. Please go in.'

Schwartz, making an indefinite bow, stood still, evidently neither accepting nor declining this invitation. Praskóvya Fëdorovna recognizing Peter Ivánovich, sighed, went close up to him, took his hand, and said: 'I know you were a true friend to Iván Ilých . . .' and looked at him awaiting some suitable response. And Peter Ivánovich knew that, just as it had been the right thing to cross himself in that room, so what he had to do here was to press her hand, sigh, and say, 'Believe me . . .'. So he did all this and as he did it felt that the desired result had been achieved: that both he and she were touched.

'Come with me. I want to speak to you before it begins,' said the widow. 'Give me your arm.'

Peter Ivánovich gave her his arm and they went to the inner rooms, passing Schwartz who winked at Peter Ivánovich compassionately.

'That does for our bridge! Don't object if we find another player. Perhaps you can cut in when you do escape,' said his playful look.

Peter Ivánovich sighed still more deeply and despondently, and Praskóvya Fëdorovna pressed his arm gratefully. When they reached the drawing-room, upholstered in pink cretonne and lighted by a dim lamp, they sat down at the table—she on a sofa and Peter Ivánovich on a low pouffe, the springs of which yielded spasmodically under his weight. Praskóvya Fëdorovna had been on the point of warning him to take another seat, but felt that such a warning was out of keeping with her present condition and so changed her mind. As he sat down on the pouffe Peter Ivánovich recalled how Iván Ilých had arranged this room and had consulted him regarding this pink cretonne with green leaves. The whole room was full of furniture and knick-knacks, and on her way to the sofa the lace of the widow's black shawl caught on the carved edge of the table. Peter Ivánovich rose to detach it, and the springs of the pouffe, relieved of his weight, rose also and gave him a push. The widow began detaching her shawl herself, and Peter Ivánovich again sat down, suppressing the rebellious springs of the pouffe under him. But the widow had not quite freed herself and Peter Ivánovich got up again, and again the pouffe rebelled and even creaked. When this was all over she took out a clean cambric handkerchief and began to weep. The episode with the shawl and the struggle with the pouffe had cooled Peter Ivánovich's emotions and he sat there with a sullen look on his face. This awkward situation was interrupted by Sokolóv, Iván Ilých's butler, who came to report that the plot in the cemetery that Praskóvya Fëdorovna had chosen would cost two hundred rubles. She stopped weeping and, looking at Peter Ivánovich with the air of a victim, remarked in French that it was very hard for her. Peter Ivánovich made a silent gesture signifying his full conviction that it must indeed be so.

'Please smoke,' she said in a magnanimous yet crushed voice, and turned to discuss with Sokolóv the price of the plot for the grave.

Peter Ivánovich while lighting his cigarette heard her inquiring very circumstantially into the price of different plots in the cemetery and finally decide which she would take. When that was done she gave instructions about engaging the choir. Sokolóv then left the room.

'I look after everything myself,' she told Peter Ivánovich, shifting the albums that lay on the table; and noticing that the table was endangered by his cigarette-ash, she immediately passed him an ash-tray, saying as she did so: 'I consider it an affectation to say that my grief prevents my attending to practical affairs. On the contrary, if anything can—I won't say console me, but—distract me, it is seeing to everything concerning him.' She again took out her handkerchief as if preparing to cry, but suddenly, as if mastering her feeling, she shook herself and began to speak calmly. 'But there is something I want to talk to you about.'

Peter Ivánovich bowed, keeping control of the springs of the pouffe, which immediately began quivering under him.

'He suffered terribly the last few days.'

'Did he?' said Peter Ivánovich.

'Oh, terribly! He screamed unceasingly, not for minutes but for hours. For the last three days he screamed incessantly. It was unendurable. I cannot understand how I bore it; you could hear him three rooms off. Oh, what I have suffered!'

'Is it possible that he was conscious all that time?' asked Peter Ivánovich.

'Yes,' she whispered. 'To the last moment. He took leave of us a quarter of an hour before he died, and asked us to take Volódya away.'

The thought of the sufferings of this man he had known so intimately, first as a merry little boy, then as a school-mate, and later as a grown-up colleague, suddenly struck Peter Ivánovich with horror, despite an unpleasant consciousness of his own and this woman's dissimulation. He again saw that brow, and that nose pressing down on the lip, and felt afraid for himself.

'Three days of frightful suffering and then death! Why, that might suddenly, at any time, happen to me,' he thought, and for a moment felt terrified. But—he did not himself know how—the customary reflection at once occurred to him that this had happened to Iván Ilých and not to him, and that it should not and could not happen to him, and that to think that it could would be yielding to depression which he ought not to do, as Schwartz's expression plainly showed. After which reflection Peter Ivánovich felt reassured, and began to ask with interest about the details of Iván Ilých's death, as though death was an accident natural to Iván Ilých but certainly not to himself.

After many details of the really dreadful physical sufferings Iván Ilých had endured (which details he learnt only from the effect those sufferings had produced on Praskóvya Fëdorovna's nerves) the widow apparently found it necessary to get to business.

'Oh, Peter Ivánovich, how hard it is! How terribly, terribly hard!' and she again began to weep.

Peter Ivánovich sighed and waited for her to finish blowing her nose. When she had done so he said, 'Believe me . . .', and she again began talking and brought out what was evidently her chief concern with him— namely, to question him as to how she could obtain a grant of money from the government on the occasion of her husband's death. She made it appear that she was asking Peter Ivánovich's advice about her pension, but he soon saw that she already knew about that to the minutest detail, more even than he did himself. She knew how much could be got out of the government in consequence of her husband's death, but wanted to find out whether she could not possibly extract something more. Peter Ivánovich tried to think of some means of doing so, but after reflecting for a while and, out of propriety, condemning the government for its niggardliness, he said he thought that nothing more could be got. Then she sighed and evidently began to devise means of getting rid of her visitor. Noticing this, he put out his cigarette, rose, pressed her hand, and went out into the anteroom.

In the dining-room where the clock stood that Iván Ilých had liked so much and had bought at an antique shop, Peter Ivánovich met a priest and a few acquaintances who had come to attend the service, and he recognized Iván Ilých's daughter, a handsome young woman. She was in black and her slim figure appeared slimmer than ever. She had a gloomy, determined, almost angry expression, and bowed to Peter Ivánovich as though he were in some way to blame. Behind her, with the same offended look, stood a wealthy young man, an examining magistrate, whom Peter Ivánovich also knew and who was her fiancé, as he had heard. He bowed mournfully to them and was about to pass into the death-chamber, when from under the stairs appeared the figure of Iván Ilých's schoolboy son, who was extremely like his father. He seemed a little Iván Ilých, such as Peter Ivánovich remembered when they studied law together. His tear-stained eyes had in them the look that is seen in the eyes of boys of thirteen or fourteen who are not pure-minded. When he saw Peter Ivánovich he scowled morosely and shame-facedly. Peter Ivánovich nodded to him and entered the death-chamber. The service began: candles, groans, incense, tears, and sobs. Peter Ivánovich stood looking gloomily down at his feet. He did not look once at the dead man, did not yield to any depressing influence, and was one of the first to leave the room. There was no one in the anteroom, but Gerásim darted out of the dead man's room, rummaged with his strong hands among the fur coats to find Peter Ivánovich's and helped him on with it.

'Well, friend Gerásim,' said Peter Ivánovich, so as to say something. 'It's a sad affair, isn't it?'

'It's God's will. We shall all come to it some day,' said Gerásim, displaying his teeth—the even, white teeth of a healthy peasant—and, like a man in the thick of urgent work, he briskly opened the front door, called the coachman, helped Peter Ivánovich into the sledge, and sprang back to the porch as if in readiness for what he had to do next.

Peter Ivánovich found the fresh air particularly pleasant after the smell of incense, the dead body, and carbolic acid.

'Where to, sir?' asked the coachman.

'It's not too late even now. . . . I'll call round on Fëdor Vasílievich.'

He accordingly drove there and found them just finishing the first rubber, so that it was quite convenient for him to cut in.

II

Iván Ilých's life had been most simple and most ordinary and therefore most terrible.

He had been a member of the Court of Justice, and died at the age of forty-five. His father had been an official who after serving in various ministries and departments in Petersburg had made the sort of career which brings men to positions from which by reason of their long service they cannot be dismissed, though they are obviously unfit to hold any responsible position, and for whom therefore posts are specially created, which though fictitious carry salaries of from six to ten thousand rubles that are not fictitious, and in receipt of which they live on to a great age.

Such was the Privy Councillor and superfluous member of various superfluous institutions, Ilyá Epímovich Golovín.

He had three sons, of whom Iván Ilých was the second. The eldest son was following in his father's footsteps only in another department, and was

already approaching that stage in the service at which a similar sinecure
would be reached. The third son was a failure. He had ruined his prospects
in a number of positions and was now serving in the railway department.
His father and brothers, and still more their wives, not merely disliked
meeting him, but avoided remembering his existence unless compelled to
do so. His sister had married Baron Greff, a Petersburg official of her father's
type. Iván Ilých was *le phénix de la famille* as people said. He was neither
as cold and formal as his elder brother nor as wild as the younger, but was
a happy mean between them—an intelligent, polished, lively and agreeable
man. He had studied with his younger brother at the School of Law, but the
latter had failed to complete the course and was expelled when he was in
the fifth class. Iván Ilých finished the course well. Even when he was at the
School of Law he was just what he remained for the rest of his life: a
capable, cheerful, good-natured, and sociable man, though strict in the
fulfilment of what he considered to be his duty: and he considered his duty
to be what was so considered by those in authority. Neither as a boy nor
as a man was he a toady, but from early youth was by nature attracted to
people of high station as a fly is drawn to the light, assimilating their ways
and views of life and establishing friendly relations with them. All the
enthusiasms of childhood and youth passed without leaving much trace on
him; he succumbed to sensuality, to vanity, and latterly among the highest
classes to liberalism, but always within limits which his instinct unfailingly
indicated to him as correct.

At school he had done things which had formerly seemed to him very
horrid and made him feel disgusted with himself when he did them; but
when later on he saw that such actions were done by people of good position and that they did not regard them as wrong, he was able not exactly to
regard them as right, but to forget about them entirely or not be at all
troubled at remembering them.

Having graduated from the School of Law and qualified for the tenth
rank of the civil service, and having received money from his father for his
equipment, Iván Ilých ordered himself clothes at Scharmer's, the fashionable tailor, hung a medallion inscribed *respice finen* on his watch-chain,
took leave of his professor and the prince who was patron of the school,
had a farewell dinner with his comrades at Donon's first-class restaurant,
and with his new and fashionable portmanteau, linen, clothes, shaving and
other toilet appliances, and a travelling rug, all purchased at the best shops,
he set off for one of the provinces where, through his father's influence, he
had been attached to the Governor as an official for special service.

In the province Iván Ilých soon arranged as easy and agreeable a position
for himself as he had had at the School of Law. He performed his official
tasks, made his career, and at the same time amused himself pleasantly and
decorously. Occasionally he paid official visits to country districts, where he
behaved with dignity both to his superiors and inferiors, and performed

the duties entrusted to him, which related chiefly to the sectarians, with an exactness and incorruptible honesty of which he could not but feel proud.

In official matters, despite his youth and taste for frivolous gaiety, he was exceedingly reserved, punctilious, and even severe; but in society he was often amusing and witty, and always good-natured, correct in his manner, and *bon enfant,* as the governor and his wife—with whom he was like one of the family—used to say of him.

In the provinces he had an affair with a lady who made advances to the elegant young lawyer, and there was also a milliner; and there were carousals with aides-de-camp who visited the district, and after-supper visits to a certain outlying street of doubtful reputation; and there was too some obsequiousness to his chief and even to his chief's wife, but all this was done with such a tone of good breeding that no hard names could be applied to it. It all came under the heading of the French saying: *'Il faut que jeunesse se passe.'*[1] It was all done with clean hands, in clean linen, with French phrases, and above all among people of the best society and consequently with the approval of people of rank.

So Iván Ilých served for five years and then came a change in his official life. The new and reformed judicial institutions were introduced, and new men were needed. Iván Ilých became such a new man. He was offered the post of Examining Magistrate, and he accepted it though the post was in another province and obliged him to give up the connexions he had formed and to make new ones. His friends met to give him a send-off; they had a group-photograph taken and presented him with a silver cigarette-case, and he set off to his new post.

As examining magistrate Iván Ilých was just as *comme il faut* and decorous a man, inspiring general respect and capable of separating his official duties from his private life, as he had been when acting as an official on special service. His duties now as examining magistrate were far more interesting and attractive than before. In his former position it had been pleasant to wear an undress uniform made by Scharmer, and to pass through the crowd of petitioners and officials who were timorously awaiting an audience with the governor, and who envied him as with free and easy gait he went straight into his chief's private room to have a cup of tea and a cigarette with him. But not many people had then been directly dependent on him— only police officials and the sectarians when he went on special missions —and he liked to treat them politely, almost as comrades, as if he were letting them feel that he who had the power to crush them was treating them in this simple, friendly way. There were then but few such people. But now, as an examining magistrate, Iván Ilých felt that everyone without exception, even the most important and self-satisfied, was in his power, and that he need only write a few words on a sheet of paper with a certain heading, and this or that important, self-satisfied person would be brought be-

[1] Youth must have its fling.

fore him in the role of an accused person or a witness, and if he did not choose to allow him to sit down, would have to stand before him and answer his questions. Iván Ilých never abused his power; he tried on the contrary to soften its expression, but the consciousness of it and of the possibility of softening its effect, supplied the chief interest and attraction of his office. In his work itself, especially in his examinations, he very soon acquired a method of eliminating all considerations irrelevant to the legal aspect of the case, and reducing even the most complicated case to a form in which it would be presented on paper only in its externals, completely excluding his personal opinion of the matter, while above all observing every prescribed formality. The work was new and Iván Ilých was one of the first men to apply the new Code of 1864.[2]

On taking up the post of examining magistrate in a new town, he made new acquaintances and connexions, placed himself on a new footing, and assumed a somewhat different tone. He took up an attitude of rather dignified aloofness towards the provincial authorities, but picked out the best circle of legal gentlemen and wealthy gentry living in the town and assumed a tone of slight dissatisfaction with the government, of moderate liberalism, and of enlightened citizenship. At the same time, without at all altering the elegance of his toilet, he ceased shaving his chin and allowed his beard to grow as it pleased.

Iván Ilých settled down very pleasantly in this new town. The society there, which inclined towards opposition to the Governor, was friendly, his salary was larger, and he began to play *vint* [a form of bridge], which he found added not a little to the pleasure of life, for he had a capacity for cards, played good-humouredly, and calculated rapidly and astutely, so that he usually won.

After living there for two years he met his future wife, Praskóvya Fëdorovna Míkhel, who was the most attractive, clever, and brilliant girl of the set in which he moved, and among other amusements and relaxations from his labours as examining magistrate, Iván Ilých established light and playful relations with her.

While he had been an official on special service he had been accustomed to dance, but now as an examining magistrate it was exceptional for him to do so. If he danced now, he did it as if to show that though he served under the reformed order of things, and had reached the fifth official rank, yet when it came to dancing he could do it better than most people. So at the end of an evening he sometimes danced with Praskóvya Fëdorovna, and it was chiefly during these dances that he captivated her. She fell in love with him. Iván Ilých had at first no definite intention of marrying, but when the girl fell in love with him he said to himself: 'Really, why shouldn't I marry?'

[2]The emancipation of the serfs in 1861 was followed by a thorough all-round reform of judicial proceedings.—A. M.

Praskóvya Fëdorovna came of a good family, was not bad looking, and had some little property. Iván Ilých might have aspired to a more brilliant match, but even this was good. He had his salary, and she, he hoped, would have an equal income. She was well connected, and was a sweet, pretty, and thoroughly correct young woman. To say that Iván Ilých married because he fell in love with Praskóvya Fëdorovna and found that she sympathized with his views of life would be as incorrect as to say that he married because his social circle approved of the match. He was swayed by both these considerations: the marriage gave him personal satisfaction, and at the same time it was considered the right thing by the most highly placed of his associates.

So Iván Ilých got married.

The preparations for marriage and the beginning of married life, with its conjugal caresses, the new furniture, new crockery, and new linen, were very pleasant until his wife became pregnant—so that Iván Ilých had begun to think that marriage would not impair the easy, agreeable, gay and always decorous character of his life, approved of by society and regarded by himself as natural, but would even improve it. But from the first months of his wife's pregnancy, something new, unpleasant, depressing, and unseemly, and from which there was no way of escape, unexpectedly showed itself.

His wife, without any reason—*de gaieté de cœur* as Iván Ilých expressed it to himself—began to disturb the pleasure and propriety of their life. She began to be jealous without any cause, expected him to devote his whole attention to her, found fault with everything, and made coarse and ill-mannered scenes.

At first Iván Ilých hoped to escape from the unpleasantness of this state of affairs by the same easy and decorous relation to life that had served him heretofore: he tried to ignore his wife's disagreeable moods, continued to live in his usual easy and pleasant way, invited friends to his house for a game of cards, and also tried going out to his club or spending his evenings with friends. But one day his wife began upbraiding him so vigorously, using such coarse words, and continued to abuse him every time he did not fulfil her demands, so resolutely and with such evident determination not to give way till he submitted—that is, till he stayed at home and was bored just as she was—that he became alarmed. He now realized that matrimony—at any rate with Praskóvya Fëdorovna—was not always conducive to the pleasures and amenities of life but on the contrary often infringed both comfort and propriety, and that he must therefore entrench himself against such infringement. And Iván Ilých began to seek for means of doing so. His official duties were the one thing that imposed upon Praskóvya Fëdorovna, and by means of his official work and the duties attached to it he began struggling with his wife to secure his own independence.

With the birth of their child, the attempts to feed it and the various failures in doing so, and with the real and imaginary illnesses of mother and child, in which Iván Ilých's sympathy was demanded but about which he understood nothing, the need of securing for himself an existence outside his family life became still more imperative.

As his wife grew more irritable and exacting and Iván Ilých transferred the centre of gravity of his life more and more to his official work, so did he grow to like his work better and became more ambitious than before.

Very soon, within a year of his wedding, Iván Ilých had realized that marriage, though it may add some comforts to life, is in fact a very intricate and difficult affair towards which in order to perform one's duty, that is, to lead a decorous life approved of by society, one must adopt a definite attitude just as towards one's official duties.

And Iván Ilých evolved such an attitude towards married life. He only required of it those conveniences—dinner at home, housewife, and bed—which it could give him, and above all that propriety of external forms required by public opinion. For the rest he looked for light-hearted pleasure and propriety, and was very thankful when he found them, but if he met with antagonism and querulousness he at once retired into his separate fenced-off world of official duties, where he found satisfaction.

Iván Ilých was esteemed a good official, and after three years was made Assistant Public Prosecutor. His new duties, their importance, the possibility of indicting and imprisoning anyone he chose, the publicity his speeches received, and the success he had in all these things, made his work still more attractive.

More children came. His wife became more and more querulous and ill-tempered, but the attitude Iván Ilých had adopted towards his home life rendered him almost impervious to her grumbling.

After seven years' service in that town he was transferred to another province as Public Prosecutor. They moved, but were short of money and his wife did not like the place they moved to. Though the salary was higher the cost of living was greater, besides which two of their children died and family life became still more unpleasant for him.

Praskóvya Fëdorovna blamed her husband for every inconvenience they encountered in their new home. Most of the conversations between husband and wife, especially as to the children's education, led to topics which recalled former disputes, and those disputes were apt to flare up again at any moment. There remained only those rare periods of amorousness which still came to them at times but did not last long. These were islets at which they anchored for a while and then again set out upon that ocean of veiled hostility which showed itself in their aloofness from one another. This aloofness might have grieved Iván Ilých had he considered that it ought not to exist, but he now regarded the position as normal, and even made it the goal at which he aimed in family life. His aim was to free himself more and more from those unpleasantnesses and to give them a semblance of harmlessness and propriety. He attained this by spending less and less time with his family, and when obliged to be at home he tried to safeguard his position by the presence of outsiders. The chief thing however was that he had his official duties. The whole interest of his life now centred in the official world and that interest absorbed him. The consciousness of his power, being able to ruin anybody he wished to ruin, the importance, even the external dignity of his entry into court, or meetings with his subordinates, his success with superiors and inferiors, and above all his masterly handling of cases, of which he was conscious—all this gave him pleasure and filled his life, together with chats with his colleagues, dinners, and bridge. So that on the whole Iván Ilých's life continued to flow as he considered it should do—pleasantly and properly.

So things continued for another seven years. His eldest daughter was already sixteen, another child had died, and only one son was left, a schoolboy and a subject of dissension. Iván Ilých wanted to put him in the School of Law, but to spite him Praskóvya Fëdorovna entered him at the High School. The daughter had been educated at home and had turned out well: the boy did not learn badly either.

III

So Iván Ilých lived for seventeen years after his marriage. He was already a Public Prosecutor of long standing, and had declined several proposed transfers while awaiting a more desirable post, when an unanticipated and unpleasant occurrence quite upset the peaceful course of his life. He was expecting to be offered the post of presiding judge in a University town, but Happe somehow came to the front and obtained the appointment instead. Iván Ilých became irritable, reproached Happe, and quarrelled both with him and with his immediate superiors—who became colder to him and again passed him over when other appointments were made.

This was in 1880, the hardest year of Iván Ilých's life. It was then that it became evident on the one hand that his salary was insufficient for them to live on, and on the other that he had been forgotten, and not only this, but that what was for him the greatest and most cruel injustice appeared to others a quite ordinary occurrence. Even his father did not consider it his duty to help him. Iván Ilých felt himself abandoned by everyone, and that they regarded his position with a salary of 3,500 rubles [about £350] as quite normal and even fortunate. He alone knew that with the consciousness of the injustices done him, with his wife's incessant nagging, and with the debts he had contracted by living beyond his means, his position was far from normal.

In order to save money that summer he obtained leave of absence and went with his wife to live in the country at her brother's place.

In the country, without his work, he experienced *ennui* for the first time in his life, and not only *ennui* but intolerable depression, and he decided that it was impossible to go on living like that, and that it was necessary to take energetic measures.

Having passed a sleepless night pacing up and down the veranda, he decided to go to Petersburg and bestir himself, in order to punish those who had failed to appreciate him and to get transferred to another ministry.

Next day, despite many protests from his wife and her brother, he started for Petersburg with the sole object of obtaining a post with a salary of five thousand rubles a year. He was no longer bent on any particular department, or tendency, or kind of activity. All he now wanted was an appointment to another post with a salary of five thousand rubles, either in the administration, in the banks, with the railways, in one of the Empress Márya's Institutions, or even in the customs—but it had to carry with it a salary of five thousand rubles and be in a ministry other than that in which they had failed to appreciate him.

And this quest of Iván Ilých's was crowned with remarkable and unexpected success. At Kursk an acquaintance of his, F. I. Ilyín, got into the first-class carriage, sat down beside Iván Ilých, and told him of a telegram just received by the Governor of Kursk announcing that a change was about to take place in the ministry: Peter Ivánovich was to be superseded by Iván Semënovich.

The proposed change, apart from its significance for Russia, had a special significance for Iván Ilých, because by bringing forward a new man, Peter Petróvich, and consequently his friend Zachár Ivánovich, it was highly favourable for Iván Ilých, since Zachár Ivánovich was a friend and colleague of his.

In Moscow this news was confirmed, and on reaching Petersburg Iván Ilých found Zachár Ivánovich and received a definite promise of an appointment in his former department of Justice.

A week later he telegraphed to his wife: 'Zachár in Miller's place. I shall receive appointment on presentation of report.'

Thanks to this change of personnel, Iván Ilých had unexpectedly obtained an appointment in his former ministry which placed him two stages above his former colleagues besides giving him five thousand rubles salary and three thousand five hundred rubles for expenses connected with his removal. All his ill humour towards his former enemies and the whole department vanished, and Iván Ilých was completely happy.

He returned to the country more cheerful and contented than he had been for a long time. Praskóvya Fëdorovna also cheered up and a truce was arranged between them. Iván Ilých told of how he had been fêted by everybody in Petersburg, how all those who had been his enemies were put to shame and now fawned on him, how envious they were of his appointment, and how much everybody in Petersburg had liked him.

Praskóvya Fëdorovna listened to all this and appeared to believe it. She did not contradict anything, but only made plans for their life in the town to which they were going. Iván Ilých saw with delight that these plans were his plans, that he and his wife agreed, and that, after a stumble, his life was regaining its due and natural character of pleasant lightheartedness and decorum.

Iván Ilých had come back for a short time only, for he had to take up his new duties on the 10th of September. Moreover, he needed time to settle into the new place, to move all his belongings from the province, and to buy and order many additional things: in a word, to make such arrangements as he had resolved on, which were almost exactly what Praskóvya Fëdorovna too had decided on.

Now that everything had happened so fortunately, and that he and his wife were at one in their aims and moreover saw so little of one another, they got on together better than they had done since the first years of marriage. Iván Ilých had thought of taking his family away with him at once, but the insistence of his wife's brother and her sister-in-law, who had suddenly become particularly amiable and friendly to him and his family, induced him to depart alone.

So he departed, and the cheerful state of mind induced by his success and by the harmony between his wife and himself, the one intensifying the other, did not leave him. He found a delightful house, just the thing both he and his wife had dreamt of. Spacious, lofty reception rooms in the old style, a convenient and dignified study, rooms for his wife and daughter, a study for his son—it might have been specially built for them. Iván Ilých himself superintended the arrangements, chose the wall-papers, supplemented the furniture (preferably with antiques which he considered particularly *comme il faut*), and supervised the upholstering. Everything progressed and progressed and approached the ideal he had set himself: even when things were only half completed they exceeded his expectations. He saw what a refined and elegant character, free from vulgarity, it would all have when it was ready. On falling asleep he pictured to himself how the reception-room would look. Looking at the yet unfinished drawing-room he could see the fireplace, the screen, the what-not, the little chairs dotted here and there, the dishes and plates on the walls, and the bronzes, as they would be when everything was in place. He was pleased by the thought of how his wife and daughter, who shared his taste in this matter, would be impressed by it. They were certainly not expecting as much. He had been particularly successful in finding, and buying cheaply, antiques which gave a particularly aristocratic character to the whole place. But in his letters he intentionally understated everything in order to be able to surprise them. All this so absorbed him that his new duties—though he liked his official work—interested him less than he had expected. Sometimes he even had moments of absent-mindedness during the Court Sessions, and would consider whether he should have straight or curved cornices for his curtains. He was so interested in it all that he often did things himself, rearranging the furniture, or rehanging the curtains. Once when mounting a step-ladder to show the upholsterer, who did not understand, how he wanted the hangings draped, he made a false step and slipped, but being a strong and agile man he clung on and only knocked his side against the knob of the window frame. The bruised place was painful but the pain soon passed, and he felt particularly bright and well just then. He wrote: 'I feel fifteen years younger.' He thought he would have everything ready by September, but it dragged on till mid-October. But the result was charming not only in his eyes but to everyone who saw it.

In reality it was just what is usually seen in the houses of people of moderate means who want to appear rich, and therefore succeed only in resembling others like themselves: there were damasks, dark wood, plants, rugs, and dull and polished bronzes—all the things people of a certain class have in order to resemble other people of that class. His house was so like the others that it would never have been noticed, but to him it all seemed to be quite exceptional. He was very happy when he met his family at the station and brought them to the newly furnished house all lit up, where a footman in a white tie opened the door into the hall decorated with plants, and when they went on into the drawing-room and the study uttering exclamations of delight. He conducted them everywhere, drank in their praises eagerly, and beamed with pleasure. At tea that evening, when Praskóvya Fëdorovna among other things asked him about his fall, he laughed, and showed them how he had gone flying and had frightened the upholsterer.

'It's a good thing I'm a bit of an athlete. Another man might have been killed, but I merely knocked myself, just here; it hurts when it's touched, but it's passing off already—it's only a bruise.'

So they began living in their new home—in which, as always happens, when they got thoroughly settled in they found they were just one room short—and with the increased income, which as always was just a little (some five hundred rubles) too little, but it was all very nice.

Things went particularly well at first, before everything was finally arranged and while something had still to be done: this thing bought, that thing ordered, another thing moved, and something else adjusted. Though there were some disputes between husband and wife, they were both so well satisfied and had so much to do that it all passed off without any serious quarrels. When nothing was left to arrange it became rather dull and something seemed to be lacking, but they were then making acquaintances, forming habits, and life was growing fuller.

Iván Ilých spent his mornings at the law court and came home to dinner, and at first he was generally in a good humour, though he occasionally became irritable just on account of his house. (Every spot on the tablecloth or the upholstery, and every broken window-blind string, irritated him. He had devoted so much trouble to arranging it all that every disturbance of it distressed him.) But on the whole his life ran its course as he believed life should do: easily, pleasantly, and decorously.

He got up at nine, drank his coffee, read the paper, and then put on his undress uniform and went to the law courts. There the harness in which he worked had already been stretched to fit him and he donned it without a hitch: petitioners, inquiries at the chancery, the chancery itself, and the sittings public and administrative. In all this the thing was to exclude everything fresh and vital, which always disturbs the regular course of official business, and to admit only official relations with people, and then only on official grounds. A man would come, for instance, wanting some information. Iván Ilých, as one in whose sphere the matter did not lie, would have nothing to do with him: but if the man had some business with him in his official capacity, something that could be expressed on officially stamped paper, he would do everything, positively everything he could within the limits of such relations, and in doing so would maintain the semblance of friendly human relations, that is, would observe the courtesies of life. As soon as the official relations ended, so did everything else. Iván Ilých possessed this capacity to separate his real life from the official side of affairs and not mix the two, in the highest degree, and by long practice and natural aptitude had brought it to such a pitch that sometimes, in the manner of a virtuoso, he would even allow himself to let the human and official relations mingle. He let himself do this just because he felt that he could at any time he chose resume the strictly official attitude again and drop the human relation. And he did it all easily, pleasantly, correctly, and even artistically. In the intervals between the sessions he smoked, drank tea, chatted a little about politics, a little about general topics, a little about cards, but most of all about official appointments. Tired, but with the feelings of a virtuoso— one of the first violins who has played his part in an orchestra with precision—he would return home to find that his wife and daughter had been out paying calls, or had a visitor, and that his son had been to school, had done his homework with his tutor, and was duly learning what is taught at High Schools. Everything was as it should be. After dinner, if they had no visitors, Iván Ilých sometimes read a book that was being much discussed at the time, and in the evening settled down to work, that is, read official papers, compared the depositions of witnesses, and noted paragraphs of the Code applying to them. This was neither dull nor amusing. It was dull when he might have been playing bridge, but if no bridge was available it was at any rate better than doing nothing or sitting with his wife. Iván Ilých's chief pleasure was giving little dinners to which he invited men and women of good social position, and just as his drawing-room resembled all other drawing-rooms so did his enjoyable little parties resemble all other such parties.

Once they even gave a dance. Iván Ilých enjoyed it and everything went off well, except that it led to a violent quarrel with his wife about the cakes

and sweets. Praskóvya Fëdorovna had made her own plans, but Iván Ilých
insisted on getting everything from an expensive confectioner and ordered
too many cakes, and the quarrel occurred because some of those cakes were
left over and the confectioner's bill came to forty-five rubles. It was a great
and disagreeable quarrel. Praskóvya Fëdorovna called him 'a fool and an
imbecile', and he clutched at his head and made angry allusions to divorce.

But the dance itself had been enjoyable. The best people were there, and
Iván Ilých had danced with Princess Trúfonova, a sister of the distinguished
founder of the Society 'Bear my Burden'.

The pleasures connected with his work were pleasures of ambition; his
social pleasures were those of vanity; but Iván Ilých's greatest pleasure was
playing bridge. He acknowledged that whatever disagreeable incident happened in his life, the pleasure that beamed like a ray of light above everything else was to sit down to bridge with good players, not noisy partners,
and of course to four-handed bridge (with five players it was annoying to
have to stand out, though one pretended not to mind), to play a clever and
serious game (when the cards allowed it) and then to have supper and drink
a glass of wine. After a game of bridge, especially if he had won a little (to
win a large sum was unpleasant), Iván Ilých went to bed in specially good
humour.

So they lived. They formed a circle of acquaintances among the best people and were visited by people of importance and by young folk. In their
views as to their acquaintances, husband, wife and daughter were entirely
agreed, and tacitly and unanimously kept at arm's length and shook off the
various shabby friends and relations who, with much show of affection,
gushed into the drawing-room with its Japanese plates on the walls. Soon
these shabby friends ceased to obtrude themselves and only the best people
remained in the Golovíns' set.

Young men made up to Lisa, and Petríschhev, an examining magistrate
and Dmítri Ivánovich Petríshchev's son and sole heir, began to be so attentive to her that Iván Ilých had already spoken to Praskóvya Fëdorovna about
it, and considered whether they should not arrange a party for them, or get
up some private theatricals.

So they lived, and all went well, without change, and life flowed pleasantly.

IV

They were all in good health. It could not be called ill health if Iván Ilých
sometimes said that he had a queer taste in his mouth and felt some discomfort in his left side.

But this discomfort increased and, though not exactly painful, grew into
a sense of pressure in his side accompanied by ill humour. And his irritability became worse and worse and began to mar the agreeable, easy, and
correct life that had established itself in the Golovín family. Quarrels be-

tween husband and wife became more and more frequent, and soon the
ease and amenity disappeared and even the decorum was barely maintained.
Scenes again became frequent, and very few of those islets remained on
which husband and wife could meet without an explosion. Praskóvya
Fëdorovna now had good reason to say that her husband's temper was trying. With characteristic exaggeration she said he had always had a dreadful
temper, and that it had needed all her good nature to put up with it for
twenty years. It was true that now the quarrels were started by him. His
bursts of temper always came just before dinner, often just as he began to
eat his soup. Sometimes he noticed that a plate or dish was chipped, or the
food was not right, or his son put his elbow on the table, or his daughter's
hair was not done as he liked it, and for all this he blamed Praskóvya
Fëdorovna. At first she retorted and said disagreeable things to him, but
once or twice he fell into such a rage at the beginning of dinner that she
realized it was due to some physical derangement brought on by taking
food, and so she restrained herself and did not answer, but only hurried to
get the dinner over. She regarded this self-restraint as highly praiseworthy.
Having come to the conclusion that her husband had a dreadful temper and
made her life miserable, she began to feel sorry for herself, and the more
she pitied herself the more she hated her husband. She began to wish he
would die; yet she did not want him to die because then his salary would
cease. And this irritated her against him still more. She considered herself
dreadfully unhappy just because not even his death could save her, and
though she concealed her exasperation, that hidden exasperation of hers
increased his irritation also.

After one scene in which Iván Ilých had been particularly unfair and after
which he had said in explanation that he certainly was irritable but that it
was due to his not being well, she said that if he was ill it should be
attended to, and insisted on his going to see a celebrated doctor.

He went. Everything took place as he had expected and as it always
does. There was the usual waiting and the important air assumed by the
doctor, with which he was so familiar (resembling that which he himself
assumed in court), and the sounding and listening, and the questions which
called for answers that were foregone conclusions and were evidently unnecessary, and the look of importance which implied that 'if only you put
yourself in our hands we will arrange everything—we know indubitably
how it has to be done, always in the same way for everybody alike.' It was
all just as it was in the law courts. The doctor put on just the same air
towards him as he himself put on towards an accused person.

The doctor said that so-and-so indicated that there was so-and-so inside
the patient, but if the investigation of so-and-so did not confirm this, then
he must assume that and that. If he assumed that and that, then . . . and
so on. To Iván Ilých only one question was important: was his case serious
or not? But the doctor ignored that inappropriate question. From his point

of view it was not the one under consideration, the real question was to decide between a floating kidney, chronic catarrh, or appendicitis. It was not a question of Iván Ilých's life or death, but one between a floating kidney and appendicitis. And that question the doctor solved brilliantly, as it seemed to Iván Ilých, in favour of the appendix, with the reservation that should an examination of the urine give fresh indications the matter would be reconsidered. All this was just what Iván Ilých had himself brilliantly accomplished a thousand times in dealing with men on trial. The doctor summed up just as brilliantly, looking over his spectacles triumphantly and even gaily at the accused. From the doctor's summing up Iván Ilých concluded that things were bad, but that for the doctor, and perhaps for everybody else, it was a matter of indifference, though for him it was bad. And this conclusion struck him painfully, arousing in him a great feeling of pity for himself and of bitterness towards the doctor's indifference to a matter of such importance.

He said nothing of this, but rose, placed the doctor's fee on the table, and remarked with a sigh: 'We sick people probably often put inappropriate questions. But tell me, in general, is this complaint dangerous, or not? . . .'

The doctor looked at him sternly over his spectacles with one eye, as if to say: 'Prisoner, if you will not keep to the questions put to you, I shall be obliged to have you removed from the court.'

'I have already told you what I consider necessary and proper. The analysis may show something more.' And the doctor bowed.

Iván Ilých went out slowly, seated himself disconsolately in his sledge, and drove home. All the way home he was going over what the doctor had said, trying to translate those complicated, obscure, scientific phrases into plain language and find in them an answer to the question: 'Is my condition bad? Is it very bad? Or is there as yet nothing much wrong?' And it seemed to him that the meaning of what the doctor had said was that it was very bad. Everything in the streets seemed depressing. The cabmen, the houses, the passers-by, and the shops, were dismal. His ache, this dull gnawing ache that never ceased for a moment, seemed to have acquired a new and more serious significance from the doctor's dubious remarks. Iván Ilých now watched it with a new and oppressive feeling.

He reached home and began to tell his wife about it. She listened, but in the middle of his account his daughter came in with her hat on, ready to go out with her mother. She sat down reluctantly to listen to this tedious story, but could not stand it long, and her mother too did not hear him to the end.

'Well, I am very glad,' she said. 'Mind now to take your medicine regularly. Give me the prescription and I'll send Gerásim to the chemist's.' And she went to get ready to go out.

While she was in the room Iván Ilých had hardly taken time to breathe, but he sighed deeply when she left it.

'Well,' he thought, 'perhaps it isn't so bad after all.'

He began taking his medicine and following the doctor's directions, which had been altered after the examination of the urine. But then it happened that there was a contradiction between the indications drawn from the examination of the urine and the symptoms that showed themselves. It turned out that what was happening differed from what the doctor had told him, and that he had either forgotten, or blundered, or hidden something from him. He could not, however, be blamed for that, and Iván Ilých still obeyed his orders implicitly and at first derived some comfort from doing so.

From the time of his visit to the doctor, Iván Ilých's chief occupation was the exact fulfilment of the doctor's instructions regarding bygiene and the taking of medicine, and the observation of his pain and his excretions. His chief interests came to be people's ailments and people's health. When sickness, deaths, or recoveries, were mentioned in his presence, especially when the illness resembled his own, he listened with agitation which he tried to hide, asked questions, and applied what he heard to his own case.

The pain did not grow less, but Iván Ilých made efforts to force himself to think that he was better. And he could do this so long as nothing agitated him. But as soon as he had any unpleasantness with his wife, any lack of success in his official work, or held bad cards at bridge, he was at once acutely sensible of his disease. He had formerly borne such mischances, hoping soon to adjust what was wrong, to master it and attain success, or make a grand slam. But now every mischance upset him and plunged him into despair. He would say to himself: 'There now, just as I was beginning to get better and the medicine had begun to take effect, comes this accursed misfortune, or unpleasantness . . .' And he was furious with the mishap, or with the people who were causing the unpleasantness and killing him, for he felt that this fury was killing him but could not restrain it. One would have thought that it should have been clear to him that this exasperation with circumstances and people aggravated his illness, and that he ought therefore to ignore unpleasant occurrences. But he drew the very opposite conclusion: he said that he needed peace, and he watched for everything that might disturb it and became irritable at the slightest infringement of it. His condition was rendered worse by the fact that he read medical books and consulted doctors. The progress of his disease was so gradual that he could deceive himself when comparing one day with another—the difference was so slight. But when he consulted the doctors it seemed to him that he was getting worse, and even very rapidly. Yet despite this he was continually consulting them.

That month he went to see another celebrity, who told him almost the same as the first had done but put his questions rather differently, and the interview with this celebrity only increased Iván Ilých's doubts and fears. A friend of a friend of his, a very good doctor, diagnosed his illness again quite differently from the others, and though he predicted recovery, his questions and suppositions bewildered Iván Ilých still more and increased his doubts. A homoeopathist diagnosed the disease in yet another way, and prescribed medicine which Iván Ilých took secretly for a week. But after a week, not feeling any improvement and having lost confidence both in the former doctor's treatment and in this one's, he became still more despondent. One day a lady acquaintance mentioned a cure effected by a wonder-working icon. Iván Ilých caught himself listening attentively and beginning to believe that it had occurred. This incident alarmed him. 'Has my mind really weakened to such an extent?' he asked himself. 'Nonsense! It's all rubbish. I mustn't give way to nervous fears but having chosen a doctor must keep strictly to his treatment. That is what I will do. Now it's all settled. I won't think about it, but will follow the treatment seriously till summer, and then we shall see. From now there must be no more of this wavering!' This was easy to say but impossible to carry out. The pain in his side oppressed him and seemed to grow worse and more incessant, while the taste in his mouth grew stranger and stranger. It seemed to him that his breath had a disgusting smell, and he was conscious of a loss of appetite and strength. There was no deceiving himself: something terrible, new, and more important than anything before in his life, was taking place within him of which he alone was aware. Those about him did not understand or would not understand it, but thought everything in the world was going on as usual. That tormented Iván Ilých more than anything. He saw that his household, especially his wife and daughter who were in a perfect whirl of visiting, did not understand anything of it and were annoyed that he was so depressed and so exacting, as if he were to blame for it. Though they tried to disguise it he saw that he was an obstacle in their path, and that his wife had adopted a definite line in regard to his illness and kept to it regardless of anything he said or did. Her attitude was this: 'You know,' she would say to her friends, 'Iván Ilých can't do as other people do, and keep to the treatment prescribed for him. One day he'll take his drops and keep strictly to his diet and go to bed in good time, but the next day unless I watch him he'll suddenly forget his medicine, eat sturgeon—which is forbidden—and sit up playing cards till one o'clock in the morning.'

'Oh, come, when was that?' Iván Ilých would ask in vexation. 'Only once at Peter Ivánovich's.'

'And yesterday with Shébek.'

'Well, even if I hadn't stayed up, this pain would have kept me awake.'

'Be that as it may you'll never get well like that, but will always make us wretched.'

Praskóvya Fëdorovna's attitude to Iván Ilých's illness, as she expressed it both to others and to him, was that it was his own fault and was another of the annoyances he caused her. Iván Ilých felt that this opinion escaped her involuntarily—but that did not make it easier for him.

At the law courts too, Iván Ilých noticed, or thought he noticed, a strange attitude towards himself. It sometimes seemed to him that people were watching him inquisitively as a man whose place might soon be vacant. Then again, his friends would suddenly begin to chaff him in a friendly way about his low spirits, as if the awful, horrible, and unheard-of thing that was going on within him, incessantly gnawing at him and irresistibly drawing him away, was a very agreeable subject for jests. Schwartz in particular irritated him by his jocularity, vivacity, and *savoir-faire,* which reminded him of what he himself had been ten years ago.

Friends came to make up a set and they sat down to cards. They dealt, bending the new cards to soften them, and he sorted the diamonds in his hand and found he had seven. His partner said 'No trumps' and supported him with two diamonds. What more could be wished for? It ought to be jolly and lively. They would make a grand slam. But suddenly Iván Ilých was conscious of that gnawing pain, that taste in his mouth, and it seemed ridiculous that in such circumstances he should be pleased to make a grand slam.

He looked at his partner Mikháil Mikháylovich, who rapped the table with his strong hand and instead of snatching up the tricks pushed the cards courteously and indulgently towards Iván Ilých that he might have the pleasure of gathering them up without the trouble of stretching out his hand for them. 'Does he think I am too weak to stretch out my arm?' thought Iván Ilých, and forgetting what he was doing he over-trumped his partner, missing the grand slam by three tricks. And what was most awful of all was that he saw how upset Mikháil Mikháylovich was about it but did not himself care. And it was dreadful to realize why he did not care.

They all saw that he was suffering, and said: 'We can stop if you are tired. Take a rest.' Lie down? No, he was not at all tired, and he finished the rubber. All were gloomy and silent. Iván Ilých felt that he had diffused this gloom over them and could not dispel it. They had supper and went away, and Iván Ilých was left alone with the consciousness that his life was poisoned and was poisoning the lives of others, and that this poison did not weaken but penetrated more and more deeply into his whole being.

With this consciousness, and with physical pain besides the terror, he must go to bed, often to lie awake the greater part of the night. Next morning he had to get up again, dress, go to the law courts, speak, and write; or if he did not go out, spend at home those twenty-four hours a day each of which was a torture. And he had to live thus all alone on the brink of an abyss, with no one who understood or pitied him.

v

So one month passed and then another. Just before the New Year his brother-in-law came to town and stayed at their house. Iván Ilých was at the law courts and Praskóvya Fëdorovna had gone shopping. When Iván Ilých

came home and entered his study he found his brother-in-law there—a
healthy, florid man—unpacking his portmanteau himself. He raised his head
on hearing Iván Ilých's footsteps and looked up at him for a moment without a word. That stare told Iván Ilých everything. His brother-in-law opened
his mouth to utter an exclamation of surprise but checked himself, and that
action confirmed it all.

'I have changed, eh?'

'Yes, there is a change.'

And after that, try as he would to get his brother-in-law to return to the
subject of his looks, the latter would say nothing about it. Praskóvya
Fëdorovna came home and her brother went out to her. Iván Ilých locked
the door and began to examine himself in the glass, first full face, then in
profile. He took up a portrait of himself taken with his wife, and compared it with what he saw in the glass. The change in him was immense.
Then he bared his arms to the elbow, looked at them, drew the sleeves
down again, sat down on an ottoman, and grew blacker than night.

'No, no, this won't do!' he said to himself, and jumped up, went to the
table, took up some law papers and began to read them, but could not
continue. He unlocked the door and went into the reception-room. The
door leading to the drawing-room was shut. He approached it on tiptoe and
listened.

'No, you are exaggerating!' Praskóvya Fëdorovna was saying.

'Exaggerating! Don't you see it? Why, he's a dead man! Look at his eyes
—there's no light in them. But what is it that is wrong with him?'

'No one knows. Nikoláevich [that was another doctor] said something,
but I don't know what. And Leshchetítsky [this was the celebrated special-
ist] said quite the contrary . . .'

Iván Ilých walked away, went to his own room, lay down, and began
musing: 'The kidney, a floating kidney.' He recalled all the doctors had told
him of how it detached itself and swayed about. And by an effort of imagination he tried to catch that kidney and arrest it and support it. So little
was needed for this, it seemed to him. 'No, I'll go to see Peter Ivánovich
again.' [That was the friend whose friend was a doctor.] He rang, ordered
the carriage, and got ready to go.

'Where are you going, Jean?' asked his wife, with a specially sad and
exceptionally kind look.

This exceptionally kind look irritated him. He looked morosely at her.

'I must go to see Peter Ivánovich.'

He went to see Peter Ivánovich, and together they went to see his friend,
the doctor. He was in, and Iván Ilých had a long talk with him.

Reviewing the anatomical and physiological details of what in the doctor's
opinion was going on inside him, he understood it all.

There was something, a small thing, in the vermiform appendix. It might
all come right. Only stimulate the energy of one organ and check the activity

of another, then absorption would take place and everything would come right. He got home rather late for dinner, ate his dinner, and conversed cheerfully, but could not for a long time bring himself to go back to work in his room. At last, however, he went to his study and did what was necessary, but the consciousness that he had put something aside—an important, intimate matter which he would revert to when his work was done—never left him. When he had finished his work he remembered that this intimate matter was the thought of his vermiform appendix. But he did not give himself up to it, and went to the drawing-room for tea. There were callers there, including the examining magistrate who was a desirable match for his daughter, and they were conversing, playing the piano, and singing. Iván Ilých, as Praskóvya Fëdorovna remarked, spent that evening more cheerfully than usual, but he never for a moment forgot that he had postponed the important matter of the appendix. At eleven o'clock he said good-night and went to his bedroom. Since his illness he had slept alone in a small room next to his study. He undressed and took up a novel by Zola, but instead of reading it he fell into thought, and in his imagination that desired improvement in the vermiform appendix occurred. There was the absorption and evacuation and the re-establishment of normal activity. 'Yes, that's it!' he said to himself. 'One need only assist nature, that's all.' He remembered his medicine, rose, took it, and lay down on his back watching for the beneficent action of the medicine and for it to lessen the pain. 'I need only take it regularly and avoid all injurious influences. I am already feeling better, much better.' He began touching his side: it was not painful to the touch. 'There, I really don't feel it. It's much better already.' He put out the light and turned on his side . . . 'The appendix is getting better, absorption is occurring.' Suddenly he felt the old, familiar, dull, gnawing pain, stubborn and serious. There was the same familiar loathsome taste in his mouth. His heart sank and he felt dazed. 'My God! My God!' he muttered. 'Again, again! And it will never cease.' And suddenly the matter presented itself in a quite different aspect. 'Vermiform appendix! Kidney!' he said to himself. 'It's not a question of appendix or kidney, but of life and . . . death. Yes, life was there and now it is going, going and I cannot stop it. Yes. Why deceive myself? Isn't it obvious to everyone but me that I'm dying, and that it's only a question of weeks, days . . . it may happen this moment. There was light and now there is darkness. I was here and now I'm going there! Where?' A chill came over him, his breathing ceased, and he felt only the throbbing of his heart.

'When I am not, what will there be? There will be nothing. Then where shall I be when I am no more? Can this be dying? No, I don't want to!' He jumped up and tried to light the candle, felt for it with trembling hands, dropped candle and candlestick on the floor, and fell back on his pillow.

'What's the use? It makes no difference,' he said to himself, staring with wide-open eyes into the darkness. 'Death. Yes, death. And none of them know or wish to know it, and they have no pity for me. Now they are playing.' (He heard through the door the distant sound of a song and its accompaniment.) 'It's all the same to them, but they will die too! Fools! I first, and they later, but it will be the same for them. And now they are merry . . . the beasts!'

Anger choked him and he was agonizingly, unbearably miserable. 'It is impossible that all men have been doomed to suffer this awful horror!' He raised himself.

'Something must be wrong. I must calm myself—must think it all over from the beginning.' And he again began thinking. 'Yes, the beginning of my illness: I knocked my side, but I was still quite well that day and the next. It hurt a little, then rather more. I saw the doctors, then followed despondency and anguish, more doctors, and I drew nearer to the abyss. My strength grew less and I kept coming nearer and nearer, and now I have wasted away and there is no light in my eyes. I think of the appendix—but this is death! I think of mending the appendix, and all the while here is death! Can it really be death?' Again terror seized him and he gasped for breath. He leant down and began feeling for the matches, pressing with his elbow on the stand beside the bed. It was in his way and hurt him, he grew furious with it, pressed on it still harder, and upset it. Breathless and in despair he fell on his back, expecting death to come immediately.

Meanwhile the visitors were leaving. Praskóvya Fëdorovna was seeing them off. She heard something fall and came in.

'What has happened?'

'Nothing. I knocked it over accidentally.'

She went out and returned with a candle. He lay there panting heavily, like a man who has run a thousand yards, and stared upwards at her with a fixed look.

'What is it, Jean?'

'No . . . o . . . thing. I upset it.' ('Why speak of it? She won't understand,' he thought.)

And in truth she did not understand. She picked up the stand, lit his candle, and hurried away to see another visitor off. When she came back he still lay on his back, looking upwards.

'What is it? Do you feel worse?'

'Yes.'

She shook her head and sat down.

'Do you know, Jean, I think we must ask Leshchetítsky to come and see you here.'

This meant calling in the famous specialist, regardless of expense. He smiled malignantly and said 'No.' She remained a little longer and then went up to him and kissed his forehead.

While she was kissing him he hated her from the bottom of his soul and with difficulty refrained from pushing her away.

'Good-night. Please God you'll sleep.'

'Yes.'

VI

Iván Ilých saw that he was dying, and he was in continual despair.

In the depth of his heart he knew he was dying, but not only was he not accustomed to the thought, he simply did not and could not grasp it.

The syllogism he had learnt from Kiezewetter's Logic: 'Caius is a man, men are mortal, therefore Caius is mortal', had always seemed to him correct as applied to Caius, but certainly not as applied to himself. That Caius—man in the abstract—was mortal, was perfectly correct, but he was not Caius, not an abstract man, but a creature quite quite separate from all others. He had been little Ványa, with a mamma and a papa, with Mitya and Volódya, with the toys, a coachman and a nurse, afterwards with Kátenka and with all the joys, griefs, and delights of childhood, boyhood, and youth. What did Caius know of the smell of that striped leather ball Ványa had been so fond of? Had Caius kissed his mother's hand like that, and did the silk of her dress rustle so for Caius? Had he rioted like that at school when the pastry was bad? Had Caius been in love like that? Could Caius preside at a session as he did? 'Caius really was mortal, and it was right for him to die; but for me, little Ványa, Iván Ilých, with all my thoughts and emotions, it's altogether a different matter. It cannot be that I ought to die. That would be too terrible.'

Such was his feeling.

'If I had to die like Caius I should have known it was so. An inner voice would have told me so, but there was nothing of the sort in me and I and all my friends felt that our case was quite different from that of Caius. And now here it is!' he said to himself. 'It can't be. It's impossible! But here it is. How is this? How is one to understand it?'

He could not understand it, and tried to drive this false, incorrect, morbid thought away and to replace it by other proper and healthy thoughts. But that thought, and not the thought only but the reality itself, seemed to come and confront him.

And to replace that thought he called up a succession of others, hoping to find in them some support. He tried to get back into the former current of thoughts that had once screened the thought of death from him. But strange to say, all that had formerly shut off, hidden, and destroyed, his consciousness of death, no longer had that effect. Iván Ilých now spent most of his time in attempting to re-establish that old current. He would say to himself: 'I will take up my duties again—after all I used to live by them.' And banishing all doubts he would go to the law courts, enter into conversation with his colleagues, and sit carelessly as was his wont, scanning the crowd with a thoughtful look and leaning both his emaciated arms on the arms of his oak chair; bending over as usual to a colleague and drawing his papers nearer he would interchange whispers with him, and then suddenly raising his eyes and sitting erect would pronounce certain words and open the proceedings. But suddenly in the midst of those proceedings the pain in his side, regardless of the stage the proceedings had reached, would begin its own gnawing work. Iván Ilých would turn his attention to it and try to drive the thought of it away, but without success. *It* would come and stand before him and look at him, and he would be petrified and the light would die out of his eyes, and he would again begin asking himself whether *It* alone was true. And his colleagues and subordinates would see with surprise and distress that he, the brilliant and subtle judge, was becoming confused and making mistakes. He would shake himself, try to pull himself together, manage somehow to bring the sitting to a close, and return home with the sorrowful consciousness that his judicial labours could not as formerly hide from him what he wanted them to hide, and could not deliver him from *It*. And what was worst of all was that *It* drew his attention to itself not in order to make him take some action but only that he should look at *It*, look it straight in the face: look at it and without doing anything, suffer inexpressibly.

And to save himself from this condition Iván Ilých looked for consolations —new screens—and new screens were found and for a while seemed to save him, but then they immediately fell to pieces or rather became transparent, as if *It* penetrated them and nothing could veil *It*.

In these latter days he would go into the drawing-room he had arranged —that drawing-room where he had fallen and for the sake of which (how bitterly ridiculous it seemed) he had sacrificed his life—for he knew that his illness originated with that knock. He would enter and see that something had scratched the polished table. He would look for the cause of this and find that it was the bronze ornamentation of an album, that had got bent. He would take up the expensive album which he had lovingly arranged, and feel vexed with his daughter and her friends for their untidiness—for the album was torn here and there and some of the photographs turned upside down. He would put it carefully in order and bend the ornamentation back into position. Then it would occur to him to place all those things in another corner of the room, near the plants. He would call the footman, but his daughter or wife would come to help him. They would not agree, and his wife would contradict him, and he would dispute and grow angry. But that was all right, for then he did not think about *It*. *It* was invisible.

But then, when he was moving something himself, his wife would say: 'Let the servants do it. You will hurt yourself again.' And suddenly *It* would flash through the screen and he would see it. It was just a flash, and he hoped it would disappear, but he would involuntarily pay attention to his side. 'It sits there as before, gnawing just the same!' And he could no longer forget *It*, but could distinctly see it looking at him from behind the flowers. 'What is it all for?'

'It really is so I lost my life over that curtain as I might have done when storming a fort. Is that possible? How terrible and how stupid. It can't be true! It can't, but it is.'

He would go to his study, lie down, and again be alone with *It*: face to face with *It*. And nothing could be done with *It* except to look at it and shudder.

VII

How it happened it is impossible to say because it came about step by step, unnoticed, but in the third month of Iván Ilých's illness, his wife, his daughter, his son, his acquaintances, the doctors, the servants, and above all he himself, were aware that the whole interest he had for other people was whether he would soon vacate his place, and at last release the living from the discomfort caused by his presence and be himself released from his sufferings.

He slept less and less. He was given opium and hypodermic injections of morphine, but this did not relieve him. The dull depression he experienced in a somnolent condition at first gave him a little relief, but only as something new, afterwards it became as distressing as the pain itself or even more so.

Special foods were prepared for him by the doctors' orders, but all those foods became increasingly distasteful and disgusting to him.

For his excretions also special arrangements had to be made, and this was a torment to him every time—a torment from the uncleanliness, the unseemliness, and the smell, and from knowing that another person had to take part in it.

But just through this most unpleasant matter, Iván Ilých obtained comfort. Gerásim, the butler's young assistant, always came in to carry the things out. Gerásim was a clean, fresh peasant lad, grown stout on town food and always cheerful and bright. At first the sight of him, in his clean Russian peasant costume, engaged on that disgusting task embarrassed Iván Ilých.

Once when he got up from the commode too weak to draw up his trousers, he dropped into a soft armchair and looked with horror at his bare, enfeebled thighs with the muscles so sharply marked on them.

Gerásim with a firm light tread, his heavy boots emitting a pleasant smell of tar and fresh winter air, came in wearing a clean Hessian apron, the sleeves of his print shirt tucked up over his strong bare young arms; and refraining from looking at his sick master out of consideration for his feelings, and restraining the joy of life that beamed from his face, he went up to the commode.

'Gerásim!' said Iván Ilých in a weak voice.

Gerásim started, evidently afraid he might have committed some blunder, and with a rapid movement turned his fresh, kind, simple young face which just showed the first downy signs of a beard.

'Yes, sir?'

'That must be very unpleasant for you. You must forgive me. I am helpless.'

'Oh, why, sir,' and Gerásim's eyes beamed and he showed his glistening white teeth, 'what's a little trouble? It's a case of illness with you, sir.'

And his deft strong hands did their accustomed task, and he went out of the room stepping lightly. Five minutes later he as lightly returned.

Iván Ilých was still sitting in the same position in the armchair.

'Gerásim,' he said when the latter had replaced the freshly-washed utensil. 'Please come here and help me.' Gerásim went up to him. 'Lift me up. It is hard for me to get up, and I have sent Dmítri away.'

Gerásim went up to him, grasped his master with his strong arms deftly but gently, in the same way that he stepped—lifted him, supported him with one hand, and with the other drew up his trousers and would have set him down again, but Iván Ilých asked to be led to the sofa. Gerásim, without an effort and without apparent pressure, led him, almost lifting him, to the sofa and placed him on it.

'Thank you. How easily and well you do it all!'

Gerásim smiled again and turned to leave the room. But Iván Ilých felt his presence such a comfort that he did not want to let him go.

'One thing more, please move up that chair. No, the other one—under my feet. It is easier for me when my feet are raised.'

Gerásim brought the chair, set it down gently in place, and raised Iván Ilých's legs on to it. It seemed to Iván Ilých that he felt better while Gerásim was holding up his legs.

'It's better when my legs are higher,' he said. 'Place that cushion under them.'

Gerásim did so. He again lifted the legs and placed them, and again Iván Ilých felt better while Gerásim held his legs. When he set them down Iván Ilých fancied he felt worse.

'Gerásim,' he said. 'Are you busy now?'

'Not at all, sir,' said Gerásim, who had learnt from the townsfolk how to speak to gentlefolk.

'What have you still to do?'

'What have I to do? I've done everything except chopping the logs for to-morrow.'

'Then hold my legs up a bit higher, can you?'

'Of course I can. Why not?' And Gerásim raised his master's legs higher and Iván Ilých thought that in that position he did not feel any pain at all.

'And how about the logs?'

'Don't trouble about that, sir. There's plenty of time.'

Iván Ilých told Gerásim to sit down and hold his legs, and began to talk to him. And strange to say it seemed to him that he felt better while Gerásim held his legs up.

After that Iván Ilých would sometimes call Gerásim and get him to hold his legs on his shoulders, and he liked talking to him. Gerásim did it all easily, willingly, simply, and with a good nature that touched Iván Ilých. Health, strength, and vitality in other people were offensive to him, but Gerásim's strength and vitality did not mortify but soothed him.

What tormented Iván Ilých most was the deception, the lie, which for some reason they all accepted, that he was not dying but was simply ill, and that he only need keep quiet and undergo a treatment and then something very good would result. He however knew that do what they would nothing would come of it, only still more agonizing suffering and death. This deception tortured him—their not wishing to admit what they all knew and what he knew, but wanting to lie to him concerning his terrible condition, and wishing and forcing him to participate in that lie. Those lies—lies enacted over him on the eve of his death and destined to degrade this awful, solemn act to the level of their visitings, their curtains, their sturgeon for dinner—were a terrible agony for Iván Ilých. And strangely enough, many times when they were going through their antics over him he had been within a hairbreadth of calling out to them: 'Stop lying! You know and I know that I am dying. Then at least stop lying about it!' But he had never had the spirit to do it. The awful, terrible act of his dying was, he could see, reduced by those about him to the level of a casual, unpleasant, and almost indecorous incident (as if someone entered a drawing-room diffusing an unpleasant odour) and this was done by that very decorum which he had served all his life long. He saw that no one felt for him, because no one even wished to grasp his position. Only Gerásim recognized it and pitied him. And so Iván Ilých felt at ease only with him. He felt comforted when Gerásim supported his legs (sometimes all night long) and refused to go to bed, saying: 'Don't you worry, Iván Ilých. I'll get sleep enough later on,' or when he suddenly became familiar and exclaimed: 'If you weren't sick it would be another matter, but as it is, why should I grudge a little trouble?' Gerásim alone did not lie; everything showed that he alone understood the facts of the case and did not consider it necessary to disguise them, but simply felt sorry for his emaciated and enfeebled master. Once when Iván Ilých was sending him away he even said straight out: 'We shall all of us die, so why should I grudge a little trouble?'—expressing the fact that he did not think his work burdensome, because he was doing it for a dying man and hoped someone would do the same for him when his time came.

Apart from this lying, or because of it, what most tormented Iván Ilých was that no one pitied him as he wished to be pitied. At certain moments after prolonged suffering he wished most of all (though he would have been ashamed to confess it) for someone to pity him as a sick child is pitied. He

longed to be petted and comforted. He knew he was an important functionary, that he had a beard turning grey, and that therefore what he longed
for was impossible, but still he longed for it. And in Gerásim's attitude
towards him there was something akin to what he wished for, and so that
attitude comforted him. Iván Ilých wanted to weep, wanted to be petted and
cried over, and then his colleague Shébek would come, and instead of
weeping and being petted, Iván Ilých would assume a serious, severe, and
profound air, and by force of habit would express his opinion on a decision
of the Court of Cassation and would stubbornly insist on that view. This
falsity around him and within him did more than anything else to poison
his last days.

VIII

It was morning. He knew it was morning because Gerásim had gone, and
Peter the footman had come and put out the candles, drawn back one of the
curtains, and begun quietly to tidy up. Whether it was morning or evening,
Friday or Sunday, made no difference, it was all just the same: the gnawing,
unmitigated, agonizing pain, never ceasing for an instant, the consciousness
of life inexorably waning but not yet extinguished, the approach of that
ever dreaded and hateful Death which was the only reality, and always the
same falsity. What were days, weeks, hours, in such a case?

'Will you have some tea, sir?'

'He wants things to be regular, and wishes the gentlefolk to drink tea in
the morning,' thought Iván Ilých, and only said 'No'.

'Wouldn't you like to move onto the sofa, sir?'

'He wants to tidy up the room, and I'm in the way. I am uncleanliness
and disorder,' he thought, and said only:

'No, leave me alone.'

The man went on bustling about. Iván Ilých stretched out his hand. Peter
came up, ready to help.

'What is it, sir?'

'My watch.'

Peter took the watch which was close at hand and gave it to his master.
'Half-past eight. Are they up?'

'No sir, except Vladímir Ivánich' (the son) 'who has gone to school.
Praskóvya Fëdorovna ordered me to wake her if you asked for her. Shall I
do so?'

'No, there's no need to.' 'Perhaps I'd better have some tea,' he thought,
and added aloud: 'Yes, bring me some tea.'

Peter went to the door but Iván Ilých dreaded being left alone. 'How
can I keep him here? Oh yes, my medicine.' 'Peter, give me my medicine.'
'Why not? Perhaps it may still do me some good.' He took a spoonful and
swallowed it. 'No, it won't help. It's all tomfoolery, all deception,' he decided
as soon as he became aware of the familiar, sickly, hopeless taste. 'No, I can't

believe in it any longer. But the pain, why this pain? If it would only cease just for a moment!' And he moaned. Peter turned towards him. 'It's all right. Go and fetch me some tea.'

Peter went out. Left alone Iván Ilých groaned not so much with pain, terrible though that was, as from mental anguish. Always and for ever the same, always these endless days and nights. If only it would come quicker! If only *what* would come quicker? Death, darkness? . . . No, no! Anything rather than death!

When Peter returned with the tea on a tray, Iván Ilých stared at him for a time in perplexity, not realizing who and what he was. Peter was disconcerted by that look and his embarrassment brought Iván Ilých to himself.

'Oh, tea! All right, put it down. Only help me to wash and put on a clean shirt.'

And Iván Ilých began to wash. With pauses for rest, he washed his hands and then his face, cleaned his teeth, brushed his hair, and looked in the glass. He was terrified by what he saw, especially by the limp way in which his hair clung to his pallid forehead.

While his shirt was being changed he knew that he would be still more frightened at the sight of his body, so he avoided looking at it. Finally he was ready. He drew on a dressing-gown, wrapped himself in a plaid, and sat down in the armchair to take his tea. For a moment he felt refreshed, but as soon as he began to drink the tea he was again aware of the same taste, and the pain also returned. He finished it with an effort, and then lay down stretching out his legs, and dismissed Peter.

Always the same. Now a spark of hope flashes up, then a sea of despair rages, and always pain; always pain, always despair, and always the same. When alone he had a dreadful and distressing desire to call someone, but he knew beforehand that with others present it would be still worse. 'Another dose of morphine—to lose consciousness. I will tell him, the doctor, that he must think of something else. It's impossible, impossible, to go on like this.'

An hour and another pass like that. But now there is a ring at the door bell. Perhaps it's the doctor? It is. He comes in fresh, hearty, plump, and cheerful, with that look on his face that seems to say: 'There now, you're in a panic about something, but we'll arrange it all for you directly!' The doctor knows this expression is out of place here, but he has put it on once for all and can't take it off—like a man who has put on a frock-coat in the morning to pay a round of calls.

The doctor rubs his hands vigorously and reassuringly.

'Brr! How cold it is! There's such a sharp frost; just let me warm myself!' he says, as if it were only a matter of waiting till he was warm, and then he would put everything right.

'Well now, how are you?'

Iván Ilých feels that the doctor would like to say: 'Well, how are our affairs?' but that even he feels that this would not do, and says instead: 'What sort of a night have you had?'

Iván Ilých looks at him as much as to say: 'Are you really never ashamed of lying?' But the doctor does not wish to understand this question, and Iván Ilých says: 'Just as terrible as ever. The pain never leaves me and never subsides. If only something . . .'

'Yes, you sick people are always like that. . . . There, now I think I am warm enough. Even Praskóvya Fëdorovna, who is so particular, could find no fault with my temperature. Well, now I can say good-morning,' and the doctor presses his patient's hand.

Then, dropping his former playfulness, he begins with a most serious face to examine the patient, feeling his pulse and taking his temperature, and then begins the sounding and auscultation.

Iván Ilých knows quite well and definitely that all this is nonsense and pure deception, but when the doctor, getting down on his knee, leans over him, putting his ear first higher then lower, and performs various gymnastic movements over him with a significant expression on his face, Iván Ilých submits to it all as he used to submit to the speeches of the lawyers, though he knew very well that they were all lying and why they were lying.

The doctor, kneeling on the sofa, is still sounding him when Praskóvya Fëdorovna's silk dress rustles at the door and she is heard scolding Peter for not having let her know of the doctor's arrival.

She comes in, kisses her husband, and at once proceeds to prove that she has been up a long time already, and only owing to a misunderstanding failed to be there when the doctor arrived.

Iván Ilých looks at her, scans her all over, sets against her the whiteness and plumpness and cleanness of her hands and neck, the gloss of her hair, and the sparkle of her vivacious eyes. He hates her with his whole soul. And the thrill of hatred he feels for her makes him suffer from her touch.

Her attitude towards him and his disease is still the same. Just as the doctor had adopted a certain relation to his patient which he could not abandon, so had she formed one towards him—that he was not doing something he ought to do and was himself to blame, and that she reproached him lovingly for this—and she could not now change that attitude.

'You see he doesn't listen to me and doesn't take his medicine at the proper time. And above all he lies in a position that is no doubt bad for him—with his legs up.'

She described how he made Gerásim hold his legs up.

The doctor smiled with a contemptuous affability that said: 'What's to be done? These sick people do have foolish fancies of that kind, but we must forgive them.'

When the examination was over the doctor looked at his watch, and then Praskóvya Fëdorovna announced to Iván Ilých that it was of course as he pleased, but she had sent to-day for a celebrated specialist who would examine him and have a consultation with Michael Danílovich (their regular doctor).

'Please don't raise any objections. I am doing this for my own sake,' she said ironically, letting it be felt that she was doing it all for his sake and only said this to leave him no right to refuse. He remained silent, knitting his brows. He felt that he was so surrounded and involved in a mesh of falsity that it was hard to unravel anything.

Everything she did for him was entirely for her own sake, and she told him she was doing for herself what she actually was doing for herself, as if that was so incredible that he must understand the opposite.

At half-past eleven the celebrated specialist arrived. Again the sounding began and the significant conversations in his presence and in another room, about the kidneys and the appendix, and the questions and answers, with such an air of importance that again, instead of the real question of life and death which now alone confronted him, the question arose of the kidney and appendix which were not behaving as they ought to and would now be attacked by Michael Danílovich and the specialist and forced to amend their ways.

The celebrated specialist took leave of him with a serious though not hopeless look, and in reply to the timid question Iván Ilých, with eyes glistening with fear and hope, put to him as to whether there was a chance of recovery, said that he could not vouch for it but there was a possibility. The look of hope with which Iván Ilých watched the doctor out was so pathetic that Praskóvya Fëdorovna, seeing it, even wept as she left the room to hand the doctor his fee.

The gleam of hope kindled by the doctor's encouragement did not last long. The same room, the same pictures, curtains, wall-paper, medicine bottles, were all there, and the same aching suffering body, and Iván Ilých began to moan. They gave him a subcutaneous injection and he sank into oblivion.

It was twilight when he came to. They brought him his dinner and he swallowed some beef tea with difficulty, and then everything was the same again and night was coming on.

After dinner, at seven o'clock, Praskóvya Fëdorovna came into the room in evening dress, her full bosom pushed up by her corset, and with traces of powder on her face. She had reminded him in the morning that they were going to the theatre. Sarah Bernhardt was visiting the town and they had a box, which he had insisted on their taking. Now he had forgotten about it and her toilet offended him, but he concealed his vexation when he remembered that he had himself insisted on their securing a box and going because it would be an instructive and aesthetic pleasure for the children.

Praskóvya Fëdorovna came in, self-satisfied but yet with a rather guilty

air. She sat down and asked how he was but, as he saw, only for the sake of
asking and not in order to learn about it, knowing that there was nothing to
learn—and then went on to what she really wanted to say: that she would
not on any account have gone but that the box had been taken and Helen
and their daughter were going, as well as Petríshchev (the examining magistrate, their daughter's fiancé) and that it was out of the question to let them
go alone; but that she would have much preferred to sit with him for a
while; and he must be sure to follow the doctor's orders while she was
away.

'Oh, and Fëdor Petróvich' (the fiancé) 'would like to come in. May he?
And Lisa?'

'All right.'

Their daughter came in in full evening dress, her fresh young flesh exposed (making a show of that very flesh which in his own case caused so
much suffering), strong, healthy, evidently in love, and impatient with
illness, suffering, and death, because they interfered with her happiness.

Fëdor Petróvich came in too, in evening dress, his hair curled *à la Capoul*,
a tight stiff collar round his long sinewy neck, an enormous white shirt-
front and narrow black trousers tightly stretched over his strong thighs. He
had one white glove tightly drawn on, and was holding his opera hat in his
hand.

Following him the schoolboy crept in unnoticed, in a new uniform, poor
little fellow, and wearing gloves. Terribly dark shadows showed under his
eyes, the meaning of which Iván Ilých knew well.

His son had always seemed pathetic to him, and now it was dreadful to
see the boy's frightened look of pity. It seemed to Iván Ilých that Vásya was
the only one besides Gerásim who understood and pitied him.

They all sat down and again asked how he was. A silence followed. Lisa
asked her mother about the opera-glasses, and there was an altercation between mother and daughter as to who had taken them and where they had
been put. This occasioned some unpleasantness.

Fëdor Petróvich inquired of Iván Ilých whether he had ever seen Sarah
Bernhardt. Iván Ilých did not at first catch the question, but then replied:
'No, have you seen her before?'

'Yes, in *Adrienne Lecouvreur*.'

Praskóvya Fëdorovna mentioned some rôles in which Sarah Bernhardt
was particularly good. Her daughter disagreed. Conversation sprang up as
to the elegance and realism of her acting—the sort of conversation that is
always repeated and is always the same.

In the midst of the conversation Fëdor Petróvich glanced at Iván Ilých
and became silent. The others also looked at him and grew silent. Iván
Ilých was staring with glittering eyes straight before him, evidently indignant with them. This had to be rectified, but it was impossible to do so.
The silence had to be broken, but for a time no one dared to break it and

they all became afraid that the conventional deception would suddenly become obvious and the truth become plain to all. Lisa was the first to pluck up courage and break that silence, but by trying to hide what everybody was feeling, she betrayed it.

'Well, if we are going it's time to start,' she said, looking at her watch, a present from her father, and with a faint and significant smile at Fëdor Petróvich relating to something known only to them. She got up with a rustle of her dress.

They all rose, said good-night, and went away.

When they had gone it seemed to Iván Ilých that he felt better; the falsity had gone with them. But the pain remained—that same pain and that same fear that made everything monotonously alike, nothing harder and nothing easier. Everything was worse.

Again minute followed minute and hour followed hour. Everything remained the same and there was no cessation. And the inevitable end of it all became more and more terrible.

'Yes, send Gerásim here,' he replied to a question Peter asked.

IX

His wife returned late at night. She came in on tiptoe, but he heard her, opened his eyes, and made haste to close them again. She wished to send Gerásim away and to sit with him herself, but he opened his eyes and said: 'No, go away.'

'Are you in great pain?'

'Always the same.'

'Take some opium.'

He agreed and took some. She went away.

Till about three in the morning he was in a state of stupefied misery. It seemed to him that he and his pain were being thrust into a narrow, deep black sack, but though they were pushed further and further in they could not be pushed to the bottom. And this, terrible enough in itself, was accompanied by suffering. He was frightened yet wanted to fall through the sack, he struggled but yet co-operated. And suddenly he broke through, fell, and regained consciousness. Gerásim was sitting at the foot of the bed dozing quietly and patiently, while he himself lay with his emaciated stockinged legs resting on Gerásim's shoulders; the same shaded candle was there and the same unceasing pain.

'Go away, Gerásim,' he whispered.

'It's all right, sir. I'll stay a while.'

'No. Go away.'

He removed his legs from Gerásim's shoulders, turned sideways onto his arm, and felt sorry for himself. He only waited till Gerásim had gone into the next room and then restrained himself no longer but wept like a child.

He wept on account of his helplessness, his terrible loneliness, the cruelty of man, the cruelty of God, and the absence of God.

'Why hast Thou done all this? Why hast Thou brought me here? Why, why dost Thou torment me so terribly?'

He did not expect an answer and yet wept because there was no answer and could be none. The pain again grew more acute, but he did not stir and did not call. He said to himself: 'Go on! Strike me! But what is it for? What have I done to Thee? What is it for?'

Then he grew quiet and not only ceased weeping but even held his breath and became all attention. It was as though he were listening not to an audible voice but to the voice of his soul, to the current of thoughts arising within him.

'What is it you want?' was the first clear conception capable of expression in words, that he heard.

'What do you want? What do you want?' he repeated to himself.

'What do I want? To live and not to suffer,' he answered.

And again he listened with such concentrated attention that even his pain did not distract him.

'To live? How?' asked his inner voice.

'Why, to live as I used to—well and pleasantly.'

'As you lived before, well and pleasantly?' the voice repeated.

And in imagination he began to recall the best moments of his pleasant life. But strange to say none of these best moments of his pleasant life now seemed at all what they had then seemed—none of them except the first recollections of childhood. There, in childhood, there had been something really pleasant with which it would be possible to live if it could return. But the child who had experienced that happiness existed no longer, it was like a reminiscence of somebody else.

As soon as the period began which had produced the present Iván Ilých, all that had then seemed joys now melted before his sight and turned into something trivial and often nasty.

And the further he departed from childhood and the nearer he came to the present the more worthless and doubtful were the joys. This began with the School of Law. A little that was really good was still found there— there was light-heartedness, friendship, and hope. But in the upper classes there had already been fewer of such good moments. Then during the first years of his official career, when he was in the service of the Governor, some pleasant moments again occurred: they were the memories of love for a woman. Then all became confused and there was still less of what was good; later on again there was still less that was good, and the further he went the less there was. His marriage, a mere accident, then the disenchantment that followed it, his wife's bad breath and the sensuality and hypocrisy: then that deadly official life and those preoccupations about money, a year of it, and two, and ten, and twenty, and always the same thing. And the longer it lasted the more deadly it became. 'It is as if I had been going downhill while I imagined I was going up. And that is really what it was. I was going up in public opinion, but to the same extent life was ebbing away from me. And now it is all done and there is only death.'

'Then what does it mean? Why? It can't be that life is so senseless and horrible. But if it really has been so horrible and senseless, why must I die and die in agony? There is something wrong!'

'Maybe I did not live as I ought to have done,' it suddenly occurred to him. 'But how could that be, when I did everything properly?' he replied, and immediately dismissed from his mind this, the sole solution of all the riddles of life and death, as something quite impossible.

'Then what do you want now? To live? Live how? Live as you lived in the law courts when the usher proclaimed "The judge is coming!" The judge is coming, the judge!' he repeated to himself. 'Here he is, the judge. But I am not guilty!' he exclaimed angrily. 'What is it for?' And he ceased crying, but turning his face to the wall continued to ponder on the same question: Why, and for what purpose, is there all this horror? But however much he pondered he found no answer. And whenever the thought occurred to him, as it often did, that it all resulted from his not having lived as he ought to have done, he at once recalled the correctness of his whole life and dismissed so strange an idea.

x

Another fortnight passed. Iván Ilých now no longer left his sofa. He would not lie in bed but lay on the sofa, facing the wall nearly all the time. He suffered ever the same unceasing agonies and in his loneliness pondered always on the same insoluble question: 'What is this? Can it be that it is Death?' And the inner voice answered: 'Yes, it is Death.'

'Why these sufferings?' And the voice answered, 'For no reason—they just are so.' Beyond and besides this there was nothing.

From the very beginning of his illness, ever since he had first been to see the doctor, Iván Ilých's life had been divided between two contrary and alternating moods: now it was despair and the expectation of this uncomprehended and terrible death, and now hope and an intently interested observation of the functioning of his organs. Now before his eyes there was only a kidney or an intestine that temporarily evaded its duty, and now only that incomprehensible and dreadful death from which it was impossible to escape.

These two states of mind had alternated from the very beginning of his illness, but the further it progressed the more doubtful and fantastic became the conception of the kidney, and the more real the sense of impending death.

He had but to call to mind what he had been three months before and what he was now, to call to mind with what regularity he had been going downhill, for every possibility of hope to be shattered.

Latterly during that loneliness in which he found himself as he lay facing the back of the sofa, a loneliness in the midst of a populous town and surrounded by numerous acquaintances and relations but that yet could not have been more complete anywhere—either at the bottom of the sea or under the earth—during that terrible loneliness Iván Ilých had lived only in memories of the past. Pictures of his past rose before him one after another. They always began with what was nearest in time and then went back to what was most remote—to his childhood—and rested there. If he thought of the stewed prunes that had been offered him that day, his mind went back to the raw shrivelled French plums of his childhood, their peculiar flavour and the flow of saliva when he sucked their stones, and along with the memory of that taste came a whole series of memories of those days: his nurse, his brother, and their toys. 'No, I mustn't think of that. . . . It is too painful,' Iván Ilých said to himself, and brought himself back to the present—to the button on the back of the sofa and the creases in its morocco. 'Morocco is expensive, but it does not wear well: there had been a quarrel about it. It was a different kind of quarrel and a different kind of morocco that time when we tore father's portfolio and were punished, and mamma brought us some tarts. . . .' And again his thoughts dwelt on his childhood, and again it was painful and he tried to banish them and fix his mind on something else.

Then again together with that chain of memories another series passed through his mind—of how his illness had progressed and grown worse. There also the further back he looked the more life there had been. There had been more of what was good in life and more of life itself. The two merged together. 'Just as the pain went on getting worse and worse so my life grew worse and worse,' he thought. 'There is one bright spot there at the back, at the beginning of life, and afterwards all becomes blacker and blacker and proceeds more and more rapidly—in inverse ratio to the square of the distance from death,' thought Iván Ilých. And the example of a stone falling downwards with increasing velocity entered his mind. Life, a series of increasing sufferings, flies further and further towards its end—the most terrible suffering. 'I am flying. . . .' He shuddered, shifted himself, and tried to resist, but was already aware that resistance was impossible, and again with eyes weary of gazing but unable to cease seeing what was before them, he stared at the back of the sofa and waited—awaiting that dreadful fall and shock and destruction.

'Resistance is impossible!' he said to himself. 'If I could only understand what it is all for! But that too is impossible. An explanation would be possible if it could be said that I have not lived as I ought to. But it is impossible to say that,' and he remembered all the legality, correctitude, and propriety of his life. 'That at any rate can certainly not be admitted,' he thought, and his lips smiled ironically as if someone could see that smile and be taken in by it. 'There is no explanation! Agony, death. . . . What for?'

XI

Another two weeks went by in this way and during that fortnight an event occurred that Iván Ilých and his wife had desired. Petríshchev formally proposed. It happened in the evening. The next day Praskóvya Fëdorovna came into her husband's room considering how best to inform him of it, but that very night there had been a fresh change for the worse in his condition. She found him still lying on the sofa but in a different position. He lay on his back, groaning and staring fixedly straight in front of him.

She began to remind him of his medicines, but he turned his eyes towards her with such a look that she did not finish what she was saying; so great an animosity, to her in particular, did that look express.

'For Christ's sake let me die in peace!' he said.

She would have gone away, but just then their daughter came in and went up to say good morning. He looked at her as he had done at his wife, and in reply to her inquiry about his health said dryly that he would soon free them all of himself. They were both silent and after sitting with him for a while went away.

'Is it our fault?' Lisa said to her mother. 'It's as if we were to blame! I am sorry for papa, but why should we be tortured?'

The doctor came at his usual time. Iván Ilých answered 'Yes' and 'No', never taking his angry eyes from him, and at last said: 'You know you can do nothing for me, so leave me alone.'

'We can ease your sufferings.'

'You can't even do that. Let me be.'

The doctor went into the drawing-room and told Praskóvya Fëdorovna that the case was very serious and that the only resource left was opium to allay her husband's sufferings, which must be terrible.

It was true, as the doctor said, that Iván Ilých's physical sufferings were terrible, but worse than the physical sufferings were his mental sufferings which were his chief torture.

His mental sufferings were due to the fact that that night, as he looked at Gerásim's sleepy, good-natured face with its prominent cheek-bones, the question suddenly occurred to him: 'What if my whole life has really been wrong?'

It occurred to him that what had appeared perfectly impossible before, namely that he had not spent his life as he should have done, might after all be true. It occurred to him that his scarcely perceptible attempts to struggle against what was considered good by the most highly placed people, those scarcely noticeable impulses which he had immediately suppressed, might have been the real thing, and all the rest false. And his professional duties and the whole arrangement of his life and of his family, and all his social and official interests, might all have been false. He tried to defend all those things to himself and suddenly felt the weakness of what he was defending. There was nothing to defend.

'But if that is so,' he said to himself, 'and I am leaving this life with the consciousness that I have lost all that was given me and it is impossible to rectify it—what then?'

He lay on his back and began to pass his life in review in quite a new way. In the morning when he saw first his footman, then his wife, then his daughter, and then the doctor, their every word and movement confirmed to him the awful truth that had been revealed to him during the night. In them he saw himself—all that for which he had lived—and saw clearly that it was not real at all, but a terrible and huge deception which had hidden both life and death. This consciousness intensified his physical suffering tenfold. He groaned and tossed about, and pulled at his clothing which choked and stifled him. And he hated them on that account.

He was given a large dose of opium and became unconscious, but at noon his sufferings began again. He drove everybody away and tossed from side to side.

His wife came to him and said:

'Jean, my dear, do this for me. It can't do any harm and often helps. Healthy people often do it.'

He opened his eyes wide.

'What? Take communion? Why? It's unnecessary! However. . . .'

She began to cry.

'Yes, do, my dear. I'll send for our priest. He is such a nice man.'

'All right. Very well,' he muttered.

When the priest came and heard his confession, Iván Ilých was softened and seemed to feel a relief from his doubts and consequently from his sufferings, and for a moment there came a ray of hope. He again began to think of the vermiform appendix and the possibility of correcting it. He received the sacrament with tears in his eyes.

When they laid him down again afterwards he felt a moment's ease, and the hope that he might live awoke in him again. He began to think of the operation that had been suggested to him. 'To live! I want to live!' he said to himself.

His wife came in to congratulate him after his communion, and when uttering the usual conventional words she added:

'You feel better, don't you?'

Without looking at her he said 'Yes'.

Her dress, her figure, the expression of her face, the tone of her voice, all revealed the same thing. 'This is wrong, it is not as it should be. All you have lived for and still live for is falsehood and deception, hiding life and death from you.' And as soon as he admitted that thought, his hatred and

his agonizing physical suffering again sprang up, and with that suffering a
consciousness of the unavoidable, approaching end. And to this was added
a new sensation of grinding shooting pain and a feeling of suffocation.

The expression of his face when he uttered that 'yes' was dreadful. Having
uttered it, he looked her straight in the eyes, turned on his face with a
rapidity extraordinary in his weak state and shouted:

'Go away! Go away and leave me alone!'

XII

From that moment the screaming began that continued for three days,
and was so terrible that one could not hear it through two closed doors
without horror. At the moment he answered his wife he realized that he
was lost, that there was no return, that the end had come, the very end,
and his doubts were still unsolved and remained doubts.

'Oh! Oh! Oh!' he cried in various intonations. He had begun by screaming 'I won't!' and continued screaming on the letter 'o'.

For three whole days, during which time did not exist for him, he
struggled in that black sack into which he was being thrust by an invisible,
resistless force. He struggled as a man condemned to death struggles in the
hands of the executioner, knowing that he cannot save himself. And every
moment he felt that despite all his efforts he was drawing nearer and nearer
to what terrified him. He felt that his agony was due to his being thrust
into that black hole and still more to his not being able to get right into it.
He was hindered from getting into it by his conviction that his life had
been a good one. That very justification of his life held him fast and prevented his moving forward, and it caused him most torment of all.

Suddenly some force struck him in the chest and side, making it still
harder to breathe, and he fell through the hole and there at the bottom was
a light. What had happened to him was like the sensation one sometimes
experiences in a railway carriage when one thinks one is going backwards
while one is really going forwards and suddenly becomes aware of the real
direction.

'Yes, it was all not the right thing,' he said to himself, 'but that's no
matter. It can be done. But what *is* the right thing?' he asked himself, and
suddenly grew quiet.

This occurred at the end of the third day, two hours before his death. Just
then his schoolboy son had crept softly in and gone up to the bedside. The
dying man was still screaming desperately and waving his arms. His hand
fell on the boy's head, and the boy caught it, pressed it to his lips, and
began to cry.

At that very moment Iván Ilých fell through and caught sight of the
light, and it was revealed to him that though his life had not been what it
should have been, this could still be rectified. He asked himself, 'What *is*

the right thing?' and grew still, listening. Then he felt that someone was kissing his hand. He opened his eyes, looked at his son, and felt sorry for him. His wife came up to him and he glanced at her. She was gazing at him open-mouthed, with undried tears on her nose and cheek and a despairing look on her face. He felt sorry for her too.

'Yes, I am making them wretched,' he thought. 'They are sorry, but it will be better for them when I die.' He wished to say this but had not the strength to utter it. 'Besides, why speak? I must act,' he thought. With a look at his wife he indicated his son and said: 'Take him away . . . sorry for him . . . sorry for you too. . . .' He tried to add, 'forgive me', but said 'forego' and waved his hand, knowing that He whose understanding mattered would understand.

And suddenly it grew clear to him that what had been oppressing him and would not leave him was all dropping away at once from two sides, from ten sides, and from all sides. He was sorry for them, he must act so as not to hurt them: release them and free himself from these sufferings. 'How good and how simple!' he thought. 'And the pain?' he asked himself. 'What has become of it? Where are you, pain?'

He turned his attention to it.

'Yes, here it is. Well, what of it? Let the pain be.'

'And death . . . where is it?'

He sought his former accustomed fear of death and did not find it. 'Where is it? What death?' There was no fear because there was no death. In place of death there was light.

'So that's what it is!' he suddenly exclaimed aloud. 'What joy!'

To him all this happened in a single instant, and the meaning of that instant did not change. For those present his agony continued for another two hours. Something rattled in his throat, his emaciated body twitched, then the gasping and rattle became less and less frequent.

'It is finished!' said someone near him.

He heard these words and repeated them in his soul.

'Death is finished,' he said to himself. 'It is no more!'

He drew in a breath, stopped in the midst of a sigh, stretched out, and died.

THE TOUPEE ARTIST

A STORY TOLD ON A GRAVE
IN SACRED MEMORY OF THE BLESSED DAY
THE 19TH FEBRUARY, 1861[1]

Nicolai Lyeskov

(1831–1896)

TRANSLATED BY A. E. CHARMOT

THERE ARE MANY PEOPLE in our country who think that only painters and sculptors are "artists", and indeed only those who have been found worthy of that title by the Academies—no others will they admit to be artists at all. For many Sazikov and Ovchinnikov are nothing more than silversmiths. Other peoples think differently: Heine mentions a tailor who "was an artist" and "had ideas", and ladies' dresses made by Worth are even now spoken of as "artistic creations". It was recently written about one of these dresses, that it "concentrated a world of imagination in the point of the bodice".

In America the domain of art is considered still wider. The celebrated American author, Bret Harte, tells of an artist who was greatly renowned among them for "working on the dead". He imparted to the faces of the deceased various consoling expressions testifying to the more or less happy state of their departed souls.

There were several grades of this art. I remember three: (1), calmness; (2), exalted contemplation; and (3), the beatitude of the direct intercourse with God. The fame of the artist corresponded to the great perfection of his work, that is to say it was immense, but unfortunately the artist himself perished, falling a victim to the coarse mob, who set no value on the freedom of artistic creation. He was stoned to death because he had communicated the expression of the "beatific intercourse with God" to the face of a deceased defaulting banker who had swindled the whole town. The happy heirs of this scoundrel had hoped to show their gratitude to their late relative by giving this order, but the artistic executor thereof paid for it with his life. . . .

In Russia we too had a master of a similarly unusual artistic nature.

[1] The date of the emancipation of the serfs.

II

My younger brother had as nurse a tall, thin, but very fine old woman, who was called Lyubov Onisimovna. She had once been an actress of the former Orel Theatre belonging to Count Kamensky, and all I am about to relate happened in Orel during the days of my childhood.

My brother is seven years younger than I am, so that when he was two years old, and in Lyubov Onisimovna's arms, I had just completed my ninth year and was quite able to understand the stories that were told me.

Lyubov Onisimovna was at that time not very old, but she was as white as the moon. Her features were fine and delicate, her tall figure was erect and as wonderfully well-proportioned as a young girl's.

My mother and aunt, looking at her, often said she must have been a beauty in her day.

She was honesty and kindness itself, and very sentimental; she loved the tragic side of life but . . . sometimes drank.

She used to take us for walks in the Trinity Cemetery, where, sitting down on a common grave with an old wooden cross, she would relate to me some story.

It was here that I heard the history of the Toupee Artist.

III

He was our nurse's colleague in the theatre; the difference was only that she "acted on the stage and danced dances", while he was the "Toupee Artist", that is, the hairdresser and maker-up, who painted and dressed the hair of all the Count's serf actresses. But he was no ordinary commonplace barber with a hairdresser's comb behind his ear and a tin pot of rouge and tallow; he was a man with ideas—in a word, an artist.

According to Lyubov Onisimovna's words no one could "make imagination in a face" better than he.

I am unable to say exactly at the time of which Count Kamensky these two artistic natures flourished. Three Counts Kamensky are known, and they were all called by the old inhabitants of Orel: "Unparalleled tyrants". Field-marshal Michail Fedotovich was killed by his serfs for his cruelty in the year 1809, and he had two sons, Nikolai, who died in 1811, and Sergei, who died in 1835.

I was a child in the forties, but can still remember a huge wooden building with imitation windows painted with soot and ochre, surrounded by an extremely long half-ruined fence. This was the sinister residence of Count Kamensky; and here, too, was his theatre. The property was situated in such a position that it was very well seen from the Trinity Cemetery, and, therefore, whenever Lyubov Onisimovna wanted to relate something, she almost always began with these words:

"Look yonder, dear; do you see how terrible it is?"

"Yes, it is terrible, nurse."

"Well, and what I am going to tell you is even more terrible!"

This is one of her stories about the hairdresser Arkadie, a tender and brave young man, who was very dear to her heart.

IV

"Arkadie dressed the hair and painted the faces of the actresses only. For the men there was another hairdresser, and if Arkadie went to the men's side it was only on occasions when the Count himself ordered him to paint someone in a very noble manner. The chief speciality of the touch of this artist consisted in 'ideas', thanks to which he was able to give to faces the finest and most varied expressions.

"He was sometimes sent for and told," said Lyubov Onisimovna, "this face must have such or such an expression." Arkadie would then step back, order the actor or actress to stand or sit before him, while he stood, with arms folded over his breast, looking at them and thinking. And all the time he himself was more beautiful than the handsomest among them, because though of middle height he was indescribably well-proportioned—his little nose was thin and proud; his eyes were kind like an angel's—and a thick curl of his hair hung beautifully over his eyes, so that he appeared to be looking out of a misty cloud.

In a word, the toupee artist was handsome and "pleased everybody." Even the Count was fond of him and distinguished him above all others. He clothed him very well, but kept him with the greatest strictness. He would not allow Arkadie to shave or cut and dress the hair of anyone but himself, and, for that reason, always kept him near his dressing-room, and Arkadie was not allowed to go anywhere, except to the theatre.

He was not even allowed to go to church, to confession or to Holy Communion, because the Count himself did not believe in God, and could not bear the clergy. Once at Easter-time he had set the wolf hounds at the Borisoglebsk priests, who had come to him with the cross.[2]

The Count, according to Lyubov Onisimovna, was so horribly ugly in consequence of his constant wickedness, that he was like all sorts of animals at the same time. But Arkadie was able to give, even to this bestial visage, though only for a time, such an expression that, when the Count sat of an evening in his box at the theatre, he appeared more imposing than many.

[2] The occurrence narrated above was known to many in Orel. I heard of it from my grandmother Alferiev, and from the merchant Ivan Ivanovich Androsov, who was known for his infallible truthfulness, and had seen the wolf-hounds baiting the priests and had only been able to save himself by "taking sin upon his soul." When the Count had ordered him to be fetched and had asked him: "Are you sorry for them?" Androsov had answered: "Not at all, your Excellency, they deserve it, it will teach them not to loaf about." For this the Count had spared him.

But in reality what the Count, to his great vexation, chiefly lacked, was an imposing and military expression.

In order that nobody else should have the advantage of the services of such an inimitable artist as Arkadie, "all his life he had to sit at home and never had any money given to him since he was born." Arkadie was at that time twenty-five years of age and Lyubov Onisimovna was nineteen. Of course they were acquainted, and it happened with them, as it often does at their age, that they fell in love with each other. But they were only able to speak of their love in vague hints, spoken too before all, while he was making her up.

Tête-à-tête meetings were quite impossible and could not even be thought of.

"We actresses," said Lyubov Onisimovna, "were taken care of in the same way as wet-nurses are looked after in the houses of illustrious personages: we were in charge of elderly women, who had children of their own, and if, God forbid! anything happened to one of us, those women's children were subjected to the most dreadful tyranny.

"The covenant of virginity could only be broken by 'the master' who had ordained it."

v

Lyubov Onisimovna was at that time not only in the full bloom of her maiden beauty, but also at the most interesting point of the development of her many-sided talents: she sang in "The Pot-Pourri Chorus", danced the chief dances in "The Chinese Kitchen Gardener", and feeling a vocation for tragedy, "knew all the parts at first sight".

I do not know for certain in which year it was that the Tzar (I cannot say if it was the Emperor Alexander I or Nikolai I) happened to pass through Orel and remained the night there, and in the evening was expected to come to Count Kamensky's theatre.

The Count invited all the notabilities of the place to come to his theatre (no tickets were sold), and the performance was to be of the best. Lyubov Onisimovna was to sing in "The Pot-Pourri Chorus" and dance in "The Chinese Kitchen Gardener", when suddenly during the last rehearsal some scenery fell down and crushed the foot of the actress who was to act the part of the Duchess de Bourblanc.

I have never heard of nor even come across such a part, but that is just how Lyubov Onisimovna pronounced the name.

The carpenter who had let the scenery fall was sent to the stables to be punished, and the injured actress was carried to her closet, but there was nobody to take the part of the Duchess de Bourblanc.

"Then," said Lyubov Onisimovna, "I offered myself, because the part pleased me very much, especially where the Duchess de Bourblanc begs forgiveness at her father's feet, and dies with dishevelled hair. I had wonderfully long fair hair, which Arkadie dressed enchantingly."

The Count was delighted with the girl's unexpected offer to take the part, and having received the assurance of the director that "Lyubov would not spoil the part", he said:

"If she spoils it you will have to answer for it with your back. But now take her the 'aquamarine ear-rings' from me."

The "aquamarine ear-rings" was both a flattering and loathsome present to receive. It was the first mark of having been chosen for the special honour of being elevated, for a short moment, to be the odalisque of the master. Soon after that, or even sometimes at once, an order was given to Arkadie to make up the doomed girl, after the play, in the innocent guise of St. Cecilia; and dressed all in white, with a wreath on her head and a lily in her hand, to symbolize innocence, she was conducted to the Count's apartments.

"That," said Nurse, "you cannot understand at your age—but it was the most terrible thing, especially for me, because I was thinking of Arkadie. I began to cry. I threw the ear-rings on the table and wept. I could not even imagine how I would be able to act in the evening."

VI

In those same fatal hours Arkadie, too, was being beguiled into an equally fatal action.

The Count's brother arrived from his estate to present himself to the Emperor. He was even uglier than the Count. He had lived long in the country and had never put on a uniform or shaved, because "his whole face had grown covered with furrows and protuberances." Now on such a special occasion it was obligatory to appear in uniform, to put one's whole person in order, and produce the military expression that was required for full dress.

And much was required.

"People now do not understand how strict one was in those days," said Nurse. "Formality was observed in everything then, and there was a form for the faces of important personages as well as for the way their hair was dressed, which was for some terribly unbecoming. If their hair was dressed in the formal way, with a high top-knot and roundlets of curls, the whole face would look like a peasant's balalaika without strings. Important personages were horribly afraid of this appearance. To avoid it much depended on the masterly way in which the hair was cut, and in which they were shaved—how the space was left between the whiskers and the moustaches and how the curls were formed, and where they were combed out—and from this—from the slightest trifle the whole expression of the face could be changed."

For civilians, according to Nurse, it was not so difficult, because they were not subjected to such close scrutiny. From them only meekness was required, but from the military more was demanded—before their superiors they had to appear meek—but before everybody else they had to look fierce and stern.

"This is just what Arkadie, with his wonderful art, knew how to impart to the Count's ugly and insignificant face."

VII

The brother from the country was much uglier than the town Count, and besides, in the country, he had become quite "shaggy" and had "let such coarseness find its way into his face" that he himself was conscious of it, but there was nobody who could trim him because being stingy in every way he had sent his own hairdresser to Moscow into service, and even if he had not done so the face of the younger Count was covered with pimples, so that it was impossible to shave him without cutting him all over.

When he arrived in Orel he sent for the town barbers and said to them:

"To the one who can make me look like my brother, the Count Kamensky, I will give two gold pieces, but for him who cuts me, I have placed two pistols here on the table. If it is well done he may take the gold and depart—but if even one little pimple is cut, or if the whiskers are trimmed a hair's breadth wrong—I will kill him on the spot."

But this was only to frighten them, as the pistols were only charged with blank cartridges.

At that time there were but few barbers in Orel, and even they only went about the public baths with basins applying cups and leeches, and possessed neither taste nor imagination. They knew it and refused to "transform" Kamensky. "The devil take you," they thought, "both you and your gold."

"We can't do what you require," they said, "because we are unworthy to touch such a personage, nor have we the proper razors. We have only common Russian razors, and for your Excellency's face English razors are wanted. It is only the Count's Arkadie who could do it."

The Count ordered the barbers to be kicked out, but they were pleased to have got away so easily. Then he drove to his elder brother's and said:

"Now listen to me, brother! I have come to ask you a great favour. Lend me your Arkadie before evening, to trim me properly and get me into a presentable condition. It is a long time since I shaved, and your town barbers don't know how to do it."

The Count answered his brother:

"The town barbers are naturally not worth anything. I did not know there were any, because even my dogs are shorn by my own hairdressers.

As for your request, you are asking me for an impossibility, for I have sworn that as long as I live Arkadie shall not dress anybody but me. Do you think I can break my word before my own slaves?"

The other answered:

"Why not? You have laid down the law, you may change it."

The Count, our master, replied that for him such reasoning was strange.

"If I began to act in that way, I should never be able to demand anything more from my people. Arkadie has been told that such is my decree, and all know it, and for that reason he is better kept than the others, but if he ever dare to apply his art to anybody but me—I will have him thrashed to death and send him as a soldier."

"One or the other," his brother said. "Either thrash him to death or send him as a soldier. You can't do both."

"Very well," answered the Count, "let it be as you wish. He shall not be thrashed to death, but almost to death, and then he shall be sent as a soldier."

"Is that your last word, brother?"

"Yes, that is my last word."

"Is this the only reason?"

"Yes, the only one."

"Well, in that case it is all right. I was beginning to think that your brother was worth less to you than a village serf. You need not break your word, simply send Arkadie to me to shave my poodle. Once there it will be my affair to see what he does."

It was awkward for the Count to refuse this.

"Very well," he said, "I will send him to shave the poodle."

"Well, that's all I want."

He pressed the Count's hand and drove away.

VIII

It was at the hour of twilight before the winter evening had set in, when they were lighting up, that the Count summoned Arkadie and said:

"Go to my brother's house and shave his poodle."

"Is that all I shall have to do?" asked Arkadie.

"Nothing more," said the Count, "but return quickly to dress the hair of the actresses. Lyubov must be made up for three different parts, and after the performance, present her to me as St. Cecilia."

Arkadie staggered.

"What is the matter with you?" the Count asked.

"Pardon me," Arkadie answered, "I slipped on the carpet."

"Take care," remarked the Count, "that bodes no good!"

But to Arkadie's sinking heart it was all the same if the omen were good or bad.

After the order to adorn me as St. Cecilia was given, he could hear and see nothing; he took up his leather case of implements and went out.

IX

He came to the Count's brother, who had already had candles lighted at the mirror, and again two pistols were placed side by side, but this time there were not two but ten gold pieces laid beside them, and the pistols were not charged with blank cartridges but with Circassian bullets.

The Count's brother said:

"I have no poodle, but this is what I require: make my toilet and give me the most audacious mien and you shall have ten gold pieces, but if you cut me I will kill you."

Arkadie stared before him, and stared at the gold, and then God only knows what happened to him—he began to shave the Count's brother and trim his hair. In a few moments he had transformed him in his best style, then he slipped the gold into his pocket and said:

"Good-bye!"

"Go," answered the Count's brother, "but first I would like to know why you are so desperate. Why did you decide to do it?"

Arkadie answered:

"Why I decided is the profoundest secret of my soul."

"Or perhaps you are charmed against bullets, and therefore are not afraid of pistols."

"Pistols are trifles," answered Arkadie, "I did not even think of them."

"How so? Is it possible that you dared to think your Count's word is more sacred than mine, and that I would not have shot you if you had cut me? If you are not charmed, you would have lost your life."

At the mention of the Count, Arkadie staggered again, and said as if half in a dream:

"I am not charmed against bullets, but God has given me sense. Before you had had time to take the pistol in your hand to shoot me, I would have cut your throat with the razor."

With that he rushed out of the house and returned to the theatre, just in time to dress my hair. He was trembling all over. As he arranged each curl he bent over me to blow it into its place, and always whispered the same words in my ear:

"Don't be afraid, I will carry you off."

X

The performance went off well, because we were all as if made of stone; inured to fear and to suffering: whatever was in our hearts we had to act so that nothing should be noticed.

From the stage we could see the Count and his brother—they looked just alike. When they came behind the scenes it was difficult to distinguish the one from the other. Only our Count was quite quiet, as if he had become kind. He was always so before the greatest ferocity.

We all were stupefied and crossed ourselves:

"Lord have mercy, and save us! Upon whom will his brutality fall this time?"

We did not know as yet of Arkadie's mad act of desperation, nor what he had done, but Arkadie himself knew that he would not be pardoned, and he was pale when the Count's brother glanced at him, and mumbled something in a low voice in our Count's ear. But I had very sharp ears, and heard what he said:

"As a brother, I give you this advice: fear him when he is shaving you with a razor!"

Our Count only smiled slightly.

I think that Arkadie heard too, because when he was making me up for the part of the Duchess in the last play he put, as he had never done before, so much powder on me that the costumier, who was a Frenchman, began to shake it off and said:

"Trop beaucoup, trop beaucoup," and taking a brush he flicked it away.

XI

When the whole performance was over, the robe of the Duchess de Bourblanc was taken off and the dress of St. Cecilia was put on me. This was a simple white gown without sleeves, fastened only with little bows on the shoulders; we could not bear this costume. Well, and then Arkadie came to dress my hair in an innocent fashion, with a thin chaplet surrounding the head, as St. Cecilia is portrayed in pictures, and he saw six men standing outside the door of my closet. This meant that as soon as he had made me up and returned to the door, he would be seized and taken to be tortured. And the tortures in store for us were such that it was a hundred times better to be condemned to death. There was the strappado and the cord; the head-vices and the thumb-screws; all these and many more. The state punishments were as nothing compared to them. Under the whole of the house there were secret cellars in which living men were kept chained up like bears. When you had to pass near them it sometimes happened that you heard the sounds of chains and the groans of men in fetters. They probably desired that news of their condition should reach the world, or that the authorities should take their part—but the authorities did not even dare to think of intervening. People were made to suffer long in those cellars; some all their lives. One lay there very long and composed some lines:

"Serpents will crawl on you and suck out your eyes,
Scorpions will shed poison over your face."

This verse he would repeat to himself until he had made himself quite terrified.

Others were chained up together with bears in such a way that the man was only one inch out of reach of the bear's claws.

But nothing of this happened to Arkadie Il'ich, because when he rushed back into my closet he seized a table and in a moment had shattered the window—more than this I cannot remember ....

When I began to regain my senses, my feet were icy cold. I moved my legs and found that I was wrapped up in a large bear or wolf skin, and around me was complete darkness. The fast horses of the troika[3] whisked along I knew not whither. Two men were alongside of me, we were all three huddled together in the broad sledge in which we were sitting—one was holding me—that was Arkadie Il'ich, the other was the driver, who hurried the horses on with all his might. The snow flew in clouds from under the horses' hoofs, while the sledge bent over first on one side, and then on the other. If we had not been sitting in the bottom of the sledge holding on with our hands, it would have been impossible to survive.

I heard their anxious talk, as if they expected something. I could only understand:

"They're coming! they're coming! Hurry up! hurry up!" and nothing more.

As soon as Arkadie Il'ich noticed I was conscious he bent over me and said:

"Lyuboshka, my little dove, they are chasing us; are you willing to die, if we cannot get away?"

I answered that I would consent with joy.

He had hoped to reach the Turkish village, Khrushchuk, where many of our people had taken refuge from the Count.

Suddenly we sped across the ice of a river, and then something like a dwelling appeared dimly before us, and the dogs began to bark. The driver whipped up his horses, and turned the sledge sharply to one side, so that it tilted over and Arkadie and I were thrown into the snow, while the driver, the sledge and the horses disappeared from our sight.

"Don't be afraid," Arkadie said, "this might have been expected, because the yamshchik[4] who drove us does not know me, and I do not know him. He agreed to help me carry you off for three gold pieces, but on condition of saving his own skin. Now we are in the hands of God. This is the village of Sukhaya Orlitsa—a bold priest lives here, who marries desperate couples and has buried many of our people. We will make him a present and he will hide us until evening, and marry us too, and in the evening the yamshchik will come for us and we shall steal away."

[3] Any vehicle drawn by three horses harnessed abreast.
[4] The driver of a troika or any post vehicle.

XII

We knocked at the door and went into the passage. The priest himself opened the door. He was old, of small stature, and had one front tooth missing. His wife, a little old woman, began to blow up the fire. We both fell at his feet.

"Save us, let us warm ourselves, and hide us until evening."

The Reverend asked:

"Who are you, my dear children? Have you booty, or are you only fugitives?"

"We have taken nothing from anybody," answered Arkadie, "we are fleeing from the brutality of Count Kamensky, and want to go to the Turkish village, Khrushchuk, where many of our people are already living. They will not find us there. We have got our own money, and we will give you a piece of gold for one night's lodging, and if you marry us three pieces of gold. Marry us if you can; if not we can be wedded in Khrushchuk."

"No, no, why can't I marry you?" said the priest. "I can do so. What is the good of being married in Khrushchuk? Give me five pieces of gold altogether—I will marry you here."

Arkadie handed him five gold pieces, and I took the "aquamarine earrings" out of my ears and gave them to the priest's wife.

The priest took the gold and said:

"Oh, my dear children, it would be easy. I have bound together all sorts of people, but it is not well that you are the Count's. Though I am a priest, still I fear his brutality. Well, never mind him, what God ordains, will be! Add another piece, or half a one, and hide yourselves."

Arkadie gave him a sixth gold piece, and then he said to his wife:

"Why are you standing there, old woman? Give the fugitive a petticoat and some sort of jacket; one is ashamed to look at her, she is almost naked." Then he wanted to take us to the church and hide us in the trunk among the vestments. The priest's wife took me behind the partition, and was just about to clothe me, when we heard a jingling outside the door and somebody knocked.

XIII

Our hearts sank within us, and the Reverend Father whispered to Arkadie:

"It is evident, my dear child, you are not to be hidden in the trunk with the vestments. Get quickly under the feather-bed."

And he said to me:

"You, my dear child, get in here," saying which he locked me up in the clock-case, put the key in his pocket and then went to open the door to the new arrivals. One could hear that there were many people outside. Some stood at the door, and two men were already looking in at the windows.

Seven men entered the room, all beaters from the Count's hunt, with their iron balls and straps, long whips in their hands and rope leashes in their girdles. The eighth who followed them was the Count's steward, in a long wolfskin coat and high fur cap.

The clock-case I was hidden in had a grating in front with a thin old muslin curtain behind it, through which I was able to see all that was going on in the room.

The old priest lost courage, perhaps, because he thought it a bad case. He trembled at sight of the steward, crossed himself and cried hastily:

"Ah, my dear children. Oh, my dear children, I know; I know what you are looking for, but I am in no way in fault towards the most serene Count, indeed I'm not in fault, in truth I'm not in fault!"

And each time he crossed himself, he pointed with his finger over his left shoulder at the clock-case in which I was hidden.

"All is lost," I thought, when I saw this extraordinary behaviour.

The steward noticed this too, and said:

"We know everything. Give me the key of this clock-case."

But the priest only crossed himself all the more.

"Indeed, my children, truly, my dear children. Pardon me, do not punish me! I have forgotten where I put the key. Verily, I have forgotten; in truth I have forgotten!"

And all the time with the other hand he stroked his pocket.

The steward too saw his incredible action, and took the key from the pocket and opened the clock-case.

"Crawl out, my pretty falcon—now I have caught you, your mate will soon appear."

Indeed, Arkadie had already shown himself; he had thrown off the priest's feather-bed and stood before us.

"Yes, there is nothing more to be done," said he. "You have won; you can take me to the torture, but she is in no way to blame. I carried her off by force."

Then he turned to the priest, and all he did was to spit in his face.

"My dear children," said the priest, "do you see how my sacred office and faithfulness are outraged? Report this to the most serene Count."

The steward answered him:

"Never mind, you need not fear, he will have to answer for all this." And then he ordered Arkadie and me to be led away.

We were all placed in three sledges: in the first Arkadie, with arms and legs bound fast, was seated with the huntsmen, and I with a similar guard was driven off in the last sledge while the rest of the party were in the middle one.

All the people we met made way for us; perhaps they thought it was a wedding.

XIV

We soon arrived, and when we entered the Count's yard I lost sight of the sledge in which Arkadie had been brought. I was taken to my former room, and questioned by one after another:

"How long had I been alone with Arkadie?"

I told every one:

"Oh, not at all!"

Then I did not escape the fate for which I had probably been destined from my birth; not with love, but with aversion, and when I came to afterwards, in my little room, and buried my head in the pillow, to weep over my misfortune, I suddenly heard terrible groans under the floor.

We girls lived in the second story of a wooden building, and below there was a large lofty room, where we learned to sing and dance. From thence every sound could be heard in our rooms. The hellish King Satan had suggested the cruel idea that they should torture Arkadie under my room.

When I realized they were torturing him, I rushed to the door to go to him, but the door was locked. . . . I don't know what I wanted to do . . . I fell down . . . on the floor the sounds were still more distinct . . . there was neither a knife nor a nail at hand . . . there was nothing with which to end it . . . I took my own plait, wound it round my neck—wound it round . . . tighter and tighter, till I only heard ringing in my ears and saw circles before my eyes, then everything ceased . . . When I came to myself again I felt I was in a strange place in a large light hut. There were many calves round me—more than ten—such caressing little calves; they came up and licked me with their cool tongues—they thought they were suckling their mother—I awoke because they tickled. I looked round and thought, "Where am I?" Then I saw a woman come into the room, a tall, elderly woman dressed in striped blue linen with a striped linen handkerchief on her head. She had a kind face.

The woman noticed I had come to my senses and began caressing me and told me I was still on the Count's estate but in the calves' house.

"It was there," explained Lyubov Onisimovna, pointing with her hand to the very furthest corner of the grey half-ruined fence.

XV

Her appearance in the farmyard was due to the suspicion that, perhaps, she was out of her mind. Such people, who were regarded as cattle, were sent to the farmyard to be observed, because the cow-herds and dairymaids, being elderly and sedate people, it was thought, could best watch over mental diseases.

The old woman in the striped linen dress whom Lyubov Onisimovna first saw on her awakening, was very kind, and was called Drosida.

"In the evening, when she had finished her work," Nurse continued, "she made up a bed for me of fresh oaten straw. She spread it out so well that it was as soft as a feather-bed, and then she said: 'My girl, I will explain everything to you. Whatever may have happened you can tell me. I, too, am like you, and have not worn this striped dress all my days, but have also known another life, though God forbid I should think of it now. All I say is, don't break your heart because you have been banished to the cattle-yard; it is better in banishment—only avoid this terrible flagon . . .'"

And she took out of the kerchief she wore round her neck, and over her bosom, a small white glass phial and showed it me.

"What is it?" I asked.

"This is a terrible flagon," she answered, "and the poison of forgetful-ness is in it."

"Give me the poison of forgetfulness," I said, "I want to forget every-thing."

"Don't drink—it is vodka," she said. "Once I lost command of myself and drank—good people gave it to me. . . . Now I can't help it—I must have it. Don't drink as long as you can help it; and don't judge me that I take a sip—I am in great pain. You have still a comfort in the world. The Lord has released him from tyranny!"

"He is dead!" I shrieked, clutching hold of my hair, and I saw it was not my hair—it was white.

"What does this mean?"

"Don't be afraid, don't be afraid," she said, "your head had become white already when they released your neck from the plait. He is alone and saved from all further tyranny. The Count showed him such mercy as nobody had known before. When night comes I shall tell you all; but now I must take a sip—I must take a sip to stop this burning—this heart-ache."

And she sipped and sipped and at last went to sleep.

At night, when all were sleeping, Aunt Drosida again got up, went to the window in the dark, and I saw her standing there, sipping at her flagon, and then she hid it once more and asked in a whisper:

"Does grief sleep or not?"

"Grief does not sleep," I answered.

Then she came to my bed and told me that the Count had sent for Arkadie after his punishment and said:

"You ought to have suffered all that I had threatened, but as you were my favourite, I will now show you mercy. Tomorrow I shall send you to be a soldier, as supernumerary, but as you were not afraid of the noble count, my brother, with his pistols, I shall open the path of honour for you. I do not wish you to be lower than your noble spirit deserves. I will write a letter asking that you should be sent at once to the war. You will not have to serve as a private soldier, but as a regimental sergeant—so show your courage. From this time you are no longer subject to my will, but to the Tzar's."

"He is better off now," said the old woman, "he need not fear anything; he has only one authority over him; he need only fear falling in battle, and not the master's tyranny."

I believed her, and for three years dreamed every night of Arkadie fighting.

In this way three years passed. God was merciful to me. I was not re-called to the theatre, but I remained all the time living in the calves' hut as Aunt Drosida's assistant. I was very happy there, because I was sorry for this woman, and when, at night, she had not had too much to drink, I liked to listen to her. She could remember how the old Count had been slaughtered by our people—and his own valet was the chief instigator—as nobody could endure his hellish cruelty any more. All this time I didn't drink and did much work for Aunt Drosida, and with pleasure too; the young cattle were like my children. I became so attached to the calves that when they had been fattened up and were taken away to be slaughtered for the table, I would make the sign of the cross over them, and for three days after could not cease crying. I was no longer of any use for the theatre because my legs refused to work properly; I began to be shaky on them. Formerly my gait was of the lightest, but now, ever since Arkadie Il'ich had carried me off senseless in the cold, where I must have frozen them, I had no longer any strength in the toes for dancing. I became the same sort of woman in striped linen that Drosida was. God only knows how long I would have lived on in this melancholy way if something had not hap-pened. One evening, when I was sitting in my hut, just before sunset, look-ing out of the window at the calves, suddenly a small stone fell into the room through the window. The stone was wrapped up in paper.

XVI

I looked round, to one side and to the other, and out of the window—nobody was to be seen. "Some one has thrown it over the fence," I thought, "and it did not go where he wanted, but has fallen into our room." Then I thought: "Shall I undo this paper or not? Perhaps it is better to unwrap it, because something is sure to be written on it. And it is sure to be some-thing that somebody requires. I may be able to find it out and keep the secret, but I will throw the note with the stone in the same way to the per-son it concerns."

I unwrapped it and began to read—I could not believe my own eyes.

XVII

The letter ran thus:

"My Faithful Lyubu:

"I have fought for the Tzar. I have shed my blood more than once, and have therefore been made an officer and gained honourable rank. Now I have come on leave to recover from my wounds, and am staying in the inn of the Push-karsky suburb, with the innkeeper. Tomorrow I shall put on my decorations and crosses and appear before the Count, with all the money I was given to continue my cure: five hundred roubles, and I shall ask to be allowed to ransom you for myself, in the hope of being married at the altar of the Most High Creator.

"And then," continued Lyubov Onisimovna, with suppressed emotion, "he wrote:

"Whatever misery you have gone through, and whatever you may have had to submit to, I will look upon as your affliction, and not as sin, nor do I consider it as weakness, but leave it to God, and I have only feelings of respect for you.

"It was signed Arkadie Il'ich."

Lyubov Onisimovna burnt the letter to ashes at once, and told nobody about it, not even the old woman, but prayed to God the whole night, not saying many words about herself, but always about him, because she said, "Although he had written that he was now an officer with decorations and wounds, I was still unable to imagine that the Count would behave to him any differently from before. I might even say I feared he would beat him again."

XVIII

Early next morning Lyubov Onisimovna took the calves out into the sun and began feeding them out of a trough with crusts and milk, when suddenly sounds reached her from outside, that people "in freedom" were hurrying somewhere; they were running and talking quickly to each other.

"I could not distinguish a word of what they were saying," she continued, "but their words seemed to pierce my heart like a knife. When our labourer, Filip, who was carting dung, came into the yard, I said to him:

"'Filipushka batushka [little father], have you heard where all the people are going and what they are about, talking so curiously to each other?'

"'They are going,' he said, 'to see the officer whose throat was cut while he slept by the innkeeper of the Pushkarsky Inn. They say that his throat was cut quite through,' he said, 'and five hundred roubles were stolen from him. The innkeeper was caught all blood,' they say, 'and the money was on him.'

"And as he told me this I felt my legs give way.

"It was quite true: that innkeeper had cut Arkadie Il'ich's throat . . . and he was buried here . . . in this very grave on which we are sitting . . . And there he is now beneath us . . . he is lying under this mound . . . You may have wondered why I always come here in our walks . . . I don't want to look there [she pointed to the dark grey ruins], but to sit here near him and . . . drink a drop for the good of his soul . . ."

XIX

Here Lyubov Onisimovna paused and, considering her story finished, took the little flagon out of her pocket and either "drank to his memory" or "took a sip", but I asked her:

"Who buried the famous artist here?"

"The Governor, my little dove, the Governor himself came to the funeral. Yes, indeed. He was an officer! At the funeral the deacon and the reverend father called him the 'boyard Arkadie', and when the coffin was lowered into the grave the soldiers fired blank shots into the air. A year later in the market-place of Il'inka the innkeeper was punished with the knout by the executioner. He received forty-three strokes of the knout for Arkadie Il'ich and bore it—he remained alive, was branded, and sent to penal servitude. All our people who were able went to see it, but the old men, who could remember how the man was punished for the cruel Count, said that these forty-three lashes were so little because Arkadie was of the common people, and that for the Count the other man received a hundred and one lashes. By law, you know, an even number of blows cannot be given, but it must always be an uneven number. The executioner from Tula was fetched on purpose then, and before the work he was given three tumblers of rum. Then he beat him so that the hundred strokes were only for torture, and the man remained alive, but the hundredth and first lash shattered his back-bone. When he was lifted up from the boards he was already dying. . . . They covered him with a mat, and took him to the prison, but he died on the way. And the Tula executioner, they say, still continued to shout: 'Give me another. . . . Let me kill all you Orel fellows!'"

"Well, and you yourself?" I asked; "did you go to the funeral?"

"Yes, I went. I went with all the others. The Count ordered that all from the theatre should be taken there, to see how one of our people could be worthy of so much honour."

"Did you take leave of him?"

"Yes, certainly. All approached and took leave of him, and I . . . he was changed . . . so much changed . . . I would not have known him . . . thin and very pale . . . they said that all the blood had run out, because his throat had been cut at about midnight. . . . Ah, the blood that he shed!"

She sat silent and pensive.

"And you yourself," I asked, "what happened to you?"

She seemed to recover her senses and passed her hand over her brow.

"I can't remember what happened at first," she answered, "or how I went home. With all the others, of course . . . somebody must have led me . . . and in the evening Drosida Petrovna said:

"'Now this mustn't be—you don't sleep, and at the same time you lie there as if made of stone. That's not right—cry—there must be relief—your heart must have relief.'

"'I can't, Auntie,' I said, 'my heart burns like a live coal, and there is no relief.'

"'Well,' she said, 'then the flagon can't be avoided.'

"She filled a glass out of her bottle for me.

"'Till now I did not allow you to have it, and dissuaded you, but now it can't be avoided. Pour it on the coal—take a sip.'

"'I don't want to,' I said.

"'Little fool! Who wants it at first? It is bitter—bitter. But the poison of sorrow is more bitter. The coal must be drenched with this poison—it will be slaked for a moment—sip, sip quickly.'

"I emptied the whole flagon. It was disgusting, but I could not sleep without it, and the next night again . . . I drank . . . and now I can't go to sleep without it . . . I get my own flagon and buy vodka . . . You are a good boy, you will never tell Mother about it, you must never betray poor people, because one must take care of poor people; poor people are all sufferers. On the way home I shall go round the corner to the dram-shop, and knock at the window. We shall not go into it, but I shall give my empty flagon, and they will shove me out a new one."

I was touched and promised that I would tell no one, on any account, of her flagon.

"Thank you, little dove, never tell anyone; it is necessary for me."

I can see her, and hear her, as if she were before me even now. Every night, when all were asleep, she would rise from her bed, so quietly that not even a bone cracked; she would listen, then creep on her long frozen legs to the window. There she would stand for a minute looking round, listening to see if Mother were not coming from her bedroom, then she tapped the neck of the flagon gently on her teeth, put it to her mouth and sipped . . . one drop, another and another. Was it coal that was being drenched? or Arkadie's memory commemorated? Then she returned to her bed, slipped under the bed-clothes, and soon she began to wheeze—gently, very gently—fu-fu, fu-fu, fu-fu—and fell asleep.

A more terrible and soul-harrowing commemoration of the dead, I have never seen in all my life.

MOUZHIKS

Anton Chekhov

(1860–1904)

TRANSLATED BY ALEC BROWN

Nikolai chikildeyev, a waiter employed by the Moscow hotel, Slavianski Bazar, was taken ill. His legs went numb and refused to serve him, so that one day as he was going along the passage he tripped and fell down, together with a tray on which he was carrying boiled bacon and peas. He had to give up the job. What money he had, his own and his wife's, all went on doctors and chemists, there was not a penny left for board, his idleness weighed heavy, so he came to the conclusion that no doubt the best thing to do would be to go home, to his native village. It was easier to be ailing at home, and life would be cheaper; not for nothing the adage runs "home walls work wonders."

He arrived in Zhoukovo in the evening. Childhood memories made his native nest out to be all brightness and cosiness and comfort; but now when he entered the one-roomed cottage he was quite frightened, it was so dark and poky and dirty. Olga, his wife, and Sasha, his daughter, who had come down with him, cast bewildered glances at the immense ramshackle stove, which occupied nearly half the cottage and was black with smoke and flies. What flies! The stove was lopsided, the timbers in the walls were cock-eyed, it looked as if the cottage might collapse any minute. In the front corner, near the eikons, bottle bottoms and scraps of newspaper were stuck up, in place of pictures. What poverty! None of the grown-ups were at home, they were in the harvest field. On the stove sat a little girl of about eight, flaxen-haired, unwashed, apathetic; she did not even look up when they came in. On the floor was a white cat, rubbing its back on an oven peel.

"Puss, puss!" Sasha beckoned it. "Pussy!"

"That cat can't hear," the little girl said, "it's gone deaf."

"Why?"

"Huh! We hit it."

At first glance Nikolai and Olga saw what things were like, but they did not say a word to one another; without speaking they dropped their bundles and without speaking they went outside again. Their cottage was the third from the end and it looked the oldest and the poorest; the next was no better, but the end one had an iron roof and curtains at the windows. That house stood by itself, and was not fenced round; it was the inn. The cottages were all in a row, and the whole little village, with its pensive calm, and the willows and mountain ash and elder peeping over the courtyard fences, looked very nice.

Beyond the peasant homesteads the ground fell away to the river, suddenly and sharply, so that here and there huge rocks stuck out of the clay. Up the steep slope, winding round those rocks and the pits dug by the potters, wriggled pathways, and there were heaps of potsherds, brown and red; down below reached the broad, level, brilliant green meadowlands, already mown, where the village cattle were now cropping. The river lay a verst out of the village, a winding river with wonderful overgrown banks, and beyond it was another wide reach of meadowland, with cattle, and long strings of white geese, and then another steep rise of land, like the Zhoukovo side, and at the top, on the ridge, a village with a five-domed church and a little further a gentleman's mansion.

"It is nice here!" Olga said, looking at the church and crossing herself. "Heavens, what space!"

At that very minute the bell had begun to ring for vespers (it was Saturday evening). Two little girls, lugging a bucket of water, looked round at the church, to listen to the bell.

"Dinner's just coming on at the Slavianski Bazar. . . ." Nikolai said, pensively.

Nikolai and Olga sat down on the edge of the cliff and watched the sun set, the sky, gold and crimson, reflected in the river, in the windows of the church, in the very atmosphere, delicate, full of calm, inexpressibly limpid, such as it never was in Moscow. And when the sun had sunk, the stock, large and small, went past them, bleating and lowing, and the geese flew over the river homeward—and then every voice was hushed, that tranquil light died out of the air, and evening darkness swooped swiftly down.

Meanwhile the old folk had come home, Nikolai's father and mother, emaciated, bent, toothless, both the same height. The two daughters-in-law, Maria and Fiokla, had come too; they were working for the squire over the river. Maria, his brother Kiriak's wife, had six children, Fiokla, wife of Denis, who was in the army, a couple, and when Nikolai stepped indoors and saw that family establishment, all those large and small bodies, stirring on the plank bed, in cradles, everywhere, and saw how greedily the old man and the peasant women ate the black bread, sopping it in water, he saw he had made a mistake coming there, ill and penniless, with wife and child too—a great mistake!

"But where's Kiriak?" he asked, when he had exchanged greetings with all of them.

"He's watchman to a merchant," his father said, "he lives there, in the forest. Not a bad worker he isn't, if it wasn't for the drink."

"He's not an earner," the old woman whimpered, "our menfolk haven't turned out good, they don't bring anything in, they only drain. Kiriak drinks, so does our old man, what's the use of hiding it, he knows the road to the pub too. The wrath of the Mother of God is on us."

Because of their arrival, the samovar was put on. The tea tasted fishy and the sugar was mouse-nibbled and grey, and there were cockroaches all over the bread and the crockery. The tea made them feel sick; and the talk made them feel sick too—all about want and illnesses. But before they had finished even half a cup there was a loud, drawn-out tipsy shout from the yard—"Mar-i-aaa!"

"It looks as if Kiriak's there; talk of the devil . . ."

There was a general silence. A moment later the shout was repeated, a savage, drawn-out cry; it might have come from under the ground. "Ma-a-riaaa!"

Maria, the elder daughter-in-law, went pale and hugged close to the stove. It was somehow strange to see that broad-shouldered, powerful, ugly woman's face full of fear. Her daughter, the child who had been sitting on the stove, and seemed so apathetic, suddenly began to cry loudly.

"And what's the matter with you, you cholera?" Fiokla, a good-looking peasant wench, also powerful and broad-shouldered, shouted over to her. "Don't you fret, he won't kill you."

From the old man Nikolai learned that Maria was afraid to live in the forest with Kiriak, also that whenever he was drunk he came for her and made a great to-do and thrashed her.

"Ma-a-riaa!" came the cry, right at the door now.

"In Jesus's name, help me, dear ones," Maria stammered, breathing as if she had just been dipped into icy-cold water, "help me, dear ones. . . ."

All the children in the cottage now began to cry together, and seeing them, Sasha did the same. Drunken coughing was to be heard, and a tall, black-bearded mouzhik in winter fur cap came in, and because his face could not be distinguished in the dim light of the little lamp, he seemed terrible. This was Kiriak. He went up to his wife, and gave her a swinging blow in the face with his fist, but she did not utter a sound, though the blow staggered her; she only crouched down, and blood sprang from her nose.

"Ahhh! What shame of it, ahhh! what shame!" the old man muttered, climbing on the stove, "and with visitors in the house, too! What sin!"

Meanwhile the old woman sat silent, bent, thinking of something; Fiokla rocked the cradle. . . . Obviously Kiriak realised he seemed terrible, and this pleased him. He snatched Maria's hand, dragged her to the door, and bellowed like a beast, to appear more terrible, but at this point he caught sight of the visitors and stood still.

"Ah, visitors . . ." he muttered at last, and let go his wife. "My dear brother and his family. . . ."

He turned to the eikon and muttered a prayer, with his drunken, inflamed eyes goggling, and went on, "My brother dear, and his family, come to the paternal home . . . from Moscow, I suppose. The great Capital City of Moscow, mother of all cities. . . . Sorry . . ."

He sank to the bench near the samovar and poured out tea for himself, and sucked it down noisily from a saucer, amid general silence. . . . Having drunk a dozen cups of tea he lay down on the bench and began to snore.

They got ready for bed. As Nikolai was ill he was to sleep with his old father on the stove; Sasha lay down on the floor, and Olga joined the young women in the outhouse.

"Ah, dearie," she said, lying down in the hay next to Maria, "tears won't help. You must bear your cross, that's all. Doesn't Holy Writ say 'Whosoever shall smite thee on thy right cheek, turn to him the other cheek also'? A-ah, dearie! . . ."

Then, in a low sing-song voice, she told them all about Moscow and her own life, how she had worked as maid in furnished lodgings.

"In Moscow, you know, the houses are big and built of stone," she said, "and there are churches and churches, forty times forty, and such lovely churches, so very nice."

Maria said that not only had she never been to Moscow, she had not even been to the local market town; she couldn't read or write, she knew no prayers, not even "Our Father." She and the other one, Fiokla, who was now sitting a little way from them listening, were both extremely rustic, and knew absolutely nought. Neither loved her husband; Maria was afraid of Kiriak, and when he stayed with her she shivered from fear and was in a fever beside him, because he stank so of vodka and tobacco. And when she asked Fiokla if she didn't miss hers, she answered sourly "Let the devil take him. . . ."

They had a good talk and then there was quiet.

It was cool, and just outside the outhouse there was a cock crowing at the top of his voice, keeping them awake. When the bluish morning light was peeping through every crack, Fiokla quietly got up and went out; a moment later they heard her running somewhere, barefoot.

II

Olga went to church and took Maria with her. As they made their way together down the path to the meadows, both were glad at heart. Olga liked the spaciousness, and Maria felt her sister-in-law was understanding and kind. The sun was rising. Low down over the meadowland a hawk was winging drowsily, and the river water was dull, with wisps of mist still hanging about, but on the ridge opposite there was now a band of bright light, the church was gleaming, and the rooks in the squire's park were noisy.

"The old man isn't so bad," Maria said, "but the old woman's a hard one, always scolding. Our own corn lasted till Shrovetide, now we're buying flour at the inn—and she's always angry; you eat too much, she says."

"Ohhh, dearie! Bear it, that is everything. As 'tis said 'Come unto Me, all ye that labour and are heavy laden.' "

Olga spoke with dignity, sing-song, and she walked as a woman going to pray should, with lively, quick steps. She read her Gospel every day, read it aloud, like a priest reading, and though there was a lot she did not understand, the sacred words touched her to tears, and when she came to old-fashioned words like *receiveth* and *verily* she let her lips play on them with a swooning sensation at heart. She believed in God and the Mother of God and the saints; she believed it was wrong to offend anyone on earth, even common people, or Dutchmen, or Gypsies, or Jews, and that misfortune awaited even those who were not kind to animals; she believed this was laid down in Holy Writ, and this was why, when she was pronouncing words of Holy Writ, even if she did not understand them, her face took on an expression of great bliss and pity and clarity.

"Where were you born?" Maria asked.

"I'm from Vladimir country. Only I was taken to Moscow a long time ago, when I was only eight."

They reached the river. On the other side, by the water's edge, a woman stood taking off her clothes.

"That's our Fiokla," Maria said, recognizing her, "she's been over there to the squire's men. She's a hussy, and a swearer, she is."

Fiokla, black-browed, with hair undone, young still and firm as a girl, leapt off the bank and thrashed the water with her legs, sending the ripples going all round her. "A hussy," Maria repeated, "she is, and no mistake."

The river was spanned by a rickety hewn plank bridge, and as they crossed it shoals of squat chub passed underneath in the clear, transparent water. The green thickets overhanging the water were glittering with dew. Then came a breath of warm air, pleasantly soft. What a magnificent morning it was! And no doubt what a magnificent thing life in this world would be, were there not want, terrible, inescapable want, from which you can hide nowhere. She only had to glance back at the village now, and how clearly she recalled the events of last night—and the enchantment of the happiness she thought she saw about her disappeared in an instant.

They reached the church. Maria stayed near the door, afraid to go right inside; nor did she dare sit down, though they never rang for communion till after nine. So she stood through it all.

After the reading from the Gospel the congregation suddenly moved aside and let the squire's family go by; two young ladies in white frocks and picture hats came in, and with them a fat, rosy-cheeked boy in sailor suit. Their appearance moved Olga; at first glance she was quite sure they were decent, cultured handsome people. But Maria glared sullenly at them, dour and frowning, as if they were not human beings at all, but monsters which might crush her if she did not move to one side.

And whenever the deacon intoned in his deep bass voice, she seemed to hear her name called—"*Mar-ia*"—and started timidly.

III

News of the arrival of the visitors spread through the village, and after communion there was a great gathering in the cottage. The Leonychevs and the Matveichevs and the Ilichovs all came to learn about their relatives who worked in Moscow. The Zhoukovo kids who could read and write were all taken to Moscow, and all to be waiters or boots-boys (just as those from the village over the river all went into the baker's trade) and that custom had been established long ago, in the days of serfdom, when a certain Louka Ivanich, a Zhoukovo peasant, now a legendary figure, being Buffet attendant in a Moscow club, started taking on only his own villagers as assistants, and as they got on, they sent for their own relatives and got them jobs in hotels and restaurants, from which time the village had been known to folk round about not as Zhoukovo, but *Khamskaia* or *Kholouievka*, meaning Bounderfield or Muckham. Nikolai had been taken to Moscow when he was eleven, and got his job by Ivan Makarich, one of the Matveichevs, who was at the time chief waiter at the Hermitage Gardens restaurant. And now Nikolai addressed the Matveichevs most edifyingly as follows: "Ivan Makarich is my benefactor, and it is my duty to pray for him day and night, as he made a fine man of me."

"Ah, dear man," a tall old woman, Ivan Makarich's sister, said in a tearful voice, "but there's never any news now of that dear fellow."

"Last winter he was working at Omon's, and this summer I did hear he had a job somewhere out of town, in a garden restaurant. . . . He's getting on in years now! Why there was a time when in the summer he'd bring home ten rubles a day, but trade is slow altogether now, and the old fellow's getting a bit doddery."

The old women and the young peasant women too stared at the felt boots on Nikolai's feet and at his pale face, and said sorrowfully, "You're no earner, Nikolai Ossipich, you're no earner! That you aren't!"

And everybody petted Sasha. She had just turned ten, but she was small and very thin and looked more like seven, no more. Amid the other little girls, with their sun-tanned faces and rough-cropped hair, and their long faded smocks, she was quite a curiosity with her pale little face and her large sombre eyes and the red ribbon in her hair; she might have been a strange little animal caught in the fields and brought home.

"My pet knows how to read!" Olga boasted, with tender eyes on her child. "Read them something, my pet!" she said, and from a corner produced a New Testament. "Read a few lines, for these God-fearing good folk to hear."

The Testament was old and heavy, bound in leather, grubby at the edges, and smelt as if monks had invaded the hut. Sasha raised her eyebrows and began in a loud sing-song voice, in the old Church language, *"And when they were departed, behold, the angel of the Lord . . . appeareth to Joseph in a dream, saying: Arise and take the young child and his mother. . . ."*

"*The young child and his mother,*" Olga repeated, scarlet with excitement.

"*And flee into Egypt, and be thou there, until I bring thee word. . . ."*

But the old word for "*until*" in the old Church language was too much for Olga, and she burst into tears. Looking at her, Maria began to whimper, and then Ivan Makarich's sister. The old man cleared his throat and began to fuss round, wanting to give his grand-daughter a present, but he failed to find anything and ended up by a gesture of resignation. And when the reading ended the neighbours all went home, very touched and most satisfied with Olga and Sasha.

Through it being a holiday, the family stayed at home the whole day. The old woman, called *grandma* by husband and daughters-in-law and grandchildren alike, tried to do everything herself; lit the stove and put the samovar on all by herself, and even carried the dinner, and then complained they made her work her life away. And all the time she had her weather eye open to see nobody ate a mouthful too much, or that the old man or her daughters-in-law were not idle. One minute she thought she heard the innkeeper's geese at the back getting into her garden, and went haring out with a stick and spent half an hour yelling about patrolling her cabbages which were just about as spindly and decrepit as she was herself; then again she got the idea a crow was after her chicks and off she went swearing in pursuit of the crow. From morning to night she was ill-tempered and grousing and at times raised her voice to such a pitch that passers-by stopped to listen.

She was most unkind to her old man, having two names for him, either *lazybones* or *cholera*. He was a characterless, hopeless peasant, and perhaps if she had not constantly nagged him he would not have worked at all, but merely sat about, on the stove, talking. He told his son a longwinded yarn about enemies he had, and complained about the insults he said he had to suffer every day from his neighbours, and it was sickening listening to him.

"Yes," he said, clutching his loins, "yes . . . a week after the Elevation of the Cross, I sold my hay at thirty copecks the *poud*, of my own good will. . . . Yes. . . . Very well. . . . Only, I mean, there was I carting the hay of my own good will one morning, not interfering with anyone; and then what do I see, you wouldn't believe it, the headman comes out of the inn, Antip Sedelnikov, and 'Where do you think you're taking that hay?' he says, and a lot more, and boxed my ears."

As for Kiriak, he had a splitting headache, through having been drunk, and was ashamed for his brother to have seen it. "You see what vodka will do," he muttered, shaking his aching head. "Oh my God! Do forgive me, brother and sister, for Jesus' sake, I am angry enough with myself."

Because it was such a holiday they bought a salt herring at the inn and out of the head made a potage. At midday they all sat down to drink tea and drank on and on till they sweated, and felt they would burst with it, and then they set to work on the potage, all eating out of one bowl. But the old woman hid the herring itself away.

In the evening the potter, down the cliff, baked his pots. Down below, in the pasture, the girls danced and sang, and there was an accordion. On the far side of the river too there was stoving going on and girls singing, and from the distance the singing sounded harmonious and gentle. In and round the inn were peasants making a great din; singing in tipsy voices, all at sixes and sevens, and swearing so terribly that all Olga could do was shiver and say "Oh Lord God, oh Lord God!"

What amazed her was that the swearing never stopped, and that the old men, who had not long to live now, swore more persistently and louder than the others. The children and the girls listened to it too without turning a hair, and it was clear they were used to it from birth.

Midnight passed, and the fires on either side of the river had died down, but still there were people about on the pasture-land and in the inn. The old man and Kiriak, both drunk, arm in arm, jostling one another, came up to the outhouse where Olga and Maria were lying.

"Let her be," the old man tried to persuade him, "let her be. . . . She's a harmless wench. . . . It's a sin. . . ."

"Ma-ariaaa!" Kiriak shouted.

"Let her be . . . It's a sin. . . . She's not a bad wench."

They stood there about a minute, then went away.

"I lo-ove the flow-ers of the fii-i-eld," the old man suddenly sang, in a high, penetrating tenor. ". . . Gather the flowers of the field. . . ."

He cleared his throat and spat, swore vilely, and went indoors.

IV

Grandma put Sasha in her garden and gave her orders to see the geese didn't get in. It was a sultry August day. The innkeeper's geese could get in the back way to the garden, but at the moment they were busy: they were gleaning the oats round the inn and chatting quietly together, only the gander kept raising his head high as if he wanted to make sure the old woman wasn't coming with her stick; other geese could get there from down below, but those geese at the moment were cropping grass a long way on the other side of the river, reaching out over the meadow in a long garland of white. Sasha stood awhile at her post, but it was very dull, and seeing the geese were not coming, she went up to the edge of the cliff.

There she discovered Maria's eldest daughter, Mot'ka. She was standing quite still on a large rock, and looking at the church. Maria had had thirteen altogether but only six were alive, and they were all daughters, not one boy, and the eldest was eight. Mot'ka was barefoot, with only a smock on, and she was standing in the sun, the sun burning right on the back of her head, but she did not notice it and might have been turned to stone. Sasha stood beside her and looked at the church and said "God lives in the church. People have lamps and candles, but God has lovely little eikon lamps, red and green and blue, like little eyes. In the night-time God walks about in the church, and the Holy Virgin goes with Him and Saint Nicholas—tap-tap-tap they go. . . . And the caretaker gets so frightened, ever so frightened. Ah, dearie," she added, imitating her mother, "and when Judgment Day comes, all the churches will be taken up to Heaven."

"And—the—bel—fries—too?" asked Mot'ka, in her bass voice, every syllable by itself.

"And the belfries too. And when Judgment Day comes, all good people will go to Paradise, and the bad ones will burn for ever in the eternal fire, dearie. God will tell my Mummy and Maria too 'you have done nobody any harm, so you go to the right, to Paradise' but to Kiriak and Grandmother he will say, 'you go to the left, into the fire.' People who have eaten meat during fast will go into the fire too."

She then looked up at the sky, opened her eyes wide, and said, "You look at the sky, don't blink, you can see the angels."

Mot'ka too now looked at the sky, and a minute passed without a word.

"See?" Sasha asked.

"No, I can't," Mot'ka growled, in her bass.

"I can. There are tiny little angels flying about the sky flit-flit with their little wings like gnats."

Mot'ka thought awhile, eyes on the ground, then she asked, "So Grandma will burn?"

"Yes, dearie."

From the rock to the bottom the slope was gentle and uninterrupted, and covered with soft green grass that you wanted to stroke or lie on. Sasha lay down and rolled to the bottom. With a serious, severe expression on her face, Mot'ka puffed and lay down too and rolled to the bottom, and as she did so her smock pulled up onto her shoulders.

"Oh how I laughed!" Sasha cried, in delight.

They both went up to the top again to roll down once more, but at that moment they heard a familiar whining voice. Oh, how awful! Grandma, toothless, bony, hunchbacked, with short grey hair blowing in the wind, with a long stick in her hand, was driving the geese out of the garden and shouting "Blast you, trampled all my cabbage plants, may your throats be cut, thrice cursed, you sores, there's no striking you down."

She caught sight of the little girls, and threw down her stick, picked up a whippy branch and, grabbing Sasha by the scruff of her neck in her fingers, dry and hard as iron spikes, began to flog her. Sasha cried from the pain and from fright, while the gander, rocking to and fro from leg to leg and stretching out its neck, came up to the old woman and hissed something at her, and when he went back to his flock all the geese greeted him with an approving chatter—ho-ho-ho. Then Grandma set about Mot'ka and once again Mot'ka's shift slipped up. With sensations of despair, crying at the top of her voice, Sasha went indoors to complain; Mot'ka at her heels, crying too, but on a bass note, without wiping away the tears, so that her face was as wet as if she had dipped it in the water.

"God almighty!" Olga cried in amazement, when the two of them came into the house, "Mother of God!"

Sasha had begun to tell about it, when with a piercing yell and oaths in came Grandma, Fiokla lost her temper, and there was a hullabaloo in the room.

"No matter, no matter!" Olga, pale, upset, consoled Sasha and stroked her head. "She's your granny, it's sin to be angry with her. No matter, my pet."

Nikolai, who was already at the end of his tether through the incessant shouting and hunger, drunkenness and stink, who knew now that he hated and despised poverty, who was ashamed of his father and mother, dangled his legs off the stove and in an exasperated, whining voice, turned to his mother and said, "You can't beat her! You have absolutely no right to beat her!"

"Bah! you there on the stove, kick up your heels for once, you weak rat!" Fiokla snapped savagely at him. "What devil brought you here, you spongers!"

Sasha and Mot'ka and all the little girls, the whole lot of them, huddled into a corner on the stove, behind Nikolai's back, and listened to it all from there, without a word, in terror, and you could hear their little hearts beating. When a household has an invalid who has been hopelessly ill a long time, there are awful moments when all the family, secretly, in their heart of hearts, long for his death; only the children fear the death of one of their own, and are always filled with horror at thought of it. And now the little girls held their breath, with faces full of grief, and watched Nikolai and thought of how he was soon going to die, and they felt they wanted to cry and to say something kind and sorrowful to him.

He pressed close to Olga, as if looking for protection from her, and in a low, quavering voice said, "Olga my dear, my darling, I can't bear this any longer. It's beyond me. For Heaven's sake, for the sake of Our Lord, do write to your sister Claudia Abramovna, beg her to sell or pawn everything she has and send us the money to get away from here. Oh Christ," he went on, miserably, "just for one glance of Moscow! Merely to dream of it, my own town!"

And when evening came and it was dark in the cottage, it was all so miserable that it was difficult to say anything. The savage old woman soaked some rye crusts in a cup and sucked at them a long time, quite an hour. Maria milked the cow and then brought a pail of milk and put it on the bench; after that the old woman poured the milk from the pail into bowls, taking a long time over that too, not hurrying herself, clearly very glad that now, the Fast of the Assumption having arrived, nobody would touch the milk and it would all be saved. And only a trifle, just a drop, she poured into a saucer for Fiokla's child. When she and Maria took the bowls to carry them into the cellar, Mot'ka started up like a dart, slipped to the ground, went up to the bench, where the wooden bowl of crusts was, and splashed some milk from the saucer onto them.

When the old woman came back, she settled down to her crusts again, and Sasha and Mot'ka, seated on the stove, watched her, and were happy now that she had broken her fast and could no longer escape going to hell. That was consolation, and so they lay down and went to sleep. As she fell asleep Sasha pictured Judgment Day: a huge oven, not unlike the potter's, was alight, and an imp of hell, with horns like a cow's, and black as pitch, drove Grandmother into the fire with a long stick, just as that afternoon she herself had driven the geese.

V

On Assumption Day, at eleven in the evening, the girls and the young men, all strolling about the pasture, suddenly began to shout and scream and run towards the village, and those who were sitting up on the edge of the cliff could not make out the reason for it.

"Fire! Fire!" rang out the desperate cry. "We're on fire!"

Those sitting up top looked about them and they saw a terrible, extraordinary sight. On one of the end cottages, on its thatched roof, stood a pillar of fire six feet high, a pillar which turned on itself and scattered sparks on all sides, like a fountain playing. The next instant the whole roof was one mass of bright flames and the crackling of the fire could be heard.

The moonlight went dim, and the whole village was now alight with the ruddy glow; black shadows crept about the ground, there was a smell

of burning, and those who had come running up from down below, all out
of breath, could not speak, quivering as they were, jostling one another,
dropping down, and not recognizing one another through seeing badly in
the bright light. It was frightful. Particularly frightful was the way the
pigeons kept flying about in the smoke, and the way the men in the inn,
unaware so far what was happening, went on singing and playing the
accordion, as if nothing was amiss.

"It's Uncle Semyon's," shouted a rough, ringing voice.

Maria rushed round and round her own house, weeping and wringing her
hands, teeth chattering, though the fire was a long way from her, at the
other end; Nikolai came out, in his felt boots, and the children ran out in
their little shirts. Outside the headman's house they were beating the
tocsin. Bim, bim, bim . . . rang through the air, and that incessant quick
jangle clutched at their hearts, and chilled. Old women stood about with
eikons in their hands. Sheep and calves and cows were being driven out
of yards, chests were brought out and sheepskins and tubs. The black
stallion that was never let out with the other horses, because he was
vicious, but now was let out, went pawing the earth and whinnying and
galloping through the village, and then stopped by a waggon and began
kicking it with his hind legs.

Now the tocsin rang over the river, at the church.

Near the burning house it was hot and so bright that you could distinguish every blade of grass. On one of the chests they had managed to
salvage, Semyon was sitting, a ginger-haired peasant with a big nose, a
peaked cap pulled right down on his head, to his ears, and wearing a
jacket; his wife was lying face downwards, groaning. There was also an
old man of about eighty, a little old fellow with a huge beard—like a
gnome—a stranger, but evidently having some connection with the fire,
since he walked up and down near it, bare-headed, with a white bundle
in his hand; the flames gleamed on his bald pate. The village headman,
Antip Sedelnikov, a swarthy black-haired man, like a gypsy, went up to the
house and with a hatchet smashed the windows, one by one, nobody
could quite tell why—after which he set about the verandah.

"Hey, you women, water!" he shouted. "Bring the engine up here.
Look sharp there!"

The peasants who a minute or so back were amusing themselves in the
inn, came dragging up the fire engine. They were all tipsy, and kept
stumbling and falling down; there was a helpless expression on every face
and tears in their eyes.

"Lasses, water!" the headman shouted; he too was tight. "Look sharp
there, lasses!"

The women and the girls ran down below to the spring and brought up
buckets and tubs full of water, poured them into the fire engine and ran
off again. Olga too brought water, and Maria, and Sasha, and Mot'ka. The

elder women and the mere lads did the pumping, and the hose hissed away, with the headman directing it, one minute into the doorway, the next into the windows, partly stemming the stream with his finger, to make it hiss harder.

"Bravo, Antip!" came shouts of approval. "Go it, Antip!"

Now Antip had made his way into the hall, into the fire, and from thence came his voice: "Pump away! Put your backs into it, good orthodox folk, being such a misfortunate occurrence!"

The men stood in a crowd to one side, doing nothing, staring into the fire. Nobody knew what he should do, not one of them could do anything, though all round them were stacks of hay and wheat and outhouses and heaps of dry brushwood. There stood Kiriak, and old Osip, his father, both of them half tipsy. And, as if anxious to justify standing empty-handed like that, the old man turned to the peasant's wife lying on the ground. "Good woman," he said, "why take on so? It's the house being punished, ain't it, not you?"

Semyon kept turning first to one, then another, explaining how it happened.

"That old man there, with the bundle, that's General Zhoukov's man. . . . He was cook to His Excellency, may His Excellency's soul rest in peace. Turned up this evening. 'Can you let me have a night's lodging?' he says. . . . Well, we had a tot each, of course. . . . My missus was busy about the samovar, to make a cup of tea for the old gentleman, and then something made her go and put the samovar out in the hall, and the fire went right up the pipe straight on to the roof and into the thatch, you see, and there we were. We nearly got caught ourselves. And the old gentleman lost his fur cap, poor old fellow."

Meanwhile they were still beating the tocsin and kept ringing in the church over the river. Olga, all lit up, and breathless, eyes in horror on the ruddy sheep and the ruddy pigeons flying about in the smoke, still kept running down the hill for water. That ringing seemed like a sharp spike driven into her heart, she thought the fire would never end, and that Sasha was lost. . . . And when the ceiling of the house fell in, the thought that now the whole village would be bound to be burnt out weakened her and she could bring water no more, but sat on the edge of the cliff with her buckets beside her; next her and down the slope below her were other women wailing as if for the dead.

Then from over the river, from the squire's mansion, two waggons of his men came bringing another fire engine with them. On horseback came a student in white unbuttoned uniform tunic, a quite young fellow. Then hatchets got busy, they put a ladder against the burning house frame and five men ran up it at once, the student first, red-faced and shouting in a sharp but hoarse voice and in a tone which suggested that putting out fires was his usual job. They took the house to pieces timber by timber; they stripped the styes and the byres and the wattle fencing and the nearest stack.

"Stop them smashing things!" rang stern voices from the crowd. "Stop them!"

Kiriak made for the house with determined face, as if he meant to stop the newcomers' breaking, but one of the workmen swung him round and gave him a punch in the back. There was a gust of laughter, then another blow, and Kiriak fell on all fours and crept back to the crowd.

From over the other side came two pretty girls in hats—they must have been the sisters of the student. They stood some way off and watched the fire. The timbers that had been saved were no longer burning, though still smoking heavily; the student, working with the hose, directed the jet; he aimed at the timbers, then caught some of the peasants, then the peasant women who were bringing the water up. *"Georges,"* the girls called, disapprovingly and worried, in a French way, *"Georges!"*

The fire was out. And it was only when people began to go home that they noticed that it was already daybreak, and they were all pale and a little sooty. It always looks like that in the early morning when the last stars go out. As they dispersed, the peasants laughed and joked about General Zhoukov's cook and the fur cap which had been burnt; they already wanted to make a joke of the fire, and even seemed sorry it had ended so soon.

"You put that out well, sir," said Olga to the student. "You ought to come to Moscow to help us, we have a fire there every day."

"What, are you from Moscow?" one of the young ladies asked.

"I am. My husband used to work in the Slavianski Bazar. And this is my daughter," and she pointed to Sasha, who was feeling cold and clinging close to her. "Moscow-born too, Miss."

The two young ladies said something in French to the student, and he gave Sasha a twenty-copeck piece. Old Osip saw this, and his face instantly lit up with hope.

"We must thank God, sir," he said, to the student, "there was no wind, or it would have burned us up in a jiffy." Then, in a lower voice, and somewhat shamefaced, he said, "It's cold in the small hours, sir; now, something to warm us . . . half a bottle, say . . ."

They gave him nothing, and so he cleared his throat and tottered off home. Then Olga stood on the edge of the cliff and watched the two waggons ford the river, and the gentry making their way across the pasture; on the other side a carriage was awaiting them. Then she went indoors and told her husband with pride, "Such nice people; such pretty girls; like cherubim."

"Damnation to them!" muttered Fiokla, sleepily and sourly.

Maria thought she was unhappy and said she very much wanted to die; on the other hand, Fiokla found life very much to her taste: even the poverty and the dirt and the incessant swearing. She ate what she was given, without thought, and slept wherever or on whatever it might be; the slops she poured out right under the front porch of the house, just swilled them out, from the doorsteps, and then would walk barefoot through it. And from the very first day she had hated Olga and Nikolai because they did not like that life.

"I was wondering what you Moscow nobility are going to eat," she would say with open malice, "I was just wondering."

One morning—this was early in September—Fiokla, rosy-cheeked from the cold, healthy and beautiful, had brought up two buckets of water; Maria and Olga were seated at table, drinking tea.

"Tea with sugar!" Fiokla declared, mockingly. "What fine ladies," she added, putting down her buckets, "taken on the fashion of drinking tea every day. Take care you don't burst with that tea," she went on, looking at Olga with hatred. "Filled your fat face, to no good, in Moscow, didn't you, you sow!"

She swung the yoke and brought it down on Olga's shoulders, so that both daughters-in-law wrung their hands and cried "Oh Lord God!"

Then Fiokla went down to the river to wash linen and all the way there swore so loudly that they could hear her in the house.

The day went by. The long autumn evening arrived. In the cottage they were spinning silk, all except Fiokla: she had gone down to the river. They got the silk from a nearby factory, and the whole household earned a little on it—some twenty copecks a week.

"Working for the gentry was better," the old man said, as he wound the silk. "There's a time for working and for eating and for sleeping. For dinner *shchi* and *kasha,* supper too. And gherkins and cabbage as much as you wanted; free to eat as much as your heart's content. There was more discipline too. Everybody knew his place."

There was only one small lamp for light, and it burned badly and smoked. If any of them got between the lamp and a large shadow fell on the window, the brilliant moonlight showed. Old Osip, without hurrying, told the story of how they lived in the serfdom days, in those same parts where it was now so dull and everything so poor, they used to go hunting with hounds, borzois and Pskov hounds, and when beating the peasants got plenty of vodka; and how whole caravans used to go to Moscow with slaughtered fowl for the young gentry; and how those who were bad were flogged or sent to the Tver estate, but those who were good were rewarded. And the old woman too had some things to tell of. She had forgotten nothing, absolutely nothing. She had to tell about her mistress, who was a good and God-fearing woman, the husband a debaucher, and how all the daughters married badly, one to a drunkard, another to a commoner, and the third eloped (Grandmother herself, being a girl then, helped her to elope) and they all died very early from sorrow, like their mother. And, recalling all that, Grandmother actually cried.

There was a sudden rat-rat on the door. They all started.

"Uncle Osip, let me in for the night!"

The little bald old man, General Zhoukov's cook, the one whose hat got burnt, appeared. He sat down and listened awhile, and then he too began reminiscing and telling them various yarns. Nikolai, sitting on the stove, with legs dangling, listened and kept asking him about what things the gentry had cooked. There was talk of *cotelettes farcies* and *rissoles* and all manner of soups and sauces, and the cook, whose memory too was very good, mentioned dishes which have quite gone out now, such as one made of bull's eyes and known as "Morning Glory."

"And did you used to do *Cotelettes Maréchal?*" Nikolai asked.

"No."

Nikolai shook his head disapprovingly. "Fine cook you are," he said.

The little girls, sitting and lying up on the stove, looked down with fixed eyes. They looked innumerable, like cherubs in the clouds. They liked the stories; they kept sighing and giving little shudders and going pale from enchantment or fear, and to Granny, who told more interesting stories than any, they listened without breathing or stirring.

They all lay down to sleep without a word, and the old men, moved by their stories, and stirred up, were full of thoughts of how fine their youth had been, for whatever it was like, when youth is over all you remember is something full of life, troubling, glad—and how terribly cold death which was so near—better not to think of that at all! The little lamp went out. And the darkness and the two little windows, brightly lit by the moon, and the silence, and the creaking of the cradle, somehow only seemed to be reminders that life was already over, and nothing would bring it back. . . . You doze off and begin to dream, and immediately someone touches you on the shoulder, or breathes in your face—and sleep is gone, and your body seems to have got past it, and your head fills, in a rush, with thoughts of death; turn on your other side—you have already forgotten it, but through your thoughts slink old, old, deadening, nagging thoughts of want, of foodstuffs, that flour has gone up—and then again, there it is, remembering that life is done now, you can't get it back. . . .

"Oh Lord God!" the cook sighed.

There was a quiet tap on the window. That must be Fiokla back. Olga got up yawning and, whispering a prayer, unlocked the door, and then slipped the bolt of the outer door. But nobody came in, only a breath of icy air from the street, and sudden moonlight. She could see through the door into the street—tranquil, deserted—see the moon itself, sailing through the sky.

"Who is there?" Olga cried.

"I am," came the answer. "It's me."

Beside the door, pressed against the wall, was Fiokla, stark naked. She was shivering from cold, her teeth were chattering, and in the bright moonlight she looked very white, and beautiful and strange. The shadows on her and the gleam of the moonlight on her flesh made a striking sight, most prominent her dark eyebrows and her firm, young breasts.

"Hooligans," she said, "over yonder, stripped me and left me like that. . . . I've come home all the way naked . . . mother naked. Bring me something to put on."

"But come inside," Olga said softly; she began shivering herself.

"I don't want to risk the old folks seeing me."

Indeed, the grandmother was already on the alert, grousing, and the old man asked "Who's that there?" Olga brought out her own shift and skirt and dressed Fiokla and then, quietly, trying not to make any noise with the doors, they went inside.

"That's you, you slippery one, is it?" the grandmother growled, sourly, guessing who it was. "Ouch, you night bird . . . there's nothing'll tame you."

"Don't fret, don't fret," Olga whispered, with her arms round Fiokla, "don't fret, dearie."

It was all quiet again. They never slept well in that house; every one of them had some persistent thing pestering him—the old man's pain in his loins, the old woman's cares and ill-humour, Maria's fear, and the children's itch and the hunger of them all. This night too their sleep was broken; they kept turning and tossing, muttering in their sleep, getting up for drinks of water.

All at once Fiokla began desperate weeping, in her coarse voice, yet the next moment had mastered herself, only rare sobs escaping, and they growing quieter and quieter, till she was still. From time to time the sound of the clock over the river came, but striking queerly, first five, then three.

"Lord God!" the old cook sighed.

Looking at the window it was difficult to know whether it was still the moonlight or dawn at last. Maria got up and went out, and she could be heard in the yard milking the cow and saying "Stead-y!" The grandmother went out. It was still dark in the house, but objects could now be distinguished.

Nikolai, who had not slept all night, got down from the stove. He opened his green chest and took out his tail suit, and put it on, and went to the window, stroking the sleeves and plucking at the tails—and he smiled. Then he cautiously took it off again, put it away in the chest and lay down once more.

Maria came back and set about lighting the stove. She looked as if she was still not fully awake, and was only coming to full wakefulness as she moved about. She must have had some dream, or else recalled the stories of yester-eve, because as she stretched luxuriously in front of the stove she said "No, better not serfs."

VII

The "master" had come—that was what the village called the local police prefect. The date and purpose of his coming had been known for a week. There were only forty households in Zhoukovo, but there was more than two thousand rubles of tax arrears, both central and local government taxes.

The prefect put up at the inn, where he "took" two glasses of tea, after which he walked to the headman's house, outside which a crowd of tax debtors was awaiting him. The headman, Antip Sedelnikov, in spite of his youth—he was only a little over thirty—was harsh, and always took the part of authority, though he was poor himself and always in arrears with his own taxes. Evidently he enjoyed being headman, enjoyed the feeling of power, which he could not realise otherwise but by harshness. At village meetings the peasants were afraid of him and obeyed him. If he came on anyone tipsy in the street or at the inn, he was capable of tying his hands behind his back there and then and putting him under arrest; once he even put Grandmother under arrest, for coming to village meeting in Osip's stead and using foul language there, and kept her in the lock-up overnight. He had never lived in a town and never read a book, but somewhere he had acquired a number of scholarly words, which he loved using in his talk, and though the peasants did not always understand what he said, this language of his earned their respect.

When Osip took his tax-book into the headman's house, the prefect, a wiry old man with long grey side-whiskers and a grey tunic, was seated at the table in the front of the room and writing something down. The room was very clean, and the walls were bright with pictures cut out of magazines, and in a most prominent place, near the eikons, hung a portrait of the ex-Prince of Bulgaria, Battenberg. By the table stood Antip Sedelnikov, arms folded.

"This man, Your Excellency," he said, when Osip's turn came, "owes 119 rubles. He paid one ruble just before Easter, but since that date hasn't paid a penny."

The prefect raised his eyes at Osip and asked, "Well, old chap, why is this?"

"Your Excellency," Osip began, in great nervousness, "show me divine mercy and permit me to say that this season now, this year, the Master of Lutoretzki said to me, 'Osip,' he said, 'sell me your hay . . . come on,' he said, 'sell it me.' And why not? I had about one hundred *pouds* to sell,

what the women cut down the lows. . . . Well, and we made a deal. . . .
All nice and proper we agreed. . . ."

His complaint was of the headman, and he kept turning round to the
other peasants as if inviting them to give witness; his face turned red and
beads of sweat appeared on it, and his eyes were like gimlets, and angry.

"I don't see the point of all this," the prefect said, "I am asking you. . . .
I am asking you—why haven't you paid up the arrears? You don't pay and
I have to answer for it, eh?"

"It's beyond me powers!"

"These words are without consequence, Your Honour," the headman
said. "It is true that the Chikildeyevs are of insufficient standing, but if you
enquire, Your Honour, everyone will tell you the real cause—vodka and
loose ways, Your Honour. No comprehension whatsoever. . . ."

The prefect wrote something down and then, in a calm, even tone of
voice, just as if asking for a glass of water, he said "Get outside!"

Shortly after he drove off, and when he was getting into his cheap
buggy, and coughed, even by the expression of his tall, bony back you
could see that his thoughts were far away from Osip or the headman, or the
Zhoukovo arrears, on something of his own. He had not got a mile away
from the village when Antip Sedelnikov was already carrying the samovar
out of the Chikildeyevs' house, with the grandmother at his heels yelling
in a shrill voice and puffing out her bosom. "You accursed creature, you,
I won't let you have it!"

He walked swiftly, with long strides, while she chased after him, out of
breath, nearly dropping, hunch-backed and infuriated; her kerchief slipped
back to her shoulders and her grey hair with its greenish tint blew in the
wind. Then all at once she stood still, and like a real rioter, began thumping
her chest with her fists and yelling still louder, in a singing voice, half
sobbing, "Good Orthodox Christians, all ye who believe in the Lord. How
cruel I'm done by. Dear beloved brothers and sisters, what oppression!
Oi, oi, darlings, do help me!"

"Granny, Granny," the headman said severely, "do have a little sense in
your head."

With no samovar the Chikildeyev household's life became completely
dismal. There was something degrading in that deprivation, something
insulting, as if the honour of the house was besmirched. Far better had the
headman taken the table and all the benches and all the crocks—the house
would not have looked so bare. The old woman yelled, Maria wept, and,
seeing her weep, the little girls wept too. The old man felt he was to
blame, and sat in one corner, crushed, without a word to say. Nikolai too
said nothing. The grandmother was fond of him and sorry for him, but
now she forgot she was sorry for him and attacked him all at once, with
oaths and reproaches, sticking her angry fists right under his nose. She
shouted that he was to blame for everything. Why indeed had he sent

home so little money when in his own letters he was always boasting that at the Slavianski Bazar he earned fifty rubles a month? Why did he come here, and bring a family into the bargain? If he died on them, where was the money coming from to bury him? It was pitiful then to see them, Nikolai, Olga and Sasha.

The old man cleared his throat of phlegm, took his cap and went to see the headman. It was quite dark. Antip Sedelnikov was busy, with distended cheeks, soldering something at the stove; the air was choking. His children, emaciated and dirty—no better than the Chikildeyev kids—were swarming about the floor, and his ugly, freckly wife, her belly big, was winding silk. Antip was the only one to look smart, handsome. On the bench was a row of five samovars. The old man crossed himself and muttered a prayer to Battenberg and then said, "Antip, show divine mercy, man, give me back that samovar! For Jesus' sake!"

"Bring me three rubles, and you shall have it!"

"It's beyond me powers!"

Antip's cheeks puffed out, the flame roared and hissed, gleaming on the samovars. The old man crushed his cap in his hands and after a bit said, "Give it me!"

The swarthy headman by now seemed quite black, like a wizard; he turned to Osip and roughly barked, "It all depends on the zemstvo authorities. At the administrational sitting of the twenty-sixth instanter you are at liberty to appeal to your own satisfaction either in writing or in person."

Osip did not understand, but that satisfied him and he went home.

About ten days later the prefect came again, spent an hour in the place, and left. It was windy and cold weather, and the river was frozen hard, but there had been no snow yet, and the folk were having a hard time, with no road. Then on the holiday in the early evening the neighbours went in to Osip's to sit and have a chat. They talked in low voices, as it was sinful to work, and lit no light. There was news—not too good either. From two or three houses, through arrears of taxes, they had taken their poultry and sent to the district government offices, and there, having nothing to feed them with, they had slaughtered them; sheep too had been taken, and roped up, and carted, and from being shifted from one cart to another at every village, one had died. And now they were arguing about who was to blame.

"The local government people," said Osip, "what do you think!"

"Of course the local government people."

They blamed the local government for everything—for their arrears, for all oppressive measures, for the bad harvests, though there was not one who had the slightest idea what the local government, the zemstvo, really meant. And it had begun with some of the rich peasants, who owned manufactories and stores and inns, being voters, and then getting dissatisfied, after which they started cursing the zemstvo in their factories and inns.

There was talk too of God, for not giving any snow. It was high time they carted firewood, and you could neither drive nor walk over the rough country. Fifteen to twenty years earlier, and before that, the conversations at Zhoukovo were far more interesting. Then every old man looked as if he was keeping a secret, knew something and was expecting something; there was talk of a Charter printed in gold, of land division, of new lands, of capital, hints of something coming; now the Zhoukovo folk had no secrets: all the cards of their life were on the table, and so talk was whittled down to want and foodstuffs and there being no snow. . . . For some time nobody spoke. Then again the poultry and the sheep came up, and they argued about who was to blame.

"The local government people, of course," Osip declared, in weary tones.

VIII

The parish church was six versts away, in Kosogorovo, and they never went there but needs drove them, for christenings or marryings or funerals; ordinary worship could be done in the church over the river. On Sundays and feast days, when the weather was fine, the girls dressed up and all of them together went down to communion, and it was a gay sight, to see them in their red and yellow and green frocks crossing the low pastures; when the weather was bad they stayed at home. But before the big feasts they had to go to the parish church; those who couldn't find time in Lent to prepare properly for the sacrament had to pay the parson fifteen copecks when at Easter he came round with the cross.

The old man did not believe in God because he had scarcely ever given it a thought; he recognized the supernatural, but his opinion was that the supernatural could only be women's business, and whenever religion was mentioned in his presence, or any miraculous thing, and a question was put to him, he would scratch his head and answer unwillingly, "How the devil should I know?"

The grandmother did believe, if rather dimly; things were always very mixed in her thoughts, and she never started thinking of sins or death or the salvation of the soul but want and cares would take possession of her mind and she forgot all about what she had started with. She remembered no prayers, and usually, before going to bed in the evening, went to the eikons and whispered at them, "Mother of God of Kazan, Mother of God of Smolensk, thrice eikons of the Mother of God. . . ."

Maria and Fiokla used to cross themselves regularly, and they fasted and took the big sacrament every year, but they did not understand a thing. The children were not taught to pray, nor told anything about God, nor given any principles, except not to eat this, that and the other during fast. Other families were much the same; very few believed and very few understood. At the same time they were all very fond of Holy Writ, tenderly and piously fond of it, but they had no books, and nobody to read and explain, and because she sometimes read the Gospel, Olga was respected, and both she and Sasha were addressed in the polite plural.

Olga frequently went to the patron feasts and special celebrations in the parishes round and to churches in the district town, which contained two monasteries and twenty-seven churches. She was an absent-minded woman, and while engaged in those expeditions would completely forget her family, and when she was on the way home would discover with delight that she had a husband and daughter, and then she would smile and be radiant and say, "God's mercy is great."

The village ways were disgusting to her and oppressive. At St. Elijah they drank, at the Assumption they drank, at Ascension Day they drank. The Zhoukovo patron feast was the Intercession of the Virgin, and on this occasion the mouzhiks drank three days. They drank fifty rubles of the parish council money and then on top of that made a house-to-house collection. The first day the Chikildeyevs killed a sheep and ate it morning, noon, and night, and the children got up during the night to eat some more. Those three days Kiriak was terribly drunk all the time, sold everything he had, to drink, down to even his fur cap and his boots, and thrashed Maria so that they had to pour water over her to bring her round. After which they were all ashamed and felt sickish.

Yet Zhoukovo—Kholouievka, or Muckham—once saw a genuine religious celebration. It was in August, when the miraculous Holy Eikon was being taken through the whole district, village to village. That day on which they expected it to arrive at Zhoukovo was without wind and overcast. Early in the morning the girls set out to meet the procession, dressed in their bright-coloured holiday frocks, and they arrived with it in the evening, a procession of the cross, chanting, and the bells pealing in the church over the river. The vast throng, their own folk and the strangers, blocked the broad village street; there was great noise and dust and press. . . . The old man too, and the grandmother, and Kiriak, all reached out their hands to the eikon, their eyes greedily fastened on it, and tears trickled down their cheeks and they cried, "Pray for us, dear Mother, pray for us and protect us!"

They all seemed suddenly to grasp that there was some connection between heaven and earth, that the rich and powerful still had not everything in their hands, that some protection from ill-usage, from slavish poverty, from cruel, unbearable want, from the terrible vodka did exist. "Protect us, Mother dear!" Maria sobbed. "Dear Mother of God!"

But that service came to its end, the eikon was borne away, and the old order returned, once more from the inn came the coarse, drunken voices. Only the rich mouzhiks were afraid of death, as the richer they became the less they believed in God and the salvation of the soul; only at the very end, out of fear, did such light candles and pay for prayers. The poorer mouzhiks were not afraid of death. They used to tell the old man and the grandmother straight in the face that they had had their day, and it was time they died, and neither of them ever turned a hair. They did not think there was anything strange in remarking to Fiokla, in Nikolai's hearing, that when Nikolai died her husband, Denis, would get exemption and come home. As for Maria, not only did she not fear death, she was even sorry it was so long coming, and she was glad when any of her children died.

Death they were not afraid of, but on the other hand they had an exaggerated fear of illness. A slight indigestion or a trifling chill was enough to have the grandmother lying down on the stove, groaning loudly and incessantly, "My hour has come!" The old man would hurry off for the priest and the grandmother would be given communion, and anointed. There was much talk of chills and worms and tumours shifting about in the stomach and threatening the heart. Chills they feared more than anything else, so even in summer they dressed in warm clothes and heated themselves on the stove. The grandmother was fond of being ill and often went to the hospital, where she always said she was fifty-eight years old, instead of seventy. She thought that if the doctor learned her real age he would not treat her, but would tell her it was high time for her to die, not consult doctors. She usually rode off to the hospital early in the morning, taking two or three of the grandchildren with her, and came home in the evening, hungry and out of temper—bearing medicine for herself and ointments for the little girls. Once she took Nikolai there and for a fortnight after that he took medicine too, and said he felt better.

The grandmother knew all the doctors and surgeons' dressers and quacks for thirty versts around, and there wasn't one she liked. At the Intercession of the Virgin, the deacon, coming round with the parson blessing the homes, told her that near the prison in the town there was a little old man who had been an army dresser and was doing a lot of curing now, and he advised her to go to him. The grandmother did so. When the first snow had fallen she drove down to the town and brought back a little old man with a beard, a long-skirted proselyte, whose face was one network of little blue veins. Just then there were men working in the house: an old tailor wearing frightful spectacles was making a waistcoat out of fragments, and two lads were beating wool into felt for boots. Kiriak, who had been given the sack for drunkenness, and now lived at home, was sitting next the tailor, mending harness, and it was very cramped and stuffy and stinking in the house. The proselyte examined Nikolai and said that he absolutely must be cupped.

He cupped him, and the old tailor and Kiriak and the children stood and watched; they thought they could see the illness coming out of

Nikolai. Nikolai too watched, watched the cups suck into his chest and gradually fill with dark blood, and he felt that something really was leaving his system, and smiled with satisfaction.

"That's good," the tailor said, "God grant it do good."

The proselyte chap put on twelve cups and then another dozen, had his fill of tea, and left. Nikolai suddenly began to shiver violently; his face drooped and, as our peasant women say, crumpled into a little fist, and his fingers turned blue. He wrapped himself in a coverlet and a fur driving coat, but felt colder and colder. As evening drew near he began to be distressed in spirit, asked them to put him on the floor, then asked the tailor not to smoke; then he fell quiet under the coat, and towards morning he died.

IX

Oh, what a fierce and what a long winter it was!

Their own flour gave out at Christmas, and they had to buy. Kiriak, living at home now, rowed in the evenings, making them all afraid, and in the morning was in agony from headaches and shame, and it was pitiful to see him. Day and night the starving cow bellowed in its byre and tore the heart of the grandmother and of Maria. And all the time the cracking cold never slackened, as if to spite them; the snowdrifts were mountainous; and still the winter dragged on. On the Annunciation there was a real winter blizzard, and snow at Easter.

But even so the winter did end at last. The first part of April was warm by day, though still frosty at night, the winter being tenacious; but then one warm day managed to get the mastery, and at last the thaw really began and the birds were singing. The whole pasture lows and the riverside thickets were under the spring waters, and the whole area between Zhoukovo and the other side was one vast gulf on which here and there were fluttering flocks of wild duck. The spring sunsets, fiery, with voluminous clouds, every evening were remarkable, new, unbelievable, the sort of sunsets that afterwards seem unreal, when you see pictures of them.

The storks flew swift, with their mournful cries, as if calling you with them. Standing on the edge of the cliff, Olga looked for long spaces at the floods and the sun and the church, bright, as if young again, and her tears flowed and she choked because she so desperately longed to go away somewhere, go on and on, to the end of the world. It was indeed decided that she should go back to Moscow, into service, and Kiriak would go with her to get a job somewhere as yardman. Oh, let it be soon she went!

When the roads had dried up and it was warm, they prepared for departure. Olga and Sasha, bundles on their backs, bast sandals on their feet, set out before it was properly light, and Maria went with them to see them well on the road. Kiriak was not well, so he was staying at home another week. For the last time Olga prayed at the church, thinking of her husband, and she did not cry, only her face wrinkled and turned ugly, like an old woman's. That winter had thinned her and she had lost her looks and gone grey a bit, and her former charm and pleasant smile had now finally given place to a humble, sorrowful expression of suffered grief, and there was something quite stupid and wooden in her glance, just as if she was deaf.

She was sorry to leave the village and the mouzhiks. Thoughts kept coming to her of how they had carried Nikolai, how they had sung the service outside every house, how they had all wept, feeling her grief. During the summer and the winter there had been moments when she had thought that those folk lived worse than animals, and living with them was terrible; they were coarse and dishonest and dirty and drunken and lived at cross purposes, incessantly quarrelling with each other, because they had no respect for each other, feared each other, and had no trust in each other. Who kept the inn and made them drunk? A mouzhik. Who squandered the village and the school and the church money in drink? The mouzhiks. Who stole from his neighbour, fired his neighbour, sneaked to the authorities against his neighbour for a bottle of vodka? Who was the first to talk against the mouzhiks before the local government and other assemblies? The mouzhiks. Yes, living with them was terrible, but yet they were human creatures and suffered and wept like human creatures, and there was not a thing in their lives for which there was not good excuse. Cruel labour, such that all night their bodies ached, bitter winters, meagre crops, scarcity which crushed them, and no help, nor hope of help. Those richer and more powerful could not help, as they themselves were coarse and dishonest and drunken, and just as foul-mouthed as the others; the merest whipper-snapper of a civil servant or a squire's man treated them all like vagabonds, even talking to the village headmen or the elders of the churches in the singular, like underlings, and thought too that they had a right to do so. But anyway could you hope for a breed that is self-seeking, greedy, debauched, lazy and descends on a village solely to outrage and pillage and terrorise—could you hope for such a breed to set an example? Olga recalled the pitiful, humbled expression on the faces of the old people that winter when Kiriak was taken away to be flogged. . . . And now she was sorry for all of them and her heart ached for them, and as she paced on her way, from time to time she turned to look back at the miserable cottages.

Having accompanied them three versts, Maria said good-bye, and then fell on her knees and began to lament and beat her face on the earth. "Now I am all alone again, oh alas my poor little head, alas, poor me . . ."

She lamented thus for a long time, and for a long time Olga and Sasha could see her kneeling there, bowing down to somebody away yonder, and clutching her head in her hands, and the rooks flying overhead.

The sun rose high in the sky and it became hot. Zhoukovo was far behind them. It was a pleasure walking. Olga and Sasha even soon forgot the village, and Maria; their hearts were glad and everything interested them. A burial mound; a row of telegraph poles, reaching one after another they knew not where, and vanishing on the horizon, with their wires buzzing mysteriously; a farm in the distance, lost in greenery, and an odour of damp and of hemp coming from it, and for some reason it seemed that the people there must be happy. Then the skeleton of a horse, whitening out in the fields. And there were the tireless skylarks, pouring forth their song, and the quails calling one to another; and a landrail croaking, just as if somebody was croaking on an old iron rake.

At midday Olga and Sasha reached a large village. There, in the main street, they came on the little old man who had been cook to General Zhoukov. He was feeling the heat, and his scarlet perspiring bald head shone in the sun. He and Olga failed to recognize one another, then both turned round at the same time and recognized each other and then, without a word, went on, each their own road. Olga stopped outside a house which seemed better off, newer than the others, and bowed down under the windows and in a loud, thin sing-song voice said "Good Orthodox Christian folk, please help with alms for the sake of Jesus our Lord, give what you can, and may your parents dwell in the Heavenly Kingdom, in eternal peace . . ."

"Good Orthodox Christian folk," rang out Sasha's voice, "please help with alms for the sake of Jesus our Lord, give what you can, and the Heavenly Kingdom . . ."

TWENTY–SIX AND ONE

Maxim Gorky (Peshkov)
(1868–1936)

TRANSLATED BY NISBET BAIN

THERE WERE TWENTY-SIX of us—twenty-six living machines shut up in a damp cellar, where from morning to evening we kneaded dough to make cakes and biscuits. The windows of our cellar looked upon a ditch yawning open before them and crammed full of bricks, green with damp; the window-frames were partly covered from the outside by an iron grating, and the light of the sun could not reach us through the window-panes covered with flour dust. Our master had closed up the windows with iron in order that we might not give away a morsel of his bread to the poor, or to those of our comrades who were living without work, and therefore starving; our master called us galley-slaves, and gave us rotten entrails for dinner instead of butcher's meat.

It was a narrow, stuffy life we lived in that stone cage beneath the low and heavy rafters covered with soot and cobwebs. It was a grievous evil life we lived within those thick walls, plastered over with patches of dirt and mould. . . . We rose at five o'clock in the morning, without having had our sleep out, and—stupid and indifferent—at six o'clock we were sitting behind the table to make biscuits from dough already prepared for us by our comrades while we were still sleeping. And the whole day, from early morning to ten o'clock at night, some of us sat at the table kneading the yeasty dough and rocking to and fro so as not to get benumbed, while the others mixed the flour with water. And all day long, dreamily and wearily, the boiling water hummed in the cauldron where the biscuits were steamed, and the shovel of the baker rasped swiftly and evilly upon our ears from beneath the oven as often as it flung down baked bits of dough on the burning bricks. From morning to evening, in one corner of the stove, they burned wood, and the red reflection of the flames flickered on the wall of the workshop as if silently laughing at us. The huge stove was like the mis-shapen head of some fairy-tale monster—it seemed to stick out from under the ground, opening its wide throat full of bright fire, breathing hotly upon us, and regarding our endless labour with its two black vent-holes just over its forehead. Those two deep cavities were like eyes—the passionless and pitiless eyes of a monster; they always regarded us with one and the same sort of dark look, as if they were weary of looking at their slaves and, not expecting anything human from us, despised us with the cold contempt of worldly wisdom.

From day to day in tormenting dust, in dirt brought in by our feet from the yard, in a dense malodorous steaming vapour, we kneaded dough and made biscuits, moistening them with our sweat, and we hated our work with a bitter hatred; we never ate of that which came forth from our hands, preferring black bread to the biscuits. Sitting behind the long table face to face with each other, nine over against nine, we mechanically used our arms and fingers during the long hours, and were so accustomed to our work that we no longer noticed our own movements. And we had examined one another so thoroughly that everyone of us knew all the wrinkles in the faces of his comrades. We had nothing to talk about, so we got accustomed to talking about nothing, and were silent the whole time unless we quarrelled—there is always a way to make a man quarrel, especially if he be a comrade. But it was rarely that we even quarrelled—how can a man be up to much if he is half dead, if he is like a figure-head, if his feelings are blunted by grievous labour? But silence is only a terror and a torture to those who have said everything and can have nothing more to say; but for people who have not begun to find their voices, silence is simple and easy. . . . Sometimes, however, we sang; it came about in this way. One of us in the midst of his work would suddenly whinny like a tired horse and begin to croon very softly one of those protracted ditties, the sadly caressing *motif* of which always lightens the heaviness of the singer's soul. One of us would begin singing, I say, and the rest would, at first, merely listen to his lonely song, and beneath the heavy roof of the cellar his song would flicker and die out like a tiny camp-fire in the steppe on a grey autumn night when the grey sky hangs over the earth like a leaden roof. Presently the first singer would be joined by another, and then two voices, softly and sadly, would float upwards from the stifling heat of our narrow ditch. And then, suddenly, several voices together would lay hold of the song, and the song would swell forth like a wave, and become stronger and more sonorous, and seem to amplify the heavy grey walls of our stony prison.

And so it came about that the whole six-and-twenty of us would find ourselves singing—our sustained, sonorous concert would fill the work-room, and the song would seem not to have room enough therein. It would beat against the stone wall, wail, weep, stir within the benumbed heart the sensation of a gentle tickling ache, reopen old wounds in it, and awake it to anguish. The singers would sigh deeply and heavily; one of them would unexpectedly break off his own song and listen to the singing of his comrades, and then his voice would blend once more with the common billow of sound. Another of us, perhaps, would utter an anguished "Ah!" and then continue singing with fast-closed eyes. No doubt the broad, dense wave of sound presented itself to his mind as a road stretching far, far away—a broad road lit up by the bright sun, with he himself walking along that road. . . .

And all the time the flame of the furnace was flickering and the baker's shovel was harshly scraping the brick floor, and the boiling water was humming in the cauldron, and the reflection of the fire was quivering on the wall and laughing at us noiselessly. . . . And we were wailing forth in the words of others our dull misery, the heavy anguish of living beings deprived of the sun, the anguish of slaves. Thus we lived, twenty-six of us, in the cellar of a large stone house, and life was as grievous to us as if all the three upper stories of this house had been built right upon our very shoulders.

But, besides the singing, we had one other good thing—a thing we set great store by and which, possibly, stood to us in the place of sunshine. In the second story of our house was a gold-embroidery factory, and amongst the numerous factory girls employed there was a damsel sixteen years old, Tanya by name. Every morning she would come to the little window pierced through the door in the wall of our workshop, and pressing against it her tiny rosy face, with its merry blue eyes, would cry to us with a musical, friendly voice: "Poor little prisoners! give me some little biscuits!"

All of us would instantly turn round at the familiar sound of that bright voice, and gaze good-naturedly and joyously at the pure virginal little face smiling upon us so gloriously. It became a usual and very pleasant thing for us to see the little nose pressed against the window-pane, to see the tiny white teeth gleaming from under the rosy lips parted by a smile. There would then be a general rush to open the door, each one trampling upon his fellows in his haste, and then in she would come, always so bright and pleasant, and stand before us, her head perched a little on one side, holding up her apron and smiling all the time. The long thick locks of her chestnut hair, falling across her shoulders, lay upon her breast. We dirty, grimy, misshapen wretches stood there looking up at her—the threshold of the door was four steps above the level of the floor—we had to raise our heads to look at her, we would wish her good-morning, and would address her in especial language—the words seemed to come to us expressly for her and for her alone. When we conversed with her our voices were gentler than usual, and our jests were less rough. We had quite peculiar and different manners—and all for her. The baker would take out of the oven a shovelful of the ruddiest, best-toasted biscuits, and skilfully fling them into Tanya's apron.

"Take care you don't fall into the clutches of the master!" we would always caution her. And she, roguishly laughing, would call to us: "Good-bye, little prisoners," and vanish as quickly as a little mouse.

Only—long after her departure, we would talk pleasantly about her among ourselves; we always said the same thing, and we said it late and early, because she and we and everything around us was always the same early and late. It is a heavy torment for a man to live where everything around him is unchanging, and if this does not kill the soul within him, the longer he lives the more tormenting will the immobility of his environment become. We always spoke of women in such a way that sometimes it went against the grain with us to listen to our own coarse, shameful speeches, and it will be understood that the sort of women we knew were unworthy to be alluded to in any other way. But we never spoke ill of Tanya. None of us ever permitted himself to lay so much as a finger upon her; nay, more, she never heard a loose jest from any of us. Possibly this was because she never remained very long with us: she twinkled before our eyes like a star falling from heaven and vanished; but, possibly also, it was because she was so tiny and so very pretty, and everything beautiful awakens respect for it even in coarse people. And there was something else. Although our prison-like labour had made dull brutes of us, for all that we were still human beings, and, like all human beings, we could not live without worshipping something or other. We had nothing better than she, and nobody but she took any notice of us who lived in that vault; nobody, though scores of people lived in that house. And finally—and that, after all, was the chief thing—we all of us accounted her as in some sort our own, as, in some sort, only existing thanks to our biscuits; we looked upon it as our duty to give her biscuits piping hot, and this became to us a daily sacrifice to our idol; it became almost a sacred office, and every day bound us to her more and more. Besides the biscuits we gave to Tanya a good deal of advice—she was to put on warmer clothes, not run rapidly upstairs, not to carry heavy loads of wood. She listened to our advice with a smile, responded to it with laughter, and never followed it at all; but we were not offended with her on that account, we only wanted to show her that we were taking care of her.

Sometimes she asked us to do different things for her; such, for instance, as to open the heavy cellar door, to chop up wood and so on, and we joyfully, nay, with a sort of pride, did for her all that she asked us to do.

But once, when one of us asked her to mend his only shirt, she sniffed contemptuously and said: "What next! do you think I've nothing better to do?"

We laughed heartily at the silly fellow—and never asked her to do anything more. We loved her—and when that is said all is said. A man always wants to lay his love upon someone, although sometimes he may crush her beneath the weight of it, and sometimes he may soil her; he may poison the life of his neighbour with his love, because in loving he does not revere the beloved. We were obliged to love Tanya because we had none else to love.

At times one or other of us would begin to reason about it like this: "Why are we spoiling the wench like this? What is there in her after all? Eh? We are making a great deal of fuss about her!"

The fellow who ventured to use such language was pretty roughly snubbed, I can tell you. We wanted something to love, we had found what we wanted, and we loved it; and what we six-and-twenty loved was bound to be inviolate, because it was our holy shrine, and everyone who ran contrary to us in this matter was our enemy. No doubt people often love what is not really good—but here we were, all twenty-six of us, in the same boat, and therefore what we considered dear we would have others regard as sacred.

Besides the biscuit factory our master had a fancy-bakery; it was located in the same house, and only separated from our hole by a wall; but the fancy-bakers—there were four of them—kept us at arm's length, considering their work as cleaner than ours, and for that reason considering themselves as better than we. So they did not come into our workshop, and laughed contemptuously at us when they met us in the yard. We, too, did not go to them; our master had forbidden us to do so for fear we should steal the milk scones. We did not like the fancy-bakers because we envied them. Their work was lighter than ours; they got more than we did and were better fed; they had a spacious, well-lighted workshop, and they were all so clean and healthy—quite the opposite to us. We indeed, the whole lot of us, looked greyish or yellowish; three of us were suffering from disease, others from consumption, one of us was absolutely crippled by rheumatism. They, on feast-days and in their spare time, put on pea-jackets and boots that creaked; two of them had concertinas, and all of them went strolling in the Park—we went about in little better than dirty rags, with down-at-heel slippers or bast shoes on our feet, and the police would not admit us into the Park—how could we possibly love the fancy-bakers?

Presently we heard that their overseer had taken to drink, that the master had dismissed him and hired another, and that this other was a soldier who went about in a rich satin waistcoat, and on great occasions wore a gold chain. We were curious to see such a toff, and, in the hope of seeing him, took it in turns to run out into the yard one after the other.

But he himself appeared in our workshop. He kicked at the door, it flew open, and, keeping it open, he stood on the threshold, smiled, and said to us: "God be with you! I greet you, my children!"

The frosty air, rushing through the door in thick smoky clouds, whirled round his feet, and there he stood on the threshold looking down upon us from his eminence, and from beneath his blond, skilfully twisted moustaches gleamed his strong yellow teeth. His vest really was something quite out of the common—it was blue, embroidered with flowers, and had a sort of sparkle all over it, and its buttons were made of pretty little pearls. And the gold chain *was* there.

He was handsome, that soldier was, quite tall, robust, with ruddy cheeks, and his large bright eyes looked good and friendly and clear. On his head was a white stiffly starched cap, and from beneath his clean spotless spats appeared the bright tops of his modish, brilliantly polished boots.

Our baker asked him, respectfully, to shut the door. He did so, quite deliberately, and began asking us questions about our master. We outdid each other in telling him that our master was a blood-sucker, a slave-driver, a malefactor, and a tormentor; everything in short that we could and felt bound to say about our master, but it is impossible to write it down here. The soldier listened, twirled his moustache, and regarded us with a gentle, radiant look.

"And I suppose now you've a lot of little wenches about here?" he suddenly said.

Some of us laughed respectfully, others made languishing grimaces; one of us made it quite clear to the soldier that there *were* wenches here—a round dozen of them.

"Do you amuse yourselves?" asked the soldier, blinking his eyes.

Again we laughed, not very loudly, and with some confusion of face. . . . Many of us would have liked to show the soldier that they were as dashing fellows as himself, but none dared to do so; no, not one. One of us indeed hinted as much by murmuring: "Situated as we are . . ."

"Yes, of course, it would be hard for you!" observed the soldier confidentially, continuing to stare at us. "You ought to be—well, not what you are. You're down on your luck—there's a way of holding one's self—there's the look of the thing—you know what I mean! And women, you know, like a man with style about him. He must be a fine figure of a man—everything neat and natty, you know. And then, too, a woman respects strength. Now what do you think of that for an arm, eh?"

The soldier drew his right arm from his pocket, with the shirt-sleeve stripped back, bare to the elbow, and showed it to us. It was a strong, white arm, bristling with shiny, gold-like hair.

"Legs and breast the same—plenty of grit there, eh? And then, too, a man must be stylishly dressed, and must have nice things. Now look at me—all the women love me! I neither call to them nor wink at them—they come falling on my neck by the dozen."

He sat down on a flour-basket and discoursed to us for a long time about how the women loved him, and how valiantly he comported himself with them. After he had gone, and when the creaking door had closed behind him, we were silent for a long time, thinking of him and of his yarns. And after a bit we suddenly all fell a-talking at once, and agreed unanimously that he was a very pleasant fellow. He was so straightforward and jolly—he came and sat down and talked to us just as if he were one of us. No one had ever come and talked to us in such a friendly way before. And we talked of him and of his future successes with the factory girls at the gold-embroiderer's, who, whenever they met us in the yard, either curled their lips contemptuously, or gave us a wide berth, or walked straight up to us as if we were not in their path at all. And as for us, we only feasted our eyes upon them when we met them in the yard, or when they passed by our window, dressed in winter in peculiar little fur caps and fur pelisses, and in summer in hats covered with flowers, and with sunshades of various colours in their hands. But, on the other hand, among ourselves, we talked of these girls in such a way that, had they heard it, they would have gone mad with rage and shame. . . .

"But how about little Tanya—I hope he won't spoil her!" said our chief baker suddenly with a gloomy voice.

We were all silent, so greatly had these words impressed us. We had almost forgotten about Tanya: the soldier had shut her out from us, as it were, with his fine burly figure. Presently a noisy dispute began. Some said that Tanya would not demean herself by any such thing; others maintained that she would be unable to stand against the soldier; finally, a third party proposed that if the soldier showed any inclination to attach himself to

Tanya, we should break his ribs. And, at last, we all resolved to keep a watch upon the soldier and Tanya, and warn the girl to beware of him. . . . And so the dispute came to an end.

A month passed by. The soldier baked his fancy-rolls, walked out with the factory girls, and frequently paid us a visit in our workshop, but of his victories over the wenches he said never a word, but only twirled his moustaches and noisily smacked his lips.

Tanya came to us every morning for her "little biscuits," and was always merry, gentle and friendly with us. We tried to talk to her about the soldier—she called him "the goggle-eyed bull-calf," and other ridiculous names, and that reassured us. We were proud of our little girl when we saw how the factory girls clung to the soldier. Tanya's dignified attitude towards him seemed to raise the whole lot of us, and we, as the directors of her conduct, even began to treat the soldier himself contemptuously. But her we loved more than ever, her we encountered each morning more and more joyfully and good-humouredly.

But one day the soldier came to us a little the worse for liquor, he sat him down, began laughing, and when we asked him what he was laughing about, he explained:

"Two of the wenches have been quarrelling about me, Liddy and Gerty," said he. "How they did blackguard each other! Ha, ha, ha! They caught each other by the hair, and were down on the floor in a twinkling, one on the top of the other; ha, ha, ha! And they tore and scratched like anything, and I was nearly bursting with laughter. Why can't women fight fair? Why do they always scratch, eh?"

He was sitting on the bench; there he sat so healthy, clean, and light-hearted, and roared with laughter. We were silent. Somehow, or other, he was disagreeable to us at that moment.

"No, I can't make it out. What luck I do have with women, it is ridiculous. I've but to wink, and—she is ready. The d-deuce is in it."

His white arms, covered with shining gold down, rose in the air and fell down again on his knees with a loud bang. And he regarded us with such a friendly look of amazement, just as if he himself were frankly puzzled by the felicity of his dealings with women. His plump, ruddy face regularly shone with happiness and self-complacency, and he kept on noisily smacking his lips.

Our chief baker scraped his shovel along the hearth violently and angrily, and suddenly remarked, with a sneer:

"It is no great feat of strength to fell little fir trees, but to fell a full-grown pine is a very different matter. . . ."

"Is that meant for me, now?" queried the soldier.

"It is meant for you."

"What do you mean?"

"Nothing. . . . Never mind."

"Nay, stop a bit! What's your little game? What pine tree do you mean?"

Our master-baker didn't answer, he was busily working with his shovel at the stove, shovelled out the well-baked biscuits, sifted those that were ready, and flung them boisterously on to the floor to the lads who were arranging them in rows on the bast wrappings. He seemed to have forgotten the soldier and his talk with him. But the soldier suddenly became uneasy. He rose to his feet and approached the stove, running the risk of a blow in the chest from the handle of the shovel which was whirling convulsively in the air.

"Come, speak—what *she* did you mean? You have insulted me. Not a single she shall ever get the better of me, n-no—I say. And then, too, you used such offensive words to me. . . ."

He really seemed to be seriously offended. No doubt he had but a poor opinion of himself except on this one point: his ability to win women. Possibly, except this one quality, there was nothing really vital in the man at all, and only this single quality allowed him to feel himself a living man.

There are people who look upon some disease, either of the body or of the soul, as the best and most precious thing in life. They nurse it all their lives, and only in it do they live at all. Though they suffer by it, yet they live upon it. They complain of it to other people, and by means of it attract to themselves the attention of their neighbours. They use it as a means of obtaining sympathy, and without it—they are nothing at all. Take away from them this disease, cure them, and they will be unhappy because they are deprived of the only means of living—there they stand empty. Sometimes the life of a man is poor to such a degree that he is involuntarily obliged to put a high value on some vice, and live thereby; indeed, we may say straight out that very often people become vicious from sheer ennui.

The soldier was offended, rushed upon our master-baker, and bellowed: "Come, I say—speak out! Who was it?"

"Speak out, eh?" and the master-baker suddenly turned round upon him.

"Yes! Well?"

"Do you know Tanya?"

"Well!"

"Well, there you are!—try her!"

"I?"

"You."

"Pooh! That's nothing."

"Let us see!"

"You shall see. Ha-ha-ha!"

"She look at you!"

"Give me a month!"

"What a braggart you are, soldier!"

"A fortnight! I'll show you. Who's she? Little Tanya! Pooh!"

"And now be off!—you're in the way."

"A fortnight, I say—and the thing's done. Poor you, I say!"

"Be off, I say."

Our baker suddenly grew savage, and flourished his shovel. The soldier backed away from him in astonishment, and observed us in silence. "Good!" he said at last with ominous calmness—and departed.

During the dispute we all remained silent, we were too deeply interested in it to speak. But when the soldier departed, there arose from among us a loud and lively babble of voices.

Someone shrieked at the baker: "A pretty business you've set a-going, Paul!"

"Go on working, d'ye hear?" replied the master-baker fiercely.

We felt that the soldier would make the assault, and that Tanya was in danger. We felt this, and yet at the same time we were all seized by a burning curiosity that was not unpleasant—what would happen? Would Tanya stand firm against the soldier? And almost all of us cried, full of confidence:

"Little Tanya? She'll stand firm enough!"

We had all of us a frightful longing to put the fortitude of our little idol to the test. We excitedly proved to each other that our little idol was a strong little idol, and would emerge victorious from this encounter. It seemed to us, at last, that we had not egged on our soldier enough, that he was forgetting the contest, and that we ought to spur his vanity just a little bit. From that day forth we began to live a peculiar life, at high nervous tension, such as we had never lived before. We quarrelled with each other for days together, just as if we had all grown wiser, and were able to talk more and better. It seemed to us as if we were playing a sort of game with the devil, and the stake on our part was—Tanya. And when we heard from the fancy-bread-bakers that the soldier had begun "to run after our little Tanya," it was painfully well with us, and so curious were we to live it out, that we did not even observe that our master, taking advantage of our excitement, had added 14 poods[1] of paste to our daily task. We practically never left off working at all. The name of Tanya never left our tongues all day. And every morning we awaited her with a peculiar sort of impatience.

Nevertheless we said not a word to her of the contest actually proceeding. We put no questions to her, and were kind and affectionate to her as before. Yet in our treatment of her there had already crept in something new and strangely different to our former feeling for Tanya—and this new thing was a keen curiosity, keen and cold as a steel knife.

"My friends, the time's up to-day," said the master-baker one morning as he set about beginning his work.

[1] 560 lbs.

We knew that well enough without any reminder from him, but we trembled all the same.

"Look at her well, she'll be here immediately," continued the baker. Someone exclaimed compassionately:

"As if eyes could see anything!"

And again a lively, stormy debate arose among us. To-day we were to know at last how clean and inviolable was the vessel in which we had placed our best. That morning, all at once and as if for the first time, we began to feel that we were really playing a great game, and that this test of the purity of our divinity might annihilate it altogether so far as we were concerned. We had all heard during the last few days that the soldier was obstinately and persistently persecuting Tanya, yet how was it that none of us asked her what her relations with him were? And she used to come to us regularly, every morning, for her little biscuits, and was the same as ever....

And this day also we very soon heard her voice.

"Little prisoners, I have come...."

We crowded forward to meet her, and when she came in, contrary to our usual custom, we met her in silence. Looking at her with all our eyes, we knew not what to say to her, what to ask her. We stood before her a gloomy, silent crowd. She was visibly surprised at this unusual reception—and all at once we saw her grow pale, uneasy, fidget in her place, and inquire in a subdued voice:

"What's the matter with you?"

"And how about yourself?" the master-baker sullenly said, never taking his eyes off her.

"Myself? What do you mean?"

"Oh, nothing, nothing."

"Come, give me the biscuits!—quick!"

Never before had she been so sharp with us.

"You're in a hurry," said the baker, not moving and never taking his eyes from her face.

Then she suddenly turned round and disappeared through the door.

The baker caught up his shovel and, turning towards the stove, remarked quietly:

"It means—she's all ready for him. Ah, that soldier ... the scoundrel ... the skunk!"

We, like a flock of sheep, rubbing shoulders with each other, went to our table, sat down in silence, and wearily began to work. Presently, someone said: "Yet it is possible ...?"

"Well, well, what's the good of talking?" screeched the baker.

We all knew that he was a wise man, far wiser than we. And we understood his exclamation as a conviction of the victory of the soldier.... We felt miserable and uneasy.

At twelve o'clock—dinner-time—the soldier arrived. He was, as usual, spruce and genteel and—as he always did—looked us straight in the eyes. But we found it awkward to look at *him*.

"Well, my worthy gentlemen, if you like, I'll show you a bit of martial prowess," said he, laughing proudly. "Just you come out into the outhouse and look through the crevices—do you understand?"

Out we went, elbowing each other on the way, and glued our faces to the crevices in the boarded-up wall of the outhouse looking upon the court-yard. We had not long to wait. Very soon, at a rapid pace, and with a face full of anxiety, Tanya came tearing through the yard, springing over the puddles of stale snow and mud. Shortly afterwards, in not the least hurry and whistling as he went, appeared the soldier, making his way in the same direction as Tanya, evidently they had arranged a rendezvous. His arms were thrust deep down in his pockets, and his moustaches were moving up and down. . . . He also disappeared. . . . Then the rain came and we watched the raindrops falling into the puddles, and the puddles wrinkle beneath their impact. The day was damp and grey—a very weary-ing day. Snow still lay upon the roofs, and on the earth dark patches of mud were already appearing. And the snow on the roofs also got covered with dirty dark-brown smuts. The rain descended slowly with a melancholy sound. We found it cold and unpleasant to stand waiting there, but we were furious with Tanya for having deserted us, her worshippers, for the sake of a common soldier, and we waited for her with the grim delight of executioners.

After a while—we saw Tanya returning. Her eyes—yes, *her* eyes, actually sparkled with joy and happiness, and her lips—were smiling. And she was walking as if in a dream, rocking a little to and fro, with uncertain foot-steps. . . .

We could not endure this calmly. The whole lot of us suddenly burst through the door, rushed into the yard, and hissed and yelled at her with evil, bestial violence.

On perceiving us she trembled—and stood as if rooted in the mud beneath her feet. We surrounded her and, maliciously, without any cir-cumlocution, we reviled her to our hearts' content, and called her the most shameful things.

We did not raise our voices, we took our time about it. We saw that she had nowhere to go, that she was in the midst of us, and we might vent our rage upon her as much as we liked. I don't know why, but we did not beat her. She stood in the midst of us, and kept turning her head now hither, now thither, as she listened to our insults. And we—bespattered her, more and more violently, with the mud and the venom of our words.

The colour quitted her face, her blue eyes, a minute before so radiant with happiness, opened widely, her bosom heaved heavily, and her lips trembled.

And we, surrounding her, revenged ourselves upon her, for she had robbed us. She had belonged to us, we had expended our best upon her, and although that best was but a beggar's crumb, yet we were six-and-twenty and she was but one, therefore we could not devise torments worthy of her fault. How we did abuse her! She was silent all along—all along she looked at us with the wild eyes of a hunted beast, she was all of a tremble.

We ridiculed, we reviled, we baited her. . . . Other people came running up to us. . . . One of us pulled Tanya by the sleeve.

Suddenly her eyes gleamed, she leisurely raised her hands to her head and, tidying her hair, looked straight into our faces, and ejaculated loudly but calmly:

"Ugh! you miserable gaol-birds!"

And she walked straight up to us, unhesitatingly as if we were not standing there in front of her at all, as if we were not obstructing her way. And for that very reason not one of us was actually standing in her way when she came up to us.

And as she passed by, without so much as turning her face towards us, she added as loudly and as haughtily:

"Oh you riff-raff! you . . . you filth!"

And—away she went, erect, beautiful, haughty.

We remained standing in the yard, in the midst of the mud, beneath the pouring rain and the grey, sunless sky.

Presently we returned in silence to our grey, stony dungeon. As before, the sun never looked through our window to us, and—Tanya did not come again.

SUNSTROKE

Ivan Bunin

(1870–   )

TRANSLATED BY HELEN MATHESON

LEAVING the hot, brightly lighted dining saloon after dinner, they went on deck and stood near the rail. She closed her eyes, leant her cheek on the back of her hand, and laughed—a clear, charming laugh—everything about this little woman was charming.

"I am quite drunk," she said. "In fact I have gone mad. Where did you come from? Three hours ago I did not know of your existence. I don't even know where you got on the boat. Was it Samara? But it doesn't matter, you're a dear. Am I dizzy, or is the boat really turning round?"

In front of them lay darkness and the light of lamps. A soft wind blew strongly against their faces and carried the light to one side. With the smartness characteristic of the Volga boats, the steamer was making a wide curve towards the small wharf.

The lieutenant took her hand and raised it to his lips. The firm little fragrant hand was tanned. His heart became faint with fear and ecstasy as he thought how strong and bronzed must be the body under the light linen dress after having basked in the Southern sun on the hot beach for a whole month. (She had told him that she was on her way from Anapi.)

"Let's get off," he murmured.

"Where?" she asked in surprise.

"At this wharf."

"What for?"

He was silent. She raised her hand to her hot cheek again.

"You are mad."

"Let's get off," he repeated stubbornly. "I implore you——"

"Oh, do as you like," she said, turning from him.

With its final impetus, the steamer bumped gently against the dimly lit wharf, and they nearly fell over each other. The end of a rope flew over their heads, the boat heaved back, there was a foam of churning waters, the gangways clattered. The lieutenant rushed away to collect their things.

A moment later they passed through the sleepy ticket office into the ankle-deep sand of the road, and silently got into a dusty open cab. The soft, sandy road sloping gradually uphill, lit by crooked lamp-posts at long intervals on either side, seemed unending, but they reached its top and clattered along a high-road until they came to a sort of square with municipal buildings and a watch-tower. It was all full of warmth and the smells peculiar to a hot night in a small provincial town. The cab drew up at a lighted portico, behind the door of which a steep old wooden stairway was visible, and an old unshaven waiter, in a pink shirt and black coat, reluctantly took their luggage, and led the way in his down-at-heel slippers. They entered a large room stuffy from the hot sun which had beaten on it all day, its white curtains drawn. On the toilet table were two unlit candles.

The instant the door closed on the waiter, the lieutenant sprang towards her with such impetuosity, and they were carried away by a breathless kiss of such passion, that they remembered it for many, many years. Neither of them had ever before experienced anything like it.

At ten o'clock next morning the little, nameless woman left. She never told him her name, and referred to herself jokingly as "the fair stranger." It was a hot, sunny morning. Church bells were ringing, and a market was in full swing in the square in front of the hotel. There were scents of hay and tar and all the odours characteristic of a Russian provincial town.

They had not slept much, but when she emerged from behind the screen, where she had washed and dressed in five minutes, she was as fresh as a girl of seventeen. Was she embarrassed? Very little, if at all. She was as simple and gay as before, and—already rational. "No, no, dear," she said in reply to his request that they should continue the journey together. "No, you must wait for the next boat. If we go together, it will spoil it all. It would be very unpleasant for me. I give you my word of honour that I am not in the least what you may think I am. Nothing at all like this has ever happened to me before or will ever happen again. I seem to have been under a spell. Or, rather, we both seem to have had something like sunstroke."

The lieutenant readily agreed with her. In a bright, happy mood he drove her to the wharf—just before the pink steamer of the Samolet Line started. He kissed her openly on the deck, and had barely time to get ashore before the gangway was lowered. He returned to the hotel in the same care-free, easy mood. But something had changed. The room without her seemed quite different from what it had been with her. He was still full of her; he did not mind, but it was strange. The room still held the scent of her excellent English lavender water, her unfinished cup of tea still stood on the tray, but she was gone. . . . The lieutenant's heart was suddenly filled with such a rush of tenderness that he hurriedly lit a cigarette and began to pace the room, switching his top-boots with his cane.

"A strange adventure," he said aloud, laughing and feeling tears well up in his eyes. "'I give you my word of honour that I am not in the least what you think I am,' and she's gone. Absurd woman!"

The screen had been moved—the bed had not been made. He felt that he had not the strength to look at that bed. He put the screen in front of it, closed the window to shut out the creaking of the wheels and the noisy chatter of the market, drew the white billowing curtains, and sat down on the sofa. Yes, the roadside adventure was over. She was gone, and now, far away, she was probably sitting in the windowed saloon, or on deck, gazing at the enormous river glittering in the sun, at the barges drifting down-stream, at the yellow shoals, at the shining horizon of sky and water, at the immeasurable sweep of the Volga. And it was good-bye for ever and ever. For where could they possibly meet again? "For," he thought, "I can hardly appear on the scene without any excuse, in the town where she lives her everyday life with her husband, her three-year-old daughter and all her family."

The town seemed to him a special, a forbidden town. He was aggravated and stunned by the thought that she would live her lonely life there, often perhaps remembering him, recalling their brief encounter, that he would never see her again. No, it was impossible. It would be too mad, too un-natural, too fantastic. He suffered and was overwhelmed by horror and despair in feeling that without her his whole life would be futile. "Damn it all!" he thought, as he got up and began to pace the room again, trying not to look at the bed behind the screen. "What in the world's the matter with me? It's not the first time, is it? And yet—— Was there anything very special about her, or did anything very special happen? It really is like sun-stroke. And how on earth am I to spend a whole day in this hole without her?"

He still remembered all of her, down to the minutest detail: her sun-burn, her linen frock, her strong body, her unaffected, bright, gay voice. The sense of ecstatic joy which her feminine charm had given him was still extraordinarily strong, but now a second feeling rose uppermost in his mind—a new, strange, incomprehensible feeling, which had not been there while they had been together, and of which he would not, the day before, have believed himself capable when he had started what he had thought to be the amusement of a passing acquaintance. And now there was no one, no one, whom he could tell. "And the point is," he thought, "that I never shall be able to tell anyone! And how am I to get through this endless day with these memories, this inexplicable agony, in this god-forsaken town on the banks of that same Volga along which the steamer is carrying her away?" He must do something to save himself, something to distract him, he must go somewhere. He put on his hat with an air of determination, took his stick and walked along the corridor with his spurs jingling, ran down the stairs and out on to the porch. But where should he go? A cab was drawn up in front of the hotel. A young, smartly-dressed driver sat on the box calmly smoking a cigar. He was obviously waiting for someone. The lieutenant stared at him, bewildered and astonished: How could any-one sit calmly on a box and smoke and in general be unmoved and in-different? "I suppose that in the whole town there is no one so miserably unhappy as I am," he thought, as he went towards the market.

It was already breaking up. For some unknown reason he found himself making his way over fresh droppings, among carts, loads of cucumbers, stacks of pots and pans, and women seated on the ground who outdid each other in their efforts to attract his attention. They lifted basins and tapped them that he might hear how sound they were, while the men deafened him with cries of "First-class cucumbers, your honour." It was all so stupid, so ridiculous that he fled from the square. He went into the cathedral, where the choir was singing loudly, resolutely, as though conscious of fulfill-ing a duty; then he strolled aimlessly about a small, hot, unkempt garden on the edge of a cliff overhanging the silvery steel breadth of the river.

The epaulettes and buttons of his linen uniform were unbearably hot to the touch. The inside of his hat was wet, his face was burning. He returned to the hotel and was delighted to get into the large, empty, cool dining-room, delighted to take off his hat and seat himself at a small table near the open window. The heat penetrated from outside, but it was airy. He ordered iced soup.

Everything was all right in this unknown town, happiness and joy emanated from everything, from the heat and the market smells. Even this old provincial hotel seemed full of gladness, and yet his heart was being torn to pieces. He drank several glasses of vodka and ate a salted cucumber with parsley. He felt that he would unhesitatingly die to-morrow if, by some miracle, he could achieve her return and spend to-day, only this one day, with her, solely, solely in order that he might tell her and prove to her and convince her somehow of his agonising and exalted love for her. "Why prove? Why convince?" He did not know why, but it was more essential than life.

"My nerves have all gone to pieces," he said, pouring out his fifth glass of vodka. He drank the entire contents of the small decanter, hoping to stupefy, to benumb himself, hoping to get rid at last of this agonising and exalted feeling. But, instead, it increased. He pushed away the soup, ordered black coffee, and began to smoke and to think with intensity. What was he to do now, how was he to free himself from this sudden and unexpected love? To free himself—but he felt only too clearly that that was impossible. He rose abruptly, quickly, took his hat and his stick, asked the way to the post office and hurried off, the text of the telegram already composed in his mind: "Henceforth all my life, for all time till death, is yours, in your power." But on reaching the thick-walled old building which housed the post and telegraph, he stopped in dismay. He knew the name of her town, he knew that she had a husband and a child of three, but he knew neither her first name nor her surname. Last night, while they were dining at the hotel, he had asked her several times, and each time she had answered with a laugh: "Why do you want to know who I am? I am Marie Marevna, the mysterious princess of the fairy story; or the fair stranger; isn't that enough for you?"

At the corner of the street, near the post office, was a photographer's window. He stared for a long time at the portrait of an officer in braided epaulettes, with protruding eyes, a low forehead, unusually luxuriant whiskers, and a very broad chest entirely covered with orders. How mad, how ridiculous, how terrifyingly ordinary, everyday things appear when the heart is struck—yes, *struck*, he understood it now, by the "sunstroke" of a love too great, a joy too immense. He looked at the picture of a bridal couple—a young man in a frock-coat and white tie, with closely-cropped hair, very erect, arm-in-arm with a girl in white tulle. His gaze wandered to a pretty piquant girl wearing a student's cap on the back of her head.

Then, filled with envy of all these unknown people who were not suffering, he stared fixedly down the street. "Where shall I go? What shall I do?" The difficult, unanswerable questions occupied both mind and soul.

The street was completely empty. All the houses were alike middle-class, two-storied white houses with large gardens, but they were lifeless; the pavement was covered with thick white dust; it was all blinding, all bathed in hot, flaming, joyful sun which now somehow seemed futile. In the distance the street rose, humped and ran into the clear, cloudless, grey-mauve horizon. There was something southern about it; it reminded one of Sebastopol, Kertch—Anapi. This was more than he could bear. With eyes half closed and head bowed from the light, staring intently at the pavement, staggering, stumbling, catching one spur in the other, the lieutenant retraced his steps.

He returned to the hotel worn out with fatigue, as though he had done a long day's march in Turkestan or the Sahara. With a final effort he got to his large empty room. It had been "done." The last traces of her were gone except for one hairpin forgotten by her on the table. He took off his coat and looked at himself in the mirror. He saw reflected, skin bronzed and moustache bleached by the sun, the bluish whites of the eyes looking so much whiter on account of the tan, an ordinary enough officer's face, but now wild and excited. And about the whole figure standing there in the thin white shirt and stiff collar was something pathetically young and terribly unhappy. He lay down on the bed, on his back, resting his dusty boots on the footrail. The windows were open, the blinds were lowered. From time to time a slight wind billowed them out, letting in the heat, the smell of hot roofs and of all the radiant, but now empty, silent, deserted Volga country-side. He lay there, his hands under his head, and stared into space. In his mind he had a vague picture of the far-away south: sun and sea, Anapi. Then arose something fantastic, a town unlike any other town— the town in which she lived, which she had probably already reached. The thought of suicide stubbornly persisted. He closed his eyes and felt hot, smarting tears well up under his eyelids. Then at last he fell asleep, and when he woke he could see by the reddish-yellow light of the sun that it was evening. The wind had died down, the room was as hot and dry as an oven. Yesterday and this morning both seemed ten years ago. Unhurriedly he rose, unhurriedly he washed, drew up the blinds and rang for a samovar and his bill, and for a long time sat there drinking tea with lemon. Then he ordered a cab to be called and his things to be carried down. As he got into the cab with its faded red seat, he gave the waiter five roubles. "I believe I brought you here last night, your honour," said the driver gaily as he gathered up the reins.

By the time they reached the wharf, the Volga was roofed by the blue of the summer night. Multitudes of many-tinted lights were dotted along the river, and bright lamps shone from the masts of the ships.

"I got you here in the nick of time," said the cabdriver ingratiatingly.

The lieutenant gave five roubles to him also, took his ticket and went to the landing-place. Just as it had done yesterday, the boat bumped gently as it touched the wharf, there was the same slight dizziness from the unsteadiness underfoot, the end of a rope was thrown, there was a sound of foaming and rushing water under the paddles as the steamer backed a little.

The brightly lighted, crowded steamer, smelling of food, seemed unusually friendly and agreeable, and in a few minutes it was speeding
forward up the river, whither in the morning she had been carried.
The last glimmer of summer twilight gradually faded on the far horizon;
capriciously, lazily reflecting their varied hues in the river, making here
and there bright patches on the rippling surface under the dim dome of
blue, the gleaming lights everywhere sprinkled in the darkness seemed to
be swimming, swimming back.
Under an awning on deck sat the lieutenant. He felt older by ten years.

Alpes Maritimes, 1925.

CAPTAIN RIBNIKOV

Alexander Kuprin

(1870–1938)

TRANSLATED BY S. S. KOTELIANSKY AND J. MIDDLETON MURRY

O N THE VERY DAY when the awful disaster to the Russian fleet at Tsushima
was nearing its end, and the first vague and alarming reports of that bloody
triumph of the Japanese were being circulated over Europe, Staff-Captain
Ribnikov, who lived in an obscure alley in the Pieski quarter, received the
following telegram from Irkutsk: *Send lists immediately watch patient pay
debts.*

Staff-Captain Ribnikov immediately informed his landlady that he was
called away from Petersburg on business for a day or two, and told her not
to worry about his absence. Then he dressed himself, left the house, and
never returned to it again.

Only five days had passed when the landlady was summoned to the police
station to give evidence about her missing lodger. She was a tall woman of
forty-five, the honest widow of an ecclesiastical official, and in a simple and
straightforward manner she told all that she knew of him. Her lodger was
a quiet, poor, simple man, a moderate eater, and polite. He neither drank
nor smoked, rarely went out of the house, and had no visitors. She could
say nothing more, in spite of all her respectful terror of the inspector of
gendarmerie, who moved his luxurious moustaches in a terrifying way and
had a fine stock of abuse on hand.

During this five days' interval Staff-Captain Ribnikov ran or drove over the whole of Petersburg. Everywhere, in the streets, restaurants, theatres, tramcars, the railway stations, this dark lame little officer appeared. He was strangely talkative, untidy, not particularly sober, dressed in an infantry uniform, with an all-over red collar—a perfect type of the rat attached to military hospitals, or the commissariat, or the War Office. He also appeared more than once at the Staff Office, the Committee for the Care of the Wounded, at police stations, at the office of the Military Governor, at the Cossack headquarters, and at dozens of other offices, irritating the officials by his senseless grumbling and complaints, by his abject begging, his typical infantry rudeness, and his noisy patriotism. Already every one knew by heart that he had served in the Army Transport, had been wounded in the head at Liao-Yang, and touched in the leg in the retreat from Mukden. 'Why the devil hasn't he received a gratuity before now! Why haven't they given him his daily money and his travelling expenses! And his last two months pay! He is absolutely ready to give his last drop of blood—damn it all—for the Czar, the throne, and the country, and he will return to the Far East the moment his leg has healed. But the cursed leg won't heal—a hundred devils take it. Imagine only—gangrene! Look yourself——' and he put his wounded leg on a chair, and was already eagerly pulling up his trouser; but he was stopped every time by a squeamish and compassionate shyness. His bustling and nervous familiarity, his startled, frightened look, which bordered strangely on impertinence, his stupidity, his persistent and frivolous curiosity taxed to the utmost the patience of men occupied in important and terribly responsible scribbling.

In vain it was explained to him in the kindest possible way that he had come to the wrong place; that he ought to apply at such and such a place; that he must produce certain papers; that they will let him know the result. He understood nothing, absolutely nothing. But it was impossible to be very angry with him; he was so helpless, so easily scared and simple, and if any one lost patience and interrupted him, he only smiled and showed his gums with a foolish look, bowed hastily again and again, and rubbed his hands in confusion. Or he would suddenly say in a hoarse ingratiating tone: 'Couldn't you give me one small smoke? I'm dying to smoke. And I haven't a cent to buy them. "Blessed are the poor. . . . Poverty's no crime," as they say—but sheer indecency.'

With that he disarmed the most disagreeable and dour officials. He was given a cigarette, and allowed to sit by the extreme corner of the table. Unwillingly, and of course in an off-hand way, they would answer his importunate questions about what was happening at the war. But there was something very affecting and childishly sincere in the sickly curiosity with which this unfortunate, grubby, impoverished wounded officer of the line followed the war. Quite simply, out of mere humanity, they wanted to reassure, to inform, and encourage him; and therefore they spoke to him more frankly than to the rest.

His interest in everything which concerned Russo-Japanese events was so deep that while they were making some complicated inquiry for him he would wander from room to room, and table to table, and the moment he caught a couple of words about the war he would approach and listen with his habitual strained and silly smile.

When he finally went away, as well as a sense of relief he would leave a vague, heavy and disquieting regret behind him. Often well-groomed, dandified staff-officers referred to him with dignified acerbity:

'And that's a Russian officer! Look at that type. Well, it's pretty plain why we're losing battle after battle. Stupid, dull, without the least sense of his own dignity—poor old Russia!'

During these busy days Captain Ribnikov took a room in a dirty little hotel near the railway station.

Though he had with him a Reserve officer's proper passport, for some reason he found it necessary to declare that his papers were at present in the Military Governor's office. Into the hotel he took his things, a hold-all containing a rug and pillow, a travelling bag, and a cheap, new box, with some underclothing and a complete outfit of mufti.

Subsequently, the servants gave evidence that he used to come to the hotel late and as if a little the worse for drink, but always regularly gave the door porter twopence for a tip. He never used to sleep more than three or four hours, sometimes without undressing. He used to get up early and pace the room for hours. In the afternoon he would go off.

From time to time he sent telegrams to Irkutsk from various post offices, and all the telegrams expressed a deep concern for some one wounded and seriously ill, probably a person very dear to the captain's heart.

It was with this same curious busy, uncouth man that Vladimir Ivanovich Schavinsky, a journalist on a large Petersburg paper, once met.

II

Just before he went off to the races, Schavinsky dropped into the dingy little restaurant called 'The Glory of Petrograd,' where the reporters used to gather at two in the afternoon to exchange thoughts and information. The company was rough and ready, gay, cynical, omniscient, and hungry enough; and Schavinsky, who was to some degree an aristocrat of the newspaper world, naturally did not belong to it. His bright and amusing Sunday articles, which were not too deep, had a considerable success with the public. He made a great deal of money, dressed well, and had plenty of friends. But he was welcome at 'The Glory of Petrograd' as well, on account of his free sharp tongue and the affable generosity with which he lent his fellow-writers half-sovereigns. On this day the reporters had promised to procure a race-card for him, with mysterious annotations from the stable.

Vassily, the porter, took off Schavinsky's overcoat, with a friendly and respectful smile.

'If you please, Vladimir Ivanovich, company's all there. In the big saloon, where Prokhov waits.'

And Prokhov, stout, close-cropped, and red-moustached, also gave him a kindly and familiar smile, as usual not looking straight into the eyes of a respectable customer, but over his head.

'A long time since you've honoured us, Vladimir Ivanovich! This way, please. Everybody's here.'

As usual his fellow-writers sat round the long table hurriedly dipping their pens in the single inkpot and scribbling quickly on long slips of paper. At the same time, without interrupting their labours, they managed to swallow pies, fried sausages and mashed potatoes, vodka and beer, to smoke and exchange the latest news of the town and newspaper gossip that cannot be printed. Some one was sleeping like a log on the sofa with his face in a handkerchief. The air in the saloon was blue, thick and streaked with tobacco smoke.

As he greeted the reporters, Schavinsky noticed the captain, in his ordinary army uniform, among them. He was sitting with his legs apart, resting his hands and chin upon the hilt of a large sword. Schavinsky was not surprised at seeing him, as he had learned not to be surprised at anything in the reporting world. He had often seen lost for weeks in that reckless noisy company,—landowners from the provinces, jewellers, musicians, dancing-masters, actors, circus proprietors, fishmongers, café-chantant managers, gamblers from the clubs, and other members of the most unexpected professions.

When the officer's turn came, he rose, straightened his shoulders, stuck out his elbows, and introduced himself in the proper hoarse, drink-sodden voice of an officer of the line:

'H'm! . . . Captain Ribnikov. . . . Pleased to meet you. . . . You're a writer too? . . . Delighted. . . . I respect the writing fraternity. The press is the sixth great power. Eh, what?'

With that he grinned, clicked his heels together, shook Schavinsky's hand violently, bowing all the while in a particularly funny way, bending and straightening his body quickly.

'Where have I seen him before?' the uneasy thought flashed across Schavinsky's mind. 'He's wonderfully like some one. Who can it be?'

Here in the saloon were all the celebrities of the Petersburg reporting world. The Three Musketeers—Kodlubtzov, Riazhkin, and Popov—were never seen except in company. Even their names were so easily pronounced together that they made an iambic tetrameter. This did not prevent them from eternally quarrelling, and from inventing stories of incredible extortion, criminal forgery, slander, and blackmail about each other. There was present also Sergey Kondrashov, whose unrestrained voluptuousness had gained him the name of 'A Pathological Case, not a man'. There was also a man whose name had been effaced by time, like one side of a worn coin, to whom remained only the general nickname 'Matanya,' by which all Petersburg knew him. Concerning the dour-looking Svischov, who wrote paragraphs 'In the police courts,' they said jokingly: 'Svischov is an awful blackmailer—never takes less than three roubles.' The man asleep on the sofa was the long-haired poet Piestrukhin, who supported his fragile, drunken existence by writing lyrics in honour of the imperial birthdays and the twelve Church holidays. There were others besides of no less celebrity, experts in municipal affairs, fires, inquests, in the opening and closing of public gardens.

Said lanky, shock-headed, pimply Matanya: 'They'll bring you the card immediately, Vladimir Ivanovich. Meanwhile, I commend our brave captain to your attention. He has just returned from the Far East, where, I may say, he made mince-meat of the yellow-faced, squinting, wily enemy. . . . Now, General, fire away!'

The officer cleared his throat and spat sideways on the floor.

'Swine!' thought Schavinsky, frowning.

'My dear chap, the Russian soldier's not to be sneezed at!' Ribnikov bawled hoarsely, rattling his sword. '"Epic heroes!" as the immortal Suvorov said. Eh, what? In a word, . . . but I tell you frankly, our commanders in the East are absolutely worthless! You know the proverb: "Like master, like man." Eh, what? They thieve, play cards, have mistresses . . . and every one knows, where the devil can't manage himself he sends a woman.'

'You were talking about plans, General,' Matanya reminded him.

'Ah! Plans! Merci! . . . My head. . . . I've been on the booze all day.' Ribnikov threw a quick, sharp glance at Schavinsky. 'Yes, I was just saying. . . . They ordered a certain colonel of the general staff to make a recon-naissance, and he takes with him a squadron of Cossacks—dare-devils. Hell take 'em! . . . Eh, what? He sets off with an interpreter. Arrives at a vil-lage, "What's the name?" The interpreter says nothing. "At him, boys!" The Cossacks instantly use their whips. The interpreter says: "Butundu!" And "Butundu" is Chinese for "I don't understand." Ha-ha! He's opened his mouth—the son of a bitch! The colonel writes down "village, Butundu." They go further to another village. "What's the name?" "Butundu." "What! Butundu again?" "Butundu." Again the colonel enters it "village, Butundu." So he entered ten villages under the name of "Butundu," and turned into one of Tchekhov's types—"Though you are Ivanov the seventh," says he, "you're a fool all the same."'

'Oh, you know Tchekhov?' asked Schavinsky.

'Who? Tchekhov? Old Anton? You bet—damn him. . . . We're friends —we're often drunk together. . . . "Though you are the seventh," says he, "you're a fool all the same."'

'Did you meet him in the East?' asked Schavinsky quickly.

'Yes, exactly, in the East, Tchekhov and I, old man. . . . "Though you are the seventh——" '

While he spoke Schavinsky observed him closely. Everything in him agreed with the conventional army type: his voice, manner, shabby uniform, his coarse and threadbare speech. Schavinsky had had the chance of observing hundreds of such debauched captains. They had the same grin, the same 'Hell take 'em', twisted their moustaches to the left and right with the same bravado; they hunched their shoulders, stuck out their elbows, rested picturesquely on their sword and clanked imaginary spurs. But there was something individual about him as well, something different, as it were locked away, which Schavinsky had never seen, neither could he define it—some intense, inner, nervous force. The impression he had was this: Schavinsky would not have been at all surprised if this croaking and drunken soldier of fortune had suddenly begun to talk of subtle and intellectual matters, with ease and illumination, elegantly; neither would he have been surprised at some mad, sudden, frenzied, even bloody prank on the captain's part.

What struck Schavinsky chiefly in the captain's looks was the different impressions he made full face and in profile. Side face, he was a common Russian, faintly Kalmuck, with a small, protruding forehead under a pointed skull, a formless Russian nose, shaped like a plum, thin stiff black moustache and sparse beard, the grizzled hair cropped close, with a complexion burnt to a dark yellow by the sun. . . . But when he turned full face Schavinsky was immediately reminded of some one. There was something extraordinarily familiar about him, but this 'something' was impossible to grasp. He felt it in those narrow coffee-coloured bright eagle eyes, slit sideways; in the alarming curve of the black eyebrows, which sprang upwards from the bridge of the nose; in the healthy dryness of the skin strained over the huge cheekbones; and, above all, in the general expression of the face—malicious, sneering, intelligent, perhaps even haughty, but not human, like a wild beast rather, or, more truly, a face belonging to a creature of another planet.

'It's as if I'd seen him in a dream!' the thought flashed through Schavinsky's brain. While he looked at the face attentively he unconsciously screwed up his eyes, and bent his head sideways.

Ribnikov immediately turned round to him and began to giggle loudly and nervously.

'Why are you admiring me, Mr. Author? Interested? I!' He raised his voice and thumped his chest with a curious pride. 'I am Captain Ribnikov. Rib-ni-kov! An orthodox Russian warrior who slaughters the enemy, without number. That's a Russian soldier's song. Eh, what?'

Kodlubtzov, running his pen over the paper, said carelessly, without looking at Ribnikov, 'And without number, surrenders.'

Ribnikov threw a quick glance at Kodlubtzov, and Schavinsky noticed that strange yellow green fires flashed in his little brown eyes. But this lasted only an instant. The captain giggled, shrugged, and noisily smacked his thighs.

'You can't do anything; it's the will of the Lord. As the fable says, Set a thief to catch a thief. Eh, what?'

He suddenly turned to Schavinsky, tapped him lightly on the knee, and with his lips uttered a hopeless sound: 'Phwit! We do everything on the off-chance—higgledy-piggledy—anyhow! We can't adapt ourselves to the terrain; the shells never fit the guns; men in the firing line get nothing to eat for four days. And the Japanese—damn them—work like machines. Yellow monkeys—and civilisation is on their side. Damn them! Eh, what?'

'So you think they may win?' Schavinsky asked.

Again Ribnikov's lips twitched. Schavinsky had already managed to notice this habit of his. All through the conversation, especially when the captain asked a question and guardedly waited the answer, or nervously turned to face a fixed glance from some one, his lips would twitch suddenly, first on one side then on the other, and he would make strange grimaces, like convulsive malignant smiles. At the same time he would hastily lick his dry, cracked lips with the tip of his tongue—thin bluish lips like a monkey's or a goat's.

'Who knows?' said the captain. 'God only. . . . You can't set foot on your own doorstep without God's help, as the proverb goes. Eh, what? The campaign isn't over yet. Everything's still to come. The Russian's used to victory. Remember Poltava and the unforgettable Suvorov. . . . And Sebastopol! . . . And how we cleared out Napoleon, the greatest captain in the world, in 1812. Great is the God of Russia. What?'

As he began to talk the corners of his lips twitched into strange smiles, malignant, sneering, inhuman, and an ominous yellow gleam played in his eyes, beneath the black frowning eyebrows.

At that moment they brought Schavinsky coffee.

'Wouldn't you like a glass of cognac?' he asked the captain.

Ribnikov again tapped him lightly on the knee. 'No thanks, old man. I've drunk a frightful lot to-day, damn it. My noddle's fairly splitting. Damn it all, I've been pegging since the early morning. "Russia's joy's in the bottle!" Eh, what?' he cried suddenly, with an air of bravado and an unexpectedly drunken note in his voice.

'He's shamming,' Schavinsky instantly thought. But for some reason he did not want to leave off, and he went on treating the captain.

'What do you say to beer . . . red wine?'

'No thanks. I'm drunk already without that. Gran' merci.'

'Have some soda?'

The captain cheered up.

'Yes, yes, please. Soda, certainly. I could do with a glass.'

They brought a siphon. Ribnikov drank a glass in large greedy gulps.

Even his hands began to tremble with eagerness. He poured himself out another immediately. At once it could be seen that he had been suffering a long torment of thirst.

'He's shamming,' Schavinsky thought again. 'What an amazing man! Excited and tired, but not the least bit drunk.'

'It's hot—damn it,' Ribnikov said hoarsely. 'But I think, gentlemen, I'm interfering with your business.'

'No, it's all right. We're used to it,' said Riazhkin shortly.

'Haven't you any fresh news of the war?' Ribnikov asked. 'A-ah gentlemen,' he suddenly cried and banged his sword. 'What a lot of interesting copy I could give you about the war! If you like, I'll dictate, you need only write. You need only write. Just call it: Reminiscences of Captain Ribnikov, returned from the Front. No, don't imagine—I'll do it for nothing, free, gratis. What do you say to that, my dear authors?'

'Well it might be done,' came Matanya's lazy voice from somewhere. 'We'll manage a little interview for you somehow. Tell me, Vladimir Ivanovich, do you know anything of the Fleet?'

'No, nothing. . . . Is there any news?'

'There's an incredible story, Kondrashov heard from a friend on the Naval Staff. Hi! Pathological Case! Tell Schavinsky.'

The Pathological Case, a man with a black tragedy beard and a chewed-up face, spoke through his nose:

'I can't guarantee it, Vladimir Ivanovich. But the source seems reliable. There's a nasty rumour going about the Staff that the great part of our Fleet has surrendered without fighting—that the sailors tied up the officers and ran up the white flag—something like twenty ships.'

'That's really terrible,' said Schavinsky in a quiet voice. 'Perhaps it's not true, yet? Still—nowadays, the most impossible things are possible. By the way, do you know what's happening in the naval ports—in all the ships' crews there's a terrible underground ferment going on. The naval officers ashore are frightened to meet the men in their command.'

The conversation became general. This inquisitive, ubiquitous, cynical company was a sensitive receiver, unique of its kind, for every conceivable rumour and gossip of the town, which often reached the private saloon of 'The Glory of Petrograd' quicker than the minister's sanctum. Each one had his news. It was so interesting that even the Three Musketeers, who seemed to count nothing in the world sacred or important, began to talk with unusual fervour.

'There's a rumour going about that the reserves in the rear of the army refuse to obey orders. The soldiers are shooting the officers with their own revolvers.'

'I heard that the general in command hanged fifty sisters of mercy. Well, of course, they were only dressed as sisters of mercy.'

Schavinsky glanced round at Ribnikov. Now the talkative captain was silent. With his eyes screwed and his chest pressed upon the hilt of his sword, he was intently watching each of the speakers in turn. Under the tight-stretched skin of his cheekbones the sinews strongly played, and his lips moved as if he were repeating every word to himself.

'My God, whom does he remind me of?' the journalist thought impatiently for the tenth time. This so tormented him that he tried to make use of an old familiar trick . . . to pretend to himself that he had completely forgotten the captain, and then suddenly to give him a quick glance. Usually that trick soon helped him to recall the name or a meeting-place, but now it was quite ineffective.

Under his stubborn look, Ribnikov turned round again, gave a deep sigh and shook his head sadly.

'Awful news! Do you believe it? What? Even if it is true we need not despair. You know what we Russians say. "Whom God defends the pigs can't eat,"—that's to say, I mean that the pigs are the Japanese, of course.'

He held out stubbornly against Schavinsky's steady look, and in his yellow animal eyes the journalist noticed a flame of implacable inhuman hatred.

Piestrukhin, the poet asleep on the sofa, suddenly got up, smacked his lips, and stared at the officer with dazed eyes.

'Ah! . . . you're still here, Jap mug,' he said drunkenly, hardly moving his mouth. 'You just get out of it!'

And he collapsed on the sofa again, turning on to his other side.

'Japanese!' Schavinsky thought with anxious curiosity. 'That's what he's like,' and drawled meaningly: 'You are a jewel, Captain!'

'I?' the latter cried out. His eyes lost their fire, but his lips still twitched nervously. 'I am Captain Ribnikov!' He banged himself on the chest again with curious pride. 'My Russian heart bleeds. Allow me to shake your hand. My head was grazed at Liao-Yang, and I was wounded in the leg at Mukden. You don't believe it? I'll show you now.'

He put his foot on a chair and began to pull up his trousers.

'Don't! . . . stop! we believe you,' Schavinsky said with a frown. Nevertheless, his habitual curiosity enabled him to steal a glance at Ribnikov's leg and to notice that this infantry captain's underclothing was of expensive spun silk.

A messenger came into the saloon with a letter for Matanya.

'That's for you, Vladimir Ivanovich,' said Matanya, when he had torn the envelope. 'The race-card from the stable. Put one on Zenith both ways for me. I'll pay you on Tuesday.'

'Come to the races with me, Captain?' said Schavinsky.

'Where? To the races? With pleasure.' Ribnikov got up noisily, upsetting his chair. 'Where the horses jump? Captain Ribnikov at your service. Into battle, on the march, to the devil's dam! Ha, ha, ha! That's me! Eh, what?'

When they were sitting in the cab, driving through Cabinetsky Street, Schavinsky slipped his arm through the officer's, bent right down to his ear, and said, in a voice hardly audible:

'Don't be afraid. I shan't betray you. You're as much Ribnikov as I am Vanderbilt. You're an officer on the Japanese Staff. I think you're a colonel at least, and now you're a military agent in Russia. . . .'

Either Ribnikov did not hear the words for the noise of the wheels or he did not understand. Swaying gently from side to side, he spoke hoarsely with a fresh drunken enthusiasm:

'We're fairly on the spree now! Damn it all, I adore it. I'm not Captain Ribnikov, a Russian soldier, if I don't love Russian writers! A magnificent lot of fellows! They drink like fishes, and know all about life. "Russia's joy is in the bottle." And I've been at it from the morning, old man!'

III

By business and disposition Schavinsky was a collector of human documents, of rare and strange manifestations of the human spirit. Often for weeks, sometimes for months together, he watched an interesting type, tracking him down with the persistence of a passionate sportsman or an eager detective. It would happen that the prize was found to be, as he called it, 'a knight of the black star'—a sharper, a notorious plagiarist, a pimp, a souteneur, a literary maniac, the terror of every editor, a plunging cashier or bank messenger, who spends public money in restaurants and gambling hells with the madness of a man rushing down the steep; but no less the objects of his sporting passion were the lions of the season—pianists, singers, littérateurs, gamblers with amazing luck, jockeys, athletes, and cocottes coming into vogue. By hook or crook Schavinsky made their acquaintance and then, enveloping them in his spider's toils, tenderly and gently secured his victim's attention. Then he was ready for anything. He would sit for whole sleepless nights with vulgar, stupid people, whose mental equipment, like the Hottentots', consisted of a dozen or two animal conceptions and clichés; he stood drinks and dinners to damnable fools and scoundrels, waiting patiently for the moment when in their drunkenness they would reveal the full flower of their villainy. He flattered them to the top of their bent, with his eyes open; gave them monstrous doses of flattery, firmly convinced that flattery is the key to open every lock; he lent them money generously, knowing well that he would never receive it back again. In justification of this precarious sport he could say that the inner psychological interest for him considerably surpassed the benefits he subsequently acquired as a realistic writer. It gave him a subtle and obscure delight to penetrate into the mysterious inaccessible chambers of the human soul, to observe the hidden springs of external acts, springs sometimes petty, sometimes shameful, more often ridiculous than affecting—as it were, to hold in his hand for a while, a live, warm human heart and touch its very pulse. Often in this inquisitive pursuit it seemed to him that he was completely losing his own 'ego,' so much did he begin to think and feel with another's soul, even speaking in his language with his peculiar words until at last he even caught himself using another's gesture and tone. But when he had saturated himself in a man he threw him aside. It is true that sometimes he had to pay long and heavily for a moment's infatuation.

But no one for a long time had so deeply interested him, even to agitation, as this hoarse, tippling infantry captain. For a whole day Schavinsky did not let him go. He sat by the table and looked into Ribnikov's very pupils.

'Listen, Captain. No one can hear us now. . . . What's the strongest oath I can give you that no one will ever hear of our conversation? . . . I am convinced, absolutely and beyond all doubt, that you're a Japanese.'

'I am Capt——'

'No, no. Let's have done with these tricks. You can't hide your face, however clever you are. The line of your cheekbones, the cut of your eyes, your peculiar head, the colour of your skin, the stiff, straggling growth on your face—everything points beyond all shadow of doubt to you belonging to the yellow race. But you're safe. I shan't tell on you, whatever offers they make me, however they threaten me for silence. I shan't do you any harm, if it's only because I'm full of admiration for your amazing courage. I say more—I'm full of reverence, terror if you like. I'm a writer—that's a man of fancy and imagination. I can't even imagine how it's possible for a man to make up his mind to it: to come thousands of miles from your country to a city full of enemies that hate you, risking your life every second— you'll be hanged without a trial if you're caught, I suppose you know? And then to go walking about in an officer's uniform, to enter every possible kind of company, and hold the most dangerous conversations. The least mistake, one slip will ruin you in a second. Half an hour ago you used the word "holograph" instead of "manuscript." A trifle, but very characteristic. An army captain would never use this word of a modern manuscript, but only of an archive or a very solemn document. He wouldn't even say "manuscript," but just a "book"—but these are trifles. But the one thing I don't understand is the incessant strain of the mind and will, the diabolical waste of spiritual strength. To forget to think in Japanese, to forget your name utterly, to identify yourself completely with another's personality—no, this is surely greater than any heroism they told us of in school. My dear man, don't try to play with me. I swear I'm not your enemy.'

He said all this quite sincerely, for his whole being was stirred to flame by the heroic picture of his imagination. But the captain would not let himself be flattered. He listened to him, and stared with eyes slightly closed at his glass, which he quietly moved over the tablecloth, and the corners of his blue lips twisted nervously. And in his face Schavinsky recognised the same hidden mockery, the same deep, stubborn, implacable hatred, the peculiar hatred that a European can perhaps never understand, felt by a wise, cultured, civilised beast, made man, for a being of another species.

'Keep your kindness in your pocket,' replied Ribnikov carelessly. 'Let it go to hell. They teased me in the regiment too with being a Jap. Chuck it! I'm Captain Ribnikov. You know there's a Russian proverb, "The face of a beast with the soul of a man." I'll just tell you there was once a case in our regiment——'

'What was your regiment?' Schavinsky asked suddenly.

But the captain seemed not to have heard. He began to tell the old threadbare dirty stories that are told in camp, on manœuvres, and in barracks, and in spite of himself Schavinsky began to feel insulted. Once during the evening as they sat in the cab Schavinsky put his arm round his waist, and drew him close and said in a low voice:

'Captain . . . no, Colonel, at least, or you would never have been given such a serious mission. Let's say Colonel, then. I do homage to your daring, that is to the boundless courage of the Japanese nation. Sometimes when I read or think of individual cases of your diabolical bravery and contempt of death, I tremble with ecstasy. What immortal beauty, what divine courage there is, for instance, in the action of the captain of the shattered warship who answered the call to surrender by quietly lighting a cigarette, and went to the bottom with a cigarette in his lips! What titanic strength, what thrilling contempt for the enemy! And the naval cadets on the fire-ships who went to certain death, delighted as though they were going to a ball! And do you remember how a lieutenant, all by himself, towed a torpedo in a boat at night to make an end of the mole at Port Arthur? The searchlights were turned on and all there remained of the lieutenant and his boat was a bloody stain on the concrete wall. But the next day all the midshipmen and lieutenants of the Japanese Fleet overwhelmed Admiral Togo with applications, offering to repeat the exploit. What amazing heroes! But still more magnificent is Togo's order that the officers under him should not so madly risk their lives, which belong to their country and not to them. It's damnably beautiful, though!'

'What's this street we're in?' interrupted Ribnikov, yawning. 'After the dug-outs in Manchuria I've completely lost my sense of direction in the street. When we were in Kharbin . . .'

'Do you remember the case of an officer who was taken prisoner and battered his head to pieces on a stone? But the most wonderful thing is the signatures of the Samurai. Of course you've never heard of it, Captain Ribnikov?' Schavinsky asked with sarcastic emphasis. 'It's understood, you haven't heard of it. . . . You see General Nogi asked for volunteers to march in the leading column in a night attack on the Port Arthur forts. Nearly the whole brigade offered themselves for this honourable death.

Since there were too many and they pressed in front of each other for the opportunity of death, they had to make application in writing, and some of them, according to an old custom, cut off the first finger of their left hand and fixed it to their signature for a seal of blood. That's what the Samurai did!'

'Samurai,' Ribnikov dully repeated. There was a noise in his throat as if something had snapped and spread. Schavinsky gave a quick glance to his profile. An expression such as he had never seen in the captain's face before suddenly played about his mouth and on his chin, which trembled once; and his eyes began to shine with the warm, tremulous light which gleams through sudden, brimming tears. But he pulled himself together instantly, shut his eyes for a second, and turned a naïve and stupid face to Schavinsky, and suddenly uttered a long, filthy, Russian oath.

'Captain, Captain, what's the matter with you?' Schavinsky cried, almost in fright.

'That's all newspaper lies,' Ribnikov said unconcernedly. 'Our Russian Tommy is not a bit behind. There's a difference, of course. They fight for their life, however,—independence—and what have we mixed ourselves up in it for? Nobody knows! The devil alone knows why. "There was no sorrow till the devil pumped it up," as we say in Russian. What! Ha, ha!'

On the race-course the sport distracted Schavinsky's attention a little, and he could not observe the captain all the while. But in the intervals between the events, he saw him every now and then in one or another of the stands, upstairs or downstairs, in the buffet or by the pari-mutuel. That day the word Tsuchima was on everybody's lips—backers, jockeys, book-makers, even the mysterious, ragged beings that are inevitable on every race-course. The word was used to jeer at a beaten horse, by men who were annoyed at losing, with indifferent laughter and with bitterness. Here and there it was uttered with passion. Schavinsky saw from a distance how the captain in his easy, confident way picked a quarrel with one man, shook hands with others, and tapped others on the shoulder. His small, limping figure appeared and disappeared everywhere.

From the races they drove to a restaurant, and from there to Schavinsky's house. The journalist was rather ashamed of his role of voluntary detective; but he felt it was out of his power to throw it up, though he had already begun to feel tired, and his head ached with the strain of this stealthy struggle with another man's soul. Convinced that flattery had been of no avail, he now tried to draw the captain to frankness, by teasing and rousing his feelings of patriotism.

'Still, I'm sorry for these poor Japs,' he said with ironical pity. 'When all is said, Japan has exhausted all her national genius in this war. In my opinion she's like a feeble little man who lifts a half dozen hundredweight on his shoulders, either in ecstasy or intoxication, or out of mere bravado, and strains his insides, and is already beginning to die a lingering death.

You see Russia's an entirely different country. She's a Colossus. To her the Manchurian defeats are just the same as cupping a full-blooded man. You'll see how she will recover and begin to blossom when the war is over. But Japan will wither and die. She's strained herself. Don't tell me they have civilisation, universal education, European technique: at the end of it all, a Japanese is an Asiatic, half-man, half-monkey. Even in type he approaches a Bushman, a Touareg, or a Blackfellow. You have only to look at his facial angle. It all comes to this, they're just Japs! It wasn't your civilisation or your political youth that conquered us at all, but simply a fit of madness. Do you know what a seizure is, a fit of frenzy? A feeble woman tears chains to pieces and tosses strong men about like straws. The next day she hasn't even the power to lift her hand. It's the same with Japan. Believe me, after the heroic fit will follow impotence and decay; but certainly before that she will pass through a stage of national swagger, outrageous militarism and insane Chauvinism.'

'Really?' cried Ribnikov in stupid rapture. 'You can't get away from the truth. Shake hands, Mr. Author. You can always tell a clever man at once.'

He laughed hoarsely, spat about, tapped Schavinsky's knee, and shook his hand, and Schavinsky suddenly felt ashamed of himself and the tricks of his stealthy searching into human souls.

'What if I'm mistaken and this Ribnikov is only the truest type of the drunken infantry-man. No, it's impossible. But if it is possible, then what a fool I'm making of myself, my God!'

At his house he showed the captain his library, his rare engravings, a collection of old china, and a couple of small Siberian dogs. His wife, who played small parts in musical comedy, was out of town. Ribnikov examined everything with a polite, uninterested curiosity, in which his host caught something like boredom, and even cold contempt. Ribnikov casually opened a magazine and read some lines aloud.

'He's made a blunder now,' Schavinsky thought, when he heard his extraordinary correct and wooden reading, each separate letter pronounced with exaggerated precision like the head boy in a French class showing off. Evidently Ribnikov noticed it himself, for he soon shut the book and asked:

'But you're a writer yourself?'

'Yes. . . . I do a bit.'

'What newspapers do you write for?'

Schavinsky named them. It was the sixth time he had been asked that question that day.

'Oh, yes, yes, yes. I forgot, I've asked you before. D'you know what, Mr. Author?'

'What is it?'

'Let us do this. You write and I'll dictate. That is, I won't dictate . . . oh, no, I shall never dare.' Ribnikov rubbed his hands and bowed hurriedly. 'You'll compose it yourself, of course. I'll only give you some thoughts and—what shall I call them—reminiscences of the war? Oh, what a lot of interesting copy I have! . . .'

Schavinsky sat sideways on the table and glanced at the captain cunningly screwing up one eye.

'Of course, I shall give your name?'

'Why, you may. I've no objection. Put it like this: "This information was supplied to me by Captain Ribnikov who has just returned from the Front."'

'Very well. Why do you want this?'

'What?'

'Having your name in it. Do you want it for future evidence that you inspired the Russian newspapers? What a clever fellow I am, eh?'

But the captain avoided a direct answer, as usual.

'But perhaps you haven't time? You are engaged in other work. Well, let the reminiscences go to hell! You won't be able to tell the whole story. As they say: "There's a difference between living a life and crossing a field." Eh, what? Ha, ha, ha!'

An interesting fancy came into Schavinsky's head. In his study stood a big, white table of unpainted ash. On the clean virgin surface of this table all Schavinsky's friends used to leave their autographs in the shape of aphorisms, verses, drawings, and even notes of music. He said to Ribnikov: 'See, here is my autograph-book, Captain. Won't you write me something in memory of your pleasant meeting, and our acquaintance which'—Schavinsky bowed politely—'I venture to hope will not be short-lived?'

'With pleasure,' Ribnikov readily agreed. 'Something from Pushkin or Gogol?'

'No . . . far better something of your own.'

'Of my own? Splendid.'

He took the pen and dipped it, thought and prepared to write, but Schavinsky suddenly stopped him.

'We'd better do this. Here's a piece of paper. There are drawing-pins in the box at the corner. Please write something particularly interesting and then cover it with the paper and fasten the corners with the drawing-pins. I give you my word of honour as an author, that for two months I won't put a finger on the paper and won't look at what you've written. Is that all right? Well, write then. I'll go out of the room so as not to hinder you.'

After five minutes Ribnikov shouted to him: 'Please come in.'

'Ready?' Schavinsky asked, entering.

Ribnikov drew himself up, put his hand to his forehead in salute and shouted like a soldier: 'Very good, sir.'

'Thanks. Now we'll go to the "Buff," or somewhere else,' Schavinsky said. 'There we'll think what we'll do next. I shan't let you out of my sight to-day, Captain.'

'With the greatest pleasure,' Ribnikov said in a hoarse bass, clicking his heels. He lifted up his shoulders and gave a military twist to his moustaches on either side.

But Schavinsky, against his own will, did not keep his word. At the last moment before leaving his house the journalist remembered that he had left his cigarette-case in the study and went back for it, leaving Ribnikov in the hall. The piece of white paper, carefully fastened with drawing-pins, aroused his curiosity. He could not resist his temptation; he turned back stealthily and after lifting a corner of the paper quickly read the words written in a thin, distinct and extraordinary elegant hand: 'Though you are Ivanov the seventh, you're a fool all the same.'

IV

Long after midnight they were coming out of a suburban café-chantant accompanied by the well-known musical comedy actor Zhenin-Lirsky, the young assistant Crown-Prosecutor Sashka Strahlmann, who was famous all over Petersburg for his incomparable skill in telling amusing stories about the topic of the day, and Karyukov, the merchant's son, a patron of the arts.

It was neither bright nor dark. It was a warm, white, transparent night. with soft *chatoyant* colours and water like mother-of-pearl in the calm canals, which plainly reflected the grey stone of the quay and the motionless foliage of the trees. The sky was pale as though tired and sleepless, and there were sleepy clouds in the sky, long, thin and woolly like clews of ravelled cotton-wool.

'Where shall we go, now?' said Schavinsky, stopping at the gate of the gardens. 'Field-Marshal Oyama! Give us your enlightened opinion.'

All five lingered on the pavement for a while, caught by a moment of the usual early morning indecision, when the physical fatigue of the reveller struggles with the irresistible and irritating yearning after new and piquant sensations. From the garden continually came patrons, laughing, whistling, noisily shuffling their feet over the dry, white cobble-stones. Walking hurriedly, boldly rustling the silk of their petticoats emerged the artistes wearing huge hats, with diamonds trembling in their ears, escorted by dashing gentlemen, smartly dressed, with flowers in their buttonholes. With the porter's respectful assistance these ladies fluttered into carriages and panting automobiles, freely arranging their dresses round their legs, and flew away holding the brims of their hats in their hands. The chorus-girls and the *filles du jardin* of the higher class drove off alone or two together in ordinary cabs with a man beside them. The ordinary women of the street appeared everywhere at once, going round the wooden fence, following close on the men who left on foot, giving special attention to the drunken. They ran beside the men for a long while, offering themselves in a whisper with impudent submissiveness, naming that which was their profession with blunt, coarse, terrible words. In the bright, white twilight of May, their faces seemed like coarse masks, blue from the white of their complexions, red with crimson colour, and one's eyes were struck with the blackness, the thickness and the extraordinary curve of their eyebrows. These naïvely bright colours made the yellow of their wrinkled temples appear all the more pitiable, their thin, scraggy necks, and flabby, feeble chins. A couple of mounted policemen, obscenely swearing, rode them down now and then with their horses' mouths afoam. The girls screamed, ran away, and clutched at the sleeves of the passers-by. Near the railing of the canal was gathered a group of about twenty men—it was the usual early morning scandal. A short, beardless boy of an officer was dead-drunk and making a fuss, looking as though he wanted to draw his sword; a policeman was assuring him of something in an unconvincing falsetto with his hand on his heart.

A sharp, suspicious-looking type, drunk, in a cap with a ragged peak, spoke in a sugary, obsequious voice: 'Spit on 'em, yer honour. They ain't worth looking at. Give me one in the jaw, if you like. Allow me to kiss yer 'and.'

A thin, stern gentleman at the back, whose thick, black whiskers could alone be seen, because his bowler was tilted over his face, drawled in a low, indistinct voice: 'What do you stand about talking for? Pitch him into the water and have done with it!'

'But really, Major Fukeshima,' said the actor, 'we must put a decent finish to the day of our pleasant acquaintance. Let's go off with the little ladies. Where shall it be, Sashka?'

'Bertha?' Strahlmann asked in reply.

Ribnikov giggled and rubbed his hands in joyful agitation.

'Women? "Even a Jew hanged himself for company's sake," as the Russian proverb says. Where the world goes there go we. Eh, what? "If we're going, let's go," as the parrot said. What? Ha, ha, ha!'

Schavinsky had introduced him to the young men, and they had all had supper in the café-chantant, listened to the Roumanian singers, drinking champagne and liqueurs. At one time they found it amusing to call Ribnikov by the names of different Japanese generals, particularly because the captain's good nature was evidently unlimited. Schavinsky it was who began this rude, familiar game. True he felt at times that he was behaving in an ugly, perhaps even treacherous, way to Ribnikov, but he calmed his conscience by the fact that he had not breathed a word of his suspicions, which never entered his friends' heads at all.

At the beginning of the evening he was watching Ribnikov. The captain was noisier and more talkative than anybody: he was incessantly drinking healths, jumping up, sitting down, pouring the wine over the tablecloth, lighting his cigarette the wrong end. Nevertheless, Schavinsky noticed that he was drinking very little.

Ribnikov had to sit next the journalist again in the cab. Schavinsky was almost sober. He was generally distinguished for a hard head in a spree, but it was light and noisy now, as though the foam of the champagne was bubbling in it. He gave the captain a side-glance. In the uncertain, drowsy light of the white night Ribnikov's face wore a dark, earthy complexion. All the hollows were sharp and black, the little wrinkles on his forehead and the lines round his nose and mouth were deepened. The captain himself sat with a weary stoop, his hands tucked into the sleeves of his uniform, breathing heavily through his open mouth. Altogether it gave him a worn, suffering look. Schavinsky could even smell his breath, and thought that gamblers after several nights at cards have just the same stale, sour breath as men tired out with insomnia or the strain of long brain work. A wave of kindly emotion and pity welled up in Schavinsky's heart. The captain suddenly appeared to him very small, utterly worn out, affecting and pitiable. He embraced Ribnikov, drew him close, and said affably: 'Very well, Captain, I surrender. I can't do anything with you, and I apologise if I've given you some uncomfortable minutes. Give me your hand.'

He unfastened the rose he wore in his coat which a girl in the garden had made him buy, and fixed it in the buttonhole of the captain's great-coat.

'This is my peace-offering, Captain. We won't tease each other any more.'

The cab drew up at a two-storied stone house standing apart in a pleasant approach. All the windows were shuttered. The others had gone in advance and were waiting for them. A square grille, a handsbreadth wide, set in the heavy door, was opened from inside, and a pair of cold searching grey eyes appeared in it for a few seconds. Then the door was opened.

This establishment was something between an expensive brothel and a luxurious club. There was an elegant entrance, a stuffed bear in the hall, carpets, silk curtains and lustre-chandeliers, and lackeys in evening dress and white gloves. Men came here to finish the night after the restaurants were shut. Cards were played, expensive wines kept, and there was always a generous supply of fresh, pretty women who were often changed.

They had to go up to the first floor, where was a wide landing adorned by palms in tubs and separated from the stairs by a balustrade. Schavinsky went upstairs arm-in-arm with Ribnikov. Though he had promised himself that he would not tease him any more, he could not restrain himself: 'Let's mount the scaffold, Captain!'

'I'm not afraid,' said he lazily. 'I walk up to death every day of my life.'

Ribnikov waved his hand feebly and smiled with constraint. The smile made his face suddenly weary, grey and old.

Schavinsky gave him a look of silent surprise. He was ashamed of his importunity. But Ribnikov passed it off immediately.

'Yes to death. . . . A soldier's always ready for it. There's nothing to be done. Death is the trifling inconvenience attached to our profession.'

Schavinsky and Karyukov the art-patron were assiduous guests and honoured habitués of the house. They were greeted with pleasant smiles and low bows.

A big, warm cabinet was given them, in red and gold with a thick, bright green carpet on the floor, with sconces in the corners and on the table. They were brought champagne, fruit and bonbons. Women came—three at first, then two more—then they were passing in and out continually. Without exception they were pretty, well provided with bare, white arms, neck, bosom, in bright, expensive, glittering dresses. Some wore ballet skirts; one was in a schoolgirl's brown uniform, another in tight riding-breeches and a jockey's cap. A stout elderly lady in black also came, rather like a landlady or a housekeeper. Her appearance was decent; her face flabby and yellow. She laughed continually the pleasant laugh of an elderly woman, coughed continually and smoked incessantly. She behaved to Schavinsky, the actor, and the art-patron with the unconstrained coquetry of a lady old enough to be their mother, flicking their hands with her handkerchief, and she called Strahlmann, who was evidently her favourite, Sashka.

'General Kuroki, let's drink to the success of the grand Manchurian army. You'll be getting mildewy, sitting in your corner,' said Karyukov.

Schavinsky interrupted him with a yawn: 'Steady, gentlemen. I think you ought to be bored with it by now. You're just abusing the captain's good nature.'

'I'm not offended,' replied Ribnikov. 'Gentlemen! Let us drink the health of our charming ladies.'

'Sing us something, Lirsky!' Schavinsky asked.

The actor cheerfully sat down to the piano and began a gipsy song. It was more recitation than singing. He never moved the cigar from his lips, stared at the ceiling, with a parade of swinging to and fro on his chair. The women joined in, loud and out of tune. Each one tried to race the others with the words. Then Sashka Strahlmann gave an admirable imitation of a gramophone, impersonated an Italian opera, and mimicked animals. Karyukov danced a fandango and called for bottle after bottle.

He was the first to disappear from the room, with a red-haired Polish girl. After him followed Strahlmann and the actor. Only Schavinsky remained, with a swarthy, white-toothed Hungarian girl on his knees, and Ribnikov, by the side of a tall blonde in a blue satin blouse, cut square and open half-way down her breast.

'Well, Captain, let's say goodbye for a little while,' said Schavinsky, getting up and stretching himself. 'It's late—we'd better say early. Come and have breakfast with me at one o'clock, Captain. Put the wine down to Karyukov, Madame. If he loves sacred art, then he can pay for the honour of having supper with its priests. *Mes compliments!*'

The blonde put her bare arm round the captain's neck and kissed him, and said simply: 'Let us go too, darling. It really is late.'

V

She had a little gay room with a bright blue paper, a pale blue hanging lamp. On the toilet-table stood a round mirror in a frame of light blue satin. There were two oleographs on one wall, 'Girls Bathing' and 'The Royal Bridegroom,' on the other a hanging, with a wide brass bed alongside.

The woman undressed, and with a sense of pleasant relief passed her hands over her body, where her chemise had been folded under her corset. Then she turned the lamp down and sat on the bed, and began calmly to unlace her boots.

Ribnikov sat by the table with his elbows apart and his head resting in his hands. He could not tear his eyes from her big, handsome legs and plump calves, which her black, transparent stockings so closely fitted.

'Why don't you undress, officer?' the woman asked. 'Tell me, darling, why do they call you Japanese General?'

Ribnikov gave a laugh, with his eyes still fixed upon her legs.

'Oh, it's just nonsense. Only a joke. Do you know the verses:

"It hardly can be called a sin,
    If something's funny and you grin! . . ."'

'Will you stand me some champagne, darling. . . . Since you're so stingy, oranges will do. Are you going soon or staying the night?'

'Staying the night. Come to me.'

She lay down with him, hastily threw her cigarette over on to the floor and wriggled beneath the blanket.

'Do you like to be next to the wall?' she asked. 'Do if you want to. O-oh, how cold your legs are! You know I love army men. What's your name?'

'Mine?' He coughed and answered in an uncertain tone: 'I am Captain Ribnikov. Vassily Alexandrovich Ribnikov!'

'Ah, Vasya! I have a friend called Vasya, a little chap from the Lycée. Oh, what a darling he is!'

She began to sing, pretending to shiver under the bedclothes, laughing and half-closing her eyes:

"Vasya, Vasya, Vasinke,
    It's a tale you're telling me."

'You *are* like a Japanese, you know, by Jove. Do you know who? The Mikado. We take in the *Niva* and there's a picture of him there. It's late now—else I'd get it to show you. You're as like as two peas.'

'I'm very glad,' said Ribnikov, quietly kissing her smooth, round shoulder.

'Perhaps you're really a Japanese? They say you've been at the war. Is it true? O-oh, darling, I'm afraid of being tickled. Is it dreadful at the war?'

'Dreadful . . . no, not particularly. . . . Don't let's talk about it,' he said wearily. 'What's your name?'

'Clotilde. . . . No, I'll tell you a secret. My name's Nastya. They only called me Clotilde here because my name's so ugly. Nastya, Nastasya—sounds like a cook.'

'Nastya,' he repeated musingly, and cautiously kissed her breast. 'No, it's a nice name. Na-stya,' he repeated slowly.

'What is there nice about it? Malvina, Wanda, Zhenia, they're nice names —especially Irma. . . . Oh, darling,' and she pressed close to him. 'You are a dear . . . so dark. I love dark men. You're married surely?'

'No, I'm not.'

'Oh, tell us another. Every one here says he's a bachelor. You've got six children for sure!'

It was dark in the room, for the windows were shuttered and the lamp hardly burned. Her face was quite close to his head, and showed fantastic and changing on the dim whiteness of the pillow. Already it was different from the simple, handsome, round grey-eyed, Russian face of before. It seemed to have grown thinner, and strangely changing its expression every minute, seemed now tender, kind, mysterious. It reminded Ribnikov of some one infinitely familiar, long beloved, beautiful and fascinating.

'How beautiful you are!' he murmured. 'I love you. . . . I love you!'

He suddenly uttered an unintelligible word, completely foreign to the woman's ear.

'What did you say?' she asked in surprise.

'Nothing. . . . Nothing. . . . Nothing at all. . . . My dear! Dear woman . . . you are a woman. . . . I love you. . . .'

He kissed her arms, her neck, trembling with impatience, which it gave him wonderful delight to suppress. He was possessed by a tender and tempestuous passion for the well-fed, childless woman, for her big young body, so cared for and beautiful. His longing for woman had been till now suppressed by his austere, ascetic life, his constant weariness, by the intense exertion of his mind and will: now it devoured him suddenly with an intolerable, intoxicating flame.

'Your hands are cold,' she said, awkward and shy. In this man was something strange and alarming which she could in no way understand. 'Cold hands and a warm heart.'

'Yes, yes, yes. . . . My heart,' he repeated it like a madman, 'My heart is warm, my heart. . . .'

Long ago she had grown used to the outward rites and the shameful details of love; she performed them several times every day—mechanically, indifferently, and often with silent disgust. Hundreds of men, from the aged and old, who put their teeth in a glass of water for the night, to youngsters whose voice was only beginning to break and was bass and soprano at once, civilians, army men, priests in mufti, baldheads and men overgrown with hair from head to foot like monkeys, excited and impotent, morphomaniacs who did not conceal their vice from her, beaux, cripples, rakes, who sometimes nauseated her, boys who cried for the bitterness of their first fall—they all embraced her with shameful words, with long kisses, breathed into her face, moaned in the paroxysm of animal passion, which, she knew beforehand, would then and there be changed to unconcealed and insuperable disgust. Long ago all men's faces had in her eyes lost every individual trait—as though they had united into one lascivious, inevitable face, eternally bent over her, the face of a he-goat with stubbly, slobbering lips, clouded eyes, dimmed like frosted glass, distorted and disfigured by a voluptuous grimace, which sickened her because she never shared it.

Besides, they were all rude, exacting and devoid of the elements of shame. They were ludicrously ugly, as only the modern man can be in his under-clothes. But this elderly little officer made a new, peculiar, attractive impres-sion on her. His every movement was distinguished by a gentle, insinuating discretion. His kiss, his caress, and his touch were strangely gentle. At the same time he surrounded her imperceptibly with the nervous atmosphere of real and intense passion which even from a distance and against her will arouses a woman's sensuality, makes her docile, and subject to the male's desire. But her poor little mind had never passed beyond the round of everyday life in the house, and could not perceive this strange and agitating spell. She could only whisper shyly, happy and surprised, the usual trivial words: 'What a nice man you are! You're my sweet, aren't you?'

She got up, put the lamp out, and lay beside him again. Through the chinks between the shutters and the wall showed thin threads of the whiten-ing dawn, which filled the room with a misty blue half-light. Behind the partition, somewhere an alarm-clock hurriedly rang. Far away some one was singing sadly in the distance.

'When will you come again?' the woman asked.

'What?' Rubnikov asked sleepily, opening his eyes. 'When am I coming? Soon—tomorrow. . . .'

'I know all about that. Tell me the truth. When are you coming? I'll be lonely without you.'

'M'm. . . . We will come and be alone. . . . We will write to them. They will stay in the mountains . . .' he murmured incoherently.

A heavy slumber enlocked his body; but, as always with men who have long deprived themselves of sleep, he could not sleep at once. No sooner was his consciousness overcast with the soft, dark, delightful cloud of oblivion than his body was shaken by a terrible inward shock. He moaned and shuddered, opened his eyes wide in wild terror, and straightway plunged into an irritating, transitory state between sleep and wakefulness, like a delirium crowded with threatening and confused visions.

The woman had no desire to sleep. She sat up in bed in her chemise clasping her bended knees with her bare arms, and looked at Ribnikov with timid curiosity. In the bluish half-light his face grew sharper still and yellower, like the face of a dead man. His mouth stood open, but she could not hear his breathing. All over his face, especially about the eyes and mouth, was an expression of such utter weariness and profound human suffering as she had never seen in her life before. She gently passed her hand back over his stiff hair and forehead. The skin was cold and covered all over with clammy sweat. Ribnikov trembled at the touch, cried out in terror, and with a quick movement raised himself from the pillow.

'Ah! Who's that, who?' he cried abruptly, wiping his face with his shirt-sleeve.

'What's the matter, darling?' the woman asked with sympathy. 'You're not well? Shall I get you some water?'

But Ribnikov had mastered himself, and lay down once more.

'Thanks, it's all right now. I was dreaming. . . . Go to sleep, dear, do.'

'When do you want me to wake you, darling?' she asked.

'Wake. . . . In the morning. . . . The sun will rise early. . . . And the horsemen will come. . . . We will go in a boat. . . . And sail over the river. . . .' He was silent and lay quiet for some minutes. Suddenly his still, dead face was distorted with terrible pain. He turned on his back with a moan, and there came in a stream from his lips mysterious, wild-sounding words of a strange language.

The woman held her breath and listened, possessed by the superstitious terror which always comes from a sleeper's delirium. His face was only a couple of inches from hers, and she could not tear her eyes away. He was silent for a while and then began to speak again, many words and unintelligible. Then he was silent again, as though listening attentively to some one's speech. Suddenly the woman heard the only Japanese word she knew, from the newspapers, pronounced aloud with a firm, clear voice:

'Banzai!'

Her heart beat so violently that the velvet coverlet lifted again and again with the throbbing. She remembered how they had called Ribnikov by the names of Japanese generals in the red cabinet that day, and a far faint suspicion began to stir in the obscurity of her mind.

Some one lightly tapped on the door. She got up and opened.

'Clotilde dear, is that you?' a woman's gentle whisper was heard. 'Aren't you asleep? Come in to me for a moment. Leonka's with me, and he's standing some apricot wine. Come on, dear!'

It was Sonya, the Karaim,[1] Clotilde's neighbour, bound to her by the cloying, hysterical affection which always pairs off the women in these establishments.

---

[1] The Karaim are Jews of the pure original stock who entered Russia long before the main immigration and settled in the Crimea. Under the Tsarist regime, they were free from the ordinary Jewish restrictions.

'All right. I'll come now. Oh, I've something very interesting to tell you. Wait a second. I'll dress.'

'Nonsense. Don't. Who are you nervous about? Leonka? Come, just as you are!'

She began to put on her petticoat.

Ribnikov roused in his sleep.

'Where are you going to?' he asked drowsily.

'Only a minute. . . . Back immediately. . . . I must . . .' she answered hurriedly tying the tape round her waist. 'You go to sleep. I'll be back in a second.'

He had not heard her last words. A dark heavy sleep had instantly engulfed him.

VI

Leonka was the idol of the whole establishment, beginning with Madame, and descending to the tiniest servant. In these places where boredom, indolence, and cheap literature produce feverishly romantic tastes, the extreme of adoration is lavished on thieves and detectives, because of their heroic lives, which are full of fascinating risks, dangers and adventures. Leonka used to appear in the most varied costumes, at times almost made up. Sometimes he kept a meaning and mysterious silence. Above all every one remembered very well that he often proclaimed that the local police had an unbounded respect for him and fulfilled his orders blindly. In one case he had said three or four words in a mysterious jargon, and that was enough to send a few thieves who were behaving rowdily in the house crawling into the street. Besides there were times when he had a great deal of money. It is easy to understand that Henrietta, whom he called Genka and with whom he had an assiduous affair, was treated with a jealous respect.

He was a young man with a swarthy, freckled face, with black moustaches that pointed up to his very eyes. His chin was short, firm and broad; his eyes were dark, handsome and impudent. He was sitting on the sofa in his shirt-sleeves, his waistcoat unbuttoned and his necktie loose. He was small but well proportioned. His broad chest and his muscles, so big that his shirt seemed ready to tear at the shoulder, were eloquent of his strength. Genka sat close to him with her feet on the sofa; Clotilde was opposite. Sipping his liqueur slowly with his red lips, in an artificially elegant voice he told his tale unconcernedly:

'They brought him to the station. His passport—Korney Sapietov, resident in Kolpin or something of the kind. Of course the devil was drunk, absolutely. "Put him into a cold cell and sober him down." General rule. That very moment I happened to drop into the inspector's office. I had a look. By Jove, an old friend: Sanka the Butcher—triple murder and sacrilege. Instantly I gave the constable on duty a wink, and went out into the corridor as though nothing had happened. The constable came out to me.

"What's the matter, Leonti Spiridonovich?" "Just send that gentleman round to the Detective Bureau for a minute." They brought him. Not a muscle in his face moved. I just looked him in the eyes and said':—Leonka rapped his knuckles meaningly on the table—' "Is it a long time, Sanka, since you left Odessa and decided to honour us here?" Of course he's quite indifferent—playing the fool. Not a word. Oh, he's a bright one, too. "I haven't any idea who Sanka the Butcher is. I am . . . so and so." So I come up to him, catch hold of him by the beard—hey, presto—the beard's left in my hand. False! . . . "Will you own up now, you son of a bitch?" "I haven't any idea." Then I let fly straight at his nose—once, twice—a bloody mess. "Will you own up?" "I haven't any idea." "Ah, that's your game, is it? I gave you a decent chance before. Now, you've got yourself to thank. Bring Arsenti the Flea here." We had a prisoner of that name. He hated Sanka to death. Of course, my dear, I knew how they stood. They brought the Flea. "Well, Flea, who's this gentleman?" The Flea laughs. "Why Sanka the Butcher, of course! How do you do, Sanichka? Have you been honouring us a long while? How did you get on in Odessa?" Then the Butcher gave in. "All right, Leonti Spiridonovich. I give in. Nothing can get away from you. Give us a cigarette." Of course I gave him one. I never refuse them, out of charity. The servant of God was taken away. He just looked at the Flea, no more. I thought, well, the Flea will have to pay for that. The Butcher will do him in for sure.'

'Do him in?' Genka asked with servile confidence, in a terrified whisper.

'Absolutely. Do him in. That's the kind of man he is!'

He sipped his glass complacently. Genka looked at him with fixed, frightened eyes, so intently that her mouth even opened and watered. She smacked her hands on her lips.

'My God, how awful! Just think, Clotilduchka! And you weren't afraid, Leonya?'

'Well, am I to be frightened of every vagabond?'

The rapt attention of the woman excited him, and he began to invent a story that students had been making bombs somewhere on Vassiliev Island, and that the Government had instructed him to arrest the conspirators. Bombs there were—it was proved afterwards—twelve thousand of them. If they'd all exploded then not only the house they were in, but half Petersburg, perhaps, would have been blown to atoms. . . . Next came a thrilling story of Leonka's extraordinary heroism, when he disguised himself as a student, entered the 'devil's workshop,' gave a sign to some one outside the window, and disarmed the villains in a second. He caught one of them by the sleeve at the very moment when he was going to explode a lot of bombs.

Genka groaned, was terror-stricken, slapped her legs, and continually turned to Clotilde with exclamations:

'Ah! what do you think of all that? Just think what scoundrels these students are, Clotilduchka! I never liked them.'

At last, stirred to her very depths by her lover, she hung on his neck and began to kiss him loudly.

'Leonichka, my darling! It's terrible to listen to, even! And you aren't frightened of anything!'

He complacently twisted his left moustache upwards, and let drop carelessly: 'Why be afraid? You can only die once. That's what I'm paid for.'

Clotilde was tormented all the while by jealous envy of her friend's magnificent lover. She vaguely suspected that there was a great deal of lying in Leonka's stories; while she now had something utterly extraordinary in her hands, such as no one had ever had before, something that would immediately take all the shine out of Leonka's exploits. For some minutes she hesitated. A faint echo of the tender pity for Ribnikov still restrained her. But a hysterical yearning to shine took hold of her, and she said in a dull, quiet voice: 'Do you know what I wanted to tell, Leonya? I've got such a queer visitor to-day.'

'H'm. You think he's a sharper?' he asked condescendingly. Genka was offended.

'A sharper, you say! That's your story. Some drunken officer.'

'No, you mustn't say that,' Leonka pompously interrupted. 'It happens that sharpers get themselves up as officers. What was it you were going to say, Clotilde?'

Then she told the story of Ribnikov with every detail, displaying a petty and utterly feminine talent for observation: she told how they called him General Kuroki, his Japanese face, his strange tenderness and passion, his delirium, and finally how he said 'Banzai!'

'You're not lying?' Leonka said quickly. Keen points of fire lit in his eyes.

'I swear it's true! May I be rooted to the ground if it's a lie! You look through the keyhole, I'll go in and open the shutter. He's as like a Japanese as two peas.'

Leonka rose. Without haste, with a serious look, he put on his overcoat, carefully feeling his left inside pocket.

'Come on,' he said resolutely. 'Who did he arrive with?'

Only Karyukov and Strahlmann remained of the all-night party. Karyukov could not be awakened, and Strahlmann muttered something indistinctly. He was still half drunk and his eyes were heavy and red.

'What officer? Blast him to hell! He came up to us when we were in the "Buff," but where he came from nobody knows.'

He began to dress immediately, snorting angrily. Leonka apologised and went out. He had already managed to get a glimpse of Ribnikov's face through the keyhole, and though he had some doubts remaining, he was a good patriot, distinguished for impertinence and not devoid of imagination. He decided to act on his own responsibility. In a moment he was on the balcony whistling for help.

VII

Ribnikov woke suddenly as though an imperative voice within him had said 'Wake up'. An hour and a half of sleep had completely refreshed him. First of all he stared suspiciously at the door: it seemed to him that some one was watching him from there with a fixed stare. Then he looked round. The shutter was half open so that every little thing in the room could be seen. The woman was sitting by the table opposite the bed, silent and pale, regarding him with big, bright eyes.

'What's happened?' Ribnikov asked in alarm. 'Tell me, what's been happening here?'

She did not answer, but her chin began to tremble and her teeth chattered.

A suspicious, cruel light came into the officer's eyes. He bent his whole body from the bed with his ear to the door. The noise of many feet, of men evidently unused to moving cautiously, approached along the corridor, and suddenly was quiet before the door.

Ribnikov with a quick, soft movement leapt from the bed and twice turned the key. There was an instant knock at the door. With a cry the woman turned her face to the table and buried her head in her hands.

In a few seconds the captain was dressed. Again they knocked at the door. He had only his cap with him; he had left his sword and overcoat below. He was pale but perfectly calm. Even his hands did not tremble while he dressed himself, and all his movements were quite unhurried and adroit. Doing up the last button of his tunic, he went over to the woman, and suddenly squeezed her arm above the wrist with such terrible strength that her face purpled with the blood that rushed to her head.

'You!' he said quietly, in an angry whisper, without moving his jaws. 'If you move or make a sound, I'll kill you. . . .'

Again they knocked at the door, and a dull voice came: 'Open the door, if you please.'

The captain now no longer limped. Quickly and silently he ran to the window, jumped on to the window-ledge with the soft-spring of a cat, opened the shutters and with one sweep flung wide the window frames. Below him the paved yard showed white with scanty grass between the stones, and the branches of a few thin trees pointed upwards. He did not hesitate for a second; but at the very moment that he sat sideways on the iron frame of the window-sill, resting on it with his left hand, with one foot already hanging down, and prepared to leap with his whole body, the woman threw herself upon him with a piercing cry and caught him by the left arm. Tearing himself away, he made a false movement and suddenly, with a faint cry as though of surprise, fell in an awkward heap straight down on the stones.

Almost at the very second the old door fell flat into the room. First

Leonka ran in, out of breath, showing his teeth; his eyes were aflame. After him came huge policemen, stamping and holding their swords in their left hands. When he saw the open window and the woman holding on the frame and screaming without pause, Leonka quickly understood what had happened. He was really a brave man, and without a thought or a word, as though he had already planned it, he took a running leap through the window.

He landed two steps away from Ribnikov who lay motionless on his side. In spite of the drumming in his head, and the intense pain in his belly and his heels from the fall, he kept his head, and instantly threw himself heavily with the full weight of his body on the captain.

'Ah. I've got you now,' he uttered hoarsely, crushing his victim in mad exasperation.

The captain did not resist. His eyes burned with an implacable hatred. But he was pale as death, and a pink froth stood in bubbles on his lips. 'Don't crush me,' he whispered. 'My leg's broken.'

HYDROMEL

Vassili Iretsky

(1882–   )

TRANSLATED BY D. C. ANDERSON

FROM his long-legged English father Bromley had inherited obstinacy and perseverance, from his Cossack mother a poetic love for the open vastness of the black-soil plains. These strangely dissimilar qualities managed somehow to blend without friction: so an individual was formed.

When his education at a forestry school was completed, Bromley negotiated for a plot of land in the province of Viatka. While waiting for the official documents confirming his purchase, he established himself on the plot with his wife and two-year-old child.

The property comprised a meadow not yet fully cleared, a tiny copse of half a score pine trees, and an insignificant little stream without source or end, which lost itself ineffectually somewhere in the valley below.

Bromley pitched his tent in the meadow, installed his family and effects, and set to work. Almost entirely with his own hands he built a small house in the Tyrolean style. He bought a horse, small but sturdy and stout-hearted; and two cows. He erected a greenhouse and, last of all, some bee-hives. Thus, in four years he became a person of consequence in the eyes of his neighbours. They looked at his little six-hectares estate, a neat patch-work of natural colours—like a picture in a children's story-book—and said "There's a nice job done!"

It was not easy to astonish the bee-keepers of that district, a district which might have been created especially for apiculture, under the direct protection too of St. Sosima and St. Savati; nevertheless Bromley aston-ished them. Except perhaps in the Caucasus there were no bees like his in the whole country.

And the variety of gear he had! Smokers, feeding troughs, baskets for catching the swarms: there was no end to it all; like a museum it was. The whole of Bromley's time was spent on this work; and he never rested con-tent till everything down to the last little detail was perfection itself. More-over his bees paid him handsomely. Fifty-two hives yielded him ten quin-tals of honey, to say nothing of the wax.

With his flaming mop of red hair, Bromley bore himself with an air of proud independence. "Like a Greek god" the neighbours said; and they called him Jupiter, a nickname, sadly inappropriate though it was, which stuck to him to the end of his life. His eyes shone with the concentrated light of a man completely absorbed in his work; their restlessness was all too human to justify the divinity attributed to him.

Each year the mottled mosaic of Bromley's enclosure acquired some new splash of colour. One year the hives would be repainted; another year there might be a new fence; or even the pink and white of a chubby baby mak-ing its first experiments in crawling against the brilliant green carpet of the lawn.

On the holding now lived three little girls, as slender, supple and ruddy as fox cubs. And on one fine day arrived a stiff-backed lady with unsmiling eyes and a fringed parasol, the English governess Bromley had engaged for his children.

The varied sounds carried by the hot summer wind across the holding—the chirping of crickets, the buzzing of bees, the lowing of cows, the cluck-ing of hens, the squeaking of the windlass of the well, were now added to by the rise and fall of scales played listlessly on a piano.

Now and then Bromley would pause from his cares as head of a family and survey his little kingdom. He would listen to all these sounds, breathe deep the scents of the earth, and let his whole being fill with a sense of the goodness of things that told him beyond doubt that he was a happy man. Then, after a quick look round to make sure no one was near to spy on his idleness, he would throw himself down in the long grass and a benign smile would curl his lips as he lent his ear to the eternal language of the countryside. Suddenly, close at hand he might hear the furious buzzing of a bee trapped in the tangled grass; he would seek it out, then help it to free itself from its green snare, and watch it fly away free again. With its sac full of honey, it would make for its home in the hive; and Bromley would remember his duties. He would jump to his feet and set his hand once more to those labours which made him too resemble a busy bee.

According to his passport, Bromley's religion was orthodox; but he never went to church. He believed in God and loved Him: he looked on Him as the great calm source of all power, as the designer of that great pulse-beat which controls all living things.

From time to time he would open his heart about such matters to his wife. Quiet and thoughtful, she would listen; but she did not share his beliefs. Her conception of God was peace and silence: all uncertainty, change, and unrest were hostile to Him. Such things, she asserted, were in the dominion of the Devil. With an indulgent smile Bromley gave his considered opinion: "Peace and silence form a rest from trouble. This rest must be earned: to have value it must be preceded by anxiety. At the same time, if this rest never came to us, all trouble and anxiety would have been suffered in vain."

Late one night Bromley was wakened by noises made by the horses in the stable. He put on his dressing-gown and went out on to the balcony to investigate. The noises ceased; but Bromley stayed outside to listen to the silence of the close night. Presently he became aware of a deep rhythmical breathing. He whispered to himself: "It is the earth breathing in deep sleep at the end of her hard day's work". Then, added to this thought, came unbidden the secret suspicion that what he heard was the breathing of God himself enjoying a sweet repose.

One winter's day grim-visaged trouble made its entrance into the clearing. Against the white carpet of wind-swept snow appeared first one horse, then a second, then a third. The horses, spattered with snow-flakes and smelling of their stables, carried each a surly-looking man wearing epaulettes and a fur cap. Under their arms were black portfolios crammed to bursting-point with papers. The hinges of the gate groaned mournfully as they threw it open. This groaning started other harsh noises. The old dog Rex echoed it with a bark; then, fearing his own temerity, put his tail between his legs and slunk into his kennel from whose shelter he could inspect these uninvited guests with more safety. The purpose of their visit was unknown to him, but he feared it deeply: he set up a plaintive howling as they disappeared one by one through the porch of the house, without even troubling to brush the snow off their coats. When Bromley saw his visitors he too could have howled had he not inherited his English father's self-control.

One of the men, in a tone needlessly loud for the little dining-room, bawled at him: "In accordance with the orders of the Ispolkom,[1] you are to

[1] Executive Committee.

submit yourself unquestioningly to my authority. Here is the Warrant and the Party Certificate. You are understood to own a number of hives: the whole lot are to be nationalized for the benefit of the workers: that goes for all the honey and wax you've got too." Then one of the others, a man wearing a stoker's gloves, added: "For your own good I advise you not to try on any bluff or to waste our time. Hand over everything you've got; if you don't—you'll be shot. We aren't leaving here empty-handed."

Bromley clenched his teeth, and said: "I can see it's useless for me to dispute your power to carry out what you threaten. I'll give you some honey and wax; but you mustn't take all I've got of it; you must leave me some to feed the swarms on. Even you can understand they'd all be dead in a week without food."

"Comrade," answered the first speaker, "we've got our orders and we're going to carry them out. The workers' and peasants' government commands you categorically to hand back everything you've filched from them. Don't start arguing the point. If you don't hand over your stuff with good grace it won't make any difference: we'll take it all the same. As to what you say about the bees, you can put in a special petition."

Bromley saw it was futile to oppose them further. He went to his study, took a large bunch of keys from a hook on the wall, threw a sheep-skin cloak round his shoulders, and strode to the front-door.

His wife and daughters were terror-struck when they saw the look on his face. All four of them stood trembling with fright.

So disaster began.

In the heated shed where the hives were kept, unqualified hostility was established at once. In ordinary business dealings Bromley was apt to be curt; now he was very brusque: to every word addressed to him he replied aggressively. He pointed to the kegs of honey, and gruffly suggested they be carried out into the yard; then he stood back to watch with a cold eye while his property was taken from him. The five intruders sweated and grunted as they carried out the heavy kegs. Soon they were tired. Bromley still watched them motionless.

"Eh, citizen," one of the men said, straightening his back, "you look as if you thought rather a lot of yourself. We may have to teach you a sharp lesson. How d'you fancy the idea of finding out what it's like to spend three months in an underground prison?"

Then the leader addressed him. "My friend's right," he said. "You just stop standing there plotting sabotage. Send for someone to help us. You're bound to have got some poor proletarian employed on the place."

"I have no one," Bromley answered quietly. "The man I had left me last autumn."

"Then you can do the job yourself! For once in a way you can work for the proletariat, instead of the other way on. And, anyhow, parasites have been formally prohibited."

Bromley threw him a contemptuous look. "Parasites," he said looking him up and down, "are people who live by the honest labour of others. All my life I have never worked less hard than any ordinary workman, and perhaps a good deal harder. This honey was produced by my labour, certainly not by yours; yet you assume the——" He was not given time to finish. An obscene oath burst from the leader, followed by: "In accordance with my powers I have the right in the event of resistance to arrest and shoot you. You are resisting: I arrest you!"

Bromley spent the next few days in an underground cellar. What impressed itself deepest on his memory of that time was not the prison bars nor the damp walls, but the never-ceasing tramp of feet from one part of the building to another across piles of broken furniture, smashed crockery, and an ankle-deep litter of paper.

In addition to the soldiers guarding him, there were numbers of officials who bustled here and there as busy as flees, bawling at each other as they clumped about. And as they clumped about they ate.

At the prison gates, in a cloud of thick yellowish steam, a crowd of men and women shoved and buzzed like a swarm of hungry bees. "What about those warrants?" "Can I buy one?" "Where?" "Who from?" "Mister comrade, can we get anything to eat here? We've just come from Glasovo." "My horse was commandeered five days ago; no one's paid me a cent." "Who can tell me anything?"

"Comrades," shouted one of the officials, "the information bureau is opposite. This office is only for the verification of warrants."

"Tell me, my dear," babbled one old woman, "which of these gentlemen are the Commissars?"

After many postponements Bromley's interrogation unexpectedly began. "Are you the proprietor Bromley?"

"Proprietor? When I own only six and a half hectares and not a single labourer? I did have one, but he left me a long while ago."

"Henceforward you will exploit no one. You are a proletarian now."

"Not a proletarian, a peasant."

"A peasant, and you wear a tie? Don't tell stupid lies!"

His questioners were three in number: a jolly-looking sailor, a scowling mistrustful workman with tired and crafty eyes, and a third man who was difficult to place. He wore a leather cap and his face was clean-shaven; he sat silent and there was a cruel twist to his mouth.

On the table, which was littered with papers, were a hunk of bread, a sausage, and a lady's mother-of-pearl handbag.

The sailor, apparently taking no interest in the talk, was cleaning his nails with a bent fork. Suddenly, with a child-like grin, he exclaimed: "Comrade, you're talking rot! You've made profits out of your land. That sort of thing's been stopped. Now's the time for the workers to make a bit of profit for a change. That's all there is to it."

Bromley spoke up. "The only thing that matters is the bees. The land's not worth enough to worry about."

With his mind occupied only with the welfare of his little buzzing friends, he began to explain quietly and clearly how bees should be looked after. The sailor stopped cleaning his nails and listened attentively. It amused him to hear that such tiny creatures needed so much care. He lit a cigarette, shut his eyes, and imagined this strange kingdom of the insect world laid out before him.

The workman pretended not to be interested in anything Bromley was saying. In reality he was much interested and much surprised.

The silent man in the leather cap was waiting impatiently for Bromley to finish; only then would his role begin. His ill-nature got the better of him; interrupting Bromley in the middle of a sentence, he stuttered out in a monotonous foreign accent: "All that's got nothing to do with the case." The sailor put his hand on Bromley's arm to restrain him. The three interrogators exchanged glances, then took up pens and wrote:

"The land of the proprietor Bromley is nationalized for the benefit of the working-class, furthermore it will provide accommodation for the children. Comrade Tchelishkin is appointed Commissar over the property. A proportion of the honey not to exceed four pounds per month will be granted to Bromley on the condition that he behaves properly. Comrade Tchelishkin will live on the property in a style calculated to provide him with substantial nourishment corresponding to human needs."

Bromley set out for his home accompanied by Tchelishkin and the latter's strange-looking mistress, a lethargic and discontented woman. After the bustle of the big government headquarters which the whole town had become, the open country slowly helped his troubled spirits to grow calmer.

For some way the three of them walked in silence, with occasional furtive glances at each other. When they had covered seven kilometres Tchelishkin could stand the silence no longer. He started a conversation with his mistress, though his words were really addressed at the frowning Bromley. After a bit he spoke to him direct. "You'll find me a strict man," he said, "and they've given me my instructions and a copy of the proceedings in your case: I'm going to abide by them. But if you on your side will fall in with the instructions I shan't have anything against you, and we'll get on all right together. What d'you say about it?"

"What can I say?" replied Bromley. "Your idea's quite sensible—in the circumstances."

"The situation's like this, it seems to me," went on Tchelishkin, "you'll do your work conscientiously; and I'll just keep an eye on things as an accredited representative of the people. That way we won't have any cause to quarrel. But the first thing to be done is to form a servants' committee."

Bromley chuckled. "How can we form a servants' committee? The only people on the whole place are myself, my wife, and an old nurse."

Tchelishkin felt the irony and resented it; but it did not defeat him. "That's just like your sort of people," he said with as much contempt as he could put into his tone. "That's just how you intellectuals argue, like a lot of wriggling snakes! You say there's no committee; well, I'm telling you there's jolly well got to be one! You're behind the times with all your silly excuses. A servants' committee there's got to be! This show's going to be run properly."

"All right; but where shall I find the members?"

"Organize them."

Tchelishkin's mistress had been listening quietly; her silence became unbearable to her: she chipped in with: "See he does it without any monkey-business, though. We all know what these bourgeois are like!"

Bromley sighed. He thought: "This is going to be a tussle to see which of us can hold out longest."

The days that followed were filled with irritating fuss.

"I may not have had a grand education like some people," declared Tchelishkin, "but I do know something about bees." And he demanded the keys of the bee-house, the wood-shed, and the provision store. He reckoned up the amount of honey in stock, and calculated that half the quantity would suffice to feed the bees during the winter: so he took two full casks into town. When he got back he had a requisition order for hay in his pocket.

Thus were sown the seeds of discord; they germinated on the question of living-quarters.

Tchelishkin's mistress took a fancy to the study: for nothing in the world would Bromley give it up. From morning to night their wrangling was heard from one end of the house to the other. The frightened children, too terrified to speak, hid in corners. Bromley's wife hated rows: she would have preferred martyrdom to them any day. Now she counselled concession to all demands; but Bromley would not give in.

"You've shown quite plainly," said Tchelishkin, "that you have the true instincts of a capitalist; therefore I arrest you."

He took him into town.

They set out scowling and muttering at each other; but after a while the snow and ice on the road cooled their tempers. Tchelishkin was the first to speak.

"You've been behaving like an owl—if I may use the expression. I know what you're thinking, you're thinking I'm being unreasonable. It's obvious you never heard I was made a chevalier of the order of St. George. No; you're the one who's being unreasonable. Why? I'll tell you. Simply because you refuse to acknowledge the Revolution. Hasn't the Revolution happened? It certainly has! From the moment it happened, you should have realized you'd got to reckon with it, and give up all these silly airs and graces. But no; you must go on acting like a perfect specimen of the ancient regime."

Bromley looked at him, but made no answer. He thought: "The fellow's out of his mind. Some devil has possessed him."

Once again they found themselves in the yellow fog of the government office. Officials still strode about, and as they strode they shouted and chewed. The air smelt of ink, sweat, and soot.

The interrogation was peaceable, and even had a feeling of lazy good-nature to it; but the verdict surprised even Tchelishkin.

"The horse belonging to the proprietor Bromley shall be entered on the register and put at the disposal of the transport service. His hay, flour, and cattle are requisitioned."

Tchelishkin was extremely put out by the turn events had taken, for it struck at his own comfort. He was in a murderous mood. Once outside the office, he threw all the blame on Bromley.

"Call yourself an intellectual?" he shouted at him. "Not enough intelligence even to get us out of a mess like this!"

Bromley said nothing, and brooded. "If only they'll leave the bees alone!" he prayed. And the bees with their long hungry proboscides knew not a word of what was going on. Their thoughts and dreams and hopes were centred only on the returning sunshine which soon would warm their wings again.

The high snow-drifts lost their dazzling whiteness, then melted; the black earth began to peep out again; and the scent of last year's rotting vegetation struck the nostrils: Spring was announcing herself.

Bromley had just started on cleaning out the hives when the order arrived: "Deliver up half your hives to be distributed among more needy people." He sighed and resigned himself to the inevitable. In the order nothing was said about sending honey as feed for the confiscated bees, and anyhow he could not spare it; yet compassion smote him for the defence-less little creatures. He packed some honey to go with them, though he knew quite well that the bees' new masters would simply eat it with their teas. He had given it, however; what more could he do?

All of them were needed to carry the bees to town—his wife, his daughters, and Bromley himself. Bromley seemed to have become taller and thinner; and, as he strode along with his copper hair bared to the wind and his eyes fixed on the far horizon, he resembled nothing less than a Viking. To cheer himself up he thought: "I will breed fresh swarms."

Then summer came. Once more the sun's rays made heavy the atmosphere, the music of bees was heard, and the sweet scent of rye in the ear was carried on the breeze. At moments Bromley felt that everything was back where it had been in the good old days. The eternal regular movement animating all living matter! What was it? God? But no; the strength-giving spirit was divine no longer, for everything Bromley knew and loved was slowly being destroyed.

At the end of June the bees began to swarm. Tchelishkin, in the pride of his commanding position, pipe in mouth, strolled masterfully about the holding. He watched very closely the detail of all work going on. His mind was made up to learn this job of bee-keeping against the coming day when this red-headed bourgeois should finally give him cause to chase him out. Then he would be proprietor.

Bromley looked up from his work in the bee-house. "For the love of God, don't smoke!" he pleaded. "Bees can't bear tobacco smoke."

"Well, I never!" rejoined Tchelishkin.

"I tell you it's true! Not only smoking either! Onions and garlic as well. If they smell them on your breath, they get terribly upset; and they may get all out of condition."

Tchelishkin laughed. "Is that so? Sounds to me like sabotage on their part. Perhaps they've formed a committee." Tchelishkin laughed again.

A new order came: "Dispatch your new hives to the agricultural bureau without delay."

Bromley paled as he read it; then he stroked his chin. An idea came to him, a brilliant idea; a smile quivered in the corners of his mouth; only just in time did he screen it from Tchelishkin's watching eye. "No," thought Bromley, "the agricultural bureau shan't have all the profits of all my labour!" He would hide the swarms in the woods—in boxes fitted into hollow trees far from the prying eyes of treacherous men. "God help me in this!"

Early next morning, while Tchelishkin still snored into his mistress's ear, Bromley scoured the forest for the most hidden and inaccessible places. On the tops of trees he placed hives, and there carried the swarms. Tchelishkin noticed nothing, neither bees full of honey flying into the woods, nor that the swarms had mysteriously disappeared. True he did ask once or twice why fewer bees were about. Then Bromley would scrutinize the hives with care, and scratch his head. "Have you smoked in here?" he asked. "You must have done! That's a thing bees never forgive. Is there no way of convincing you that that is not just an idea of my own?" Bromley rejoiced at the easy success of his stratagem.

In the autumn, when Bromley was gathering in the honey, a District Committee arrived at the house followed closely by a Commission from the town. Both stayed for two days.

In the morning they quarrelled rowdily, after noon they gave themselves up to a plentiful and pacific meal, and in the evening they set to quarrelling again: each party threatening to arrest the other. In the end they divided the honey among themselves and decamped, taking all the poultry with them.

In their quarrels the townsmen ranged themselves against the villagers.

"You rascals, how dare you let him keep a piano? What right has he to have one? What have you got to say about it? What times d'you think we're living in? The old regime? Is Proletariat only an empty word to you? And you say political power's been put into better hands!"

The villagers were abashed, and decided without further parley that the piano be requisitioned for the Youth Circle. Tchelishkin was as furious as a polecat; his mistress abandoned her role of lady and swore like a peasant; as for Bromley . . .

The imperturbability he had inherited from his father stood him now in good stead: without it he would have sobbed like a child. But he was a strong man, energetic and enduring, and had never known the meaning of the word despair. But his poor wife wept silently and in secret: to hide her tears from her children she retired to her bedroom and cried into her pillow. Yes, Bromley had never known despair; but it was not far off now.

Although it was only autumn, hunger was beginning to make itself felt. With a sigh and a frown, Bromley sent the children out to gather mushrooms, while he himself ventured into the villages to try to barter household ornaments for flour. As for Tchelishkin, realizing what winter would be like on that place, he hurried back into town to get some other post there. On taking his leave of Bromley, he handed him an order allowing him to remove all the blankets, pillows and curtains.

The concealed hives yielded good honey: the breed had not deteriorated. Above all Tchelishkin was gone, Tchelishkin who for so many long unhappy days had strode about to remind them of their misfortunes; now they could collect their thoughts and reflect; fill their hearts with hope, and plan for the future. They will never come here again! They will forget us! They will leave us in peace while our wounds heal! Keep quiet and don't talk about them! Keep still and hide like a field-mouse when it sees a bird of prey wheeling against the sky above it!

The hives were still out in the woods, where Bromley had to go secretly, noiselessly, to tend them, under the shielding silence of the forest. He was thinking of bringing them back again to the warm for the winter when a man came looking for him. The executive committee wished to see him, he was told: they had come to a decision.

He walked to the town with anxiety gnawing at his heart, like a man on the watch for a bear. What new catastrophe could be waiting for him? But how hard it was to divine what those savage disturbers of the peace might want! The meaning of frost-feathers on window panes was easier to decipher.

Once again he was in the presence of those untidy piles of scribbled paper, those ink-stains, that irritating uproar which seemed to lead nowhere. There was a smell of decay and cheap tobacco. From behind the table tired eyes stared at him, then dropped uneasily to a portfolio of papers.

"It is proposed," he heard said, "to set up a children's colony in your district. To be precise, in the words of the written order: 'On the holding of the proprietor Bromley'. The order also says: 'Expropriate the house within twenty-four hours'." Bromley bowed his head: the inevitable and irrevocable was coming about. The tired eyes fixed their attention on a blot of ink, and their owner went on hurriedly: "From the humanitarian point of view you have all my sympathy; but what else can I do? We must find somewhere to put the children. As to the 'twenty-four hours', don't let that worry you too much: it's only put in to make it sound important. Everyone who writes tries to make himself sound important; that's what paper's for. But there's always a way to get round the law. You will have three days' grace. Three days, but no longer. Bear that in mind."

Bromley strode home with paces as long as if he were walking on stilts. He accepted the fact that he must now depart; and his mind was occupied only by the consideration of what articles of his moveable property he should take with him, what leave, what hide. The nearer he got to his home, the more eager he was to arrive so that he might have done with this sorry business.

Sad hours followed. His wife's first thought was for the ikons, which she took from the walls and crammed tightly into a hamper. Bromley had always carefully refrained from references to her piety; now restraint was thrown to the winds. "What d'you want with all that rubbish?" he cried. "You're mad!"

With a look of horror his wife turned her meek blue eyes to him and murmured in anguish: "You too? You've become a bolshevik! At last they've succeeded in contaminating even you!"

Yes, yes, anything you like! But was this a time for praying and weeping? The enemy was at the gate; they must hurry. In a stony silence he emptied cupboards, chests of drawers, trunks, of all their contents; and packed the most essential things in hampers. His dry lips were tight-pressed for he too hated parting with so many things they had known and lived with for many years. His wife's dresses seemed to him a superfluous encumbrance, yet from consideration for her he packed them too.

The household packing done, he went to the apiary, to bid a last sad farewell to all the bulky and diverse apicultural implements he would have to leave behind. In orderly rows on the shelves stood the smokers, clean and burnished; next to them the baskets for taking up the swarms, the feeding-troughs, the graters, funnels for straining the wax, tea-pots, syringes, frames, basins for heating the wax, buckets, honey-strainers, coarse and fine; an army of utensils he had chosen with so much care and which had served him well for so many years. All now to be left behind, all to be abandoned! O dear God! For the last time he touched them, caressed them. There stood the Vingham smoker, shaped like a torpedo, shining even in the gloom; how often had his loving fingers unscrewed its parts, cleaned and reassembled them with care and precision! There too stood the Dultia feeder. Shall I take it with me, shall I take them all?

His wife entered the bee-shed and watched him as he quickly set to work. "Why take all these things," she inquired, "when the bees must stay behind?"

"The bees stay behind? How can you imagine such a thing? You must be mad!"

She asked no more questions, merely wondered how they were to carry such a load, how house it in an already over-crowded flat in town? She was surprised still more later, when he loaded not one single hive onto the wagonette.

They set out in the night along the rough country roads, their ears straining for hostile noises in the darkness. The cloudy shadows of that autumn night made them imagine almost they were fleeing from the shame of some misdeed.

At dawn they reached the house of Bromley's sister-in-law. Creeping like thieves, so as not to be seen by other tenants, they climbed the stairs. The children were wrapped in shawls and sent to lie in a dark corner, where they soon dropped off to sleep. The two women—Bromley's wife and sister-in-law—wandered distracted from room to room, their eyes streaming with tears: like dripping candles, Bromley thought. But he was calm: a practical idea, tempering the gloom of his misfortunes, lay at the back of his mind. He sat busy thinking it over.

For several days they talked only in undertones, as if some dread disease were in their midst; and the women arranged and rearranged the furniture, taking care to make no noise in doing it. They were surprised and alarmed at Bromley's air of having nothing to fear. He spoke in normal tones, tramped about the house without a thought for the noise he made, and even chatted loudly with the neighbours. Then one fine day he disappeared.

Late next night he returned to them. His clothes were sodden and mud-smeared as if he had been through a marsh. On his back was a great bundle of firewood; but when the bundle was untied out came four of his precious hives. The whole operation was carried out so secretly that, save his wife, no one was aware of it. She asked him where he had found the bees. With a knowing look he answered: "Where from but the hives I hid in the woods?" The others had been too dangerous to approach.

Bromley's active nature was satisfied only when he was sure of constant work; this satisfaction he thought to get by taking a job in an office; but it turned out to be sadly incomplete. Days passed and he grew morose. There was nothing now to hope for but a miracle.

Bromley hated idle chatter. Unless the talk concerned a practical matter, of vital interest to himself, he let his attention wander to reveries of ownership, past and, possibly, to come. It was bad for him to have ample time now for such reveries. It led to his putting off of urgent duties. A pair of shoes needed soling? Ah well, what does it matter? Later on when times are better I'll buy a new pair. So he waited, fabricating comfortable fictions to excuse his idleness.

Suddenly his mood changed: the sharp goad of conscience pricked him; he jumped to his feet. "Work, work, work!" he exclaimed. "I must work!" He threw back his shoulders and grappled with life anew.

Telling no one of his purpose he settled to a task of sawing, planing, and boring, with a stubbornness which was all his own. His duties at the office —making entries in pale thin ink in ledgers, and adding columns of figures under the heading "Current and distributing account"—hindered him not at all. His boring, sawing, and planing went on.

Then spring came again to give warmth to the air, cockchafers started their singing; and the bees, drunk with liberty, took flight from the home Bromley had built them and buzzed happily under the sky-light of the attic.

Bromley too was drunk, drunk with joy. He looked quite youthful again as he smiled and said: "We had to go through with it, but here we still are!" Everything now seemed to him as it had been in the happy past, for could he not listen all day to the music produced against the blue sky by those cheerful little creatures who worked only to make themselves useful to others? Misfortunes were forgotten; no more notice was taken of over-crowding, insufficient food, nightly intrusions, or worn-out shoes. Summer passed at a gallop; the sunshine quickly healed the wounds of winter and gave strength to the belief: "Everything will be all right. Perhaps not to-day, nor tomorrow, nor even the day after tomorrow; but for certain a time is coming when everything will be all right."

One thing only made Bromley uneasy. A lot of talk was going around about bees being kept in the attic of a certain house. People were aston-ished when they heard such a thing was being done; they got excited about it; they envied. "That chap will be a bee-keeper till he dies," they said. "For two pins he'd set up a hive on the church steeple." But Bromley was bothered by this talk. He wished he could shield his bees from all those curious eyes and dangerous tongues. They will destroy my work with their chatter, he said to himself. Yet, though he pondered on the problem at his work, at his leisure, he could find no way to silence the chatterers. His fears were well-founded for, sure enough, the talk reached the ears of the authori-ties; and soon some uninvited guests presented themselves at his front door.

They searched the whole house, then reached the attic.

"Where did you get these bees?" they wanted to know.

"From the woods. They are half-wild."

"What right have you to keep them?"

"Since when has it been forbidden? Can you show me the decree?" He spoke calmly, but only because he was keeping a tight hold on his temper and his fears. The men exchanged looks, and appeared to agree with his argument. With a nod they left him.

Then autumn came and the time for gathering the honey. Now he was to see the real significance of the men's silent and empty-handed departure. No sooner had he gathered all the honey than they called again. This time they did not leave behind them even enough honey to feed the bees during the coming winter.

So the light of day went out for Bromley. His last defences had been carried; this final pillaging had broken his spirit. His shoulders drooped, his mouth sagged, his whole being pictured dumb wretchedness. Somehow he contrived to feed the bees—they could hardly be left to die—but his sawing and planing were heard no more. Why work hard for nothing? He let his arms drop to his sides: for the whole winter they hung limp like wet whip thongs. Wounded to the innermost core of his being, he mooned silently about the house without appearing even to notice his wife and children.

At last the day came when he bethought himself of two hives which he had once made for travelling. He fixed them with a strap to his shoulders, packed a change of linen and a little food in his haversack, and set out for Petrograd. There, surely in the general turmoil of a great city he would be able to pass unnoticed; there people would leave him in peace. Pray God they would!

It was not a long journey, two and a half days to be exact; yet a terrible anxiety lay on Bromley every foot of the way, with every telegraph pole that flashed by, at every station. Six times armed bands swept like snowstorms down upon the train and invaded the carriages. On the pretext of searching for contraband goods they clawed over everything. They smashed in boxes, thrust their ramrods through pillows, ripped, scattered, and swore; and finally took to themselves what they wanted—bread, butter, a sucking-pig, but above all flour: when they found it a white cloud would arise, and some poor traveller would scowl in impotent rage.

Bromley's bees always provoked suspicion. "Bees? What d'you want with bees? I expect it's really alcohol you're carrying. Or even brandy; eh, comrade? You'd better open it up."

Each time the same argument would follow.

"What's the good of opening it? I tell you it's only bees! If I open the hive the whole swarm will die. Your smoke will get at them. Bees can't abide smoke."

"Oh, they can't abide smoke, can't they? Then they'll have to get used to it. And we still don't know they really are bees. Look here, comrade, you'd better stop this funny game, and show us what you've got. It's our duty to make sure; we've got our orders; and we're used to tricks like yours."

"I give you my word of honour they're nothing but bees."

"Word of honour! You've thought of a fine way of convincing us! Word of honour indeed! A word of honour nowadays is worth less than a Soviet rouble. Stop wasting our time!"

"All right; put your ear against the hive: you'll hear them buzzing."

"I can't hear any buzzing. What a daft trick! Here, Karatkoff, break open this musical box. We'll get at the truth all right."

Six times this scene was re-enacted. Six times Bromley's heart stopped beating and froze with fear. The bees would perish, tobacco smoke would poison them, they would weaken and fall sick. And, in the intervals when he dropped off, nightmares haunted and followed him. He saw before him great red hands with dirty fingers. Take them away! Take them away!

After the sixth search he became calmer, and was settling himself down to sleep when someone shouted to him: "You just wait a bit! There's still the stop at Mga. That's where you'll find you'll really sweat."

"What is there special about that station?"

"Special?" The man laughed loosely, tapped his nose, and gave a knowing wink to his neighbours. "You're not telling me you haven't heard! You've never heard about Liga? You'll soon find out about him. There's a brigand for you. Not a man, he isn't. He's a devil, an imp of hell, the strangler of speculators—Anathase Liga!" The passengers trembled. "Even if you've got a trading-permit, he just spits on it. The authorities are too far away to touch him. There's not a trick he's not up to. He can twist anything you say to make it mean what he wants it to mean. He could prove that the good God himself was a speculator. That's the sort of a fellow Liga is!"

Hearts beat faster or slower according to their habit under the stress of fear. Then—Liga appeared.

He was thin, consumptive, and sharp-featured as a hawk. Entering a carriage like a general at a review, he made a haughty inspection of all those who were delivered into his power, and at once began to shout. Like Julius Caesar he referred to himself in the third person, and took no trouble to hide the admiration he felt for himself.

"Good morning, citizens! I, Anathase Liga, chief of the demarcation line, have the honour to salute you. No doubt you've heard of me already. Allow me to feel you all over a little. So as not to waste time, don't bother to do any unnecessary undressing; and don't try to think of any tricks to play on me. If any of you have got contraband goods in here, declare them. You know quite well you can't fool me."

He spoke fast, and all the time his sharp little eyes were untying all the knots, piercing into valises, hampers, bales, and penetrating to the bottom of portfolios, into bags hung round necks, into waistcoat-pockets.

Sometimes speculators and peasants travelling with provisions, especially when they belonged to the red army, tipped each other the wink, and so crowded up a carriage that it was difficult for inspectors to get into it;

indeed they took a grave risk in going in, for a serious assault was easy in such dark and crowded conditions.

In cases like that Liga would stand at the door glaring at the heads, feet, and buttocks protruding from the benches. He would let out a contemptuous roar: "Ha, you thought you'd made a nice little trap for Liga! You said to yourselves he'll be too frightened to come in! Never! Liga is afraid of no man. Liga has ten hefty bodyguards round him. Would anyone care to feel their muscles? You'll find Liga a pretty shrewd fellow; and the luck is generally on his side, what's more. You enjoy being crowded like this, do you? Well, move up a bit closer: you'll keep warmer."

His fearless energy was born of a consumptive's impetuosity, the impetuosity which had won him three St. George's Crosses in the war, and afterwards had helped him to climb the steep ladder of executive power. He revelled in enterprises of danger and difficulty, missions impossible of achievement; and real enjoyment came to him when he could bring to his activities his powers of subtle imagination. For example, his imagination once prompted him to stop in front of a sleepy and demure-looking lady, and say: "I hope madam will forgive me, but the exigencies of the service compel me to undress her." To the accompaniment of a chorus of laughter mixed with a few muttered expressions of outraged sensibility, he graciously led his victim out of the carriage, with an invitation to step into his office. There on the spittle-covered floor he made her undress. As he expected, a small bag of diamonds fell from her corset, some gold ten-rouble pieces nestled in her stockings, and a belt containing alcohol was round her waist. Leaving to an underling the task of drawing up a report, he returned to the carriage to acquaint the uneasy ant-hill there with all that had just happened.

"I beg you all to be calm. You know Liga will never cheat you of a little entertainment. Liga has just had the good luck to find twenty-two diamonds and the equivalent of six million roubles which will go to Moscow to be shared out among the poor. Now who else would like to undress? Whose turn is it?"

Under the flash of his penetrating little blood-shot eyes heads were lowered—as birds try to hide themselves at the sight of a gun—but sometimes too late; sometimes a victim hid a guilty look too slowly.

There were times, of course, when Liga was not so lucky. On some occasions his imagination led him too far; but these did not trouble him greatly: he knew all the ways of getting out of a predicament.

Once he undressed an engineer, and found nothing. He felt him all over, ripped the lining of his coat, ransacked his luggage; there was no contraband. He decided to let the man go in peace, but this engineer had other ideas. He explained himself as a person of importance, charged by Lenin himself with a task of electrification.

"I demand an enquiry," he said with indignation. "What right had you to undress me? What cause was there? The matter shall not rest at this!"

Liga snorted; for a moment he was worried; then quickly calm came back to him: he had thought of a way out; a look as if he had just remembered something crossed his thin face. He opened the engineer's valise again, and rummaged inside it. He found what he wanted, a small envelope which he now rapped on the table. "Tchourakoff," he ordered, "write down this report. On such and such a date, in such and such a month, in the presence of so and so . . . and all the rest of it . . . then: 'In the suspected valise were found four improper drawings and three pornographic photographs. This constitutes an offence against the morals of the workers and peasants. The said drawings and photographs have been confiscated to the State. They are forwarded herewith. I await your necessary instructions.'" Then he turned to the discomforted engineer. "Are you satisfied, citizen? Sign here, and you will receive a copy."

Several times people warned Liga to take care. "One day you will get caught," they said. "Someone will denounce you. Your conduct is not always—shall we say?—quite correct. You haven't done so badly out of all those diamonds and gold bracelets and millions; you make a pretty good thing too out of all the flour and butter. Take care, you may find yourself put up against a wall."

Liga laughed. "Don't you worry about Liga! Liga could clear himself of anything. Just try and see if you can prove I've made a profit out of my job. You think someone may denounce me, someone may say: 'He has hidden a hundred million roubles'? Suppose they do. What then? Where are those millions? I've been in the hands of the Cheka once already. For three months they kept me in a dungeon and grilled me; and what came of it? I'd got into their hands through the cleverest of all examining magistrates, Lekasse himself. There's a man for you! Not one scrap of pity! He boasts that no one ever gets away from him: they all go to the wall—but not Liga. I just talked to him as if I were talking to a father confessor."

"You confessed?"

"I confessed nothing, I denied everything. 'What have I done wrong?' I said to him. 'All you can say is I have a rather hasty temper. What does that matter to the government of workers and peasants? They've got a hasty temper themselves.' The magistrate laughed and released me."

"Excuse me, but what have you got there, citizen?" he asked Bromley.

"Bees, honey-bees."

"Carrying a swarm, are you? Now isn't that nice! All the same I think you'd better show it to me."

"How can I show it to you?"

"In whatever way you please, but show it. Bees are fond of honey and have no marked objection to sugar. Perhaps it's really sugar you're carrying. What makes you hesitate? You can be quite frank about your possessions with me. That's what I'm here for, to help people to be frank.'"

"As God is my witness, these are bees and only bees!"

"Look here, citizen, why drag God into this dirty company?" He swept his arm round the carriage. "You can see for yourself all these people are nothing but speculators and traders. And I'm not so sure about you. To put it plainly, I don't believe a word you're saying."

"Very well. Have the goodness to put your ear here. . . . Now can you hear them buzzing?"

"Not yet. We'd better stir them up a bit to verify your story. From the little education I had I seem to remember that bees are afraid of smoke. We'll just blow a little in through this hole."

Bromley shuddered. "Please, please! They'll all die! They're almost dead now, in this suffocating atmosphere."

Liga must have heard the ring of truth in that cry, for he made no more effort to verify Bromley's story; yet he was never very willing to concede a point. Carefully watching the effect of his words, he said slowly: "All right, I believe you; but why haven't you taken out a permit? It appears that these bees are not government property; perhaps they belong to the workers and peasants . . . Ah, you see what I'm getting at? Yes, it'll be best for all parties if you come with me while I write out a report. I'm sure you won't mind waiting here till I receive the necessary instructions and the matter can be fully cleared up. That'll be better for the bees too; they'll be glad of a rest after travelling so far."

Bromley stood up. In a resigned but dignified manner he passed the strap of the hives across his shoulders; then said, weighing every word: "I must obey your orders; but I'd like you to know what I think of you. You are behaving wickedly, inhumanely. I am carrying these bees because I am a specialized bee-keeper. For no reason I can understand you want to harm me. The bees will die, I know that: I've been breeding this sort for eight years now; then, through a caprice of yours . . ."

"Cut it short, citizen. They'll be worrying at Petrograd why the train's late."

"Through a caprice of yours all my hard work will be undone. I am ready." Then he remembered something. He stooped down and drew from under the seat a black earthenware pot. "You'd better have the honey too. It was food for the bees. Six times I've managed to hide it from the bandits. Now I give it to you quite willingly."

Liga blinked his eyes and looked at him closely. Then in a tone no one had ever heard him use before he said: "All right, all right! Liga is not a dog. He knows how to give way when he comes up against someone honest. Bon voyage, citizen."

A voice from the corner of the carriage said: "Bravo, Liga! You're not such a bad fellow after all." Then when Liga had disappeared the same voice said: "This chap here's a lucky chap all right! He's got the knack of getting what he wants."

In the gloomy twilight could be heard cries of anger coming from pillaged carriages further along the train; then the train moved, gathered speed laboriously, and with many grating sounds proceeded on its way.

Is that the last of it? wondered Bromley to himself. Can I dare hope my troubles are at an end?

When, five hours later, the long lines of the houses of the capital came into view, he drew a deep sigh of relief. Arrived! God be praised!

The train with passengers leaning like a long row of mud-splashes from every window steamed into Petrograd station soon after night had descended. Bromley made his way irresolutely through the crowd, then had difficulty in convincing himself that there were no cabs or trams to carry him the remainder of his journey. With a heavy heart he set out on foot for Lesnoi. He had not walked many paces through the soggy slush of snow before he realized it would be next to impossible for him to reach the suburbs of the city that night. Two hives weighing fifty kilos, and a heavy sack on shoulders already loaded down with the weariness of three days sitting in a train with no continuous sleep made his footsteps lag. He halted, swung the load from his shoulders, and sat himself down on the granite pedestal of a monument. Where, he wondered, could he pass the night?

After a few seconds he became conscious of someone sitting beside him. He looked down and saw a quite tiny person muttering and swearing over the contents of a large sack, a child of perhaps thirteen years.

"Could you tell me of somewhere to sleep tonight?" Bromley asked.

"Sorry, I can't," the urchin answered dryly as he busied himself in emptying his pockets. "As a matter of fact I've got some lodgings not far from here, though I don't know if they'll let me in again. Anyhow it's not lodgings I've got really; it's more like a corner of a room."

"D'you think they'd let me in? I will pay. I'll pay with bread. I've got a long way to go, to Lesnoi."

The boy was silent for a moment. "My landlady's a pretty hard woman, what you might call a Tartar. I shouldn't think she'd let you in: she's too afraid of typhoid. Where d' you come from? . . . Oh, from Viatka! It might do the trick if you said you came from Zvanka."

They set off side by side. For twenty paces there was silence; then Bromley asked: "What d'you do for an occupation?"

"Same as everyone else, I speculate. I've just been to Vologda looking for butter."

"Did you get much?"

"I got a lot of it, though there's not much left with me now. Thirty-five pounds I bought; but train thieves stole fifteen, and the curds I had as well. But that's what speculation's like. Tell me, citizen, what's butter worth in Viatka now? Is there a shortage there?"

"I can't really say," replied Bromley a little ashamed of his ignorance of commerce. "I think it's a thousand." Then he added: "Have you any parents?"

"Not now," the boy replied. "All I've got's an invalid brother. He's eight, but he can't use his legs. I have to find food for him: I pay for his board and lodging. It'd be best for him if he died soon; I shan't be able to do much more for him. I've been arrested four times. I go to Vologda every week, or to Tcherepovetz or Viatka. I've had typhus. It got me at Vologda. I was in bed a month and a half, and ever since then my legs have been weak and I've had a cough. I'll die soon. What'll happen to my little brother? That bothers me. Look here, citizen, don't go and tell my land-lady he's my brother. I pretend he's only my cousin. My surname's differ-ent from his."

"How did that happen?"

"It was just a bit of necessity." He stepped over a gutter, then added carelessly: "I stabbed one of the brigands in the hand. I meant to get him in the side, but I only cut his hand. They put me down to go to a peni-tentiary colony, but I slipped out of that all right, then I changed my name. That's to say, I didn't really change my name. What I did was to buy an identification card for a pound of butter." He laughed. "Now I'm like an actor, I go about with someone else's name. D'you think it matters? Before I die I'll confess about it. The long and short of it is, I'm a globe-trotter."

Shifting his sack onto the other shoulder the boy asked gently: "Tell me, citizen, can you think out a way of making sure my little brother gets what he needs? You see, when I'm dead there'll be no one to get food for him. He can't look after himself. I've just been to a fortune-teller. I gave her half a pound of butter to tell me without any mincing of words what my future was. She said I'd die soon. That's all right for me, but there's my brother. I once won a million and a half at cards. I thought it'd do to fix little brother's life for him, but it didn't work out like th— went on caramels and chocolate. I bought him else. D'you think you could advise —

"How old are you?" B

"Twelve," answered the
write."

Bromley had no time to
to duck his head to enter t
feet dragged in mud below
Then they crossed a dismal
and bathed with the rank eff

"What's your name?" asked

"Gania, Gabriel."

"Well, Gabriel, plead my ca
Lesnoi."

Gania clicked his tongue with compassion and said: "Yes, that's a long long way, and a state of siege has been declared. You're forbidden to be out after eleven." Then he pulled hard at a cracked bell. A dog barked. Footsteps dragged themselves nearer. A cautious unfriendly voice asked: "Who's there?"

"Me."

"Me who?"

"Me, of course!"

Cautiously the door was opened. The landlady listened to Bromley's request with a half-hostile attitude, and refused firmly. "I've no rooms vacant. You can't have lodgings if you're not registered. Etc. Etc."

Since he was on the point of collapse with fatigue, Bromley pleaded humbly with no effort to conceal his misery. "No, no, I won't let you in!" the landlady screamed. Then she turned angrily to Gania: "As for you, you have no right to live here at all. In future you can find somewhere else. D'you think this is a hotel?"

Bromley sighed. He was by now resigned to having to move on somewhere else, but he ventured questioningly: "A pound of honey?"

The landlady reflected for an instant, then to confirm what she thought she had heard, asked: "What d'you say?"

"I will give you one pound of honey for a night's lodging."

"In advance?"

"Yes, yes!" Bromley exclaimed excitedly. With great relief he slipped the strap of the hives from his shoulder: he felt that in another moment he would have fallen where he stood. Half an hour later he was stretched his full length on a straw mat and his cloak was over him. A night-light burned brightly, till by-and-by it spluttered out. The bees were out in the corridor. Gania was sitting on the foot of his brother's bed. While waiting for sleep to claim him, Bromley listened to the little globe-trotter's soft voice telling his ailing brother all about his expedition in search of butter and all his grand plans for the future. He remembered the words of his wife, "Unrest and uncertainty are the opposites of God: they lie in the domination of the Devil." Then, his imagination half paralysed by drowsiness presented to him, not Gania sitting on the foot of the bed, but a perky little imp possessed of the spirit of cunning and knowing well how to use it further his mischievous ends. Suddenly a torturing thought came to him: bees? Were they still alive? Would they die in this used-up air? Would ld and the jolting of their journey prove too much for their re- Was all his work to be brought to nothing? Were all his hopes to ? If only the good God had not planned that for him! as sound, though punctuated by a short and vivid dream. He is old home taking up a new swarm, while beyond him the s three little girls frisked in and out of the hives against green of the grass.

g globe-trotter, "but even so I can read and over the boy's question. He had sudde k passage of a porter's lodge in whi water dripped down his neck from ward impregnated with the sti n of an ancient dwelling. nley. ll, I'm very tired.

In the morning he had a quick conference with Gania. If the latter went to Viatka, he would go and see Bromley's wife, and hand her a letter asking her to provide him with shelter and tell him all the news. Then Bromley threw the strap of the hives across his shoulders, and set out for Lesnoi.

As he trudged by muddy pavements and snow-strewn streets he wondered whether he would find the landlady he had known still in charge of his old apartments. When he had known her she was fifty: that was ten years ago. Perhaps she had died? Perhaps she had moved? Alternately he felt convinced: "She will still be there"; "She will be gone". He tried to tell his fortune in this by counting the numbers of the windows in the houses he passed: an even number would mean he found his old landlady, an odd number—the dreaded reverse. Seven times he tempted providence. Six houses in Viborg Road gave a favourable result. His anxiety assuaged, he gave his mind to other matters. "When I've got myself settled in, I'll sell my gold watch; then I'll be able to buy a board and fix the hives by the window. There'll be a little hole in the window they can fly out by."

The melting snow around him stank putrid from the rotting rubbish it contained; yet in the midst of this miasma of decay he imagined suddenly he smelt the sweet perfume of acacias. He remembered there were acacias at the house he was making for. Was this sudden feeling that he smelt them a kindly message that after all his troubles his quest would be successful? Or was it trying to tell him the acacias had been cut down, cut down as the fence would have been to feed the stove? Derelict and forlorn the house rose before his imagination like a plucked fowl. Pray God this had not happened! His misgivings grew as he trudged forward.

. His anxiety was not justified. He found everything he had hoped for: his old landlady, the acacias, and even a room free. True the room was empty of furniture, there was no glass in the windows, the skirting had been torn away, but—it was a room. The landlady too had the same pillaged and patched appearance. Instead of shoes on her feet was a multiplicity of thick old socks, and the rest of her resembled a busted pillow.

When she first opened the door to Bromley she eyed him with a cold suspicious eye; then recognition twisted her wrinkles into smiles; in a shrill voice, which matched ill with her thick curves, she welcomed him: "You? It's not possible!"

"Yes, it is me."

Yes, yes, she thought, Mr. Bromley it certainly is, but a changed Mr. Bromley: his bearing was different and his eyes were tired now and yellow, sad, and a little dim. His red hair too had lost its golden sheen. One thing however remained the same—the stubborn line of his eyebrows. That still showed vigour, youth, and staying-power. As she looked at him her memories made her blush. She recollected shamefacedly the love she had felt for this bright student, the advances she had been the first to make, the cold dignity of his rebuff.

Bromley quickly told the story of his misfortunes, and ended: "I want to try my luck in Petrograd. Can you take me in? It's my last throw."

The landlady glanced at the bees and nodded her shawl-covered head. "You stay here with me and do what you like. I know you, you're one of the obstinate ones."

Her words seemed to lighten by a thousand kilos the weight on Bromley's back. He threw back his shoulders, and his heart beat normally again. The memory of his troubles slipped from him. He felt an urge to shout with joy! But no, the blows fate had dealt him had taught him not to be excited by a trifling triumph. Now that the problem of where to live was solved, his mind flicked back to his bees; but it was quickly recalled by the demands of friendship: he told his landlady about his three red-headed little girls, his quiet and thoughtful wife, and the fresh green meadow where he had pitched his tent those long years ago. Then he fell silent and went up to his room.

In solitude there he set himself to the labours he had planned. He bought some planks and carpenter's tools, mended the windows and stove, and above all fed his bees. Their need of care was great: the journey had upset them more than even he had feared. They shivered as if frozen; they seemed almost to want to die. But Bromley knew he would pull them through, and everything would come right again as it had been in the long-distant past. An almost heavenly strength possessed him as his spirits rose.

In his mind's eye he saw the arrival in Petrograd of his quiet wife and noisy children. Then he saw himself accepting a nice comfortable job in the pine forest; there they would all live in a little wooden house, and a meadow could be seen through the windows (how could anyone live without a green meadow?) and also this was the most important thing—on the grass would be a mottled mosaic of bee-hives. He thought he could already feel the waving steamy heat of the burning summer sun, and hear the most beautiful music in the world, the buzzing music of those industrious little creatures which God had sent onto earth to set an example to us all. Already too he was inhaling the sweet aromas of evening as they lapped against his face like rollers of the ocean; he saw the bees at the close of day, tired, with their full honey-sacs flying slowly home to their hives; and he heard the sonorous timbre of his daughters' laughter. This last thought brought him back from his reverie. What was happening to his wife and daughters?

Remembering Gania's promise to call at his home in Viatka, he hurried across the city. As he strode along he thought out the best way of placing the feeding-troughs and wondered whether it would be necessary to plant some mignonette.

Gania was not at home when he arrived; but his little paralysed brother foraged in a mess of broken chocolate and sunflower seeds under his pillow, and produced a crumpled envelope. Bromley tore it open, and the meaning of the few words he read in a clumsy, childish hand surged over him

like a flood of corroding poison: "Our darling mother died yesterday of
Spanish flu."

For once the fortitude and self-control he had inherited from his father
did not serve him. He let out a roar of anguish. A fierce hatred shook his
whole body. Against whom? He could not have said. The little invalid
gazed at him with the big compassionate eyes of an ikon, and sensed the
presence of grief. Although this was a stranger's grief and he was ignorant
of its cause, he began sobbing silently.

Bromley regained control of himself. A decision was called for. His children were there in Viatka with no one to look after them: here were his
bees in the same condition. His blood was there: here was the altar of his
hopes. He clenched his teeth, and set himself to unravel the knot. The two
possible solutions to the dilemma inevitably clashed.

Because bees do not like smoke, Bromley had never tasted tobacco; now
he felt an irresistible envy for all smokers. As soon as he was out again in
the street he bought himself a packet of cigarettes; then he said to himself:
"Before I have finished the packet, I must have made up my mind."

He set out on the streets to Lesnoi as he had done twelve days before.
Again he sought to discover his fate by counting the windows of the
houses: even numbers, he would go back to Viatka; odd numbers, he
would stay in Petrograd. He had not walked half the way, however, nor
finished the cigarettes before he made the sudden and irrevocable decision
to stay. He had left Viatka without a thought about whether he had the
right to leave or not; perhaps a second time he would not be allowed to
leave. In that event the bees in Petrograd would certainly perish. He must
stay here and send for his children.

When he got home he went straight up to bed, without seeing his landlady. After any deep emotion he usually slept heavily and long—like a new-
born baby, as they say in story-books. Now he slept for fifteen hours on
end. When he woke again he had a racking headache and his legs were
weak. The calm assurance he had felt when he took his decision to stay in
Petrograd had somewhat waned. However he sat down and wrote a letter
to friends at Viatka about his children; but a dull indifference to what
might happen had got him in its clutches. Nevertheless he attended to his
bees with his usual affection: he filled their feeder with sugared water, then
lighted the stove with care not to make a smoke. This duty done, he set
himself to planing a piece of wood, for some small boxes were needed. But
he groaned at his work. A clogging tiredness weighed him down. Was it
from grief? he wondered.

The tiredness became too much for him. He put his tools aside, and lay
down on the pallet, pulling his cloak around him; quickly he fell into a
light disturbed sleep.

It was as if only one half of his consciousness slept. The waking part
stood watching everything that happened to the other. Fantastic appari-

tions went in and out of it illuminated by a red-hot fire; then they piled
themselves together into heavy round blocks of varying sizes. They made
noises too. At first they resounded like balls in a skittle-alley, then they
tinkled, then, when they struck his skull and started spinning, they made
a rattling sound. It was incomprehensible and meaningless; but his waking
part went on watching closely while the little blocks swallowed the big
ones and hungrily chewed them into tiny pieces. Still unsatiated they attacked his head from every side, sometimes coming near his teeth. Then
he snapped at them and tried to chew them to ease the pressure on his
skull. He did not succeed in this; but soon some large grindstones came
to his aid. They had no difficulty in crushing all the blocks, but they went
further: as if by accident, they swallowed the side of his head which lay on
the pillow. Then followed terrible minutes, terrible because each grind-
stone had a face at the base of which waggled a jaw resembling the snout
of a pig. But eventually everything ended well: the grindstones started
turning, the faces moved, and the jaws chewed and gnashed with fury.
Occupied with their own work, they paid no more attention to Bromley. He
sighed with relief, sat up quickly, and looked around him. His room was
in darkness, and his head seemed not to belong to him: it had become horribly heavy, and pivoted as if it had been set in motion by invisible pistons.

"I must have caught cold," thought Bromley, vexed. He remembered a
tin of aspirin he had put on a shelf soon after he arrived there two weeks
ago. He would take some now. He tried to rise, but the effort required was
too much for him: his head fell back on the pillow, the last ounce of
strength left his body, and dreams recaptured him.

This time the dream was of a snow-storm with mounted men in great
fur caps riding through it. Then everything became a blank.

Four days later the landlady knocked timidly on his door. She knew his
liking for solitude, and would never enter his room without being called,
even to make the bed. Now, getting no answer to her knocking, she
knocked again, and again and again and again. Then she cautiously opened
the door, and threw a quick look round the room. She saw Bromley lying
with his eyes open, wild, and bloodshot. On the bare floor he was lying: the
mattress, blankets, and pillow had been tossed aside. Great runnels of hot
dirty sweat trickled across his temples and splashed to the floor boards,
whence rose a thin thread of steam.

The landlady looked at his eyes, and fled the room terrified. A few
minutes passed and she returned accompanied by a white-coated student.
In silence and with every care they tried to get him back into bed. He resisted them: he shouted, kicked, and threw off again the pillow they had
placed under his head. So they tied his body and legs in the bedding; then
they left the room.

For several minutes Bromley lay still uttering incoherent groans. Suddenly he sat up, shook himself, and placed his elbows on a chair beside

him. With a great effort he succeeded in standing to his full height, dragging with him the blankets, mattress, and pillow which were tied to him. He took a step forward, panted, and stood still. He seemed to be listening for something, and his face shone with the gleam of happy madness.

The hot rays of the spring sunshine had set the bees in a flutter and were calling them out of doors. They buzzed feverishly in their hives and crowded in and out through the hole in the window. Listening to the familiar happy sound, Bromley, hobbled like a horse, tottered to greet them, his face glowing with joy.

Standing there in the sunshine he once again resembled a Greek god. Tall and defiant, his copper-coloured hair shining like an aureole round his head, his body swathed in steam from the feverish sweat: the picture was of a divine being hovering in the clouds.

But a weight on his back and on his legs, an insupportable weight, anchored him to the earth and made him powerless. With growing irritation he shook himself, he threatened some invisible enemy with his bony fists, then, with the violence of despair, tried to throw off his ridiculous bonds, a pillow, a mattress, and a quilt. For a moment his arms thrashed like flails, then slowly grew feeble, and his strength ebbed never to rise again.

The famished bees, now four days without food, crept for the thousandth time sadly, hopefully, and uselessly along their empty feeding-trough. Then they dragged themselves across the floor towards their master, and there they stood perplexed in front of his cold and glazing eyes.

WITHOUT CHERRY BLOSSOM

Pantaleimon Romanof

(1884–)

TRANSLATED BY STEPHEN GRAHAM

IT SEEMS as if there never had been so magnificent a spring before.

But, dear Verusha, I feel sad.

Sad, ill, as if I'd done something rather second-rate. . . .

I've a bottle with a broken neck in my window at the hostel, and a broken withered little branch of bird cherry in it. I brought it home last night. . . . And when I look at that bottle, somehow I want to cry.

I'll be brave and tell you all. I lately made the acquaintance of a comrade from another faculty. I am far removed from sentiment of any kind, as he would say; far from bewailing lost innocence, and even further from any gnawing of conscience over my first "fall." But there is something that rubs me up the wrong way, not clear, confused, ever present.

I'll tell you later, with "shameless" frankness, how it all happened. But first of all I would like to put some questions to you.

When you and Paul were united, for the first time, didn't you wish that the day of your first love might be to you a sort of festival day, somehow or other different from the everyday?

For instance, would it have seemed humiliating to you, on that spring festival day of your life, to go out of doors in dirty boots, or to wear a torn or soiled blouse?

I ask you because all my acquaintances, the folk of my own age, look on the matter differently. I do not seem to have sufficient pluck to think and act just as I feel.

It needs a good deal of effort to go against the accepted opinion of those among whom one lives.

With us the accepted attitude towards the beautiful is one of youthful disdain, and it is the same with regard to any daintiness or correctness of attire or fastidiousness in the home.

Our hostel is all dirt, filth, disorder, tumbled beds. Cigarette ends on the window ledges, flimsy partitions between the cubicles all covered with torn placards and advertisements. There is not one of us who tries to beautify his dwelling, and as there is a rumour that we are going to be transferred to another building, the students are even more careless than they would be ordinarily, and frequently do deliberate damage to the place.

It is as if there were someone or other before whom we are ashamed to be seen occupying ourselves with such trifles as a clean and beautiful room and healthy fresh air in it. It is not because we have serious business on hand and no time, but because we feel obliged to despise everything connected with care for beauty.

That is the more strange because we all know that the powers that be, our poverty-stricken proletarian powers, spend a vast amount of money and energy simply to make everything beautiful, putting flower-gardens all over the place, the like of which was unknown under the old régime of squires and capitalists, though they prided themselves on their love of an elegant, beautiful life. All Moscow gleams with stucco, and our university, which stood a hundred years looking like a tumble-down police station, has now been converted into the most beautiful building in Moscow.

And we . . . feel an involuntary pride in the fact that it is so beautiful. But for all that, our own life inside these walls, purified by our new government, our own life is dominated by filth and disorder.

All the girls and our men-comrades behave as if they were afraid of being accused of delicacy and good manners. They deliberately cultivate a coarse and debauched way of talking and slap one another on the hips. And when they refer to sex they make use of the most coarse expressions, the most disgusting street slang.

The most abominable epithets have with us full civic rights. And when some of our girls, I will not say all, a few, feel mortified, something even worse sets in. The rest try to accustom them "to the mother tongue."

Cynicism, the tone of coarse debauch and the trampling underfoot of all fastidiousness alone have success. Perhaps it is because we are a poverty-stricken lot, and having nothing to spend on dress, we just spit upon the whole business or like to pretend that we do. Or it may be that we think of ourselves as the soldiers of the revolution, for whom naturally senti-mental notions and fastidiousness have no place. But if we are soldiers of the revolution we ought somehow to take an example from the power we have set up, and strive for beauty in life not simply for the sake of the beautiful, but for the sake of cleanliness and health. For that reason it seems about time that we decided to give up this exaggerated, over-emphasised barracks style.

But, you know, the majority like it. To say nothing of our men, our girls like it; it gives them more freedom and demands little exercise of will on their part.

But this neglect of the beautiful, the pure and the healthy leads to an appalling hooliganism in our intimate relationships. It begets a coarseness, a lack of ceremony, a fear of showing the least human delicacy of feeling or of sensibility or care towards one's woman friend or any of the girls.

It all comes from the fear of infringing the unwritten moral code.

Things are different with you at the academy. I am sometimes sorry that I entered the university. My mother, who is a village midwife, looks up to me with a sort of pious respect as to a higher being, but I often wonder what she would think if she saw the filth in which we live and heard the latest bad language that we habitually use.

For us love does not exist; we have only sexual relationships. And so, love is scornfully relegated to the realm of "psychology," and our right to existence is only understood physiologically.

The girls live with their men friends, and it is a small matter to go with them for a week or a month, or promiscuously, for one night only. And anyone who is trying to find in love anything beyond the physiological is laughed down as mental or a bad case.

II

What does he think he is? An ordinary student in high boots and a blue blouse unbuttoned at the neck. He always pushes back his untidy locks from his brow with his hands.

His eyes attracted me. When he is by himself and is walking along the corridors one feels a great seriousness and calm in his eyes.

But directly he fell in with any of his fellow-students he became, it seemed to me, exaggeratedly noisy, loose and coarse. The girls inspired him with self-confidence because he was handsome, the men because he was clever. He seemed to be afraid to lose the sort of leadership which he had.

I saw two men in him, one possessing a good deal of inner strength and seriousness of mind, the other a vulgar wag who irritated you by the way he had of showing off and impressing others with the appearance of being very coarse, much more coarse than, in fact, he is.

Yesterday at sunset we went out for the first time together. Evening stillness had settled on the city and the street noises were subdued. The air was fresh and there was a pleasant odour of the damp earth coming from the squares.

"Come along to my place, I don't live far from here," said he.

"No, I'm not coming."

"What's that? Etiquette?"

"It's not etiquette at all. That, in the first place. In the second place, it's very pleasant out of doors at the moment."

He shrugged his shoulders.

We walked along the quay and stood for a while at the drawbridge. A girl came selling branches of bird cherry blossom. I bought a spray of it and had to wait a long while for my change. He stood to one side, looking at me and frowning slightly.

"Can't you get on without cherry blossom?"

"I can. But it's better with cherry blossom than without."

"I manage always without cherry blossom, and somehow it does not turn out badly," said he, grinning unpleasantly.

Two girls were ahead of us. A whole crowd of students were mauling them, and when they tore themselves away the students burst into fits of laughter, stared after the girls and called out things after them.

"They've put the girls in a bad temper. Went to them without cherry blossom, and the girls took fright," said my companion.

"Why do you dislike cherry blossom so much?" I asked.

"Well, it all ends the same way, cherry blossom or no cherry blossom. . . . Why mince matters?"

"You speak in that way because you have never loved."

"Why is that necessary?"

"Then what is there in a woman for you?"

"Oh, drop this Chinese ceremoniousness and call me thou, don't call me you! As for woman, there is something there for me, and I dare say it amounts to a good deal."

"I shan't call you you. If everyone uses thou there is no pleasure in it."

We passed some lilac bushes. I stopped a moment to pin the cherry blossom to my blouse. He made a sudden movement, pushed back my head and tried to kiss me.

I pushed him back.

"Don't want to; all right, don't!" said he calmly.

"I don't want it. As you don't love anyone, it's all the same to you what woman you kiss. If instead of me it had been someone else, you'd have wanted to kiss her just the same."

"Quite right. A woman also kisses whom she wants to, and does not confine herself to one. We had a little beano lately, and the fiancée of a friend of mine who was there kissed me with as much gusto as she did him. And if it had been someone else near her, she'd have done the same by him. And that couple are marrying for love at the registration office and the rest of it."

I was annoyed in the depths of myself when I heard him speak thus. I had fancied that he was not entirely indifferent to me. How many times had he sought my glance even when I was in a dense crowd of other students! And why should he spoil this delightful spring evening with licentious and coarse ideas, when one craved tenderness and quiet conversation?

I hated him at that moment. We were passing a bench on which a lady of a kind was sitting. She wore silk stockings and her legs were crossed above the knees. She raised her eyes whenever anyone went by.

My companion stared fixedly at her. And having gone on a few steps he turned round and stared at her again. I felt as if I had been stung.

"Let's sit down here," said he at the next bench. He wanted to sit down there so that he could continue to stare at her.

All at once I felt so upset that I felt I might begin to cry. Fearing lest I should break down, I told him I did not want to be with him any longer and said good-bye.

He was taken aback, and evidently bewildered.

"Why?" he asked. "Don't you like me to be sincere? Would it be better if I dressed my ideas up and lied?"

"I'm sorry you do not possess anything that does not need to be dressed up."

"Well, what are you going to do about it?" said he, as if not at first grasping what I meant. "In that case I'll be going also. Good-bye." He held my hand in his for a moment. "Only it's foolish, it's foolish," he repeated, and threw my hand down and strode away towards his home.

I also was taken by surprise. I did not think that he would go away.

I stopped on the corner of the boulevard and looked round. It was one of those May nights when you feel that the life encompassing you is for that night only and never to be repeated. The moon, with wisps of cloud about her, stood on high in a warm, cloudy yellow haze. The far-distant sunset tones were lost behind the roofs of many houses and the Kremlin towers. And the infrequent street lights were dimmed by the moonlight.

And there were gay crowds of young men and girls in the brightly lighted square in front of the cathedral, and loving couples on the garden seats under low-branching, close-cropped trees and lilac bushes.

There was a murmur of light conversation and laughter; one saw the glowing ends of cigarettes. Everyone seemed affected, intoxicated by the awakening warmth of the night and eager not to lose a moment of it.

But when such a night strikes no chord in your soul, when you are lonely and miserable and have no companion, you feel very sad, you could not feel worse.

A few moments earlier I had been indifferent whether he was with me or not. But the thought of his staring at that woman on the bench preyed on my mind. I felt a tearful anxiety, and I weakened to such an extent that I wanted nothing else in the world but that he should be with me.

In a word—don't condemn me—I could not bear to be like one who has been expelled from the glad company, thrown out from the choir, this spring festival night.

And without considering what it might mean, I retraced my steps and hurried towards his house.

III

There was but one thought in my head: he might have gone out, I might be late, I might remain solitary. And then I reproached myself for breaking away from him so ridiculously without making the slightest effort to bring out the good side of his character.

I reflected that in this I had behaved in just the same way as those who shrug their shoulders at unpleasant conditions and do nothing to better them. It meant that I wanted to get something better without any expense of energy on my part.

I went under the gateway of the old stone house and felt the strange contrast of the air of the warm May night out of doors and the cold reek of unheated walls.

There are still many entrances like this in Moscow, with unwashed doors and rags of old advertisements hanging from them, filthy outer stairways scribbled over and unswept.

He didn't at all expect to see me again. Apparently he was about to sit down to work. There was a slight table that looked like a plasterer's trestles set up against one of the walls. An electric lamp bulb hung on a cord from the ceiling, but had been pulled over to the table and was fixed there by a nail.

"So, the heroine has returned!" he exclaimed. "Evidently thought better of it. So much the better."

He came up to me grinning and took me by the arm. Perhaps he was going to kiss me or stroke me, but he did neither.

"I was sorry we quarrelled and I wanted to put it right," said I.

"What was there to put right? Wait a moment, I'll put a notice on the door that I'm not at home. Otherwise someone may come."

He wrote out the notice, standing at the table, and then went out with it. Alone in the room, I had a look round.

This room of his had the same general character as that staircase. The walls were scrawled with telephone numbers; cigarette ends and scraps of paper littered the unswept floor. There was a tumbled, unmade bed alongside one of the walls, just as in one of our rooms at the hostel; dirty dishes on the window-ledge, empty bottles, butter-paper, egg-shells, cans.

I felt somewhat embarrassed and could not think what I would say to him when he came back. It would not be very wise to be silent, as that might be construed to mean something quite different.

Then it occurred to me to ask myself why he had gone out to fix that notice on the door. What if someone did come?

Suddenly I understood, and at the thought I went dizzy and caught my breath. With a beating heart I went to the window-ledge, having the intention of clearing away the bottle and cigarette boxes to make a place to sit down. I saw that my hand trembled. All the same I did clear the ledge and lay down on it on my stomach.

I had never felt before such an agitated tension of expectation as I did as I lay there listening for what might happen behind my back.

My only regret was that the best minutes of my life and happiness, perhaps of my first day of love, must be accomplished in the midst of the leavings of yesterday's food in this bespattered, dirty room.

That was why, when he came back into the room, I suggested we go out for some fresh air.

An expression of surprise and vexation flitted across his face.

"Why?" he asked. "Haven't you just come from out there?"

Then his voice changed.

"I've fixed it so that nobody is likely to disturb us. Don't talk nonsense. I'm not going to let you out anywhere now," said he hurriedly.

"I don't like being here."

"Ah, beginning all that over again . . ." said he crossly. "What's the matter? Where do you want to go to?"

His speech was choking and rapid, and his hands trembled when he thought to restrain me from going.

My hands also trembled, and my heart beat so violently it was dark before my eyes. A conflict was raging in my mind, the mood of surrender, the feeling that no one would disturb us, and the mood of protest, engendered by his thievish hurried whispering, his greedy haste and the loss of his calm and self-restraint. He seemed to have only one thing at heart, to succeed before any of his comrades burst in upon him. He showed impatience and irritation at the slightest show of resistance on my part.

We women even in free love cannot look too squarely at the actual Fact. For us the fact is always at the end of the chapter, while at the beginning we are charmed by the man himself, his mind, his talents, his soul, his tenderness. We always begin by desiring something other than physical union. When this other desire has not been satisfied and a woman falls a victim to the momentary impulse of her senses, she experiences a disgust with herself instead of a fullness and happiness. She becomes hostile to the man as towards an accomplice in her fall, as towards a gross being who has forced her to have disagreeable and abominable sensations.

The unmade bed, those egg-shells in the window, the dirt, his furtive glances, and the feeling that things were not going the way they should, had already discountenanced me.

"I can't remain!" I exclaimed, almost in tears.

"Now what's the matter? Don't you like the furniture? Not enough poetry in it? But I'm not some baron . . ." he cried with ill-concealed vexation.

I suppose the expression on my face changed at his shouting, for, as if anxious to undo the impression he might have made by these words, he began to calm me in hurried whispers.

"That's all right, dear, stop . . . it's quite true someone might come in."

I ought most certainly to have gone away then. But the fact of being alone with him there enkindled such sheer desire in me as in him. I chose to deceive myself and stayed on in the false expectation that something would intervene. . . .

"Wait, I'll make some poetry for you," said he, and turned out the light.

That was better truly, for one did not see the dirty bed nor the bottles nor the cigarette ends on the floor.

I stood at the window with my back to him. He came up behind me and put an arm round my neck while I remained looking out at the window. I could not see the expression of his face, but I was grateful to him for that embrace. I would have liked to stand there for a long, long while.

But his impatience got the better of him. He kept thinking that his comrades might come in. "How long will you stand there?" he asked, leading me away from the window with his arm.

When we got up he first of all turned on the light.

"Oh, I don't want any light," I cried in misery and alarm.

He looked at me with astonishment, and shrugging his shoulders, turned the light out again. Then he went back to the bed and began to tidy it.

"I must put my room-mate's bed straight, otherwise Vanya'll guess right away that I've had a lady in the room," said he.

He was fussing around the bed and was on all-fours on the floor, evidently looking for something. I was left alone. Presently he came up to me. Almost against my will I gave a deep sigh and turned my head round to see him. I was struggling with all my strength to overcome my feelings. He stretched out a hand.

"There," said he, "your hairpins. I crawled and crawled about the floor. Why must you be absolutely without light? You'd better be off now or somebody will be along. I'll see you out by the back way. The front door will be shut now."

We did not say a word to one another, and somehow seemed to be avoiding one another's eyes.

When I got into the street I walked some way mechanically, without a thought. Then suddenly I felt something metallic in my hand and I shuddered, remembering that it was the hairpins which he had put in my palm. I even stood and gazed at them. They were certainly hairpins, nothing more or less.

Still holding them in my hand, I staggered home. I still had that spray of crumpled blossom on my blouse, and it hung loose like a rag.

And the same wonderful night held sway over the town. The moon stood high over the masses of buildings, and the little clouds were like curling smoke. The same vague, misty horizon lay far away over the city.

And there was the same aroma of apple blossom, bird cherry and grass. . . .

IN THE TOWN OF BERDICHEV

Vassili Grossman

(1908–   )

TRANSLATED BY JOHN RODKER

IT WAS STRANGE to see Vavilova's dark weather-beaten face turn red.

'What are you laughing at?' she said at last. 'Don't be silly.'

Koziriov took a paper from the table, looked at it and, shaking his head, burst out laughing again.

'Oh, I can't help it,' he said laughing, '. . . report . . . of the Commissar of the first battalion . . . forty days' leave because of pregnancy.'

He became serious.

'Well, all right. But who will take your place? Perelmutter, of the political section?'

'Perelmutter is a staunch Communist,' said Vavilova.

'You're all staunch,' remarked Koziriov, and, lowering his voice, as though he were talking about something shameful, asked:

'Are you going to have the baby soon, Claudia?'

'Yes, soon,' answered Vavilova and, taking off her fur cap, wiped the perspiration off her forehead.

'I would have got rid of it,' she said in a bass voice. 'But I waited too long: you know yourself that at Groubeshov I never got off my horse for three months. And when I went to the hospital the doctor refused to do it.'

The corners of her lips drooped as though she were going to cry.

'I even threatened the damned fellow with my Mauser, but he refused—he said it was too late.'

She went out, and Koziriov remained sitting at the table and looking at the report.

'So this is Vavilova,' thought he. 'Nothing very womanish about her—carries a Mauser, wears leather breeches, has led her battalion in the attack any number of times, and even her voice is not a woman's—yet Nature must tell in the end, apparently.'

And for some reason he was resentful and felt a little sad.

On the report he wrote 'Order,' and waving his nib hesitatingly over the paper, sat frowning—how should he word it?

'Leave of forty days to be given from this day': he pondered a little and added 'On account of illness,' then above that scribbled in 'woman's illness,' swore to himself, and crossed out 'woman's illness.'

'Now make soldiers of them!' he said, and called his orderly.

'Our Vavilova, eh?' he said loudly and angrily. 'You've heard, I suppose?'

'Yes, I've heard,' answered the orderly, and shaking his head spat on the ground.

Together they condemned Vavilova and all women generally, made a few jokes, laughed, and then Koziriov ordered him to fetch the Staff Commander and said:

'You must go and see her—tomorrow, I should say; find out whether she is in a private house or in hospital, and how she's getting on.'

Then he and the Staff Commander hung over the table till next morning, their fingers moving over the map, speaking in short abrupt sentences —the Poles were approaching.

Vavilova went to live in a room requisitioned for her.

The little house stood in the Yatki, as the market-place was called, and belonged to Chaim Abraham Leibovich Magazannik, whom the neighbours and even his own wife called Chaim Tuter, which means Tartar.

Vavilova's entry into the house was not effected without a scandal. She was brought to the house by an employee of the communal department, a thin lad in a leather jacket and Red Army helmet. Magazannik swore at him in Jewish: the youth was silent and shrugged his shoulders.

Then Magazannik went over to the Russian language.

'What impudence these whipper-snappers have,' he shouted to Vavilova, as though he expected her to share his indignation. 'That's all they could think of. Of course, there are no bourgeois in the town. There's only one room left for the Soviet, and that one belongs to the poor man Magazannik. Only from a working-man with seven children can they take a room. What about Litvak the grocer? And Khodorov the clothier? And Ashkenazi, the leading millionaire in the town?'

Around him stood Magazannik's children, seven ragged curly-pated angels gazing at Vavilova with their coal-black eyes. As big as a house, she was twice as tall as their father. They thought it all terribly funny and very interesting.

Finally Magazannik was pushed aside, and Vavilova passed into her room.

Such a concentrated smell of human beings coming from the sideboard, the flat feather beds which were as dark and flabby as the breasts of the old women who had once received those feather beds as part of their dowry, and the chairs with their gaping seats, assailed her nostrils, that she took a deep breath as though she were going to plunge into deep water.

At night she could not sleep. The Magazannik family snored on the other side of the wall like an orchestra composed of many instruments, from the droning double-bass to the high flutes and violins. The closeness of the summer night, the heavy smells—everything seemed to suffocate her.

What smells there were in the room!

Of kerosene, of garlic, of perspiration, of goose dripping, of unwashed linen. The odours of the human animal.

She felt her swollen dilated belly; at times the living being within her kicked and turned round.

For months she had struggled with it, honestly and persistently: sprung heavily from her horse; at 'Subotniks'[1] in the towns, silent and strenuous, she rolled about pine blocks weighing many poods; drank herbs and infusions in the villages; used up so much of the iodine belonging to the regimental chemical stores that the surgeon thought of sending a complaint to the sanitary department of the brigade; scalded herself with boiling water in the bath-house until she was covered with blisters.

But it obstinately went on growing, preventing her from walking and from riding; she suffered from nausea, vomited, and was drawn down to the earth.

At first she laid all the blame on that sad and ever-silent man who had been stronger than herself, and had found a way through her thick leather jacket and cloth tunic to her woman's heart. She saw how he was the first to run on the little wooden bridge which was so terrible in its simplicity, how the enemy's machine-gun crackled, and how he seemed to vanish: the empty greatcoat threw its arms up and falling, hung over the brook.

[1]Saturday (Sabbath). A collective voluntary effort to hasten the completion of some job.

She flew past him on her ardent little horse and the battalion, as though it were pushing her, poured after her.

After this it remained. It was to blame for everything. And now Vavilova lay conquered, and it victoriously kicked her with its heels, and lived in her.

In the morning, when Magazannik was getting ready to go to work, and his wife was giving him breakfast, driving away flies, children, and the cat, he said, speaking in a low voice and glancing at the wall of the requisitioned room:

'Give her some tea, a plague on her.'

He basked in the sunlit columns of dust, the smells, the children's cries, the cat's miaowing, the grumbling of the samovar. He did not feel like going to the workshop: he loved his wife, his children, his old mother, and he loved his home.

He went away sighing, and in the house only women and children remained.

The Yatki market-place seethed the whole day long. Peasants were selling birchwood, white as though it had been chalked all over; peasant-women were rustling their wreaths of onions; old Jewish women sat over fluffy hills made of geese with their legs tied together. Out of this luxuriant white flower the goose-seller would pull out a living petal with a sinuous neck and her customers would blow on the tender fluff between its legs and feel the yellow fat under the soft warm skin.

Dark-legged girls in coloured kerchiefs carried tall red pots full to the brim with wild strawberries, and timidly, as though they were going to run away, looked at their customers. Moist yellow lumps of butter wrapped in downy leaves of green burdock were being sold from carts.

A blind beggar, with the white beard of a wizard, wept tragically and as though in prayer as he held out his hand, but his terrible grief touched no one: everybody passed him with indifference. A peasant-woman tore the smallest onion off her wreath and threw it into the old man's iron basin. He felt it all over, and leaving off his prayers, said angrily:

'May your children provide for you like this in your old age,' and once again started crooning his prayer, the prayer which was as ancient as the Jewish people.

People were selling, buying, touching, feeling, raising their eyes thoughtfully to the heavens as though they expected somebody in the tender blue sky to advise them whether they should buy a pike or whether it were better to buy a carp. Meanwhile everybody went on making a deafening noise, swearing, abusing each other, and laughing.

Vavilova tidied up and swept the room. She put away her greatcoat, fur cap, and boots. Her head was bursting from the street noises. The little Tuters were making a noise inside the house, and she seemed to be asleep and having an unpleasant strange dream.

When Magazannik came in the evening after work, he stood amazed in the doorway: at the table sat his wife Beila and by her side sat a huge woman in a wide dress, with loose slippers on her bare feet, and a bright kerchief tied round her head; they were laughing together softly, talking to each other, and holding up tiny toy-like baby clothes in their big fat hands.

In the day-time Beila had gone into Vavilova's room. Vavilova was standing by the window, and Beila's sharp woman's eye saw her condition.

'I beg your pardon,' said Beila with determination, 'but you're pregnant.'

And Beila, throwing up her hands, laughing and lamenting, started fussing round her.

'Yes,' said she. 'Children—you don't know yet what a misfortune they are,' and she pressed and squeezed the youngest Tuter against her bosom. 'They're such a misfortune, such a calamity, such a nuisance. Every day they want to eat, and not one week passes but one has a rash, or another the fever, or another an abscess. And Doctor Baraban, God bless him, takes ten pounds of the best rye flour for every visit.'

She stroked little Sonia's head.

'And they're all alive—I haven't lost one.'

She discovered that Vavilova knew nothing, did not know how to do anything, and understood nothing. She bent down immediately before Beila's great knowledge. She listened to Beila and asked her questions, and Beila, laughing with pleasure at the Commissar's knowing nothing, told her about everything.

How to feed and bath the baby and put him to sleep, what must be done to prevent his crying at night, how many napkins and shirts one must have, how new-born babies scream themselves hoarse, turn blue, and it seems as though one's heart must stop beating for fear that the baby may die, how to cure diarrhoea, what causes the itch, how the spoon suddenly begins to make a noise in the baby's mouth and by that you can tell that he is beginning to cut his teeth.

A complicated world with its own laws, customs, joys, and sorrows.

Vavilova knew nothing of this world. And Beila condescendingly, like an elder sister, introduced her to it.

'Get out of the way,' she screamed at the children, 'out into the yard!' And when only the two of them were left in the room, Beila, her voice lowered to a whisper, started telling her about the confinement. O, this was not a simple thing. Like an old soldier, Beila told the young recruit about the great pangs and joys of childbirth.

'Giving birth to children,' said she, 'you think is a simple matter, like a war: bang-bang and it's all over; oh no, by no means, it's not nearly as simple.'

Vavilova listened to her. For the first time, during the whole of her pregnancy, she had met a person who spoke about this accidental and unpleasant thing which had overtaken her as a happy event which would be the most important and necessary occurrence in Vavilova's life.

And in the evening the discussion was continued this time with Tuter participating. No time was to be lost: after supper Tuter took a candle and climbed up to the attic and making a great din, dragged down an iron cradle and a bath for the new human being.

'Don't worry, Comrade Commissar,' he said laughingly, his eyes sparkling. 'Our business, which you are taking on, is in full swing.'

'Be quiet, be quiet, you rascal,' uttered his wife. 'It's not for nothing that people call you the Tartar.'

At night Vavilova lay in her bed. The heavy smells no longer oppressed her as they had done the night before. She had become used to them, and did not even notice them. She did not want to think about anything.

She seemed to hear horses neighing somewhere, and to see a long line of brown horses' heads: each had a white patch on the forehead. The heads were incessantly moving, nodding, and baring their teeth. She thought about the battalion, and remembered Kirpichov, the political instructor of the second company. All was quiet on the Front. Who was lecturing about the July days? The surveyor must be rated soundly for having delayed the arrival of the boots. And then they could cut up cloth themselves for puttees. In the second company there were a good many dissatisfied men, especially that curly-headed fellow who sang songs of the Don. Vavilova yawned and closed her eyes. The battalion went away far far into the distance, into the pink corridor of the dawn, between the wet stacks of snow. And her thoughts about it were somehow unreal.

It pushed her impatiently with its little heels. Vavilova opened her eyes and sat up in bed.

'A girl or a boy?' she asked aloud. And she suddenly felt how the heart in her bosom became big and warm and began to throb.

'A girl or a boy?'

The confinement began in the day-time.

'Oh!' screamed Vavilova hoarsely, woman-like, as she felt a sharp, all-penetrating pain seize her suddenly.

Beila put her to bed. Sioma ran gaily for the midwife.

Vavilova held Beila's hand and said quietly and rapidly:

'It's begun, Beila, and I thought it would start only in ten days. It's begun, Beila.'

Then the pains passed away, and to Vavilova it seemed that they need not have sent so quickly for the midwife.

But half an hour later the pains started again. Vavilova's face turned quite dark and the sunburn on it looked dead: as though it had been laid on by accident. Vavilova lay with clenched teeth; she looked as if she were thinking of something shameful and painful, as if she were about to jump up and cry 'What have I done, what have I done?' as she covered her face with her hands in despair.

The children were peeping into the room, the blind grandmother was

heating a large saucepan of water on the stove. Beila kept looking at the
door: the expression of anguish on Vavilova's face frightened her. At last
the midwife came. Her name was Rosalia Samoilovna. Her hair was cut
short and she was stocky and red-faced. The house was immediately filled
with her querulous penetrating voice. She scolded Beila, the children, and
the old grandmother. Everybody started running around her. The primus
stove in the kitchen started humming. The table and chairs were taken out
of the room; Beila washed the floor with as much haste as though she were
putting out a fire; Rosalia Samoilovna herself drove the flies away with a
towel. Vavilova watched her and it seemed to her as though the Commander of the army had arrived at Staff Headquarters. He was also stocky,
red-faced, and querulous, and he used to come when something had gone
wrong at the Front, and everybody would read the communiqués and look
at each other and whisper, as though a dead or dangerously sick man lay
there. And the Commander would brutally tear aside this veil of mystery
and silence—shouting, abusing, giving orders and laughing, as though baggage trains cut off and regiments surrounded by the enemy were none of
his business.

She submitted to Rosalia Samoilovna's dictatorial voice, answered her
questions, turned round, and did everything she ordered her to do. At
times she seemed to be losing consciousness; the walls and ceiling seemed
to lose their sharpness of surface and outline, to be breaking and falling
on her in waves. The midwife's loud voice would bring her to herself again
and she could see her red perspiring face and the white tail-ends of the
kerchief round her neck. She thought of nothing now. She wanted to howl
like a wild beast and to bite the pillow. Her bones seemed to crack and to
break, and the clammy sickening perspiration stood out in drops on her
forehead. She did not scream, however, but only ground her teeth and, convulsively tossing her head about from side to side, gulped in the air.

Now and again the pains left her as though she had never had any, and
in astonishment she would look about her, listen to the noise of the market,
and gaze with wonder at the glass on the stool and the picture on the wall.

But when the child, furious in his desire to live, started tearing at her
again, she felt the horror of the renewed pangs and a confused feeling of
joy: let it be as soon as possible—after all it was inevitable.

Rosalia Samoilovna said in a low voice to Beila:

'If you think that I should have liked to have my first child at thirty-six,
you're mistaken, Beila.'

Vavilova did not hear her words, but she felt frightened because the
midwife had spoken in a low voice.

'What, shan't I live?' she asked.

She did not catch Rosalia Samoilovna's answer.

Beila stood in the door pale and flustered, and said, shrugging her shoulders:

'Well, well. And who wants this torture—neither she, nor the child, nor the father, may he perish, nor God in Heaven. Who was the clever person who invented it for our misfortune?'

The confinement lasted for many hours.

When Magazannik came home he sat on the steps outside. He was as worried as though it was his Beila who was in childbirth. The twilight deepened, and the windows were lit up. Jews were returning from synagogue, carrying their prayer clothes under their arm. In the moonlight the empty Yatki market-place, the little houses, and the streets seemed picturesque and mysterious. Cavalry-men in riding-breeches marched about the brick pavements clinking their spurs. Girls were eating sunflower seeds and laughing at the Red Army men. One of them was saying in a quick patter:

'And I eat sweets and throw the papers at him, and I eat and throw the papers at him.'

'Ay,' said Magazannik, 'we didn't have enough troubles of our own, but the whole Partisan Brigade must come and be confined in my house.' Suddenly he began to listen intently and half rose from where he was sitting. From behind the door he heard a man's hoarse voice.

The voice was shouting such violent obscene oaths that Magazannik, after listening for a while, shook his head and spat on the ground: it was Vavilova, mad with pain in the final phase of labour, fighting with God, with woman's cursed lot.

'That I understand,' said Magazannik, 'that I understand: a Commissar is having a baby; while Beila can only say one thing "Oh mother, oh mother?"'

Rosalia Samoilovna slapped the new-born baby on his wrinkled damp buttocks and announced:

'A boy!'

'What did I say!' exclaimed Beila triumphantly, and opening the door, cried out exultantly:

'Chaim, children, a boy!'

And the whole family clustered in the doorway and talked excitedly to Beila. Even the blind grandmother felt her way to her son and smiled at the great miracle. She moved her lips, her head trembled, her dead hands felt their way over her black kerchief. She was smiling and whispering silently. The children pushed her away from the door but she stretched out her neck and tried to get in: she wanted to hear the voice of ever-triumphant life.

Vavilova looked at the new-born child. She was surprised that such an insignificant bit of reddish-blue flesh could have caused such terrible suffering.

She had imagined that her child would be big, freckly, and snub-nosed, with a bristling red head, and that he would immediately start fighting and kicking, crying loudly, and trying to get away. But he was a weak little fellow, like an oat-stem grown up in a cellar; he could not keep his little head up; his small crooked legs moved about as though they were dried up; his whitish-blue eyes were blind; and his whimper could hardly be heard. It seemed as though, if the door were suddenly opened, he would be extinguished like the thin bent candle that Beila had fastened to the edge of the cupboard.

And although it was like a hot-house in the room, she stretched out her arms and said:

'He is cold: give him to me.'

The little man whimpered, moving his head about. Vavilova was afraid to move, but she looked at him sideways and watched his movements.

'Eat, eat, little son,' she said, and began to cry.

'Sonny, sonny,' she murmured, and one by one the tears fell from her eyes, and the transparent drops ran down her dark cheeks and over the pillow.

She remembered the silent man, and felt pity for them both with a sharp maternal pang. For the first time she wept for him who was killed in the battle at Korosten: for he would never see his son.

And this tiny helpless creature was born without his father, and she covered him up with her blanket so that he should not feel cold.

But perhaps she was crying for quite a different reason. At any rate Rosalia Samoilovna, smoking a cigarette and sending the smoke through the open window-pane, said:

'Let her cry, let her cry. That calms the nerves better than bromide. My patients always cry after childbirth.'

On the third day after the baby was born, Vavilova got up. Her strength returned to her rapidly: she walked about a great deal, and helped Beila in the house. When no one was at home she would sing softly to the little man: the little man was called Aliosha, Alioshenka.

'You ought to see,' Beila said to her husband, 'this Russian woman is quite mad. She has already been three times to the doctor with him. The door mustn't be opened in the house, because he might catch cold, or be woken up, or he's feverish. In fact, she's just like a good Jewish mother.'

'Well, why not?' answered Magazannik. 'If a woman puts on leather breeches do you think she turns into a man?' And he shrugged his shoulders and closed his eyes.

A week later Koziriov and the chief of staff came to see Vavilova. They smelt of leather, tobacco, and horse sweat. Aliosha was asleep in his cradle, which was covered by a piece of muslin to protect him from the flies. Creaking in a most deafening manner, like two new boots, they went up to the cradle and looked at the thin little face of the sleeping child. His face was twitching in his sleep: the twitching was due only to movements of the skin, but these movements gave the face various expressions—sometimes of melancholy, sometimes of anger, and sometimes a smile.

The two commanders exchanged a look.

'Yes,' said Koziriov.

'Yes, indeed,' said the Chief of Staff.

Then they sat down and started telling Vavilova the latest news. The Poles had taken the offensive, and our forces were retreating. Of course this was temporary. The fourteenth army was rallying at Zhmerinka. Divisions were approaching from the Urals. The Ukraine would be ours. In a month's time a change would probably take place. But meanwhile the Poles were making themselves unpleasant.

Koziriov uttered an oath.

'Shut up,' said Vavilova. 'Don't make such a noise—you'll wake him.'

'Yes, our blood is always up,' said the Chief of Staff, and burst out laughing.

'You're always ready with your jokes,' said Vavilova and added with the air of a martyr: 'You might leave off smoking too: you're smoking like a chimney.'

The two army men suddenly felt bored. Koziriov yawned. The Chief of Staff looked at his watch and said:

'We mustn't be late at Lissaya Gora.'

'And his watch is a gold one,' she thought to herself with exasperation.

'Well, good-bye, Claudia,' said Koziriov, and got up. 'I've ordered them to send you a sack of flour, some sugar and fat: they'll bring it to you to-day in a trap.'

They went out into the street. The little Magazanniks stood round the horses. Koziriov climbed into the saddle with a groan. The Chief of Staff clicked with his tongue and jumped on his horse as it was moving.

When they came to the corner, they both unexpectedly, as though by common consent, drew in their reins and stopped.

'Yes,' said Koziriov.

'Yes, indeed,' answered his chief. They laughed, struck their horses, and galloped to Lissaya Gora.

The trap arrived that evening. Magazannik dragged in the sacks of food, and going into Vavilova's room, said in a mysterious whisper:

'What do you think of this news, Comrade Vavilova: Tsesarsky's brother-in-law came to our workshop—,' he looked about him, as though he were excusing himself before Vavilova, and said in a surprised tone of voice:

'The Poles are in Choudnov, and Choudnov is forty versts away from here.'

Beila came into the room. She listened for a while, and then said with determination:

'What's the use of talking? The Poles will be here to-morrow. So I want to tell you this. Poles, Austrians, Galicians, whoever they are, you can remain with us. You have been sent enough food, thank God, to last you three months.'

Vavilova was silent. For the first time in her life she did not know what to do.

'Beila,' she said, and stopped.

'I'm not afraid,' said Beila, 'do you think I'm afraid? Give me five like them, and I'll not be afraid. But have you ever seen a mother who left her child when he was a week and a half old?'

All night long outside the windows there could be heard the neighing of horses, the rumbling of wheels, and excited angry voices. Baggage trains were going from Shepetovka to Kazatin.

Vavilova sat by the cradle. The child was asleep. She looked at the little yellow face, and thought to herself that after all nothing special would happen, Koziriov said that they would return in a month's time. Just as long as she had intended to be on leave. But if she were cut off for longer? Even that did not worry her.

When Aliosha became a little stronger, they would make their way through the front.

Who would touch them—a peasant-woman and a baby-in-arms? And Vavilova pictured how one early summer morning she would cross the fields, a coloured kerchief round her head, with Aliosha in her arms, gazing around him and holding out his little arms. How delightful! She started singing in a thin voice:

'Sleep, sonny, sleep,' and rocking the cradle, fell into a doze.

In the morning the market was busy as usual. People seemed particularly excited that day. Some were watching the unending chain of military carts and laughing happily. But soon the baggage train had passed. The streets were full of people. The inhabitants—'the population,' as the commandants called them in their orders, stood at the gates. Everybody was talking in an excited whisper and looking over his shoulder. It was said that the Poles had already occupied the small town of Piatka, fifteen versts away. Magazannik did not go to work. He sat in Vavilova's room and philosophized to his heart's content.

An armoured car thundered past in the direction of the railway station: it was thickly covered with dust and it seemed as though the steel had become tarnished as a result of weariness and many sleepless nights.

'I'll tell you the truth,' said Magazannik, 'this is the best time for people: one rule has gone, and the other hasn't come yet. No requisitions, no contributions, no pogroms.'

'It's only in the daytime that he's so clever,' said Beila. 'But when at night the whole town is in a hubbub, shrieking for help from the bandits, he sits as pale as death and trembles with fear.'

'Don't keep on interrupting,' said Magazannik, angrily.

He kept running out into the street and returning with the latest news. The Revolutionary Committee had already evacuated the town during the night, the Party Committee had followed it, and the staff had left in the morning. The station was already empty. The last division had gone.

Suddenly cries were heard in the street. An aeroplane was in sight. Vavilova went to the window. Although the aeroplane was flying high, white and red circles on the wings could be seen distinctly. It was a Polish observation aeroplane. The machine made a circle over the town and then flew towards the station. Guns began to be heard booming from the direction of Lissaya Gora: shells flew over the town, and from somewhere in the distance, beyond the level crossing, came the sound of exploding missiles.

First the shells wailed like the wind, then the guns sighed heavily, and a few seconds later the explosions rang out joyously. The Bolsheviks were hindering the advance of the Poles. Soon the Poles started replying: shells burst in different parts of the town.

Bang! went the exploding air with a deafening roar; bricks fell and scattered, smoke and dust hung over the shattered walls of houses. Silence descended on the streets, severe and deserted, as in a picture. Each explosion was followed by such quiet that the hearts of the inhabitants were struck with terror. And all the time the sun shone in the cloudless sky and radiantly lit up the town which lay prostrate beneath it like a corpse.

The whole town lay hidden in cellars and basements, sighed and groaned with terror, shut its eyes, and held its breath without knowing why.

Everybody, even the children, knew that this bombardment was called artillery preparation, and that before entering the town, the troops would send out a few more dozen shells. And then everybody knew it would become incredibly quiet and that suddenly, their horses' hoofs ringing, a reconnoitring party would gallop along the wide street from the direction of the level crossing. And then, dying of fear and curiosity, everybody would peep from behind their doors, curtains, and cracks in the shutters, and covered with perspiration, would come out on tip-toe into the street.

A detachment would arrive in the square. The horses would stoop and snort; their riders would talk excitedly to each other in a marvellously simple human tongue, and the Commander, delighted at the total submission of the prostrate conquered town, would shout in a drunken voice, discharge his revolver into the muzzle of silence, and draw up his horse.

And then from every direction infantry and cavalry would pour in; dusty tired men, thrifty peasants in blue greatcoats, good-natured but capable of murder, would run about from house to house, searching greedily for the population's chickens, towels and boots.

Everyone knew this, because the town had changed hands fourteen times already, had been occupied by Petlura, Denikin, the Bolsheviks, Galicians, Poles, Tutunik's, and Maroussia's bands, and 'nobody's' Ninth Regiment. And each time it was the same as before.

'They're singing!' cried Magazannik. 'They're singing!'

And forgetting his fear, he ran out into the street. Vavilova followed him.

After the stuffiness of the dark room Vavilova breathed the light and warmth of the summer day with particular pleasure. She had awaited the Poles with much the same feeling as she had experienced during her confinement: let them come quickly. The explosions had frightened her: she was afraid that they would waken Aliosha; she brushed aside the whistle of the shells as she would have brushed aside flies.

'Be quiet, be quiet,' she sang over the cradle. 'You'll wake Aliosha.'

She had tried not to think about anything just then. She had made up her mind already: in a month's time either the Bolsheviks would return or she and the baby would make their way to them through the Front.

'I can't understand anything,' said Magazannik. 'Have a look.'

Marching along the wide and empty street in the direction of the level crossing, from which the Poles were to have come, was a detachment of military cadets. They were dressed in white canvas trousers and tunics.

'May the Red Flag be the symbol of the working people,' they sang slowly as if sadly.

They were marching towards the Poles.

Why? For what reason?

Vavilova watched them. And suddenly she remembered: the great Red Square, several thousand volunteers of the working-classes who were going to the front thronging round a hastily set-up wooden platform. A bald man, waving his cap, was making a speech. Vavilova stood quite near him.

She was so agitated that she could not understand half the words the man was saying in his clear though slightly guttural voice. The people standing near her listened to him and breathed heavily. An old man in a wadded coat for some reason or other was weeping.

What had happened to her in the square, under the dark walls, she did not know. Once in the night she had wanted to tell that silent man about it. She thought he would understand. But she was unable to explain anything. But when they marched from the square to the Briansk railway station, they sang that song.

And as she watched the faces of these singing cadets, she again felt what she had felt two years ago.

Now in the street Magazannik saw a woman in a fur hat and greatcoat following the cadets and fitting an iron ring into her big tarnished Mauser as she went.

Magazannik followed her with his eyes and said:

'These were the sort of people who used to be in the Bund. These are real people, Beila. Are we real people? We're just scum.'

Aliosha had woken up and was crying and trying to kick off his napkin. Coming to herself, Beila said to her husband:

'Listen, the baby is awake. You had better light the primus—I must heat up some milk.'

The detachment disappeared round the corner.

HUNGER

Alexander Neweroff

(1886–1923)

TRANSLATED BY BASIL CREIGHTON

LITTLE CLUSTERS OF MILLET grew here and there. Their long, dry stalks gave the plants the look of open scissors. They lay heeled over under the stress of drought and wind with their bare roots showing. Though maimed they still wanted to live and drag out a wretched existence on the black, parched earth. When the late June rain came and washed down their dusty stalks, they recovered a little and reared themselves obliquely in the air without the strength to stand upright. Their stalks sprawled piteously in all directions and produced frail, thin blossoms—and died, scorched up by the heat.

The oats were thin and scanty and after pushing up their sharp blades in early spring had stopped growing. The haulm grew pale and wrinkled and changed by degrees into dry and prickly straw. Only a very few stalks formed ears, and in these the grain had no time to ripen and the husks were empty.

Barley had come up here and there. Its thin, beardless ears contained nothing but withered, shrunken seeds.

The twining bean vines bore thin, flat pods and curled about one another in a tangle. A solitary, belated dark red blossom opened here and there beneath its pale pink hood. They unfolded feebly and slowly while a corrosive rust covered them by degrees.

Blue campanulas and weeds of all sorts decked out the breathless fields for an hour or two in the early morning. Wild flax embraced the flowering stalks in a death-grapple and both died a common death.

Happy families of wild dill flowered in the morning, round caps on their heads. Towards midday the wind blew their caps off and the cheery white-headed companies perished.

Hot winds blew at midday—whirling, tousle-headed horrors. They reared up and chased over the fields like wild, runaway horses with flowing tails and greedily licked up the dust. Lambs fell down dead. The herds of cattle stood all day long in the dried-up lakes and then crept slowly back up the naked, trodden hills.

II

First Jemeljan's cow, Burjonushka, fell helplessly to the ground. Her nostrils were dirty and choked with dust. They got her on to the middle of the road, bound her sprawling legs with ropes and so dragged her home to the village. She did not bellow nor make any resistance. She lay despondently where she was with her small head turned to one side. Only her stricken eyes were glazed in the agony of death. At home Annushka and her three children cried over her; grandfather Vassili gave a sad little cough and tapped the dead beast's flanks with his stick. Jemeljan was whetting a knife. When they laid out the emaciated, red-haired carcase to drag it behind the barn for the dogs to devour, Jemeljan suddenly said to grandfather:

"Father, cut her belly open."

Grandfather Vassili understood. He rolled up the sleeves of his linen shirt and thrust his arm as high as the shoulder into the belly when he had cut it open. He drew out the empty guts, cut out lungs, heart, liver and kidneys and laid them all out carefully on the straw. Jemeljan hacked Burjonka's rump into small pieces and put the pieces in a barrel and threw the lungs, heart and liver, all gory as they were, into the kitchen where his wife was standing.

"Cook that!"

Burjonka's hide was hung up in the cart-shed. The dog licked up the blood. When they sat at table round a dish of Burjonka's flesh, not a sound was made and not a word was spoken. Not one made a face or mentioned that Burjonka had been slaughtered after she was dead. There was no bread on the table. The children looked at their father, who sat in this unwonted silence with a stern frown on his face. Grandfather Vassili suddenly began to cough and let his spoon drop. A little piece of Burjonka had stuck in his throat. He got up from the table before the end of the meal. His legs went weak and his heart thumped. He wanted to go out, but before he reached the threshold he had to put both hands over his mouth to keep it shut. As though joking or up to some mischief, he bent over a broken jar and shook his head.

Jemeljan shouted crossly:

"Go outside!"

He too got up without finishing his supper. Anna spat secretly under the bench. That night she talked to her little one in its cradle:

"Die now, Petjenka. Cow gone. Milk all gone. How am I going to feed you?"

Jemeljan could not sleep. He sat for a long time on the edge of the bed, with sunken head and eyes tight shut, and saw famine as it slowly approached. It came without haste, long arms outstretched. The circle closed in, the misery that stalked them grew ever nearer. Jemeljan sat enclosed

within this circle and did not know what to do, whither to go or to whom
to bend the knee.

III

In the morning grandfather Vassili went into the fields. He went in a
long linen smock without a cap and hit at the hard clods with his stick.
The path cracked in deep cracks. The squirrels whistled monotonously.
Green, large-headed locusts with round blind eyes fell at his feet like dry
rain. The old man turned to pluck some tiny ears of barley and rubbed
them in his palm and felt for the grain. He stood looking at the oats for a
long time, and then tortured with anxiety he shook his head:
Death!

IV

A week later a linen bag with two shoulder straps was stitched together
for him, and Jemeljan said in a low voice without looking his father in the
face:
"Father, you must go begging!"
Grandfather Vassili cut himself a stick to keep off the dogs and shod
it with an iron tip and began practising: "Help—there is no other help
for us . . ." His voice trembled. Tears dimmed his eyes. When Jemeljan
and his wife were out of the house he sat by the fire against the chimney
and droned sadly and monotonously the beggars' chant:
"There is no other help for us . . ."
He got nothing in his own village. He had to set off for Smolnoje. It was
a hot, still morning. Light puffs of cloud which the wind had not yet
scattered, hung high overhead. There was the fragrance of early morning
coolness in the air. When he had climbed the hill beyond the village he
took off his old cap and looked joyfully up at the clouds: perhaps it
would rain. All alone among the fields he raised his shame-faced moan:
"For there's no other help for us——"
Chanted and wept.
The sun rose. The clouds melted away. Grandfather, bent with care,
swallowed the dust of the road which the wind blew in his face. He did
not reach Smolnoje. He sat down in the middle of the road and crossed
himself in terror. He put his cap under his head and spread out his sack. A
long-legged fly jumped onto his face. A squirrel whistled close to his ear.
There was a pungent smell of camomile. Turning his head an inch or so
he said in a low voice:
"Death has overtaken me. I can go no farther."
He plucked a dusty stalk of grass, chewed it and spat. He said nothing
but only thought:
"Glad to chew grass like a cow."
At midday Jemeljan came along with a cart. Grandfather lay in the

middle of the road as Burjonka had. Shod in bast shoes, he lay with his legs splayed out in mute and melancholy resignation. The horse kept stopping every moment, his head between his knees. It seemed an almost hopeless task to get the old man home. Jemeljan walked beside the shaft trying not to think and seeing all the time the long bony arms outstretched to throttle him.

The children lay about at home with swollen limbs. Their mother wept at the sight of them and sat by the empty hearth.

The old man was laid in the passage and covered with a skin. When he saw the stern frown on his son's face he whispered hurriedly:

"Don't be angry, my son. I'll soon be dead."

V

In August the two Lugin brothers left the village. They slaughtered two cows, made two waggons, covered them with cow hides and loaded up their children, their rags and gear of all sorts. The waggons set off at night through the warm, steamy meadows and to the music of prattling children made for the distant places where bread was still to be had.

Jemeljan made a plan. The old man and two of the children had to die. The third child might be got into an orphanage. He would build a waggon, cover it over with Burjonka's hide and flee with his wife from the long outstretched arms. He weighed this plan in his mind for long, as a good father of a family should, and came back always to the same conclusion.

"There's nothing else for it."

He hid his agony of mind. It tugged at his heart and hammered in his temples in short, dull throbs. Jemeljan clenched his teeth and waited for the death of three people and looked at them with angry, longing eyes.

Grandfather still did not die.

They carried him from the passage into the yard, from the yard onto the stove, and back into the passage. They dragged him to and fro like an old rotten log, but he only groaned and huddled himself together. Jemeljan took hold of his swollen legs and when he felt their gruesome deathly chill he rejoiced that his miseries were drawing to an end. Yet the old man opened his heavy eyelids and painfully muttered with black, decayed lips: "I'm still alive."

Petka lay in his cradle like a corpse dug up out of the grave. Hunger hollowed his eyes and bared ribs as frail and soft as a newly born lamb's. There was nothing left of him but his head on the thin, wobbling neck and his little arms and legs. He did not cry. He only rattled in his throat, gave spasmodic jerks and opened his large famished mouth. Mishka and Serjoshka lay on the floor beside the bed with swollen bellies, incapable of movement. Anna fed them on grass and baked cakes of clay mixed with clover.

Jemeljan repaired the waggon. He made new axles and an awning of Burjonka's hide. It looked like a little house without windows. It was time to be off before winter came.

Pavel Mitrochin joined him in the yard one night and sat on the axle as though at a funeral—no smile on his face.

"Where are you off to?"

"Somewhere or other."

They were silent for a long time.

"Where's there to go?"

"Perhaps I'll get to Siberia."

"You'll never get as far. We'd better go and steal."

Jemeljan shook his head.

"How can I steal? My eyes would betray me."

"Then—die."

Again they said nothing for a long time.

VI

Grandfather died on Friday evening. They carried him to the grave-yard on Saturday. They did not even make a coffin for him. They dug a large, roomy grave, big enough for three.

Jemeljan remembered that two more of his family were due to die soon. He was happier when he left the grave-yard.

"Thank God for that!"

When he got home, Anna took him out to the shed where the horse was dying. It lay on its left side with its neck stretched out, feebly kicking and looking at his master and mistress with wide eyes that understood. Jemeljan knelt down and clasped its head in both hands and burst into tears.

"What are you doing to me?"

VII

That night there was horse-flesh to cook. Jemeljan sat on the bed with reddened, baffled eyes and clenched teeth.

"Where can we go on foot?"

Jelisarov came in with an earthenware plate in his hand and fell on his knees.

"Give me a bone. I'm finished."

They sat him down at the table. He couldn't get his spoon to his mouth without spilling it. He cried and whimpered and then put out his tongue and lapped from the plate like a dog. Then he crawled to the stove.

"Where are you going, Grandfather?"

The old man's eyes went green. He opened his mouth and showed his large, broad teeth.

"I'll stay here. I'll lie here a bit."

"Are you quite crazy?"

"Yes, yes, I'll stay here. I get nothing to eat at home."

VIII

Pavel Mitrochin came into the yard that night and stood for a long time at the window, looking in. He retreated a few steps, returned and fingered the latch of the door.

"Jemeljan, Jemeljan, I'm going to rob you."

It was dark in the passage. The floor cracked softly under his feet. Unseen arms groped after him from every side. Eyes peered from every corner. His feet got entangled in unseen ropes. The pail he overturned in the corner made a clatter. Anna whispered in terror:

"A thief!"

Jemeljan seized an axe and ran out.

"Who's there?"

There was not a sound in the passage. A low moon looked in at the open door. The waggon stood ready in the yard, covered over with Burjonka's hide. The little horns stood out stark in the moonlight. The tail hung behind.

Anna screamed from the passage.

"We've been robbed!"

Jemeljan's mind was a blank. He stood by the waggon, axe in hand, and felt that a whirlwind carried him aloft, that he flew on wings of rage and torment and despair. He did not know whither he flew. Black specks were in front of his eyes. Someone gave him a merciless whack on the side of the head.

IX

Next morning he complained to Pavel: "I've been robbed. On top of all else."

Pavel said grimly:

"I'd have murdered the man."

"Yes, if I could catch him."

"Yes, that's the difficulty."

They said nothing for a long time after this.

"What are we to do to live, Pavel?"

"I'm going to take my boy to the town."

"What's the good of that?"

"I'll leave him there. He'll be fed there."

"Will anyone take him in, then?"

"What else can I do?"

A glimmer of hope. Jemeljan went in.

"Anna, children are given something to eat in the town. I'll take one of ours there."

"And if nobody'll take him?"

"What else can we do? The horse-flesh is nearly finished."

Anna began to cry.

"Which of them?"

"Mishka. I couldn't get Serjoshka so far. Petka will die in any case, perhaps. When I get home again I'll make a little two-wheeled cart."

Mishka was seized with a fit of shivers as Jemeljan's sombre eyes rested on him.

"Little Father, don't take me to the town."

"How can I find food for you here?"

"I won't eat any more. Not another mouthful!"

Jemeljan tried to persuade him:

"You are little, Mishka, you're not old enough to understand. I don't do it of my own free will. Silly child! I have nothing to give you to eat. The cow has been eaten. The horse is nearly eaten up too. What are we to do next? It isn't so bad in the town. You'll be kept alive there. If you miss us we'll come and see you. You needn't be afraid of the town."

Jemeljan sat on the floor and his eyes were kindly and full of sorrow. The children lay beside him. He told them about starvation striding from village to village and about the great town with great houses and his heart warmed with joy. Petka was certain to die. Mishka would find a refuge in the town. He and Anna would put Serjoshka in a little two-wheeled cart and set off, all three, to find a place where there was bread. If Serjoshka could not last out, he would just have to die. The cart would be all the lighter to push without him.

x

Mishka was shod with Grandfather's bast shoes and Grandfather's cap was pulled down over his head. He stood in the middle of the room, small and listless, with legs thickly wrapped about, and gazed apathetically at his father.

Anna burst into tears.

"Mishenka, son of my heart!"

Jemeljan besought her:

"Don't, Anna. It's bad enough as it is."

When it was time to go, Mishka suddenly sat down on the floor.

"Little Father, don't send me away to the town!"

Pavel came in with a stout stick in his hand.

"Come along. Let's be off!"

Pavel's wife, her eyes dark and sunken, stood in the doorway, looking at her Wolodjka, who was quite wasted away. He tottered, licked his parched, bloodless lips and coughed like an old man.

A huge cloud blew up from the west. Another crept up from the north. Between them there was an arch of clear sky into which puffs of cloud drifted. There was still this green clearing in the sky, but the cloud in the west was piling up slowly. A wind sprang up and soon the cloud filled all the horizon. A few drops pattered down like dried peas. The untrammelled wind of the steppes arose in its might. Jemeljan and Pavel walked on under the great cloud into the darkness and the children staggered after. Mishka was always behind, crying silently. Not a village nor any habitation was to be seen. Only bare fields and the black cloud. Wolodjka clutched his chest.

"Father, stop!"

"What's the matter now?"

"I can't go any farther."

Pavel took a long look at Wolodjka's blackened lips and his sharp famished nose and took him on his back.

"Hold on tight."

Jemeljan encouraged Mishka to keep going.

"Don't hurry. We'll go as slow as you like. We'll eat something at the station. Then the train will come and we'll set off. There's nothing to be afraid of. Are your feet tired?"

"Tired."

"Never mind, Mishka, never mind. Patience, little son!"

The water tower of the wayside station came into sight. The smoke of a passing train streamed past. Mishka cried bitterly.

"I can't go another step."

"Right. Then we'll have a rest. Pavel, wait a bit!"

Mitrochin answered grimly.

"We'll miss the train."

"Get up, Mishka. We'll go on slowly."

Mishka kept repeating piteously:

"I can't go another step."

Jemeljan screamed fiercely at him:

"Oh, hell! Then I'll leave you behind!"

As Pavel had done, he took his son on his back and in a daze plodded on with bent head. Like a horse with a heavy load he plodded on over the slippery, sun-baked earth.

XI

Children, abandoned like stray dogs to their fate, wandered the length of the train. Women lay about in the last stages of exhaustion. The dying gazed out from beneath coarse sheeting. Tears and groans and a cold wind. The devil was regaling himself as never before. Prayers and curses, love and hate, hope and despair—all mixed up together. A peasant, whose face was blotched and black, said:

"I run with death on my heels. We had a black cat. We've eaten it now."

"Eaten it?"

"To the last bone. There's a howling in your ears if you go out into the road—many have gone out of their minds. A neighbour of mine—a little girl of his died—he dragged her body into the cellar and hacked it in pieces with a hatchet."

"He did?"

"Yes, like an ox."

A woman wailed.

"I've been to the town too, been to the town too. And there's nothing, nothing, nothing."

"Is there no food to be had there?"

"Nothing, nothing, nothing, nothing. I put my child down and went away. Put it down and went away. Hid behind a house to see what would happen. Went back. There it lay in its swaddling clothes, looking at me. I picked it up. It was dead."

XII

Jemeljan had no strength left. He set Mishka down in a corner in the station and gave him a bit of horse-flesh. Mishka did not eat it. He licked it, smelt it, rolled it into a ball. Wolodjka lay huddled beside him.

"Mishka, blow on me!"

"Are you cold?"

"I'm hungry!"

"Take a bite! Here!"

"I'll eat it all!"

"Not all. Father'll be cross."

Jemeljan stood near the telegraph office. A long white strip crept on endlessly and just such a long white strip was wound up in his head.

"The train will be here soon."

"They won't take us on board."

"We'll try hard!"

"It's just as bad in the town."

"It's only fools say so. If no one will take the children in, we'll leave them somewhere. It's better than having them under your eyes."

Jemeljan was grieved for Mishka. He was like a nail in his heart. It would hurt to pull it out. And yet it had to be pulled out. Jemeljan lay down. He was done for. His bones were water. His head reeled. He was weary. He put his arm round Mishka and covered him with the flap of his coat.

"Asleep, Mishka?"

"I feel so bad!"

"We'll go to sleep. The train will be here soon."

XIII

The train was late. Pavel gave Jemeljan a shake. Jemeljan looked at him
with weak and failing eyes and said after thinking it over:

"I'm dying, brother. I can do no more."

"You'll soon come round."

"No. Take Mishka with you."

"What shall I do with him?"

"Put him in a home for children."

"Can't. My own boy is like a knife in my throat."

XIV

Jemeljan lay for three days in the little station. Mishka went from coach
to coach along the train. His eyes were dry, his voice too was gone. He could
scarcely stretch out his hands or open his gaping, ghastly mouth.

"Little uncle!"

A wind blew. Rain fell. Jemeljan lay there with black and swollen face.
In the peace and relief of delirium he talked to Anna:

"Don't cry. I shan't die. What are you crying for?"

He waited long for Mishka. He groped about him with his hands.
For brief intervals he opened his eyes. Mishka did not come. Early one
morning he crept out of the station building. Somebody shouted:

"Where are you off to, peasant?"

Jemeljan did not hear. He crept on to the track, sat there for a while
and then lay down on his face. The engine whistled shrilly. Anna came to
him, the three children too: Mishka, Serjoshka, Petka. Jemeljan pressed
them feebly to his warm and throbbing heart and thought tenderly:

"Now we're there."

ROMANCE

Vera Inber

(1891–   )

TRANSLATED BY JOHN RODKER

A ND THEN CAME the autumn twilight, bringing to the earth the silence that
pervades a room before one goes to sleep. The train travelled through the
quiet, rustling the leaves. Now and then small stations, dimly lighted, halted
its progress for a few minutes. All at once the Shaturka power-station came

into view, its round lights reflected in the artificially raised water. Full of energy, steel masts marched off into the horizon with powerful strides. Their strong legs did not know what it was to be tired.

Evgenia Bart, newspaper woman, was reclining on the upper berth of an old-fashioned car that belonged to the naïve times when there was as yet no division into compartments. In its youth this railway car had shone brightly; illuminated with thick candles, it coursed along the main lines. But now it lumbered slowly on the Kazan railroad, the worst of all lines. Clean and proper like elderly people, garrulous and good-natured, with a woman conductor to tend it like a nurse, it carried engineers and technicians to the different plants and construction enterprises.

Evgenia lay silent. From time to time she said aloud: "But what of it!", or "Well, well, well," or "Now, for a smoke."

She took out a match-box in which green matches with yellow heads huddled together like birds, and she smiled to think how nice they looked. She read the inscription on the box and burst out laughing at the blithe ring of the Latin word.[1]

An elderly engineer, who was sitting below, looked up at her. He did not approve of women smoking, travelling alone, and laughing for no apparent reason.

Genya now stared out of the window and now peered down into the car. Outside, night was coming on. The wind, blowing over the earth, caused the little stations to tremble. From her upper berth Genya could see how heads were beginning to grow bald; but their owners were happily ignorant of it.

"It's now seven o'clock. Soon I'll be seeing Shirokov," she said to herself. "But what of it? I'm only going for a couple of days. I'm a journalist by profession, and I'm going to see the new plant on the Oka where Shirokov is chief engineer. I've been following up the plant and that's why I'm going. And now for a smoke."

Meanwhile the conversation in the lower berths was about bridges and viaducts, about the overflowing of the rivers in spring, when in the city one can see wooden pavements swelling and floating, and, in the country, the willows wear a silver sheen and brooks mirror the turbulent flight of the clouds.

They spoke about ice floes and ice blockages, about their importance for the life of bridges, about the professional conceit of one well-known diver who despised all other trades but was willing to concede that an aviator might be worthy of a diver's friendship.

"One of the intelligentsia, I suppose," said a young electrician.

But the elderly engineer resented this insult and took up the cudgels on behalf of the diver. "That's not so, young man. Diver Brichkin was no

[1] Lucifer?

intellectual in the rotten sense in which you understand the word. But he was a romantic. Oh, I see you're smiling. Let me tell you, I feel sorry for you all. To surround the work one loves with a pedestal, to raise it on a halo . . ."

"The other way about," they corrected him.

"That's unimportant. That isn't the point. What I'm driving at is that you're incapable of the ardour and the enthusiasm with which we worked, each on his own hook, instead of hiding behind the backs of the brigade. With what ardour and enthusiasm I worked, building my first bridge over the river Dymka!"

Genya pictured the young engineer to herself as a young toreador advancing to meet a bull in the form of the bridge. She had a journalist's quick imagination.

"We were like this both in our work and in our private life," continued the engineer, giving a sharp glance at Genya. "In love we were like the knights of olden times. I remember that once in Persia I rode a horse to death just in order to bring a girl a bouquet."

"You, riding a horse like that," his companions said. "Your name should be put on the blackboard."

But the engineer paid no heed. He flew away at top speed on his Persian steed into the land of past memories. He recalled the quiet provinces covered with a cloth of snow. Winter with the sun, newly burnished, on the horizon. What warm-skinned women awaited there the builders of bridges! What tenderness was in their eyes! Women's charm then was an object of love but now it perishes without attention. Formerly there were engineers, but now there is the I. T. R. (Engineering and Technical Workers). Now romance is a thing of the past. Is there even one person sitting here, he asked, who can appreciate the length of a woman's eyelashes, the swan-like warmth of honey locks or the colour of a woman's cheeks like the colour and the odour of a rose?

At this stage a woman conductor, encased in straps and smelling like a hospital ward, traversed the length of the car with a lantern in her hands.

"The old man is right," Genya mused, "to the extent that this is not an epoch of laughing dimples. The old regime exploited feminine beauty, but we do not. What we need is a good brain, and we are quite indifferent as to the outer shape of the brain box. What we need is keen eyes—who stops to think of the colour of these eyes? And as for these I.T.R.ites—oh, how well I know this martial crew. You won't find your I.T.R.ites studying the length of a woman's eyelashes. Your I.T.R.ite is often brusque and sometimes goes about unshaved. He won't call a woman 'ducky' or 'love.' He'll call her by some other name, sometimes a really terrible name."

Genya recalled one of Shirokov's few letters. "Good old Bullard," wrote Shirokov. "The factory and I are looking forward to you. Come quick."

Eager to discover the meaning of this funny-sounding word, Genya asked an old friend of hers, also an I.T.R.ite, who told her, "A Bullard is a huge six-spindle semi-automatic verticle boring mill."

Forty minutes late, Genya jumped from the car on to the low, wet ground.

The station stood solitary. The living quarters of the plant's workers were not far distant. Genya was encompassed by this strange night filled with the barking of dogs, lighted up with a few lone lamps, so unlike night in great cities, and her heart beat much faster than newspaper women's hearts are supposed to do.

She saw Shirokov. He advanced to meet her, wearing a dogskin coat and Wellington boots. Beneath his cap glittered two Tartar eyes. His face was wreathed in smiles. He was happy and couldn't conceal it.

"So there you are," he said. "Come along. I have a horse waiting. I'm straight from the plant and have had no time to shave. So you'll excuse me, Bullard, won't you?"

They sat in the droshky. An almost-Persian steed drove them recklessly over the unpaved ground full of bottomless puddles. Small houses flew by on both sides. An occasional lantern lit their way.

"Put on speed, Nikifor," shouted Shirokov. "Give our Moscow friend an exhibition of first-class horsemanship."

"For beating the horse, you should be put up on the blackboard," Bullard laughed. She was happy and couldn't conceal it.

"We have the evening to ourselves," Shirokov said, covering Genya with the bottom of his dogskin coat. "You're not cold, are you? To-morrow I'll show you the forge we're building. One hundred and twenty metres long and forty-five metres wide. Quite a large forge. You're not hot, are you? Only somehow we can't put the workers' dining-hall in order. That's my big trouble. By the way, what colour eyes have you, Bullard? I once knew but I've forgotten."

"Hazel, according to a rough estimate, but that's unimportant. It isn't eyes that decide things now . . ."

Just then the right side of the droshky flew upwards like the wing of an airplane, and the left one plunged into the water. Their faces were spattered with mud and their feet all at once were soaked.

"Ai, ai, ai, what's wrong?" asked Bullard.

"The trace broke. There's your 'ai, ai, ai,' for you," answered Shirokov.

The rest of the way the droshky drove smoothly. Shirokov chaffed Nikifor, the plant's driver, about the puddles: "After this I won't be able to bear the sight of you any more. You almost killed our Moscow friend. You're no longer my friend, or a shock-worker. A shock-driver ought to know the road like his own boots—every hole by heart. But you!"

"Yes, I, Peter Efimovitch, I know it by day. But nights . . ."

"Shut up, who stuck up for you when you got dead drunk? Who but I? And you?"

"I'll make up for this wrong I've done you. I'll do something for you too. Really, I promise you."

"The trace broke. Ho, ho, ho. It won't be an easy job making up for such a grievous wrong," said Bullard.

"Never mind, I'll make up for it," Nikifor answered.

Genya and Shirokov climbed up to the second story. The pinewood house, where the I.T.R.ites dwelt, had been built only recently. Warm and cozy like a bed in winter, it smelt like a pine forest and clung to the fingers. From behind one of the walls could be heard a German lullaby. The singer was a Bavarian woman who had come out here with her husband. She was singing her little I.T.R.ite to sleep in its native language, worrying whether he had a fever or had caught cold.

Shirokov and Genya were met by the bashful Vasunin, Shirokov's assistant. The whole evening he had fussed with the samovar, worrying whether it had a fever or had caught cold. And the grateful samovar had gurgled in its native language.

A severe masculine cleanliness ruled the apartment of the Chief Engineer and his assistants. Over the sofa hung the plan of the plant, white on blue. The future forge stood out, ready for the workmen to enter. The plant builders, present and future, were working at top speed, fulfilling the production plan. The workers' dining-hall, spick-and-span as a laboratory, warmed one's heart. The workers thronged into it merrily, carefully wiping their boots at the entrance, and not a single swear word hung in the well-ventilated air. Everything was in its place. Everything ran smoothly.

"How quiet it is," said Bullard, while being shown over the apartment. "No visitors, no telephone going. Just to think of Moscow at this time!"

At this stage there was a knock at the hall door and Vasunin went to open it.

Left alone with Bullard, Shirokov did something that was beneath the dignity of an I.T.R.ite. He took one of Bullard's hands and pressed it to his unshaved cheek.

"Well, come to-morrow," Vasunin was saying in the entry. "Peter Efimovitch is busy just now. He's taking a rest. He has someone to see him. Surely you understand . . . Sh, sh," said Vasunin.

"It's all right, I'm not making a noise. Maybe she's asleep now, dozing you know, for all I can tell. It would be good to try her again. Maybe she'd consent."

"Sh, sh," Vasunin repeated, and from his voice it was clear that he glanced toward the door.

"The beauty of the district, I'm telling you," Nikifor hissed. "And you know what a large district ours is. Such eyes, Sergei Sergeivich, they're beyond words. They reach my very heart. Such shoulders—Oh, boy!"

Nikifor apparently was showing what kind of shoulders she had because something fell down from the hall rack.

Genya looked at Shirokov. He screwed up his eyes and his nostrils distended. Unthinking, he had continued to hold Genya's hand in his. Suddenly he placed it on the table and made a bee-line for the entry.

"Such breasts," Nikifor said at the top of his voice. "She weighs every bit of a hundred kilos. I know his taste all right. Skin like kid."

"Is that you, Peter?" said Vasunin, "I just wanted . . ."

But Shirokov wouldn't listen to him.

"Bring her here, Nikifor," he said. "Hold on there, though, I must have a shave first, otherwise she'll think I'm too rough. Where's our foreign soap? Hold on there. First of all bring me some candy. What's her name, Nikifor?"

"Kovrova Stepanida," Nikifor sang gently.

"And her patronymic?"

"Egorovna," cooed Nikifor.

"Calm, absolutely calm," Bullard reassured herself. "Nothing terrible has happened. A mere misunderstanding. His taste is a hundred kilos and I weigh only forty-five. Who could have forseen this? Tomorrow I leave for Moscow and I shall have forgotten about it the day after."

But in thinking with what difficulty she had squeezed out these two days, these two valuable evenings, Bullard understood that she would not forget it so soon. In order not to hear Shirokov say: "How do you do, my darling," Genya put on the earphones and heard Lenski sing from Moscow: "How long, my foes, has thirst of blood us parted."[2]

"No, not long ago. Only just now," Bullard answered. She covered her face with her hands.

Thus the time passed.

Shirokov entered the room with the air of a conqueror.

"What a Jane!" he exclaimed, drinking down the glass of cold tea in one gulp. "I have been dreaming of such a Jane for half a year. What shoulders. What . . ."

Bullard, all pale, advanced to meet him. "You're rotten, Mister I. T. R.," she said.

"Oh!" said Shirokov.

"You've rotted into your constituent elements: cynicism, profligacy and a cold disregard of human beings. Where's my hat?"

"Oh," said Shirokov. He pressed his lips tightly. Bullard became silent. Her heart froze. Shirokov paced the room and stopped in front of the plan.

"Just try to imagine a seasonal worker going into the dining-hall for the first time," he said. "He finds the floor dirty, the tablecloth sticky and the air greasy. This often happens. The waitress combs her hair with the spoon as she hands him the *shchi*. To make things worse, Bullard, this seasonal worker chances to see in the kitchen window the leading personage of the

[2]*Eugen Onegin* by Tchaikovsky.

place. He sees the cook. And then, Bullard, it becomes clear to the seasonal worker that she, this thin, weak-willed woman with a running nose, is the cause of all the gloom, contamination and dirt. So our seasonal worker, with his mental waverings, pictures himself back on his farm, sitting in the glow of the stove. As a result, his work on the job suffers, and the job, mind you, is no easy one. Then the chief engineer, whose eyes must be all-seeing, takes note of the poor work. He puts himself in the place of the seasonal worker, traversing all his daily paths until he comes to the cook. He sees that what is needed is a jolly, broadshouldered, tidy and skillful woman. He seeks out this woman. He searches high and low for her and at last he finds her, my darling Bullard."

Bullard looked at Shirokov and her heart warmed. Shirokov smiled. His Tartar eyes glistened. He was terribly happy and couldn't conceal it.

EARTH ON THE HANDS

Boris Pilnjak

(1894–)

TRANSLATED BY BASIL CREIGHTON

I N SUMMER, when the first days of June have come, if you live in a country town in Russia, you must open the windows first thing in the morning, to let the soft June wind blow through the rooms. Then they will be filled with coolness and the green light from the limes and maples. The wild vine on the terrace smothers the gold of day in its greenery. On such days man and earth are one.

It was on just such a morning that a man sat at his writing table in the corner by the open window opposite the terrace door, buried in his papers and his thoughts, while his wife grubbed about in the golden light of morning in the flower beds among the lilacs. Every now and then she came back onto the terrace, with a scarf round her neck and her hands held away from her body in case she dirtied her dress. Rare, rare and precious, is the joy of being bound in friendship with the earth . . . ! Rare, rare and precious, is the joy of a marriage fortified with love and confidence and loyalty. This joy of friendship, trust and love and fellowship in work, was at home in that house. It is to be found only among people of cultured minds and interests—and these two were good, simple, industrious people:

he was a writer on sociological subjects and she a painter. They had met when he was over thirty-five and she over thirty.

There is nothing like turning over the soil for healthful exercise of the muscles, planting out tobacco and mignonette in the beds and weeding as you go; it is wonderful to think as you bend over the earth that what you plant will thrive and grow. Her husband had been at work on the beds with her before sitting down to his books. Once he got down to them at his desk the familiar trains of thought came back—figures, comparisons, quotations, arguments and formulas. Now work began in earnest and the hours when the eyes of learned men and artists are utterly absent-minded, indifferent and blind to the world that lies outside their books.

While he was in this state of trance Andreieva became aware of a stranger coming through the gate into the courtyard. He was wearing a wide-brimmed hat and carrying a small bag. The intruder came up to the window and said he wanted Anna Andreieva. Without raising his eyes from the paper her husband replied that she was in the garden.

He had no idea how many minutes had gone by when his wife came in through the terrace door, her hands covered with earth, accompanied by the stranger. He did not see his wife's face.

The stranger bowed and said: "If you don't mind I would like to have a few more minutes alone with Anna."

And Anna said: "Yes, I'm taking Sergei into my room, Paul."

Again he did not see his wife's face and again minutes passed during which his eyes saw nothing of the world except the world in his books. Anna came back out of her room. Paul raised vacant eyes and noticed that his wife's hands—covered with earth as before—hung down helplessly and that her eyes were full of helplessness. Paul came back to reality.

Then the stranger began speaking. Anna was standing in the terrace door with her back to them both—the gold light of day touched the edges of the vine and her shoulders.

"Paul Andreievitch," the stranger said and then made a long pause. "Paul Andreievitch, we are no thieves—you and I. It's simply my feelings as a human being." He paused again to collect his thoughts. "I have not seen Anna for thirteen years—but for all these thirteen years I have been dreaming of her and thinking of her. You know that I parted from her in Paris and went as a Russian to fight on the French front. You know that Anna lived with me in her youth—but you know, too, that Anna has nothing to reproach herself with on that account and that you cannot reproach her either. The world is large enough to lose one's way in. I have come back to Anna, and now you two have been married for eight years. We are all getting on in life. I did not know that Anna was married."

Paul saw before him the man whose memory their marriage had kept sacred—Anna's first husband, a man worthy of esteem. An old man now, grey-haired, an artist; in other days when Anna was a girl he had taught

her the art of painting and the value of life. The old man's eyes were
honest and good; they looked at Paul kindly and disconcertedly. They
could not have looked at him in any other way, for in the room was the
only woman he loved and if his eyes were good so was he. Paul reflected
that he too was grey, grey before his time, aged by the years of the Russian
upheavals, and that his eyes too were good and disarmed by a natural
goodness of heart.

Two men, the one very like the other, for it was not for nothing that Anna
loved them both, confronted each other. Paul remembered Anna's descriptions of Sergei as a young and good-looking artist, warmhearted,
brilliant and alive. And the picture she had drawn of him got mixed
up with the picture of the man before him, an old man with kindly and
tired eyes. A man who had come back out of the jaws of death.

"How you have altered, Sergei—Sergei Ivanovitch," Paul said absently.

The two men smiled, almost unconsciously. Paul put out his hand. And
as he grasped the hand of the other man he was aware in his spine, in the
nervous tremor in his chest and shoulder-blades, of himself and Anna and
the intruder. Anna all her life had loved only these two. She honoured
Sergei's memory, and he too honoured it as the memory of a man who
had loved Anna, a man whose death certificate was in Anna's hands,
sent her from a French infantry regiment, stating that the Russian painter,
Sergei Ivanovitch Lavrenjov, private, had fallen "before Verdun." This
memory—sacred and secret, and all the more sacred and secret because
honoured—lay between them. Not once since he had loved Anna had
he questioned her about her feelings for Sergei, and never had he set
himself over against him—because he wished above all to guard his memory.
Paul held Sergei's hand. And in his spine and from the tremor in his
chest he felt that from this moment onwards he could not—even in his
thoughts—call Anna his wife; for he too, as Sergei had said, was no—thief.

He held Sergei's hand for a long time. Sergei's eyes did not move. "Yes,
Sergei. Yes, you are right. I am no thief."

Anna turned round to them. She walked up to them. Her hands, held
far from her body, were turned to stone. Tears were in her eyes. Sergei
stretched his hands out towards her, palms upwards—and Anna's eyes fell.
Paul knew that this must be a characteristic gesture of Sergei's, which
Anna remembered from the days gone by. And he let his eyes fall as
people do who let their eyes fall from shame lest they should see what they
ought not to see. Anna saw Paul's averted eyes and she put out her
hands to him. He did not see and Anna was left with her hands in the
air.

"I'll go and wash my hands," she exclaimed.

"Yes, go," Paul said.

"Anna, Paul Andreievitch," Sergei began and his lips grinned in physical
pain, "Anna, Annushka, my darling . . . . if you wish, I will go away at once

and for ever, Annushka . . . Yes, I have aged very much, Paul Andreievitch, I have aged very much."

Anna sank weakly onto the chair at the table and forgot all about her
hands.

"No, no. That's nonsense," Paul said. "Anna has always spoken of you
with such affection. We have photographs of you and you see—the picture,
I mean, I had formed of you . . . Nonsense, Seriosha!" Paul called Sergei
by the name he and Anna had always used when he was in their thoughts.
"No, listen to me, Seriosha, it is only in comparison with your photograph
that you have altered . . ."

Anna stretched her hands out to Paul with the same gesture with which
Sergei had stretched his out to her. Anna must, he saw, have picked it up
from Sergei. Paul took both her hands in his and kissed the earth on
them; he kissed the moist dark earth with all the tenderness he felt for
the woman. Wiping the soil from his lips he said: "No, Annushka," (he
caught himself calling Anna by the name Sergei had given her) "No, Anna,
I am no thief. I know I cannot call you my wife—not unless you call me
your husband." Paul again wiped the soil from his lips. "What strange
things time hides! Here we are, the three of us, how can I say it? The most
wonderful thing in my life—you knew it before me, Seriosha—and I have
got to know what was for you the most sacred of all things on earth, your
own exclusive mystery. I can find no words for it."

Anna stood up. For a second she stood there motionless. All the strength
ebbed from her will. Her neck trembled like a string of an instrument. Her
head sank between her shoulders. She went to Sergei—and embraced him.
Paul understood: when Anna stretched her hands out to Paul, she defended Sergei—and now when she went to Sergei, she defended Paul. And
with her head sunk and her cheek on Sergei's breast Anna said:

"I am afraid, Seriosha—I am afraid, Paul. How I waited for you, Seriosha,
when you went to the front! What torments I suffered when here in Russia I got the news of your death! You know how I loved you. Now you
have come—and how glad I am! No, that is not the way to express it. You
have returned—and I—love you. But—I love Paul too. I have a son. We
have a son; he is my only son, and I shall have no more children. I am in
great dread. I do not know! Paul, do you hear? . . . . I do not know . . . ."

Paul went to Anna and put his arms round Sergei and her, leaning his
head on Anna's shoulder.

"Annushka," he said—again he called her by Sergei's name for her, but
he did not correct himself—"Annushka, darling, you know, darling, you
know that Sergei and I, that we think of your happiness and your happiness only . . . You know—that we wait for what you say."

Paul was speechless. The depth of his love for Anna overpowered him,
and gratitude for the humanity of her conduct filled him to overflowing.
He was silent and let his head fall. He tried to look at Anna's face, but for

a moment her features swam before his eyes. The dusk came into the room, the daylight failed outside the windows. The self-forgetfulness, the indifference to the passage of time which came over Paul while he was at work now came over them all. They stood there with their arms about each other and time stood still. The whitish dusk of a white June night in Russia was around them. The earth radiated its gold. The scent of stocks was in the room. Gnats sang in the garden. Anna's face was strengthless and her eyes were shut. Her earth-soiled hands hung on Sergei's shoulders so as not to soil his coat.

"It is night already," Paul said in amazement. "Annushka, go and wash your hands. They are covered with earth."

Paul took hold of Anna's hands. He kissed the earth on her hands tenderly. Anna's face was happy. She walked to the door of her room to wash the earth from her hands. All the windows were open and the green evening air blew through the house. In hours like these man is one with the earth.

A LETTER

Isaac Babel

(1894–   )

TRANSLATED BY ALEC BROWN

H ERE IS A LETTER HOME which I wrote for a lad of our detachment, named Kourdioukov, at his dictation. It deserves recording, I have copied it out without any touching up, and give it, word for word, exactly as it stood.

"My dear Mother, Evdokia Fiodorovna. In the first lines of the present letter in all haste I inform you that, thanks to the Lord, I find myself alive and well, which same I hope to hear from you. Also most humbly I bow down to you, from white face to damp earth. . . . [Here follows a list of all relations, blood and marriage, and spiritual relations—god-fathers, etc. Let us leave them out and pass to the second section.]

"My dear Mother, Evdokia Fiodorovna Kourdioukov. In great haste I write to tell you that I am in Comrade Boudyonny's Cavalry Army, where also is your relation in God Nikon Vassilievich, who at present is a Red Hero. He took me on as his companion for this expedition of the Political Department, where we take literature and newspapers about the front,

namely the Moscow *Izvestia,* the Moscow *Pravda* and our own newspaper
which shows no mercy, *The Red Cavalryman,* which every single fighter
in the advanced positions wants to be able to read, whereupon with heroic
spirit he cuts down these scum the Polish squires, and so I'm getting on
very firstrate here with Nikon Vassilievich.

"My dear Mother Evdokia Fiodorovna. Please send me whatever you can
manage, what you have to send. Will you please kill the young black and
white hog and make me up a parcel to the Political Section of Comrade
Boudyonny, for Vassili Kourdioukov. Every night I lie down on an empty
stomach and without anything to cover myself with, so that I am terrible
cold. Write me a letter and tell me about my Steve, is he alive or dead, I
beg you please look after him well and write to me about him, does he
still over-reach or has he stopped that, and how about the itch in his front
feet and have you had him shoed or not? I beg you, my dear Mother
Evdokia Fiodorovna, don't fail to wash his front feet with the soap I left,
it's behind the eikons, and if Father has used it all up, buy some more in
Krasnodar and God will be with you. I can also inform you that it's very
poor country in these parts, the peasants take their horses and hide from
our red eagles in the woods, there is little corn to be seen and what there
is, it's very stunted, we laugh at it. The farmers in these parts sow rye and
likewise oats. There are hops too in these parts growing on poles, so that
it's all very neat and trim and they make homemade spirits with them.

"And now I write a few more lines to hasten to describe to you about
Father, as he cut down my brother Fiodor Timofeich Kourdioukov a
year ago today. Our Red Brigade under Comrade Pavlichenko was advancing on the town of Rostov when there was treachery in our ranks.
Now at that time Father was in Denikin's army, he was Company Commander. Those who saw them say they were wearing medals and all like
in the old days. And as a result of the treachery we were all taken
prisoner and so Father saw brother Fiodor Timofeich. And Father he
began cutting Fiodia about and calling him a cur and a red scum and a son
of a bitch and a lot more and cut him about till dark, until Brother
Fiodor Timofeich passed away. I wrote you a letter at the time to tell you
how your Fiodia was buried without a cross, but Father caught me with the
letter and said you mother's whelps you . . . . spawn, that whore's, I
bellied your mother and I'll belly her again, my life's ruined, I'll bring my
seed up the way it should go and a lot more. I suffered at his hands like
our Saviour Jesus Christ, only I got away from Father quickly and ran
away and got through to my unit under Comrade Pavlichenko.

"Our Brigade then got orders to proceed to the town of Voronezh to fill
its ranks and when we got there we did get reinforcements, also horses and
haversacks and revolvers and all we needed. As for Voronezh, my dear
Mother, Evdokia Fiodorovna, I can tell you that it's a very fine little town,
a bit bigger than Krasnodar, and the people are very handsome, with a

river capable for bathing. There we received two pounds of bread each a day, half a pound of meat and the sugar we needed, so that when we got up in the mornings we could drink sweetened tea, and sup the same and so we forgot being hungry, and to dinner I used to go to Brother Semyon Timofeich to eat pancakes and roast goose, after which I used to lie down to rest. At that time on account of his desperation the whole regiment wanted Semyon Timofeich for Commander and orders were issued by Comrade Boudyonny and he got two horses, proper uniform, a cart for his gear separately and the order of the Red Banner and I was recognized as his brother. So now if any of the neighbours takes it in his head to get uppish with you, Semyon Timofeich can slit his throat for him proper. Then we began to push General Denikin back, cut down thousands of them and drove them into the Black Sea, only no sign of Father, and Semyon Timofeich looked for him everywhere, because he was very cut up about Brother Fiodia. Only, dear Mother, as you know what our Father's like, what a stubborn man he is, so what did he do—he had the impudence to dye his beard from ginger to black and he was living in the town of Maikop in civvies, so nobody there had any idea that he was nobody else but an old Tsarist mounted gendarme. Only truth will out and Nikon Vassilich caught sight of him one day quite by chance in a cottage and wrote to Semyon Timofeich to tell him. Then he got our horses and covered those hundred and fifty miles in no time, I, Brother Sim and some lads from our outpost who wanted to go with us.

"And what did we find in the town of Maikop? We found that the rear of the armies was all out of sympathy with the front lines and in that town there was treachery all over, and large numbers of Jews, like under the Tsar. And Semyon Timofeich in Maikop had a stand-up row with those Jewboys, because they wouldn't let Father out of their hands, but locked him up in the prison and said there were orders from Comrade Trotsky that no prisoners were to be killed; we'll try him ourselves, they said, you keep calm, he'll get his deserts. Only, Semyon Timofeich had his own way and proved that he was Commander of a Regiment and had all the Orders of the Red Banner from Comrade Boudyonny, and threatened to cut down anybody who stood out for Father's person and refused to give him up, and all the boys stood for Semyon Timofeich. Only when Semyon Timofeich got hold of Father he began flogging Father and all the boys were paraded in the courtyard in proper formation. And then Sim splashed some water on Father Timofey Rodionich's beard and the dye ran out of it. And Sim asked Timofey Rodionich:

" 'Do you feel all right in my hands, Father?'

" 'No,' said Father, 'rotten.'

"Then Sim asked:

" 'And when you cut Fiodia up did he feel all right, in your hands?'

" 'No,' said Father, 'rotten.'

"Then Sim asked:

" 'And, Father, did you never think you'd feel rotten some day too?'

" 'No,' Father said, 'I never thought I'd feel rotten.'

"Then Sim turned right round to the crowd there and said, 'Whereas I do think that if I get into the hands of your people there'll be no mercy for me. And now, Father, we're going to put an end to you. . . .'

"And Timofey Rodionich then began insolently cursing Sim and swearing at him, ... his mother and the Virgin, and hitting Sim in the jaws, and Sim sent me out of the yard, so, dear Mother, Evdokia Fiodorovna, I cannot give you any description of how they finished off Father, because I was sent out of the yard.

"After that we were stationed in Novorossiysk. As for this town, I can tell you that the dry land ends there, and further on there's nought but water, the Black Sea, and we stayed there right through till May, when we came out on the Polish front, where we're knocking the stuffing out of the Polish squires. . . .

"I remain your Loving Son, Vassili Timofeich Kourdioukov. Mother, do keep your eye on my Stevie and God will be with you. . . ."

There is Kourdioukov's letter, not a word in it changed. When I had finished writing it, he took it and tucked it away under his shirt, next to his skin.

"Kourdioukov," I asked the lad, "your father was a tyrant, was he?"

"My father was a devil," he said sullenly.

"And your mother's better?"

"Mother's all right. If you'd like, here's our family . . ."

He handed me a dog-eared photograph. It showed Timofey Kourdioukov, a broad-shouldered mounted gendarme, wearing his uniform cap and with well combed-out beard, stolid, high-cheekboned, with a harsh glint in his stupid, colourless eyes. Beside him, in a basket chair, was a frail little peasant woman with loose-hanging blouse and a consumptive, clear-skinned, timorous face. And behind, against the wall, one of those miserable country-photographer back-cloths with flowers and pigeons, were two tall lads, monstrously stalwart and stupid-looking, standing stiff and gawky—with broad faces and staring eyes, as if being drilled—the two other sons, Fiodor and Semyon.

THE CHILD

Vsevolod Ivanov

(1895–   )

TRANSLATED BY JOHN COURNOS

Mongolia is a wild beast, and a gloomy one! Its stone is a wild beast, and its water is a wild beast; even its ladybird watches for an opportunity to bite.

No one knows the heart of the Mongolian—he walks about in skins, he looks like a Chinaman and, very remote from the Russians, across the desert of Nor-Koi, he has made his home. And it is said that he will go beyond China into India, into the unknown blue lands on the seven shores. . . .

Many Kirghis who had left Irtish during the Russian war and trekked to Mongolia, had pitched their tents near the Russians. Their heart is well-known—it can be seen through and through. They wandered here in no undue haste—and they brought their beasts and their children, and even their sick.

The Russians were being driven hither without mercy—but then they were moujiks, and sturdy fellows. On the mountain stones they left their superfluous weakness—here one fellow died, there another was beaten to death. The families and the tools and the domestic beasts had been left to the Whites. The moujiks were malignant like wolves during the spring. They lay in their tents and thought about the steppe, about Irtish. . . .

There were about fifty of them. Sergey Selivanov acted as their head, and the detachment was called: "The partisan detachment of the Red Guard of Comrade Selivanov."

They were bored.

While they were being driven across the mountains, their hearts had been in fear of the black stoniness over which they had to pass. They reached the steppe—and they found it tedious here; because the steppe was like their own Irtish steppe: there was sand, harsh grass, a hard-forged sky. Everything was alien, not one's own, and the land was unploughed and wild.

And it was hard without women.

At night they sat around and told soldiers' tales about women, and when it became unbearable they saddled their horses and caught Kirghis women in the steppe.

And the Kirghis women submitted to their Russian captors.

It was loathsome to take them, for they were still and never opened their tightly closed eyes. It was as if you had sinned with domestic cattle.

The Kirghis feared the moujiks, and would wander away further into the steppe. When they saw a Russian they threatened him with a rifle or with a sling; they raised whoops, but they did not shoot. Perhaps, they couldn't? . . .

II

The paymaster of the detachment, Afanasy Petrovitch, was tearful, like an infant. And his face was like an infant's: it was small, hairless and rosy. But his legs were long and strong, like a camel's.

When he mounted a horse, he was forbidding. His face seemed hidden, and he sat there looking grey, angry and terrifying.

On Trinity day three men were ordered out into the steppe to find good meadows. They were Selivanov himself, paymaster Afanasy Petrovitch, and secretary Drevesinin.

The sand rose in the sun like a cloud of smoke.

From on high the wind blew. While from the earth, toward the tremulous sky, the warmth rose. The bodies of the men and the beasts were hard and heavy, like stones. It was tedious.

And Selivanov hoarsely said:

"What sort of meadows are there out there? . . ."

The others knew: he was speaking of Irtish. But the beardless faces were mute. It was as if the sun had burnt out their hair, as it burns out the grass in the steppe. Their narrow eyes, like wounds from a fish-hook, were inflamed red. It was hot.

Afanasy Petrovitch responded at last in a lamenting voice:

"Surely everything hasn't dried up there too?"

His slender voice was tearful, but there were no tears on his face. Only the horse under him, tired and panting, showed a trickle in its great long eyes.

Thus, one after the other, along paths traced by wild goats, the partisans rode into the steppe. . . .

The sand glowed hot, in endless monotony. A stifling wind blew. The sweat struggled within the body, unable to break through the dry skin. . . .

Towards evening, just as they were issuing out of a valley, Selivanov said, pointing to the west:

"Look! There are riders out there!"

It was true: on the remote horizon rosy clouds of sand could be seen.

"It must be Kirghis."

A dispute arose. Drevesinin said that the Kirghis wandered afar and dared not approach Selivanov's camp. Afanasy Petrovitch said, it was certainly Kirghis. It was the sort of thick dust the Kirghis usually raised.

But when they got nearer to the dust, they all decided:

"Strangers . . . unknown folk. . . ."

From the voices of their riders the horses sniffed something strange in the air. They pricked up their ears, and fell to the earth long before the command. They lay there, in the hollows, these grey and yellow horses, still as corpses. They were helpless and laughable, with their legs as thin as poles. Was it from shame, then, they closed their large frightened eyes and breathed panting?

Selivanov and paymaster Afanasy Petrovitch lay beside their horses. The paymaster, his nose sniffing, was crying. To make it easier for him, Selivanov always placed him by his side, and from this childish crying the heavy moujik's heart felt almost cheered and incited to mischief.

The pathway was lost in the dust. The beat of wheels was audible. The long black manes of horses could be seen wavering in the dust.

Selivanov said with assurance:

"Russians. . . . Officers."

Two persons in hats with red bands were sitting in the new plaited waggon. Their faces were invisible through the dust. It was as if the red bands shimmered in a yellow cloud. The muzzle of a gun could be seen thrust upward each time a hand with a whip was flung out above the dust.

Drevesinin reflected and said:

"Officers . . . on business, of course. An expedition is on foot. . . . That's clear."

He winked an insolent eye, and added:

"We'll prescribe for them, won't we, Selivanchik?"

The waggon with its passengers firmly goes on. They have good horses. Merrily they go on, and behind them, as with a foxen tail, the waggon hides its traces under the falling Mongolian dust.

Afanasy Petrovitch drawled in his lachrymose way:

"It's not necessary, brothers. . . . Better put them in prison. . . . Wait before you must beat them."

"Aren't you sorry for your own head . . . d'you want a beating?"

Selivanov grew angry and snapped at him:

"It is not necessary to cry here, paymaster!"

What, above all, provoked them to anger was that the officers should have ventured to appear alone, without a convoy. It was as if their strength was considered as nothing, as if death were to be meted out to the moujiks as a matter of course. At that moment one officer actually had risen to his height and was looking round the steppe; but it was hard for him to see:

there was the dust; there was the evening wind on the red burned grass; there were the two stones by two hollows in the ground resembling corpses of horses. . . . What sort of stones were they? . . . Were these corpses? . . .

The waggon, the wheels, the passengers, their thoughts. . . . They ride on in the red dust.

The men in ambush fired their rifles. . . . They raised a whoop. Then again fired.

At the same moment the two hats, one hitting against the other, fell into the waggon.

The reins had suddenly been dropped. . . .

The horses tore forward . . . fell. There was white froth at their manes . . . Their muscles trembling, they lowered their heads, and rose to their feet.

Afanasy Petrovitch said:

"They must be dead. . . ."

The moujiks walked up, looked in,

The two passengers with the red bands in their hats were dead. They were sitting shoulder to shoulder, their heads thrown back. One of the dead was a woman. Her hair had fallen apart; her military tunic outlined her high woman's breasts.

"It's odd," said Drevesinin. "She has herself to blame. She had no right to wear that hat. Who wants to kill a woman? . . . Women are necessary to society."

Afanasy Petrovitch spat.

"You're a monster and a boorjooy.[1] . . . There's nothing in your head . . . just trash. . . ."

"Don't go so fast," Selivanov interrupted them. "We're not robbers, we must write it all down—it's all national property now. Give me some paper."

The first thing they saw among other articles of "national property" was a light-eyed, fair-haired infant, lying in a plaited Chinese basket. In his small hand he tightly clutched a corner of the brown blanket. A suckling, he was tiny and he squealed in a slender voice.

With much feeling, Afanasy Petrovitch said:

"So there . . . he's got to have his say . . . and all about it."

They took pity on the woman and did not deprive her of her clothes, but the man they buried naked in the sand.

III

Afanasy Petrovitch journeyed back in the seized waggon, he held the infant in his arms and, rocking him, he sang quietly:

[1] A bourgeois.

The nightingale bird
Sings its sad song . . .
The canary bird
Too . . . how my heart's wrung . . .

He remembered the small village Lebiajy—his native home; the droves of cattle; his family; the little children—and he cried in subdued tones.

The infant also cried.

The heated sand, dry and friable, also seemed to cry subduedly, as the waggon ran over it. The partisans rode on their low, firm-fleshed Mongolian horses. Their faces were burning and their souls were burning.

Near the pathways stifled by the sun there were stretches of wormwood, resembling sand—very fine and almost invisible to the eye.

And the sand is wormwood, fine and bitter.

Oh, pathways, goat pathways! Oh, sands, bitter sands! Mongolia is a wild beast, and a gloomy one! . . .

They examined the officer's property. There were books, a box containing tobacco, and gleaming steel instruments. One of these was a small four-cornered brass case standing on three long legs and divided into several compartments.

The partisans examined the various objects, felt them with their hands, again and again tried their weight.

The moujiks smelt of sheep's fat—from sheer tedium they ate a great deal, and the fat had gotten on to their clothes. Big-cheek-boned and thin-lipped, they had come from a Cossack village on the Don; with long black hair and dark faces, they had known the lime mines. And they all had bow-legs and guttural steppe voices.

Afanasy Petrovitch lifted the brass-topped tripod and said:

"It's a telescope. . . ." And he half closed his eyes. "It's a good telescope, must cost more than a million. They've looked at the moon through it, fellows, and they've found gold sand on it. . . . It isn't necessary to wash it. . . . It pours like flour, and all of it the purest gold. All you've got to do is to pour it into a sack. . . ."

One of the others, who had lived in a town, roared with laughter.

"A cock and bull story. . . ."

Afanasy Petrovitch got angry.

"A cock and bull story, is it, you filthy carrion? . . . Just wait. . . ."

"Wait for whom?"

Afanasy Petrovitch seized a revolver.

"Sh-h!" Selivanov quieted them.

They shared the tobacco, and they handed over the instrument to Afanasy Petrovitch—as paymaster he would wait for an opportunity to give it in exchange for something from the Kirghis.

He placed the instrument before the infant.

"Here's something to play with. . . ."

The infant paid no attention to the offering. He was crying. Afanasy Petrovitch tried this and that, even worked himself into a sweat; but the infant, unappeased, went on whimpering.

The cooks brought in dinner. There was a thick odour of butter, of gruel, of cabbage-soup. Huge wooden spoons were drawn from the boot-legs. The grass had been stamped down by the campers. Higher up, on the cliffs, the sentinel shouted:

"Hurry up! . . . I want some grub. . . . Send up a fellow to take my place!"

They had their dinner, then remembered: the infant wanted food. He had not ceased crying.

Afanasy masticated a mouthful of bread. He thrust a bit of the wet bread into the open tiny mouth, to the accompaniment of:

"Pp-i-pi . . . little fellow . . . get it down, young 'un. . . . It's tasty."

But the infant turned away his head and shut his mouth—he simply wouldn't have any of it. He was whimpering through his nose, in low but piercing tones.

The moujiks came up, surrounding them. Heads looked above heads at the infant. All were silent.

It was hot. The cheeks and the lips looked greasy from the mutton they had eaten. The shirts were open. The feet were bare, yellow—like the Mongolian soil.

One of the moujiks proposed:

"Try the cabbage-soup on him. . . ."

They cooled the soup. Afanasy Petrovitch dipped a finger into it and stuck it into the infant's mouth. The good fat cabbage-soup ran down from his lips on to his little rose-coloured shirt and baize blanket.

He refused it. He went on whimpering.

"A puppy is more clever—he'll eat off your finger. . . ."

"One's a dog, the other a human being. . . ."

"Thinking won't help here! . . ."

There was no cow's milk in the camp. They thought of feeding the infant on mare's milk. That too was impossible. The child might die.

The moujiks scattered among their carts. Disturbed, they talked it over in groups. Afanasy Petrovitch wandered among the carts, a torn under-tunic over his shoulders, his small eyes also looking ragged. His voice was thin, perturbed, like a child's; it was as if the infant himself was running about, complaining.

"What's to come of it? . . . What's the way out, moujiks? . . . There must be a way out, eh? . . . Can't you think up something, you sons of dogs? . . ."

They stood about, these broad-shouldered, mighty fellows, and looked helpless.

"It's a woman's business. . . ."

"To be sure. . . ."

"From a woman's hands he would have eaten a whole sheep. . . ."

"That's how it is."

Selivanov collected a crowd and announced:

"It's impossible to let the little Christian fellow die like a beast. Let's say, the father was a boorjoy, but the baby—what about him? He's not to blame."

The moujiks agreed.

"It's nothing to do with the child. He's innocent."

Drevesinin broke into a loud laugh:

"Let the child grow up! He'll grow up with us—and he'll fly up to the moon. . . . To pick up the golden dust. . . ."

The moujiks did not laugh. Afanasy Petrovitch raised a fist and shouted:

"You're an ignorant dog—that's what you are! The only one in camp that makes mock!"

He stamped his feet, waved his arms, then suddenly raised the piercing cry:

"A cow. . . . A cow is what we want for him!"

They responded in one voice:

"Without a cow it means death. . . ."

"We must have a cow. . . ."

"Without a cow he'll die!"

Afanasy Petrovitch said with decision:

"Fellows, I intend going for a cow. . . ."

Drevesinin insolently interrupted him:

"Are you going to Irtish, to the Lebiajy village? . . ."

"It's no good my going to Irtish, unspeakable monster! I'm going to the Kirghis!"

"You'll exchange the telescope for a cow, I s'pose! Go, then, benefactor!"

Afanasy Petrovitch turned on him and cried savagely:

"You carrion! D'you want to smell my fist?"

The chairman of the gathering, Selivanov, called for order:

"Enough!"

A vote was taken. It was decided that Drevesinin, Afanasy Petrovitch and three others should mount their horses and go to a Kirghis village, in the steppe, and drive back a cow. With luck, they might bring two or five cows, as the cooks were complaining that their meat supply was becoming exhausted.

They attached rifles to their saddles, and donned caps of fox fur, so as to give the appearance at a distance of being Kirghis.

They wound the blanket round the baby and put it in the shadow under a cart. A young moujik sat at his side, and for his own amusement and the baby's fired intermittently into a bush of wormwood.

IV

Oh, sands—joyless, Mongolian! Oh, stone—blue, unhappy! The hands here are deep in the soil, evil!

The Russians ride on the sands. It is night.

The sands smell of heat, of wormwood.

The dogs in the acolas[2] bark at the wolf, at the darkness.

The wolves howl in the darkness at hunger, at death.

The Kirghis ran to escape death.

Will the droves of cattle escape death?

The Kirghis village smelt of sour milk. Lean and hungry children sat by bonfires. Near them were several bare-ribbed, sharp-muzzled dogs. The tents looked like hay-ricks. Beyond the tents was a lake and rushes. Suddenly, shots rang out, from the rushes, aimed at the bonfires. There were cries: "O-o-a-at! . . ."

The Kirghis all at once rushed from their felt huts. They raised cries of fear. They sprang on their horses. The horses were kept bridled day and night. They trampled on their tents. They trampled on the steppe. Wild cries came from the rushes:

"Ai-ai, the Reds—the Whites—Russians—ai-ai. . . ."

One grey-bearded fellow fell from his horse, his head landing in the huge boiling kettle, which was upset. Scalded, he whimpered in a thick voice. Its tail between its legs, a hungry, shaggy dog cautiously dipped its muzzle into the hot milk.

The mares neighed shrilly. Frightened, as if they were threatened by wolves, the sheep in the fold were panicky. The cows panted.

The Kirghis women, seeing the Russians, humbly submitted to them.

Drevesinin laughed lewdly:

"We are stallions, then, are we? . . . We shan't always . . ."

Quickly filling his flat Austrian flask with milk and, cracking his whip, he drove some cows and calves towards a tent. The calves, loosed from their leash, made at once for the cows' udders, and joyously, with their large soft lips, seized the teats.

"They look mighty hungry, I say . . ."

And Drevesinin fired his revolver at the calves.

Afanasy Petrovitch made a circuit of the village and was about to follow Drevesinin on his horse, when he suddenly remembered:

"Why, we must have a sucking-bottle. The deuce take it, we've almost forgotten it!"

[2]Kirghis villages.

He rushed in and out of the tents in search of a sucking-bottle. The fires in the tents were almost extinguished. Afanasy Petrovitch seized a firebrand and, flourishing it so that the sparks flew, and coughing from the smoke, he searched for a sucking-bottle. In one hand the firebrand crackled, in the other he held a revolver. He could find no sucking-bottle. The submissive Kirghis women sprawled about on their beds of felt. The children were bawling.

Afanasy Petrovitch grew angry and, in one tent, he shouted at a young Kirghis woman:

"A sucking-bottle, you good-for-nothing, I want a sucking-bottle!"

The Kirghis woman wept and began to undo her silk caftan . . . At her side cried an infant, wrapped in rags.

At that moment Afanasy Petrovitch seized her breast and pressed it. He whistled and cried joyously:

"Woh . . . A sucking-bottle! Ah, a good one! . . . Don't make that noise! It's a good one!"

And he seized the woman by the hand and dragged her after him.

In the darkness he placed the woman in the saddle, and from time to time he felt her breast until he brought her to Selivanov's camp.

"I've found what I wanted," he said, overjoyed, and there were tears in his eyes. "When I say I'll find a thing, I'll find it if if I have to dig in the earth for it."

V

Once in camp, Afanasy Petrovitch discovered that, in the darkness, the Kirghis woman had managed to bring her own child with her.

"Never mind," the moujiks said. "There'll be enough milk for both. There are cows, and she's a healthy wench."

The Kirghis woman was taciturn and strict, and she fed the infants when no one was looking on. The two of them lay on the felt bed in the tent— one of them all white, the other a little yellow fellow—and they whimpered in one voice.

In the course of a week, at the common gathering, Afanasy Petrovitch complained:

"Comrades, I don't like this hiding game. The Kirghis woman is cheating us. She's giving all her milk to her own. As for ours, she sometimes lets him have a drop or two. Brothers, I know, for I've peeped. Just have a look for yourselves . . ."

The moujiks went and looked. The infants were like all infants. One was a little white fellow, the other a yellow, like a ripe melon. But it was clearly to be seen that the Russian was meagre compared to the Kirghis.

Afanasy Petrovitch gesticulated with his hands.

"I've given him a name—Vaska. . . . But when you take a look at him . . . Cheating, I call it!"

Then spoke Drevesinin, without his usual smile:

"Oh, you Vaska, you look as if you had a foot in the other world. . . ."

They found a stick, and they arranged it on a waggon shaft to make sure that one half did not outweigh the other.

They suspended the infants, one at either end, to see which outweighed the other.

The infants tied in hanging rags whimpered. The faint odour of babies came from them. The Kirghis woman was standing near the waggon and, understanding nothing, was crying.

The moujiks were silently looking on.

"Let it go!" said Selivanov. "We'll see what the scales say!"

Afanasy Petrovitch removed his hands from the stick, and immediately the Russian youngster rose high.

"Oh, you yellow-mouthed wretch!" said Afanasy Petrovitch wrathfully.

He lifted a sheep's skull lying on the ground and placed it on the Russian child's side of the scales. The two infants were then even.

The moujiks raised a din.

"She has overfed her own by a whole sheep's head, eh?"

"No one's watched her!"

"What a beast! Not to have fed ours!"

"Who's watched her?"

"There're other things to do besides watching her!"

A few of the more sedate moujiks confirmed this view:

"How's one to watch her!"

"Besides—she's the other babe's mother. . . ."

Afanasy Petrovitch stamped his feet, and shouted:

"I s'pose you think a Russian human being must perish for some sort of foreign trash. . . . Is my Vaska to perish then? . . ."

They looked at Vaska. He was lying there, looking pale and meagre.

The moujiks felt perturbed.

Said Selivanov to Afanasy Petrovitch:

"Why don't you get rid of him . . . of the other, I mean. God be with him, let him die . . . the little Kirghis fellow. We've beat up a lot of them. And what's one more or less to answer for?"

The moujiks gave a look at Vaska and, without another word, went their ways.

Afanasy Petrovitch took the little Kirghis and put him into a torn sack.

The mother began to weep. Afanasy Petrovitch hit her lightly on her jaw and went to the steppe.

VI

Two days later the moujiks stood on their tip-toes near the tent and looking over each other's shoulder, peeped inside, where on the felt bed the Kirghis woman was feeding the white child.

The woman had a submissive face with narrow eyes, like seeds of oats; she wore her purple silk caftan and boots of morocco leather.

The infant had his face snuggled against her breast, and he played with his hands on the caftan, while his legs pranced about with ridiculous awkwardness.

The moujiks looked on and laughed uproariously.

And more tender than anyone else was Afanasy Petrovitch. Sniffing, he said in a tearful voice:

"Ain't he a fine youngster!"

Beyond the linen tent there ran, no one knew whither: dales, cliffs, the steppe, alien Mongolia.

No one knew whither ran Mongolia—a wild beast, and a gloomy one.

THE CUSTOMER

Georgy Peskov

TRANSLATED BY GLEB STRUVE

NADEZHDA ALEXEYEVNA was going to the Smolensky Market. She held a basket covered with oil-cloth, and a little folding-stool.

Both the girls were staying at home. She would lock them in. It couldn't be helped . . . the flat was full of every kind of rabble.

Nathalie, the elder, said nothing, looking on with wide, anxious eyes.

Vera was pestering her: "Will you buy some bread to-day? Do buy as much as you can."

"There is some dough-cake left and a little milk. Have it when you feel hungry," said Nadezhda Alexeyevna.

Nathalie made up her mind to ask, almost in a whisper: "And when will you be back, mummy?"

"Don't be afraid. I'll try to be back early to-day."

"Do buy some bread!"

The key clicked. "Like little birds in a cage," thought Nadezhda Alexeyevna as she made her way through the foul-smelling, bespitted passage. "Poor darlings! Why must it be?" It was a question she was always asking lately. But who was there to answer it? She believed in God, she went to Church, she taught her children to pray, but what had all that to do with her present circumstances, with the girls having to remain the whole day alone, among strange, unkind people? What had it to do with the fact that she, who had been spoilt, used to wearing bracelets and silk underclothes, had now to drag herself through the rain to the Smolensky Market, her skirts spattered with mud? Even when she did pray to God for help, it was rather through habit. Only a miracle could help them. Like the miracle of Arisha, the nanny, who used to say: "My purse is never empty. Nicholas the Miracle-worker sees to that." But Nadezhda Alexeyevna did not believe in miracles. Nor did Arisha for that matter. She simply humbugged her employers.

Nadezhda Alexeyevna had her own permanent place at the Market, but she dared not be late, or the bookseller would spread his books over it.

Already there was a crowd in the Square. The Princess, Nadezhda Alexeyevna's invariable neighbour, a stately old woman who looked elegant even in her rags, was seated on a stool, and had spread out on her knees and on the ground near her all her goods—a pair of mother-of-pearl opera-glasses, a heavy silver bowl, a bundle of ostrich feathers, some ribbons, a few bronze knick-knacks. Several chains, a lorgnette, an ivory rosary hung round her neck.

"You're late to-day," she said. Her low voice was a little husky with the dampness of the autumn morning. "I had to fight for your place."

The old bookseller, a professional, looked at them disapprovingly. In his opinion they had no business to be there at all, and he didn't care whose fault it was that they had been brought to this plight.

"Well, did you sell your statuette yesterday?" Nadezhda Alexeyevna asked.

"I did. To that one-eyed man. Nobody offered more."

"Cigarettes . . . in packets and loose! Cigarettes!" shouted a boy as he passed along the rows of sellers.

"Seeds! Roasted seeds! Anyone want seeds?"

"Give some here."

The fat peasant-woman emptied a glass of sunflower seeds into the book-seller's bulging pocket.

"Want some more?"

"That'll do."

"Want much for that tray?" asked a man in a shabby military tunic, of the Princess, as he passed.

In an edifying tone she corrected him: "It's not a tray, it's a vase."

Every word of theirs was a shock to her, she could not accustom herself to this new society.

"What do I care about that? How much d'you want for it?"

"It costs fifty thousand."

"This ——," he added an unprintable word. "Take twenty-five. . . ."

A handsome young woman passed by, a luxurious fur coat thrown over her shoulders. A leather-jacketed individual tugged with both hands at the beaver collar.

"How much?"

"Three million."

"Three 'lemons' . . . what for?"

"For the coat."

"And how much what's inside?"

The people round them laughed.

Opposite Nadezhda Alexeyevna sat an old nurse selling her masters' things. She wore a white kerchief, printed with black birdseyes and a yellow border, and over it a bowler hat which she could not manage to sell. From time to time all sorts of remarks were made about it but she refused to take it off; it could better be seen as it was.

"Things don't seem to be going well to-day," said Nadezhda Alexeyevna.

The Princess looked at her watch. "It's still early. You'll have time. Your little ones are locked in so that nobody can do them any harm."

They had long since told each other the mirthless tales of their lives and griefs. There were no joys. Where would joys come from?

"Why haven't you brought your Lembrandt to-day?" asked the Princess of the nurse, imitating her pronunciation.

"The master said he'll take it to the antique dealer."

"What master? There aren't any masters left," said the cigarette boy, trying to ingratiate himself with the militiaman.

"Take your things out of the road," ordered the latter.

"Shall I hold them between my teeth then?" shouted back the nurse.

"Go on. Quick. No talking!"

They all hurried to collect their things. The bookseller alone did not move. He had a permit.

The militiaman passed on, and once more the goods were displayed.

"How much for a slice of bread, citizen?" asked a hungry-looking man in a long-coated soldier's uniform.

"Five roubles," replied the short, sturdy sandwich-seller, "only you can't have it without the sausage."

The other man's eyes flared.

"And how much sausage d'ye give?"

"You pay separately for the sausage, my dear fellow," explained the seller imperturbably.

The uniformed man moved off.

Several country girls with tin milk-cans surrounded the Princess. They had sold their milk and were buying new clothes for themselves.

"Look, Pollie, that blue one doesn't look bad."

"Oh, what a nice jacket!"

She took the silk knitted jacket and tried to pull it on. It was much too tight.

"Mind you don't tear it," said the Princess. The girl dragged the jacket over her fat stomach and turned round in front of her friends. They all thought it fitted her to perfection.

"How much?"

"Seventy-five thousand."

"Good heavens!" was the horrified rejoinder. "Why, the jacket's no good. Will you take less?"

"No."

The girl pulled it off, threw it on to the rest of the goods, and walked away, consulting her friends.

"*Très-distinguées.*" The Princess laughed maliciously. "They smell of dung but they adorn their fingers with rings."

Nadezhda Alexeyevna had sold nothing so far. She felt peculiarly restless. All the time she fancied that something was wrong at home. She had forgotten to hide the matches when she came away. Vera always tried to play with them. Suppose a fire should break out and they were locked in! Nobody came to buy, as though on purpose. She was willing to sell her things for a song. And Nathalie was so fond of opening the window. What if she fell out? How terrible! Nadezhda Alexeyevna made the sign of the Cross by force of habit, and whispered: "Lord have mercy on us."

"You don't look your usual self. Don't you feel well?" the Princess asked.

"I am afraid for the girls."

"Don't be afraid. There is no need."

"I wish I could sell something so that I should have enough to buy some bread. I'd go immediately then. I feel more anxious than I have ever done before."

The Princess looked at her with earnest sympathy.

"Wait . . . those girls will come and buy the jacket, and then I'll give you half the money and you can go. You can give it back to me to-morrow."

"Oh no, thanks."

"Nonsense!" said the Princess severely. "If it's a premonition you must go. A mother's heart never lies."

"Anybody want seeds? Roasted seeds!"

"Come here, dearie."

A gloomy Tartar stopped in front of Nadezhda Alexeyevna.

"Is the trousers dear?" He took the trousers, unfolded them, held them up against the light.

"I can't sell them separately, it's a whole suit."

"And where's the coat? Shabby. How much d'you want?"

"Five hundred thousand."

"Too much. Will you take two hundred?"

"Don't let him have it," whispered the Princess.

"Take the money," said the Tartar fetching a fat purse from under his coat.

"Four hundred and fifty."

"I pay you two hundred."

"All right, four hundred."

Next to the Tartar, Nadezhda Alexeyevna suddenly saw a pale-faced lady dressed in poor and slovenly fashion.

"How much are you asking?" the lady enquired in a strangely hurried tone. It was obvious that she was anxious to buy the suit and was afraid of letting it go.

"Four hundred and fifty . . . but I'll let you have it for four hundred."

"I'll give you four hundred and fifty. But I haven't got the money on me. Could you come with me?"

"I am giving you two hundred. Here's the money," said the Tartar.

"It's quite near," went on the lady beseechingly. "I'll be back in a moment. I must buy some bread. Will you wait for me?"

"Don't go with her," the Princess whispered. "Better sell it to that Tartar."

Nadezhda Alexeyevna looked at the lady. Her face, too pale, seemed to bear the traces of an old and deep-rooted grief. Her grey restless eyes were so wide open that their whites could be seen all round the iris. The finely shaped mouth was restless, too, and twitched all the time.

"All right, I'll wait for you," said Nadezhda Alexeyevna.

"*Merci*," and the lady hurried away.

"You shouldn't, you shouldn't, how could you?" said the Princess. "Didn't I tell you to refuse?"

"But why?"

"How could you? Going to a young woman you know nothing about! She's lying, I feel certain. Where should she get all that money from? She's dressed worse than you and I."

Nadezhda Alexeyevna's heart beat so that she could hardly breathe. Four hundred and fifty thousand! It would feed the three of them for a week and pay off her debts.

"Give it to that Tartar! There he is! Call him!" the Princess insisted.

Nadezhda Alexeyevna said nothing, and waited for the lady as the dying man awaits the priest.

"She won't come, you'll see," the Princess said angrily. "It'll be all to the good. At least she won't lure you into a trap. Did you notice? She has the eyes of an adventuress."

Time passed. The lady did not come back. Nadezhda Alexeyevna was in despair, soon the whistle would be blown, and she had no money even to buy bread.

The milk girls came back for the jacket. The one who bought it unwrapped the money from her handkerchief and handed it out note by note, saying: "There, hold on to it."

As soon as they had gone, the Princess offered the money to Nadezhda Alexeyevna.

"Take it please, and go to your children. I'll tell her that you waited for her and then went."

"Thank you, but I think I had better wait a little longer."

The Princess felt offended. Without looking at Nadezhda Alexeyevna she began packing her things into a yellow travelling bag.

The whistle went.

"She hasn't come!" thought Nadezhda Alexeyevna, horrified, and in that moment saw the lady hurrying towards her. She was not carrying anything. "She said she would go and buy some bread," thought Nadezhda Alexeyevna, and was unpleasantly struck because it had turned out to be a lie. But she hastened to re-assure herself.

"I was afraid you would be gone," said the lady. "My husband has been intending to buy a suit for a long time and I am so glad I have managed to find one that would fit."

Nadezhda Alexeyevna remembered that the lady had hardly seen it.

"Would you like to have another look at it?" she asked.

"Oh no, what's the good? I have seen it. It will fit him all right. Provided that the trouser-legs aren't too short. My husband is very tall."

"This was made for a tall man."

"Splendid! Let's go. Is your *maman* coming with us?"

"This lady isn't my mother." Nadezhda Alexeyevna smiled. The customer obviously did not mind *maman* going with them, and this re-assured her.

She leaned towards the Princess and whispered: "Don't be cross, see you to-morrow," and, taking up her stool and the basket on her arm, followed the lady.

"May I help you?" asked the latter, kindly.

"Oh no, don't bother. Thank you."

"Why not? Please. I do understand your position," said the lady with what seemed to Nadezhda Alexeyevna real and sincere emotion. "I was in the same position until quite recently. Heavens! It's terrible to think about what one has to go through." Her eyes grew still wider, and their whites showed even more clearly. "What a blessing it's all over! Have you any children?"

"Two girls."

"And I have a little boy . . . eighteen months old. He's called Leo. . . . You'll see him . . . with fair curls. Such a darling!"

It would have been ridiculous to be afraid of this kind and loving mother whose face brightened up the very moment she began to talk of her Leo.

"My husband has a very good job now," she continued, "and we have everything we want. Everything. But before this it was a nightmare. When Leo had dysentery . . . no doctor . . . nothing to feed him on. . . ."

Her mobile face constantly changed its expression. When she referred to the past she felt so strongly that one would have thought she was referring to the present. When she spoke of the present, on the other hand, it was as though she were talking of a long-forgotten, happy dream. Nadezhda Alexeyevna was not actually conscious of this, but she somehow sensed it unpleasantly.

"Is there far to go still?" she asked. They had passed several streets already.

"No, no, we're almost there. One more turning and then straight on. My husband will be delighted. He wanted a dinner jacket and striped trousers. It's very smart. And not expensive either. I am glad that Tartar hadn't bought it of you."

"So am I," said Nedezhda Alexeyevna. The lady's obvious sincerity disarmed her.

"We'll be there in a moment, you'll sit with us for a while and have a rest. . . ."

"No, I can't. I am in a hurry to get back to my children."

"Never mind. You can always stop for a cup of tea or coffee. My husband will try it on in the meantime. You'll see how comfortable it is at our place."

They turned off several times, and Nadezhda Alexeyevna did not know the streets along which they were walking. The houses were all alike, two-storeyed, wooden. She was terribly tired and, despite her sympathy for her companion, felt vaguely anxious. She tried to persuade herself that she was afraid simply because the lady's husband might refuse to take the suit; but she was afraid of something else. She could not have named it, but her fear was such that her hands shook and her feet felt weak.

"What a long way it is!"

"It only seems a long way to you. We haven't been walking more than ten minutes."

Through all her anxiety and worry Nadezhda Alexeyevna realised clearly that they had been walking for at least half an hour. The lady's strange, unnecessary lying added to her anxiety. By now it was almost dark. They turned off again.

"Here we are!" said the lady, stopping in front of the only four-storeyed brick house in the whole street. She opened the door and let Nadezhda Alexeyevna pass in first. Then she came in and slammed the door behind her. The staircase was not lit up, and Nadezhda Alexeyevna stretched out her hands in front of her. For a moment she thought: "Back I go!" but she at once remembered her little girls who were awaiting her, hungry.

"For some reason they haven't switched on the light to-day," said the lady. "Usually there is a light. Let me go on in front."

She ran up the stairs, and Nadezhda Alexeyevna, noticing the agility with which she found her way in the darkness, suspected that she had once more lied, this time about the light.

Gropingly, she began mounting the stairs, clutching the cold iron railings. When she reached the top landing, the lady had already opened the door and lit a small oil lamp. The wick was badly trimmed. A narrow strip of flame licked at the glass and smoked.

"Please come in and take off your things," said the lady in the amiable tones of a hostess who invites guests into a cosy, brightly-lit room.

Nadezhda Alexeyevna felt immediately that the flat was damp and unheated. By now she could hardly control the fear which almost impelled her to rush out of the room.

From the hall which was encumbered with trunks, the lady passed into a corridor and from there into a long narrow room with one uncurtained window. Nadezhda Alexeyevna followed her.

The hostess put the unshaded tin lamp on the table. It was an ordinary bare kitchen table. There was nothing on it apart from an ash-tray with a few cigarette stumps. The walls were bare, no pictures, no photographs. The furniture consisted of a couple of bentwood chairs and a shabby sofa.

Nadezhda Alexeyevna remembered "It's comfortable at our place," and stood rigid with horror.

Something stirred in a corner. A dishevelled white lap-dog with long body and short legs came out. Old age had caused it to lose all the prettiness proper to its breed. It had melancholy, bleary eyes. Inordinately long teeth protruded over its hanging lip. The hair on its face was brown as though tobacco-stained. It stopped in front of Nadezhda Alexeyevna and looked at her sadly, without barking, as if to say: "You see, this is rather a miserable place."

"Go to your place, Fleuerette," said the hostess without raising her voice, as if talking to a human being. The dog turned and went back to its rug in the corner. Looking there, Nadezhda Alexeyevna saw a perambulator, almost hidden behind the door. She felt relieved. This time the lady had not lied.

"I'll just tell them to put on the samovar," said the lady, going into the corridor and closing the door behind her.

The fact that she did not go to the perambulator seemed again unnatural, terrifying. The perambulator itself, in the corner behind the door, was terrifying. In a flash, she thought that it might contain the solution of the whole puzzle. A terrible solution. "It's just nerves," she thought, trying to reassure herself.

The lamp still smoked. Nadezhda Alexeyevna reduced the flame, but then it was too dark. She turned it up again and it smoked. The hostess came in.

"Tea will be brought in a moment."

"But where is your husband?" asked Nadezhda Alexeyevna.

Her words strayed about the empty room, finding nowhere to lodge.

"He is not back from his office yet," said the hostess in a carefree voice. "He'll be here presently."

For some reason she would not sit down, moving about the room all the time, noiselessly and suddenly changing her direction, like a bat. Not once did she go near the perambulator.

Fleurette still lay huddled on the rug.

With hideous slowness time dragged on.

"I can't wait any longer," said Nadezhda Alexeyevna at last, and rose resolutely. She felt that something irreparable would happen if she stayed a moment longer. She thought neither of the children nor of the money. She had but one idea . . . to get away.

"Oh please," said the lady, taking her gently by the shoulders and looking into her face, "you will offend me by not staying to tea."

Her words, in themselves so ordinary and pleasant, seemed now incongruous and frightening. "No tea, no servants" flashed through Nadezhda Alexeyevna's mind.

"No, I can't!" she said, extricating herself impatiently from the embrace.

The other suddenly put her finger to her lips—the studied gesture of a bad actress.

"Hush! I think he's here. Fleurette, come and meet your master," she said, again addressing the dog as though it were a human being, and running lightly to the door.

The dog rose slowly, reluctantly, and crawled after her. They both went into the passage.

Nadezhda Alexeyevna went suddenly to the perambulator, wheeled it from the corner and turned it to the light. Contrary to her expectations it was not empty. A child, thickly wrapped up, its head covered with a cap, lay so that its face could not be seen.

For a second, Nadezhda Alexeyevna hesitated. Then something snapped in her mind. With a shudder she seized the child, turned it face upwards, and started back. Among the clothes which she had unwrapped lay a yellow Teddy bear.

Backing away from the perambulator as though it contained a dead child, she leant against the wall.

Something scratched the floor. Fleurette stood in front of her licking her rusty face with her pale tongue. "Didn't you realise?" asked her tired, old, knowing eyes.

Suddenly her mistress came into the room, alone. She looked towards the corner where Nadezhda Alexeyevna stood. There seemed to be nothing but whites to her eyes. A pitiful, guilty smile crept into them and vanished.

"Yes, you see . . . we are alone with him," she said in a new, weary voice, no longer unnaturally gay. "Alone, we two . . . and Fleurette. Nobody knew little Leo besides us, and we all three loved him." She went up to Nadezhda Alexeyevna and took her timidly by the shoulders. There was nothing affected now in her embrace. She wiped her eyes with the palm of her hand. Then she took the Teddy bear carefully from the perambulator and wrapped him up.

"Do you remember Leo? Do you remember how he used to call you Teddy?"

She sat on a chair with it and began to rock slowly to and fro, singing a lullaby in an undertone.

Fleurette went up to her, put her front paws on her knees and stared at her with old, tired, knowing eyes.

Nadezhda Alexeyevna picked up her things quietly, as though afraid of wakening a child, stole into the hall, leapt on to the landing and rushed downstairs.

THE KNIVES

Valentine Katayev

(1897–   )

TRANSLATED BY BASIL CREIGHTON

A SUNDAY'S STROLL in the public gardens is the very thing to show what a man's good for.

Pashka Kokushkin began his Sunday's stroll in the Fresh Ponds at six in the evening. First of all he went to the open-air Mosselprom Pavilion and drank a bottle of beer. That at once showed a proper attitude to life and also his moderation.

Then he bought two packets of roasted sunflower seeds from a woman and walked at a leisurely pace along the main avenue. On the way he spoke to a gipsy.

"Let me read your hand, my fine young gentleman. I'll tell you all the truth. I'll tell you what your heart is set on and I'll tell you what's on your mind. I'll tell you it all and hide nothing, and you've only to give the old gipsy ten kopeks for the pleasure it'll be to you. If I tell your fortune, all will be well with you. If I don't, you'll be sorry."

Pashka thought it over.

"Fortune telling is rubbish and—a silly superstition. All the same, here's a copper for you. You can carry on, though you'll only tell a pack of lies."

The gipsy put the coin in the pocket of her garish skirt and showed her black teeth.

"There's a pleasant meeting in store for you, young man, and because of this meeting your heart will have sorrow. An old man stands in your way, but don't fear anything. Fear only the knife. The knife will cause you a lot of trouble. Don't fear your friends—fear your enemies, and the green parrot will bring you luck. Go on your way with a brave heart!"

The gipsy bent her lean body forward and walked away with dignity, shuffling the soles of her dusky feet over the ground.

"Lies well, the rascal," Pashka said, winked, laughed out loud and went on his way.

As he went he sampled all the pleasures life had to offer. First he weighed himself on a rickety weighing machine; it registered a hundred and seventy-five pounds. Then he tried his strength and, nearly sinking to his knees with the exertion, he made the quivering pointer reach "strong man." After this he strolled on for a while and tested his nerves with electricity. He grasped the brass rod with both hands; there was a tingling in his wrists and a tickling as of ants, his wrists filled with soda water, his palms stuck to the brass rod—but his nerves were proved to be strong.

Finally he sat on a chair in front of a back-cloth suspended from a tree and displaying the Kremlin as seen from the Stone Bridge, crossed his legs, made a very fierce face and had his photograph taken. In ten minutes Pashka received the still wet print and gazed upon it for a long time with great satisfaction: his check cap, his own familiar nose, his Apache shirt with open collar, his coat—all faultless—pleased him well. It was not easy to believe that this strikingly handsome fellow and himself were one and the same.

"Not bad," he said as he carefully rolled up the sticky photograph and marched off to the landing stage.

To exhaust the stock of Sunday delights Pashka had now only to ogle some girls as they passed and take them for a row. Meanwhile he walked on and arrived at an unusually popular booth. A crowd blocked its wide-open doors. The ring of metal and loud laughter could be heard from within.

"What's going on here?" Pashka asked an undersized Red Guardsman who was pushing his way in.

"Throwing rings. It's a game. If you throw straight you get a samovar."

Pashka peered inquisitively into the brilliantly lighted interior over the heads of the crowd. The whole of the back wall was hung with red cotton. In front of it were three tiers of knives stuck on end. Among the knives enticing prizes were displayed. On the lowest tier—boxes, sweetmeats, cakes; on the middle one—alarum clocks, casseroles, caps; and on the top one, just below the roof in semi-darkness, particularly seductive articles—two balalaikas, a Tula samovar, yellow elastic-sided boots, an Italian concertina, a cuckoo-clock and a gramophone. You threw the rings and if you got one over a knife you won the article lying beside it. But it was almost impossible to throw a ring over a knife, for the knives were very flexible and the rings rebounded from them. Most amusing!

Pashka elbowed his way into the booth. A little old man with silver spectacles on his nose stood behind the counter, giving out the rings, forty throws for twenty-five kopeks. A heated young man with a moist shock of hair was laughing uproariously as he threw his last five rings. His coat flapped, the metal rings flew from his clumsy fingers, struck against the knives and fell with a clatter into the sack hanging beneath. The gaping throng laughed. The young fellow's face flushed. The knives rang and vibrated in ever-widening circles as the rings struck them.

"To hell with the knives and the rings too," the fellow cried out at last. "There's a ruble and a half chucked away. I might at least have got a Balaev cake!" And he vanished crestfallen among the crowd.

"Last Sunday someone won a pair of boots," said a youth in patched trousers, "and spent ten rubles to get them."

"Let me have a go," Pashka said, pushing his way up to the counter. "Just for the fun of the thing."

The old man handed him the rings.

"Now then," Pashka asked prosily, "if you hit a knife at the bottom, you win a Balaev cake. Is that it?"

"That's so," the old man said with indifference.

"And next row, an alarum clock?"

The old man nodded.

"Fine. And for a samovar, I suppose, you have to aim right under the roof?"

"Get your cake first. Then you can start talking," someone in the crowd remarked impatiently. "Get on! Make a start!"

Pashka put his photograph down on the counter, pushed the crowd aside with his elbows, took his stance, aimed—but suddenly the ring flew from his grasp, fell on its side and rolled away. Pashka had turned to stone. On a chair beside the shelves, with her hands demurely folded in her lap, sat a young, smartly-dressed girl, whose beauty was such that his eyes were blinded. The girl got up quickly from her chair, picked up the ring and handed it back to Pashka without raising her eyes; but at the last moment she smiled faintly and stealthily, only with the corners of her mouth—and Pashka was a lost man.

"Now then, what's up with you? Get on and win your samovar," the eager onlookers shouted behind him.

Pashka awoke and began to sling the rings one after the other, seeing nothing but the girl's lowered eyelids and her little mouth arched in the middle like a cherry. When he had thrown all forty rings she collected them and put them silently on the counter. But this time she did not smile. She only raised her grey eyes to Pashka and stroked back an ash-blonde lock that had fallen forward from behind her ear. Pashka paid another twenty-five kopeks. The rings flew at random. The gaping crowd laughed and surged at his back. The knives hummed like bees. The old man scratched his nose in complete indifference with a hooked forefinger.

When he had squandered a ruble and not made a single hit Pashka forlornly left the crowd and walked under the lime trees along by the water which was dyed a rosy pink with the sunset. A light mist lay over the pond. The air was cool about his ears. The lights of a cinema were reflected as pillars of flame in the tinted water. Girls in twos with short-cropped heads and green and blue combs in their hair and their arms round each other's waists passed Pashka and nudged each other and turned round to giggle at him, "Isn't he too lovely, that boy." But Pashka went on without paying any attention and hummed to himself in a dream:

"The gipsy told your fortune, the gipsy told your fortune, the gipsy told your fortune, gazing on your hand."

Before the night was over he had lost his heart finally and irrevocably.

For a whole month Pashka went to the booth every Sunday to throw the rings. He threw half his earnings away. He did not take his holiday—he had quite forgotten it was his turn. He became quite crazy. The girl handed him the rings with lowered eyes as before. Only sometimes she smiled as if to herself. And sometimes when she suddenly caught sight of Pashka in the crowds she blushed so deeply that even her shoulders through the thin muslin seemed to glow like dark-cheeked peaches. In spite of all he could do, Pashka never succeeded in having a private word with her; either people got in the way or else the old man was watching them over his spectacles with angry eyes, scratching his nose at the same time with his hooked finger, as though threatening and warning Pashka: "Keep your hands off the girl. She is not for you. Get out of it." But once Pashka did succeed in speaking to her for one second. There were not many people there and the old man had just run round to the back of the booth with a birch to chase away the ragged children.

"Pardon me," Pashka said and his heart stood still, "what is your name?"

"Ludmilla," the girl whispered quickly with glowing cheeks. "I know you well. You once left your photograph behind on the counter and I've kept it. I've lost my heart completely—it's so beautiful."

She put one finger to her neck and pointed to the corner of the crumpled print against her collar bone. When she looked up she was blushing like a rose. "And what's your name?"

"Pashka. Won't you come to the Coliseum with me? It's quite a good piece: The Woman With the Milliards."

"I couldn't. Father never lets me out of his sight."

"Come all the same."

"God forbid! If I went out he would never let me in again. And Mother is even worse. She has a stall at Sucharev Market in her own name. It's horrible how strict parents are. Simply frightful. We live in the Sretenka, Prosvirin Street, not far from here, number two, in the yard to the left as you go in."

"What are we to do, then, Ludmillotchka?"

"We can't do anything. Quick, throw your rings. Father's coming."

Pashka had hardly begun throwing when her father came in with the birch in his hand. He gave his daughter an angry look. So Pashka went away without having come to any arrangement. And when he went the Sunday after—the booth was shut and barred. On the signboard was: "Champion American Quoits, 40 throws 25 kopeks." A green parrot with a red tail was painted on a blue background. In his beak he held a ring, and the wind blew the yellow leaves of the lime trees past the parrot and whirled them all round the booth; the flowerbeds were over and done, not a soul was to be seen. Autumn had come.

Then Pashka remembered the gipsy's words: "An old man stands in your way . . . the knife will cause you a lot of trouble . . . the green parrot will bring you luck"—and the fury of rage he got into with the old crone passes description. He shook his fist at the parrot and went on through the dreary, yellowing gardens in a gusty wind that blew from all sides at once. He went to the Sretenka and found Prosvirin Street. It was a sombre day, grey and autumnal. Number two—there it was, green and white, with a small, poverty-stricken church opposite. Pashka entered the courtyard and turned to the left. But he had no idea where to go next. Then a street organ began to play in the middle of the yard; on it was perched a green parrot with a red tail, and it looked at Pashka out of round, unabashed and heavily lidded eyes. Then a little window opened on the second floor. A delicate little hand emerged and threw a coin wrapped in paper into the yard below. Through the double window over the padding of felt, decorated with gaily coloured snippets of wool, between the curtains and the pot-plants, Pashka caught sight of Ludmilla. She looked joyfully down at him, caressed the window with her pretty cheeks, made signs with her dainty little fingers, extended her arms, shook her head, nodded—there was no making head or tail of what she meant. Pashka too began to talk with his hands: "Come down, never mind your parents; I cannot live without you," but then a fat, moustachio'd woman in a Turkish shawl blotted Ludmilla out, shut the window with a bang and menaced Pashka with her finger.

Pashka dragged himself home, spent two weeks of torment, prowled round Prosvirin Street by night and terrified passers-by, who took him for a thief, got into desperate straits; and on the third Sunday cleaned his coat and trousers with cold tea, put on a pink tie, polished his shoes and went straight to beard the lion in his den—to offer his heart and hand.

Ludmillotchka herself opened the door, gasped with astonishment and clutched at her heart; but Pashka marched straight past her into the room where her parents were drinking tea with milk after their devotions and said:

"Bon appetit and your pardon, little Father, and yours, little Mother, but I cannot live without Ludmillotchka. I was lost the moment I set eyes on her. Do as you please—here I am, master smith of the 6th class, plus bonuses, member of the union since 1917, drink no spirits, pay alimony to nobody, so there's no trouble in that way either."

"I am no little Father to you," the old man screamed in an inhuman voice, "and my wife is not your little Mother. Do you understand that?"

"And what do you mean by listening to the street organ in the yard under the windows and bursting in on strangers in their own house?" the wife added in a bass voice. "So take that. The idea! We have very different suitors in mind. Think of it, 6th class! Last year even a house-owner from Miasnitzkya spoke for Ludmilla and we turned him down. Kindly leave the house, comrade! And the girl—under lock and key is well enough. We want no smiths here, not to mention Reds."

"I make up to a thousand rubles in hard cash by the Champion Quoits alone in the season," the father put in pugnaciously, "and the prizes alone are worth four hundred rubles. Ludmillotchka wants a husband with capital to extend the business. So—good day. Do you hear?"

"Then you won't let me have her?" Pashka asked in a voice of despair.

"No," the old man squealed.

"Very well," Pashka said threateningly. "If it's a matter of capital to extend the business, that puts the stopper on it. But you haven't heard the last of me. I'll lead you a dance yet. Good-bye, Ludmillotchka, hold on and—wait!"

Ludmillotchka, however, was sitting in the passage on a chest, wringing her hands.

Pashka set his teeth and went to Sucharev Market and bought himself a sharp kitchen knife. When he got home he shut himself up. Winter came and went. The ice was removed on sledges from the Fresh Ponds. Pashka went deliberately to work. Not an hour was given up to frivolity; at nights he lay low at home and his neighbours heard a subdued ringing noise proceeding from his room. Perhaps he was learning to play the guitar. No one could say. The river rose. The sun got warmer, the trees budded and put on their greenery, the rowing boats were transported on lorries to the Fresh Ponds. The photographers hung their Kremlins and moonlit nights in the walks. Of an evening the gardens were frequented by strolling couples.

Pashka went regularly Sunday by Sunday to see whether the booth was open yet. It was shut. The green parrot with a red tail sat against its blue weathered background, holding a ring in its beak, and the fresh

green of the lime trees waved above it. Pashka was lean and sombre. One
fine Sunday the booth was open. The gaping crowd surged round the
entrance. The lights shone brightly within, the ring of metal and bursts of
laughter could be heard.

Pashka shouldered his way through the crowd and stepped politely up
to the counter. His eyes shone like steel above his strong cheek bones.
Ludmilla was collecting the rings. No sooner had he entered than all the
colour left her face and she went a transparent white. Her eyes were dark
and her little mouth no longer resembled a cherry. Her father adjusted his
spectacles and took a step back.

"By your leave, friends," Pashka said gruffly, shouldering a fellow aside
who was throwing his rings, and without a glance at the old man he
made a sign to the girl. She handed him the rings as though she were
nearly fainting. He touched her cold fingers and tossed a three rouble piece
down on the counter.

"You ought to have hired a cart, friend, for the samovar." There was a
titter at his back.

Without turning round, Pashka took hold of the ring and flung it
negligently. A brief tinkle was heard. The ring had fallen over the knife
without so much as touching it. The old man scratched his nose hurriedly
and uneasily put a box of Balaev sweetmeats down in front of Pashka.
Pashka pushed it aside and threw his second ring as casually as he had the
first. It fell just as easily and surely over the second blade. The old man
scarcely had time to trot to the shelves before three more rings lightly
skimmed the air and with scarcely a sound encircled three more knives. The
crowd was dumb.

The old man turned his little face to Pashka and blinked. A dark drop
of sweat stood out like a wart on his forehead. His trousers slipped down a
little and bagged out. Pashka stood leaning elegantly on the counter with
feet crossed and jingled his handful of rings.

"Well, Papa, what about Ludmillotchka now?" he asked quietly, looking aside with an air of indifference.

"I won't let you have her," her father answered in his treble pipe.

"You won't," Pashka said sleepily. "Right. Hey, you," he called out to a
boy, "run to the Pokrovski gate for a cart and you shall have the samovar.
Out of the way, Papa."

Pashka's face went steely. The veins stood out and branched on his
brow. He braced himself and lightly raised his arm. Sparks shot from his
finger tips. The knives quivered and sang under the assault of the rings.
The crowd roared and raged and grew to a mob. People ran to the booth
from all sides. Pashka scarcely troubled to take aim. He was frightful to
look upon. Not a ring fell into the sack. In five minutes all was over.
Pashka wiped his forehead with his sleeve. The crowd made way. The
cart was drawn up outside the booth.

"Load up," Pashka said.

"What do you mean to do?" the old man asked in agony, hopping from one foot to another round the shelves.

"Do? Nothing. Chuck 'em all into the pond and have done with it."

"Yes, but why, comrade?" the old fellow whimpered like a woman. "The goods alone are worth four hundred rubles, let alone the business."

"To hell with it—even if they were worth a thousand. The plunder belongs to me. I haven't stolen it. I won it honestly. The people here are my witnesses. I practised all winter and not a wink of sleep have I had. I do what I like. If I like, I keep the loot. If I don't like, I chuck it into the water."

"That's quite right," the crowd roared enthusiastically. "Take your oath on it! But not the gramophone. Don't chuck that in too."

Volunteers soon had the cart loaded to the very top.

"Off you go," Pashka commanded.

"Where are you going?" the old man blubbered. "I shan't dare show my nose at my home again after this. . . . Are you really going to sink the lot?"

"Yes," Pashka said. "Drive onto the landing stage."

"Have you no shame in the sight of God?"

"God—that's a survival of the dark ages, Papa, a painted effigy like that green parrot. But this here is—fact," and he braced his brawny arm.

The cart moved off surrounded by a living ring of cheering people and did not stop until it reached the landing stage. Pashka took the leather boots from the top of the pile and threw them into the water. The crowd gasped.

"Stop," the old man cried in a voice not his own. "Don't throw them in the water."

Pashka laid his hand on top of the loot and said quietly, lowering his eyes:

"For the last time, Papa, I speak to you frankly, as man to man. Let all here bear me witness. Give me the girl and you can have your junk and I'll never again come within a hundred yards of your booth as long as I live. But otherwise I'll blow your whole show sky-high, Papa. I cannot live a day longer without Ludmillotchka."

"Take her!" the old man squealed. "Curse you—take her!"

"Ludmillotchka," Pashka said as he left the cart. His face was pale.

She stood beside him, hiding her face in her sleeve in her embarrassment. Even her little hands were red with shame.

"The show is over, comrades. You can go," Pashka said, taking the girl by the arm as carefully as if she were made of porcelain.

The scent of lilac filled the whole gardens. Lilac was everywhere, lilac petals in the hair, lilac petals in the water. The moon, high in the dark violet-blue of the sky above the lime trees, was as sharp as a knife. And its new-born light broke in reflections on the water, melting into rings large and small, just like gold wedding rings, come to life.

PIPPO SPANO

Heinrich Mann

(1871–   )

TRANSLATED BY BASIL CREIGHTON

I: THE COMEDY

"AND DON'T BETRAY ME," Mario Malvolto told his two friends. "Let them think I am coming back."

"You're not coming back?"

"I must go home. I've a headache. No, the truth is, I want to be alone."

"To reflect on your triumph. Good-night, you happy poet."

"You'll never sleep."

"Who knows? Good-night."

The other two went in. Mario Malvolto stood for a moment at the top of the stairs. At his back the noise of the banquet held in his honour died away. To left and right of him a gold-braided lackey bowed low. Holding his slight figure erect he went step by step down the rich, pale stair-carpet between the gilded rails.

"I must roll these vanities on the tongue," he thought as he went. "In there I was too much taken up with my part. Now I am master of the situation."

"Where are we driving to, Signore Malvolto?" the coachman asked.

"To Settignano."

"Why did he ask? Did he think I was going to Mimi—now? Oh, Mimi, you flapping silken flag! Fluttering now round one neck, now round another. I have kissed it whenever it came to my turn, even embroidered romance upon it. Yes, Mimi, you little cocotte of fleeting impulses, but without a trace of greatness in your sensuality, I have endowed you with passions you never had, given you, to my own satisfaction, out of vanity, out of desire, a whole life to live, as puppets are twitched into grandiloquent attitudes. You were only a girl. Adieu, Mimi.

"We want more, something stronger. A thing like Mimi can be loved in the intervals of writing a tragedy. It takes so little of the heart. My tragedy won the prize tonight. Yes, I am strong. But it is time to shun for good and all the little satisfactions that tend to weakness, and that you, who from my study wall challenge me with a look over your iron shoulder, forbid."

Would the cramping streets of Florence never come to an end? He suddenly felt a violent longing for the air of the hills, the air that shimmered with the glitter of olive trees, that was spiced with bay and left softly pungent kisses on his lips. Still the narrow streets echoed in the silence of the night and still the shadow of horse and coachman climbed up and down the walls. Then the houses of the suburbs came into view. The moonlight shone out over the first gardens.

"I have conquered that hill over there on which my house stands. And not only it—I have conquered all these hills."

His hand made a half-circle; it moved over the distant shape of a hill as over a woman's breast.

"The whole of this country, all its towns, every house to the very last of them I have had to conquer. For nothing of it all belonged to me. No hidden path in any corner of the land knew me from my start. Consider this today. You were born at sea of a mother of a foreign race. With your art as a maker of tragedies you have striven for this country, for every furrow of it, like an eager pilgrim in a coat of mail who sheds his blood in his fervour.

"Now I have a footing. Everyone in Italy knows in what village and on what table the sheet of paper lies which I cover with the written word. This evening the defeated passed me in procession, a whole theatreful, whom I had overthrown. What have I to reckon? Eleven calls. Spoken to by the Queen. Shaken hands with by the Count of Turin. Then the banquet. The two deputies, the Minister's telegram. The Mayor's speech. My rivals consoling themselves with ironical comments. What else? Nothing. There were no women at the banquet. No women—so what good is all the rest?"

Leaning out of the carriage, chin in hand, Mario Malvolto watched the blossoming trees swim far and near in pale moonlight. Before Ponte a Mensola he thought he caught a glimpse of another carriage high up ahead of his own. It vanished again instantly. Its hood was up. His coachman had seen nothing and who could be on the road at that time of night?

"Do women really know that at bottom everything is done for them alone? Many behave as though they believed in the intellect—the intellect, that helpless child, which can neither stand nor walk without the senses. We have only our sensuality; and to what purpose is it, what is its chief reward? The hours spent at the writing-table are hours squandered in the pursuit of women, a night dedicated to the Muses is a barren night of love. Do they know it? Why ask? Their distrust of talent says all and their preference for the dolt who belongs only to them, not to the book. The woman and the book are foes.

"A poet of twenty, as I well remember, has too much to say to them —that is why he is clumsy, silent, tongue-tied by his passion. This does not suit the creatures who know no delights but those of vanity. In those days each one of them set me dreaming as they sat in a salon or drove along the Corso. I would have thrown myself at the feet of her who rewarded me with a glance, at any cost, with a fanatic's resolution. They are not so foolish. Not one of them is tempted to console our neurasthenic extravagances of feeling. They are never drawn to our self-centred rhapsodies: it is success that inevitably attracts them. They rally to it; that is their métier. Fulfilling their function without a thought, they look on while we love-stricken ones perish for them. But they are the indestructible part of humanity. And I pray to them because I pray for strength!

"Then suddenly I gave my shyness of those days the slip—I and the little Princess Nora. What a surprise! A tutor of no position whatever, whom the ladies did not even give a parcel to carry! That desperate deed at once exalted me above them one and all. An elopement with Princess Gallipoli —where was the woman before whom I need drop my eyes? Ah, but I still had the old inclination to look to the ground. Since then there is no audacity with women I have not dared; but I have had to force myself to it every time.

"I am accused of callousness, of something worse than audacities. A man in society declined to fight a duel with me and a court of honour upheld him. The fools, they little dream that my callousness proceeds from my fear of my own tenderness. I suffer from excess of understanding, from too much reflection, too keen a foreknowledge of another's sorrow. I have every disposition to end up as a victim. What compulsion I had to put on myself to abandon little Princess Nora, to leave her dishonoured and outcast. Even today when I meet her in Rome in the higher circles of the demi-monde, I feel a sort of anguish. . . .

"Do I not often feel anguish over Tina, great tragic actress though she is, who suffers on my account?"

Mario Malvolto leant back again in the seat and scanned the top of a distant hill, where a villa rose moon-grey from the moon-grey billows of foliage. A light, a small light, like a needle or a thought, pierced the crown of a tree and transformed it to a burnished cloud.

"Where in the world is she now? How long I have been without news of her. It is bad this time, now that she declined to create the part of my Arachne tonight. Have I ever caused her a pain I have not suffered at her hands? Who can hold a candle to us two in hurting and being hurt? We know that we never work so well, are never such artists as we are in and for each other. And in spite of all angry words, all satiety and all hate we always rush together again. There is not a comedy in the world to match our love. Behind all our passions—fantastic emanations of our love —art is ambushed in the wings, ironically smiling and intent only on picking up a hint for a new part.

"From time to time one of us divines that the other is merely playing a comedy. And suddenly we are nauseated and fly apart. But four months later we meet again at a rehearsal. That is an accident of our profession. It has nothing to do with love—not with the love for whose sake in youth one toils all night and longs for fame. For I should like to know of what use fame is if it does not bring love with it. . . . Ah, it too is a phantom. The more hotly it is pursued the farther it retreats. When I was utterly unknown it had a corporal form: a king who poised a wreath of gold. Now that I have bought it up bit by bit and know of what it consists, what feelings can it any longer inspire? Celebrity is a gilded lie about myself that I myself have disseminated far and wide. It answers to someone who is not me. No one may know the truth about me.

"People have got to say: Malvolto has his way with women and life too; his reputation is not of the best. He's a man of steel, a realist and there you have the core of his work. The greatness and the strength of the race have come to life in a poet. He shows that even a slight frame can bear their weight. The Renaissance has returned, fully armed. . . . That is how people must talk; they must not have the faintest suspicion of my dark fears and of the diffidence that every woman, every great work of art, every robust man inspires in me; they must not dream that if my pages pulsate with life I pay for them with days of depression and hours of physical exercise. I do not wish them to dream it. Pain stands, chisel in hand, behind every perfected beauty. Have I not the right to be proud?

"I feel the melancholy pride that comes of work done not by strength but by merely willing it; of a life without native vigour that reaches up only in urgent desire, as a Niobe raises her arms. After all I have had, still today I yearn after women. I dream of them as I did when I was twenty— only more hopelessly. For I have put them to the proof since then and learn that they are no companions for the player. They are too like me— what have they to offer me or I them? They too wish for applause. They wish to be paid in the coin of passion: they cost me too much. I need my feelings—for my public. I have to harvest my soul so that others may drink the vintage. The more life I share out the poorer my own must be.

"But that rare Phoenix among women, who simply gives herself in reckless passion; who doubts nothing, demands nothing, not approbation, not martyrdom; who rolls up all her life and without a quaver, without a thought for the world or reputation or the future, casts it into mine, breathes with my breath and goes under in my doom—such a woman naturally is not for me. Even if she were to come in at my door in bodily form the miracle would be incomplete. For there would be no room for her in me and my daily life: she would be too large and too strong. There is room only for the longing she inspires.

"I longed for her again tonight—on the stage, through the hole in the curtain behind which I belong! I longed for all of them!"

Mario Malvolto laid his head back with a groan and plumbed the pale flood of the stars.

"I knew them nearly all. A few had been mine, a few more might be if I chose. What good would it be? Am I to use them for my sentimental education or my social advancement, as I did the little Princess Nora, or as studies for twenty different parts, as I have Tina, the tragedy actress? Or are they to be poor lifeless puppets like Mimi for me to dress up in fancied passions which are as false to them as they are to me? Or are they in the long run to find me out and send me away with a flea in my ear? . . . You get tired of plucking the stars up there with your eyes, one after one, and in the end your hands are empty. . . .

"That is how they shone in the circle tonight."

He looked at a large ripe star.

"The Linozzo. Long, flat Egyptian nose, long eyes close together. Black gleaming waves of hair just above her eyebrows. Wide soft mouth, moist, sinuous, darkly painted. She is desirable above all when she holds a gleaming fan to the corner of her mouth or when with her head thrust back she smiles over her shoulder out of the corner of her eyes. . . . She never took her eyes off me all the time I was in the Queen's box. She is ambitious —I could have her."

His eyes were caught by another luminary.

"The Borgofinale. A full profile, with rounded chin, staring out wild-eyed from a luxuriant mass of auburn hair above the sumptuous ermine collar of her cloak. She was one of the first to set me on fire. Her distracted face calls up a whole train of bogus emotions. But was she virtuous perhaps?

"An impossible one—the Lancredoni. Lean swarthy-skinned princess. Her small, Gorgon head with the fleeting lines of nose and forehead is borne on the stiff stalk of her neck. Her lace sleeve leaves her sloping shoulder, fragile and pure as porcelain, bare. The Princess yawns beneath the cold gleam of her tiara. . . . And tonight from behind my curtain I prevailed upon her! I gloried over her, knowing that I had more delight in her than he who held her every night in his arms! What is left to me? Perhaps a few lines that will appear in print. But for me, in my soul? . . .

"Then the young girls! There they sat, just in front of me, peering bright-eyed out of a world into which no path leads. The Cantoggi caught my eye once in the hole in the curtain. I started back at this look she shot without knowing where it found its mark.

"Which of them will come and take me by the hand and lead me homewards into that country of hers where one is strong with the strength of innocent emotion?

"Not one. For they have nothing more pressing to do than to learn their parts in the comedy. Gemma Cantoggi, a child, fresh from the country, is to marry Lanti, a voluptuary past his prime. Charming!

"Suppose I asked of one of them the boon of self-oblivion—probably I should not be allowed to know anything of her either. There was a foreigner in the stalls, a strong and beautiful profile beneath the velvet knot of her large hat. A billowy scarf enveloped her to the lips in rosy chiffon. . . ."

Mario Malvolto dreamed on as he turned into the piazza of Settignano. The low, flatly curving gable of the church was powdered blue by the moon, A single lamp twinkled feebly in the wide starry night, in the midst of which, on its hill, the little town was sleeping.

Mario Malvolto heard a faint sound and saw a dark object moving at the end of the long narrow street. It could only be the carriage he had seen just now; its hood was up. A moonbeam fell suddenly across it; something white leant out. Where in the neighbourhood did that vehicle belong? Nowhere, the coachman replied. It vanished into the shadow.

They emerged from the narrow street and drove downhill for a short way. Mario Malvolto got out, walked for a few yards between two hedges and up eleven steps to his door. It was open and his servant lay asleep in front of it.

Mario Malvolto stepped over him and taking the lamp from a table in the hall went up the steps into his study. The busts of women on the bookcase in their close-fitting dresses of a long-past day smiled whitely from the sharp confines of their dreams; the large threaded pearls that encircled their foreheads seemed to quiver in the light of the moon.

It was so light in the room that Malvolto put out the lamp. He leaned against the open terrace door. How white the garden! All the dense, dark foliage over the whole ridge of the hill and right down to the wall with its ilex canopy shone in pale enchanted loveliness. The wistaria hung in a silver mantle round the bleached dead cypress. And even the camellias bloomed only as ghosts.

He looked into the room again and gave a start. For a moment it seemed to him that the more than life-size man there on the brightly lighted wall had brandished his sword in the air. Mario Malvolto, speaking in thought, addressed the man whose portrait was the only picture that looked down daily on his work:

"So we meet again. When I left you this evening I was eager for battle, strung up for resounding victory or for crushing defeat. It is victory. Wine and speeches swelled it out. I left them to it—secure in my triumph. I only need to draw it from my breast and look upon it, you see. And on my way home, moonstruck with ghostly musings, I found it a defeat—oh yes, a pale stillness of defeat, a worse one than if I had been whistled noisily off the stage.

"Have you too ever known a victory turn suddenly to defeat and elude your grasp at the moment when it rang loudest in your ears? War and art, they are both the same superhuman exaggeration. Do you know the nausea after an orgy? Answer, Pippo Spano!

"There you stand, erect, your iron legs astride, your gigantic blade athwart them in your hands of bronze. Your limbs are agile, ready alike for the assault, the chase, for hot embrace and thrust of cold steel, ready for wine and for blood. In the very sound of your name there is the whistle of a brandished blade and then a cleaving blow. Iron is arched over your broad chest and a golden girdle encircles your slender hips over the joyous blue of your doublet. You have a short, forked beard, your mouth stands out brutally in your lean face and dull blond locks of hair hang about it. You look over your shoulder with head thrown back and blazing eyes, alert and terrible. On closer scrutiny, a smile can be seen: a smile born of an excess of ruthless self-confidence; a smile that refuses to be questioned; the mere hint of a smile that causes a profound dismay, overwhelms with sudden dread, rivets the eyes, excites defiance and at last extorts respect.

"Since you know so unutterably how to triumph, how fearfully you must often have known defeat! Yes, how you must have suffered, you and the painter of your portrait, who was as strong as you. Great works of art— your life or your portrait—only rise to such glamorous heights because they have known the abyss. Ah, you smiter of the Turks, don't try to deceive me —I hear your shout of rage when a blow got home. I see you bleed when a friend betrayed you. I can almost imagine the orgy of pain you suffered whenever a woman dug into your heart with her sharp finger-tips."

Mario Malvolto folded his arms. Still with his eyes on the condottiere's face he drew nearer and said in a whisper:

"You see, I pine for such orgies too. I am too fragile for them and too diffident, that is why I create characters who are otherwise. That is why you stand there to be my conscience, my compulsion to greatness. You are to give me a loathing of the measured joys, of that economy in suffering with which we poor moderns content ourselves. Our art represents the bourgeoisie of the soul. Paltry neurasthenics live out their seventy years of humdrum life, indulging daily in a pennyworth of pain and six pennyworth of comfort. The artist burrows laboriously in his constipated soul, in his own exclusively, and proudly displays the sorry stuff he brings to light. Rancorously he shuts his eyes to all that has strength or vivid colour.

"But I mean to live! I want to be lavish; in my brief span my art shall make me a second, mightier life. I will know nothing of the weakling that I am; I know enough of him already. I will experience alien beauties, alien pains. Really alien. Women who die for love, exquisites of exorbitant desires, sculptors who chip their hearts out on a block of marble. They dig the phantoms of hell out of the rock and their pain is the whirlwind that blows souls through the purple gloom. . . . To such as these I will go out, who do not play eavesdropper to their own peevish moods, whose destiny is not chained to the poverty of their own blood. No, they are called to battle in the world outside them and they must fling themselves into the fray!

"I will force my way into their life, as though it were encompassed with a quick-set hedge, a prouder, more impulsive world, where violence and the intoxication of surrender reign, where unutterable defeat is drunk to the dregs and splendours without a name, where life is lived to the full and death comes once for all.

"And the woman whom you, Pippo Spano, could love, she is the goal of all my longing. She comes to meet me as the sum and end out of the world I conjure up. Is it not so——"

And Mario Malvolto, forgetting himself, spoke louder:

"Is it not so, she comes to meet me? Do you believe it, Pippo Spano! She comes——"

He broke off: there she stood.

She stood on the threshold of the little white drawing room, whose shadows were suddenly illumined by the moon. She herself was white and clothed in moonlight. Her pale face, short nose, vigorous lips were framed in heavy black coils of hair. At every breath she took embroidered silver flowers were shed from her small slight figure, from her shoulders and her neck; her life was in her breathing. She lifted her arms to the curtain of the door and her sleeves, made entirely of the petals of the flowers, fell in a shower of pale leaves. Her arm, the pistil within them, shimmered in the moon.

Mario Malvolto had drawn back. He clasped his forehead. A hallucination? He had drunk a lot of wine and even more deeply of rhapsody. But his heart beat quietly and firmly, his spirit was unusually clear and unencumbered. Would that spectre never go? . . . He took two quick steps towards it. But it held its ground, it even spoke.

The girl said quietly and simply:

"Mario Malvolto, I love you. I am here for us to love each other."

II: THE MIRACLE

THEN HE RECOGNISED Gemma Cantoggi.

"You—here! But a word, Contessa, would have sufficed," he stammered. "I would have hastened to you."

"Yes, but I have come to you instead," she replied.

"But you compromise yourself."

"Oh, no. We have a house quite near. They think I am spending the night there. I often leave our town house at night when the mood takes me. My maid came with me. She is in the secret."

He looked dubiously at her. This was the Cantoggi who was to marry Lanti, the voluptuary who was past his prime; one of those unusually beautiful women whom in their day all men desire and all women hate; for whom a boy takes his life; who for twenty years dance in the van of fashion and who when their day is done have promised happiness to a thousand and kept their promise to six or seven, and left a lingering and intoxicating fragrance behind them in the memory of a few old gentlemen. What were they in themselves? What did their lives mean? He knew: the influence they exercised, the martyrdom of the man and the applause of the crowd.

Was she here as a colleague, the actress to the playwright? Did she seek advice how to reach the pinnacle of success? He had scarcely grasped and did not believe one word of what she had said.

"But what brings you here?" he asked in agitation.

"Love of you, Mario Malvolto," she replied, and her voice trembled slightly.

"Contessina, you are a child. If you love me why did you not ask some friend of yours to introduce me to you? I should have fallen at your feet."

"We should have had no freedom at home. We should have had to marry in order to love each other."

"Ah!"

He felt a wicked satisfaction.

"The Contessina Cantoggi would not want me for a husband!"

"You would have engaged yourself to me, Mario," she said without understanding what he meant, "before you knew what I was like. You would have sworn you loved me and perhaps it would have been a pretence. As soon as I saw it, all would have been over. I want us to love each other without anyone's knowing. You are not to flatter yourself: I am loved by the beautiful Cantoggi and all Florence knows it. Do you hear? You are not to do that."

"Do you think I am so sunk in vanity?" he muttered.

"No, I do not. Forgive me. I am jealous in advance. I want to shut you up here."

She crossed the threshold into his study and went impulsively up to him.

"And I could not bear it if we saw each other before strangers and had to speak to each other with reserve. I want to be always—— Listen, I love you!"

She suddenly opened her arms, casting off a last shred of modesty:

"I want to be always naked with you!"

A wave of emotion swept over him; he took her in his arms.

"If I could believe that you were really in my arms!"

He groaned, with his mouth in her hair. The Phoenix of a woman who wished to make him rich with reckless passion: there she was, there was the miracle. One of those young girls who peered out clear-eyed from their world into which no path led: there she was, there was the miracle.

"If I could believe it!"

"You feel me," she said quivering. "And you must surely feel that I love you."

"I do feel it," he said, in pity more for himself than her.

"And you will love me?"

"I will, I will indeed!" he cried in pain.

With her face buried in his neck she asked: "Have you ever thought me beautiful before? Would you have wanted me?"

"You—only you."

And he knew he lied and yet was honest. He had desired all women and would always desire them. But did he not now hold them all in this one girl? Perhaps, perhaps.

"I too," she said, looking up with wide eyes. "You—only you."

"Then you knew that you caught an eye through the hole in the curtain tonight and whose eye it was?"

"No."

"Not? Have you not often caught sight of me in a box? And tonight on the stage when I was called before the curtain?"

"No. I didn't really know you by sight. I trembled when you came on to the stage. It might have been someone else, a friend of yours."

He was speechless.

"We have lived so long in San Gimignano," she explained. "I have only lived here since my father died and my brother was in garrison in Florence."

"Then you came because I am famous."

"Famous? I don't know. Perhaps I've heard people talking a lot of nonsense about you; but I didn't know it was you they meant. I had read your books, but I never noticed the name."

Mario Malvolto thought: So much for fame.

"There were people in them I could understand. I said to myself: I should have behaved and felt like that, if——"

"If——"

"If I came across that man. With my fiancé, I knew, I could never experience anything of the sort."

"Yes, you are engaged."

"I was. I broke it off before coming to you."

"I don't understand all that."

"It's so simple. Tonight in your play I saw the same people living and dying as those I knew in your books. They were more vivid than the people with whom I dine and drive in the Corso. They did not smile so much and I could believe them—because they died!"

"Because they died."

"When I got home I looked at the name of the author of the novels. It was yours. Then I drove up here."

He was enchanted. How trusting, how resolute a passion! To think that it was before his eyes, within his grasp! But he bethought himself: she wanted more of him. He had suddenly to repress a pang.

"Do you suppose then that I resemble my creations? Perhaps I make them so because I am otherwise."

"But you have made them. You must have carried them in your heart. . . . It is so simple; tonight I suddenly saw it all so clearly. If the people we might love do not exist in our world, if they do not exist anywhere at all—still we seek them in the heart of him who has created them! Why don't women do that? It would be too silly not to come to you."

"I am not so strong. . . ."

It seemed to him as though he wrestled with this seventeen-year-old girl, as though his life were at stake.

"Your betrothed, Contessina, is a hero compared to me. I know he has the show of vigour rather than the reality, more of the swordsman's alertness than nerve and muscle. But judging from his looks, at least, I'm sure he is no backward cavalier. You have much to expect from him, after all."

"I know pretty well what I have to expect," she said with a shrug of her shoulders. She sat down at his table in the chair he sat in when he worked. She played with his pen, threw a notebook to the floor and propped her chin on her hands.

"When he used to visit me at San Gimignano, when I walked with him on the crumbling watch-tower, high amidst the ivy with the blue landscape beneath—do you know what he reminded me of? Of an Englishman taking photographs of it. Do you suppose he had the haziest notion of all I had felt there, all one can feel in sixteen years in those ivied turrets, on those warm ruinous walls among the ilex trees? I would have been ashamed to utter one word of it . . . but to you——"

"To me?" Mario Malvolto said, stretching out his hands with a sense of guilt for the gift she offered.

"To you I can tell it all."

And she sprang to her feet.

"Or rather, you know it already. You have felt it too, it is from you I learnt it!"

He flinched away from her.

"We writers drive a shady trade. We procure you pleasures, but that does not mean that our . . ."

"You're being modest. You're playing the coquette." And when he made a deprecating gesture: "Or else you don't believe me."

They both stretched out their arms simultaneously.

"Not believe you!"

That was not possible. Her breath, her look, and the very lines of her body were truth itself. The tender lines of her body, a soul incarnate, swept through him, vibrant with passion. He throbbed with them; he wished with all his heart they might enwrap his heart and break it together with every artifice within it; overpower it and enslave it. Never to feel anything but her! That was his goal—a goal to reach in swoon.

"Listen," he begged, hoarse with torment, "you are deceived in me. I am not so honest as you. I cannot be."

"Would you say so if you were not?"

"I am trying to be at this moment. But you must not try me too far. Believe me—your betrothed, he may be cold—but even so he has more good feeling than I have. He is, after all, nearer to you."

And when she denied it with a look:

"He may not be able to look backward into your childhood's dreams. Be glad that he cannot. He will be able to love you all the more truthfully as you are if he lacks the gift of imputing to you what never was, or is no longer."

She walked away and sat down on the ottoman and folding her arms over the cushion leant her breast against it.

"I know more about him than that," she said slowly, looking far away into the moonlight. "His mistress has told me about him."

"The Traffetti?" he asked quickly.

"I went to her. Does that surprise you? She is a great singer and a beautiful woman. I considered how little reason she could have to withhold the truth. And she was the only person who could tell it me. . . . Well, he is weak, he . . . can do very little. How can I put it? . . ."

He started back: "Does she take me for a bull?" She read his gesture.

"I am not a child. I can make up my own mind. He needs artificial stimulus and expedients, he asks things of his mistresses that—that the Traffetti had to explain to me."

"Oh—oh—she explained all that to you?"

He thought: "A young girl going to a whore to be put right about the capacities of her betrothed—— No, I should never have imagined that. Who could?"

She looked at him wide-eyed.

"And you—you don't need that."

"No," he admitted in astonishment.

She went on with vehemence:

"You suspected me just now of base desires. Yes, I know you did. Don't deny it. You little know me . . . The worst is not his lack of robustness, but that he has no love. The Traffetti loves him. She cried when she told me about him."

"But he fought a duel on your account the other day," Malvolto said without thinking.

"I don't want anyone to fight for me as he did. He held his ground calmly and coldly the whole time, keeping his opponent's fury at a distance —his eye always on the other's sword-point—until at last he could pass his guard. . . . A man who avenges an insult to his beloved does not look so! There is no love in him, I tell you."

Very well, Malvolto thought and gave up the defence of her bridegroom. He watched her as she undid her tightly fitting bodice. A brooch rolled on to the carpet. He caught a glimpse of blue-veined flesh shimmering through the lace. She was behaving like a child who had got home, tired and happy, after a long day.

"I shall never get to feel his soul. Yours I have often felt. I bring you mine."

She stood up.

"And my body."

He rushed to her, fell on his knees, rained kisses on her arms and her hands. All at once he was warmed through and through by the sense of her soul that for months had thought of his and now had freed itself from captivity, from alien toils; feeling its way, a passionate somnambulist, through the moonlit woods of its own profound premonition—to him! She had come—she had stepped out of the white parlour in a shaft of moonlight. There she stood, created for him and, without him, incomprehensible. There she lay on his breast to release him, to induct him into the sacredness of life, to fill his lungs with her breath and teach him how in forgetfulness of all else to feel and live with strength!

"I love you, Gemma!"

She only smiled with her hands on his hair.

"But I believe," he cried out within himself. "The miracle has come to me. I am strong enough to believe it and find salvation in it."

He jumped up and put his arm round her. . . . Suddenly his blood ran cold. "Yes, you believe, you actor. And first thing tomorrow morning you will be wondering what artistic use to make of your moment of belief!

"But I love her," he protested to his adversary, "and she me. Am I not a human being?

"No, you are not. You only play at being one. Forego your effect for once, just this once out of pity for a child. Think——

"Oh, I know and I am afraid. This is not just a romantic episode to take up and drop as soon as one is tired of it. It is not a house with two entrances. It is a defile and once within it there is no issue but there where the torrent pours over the rock."

Reluctantly he let go of her. His eyes, distraught with pain, wandered round the walls and suddenly met those of Pippo Spano. Pippo Spano was smiling now. His terrible smile, inscrutable hitherto, now said in so many words:

"Is this the strength which I, your conscience, was to wring from you? A woman throws herself at your feet. You go to her on the current of your blood. And are you going to allow the pale cast of thought to show that life the door? Do so—but never again seek to smuggle yourself out of the world of weaklings into mine, where men love and rob and, if it must be, die."

Mario Malvolto snatched Gemma from the floor. All his blood rushed to his head and, like a warrior whose booty clasps his neck with her white arms, he carried her into his bedroom.

III: BELIEF

Mario malvolto stood alone on his terrace and watched the sun come up. Gemma had gone. He listened to the last echoes of the storm of joy she had aroused in him. Soon it would have died away. If she came back that evening still in the same glory of passion, how would she find him? He did not know. Twenty hours might sweep him far away. He would make an effort to get back to her. Perhaps he would succeed.

"No, no. We'll part at once. I will not see her again. That is the strong thing to do, for I still desire her and ever shall. . . . I will write to her. She will suffer. It will be a clean cut, as swift as our happiness. Unless one died of it, it is bound to pass. If I gave way to pity now and tried to deceive her, I should only be opening the way to long anguish, quivering resuscitations of what must die in the end."

He went down the steps into the garden and as he walked along the paths between the trees and bushes he wrote in his head:

"My adored Gemma!

"I still have the right to call you so today. If you came back again tonight, it would perhaps already have become a lie—the first of all the many lies with which I should seek to reprieve our love. I will not have that. We were too strong and too happy. I want to repay the truth of your feeling with the utmost truth that is in me. Listen, my Gemma.

"You love me still, I know. You are convinced that you love me for ever. And you would consider a feeling null and void that foresaw its own death. But that, Gemma, is the case with mine. Oh, it is not that in the years to come I shall not wish you here as ardently as I do now at this moment! But if you came in two hours, perhaps even so you would come too late. Perhaps, beloved, even in the closeness of your embraces last night I was already untrue to you. Who knows whether I may not have sought out words with which to describe them? Art is your rival, Gemma, and one you may not lightly challenge.

"Sometimes you would find me clasped to her hard breast when you came with open arms into my room."

Mario Malvolto watched a tress of wistaria slip through the hollow of his hand and wondered: "Hard breast? Has art a hard breast?" He let it pass for the moment.

"You do not understand me, I know. You think one can drop one's occupations when a woman comes in. Lanti, if you married him, would send his horse away the moment you asked. A stockbroker would finish with his clients. Money is a passion that seldom holds its ground against a woman. With art, Gemma, it is another matter. It alone and war and power are superhuman exaggerations that claim the body and soul. But art is the most ravenous of the three, it engrosses the other two. It alone so hollows out its victim that he is left forever incapable of a genuine feeling, of frank surrender. Think—the whole world to me is only raw material for a phrase. All you see and enjoy—those walls of San Gimignano, over which your childish dreams ran like squirrels, would be no joy to me unless they evoked the words that mirrored them. Every golden evening, every weeping friend, all my feelings and even my pain over their decay are all only matter for words. And so would you be too. Gemma, that is intolerable.

"I shall never sit with my wife and be happy in the sight of her. I should be thinking how her features could best be described, how and in what original way they had to be looked at to take me by surprise and compel the arresting word. When I had your wonderful flesh—I use a really banal word, wonderful—when I felt it within my hands, I should be seeking out a better, a word that captured the essence of your flesh and yours alone.

"I should be assiduous enough: you would often see me in a fever of uncontrollable emotion. Do not mistake that for love. It is essential to me to cheat myself into states of feeling in order that I may be able to represent them. I have to enter into people who are strong and beautiful as you are, vibrate with their nerves, riot in their pleasures, be damned with their damnation and share their downfall. I cannot know people out of myself, for I am not a person: I am a player.

"Think of all the women you meet in society and with whom you exchange a word or a smile; think of each single one and know that I have already been unfaithful to you with her and will be so again—in my heart. And yet nothing ought to go on in it but you! But there is worse still: I shall be unfaithful to you with yourself, with a counterfeit Gemma.

"Those creations of mine you love, for whose sake you threw yourself into my arms, Gemma, they were all once real people. I have falsified them to gain my artistic ends. I shall falsify you too. I am on the way to it already. This letter is the first of the artistic uses I shall put you to."

Mario Malvolto had tears in his eyes. He was genuinely suffering; but it was to his advantage to suffer. "My letter will be good," he told himself.

"You, Gemma, are a woman and there would of necessity be times when you were moody, sick and sad at heart; you would come to your beloved for consolation. I would lavish it on you, do not doubt. From selfishness—to learn more of life. Your sufferings and my sympathy would both serve my turn. . . . Yes, if you died, my beautiful Gemma, I would despair, you may be sure. But even before you had breathed your last, your death and my despair would furnish me with two characters for a play.

"Do not hate me for it! I live condemned to loneliness behind the glare of the footlights that separate me from all spontaneous, unexploited feelings. How I should love it to be otherwise—and that the heart-throbs that beset me in the intoxication of your warm blood were not a substitute for the agitations that rise from an ink-pot.

"If I could but give myself to you utterly, once and for all! Renounce all I have won, all that the long pursuit of art has made of me, and lay it all on your knees! No more would be known of me but that I had vanished for love of a woman. And I would make of the whole country as far as my fame has gone only one single laurel-grove for your little feet!

"All my desire is to be numbered with the strong ones who could do thus, those condottieri of life who gulp their whole lives in a single hour and die happy. Instead of facing this forlorn parting, we ought to have died together, Gemma, this very dawn!"

Mario Malvolto broke off.

"And why not tonight?" he cried out as he stood in the sun-flecked shadows of two rose bushes. "Why not the day after tomorrow or any other day when we were happy?

"Mark, my friend, what a shabby commonplace trick you are playing! You would like in due course to be quit of the girl you have enjoyed; you uncover her little secrets, which are your concern alone. You have no right to. Now that you have once taken her with a high hand, now that you have carried her off as plunder to your bed—do your duty and be strong to the end. She came to you as to an artist of other days who gave two women their due, one on canvas and one in bed. At bottom you are afraid that one or the other may prove too much for you. Then die of her. The miracle has happened. This miracle called woman arose from a prouder, more impulsive world conjured up by your longing and stepped into your room. You gave it welcome; now believe it. Now believe it your release. And if you are too weak to believe, then die for it notwithstanding, as a martyr is nailed in silence even though without conviction to the cross."

Mario Malvolto took his resolve. He tore the letter he had written in his head to pieces. Then he went in and stood with folded arms in front of the portrait of Pippo Spano. No, Pippo Spano did not smile. Or perhaps he did? But his smile had never been so inscrutable.

Gemma came to her lover that night and the next night and every night. It seemed to him that belief was within his grasp. You had to go through the motions, live in its rites, follow its dietetic prescriptions. At last it came. The problem was to conquer art that pressed a mask upon the face of love, to wrench one's own spirit round as though it were a horse, to turn away one's creative curiosity from all the world and concentrate it on a woman with the sole ambition of fashioning within oneself a perfect love.

"Occasional excesses," he told himself, "are not so dangerous to the state of mind required for artistic effort as the slow flooding of the system with small doses of alcohol. From now onwards I will drink wine every day.

"I will go visiting at the hours when I might be working and I will choose the houses of the least intelligent people."

"It was a mistake," he confessed a few days later, "for I had time, the way they talked there, to think out a story between two of their remarks."

But he returned just as dissatisfied from houses of greater pretensions.

"These two weeks of idleness have given me a frightful alertness. Everything that an artist experiences in society touches me to the quick: the prick of conscience at the sight of beauty, the exasperation at the least sign of indifference, the discouragement caused by the success of talented mediocrity, the paean that greets a woman's friendly glance and the deep melancholy if he fails to please. My sensibilities react instantaneously to all that provokes the busy instincts of us artists—our vindictiveness, our urge to put a bridle on nature, to impose ourselves on the world, our ostentation and our thirst for self-glorification.

"I will stay at home."

He tried reading a book for the sake of its contents. Up to now he had opened one only to appropriate something as his own. The experiment prostrated him with unutterable boredom. So he went for walks.

He laid it down as a law that the hazy line of the hills on the horizon had no name; that no words corresponded to the silver eyes the olive yards opened when the sunlight flitted over them. Mostly he lay down in the open country beneath a tree and closed his eyes, as a sick man who hopes to gain courage from the measured breathing of nature and who must not be exposed to the shock of its light and stir. "Nature will heal me. I am a sick man, obsessed by art."

If ever he ventured to look on nature, it seemed to him to have a new tenderness. The kindly earth gave herself shyly to him again as to a convalescent. Never had he encountered her so calmly, so undemandingly as now; never since, when he was a boy, the fearful desire had seized him to wrestle with her and bend her beneath the yoke of words. Now at last this fear relaxed, daily a little more. The earth would no longer be conquered; the distant scene nodded kindly and that grassy mound pressed him as a friend to its breast.

Once in mid June he was standing in the pinewood above Settignano on a stony track, brown with pine needles, looking down into a valley over which a sudden artillery of clouds shot beams of light. Now a river sparkled out on the edge of the dark arable; now an impetuous green flame leapt at the steep wall of a wood; now a house blazed white from the massed shadow of cypresses. Mario Malvolto savoured the pleasure of being allowed to see it all without having to depict it in words.

Suddenly the light that leapt a distant meadow and caught a flock of sheep, a rock, a man, suddenly the light became a figure and the figure drew nearer. It was white and nimble. It hastened between the dry branches at the bottom of the wood from which Malvolto looked down. His heart beat faster: he knew who it was. It was she now who lived in the coppices where for so long only words had roosted! Her limbs flashed in the stream; that flickering flight of birds bore the desire of her on to love's horizon.

"The earth is full of her! My senses encounter nothing that does not breathe with her breath. And I clothe her, not in a garment of words but in kisses. She brings no masterpiece to birth in me—only love. I love her, I love her!"

He ran home, thinking he would find her there also.

"I'm a fool. She has only just gone."

Nevertheless he leant over the garden wall, keeping a look out for her. And there she was. She sprang white and nimbly from a thicket, caught in a noose of light, as he had seen her just a moment before far away between the fields in the valley. She was chasing a fledged nestling that fluttered on to a branch behind the well. She jumped up on to the narrow rim of the deep well and ran round it without so much as a glance at her feet. The wind of her sleeve made the branch quiver and the light that shot from the clouds seemed to run with her. She was herself a feathered creature balanced in air and the garden enticed her to all its secret haunts. She was just stretching out her hand to catch the little siskin . . . but Mario saw her danger and was alarmed; she heard his shout and looked round, shading her eyes with one hand. She gave a choking cry of joy, the cry of an up-springing bird, and jumped down from the well. She ran with flying skirt to the wall, caught his hand, felt with her feet for the footholds between the stones and so reached his kisses. They curled up together like two squirrels on the warm wide top of the wall and their kisses were playful and impulsive. Gemma, mute and fierce, bit her lover in the neck and all the while her eyes, darkly wavering with passion, looked back into the garden. Her desire drew her there and she let herself down and pulled him after into her lawless realm, among bushes laden with crimson flowers that nodded and bled as the lovers sank entwined between them.

Mario Malvolto felt that he had embraced a woman for the first time. He, and the whole world with him, had been for the first time entirely consumed by a woman, translated body and soul into the strength of a woman's being. And from these seconds of boundless life it was bitter to turn back; it was as though he left years of vigorous and lavish life behind him. Still— he had loved. Gemma had made a man of a player. She had led him with her light and noiseless tread so far back into nature that new horizons dawned. He to whom life had ever been but a pretext, who had merely experimented with all that causes suffering or joy, who had believed in nothing and attached himself to nothing; he who had sat in the next room without presentiment while his mother died—it was to him that Gemma had called from afar. He could not assess his gratitude: there were no words to describe his happiness. He sought for none and had none—only the name he suddenly found for her, Santa Venere.

She had come to announce very good news: her brother had been ordered on manoeuvres. He was leaving in three days and perhaps they would be left alone for months together. Gemma was now moving into her villa near by and she had put off all possible visitors by saying that she would always be out for long walks. What bliss opened before them! Suddenly they looked down a magic avenue of days whose green, luxuriant perspective was shot with gold; and, far down the black marble galleries of the nights ahead, gleamed delight.

When she had gone, all at once he felt empty; he came back bitter and empty out of another life. He wandered aimlessly from room to room. Here lay one of her gloves, there some flowers, picked and thrown down. A book of pictures lay on its crumpled face in a corner. One of the Florentine ladies of a past century wore a huge collar round her neck that was now once more the latest fashion. Malvolto put on his hat as though he were in a café or in any other place where by chance he had an hour to while away. He was no longer at home; the house was hers, that alien creature of lawless energies who came on wings, embraced and flew away. She had leagued herself with Pippo Spano to introduce love's martial law within his walls. Pippo Spano drew himself up against the crimson arras, resolute and alert. Mario Malvolto did not feel equal to this perpetual battle-alarm. He gave a sad look into the devastation of his bedroom and into the bathroom, where the taps were dripping. Only the little white drawing room where she had first appeared to him in the moonlight was undisturbed. She never entered it—it was too fragile and soft for her. Tina, his great tragedienne, used to sit there when she came and when they roamed hand in hand as friends through long days devoted to the Muses. "Yes—she left me time to work. In fact, we loved each other in order to work. Was that so very awful, after all?"

With a sigh he unlocked the drawer of his writing-table where the manuscript of the work he had been busy upon lay hidden. This was the only spot in the whole room on which Gemma had not yet laid her despotic little hand.

"My God, how long since I wrote! I cannot imagine now how I ever wrote this at all. I couldn't write a page more of it now. My talent has gone!"

He held his head in his hands.

"When we've done with each other, this girl and I—we must after all be done some day—what months of hygiene, what a regime of boredom I shall need to get me up to scratch again. I wonder whether she has the faintest notion that she has already cost me half a novel? She is expensive; but it's incredible the value women put upon themselves, what they accept without a thought. It's well known, of course; only moments come when the discovery is made afresh. Oh, well. No doubt the affair will give my mind a lot to feed on. Perhaps I was in need of a strong dose of real life; otherwise

art is left to fertilize itself. I shall find out later what use the girl has been
to me. Later . . ."

He tossed the manuscript back into the drawer and went out on to the
terrace, forgetting the key for the first time. He drew a deep breath. Already he desired her again.

Next day a letter came in place of her. She said she was moving house
and her brother was giving her a lot to do before he left. Three days more!

Mario Malvolto spent those three days in his room doing nothing, ever
on the alert. She might be meaning to take him by surprise. Any moment
a twig might snap down there in the garden as she pushed her way in at
the secret little gate. But the days had run out before she came. She laughed
slyly. "How the waiting must have sharpened your appetite . . . and
mine!" she said frankly, as her arms quivered round his neck.

She had had an idea since seeing him last.

"Tell me, do you ever work?"

He drew back.

"No, but I want to know. Whenever I've come you've just been waiting.
Or roaming the country. You look very well, better than at first. But I have
never found you at your desk. You don't think I want to keep you from it?"

He understood. She wanted him altogether and everywhere—even at his
writing-table. "She's afraid I write in secret and live a double life. If she only
knew how mistaken she was!"

She had observed the key in the lock of the drawer and fell upon it and
took out his manuscript.

"Now I've got you! So you've never shown me this. And something so
precious!"

It was the first time he had seen her touch any object with reverence.
She put the pages carefully on the table without disarranging them.

"Sit down!"

"I am to write? Gemma, what are you thinking of? I have been longing
for you for three days!"

"I don't want you—unless you write!"

He obeyed. Confusedly he turned the written pages and recalled with an
effort the next sentence he had had ready in his head. He wrote it down
and could not get any further. When he looked up Gemma stood there
naked, holding her arms level with her shoulders.

"Now write," she said softly and with a menace in her softness.

He sat upright and changed colour and bit his lip. She began to dance;
he felt her wafted about him like a large, very white flower, stirred by a hot
breeze.

"I want your genius to live in me," she whispered.

She gazed past him. All the blood rushed to his head. Visions of un-
imagined creations came to birth in him, a true primeval forest of the spirit,
glowing with petals, succulent with sap, howling with wild beasts, and

impenetrable. He saw that he was helpless; he could not master a single feeling, carve one clear-cut image, light on one word. "It will all come later. Later . . ."

He caught sight of her facing him on the threshold of the terrace. Her outline was touched with pink and a lustre of gold veiled her body. She was a shell precious for its rarity; her hair fell about her like seaweed.

She was a nymph who flitted past him like a beam of light, too swift for recognition, peeping for a moment slyly and wildly over his shoulder and the next moment nothing was left of her but the faint fragrance lingering as the echo of a fairy dream.

"Unless you write——" she said at last.

He wrote the first words that came into his head. She approached inquisitively and sat on the arm of his chair and looked over his shoulder. He saw the muscles of her graceful legs ripple and wrote on. What did it matter? He rode for a fall with a thrill of satisfaction. He felt he was far beyond all that once he had prized most highly. Art? The sheer loneliness of art? Art one drained one's life blood to nourish, for which one beggared oneself, for whose sake one put off the man and put on the player? Ah—now he was playing a comedy. But his work, his work at his desk, art itself was the comedy and he played it for love to see!

Now Gemma took his head in her arms and bent it back, just as though she took a child home who had played about long enough. It had all been only the battle between the woman and the book. "How I love her for having won!"

She let herself slowly down upon him in eager, full and deep-red kisses that smelt of iris, her native perfume. When he shut his eyes it seemed that the great blue petals closed over him for ever.

She had to go home. A moment later he gave a start. "I see her at this moment as distinctly as if she had never gone. My brain and all my blood are so full of her body, of her flower-coloured arm round my neck, of her long, softly rounded thighs, of her danced caresses. I am brim full of her every movement! I, my house, my garden, this hill—everything is charged with her life. It lies littered about as flowering branches torn from the tree and I see them and seize them and inhale their scent! Poetry is dumb—I have only living images of incarnate beauty."

When she came back in the evening he took her to the long loggia on the shadowed side of the house, on whose walls Orpheus, young and lean, strode between slim and scarcely budding trees and Galatea poised bright limbs over a deep blue sea. The olive yard intruded its pale clouds of leaves almost under the arches.

"It is not impossible that Pan may be watching from the field out there. No one else."

"Let's hope not," she said lightly with a smile.

"The peasant only comes out to work in the cool of the evening and his vineyard is locked. In the garden there is not a spot overlooked from any house near by. It is your people I am anxious about. How do you explain your long absences?"

"I? I don't. That is my companion's business. She can surely think of some place where I might be."

And the girl's passion that threw prudence to the winds and scorned all stratagem struck him in the face with the force of a tornado. His heart stopped.

The sun was just rising when they woke. The first sharp beams pierced the open window and were shivered to gold-dust in the long peacock-blue curtains. Gemma held out her hand to catch it. She jumped out of bed and climbed with the thin cloud of her nightdress floating about her impetuous limbs on to the foot-end of the bed and stood there in an aureole of blue-green light. It was the light on the floor of fabulous seas. The whole room, tiled floor, walls and furniture, was sea-green, and on the bed, chest, cupboard and mirror in the severe style of Renaissance Siena the gilded carved work took on a fitful shimmer, while all the space between was dim. Only in the corner of the window the one picture was splashed with the red of dawn.

"What is that?"

And Gemma raised her arm in the light that came seeping through—a mermaid rising from the deep to ask about a marvel far across the water. "I have never seen that before."

"Because you were never here until sunrise before. That picture only strikes the eye at dawn."

"I see a semicircular colonnade and from its two gateways swarm a troop of genii with ghostly wings and serpents' tails, little dragons, monsters that blow out their bellies and women, tall women with their hair full of ripe, dark fruit or with forked locks—women with long narrow breasts like udders. They dance a weird dance, wreathing garlands of flesh, no, of lustrous flowers amid the bright clouds of their robes, whirling discs of green air, while an owl looks on. . . . I'd like to have a dream like that," Gemma said. "And there at the back of the colonnade is a couch where the dreamer lies!"

"That is me, Gemma. For I am the only one to feel the charm of this picture. The original hangs unnoticed in a gallery somewhere. I am vain of the pictures no one else has eyes for: they belong exclusively to me! . . . How often," Malvolto said starting up and speaking to himself, "how often I used to wake up at dawn to interview my dreams and found them all ushered in and ordered by that picture."

Gemma gave a cry and fled for refuge into her lover's arms.

"Horrible—oh, how horrible! A mask—a mask with a huge nose, and red, it might be alive; and it's made of skin, the skin of a human face!"

After a moment, still shuddering, she asked: "What is it?"

"I have always taken it to be a symbol of art," he replied. "The flayed skin that still boasts the features of the vanished body and is still miraculously coloured by the blood that has long since ceased to pulse—that to me is art. I grope behind the skin whose nostrils still expand as though informed with life and whose eyelids still wink; I grope for the body behind, for life itself. It was never there—not for me. . . . But now I have it in my arms!"

And he drew her to him. Gemma went up to the picture again.

"It is really horrible. But I want it. I'll have a mask made like it to frighten you with. You must make a copy of it for me. Quick—get some paper."

They ran into his study and hunted about in the drawers and came on the manuscript.

"There doesn't seem to be anything else here," Gemma said, hesitating.

He took a page of it and pressed it so tightly against her face that her nose broke through.

"What are you doing?"

"Don't you see what that is? It is the skin—the skin beneath which the blood seems to course. There is your mask!"

She held the torn paper in her hand. He lit a wax taper and let the flame creep up and devour the written lines. When it got near her fingers he took the sheet from her and put it in the hearth.

He went back for another sheet. She had gone white. She divined, without fully realizing, her last, decisive victory.

"What are you doing?" she asked again. "You surely don't mean to burn your story, your precious story? You were going to go on with it—later."

"Later? When?"

She did not know.

"For us, Gemma, there is no later. We love each other and then comes death."

She trembled. She threw her arms round his neck. With his face against hers, he said:

"My dreams are over. The dreams in that picture have all vanished down the dark perspective of the colonnade whence they issued. Instead of dreams I have you. You are the substance behind them all, the goal of all my longing. You have pulled me over into your life——"

"Yes!"

She kissed him without comprehending what he went on to say:

"—into a prouder, more impulsive world encompassed by a quick-set hedge, where violence and the intoxication of surrender reign, where unutterable defeat is drunk to the dregs and splendours without a name, where life is lived to the full and death comes once for all."

"And death comes once for all," she echoed with wide eyes. She had only heard the final words fall from his lips and uttered them as her own. "Yes, I feel it—I feel it coming," she said.

She slowly took a page, let it flame up and put it on the hearth. She took another and another; the flames rose higher and their reflections danced on her white skin and ran along the narrow folds of her nightdress. As her small hands made a funeral pyre of thoughts, perceptions, aspirations and wrestlings for the truth, her lips wore a two-edged smile, sweet and cruel.

Mario Malvolto stood with folded arms. He said to himself with suicidal joy:

"I believe."

IV: THE DEED

HE SAT WAITING for her in the dusk. She had gone home for an hour or so to speak to her companion, whom she had sent to the town on an errand.

The summer was over; a cool breath came from the garden; the withered cypress stood up bared and menacing, stripped of its veil of wistaria. Malvolto lay on his face, his face in his hands and thought of Gemma, in a mood of incomprehensible gloom.

Suddenly he knew that she had come. She was silhouetted in the pale frame of the open terrace door.

She approached slowly—he took a breath at each step she took—and came to a stop between his knees without touching him, her arms hanging at her sides. He saw her face hover above his, remotely shimmering in the dusk of the evening, an evening that clutched at his heart with the dread that no dawn would ever follow it. And her two eyes above him, large and dark, blinded by night and hot with banked fire—he took them for two craters gaping over him. They came slowly nearer, so near that they became one crater over whose rim he bent, dizzy yet allured. Then Gemma's cheek touched his and she whispered:

"Darling, we must die."

He only pressed his cheek a little closer to hers in reply. She had said nothing new. He had felt her words coming all the way from her house to his. No, they came from even further back: from the first night when she gave herself to him! They had both known long ago that after their embraces nothing was left them but to die. From the very beginning death was enfolded in their love. They had said "for ever" and to that "ever" death alone could give a name.

She clasped him round the shoulders and he her. They felt themselves rocked, drowned and dissolved away in the enchantment of a deathly sea. All around them the forms and colours that a day had lent to things dissolved away.

Malvolto fought his way to the surface of a flood of blackness. He asked:

"But why? What has happened?"

Gemma smiled; she walked away and said lightly:

"Well, we've been photographed."

"We——"

"Yes. It's all over the town. It's an excellent likeness, I'm told. I am standing on the terrace and you are lying at my feet."

"You are—naked?"

"And you, poor dear, have not much on."

"Appalling! This is appalling. And I made absolutely certain that the terrace could not be overlooked from any single point in the whole neighbourhood! It must have been taken from the garden. It can only have been my servant, Niccolo—or else your companion. I'll——"

And he made for the door. But Gemma seized him by the arm.

"What does it matter who did it? Some passer-by or other. Don't let's waste time that is better spent on love."

He came back, suddenly calmed.

"You are right. How did you find out?"

"My companion saw it in a friend's house and also in a shop where she was not known. It's being sold on the sly and having a great sale, I hear. You can imagine it, I, the Cantoggi and you, Mario Malvolto . . ."

He felt a fleeting vanity, but instantly he was overwhelmed with shame and rage at himself. He flung himself at her feet.

"You, Gemma—all your hidden beauties that have seen the light for my eyes alone are now hawked round and shown in drawing-rooms and clubs and in the wings of theatres—yes, we must die. It is intolerable."

"I could tolerate that," she said, still smiling.

"I have destroyed your reputation. Everyone in the town calls me a lucky fellow, everyone envies me. It's unspeakable."

He struck his forehead with his fists.

"We must die!"

"Not for that," she said gently. "I don't mind about all that. But they would separate us."

"They would——"

He stood up.

"Does your brother know? Has he come back?"

"Not until next week. But he might hear about it any day."

"They won't tell him."

"Not if he were my husband," Gemma said and her smile died away. Malvolto bowed his head.

"You are right. They will tell a brother."

Suddenly he drew himself up.

"Then I'll fight him!"

Gemma shook her head.

"You mean he'll kill me?" he shouted. "Four months ago perhaps. I'm a practised swordsman now."

"If you did kill him, I have other relations and they will separate us. I'm only seventeen."

And when he made no reply she went on in a colourless tone: "And then, you see, we should still have to die. Why should you kill my poor brother first? Better die now—at once."

Malvolto gave a rapid glance about him: no, there was no other way out. Gemma, standing there, her slender figure hazily outlined, her face floating like a water-lily on the night and her eyes that were darker even than it— Gemma had now become a childlike Judith and round one of her flowerlike fingers she wound a lock of hair and by it hung a head and that head was his.

But she died with him—he maligned her: she walked to her death in the strength of martyrdom, coolly and with courageous step, whereas he, for whose sake she went, still sought for a way of escape. He took her in his arms.

"Gemma—the world's only lover—your strength and calm raises me up. It is I who kill you. Do you not hate me for it?"

"Hate you?" she exclaimed with the first trace of emotion. "I feel I love you for the first time. When I came in just now and you were there in the dusk and I stood between your knees and we looked at each other—yes, we looked at each other. Had you ever looked at me like that before? I never had at you. I should never have believed it was possible to be happier than we have been. Now there is something there that makes me happier still. . . . Let us taste it," she whispered with her eyes closed.

He caught her up as wildly as on the first night. Yes, she had all desire at her command: she drove him on all through her proud, impulsive realm to the last thicket where the utmost joy was hidden. Stung by the lash of death he carried her into the bedroom.

The moon had risen when they came back. They leaned together, their arms round each other, their temples touching, their feet weary. As they stepped into the sharp band of light that fell across the room from the terrace door they started as though at a cold shower and separated. Gemma went to the door and leaning against the frame pressed her forehead on it. She heard Mario restlessly pacing the carpet. He looked about him. How the room had altered. It belonged to love no longer; this very room was to see them die. The wide couch offered itself no longer to their embraces; it looked like an operation table. Gemma turned abruptly and said:

"Do it."

He stopped short in sudden anguish.

"I—have I got to?"

"Yes. Do you expect me to?"

They looked each other straight in the eyes and saw a gleam of enmity flame up in their depths. The next moment they ran to each other with open arms. They felt each other's tears on their cheeks.

"We who still have a life to live——"

"And we must kill each other."

"Was anyone ever so unhappy as we——"

They remained for a long time motionless. Then Gemma sobbed.

"I shall never embrace you again—never again."

"I shall never kiss your thighs again," Mario said, "and never measure their little hollows again with my lips. Never bury my face again in your hair or on your knees——"

He clung to her in an agony of devotion. He filled the delicate pink shell of her ear for the last time with the burden of his whispered desires; arraigned her, limb by limb, because she betrayed him and had no more joys to lavish on him.

At last she freed herself and going with her gliding step to the couch lay down upon it and said with a smile: "I am ready."

He passed his hand over his forehead and then walked quickly to his writing-table. She looked away. She heard the ring of steel. He came up to her, one hand behind his back.

"Your murderer is here," he stammered. "He is stealing upon you."

He collapsed when he reached her, his forehead on her knees.

"I can't do it, Gemma. You are the stronger."

He held the dagger out to her.

"You do not love me as I do you—to the last quiver of my hand."

"I love you so much," she said, folding his head once more in her arms, "that the only happiness left me is to die by your hand! Think—death alone gives you to me altogether. It makes us inseparable. Kiss me—kiss me while you stab."

But he tore himself loose.

"You must live," he cried. "What does my fate matter to you? I am content and I—I thank you!"

She fell in his arms—deathly pale.

"What are you thinking of? You want to leave me alone? How can you?"

And she sobbed bitterly.

"Your coat is torn, your shirt too. Good God, you're bleeding!"

"Only a scratch," he muttered. "That way is barred."

"Be good to me," she whispered as she drew him to her on the couch as though asking an embrace. "All good, all light of the sun has come to me only from you. Don't you know what it was I dreamt of as a child on my ivied walls at San Gimignano? Of you, my dearest."

She laid her head dreamily back with a tremulous smile of desire and guided the dagger in his shuddering grasp to the place where he was to plunge it in, and since her loveliness so lusted after death the most heroic gesture of her life was also the most lascivious. He stabbed with tight-shut eyes, in a spasm of horror, against his will and before she expected it. She cried out.

When he opened his eyes he was in a daze. Where was she? He could not find her head. It was lolling over the edge of the couch. He put it back on the cushion. A piece of white flesh fell on his knee. What was it? A finger. He had cut off one of her fingers. He leapt up, pierced with terror. The weapon clattered to the floor.

"What have I done? Did I do that? I? There she lies—blood on her lips, what is all this—she is contorted, writhing. Why? My God, her breast gapes! . . . Gemma!"

He bent over her, weeping aloud. She looked in his eyes with a forlorn and questioning look. Suddenly he understood. She wanted him now to plunge the blade into his own breast. He stood up swaying on his feet, and a cold shudder swept through him. A gulf had abruptly opened between her and him; the abyss that parted the living, who had all before him, and her, whom death left no more choice, yawned before his eyes. "What part have I in this dying woman?" And he remembered with a dull throb of memory how a few moments ago he had said to her: "What does my fate matter to you?" And he had tried to rescue her and turned the dagger against himself. And now there she lay. . . .

He bent down for the dagger and her quivering eyes followed him.

No! If he did do it—he would not be dying with her. Their deaths were too unequal. Dying, for her, was a simple, easy matter. She died as a child. What did she know? What had she ever doubted? No disillusionments riveted her to the martyrdom of living. She had appeared on the earth at the beck of a single passion. All her life, all her brief years had led—down a short avenue, where at the end a Hermes stood—to him, to him and that moonlit night when she flung herself into his arms. Between that full moon and this in which she died lay all that gave her meaning, all she was capable of feeling, all of her. Dying now, dying with him she left nothing behind, had nothing to regret.

But he—oh, he! He had broken out this very moment from a tangled and luxuriant garden and saw again the wide world before him. What joys and sufferings and what goals beckoned him! Women and words and warfares rang out a clarion note. He seethed with new ideas. Now his art could illumine the visions which had shot up in him in tropical profusion when Gemma, a little naked Muse, danced about him. She had fulfilled her mission as love's ambassador and now returned where she belonged. And her death—of what use was it if he was to make no more of her?

But her eyes were on him; the whites were turned up, leaving only a narrow strip of the pupils.

"What am I thinking of? What am I doing? I'm out of my mind. How can I look on and watch her suffer and do nothing?"

He turned away and rang the bell in a panic. He ran to the door. The dying girl struggled for breath. With a piercing scream she cried out: "Murderer—you murderer!"

He whipped round, white and wide-eyed as she, and met her full gaze once more.

There were steps outside. Old Niccolo stood in the doorway, uttered a loud cry and turned and ran. The door was left open and sounds came from the house.

Mario Malvolto was still gazing into Gemma's dying eyes. "Murderer," he muttered with blanched lips. "You are right. I stole upon you, I stole my way into your life, the life of the strong. I wanted to live to the full, to love regardlessly, to be a man at last. I wanted, too, to die as the strong die—once and for all. Forgive me: it was a mistake. I did not deceive you. I did not know until my life was demanded of me that it was play-acting, like all the rest. Forgive me, darling girl. It is not mere cowardice; it is only that one does not really kill oneself in the last act of a comedy."

But then he picked up the dagger from the floor.

"I'll do it all the same. Look, I am going to do it!"

He tore his shirt open and showed her the point on his chest.

"Do you see it? And realize what I am doing? I do it because you are watching and only for you!"

But he saw that her eyes were glazed.

"You are dead? But we were to die together and now you forsake me? Now when I am ready, now when I sacrifice all to you, not just the one life you sacrifice for me but all the hundreds of uncreated lives within me —do you vanish now? Have you gone for ever? Then—what am I doing? What is left me to do? I know nothing any more."

He raised his arms and let them fall again. His eyes wandering distractedly round encountered the eyes of Pippo Spano.

"You! What would you do now? Did such defeat ever come your way? It is your strength that seduced me. You were my conscience. It is your fault. What am I to do?"

Pippo Spano smiled. Etched by the moonlight, his smile, born of an excess of ruthless self-confidence, fascinated Mario Malvolto and at the same time overwhelmed him with sudden dread. He stood transfixed. He questioned it with all the strength of his being; he supplicated it with folded hands, swaying on his feet, gasping for breath, now in a fever, now in a cold sweat, distraught and plunged in misery—a player on whom the curtain would not fall.

OLD ROGAUM AND HIS THERESA

Theodore Dreiser

(1871–)

IN ALL BLEECKER STREET was no more comfortable doorway than that of the butcher Rogaum, even if the first floor was given over to meat market purposes. It was to one side of the main entrance, which gave ingress to the butcher shop, and from it led up a flight of steps, at least five feet wide, to the living rooms above. A little portico stood out in front of it, railed on either side, and within was a second or final door, forming, with the outer or storm door, a little area, where Mrs. Rogaum and her children frequently sat of a summer's evening. The outer door was never locked, owing to the inconvenience it would inflict on Mr. Rogaum, who had no other way of getting upstairs. In winter, when all had gone to bed, there had been cases in which belated travelers had taken refuge there from the snow or sleet. One or two newsboys occasionally slept there, until routed out by Officer Maguire, who, seeing it half open one morning at two o'clock, took occasion to look in. He jogged the newsboys sharply with his stick, and then, when they were gone, tried the inner door, which was locked.

"You ought to keep that outer door locked, Rogaum," he observed to the phlegmatic butcher the next evening, as he was passing, "people might get in. A couple o' kids was sleepin' in there last night."

"Ach, dot iss no difference," answered Rogaum pleasantly. "I haf der inner door locked, yet. Let dem sleep. Dot iss no difference."

"Better lock it," said the officer, more to vindicate his authority than anything else. "Something will happen there yet."

The door was never locked, however, and now of a summer evening Mrs. Rogaum and the children made pleasant use of its recess, watching the rout of street cars and occasionally belated trucks go by. The children played on the sidewalk, all except the budding Theresa (eighteen just turning), who, with one companion of the neighborhood, the pretty Kenrihan girl, walked up and down the block, laughing, glancing, watching the boys. Old Mrs. Kenrihan lived in the next block, and there, sometimes, the two stopped. There, also, they most frequently pretended to be when talking with the boys in the intervening side street. Young "Connie"

Almerting and George Goujon were the bright particular mashers who held the attention of the maidens in this block. These two made their acquaintance in the customary bold, boyish way, and thereafter the girls had an urgent desire to be out in the street together after eight, and to linger where the boys could see and overtake them.

Old Mrs. Rogaum never knew. She was a particularly fat, old German lady, completely dominated by her liege and portly lord, and at nine o'clock regularly, as he had long ago deemed meet and fit, she was wont to betake her way upward and so to bed. Old Rogaum himself, at that hour, closed the market and went to his chamber.

Before that all the children were called sharply, once from the doorstep below and once from the window above, only Mrs. Rogaum did it first and Rogaum last. It had come, because of a shade of lenience, not wholly apparent in the father's nature, that the older of the children needed two callings and sometimes three. Theresa, now that she had "got in" with the Kenrihan maiden, needed that many calls and even more.

She was just at that age for which mere thoughtless, sensory life holds its greatest charm. She loved to walk up and down in the as yet bright street where were voices and laughter, and occasionally moonlight streaming down. What a nuisance it was to be called at nine, anyhow. Why should one have to go in then, anyhow. What old fogies her parents were, wishing to go to bed so early. Mrs. Kenrihan was not so strict with her daughter. It made her pettish when Rogaum insisted, calling as he often did, in German, "Come you now," in a very hoarse and belligerent voice.

She came, eventually, frowning and wretched, all the moonlight calling her, all the voices of the night urging her to come back. Her innate opposition due to her urgent youth made her coming later and later, however, until now, by August of this, her eighteenth year, it was nearly ten when she entered, and Rogaum was almost invariably angry.

"I vill lock you oudt," he declared, in strongly accented English, while she tried to slip by him each time. "I vill show you. Du sollst come ven I say, yet. Hear now."

"I'll not," answered Theresa, but it was always under her breath.

Poor Mrs. Rogaum troubled at hearing the wrath in her husband's voice. It spoke of harder and fiercer times which had been with her. Still she was not powerful enough in the family councils to put in a weighty word. So Rogaum fumed unrestricted.

There were other nights, however, many of them, and now that the young sparks of the neighborhood had enlisted the girls' attention, it was a more trying time than ever. Never did a street seem more beautiful. Its shabby red walls, dusty pavements and protruding store steps and iron railings seemed bits of the ornamental paraphernalia of heaven itself. These lights, the cars, the moon, the street lamps! Theresa had a tender eye for the dashing Almerting, a young idler and loafer of the district, the son of a stationer farther up the street. What a fine fellow he was, indeed! What a handsome nose and chin! What eyes! What authority! His cigarette was always cocked at a high angle, in her presence, and his hat had the least suggestion of being set to one side. He had a shrewd way of winking one eye, taking her boldly by the arm, hailing her as, "Hey, Pretty!" and was strong and athletic and worked (when he worked) in a tobacco factory. His was a trade, indeed, nearly acquired, as he said, and his jingling pockets attested that he had money of his own. Altogether he was very captivating.

"Aw, whaddy ya want to go in for?" he used to say to her, tossing his head gayly on one side to listen and holding her by the arm, as old Rogaum called. "Tell him yuh didn't hear."

"No, I've got to go," said the girl, who was soft and plump and fair—a Rhine maiden type.

"Well, yuh don't have to go just yet. Stay another minute. George, what was that fellow's name that tried to sass us the other day?"

"Theresa!" roared old Rogaum forcefully. "If you do not now come! Ve vill see!"

"I've got to go," repeated Theresa with a faint effort at starting. "Can't you hear? Don't hold me. I haf to."

"Aw, whaddy ya want to be such a coward for? Y' don't have to go. He won't do nothin' tuh yuh. My old man was always hollerin' like that up tuh a coupla years ago. Let him holler! Say, kid, but yuh got sweet eyes! They're as blue! An' your mouth——"

"Now stop! You hear me!" Theresa would protest softly, as, swiftly, he would slip an arm about her waist and draw her to him, sometimes in a vain, sometimes in a successful effort to kiss her.

As a rule she managed to interpose an elbow between her face and his, but even then he would manage to touch an ear or a cheek or her neck—sometimes her mouth, full and warm—before she would develop sufficient energy to push him away and herself free. Then she would protest mock earnestly or sometimes run away.

"Now, I'll never speak to you any more, if that's the way you're going to do. My father don't allow me to kiss boys, anyhow," and then she would run, half ashamed, half smiling to herself as he would stare after, or if she lingered, develop a kind of anger and even rage.

"Aw, cut it! Whaddy ya want to be so shy for? Dontcha like me? What's gettin' into yuh, anyhow? Hey?"

In the meantime George Goujon and Myrtle Kenrihan, their companions, might be sweeting and going through a similar contest, perhaps a hundred feet up the street or near at hand. The quality of old Rogaum's voice would by now have become so raucous, however, that Theresa would have lost all comfort in the scene and, becoming frightened, hurry away. Then it was often that both Almerting and Goujon as well as Myrtle Kenrihan would follow her to the corner, almost in sight of the irate old butcher.

"Let him call," young Almerting would insist, laying a final hold on her soft white fingers and causing her to quiver thereby.

"Oh, no," she would gasp nervously. "I can't."

"Well, go on, then," he would say, and with a flip of his heel would turn back, leaving Theresa to wonder whether she had alienated him forever or no. Then she would hurry to her father's door.

"Muss ich all my time spenden calling, mit you on de streeds oudt?" old Rogaum would roar wrathfully, the while his fat hand would descend on her back. "Take dot now. Vy don'd you come ven I call? In now. I vill show you. Und come you yussed vunce more at dis time—ve vill see if I am boss in my own house, aber! Komst du vun minute nach ten to-morrow und you vill see vot you vill get. I vill der door lock. Du sollst not in kommen. Mark! Oudt sollst du stayen—oudt!" and he would glare wrathfully at her retreating figure.

Sometimes Theresa would whimper, sometimes cry or sulk. She almost hated her father for his cruelty, "the big, fat, rough thing," and just because she wanted to stay out in the bright streets, too! Because he was old and stout and wanted to go to bed at ten, he thought every one else did. And outside was the dark sky with its stars, the street lamps, the cars, the tinkle and laughter of eternal life!

"Oh!" she would sigh as she undressed and crawled into her small neat bed. To think that she had to live like this all her days! At the same time old Rogaum was angry and equally determined. It was not so much that he imagined that his Theresa was in bad company as yet, but he wished to forefend against possible danger. This was not a good neighborhood by any means. The boys around here were tough. He wanted Theresa to pick some nice sober youth from among the other Germans he and his wife knew here and there—at the Lutheran Church, for instance. Otherwise she shouldn't marry. He knew she only walked from his shop to the door of the Kenrihans and back again. Had not his wife told him so? If he had thought upon what far pilgrimage her feet had already ventured, or had even seen the dashing Almerting hanging near, then had there been wrath indeed. As it was, his mind was more or less at ease.

On many, many evenings it was much the same. Sometimes she got in on time, sometimes not, but more and more "Connie" Almerting claimed her for his "steady," and bought her ice-cream. In the range of the short block and its confining corners it was all done, lingering by the curbstone and strolling a half block either way in the side streets, until she had offended seriously at home, and the threat was repeated anew. He often tried to persuade her to go on picnics or outings of various kinds, but this, somehow, was not to be thought of at her age—at least with him. She knew her father would never endure the thought, and never even had the courage to mention it, let alone run away. Mere lingering with him at the adjacent street corners brought stronger and stronger admonishments—even more blows and the threat that she should not get in at all.

Well enough she meant to obey, but on one radiant night late in June the time fled too fast. The moon was so bright, the air so soft. The feel of far summer things was in the wind and even in this dusty street. Theresa, in a newly starched white summer dress, had been loitering up and down with Myrtle when as usual they encountered Almerting and Goujon. Now it was ten, and the regular calls were beginning.

"Aw, wait a minute," said "Connie." "Stand still. He won't lock yuh out."

"But he will, though," said Theresa. "You don't know him."

"Well, if he does, come on back to me. I'll take care of yuh. I'll be here. But he won't though. If you stayed out a little while he'd letcha in all right. That's the way my old man used to try to do me but it didn't work with me. I stayed out an' he let me in, just the same. Don'tcha let him kidja." He jingled some loose change in his pocket.

Never in his life had he had a girl on his hands at any unseasonable hour, but it was nice to talk big, and there was a club to which he belonged, The Varick Street Roosters, and to which he had a key. It would be closed and empty at this hour, and she could stay there until morning, if need be or with Myrtle Kenrihan. He would take her there if she insisted. There was a sinister grin on the youth's face.

By now Theresa's affections had carried her far. This youth with his slim body, his delicate strong hands, his fine chin, straight mouth and hard dark eyes—how wonderful he seemed! He was but nineteen to her eighteen but cold, shrewd, daring. Yet how tender he seemed to her, how well worth having! Always, when he kissed her now, she trembled in the balance. There was something in the iron grasp of his fingers that went through her like fire. His glance held hers at times when she could scarcely endure it.

"I'll wait, anyhow," he insisted.

Longer and longer she lingered, but now for once no voice came.

She began to feel that something was wrong—a greater strain than if old Rogaum's voice had been filling the whole neighborhood.

"I've got to go," she said.

"Gee, but you're a coward, yuh are!" said he derisively. "What 'r yuh always so scared about? He always says he'll lock yuh out, but he never does."

"Yes, but he will," she insisted nervously. "I think he has this time. You don't know him. He's something awful when he gets real mad. Oh, Connie, I must go!" For the sixth or seventh time she moved, and once more he caught her arm and waist and tried to kiss her, but she slipped away from him.

"Ah, yuh!" he exclaimed. "I wish he would lock yuh out!"

At her own doorstep she paused momentarily, more to soften her progress than anything. The outer door was open as usual, but not the inner. She tried it, but it would not give. It was locked! For a moment she paused, cold fear racing over her body, and then knocked.

No answer.

Again she rattled the door, this time nervously, and was about to cry out.

Still no answer.

At last she heard her father's voice, hoarse and indifferent, not addressed to her at all, but to her mother.

"Let her go, now," it said savagely, from the front room where he supposed she could not hear, "I vill her a lesson teach."

"Hadn't you better let her in now, yet?" pleaded Mrs. Rogaum faintly.

"No," insisted Mr. Rogaum. "Nefer! Let her go now. If she vill alvays stay oudt, let her stay now. Ve vill see how she likes dot."

His voice was rich in wrath, and he was saving up a good beating for her into the bargain, that she knew. She would have to wait and wait and plead, and when she was thoroughly wretched and subdued he would let her in and beat her—such a beating as she had never received in all her born days.

Again the door rattled, and still she got no answer. Not even her call brought a sound.

Now, strangely, a new element, not heretofore apparent in her nature but nevertheless wholly there, was called into life, springing in action as Diana, full formed. Why should he always be so harsh? She hadn't done anything but stay out a little later than usual. He was always so anxious to keep her in and subdue her. For once the cold chill of her girlish fears left her, and she wavered angrily.

"All right," she said, some old German stubbornness springing up, "I won't knock. You don't need to let me in, then."

A suggestion of tears was in her eyes, but she backed firmly out onto the stoop and sat down, hesitating. Old Rogaum saw her, lowering down from the lattice, but said nothing. He would teach her for once what were proper hours!

At the corner, standing, Almerting also saw her. He recognized the simple white dress, and paused steadily, a strange thrill racing over him. Really they had locked her out! Gee, this was new. It was great, in a way. There she was, white, quiet, shut out, waiting at her father's doorstep.

Sitting thus, Theresa pondered a moment, her girlish rashness and anger dominating her. Her pride was hurt and she felt revengeful. They would shut her out, would they? All right, she would go out and they should look to it how they would get her back—the old curmudgeons. For the moment the home of Myrtle Kenrihan came to her as a possible refuge, but she decided that she need not go there yet. She had better wait about awhile and see—or walk and frighten them. He would beat her, would he? Well, maybe he would and maybe he wouldn't. She might come back, but still that was a thing afar off. Just now it didn't matter so much. "Connie" was still there on the corner. He loved her dearly. She felt it.

Getting up, she stepped to the now quieting sidewalk and strolled up the street. It was a rather nervous procedure, however. There were street cars still, and stores lighted and people passing, but soon these would not be, and she was locked out. The side streets were already little more than long silent walks and gleaming rows of lamps.

At the corner her youthful lover almost pounced upon her.

"Locked out, are yuh?" he asked, his eyes shining.

For the moment she was delighted to see him, for a nameless dread had already laid hold of her. Home meant so much. Up to now it had been her whole life.

"Yes," she answered feebly.

"Well, let's stroll on a little," said the boy. He had not as yet quite made up his mind what to do, but the night was young. It was so fine to have her with him—his.

At the farther corner they passed Officers Maguire and Delahanty, idly swinging their clubs and discussing politics.

" 'Tis a shame," Officer Delahanty was saying, "the way things are run now," but he paused to add, "ain't that old Rogaum's girl over there with young Almerting?"

"It is," replied Maguire, looking after.

"Well, I'm thinkin' he'd better be keepin' an eye on her," said the former. "She's too young to be runnin' around with the likes o' him."

Maguire agreed. "He's a young tough," he observed. "I never liked him. He's too fresh. He works over here in Myer's tobacco factory, and belongs to The Roosters. He's up to no good, I'll warrant that."

"Teach 'em a lesson, I would," Almerting was saying to Theresa as they strolled on. "We'll walk around a while an' make 'em think yuh mean business. They won't lock yuh out any more. If they don't let yuh in when we come back I'll find yuh a place, all right."

His sharp eyes were gleaming as he looked around into her own. Already he had made up his mind that she should not go back if he could help it. He knew a better place than home for this night, anyhow—the club room of the Roosters, if nowhere else. They could stay there for a time, anyhow.

By now old Rogaum, who had seen her walking up the street alone, was marveling at her audacity, but thought she would soon come back. It was amazing that she should exhibit such temerity, but he would teach her! Such a whipping! At half-past ten, however, he stuck his head out of the open window and saw nothing of her. At eleven, the same. Then he walked the floor.

At first wrathful, then nervous, then nervous and wrathful, he finally ended all nervous, without a scintilla of wrath. His stout wife sat up in bed and began to wring her hands.

"Lie down!" he commanded. "You make me sick. I know vot I am doing!"

"Is she still at der door?" pleaded the mother.

"No," he said. "I don't tink so. She should come ven I call."

His nerves were weakening, however, and now they finally collapsed.

"She vent de stread up," he said anxiously after a time. "I vill go after."

Slipping on his coat, he went down the stairs and out into the night. It was growing late, and the stillness and gloom of midnight were nearing. Nowhere in sight was his Theresa. First one way and then another he went, looking here, there, everywhere, finally groaning.

"Ach, Gott!" he said, the sweat bursting out on his brow, "vot in Teufel's name iss dis?"

He thought he would seek a policeman, but there was none. Officer Maguire had long since gone for a quiet game in one of the neighboring saloons. His partner had temporarily returned to his own beat. Still old Rogaum hunted on, worrying more and more.

Finally he bethought him to hasten home again, for she must have got back. Mrs. Rogaum, too, would be frantic if she had not. If she were not there he must go to the police. Such a night! And his Theresa—— This thing could not go on.

As he turned into his own corner he almost ran, coming up to the little portico wet and panting. At a puffing step he turned, and almost fell over a white body at his feet, a prone and writhing woman.

"Ach, Gott!" he cried aloud, almost shouting in his distress and excitement. "Theresa, vot iss dis? Wilhelmina, a light now. Bring a light now, I say, for himmel's sake! Theresa hat sich *umgebracht*. Help!"

He had fallen to his knees and was turning over the writhing, groaning figure. By the pale light of the street, however, he could make out that it was not his Theresa, fortunately, as he had at first feared, but another and yet there was something very like her in the figure.

"Um!" said the stranger weakly. "Ah!"

The dress was gray, not white as was his Theresa's, but the body was round and plump. It cut the fiercest cords of his intensity, this thought of death to a young woman, but there was something else about the situation which made him forget his own troubles.

Mrs. Rogaum, loudly admonished, almost tumbled down the stairs. At the foot she held the light she had brought—a small glass oil-lamp—and then nearly dropped it. A fairly attractive figure, more girl than woman, rich in all the physical charms that characterize a certain type, lay near to dying. Her soft hair had fallen back over a good forehead, now quite white. Her pretty hands, well decked with rings, were clutched tightly in an agonized grip. At her neck a blue silk shirtwaist and light lace collar were torn away where she had clutched herself, and on the white flesh was a yellow stain as of one who had been burned. A strange odor reeked in the area, and in one corner was a spilled bottle.

"Ach, Gott!" exclaimed Mrs. Rogaum. "It iss a vooman! She haf herself gekilt. Run for der police! Oh, my! oh, my!"

Rogaum did not kneel for more than a moment. Somehow, this creature's fate seemed in some psychic way identified with that of his own daughter. He bounded up, and jumping out his front door, began to call lustily for the police. Officer Maguire, at his social game nearby, heard the very first cry and came running.

"What's the matter here, now?" he exclaimed, rushing up full and ready for murder, robbery, fire, or, indeed, anything in the whole roster of human calamities.

"A vooman!" said Rogaum excitedly. "She haf herself *umgebracht*. She iss dying. Ach, Gott! in my own doorstep, yet!"

"Vere iss der hospital?" put in Mrs. Rogaum, thinking clearly of an ambulance, but not being able to express it. "She iss gekilt, sure. Oh! Oh!" and bending over her the poor old motherly soul stroked the tightened hands, and trickled tears upon the blue shirtwaist. "Ach, vy did you do dot?" she said. "Ach, for vy?"

Officer Maguire was essentially a man of action. He jumped to the sidewalk, amid the gathering company, and beat loudly with his club upon the stone flagging. Then he ran to the nearest police phone, returning to aid in any other way he might. A milk wagon passing on its way from the Jersey ferry with a few tons of fresh milk aboard, he held it up and demanded a helping.

"Give us a quart there, will you?" he said authoritatively. "A woman's swallowed acid in here."

"Sure," said the driver, anxious to learn the cause of the excitement. "Got a glass, anybody?"

Maguire ran back and returned, bearing a measure. Mrs. Rogaum stood looking nervously on, while the stocky officer raised the golden head and poured the milk.

"Here, now, drink this," he said. "Come on. Try an' swallow it."

The girl, a blonde of the type the world too well knows, opened her eyes, and looked, groaning a little.

"Drink it," shouted the officer fiercely. "Do you want to die? Open your mouth!"

Used to a fear of the law in all her days, she obeyed now, even in death. The lips parted, the fresh milk was drained to the end, some spilling on neck and cheek.

While they were working old Rogaum came back and stood looking on, by the side of his wife. Also Officer Delahanty, having heard the peculiar wooden ring of the stick upon the stone in the night, had come up.

"Ach, ach," exclaimed Rogaum rather distractedly, "und she iss oudt yet. I could not find her. Oh, oh!"

There was a clang of a gong up the street as the racing ambulance turned rapidly in. A young hospital surgeon dismounted, and seeing the woman's condition, ordered immediate removal. Both officers and Rogaum, as well as the surgeon, helped place her in the ambulance. After a moment the lone bell, ringing wildly in the night, was all the evidence remaining that a tragedy had been here.

"Do you know how she came here?" asked Officer Delahanty, coming back to get Rogaum's testimony for the police.

"No, no," answered Rogaum wretchedly. "She vass here alretty. I vass for my daughter loog. Ach, himmel, I haf my daughter lost. She iss avay."

Mrs. Rogaum also chattered, the significance of Theresa's absence all the more painfully emphasized by this.

The officer did not at first get the import of this. He was only interested in the facts of the present case.

"You say she was here when you come? Where was you?"

"I say I vass for my daughter loog. I come here, und der vooman vass here now alretty."

"Yes. What time was this?"

"Only now yet. Yussed a half-hour."

Officer Maguire had strolled up, after chasing away a small crowd that had gathered with fierce and unholy threats. For the first time now he noticed the peculiar perturbation of the usually placid German couple.

"What about your daughter?" he asked, catching a word as to that.

Both old people raised their voices at once.

"She haf gone. She haf run avay. Ach, himmel, ve must for her loog. Quick—she could not get in. Ve had der door shut."

"Locked her out, eh?" inquired Maguire after a time, hearing much of the rest of the story.

"Yes," explained Rogaum. "It was to schkare her a liddle. She vould not come ven I called."

"Sure, that's the girl we saw walkin' with young Almerting, do ye mind? The one in the white dress," said Delahanty to Maguire.

"White dress, yah!" echoed Rogaum, and then the fact of her walking with some one came home like a blow.

"Did you hear dot?" he exclaimed even as Mrs. Rogaum did likewise. *"Mein Gott, hast du das gehoert?"*

He fairly jumped as he said it. His hands flew up to his stout and ruddy head.

"Whaddy ya want to let her out for nights?" asked Maguire roughly, catching the drift of the situation. "That's no time for young girls to be out, anyhow, and with these toughs around here. Sure, I saw her, nearly two hours ago."

"Ach," groaned Rogaum. "Two hours yet. Ho, ho, ho!" His voice was quite hysteric.

"Well, go on in," said Officer Delahanty. "There's no use yellin' out here. Give us a description of her an' we'll send out an alarm. You won't be able to find her walkin' around."

Her parents described her exactly. The two men turned to the nearest police box and then disappeared, leaving the old German couple in the throes of distress. A time-worn old church-clock nearby now chimed out one and then two. The notes cut like knives. Mrs. Rogaum began fearfully to cry. Rogaum walked and blustered to himself.

"It's a queer case, that," said Officer Delahanty to Maguire after having reported the matter of Theresa, but referring solely to the outcast of the doorway so recently sent away and in whose fate they were much more interested. She being a part of the commercialized vice of the city, they were curious as to the cause of her suicide. "I think I know that woman. I think I know where she came from. You do, too—Adele's, around the corner, eh? She didn't come into that doorway by herself, either. She was put there. You know how they do."

"You're right," said Maguire. "She was put there, all right, and that's just where she come from, too."

The two of them now tipped up their noses and cocked their eyes significantly.

"Let's go around," added Maguire.

They went, the significant red light over the transom at 68 telling its own story. Strolling leisurely up, they knocked. At the very first sound a painted denizen of the half-world opened the door.

"Where's Adele?" asked Maguire as the two, hats on as usual, stepped in.

"She's gone to bed."

"Tell her to come down."

They seated themselves deliberately in the gaudy mirrored parlor and waited, conversing between themselves in whispers. Presently a sleepy-looking woman of forty in a gaudy robe of heavy texture, and slippered in red, appeared.

"We're here about that suicide case you had tonight. What about it? Who was she? How'd she come to be in that doorway around the corner? Come, now," Maguire added, as the madam assumed an air of mingled injured and ignorant innocence, "you know. Can that stuff! How did she come to take poison?"

"I don't know what you're talking about," said the woman with the utmost air of innocence. "I never heard of any suicide."

"Aw, come now," insisted Delahanty, "the girl around the corner. You know. We know you've got a pull, but we've got to know about this case, just the same. Come across now. It won't be published. What made her take the poison?"

Under the steady eyes of the officers the woman hesitated, but finally weakened.

"Why—why—her lover went back on her—that's all. She got so blue we just couldn't do anything with her. I tried to, but she wouldn't listen."

"Lover, eh?" put in Maguire as though that were the most unheard-of thing in the world. "What was his name?"

"I don't know. You never can tell that."

"What was her name—Annie?" asked Delahanty wisely, as though he knew but was merely inquiring for form's sake.

"No—Emily."

"Well, how did she come to get over there, anyhow?" inquired Maguire most pleasantly.

"George took her," she replied, referring to a man-of-all-work about the place.

Then little by little as they sat there the whole miserable story came out, miserable as all the wilfulness and error and suffering of the world.

"How old was she?"

"Oh, twenty-one."

"Well, where'd she come from?"

"Oh, here in New York. Her family locked her out one night, I think."

Something in the way the woman said this last brought old Rogaum and his daughter back to the policemen's minds. They had forgotten all about her by now, although they had turned in an alarm. Fearing to interfere too much with this well-known and politically controlled institution, the two men left, but outside they fell to talking of the other case.

"We ought to tell old Rogaum about her some time," said Maguire to Delahanty cynically. "He locked his kid out tonight."

"Yes, it might be a good thing for him to hear that," replied the other. "We'd better go round there an' see if his girl's back yet. She may be back by now," and so they returned but little disturbed by the joint miseries.

At Rogaum's door they once more knocked loudly.

"Is your daughter back again?" asked Maguire when a reply was had.

"Ach, no," replied the hysterical Mrs. Rogaum, who was quite alone now. "My husband he haf gone oudt again to loog vunce more. Oh, my! Oh, my!"

"Well, that's what you get for lockin' her out," returned Maguire loftily, the other story fresh in his mind. "That other girl downstairs here tonight was locked out too, once." He chanced to have a girl-child of his own and somehow he was in the mood for pointing a moral. "You oughtn't to do anything like that. Where d'yuh expect she's goin' to if you lock her out?"

Mrs. Rogaum groaned. She explained that it was not her fault, but anyhow it was carrying coals to Newcastle to talk to her so. The advice was better for her husband.

The pair finally returned to the station to see if the call had been attended to.

"Sure," said the sergeant, "certainly. Whaddy ya think?" and he read from the blotter before him:

"'Look out for girl, Theresa Rogaum. Aged 18; height, about 5, 3; light hair, blue eyes, white cotton dress, trimmed with blue ribbon. Last seen with lad named Almerting, about 19 years of age, about 5, 9; weight 135 pounds.'"

There were other details even more pointed and conclusive. For over an hour now, supposedly, policemen from the Battery to Harlem, and far beyond, had been scanning long streets and dim shadows for a girl in a white dress with a youth of nineteen,—supposedly.

Officer Halsey, another of this region, which took in a portion of Washington Square, had seen a good many couples this pleasant summer evening since the description of Theresa and Almerting had been read to him over the telephone, but none that answered to these. Like Maguire and Delahanty, he was more or less indifferent to all such cases, but idling on a corner near the park at about three a.m., a brother officer, one Paisly by name, came up and casually mentioned the missing pair also.

"I bet I saw that couple, not over an hour ago. She was dressed in white, and looked to me as if she didn't want to be out. I didn't happen to think at the time, but now I remember. They acted sort o' funny. She did, anyhow. They went in this park down at the Fourth Street end there."

"Supposing we beat it, then," suggested Halsey, weary for something to do.

"Sure," said the other quickly, and together they began a careful search, kicking around in the moonlight under the trees. The moon was leaning moderately toward the west, and all the branches were silvered with light and dew. Among the flowers, past clumps of bushes, near the fountain, they searched, each one going his way alone. At last, the wandering Halsey paused beside a thick clump of flaming bushes, ruddy, slightly, even in the light. A murmur of voices greeted him, and something very much like the sound of a sob.

"What's that?" he said mentally, drawing near and listening.

"Why don't you come on now?" said the first of the voices heard. "They won't let you in any more. You're with me, ain't you? What's the use cryin'?"

No answer to this, but no sobs. She must have been crying silently.

"Come on. I can take care of yuh. We can live in Hoboken. I know a place where we can go tonight. That's all right."

There was a movement as if the speaker were patting her on the shoulder.

"What's the use cryin'? Don't you believe I love yuh?"

The officer who had stolen quietly around to get a better view now came closer. He wanted to see for himself. In the moonlight, from a comfortable distance, he could see them seated. The tall bushes were almost all about the bench. In the arms of the youth was the girl in white, held very close. Leaning over to get a better view, he saw him kiss her and hold her—hold her in such a way that she could but yield to him, whatever her slight disinclination.

It was a common affair at earlier hours, but rather interesting now. The officer was interested. He crept nearer.

"What are you two doin' here?" he suddenly inquired, rising before them, as though he had not seen.

The girl tumbled out of her compromising position, speechless and blushing violently. The young man stood up, nervous, but still defiant.

"Aw, we were just sittin' here," he replied.

"Yes? Well, say, what's your name? I think we're lookin' for you two, anyhow. Almerting?"

"That's me," said the youth.

"And yours?" he added, addressing Theresa.

"Theresa Rogaum," replied the latter brokenly, beginning to cry.

"Well, you two'll have to come along with me," he added laconically. "The Captain wants to see both of you," and he marched them solemnly away.

"What for?" young Almerting ventured to inquire after a time, blanched with fright.

"Never mind," replied the policeman irritably. "Come along, you'll find out at the station house. We want you both. That's enough."

At the other end of the park Paisly joined them, and, at the station house, the girl was given a chair. She was all tears and melancholy with a modicum possibly of relief at being thus rescued from the world. Her companion, for all his youth, was defiant if circumspect, a natural animal defeated of its aim.

"Better go for her father," commented the sergeant, and by four in the morning old Rogaum, who had still been up and walking the floor, was rushing stationward. From an earlier rage he had passed to an almost killing grief, but now at the thought that he might possibly see his daughter alive and well once more he was overflowing with a mingled emotion which contained rage, fear, sorrow, and a number of other things. What should he do to her if she were alive? Beat her? Kiss her? Or what? Arrived at the station, however, and seeing his fair Theresa in the hands of the police, and this young stranger lingering near, also detained, he was beside himself with fear, rage, affection.

"You! You!" he exclaimed at once, glaring at the imperturbable Almerting, when told that this was the young man who was found with his girl.

Then, seized with a sudden horror, he added, turning to Theresa, "Vot haf you done? Oh, oh! You! You!" he repeated again to Almerting angrily, now that he felt that his daughter was safe. "Come not near my tochter any more! I vill preak your effery pone, du teufel, du!"

He made a move toward the incarcerated lover, but here the sergeant interfered.

"Stop that, now," he said calmly. "Take your daughter out of here and go home, or I'll lock you both up. We don't want any fighting in here. D'ye hear? Keep your daughter off the streets hereafter, then she won't get into trouble. Don't let her run around with such young toughs as this." Almerting winced. "Then there won't anything happen to her. We'll do whatever punishing's to be done."

"Aw, what's eatin' him!" commented Almerting dourly, now that he felt himself reasonably safe from a personal encounter. "What have I done? He locked her out, didn't he? I was just keepin' her company till morning."

"Yes, we know all about that," said the sergeant, "and about you, too. You shut up, or you'll go downtown to Special Sessions. I want no guff out o' you." Still he ordered the butcher angrily to be gone.

Old Rogaum heard nothing. He had his daughter. He was taking her home. She was not dead—not even morally injured in so far as he could learn. He was a compound of wondrous feelings. What to do was beyond him.

At the corner near the butcher shop they encountered the wakeful Maguire, still idling, as they passed. He was pleased to see that Rogaum had his Theresa once more. It raised him to a high, moralizing height.

"Don't lock her out any more," he called significantly. "That's what brought the other girl to your door, you know!"

"Vot iss dot?" said Rogaum.

"I say the other girl was locked out. That's why she committed suicide."

"Ach, I know," said the husky German under his breath, but he had no intention of locking her out. He did not know what he would do until they were in the presence of his crying wife, who fell upon Theresa, weeping. Then he decided to be reasonably lenient.

"She vass like you," said the old mother to the wandering Theresa, ignorant of the seeming lesson brought to their very door. "She vass loog like you."

"I vill not vip you now," said the old butcher solemnly, too delighted to think of punishment after having feared every horror under the sun, "aber, go not oudt any more. Keep off de streads so late. I von't haf it. Dot loafer, aber—let him yussed come here some more! I fix him!"

"No, no," said the fat mother tearfully, smoothing her daughter's hair. "She vouldn't run away no more yet, no, no." Old Mrs. Rogaum was all mother.

"Well, you wouldn't let me in," insisted Theresa, "and I didn't have any place to go. What do you want me to do? I'm not going to stay in the house all the time."

"I fix him!" roared Rogaum, unloading all his rage now on the recreant lover freely. "Yussed let him come some more! Der penitentiary he should haf!"

"Oh, he's not so bad," Theresa told her mother, almost a heroine now that she was home and safe. "He's Mr. Almerting, the stationer's boy. They live here in the next block."

"Don't you ever bother that girl again," the sergeant was saying to young Almerting as he turned him loose an hour later. "If you do, we'll get you, and you won't get off under six months. Y' hear me, do you?"

"Aw, I don't want 'er," replied the boy truculently and cynically. "Let him have his old daughter. What'd he want to lock 'er out for? They'd better not lock 'er out again though, that's all I say. I don't want 'er."

"Beat it!" replied the sergeant, and away he went.

A. V. LAIDER

Max Beerbohm

(1872–   )

I UNPACKED MY THINGS and went down to await luncheon.

It was good to be here again in this little old sleepy hostel by the sea. Hostel I say, though it spelt itself without an s and even placed a circumflex above the o. It made no other pretension. It was very cosy indeed.

I had been here just a year before, in mid-February, after an attack of influenza. And now I had returned, after an attack of influenza. Nothing was changed. It had been raining when I left, and the waiter—there was but a single, a very old waiter—had told me it was only a shower. That waiter was still here, not a day older. And the shower had not ceased.

Steadfastly it fell on to the sands, steadfastly into the iron-grey sea. I stood looking out at it from the windows of the hall, admiring it very much. There seemed to be little else to do. What little there was I did. I mastered the contents of a blue hand-bill which, pinned to the wall just beneath the framed engraving of Queen Victoria's Coronation, gave token of a concert that was to be held—or rather, was to have been held some weeks ago—in the Town Hall, for the benefit of the Life-Boat Fund. I looked at the barometer, tapped it, was not the wiser. I glanced at a pamphlet about Our Dying Industries (a theme on which Mr. Joseph Chamberlain was at that time trying to alarm us). I wandered to the letter-board.

These letter-boards always fascinate me. Usually some two or three of the envelopes stuck into the cross-garterings have a certain newness and freshness. They seem sure they will yet be claimed. Why not? Why *shouldn't* John Doe, Esq., or Mrs. Richard Roe, turn up at any moment? I do not know. I can only say that nothing in the world seems to me more unlikely. Thus it is that these young bright envelopes touch my heart even more than do their dusty and sallow seniors. Sour resignation is less touching than impatience for what will not be, than the eagerness that has to wane and wither. Soured beyond measure these old envelopes are. They are not nearly so nice as they should be to the young ones. They lose no chance of sneering and discouraging. Such dialogues as this are only too frequent:

A VERY YOUNG ENVELOPE: Something in me whispers that he will come to-day!

A VERY OLD ENVELOPE: He? Well, that's good! Ha, ha, ha! Why didn't he come last week, when *you* came? What reason have you for supposing he'll ever come *now*? It isn't as if he were a frequenter of the place. He's never been here. His name is utterly unknown here. You don't suppose he's coming on the chance of finding *you*?

A. V. Y. E.: It may seem silly, but—something in me whispers——

A. V. O. E.: Something in *you*? One has only to look at you to see there's nothing in you but a note scribbled to him by a cousin. Look at *me*! There are three sheets, closely written, in *me*. The lady to whom I am addressed——

A. V. Y. E.: Yes, sir, yes; you told me all about her yesterday.

A. V. O. E.: And I shall do so to-day and to-morrow and every day and all day long. That young lady was a widow. She stayed here many times. She was delicate, and the air suited her. She was poor, and the tariff was just within her means. She was lonely, and had need of love. I have in me for her a passionate avowal and strictly honourable proposal, written to her, after many rough copies, by a gentleman who had made her acquaintance under this very roof. He was rich, he was charming, he was in the prime of life. He had asked if he might write to her. She had flutteringly granted his request. He posted me to her the day after his return to London. I looked forward to being torn open by her. I was very sure she would wear me and my contents next to her bosom. She was gone. She had left no address. She never returned. . . . This I tell you, and shall continue to tell you, not because I want any of your callow sympathy—no, *thank* you!—but that you may judge how much less than slight are the chances that you yourself——

But my reader has overheard these dialogues as often as I. He wants to know what was odd about this particular letter-board before which I was standing. At first glance I saw nothing odd about it. But presently I distinguished a handwriting that was vaguely familiar. It was mine. I stared, I wondered. There is always a slight shock in seeing an envelope of one's own after it has gone through the post. It looks as if it had gone through so much. But this was the first time I had ever seen an envelope of mine eating its heart out in bondage on a letter-board. This was outrageous. This was hardly to be believed. Sheer kindness had impelled me to write to "A. V. Laider, Esq.," and this was the result! I hadn't minded receiving no answer. Only now, indeed, did I remember that I hadn't received one. In multitudinous London the memory of A. V. Laider and his trouble had soon passed from my mind. But—well, what a lesson not to go out of one's way to write to casual acquaintances!

My envelope seemed not to recognise me as its writer. Its gaze was the more piteous for being blank. Even so had I once been gazed at by a dog that I had lost and, after many days, found in the Battersea home. "I don't know who you are, but whoever you are, claim me, take me out of this!" That was my dog's appeal. This was the appeal of my envelope.

I raised my hand to the letter-board, meaning to effect a swift and lawless rescue, but paused at sound of a footstep behind me. The old waiter had come to tell me that my luncheon was ready. I followed him out of the hall, not, however, without a bright glance across my shoulder to reassure the little captive that I should come back.

I had the sharp appetite of the convalescent, and this the sea-air had whetted already to a finer edge. In touch with a dozen oysters, and with stout, I soon shed away the unreasoning anger I had felt against A. V. Laider. I became merely sorry for him that he had not received a letter which might perhaps have comforted him. In touch with cutlets, I felt how sorely he had needed comfort. And anon, by the big bright fireside of that small dark smoking-room where, a year ago, on the last evening of my stay here, he and I had at length spoken to each other, I reviewed in detail the tragic experience he had told me; and I fairly revelled in reminiscent sympathy with him. . . .

A. V. LAIDER—I had looked him up in the visitors' book on the night of his arrival. I myself had arrived the day before, and had been rather sorry there was no one else staying here. A convalescent by the sea likes to have some one to observe, to wonder about, at meal-time. I was glad when, on my second evening, I found seated at the table opposite to mine another guest. I was the gladder because he was just the right kind of guest. He was enigmatic. By this I mean that he did not look soldierly nor financial nor artistic nor anything definite at all. He offered a clean slate for speculation. And thank heaven! he evidently wasn't going to spoil the fun by engaging me in conversation later on. A decently unsociable man, anxious to be left alone.

The heartiness of his appetite, in contrast with his extreme fragility of aspect and limpness of demeanour, assured me that he, too, had just had influenza. I liked him for that. Now and again our eyes met and were instantly parted. We managed, as a rule, to observe each other indirectly. I was sure it was not merely because he had been ill that he looked interesting. Nor did it seem to me that a spiritual melancholy, though I imagined him sad at the best of times, was his sole asset. I conjectured that he was clever. I thought he might also be imaginative. At first glance I had mistrusted him. A shock of white hair, combined with a young face and dark eyebrows, does somehow make a man look like a charlatan. But it is foolish to be guided by an accident of colour. I had soon rejected my first impression of my fellow-diner. I found him very sympathetic.

Anywhere but in England it would be impossible for two solitary men, howsoever much reduced by influenza, to spend five or six days in the same hostel and not exchange a single word. That is one of the charms of England. Had Laider and I been born and bred in any other land we should have become acquainted before the end of our first evening in the small smoking-room, and have found ourselves irrevocably committed to go on talking to each other throughout the rest of our visit. We might, it is true, have happened to like each other more than any one we had ever met. This off-chance may have occurred to us both. But it counted for nothing as against the certain surrender of quietude and liberty. We slightly bowed to each other as we entered or left the dining-room or smoking-room, and as we met on the widespread sands or in the shop that had a small and faded circulating library. That was all. Our mutual aloofness was a positive bond between us.

Had he been much older than I, the responsibility for our silence would of course have been his alone. But he was not, I judged, more than five or six years ahead of me, and thus I might without impropriety have taken it on myself to perform that hard and perilous feat which English people call, with a shiver, "breaking the ice." He had reason, therefore, to be as grateful to me as I to him. Each of us, not the less frankly because silently, recognised his obligation to the other. And when, on the last evening of my stay, the ice actually was broken no ill-will rose between us: neither of us was to blame.

It was a Sunday evening. I had been out for a long last walk and had come in very late to dinner. Laider left his table almost immediately after I sat down to mine. When I entered the smoking-room I found him reading a weekly review which I had bought the day before. It was a crisis. He could not silently offer, nor could I have silently accepted, sixpence. It was a crisis. We faced it like men. He made, by word of mouth, a graceful apology. Verbally, not by signs, I besought him to go on reading. But this, of course, was a vain counsel of perfection. The social code forced us to talk now. We obeyed it like men. To reassure him that our position was not so desperate as it might seem, I took the earliest opportunity to mention that I was going away early next morning. In the tone of his "Oh, are you?" he tried bravely to imply that he was sorry, even now, to hear that. In a way, perhaps, he really was sorry. We had got on so well together, he and I. Nothing could efface the memory of that. Nay, we seemed to be hitting it off even now. Influenza was not our sole theme. We passed from that to the aforesaid weekly review, and to a correspondence that was raging therein on Faith and Reason.

This correspondence had now reached its fourth and penultimate stage—its Australian stage. It is hard to see why these correspondences spring up; one only knows that they do spring up, suddenly, like street crowds. There comes, it would seem, a moment when the whole English-speaking race is unconsciously bursting to have its say about some one thing—the split infinitive, or the habits of migratory birds, or faith and reason, or what-not. Whatever weekly review happens at such a moment to contain a reference, however remote, to the theme in question reaps the storm. Gusts of letters blow in from all corners of the British Isles. These are presently reinforced by Canada in full blast. A few weeks later the Anglo-Indians weigh in. In due course we have the help of our Australian cousins. By that time, however, we of the Mother Country have got our second wind, and so determined are we to make the most of it that at last even the Editor suddenly loses patience and says "This correspondence must now cease.—Ed." and wonders why on earth he ever allowed anything so tedious and idiotic to begin.

I pointed out to Laider one of the Australian letters that had especially pleased me in the current issue. It was from "A Melbourne Man," and was of the abrupt kind which declares that "all your correspondents have been groping in the dark" and then settles the whole matter in one short sharp flash. The flash in this instance was "Reason is faith—faith reason—that is all we know on earth and all we need to know." The writer then inclosed his card and was, etc., "A Melbourne Man." I said to Laider how very restful it was, after influenza, to read anything that meant nothing whatsoever. Laider was inclined to take the letter more seriously than I, and to be mildly metaphysical. I said that for me faith and reason were two separate things, and (as I am no good at metaphysics, however mild) I offered a definite example, to coax the talk on to ground where I should be safer. "Palmistry, for example," I said. "Deep down in my heart I believe in palmistry."

Laider turned in his chair. "You believe in palmistry?"

I hesitated. "Yes, somehow I do. Why? I haven't the slightest notion. I can give myself all sorts of reasons for laughing it to scorn. My common sense utterly rejects it. Of course the shape of the hand means something—

is more or less an index of character. But the idea that my past and future are neatly mapped out on my palms——" I shrugged my shoulders.

"You don't like that idea?" asked Laider in his gentle, rather academic voice.

"I only say it's a grotesque idea."

"Yet you do believe in it?"

"I've a grotesque belief in it, yes."

"Are you sure your reason for calling this idea 'grotesque' isn't merely that you dislike it?"

"Well," I said, with the thrilling hope that he was a companion in absurdity, "doesn't it seem grotesque to *you*?"

"It seems strange."

"You believe in it?"

"Oh, absolutely."

"Hurrah!"

He smiled at my pleasure, and I, at the risk of re-entanglement in metaphysics, claimed him as standing shoulder to shoulder with me against "A Melbourne Man." This claim he gently disputed. "You may think me very prosaic," he said, "but I can't believe without evidence."

"Well, I'm equally prosaic and equally at a disadvantage: I can't take my own belief as evidence, and I've no other evidence to go on."

He asked me if I had ever made a study of palmistry. I said I had read one of Desbarolles' books years ago, and one of Heron-Allen's. But, he asked, had I tried to test them by the lines on my own hands or on the hands of my friends? I confessed that my actual practice in palmistry had been of a merely passive kind—the prompt extension of my palm to any one who would be so good as to "read" it and truckle for a few minutes to my egoism. (I hoped Laider might do this.)

"Then I almost wonder," he said, with his sad smile, "that you haven't lost your belief, after all the nonsense you must have heard. There are so many young girls who go in for palmistry. I am sure all the five foolish virgins were 'awfully keen on it' and used to say 'You can be led, but not driven,' and 'You are likely to have a serious illness between the ages of forty and forty-five,' and 'You are by nature rather lazy, but can be very energetic by fits and starts.' And most of the professionals, I'm told, are as silly as the young girls."

For the honour of the profession, I named three practitioners whom I had found really good at reading character. He asked whether any of them had been right about past events. I confessed that, as a matter of fact, all three of them had been right in the main. This seemed to amuse him. He asked whether any of them had predicted anything which had since come true. I confessed that all three had predicted that I should do several things which I had since done rather unexpectedly. He asked if

I didn't accept this as at any rate a scrap of evidence. I said I could only regard it as a fluke—a rather remarkable fluke.

The superiority of his sad smile was beginning to get on my nerves. I wanted him to see that he was as absurd as I. "Suppose," I said, "suppose for sake of argument that you and I are nothing but helpless automata created to do just this and that, and to have just that and this done to us. Suppose, in fact, we *haven't* any free will whatsoever. Is it likely or conceivable that the Power that fashioned us would take the trouble to jot down in cipher on our hands just what was in store for us?"

Laider did not answer this question, he did but annoyingly ask me another. "You believe in free will?"

"Yes, of course. I'll be hanged if I'm an automaton."

"And you believe in free will just as in palmistry—without any reason?"

"Oh, no. Everything points to our having free will."

"Everything? What, for instance?"

This rather cornered me. I dodged out, as lightly as I could, by saying "I suppose *you* would say it was written in my hand that I should be a believer in free will."

"Ah, I've no doubt it is."

I held out my palms. But, to my great disappointment, he looked quickly away from them. He had ceased to smile. There was agitation in his voice as he explained that he never looked at people's hands now. "Never now —never again." He shook his head as though to beat off some memory.

I was much embarrassed by my indiscretion. I hastened to tide over the awkward moment by saying that if *I* could read hands I wouldn't for fear of the awful things I might see there.

"Awful things, yes," he whispered, nodding at the fire.

"Not," I said in self-defence, "that there's anything very awful, so far as I know, to be read in *my* hands."

He turned his gaze from the fire to me. "You aren't a murderer, for example?"

"Oh, no," I replied, with a nervous laugh.

"*I* am."

This was a more than awkward, it was a painful, moment for me; and I am afraid I must have started or winced, for he instantly begged my pardon. "I don't know," he exclaimed, "why I said it. I'm usually a very reticent man. But sometimes——" He pressed his brow. "What you must think of me!"

I begged him to dismiss the matter from his mind.

"It's very good of you to say that; but—I've placed myself as well as you in a false position. I ask you to believe that I'm not the sort of man who is 'wanted' or ever was 'wanted' by the police. I should be bowed out of any police-station at which I gave myself up. I'm not a murderer in any bald sense of the word. No."

My face must have perceptibly brightened, for "Ah," he said, "don't imagine I'm not a murderer at all. Morally, I am." He looked at the clock. I pointed out that the night was young. He assured me that his story was not a long one. I assured him that I hoped it was. He said I was very kind. I denied this. He warned me that what he had to tell might rather tend to stiffen my unwilling faith in palmistry, and to shake my opposite and cherished faith in free will. I said "Never mind." He stretched his hands pensively toward the fire. I settled myself back in my chair.

"My hands," he said, staring at the backs of them, "are the hands of a very weak man. I dare say you know enough of palmistry to see that for yourself. You notice the slightness of the thumbs and of the two 'little' fingers. They are the hands of a weak and over-sensitive man—a man without confidence, a man who would certainly waver in an emergency. Rather Hamlet-ish hands," he mused. "And I'm like Hamlet in other respects, too: I'm no fool, and I've rather a noble disposition, and I'm unlucky. But Hamlet was luckier than I in one thing: he was a murderer by accident, whereas the murders that I committed one day fourteen years ago—for I must tell you it wasn't one murder, but many murders that I committed—were all of them due to the wretched inherent weakness of my own wretched self.

"I was twenty-six—no, twenty-seven years old, and rather a nondescript person, as I am now. I was supposed to have been called to the Bar. In fact, I believe I *had* been called to the Bar. I hadn't listened to the call. I never intended to practise, and I never did practise. I only wanted an excuse in the eyes of the world for existing. I suppose the nearest I have ever come to practising is now at this moment: I am defending a murderer. My father had left me well enough provided with money. I was able to go my own desultory way, riding my hobbies where I would. I had a good stableful of hobbies. Palmistry was one of them. I was rather ashamed of this one. It seemed to me absurd, as it seems to you. Like you, though, I believed in it. Unlike you, I had done more than merely read a book or so about it. I had read innumerable books about it. I had taken casts of all my friends' hands. I had tested and tested again the points at which Desbarolles dissented from the gypsies, and—well, enough that I had gone into it all rather thoroughly, and was as sound a palmist as a man may be without giving his whole life to palmistry.

"One of the first things I had seen in my own hand, as soon as I had learned to read it, was that at about the age of twenty-six I should have a narrow escape from death—from a violent death. There was a clean break in the life-line, and a square joining it—the protective square, you know. The markings were precisely the same in both hands. It was to be the narrowest escape possible. And I wasn't going to escape without injury, either. That is what bothered me. There was a faint line connecting the break in the life-line with a star on the line of health. Against that star

was another square. I was to recover from the injury, whatever it might be.
Still, I didn't exactly look forward to it. Soon after I had reached the age
of twenty-five, I began to feel uncomfortable. The thing might be going
to happen at any moment. In palmistry, you know, it is impossible to pin
an event down hard and fast to one year. This particular event was to be
when I was *about* twenty-six; it mightn't be till I was twenty-seven; it
might be while I was only twenty-five.

"And I used to tell myself that it mightn't be at all. My reason rebelled
against the whole notion of palmistry, just as yours does. I despised my
faith in the thing, just as you despise yours. I used to try not to be so
ridiculously careful as I was whenever I crossed a street. I lived in London
at that time. Motor-cars had not yet come in, but—what hours, all told, I
must have spent standing on curbs, very circumspect, very lamentable! It
was a pity, I suppose, that I had no definite occupation—something to take
me out of myself. I was one of the victims of private means. There came
a time when I drove in four-wheelers rather than in hansoms, and was
doubtful of four-wheelers. Oh, I assure you, I was very lamentable indeed.

"If a railway-journey could be avoided, I avoided it. My uncle had a place
in Hampshire. I was very fond of him and of his wife. Theirs was the only
house I ever went to stay in now. I was there for a week in November, not
long after my twenty-seventh birthday. There were other people staying
there, and at the end of the week we all travelled back to London together.
There were six of us in the carriage: Colonel Elbourn and his wife and
their daughter, a girl of seventeen; and another married couple, the Blakes.
I had been at Winchester with Blake, but had hardly seen him since that
time. He was in the Indian Civil, and was home on leave. He was sailing
for India next week. His wife was to remain in England for some months,
and then join him out there. They had been married five years. She was
now just twenty-four years old. He told me that this was her age.

"The Elbourns I had never met before. They were charming people. We
had all been very happy together. The only trouble had been that on the
last night, at dinner, my uncle asked me if I still went in for 'the gypsy
business,' as he always called it; and of course the three ladies were immensely excited, and implored me to 'do' their hands. I told them it was
all nonsense, I said I had forgotten all I once knew, I made various
excuses; and the matter dropped. It was quite true that I had given up reading hands. I avoided anything that might remind me of what was in my
own hands. And so, next morning, it was a great bore to me when, soon
after the train started, Mrs. Elbourn said it would be 'too cruel' of me if
I refused to do their hands now. Her daughter and Mrs. Blake also said
it would be 'brutal'; and they were all taking off their gloves, and—well, of
course I had to give in.

"I went to work methodically on Mrs. Elbourn's hands, in the usual way,
you know, first sketching the character from the backs of them; and there

was the usual hush, broken by the usual little noises—grunts of assent from the husband, cooings of recognition from the daughter. Presently I asked to see the palms, and from them I filled in the details of Mrs. Elbourn's character before going on to the events of her life. But while I talked I was calculating how old Mrs. Elbourn might be. In my first glance at her palms I had seen that she could not have been less than twenty-five when she married. The daughter was seventeen. Suppose the daughter had been born a year later—how old would the mother be? Forty-three, yes. Not less than that, poor woman!"

Laider looked at me. "Why 'poor woman,' you wonder? Well, in that first glance I had seen other things than her marriage-line. I had seen a very complete break in the lines of life and of fate. I had seen violent death there. At what age? Not later, not possibly *later,* than forty-three. While I talked to her about the things that had happened in her girlhood, the back of my brain was hard at work on those marks of catastrophe. I was horribly wondering that she was still alive. It was impossible that between her and that catastrophe there could be more than a few short months. And all the time I was talking; and I suppose I acquitted myself well, for I remember that when I ceased I had a sort of ovation from the Elbourns.

"It was a relief to turn to another pair of hands. Mrs. Blake was an amusing young creature, and her hands were very characteristic, and prettily odd in form. I allowed myself to be rather whimsical about her nature, and having begun in that vein, I went on in it—somehow—even after she had turned her palms. In those palms were reduplicated the signs I had seen in Mrs. Elbourn's. It was as though they had been copied neatly out. The only difference was in the placing of them; and it was this difference that was the most horrible point. The fatal age in Mrs. Blake's hands was —not past, no, for here *she* was. But she might have died when she was twenty-one. Twenty-three seemed to be the utmost span. She was twenty-four, you know.

"I have said that I am a weak man. And you will have a good proof of that directly. Yet I showed a certain amount of strength that day—yes, even on that day which has humiliated and saddened the rest of my life. Neither my face nor my voice betrayed me when in the palms of Dorothy Elbourn I was again confronted with those same signs. She was all for knowing the future, poor child! I believe I told her all manner of things that were to be. And she had no future—none, none in *this* world—except——

"And then, while I talked, there came to me suddenly a suspicion. I wondered it hadn't come before. You guess what it was? It made me feel very cold and strange. I went on talking. But, also, I went on—quite separately —thinking. The suspicion wasn't a certainty. This mother and daughter were always together. What was to befall the one might anywhere—anywhere—befall the other. But a like fate, in an equally near future, was in store for that other lady. The coincidence was curious, very. Here we all were together—here, they and I—I who was narrowly to escape, so soon now, what they, so soon now, were to suffer. Oh, there was an inference to be drawn. Not a *sure* inference, I told myself. And always I was talking, talking, and the train was swinging and swaying noisily along—to what? It was a fast train. Our carriage was near the engine. I was talking loudly. Full well I had known what I should see in the Colonel's hands. I told myself I had not known. I told myself that even now the thing I dreaded was not sure to be. Don't think I was dreading it for myself. I wasn't so 'lamentable' as all that—now. It was only of them that I thought—only for them. I hurried over the Colonel's character and career; I was perfunctory. It was Blake's hands that I wanted. *They* were the hands that mattered. If *they* had the marks—— Remember, Blake was to start for India in the coming week, his wife was to remain in England. They would be apart. Therefore——

"And the marks were there. And I did nothing—nothing but hold forth on the subtleties of Blake's character. There was a thing for me to do. I wanted to do it. I wanted to spring to the window and pull the communication-cord. Quite a simple thing to do. Nothing easier than to stop a train. You just give a sharp pull, and the train slows down, comes to a standstill. And the Guard appears at your window. You explain to the Guard.

"Nothing easier than to tell him there is going to be a collision. Nothing easier than to insist that you and your friends and every other passenger in the train must get out at once. . . . There *are* easier things than this? Things that need less courage than this? Some of *them* I could have done, I daresay. This thing I was going to do. Oh, I was determined that I would do it—directly.

"I had said all I had to say about Blake's hands. I had brought my entertainment to an end. I had been thanked and complimented all round. I was quite at liberty. I was going to do what I had to do. I was determined, yes.

"We were nearing the outskirts of London. The air was grey, thickening; and Dorothy Elbourn had said, 'Oh, this horrible old London! I suppose there's the same old fog!' And presently I heard her father saying something about 'prevention' and 'a short act of Parliament,' and 'anthracite.' And I sat and listened and agreed and——'"

Laider closed his eyes. He passed his hand slowly through the air.

"I had a racking headache. And when I said so, I was told not to talk. I was in bed, and the nurses were always telling me not to talk. I was in a hospital. I knew that. But I didn't know why I was there. One day I thought I should like to know why, and so I asked. I was feeling much better now. They told me, by degrees, that I had had concussion of the brain. I had been brought there unconscious, and had remained unconscious for forty-eight hours. I had been in an accident—a railway accident. This seemed to me odd. I had arrived quite safely at my uncle's place, and I had no memory of any journey since that. In cases of concussion, you know, it's not uncommon for the patient to forget all that happened just before the accident; there may be a blank of several hours. So it was in my case. One day my uncle was allowed to come and see me. And somehow, suddenly at sight of him, the blank was filled in. I remembered, in a flash, everything. I was quite calm, though. Or I made myself seem so, for I wanted to know how the collision had happened. My uncle told me that the engine-driver had failed to see a signal because of the fog, and our train had crashed into a goods-train. I didn't ask him about the people who were with me. You see, there was no need to ask. Very gently my uncle began to tell me, but—I had begun to talk strangely, I suppose. I remember the frightened look of my uncle's face, and the nurse scolding him in whispers.

"After that, all a blur. It seems that I became very ill indeed, wasn't expected to live. However, I live."

There was a long silence. Laider did not look at me, nor I at him. The fire was burning low, and he watched it.

At length he spoke. "You despise me. Naturally. I despise myself."

"No, I don't despise you; but——"

"You blame me." I did not meet his gaze. "You blame me," he repeated.

"Yes."

"And there, if I may say so, you are a little unjust. It isn't my fault that I was born weak."

"But a man may conquer weakness."

"Yes, if he is endowed with the strength for that."

His fatalism drew from me a gesture of disgust. "Do you really mean," I asked, "that because you didn't pull that cord, you *couldn't* have pulled it?"

"Yes."

"And it's written in your hands that you couldn't?"

He looked at the palms of his hands. "They are the hands of a very weak man," he said.

"A man so weak that he cannot believe in the possibility of free will for himself or for any one?"

"They are the hands of an intelligent man, who can weigh evidence and see things as they are."

"But answer me: Was it fore-ordained that you should not pull that cord?"

"It was fore-ordained."

"And was it actually marked in your hands that you were not going to pull it?"

"Ah, well you see, it is rather the things one *is* going to do that are actually marked. The things one *isn't* going to do—the innumerable negative things—how could one expect *them* to be marked?"

"But the consequences of what one leaves undone may be positive?"

"Horribly positive," he winced. "My hand is the hand of a man who has suffered a great deal in later life."

"And was it the hand of a man *destined* to suffer?"

"Oh, yes. I thought I told you that."

There was a pause.

"Well," I said, with awkward sympathy. "I suppose all hands are the hands of people destined to suffer."

"Not of people destined to suffer so much as *I* have suffered—as I still suffer."

The insistence of his self-pity chilled me, and I harked back to a question he had not straightly answered. "Tell me: Was it marked in your hands that you were not going to pull that cord?"

Again he looked at his hands, and then, having pressed them for a moment to his face, "It was marked very clearly," he answered, "in *their* hands."

Two or three days after this colloquy there had occurred to me in London an idea—an ingenious and comfortable doubt. How was Laider to be sure that his brain, recovering from concussion, had *remembered* what happened in the course of that railway-journey? How was he to know that his brain hadn't simply, in its abeyance, *invented* all this for him? It might be that he had never seen those signs in those hands. Assuredly, here was a bright loop-hole. I had forthwith written to Laider, pointing it out.

This was the letter which now, at my second visit, I had found miserably pent on the letter-board. I remembered my promise to rescue it. I arose from the retaining fireside, stretched my arms, yawned, and went forth to fulfil my Christian purpose. There was no one in the hall. The "shower" had at length ceased. The sun had positively come out, and the front door had been thrown open in its honour. Everything along the sea-front was beautifully gleaming, drying, shimmering. But I was not to be diverted from my errand. I went to the letter-board. And—my letter was not there! Resourceful and plucky little thing—it had escaped! I did hope it would not be captured and brought back. Perhaps the alarm had already been raised by the tolling of that great bell which warns the inhabitants for miles around that a letter has broken loose from the letter-board. I had a vision of my envelope skimming wildly along the coast-line, pursued by the old but active waiter and a breathless pack of local worthies. I saw it out-distancing them all, dodging past coast-guards, doubling on its tracks, leaping break-waters, unluckily injuring itself, losing speed, and at last, in a splendour of desperation, taking to the open sea. But suddenly I had another idea. Perhaps Laider had returned?

He had. I espied afar on the sands a form that was recognisably, by the listless droop of it, his. I was glad and sorry—rather glad, because he completed the scene of last year; and very sorry, because this time we should be at each other's mercy: no restful silence and liberty, for either of us, this time. Perhaps he had been told I was here, and had gone out to avoid me while he yet could. Oh weak, weak! Why palter? I put on my hat and coat, and marched out to meet him.

"Influenza, of course?" we asked simultaneously.

There is a limit to the time which one man may spend in talking to another about his own influenza; and presently, as we paced the sands, I felt that Laider had passed this limit. I wondered that he didn't break off and thank me now for my letter. He must have read it. He ought to have thanked me for it at once. It was a very good letter, a remarkable letter. But surely he wasn't waiting to answer it by post? His silence about it gave me the absurd sense of having taken a liberty, confound him. He was evidently ill at ease while he talked. But it wasn't for me to help him out of his difficulty, whatever that might be. It was for him to remove the strain imposed on myself.

Abruptly, after a long pause, he did now manage to say, "It was—very good of you to—to write me that letter." He told me he had only just got it, and he drifted away into otiose explanations of this fact. I thought he might at least say it was a remarkable letter; and you can imagine my annoyance when he said, after another interval, "I was very much touched indeed." I had wished to be convincing, not touching. I can't bear to be called touching.

"Don't you," I asked, "think it *is* quite possible that your brain invented all those memories of what—what happened before that accident?"

He drew a sharp sigh. "You make me feel very guilty."

"That's exactly what I tried to make you *not* feel!"

"I know, yes. That's why I feel so guilty."

We had paused in our walk. He stood nervously prodding the hard wet sand with his walking-stick. "In a way," he said, "your theory was quite right. But—it didn't go far enough. It's not only possible, it's a fact, that I didn't see those signs in those hands. I never examined those hands. They weren't there. *I* wasn't there. I haven't an uncle in Hampshire, even. I never had."

I too, prodded the sand. "Well," I said at length, "I do feel rather a fool."

"I've no right even to beg your pardon, but——"

"Oh, I'm not vexed. Only—I rather wish you hadn't told me this."

"I wish I hadn't had to. It was your kindness, you see, that forced me. By trying to take an imaginary load off my conscience, you laid a very real one on it."

"I'm sorry. But you, of your own free will, you know, exposed your conscience to me last year. I don't yet quite understand why you did that."

"No, of course not. I don't deserve that you should. But I think you will. May I explain? I'm afraid I've talked a great deal already about my influenza, and I shan't be able to keep it out of my explanation. Well, my weakest point—I told you this last year, but it happens to be perfectly true that my weakest point—is my will. Influenza, as you know, fastens unerringly on one's weakest point. It doesn't attempt to undermine my imagination. That would be a forlorn hope. I have, alas! a very strong imagination. At ordinary times my imagination allows itself to be governed by my will. My will keeps it in check by constant nagging. But when my will isn't strong enough even to nag, then my imagination stampedes. I become even as a little child. I tell myself the most preposterous fables, and—the trouble is—I can't help telling them to my friends. Until I've thoroughly shaken off influenza, I'm not fit company for any one. I perfectly realise this, and I have the good sense to go right away till I'm quite well again. I come here usually. It seems absurd, but I must confess I was sorry last year when we fell into conversation. I knew I should very soon be letting myself go, or rather, very soon be swept away. Perhaps I ought to have warned you; but—I'm a rather shy man. And then you mentioned the subject of palmistry. You said you believed in it. I wondered at that. I had once read Desbarolles' book about it, but I am bound to say I thought the whole thing very great nonsense indeed."

"Then," I gasped, "it isn't even true that you believe in palmistry?"

"Oh, no. But I wasn't able to tell you that. You had begun by saying that you believed in palmistry, and then you proceeded to scoff at it. While you scoffed I saw myself as a man with a terribly good reason for *not* scoffing; and in a flash I saw the terribly good reason; I had the whole story—at least I had the broad outlines of it—clear before me."

"You hadn't ever thought of it before?" He shook his head. My eyes beamed. "The whole thing was a sheer improvisation?"

"Yes," said Laider, humbly, "I am as bad as all that. I don't say that all the details of the story I told you that evening were filled in at the very instant of its conception. I was filling them in while we talked about palmistry in general, and while I was waiting for the moment when the story would come in most effectively. And I've no doubt I added some extra touches in the course of the actual telling. Don't imagine that I took the slightest pleasure in deceiving you. It's only my will, not my conscience, that is weakened after influenza. I simply can't help telling what I've made up, and telling it to the best of my ability. But I'm thoroughly ashamed all the time."

"Not of your ability, surely?"

"Yes, of that, too," he said with his sad smile. "I always feel that I'm not doing justice to my idea."

"You are too stern a critic, believe me."

"It is very kind of you to say that. You are very kind altogether. Had I known that you were so essentially a man of the world—in the best sense of that term—I shouldn't have so much dreaded seeing you just now and having to confess to you. But I'm not going to take advantage of your urbanity and your easy-going ways. I hope that some day we may meet somewhere when I haven't had influenza and am a not wholly undesirable acquaintance. As it is, I refuse to let you associate with me. I am an older man than you, and so I may without impertinence warn you against having anything to do with me."

I deprecated this advice, of course; but, for a man of weakened will, he showed great firmness. "You," he said, "in your heart of hearts don't want to have to walk and talk continually with a person who might at any moment try to bamboozle you with some ridiculous tale. And I, for my part, don't want to degrade myself by trying to bamboozle any one—especially one whom I have taught to see through me. Let the two talks we have had be as though they had not been. Let us bow to each other, as last year, but let that be all. Let us follow in all things the precedent of last year."

With a smile that was almost gay he turned on his heel, and moved away with a step that was almost brisk. I was a little disconcerted. But I was also more than a little glad. The restfulness of silence, the charm of liberty— these things were not, after all, forfeit. My heart thanked Laider for that; and throughout the week I loyally seconded him in the system he had laid down for us. All was as it had been last year. We did not smile to each other, we merely bowed, when we entered or left the dining-room or smoking-room, and when we met on the widespread sands or in that shop which had a small and faded, but circulating, library.

Once or twice in the course of the week it did occur to me that perhaps Laider had told the simple truth at our first interview and an ingenious lie at our second. I frowned at this possibility. The idea of any one wishing to be quit of *me* was most distasteful. However, I was to find reassurance. On the last evening of my stay, I suggested, in the small smoking-room, that he and I should, as sticklers for precedent, converse. We did so, very pleasantly. And after a while I happened to say that I had seen this afternoon a great number of sea-gulls flying close to the shore.

"Sea-gulls?" said Laider, turning in his chair.

"Yes. And I don't think I had ever realised how extraordinarily beautiful they are when their wings catch the light."

"Beautiful?" Laider threw a quick glance at me and away from me. "You think them beautiful?"

"Surely."

"Well, perhaps they are, yes; I suppose they are. But—I don't like seeing them. They always remind me of something—rather an awful thing—that once happened to me. . . ."

It was a very awful thing indeed.

THE AMULET

Jacob Wassermann

(1873–1934)

TRANSLATED BY BASIL CREIGHTON

When you think of the lives some people have to live, lives of nothing but want and care, destitute of all joy, without a moment's repose, without beauty and almost without hope, it makes you wonder why they do not simply go out, like flames with nothing to feed them. Man is a patient creature, born to suffering, and what he endures is often out of all proportion to the resources nature has endowed him with. And many endure it without even grumbling. Is it because they do not know that others have a different lot, or are they too much preoccupied by their own fate? What is it prevents them from resigning themselves in silent passivity to the dark, inevitable end, and taking the path to the grave—to death which they understand as little as they do their wretched existence?

Christine Schierling grew up in the grimy back streets of a large town and had never known father or mother. She began her life in an orphanage; then her guardian took her to live with him; then her guardian died; then she had to go into service with a rent-collector. She had to carry water, wash clothes, light fires, look after children, scrub floors—that was her life from early in the morning until late at night.

Innumerable were the houses in which she toiled, the families whose bread she ate, the stairs she ran up and down, the scoldings she was given by her mistresses. She was always changing situations, not because of the hardships she suffered, for these she could not escape wherever she went, but because every now and then the thought came to her that she might better herself.

But this turned out to be an illusory hope. The mistress of a prosperous household looked askance at a girl who came from a poor one and so she always had to seek refuge again with lower class people. Sometimes they were good people, sometimes bad, just as it might happen. Sometimes her wages were in arrear, sometimes she was half-starved. In one place there were ill-natured children who tormented and persecuted her, in others lodgers who took liberties when they came home at night. In one place the wife was in poor health, in another she was a termagant, for whom you could do nothing right; and sometimes the husband was a drunkard, who deceived his wife with other women and there was everlasting quarrelling and bickering.

She got to know every sort of person and every sort of family life. She knew the shamefaced brand of poverty which is slovenly, and the industrious brand which defies every assault of fate. She had seen love under the piteous ruins of lost happiness and hate that infests the air with its pestilence, hate between father and son, between man and wife, between brother and sister. She knew the language of envy, the poison of scandal, the rage of despair, tongue-tied melancholy and the horrors that bring crime to birth. She had been with a confectioner, a shoemaker, a procuress, a bankrupt manufacturer, a midwife, a woman who kept a tobacconist's shop, a retailer of brandy. She often dreamed of the houses in which she had sojourned, but she did not see them one after the other, or now one and now another, but all at once in a nightmare conglomeration—like the cells of a honeycomb. She saw steps without end and innumerable doors. She smelt a smell of beds, fat and bad coffee. She heard a ceaseless noise, noise everywhere, singing, whistling, hammering, shouting and laughing; the crying of children, the barking of dogs, thumping and shovelling, cursing and groaning. And all without a sun and without a sky.

She had only rarely slept in a bed, usually on a sack of straw or a mattress beside the kitchen fire. Vermin crawled over her hands and face as soon as it was dark. It was only when she was with the manufacturer that she had a room to herself, but it was a cupboard in the attic where the wind blew in and on cold nights she froze to the marrow of her bones.

Between her twentieth and twenty-first year she was with a Major. He was addressed as Major, but in reality he was a dilapidated old man who made his living out of petty agencies eked out with a scanty pension. As long as he was well she never had a kind word from him, but when he was taken bad and Christine had to look after him he got down in the mouth and as soon as she left the room he whined until she came back. Christine heard his moans and complaints and saw that it was all up with him. When he felt that he was at death's door he called the girl to his bedside and said: "May God reward you for all you have done for me. I cannot. But, so that you shan't go away empty-handed from my deathbed, I will give you the amulet my mother, now with God, hung round my neck when I went to fight against the Italians. Perhaps it will bring you better luck than it has me." Saying this he felt under his woollen nightshirt and after undoing the catch he brought out a steel chain with a coin attached to it. It was as large as a florin piece and the colour of verdigris. Christine thanked him. Immediately afterwards the Major breathed his last.

Ever after she always wore the chain round her neck. Ten years later she at last reached a higher station in life: she went into service with a Jewish couple. The man's name was Simon Laubeseder and he had originally been a rag-and-bone man; then he started an old clothes shop in the outskirts of the town, where he supplied the artisans with cheap clothing, and it was not long before he opened a business in the Stiftgasse, which boasted the name of Warehouse of the Emperor of Austria. They were a childless couple and the work was not too hard; also they were quiet people and Christine learnt from them what decent ways were. But the most important thing of all was that she had a bedroom of her own.

She decorated the bare walls with illustrations from newspapers. There were the Crown Prince Rudolph, Prince Bismarck with his dog, Tyras, and a picture of the battle of Trafalgar; the pictures were tacked up and fir twigs and dried flowers were stuck in behind them. The photograph of the Major hung over her bed; it showed him as a young lieutenant and it likewise was framed in foliage. A long-legged table, covered with a tablecloth displayed in loving array all kinds of mementoes and presents collected during her past life—a wax peach, a thimble in a red silk case, a china dwarf crouching under a toadstool, a prayer book with a gilt cross and a necklace of glass beads. Sometimes when she went out shopping she met a soldier in the passage or on the stairs, a corporal of the German Masters of the Teutonic Order. He had a black, turned-up moustache, thick lips, a close-shaven round chin and a merry gleam in his eye. The second time she encountered him he gave her a salute; the third time he laughed; the fourth time he entered into conversation and she learned that he was paying a visit to his sister who lived in the house and was married to Grieshacker, the haulage contractor. The corporal's name was Kalixtus Zoff and he had got himself put on the active list of his regiment and hoped soon to be promoted sergeant major.

By degrees Christine became friendly with him and they agreed to go for a walk together one Sunday. They took the train to Sievering, walked through the Frühlingswald to Weidling and returned on foot to the town as dusk was falling. The corporal was going to meet his sister and her husband and they went to a small public house and sat down at a table at which eight or ten people were already seated. Christine knew Frau Grieshacker by sight and she sat down beside her and shyly said good evening. The corporal soon began to talk big and got into a violent argument with Grieshacker about whether the Salzburg express stopped at Neulengbach or not.

Kalixtus Zoff gave Christine his arm on the way home and made a few clumsy advances under cover of the darkness. But Christine was tired. It was the first time in years she had been for a long walk. Her eyes were dropping before she got in, and when the corporal asked for a kiss as he said good night she complied without thinking much about it. She kissed him on his thick lips and his moustache tickled her under her nose. Frau Grieshacker laughed and the lorryman whistled meaningly.

Christine kept company with the corporal for a long time without giving way to him, as, of course, it was his object she should; and she resisted not because she was afraid or because she set any value on her surrender, but because she had little inclination for what to him seemed so desirable.

Kalixtus Zoff was annoyed; he said she was making a fool of him and threatened to break with her. Yet he always came back, armed each time with new weapons of attack. He boasted of his manly vigour, hinted at secret advantages of which he was the possessor and spoke contemptuously of other men who had only the outward appearance of virility. When Christine assured him that she believed him and yet remained unmoved, he got wild and placing his right hand on the breast of his tunic and his left on the hilt of his side arm, he swore that unless she would be his he would put a bullet through himself and her as well.

She displayed great calm when he raved and this impressed him. He had formed the opinion that her obstinacy must be due to her earlier experiences with men and he did everything possible to convince her that he was quite an exception to the common run of males. Hence his astonishment was unbounded when he was forced to see his mistake and learned that her past was not at all what he had supposed it.

It was on a summer evening and they were walking from Kahlenberg over the hills towards Nussdorf. There were other loving couples walking in front of them and behind them; some were singing, some whispering and sometimes a couple left the road and disappeared from view. The voices of Sunday holiday makers resounded from the woods and from the edges of the vineyards and the numerous wayside inns. The moon rose above the town and the air was sultry. As they walked along, Christine by degrees began to talk. Her tongue was loosened and her dulled senses escaped from the shackles which since her childhood had never relaxed their grip. She told him the story of her life and all the places she had been and how hard a time she had had of it. Kalixtus Zoff listened at first with indulgent condescension, but when that part of the story he was waiting for never came he decided to come to the rescue of his own impatience and her forgetfulness with a plain question. She answered with a shake of her head that nothing of that sort had ever occurred. He was so taken aback that he stood still and looked at her with his mouth open, for the very idea of such a thing was not only new to him but at the first flush incomprehensible; so incomprehensible that he tried to combat it with a contemptuous gesture; and only the sombre melancholy of her demeanour and her voice prevented him giving more energetic expression to his incredulity.

She again couldn't understand his astonishment. She was not aware of ever having told a lie or made herself out other than she was. "Oh, yes," she went on, "you see more than enough, more than you want to, and all feeling for it goes."

That's how it was with her. She had seen too much; and her "Oh yes" said everything. In the houses she had been in the walls were thin, the bed springs rusty and nobody felt any shame in the eyes of another; sanctity was sunk in brute necessity, the most intimate tenderness in grim compulsion. When they lay in each other's arms, their wretchedness still pursued them; and when one night raised them above the drab level, how friendless they were all the nights after! Marriage was like death, the veil was lifted; childbirth a terror. Money—everybody squabbled over, clutched at, sold their souls for money. Without money—hunger, horror, despair and murder. Once a prostitute, who had managed to save a hundred crowns, was stabbed near the kitchen where Christine slept. She saw the murdered woman's face. Nobody's resources for love could be great enough not to be beggared of all hope, of every innocent anticipation and secretly treasured belief after a sight like that. It was the opened sewer of the underworld; inevitable, incarnate doom.

Christine told him all this too in her own simple words; and how she had to give evidence afterwards in court; and how her evidence told against her mistress, the procuress. In consequence of this two pimps enticed her one night on to a derelict building plot and beat her and she lay there until midnight in a pool of blood.

Kalixtus Zoff gradually began to feel small. He detected the ring of truth in her words and, further, it was borne in upon him that this girl was altogether incapable of untruth. The suspicion came to him that she was as far above him as he, up to now, had imagined himself to be above her and, in spite of his martial prowess, he felt overawed.

His silence touched Christine, for she guessed the cause of it. "I don't want to go home yet," she begged of a sudden and looked round about her. Absorbed in their talk, they had got off the road and now they were all by themselves. The moon had glided behind a bank of clouds and far down in the plain of the Danube the lights of the town gleamed dimly, veiled in mist. Christine sank down on the grass, Kalixtus sat down beside her and began softly whistling a tune.

"How well you whistle," Christine said.

"Yes, I can whistle," he replied as he leaned his head on her breast.

Christine was able to conceal her pregnancy until about Christmas time. Frau Laubeseder gave her a good talking to when she noticed her condition, but Christine was obstinately dumb. She admitted what there was no denying, but little else could be dragged out of her. She didn't know where she meant to go when her time came and she didn't want any well-meant advice.

The people in the house and the street looked at her inquisitively: she read pity in some faces, scorn in others. Kalixtus Zoff was a little disconcerted at first, but when Christine neither reproached him nor pulled a long face, nor asked him for money, he worried no more and was honestly grateful to her for behaving in a way that excused him from the necessity of making even the show of a bad conscience.

One night in March Christine gave birth to a boy. That evening, when she felt the first pains, she went to a midwife in the neighbourhood with whom she had made arrangements some days before. She had to pay fifteen crowns the moment she arrived and then she was allowed to stay there and the woman made a bed ready for her.

She lay in bed for four days and then the midwife said she was well enough to get up. She got up, but she still felt very weak. She had to leave the infant with the midwife for the time; she was to come back on Sunday and then they would discuss what was to be done with the child. "What are you going to call him?" the midwife asked. Christine replied that he was to be called Joseph.

Through the midwife she heard of a woman at Erdberg who was prepared to take the child in return for a small payment. The midwife took him there herself and on the next Sunday Christine went to Erdberg with the corporal to make sure that the baby was in good hands. The woman whose charge he was in was a laundress and Christine was not at all pleased with her. She had four small children of her own and the house was dirty and dark.

Two days later Christine went out to Erdberg again and, without making many words of it, demanded to have the child given up to her and took him to the Laubeseders'. But he cried piteously half the night and Simon Laubeseder's sleep was disturbed and he forbade her to keep the child in the house. And so Christine had to look about for another home for him and she remembered the widow of a gardener, whom she had got to know in one of her former places and who had done her a few kindnesses. She went to her and she agreed to mother the child in return for a moderate sum. The child was christened, the court appointed a guardian for him and Kalixtus Zoff would have had to pay for his maintenance, but he had no money and so Christine had to take it all on herself.

As the gardener's widow lived near by, Christine often ran along in the evenings to see how Joseph was getting on. As far as she could see and from what the woman said, the child had nothing to complain of, but every time Christine saw him her heart stood still: he looked so bad and his skin was yellow and his eyes big. When a year had gone by and the child was still sickly, she put him in charge of a woman who kept a dairy in Hetzendorf, a certain Frau Tomasek, and there he stayed, for she was better than her predecessors and had some little love for the homeless creature.

The corporal took Christine out every Sunday just as he had before, but now they did not often go out into the country, though this was what Christine liked best. Instead they paid Joseph a visit and then Zoff headed for a pub in the newly built outskirts of the town, where it was his custom to meet his friend, Polivka, who was a barber.

Polivka and Zoff had got to know one another in a dance bar at Prater not long before. They had had a quarrel over a girl, as Kalixtus made no bones about telling Christine; but then they came to the conclusion that the girl was no great catch and went off together; and as they strolled along late at night they opened their hearts to one another.

Polivka the barber was always dinning it into the corporal's ears that he ought to give up the army; and for this reason Christine, who at first could not put up with the man, began by degrees to look on him more favourably. Polivka's contention was debated at great length, but Kalixtus Zoff was deaf to the voice of reason.

He kept saying that he was born to be a soldier and that his heart and soul were in it. Polivka, who had the reputation among his acquaintances of being a well-read and educated fellow and whose command of words fully bore out his reputation, maintained on the other hand that times being what they were, a soldier's life was merely idleness and folly and that a man of Kalixtus Zoff's physical and mental gifts—and here Polivka winked slyly at Christine, who was listening with all her ears—could show up to greater advantage in any other line of life and even make a comfortable position for himself.

"All that's a lot of nonsense," Kalixtus Zoff replied. "I wear the Emperor's uniform and that's the end of it. If the Emperor did not need soldiers he would let us know it himself. Why should I sweat my guts out all the week for a few lousy crowns? I have my bed and board, my drink and my uniform and, over and above that, there's something else to be taken into account. There's not a man so smart and well turned out as one of us when he leaves barracks to walk out with his girl." He put his arm roughly round Christine's shoulders and pinched her arm so hard that she cried out.

"And what about you, Polivka?" he asked, turning to the barber. "You don't do so mighty well even though you have supped up wisdom with a spoon."

"That's true," Polivka said, looking somewhat nettled, as he swept his barbered locks from his forehead. "But that is up to me personally, to put it that way. If I were no more than a barber I should long since have had my saloon in the Ringstrasse with half-a-dozen assistants and a wife. But I was born for something better. I have my ambitions. Fortune did not put the shaving brush and razor in my cradle." He rested his chin in his hand and his little twinkling boot-button eyes gazed sadly into space.

Christine did not understand what he was talking about. But she felt sure that she was destined to know him better. During the next week but one she received a rosy pink note with his signature, in which he invited her and her friend Kalixtus to a dramatic performance to be given by "The Blackbirds" on the following Sunday. They were going to give "The Robbers" and Polivka was taking the part of Karl. Christine and Kalixtus betook themselves to the "Golden Pear" at the hour appointed. She had never been to a theatre before and the auditorium and all the lights and the well-dressed people and the painted curtain made a deep impression on her. When the curtain went up and the performance began and a space hitherto invisible, was revealed, where strangely dressed and strangely speaking persons moved about, she involuntarily seized Kalixtus's arm and sighed and marvelled and felt afraid.

It was some time before she formed a clear idea of what was going on. By degrees she got hold of the story and as she held her breath in rapt attention her heart went out to the unhappy and magnificent Karl Moor. When he came on the stage in his might, wearing a hat with nodding plume, his eyes darting lightning, his arms waving like the sails of a windmill; when he stormed against mankind in a voice that made the air quiver, Kalixtus Zoff gave Christine a nudge and whispered: "There he is. That's Polivka."

Christine could hardly believe it. Yet doubt and amazement ran into one in the stress of her emotion and towards the end of the piece she could no longer restrain her tears and sobbed so loudly that people turned round and looked at her and the corporal felt embarrassed. She felt strangely happy as her grief welled out; it came dimly to her mind how seldom she had cried; in fact, she could not remember having ever done so and it gave her a feeling of luxury and joy.

"Well, now we'll go and fetch Polivka," Kalixtus Zoff said in a loud voice at the end of the fifth act, getting up and gazing proudly round to let all the world know that he was a friend of the much-admired actor. "He made a proper job of it. Grand! Why, a general might envy him lungs like that!"

Christine wanted to go home. She said in excuse that she felt bad and when Kalixtus Zoff got annoyed she pleaded with him and looked at him with imploring eyes. He shrugged his shoulders and left her. He turned with his noisy cheeriness to a group of Polivka's friends and a moment later Polivka himself joined them, clad once more in his everyday clothes and with his face clean of paint and rather pale. He shook hands all round and laughed conceitedly.

Christine was glad to have seen him after all and then she hurried away. A cold wind swept along in the street, but she did not feel it. She was warmed within by veneration, and fortified by aspirations she had never known before.

Polivka observed Christine's altered demeanour, but he put a wrong construction on it.

"What's the matter with Christine? What is she cross with me for?" he enquired of Kalixtus Zoff one day.

"Christine? You turned her head with your play-acting," the corporal answered. "She's been up in the air ever since, I tell you."

The barber then saw how the land lay. And he took a closer look at Christine. She was not bad, even if she was thirty-three. Her way of dressing and behaving was certainly unpretentious and too modest by far, but her face, her soft lips and her sad eyes were more attractive than was usual in girls of her station. Polivka felt the desire to fulfil expectations of which his person, idolised even by himself, was the object. With pleasing tremors he pictured himself as lord and master of the poor servant girl and while he lathered his clients' stubbly chins he closed his eyes in a poetic dream. He no longer felt any scruples about having to go behind his friend in order to win Christine.

Hence his mortification was great when the first advance he made met with an insulting rebuff. She gazed at him with astonishment and he was completely cowed.

Next Sunday Kalixtus Zoff greeted him with a friendly dig in the ribs and shouted out with a laugh: "Polivka, you're a dirty dog."

The barber went green and yellow with embarrassment and annoyance and racked his brains what to do next. The corporal seemed to be confoundedly sure of the girl and she instantly rose in his estimation now that he found she was far from being so willing as he had supposed. He therefore lay in ambush and resolved to go to work with more circumspection.

He had offended Christine by his clumsy overtures. There was a contradiction in her feelings for Polivka: she had a vision of him in her own mind that awed and affected her; when she thought of him her breast expanded and her soul warmed; but in his actual presence she was shocked and disillusioned and she looked in vain for the other Polivka of whom she dreamed. In all this the idea of being untrue to Kalixtus never entered her head. She considered herself bound to him for good, or until he himself cast her off. She knew that he was not so particular, but she did not pass judgment on him for that; she did not take it on herself to judge him. She regarded herself as his property, of which he could dispose as he saw fit or even as his fancy dictated.

Meanwhile the time came when the Emperor, as Kalixtus had said, found a use for his soldiers. The archduke and heir to the throne was murdered and the Serbs challenged the Empire and challenged the whole world. Russia mobilised, England rose up in menace and countries where peace had long been at home shuddered in anticipation of slaughter without end.

Even Polivka had to realise at last what a soldier was and what he was

good for. Everyone else realised it likewise and put all his trust in the
defenders of his property. The soldier, too, now became conscious of his
destiny and prepared in the time-honoured manner to welcome war as a
glorious adventure. It had never of course entered his head that things
would come to such a pass and he did not grasp the full seriousness of
it yet.

It was the women who were filled with apprehension; the shadow of the
future already fell on their hearts. Pain and astonishment took possession
of them and unconsciously they sundered their daily activities from those
of the men, which seemed to them mysterious and atrocious.

Many a man became a hero who had little foreseen such a transformation
and many a love became new again which had seemed staled by custom.
Christine sat up for the whole of one night mending the clothes Kalixtus
was taking with him on active service. There was haste, for the regiment
was marching to the station to entrain on the following day. She would
have liked to do a great deal more for him and, if loving care could have
made her sewing any firmer, his shirts and handkerchiefs would have
been imperishable. Yes, she was filled with apprehension and her heart was
overshadowed; yet she thought with tenderness of the man to whose fate
her own was bound and who was going to war, perhaps never to return.

She too had never connected his profession, even remotely, with danger.
So easy a life, so untroubled, so leisurely; and hers, in comparison, so hard,
so full of drudgery and toil. She had had it against him that he laughed his
way through life and refused to take any thought for the morrow, and now
he had to pay the price. From one day to another it might be all over with
him and the bullet that might hit him was already cast. How good and
right it was, then, that no sorrows had so far darkened his existence.

She told herself ten times over that she would be true to him. Why? She
had no guilty thought when she said it. She was not afraid of herself. She
said it only to give herself the assurance and him peace of mind. Her fond
longing was far away from her: Karl Moor beckoned only on the farthest
outskirts of her dreams. She was staid and unruffled; awed and stilled by
the dread disaster of a whole world's collapse. And yet the mysterious
evolution of a human destiny embraces, is already embraced by, all that
lies merely as an embryo within it.

Kalixtus Zoff was able to snatch half an hour early in the morning and
pay the boy a visit with her. He was four years old by this time. His face
was yellow and when his father gave him a piece of chocolate he had
brought for him his eyes lit up greedily. Frau Tomasek said he was never
satisfied and Kalixtus Zoff laughed, but Christine felt a stab of doubt when
she heard it. The neglected child went to her heart, the word mother
sounded so strange on his lips; and she wondered how she could contrive
to take the child into her own keeping. At midday she went to the station

and the barber escorted her. With a frown of uneasiness he studied the calling-up notices on the walls.

"Keep your heart up, Zoff," he said to Kalixtus by way of good-bye.

"Servus, Polivka, you old froth-blower," the corporal replied cheerily and turned to Christine and, opening his eyes very wide, he said in a severe tone: "Good-bye, Tiny, and see you're true to me."

"And you, see you keep safe," she stammered and looked at him and looked away again, and then lost sight of him in the crowd of soldiers.

Polivka, as a man bent on profit, lost no time in trying to occupy the place Kalixtus Zoff had left vacant, in so far at least as he laid claim to the superfluous victuals from the kitchen which the corporal had had the enjoyment of. Every evening he came to the door at the time when Christine went out to the grocer's and approached his goal by the winding paths of eloquence, by playful and poetical allusions, as though his stomach were the keeper of his heart and the guardian angel of the absent.

There was no occasion for all this with Christine. She saw no need for mystery or cunning. She had saved the eatables she had given Kalixtus from what she was allowed for herself and she would never have thought of taking advantage of her master and mistress by thieving and pilfering. She ate sparingly, even more so now than before. He who cooks himself is soon satisfied. But she would never have ventured to offer the barber what the corporal had for so long enjoyed; he seemed to her too superior and too proud for that, and when he raised the question she was surprised, though she gladly consented.

Polivka was a dainty feeder. Meat had not to be too fat, nor too lean either; bread he despised and liked only crisp pastries. Sausage and cheese were beneath his notice.

One day he asked Christine for a loan of forty crowns. His business had fallen off owing to the war. Receipts diminished week by week.

He knew from Kalixtus Zoff that Christine had saved about five hundred crowns. But he knew also that the corporal, easygoing though he was, had made it a point of honour to keep his fingers off her hard-earned savings. Polivka was less scrupulous. At the best of times he always had his eye out for anything that might add to his enjoyment of life and, now that he was in want, he was even greedier and more ruthless.

Christine was too good-natured to distrust him and, so far from meeting his haughty demand with a point-blank refusal, she did not even think twice about it. When she handed out the money he crumpled up the two notes and stuffed them into his waistcoat pocket just as though he were being paid a debt which was long overdue.

The date when the loan was to be repaid passed by and instead of keeping his word he asked for a further sum of twenty crowns. The sixty soon became a hundred, then three hundred, and so it went on until he had cleaned her out. It had taken her fifteen years to amass her capital: it only took four months to dispose of it. There was always some fresh circumstance which compelled Polivka to come down upon her: taxes were due, his landlord would wait no longer, the tailor was going to sell him up. At first he was in real need of the money, but when he found how easy it was to get possession of Christine's savings he fancied the source must be inexhaustible and spent what she gave him in riotous living.

He was one of the regular patrons of the lottery and spoke of the winning ticket he was soon going to draw with the same confidence as he might have of money in the bank. Also he told her about a sick but miserly uncle in Bohemia, who had sacks of gold buried in his cellar and whose death might be expected any day. He drew a glowing picture of the fine life he would then lead and one Sunday he even took Christine to see over a villa in Hietzing and smacked his lips as he said that he had long had his eye on the place and would buy it as soon as his uncle in Bohemia was off the hooks.

Christine believed it all; that is to say, she believed as people do when they are afraid of the truth. When she had handed over the greater part of her fortune to Polivka she had a pretty good notion what his promises and solemn oaths were worth. She saw that he did no work and that things were going from bad to worse with him. He spent his nights drinking and his days in bed.

When she became a mother Christine began for the first time to rejoice in her savings; it was her dearest thought that one day the money would be of use to Joseph and ease his first steps on the hard road of life. How could she look the boy in the face if he wanted clothes and shoes and books and she had nothing to give him and was as poor as a mouse? What would she say to him, what would the boy think of her and what would become of him?

She did not upbraid Polivka. He was still the object of her deep veneration, owing to a law of her nature and by virtue of a secret steadfastness in her very soul. Once she had received the vision of higher things in a moment of uplifted happiness she could not let it go. Against this even the loss of her money could not prevail, bitter as it was. She lulled herself with the idea that Kalixtus would recover the money for her when he came back; Polivka would not have the face to brazen it out then and he would have to pay her back.

Meanwhile, Kalixtus only added to her cares, for though he had promised to write regularly she had not had a single word from him. Her letters remained unanswered. Many wounded soldiers were to be seen in the streets. They all looked tired and sad. Often she longed to question one of them, but she was afraid to. Disquieting rumours were abroad and at the grocer's in the evenings people said openly that things were going badly at the front; and when she talked to Polivka about it he made a face, which suggested that he received the most important despatches every morning from the General Staff, and remarked with Austrian relish of misfortune that it would all end badly.

She searched the dim future in her dread and prayed at night that Kalixtus might be spared. Her heart beat dully when she thought of him, as though she already half gave him up for lost. If ever her despondence lifted, the thought of Joseph filled her heart to overflowing and she hastened to Frau Tomasek to see the child. Instead of the rickety, pale and cowed little boy he actually was, she saw in him a flower of promise; the one living being on whom her hopes could rest, who was incontestably and utterly her own, and suddenly she loved him with a boundless love.

She now resolved to speak to Polivka once more about the money. She went to see him one afternoon in December when a moist grey mist shrouded the streets. Polivka's shop was shut and she went next door where the barber lived in a basement room.

She entered and found Polivka lying dressed on his bed, smoking. The walls were covered with photographs of actors and actresses. Empty beer bottles and coffee cups, a lamp with a broken chimney and a pair of dirty boots littered the table.

Polivka raised his head inquisitively and asked what she had come for. Christine's courage failed her and she said nothing about the money. He clasped his hands behind his head and stared at the ceiling. "Kalixtus is dead," he said abruptly.

Christine felt as if all the blood was drained from her brain. Frau Grieshacker had told him so, Polivka said, and she had had the news from a platoon sergeant in the same regiment. He sighed and shut his eyes.

Christine did not move. After a while she turned round and silently left the room. Polivka jumped up from his bed, tore the door open and called after her.

She came back and stood with limp arms.

"Now you belong to me," he said.

She did not answer and went away.

The Grieshackers had moved and now lived at Meidling. Christine went out there that night. Frau Grieshacker welcomed her very kindly. Her husband too was at the front and she had had no news of him for a long time. As for Kalixtus she could only repeat what the sergeant had told her. She sat down at the table and buried her face in her apron and wept.

Then she asked where the child was and how he was getting on. When Christine only looked sadly in front of her, she said she could bring him to her. Christine promised she would.

At this very hour Kalixtus Zoff was lying out on a battlefield in Poland. A shell splinter had torn off his right arm. The field dressing a wounded

comrade had bound round him had not stopped the bleeding. Tortured
with throbbing pain he lay in a wet hollow, waiting to be picked up and
taken to a dressing station. The guns were silent. All around him he heard
groans and cries of pain.

He thought of Vienna where he had led such a jolly and careless life; of
Christine and their walks together and of his little son with his enormous
head and great staring eyes. But the thought of Christine crowded out all
else. He saw her as clearly and vividly as if he had been talking to her
an hour before. She had never been so near to him during all the six
months since he left her as now when he lay in the mud, unable to
move.

She looked at him with reproachful eyes which frightened him. It came
over him that he had behaved badly to her, but just how and why he
could not make out.

When night fell he lifted his head and saw dim figures against the overcast sky. They were stretcher-bearers. He tried to shout and could not.
They went past. His forehead broke out in a cold sweat.

The wound began to pulse more feverishly. He touched it with his left
hand and his fingers were soaked in blood. What will happen to me, he
thought. And what will happen to her? His heart was suddenly filled with
a tenderness for Christine he had never known before.

With an effort he raised his head once more. It was a dreary scene. Pale
moonlight glimmered over the river through the drifting clouds. Then an
unwieldy lump came shuffling over the ground, a lump that breathed
stertorously, snuffled loudly and grunted hoarsely and greedily.

It was a black pig, as large as a bear, with pendulous chops, stark bristles
and savagely gleaming eyes. Probably it had been starving in its sty and
had broken out to seek for food on the field of battle.

The clumsy brute came panting up to him. Kalixtus Zoff felt hot breath
in his face. Its snuffling sounded gleeful and impatient. The smell of fresh
blood had an intoxicating effect on it. Kalixtus was transfixed with horror
as he wondered how to defend himself. None of the battles in which he
had fought had roused him to this pitch of terror.

What does it all mean, he thought. Why must I lie here and perish like
a beast? Why is my arm torn away? I am a cripple, a cripple for the rest
of my days. What is the meaning of all this frightful misery that has suddenly come down on the world?

He made a movement of his shoulders. The pig started. Then it came
on again more savagely. He moved again and it grunted angrily and stuck
its snout in his face. Then with a grisly noise it began to lap the blood; in
a moment it would dig its tusks in his flesh. Nausea and despair roused
Kalixtus to a last effort. He felt along his side with his left hand and
grasped his yataghan and drawing it from the scabbard plunged the steel
deep into the animal's belly.

The beast uttered a piercing shriek. It was a shriek that filled the silence of the night and the whole vault of the sky. It sounded like a frantic scream of the demon who held all humanity in his claws. Kalixtus Zoff swooned, but the doctor and his orderlies, hearing the noise, crossed the narrow stream at once, found the animal writhing in its death throes and the unconscious body of the wounded man.

Christine kept her promise and took Joseph to Frau Grieshacker and he remained in her charge. Frau Tomasek was very angry and suddenly demanded to be paid back for all kinds of expenses she pretended she had incurred. Christine had to argue for a long time until at last the woman contented herself with a part of her unjust demands and, as she seemed to have a genuine affection for her foster child, Christine asked Frau Grieshacker to allow her to visit the child on Sundays.

Frau Grieshacker was glad to take the child and said he was like Kalixtus. She had a sister living with her, Frau Wandl by name, a lean and silent person, who did a great deal for the boy with the air of being unable to endure him.

When the four women sat together and talked they kept their eyes on the boy all the time as he played on the floor, each with different feelings. Sometimes Polivka was there too, but he was no longer the gay spark of other days. He brooded darkly within his soul or picked up Herr Grieshacker's concertina and gave musical expression to his bad temper and his pessimism. Then he urged Christine to go with him to the public house and when she refused he went off by himself in a rage.

Once she followed him and begged him not to go. He asked malignantly what life had to offer him except the public house. If she wanted him to give up anything for her sake she ought to do something for his sake. Christine said he was not to start on that again when she was in such sorrow and he ought to think of poor Kalixtus. Oh, said he, dead was dead, and once under the ground no one came back. If she kept on refusing him, what could he do but drink? Christine was tired of all this talk and she asked herself why she made so much of a matter of no importance. Who was any the better? Ought she to think such a lot of herself and put on airs when the man was desperate and had set his whole heart on it?

Sensing her change of mind, Polivka took hold of her arm and his voice became cajoling. But in his words there was the cynical indifference of a wastrel, who had no aim and no belief left and made the common plight of humanity merely an excuse for poaching the small game of sensual indulgence.

Christine went with him to his dirty room and lay down in his dirty bed. She gave herself to him as a martyr and her heart was heavy, for the ideal longing he had once inspired in her went pale and vanished away as she did it. And when she left the man, she felt a gnawing uneasiness take hold of her on Joseph's account. She felt she had done the child a mortal harm. Her thoughts became confused and she had no sleep and no peace of mind left. She no longer ventured to enter the house where he was; every day she set out, but when she got near she turned back. She was afraid of reading in his face all the sufferings and privations that haunted her mind; she lost all joy in her work and things got so bad that Frau Laubeseder, for all her patience, gave her notice; and on the top of that she discovered to her horror that she was pregnant.

The day before her notice expired Frau Laubeseder, who was sorry for her, said that she could stay on until she found a new situation. But Christine replied that she was not going to take another place. She was going to have Joseph to live with her. She did not say how she proposed to do so if she was not earning anything and probably she did not know herself.

Next morning she packed up her possessions in her wooden boxes; clothes, aprons, underclothes and stockings, the pictures on the wall, the wax peach, the red silk case containing the thimble, the china dwarf, the prayer book and the beads. Then she took her wages and said good-bye to her master and mistress, who had been so good to her, and called to the porter's son to help her down with her boxes. He asked her where she was going and she said to Polivka, the barber.

Polivka was not at all sorry to see her, as she brought some money with her, not to mention her few possessions, which were of sufficient value to pawn.

He kept his ears open for what she might say, for he was determined not to put up with good advice or reproaches.

When she got to work at once tidying up the dirt and confusion of his room, he watched her with disapproving eyes.

That evening Christine told him that she was going to fetch Joseph from Frau Grieshacker's. He flared up and said he would not have the bastard in the house. Christine went pale and replied quietly that she would have to go somewhere else with Joseph in that case. Polivka was silenced by this and a little later he asked her how much she had in cash. Christine said she had thirty-five crowns and a few coppers. He seemed to be taken aback and asked again whether that was all. She nodded. Well, anyway, he said, she could lend him the money for the rent. She made no objection.

"Curse it, curse it, what'll become of us!" the barber muttered.

Oh, that night, side by side, want by want! That frosty, damp, leaden, endless night!

"Curse it, curse it," Polivka muttered again before he fell asleep, as he scratched his abundant locks. But Christine looked at her red hands and thought of all the work they had got through already and could still get through. Then she did not feel so frightened.

At six in the morning she got up silently, but Polivka heard her and seized her roughly by the arm. Why the devil couldn't she leave her bastard where he was? Christine glanced round and answered with passion that she would rather die than leave the child another day in the hands of strangers.

She washed and dressed and when she was ready to go she said she had slaved all her life for strangers and now she would have a try and see what it was like slaving for her own flesh and blood for a change. As she said this her face lit up with a glow of tenderness.

Polivka, however, was already asleep again.

It was eight o'clock when she entered Frau Grieshacker's room. Frau Grieshacker met her with the news that Kalixtus had unexpectedly returned. And she sat down at the table and cried into her apron, as she had done before, when she had had to announce the news of his death.

Her tears were not due to excess of joy. Her expression betrayed something other than joy over her brother's return.

When she had recovered she told Christine that there had been a ring at the door at about seven the night before, and there he was. He had asked at once where Christine was. A friend he had sent to the Laubeseders' had told him she was no longer in service with them. He was now going there himself. Perhaps the porter could tell him where she was.

Christine who up to now had stood like a stone began to tremble and had to hold onto the wall. Frau Grieshacker went on to say that he had spent five months in a hospital on the frontier. He had not wanted anyone to write for him and he could not write himself. She sighed. It was not a pleasant sigh.

Suddenly Christine cried out: "Joseph!" and again: "Joseph!"

The boy appeared in the doorway. He had an abnormally large head and his expression as he looked at his mother was stupid.

Christine kneeled down and flung her arms round him. Then she picked him up and looked wildly round and, before Frau Grieshacker could ask her where she was off to or get between her and the door, she was out of the room and out of the house with the boy in her arms.

Only to get away, away out of this life, out of this world. That was the one thought in her seething brain.

When she got back to Polivka the landlord had just been. Polivka had paid the rent with the money Christine had given him the night before. He was sitting in his pants at the table with the newspaper in front of him, reading the latest army orders, which meant that he too would be conscripted at last.

He had been fearing this for weeks. Now it had come; and he thought of the monotonous and fatiguing life in barracks and of the grim fate against which there was no appeal: he would be sent to the front and killed. He had got an old rusty revolver out of a drawer and put it on the table beside the newspaper.

He looked gloomily at Christine as she came hurriedly in with the boy on her arm. He was going to abuse her for going out without seeing to his breakfast, but she got in first and what she said in a hoarse voice smote him dumb.

For a while he stared blankly at her and then he said it was a lie. He had it on the best authority that Kalixtus was dead. Christine shook him by the shoulder with her free hand and breathlessly told him what she had heard from Frau Grieshacker. Her agitation, her dismay and the agony she was obviously in would have convinced him if her words had not. The corporal's revenge was a thing to fear. A man who had seen all the blood flow that he had seen would not think twice about adding one more dead man to the list.

"Get up—get up—we must go," Christine said, wild-eyed. She added that Kalixtus might come in at the door any moment. The porter at the Laubeseders' knew where she was.

While Polivka was getting ready Christine took the revolver and put it in the pocket of her dress.

Soon they were in the street. Christine still carried the boy, although her arm ached. Polivka bought some bread and bacon at a grocer's and ate as he walked.

When they got to the edge of the town Christine could carry the child no longer. She put him down and led him by the hand. Polivka asked gruffly what the hurry was. She gave him no answer. He followed her because he had no idea what he would do on his own and because her stronger will imposed on his cowardice and indecision. He hated her, but he did not dare to cross her. He told her she had made life a weariness to him and brought him to ruin; and yet when she walked even faster he quickened his pace likewise.

Christine sank down exhausted in a meadow near the Steinhof. The day was drawing in, rain fell from a grey March sky, Joseph cried himself to sleep, Polivka lay down in the shelter of a stack of wood near by.

Despair took hold of Christine's soul and swept through her like a storm, like a blazing fire. She looked in the face of her boy and shuddered at the life she saw in it. All that had been rose again before her eyes and she shuddered at the black hopelessness that streamed from it. It seemed to her as though devouring jaws opened over the boy's head and this vision was so distinct that she cried out. Taking the revolver from her pocket, she tried cocking it and suddenly a shot rang out.

The bullet had hit her. Blood trickled from her left ear. Polivka leapt to his feet. She was seized with a frantic terror that she might die before she had done her child the last service love could do and took hold of the revolver as she had held it before. Before Polivka could reach her, she had put the muzzle to the boy's temple and a second shot rang out.

Polivka snatched the revolver from her grasp. She spread her arms over the boy's body and fainted away. But even while she was unconscious, she knew that Joseph was dead. When she came round and opened her eyes she saw the pale child beside her in spite of the darkness. Polivka stood there weeping. She only said: "We must bury him."

Polivka looked at her in fright and replied that he would have nothing to do with it. He was going back to tell the police.

But it appeared that he was still spellbound by her. He said that he was innocent and that she would have to swear it. Meanwhile she dug a hole with a piece of wood in the moist leaf mold. She laid the child in it and covered him with earth and leaves. Then she prayed with folded hands and when she got up she wondered that she was still alive.

They left the wood and came to a spring. There Christine washed the blood from her cheek. The thought of the murder drove them both back to mankind. They reached the inner town at dawn and went into a small coffee house to refresh themselves. Then they got up again and went to Franz-Joseph's Land and aimlessly traversed the Prater water meadows without exchanging a word. They bought some bread and cheese. Christine could eat nothing. They spent the night in the open and in the morning they wandered wretchedly on. So it went on for five days and nights. On the fifth night they took shelter in a barn. A dog barked. The farmer found them and was going to fetch the constable, so they hurried off as fast as they could go.

Christine fell down. She felt at that moment that the child in her womb lived no longer, and now she knew what it was that had kept her alive since Joseph's death. She could not get up. Polivka looked at her and did not stir a finger.

"Do you call yourself a man?" she groaned.

He was seized with senseless rage and beat her with his fists. She screamed and screamed and at last he stopped and helped her up. When they got back to the town he led her to the steps of a shop and told her to sit down and wait for him. He went away and never came back.

Christine was in great pain. An old labouring man stopped and asked her what was wrong. She asked him to help her into the tram. As they went along he told her that he had had two sons killed at the front.

With a superhuman effort she got to the house in which the Grieshackers lived, and then collapsed.

She was asked while she was delirious where her child was and in her delirium she confessed what had happened to him.

Frau Grieshacker informed the police.

Why not end her story here? Can any ray of hope lighten such darkness? No spirits watch over her fate, the stars circle cold and strange above it. And yet a light, almost of another world, is shed about its final moments. Ghosts and goblins flee in terror before it, as though Justice uncovered her face and spat flames at them.

Christine lay in the prison hospital and when she opened her eyes after days of deathly trance she saw a man in uniform, who had only one arm, sitting by her bed. She saw that it was Kalixtus Zoff. There was a grave look in his face which had never been there before. His cheeks were no longer plump, his chin was no longer round and shining and his moustache no longer twirled in the air. He was pale and he wore a look of puzzled surprise, as if an unfathomable mystery yawned between him and the Kalixtus Zoff of other days.

Christine felt shyly for his hand. Her lips quivered and she looked at him as at the Judge on the Day of Judgment.

"Keep still," Kalixtus Zoff said. "I know all about it." All the colour left her face; it went as white as the pillow on which it lay. Raising her right hand she pointed ghostily upwards. Kalixtus Zoff nodded. "Don't worry yourself, Tiny," he said. "I know all about it." His voice did not sound the same.

She searched his eyes in dread and trembled beneath the bedclothes.

He bent down to her and went on: "I'm going to be good to you again." She trembled more violently and clasped his hand in both of hers.

"I'm going to be good to you again," he said. "And when you've done your time I'll marry you."

Christine's head fell back. A glow of holiness, of sweetness and warmth suffused her.

They were the first words of human kindness she had heard, the first human goodness she had experienced, the first pure happiness she had tasted. It made it worth while to have lived and suffered as she had lived and suffered. Now a new state of being began.

But as she knew that her death was near she took the amulet she had worn all these years round her neck and gave the coin and the chain to Kalixtus with a look of grateful tenderness and the smile of a woman who, if only at death's door, has been touched at last by the ray of love.

CAVALRY PATROL

Hugo von Hofmannsthal

(1874–1929)

TRANSLATED BY BASIL CREIGHTON

On THE 22ND OF JULY, 1848, between five and six in the morning, the
second squadron of Wallmoden cuirassiers, one hundred and seven strong,
under the command of Captain Baron Rofrano, left the Casino San Ales-
sandro on a reconnaissance and rode towards Milan. An indescribable stillness lay over the gleaming, open country; the clouds of morning rose in
smoke drifts into the radiant sky from the peaks of the distant mountains;
the maize stood motionless and farmhouses and churches shone out amidst
groups of trees that looked as if they had been freshly washed. The patrol
had scarcely gone a mile beyond the last outposts when it was fired on
from the cover of the maize-fields and the advance guard reported enemy
foot soldiers. The squadron formed line along the side of the road and a
hail of bullets that made a peculiarly loud noise whizzed over their heads.
Then they charged across the open and drove a party armed with miscellaneous firearms before them as if they were quail. They belonged to the
Legion Manaras and wore strange headgear. The prisoners were put in
charge of a corporal and eight men and sent back. The advance guard next
reported suspicious figures in front of a fine country house approached by
an avenue of cypresses. The squadron sergeant-major, Anton Lerch, dismounted and posted twelve men armed with carbines to cover all the windows and took prisoner eighteen students belonging to the Pisan Legion,
well-educated and good-looking young fellows with white hands and long
hair. Half an hour later the squadron captured a man, dressed as a native
of Bergamo, whose exaggeratedly simple and unassuming air aroused suspicion. The man had detailed plans of the utmost importance, concerning
the raising of volunteers in the Giudicaria and their co-operation with the
Piedmontese Army, sewn into the lining of his coat. At about ten o'clock
in the morning a herd of cattle fell into their hands. Immediately after
this they were engaged by a strong party of the enemy, who opened fire on
the advance guard from behind the wall of a cemetery. The leading
troopers under Lieutenant Count Trautsohn leapt the low wall and

charging across the graves fell on the panic-stricken enemy, most of whom escaped into the church and from there by the door of the sacristy into a dense wood. The twenty-seven prisoners said they were Neapolitan irregulars under Papal officers. The squadron lost one man killed. A party composed of Lance-corporal Wotrubek and Troopers Holl and Haindl rode round the wood and came upon a light howitzer drawn by two cart horses; they fell upon the gun-team, seized the horses by their bridles and turned them round. Lance-corporal Wotrubek, who was slightly wounded, was sent back to headquarters with a report of the encounters with the enemy and the other incidents of the day; the prisoners were marched off to the rear likewise, but the howitzer accompanied the squadron, which after supplying escorts for the prisoners was still seventy-eight strong.

As all the prisoners were emphatic in declaring that Milan had been entirely abandoned by enemy troops, both regulars and irregulars, and was also denuded of artillery and military stores, the captain himself, let alone the squadron, found the temptation to ride through this large, fine town lying defenceless in their path too strong to resist. The clocks struck twelve as the four trumpeters blared out the regimental call into the brazen glare of the sky, making a thousand windows rattle and flashing back on eight and seventy cuirasses and eight and seventy erect and naked blades; streets to right and streets to left became a turmoil of scurrying feet and astonished faces; blanched faces vanished with a curse into doorways, drowsy windows were thrown open by the bare arms of beauty, as on they rode past Santa Babila, San Fedele, San Carlo, past the world-famous marble Duomo, past San Satiro, San Giorgio, San Lorenzo, San Eustorgio, whose ancient west doors, all wide open, gave glimpses of candle-lighted altars through a haze of incense, of silver saints and bright-eyed Madonnas robed in silk brocade; from a thousand attics, sombre doorways and tiny cabins a shot might have rung out and still they saw nothing but half-grown girls and children, with white teeth and black hair; on they rode at the trot looking out on all this with eyes shining in a mask of blood and dust; in at the Porta Venezia, out by the Porta Ticinese the beautiful squadron rode through Milan.

Not far from the last-mentioned gateway, where a glacis extended, shadowed by some fine plane trees, Sergeant-major Anton Lerch thought he caught sight of a woman's face he knew at the ground-floor window of a newly built, bright yellow house. He turned round in the saddle to take another look; at the same moment his horse seemed to him to go lame in one of his fore feet, as if he had just got a stone in his shoe, and as he was bringing up the rear and could fall out without breaking the ranks he decided to dismount, but not before he had reined his horse half-way into the passage of the house in question. He had scarcely picked up the second of his bay's white stockinged feet to examine the hoof when a door in the passage near the entrance opened and a buxom young woman

in rather dishevelled morning attire appeared. Through the open door the
sergeant-major caught a glimpse of a sun-lit room with windows on to a
garden; also of some pots of basil and red geraniums on the window sill
and, further, a mahogany cupboard and a mythological group in biscuit
porcelain. At the same moment a pierglass revealed the opposite wall
to his sharp eyes; its whole extent was occupied by a large white bed and
a wallpapered door, through which a corpulent, clean-shaven elderly man
was in the act of retreating.

Meanwhile, the woman's name came back into his head and with it a lot
else: that she was the widow or divorced wife of a Croat paymaster-
sergeant; that nine or ten years before in Vienna he had spent evenings
with her, often until late at night, in the company of another man, who
was at that time her lover; and while he thought of all this he tried to see
beneath her present fullness of figure the slender luxuriance it used to have.
But she, as she stood there, only smiled at him as if flattered and her Slav
smile drove the blood into his strong neck and up to his eyes, while a certain coyness in her way of accosting him, as well as her morning attire and
his glimpse into the bedroom, made him confused. Just then his dulled
eyes fell on a large fly crawling over the comb in her hair and just as he was
consciously thinking of nothing but how his hand, after flicking away the
fly, would come to rest on the warm white coolness of the nape of her
neck, the thought of the day's fights and other happenings rushed through
him and he pulled her head clumsily forward and said: "Vuic,"—her name
had never once passed his lips for ten years and her Christian name he had
entirely forgotten—"in a week we're moving in and then my billet will be
there," and he pointed to the half-open door. As he spoke he heard several doors in the house shutting and then felt a mute pull on the reins,
which became a strong tug as his horse neighed loudly after its companions.
He mounted and trotted after the squadron without having had from
Vuic any answer but an embarrassed smile as her head was bent back on
her neck. But he had said enough to make his meaning plain.

As the sergeant-major rode, now at a slower pace, beside the column
beneath the oppressive metallic glare of the sky with his eyes blinded by
the cloud of dust that accompanied them, his fancy dwelt more and
more closely on the room with the mahogany furniture and the pot of
basil and, at the same time, he conjured up an atmosphere of civil life with
just a dash or tinge of military service, an atmosphere of comfort and
pleasant brutality without duties, a slippered existence, with the basket
hilt of his sabre protruding from the left pocket of his dressing-gown. The
clean-shaven, corpulent man, who had vanished through the wallpapered
door, a cross between a priest and a pensioned-off butler, played an important part in this dream, almost more important than the lovely broad
bed and Vuic's beautiful white skin. *First* the clean-shaven man took the
part of an obsequious friend on a confidential footing, who retailed society

tittle-tattle and was sent out for tobacco and capons; next he was pushed to the wall, forced to pay hush-money, mixed up in every sort of intrigue, a Piedmontese agent, a popish cook, a go-between, an owner of suspicious houses with dark rooms giving onto gardens, where conspirators hatched their plots, and grew like a sponge to gigantic proportions, a barrel of a man in whom you could pierce twenty bung-holes and draw off gold instead of blood.

The patrol met with no adventures during the afternoon and there was nothing to interfere with the sergeant-major's day-dreaming. He was obsessed by a thirst for unforeseen windfalls, for gratuities, for pockets bulging with unawaited ducats. For the thought of the moment when for the first time he was to set foot in the room with the mahogany furniture was the prick in his flesh that set him tingling with a thousand wishes and covetous desires.

Towards evening, when after a halt to feed and partly rest the horses the column swung round with the intention of pressing on to Lodi and the Adda bridge, where, however, there was good reason to expect that they would make contact with the enemy, the sergeant-major caught sight of a village, with a half-ruinous church tower, lying off the road in a hollow already shadowed by the dusk. It aroused his suspicions so enticingly that he beckoned to Troopers Holl and Scarmolin to follow him and, leaving the squadron's line of march, made for the village, hoping to drop right on an enemy general and his handful of men, to make a surprise attack, or in some way or another to earn a quite exceptional reward: such was the heated state of his imagination. When he was close to the wretched and apparently deserted little place he ordered Scarmolin to skirt the houses to the right and Holl those to the left, while he himself, pistol in hand, proposed to gallop straight through the middle of it. But soon, finding himself on hard flagstones, over which, to make it worse, some sort of slippery grease had been spilt, he had to rein his horse in to a walk. The village was as still as death: not a child, not a bird, not a breath of air. To right and left were dirty hovels, whose walls had shed their plaster, and on the naked bricks obscenities were scrabbled in charcoal; and looking through the bare door-posts the sergeant-major saw now and then a comatose, half-naked form prostrate on a bed or limping across the room as though with a hip out of joint. His horse moved with difficulty, bringing his hind legs forward as heavily as if they were of lead. He turned in the saddle to look down at the shoes of its hind feet and just as he straightened himself again a female, whose face he could not see, passed immediately in front of his horse. She was only half clothed; her torn and dirty skirt of flowered silk trailed in the gutter, her bare feet were in dirty slippers; she passed so close in front of the horse that the breath of its nostrils stirred the greasily shining knot of hair that hung over her bare neck under an old straw hat; and yet she did not quicken her pace or get out of the horseman's way. From under a door sill on the left of the road two bleeding rats, with their teeth gripped in one another, rolled into the middle of the street, and the under one gave such a piercing scream that the horse stopped and with ears pricked stared snorting at the ground. The sergeant-major urged it on with a pressure of his knees and by this time the woman had vanished into the passage of a house without giving him time to see her face. A dog ran hurriedly out of the house next door with its head in the air, dropped a bone in the middle of the street and tried to bury it in a crevice between the paving stones. It was a white unclean bitch with hanging teats; she scratched at the ground with the fury of the damned, then seized the bone in her teeth and carried it a little way further. As she was beginning to dig again three other dogs joined her: two of them were puppies, with weak joints and flabby skin; unable to bark or bite, they pulled at each other's lips with their blunt teeth. The third was a light-fawn greyhound, whose body was so blown out that it could hardly drag itself along on its four thin legs. Its head looked far too small for its body, which was distended as tightly as a drum; in its small restless eyes there was a terrible expression of pain and uneasiness. The next moment two more dogs came running up: one was lean and white; it had a hideous look of insensate greed in its inflamed eyes, which had trickles of black running from them; the other was a mongrel dachshund on long legs. It raised its head and looked at the sergeant-major. Its eyes were unutterably tired and sad. The bitch meanwhile ran hither and thither in front of the horse in senseless haste; the two puppies snapped with feeble jaws at the horse's fetlocks and the greyhound dragged its horrible carcase at his heels. The bay was now almost at a standstill. But when his master, after trying to fire his pistol at one of the curs and finding it misfire, touched him with his spurs, he lurched heavily on. After a few paces, however, he came to a stop, for a cow, which a yokel was tugging along on a rope to the slaughter-house, barred the way. The cow, starting back in terror at the smell of blood and the sight of the freshly flayed hide of a black calf nailed up at the doorway, planted her feet firmly and blowing out her nostrils took a deep breath of the hazy sunset air. The yokel gave a tug at the rope and applied his stick, but before he got the beast to go on, she turned her mournful eyes and snatched a mouthful of the hay tied to the sergeant-major's saddle bow. The sergeant-major was now at the end of the village street; there were low, crumbling walls on each side of the road and he could see it stretching on beyond a stone bridge that crossed an apparently dry channel, but his mount moved so leadenly, as though scarcely able to put one foot before another, that every inch of the walls to right and left and every one of the millepedes and woodlice upon them moved past him at a laborious crawl; and it seemed to him that it had taken whole centuries to ride through this abhorrent village. Just then he heard a hollow, laboured gasp, which came from his horse's chest; but, as he could not at first believe it was his horse that made this strange noise, he looked all around him for the cause of it, first near at hand and then in the distance, and saw on the far side of the bridge and, as it happened, at the same distance from it as he was himself, a cuirassier of his own regiment advancing towards him, a sergeant-major mounted on a bay with white socks to its fore feet. Now he knew very well that in the whole squadron there was only one such horse, and that was the one that he himself bestrode at that very moment. He was still too far off to recognise the other rider, so he dug his spurs impatiently into his horse's sides and put him to a brisk trot; whereupon the other came on at the very same pace until only a stone's throw parted them, and now as the two horses, from opposite sides, each at the same moment, each with white stockinged fore feet, set foot on the bridge, the sergeant-major, seeing in a glassy stare that the other was himself, reined in his horse in a frenzy and put up his right hand with outspread fingers to ward the apparition off. Whereupon the other, checking his horse and raising his hand in the same manner, suddenly vanished; and as Troopers Holl and Scarmolin emerged unconcernedly from the dry ditch on either side, the squadron's trumpeter could be distinctly heard sounding the charge at no great distance across the pastures. The sergeant-major put his horse to a headlong gallop and breasting a rise saw the squadron already charging at the gallop towards a wood from which enemy horsemen, armed with pikes, were hurriedly deploying; saw, as he gathered up the four loose reins in his left hand and wound the sword-knot round his right, the fourth section detach itself from the squadron and check its speed; found himself suddenly amidst the thunder of hoofs, then in a cloud of dust, then face to face with the enemy; struck at a blue arm that levelled a pike at him; saw the captain's face close beside him with staring eyes and teeth grimly bared and next moment was wedged in among nothing but enemy faces and strange colours; dived into a mêlée of brandished steel, ran the nearest man through the neck and thrust him from the saddle, saw Trooper Scarmolin at his side laughing as he cleft the bridle-hand of one of the enemy with a blow that lodged deep in the horse's neck, felt the press about him give way and was suddenly alone at the edge of a small stream behind an enemy officer mounted on a grey horse. The officer put his horse at the stream, but the horse refused. He pulled him round with a jerk and, as he turned his young and very pale face, and also the mouth of a pistol, to the sergeant-major, he was run through the gullet by a sabre which had the whole weight of a galloping horse behind its small sharp point. The sergeant-major withdrew his sabre and seized the bridle rein of the grey at the very place where it had been grasped by the fingers of the fallen rider; and the horse stepped over his dying master as lightly and gracefully as a deer.

As the sergeant-major rode back with his beautiful prize, the sun, sinking to the horizon in thick haze, cast an unearthly glow over the pastures. Even where not a hoof-mark was to be seen there seemed to be whole pools of blood. There was a red light on the white uniforms and laughing faces; cuirasses and saddlecloths shone in the glow and brightest of all shone three small fig trees, on whose soft leaves the troopers wiped the blood from their swords. The captain halted near the red-stained trees and the trumpeter at his side put the trumpet, which seemed to have been dipped in a red juice, to his lips and blew the rally. The sergeant-major rode from troop to troop and found that the squadron had not lost a man and had captured nine horses. He rode up to the captain to make his report, still leading the grey, who threw up his head and capered and sniffed the air, like the beautiful, vain young animal he was. The captain scarcely listened to the report. He beckoned to Lieutenant Count Trautsohn, who thereupon dismounted and, taking with him six troopers, also on foot, unharnessed the captured light howitzer, which was halted behind the squadron's front. The gun was then hauled to one side by the six men and submerged in a small marshy backwater of the stream. The lieutenant then mounted again after giving the two team horses, who were now no longer needed, a slap on the hindquarters with the flat of his sword and silently resumed his position in front of the first troop. Meanwhile the squadron, which was drawn up in two ranks, showed signs, without any actual breach of discipline, of being affected by the excitement of four victorious engagements in one day; there were outbursts of smothered laughter and remarks were exchanged in undertones. The horses too were restless, particularly those between which the horses captured as booty from the enemy were standing. After the adventures of the day they all felt it cramping to be drawn up in parade order; their minds were on the victorious charge and they longed to ride again helter skelter upon a new enemy with drawn swords and to capture more horses as booty. At this moment Captain Baron Rofrano rode close along the squadron's front and raising his heavy eyelids from his rather sleepy blue eyes gave the order, clearly but without raising his voice: "All led horses to be let go." The squadron sat as though carved in stone. Only the grey at the sergeant-major's side stretched out his head until his nostrils almost touched the forehead of the horse on which the captain sat. The captain returned his sword and took one of his pistols from the holster; wiping a speck of dust from the shining barrel with the back of his bridle hand, he repeated the order in a louder voice and followed it up by counting: "One—two——" After counting two he fixed his heavy-lidded eye on the sergeant-major, who sat motionless in his saddle and stared him in the face. While Anton Lerch's steady and unblinking gaze, in which only now and then something doglike and submissive flickered up and vanished again, might express a sort of trust and devotion born of many years of military service, he was almost completely unconscious of the tremendous tension of this critical moment; for his consciousness was flooded by visions of luxury and ease quite foreign to his life and, from depths utterly unknown even to himself, there rose an animal rage against the man before him, who wanted to take away his horse. His face, his voice, his bearing, his whole being aroused a rage so terrible that it could only have ripened in secret from long years of close and daily association. But whether the captain experienced anything of the sort or whether this moment of stubborn insubordination seemed to him to condense the silent and pervasive danger inherent in all critical situations cannot be said. He raised his arm with a casual almost foppish air and, as he contemptuously lifted his upper lip and counted three, the shot rang out and the sergeant-major, hit in the forehead, reeled over on his horse's neck and fell to the ground between the bay and the grey.

But before his body hit the ground, all ranks, with a shake of the reins or the kick of a boot, had got rid of their prizes, and the captain, quietly restoring his pistol to the holster as he observed the quiver that ran through the squadron after his lightning stroke, could now put himself at its head again; for the enemy, as far as could be made out at that distance in the failing light, appeared to be rallying. The enemy, however, did not venture on a fresh attack and soon afterwards, when night had fallen, the patrol reached the southern outpost of their own army.

SEEDS

Sherwood Anderson

(1876–   )

H E WAS A SMALL MAN with a beard and was very nervous. I remember how the cords of his neck were drawn taut.

For years he had been trying to cure people of illness by the method called psychoanalysis. The idea was the passion of his life. "I came here because I am tired," he said dejectedly. "My body is not tired but something inside me is old and worn-out. I want joy. For a few days or weeks I would like to forget men and women and the influences that make them the sick things they are."

There is a note that comes into the human voice by which you may know real weariness. It comes when one has been trying with all his heart and soul to think his way along some difficult road of thought. Of a sudden he finds himself unable to go on. Something within him stops. A tiny explosion takes place. He bursts into words and talks, perhaps fool-ishly. Little side currents of his nature he didn't know were there run out and get themselves expressed. It is at such times that a man boasts, uses big words, makes a fool of himself in general.

And so it was the doctor became shrill. He jumped up from the steps where we had been sitting, talking and walked about. "You come from the West. You have kept away from people. You have preserved yourself—damn you! I haven't——" His voice had indeed become shrill. "I have entered into lives. I have gone beneath the surface of the lives of men and women. Women especially I have studied—our own women, here in America."

"You have loved them?" I suggested.

"Yes," he said. "Yes—you are right there. I have done that. It is the only way I can get at things. I have to try to love. You see how that is? It's the only way. Love must be the beginning of things with me."

I began to sense the depths of his weariness. "We will go swim in the lake," I urged.

"I don't want to swim or do any damn plodding thing. I want to run and shout," he declared. "For a while, for a few hours, I want to be like a dead leaf blown by the winds over these hills. I have one desire and one only—to free myself."

We walked in a dusty country road. I wanted him to know that I thought I understood, so I put the case in my own way.

When he stopped and stared at me I talked. "You are no more and no better than myself," I declared. "You are a dog that has rolled in offal, and because you are not quite a dog you do not like the smell of your own hide."

In turn my voice became shrill. "You blind fool," I cried impatiently. "Men like you are fools. You cannot go along that road. It is given to no man to venture far along the road of lives."

I became passionately in earnest. "The illness you pretend to cure is the universal illness," I said. "The thing you want to do cannot be done. Fool —do you expect love to be understood?"

We stood in the road and looked at each other. The suggestion of a sneer played about the corners of his mouth. He put a hand on my shoulder and shook me. "How smart we are—how aptly we put things!"

He spat the words out and then turned and walked a little away. "You think you understand, but you don't understand," he cried. "What you say can't be done can be done. You're a liar. You cannot be so definite without missing something vague and fine. You miss the whole point. The lives of people are like young trees in a forest. They are being choked by climbing vines. The vines are old thoughts and beliefs planted by dead men. I am myself covered by crawling creeping vines that choke me."

He laughed bitterly. "And that's why I want to run and play," he said.

"I want to be a leaf blown by the wind over hills. I want to die and be born again, and I am only a tree covered with vines and slowly dying. I am, you see, weary and want to be made clean. I am an amateur venturing timidly into lives," he concluded. "I am weary and want to be made clean. I am covered by creeping crawling things."

A woman from Iowa came here to Chicago and took a room in a house on the west-side. She was about twenty-seven years old and ostensibly she came to the city to study advanced methods for teaching music.

A certain young man also lived in the west-side house. His room faced a long hall on the second floor of the house and the one taken by the woman was across the hall facing his room.

In regard to the young man—there is something very sweet in his nature He is a painter but I have often wished he would decide to become a writer. He tells things with understanding and he does not paint brilliantly.

And so the woman from Iowa lived in the west-side house and came home from the city in the evening. She looked like a thousand other women one sees in the streets every day. The only thing that at all made her stand out among the women in the crowds was that she was a little lame. Her right foot was slightly deformed and she walked with a limp. For three months she lived in the house—where she was the only woman except the landlady—and then a feeling in regard to her began to grow up among the men of the house.

The men all said the same thing concerning her. When they met in the hallway at the front of the house they stopped, laughed and whispered. "She wants a lover," they said and winked. "She may not know it but a lover is what she needs."

One knowing Chicago and Chicago men would think that an easy want to be satisfied. I laughed when my friend—whose name is LeRoy—told me the story, but he did not laugh. He shook his head. "It wasn't so easy," he said. "There would be no story were the matter that simple."

LeRoy tried to explain. "Whenever a man approached her she became alarmed," he said. Men kept smiling and speaking to her. They invited her to dinner and to the theatre, but nothing would induce her to walk in the streets with a man. She never went into the streets at night. When a man stopped and tried to talk with her in the hallway she turned her eyes to the floor and then ran into her room. Once a young drygoods clerk who lived there induced her to sit with him on the steps before the house.

He was a sentimental fellow and took hold of her hand. When she began to cry he was alarmed and arose. He put a hand on her shoulder and tried to explain, but under the touch of his fingers her whole body shook with terror. "Don't touch me," she cried, "don't let your hands touch me!" She began to scream and people passing in the street stopped to listen. The drygoods clerk was alarmed and ran upstairs to his own room. He bolted the door and stood listening. "It is a trick," he declared in a trembling voice. "She is trying to make trouble. I did nothing to her. It was an accident and anyway what's the matter? I only touched her arm with my fingers."

Perhaps a dozen times LeRoy has spoken to me of the experience of the Iowa woman in the west-side house. The men there began to hate her. Although she would have nothing to do with them she would not let them alone. In a hundred ways she continually invited approaches that when made she repelled. When she stood naked in the bathroom facing the hallway where the men passed up and down she left the door slightly ajar. There was a couch in the living room downstairs, and when men were present she would sometimes enter and without saying a word throw herself down before them. On the couch she lay with lips drawn slightly apart. Her eyes stared at the ceiling. Her whole physical being seemed to be waiting for something. The sense of her filled the room. The men standing about pretended not to see. They talked loudly. Embarrassment took possession of them and one by one they crept quietly away.

One evening the woman was ordered to leave the house. Someone, perhaps the drygoods clerk, had talked to the landlady and she acted at once. "If you leave tonight I shall like it that much better," LeRoy heard the elder woman's voice saying. She stood in the hallway before the Iowa woman's room. The landlady's voice rang through the house.

LeRoy the painter is tall and lean and his life has been spent in devotion to ideas. The passions of his brain have consumed the passions of his body. His income is small and he has not married. Perhaps he has never had a sweetheart. He is not without physical desire but he is not primarily concerned with desire.

On the evening when the Iowa woman was ordered to leave the west-side house, she waited until she thought the landlady had gone downstairs, and then went into LeRoy's room. It was about eight o'clock and he sat by a window reading a book. The woman did not knock but opened the door. She said nothing but ran across the floor and knelt at his feet. LeRoy said that her twisted foot made her run like a wounded bird, that her eyes were burning and that her breath came in little gasps. "Take me," she said, putting her face down upon his knees and trembling violently. "Take me quickly. There must be a beginning to things. I can't stand the waiting. You must take me at once."

You may be quite sure LeRoy was perplexed by all this. From what he has said I gathered that until that evening he had hardly noticed the woman. I suppose that of all the men in the house he had been the most indifferent to her. In the room something happened. The landlady followed the woman when she ran to LeRoy, and the two women confronted him. The woman from Iowa knelt trembling and frightened at his feet. The landlady was indignant. LeRoy acted on impulse. An inspiration came to him. Putting his hand on the kneeling woman's shoulder he shook her violently. "Now behave yourself," he said quickly. "I will keep my promise." He turned to the landlady and smiled. "We have been engaged to be married," he said. "We have quarrelled. She came here to be near me. She has been unwell and excited. I will take her away. Please don't let yourself be annoyed. I will take her away."

When the woman and LeRoy got out of the house she stopped weeping and put her hand into his. Her fears had all gone away. He found a room for her in another house and then went with her into a park and sat on a bench.

Everything LeRoy has told me concerning this woman strengthens my belief in what I said to the man that day in the mountains. You cannot venture along the road of lives. On the bench he and the woman talked until midnight and he saw and talked with her many times later. Nothing came of it. She went back, I suppose, to her place in the West.

In the place from which she had come the woman had been a teacher of music. She was one of four sisters, all engaged in the same sort of work and, LeRoy says, all quiet capable women. Their father had died when the eldest girl was not yet ten, and five years later the mother died also. The girls had a house and a garden.

In the nature of things I cannot know what the lives of the women were like but of this one may be quite certain—they talked only of women's affairs, thought only of women's affairs. No one of them ever had a lover. For years no man came near the house.

Of them all only the youngest, the one who came to Chicago, was visibly affected by the utterly feminine quality of their lives. It did something to her. All day and every day she taught music to young girls and then went home to the women. When she was twenty-five she began to think and to dream of men. During the day and through the evening she talked with women of women's affairs, and all the time she wanted desperately to be loved by a man. She went to Chicago with that hope in mind. LeRoy explained her attitude in the matter and her strange behavior in the westside house by saying she had thought too much and acted too little. "The life force within her became decentralized," he declared. "What she wanted she could not achieve. The living force within could not find expression. When it could not get expressed in one way it took another. Sex spread itself out over her body. It permeated the very fibre of her being. At the last she was sex personified, sex become condensed and impersonal. Certain words, the touch of a man's hand, sometimes even the sight of a man passing in the street did something to her."

Yesterday I saw LeRoy and he talked to me again of the woman and her strange and terrible fate.

We walked in the park by the lake. As we went along the figure of the woman kept coming into my mind. An idea came to me.

"You might have been her lover," I said. "That was possible. She was not afraid of you."

LeRoy stopped. Like the doctor who was so sure of his ability to walk into lives he grew angry and scolded. For a moment he stared at me and then a rather odd thing happened. Words said by the other man in the dusty road in the hills came to LeRoy's lips and were said over again. The suggestion of a sneer played about the corners of his mouth. "How smart we are. How aptly we put things," he said.

The voice of the young man who walked with me in the park by the lake in the city became shrill. I sensed the weariness in him. Then he laughed and said quietly and softly, "It isn't so simple. By being sure of yourself you are in danger of losing all of the romance of life. You miss the whole point. Nothing in life can be settled so definitely. The woman—you see—was like a young tree choked by a climbing vine. The thing that wrapped her about had shut out the light. She was a grotesque as many trees in the forest are grotesques. Her problem was such a difficult one that thinking of it has changed the whole current of my life. At first I was like you. I was quite sure. I thought I would be her lover and settle the matter."

LeRoy turned and walked a little away. Then he came back and took hold of my arm. A passionate earnestness took possession of him. His voice trembled. "She needed a lover, yes, the men in the house were quite right about that," he said. "She needed a lover and at the same time a lover was not what she needed. The need of a lover was, after all, a quite secondary thing. She needed to be loved, to be long and quietly and patiently loved. To be sure she is a grotesque, but then all the people in the world are grotesques. We all need to be loved. What would cure her would cure the rest of us also. The disease she had is, you see, universal. We all want to be loved and the world has no plan for creating our lovers."

LeRoy's voice dropped and he walked beside me in silence. We turned away from the lake and walked under trees. I looked closely at him. The cords of his neck were drawn taut. "I have seen under the shell of life and I am afraid," he mused. "I am myself like the woman. I am covered with creeping crawling vine-like things. I cannot be a lover. I am not subtle or patient enough. I am paying old debts. Old thoughts and beliefs—seeds planted by dead men—spring up in my soul and choke me."

For a long time we walked and LeRoy talked, voicing the thoughts that came into his mind. I listened in silence. His mind struck upon the refrain voiced by the man in the mountains. "I would like to be a dead dry thing," he muttered looking at the leaves scattered over the grass. "I would like to be a leaf blown away by the wind." He looked up and his eyes turned to where among the trees we could see the lake in the distance. "I am weary and want to be made clean. I am a man covered by creeping crawling things. I would like to be dead and blown by the wind over limitless waters," he said. "I want more than anything else in the world to be clean."

THE OTHER WOMAN

Sherwood Anderson

(1876–   )

I AM IN LOVE with my wife," he said—a superfluous remark, as I had not questioned his attachment to the woman he had married. We walked for ten minutes and then he said it again. I turned to look at him. He began to talk and told me the tale I am now about to set down.

The thing he had on his mind happened during what must have been the most eventful week of his life. He was to be married on Friday afternoon. On Friday of the week before he got a telegram announcing his appointment to a government position. Something else happened that made him very proud and glad. In secret he was in the habit of writing verses and during the year before several of them had been printed in poetry magazines. One of the societies that give prizes for what they think the best poems published during the year put his name at the head of its list. The story of his triumph was printed in the newspapers of his home city and one of them also printed his picture.

As might have been expected he was excited and in a rather highly strung nervous state all during that week. Almost every evening he went to call on his fiancée, the daughter of a judge. When he got there the house was filled with people and many letters, telegrams and packages were being received. He stood a little to one side and men and women kept coming up to speak to him. They congratulated him upon his success in getting the government position and on his achievement as a poet. Everyone seemed to be praising him and when he went home and to bed he could not sleep. On Wednesday evening he went to the theatre and it seemed to him that people all over the house recognized him. Everyone nodded and smiled. After the first act five or six men and two women left their seats to gather about him. A little group was formed. Strangers sitting along the same row of seats stretched their necks and looked. He had never received so much attention before, and now a fever of expectancy took possession of him.

As he explained when he told me of his experience, it was for him an altogether abnormal time. He felt like one floating in air. When he got into bed after seeing so many people and hearing so many words of praise his head whirled round and round. When he closed his eyes a crowd of people invaded his room. It seemed as though the minds of all the people of his city were centred on himself. The most absurd fancies took possession of him. He imagined himself riding in a carriage through the streets of a city. Windows were thrown open and people ran out at the doors of houses. "There he is. That's him," they shouted, and at the words a glad cry arose. The carriage drove into a street blocked with people. A hundred thousand pairs of eyes looked up at him. "There you are! What a fellow you have managed to make of yourself!" the eyes seemed to be saying.

My friend could not explain whether the excitement of the people was due to the fact that he had written a new poem or whether, in his new government position, he had performed some notable act. The apartment where he lived at that time was on a street perched along the top of a cliff far out at the edge of his city, and from his bedroom window he could look down over trees and factory roofs to a river. As he could not sleep and as the fancies that kept crowding in upon him only made him more excited, he got out of bed and tried to think.

As would be natural under such circumstances, he tried to control his thoughts, but when he sat by the window and was wide awake a most unexpected and humiliating thing happened. The night was clear and fine. There was a moon. He wanted to dream of the woman who was to be his wife, to think out lines for noble poems or make plans that would affect his career. Much to his surprise his mind refused to do anything of the sort.

At a corner of the street where he lived there was a small cigar store and newspaper stand run by a fat man of forty and his wife, a small active woman with bright grey eyes. In the morning he stopped there to buy a paper before going down to the city. Sometimes he saw only the fat man, but often the man had disappeared and the woman waited on him. She was, as he assured me at least twenty times in telling me his tale, a very ordinary person with nothing special or notable about her, but for some reason he could not explain, being in her presence stirred him profoundly. During that week in the midst of his distraction she was the only person he knew who stood out clear and distinct in his mind. When he wanted so much to think noble thoughts he could think only of her. Before he knew what was happening his imagination had taken hold of the notion of having a love affair with the woman.

"I could not understand myself," he declared, in telling me the story. "At night, when the city was quiet and when I should have been asleep, I thought about her all the time. After two or three days of that sort of thing the consciousness of her got into my daytime thoughts. I was terribly muddled. When I went to see the woman who is now my wife I found that my love for her was in no way affected by my vagrant thoughts. There was but one woman in the world I wanted to live with and to be my comrade in undertaking to improve my own character and my position in the world, but for the moment, you see, I wanted this other woman to be in my arms. She had worked her way into my being. On all sides people were saying I was a big man who would do big things, and there I was. That evening when I went to the theatre I walked home because I knew I would be unable to sleep, and to satisfy the annoying impulse in myself I went and stood on the sidewalk before the tobacco shop. It was a two-story building, and I knew the woman lived upstairs with her husband. For a long time I stood in the darkness with my body pressed against the wall of the building, and then I thought of the two of them up there and no doubt in bed together. That made me furious.

"Then I grew more furious with myself. I went home and got into bed, shaken with anger. There are certain books of verse and some prose writings that have always moved me deeply, and so I put several books on a table by my bed.

"The voices in the books were like the voices of the dead. I did not hear them. The printed words would not penetrate into my consciousness. I tried to think of the woman I loved, but her figure had also become something far away, something with which I for the moment seemed to have nothing to do. I rolled and tumbled about in the bed. It was a miserable experience.

"On Thursday morning I went into the store. There stood the woman alone. I think she knew how I felt. Perhaps she had been thinking of me as I had been thinking of her. A doubtful hesitating smile played about the corners of her mouth. She had on a dress made of cheap cloth and there was a tear on the shoulder. She must have been ten years older than myself. When I tried to put my pennies on the glass counter, behind which she stood, my hand trembled so that the pennies made a sharp rattling noise. When I spoke the voice that came out of my throat did not sound like anything that had ever belonged to me. It barely arose above a thick whisper. 'I want you,' I said. 'I want you very much. Can't you run away from your husband? Come to me at my apartment at seven tonight.'

"The woman did come to my apartment at seven. That morning she didn't say anything at all. For a minute perhaps we stood looking at each other. I had forgotten everything in the world but just her. Then she nodded her head and I went away. Now that I think of it I cannot remember a word I ever heard her say. She came to my apartment at seven and it was dark. You must understand this was in the month of October. I had not lighted a light and I had sent my servant away.

"During that day I was no good at all. Several men came to see me at my office, but I got all muddled up in trying to talk with them. They attributed my rattle-headedness to my approaching marriage and went away laughing.

"It was on that morning, just the day before my marriage, that I got a long and very beautiful letter from my fiancée. During the night before she also had been unable to sleep and had got out of bed to write the letter. Everything she said in it was very sharp and real, but she herself, as a living thing, seemed to have receded into the distance. It seemed to me that she was like a bird, flying far away in distant skies, and that I was like a perplexed bare-footed boy standing in the dusty road before a farm house and looking at her receding figure. I wonder if you will understand what I mean?

"In regard to the letter. In it she, the awakening woman, poured out her heart. She of course knew nothing of life, but she was a woman. She lay, I suppose, in her bed feeling nervous and wrought up as I had been doing. She realized that a great change was about to take place in her life and was glad and afraid too. There she lay thinking of it all. Then she got out of bed and began talking to me on the bit of paper. She told me how afraid she was and how glad too. Like most young women she had heard things whispered. In the letter she was very sweet and fine. 'For a long time, after we are married, we will forget we are a man and woman,' she wrote. 'We will be human beings. You must remember that I am ignorant and often I will be very stupid. You must love me and be very patient and kind. When I know more, when after a long time you have taught me the way of life, I will try to repay you. I will love you tenderly and passionately. The possibility of that is in me or I would not want to marry at all. I am afraid but I am also happy. O, I am so glad our marriage time is near at hand!'

"Now you see clearly enough what a mess I was in. In my office, after I had read my fiancée's letter, I became at once very resolute and strong. I remember that I got out of my chair and walked about, proud of the fact that I was to be the husband of so noble a woman. Right away I felt concerning her as I had been feeling about myself before I found out what a weak thing I was. To be sure I took a strong resolution that I would not be weak. At nine that evening I had planned to run in to see my fiancée. 'I'm all right now', I said to myself. 'The beauty of her character has saved me from myself. I will go home now and send the other woman away.' In the morning I had telephoned to my servant and told him that I did not want him to be at the apartment that evening and I now picked up the telephone to tell him to stay at home.

"Then a thought came to me. 'I will not want him there in any event,' I told myself. 'What will he think when he sees a woman coming in my place on the evening before the day I am to be married?' I put the telephone down and prepared to go home. 'If I want my servant out of the apartment it is because I do not want him to hear me talk with the woman. I cannot be rude to her. I will have to make some kind of an explanation, I said to myself.

"The woman came at seven o'clock, and, as you may have guessed, I let her in and forgot the resolution I had made. It is likely I never had any intention of doing anything else. There was a bell on my door, but she did not ring, but knocked very softly. It seems to me that everything she did that evening was soft and quiet, but very determined and quick. Do I make myself clear? When she came I was standing just within the door where I had been standing and waiting for a half hour. My hands were trembling as they had trembled in the morning when her eyes looked at me and when I tried to put the pennies on the counter in the store. When I opened the door she stepped quickly in and I took her into my arms. We stood together in the darkness. My hands no longer trembled. I felt very happy and strong.

"Although I have tried to make everything clear I have not told you what the woman I married is like. I have emphasized, you see, the other woman. I make the blind statement that I love my wife, and to a man of your shrewdness that means nothing at all. To tell the truth, had I not started to speak of this matter I would feel more comfortable. It is inevitable that I give you the impression that I am in love with the tobacconist's wife. That's not true. To be sure I was very conscious of her all during the week before my marriage, but after she had come to me at my apartment she went entirely out of my mind.

"Am I telling the truth? I am trying very hard to tell what happened to me. I am saying that I have not since that evening thought of the woman who came to my apartment. Now, to tell the facts of the case, that is not true. On that evening I went to my fiancée at nine, as she had asked me to do in her letter. In a kind of way I cannot explain the other woman went with me. This is what I mean—you see I had been thinking that if anything happened between me and the tobacconist's wife I would not be able to go through with my marriage. 'It is one thing or the other with me,' I had said to myself.

"As a matter of fact I went to see my beloved on that evening filled with a new faith in the outcome of our life together. I am afraid I muddle this matter in trying to tell it. A moment ago I said the other woman, the tobacconist's wife, went with me. I do not mean she went in fact. What I am trying to say is that something of her faith in her own desires and her courage in seeing things through went with me. Is that clear to you? When I got to my fiancée's house there was a crowd of people standing about. Some were relatives from distant places I had not seen before. She looked up quickly when I came into the room. My face must have been radiant. I never saw her so moved. She thought her letter had affected me deeply, and of course it had. Up she jumped and ran to meet me. She was like a glad child. Right before the people who turned and looked inquiringly at us, she said the thing that was in her mind. 'O, I am so happy,' she cried. 'You have understood. We will be two human beings. We will not have to be husband and wife.'

"As you may suppose everyone laughed, but I did not laugh. The tears came into my eyes. I was so happy I wanted to shout. Perhaps you understand what I mean. In the office that day when I read the letter my fiancée had written I had said to myself, 'I will take care of the dear little woman.' There was something smug, you see, about that. In her house when she cried out in that way, and when everyone laughed, what I said to myself was something like this: 'We will take care of ourselves.' I whispered something of the sort into her ears. To tell you the truth I had come down off my perch. The spirit of the other woman did that to me. Before all the people gathered about I held my fiancée close and we kissed. They thought it very sweet of us to be so affected at the sight of each other. What they would have thought had they known the truth about me God only knows!

"Twice now I have said that after that evening I never thought of the other woman at all. That is partially true but, sometimes in the evening when I am walking alone in the street or in the park as we are walking now, and when evening comes softly and quickly as it has come to-night, the feeling of her comes sharply into my body and mind. After that one meeting I never saw her again. On the next day I was married and I have never gone back into her street. Often however as I am walking along as I am doing now, a quick sharp earthy feeling takes possession of me. It is as though I were a seed in the ground and the warm rains of the spring had come. It is as though I were not a man but a tree.

"And now you see I am married and everything is all right. My marriage is to me a very beautiful fact. If you were to say that my marriage is not a happy one I could call you a liar and be speaking the absolute truth. I have tried to tell you about this other woman. There is a kind of relief in speaking of her. I have never done it before. I wonder why I was so silly as to be afraid that I would give you the impression I am not in love with my wife. If I did not instinctively trust your understanding I would not have spoken. As the matter stands I have a little stirred myself up. To-night I shall think of the other woman. That sometimes occurs. It will happen after I have gone to bed. My wife sleeps in the next room to mine and the door is always left open. There will be a moon to-night, and when there is a moon long streaks of light fall on her bed. I shall awake at midnight to-night. She will be lying asleep with one arm thrown over her head.

"What is it that I am now talking about? A man does not speak of his wife lying in bed. What I am trying to say is that, because of this talk, I shall think of the other woman to-night. My thoughts will not take the form they did during the week before I was married. I will wonder what has become of the woman. For a moment I will again feel myself holding her close. I will think that for an hour I was closer to her than I have ever been to anyone else. Then I will think of the time when I will be as close as that to my wife. She is still, you see, an awakening woman. For a moment I will close my eyes and the quick, shrewd, determined eyes of that other woman will look into mine. My head will swim and then I will quickly open my eyes and see again the dear woman with whom I have undertaken to live out my life. Then I will sleep and when I awake in the morning it will be as it was that evening when I walked out of my dark apartment after having had the most notable experience of my life. What I mean to say, you understand, is that, for me, when I awake, the other woman will be utterly gone."

EARLY SORROW

Thomas Mann

(1875-   )

TRANSLATED BY H. T. LOWE-PORTER

THE PRINCIPAL DISH at dinner had been croquettes made of turnip greens. So there follows a trifle, concocted out of one of those dessert powders we use nowadays, that taste like almond soap. Xaver, the youthful man-servant, in his outgrown striped jacket, white woollen gloves, and yellow sandals, hands it round, and the "big folk" take this opportunity to remind their father, tactfully, that company is coming to-day.

The "big folks" are two, Ingrid and Bert. Ingrid is brown-eyed, eighteen and perfectly delightful. She is on the eve of her exams; and will probably pass them, if only because she knows how to wind masters, and even head-masters, round her finger. She does not, however, mean to use her certificate once she gets it; having leanings towards the stage, on the ground of her ingratiating smile, her equally ingratiating voice, and a marked and irresistible talent for burlesque. Bert is blond and seventeen. He intends to get done with school somehow, anyhow, and fling himself into the arms of life. He will be a dancer, or a cabaret actor, possibly even a waiter—but not a waiter anywhere else save at "Cairo," the night club, whither he has once already taken flight, at five in the morning, and been brought back crest-fallen. Bert bears a strong resemblance to the youthful manservant, Xaver Kleinsgutl, of about the same age as himself; not because he looks common

—in features he is strikingly like his father, Professor Cornelius—but by reason of an approximation of types, due in its turn to far-reaching compromises in matters of dress and bearing generally. Both lads wear their heavy hair very long on top, with a cursory parting in the middle; and give their heads the same characteristic toss to throw it off the forehead. When one of them leaves the house, by the garden gate, bareheaded in all weathers, in a blouse coquettishly girt with a leather strap, and sheers off bent well over with his head on one side; or else mounts his push-bike— Xaver makes free with his employers', of both sexes, or even, in acutely irresponsible mood, with the professor's own—Dr. Cornelius from his bedroom window cannot, for the life of him, tell whether he is looking at his son or his servant. Both, he thinks, look like young moujiks. And both are impassioned cigarette-smokers; though Bert has not the means to compete with Xaver, who smokes as many as thirty a day, of a brand named after a popular cinema star. The big folk call their father and mother the "old folk"—not behind their backs, but as a form of address and in all affection: "Hullo, old folks," they will say; though Cornelius is only forty-seven years old and his wife eight years younger. And the professor's parents, who lead in his household the humble and hesitant life of the veritably old, are on the big folk's lips the "ancients." As for the "little folk," Ellie and Snapper, who take their meals upstairs with blue-faced Ann—so-called because of her prevailing facial hue—Ellie and Snapper follow their mother's example and address their father by his first name, Abel. Unutterably comic it sounds, in its pert, confiding familiarity; particularly on the lips, in the sweet accents, of five-year-old Eleanor, who is the image of Frau Cornelius' baby pictures, and whom the professor loves above everything else in the world.

"Darling old thing," says Ingrid affably, laying her large but shapely hand on his, as he presides in proper middle-class style over the family table, with her on his left and the mother opposite: "Parent mine, may I ever so gently jog your memory, for you have probably forgotten: this is the afternoon we were to have our little jollification, our turkey-trot with eats to match. You haven't a thing to do but just bear up and not funk it; everything will be over by nine o'clock."

"Oh—ah!" says Cornelius, his face falling. "Good!" he goes on, and nods his head to show himself in harmony with the inevitable. "I only meant— is this really the day? Thursday, yes. How time flies! Well, what time are they coming?"

"Half-past four they'll be dropping in, I should say," answers Ingrid, to whom her brother leaves the major rôle in all dealings with the father. Upstairs, while he is resting, he will hear scarcely anything, and from seven to eight he takes his walk. He can slip out by the terrace if he likes.

"Tut!" says Cornelius deprecatingly, as who should say, "You exaggerate." But Bert puts in: "It's the one evening in the week Wanja doesn't have to play. Any other night he'd have to leave by half-past six, which would be painful for all concerned."

Wanja is Ivan Herzl, the celebrated young leading man at the Stadt-theater. Bert and Ingrid are on intimate terms with him, they often visit him in his dressing-room and have tea. He is an artist of the modern school, who stands on the stage in strange and, to the Professor's mind, utterly affected dancing attitudes, and shrieks lamentably. To a professor of history, all highly repugnant; but Bert has entirely succumbed to Herzl's influence, blackens the lower rim of his eyelids—despite painful but fruitless scenes with his father—and with youthful carelessness of the ancestral anguish declares that not only will be take Herzl for his model if he becomes a dancer, but in case he turns out to be a waiter at "Cairo" he means to walk precisely thus.

Cornelius slightly raises his brows and makes his son a little bow—in-dicative of the unassumingness and self-abnegation befitting his age. You could not call it a mocking bow, or suggestive in any special sense. Bert may refer it to himself, or equally to his so talented friend.

"Who else is coming?" next inquires the master of the house. They men-tion various people, names all more or less familiar, from the city, from the suburban colony, from Ingrid's school. They still have some telephon-ing to do, they say. They have to phone Max. This is Max Hergesell, an engineering student; Ingrid utters his name in the nasal drawl which ac-cording to her is the traditional intonation of all the Hergesells. She goes on to parody it in the most abandonedly funny and life-like way, and the parents laugh until they nearly choke over the wretched trifle. For even in these times when something funny happens people have to laugh.

From time to time the telephone bell rings in the Professor's study, and the big folk run across knowing it is their affair. Many people had to give up their telephones, the last time the price rose; but so far the Corneliuses have been able to keep theirs, just as they have kept their villa, which was built before the war, by dint of the salary Cornelius draws as Professor of History—a million marks, and more or less adapted to the chances and changes of post-war life. The house is comfortable, even elegant, though sadly in need of repairs that cannot be made for lack of materials, and at present disfigured by iron stoves with long pipes. Even so, it is still the proper setting of the upper middle class, though they themselves look odd enough in it, with their worn and turned clothing and altered way of life. The children, of course, know nothing else; to them it is normal and reg-ular, they belong by birth to the "villa proletariat." The problem of clothing troubles them not at all. They and their like have evolved a costume to fit the time, by poverty out of taste for innovation: in summer it consists of scarcely more than a belted linen smock and sandals. The middle-class parents find things rather more difficult.

The big folks' table napkins hang over their chair-backs, they talk with their friends over the telephone. These friends are the invited guests who have rung up to accept or decline or arrange: and the conversation is carried on in the jargon of the clan, full of slang and high spirits, of which the old folk understand hardly a word. These consult together meantime about the hospitality to be offered to the impending guests. The Professor displays a middle-class ambitiousness: he wants to serve a sweet—or something that looks like a sweet—after the Italian salad and brown bread sandwiches. But Frau Cornelius says that would be going too far. The guests would not expect it, she is sure—and the big folk, returning once more to their trifle, agree with her.

The mother of the family is of the same general type as Ingrid, though not so tall. She is languid, the fantastic difficulties of the housekeeping have broken and worn her. She really ought to go and take a cure, but feels incapable; the floor is always swaying under her feet, and everything seems upside down. She speaks of what is uppermost in her mind: the eggs, they simply must be bought to-day. Six thousand marks apiece they are, and just so many are to be had on this one day of the week at one single shop fifteen minutes' journey away. Whatever else they do, the big folk must go and fetch them immediately after luncheon, with Danny, their neighbour's son, who will soon be calling for them; and Xaver Kleinsgutl will don civilian garb and attend his young master and mistress. For no single household is allowed more than five eggs a week; therefore the young people will enter the shop singly, one after another, under assumed names, and thus wring twenty eggs from the shopkeeper for the Cornelius family. This enterprise is the sporting event of the week for all participants, not excepting the moujik Kleinsgutl, and most of all for Ingrid and Bert, who delight in misleading and mystifying their fellow-men, and would revel in the performance even if it did not achieve one single egg. They adore impersonating fictitious characters; they love to sit in a bus and carry on long life-like conversations in a dialect which they otherwise never speak, the most commonplace dialogue about politics and people and the price of food, while the whole bus listens open-mouthed to this incredibly ordinary prattle, though with a dark suspicion all the while that something is wrong somewhere. The conversation waxes ever more shameless, it enters into revolting detail about these people who do not exist. Ingrid can make her voice sound ever so common and twittering and shrill as she impersonates a shop girl with an illegitimate child, said child being a son with sadistic tendencies, who lately out in the country treated a cow with such unnatural cruelty that no Christian could have borne to see it. Bert nearly explodes at her twittering, but restrains himself and displays a grisly sympathy; he and the unhappy shop girl entering into a long stupid, depraved and shuddery conversation over the particular morbid cruelty involved; until an old gentleman opposite, sitting with his ticket folded between his index finger and his seal ring, can bear it no more and makes

public protest against the nature of the themes these young folk are discussing with such particularity. He uses the Greek plural: "themata."
Whereat Ingrid pretends to be dissolving in tears, and Bert behaves as
though his wrath against the old gentleman was with difficulty being held
in check and would probably burst out before long. He clenches his fists, he
gnashes his teeth, he shakes from head to foot; and the unhappy old gentleman, whose intentions had been of the best, hastily leaves the bus at the
next stop.

Such are the diversions of the big folk. The telephone plays a prominent
part in them: they ring up any and everybody—members of government,
opera singers, dignitaries of the Church—in the character of shop assistants,
or perhaps as Lord or Lady Doolittle. They are only with difficulty persuaded that they have the wrong number. Once they emptied their parents'
card-tray and distributed its contents among the neighbours' letter-boxes,
wantonly, yet not without enough impish sense of the fitness of things to
make it highly upsetting, God only knowing why certain people should
have called where they did.

Xaver comes in to clear away, tossing the hair out of his eyes. Now that
he has taken off his gloves you can see the yellow chain-ring on his left
hand. And as the Professor finishes his watery eight-thousand-mark beer
and lights a cigarette, the little folk can be heard scrambling down the
stair, coming, by established custom, for their after-dinner call on Father
and Mother. They storm the dining-room, after a struggle with the latch,
clutched by both pairs of little hands at once; their clumsy small feet
twinkle over the carpet, in red felt slippers with the socks falling down on
them. With prattle and shoutings each makes for his own place: Snapper
to Mother, to climb on her lap, boast of all he has eaten, and thump his
fat little tum; Ellie to her Abel, so much hers because she is so very much
his; because she consciously luxuriates in the deep tenderness—like all deep
feeling, concealing a melancholy strain—with which he holds her small
form embraced; in the love in his eyes as he kisses her little fairy hand or
the sweet brow with its delicate tracery of tiny blue veins.

The little folk look like each other, with the strong undefined likeness
of brother and sister. In clothing and hair-cut they are twins. Yet they are
sharply distinguished after all, and quite on sex lines. It is a little Adam and
a little Eve. Not only is Snapper the sturdier and more compact, he appears
consciously to emphasise his four-year-old masculinity in speech, manner
and carriage, lifting his shoulders and letting the little arms' hang down
quite like a young American athlete, drawing down his mouth when he
talks and seeking to give his voice a gruff and forthright ring. But all this
masculinity is the result of effort rather than natively his. Born and brought
up in these desolate, distracted times, he has been endowed by them with
an unstable and hypersensitive nervous system, and suffers greatly under
life's disharmonies. He is prone to sudden anger and outbursts of bitter

tears, stamping his feet at every trifle; for this reason he is his mother's special nursling and care. His round, round eyes are chestnut brown, and already inclined to squint, so that he will need glasses in the near future. His little nose is long, the mouth small—the father's nose and mouth they are, more plainly than ever since the Professor shaved his pointed beard and goes smooth-faced. The pointed beard had become impossible—even professors must make some concession to the changing times.

But the little daughter sits on her father's knee, his Eleonorchen, his little Eve, so much more gracious a little being, so much sweeter-faced than her brother—and he holds his cigarette away from her while she fingers his glasses with her minute and dainty hands. The lenses are divided for reading and distance, and each day they tease her curiosity afresh.

At bottom he suspects that his wife's partiality may have a firmer basis than his own: that Snapper's refractory masculinity perhaps is solider stuff than his own little girl's more explicit charm and grace. But the heart will not be commanded, that he knows; and once and for all his heart belongs to the little one, as it has since the day she came, since the first time he saw her. Almost always, when he holds her in his arms, he remembers that first time: remembers the sunny room in the Women's Hospital, where Ellie first saw the light, twelve years after Bert was born. He remembers how he drew near, the mother smiling the while, and cautiously put aside the canopy of the diminutive bed that stood beside the large one. There lay the little miracle among the pillows: so well-formed, so encompassed, as it were, with the harmony of sweet proportions, with little hands that even then, though so much tinier, were beautiful as now; with wide-open eyes blue as the sky and brighter than the sunshine—and almost in that very second he felt himself captured and held fast. This was love at first sight, love everlasting: a feeling unknown, unhoped for, unexpected—in so far as it could be a matter of conscious awareness; it took entire possession of him, and he understood, with joyous amazement, that this was for life.

But he understood more. He knows, does Dr. Cornelius, that there is something not quite right about this feeling, so unaware, so undreamed of, so involuntary. He has a shrewd suspicion that it is not by accident it has so utterly mastered him and bound itself up with his existence; that he had—even subconsciously—been preparing for it, or, more precisely, been prepared for it. There is, in short, something in him which at a given moment was ready to issue in such a feeling; and this something, highly extraordinarily to relate, is his essence and quality as a professor of history. Dr. Cornelius, however, does not actually say this, even to himself; he merely realises it, at odd times, and smiles a private smile. He knows that history professors do not love history because it is something that comes to pass, but only because it is something that *has* come to pass; that they hate a revolution like the present one, because they feel it is lawless, incoherent, irrelevant, in a word unhistoric; that their hearts belong to the coherent, disciplined, historic past. For the temper of timelessness, the temper of eternity—thus the scholar communes with himself, when he takes his walk by the river, before supper—that tempers brood over the past; and it is a temper much better suited to the nervous system of a history professor than are the excesses of the present. The past is immortalised, that is to say it is dead; and death is the root of all godliness and all abiding significance. Dr. Cornelius, walking alone in the dark, has a profound insight into this truth. It is this conservative instinct of his, his sense of the eternal, that has found in his love for his little daughter a way to save itself from the wounding inflicted by the times. For father love, and a little child on its mother's breast—are not these timeless, and so very, very holy and beautiful? Yet Cornelius, pondering there in the dark, descries something not perfectly right and good in his love. Theoretically, in the interests of science, he admits it to himself. There is something ulterior about it, in the nature of it: that something is hostility, hostility against the history of to-day, which is still in the making and thus not history at all, in behalf of the genuine history that has already happened, that is to say, death. Yes, passing strange though all this is, yet it is true; true in a sense, that is. His devotion to this priceless little morsel of life and new growth has something to do with death, it clings to death as against life; and that is neither right nor beautiful—in a sense. Though only the most fanatical asceticism could be capable, on no other ground than such casual scientific perception, of tearing this purest and most precious of feelings out of his heart.

He holds his darling on his lap and her slim rosy legs hang down. He raises his brows as he talks to her, tenderly, with a half-teasing note of respect, and listens enchanted to her high, sweet little voice calling him Abel. He exchanges a look with the mother, who is caressing her Snapper and reading him a gentle lecture. He must be more reasonable, he must learn self-control; to-day again, under the manifold exasperations of life, he has given way to rage and behaved like a howling dervish. Cornelius casts a mistrustful glance at the big folk now and then, too; he thinks it not unlikely they are not unaware of those scientific preoccupations of his evening walks. If such be the case they do not show it. They stand there, leaning their arms on their chair-backs, and, with a benevolence not untinctured with irony, look on at the parental happiness.

The children's frocks are of a heavy, brick-red stuff, embroidered in modern "arty" style. They once belonged to Ingrid and Bert and are precisely alike, save that little knickers come out beneath Snapper's smock. And both have their hair bobbed. Snapper's is a streaky blond, inclined to turn dark. It is bristly and sticky, and looks for all the world like a droll, badly-fitting wig. But Ellie's is chestnut brown, glossy and fine as silk, as pleasing as her whole little personality. It covers her ears—and these ears are not a pair, one of them being the right size, the other distinctly too large. Her father will sometimes uncover this little abnormality and exclaim over it as though he had never noticed it before, which both makes Ellie giggle and covers her with shame. Her eyes are now golden-brown, set far apart and with sweet gleams in them—such a clear and lovely look! The brows above are blond; the nose still unformed, with thick nostrils and almost circular holes; the mouth large and expressive, with a beautifully arching and mobile upper lip. When she laughs, dimples come in her cheeks, and she shows her teeth like loosely strung pearls. So far she has lost but one tooth, which her father gently twisted out with his handkerchief after it had grown very wobbling. During this small operation she had paled and trembled very much. Her cheeks have the softness proper to her years; but they are not chubby; indeed they are rather concave, due to her facial structure, with its somewhat prominent jaw. On one, close to the soft fall of her hair, is a downy freckle.

Ellie is not too well pleased with her looks—a sign that already she troubles about such things. Sadly she thinks it is best to admit it once for all, her face is "homely"; though the rest of her, "on the other hand," is not bad at all. She loves expressions like "on the other hand"; they sound choice and grownup to her, and she likes to string them together, one after the other: "very likely," "probably," "after all." Snapper is self-critical too, though more in the moral sphere: he suffers from remorse for his attacks of rage, and considers himself a tremendous sinner. He is quite certain that heaven is not for such as he; he is sure to go to "the bad place" when he dies, and no persuasions will convince him to the contrary—as that God sees the heart and gladly makes allowances. Obstinately he shakes his head, with the comic, crooked little peruke, and vows there is no place for him in heaven. When he has a cold he is immediately quite choked with mucus; rattles and rumbles from top to toe if you even look at him; his temperature flies up at once and he simply puffs. Nursey is pessimistic on the score of his constitution: such fat-blooded children as he might get a stroke any minute. Once she even thought she saw the moment at hand: Snapper had been in one of his berserker rages, and in the ensuing fit of penitence stood himself in the corner with his back to the room. Suddenly Nurse noticed that his face had gone all blue, far bluer, even, than her own. She raised the alarm, crying out that the child's all-too-rich blood had at length brought him to his final hour; and Snapper, to his vast astonishment, found himself, so far from being rebuked for evil-doing, encompassed in tenderness and anxiety—until it turned out that his colour was not caused by apoplexy but by the distempering on the nursery wall, which had come off on his tear-wet face.

Nursey has come downstairs too, and stands by the door, sleek-haired, owl-eyed, with her hands folded over her white apron, and a severely dignified manner born of her limited intelligence. She is very proud of the care and training she gives her nurslings and declares that they are "en-

veloping wonderfully." She has had seventeen suppurated teeth lately removed from her jaws, and been measured for a full set of symmetrical yellow ones in dark rubber gums; these now embellish her peasant face. She
is obsessed with the strange conviction that these teeth of hers are the subject of general conversation, that, as it were, the sparrows on the house-tops
chatter of them. "Everybody knows I've had a false set put in," she will say;
"there has been a great deal of foolish talk about them." She is much given
to dark hints and veiled innuendo: speaks for instance of a certain Dr.
Bleifuss, whom every child knows, and "there are even some in the house
who pretend to be him." All one can do with talk like this is charitably to
pass it over in silence. But she teaches the children nursery rhymes: gems
like

> "Puff, puff, here comes the train!
> Puff, puff, toot, toot,
> Away it goes again."

or that gastronomical jingle, so suited, in its sparseness, to the times, and
yet seemingly with a blitheness of its own:

> "Monday we begin the week,
> Tuesday there's a bone to pick.
> Wednesday we're half way through,
> Thursday what a great to-do!
> Friday we eat what fish we're able,
> Saturday we dance round the table.
> Sunday brings us pork and greens—
> Here's a feast for kings and queens!"

Also a certain four-line stanza with a romantic appeal, unutterable and
unuttered:

> "Open the gate, open the gate
> And let the carriage drive in.
> Who is it in the carriage sits?
> A lordly sir with golden hair."

Or, finally, that ballad about golden-haired Marianne who sat on a, sat on a,
sat on a stone, and combed out her, combed out her, combed out her hair;
and about bloodthirsty Rudolph, who pulled out a, pulled out a, pulled out
a knife—and his ensuing direful end. Ellie enunciates all these ballads
charmingly, with her mobile little lips, and sings them in her sweet little
voice—much better than Snapper. She does everything better than he does,
and he pays her honest admiration and homage, and obeys her in all things
except when visited by one of his attacks. Sometimes she teaches him, in-
structs him upon the birds in the picture-book and tells him their proper
names: "This is a chaffinch, Buddy, this is a bullfinch, this is a cowfinch."

He has to repeat them after her. She gives him medical instruction too, teaches him the names of diseases, such as infammation of the lungs, infammation of the blood, infammation of the air. If he does not pay attention and cannot say the words after her, she stands him in the corner. Once she even boxed his ears, but was so ashamed that she stood herself in the corner for a long time. Yes, they are fast friends, two souls with but a single thought, and have all their adventures in common. They come home from a walk and relate as with one voice that they have seen two moollies and a teenty-weenty baby calf. They are on familiar terms with the kitchen, which consists of Xaver and the ladies Hinterhofer, two sisters once of the lower middle class, who, in these evil days, are reduced to living "au pair" as the phrase goes and officiating as cook and housemaid for their board and keep. The little ones have a feeling that Xaver and the Hinterhofers are on much the same footing with their father and mother as they are themselves. At least sometimes, when they have been scolded, they go downstairs and announce that the master and mistress are cross. But playing with the servants lacks charm, compared with the joys of playing upstairs. The kitchen could never rise to the height of the games their father can invent. For instance there is "four gentlemen taking a walk." When they play it Abel will crook his knees until he is the same height with themselves, and go walking with them, hand in hand. They never get enough of this sport; they could walk round and round the dining-room a whole day on end, five gentlemen in all, counting the diminished Abel.

Then there is the thrilling cushion game. One of the children, usually Ellie, seats herself, unbeknownst to Abel, in his seat at table. Still as a mouse she awaits his coming. He draws near with his head in the air, descanting, in loud, clear tones, upon the surpassing comfort of his chair; and sits down on top of Ellie. "What's this, what's this?" says he. And bounces about, deaf to the smothered giggles exploding behind him. "Why have they put a cushion in my chair? And what a queer, hard, awkward-shaped cushion it is!" he goes on. "Frightfully uncomfortable to sit on!" And keeps pushing and bouncing about more and more on the astonishing cushion, and clutching behind him into the rapturous giggling and squeaking, until at last he turns round, and the game ends with a magnificent climax of discovery and recognition. They might go through all this a hundred times without diminishing by an iota its power to thrill.

To-day is no time for such joys. The imminent festivity disturbs the atmosphere, and besides there is work to be done, and, above all, the eggs to be got. Ellie has just time to recite "Puff, puff," and Cornelius to discover that her ears are not mates, when they are interrupted by the arrival of Danny, come to fetch Bert and Ingrid. Xaver, meantime, has exchanged his striped livery for an ordinary coat, in which he looks rather rough-and-ready, though as brisk and attractive as ever. So then Nursey and the children ascend to the upper regions, the Professor withdraws to his study to read, as always after dinner, and his wife bends her energies upon the sandwiches and salad that must be prepared. And she has another errand as well. Before the young people arrive she has to take her shopping basket and dash into town on her bicycle, to turn into provisions a sum of money she has in hand, which she dares not keep lest it lose all value.

Cornelius reads, leaning back in his chair, with his cigar between his middle and index fingers. First he reads Macaulay on the origin of the English public debt at the end of the seventeenth century: then an article in a French periodical on the rapid increase in the Spanish debt towards the end of the sixteenth. Both these for his lecture on the morrow. He intends to compare the astonishing prosperity which accompanied the phenomenon in England with its fatal effects a hundred years earlier in Spain, and to analyse the ethical and psychological grounds of the difference in results. For that will give him a chance to refer back from the England of William III, which is the actual subject in hand, to the time of Philip II and the counter-Reformation, which is his own special field. He has already written a valuable work on this period; it is much cited and got him his professorship. While his cigar burns out and gets strong, he excogitates a few pensive sentences in a key of gentle melancholy, to be delivered before his class next day: about the practically hopeless struggle carried on by the belated Philip against the whole trend of history: against the new, the kingdom-disrupting power of the Germanic ideal of freedom and individual liberty. And about the persistent, futile struggle of the aristocracy, condemned by God and rejected of man, against the forces of progress and change. He savours his sentences; keeps on polishing them while he puts back the books he has been using; then goes upstairs for the usual pause in his day's work, the hour with drawn blinds and closed eyes, which he so imperatively needs. But to-day, he recalls, he will rest under disturbed conditions, amid the bustle of preparations for the feast. He smiles to find his heart giving a mild flutter at the thought. Disjointed phrases on the theme of black-clad Philip and his times mingle with a confused consciousness that they will soon be dancing down below. For five minutes or so he falls asleep.

As he lies and rests he can hear the sound of the garden gate and the repeated ringing at the bell. Each time a little pang goes through him, of excitement and suspense, at the thought that the young people have begun to fill the floor below. And each time he smiles at himself again—though even his smile is slightly nervous, is tinged with the pleasurable anticipations people always feel before a party. At half-past four—it is already dark—he gets up and washes at the wash-hand stand. The basin has been out of repair for two years. It is supposed to tip, but has broken away from its socket on one side, and cannot be mended because there is nobody to mend it, neither replaced because no shop can supply another. So it has to be hung up above the vent and emptied by lifting in both hands and pouring out the water. Cornelius shakes his head over this basin, as he does several times a day—whenever, in fact, he has occasion to use it. He finishes his toilet with care, standing under the ceiling light to polish his glasses till they shine. Then he goes downstairs.

On his way to the dining-room he hears the gramophone already going, and the sound of voices. He puts on a polite, society air; at his tongue's end is the phrase he means to utter: "Pray don't let me disturb you," as he passes directly into the dining-room for his tea. "Pray don't let me disturb you"—it seems to him precisely the *mot juste:* towards the guests cordial and considerate, for himself a very bulwark.

The lower floor is lighted up, all the bulbs in the chandelier are burning save one that has burned out. Cornelius pauses on a lower step and surveys the entrance hall. It looks pleasant and cosy in the bright light, with its copy of Marée over the brick chimney-piece, its wainscoted walls—wainscoted in soft wood—and red-carpeted floor, where the guests stand in groups, chatting, each with his tea-cup and slice of bread-and-butter spread with anchovy paste. There is a festal haze, faint scents of hair and clothing and human breath come to him across the room, it is all characteristic, and familiar, and highly evocative. The door into the dressing-room is open, guests are still arriving.

A large group of people is rather bewildering at first sight. The Professor takes in only the general scene. He does not see Ingrid, who is standing just at the foot of the steps, in a dark silk frock with a pleated collar falling softly over the shoulders, and bare arms. She smiles up at him, nodding and showing her lovely teeth.

"Rested?" she asks, for his private ear. With a quite unwarranted start he recognises her, and she presents some of her friends.

"May I introduce Herr Zuber?" she says. "And this is Fräulein Plaichinger."

Herr Zuber is insignificant. But Fräulein Plaichinger is a perfect Germania, blonde and voluptuous, arrayed in floating draperies. She has a snub nose, and answers the Professor's salutation in the high, shrill pipe so many stout women have.

"Delighted to meet you," he says. "How nice of you to come! A classmate of Ingrid's, I suppose?"

And Herr Zuber is a golfing partner of Ingrid's. He is in business; he works in his uncle's brewery. Cornelius makes a few jokes about the thinness of the beer and professes to believe that Herr Zuber could easily do something about the quality if he would. "But pray don't let me disturb you," he goes on, and turns toward the dining-room.

"There comes Max," says Ingrid. "Max, you sweep, what do you mean by rolling up at this time of day?" For such is the way they talk to each other, offensively to an older ear: of social forms, of hospitable warmth, there is no faintest trace. They all call each other by their first names.

A young man comes up to them out of the dressing-room, and makes his bow: he has an expanse of white shirt-front and a little black string tie. He is as pretty as a picture, dark, with rosy cheeks, clean-shaven of course, but with just a sketch of side-whisker. Not a ridiculous or flashy beauty, not like a gypsy fiddler, but just charming to look at, in a winning, well-bred way, with kind dark eyes. He even wears his dinner-jacket a little awkwardly.

"Please don't scold me, Cornelia," he says; "it's the idiotic lectures." And Ingrid presents him to her father as Herr Hergesell.

Well, and so this is Herr Hergesell. He knows his manners, does Herr Hergesell, and thanks the master of the house quite ingratiatingly for his invitation, as they shake hands. "I certainly seem to have missed the bus," says he, jocosely. "Of course I have lectures to-day up to four o'clock; I would have; and after that I had to go home to change." Then he talks about his pumps, with which he has just been struggling in the dressing-room.

"I brought them with me in a bag," he goes on. "Mustn't tramp all over the carpet in our brogues—it's not done. Well, I was ass enough not to fetch along a shoe-horn, and I find I simply can't get in! What a sell! They are the tightest I've ever had, the numbers don't tell you a thing, and all the leather to-day is just cast iron. It's not leather at all. My poor finger"—he confidingly displays a reddened digit and once more characterises the whole thing as a "sell," and a putrid sell into the bargain. He really does talk just as Ingrid said he did, with a peculiar nasal drawl, not affectedly in the least, but merely because that is the way of all the Hergesells.

Dr. Cornelius says it is very careless of them not to keep a shoe-horn in the dressing-room, and displays proper sympathy with the mangled finger. "But now you *really* must not let me disturb you any longer," he goes on. *"Auf wiedersehen!"* And he crosses the hall into the dining-room.

There are guests there too, drinking tea, the family table is pulled out. But the Professor goes at once to his own little upholstered corner with the electric light bulb above it: the nook where he usually drinks his tea. His wife is sitting there talking with Bert and two other young men, one of them Herzl, whom Cornelius knows and greets; the other a typical "Wandervogel" named Möller, a youth who obviously neither owns nor cares to own the correct evening dress of the middle classes (in fact there is no such thing any more), nor to ape the manners of a gentleman (and, in fact, there is no such thing any more either). He has a wilderness of hair, horn spectacles, and a long neck, and wears golf stockings and a belted blouse. His regular occupation, the Professor learns, is banking, but he is by way of being an amateur folk-lorist, and collects folk songs from all localities and in all languages. He sings them, too, and at Ingrid's command has brought his guitar; it is hanging in the dressing-room in an oiled-cloth case. Herzl the actor is small and slight, but he has a strong growth of black beard, as you can tell by the thick coat of powder on his cheeks. His eyes are larger than life, with a deep and melancholy glow. He has put on rouge besides the powder—those dull carmine high-lights on the cheeks can be nothing but a cosmetic. "Queer," thinks the Professor. "You would think a man would be one thing or the other—not melancholic and use face paint at the same time. It's a psychological contradiction. How can a melancholy man rouge? But here we have a perfect illustration of the ab-normality of the artist soul-form. It can make possible a contradiction like this—perhaps it even consists in the contradiction. All very interesting— and no reason whatever for not being polite to him. Politeness is a primi-tive convention—and legitimate. . . . Do take some lemon, Herr Hofs-chauspieler!"

Court actors and court theatres—there are no such things any more, really. But Herzl relishes the sound of the title, notwithstanding he is a revolutionary artist. This must be another contradiction inherent in his soul-form; so, at least, the Professor assumes, and he is probably right. The flattery he is guilty of is a sort of atonement for his previous hard thoughts about the rouge.

"Thank you so much—it's really too good of you, sir," says Herzl, quite embarrassed. He is so overcome that he almost stammers; only his perfect enunciation saves him. His whole bearing towards his hostess and the master of the house is exaggeratedly polite. It is almost as though he has a bad conscience in respect of his rouge; as though an inward compulsion had driven him to put it on, but now, seeing it through the Professor's eyes, he disapproves of it himself, and thinks, by an air of humility toward the whole of unrouged society, to mitigate its effect.

They drink their tea and chat: about Möller's folk-songs, about Basque folk-songs and Spanish folk-songs; from which they pass to the new pro-duction of "Don Carlos" at the Stadttheater, in which Herzl plays the title-rôle. He talks about his own rendering of the part, and says he hopes his conception of the character has unity. They go on to criticise the rest of the cast, the setting and the production as a whole; and Cornelius is struck, rather painfully, to find the conversation trending towards his own special province, back to Spain and the counter-Reformation. He has done noth-ing at all to give it this turn, he is perfectly innocent; and hopes it does not look as though he had sought an occasion to play the professor. He wonders, and falls silent, feeling relieved when the little folk come up to the table. Ellie and Snapper have on their blue velvet Sunday frocks; they are permitted to partake in the festivities up to bedtime. They look shy and large-eyed as they say how-do-you-do to the strangers, and, under pressure, repeat their names and ages. Herr Möller does nothing but gaze at them solemnly, but Herzl is simply ravished. He rolls his eyes up to heaven and puts his hands over his mouth, he positively blesses them. It all, no doubt, comes from his heart; but he is so addicted to theatrical methods of making an impression and getting an effect, that both words and behaviour ring frightfully false. And even his enthusiasm for the little folk looks too much like part of his general craving to make up for the rouge on his cheeks.

The tea-table has meanwhile emptied of guests, and dancing is going on in the hall. The children run off, the Professor prepares to retire. "Go and enjoy yourselves," he says to Möller and Herzl, who have sprung from their chairs as he rises from his. They shake hands and he withdraws into his study, his peaceful kingdom, where he lets down the blinds, turns on the desk lamp, and sits down to his work.

It is work which can be done, if necessary, under disturbed conditions: nothing but a few letters and a few notes. Of course, Cornelius' mind wanders. Vague impressions float through it: Herr Hergesell's refractory pumps, the high pipe in that plump body of the Plaichinger female. As he writes, or leans back in his chair and stares into space, his thoughts go back to Herr Möller's collection of Basque folk-songs, to Herzl's posings and humility; to "his" Carlos and the court of Philip II. There is something strange, he thinks, about conversations. They are so ductile, they will go of their own accord in the direction of one's dominating interest. Often and often he has seen this happen. And while he is thinking, he is listening to the sounds next door—rather subdued, he finds them. He hears only voices, no sound of footsteps. The dancers do not glide or circle round the room; they merely walk about over the carpet, which does not hamper their movements in the least. Their way of holding each other is quite different and strange, and they move to the strains of the gramophone, to the weird music of the new world. He concentrates on the music and makes out that it is a jazz-band record, with various percussion instruments and the clack and clatter of castanets, which, however, are not even faintly suggestive of Spain, but merely jazz with the rest. No, not Spain. . . . His thoughts are back at their old round.

Half an hour goes by. It occurs to him it would be no more than friendly to go and contribute a box of cigarettes to the festivities next door. Too bad to ask the young people to smoke their own—though they have probably never thought of it. He goes into the empty dining-room and takes a box from his supply in the cupboard: not the best ones, nor yet the brand he himself prefers, but a certain long, thin kind he is not averse to getting rid of—after all, they are nothing but youngsters. He takes the box into the hall, holds it up with a smile, and deposits it on the mantel-shelf. After which he gives a look round and returns to his own room.

There comes a lull in dance and music. The guests stand about the room in groups, or round the table at the window, or seated in a circle by the fireplace. Even the built-in stairs, with their worn velvet carpet, are crowded with young folk as in an amphitheatre: Max Hergesell is there, leaning back with one elbow on the step above and gesticulating with his free hand as he talks to the shrill, voluptuous Plaichinger. The floor of the hall is nearly empty, save just in the centre: there, directly beneath the chandelier, the two little ones in their blue velvet frocks clutch each other in an awkward embrace, and twirl silently round and round, oblivious of all else. Cornelius, as he passes, strokes their hair, with a friendly word; it does not distract them from their small solemn preoccupation. But at his own door he turns to glance round and sees young Hergesell push himself off the stair by his elbow—probably because he noticed the Professor. He comes down into the arena, takes Ellie out of her brother's arms, and dances with her himself. It looks very comic, without the music, and he crouches down just as Cornelius does when he goes walking with the four gentlemen, holding the fluttered Ellie as though she were grown up, and taking little "shimmying" steps. Everybody watches with huge enjoyment, the gramophone is put on again, dancing becomes general. The Professor stands and looks with his hand on the door-knob. He nods and laughs; when he finally shuts himself into his study the mechanical smile still lingers on his lips.

Again he turns over pages by his desk lamp; takes notes, attends to a few simple matters. After a while he notices that the guests have forsaken the entrance hall for his wife's drawing-room, into which there is a door from his own study as well. He hears their voices, and the sounds of a guitar being tuned. Herr Möller, it seems, is to sing—and does so. He twangs the strings of his instrument, and sings in a powerful bass a ballad in a strange tongue, possibly Swedish. The Professor does not succeed in identifying it, though he listens attentively to the end, after which there is great applause. The sound is deadened by the portière that hangs over the dividing door. The young bank clerk begins another song. Cornelius goes softly in.

It is half-dark in the drawing-room; the only light is from the shaded standard lamp, beneath which Möller sits, on the divan, with his legs crossed, picking his strings. His audience is grouped easily about; as there are not enough seats, some stand, and more, among them many young ladies, are simply sitting on the floor with their hands clasped round their knees, or even with their legs stretched out before them. Hergesell sits thus, in his dinner jacket, next the piano, with Fräulein Plaichinger beside him. Frau Cornelius is holding both children on her lap, as she sits in her easy-chair opposite the singer. Snapper, the Bœotian, begins to talk loud and clear in the middle of the song, and has to be intimidated with hushings and finger-shakings. Never, never would Ellie allow herself to be guilty of such conduct. She sits there daintily erect and still on her mother's knee. The Professor tries to catch her eye and exchange a private signal with his little girl; but she does not see him. Neither does she seem to be looking at the singer. Her gaze is directed lower down.

Möller sings the "joli tambour":

"Sire, mon roi, donnez-moi votre fille,—"

They are all enchanted. "How good," Hergesell is heard to say, in the odd, nasally-condescending Hergesell tone. The next one is a beggar ballad, to a tune composed by young Möller himself; it elicits a storm of applause:

> "Gypsy lassie a-going to the fair
> Huzza!
> Gypsy laddie a-goin' to be there—
> Huzza, diddlety umpty dido!"

Laughter and high spirits, sheer reckless hilarity, reigns after this jovial ballad. "Frightfully good!" Hergesell comments again, as before. Follows another popular song, this time a Hungarian one; Möller sings it in its own outlandish tongue, and most effectively. The Professor applauds with ostentation. It warms his heart, and does him good, this outcropping of artistic, historic, and cultural elements all amongst the shimmying. He goes up to young Möller and congratulates him, talks about the songs and their sources, and Möller promises to lend him a certain annotated book of folk-songs. Cornelius is the more cordial because all the time, as fathers do, he has been comparing the parts and achievements of this young stranger with those of his own son, and being gnawed by envy and mortification. This young Möller, he is thinking, is a capable bank clerk (though about Möller's capacity he knows nothing whatever) and has this special gift besides, which must have taken talent and energy to cultivate. "And here is my poor Bert, who knows nothing and can do nothing, and thinks of nothing except playing the clown, without even talent for that!" He tries to be just; he tells himself that after all Bert has innate refinement; that probably there is a good deal more to him than there is to the successful Möller; that perhaps he has even something of the poet in him, and his dancing and table-waiting are due to mere boyish folly and the distraught times. But paternal envy and pessimism win the upper hand; when Möller begins another song, Dr. Cornelius goes back to his room.

He works as before, with divided attention, at this and that, while it gets on for seven o'clock. Then he remembers a letter he may just as well write, a short letter and not very important, but letter-writing is wonderful for the way it takes up the time, and it is almost half-past when he has finished. At half-past eight the Italian salad will be served; so now is the prescribed moment for the Professor to go out into the wintry darkness to post his letters, and take his daily quantum of fresh air and exercise. They are dancing again, and he will have to pass through the hall to get his hat and coat; but they are used to him now, he need not stop and beg them not to be disturbed. He lays away his papers, takes up the letters he has written, and goes out. But he sees his wife sitting near the door of his room, and pauses a little by her easy-chair.

She is watching the dancing. Now and then the big folk or some of their guests stop to speak to her; the party is at its height, and there are more onlookers than these two: blue-faced Ann is standing at the bottom of the stairs, in all the dignity of her limitations. She is waiting for the children, who simply cannot get their fill of these unwonted festivities, and watching over Snapper, lest his all-too-rich blood be churned to the danger point by too much twirling round. And not only the nursery but the kitchen takes an interest: Xaver and the two ladies Hinterhofer are standing by the pantry door looking on with relish. Fräulein Walburga, the elder of the two sunken sisters (the culinary section—she objects to being called a cook), is a whimsical, good-natured sort, brown-eyed, wearing glasses with thick circular lenses; the nosepiece is wound with a bit of rag to keep it from pressing on her nose. Fräulein Cecilia is younger, though not so precisely young either. Her bearing is as self-assertive as usual: this being her way of sustaining her dignity as a former member of the middle class. For Fräulein Cecilia feels acutely her descent into the ranks of domestic service. She positively declines to wear a cap or other badge of servitude; and her hardest trial is on the Wednesday evening when she has to serve the dinner while Xaver has his afternoon out. She hands the dishes with averted face and elevated nose—a fallen queen; and so distressing is it to behold her degradation that one evening when the little folk happened to be at table and saw her they both with one accord burst into tears. Such anguish is unknown to young Xaver. He enjoys serving, and does it with an ease born of practice as well as talent, for he was once a "piccolo." But otherwise he is a thorough-paced good-for-nothing and wind-bag—with quite distinct traits of character of his own, as his long-suffering employers are always ready to concede, but perfectly impossible and a bag of wind for all that. One must just take him as he is, they think, and not expect figs from thistles. He is the child and product of the disrupted times, a perfect specimen of his generation, follower of the revolution, bolshevist sympathiser. The Professor's name for him is the "minute-man," because he is always to be counted on in any sudden crisis, if only it address his sense of humour or love of novelty; and will display therein amazing readiness and resource. But he utterly lacks a sense of duty, and can as little be trained to the performance of the daily round and common task as some kinds of dog can be taught to jump over a stick. It goes so plainly against the grain that criticism is disarmed. One becomes resigned. On grounds that appealed to him as unusual and amusing he would be ready to turn out of his bed at any hour of the night. But he simply cannot get up before eight in the morning, he cannot do it, he will not jump over the stick. Yet all day long the evidence of this free and untrammelled existence, the sound of his mouth-organ, his joyous whistle, or his raucous but expressive voice lifted in song, rises to the hearing of the world above-stairs; and the smoke of his cigarettes fills the pantry. While the Hinterhofer ladies work he stands and looks on. Of a morning while the Professor is breakfasting, he tears the leaf off the study calendar

—but does not lift a finger to dust the room. Dr. Cornelius has often told him to leave the calendar alone, for he tends to tear off two leaves at a time, and thus to add to the general confusion. But young Xaver appears to find joy in this activity, and will not be deprived of it.

Again, he is fond of children, a winning trait. He will throw himself into games with the little folk in the garden, make and mend their toys with great ingenuity, even read aloud from their books—and very droll it sounds in his thick-lipped pronunciation. With his whole soul he loves the cinema; after an evening spent there he inclines to melancholy and yearning and talking to himself. Vague hopes stir in him that some day he may make his fortune in that gay world and belong to it by rights; hopes based on his shock of hair and his physical agility and daring. He likes to climb the ash tree in the front garden, mounting branch by branch to the very tip, and frightening everybody to death who sees him. Once there he lights a cigarette and smokes it as he sways to and fro, keeping a look out for a cinema director who might chance to come along and engage him.

If he changed his striped jacket for mufti, he might easily dance with the others, and no one would notice the difference. For the big folks' friends are rather anomalous in their clothing: evening dress is worn by a few, but it is by no means the rule. There is quite a sprinkling of guests, both male and female, in the same general style as Möller the ballad singer. The Professor is familiar with the circumstances of most of this young generation he is watching as he stands beside his wife's chair; he has heard them spoken of by name. They are students at the High School, or at the School of Applied Art; they lead, at least the masculine portion, that precarious and scrambling existence which is purely the product of the time. There is a tall, pale, spindling youth, the son of a dentist, who lives by speculation. From all the Professor hears, he is a perfect Aladdin. He keeps a car, treats his friends to champagne suppers, and showers presents upon them on every occasion, costly little trifles in mother-of-pearl and gold. So to-day he has brought gifts to the young givers of the feast: for Bert a gold lead-pencil, and for Ingrid a pair of earrings of barbaric size, great gold circlets that fortunately do not have to go through the little ear-lobe, but are fastened over it by means of a clip. The big folk come laughing to their parents to display these trophies; and the parents shake their heads even while they admire—Aladdin bowing over and over from afar.

The young people appear to be absorbed in their dancing—if the performance they are carrying out with so much still concentration can be called dancing. They stride across the carpet, slowly, according to some unfathomable prescript, strangely embraced; in the newest attitude, tummy advanced and shoulders high, waggling the hips. They do not get tired, because nobody could. There is no such thing as heightened colour, or heaving bosoms. Two girls may dance together, or two young men—it is all the same. They move to the exotic strains of the gramophone, played with the loudest needles to procure the maximum of sound: shimmeys, foxtrots, one-steps, double foxes, African shimmeys, Java dances and Creole polkas, the wild musky melodies follow one another, now furious, now languishing, a monotonous negro programme in unfamiliar rhythm, to a clacking, clashing and strumming orchestral accompaniment.

"What is that record?" Cornelius inquires of Ingrid, as she passes him by in the arms of the pale young speculator, with reference to the piece then playing, whose alternate languors and furies he finds comparatively pleasing and showing a certain resourcefulness in detail.

"'Prince of Pappenheim: Console thee, dearest child,'" she answers and smiles pleasantly back at him with her white teeth.

The cigarette smoke wreathes beneath the chandelier. The air is blue with a festal haze compact of sweet and thrilling ingredients, that stir the blood with memories of green-sick pains, and are particularly poignant to those whose youth—like the Professor's own—has been over-sensitive. . . . The little folk are still on the floor. They are allowed to stop up until eight—so great is their delight in the party. The guests have got used to their presence; in their own way, they have their place in the doings of the evening. They have separated, anyhow: Snapper revolves all alone in the middle of the carpet, in his little blue velvet smock; while Ellie is running after one of the dancing couples, trying to hold the man fast by his coat. It is Max Hergesell and Fräulein Plaichinger. They dance well, it is a pleasure to watch them. One has to admit that these mad modern dances, when the right people dance them, are not so bad after all—they have something quite taking. Young Hergesell is a capital leader, dances according to rule, yet with individuality. So it looks. With what aplomb can he walk backwards—when space permits! And he knows how to be graceful standing still in a crowd. And his partner supports him well, being unsuspectedly lithe and buoyant, as fat people often are. They look at each other, they are talking, paying no heed to Ellie, though others are smiling to see the child's persistence. Dr. Cornelius tries to catch up his little sweetheart, as she passes, and draw her to him. But Ellie eludes him, almost peevishly, her dear Abel is nothing to her now. She braces her little arms against his chest, and turns her face away with a persecuted look. Then escapes to follow her fancy once more.

The Professor feels an involuntary twinge. Uppermost in his heart is hatred for this party, with its power to intoxicate and estrange his darling child. His love for her—that not quite disinterested, not quite unexceptionable love of his—is easily wounded. He wears a mechanical smile, but his eyes have clouded, and he stares fixedly at a point in the carpet, between the dancers' feet.

"The children ought to go to bed," he tells his wife. But she pleads for another quarter of an hour; she has promised already, and they do love it so! He smiles again and shakes his head, stands so a moment and then goes across to the dressing-room, which is full of coats and hats and scarves and overshoes. He has trouble in rummaging out his own coat, and Max Hergesell comes out of the hall, wiping his brow.

"Going out, sir?" he asks, in Hergesellian accents, dutifully helping the older man on with his coat. "Silly business this, with my pumps," he says. "They pinch like hell. The brutes are simply too tight for me, quite apart from the bad leather. They press just here on the ball of my great toe"— he stands on one foot and holds the other in his hand—"it's simply unbearable. There's nothing for it but to take them off; my brogues will have to do the business. . . . Oh, let me help you, sir."

"Thanks," says Cornelius. "Don't trouble. Get rid of your own tormentors. . . . Oh, thanks very much!" For Hergesell has gone on one knee to snap the fasteners of his snow boots.

Once more the Professor expresses his gratitude; he is pleased and touched by so much sincere respect and youthful readiness to serve. "Go and enjoy yourself," he counsels. "Change your shoes, and make up for what you have been suffering. Nobody can dance in shoes that pinch. Good-bye, I must be off to get a breath of fresh air."

"I'm going to dance with Ellie now," calls Hergesell after him. "She'll be a first-rate dancer when she grows up, and that I'll swear to."

"Think so?" Cornelius answers, already half out. "Well, you are a connoisseur, I'm sure. Don't get curvature of the spine with stooping."

He nods again and goes. "Fine lad," he thinks as he shuts the door. "Student of engineering. Knows what he's bound for, got a good clear head, and so well set up and pleasant too." And again paternal envy rises, as he compares his poor Bert's status with this young man's, which he puts in the rosiest light that his son's may look the darker. Thus he sets out on his evening walk.

He goes up the avenue, crosses the bridge and walks along the bank on the other side as far as the next bridge but one. The air is wet and cold, with a little snow now and then. He turns up his coat collar and slips the crook of his cane over the arm behind his back. Now and then he ventilates his lungs with a long deep breath of the night air. As usual when he walks, his mind reverts to his professional preoccupations, he thinks about his lectures and the things he means to say to-morrow about Philip's struggle against the Germanic revolution, things steeped in melancholy and penetratingly just. Above all just, he thinks. For in one's dealings with the young, it behoves one to display the scientific spirit, to exhibit the principles of enlightenment—not only for purposes of mental discipline but on the human and individual side, in order not to wound them or indirectly offend their political sensibilities; particularly in these days, when there is so much tinder in the air, opinions are so frightfully split up and chaotic, and you may so easily incur attacks from one party or the other, or even give rise to scandal, by taking sides on a point of history.

"And taking sides is unhistoric anyhow," so he muses. "Only justice, only impartiality is historic." And could not, properly considered, be otherwise. . . . For justice can have nothing of youthful fire, and blithe, fresh, loyal conviction. It is by nature melancholy. And being so, has secret affinity with the lost cause and the forlorn hope rather than with the fresh and blithe and loyal—perhaps this affinity is its very essence and without it it would not exist at all! . . . "And is there then no such thing as justice?" the Professor asks himself; and ponders the question so deeply that he absently posts his letters in the next box and turns round to go home. This thought of his is unsettling and disturbing to the scientific mind—but is it not after all itself scientific, psychological, conscientious, and therefore to be accepted without prejudice, no matter how upsetting? In the midst of which musings Dr. Cornelius finds himself back at his own door.

On the outer threshold stands Xaver, and seems to be looking for him.

"Herr Professor," says Xaver, tossing back his hair, "go upstairs to Ellie at once. She's in a bad way."

"What's the matter?" asks Cornelius in alarm. "Is she ill?"

"No-o, not to say ill," answers Xaver. "She's just in a bad way and crying fit to bust her little heart. It's along o' that chap with the shirt-front that danced with her—Herr Hergesell. She couldn't be got to go upstairs peaceably, not at no price at all, and she's b'en crying bucketfuls."

"Nonsense," says the Professor, who has entered and is tossing off his things in the dressing-room. He says no more; opens the glass door and without a glance at the guests turns swiftly to the stairs. Takes them two at a time, crosses the upper hall and the small room leading into the nursery. Xaver follows at his heels, but stops at the nursery door.

A bright light still burns within, showing the gay frieze that runs all round the room, the large row of shelves heaped with a confusion of toys, the rocking-horse on his swaying platform, with red varnished nostrils and raised hoofs. On the linoleum lie other toys—building blocks, railway trains, a little trumpet. The two white cribs stand not far apart, Ellie's in the window corner, Snapper's out in the room.

Snapper is asleep. He has said his prayers in loud, ringing tones, prompted by Nurse, and gone off at once into vehement, profound and rosy slumber—from which a cannon-ball fired at close range could not rouse him. He lies with both fists flung back on the pillows on either side of the tousled head with its funny crooked little slumber-tossed wig.

A circle of females surrounds Ellie's bed: not only blue-faced Ann is there but the Hinterhofer ladies too, talking to each other and to her. They make way as the Professor comes up, and reveal the child sitting all pale among her pillows, sobbing and weeping more bitterly than he has ever seen her sob and weep in her life. Her lovely little hands lie on the coverlet in front of her, the nightgown with its narrow lace border has slipped down from her shoulder—such a thin, bird-like little shoulder—and the

sweet head Cornelius loves so well, set on the neck like a flower on its
stalk, her head is on one side, with the eyes rolled up to the corner between
wall and ceiling above her head. For there she seems to envisage the
anguish of her heart, and even to nod to it—either on purpose or because
her head wobbles as her body is shaken with the violence of her sobs. Her
eyes rain down tears. The bow-shaped lips are parted, like a little *mater
dolorosa's,* and from them issue long, low wails that in nothing resemble
the unnecessary and exasperating shrieks of a naughty child, but rise from
the deep extremity of her heart and wake in the Professor's own a sympathy that is well-nigh intolerable. He has never seen his darling so before.
His feelings find immediate vent in an attack on the ladies Hinterhofer.

"What about my supper?" he asks sharply. "There must be a great deal
to do. Is my wife being left to do it alone?"

For the acute sensibilities of the former middle class, this is quite enough.
The ladies withdraw in righteous indignation, and Xaver Kleinsgutl jeers
at them as they pass out. Having been born to low life instead of achieving
it, he never loses a chance to mock at their fallen state.

"Childie, childie," murmurs Cornelius, and sitting down by the crib en-
folds the anguished Ellie in his arms. "What is the trouble with my
darling?"

She bedews his face with her tears.

"Abel. . . . Abel . . ." she stammers between sobs. "Why—isn't Max—
my brother? Max ought to be—my brother!"

Alas, alas! What mischance is this? Is this what the party has wrought,
with its fatal atmosphere? Cornelius glances helplessly up at blue-faced
Ann standing there in all the dignity of her limitations with her hands
before her on her apron. She purses up her mouth and make a long face.
"It's pretty young," she says, "for the female instincts to be showing up."

"Hold your tongue," snaps Cornelius, in his agony. He has this much to
be thankful for, that Ellie does not turn from him now; she does not push
him away as she did downstairs, but clings to him in her need, while she
reiterates her absurd, bewildered prayer that Max might be her brother, or
with a fresh burst of desire demands to be taken downstairs so that he can
dance with her again. But Max, of course, is dancing with Fräulein
Plaichinger, that behemoth who is his rightful partner and has every claim
upon him; whereas Ellie—never, thinks the Professor, his heart torn with
the violence of his pity, never has she looked so tiny and birdlike as now,
when she nestles to him shaken with sobs and all unaware of what is
happening in her little soul. No, she does not know. She does not comprehend that her suffering is on account of Fräulein Plaichinger, fat, overgrown and utterly within her rights in dancing with Max Hergesell,
whereas Ellie may only do it once, by way of a joke, although she is
incomparably the more charming of the two. Yet it would be quite mad
to reproach young Hergesell with the state of affairs, or to make fantastic

demands upon him. No, Ellie's suffering is without help or healing and must be covered up. Yet just as it is without understanding, so it is also without restraint—and that is what makes it so horribly painful. Xaver and blue-faced Ann do not feel this pain, it does not affect them—either because of native callousness or because they accept it as the way of nature. But the Professor's fatherly heart is quite torn by it, and by a mortifying horror of this passion, so hopeless and so absurd.

Of no avail to hold forth to poor Ellie on the subject of the perfectly good little brother she already has. She only casts a distraught and scornful glance over at the other crib where Snapper lies vehemently slumbering, and with fresh tears calls again for Max. Of no avail either the promise of a long, long walk to-morrow, all five gentlemen, round and round the dining-room table; or a dramatic description of the thrilling cushion games they will play. No, she will listen to none of all this, nor to lying down and going to sleep. She will not sleep, she will sit bolt upright and suffer. . . . But on a sudden they stop and listen, Abel and Ellie; listen to something miraculous, that is coming to pass, that is approaching by strides, two strides, to the nursery door, that now overwhelmingly appears. . . .

It is Xaver's work, not a doubt of that. He has not remained by the door where he stood to gloat over the ejection of the Hinterhofers. No, he has bestirred himself, taken a notion, likewise steps to carry it out. Downstairs he has gone, twitched Herr Hergesell's sleeve and made a thick-lipped request. So here they both are. Xaver, having done his part, remains by the door; but Max Hergesell comes up to Ellie's crib: in his dinner-jacket, with his sketchy side-whisker and charming black eyes; obviously quite pleased with his rôle of swan knight and fairy prince, as one who should say: "See, here am I, now all losses are restored and sorrows end."

Cornelius is almost as much overcome as Ellie herself.

"Just look," he says feebly, "look who's here. This is uncommonly good of you, Herr Hergesell."

"Not a bit of it," says Hergesell. "Why shouldn't I come to say good-night to my fair partner?"

And he approaches the bars of the crib, behind which Ellie sits struck mute. She smiles blissfully through her tears. A funny, high little note that is half a sigh of relief comes from her lips, then she looks dumbly up at her swan knight with her golden-brown eyes—tear-swollen though they are, so much more beautiful than the fat Plaichinger's. She does not put up her arms. Her joy, like her grief, is without understanding; but she does not do that. The lovely little hands lie quiet on the coverlet, and Max Hergesell stands with his arms leaning over the rail as on a balcony.

"And now," he says smartly, "she need not 'sit the livelong night and weep upon her bed!'" He looks at the Professor to make sure he is receiving due credit for the quotation. "Ha, ha!" he laughs, "she's beginning

young. 'Console thee, dearest child!' Never mind, you're all right! Just as
you are you'll be wonderful! You've only got to grow up. . . . And you'll
lie down and go to sleep like a good girl, now I've come to say good-night?
And not cry any more, little Lorelei?"

Ellie looks up at him, transfigured. One birdlike shoulder is bare, the
Professor draws the lace-trimmed nightie over it. There comes into his
mind a sentimental story he once read about a dying child who longs to
see a clown he had once, with unforgettable ecstasy, beheld in a circus.
And they bring the clown to the bedside marvellously arrayed, embroidered
before and behind with silver butterflies; and the child dies happy. Max
Hergesell is not embroidered, and Ellie, thank God, is not going to die,
she has only "been in a bad way." But after all, the effect is the same.
Young Hergesell leans over the bars of the crib and rattles on, more for
the father's ear than the child's, but Ellie does not know that—and the
father's feelings toward him are a most singular mixture of thankfulness,
embarrassment, and hatred.

"Good-night, little Lorelei," says Hergesell, and gives her his hand
through the bars. Her pretty, soft, white little hand is swallowed up in the
grasp of his big, strong, red one. "Sleep well," he says, "and sweet dreams!
But don't dream about me—God forbid! Not at your age—ha, ha!" And
then the fairy clown's visit is at an end. Cornelius accompanies him to the
door. "No, no, positively, no thanks called for, don't mention it," he large-
heartedly protests; and Xaver goes downstairs with him, to help serve the
Italian salad.

But Dr. Cornelius returns to Ellie, who is now lying down, with her
cheek pressed into her flat little pillow.

"Well, wasn't that lovely?" he says, as he smooths the covers. She nods,
with one last little sob. For a quarter of an hour he sits beside her and
watches while she falls asleep in her turn, beside the little brother who
found the right way so much earlier than she. Her silky brown hair takes
the enchanting fall it always does when she sleeps; deep, deep lie the lashes
over the eyes that late so abundantly poured forth their sorrow; the angelic
mouth with its bowed upper lip is peacefully relaxed and a little open.
Only now and then comes a belated catch in her slow breathing.

And her small hands, like pink and white flowers, lie so quietly, one on
the coverlet, the other on the pillow by her face—Dr. Cornelius, gazing,
feels his heart melt with tenderness as with strong wine.

"How good," he thinks, "that she breathes in oblivion with every breath
she draws! That in childhood each night is a deep, wide gulf between one
day and the next. To-morrow, beyond all doubt, young Hergesell will be
a pale shadow, powerless to darken her little heart. To-morrow, forgetful of
all but present joy, she will walk with Abel and Snapper, all five gentlemen,
round and round the table, will play the ever-thrilling cushion game."

Heaven be praised for that!

MR. AND MRS. ABBEY'S DIFFICULTIES

E. M. Forster

(1879-)

THE DEATH OF MRS. RAWLINGS, followed four years afterwards by that of Mrs. Jennings, her respectable parent, involved Mr. and Mrs. Abbey in appreciable difficulties finally. They did not at first realize the possible consequences of becoming guardian to the four children—John, George, Tom, and Fanny—the offspring of Mrs. Rawlings by a previous union; indeed, Mr. Abbey acted with unusual precipitancy, and, without troubling Mr. Sandall, his co-executor under Mrs. Jennings' will, undertook sole charge even in the grandmother's lifetime. The sum of £8,000—and £8,000 was a substantial sum a hundred years ago—passed into his control, and he proceeded to administer it for the benefit of the young people as only a business man can.

The connection of the two deceased ladies had been with the livery trade. They had kept the stables attached to the Swan and Hoop, Finsbury Pavement, and the first husband of Mrs. Rawlings had actually been killed by falling off one of his own horses on a dark night not far from Southgate. Mr. Abbey's own position was more secure. A broker in tea, and in coffee also, although scarcely in coffee to an equal extent, he had added to his office in Pancras Lane a residence at Walthamstow, and to the latter a conservatory, and to everything that he undertook the conviction of some ultimate issue. It was at Walthamstow that he made provision for the child Fanny, who was aged but seven years only when she came under his charge. He arranged that she should live with Mrs. and Miss Abbey, she should attend a young ladies' school where she might acquire such education as her sex necessitated. The education of her brother John was already complete, for he had attained his sixteenth year, and Mr. Abbey was prompt to remove him from his studies and to apprentice him to a surgeon. George (aged thirteen) and Tom (eleven) were received as clerks into his own office. Thus suitable provision for all concerned was rapidly and adequately made.

Unfortunately the children were restless—a defect inherited from their father, who had been of rustic origin. John would not stick to his gallipots, nor George and Tom to their stools; and Fanny wished to learn the flageolet. They were always asking for money to satisfy their whims, and since Mr. Abbey had in view their ultimate good alone and had reinvested the £8,000 to that end, he negatived all such demands. What they wasted on letter-paper alone was deplorable, for, as the three boys grew up, they were in constant correspondence with one another and with their sister. Mr. and Mrs. Abbey valued a united family highly, none higher; but saw no advantage in Tom communicating with George that it was raining in Devonshire, or in John informing Fanny that he had counted the buns and tarts in a pastry-cook's window, and 'was just beginning with the jellies.' Mrs. Abbey, in particular, felt that family affection was used as a cloak for something else: that they communicated, as she expressed it, 'behind my back,' and were not so much devoted to each other, which is all very proper and well, as interested in what each other thought. An unfortunate discovery gave her some pain. Fanny left her letters lying about, as young girls will, and Mrs. Abbey's eye was caught by the strange appearance of one of them. It was written in short lines, certainly just nonsense, yet she did not relish it, the more so since it was in John's hand-writing, and he a notorious makegame.

Two or three Posies
With two or three simples—
Two or three Noses
With two or three pimples—
Two or three sandies
And two or three tabbies—
Two or three dandies
And two Mrs. —— mum!

Who might 'Mrs. —— mum!' be? Mrs. Abbey reread the paragraph and then saw that it was a crambo or forfeit, the last line of which concealed her own name. She was affronted, the more so since the name must be in the plural gender. 'Two Mrs. Abbeys,' she repeated to herself. 'And why two?' She inquired of her husband next time he came down from Pancras Lane, of Miss Caley, the headmistress of Fanny's school, of Miss Tucker, the headmistress of the school to which she was subsequently transferred. They all agreed that an unkindness was intended. She kept a look-out for John's letters in the future, and discovered in another that she was to be sent up to the London office 'to count coffee-berries,' while the grass plot was used for dancing. Elsewhere Fanny was to 'pay no attention to Mrs. Abbey's unfeeling and ignorant gabble. You can't stop an old woman's crying any more than you can a child's. The old woman is the greatest nuisance, because she is too old for the rod. Many people live opposite a blacksmith's till they cannot hear the hammer.' Here all was too plain, except, indeed, the blacksmith, whose forge was at the farther extremity of the village; and Mrs. Abbey was obliged to take up a different line with Fanny. She would not allow the girl to go up to see her brother in town, and she discouraged his visiting Walthamstow.

How necessary her strictness was, the following anecdote will evince. While the children were deficient in character and breeding on the one side, they had inherited from their mother, Mrs. Rawlings, on the other, a tendency to consumption, and Tom was the first to sicken. Fanny professed to be heart-broken, and permission for a visit to his bedside could not well be withheld. She went up to Hampstead, and saw him, thus paying lip service to truth, but afterwards proceeded to act the fine lady, and made a round of calls with her brother John. She returned to Walthamstow in an unseemly state, could give Mrs. Abbey no interesting details as to the progress of Tom's malady, nothing but chatter about Mr. So-and-so and Miss T'other, what they said and ate and wore and contributed to the newspapers, and might she buy a magazine once a month, even if it meant giving up her spaniel, and she did not think Miss Tucker would object, for newspapers opened the world as Mr. Dilke had remarked, and Mrs. Dilke was at Brighton. She was easily silenced, but the Abbeys realized how susceptible she was to bad influences, and how sternly they must guard her against them. Letters like the following could not be indefinitely allowed to arrive:

'MY DEAR FANNY—

'I called on Mr. Abbey in the beginning of last week, when he seemed averse to letting you come again from having heard that you had been to other places besides Well Walk. I do not mean to say you did wrongly in speaking of it, for there should rightly be no objection to such things: but you know with what People we are obliged in the course of Childhood to associate, whose conduct forces us into duplicity and falsehood to them. . . . Perhaps I am talking too deeply for you: if you do not know, you will understand what I mean in the course of a few years. I think poor Tom is a little Better, he sends his love to you. I shall call on Mr. Abbey to-morrow: when I hope to settle when to see you again. Mrs. Dilke is expected home in a day or two. She will be pleased, I am sure, with your present. I will try for permission for you to remain all Night should Mrs. D. return in time.

'Your affectionate brother
'JOHN'

Permission was refused. The Dilkes and their set were no companions for a growing girl of fourteen, and Fanny remained under discipline at the time of Tom's death. The discipline had even to be increased, as the following letter, dated four months later, indicates; it had proved impossible to keep her in a healthy and modest frame of mind without almost entirely forbidding any intercourse between her and the rest of her family; it had also proved desirable to remove her from Miss Tucker's, owing to the expense:

'MY DEAR FANNY—

'Your letter to me at Bedhampton hurt me very much. What objection can there be to your receiving a letter from me? At Bedhampton I was unwell and did not go out of the Garden Gate but twice or thrice during the fortnight I was there—Since I came back I have been taking care of myself—I have been obliged to do so, and am now in hopes that by this care I shall get rid of a sore throat which has haunted me at intervals nearly a twelvemonth. I always had a presentiment of not being able to succeed in persuading Mr. Abbey to let you remain longer at School—I am very sorry that he will not consent. I recommend you to keep up all that you know and to learn more by yourself, however little. The time will come when you will be more pleased with Life—look forward to that time, and though it may be a trifle be careful not to let the idle and retired Life you lead fix any awkward habit or behaviour on you—whether you sit or walk endeavour to let it be in a seemly and, if possible, a graceful manner. We have been very little together: but you have not the less been with me in thought. You have no one in the world besides me who would sacrifice any-thing for you—I feel myself the only Protector you have. In all your little troubles think of me with the thought that there is at least one person in Eng-land who, if he could, would help you out of them—I live in hopes of being able to make you happy—I should not perhaps write in this manner if it were not for the fear of not being able to see you often or long together. I am in hopes that Mr. Abbey will not object any more to your receiving a letter now and then from me. How unreasonable! . . .

'Your affectionate brother
'JOHN'

Though less coarse in tone than its predecessors, this letter was even more calculated to undermine authority. O mark the impudence of calling life at Walthamstow 'idle'—he who had never done a stroke of real work for years, had weakened his constitution by dissipation and drift, falling in love with his landlady's daughter, and had vainly tried, when it was too late, to continue his medical career and obtain a post as surgeon upon an East Indiaman! The 'sore-throat' of which he complained was the precursor of the usual hereditary trouble, its later developments proving fatal. Kindly Mr. and Mrs. Abbey were distressed, and, Fanny herself falling ill, called in the family practitioner to attend her. Yet they could not but feel that sickness had all along been used to claim illicit privileges and to undermine their authority as guardians, and that just as in the case of Tom so in the case of John there had been duplicity. In view of his departure abroad, John was permitted to write his sister as often as he wished, and almost his last letter to her contained the venomous sentence, 'In case my strength returns, I will do all in my power to extricate you from the Abbies.' He could not even spell.

Blessed with excellent health himself, Mr. Abbey left illness to doctors. But in money matters he felt himself on firmer ground, and, a man of business through and through, brooked no interference in his own domain. When the three boys had abandoned the professions assigned to them, he could not prevent them, but he could cut off their supplies whenever fit without giving a reason. There was so much that boys could not understand. In the first place, the reinvestment of the £8,000 had, he owned frankly to himself, not been a success. In the second place, old Mr. Jennings, the original stableman, had left a confused will. He had died worth £13,160 19s. 5d., £9,343 2s. of which had gone to his widow and thence in more compact form to the grandchildren as £8,000; but he had also left his grandchildren £1,000 direct and £50 a year besides in reversion after their mother's death.

Mr. Abbey was aware of these additional legacies, but they were not often in his mind, for, like all city men, he had much to think about, and he deemed it fitter to leave them alone; they would do no harm, the interest would accumulate in Chancery, and when documents came about them it was his habit to clear his throat and drop everything together into a safe. And as years went on and the children failed to mention the legacies to him he ceased mentioning them to himself. He had so much to think about. After the first excitement of guardianship, he had done what nine men out of ten of substance would do in his place: nothing; so he said nothing. When John and George called with troubled faces at Pancras Lane and asked exactly how poor they were, he rightly replied, 'This is no ordinary question,' and silenced them by some reference to their own inexperience. Or, 'Ask your Aunt Midgely,' he would say. They knew not what he meant, nor did he, for Mrs. Midgely Jennings was unlikely to afford information, since she was herself dissatisfied with her income, and periodically threatened to bring suits, against whom or for what Mr. Abbey was not quite cognizant.

He was not clear either about the great Chancery suit, Rawlings v. Jennings, which the mother and grandmother had initiated by mutual consent in their lifetimes in order to clear up in an amicable spirit the obscurities of Mr. Jennings' will. Not one to interfere with another man's job, Mr. Abbey left law to the lawyers, and thanks to his attitude the Chancery suit lasted twenty years. Ah, he did not know much, but he always knew a little more than his wards; he performed that duty, and Tom and John remained ignorant until the day of their death, while Fanny believed for many years that she was a pauper and owed Mrs. Abbey for her board and lodging. Much extravagance was averted by this timely reticence, many loans to undesirable friends, and tours both in England and on the Continent, which could have led to no useful purposes. 'Ever let the fancy roam, pleasure never is at home,' wrote John to George openly in one of his letters; atrocious advice as coming from an elder brother to a younger, and alluding to the fact that George had decamped with the daughter of a sea-captain to America. All this Mr. Abbey realized, deprecated, and strove to check, and it was not his fault when Fanny terminated her connection with Walthamstow in the arms of a Spaniard.

The last years of the stewardship were very painful. Being small and sickly, and two of her brothers dead and the third abroad, Fanny seemed inclined to settle down. She spoke little, she dressed plainly, and never tossed her head when Mrs. Abbey repeated that she resembled her father, who had fallen off the horse, and that naught but idleness had ever been found on that side of the family. But, unfortunately, George came from America on a visit. Fanny was upset again, and all the careful accumulations of so many years came tumbling down. George was more robust than his brothers, had married, and had acquired a hard effrontery which passed for business ability among the Yankees, though it was not so estimated by Mr. Abbey. Retrenchment and deliberation were to Mr. Abbey the twin pillars of commercial achievement, he never hurried others and he did not expect to be hurried. He greeted the prodigal in measured tones, and received in reply a point-blank demand that the trust should be wound up. 'Ask your Aunt Midgely,' he said; but retorting that he knew whom to ask, George prepared to take the case into court. He insisted on the safe being opened, he discovered that the two additional legacies, ever Mr. Abbey's weak point, had been invested twenty years previously in Consols by order of the court, £1,550 7s. 10d. of Consols in the one case and £1,666 13s. 4d. in the other, and that the interest had been accumulating ever since his mother's death. He dragged every detail, including what had been paid as lawyers' fees, to the light, and before Mr. Abbey could collect himself had returned to America with £1,147 5s. 1d. in his pocket.

Worse was to follow; when Fanny came of age, which she did two years after George's visit, she claimed her share also. Mr. Abbey might have ceded it without protest, had she not claimed in addition the shares of her two dead brothers. Such rapacity was childish, and Mr. Abbey was quick to reply that the arrangement would be unfair to George. Fanny retorted 'No, George's own wish!' and she applied to Mr. Dilke, who produced the necessary documents. Fanny annexed the balance, no less than £3,375 5s. 7d., and quitted Walthamstow. Her Spanish adventurer married her soon afterwards, but Mr. and Mrs. Abbey could never feel it retribution sufficient. Although the money was not theirs to spend, they had come to feel that it was theirs to keep, and they would have liked it to accumulate at compound interest for ever. Bitter words had passed, Fanny insolently hinting that if Tom and John had been given their proper dues, the additional procurable comfort might have prolonged their lives.

Of course it would not have, and in any case what is the use of such people, Mr. Abbey could not help thinking as he sat at Walthamstow in the evening of his own life. Now that the worrying and badgering was over and the trust that he had so faithfully administered was filched from him, now that Rawlings v. Jennings was wound up, and idle verses about his wife no longer fell through the letter-box, he could not feel that his four wards had ever existed in the sense in which he, in which Mrs. Abbey, in which Miss Abbey and the conservatory existed. Already were they forgotten—George in America, Fanny in Spain, Tom in the graveyard of St.

Stephen's, Coleman Street, John at Rome. On the tomb of the last-mentioned had been placed a text which rather pleased the old gentleman, despite its fanciful wording. He found it appropriate to the whole family. 'Here lies one whose name was writ in water,' it said. He had written in water himself once with the point of a wet umbrella, and he remembered that almost before the servant arrived to open the door, his signature had evaporated. He himself has expressed the same truth in sounder English in the one letter of his that has been preserved, a business letter addressed to Messrs. Taylor and Hessey, publishers, Waterloo Place; he has summed up once for all the world's judgment upon inefficiency:

Pancras Lane,
Cheapside.
April 18, 1821.

Sir—

'I beg pardon for not replying to your favour of the 30th ult. respecting the late Mr. Jno. Keats.

'I am obliged by your note, but he having withdrawn himself from my controul, and acted contrary to my advice, I cannot interfere with his affairs.

'I am, Sir,
'Yr. mo. Hble. St.
'RICHARD ABBEY'
[1925]

THE INVISIBLE COLLECTION

AN EPISODE OF THE INFLATION PERIOD IN GERMANY

Stefan Zweig

(1881–)

TRANSLATED BY EDEN AND CEDAR PAUL

AT THE FIRST JUNCTION beyond Dresden, an elderly gentleman entered our compartment, smiled genially to the company, and gave me a special nod, as if to an old acquaintance. Seeing that I was at a loss, he mentioned his name. Of course I knew him! He was one of the most famous connoisseurs and art-dealers in Berlin. Before the war, I had often purchased autographs and rare books at his place. He took the vacant seat opposite me, and for a while we talked of matters not worth relating. Then, changing the conversation, he explained the object of the journey from which he was returning. It had, he said, been one of the strangest of his experiences in the thirty-seven years he had devoted to the occupation of artpedlar. Enough introduction. I will let him tell the story in his own words, without using quote-marks—to avoid the complication of wheels within wheels.

You know [he said] what has been going on in my trade since the value of money began to diffuse into the void like gas. War profiteers have developed a taste for old masters (Madonnas and so on), for incunabula, for ancient tapestries. It is difficult to satisfy their craving; and a man like myself, who prefers to keep the best for his own use and enjoyment, is hard put to it not to have his house stripped bare. If I let them, they would buy the cuff-links from my shirt and the lamp from my writing-table. Harder and harder to find wares to sell. I'm afraid the term "wares" may grate upon you in this connexion, but you must excuse me. I have picked it up from customers of the new sort. Evil communications . . . Through use and wont I have come to look upon an invaluable book from one of the early Venetian presses much as the philistine looks upon an overcoat that cost so or so many hundred dollars, and upon a sketch by Guercino as animated by nothing more worthy of reverence than the transmigrated soul of a banknote for a few thousand francs.

Impossible to resist the greed of these fellows with money to burn. As I looked round my place the other night, it seemed to me that there was so little left of any real value that I might as well put up the shutters. Here was a fine business which had come down to me from my father and my grandfather; but the shop was stocked with rubbish which, before 1914, a street-trader would have been ashamed to hawk upon a hand-cart.

In this dilemma, it occurred to me to flutter the pages of our old ledgers. Perhaps I should be put on the track of former customers who might be willing to resell what they had bought in prosperous days. True, such a list of sometime purchasers has considerable resemblance to a battlefield laden with the corpses of the slain; and in fact I soon realized that most of those who had purchased from the firm when the sun was shining were dead or would be in such low water that it was probable they must have sold anything of value among their possessions. However, I came across a bundle of letters from a man who was presumably the oldest yet alive—if he was alive. But he was so old that I had forgotten him, since he had bought nothing after the great explosion in the summer of 1914. Yes, very, very old. The earliest letters were dated more than half a century back, when my grandfather was head of the business. Yet I could not recall having had any personal relationships with him during the thirty-seven years in which I had been an active worker in the establishment.

All indications showed that he must have been one of those antediluvian

eccentrics, a few of whom survive in German provincial towns. His writing
was copperplate, and every item in his orders was underlined in red ink.
Each price was given in words as well as figures, so that there could be no
mistake. These peculiarities, and his use of torn-out fly-leaves as writing
paper, enclosed in a scratch assortment of envelopes, hinted at the penuri-
ousness of a confirmed backwoodsman. His signature was always followed
by his style and title in full: "Forest Ranger and Economic Councillor,
Retired; Lieutenant, Retired; Holder of the Iron Cross First Class." Since
he was obviously a veteran of the war of 1870–1871, he must by now be
close on eighty.

For all his cheese-paring and for all his eccentricities, he had manifested
exceptional shrewdness, knowledge, and taste as collector of prints and
engravings. A careful study of his orders, which had at first totalled very
small sums indeed, disclosed that in the days when a taler could still pay
for a pile of lovely German woodcuts, this country bumpkin had got together a collection of etchings and the like outrivalling the widely trum-
peted acquisitions of war profiteers. Merely those which, in the course of
decades, he had bought from us for trifling sums would be worth a large
amount of money today; and I had no reason to suppose that he had
failed to pick up similar bargains elsewhere. Was his collection dispersed?
I was too familiar with what had been going on in the art trade since the
date of his last purchase not to feel confident that such a collection could
scarcely have changed hands entire without my getting wind of the event.
If he was dead, his treasures had probably remained intact in the hands
of his heirs.

The affair seemed so interesting that I set forth next day (yesterday evening) on a journey to one of the most out-of-the-way towns in Saxony.
When I left the tiny railway station and strolled along the main street, it
seemed to me impossible that anyone inhabiting one of these gimcrack
houses, furnished in a way with which you are doubtless familiar, could
possibly own a full set of magnificent Rembrandt etchings together with
an unprecedented number of Dürer woodcuts and a complete collection of
Mantegnas. However, I went to the post-office to inquire, and was astonished to learn that a sometime Forest Ranger and Economic Councillor of
the name I mentioned was still living. They told me how to find his house,
and I will admit that my heart beat faster than usual as I made my way
thither. It was well before noon.

The connoisseur of whom I was in search lived on the second floor of
one of those jerry-built houses which were run up in such numbers by
speculators during the sixties of the last century. The first floor was occupied by a master tailor. On the second landing to the left was the name-
plate of the manager of the local post-office, while the porcelain shield on
the right-hand door bore the name of my quarry. I had run him to earth!
My ring was promptly answered by a very old, white-haired woman wear-

ing a black lace cap. I handed her my card and asked whether the master was at home. With an air of suspicion she glanced at me, at the card, and then back at my face once more. In this God-forsaken little town a visit from an inhabitant of the metropolis was a disturbing event. However, in as friendly a tone as she could muster, she asked me to be good enough to wait a minute or two in the hall, and vanished through a doorway. I heard whispering, and then a loud, hearty, masculine voice: "Herr Rackner from Berlin, you say, the famous dealer in antiquities? Of course I shall be delighted to see him." Thereupon the old woman reappeared and invited me to enter.

I took off my overcoat, and followed her. In the middle of the cheaply furnished room was a man standing up to receive me. Old but hale, he had a bushy moustache and was wearing a semi-military frogged smoking-jacket. In the most cordial way, he held out both hands towards me. But though this gesture was spontaneous and nowise forced, it was in strange contrast with the stiffness of his attitude. He did not advance to meet me, so that I was compelled (I must confess I was a trifle piqued) to walk right up to him before I could shake. Then I noticed that his hand, too, did not seek mine, but was waiting for mine to clasp it. At length I guessed what was amiss. He was blind.

Ever since I was a child I have been uncomfortable in the presence of the blind. It embarrasses me, produces in me a sense of bewilderment and shame to encounter anyone who is thoroughly alive, and yet has not the full use of his senses. I feel as if I were taking an unfair advantage, and I was keenly conscious of this sensation as I glanced into the fixed and sightless orbs beneath the bristling white eyebrows. The blind man, however, did not leave me time to dwell upon this discomfort. He exclaimed, laughing with boisterous delight:

"A red-letter day, indeed! Seems almost a miracle that one of the big men of Berlin should drop in as you have done. There's need for us provincials to be careful, you know, when a noted dealer such as yourself is on the war-path. We've a saying in this part of the world: 'Shut your doors and button up your pockets if there are gipsies about!' I can guess why you've taken the trouble to call. Business doesn't thrive, I've gathered. No buyers or very few, so people are looking up their old customers. I'm afraid you'll draw a blank. We pensioners are glad enough to find there's still some dry bread for dinner. I've been a collector in my time, but now I'm out of the game. My buying days are over."

I hastened to tell him he was under a misapprehension, that I had not called with any thought of effecting sales. Happening to be in the neighbourhood I felt loath to miss the chance of paying my respects to a long-standing customer who was at the same time one of the most famous among German collectors. Hardly had the phrase passed my lips when a remarkable change took place in the old man's expression. He stood stiffly in the middle of the room, but his face lighted up and his whole aspect was suffused with pride. He turned in the direction where he fancied his wife to be, and nodded as if to say, "D'you hear that?" Then, turning back to me, he resumed—having dropped the brusque, drill-sergeant tone he had previously used, and speaking in a gentle, nay, almost tender voice:

"How charming of you. . . . I should be sorry, however, if your visit were to result in nothing more than your making the personal acquaintanceship of an old buffer like myself. At any rate I've something worth while for you to see—more worth while than you could find in Berlin, in the Albertina at Vienna, or even in the Louvre (God's curse on Paris!). A man who has been a diligent collector for fifty years, with taste to guide him, gets hold of treasures that are not to be picked up at every street-corner. Lisbeth, give me the key of the cupboard, please."

Now a strange thing happened. His wife, who had been listening with a pleasant smile, was startled. She raised her hands towards me, clasped them imploringly, and shook her head. What these gestures signified was a puzzle to me. Next she went up to her husband and touched his shoulder, saying:

"Franz, dear, you have forgotten to ask our visitor whether he may not have another appointment; and, anyhow, it is almost dinner-time.—I am sorry," she went on, looking to me, "that we have not enough in the house for an unexpected guest. No doubt you will dine at the inn. If you will take a cup of coffee with us afterwards, my daughter Anna Maria will be here, and she is much better acquainted than I am with the contents of the portfolios."

Once more she glanced piteously at me. It was plain that she wanted me to refuse the proposal to examine the collection there and then. Taking my cue, I said that in fact I had a dinner engagement at the Golden Stag, but should be only too delighted to return at three, when there would be plenty of time to examine anything Herr Kronfeld wanted to show me. I was not leaving before six o'clock.

The veteran was as pettish as a child deprived of a favourite toy.

"Of course," he growled, "I know you mandarins from Berlin have extensive claims on your time. Still, I really think you will do well to spare me a few hours. It is not merely two or three prints I want to show you, but the contents of twenty-seven portfolios, one for each master, and all of them full to bursting. However, if you come at three sharp, I dare say we can get through by six."

The wife saw me out. In the entrance hall, before she opened the front door, she whispered:

"Do you mind if Anna Maria comes to see you at the hotel before you return? It will be better for various reasons which I cannot explain just now."

"Of course, of course, a great pleasure. Really, I am dining alone, and your daughter can come along directly you have finished your own meal."

An hour later, when I had removed from the dining-room to the parlour of the Golden Stag, Anna Maria Kronfeld arrived. An old maid, wizened and diffident, plainly dressed, she contemplated me with embarrassment. I did my best to put her at her ease, and expressed my readiness to go back with her at once, if her father was impatient, though it was short of the appointed hour. At this she reddened, grew even more confused, and then stammered a request for a little talk before we set out.

"Please sit down," I answered. "I am entirely at your service."

She found it difficult to begin. Her hands and her lips trembled. At length:

"My mother sent me. We have to ask a favour of you. Directly you get back, Father will want to show you his collection; and the collection . . . the collection. Well, there's very little of it left."

She panted, almost sobbed, and went on breathlessly:

"I must be frank. . . . You know what troublous times we are passing through, and I am sure you will understand. Soon after th[e] my father became completely blind. His sight had alrea[dy] Agitation, perhaps, contributed. Though he was over seventy, he wanted to go to the front, remembering the fight in which he had taken part so long ago. Naturally there was no use for his services. Then, when the advance of our armies was checked, he took the matter very much to heart, and the doctor thought that may have precipitated the oncoming of blindness. In other respects, as you will have noticed, he is vigorous. Down to 1914 he could take long walks, and go out shooting. Since the failure of his eyes, his only pleasure is in his collection. He looks at it every day. 'Looks at it,' I say, though he sees nothing. Each afternoon he has the portfolios on the table, and fingers the prints one by one, in the order which many years have rendered so familiar. Nothing else interests him. He makes me read reports of auctions; and the higher the prices, the more enthusiastic does he become.

"There's the dreadful feature of the situation. Father knows nothing about the inflation; that we are ruined; that his monthly pension would not provide us with a day's food. Then we have others to support. My sister's husband was killed at Verdun, and•there are four children. These money troubles have been kept from him. We cut down expenses as much as we can, but it is impossible to make ends meet. We began to sell things, trinkets and so on, without interfering with his beloved collection. There was very little to sell, since Father had always spent whatever he could scrape together upon woodcuts, copperplate engravings, and the like. The collector's mania! Well, at length it was a question whether we were to touch the collection or to let him starve. We didn't ask permission. What would have been the use? He hasn't the ghost of a notion how hard food is to come by, at any price; has never heard that Germany was defeated and surrendered Alsace-Lorraine. We don't read him items of that sort from the newspapers!

"The first piece we sold was a very valuable one, a Rembrandt etching, and the dealer paid us a long price, a good many thousand marks. We thought it would last us for years. But you know how money was melting away in 1922 and 1923. After we had provided for our immediate needs, we put the rest in a bank. In two months it was gone! We had to sell another engraving, and then another. That was during the worst days of inflation, and each time the dealer delayed settlement until the price was not worth a tenth or a hundredth of what he had promised to pay. We tried auction-rooms, and were cheated there too, though the bids were raised by millions. The million- or milliard-mark notes were waste-paper by the time we got them. The collection was scattered to provide daily bread, and little of that.

"That was why Mother was so much alarmed when you turned up to-day. Directly the portfolios are opened, our pious fraud will be disclosed. ⟨...⟩ item by touch. You see, every print we disposed of was ⟨repla⟩ced by a sheet of blank cartridge-paper of the same size and thickness, so that he would notice no difference when he handled it. Feeling them one by one, and counting them, he derives almost as much pleasure as if he could actually see them. He never tries to show them to anyone here, where there is no connoisseur, no one worthy to look at them; but he loves each of them so ardently that I think his heart would break if he knew they had been dispersed. The last time he asked someone to look at them, it was the curator of the copperplate engravings in Dresden, who died years ago.

"I beseech you"—her voice broke—"not to shatter his illusion, not to undermine his faith, that the treasures he will describe to you are there for the seeing. He would not survive the knowledge of their loss. Perhaps we have wronged him; yet what could we do? One must live. Orphaned children are more valuable than old prints. Besides, it has been life and happiness to him to spend three hours every afternoon going through his imaginary collection, and talking to each specimen as if it were a friend. Today may be the most enthralling experience since his sight failed. How he has longed for the chance of exhibiting his treasures to an expert! If you will lend yourself to the deception . . ."

In my cold recital, I cannot convey to you how poignant was this appeal. I have seen many a sordid transaction in my business career; have had to look on supinely while persons ruined by inflation have been diddled out of cherished heirlooms which they were compelled to sacrifice for a crust. But my heart has not been utterly calloused, and this tale touched me to the quick. I need hardly tell you that I promised to play up.

We went to her house together. On the way I was grieved (though not surprised) to learn for what preposterously small amounts these ignorant though kind-hearted women had parted with prints many of which were extremely valuable and some of them unique. This confirmed my resolve to give all the help in my power. As we mounted the stairs we heard a jovial shout: "Come in! Come in!" With the keen hearing of the blind, he had recognized the footsteps for which he had been eagerly waiting.

"Franz usually takes a siesta after dinner, but excitement kept him awake today," said the old woman with a smile as she let us in. A glance at her daughter showed her that all was well. The stack of portfolios was on the table. The blind collector seized me by the arm and thrust me into a chair which was placed ready for me.

"Let's begin at once. There's a lot to see, and time presses. The first portfolio contains Dürers. Nearly a full set, and you'll think each cut finer than the others. Magnificent specimens. Judge for yourself."

He opened the portfolio as he spoke, saying:

"We start with the Apocalypse series, of course."

Then, tenderly, delicately (as one handles fragile and precious objects), he picked up the first of the blank sheets of cartridge-paper and held it admiringly before my sighted eyes and his blind ones. So enthusiastic was his gaze that it was difficult to believe he could not see. Though I knew it to be fancy, I found it difficult to doubt that there was a glow of recognition in the wrinkled visage.

"Have you ever come across a finer print? How sharp the impression. Every detail crystal-clear. I compared mine with the one at Dresden; a good one, no doubt, but 'fuzzy' in contrast with the specimen you are looking at. Then I have the whole pedigree."

He turned the sheet over and pointed at the back so convincingly that involuntarily I leaned forward to read the nonexistent inscriptions.

"The stamp of the Nagler collection, followed by those of Remy and Esdaille. My famous predecessors never thought that their treasure would come to roost in this little room."

I shuddered as the unsuspecting enthusiast extolled the blank sheet of paper; my flesh crept when he placed a fingernail on the exact spot where the alleged imprints had been made by long-dead collectors. It was as ghostly as if the disembodied spirits of the men he named had risen from the tomb. My tongue clave to the roof of my mouth—until once more I caught sight of the distraught countenances of Kronfeld's wife and daughter. Then I pulled myself together and resumed my role. With forced heartiness, I exclaimed:

"Certainly you are right. This specimen is peerless."

He swelled with triumph.

"But that's nothing," he went on. "Look at these two, the *Melancholia,* and the illuminated print of the *Passion.* The latter, beyond question, has no equal. The freshness of the tints! Your colleagues in Berlin and the custodians of the public galleries would turn green with envy at the sight."

I will not bore you with details. Thus it went on, a pæan, for more than two hours, as he ransacked portfolio after portfolio. An eerie business to watch the handling of these two or three hundred blanks, to chime in at appropriate moments with praise of merits which for the blind collector were so eminently real that again and again (this was my salvation) his faith kindled my own.

Once only did disaster loom. He was "showing" me a first proof of Rembrandt's *Antiope,* which must have been of inestimable value and which had doubtless been sold for a song. Again he dilated on the sharpness of the print, but as he passed his fingers lightly over it the sensitive tips missed some familiar indentation. His face clouded, his mouth trembled, and he said:

"Surely, surely it's the *Antiope?* No one touches the wood-cuts and etchings but myself. How can it have got misplaced?"

"Of course it's the *Antiope,* Herr Kronfeld," I said, hastening to take the "print" from his hand and to expatiate upon various details which my own remembrance enabled me to conjure up upon the blank surface.

His bewilderment faded. The more I praised, the more gratified he became, until at last he said exultantly to the two women:

"Here's a man who knows what's what! You have been inclined to grumble at my 'squandering' money upon the collection. It's true that for half a century and more I denied myself beer, wine, tobacco, travelling, visits to the theatre, books, devoting all I could spare to these purchases you have despised. Well, Herr Rackner confirms my judgment. When I am dead and gone, you'll be richer than anyone in the town, as wealthy as the wealthiest folk in Dresden, and you'll have good reason for congratulating yourself on my 'craze.' But so long as I'm alive, the collection must be kept together. After I've been boxed and buried, this expert or another will help you to sell. You'll have to, since my pension dies with me."

As he spoke, his fingers caressed the despoiled portfolios. It was horrible and touching. Not for years, not since 1914, had I witnessed an expression of such unmitigated happiness on the face of a German. His wife and daughter watched him with tear-dimmed eyes, yet ecstatically, like those women of old who—affrighted and rapturous—found the stone rolled away and the sepulchre empty in the garden outside the wall of Jerusalem. But the man could not have enough of my appreciation. He went on from portfolio to portfolio, from "print" to "print," drinking in my words, until, outwearied, I was glad when the lying blanks were replaced in their cases and room was made to serve coffee on the table.

My host, far from being tired, looked rejuvenated. He had story after story to tell concerning the way he had chanced upon his multifarious treasures, wanting, in this connexion, to take out each relevant piece once more. He grew peevish when I insisted, when his wife and daughter insisted, that I should miss my train if he delayed me any longer. . . .

In the end he was reconciled to my going, and we said good-bye. His voice mellowed; he took both my hands in his and fondled them with the tactile appreciation of the blind.

"Your visit has given me immense pleasure," he said with a quaver in his voice. "What a joy to have been able at long last to show my collection to one competent to appreciate it. I can do something to prove my gratitude, to make your visit to a blind old man worth while. A codicil to my will shall stipulate that your firm, whose probity everyone knows, will be entrusted with the auctioning of my collection."

He laid a hand lovingly upon the pile of worthless portfolios.

"Promise me they shall have a handsome catalogue. I could ask no better monument."

I glanced at the two women, who were exercising the utmost control, fearful lest the sound of their trembling should reach his keen ears. I promised the impossible, and he pressed my hand in response.

Wife and daughter accompanied me to the door. They did not venture to speak, but tears were flowing down their cheeks. I myself was in little better case. An art-dealer, I had come in search of bargains. Instead, as events turned out, I had been a sort of angel of good-luck, lying like a trooper in order to assist in a fraud which kept an old man happy. Ashamed of lying, I was glad that I had lied. At any rate I had aroused an ecstasy which seems foreign to this period of sorrow and gloom.

As I stepped forth into the street, I heard a window open, and my name called. Though the old fellow could not see me, he knew in which direction I should walk, and his sightless eyes were turned thither. He leaned out so far that his anxious relatives put their arms round him lest he should fall. Waving a handkerchief, he shouted:

"A pleasant journey to you, Herr Rackner."

His voice rang like a boy's. Never shall I forget that cheerful face, which contrasted so grimly with the careworn aspect of the passers-by in the street. The illusion I had helped to sustain made life good for him. Was it not Goethe who said:

"Collectors are happy creatures"?

UNCLE FRED FLITS BY

P. G. Wodehouse

(1881–   )

In order that they might enjoy their after-luncheon coffee in peace, the Crumpet had taken the guest whom he was entertaining at the Drones Club to the smaller and less frequented of the two smoking-rooms. In the other, he explained, though the conversation always touched an exceptionally high level of brilliance, there was apt to be a good deal of sugar thrown about.

The guest said he understood.

"Young blood, eh?"

"That's right. Young blood."

"And animal spirits."

"And animal, as you say, spirits," agreed the Crumpet. "We get a fairish amount of those here."

"The complaint, however, is not, I observe, universal."

"Eh?"

The other drew his host's attention to the doorway, where a young man in form-fitting tweeds had just appeared. The aspect of this young man was haggard. His eyes glared wildly and he sucked at an empty cigarette-holder. If he had a mind, there was something on it. When the Crumpet called to him to come and join the party, he merely shook his head in a distraught sort of way and disappeared, looking like a character out of a Greek tragedy pursued by the Fates.

The Crumpet sighed.

"Poor old Pongo!"

"Pongo?"

"That was Pongo Twistleton. He's all broken up about his Uncle Fred."

"Dead?"

"No such luck. Coming up to London again to-morrow. Pongo had a wire this morning."

"And that upsets him?"

"Naturally. After what happened last time."

"What was that?"

"Ah!" said the Crumpet.

"What happened last time?"

"You may well ask."

"I do ask."

"Ah!" said the Crumpet.

Poor old Pongo (said the Crumpet) has often discussed his Uncle Fred with me, and if there weren't tears in his eyes when he did so, I don't know a tear in the eye when I see one. In round numbers the Earl of Ickenham, of Ickenham Hall, Ickenham, Hants, he lives in the country most of the year, but from time to time has a nasty way of slipping his collar and getting loose and descending upon Pongo at his flat in the Albany. And every time he does so, the unhappy young blighter is subjected to some soul-testing experience. Because the trouble with this uncle is that, though sixty if a day, he becomes on arriving in the metropolis as young as he feels—which is, apparently, a youngish twenty-two. I don't know if you happen to know what the word "excesses" means, but those are what Pongo's Uncle Fred from the country, when in London, invariably commits.

It wouldn't so much matter, mind you, if he would confine his activities to the club premises. We're pretty broad-minded here, and if you stop short of smashing the piano, there isn't much that you can do at the Drones that will cause the raised eyebrow and the sharp intake of breath. The snag is that he will insist on lugging Pongo out in the open and there, right in the public eye, proceeding to step high, wide and plentiful.

So when, on the occasion to which I allude, he stood pink and genial on Pongo's hearth-rug, bulging with Pongo's lunch and wreathed in the smoke of one of Pongo's cigars, and said: "And now, my boy, for a pleasant and instructive afternoon," you will readily understand why the unfortunate young clam gazed at him as he would have gazed at two-penn'orth of dynamite, had he discovered it lighting up in his presence.

"A what?" he said, giving at the knees and paling beneath the tan a bit.

"A pleasant and instructive afternoon," repeated Lord Ickenham, rolling the words round his tongue. "I propose that you place yourself in my hands and leave the programme entirely to me."

Now, owing to Pongo's circumstances being such as to necessitate his getting into the aged relative's ribs at intervals and shaking him down for an occasional much-needed tenner or what not, he isn't in a position to use the iron hand with the old buster. But at these words he displayed a manly firmness.

"You aren't going to get me to the dog races again."

"No, no."

"You remember what happened last June."

"Quite," said Lord Ickenham, "quite. Though I still think that a wiser magistrate would have been content with a mere reprimand."

"And I won't——"

"Certainly not. Nothing of that kind at all. What I propose to do this afternoon is to take you to visit the home of your ancestors."

Pongo did not get this.

"I thought Ickenham was the home of my ancestors."

"It is one of the homes of your ancestors. They also resided rather nearer the heart of things, at a place called Mitching Hill."

"Down in the suburbs, do you mean?"

"The neighbourhood is now suburban, true. It is many years since the meadows where I sported as a child were sold and cut up into building lots. But when I was a boy Mitching Hill was open country. It was a vast, rolling estate belonging to your great-uncle, Marmaduke, a man with whiskers of a nature which you with your pure mind would scarcely credit, and I have long felt a sentimental urge to see what the hell the old place looks like now. Perfectly foul, I expect. Still, I think we should make the pious pilgrimage."

Pongo absolutely-ed heartily. He was all for the scheme. A great weight seemed to have rolled off his mind. The way he looked at it was that even an uncle within a short jump of the looney bin couldn't very well get into much trouble in a suburb. I mean, you know what suburbs are. They don't, as it were, offer the scope. One follows his reasoning, of course.

"Fine!" he said. "Splendid! Topping!"

"Then put on your hat and rompers, my boy," said Lord Ickenham, "and let us be off. I fancy one gets there by omnibuses and things."

Well, Pongo hadn't expected much in the way of mental uplift from the sight of Mitching Hill, and he didn't get it. Alighting from the bus, he tells me, you found yourself in the middle of rows and rows of semi-detached villas, all looking exactly alike, and you went on and you came to more semi-detached villas, and those all looked exactly alike, too. Nevertheless, he did not repine. It was one of those early spring days which suddenly change to mid-winter and he had come out without his overcoat, and it looked like rain and he hadn't an umbrella, but despite this his mood was one of sober ecstasy. The hours were passing and his uncle had not yet made a goat of himself. At the Dog Races the other had been in the hands of the constabulary in the first ten minutes.

It began to seem to Pongo that with any luck he might be able to keep the old blister pottering harmlessly about here till nightfall, when he could shoot a bit of dinner into him and put him to bed. And as Lord Ickenham had specifically stated that his wife, Pongo's Aunt Jane, had expressed her intention of scalping him with a blunt knife if he wasn't back at the Hall by lunch time on the morrow, it really looked as if he might get through this visit without perpetrating a single major outrage on the public weal. It is rather interesting to note that as he thought this Pongo smiled, because it was the last time he smiled that day.

All this while, I should mention, Lord Ickenham had been stopping at intervals like a pointing dog and saying that it must have been just about here that he plugged the gardener in the trousers seat with his bow and arrow and that over there he had been sick after his first cigar, and he now paused in front of a villa which for some unknown reason called itself The Cedars. His face was tender and wistful.

"On this very spot, if I am not mistaken," he said, heaving a bit of a sigh, "on this very spot, fifty years ago come Lammas Eve, I . . . Oh, blast it!"

The concluding remark had been caused by the fact that the rain, which had held off until now, suddenly began to buzz down like a shower-bath. With no further words, they leaped into the porch of the villa and there took shelter, exchanging glances with a grey parrot which hung in a cage in the window.

Not that you could really call it shelter. They were protected from above all right, but the moisture was now falling with a sort of swivel action, whipping in through the sides of the porch and tickling them up properly. And it was just after Pongo had turned up his collar and was huddling against the door that the door gave way. From the fact that a female of general-servant aspect was standing there he gathered that his uncle must have rung the bell.

This female wore a long mackintosh, and Lord Ickenham beamed upon her with a fairish spot of suavity.

"Good afternoon," he said.

The female said good afternoon.

"The Cedars?"

The female said yes, it was The Cedars.

"Are the old folks at home?"

The female said there was nobody at home.

"Ah? Well, never mind. I have come," said Lord Ickenham, edging in, "to clip the parrot's claws. My assistant, Mr. Walkinshaw, who applies the anæsthetic," he added, indicating Pongo with a gesture.

"Are you from the bird shop?"

"A very happy guess."

"Nobody told me you were coming."

"They keep things from you, do they?" said Lord Ickenham, sympathetically. "Too bad."

Continuing to edge, he had got into the parlour by now, Pongo following in a sort of dream and the female following Pongo.

"Well, I suppose it's all right," she said. "I was just going out. It's my afternoon."

"Go out," said Lord Ickenham cordially. "By all means go out. We will leave everything in order."

And presently the female, though still a bit on the dubious side, pushed off, and Lord Ickenham lit the gas-fire and drew a chair up.

"So here we are, my boy," he said. "A little tact, a little address, and here we are, snug and cosy and not catching our deaths of cold. You'll never go far wrong if you leave things to me."

"But, dash it, we can't stop here," said Pongo.

Lord Ickenham raised his eyebrows.

"Not stop here? Are you suggesting that we go out into that rain? My dear lad, you are not aware of the grave issues involved. This morning, as I was leaving home, I had a rather painful disagreement with your aunt. She said the weather was treacherous and wished me to take my woolly muffler. I replied that the weather was not treacherous and that I would be dashed if I took my woolly muffler. Eventually, by the exercise of an iron will, I had my way, and I ask you, my dear boy, to envisage what will happen if I return with a cold in the head. I shall sink to the level of a fifth-class power. Next time I came to London, it would be with a liver pad and a respirator. No! I shall remain here, toasting my toes at this really excellent fire. I had no idea that a gas-fire radiated such warmth. I feel all in a glow."

So did Pongo. His brow was wet with honest sweat. He is reading for the Bar, and while he would be the first to admit that he hasn't yet got a complete toe-hold on the Law of Great Britain he had a sort of notion that oiling into a perfect stranger's semi-detached villa on the pretext of pruning the parrot was a tort or misdemeanour, if not actual barratry or soccage in fief or something like that. And apart from the legal aspect of the matter there was the embarrassment of the thing. Nobody is more of a whale on correctness and not doing what's not done than Pongo, and the situation in which he now found himself caused him to chew the lower lip and, as I say, perspire a goodish deal.

"But suppose the blighter who owns this ghastly house comes back?" he asked. "Talking of envisaging things, try that one over on your pianola."

And, sure enough, as he spoke, the front door bell rang.

"There!" said Pongo.

"Don't say 'There!' my boy," said Lord Ickenham reprovingly. "It's the sort of thing your aunt says. I see no reason for alarm. Obviously this is some casual caller. A ratepayer would have used his latchkey. Glance cautiously out of the window and see if you can see anybody."

"It's a pink chap," said Pongo, having done so.

"How pink?"

"Pretty pink."

"Well, there you are, then. I told you so. It can't be the big chief. The sort of fellows who own houses like this are pale and sallow, owing to working in offices all day. Go and see what he wants."

"You go and see what he wants."

"We'll both go and see what he wants," said Lord Ickenham.

So they went and opened the front door, and there, as Pongo had said, was a pink chap. A small young pink chap, a bit moist about the shoulder-blades.

"Pardon me," said this pink chap, "is Mr. Roddis in?"

"No," said Pongo.

"Yes," said Lord Ickenham. "Don't be silly, Douglas—of course I'm in. I am Mr. Roddis," he said to the pink chap. "This, such as he is, is my son Douglas. And you?"

"Name of Robinson."

"What about it?"

"My name's Robinson."

"Oh, *your* name's Robinson? Now we've got it straight. Delighted to see you, Mr. Robinson. Come right in and take your boots off."

They all trickled back to the parlour, Lord Ickenham pointing out objects of interest by the wayside to the chap, Pongo gulping for air a bit and trying to get himself abreast of this new twist in the scenario. His heart was becoming more and more bowed down with weight of woe. He hadn't liked being Mr. Walkinshaw, the anæsthetist, and he didn't like it any better being Roddis Junior. In brief, he feared the worst. It was only too plain to him by now that his uncle had got it thoroughly up his nose and had settled down to one of his big afternoons, and he was asking himself, as he had so often asked himself before, what would the harvest be?

Arrived in the parlour, the pink chap proceeded to stand on one leg and look coy.

"Is Julia here?" he asked, simpering a bit, Pongo says.

"Is she?" said Lord Ickenham to Pongo.

"No," said Pongo.

"No," said Lord Ickenham.

"She wired me she was coming here to-day."

"Ah, then we shall have a bridge four."

The pink chap stood on the other leg.

"I don't suppose you've ever met Julia. Bit of trouble in the family, she gave me to understand."

"It is often the way."

"The Julia I mean is your niece Julia Parker. Or, rather, your wife's niece Julia Parker."

"Any niece of my wife is a niece of mine," said Lord Ickenham heartily. "We share and share alike."

"Julia and I want to get married."

"Well, go ahead."

"But they won't let us."

"Who won't?"

"Her mother and father. And Uncle Charlie Parker and Uncle Henry Parker and the rest of them. They don't think I'm good enough."

"The morality of the modern young man is notoriously lax."

"Class enough, I mean. They're a haughty lot."

"What makes them haughty? Are they earls?"

"No, they aren't earls."

"Then why the devil," said Lord Ickenham warmly, "are they haughty? Only earls have a right to be haughty. Earls are hot stuff. When you get an earl, you've got something."

"Besides, we've had words. Me and her father. One thing led to another, and in the end I called him a perishing old—— Coo!" said the pink chap, breaking off suddenly.

He had been standing by the window, and he now leaped lissomely into the middle of the room, causing Pongo, whose nervous system was by this time definitely down among the wines and spirits and who hadn't been expecting this *adagio* stuff, to bite his tongue with some severity.

"They're on the doorstep! Julia and her mother and father. I didn't know they were all coming."

"You do not wish to meet them?"

"No, I don't!"

"Then duck behind the settee, Mr. Robinson," said Lord Ickenham, and the pink chap, weighing the advice and finding it good, did so. And as he disappeared the door bell rang.

Once more, Lord Ickenham led Pongo out into the hall.

"I say!" said Pongo, and a close observer might have noted that he was quivering like an aspen.

"Say on, my dear boy."

"I mean to say, what?"

"What?"

"You aren't going to let these bounders in, are you?"

"Certainly," said Lord Ickenham. "We Roddises keep open house. And as they are presumably aware that Mr. Roddis has no son, I think we had better return to the old layout. You are the local vet, my boy, come to minister to my parrot. When I return, I should like to find you by the cage, staring at the bird in a scientific manner. Tap your teeth from time to time with a pencil and try to smell of iodoform. It will help to add conviction."

So Pongo shifted back to the parrot's cage and stared so earnestly that it was only when a voice said "Well!" that he became aware that there was anybody in the room. Turning, he perceived that Hampshire's leading curse had come back, bringing the gang.

It consisted of a stern, thin, middle-aged woman, a middle-aged man and a girl.

You can generally accept Pongo's estimate of girls, and when he says that this one was a pippin one knows that he uses the term in its most exact sense. She was about nineteen, he thinks, and she wore a black béret, a dark-green leather coat, a shortish tweed skirt, silk stockings and high-heeled shoes. Her eyes were large and lustrous and her face like a dewy rosebud at daybreak on a June morning. So Pongo tells me. Not that I suppose he has ever seen a rosebud at daybreak on a June morning, because it's generally as much as you can do to lug him out of bed in time for nine-thirty breakfast. Still, one gets the idea.

"Well," said the woman, "you don't know who I am, I'll be bound. I'm Laura's sister Connie. This is Claude, my husband. And this is my daughter Julia. Is Laura in?"

"I regret to say, no," said Lord Ickenham.

The woman was looking at him as if he didn't come up to her specifications.

"I thought you were younger," she said.

"Younger than what?" said Lord Ickenham.

"Younger than you are."

"You can't be younger than you are, worse luck," said Lord Ickenham. "Still, one does one's best, and I am bound to say that of recent years I have made a pretty good go of it."

The woman caught sight of Pongo, and he didn't seem to please her, either.

"Who's that?"

"The local vet, clustering round my parrot."

"I can't talk in front of him."

"It is quite all right," Lord Ickenham assured her. "The poor fellow is stone deaf."

And with an imperious gesture at Pongo, as much as to bid him stare less at girls and more at parrots, he got the company seated.

"Now, then," he said.

There was silence for a moment, then a sort of muffled sob, which Pongo thinks proceeded from the girl. He couldn't see, of course, because his back was turned and he was looking at the parrot, which looked back at him—most offensively, he says, as parrots will, using one eye only for the purpose. It also asked him to have a nut.

The woman came into action again.

"Although," she said, "Laura never did me the honour to invite me to her wedding, for which reason I have not communicated with her for five years, necessity compels me to cross her threshold to-day. There comes a time when differences must be forgotten and relatives must stand shoulder to shoulder."

"I see what you mean," said Lord Ickenham. "Like the boys of the old brigade."

"What I say is, let bygones be bygones. I would not have intruded on you, but needs must. I disregard the past and appeal to your sense of pity."

The thing began to look to Pongo like a touch, and he is convinced that the parrot thought so, too, for it winked and cleared its throat. But they were both wrong. The woman went on.

"I want you and Laura to take Julia into your home for a week or so, until I can make other arrangements for her. Julia is studying the piano, and she sits for her examination in two weeks' time, so until then she must remain in London. The trouble is, she has fallen in love. Or thinks she has."

"I know I have," said Julia.

Her voice was so attractive that Pongo was compelled to slew round and take another look at her. Her eyes, he says, were shining like twin stars and there was a sort of Soul's Awakening expression on her face, and what the dickens there was in a pink chap like the pink chap, who even as pink chaps go wasn't much of a pink chap, to make her look like that, was frankly, Pongo says, more than he could understand. The thing baffled him. He sought in vain for a solution.

"Yesterday, Claude and I arrived in London from our Bexhill home to give Julia a pleasant surprise. We stayed, naturally, in the boarding-house where she has been living for the past six weeks. And what do you think we discovered?"

"Insects."

"Not insects. A letter. From a young man. I found to my horror that a young man of whom I knew nothing was arranging to marry my daughter. I sent for him immediately, and found him to be quite impossible. He jellies eels!"

"Does what?"

"He is an assistant at a jellied eel shop."

"But surely," said Lord Ickenham, "that speaks well for him. The capacity to jelly an eel seems to me to argue intelligence of a high order. It isn't everybody who can do it, by any means. I know if someone came to me and said 'Jelly this eel!' I should be nonplussed. And so, or I am very much mistaken, would Ramsay MacDonald and Winston Churchill."

The woman did not seem to see eye to eye.

"Tchah!" she said. "What do you suppose my husband's brother Charlie Parker would say if I allowed his niece to marry a man who jellies eels?"

"Ah!" said Claude, who, before we go any further, was a tall, drooping bird with a red soup-strainer moustache.

"Or my husband's brother, Henry Parker."

"Ah!" said Claude. "Or Cousin Alf Robbins, for that matter."

"Exactly. Cousin Alfred would die of shame."

The girl Julia hiccoughed passionately, so much so that Pongo says it was all he could do to stop himself nipping across and taking her hand in his and patting it.

"I've told you a hundred times, mother, that Wilberforce is only jellying eels till he finds something better."

"What is better than an eel?" asked Lord Ickenham, who had been following this discussion with the close attention it deserved. "For jellying purposes, I mean."

"He is ambitious. It won't be long," said the girl, "before Wilberforce suddenly rises in the world."

She never spoke a truer word. At this very moment, up he came from behind the settee like a leaping salmon.

"Julia!" he cried.

"Wilby!" yipped the girl.

And Pongo says he never saw anything more sickening in his life than the way she flung herself into the blighter's arms and clung there like the ivy on the old garden wall. It wasn't that he had anything specific against the pink chap, but this girl had made a deep impression on him and he resented her glueing herself to another in this manner.

Julia's mother, after just that brief moment which a woman needs in which to recover from her natural surprise at seeing eel-jelliers pop up from behind sofas, got moving and plucked her away like a referee breaking a couple of welter-weights.

"Julia Parker," she said, "I'm ashamed of you!"

"So am I," said Claude.

"I blush for you."

"Me, too," said Claude. "Hugging and kissing a man who called your father a perishing old bottle-nosed Gawd-help-us."

"I think," said Lord Ickenham, shoving his oar in, "that before proceeding any further we ought to go into that point. If he called you a perishing old bottle-nosed Gawd-help-us, it seems to me that the first thing to do is to decide whether he was right, and frankly, in my opinion . . ."

"Wilberforce will apologize."

"Certainly I'll apologize. It isn't fair to hold a remark passed in the heat of the moment against a chap . . ."

"Mr. Robinson," said the woman, "you know perfectly well that whatever remarks you may have seen fit to pass don't matter one way or the other. If you were listening to what I was saying you will understand . . ."

"Oh, I know, I know. Uncle Charlie Parker and Uncle Henry Parker and Cousin Alf Robbins and all that. Pack of snobs!"

"What!"

"Haughty, stuck-up snobs. Them and their class distinctions. Think themselves everybody just because they've got money. I'd like to know how they got it."

"What do you mean by that?"

"Never mind what I mean."

"If you are insinuating——"

"Well, of course, you know, Connie," said Lord Ickenham mildly, "he's quite right. You can't get away from that."

I don't know if you have ever seen a bull-terrier embarking on a scrap with an Airedale and just as it was getting down nicely to its work suddenly having an unexpected Kerry Blue sneak up behind it and bite it in the rear quarters. When this happens, it lets go of the Airedale and swivels round and fixes the butting-in animal with a pretty nasty eye. It was exactly the same with the woman Connie when Lord Ickenham spoke these words.

"What!"

"I was only wondering if you had forgotten how Charlie Parker made his pile."

"What are you talking about?"

"I know it is painful," said Lord Ickenham, "and one doesn't mention it as a rule, but, as we are on the subject, you must admit that lending money at two hundred and fifty per cent interest is not done in the best circles. The judge, if you remember, said so at the trial."

"I never knew that!" cried the girl Julia.

"Ah," said Lord Ickenham. "You kept it from the child? Quite right, quite right."

"It's a lie!"

"And when Henry Parker had all that fuss with the bank it was touch and go they didn't send him to prison. Between ourselves, Connie, has a bank official, even a brother of your husband, any right to sneak fifty pounds from the till in order to put it on a hundred to one shot for the Grand National? Not quite playing the game, Connie. Not the straight bat. Henry, I grant you, won five thousand of the best and never looked back afterwards, but, though we applaud his judgment of form, we must surely look askance at his financial methods. As for Cousin Alf Robbins . . ."

The woman was making rummy stuttering sounds. Pongo tells me he once had a Pommery Seven which used to express itself in much the same way if you tried to get it to take a hill on high. A sort of mixture of gurgles and explosions.

"There is not a word of truth in this," she gasped at length, having managed to get the vocal cords disentangled. "Not a single word. I think you must have gone mad."

Lord Ickenham shrugged his shoulders.

"Have it your own way, Connie. I was only going to say that, while the jury were probably compelled on the evidence submitted to them to give

Cousin Alf Robbins the benefit of the doubt when charged with smuggling
dope, everybody knew that he had been doing it for years. I am not blaming him, mind you. If a man can smuggle cocaine and get away with it,
good luck to him, say I. The only point I am trying to make is that we
are hardly a family that can afford to put on dog and sneer at honest suitors
for our daughters' hands. Speaking for myself, I consider that we are very
lucky to have the chance of marrying even into eel-jellying circles."

"So do I," said Julia firmly.

"You don't believe what this man is saying?"

"I believe every word."

"So do I," said the pink chap.

The woman snorted. She seemed overwrought.

"Well," she said, "goodness knows I have never liked Laura, but I would
never have wished her a husband like you!"

"Husband?" said Lord Ickenham, puzzled. "What gives you the impression that Laura and I are married?"

There was a weighty silence, during which the parrot threw out a general invitation to the company to join it in a nut. Then the girl Julia spoke.

"You'll have to let me marry Wilberforce now," she said. "He knows too
much about us."

"I was rather thinking that myself," said Lord Ickenham. "Seal his lips, I
say."

"You wouldn't mind marrying into a low family, would you, darling?"
asked the girl, with a touch of anxiety.

"No family could be too low for me, dearest, if it was yours," said the
pink chap.

"After all, we needn't see them."

"That's right."

"It isn't one's relations that matter: it's oneselves."

"That's right, too."

"Wilby!"

"Julia!"

They repeated the old ivy on the garden wall act. Pongo says he didn't
like it any better than the first time, but his distaste wasn't in it with the
woman Connie's.

"And what, may I ask," she said, "do you propose to marry on?"

This seemed to cast a damper. They came apart. They looked at each
other. The girl looked at the pink chap, and the pink chap looked at the
girl. You could see that a jarring note had been struck.

"Wilberforce is going to be a very rich man some day."

"Some day!"

"If I had a hundred pounds," said the pink chap, "I could buy a half-
share in one of the best milk walks in South London to-morrow."

"If!" said the woman.

"Ah!" said Claude.

"Where are you going to get it?"

"Ah!" said Claude.

"Where," repeated the woman, plainly pleased with the snappy crack and loath to let it ride without an encore, "are you going to get it?"

"That," said Claude, "is the point. Where are you going to get a hundred pounds?"

"Why, bless my soul," said Lord Ickenham jovially, "from me, of course. Where else?"

And before Pongo's bulging eyes he fished out from the recesses of his costume a crackling bundle of notes and handed it over. And the agony of realizing that the old bounder had had all that stuff on him all this time and that he hadn't touched him for so much as a tithe of it was so keen, Pongo says, that before he knew what he was doing he had let out a sharp, whinnying cry which rang through the room like the yowl of a stepped-on puppy.

"Ah," said Lord Ickenham. "The vet wishes to speak to me. Yes, vet?"

This seemed to puzzle the cerise bloke a bit.

"I thought you said this chap was your son."

"If I had a son," said Lord Ickenham, a little hurt, "he would be a good deal better-looking than that. No, this is the local veterinary surgeon. I may have said I *looked* on him as a son. Perhaps that was what confused you."

He shifted across to Pongo and twiddled his hands enquiringly. Pongo gaped at him, and it was not until one of the hands caught him smartly in the lower ribs that he remembered he was deaf and started to twiddle back. Considering that he wasn't supposed to be dumb, I can't see why he should have twiddled, but no doubt there are moments when twiddling is about all a fellow feels himself equal to. For what seemed to him at least ten hours Pongo had been undergoing great mental stress, and one can't blame him for not being chatty. Anyway, be that as it may, he twiddled.

"I cannot quite understand what he says," announced Lord Ickenham at length, "because he sprained a finger this morning and that makes him stammer. But I gather that he wishes to have a word with me in private. Possibly my parrot has got something the matter with it which he is reluctant to mention even in sign language in front of a young unmarried girl. You know what parrots are. We will step outside."

"*We* will step outside," said Wilberforce.

"Yes," said the girl Julia. "I feel like a walk."

"And you?" said Lord Ickenham to the woman Connie, who was looking like a female Napoleon at Moscow. "Do you join the hikers?"

"I shall remain and make myself a cup of tea. You will not grudge us a cup of tea, I hope?"

"Far from it," said Lord Ickenham cordially. "This is Liberty Hall. Stick around and mop it up till your eyes bubble."

Outside, the girl, looking more like a dewy rosebud than ever, fawned on the old buster pretty considerably.

"I don't know how to thank you!" she said. And the pink chap said he didn't, either.

"Not at all, my dear, not at all," said Lord Ickenham.

"I think you're simply wonderful."

"No, no."

"You are. Perfectly marvellous."

"Tut, tut," said Lord Ickenham. "Don't give the matter another thought."

He kissed her on both cheeks, the chin, the forehead, the right eyebrow, and the tip of the nose, Pongo looking on the while in a baffled and discontented manner. Everybody seemed to be kissing this girl except him.

Eventually the degrading spectacle ceased and the girl and the pink chap shoved off, and Pongo was enabled to take up the matter of that hundred quid.

"Where," he asked, "did you get all that money?"

"Now, where did I?" mused Lord Ickenham. "I know your aunt gave it to me for some purpose. But what? To pay some bill or other, I rather fancy."

This cheered Pongo up slightly.

"She'll give you the devil when you get back," he said, with not a little relish. "I wouldn't be in your shoes for something. When you tell Aunt Jane," he said, with confidence, for he knew his Aunt Jane's emotional nature, "that you slipped her entire roll to a girl, and explain, as you will have to explain, that she was an extraordinarily pretty girl—a girl, in fine, who looked like something out of a beauty chorus of the better sort, I should think she would pluck down one of the ancestral battle-axes from the wall and jolly well strike you on the mazzard."

"Have no anxiety, my dear boy," said Lord Ickenham. "It is like your kind heart to be so concerned, but have no anxiety. I shall tell her that I was compelled to give the money to you to enable you to buy back some compromising letters from a Spanish *demi-mondaine*. She will scarcely be able to blame me for rescuing a fondly-loved nephew from the clutches of an adventuress. It may be that she will feel a little vexed with you for a while, and that you may have to allow a certain time to elapse before you visit Ickenham again, but then I shan't be wanting you at Ickenham till the ratting season starts, so all is well."

At this moment, there came toddling up to the gate of The Cedars a large red-faced man. He was just going in when Lord Ickenham hailed him.

"Mr. Roddis?"

"Hey?"

"Am I addressing Mr. Roddis?"

"That's me."

"I am Mr. J. G. Bulstrode from down the road," said Lord Ickenham. "This is my sister's husband's brother, Percy Frensham, in the lard and imported-butter business."

The red-faced bird said he was pleased to meet them. He asked Pongo if things were brisk in the lard and imported-butter business, and Pongo said they were all right, and the red-faced bird said he was glad to hear it.

"We have never met, Mr. Roddis," said Lord Ickenham, "but I think it would be only neighbourly to inform you that a short while ago I observed two suspicious-looking persons in your house."

"In my house? How on earth did they get there?"

"No doubt through a window at the back. They looked to me like cat burglars. If you creep up, you may be able to see them."

The red-faced bird crept, and came back not exactly foaming at the mouth but with the air of a man who for two pins would so foam.

"You're perfectly right. They're sitting in my parlour as cool as dammit, swigging my tea and buttered toast."

"I thought as much."

"And they've opened a pot of my raspberry jam."

"Ah, then you will be able to catch them red-handed. I should fetch a policeman."

"I will. Thank you, Mr. Bulstrode."

"Only too glad to have been able to render you this little service, Mr. Roddis," said Lord Ickenham. "Well, I must be moving along. I have an appointment. Pleasant after the rain, is it not? Come, Percy."

He lugged Pongo off.

"So that," he said, with satisfaction, "is that. On these visits of mine to the metropolis, my boy, I always make it my aim, if possible, to spread sweetness and light. I look about me, even in a foul hole like Mitching Hill, and I ask myself—How can I leave this foul hole a better and happier foul hole than I found it? And if I see a chance, I grab it. Here is our omnibus. Spring aboard, my boy, and on our way home we will be sketching out rough plans for the evening. If the old Leicester Grill is still in existence, we might look in there. It must be fully thirty-five years since I was last thrown out of the Leicester Grill. I wonder who is the bouncer there now."

Such (concluded the Crumpet) is Pongo Twistleton's Uncle Fred from the country, and you will have gathered by now a rough notion of why it is that when a telegram comes announcing his impending arrival in the great city Pongo blenches to the core and calls for a couple of quick ones.

The whole situation, Pongo says, is very complex. Looking at it from one angle, it is fine that the man lives in the country most of the year. If he didn't he would have him in his midst all the time. On the other hand, by living in the country he generates, as it were, a store of loopiness which expends itself with frightful violence on his rare visits to the centre of things.

What it boils down to is this—Is it better to have a loopy uncle whose loopiness is perpetually on tap but spread out thin, so to speak, or one who lies low in distant Hants for three hundred and sixty days in the year and does himself proud in London for the other five? Dashed moot, of course, and Pongo has never been able to make up his mind on the point.

Naturally, the ideal thing would be if someone would chain the old hound up permanently and keep him from Jan. One to Dec. Thirty-one where he wouldn't do any harm—viz. among the spuds and tenantry. But this, Pongo admits, is a Utopian dream. Nobody could work harder to that end than his Aunt Jane, and she has never been able to manage it.

IN THE LAST COACH

Leonhard Frank

(1882–   )

TRANSLATED BY CYRUS BROOKS

REFRESHED BY A MONTH'S HOLIDAY in the mountains, the banker, still a young man, was sauntering along between a trout-stream and a wet wall of rock, making for a café in the woods. Here, sitting on a terrace built out against the wall of the café, he could enjoy for the last time the aromatic strawberries and listen to the stimulating sound of the engines in the great saw-mill.

He hummed contentedly to himself, as he strode through the green and blue, thinking of the delightful journey down into the valley, of the famous viaduct that soared through the air eighty feet above the ground, and of the far-distant plains and mountains he would see from it. He lifted his hat with a vertical movement, as though it were a dumb-bell, in spritely acknowledgment of the sweeping curve described by the straw hat of the hardware traveller. Satisfied with the order he had received, the traveller had just left a shop which clung close to the cliff-face.

"What clear air! What wonderful flowers! What a marvellous scent there is here!" cried the hardware traveller. "And that cliff! It's quite a symbol of Germany."

"Because it's always dripping with water?"

"No, because of its defiant strength!"

They had first met while sunbathing a few days before.

'I'll take good care I never get so worn and skinny, nor acquire such a fat, pimply belly!' So the sturdy banker had thought, standing there firmly with legs apart, his hands on his hips and the thumbs turned down in front. He had been shocked and amused by the pitiable figure of the commercial traveller, and had tried in vain to get him under the cold shower.

"I'll see to that."

"See to what?"

"Exercise. You must have exercise. Arms—raise! Arms—lower! . . . Knees—bend! Knees—stretch!" He bent his knees once more and shot his arms forward till the shoulder-joints cracked. "There, sir, that's the way to keep young."

"That varies," answered the workman, standing in the open shed of the saw-mill beside his circular-saw. "Yesterday they sacked a hundred at one go. Now we've got close on seven hundred. We've got ten foremen."

"And the owner?" asked the banker.

"He came here once. That'll be five years ago. He was touring the mountains with his car and dropped in at the mill. He lives in Berlin. I read in the paper the other day that he'd given two hundred thousand marks for cultural developments. It was a theatre!"

"I can assure you it's months since I had time to go to the theatre," said the traveller in hardware. "Our trade is booming."

"Yes, things seem to be improving a little. . . . Did you get your arm in the machine?" The banker laid his hand on the fair head of a little girl, whose left hand was missing.

"No, I was born like that," said the child, readily, as though she had often answered the same question, and hid the thin stump under her pinafore.

"Her mother had a shock before the child was born. That often happens about here; you see, a good few accidents happen in the saw-mills. The safety appliances are not too good."

"That will improve now, too," said the banker, reassuringly. "Times are changing, and those things will be looked after."

The traveller threw out his hand: "Have you ever been to the theatre? Do you ever——" He looked round, as though the heap of sawdust or the roof of the shed would inform him whether people hereabouts went to the theatre.

"Theatre!" The workman turned a handle, the circular-saw began to scream and wrapped him in a cloud of sawdust.

"Here, child, take that to your mother." The banker pressed a note into the little girl's right hand, and walked with springy tread through the gate.

Suddenly he turned back and patted the little girl's cheek. "What's your name? . . .

"Bärbelchen, is it? I see."

Taking one small step after another, he climbed peacefully café-wards in the wake of the panting hardware traveller.

As the waiter was bringing the second portion of strawberries, disconnected fragments of speech came up from the great yard of the saw-mill, which was now black with people.

"The meeting was probably called because a hundred workmen have been discharged," answered the waiter.

The traveller put down a spoonful of strawberries. "What, in broad daylight?"

"They never work on a Saturday afternoon."

"And why don't they work, I should like to know. Look at me—I've still got two customers to see and I'm leaving this afternoon."

The chairman was seated at a little table, placed on a pile of planks; he had a bell in front of him. The district secretary of the party was leaning forward at his side, speaking of the basic principles of Social Democracy, of the eventual triumph of Socialism by the gradual attainment of a parliamentary majority.

The audience—all the mill-hands and a number of woodcutters—were standing or sitting on piles of planks. Some were counting their money. It was pay-day. Many were grumbling.

The traveller turned sharply round and listened to the shouting that came up from the saw-mill. The excitement of the discharged workmen had suddenly exploded.

"That is the only way we can build up trade," shouted the secretary, through the noise, "and at the same time retain all the achievements of civilization and, so to speak, carry them with us. Comrades, may this beautiful valley of ours be saved from Asiatic excesses. In this beauteous vale——"

"A virgin went to the well with a pail!" cried one of the discharged workmen.

Many were mopping their faces with their handkerchiefs. There was a smell of sweat. The sun burned vertically down on the snowy peaks, which glittered like diamonds.

A discussion followed. While the first speaker was declaring that he was not quite in agreement with the secretary, but thought the interruption about the virgin going to the well with a pail to be unjustified, a bent, hoary, old woodcutter was showing his boot to one of his colleagues. The upper had been cut deep by an axe. "If I'd been barefoot there'd have been nothing left but a stump. It'll heal up. That boot's finished. That won't heal."

Just then his name was called. He pushed his way through and scrambled on to the stacked boards. "We old members of the party have been organized for thirty years. There's no need to explain the policy to us. We

know all about it already. It's quite right. Everything evolves. And of
course trade has got to be built up again. Our wages are not even enough
to buy food. And nobody can afford a pair of boots. But I ask you this: I
should like to send my two boys to the secondary school so that they'll
learn something, and have a better time of it than their father. But I ask
you: who's going to pay for it? What are you to do?—— As soon as the
lads come out of school and have had their plate of soup they have to be
off to work. So how can they learn? I can reckon it out to the last pfennig.
Without counting anything for clothes and boots, my wages——"

"I must ask the speaker to keep to the point." The chairman sat down
again. The discreet tinkle of the bell still hung in the air.

The stiff-jointed old woodcutter turned and looked helplessly at the
chairman: "Well, that's what I had to say about the subject and about the
policy." He stood still for a moment, added suddenly: "That's the great
point." And scrambled down.

A gentleman with knock-knees and yellow gaiters was standing outside
the fence. He had a large notebook in his hand and was looking with
dreamy eyes at the distant mountains, as though he were sketching or writing verse.

A stranger, a well-known labour leader from the capital, an agitator
whose name they had often seen in the papers and who had been sent here
by his party, climbed on to the pile of planks.

In his first few sentences he dealt with the day's struggle and went on to
the great aim for which the workers had been fighting for generations.
The chairman then asked the agitator to keep to the point, and when the
workmen raised violent objections, as though this were what they wanted
to hear, he swung his bell vigorously.

The agitator, a man of not more than thirty, stood there on the piled
planks with the bearing of a man of sixty, and, letting his thick lower lip
droop down, waited, apparently unseeing, until the hubbub had died down.
The knees of his trousers were baggy, his thin shoulder-blades protruded
visibly.

Blue-black clouds hung over the end of the valley. The agitator spoke
more quickly and without pauses, stepped forward to the edge of his
crude platform and drove home his words with gestures. The workmen,
sitting and standing, watched him, motionless.

The first dry lightning-flash spanned the whole valley, as though one
peak were sending a signal to its fellow.

Outside the fence the gaitered gentleman was still standing on the same
spot in the same dreamy posture.

In the storm-zone diagonal spears of rain were falling; the café-terrace
was still in sunshine. "I'm Conservative. Very Conservative. That's the only
party that will make Germany great again."

"Well, you see, I'm a Democrat," said, with a smile, the banker, reposing deep within himself. "The most capable men, those who have learned something, ought to be the leaders of the nation."

The traveller listened to the applause that ascended from the yard: "Well, have it your own way."

Large, separate raindrops spattered on the chairman's table and evaporated.

His arms level with his chest, the banker trotted down the zigzag path to the mill-yard.

"They don't trouble about their meeting now," panted the hardware traveller. Many of the audience were running with turned-up coat collars through the gate.

The whole sky was blue-black. Fiery serpents of lightning sprang at each other, struck and became wildly entangled; every second the accompanying thunder-claps burst forth.

At last the gaitered gentleman retired from the fence, soaked to the skin, and hastened away with long strides through the downpouring, vertical masses of water.

The banker had reached his hotel. The mill-yard was deserted.

A few minutes later, tatters of cloud, like huge frightened birds, were sailing high across the valley to vanish beyond the snowy peaks, where in places the sun was already shining. The sparrows began to chirp noisily. Everything sparkled with moisture.

The hotel coach, laden with yellow trunks, the owners of which were still sitting at dinner, passed a slowly revolving turn-table, on which stood the last coach, shining in its fresh coat of paint.

II

The drunken shunter reeled so unsteadily between the buffers that his arm, equally inebriated, was almost crushed as the last coach moved into place.

His voice, bawling a song, rose through the clang of the buffers. His hand went out by habit towards the couplings. Then he shouted to the engine-driver a word that came back, swollen to a cry of rage, from the mountain-cliffs; he reeled towards the station bar.

"That looks a bit like Socialism, too," said an army officer, as he got into the last coach.

"By the way, I did not know your father had two sons." The speaker, a public prosecutor, bowed and stepped aside to allow the agitator to precede him into the last coach. "I'm very glad to have met you. What a coincidence!"

The agitator let his heavy lower lip droop down. 'During the revolution he got working men condemned to more than three hundred years' penal servitude; no doubt he knows all about the leaders; he must have my photograph in his files. . . . He knows I know all that. So why is he fabricating another son for my father? Is he trying to be funny? Good, let's have a little joke together. We've a long journey before us!'

By his tone, almost imperceptibly ironic, the public prosecutor had conveyed that he knew no second son existed.

"And how do you explain the shocking fact that your brother, who no doubt has enjoyed the same careful, conventional education as you have had yourself, could possibly have strayed into such paths?" he asked, and smiled.

With the same calm he had revealed on the pile of planks, while waiting for the hubbub to die down, the agitator allowed a few seconds to pass before he answered, with the same smile: "Let us assume that two sons of a highly-respected man have had the same mother and the same nurse, have been brought up with the same strictness by the same teachers and have been through the same experiences, so to speak, from the cradle upwards."

"Well?" asked the public prosecutor, in an interested voice, as the agitator paused. Both were leaning back on their seats.

"Paul adapts himself to life while still a child, and receives as a reward the privileges and enjoyments of his class; he grows up like his father, and becomes, like him, a highly-respected man; Eugen, on the other hand, rebels almost from infancy, refuses to give up his individuality, gets right out of the rut, and finally goes over to the working class. That is how my brother explains the reaction of us two to our environment. You see I get the worst of it, though he is the one who has gone off the rails."

"Off the rails! If that were all—if he were just a mettlesome young fellow who did nothing but play around and run into debt—well, that happens in the best families. But to forget his social obligations, to forget what a member of our class owes to his education and position in life, to join elements that are driving the nation headlong to perdition, that, really, that is incredible in a man of good family. You must pardon my speaking so frankly about your brother, doctor. Excuse me, you did take your degree, didn't you?"

"I am a doctor of economics."

"Your brother, too, unless I'm mistaken?"

"My brother is also a doctor of economics. We are twins."

"I was discussing this painful case only recently with your father, and he——"

"——agreed with you completely. I thought so. But my brother—we still meet occasionally—believes that the nation has already descended to the state you mentioned, owing to the war, and that there will always be wars so long as the means of production are not transferred to the nation."

"But your brother is not one of those who believe that this transfer can be made peaceably, when the time and economic conditions and capitalism and the working classes are ripe for it, and the international situation and a few dozen other things just happen to be favourable for the change, is he?" asked the public prosecutor, smiling and turning to the knock-kneed gentleman in gaiters, who was standing half in the corridor and half in the compartment, his ear turned towards the speaker. He signalled to him with an imperceptible shake of his head to go away, then he went to the window to see how long it would be before the train started.

'I've seen that six-foot ear somewhere before. . . . Has my special detective been promoted *agent provocateur* and this amateur appointed to watch over me?' reflected the agitator, and gave the gaitered gentleman that cheery smile which acts like the threat of a revolver on all spies who have not yet achieved complete cold-bloodedness.

The spy smiled cheerfully back.

'Not an amateur after all!'

"We love each other so dearly," said the banker to his young wife, who was in the final stages of pregnancy, "that nothing on earth could seriously threaten to come between us. The world is redeemed in us and in our love." He supported her with the utmost gentleness towards the last coach. "What bliss to work for you, to live and die for you!"

In addition to this couple the following passengers were seated in the same compartment of the last coach: a priest, the army officer, a university professor, a newspaper editor and the hardware traveller, who kindly gave up his corner-seat to the banker's wife. Might he offer her his travelling-cushion?

She thanked him with a smile, and drew a cushion out of her own case. Then her eyes went back at once to her husband, and seemed at the same time to be looking into her own body.

"I should have been delighted," added the traveller, and seemed to screw himself up in order to leave more room for the pregnant woman. His voice was so harsh that the agitator, who was alone with the public prosecutor in the next compartment, thought he was listening to the croakings of a flight of ravens.

The professor was leaning back in the corner next to the door, a Scotch plaid over his knees. He watched through his bright glasses, from under his plaid cap, the little interchange of courtesies which had just taken place, and smiled benevolently. All were silent now, but it seemed that he was quite exceptionally silent and would remain so during the whole journey.

The commercial traveller's solicitude for the banker's wife had created a pleasant, communal feeling in the compartment. Even the officer, while maintaining a proper reserve, had a friendly expression around his lips—though of course he had not yet been introduced. And the sad but kindly look on the face of the priest proclaimed unreservedly that nothing but mutual kindness and love could soften the inevitable hardships of life.

The banker, who had resolved to be an affectionate father, did all he could for his young wife, who expected to bear her child in the course of the following week. And she withdrew her glance from his face only to bury it in herself.

"Presumably I shall again lead for the prosecution in the sensational political trials which are still pending. Just imagine what my situation would be if the workers, instigated and led on by your brother, should again indulge in strikes or demonstrations, should plunder or come into conflict with the police or military. I should be compelled to demand, for the son of your highly-respected father, an exemplary sentence, possibly fifteen years——"

"——Or even death?"

"——Certainly, under certain conditions and if malicious intent were proven, even death."

'For me! Very nice.'

"What a situation for me to be in! You can see that?"

"I see. You deserve the deepest sympathy."

"And still more your father."

"And what about my brother?"

"He too, if you like! But revolution is warfare——"

"That is precisely what my brother says."

"——and if a man exposes himself to danger he must reckon with the possibility of death. . . . From what I know of your brother he would refuse the services of a psychiatrist; he would be more likely to use the court as a platform from which to make some violent speech, to take the last opportunity of serving the cause he has at heart."

"With the possibility of the death sentence before his eyes! . . . And yet under certain conditions and with the proof of malicious intent, sentence of death might be passed on—me!"

"Yes! For leaders of your sort are exceptionally dangerous."

"And must be removed, I suppose?"

"That is so."

III

The train began to move. A goods train, loaded with logs, had left this station, the highest in the whole country, a short time before. Bark was still lying between the rails at the siding. Long, thin wisps of smoke still clung to the damp cliffs.

An ex-student was standing alone in the corridor. His ambition was to become a public prosecutor. A vigorous, black moustache, curled up at the ends, on a pale face covered with duelling scars. He looked up at the wet, perpendicular walls of rock and down far below, where the little hamlets lay blue on green silk, as though strewn from a box of toys.

The ex-student thrust out his lower lip and let it slip back approximately each time a telegraph-pole flew by. He suffered from boredom. And from an affection of the bladder. That was why he was standing in the corridor.

A workman had strayed into the corridor of the second-class coach and was leaning against the next window, eating a green apple. He was one of the hundred who had been dismissed from the saw-mill and was going to the city in the hope of finding work.

"Rich crops."

"But coal! Coal is what we need," repeated the hardware traveller, obstinately.

And the clergyman: "If it is God's will, we shall soon have coal again, too."

'God' produced no response from the traveller; he said: "Without coal, no production. Without production, no export. Without export, no payment of debts and no boom. That's clear. Coal is everything."

The banker's wife had closed her eyes. She was living her two lives to herself.

The banker said, "Yes, coal! And big, long-term credits. And work, of course, only work——"

"——can save us. That's clear. Work's everything."

"The return to the old German discipline," said the university professor, to everyone's surprise.

The officer's body automatically expressed approval by moving from the hips upward, as though driven by electricity.

"Then we should soon be back where we were before the war. We could—begin all over again. We'd show the world what we're made of. We should be able to work again. And we *can* work. Better than anyone else."

"We've proved that."

"We've proved it."

The priest said flatly: "This nation cannot be broken."

'It'll be hard to find a job; there are too many unemployed,' thought the discharged mill-hand. 'What are they talking about in there?'

"If you would like to know why I was entrusted with the prosecution in those sensational political trials—if you are interested——"

"I am very deeply interested."

"Then I will explain it to you with pleasure," cried the public prosecutor. He shouted the words aloud. And the ardour of a youth of seventeen revived in his eyes.

"You see, some boys are interested in nothing but football. Life to them is just a football-field. Others long for the open road, for a life of freedom on the high seas, and cannot understand the ambition of a boy who, God knows why, is determined to be the best lithographer in his native town and marry his neighbour's daughter Lenchen. But the latter suddenly becomes a ship's boy on a boat bound for India, while the one who dreamed of freedom is cooped up as a clerk in the municipal offices."

The detective appeared in the doorway and examined the luggage rack with great interest. The public prosecutor laughed frankly and waved him away.

"The boy on the ground floor spends his youth building model steam-engines; the one on the floor above collects snakes; some people will collect anything, and others make it a principle to collect nothing but what they find in the streets. . . . My youthful passion was the study of the political trials and revolutionary movements of all times and peoples. To-day I am a public prosecutor. My life is entirely consistent."

The train was late. It stopped. Only for a half minute. And, as it moved slowly forward again, a breathless peasant, scythe in hand, scrambled on to the running-board and entered the last coach.

"I had all the books on the subject—every one of them! And I studied them, read them and read them again and again, full of revolt against the savage injustice of the rulers, full of passion and determination to become an avenger of the poor, a revolutionary such as the world had never seen before."

"That sounds as though you were describing my own youth rather than your own."

"But one day I realized that all I had been doing was, so to speak, to collect revolutions and attempts to save humanity."

"And yet you think your life is consistent?"

The public prosecutor was silent for a second. And during that long second, there appeared on his face the phantom of his submerged self; it stood on the frontier of life and could not step over it.

Then he drew back his lips, and his face resembled a plaster mask, hanging on the wall, which suddenly begins to smile. "Well, my case was like that of the lover of freedom, who longs for the high seas, and is placed by Fate in the municipal offices. . . . What of it? There are so many who want to save the world while they are young. There may even be one in the next compartment among those representatives of our national life—the church, science, finance, the army, the press, education. And who knows? Perhaps at one time in his life even that detective—Life is not easy."

"But, my dear, you have no idea of the cost of such a school. 'An open-air school with boarding facilities for gifted children of the working classes'—I know, it sounds very nice," whispered the banker. "There are buildings to be put up and furnished! Salaries for long-haired teachers and young women in sandals! And think of how much your gifted children of the working classes will eat, when they spend long days in the clear, fresh air!"

The banker was irritated by the look which was his wife's first response. He knew that look: it said more plainly than words that a clear conscience is worth more than money.

"And what are your gifted working-class children to learn in this open-air school? To grow vegetable-marrows? To make chests of drawers?"

"Everything, everything. . . . A complete development of the faculties of mind and body. According to their ability. . . . Of course we should grow all we needed."

"Of course!"

"Vegetables and such things."

"Oh, yes, vegetables! . . . You would grow nothing, believe me." And suddenly, in a low, caressing voice: "All right—if it's a boy."

A train, packed with incoming visitors, crawled up the steep mountain-line so slowly that a dog would have had no difficulty in keeping up with it. It passed the other train, which was boring its way with screeching brakes and reversed power towards the valley, passed it so slowly that the agitator could see the passengers buttering their rolls in the dining-car and raising white coffee-cups to their lips; he saw the waiter spread out his hands and shrug his shoulders regretfully because a diner had asked for something he could not supply.

"Yes, Socialism is my passion. Or anything connected with revolution! And that's as true to-day as when I was a young man!"

"Why are you displaying your cynicism to me of all people?" asked the agitator, in an indifferent voice.

The public prosecutor shook his head as though in surprise. "You are busy all day long with Socialism, devotion, loyalty and similar virtuous ideas, and you evidently cannot imagine what a relief it is for one of us to be able to tell the truth occasionally."

"At all events you differ in one pleasing respect from other members of your class, for you know that your views are a swindle."

"You are not very polite. And you seem to be a cynic too. At least I've not noticed so far that you showed any moral indignation at my insincerity; I have however noticed a sturdy cynicism in many of your remarks."

"Cynicism is in the thing itself and not in the words that designate it."

"Says Marx in his excellent work *Das Elend der Philosophie,* page 17," said the prosecutor fluently, and, since the agitator did not conceal his surprise:

"Few of your comrades have studied the life work of that great man as passionately as I—of course, in my youth."

The public prosecutor had lost something of his reserve. His calm had left him. His brow was flushed. It had an unhealthy look. The public prosecutor was in the grip of an idea. Like a boy sorting his collection of snakes.

"Did you notice the famous viaduct as you came up?" began the banker, in the next compartment.

"Marvellous piece of work," said the commercial traveller, promptly. "And the view! Magnificent!"

"Yes, it reminded me of those religious paintings by the old masters."

And as the priest, favourably affected, threw a friendly, questioning look at the banker:

"In about an hour we shall cross the viaduct. You ought really to take a good look at it. . . . Just imagine a mountain valley bounded by the steep cliffs of sublime, snow-covered alpine giants; on all sides romantic, jagged mountain-chains extend to remote distances, and in the middle of this mighty, and, I must admit, rather grim valley, a lovely green hill in the shape of a pointed cone, quite idyllic, like the background of some old, religious painting."

"There's really no need," said the public prosecutor, with a smile, to the detective, who had been standing within hearing, his shorthand-notebook in his hand. A sudden backward jerk of the train had brought him into view.

"That's it. You have described it very well," said the editor. He took a bottle of wine and a corkscrew from his suit case, and looked inquiringly at the detective, who had now thrust his ear into this compartment.

"He was only sent here for my personal safety. But he can't help it. I never met a more conscientious man in my life." The public prosecutor took several pages of notes from his attaché case. "Would you like to read the verbatim report of the speech you made to-day at the saw-mill? I have put brackets round the passages he made up. 'The capitalists must be swept away with fire and sword, poison and the knife. . . . To the lamp-posts with every one of them!' I'm sure you didn't say that."

"Perhaps I did. Who knows?"

"This conical hill has been cleverly exploited by engineers as a base for the iron supports of the viaduct. The rails run through the air at a dizzy height, crossing the gulf to the top of the cone. You will see: we shall travel round a very small circle—actually a spiral—encircling the little green summit of the cone. And, as we are sitting in the last coach and the train happens to be a very long one, we shall see the engine of our own train coming towards us. The engine of our own train! Extraordinary, isn't it?"

The editor's tone suggested that he was quoting from something he had previously written: "American engineers came over on purpose to study this masterpiece of German railway construction." And he inserted the corkscrew into the cork.

"But why?" asked the banker, as his wife took off her heavy diamond rings, two from each hand.

"You take them." She showed the anticipatory maternal smile he already knew.

The banker had always accepted such actions without contradiction, when they seemed in some unaccountable way to be connected with the coming child.

Amidst the silence of his fellow-travellers, he carefully placed the rings in a little pigskin jewel-case, in which several valuable pendants, a diamond necklace and a long coiled chain of big pearls already lay on the white silk. As he did so, he went on:

"When we cross the viaduct we shall be sixteen hundred feet above the bottom of the valley. We travel, so to speak, through the air. The sides of this valley are so precipitous, so precipitous, that a chamois perhaps might manage to climb down them, but certainly not a human being. You can see everything quite clearly, for the circle, that is to say the spiral, is so small that the train, to avoid jumping the rails and hurtling down into the valley——"

"Sixteen hundred feet—that's quite enough for me!"

"——has to move exceptionally slowly."

At last the priest began to look a little perturbed. All fell silent. All saw the viaduct soaring through the air across the chasm; all watched the train move very, very slowly round the narrow spiral of rails that encircled the top of the conical hill.

The generous dinner they had just eaten and the regular rhythm of the train made the passengers feel sleepy.

The professor, already dozing, heard the train singing ceaselessly and monotonously: 'When the dog . . . with the bone . . . jumped o—ver the hedge . . . when the dog . . . with the bone . . . jumped o—ver the hedge.'

'That caper sauce was delicious at lunch to-day,' thought the banker. 'Yes, man's striving after perfection expresses itself in many forms.'

'. . . with the bone . . . jumped o—ver the hedge.'

And, since his fellow-passengers were all more or less asleep, the editor considered all to himself the accuracy of a statement he had recently made to the effect that the Press in the twentieth century was no trifle.

"Only work can save us and coal," murmured the priest, half asleep.

'. . . jumped o—ver the hedge.'

"This nation . . . cannot be broken."

'When the dog. . . .'

Meanwhile the discharged mill-hand was mending the wide corridor-window. It was half open, and—so the guard had told him—had not opened properly since the coach was repainted.

IV

A man was leaning against the back end of the coach. He had been busy throughout the journey: first he had been writing figures in a note-book; then he had counted a number of bank-notes of high value, and a very large number of bank-notes of low value, and finally had compared the total with the sum of the figures in his notebook.

Suddenly his eyes opened wide. He wrenched open the door of the coach, jumped out, and rolled down the high embankment. He got up and stood staring after the last coach, which had become disconnected from the rest of the train and was moving at a moderate speed through the rugged landscape.

At this point the line was almost level; if anything it rose, so that the distance between the uncoupled last coach and the train grew rapidly greater.

The train moved on. And vanished behind the spur of a hill.

When the train had passed the pointsman's hut and was slowly boring its way with screaming brakes into the wide main valley, the pointsman switched over the points for the next timber-train.

From this spot, the timber-trains travelled by a rack and pinion through a branch valley, narrow and fissured, that led to the chief saw-mill at the foot of the mountains.

The pointsman whistled to his dog and walked towards his hut. He examined the condition of ten meagre heads of red cabbage, which grew in a patch of garden surrounded by a toy-like fence no higher than a man's knee. He leapt up and round.

He was just in time to see a second-class coach, its fresh paintwork glinting in the sun, pass slowly over the points and, propelled by its own weight, shoot down the steep decline of the branch-valley at a rapidly increasing speed.

He uttered a cry of horror. The dog barked. The coach had vanished.

The discharged mill-hand had been looking out of the rear window of the coach, vainly trying to catch sight of the man who had jumped out. At that moment he remembered that once as a boy he had been very anxious to pull the communication cord, which his father had strictly forbidden him to do. His feet were still by the door though his hands had already reached the window, as he threw himself with a wild vehemence across the compartment. It was as though, after thirty years, his father had at last given him permission to pull the communication cord. The passengers started out of their slumber.

His right hand raised to the cord, his left grasping the edge of the open window, he drew his body after him through the atmosphere of startled annoyance. As he did so, his head popped through the window and he saw that the coach was uncoupled.

The student appeared in the doorway. "A gentleman out here has just jumped out of the train."

Without a second's hesitation, the hardware traveller said: "If he likes to do that, it's his affair! Besides, he was a competitor of mine." His smartness caused some amusement among his fellow-passengers. It was the considered opinion of the banker, and he always carefully practised it, that nothing was better for an expectant mother than a cheerful frame of mind; he therefore smiled affectionately at his wife, encouraging her to join in the general amusement, and she produced a short, faint smile which broke almost before it had formed, and for a while the fragments remained in the neighbourhood of her lips.

The professor, reclining with crossed arms deep in his corner, showed that he could smile, even if the joke were a little banal. . . .

The officer was a uniformed dummy with eyes, a mouth and a forehead, correct poise with a stiff smile adhering to it.

"We're making up for lost time. Travelling like the devil after a pretty nun, what?"

The priest drew up his travelling-rug, leaned back more comfortably in his seat, and said with mild sympathy: "May God protect him! Why did this gentleman jump out?"

The face of the workman was quite colourless. He turned round very slowly. Shock had robbed him of speech.

"That queer fellow spent the whole time counting money," said the student, suspiciously. "You never know what would make a man like that jump out."

With a rapid glance, the banker assured himself that the valuable jewel-case was still on the folding-table.

The workman's eyes stared like glass. His little, dusty moustache was trembling. His white lips said: "We're uncoupled."

This flash of truth did not strike home at once. The hardware traveller, still indignant and yet already moved, as though death had touched him from a distance, said harshly: "What do you mean—uncoupled?"

The coach sped with violent jerks down the steep, cogged line.

"There's—there's—there's nothing we can do. There's—there's nothing we can do. It's all up."

He turned sideways and went through the door as slowly as though he had never in his life had so much time. "What? What can we do?"

The professor turned his head: "Has anything happened?"

Seen from a distant point outside the train: the mountain landscape in its vast dimensions—and on that line of rails with its toothed rack that dropped so steeply towards the valley, a dark, tiny, tiny speck that did not move, did not rush, but hurtled between the mountains into the depths.

"There's no way of stopping this coach," said the workman, still speaking into the compartment. "There's no way in the world." And, with lips white and a heart that scarcely beat, he stepped into the corridor. "We're all dead men."

"What's happened then? Has something happened? Something happened?" The professor had got up from his place.

The priest, still incredulous: "They say we are uncoupled."

The banker, at this moment still far from admitting the deadly fact even to himself, yet white in the face, began indignantly: "The authorities ought to——"

The officer and the hardware traveller had both looked out simultaneously: their faces reappeared. Colourless. White.

The truth struck home. All rose. Speechless. Without a word, the traveller dashed into the corridor, blindly seeking salvation.

A curve: the flying coach sprang a yard above the rails—those standing were mowed, falling across each other, on to the seats—and crashed back, while a scream of fear arose from many throats, on to the rails.

If the next curve were but a few degrees sharper, the coach would shoot off the track—fly straight through the air and explode like a shell.

Six pairs of glazed eyes.

Only the woman with child looked forward with soft, impressionable eyes to this frightful catastrophe, sent more and more intent and gentle looks pressing upon the first, till the disaster burnt itself into her eyes, and the child, if ever it were born, would come into the world with that horrid vision upon its skin.

The professor also had completely changed. He was no longer a professor. Glasses, cap, plaid travelling-rug lay on the floor. His face had grown angular and smaller. He had not yet accepted the inevitability of death.

None of them had accepted it yet. The banker asked: "You're not afraid, are you, dear? There's nothing to be afraid of?"

Has any man, however desperate his situation, ever given up his belief in life before the last second?

Voices shouting counsel, which the counsellors did not believe. The coach must be stopped. The passengers must jump out.

They could not even *look* out. The speed numbed their brains.

A short, sharp bang and black lightning—the sky again in a second: the flying coach had passed through a tunnel.

The officer, a brave man, who had resolutely risked his life in the war, always with the hope of saving it, had not yet lost his nerve. He was searching for some possible means of escape—searching with every muscle tense, the veins swollen on his forehead, for a possibility that did not exist. This was no enemy to be overcome by strength, courage and determination.

The woman dropped her face into her hands. Slowly a cry arose from deep in her womb, swelled upward—no one noticed it—welled out through her fingers, became sharp and guttural and broke in a scream: she had given up her own life and her child's for lost.

She withdrew her hands from her face, which was still mobile. Moaning, she lamented her own full life and the still unlived one.

This did not attract for a moment the attention of the banker and the rest. For in just that moment death might seize any man whose mind relaxed or whose muscles were unready to jump. After all, there must be some possibility of salvation. Death was itself an impossibility.

An axle had run hot and was whistling shrilly. The intervals between its whistlings grew shorter and shorter till it whistled continuously; a noise that permeated and drowned all other noises, like a human cry driven to its topmost pitch, went with them as they rushed into the valley.

Dull thudding of rails; the coach leaped and crashed down again.

The professor repeatedly raised both hands to his temples; he felt the horror lie cold in his hair; in terror of death he exorcised his terror with a lie: he entered his flat in the best part of the town, went into his cheerful study, sat down at his desk: the green lamp-shade shone up.

His impotent will to live caused the banker to get out of the train, which had just steamed punctually into the valley station.

At intervals the old priest was no longer alive; his face was dead. But, in between, the will to live wrenched him back to his sense of horror.

At the door stood the student, staring inquiringly with dull eyes at those older than himself, who ought to know better than he by what means he could be saved. He got no answer.

The saliva was dripping from the editor's mouth.

The hardware traveller threw himself through the woman's ebbing cry towards the window, then immediately back into the corridor, and thence into the next compartment. From one compartment to another. From end to end of the coach. Up and down. There was no way out.

Into the compartment where the public prosecutor, the agitator and the detective stood clinging to each other and the luggage rack, tossed from side to side. The woman's face had turned green. Her labour had begun.

A hand still lay on her shoulder; it seemed to be independent of the banker's arm, to lie independently on her shoulder; for the banker was staring at the valley-station, where the train was just running in, just running in, over and over again.

He would finance the forest school for workmen's children. That was a vow.

Each made his own vow. Each had already made it, and repeated it and enlarged it.

All his life the mill-hand had worked in order to eat and eaten in order to work.

His mother is bleaching washing on the lawn for the gentlefolk. The cook from the big house gives the washerwoman's little boy, as he sits there beside the laundry, a hunk of fresh, white bread, thickly spread with butter. Again and again, this most beautiful of all his childhood's memories comes back. White laundry, white bread, shining butter, shining sun—again and again. And flits away. More quickly than the coach rushes valley-ward.

Did something flash past? Was that a station? A halt? An Alpine hut?

Green pastures, rocks. White waterfall. Mountain torrent. The thunder boomed louder over a little iron bridge. Forest. Another bridge. Green pastures. Yellow: a group of grazing cows.

Any tune can be set to the speed of a train; this projectile flew so fast that there were no joints between rails that could supply the beats.

The landscape roared by.

Now there was no one left in the compartments. All were in the corridor. They ran shouting up and down, seeking deliverance. Only the pregnant woman half sat, half lay, upon a seat, forsaken, moaning, throbbing with pain.

The workman was still listening—listening to the screaming, smoking whistle of the axle—still thinking. He thought the coach would catch fire at any minute. Burn to ashes!

Then death put its hand into the frenzied coach and strangled hope, which was as large as life and yet as minute as a speck of dust: with his mind's eye the banker saw the viaduct.

His lips framed the words: "The viaduct!" Yelled, "viaduct, the viaduct!" He fell on his hands and knees. Scrambled on all fours, uttering hoarse, animal sounds.

In a blue flash that struck hope dead, all saw the viaduct spanning the empty air, sixteen hundred feet above the valley, the narrow, deadly ring from which the frenzied coach must leap! Must!

"The viaduct. Viaduct!"

"Viaduct?"

Those were the last sounds of human speech, already drowned by cries of deadly terror, for which there are no words in any language.

The last vestiges of human masks, masks which in the course of life had grown into faces again, fell away, vanished: the primal face appeared.

All pressed back, retreating from the viaduct, stumbling over each other, wildly fighting each other, screaming in deadly terror, against the back of the coach—to be twenty-five feet farther away from the death leap.

Even the officer. Courage had ceased to exist, even for him, in face of inevitable and certain death. His temples turned cold and seemed to climb up over his head.

The detective's shorthand-notebook and a gold watch with a broken chain lay side by side in the corridor. The professor's plaid cap was propped against the wall by the window.

Faith, God, Jesus and the Virgin Mary, whose omnipotence the priest had been proclaiming for forty years, existed no longer: the Church collapsed without a sound.

"Holy Mary, Mother of God, pray for us poor sinners, now and in the hour of our death. Amen," muttered the pious peasant on his knees.

The woman had fallen from the seat and was writhing with upraised legs on the floor. Her piercing cries rose through the tumult. She had no husband now.

The workman was standing with knees half-bent, ready to jump, his hands clasping the edge of the window he had mended; several times he had noticed that, close beside him, life was wrestling for a life.

And, when he was spun round and thrown half into the compartment, he did what lay to hand with the same simple directness he had shown in mending the window: he knelt down and set to work: "Press! Press, I tell you! Keep on pressing!" And with his left hand braced against her chest he used his right to bring forth the child.

Past the agitator, who was half-lying in the doorway, pressing both fists into his eyes, rigid with horror at this meaningless death, the public prosecutor staggered, hurled violently to and fro between window and door, and joined the huddled throng.

The professor lay on his belly, his mouth on the floor, screaming convulsively.

A long swaying thread of saliva dripped on to him from the corner of the editor's mouth, which was drawn far back into his cheeks; his glassy eyes stared forward like all the rest, to the shattering end.

An amusement-contractor, whose roundabouts were at that moment revolving in a remote mountain-village, suddenly became insane. He ran out of the front compartment and down the corridor, wrenched open the door at the farther end and sprang out. Flew out.

The huddled group at the back of the coach saw the arm of the amusement-contractor torn from the body at the shoulder-joint, saw the body fly past. It was half a second before the hand loosed its grip on the door handle; then the arm was flung high in the air towards a freshly-ploughed field, dug itself in, and stood with the clenched fingers pointing towards the sky.

The door remained open, forged to the outside of the coach by the air-pressure.

Green, dark, sunny, dark, sky-blue.

A sparrow, not reckoning with this monstrous speed as it flew across the track, darted in through the open doorway, thudded against the panelling and fell dead on the floor.

The huddled group recoiled from the suction of that dangerous open door, fought with fists and feet, hissing between clenched teeth, for the safest place, scrambled over each other on hands and knees.

They did not resume the postures of human beings.

The mother on the seat, bare and bleeding, with the quiet baby in her hands moving its lips and bloody finger-tips, was borne with frantic speed through the landscape. The workman knelt in the blood, the jewel-case at his side and around him scattered diamond rings and the pearl necklace. The woman was not ashamed. We feel no shame when face to face with life and death.

A black pencil line became visible in the sunny distance ahead; in a few seconds it had grown into a horizontal walking stick moving slowly forward; then the agitator saw that it was a train: the goods train, laden with logs, which had left the terminus in the mountains before the passenger train.

Some enigmatic scruple had prevented the public prosecutor from taking part in the fight for the safest place; he looked back into his past, as though he had suddenly encountered a firm point within himself which arrested his fall into the chasm of fear. His face was transfigured as he pressed to his breast the youth he saw before him in flesh and blood, and held him tightly clasped, till the youth had finally entered into the man of thirty-four, to be carried within him as a talisman for the rest of his life.

In the mother's eyes as she looked at the workman was a happiness that could not be darkened even by the certain approach of death.

Suddenly she was holding a strange musical instrument in her hands. She was in darkness. Soft, wonderful music filled the air, never heard before: Death, a little man in a long coat, stepped quickly and noiselessly into the middle of the room. 'Death?' Then, as though in a theatre, the curtain fell. The woman had lost consciousness.

The agitator's brain had begun to work again: "If only that train would move faster, if only it would fly! . . . Unless the driver puts on full-steam we shall be shattered to pieces." And he shouted through the open window of the door at the front of the coach.

Suddenly every sound stopped. The whistling of the hot axle died out. The coach rose, sped through the air, noiseless. A silence of death. In which terrified screams burst out. Still flying. Human eyes, already lifeless, stared at the bloody mush of wood, limbs, bones, iron, flesh.

Once more the coach crashed back on to the rails.

"Holy Mary, Mother of God, pray for us poor sinners, now and in the hour of our death. Amen."

And the agitator shouted again through the open window of the door at the front. His shouts struck against the wall of air and recoiled into the coach.

The engine-driver heard nothing. All the brakes of the timber-train were grating. Pipe in mouth, his bare forearms resting comfortably on the iron door, he looked out over the passing landscape.

The rails flashed like streaks of lightning back under the coach. On each side, rocks, telegraph poles, trees, huts, reeled, merged and sped thundering past. Even the farthest peaks were in motion. The mountains turned slowly but visibly around the tiny projectile.

The engine-driver straightened his back and caught sight of the coach shooting towards him. Still nearly a mile away. No time for thought: the branch line had but a single track. Brakes off. Full steam.

In the next few seconds the space between the train and the projectile rapidly diminished; but the track was steep and the timber-train many times heavier than the coach.

Never had a train swooped so madly towards the valley.

After an immeasurable half-minute the two projectiles were travelling at the same speed, a few coach-lengths away from each other.

The brakes stole imperceptibly towards the wheels of the flying train, inaudibly, cautiously, like the hand of a pickpocket. Presently a hissing sound arose; gradually it grew louder and turned into a rising scream that drowned the noise of the train, deafened the ears, and filled the whole valley: the train stopped.

V

Silence. Through which came the hammering of a woodpecker. The new-born child had ceased to cry; in the midst of a cry it had fallen asleep. It lay, with both little legs drawn up, between the cushioned back of the seat and its unconscious mother.

So gently had buffer met buffer, despite the wild speed, that the men who crouched on hands and knees at the rear of the coach were still expecting a bloody fate though already they were saved.

Their numbed senses failed to react to silence and life; they still reproduced the catastrophic crashes and whistlings; like the mountains, which hum throughout eternity with the thousandfold echoes they hold imprisoned within themselves.

Twelve yards away a cow lay on the grass watching and chewing the cud. The whisper of grasses, the chatter and roar of distant brooks and falls, the buzz of myriads of gnats, caught up by the vibrating membranes of rocky cliffs and chasms, and thrown back across the quivering air of the valley, produced the great voice, the great audible silence of the mountains, in which the melodious twitter of a bird was the only living and immediate note.

That cow was not flashing past; it was lying still. This was no dream. The cow was reality, life. The bird, too, was twittering again.

Escaped from death, numb and terrified, they returned to life; feeling came back to their limbs. It was both painful and pleasant. Their heavy limbs refused to obey them.

Their helpless bodies slumped down over the running-board. They sat or lay outstretched: a little dark heap in a field.

Saved, released from the excess of fear they had experienced, breathing again in an excess of life, which came storming in upon them suddenly, confusing in its mighty power and millionfold variety, they could not apprehend the fields, the sun, the sky, the train, the greenness, the cow; for to apprehend these things man has a whole life at his disposal.

The agitator, too, had let himself sink down into the grass. The public prosecutor was sitting alone in the compartment, unaccountably transfigured.

The short, stumpy engine-driver walked slowly along the dark train, which was laden from the tender to the last truck with peeled fir trunks, shining in the sun; he walked like a man momentarily indifferent to his surroundings, who has just exerted all his energies to finish a hard job of work. He looked down at the ground, and wiped his hot, perspiring face with a red handkerchief.

The breathless cry of the child broke out again and died back upon itself. The woman awoke from her swoon, her eyes full of inquiry. Her groping hand found the baby. She closed her eyes again.

The banker had turned his head and listened. Then with his mind's eye he saw his wife, and his head jerked round again. His shoulders were glowing. That was good. And down his spine he felt a beneficent tingling of warmth, as after a cold shower-bath.

Willingly he helped the exhausted priest, who could not rise from the grass without his aid, and felt as he did so a melting tenderness in his breast.

"The coupling's not damaged. . . . Probably he forgot to fasten the catch," said the engine-driver, standing bent forward between the buffers. He fastened the catch and called on the passengers to get in.

"Well, I've got nothing to say," remarked the hardware traveller. He was the first to find his tongue.

The officer held out the palm of his hand: "After you, sir."

Brains began to function again. Knees were still shaking. Each helped the other to get in. The student appeared to think to himself: 'They ought to know.' And followed the others.

The banker leaned down and put out his hand. "Up!" he cried, jokingly. His smiling lips were trembling.

The engine-driver wiped his neck with his handkerchief as he walked back to his engine. There he found the workman, squatting in the grass, his head in his right hand, looking at the dripping, oily wheels. The boiler appeared to be sweating.

"We're off now. Jump in! You can come up with me."

The workman looked up inquiringly, as though he did not know where he was.

The peasant was already trudging across country towards the mountain-side. Scythe on shoulder, he was making for a meadow that lay higher up in the main valley. He and ten others had to mow that meadow during the evening and the cool moonlit night that would follow. His sunken lips were muttering. His left hand was counting on the fingers of the right, reckoning how much money he had lost through the delay.

Then there were his hopes for the child. . . . Our child! . . . We have been so near to each other . . . so near! thought the banker. 'And now . . . now. . . . Just because that drunken scoundrel failed to fasten the catch!'

At last he entered the compartment where his wife was lying in blood-stained desolation, the blood-stained child in her arms. "Now it's all over," he said, in a comforting tone. "You were so frightened of it. And now it's all over. There's the baby."

She shut her eyes—her hand moved as it lay on the child—and opened

them again. 'Has nothing happened? Has not something occurred, something decisive, which you must admit unless our whole life from this moment on is to be a single, unbroken lie?' asked the exhausted woman with
her eyes.

He spread the travelling-rug carefully and solicitously across her knees,
bent on tiptoe to pick up the jewellery, and closed the pigskin case.

Our life *before* must have been a single unbroken lie, she thought, or
this could not have happened. 'Between then and now are fifteen minutes
of truth. His truth—Each for himself!'

"We shall soon be there. Then I'll see you get a bath, a bed, midwife, doctor, everything you want."

It was as though a planet spoke to another, which did not hear its voice.
And yet again there lay that broken smile about her mouth.

The engine let off steam and half the train vanished in white; it moved
and all the buffers groaned; the backward jerk ran through the trucks, the
coach and all the passengers, and life had begun again: rattling, groaning
and lamenting like the belts, hammers and files of a great factory, the
timber-train crept cautiously and surely down into the valley.

The passengers who had been saved stood in the corridor, talking excitedly. All spoke together; all agreed with each other. They had the joy
and splendour of life in their eyes and caresses that were never performed.

The public prosecutor sat motionless in his compartment, his eyes fixed
on the distant past.

The hardware-traveller appeared in the doorway, took one step and laid
his hand inquiringly on the shoulder of the man with the transfigured face.

He came out again on tiptoe. "That gentleman in there is crying."

"Crying?"

"Yes, he's crying."

"A man's crying." The professor passed the word along.

They spoke more quietly. And suddenly all fell silent, looking out.

How good the landscape was! The lovely fields. The bare fields in the
sunshine. And birds were sitting on the telegraph wires. Close together.
They flew up and flew down again. They opened their beaks and twittered;
but one could not hear them.

"How cheerfully we all started out! . . . . Who could have expected it!"

All looked at the editor. "Yes, things happen so suddenly," said the professor. "You are sitting quietly in your study—and suddenly a tiny vein
bursts in your brain . . . and it's all up: tongue and limbs paralysed; you
can't tell a goose from a child."

"What a hell of a speed!"

And the priest said: "We are always in God's hand."

"And now we're going so slowly that if the human eye was built to see
round corners we should still be able to see that cow!"

They smiled happily. They breathed and smiled.

"Quite a difference in the speed, what?" joked the hardware-traveller. And began to describe his feelings during that wild downward rush.

"But one can't see round corners. I don't suppose they will ever discover how to see round corners," said the student, half inquiringly. His mind had moved rather slowly. He bent down and took up his gold watch. He held it to his left ear. He held it to his right ear. It was still going.

The detective had already picked up his shorthand-notebook. He shook off the dust and smoothed out two leaves that were covered with writing.

The agitator looked on in surprise. "Have you got it all down?"

"You've got to keep things tidy," said the detective, and carefully inserted the mauve carbon-paper between the cover and the first page.

"He lost both his sons. Just before the end of the war. It killed his wife. Since then he's been boozing," explained the engine-driver, and offered the workman his blue enamelled can, in which there was still a little coffee.

"Now they'll give him the sack." The workman handed back the can. "Then it's all over with him."

"Yes, all over with him then." The engine-driver drank the rest of the coffee.

"I've called it *The Death Ride* . . . That's the title. That's it. To-morrow afternoon you will find the whole story in my paper. To-morrow morning, if possible."

"Shall you print the names?" asked the hardware-traveller, eagerly.

So they began to introduce themselves. The student clapped his heels together twice, for he also gave the name of the corps he belonged to.

"He didn't fasten the safety-catch. He's——"

"Of course the man must——"

"——an absolute danger to life."

"——be discharged immediately."

"Of course."

"And he seems to be Socialistic," put in the officer. They were all speaking together.

The banker went into the corridor, met their questioning eyes and announced, the banker announced: "A healthy boy."

Amidst their congratulations—the officer was just introducing himself— he explained: "And we had got everything ready so carefully: midwife, doctor, nursery, with bath and everything complete. All the woodwork white enamelled—not just painted—and the dear little garments! Only the cradle is dark—a wonderful, seventeenth-century piece. And now—this surprise! Any poor woman, lying in a damp cellar, perhaps not even knowing where she can get food for her baby, would have had an easier and more comfortable time."

The priest said with mild gravity that God's ways were inscrutable.

And the traveller—he hesitated before deciding to say it: "One passenger gone west, and a new one come in his place."

At first they did not understand, but when they remembered the amusement contractor the expression of all their faces indicated that flippancy
was in bad taste.

"We must see about searching for his body."

"Yes, his body must be found at once."

"It can't be left lying out there."

"Certainly not! I'll see to that. I'm a traveller; I know this part of the
world. There's a motor lorry at the saw-mill. The manager wouldn't give
up his car for a job like that."

"A good thing your wife didn't see that frightful incident. In her condition! . . . Did you see the way his hand still clung to the door-handle
after his body had been torn off? Horrible!"

"The body must be somewhere between—I say, tell me, what became
of——?"

"Wherever it is, it must be found at once."

"——the viaduct?"

"The viaduct?—It's on the main line—it didn't occur to me till later—
our coach, this damned old 'bus, shot down into another valley. . . . But
still, I had quite enough of it, thank you, without a viaduct!"

The professor put up his forefinger level with his eyes. "From a scientific
standpoint it is an interesting fact that, when the body had already gone,
the muscular strength of the arm still functioned sufficiently to enable it to
cling to the handle."

For some little time the public prosecutor had been standing in the
doorway, looking at the company as though at his own past.

As the timber-train ran into the saw-mill, for the track ended in the yard
—the banker was sitting with his wife, holding her gently in his arms—the
priest said: "When a man has been beheaded, they say his eyes still open
and shut: I wonder whether he can still see what is happening?" And he
gave the professor a modest smile, intending to convey that the subject in
which he was expressing an interest did not really concern him as a tyro
in the sciences and a shepherd of souls.

"You are the man who saved us. I thank you. . . . I haven't enough
change, so take this." The banker looked on sympathetically as the engine-
driver, his oily fingers outspread, folded the cheque with great care, and
put it in his time-book.

Ten minutes later the woman was lying in a clean bed. She had everything; even the doctor and the midwife were there. She had everything.
Except her faith in her husband.

"And now let us all thank God who has saved us from a great peril. . . .
I wonder whether there is a priest in this charming village?"

"I know this part of the world. He lives in that big house among the trees.
But he's a competitor of yours unless I'm mistaken, and I don't think I am
mistaken."

The priest smiled wryly. "There are cases—there are cases in human experience," he said, more to himself than to the others; he took his handbag and walked away, his umbrella under his arm.

The motor-lorry clattered off up the mountain-side, past the house where the mother lay, which much resembled a shooting-gallery. Targets were painted over and on the door, on the green window-shutters, on the gable, on the weather-vane, over and between all the windows, till there was not a member of the ex-soldiers' association who could walk past the house without being overcome with a desire to shoot.

The midwife and the doctor were busy in the kitchen. The banker stood in the bedroom, beside the white bed. "I should so much like to stay with you. I'm so happy. But I simply can't do it. At the general meeting of the shareholders to-day—I represent forty per cent. of the capital—we are to deal with the old amalgamation scheme. The new company we should form, you know, would be far and away the biggest financial force in this part of the country, and would have the necessary power and resources. We should be able to control prices. But you understand, dear?"

"Yes, I won't keep you." She spoke as though she had realized that those laws which also express themselves in the furious downward rush of an uncoupled railway-coach cannot be set aside by the wish of one of the occupants to stay quietly at his wife's bedside.

"You can begin to collect your long-haired teachers, who know everything and have everything, except the money required to realize their ideals."

She made no reply to that. She thought with sympathy, which found in her weakness a proof of its depth, of the workman, and looked at her child as though it were the workman's child.

"I wonder whether the manager of the mill would lend me his car. Then I could still catch the train—you know, the train from which our coach was uncoupled."

The others had already set off on foot, through the lesser valley, across into the main valley to the station.

'It's like driving down the High Street,' thought the banker, sitting in the car; past the officer, who waved his hand, as he walked alone under the apple-trees, bare of any contact with the landscape; past the student who bowed, already telling his adventure to the members of his corps: 'A sticky business in one carriage: some woman had a kid.'

Past the editor and the professor: this time three black hats floated through the blue evening air.

'And that man with the gaiters touched his hat too. . . . . We might just as well (as though I'm a sort of royalty!) have motored over to the station together.'

Up a steep hill, and slowly past the agitator and the public prosecutor. The banker leaned back. 'Father! . . . The little beggar will grow up some day. . . . I wonder if she's got all she wants. Good girl! . . . I'll send some flowers at once. And the family doctor. Heaps of flowers! But without scent! And sterilized milk. . . . What became of that workman who happened to be there, and was able to help her when the child was born? . . . Lucky chance! Lucky, when all's said and done! I'll send him something extra. . . . If only one could make everybody happy,' yearned the banker, suddenly, and immersed himself in his notes for the shareholders' meeting.

"Have you ever thought about it?" asked the agitator of the public prosecutor, and stood still.

(The detective also stood still.)

"What shall you do now?"

The ebb of the noisy day, the first descending veils of evening, sharpened the ears of the valley. The chirp of grasshoppers, the voices of animals, had grown stronger. In the distance, a little dark group of labourers trudged heavily across a field towards the village, and with them the cattle, whose tinkling bells sounded from the distance, as they were driven home from the pasturage. Here and there a peasant was still at work, kneeling in the fields. And a ploughman, whose silhouette rose black from the darkening hill against the white, sleeping mountainside, sank slowly downhill again, dissolved in the dark and was absorbed into his valley.

The public prosecutor had made no answer. He walked in silence beside the agitator, bound by the yoke of his opinions.

The manner in which they walked beside each other strengthened the detective's suspicions. 'If it turned out that he was a first-rate actor, a super spy, and I was a fool, they'd kick me out. . . . But if——'

Hesitating, the detective left the road and walked thoughtfully through the woods. He, too, had a mother and a wife and two little children; and when their father came home from a journey, they asked: "Have you brought us anything, daddy?" At which he started and said regretfully: "Goodness, fancy my forgetting!" and then winked slyly with his left eye.

The manager's car sped past, filled with flowers, returning from the station to the mill. The well-fed liveried chauffeur was whistling like a blackbird. A few minutes later a straw-hat was raised: the hardware-traveller, who had come to terms with the chauffeur, went riding past. He had paid a profitable visit to three retailers in the village, and finished up by inquiring after his fellow-traveller, the priest. In the living-room two sky-blue, glass vases of gentian were standing on the sideboard, and the two shepherds of souls were sitting in the twilight at a window-table, being served by an elderly woman with thin, yellow hands and hair combed smoothly back. On the wall above the bookshelf was ticking a finely-built clock, and presently the lamp would be brought in. 'Very nice, too!' the traveller had thought to himself.

All were seated at the same table in the waiting-room. The editor was writing his descriptive article. The banker was drinking water with a little red wine, and scanning the latest financial news in a paper he had bought at the station bookstall. Now and then he exchanged a word with the hardware-traveller, who was cracking jokes and writing figures in his notebook, or thought affectionately of his wife.

She had sent word to the priest, who had gone to the shooting-gallery house after dinner, prepared to baptize the child, that she was a Jewess.

The agitator and the public prosecutor were pacing up and down the platform. The train from which the last coach had become detached had just been signalled.

The detective watched the two men reflectively. At last he determined to communicate his suspicions to the political department, but only verbally and with much discretion.

The workman was standing on the quay by the wharf, looking across the river, immersed in memories; as though the river, and that alone, were his home, his childhood. He withdrew his glance, and asked an old boat-man who was swilling the deck of a barge: "Is she yours?"

"Mine? She belongs to the saw-mill."

"I grew up by the water, too. Down at my home they've given up building boats of anything but iron. They last longer."

"Well, he's got plenty of wood. And these last too. We built this one in '86, down there at the yard. I can still remember it. . . . In the boat-yard. It belongs to the saw-mill now, too."

"There's something grand about flowing water. . . . That's the train at last."

"That's right."

From here onward the train was an express; it raced into the plain, moving irresistibly towards the capital.

COUNTERPARTS

James Joyce

(1882–   )

Tʜᴇ ʙᴇʟʟ ʀᴀɴɢ furiously and, when Miss Parker went to the tube, a furious voice called out in a piercing North of Ireland accent:

"Send Farrington here!"

Miss Parker returned to her machine, saying to a man who was writing at a desk:

"Mr. Alleyne wants you upstairs."

The man muttered *"Blast* him!" under his breath and pushed back his chair to stand up. When he stood up he was tall and of great bulk. He had a hanging face, dark wine-coloured, with fair eyebrows and moustache: his eyes bulged forward slightly and the whites of them were dirty. He lifted up the counter and, passing by the clients, went out of the office with a heavy step.

He went heavily upstairs until he came to the second landing, where a door bore a brass plate with the inscription *Mr. Alleyne.* Here he halted, puffing with labour and vexation, and knocked. The shrill voice cried:

"Come in!"

The man entered Mr. Alleyne's room. Simultaneously Mr. Alleyne, a little man wearing gold-rimmed glasses on a clean-shaven face, shot his head up over a pile of documents. The head itself was so pink and hairless it seemed like a large egg reposing on the papers. Mr. Alleyne did not lose a moment:

"Farrington? What is the meaning of this? Why have I always to complain of you? May I ask you why you haven't made a copy of that contract between Bodley and Kirwan? I told you it must be ready by four o'clock."

"But Mr. Shelley said, sir——"

"Mr. Shelley said, sir. . . . Kindly attend to what I say and not to what *Mr. Shelley says, sir.* You have always some excuse or another for shirking work. Let me tell you that if the contract is not copied before this evening I'll lay the matter before Mr. Crosbie. . . . Do you hear me now?"

"Yes, sir."

"Do you hear me now? . . . Ay and another little matter! I might as well be talking to the wall as talking to you. Understand once for all that you get a half an hour for your lunch and not an hour and a half. How many courses do you want, I'd like to know. . . . Do you mind me now?"

"Yes, sir."

Mr. Alleyne bent his head again upon his pile of papers. The man stared fixedly at the polished skull which directed the affairs of Crosbie & Alleyne, gauging its fragility. A spasm of rage gripped his throat for a few moments and then passed, leaving after it a sharp sensation of thirst. The man recognised the sensation and felt that he must have a good night's drinking. The middle of the month was passed and, if he could get the copy done in time, Mr. Alleyne might give him an order on the cashier. He stood still, gazing fixedly at the head upon the pile of papers. Suddenly Mr. Alleyne began to upset all the papers, searching for something. Then, as if he had been unaware of the man's presence till that moment, he shot up his head again, saying:

"Eh? Are you going to stand there all day? Upon my word, Farrington, you take things easy!"

"I was waiting to see . . ."

"Very good, you needn't wait to see. Go downstairs and do your work."

The man walked heavily towards the door and, as he went out of the room, he heard Mr. Alleyne cry after him that if the contract was not copied by evening Mr. Crosbie would hear of the matter.

He returned to his desk in the lower office and counted the sheets which remained to be copied. He took up his pen and dipped it in the ink but he continued to stare stupidly at the last words he had written: *In no case shall the said Bernard Bodley be* . . . The evening was falling and in a few minutes they would be lighting the gas: then he could write. He felt that he must slake the thirst in his throat. He stood up from his desk and, lifting the counter as before, passed out of the office. As he was passing out the chief clerk looked at him inquiringly.

"It's all right, Mr. Shelley," said the man, pointing with his finger to indicate the objective of his journey.

The chief clerk glanced at the hat-rack, but, seeing the row complete, offered no remark. As soon as he was on the landing the man pulled a shepherd's plaid cap out of his pocket, put it on his head and ran quickly down the rickety stairs. From the street door he walked on furtively on the inner side of the path towards the corner and all at once dived into a doorway. He was now safe in the dark snug of O'Neill's shop, and, filling up the little window that looked into the bar with his inflamed face, the colour of dark wine or dark meat, he called out:

"Here, Pat, give us a g.p., like a good fellow."

The curate brought him a glass of plain porter. The man drank it at a gulp and asked for a caraway seed. He put his penny on the counter and, leaving the curate to grope for it in the gloom, retreated out of the snug as furtively as he had entered it.

Darkness, accompanied by a thick fog, was gaining upon the dusk of February and the lamps in Eustace Street had been lit. The man went up by the houses until he reached the door of the office, wondering whether he could finish his copy in time. On the stairs a moist pungent odour of perfumes saluted his nose: evidently Miss Delacour had come while he was out in O'Neill's. He crammed his cap back again into his pocket and re-entered the office, assuming an air of absent-mindedness.

"Mr. Alleyne has been calling for you," said the chief clerk severely. "Where were you?"

The man glanced at the two clients who were standing at the counter as if to intimate that their presence prevented him from answering. As the clients were both male the chief clerk allowed himself a laugh.

"I know that game," he said. "Five times in one day is a little bit. . . . Well, you better look sharp and get a copy of our correspondence in the Delacour case for Mr. Alleyne."

This address in the presence of the public, his run upstairs and the porter he had gulped down so hastily confused the man and, as he sat down at his desk to get what was required, he realised how hopeless was the task of finishing his copy of the contract before half past five. The dark damp night was coming and he longed to spend it in the bars, drinking with his friends amid the glare of gas and the clatter of glasses. He got out the Delacour correspondence and passed out of the office. He hoped Mr. Alleyne would not discover that the last two letters were missing.

The moist pungent perfume lay all the way up to Mr. Alleyne's room. Miss Delacour was a middle-aged woman of Jewish appearance. Mr. Alleyne was said to be sweet on her or on her money. She came to the office often and stayed a long time when she came. She was sitting beside his desk now in an aroma of perfumes, smoothing the handle of her umbrella and nodding the great black feather in her hat. Mr. Alleyne had swivelled his chair round to face her and thrown his right foot jauntily upon his left knee. The man put the correspondence on the desk and bowed respectfully but neither Mr. Alleyne nor Miss Delacour took any notice of his bow. Mr. Alleyne tapped a finger on the correspondence and then flicked it towards him as if to say: *"That's all right: you can go."*

The man returned to the lower office and sat down again at his desk. He stared intently at the incomplete phrase: *In no case shall the said Bernard Bodley be* . . . and thought how strange it was that the last three words began with the same letter. The chief clerk began to hurry Miss Parker, saying she would never have the letters typed in time for post. The man listened to the clicking of the machine for a few minutes and then set to work to finish his copy. But his head was not clear and his mind wandered away to the glare and rattle of the public-house. It was a night for hot punches. He struggled on with his copy, but when the clock struck five he had still fourteen pages to write. Blast it! He couldn't finish it in time. He longed to execrate aloud, to bring his fist down on something violently. He was so enraged that he wrote *Bernard Bernard* instead of *Bernard Bodley* and had to begin again on a clean sheet.

He felt strong enough to clear out the whole office single-handed. His body ached to do something, to rush out and revel in violence. All the indignities of his life enraged him. . . . Could he ask the cashier privately for an advance? No, the cashier was no good, no damn good: he wouldn't give an advance. . . . He knew where he would meet the boys: Leonard and O'Halloran and Nosey Flynn. The barometer of his emotional nature was set for a spell of riot.

His imagination had so abstracted him that his name was called twice before he answered. Mr. Alleyne and Miss Delacour were standing outside the counter and all the clerks had turned round in anticipation of something. The man got up from his desk. Mr. Alleyne began a tirade of abuse, saying that two letters were missing. The man answered that he knew nothing about them, that he had made a faithful copy. The tirade continued: it was so bitter and violent that the man could hardly restrain his fist from descending upon the head of the manikin before him:

"I know nothing about any other two letters," he said stupidly.

"*You—know—nothing.* Of course you know nothing," said Mr. Alleyne. "Tell me," he added, glancing first for approval to the lady beside him, "do you take me for a fool? Do you think me an utter fool?"

The man glanced from the lady's face to the little egg-shaped head and back again; and, almost before he was aware of it, his tongue had found a felicitous moment:

"I don't think, sir," he said, "that that's a fair question to put to me."

There was a pause in the very breathing of the clerks. Everyone was astounded (the author of the witticism no less than his neighbours) and Miss Delacour, who was a stout amiable person, began to smile broadly. Mr. Alleyne flushed to the hue of a wild rose and his mouth twitched with a dwarf's passion. He shook his fist in the man's face till it seemed to vibrate like the knob of some electric machine:

"You impertinent ruffian! You impertinent ruffian! I'll make short work of you! Wait till you see! You'll apologise to me for your impertinence or you'll quit the office instanter! You'll quit this, I'm telling you, or you'll apologise to me!"

. . .

He stood in a doorway opposite the office watching to see if the cashier would come out alone. All the clerks passed out and finally the cashier came out with the chief clerk. It was no use trying to say a word to him when he was with the chief clerk. The man felt that his position was bad enough. He had been obliged to offer an abject apology to Mr. Alleyne for his impertinence but he knew what a hornet's nest the office would be for him. He could remember the way in which Mr. Alleyne had hounded little Peake out of the office in order to make room for his own nephew. He felt savage and thirsty and revengeful, annoyed with himself and with everyone else. Mr. Alleyne would never give him an hour's rest; his life would be a hell to him. He had made a proper fool of himself this time. Could he not keep his tongue in his cheek? But they had never pulled together from the first, he and Mr. Alleyne, ever since the day Mr. Alleyne had overheard him mimicking his North of Ireland accent to amuse Higgins and Miss Parker: that had been the beginning of it. He might have tried Higgins for the money, but sure Higgins never had anything for himself. A man with two establishments to keep up, of course he couldn't. . . .

He felt his great body again aching for the comfort of the public-house. The fog had begun to chill him and he wondered could he touch Pat in O'Neill's. He could not touch him for more than a bob—and a bob was no use. Yet he must get money somewhere or other: he had spent his last

penny for the g.p. and soon it would be too late for getting money anywhere. Suddenly, as he was fingering his watch-chain, he thought of Terry
Kelly's pawn-office in Fleet Street. That was the dart! Why didn't he think
of it sooner?

He went through the narrow alley of Temple Bar quickly, muttering to
himself that they could all go to hell because he was going to have a good
night of it. The clerk in Terry Kelly's said *A crown!* but the consignor held
out for six shillings; and in the end the six shillings was allowed him
literally. He came out of the pawn-office joyfully, making a little cylinder
of the coins between his thumb and fingers. In Westmoreland Street the
footpaths were crowded with young men and women returning from business and ragged urchins ran here and there yelling out the names of the
evening editions. The man passed through the crowd, looking on the spectacle generally with proud satisfaction and staring masterfully at the office-
girls. His head was full of the noises of tram-gongs and swishing trolleys
and his nose already sniffed the curling fumes of punch. As he walked on he
preconsidered the terms in which he would narrate the incident to the
boys:

"So, I just looked at him—coolly, you know, and looked at her. Then I
looked back at him again—taking my time, you know. 'I don't think that
that's a fair question to put to me,' says I."

Nosey Flynn was sitting up in his usual corner of Davy Byrne's and, when
he heard the story, he stood Farrington a half one, saying it was as smart
a thing as ever he heard. Farrington stood a drink in his turn. After a
while O'Halloran and Paddy Leonard came in and the story was repeated
to them. O'Halloran stood tailors of malt, hot, all round and told the story
of the retort he had made to the chief clerk when he was in Callan's of
Fownes's Street; but, as the retort was after the manner of the liberal shepherds in the eclogues, he had to admit that it was not as clever as Farrington's retort. At this Farrington told the boys to polish off that and have another.

Just as they were naming their poisons who should come in but Higgins!
Of course he had to join in with the others. The men asked him to give his
version of it, and he did so with great vivacity for the sight of five small
hot whiskies was very exhilarating. Everyone roared laughing when he
showed the way in which Mr. Alleyne shook his fist in Farrington's face.
Then he imitated Farrington, saying, *"And here was my nabs, as cool as
you please,"* while Farrington looked at the company out of his heavy dirty
eyes, smiling and at times drawing forth stray drops of liquor from his
moustache with the aid of his lower lip.

When that round was over there was a pause. O'Halloran had money but
neither of the other two seemed to have any; so the whole party left the
shop somewhat regretfully. At the corner of Duke Street Higgins and
Nosey Flynn bevelled off to the left while the other three turned back

towards the city. Rain was drizzling down on the cold streets and, when they reached the Ballast Office, Farrington suggested the Scotch House. The bar was full of men and loud with the noise of tongues and glasses. The three men pushed past the whining match-sellers at the door and formed a little party at the corner of the counter. They began to exchange stories. Leonard introduced them to a young fellow named Weathers who was performing at the Tivoli as an acrobat and knockabout *artiste*. Farrington stood a drink all round. Weathers said he would take a small Irish and Apollinaris. Farrington, who had definite notions of what was what, asked the boys would they have an Apollinaris too; but the boys told Tim to make theirs hot. The talk became theatrical. O'Halloran stood a round and then Farrington stood another round, Weathers protesting that the hospitality was too Irish. He promised to get them in behind the scenes and introduce them to some nice girls. O'Halloran said that he and Leonard would go, but that Farrington wouldn't go because he was a married man; and Farrington's heavy dirty eyes leered at the company in token that he understood he was being chaffed. Weathers made them all have just one little tincture at his expense and promised to meet them later on at Mulligan's in Poolbeg Street.

When the Scotch House closed they went round to Mulligan's. They went into the parlour at the back and O'Halloran ordered small hot specials all round. They were all beginning to feel mellow. Farrington was just standing another round when Weathers came back. Much to Farrington's relief he drank a glass of bitter this time. Funds were getting low but they had enough to keep them going. Presently two young women with big hats and a young man in a check suit came in and sat at a table close by. Weathers saluted them and told the company that they were out of the Tivoli. Farrington's eyes wandered at every moment in the direction of one of the young women. There was something striking in her appearance. An immense scarf of peacock-blue muslin was wound round her hat and knotted in a great bow under her chin; and she wore bright yellow gloves, reaching to the elbow. Farrington gazed admiringly at the plump arm which she moved very often and with much grace; and when, after a little time, she answered his gaze he admired still more her large dark brown eyes. The oblique staring expression in them fascinated him. She glanced at him once or twice and, when the party was leaving the room, she brushed against his chair and said *"O, pardon!"* in a London accent. He watched her leave the room in the hope that she would look back at him, but he was disappointed. He cursed his want of money and cursed all the rounds he had stood, particularly all the whiskies and Apollinaris which he had stood to Weathers. If there was one thing that he hated it was a sponge. He was so angry that he lost count of the conversation of his friends.

When Paddy Leonard called him he found that they were talking about feats of strength. Weathers was showing his biceps muscle to the company

and boasting so much that the other two had called on Farrington to up-
hold the national honour. Farrington pulled up his sleeve accordingly and
showed his biceps muscle to the company. The two arms were examined
and compared and finally it was agreed to have a trial of strength. The table
was cleared and the two men rested their elbows on it, clasping hands.
When Paddy Leonard said *"Go!"* each was to try to bring down the other's
hand on to the table. Farrington looked very serious and determined.

The trial began. After about thirty seconds Weathers brought his opponent's hand slowly down on to the table. Farrington's dark wine-coloured
face flushed darker still with anger and humiliation at having been defeated
by such a stripling.

"You're not to put the weight of your body behind it. Play fair," he said.

"Who's not playing fair?" said the other.

"Come on again. The two best out of three."

The trial began again. The veins stood out on Farrington's forehead, and
the pallor of Weathers' complexion changed to peony. Their hands and
arms trembled under the stress. After a long struggle Weathers again
brought his opponent's hand slowly on to the table. There was a murmur of
applause from the spectators. The curate, who was standing beside the
table, nodded his red head towards the victor and said with stupid familiarity:

"Ah! that's the knack!"

"What the hell do you know about it?" said Farrington fiercely, turning
on the man. "What do you put in your gab for?"

"Sh, sh!" said O'Halloran, observing the violent expression of Farrington's face. "Pony up, boys. We'll have just one little smahan more and then
we'll be off."

A very sullen-faced man stood at the corner of O'Connell Bridge waiting
for the little Sandymount tram to take him home. He was full of smouldering anger and revengefulness. He felt humiliated and discontented; he did
not even feel drunk; and he had only twopence in his pocket. He cursed
everything. He had done for himself in the office, pawned his watch, spent
all his money; and he had not even got drunk. He began to feel thirsty
again and he longed to be back again in the hot reeking public-house. He
had lost his reputation as a strong man, having been defeated twice by a
mere boy. His heart swelled with fury and, when he thought of the woman
in the big hat who had brushed against him and said *Pardon!* his fury
nearly choked him.

His tram let him down at Shelbourne Road and he steered his great body
along in the shadow of the wall of the barracks. He loathed returning to his
home. When he went in by the side-door he found the kitchen empty and
the kitchen fire nearly out. He bawled upstairs:

"Ada! Ada!"

His wife was a little sharp-faced woman who bullied her husband when he was sober and was bullied by him when he was drunk. They had five children. A little boy came running down the stairs.

"Who is that?" said the man, peering through the darkness.

"Me, pa."

"Who are you? Charlie?"

"No, pa. Tom."

"Where's your mother?"

"She's out at the chapel."

"That's right. . . . Did she think of leaving any dinner for me?"

"Yes, pa. I——"

"Light the lamp. What do you mean by having the place in darkness? Are the other children in bed?"

The man sat down heavily on one of the chairs while the little boy lit the lamp. He began to mimic his son's flat accent, saying half to himself: *"At the chapel. At the chapel, if you please!"* When the lamp was lit he banged his fist on the table and shouted:

"What's for my dinner?"

"I'm going . . . to cook it, pa," said the little boy.

The man jumped up furiously and pointed to the fire.

"On that fire! You let the fire out! By God, I'll teach you to do that again!"

He took a step to the door and seized the walking-stick which was standing behind it.

"I'll teach you to let the fire out!" he said, rolling up his sleeve in order to give his arm free play.

The little boy cried *"O, pa!"* and ran whimpering round the table, but the man followed him and caught him by the coat. The little boy looked about him wildly but, seeing no way of escape, fell upon his knees.

"Now, you'll let the fire out the next time!" said the man, striking at him vigorously with the stick. "Take that, you little whelp!"

The boy uttered a squeal of pain as the stick cut his thigh. He clasped his hands together in the air and his voice shook with fright.

"O, pa!" he cried. "Don't beat me, pa! And I'll . . . I'll say a *Hail Mary* for you. . . . I'll say a *Hail Mary* for you, pa, if you don't beat me. . . . I'll say a *Hail Mary*. . . ."

THE TRAGEDY OF GOUPIL

Louis Pergaud

(1882–1915)

TRANSLATED BY VYVYAN HOLLAND

<hr>

IT WAS A SPRING EVENING, a warm March evening no different from any other, an evening with a full moon and a high wind which kept the reluctant buds in their resinous prisons for fear of a possible frost.

But for Goupil it was not like any other evening.

That twilight hour which spreads its shadowy film over the countryside, making the peaks seem higher and deepening the valleys, had already brought the woodland beasts from their lairs. But he, apparently insensible to the mysterious life which stirred these familiar shadows, lay hidden in the hole in the Moraies rock, whither, closely pressed by the poacher Lisée's dog, he had taken refuge in the morning, and was not getting ready to mingle with it as he usually did each evening.

Yet it was not because he felt that an expedition into the clearing along the edge of the wood would prove fruitless; for the fox knew quite well that on windy nights, under the full moon, the timid hares, deluded by the moonlight and frightened by the noise made by the swaying branches, did not leave their forms until late at night; nor was it the rustling of the leaves stirred by the wind, for the old forester with his practised ear was quite capable of distinguishing between human and woodland sounds. Neither could his long reverie and his strange inaction be explained by weariness, since he had been resting all day, first of all stretched out like a corpse in the exhaustion following upon the determined pursuit of which he had been the object, and afterwards curled into a circle, his sensitive black muzzle resting on his hind paws to protect it from any unpleasant or irksome contact.

He was now lying in a heraldic attitude, his legs folded beneath him, his eyes half closed and his ears pricked, allowing his brain to grasp, according to the dictates of an instinctive, mysterious and all powerful logic, sensations and ideas powerful enough to keep him, without the restraint of any tangible barrier, behind the rock through a cleft in which he had crawled.

This Moraies cave was not Goupil's usual earth: it corresponded to the keep in which a beleaguered garrison seeks its last refuge, the last asylum in case of extreme peril.

At dawn on that same day he had gone to sleep in a bramble thicket at the very spot at which, with one masterly snap of his jaws, he had broken the back of a leveret returning to its form and with whose flesh he had appeased his hunger.

He had been dozing there when the bell on Miraut's collar had unceremoniously roused him from the torpor into which the warmth of the spring sun and the tranquillity of a sated appetite had plunged him. Miraut was Lisée's dog.

Among all the dogs in the neighbourhood which in turns, when the morning conditions happened to be favourable and the autumn dew lay on the ground, had given him chase, Goupil knew of no more relentless enemy than Miraut. He knew by costly and bitter experience that no amount of cunning was of any use against him; so, as soon as the sound of his bark or the tinkle of his bell announced his approach, the fox fled as fast as his swift feet could carry him and, in order to put Miraut off the scent, contrary to the natural instinct of all foxes and contrary to his own habits, he would travel a great distance and describe a huge circle, following roads after the fashion of hares and then, returning to Moraies, would slide down the bank of rolling stones leading to his earth as quickly as possible, certain that his paws had not left his enemy sufficient scent to smell him out.

This was his last tactical resource which no untoward event had ever made him modify so far, and today it had succeeded as usual. Yet Goupil was not quiet in his mind for, at a few dozen yards from the path he seemed to have seen, concealed behind the bole of a beech tree, the form of Lisée, Miraut's master.

Goupil knew him well, but this time he had not leaped with fear at the thundering report which always marked the meeting of the two enemies; he had not heard the swift whistling lash of the pellets past his ears, those leaden pellets which, in spite of your winter coat, could bite into you more stingingly and deeper than even the great blackthorns. He was suspicious and from that suspicion there grew a vague alarm, the instinct of preservation which, even before he received painful evidence of its truth, kept him in the cave on the border line of the danger which threatened him.

Crouching in the depths of his lair, he heard suspicious sounds which might possibly have been nothing but the rolling of the last stones disturbed by his feet, but a strange framework, which he had never noticed before seemed to belie this easy explanation.

Goupil scented a trap. Goupil was Lisée's prisoner.

II

He seemed to be frozen into an apathetic sphinxlike attitude. But the shivers running through the fur on his front paws, the tips of his ears

trembling at every sound that rose out of the night, and the fleeting glint
in his eyes as his oblong pupils dilated beneath the half-lowered curtains
of his eyelids, showed that every nerve in his body was intensely alert.

The old stager's deep meditation lasted throughout the night. Indeed
there was nothing to compel him to leave his lair. On the contrary his
stomach, accustomed to frequent and prolonged fasts and sufficiently bal-
lasted that morning with the food supplied by the leveret's flesh, urged him
not to leave the chosen refuge which had so often sheltered him during the
more perilous moments of his life.

Even though the night was really his accomplice, he was too distrustful
to dare to profit by the insidious protection of its silence and its darkness.
He awaited the dawn with a premonition that it would produce some new
fact which, either confirming his suspicions or buoying up his hopes, would
decide him on the course of action to be adopted.

Hour succeeded hour. The moonlight seemed to grow brighter and
outlined against the black sky the even blacker branches of the trees, at the
ends of which the swollen buds at the invisible tips of the twigs formed a
sort of light mist over the forest.

Long rows of boughs, all aligned parallel to one another and cut by the
woodmen after the rising of the sap, stretched out in infinite perspectives
of dying shoots.

The blackbirds, which at dusk vied with one another in liveliness and
cast the harmony of their notes to the four winds of heaven, had long been
silent. Only the drumming of the wind rolled deliberately and continuously
through the branches, punctuated now and then by the hooting of the
little owls and the screeching of the screech owls, whilst from the fertile
earth rose an indefinite, subtle and penetrating fragrance which seemed to
contain in germ that of all woodland scents.

As dawn broke the man appeared, preceded by Miraut. Goupil heard the
snuffling of the dog winding him at the entrance to his lair, and the violent
oaths of the poacher as he calculated that the well-known patience and
endurance of foxes would cause grave depreciation in the value of the
silvery pelt which he expected to take from his victim when he was finally
captured.

In the meantime Goupil, passing his long red tongue over his cunning
old muzzle, congratulated himself on having escaped immediate danger
and began to try to discover some means of giving his enemy the slip.

There seemed to be only two alternatives. He must either make a dash
for it or, braving the pangs of hunger, try to exhaust the patience of his
gaoler, who might eventually think that he had escaped and would then
remove the trap. This second alternative was only to be resorted to in the
last instance and it was to the first that the fox turned his attention.

As the trap barred the entry to the cave, Goupil carefully sounded the
walls of his prison with his paws and his muzzle. The inspection did not

take long: there was rock behind, rock above, to the right and to the left. There was no chance of escape there. Beneath him his claws made semicircular patterns in the dark soil: perhaps salvation lay in that direction. And immediately, with the courage and tenacity of despair, he began to burrow into the soft earth.

At the end of the day he had dug a hole a good foot deep and as large as his body, when his claws scraped against something hard. He had reached rock again. Goupil tried digging further on, but with the same result; he kept on scratching, he scratched all night, ever hoping to come across a fault in the rock which would give him his freedom.

Slowly, following a cruel, relentless curve, the bedrock rose until it reached the level of the ground at the entrance to the cave; but in his feverish state the fox did not notice this. He kept on scratching, frantically scratching.

He scratched for three days and three nights, biting the earth with rage, a blackish saliva dripping from his jowl. He wore down his claws, broke his teeth and bruised his muzzle. He dug up all the earth in his cave. The impenetrable wall of rock still remained intact and the wretched prisoner, starved and feverish among the lamentable chaos of the tumbled earth, after struggling until his strength was completely exhausted, fell down and slept for twelve hours on end with that leaden sleep that follows a great defeat.

III

Under the violent pangs of his long-empty stomach, Goupil awoke among the wretched disorder of the earth. The clear dawn rose through the cleft in the rock; the buds were beginning to burst; every shade of green was spreading the joy of life in the sunlight and the song of the robins and of the blackbirds filled the air with a symphony of liberty which must have sounded terrible to the prisoner's ears. The knowledge of the truth returned to his mind like a tooth ripping up a hare's stomach and, resigned to his fate now, he settled himself down in the most convenient position in which to dream, to fast and to wait. And there before him, like an appalling nightmare, ironically defying his patience, rose the trap.

It was a rudimentary affair invented by Lisée: two uprights, like those of a scaffold, supported an oak plank which seemed to prolong them. But, owing to an ingenious piece of mechanism, when any intruder entered the fatal passage the oak plank, shaved away at each side, would slide treacherously down like a guillotine along grooves cut in the uprights, and break his back.

Then, excited by hunger, Goupil's brain lived again through the voluptuous memory of hearty meals he had enjoyed and conjured up pictures of orgies of flesh and blood to fall back, more modestly, on the frugal fare of wintertime, the dead moles devoured by the roadside, the red berries gleaned from the leafless bushes and the wild apples discovered beneath the damp decay of fallen leaves.

How many hares had he caught at footbridges over dykes and at places where cart tracks met, and how many leverets had he killed in fields of clover or of lucerne, how many partridges had he chased from their nests in order to devour their eggs, and how many fowls had he boldly stolen from chicken runs under the very noses of watchdogs and in constant danger from farmers' guns?

The hours dragged by, all terribly alike except that the increasing pangs of hunger kept adding to the sum total of his misery.

Stoically calm, his stomach pressed hard against the ground as though in an effort to compress it, Goupil, in order to forget his present situation, recalled to memory all the other perils he had escaped: his flights under showers of lead, the ruses he had employed to put dogs off his track, the poisoned bait tempting his hunger. But above all he saw rising before him with even more terrible precision, from among all the bad days of his life, a certain winter night whose most minute details were deeply engraved upon his memory; he lived through it again as it passed across the screen of his faithful memory:

The earth was white, the trees were white and in the clear sky the stars glittered harshly and shed a sinister, cold, almost wicked glow. The hares had not left their forms, the partridges had all crept up close to the villages and the moles slept in the most remote corners of their subterranean galleries; no more frozen sloes on the blackthorns in the valleys, no more wild apples beneath the apple trees in the woods. Nothing more anywhere, nothing but that soft glistening whiteness made up of crystalline spangles which become sharper in the frost and insinuate themselves right into the skin in spite of the thickness of one's pelt.

The valley slept in the distance beneath the aegis of its iron-roofed church tower. Goupil drew near it and cautiously crept round it, then, shortening his circles and egged on by hunger he gradually came right up to it.

There was not a sound to be heard except, every quarter of an hour, the thin note carelessly launched into the silence from the clock tower or the metallic clanking of chains rattled by oxen as they stirred in their sleep.

A strong smell of flesh reached his nostrils; no doubt some dead animal left there to rot, whose incipient decay deliciously tickled his famished sense of smell.

He continued on his way, hugging a fence until he came within a few paces of where he could see the object of his search lying as a brown mass on the virgin whiteness of the snow.

The house opposite was sleeping soundly: the quiet darkness of a large window seemed to bear witness to its emptiness or to its slumber.

But Goupil was suspicious. Impelled by his instinct, he hurled himself bravely at full speed into the open space and passed the carcass by without stopping, his eyes fixed on the suspected window. No one but he would have noticed anything; but the piercing eyes of the old savage had seen a tiny red reflection glowing in the upper corner of one of the panes and that was enough for him. He understood now.

The man behind there could load his gun and get ready to fire: the shot would not be for him. For Goupil was certain that behind that silent window a man was keeping vigil, one of his enemies, one of the murderers of his race: he had put out the lamp, pretending to have gone to bed, but the vent-hole of his stove, which he had neglected to shut, betrayed his presence and Goupil, who had already heard shots fired in the night, knew now why the man was watching. Who knows how many other animals, more trusting than himself, had paid with their lives for their rashness in exposing themselves to the assassin's shot at such close range? And Goupil reconstructed the scene: the man quietly seated in his mysterious house, meditating on the misery of wild creatures, offering them something with which to appease their hunger and, at the right moment, protected by the sheltering darkness, shooting his victims through the open window pane.

It was there that his woodland brothers perished, those who, with less self-control than he, had ventured down to the village and had never been seen again.

And as he retraced his way to his wood, keeping himself well in the shadows, the silhouette of a cat suddenly appeared on the top of a wall. His large dark eyes met the creature's phosphorescent pupils in the darkness and with a mighty bound he hurled himself in its wake.

The cat knew quite well that the menace of its claws, though quite sufficient to restrain the audacity of dogs, would not stop Goupil's rush and that neither would flight protect it from the old savage's attack. But there was an apple tree close at hand. It reached this and was already climbing it when a sudden snap stopped it and delivered it to its enemy, who finished it off. And the silence of the night was rent by a long sinister howl, a death howl which kept all the dogs in the village and in the farms in the neighbourhood barking at the doors of their kennels or in the stables far into the night.

Other memories, too, came and went in his mind while the links of the hours forged their monotonous chain and the eternal days passed.

Then Goupil's ideas became vague and confused. The memories of meals were mixed in appalling nightmares with fearful pictures: fantastic rings of hares spun around him, firing shots at him which ploughed through his skin, taking off long strips of fur without succeeding in killing him. A high fever attacked him: his cold black muzzle grew hot and his eyes red; his flanks began to throb and his long lean tongue hung from his jaws like a ragged wet cloth, on the central channel of which a drop of sweat would appear from time to time, to be licked back into his burning mouth in an effort to cool it.

Time passed. He had examined the trap and tried, in order to avoid it, to understand its danger, but his wild animal brain could not understand human mechanisms and he preferred starvation in the security of his refuge to this unknown horror full of agonising mystery.

One morning for one joyful moment he thought his deliverance had come. The man appeared. He remained there for some time, moved something and went away again; but the terrible oath which marked his departure left the fox with but very faint hope. Lisée had only been trying the trap and now he came every day at dawn, feeling that the end was at hand.

During this time Goupil was becoming more and more troubled by fever. Sometimes he lay stretched out for minutes at a time, panting desperately, sometimes he got up and walked round and round his prison, seeking for the outlet which he was always hoping to find, without success.

A crescent moon, in its last quarter, was mounting the sky. A red moon. It was like a joint of underdone meat which some cruel power was parading through the sky on a plate of clouds! Motionless, the fox stretched towards it his emaciated neck, his sunken jowl, his enormous eyes. As on the first day of his captivity, the wind howled dismally among the trees and he seemed to hear the ebb and flow of the music of a vast pack of hounds which was gradually drawing closer to him; or, again, the humming in his brain appeared to be the bubbling of a spring and, in order to try to quench his burning thirst, he kept turning round and round, looking on all sides for water, clear water which he would lap up for ever.

The dawn of the eleventh day revealed a milky brightness above the neighbouring wood. The end had got to come. Suddenly Goupil made up his mind and, without looking to either side, bracing his poor emaciated legs with a sort of despairing energy, he made a desperate bound and hurled himself into the unknown.

IV

On that day as on the preceding days, with the apparent heaviness with which he disguised the briskness of his gait, Lisée climbed the narrow gully through which his heavy hob-nailed boots had gradually worn a track ending at Goupil's prison.

As a well-trained dog, Miraut preceded him by a few yards. In the ordinary way, when hunting, the dog kept exactly the same distance from his master, a distance determined by long usage and mutual understanding. But that day Lisée had to keep on calling back his old associate by short and often repeated whistling.

With his muzzle in the air and his stern waving, Miraut scented his prey and Lisée, thinking of Goupil's fate, gleefully rubbed his great horny hands together. But he did not increase his pace and continued on his way towards the lair where the dog, his muzzle thrust forward, and his eyes staring before him, his body close to the ground and his stern stuck straight out behind him, was only waiting for the presence of his master and a signal to leap.

Beneath the weight of the oak plank which had fallen upon him, the fox, gaunt, half-flayed, lay on his right side, his hindquarters firmly fixed by the trap which had caught him just in front of his hind legs and, by throwing him a little to one side, had protected his spine from a mortal blow. A whitish mucus flowed from his nostrils, and his large, bleary eyes had closed when the shock had made him lose consciousness. He had been lying there for about a quarter of an hour when Lisée arrived.

A cruel, contemptuous smile showed that the victor's triumph was mitigated by the little he thought of the value of the vanquished. The pelt was worthless and what poor devil, however hungry he might be, would have attempted to attack such a wretched prey, even after, as usual, letting the flesh freeze to remove some of its wild-animal odour from it?

Suddenly the poacher, looking attentively at Goupil, saw a shudder pass through his frame. For, indeed, he had in fact only lost consciousness.

And then Lisée formulated in his mind a scheme of revenge, while at the same time playing a savage joke on his enemy.

Without saying a word he removed his dog's collar and immediately fastened it round Goupil's neck; he then fumbled in the pockets of his old corduroy trousers through which the bluish weft of the cotton foundation could be seen in places. Having found some pieces of string he soon made an effective muzzle which he fastened on to the old creature: then he tied his hind paws together with a handkerchief and opened the trap, which he hid in a neighbouring thicket. Lastly, seizing the fox by his four paws he flung him over his shoulders like a collar and retraced his way to the village with the same swift cumbrous gait.

Miraut followed behind, his eyes riveted on the pointed nose bumping up and down on his master's shoulder.

Lisée's rhythmic stride, the warmth of the sun and the pure balmy spring morning air gradually restored the use of his senses to Goupil.

His first sensation was a blessed feeling of relief and of lightness which contrasted with the sharp pain and the atrocious anguish which he had experienced when he was first caught in the trap; then the pleasant dilation of his lungs in the fresh, sweet-smelling air brought back to him the corresponding memory of his freedom in the woods; and, too, it was for him an unconscious delight once more to see the healthy clearness of the air through the mists of sleep and to enjoy the glorious sun appearing over the horizon.

But as he returned more fully to consciousness his sensations began to be modified: at first there was a feeling of discomfort in his legs and at his neck and a heaviness in his head; then the perception of a strange smell, the smell of man and dog, forcing itself upon his brain, rudely recalled him to reality. He opened his feverish eyes wide and saw everything: the man carrying him, the dog following him, his legs imprisoned in the poacher's rough hands and in the distance the village with its tiled roofs, that mysterious village full of traps and of enemies.

His whole body stiffened in an instinctive and desperate effort, a terrific strain in every muscle to try to make Lisée let go so that he could dash off into the forest. But the man was on his guard; he merely tightened the grip of his gnarled hands, thereby crushing the wretched creature's legs still more, and Miraut also showed his ruthless vigilance by growling significantly.

An even greater torment, which made him forget everything, hunger, thirst, and pain, now racked Goupil's mind. The danger had changed its form, but it was more imminent, more certain and more appalling. He almost regretted the atrocious hours during which he had been starving to death in his cave and he wondered what tortures he was going to be subjected to before dying.

He saw himself spreadeagled on the floor, abandoned to Miraut's teeth, or made to serve as a target for Lisée. He saw himself lying half flayed, his flesh quivering, his bones broken, and seemed to feel the pellets, coming from Heaven knew where, boring into his muscles and remaining like inextricable thorns, making holes from which the blood flowed continuously and without any possibility of being staunched.

Miraut was baring his sharp fangs and, in reply to this challenge Goupil, from behind the meshes of his muzzle, also snarled and uncovered his discoloured gums from which sprang the pointed canines. Oh, how glad he would have been to be able to bite the tormentor who was carrying him, but the man was quite confident of his immunity and went silently on his way to the village, smiling at the thought of his merciless jest.

The fox heard the various sounds of village life, many of which he recognised because he had at other times studied them from a distance: some of them meant nothing to him; some touched more particularly on his life as a hunter of cats and as a farm-yard expert, and lastly there were others, the most terrible of all, which reminded him of the fact that man and his vassal the dog were enemies upon whose clemency he could never count. He heard the lowing of cattle, the clucking of fowls, the barking of dogs and the shrill screams of children playing and quarrelling in front of houses. He saw himself already surrounded by a circle of ferocity, an unpenetrable triple hedge of enemies and he dreaded even more keenly the prospect of his unknown fate.

Luckily for Goupil, Lisée lived in a house a little way out of the village. He entered a lane bordered by two hawthorn hedges and some urchins who were gathering violets there, interested by the sight of the curious, wicked-looking beast which he was carrying, followed him as far as his home.

Lisée tied Goupil with a piece of rope to the foot of the bed in the room containing the stove, and breakfasted on a bowl of soup which his wife gave him; then he went about his day's work, leaving to the care of Miraut the old muzzled creature who expected that at any moment the dog would leap upon him and tear him to shreds.

But nothing of the sort happened, and Miraut contented himself with lying curled up before the fire on a piece of sacking, from time to time casting a look of hatred in his direction, fully conscious of the responsibility placed upon him.

The sound of childish shouts and quarrelling and laughter struck terror into the captive's brain; all the village children, informed of his presence by those who had first seen him, were hovering round the house in the hope of also catching a glimpse of him.

Sometimes one of them, bolder than the rest, would pull himself up on the window sill and take a rapid glance into the darkened room and then, when questioned by the others and not having seen anything, would take refuge in significant silence.

All this noise terrified Goupil. An overwhelming feeling of languor came over him; bewildered by so many strange adventures he could no longer grasp anything that was happening and lost consciousness again. He did not notice the approach of night, but he shuddered when the poacher returned with several other enemies with the same smell, who made large clouds of blue smoke come out of their pipes. They were laughing.

Goupil did not know the smell of tobacco: it seized him by the nose and throat like the choking advance guard of death. Neither did he understand laughter. Miraut, who was intelligent and observant, knew that this outward sign in his master meant that he would be patted and given tidbits to eat: he, too, tried, like many other dogs, to make men understand his own good humour or his submissiveness by the more or less agreeable curling back of his lips. But the old fox saw nothing in this manifestation but stumps of teeth, yellowed by tobacco, set in cruel-looking jaws, and bellies which shook as though they themselves longed to seize on some coveted prey.

The only relationship that Goupil could establish was between the protruding teeth and the shaking bellies and this was for him a terrible sign of danger and menace.

Lisée was talking and gesticulating and the men's mouths grew larger, their teeth seemed to grow longer, their bellies shook more violently and their faces became more dreadful. The end was surely at hand.

Quietly, as though to give formality to the final preparations, the men sat down while Lisée prepared the instruments which were to serve to torture the condemned animal and Goupil himself cowered by the corner of the bed, vainly trying to hide himself and only wishing he could dissolve entirely and disappear.

At last the poacher seemed to have finished. In one hand he held what appeared to be a black metal jaw and in the other a small hollow metal sphere, pierced on top by two round holes which looked like the eyes of a corpse and underneath by a wide slit like a mouth distended by a savage smile.

He suddenly seized Goupil and held him by gripping his chest and neck between his knees. The fox felt that the end had come and, after a moment's vain desire to struggle, abandoned himself to his fate, realising the utter impossibility of even the faintest hope. He felt the cold of a piece of wire about his throat, he saw the metal jaw, the steel pincers, close suddenly on the wire and felt this new collar gradually crushing his neck in its merciless grip. . . . He was going to be strangled.

But Lisée, passing his finger between the wire and Goupil's neck, interrupted the torture, took off Miraut's leather collar and threw it to one side and then, seizing the bewildered Goupil by the metal sphere, dragged him towards the door, followed by the savage, relentless chorus of the other men.

The poacher let Goupil out in the direction of the swamp from which rose the hoarse croaking of bullfrogs and, before he could realise what was happening, Lisée shot him out into the night with a brutal kick on the hindquarters.

V

The fox did not try to understand and instinctively sped as fast as he could towards his native forest, just as a fish out of water tries to leap back into the river. But, to his horror, Miraut's bell, the same fatal bell which had awakened him as he lay in the brambles with the remains of the hare, followed him as he went.

No, it was no hallucination, it was indeed the bell whose thin, irregular tinkle he could quite clearly distinguish in the silence full of humming sounds and the shrilling of insects.

Miraut was not giving tongue in that regular, protracted way which he had when following a scent and which echoed all through the wood. This silent pursuit was all the more distracting and terrifying because of the mystery with which it was surrounded. The dog must be very close behind him and was perhaps just preparing to seize him and the fox expected at any moment to feel the sharp fangs pierce his skin; he seemed to hear the rippling of the muscles of the hound's legs as it strained to reach him and the laboured breathing of his own tired lungs.

It was a battle of speed, a desperate struggle in which the stronger and the more persevering must inevitably defeat the other.

In the meantime the bell stuck resolutely to his heels, neither gaining nor losing but keeping its exact distance. It was a heroic but unequal contest: on the one side the hale, robust dog, thirsting for revenge; on the other Goupil weakened by eleven days of fasting and fever and only kept going by the instinct of self-preservation which would make him use up his last ounce of strength before abandoning himself to his fate.

Quickening his pace he sped on into the night, looking neither to right nor to left, feeling nothing, seeing nothing; neither could he hear anything but the bell, each tinkle of which lashed his failing courage like a whip, made him pick up his stumbling feet and seemed to rub soothing oil into his exhausted muscles.

He was close to the edge of the wood now, with its low wall of mossy stones which had fallen down in places, and its half-choked ditch; Goupil crossed this at a place where there was a breach in the wall, near the beginning of a ride out of which the hares came when they wanted to graze in the fields. He dived straight into it, urged on by an instinctive impulse which told him that perhaps the dog would abandon his trail to follow a hare which had bolted at their approach; but Miraut held on and the bell continued to tinkle with him.

The straight ride, which had not been cut back by the keepers, seemed to rush towards a glade like an immense arch of greenery, from which the lowest branches hung like garlands. The stars were quietly coming out behind the lattice work of these branches, the blackbirds took up their overnight song once more in a hundred different themes, and countless swarms of cockchafers rose from the fields and flew towards the young greenery of the wood, making a far-away wave-like sound which kept rising and falling in intensity.

The fox fled desperately on, passing the boundary-stones of the rides without even looking at them, cutting across one to enter another, leaving the undergrowth for the clearings and the clearings for the open country, but ever pursued by the relentless bell.

The moon rose. Goupil returned to the undergrowth and made for the dense thickets through which his skill as an old forester enabled him to glide as swiftly as a shadow on a wall and where he hoped with the aid of the brambles and the clematis to shake off the savage hound that pursued him.

He doubled round the oaks, slid under entanglements of brambles which tore at him as he passed them without succeeding in stopping or even slowing down his mad flight; he plunged into tunnels of young vegetation to reappear, five or six paces further on, in the brightness of a sudden clearing, but the tinkling of the bell pursued him like a funeral knell, a monotonous and ceaseless tolling.

Animals started up beneath his feet and birds hurriedly took flight, vanishing like black shadows in the sinister half-light of the wood; brown owls and screech owls, attracted by the sound of the bell, followed this strange career with their silent flight and mingled their wings above his head.

The fox dived resolutely into the densest thickets; at one moment a clematis tendril held him up. He broke it with a sudden bound and started off again and the noise of the bell stopped. Hope filled the fugitive's lungs and braced his muscles with fresh strength; doubtless Miraut had lost sight of him and he sped straight before him like an arrow. He ran two hundred, perhaps three hundred yards in this hopeful silence and then, to make sure that he was alone, he stopped dead and cast a glance behind him.

Hardly had he turned his head when the thin irregular note of the bell once more fell upon his ear and embarked him once more upon his race through the woods, assailed with all the agonies of uncertainty.

He ran all night without interruption until his poor stiff swollen feet collapsed beneath him and flung him on the ground, an inert wreck, a few yards from a spring where he lay without consciousness, half dead, sightless and voiceless.

And immediately, as though its work were accomplished, the bell became silent.

VI

No one could say how long Goupil remained in that state of total prostration which no longer belonged to life and yet was not death. The vital force of the old forest ranger must have been very powerful for it to have been able, after so much fasting, so many emotions, so much weariness and so much suffering, to wake him from his lethargy and cast him back into the light of day.

Nothing seemed to predominate in the chaos of his sensations. In the midst of the gentle protective silence which surrounded him, and even before his stomach recalled him too vividly to painful reality, it was a feeling of discomfort at his neck that first awakened him: that piece of wire of Lisée's on which his thoughts dwelt so strangely and on which his new life seemed to be concentrated. Indeed, two separate sensations could hardly find accommodation in his enfeebled brain. Was he awake or was he asleep? Was he dreaming? He did not know. His eyes were closed and now he opened them. He opened them slowly, without moving his body, and gazed at the peaceful landscape before him; then, with infinite caution, to which he knew how to school himself when, guided by his subtle sense of smell, he crept up to a covey of partridges at dusk, he turned his head and looked round him. There was nothing suspicious in sight; he breathed again. Where could the dog have got to? It had vanished like a bad dream. Perhaps, after all, it had only been a long nightmare? But no, the uncomfortable piece of wire remained there to witness the retrospective horror of his appalling captivity.

Goupil instinctively put his paw up to it in the hope of being able to get rid of it, but he had hardly touched it when the bell sounded again and he cowered down and a shudder of terror ran along his spine. He gave a hurried look round, but there was still nothing in sight. And yet the bell was there, quite close to him. And then suddenly Goupil grasped the situation.

The metal sphere with its jeering mouth and its death's-head eyes, which Lisée had slipped on to the wire knotted round his neck, was Miraut's bell; it was with this fateful bell that he had run all through the night, thinking himself pursued by the dog; that was Lisée's revenge which had made him drain the cup of bitter agony to its dregs through eight hours of flight and which, now that he was returning once more to hope and happiness, was going to follow him pitilessly, to poison his days and to accomplish its deadly work in face of and in spite of everything.

He stood up painfully on his thin legs, forefeet first and then hind feet, and crawled over to the spring whose continuous monotonous rippling was almost a form of silence, a singing silence with whose tones the different cries of the woodland dwellers harmonised peacefully.

He drank for a long time with a noise like the clicking of castanets, blurring his reflection in the clear water, the reflection of an emaciated Goupil whose muzzle alone seemed to be alive, and on whose head the short, pointed ears seemed to be something detached, like twin turrets, listening to the noises of the countryside with the ever-present fear of catching hostile sounds in the perspectives of silence.

Then his thoughts turned to food and, as the forest did not offer him sufficient resources, he made for the grassy plain where the larks sprang up from time to time like fountain-jets in their reeling ascent, filling the air with their trills, to fall back again intoxicated with the blueness of the sky.

There he would certainly find some of the herbs which he had always known or which he had come to know: sprigs of wild sorrel, a few mushrooms perhaps, the purgative couch-grass or even a molehill or two which he would attack resolutely and, who knows, perhaps the half-decomposed carcasses of beasts or birds who had died during the winter and had not yet been found.

But how irritating the bell was! No doubt he would soon grow accustomed to the choking wire round his neck, but this noise which stuck to him like a thorn in his flesh, reminding him only too well of the dangers he had run and had yet to fear, secretly ruined the pleasure he would have experienced in being able to enjoy life to the full. It was the price of his liberty which he was condemned to drag about with him until he died. And the desire to get rid of it grew fiercer and fiercer in his heart.

Time after time, lying on his back, his hind legs rigid with determination and rage, stuck straight up in the air, he clawed at his neck with his forepaws in strong, regular strokes to try to drag off or to break the metallic grip of Lisée's wire. He only succeeded in completely stripping the fur from both sides of his neck and in breaking his claws, but the collar which held him did not yield a fraction of an inch and at every stroke the tinkle of the bell came like an insolent or ironically defiant peal of laughter. Goupil tried to get used to it, but in vain, and terrible rages which nothing could curb would grip him by the throat and contract his muscles. And yet he had to live.

He lived.

By turns, herbs from the plain, wild fruit from the woods and cockchafers which he shook out of bushes furnished him with his daily sustenance; there were also little birds' nests which he knew where to find behind the green shields of the hedges and beneath the thorny branches of wild gooseberry bushes. Sometimes he sucked the eggs, sometimes he devoured the fledglings, little red bodies whose eyes were closed and who opened enormous beaks when they heard the rustle of the twigs being pulled aside above their heads. He could raise himself as high as the blackbirds' nests built in the low branches of the hazels, he destroyed coveys of young partridges and quails among the green corn and he could even approach farmhouses without arousing suspicion, protected by his bell.

He had a particular hatred for a certain cock of Bouloie Farm, an ancient rooster with a strident voice and heavy, feathered legs, who was as cunning as he was himself. The all-powerful and jealous pasha of a vast seraglio of hens, he seemed to divine Goupil's presence every time he approached and, raising his head and beating his wings, would utter a rallying crow, an urgent call which warned the hens of their danger and sent them scurrying back in disorder round the watchdog's kennel, where they felt they were safe.

For a long time Goupil had decided upon the death of this fowl.

For several days he watched its movements and then, having got to know its habits, he came along one fine morning, crouched behind a hedge and waited.

The rooster approached, crest waving in the wind, eyes sparkling, at the head of his clucking flock. But he had neither the easy gallantry nor the swaggering boldness of the days on which he felt confident: he clearly scented danger. Goupil made his little bell tinkle and this domestic sound reassured his enemy; then with the patience of an experienced hunter he let the fowl draw slowly near and, when it was quite close and there was no longer any chance of its escaping, he made a tremendous bound towards it, chased it, caught it, crushed its breast between his jaws and, proud of his victory and carrying his crafty head on high, carried it off into the forest where he plucked it and devoured it.

After that it was easy to decimate the stupid flock of hens belonging to his neighbour the farmer: but he went at such varied intervals and at such different times of the day, that the farmer could never hope to surprise him and, not having seen him and not having any idea of the identity of the thief except from the sound of his bell and, moreover, knowing nothing of Goupil's adventures, stoutly accused Miraut of killing his hens and even went so far as to threaten to bring an action against Lisée or to destroy his good-for-nothing dog.

In the meantime Goupil was growing fat again and even if he had largely to resign himself to leaving hares alone, the fowls of the farm offered him quite sufficient compensation and he began to recover confidence in life.

One thing, however, weighed horribly on him, and that was loneliness.

He had never set eyes on any of his brothers since the evening of his captivity and he could not without deep emotion conjure up the romping, nibbling and teasing which preceded important expeditions, nor the bitter quarrels aroused by disputes over the division of spoils which made sharp rows of fangs shoot out challengingly under black curled-back lips.

But now the forest was empty. It seemed as though his race had disappeared since his captivity.

And yet he felt its presence around him perpetually. He felt it by the traces which other foxes left in crossing the damp paths through the undergrowth, by the scent left by their feet on the grass in the glades and on the low branches of thickets, and especially by the peculiar yelping which told him of a nocturnal hunt by two friends: one acting as dog, giving tongue in a thin rather husky voice, while the other, in accordance with the direction indicated by the barking, would wait at some place by which the hare would probably pass and would kill it without having to run a yard.

He knew every run and very seldom made a mistake about direction; he had even, one day when he felt a little hungry, become bold enough to lie in wait and kill a hare which Miraut was hunting. But he never tried to do that again, because the hound, just as cunning as he, guessed what had happened and set off with fresh energy in pursuit, without wasting a moment. Weighed down by his capture, the fox would infallibly have been caught had he not been prudent enough to abandon to his enemy the stolen prey which would have furnished him with such a satisfying meal. No doubt Miraut had recovered the hare on the steep pebble bank on which he had abandoned it, for patches of fur and bloodstains on the stones told a sufficiently clear story of the savoury meal to which he had so selfishly helped himself.

Goupil naturally hoped to profit by his brothers' hunting but he very seldom succeeded, for if the bell always sent the bushy-tailed hunter lying in wait about his business, it often happened that it also turned the tawny hare, with his keen ear for forest noises, away from the run. But when this happened his most earnest desire was to meet the other foxes once more in order to make them understand that he was not their enemy; but it was labour lost, for the lonely creature could neither get his brothers to come to him nor could he get near them; his calling met with no other response than the echo which cast mockingly back at him the plaintive end of his yelpings.

One evening he recognised the voice of his old hunting companion, now hunting with another, no doubt one of his rivals, and it made him miserable because he felt that there was a ban upon him among his race and that he was, as it were, dead to all other foxes.

How often, even without any desire for plunder, had he not tried to get near the hunters! But as soon as he approached the hunt seemed to fade away and silence fell all around: the bell created mystery and emptiness about him.

VII

Then came the season of love-making.

In the trail of the vixens in the mating season Goupil sniffed marvellously voluptuous scents which made his jaws snap together and fired his blood. Then his whole being vibrated with the great courage necessary for the fights which succeeded the nuptial parade, of which they were but the supreme form, and he conjured up in his mind before his wounded, shamed and vanquished rivals the slenderest of females, docile and submissive to her master's will.

Oh, for those battles in the depths of the woods, those fierce clashes in which teeth sink into pelts and make the flesh bleed, those howling battles at the end of which the victor, himself also wounded and bleeding, enjoyed his triumph while in the distance, still menacing, the vanquished showed their teeth and prowled restless and woeful round the mating couple.

Goupil was one of the stronger ones; he had often come off best in these nocturnal tourneys and, with a rage rendered ten times greater because of the inaccessibility of the goal, he followed the multiple tracks in which his rivals' footprints were confused as they followed the path taken by the coveted females; but the goal kept moving, never to be reached because the abominable bell, warning them of the presence of an interloper, reconciled the rivals in the face of common danger and always put the mating groups to flight.

Every night he ran hither and thither, leaving one track to follow another in the hope, never to be realised, that the constant yelping which he directed towards the female would be enough to prevent her from fleeing before the approaching bell.

He was in despair. He forgot to steal chickens or to drink at springs; he was consumed by the love fever, and wild paroxysms of rage, as in the first days of his liberation, made him fling himself on his back on the ground to try once more to snap the wire which welded to his life the indelible mark of the ferocity of man.

But it was waste of labour.

One evening, however, he changed his tactics. He had just crossed the track of a rutting female and decided that he must catch up with her at all costs, concentrating all the turbulent energies of an exasperated male to this end. But he must silence the bell. He *must* be able to do so!

In order to do this he determined to thread his way through the dense tangle of the undergrowth with a slow, easy gait during which his head and neck should preserve the most complete immobility. So he started off on the tracks of Madame Vixen, his whole body taut and set, his legs arched and his muzzle following the scent close to the ground.

He advanced with infinite precaution, stifling his instinctive emotions by the strength of his desire and by sheer will power. There would, for instance, be a path or a ditch which he was forcing himself to cross slowly; when, deep inside him, a subconscious instinct of self-protection would flex the muscles of his hindquarters to clear it at a bound, or else an easy prey would suddenly appear and in spite of himself his eyes would follow its precipitous flight.

He stepped over twigs, slithered beneath the low-hanging branches of the dense shrubbery, now walking on the tips of his toes and now crouching down on his pliant hocks; he proceeded slowly, anxiously, his head in a whirl and his heart beating wildly as the delicious scent made his nerves tingle, and he got nearer and nearer to his goal. But he still took care not to move his neck the fraction of an inch or to cause the bell the slightest jar.

He was there.

In the centre of a glade brightly lit up by the moon two males were already fighting for the female who stood by watching them. Their fangs were being buried in each other's pelts with muffled snarls, their rigid legs were straining against each other's backs and hindquarters, blood was beginning to flow and the light of battle shone from the contestants' eyes.

Circling around the rivals in the narrow glade outlined by the freshly grown turf on the site of a charcoal burner's fire, the female considered them calmly through half-closed eyes, her brush trailing behind her like a lady's train.

She passed close to Goupil, winded him and turned towards him and he, emboldened and excited and disregarding the enforced stiffness of his neck, without troubling about the other two who were tearing each other to pieces, without heeding anything else, began to prepare for the love act by his preliminary caresses.

But at the supreme moment he raised himself sharply on his hindquarters and the sound of the bell rang out in the night. Immediately, as though actuated by invisible springs, both combatants and the female took to such sudden and headlong flight that before he had time to see them vanish, the bewildered Goupil found himself alone in the deserted glade.

Then the poor lonely creature began to bite the grass in the glade in uncontrollable rage, and to howl despairingly and to make the merciless bell ring unceasingly as though he were trying to tire it out. And the grinning moon made the shadows of the trees dance around him and the night birds, attracted by this unusual noise, wove the mysterious and balefully silent patterns of their flight above his head.

The dawn found him still there and, remembering the danger which he carried about him, he turned his thoughts to the question of self-preservation. Seized once more by love of life like a convalescent after a terrible crisis, he felt all the problems of existence weighing upon him and, in order to be able to solve them when the time came, he began by hiding himself in a thicket in the middle of the wood where he fell into the troubled sleep of hunted and harassed creatures.

And for a long time life went on in the same way. Forest life, so satisfying to his instincts, smiled upon him once more; he almost recaptured his forest ranger's soul, thanks to the necessity of finding his daily sustenance, and contented himself, though this was a sad form of enjoyment, a bitter pleasure, with listening from afar to the life of those of his race which their nocturnal hunting so often recalled to him, like the happy music of a lost paradise.

The oppressive heat of the month of August made him go at nightfall to the meadows beside the roads where he was certain of finding moles seeking on the surface a temporary respite from the heat which was stifling them, wandering about in the freshly mown swaths of the late crop and destined to death by the mere fact of having deserted the primitive cross-roads beneath their dried-up molehills.

This was an assured source of food for Goupil, because even if he had not found them still alive, wandering miserably beneath the double weight of their blindness and of the discomfort which drove them from the over-heated furnace of the earth, he knew that he would certainly come across them dead by the roadside, for those that leave their tunnels in this way never return and nearly all perish in the course of their first and last journey into the open.

Then autumn followed with its abundance of fruit which would have made life particularly peaceful for him if packs of hounds, rousing his domain on every side with their furious baying, had not reminded him too vividly of Lisée and Miraut and of his captivity and isolation.

Having become more cunning as a result of his experience, he used an earth with a double exit and only entered it after having, by cleverly crossing his tracks, put up a false scent which would keep even the most formidable hounds away from his trail.

Life, however, seemed easy to him and the old scavenger never gave a thought to the approaching winter which, from the premature migration of the wood pigeons and the jays, and from the sudden thickening of his own pelt, promised to be early and severe.

VIII

It came suddenly, without any transition period, as sometimes happens in the mountains, after the cold mists of the end of October and of the first days of November which stripped the forest of its autumn-tinted leaves. A few red berries still gleamed among the briars in the hedges, a few violet sloes, wrinkled by the first frosts, still clung to the blackthorns, their stalks almost severed by the ruthless bite of the frost; then one fine morning when the wind seemed to have fallen asleep, snow began to fall, treacherously, noiselessly, and without any fuss, with the quiet persistence of the good workman whom nothing discourages and nothing flurries and who knows that he has plenty of time in which to finish his task.

The snow fell for two days and two nights without a stop, levelling the hillocks and filling up the dips in the ground, flattening everything with its soft, uniform covering. And during the whole of the time it was falling none of the woodland beasts or the non-migratory birds stirred from their carefully chosen shelters.

Goupil (he would have no more to do with caves), crouching beneath the low branches of a clump of hazels had, like the rest, allowed himself to be buried beneath the shroud which gradually formed and, moulding his huddled shape, built for him a narrow kennel, a delicate, fragile shell, whose flimsy wall he would easily be able to break through when the moment came. In this shell he was warm, for his pelt was thick and the vault of the snow, moulding an arch for his back, protected it completely from the outer cold.

When he guessed that the snow had ceased to fall he waited until midday and then made a narrow exit for himself and, being careful not to damage the snow house which nature had made to his measure, he went in search of his daily food.

The bad days had returned: Goupil felt this clearly, all the more because, hampered by the bell which he was condemned to sound at every step, he found himself at a very real disadvantage in hunting and especially in hunting hares.

He knew quite well that a hare bolting before him would inevitably fall a victim to him, because when the snow was soft, the unfortunate creatures were quite incapable of competing in speed with foxes and dogs. But they were quite aware of this inferiority, so that when they heard an unfamiliar sound, such as that of a bell or of footsteps, they took the wise precaution of getting a very long start. So that Goupil was more than suspect to them.

Then the endless searching started again, the weary digging beneath the wild apple trees, the patient gleaning among bushes shaken free from their snow, all of which only half filled his stomach which was too often quite empty.

Once more he experienced foodless days, long waits by the runs used by hares and cautious ambushes at the outskirts of villages or farms in the faint hope of catching a fowl or strangling a cat.

This continued until the first days of December. But at this period the cold grew more intense and biting blizzards began to blow; the snow, broken up by the frost into tiny crystal spangles, found its way into every-thing, filling up the deepest valleys, insinuating itself into the most shel-tered places, and forming veritable white dunes and drifts which kept shifting at the will of the wind.

His snow house, however, remained intact; it had even become more substantial and he was more comfortable in it, for the warmth of his body had melted a thin layer of snow all round him and this subsequently froze and solidified and formed a harder crust, an arch of ice which easily sup-ported the varying weight of the snow above it.

All the bushes had been carefully picked bare; the birds all hovered about the villages, and hares were unapproachable. Nothing, nothing more at all, and Goupil, remembering his former adventure, hesitated to tempt Provi-dence again and to try to gain the confidence of domestic animals by means of his bell.

But it came inevitably to that. Each night he drew imperceptibly nearer to human habitations, even frightening away other foxes who, starving also, were already prowling round and had not, as he had, waited until hunger had driven them to the utmost limit before coming to hunt such dangerous quarry.

But not a single animal dreamed of leaving the warm litter in its stable or the fireside where, on warm bricks or floor-boards, the shivering cats would curl up when they were not watching the piled-up trusses of corn in the barns or holes in the walls for the lean, harried-looking mice who, also starving, had all returned to the shelter of the houses.

From time to time the furious barking of a dog would warn him that he had come too close, that he had been winded and that the time had come for him to make himself scarce with all possible speed. He never gained anything from these nocturnal expeditions. The traditional carcass which formerly tempted starving stomachs and from which one could, at the worst, by creeping up in short stages with long intervals between them, furtively seize a scrap and make off, no longer existed; the village animals obstinately refused to die. Nevertheless, Goupil kept on prowling round at a safe distance from the houses: but he carefully avoided Lisée's house and, in spite of the ferment in his brain, and in spite of his empty stomach, he fled even more quickly than usual on the night on which he heard Miraut's bark answering the bark of one of his hunting companions who was inform-ing him in his own fashion of the proximity of one of the denizens of the forest.

But Goupil was still without food. The days passed but the cold remained and fiercer and fiercer hunger gnawed at the vitals of the forest dwellers.

And he, gaunt now, a wasted shadow of his former self, even more wretched looking than he had been after the days of his imprisonment, was nothing but a poor tatterdemalion, exhausted by fever, hovering between death and madness, who, having acquired the habit of prowling round the

village, returned there inevitably each night at the same time, without knowing why, no longer trying to avoid the dogs, not even avoiding Lisée's house,
without a hope of finding anything to eat, without even looking for anything, baffled by the bell which tinkled at his neck and ripe for the final
and supreme ordeal.

IX

Christmas Eve that year had been a day of long twilight. The sun
never showed itself at all; a few grey ribbons just above the horizon at midday had borne witness to its passage behind the inky clouds which stretched
their sinister canopy above the silent, cheerless countryside.

A few mournful caws from luckless crows, and an occasional chattering
magpie searching for the last red berries of the rowans had occasionally
broken the silence, but that had been all.

The torpid village on which the motionless smoke, the feverish breath of
the cottages, seemed to weigh like a pall of misery, had given the only other
sign of life at dawn and at nightfall, when the stable doors had, at the usual
hour, belched forth the cattle full of suppressed energy, lowing and hurrying towards their watering place.

And yet everything in the village was alive and awake, for it was Christmas Eve. There was a great deal of unaccustomed bustle in the old
romanesque kitchens where the rustic pillars and smoke-blackened cross-
beams supported the spans of the immense fireplaces in which sides of
bacon and hams were being dried in the aromatic smoke of burning juniper
wood.

For Christmas Eve and Christmas Day the housewives had kneaded and
cooked a double batch of bread and of cakes whose warm smell still pervaded the whole house. Forgetting their games and their quarrels, the
children had followed all the preparations with cries of delight and
had noisily enumerated all the good things, impatiently awaiting the longed-
for moment when they were to be enjoyed: plums dried in the oven on
plaited osiers after the baking of the bread, meringues powdered with
"hundreds and thousands" and apples brought up from the cellars emitting
a subtle odour of ether.

Supper had been plentiful and full of gaiety, and, according to custom, at
midnight the whole happy family had been lit by yellow torches to the
church and back for the longed-for festivities.

They had eaten and drunk and sung and laughed and the grandmother
had begun the traditional story in her quavering, rather mysterious and
far-away voice:

"It was after midnight on one Christmas Eve many, many years ago,
when the soil we till now still belonged to the great lords and our grandfathers' grandfathers obeyed them.

"The hour of mass was approaching when a man whom no one had ever seen before came to call upon the Count at the castle whose ruins are familiar to you all. A herd of wild boar, he said, had gathered at the bottom of the Wolves Valley and in the clear moonlight they could easily be hunted. Immediately the Count, who was an ardent sportsman, forgot his religious duties, had horses saddled for himself and his servants and sent for his hounds. But his pious wife wept and besought him so earnestly that at last he consented, when the church bell pealed for mass, to take his place in church in the red armchair beneath the gilded canopy which was reserved for them.

"The chanting had already begun, but a baffled frown barred the Count's forehead when the mysterious stranger, entering the church without signing himself, once more approached him and whispered in his ear.

"The unfortunate man could no longer resist and, in spite of the imploring looks of his wife, left the church, followed by his servants. Very soon the baying of the hounds could be heard in the distance and during the whole mass the noise of the hunt moving about the countryside was like blasphemy to the ears of the faithful, all of whom had tears in their eyes and offered up fervent prayers. The hunt went on all night and then suddenly all sound of it ceased. But the Count never returned to the castle; he disappeared with his infernal pack and his menials and now, in hell, he bitterly atones for the sacrilege for which God had condemned him to return every hundred years on Christmas Day, to hunt through the night with his hounds. The wretched Countess died in a convent; as for the stranger who had tempted her husband, he was never seen again either and everyone thought that he must have been the devil himself.

"My mother never heard the hunt, but her grandmother did: it was a dark night like this. It was . . ."

At that moment a dismal howl, a howl with a ring of death in it, tragically long and drawn out, swept through the village like a trail of horror and all the dogs in the village and in the outlying farms replied to this unearthly signal with long melancholy howls. The sound rose menacingly and then died down into a sob. When it was over, it began again, or rather it did not finish, but grew lower in agonising modulations and prolonged itself in a rhythm of monotonous despair.

"Let us pray, my children, let us pray for the soul of the Count."

No one in the village slept that night. The men took down their old flintlocks from the nails from which they hung and carefully examined their priming and in their awed faces, on which the scepticism of the century had perhaps placed its seal, the signs of old superstitious terror rose like foam upon a wave.

The women and children huddled silently round the fireplace, seeking protection in the light and warmth against the unknown danger with which they thought they were being threatened. But more than anyone else in the village that night Lisée felt the agony of fear.

For the first howl had come from outside the door of the old poacher and he feared neither God nor devil. It was from there that the strange master of this great mysterious drama gave orders to his invisible pack. And so Lisée had pushed a huge oak dresser against the door, before which Miraut, his tail between his legs and his hair bristling, howled dismally. Lisée remained awake all night, his gun charged with buck-shot in his hands, ready to fire. An hour before dawn the sound of the melancholy hunt died away.

Reassured by the daylight and by the silence, the poacher slowly and silently dragged aside the heavy dresser which barricaded the door and cautiously opened it.

There before him was Goupil, like a skeleton, his eyes haggard, his legs rigid in death and stiffened by the frost, his pelt nearly bald, with the fatal bell round his neck, in the attitude of a cat preparing to spring.

Miraut sniffed at him fearfully and backed away with a silent snarl.

Lisée went back into his house with his head throbbing and his legs tottering beneath him. He fetched a spade and a sack into which he placed the body of his unhappy victim and went up to the forest, followed by his dog.

There he dug a deep hole beneath the snow, into which he placed the body of the fox, carefully filling it in afterwards.

And he returned to his house with his shoulders bowed and his eyes full of vague terrors, while Miraut, who had not his master's reasons for grave preoccupation, raised an irreverent and philosophic leg against the grey mound of earth and snow beneath which Goupil slept his last sleep.

ODOUR OF CHRYSANTHEMUMS

D. H. Lawrence

(1885–1930)

THE SMALL LOCOMOTIVE ENGINE, Number 4, came clanking, stumbling down from Selston with seven full waggons. It appeared round the corner with loud threats of speed, but the colt that it startled from among the gorse, which still flickered indistinctly in the raw afternoon, outdistanced it at a canter. A woman, walking up the railway line to Underwood, drew back into the hedge, held her basket aside, and watched the footplate of the engine advancing. The trucks thumped heavily past, one by one, with slow inevitable movement, as she stood insignificantly trapped between the jolting black waggons and the hedge; then they curved away towards the coppice where the withered oak leaves dropped noiselessly, while the birds, pulling at the scarlet hips beside the track, made off into the dusk that had already crept into the spinney. In the open, the smoke from the engine sank and cleaved to the rough grass. The fields were dreary and forsaken, and in the marshy strip that led to the whimsey, a reedy pit-pond, the fowls had already abandoned their run among the alders, to roost in the tarred fowl-house. The pit-bank loomed up beyond the pond, flames like red sores licking its ashy sides, in the afternoon's stagnant light. Just beyond rose the tapering chimneys and the clumsy black headstocks of Brinsley Colliery. The two wheels were spinning fast up against the sky, and the winding-engine rapped out its little spasms. The miners were being turned up.

The engine whistled as it came into the wide bay of railway lines beside the colliery, where rows of trucks stood in harbour.

Miners, single, trailing and in groups, passed like shadows diverging home. At the edge of the ribbed level of siding squat a low cottage, three steps down from the cinder track. A large bony vine clutched at the house, as if to claw down the tiled roof. Round the bricked yard grew a few wintry primroses. Beyond, the long garden sloped down to a bush-covered brook course. There were some twiggy apple trees, winter-crack trees, and ragged cabbages. Beside the path hung dishevelled pink chrysanthemums, like pink cloths hung on bushes. A woman came stooping out of the felt-covered fowl-house, half-way down the garden. She closed and padlocked the door, then drew herself erect, having brushed some bits from her white apron.

She was a tall woman of imperious mien, handsome, with definite black eyebrows. Her smooth black hair was parted exactly. For a few moments she stood steadily watching the miners as they passed along the railway: then she turned towards the brook course. Her face was calm and set, her mouth was closed with disillusionment. After a moment she called:

"John!" There was no answer. She waited, and then said distinctly:

"Where are you?"

"Here!" replied a child's sulky voice from among the bushes. The woman looked piercingly through the dusk.

"Are you at that brook?" she asked sternly.

For answer the child showed himself before the raspberry-canes that rose like whips. He was a small, sturdy boy of five. He stood quite still, defiantly.

"Oh!" said the mother, conciliated. "I thought you were down at that wet brook—and you remember what I told you——"

The boy did not move or answer.

"Come, come on in," she said more gently, "it's getting dark. There's your grandfather's engine coming down the line!"

The lad advanced slowly, with resentful, taciturn movement. He was dressed in trousers and waistcoat of cloth that was too thick and hard for the size of the garments. They were evidently cut down from a man's clothes.

As they went slowly towards the house he tore at the ragged wisps of chrysanthemums and dropped the petals in handfuls along the path.

"Don't do that—it does look nasty," said his mother. He refrained, and she, suddenly pitiful, broke off a twig with three or four wan flowers and held them against her face. When mother and son reached the yard her hand hesitated, and instead of laying the flower aside, she pushed it in her apron-band. The mother and son stood at the foot of the three steps looking across the bay of lines at the passing home of the miners. The trundle of the small train was imminent. Suddenly the engine loomed past the house and came to a stop opposite the gate.

The engine-driver, a short man with round grey beard, leaned out of the cab high above the woman.

"Have you got a cup of tea?" he said in a cheery, hearty fashion.

It was her father. She went in, saying she would mash. Directly, she returned.

"I didn't come to see you on Sunday," began the little grey-bearded man.

"I didn't expect you," said his daughter.

The engine-driver winced; then, reassuming his cheery, airy manner, he said:

"Oh, have you heard then? Well, and what do you think——?"

"I think it is soon enough," she replied.

At her brief censure the little man made an impatient gesture, and said coaxingly, yet with dangerous coldness:

"Well, what's a man to do? It's no sort of life for a man of my years, to sit at my own hearth like a stranger. And if I'm going to marry again it may as well be soon as late—what does it matter to anybody?"

The woman did not reply, but turned and went into the house. The man in the engine-cab stood assertive, till she returned with a cup of tea and a piece of bread and butter on a plate. She went up the steps and stood near the footplate of the hissing engine.

"You needn't 'a' brought me bread an' butter," said her father. "But a cup of tea"—he sipped appreciatively—"it's very nice." He sipped for a moment or two, then: "I hear as Walter's got another bout on," he said.

"When hasn't he?" said the woman bitterly.

"I heered tell of him in the 'Lord Nelson' braggin' as he was going to spend that b—— afore he went: half a sovereign that was."

"When?" asked the woman.

"A' Sat'day night—I know that's true."

"Very likely," she laughed bitterly. "He gives me twenty-three shillings."

"Aye, it's a nice thing, when a man can do nothing with his money but make a beast of himself!" said the grey-whiskered man. The woman turned her head away. Her father swallowed the last of his tea and handed her the cup.

"Aye," he sighed, wiping his mouth. "It's a settler, it is——"

He put his hand on the lever. The little engine strained and groaned, and the train rumbled towards the crossing. The woman again looked across the metals. Darkness was settling over the spaces of the railway and trucks: the miners, in grey sombre groups, were still passing home. The winding-engine pulsed hurriedly, with brief pauses. Elizabeth Bates looked at the dreary flow of men, then she went indoors. Her husband did not come.

The kitchen was small and full of firelight; red coals piled glowing up the chimney mouth. All the life of the room seemed in the white, warm hearth and the steel fender reflecting the red fire. The cloth was laid for tea; cups glinted in the shadows. At the back, where the lowest stairs protruded into the room, the boy sat struggling with a knife and a piece of whitewood. He was almost hidden in the shadow. It was half-past four. They had but to await the father's coming to begin tea. As the mother watched her son's sullen little struggle with the wood, she saw herself in his silence and pertinacity; she saw the father in her child's indifference to all but himself. She seemed to be occupied by her husband. He had probably gone past his home, slung past his own door, to drink before he came in, while his dinner spoiled and wasted in waiting. She glanced at the clock, then took the potatoes to strain them in the yard. The garden and fields beyond the brook were closed in uncertain darkness. When she rose with the saucepan, leaving the drain steaming into the night behind her, she saw the yellow lamps were lit along the high road that went up the hill away beyond the space of the railway lines and the field.

Then again she watched the men trooping home, fewer now and fewer.

Indoors the fire was sinking and the room was dark red. The woman put her saucepan on the hob, and set a batter pudding near the mouth of the oven. Then she stood unmoving. Directly, gratefully, came quick young steps to the door. Someone hung on the latch a moment, then a little girl entered and began pulling off her outdoor things, dragging a mass of curls, just ripening from gold to brown, over her eyes with her hat.

Her mother chid her for coming late from school, and said she would have to keep her at home the dark winter days.

"Why, mother, it's hardly a bit dark yet. The lamp's not lighted, and my father's not home."

"No, he isn't. But it's a quarter to five! Did you see anything of him?"

The child became serious. She looked at her mother with large, wistful blue eyes.

"No, mother, I've never seen him. Why? Has he come up an' gone past, to Old Brinsley? He hasn't, mother, 'cos I never saw him."

"He'd watch that," said the mother bitterly, "he'd take care as you didn't see him. But you may depend upon it, he's seated in the 'Prince o' Wales.' He wouldn't be this late."

The girl looked at her mother piteously.

"Let's have our teas, mother, should we?" said she.

The mother called John to table. She opened the door once more and looked out across the darkness of the lines. All was deserted: she could not hear the winding-engines.

"Perhaps," she said to herself, "he's stopped to get some ripping done."

They sat down to tea. John, at the end of the table near the door, was almost lost in the darkness. Their faces were hidden from each other. The girl crouched against the fender slowly moving a thick piece of bread before the fire. The lad, his face a dusky mark on the shadow, sat watching her who was transfigured in the red glow.

"I do think it's beautiful to look in the fire," said the child.

"Do you?" said her mother. "Why?"

"It's so red, and full of little caves—and it feels so nice, and you can fair smell it."

"It'll want mending directly," replied her mother, "and then if your father comes he'll carry on and say there never is a fire when a man comes home sweating from the pit. A public-house is always warm enough."

There was silence till the boy said complainingly: "Make haste, our Annie."

"Well, I am doing! I can't make the fire do it no faster, can I?"

"She keeps wafflin' it about so's to make 'er slow," grumbled the boy.

"Don't have such an evil imagination, child," replied the mother.

Soon the room was busy in the darkness with the crisp sound of crunching. The mother ate very little. She drank her tea determinedly, and sat thinking. When she rose her anger was evident in the stern unbending of her head. She looked at the pudding in the fender, and broke out:

"It is a scandalous thing as a man can't even come home to his dinner! If it's crozzled up to a cinder I don't see why I should care. Past his very door he goes to get to a public-house, and here I sit with his dinner waiting for him——"

She went out. As she dropped piece after piece of coal on the red fire, the shadows fell on the walls, till the room was almost in total darkness.

"I canna see," grumbled the invisible John. In spite of herself, the mother laughed.

"You know the way to your mouth," she said. She set the dust-pan outside the door. When she came again like a shadow on the hearth, the lad repeated, complaining sulkily:

"I canna see."

"Good gracious!" cried the mother irritably, "you're as bad as your father if it's a bit dusk!"

Nevertheless she took a paper spill from a sheaf on the mantelpiece and proceeded to light the lamp that hung from the ceiling in the middle of the room. As she reached up, her figure displayed itself just rounding with maternity.

"Oh, mother——!" exclaimed the girl.

"What?" said the woman, suspended in the act of putting the lamp glass over the flame. The copper reflector shone handsomely on her, as she stood with uplifted arm, turning to face her daughter.

"You've got a flower in your apron!" said the child, in a little rapture at this unusual event.

"Goodness me!" exclaimed the woman, relieved. "One would think the house was afire." She replaced the glass and waited a moment before turning up the wick. A pale shadow was seen floating vaguely on the floor.

"Let me smell!" said the child, still rapturously, coming forward and putting her face to her mother's waist.

"Go along, silly!" said the mother, turning up the lamp. The light revealed their suspense so that the woman felt it almost unbearable. Annie was still bending at her waist. Irritably, the mother took the flowers out from her apron-band.

"Oh, mother—don't take them out!" Annie cried, catching her hand and trying to replace the sprig.

"Such nonsense!" said the mother, turning away. The child put the pale chrysanthemums to her lips, murmuring:

"Don't they smell beautiful!"

Her mother gave a short laugh.

"No," she said, "not to me. It was chrysanthemums when I married him, and chrysanthemums when you were born, and the first time they ever brought him home drunk, he'd got brown chrysanthemums in his buttonhole."

She looked at the children. Their eyes and their parted lips were wondering. The mother sat rocking in silence for some time. Then she looked at the clock.

"Twenty minutes to six!" In a tone of fine bitter carelessness she continued: "Eh, he'll not come now till they bring him. There he'll stick! But he needn't come rolling in here in his pit-dirt, for *I* won't wash him. He can lie on the floor—— Eh, what a fool I've been, what a fool! And this is what I came here for, to this dirty hole, rats and all, for him to slink past his very door. Twice last week—he's begun now——"

She silenced herself, and rose to clear the table.

While for an hour or more the children played, subduedly intent, fertile of imagination, united in fear of the mother's wrath, and in dread of their father's home-coming, Mrs. Bates sat in her rocking-chair making a "singlet" of thick cream-coloured flannel, which gave a dull wounded sound as she tore off the grey edge. She worked at her sewing with energy, listening to the children, and her anger wearied itself, lay down to rest, opening its eyes from time to time and steadily watching, its ears raised to listen. Sometimes even her anger quailed and shrank, and the mother suspended her sewing, tracing the footsteps that thudded along the sleepers outside; she would lift her head sharply to bid the children "hush," but she recovered herself in time, and the footsteps went past the gate, and the children were not flung out of their play-world.

But at last Annie sighed, and gave in. She glanced at her waggon of slippers, and loathed the game. She turned plaintively to her mother.

"Mother!"—but she was inarticulate.

John crept out like a frog from under the sofa. His mother glanced up.

"Yes," she said, "just look at those shirt-sleeves!"

The boy held them out to survey them, saying nothing. Then somebody called in a hoarse voice away down the line, and suspense bristled in the room, till two people had gone by outside, talking.

"It is time for bed," said the mother.

"My father hasn't come," wailed Annie plaintively. But her mother was primed with courage.

"Never mind. They'll bring him when he does come—like a log." She meant there would be no scene. "And he may sleep on the floor till he wakes himself. I know he'll not go to work to-morrow after this!"

The children had their hands and faces wiped with a flannel. They were very quiet. When they had put on their nightdresses, they said their prayers, the boy mumbling. The mother looked down at them, at the brown silken bush of intertwining curls in the nape of the girl's neck, at the little black head of the lad, and her heart burst with anger at their father who caused all three such distress. The children hid their faces in her skirts for comfort.

When Mrs. Bates came down, the room was strangely empty, with a tension of expectancy. She took up her sewing and stitched for some time without raising her head. Meantime her anger was tinged with fear.

II

The clock struck eight and she rose suddenly, dropping her sewing on her chair. She went to the stairfoot door, opened it, listening. Then she went out, locking the door behind her.

Something scuffled in the yard, and she started, though she knew it was only the rats with which the place was overrun. The night was very dark. In the great bay of railway lines, bulked with trucks, there was no trace of light, only away back she could see a few yellow lamps at the pit-top, and the red smear of the burning pit-bank on the night. She hurried along the edge of the track, then, crossing the converging lines, came to the stile by the white gates, whence she emerged on the road. Then the fear which had led her shrank. People were walking up to New Brinsley; she saw the lights in the houses; twenty yards further on were the broad windows of the "Prince of Wales," very warm and bright, and the loud voices of men could be heard distinctly. What a fool she had been to imagine that anything had happened to him! He was merely drinking over there at the "Prince of Wales." She faltered. She had never yet been to fetch him, and she never would go. So she continued her walk towards the long straggling line of houses, standing blank on the highway. She entered a passage between the dwellings.

"Mr. Rigley?—Yes! Did you want him? No, he's not in at this minute." The raw-boned woman leaned forward from her dark scullery and peered at the other, upon whom fell a dim light through the blind of the kitchen window.

"Is it Mrs. Bates?" she asked in a tone tinged with respect.

"Yes. I wondered if your Master was at home. Mine hasn't come yet."

" 'Asn't 'e! Oh, Jack's been 'ome an' 'ad 'is dinner an' gone out. 'E's just gone for 'alf an hour afore bedtime. Did you call at the 'Prince of Wales'?"

"No——"

"No, you didn't like——! It's not very nice." The other woman was indulgent. There was an awkward pause. "Jack never said nothink about—about your Mester," she said.

"No!—I expect he's stuck in there!"

Elizabeth Bates said this bitterly, and with recklessness. She knew that the woman across the yard was standing at her door listening, but she did not care. As she turned:

"Stop a minute! I'll just go an' ask Jack if 'e knows anythink," said Mrs. Rigley.

"Oh, no—I wouldn't like to put——!"

"Yes, I will, if you'll just step inside an' see as th' childer doesn't come downstairs and set theirselves afire."

Elizabeth Bates, murmuring a remonstrance, stepped inside. The other woman apologized for the state of the room.

The kitchen needed apology. There were little frocks and trousers and childish undergarments on the squab and on the floor, and a litter of playthings everywhere. On the black American cloth of the table were pieces of bread and cake, crusts, slops, and a teapot with cold tea.

"Eh, ours is just as bad," said Elizabeth Bates, looking at the woman, not at the house. Mrs. Rigley put a shawl over her head and hurried out, saying:

"I shanna be a minute."

The other sat, noting with faint disapproval the general untidiness of the room. Then she fell to counting the shoes of various sizes scattered over the floor. There were twelve. She sighed and said to herself, "No wonder!"—glancing at the litter. There came the scratching of two pairs of feet on the yard, and the Rigleys entered. Elizabeth Bates rose. Rigley was a big man, with very large bones. His head looked particularly bony. Across his temple was a blue scar, caused by a wound got in the pit, a wound in which the coal-dust remained blue like tattooing.

"'Asna 'e come whoam yit?" asked the man, without any form of greeting, but with deference and sympathy. "I couldna say wheer he is—'e's non ower theer!"—he jerked his head to signify the "Prince of Wales."

"'E's 'appen gone up to th' 'Yew,'" said Mrs. Rigley.

There was another pause. Rigley had evidently something to get off his mind:

"Ah left 'im finishin' a stint," he began. "Loose-all 'ad bin gone about ten minutes when we com'n away, an' I shouted, 'Are ter comin', Walt?' an' 'e said, 'Go on, Ah shanna be but a'ef a minnit,' so we com'n ter th' bottom, me an' Bowers, thinkin' as 'e wor just behint, an' 'ud come up i' th' next bantle——"

He stood perplexed, as if answering a charge of deserting his mate. Elizabeth Bates, now again certain of disaster, hastened to reassure him:

"I expect 'e's gone up to th' 'Yew Tree,' as you say. It's not the first time. I've fretted myself into a fever before now. He'll come home when they carry him."

"Ay, isn't it too bad!" deplored the other woman.

"I'll just step up to Dick's an' see if 'e *is* theer," offered the man, afraid of appearing alarmed, afraid of taking liberties.

"Oh, I wouldn't think of bothering you that far," said Elizabeth Bates, with emphasis, but he knew she was glad of his offer.

As they stumbled up the entry, Elizabeth Bates heard Rigley's wife run across the yard and open her neighbour's door. At this, suddenly all the blood in her body seemed to switch away from her heart.

"Mind!" warned Rigley. "Ah've said many a time as Ah'd fill up them ruts in this entry, sumb'dy 'll be breakin' their legs yit."

She recovered herself and walked quickly along with the miner.

"I don't like leaving the children in bed, and nobody in the house," she said.

"No, you dunna!" he replied courteously. They were soon at the gate of the cottage.

"Well, I shanna be many minnits. Dunna you be frettin' now, 'e'll be all right," said the butty.

"Thank you very much, Mr. Rigley," she replied.

"You're welcome!" he stammered, moving away. "I shanna be many minnits."

The house was quiet. Elizabeth Bates took off her hat and shawl, and rolled back the rug. When she had finished, she sat down. It was a few minutes past nine. She was startled by the rapid chuff of the winding-engine at the pit, and the sharp whirr of the brakes on the rope as it descended. Again she felt the painful sweep of her blood, and she put her hand to her side, saying aloud, "Good gracious!—it's only the nine o'clock deputy going down," rebuking herself.

She sat still, listening. Half an hour of this, and she was wearied out.

"What am I working myself up like this for?" she said pitiably to herself, "I s'll only be doing myself some damage."

She took out her sewing again.

At a quarter to ten there were footsteps. One person! She watched for the door to open. It was an elderly woman, in a black bonnet and a black woollen shawl—his mother. She was about sixty years old, pale, with blue eyes, and her face all wrinkled and lamentable. She shut the door and turned to her daughter-in-law peevishly.

"Eh, Lizzie, whatever shall we do, whatever shall we do!" she cried.

Elizabeth drew back a little, sharply.

"What is it, mother?" she said.

The elder woman seated herself on the sofa.

"I don't know, child, I can't tell you!"—she shook her head slowly. Elizabeth sat watching her, anxious and vexed.

"I don't know," replied the grandmother, sighing very deeply. "There's no end to my troubles, there isn't. The things I've gone through, I'm sure it's enough——" She wept without wiping her eyes, the tears running.

"But, mother," interrupted Elizabeth, "what do you mean? What is it?"

The grandmother slowly wiped her eyes. The fountains of her tears were stopped by Elizabeth's directness. She wiped her eyes slowly.

"Poor child! Eh, you poor thing!" she moaned. "I don't know what we're going to do, I don't—and you as you are—it's a thing, it is indeed!"

Elizabeth waited.

"Is he dead?" she asked, and at the words her heart swung violently, though she felt a slight flush of shame at the ultimate extravagance of the question. Her words sufficiently frightened the old lady, almost brought her to herself.

"Don't say so, Elizabeth! We'll hope it's not as bad as that; no, may the Lord spare us that, Elizabeth. Jack Rigley came just as I was sittin' down to a glass afore going to bed, an' 'e said, ' 'Appen you'll go down th' line, Mrs. Bates. Walt's had an accident. 'Appen you'll go an' sit wi' 'er till we can get him home.' I hadn't time to ask him a word afore he was gone. An' I put my bonnet on an' come straight down, Lizzie. I thought to myself, 'Eh, that poor blessed child, if anybody should come an' tell her of a sudden, there's no knowin' what'll 'appen to 'er.' You mustn't let it upset you, Lizzie—or you know what to expect. How long is it, six months —or is it five, Lizzie? Ay!"—the old woman shook her head—"time slips on, it slips on! Ay!"

Elizabeth's thoughts were busy elsewhere. If he was killed—would she be able to manage on the little pension and what she could earn?—she counted up rapidly. If he was hurt—they wouldn't take him to the hospital

—how tiresome he would be to nurse!—but perhaps she'd be able to get him away from the drink and his hateful ways. She would—while he was ill. The tears offered to come to her eyes at the picture. But what sentimental luxury was this she was beginning? She turned to consider the children. At any rate she was absolutely necessary for them. They were her business.

"Ay!" repeated the old woman, "it seems but a week or two since he brought me his first wages. Ay—he was a good lad, Elizabeth, he was, in his way. I don't know why he got to be such a trouble, I don't. He was a happy lad at home, only full of spirits. But there's no mistake he's been a handful of trouble, he has! I hope the Lord'll spare him to mend his ways. I hope so, I hope so. You've had a sight o' trouble with him, Elizabeth, you have indeed. But he was a jolly enough lad wi' me, he was, I can assure you. I don't know how it is. . . ."

The old woman continued to muse aloud, a monotonous irritating sound, while Elizabeth thought concentratedly, startled once, when she heard the winding-engine chuff quickly, and the brakes skirr with a shriek. Then she heard the engine more slowly, and the brakes made no sound. The old woman did not notice. Elizabeth waited in suspense. The mother-in-law talked, with lapses into silence.

"But he wasn't your son, Lizzie, an' it makes a difference. Whatever he was, I remember him when he was little, an' I learned to understand him and to make allowances. You've got to make allowances for them——"

It was half-past ten, and the old woman was saying: "But it's trouble from beginning to end; you're never too old for trouble, never too old for that——" when the gate banged back, and there were heavy feet on the steps.

"I'll go, Lizzie, let me go," cried the old woman, rising. But Elizabeth was at the door. It was a man in pit-clothes.

"They're bringin' 'im, Missis," he said. Elizabeth's heart halted a moment. Then it surged on again, almost suffocating her.

"Is he—is it bad?" she asked.

The man turned away, looking at the darkness:

"The doctor says 'e'd been dead hours. 'E saw 'im i' th' lamp-cabin."

The old woman, who stood just behind Elizabeth, dropped into a chair, and folded her hands, crying: "Oh, my boy, my boy!"

"Hush!" said Elizabeth, with a sharp twitch of a frown. "Be still, mother, don't waken th' children: I wouldn't have them down for anything!"

The old woman moaned softly, rocking herself. The man was drawing away. Elizabeth took a step forward.

"How was it?" she asked.

"Well, I couldn't say for sure," the man replied, very ill at ease. " 'E wor finishin' a stint an' th' butties 'ad gone, an' a lot o' stuff come down atop 'n 'im."

"And crushed him?" cried the widow, with a shudder.

"No," said the man, "it fell at th' back of 'im. 'E wor under th' face, an' it niver touched 'im. It shut 'im in. It seems 'e wor smothered."

Elizabeth shrank back. She heard the old woman behind her cry:

"What?—what did 'e say it was?"

The man replied, more loudly: "'E wor smothered!"

Then the old woman wailed aloud, and this relieved Elizabeth.

"Oh, mother," she said, putting her hand on the old woman, "don't waken th' children, don't waken th' children."

She wept a little, unknowing, while the old mother rocked herself and moaned. Elizabeth remembered that they were bringing him home, and she must be ready. "They'll lay him in the parlour," she said to herself, standing a moment pale and perplexed.

Then she lighted a candle and went into the tiny room. The air was cold and damp, but she could not make a fire, there was no fireplace. She set down the candle and looked round. The candlelight glittered on the lustre-glasses, on the two vases that held some of the pink chrysanthemums, and on the dark mahogany. There was a cold, deathly smell of chrysanthemums in the room. Elizabeth stood looking at the flowers. She turned away, and calculated whether there would be room to lay him on the floor, between the couch and the chiffonier. She pushed the chairs aside. There would be room to lay him down and to step round him. Then she fetched the old red tablecloth, and another old cloth, spreading them down to save her bit of carpet. She shivered on leaving the parlour; so, from the dresser-drawer she took a clean shirt and put it at the fire to air. All the time her mother-in-law was rocking herself in the chair and moaning.

"You'll have to move from there, mother," said Elizabeth. "They'll be bringing him in. Come in the rocker."

The old mother rose mechanically, and seated herself by the fire, continuing to lament. Elizabeth went into the pantry for another candle, and there, in the little penthouse under the naked tiles, she heard them coming. She stood still in the pantry doorway, listening. She heard them pass the end of the house, and come awkwardly down the three steps, a jumble of shuffling footsteps and muttering voices. The old woman was silent. The men were in the yard.

Then Elizabeth heard Matthews, the manager of the pit, say: "You go in first, Jim. Mind!"

The door came open, and the two women saw a collier backing into the room, holding one end of a stretcher, on which they could see the nailed pit-boots of the dead man. The two carriers halted, the man at the head stooping to the lintel of the door.

"Wheer will you have him?" asked the manager, a short, white-bearded man.

Elizabeth roused herself and came from the pantry carrying the unlighted candle.

"In the parlour," she said.

"In there, Jim!" pointed the manager, and the carriers backed round into the tiny room. The coat with which they had covered the body fell off as they awkwardly turned through the two doorways, and the women saw their man, naked to the waist, lying stripped for work. The old woman began to moan in a low voice of horror.

"Lay th' stretcher at th' side," snapped the manager, "an' put 'im on th' cloths. Mind now, mind! Look you now——!"

One of the men had knocked off a vase of chrysanthemums. He stared awkwardly, then they set down the stretcher. Elizabeth did not look at her husband. As soon as she could get in the room, she went and picked up the broken vase and the flowers.

"Wait a minute!" she said.

The three men waited in silence while she mopped up the water with a duster.

"Eh, what a job, what a job, to be sure!" the manager was saying, rubbing his brow with trouble and perplexity. "Never knew such a thing in my life, never! He'd no business to ha' been left. I never knew such a thing in my life! Fell over him clean as a whistle, an' shut him in. Not four foot of space, there wasn't—yet it scarce bruised him."

He looked down at the dead man, lying prone, half naked, all grimed with coal-dust.

"'Sphyxiated,' the doctor said. It *is* the most terrible job I've ever known. Seems as if it was done o' purpose. Clean over him, an' shut 'im in, like a mouse-trap"—he made a sharp, descending gesture with his hand.

The colliers standing by jerked aside their heads in hopeless comment.

The horror of the thing bristled upon them all.

Then they heard the girl's voice upstairs calling shrilly: "Mother, mother—who is it? Mother, who is it?"

Elizabeth hurried to the foot of the stairs and opened the door:

"Go to sleep!" she commanded sharply. "What are you shouting about? Go to sleep at once—there's nothing——"

Then she began to mount the stairs. They could hear her on the boards, and on the plaster floor of the little bedroom. They could hear her distinctly:

"What's the matter now?—what's the matter with you, silly thing?"— her voice was much agitated, with an unreal gentleness.

"I thought it was some men come," said the plaintive voice of the child. "Has he come?"

"Yes, they've brought him. There's nothing to make a fuss about. Go to sleep now, like a good child."

They could hear her voice in the bedroom, they waited whilst she covered the children under the bedclothes.

"Is he drunk?" asked the girl, timidly, faintly.

"No! No—he's not! He—he's asleep."

"Is he asleep downstairs?"

"Yes—and don't make a noise."

There was silence for a moment, then the men heard the frightened child again:

"What's that noise?"

"It's nothing, I tell you, what are you bothering for?"

The noise was the grandmother moaning. She was oblivious of everything, sitting on her chair rocking and moaning. The manager put his hand on her arm and bade her "Sh—sh!!"

The old woman opened her eyes and looked at him. She was shocked by this interruption, and seemed to wonder.

"What time is it?"—the plaintive thin voice of the child, sinking back unhappily into sleep, asked this last question.

"Ten o'clock," answered the mother more softly. Then she must have bent down and kissed the children.

Matthews beckoned to the men to come away. They put on their caps and took up the stretcher. Stepping over the body, they tiptoed out of the house. None of them spoke till they were far from the wakeful children.

When Elizabeth came down she found her mother alone on the parlour floor, leaning over the dead man, the tears dropping on him.

"We must lay him out," the wife said. She put on the kettle, then returning knelt at the feet, and began to unfasten the knotted leather laces. The room was clammy and dim with only one candle, so that she had to bend her face almost to the floor. At last she got off the heavy boots and put them away.

"You must help me now," she whispered to the old woman. Together they stripped the man.

When they arose, saw him lying in the naïve dignity of death, the women stood arrested in fear and respect. For a few moments they remained still, looking down, the old mother whimpering. Elizabeth felt countermanded. She saw him, how utterly inviolable he lay in himself. She had nothing to do with him. She could not accept it. Stooping, she laid her hand on him, in claim. He was still warm, for the mine was hot where he had died. His mother had his face between her hands, and was murmuring incoherently. The old tears fell in succession as drops from wet leaves; the mother was not weeping, merely her tears flowed. Elizabeth embraced the body of her husband, with cheek and lips. She seemed to be listening, inquiring, trying to get some connection. But she could not. She was driven away. He was impregnable.

She rose, went into the kitchen, where she poured warm water into a bowl, brought soap and flannel and a soft towel.

"I must wash him," she said.

Then the old mother rose stiffly, and watched Elizabeth as she carefully washed his face, carefully brushing the big blond moustache from his mouth with the flannel. She was afraid with a bottomless fear, so she ministered to him. The old woman, jealous, said:

"Let me wipe him!"—and she kneeled on the other side drying slowly as Elizabeth washed, her big black bonnet sometimes brushing the dark head of her daughter-in-law. They worked thus in silence for a long time. They never forgot it was death, and the touch of the man's dead body gave them strange emotions, different in each of the women; a great dread possessed them both, the mother felt the lie was given to her womb, she was denied; the wife felt the utter isolation of the human soul, the child within her was a weight apart from her.

At last it was finished. He was a man of handsome body, and his face showed no traces of drink. He was blond, full-fleshed, with fine limbs. But he was dead.

"Bless him," whispered his mother, looking always at his face, and speaking out of sheer terror. "Dear lad—bless him!" She spoke in a faint, sibilant ecstasy of fear and mother love.

Elizabeth sank down again to the floor, and put her face against his neck, and trembled and shuddered. But she had to draw away again. He was dead, and her living flesh had no place against his. A great dread and weariness held her: she was so unavailing. Her life was gone like this.

"White as milk he is, clear as a twelve-month baby, bless him, the darling!" the old mother murmured to herself. "Not a mark on him, clear and clean and white, beautiful as ever a child was made," she murmured with pride. Elizabeth kept her face hidden.

"He went peaceful, Lizzie—peaceful as sleep. Isn't he beautiful, the lamb? Ay—he must ha' made his peace, Lizzie. 'Appen he made it all right, Lizzie, shut in there. He'd have time. He wouldn't look like this if he hadn't made his peace. The lamb, the dear lamb. Eh, but he had a hearty laugh. I loved to hear it. He had the heartiest laugh, Lizzie, as a lad——"

Elizabeth looked up. The man's mouth was fallen back, slightly open under the cover of the moustache. The eyes, half shut, did not show glazed in the obscurity. Life with its smoky burning gone from him, had left him apart and utterly alien to her. And she knew what a stranger he was to her. In her womb was ice of fear, because of this separate stranger with whom she had been living as one flesh. Was this what it all meant—utter, intact separateness, obscured by heat of living? In dread she turned her face away. The fact was too deadly. There had been nothing between them, and yet they had come together, exchanging their nakedness repeatedly. Each time he had taken her, they had been two isolated beings, far apart as now. He was no more responsible than she. The child was like ice in her womb. For as she looked at the dead man, her mind, cold and detached, said clearly: "Who am I? What have I been doing? I have been fighting a husband who did not exist. *He* existed all the time. What wrong have I done? What was that I have been living with? There lies the reality, this man." And her soul died in her for fear: she knew she had never seen him, he had never seen her, they had met in the dark and had fought in the dark, not knowing whom they met nor whom they fought. And now she saw, and turned silent in seeing. For she had been wrong. She had said he was something he was not; she had felt familiar with him. Whereas he was apart all the while, living as she never lived, feeling as she never felt.

In fear and shame she looked at his naked body, that she had known falsely. And he was the father of her children. Her soul was torn from her body and stood apart. She looked at his naked body and was ashamed, as if she had denied it. After all, it was itself. It seemed awful to her. She looked at his face, and she turned her own face to the wall. For his look was other than hers, his way was not her way. She had denied him what he was—she saw it now. She had refused him as himself. And this had been her life, and his life. She was grateful to death, which restored the truth. And she knew she was not dead.

And all the while her heart was bursting with grief and pity for him. What had he suffered? What stretch of horror for this helpless man! She was rigid with agony. She had not been able to help him. He had been cruelly injured, this naked man, this other being, and she could make no reparation. There were the children—but the children belonged to life. This dead man had nothing to do with them. He and she were only channels through which life had flowed to issue in the children. She was a mother— but how awful she knew it now to have been a wife. And he, dead now, how awful he must have felt it to be a husband. She felt that in the next world he would be a stranger to her. If they met there, in the beyond, they would only be ashamed of what had been before. The children had come, for some mysterious reason, out of both of them. But the children did not unite them. Now he was dead, she knew how eternally he was apart from her, how eternally he had nothing more to do with her. She saw this episode of her life closed. They had denied each other in life. Now he had withdrawn. An anguish came over her. It was finished then: it had become hopeless between them long before he died. Yet he had been her husband. But how little!

"Have you got his shirt, 'Lizabeth?"

Elizabeth turned without answering, though she strove to weep and behave as her mother-in-law expected. But she could not, she was silenced. She went into the kitchen and returned with the garment.

"It is aired," she said, grasping the cotton shirt here and there to try. She was almost ashamed to handle him; what right had she or any one to lay hands on him; but her touch was humble on his body. It was hard work to clothe him. He was so heavy and inert. A terrible dread gripped her all the while: that he could be so heavy and utterly inert, unresponsive, apart. The horror of the distance between them was almost too much for her— it was so infinite a gap she must look across.

At last it was finished. They covered him with a sheet and left him lying, with his face bound. And she fastened the door of the little parlour, lest the children should see what was lying there. Then, with peace sunk heavy on her heart, she went about making tidy the kitchen. She knew she submitted to life, which was her immediate master. But from death, her ultimate master, she winced with fear and shame.

THE CHINK

Alexandre Arnoux

(1884–   )

TRANSLATED BY VYVYAN HOLLAND

WE HAD LEFT the trenches at dawn, with empty wicker cages fastened to our shoulders. It was the hour at which the war seemed to doze, overcome by weariness at the end of the night; the sentries' heads began to nod as they leaned against their armoured parapets with half-closed eyes and the guns seemed to yawn on their carriages. . . . It was also the hour of raids and surprise attacks, of sudden bombardments which stupefy men and seem to rob them of all will-power. But on that particular day all was quiet in the cheerless trenches, after a feverish, jumpy night in which sudden bursts of fire disturbed the flat calm, in which rockets called for barrages and stopped them again almost as soon as they had begun, and in which the men hurriedly put on their gas-masks at the sound of Klaxon-horns without anyone knowing why or whence the sound had come. A sleepy machine-gun spread its bullets around, and fatigue-parties, their pipes between their teeth, came down communication trenches in smoky processions, swinging water-bottles full of coffee in their hands. We were already walking in the open, passing through the barbed wire at breaches indicated by fir branches, on the backward slope of the crest, between the pale moon and the hazy sun; banks of mist wound along below us, following the course of a stream; the white frosty grass seemed to turn a mauve colour on the further slopes. Then, little by little, the sickle moon faded in the pink sky and the sun shone brightly on the black spruces on which the rime looked like a primitive form of decoration, composed of sugar or spun glass. My companion, the Chink, began to roll himself a cigarette and to talk interminably, scarcely pausing even for breath.

He was tall and sturdy, with shiny black hair and a short thin moustache. Beneath the grime on his face his skin was yellow; he never washed this, but after being soaped it would probably have shone like a ball of polished box-wood. And finally there were his eyes, elongated towards the temples, which, added to his colour and a certain indefinite air of mystery and drollery, had earned him the nickname of "The Chink", of which he was rather proud. Whence did he come? What was his family? What was his trade? An imaginative liar, he often told us the story of his life, but it was never the same story. His boasting used to amaze and disconcert and attract us; he was agreeable enough, a bit of a wag and rather domineering; when he talked the others used to gather round him, the simple ones open-mouthed and the more sophisticated incredulous. If some sceptic were to point out contradictions or gross improbabilities in any of his statements, he would either reply by some coarsely facetious remark or by insults, according to his mood, or by blows which were formidable enough in themselves and to which he gave English names which added to their moral effect. From the general basis of his stories and of his vocabulary one could deduce that he had once served in a disciplinary battalion and had worked irregularly as an electrician and as a printer and had been in all sorts of vague professions and had done all sorts of odd jobs. A "god-mother" who lived in a dingy house near the Montparnasse railway-station sent him a postal-order for ten francs every fortnight and a picture-postcard every Sunday; he seemed to have no other correspondent. He himself sometimes claimed to be the son of a cook in the Chinese Embassy and a show-girl at a low music-hall in Montparnasse, an illusion born of his nickname, and sometimes the son of a priest from the Yonne district who very nearly became a bishop. His popularity in the company was founded, apart from the respect he commanded by his "swings" and "uppercuts", on the dual faculty of being able to belch at will and to light his effluvia at a candle flame. He owed his lucky position to these two talents; I owed mine to a certain skill at poker, at which the quartermaster-sergeant, who was always hard up, was worth forty or fifty francs a month to me.

So we had a "cushy job", and we were the objects of envy and contempt on the part of our comrades. Every morning we trudged eight miles with our wicker baskets on our backs to the divisional pigeon-loft and eight miles back with the pigeons, which would be released in the line and, after circling three times in the sky, would return to their home, lit up by a red light in the highest attic of the village in which they lived. Having delivered our cooing burden we were exempt from patrols, fatigues and guards and spent the rest of the time in telling stories, playing cards and sleeping until the following morning in our bunks made of woven wire, unless, of course, there was a bombardment, a gas-attack or a raid. But that, as the Chink said, was no longer soldiering, it was war.

II

My companion looked at the clouds scurrying towards the East and rambled on in his usual way. I liked the unexpectedness and the incongruity of his associations of ideas and his mobile imagination which touched on everything but settled on nothing.

"Yes, my boy, it's a good job, a cushy job. . . . Just walking about like tourists with a wicker knapsack on one's back. There are always jobs in wartime for intellectuals and people with influence and independent people. Why, I could have been an N.C.O. myself but I didn't trouble about it: in spite of my education I like freedom. I've often been offered stripes. I commanded the section in the Faubourg St.-Laurent at Arras. The major gave me some champagne, a bottle of gooseberry wine which didn't cost him much, out of a cellar as big as the Pantheon. I drank it, but I didn't take the stripes. I told him that I was working for the glory and the fraternity of peoples, for the crushing of militarism and for the League of Nations, not for ambition. The old man was rather sour and asked me if I was a Socialist. "Definitely," I replied. " 'Definitely' is a word which means that one's serious. That shut him up: the shock killed him three days later, that and a shrapnel splinter in the navel which gave him appendicitis, which was the fashionable disease then. Corporal! Sergeant! Sergeant-major! All a lot of humbug! We're stretcher-bearers for pigeons, that's the job for me! Oh, look at those clouds, one black and one white. They're going to box. The nigger Sam MacVea against Carpentier, four-ounce gloves, middle-weights, forty rounds. Time! The coloured man knows a thing or two. Right in the solar plexus! One, two, three! . . . The gong! . . . I tell you the paleface has taken the count! Filthy greasy nigger! Now there's a jockey in orange and blue coming past the post, riding in the American style, laughing at the rest of the field. I've bet fifteen francs on the rails and a hundred and twenty in the paddock. Where's my bookie gone? I want my money. And there's the Nesle Tower over there, above that shattered tree. 'It was a noble old man's head!' Oh, my friend, what a job, what a cushy job! The pigeon-fancier, little old Van de Putte, will give us a glass of spirits behind the wood-pile while he's smoking his half-penny pipe which stinks of nicotine and is as filthy as a Corsican's sock. There's always a place for intellectuals in wartime, independent people like you and me. . . ."

He went on talking, suiting his imaginary life and exploits to the undulations of the landscape and the changes in the sky. I did not listen to him, but I allowed myself to be lulled by his verbiage, which conjured up in my mind obscure pictures which dissolved as soon as they had formed; and the movement of my legs sent me off, so to speak, into a state of waking coma. We were now travelling through woods white with rime whose branches

swept our cloaks and covered them with shining crystals. We broke through
the gossamers stretched from one side of the rides to the other, between
the leafless briars with their red berries and the fleecy viburnums. I never
opened my mouth. Sometimes the Chink interrupted my vague meditations:

"I'll bet you don't believe me."

I replied mechanically:

"Yes. I believe you."

"Then you're a fool, because I've been talking rot and pulling your leg.
But what I'm going to tell you now is gospel truth. The insoluble and un-
amalgamated truth. Sometimes one gasses away for the sake of gassing, at
others one talks in order to think. That's the difference. Now listen to me."

What he likes about words is their resounding value, quite independently
of their meaning; verbal explanations enchant him; he neither looks for nor
understands any other sort. He says things like "This stuff must be incom-
bustible because it is an ignifuge." He has picked up a compendious vocabulary in all manner of different places; "short-circuit" for anything to do
with electricity, "the force of inertia" for the rest of physics. As for the
fluctuations of the war, sometimes he sums them up with a casual: "What
we need is better communications for the distribution of our effectives,"
and sometimes his only comment is a single cabalistic word, screwing up
his slanting eyes and assuming an air of importance behind his rough
greenish muffler, a single word framed by two periods of sybilline silence:
"Treachery."

The Chink continued:

"Do you see that little bit of abandoned trench in the clearing there,
behind those ash-trees? It reminds me of an adventure which disgusted me
with militarism and glory from the first. We had attacked, in the Forest of
Champenoux, a little ditch like that. It was more of a reconnaissance than
an attack, as we did not quite understand the situation. I had got a little
in advance of the others and when I jumped into the trench there was
nothing there but a tin of canned peas, a hymn-book and a German helmet.
So I put on the helmet and I started doing my job, walking up and down
with my rifle at the slope, like a sentinel outside the Elysée. The section
approached crawling on its stomach; the platoon officer saw my helmet and
gave the order to fire. But one of the men cried: 'Don't shoot, it's the
Chink!' They all laughed a lot, but the officer was furious: he gnawed his
moustache and looked at me with eyes like a baboon: and I got a fortnight's
fatigues. Then I said: 'Treachery!' After that I lost all interest in the war.
. . . Sometimes, however, nature got the upper hand, in spite of my being
fed up; then I outdid them all, the patrols, the snipers, all the volunteers for
the dirty jobs. One day I raked the German wire with a rake pinched from
the colonel's gardener to see if they'd electrified their entanglements, as
people said they had. There was a moon shining as large as my bottom: all
the others got the wind up merely from watching me. But that was only a

flash in the pan. I never really put my heart into anything after the Champenoux affair."

I knew him to be brave enough, with a rather stupid, theatrical, completely useless, but on the whole seasoned kind of bravery, which very few people possess, even as a vice.

"I'm not a fire-eater, you understand. So, in order to avoid trouble, they made me a stretcher-bearer. Me a stretcher-bearer! I earned a lot of money in that job. We were holding a trench sector where there had been a battle and where a lot of corpses had remained between the lines, in no-man's land. The colonel mentioned all those who brought any back in regimental orders. Civilians all long to get the Croix de Guerre so as to dazzle their neighbours and fascinate their women with it; so they volunteered in crowds; only the miserable fellows dared not risk their precious skins. So I used to collect the stiffs, at night, for thirty or forty francs, according to my client's purse. Afterwards they wrote to their Member of Parliament to have them taken out of the line; that banished their remorse. Oh, those were good times. Pockets full of money . . . I'll tell you something: the only industries that really pay are those which depend on the meanness of humanity. It's as rich as the Klondike and is quite inexhaustible."

We were descending a steep slope into a valley; in front and on a level with us rose the hutments of Camp-de-la-Fille-Verte, whose smoke floated peacefully up into the air. The Chink picked the over-ripe rowan-berries as he went along and jumped with both feet together on the huge white, black and orange slugs which crawled among the dead leaves like india-rubber lanyards.

"You're a pal, you are. You never say anything. You believe everything I tell you. It never seems to bore you. You're either too polite or too superior, too intelligent or too stupid, I never know which. You disgust me and yet I like you. One of these days I'll put your jaw out with a cross-hook. Recite me a Chinese poem, you old fool, a poem where marvellous things happen and there are wonderful words."

So I improvised, suiting the words and the rhythm to our pace:

"The wise Confucius lives
In his bath of asses' milk
Like the full moon
In the midst of the Milky Way."

The Chink was delighted; he laughed, screwed up his slanting eyes and put his two index fingers in the air like a cheap Chinese figure. I went on:

"The Celestial who reigns over the towns,
The rivers, the rice-field and the junks,
The supreme being whose ensign is a yellow dragon,
Eats, with four-sided scarlet chopsticks,
Ducks' eggs laid seven generations ago."

"I like that, I like that! It makes my liver swell!" cried my companion.

> "The eye of the Sun dominates the peaceful sea,
> The flower called Ho-to-ho gives out its scent,
> The jackdaw does not interrupt the music of the flutes,
> The Prince is beloved by his wives and the neat-herd by his oxen.
> Here is the Empire of the Calm Morning
> And of the Benevolent Afternoon."

The Chink beheaded the dry yellow toad-stools that lay in his path with his stick and continued, doggedly:

"I like those. . . . They're the songs of my own country. I tell you, my old friend, I ought to have been a mandarin with moustaches down to my navel and nails like bayonets. If you wanted, we could find an even better job than that of pigeon-carriers; a job compared with which that of chauffeur to the general at Limoges would seem like the smell of a dung-hill. Listen. You've got education and imagination and I'm a printer, and a good one at that. I've worked on *Paris-Sport* and on *Gil-Blas,* at the time when the press wasn't rotten as it is now. I know the alphabets of every language, even that of Hebrew, which is printed the wrong way round. I composed the Greek text of Abbé Pascal's *Paroissiales,* who wrote about priests and medical theses in which there were so many names of diseases that after reading them you were surprised to find yourself still alive and kicking. Well, we two can get together and start a trench newspaper, something with a good title that will please the colonel and the divisional commander. It's bound to succeed. You can write the stories, heroic stories, naturally, and jokes by soldiers when they sink into the mud up to the waist, when they're getting rained on or trench-mortared or shrapnelled or gassed and taking it all as a jest, and ragging everyone just as if they were among the girls at La Fauvette or the Gaieté-Montparnasse. Naturally, you'll make all this up behind the line, in a pub with a quart of red wine in front of you, and a fire at your back. I'll set up your articles. Oh, I can see myself, whistling while I pick out the letters; and of course I'll correct your spelling mistakes, because everyone knows that journalists can't spell. We'll be keeping up the morale of the troops. Even the officers would want to place copy with us, impressions of battles and diaries; it flatters them. But they'll have to coax us, and pay us. You see, my boy, we'll be like kings!"

"Don't dawdle, Chink. We're none too early as it is; and in any case we ought to hurry just here. They always pepper this place with shells every day at this time. It's a habit they've got. The big ones have even dug up the old men's potatoes and knocked their cabbages down."

It was quite sufficient for me to advise my companion to do something for him immediately to do the opposite. He leaned up against a beech-tree and rolled a cigarette, carefully removing, one by one, the pieces of wood which he always claims to find in Government tobacco, bits of wood big enough to build a corps observation station; and then he caught sight of a party of army telegraphists laying an underground cable in a fairly deep brick-lined trench.

"Hi, there, the Eighth Mudlarks! You've never been so near the line before; you'd better look out and keep your eyes skinned; one's all right here, five miles behind the reserve line. There'd have to be a successful attack for you to be sent to drive trams in Magdeburg. If there are any storm-troops in the sector and the sentries have gone to sleep you're boiled, cleaned up, done for!"

The engineer corporal, a lean man with a goatee and glasses, shrugged his shoulders.

"If you're drunk, buzz off or else put a cork in it!"

"Me buzz off? Me drunk? He insults the infantry and thinks himself a specialist. Specialist in what? A specialist in bloodiness. Why don't they put the engineers, the technicians, the clever people, like me for instance, in the intelligent branches of the army? Do you even know what the cable you are laying is called? Do you know its scientific name? Yes, scientific?"

"I tell you to buzz off and go and sleep it off somewhere."

"Well, specialist, it's called a *triphrased* cable, because there are three in each. Remember that; it may help you when you try to become a captain."

The Chink impudently enjoyed the effect of his words, his cap on the back of his head, his cigarette stuck in the corner of his mouth, smoking in short puffs; I called to him in vain to come on in order to avoid a brawl. The little corporal had already turned back his sleeves and seized a crowbar. My companion jeered at him:

"You've only to fasten claws on your legs to make you look like a daddy longlegs."

At that moment two almost simultaneous reports were carried to us by the wind; I shouted:

"Look out! Take cover, they're always on time!"

I made for a sort of cave beneath a rock overhanging the path, a disused ammunition dump, among abandoned tools and drums of rusty barbed wire. The engineers lay down at the bottom of the trench into which their corporal disappeared with diabolic speed. The shells came whining towards us. I yelled to the Chink:

"Don't be a fool! Get down!"

He replied, without budging, while relighting his cigarette, which had gone out, in that modest, bantering, doubtful tone of voice which he assumed when he wanted to swagger more effectively, and to appear not to be swaggering:

"They're firing on the batteries."

"You're kidding yourself."

"I'm inoculated against shells."

"You're trying to impress the sappers."

"I don't have to do what you tell me. You're not an N.C.O."

The two shells burst, rather short, shooting out a torrent of shrapnel which rained down like water out of a watering-can, sang through the air and hit the ground with a sharp thud; ragged wisps of black smoke floated in the air, wafted along by the wind. The Chink remained standing and, watching the direction in which the invisible sappers lay out of the corner of his eye, hummed villainously, to the air of a popular tune:

> "A corporal is a vegetable
> Which drinks and sleeps and smokes.
> It cannot even sign its name;
> It's as stupid as a pig."

The corporal brandished a wooden sledge-hammer, describing circles with it above the parapet of the trench. The Chink defied him homerically:

"Come out of that, capon, scum of the earth, defeatist! Come, Trotsky, take off your jacket and let's see if you've got a heart or a calf's liver in your chest!"

I made a megaphone of my hands and cried:

"There's a lull. Let's run for it!"

And I set off at the double for the steep road round the corner by which the camp was approached from the far side. Here one could breathe more easily; the road was built below the bluff, through a piece of dead ground which the enemy batteries could not reach. I waited there for my companion, who came strolling along a few minutes later whistling to himself. The bombardment grew fiercer; a droning aeroplane was directing the fire, followed by our anti-aircraft guns, which made a ring of white fluff balls round it: the bases of their shells fell to the right among the dried branches of the undergrowth, making a noise like squashed bees.

"Mind the flies!" said a venerable-looking territorial who had been breaking stones beside the road and was profiting by the enforced interruption to read his newspaper in a gap in the rock wall.

We walked along at a faster pace to make up for lost time. The Chink was capering along in front of me; his jovial face shone in the sunlight, covered with a fine network of wrinkles.

"I've shut the Eighth Mudlarks up: I've ruffled their smugness for them. Listen, I like that. There are plenty of shells falling now, light howitzers, perfect brutes. The game's warming up. They're hidden there among the bricks; it makes those pimps' hair stand on end. Calling themselves specialists and not even knowing what a triphrased underground cable is! The bombardment polarizes them. A fine lot of technicians! Technicians of nothing at all, only fit to strap clamps on their boots and climb telegraph poles and screw insulators on to them, monkeys who unwind cables from their drums with hands sticky with insulating tape. Nothing but mechanical rabbits. It's heart-breaking! And we, who are so competent, are choked and massacred in the infantry!"

A French fighting plane, predatory and active, turned and dived at the German observer; the anti-aircraft guns ceased fire; a few tufts of snowy cotton-wool still floated gently in the sky before dissolving; up above, the machine-guns rattled off in bursts; then the wooded hill-crest cut off the fight from us. The Chink walked sturdily on without saying any more.

III

When we reached Saint-Anthelme-de-Noroy, a small collection of houses lost in its swampy surroundings and inhabited by an artillery waggon-line and a road-making company, the Chink stopped in front of the second house on the left, the only one that remained intact in the hamlet. It stood in front of the drinking-fountain, from which a canvas trough extended, between the skeleton of a burnt-out barn and the blackened, empty stumps of what had been the town-hall before it was bombarded; three Portland stone steps gave evidence of its former splendour. But my companion had no intention of philosophising on the fate of this public building; he was scanning the sound house with its festoons of clay sparrows' nests, shaped like inverted tiaras. Above the window the words "Grocery, Wine, Beer. No Credit Given" were awkwardly scrawled in a handwriting like that of a giant learning his alphabet. A tariff-list was pasted on the closed shutters and on the worm-eaten door an official hand had written in chalk in a beautiful copper-plate: "Out of Bounds for Troops."

A gunner who was washing his leggings in a dixie enlightened us:

"It's no good knocking: they've shut the place up for a month. Some story of serving drinks after closing time and that a lance-corporal knocked out the pot-boy in the back premises when he was tight. The landlord's working in the fields and his wife has gone to stay with her cousin at Nancy. She'll come back at the end of the month with masses of fresh provisions in her kick."

"And the girl?" asked the Chink, eagerly.

"The girl's gone to Nancy as well. She's got a chap there. They say she's going to marry a sergeant in a regiment who was billeted in the village. He's said to come from a decent family and to have money."

My companion gave a hollow groan and we went on. He relapsed into glum silence and I let my thoughts wander. We passed through heath and fallow land and narrow strips of plough which wound round the hills like sashes and accentuated the contours of the ground. A black-and-white magpie clinging to the trunk of a horn-beam fled at our approach and fluttered away over the fields. We could hear a peasant's voice shouting to his horse as he guided his plough for the Autumn crop; a dog barked some-

where and there was the sound of a creaking wheel; solitary sounds filtering
through the light mist, which seemed to accentuate the silence.

Suddenly the Chink, between his teeth, muttered:

"Do you know her name?"

"Whose name?"

"Not the Pope's anyway. The woman at the inn."

"I'm not interested in disused women."

"Not the old woman, for the love of Mike, the girl!"

"I don't know it."

"You're silly. It's a pretty name."

"Wait. Flourette was dreaming of it out loud in the dugout while the
bomb splinters danced a tango on the corrugated iron roof——"

"Flourette . . . Oh, no, I hate Flourette. He's a bluffer and he's always
broke. He hasn't got a bean in spite of the fact that he reshapes government uniforms into a cross between a ballet-skirt and an airman's tunic. If I
were the sergeant-major I'd jug him. Shaping tunics at ten francs a time to
attract the women! Hell take him! I'll tell you her name: it's Mary, with a
y, like the nobs spell it."

"Toadie, also, because she's short and thickset. Two inches of leg and
then her bottom."

"And who gave her that nickname? A lot of scrimshankers and good-for-
nothings. She's called Mary with a *y*, in the English way. She's white and
plump, well curved without being blubbery, with violet eyes and hair. . . .
Hair like one sees on naked women in museums, right down to her
knees and the colour of ripe corn, and so soft to touch that one feels as
though one had a river of silk running through one's hands."

"Oh, so you've felt it."

"Yes, once, by accident."

I smiled and hummed the sentimental and rather vulgar waltz:

"You Gave Me the Greatest Thrill in Life."

The Chink broke off the reddish-brown branch of an oak and said,
roughly:

"Don't jeer, you fool, you don't understand."

We kept silence after this; besides, the track began to rise; the clay,
moistened by the rain and kneaded by the horses' hoofs, clung to the soles
of our boots; I was trying to get back my breath on the top of the hill
when my companion seized me violently by the arm.

"Listen, sonny," he said. "Listen and look. Look at the plains, the hills,
the black and red forests and the rivers bordered by golden poplars. I
myself like nature and clouds and wind. I've known people in the newspaper offices for which I worked who earned as much as twopence-
halfpenny a line and got no kick at all out of nature. If I had been born in
the middle-classes, instead of becoming a waster I should have been a

novelist, a poet or an electrical inventor. I wouldn't have liked too narrow or too quiet a profession, but something slightly adventurous, and rather leisurely. I've been a type-setter; it's not quite the same thing, perhaps, but they're down the same street. Imagination, nature and women, those are the bees in my bonnet, my diseases."

"But your 'god-mother' in the Hotel de l'Occident et du Brésil. Isn't she enough for you?"

"Oh, you know . . . Don't talk about that, my boy. Chuck it. When I was in the hospital, after my wound, there was a sister there, a little pink-and-white thing, who was always on the move like a water-wagtail. She took an interest in me, this nun did, and then, out of deviltry, I used to swear and put forward scandalous theories of life: I influenced others, I stole, I made myself out even worse than I am, and I laughed at her when she came to pray for me. She prayed for my sins, all by herself, at least so she said. Perhaps she was laughing at me; but all the same it made me happy to think this little wagtail twittered 'Hail Marys' for me; it had never happened to me before. When I left she gave me a holy medal. I never dared write to her to tell her how I was getting on. During my convalescence in Paris I found my girl again, my real, regular girl; I beat her when I thought of that nun praying for my sins. It relieved me and seemed to me to be a good action. . . . I tell you once more that I don't belong to the same race as other men, labourers and peasants and shop-keepers and clerks. I am outside the law."

He walked on pensively for a while, then squirted a jet of tobacco-juice at a mound of earth at the edge of the wood bordering the path.

"Look," he observed, "there's a fine place to set rabbit-snares. Let's pinch some wire from those telephone chaps. You can see their runs; they come out of the wood by them to go and lie in the fields."

"Oh, Chink, don't dawdle; Van de Putte is waiting for us!"

He ran and caught me up:

"Mary with a *y*, brother . . . Violet eyes and hair down to her knees. The last woman one saw when one went into the line, at the bend in the road, framed in the window; beyond that there are no more civilians. The first woman, too, whom one saw when one came back from the trenches. How many men in the sector are thinking of her at this moment! And how many dead are there to whom she waved and smiled as they passed? And from afar those that return search eagerly for the hovel with its sign. The battalion marches past, rifles slung over shoulders, and the battalion makes eyes at her; for this is the beginning of the world in which there are gardens and children and lovely things which are not only meant to kill. The battalion cook on the field-kitchen presents his ladle; the machine-gunner, the one who sits at the back of the gun-carriage and has no need to turn round, waves his helmet at her for a long time, as far as the bridge. The boys begin to understand that they're going on living; they're no longer afraid, they sing, they groom their mules, they breathe the fresh air deep into their lungs. And all because of her. I myself can only love women whom other men want. It's a fancy of mine. It excites me."

He swept his arm round in a vague circle as though calling Heaven and Earth to witness his words and then he stared me straight in the eye. The walk, the keen wind and the autumn sun filled me with a sort of cheerful mischief, which made me mow down the grass with my stick and kick at any unevenness in the ground. I do not know what put it into my mind to contradict the Chink and to draw his insults down on my head. Perhaps I was unconsciously getting a little tired of his verbosity; perhaps the demon of curiosity made me want to penetrate his thoughts and to strike a spark of conflict and discussion from him. So after a short pause I replied, with deliberately aggressive coldness:

"You're lying, Chink, and you know it. You bore me and disgust me."

"I'm lying? Say that again, you stinker! Say it again."

"You're lying. You're making all this humbug up to try to impress me and make me think what a fine fellow you are. But it's no good: I'm proof against that sort of thing. You can swear yourself to death with your hand on your heart and your eyes rolling like those of an old tom-cat. I don't care a damn. I just don't believe you."

"Curse and blast it! The one time I'm telling the truth! And to think how often I've made up stories which you swallowed with about as much subtlety as a ploughboy. I've had you often in spite of your being an intellectual. I've had you on toast. But to-day I don't want you to disbelieve me. I forbid you to! Or else . . ."

His face grew purple with fury; a mahogany-coloured gleam shone through the coat of filth which covered it. He took guard, his left arm bent on a level with his eyes and his right fist clenched. He was stamping with rage.

"Come and fight, you dirty dog! I'm going to knock your teeth out."

"Don't be silly; the pigeon-fancier is waiting for us; we've got to hurry. You waste half the day in talking rot and in stupid quarrelling——"

"You swine! You're taking sides with the Eighth Mudlarks now."

"You're begging the question."

"Me? Put 'em up, you mug, do you hear?"

"I'm not going to fight you, my son."

"Then look out for yourself. I'm going to give it to you."

"No, you brute. In the first place we're not in the same class. You weigh fifteen pounds more than I do. And in any case you're only a mountebank, a filthy mountebank."

This last insult flattered and appeased him and put him in a good temper. My mischievous gaiety was satisfied with this altercation; I preferred not to run the risk of being beaten up, which was inevitable if I could not avoid coming to blows with him; I could keep the upper hand so long as we stuck to insults. He kicked the mud that stuck to his boots in my direction, then he slapped me on the shoulder and we went on, side by side.

"You sly old rascal! You're the only man with any brains in the company, you and the company clerk, the one who once said: 'I'm not going to get married during the war because if my wife became a widow I should regret it all my life.' He's a one, he is, and no mistake. All the rest are bits of machinery, connecting-rods, driving-belts and the force of inertia."

His joviality suddenly deserted him and after a moment he said in a humble, crushed voice:

"Poor, feckless, drunken, lazy and yet with aspirations. Never a penny in one's pocket; as soon as one earns anything it's either drunk or gambled away. No chance of getting out of the rut. The man who comes into the world square can't leave it pointed. One never settles down; one eats and goes on the burst, vegetates, eats again and goes on the burst again. Life! It's a bloody life really. . . . Emotions which upset your brain, the need one feels of telling tales . . . One lies, just as much for oneself as for other people. One needs a woman to restrain one, to mould one. You can't understand that. You've never known what it is to be destitute. Destitution in itself is nothing. It is far worse to like it, not to try to get out of it, to consent to it and to enjoy it. One is perfectly free and depends on nothing; men admire that; they despise one, but they admire one, especially when one has the gift of the gab, and pretends to revolt against it and leans against the bar in a pub and stares at them with one's cigarette hanging from one's mouth and one's cap over one's eyes. Why didn't you believe me? Why did you call me a mountebank?"

"Listen, Chink, when you tell me stories, either true ones or false ones, I don't care: I take what amuses me and I let the rest go. But I will not, do you hear me, I will not stand it when you overstep the mark, when you try to rouse my pity for you and to interest me in your sentimental quibbles. That I won't accept."

His mouth pursed up in a spasm of rage and he leaned towards me, barring the way.

"Why not? Why not?"

I replied slowly, pausing between my words:

"Because it bores me. That's why."

I expected an explosion of rage, insults, even a fight perhaps, and I watched the Chink carefully, prepared for anything. I took an intense delight in the sight of that rich, undisciplined nature, that mobile, brutal character, and in this cruel game to which the very risk added piquancy. But my companion made no rejoinder; he merely shrugged his shoulders and quickened his pace. I wondered whether he was suddenly going to explode, whether he was turning some subtle revenge over in his mind, and whether he was thinking out some bold plan for retaliation which would be impossible to foresee and to guard against. He walked along

silently, chewing his cigarette and jolting his wicker cage with sudden
nervous spasms. We were approaching the end of our journey; we could
already see the pigeon-loft perched on top of a barn; pigeons were flying
round us in strictly symmetrical patterns; we could hear the rustle of their
wings as they approached us, moved away again and returned, describing
great circles in the pale light of the October morning. I ventured a remark:

"They're manœuvring, the little beasts. See how they turn, Chink. The
inside ones hug the centre of the track and slow down, the middle ones
keep on at the same speed and the outside ones increase theirs; the alignment remains the same always. It's like a bicycle race at the Buffalo
Velodrome on a Sunday in peacetime; except that there's no money on it
and no one gets left behind."

The Chink gave no sign that he had heard; even this reference to bicycle
racing, so dear to his suburban heart, did not succeed in making him un-
bend. The shadow of the pigeon's flight, mottled like the shadow thrown
by an almond-tree in blossom, was upon us now; then it moved away from
us, across the fields, gradually becoming more compact, crossed the road,
climbed the wall and lost itself in the dwarf vines twisted as though with
scrofula. My companion did not deign either to look or to reply. A girl
carrying a basketful of grass nodded to us; the Chink scowled at her. I bade
her a friendly good-morning myself and said to him:

"There! And the first woman you see you ignore and scowl at."

Between his teeth he muttered:

"The first one is that other one, in the window."

"The window's closed and the bird has flown."

"That doesn't matter. She's still the first, even when there's nobody
there."

He stamped on the ground and shortened his steps as though he was
trapped by violent feelings from which he could not free himself. A
preposterous idea occurred to me and stuck in my mind. Could he, by any
possible chance, be sincere? Had he not invented it all, talked just for the
sake of talking? Did he really, in his nebulous and contradictory way which
always needed applause and a gallery, did he really love the grocer's
daughter of Saint-Anthelme-de-Noroy, the first woman seen by those who
come down from the deserted regions in which there are only men thirsting for blood and death?

IV

Old Van de Putte, the chief divisional pigeon-fancier, received us
smoking his clay pipe, which bubbled in time with the heavy placid breathing of its owner, emitting at each rumbling a cloud of smoke and a smell
of burnt earth and nicotine.

"Ah, my lads! So you're here, are you, you couple of bandits! Always
late, never on time. A drink at every pub and a pinch for every girl you

meet. It's utter destruction. No longer any discipline. Just going where the wind blows them. Disaster in the long run. Drunken, bottle-nosed, gallows-bird faces, with the shifty eye of the libertine. . . . Bandits . . . and they trust pigeons to them. Desolation, desolation!"

He laughed and his eyes softened as, with his hands clasped over his paunch, he said:

"The pigeons came home all right yesterday. Dudule the first and Marouf the last, as usual. You're going to take up the reliefs. Mind you don't shake them about too much! Fancy confiding these gentle birds to a couple of thugs, a couple of gin-vats like you! Little birds brought up like girls at the Sacré-Cœur handed over to a couple of pimps! Damnation! *Damnation!* Have you still got plenty of rice up there? Another bagful? Good. Don't stuff them too much. A few grains only, not more, or they may not come back. They don't know anything about war or about danger, the pretty dears; all that passes over their heads. And don't forget to release them at once in case of gas, so that they can get well up into the air. Don't let them die in their baskets like Fanfan and Coco, the victims of your predecessors. . . . Wait a minute, wait a minute! Don't put the cages on yet. You lads must be thirsty; you've come a long way. A couple of bad lots but not idlers with all that walking. You'll take a glass of coffee, eh, lads? And a little spirit with it, some mirabelle, extra special, at six francs a pint. You're not going to refuse? No, I see you're not. I always had an idea you wouldn't refuse, you young rascals!"

The old man winked his eye and jovially patted his rounded belly. We entered his low-roofed room; the coffee was warming in a dented saucepan over a fire of pine cones and vine branches. We drank the steaming brew in luxurious little sips. Then the pigeon-fancier tiptoed stealthily up carrying a bottle with an air of mystery and reverence and poured us each out a bumper of that colourless spirit which fills one with a taste of sun-warmed fruit and burning honey.

"Don't be nervous," he went on; "don't be shy. You don't want wrinkles in your stomach. It's ten years, my lads, since I saw my own toes. Have a drink from time to time and beware of women, the best of whom isn't worth a rap. They're a destructive breed."

"You're right there, Van de Putte, a thousand times right. You tell the Chink all about it; he's in love."

"That scoundrel in love?"

"Yes, with the grocer's daughter at Saint-Anthelme."

"It's a bad business, Chink, the shortest cut to unhappiness and trouble. I once had a big wife with teeth like pearls and a crupper like that of a fifteen-hundred-franc mare. I had a wife and a pigeon-loft. The pigeons always came back; they never got lost and brought me in a tidy sum in bets. They would be released at Bordeaux, at Toulouse, anywhere in the world, Chink. It was like having a racing stable. Everyone knew Van de

Putte's pigeon-loft, even as far away as the Campine. A hundred pigeons that always came back and a single wife named Marie——"

"With a *y*?" the Chink interrupted eagerly.

"*Y*? No, no *y*. Why the hell with a *y*? Well, anyway, she went away one day to Lille, only forty kilometres from the pigeon-loft, and she never found the way back again. Pigeons have got compasses in their heads, not so women. Damnation! A great misfortune but a good riddance. Let's finish the mirabelle, lads! Look here, Chink, listen to the advice of an old man who was a cuckold before you drank your first glass of beer. . . . Don't let yourself be seduced by their wiles; enjoy them when they're in the mood for it, but always keep your liberty."

"How can I help it?" the other replied glumly. "I love women; it's my nature."

"It's a bad nature, then. A disgusting vice. Everyone's getting like that since the war started. They get engaged, get married, write to 'god-mothers.' As if there wasn't enough catastrophe in the world they've to go making love. They're all mad, all crazy. They escape from machine-guns and bombs to fall into the clutches of women. I tell you, death seems to excite their passions; as for women, there's no longer any holding them. A philosopher explained this to me. He was the local scavenger, but he knew more than an officer of the Academy. It's the species, he explained to me, which insists on this; lots of men die, but the species doesn't want to die, it wants to perpetuate itself; so it sends men and women crazy with passion and forces them to procreate brats. The more carnage there is the more the species gingers up those that remain. This species is a strumpet, a pimp! But my friend was a philosopher; there wasn't much he didn't know. I've got a cousin who's a hospital-nurse. Her favourite expression is, 'I only look after the badly wounded.' You ought to see her when she says it; she rolls her eyes and wriggles her bottom just as if someone were tickling her with a feather. And yet she's long past the age for that sort of thing. Don't fall into degradation, Chink."

The Chink smiled with a superior air; he gave me a meaning look and casually observed to the pigeon-fancier: . . .

"You're a misogynist."

"Ah!" replied Van de Putte. "Always using long words and humbugging. Go on! Be off with you! Get on with the job, you ruffians! And don't shake the poor innocents up too much."

v

On the road back, now crowded with transport and people on foot, rumbling supply-wagons, low-slung ambulances, companies of African donkeys loaded with faggots and soldiers going on leave with heavily loaded knapsacks, the Chink kept growling out disconnected phrases:

"Old fool . . . Just a doves' innkeeper . . . He doesn't understand anything else. . . . Ha-ha! Misogynist! That took his breath away. He's just a vulgarian trying to impress people, without knowing anything about life. Misogynist!"

The soldiers we met gave us friendly looks; the pigeons attracted a kind of sympathy which was reflected on their carriers and evoked ideas of soaring flight, of fidelity and of tenderness in men's minds. Their beaks pecked at my shoulders in a way that was not at all unpleasant; behind my back I could hear the cooing from their fine full chests beneath the water-proof cover on their cage, and I quoted, gazing into the distance:

" 'Two pigeons loved each other tenderly.' "

The Chink looked me up and down and spat out of the corner of his mouth: he had not yet forgiven my incredulity. I grew rather exasperated in my turn, and I tried to concoct some scheme which would make me complete master of his secret. I knew my companion to be far too loquacious to be able to walk eight miles without speaking; so I decided to let the conversation take its course and to rely on some sudden inspiration to gain my ends.

We made good progress with the wind at our backs; I chewed over-ripe rowan-berries which tasted of decayed leaves and autumn, and I watched the flight of the plovers as they wheeled in the air and uttered their plaintive cries. A strange, nostalgic harmony which bathed the perspective of a war winter with its deadly hours of cold and rain and night and mud. And I spat out the shining pips in the reddish ruts of the unmetalled road with a kind of bitter melancholy.

When we came in sight of the houses of Saint-Anthelme-de-Noroy, at the bottom of the basin through which a narrow stream ran between golden aspens, the Chink exclaimed:

"Curse and blast it! They've put the pub out of bounds. The slops have shut the place up and the girl has gone away by train. There was a woman there and now there isn't one any more. I've been thinking, sonny, the old doves' hotel proprietor was talking through his hat; he knows nothing about the feelings of the heart . . . and yet his reasoning was sound. We're all crazy, all mad; the war has altered all our ideas on the subject of love; everyone has completely changed. It is true that risk and death excite people's passions, as he said. I've seen old men become amorous of their wives after years of marriage and dozens of children; they wrote them eight-page letters every day and when they got tight in billets they maundered on about them, crying and showing their friends the photographs of their old Dutches, fat ones, thin ones, some with snub-noses, and some with noses as thin as razor-blades. And everyone thought it was all quite natural. And the younger ones' fiancées and 'god-mothers'! And those who become jealous, and those who let their hearts run away with them and don't know what they're doing and make women promises, chuck them over and then start all over again right and left! I knew an ex-colonial soldier, now dead, who had racketed about all the brothels in the four corners of the world without ever having given it a thought. Well, this man began to get ideas into his head after the war started; he complained; he was no longer content with physical contact. 'When I give a girl ten francs,' he said, 'she still doesn't give me her friendship.' This depressed him very much, poor devil, and before the war he had never so much as thought of anything but the colour of a girl's skin and the jut of her buttocks. And with women it's the same story, only worse. It's the will of the species, as the old scavenger philosopher used to say, the general upheaval all over the world. There are no longer any rules or morals; passions have turned everything topsy-turvy. Life nowadays is like a chaotic film exhibited by a mad operator on a warped screen."

"You're talking nonsense again, Chink. Have I changed, for instance?"

"You hide your feelings because you're an intellectual and are therefore more of a hypocrite than other people; besides, you don't drink. I've seen you waiting for your letters with the large sloping blue handwriting, pressing your thighs together and dilating your nostrils as though you were gambling your fortune on the spin of a coin, and the coin was actually in the air; I've pretended not to notice, out of tact. I could go on about it for seven years. Have you ever seen Sergeant Coudure, a sober-minded business man, with a nose like a searchlight and a belch like an eight-inch howitzer and very fond of his glass, when he says: 'The old girl has been swearing at me again'? His face gets long, his voice gets sloppy and one would think he was Romeo listening to the blackbird on his rope-ladder. And look at Corporal Joron, the man who's always talking of the open country: 'At the time when we weren't yet tucked away into mole-hills . . . At the time when we were cavaliers and not field-mice . . .' He used to go about asking every man he saw if he couldn't get his sister or his cousin or his niece to start a correspondence with him and marry him. One day he wrote to a young virgin whom he had met at some time or other; he came back from leave engaged to be married to her; he no longer spoke of the open country but spent all day composing long screeds on mauve paper at four francs a box. It needed a terrific emotion to cure him of his mania, a flash of lightning and God's thunder on top of it. Mourargue found out that he was a cuckold by accident; his wife gave birth to twins, an Indian and a Senegalese some people said, but that was an exaggeration. In peacetime he would have swallowed his shame, bumped the wench off or got divorced, or perhaps he would just simply have got tight and fed the little strangers without making too much fuss. But no—and as he was known to be a funk it makes it all the more meritorious—no, he volunteered for the advance-guard and during the attack on the 11th he got himself cut in half on a machine-gun by the fellow who was chained to it. Passion! Have you ever seen cuckolds in civil life dashing themselves against coffee-mills? They're all the same, all bewitched by that strumpet the Species. Saumoire fell in love with the two sisters who kept the café at Pou-Volant, he never quite knew which. The girls were jealous and there were sentimental complications with the fellow, who was already crazy: scenes, tears, makings up, moonlight walks, blows. He couldn't make up his mind; so at the first chance he got he volunteered for Salonica, where he caught fever. He spent his sick-leave at Pou-Volant. There he had an attack of malaria complicated with madness; following on a general row he blacked the mother's eye, locked the girls in the bakehouse, drank all the good wine in the cellar, took a pot shot at himself which missed because his hand was trembling so much and only removed the tip of his ear. And you think that's natural! The only explanation is the topsy-turvydom of the age. My girl, the one in Montparnasse, confirmed this to me; she's not very bright, but she prowls about round the railway stations where one sees everyone. She maintains that men have been changed; before, they used to make love in a straightforward manner; now they've got ideas, they either want to beat people or to cry; they're looking for they don't know what; they puzzle one, even though one is used to them. They've been mechanised by circumstances."

We were descending the slope into the hamlet whose ruins, mended with planks of wood and patched with sheets of tarred paper, sheltered the personnel and the horses of the artillery waggon-line. Field-kitchens were smoking between the breached walls and sent the acrid smell of damp wood up to us. The roofless belfry brooded over the misery of its flock like an old man over the corpses of his little ragged children. A driver was singing at the top of his voice as he washed his shirt on a flat stone by the stream, and every time he slapped it down it seemed as if the front of the church tower leaned further over. With my pipe stem I drew the Chink's attention to Mary's house at the crossroads, with its black door, its green shutters and its clay tiaras. He went on, suddenly affected by the desolation of the scene:

"I once saw at the Clichy fair a booth over which was written: 'American Eye-opener.' Inside all sorts of curiosities and catastrophes were displayed in glass cases. But they were not to be compared with what we can see nowadays for nothing."

Suddenly he shouted:

"What on earth's up, old son? There's someone there. . . ."

He began to run at full speed; the wicker hamper bumped against his shoulders and the scared pigeons flapped their wings and made anguished cooing noises. The grocery window was open and the shutters were fastened back to the wall. I only caught the Chink up at the door, on which he was beating furiously. At last an old peasant cautiously opened it a few inches. The Chink whispered to me that he was going to have a word with him and greeted the owner politely.

"What do you fellows want?"

"Just a glass of wine to help us on our way."

"It's out of bounds; I can't serve you."

"We'll come in behind, through the pig-sty. Come on! A quick one, with a bit of saveloy."

"I tell you it's out of bounds to troops."

"The landlady knows me well."

"Well, I don't know you."

"Call her then."

"She's a long way away. I should have to shout pretty loud for her to hear me."

"In the vineyard?"

"No, at Nancy."

"And the girl? Mademoiselle Mary wouldn't refuse me. I gave her an aluminum ring and a cartridge case with a thistle pattern and her name engraved on it."

"Our daughter won't be back for some time. She's being married in three days. I'm going to the wedding myself and I'm taking the litter of pigs with me to sell it."

The old man shut the door again; the Chink leaned against the door-jamb with his eyes half closed. The man washing his shirt was still singing on the river-bank and from time to time a horse neighed; no other sound broke the silence. My companion passed the back of his hand over his forehead, ejected a long stream of saliva into the middle of the road and repeated three times without my being able to discover to whom his insult referred:

"Filthy beast! Filthy beast! Filthy beast!"

VI

The Fille-Verte camp was still being bombarded when we passed through it in short rushes between which we lay flat in the mud of the trenches. We were in a hurry and were both rather upset. The Chink was brooding over his heart troubles; I was indignant at the enemy sprinkling our path with shells at unexpected times. When one is accustomed to expect a bombardment at a certain time of day, one relies upon it; it seemed to me that the Germans were lacking in the courtesies of war. I was also irritated with my companion; I was convinced that he was lying to me; there was nothing to prove that he was just giving himself airs and there was nothing in his words to confirm the first theory I had formed, but instead of submitting to the facts I fought against them; such is the ordinary human attitude of mind; and I nursed a grudge against the Chink for having shown himself to be sincere and for having frustrated my knowledge of psychology and my insight into human nature. These rather nebulous feelings were complicated by the annoyance of finding myself bombarded, of being forced to play hide-and-seek with unexpected shells and of having to drag my cloak in the mud after having washed it the previous day.

It was some time before we were able to leave the redoubt; the shrapnel and high-explosive shells made the sunken road impassable; we lay side by side under a wretched battered tunnel of corrugated iron camouflaged with pine needles. The pigeons were gurgling behind our shoulders and pecked at us with their beaks and scratched us with their claws. A motor-cycle passed us like a flash at full speed, between two bursts of fire, crashed into a shell-hole, leaped into the air with its wheels racing and only came to earth some yards further on. The Chink, roused to curiosity, called out:

"He's crashed! No, he's all right! He's off again!"

A short sharp burst of fire from a high-velocity gun sent my companion back to cover; I heard a tearing sound and he chuckled:

"I've caught my trousers on a bit of barbed wire. Hell's bells! And I've got a gash in my thigh. And the bloody pigeons are pecking me. Let's buzz off. I'm not going to stay in this tunnel any more."

"Wait a minute, Chink; there's sometimes a belated shell or two."

"You've got the wind up too. I'm not going to stay and rot in here any more. I'm buzzing off."

"I forbid you to go."

"I don't take orders from a private soldier. Come along. Up with you!"

"If you move I'll hit you. You're getting on my nerves."

A last burst of fire put an end to our discussion; we waited a few minutes more and, as no more shells whistled through the pale sky, I started off. But the Chink, squatting on his haunches with a far-away look in his eyes, seemed not to be paying attention to anything. Finally he said, in a slow, solemn voice:

"An extraordinary thing once happened to me; I've suddenly remembered it, I don't exactly know why."

"You can think about it as you go along."

He smiled and replied quietly, with a shrug of indifference:

"Shut up! I'm not talking to you, I'm talking to myself."

He went on rolling his cigarette with his hands on a level with his waist in a Buddha-like pose. The pigeons were cooing softly; I suggested, ironically:

"The doves are playing the incidental music to the drama. *Tremolo,* enter the leading man."

He did not fly into a temper, as I expected him to do, but went on:

"There's nothing so dreary as a cinema without an orchestra. Yes, an adventure of which even the smartest couldn't make head or tail and for which I got a court-martial and two years' hard."

"You never told me about that."

"Yes." And he smote himself proudly on the chest. "Yes, I'm an old lag. In those days I belonged to an army for the *exploitation of tactical success*. Staff-officers' jargon. As there were no tactical successes, we hadn't got anything to exploit; we were like a lot of pastry-cooks without sugar or butter. So we didn't do anything. We just loafed and cleaned our rifles and played football in the back areas. They were happy enough days. Unfortunately an idle life never suited me; I felt at a loose end and I thought of writing to the nun at the hospital, the little creature who prayed for my sins, to tell her about myself. I cut parades and fatigues and broke camp whenever I could manage it, which was pretty often. You ought to have seen me, crouching beneath a tree with a board across my knees and holding a fountain-pen I had scrounged in an empty dugout between my first and second fingers. It was the beginning of Spring, when the leaves start coming out and the days start growing longer; I inhaled the balmy air with half-closed eyes; you would have thought I was a novelist."

"Chink," I said, "I'm making a dash for it. Who loves me follows me."

He never moved a muscle but lit his cigarette without seeming to have heard me and went on, lost in his memories:

"A fine time it was. I didn't really know whether I was happy or unhappy. When I wanted to write I couldn't. When I felt that I could I no longer wanted to. Added to which, the Spring was working in my blood and made me gay because the air was so bright and sad because I had grown unaccustomed to the sun. I spent days on end making resolutions."

With a heave of my shoulders I settled by pigeon basket on my back and then I left my companion after a short, rather disdainful "See you later" to which he made no reply. He did not catch me up again till I reached the field-kitchens; he was running, and I pretended not to recognise his step. He passed me and planted himself before me; I whistled under my breath and he shook his fists at me in a rage and shouted:

"Will you shut up! Stop that row or I'll spoil your beauty for you."

I replied in a superior, taunting voice:

"You inhaled the balmy air with half-closed eyes: one would have thought that you were a novelist. To be continued in our next."

He stamped his foot menacingly. A strange green glow came into his slanting eyes; his charred cigarette-end dangled from the yellow corner of his smoker's mouth and he went on, feverishly:

"Listen. One day I wrote perhaps ten letters, all of which I destroyed. So I went along to the café to get tight. There I found a sergeant molesting a girl; I didn't like it and I had to relieve my feelings somehow. I told the N.C.O. to let the wench go; he replied by telling me to go to hell; so I knocked out two of his teeth and cut his eyebrow open to lift me out of my depression. I got off cheaply with two years' hard. You see the sort of man I am. Now do you believe that I love the girl from Saint-Anthelme-de-Noroy, in life and in death?"

He held up his hand and spat on the ground to give weight to his words. I half closed my eyes so that he should not be able to read my thoughts. The note of truth which he had put into his brief speech, all delivered in a single breath, shook me for a moment; I was tempted to smile and to open my heart to him; but I kept control of myself. I had begun a game which I did not want to stop and I bluffed, as I did when I played poker with the quartermaster-sergeant. My inexorable curiosity struggled within me against all human weakness. Inscrutable and expressionless, therefore, I looked him straight in the eyes and answered in a voice which was neither sympathetic nor credulous nor hostile, nor even indifferent, a voice modulated by a succession of syllables and nothing more:

"I've already told you what I think about it. If it gives you any pleasure for me to believe you, I believe you. Let me know once for all and stop boring me."

"You swine!" he shouted. "Someone must understand me and appreciate me! I can't live alone in a hole; I need expansion and a pal who shares things with me; I can't just bury myself in my sentiments and go to sleep in them; I need you; your nature supplements mine. That's why I love the woman whom the whole sector has seen at her window and who has smiled at those who were about to die."

"That's all very fine, Chink, but it's just gallery stuff."

"I can prove it to you."

"How?"

"By material proof."

He searched his mind for a moment, his forehead wrinkled and his mouth set in a hard line.

"Proof? Oh, Mourargue was mown down by a Bavarian machine-gun. Saumoire returned from Salonica and had a shot at himself and took off the end of his ear. I myself have knocked out a sergeant for the nun at the hospital and got two years' hard for it. And all the others one has never heard of."

I retorted, with abusive familiarity:

"No more of that, my lad. You'd do better to do more and not talk so much; you've said too much already. It only makes me think your boasting has driven you mad. Don't count on me as a gallery to weep over your corpse. That's not in my line; you'll never be able to convince me."

We entered the windings of a communication trench from the walls of which the thaw was flaking pieces off; telegraph wires whose staples had fallen out formed dangerous entanglements; the broken duck-boards were full of snares; conversation died down automatically. I walked in front, without troubling my head about my companion, only paying attention to where I was placing my huge, mud-laden boots.

VII

That evening, as usual on quiet days, we played cards in the company office, a well-built sap protected by iron girders and rough pit-props covered with eight feet of packed earth. The quartermaster-sergeant, who had pretentions to fastidiousness, cut the cards absently with rather a wry face because the sergeant-major, who was his partner, had insisted on playing "manille", a plebeian game which was, he considered, only played by common people in remote provincial inns. The "major" was thoroughly enjoying himself; an extra orderly, who never spoke, made the fourth. Salvoes of artillery fire occasionally shook our mole-hill; the candle flame flickered and straightened up again; the scared rats were quiet for a few seconds and then resumed their noisy aimless scurrying over the corrugated iron, uttering sharp squeaks all the time.

The sergeant-major paused for thought, running his forefingers over his fanned-out cards; the quartermaster scornfully toyed with his knife-chain; the orderly was intent on his hand, anxious not to make a mistake in front of these high and mighty dispensers of favours and "cushy" jobs. In those days a man's life might depend upon a badly played hand at cards.

There was a knock on the door and the Chink appeared. He saluted formally, which in itself rather astonished me, as he always prided himself on his lack of discipline. He pretended not to see me.

"Sergeant-major," he said, "I hear they asked for volunteers for the tanks this morning."

"Quite right, they did."

"I want you to put my name down."

The quartermaster-sergeant interrupted him.

"Why, Chink, you're crazy! You've got a job——"

"Don't bother about me!"

"Do you want to be killed? You'll never find a job like being a pigeon-carrier again, especially in the tanks."

"I tell you to put me down."

"But why the devil are you deserting us?"

"For . . ."

He hesitated a little and finally cast a glance in my direction, a glance which he shifted almost at once. Then, after a further pause, he went on:

"For entirely personal reasons."

The quartermaster-sergeant guffawed.

"I'll bet it's something to do with women again, you old rip!"

"Perhaps. Well, yes. Exactly."

"Oh, women! Women!" muttered the quartermaster, in a far-away voice, absent-mindedly taking a Virginian cigarette from my case lying open on the table. "Women! Nothing but heart burnings! Before the war I followed a little actress all over the place, as far as Morocco, with two celluloid collars and a father's curses in my suit-case. I'll tell you all about it some day. Folly! Nothing but folly! Have you got a light?"

The sergeant-major, having decided upon his plan of attack, was getting impatient; he had already made three francs at twenty-five centimes per form sent in, and he was longing to make it up to five francs. Besides, he had a horror of *nil* returns.

"Put him down, Quartermaster, put him down; don't discourage volunteers. Congratulations, Chink, and a thousand regrets at losing you. You've got guts; you're a real *poilu*. Put him down, Quartermaster. Good luck, Chink; we'll fix it for you. It's you to play."

I was troubled and torn by a sort of remorse. I wanted to speak, to detain my comrade; but I suddenly felt embarrassed and I could not make up my mind to do so; my feelings were overcome by my vanity. Finally I made an effort and blurted out:

"Chink!"

I stopped short. The Chink already had his hand on the door-latch, and he turned round; the light from the candle clearly lit up his slanting eyes, shaded by their thick lashes. The simplicity of the attitude and of the speech of a man whose nature was composed of boasting and excess, this very simplicity seemed to me to be a provocation and a mockery. Which of us was fooling the other? His mouth was twisted and contracted and seemed to be mocking me, yes, really enjoying the success of a tremendous farce pushed to extreme limits and capable of resolving itself in blood.

At that moment a bursting shell shook the dugout. The candle flame flickered and a wavering light passed across the Chink's eyes; his eyelids fluttered once and in the depths of those eyes I saw an unreal, supernatural fire, the kind with which we endow the looks of legendary lovers who exalt the power of passion in themselves to an almost limitless degree, and who accomplish themselves in death. And why not believe it? Because of his squalor and his bragging? The incidence of passion is a haphazard one and its devastations are not concerned with logical convention. I coughed once or twice and resumed:

"Chink. Chink, old boy!"

But the spell was broken, the flame had died down in his eyes, and they were but wretched human eyes, greenish circles in the centre of a ball of cornea criss-crossed with red lines. His hard, vulgar mouth no longer expressed anything but the obstinacy of a man who wanted to get the better of me, at no matter how great a price.

"Leave the Chink alone," said the sergeant-major. "Your turn, Quartermaster, and don't play your cards in that overbearing way."

The quartermaster-sergeant let a card fall on the table.

"I trump," proclaimed the sergeant-major in a triumphant voice. "I trump and it's a club. Queen wins, knave wins, seven wins!"

When I raised my head the Chink had gone.

That very evening he left for the divisional troop-lines and from there he
went to an instructional camp. I never saw him again. A long time afterwards I heard of his death in a burning tank, in which he was roasted
alive. I have never been able to decide whether he died for the girl from
Saint-Anthelme or in order to get the better of me. The heart of man
nearly always remains unfathomable. When I informed old Van de Putte
of the Chink's caprice he thought for a while whilst sipping his mirabelle
and murmured, with a wise look in his eye:

"It's the species that does that. We must believe what the scavenger said.
Individual man no longer exists. There is only the species."

HAIRCUT

Ring Lardner
(1885–1933)

I GOT ANOTHER BARBER that comes over from Carterville and helps me out
Saturdays, but the rest of the time I can get along all right alone. You can
see for yourself that this ain't no New York City and besides that, the most
of the boys works all day and don't have no leisure to drop in here and get
themselves prettied up.

You're a newcomer, ain't you? I thought I hadn't seen you round before.
I hope you like it good enough to stay. As I say, we ain't no New York City
or Chicago, but we have pretty good times. Not as good, though, since Jim
Kendall got killed. When he was alive, him and Hod Meyers used to keep
this town in an uproar. I bet they was more laughin' done here than any
town its size in America.

Jim was comical, and Hod was pretty near a match for him. Since Jim's
gone, Hod tries to hold his end up just the same as ever, but it's tough
goin' when you ain't got nobody to kind of work with.

They used to be plenty fun in here Saturdays. This place is jam-packed
Saturdays, from four o'clock on. Jim and Hod would show up right after
their supper, round six o'clock. Jim would set himself down in that big
chair, nearest the blue spittoon. Whoever had been settin' in that chair,
why they'd get up when Jim come in and give it to him.

You'd of thought it was a reserved seat like they have sometimes in a
theayter. Hod would generally always stand or walk up and down, or some

Saturdays, of course, he'd be settin' in this chair part of the time, gettin' a haircut.

Well, Jim would set there a w'ile without openin' his mouth only to spit, and then finally he'd say to me, "Whitey,"—my right name, that is, my right first name, is Dick, but everybody round here calls me Whitey—Jim would say, "Whitey, your nose looks like a rosebud tonight. You must of been drinkin' some of your aw de cologne."

So I'd say, "No, Jim, but you look like you'd been drinkin' somethin' of that kind or somethin' worse."

Jim would have to laugh at that, but then he'd speak up and say, "No, I ain't had nothin' to drink, but that ain't sayin' I wouldn't like somethin'. I wouldn't even mind if it was wood alcohol."

Then Hod Meyers would say, "Neither would your wife." That would set everybody to laughin' because Jim and his wife wasn't on very good terms. She'd of divorced him only they wasn't no chance to get alimony and she didn't have no way to take care of herself and the kids. She couldn't never understand Jim. He *was* kind of rough, but a good fella at heart.

Him and Hod had all kinds of sport with Milt Sheppard. I don't suppose you've seen Milt. Well, he's got an Adam's apple that looks more like a mushmelon. So I'd be shavin' Milt and when I'd start to shave down here on his neck, Hod would holler, "Hey, Whitey, wait a minute! Before you cut into it, let's make up a pool and see who can guess closest to the number of seeds."

And Jim would say, "If Milt hadn't of been so hoggish, he'd of ordered a half a cantaloupe instead of a whole one and it might not of stuck in his throat."

All the boys would roar at this and Milt himself would force a smile, though the joke was on him. Jim certainly was a card!

There's his shavin' mug, settin' on the shelf, right next to Charley Vail's. "Charles M. Vail." That's the druggist. He comes in regular for his shave, three times a week. And Jim's is the cup next to Charley's. "James H. Kendall." Jim won't need no shavin' mug no more, but I'll leave it there just the same for old time's sake. Jim certainly was a character!

Years ago, Jim used to travel for a canned goods concern over in Carterville. They sold canned goods. Jim had the whole northern half of the State and was on the road five days out of every week. He'd drop in here Saturdays and tell his experiences for that week. It was rich.

I guess he paid more attention to playin' jokes than makin' sales. Finally the concern let him out and he come right home here and told everybody he'd been fired instead of sayin' he'd resigned like most fellas would of.

It was a Saturday and the shop was full and Jim got up out of that chair and says, "Gentlemen, I got an important announcement to make. I been fired from my job."

Well, they asked him if he was in earnest and he said he was and nobody could think of nothin' to say till Jim finally broke the ice himself. He says, "I been sellin' canned goods and now I'm canned goods myself."

You see, the concern he'd been workin' for was a factory that made canned goods. Over in Carterville. And now Jim said he was canned himself. He was certainly a card!

Jim had a great trick that he used to play w'ile he was travelin'. For instance, he'd be ridin' on a train and they'd come to some little town like, well, like, we'll say, like Benton. Jim would look out the train window and read the signs on the stores.

For instance, they'd be a sign, "Henry Smith, Dry Goods." Well, Jim would write down the name and the name of the town and when he got to wherever he was goin' he'd mail back a postal card to Henry Smith at Benton and not sign no name to it, but he'd write on the card, well, somethin' like "Ask your wife about that book agent that spent the afternoon last week," or "Ask your Missus who kept her from gettin' lonesome the last time you was in Carterville." And he'd sign the card, "A Friend."

Of course, he never knew what really come of none of these jokes, but he could picture what *probably* happened and that was enough.

Jim didn't work very steady after he lost his position with the Carterville people. What he did earn, doin' odd jobs round town, why he spent pretty near all of it on gin and his family might of starved if the stores hadn't of carried them along. Jim's wife tried her hand at dressmakin', but they ain't nobody goin' to get rich makin' dresses in this town.

As I say, she'd of divorced Jim, only she seen that she couldn't support herself and the kids and she was always hopin' that some day Jim would cut out his habits and give her more than two or three dollars a week.

They was a time when she would go to whoever he was workin' for and ask them to give her his wages, but after she done this once or twice, he beat her to it by borrowin' most of his pay in advance. He told it all round town, how he had outfoxed his Missus. He certainly was a caution!

But he wasn't satisfied with just outwittin' her. He was sore the way she had acted, tryin' to grab off his pay. And he made up his mind he'd get even. Well, he waited till Evans's Circus was advertised to come to town. Then he told his wife and two kiddies that he was goin' to take them to the circus. The day of the circus, he told them he would get the tickets and meet them outside the entrance to the tent.

Well, he didn't have no intentions of bein' there or buyin' tickets or nothin'. He got full of gin and laid round Wright's poolroom all day. His wife and the kids waited and waited and of course he didn't show up. His wife didn't have a dime with her, or nowhere else, I guess. So she finally had to tell the kids it was all off and they cried like they wasn't never goin' to stop.

Well, it seems, w'ile they was cryin', Doc Stair came along and he asked what was the matter, but Mrs. Kendall was stubborn and wouldn't tell him, but the kids told him and he insisted on takin' them and their mother in the show. Jim found this out afterwards and it was one reason why he had it in for Doc Stair.

Doc Stair come here about a year and a half ago. He's a mighty handsome young fella and his clothes always look like he has them made to order. He goes to Detroit two or three times a year and w'ile he's there he must have a tailor take his measure and then make him a suit to order. They cost pretty near twice as much, but they fit a whole lot better than if you just bought them in a store.

For a w'ile everybody was wonderin' why a young doctor like Doc Stair should come to a town like this where we already got old Doc Gamble and Doc Foote that's both been here for years and all the practice in town was always divided between the two of them.

Then they was a story got round that Doc Stair's gal had throwed him over, a gal up in the Northern Peninsula somewheres, and the reason he come here was to hide himself away and forget it. He said himself that he thought they wasn't nothin' like general practice in a place like ours to fit a man to be a good all round doctor. And that's why he'd came.

Anyways, it wasn't long before he was makin' enough to live on, though they tell me that he never dunned nobody for what they owed him, and the folks here certainly has got the owin' habit, even in my business. If I had all that was comin' to me for just shaves alone, I could go to Carterville and put up at the Mercer for a week and see a different picture every night. For instance, they's old George Purdy—but I guess I shouldn't ought to be gossipin'.

Well, last year, our coroner died, died of the flu. Ken Beatty, that was his name. He was the coroner. So they had to choose another man to be coroner in his place and they picked Doc Stair. He laughed at first and said he didn't want it, but they made him take it. It ain't no job that anybody would fight for and what a man makes out of it in a year would just about buy seeds for their garden. Doc's the kind, though, that can't say no to nothin' if you keep at him long enough.

But I was goin' to tell you about a poor boy we got here in town—Paul Dickson. He fell out of a tree when he was about ten years old. Lit on his head and it done somethin' to him and he ain't never been right. No harm in him, but just silly. Jim Kendall used to call him cuckoo; that's a name Jim had for anybody that was off their head, only he called people's head their bean. That was another of his gags, callin' head bean and callin' crazy people cuckoo. Only poor Paul ain't crazy, but just silly.

You can imagine that Jim used to have all kinds of fun with Paul. He'd send him to the White Front Garage for a left-handed monkey wrench. Of course they ain't no such a thing as a left-handed monkey wrench.

And once we had a kind of a fair here and they was a baseball game between the fats and the leans and before the game started Jim called Paul over and sent him way down to Schrader's hardware store to get a key for the pitcher's box.

They wasn't nothin' in the way of gags that Jim couldn't think up, when he put his mind to it.

Poor Paul was always kind of suspicious of people, maybe on account of how Jim had kept foolin' him. Paul wouldn't have much to do with anybody only his own mother and Doc Stair and a girl here in town named Julie Gregg. That is, she ain't a girl no more, but pretty near thirty or over.

When Doc first come to town, Paul seemed to feel like here was a real friend and he hung round Doc's office most of the w'ile; the only time he wasn't there was when he'd go home to eat or sleep or when he seen Julie Gregg doin' her shoppin'.

When he looked out Doc's window and seen her, he'd run downstairs and join her and tag along with her to the different stores. The poor boy was crazy about Julie and she always treated him mighty nice and made him feel like he was welcome, though of course it wasn't nothin' but pity on her side.

Doc done all he could to improve Paul's mind and he told me once that he really thought the boy was gettin' better, that they was times when he was as bright and sensible as anybody else.

But I was goin' to tell you about Julie Gregg. Old Man Gregg was in the lumber business, but got to drinkin' and lost the most of his money and when he died, he didn't leave nothin' but the house and just enough insurance for the girl to skimp along on.

Her mother was a kind of a half invalid and didn't hardly ever leave the house. Julie wanted to sell the place and move somewheres else after the old man died, but the mother said she was born here and would die here. It was tough on Julie, as the young people round this town—well, she's too good for them.

She's been away to school and Chicago and New York and different places and they ain't no subject she can't talk on, where you take the rest of the young folks here and you mention anything to them outside of Gloria Swanson or Tommy Meighan and they think you're delirious. Did you see Gloria in Wages of Virtue? You missed somethin'!

Well, Doc Stair hadn't been here more than a week when he come in one day to get shaved and I recognized who he was as he had been pointed out to me, so I told him about my old lady. She's been ailin' for a couple years and either Doc Gamble or Doc Foote, neither one, seemed to be helpin' her. So he said he would come out and see her, but if she was able to get out herself, it would be better to bring her to his office where he could make a completer examination.

So I took her to his office and w'ile I was waitin' for her in the reception room, in come Julie Gregg. When somebody comes in Doc Stair's office, they's a bell that rings in his inside office so as he can tell they's somebody to see him.

So he left my old lady inside and come out to the front office and that's the first time him and Julie met and I guess it was what they call love at first sight. But it wasn't fifty-fifty. This young fella was the slickest lookin' fella she'd ever seen in this town and she went wild over him. To him she was just a young lady that wanted to see the doctor.

She'd came on about the same business I had. Her mother had been doctorin' for years with Doc Gamble and Doc Foote and without no results. So she'd heard they was a new doc in town and decided to give him a try. He promised to call and see her mother that same day.

I said a minute ago that it was love at first sight on her part. I'm not only judgin' by how she acted afterwards but how she looked at him that first day in his office. I ain't no mind reader, but it was wrote all over her face that she was gone.

Now Jim Kendall, besides bein' a jokesmith and a pretty good drinker, well, Jim was quite a lady-killer. I guess he run pretty wild durin' the time he was on the road for them Carterville people, and besides that, he'd had a couple little affairs of the heart right here in town. As I say, his wife could of divorced him, only she couldn't.

But Jim was like the majority of men, and women, too, I guess. He wanted what he couldn't get. He wanted Julie Gregg and worked his head off tryin' to land her. Only he'd of said bean instead of head.

Well, Jim's habits and his jokes didn't appeal to Julie and of course he was a married man, so he didn't have no more chance than, well, than a rabbit. That's an expression of Jim's himself. When somebody didn't have no chance to get elected or somethin', Jim would always say they didn't have no more chance than a rabbit.

He didn't make no bones about how he felt. Right in here, more than once, in front of the whole crowd, he said he was stuck on Julie and anybody that could get her for him was welcome to his house and his wife and kids included. But she wouldn't have nothin' to do with him; wouldn't even speak to him on the street. He finally seen he wasn't gettin' nowheres with his usual line so he decided to try the rough stuff. He went right up to her house one evenin' and when she opened the door he forced his way in and grabbed her. But she broke loose and before he could stop her, she run in the next room and locked the door and phoned to Joe Barnes. Joe's the marshal. Jim could hear who she was phonin' to and he beat it before Joe got there.

Joe was an old friend of Julie's pa. Joe went to Jim the next day and told him what would happen if he ever done it again.

I don't know how the news of this little affair leaked out. Chances is that Joe Barnes told his wife and she told somebody else's wife and they told their husband. Anyways, it did leak out and Hod Meyers had the nerve to kid Jim about it, right here in this shop. Jim didn't deny nothin' and kind of laughed it off and said for us all to wait; that lots of people had tried to make a monkey out of him, but he always got even.

Meanw'ile everybody in town was wise to Julie's bein' wild mad over the Doc. I don't suppose she had any idear how her face changed when him and her was together; of course she couldn't of, or she'd of kept away from him. And she didn't know that we was all noticin' how many times she made excuses to go up to his office or pass it on the other side of the street and look up in his window to see if he was there. I felt sorry for her and so did most other people.

Hod Meyers kept rubbin' it into Jim about how the Doc had cut him out. Jim didn't pay no attention to the kiddin' and you could see he was plannin' one of his jokes.

One trick Jim had was the knack of changin' his voice. He could make you think he was a girl talkin' and he could mimic any man's voice. To show you how good he was along this line, I'll tell you the joke he played on me once.

You know, in most towns of any size, when a man is dead and needs a shave, why the barber that shaves him soaks him five dollars for the job; that is, he don't soak *him*, but whoever ordered the shave. I just charge three dollars because personally I don't mind much shavin' a dead person. They lay a whole lot stiller than live customers. The only thing is that you don't feel like talkin' to them and you get kind of lonesome.

Well, about the coldest day we ever had here, two years ago last winter, the phone rung at the house w'ile I was home to dinner and I answered the phone and it was a woman's voice and she said she was Mrs. John Scott and her husband was dead and would I come out and shave him.

Old John had always been a good customer of mine. But they live seven miles out in the country, on the Streeter road. Still I didn't see how I could say no.

So I said I would be there, but would have to come in a jitney and it might cost three or four dollars besides the price of the shave. So she, or the voice, it said that was all right, so I got Frank Abbott to drive me out to the place and when I got there, who should open the door but old John himself! He wasn't no more dead than, well, than a rabbit.

It didn't take no private detective to figure out who had played me this little joke. Nobody could of thought it up but Jim Kendall. He certainly was a card!

I tell you this incident just to show you how he could disguise his voice and make you believe it was somebody else talkin'. I'd of swore it was Mrs. Scott had called me. Anyways, some woman.

Well, Jim waited till he had Doc Stair's voice down pat; then he went after revenge.

He called Julie up on a night when he knew Doc was over in Carterville. She never questioned but what it was Doc's voice. Jim said he must see her that night; he couldn't wait no longer to tell her somethin'. She was all excited and told him to come to the house. But he said he was expectin' an important long distance call and wouldn't she please forget her manners for once and come to his office. He said they couldn't nothin' hurt her and nobody would see her and he just *must* talk to her a little w'ile. Well, poor Julie fell for it.

Doc always keeps a night light in his office, so it looked to Julie like they was somebody there.

Meanw'ile Jim Kendall had went to Wright's poolroom, where they was a whole gang amusin' themselves. The most of them had drank plenty of gin, and they was a rough bunch even when sober. They was always strong for Jim's jokes and when he told them to come with him and see some fun they give up their card games and pool games and followed along.

Doc's office is on the second floor. Right outside his door they's a flight of stairs leadin' to the floor above. Jim and his gang hid in the dark behind these stairs.

Well, Julie come up to Doc's door and rung the bell and they was nothin' doin'. She rung it again and she rung it seven or eight times. Then she tried the door and found it locked. Then Jim made some kind of a noise and she heard it and waited a minute, and then she says, "Is that you, Ralph?" Ralph is Doc's first name.

They was no answer and it must of came to her all of a sudden that she'd been bunked. She pretty near fell downstairs and the whole gang after her. They chased her all the way home, hollerin', "Is that you, Ralph?" and "Oh, Ralphie, dear, is that you?" Jim says he couldn't holler it himself, as he was laughin' too hard.

Poor Julie! She didn't show up here on Main Street for a long, long time afterward.

And of course Jim and his gang told everybody in town, everybody but Doc Stair. They was scared to tell him, and he might of never knowed only for Paul Dickson. The poor cuckoo, as Jim called him, he was here in the shop one night when Jim was still gloatin' yet over what he'd done to Julie. And Paul took in as much of it as he could understand and he run to Doc with the story.

It's a cinch Doc went up in the air and swore he'd make Jim suffer. But it was a kind of a delicate thing, because if it got out that he had beat Jim up, Julie was bound to hear of it and then she'd know that Doc knew and of course knowin' that he knew would make it worse for her than ever. He was goin' to do somethin', but it look a lot of figurin'.

Well, it was a couple days later when Jim was here in the shop again, and so was the cuckoo. Jim was goin' duck-shootin' the next day and had come in lookin' for Hod Meyers to go with him. I happened to know that

Hod had went over to Carterville and wouldn't be home till the end of the week. So Jim said he hated to go alone and he guessed he would call it off. Then poor Paul spoke up and said if Jim would take him he would go along. Jim thought a w'ile and then he said, well, he guessed a half-wit was better than nothin'.

I suppose he was plottin' to get Paul out in the boat and play some joke on him, like pushin' him in the water. Anyways, he said Paul could go. He asked him had he ever shot a duck and Paul said no, he'd never even had a gun in his hands. So Jim said he could set in the boat and watch him and if he behaved himself, he might lend him his gun for a couple of shots. They made a date to meet in the mornin' and that's the last I seen of Jim alive.

Next mornin', I hadn't been open more than ten minutes when Doc Stair come in. He looked kind of nervous. He asked me had I seen Paul Dickson. I said no, but I knew where he was, out duck-shootin' with Jim Kendall. So Doc says that's what he had heard, and he couldn't understand it because Paul had told him he wouldn't never have no more to do with Jim as long as he lived.

He said Paul had told him about the joke Jim had played on Julie. He said Paul had asked him what he thought of the joke and the Doc had told him that anybody that would do a thing like that ought not to be let live.

I said it had been a kind of a raw thing, but Jim just couldn't resist no kind of a joke, no matter how raw. I said I thought he was all right at heart, but just bubblin' over with mischief. Doc turned and walked out.

At noon he got a phone call from old John Scott. The lake where Jim and Paul had went shootin' is on John's place. Paul had came runnin' up to the house a few minutes before and said they'd been an accident. Jim had shot a few ducks and then give the gun to Paul and told him to try his luck. Paul hadn't never handled a gun and he was nervous. He was shakin' so hard that he couldn't control the gun. He let fire and Jim sunk back in the boat, dead.

Doc Stair, bein' the coroner, jumped in Frank Abbott's flivver and rushed out to Scott's farm. Paul and old John was down on the shore of the lake. Paul had rowed the boat to shore, but they'd left the body in it, waitin' for Doc to come.

Doc examined the body and said they might as well fetch it back to town. They was no use leavin' it there or callin' a jury, as it was a plain case of accidental shootin'.

Personally I wouldn't never leave a person shoot a gun in the same boat I was in unless I was sure they knew somethin' about guns. Jim was a sucker to leave a new beginner have his gun, let alone a half-wit. It probably served Jim right, what he got. But still we miss him round here. He certainly was a card!

Comb it wet or dry?

CHAMPION

Ring Lardner

(1885–1933)

Mɪᴅɢᴇ ᴋᴇʟʟʏ scored his first knockout when he was seventeen. The knockee was his brother Connie, three years his junior and a cripple. The purse was a half dollar given to the younger Kelly by a lady whose electric had just missed bumping his soul from his frail little body.

Connie did not know Midge was in the house, else he never would have risked laying the prize on the arm of the least comfortable chair in the room, the better to observe its shining beauty. As Midge entered from the kitchen, the crippled boy covered the coin with his hand, but the movement lacked the speed requisite to escape his brother's quick eye.

"Watcha got there?" demanded Midge.

"Nothin'," said Connie.

"You're a one legged liar!" said Midge.

He strode over to his brother's chair and grasped the hand that concealed the coin.

"Let loose!" he ordered.

Connie began to cry.

"Let loose and shut up your noise," said the elder, and jerked his brother's hand from the chair arm.

The coin fell onto the bare floor. Midge pounced on it. His weak mouth widened in a triumphant smile.

"Nothin', huh?" he said. "All right, if it's nothin' you don't want it."

"Give that back," sobbed the younger.

"I'll give you a red nose, you little sneak! Where'd you steal it?"

"I didn't steal it. It's mine. A lady give it to me after she pretty near hit me with a car."

"It's a crime she missed you," said Midge.

Midge started for the front door. The cripple picked up his crutch, rose from his chair with difficulty, and, still sobbing, came toward Midge. The latter heard him and stopped.

"You better stay where you're at," he said.

"I want my money," cried the boy.

"I know what you want," said Midge.

Doubling up the fist that held the half dollar, he landed with all his strength on his brother's mouth. Connie fell to the floor with a thud, the crutch tumbling on top of him. Midge stood beside the prostrate form.

"Is that enough?" he said. "Or do you want this, too?"

And he kicked him in the crippled leg.

"I guess that'll hold you," he said.

There was no response from the boy on the floor. Midge looked at him a moment, then at the coin in his hand, and then went out into the street, whistling.

An hour later, when Mrs. Kelly came home from her day's work at Faulkner's Steam Laundry, she found Connie on the floor, moaning. Dropping on her knees beside him, she called him by name a score of times. Then she got up and, pale as a ghost, dashed from the house. Dr. Ryan left the Kelly abode about dusk and walked toward Halsted Street. Mrs. Dorgan spied him as he passed her gate.

"Who's sick, Doctor?" she called.

"Poor little Connie," he replied. "He had a bad fall."

"How did it happen?"

"I can't say for sure, Margaret, but I'd almost bet he was knocked down."

"Knocked down!" exclaimed Mrs. Dorgan.

"Why, who—?"

"Have you seen the other one lately?"

"Michael? No, not since mornin'. You can't be thinkin'——"

"I wouldn't put it past him, Margaret," said the doctor gravely. "The lad's mouth is swollen and cut, and his poor, skinny little leg is bruised. He surely didn't do it to himself and I think Helen suspects the other one."

"Lord save us!" said Mrs. Dorgan. "I'll run over and see if I can help."

"That's a good woman," said Doctor Ryan, and went on down the street.

Near midnight, when Midge came home, his mother was sitting at Connie's bedside. She did not look up.

"Well," said Midge, "what's the matter?"

She remained silent. Midge repeated his question.

"Michael, you know what's the matter," she said at length.

"I don't know nothin'," said Midge.

"Don't lie to me, Michael. What did you do to your brother?"

"Nothin'."

"You hit him."

"Well, then, I hit him. What of it? It ain't the first time."

Her lips pressed tightly together, her face like chalk, Ellen Kelly rose from her chair and made straight for him. Midge backed against the door.

"Lay off'n me, Ma. I don't want to fight no woman."

Still she came on breathing heavily.

"Stop where you're at, Ma," he warned.

There was a brief struggle and Midge's mother lay on the floor before him.

"You ain't hurt, Ma. You're lucky I didn't land good. And I told you to lay off'n me."

"God forgive you, Michael!"

Midge found Hap Collins in the showdown game at the Royal.

"Come on out a minute," he said.

Hap followed him out on the walk.

"I'm leavin' town for a w'ile," said Midge.

"What for?"

"Well, we had a little run-in up to the house. The kid stole a half buck off'n me, and when I went after it he cracked me with his crutch. So I nailed him. And the old lady came at me with a chair and I took it off'n her and she fell down."

"How is Connie hurt?"

"Not bad."

"What are you runnin' away for?"

"Who the hell said I was runnin' away? I'm sick and tired o' gettin' picked on; that's all. So I'm leavin' for a w'ile and I want a piece o' money."

"I ain't only got six bits," said Happy.

"You're in bad shape, ain't you? Well, come through with it."

Happy came through.

"You oughtn't to hit the kid," he said.

"I ain't astin' you who can I hit," snarled Midge. "You try to put some-thin' over on me and you'll get the same dose. I'm goin' now."

"Go as far as you like," said Happy, but not until he was sure that Kelly was out of hearing.

Early the following morning, Midge boarded a train for Milwaukee. He had no ticket, but no one knew the difference. The conductor remained in the caboose.

On a night six months later, Midge hurried out of the "stage door" of the Star Boxing Club and made for Duane's saloon, two blocks away. In his pocket were twelve dollars, his reward for having battered up one Demon Dempsey through the six rounds of the first preliminary.

It was Midge's first professional engagement in the manly art. Also it was the first time in weeks that he had earned twelve dollars.

On the way to Duane's he had to pass Niemann's. He pulled his cap over his eyes and increased his pace until he had gone by. Inside Niemann's stood a trusting bartender, who for ten days had staked Midge to drinks and allowed him to ravage the lunch on a promise to come in and settle the moment he was paid for the "prelim."

Midge strode into Duane's and aroused the napping bartender by slap-ping a silver dollar on the festive board.

"Gimme a shot," said Midge.

The shooting continued until the wind-up at the Star was over and part of the fight crowd joined Midge in front of Duane's bar. A youth in the early twenties, standing next to young Kelly, finally summoned sufficient courage to address him.

"Wasn't you in the first bout?" he ventured.

"Yeh," Midge replied.

"My name's Hersch," said the other.

Midge received the startling information in silence.

"I don't want to butt in," continued Mr. Hersch, "but I'd like to buy you a drink."

"All right," said Midge, "but don't overstrain yourself."

Mr. Hersch laughed uproariously and beckoned to the bartender.

"You certainly gave that wop a trimmin' tonight," said the buyer of the drink, when they had been served. "I thought you'd kill him."

"I would if I hadn't let up," Midge replied. "I'll kill 'em all."

"You got the wallop all right," the other said admiringly.

"Have I got the wallop?" said Midge. "Say, I can kick like a mule. Did you notice them muscles in my shoulders?"

"Notice 'em? I couldn't help from noticin' 'em," said Hersch. "I says to the fella settin' alongside o' me, I says: 'Look at them shoulders! No wonder he can hit,' I says to him."

"Just let me land and it's good-by, baby," said Midge. "I'll kill 'em all."

The oral manslaughter continued until Duane's closed for the night. At parting, Midge and his new friend shook hands and arranged for a meeting the following evening.

For nearly a week the two were together almost constantly. It was Hersch's pleasant rôle to listen to Midge's modest revelations concerning himself, and to buy every time Midge's glass was empty. But there came an evening when Hersch regretfully announced that he must go home to supper.

"I got a date for eight bells," he confided. "I could stick till then, only I must clean up and put on the Sunday clo'es, 'cause she's the prettiest little thing in Milwaukee."

"Can't you fix it for two?" asked Midge.

"I don't know who to get," Hersch replied. "Wait, though. I got a sister and if she ain't busy, it'll be O. K. She's no bum for looks herself."

So it came about that Midge and Emma Hersch and Emma's brother and the prettiest little thing in Milwaukee foregathered at Wall's and danced half the night away. And Midge and Emma danced every dance together, for though every little onestep seemed to induce a new thirst of its own, Lou Hersch stayed too sober to dance with his own sister.

The next day, penniless at last in spite of his phenomenal ability to make someone else settle, Midge Kelly sought out Doc Hammond, matchmaker for the Star, and asked to be booked for the next show.

"I could put you on with Tracy for the next bout," said Doc.

"What's they in it?" asked Midge.

"Twenty if you cop," Doc told him.

"Have a heart," protested Midge. "Didn't I look good the other night?"

"You looked all right. But you aren't Freddie Welsh yet by a consid'able margin."

"I ain't scared of Freddie Welsh or none of 'em," said Midge.

"Well, we don't pay our boxers by the size of their chests," Doc said. "I'm offerin' you this Tracy bout. Take it or leave it."

"All right; I'm on," said Midge, and he passed a pleasant afternoon at Duane's on the strength of his booking.

Young Tracy's manager came to Midge the night before the show.

"How do you feel about this go?" he asked.

"Me?" said Midge, "I feel all right. What do you mean, how do I feel?"

"I mean," said Tracy's manager, "that we're mighty anxious to win, 'cause the boy's got a chanct in Philly if he cops this one."

"What's your proposition?" asked Midge.

"Fifty bucks," said Tracy's manager.

"What do you think I am, a crook? Me lay down for fifty bucks. Not me!"

"Seventy-five, then," said Tracy's manager.

The market closed on eighty and the details were agreed on in short order. And the next night Midge was stopped in the second round by a terrific slap on the forearm.

This time Midge passed up both Niemann's and Duane's, having a sizable account at each place, and sought his refreshment at Stein's farther down the street.

When the profits of his deal with Tracy were gone, he learned, by first-hand information from Doc Hammond and the matchmakers at the other "clubs," that he was no longer desired for even the cheapest of preliminaries. There was no danger of his starving or dying of thirst while Emma and Lou Hersch lived. But he made up his mind, four months after his defeat by Young Tracy, that Milwaukee was not the ideal place for him to live.

"I can lick the best of 'em," he reasoned, "but there ain't no more chanct for me here. I can maybe go east and get on somewheres. And besides——"

But just after Midge had purchased a ticket to Chicago with the money he had "borrowed" from Emma Hersch "to buy shoes," a heavy hand was laid on his shoulders and he turned to face two strangers.

"Where are you goin', Kelly?" inquired the owner of the heavy hand.

"Nowheres," said Midge. "What the hell do you care?"

The other stranger spoke:

"Kelly, I'm employed by Emma Hersch's mother to see that you do right by her. And we want you to stay here till you've done it."

"You won't get nothin' but the worst of it, monkeying with me," said Midge.

Nevertheless, he did not depart for Chicago that night. Two days later, Emma Hersch became Mrs. Kelly, and the gift of the groom, when once they were alone, was a crushing blow on the bride's pale cheek.

Next morning, Midge left Milwaukee as he had entered it—by fast freight.

"They's no use kiddin' ourself any more," said Tommy Haley. "He might get down to thirty-seven in a pinch, but if he done below that a mouse could stop him. He's a welter; that's what he is and he knows it as well as I do. He's growed like a weed in the last six mont's. I told him, I says, 'If you don't quit growin' they won't be nobody for you to box, only Willard and them.' He says, 'Well, I wouldn't run away from Willard if I weighed twenty pounds more.'"

"He must hate himself," said Tommy's brother.

"I never seen a good one that didn't," said Tommy. "And Midge is a good one; don't make no mistake about that. I wisht we could of got Welsh before the kid growed so big. But it's too late now. I won't make no holler, though, if we can match him up with the Dutchman."

"Who do you mean?"

"Young Goetz, the welter champ. We mightn't not get so much dough for the bout itself, but it'd roll in afterward. What a drawin' card we'd be, 'cause the people pays their money to see the fella with the wallop, and that's Midge. And we'd keep the title just as long as Midge could make the weight."

"Can't you land no match with Goetz?"

"Sure, 'cause he needs the money. But I've went careful with the kid so far and look at the results I got! So what's the use of takin' a chanct? The kid's comin' every minute and Goetz is goin' back faster'n big Johnson did. I think we could lick him now; I'd bet my life on it. But six mont's from now they won't be no risk. He'll of licked hisself before that time. Then all as we'll have to do is sign up with him and wait for the referee to stop it. But Midge is so crazy to get at him now that I can't hardly hold him back."

The brothers Haley were lunching in a Boston hotel. Dan had come down from Holyoke to visit with Tommy and to watch the latter's protégé go twelve rounds, or less, with Bud Cross. The bout promised little in the way of a contest, for Midge had twice stopped the Baltimore youth -and Bud's reputation for gameness was all that had earned him the date. The fans were willing to pay the price to see Midge's hay-making left, but they wanted to see it used on an opponent who would not jump out of the ring the first time he felt its crushing force. But Cross was such an opponent, and his willingness to stop boxing-gloves with his eyes, ears, nose and throat had long enabled him to escape the horrors of honest labor. A game boy was Bud, and he showed it in his battered, swollen, discolored face.

"I should think," said Dan Haley, "that the kid'd do whatever you tell him after all you done for him."

"Well," said Tommy, "he's took my dope pretty straight so far, but he's so sure of hisself that he can't see no reason for waitin'. He'll do what I say, though; he'd be a sucker not to."

"You got a contrac' with him?"

"No, I don't need no contrac'. He knows it was me that drug him out o' the gutter and he ain't goin' to turn me down now, when he's got the dough and bound to get more. Where'd he of been at if I hadn't listened to him when he first come to me? That's pretty near two years ago now, but it seems like last week. I was settin' in the s'loon acrost from the Pleasant Club in Philly, waitin' for McCann to count the dough and come over, when this little bum blowed in and tried to stand the house off for a drink. They told him nothin' doin' and to beat it out o' there, and then he seen me and come over to where I was settin' and ast me wasn't I a boxin' man and I told him who I was. Then he ast me for money to buy a shot and I told him to set down and I'd buy it for him.

"Then we got talkin' things over and he told me his name and told me about fightin' a couple o' prelims out to Milwaukee. So I says, 'Well, boy, I don't know how good or how rotten you are, but you won't never get no-wheres trainin' on that stuff.' So he says he'd cut it out if he could get on in a bout and I says I would give him a chanct if he played square with me and didn't touch no more to drink. So we shook hands and I took him up to the hotel with me and give him a bath and the next day I bought him some clo'es. And I staked him to eats and sleeps for over six weeks. He had a hard time breakin' away from the polish, but finally I thought he was fit and I give him his chanct. He went on with Smiley Sayer and stopped him so quick that Smiley thought sure he was poisoned.

"Well, you know what he's did since. The only beatin' in his record was by Tracy in Milwaukee before I got hold of him, and he's licked Tracy three times in the last year.

"I've gave him all the best of it in a money way and he's got seven thousand bucks in cold storage. How's that for a kid that was in the gutter two years ago? And he'd have still more yet if he wasn't so nuts over clo'es and got to stop at the good hotels and so forth."

"Where's his home at?"

"Well, he ain't really got no home. He came from Chicago and his mother canned him out o' the house for bein' no good. She give him a raw deal, I guess, and he says he won't have nothin' to do with her unless she comes to him first. She's got a pile o' money, he says, so he ain't worryin' about her."

The gentleman under discussion entered the café and swaggered to Tommy's table, while the whole room turned to look.

Midge was the picture of health despite a slightly colored eye and an ear that seemed to have no opening. But perhaps it was not his healthiness that drew all eyes. His diamond horse-shoe tie pin, his purple cross-striped shirt, his orange shoes and his light blue suit fairly screamed for attention.

"Where you been?" he asked Tommy. "I been lookin' all over for you."

"Set down," said his manager.

"No time," said Midge. "I'm goin' down to the w'arf and see 'em unload the fish."

"Shake hands with my brother Dan," said Tommy.

Midge shook with the Holyoke Haley.

"If you're Tommy's brother, you're O. K. with me," said Midge, and the brothers beamed with pleasure.

Dan moistened his lips and murmured an embarrassed reply, but it was lost on the young gladiator.

"Leave me take twenty," Midge was saying. "I prob'ly won't need it, but I don't like to be caught short."

Tommy parted with a twenty-dollar bill and recorded the transaction in a small black book the insurance company had given him for Christmas.

"But," he said, "it won't cost you no twenty to look at them fish. Want me to go along?"

"No," said Midge hastily. "You and your brother here prob'ly got a lot to say to each other."

"Well," said Tommy, "don't take no bad money and don't get lost. And you better be back at four o'clock and lay down a w'ile."

"I don't need no rest to beat this guy," said Midge. "He'll do enough layin' down for the both of us."

And laughing even more than the jest called for, he strode out through the fire of admiring and startled glances.

The corner of Boylston and Tremont was the nearest Midge got to the wharf, but the lady awaiting him was doubtless a more dazzling sight than the catch of the luckiest Massachusetts fisherman. She could talk, too— probably better than the fish.

"O you Kid!" she said, flashing a few silver teeth among the gold. "O you fighting man!"

Midge smiled up at her.

"We'll go somewheres and get a drink," he said. "One won't hurt."

In New Orleans, five months after he had rearranged the map of Bud Cross for the third time, Midge finished training for his championship bout with the Dutchman.

Back in his hotel after the final workout, Midge stopped to chat with some of the boys from up north, who had made the long trip to see a champion dethroned, for the result of this bout was so nearly a foregone conclusion that even the experts had guessed it.

Tommy Haley secured the key and the mail and ascended to the Kelly suite. He was bathing when Midge came in, half an hour later.

"Any mail?" asked Midge.

"There on the bed," replied Tommy from the tub.

Midge picked up the stack of letters and postcards and glanced them over. From the pile he sorted out three letters and laid them on the table. The rest he tossed into the waste-basket. Then he picked up the three and sat for a few moments holding them, while his eyes gazed off into space. At length he looked again at the three unopened letters in his hand; then he put one in his pocket and tossed the other two at the basket. They missed their target and fell on the floor.

"Hell!" said Midge, and stooping over picked them up.

He opened one postmarked Milwaukee and read:

DEAR HUSBAND:

I have wrote to you so manny times and got no anser and I dont know if you ever got them, so I am writeing again in the hopes you will get this letter and anser. I dont like to bother you with my trubles and I would not only for the baby and I am not asking you should write to me but only send a little money and I am not asking for myself but the baby has not been well a day since last Aug. and the dr. told me she cant live much longer unless I give her better food and thats impossible the way things are. Lou has not been working for a year and what I make dont hardley pay for the rent. I am not asking for you to give me any money, but only you should send what I loaned when convenient and I think it amts. to about $36.00. Please try and send that amt. and it will help me, but if you cant send the whole amt. try and send me something.

Your wife,

EMMA

Midge tore the letter into a hundred pieces and scattered them over the floor.

"Money, money, money!" he said. "They must think I'm made o' money. I s'pose the old woman's after it too."

He opened his mother's letter:

dear Michael Connie wonted me to rite and say you must beet the dutchman and he is sur you will and wonted me to say we wont you to rite and tell us about it, but I gess you havent no time to rite or we herd from you long beffore this but I wish you would rite jest a line or 2 boy becaus it wuld be better for Connie then a barl of medisin. It wuld help me to keep things going if you send me money now and then when you can spair it but if you cant send no money try and fine time to rite a letter onley a few lines and it will please Connie. jest think boy he hasent got out of bed in over 3 yrs. Connie says good luck.

Your Mother,

ELLEN F. KELLY

"I thought so," said Midge. "They're all alike."

The third letter was from New York. It read:

Hon:—This is the last letter you will get from me before your champ, but I will send you a telegram Saturday, but I can't say as much in a telegram as in a letter and I am writing this to let you know I am thinking of you and praying for good luck.

Lick him good hon and don't wait no longer than you have to and don't forget to wire me as soon as its over. Give him that little old left of yours on the nose hon and don't be afraid of spoiling his good looks because he couldn't be no homlier than he is. But don't let him spoil my baby's pretty face. You won't will you hon.

Well hon I would give anything to be there and see it, but I guess you love Haley better than me or you wouldn't let him keep me away. But when your champ hon we can do as we please and tell Haley to go to the devil.

Well hon I will send you a telegram Saturday and I almost forgot to tell you I will need some more money, a couple hundred say and you will have to wire it to me as soon as you get this. You will won't you hon.

I will send you a telegram Saturday and remember hon I am pulling for you. Well good-by sweetheart and good luck.

GRACE

"They're all alike," said Midge. "Money, money, money."

Tommy Haley, shining from his ablutions, came in from the adjoining room.

"Thought you'd be layin' down," he said.

"I'm goin' to," said Midge, unbuttoning his orange shoes.

"I'll call you at six and you can eat up here without no bugs to pester you. I got to go down and give them birds their tickets."

"Did you hear from Goldberg?" asked Midge.

"Didn't I tell you? Sure; fifteen weeks at five hundred, if we win. And we can get a guarantee o' twelve thousand, with privileges either in New York or Milwaukee."

"Who with?"

"Anybody that'll stand up in front of you. You don't care who it is, do you?"

"Not me. I'll make 'em all look like a monkey."

"Well you better lay down aw'ile."

"Oh, say, wire two hundred to Grace for me, will you? Right away; the New York address."

"Two hundred! You just sent her three hundred last Sunday."

"Well, what the hell do you care?"

"All right, all right. Don't get sore about it. Anything else?"

"That's all," said Midge, and dropped onto the bed.

"And I want the deed done before I come back," said Grace as she rose from the table. "You won't fall down on me, will you, hon?"

"Leave it to me," said Midge. "And don't spend no more than you have to."

Grace smiled a farewell and left the café. Midge continued to sip his coffee and read his paper.

They were in Chicago and they were in the middle of Midge's first week in vaudeville. He had come straight north to reap the rewards of his glorious victory over the broken-down Dutchman. A fortnight had been spent in learning his act, which consisted of a gymnastic exhibition and a ten-minutes' monologue on the various excellences of Midge Kelly. And now he was twice daily turning 'em away from the Madison Theatre.

His breakfast over and his paper read, Midge sauntered into the lobby and asked for his key. He then beckoned to a bell-boy, who had been hoping for that very honor.

"Find Haley, Tommy Haley," said Midge. "Tell him to come up to my room."

"Yes, sir, Mr. Kelly," said the boy, and proceeded to break all his former records for diligence.

Midge was looking out of his seventh-story window when Tommy answered the summons.

"What'll it be?" inquired his manager.

There was a pause before Midge replied.

"Haley," he said, "twenty-five per cent's a whole lot o' money."

"I guess I got it comin', ain't I?" said Tommy.

"I don't see how you figger it. I don't see where you're worth it to me."

"Well," said Tommy, "I didn't expect nothin' like this. I thought you was satisfied with the bargain. I don't want to beat nobody out o' nothin', but I don't see where you could have got anybody else that would of did all I done for you."

"Sure, that's all right," said the champion. "You done a lot for me in Philly. And you got good money for it, didn't you?"

"I ain't makin' no holler. Still and all, the big money's still ahead of us yet. And if it hadn't of been for me, you wouldn't of never got within grabbin' distance."

"Oh, I guess I could of went along all right," said Midge. "Who was it that hung that left on the Dutchman's jaw, me or you?"

"Yes, but you wouldn't been in the ring with the Dutchman if it wasn't for how I handled you."

"Well, this won't get us nowheres. The idear is that you ain't worth no twenty-five per cent now and it don't make no diff'rence what come off a year or two ago."

"Don't it?" said Tommy. "I'd say it made a whole lot of difference."

"Well, I say it don't and I guess that settles it."

"Look here, Midge," Tommy said, "I thought I was fair with you, but if you don't think so, I'm willin' to hear what you think is fair. I don't want nobody callin' me a Sherlock. Let's go down to business and sign up a contrac'. What's your figger?"

"I ain't namin' no figger," Midge replied. "I'm sayin' that twenty-five's too much. Now what are you willin' to take?"

"How about twenty?"

"Twenty's too much," said Kelly.

"What ain't too much?" asked Tommy.

"Well, Haley, I might as well give it to you straight. They ain't nothin' that ain't too much."

"You mean you don't want me at no figger?"

"That's the idear."

There was a minute's silence. Then Tommy Haley walked toward the door.

"Midge," he said, in a choking voice, "you're makin' a big mistake, boy. You can't throw down your best friends and get away with it. That damn woman will ruin you."

Midge sprang from his seat.

"You shut your mouth!" he stormed. "Get out o' here before they have to carry you out. You been spongin' off o' me long enough. Say one more word about the girl or about anything else and you'll get what the Dutchman got. Now get out!"

And Tommy Haley, having a very vivid memory of the Dutchman's face as he fell, got out.

Grace came in later, dropped her numerous bundles on the lounge and perched herself on the arm of Midge's chair.

"Well?" she said.

"Well," said Midge, "I got rid of him."

"Good boy!" said Grace. "And now I think you might give me that twenty-five per cent."

"Besides the seventy-five you're already gettin'?" said Midge.

"Don't be no grouch, hon. You don't look pretty when you're grouchy."

"It ain't my business to look pretty," Midge replied.

"Wait till you see how I look with the stuff I bought this mornin'!"

Midge glanced at the bundles on the lounge.

"There's Haley's twenty-five per cent," he said, "and then some."

The champion did not remain long without a manager. Haley's successor was none other than Jerome Harris, who saw in Midge a better meal ticket than his popular-priced musical show had been.

The contract, giving Mr. Harris twenty-five per cent of Midge's earnings, was signed in Detroit the week after Tommy Haley had heard his dismissal read. It had taken Midge just six days to learn that a popular actor cannot get on without the ministrations of a man who thinks, talks and means business. At first Grace objected to the new member of the firm, but when Mr. Harris had demanded and secured from the vaudeville people a one-hundred-dollar increase in Midge's weekly stipend, she was convinced that the champion had acted for the best.

"You and my missus will have some great old times," Harris told Grace. "I'd of wired her to join us here, only I seen the Kid's bookin' takes us to Milwaukee next week, and that's where she is."

But when they were introduced in the Milwaukee hotel, Grace admitted to herself that her feeling for Mrs. Harris could hardly be called love at first sight. Midge, on the contrary, gave his new manager's wife the many times over and seemed loath to end the feast of his eyes.

"Some doll," he said to Grace when they were alone.

"Doll is right," the lady replied, "and sawdust where her brains ought to be."

"I'm li'ble to steal that baby," said Midge, and he smiled as he noted the effect of his words on his audience's face.

On Tuesday of the Milwaukee week the champion successfully defended his title in a bout that the newspapers never reported. Midge was alone in his room that morning when a visitor entered without knocking. The visitor was Lou Hersch.

Midge turned white at sight of him.

"What do you want?" he demanded.

"I guess you know," said Lou Hersch. "Your wife's starvin' to death and your baby's starvin' to death and I'm starvin' to death. And you're dirty with money."

"Listen," said Midge, "if it wasn't for you, I wouldn't never saw your sister. And, if you ain't man enough to hold a job, what's that to me? The best thing you can do is keep away from me."

"You give me a piece o' money and I'll go."

Midge's reply to the ultimatum was a straight right to his brother-in-law's narrow chest.

"Take that home to your sister."

And after Lou Hersch had picked himself up and slunk away, Midge thought: "It's lucky I didn't give him my left or I'd of croaked him. And if I'd hit him in the stomach, I'd of broke his spine."

There was a party after each evening performance during the Milwaukee engagement. The wine flowed freely and Midge had more of it than Tommy Haley ever would have permitted him. Mr. Harris offered no objection, which was possibly just as well for his own physical comfort.

In the dancing between drinks, Midge had his new manager's wife for a partner as often as Grace. The latter's face as she floundered round in the arms of the portly Harris, belied her frequent protestations that she was having the time of her life.

Several times that week, Midge thought Grace was on the point of starting the quarrel he hoped to have. But it was not until Friday night that she accommodated. He and Mrs. Harris had disappeared after the matinee and when Grace saw him again at the close of the night show, she came to the point at once.

"What are you tryin' to pull off?" she demanded.

"It's none o' your business, is it?" said Midge.

"You bet it's my business; mine and Harris's. You cut it short or you'll find out."

"Listen," said Midge, "have you got a mortgage on me or somethin'? You talk like we was married."

"We're goin' to be, too. And to-morrow's as good a time as any."

"Just about," Midge said. "You got as much chanct o' marryin' me to-morrow as the next day or next year and that ain't no chanct at all."

"We'll find out," said Grace.

"You're the one that's got somethin' to find out."

"What do you mean?"

"I mean I'm married already."

"You lie!"

"You think so, do you? Well, s'pose you go to this here address and get acquainted with my missus."

Midge scrawled a number on a piece of paper and handed it to her. She stared at it unseeingly.

"Well," said Midge, "I ain't kiddin' you. You go there and ask for Mrs. Michael Kelly, and if you don't find her, I'll marry you to-morrow before breakfast."

Still Grace stared at the scrap of paper. To Midge it seemed an age before she spoke again.

"You lied to me all this w'ile."

"You never ast me was I married. What's more, what the hell diff'rence did it make to you? You got a split, didn't you? Better'n fifty-fifty."

He started away.

"Where you goin'?"

"I'm goin' to meet Harris and his wife."

"I'm goin' with you. You're not goin' to shake me now."

"Yes, I am, too," said Midge quietly. "When I leave town to-morrow night, you're going to stay here. And if I see where you're goin' to make a fuss, I'll put you in a hospital where they'll keep you quiet. You can get your stuff to-morrow mornin' and I'll slip you a hundred bucks. And then I don't want to see no more o' you. And don't try and tag along now or I'll have to add another K. O. to the old record."

When Grace returned to the hotel that night, she discovered that Midge and the Harrises had moved to another. And when Midge left town the following night, he was again without a manager, and Mr. Harris was without a wife.

Three days prior to Midge Kelly's ten-round bout with Young Milton in New York City, the sporting editor of *The News* assigned Joe Morgan to write two or three thousand words about the champion to run with a picture lay-out for Sunday.

Joe Morgan dropped in at Midge's training quarters Friday afternoon. Midge, he learned, was doing road work, but Midge's manager, Wallie Adams, stood ready and willing to supply reams of dope about the greatest fighter of the age.

"Let's hear what you've got," said Joe, "and then I'll try to fix up something."

So Wallie stepped on the accelerator of his imagination and shot away.

"Just a kid; that's all he is; a regular boy. Get what I mean? Don't know the meanin' o' bad habits. Never tasted liquor in his life and would prob'ly get sick if he smelled it. Clean livin' put him up where he's at. Get what I mean? And modest and unassumin' as a school girl. He's so quiet you wouldn't never know he was round. And he'd go to jail before he'd talk about himself.

"No job at all to get him in shape, 'cause he's always that way. The only trouble we have with him is gettin' him to light into these poor bums they match him up with. He's scared he'll hurt somebody. Get what I mean? He's tickled to death over this match with Milton, 'cause everybody says Milton can stand the gaff. Midge'll maybe be able to cut loose a little this time. But the last two bouts he had, the guys hadn't no business in the ring with him, and he was holdin' back all the w'ile for the fear he'd kill somebody. Get what I mean?"

"Is he married?" inquired Joe.

"Say, you'd think he was married to hear him rave about them kiddies he's got. His fam'ly's up in Canada to their summer home and Midge is wild to get up there with 'em. He thinks more o' that wife and them kiddies than all the money in the world. Get what I mean?"

"How many children has he?"

"I don't know, four or five, I guess. All boys and every one of 'em a dead ringer for their dad."

"Is his father living?"

"No, the old man died when he was a kid. But he's got a grand old mother and a kid brother out in Chi. They're the first ones he thinks about after a match, them and his wife and kiddies. And he don't forget to send the old woman a thousand bucks after every bout. He's going to buy her a new home as soon as they pay him off for this match."

"How about his brother? Is he going to tackle the game?"

"Sure, and Midge says he'll be a champion before he's twenty years old. They're a fightin' fam'ly and all of 'em honest and straight as a die. Get what I mean? A fella that I can't tell you his name come to Midge in Milwaukee onct and wanted him to throw a fight and Midge give him such

a trimmin' in the street that he couldn't go on that night. That's the kind
he is. Get what I mean?"

Joe Morgan hung around the camp until Midge and his trainers returned.

"One o' the boys from *The News*," said Wallie by way of introduction.
"I been givin' him your fam'ly hist'ry."

"Did he give you good dope?" he inquired.

"He's some historian," said Joe.

"Don't call me no names," said Wallie smiling. "Call us up if they's anything more you want. And keep your eyes on us Monday night. Get what
I mean?"

The story in Sunday's *News* was read by thousands of lovers of the manly
art. It was well written and full of human interest. Its slight inaccuracies
went unchallenged, though three readers, besides Wallie Adams and Midge
Kelly, saw and recognized them. The three were Grace, Tommy Haley and
Jerome Harris and the comments they made were not for publication.

Neither the Mrs. Kelly in Chicago nor the Mrs. Kelly in Milwaukee knew
that there was such a paper as the New York *News*. And even if they had
known of it and that it contained two columns of reading matter about
Midge, neither mother nor wife could have bought it. For *The News* on
Sunday is a nickel a copy.

Joe Morgan could have written more accurately, no doubt, if instead of
Wallie Adams, he had interviewed Ellen Kelly and Connie Kelly and
Emma Kelly and Lou Hersch and Grace and Jerome Harris and Tommy
Haley and Hap Collins and two or three Milwaukee bartenders.

But a story built on their evidence would never have passed the sporting
editor.

"Suppose you can prove it," that gentleman would have said. "It wouldn't
get us anything but abuse to print it. The people don't want to see him
knocked. He's champion."

A BALAAM

Arnold Zweig

(1887–   )

TRANSLATED BY BASIL CREIGHTON

NOTHING IN LIFE is more forlorn than looking back in vain regret. And,
worse, to be an aging woman without a future and to sit on an afternoon of
cold and drizzling rain, when it is neither autumn nor winter, looking out

of a window in a provincial town on a street that apes the ostentation of a capital city; and to see it all in the naked dreariness and desolation of a ghoulish shadow-world, on whose altar you have a short while ago sacrificed a daughter . . . a young and lovely and unreflecting life cut short by a sudden, shamefaced, senseless death, a death caused by the attempt to procure an abortion, a painful, backstairs death, "as the law enjoined." She had yielded to the fear of people's tongues, in the pitiful and yet so human shrinking from scandal, meaning glances, pointing fingers, gossip. And to have to realise over and over again that this human frailty had instantly taken its revenge upon her, at once and unforeseeably; and her husband chose this very moment to leave her, to cast off the last shreds of a common life, as he might the bed-clothes of a bed in which he had slept too long, jumped up and went off and was no more heard of . . . and free now to live a new life, left his discarded wife behind as an empty oyster-shell fit only for the rubbish-heap where it properly belonged—without urgent cares or urgent needs, without joy or occupation or point or meaning . . . A bulky letter had lain unopened on the table for the last two days—perhaps anonymous and stuffed full of slander or hideous congratulations on being quit of a husband who—and then a torrent of gossip like an opened sewer, giving the names of waitresses and prostitutes and barmaids in the neighbouring town with the exact day and time, which enabled her to detect the barefaced lies; for they were often the very nights on which she and her husband had been accusing each other of Ilse's death in violent storms of mutual recrimination . . . Well, she would drain the cup to the dregs. Better the acrid stench of gossip than this grey and dreary drizzle against a background of stucco caryatids and stucco façades and shop-windows full of objects in whose motionless immutability she saw her own life staring out at her: a life of marking time, a life that numbly ran to waste. For such a life it was indeed worth while to suffer birth and death!

She looked first at the signature: the letter was from a young medical student who three days before had chosen not to take off his hat to her. She had sadly mentioned his rudeness to his mother when she met her at church the day before yesterday. But he was a good fellow, a friend of Ilse's, and she could read his letter with a quiet mind:—

"Dear Madam,

"My mother tells me you complained to her of my rudeness in not taking my hat off to you. You were kind enough to add that possibly it was my first term at the university that encouraged me to forget my manners and how to behave to a lady. This gives me the right to explain myself and I shall do so; but I warn you that my explanation will be a counter-attack, and a bitter one, which will give you further cause to complain of my manners. But I don't care a hang for good manners and if you don't like it you are not compelled to read this letter, which will possibly be a long one.

"I refused to take my hat off to you yesterday before my departure, as in the ordinary course of things I should have done, because my bile rose at the sight of your mourning and long black veil; I felt a hatred of you that no words can express and tonight, as I write, it makes me shudder as if I were in a fever. I have before my eyes at this moment the last (and very charming) photograph taken of your daughter, whom you lost five months ago. She is smiling, dressed in white and holding her tennis racket, and she looks triumphantly out at me as she used to do when playing with Egon B. against me and someone else. Now you can go and plant roses on her grave out there in the cemetery. Yes, I don't spare you and I shall not spare you; you deserve all this and more. Don't imagine I am so childish as to think you neglected to do everything in your power to save the dear girl's life. You were much too fond of her for that and you would not have spared yourself even if she had not been your only child, for no one could accuse you of not having been 'a good mother.'

"But I am forgetting to account clearly and precisely for my behaviour. It is on that and not on an apology that this letter turns. You are not a person one *can* take one's hat off to."

She raised her eyes from the paper: he knows nothing, poor fool; but what is he driving at? Has he some dim suspicion? Oh no, this Quixotic childishness is a thrust in the dark and yet it strikes home: it is true I deserve to be cut, for I have been cowardly, oh, so cowardly . . . She read on in resignation.

"Bear with me if I now recall things you know already—the years our families have been acquainted and how young Ilse and I were when we first played croquet together under the old chestnut trees in our garden. She was nine and wore short dresses and her beautiful brown hair was loose for the wind or the reverent hands of a boy to play with. It came on to rain and then we both took shelter under the trees or flattened our noses against a window-pane and Ilse told me she wanted to die very, very young and then she would not have to leave school, and she was going to die on her feet, struck by lightning; for she had heard some such alarming tale in the history lesson. I was only twelve then and I listened with awe and my flesh crept. I remember all this and much more, for my head is a whole gallery of such pictures.

"Later on, my mother used to say in joke that she had arranged our future for us and I confess it was my greatest delight to imagine what it would be like when we were married. Ilse quite approved of the scheme; she thought we suited each other very well because I was the taller and an obliging playfellow (I used always to pick up her balls for her at tennis);

and when I once hotly took up the defence of blue eyes against all others
in the world, she gave me afterwards our one and only kiss. You remember those blue eyes of hers. She was fourteen by that time and when she
was fifteen she got to know Egon Bucksbach on my birthday in my room.
I was eighteen and up to six months ago I often had good reason to curse
that occasion. I do so no longer.

"I grant that even in those days I shared your dislike of that elegant and
precocious youth; but Ilse loved him. He was her first love. Do you remember what that means? Can you imagine with what eyes she saw him?
Her first . . . For as for loving me—it never occurred to her; I was always
there, her playfellow and brother. She did not even notice that I felt differently. What would have been the point? I soon knew all about it. Even
today when I am twenty and should look back on that time with detachment, even today I am amazed to see how much one could suffer over so
little. It is that time which makes me your enemy. Not on my account.
You wished me well; you regarded us as engaged—but you were deceived.
It was then that I began to hate you; for, listen, I was the confidant of both
. . . Ilse came to me, naturally, and he . . . he did the same as a matter
of course.

"Do you begin to see now what the crime is I accuse you of? From the
day you first tumbled to it that Ilse took to Bucksbach (it needed marvellous penetration to tumble to it with a child of her age) you treated
her as though she were a thief or had gone on the streets. You used words
to her that the child only dimly understood. You looked at her in ways
that made her wretched. You didn't beat her—that is not done nowadays,
of course—but in her hearing you called down God's mercy on 'this creature'. Ilse still believed in God. You locked her in her room; you crept in
on tiptoe to take her by surprise; you stole her diary; you rummaged
through her bed and cupboards for letters. You forced her to swear never
to speak or write to him again; and then never dreamt of trusting to her
word.

"You did all this to her, not to mention all the pinpricks, looks and
glances with which one woman can torture another who has to live with
her on the closest terms without any means of defence. In any case, Ilse had
no wish to defend herself, for she thought herself very sinful.

"How do I know all this? From her tears and all she told me. It lessens
your guilt in my eyes that tears mean little to a woman, because from an
early age they are easily at her command; besides that, your unhappy marriage and your jealousy—for the motive of what you did was not maternal
solicitude but jealousy—disposed you early on to read a vulgar meaning
into anything that happened; but I who was a boy at that time could see
how terribly you upset her and how bitterly her young heart suffered. Ilse
came to me to weep her heart out, to lean upon me for sympathy and
consolation, to hear from my lips whether she had really been so low a

creature as you never tired of reproaching her with being. And once, when
you had shed tears over her, it took me all my time to restrain her from an
act of desperation; the poor child was so shattered and tortured. A
mother's tears! You should have seen her! You should have heard her! How
humbly she bowed before you, how she accused herself, how she acknowledged you were right. She never disputed your authority, never complained of you, never got indignant—she was only miserably unhappy.

"The affair with him lasted three months, her martyrdom fifteen. I know
she let him kiss her, but only at the very end and very shyly; as far as I
know it happened on eight or nine occasions. You see how deeply I was in
their confidence; they hid nothing from me. Not even he. I heard his confession, I cheered him up when he flung himself in despair in the corner
of the sofa, I bore with his self-accusations when he put all the blame on
himself and said he was not worth suffering so much for . . . This conceited fop knew his own worthlessness compared with our little girl . . .

" 'Oh, God,' he used to groan, 'I do not deserve her. She is far above me
and now she has to go through all this.'

"He read me her letters; as I said before, he was a cad. Well, even if
I had not always known what a wonderful child Ilse was those fifteen letters and notes would have opened my eyes. I have them still. He had to
hand them over to me so that Ilse could truthfully assure you that he had
not a line of hers in his possession. This precious treasure is in my hands
and it is a real treasury of her beloved soul for ever. I would not part with
it for anything in the world and if I thought I could ever smile over it I
would prefer not to live. But I shall never sink so low.

"I know that all your hatred condensed to a fear lest Ilse and Bucksbach might reach the point that experienced and sex-conscious women
almost take for granted in every affair between young people. I hardly
need assure you that no such thought ever entered either Ilse's head or his,
although to you it seemed so likely. For the child's innocence was so complete that it put even him far from any idea of endangering it.

"I know all about schoolgirls nowadays. I know what they talk about
when they get together in dark corners. And I know how they talk about
it. One often shudders at the thought of marrying such girls. Ilse was never
one of them; her innocence passed by such things unscathed.

"And yet for the last fifteen months of her life you filled her tender heart
with unhappiness to overflowing. Perhaps you did not know that there
were children who died of wounds which others scarcely feel. You drove her
to despair, you laid her happy life waste, you brought her feelings to confusion and made her long for release. She did not kill herself—but when
her terrible illness came I can well believe she gave way to it with relief
and without a struggle. She died—a darling beautiful girl who had not
harmed a soul and who gladdened every eye with the sight of her flying
hair. She died at the age of seventeen and a half before she had tasted the

happiness of life or known more of love than its torment . . . I was far away when she died.

"I knew nothing of her illness; when at last I heard from home that Ilse Arlesius was ill it was too late to do anything. I have often blamed myself since for not having been more comfort to her during her brief existence. It is true that after her last meeting with Bucksbach (it was a heart-rending parting in sobs and tears) she made me swear never to speak of their meeting again; but perhaps she might have consented to it if I had been more persistent. It was my luke-warmness, my indolence, my ridiculous egoism that persuaded me my turn would perhaps come if only the other were forgotten. I have really no right to write this letter.

"I was told (when I went home a few days ago) that Ilse often spoke of me in her last painful and feverish hours, that she asked for me and hoped—it fills me with joy and despair to think of it—I might in some way alleviate her suffering. Perhaps it was because she never omitted in childish solemnity to put my 'stud: med:' on the cards she sent me. Perhaps it was because she knew from of old that I always did what I could to spare her suffering or to lessen it. Ah yes . . . Now all that is over and there is nothing left but the mound of her grave, where the wreathes and flowers wither. It is somewhat of a shock to me to find myself incapable of accepting a fact: I would gladly dispute the logical conclusion of an indisputable proposition, namely, that the dead are dead and that I shall never see her again or hear her voice, whereas I still have all her movements, every tone of her voice, whether vexed or sad or playful, so clearly in my memory that some remote resemblance often makes me start, and hope that it is she who is speaking . . . which, as you will admit, is somewhat crazed . . .

"And I will confess, too, that during the first months of bitter affliction I regretted that my medical scepticism had forced me to regard spiritualism and everything of the sort once and for all as rubbish, fraud and self-deception.

"We have lost her, you and I. Perhaps when the year comes to an end you and I will be the only ones to remember her at all. We are united in that. Believe me, I shudder to think of your last few months—walking all alone through the rooms where every inch was loaded with memories of your child, opening and shutting doors whose cool metal handles were so often warmed by Ilse's hand, going up to cupboards where her pretty dresses hung, untouched and folded, the white ones and the brown and the sea-blue trimmed with fur that I loved so much. Oh no, I do not envy you all you have suffered! And the weeks of nursing and the three days afterwards; and what you must have had to bear, strong as you are, when Ilse's death hastened the separation from your husband; and then your sleepless nights, while the past twitched picture after picture before your eyes . . . To what loneliness we are left, you and I. How sadly we miss the delightful

laughter and the darling solemnness of our Ilse! I, at least, know that life
will bring new claims on my affections, that youth and its desires will
unite to dim my memories and arouse new feelings. I shall never forget
Ilse, for she is part, and the loveliest part, of my boyhood, but I shall think
of her more calmly, more seldom—in time. But you! I shudder to think of
your evenings, to think that your future is nothing but a chain of grief, a
glaring mirror of the past, as you sit alone and hemmed in by pain within
your four walls, where the presence of your husband had become intolerable. Oh, if I could only be of some help to you. Couldn't we talk sometimes of her whom we have lost? Couldn't we comfort each other by recalling our happy memories of her, now she is far removed from all pain?
We human beings are so irresponsible in what we do, so innocent of what
we suffer . . . All we do to make others suffer is so full of the best intentions, so overborne by forces over which we have no control. Do we hate?
Do we love? I do not know. I feel it is something outside us that makes us
love and hate, makes us do things that give us pleasure, things of which we
suffer, things of which we perish. Perhaps it is in our blood; perhaps it is
only something that has happened to us, or somewhere near us, days
before. Then influences of all sorts come to us in dreams. And so, do not
take too hardly all that came to you and Ilse. Perhaps years of sorrow and
bitter tears and sadness might have been her lot—perhaps we can be happy
in her death. It is never safe to be alive.

"My mother and I will always be glad to see you, I in any case. I may be
young but I have suffered. And suffering brings people together. Do not
refuse me, let me still enjoy in days of sorrow the friendship you showed
me in happier ones.

"Yours,
"Joachim."

"P.S.

"Now that I have finished this wild letter in the wrought-up state I am
in tonight, I remember that I began in quite another mood, a mood of hostility. I cannot bring myself to read it through; it called up what has been
too vividly, too violently. I leave myself and my perhaps brutal tactlessness
to your mercy. I beg you from my heart to forgive me all . . . I will call
tomorrow afternoon to know whether you forgive me. I will bring Ilse's letters with me and I beseech you urgently to pardon me.

"Yours J."

A man of God! As soon as she had put the letter down on the window-
ledge she laughed—a bitter, noiseless laugh—over this Balaam who set out
to curse and ended by blessing and whose curse and blessing were equally
and touchingly wide of the mark—a laugh that dissolved her bitterness in
tears. Suddenly she saw herself with alarming clearness. She saw a woman
who had been guilty of much petty malice in the name of love. A woman

who had known as little of her daughter as this boy had, whose love spoke in every line as clearly as the chirping of the grasshoppers from the grass at the edge of a field, incessant, scarcely audible above other sounds, but in the silence as loud as a surging sea. Oh yes, what horror and misery to be young in the world today, at a time when old conventions were no longer binding and new ones were not yet taken for granted: the loneliness and sorrow that fell to that child's, her Ilse's, lot, thousands of Ilses, thousands of Joachims were suffering at that very moment. They were no exception to the common run; it was simply that new ideas took possession of good and bad alike—and it was just the best that suffered because they could not bear the break with the past . . . But, if the young had these problems, a woman who had no ties could find work to do. She must learn to help people. She must learn midwifery and the care of children and all that went with it. Then her martyrdom would not have been in vain: she had learnt her lesson and could teach others; she could teach the old to have more discernment and youth to show more trust.

The rain came drearily down, but she saw it no longer with the listless eyes of one whose purpose in life had gone; she had received a blessing from the letter of a sorrowing lover and found her calling—the conversion of youth, perhaps, from its furtive precocity. She had been given strength to break away from her ladylike existence, to atone for the sin of cowardice by practical work in a place where no one knew her. She would dedicate her daily labours to youth here and now in the harshness of city life, where men lived and died unregarded, callously exploited as a piece of wood in which ants hollow out their tunnels and rear their broods and have their being, until at last it moulders away.

OLD MAN MINICK

Edna Ferber

His wife had always spoiled him outrageously. No doubt of that. Take, for example, the matter of the pillows merely. Old man Minick slept high. That is, he thought he slept high. He liked two plump pillows on his side of the great, wide, old-fashioned cherry bed. He would sink into them with a vast grunting and sighing and puffing expressive of nerves and muscles relaxed and gratified. But in the morning there was always one pillow on the floor. He had thrown it there. Always, in the morning, there it lay, its plump white cheek turned reproachfully up at him from the side of the bed. Ma Minick knew this, naturally, after forty years of the cherry bed. But she never begrudged him that extra pillow. Each morning, when she arose, she picked it up on her way to shut the window. Each morning the bed was made up with two pillows on his side of it, as usual.

Then there was the window. Ma Minick liked it open wide. Old man Minick, who rather prided himself on his modernism (he called it being up to date) was distrustful of the night air. In the folds of its sable mantle lurked a swarm of dread things—colds, clammy miasmas, fevers.

"Night air's just like any other air," Ma Minick would say, with some asperity. Ma Minick was no worm; and as modern as he. So when they went to bed the window would be open wide. They would lie there, the two old ones, talking comfortably about commonplace things. The kind of talk that goes on between a man and a woman who have lived together in wholesome peace (spiced with occasional wholesome bickerings) for more than forty years.

"Remind me to see Gerson to-morrow about that lock on the basement door. The paper's full of burglars."

"If I think of it." She never failed to.

"George and Nettie haven't been over in a week now."

"Oh, well, young folks . . . Did you stop in and pay that Koritz the fifty cents for pressing your suit?"

"By golly, I forgot again! First thing in the morning."

A sniff. "Just smell the Yards." It was Chicago.

"Wind must be from the west."

Sleep came with reluctant feet, but they wooed her patiently. And presently she settled down between them and they slept lightly. Usually, some time during the night, he awoke, slid cautiously and with infinite stealth from beneath the covers and closed the wide-flung window to within a bare two inches of the sill. Almost invariably she heard him; but she was a wise old woman; a philosopher of parts. She knew better than to allow a window to shatter the peace of their marital felicity. As she lay there, smiling a little grimly in the dark and giving no sign of being awake, she thought, "Oh, well, I guess a closed window won't kill me either."

Still, sometimes, just to punish him a little, and to prove that she was nobody's fool, she would wait until he had dropped off to sleep again and then she, too, would achieve a stealthy trip to the window and would raise it slowly, carefully, inch by inch.

"How did that window come to be open?" he would say in the morning, being a poor dissembler.

"Window? Why, it's just the way it was when we went to bed." And she would stoop to pick up the pillow that lay on the floor.

There was little or no talk of death between this comfortable, active, sound-appearing man of almost seventy and this plump capable woman of sixty-six. But as always, between husband and wife, it was understood wordlessly (and without reason) that old man Minick would go first. Not that either of them had the slightest intention of going. In fact, when it happened they were planning to spend the winter in California and perhaps live there indefinitely if they liked it and didn't get too lonesome for George and Nettie, and the Chicago smoke, and Chicago noise, and Chicago smells and rush and dirt. Still, the solid sum paid yearly in insurance premiums showed clearly that he meant to leave her in comfort and security. Besides, the world is full of widows. Everyone sees that. But how many widowers? Few. Widows there are by the thousands; living alone; living in hotels; living with married daughters and sons-in-law or married sons and daughters-in-law. But of widowers in a like situation there are bewilderingly few. And why this should be no one knows.

So, then. The California trip never materialized. And the year that followed never was quite clear in old man Minick's dazed mind. In the first place, it was the year in which stocks tumbled and broke their backs. Gilt-edged securities showed themselves to be tinsel. Old man Minick had retired from active business just one year before, meaning to live comfortably on the fruit of a half-century's toil. He now saw that fruit rotting all about him. There was in it hardly enough nourishment to sustain them. Then came the day when Ma Minick went downtown to see Matthews about that pain right here and came home looking shrivelled, talking shrilly about nothing, and evading Pa's eyes. Followed months that were just a jumble of agony, X-rays, hope, despair, morphia, nothingness.

After it was all over: "But I was going first," old man Minick said, dazedly.

The old house on Ellis near Thirty-ninth was sold for what it would bring. George, who knew Chicago real-estate if any one did, said they might as well get what they could. Things would only go lower. You'll see. And nobody's going to have any money for years. Besides, look at the neighborhood!

Old man Minick said George was right. He said everybody was right. You would hardly have recognized in this shrunken figure and wattled face the spruce and dressy old man whom Ma Minick used to spoil so delightfully. "You know best, George. You know best." He who used to stand up to George until Ma Minick was moved to say, "Now, Pa, you don't know everything."

After Matthews' bills, and the hospital, and the nurses and the medicines and the thousand and one things were paid there was left exactly five hundred dollars a year.

"You're going to make your home with us, Father," George and Nettie said. Alma, too, said this would be the best. Alma, the married daughter, lived in Seattle. "Though you know Ferd and I would be only too glad to have you."

Seattle! The ends of the earth. Oh, no. No! he protested, every fibre of his old frame clinging to the accustomed. Seattle, at seventy! He turned piteous eyes on his son George and his daughter-in-law Nettie. "You're going to make your home with us, Father," they reassured him. He clung to them gratefully. After it was over Alma went home to her husband and their children.

So now he lived with George and Nettie in the five-room flat on South Park Avenue, just across from Washington Park. And there was no extra pillow on the floor.

Nettie hadn't said he couldn't have the extra pillow. He had told her he used two and she had given him two the first week. But every morning she had found a pillow cast on the floor.

"I thought you used two pillows, Father."

"I do."

"But there's always one on the floor when I make the bed in the morning. You always throw one on the floor. You only sleep on one pillow, really."

"I use two pillows."

But the second week there was one pillow. He tossed and turned a good deal there in his bedroom off the kitchen. But he got used to it in time. Not used to it, exactly, but—well——

The bedroom off the kitchen wasn't as menial as it sounds. It was really rather cosy. The five-room flat held living room, front bedroom, dining room, kitchen, and maid's room. The room off the kitchen was intended as a maid's room but Nettie had no maid. George's business had suffered with the rest. George and Nettie had said, "I wish there was a front room for you, Father. You could have ours and we'd move back here, only this room's too small for twin beds and the dressing table and the chiffonier." They had meant it—or meant to mean it.

"This is fine," old man Minick had said. "This is good enough for anybody." There was a narrow white enamel bed and a tiny dresser and a table. Nettie had made gay cretonne covers and spreads and put a little reading lamp on the table and arranged his things. Ma Minick's picture on the dresser with her mouth sort of pursed to make it look small. It wasn't a recent picture. Nettie and George had had it framed for him as a surprise. They had often urged her to have her picture taken, but she had dreaded it. Old man Minick didn't think much of that photograph, though he never said so. He needed no photograph of Ma Minick. He had a dozen of them; a gallery of them; thousands of them. Lying on his one pillow he could take them out and look at them one by one as they passed in review, smiling, serious, chiding, praising, there in the dark. He needed no picture on his dresser.

A handsome girl, Nettie, and a good girl. He thought of her as a girl, though she was well past thirty. George and Nettie had married late. This was only the third year of their marriage. Alma, the daughter, had married young, but George had stayed on, unwed, in the old house on Ellis until he was thirty-six and all Ma Minick's friends' daughters had had a try at him in vain. The old people had urged him to marry, but it had been wonderful to have him around the house, just the same. Somebody young around the house. Not that George had stayed around very much. But when he was there you knew he was there. He whistled while dressing. He sang in the bath. He roared down the stairway, "Ma, where's my clean shirts?" The telephone rang for him. Ma Minick prepared special dishes for him. The servant girl said, "Oh, now, Mr. George, look what you've done! Gone and spilled the grease all over my clean kitchen floor!" and wiped it up adoringly while George laughed and gobbled his bit of food filched from pot or frying pan.

They had been a little surprised about Nettie. George was in the bond business and she worked for the same firm. A plump, handsome, eye-glassed woman with fine fresh coloring, a clear skin that old man Minick called appetizing, and a great coil of smooth dark hair. She wore plain tailored things and understood the bond business in a way that might have led you to think hers a masculine mind if she hadn't been so feminine, too, in her manner. Old man Minick had liked her better than Ma Minick had.

Nettie had called him Pop and joked with him and almost flirted with him in a daughterly sort of way. He liked to squeeze her plump arm and pinch her soft cheek between thumb and forefinger. She would laugh up at him and pat his shoulder and that shoulder would straighten spryly and he would waggle his head doggishly.

"Look out there, George!" the others in the room would say. "Your dad'll cut you out. First thing you know you'll lose your girl, that's all."

Nettie would smile. Her teeth were white and strong and even. Old man Minick would laugh and wink, immensely pleased and flattered. "We understand each other, don't we, Pop?" Nettie would say.

During the first years of their married life Nettie stayed home. She fussed happily about her little flat, gave parties, went to parties, played bridge. She seemed to love the ease, the relaxation, the small luxuries. She and George were very much in love. Before her marriage she had lived in a boarding house on Michigan Avenue. At mention of it now she puckered up her face. She did not attempt to conceal her fondness for these five rooms of hers, so neat, so quiet, so bright, so cosy. Over-stuffed velvet in the living room, with silk lamp-shades, and small tables holding books and magazines and little boxes containing cigarettes or hard candies. Very modern. A gate-legged table in the dining room. Caramel-colored walnut in the bedroom, rich and dark and smooth. She loved it. An orderly woman. Everything in its place. Before eleven o'clock the little apartment was shining, spotless; cushions plumped, crumbs brushed, vegetables in cold water. The telephone. "Hello! . . . Oh, hello, Bess! Oh, hours ago . . . Not a thing . . . Well, if George is willing . . . I'll call him up and ask him. We haven't seen a show in two weeks. I'll call you back within the next half hour . . . No, I haven't done my marketing yet. . . . Yes, and have dinner downtown. Meet at seven."

Into this orderly smooth-running mechanism was catapulted a bewildered old man. She no longer called him Pop. He never dreamed of squeezing the plump arm or pinching the smooth cheek. She called him Father. Sometimes George's Father. Sometimes, when she was telephoning, there came to him—"George's father's living with us now, you know. I can't."

They were very kind to him, Nettie and George. "Now just you sit right down here, Father. What do you want to go poking off into your own room for?"

He remembered that in the last year Nettie had said something about going back to work. There wasn't enough to do around the house to keep her busy. She was sick of afternoon parties. Sew and eat, that's all, and gossip, or play bridge. Besides, look at the money. Business was awful. The two old people had resented this idea as much as George had—more, in fact. They were scandalized.

"Young folks nowdays!" shaking their heads. "Young folks nowdays. What are they thinking of! In my day when you got married you had babies."

George and Nettie had had no babies. At first Nettie had said, "I'm so happy. I just want a chance to rest. I've been working since I was seventeen. I just want to rest, first." One year. Two years. Three. And now Pa Minick.

Ma Minick, in the old house on Ellis Avenue, had kept a loose sort of larder; not lavish, but plentiful. They both ate a great deal as old people are likely to do. Old man Minick, especially, had liked to nibble. A handful of raisins from the box on the shelf. A couple of nuts from the dish on the sideboard. A bit of candy rolled beneath the tongue. At dinner (sometimes, towards the last, even at noon-time) a plate of steaming soup, hot, revivifying, stimulating. Plenty of this and plenty of that. "What's the matter, Jo? You're not eating." But he was, amply. Ma Minick had liked to see him eat too much. She was wrong, of course.

But at Nettie's things were different. Hers was a sufficient but stern ménage. So many mouths to feed; just so many lamb chops. Nettie knew about calories and vitamins and mysterious things like that, and talked about them. So many calories in this. So many calories in that. He never was quite clear in his mind about these things said to be lurking in his food. He had always thought of spinach as spinach, chops as chops. But to Nettie they were calories. They lunched together, these two. George was, of course, downtown. For herself Nettie would have one of those feminine pick-up lunches; a dab of apple sauce, a cup of tea, and a slice of cold toast left from breakfast. This she would eat while old man Minick guiltily supped up his cup of warmed-over broth, or his coddled egg. She always pressed upon him any bit of cold meat that was left from the night before, or any remnants of vegetable or spaghetti. Often there was quite a little fleet of saucers and sauce plates grouped about his main plate. Into these he dipped and swooped uncomfortably, and yet with a relish. Sometimes, when he had finished, he would look about, furtively.

"What'll you have, Father? Can I get you something?"

"Nothing, Nettie, nothing. I'm doing fine." She had finished the last of her wooden toast and was waiting for him, kindly.

Still, this balanced and scientific fare seemed to agree with him. As the winter went on he seemed actually to have regained most of his former hardiness and vigor. A handsome old boy he was, ruddy, hale, with the zest of a juicy old apple, slightly withered but still sappy. It should be mentioned that he had a dimple in his cheek which flashed unexpectedly when he smiled. It gave him a roguish—almost boyish—effect most appealing to the beholder. Especially the feminine beholder. Much of his spoiling at the hands of Ma Minick had doubtless been due to this mere depression of the skin.

Spring was to bring a new and welcome source of enrichment into his life. But these first six months of his residence with George and Nettie were hard. No spoiling there. He missed being made much of. He got kindness, but he needed love. Then, too, he was rather a gabby old man. He liked to hold forth. In the old house on Ellis there had been visiting back and forth between men and women of his own age, and Ma's. At these gatherings he had waxed oratorical or argumentative, and they had heard him, some in agreement, some in disagreement, but always respectfully, whether he prated of real estate or social depravity; prohibition or European exchange.

"Let me tell you, here and now, something's got to be done before you can get a country back on a sound financial basis. Why, take Russia alone, why . . ." Or: "Young people nowdays! They don't know what respect means. I tell you there's got to be a change and there will be, and it's the older generation that's got to bring it about. What do they know of hardship! What do they know about work—real work. Most of 'em's never done a real day's work in their life. All they think of is dancing and gambling and drinking. Look at the way they dress! Look at . . ."

Ad lib.

"That's so," the others would agree. "I was saying only yesterday . . ."

Then, too, until a year or two before, he had taken active part in business. He had retired only at the urging of Ma and the children. They said he ought to rest and play and enjoy himself.

Now, as his strength and good spirits gradually returned he began to go downtown, mornings. He would dress, carefully, though a little shakily. He had always shaved himself and he kept this up. All in all, during the day, he occupied the bathroom literally for hours, and this annoyed Nettie

to the point of frenzy, though she said nothing. He liked the white cheerfulness of the little tiled room. He puddled about in the water endlessly.
Snorted and splashed and puffed and snuffled and blew. He was one of
those audible washers who emerge dripping and whose ablutions are distributed impartially over ceiling, walls, and floor.

Nettie, at the closed door: "Father, are you all right?"

Splash! Prrrf! "Yes. Sure. I'm all right."

"Well, I didn't know. You've been in there so long."

He was a neat old man, but there was likely to be a spot or so on his
vest or his coat lapel, or his tie. Ma used to remove these, on or off him, as
the occasion demanded, rubbing carefully and scolding a little, making a
chiding sound between tongue and teeth indicative of great impatience of
his carelessness. He had rather enjoyed these sounds, and this rubbing and
scratching on the cloth with the fingernail and a moistened rag. They
indicated that someone cared. Cared about the way he looked. Had pride
in him. Loved him. Nettie never removed spots. Though infrequently she
said, "Father, just leave that suit out, will you? I'll send it to the cleaner's
with George's. The man's coming tomorrow morning." He would look
down at himself, hastily, and attack a spot here and there with a futile
fingernail.

His morning toilette completed, he would make for the Fifty-first Street
L. Seated in the train he would assume an air of importance and testy
haste; glance out of the window; look at his watch. You got the impression
of a handsome and well-preserved old gentleman on his way downtown to
consummate a shrewd business deal. He had been familiar with Chicago's
downtown for fifty years and he could remember when State Street was a
tree-shaded cottage district. The noise and rush and clangor of the Loop
had long been familiar to him. But now he seemed to find the downtown
trip arduous, even hazardous. The roar of the elevated trains, the hoarse
hoots of the motor horns, the clang of the street cars, the bedlam that is
Chicago's downtown district bewildered him, frightened him almost. He
would skip across the street like a harried hare, just missing a motor truck's
nose and all unconscious of the stream of invective directed at him by his
charioteer. "Heh! Whatcha! . . . Look!"— Sometimes a policeman came
to his aid, or attempted to, but he resented this proffered help.

"Say, look here, my lad," he would say to the tall, tired, and not at all
burly (standing on one's feet directing traffic at Wabash and Madison for
eight hours a day does not make for burliness) policeman, "I've been coming downtown since long before you were born. You don't need to help
me. I'm no jay from the country."

He visited the Stock Exchange. This depressed him. Stocks were lower
than ever and still going down. His five hundred a year was safe, but the
rest seemed doomed for his lifetime, at least. He would drop in at George's
office. George's office was pleasantly filled with dapper, neat young men

and (surprisingly enough) dapper, slim young women, seated at desks in the big light-flooded room. At one corner of each desk stood a polished metal placard on a little standard, and bearing the name of the desk's occupant. Mr. Owens. Mr. Satterlee. Mr. James. Miss Rauch. Mr. Minick.

"Hello, Father," Mr. Minick would say, looking annoyed. "What's bringing you down?"

"Oh, nothing. Nothing. Just had a little business to tend to over at the Exchange. Thought I'd drop in. How's business?"

"Rotten."

"I should think it was!" Old man Minick would agree. "I—should—think —it—was! Hm."

George wished he wouldn't. He couldn't have it, that's all. Old man Minick would stroll over to the desk marked Satterlee, or Owens, or James. These brisk young men would toss an upward glance at him and concentrate again on the sheets and files before them. Old man Minick would stand, balancing from heel to toe and blowing out his breath a little. He looked a bit yellow and granulated and wavering, there in the cruel morning light of the big plate glass windows. Or perhaps it was the contrast he presented with these slim, slick young salesmen.

"Well, h'are you to-day, Mr.—uh—Satterlee? What's the good word?"

Mr. Satterlee would not glance up this time. "I'm pretty well. Can't complain."

"Good. Good."

"Anything I can do for you?"

"No-o-o. No. Not a thing. Just dropped in to see my son a minute."

"I see." Not unkindly. Then, as old man Minick still stood there, balancing, Mr. Satterlee would glance up again, frowning a little. "Your son's desk is over there, I believe. Yes."

George and Nettie had a bedtime conference about these visits and Nettie told him, gently, that the bond house head objected to friends and relatives dropping in. It was against office rules. It had been so when she was employed there. Strictly business. She herself had gone there only once since her marriage.

Well, that was all right. Business was like that nowdays. Rush and grab and no time for anything.

The winter was a hard one, with a record snowfall and intense cold. He stayed indoors for days together. A woman of his own age in like position could have occupied herself usefully and happily. She could have hemmed a sash-curtain; knitted or crocheted; tidied a room; taken a hand in the cooking or preparing of food; ripped an old gown; made over a new one; indulged in an occasional afternoon festivity with women of her own years. But for old man Minick there were no small tasks. There was nothing he could do to make his place in the household justifiable. He wasn't even particularly good at those small jobs of hammering, or painting, or general "fixing." Nettie could drive a nail more swiftly, more surely than he. "Now, Father, don't you bother. I'll do it. Just you go and sit down. Isn't it time for your afternoon nap?"

He waxed a little surly. "Nap! I just got up. I don't want to sleep my life away."

George and Nettie frequently had guests in the evening. They played bridge, or poker, or talked.

"Come in, Father," George would say. "Come in. You all know Dad, don't you, folks?" He would sit down, uncertainly. At first he had attempted to expound, as had been his wont in the old house on Ellis. "I want to say, here and now, that this country's got to . . ." But they went on, heedless of him. They interrupted or refused, politely, to listen. So he sat in the room, yet no part of it. The young people's talk swirled and eddied all about him. He was utterly lost in it. Now and then Nettie or George would turn to him and with raised voice (he was not at all deaf and prided himself on it) would shout, "It's about this or that, Father. He was saying . . ."

When the group roared with laughter at a sally from one of them he would smile uncertainly but amiably, glancing from one to the other in complete ignorance of what had passed, but not resenting it. He took to sitting more and more in his kitchen bedroom, smoking a comforting pipe and reading and re-reading the evening paper. During that winter he and Canary, the negro washwoman, became quite good friends. She washed down in the basement once a week but came up to the kitchen for her massive lunch. A walrus-waisted black woman, with a rich throaty voice, a rolling eye, and a kindly heart. He actually waited for her appearance above the laundry stairs.

"Weh, how's Mist' Minick to-day! Ah nev' did see a gemun spry's you ah fo' yo' age. No, suh! nev' did."

At this rare praise he would straighten his shoulders and waggle his head. "I'm worth any ten of these young sprats to-day." Canary would throw back her head in a loud and companionable guffaw.

Nettie would appear at the kitchen swinging door. "Canary's having her lunch, Father. Don't you want to come into the front room with me? We'll have our lunch in another half-hour."

He followed her obediently enough. Nettie thought of him as a troublesome and rather pathetic child—a child who would never grow up. If she attributed any thoughts to that fine old head they were ambling thoughts, bordering, perhaps, on senility. Little did she know how expertly this old one surveyed her and how ruthlessly he passed judgment. She never suspected the thoughts that formed in the active brain.

He knew about women. He had married a woman. He had had children by her. He looked at this woman—his son's wife—moving about her little five-room flat. She had theories about children. He had heard her expound them. You didn't have them except under such and such circumstances. It wasn't fair otherwise. Plenty of money for their education. Well. He and his wife had had three children. Paul, the second, had died at thirteen. A blow, that had been. They had not always planned for the coming of the three but they always had found a way, afterward. You managed, somehow, once the little wrinkled red ball had fought its way into the world. You managed. You managed. Look at George! Yet when he was born, thirty-nine years ago, Pa and Ma Minick had been hard put to it.

Sitting there, while Nettie dismissed him as negligible, he saw her clearly, grimly. He looked at her. She was plump, but not too short, with a generous width between the hips; a broad full bosom, but firm; round arms and quick slim legs; a fine sturdy throat. The curve between arm and breast made a graceful gracious line . . . Working in a bond office . . . Working in a bond office . . . There was nothing in the Bible about working in a bond office. Here was a woman built for child-bearing.

She thought him senile, negligible.

In March Nettie had in a sewing woman for a week. She had her two or three times a year. A hawk-faced woman of about forty-nine, with a blue-bottle figure and a rapacious eye. She sewed in the dining room and there was a pleasant hum of machine and snip of scissors and murmur of conversation and rustle of silky stuff; and hot savory dishes for lunch. She and old man Minick became great friends. She even let him take out bastings. This when Nettie had gone out from two to four, between fittings.

He chuckled and waggled his head. "I expect to be paid regular assistant's wages for this," he said.

"I guess you don't need any wages, Mr. Minick," the woman said. "I guess you're pretty well fixed."

"Oh, well, I can't complain." (Five hundred a year.)

"Complain! I should say not! If I was to complain it'd be different. Work all day to keep myself; and nobody to come home to at night."

"Widow, ma'am?"

"Since I was twenty. Work, work, that's all I've had. And lonesome! I suppose you don't know what lonesome is."

"Oh, don't I!" slipped from him. He had dropped the bastings.

The sewing woman flashed a look at him from the cold hard eye. "Well, maybe you do. I suppose living here like this, with sons and daughters, ain't so grand, for all your money. Now me, I've always managed to keep my own little place that I could call home, to come back to. It's only two rooms, and nothing to rave about, but it's home. Evenings I just cook and fuss around. Nobody to fuss for, but I fuss, anyway. Cooking, that's what I love to do. Plenty of good food, that's what folks need to keep their strength up." Nettie's lunch that day had been rather scant.

She was there a week. In Nettie's absence she talked against her. He protested, but weakly. Did she give him egg-nogs? Milk? Hot toddy? Soup?

Plenty of good rich gravy and meat and puddings? Well! That's what folks needed when they weren't so young any more. Not that he looked old. My, no. Sprier than many young boys, and handsomer than his own son if she did say so.

He fed on it, hungrily. The third day she was flashing meaning glances at him across the luncheon table. The fourth she pressed his foot beneath the table. The fifth, during Nettie's afternoon absence, she got up, ostensibly to look for a bit of cloth which she needed for sewing, and, passing him, laid a caressing hand on his shoulder. Laid it there and pressed his shoulder ever so little. He looked up, startled. The glances across the luncheon had largely passed over his head; the foot beneath the table might have been an accident. But this—this was unmistakable. He stood up, a little shakily. She caught his hand. The hawk-like face was close to his.

"You need somebody to love you," she said. "Somebody to do for you, and love you." The hawk face came nearer. He leaned a little toward it. But between it and his face was Ma Minick's face, plump, patient, quizzical, kindly. His head came back sharply. He threw the woman's hot hand from him.

"Woman!" he cried. "Jezebel!"

The front door slammed. Nettie. The woman flew to her sewing. Old man Minick, shaking, went into his kitchen bedroom.

"Well," said Nettie, depositing her bundles on the dining room table, "did you finish that faggoting? Why, you haven't done so very much, have you!"

"I ain't feeling so good," said the woman. "That lunch didn't agree with me."

"Why, it was a good plain lunch. I don't see——"

"Oh, it was plain enough, all right."

Next day she did not come to finish her work. Sick, she telephoned. Nettie called it an outrage. She finished the sewing herself, though she hated sewing. Pa Minick said nothing, but there was a light in his eye. Now and then he chuckled, to Nettie's infinite annoyance, though she said nothing.

"Wanted to marry me!" he said to himself, chuckling. "Wanted to marry me! The old rip!"

At the end of April, Pa Minick discovered Washington Park, and the Club, and his whole life was from that day transformed.

He had taken advantage of the early spring sunshine to take a walk, at Nettie's suggestion.

"Why don't you go into the Park, Father? It's really warm out. And the sun's lovely. Do you good."

He had put on his heaviest shirt, and a muffler, and George's old red sweater with the great white "C" on its front, emblem of George's athletic prowess at the University of Chicago; and over all, his greatcoat. He had taken warm mittens and his cane with the greyhound's head handle, carved. So equipped he had ambled uninterestedly over to the Park across the way. And there he had found new life.

New life in old life. For the Park was full of old men. Old men like himself, with greyhound's-head canes, and mufflers and somebody's sweater worn beneath their greatcoats. They wore arctics, though the weather was fine. The skin of their hands and cheek-bones was glazed and had a tight look though it lay in fine little folds. There were splotches of brown on the backs of their hands, and on the temples and forehead. Their heavy grey or brown socks made comfortable folds above their ankles. From that April morning until winter drew on the Park saw old man Minick daily. Not only daily but by the day. Except for his meals, and a brief hour for his after-luncheon nap, he spent all his time there.

For in the Park old man Minick and all the old men gathered there found a Forum—a safety valve—a means of expression. It did not take him long to discover that the Park was divided into two distinct sets of old men. There were the old men who lived with their married sons and daughters-in-law or married daughters and sons-in-law. Then there were the old men who lived in the Grant Home for Aged Gentlemen. You saw its fine red-brick façade through the trees at the edge of the Park.

And the slogan of these first was:

"My son and my da'ter they wouldn't want me to live in any public Home. No, siree! They want me right there with them. In their own home. That's the kind of son and daughter I've got!"

The slogan of the second was:

"I wouldn't live with any son or daughter. Independent. That's me. My own boss. Nobody to tell me what I can do and what I can't. Treat you like a child. I'm my own boss! Pay my own good money and get my keep for it."

The first group, strangely enough, was likely to be spotted of vest and a little frayed as to collar. You saw them going on errands for their daughters-in-law. A loaf of bread. Spool of white No. 100. They took their small grandchildren to the duck pond and between the two toddlers hand in hand—the old and infirm and the infantile and infirm—was hard to tell which led which.

The second group was shiny as to shoes, spotless as to linen, dapper as to clothes. They had no small errands. Theirs was a magnificent leisure. And theirs was magnificent conversation. The questions they discussed and settled there in the Park—these old men—were not international merely. They were cosmic in scope.

The War? Peace? Disarmament? China? Free love? Mere conversational bubbles to be tossed in the air and disposed of in a burst of foam. Strong meat for old man Minick who had so long been fed on pap. But he soon got used to it. Between four and five in the afternoon, in a spot known as Under The Willows, the meeting took the form of a club—an open forum. A certain group made up of Socialists, Free Thinkers, parlor anarchists, bolshevists, had for years drifted there for talk. Old man Minick learned high-sounding phrases. "The Masters . . . democracy . . . toil of the many for the good of the few . . . the ruling class . . . free speech . . . the People. . . ."

The strong-minded ones held forth. The weaker ones drifted about on the outskirts, sometimes clinging to the moist and sticky paw of a round-eyed grandchild. Earlier in the day—at eleven o'clock, say—the talk was not so general nor so inclusive. The old men were likely to drift into groups of two or three or four. They sat on sun-bathed benches and their conversation was likely to be rather smutty at times, for all they looked so mild and patriarchal and desiccated. They paid scant heed to the white-haired old women who, like themselves, were sunning in the park. They watched the young women switch by, with appreciative glances at their trim figures and slim ankles. The day of the short skirt was a grand time for them. They chuckled among themselves and made wicked comment. One saw only white-haired, placid, tremulous old men, but their minds still worked with belated masculinity like naughty small boys talking behind the barn.

Old man Minick early achieved a certain leadership in the common talk. He had always liked to hold forth. This last year had been one of almost unendurable bottling up. At first he had timidly sought the less as-sertive ones of his kind. Mild old men who sat in rockers in the pavilion waiting for lunch time. Their conversation irritated him. They remarked everything that passed before their eyes.

"There's a boat. Fella with a boat."

A silence. Then, heavily: "Yeh."

Five minutes.

"Look at those people laying on the grass. Shouldn't think it was warm enough for that . . . Now they're getting up."

A group of equestrians passed along the bridle path on the opposite side of the lagoon. They made a frieze against the delicate spring greenery. The coats of the women were scarlet, vivid green, arresting, stimulating.

"Riders."

"Yes."

"Good weather for riding."

A man was fishing near by. "Good weather for fishing."

"Yes."

"Wonder what time it is, anyway." From a pocket, deep-buried, came forth a great gold blob of a watch. "I've got one minute to eleven."

Old man Minick dragged forth a heavy globe. "Mm. I've got eleven."

"Little fast, I guess."

Old man Minick shook off this conversation impatiently. This wasn't con-versation. This was oral death, though he did not put it thus. He joined

the other men. They were discussing Spiritualism. He listened, ventured
an opinion, was heard respectfully and then combated mercilessly. He rose
to the verbal fight, and won it.

"Let's see," said one of the old men. "You're not living at the Grant
Home, are you?"

"No," old man Minick made reply, proudly. "I live with my son and his
wife. They wouldn't have it any other way."

"Hm. Like to be independent myself."

"Lonesome, ain't it? Over there?"

"Lonesome! Say, Mr.—what'd you say your name was? Minick? Mine's
Hughes—I never was lonesome in my life 'cept for six months when I lived
with my daughter and her husband and their five children. Yes, sir. That's
what I call lonesome, in an eight-room flat."

George and Nettie said, "It's doing you good, Father, being out in the
air so much." His eyes were brighter, his figure straighter, his color better. It was that day he had held forth so eloquently on the emigration question. He had to read a lot—papers and magazines and one thing and another—to keep up. He devoured all the books and pamphlets about bond
issues and national finances brought home by George. In the Park he was
considered an authority on bonds and banking. He and a retired real-
estate man named Mowry sometimes debated a single question for weeks.
George and Nettie, believed, thought he ambled to the Park and spent
senile hours with his drooling old friends discussing nothing amiably and
witlessly. This while he was eating strong meat, drinking strong drink.

Summer sped. Was past. Autumn held a new dread for old man Minick.
When winter came where should he go? Where should he go? Not back to
the five-room flat all day, and the little back bedroom, and nothingness. In
his mind there rang a childish old song they used to sing at school. A silly
song:

Where do all the birdies go?
I know. *I* know.

But he didn't know. He was terror-stricken. October came and went.
With the first of November the Park became impossible, even at noon, and
with two overcoats and the sweater. The first frost was a black frost for
him. He scanned the heavens daily for rain or snow. There was a cigar
store and billiard room on the corner across the boulevard and there he
sometimes went, with a few of his Park cronies, to stand behind the players'
chairs and watch them at pinochle or rum. But this was a dull business.
Besides, the Grant men never came there. They had card rooms of their
own.

He turned away from this smoky little den on a drab November day,
sick at heart. The winter. He tried to face it, and at what he saw he shrank
and was afraid.

He reached the apartment and went around to the rear, dutifully. His rubbers were wet and muddy and Nettie's living-room carpet was a fashionable grey. The back door was unlocked. It was Canary's day downstairs, he remembered. He took off his rubbers in the kitchen and passed into the dining room. Voices. Nettie had company. Some friends, probably, for tea. He turned to go to his room, but stopped at hearing his own name. Father Minick. Father Minick. Nettie's voice.

"Of course, if it weren't for Father Minick I would have. But how can we as long as he lives with us? There isn't room. And we can't afford a bigger place now, with rents what they are. This way it wouldn't be fair to the child. We've talked it over, George and I. Don't you suppose? But not as long as Father Minick is with us. I don't mean we'd use the maid's room for a—for the—if we had a baby. But I'd have to have someone in to help, then, and we'd have to have that extra room."

He stood there in the dining room, quiet. Quiet. His body felt queerly remote and numb, but his mind was working frenziedly. Clearly, too, in spite of the frenzy. Death. That was the first thought. Death. It would be easy. But he didn't want to die. Strange, but he didn't want to die. He liked Life. The Park, the trees, the Club, the talk, the whole show. . . . Nettie was a good girl . . . The old must make way for the young. They had the right to be born . . . . Maybe it was just another excuse. Almost four years married. Why not three years ago? . . . The right to live. The right to live. . . .

He turned, stealthily, stealthily, and went back into the kitchen, put on his rubbers, stole out into the darkening November afternoon.

In an hour he was back. He entered at the front door this time, ringing the bell. He had never had a key. As if he were a child they would not trust him with one. Nettie's women friends were just leaving. In the air you smelled a mingling of perfume, and tea, and cakes, and powder. He sniffed it, sensitively.

"How do you do, Mr. Minick!" they said. "How are you! Well, you certainly look it. And how do you manage these gloomy days?"

He smiled genially, taking off his greatcoat and revealing the red sweater with the big white "C" on it. "I manage. I manage." He puffed out his cheeks. "I'm busy moving."

"Moving!" Nettie's startled eyes flew to his, held them. "Moving, Father?"

"Old folks must make way for the young," he said, gaily. "That's the law of life. Yes, sir! New ones. New ones."

Nettie's face was scarlet. "Father, what in the world——"

"I signed over at the Grant Home to-day. Move in next week." The women looked at her, smiling. Old man Minick came over to her and patted her plump arm. Then he pinched her smooth cheek with a quizzical thumb and forefinger. Pinched it and shook it ever so little.

"I don't know what you mean," said Nettie, out of breath.

"Yes, you do," said old man Minick, and while his tone was light and jesting there was in his old face something stern, something menacing. "Yes, you do."

When he entered the Grant Home a group of them was seated about the fireplace in the main hall. A neat, ruddy, septuagenarian circle. They greeted him casually, with delicacy of feeling, as if he were merely approaching them at their bench in the Park.

"Say, Minick, look here. Mowry here says China ought to have been included in the four-power treaty. He says——"

Old man Minick cleared his throat. "You take China, now," he said, "with her vast and practically, you might say, virgin country, why——"

An apple-cheeked maid in a black dress and a white apron stopped before him. He paused.

"Housekeeper says for me to tell you your room's all ready, if you'd like to look at it now."

"Minute. Minute, my child." He waved her aside with the air of one who pays five hundred a year for independence and freedom. The girl turned to go. "Uh—young lady! Young lady!" She looked at him. "Tell the housekeeper two pillows, please. Two pillows on my bed. Be sure."

"Yes, sir. Two pillows. Yes, sir. I'll be sure."

THE GOLDEN BEETLE

Bruno Frank

(1887–   )

TRANSLATED BY BASIL CREIGHTON

JOHN ABRECHT, assistant district surveyor, was a tall young man of powerful build. One afternoon between three and four o'clock on a hot and cloudless day in July he was walking from Lengenau to Diesbach to make a survey. The road was shadeless and the heat made his blood pulse through his veins. His dark clothes were not very suitable for such weather, but it made him happy to feel the sweat trickling down his chest.

He had got about half way to his destination and just passed the turn to Hochberg when he caught sight of a girl working in the fields. She was all alone in the sultry solitude beneath the shining vault of the sky. As

soon as she heard his footsteps on the road she stood erect and looked at
him, shading her eyes with her hand. She was only a young girl, and yet
a woman too, sunburnt, stalwart and provocative. She laughed and waved
to him. The blood rushed up to his eyes and before he knew what he was
doing he was walking over the stubble towards her like a drunken man.
What first passed between them he was never able to say, even later
under interrogation in court. He let his bag of instruments fall to the
ground and put his arm round her waist. She had nothing on beneath her
blouse, which was hot and moist. Her healthy young body breathed out a
breath that bereft him of his senses; it was the breath of the ever young
and fruitful earth and he drew it in as he kissed her. She laughed and made
no resistance and unthinkingly surrendered her large wide lips. He tore
open the buttons of her blouse and uncovered her breasts, which were
already ripe, firm and proud. The rigid restraint which prudence imposed
on him as an official in a small town, was now his undoing and the natural
instincts of a normal young man in one moment laid his life in ruins. He
bent over her with his face buried in her breast, bathing his eyes and mouth
in the fragrance of her youth. Next she was lying on the ground between
two sheaves and he on the top of her; he was not so much resolved to
possess her as rushed on by the irresistible wheels of fate. It was only then
that she began to defend herself vigorously. But it was beyond him to see
that her resistance was in earnest; the blood throbbed like a hammer in his
ears, his eyes were shut, his mouth uttered unintelligible words, his hands
gripped the quivering prey as in a vise. He no longer knew where he was
nor what he did nor whom he embraced beneath the burning arc of the
sky.

II

Next day the girl's father went to the police and lodged a charge. He
was deaf to all reason, and even when the guilty man, overcome by shame
and remorse, offered to make all amends in his power and promised to
make the wronged girl his wife in a few years' time, he remained obdurate.
It made no difference to the pig-headed farmer that the child quickly
recovered and the very next morning called herself a silly little fool for
rushing home in a storm of tears.

What finished John Abrecht was the unfortunate coincidence that the
farmer had recently been worsted by the surveyor's office over a disputed
boundary and no entreaties, least of all any appeal to his feelings, could
have induced him to forego his unhoped for revenge.

So destiny took its course. The local police did not at first wish to proceed to an arrest, but they had to do so on receipt of telegraphic orders.
John Abrecht was taken to the town and stood his trial seven weeks later.

He had no luck, for the girl, whose evidence might have got him off with
a light sentence or perhaps even with an acquittal, was lying at home in a

great feather bed with a temperature; and so instead of hearing what she had to say the court had only her first written evidence before it. And there was no getting over this bald account. Her extreme youth and even more her subsequent indisposition told heavily against the prisoner; for although she had merely caught a chill through bathing late on a cool September evening the prosecution deliberately led the jury astray by attributing her fever to Abrecht's assault, which her robust physique had long since got over.

John Abrecht was sentenced to two years' imprisonment with hard labour.

III

He came of a strict Protestant family and took his imprisonment as a just and not too harsh penance. His parents were no longer living and his only sister was married and lived in a distant part of the country, so her respectability would not be outraged, a thought that gave him some consolation.

The loss of his job was no great sorrow to him. He was robust and optimistic by nature and had never liked his humdrum duties. It was a fine life tramping the roads from village to village whether in the blaze of summer or through deep snowdrifts; but the tiresome work in the office over title deeds was not at all to his taste, and defining crooked boundaries between the properties of quarrelsome, petty-minded land owners was no profession for him. The fruitful steaming earth belonged to all and it was ridiculous presumption to cut it up into parcels and designate these parcels with numbers and letters. He was born to be a farmer, for he loved the earth and would have liked nothing better than to give all his energies to making it fruitful. He had often, while treading the daily round of official work, dreamt of emigrating to undeveloped countries oversea and wrestling alone with the untilled virgin soil.

These dreams inspired him now and made the dreary days of imprisonment seem shorter. He sat silent among the others in the gloomy workroom, cutting out boot soles with his strong fingers, and while his eyes seemed to be glumly·fixed only on the hacked and dirty surface of the bench they saw his domain beneath a tropical sun: a long low white house, with a swiftly flowing stream near by and all around him fields of standing crops, bushes and large-leaved plants, his property, won by him from the primeval wilderness, and at evening when the sky was a blaze of red, herds of cattle and flocks of sheep, larger and finer than ours and with magnificently curved and bending horns, moved on towards him.

IV

The beasts he would own and look after often filled his mind. He was a good-natured fellow and had always loved animals; but now he felt that

his act of folly had parted him from his fellow men and put him still
nearer to the beasts of the field. His future was not peopled with friends; it
scarcely included a woman; in his dreams he plunged his hands into the
thick fleeces of rams, the oxen lowed softly as he pulled them familiarly
by the tuft of hair on their foreheads, and a large black Newfoundland
dog kept faithfully to his heels as he walked over the acres he had won
beneath a southern sun.

Such fancies were not enough to prevent him suffering from his loneliness, yet he never tried to get into touch with the other prisoners. What he
had done was the madness of a moment, the compulsion of an evil spirit; it
had nothing to do with the kernel of his being and he had no wish to
know or to realize at first hand what evil deeds had brought them all
together in that place. He had made a slip and now he paid for it; he
went through a two years' death in which he was alone with his conscience.
New life beckoned from the other side. They let him go his way and gave
up all attempts at whispered communication with him when they had
their half hour's walk in the prison yard in single file. They even forgot his
presence. The only man who seemed to have an active dislike for him was
his warder. This was very soon brought home to him. Many of the con-
victs, if they earned it by good behaviour, were taken out on navvy work
outside the town, and John, who longed for air and exercise, asked permission to be one of them. For three days he lived in a whirl of hope. Then
his request was refused.

"You'll stay at home with us," the warder told him when he unlocked
his cell in the morning to march him off to the workroom. He looked at
Abrecht for a moment and then added malevolently, "You swine."

v

The warder was a small, thick-set fellow with short arms and enormous
hands. He had a very low forehead, which was always red, and above it his
tow-coloured hair stood up like a brush; his yellow eyes were set flatly in
his face. But the most horrible thing about him was his narrow streak of a
mouth between his dogged chin and his military moustache, a hard, colourless streak in the middle of his common, brutal face. It had no relation to
the rest of his features; it seemed to be there by stealth. There was something sinister when this diminutive mouth opened to let out an abusive
word, revealing two rows of small, pointed, regular teeth, which were
always dirty.

This turn-key was a married man without children; he had passed
middle-age and his long years of service had brought him no promotion.
He was harsh, but not equally harsh to all the prisoners in his charge.
There were ways of establishing a degrading sort of intimacy with him. It
gave him satisfaction to make life easier for his favourites, but servility was

essential. It was even said that he got in white bread, wine and cigars for an habitual swindler and that he was on friendly terms with this wrecker of widows and orphans during the periods he was not in prison. John Abrecht had never really taken his jailer into account. He was obedient and submissive, but there was nothing personal in his submissiveness; he was on the same terms with the man as with the thick walls and the lock of his cell, any feeling for which would have seemed equally absurd. Perhaps it was just this attitude that enraged the warder, for it gave him particular satisfaction to have his importance recognized by his educated victims. It may be that Abrecht's crime stirred the envy of a man who had a scraggy, unappetizing and cantankerous wife in his basement dwelling. But it is just as likely that the malice and cruelty of his nature fixed on Abrecht at random when he saw how resolutely and unassailably he bore his punishment. He watched for an opportunity to do him an injury, to show his contempt of him. One evening in the second spring he went to the peephole to observe the object of his hatred. It was half-past seven and it was still light in the cell. John was standing in his striped uniform in the middle of the cell with his shaven head turned away. He was looking up at the slit of window high up in the wall and through the grating the branch of a tree with serrated leaves could be seen against the red glow of the evening sky. It was one of the two or three trees that grew in the yard, a tall elm, which rose in the air at a short distance from the window. And John Abrecht was looking at it with his head raised and even from the back view of him it could be seen that he was intently listening.

The jailer put his ear to the opening and heard the song of birds in loud and rhythmic chant.

The prisoner stood lost in the sound. For weeks past it had been his joy morning and evening. Ever since the autumn he had been waiting for the singing of the birds to begin again, all through the long, dark and silent winter. It was not only the song of the small birds he heard as he stood there; the forests and gardens and plains of the whole earth sang to him and the beasts of the earth greeted him. He heard it in the barking of dogs, the crowing of cocks, the tender bleating of lambs, the neighing of wild horses and the dull bellow of the buffaloes in a far off, dreamed of home beyond the seas. He heard his freedom in it and the life to be when his penalty had been paid.

The warder turned the key and went in. "Oh, so you're enjoying a concert, are you?" he said after a pause. "Now then, lie down and be quick about it." And he pointed to the bunk, which he had let down from the wall an hour before when he locked the cells.

The prisoner obeyed. The warder left the cell and came back almost immediately with a ladder, climbed up and closed the shutter with a bang. Then he listened intently and made a sour grimace when the song of the birds was still faintly audible.

"We'll do something about that," he said spitefully. "You can say good-bye to your concert-party, you skunk."

Two days later Abrecht was put into another cell, from which nothing but the vacant sky was to be seen. He could only see, at heartbreaking intervals, a swallow flicker past in the bright vacancy of the sky.

VI

There were still six months to go before his release and now at last his sentence began to torture him in earnest. Now at last he knew the hideous waking, the first look into the intolerable loneliness and horror of each day, which so many identical days were to follow until the day of his release came. His plan for this day never altered. He was going to go to the girl whom he had assaulted and ask her and her parents for her hand. If they said yes, he would not mind; if they said no, as was more likely, he would make over to her as dowry the half of what little he possessed. With what remained to stand between him and destitution at the outset, he would start a new life beyond the sea and work as a free man. He would leave as little trace behind him as the ship that took him left in the sea.

What he wished remained steadfast, but in his longing for freedom, which was so constant and innocuous, there was mixed despair and hate. He wanted to outrun this hate for the man who tortured and injured him; it was of this rather than of remorse and regret and the blot on his name that he hoped to be cured in the air of the sea and a southern land. He scarcely dared to look at the man now for fear of his own uncontrollable nature, which had once already got the better of him so disastrously. He stood before him with lowered eyes, disciplined and submissive. And almost every hour he repeated the words that gave him comfort and self-control: "Once I am free I shall never see that man again, never, never."

Meanwhile his longing for the warm proximity of another human being increased. He yearned for the presence of a woman. But the desire that overwhelmed him was not merely sensual: it was the need for tenderness, gentle communion, the mutual exchange of kindness that enthralled him. If the little sunburnt girl in that harvest field allowed him to make good the wrong he had done her, what a life he would make for her, how his arms would protect her! She was often in his thoughts, he imagined he knew and loved her, feature by feature, though he had scarcely noticed her in the white glare of the sun and the tumult of his feelings. But if it was not to be her—well, he would find another over there in the new country. And his desire called up a slender, gentle creature with fragrant, dark hair, looking up at him confidingly, with large and gentle eyes. But it needn't be a woman at all, not even a human being, only some living thing that he could watch over and protect. It need only be a dog that pressed against his knees, only a tame bird that liked to perch on his hand.

Only the tiniest heart that beat trustfully in his presence. Anything not to be alone with these dead walls and that hellish jailer. He got to such a pitch that in the night he put his right hand to his heart and felt his pulse at the same time, so as to have the sense of life twice over.

Summer came and every day John Abrecht believed that now his cup was full, now his craving for a living being could rise to no higher pitch, now the utmost limit of human suffering was reached. He might tell himself that soon, in little more than a hundred days the end was certain, he might contrast his fate with the thousands who had to suffer longer, suffer to all eternity, but for all that he felt no better off and his suffering grew. It was no relief to look at the mute and evil heads in the workroom; besides, his enemy had succeeded in getting him solitary confinement for three days out of the seven.

And then the miracle happened.

VII

He came back one evening from the workroom, the warder entered his cell with him, let the bunk down with a crash from the wall, looked round and, finding no cause for reprimand, shut the heavy door behind him and his vengeful footsteps died away.

John Abrecht stood a moment with his face turned to the square of paling summer sky, in which no living creature was to be seen, and then turned despondently to the dreary loneliness of his cell. His eye fell on the comfortless bunk.

Then he saw in the middle of the coarse grey blanket a moving particle of life, shining green and gold. John pressed both hands to his heart.

It was a mystery how the beetle could have got in. He could not have flown in through the window; John knew enough of the species to know that. But how unlikely it was, how astonishing and wonderful, that it should have found its way over the threshold of his cell, the door of which was so seldom open. It was a miracle.

John approached carefully in order not to frighten the tiny object. He silently let himself down on the wretched bed, knelt down in his prison trousers and looked closely at this living thing which had been given him for his delight. The little creature moved his six, finely articulated little brown legs one after the other and struggled on over the rough pile of the blanket. Sometimes he patiently stopped to rest. His green-gold wing cases shone in the evening light, the little shield on his neck glanced and shimmered like a precious jewel, his feelers moved more tenderly and silently than anything in the world and his projecting eyes peered about him.

You can't possibly see me, John thought, I am like a mountain to you, like a whole range of mountains, you little, little one. But I can see you, you bring me joy and a hint of liberty and you are so beautiful. But even if you were ugly and stank and stung me, I would still be kind to you, and you would still lie in my heart. Let me touch you, let me feel the living gold on your wings, my saviour, my beauty—and he carefully stretched out a trembling finger.

Then the second miracle happened. The beetle seemed to realize his presence, to feel that he was a man. It seemed dismayed. Then it made a clumsy turn in the heavy wool and came straight towards John Abrecht, straight towards his breast, as he knelt there.

VIII

Who can say whether it is possible or merely a childish dream, to tame an insect, to win its love and to make it one's friend? What do we know? We do not know what passes in the fibre of the branch that we break across our knees, we do not know what repercussions follow from the splintering of a stone, thrown by a child. We know nothing. We wash the sleep out of our eyes and go on with our concerns in deadly earnest, we warm our bodies with food and embrace a woman whose warmth pleases us and who is as strange to us as a tree or stone or an animal, we get up and go to bed again in ignorance deeper than before. We know nothing.

It was enough for John Abrecht to believe that he had won the affection of the little gold beetle. It was now his whole life. The days he had to spend in solitary confinement were now the best. But even the other days when he only returned to his cell at evening were tolerable, for they were shortened by anticipation.

He had to fight for his gleaming treasure. He listened, tense in every nerve for the warder's step in case he might take them both by surprise; and he suffered thirst in doing without his drink of water, for the water jug was the only hiding place the cell contained. He emptied it secretly and silently and in its moist earthenware depth the gold beetle sat all day long, waiting for him. He sat among the grasses and faded flowers which his human friend secretly brought up to him from his walks in the prison yard. They played together. The tiny creature clambered gently over the man's finger; its touch was soft, it was never afraid. And it nibbled at a grass stalk or sucked at a dandelion which the man held out to him.

John Abrecht was perfectly right in his head. He knew what it was he loved: just a little beetle, whose life would end with the summer. But his own torment would end with the summer too and then his tiny companion would lead him to the threshold of life and hand him over to all those creatures to whom John had dedicated his energies of love. What did it matter whence the joy came? It had come to him on the verge of his blackest despair, and why should he analyze it and ask more of this particle of life that gleamed so consolingly in the light of the estranging summer days?

I cannot show you enough love, precious little one, he thought, I cannot be kind enough to you, for you do not understand all. But even if you no longer lived and moved your little legs, my jewel, I would still stretch out my arms to love and cherish the earth to which you had returned.

IX

On one of his days of solitary confinement, John Abrecht was kneeling with his friend on the stone floor. It was about noon and he had put his bowl down in front of him and the beetle was amusing himself by making the circuit of its edge. Sometimes John held his forefinger across his path; then the little creature stopped, seemed to glance sideways and moved his foremost and shortest pair of legs as though in fun.

The door creaked and shut again. John jumped up and looked with mortal dread into the warder's angry face. His forehead was redder than usual and his flat eyes gleamed and his little mouth was nothing but a pinched white streak. Abrecht knew at once that concealment was over and that the man had been watching him. He raised his hands in clumsy supplication and looked not unlike the little creature he wanted to protect. He tried to speak.

"Shut your mouth," the warder said. "Show me what you've got there."

"Don't, don't!" Abrecht stammered. "Don't hurt him!"

The warden bent down and picked up the little creature, who had sat waiting on the edge of the bowl, gave a passing glance at the creeping thing in his hand, then let it fall to the ground and squashed it with his boot. You could hear the crunch.

"That will teach you to amuse yourself."

John Abrecht sank down on the stool in the corner. He sat with his face in his hands and did not move. He sat for half a minute with his nails boring into his temples, holding himself in with all his strength.

"Jump to it and clean it up," the warder said, giving him a push. Abrecht got up with his eyes fixed to the ground and obediently took the floor cloth from the corner. The boot had done its business well. There was only a patch on the floor, black mangled limbs and a little discoloured blood. A single scrap of one wing case could be distinguished and the gilded lacquer gleamed out from the darkness of destruction.

John carefully wiped it all up, without raising his eyes. The warder found nothing further to say and with another glance round went out, not satisfied even yet.

X

The man little knew how near death had been to his hairy throat in that half minute. He little knew why Abrecht's hands had bored so furiously into his temples. He had deprived a prisoner of a pastime. Duty was duty. Basta!

But the best pastime on this earth is hatred. Everybody knows that. The blockheads of every nation have known that since time immemorial. They occupy their vacant hours in hating and abusing other nations, and how can a man be aware of monotony or even of the passing of the days when his heart has once penetrated to the hellish depths of another's heart and come up again from that deep shaft like a bucket filled to the brim with the lust for revenge?

Two months lay between Abrecht and his release. They were no more to him than one brief torch-lit night. He stood and walked and worked and cleaned himself and his cell automatically and without a care, feeling with a terrible joy how the flames ate deeper and deeper into his vitals. He could crouch hour after hour on his stool, or lie in the dark under his blanket, revolving the same words, the same thoughts in his mind. Fifty and five hundred times over he could mutely repeat the same words: "How can a human being do that? A man like that must not live. A man like that contaminates the world."

But he knew too that the man no longer lived. His doom was sealed. It had been all he could do in that half minute not to kill him. But now it was easy; it cost him no trouble at all to wait. Now there was even a sort of bitter satisfaction in letting Satan enjoy his bail in the arrogant belief that no danger threatened him.

Imprisonment had not in the least turned his brain. When he cherished and loved the gilded beetle he had been perfectly sane. He had always been perfectly clear about what he felt: he loved a little gleaming beetle, which was no longer there and yet stood for everything. Even now he knew quite well what a little thing it was that had happened: someone had trodden on an insect. He was quite able to realize that there was very little in a defenceless prisoner's being deprived, for no reason but spite, of the one wretched joy he possessed.

Nevertheless it typified all that was hateful, despicable and worthy of destruction on earth. Nothing more insignificant and unimportant could be imagined and yet nothing more tremendous and evil and horrible; and if he killed that warder, if he broke his contemptible neck for him or stuck a knife into his gullet, he would still be killing the devil and bruising the serpent's head; and it had to happen and that was why it would happen, for he neither knew nor cared what awaited him when the deed was done and that was why he hungered and thirsted for that moment and would not fail it. Amen. Amen. Amen.

XI

John Abrecht made for the centre of the town, uncertain of his way and what to do. His clothes hung loosely on him. His boots felt heavy. His felt hat was too large for his shaven head. He carried a small leather suitcase in his hand.

It was a fine sunny autumn morning and even the outskirts of the town had a friendly air. Everyone looked happy and the trams clanked cheerfully by. Before he had crossed more than a street or two he felt that he had come a long way: no one by that time would dream where he had come from. Taking care not to remove his hat, he stopped a young fellow and asked him the time. "Would you mind telling me the date as well?" he added in an undertone. "It's the 29th of September," the man said and hurried on.

So they had let him out two days before his time. What generosity after those two years! And he walked on lost in thought. Finally he stood, clasping his suitcase, on the front platform of a tram. People got on and off, nobody noticed him, the streets grew more crowded and lively. His eyes rested on a hand-cart heaped with ripe peaches long after they passed it. Anyone could go up and buy some of the luscious fruit for a few pence. He glanced into his pocketbook, in which he had a good number of folded notes. He had provided for himself well—in those days.

Perhaps it was the fruit-vendor's barrow that decided him to get out in the large market place and take a room in one of the hotels there. The boots took him up the narrow winding staircase, smelling of vegetables and spirits and wine, to a plainly furnished room high up under the roof. Then there was another interruption: it was the boots, panting in with a registration paper in his hand. He filled it in carefully and deliberately, giving a false name and a false address in another town. He noticed he had almost forgotten how to write.

Then he started to unpack his suitcase and it gave him an odd feeling as he took out his washing things, his two brushes and soap and comb and a little shaving mirror and razor and all that he had so carefully packed as though for a two days' holiday. Everything had been taken from him when he entered the prison and for seven hundred days his suitcase had lain untouched in store, provided with a label, on which were written the number of a cell and the date.

Dazed by his sudden release he idly reflected that he, as well as his suitcase, had been laid on one side all this time, waiting in a state of suspended animation. Now, surely, it must be possible to take up the thread of his life where he had let it drop.

But no, it was not.

XII

He walked to the open window and put both his hands on the iron rail of the low balustrade. Below there was a happy turmoil of colour and noise. The square between the old gabled town hall and the irregular rows of houses to which his inn belonged was alive with the coming and going of market day; people were going cheerfully about their business in the sunshine, all the stalls were gay with fruit and flowers and leafy plants; everyone was happy, want was far away and life seemed easy.

All this lay beneath John's eyes and at the same time sharply separate from him; it was real and only a few steps parted him from it, and yet it seemed intangible and unsubstantial. It was the world, actual human existence, but he had no part in it, not yet. If he had descended the old inn stairs to the sunny square, it would all have retreated before him and the busy stir of life would still have gone on in the distance.

There was fruit in plenty: the sun had been busy while he had been banished from it. And even now he could not buy any of that lovely fruit heaped up like solid sunlight—not yet. His eye caught sight of more peaches in a basket. A peach seemed to him the perfect work of nature. Nature wanted to show once and for all what it was capable of and so it produced its best in a playful mood—a peach or a swan or a piece of rose-coloured crystal. At school one day he had been taught the meaning of the word peach. It meant Persian fruit. Persia! The dream of a sea voyage, foreign lands and southern suns passed dimly before his eyes. He might not stretch out his hands to part the veil yet, but the hour was near.

His spirits rose and he looked more closely at the gay scene below him. He saw a stall-holder playing with his dog. He was a robust man of fifty in a sweater with a tweed cap on his head; the dog, a playful little animal with flop ears that were much too big for it and too long a tail. Its forefeet were on a vegetable basket and the man was teasing it with a bunch of carrots. The dog enjoyed the game; it lifted first one and then the other of its short front legs to pat comically at the yellow bundle. Suddenly its master threw the carrots away, grasped him by one ear and laughed right in his black face. At that he broke loose and began to bark with all his might and ran excitedly round and round the stall.

But John was no longer looking. As he watched the dog playfully patting with its front legs, the veil was suddenly torn from his eyes and his actual situation rose before him. He knew what it was that still parted him from the world and from the future. He heard the crunching on the stone floor; he heard those pitiless and unspeakably brutal words; he saw those yellow eyes and that boot grinding on the floor. The world was full again of the pestilential breath of the most evil, the lowest of mankind; and his pulses throbbed again with a terrible hatred and an indeflectible lust of vengeance. No consideration, no thoughts of prudence could stem the vehemence of that necessity. It would be easier to hold back the sea with a rope.

"I shall kill him," he told himself. For the first time he uttered what he had known for weeks was his resolve. He carefully shut the window and bolted the door as though someone outside might break in on his thoughts. Then he sat down in the middle of the room at the empty table and leaning his forehead in one hand he began methodically and calmly to make his plans.

XIII

Next day he had an exhaustive interview at the Emigration Office. From there he went to the Consulate of a South American State and was politely given full details by the official, an elderly German. There he booked his passage for a not far distant date and made arrangements with the depository where his things were stored. That night he began to make investigations. There was need of much methodical reconnaissance before he could be certain of achieving his aim. Not far from the prison, a little further out along the uncompleted suburban road, there was an inn called the Concord, frequented by the prison staff. It was here that the warders sat over beer and cards; and from this low-ceilinged and stuffy inn-parlour, where they sat in comfort, they returned to carry out their duties or to the cowardly satisfaction of their worst instincts. Night after night John hung about the place; twice he even went in and quietly drank his beer without being recognized and listened to the jailers' commonplace talk—to judge from which they might just as well have been rate-collectors or tobacconists.

He examined with particular care the stretch of road that led to the prison. After a short distance, in the direction of the town, a narrow lane went off to the left, leading between the outer wall of the prison and a long black warehouse. It was by this lane that the warders reached the back entrance of the prison.

John knew the daily routine of the prison and soon he had ascertained the rotation in which they went for their nightly refreshment in the public house. Only one thing remained—to come upon his victim when he was unaccompanied. In order to be sure, he made a test ambush.

He took up his station in the lane towards nine o'clock, squeezing himself up against the darkness of the warehouse door, and waited. Not far from him there was a dim oil lamp projecting from the prison wall on an iron bracket. Anyone who turned off the road along the lane could be clearly recognized. Soon a warder came along, a tall lean fellow. As soon as he passed under the light of the lamp, John noticed the grave and decent expression of his long face.

Why couldn't he have been my warder, he thought quietly, and then this load would not have lain on my heart. The man walked steadily on and rang the bell at the gate. The gate opened and shut behind him.

"Yes, I should not have had to kill him," he said to himself as he lay in wait. The thought inspired a calm regret for the part he had to play but not any pity at all for the condemned man. What lay before him did not follow from a resolve which he could alter at will: there was no choice. That man and the nameless evil he represented stood between John and the world. It was impossible to advance one single step into real life before this barrier had been overthrown. Actually, this barrier was not outside him at all; it was not a man with his feet on the ground; it was in Abrecht's blood as a terrible clot of hatred and nausea and contempt. His life was held from day to day only on that condition. Strength was given him only to do that deed. Only when that clot had been dispersed and washed away would he be free to breathe and live his life and love. Only then would his blood course calmly and gently through his veins.

He remembered a school friend of his, who had been dangerously ill; the doctor had diagnosed blood-poisoning and given him a mercury injection and cured him. John remembered distinctly what an impression it had made on him; he had imagined the cooling stream of dimly shining silver coursing through the boy's blood and gently carrying away all the poisonous germs. That's how it would be with him when his deed was done.

At that moment he saw his victim coming. A short heavy tread came along the lane and soon Abrecht saw the flat brutal face, the eyes, the moustache and the chin lit up for a moment by the lamp. He came on singing and suspecting nothing. John heard the words of a popular song in that hideous voice. "It needn't be flannel," he sang as he passed Abrecht's motionless figure.

"Though I daresay it will be," the voice went on. He laughed at the absurdity of the words, which the filthy idiot had no doubt got wrong; he laughed silently from scorn and hatred and the luxury of triumph as he thought how the man had brushed shoulders in his besotted complacency with his irrevocable doom.

There was a ring at the bell, the gate opened and slammed to again with a dull echo.

XIV

Next morning he took a local train. First it went through the ugly industrial outskirts and then for nearly an hour through pleasant rolling country. He got out and took the road for Hochberg.

The autumn fields lay brown and deserted in the clear air and John quite enjoyed the walk in spite of his thick dark suit. Soon he came to the spot where the road turned off and ascended a gentle hill towards Hochberg.

This was the place, he thought, as he looked at the empty silent field, on which then the sheaves had been standing and where his fate had overtaken him.

If I had only passed an hour later, he thought, my life would have gone on as usual; or if I had taken another road, or if it had not been so hot, or if the girl had had to stay at home peeling potatoes. It is on such things a man's destiny turns; everything is luck, whether good or bad.

But even while he thought this and looked at the reaped stubble field he knew that it was foolish to talk of luck. It was utterly impossible to think away that disaster or to cancel those two years in prison; his life had been directed and turned aside by some higher power, by some obscure and all powerful decree. Even if it was open to him to wish what was done undone, did not a secret instinct of his being accept and endorse every turn of fate? Did he not meet with composure his crime and his punishment, his imprisonment and his liberty, his homelessness and the promise of the unknown? He welcomed all, good and bad alike.

But no, not one thing—not the heartless cruelty of that malicious devil who murdered the defenceless. Room could be found for all in a heart which did not quail, which was ready to be overthrown, to suffer hunger, sorrow and pain, to be forsaken and lost and repulsed. But one thing alone could not be tolerated. That man must die. A red mist rose before John's eyes. He no longer saw the place where his destiny had been accomplished: the field had vanished from his eyes.

He broke off and took the road to Hochberg. When he got there he enquired his way to the farm and nobody noticed him as he went along the road. Only a few there had ever known him and people quickly forget. Soon he arrived at the farm, which had a moderately prosperous air.

The farmer was sitting at a table in the kitchen. John gave his name quietly, ready for a rough reception. But nothing of the sort occurred. The man only said yes and what did he want.

John put his question in few words.

"Well," the farmer said, still without getting up, "well, I don't know. The story's all forgotten now and it would be a pity perhaps to rake it up again, and you won't get your job back again, I suppose?"

"No, that's true," Abrecht said, surprised at the man's composure. Where had the anger gone that had flung him into a criminal's cell? Two years were an eternity. Was one still the same person after two years? He too was quite unmoved at the sight of his former enemy.

"Would you like to see Joanna?" he went on to ask. "I'll call her." He got up and crossed the yard to the door of a barn and John could see through the window that he stood still and said something through the door.

So her name was Joanna. He had forgotten that or never known it. But now it seemed to him that having the same names was a barrier to their union. It was certainly a foolish notion but it seemed to rule out all idea of their marrying. It was not to be.

The girl came in with her father. Abrecht would scarcely have recognized her. He would very likely not have noticed her in a crowd. She had grown into a lanky girl, neither pretty nor plain. Now that autumn had come she was not even particularly sunburnt and it was her sunburnt complexion that his memory had so long held fast. She looked aside in embarrassment as she held out her hand.

"I wanted to ask your forgiveness, Miss Joanna," he said.

She obviously did not know what to reply and muttered almost unintelligibly: "Oh, it doesn't matter."

"I have already told your father that I would gladly make you all amends. I asked him whether he would like us to marry."

She looked up at him for the first time; she too had never realized what he looked like and she was surprised by his grave lean face.

"I don't know, Mr. Abrecht," she murmured. "People have pretty well forgotten all about it now."

"Besides, there's another man who wants to marry her," her father said from his chair. "She's young yet, only seventeen."

"I see," said Abrecht. "Well, I wish you happiness. I am very glad that I have not ruined your life. I thought a lot about you, in there, Miss Joanna."

At this she looked him full in the face. "Did you have a very bad time?" she asked gently.

"Oh no," he replied vaguely.

He was now a free man and there was little more to detain him in the room; he had only his further offer of a sum of money to make. And he had to ask twice whether this was agreeable to them. Joanna's only reply was to look at him curiously and with bewilderment, but her father went into the proposal without thanking him or expressing any surprise, just as though it was a matter he had been counting on all the time. When it was settled, there seemed nothing further to say.

"My wife and son have gone to Lengenau market," her father said at last. "But will you have a cup of coffee, Mr. Abrecht?"

John declined, but the girl had already gone out, apparently relieved that the interview was over. After a few minutes she came back with two jugs and a cup and a loaf of very white, fragrant, milk bread. John ate and drank while the other two looked on. Scarcely anything more was said, for there was nothing more to say.

At last Abrecht took out his time-table from his pocket. "If I drive you to the station you can catch the three-sixteen," the farmer said. John again tried to decline, feeling rather sadly what a mockery it all was. But again the farmer had already left the room to put the horse in.

"I'll come with you, Father," his daughter called after him.

They drove to the station, the farmer smoking, the girl beside him and John on the back seat all by himself like a gentleman. He looked at the farmer's broad back and his daughter's narrower shoulders, wrapped in a shawl, and her hat adorned with yellow flowers, put on in his honour, and perched awkwardly on the top of her head like a plate. They drove through the village and on to the cross roads. They came to the undulating field. But neither father nor daughter looked at that stretch of fallow of theirs and John, who was lost in thought with his chin on his chest, did not notice till long afterwards that they had passed it.

XV

At five o'clock he was back again in his inn and at eight he went his
way through the dusk. He did not notice the coolness of the evening, he
did not notice the passers-by who were off to rest or amuse themselves
after the toils of the day. He walked all the way to give his limbs occupation and even so it was all he could do not to run headlong to his destination.

He had had to put restraint and compulsion on himself day after day; he
had had to damp down the furnace within him in order to arrange everything with composure. But now that he gave the flames their head, now that
they might leap up and destroy, every moment of waiting cramped and
tortured him. His whole body now was nothing but the instrument of
revenge, his eyes were riveted on their mark, and his hands were only
weapons of destruction. His whole being ached with the lust to destroy. So
longs a man on the rack for the end of his torture, so longs the lover for
the arms of one woman alone, so longs the dying man in the glare of the
desert for the water he cannot find. But Abrecht knew where to find it;
the cure of his raging fever was certain and the cure was near at hand.
He broke into a run and reached his destination long before it was prudent.
But the dusk concealed him as he stood motionless at his post and at last
he controlled even his breath and his thumping heart so that he could listen
with all his ears. No one came past. He saw the gloomy prison wall and
the dreary light of the lamp. He felt in his pocket for the strong-handled
knife but as soon as his hand closed on it he knew that he would not need
it. Nothing, not even steel should come between him and his vengeance.

"I shall strangle him," he told himself in a whisper. In the darkness he
clenched his right hand with all the strength that possessed him. "I am
strong enough to split a rock," he went on without knowing whether his
lips had formed the words.

It occurred to him that he was not carrying out his plans after all. He
had left his disguise behind in his room over the market place, a false
beard and a mask of black cloth. But even if he had remembered them he
would not have made use of them. He confronted his fate on the great
day, the day of fulfilment: he would have gone to meet it naked.

In his frenzy he listened backwards into time and that brutal voice spoke
in his ear, straight into his brain. He heard it saying: "I'll teach you to
amuse yourself, you skunk. We'll see about that. Jump to it and clean it
up——" And the sound of crunching.

Then there were footfalls in the lane, hurried and out of step, and in the
light of the lamp Abrecht saw two of the warders on their way back to the
prison, talking as they walked along.

One was the man with the long kindly face; the other he did not know.
They passed, rang the bell, and vanished.

Supposing the man he waited for was not alone. How easily it might happen in spite of all his foresight! It was a possibility, but it would not happen. The tremendous tension of the last hours could never be repeated, could not come and go in vain. The world was not so lavish.

From that moment onwards he stood in complete composure, in the stillness of death, and waited. He was nothing but one iron muscle, taut and ready for the spring.

XVI

He was coming. He heard the step he knew from the dreary days of imprisonment, short, hard and hostile. Yes, there he came and alone. John saw him pass beneath the lamp and now he had only twenty paces to go, now only five. John stood there—nothing but a tool, ready to seize and clench. Now he had him, heaven be praised, at last, at last!

In one leap he was out of his hiding place and both his hands were round his enemy's throat, wrenching him round. The man tried to cry out in his mortal terror, but the sound was throttled in his throat; he fought, tried to get a grip, tried to get in a blow, but the iron hands kept their throttle-hold and held him at arms' length, and his short arms beat the air. His cap fell to the ground and the light of the lamp lit up his short hair, standing up like a brush, and his contorted face.

And John saw him. His whole strength was concentrated in the clench of his hands, but his eye remained clear and his mind kept its sinister composure.

Silence fell. Scarcely a gurgle came from his throat. A squeak like that of a mouse or some tiny animal was all he could get out. His small mouth was open and his tongue quivered in the small opening between his sharp, dirty teeth. But those flat eyes protruded as though at any moment they would be squeezed from his head. John saw all this; he saw the man wilt and he knew that the end and unconsciousness would be the work of a moment and that his strength amply sufficed to bring this end about. But he did not relent. He, with his hands round the throat of the beast, was more than just an individual person taking his revenge.

There was an oppressive calm in John's heart. The impulse, the tremendous and agonizing impulse, the urge for release through an act of revenge was still there; only death, with its last gurgle, its last quiver, could do away with it. It was this frenzied speechless longing that gave his throttling hands their strength. He must press on to the end, he must finish it off, he must kill.

But then John began to speak. Holding the man at arms' length, he spoke into his tortured jowl in a cold, clear and controlled voice and heard his own words as though they were another's.

"I have got you. Do you hear? Do you know who I am? You have got

to die. Do you see what I am doing to you? I am squeezing your life out in
my hands. You will live only a few seconds more and they will be frightful.
But not half frightful enough. For you are a devil, the lowest and filthiest
of God's creatures. A bit of filth, so cruel and horrible that there is no
punishment meet for you. Strangling is not bad enough, nothing is bad
enough for you. You deserve to have every one of your bones broken one
by one. Your hide ought to be cut in strips. Your flesh ought to be plucked
from you with pincers, you torturer, you hangman, you cowardly brute.
What have they, who serve their sentences in there, done to you? What
have I done to you? Do you think, you devil, that there is no justice in the
world? Did you think you could go on doing as you pleased? No, your end
has come. You have done too much evil. You are not a human being, you
are the serpent, you are all that is vile and evil in the world. Your pestilential breath fills the world and there is no breathing as long as you are in it.
But I shall put you out, I shall strangle you. You shall be no more."

He was pulled forward and this told him that the man's knees had given
way. He lay at his feet with his bloated face turned upwards in bestial
despair, his eyes turned up and nearly extinct, his parched mouth open and
his tongue protruding. John was neither shaken nor moved by the sight: his
rage even increased. He tried to tighten the clench of his deadly grip with
all the force of hatred, contempt and suffering that he had gone through.
He bent down and spat out his words against the dying mask and now his
voice was no longer clear, no longer controlled: it was an inhuman voice
that screamed and broke.

"Do you still know me or have you passed out? Open your eyes and look
at me. I am the man you tormented and now I am doing you in. I am the
prisoner in cell 93. Do you remember the birds? Yes, I used to listen to
them singing. That was me and it gave me pleasure and it's me who is
murdering you now. And then you went and covered the grating and as
you could still hear them you went to the Governor and had me moved
to another cell and you pushed me and you insulted me and you shouted at
me and you mocked me and you chucked my food at me and you reviled
me and tortured and tormented me—me, a defenceless man. There, now
die, now gasp and struggle for your last mouthful of air. There, there, do
you feel me? But you shall know exactly what you are dying for. Shall I tell
you? You are dying for a beetle, a little beetle . . . What was I but a poor
miserable wretch? I had nothing in the world. I was next door to going
crazy. Another day or two and I should have gone crazy. And then a joy
came to me, a little joy that rescued me. What was that joy, eh? It was a
beetle, an insect, a thing so small you could scarcely see it. And I loved it
and rejoiced in it. I played with it and spoke to it and taught it to know
me and that poor little thing was my whole world. In my wretchedness,
it was all, everything. And it was that you took from me. It was that you
flung on the ground and trod on with your dirty boot. Can God have made

a man like you? Is he to live? No. He must get out of it. His breath must cease. So give it up now, your last, last gasp. . . ."

And with his iron grip round the dying jailer's throat he hissed in his face in a ghastly imitation of his voice: "What have you got there? Give it up! I'll teach you. There, clean it up."

But suddenly in the midst of the thunderous haze of his vengeance, a great light came to John Abrecht, a light from God. He saw the man beneath him, now weak with his agony, unconscious, sinking fast, move his two arms. He saw those two short arms signalling for help, imploring mercy, moving uncertainly and feebly, two feelers of a dying creature. A sick child moves its arms like that when it wants something or a tiny, unconscious insect its thin legs.

A gentle current streamed through John's hair and body and hands. His grasp loosened, his muscles all relaxed and a cool air of sea and stars blew through his breast. The man at his feet sank speechless to the ground and John stood up and took a deep breath, a quiver between tears and laughter ran over his lank face and he leaned upright against the prison wall.

He stood there with his murderous hands pressed flatly to his chest. It was only for a few moments, which, for all he knew, might have been an instant or an age, and his whole being was released and renewed by a gentle and magical power, by a current of silver in his veins. He was unable to think; later, later on he would be able to think. He resigned himself and was healed and overwhelmed by a happiness beyond words—illumination, release and mercy.

He opened his eyes and bent over a lifeless form lying on its face. He took it carefully by the shoulders and raised it up. The man's breast rose and fell and his features, though his eyes were shut, stirred. John knelt over him, resting his weight on his arm, and watched him as he came back to life in the dreary light of the lamp.

Abrecht held the man's body with hands that forgot what they had done; he saw the man with eyes that had never seen him before. He had a funny little mouth half open, a childish little mouth with small sharp teeth and an underlip that drooped pathetically.

He began cautiously massaging his temples while he supported him with his left arm. And after a few moments he opened his eyes. They were dim and saw nothing as yet and shut again. His breath came in gasping spasms. John went quietly and slowly and methodically on with his task, as though he were alone in the world with his patient, as though no path led back to the ways of mankind. Sometimes he had to stop and draw in his breath to master a sense of bliss that threatened to reduce him to weakness.

Suddenly he noticed that the man was looking at him. He had come back to life and his whole body revived and gained resistance. Abrecht let him go and getting slowly to his feet retreated a step or two. He saw the look of mortal fear in the other man's eyes; he would gladly have reassured and consoled him, but he knew that this could not be and so he left him there with a rueful smile.

The jailer got shakily to his feet. He leant against the wall of the shed with gaping eyes and hands splayed out behind him. Then he staggered on his way, still expecting his assailant to follow him, and slowly made for the prison gate. John too walked away, lost in thought, still incapable of grasping the situation—back into the world.

XVII

But as he went back into the town his thoughts still remained behind and dwelt on his victim with feelings of mercy, and joy that he was alive after all. No anxiety was mingled with his feelings. The man might raise a hue and cry, hunt him down and have him imprisoned; but that fateful night would not end so. Even if it did he would accept it. Nothing could take away what it had given him. He went on his way without fear even though he did not know how ample his protection was.

For the jailer when he reached the little gate in the wall and gained his quarters had no thought of pursuit. He lay down, shivering with fright and cold. His wife gave him some tea and as she grumblingly brought it to him in bed she saw for the first time the piteous expression of his face. She questioned him, rather casually, it is true, for his goings-on interested her very little. But he did not dare tell her what had happened. He still felt that the horror might rise up again and stand before him if he mentioned it; he still felt the iron grip at his throat and hid himself in the bedclothes, pursued even into his bed by anguish and terror.

But in the middle of the night when he woke from sleep with a scream, he told her all about it. His wife was indignant at the assault and insisted that the man should be caught and punished. But he protested with horror and raised his cowardly hands in the flickering candle-light.

"No, no," he screamed. "If they catch him he'll come back and murder me in his cell." And he made his wife swear not to breathe a word of what had happened. She gave him her promise for the sake of peace.

Next day he was sick and unable to get up. He trembled when he saw the branches of the elm stirring in the breeze outside the window. He screamed when the door opened and his wife and the prison doctor came in. And even when after a few days he left his bed and tried to resume his duties he was no longer the same man. He was afraid of the prisoners and scarcely dared to be alone with any one of them; he started when a bunk he had himself let down fell with a clatter into its socket.

It soon became obvious that he was no longer fit to carry out his duties. The authorities, who considered that his conduct as a warder had been exemplary, took the trouble to get a post for him in the war museum. There he wandered round, silent and apprehensive, amidst the symbols of faded glory and the instruments of another kind of brutality. His duties were light and he had more leisure than before, but this was no consolation to him. It was no pleasure to him to get home early to the even more confined quarters he now occupied. His wife, loveless and cantankerous before, was short-tempered and felt bitter resentment against him now that, having lost his only redeeming quality of a semi-military status, he sat moodily and broken-spirited in their wretched dwelling, preventing her by his presence from indulging in those endless hours of gossip with the neighbours which had been her one delight.

She was angry with him also because his collapse forced her to look to every penny. His new post was easier but worse paid, and what he could earn in tips was not worth mentioning. Those who visited the war museum were not the sort of people to be free with their money. They were chiefly school children, herded round by their teachers or else in little troops on their own and up to any mischief; or lower middle-class people and junior officials, chiefly concerned in detecting stains of dried blood and deciphering the heroic emblems on the banners; or soldiers with their servant-girls. If by any chance a prosperous stranger came along and looked with interest at the rubbish-heap of glory and asked a question, he found that the attendant only gave a brief, confused and taciturn reply which showed very clearly that he knew nothing about it. The visitor then went on with a nod, and the wretched man shambled through the cold rooms beneath the bright tatters of standards and flags, among pikes and cannon and all the other moulder-ing instruments of death.

XVIII

When John Abrecht reached the middle of the town he sat down on a bench in the garden of a large cheerful square. It had been a fine, hot day, one of those with which summer takes its leave, and many people were still up and enjoying the cool night air. There were only a few couples strolling along the paths and talking in whispers, but in the streets outside people were sitting in front of the cafés with variously coloured drinks in front of them, talking and laughing. The distance lent beauty to the scene and the sound of a violin accompanied the voices and gave them harmony. The sun blinds of the cafés and the large-leaved exotic plants in the garden gave the square a foreign look and the emerald of the mown grass had an exotic luxuriance, lit up by the unnatural light of the tall arc lamps.

As John sat looking at all this there was peace in his heart; he had come a tremendous distance on his way, he had reached his goal and now enjoyed a brief, delicious rest; the luxury of release after long torture filled his heart and the singing tones of the distant violin and the subdued richness of the turf were one with it. He looked across the expanse of exotic-looking grass and smiled, and a verse came to his mind which he had learnt as a child: "Here Peace herds her white lambs."

He sat and rested. The night wore on; the voices died away one by one, the music ceased without his noticing, the light of some of the tall lamps was extinguished, dark shadows stretched across the emerald grass and a cool breeze stroked the bushes.

What was it I went through tonight, there in that lane, he thought to himself as he got up. What a moment it was! I shall never forget it. It is something that exceeds all thought. Besides, I have never learnt to think. But even if I were learned and wise I could never get to the bottom of it, for it lies beyond all words and beyond all thought.

What was it? I hated him and meant to kill him and then he raised his arms, moved them like this . . . and then I understood it all. Was it because he reminded me of the gilded beetle? Yes, that was it partly. The beetle moved his brown legs like that when we played together and then he crushed him with his boot. But it was not only that. As he raised his arms in that imploring way he looked like a little child in its cot. I too must have done the same at home when I was little. We are all more alike than we think, and where is the dividing line? Who can take his own measure and separate and distinguish himself or say he is this or that and this is good and that is bad? Yes, that, more or less, is what I felt there in the lane suddenly entering into me and gently coursing through my veins. But it was something even better and greater, I believe, only there are no words for it. . . .

That jailer was once a little child and at the moment of death he became a child again and he cannot help all that lies between. Probably he does not know he is evil and cruel. Probably he thinks he does right. And the little beetle that comforted me in my cell, he too is not there only for consolation and beauty; I know quite well he does not live on the flowers one brings him and does not endure captivity in a water-jug with patience. He hunts little beetles and eats caterpillars and tiny snails and defenceless naked worms and who am I to judge and say this is good and that is bad and set myself up as a judge and an avenger? I assaulted a girl in a field on a hot day and today I have nearly committed a murder. I did not commit it, but what held me back? A miracle, the grace of God. Certainly I think that, in spite of lust and murder, I am a little better than that man. Possibly I would not torture a defenceless man, but what authority can I claim, what judgment can I invoke, where is the judge's bench to which one can appeal?

Is there such a court? Who knows in whose ear all voices make a concord? There the good is a high, clear note, the bad a deep and mighty bass. Who knows, who knows? Do we not think sometimes, did I not think, tonight in the lane, that I suddenly heard that harmony? As though a brief burst of music came through a suddenly opened door. Then we know at once how small and narrow and stupid all our thoughts and judgments are.

Yes, I felt tonight that I knew where my path led and could never lose it again. As though the silver current of truth coursed in my blood and would never fail me all my life. But is it so? Do I now know more of the forces that are at work in me, do I know better my place in the great plan?

Do I know his? Why was he made as he was, that man I wanted to kill? Why has he that mouth, that chin and that eye? Who is he? What is his business here? He lives his life knowing nothing of himself, and when he vanishes what does it amount to? It amounts to life, life! Welcome bad and good alike!

A gust blew through the bushes and trees. John took a deep breath.

Yes, that is it. Ugly and beautiful, good, bad, all is welcome! Oh life! I am still young. You spread out before me, a vast and radiant expanse with all your vicissitudes and terrors. I set out on my voyage with the strength of youth still in me and with a new blessing, ready to meet you in your might, you and all your creatures, and call you friend.

THE CATALAN NIGHT

Paul Morand
(1889–   )

TRANSLATED BY VYVYAN HOLLAND

I WAS TO HAVE a lady as a travelling companion. One half of her already graced the compartment in which I sat. The other half, leaning out of the window, still belonged to Lausanne station and to a delegation of men of various nationalities, welded together by the same shadow on the platform, linked by the same wild rose in the buttonhole of each of them. Bells began to ring. Passengers ran about on the asphalt platform. As though at the tacit bidding of the time-table, the signal drooped like a scarlet fruit at the top of its latticed trunk. A whistle blew. The lady shook hands over the lowered window; a freckled British hand; a pulpy German hand; a Russian hand with a parchment-like skin; the slim fingers of a Japanese. And lastly a young Spaniard, with a stock hiding a boil on his neck, stretched out a grimy paw covered with copper rings and said:

"Good-bye, Doña Remedios!"

Then the crowd parted and through the gap a mauve star twinkled, followed by a soft flare and a cloud of smoke through which a film camera immediately began to perform its desperate duties.

The train broke, one by one, from the handshakes that were anchoring it and, having gained its freedom, sped on its way. A shout went up:

"Long live the International!" but it was instantly smothered by the clatter of the turntables and the velvety darkness of a tunnel.

The lady still leaned rashly out of the window, waving her hand. I prevailed upon her to stop by placing a hand on her plump shoulder, and I drew her attention to an enamelled notice on which was written:

IT IS DANGEROUS TO ALLOW CHILDREN TO LEAN OUT OF THE WINDOWS

at which she smiled, turning towards me.

Beautiful, handsome, pretty, intriguing. In that moment Fate made amends for the disappointments of so many other train departures, in which it is the woman with whom one would like to travel who remains on the platform, while the man who was with her sits beside one, without any indication until that moment as to which of the two was going to travel, so equally affected were they by the parting, so equally full of emotion, and wrapped in their dreams.

There was no disillusionment when the train came out of the tunnel. Under cover of a drowsiness with which I pretended to be overcome I began to study my companion's face as though it were a map, so that I should be in no danger of taking the wrong turning. A charming and undulating landscape bounded by shoes and a hat. I always envy those passport officials whose daily task enables them to make a record on their forms of so many human faces, cold, warm, as different from one another as the flower-like imprints of finger-tips.

In this face, with its soft curves, frankly no feature was remarkable; her full lips, her forehead, her high cheekbones which, seen three-quarter face, hid her eyes from one's gaze, cutting one's glance off slantwise in an irresistible way and sending it off in one of those theatrical exits known as "into the wings" which deceive no one but are none the less charming. Her bosom rose in a gentle slope to her rounded neck, encircled by a plain rope of imitation pearls, and shaded by a youthful and determined chin. On her first finger shone a sapphire set in brilliants; her thin silk dress fell in a fold between her short thighs. In the mittened hands spread flat upon her knees, in her feet, so arched that they almost seemed swollen and which did not quite reach the floor, in her hair tightly stretched back to her ears where it was allowed to escape in frothy waves, so oiled that it ceased to be black and reflected every colour of its surroundings, in the bun twisted like a wrung-out cloth and glistening with brilliantine, in all these things one's memory was taken irresistibly back to Spain.

She leaned her head against the railway embroidery on the head-rest and went to sleep quite naturally. Perhaps I had hypnotised her.

As we approached Morges a storm suddenly burst over us. Terrific thunder-claps crashed against the mountain peaks, drowning the rattle of the train. A whimper came from somewhere. My companion woke with a start and absent-mindedly made the sign of the cross. Taken unawares, she wore that look of a bird with ruffled plumage which Southern European women get when travelling. The young ones lose their composure and become wooden, whilst the older ones turn a lead-grey colour and sag beneath the sparkle of their jewels. The sky split like a piece of silk. The lightning struck the railway track with a suddenness that was even more abrupt than a Press photographer's flashlight. I offered to pull down the blind.

"I'm not frightened of the storm, but my dog, who is in her basket, can't bear it."

Then, as though her face had been stripped by the thunder, she opened her bag and reconstructed it behind a cloud of powder. There was a white lock among her black hair, like a jet of steam in a puff of coal smoke. The whimpering started again under the seat and went on until she decided to take a mongrel fox-terrier with fawn-coloured ears out of a gilt basket on which was written "Souvenir of the Rigi." To put her more at her ease I opened my bag and took out a teddy-bear and a red donkey. She complimented me on my menagerie. On my side I showered praises on her dog in a way which is usually only considered correct on suburban railway trains.

"Trick is ugly, Monsieur, but I love her because she is all I have left in the world."

"Nevertheless, the leave-takings which I witnessed at the station a little while ago seemed to me to be extraordinarily warm. Having only been in Lausanne a few hours myself, I know nothing at all of a person worthy of being photographed by flashlight. Perhaps you've been giving a charity performance at the Casino?"

"I am not, Monsieur, altogether an actress," she replied. As she finished the word "actress", lisping it slightly, her tongue appeared for a moment between her closed teeth which were like minute grains of rice. She favoured me with a tired smile. "Even though I have played a part in the most terrible parody of justice of this century. My name is Remedios Sirvent and I was the companion of Esteban Puig, the Catalan champion of liberty, legally assassinated at Barcelona last spring by the police, militarist and clerical reaction."

I had, like everyone else, taken a passing interest in that event, which some considered to be a just punishment and others looked upon as a martyrdom, but which had subsequently been relegated to oblivion. Consequently I was greatly surprised at the description which she gave me of the gathering at Lausanne, at the thought of which—here she beat her breast—she still thrilled.

In order that all restrictions on individual action should cease, and with the object of bringing pressure to bear on the Spanish Government, the International Socialist Bureau had organised a monster demonstration.

The mass meeting, she explained to me, took place in the rain, on the borders of the lake, in close, serried ranks. A seething mass of humanity stretched as far as the balconies of the villas and the hotel terraces; the roofs were packed with sight-seers. Souvenir cards were sold; subscription lists were filled with names; preceded by their silken ensigns the delegates marched past; anarchist contingents from Zurich and Lugano beneath their black banners; Russian social-revolutionaries, Indian nationalists, American Zionists, the General Unions of French and Belgian workers; the officials of the Independent Labour Party and of the Second International sang hymns. All the comrades were there: Rosario, Rakovski, Vandervelde, Luxembourg, Jaurès, Burns, Thomas, Lippovici. A never-to-be-forgotten moment. What mattered it that one no longer possessed a country, when one was received as she had been received, at the threshold of Humanity? She would do her duty now with renewed strength of purpose, pushing aside all obstacles in her path, striving to banish the languor which over-comes one after a great sorrow, and during which one's nature recovers its strength. She wanted to remain bruised, both in her opinions and in her affections, and to work tirelessly to the end that the work to which Puig had devoted his life should be continued and the Cause fostered. He had left her sufficient money for her needs. She belonged to the lower middle classes and was naturally inclined to a life of luxury and ease beneath a tranquil sky. But she could not drift into becoming the charming widow, absorbed in her white rabbits and her vineyards, taking the air in her carriage in her widow's weeds. She felt the need of great international con-flicts, of European upheavals, of rugged climates, of propaganda voyages and lectures, and wanted to compel attention, to win the hearts of the people, to obtain a revision of his shameful trial.

Enthusiasm radiated from her eyes, her lips and the palms of her hands, with something playful and childish which was particularly attractive; sometimes she interpreted her thoughts seriously, announcing its degeneracy to a decadent world; sometimes she started off on a frantic and confused flow of invective without, however, losing any of her charm in the process.

The idea of a new order of Society enraptured her so much that beads of moisture stood out on her forehead. The natural passionate good-nature of the Spaniard gave way before a fervour of despotism which her eloquence alone held in check. But at the back of everything there remained the cold and austere religious sense and the respect for established order which are the nearest kin to prayer. Her marvellous credulity was a great asset, egging her on to romantic sacrilege and above all giving her the strength to be insatiable, which is usually lacking in revolutionaries of the Latin races, who are satisfied with so little.

"*Hombre*," she said, "my life is expressed in four words: service, knowl-edge, faith, love."

She enlarged upon this idea, but, before explaining it, insisted on defining her position in relation to the different political parties in Spain. For my part, I listened with such good will that I fell asleep.

We were approaching the frontier.

The lightning still accompanied us, punctuated by desultory thunder-claps, like an endless argument among the mountain tops. Doña Remedios still nursed her dog which, covering its mistress's knees with its ears, gloomily surveyed her little feet adorned with tastefully designed buckles, shaped like pieces of barbaric jewelry.

The daylight grew fainter and the sky seemed gradually to become charred like a smoking lamp in the rays of the setting sun. Eau de Cologne was shaking monotonously about in its bottles at the bottom of bags with the gurgling sound of subterranean springs; my companion, comfortably ensconced in the corner of that one-night travelling home, pickled in smoke and smelling of hot leather, was reading "Les Samedis de Chiffonnette."

The sound of iron-shod boots on the heating apparatus announced the arrival of the customs officials. Doña Remedios raised her eyes.

"Nothing to declare," she said.

A southern French customs officer, accompanied by a Swiss soldier, on whose cap one noticed with surprise the absence of the word "Lift", pointed to a parcel of some size lying in the rack.

"What have you got in that basket?" he asked.

With a mixture of irritation and embarrassment my companion rose and lifted down a thick bunch of palm-leaves tied in a sheaf with a red silk ribbon. She opened it and I saw in the midst of the foliage a plaster gentle-man with empty eye-sockets who looked like President Carnot.

"There!" she said, proudly. "That is a bust of Estebán Puig which was presented to me this afternoon by the B.I.L. [Bureau Internationale de Lausanne]. Must one pay duty on one's memory of the dead on entering France?"

And she wiped away a tear with a lace handkerchief the size of a postage-stamp.

.   .

Samuel Pacifico, professor of history at the Louis-le-Grand college, was at home to his friends every Sunday in his sixth-floor attic in the Rue Saint-Jacques. Since leaving school we had always kept up the custom of visiting our old master. The author of "The History of the Working-Classes" was a timid, shaggy dwarf whose face was a network of blue veins, who smelled of the Saint-Paul quarter, made his own shoes and cut his own hair with a machine of his own invention. He used to walk down the Boulevard Saint-Michel, hugging the wall, talking to himself and scrutinis-ing everyone with his grey and black eyes which reminded one of a photographic plate in a yellow developer. He had preserved for us that

affection which had formerly deprived our lessons of much of their tedious-
ness, and which later we had fostered and returned, no subsequent experience having ever again brought the good luck which was ours from
childhood, namely that of finding a man who did not mind corrupting the
youth of a generation which was no longer worthy of corruption. His intelligence, which was profound enough to have overthrown a nation, was
entirely at the service of Science. He imposed a discipline and austere
habits on himself which he did not even wish us to adopt, holding himself,
as it were, responsible for our happiness. The Jesuits, against their inclination, took us, their boarders, to Pacifico's classes, disapproving all the time
of his diabolic humour; later, at the Political Science lectures, Monsieur
Laguillère-Desveaux would interrupt his polished and colourless discourse
in order to put us on our guard against "the anti-liberal licentiousness with
which nowadays people proceed to the study of Social Science."

Pacifico never went out to dinner, never set foot in a drawing-room and
never crossed the Seine except to go to the Rue de la Paix to buy rings, of
which he had a collection which drove women to distraction. But that was
the only Eastern taste he possessed. He commanded respect as having
played his part in the pomps (and also in some of the shady intrigues) of
the Third Republic, an active part which will never be accredited to him by
history, exerting his influence on behalf of his friends, avenging them,
bringing to bear a subtle pressure which ministerial offices rarely resisted
for more than a few hours, seeking no personal advancement and having
for recreation nothing but his weekly receptions.

It would have been useless to try to open one of Bayle's folios in
the room in the Rue Saint-Jacques on Sunday evenings towards six o'clock;
there would have been no room. In an atmosphere of tobacco and sealing-
wax, one found university students in dinner-jackets and ready-made ties,
examination coaches with their acid-stained fingers, an unfrocked priest, a
painted female lawyer or two, a few members of the communist colonies of
Draveil who stole the teaspoons, and an actress from the Théâtre-Français
converted to modern art, who had refused the Legion of Honour and talked
of acting only for the lower classes.

Nevertheless, I was amazed to see my travelling companion of the previous
week walk into the circular study, picking her way between the books and
manuscripts. I wondered why it had not struck me before that I should
meet her here. For was not this room—as unpretending as a railway turn-
table on a branch line, the abode of a scholar and recluse, unknown to Paris
as is indeed everything else—was it not famous abroad? On crossing the
frontier, on the threshold of France, the first enquiry is for a hotel and for
this address. Wells, Unamuno, Gorki, Wedekind (Shaw simply put, "G.B.S.
Irishman") have signed their names in the master's visitors' book. The
leaders of Europe have come here to pick up hints about the governing of
their countries. It was natural that Doña Remedios, in her turn, should

continue her work close to the man who could drown his burning thoughts in wisdom in the same way that, after a war, explosives are relegated to the bottom of the sea. There she sat, draped in a graduate's gown lined with white satin, gazing around her, accompanying her replies with little grimaces and mechanically turning over the pages of Jaurès's "Social History of the French Revolution" as though it were a warrant for her presence there.

"We are old friends," she said, when Pacifico introduced me. "A storm brought us together."

She reminded me of the station, the thunder and the whining of her dog Trick.

"That journey," I said, "seems almost mythical to me now, and Switzerland has assumed a dignity which has not really been hers for a hundred years. The loyalty of atmosphere, the eloquence of the mountain torrents, the red elegy of your widowhood and that precious train of ours with its two engines, which bore us through such forests of symbols and of pines [Remedios never flinched], these I shall treasure in my mind for ever."

How satisfying she looked, braving in Paris the creations of the best dress-maker of the Paralelo—an unrelieved black—a pretentious hat with a feather in it, a silver-fox fur, a little colour in her cheeks and a little blood on her hands, brooding on vengeance through those autumn days during which, at the call of the chrysanthemums, one passes so imperceptibly into the winter.

Pacifico begged her to write something in his visitors' book.

"Will a quotation do?"

When she had put on her spectacles and taken up the pen, I suggested: "Why not a thought of your own?"

She laughed and held the book out:

"It's a quotation from our Moratín."

We read:

Being young and thoughtless she was therefore a charming woman.

Remedios.

My confusion made her laugh and she observed that it would be a lesson to me not to make fun of her in the future.

"In the first place," I said, "I met you in Helvetia, where one is allowed to think, and, besides, I can assure you that in Paris general ideas are no longer possible; every thought must be expressed in anecdote."

The master took up the cudgels for Remedios and denounced me as having a purely literary turn of mind. We passed the time in this way until dinner to which we were asked to stay: for these gatherings added to their other attractions that of being far from unfriendly to laughter, particularly when the Collège de France made way for the younger generation which, Pacifico declared, "prolonged his life." The food was good and the wine carefully chosen, our host having entrusted the care of his establishment to a housekeeper who had at one time made the Bishop's palace at Toulouse the best pot-house in south-west France.

A few of us remained that evening under the vanilla-tinted light of the gothic bronze chandelier, surrounded by the illusive pastures of the tapestries on which, facing each other, were hung portraits of Renan and Berthelot, who continued their conversation above the fumes of turkey and cabbage. Remedios's prominent bust presided over this family dinner.

Pacifico held a glass of sherry to the light and then presented it to Remedios, saying:

"To the health and to the glory of Puig."

"I thank you and I believe that you mean it. In rushing headlong to his death, Esteban did nothing more than to answer the call of the oppressed with the heart of a hero."

"And now darkness is spreading over Spain once more," added Pacifico.

"So it will always be, *hombre,* each time anyone tries to awaken to class-consciousness a proletariat which has stagnated for centuries in monastic ignorance and in barbarism," declared Remedios with her thick Spanish accent. "Esteban realised the futility of violence after the attempt of 1905, and he explained to me that the problem would have to be approached from a greater distance. 'We are working for thirty, for fifty years hence,' he said. But as soon as he revealed his plans they made away with him."

One of the guests, a professor of semasiology, asked her to explain.

Full of her subject, Remedios considered us with the challenging air of a great pianist who is about to attack the *Symphonic Variations*. But she must have seen the look I gave her, devoid of all interest and enthusiasm, for she cut out the peroration and, in a rapid voice, laid down her conclusions.

"There's nothing to say that you don't already know," she said. "To the traveller, Spain is just like any other country, with lottery tickets, watering places, life insurance, members of parliament who kiss each other on the mouth after debates and lifts whose floors light up as soon as one sets foot in them. A picturesque cesspool. Barcelona is cast in a South American mould and there the sleeping cars break into flower at the end of their stalks in hotels which are blossoms of mahogany and blue velvet. One goes through the streets on metal wires, one paints as at Schwabing, one only applauds bull-fighters when they return from Buenos Aires and one constructs buildings with enamelled bricks in which one can drive a motor car up to the fifth floor. Then suddenly, round a bend in the road, appears the Blessed Sacrament, that obsolete coinage which still circulates among us; the people fall on their knees (they are fined if they don't) and one sees officials in blue silk belts carrying candles, followed by officers in cassocks and field-boots. The over-loaded tramcars stop, surrounded by yoked oxen and Hispano-Suiza cars, to make room for those people with the heads of Inquisitors, these mitred vultures, these mean old peasant faces issuing from priceless lace, the lackeys of a God who abandons the poor in order to fawn upon the rich. Or else, if the traveller doesn't read the papers and therefore doesn't know that a strike is imminent, he is surprised one morning, on waking, to see from the windows of his hotel the civil guard with their yellow bandoliers lying in ambush at the corners of the streets, waiting for the trades union worker to show himself. The town, haughty yesterday beneath its diadem of electric light, and distributing alms to the rest of Spain, is thenceforth as empty as the Sepulchre on the third day. The civil population is driven to work before the muzzles of the mercenaries' rifles. Constitutional guarantees are suspended and a police of hired assassins carries out a systematic search in those suburbs of ours smelling of charred bones, essence of cesspool and resin. Everything now proceeds according to an abominable, preconceived plan. The civil authority resigns and martial law is declared; following a telegram which is said to come from Madrid but which in actual fact the governor always keeps in his safe, the government passes into the hands of the most backward beings that exist on the face of the earth, only equalled, perhaps, by some of the Russian governors in the Caucasian provinces. The artillery takes up its position in the public squares, machine-guns are placed on the monuments. The troops shoot without orders. People are arrested in their homes, searches are carried out at all hours of the day and night, trials take place without counsel or witnesses, affidavits read out being a parody of justice. Then one day at dawn, in the fortress moat, they kill. It's all over: Truth covers her face for another fifty years."

She took a cigar, lit it and blew a long cloud of smoke beneath the chandelier. Then she hummed a tune they play in Spain to herald the entry of the bull.

"Don't let my excitement worry you. Actually these memories are a consolation to me. In Paris people work well, but they forget too soon. There is no time here to think of death, which is an ordinary Spanish amusement. One ought to think of it; it helps to keep things in their proper perspective. Either the present order of Society must change or I must leave my bones on it. I don't want to die until the great fictions of life, Religion, Authority, Family, which with us still retain all their evil influence, have had their emptiness exposed, nor do I want to die without having helped my brothers and sisters to rid themselves of the burden of 'pobreness,' and of the yoke of the capitalist and of the 'padrón.' Of all those who exploit the poor, the Catalans are the most bitter, the most cruel and the most unjust. Oh, how wonderful it would be to exterminate them all!"

And she banged her fist on the table, not with her thumb inside her fingers, as women generally do, but placed correctly over the fingers like a lid. Her breasts and the glasses shook.

Suddenly her mood changed to one of gaiety and she pushed her chair away from the table and addressed herself to Pacifico:

"Thank you, foster-father, for my good dinner."

"My little red child, this is your home, as they say in your country."

"For a moment," she said, "we swerve from our purpose and neglect our duty. That is the whole treacherous cunning of Paris. But to-morrow we resume our labours until the moment comes for the prison gates to fly open and for the whole fabric of prolific and radiant Spain to crumble to the ground."

She was exquisite in this mood, in her ardour and her strength; in her moments of repose she seemed detached, affected, out of touch with things and rather ridiculous. To think in capitals and to fly to extremes suited her, even though after being swept away by her one had, as a sort of self-punishment, a distinct tendency to look upon her as a character in a Spanish tragi-comedy. Looking at her under the chandelier, wasting herself in extravagant phrases, a well-built woman with a firm, calm body and the sturdy limbs of a well-fed shopkeeper's wife, one hesitated or indeed refused altogether to share her enthusiasm. But she had less charm when she became once more a nice, simple, naturally fresh young woman. She reminded me alternately of an eagle and a hen. In any case, she was a graceful figure, not particularly gifted and with nothing of the *femme fatale* about her. Affliction had left no mark of bitterness on her soft childish nose or on her full lips; no wrinkles furrowed her low forehead or the eyelids stretched over her wide eyes filled with perpetual but harmless fire.

I went on studying her. She had dispensed with all creeds and had freed herself from human ties and divine pledges; one expected that of her. But when all was said, what one felt most about this rebel girl was her sense of well-being, the integrity of her ideas, her catholic ancestry, mixed with that middle-class Spanish attitude of grateful respect towards the male which is a legacy from the Moors. As we sat round her we were all conscious of these things, but we were all inclined to want to put her beliefs to the test, watching for any sign of weakening, believing that hers was more a sentimental escapade into the world of anarchism than a true vocation.

"Remedios," said one of the guests, as we left the table, "is an idyl of a thoroughly domestic kind. She is a mermaid in the sea of Marxism."

"It would be interesting to see into her future," said Pacifico, who had leanings towards occultism.

Everyone had something to say:

"I think her end will come in days of violence, full of bloodshed in spite of her."

"She will marry a bull-fighter who has retired on his wounds and will keep a hotel in Algeciras."

"She will give lectures in the Argentine or go on the films."

"Has she any literary talent?"

"No, I believe she's quite a good girl."

From this point onwards all seriousness ceased. A friend of Pacifico's childhood, an old gentleman with rouged cheeks who played chess and repaired old lace, offered to tell our fortunes by cards. But we preferred the game which consists in giving each person a list of qualities or defects against which he has to give himself marks ranging from 0 to 20. We were soon pencilling away on our knees. The old gentleman established himself at the piano and played the overture to *Les Indes galantes*. The autumn wind blew white ash from the fire all over the carpet.

Remedios moistened her pencil with a look of perplexity and asked the difference between sensuality and temperament, maintaining that in Spanish there was only one word for both and that she, for her part, saw no difference between them. Pacifico, in his precise way, got the uncompromising idea of "goodness" changed to "niceness." Someone else pointed out that we had forgotten "snobbishness." Some of them cheated, others, seized with remorse, scratched out their marks, or, after a brief examination of conscience, increased them. Remedios proceeded hesitatingly, indiarubber in hand, full of concentrated sincerity. I asked if one could give oneself more than 20 marks for anything.

There was no sound but that made by the housekeeper clearing the table, the creaking of the furniture and the regular ticking of the clock. When the lists were complete, Pacifico called out each quality or defect and each person in turn, either boldly or sheepishly, called out the number of marks he had given himself for it.

"Man, know thyself," said Pacifico. And so we did, extraordinarily well. The younger ones were, I must admit, sometimes rather wide of the mark, but for those who had reached a certain age there were clearly no illusions left.

We then went on to the second part of the game, which consisted in taking one's neighbour's list and substituting for his marks the marks which we thought he really deserved.

"But you know nothing at all about me," exclaimed Remedios, as I took possession of her moral inventory.

I answered that I could always guess and that in any case I had drunk out of her glass in the dining-car when she was not looking.

Many days have passed since that happy Sunday. But I still possess Remedios's list, carefully drawn up by her and corrected by me. I give here, for what it is worth, this precious document which, beneath its dry figures, seems to me now to be full of admissions:

REMEDIOS

Qualities or defects.	Marks given by her.	Marks as amended by me.
Beauty	18	14
Charm	9	17
Elegance	20	8

Qualities or defects.	Marks given by her.	Marks as amended by me.
Intelligence	2	7
Genius	3	?
Sensitiveness	8	19
Business sense	1	18
Sensuality	0	19
Temperament	2	15
Modesty	20	10
Political sense	19	3
Judgment	8	4
Wit	10	10
Religious feeling	0	20
Snobbishness	7	17
Luck	0	19
Sense of humour	1	18
Will power	16	5
Selfishness	19	4
Greed	18	18

"If you like, Remedios, we could dine together one evening, without dressing, and go to a cinema."

"I should love to. I hate being alone. I hear mysterious knockings on my shutters every evening and the ghost of a nun appears from the back of my wardrobe every time I open it to get out my nightgown."

"And I'm afraid of dying when I sleep alone."

"Who wrote that?"

"Mallarmé, but it should have been Baudelaire."

"Come and fetch me on Tuesday at seven o'clock at the Hôtel du Mexique in the Rue Servandoni."

I had to wait for Remedios in the palm-filled hall, seated in a blue cane armchair, until the hands of the cuckoo clock pointed to a quarter to nine. Dinner, which was served on linoleum table-cloths with a Persian design, had been cleared away for two hours. The ecclesiastic contingent of the establishment had fondled the cat and read the advertisements in *La Croix* and the games of piquet were coming to an end. People were beginning to go to bed. At last Remedios came down, glistening with diamonds beneath a cloak of black Liberty silk, through which one caught a glimpse of full evening dress, with the key of her room and her candlestick in her hand. An elaborately cut tortoise-shell comb a foot high towered above her and knocked against the top of the carriage. At the sight of these things I changed my mind about taking her to a café and ran my mind along the Grands Boulevards to try to think of a restaurant in which a cloak like this would be admitted.

In spite of all my precautions, our entry did not pass altogether un-noticed.

"Please get it firmly into your mind that I want nothing but vegetables and a glass of water."

"Remedios, wonderful woman of a wonderful evening, do be serious. Do you like it dry or sweet?"

Between the salt cellar and the pepper-mill she deposited her white gloves twisted together, a velvet bag on which the following motto was worked in diamonds:

REMEDIOS
SIN DIOS

and a fan made of green feathers.

"I'll have some oysters," she declared resignedly, "if you will ask them to do one up in paper for me to take home to my Chinese gold fish. I should also like the outside slice of the saddle for Trick. You are dining with a woman who was rich this morning and who is penniless to-night. I think I told you in the train—in that spontaneous impulse to talk of oneself which is evoked by sympathy—that by his will Estebán Puig had left me sufficient for my needs. Actually he left me two houses let on lease at Biarritz. In point of fact, rumour attributed a much larger fortune to me. This gave me a great deal of pain. Buying *El Debate,* the organ of the Jesuits, at a kiosk in the Boulevard Saint-Michel this morning, I realised how much use our enemies were making of this. So I went straight to my lawyer and made him draw up a formal deed of renunciation which I signed there and then and which will be published in to-morrow's *Humanité.* The whole of Puig's gift will pass to his Socialist Institute. Which explains why I am penniless this evening."

She laughed and stirred her wine with a fork.

"No, there is nothing praiseworthy about this renunciation. It was wrong of me ever to have accepted it. I can never lose the real gifts I received from Puig. He found me, chose me and raised me to his level when I was nothing but a pupil teacher in a suburban school. He made me read, think; until the very day of his death his one desire for me was to make me a com-panion worthy of him. He was twenty years my senior, tall, with a head like a boulder and the eyes of a basilisk, but the lower part of his face and his hands were calm and full of wisdom. That is how he struck me when he came to my home one evening to ask me if I would take night-school for working-class children. His voice shook and seemed to issue from some secret hiding-place. He told me that he needed me. His face was as white as an altar cloth. I followed him."

The dress she was wearing fitted her closely and was cut low, her bosom swelling above it like an overflowing cup.

"Where did you get your dress?"

"At Worth's," she said, "they called it 'Eastern Night.' It can't be helped.
. . . In future I shall copy the dresses in the woman's supplement of the
Vanguardia."

She went on speaking:

"Just think. Puig was the soul of the Socialist Institute. It was created by
him in 19— on an entirely new basis of teaching, at any rate in Spain, and
there (you can imagine how revolutionary it was) he gave a mixed education both in the social and in the sexual sense of the word. In addition he
insisted on moral and material cleanliness, teaching truth without either
rewards or punishments, and knowledge without religion, making a fair
distribution of mental and manual labour. In a word, the system consisted
of the admirable scholastic enactments of your Convention, the ideas of
Lavoisier put into practice, to quote Puig, as they have never been in
France. Reclus and Kropotkin helped. I've got a wonderful correspondence
with them in one of my hat boxes. But to create all this was to wage the
battle of light against darkness and this cannot be done with impunity.
Puig was crushed. In my country one must not take the children away from
the priests, who want to make a saint of everyone."

She stopped talking, absorbed in her pocket mirror.

"How dark my complexion is! I wonder why?"

"A woman's complexion, Remedios, is her conscience."

"I am upsetting myself too much. Please forgive me, but I must keep on
reminding myself of these things. Even though the head-waiter is listening
to us with such horror, you must hear the exordium of Puig's funeral oration as it was delivered over his grave by Portet. It went like this: 'The
reputed son of one of those innumerable gods created by man is condemned
to death because he wished to be proclaimed king. He is about to die. Born,
as are all gods, of ignorance and fear, he falters when face to face with
death, loses confidence and cries tremulously: "Father, why hast thou forsaken me?" On the other hand, look at Puig, the son of free thought and
of morality without sanctions; he also is about to die. Does he flinch? Does
he lose his freedom of thought? No! He stands proudly erect to the end,
crying as he falls: "Long live the International!" '"

Remedios' eyes are black or grey or blue. How can one tell? All eyes are
of all colours. My feeling of happiness suddenly dissolves. With hands as
clumsy as wooden splints I take her hand. On her wrist she is wearing a
bracelet of graduated sapphires. I feel I want to leave the place, but everything seems to have taken root. It is all a dream. My heart aches as though
someone were extracting teeth from it.

"Remedios!"

"*Por favor?*"

"As a favour, let me love you."

I had not chosen my moment well, but the night before I had decided to make this declaration to her. She attracted me immeasurably, and her attraction seemed to increase daily.

"You would be making a great mistake if you did," she replied, shrugging her shoulders in little quick movements which had the effect of entirely obliterating her already short neck.

"It is principally to avoid it that I say it, dear remedy."

This talk of love gave the coffee back its taste and restored that equipoise which procures for us the sympathy of tradesmen and the collaboration of Fate.

"The fact is that when I am not violent and weak and overcome by the withering emotion of love, as I am this evening, my wickedness, Remedios, knows no bounds."

"Yes, I've noticed that," she replied, "and to be quite frank, for my part, I am quite certain that I shall never love anyone again. That side of my life is finished. Physical love is nothing but a magnificent debauch which time can, if necessary, replace. But when the bonds that bind two hearts are once broken, it is different."

She quoted some grossly sentimental Andalusian proverb which I have forgotten and which suddenly diminished her beauty.

After a moment's silence she went on:

"I'm going to make my living by giving Spanish lessons."

"May I be one of your pupils?"

"My first and my favourite one."

The revolving door of the restaurant turned its pink silk paddle-boards in the concave water of its glass sides. The tables were emptying. Women were going downstairs in their brightly lined cloaks like statues in coloured alcoves; men were looking excitedly for their companions or their hats.

Remedios exuded a fragrance in the close room like warmed wine. The last diners also exuded an atmosphere of delightful well-being. The wine-waiter became god-like. A lady who was drinking with one finger in the air remarked as she finished:

"Yes, it's very good, it leaves a slight taste in the mouth."

The radiators were cooling with a sound of cracking joints.

Remedios pushed aside her plate and her glass, took her lip-salve from her bag and drew a *jota* on the table cloth.

"First steps. The alphabet is A B C D E F G H I *J* . . . and that's the *jota*. No, it isn't a dance, it's the first difficulty that besets you when you cross the Pyrenees."

For a moment I tried to pronounce it.

"Your progress surprises me," said Remedios, flatteringly. "Now let's choose a phrase in which the r's and j's are well distributed,

"El pajarito de la caja roja."

"What does that purring sound mean, Remedios?"

"It means: 'The little bird in the red cage.' "

"But, Remedios, that's you!"

It was late. We rose. The restaurant was empty. I loved her for life. While she went to the cloak-room I returned to our little table and furtively licked her spoon.

I had patiently accustomed my tongue to rolling r's on my teeth from which I threw them back with a sudden movement on to the glottis in the pronunciation of a not too imperfect *jota*. On my way to the Rue Servandoni I set myself the task of repeating a hundred times the phrase which Remedios had taught me two days before.

At the hotel I found a note waiting for me. Remedios had left France the day before by the Barcelona express. The red cage was empty. All that was left was this revolting hall decorated with lizard skins, with coloured glass and with the cat which was devouring a sort of brain pudding out of an imitation Rouen plate. The autumn day was dying peacefully away under the canopy of an orange-coloured storm, and was being momentarily prolonged by the coat which painters, singing at their work, were putting on the house-fronts.

Crushed beneath the habits of two long days and suddenly crystallised into a fidelity that was new to me, I stood in the Luxembourg like a monolith. I had keyed myself up to meet Remedios again, to beset her with childish excitements as one does to stop hiccoughs, to put a thousand questions of grammar to her, to create quaint fancies for her, without ever revealing to her my purpose, which was to keep her thoughts on myself, to persuade her that all the refinements of Paris, the atmosphere of the Seine, the genius of the Saint-Michel fountain from which the water overflows like a bath in which one has fallen asleep with the tap on, the statement of the programme girl offering you a programme: "It cost *me* a franc," the charm of private rooms in restaurants, the broad outlook of the big Stores where the remnants unroll in little waves beneath the arc lamps of the central hall like dazzling orchids, were all nothing but different forms of love, a love in which the cafés also played their part when the hour of a quarter to eight brought its delicious relaxation with it.

By this unpremeditated departure I saw her, on the contrary, freed, in more peaceful possession of herself even than before, and gone from me for ever. It was still daylight and the only stars were those of the trams, when I began to realise how complete was my subjection and how sudden an end had been put to my happiness, and that this state of affairs continued even after sunset. Why this sudden departure, leaving no trace? Was not Spain barred to her? Or had she perhaps concealed the truth from me and set out for Italy and a mad round of excitements, or for America from a desire either for self-effacement or for notoriety?

It was indeed towards Spain that she had gone, for on the following day I received a postcard from the frontier. On it were depicted the docks of Port-Vendres with a row of large casks and a view of the town-hall above which rose a fort. On the back of the card were these words: "The decree of Fate," the proud Spanish brevity of which was spoilt by the fact that the handwriting was that of a servant girl and by the ending: *A greeting from Port-Vendres*. I hoped that Remedios had been unable to cross the frontier. But a few days later Pacifico told me that she had reached Barcelona.

Paris was flooded by an enervating November rain in which houses were reflected right up to the roof in the asphalt. The spray round the street lamps turned into a sort of pink dust. Along the soaking pavements the stunted trees bore the full brunt of the wind. At night-time a rush of waters beneath the roads came from the sewer outfalls. The need I felt for Remedios did not cease, nor did it even diminish. Our first meetings seemed now to have been specially arranged by destiny to ensure that at any rate our two lives should not remain apart for ever. I went over in my mind all the circumstances of our acquaintance. In the beginning I had loved her voice, coarsened by public meetings, her short hands, shorter still in their mittens, her murderer's thumb, her adventures in which lethargy always seemed to play a part, her escapade into anarchy; then I had come to love the narrow limits of her ideas, the chronicle of her sufferings, her goodness and also the perpetual amusement afforded by her love of pleasure, her natural sense of duty and the rebelliousness which made her swerve continually from the path of her destiny. I conjured her up again, irresponsible, romantic and always smiling. Was it possible that our meeting was merely one of those incidents which, judging from their results, Remedios accused of uniting against her peace of mind, declaring them at the same time to be inevitable? Everything began to hold evil omens; the shape of the clouds and of coffee-grounds began to be unfavourable. The loneliness of the evenings, and even of the mornings which were too brilliant for me to submit to Fate and to live sensibly, urged me to follow her. The newspapers announced grave reactionary measures in Catalonia. I could not bear the thought that, all because of me, Remedios was perhaps hurtling headlong towards disaster, and I in my turn took the evening express.

I was in a circus with an arena of sand, an unbroken beach in which the forces of sunlight and shadow held equal sway. Above was a circus of blue sky across which the fierce sun moved without encountering the outspread cape of a single cloud. A dense crowd was suspended midway between these two empty circuses, like a frame of dark wood dividing two mirrors which reflect each other. The countless pale smudges of the closely packed faces quivered in the heat-haze which made individual sounds vibrate and unite into a single harmony. Could one of these smudges, one of these sounds, be

Remedios? It was the Fiesta de la Prensa and on the glaring posters we were promised eight Sottomayor bulls. In the space of an hour the town had emptied itself into this Moorish basin. I carefully scanned the tiers, stripping them like a corn-cob. I rid the circus of everything that was not a brilliant, eloquent mouth, a shapely body moulding a silk dress and two eyes as open as a book. Were you there, Remedios, you precious thing, you indispensable object? Perhaps, but not recognisable, because you were no longer that preposterous and provoking figure, that tongue of flame which one would have picked out instantly from a grey Parisian crowd; here you were merely one of these thousand glimmering lights, one of these bodies satiated with siestas, bloated with sweetmeats, dominated by religion and superstition, a Spanish woman.

One saw the civil guard in their top boots, the military band in their canvas shoes. In his box the president was holding forth to some women who looked like fondants. He cast his gestures to the crowd like handfuls of coppers. Piercing whistles rose up and gradually died down again. Then the president rose. So violently did he wave his handkerchief that it started the brazen notes of a trumpet into life. The trumpet in turn set in motion the gate of the toril, revealing a dark passage at the end of which was a glimmer of blue sky.

The bull came out into the light. Bewildered, he stopped at the edge of the shaded portion of the arena. His coat was dirty, his flanks were mottled. His horns were covered with plaster from the walls. He was alone, the single point on which the two halves of the ring were strained like bows. He was attracted by a horse kicking against the barrier. He trotted towards it. It was a decrepit old grey screw. Its stomach was patched like a poor man's coat and its legs tottered beneath the weight of the upholstered picador flourishing his lance. The bull halted for a moment and bellowed; then, attracted by the dull gleam of the steel that menaced him, he charged, his muzzle close to the ground. The lance entered between his shoulders, bent like a rapier and broke. A thrust from his hindquarters and his horns penetrated the horse's stomach with a squelching sound. The horse appeared to jump; it remained suspended in the air, its legs apart, while the bull, blinded with blood, gored its stomach. Then the horse crashed down like an old wall, smothering its rider, hampered by his horsehair armour. The picador's head emerged from a jumble of harness and entrails. His hat with its gaudy rosettes had fallen off, revealing a fat face like that of a terrified monk, glistening with sweat. The horse scrambled up and staggered off, shedding its bowels round the arena. Other horses were lying beside the barrier; the absence of saddles accentuated the prominence of their bones. Their yellow teeth were bared.

Remedios? Not one of those fans was cooling that beloved neck into which, in Paris, her veil used to dig so deep a furrow. No eyebrow was plastered down as much as hers, which she used to smooth with a little brush meant for glazing pastry. None of the women round me possessed that husky voice which enthralled me so. Remedios was not here. Remedios couldn't bear the sight of blood.

The bull now became the sport of men dressed in silver, arranged in a row like chessmen. One after the other they spread their wings, set flight and settled before the crimson horns. One swathed his hips in his cape, his foolish pink stockings emerging from below the skirt thus formed. Another held up a bright cape spotted with dried blood stains. He dragged this cape along the ground like a net and then spread it out like a curtain. The curtain parted and behold! A man had flashed across the sun, leaving in the bull two pairs of banderillas decorated with tin foil, like silver flowers from the roots of which the blood bubbled, already turning black.

The bull was getting slow. He was now the property of the man dressed in gold. From the crowd there gradually rose a low rumbling growl which the first clever pass would break into a thousand separate sounds. The killer was a small man. His hair was like the patent leather of his pumps. The bull rent the red cloth and the man's silk sleeves. He grew weary, his head drooped lower and lower towards the earth on which he slowly slobbered. The man retired three paces, wiped the sweat from his blue and yellow face and threw off his hat with a theatrical toss of the head; he was bald. He rose up on tiptoe like a tenor. A sudden momentary effort and a backward leap; he waited, hands on hips; a smile wrinkled his thin cheeks. He signed to the crowd to keep quiet for a moment. The bull receded obliquely, his muzzle in the sand; his legs bent; he fell on his knees. His feet stiffened and his head fell backwards.

The president awarded the ear.

Nothing remained in the empty arena but a trampled place with a jumble of footprints and hoof-marks round a dark stain.

Was it the aniseed-scented afternoon, my lack of love, or this harrowing butchery that made me feel so **sick**?

My search lasted two days. In the end I got Remedios's telephone number from the Socialist Institute. Her voice! She made an appointment to meet me at seven o'clock next morning on the outskirts of the town.

I tried to sleep, without success. My window looked out over a flat boulevard bedecked with palm trees. Children played there until two in the morning, digging with their spades in the electrically lit sand beneath the street lamps, enjoying themselves in the middle of the night of which other European children only know the borders. Electric signs flickered. A soap advertisement traced its crimson path across a house-front and went out, only to reappear an instant later to greet one in blue and then in green, just as theatrical stars take each call before the curtain wearing a different shawl. Above this domestic conflagration the fortress of Montjuich pursued its relentless vigil from the top of its rock, swept four times every minute by the lighthouse.

When three o'clock struck, the square was empty. The trente et quarante rooms still glowed on the first floors of the houses. Some of the players came out on the balconies while the cards were being shuffled and leaned their elbows on the plush-covered rails. In the streets below the cabmen were also playing cards in their carriages. With the first signs of dawn above the horizon, even the hairdressers, in whose shops the customers had been suffering a kind of cosmetic trepanning, covered up their hot water apparatus, and the town entered on a brief period of rest.

A little later a taxi came to take me to the Parque de Vich where Remedios had asked me to meet her. In the Plaza de Colón the confraternity of beggars was sleeping, each member stretched out on two iron chairs. There were about a hundred of them, their faces black, their feet wrapped in evening papers, under the pachydermatous palm trees, scratching themselves even in their dreams. Amongst them a gentleman in a dinner jacket, with a flower in his buttonhole, having decided against going home, was snoring with his mouth open.

The carriage passed through the Argüelles district, the quarter inhabited by rich cotton-brokers. To tell the truth I was not sure that I was yet awake. It was an endless series of villas twisted like marshmallow stalks, lit by windows which resembled chain-armour, railed off by metallic seaweed and zinc creepers painted green or pale pink. Under corrugated iron roofs sagged indiarubber houses, pierced by gaping doors through which the road seemed to continue, rising in a gentle slope to the roofs. At their sides the porters' lodges bulged like tumours, and chimneys rose like vines swollen with varicocele at the tops of walls where rabbit-fishes were fighting in thickets of wrought-iron irises. Then, the imagination of the architects having apparently come to an end, the avenues no longer existed except in their name plates, hidden amongst the featureless country. Here and there between the market gardens a private house still thrust up its silhouette of a mounted gun, with its burnt almond stucco, bristling with burr-stones, looking like unappetising praliné cakes. At last the carriage came to a halt before a tiled terrace decorated with china fruits on the top of twelve staggering cromlechs. This platform must also have served as a roof, for pierced japanned pipes, reminding one of pepper pots, sprouted from it like trees. I dived into the path which wriggled like a severed worm and I reached, in spirals, the chequered summer house where Remedios was waiting for me, smiling among the aloes. She looked as though she had nothing on beneath her lilac dust coat from Valentin's, the rubber king. The sky was reflected in her oiled hair. She turned her great eyes to me and pursing up her lips in that barren kiss which is called a pout, she said:

"Well, *simpático*, are you satisfied?"

"It's like a dream, I adore you so."

She patted my shoulder and then my back with her hand, showing her delight at seeing me in the Spanish fashion, in one of those embraces which one still sees in classic comedy at the Théâtre Français.

"How can I ever tell you," she said, "the sacrifice I am making in giving up my resistance? You have come at a terrible moment, when I ought to see no one, but providence . . . This is the Parque de Vich, given to the town by a Catalan who made his fortune in Chili. A mixture of Bagatelle and Luna Park. You must admit that it is idyllic with its banks, its powdered glass designs; in the evening a steam orchestra plays in the grotto. I am happy here; as in the well-known tango: *'I wish I were a bee, to die among the flowers.'*

"Instead of that one must always be fighting. Oh, yes, I don't mind admitting to you that I wasn't made for this sort of thing. I am the secretary of the Party and honorary president with Anatole France of a League of Freedom, in addition to being traveller, lecturer and propagandist. But what I really love, you know, is to be able to lunch in my dressing-gown, to have a maid and keep birds, to have the hair-dresser in every day, to sleep in the shelter of two strong arms, to drink my chocolate in bed, to go to the cinema at the cocktail hour, the *función-vermouth* as we call it, to dine with my sisters among my nephews and nieces and to find a bowl of roses at my bedside when I go home. I have never admitted this to anyone else; take it with you as a secret to the grave. You must go now. I can't be sure I haven't been followed, even though I came straight here after getting up. Take the train back to France this evening."

"I came here to see you."

She became insistent.

"There's going to be a general strike in Barcelona at any moment, perhaps even to-morrow. All foreigners will be suspect; people will be ruthlessly shot. I can't say more than that."

"My only desire, Remedios, is to love you, and my only mistake is to want to seduce you. If I am plunged into danger with you it won't be from imprudence or gallantry or jocularity on my part, but because the need of being near you keeps me here."

Having said this, I took her into my arms.

She deposited face-powder and dried cosmetic on my clothes, grew sentimental and put on her spectacles.

From the summit of this calvary of ours with its border of fantastic shrubbery, amongst which beds of heliotrope were laid out in the form of the insignia of the Order of Alfonso XII, between the embrasures adorned with breast plates, the town appeared in the tense atmosphere, fined down like a model in an architectural exhibition. A thick haze hung over the sea and joined it to the sky. The funicular railway began to move; a dynamo purred somewhere.

"You see the awakening of Barcelona," said Remedios, "with her

luxurious houses, her peaceful tramways, her civic amenities, all eloquent
of her industry; but you have not seen her in her hours of bloodshed, with
her torn-down shutters, her twisted and broken pipes, and just beneath
my window, caressed by the sun, a single blot—the body of a little girl
killed as she was leaving school, sprawling on the ground, her head covered
with flies." When she was carried away by her subject little silver bubbles
blew from her mouth and floated for a moment in the sunlight.

"Yes, *mono*. Less than a year ago it began with a meeting of protest
against the despatch of reservists to Morocco, that cancer which gnaws at
the vitals of Spain. Opposite the station over there on the right, from which
smoke is rising as from a cauldron, a watch was kept from the sinister
windows of the Capitanía General. The rails had been torn up to prevent
the arrival of reinforcements from Valencia and Madrid. It was a
Wednesday. Paving stones were being taken up and trees felled. At midday the sack of the convents began. The first one was that of San Martin
de Provensals, if I remember rightly. Puig, who had gone out at dawn,
had not returned. At midnight I ventured out. The populace was converging towards the centre of the town, after rifling the armouries. I found out
that Puig was remaining permanently at the People's House.

"The churches of Maristes, San Antonio, San Pablo, the convents and
the parish churches were burning one by one. Forty-nine churches were
roasted in this way. Machine-guns swept the city from the top of the
Columbus column. The infantry refused to fire. The Jesuits of Sarría, that
barrack-like building over there by the gasometer, defended themselves
with rifles. At length the batteries of Montjuich trained their guns on the
revolutionary party. From my room I heard muffled reports, the explosion
of hidden syndicalist or clerical bomb stores. Then the reinforcements
arrived. General Santiago had terrifying proclamations put up. There was
a stampede and the ringleaders made for the Pyrenees. At last the detona-
tions died down and ceased altogether. . . . Barcelona became once more
as you see it there, a city of wealth and vice, the town of child prostitution,
obscene photographs and 'fancy goods,' preserving the spirit of the Inquisition behind a screen of electric signs, with its fortified convents and banks,
its patchwork houses with their strong-rooms and their cellars protected by
bars, of which those which keep the poor from the confessionals are but
gilded replicas. In the meantime Puig had been arrested and imprisoned up
there.

"They had got him. They had at last laid their hands on this dangerous
anarchist. No civil lawyer was allowed to cross the threshold of his cell.
And yet you remember the indignation of Europe and the way in which
every lover of justice had his eyes focussed on that dungeon, in which the
greatest heart in the world was waiting without faltering for a single
moment. Socrates, Christ, the Chevalier du Barreau, Bismarck, Ravachol, all
the great adventurers into the realm of thought, have met their death like

that. As for me, I never saw him again alive. Puig wrote to me every day, I know, but I never got his letters. I was myself placed secretly in a cabin of the Pelayo, that old cruiser which sleeps its crocodile sleep in the harbour basin, ready at any moment to serve as a gaol.

"Look, they are decking it with flags. To-day triumphal arches of silver paper will be erected all over the town. This evening there will be a candle in every window, for the King is coming to-morrow to review the troops who are going to Tetuan. Everything is beginning all over again, and will go on until the time when . . ."

An appetising domestic smell of chocolate rose in the morning air.

Remedios sucked her pendant with a far-away look. Then she went on speaking, as though in a dream:

"Puig was put into the chapel at six o'clock in the evening. All night long he remained awake, refusing to kneel, standing between two brothers of Charity. . . . He died shot in the back. For another whole day he remained on view in his black deal coffin, his head swathed in bandages, his face bloodless, and a wound in his throat plugged with lime."

Suddenly she threw her arms round my neck:

"What a little ragamuffin I am, aren't I?"

I went to the window to open it, but Remedios threw herself on the curtain and pulled it right across.

"Is that because of the man who is patrolling up and down outside?" I asked.

For some time I had noticed that a very tall man with a stoop and a complexion like fine porcelain framed in a beard was watching us.

"Yes, that is José Salt."

"Police?"

"No."

"Jealous?"

"It's rather sad. Salt was formerly professor of history at the Institute. He was one of Puig's most ardent supporters and served him with intelligence, delight and vanity. I in my turn took a class, as you know, and became Puig's companion. Salt fell in love with me and lost his peace of mind. He spied on us, followed us about, plagued us with anonymous letters, probably denounced us to the police, in short became such a nuisance that Puig, in spite of his gentleness and self-control, quarrelled with him, with the result that Salt had to leave the Institute. He was in the Argentine when the trouble occurred. I found him here on my return, avoiding me, dedicating poetry to me. He is lecturing again—the preachings of a visionary which no one listens to—passes his nights in churches and takes cocaine. Yesterday he came up to me in the street and asked me to live with him; when I tried to move away he swore that to-morrow he would put a bomb inside a bouquet of the flowers I like best and throw it from a window into the King's carriage on his return from the review."

"That is the sort of romantic venture that makes anarchy intolerable. Anarchy should above all be an exact science. But Spaniards have lost all sense of the fitness of things since they have given up the study of theology."

"It is quite true, *amor simpático*. You talk like a bird."

I suddenly heard my neck crack; against my lips I found teeth which were not my own. A heat greater than that of the mid-day sun pervaded me. I couldn't breathe; close to my eyes I saw a single shining eye which gazed at me, gave me a feeling of intense discomfort, and went out.

"What has suddenly changed me like this?" asked Remedios after the kiss. "I can assure you it isn't a passing fancy on my part—that's what you say, what you do in Paris, isn't it? No. I've no desire for pleasure left. But you were so unhappy that I couldn't resist you. That is my weak spot."

"In the first place, I am that sad brute . . ."

"Yes, I felt that about you when we first dined together, and you let me ask the gipsy band to play the music of Lakmé. I remember: *'It is that God is deserting us.'* Just at that moment someone was cracking lobster claws. I felt it was my heart that was being crushed. You see, something goes on throbbing beneath all this. In France your votive offerings take the shape of election cards, academic palms and dentists' diplomas. In Spain, round the statue of the Virgin hang hearts, bunches of hearts . . ."

"Yes, and diseased eyes, tumours and, especially at Toledo, sexual organs, all modelled in wax."

"In any case, why should I invoke the Fates when we are together again? We have been separated for so long . . ."

"And you've got thinner," I continued flatteringly.

"Then you will love me always?"

"Of course."

"I should like you to be a cat," said Remedios, playing with my watch-chain. "You would never leave me then. In the daytime you would be put into a little basket and in the evening I would take you out and you would become a man again."

Her satin blouse was covered with big foolish dots and had a sailor collar with a white crêpe-de-chine scarf. I felt I wanted to bite her little feet to stop them swinging to and fro. What numberless seated ancestors she must have had to be what she was! Except for the flies we were alone in the tea shop. Half a Dutch cheese, like a severed breast, shared its glass cover with a raw ham which smelled of tallow and was turning black.

"When are we going on with our lessons? The irregular verbs?"

Remedios studied the lines round my eyes. I no longer saw anything but her round powdered nose protruding from her plump face.

"I think you are hypersensitive," she explained, "and capable of very deep affection. You ought to get to know me better. Personally I am hyperneurotic."

All the same I opened the window, so that she could call for help if I tried to kill her.

"You cannot often have been accused of coldness of heart," she said. "And yet you are not very demonstrative."

Her body was too long and from it she emitted a sigh which filled the whole room.

Beyond the pavement lay an imitation wharf. Barcelona was a monstrous town. All the women who went past seemed to have thick eyelashes and large thighs; they were followed by thin Jesuits who went along in threes, holding each other's little fingers. In the background there was the inevitable Montjuich, a sheer rock with palms growing out of its crevices like hairs and dotted with little houses clinging on like limpets. The view from the other window consisted of a woman selling dyed feathers and, in the distance, the modern cathedral of Soller, with its four reinforced concrete towers and its merry-go-round organ. Remedios was dwindling. She was becoming just an ordinary companion. That display of authority by which she asserted herself in Switzerland and France had gone. Her own country seemed to tone her down. Was that the reason she no longer wanted to have one? She used to be the personification of glory and love. But now she had become comfortable, cheerful and docile; a kind of domestic utensil. She had eyes for no one but me and her looks seemed to say: "After all one must live, so why not enjoy one's life?" She forgot the dead in the living, and used her old expression, "My sacrifice," to excuse herself. She really believed it, too; and not altogether without reason. I was only annoyed that I could not be grateful to her for it. Or was it her spotted blouse and the white crêpe-de-chine scarf that irritated me? How she used to attract me in Paris in her mourning! (There was, for instance, the silver veil she kept for interviews.) She climbed up the Rue Saint-Jacques as though it were a Calvary. What a crowd of idlers were always after her! I thought, as one always does, that I had found something quite extraordinary. To-day, without hypocrisy to myself, just as without any irony towards her . . .

"Let's take the funicular up to the Tibidabo this evening," she said. "I'll bring Trick and we can dine à la carte. The view stretches as far as the Palma lighthouse. I will rest my head softly on your shoulder and we will be wafted to the country of conventional dreams, in which heroism does not exist. I will bring a nightdress."

Her jet-black earrings trembled submissively.

I had room number 217. It was a new room and smelled of size. A black-beetle crawled leisurely across the carpet. Someone had left an ace of clubs in one of the drawers. I ordered dinner for two. At that moment there was an explosion in the distance. The electric light went out and I lit three candles.

I opened the window. It looked out over a courtyard from which rose the smell of bisque d'écrevisse and soapsuds. I counted the flowers on the counterpane, polished the tarnished bottles of my dressing-case on the curtains and put my slippers away. Lastly, I placed some flowers in a waterless vase as they do on the stage.

Remedios wanted me to be a cat in a little basket. She had promised to give me a cigarette-case with an enamelled cover representing a naked blonde on the sea-shore. For some obscure reason she had the bust of Esteban Puig with its gouged-out eyes brought to my hotel, wrapped in oil-cloth. I had put it under my bed. What was I to do? One must either live alone or take people as one finds them. Why do the Spanish news-papers devote the whole of their front pages to obituary notices? There is something so sinister in their daily lament.

I made new resolutions. I must be more ardent. I must be more carried away, more emotional. Perhaps I should exhibit chronic enthusiasm. How exquisite, how radiant Remedios was!

Tired of waiting for her, I dined alone. Every twenty minutes the funicular announced its arrival by a jar which made the mountain shake, followed by a noise of rushing water. Then my anxiety redoubled. I strained my ears. But Remedios was still not in that one. I dared not try to explain her lateness to myself or to think of what would happen if she did not come at all, out of fear of arousing hostile forces which would prevent her from reaching me. I wanted Remedios with all my heart and I longed to see her safe with me between these four smooth, sanatorium-like walls. I forgot that on that very morning I would have given anything to be back in Paris.

Gradually I compelled myself to believe that Remedios would certainly not come, but that I should pass just as good a night stretched diagonally or right across the bed.

The hotel was 800 metres above the sea-level. The sound of country life had not yet begun there and the hum of the town was too far away to reach me. Either would have lulled me into a sleep which was denied me and there was nothing left for me to do but to wait.

I lay down fully dressed. Towards two in the morning my neighbours, who had been carrying on an excited conversation for hours without a stop, sent for a steak and a bottle of manzanilla. Then a child began to cry, heralding the dawn. Another child answered it.

I had left the door ajar and I trembled at every sound. A hundred times I dozed for a moment. The telephone bell kept ringing in the corridor, but the floor waiter, dozing beneath a red lamp, paid no attention to it. The panels of the imported English furniture kept cracking all through the night. Every time I started up I saw the other pillow lying there swollen and cold and the infinitely big room, lit only by the moon which an obliging mirror deflected on to the dusty water of a fire bucket.

Then, suddenly, I sank into sleep.

It was not until the following morning that I heard of the outrage committed by Remedios and of her arrest.

SILENT SNOW, SECRET SNOW

Conrad Aiken

(1889-   )

Just why it should have happened, or why it should have happened just when it did, he could not, of course, possibly have said; nor perhaps could it even have occurred to him to ask. The thing was above all a secret, something to be preciously concealed from Mother and Father; and to that very fact it owed an enormous part of its deliciousness. It was like a peculiarly beautiful trinket to be carried unmentioned in one's trouser-pocket—a rare stamp, an old coin, a few tiny gold links found trodden out of shape on the path in the park, a pebble of carnelian, a sea shell distinguishable from all others by an unusual spot or stripe—and, as if it were anyone of these, he carried around with him everywhere a warm and persistent and increasingly beautiful sense of possession. Nor was it only a sense of possession—it was also a sense of protection. It was as if, in some delightful way, his secret gave him a fortress, a wall behind which he could retreat into heavenly seclusion. This was almost the first thing he had noticed about it—apart from the oddness of the thing itself—and it was this that now again, for the fiftieth time, occurred to him, as he sat in the little schoolroom. It was the half hour for geography. Miss Buell was revolving with one finger, slowly, a huge terrestrial globe which had been placed on her desk. The green and yellow continents passed and repassed, questions were asked and answered, and now the little girl in front of him, Deirdre, who had a funny little constellation of freckles on the back of her neck, exactly like the Big Dipper, was standing up and telling Miss Buell that the equator was the line that ran round the middle.

Miss Buell's face, which was old and grayish and kindly, with gray stiff

curls beside the cheeks, and eyes that swam very brightly, like little min-
nows, behind thick glasses, wrinkled itself into a complication of amusements.

"Ah! I see. The earth is wearing a belt, or a sash. Or someone drew a
line round it!"

"Oh, no—not that—I mean—"

In the general laughter, he did not share, or only a very little. He was
thinking about the Arctic and Antarctic regions, which of course, on the
globe, were white. Miss Buell was now telling them about the tropics, the
jungles, the steamy heat of equatorial swamps, where the birds and butterflies, and even the snakes, were like living jewels. As he listened to these
things, he was already, with a pleasant sense of half-effort, putting his
secret between himself and the words. Was it really an effort at all? For
effort implied something voluntary, and perhaps even something one did
not especially want; whereas this was distinctly pleasant, and came almost
of its own accord. All he needed to do was to think of that morning, the
first one, and then of all the others—

But it was all so absurdly simple! It had amounted to so little. It was
nothing, just an idea—and just why it should have become so wonderful,
so permanent, was a mystery—a very pleasant one, to be sure, but also, in
an amusing way, foolish. However, without ceasing to listen to Miss Buell,
who had now moved up to the north temperate zones, he deliberately invited his memory of the first morning. It was only a moment or two after
he had waked up—or perhaps the moment itself. But was there, to be
exact, an exact moment? Was one awake all at once? or was it gradual?
Anyway, it was after he had stretched a lazy hand up towards the headrail,
and yawned, and then relaxed again among his warm covers, all the more
grateful on a December morning, that the thing had happened. Suddenly,
for no reason, he had thought of the postman, he remembered the postman. Perhaps there was nothing so odd in that. After all, he heard the postman almost every morning in his life—his heavy boots could be heard
clumping round the corner at the top of the little cobbled hill-street, and
then, progressively nearer, progressively louder, the double knock at each
door, the crossings and re-crossings of the street, till finally the clumsy steps
came stumbling across to the very door, and the tremendous knock came
which shook the house itself.

(Miss Buell was saying "Vast wheat-growing areas in North America
and Siberia.")

Deirdre had for the moment placed her left hand across the back of her
neck.)

But on this particular morning, the first morning, as he lay there with his
eyes closed, he had for some reason *waited* for the postman. He wanted to
hear him come round the corner. And that was precisely the joke—he never
did. He never came. He never had come—*round the corner*—again. For

when at last the steps *were* heard, they had already, he was quite sure, come a little down the hill, to the first house; and even so, the steps were curiously different—they were softer, they had a new secrecy about them, they were muffled and indistinct; and while the rhythm of them was the same, it now said a new thing—it said peace, it said remoteness, it said cold, it said sleep. And he had understood the situation at once—nothing could have seemed simpler—there had been snow in the night, such as all winter he had been longing for; and it was this which had rendered the postman's first footsteps inaudible, and the later ones faint. Of course! How lovely! And even now it must be snowing—it was going to be a snowy day—the long white ragged lines were drifting and sifting across the street, across the faces of the old houses, whispering and hushing, making little triangles of white in the corners between cobblestones, seething a little when the wind blew them over the ground to a drifted corner; and so it would be all day, getting deeper and deeper and silenter and silenter.

(Miss Buell was saying "Land of perpetual snow.")

All this time, of course (while he lay in bed), he had kept his eyes closed, listening to the nearer progress of the postman, the muffled footsteps thumping and slipping on the snow-sheathed cobbles; and all the other sounds—the double knocks, a frosty far-off voice or two, a bell ringing thinly and softly as if under a sheet of ice—had the same slightly abstracted quality, as if removed by one degree from actuality—as if everything in the world had been insulated by snow. But when at last, pleased, he opened his eyes, and turned them towards the window, to see for himself this long-desired and now so clearly imagined miracle—what he saw instead was brilliant sunlight on a roof; and when, astonished, he jumped out of bed and stared down into the street, expecting to see the cobbles obliterated by the snow, he saw nothing but the bare bright cobbles themselves.

Queer, the effect this extraordinary surprise had had upon him—all the following morning he had kept with him a sense as of snow falling about him, a secret screen of new snow between himself and the world. If he had not dreamed such a thing—and how could he have dreamed it while awake?—how else could one explain it? In any case, the delusion had been so vivid as to affect his entire behavior. He could not now remember whether it was on the first or the second morning—or was it even the third?—that his mother had drawn attention to some oddness in his manner.

"But my darling—" she had said at the breakfast table—"what has come over you? You don't seem to be listening. . . ."

And how often that very thing had happened since!

(Miss Buell was now asking if anyone knew the difference between the North Pole and the Magnetic Pole. Deirdre was holding up her flickering brown hand, and he could see the four white dimples that marked the knuckles.)

Perhaps it hadn't been either the second or third morning—or even the fourth or fifth. How could he be sure? How could he be sure just when the delicious *progress* had become clear? Just when it had really *begun?* The intervals weren't very precise. . . . All he now knew was, that at some point or other—perhaps the second day, perhaps the sixth—he had noticed that the presence of the snow was a little more insistent, the sound of it clearer; and, conversely, the sound of the postman's footsteps more indistinct. Not only could he not hear the steps come round the corner, he could not even hear them at the first house. It was below the first house that he heard them; and then, a few days later, it was below the second house that he heard them; and a few days later again, below the third. Gradually, gradually, the snow was becoming heavier, the sound of its seething louder, the cobblestones more and more muffled. When he found, each morning, on going to the window, after the ritual of listening, that the roofs and cobbles were as bare as ever, it made no difference. This was, after all, only what he had expected. It was even what pleased him, what rewarded him: the thing was his own, belonged to no one else. No one else knew about it, not even his mother and father. There, outside, were the bare cobbles; and here, inside, was the snow. Snow growing heavier each day, muffling the world, hiding the ugly, and deadening increasingly—above all—the steps of the postman.

"But my darling—" she had said at the luncheon table—"what has come over you? You don't seem to listen when people speak to you. That's the third time I've asked you to pass your plate. . . ."

How was one to explain this to Mother? or to Father? There was, of course, nothing to be done about it: nothing. All one could do was to laugh embarrassedly, pretend to be a little ashamed, apologize, and take a sudden and somewhat disingenuous interest in what was being done or said. The cat had stayed out all night. He had a curious swelling on his left cheek—perhaps somebody had kicked him, or a stone had struck him. Mrs. Kempton was or was not coming to tea. The house was going to be house cleaned, or "turned out," on Wednesday instead of Friday. A new lamp was provided for his evening work—perhaps it was eye-strain which accounted for this new and so peculiar vagueness of his—Mother was looking at him with amusement as she said this, but with something else as well. A new lamp? A new lamp. Yes Mother, No Mother, Yes Mother. School is going very well. The geometry is very easy. The history is very dull. The geography is very interesting—particularly when it takes one to the North Pole. Why the North Pole? Oh, well, it would be fun to be an explorer. Another Peary or Scott or Shackleton. And then abruptly he found his interest in the talk at an end, stared at the pudding on his plate, listened, waited, and began once more—ah how heavenly, too, the first beginnings—to hear or feel—for could he actually hear it?—the silent snow, the secret snow.

(Miss Buell was telling them about the search for the Northwest Passage, about Hendrik Hudson, the Half Moon.)

This had been, indeed, the only distressing feature of the new experience: the fact that it so increasingly had brought him into a kind of mute misunderstanding, or even conflict, with his father and mother. It was as if he were trying to lead a double life. On the one hand he had to be Paul Hasleman, and keep up the appearance of being that person—dress, wash, and answer intelligently when spoken to—; on the other, he had to explore this new world which had been opened to him. Nor could there be the slightest doubt—not the slightest—that the new world was the profounder and more wonderful of the two. It was irresistible. It was miraculous. Its beauty was simply beyond anything—beyond speech as beyond thought— utterly incommunicable. But how then, between the two worlds, of which he was thus constantly aware, was he to keep a balance? One must get up, one must go to breakfast, one must talk with Mother, go to school, do one's lessons—and, in all this, try not to appear too much of a fool. But if all the while one was also trying to extract the full deliciousness of another and quite separate existence, one which could not easily (if at all) be spoken of—how was one to manage? How was one to explain? Would it be safe to explain? Would it be absurd? Would it merely mean that he would get into some obscure kind of trouble?

These thoughts came and went, came and went, as softly and secretly as the snow; they were not precisely a disturbance, perhaps they were even a pleasure; he liked to have them; their presence was something almost palpable, something he could stroke with his hand, without closing his eyes, and without ceasing to see Miss Buell and the school-room and the globe and the freckles on Deirdre's neck; nevertheless he did in a sense cease to see, or to see the obvious external world, and substituted for this vision the vision of snow, the sound of snow, and the slow, almost soundless, approach of the postman. Yesterday, it had been only at the sixth house that the postman had become audible; the snow was much deeper now, it was falling more swiftly and heavily, the sound of its seething was more distinct, more soothing, more persistent. And this morning, it had been—as nearly as he could figure—just above the seventh house—perhaps only a step or two above: at most, he had heard two or three footsteps before the knock had sounded. . . . And with each such narrowing of the sphere, each nearer approach of the limit at which the postman was first audible, it was odd how sharply was increased the amount of illusion which had to be carried into the ordinary business of daily life. Each day, it was harder to get out of bed, to go to the window, to look out at the— as always—perfectly empty and snowless street. Each day it was more difficult to go through the perfunctory motions of greeting Mother and Father at breakfast, to reply to their questions, to put his books together and go to school. And at school, how extraordinarily hard to conduct with success simultaneously the public life and the life that was secret. There were times when he longed—positively ached—to tell everyone about it—to burst out with it—only to be checked almost at once by a far-off feeling as of some faint absurdity which was inherent in it—but *was* it absurd?—and more importantly by a sense of mysterious power in his very secrecy. Yes: it must be kept secret. That, more and more, became clear. At whatever cost to himself, whatever pain to others—

(Miss Buell looked straight at him, smiling, and said, "Perhaps we'll ask Paul. I'm sure Paul will come out of his day-dream long enough to be able to tell us. Won't you, Paul." He rose slowly from his chair, resting one hand on the brightly varnished desk, and deliberately stared through the snow towards the blackboard. It was an effort, but it was amusing to make it. "Yes," he said slowly, "it was what we now call the Hudson River. This he thought to be the Northwest Passage. He was disappointed." He sat down again, and as he did so Deirdre half turned in her chair and gave him a shy smile, of approval and admiration.)

At whatever pain to others.

This part of it was very puzzling, very puzzling. Mother was very nice, and so was Father. Yes, that was all true enough. He wanted to be nice to them, to tell them everything—and yet, was it really wrong of him to want to have a secret place of his own?

At bedtime, the night before, Mother had said, "If this goes on, my lad, we'll have to see a doctor, we will! We can't have our boy—" But what was it she had said? "Live in another world"? "Live so far away"? The word "far" had been in it, he was sure, and then Mother had taken up a magazine again and laughed a little, but with an expression which wasn't mirthful. He had felt sorry for her. . . .

The bell rang for dismissal. The sound came to him through long curved parallels of falling snow. He saw Deirdre rise, and had himself risen almost as soon—but not quite as soon—as she.

II

On the walk homeward, which was timeless, it pleased him to see through the accompaniment, or counterpoint, of snow, the items of mere externality on his way. There were many kinds of bricks in the sidewalks, and laid in many kinds of pattern. The garden walls too were various, some of wooden palings, some of plaster, some of stone. Twigs of bushes leaned over the walls; the little hard green winter-buds of lilac, on gray stems, sheathed and fat; other branches very thin and fine and black and desiccated. Dirty sparrows huddled in the bushes, as dull in color as dead fruit left in leafless trees. A single starling creaked on a weather vane. In the gutter, beside a drain, was a scrap of torn and dirty newspaper, caught in a little delta of filth: the word ECZEMA appeared in large capitals, and below it was a letter from Mrs. Amelia D. Cravath, 2100 Pine Street, Fort Worth, Texas, to the effect that after being a sufferer for years she had been cured by Caley's Ointment. In the little delta, beside the fan-shaped and deeply runneled continent of brown mud, were lost twigs, descended from their parent trees, dead matches, a rusty horse-chestnut burr, a small concentration of sparkling gravel on the lip of the sewer, a fragment of eggshell, a streak of yellow sawdust which had been wet and was now dry and congealed, a brown pebble, and a broken feather. Further on was a cement sidewalk, ruled into geometrical parallelograms, with a brass inlay at one end commemorating the contractors who had laid it, and, halfway across, an irregular and random series of dog-tracks, immortalized in synthetic stone. He knew these well, and always stepped on them; to cover the little hollows with his own foot had always been a queer pleasure; today he did it once more, but perfunctorily and detachedly, all the while thinking of something else. That was a dog, a long time ago, who had made a mistake and walked on the cement while it was still wet. He had probably wagged his tail, but that hadn't been recorded. Now, Paul Hasleman, aged twelve, on his way home from school, crossed the same river, which in the meantime had frozen into rock. Homeward through the snow, the snow falling in bright sunshine. Homeward?

Then came the gateway with the two posts surmounted by egg-shaped stones which had been cunningly balanced on their ends, as if by Columbus, and mortared in the very act of balance: a source of perpetual wonder. On the brick wall just beyond, the letter H had been stenciled, presumably for some purpose. H? H.

The green hydrant, with a little green-painted chain attached to the brass screw-cap.

The elm tree, with the great gray wound in the bark, kidney-shaped, into which he always put his hand—to feel the cold but living wood. The injury, he had been sure, was due to the gnawings of a tethered horse. But now it deserved only a passing palm, a merely tolerant eye. There were more important things. Miracles. Beyond the thoughts of trees, mere elms. Beyond the thoughts of sidewalks, mere stone, mere brick, mere cement. Beyond the thoughts even of his own shoes, which trod these sidewalks obediently, bearing a burden—far above—of elaborate mystery. He watched them. They were not very well polished; he had neglected them, for a very good reason: they were one of the many parts of the increasing difficulty of the daily return to daily life, the morning struggle. To get up, having at last opened one's eyes, to go to the window, and discover no snow, to wash, to dress, to descend the curving stairs to breakfast—

At whatever pain to others, nevertheless, one must persevere in severance, since the incommunicability of the experience demanded it. It was desirable of course to be kind to Mother and Father, especially as they seemed to be worried, but it was also desirable to be resolute. If they should decide—as

appeared likely—to consult the doctor, Doctor Howells, and have Paul inspected, his heart listened to through a kind of dictaphone, his lungs, his
stomach—well, that was all right. He would go through with it. He would
give them answer for question, too—perhaps such answers as they hadn't
expected? No. That would never do. For the secret world must, at all costs,
be preserved.

The bird-house in the apple-tree was empty—it was the wrong time of
year for wrens. The little round black door had lost its pleasure. The wrens
were enjoying other houses, other nests, remoter trees. But this too was a
notion which he only vaguely and grazingly entertained—as if, for the moment, he merely touched an edge of it; there was something further on,
which was already assuming a sharper importance; something which already teased at the corners of his eyes, teasing also at the corner of his mind.
It was funny to think that he so wanted this, so awaited it—and yet found
himself enjoying this momentary dalliance with the bird-house, as if for a
quite deliberate postponement and enhancement of the approaching pleasure. He was aware of his delay, of his smiling and detached and now almost
uncomprehending gaze at the little bird-house; he knew what he was
going to look at next: it was his own little cobbled hill-street, his own
house, the little river at the bottom of the hill, the grocer's shop with the
cardboard man in the window—and now, thinking of all this, he turned his
head, still smiling, and looking quickly right and left through the snow-
laden sunlight.

And the mist of snow, as he had foreseen, was still on it—a ghost of snow
falling in the bright sunlight, softly and steadily floating and turning and
pausing, soundlessly meeting the snow that covered, as with a transparent
mirage, the bare bright cobbles. He loved it—he stood still and loved it.
Its beauty was paralyzing—beyond all words, all experience, all dream. No
fairy-story he had ever read could be compared with it—none had ever
given him this extraordinary combination of ethereal loveliness with a
something else, unnameable, which was just faintly and deliciously terrifying. What was this thing? As he thought of it, he looked upward toward
his own bedroom window, which was open—and it was as if he looked
straight into the room and saw himself lying half awake in his bed. There
he was—at this very instant he was still perhaps actually there—more truly
there than standing here at the edge of the cobbled hill-street, with one
hand lifted to shade his eyes against the snow-sun. Had he indeed ever left
his room, in all this time? since that very first morning? Was the whole
progress still being enacted there, was it still the same morning, and himself
not yet wholly awake? And even now, had the postman not yet come
round the corner? . . .

This idea amused him, and automatically, as he thought of it, he turned
his head and looked toward the top of the hill. There was, of course,
nothing there—nothing and no one. The street was empty and quiet. And

all the more because of its emptiness it occurred to him to count the houses
—a thing which, oddly enough, he hadn't before thought of doing. Of
course, he had known there weren't many—many, that is, on his own side
of the street, which were the ones that figured in the postman's progress
—but nevertheless it came to him as something of a shock to find that
there were precisely *six,* above his own house—his own house was the
seventh.

Six!

Astonished, he looked at his own house—looked at the door, on which
was the number thirteen—and then realized that the whole thing was exactly and logically and absurdly what he ought to have known. Just the
same, the realization gave him abruptly, and even a little frighteningly, a
sense of hurry. He was being hurried—he was being rushed. For—he knit
his brows—he couldn't be mistaken—it was just above the *seventh* house,
his *own* house, that the postman had first been audible this very morning.
But in that case—in that case—did it mean that tomorrow he would hear
nothing? The knock he had heard must have been the knock of their own
door. Did it mean—and this was an idea which gave him a really extraordinary feeling of surprise—that he would never hear the postman again?—
that tomorrow morning the postman would already have passed the house,
in a snow by then so deep as to render his footsteps completely inaudible?
That he would have made his approach down the snow-filled street so
soundlessly, so secretly, that he, Paul Hasleman, there lying in bed, would
not have waked in time, or, waking, would have heard nothing?

But how could that be? Unless even the knocker should be muffled in
the snow—frozen tight, perhaps? . . . But in that case—

A vague feeling of disappointment came over him; a vague sadness, as
if he felt himself deprived of something which he had long looked forward
to, something much prized. After all this, all this beautiful progress, the
slow delicious advance of the postman through the silent and secret snow,
the knock creeping closer each day, and the footsteps nearer, the audible
compass of the world thus daily narrowed, narrowed, narrowed, as the
snow soothingly and beautifully encroached and deepened, after all this,
was he to be defrauded of the one thing he had so wanted—to be able to
count, as it were, the last two or three solemn footsteps, as they finally
approached his own door? Was it all going to happen, at the end, so suddenly? or indeed, had it already happened? with no slow and subtle grada-
tions of menace, in which he could luxuriate?

He gazed upward again, toward his own window which flashed in the
sun: and this time almost with a feeling that it would be better if he *were*
still in bed, in that room; for in that case this must still be the first morning, and there would be six more mornings to come—or, for that matter,
seven or eight or nine—how could he be sure?—or even more.

III

After supper, the inquisition began. He stood before the doctor, under the lamp, and submitted silently to the usual thumpings and tappings.

"Now will you please say 'Ah!'?"

"Ah!"

"Now again please, if you don't mind."

"Ah."

"Say it slowly, and hold it if you can—"

"Ah-h-h-h-h-h—"

"Good."

How silly all this was. As if it had anything to do with his throat! Or his heart or lungs!

Relaxing his mouth, of which the corners, after all this absurd stretching, felt uncomfortable, he avoided the doctor's eyes, and stared towards the fireplace, past his mother's feet (in gray slippers) which projected from the green chair, and his father's feet (in brown slippers) which stood neatly side by side on the hearth rug.

"Hm. There is certainly nothing wrong there . . ."

He felt the doctor's eyes fixed upon him, and, as if merely to be polite, returned the look, but with a feeling of justifiable evasiveness.

"Now, young man, tell me,—do you feel all right?"

"Yes, sir, quite all right."

"No headaches? no dizziness?"

"No, I don't think so."

"Let me see. Let's get a book, if you don't mind—yes, thank you, that will do splendidly—and now, Paul, if you'll just read it, holding it as you would normally hold it—"

He took the book and read:

"And another praise have I to tell for this the city our mother, the gift of a great god, a glory of the land most high; the might of horses, the might of young horses, the might of the sea. . . . For thou, son of Cronus, our lord Poseidon, hast throned herein this pride, since in these roads first thou didst show forth the curb that cures the rage of steeds. And the shapely oar, apt to men's hands, hath a wondrous speed on the brine, following the hundred-footed Nereids. . . . O land that art praised above all lands, now is it for thee to make those bright praises seen in deeds."

He stopped, tentatively, and lowered the heavy book.

"No—as I thought—there is certainly no superficial sign of eye-strain."

Silence thronged the room, and he was aware of the focused scrutiny of the three people who confronted him. . . .

"We could have his eyes examined—but I believe it is something else."

"What could it be?" This was his father's voice.

"It's only this curious absent-minded—" This was his mother's voice.

In the presence of the doctor, they both seemed irritatingly apologetic.

"I believe it is something else. Now Paul—I would like very much to ask you a question or two. You will answer them, won't you—you know I'm an old, old friend of yours, eh? That's right! . . . ."

His back was thumped twice by the doctor's fat fist,—then the doctor was grinning at him with false amiability, while with one finger-nail he was scratching the top button of his waistcoat. Beyond the doctor's shoulder was the fire, the fingers of flame making light prestidigitation against the sooty fireback, the soft sound of their random flutter the only sound.

"I would like to know—is there anything that worries you?"

The doctor was again smiling, his eyelids low against the little black pupils, in each of which was a tiny white bead of light. Why answer him? why answer him at all? "At whatever pain to others"—but it was all a nuisance, this necessity for resistance, this necessity for attention: it was as if one had been stood up on a brilliantly lighted stage, under a great round blaze of spotlight; as if one were merely a trained seal, or a performing dog, or a fish, dipped out of an aquarium and held up by the tail. It would serve them right if he were merely to bark or growl. And meanwhile, to miss these last few precious hours, these hours of which every minute was more beautiful than the last, more menacing—? He still looked, as if from a great distance, at the beads of light in the doctor's eyes, at the fixed false smile, and then, beyond, once more at his mother's slippers, his father's slippers, the soft flutter of the fire. Even here, even amongst these hostile presences, and in this arranged light, he could see the snow, he could hear it—it was in the corners of the room, where the shadow was deepest, under the sofa, behind the half-opened door which led to the dining room. It was gentler here, softer, its seethe the quietest of whispers, as if, in deference to a drawing room, it had quite deliberately put on its "manners"; it kept itself out of sight, obliterated itself, but distinctly with an air of saying, "Ah, but just wait! Wait till we are alone together! Then I will begin to tell you something new! Something white! something cold! something sleepy! something of cease, and peace, and the long bright curve of space! Tell them to go away. Banish them. Refuse to speak. Leave them, go upstairs to your room, turn out the light and get into bed—I will go with you, I will be waiting for you, I will tell you a better story than Little Kay of the Skates, or The Snow Ghost—I will surround your bed, I will close the windows, pile a deep drift against the door, so that none will ever again be able to enter. Speak to them! . . . ." It seemed as if the little hissing voice came from a slow white spiral of falling flakes in the corner by the front window —but he could not be sure. He felt himself smiling, then, and said to the doctor, but without looking at him, looking beyond him still—

"Oh, no, I think not—"

"But are you sure, my boy?"

His father's voice came softly and coldly then—the familiar voice of silken warning. . . .

"You needn't answer at once, Paul—remember we're trying to help you —think it over and be quite sure, won't you?"

He felt himself smiling again, at the notion of being quite sure. What a joke! As if he weren't so sure that reassurance was no longer necessary, and all this cross-examination a ridiculous farce, a grotesque parody! What could they know about it? These gross intelligences, these humdrum minds so bound to the usual, the ordinary? Impossible to tell them about it! Why, even now, even now, with the proof so abundant, so formidable, so imminent, so appallingly present here in this very room, could they believe it? —could even his mother believe it? No—it was only too plain that if anything were said about it, the merest hint given, they would be incredulous —they would laugh—they would say "Absurd!" think things about him which weren't true. . . .

"Why no, I'm not worried—why should I be?"

He looked then straight at the doctor's low-lidded eyes, looked from one of them to the other, from one bead of light to the other, and gave a little laugh.

The doctor seemed to be disconcerted by this. He drew back in his chair, resting a fat white hand on either knee. The smile faded slowly from his face.

"Well, Paul!" he said, and paused gravely, "I'm afraid you don't take this quite seriously enough. I think you perhaps don't quite realize—don't quite realize—" He took a deep quick breath, and turned, as if helplessly, at a loss for words, to the others. But Mother and Father were both silent—no help was forthcoming.

"You must surely know, be aware, that you have not been quite yourself, of late? don't you know that? . . ."

It was amusing to watch the doctor's renewed attempt at a smile, a queer disorganized look, as of confidential embarrassment.

"I feel all right, sir," he said, and again gave the little laugh.

"And we're trying to help you." The doctor's tone sharpened.

"Yes sir, I know. But why? I'm all right. I'm just *thinking,* that's all."

His mother made a quick movement forward, resting a hand on the back of the doctor's chair.

"Thinking?" she said. "But my dear, about what?"

This was a direct challenge—and would have to be directly met. But before he met it, he looked again into the corner by the door, as if for reassurance. He smiled again at what he saw, at what he heard. The little spiral was still there, still softly whirling, like the ghost of a white kitten chasing the ghost of a white tail, and making as it did so the faintest of whispers. It was all right! If only he could remain firm, everything was going to be all right.

"Oh, about anything, about nothing,—*you* know the way you do!"

"You mean—day-dreaming?"

"Oh, no—thinking!"

"But thinking about *what?*"

"Anything."

He laughed a third time—but this time, happening to glance upward towards his mother's face, he was appalled at the effect his laughter seemed to have upon her. Her mouth had opened in an expression of horror. . . . This was too bad! Unfortunate! He had known it would cause pain, of course—but he hadn't expected it to be quite so bad as this. Perhaps—perhaps if he just gave them a tiny gleaming hint—?

"About the snow," he said.

"What on earth!" This was his father's voice. The brown slippers came a step nearer on the hearth rug.

"But my dear, what do you mean?" This was his mother's voice.

The doctor merely stared.

"Just *snow,* that's all. I like to think about it."

"Tell us about it, my boy."

"But that's all it is. There's nothing to tell. *You* know what snow is?"

This he said almost angrily, for he felt that they were trying to corner him. He turned sideways so as no longer to face the doctor, and the better to see the inch of blackness between the window-sill and the lowered curtain,—the cold inch of beckoning and delicious night. At once he felt better, more assured.

"Mother—can I go to bed, now, please? I've got a headache."

"But I thought you said—"

"It's just come. It's all these questions—! Can I, Mother?"

"You can go as soon as the doctor has finished."

"Don't you think this thing ought to be gone into thoroughly, and *now?*" This was Father's voice. The brown slippers again came a step nearer, the voice was the well-known "punishment" voice, resonant and cruel.

"Oh, what's the use, Norman—"

Quite suddenly, everyone was silent. And without precisely facing them, nevertheless he was aware that all three of them were watching him with an extraordinary intensity—staring hard at him—as if he had done something monstrous, or was himself some kind of monster. He could hear the soft irregular flutter of the flames; the cluck-click-cluck-click of the clock; far and faint, two sudden spurts of laughter from the kitchen, as quickly cut off as begun; a murmur of water in the pipes; and then, the silence seemed to deepen, to spread out, to become worldlong and worldwide, to become timeless and shapeless, and to center inevitably and rightly, with a slow and sleepy but enormous concentration of all power, on the beginning of a new sound. What this new sound was going to be, he knew perfectly well. It might begin with a hiss, but it would end with a roar—there was no time to lose—he must escape. It mustn't happen here—

Without another word, he turned and ran up the stairs.

IV

Not a moment too soon. The darkness was coming in long white waves. A prolonged sibilance filled the night—a great seamless seethe of wild influence went abruptly across it—a cold low humming shook the windows. He shut the door and flung off his clothes in the dark. The bare black floor was like a little raft tossed in waves of snow, almost overwhelmed, washed under whitely, up again, smothered in curled billows of feather. The snow was laughing: it spoke from all sides at once: it pressed closer to him as he ran and jumped exulting into his bed.

"Listen to us!" it said. "Listen! We have come to tell you the story we told you about. You remember? Lie down. Shut your eyes, now—you will no longer see much—in this white darkness who could see, or want to see? We will take the place of everything. . . . Listen—"

A beautiful varying dance of snow began at the front of the room, came forward and then retreated, flattened out toward the floor, then rose fountain-like to the ceiling, swayed, recruited itself from a new stream of flakes which poured laughing in through the humming window, advanced again, lifted long white arms. It said peace, it said remoteness, it said cold —it said—

But then a gash of horrible light fell brutally across the room from the opening door—the snow drew back hissing—something alien had come into the room—something hostile. This thing rushed at him, clutched at him, shook him—and he was not merely horrified, he was filled with such a loathing as he had never known. What was this? this cruel disturbance? this act of anger and hate? It was as if he had to reach up a hand toward another world for any understanding of it,—an effort of which he was only barely capable. But of that other world he still remembered just enough to know the exorcising words. They tore themselves from his other life suddenly—

"Mother! Mother! Go away! I hate you!"

And with that effort, everything was solved, everything became all right: the seamless hiss advanced once more, the long white wavering lines rose and fell like enormous whispering sea-waves, the whisper becoming louder, the laughter more numerous.

"Listen!" it said. "We'll tell you the last, the most beautiful and secret story—shut your eyes—it is a very small story—a story that gets smaller and smaller—it comes inward instead of opening like a flower—it is a flower becoming a seed—a little cold seed—do you hear? we are leaning closer to you—"

The hiss was now becoming a roar—the whole world was a vast moving screen of snow—but even now it said peace, it said remoteness, it said cold, it said sleep.

THE LOVELY DAY

Jacques de Lacretelle

(1888–   )

TRANSLATED BY VYVYAN HOLLAND

Let's hide the case under his napkin to give him a surprise."

"No. I'll take him to one side and give him the watch and tell him: 'Here's a present for your eleventh birthday from your grandmother and me, Henri.' You see, we mustn't treat him like a child. It only annoys him when we do; I noticed that last time."

The grandfather wandered round the table laid for luncheon and inspected it carefully. Suddenly he stopped and, pointing with his finger, said:

"It's the same with that mug. Why not give him a proper glass?"

"Don't you recognise it? It's the one that Louise used to use when she was a little girl. I thought it might amuse him. Besides, he'll see that we think of his mother and still love her."

She uttered these last words almost in a whisper, turning away her head as she did so. He made no reply and started off again.

This little old couple were curiously alike. They were both the same height and they both looked delicate; their faces were thin and their eyes dull. One might have thought that the same wear and tear had effaced all the outward signs of their original character. And yet, from a certain agitation and a peculiar manner of tossing her head, it was evident that she had a certain will of her own and did not take things lying down. He, on the other hand, walked with a measured step, with a thoughtful, preoccupied air, nodding his head methodically as though he were doing an endless sum in mental arithmetic. Sometimes he halted, placed his hands one on each side of his face like blinkers and then brought them forward with a jerk in order better to limit his field of vision.

She picked up the mug, turned it over in her hands and gazed at the monogram engraved on its side.

"Do you remember, when Louise had her long illness and would scarcely eat anything at all, how I used to put meat jelly into it? I can see her now bending her poor thin little face over the mug."

He nodded, blinked his eyes and continued his walk round the table.

"Is it possible," she went on, gazing at the mug in a sort of reverie, "that the woman who now hates us so much and is always looking for some means of tormenting us is really the same person as that child? Sometimes, when I think about it, I can't believe that it's true. She does everything she can to make us suffer. For instance, why did she forbid us to go and meet Henri at the station this morning?"

She replaced the mug by a glass. There was a moment's silence.

"Why," cried the grandfather, "you've put a cushion on his chair! That's silly. He's taller than you are, my dear!"

"Oh, do let me arrange things in my own way!"

"I repeat that a boy doesn't like all these little attentions; they humiliate him."

He made his protest with a sort of quiet stubbornness, raising both hands together in his favourite gesture.

"A boy, a boy? . . . He's only a child . . . a child whom no one looks after and who never gets any affection or care. When he comes here I like him to feel some of the tenderness which his mother denies him now that she has no eyes for anyone but that wretched man."

"For Heaven's sake don't talk like that in front of him."

"And why not? Do you think that other fellow makes any bones about jeering at us and insulting us?"

"Very likely," he replied with a sigh, "but that doesn't mean that we must imitate him. The last time, when you told Henri that his stepfather was a bankrupt and had narrowly escaped going to prison, he blushed and I could easily see that he hated hearing about such things. I do implore you to be more careful today."

She shrugged her shoulders and retorted sharply:

"That's it! Always give in, always take everything lying down! That's your method. If, when Louise ran away with that man, we had asked the Court for the custody of our grandchild, Henri wouldn't have been brought up in the wings of a theatre by a rascally impresario. He would be living with us and I would have brought him up properly in spite of my affection for him which seems so ridiculous to you."

"I didn't say that, my dear; I only said that one must not identify Henri with the sad incidents that have estranged our daughter from us. When he is a man he will learn to distinguish of his own accord between what is decent and what is despicable. I'm confident of that."

The grandfather had drawn himself up to the full height of his small stature. His chin was twitching with emotion. His wife looked at him and replied, in a tender, rather subdued voice:

"Yes, I know, Antoine. I've let myself be carried away. Forgive me. We're both so unhappy, and today my nerves are all on edge. It's nearly five months since we've seen him. Just think of it. Isn't it wicked to keep him away from us for so long?"

Her voice broke, and she put her handkerchief up to her eyes, which had filled with tears. He took both her hands in his and pressed them.

"Now, don't distress yourself. We'll be happy today. It's going to be a lovely day. Look . . ."

He spoke to her with grave tenderness and led her gently towards the open door which led to the garden. When they reached the terrace they halted and raised their heads. The sky was a pale, pure blue. There was not a cloud to be seen. There was the same look of hope in their tired, blinking eyes. They kept hold of each other's hands and their voices mingled in soft repetition:

"A lovely day."

They were like two prison companions standing in the same narrow beam of light filtering into their cell.

The one-story house stood between two carefully tended garden plots. The front garden sloped down towards a road, beyond which flowed the Marne, like another, smoother and brighter road. The garden at the back consisted of a series of flower beds separated by a network of well-raked paths. A big lilac bush against the wall was in flower. Here and there on the horizon a factory chimney or a massive brick building rose up, reminding them that they were in a suburb of Paris. Some distance away a viaduct, straddling the river at a great height, cut the landscape in two.

"I must go into the kitchen," said the grandmother. "I want to see how Clothilde is getting along with the sweet."

Left alone, the old man walked carefully down the steps leading to the garden, went up to the lilac bush and slowly inhaled the perfume of the flowers, his hands clasped behind his back. A look of contentment appeared in his face and he stroked his little white beard. Then he seized a rake lying beneath the steps and began to rake one of the paths. Every now and then he stopped and then his expression was a mixture of happiness and resignation. From time to time he bent down to pull out a weed or to turn over a pebble. In all his movements there was a sort of humility which gave them a certain grace. He looked like some rustic saint.

Voices came from the kitchen. The grandmother appeared at the window, above the wire meat safe.

"What's the time, Antoine?" she called. "It's midday by Clothilde's clock."

He took out his watch and shook his finger in a sign of negation.

"It's thirteen minutes to. Look, the express is just passing."

He pointed in the direction of the viaduct. A short, shining train slid across it and disappeared.

The grandmother left the window and came to join her husband in the garden.

"It's just as well that I went into the kitchen," she said. "The cream was much too thin."

She tried to put her watch back into her belt, but her fingers got entangled in the guard. She tugged at the chain impatiently.

"Only a quarter of an hour more," she said. "In a quarter of an hour he will be here."

"Don't get so excited, my poor dear. You've been wearing yourself out ever since you got up."

She sighed deeply as though she really was very tired. Then she shrugged her shoulders and, firmly grasping her husband's arm, she observed in a low voice in which there was a note of anxiety:

"Look, Antoine, I only ask one thing: to live for a short while after Henri becomes free. Then he can choose his own home and he'll come and live here with us, and our last years will be the happiest of our lives.

"His mother can't love him," she went on with a sort of dull persistence. "If she did, would she drag him about in the way she does, from hotel to hotel, in her husband's trail? Neither Henri's happiness, nor his future, nor anything else has meant anything to her since she's become infatuated with that man. I may not always have got on with Louise's first husband, but at any rate the poor boy loved his son and looked after him."

He listened with a faraway, dreamy look in his eyes. Suddenly he interrupted her.

"When I think of Henri's career and when I tell myself that this bad upbringing may perhaps prevent him from becoming a respectable citizen . . . then I feel as though I could do anything . . . I even feel capable of strangling the brute!"

A wave of colour swept over his bald, sloping pate. His trembling fingers curved inwards as though about to seize something in a death grip. His wife looked on at this ineffective exhibition of fury.

"Oh, Antoine, how you love Henri!"

And she squeezed his hands in sympathy.

"Come, let's wait in front," she said.

They climbed the steps again and passed through the house. The kitchen door was open. The cook, hearing their footsteps, raised her head. She was a heavily built wench, no longer young, whose blue eyes and thick black eyebrows gave her a look which was a mixture of sensitiveness and surliness.

"Well, Master Henri won't be long now!" she called to them in a coarse, cheerful voice.

They smiled at her.

The front garden was to the south of the house. The lawn, with its bright green grass, shone in the sun. The two old people waited at the top of the steps and began to stare fixedly at the little iron gate at the end of the garden. They did not speak. Time passed. She jerked out her watch and looked at the time. Then he said, in a quiet, rather forced voice:

"What a lovely day!"

She did not appear to hear him. Then, in a sudden burst of anxious fury:

"He won't come!" she cried. "I've got a presentiment. They haven't sent him. Louise will have decided at the last moment, for no reason at all, just to be contradictory. I know her so well! She was like that as a child; she disobeyed me for the pleasure of disobeying, without any pity for the sorrow she caused me."

Her husband tried to calm her, but she would not let him speak.

"No! . . . I know her better than you do. Why did she forbid us to go and meet our darling this morning, unless it was for the pleasure of spoiling some of our happiness? 'Henri will be with you at midday. It's no use going to the station.' That's what she wrote to me, the stubborn, heartless girl!"

The little old woman stood stiffly erect, shaking as though in the presence of an enemy.

Suddenly she calmed down. Her arms fell to her sides. She instinctively turned her face towards the road, on which, however, nothing was to be seen; her eyes suddenly brightened.

"He's coming," she said eagerly.

And the next moment a boy, followed by a woman, appeared behind the bars of the gate.

He was tall, but rather thin and fragile, and from the way he pushed open the gate it seemed as though it cost him an effort. His face was round and, as he held it slightly bent down and as his complexion was pale, it appeared to be small and to present no salient feature.

He raised his face to greet his grandparents. He was not ugly, but there was nothing attractive about his listless expression. His grandmother had run across the lawn to meet him and was holding him in her arms.

"Henri, my Henri!" she kept saying, stroking his hair.

After he had returned her greeting he remained passive, staring covertly into the distance. Then it was the grandfather's turn and he took his grandson's head between his hands and kissed him tenderly and solemnly on the forehead.

The woman who had brought the child stood a little in the background. She was wearing a black dress, very short and tight-fitting. Her neck was bare and her face heavily made up. The grandmother took all this in at a glance. Nevertheless, she nodded to her graciously and said:

"Thank you for having brought our grandson. I hope it has not interfered with your day off."

"Oh, no, madame," replied the maid. "I happen to have an aunt who lives
at La Varenne whom I would like to go and see this afternoon if Madame
will allow me."

"Naturally," said the grandmother. "You can come back to fetch him for
the six o'clock train."

"Madame Louise told us to leave at about four."

"But if you go to La Varenne after luncheon you'll hardly have any time
there at all," replied the grandmother in a voice which was half con-
spiratorial and half pleading.

The maid gave a knowing little smile and made for the kitchen.

"How you've grown, Henri!" cried his grandmother, placing her arm
round his neck. "See, my arm isn't long enough to go round. Do you know,
it's nearly six months since we saw you. Have you thought of us at all?"

He nodded his head without speaking.

"And your birthday passed without us giving you a present. But we
didn't forget it. We didn't want to send it by post. Your grandfather will
give it to you now. Antoine!"

The grandfather produced the case, opened it and placed it in the child's
outstretched hand. The boy thanked him, took out the watch and examined it and then shot a pleased glance at the two old people from between his long curly lashes.

"Do you like it?" asked the grandmother, solicitously.

"Oh, yes! Is it gold?"

"Of course," replied the grandfather. "It's a real man's watch."

Grasping his present firmly in his hand, he went over to them and gave
them each a kiss.

The grandmother detained him and began to question him, stroking him
lovingly as she did so.

"Tell me what you've been doing, darling. Are you comfortable in Marseilles? Have you got a nice room?"

He answered rather shyly, letting his arms hang idly by his sides. He did
not like Marseilles, he said, but he had enjoyed himself at Nice, where they
had spent a month, and also in Italy, at San Remo and Rapallo.

He spoke slowly and without any gestures. His face remained expressionless and even his lips scarcely moved. It was the grandmother who, eagerly
following the movement of his lips, animated his recital. Her lined old face,
brimming over with warmth and passion, puckered up at the mention of
Marseilles and brightened at that of San Remo and Italy. And yet, masked
by this forced gaiety, care and sorrow seemed to lurk in the depths of her
eyes.

The grandfather stood a couple of yards away and rubbed his hands together with a complacent and wary look in his eyes. The cook appeared at

the front door and in a familiar voice announced that luncheon was ready.

"Let's go and eat!" cried the grandfather, clapping his hands.

"Sit over there, Henri, facing the window, so that we can see you better," said his grandmother as they entered the dining room.

The child sat in the place indicated, wincing slightly as though he did not like the light.

Thus lit up, his features were even more strikingly lifeless. Never for a moment did his face betray any of those eager, innocent emotions usual to children, nor even any look of awkwardness or timidity. He would turn his head slowly in the direction of the person or object that interested him and stare fixedly at it, without any change of expression. Only very occasionally would a slight contraction round the eyes or a glance shot in a rather feminine way from beneath his eyelids indicate that something had struck him as agreeable or unpleasant.

"And your studies, Henri?" asked the grandfather. "How are you getting on? Do you like them?"

The child looked at him coldly and replied shortly that he had spent three months at school in Marseilles and since then had pursued his studies by correspondence.

"And are your masters pleased with you? Have your reports been good?"

A hostile little frown appeared on his forehead and he turned his head towards the dish which the servant was bringing in. His grandfather was about to pursue the subject when he caught an impatient gesture from his wife and held his tongue.

"And now," she said, "I hope you're going to remain in Paris. What are your mother's plans?"

"Mother wants to stay, but she says we shall have to be off again soon."

"Really? Can't she do what she wants to?" cried the grandmother, in a mixture of irritation and sarcasm. "Who's to stop her?"

The boy, his head bowed over his plate, went on eating greedily without replying. His grandmother continued, with some hesitation:

"And . . . and your stepfather . . . is he kind to you? Do your mother and he ever quarrel?"

He nodded his head, bending it still lower and showing his untidy locks; then he thrust out his glass for something to drink.

As she poured it out she noticed his hands.

"Why, Henri, you bite your nails!"

The frown of resentment reappeared on the child's face, and he tried to hide his finger tips.

"I'm very distressed about that," said his grandmother. "It's a very nasty habit, Henri. But," she added gaily, "I don't want to scold you today!"

And to make amends for having reprimanded him she stroked the bitten fingernails.

"Heavens! What *have* you got on?" she cried, tugging at a piece of red-

and-green striped vest which she saw at his wrist. "It's awful. Where did you get it?"

"They bought it for me in Italy. Our trunks were left behind in the hotel at Nice, so . . ."

He became embarrassed and did not finish his sentence.

"It's terrible!" cried the grandmother. "So you hadn't any underlinen?"

"We got our luggage back when we returned."

She exchanged a long look with her husband. "What a life!" they thought. A short silence fell. Then the grandfather spoke in a voice which he tried to make sound cheerful.

"Tell me, Henri, what did you like most in your travels? You must have made some lovely excursions. And Italy is such a beautiful country! Tell me what you thought of it. What was it that amused you most?"

The child, who was drinking in long gulps, did not reply at once but looked from one to the other, his face half buried in his glass.

"When I played in comedy," he replied after a moment.

"When you played in comedy?" repeated his grandmother, raising her hands in surprise. "Where was that?"

"In a casino. But it was a real theatre and a real play."

The grandmother let her hands fall back on the table. She opened her mouth and asked mechanically:

"What play?"

"A very well-known one that has been played in Paris. My name was Charlie. I appeared in two of the scenes and in the second one I said things that made everyone laugh."

In an agonised voice the grandmother stammered:

"And did you like doing it?"

At this question the child's face suddenly changed. Dimples appeared in his cheeks and his eyes shone. He moistened his lips and made a sweeping gesture with his arm. And then the words came tumbling out:

"Oh, yes! When I came onto the stage I had a very funny feeling. I was happy, so happy, and yet my whole body trembled. I could see nothing but the row of electric lamps at the foot of the stage. Luckily the lady who was my mother in the play kept me close to her, otherwise I should not have been able to walk straight, the light was so bright. Then, after a moment, I got used to it and I was loudly applauded. I took three calls. After the performance someone told me that I could earn a lot of money later if I wanted to."

A peculiar resonance had come into his voice, and a gleam of sincerity and even a certain poetic look illuminated his features. But, catching sight of his grandmother's dismayed face, the child suddenly stopped talking, lowered his head and resumed his listless expression.

"And your mother let you do that?" the grandmother asked feebly. "Didn't she say anything when she saw you on the stage?"

"She remained in the wings all the time. I could see her clearly through the scenery. After the first scene she told me that I was too pale and put some rouge on my cheeks."

His grandmother hid her face in her hands and smothered an exasperated groan.

Luncheon proceeded. The grandmother constantly questioned the child, both about himself and about his mother and stepfather. She tried to delve into all the secrets of their lives. Her tone was urgent and sometimes bitter, but this keen curiosity was, as it were, quite ineffective, and when the child replied the old woman's face, twitching with apprehension, was like the face of a blind woman hearing a description of something she cannot see.

The grandfather did not seem to like these questions. From time to time he made discreet little signs to his wife. But she paid no attention and, indeed, at one moment shot a glance of annoyance at him. The grandfather bent his head in confusion. The child observed the whole of this incident, but he made no sign that he had done so and continued leisurely to chew his food.

"Henri," said his grandfather, as they rose from the table, "how would you like to go for a row on the river this afternoon?"

The grandmother intervened at once.

"What an idea! You're not going to take him away from me. You don't want to leave your grandmother, Henri, do you?"

She was seated on a low chair and held him tightly, as though fearing that someone would try to snatch him from her.

"I'm so glad to have you to myself today, Henri dear! I've been looking forward to it for so long."

Her voice trembled with emotion, and tears flowed down her worn cheeks. She made no attempt to dry them and indeed took a sort of pleasure in letting the child see them.

"But you mustn't be bored," she went on, briskly. "Tell us what you would like to do."

The child opened his lips as though to answer, but he changed his mind and after a moment said:

"I don't know."

"Yes, but I feel that there's something that would amuse you but that you don't like to tell us."

He denied this with a slight shake of his shoulders.

"Oh, well! We'll see about that in a moment or two," said his grandfather. "In the meantime, come and see my lilac."

They went into the garden. The lilac bush was very thick and partly concealed the window.

"Your grandmother wants to cut it back because it takes some of the light away from the drawing room; but then," explained the grandfather, "it would not bear such lovely flowers; for, you see, lilac is never more beautiful and more abundant than when one leaves it to itself."

He pulled down a branch and thrust a fully blown sprig of mauve blossom towards the child's face. The boy inhaled deeply and the sensual look returned to his face.

"And here," said the grandfather, proudly pointing to a bed full of red flowers. "What do you think of my garden, eh?"

He held his grandson by the hand. The grandmother, who had rejoined them, walked on the other side of the child. They remained silent, only raising their heads towards the tall trees which occasionally swayed in a neighbouring garden. Even though the sky was not so blue as it had been at midday, it was a splendid day. In the air, warmed by the sun, delicate odours and gentle rustlings seemed to be carrying out a quiet labour which lulled the senses. A woman's shout in the distance died away in a peal of laughter. A man's voice mimicked the shout with another and the first voice began to laugh still more loudly. Probably a couple passing down the river in a boat, with the man amusing himself by making it rock to try to frighten his companion.

The two old people enjoyed these things in a sort of gentle calm. Their heads were both inclined at the same angle and they both wore the same look of contentment. The grandmother had quietly replaced her arm round her grandson's neck.

The child was also affected by his surroundings in much the same way and made no attempt to move. But all sorts of secrets seemed to be stirring within him. His upper lip curled nervously and his teeth were clenched together, as though he had bitten into an unripe fruit. With a lithe movement of his head he broke loose from his grandmother's embrace. Then he became thoughtful again.

"Henri," said his grandmother, "do tell us what you would like to do."

He said nothing for a moment. Then a gleam came into his eyes.

"Let's go and see the thieves' house."

"The thieves' house? What do you mean?"

"The house where the band of thieves took refuge some years ago. The police besieged it, but the thieves barricaded themselves in and opened fire. The police had to blow down the walls."

"Whoever told you that tale?" asked his grandmother.

"Claire told me in the train, coming here. She told me that the house was quite close, under the viaduct. She's been there herself."

"That's absurd!" cried his grandmother in a muffled voice. Then she went on in a softer voice: "The house no longer exists, Henri, or, rather, it was rebuilt ages ago. There's nothing to see. . . . Besides, you couldn't enjoy seeing the place where something so horrible took place?"

"They held out for two days. Sometimes they fired from the windows and sometimes from the roof. And when their ammunition gave out they killed themselves. But they never gave in."

He acted the scene cleverly, pretending to hide and to take aim, as though he had given the story a great deal of thought.

The grandparents followed his movements in amazement and with a vague feeling of alarm. But the grandfather cast a reassuring glance at his wife and said:

"But of course, of course, it's only natural. . . . At his age one thinks of nothing but fighting and adventure. His muscles are beginning to develop and he's longing to use them.

"Henri," he added, feeling his arms, "would you like to play football? There's one here among your toys."

The boy nodded his head.

"That's right," said the grandmother, delighted that the idea of going for a row had been abandoned, "come and play here, on the grass."

"On the grass?" the grandfather quietly protested.

"Oh, you and your grass! Anyone would think that you loved it more than you love Henri."

She went in to fetch the ball and then came and sat in an armchair at the edge of the lawn. During her absence the goals had been marked out by driving sticks into the ground. The grandfather took off his coat and the game began.

The boy was impetuous but he lacked skill. He kicked the ball hard in such a way as to make it spin without travelling very far. He did not seem too anxious to run and preferred to wait for the ball to come to him, planted on his fragile legs, bare to the knees. Opposite him his grandfather with his precise movements seemed to be almost the more active of the two. He would go back a pace or two, raise his hands vertically to each side of his face to take better aim and then give the ball an accurate kick. He entered into the game with childish enthusiasm. With his legs slightly bent and his grey eyebrows knitted he took careful note of all his grandson's movements. Sometimes he would advance to the attack and sometimes he would retire prudently to his own ground. The grandmother's eyes never left her grandson; she encouraged him and cheered him on the whole time. This attitude seemed to provoke a fit of jealousy in her husband. He redoubled his efforts and he seemed extremely anxious to defeat his opponent. However, as the game became more lively, the child became more impetuous. His kicking became wilder and he dug up big pieces of turf with his toes. He charged his grandfather and jostled him. His grandmother, noticing these signs of impatience, began to be alarmed. She frowned at her husband as though to say: "Let him win." But the little old man, carried away by the game, pretended not to see and went on defending himself. The child was frowning with mortification. His grandmother began to be really anxious and swayed from side to side in her armchair. Suddenly, she had an idea. As the two players were struggling at the edge of a flower bed she cried:

"Look out for your flowers, Antoine!"

The grandfather raised his head and stood still. Then she went on, briskly:

"Go on, Henri, kick the ball."

The child, taking advantage of this distraction, shot forward and succeeded in steering the ball through his grandfather's goal.

"Oh!" said the grandfather, looking reproachfully in his wife's direction.

"Henri has won! Henri has won!" she cried, clapping her hands gleefully.

"But that's cheating!" the old man protested ruefully.

She shrugged her shoulders and covered her husband's voice.

"Bravo, Henri," she said. "And now come and rest beside me for a moment."

They sat down. The grandfather was slightly out of breath and held his hand up to his chest, but his wife took no notice of him and leaned over her grandson on whom she lavished praise for his skill. The child let his arms hang between his knees and picked up pebbles which he threw in front of him, aimlessly, without replying.

"Oh, look!" said his grandfather after a few moments. "I don't like the look of that sky.

"Nor of that either," he added, as a swallow flew by almost touching the lawn.

A cold breeze blew across the garden. The grandmother shivered and pressed her grandson to her as though to prevent him from shivering too. A moment later large drops of rain began to fall and they hurried back into the house.

The storm continued. It was a spring storm, interspersed with hail and lightning flashes. They had begun by playing a guessing game, but this did not seem to amuse the child; and now all three were standing by the window, gloomily watching the falling rain. The child pressed his forehead against the window and hummed a tune. His breath covered the pane with an opaque mist. Sometimes he clapped his hands when he saw large hailstones strike the leaves of the lilac bush and rebound.

From time to time the two old people glanced at him with the same anxious look. "If only he doesn't get bored," they both thought.

"Would you like to read a book until the rain stops, Henri?" asked his grandmother.

Without turning round, and with his lips pressed to the windowpane, he made a grimace of refusal.

"I can show you some books that will amuse you," said the grandfather. "Books full of adventures and fighting—just the sort that you like."

The child made another face. Then he said slowly:

"It's not the same thing, because the stories in books aren't true."

And he resumed his humming.

Low clouds covered the sky outside, and the window, already half obscured by the lilac bush, only let in a very feeble light. In this sudden darkness the silence and the lack of anything to do became even more palpable. A look of desperation came into the grandmother's eyes. She drew the curtains and moved a chair, as though to return to the world of light and sound.

"I've got an idea, Henri," she cried suddenly. "I'll show you all your things. They're in this cupboard."

The child turned round and it was evident that the idea pleased him. His grandmother immediately went to the cupboard and opened both its doors wide.

"Look, Henri, everything in here belongs to you."

It was a tall cupboard containing several shelves, and was filled with the presents which the grandparents had given their grandson. On the lower shelves were large square boxes, ninepins, a little rifle and a suit of toy armour; above, there were picture books and a stamp album. Everything was in beautifully arranged order.

The child drew near. He examined his possessions with considerable satisfaction. He raised the lids of some of the boxes and took out the toys they contained. The grandmother smilingly pointed things out to him.

"Your marionette theatre is up there, taken to pieces and carefully wrapped up so that it won't spoil. And behind there is the camera we gave you last year."

It was evident that she had arranged everything herself and that she often amused herself by handling them.

"This," she went on, as the child continued his inspection, "is my own corner. This is where I put all the things I treasure most. My jewels are in this casket. My purse is in that red bag. Here is a photograph of your mother when she was your age. And this notebook is precious to me too. You gave it to me yourself. Do you recognise it? See what's written on the cover. 'Drawings made by Henri at the age of eight and given to Grandmother.'"

Her face had become happy again. She pressed up against the child, who seemed to be attracted by the objects she was showing him. The grandfather smiled his approval of the scene and walked up and down the room. He halted for a moment by the window, opened it and announced that it had stopped raining. The grandmother suggested that they should go for a walk, but the child refused.

"I want to play with my toys," he said.

"Take some out-of-doors game and let's go into the garden. Look how clear the sky is now."

"No, I want to play here," he protested, with a sly, stubborn look.

They gave way to him eagerly. He went to the cupboard, considered all the boxes at length and indicated one of them.

"The theatre," he said.

The grandfather raised himself on tiptoe, lifted it down and brought it to him.

"I'll help you set it up, Henri."

"No," he replied quickly, "I want to do it by myself."

Kneeling on the ground, he took out the various parts of the theatre and then the scenery and the marionettes themselves. The two old people followed his movements admiringly. But the child did not seem quite happy. He looked at his grandparents out of the corners of his eyes and dawdled. After a moment or two he stood up and, going up to them, said in a pleading voice:

"Won't you leave me alone? I'll get everything ready. When I've finished I'll call you and I'll give you a performance."

And he kissed his grandmother on the cheek. Touched by this display of affection, she held him to her.

"Yes, Henri dear, we'll do just as you wish."

He quickly disengaged himself from her embrace and, as his grandparents left the room, he shook his finger at them and said:

"Don't come in until I call you!"

They went into the hall and the grandmother opened the kitchen door. Clothilde was alone.

"Has the maid gone already?" asked the grandmother.

"She has, indeed! And she was in a hurry, too."

"Of course! She asked leave to go and see her aunt at La Varenne."

"Oh, she won't go as far as that," replied the plump girl, ironically. "Her young man was waiting for her at the corner of the street and in weather like this they'll soon have got under cover. I don't know if they are all like that in Paris, but she's a real hussy. The things she told me about her house and her employers!"

"What did she say?" asked the grandmother eagerly.

"She said that her master and Madame Louise were always quarrelling, and that there's no money, and that the most extraordinary people come to the house . . ."

Such an expression of pain came over her mistress's face that she tried to modify her remarks.

"Anyway, it's probably nothing but lies. They're hardly worth repeating to Madame. One knows only too well the things a bad girl like that is capable of inventing about her employers!"

They walked along slowly without speaking, but they were clearly stunned by what they had just heard. Their eyes were lowered as though they were in the presence of something which they did not want to see. The grandmother broke the silence with a sigh.

"Louise," she said, in a voice which rose from the depths of her recollections, "Louise, who was so proud!

"And how awful to think that our little darling lives in such surroundings," she continued. "Our little darling who is so good."

She turned towards her husband as though seeking his assent, but he contented himself with nodding his head, and silence fell again.

In this silence the various incidents of the day returned to their minds. They thought of the moment at which the figure of their grandson had appeared through the bars of the garden gate. They recalled his movements and the expressions on his face, they remembered his words. Then, as though these pictures brought them back to the present, they raised their heads and looked around them. On all sides could be seen the damage done by the storm. The flowers in the flower beds had been beaten down by the hail; the gravel in the paths was streaked with muddy runnels.

The grandfather looked round his garden. He bent down to straighten a plant whose flower lay in the mud; but its stalk was broken. He sighed, took his wife's arm again, looked at the sky and said, sorrowfully shaking his head:

"We were expecting such a lovely day."

She answered him by a pressure of her arm to show that she shared his disappointment; and like a lovesick woman who has let herself be lulled by a dream and suddenly returns to reality, she leaned her head towards her husband and laid it tenderly upon his shoulder.

They had walked round the house and were now in the part of the garden onto which the drawing room opened.

"Henri must have finished his preparations by now," she said.

They crept up noiselessly and, hidden by the lilac bush, looked into the room. A painted cardboard theatre stood in the middle of it. They could see the little tragic mask above the stage. The child was at the far end of the room, with his back to the window. They could not distinguish his movements.

"What is he doing?" asked the grandmother. "Oh, yes, I see. He's looking for something in the cupboard. Now that he knows where his toys are, he'll go there often. Heavens, how wonderful it would be if we always had him with us!"

The grandfather was looking also. Suddenly he started, thrust his head forward and placed his hands on each side of it to get a better view.

"He looks as if he's hiding. Perhaps he is preparing a surprise for us," whispered the grandmother once more.

Then she recoiled abruptly. Her wide-open eyes, her gaping mouth and all her features were distorted in a sort of mute horror. It is thus, no doubt, that people look at the moment when they feel that their heart's blood is ebbing.

The child was holding up the red bag in his hands and with hurried, furtive movements, but with the utmost calm, he was stealing.

ON THE FARM

Hans Friedrich Blunck

(1888–   )

TRANSLATED BY BASIL CREIGHTON

THE COLT was an ungainly, playful creature; it took the farmer and the carter at Babenhof all their time to hold him while they gave him one more grooming and a last combing of his mane and tail. He was the pride of the farm, a two-year-old, strong-limbed, white-maned, and he was just off to the town to be shown for the first time, in the colts' class. The farmer wanted to show him himself; but a tragedy had happened on the farm a few days before and he felt it was his duty to remain on the place until things had settled down again. What he meant by settling down Kersten himself did not know: nobody can restore the dead to life.

The colt took the business of being smartened up and groomed as an invitation to play; he danced about, plucked at the young man's shirt with his lips, laid back his ears and tried to snatch the farmer's hat. "Take care he doesn't kick, Bernd!" But Bernd did not listen. He was silent and abstracted. He looked so smart in his black suit and hard hat that Kersten couldn't help smiling. Then he remembered why the man had that drawn look of suspense about his eyes: he was thinking of the tragedy that had taken place on the farm. He himself had been haunted for some days past by the thought of retribution. Perhaps both of them—they were very alike in the hard, strong set of the chin, in their hair and high-set eyebrows— were full of the same thought that would not let them rest.

"Bernd!"—Bernd turned his head towards the farmyard, where the empty waggons were coupled. Kersten too glanced across; he knew now why the young man had that look of sinister gloom, a look, rather, of one who had been roused to fury: Johann Kortmann had come to fetch the borrowed waggons.

The carter crossed the yard, leading the colt. Their neighbour at the

same moment bent over the waggon pole. It was just as well! The carter
was to have married the dead girl and it was Kortmann's fault that all was
over—it seemed to Kersten scarcely believable that a girl like her, always
busy, always looking ahead, such a capable housekeeper, should have lost
courage and taken her life. Kersten followed Bernd anxiously with his eyes
as he led the colt towards the gate. At that moment he too felt the urge
to wreak vengeance on their neighbour, even at the cost of life and liberty.
The carter turned into the road without a word to Kortmann, untied the
halter of the old chestnut mare, got on her back and rode off with the colt
on a leading rein. The farmer was relieved to see him go.

Kersten lived on very close terms with his farm hands; he knew how to
take them. As often happens in the north of Germany, he had followed a
profession before retiring to the ancestral farm: he had been a barrister and
got to know many sides of life, good and bad, just and unjust. His wife and
son had died, one after the other, a few years before, and so, finding life out
in the world distasteful, he came back to the farm with his daughter, who
was still only a child. It was a fine big farm, just the place to tempt a man
who had led a busy, varied life to try out new systems of farming. His years
in the town lay far behind him: Kersten was a farmer again, and if ever he
left the place it was either as a representative of the farming interest or to
transact some business for someone in the village.

This time it was his own farm that was overtaken by misfortune; the
maidservant—she was to have married the head-carter, Bernd Burmeister,
that year—had taken her own life. Nobody would say why, but everybody
knew.

Kersten hurried indoors as though pursued by his thoughts. He kept
accounts of certain experiments in cropping the land and made careful
reports on them to the County Council. This year he was proud of some
colts he had bred. The one Bernd was taking to the show was the pick of
them. But he wanted to report also on some other experiments he had
made at Babenhof, particularly his maize, which even up there in the north
he had sown for many years and succeeded with better every year.

He looked up from his writing table as he caught sight of an old cottage
woman, who for the last few days since the girl's death had been housekeeper at the farm; she was calling the poultry, and little Marie, Kersten's
child, was helping and shouting for joy. It was funny to see how the ducks
tumbled over themselves in their haste; and the way the pigeons called
to each other and swooped down from the dove-cote was a charming
sight, and then the behaviour of the three cocks as they displayed the corn
to their hens with as much astonishment as though they had only just discovered the providence that supplied their needs. Such a picking and
pecking, scratching and chucking, such a scuttling and flutter of wings, all
to be first where the corn fell thickest. The bright plumage and vainglory

of the lords and masters of the farmyard made a brave show. The geese were late and came up in a rush, beating their wings, and even the turkey-cock, who scorned to be seen among the common fry, led up his three wives, taking good care at the same time that they did not strut with undue haste or break into a run. He approached with dignity, gobbling as he came, his throat flushed red with exertion or self-control, but his arrogance was rewarded; besides, he knew very well that he and his wives would not be forgotten

But the child found his over-weening pride so comic that she suddenly emptied all the corn out of her skirt just to be able to laugh her fill. "Look at his lordship arriving!" she shouted, pointing with both hands.

Apparently a raised voice and laughter, even though a child's, were un-seemly; for old Frau Dierk intervened at once: "Sh, sh!" Marie nodded, looked round and then ran quickly indoors. Why had she run away? Frau Dierk too drew herself up and looked fixedly across at the cart sheds. Johann Kortmann was coming along with a lurching stride. "He walks like a mur-derer," flashed through the farmer's head. What nonsense, he thought next moment; if you don't keep an open mind, who in the whole village is going to keep his head? But he could not help clenching his fists. If only, he thought, he might just give that fellow one punch in the jaw or spit in his face or do something outrageous!

Johann Kortmann was embarrassed by the old lady's greeting. She let him come up to her without saying a word: she just stood there without winking. The young man did not know what to say; he held out a cord that had broken, smiled sheepishly at the broken ends and looked up again at Frau Dierk. "Got a rope?" he asked at last. The old woman shook her head almost imperceptibly; she neither spoke nor moved. Johann Kortmann turned away abashed.

Kersten had marked the ingratiating smile; and now he was overcome by pity. He's not to be envied either, poor devil, he thought. Next moment he felt merciless. Hadn't Johann Kortmann known that the carter and the young servant-girl were going to be married? Everyone in the village knew that the drawings for their cottage on the farm had been passed and the stonemason told to get to work. What business had this neighbour of theirs to make free with what was another's?

No doubt the girl had her share in the blame, but no one spoke ill of the dead. She was a jolly girl with a passion for dancing and Bernd, head-carter on Kersten's farm, was dour, too serious altogether; but he was far and away a better fellow than Johann Kortmann. As soon as she had realised that she had been left in the lurch she had paid the bitterest penalty that youth can exact of itself. Guilt? Kersten pleaded the case as he might have done in court in days gone by: The man has the responsi-bility and must pay the penalty. He is not lord and master for nothing.

The living bear the blame, not the dead.

A brief autumn storm broke over the village at midday. The rain pattered on the leaves of the great walnut that stretched its boughs over the farm-yard. Kersten, as he always did when a storm blew up, went anxiously to the stables and through the barns, as though that could ward off the lightning, and then went back into the farmhouse. Old Frau Dierk was in the passage holding the frightened child by the arm. "There's nothing to be afraid of," she was saying to comfort her. "The good God will protect us. And if anything did happen to us, you'd fly straight up to heaven, where Anna's gone." Kersten did not want the child to be reminded of the maid-servant. He shook his head angrily. "Yes, yes, Herr Kersten," the old lady said. "The parson's not always in the right of it. What do any of us know what the dear God has in store for us?"

"And Johann Kortmann—will he go to hell?" the child asked.

"Run along," Kersten said roughly, "you're talking nonsense." Marie rubbed her eyes and slipped away into the sitting-room. "Did you put that into her head?" Kersten asked. Mother Dierk stubbornly shook her head. She had a good conscience. She had said nothing, she had not spoken a word about the whole affair. She had kept her lips as tightly closed with every-body as she had just now when their neighbour's son came across the yard to her. "But this I do know," she permitted herself to say now, "Kortmann promised to make a farmer's wife of her and that's how he got her away from Bernd. Then left her in the lurch."

"How do you know that?" Kersten asked.

"Because she told me so herself the night before. And Bernd, who was to have married her, knows it too. You'd best keep your eyes open, Master. In case anything happens between the men-folk."

Kersten walked silently on. Once more he saw himself in court and speeches for the prosecution and the defence ran through his head. He had the uncanny feeling that he had to speak in defence of someone—in his own defence, it suddenly flashed through his mind. It might be that in thought he had killed that man as he walked across the yard.

A warm rain succeeded the storm. That was good and also bad: the maize needed sun to ripen it, the winter barley was not yet sown. Kersten threw on a coat and tramped out to the Babenhof fields to see how the work was going. His way led through an avenue of young oaks; he had planted them himself; whoever followed after him on the farm would one day take pleasure in their rustling shade. After him? And suppose his daughter when she married lived in the town. Once more he was reminded of the maidservant. What a waste! He felt a sort of shyness as the thought of what his loneliness had meant to him shot through his mind. He too at moments had wished to have a son from that young spirited girl. Vain thoughts, which all the same are never far from a farmer's mind.

And there again it was his carter whose bride he had calmly thought of having for his own. He was fond of Bernd: he was as like himself as a younger brother; only he was too slow-witted and took life too hard. They would have to keep an eye on him.

The under-carter came up with the two horses and the seed drill. He had not sown the seed yet; he had noticed the storm coming up and had waited to see how bad the rain would be. Kersten said he had done quite right. "Has Bernd got back?" the lad asked, turning round on his horse, and when the farmer looked at him in perplexity, he added: "Bernd Burmeister with the colt."

"But he can't get back before dark, man." What was the fellow thinking of? But there—they all had their share in what was to be. Each feared the living on account of the dead.

Later in the day Kersten had a strange experience for which he could find no explanation. He had been reading some agricultural journals to take his mind off what had occurred; but the whole farm lay under the ban of an oppression, a suspense, and it had him too by the throat. Again and again he found himself embarked on imaginary discourses about Bernd or Johann Kortmann, defending the one while he hated the sight of the other. As in his days of legal practice he lived through all that had happened or that might have happened, linking up and considering at the same time all the possibilities, putting himself in the place of the people concerned and trying at the same time to restrain them. The hatred and every thought that possessed his carter were revealed to him in his own soul as though in duplicate.

Just as he was about to cross the sitting-room to his bedroom it suddenly occurred to him to lock his gun-cupboard, feeling it was himself for whom the temptation might be too strong. It was dusk and as he opened the door into the next room he saw someone in front of the cupboard. As he turned, it seemed to him that the other man looked round, a bolt clicked and then the man had gone. "Bernd!" Kersten called out. "Hello, Bernd!" But by that time he was through the side door, which was ajar. Kersten followed, but heard no sound of steps. He then hurried back, turned on the light to make sure that nothing was missing and went out across the yard to find the carter. He met old Frau Dierk and hastened to ask her, but Bernd was not back yet, she said.

But he must be. He had seen him. They went together to the stable. The colt was not there and the carter could not possibly have returned. Unless of course he had stabled the colt somewhere else and stolen back and into the house. Kersten was bewildered. He decided to say nothing about what he had seen and he could not in any case think of any explanation.

He went to bed and after he had lain awake for an hour he heard the clatter of hoofs. They had come at last. He thought of getting up at once to find out whether the colt had got a prize, but he decided to put it off until the morning, because he would have to ask the man about his visit to the cupboard and it all seemed vague and baffling. Then, after all, he got up, went to his gun-cupboard and methodically examined it. Nothing was missing, nothing was out of its proper place. His over-heated brain had played a trick on him. So he changed his mind and went out to the stable, where he found the carter unsaddling the mare, and asked about the show. The colt had not got a prize, only an honourable mention.

"Well, off to bed with you now, Bernd."

"Yes—in a moment."

A new day dawned over Babenhof, a day like any other, and Kersten was inclined to take himself to task for his hours of gloomy preoccupation and agonised questioning and cross-questioning. The dawn sky was clear; cloudless sunlight lay over the yellowing leaves of bush and hedge and on the loaded fruit trees in the orchard. Nothing had happened, all was quiet.

It was not until midday when he came back from a lengthy sitting of the County Council and the inspection of a long stretch of newly made road that Kersten heard that Johann Kortmann was missing. He must have gone to the town, people said.

The winter barley had been sown hours ago. Bernd and the handy under-carter had seen to that. They greeted the farmer with a laugh when he went out to the field and were pleased to have got it done quicker than he could have expected. The head carter told a bit more about the showing of the colt. The gentry there had thought him a bit too tall; there were a lot more fine animals there and the judges had to look hard to find any they could pick holes in. Now the colt was in harness, rather bewildered and clumsy at turning, but good natured and willing.

At night a woman came over from the Kortmanns' farm to see if anyone knew where Johann had got to: nothing had been seen of him all day. Kersten happened to be standing with his head carter, discussing the lay-out of the next day's work. The farmer felt the blood rush to his head. He sent the woman roughly about her business. Then, as he turned to Bernd, the apparition at the gun-cupboard came into his mind. It must have been the shadow of his own evil wishes! He glanced uneasily at the man beside him. But he only showed his teeth in a grin. Johann must be on the roads, Bernd called out after the woman, they had better enquire in the inns in all the villages round about. There was not a trace of agitation, not the slightest concern or confusion to be seen in him.

But nothing more was seen of Kortmann, and now, without a word being said, Babenhof was enclosed within a ring of silence. In spite of all the hard things that had been said of Johann Kortmann up to now, nobody would countenance such a revenge as that. Where was Johann? Nobody knew anything of him. He had gone to the Jug and Bottle at night as usual, since when there had been no trace of him. Murder? Nobody said the word outright, but all pointed a finger at the farm which had the motive for revenge. If Johann Kortmann had been beaten and left for dead, he would have been found; but his disappearance was a mystery that lay on them with the weight of an accursed thing. However much there was to reproach the missing man with, God alone was the disposer of life and death.

Feeling in the village changed. Excuses were made for Kortmann; people were already incensed against the Babenhof folk and waited tensely to know what would come out. Old Kortmann came and had a talk with Kersten. Kersten maintained roundly that no one on his farm knew anything about the disappearance of his son, and he asked the old man irritably whether it was he whom he suspected.

As a barrister Kersten had always played the part of judge too. He condemned the murderer if murder had been committed, but he understood the urge to exact a penalty from Kortmann because that urge had been too much for him himself. What man is free of his secret thoughts?

"But if you mean someone else on the farm," he advised the old man, "then be careful what you say. My men are incapable of deceiving me. I don't know, of course, what has happened to your son; perhaps—it is no wish of mine that it should be so—he has taken his own life. Forgive me," he added quickly, "but I must say it in case injustice should be done to others."

Old Kortmann shook his head. He knew that his son had not left the district and had not laid hands on himself. The secret remained.

But the village knew that old Kortmann had been to Babenhof and rumour got busy. Whatever Johann's guilt, fresh guilt was in the air and they sought out the man who had taken a lawless revenge. When Kersten went to the Jug and Bottle that night he noticed that he was avoided. They talked of other things when he asked about the missing man and they left at an early hour.

The host could not leave and so escape being questioned. "What do people say about it then?" Kersten asked with a casual air.

"They want to set a search on foot for Johann Kortmann, the fishermen in the lake, the rest in the woods."

"Quite right," Kersten replied with conviction. "That's what ought to be done. I was with Burmeister last night myself. I saw him when he got home with the horses from the town."

The innkeeper nodded awkwardly. "The policeman is coming tomorrow. It is no business of ours to discuss the business and perhaps blame the innocent."

It was not until he was on his way home that the apparition at the gun-cupboard started to Kersten's eyes; he had completely forgotten it because he had come to the conclusion that it must have been an illusion. Now he recollected it and at the same moment everything swam before his eyes. If

Bernd had really been at the cupboard door, if he, Kersten, had been deceived by Bernd's air of trustworthiness—— Was it not unjust to act as though it were not common knowledge that Bernd Burmeister had had his life and love treacherously destroyed? Would he not in Bernd's place have wanted to square accounts with Kortmann?

Kersten stood still; the uncertainty in which he was affected his feet and knees. He was honest enough to recall the aimless fancies the dead girl had aroused. He had looked upon her with the secret thought that all men indulge in who are left without sons and who consider the women about them as possible mothers; and he would dearly have liked to call the guilty to account for her fruitless death. Then what must have been his man's state of mind?

Kersten hurried home and went straight to his gun-cupboard to give it another careful look over.

How could he possibly have failed to notice before that his revolver was missing?

The discovery made his head whirl. The cupboard seemed to shrink together. Instantly he reproached himself bitterly. Why had he even in his own mind kept silence about what he had seen at the cupboard? It was partisanship: he had wanted to shield his own people. Murder had been committed—and he, he knew who had done it.

In the first shock of dismay Kersten took refuge in his room and collapsed into a chair. He saw himself in court and saw the eyes of the judge fixed keenly on him, as he asked: "How could you, knowing the feeling there was on your farm, leave the cupboard unlocked? How could you fail to make a thorough search as soon as ever Kortmann disappeared?"

He heard the carter in the passage and got up and turned on the light and went heavily out and pulled him by the hand into the room.

"Why did you do it, Bernd?" he asked without more ado. He could scarcely get his breath, he could hardly look the man in the eyes. "How did it happen?" he groaned. "You'd better tell me."

The man went as pale as death; he clasped his hands together and raised them as though he could not breathe. "It was not I, master."

"Tell me about it. I saw you last night at my cupboard. Tell me honestly how it happened. It's the best thing you can do."

"At the cupboard?" Burmeister stammered.

Kersten pushed him into a chair. He could hear his breathing as he sat opposite him. "How could you do such a thing? Tell me about it."

The door flew open and the kitchenmaid rushed in with her face as white as chalk. "The policeman's here. He wants to speak to Herr Kersten."

"Tell him to wait," Kersten was going to say, when the carter groaned out: "No, not the police!" He jumped up abruptly as though to make his escape and one hand went to his pocket.

Kersten was able to seize his hands and push him back onto the chair.

"Tell the policeman I am coming," he called out after the girl. He felt in the carter's pocket but found nothing there.

The girl came back: "The policeman cannot wait, Herr Kersten."

He followed on her heels and after scrutinising the two men seated at the table, he cleared his throat and drew nearer with a heavy, hesitant step. "Well," he said, "you seem to know what I've come about." The tone of his voice showed he was sorry. He looked from one to the other and turning round he pulled up a chair and sat down between the farmer and his man. "Bernd Burmeister?"

Bernd shook his head again distractedly. "No, no," he almost shouted. "You try it on. You'll never prove anything."

"Don't make it worse than it is," Kersten warned him. "I shall be put on my oath, you know, and I shall have to say you went to my gun-cupboard."

The man seemed utterly distraught. "But that was not—till after-wards——"

"Afterwards—after you'd done it?" the policeman put in quickly, taking advantage of the admission.

"Not till afterwards," Burmeister stammered. "And you can see for your-self that not a shot has been fired."

It was a senseless, crazy line of defence. "And what happened first?" the knowing old sergeant-major asked. He put one hand on Bernd Burmeister's shoulder, casually passed it down his side and produced the missing revolver from one of his pockets. He laid it down on the far side of the table. "Well, we can see about that all in good time. We'll soon know whether you have fired a shot or no. Meanwhile, tell me how it all came about and what happened first?" He took hold of the carter, who was sobbing convulsively, by the arm. "There, I know the man took your girl from you. He was a swine, a bad lot. But all the same I've got to know what happened after that."

Kersten wanted to put in a word; he envied the old sergeant-major his fatherly way of dealing with people; he himself at critical moments was always the observant barrister. When he saw that Burmeister was incapable of getting a word out, he tried to gain time for him by opening the breach and the chamber of the revolver. "Sergeant-major," he brought out, "it's true it has not been fired."

The cartridges were all there. The barrel when he held it up to the light was clean. "You must witness, sergeant-major, that he has not fired a shot," Kersten said again in agitation.

"Yes, but before," the policeman insisted, turning to Burmeister again. "Something happened before that, didn't it? And then you got hold of the revolver and thought to yourself you could always do yourself in if it came out."

The carter nodded his head convulsively.

He's not speaking the truth now, Kersten thought with annoyance, I saw him at the cupboard before anything happened. He was wrought up and in his excitement he became as much a part of the other man as if he had had a share in what he had done. Thirty years younger, he thought in a flash, thirty years less master of himself and what might not he have done? But after all, he reflected next moment, he is a murderer. How could he come to steal a firearm from me? How could he do it?

The carter now brought out a few sentences by fits and starts. When he had unsaddled the horses, he went back through the village. He might have meant to run across Johann Kortmann, or he might not—he didn't know why it was he went. He did run into him, however—just on the bridge it was—and they went for each other at once. They fell over the parapet together, and as they struggled in the water he had got the other man under.

The policeman glanced at Kersten. Kersten muttered in a groan: "I don't understand a word of it."

"Would you mind leaving us alone for a moment?" the old man asked. "But don't be far away, Herr Kersten. Wait in the next room."

The farmer got up reluctantly. He was already drawing up his speech for the defence; he was going to plead self-defence. But then—Burmeister was lying. He had caught him red-handed at the cupboard. He had gone out deliberately, taking the weapon with him. Kersten opened the door in order to go into the next room. As he did so the light fell on the cupboard and suddenly he saw, exactly as he had the night before, that someone was standing there and unmistakably turning round towards him.

He caught his breath in his agitation and wanted to stop the man, but he heard no sound of a step. So he went back and opened the door again. "There's a spook here," he stammered distractedly. The policeman shook his head: he couldn't make the man out. Kersten then for the third time opened the connecting door and now he distinctly saw that, as he entered, either a draught of air or a sinking of the floor boards made the glazed cupboard door swing open so that a dim shadow seemed to turn towards him—his own shadow.

"What was that you were saying?" the sergeant-major asked on second thought.

"Nothing, nothing, it was the cupboard door, that was all," Kersten muttered. He knew that he had never in his life looked such a fool; he shut the door behind him in a rage and stood in the darkness of the bedroom.

He thought it all over: so the night before he had made an assumption that had no foundation. He had seen the reflection in the cupboard door before Bernd Burmeister had come home. A warning apparition? Rubbish! A simple reflection, which had deceived him, which—perhaps—he had been expecting. His oppression did not leave him; it was clear to him that in his heart he was not without blame. He remembered his state of mind as he went about with clenched fists, wishing in his heart that he could bring destruction on the head of the man who had brought disaster on his farm. A reflection in the door—and at the same time an image of his heart's desire! He had seen his own inmost thought there; involuntarily and from a sense of what was just, he had been awaiting what the carter subsequently did.

He was overcome by a great weariness. He waited awhile longer and then he went back into the next room as though he had been summoned and sat down at the table.

"We've just about done," the sergeant-major said, surprised that the farmer had come in without being called. Then he added reluctantly: "I'm taking him to town tonight. There's no help for it."

"I'm coming too," Kersten said shortly, and when the sergeant-major got to his feet in perplexity, he added: "I'll stay there until it comes on."

The sergeant-major's face cleared. He had understood. "Oh, I see, because you used to be a barrister," he said, nodding.

Kersten shook his head. He wanted to explain himself, but said no more.

The carter had recovered his composure. He looked straight in front of him with a stolid and obstinate expression, but when he heard Kersten say he was coming too, he glanced up and nodded his gratitude.

"Perhaps he only did more or less what all of us wanted to see happen," Kersten said to the sergeant-major, "and so we must all take our share of the blame." He added under his breath: "I felt the same as he did. I must tell the court that."

THE KILLERS

Ernest Hemingway

(1898–   )

T HE DOOR of Henry's lunch-room opened and two men came in. They sat down at the counter.

"What's yours?" George asked them.

"I don't know," one of the men said. "What do you want to eat, Al?"

"I don't know," said Al. "I don't know what I want to eat."

Outside it was getting dark. The street-light came on outside the window. The two men at the counter read the menu. From the other end of the counter Nick Adams watched them. He had been talking to George when they came in.

"I'll have a roast pork tenderloin with apple sauce and mashed potatoes," the first man said.

"It isn't ready yet."

"What the hell do you put it on the card for?"

"That's the dinner," George explained. "You can get that at six o'clock." George looked at the clock on the wall behind the counter.

"It's five o'clock."

"The clock says twenty minutes past five," the second man said.

"It's twenty minutes fast."

"Oh, to hell with the clock," the first man said. "What have you got to eat?"

"I can give you any kind of sandwiches," George said. "You can have ham and eggs, bacon and eggs, liver and bacon, or a steak."

"Give me chicken croquettes with green peas and cream sauce and mashed potatoes."

"That's the dinner."

"Everything we want's the dinner, eh? That's the way you work it."

"I can give you ham and eggs, bacon and eggs, liver——"

"I'll take ham and eggs," the man called Al said. He wore a derby hat and a black overcoat buttoned across the chest. His face was small and white and he had tight lips. He wore a silk muffler and gloves.

"Give me bacon and eggs," said the other man. He was about the same size as Al. Their faces were different, but they were dressed like twins. Both wore overcoats too tight for them. They sat leaning forward, their elbows on the counter.

"Got anything to drink?" Al asked.

"Silver beer, bevo, ginger-ale," George said.

"I mean you got anything to *drink?*"

"Just those I said."

"This is a hot town," said the other. "What do they call it?"

"Summit."

"Ever hear of it?" Al asked his friend.

"No," said the friend.

"What do you do here nights?" Al asked.

"They eat the dinner," his friend said. "They all come here and eat the big dinner."

"That's right," George said.

"So you think that's right?" Al asked George.

"Sure."

"You're a pretty bright boy, aren't you?"

"Sure," said George.

"Well, you're not," said the other little man. "Is he, Al?"

"He's dumb," said Al. He turned to Nick. "What's your name?"

"Adams."

"Another bright boy," Al said. "Ain't he a bright boy, Max?"

"The town's full of bright boys," Max said.

George put the two platters, one of ham and eggs, the other of bacon and eggs, on the counter. He set down two side-dishes of fried potatoes and closed the wicket into the kitchen.

"Which is yours?" he asked Al.

"Don't you remember?"

"Ham and eggs."

"Just a bright boy," Max said. He leaned forward and took the ham and eggs. Both men ate with their gloves on. George watched them eat.

"What are *you* looking at?" Max looked at George.

"Nothing."

"The hell you were. You were looking at me."

"Maybe the boy meant it for a joke, Max," Al said.

George laughed.

"*You* don't have to laugh," Max said to him. "*You* don't have to laugh at all, see?"

"All right," said George.

"So he thinks it's all right." Max turned to Al. "He thinks it's all right. That's a good one."

"Oh, he's a thinker," Al said. They went on eating.

"What's the bright boy's name down the counter?" Al asked Max.

"Hey, bright boy," Max said to Nick. "You go around on the other side of the counter with your boy friend."

"What's the idea?" Nick asked.

"There isn't any idea."

"You better go around, bright boy," Al said. Nick went around behind the counter.

"What's the idea?" George asked.

"None of your damn business," Al said. "Who's out in the kitchen?"

"The nigger."

"What do you mean the nigger?"

"The nigger that cooks."

"Tell him to come in."

"What's the idea?"

"Tell him to come in."

"Where do you think you are?"

"We know damn well where we are," the man called Max said. "Do we look silly?"

"You talk silly," Al said to him. "What the hell do you argue with this kid for? Listen," he said to George, "tell the nigger to come out here."

"What are you going to do to him?"

"Nothing. Use your head, bright boy. What would we do to a nigger?"

George opened the slit that opened back into the kitchen. "Sam," he called. "Come in here a minute."

The door to the kitchen opened and the nigger came in. "What was it?" he asked. The two men at the counter took a look at him.

"All right, nigger. You stand right there," Al said.

Sam, the nigger, standing in his apron, looked at the two men sitting at the counter. "Yes, sir," he said. Al got down from his stool.

"I'm going back to the kitchen with the nigger and bright boy," he said. "Go on back to the kitchen, nigger. You go with him, bright boy." The little man walked after Nick and Sam, the cook, back into the kitchen. The door shut after them. The man called Max sat at the counter opposite George. He didn't look at George but looked in the mirror that ran along back of the counter. Henry's had been made over from a saloon into a lunch-counter.

"Well, bright boy," Max said, looking into the mirror, "why don't you say something?"

"What's it all about?"

"Hey, Al," Max called, "bright boy wants to know what it's all about."

"Why don't you tell him?" Al's voice came from the kitchen.

"What do you think it's all about?"

"I don't know."

"What do you think?"

Max looked into the mirror all the time he was talking.

"I wouldn't say."

"Hey, Al, bright boy says he wouldn't say what he thinks it's all about."

"I can hear you, all right," Al said from the kitchen. He had propped open the slit that dishes passed through into the kitchen with a catsup bottle. "Listen, bright boy," he said from the kitchen to George. "Stand a little further along the bar. You move a little to the left, Max." He was like a photographer arranging for a group picture.

"Talk to me, bright boy," Max said. "What do you think's going to happen?"

George did not say anything.

"I'll tell you," Max said. "We're going to kill a Swede. Do you know a big Swede named Ole Andreson?"

"Yes."

"He comes here to eat every night, don't he?"

"Sometimes he comes here."

"He comes here at six o'clock, don't he?"

"If he comes."

"We know all that, bright boy," Max said. "Talk about something else. Ever go to the movies?"

"Once in a while."

"You ought to go to the movies more. The movies are fine for a bright boy like you."

"What are you going to kill Ole Andreson for? What did he ever do to you?"

"He never had a chance to do anything to us. He never even seen us."

"And he's only going to see us once," Al said from the kitchen.

"What are you going to kill him for, then?" George asked.

"We're killing him for a friend. Just to oblige a friend, bright boy."

"Shut up," said Al from the kitchen. "You talk too goddam much."

"Well, I got to keep bright boy amused. Don't I, bright boy?"

"You talk too damn much," Al said. "The nigger and my bright boy are amused by themselves. I got them tied up like a couple of girl friends in the convent."

"I suppose you were in a convent."

"You never know."

"You were in a kosher convent. That's where you were."

George looked up at the clock.

"If anybody comes in you tell them the cook is off, and if they keep after it, you tell them you'll go back and cook yourself. Do you get that, bright boy?"

"All right," George said. "What you going to do with us afterward?"

"That'll depend," Max said. "That's one of those things you never know at the time."

George looked up at the clock. It was a quarter past six. The door from the street opened. A street-car motorman came in.

"Hello, George," he said. "Can I get supper?"

"Sam's gone out," George said. "He'll be back in about half an hour."

"I'd better go up the street," the motorman said. George looked at the clock. It was twenty minutes past six.

"That was nice, bright boy," Max said. "You're a regular little gentleman."

"He knew I'd blow his head off," Al said from the kitchen.

"No," said Max. "It ain't that. Bright boy is nice. He's a nice boy. I like him."

At six-fifty-five George said: "He's not coming."

Two other people had been in the lunch-room. Once George had gone out to the kitchen and made a ham-and-egg sandwich "to go" that a man wanted to take with him. Inside the kitchen he saw Al, his derby hat tipped back, sitting on a stool beside the wicket with the muzzle of a sawed-off shotgun resting on the ledge. Nick and the cook were back to back in the corner, a towel tied in each of their mouths. George had cooked the sandwich, wrapped it up in oiled paper, put it in a bag, brought it in, and the man had paid for it and gone out.

"Bright boy can do everything," Max said. "He can cook and everything. You'd make some girl a nice wife, bright boy."

"Yes?" George said. "Your friend, Ole Andreson, isn't going to come."

"We'll give him ten minutes," Max said.

Max watched the mirror and the clock. The hands of the clock marked seven o'clock, and then five minutes past seven.

"Come on, Al," said Max. "We better go. He's not coming."

"Better give him five minutes," Al said from the kitchen.

In the five minutes a man came in, and George explained that the cook was sick.

"Why the hell don't you get another cook?" the man asked. "Aren't you running a lunch-counter?" He went out.

"Come on, Al," Max said.

"What about the two bright boys and the nigger?"

"They're all right."

"You think so?"

"Sure. We're through with it."

"I don't like it," said Al. "It's sloppy. You talk too much."

"Oh, what the hell," said Max. "We got to keep amused, haven't we?"

"You talk too much, all the same," Al said. He came out from the kitchen. The cut-off barrels of the shotgun made a slight bulge under the waist of his too tight-fitting overcoat. He straightened his coat with his gloved hands.

"So long, bright boy," he said to George. "You got a lot of luck."

"That's the truth," Max said. "You ought to play the races, bright boy."

The two of them went out the door. George watched them, through the window, pass under the arc-light and cross the street. In their tight overcoats and derby hats they looked like a vaudeville team. George went back through the swinging-door into the kitchen and untied Nick and the cook.

"I don't want any more of that," said Sam, the cook. "I don't want any more of that."

Nick stood up. He had never had a towel in his mouth before.

"Say," he said. "What the hell?" He was trying to swagger it off.

"They were going to kill Ole Andreson," George said. "They were going to shoot him when he came in to eat."

"Ole Andreson?"

"Sure."

The cook felt the corners of his mouth with his thumbs.

"They all gone?" he asked.

"Yeah," said George. "They're gone now."

"I don't like it," said the cook. "I don't like any of it at all."

"Listen," George said to Nick. "You better go see Ole Andreson."

"All right."

"You better not have anything to do with it at all," Sam, the cook, said. "You better stay way out of it."

"Don't go if you don't want to," George said.

"Mixing up in this ain't going to get you anywhere," the cook said. "You stay out of it."

"I'll go see him," Nick said to George. "Where does he live?"

The cook turned away.

"Little boys always know what they want to do," he said.

"He lives up at Hirsch's rooming house," George said to Nick.

"I'll go up there."

Outside the arc-light shone through the bare branches of a tree. Nick walked up the street beside the car-tracks and turned at the next arc-light down a side-street. Three houses up the street was Hirsch's rooming house. Nick walked up the two steps and pushed the bell. A woman came to the door.

"Is Ole Andreson here?"

"Do you want to see him?"

"Yes, if he's in."

Nick followed the woman up a flight of stairs and back to the end of a corridor. She knocked on the door.

"Who is it?"

"It's somebody to see you, Mr. Andreson," the woman said.

"It's Nick Adams."

"Come in."

Nick opened the door and went into the room. Ole Andreson was lying on the bed with all his clothes on. He had been a heavyweight prizefighter and he was too long for the bed. He lay with his head on two pillows. He did not look at Nick.

"What was it?" he asked.

"I was up at Henry's," Nick said, "and two fellows came in and tied up me and the cook, and they said they were going to kill you."

It sounded silly when he said it. Ole Andreson said nothing.

"They put us out in the kitchen," Nick went on. "They were going to shoot you when you came in to supper."

Ole Andreson looked at the wall and did not say anything.

"George thought I better come and tell you about it."

"There isn't anything I can do about it," Ole Andreson said.

"I'll tell you what they were like."

"I don't want to know what they were like," Ole Andreson said. He looked at the wall. "Thanks for coming to tell me about it."

"That's all right."

Nick looked at the big man lying on the bed.

"Don't you want me to go and see the police?"

"No," Ole Andreson said. "That wouldn't do any good."

"Isn't there something I could do?"

"No. There ain't anything to do."

"Maybe it was just a bluff."

"No. It ain't just a bluff."

Ole Andreson rolled over toward the wall.

"The only thing is," he said, talking toward the wall, "I just can't make up my mind to go out. I been here all day."

"Couldn't you get out of town?"

"No," Ole Andreson said. "I'm through with all that running around." He looked at the wall.

"There ain't anything to do now."

"Couldn't you fix it up some way?"

"No. I got in wrong." He talked in the same flat voice. "There ain't anything to do. After a while I'll make up my mind to go out."

"I better go back and see George," Nick said.

"So long," said Ole Andreson. He did not look toward Nick. "Thanks for coming around."

Nick went out. As he shut the door he saw Ole Andreson with all his clothes on, lying on the bed looking at the wall.

"He's been in his room all day," the landlady said downstairs. "I guess he don't feel well. I said to him: 'Mr. Andreson, you ought to go out and take a walk on a nice fall day like this,' but he didn't feel like it."

"He doesn't want to go out."

"I'm sorry he don't feel well," the woman said. "He's an awfully nice man. He was in the ring, you know."

"I know it."

"You'd never know it except from the way his face is," the woman said. They stood talking just inside the street door. "He's just as gentle."

"Well, good night, Mrs. Hirsch," Nick said.

"I'm not Mrs. Hirsch," the woman said. "She owns the place. I just look after it for her. I'm Mrs. Bell."

"Well, good night, Mrs. Bell," Nick said.

"Good night," the woman said.

Nick walked up the dark street to the corner under the arc-light, and then along the car-tracks to Henry's eating-house. George was inside, back of the counter.

"Did you see Ole?"

"Yes," said Nick. "He's in his room and he won't go out."

The cook opened the door from the kitchen when he heard Nick's voice. "I don't even listen to it," he said and shut the door.

"Did you tell him about it?" George asked.

"Sure. I told him but he knows what it's all about."

"What's he going to do?"

"Nothing."

"They'll kill him."

"I guess they will."

"He must have got mixed up in something in Chicago."

"I guess so," said Nick.

"It's a hell of a thing."

"It's an awful thing," Nick said.

They did not say anything. George reached down for a towel and wiped the counter.

"I wonder what he did?" Nick said.

"Double-crossed somebody. That's what they kill them for."

"I'm going to get out of this town," Nick said.

"Yes," said George. "That's a good thing to do."

"I can't stand to think about him waiting in the room and knowing he's going to get it. It's too damned awful."

"Well," said George, "you better not think about it."

THE STRANGER

Katherine Mansfield

(1890–1923)

It seemed to the little crowd on the wharf that she was never going to move again. There she lay, immense, motionless on the grey crinkled water, a loop of smoke above her, an immense flock of gulls screaming and diving after the galley droppings at the stern. You could just see little couples parading—little flies walking up and down the dish on the grey crinkled tablecloth. Other flies clustered and swarmed at the edge. Now there was a gleam of white on the lower deck—the cook's apron or the stewardess perhaps. Now a tiny black spider raced up the ladder on to the bridge.

In the front of the crowd a strong-looking, middle-aged man, dressed very well, very snugly in a grey overcoat, grey silk scarf, thick gloves and dark felt hat, marched up and down, twirling his folded umbrella. He seemed to be the leader of the little crowd on the wharf and at the same time to keep them together. He was something between the sheep-dog and the shepherd.

But what a fool—what a fool he had been not to bring any glasses! There wasn't a pair of glasses between the whole lot of them.

"Curious thing, Mr. Scott, that none of us thought of glasses. We might have been able to stir 'em up a bit. We might have managed a little signalling. *Don't hesitate to land. Natives harmless.* Or: *A welcome awaits you. All is forgiven.* What? Eh?"

Mr. Hammond's quick, eager glance, so nervous and yet so friendly and confiding, took in everybody on the wharf, roped in even those old chaps lounging against the gangways. They knew, every man-jack of them, that Mrs. Hammond was on that boat, and he was so tremendously excited it never entered his head not to believe that this marvellous fact meant something to them too. It warmed his heart towards them. They were, he decided, as decent a crowd of people—— Those old chaps over by the gangways, too—fine, solid old chaps. What chests—by Jove! And he squared his own, plunged his thick-gloved hands into his pockets, rocked from heel to toe.

"Yes, my wife's been in Europe for the last ten months. On a visit to our eldest girl, who was married last year. I brought her up here, as far as Salisbury, myself. So I thought I'd better come and fetch her back. Yes, yes, yes." The shrewd grey eyes narrowed again and searched anxiously, quickly, the motionless liner. Again his overcoat was unbuttoned. Out came the thin, butter-yellow watch again, and for the twentieth—fiftieth—hundredth time he made the calculation.

"Let me see, now. It was two fifteen when the doctor's launch went off. Two fifteen. It is now exactly twenty-eight minutes past four. That is to say, the doctor's been gone two hours and thirteen minutes. Two hours and thirteen minutes! Whee-ooh!" He gave a queer little half-whistle and snapped his watch to again. "But I think we should have been told if there was anything up—don't you, Mr. Gaven?"

"Oh, yes, Mr. Hammond! I don't think there's anything to—anything to worry about," said Mr. Gaven, knocking out his pipe against the heel of his shoe. "At the same time——"

"Quite so! Quite so!" cried Mr. Hammond. "Dashed annoying!" He paced quickly up and down and came back again to his stand between Mr. and Mrs. Scott and Mr. Gaven. "It's getting quite dark, too," and he waved his folded umbrella as though the dusk at least might have had the decency to keep off for a bit. But the dusk came slowly, spreading like a slow stain over the water. Little Jean Scott dragged at her mother's hand.

"I wan' my tea, mammy!" she wailed.

"I expect you do," said Mr. Hammond. "I expect all these ladies want their tea." And his kind, flushed, almost pitiful glance roped them all in again. He wondered whether Janey was having a final cup of tea in the saloon out there. He hoped so; he thought not. It would be just like her not to leave the deck. In that case perhaps the deck steward would bring her up a cup. If he'd been there he'd have got it for her—somehow. And for a moment he was on deck, standing over her, watching her little hand fold round the cup in the way she had, while she drank the only cup of tea to be got on board. . . . But now he was back here, and the Lord only knew when that cursed Captain would stop hanging about in the stream. He took another turn, up and down, up and down. He walked as far as the cab-stand to make sure his driver hadn't disappeared; back he swerved again to the little flock huddled in the shelter of the banana crates. Little Jean Scott was still wanting her tea. Poor little beggar! He wished he had a bit of chocolate on him.

"Here, Jean!" he said. "Like a lift up?" And easily, gently, he swung the little girl on to a higher barrel. The movement of holding her, steadying her, relieved him wonderfully, lightened his heart.

"Hold on," he said, keeping an arm round her.

"Oh, don't worry about *Jean*, Mr. Hammond!" said Mrs. Scott.

"That's all right, Mrs. Scott. No trouble. It's a pleasure. Jean's a little pal of mine, aren't you, Jean?"

"Yes, Mr. Hammond," said Jean, and she ran her finger down the dent of his felt hat.

But suddenly she caught him by the ear and gave a loud scream. "Lo-ok, Mr. Hammond! She's moving! Look, she's coming in!"

By Jove! So she was. At last! She was slowly, slowly turning round. A bell sounded far over the water and a great spout of steam gushed into the air. The gulls rose; they fluttered away like bits of white paper. And whether that deep throbbing was her engines or his heart Mr. Hammond couldn't say. He had to nerve himself to bear it, whatever it was. At that moment old Captain Johnson, the harbour-master, came striding down the wharf, a leather portfolio under his arm.

"Jean'll be all right," said Mr. Scott. "I'll hold her." He was just in time. Mr. Hammond had forgotten about Jean. He sprang away to greet old Captain Johnson.

"Well, Captain," the eager, nervous voice rang out again, "you've taken pity on us at last."

"It's no good blaming me, Mr. Hammond," wheezed old Captain Johnson, staring at the liner. "You got Mrs. Hammond on board, ain't yer?"

"Yes, yes!" said Hammond, and he kept by the harbour-master's side. "Mrs. Hammond's there. Hul-lo! We shan't be long now!"

With her telephone ring-ringing, the thrum of her screw filling the air, the big liner bore down on them, cutting sharp through the dark water so that big white shavings curled to either side. Hammond and the harbour-master kept in front of the rest. Hammond took off his hat; he raked the decks—they were crammed with passengers; he waved his hat and bawled a loud, strange "Hul-lo!" across the water; and then turned round and burst out laughing and said something—nothing—to old Captain Johnson.

"Seen her?" asked the harbour-master.

"No, not yet. Steady—wait a bit!" And suddenly, between two great clumsy idiots—"Get out of the way there!" he signed with his umbrella—he saw a hand raised—a white glove shaking a handkerchief. Another moment, and—thank God, thank God!—there she was. There was Janey.

There was Mrs. Hammond, yes, yes, yes—standing by the rail and smiling and nodding and waving her handkerchief.

"Well, that's first class—first class! Well, well, well!" He positively stamped. Like lightning he drew out his cigar-case and offered it to old Captain Johnson. "Have a cigar, Captain! They're pretty good. Have a couple! Here"—and he pressed all the cigars in the case on the harbour-master—"I've a couple of boxes up at the hotel."

"Thenks, Mr. Hammond!" wheezed old Captain Johnson.

Hammond stuffed the cigar-case back. His hands were shaking, but he'd got hold of himself again. He was able to face Janey. There she was, lean-ing on the rail, talking to some woman and at the same time watching him, ready for him. It struck him, as the gulf of water closed, how small she looked on that huge ship. His heart was wrung with such a spasm that he could have cried out. How little she looked to have come all that long way and back by herself! Just like her, though. Just like Janey. She had the courage of a—— And now the crew had come forward and parted the passengers; they had lowered the rails for the gangways.

The voices on shore and the voices on board flew to greet each other.

"All well?"

"All well."

"How's mother?"

"Much better."

"Hullo, Jean!"

"Hillo, Aun' Emily!"

"Had a good voyage?"

"Splendid!"

"Shan't be long now!"

"Not long now."

The engines stopped. Slowly she edged to the wharf-side.

"Make way there—make way—make way!" And the wharf hands brought the heavy gangways along at a sweeping run. Hammond signed to Janey to stay where she was. The old harbour-master stepped forward; he fol-lowed. As to "ladies first," or any rot like that, it never entered his head.

"After you, Captain!" he cried genially. And, treading on the old man's heels, he strode up the gangway on to the deck in a bee-line to Janey, and Janey was clasped in his arms.

"Well, well, well! Yes, yes! Here we are at last!" he stammered. It was all he could say. And Janey emerged, and her cool little voice—the only voice in the world for him—said,

"Well, darling! Have you been waiting long?"

No; not long. Or, at any rate, it didn't matter. It was over now. But the point was, he had a cab waiting at the end of the wharf. Was she ready to go off? Was her luggage ready? In that case they could cut off sharp with her cabin luggage and let the rest go hang until to-morrow. He bent

over her and she looked up with her familiar half-smile. She was just the
same. Not a day changed. Just as he'd always known her. She laid her
small hand on his sleeve.

"How are the children, John?" she asked.

(Hang the children!) "Perfectly well. Never better in their lives."

"Haven't they sent me letters?"

"Yes, yes—of course! I've left them at the hotel for you to digest later on."

"We can't go quite so fast," said she. "I've got people to say good-bye to
—and then there's the Captain." As his face fell she gave his arm a small
understanding squeeze. "If the Captain comes off the bridge I want you to
thank him for having looked after your wife so beautifully." Well, he'd
got her. If she wanted another ten minutes—— As he gave way she was
surrounded. The whole first-class seemed to want to say good-bye to
Janey.

"Good-bye, *dear* Mrs. Hammond! And next time you're in Sydney I'll
expect you."

"Darling Mrs. Hammond! You won't forget to write to me, will you?"

"Well, Mrs. Hammond, what this boat would have been without you!"

It was as plain as a pikestaff that she was by far the most popular woman
on board. And she took it all—just as usual. Absolutely composed. Just
her little self—just Janey all over; standing there with her veil thrown
back. Hammond never noticed what his wife had on. It was all the same
to him whatever she wore. But to-day he did notice that she wore a black
"costume"—didn't they call it?—with white frills, trimmings he supposed
they were, at the neck and sleeves. All this while Janey handed him round.

"John, dear!" And then: "I want to introduce you to——"

Finally they did escape, and she led the way to her state-room. To follow
Janey down the passage that she knew so well—that was so strange to him;
to part the green curtains after her and to step into the cabin that had
been hers gave him exquisite happiness. But—confound it!—the stewardess was there on the floor, strapping up the rugs.

"That's the last, Mrs. Hammond," said the stewardess, rising and pulling
down her cuffs.

He was introduced again, and then Janey and the stewardess disappeared into the passage. He heard whisperings. She was getting the tipping
business over, he supposed. He sat down on the striped sofa and took his
hat off. There were the rugs she had taken with her; they looked good as
new. All her luggage looked fresh, perfect. The labels were written in her
beautiful little clear hand—"Mrs. John Hammond."

"Mrs. John Hammond!" He gave a long sigh of content and leaned back,
crossing his arms. The strain was over. He felt he could have sat there for
ever sighing his relief—the relief at being rid of that horrible tug, pull,
grip on his heart. The danger was over. That was the feeling. They were on
dry land again.

But at that moment Janey's head came round the corner.

"Darling—do you mind? I just want to go and say good-bye to the doctor."

Hammond started up. "I'll come with you."

"No, no!" she said. "Don't bother. I'd rather not. I'll not be a minute."

And before he could answer she was gone. He had half a mind to run after her; but instead he sat down again.

Would she really not be long? What was the time now? Out came the watch; he stared at nothing. That was rather queer of Janey, wasn't it? Why couldn't she have told the stewardess to say good-bye for her? Why did she have to go chasing after the ship's doctor? She could have sent a note from the hotel even if the affair had been urgent. Urgent? Did it— could it mean that she had been ill on the voyage—she was keeping something from him? That was it! He seized his hat. He was going off to find that fellow to wring the truth out of him at all costs. He thought he'd noticed just something. She was just a touch too calm—too steady. From the very first moment——

The curtains rang. Janey was back. He jumped to his feet.

"Janey, have you been ill on this voyage? You have!"

"Ill?" Her airy little voice mocked him. She stepped over the rugs, and came up close, touched his breast, and looked up at him.

"Darling," she said, "don't frighten me. Of course I haven't! Whatever makes you think I have? Do I look ill?"

But Hammond didn't see her. He only felt that she was looking at him and that there was no need to worry about anything. She was here to look after things. It was all right. Everything was.

The gentle pressure of her hand was so calming that he put his over hers to hold it there. And she said:

"Stand still. I want to look at you. I haven't seen you yet. You've had your beard beautifully trimmed, and you look—younger, I think, and decidedly thinner! Bachelor life agrees with you."

"Agrees with me!" He groaned for love and caught her close again. And again, as always, he had the feeling he was holding something that never was quite his—his. Something too delicate, too precious, that would fly away once he let go.

"For God's sake let's get off to the hotel so that we can be by ourselves!" And he rang the bell hard for someone to look sharp with the luggage.

. . . . . .

Walking down the wharf together she took his arm. He had her on his arm again. And the difference it made to get into the cab after Janey—to throw the red-and-yellow striped blanket round them both—to tell the driver to hurry because neither of them had had any tea. No more going without his tea or pouring out his own. She was back. He turned to her, squeezed her hand, and said gently, teasingly, in the "special" voice he had for her: "Glad to be home again, dearie?" She smiled; she didn't even bother to answer, but gently she drew his hand away as they came to the brighter streets.

"We've got the best room in the hotel," he said. "I wouldn't be put off with another. And I asked the chambermaid to put in a bit of a fire in case you felt chilly. She's a nice, attentive girl. And I thought now we were here we wouldn't bother to go home to-morrow, but spend the day looking round and leave the morning after. Does that suit you? There's no hurry, is there? The children will have you soon enough. . . . I thought a day's sight-seeing might make a nice break in your journey—eh, Janey?"

"Have you taken the tickets for the day after?" she asked.

"I should think I have!" He unbuttoned his overcoat and took out his bulging pocket-book. "Here we are! I reserved a first-class carriage to Cooktown. There it is—'Mr. *and* Mrs. John Hammond.' I thought we might as well do ourselves comfortably, and we don't want other people butting in, do we? But if you'd like to stop here a bit longer——?"

"Oh, no!" said Janey quickly. "Not for the world! The day after to-morrow, then. And the children——"

But they had reached the hotel. The manager was standing in the broad, brilliantly lighted porch. He came down to greet them. A porter ran from the hall for their boxes.

"Well, Mr. Arnold, here's Mrs. Hammond at last!"

The manager led them through the hall himself and pressed the elevator-bell. Hammond knew there were business pals of his sitting at the little hall tables having a drink before dinner. But he wasn't going to risk inter-ruption; he looked neither to the right nor the left. They could think what they pleased. If they didn't understand, the more fools they—and he stepped out of the lift, unlocked the door of their room, and shepherded Janey in. The door shut. Now, at last, they were alone together. He turned up the light. The curtains were drawn; the fire blazed. He flung his hat on to the huge bed and went towards her.

But—would you believe it?—again they were interrupted. This time it was the porter with the luggage. He made two journeys of it, leaving the door open in between, taking his time, whistling through his teeth in the corridor. Hammond paced up and down the room, tearing off his gloves, tearing off his scarf. Finally he flung his overcoat on to the bedside.

At last the fool was gone. The door clicked. Now they *were* alone. Said Hammond: "I feel I'll never have you to myself again. These cursed people! Janey"—and he bent his flushed, eager gaze upon her—"let's have dinner up here. If we go down to the restaurant we'll be interrupted, and then there's the confounded music" (the music he'd praised so highly, applauded so loudly last night!). "We shan't be able to hear each other speak. Let's have something up here in front of the fire. It's too late for tea. I'll order a little supper, shall I? How does that idea strike you?"

"Do, darling!" said Janey. "And while you're away—the children's letters——"

"Oh, later on will do!" said Hammond.

"But then we'd get it over," said Janey. "And I'd first have time to——"

"Oh, I needn't go down!" explained Hammond. "I'll just ring and give the order . . . you don't want to send me away, do you?"

Janey shook her head and smiled.

"But you're thinking of something else. You're worrying about something," said Hammond. "What is it? Come and sit here—come and sit on my knee before the fire."

"I'll just unpin my hat," said Janey, and she went over to the dressing-table. "A-ah!" She gave a little cry.

"What is it?"

"Nothing, darling. I've just found the children's letters. That's all right! They will keep. No hurry now!" She turned to him, clasping them. She tucked them into her frilled blouse. She cried quickly, gaily: "Oh, how typical this dressing-table is of you!"

"Why? What's the matter with it?" said Hammond.

"If it were floating in eternity I should say 'John!'" laughed Janey, staring at the big bottle of hair tonic, the wicker bottle of eau-de-Cologne, the two hair-brushes, and a dozen new collars tied with pink tape. "Is this all your luggage?"

"Hang my luggage!" said Hammond; but all the same he liked being laughed at by Janey. "Let's talk. Let's get down to things. Tell me"—and as Janey perched on his knees he leaned back and drew her into the deep, ugly chair—"tell me you're really glad to be back, Janey."

"Yes, darling, I am glad," she said.

But just as when he embraced her he felt she would fly away, so Hammond never knew—never knew for dead certain that she was as glad as he was. How could he know? Would he ever know? Would he always have this craving—this pang like hunger, somehow, to make Janey so much part of him that there wasn't any of her to escape? He wanted to blot out everybody, everything. He wished now he'd turned off the light. That might have brought her nearer. And now those letters from the children rustled in her blouse. He could have chucked them into the fire.

"Janey," he whispered.

"Yes, dear?" She lay on his breast, but so lightly, so remotely. Their breathing rose and fell together.

"Janey!"

"What is it?"

"Turn to me," he whispered. A slow, deep flush flowed into his forehead. "Kiss me, Janey! You kiss me!"

It seemed to him there was a tiny pause—but long enough for him to suffer torture—before her lips touched his, firmly, lightly—kissing them as she always kissed him, as though the kiss—how could he describe it?—confirmed what they were saying, signed the contract. But that wasn't what he wanted; that wasn't at all what he thirsted for. He felt suddenly, horribly tired.

"If you knew," he said, opening his eyes, "what it's been like—waiting to-day. I thought the boat never would come in. There we were, hanging about. What kept you so long?"

She made no answer. She was looking away from him at the fire. The flames hurried—hurried over the coals, flickered, fell.

"Not asleep, are you?" said Hammond, and he jumped her up and down.

"No," she said. And then: "Don't do that, dear. No, I was thinking. As a matter of fact," she said, "one of the passengers died last night—a man. That's what held us up. We brought him in—I mean, he wasn't buried at sea. So, of course, the ship's doctor and the shore doctor——"

"What was it?" asked Hammond uneasily. He hated to hear of death. He hated this to have happened. It was, in some queer way, as though he and Janey had met a funeral on their way to the hotel.

"Oh, it wasn't anything in the least infectious!" said Janey. She was speaking scarcely above her breath. "It was *heart*." A pause. "Poor fellow!" she said. "Quite young." And she watched the fire flicker and fall. "He died in my arms," said Janey.

The blow was so sudden that Hammond thought he would faint. He couldn't move; he couldn't breathe. He felt all his strength flowing—flowing into the big dark chair, and the big dark chair held him fast, gripped him, forced him to bear it.

"What?" he said dully. "What's that you say?"

"The end was quite peaceful," said the small voice. "He just"—and Hammond saw her lift her gentle hand—"breathed his life away at the end." And her hand fell.

"Who—else was there?" Hammond managed to ask.

"Nobody. I was alone with him."

Ah, my God, what was she saying! What was she doing to him! This would kill him! And all the while she spoke:

"I saw the change coming and I sent the steward for the doctor, but the doctor was too late. He couldn't have done anything anyway."

"But—why *you*, why *you*?" moaned Hammond.

At that Janey turned quickly, quickly searched his face.

"You don't *mind*, John, do you?" she asked. "You don't—— It's nothing to do with you and me."

Somehow or other he managed to shake some sort of smile at her. Somehow or other he stammered: "No—go—on, go on! I want you to tell me."

"But, John darling——"

"Tell me, Janey!"

"There's nothing to tell," she said, wondering. "He was one of the first-class passengers. I saw he was very ill when he came on board. . . . But he seemed to be so much better until yesterday. He had a severe attack in the afternoon—excitement—nervousness, I think, about arriving. And after that he never recovered."

"But why didn't the stewardess——"

"Oh, my dear—the stewardess!" said Janey. "What would he have felt? And besides . . . he might have wanted to leave a message . . . to——"

"Didn't he?" muttered Hammond. "Didn't he say anything?"

"No, darling, not a word!" She shook her head softly. "All the time I was with him he was too weak . . . he was too weak even to move a finger. . . ."

Janey was silent. But her words, so light, so soft, so chill, seemed to hover in the air, to rain into his breast like snow.

The fire had gone red. Now it fell in with a sharp sound and the room was colder. Cold crept up his arms. The room was huge, immense, glittering. It filled his whole world. There was the great blind bed, with his coat flung across it like some headless man saying his prayers. There was the luggage, ready to be carried away again, anywhere, tossed into trains, carted on to boats.

. . . "He was too weak. He was too weak to move a finger." And yet he died in Janey's arms. She—who'd never—never once in all these years—never on one single solitary occasion——

No; he mustn't think of it. Madness lay in thinking of it. No, he wouldn't face it. He couldn't stand it. It was too much to bear!

And now Janey touched his tie with her fingers. She pinched the edges of the tie together.

"You're not—sorry I told you, John darling? It hasn't made you sad? It hasn't spoilt our evening—our being alone together?"

But at that he had to hide his face. He put his face into her bosom and his arms enfolded her.

Spoilt their evening! Spoilt their being alone together! They would never be alone together again.

THE HOUSE OF MOURNING

Franz Werfel

(1890–   )

TRANSLATED BY H. T. LOWE–PORTER

INTRODUCTION

Upon THE TRAGEDY follows the satyr-play: both equally grisly. Idea, empire, overthrow—what sounding words for a play that is always and ever the same! No downfall on earth is so great that it has not its comic side, its matter for laughter. A relief, that is all, a relief of the guard. One midday the company of the castle ward falls in with clatter and ring for the last time. The rolling drum thunders through the court; once more the snarling words of command bark like ravens through the air; once more the sentries with echoing tread parade to their last position on the stone-flagged pavement; the venerable, the glorious banner of a world-famous regiment, tattered in a hundred frays, sinks, with its golden tip pointing earthwards. Tomorrow, perhaps, it will already have begun to moulder in a museum. What has happened? Nothing. Time has cleared his throat, world-history batted an eye. But we, hurrah, we were there! Our children were not. And our brilliantly technicized grandchildren have not even an idea of the emotional experiences we went through.

The title of the following satyr-play in the form of a short story is once more a play upon words. That a house of mourning is a house where a death is being mourned goes without saying. But the German language possesses a pendant to the phrase: it speaks of a "house of joy." It might be inferred that such a place, as the literal opposite of a house of mourning, is one where a newcomer to the earthly scene is being given a joyous welcome. Not a maternity clinic, of course! No, nothing like that at all, language is not so logical. And in fact, the arrival of a new little citizen in a "house of joy" would be a painful incident and very awkward for the business. In other words, chosen with care so as not to offend fastidious ears, a house of joy is a shame-faced shelter for shameless pleasures, where one can procure at fixed prices both the joys of Bacchus and the joys of Venus. Even this definition sounds blatant and coarse, in contrast to the complacent French *"maison."* And how crude, too, as applied to the unique

and singular establishment introduced to the reader in the story which
follows!

Situated in a large provincial capital in the heart of the empire—the
identity of the city will not be given with any more particularity—secluded
in a romantic fastness, the establishment differed most emphatically from
all others called by the same name. It was not only a house of joys, but one
of intellectual pretensions too. The quite peculiar *genius loci* elevated it far
above its kind, and its own nightly activities and *raison d'être* as well. It
was more than a house, it was a meeting-place. Why should not the empire,
which after all was the fading shadow of the Roman imperium, why should
not it too possess a meeting-place which, strictly speaking, was a lupanar?
At all events, such was the fact. It was the rather extraordinary rendezvous
of both the young and the old of the upper classes—at least of such as did
not cling to a puritanical morality or languish in too austere matrimonial
bonds. Many of the guests, indeed, took small interest in the more ques-
tionable diversions of the place; they came to enjoy the relaxations of the
prevailing atmosphere, so favourable to æsthetic and philosophical discussion. After all, not the worst sayings of the great Socrates were uttered
in a group of hetæræ, flute-players, and *fils de joie*. Well, then, scholars,
writers, and philosophers paid visits to this ancient establishment, to say
nothing of the hereditary nobles, cavalry officers, officials, lawyers, and
actors who were its prescriptive guests.

This memorable lupanar often harboured for some hours of the night
the cream of the youth who would one day play an important role in the
affairs of the empire. As for the corresponding femininity there active, it
was less socially creamy, but on the other hand more highly coloured. All
the peoples of the monarchy, the freshest, most unexhausted stocks, had
sent thither their prettiest girls—many of them were peasants. The country
innocence of soul, which strangely enough, these Magdalenes often
preserved, was not inconsistent with their profession; indeed, a sturdy
naïveté, even on this plane, was one of the mysteries of the Austrian temperament—in the grosser and more grasping resorts of western Europe one
would hardly meet with their like.

Down to the very last hour before their deliverance, upon the polished
parquetry of that most singular salon, these blithe and serviceable hand-
maids of the empire shrieked and sang and ate and drank and danced and
wrangled with the guests of the house, unforced, symbolic. And destiny, in
that very hour, found an easy way past the narrow door, narrow though it
was; and, equally unforced and symbolic, turned the house of joy into a
house of mourning. As I shall now relate.

I

It would have been a night like any other if two events had not broken
into it and disturbed its course.

Four of the five tables in the Grand Salon were full at ten o'clock; also the Blue Salon, usually occupied by upper officialdom, noblemen of high rank, and the leading figures of finance and industry, was well frequented at any early hour. In the Blue Room one ordered only champagne; it was open only to guests above a certain rank, paying not less than a certain income tax. It was hung with tapestries and had an ingenious arrangement of mirrors which, so people said, were for the purpose of performance in common of the more *raffiné* kinds of vice. The guests in the Grand Salon knew only by hearsay what went on in the Blue Salon; even where they were, the drinking of a bottle of sour wine was an expensive amusement. But since the consumption of drinks was after all not the establishment's main source of income, regular habitués of the Grand Salon had certain quantities of coffee and brandy meted out to them.

This is not to dim the lustre of the Grand Salon. It was absolutely first-class: Renaissance furniture, heavily gilt; red velvet curtains and a parquetry dance floor smooth as glass. This was, in short, an establishment which could tranquilly repudiate the name applied to it by a poverty-stricken and inarticulate vocabulary. And even if you used the word, you would have to put R.-and-I. in front of it. For everything here mirrored for the beholder—if rather self-consciously in such a setting—the period of the Dual Monarchy: the plush furniture, the gilded arabesques, the etchings (which depicted not only scenes of gallantry, all quite decorous, but also the noble sport of horse-racing), the dust-traps, the moth-eaten sumptuousness, even the Imperial portrait hanging in the kitchen—all these were a survival of the Renaissance splendours of a proud and vanished decade.

Until well on in the war there had been three institutions in the city which preserved in all its purity this quasi-official character. These were the pâtisserie Stutzig; the dancing-school founded by Herr Pirnik, in a beautiful baroque palace near the famous bridge—a place of great distinction where the youth of the upper bourgeoisie could learn the waltz, the polka, Sir Roger de Coverley, the tirolienne, and even the classic quadrille—and, finally, the establishment which is the scene of our story.

It was, I believe, the last to disappear.

II

The ladies, except those on private service, were all at their posts. They paced the room with swaying step, made rapturous eyes at themselves in the mirrors, coolly helped themselves to the guests' cigarettes, and now and then with detached and condescending air sat for a while at the tables. They seemed to be full of a consciousness of their own dignity, a dignity which communicated itself to every pensionnaire of this famous and superior establishment. To be received here was to have entry to the upper circles. The sense of dignity I mean found expression in various ways: for instance, these ladies differed from the ones in most other establishments in that they did not wear short frocks, but appeared in fantastic négligées, flowing morning garments; Valeska, the most magnificent, wore a proper ball-gown, which would certainly have received comment in the newspapers if it had appeared at the carnival ball. Despite these hampering garments one did sometimes get a glimpse of their legs as they took a cigarette-case or powder-puff out of their stockings.

Only one, Ludmilla, wore a short skirt; and with her slender childish figure she could scarcely have done otherwise. She noticeably lacked the superficial restlessness, the idle unquiet, which is characteristic of the profession of such ladies, which made them sit and stand by turns and neither for long, or urged them up and down the room like caged animals. Ludmilla sat still, on the right side of the military tables, attending with the utmost seriousness to Lieutenant Kohout's exposition, as though she did not want to lose any opportunity of being instructed. She gave no sign of mental disturbance.

Lieutenant Kohout, Twenty-Third Field-Artillery Regiment, had with him two young men of the same service, both of them one-year volunteers. Their intercourse had the false and insecure familiarity which characterizes relations between superiors and inferiors when they waive distinctions of rank and sit at the same table. The manœuvres were close at hand and with them the alarming spectre of the examinations for reserve officers.

The lieutenant, staring with his watery eyes straight at Ludmilla, was encouraging the two volunteers, who faced the future with qualms.

"Let me tell you," said he, looking to Ludmilla for approval, "I did not have it so easy with the ensign's exam, and you've been at school, you are educated. Colonel von Wurmser looks me sharp in the eye: 'Deputy Cadet-Officer Kohout!' says he. 'What do you know about Julius Cæsar?' I pull myself together and shout out: 'Your obedient servant, Herr Oberst—nothing!' Second question: 'Deputy Cadet-Officer Kohout! What do you know about Charlemagne?' I pull myself together a bit more and yell: 'Obedient servant, Herr Oberst—nothing!' The Colonel waits a bit, then he says: 'Deputy Cadet-Officer Kohout! What do you know about the Emperor Joseph?' But there I've got him. I clap my heels together so they crack: 'Obedient servant, Herr Oberst, but which Kaiser Joseph? aren't there two of them?' Colonel von Wurmser says: 'Well, well!' But I got through at that! So you see, one just has to act like a soldier, not a civilian. And that's all there is to it!"

Ludmilla looked at the lieutenant with sympathy and understanding. She did not laugh. Her childish brow was sternly concentrated beneath the heavy blond hair which God had given her. She seemed to be in full agreement with the healthy attitude taken by the lieutenant: military, not civil! In every respect she inclined to strictness in her views of the world-order.

One of the volunteers began to caress her legs under the table; she submitted, only moving a little aside. The clever girl full realized that military distinctions of rank, and the mutual embarrassment between superior and inferior, would put a damper on further advances and appetites—and just that was what she needed today.

Anyhow she felt better here than she would have felt at the next table, where Ilonka, the "fat Hungarian bitch," was making up to two old men. And what old men! One of them surely came from the country, from some place that Ludmilla hated without ever having seen it. He had an enormous watch-chain across his paunch; you wondered whether the watch-chain was there for the paunch or the paunch for the watch-chain. She had seen such things before. In the hole she came from, a man was respected only after he had eaten himself a belly of the right proportions for a watch-chain. He was a proper *"Baalboth,"* that man.

It was Jenny, the Jewess, who had introduced this mysterious word: a legendary predecessor of the present ladies; she now lived in Vienna, where she owned a large coffee-house on the Franz-Josef Quay. Jenny was the pattern and prototype of a successful career in the profession. Hardly a day passed but her glorious record was cited as an example. As for the word *Baalboth,* it signified a rich man from the provinces, who came to the capital overnight to give full satisfaction to his need for "love-life," but who never paid a penny over and above the tax.

And that pig of an Ilonka was sucking around the Baalboth. He was good for ten gulden. But Ludmilla granted that neither of the two old fools (shame on these fat-gutted old fathers of families for coming to a knocking-house!) was after Ilonka. The Baalboth never looked at her; he kept rolling his eyes towards Ludmilla, but she gave him not even a haughty glance. Clients like that were nothing to her. He might talk as loud as he liked to impress her with his self-important ideas. And actually he had raised his voice so high as to be heard all over the salon:

"Organization, Herr Kraus, organization," he boomed, while his covetous eyes did not look at Herr Kraus but besought the favours of Ludmilla.

"When you look up at the sky, Herr Kraus, what do you see there? Organization! And when you look at an ant-heap? Ditto. Our German brother up in the Reich is right: Organization in economic and political life. But we here in Austria . . ."

The Baalboth sighed, depressed by the sorry state of the Fatherland and the defeat of his amorous approaches.

Herr Kraus sighed too, entirely convinced of the sad situation.

"Yes, I read something just like that in the newspaper today."

Ludmilla tried to find some other direction for her eyes. There was the "young" table, good-naturedly boycotted by most of the girls, because the youngsters never could spend very much and used the Grand Salon mainly as a place where they stimulated themselves by dancing and discussion. Those two rhinoceros-hides, Manya and Anita, were sitting there, of course, laughing with *his* friends, who had just come in. But Oscar had not come, neither today nor yesterday nor the day before. For the first time! Ludmilla would sooner have thrown herself out of the window than gone up to the table and asked about him. She did not even answer the others' greetings. Manya laughed aloud, high and clear. Let her laugh; she was nothing but the daughter of the grave-digger of Rokycany, with her huge dirty legs which the year before had most likely been running after the village geese. Grave-digger; that was only a shade better than being a hangman or a knacker.

Ludmilla preferred to look over at the clever people in the corner, the Jews, who never drank wine or brandy but only coffee. Grete, the crazy girl from Berlin, was practising her charms upon them. She nodded pleasantly at Grete, a friendly gesture which surprised the other ladies no little. They were not used to it from the reserved creature. And Grete, on account of her "education," was an object of general aversion. But Ludmilla had seen Grete embracing and kissing her Doctor Schleissner. And she had suddenly felt a sort of good-natured envy and the impulse to send a signal of understanding across to her colleague. She did not envy her Schleissner. Certainly not. How can one love a man who talks all the time, who has got such an enormous nose, and wiry black hair which he keeps twisting in his fingers? What does the man do when he isn't talking? Can he keep quiet at all, can he sleep, can he love? Certainly a man like that knows nothing about tenderness.

But Grete's room was full of pictures of writers. And she had albums full of poems and signatures, which the odious female kept thrusting under the noses of the other ladies. A daft creature!

Ludmilla regretted her friendly gesture, for Grete squealed out in rapture over something Schleissner had said:

"That such a man must die! That such a brain must rot under the earth!"

Ludmilla was relieved when Fräulein Edith, the housekeeper, came in, bringing a fresh bottle of wine for the two old men and the coffee-tray for four people at the "clever" table in the corner.

The sight of Fräulein Edith's solid, fresh, and beaming personality always had power to raise Ludmilla's spirits.

In every human activity there is a natural hierarchy and order of precedence. What the command of the regiment was to Lieutenant Kohout, that, to the ladies of the house, at least to the decent ones, was the position of housekeeper. In this case the incumbent was pretty, not old, scarcely thirty; her muscular and expansive figure was at its best. She was exempt from duty. She need not respond, she might follow the dictates of her heart. She kept all the books, the boarders' accounts, pronounced on their value to the establishment, and her contract allowed her two subscription seats in the new Deutsches Theatre.

The girls were taken only every two weeks to enjoy a Sunday afternoon performance, but Edith sat twice a week in the parquet, and the girls jealously competed for the honour of occupying the other seat.

It was on such an occasion—they were giving *The Violet Man*—that Ludmilla saw Oscar for the first time. No one could have said that the lean, hollow-cheeked novice cut a good figure in the small role of a Prussian officer. But she, in her clear-sightedness, had fallen in love with the inconspicuous youth.

She got up from the table, left the protesting lieutenant, and went to Fräulein Edith. The housekeeper took her caressingly round the waist:

"The wretch hasn't come again!"

Ludmilla overcame her tears by giving vent to a strong word, though it went to her heart as she said it. Edith consoled her:

"Silly! You'll get over that. What is a man? When he is very genteel, a hundred crowns in trousers. And anybody like you! You wouldn't let him make a fool of you! Shame on you!"

"But what shall I do, Edith, if somebody wants to go with me? . . ."

Edith was already prepared. For Ludmilla's sake she was willing to shut her managerial eye:

"You know what, Milly," she whispered, "I'll screen you. Go upstairs and lock yourself in."

Ludmilla stamped her foot. *"Jesus and Mary!* I couldn't. I couldn't stand it upstairs."

Edith soothed her, one eye on her duties:

"I know all that. Been through it, darling. Has it hurt me? Look at me, and just don't care!"

The housekeeper turned away to her duties. There were more guests come, the Grand Salon was full. Laughter and ringing of glasses sounded from the Blue Room. But there was something not in order. Fräulein Edith flew into a rage, her deep voice had a threat in it:

"Where is Nejedli?"

At that very moment Herr Nejedli bobbed up and paid his compliments to the guests:

"Beg the assembled company's pardon. But I was engaged at a children's ball. Lasted a long time. Until now."

The housekeeper's stern eye countenanced no humbug. Nejedli's hand felt eagerly and guiltily about above the floor:

"Little children, no higher'n that, I tell you, Fräulein Edith, just sweet li'l' childr'n——"

The old man hurried to the piano and began to enliven the mood of the evening by thundering out Fucik's "Gladiators' March."

III

Herr Nejedli, the pianist, had four distinguishing characteristics. In the first place he wore a "tom-cat" over his bald spot; that is to say a sort of transformation, in his case of a quite different colour from the fringe of hair round the edge. The "tom-cat" was a chestnut-brown, the fringe snow-white. Who could expect that a man who plays piano at a night club could keep himself supplied with hair of enough colours to keep pace with his advancing age?

His second peculiarity was even stranger. It consisted of a composite aura which he spread abroad, composed of the scents of greasy pomade, aniseed brandy, and old age.

The third peculiarity was the description, with variations, of the accidents to which his daughter Rosalie had fallen victim. The tragedy of these accidents grew deeper in proportion to the number of drinks Herr Nejedli had had. Never had a more pitiable creature lived than this Rosa, of whom initiated souls asserted that she had really blossomed, and was not the mere monstrous creation of the alcoholic brain.

But whatever, and whether, she had been, according to her father she had died that very day of tuberculosis; yesterday she had fallen out of the window, or else a railway accident had to be conjured up to account for her demise. Whatever the cause of death, tears of deep and genuine feeling would pour down the old man's cheeks as he told his tale.

But the most striking of Herr Nejedli's peculiarities lay in the fact that as an eight-year-old boy he had been the "royal and imperial titular prodigy" at the former court of the Emperor Ferdinand the Good up on the Hradčany—it was thus that he himself designated his extraordinary rank. This brilliant past of his was often the subject of banter.

Herr Doktor Schleissner, who loved to play the part of habitué and introducer of strangers, came up to the piano and presented a tall, gloomy, dignified man:

"May I present the gentlemen to each other? Our great virtuoso, Herr Nejedli, Herr President Moré."

"No names, I beg you," whispered the gloomy man, with a face of anguish, as though somebody had trodden on his toe.

Schleissner begged pardon:

"Forget the name, Nejedli! But do not forget that the President of the Spinoza Society and Master of the Order of Sons of the League stands before you."

Old Nejedli sprang up.

"An honour, Herr President! I know the Herr President already if I may say so. I had the honour yesterday at the funeral of Imperial Counsellor Habrda . . ."

Moré cut the interview short. He did not like to be reminded of funerals, since they stood in close connexion with his business, the nature of which he preferred to conceal. In other words, the President of the Spinoza Society was listed in trade journals as agent for gravestones and monuments. He formed a bridge between the sorrowing survivors, the monument business, and the reputation of the deceased in the community. It is not surprising that the large number of honorary offices on the one side and the business connexion with death on the other accounted for the President's serious bearing and his long priestlike coat.

He seemed to be here for the first time. He slowly carried a folded handkerchief to his mouth; the inadequate but symbolic gesture seemed to signify that a man like him, in such surroundings as these, would do well to conceal his too-familiar features.

But Doctor Schleissner wanted to give the President some entertainment. He turned to the pianist:

"Can you tell us about Kaiser Ferdinand the Good and your concerts, Nejedli?"

The old man bent nervously over the keys.

"Seems to me, gentlemen, you want me to commit high treason and *lèse-majesté*. There are nothing but *balmilchomes* here in the room——"

Moré gave him a sinister look.

Nejedli hastened to say:

"Balmilchome, Herr President, is what the Israelites call a soldier or an underling in active military service."

Schleissner tried to soothe him:

"In the first place, nobody can hear you, and in the second nobody has an idea who Kaiser Ferdinand was."

Nejedli eagerly explained:

"The dear departed uncle of our own Kaiser. They deposed him in the '48, in Olmütz. I remember him like today. He lived in the castle up there, and every day he came down in a coach and pair—Lipizzan white horses of course—and drove to the Baumgarten or in the Canal Park."

The President asked, in his deep, oratorical voice:

"And was he really so good?"

At the words his solemn countenance took on the flattered expression of a man whose thoughts are dwelling with emotion on illustrious personages.

Nejedli rolled his eyes mysteriously.

"No, he was not good, but he was cracked."

Schleissner encouraged him:

"You were an infant prodigy and gave concerts in the castle."

Nejedli's bony fingers executed a run on the piano.

"Trust me, Herr Doktor, I was in request as a prodigy. I gave concerts in the Spanish salon. The whole plenotitulo nobility was there, court and society. There was His Grace Count Kolowrat; he sat here, and over there

Her Serene Highness the Princess Lobkowitz. I can see her as though it were today. A beauty, she was, on my word. And then His Excellency the Governor of Bohemia and Corps-Commandant Count . . . Count . . . what the devil was his name?"

Doctor Schleissner bent forward inquisitively.

Nejedli's fingers trilled up the keyboard again.

"At that time, gentlemen, I had a memory; and fingers, if I may say so. I played off my whole programme by heart: 'Evening Bells,' *Mon Souvenir,* 'Overture to *Wilhelm Tell,*' and 'Arrangement from *La Juive.*' Yes, and to-day I can play only a little by heart, and not from notes at all, on account of my sight having gone wrong. I have wept my eyes out. Herr Doktor knows, since I had the misfortune with Roserl . . ."

Doctor Schleissner quickly and tactfully brought him back to his subject. Nejedli's hands executed a tune as he went on:

"Yes, gentlemen, in that day I really could play well. The court and company applauded and wanted it all *da capo*. The ladies looked at me through their glasses, all emotion. And His Majesty the Emperor applauded too and came up to me: 'Bravo, bravo!' he cried; and I make my little curtsy, small boy as I am and kiss his hand. He begins to pet me, in his condescension—but true as I am standing here, all of a sudden he jerks away his hand and fetches me a box on the ear——"

The President's eyes flashed darkly. But Nejedli went on with mild forbearance:

"Not that I mean to say anything against His Majesty. He could not help it. I could see him struggling against the blow which he had in his hand. Ear-boxings were a sort of specialty of his. His adjutant, General Herr Graf Kinsky, used to keep hold of his hand when they were driving, because you never could tell. They drove across the Stone Bridge, where the golden Lord God is, that a Jew had to put up because he had not taken off his hat to the Almighty. Though I'm not saying anything against the Jews.

" 'Let me out, Your Excellency,' says His Majesty to the adjutant. But he kept on holding the Kaiser's hand, tighter than ever. His Majesty begs and begs: 'Let me out, Excellency, I must cross myself here.' So the General can't do anything more, because of the regulations, he has to let go of the august hand. And so he gets one good and hard!"

Doctor Schleissner was enchanted with his story. But his friend, the agent for monumental stonework, President Moré, seemed less edified. Under the mask of harmless anecdote were concealed subversive opinions and Czechoslovak treason against the imperial house, of which he was a devoted adherent.

Nejedli drove Anita and Manya from the piano.

"Get away, girlies! I'll play some dance-music."

He turned to Schleissner.

"Does the Herr Doktor know the national anthem which was played at the time of the blessed Emperor Ferdinand in Vienna?"

And he sang, softly, accompanying himself only in the bass:

> "In Schönbrunn,
> He says,
> Lives an ape,
> He says,
> Got a face,
> He says,
> Like a priest,
> He says,
> Eats no sugar,
> He says,
> Drinks no wine,
> He says,
> What ape,
> He says,
> Can that be?"

The pianist looked President Moré in the eyes, shaking his head sadly.

"Disrespectful lot, the Viennese! Really loyal imperialists are to be found only here."

"What is that you are singing? Louder!" Lieutenant Kohout called to Nejedli.

But the latter took a firm line:

"Herr Leutnant, just an old popular song, it would not interest the Herr Leutnant."

The lieutenant agreed:

"I only like the new ones. Come on, Nejedli, play us something brisk!"

And Nejedli began with his gouty fingers to reel out a waltz which was at least ten years old. The ladies danced, mostly with each other. Only Grete danced with Doctor Schleissner, towering above him, holding him in abandoned embrace.

Ludmilla stood in the doorway and kept her back turned to them all.

IV

All at once the girls disappeared out of the Grand Salon. Fräulein Edith was what one might call a past mistress of such unobtrusive movements of troops.

Illustrious guests seemed to have arrived, the sort that were usually led to a still more exclusive room than even the Blue Salon. This room, the existence of which has not been mentioned before, was called the Japanese Private; it was on the ground floor, two doors right of the entrance.

This floor of the house was carefully arranged not to chill the ardours of the guest but rather to intensify them. So soon as the door opened, he was saluted by a wave of warm air and a fragrance whose individual character he would remember all his life: an odour like warm bath-water with perfume in it; of soap-suds, vaseline, face-cream, rouge, perspiration, alcohol, and highly seasoned food.

It could not remain a secret for long that very exalted personages were occupying the Japanese Private. Herr Doktor Schleissner had sharp ears; he could hear not only the thundering of *fiacre* wheels in the narrow street, but also the ringing of spurs on the ground floor. And all the girls had disappeared. Schleissner swiftly deduced: Serene Highnesses from the Brandeiser Dragoons. Moré's face wore an impenetrable expression. He looked as though he had not needed to guess, because the names of the personages who had come were already known to him. But indiscretion was not his weakness.

At that time there were none of those big dance palaces which dominate the night life of cities today. The number of "Tabarins," "Maxims," and "Alhambras" was very limited. For that reason probably it was that there was nothing very scandalous about visiting this house in the Gamsgasse. Officers could appear in full uniform; high functionaries, if they came, need encounter no reproach; guests of high station were no exception. The historical-minded explained this liberal attitude on the ground that in 1866 the Prussian generals had celebrated their victories in the Blue Salon and thus given the whole house a kind of accolade.

The ladies very soon returned to the Grand Salon. Only Anita, Valeska, and the Polish Jadwiga had had the good fortune to be invited by the elegant newcomers. Grete scolded:

"The ill-bred puppies!"

She flung herself again into the ready arms of Doctor Schleissner. But it was surprising that Ludmilla came back, she, the prize of the collection, the child-beauty of the house. It was to be hoped that none of her colleagues noticed how Edith, whose feeling heart remembered its own griefs, had hidden her away and denied her to the guests.

Ludmilla moved with her usual strikingly resolute tread across the room and made as though to sit down again at the harmless table with the artillery; but the Baalboth, that rumbling-voiced guest with the belly, the watch-chain, and the organization-mania, got up heavily and approached her, with the clumsy dancing-class bow of an elderly provincial:

"Fräulein, may I inquire after your health?"

He said that with sweat standing on his brow, the sweat of lust and self-conquest, and the sour uneasiness of a bad conscience. Ludmilla measured him up and down, like a good married woman flashing a look at a man who addresses her in the street. "Pah!" said she; and sat down in her former place. The humiliated man stood heavily, isolated, on the polished

dance floor. Then with slow feet that seemed to be ashamed of their creaking tread he went back to his place; but in his staring gaze could be read
something more than mere confusion.

Nobody had noticed this scene, for just then somebody said, in a high-
pitched, chirping drawl:

"Evening, precious children, all of you!"

The owner of the sluggish voice and still more sluggish body was welcomed with applause and lively salutations. He was no other than the
present owner and proprietor, Max Stein, a popular and an extraordinary
figure, called "Maxl" by all the friends of the house.

It is popularly supposed that all old families are decadent. And Max
came of an old family indeed, though he was hardly a scion of the aristocracy. But in the point of decadence he yielded nothing to the sons of
princes.

The house in the Gamsgasse, though not a feudal estate, had a long history, and more than that, a legend all its own.

To that day there was still an alley in the New Town called the "Extra
Street"; Charles IV, the famous city-builder, had so christened it in anger
because it had not been arranged for and set down in his plans. The order
for the building of a brothel had been issued by him in person; he had
with his own hands marked the site on the plan. The political foresight
of this great personage cannot be too highly praised; he it was who, in
order to check the persecution at the beginning of the new puritan movement, set apart for the courtesans and their establishments one of the most
charming quarters of the "little town" and named it Venice, after the city
of Venus. The real home of the growing heresy, however, was nowhere
else than in the university, which, the first to be founded on the soil of
the German Holy Roman Empire, was famous far and wide. The conclusion is not too far-fetched, that His Pious Majesty conceived the idea of
putting the Grand Salon in the immediate neighbourhood of the university, with no other aim in view than that of bringing those arrogant
and ascetic heretics to a fall and thus perhaps to their senses. A building
commission could show that subterranean passages led from the Gamsgasse
into the Carolinen; and here students in doublet and jerkin had caroused.
If one may trust the sources, even Wallenstein, when he held court in the
capital, came often to the Grand Salon to taste a little fleeting pleasure.

Old businesses possess the same mysterious value as old wine and old
violins. Rivals might give their firms the finest titles; it did not help them
to call themselves "Napoleon"; they could get only rabble and off-
scourings for clients.

The house and business had been in the Stein family for a very long
time. The grandmother, born Busch, a well-known local benefactress, had
had the establishment as part of her dowry; but before that Maxl's great-
grandfather had been proprietor and host, protected by the police authori-

ties; so that Herr Max himself might be considered the last representative of a long line.

His parents were dead. His brother, Adolf, had been in the business up to two years before; a dry, impossible sort of host, who, when things were lively in the Grand Salon but not showing any practical results, would grumble: "Come, come now, get down to business and go upstairs!" That sort of thing destroyed the romantic atmosphere. Fortunately Adolf had had the most pressing reasons for emigrating to America, and Maxl had now nobody but Edith. But Edith was a host in herself; she held the whole thing together magnificently, and as for honesty she was simply a jewel.

Maxl turned an indifferent ear to the applause which greeted him. His yellow face was like an old man's but also like a child's, so that nobody could have guessed his age. His glasses sat crooked on his bulbous, turned-up nose, and a lax, weak-willed lower lip hung down like wattles on his chin. The man was so flabby and exhausted that a stranger would have found it hard to understand why there was no compassion but simply conviviality in the welcome he got. He pushed over to the piano, with his shambling, pathetic gait, to take his place in his favourite seat on the bench next to Nejedli, followed on all sides by shouts of:

"Maxl, Maxl, tell us a joke!"

Max objected:

"Leave me out of it. I won't tell you anything today. I am too tired. I'm worn out sleeping——"

That was just artistic vanity, they paid no attention. Maxl turned to the pianist, his friend:

"Nejedli, they mustn't pick at me today. I am honestly tired. I slept wrong——"

But Nejedli gave him no sympathy either. So he began in his sickly drawl:

"Two Jews are walking along the street, they see a taking female coming along. The first says: 'I'd like to have her again.' The other says—" He broke off the tale, which they all knew by heart, and stared in the air, trying to remember. Then he finished:

"I've forgotten the point."

His audience burst into a roar, and Maxl chuckled:

"Pretty good, eh?"

They gave him no rest. Doctor Schleissner persuaded the gloomy President Moré to advance. He got up and went to the piano with his mincing, pompous walk.

"May I present myself, Sir? Will you not give us the pleasure of a song?"

Maxl made a horrified face at the black apparition:

"Herr President, you look like *malach hamoves,* the angel of death!"

The angel of death would not be denied. Maxl, vain as any artist, turned to Nejedli:

"Nejedli, you know my voice is no good today. I'm not well——"

The President encouraged him:

"We're not asking you to sing '*Celeste Aïda*'!"

The proprietor weakened.

"Well, what shall I sing?"

A chorus shouted the names of various popular songs: "Manzanares," "*Les Dessous*," "Sigismund," and "Weeping Like a Child."

Maxl chose the one whose languorous melody had special need of a powerful voice and a passionate delivery for its success. He consulted with Nejedli, cleared his throat for a whole minute, and then his low and quavering voice issued from his labouring wrinkled throat. In it trembled all the exhaustion of his ancient house, transmuted to a quality of plaintive resignation. And in that plaintive voice he sang, constantly forgetting and muddling up both words and tune:

> "He played in the flood of her gold-blond hair;
> Her eyes smiled up at him so clear—
> Come with me, you marvellous darling—
> To Manzanares, to Manza——"

The big head began to shake on the thin neck, the glasses fell ringing from the bulbous nose to the floor. Amid loud applause, Max crawled under the piano in a rage, and only came out after prolonged entreaties, pathetically wrought up. His yellow face was streaming with perspiration. He stormed:

"That's enough, that's enough! I have to kill myself, just because you are so pig-headed! I'd rather make bad business for myself: Edith, a round of cognacs on the house! And you, Nejedli, play us——"

Nejedli got up and announced:

"I will play the company the glorious aria out of the glorious opera *La Juive*."

Ludmilla, who adored sad music, approached the piano.

Max had a soft side for her; he babbled:

"Come on, Milly, sit on my lap."

But Ludmilla responded bluntly:

"Why, Herr Maxl?"

The connoisseur looked at her from head to foot, sentimentally, and issued the prophetic statement:

"One of these days, girlie, we shall all be calling you 'My Lady'!"

Nejedli burst forth, singing to his own accompaniment:

> "Almighty God, hear my prayer,
> Hear my prayer, great God,
> Give me back my child,
> Give me Recha, my child!"

"Rosa, Rosa," the initiated corrected him. Nejedli squinted venomously at them over his glasses as he made a daring and impermissible transition into Offenbach's "Barcarole":

> "Sweet night, thou night of love,
> Oh, quench my longing!"

Max began to be uneasy, wriggled in his chair, put his hands over his ears, and blubbered:

"Stop, Nejedli. I can't stand it. It makes me weep like a child."

Repeated rounds of cognac were now having their effect on the house. A mood of passive enjoyment and muddle-headed surrender to the music settled on the company. Most of the ladies had taken off the flowing garments of respectability and danced in their shifts. The noise increased, augmented by a literary argument which had broken out at the "clever" table, where Grete, Doctor Schleissner, and President Moré were sitting. A new guest had added himself to it, Municipal Accountant Eduard von Peppler, who was also an author. The unhappy man was cursed by fate with the task of reconciling two conflicting claims in his nature: those of the regular duties of an official of the "ninth grade" and the desperate compulsions of a satanic poet. He was, one might say, a Baudelaire detailed to the duties of the royal and imperial municipal presidium. Herr von Peppler's blood was brought to fever-heat at the sight of one of his colleagues at the "young" table. The aspiring young man had already had some literary success. Herr von Peppler yelled that *his* generation had tried with all their might to find life, and they had found syphilis; this cowardly young one did not try hard to find life and instead they found publishers. Fiery red in the face he parried the ironic laughter of the young generation:

"You are all bourgeois! You are all vegetarian poets! All of you shipwrecked on the paternal hearth! Shame upon you, you boarders and lodgers!" He clutched furiously to right and left at Moré's and Schleissner's cognac glasses and drained them down.

Herr Doktor Schleissner sprang into the breach. He jumped up and declared that other times had to come, that humanity consisted for the most part of repression, and that in repression, in bad sexual digestion, lay the sickness of the world. There was only one goal: erotic liberation!

And, as it were, to make a beginning of this liberating process, he began, heedless of Moré's indignant gaze, to sing the song which he called the Hymn of the League, which was unfortunately more obscene than witty:

> "As long as arses to trousers fit,
> Nobody wants to do their bit . . ."

It must be said that the singer himself belied his own song and that the statement in his mouth was pure self-advertisement; for Doctor Julius

Schleissner, partner in a very well-known firm of lawyers, was a hard-working and conscientious man, with not only juristic but also political and literary ambitions. This very year he was giving free to women artists in the public rooms of their club a course with the stimulating title: "French Immoralism from Stendhal to André Gide." After these lectures there took place a tango contest, when the exponent of immoralism took part with solemnity in the languishing contortions of the dance. President Moré, on the other hand, was neither a friend of the dance nor of French immoralism, and least of all of naked indecency. He was a confirmed student of Goethe. One of his favourite occupations was to ferret out in various editions of the first and second parts of *Faust* misprints, errors of style, negligent versification, and contradictions of thought. Schleissner's shameless song offended him; he hung his head.

With everything swaying and humming about him, Herr Maxl sat silent and sunken beside Nejedli, whose stiff-jointed fingers were pitilessly and unconsciously mangling the dance-music. The pianist listened as he laboured to the proprietor's complaining voice:

"You know, Nejedli, I sleep very fast. . . ."

Nejedli nodded to show that he understood.

But Maxl's manner displayed the mild annoyance of one who strives in vain to express a thought of peculiar subtlety:

"Please understand me, Nejedli. One can sleep slowly, one can sleep in the ordinary way, one can sleep fast, and one can sleep very fast. You know, my friend, there is no end to what one can sleep through in a quarter of an hour. . . ."

Nejedli grunted his assent, but the evidence of his understanding was insufficient. A sort of shudder passed over Maxl, a fevered dimness, like a scarcely perceptible movement over the dark surface of a pool. His eyes stared.

"You won't believe me, Nejedli. But as true as I live, I have slept ten years in a single hour, and that is why I am so tired."

Just then the Baalboth left the room with his creaking tread. The high spirits in the room were reaching their climax. A minute later Fräulein Edith came in and began to discuss something earnestly with Ludmilla.

V

In contrast to the more vulgar establishments such as the Napoleon, it was one of the sound customs of the house that the appointments were not made in public. A gentleman apparently took leave of his company, unobtrusively indicated to Edith the lady of his choice, and the housekeeper in her turn quietly arranged the blissful rendezvous, not without—in the case of a doubtful or strange guest—receiving beforehand the usual payment. It must be said that this very seldom happened, for only people of the upper classes frequented the house. Strangers hardly ever came; and Fräulein Edith had a very fair knowledge of men, relying a good deal on her own impressions. Just as seldom—this in contrast to the lower-class Napoleon—did any scandal occur. Of course, among the boarders there was faction, discord, hatred; but it was an unwritten law that peace and friendliness must prevail during business hours.

So that events like the following were practically unheard of. A discordant hubbub arose at the door of the Grand Salon. The hollow, beery voice of the clumsy provincial rose and thundered, till it seemed to shake the thin and infirm walls. At first there was the one angry voice alone; but after a while the ladies' good manners could not stand the strain: treble shrieks began to mingle with the angry bass.

Anyone who has ever seen a crowd collect, hungry for sensation, when a worn-out horse falls in the street, can imagine the avid curiosity with which, at this hour, in this place, everybody clustered round to revel in the fray. Even the patrons of the Blue Salon stuck out their heads with malicious enjoyment.

The trouble was this: the old farmer with the monstrous watch-chain had made of Fräulein Edith the customary request for Ludmilla's services. In vain Edith made excuses, brought out plausible explanations, in order to protect her young charge from the undesirable, even repellent encounter. To herself Fräulein Edith cursed Oscar's defection. There was nothing like an unhappy love to put the ladies off; it was the most frequent source of loss of discipline and neglect of duty. But all her quick-wittedness was of no avail. The Baalboth was not only knowing, he was extremely obstinate and spiteful. He was animated by the violent anger of the rejected man. Edith saw nothing else to do but put Ludmilla at his service. But Ludmilla said straight out, with the coldest indifference, to the Baalboth's face, that she would not think of acceding to his request. And then the storm broke.

The furious provincial had retreated to the landing and stood clinging to the gilt-bronze Venus posted there as the emblem of the establishment. (On the next lower landing stood an equally gilded Trumpeter of Säkkingen—not precisely as an emblem.) The girls screamed all together, the guests laughed, and the humiliated man continued to shout, despite all Edith could do to calm him, that he must see the proprietor.

Herr Maxl finally dragged himself up, followed by Nejedli. It must be said that despite a thick tongue, deathly pallor, and physical weakness he bore himself not only with quick wit but also like a knightly defender of his ladies.

The Baalboth shrieked at him:

"Herr Proprietor! What sort of house is this?"

Maxl drawled:

"Edith, go downstairs and bring up the house-number."

The angry man was not to be put off.

"If I go into a bakery and want to buy a roll——"

Maxl's weary croak interrupted him:

"Go into a bakery and buy yourself a roll."

"What do you mean?"

"What should I mean?"

The Baalboth softened his roaring bass to the mildness of condescending argument:

"Herr Proprietor! Suppose a purchaser goes into a shop and they won't serve him with a piece of goods in stock——"

Max looked at the complainant with melancholy eye and repeated with a sigh:

"In stock . . ."

Patience was exhausted; there arose a roar:

"Good Lord in heaven, I won't be made a fool of! That's no way to treat a customer! Do you think there are no other houses as good as yours? There are better. Old Aunt Pohl in Aussig—there's something to be said for hers. They have organization too. I tell you, for the last time: my train goes tomorrow morning at seven thirty-five. I intend to spend the rest of the night in this house, and spend it with the girl that I pick out and pay for."

Maxl answered the screaming with extreme humility:

"Pardon, Herr . . . Forest Inspector . . . help yourself. Are you a human being? Of course you are a human being. And is Ludmilla a human being? She is a human being. Pardon, Herr . . . Inspector of Roads . . . a human being has to understand, when a human being won't go with him . . ."

An outburst of laughter. Maxl turned triumphantly to the laughers:

"Pretty good, eh?"

Ludmilla stood there all the time as though the affair had nothing to do with her. But now opinion began to veer. The girls' excitement was becoming spiteful. This haughty piece was going too far. Edith looked anxiously about her, wondering how to cope with the rising storm. They began to take sides, their hate and envy no longer under control, their self-possession gone.

Suddenly Ilonka, the fat Hungarian, planted herself before Ludmilla.

"Say, what are you a whore for?"

Grete interrupted her ecstatically:

"Let her alone! Haven't we got the rights of human beings too?"

Ilonka grew even more venomous.

"If everybody were to do that! Fine business that would be! Why, we might pick out the guests ourselves! It isn't always a joy to me either!"

Ludmilla said quietly:

"To you it is always a joy."

Grete, to Edith's dismay, made the situation infinitely worse with her exaggerated notions:

"You ought to be ashamed of yourself. Ludmilla is right: we must fight for our freedom."

This high-flown phrase, even more than Ludmilla's obstinacy, worked the ladies up to a high pitch. They hated in the Berlin woman the most intolerable of all species of arrogance, the arrogance of education.

Ilonka shrieked:

"We've just been waiting for you, you *Meschuggene!*"

Grete made her most demure face.

"It's not my fault that I've learned something. Everybody can't be brought up in a pigsty."

And now it came: Ilonka rushed at Grete, and with her pudgy little fist struck the tall girl in the face. The fight was on. Already some of the combatants were rolling on the floor. Their silk shirts ripped at the seams and the rounded flesh bulged out. Manya, the unwieldy damsel from Rokycany, simply tore her shirt off her back before she flung herself with a joyous cry into the fray. For even in anger she remained practical. The grave-digger's daughter cared not whom she hit. She was avenging herself on the whole troop.

One or two more debauched fellows, at the sight, deliberately fanned the flames. But the original incendiary, the Baalboth, struggled gasping in Ludmilla's direction, with the idea of taking her by force. She, however, had cleverly slipped away unseen.

The gentlemen were thrilled by the priceless spectacle, which raged to and fro in the corridor between the Grand Salon and the Blue Salon. Doctor Schleissner whinnied with joy. The municipal official and satanist Peppler stared with open eyes in which the joy of destruction shone; he urged the combatants on. Only Lieutenant Kohout and President Moré withdrew. The lieutenant was mindful of the regulations, which ordered officers as much as possible to dissociate themselves from dishonourable proceedings. Moré too had his professional honour to think of. Both gentlemen silently retreated behind the piano.

Nejedli, on the other hand, was one of the few who tried to part the engaged participants. He gasped with his efforts, his tom-cat sat askew and his cravat was twisted over to one side.

Edith stared in desperation, Maxl was stunned by the fray. Anything like this had never happened before. Up to now the ladies, despite any small episodes or lack of harmony, had always been mindful of the dignity of a first-class establishment.

Who knows what the end would have been if a tremendous event had not like a stroke of lightning struck the house?

Suddenly, as though he had risen out of the earth, a messenger stood there, an orderly from the Sixth Regiment of Dragoons. Usually, when for any reason a representative of the power of the state came to the house, a gentleman from the Health Department, or a police official, he knew how to be discreet about his entrance. But this soldier, a tall, blond Czech peasant lad, had towered abruptly upon the distracted scene. Rosy-cheeked, he stood in the middle of the witches' dance and brought into the smoke- and sweat-laden atmosphere a breath of fresh air. He looked actually ready for a campaign, in field uniform, with helmet, cartridge-pouch, cavalry sword, and great spurs.

The combat broke off in a flash. The ladies reduced themselves to order as though nothing had happened. A deep stillness suddenly yawned. Every- body felt that destiny was in the air. Even Maxl's storm-shaken figure stiff- ened with life. He in person led the orderly whither he demanded to be led.

Two minutes later the swift tread of cavalry boots rang on the ground floor and the house-door slammed shut. Slowly, rigidly, breathless, Max mounted the stair. He sobbed incomprehensible lamentations. By de- grees they got out of him the frightful news. The Crown Prince had been murdered in Sarajevo.

Never had the respectable house in the Gamsgasse emptied more ex- peditiously than now. The dionysiac frenzy, the light-headed intoxication in the Grand Salon, seemed to have burned itself out; the gentlemen quickly settled down. Herr Doktor Schleissner, that intellectual corsair, became a serious person who looked with great concern into the future. He was a reserve officer. Herr President Moré brushed away the loose frivolity which, like a speck of dust on his coat, he had borne with for an hour. He murmured reproachfully: "This is what happens when one goes out nights." What he meant, or how he connected in his bitter thoughts the catastrophe with the light-hearted evening now at an end, remained un- clear.

The Baalboth no longer felt he owed it to his pride to insist on Lud- milla's services.

Lieutenant Kohout and the two volunteers looked frozen-faced, as though as they were charged with presiding over a military commission. Herr von Peppler wrapped himself romantically in his rain-coat and in earnest of future events made peace with the younger generation. Everybody hur- ried down the steps. They wanted to go to the newspaper offices to get details of the tragedy. Some few shrinking figures slipped out seeking the shadows, after the main rout, either because they were mindful of a more sensitive reputation or had a more enviable married life than most.

In the forsaken salon the head of the house sat alone with Nejedli. He squatted quite collapsed on the piano-stool. He seemed already to have forgotten the frightful event, for he stammered: "Shall I go to bed, Nejedli?"

The pianist yawned.

"Yes, go to bed, Herr Maxl, nothing else will happen today."

He gave the old man an indignant glance.

"But I sleep too fast, Nejedli, I've slept for ten years. I am afraid to sleep, Nejedli."

Nejedli gave no answer, he was busy pouring all the remains of cognac into one glass, which he providently emptied. When he found nothing more to drink and saw the proprietor sitting there with his eyes closed, he took the music money from the table and slipped on tiptoe, muttering, out of the room.

He did not hear the anxious question that followed him:

"Shall I go to sleep, Nejedli?"

The large salon was full of wreckage. Broken glasses strewed the floor, chairs were upset, everywhere was the odour of spilt wine, coffee, brandy. Maxl blinked at the desolation. He took a deep breath, to call Edith and command that order be restored. Impotent angry wrinkles suddenly showed on his brow. But he only gasped for breath and no sound came from his loose lips. At last he got up and staggered from the room. His tapping, shuffling step sounded for a long time, before it died away upstairs.

As the last noise of the departing guests died away in the narrow street, Ludmilla could no longer contain herself; she did something that was sternly forbidden: opened the door and looked out into the night.

Oscar stood before her.

She would gladly have choked it back, but she had no power over the spasmodic scream which forced itself to her lips.

VI

Ludmilla sat beside Oscar at the supper-table in the kitchen.

The kitchen was the real shrine and hearthstone of the establishment; and a very fine room it was, with its tiled stove and four tables covered with white oil-cloth. He who might enter here was no more a client, a stranger, or a victim; he was tax-free in every respect, he belonged to the clan, he shared the secrets of the wide-flung order.

The dim four-o'clock hour of the summer dawn had now broken, the time of the principal meal was come. In importance this four-o'clock hour was exceeded only by the six-o'clock evening one when the ladies got themselves ready for society and the Figaro ran from one to the other with the curling-tongs. But the early-morning meal was nicer; one washed down all the bad alcohol and tobacco fumes with hot soup and looked forward to the joy of sleep.

At each place two plates stood on top of each other, a serviette rested in its ring, and silver forks and spoons shone at either side—such as even the best establishments do not show. This silver put one under an obligation. Whoever had only for a little while used it was ennobled for all time. He could hardly sink again to the level of Napoleon. Much oftener his path lay upwards.

Ludmilla had forgiven Oscar. Forgiven him? What a pompous word! What should she have done, what else was there for her to do? Sulk perhaps, make him smart, spoil the little time that he was by her side? When he went out of the door and with ten steps was in the Eisengasse, she was so much air for him, poorer than the poorest, could not threaten him as any other woman could, not give him presents nor frighten him, had not the slightest power over him for good or bad. If she had permission to go out, did he not have to refuse—and with perfect right—to spend the afternoon with her? She could understand that. How could she show herself at the side of the promising young actor without compromising him? She did not even want to go about with him outside, either in the street or in strange rooms. This was why she always gave up her afternoon out to the other girls.

Here alone, in this house, in this kitchen, could he find her. But she could not find him anywhere. Was it not a good deal, that he had come? Who forced him to come? (But if he married, his wife could force him.) She did not even know his address, so as to write him a letter. No, she had never asked him for his address. But he never noticed that—men are pigs!

And now he was here. She must be grateful, nothing but grateful. She felt a glow of joy that she had not surrendered, that she had held out for two days, here in this house, defying all her foes, and proved her strength and will-power. She said nothing about her fight, for Oscar would not have taken any particular interest in it.

But now that he sat beside her, it was all one, she was in heaven to be able to feed the hungry man and give him her soup. Oscar, not lifting his eyes, sat, audibly eating and swallowing; Ludmilla with quick stolen glances took in the features of her beloved, storing them up that she might possess of him as much as possible.

Meanwhile the other ladies had appeared. The late violent scrimmage had left no marks. A few little bruises and scratches were not worth mentioning. Strangely enough the outburst seemed to have cleared the air of hatred, and shame over the mortifying episode united even the late foes. A friendly and obliging spirit reigned, even a somewhat watchful and exaggerated cordiality. The grumpy Manya was humming the mournful notes of a Slavic folksong, to show that she was in a reconciled and pleasant mood.

The girls had taken off their alluring evening garments and wore bedraggled nightgowns and bed-jackets; instead of gilt and silver dancing-shoes they had on down-at-heel slippers; their hair was dishevelled and their stockings wrinkled.

They ate their soup languidly, audibly, and smacked their lips. Oscar, sitting beside Ludmilla among the ladies, explained to her in a low voice why he had not come for so long. The theatre manager had asked him to take over the part of one of the actors who was taken ill. It was a good role, a classic role, which had latterly been played by Kainz, and Oscar's first big part. He could not hesitate to give the last two nights to prepare himself in it.

Ludmilla, so lately unbelieving, looked at him with adoring eyes. She trusted him, with passion. His reasons were so convincing. Word for word she repeated Oscar's justification aloud, to prove to her colleagues that she need not be ashamed of her love.

Grete asked for the name of the play and did not omit to boast:

"My father always took me with him to all the plays. Did you know Christians, Herr Oscar?"

Oscar fell prey to embarrassment and could not answer for a moment. Ludmilla had not asked him the name of his part. He gave himself away by mentioning a play which was not being given at the time. He looked quickly at her. But she was all faith. She would not have minded an even bigger lie.

By degrees Oscar himself was affected by the girl's love and the nobility it imparted to her; instead of passively letting himself be loved he himself felt tenderness and began whispering sweet hopes in her ear.

Ilonka must have caught some of the whispering, for she laughed:

"Listen! He went to set her out!"

And turning to Ludmilla: "Set you out—yes, fine he will—with your behind out of the window!"

Ludmilla, with puckered brows and eyes cast down, thought for a long time; then suddenly spoke in a strange, deep voice:

"Do you know, Oscar, what was the worst thing you have done?"

And slowly she answered her own question:

"That you came back today, that is the worst thing you have done!"

But before Oscar and the others could understand this new turn, Edith came in, and said, betraying apprehension and horror in her voice:

"Children, I don't know what the matter is, but there is such a queer groaning from Herr Maxl's room. I daren't knock, but I was so frightened . . ."

They all looked at each other, and everybody had a vision of Herr Maxl's pathetic yellow face. They all knew at once, it seemed they had always known, that Herr Maxl was a very sick man. They had never thought about it, for even the oldest in service among them had never known a Herr Maxl who was not short-winded, yellow with jaundice, utterly exhausted, and yet funny. He was like that. And nobody had ever heard a complaint out of his mouth. They believed in the old country proverb which says: "If the nag eats it doesn't need a vet."

But now they saw that they must leave their pork and greens and noodles to get cold. They responded to Fräulein Edith's words with an outpouring of feminine concern.

The whole troop got up, even Ludmilla left Oscar's side. A procession of untidy females trooped up the stair, past the guardian Venus and the Trumpeter of Säkkingen; they moved forgetful of their usual alluring gait and the provocative posturings of their feminine backsides. They looked like a lot of servantmaids and untidy shop-girls climbing the steps to an employment bureau.

But the higher they got, the nearer to their master's chamber, the heavier and more inexplicable grew the dread which they felt round their throats like a wet cloth. They pressed close together, as Edith knocked in vain, three, four, five times. At last—the groaning had stopped—she cautiously opened the door, and before her hand had even found the switch of the electric light the boldest of them pressed behind her into the gloom of the chamber.

None of them ever came here. It was a strict rule of the house.

The light revealed an extraordinary array of madonnas and saints decorating the walls. Only after that did they see their employer, whose body was hanging half out of bed, without a sign of life.

Had he fainted, was he dead?

Edith and Valeska lifted the body back on the bed. The others ran wildly to and fro, fetching Cologne water, perfume, and useless bottles of medicine, pouring them recklessly over Maxl's yellow brow and between his open lips.

Grete screamed without stopping that she could not bear to see it. Ilonka was quite in her element, saying over and over that in these cases there was only one remedy, chopped onion mixed with spit rubbed on the patient's eyelids and put up his nose. She had the recipe from her grandmother, who knew more about such things than anybody else in the world. Edith thought of the framed notice that hung in the kitchen: "First aid to the injured." But she had not the courage to touch the strange form again.

Manya, however, the grave-digger's daughter, laughed contemptuously, went up to the bed, pushing the incompetents back with her strong arms, and lifted the figure's eyelids. Then she turned round and announced, in an official tone:

"He is dead!"

And the doctor, whom Edith sent for at once, could do no more than confirm Manya's words.

VII

Difficulties of all sorts multiplied. This was the first time—aside from some legendary stabbings in ancient times—that a dead person lay in the house. And a dead person who was not a guest overtaken by some violent or irregular death, but a member of the household, who had died, according to the doctor, from entirely natural causes.

Herr Maxl had left no instructions—which could surprise nobody who had seen him even once. The deceased had often lacked energy even to eat his dinner; where would he have got enough to occupy himself with the world and its interests when he was not there at all?

Years before he had sold his share in the other property of his parents to his brother Adolf for a mess of pottage; the latter indeed had very soon given it up in turn to mysterious creditors. Nothing remained for Herr Maxl but to move into the Gamsgasse; he had lived there ever since in a room above the boarders' quarters.

For the present nobody knew how things had been left. The legal heirs, who were only distant connexions, gave no sign of life until four days later—for reasons best known to themselves. So everything fell upon Fräulein Edith's shoulders. But they were very capable ones.

Of course the police and the inheritance authorities were particularly interested in a business enterprise of this kind, so suddenly left orphaned. But Edith's relations, not only with the police but with all the state and municipal authorities, were very independent, permanent, and assured. After a cursory examination they left her a free hand, and she had enough foresight to arrange matters to her own advantage and the boarders', and to the honour of the deceased as well.

She cannot be praised too highly for her action in one matter: she faithfully set aside the large sum which she had received the day before from her employer—he was in the habit of turning over to her with careless openhandedness the daily takings from the business—and which had not been entered in the books. She put it into an envelope and wrote tenderly on it "Herr Maxl" with a pious cross after the name. She was so little self-seeking as to devote this whole sum to the expenses of a funeral worthy of the deceased. But just here came in the greatest difficulty of all.

First and foremost the religious question.

Herr Maxl's origins were Jewish. She, Edith, had been brought up by the Ursulines; she always said that, without that stern discipline and the happiness of an inward faith, she could never have become housekeeper in one of the best houses in Europe. If anyone pointed out that the profession she had adopted did not accord with her religious tenets, she would tell the story of what had happened to her in the confessional. The young priest had consoled her as follows:

"My child," he said, "your life is certainly a very sinful one. But God has distributed properties and callings among men according to His will. Even your calling—strange as it is—He has always suffered. It would be better for you to find another. But if you cannot do that, then you must ever be mindful that you are a child of the Church. And then you will never despair. And never forget that the lowest vices of which mankind is guilty are born only of despair."

Fräulein Edith did not change her profession. She went on sinning, but also clinging fanatically to the Church.

But her fanaticism, of course, was at the bottom of the tendency to proselytizing which she displayed. Who was a more likely subject for her efforts than Herr Maxl? And it is true that the first time her employer went with her to Mass in the Church of Saint Gall he was as one transformed.

After that he went every Sunday with Edith to vespers—which was no small effort, considering how prolonged and trying the Saturday night sessions were at the house. But Edith achieved still more. She brought him to an understanding of the nature of the Holy Mother of God; and he hung the walls of his room full of saintly pictures. Daily Edith spoke to him of the final step, the baptism, that must be taken before his soul could be saved. But Herr Maxl met her most affecting appeals with the same words:

"But I've always been a good child!"

And when she began to plead, he croaked in his whining apathetic voice:

"*Nebbich,* what could they do with me?"

And when the zealous woman painted in fiery colours all the unpleasant metaphysical consequences of his unbaptized state, Maxl always closed the conversation with the remark:

"Listen, Edith! Once a Jew always a Jew."

Yet it is a fact and must be told, that long before Edith's time, for reasons no longer explainable, Maxl had procured the official document which is called declaration of non-confessional status, and which frees the citizen from religious duties and observances.

It would have been Edith's dearest wish to give the master of the house a Christian burial with all due and formal rites. She ran to the parish of Saint Gall. But however willing the good priest, his hands were tied: without a certificate of baptism there could be no church burial. But there were no such restrictions, he added, on Masses for the dead, and Edith straightway arranged for three. And as she went away the Reverend, all smiling and blithe, gave her to understand that the appearance of an officiating priest in such a place and in these unregenerate times would only give rise to anger and the mockery of free-thinkers.

For good or ill, Edith was forced to seek out the Jewish religious authorities, in whose register the name of the departed was inscribed. They told her that she must buy for the dead a lot in the Mosaic quarter of the Olschan Cemetery. But even so, a ceremonial funeral was out of the question. Herr Stein was an apostate; he had broken with his ancestral faith and besides that had not been in person any sort of ornament to any communion or community. If the funeral were permitted to take place from the burial hall of the Central Cemetery, then if the authorities were willing to shut their eyes, this or that might happen. But it was not to be expected that anyone entrusted with the care of souls could enter the house in the Gamsgasse.

When Edith obtained the order for the grave, the official asked her whether Herr Stein had left any sons; for somebody would have to say the *Kaddish* for him—the prayer in memory of the dead. It was explained to him that there would be no other mourners at the grave save a few women; he looked at the housekeeper mistrustfully over his spectacles and nodded ironically, as though to say: "No sons! That is what one would expect of Herr Stein."

But the firm of François Blum made no conditions to customers. Early in the afternoon they made personal offer of their services for a good and inexpensive funeral.

Anybody who grew up in the city which is our scene will remember the large sign over the door of "François Blum, *entreprise de pompes funèbres.*" He will even remember the show-windows in black and silver which the firm had set up in various busy quarters of the town. In the middle was a huge coffin—large enough to accommodate a primeval giant in his last sleep—and on both sides others arranged according to size, down to tiny caskets for children. Effective draperies of black cloth surrounded the glittering horror, and palm branches, the dusty requisites of heavenly peace, adorned the whole.

The François Blum firm thus provided a well-assorted *memento mori* for the town as it hurried past on earthly occupations bent. The eye, after feasting on a display of lobsters, game, pineapple, and caviare, or admiring an arrangement of lingerie, jewels, or flowers, a temptation for the spirit in books or musical instruments, would suddenly recoil as black and silver death, pompous with dusty palm branches, stared at it from the show-window. It was not Thanatos, the boy with the drooping torch, not the reaper with his scythe; it was middle-class death, it was the death of the great cities, modern death, death without symbolism or image, a ridiculous thing made of silver paint, paper palms, black cloth, plaster, and decay.

But yet this death remained one of the few solemnities known to the life of man. Nobody was more aware of this than the ladies in the Gamsgasse. So that Fräulein Edith, despite considerable extra expense, resolved to order a funeral of the house of Blum.

After that first night of fear and trembling, with the knowledge of a corpse in the house, in their house, the girls managed to get adjusted to the sad situation.

The house had of course to remain closed until the evening after the funeral. The unexpected holiday, combined with all sorts of errands and issuings from the house, which upset the regular order of things, was an agreeable change and novelty. And then they had zealously set to work, within their scanty means, to make the necessary mourning garments. The kitchen was turned into a work-shop, sewing-machines rattled, scraps of stuff strewed the floor, stove and dishware retreated into the background. There was much work to do. The ladies were afraid to go upstairs, so all the noisy life collected in the lower story.

Night fell away like an illness from the denizens of this place. All these children of an early-rising folk, peasants, workmen, small business people, petty officials, conductors, waiters, eagerly enjoyed the forbidden luxury of daylight. Enfranchised by death, they ran joyously about in the streets and, mad with the joy of motion, rode recklessly in the electric street car from one end of the town to the other.

Even Ludmilla, despite her actor, was seized by the contagion. She sewed, altered, tried on with the rest. And that the slender black of a mourning maiden would become her best of all, not even Ilonka doubted in her heart.

The coffin would be set up in the Grand Salon. Though they might expect no guests, yet it was fitting that somewhere a little lunch should be ready and this was laid in the Blue Salon.

Next day workmen thumped in their big boots up the shaky stairs, and a wild clamouring and hammering began in the Grand Salon. This room had never seen daylight, it blinked uncomfortably like some sort of night animal disturbed in its lair. How little, how insignificant, in the dry light this animal seemed, that knew how to stretch itself so exuberantly at its own hour.

The ghosts of all the dances, songs, jokes good and bad, that had ever echoed in this room rose up in defiance along its walls. It was no use. The walls were covered in black, the catafalque rose by degrees from the floor, a grove of laurels and palms somewhat the worse for wear was dragged through the door, amid shouted directions. Edith even had a large un-authorized cross set up at the head of the bier.

The *pompes funèbres* did all honour to their good reputation. But it is uncertain whether it was they who inserted the notice in the newspaper, which struck some of its readers by reason of the paradox of human destiny it contained, the strange fate that had overtaken the house of joy:

"Yesterday in this city occurred the death of Herr Max Stein. The funeral will take place from the house of mourning, Number 5 Gamsgasse."

Everything followed its due course. There was only one rather untoward circumstance: the characteristic odour of the ground floor, that mingling of hot, scented bath-water, soap-suds, vaseline, face-cream, rouge, perspiration, alcohol, and highly seasoned food could not be got rid of. The ladies burned incense for hours, but the air became thereby only the more—there is only one word for it—indecent.

VIII

It belongs to the improbabilities which one admits in life but finds it hard to forgive in a story that Herr President Moré, certainly the most assiduous newspaper-reader in the city, overlooked that paradoxical death-notice. Some explanation for the circumstance lies in the fact that in those fateful and nerve-racking days all the news-sheets were full of the most crucial events and that in every line war and peace and the fate of the world were at stake.

Herr Moré had left his coffee-house deep in thought. His spirit was stirred by patriotic emotions and war floated before his mental eye. Moré's idea of war was a very backward one: there was no "modern emptiness of the battle-fields," no concrete trenches, squadrons of planes, or gas attacks; it was a tempestuous painting full of liveliness and cavalry. Glorious steeds reared heavenwards like equestrian statuary, hand-grenades burst red, green, yellow, and blue, like the most extravagant fireworks, the wounded clutched at their hearts like opera-singers reaching a high note.

Picturing the world-catastrophe in such lively colours as these, the President crossed the Fruit Market and went down the Eisengasse in front of the university; he saw on the right of the little square a third-class hearse with a team of horses and three mourning carriages. He wondered who had died hereabouts—such knowledge indeed belonged to his profession —and zealously ran through the names of the better firms and families of the district. He wondered himself that the news of a death had escaped him. But at the same time—directly he knew where he was—he was taken by a desire, to which in earlier years he had sometimes given way.

Herr Doktor Schleissner might flatter himself that it was he to whom the President owed his knowledge of "these sacred halls." It was not Moré's way to turn day into night and expose himself to the public eye. But, Lord, once in a way it might do.

And the truth was, he had known the house in the Gamsgasse a long time and in better hours than those devoted to the common herd. As a younger man he had often come here privately in the afternoon and always found satisfaction and enjoyment. His way of doing things seemed to him not only more discreet but also more moral and above all more hygienic than the usual practice.

The President stood still. He was conscious, with deep emotion, that a new day was dawning. It wore a double face. On the one side sombre, tragic, like a train of corpselike gentlemen in frock coats and top-hats; on the other very brisk, fresh, and rosy like a foot-soldier. Moré's fancy did actually conjure up foot-soldiers, and other figures out of the appropriate literature, such as *vivandières,* sergeants, dice-throwers, and camp prostitutes.

Moré looked at the hearse, thought of the hard times on the one hand and the loosening of morals on the other, and decided that, as he had nothing in particular on for the next few hours, there was nothing to stand in the way of his desires. He passed the waiting hearse and the horses with waving black plumes on their heads, and with his own mincing step entered the narrow street.

He found the always sternly closed and thick-curtained door wide open.

Meantime, in the house all was ready for the ceremony. The coffin stood on the bier, with a few loose flowers and a poverty-stricken wreath atop. Edith's money, so magnanimously put aside, had not been enough to do very much.

There had been besides a difference of opinion between Edith and the *pompes funèbres,* about the coffin. This was nothing but the simple wooden box prescribed by Jewish rites. God Himself had said: "Dust thou art, and unto dust shalt thou return." And thus every decoration or beautification of the process ordained by God is impious and blasphemous. And yet the housekeeper had other views. A coffin must be splendid, ornamented with silver, adorned with emblems, and somewhere there must be a white lace "throw." She had to pay good money to have even such a box delivered. "That is regular Jewish," she cried. Even religion served to fleece the customer. It was hard to convince her in her excitement that the earth of the Hebrew burying-ground might not receive any but the prescribed coffin.

The ladies had foregathered in their meagre but rather striking mourning garb. Some poor people had come from the neighbourhood, but moved off at once on their tiptoes to the Blue Salon, where they were served with free drinks and loaf cake. Herr Nejedli did the honours there and did not need to urge the neighbours or the undertakers' men or himself to fall to.

Unfortunately there was no guest, no dragoon of the Sixth, no artillerist, intellectual, night-bird, no Schleissner, no Peppler, no Oscar—in a word not an eye there to look with astonishment at the transformation of the Grand Salon. The dancing-floor was largely taken up by the catafalque; the shrouded electric bulbs cast a sombre glow; the amoretti over the looking-glasses had black négligées, a cross and tall candles stood at the head of the Jewish coffin, and a particularly large family of well-powdered little girls in deep mourning wept because that was the fitting thing, because they had known the deceased, because life was sad, death shattering to the feelings, and the unusual solemnity very agreeable on the whole.

Red noses were wiped and sobbings re-echoed; and amid these sights and sounds all the past of the Grand Salon was as though it had not been. And again a moment went past saturated with the lofty, the Shakespearian, inconsistencies of life.

But one could not sob and snuffle for ever or stare at the coffin. Something ought to happen, somebody must say something, make the dead a farewell address. Edith became more and more uneasy. The absence of the priest was painfully evident; it was the great gap in these arrangements to which she had sacrificed such a good round sum. She was beside herself: for without God and some sort of ceremony how were they to go on? Everything was splendid, everybody awaiting the sad final parting, yet here they were, all standing about, too long already, the air seemed thick with painful question: it was a dumb scandal. Edith bit her lips, no idea occurred to her. She glanced despairingly round.

And lo, suddenly her desperate eye fell upon President Moré, standing tall and black in the doorway. None of the "guests" had come; but his warm heart and noble mind had found the way hither. Edith thanked God for the wisdom of destiny and the soul of Moré.

His appearance fitted in marvellously with the funeral pomp; there was nothing more to be wished for, now that he had come, this incomparable functionary, whose very name reminded one of death. The housekeeper fell upon him with whispers and in ten seconds the situation was saved.

It goes without saying that the President of the Spinoza Society, the Master of Ceremonies of the Sons of the League, possessed a distinct oratorical gift. And that an agent for monumental stonework had cemetery oratory at his tongue's end was a matter of course. Besides, as a usual consequence of the talent, he had an uncontrollable itch to hold forth—on all occasions, at the opening and closing of sessions, gatherings, congresses, at solemn and not-solemn occasions, weddings, anniversaries, club meetings, and harmless parties everywhere, where a speech was indicated or not indicated. So that now Edith was not more delighted at the President's consent than he with her request.

With a swift inquiring glance round he assured himself that nobody unauthorized, above all no journalist, was present. Then only did he take his place by the bier, lift his head as though to listen for inspiration, and close his anguished eyes.

And now he began his harangue—which had just as much and just as little to do with the deceased under the pall as with anybody else in the world. But it was, and this was the main point, a fine speech.

The President began by quoting Goethe, to the effect that the suffering and struggling man was always on the way to salvation. The imminent danger, in sight of so many bayadères, to quote also the passage about "the fiery arms of the immortals" which "bear lost children up to heaven," he avoided in the nick of time and took refuge in that less suspect strophe, in which the novice at the gates of paradise challenges the houris to let him in without fear because he has always been a man. The audience, awed by the incomprehensible poetry, were not amazed by the President's invitation to picture Herr Maxl as an aspiring and struggling warrior before the gates of paradise.

Perhaps Herr Maxl himself was the only one to feel surprised at the picture—if we accept the esoteric doctrine of certain teachers, that the "intelligences" of the dead are present at their own funerals.

But the President did not stop at Goethe. He called in Spinoza, Lessing, Isaiah, and Haeckel, and on this sad occasion introduced the greatest spirits of the world into the Grand Salon in the Gamsgasse.

The speech rose to its climax; the President addressed the dead in stern and manly voice by name, making a prophecy about the stormy future; he praised in the departed the symbol of a blithe, free, and happy age, which now lay on its bier to pass away for ever. It was decreed in God's wisdom that one must now take leave of this good and kindly soul, and perhaps, who knew, also from one's own light-hearted youth for ever.

At this point the smouldering sobs burst into a conflagration of loud wails. Ludmilla, overcome by her hopeless love, screamed into her handkerchief. It was Oscar who lay there, waiting this very day to be buried.

Ilonka beat her breast in an access of frenzy. Manya, the callous daughter of grave-diggers, writhed in pain. Edith knelt with uncontrollable tears of contrition beside the catafalque. Only Grete, her eyes dry and burning, hung upon the speaker's compelling lips.

The speech ended on a solemn and consoling note.

The ladies, as though waked out of an anguished dream, behaved like awkward schoolgirls or maidservants as the President with stern sympathetic mien shook each of them by the hand.

Edith was the first to recover from her emotions. Gratefully she saw this ceremony, which was her own work and merit, take its edifying course. After such a moving discourse only music could have anything to say. The housekeeper urged Herr Nejedli towards the piano.

But it seemed that in the course of the years the repertory of the former imperial and royal titulary infant prodigy of Kaiser Ferdinand the Good had become very restricted. Dances, marches, popular songs, yes, those his fingers still knew, but it was impossible to accompany the funeral procession with the electrifying strains of the "Gladiators' March."

So they were in a quandary. Herr Nejedli's hands were not capable either of a simple choral or of a Chopin funeral march. All together his programme was limited to three numbers: the wedding procession from *Lohengrin,* the aria from *La Juive,* and the "Barcarole" from the *Tales of Hoffmann.*

The old man unhesitatingly rejected *Lohengrin* and decided on *La Juive:*

"Almighty God, hear my prayer,
Hear my prayer, great God!"

Nobody took offence at the lively, almost enlivening passion of this allegro, and when Nejedli passed over by quite unauthorized modulations into the "Barcarole," they all looked at each other; for the "Barcarole" had been Maxl's favourite piece, at which he always "had to weep like a little child." The services could not have closed more suitably or loftily than with these immortal strains, to which garlanded barks sailed over dark waters:

"Sweet night, thou night of love,
Oh, quench my longing . . ."

The bearers with the coffin groaned and blundered past the gilt-bronze Venus and the Trumpeter of Säkkingen, down the shaky, complaining stair. The ladies followed. But there were no more sounds of mourning, instead whispers and faint laughter. Had they not cried themselves out already? Tears, they quench the divine thirst of the soul, and thus we are happy and satisfied when we have wept.

The ladies were happy and satisfied. And more, they were full of the joy and pride that come from everything that has gone off well.

IX

The firm of Blum were not only very expeditious in the erection of their funeral pomp but also in taking down and dismantling the draperies, equipages, mourning-veils, and platforms. Swiftly, like good stage-managers, they accomplished the change of scene between death and life.

Particularly in the present case speed was necessary, for by evening the house must be open for pleasure and no reminder of death must oppress the spirits of the guests.

The thing happened like magic. Scarcely had the cortège set off when all the windows were flung open, calling and hammer-blows resounded, and the Grand Salon, freed from its unnatural bonds, came back to itself again. And the smell native to the house, which had been suppressed by the incense, candle-smoke, and unnatural odours, expanded to fill the lower floor as of yore. When two hours later the mourners returned in their landaus from the cemetery, no visible shadow lay upon the rooms and they were as they had always been.

With a slight feeling of strangeness the ladies passed through these rooms which were old and yet new, for every dwelling-place has its epochs and the dwellers therein feel it. Between today and today lay an abyss, the grave yawned, into which an hour ago they had seen lowered the naked unplaned box.

President Moré came back with the others from the interment. Out there in Olschan, where he was a well-known personage, he had held himself a little apart for the sake of his reputation, but his withdrawal might just as well have been accounted for by modesty.

The President received unlimited regard for his moving funeral oration. The girls looked up at him with shy respect. And besides he was the only one of all the guests who had found a human approach to themselves and their lives. He had come hither today with no other purpose than to pay reverence to the dead and express his sympathy with the survivors.

Fräulein Edith knew how to value the honour he had done them. With sincere gratitude in her eyes she went up to Moré, held his hand tenderly in hers, and declared that now she knew who of all the friends of the house was a true human being and a man with a heart.

The President gave a melancholy shrug of the shoulders and said that he knew life, he had understanding of the ways of the world. But that nobody else, not even Doctor Schleissner, had found his way hither, that surprised him. Edith expressed her view that a man was a man and pursued no other end than male beastliness. The President was an exception. She had known it all along. Nobody could fool her; she had nothing, but knowledge of mankind was not such bad capital after all.

Tears came into the eyes of the honest man, to think that fate had given him this opportunity to show himself more virtuous than his knower of men expected from them in general. The actual reason for his appearance was forgotten. He began to believe that humanity itself, the classic masters of which he served unresting, had brought him hither today.

The ladies stood round his dignified and gloomy figure as though he were a schoolmaster, listening to his words; and all the everyday phrases and sayings which had not been heard in this room for days, even now they did not dare to use them, though Ilonka felt an almost irresistible itch to fling into the talk a few professional phrases with sap and marrow.

The Grand Salon, the blinds of which were very properly closed, lay again in the light of the illumination peculiar to it, and awaited with red plush, marble tables, Renaissance mirrors, and fresh-waxed parquetry floor the nightly conviviality. By degrees, and still in their weeds, the girls began to practise the weaving gait proper to the evening, which they had intermitted three whole days.

Only Ludmilla was absent; she had remained in a suburb to visit some relatives.

The President, highly self-satisfied, considered long whether as a business man he ought not to regard the house as a prospective client. Despite certain moral objections he came to the conclusion that it would be a sign of incipient incapacity and business negligence if he let escape so favourable an opportunity. So he girded himself up and began, this time without pathos but instead in a ringing and cordial tone.

"Children," said he, making Grete and Anita sit down beside him and fetching a sigh, "children, man dies, and we must all die. What this death is, nobody knows, and he who learns knows it no longer. Good, we must come to terms with it. But the business has another hitch. . . ."

His voice now took on a tone weighted with knowledge and resignation:

"A grave, when it is not tended, falls to decay; I give my word, inside a few months it is a dung-heap. I speak from experience."

Manya confirmed this view and Moré went on:

"But the care of a grave, ladies, costs money; ugly though it may be, it costs money to remember. Who gives this money? Decent and proper survivors. But if a man has nobody, what then?"

The President looked meaningfully from one to another, before he proceeded to touch their hearts:

"What then? Ask yourselves, if some day you will have anybody?"

The argument went home. Whom would they have then? Hospital, asylum, dissection, at best a hard crust, that was the end of the story, they had heard it all so often. The President smiled a fatherly smile.

"Well, at least Herr Max Stein has somebody left, he has girls with hearts like yours. But where will you all be dispersed, in the year to come? None of us know!"

This went home too. Today they were employed in the first-class establishment in the Gamsgasse and ate with silver forks and spoons. But the years pass, and not everybody can get to be housekeeper; prizes in life or in the lottery are hard to win. There had been dozens of Manyas, Anitas, Ilonkas, who had sunk to the Napoleon and then further still and finished up in the provinces.

The President had no wish to be depressing; his face suddenly brightened.

"But I have thought of something: How would it be, if you made a little collection among you, to put up a stone with his name on it? I speak from experience. A piece of marble like that—it does not have to be marble, sandstone is very nice—but marble keeps a grave green for ever. Of course it must be nicely done—no sculpture, just simple gilt lettering. But in the years to come the passer-by reads 'Max Stein,' says 'Aha!' and remembers him. What do you say? Shall we open a little fund? That is, only if you think well of it. For it is all the same to me. But I think of everything and I happen to have a price-list with me. From three hundred kronen upwards one can get quite fair stones. . . ."

The ladies' hearts were still oppressed by the weight of the last three days. Not yet did they feel at home on the parquetry of the Grand Salon. The vision of the cemetery was before them still. The question: Whom will you have? still rang in their ears. Gladly would they have bought themselves free of the fate that threatened them more than other people. And is not death, among all primitive peoples and persons, the thought that most rouses the instinct to sacrifice?

Thus the words of Moré fell on fruitful ground. More or less eagerly they all sought their rooms. Their cash in hand and savings were counted over and over. According to the measure of generosity, faith, greed, or caprice, they gave.

Valeska, the vainest and best-natured of them all, was undressing when the collection was made; either for that reason or just to show herself in her magnificence she came downstairs stark naked, to hand in personally to death's business representative the twenty-five kronen of her tribute to death. And it was a marvel to see how, when suddenly the joyful flesh-colour of this feminine body blossomed in the lingering gloom of the Grand Salon, the room seemed for the first time since Max's death to be coming back to itself. The exhausting space smiled wanly and drew faltering breath like an invalid who has turned the corner back to life. Valeska stood there revolving self-absorbed round her own lovely axis—it was a homely and a heartening sight.

During the next fifteen minutes Moré had entered most of the girls' real names in his lists with the amount promised appended. Only Fräulein Edith, who had already done all she could, and Manya, the initiated, who saw through the game, did not contribute.

The agent for monumental stone booked the order in his note-book and actually, moved by his own magnanimity, reduced his own commission from the usual fifteen to seven and a half percent.

The dressing-hour, and the hairdresser, had arrived. The wonted excitement possessed the ladies. They all rushed screaming upstairs to the dressing-room, Ilonka's voice ringing above the others in her favourite strong language, which burst like a freed torrent from her breast.

Grete stopped in the salon with the President. She seized his hand.

"A big hole! And you are chucked down it. Just dirt and that's all."

The presiding officer of the Spinoza Society avoided any precise statement of his views:

"That is not the important thing about it."

Grete asked, astonished:

"Why, Prexy, you don't mean you believe in heaven, like Edith?"

The President contented himself with quoting Goethe:

" 'And lo, behold, we can know nothing.' "

But Grete had not got to the end of her metaphysical preoccupations; she looked sharply at Moré and emphasized each word:

"If it is true that we are going to go to heaven, then why does it rain every time anybody is buried?"

There was triumph in her voice. But the President disarmed her logic out of his professional experience:

"I have often in my practice seen funerals on beautiful days."

Grete asked suddenly:

"I say, Prexy, what did Spinoza say?"

"He said a great deal, my child."

"Did Spinoza say: 'Sire, give freedom of thought'?"

"No, that comes from Schiller. But that was just what Spinoza thought. For instance, he said: 'Happiness is virtue, not its reward.' "

"Happiness is not its reward! Nor mine either. That is divine."

Grete chuckled with satisfaction at Moré's quotation.

Her voice grew very confidential:

"Spinoza was Spanish, wasn't he? I had a Spaniard once. . . . No, two!"

The President instructed her:

"Spinoza was a Dutchman."

Grete made a disgusted face:

"A Dutchman! Disgusting. I can't stand them. In Hamburg, you know, there were always a lot of Dutch."

The President, whose mind dwelt continually on the political situation, said:

"They will probably remain neutral."

Grete pressed herself close to him.

"You know I'm crazy about you? Much more than Schleissner. How can a man be called Schleissner? It was grand of you, Prexy, to come to-day!"

The President smiled benevolently. With his large hairy hand he delicately stroked Grete's long legs. She sighed against his breast:

"You shall be my lover, and you needn't give me any money."

But she misjudged the President.

He drew himself up to his full height and declared that he was a guest of the house, like any other and would not be made an exception of. He would go up with her now to her room. But he would take nothing as a present. How could she do that and how could he? There must be order in all things.

The pair disappeared.

At the same time Edith was hearing from Ludmilla the news that she would not be returning to the Gamsgasse.

X

Here it is time to draw to a close these brief and cursory notes, for as a matter of fact the story of the old established house in the Gamsgasse ends at this point. Even what is here set down is but an inconsiderable chronicle of last days, if we are to assume, without exaggerated historical assumptions, that the famous house was founded some time after the battle on the White Mountain. The magnificent assumption that Charles the Fourth of Luxembourg had some three centuries earlier been its founder probably belongs to legend. But that is the way with fame: it ascribes to famous names the deeds of unknown men. Why should not Charles, the great city-builder, to whom we owe the New Town, the university, and the old bridge, also have laid the foundation-stone of the Grand Salon in the Gamsgasse?

At all events it had a long and splendid life between the Thirty Years' War and the Great War: a life which deserved a more romantic ending than to terminate with the death of a decadent, half-witted last survivor. But do the great kingdoms of the earth perish more grandly? They think to survive, they carry on wars, and before they know it they are dissolved and divided up as booty.

In that paradoxical moment when Herr Max lay on his bier in the large salon, the establishment had fulfilled its destiny, however long it might linger on. The heirs were no good, as is sufficiently shown by the fact that Fräulein Edith, the most pious and cautious of all housekeepers, gave notice in the early days of the new regime. This notice, and the severity of the new laws, gave the *coup de grâce*.

The building still stands; but it has been absorbed by the neighbouring leather trade; even the peculiar, once indestructible odour in the vestibule is said to have been wholly drowned out by the stench of Russian leather.

Moreover, every death is a court of last appeal; and nothing dies whose time has not come. If today one passes by night through the streets glaring with electric signs, one reads at every corner the names of places dedicated not to joy but to the dance. The Negro saxophone wails. Real ladies go in and out through the glittering portals, and their magnificent free limbs are a plainer allure than was ever allowed in the Gamsgasse of yore.

Careworn, deprived of her bread by an unlimited, unlicensed competition, the street-walker drearily makes her round. Who knows whether "houses" still exist? Perhaps this account of mine may thus possess some historical value if no other.

No one will inquire into the unimportant fates of highly unimportant persons. In this picture they played only the part of supernumeraries. And the inquiry would embarrass the answerer. Of course he would at once burst out:

"You know, Oscar has become quite prominent; he owns the finest country-house in an American film city!"

But the question itself would be silly: even a Zulu knows Oscar's face on the films.

As for Ludmilla, she is to be seen at every première in the theatres. She has not grown fatter, only in the struggle with her double chin the chin seems to have got the upper hand. She may still be called pretty. Her slender, classic legs, much advantaged by present fashions, have a daily triumph on the street.

Her old friends long ago stopped venturing to greet her. She acknowledges the bow only of the gentlemen she knows, and it is exactly her old acquaintances whom she does not know. She looks them in the face with wide, childlike eyes and, however ingratiatingly they smile, she cannot, by the greatest effort, remember them.

It happened not otherwise even to Oscar, on his late triumphal tour of the world. The staring childlike eyes did not recognize him, he read nothing there but the disdain of a lady bored by importunate glances. The incident upset him, and deprived him of speech for quite a while—which proves, once more, that a man is vainer than a woman.

Who could reproach Ludmilla for her bad memory? The war washed away in blood many other memories as well. And she has long since become the wife of an influential deputy of the Republic. Chance would have it that in the enthusiastic days of the Revolution her husband was a member of a parliamentary commission which under the leadership of a well-known feminist successfully attacked the problem of prostitution and decided the fate of the Grand Salon. Frau Ludmilla's husband passes for an idealist, he was never involved in any of the numerous financial scandals, and is, so one hears, a great political hope. For her and for the state it is sincerely to be wished that he may become a minister in the next Cabinet.

A START IN LIFE

Ruth Suckow

(1892–)

THE SWITZERS were scurrying around to get Daisy ready by the time that Elmer Kruse should get through in town. They had known all week that Elmer might be in for her any day. But they hadn't done a thing until he appeared. "Oh, it was so rainy to-day, the roads were so muddy, they hadn't thought he'd get in until maybe next week." It would have been the same any other day.

Mrs. Switzer was trying now at the last moment to get all of Daisy's things into the battered telescope that lay open on the bed. The bed had not "got made"; and just as soon as Daisy was gone, Mrs. Switzer would have to hurry off to the Woodworths, where she was to wash to-day. Daisy's things were scattered over the dark brown quilt and the rumpled sheet that were dingy and clammy in this damp weather. So was the whole bedroom, with its sloping ceiling, and old-fashioned square-paned windows, the commode that they used for a dresser littered with pin trays, curlers, broken combs, ribbons, smoky lamp, all mixed up together; the door of the closet open, showing the confusion of clothes and shabby shoes. . . . They all slept in this room—Mrs. Switzer and Dwight in the bed, the two girls in the cot against the wall.

"Mama, I can't find the belt to that plaid dress."

"Oh, ain't it somewheres around? Well, I guess you'll have to let it go. If I come across it I can send it out to you. Someone'll be going past there."

She had meant to get Daisy all mended and "fixed up" before she went out to the country. But somehow . . . oh, there was always so much to see to when she came home. Gone all day, washing and cleaning for other people; it didn't leave her much time for her own house.

She was late now. The Woodworths liked to have her get the washing out early so that she could do some cleaning too before she left. But she couldn't help it. She would have to get Daisy off first. She had already had on her wraps ready to go, when Elmer came—her cleaning cap, of a blue faded almost into gray, and the ancient black coat with gathered sleeves that she wore over her work dress when she went out to wash.

"What's become of all your underclothes? They ain't all dirty, are they?"

"They are, too. You didn't wash for us last week, mama."

"Well, you'll just have to take along what you've got. Maybe there'll be some way of getting the rest to you."

"Elmers come in every week, don't they?" Daisy demanded.

"Yes, but maybe they won't always be bringing you in."

She jammed what she could into the telescope, thinking with her helpless, anxious fatalism that it would have to do somehow.

"Daisy, you get yourself ready now."

"I am ready. Mama, I want to put on my other ribbon."

"Oh, that's 'way down in the telescope somewhere. You needn't be so anxious to fix yourself up. This ain't like going visiting."

Daisy stood at the little mirror preening herself—such a homely child, "all Switzer," skinny, with pale sharp eyes set close together and thin, stringy, reddish hair. But she had never really learned yet how homely she was. She was the oldest, and she got the pick of what clothes were given to the Switzers. Goldie and Dwight envied her. She was important in her small world. She was proud of her blue coat that had belonged to Alice Brooker, the town lawyer's daughter. It hung unevenly above her bony little knees, and the buttons came down too far. Her mother had tried to make it over for her.

Mrs. Switzer looked at her, troubled, but not knowing how she could tell her all the things she ought to be told. Daisy had never been away before except to go to her Uncle Fred's at Lehigh. She seemed to think that this would be the same. She had so many things to learn. Well, she would find them out soon enough—only too soon. Working for other people—she would learn what that meant. Elmer and Edna Kruse were nice young people. They would mean well enough by Daisy. It was a good chance for her to start in. But it wasn't the same.

Daisy was so proud. She thought it was quite a thing to be "starting in to earn." She thought she could buy herself so much with that dollar and a half a week. The other children stood back watching her, round-eyed and impressed. They wished that they were going away, like Daisy.

They heard a car come splashing through the mud on low.

"There he is back! Have you got your things on? Goldie—go out and tell him she's coming."

"No, me tell him, me!" Dwight shouted jealously.

"Well—both of you tell him. Land! . . ."

She tried hastily to put on the cover of the bulging telescope and to fasten the straps. One of them broke.

"Well, you'll have to take it the way it is."

It was an old thing, hadn't been used since her husband, Mert, had "left off canvassing" before he died. And he had worn it all to pieces.

"Well, I guess you'll have to go now. He won't want to wait. I'll try and send you out what you ain't got with you." She turned to Daisy. Her face was working. There was nothing else to do, as everyone said. Daisy would have to help, and she might as well learn it now. Only, she hated to see Daisy go off, to have her starting in. She knew what it meant. "Well—you try and work good this summer, so they'll want you to stay. I hope they'll bring you in sometimes."

Daisy's homely little face grew pale with awe, suddenly, at the sight of her mother crying, at something that she dimly sensed in the pressure of her mother's thin strong arms. Her vanity in her new importance was somehow shamed and dampened.

Elmer's big new Buick, mud-splashed but imposing, stood tilted on the uneven road. Mud was thick on the wheels. It was a bad day for driving, with the roads a yellow mass, water lying in all the wheel ruts. This little road that led past these few houses on the outskirts of town, and up over the hill, had a cold rainy loneliness. Elmer sat in the front seat of the Buick, and in the back was a big box of groceries.

"Got room to sit in there?" he asked genially. "I didn't get out, it's so muddy here."

"No, don't get out," Mrs. Switzer said hastily. "She can put this right on the floor there in the back." She added, with a timid attempt at courtesy, "Ain't the roads pretty bad out that way?"

"Yes, but farmers get so they don't think so much about the roads."

"I s'pose that's so."

He saw the signs of tears on Mrs. Switzer's face, and they made him anxious to get away. She embraced Daisy hastily again. Daisy climbed over the grocery box and scrunched herself into the seat.

"I guess you'll bring her in with you some time when you're coming," Mrs. Switzer hinted.

"Sure. We'll bring her."

He started the engine. It roared, half died down as the wheels of the car spun in the thick wet mud.

In that moment, Daisy had a startled view of home—the small house standing on a rough rise of land, weathered to a dim color that showed dark streaks from the rain; the narrow sloping front porch whose edge had a soaked gnawed look; the chickens, grayish-black, pecking at the wet

ground; their playthings, stones, a wagon, some old pail covers littered
about; a soaked, discolored piece of underwear hanging on the line in the
back yard. The yard was tussocky and overhung the road with shaggy long
grass where the yellow bank was caved in under it. Goldie and Dwight were
gazing at her solemnly. She saw her mother's face—a thin, weak, loving
face, drawn with neglected weeping, with its reddened eyes and poor teeth
. . . in the old coat and heavy shoes and cleaning cap, her work-worn hand
with its big knuckles clutching at her coat. She saw the playthings they had
used yesterday, and the old swing that hung from one of the trees, the ropes
sodden, the seat in crooked. . . .

The car went off, slipping on the wet clay. She waved frantically, suddenly understanding that she was leaving them. They waved at her.

Mrs. Switzer stood there a little while. Then came the harsh rasp of the
old black iron pump that stood out under the box elder tree. She was pumping water to leave for the children before she went off to work.

II

Daisy held on as the car skidded going down the short clay hill. Elmer
didn't bother with chains. He was too used to the roads. But her eyes
brightened with scared excitement. When they were down, and Elmer
slowed up going along the tracks in the deep wet grass that led to the main
road, she looked back, holding on her hat with her small scrawny hand.

Just down this little hill—and home was gone. The big car, the feel of her
telescope on the floor under her feet, the fact that she was going out to the
country, changed the looks of everything. She saw it all now.

Dunkels' house stood on one side of the road. A closed-up white house.
The windows stared blank and cold between the old shutters. There was a
chair with a broken straw seat under the fruit trees. The Dunkels were
old Catholic people who seldom went anywhere. In the front yard was a
clump of tall pines, the rough brown trunks wet, the green branches, dark
and shining, heavy with rain, the ground underneath mournfully sodden
and black.

The pasture on the other side. The green grass, lush, wet and cold, and
the outcroppings of limestone that held little pools of rain water in all the
tiny holes. Beyond, the low hills gloomy with timber against the lowering
sky.

They slid out onto the main road. They bumped over the small wooden
bridge above the swollen creek that came from the pasture. Daisy looked
down. She saw the little swirls of foam, the long grass that swished with
the water, the old rusted tin cans lodged between the rocks.

She sat up straight and important, her thin, homely little face strained
with excitement, her sharp eyes taking in everything. The watery mud holes

in the road, the little thickets of plum trees, low and wet, in dark inter-lacings. She held on fiercely, but made no sound when the car skidded.

She felt the grandeur of having a ride. One wet Sunday, Mr. Brooker had driven them all home from church, she and Goldie and Dwight packed tightly into the back seat of the car, shut in by the side curtains, against which the rain lashed, catching the muddy scent of the roads. Sometimes they could plan to go to town just when Mr. Pattey was going to work in his Ford. Then they would run out and shout eagerly, "Mr. Pattey! Are you going through town?" Sometimes he didn't hear them. Sometimes he said, with curt good nature, "Well, pile in"; and they all hopped into the truck back. "He says we can go along with him."

She looked at the black wet fields through which little leaves of bright green corn grew in rows, at showery bushes of sumach along the roadside. A gasoline engine pumping water made a loud desolate sound. There were somber-looking cattle in the wet grass, and lonely, thick-foliaged trees growing here and there in the pastures. She felt her telescope on the floor of the car, the box of groceries beside her. She eyed these with a sharp curiosity. There was a fresh pineapple—something the Switzers didn't often get at home. She wondered if Edna would have it for dinner. Maybe she could hint a little to Edna.

She was out in the country. She could no longer see her house even if she wanted to—standing dingy, streaked with rain, in its rough grass on the little hill. A lump came into her throat. She had looked forward to playing with Edna's children. But Goldie and Dwight would play all morning without her. She was still proud of being the oldest, of going out with Elmer and Edna; but now there was a forlornness in the pride.

She wished she were in the front seat with Elmer. She didn't see why he hadn't put her there. She would have liked to know who all the people were who lived on these farms; how old Elmer's babies were; and if he and Edna always went to the movies when they went into town on Saturday nights. Elmer must have lots of money to buy a car like this. He had a new house on his farm, too, and Mrs. Metzinger had said that it had plumbing. Maybe they would take her to the movies, too. She might hint about that.

When she had gone to visit Uncle Fred, she had had to go on the train. She liked this better. She hoped they had a long way to go. She called out to Elmer:

"Say, how much farther is your place?"

"What's that?" He turned around. "Oh, just down the road a ways. Scared to drive in the mud?"

"No, I ain't scared. I like to drive most any way."

She looked at Elmer's back, the old felt hat crammed down carelessly on his head, the back of his neck with the golden hair on the sunburned skin above the blue of his shirt collar. Strong and easy and slouched a little over the steering wheel that he handled so masterly. Elmer and Edna were just young folks; but Mrs. Metzinger said that they had more to start with than most young farmers did, and that they were hustlers. Daisy felt that the pride of this belonged to her too, now.

"Here we are!"

"Oh, is this where you folks live?" Daisy cried eagerly.

The house stood back from the road, beyond a space of bare yard with a little scattering of grass just starting—small, modern, painted a bright new white and yellow. The barn was new too, a big splendid barn of frescoed brick, with a silo of the same. There were no trees. A raw desolate wind blew across the back yard as they drove up beside the back door.

Edna had come out on the step. Elmer grinned at her as he took out the box of groceries, and she slightly raised her eyebrows. She said kindly enough:

"Well, you brought Daisy. Hello, Daisy, are you going to stay with us this summer?"

"I guess so," Daisy said importantly. But she suddenly felt a little shy and forlorn as she got out of the car and stood on the bare ground in the chilly wind.

"Yes, I brought her along," Elmer said.

"Are the roads very bad?"

"Kind of bad. Why?"

"Well, I'd like to get over to mama's some time to-day."

"Oh, I guess they aren't too bad for that."

Daisy pricked up her sharp little ears. Another ride. That cheered her.

"Look in the door," Edna said in a low fond voice, motioning with her head.

Two little round, blond heads were pressed tightly against the screen door. There was a clamor of "Daddy, daddy!" Elmer grinned with a bashful pride as he stood with the box of groceries, raising his eyebrows with mock surprise and demanding, "Who's this? What you shoutin' 'daddy' for? You don't think daddy's got anything for you, do you?" He and Edna were going into the kitchen together, until Edna remembered and called back hastily:

"Oh, come in, Daisy!"

Daisy stood, a little left out and solitary, there in the kitchen, as Billy, the older of the babies, climbed frantically over Elmer, demanding candy, and the little one toddled smilingly about. Her eyes took in all of it. She was impressed by the shining blue-and-white linoleum, the range with its nickel and enamel, the bright new woodwork. Edna was laughing and scolding at Elmer and the baby. Billy had made his father produce the candy. Daisy's sharp little eyes looked hungrily at the lemon drops until Edna remembered her.

"Give Daisy a piece of your candy," she said.

He would not go up to Daisy. She had to come forward and take one of the lemon drops herself. She saw where Edna put the sack, in a dish high in the cupboard. She hoped they would get some more before long.

"My telescope's out there in the car," she reminded them.

"Oh! Elmer, you go and get it and take it up for her," Edna said.

"What?"

"Her valise—or whatever it is—out in the car."

"Oh, sure," Elmer said with a cheerful grin.

"It's kind of an old telescope," Daisy said conversationally. "I guess it's been used a lot. My papa used to have it. The strap broke when mama was fastening it this morning. We ain't got any suitcase. I had to take this because it was all there was in the house, and mama didn't want to get me a new one."

Edna raised her eyebrows politely. She leaned over and pretended to spat the baby as he came toddling up to her, then rubbed her cheek against his round head with its funny fuzz of hair.

Daisy watched solemnly. "I didn't know both of your children was boys. I thought one of 'em was a girl. That's what there is at home now—one boy and one girl."

"Um-hm," Edna replied absently. "You can go up with Elmer and take off your things, Daisy," she said. "You can stop and unpack your valise now, I guess, if you'd like to. Then you can come down and help me in the kitchen. You know we got you to help me," she reminded.

Daisy, subdued, followed Elmer up the bright new stairs. In the upper hall, two strips of very clean rag rug were laid over the shining yellow of the floor. Elmer had put her telescope in one of the bedrooms.

"There you are!"

She heard him go clattering down the stairs, and then a kind of murmuring and laughing in the kitchen. The back door slammed. She hurried to the window in time to see Elmer go striding off toward the barn.

She looked about her room with intense curiosity. It too had a bright varnished floor. She had a bed all of her own—a small, old-fashioned bed, left from some old furnishings, that had been put in this room that had the pipes and the hot water tank. She had to see everything, but she had a stealthy look as she tiptoed about, started to open the drawers of the dresser, looked out of her window. She put her coat and hat on the bed. She would rather be down in the kitchen with Edna than unpack her telescope now.

She guessed she would go down where the rest of them were.

III

Elmer came into the house for dinner. He brought in a cold, muddy, outdoor breath with him. The range was going, but the bright little kitchen seemed chilly, with the white oilcloth on the table, the baby's varnished high chair and his little fat mottled hands.

Edna made a significant little face at Elmer. Daisy did not see. She was standing back from the stove, where Edna was at work, looking at the baby.

"He can talk pretty good, can't he? Dwight couldn't say anything but 'mama' when he was that little."

Edna's back was turned. She said meaningly:

"Now, Elmer's come in for dinner, Daisy, we'll have to hurry. You must help me get on the dinner. You can cut bread and get things on the table. You must help, you know. That's what you are supposed to do."

Daisy looked startled, a little scared and resentful. "Well, I don't know where you keep your bread."

"Don't you remember where I told you to put it this morning? Right over in the cabinet, in that big box. You must watch, Daisy, and learn where things are."

Elmer, a little embarrassed at the look that Edna gave him, whistled as he began to wash his hands at the sink.

"How's daddy's old boy?" he said loudly, giving a poke at the baby's chin.

As Edna passed him, she shook her head and her lips just formed, "Been like that all morning!"

He grinned comprehendingly. Then both their faces became expressionless.

Daisy had not exactly heard, but she looked from one to the other, silent and dimly wondering. The queer ache that had kept starting all through the morning, under her interest in Edna's things and doings, came over her again. She sensed something different in the atmosphere than she had ever known before—some queer difference between the position of herself and of the two babies, a faint notion of what mama had meant when she had said that this would not be visiting.

"I guess I'm going to have the toothache again," she said faintly.

No one seemed to hear her.

Edna whisked off the potatoes, drained the water. . . . "You might bring me a dish, Daisy." Daisy searched a long time while Edna turned impatiently and pointed. Edna put the rest of the things on the table herself. Her young, fresh, capable mouth was tightly closed, and she was making certain resolutions.

Daisy stood hesitating in the middle of the room, a scrawny, unappealing little figure. Billy—fat, blond, in funny, dark blue union-alls—was trotting busily about the kitchen. Daisy swooped down upon him and tried to bring him to the table. He set up a howl. Edna turned, looked astonished, severe.

"I was trying to make him come to the table," Daisy explained weakly.

"You scared him. He isn't used to you. He doesn't like it. Don't cry, Billy. The girl didn't mean anything."

"Here, daddy'll put him in his place," Elmer said hastily.

Billy looked over his father's shoulder at Daisy with suffused, resentful blue eyes. She did not understand it, and felt strangely at a loss. She had been left with Goldie and Dwight so often. She had always made Dwight go to the table. She had been the boss.

Edna said in a cool, held-in voice, "Put these things on the table, Daisy."

They sat down. Daisy and the other children had always felt it a great treat to eat away from home instead of at their own scanty, hastily set table. They had hung around Mrs. Metzinger's house at noon, hoping to be asked to stay, not offended when told that "it was time for them to run off now." Her pinched little face had a hungry look as she stared at the potatoes and fried ham and pie. But they did not watch and urge her to have more, as Mrs. Metzinger did, and Mrs. Brooker when she took pity on the Switzers and had them there. Daisy wanted more pie. But none of them seemed to be taking more, and so she said nothing. She remembered what her mother had said, with now a faint comprehension. "You must remember you're out working for other folks, and it won't be like it is at home."

After dinner, Edna said, "Now you can wash the dishes, Daisy."

She went into the next room with the children. Daisy, as she went hesitatingly about the kitchen alone, could hear Edna's low contented humming as she sat in there rocking, the baby in her lap. The bright kitchen was empty and lonely now. Through the window, Daisy could see the great barn looming up against the rainy sky. She hoped that they would drive to Edna's mother's soon.

She finished as soon as she could and went into the dining room where Edna was sewing on the baby's rompers. Edna went on sewing. Daisy sat down disconsolately. That queer low ache went all through her. She said in a small dismal voice:

"I guess I got the toothache again."

Edna bit off a thread.

"I had it awful hard awhile ago. Mama come pretty near taking me to the dentist."

"That's too bad," Edna murmured politely. But she offered no other condolence. She gave a little secret smile at the baby asleep on a blanket and a pillow in one corner of the shiny leather davenport.

"Is Elmer going to drive into town to-morrow?"

"To-morrow? I don't suppose so."

"Mama couldn't find the belt of my plaid dress and I thought if he was, maybe I could go along and get it. I'd like to have it."

Daisy's homely mouth drooped at the corners. Her toothache did not seem to matter to anyone. Edna did not seem to want to see that anything was wrong with her. She had expected Edna to be concerned, to mention remedies. But it wasn't toothache, that strange lonesome ache all over her. Maybe she was going to be terribly sick. Mama wouldn't come home for supper to be told about it.

She saw mama's face as in that last glimpse of it—drawn with crying, and yet trying to smile, under the old cleaning cap, her hand holding her coat together. . . .

Edna glanced quickly at her. The child was so mortally unattractive, unappealing even in her forlornness. Edna frowned a little, but said kindly:

"Now you might take Billy into the kitchen out of my way, Daisy, and amuse him."

"Well, he cries when I pick him up," Daisy said faintly.

"He won't cry this time. Take him out and help him play with his blocks. You must help me with the children, you know."

"Well, if he'll go with me."

"He'll go with you, won't he, Billy boy? Won't you go with Daisy, sweetheart?"

Billy stared and then nodded. Daisy felt a thrill of comfort as Billy put his little fat hand in hers and trotted into the kitchen beside her. He had the fattest hands, she thought. Edna brought the blocks and put the box down on the floor beside Daisy.

"Now, see if you can amuse him so that I can get my sewing done."

"Shall you and me play blocks, Billy?" Daisy murmured.

He nodded. Then he got hold of the box with one hand, tipped out all the blocks on the floor with a bang and a rattle, and looked at her with a pleased proud smile.

"Oh no, Billy. You mustn't spill out the blocks. Look, you're too little to play with them. No, now—now wait! Let Daisy show you. Daisy'll build you something real nice—shall she?"

He gave a solemn nod of consent.

Daisy set out the blocks on the bright linoleum. She had never had such blocks as these to handle before. Dwight's were only a few old, unmatched, broken ones. Her spirit of leadership came back, and she firmly put away that fat hand of Billy's whenever he meddled with her building. She could make something really wonderful with these blocks.

"No, Billy, you mustn't. See, when Daisy's got it all done, then you can see what the lovely building is."

She put the blocks together with great interest. She knew what she was going to make—it was going to be a new house; no, a new church. Just as she got the walls up, in came that little hand again, and then with a delighted grunt Billy swept the blocks pell-mell about the floor. At the clatter, he sat back, pursing his mouth to give an ecstatic "Ooh!"

"Oh, Billy—you mustn't, the building wasn't done! Look, you've spoiled it. Now you've got to sit 'way off here while I try to build it over again."

Billy's look of triumph turned to surprise and then to vociferous protest as Daisy picked him up and firmly transplanted him to another corner of the room. He set up a tremendous howl. He had never been set aside like that before. Edna came hurrying out. Daisy looked at Edna for justification, but instinctively on the defensive.

"Billy knocked over the blocks. He spoiled the building."

"Wah! Wah!" Billy gave loud heartbroken sobs. The tears ran down his fat cheeks and he held out his arms piteously toward his mother.

"I didn't hurt him," Daisy said, scared.

"Never mind, lover," Edna was crooning. "Of course he can play with his blocks. They're Billy's blocks, Daisy," she said. "He doesn't like to sit and see you put up buildings. He wants to play, too. See, you've made him cry now."

"Do' wanna stay here," Billy wailed.

"Well, come in with mother then." She picked him up, wiping his tears.

"I didn't hurt him," Daisy protested.

"Well, never mind now. You can pick up the blocks and then sweep up the floor, Daisy. You didn't do that when you finished the dishes. Never mind," she was saying to Billy. "Pretty soon daddy'll come in and we'll have a nice ride."

Daisy soberly picked up the blocks and got the broom. What had she done to Billy? He had tried to spoil her building. She always made Dwight keep back until she had finished. Of course it was Daisy, the oldest, who should lead and manage. There had been no one to hear her side. Everything was different. She winked back tears as she swept, poorly and carelessly.

Then she brightened up as Elmer came tramping up on the back porch and then through the kitchen.

"Edna!"

"She's in there," Daisy offered.

"Want to go now? What! Is the baby asleep?" he asked blankly.

Edna gave him a warning look and the door was closed.

Daisy listened hard. She swept very softly. She could catch only a little of what they said—"Kind of hate to go off . . . I know, but if we once start . . . not a thing all day . . . what we got her for . . ." She had no real comprehension of it. She hurried and put away the broom. She wanted to be sure and be ready to go.

Elmer tramped out, straight past her. She saw from the window that he was backing the car out from the shed. She could hear Edna and Billy upstairs, could hear the baby cry a little as he was wakened. Maybe she ought to go out and get on her wraps, too.

Elmer honked the horn. A moment later Edna came hurrying downstairs, in her hat and coat, and Billy in a knitted cap and a red sweater crammed over his union-alls, so that he looked like a little Brownie. The baby had on his little coat, too.

Edna called out, "Come in and get this boy, daddy." She did not look at Daisy, but said hurriedly, "We're going for a little ride, Daisy. Have you finished the sweeping? Well, then, you can pick up those pieces in the dining room. We won't be gone so very long. When it's a quarter past five, you start the fire, like I showed you this noon, and slice the potatoes that were left, and the meat. And set the table."

The horn was honked again.

"Yes! Well, we'll be back, Daisy. Come, lover, daddy's in a hurry."

Daisy stood looking after them. Billy clamored to sit beside his daddy. Edna took the baby from Elmer and put him beside her on the back seat. There was room—half of the big back seat. There wasn't anything, really, to be done at home. That was the worst of it. They just didn't want to take her. They all belonged together. They didn't want to take anyone else along. She was an outsider. They all—even the baby—had a freshened look of expectancy.

The engine roared—they had started; slipping on the mud of the drive, then forging straight ahead, around the turn, out of sight.

IV

She went forlornly into the dining room. The light from the windows was dim now in the rainy, late afternoon. The pink pieces from the baby's rompers were scattered over the gay rug. She got down on her hands and knees, slowly picking them up, sniffing a little. She heard the Big Ben clock in the kitchen ticking loudly.

That dreadful ache submerged her. No one would ask about it, no one would try to comfort her. Before, there had always been mama coming home, anxious, scolding sometimes, but worried over them if they didn't feel right, caring about them. Mama and Goldie and Dwight cared about her—but she was away out in the country, and they were at home. She didn't want to stay here, where she didn't belong. But mama had told her that she must begin helping this summer.

Her ugly little mouth contorted into a grimace of weeping. But silent weeping, without any tears; because she already had the cold knowledge that no one would notice or comfort it.

THE DESERT ISLANDER

Stella Benson

(1892–1933)

CONSTANTINE hopefully followed the Chinese servant through the unknown house. He felt hopeful of success in his plan of begging this Englishman for help, for he knew that an Englishman, alone among people of a different colour (as this Englishman was alone in this South China town), treated the helping of stray white men almost as part of the White Man's Burden. But even without his claim of one lonely white man upon another, Constantine would have felt hopeful. He knew himself to be a man of compelling manner in spite of his ugly, too long face, and his ugly, too short legs.

As Constantine stumped in on his hobnailed soles, Mr. White—who was evidently not a very tactful man—said, "Oh, are you *another* deserter from the Foreign Legion?"

"I am Constantine Andreievitch Soloviev," said Constantine, surprised. He spoke and understood English almost perfectly (his mother had been English), yet he could not remember ever having heard the word *another* applied to himself. In fact it did not—could not possibly—so apply. There was only one of him, he knew.

Of course, in a way there was some sense in what this stupid Englishman said. Constantine had certainly been a *légionnaire* in Tonkin up till last Thursday—his narrow pipe-clayed helmet, stiff khaki greatcoat, shabby drill uniform, puttees, brass buttons, and inflexible boots were all the property of the French Government. But the core—the pearl inside this vulgar, horny shell—was Constantine Andreievitch Soloviev. That made all the difference.

Constantine saw that he must take this Didymus of an Englishman in hand at once and tell him a few exciting stories about his dangerous adventures between the Tonkin border and this Chinese city. Snakes, tigers, love-crazed Chinese princesses and brigands passed rapidly through his mind, and he chose the last, because he had previously planned several impressive things to do if he should be attacked by brigands. So now, though he had not actually met a brigand, those plans would come in useful. Constantine intended to write his autobiography some day when he should have married a rich wife and settled down. Not only did his actual life seem to him a very rare one but, also, lives were so interesting to make up.

Constantine was a desert islander—a spiritual Robinson Crusoe. He made up everything himself and he wasted nothing. *Robinson Crusoe* was his favourite book—in fact, almost the only book he had ever read—and he was proud to be, like his hero, a desert islander. He actually preferred clothing his spirit in the skins of wild thoughts that had been the prey of his wits and sheltering it from the world's weather in a leaky hut of his brain's own contriving, to enjoying the good tailoring and housing that dwellers on the mainland call experience and education. He enjoyed being barbarous, he enjoyed living alone on his island, accepting nothing, imitating nothing, believing nothing, adapting himself to nothing—implacably home-made. Even his tangible possessions were those of a marooned man rather than of a civilized citizen of this well-furnished world. At this moment his only luggage was a balalaika that he had made himself out of cigar-boxes, and to this he sang songs of his own composition—very imperfect songs. He would not have claimed that either his songs or his instrument were better than the songs and instruments made by song-makers and balalaika-makers; they were, however, much more rapturously *his* than any acquired music could have been and, indeed, in this as in almost all things, it simply never occurred to him to *take* rather than *make*. There was no mainland on the horizon of his desert island.

"I am not a beggar," said Constantine. "Until yesterday I had sixty piastres which I had saved by many sacrifices during my service in the Legion. But yesterday, passing through a dark forest of pines in the twilight, about twenty versts from here, I met——"

"You met a band of brigands," said Mr. White. "Yes, I know . . . you all say that."

Constantine stared at him. He had not lived, a desert islander, in a crowded and over-civilized world without meeting many rebuffs, so this one did not surprise him—did not even offend him. On the contrary, for a minute he almost loved the uncompromising Mr. White, as a sportsman almost loves the chamois on a peculiarly inaccessible crag. This was a friend worth a good deal of trouble to secure, Constantine saw. He realized at once that the desert islander's line here was to discard the brigands and to discard noble independence.

"Very well then," said Constantine. "I did *not* meet brigands. I *am* a beggar. I started without a penny and I still have no penny. I hope you will give me something. That is why I have come." He paused, drawing long pleased breaths through his large nose. This, he felt, was a distinctly self-made line of talk; it set him apart from all previous deserting *légionnaires*.

Mr. White evidently thought so too. He gave a short grunting laugh. "That's better," he said.

"These English," thought Constantine lovingly. "They are the next best thing to *being* originals, for they *admire* originals." "I like you," he added

extravagantly, aloud. "I like the English. I am so glad I found an Englishman to beg of instead of an American—though an American would have
been much richer than you are, I expect. Still, to a beggar a little is enough.
I dislike Americans; I dislike their women's wet finger-nails."

"Wet finger-nails?" exclaimed Mr. White. "Oh, you mean their manicure
polishes. Yes . . . they *do* always have wet finger-nails . . . ha, ha . . . so
they do. I should never have thought of that myself."

"Of course not," said Constantine, genuinely surprised. "*I* thought of it.
Why should *you* have thought of it?" After a moment he added, "I am not
a gramophone."

Mr. White thought that he had said, "Have you got a gramophone?"
and replied at once with some pleasure, "Yes, I have—it is a very precious
companion. Are you musical? But of course you are, being Russian. I
should be very lonely without my daily ration of Chopin. Would you like
some music while the servants are getting you something to eat?"

"I should like some music," said Constantine, "but I should not like to
hear a gramophone. I will play you some music—some unique and only
music on a unique and only instrument."

"Thank you very much," said Mr. White, peering doubtfully through his
glasses at the cigar-box balalaika. "What good English you speak," he
added, trying to divert his guest's attention from his musical purpose. "But
all Russians, of course, are wonderful linguists."

"I will play you my music," said Constantine. "But first I must tell you
that I do not like you to say to me, 'Being Russian you are musical' or 'All
Russians speak good English.' To me it seems so stupid to see me as one
of many."

"Each one of us is one of many," sighed Mr. White patiently.

"*You*, perhaps—but *I*, not," said Constantine. "When you notice my
English words instead of my thoughts it seems to me that you are listening wrongly—you are listening to sounds only, in the same way as you
listen to your senseless gramophone——"

"But you haven't heard my gramophone," interrupted Mr. White, stung
on his darling's behalf.

"What does it matter what sounds a man makes—what words he uses?
Words are common to all men; thoughts belong to one man only."

Mr. White considered telling his guest to go to hell, but he said instead,
"You're quite a philosopher, aren't you?"

"I am not *quite an* anything," said Constantine abruptly. "I am me. All
people who like Chopin also say, 'You're quite a philosopher.'"

"Now you're generalizing, yourself," said Mr. White, clinging to his
good temper. "Exactly what you've just complained of my doing."

"Some people *are* general," said Constantine. "Now I will play you my
music, and you will admit that it is not one of many musics."

He sang a song with Russian words which Mr. White did not understand. As a matter of fact, such was Constantine's horror of imitating that the words of his song were just a list of the names of the diseases of horses, learned while Constantine was a veterinary surgeon in the Ukraine. His voice was certainly peculiar to himself; it was hoarse—so hoarse that one felt as if a light cough or a discreet blowing of that long nose would clear the hoarseness away; it was veiled, as though heard from behind an intervening stillness; yet with all its hoarseness and insonorousness, it was flexible, alive, and exciting. His instrument had the same quality of quiet ugliness and oddity; it was almost enchanting. It was as if an animal—say, a goat—had found a way to control its voice into a crude goblin concord.

"That's my music," said Constantine. "Do you like it?"

"Frankly," said Mr. White, "I prefer Chopin."

"On the gramophone?"

"On the gramophone."

"Yet one is a thing you never heard before and will never hear again—and the other is a machine that makes the same sound for millions."

"I don't care."

Constantine chewed his upper lip for a minute, thinking this over. Then he shook himself. "Nevertheless, I like you," he said insolently. "You are almost a person. Would you like me to tell you about my life, or would you rather I explained to you my idea about Zigzags?"

"I would rather see you eat a good meal," said Mr. White, roused to a certain cordiality—as almost all Anglo-Saxons are—by the opportunity of dispensing food and drink.

"I can tell you my Zigzag idea while I eat," said Constantine, leading the way towards the table at the other end of the room. "Are you not eating too?"

"I'm not in the habit of eating a meat meal at ten o'clock at night."

"Is 'not being in the habit' a reason for not doing it now?"

"To me it is."

"Oh—oh—*oh*—I wish I were like you," said Constantine vehemently. "It is so tiring being me—having no guide. I *do* like you."

"Help yourself to spinach," said Mr. White crossly.

"Now shall I tell you my Zigzag idea?"

"If you can eat as well as talk."

Constantine was exceedingly hungry; he bent low over his plate, though he sat sideways to the table, facing Mr. White, ready to launch a frontal attack of talk. His mouth was too full for a moment to allow him to begin to speak, but quick, agonized glances out of his black eyes implored his host to be silent till his lips should be ready. "You know," he said, swallowing hurriedly, "I always think of a zigzag as going *downwards*. I draw it in the air, *so* . . . a straight honest line, then—see—a diagonal subtle line cuts the air away from under it—so . . . Do you see what I mean? I will call the *zig* a *to,* and the *zag* a *from.* Now——"

"Why is one of your legs fatter than the other?" asked Mr. White.

"It is bandaged. Now, I think of this zigzag as a diagram of human minds. Always human minds are *zigs* or *zags*—a *to* or a *from*—the brave *zig* is straight, *so* . . . the cleverer, crueller *zag* cuts away below. So are men's——"

"But why is it bandaged?"

"It was kicked by a horse. Well, so are men's understandings. Here I draw the simple, faithful understanding—and here—*zag*—the easy, clever understanding that sees through the simple faith. Now below that—see—*zig* once more—the wise, the serene, and now a *zag* contradicts once more; this is the cynic who knows all answers to serenity. Then below, once more——"

"May I see your leg?" asked Mr. White. "I was in an ambulance unit during the war."

"Oh, what is this talk of legs?" cried Constantine. "Legs are all the same; they belong to millions. All legs are made of blood and bone and muscle—all vulgar things. Your ambulance cuts off legs, mends legs, fits bones together, corks up blood. It treats men like bundles of bones and blood. This is so dull. Bodies are so dull. Minds are the only onliness in men."

"Yes," said Mr. White. "But minds have to have legs to walk about on. Let me see your leg."

"Very well, then, let us talk of legs. We have at least legs in common, you and I."

"Hadn't you got more sense than to put such a dirty rag round an open wound?"

"It is not dirty; it is simply of a grey colour. I washed it in a rice field." Constantine spoke in a muffled voice from somewhere near his knee-cap, for he was now bent double, wholeheartedly interested in his leg. "I washed the wound too, and three boils which are behind my knee. This blackness is not dirt; it is a blackness belonging to the injury."

Mr. White said nothing, but he rose to his feet as though he had heard a call. Constantine, leaving his puttee in limp coils about his foot like a dead snake, went on eating. He began to talk again about the zigzag while he stuffed food into his mouth, but he stopped talking soon, for Mr. White was walking up and down the long room and not pretending to listen. Constantine, watching his host restively pacing the far end of the room, imagined that he himself perhaps smelled disagreeable, for this was a constant fear of his—that his body should play his rare personality this horrid trick. "What is the matter?" he asked anxiously, with a shamed look. "Why are you so far?"

Mr. White's lazy, mild manner was quite changed. His voice seemed to burst out of seething irritation. "It's a dam nuisance just now. It couldn't happen at a worse time. I've a great deal of work to do—and this fighting all over the province makes a journey so dam——"

"What is so dam?" asked Constantine, his bewilderment affecting his English.

"I'll tell you what," said Mr. White, standing in front of Constantine with his feet wide apart and speaking in an angry voice. "You're going to bed now in my attic, and to-morrow at daylight you're going to be waked up and driven down in my car, by me (damn it!) to Lao-chow, to the hospital—a two days' drive—three hundred miles—over the worst roads you ever saw."

Constantine's heart gave a sickening lurch. "Why to hospital? You think my leg is dangerous?"

"If I know anything of legs," said Mr. White rather brutally, "the doctor won't let you keep that one an hour longer than he has to."

Constantine's mouth began instantly to tremble so much that he could scarcely speak. He thought, "I shall die—I shall die like this—of a stupid black leg—this valuable lonely me will die." He glared at Mr. White, hungry for consolation. "He isn't valuable—he's one of many . . . of course he could easily be brave."

Mr. White, once more indolent and indifferent, led the little Russian to the attic and left him there. As soon as Constantine saw the white sheets neatly folded back, the pleasant blue rugs squarely set upon the floor, the open wardrobe fringed with hangers, he doubted whether, after all, he did value himself so much. For in this neat room he felt betrayed by this body of his—this unwashed, unshaven, tired body, encased in coarse dirty clothes, propped on an offensive, festering leg. He decided to take all his clothes off, even though he had no other garment with him to put on; he would feel more appropriate to the shiny linen in his own shiny skin, he thought. He would have washed, but his attention was diverted as he pulled his clothes off by the wound on his leg. Though it was not very painful, it made him nearly sick with disgust now. Every nerve in his body seemed on tiptoe, alert to feel agony, as he studied the wound. He saw that a new sore place was beginning, well above the knee. With only his shirt on, he rushed downstairs, and in at the only lighted doorway. "Look— look," he cried. "A new sore place. . . . Does this mean the danger is greater even than we thought?"

Mr. White, in neat blue-and-white pyjamas, was carefully pressing a tie in a tie-press. Constantine had never felt so far away from a human being in his life as he felt on seeing the tie-press, those pyjamas, those mono-grammed silver brushes, that elastic apparatus for reducing exercises that hung upon the door.

"Oh, go to bed," said Mr. White irascibly. "For God's sake, show a little sense."

Constantine was back in his attic before he thought, "I ought to have said, 'For God's sake, show a little *non*sense yourself.' Sense is so vulgar."

Sense, however, was to drive him three hundred miles to safety, next day.

All night the exhausted Constantine, sleeping only for a few minutes at a time, dreamed trivial, broken dreams about establishing his own superiority, finding, for instance, that he had after all managed to bring with him a suitcase full of clean, fashionable clothes, or noticing that his host was wearing a filthy bandage round his neck instead of a tie.

Constantine was asleep when Mr. White, fully dressed, woke him next morning. A clear, steely light was slanting in at the window. Constantine was always fully conscious at the second of waking, and he was immediately horrified to see Mr. White looking expressionlessly at the disorderly heap of dirty clothes that he had thrown in disgust on the floor the night before. Trying to divert his host's attention, Constantine put on a merry and courageous manner. "Well, how is the weather for our motorcar jaunt?"

"It could hardly be worse," said Mr. White placidly. "Sheets of rain. God knows what the roads will be like."

"Well, we are lucky to have roads at all, in this benighted China."

"I don't know about that. If there weren't any roads we shouldn't be setting off on this beastly trip."

"I shall be ready in two jiffies," said Constantine, springing naked out of bed and shuffling his dreadful clothes out of Mr. White's sight. "But just tell me," he added as his host went through the door, "why do you drive three hundred miles on a horrible wet day just to take a perfect stranger—a beggar too—to hospital?" (He thought, "Now he *must* say something showing that he recognizes my value.")

"Because I can't cut off your leg myself," said Mr. White gloomily. Constantine did not press his question because this new reference to the cutting off of legs set his nerves jangling again; his hands trembled so that he could scarcely button his clothes. Service in the Foreign Legion, though it was certainly no suitable adventure for a rare and sensitive man, had never obliged him to face anything more frightening than non-appreciation, coarse food, and stupid treatment. None of these things could humiliate him—on the contrary, all confirmed him in his persuasion of his own value. Only the thought of being at the mercy of his body could humiliate the excited and glowing spirit of Constantine. Death was the final, most loathsome triumph of the body; death meant dumbness and decay—yet even death he could have faced courageously could he have been flattered to its very brink.

The car, a ramshackle Ford, stood in the rain on the bald gravel of the compound, as Constantine, white with excitement, limped out through the front door. His limp, though not consciously assumed, had developed only since last night. His whole leg now felt dangerous, its skin shrinking and tingling. Constantine looked into the car. In the back seat sat Mr. White's coolie, clasping a conspicuously neat little white canvas kit-bag with leather straps. The kit-bag held Constantine's eye and attacked his self-respect as the tie-press had attacked and haunted him the night before. Every one of his host's possessions was like a perfectly well-balanced, indisputable statement in a world of fevered conjecture. "And a camp-bed—so nicely rolled," said Constantine, leaning into the car, fascinated and humiliated. "But only one. . . ."

"I have only one," said Mr. White.

"And you are bringing it—for me?" said Constantine, looking at him ardently, overjoyed at this tribute.

"I am bringing it for myself," said Mr. White with his unamused and short-sighted smile. "I am assuming that a *légionnaire* is used to sleeping rough. I'm not. I'm rather fixed in my habits and I have a horror of the arrangements in Chinese inns."

"He is morally brave," thought Constantine, though, for the first time, it occurred to him how satisfactory it would be to slap his host's face. "A man less brave would have changed his plans about the camp-bed at once and said, "For you, my dear man, of course—why not?" Constantine chattered nervously as he took his seat in the car next to his host, the driver. "I feel such admiration for a man who can drive a motor-car. I adore the machine when it does not—like the gramophone—trespass on matters outside its sphere. The machine's sphere is space, you see—it controls space—and that is so admirable—even when the machine is so very unimpressive as this one. Mr. White, your motor-car is *very* unimpressive indeed. Are you sure it will run three hundred miles?"

"It always seems to," said Mr. White. "I never do anything to it except pour petrol, oil, and water into the proper openings. I am completely unmechanical."

"You cannot be if you work a gramophone."

"You seem to have my gramophone on your mind. To me it doesn't answer the purpose of a machine—it simply *is* Chopin, to me."

Constantine stamped his foot in almost delighted irritation, for this made him feel a god beside this groundling. After a few minutes of self-satisfaction, however, a terrible thought invaded him. He became obsessed with an idea that he had left fleas in his bed in Mr. White's attic. That smug, immaculate Chinese servant would see them when he made the bed, and on Mr. White's return would say, "That foreign soldier left fleas in our attic bed." How bitterly did Constantine wish that he had examined the bed carefully before leaving the room, or alternatively, that he could invent some elaborate lie that would prevent Mr. White from believing this revolting accusation. Constantine's mind, already racked with the fear of pain and death and with the agony of his impotence to impress his companion, became overcast with the hopelessness and remorselessness of everything. Everything despairing seemed a fact beyond dispute; everything hopeful, a mere dream. His growing certainty about the fleas, the persistence of the rain, combined with the leakiness of the car's side-curtains, the skiddiness of the road, the festering of his leg, the thought of the surgeon's saw, the perfection of that complacent kit-bag in the back seat, with the poor cigar-box balalaika tinkling beside it, the overstability and overrightness of his friend in need—there was not one sweet or flattering thought to which his poor trapped mind could turn.

The absurdly inadequate bullock-trail only just served the purpose of a road for the Ford. The wheels slid about, wrenching themselves from groove to groove. Constantine's comment on the difficulties of the road was silenced by a polite request on the part of Mr. White. "I can't talk while I'm driving, if you don't mind. I'm not a good driver, and I need all my attention, especially on such a bad road."

"I will talk and you need not answer. That is my ideal plan of conversation. I will tell you why I joined the Foreign Legion. You must have been wondering about this. It will be a relief for me from my misfortunes, to talk."

"I'd rather not, if you don't mind," said his host serenely.

"Mean old horse," thought Constantine passionately, his heart contracting with offence. "It is so English to give away nothing but the bare, bald, stony fact of help—no decorations of graciousnesses and smilings. A Russian would be a much poorer helper, but a how much better friend."

The car ground on. Constantine turned over again and again in his mind the matter of the fleas. The wet ochre-and-green country of South China streamed unevenly past, the neat, complex shapes of rice fields altering, disintegrating and re-forming, like groups in a country dance. Abrupt horns of rock began piercing through the flat rain-striped valley, and these, it seemed, were the heralds of a mountain range that barred the path of the travellers, for soon cliffs towered above the road. A village which clung to a slope at the mouth of a gorge was occupied by soldiers. "This is where our troubles begin," said Mr. White peacefully. The soldiers were indolent, shabby, ineffectual-looking creatures, scarcely distinguishable from coolies, but their machine-guns, straddling mosquito-like about the forlorn village street, looked disagreeably wideawake and keen. Constantine felt as if his precious heart were the cynosure of all the machine-guns' waspish glances, as the car splashed between them. "Is this safe?" he asked. "Motoring through a Chinese war?"

"Not particularly," smiled Mr. White. "But it's safer than neglecting that leg of yours."

Constantine uttered a small, shrill, nervous exclamation—half a curse. "Is a man nothing more than a leg to you?"

As he spoke, from one side of the gorge along which they were now driving, a rifle shot cracked, like the breaking of a taut wire. Its echoes were overtaken by the sputtering of more shots from a higher crag.

Constantine had been tensely held for just such an attack on his courage as this—and yet he was not ready for it. His body moved instantly by itself, without consulting his self-respect; it flung its arms round Mr. White. The car, thus immobilized at its source of energy, swerved, skidded, and stood still askew upon the trail. Constantine, sweating violently, recalled his pride and reassembled his sprawling arms. Mr. White said nothing, but he looked with a cold benevolence into Constantine's face and shook his head slightly. Then he started the car again and drove on in silence. There was no more firing.

"Oh, *oh,* I do *wish* you had been a little bit frightened too," said Constantine, clenching his fists. He was too much of a desert islander to deny his own fright, as a citizen of the tradition-ruled mainland might have denied it. Brave or afraid, Constantine was his own creation; he had made himself, he would stand or fall by this self that he had made. It was indeed, in a way, more interesting to have been afraid than to have been brave. Only, unfortunately, this exasperating benefactor of his did not think so.

The noon-light was scarcely brighter than the light of early morning. The unremitting rain slanted across the grey air. Trees, skies, valleys, mountains, seen through the rain-spotted windshield, were like a distorted, stippled landscape painted by a beginner who has not yet learned to wring living colour from his palette. However, sun or no sun, noontime it was at last, and Mr. White, drawing his car conscientiously to the side of the bullock trail, as if a procession of Rolls-Royces might be expected to pass, unpacked a neat jigsaw puzzle of a sandwich-box.

"I brought a few caviare sandwiches for you," he said gently: "I know Russians like caviare."

"Are your sandwiches then made of Old England's Rosbif?" asked Constantine crossly, for it seemed to him that this man used nothing but collective nouns.

"No; of bloater paste."

They said nothing more but munched in a rather sullen silence. Constantine had lost his desire to tell Mr. White why he had joined the Foreign Legion—or to tell him anything else, for that matter. There was something about Mr. White that destroyed the excitement of telling ingenious lies—or even the common truth; and this *something* Constantine resented more and more, though he was uncertain how to define it. Mr. White leaned over the steering-wheel and covered his eyes with his hands, for driving tired him. The caviare, and his host's evident weariness, irritated Constantine more and more; these things seemed like a crude insistence on his increasing obligation. "I suppose you are tired of the very sight of me," he felt impelled to say bitterly.

"No, no," said Mr. White politely but indifferently. "Don't worry about me. It'll all be the same a hundred years hence."

"Whether my leg is off or on—whether I die in agony or live—it will all be the same a hundred years hence, I suppose you would say," said Constantine, morbidly goading his companion into repeating this insult to the priceless mystery of personality.

"My good man, I can't do more than I *am* doing about your leg, can I?" said Mr. White irritably, as he restarted the car.

"A million times more—a million times more," thought Constantine hysterically, but with an effort he said nothing.

As the wet evening light smouldered to an ashen twilight, they drove into Mo-ming, which was to be their night's stopping-place. Outside the city wall they were stopped by soldiers; for Mo-ming was being defended against the enemy's advance. After twenty minutes' talk in the clanking Cantonese tongue, the two white men were allowed to go through the city gate on foot, leaving the Ford in a shed outside, in the care of Mr. White's coolie. Mr. White carried his beautiful little kit-bag and expected Constantine to carry the camp-bed.

"What—and leave my balalaika in the car?" protested Constantine childishly.

"I think it would be safe," said Mr. White, only faintly ironic. "Hurry up. I must go at once and call on the general in charge here. I don't want to have my car commandeered."

Constantine limped along behind him, the camp-bed on one shoulder, the balalaika faintly tinkling under his arm. They found the inn in the centre of a tangle of looped, frayed, untidy streets—a box-like gaunt house, one corner of which was partly ruined, for the city had been bombarded that day. The inn, which could never have been a comfortable place, was wholly disorganized by its recent misfortune; most of the servants had fled, and the innkeeper was entirely engrossed in counting and piling up on the verandah his rescued possessions from the wrecked rooms. An impudent little boy, naked down to the waist—the only remaining servant—showed Mr. White and Constantine to the only room the inn could offer.

"One room between us?" cried Constantine, thinking of his shameful, possibly verminous, clothes and his unwashed body. He felt unable to bear the idea of unbuttoning even the greasy collar of his tunic within sight of that virgin-new kit-bag. Its luminous whiteness would seem in the night like triumphant civilization's eye fixed upon the barbarian—like the smug beam of a lighthouse glowing from the mainland upon that uncouth obstruction, a desert island. "I'm not consistent," thought Constantine. "That's my trouble. I ought to be proud of being dirty. At least that is a home-made condition."

"Yes—one room between us," said Mr. White tartly. "We must do the best we can. You look after things here, will you, while I go and see the general and make the car safe."

Left alone, Constantine decided not to take off any clothes at all—even his coarse greatcoat—but to say that he had fever and needed all the warmth he could get. No sooner had he come to this decision than he felt convinced that he actually was feverish; his head and his injured leg ached and throbbed as though all the hot blood in his body had concentrated in those two regions, while ice seemed to settle round his heart and loins. The room was dreary and very sparsely furnished with an ugly, too high table and rigid chairs to match. The beds were simply recesses in the wall, draped with dirty mud-brown mosquito-veils. Constantine, however, stepped more bravely into this hard, matted coffin than he had into Mr. White's clean attic bed. As he lay down, his leg burned and throbbed more fiercely than ever, and he began to imagine the amputation—the blood, the yawning of the flesh, the scraping of the saw upon the bone. His imagination did not supply an anaesthetic. Fever came upon him now in good earnest; he shook so much that his body seemed to jump like a fish upon the unyielding matting, he seemed to breathe in heat, without being able to melt the ice in his bones. Yet he remained artistically conscious all the time of his plight, and even exaggerated the shivering spasms of his limbs. He was quite pleased to think that Mr. White would presently return and find him in this condition, and so be obliged to be interested and compassionate. Yet as he heard Mr. White's heavy step on the stair, poor Constantine's eye fell on the fastidious white kit-bag, and he suddenly remembered all his fancies and fears about vermin and smells. By the time Mr. White was actually standing over him, Constantine was convinced that the deepest loathing was clearly shown on that superior, towering face.

"I can't help it—I can't help it," cried Constantine, between his chattering teeth.

Mr. White seemed to ignore the Russian's agitation. "I think the car'll be all right now," he said. "I left the coolie sleeping in it, to make sure. The general was quite civil and gave me a permit to get home; but it seems it's utterly impossible for us to drive on to Lao-chow. Fighting on the road is particularly hot, and the bridges are all destroyed. The enemy have reached the opposite side of the river, and they've been bombarding the city all day. I told the general about your case; he suggests you go by river in a sampan down to Lao-chow to-morrow. You may be fired on just as you leave the city, but nothing to matter, I dare say. After that, you'd be all right—the river makes a stiff bend south here, and gets right away from the country they're fighting over. It would take you only about eighteen hours to Lao-chow, going down stream. I've already got a sampan for you. . . . Oh, Lord, isn't this disgusting?" he added, looking round the dreadful room and wrinkling his nose. "How I loathe this kind of thing!"

"I can't help it. I can't help it." Constantine began first to moan and then to cry. He was by now in great pain, and he did not try to control his distress. It passed through his mind that crying was the last thing a stupid

Englishman would expect of a *légionnaire;* so far so good, therefore—he was a desert islander even in his degradation. Yet he loathed himself; all his morbid fears of being offensive were upon him, and the unaccustomed exercise of crying, combined with the fever, nauseated him. Mr. White, still wearing his expression of repugnance, came to his help, loosened that greasy collar, lent a handkerchief, ordered some refreshing hot Chinese tea.

"You should have known me in Odessa," gasped Constantine in an interval between his paroxysms. "Three of the prettiest women in the town were madly in love with me. You know me only at my worst."

Mr. White, soaking a folded silk handkerchief in cold water, before laying it on Constantine's burning forehead, did not answer. He unrolled the pillow from his camp-bed and put it under Constantine's head. As he did so, he recoiled a little, but after a second's hesitation, he pushed the immaculate little pillow into place with a heroic firmness.

"I wore only silk next the skin then," snuffled Constantine. The fever rose in a wave in his brain, and he shouted curses upon his cruelly perfect friend.

Mr. White lay only intermittently on his camp-bed that night. He was kept busy making use of his past experience as a member of an ambulance unit. Only at daylight he slept for an hour or so.

Constantine, awakened from a short sleep by the sound of firing outside, lay on his side and watched Mr. White's relaxed, sleeping face. The fever had left Constantine, and he was now sunk in cold, limp depression and fear. Luckily, he thought, there was no need to stir, for certainly he could not be expected—a sick man—to set forth in a sampan through such dangers as the persistent firing suggested. At least in this inn he knew the worst, he thought wearily, and his companion knew the worst too. "I will not leave him," Constantine vowed, "until I have somehow cured him of these frightful memories of me—somehow amputated his memory of me. . . ." He lay watching his companion's face—hating it—obscurely wishing that those eyes, which had seen the worst during this loathsome night, might remain for ever shut.

Mr. White woke up quite suddenly. "Good Lord!" he said, peering at his watch. "Nearly seven. I told the sampan man to be at the foot of the steps at daylight."

"Are you mad?" asked Constantine shrilly. "Listen to the firing—quite near. Besides—I'm a very sick man, as you should know by now. I couldn't even walk—much less dodge through a crowd of Chinese assassins."

Mr. White, faintly whistling Chopin, laboriously keeping his temper, left the room, and could presently be heard hee-hawing in the Chinese language on the verandah to the hee-hawing innkeeper.

When he came back, he said, "The sampaneer's there, waiting—only too anxious to get away from the bombing they're expecting to-day. He's tied up only about a hundred yards away. You'll be beyond the reach of the firing as soon as you're round the bend. Hurry up, man; the sooner you get down to hospital, and I get off on the road home, the better for us both."

Constantine, genuinely exhausted after his miserable night, did not speak, but lay with his eyes shut and his face obstinately turned to the wall. He certainly felt too ill to be brave or to face the crackling dangers of the battle-ridden streets, but he was conscious of no plan except a determination to be as obstructive as he could—to assert at least this ignoble power over his tyrant.

"Get up, you damn fool," shouted Mr. White, suddenly plucking the pillow from under the sick man's head, "or I'll drag you down to the river by the scruff of your dirty neck."

Dirty neck! Instantly Constantine sat up—hopeless now of curing this man's contempt, full of an almost unendurable craving to be far away from him—to wipe him from his horizon—to be allowed to imagine him dead. Invigorated by this violent impulse, he rolled out of bed and sullenly watched Mr. White settle up with the innkeeper and take a few packages out of that revoltingly refined kit-bag.

"A small tin of water-biscuits," said Mr. White, almost apologetically, "and the remains of the bloater paste. It's all I have with me, but it ought to keep you alive till you get to Lao-chow to-morrow morning. . . . I'll see you down to the river first and then pick up these things." He spoke as if he were trying to make little neat plans still against this disorderly and unwonted background. He brushed his splashed coat with a silver clothes-brush, wearing the eagerly safe expression Constantine had seen on his face as he bent over the tie-press the night before last. The orderly man was trying to maintain his quiet impersonal self-respect amid surroundings that humiliated him. Even Constantine understood vaguely that his attacker was himself being attacked. "Well, I've done my best," added Mr. White, straightening his back after buckling the last strap of the kit-bag, and looking at Constantine with an ambiguous, almost appealing look.

They left the inn. The steep street that led down to the river between mean, barricaded shops was deserted. The air of it was outraged by the whipping sound of rifle fire—echoes clanked sharply from wall to wall.

"It is not safe—it is not safe," muttered Constantine, suddenly standing rooted, feeling that his next step must bring him into the path of a bullet.

"It's safer than a gangrenous leg." With his great hand, Mr. White seized the little Russian's arm and dragged him almost gaily down the steps. Constantine was by now so hopelessly mired in humiliation that he did not even try to disguise his terror. He hung back like a rebellious child, but he was tweaked and twitched along, stumbling behind his rescuer. He was pressed into the little boat. "Here, take the biscuits—good-bye—good luck," shouted Mr. White, and a smile of real gaiety broke out at last upon his face. The strip of rainy air and water widened between the two friends.

"Strike him dead, God!" said Constantine.

The smile did not fade at once from the Englishman's face, as his legs curiously crumpled into a kneeling position. He seemed trying to kneel on air; he clutched at his breast with one hand while the other hand still waved good-bye; he turned his alert, smiling face towards Constantine as though he were going to say again—"Good-bye—good luck." Then he fell, head downward, on the steps, the bald crown of his head just dipping into the water. Mud was splashed over the coat he had brushed only five minutes before.

There was a loud outcry from the sampan man and his wife. They seemed to be calling Constantine's already riveted attention to the fallen man—still only twenty yards away; they seemed uncertain whether he would now let them row yet more quickly away, as they desired, or insist on returning to the help of his friend.

"Row on—row on," cried Constantine in Russian and, to show them what he meant, he snatched up a spare pole and tried to increase the speed of the boat as it swerved into the current. Spaces of water were broadening all about the desert islander—home on his desert island again at last. As Constantine swayed over the pole, he looked back over his shoulder and flaunted his head, afraid no more of the firing now that one blessed bullet had carried away unpardonable memory out of the brain of his friend.

BIG BLONDE

Dorothy Parker

(1893–   )

H AZEL MORSE was a large, fair woman of the type that incites some men when they use the word "blonde" to click their tongues and wag their heads roguishly. She prided herself upon her small feet and suffered for her vanity, boxing them in snub-toed, high-heeled slippers of the shortest bearable size. The curious things about her were her hands, strange terminations to the flabby white arms splattered with pale tan spots—long, quivering hands with deep and convex nails. She should not have disfigured them with little jewels.

She was not a woman given to recollections. At her middle thirties, her old days were a blurred and flickering sequence, an imperfect film, dealing with the actions of strangers.

In her twenties, after the deferred death of a hazy widowed mother, she had been employed as a model in a wholesale dress establishment—it was still the day of the big woman, and she was then prettily colored and erect and high-breasted. Her job was not onerous, and she met numbers of men and spent numbers of evenings with them, laughing at their jokes and telling them she loved their neckties. Men liked her, and she took it for granted that the liking of many men was a desirable thing. Popularity seemed to her to be worth all the work that had to be put into its achievement. Men liked you because you were fun, and when they liked you they took you out, and there you were. So, and successfully, she was fun. She was a good sport. Men like a good sport.

No other form of diversion, simpler or more complicated, drew her attention. She never pondered if she might not be better occupied doing something else. Her ideas, or, better, her acceptances, ran right along with those of the other substantially built blondes in whom she found her friends.

When she had been working in the dress establishment some years she met Herbie Morse. He was thin, quick, attractive, with shifting lines about his shiny, brown eyes and a habit of fiercely biting at the skin around his finger nails. He drank largely; she found that entertaining. Her habitual greeting to him was an illusion to his state of the previous night.

"Oh, what a peach you had," she used to say, through her easy laugh. "I thought I'd die, the way you kept asking the waiter to dance with you."

She liked him immediately upon their meeting. She was enormously amused at his fast, slurred sentences, his interpolations of apt phrases from vaudeville acts and comic strips; she thrilled at the feel of his lean arm tucked firm beneath the sleeve of her coat; she wanted to touch the wet, flat surface of his hair. He was as promptly drawn to her. They were married six weeks after they had met.

She was delighted at the idea of being a bride; coquetted with it, played upon it. Other offers of marriage she had had, and not a few of them, but it happened that they were all from stout, serious men who had visited the dress establishment as buyers; men from Des Moines and Houston and Chicago and, in her phrase, even funnier places. There was always something immensely comic to her in the thought of living elsewhere than New York. She could not regard as serious proposals that she share a Western residence.

She wanted to be married. She was nearing thirty now, and she did not take the years well. She spread and softened, and her darkening hair turned her to inexpert dabblings with peroxide. There were times when she had little flashes of fear about her job. And she had had a couple of thousand evenings of being a good sport among her male acquaintances. She had come to be more conscientious than spontaneous about it.

Herbie earned enough, and they took a little apartment far uptown. There was a Mission-furnished dining room with a hanging central light globed in liver-colored glass; in the living room were an "overstuffed suite," a Boston fern, and a reproduction of the Henner *Magdalene* with the red hair and the blue draperies; the bedroom was in gray enamel and old rose, with Herbie's photograph on Hazel's dressing table and Hazel's likeness on Herbie's chest of drawers.

She cooked—and she was a good cook—and marketed and chatted with the delivery boys and the colored laundress. She loved the flat, she loved her life, she loved Herbie. In the first months of their marriage she gave him all the passion she was ever to know.

She had not realized how tired she was. It was a delight, a new game, a holiday, to give up being a good sport. If her head ached or her arches throbbed, she complained piteously, babyishly. If her mood was quiet, she did not talk. If tears came to her eyes, she let them fall.

She fell readily into the habit of tears during the first year of her marriage. Even in her good sport days she had been known to weep lavishly and disinterestedly on occasion. Her behavior at the theater was a standing joke. She could weep at anything in a play—tiny garments, love both unrequited and mutual, seduction, purity, faithful servitors, wedlock, the triangle.

"There goes Haze," her friends would say, watching her. "She's off again."

Wedded and relaxed, she poured her tears freely. To her who had laughed so much, crying was delicious. All sorrows became her sorrows; she was Tenderness. She would cry long and softly over newspaper accounts of kidnaped babies, deserted wives, unemployed men, strayed cats, heroic dogs. Even when the paper was no longer before her, her mind revolved upon these things and the drops slipped rhythmically over her plump cheeks.

"Honestly," she would say to Herbie, "all the sadness there is in the world when you stop to think about it!"

"Yeah," Herbie would say.

She missed nobody. The old crowd, the people who had brought her and Herbie together, dropped from their lives, lingeringly at first. When she thought of this at all it was only to consider it fitting. This was marriage. This was peace.

But the thing was that Herbie was not amused.

For a time he had enjoyed being alone with her. He found the voluntary isolation novel and sweet. Then it palled with a ferocious suddenness. It was as if one night, sitting with her in the steam-heated living room, he would ask no more; and the next night he was through and done with the whole thing.

He became annoyed by her misty melancholies. At first, when he came home to find her softly tired and moody, he kissed her neck and patted her shoulder and begged her to tell her Herbie what was wrong. She loved that. But time slid by, and he found that there was never anything really, personally, the matter.

"Ah, for God's sake," he would say. "Crabbing again. All right, sit here and crab your head off. I'm going out."

And he would slam out of the flat and come back late and drunk.

She was completely bewildered by what happened to their marriage. First they were lovers; and then, it seemed without transition, they were enemies. She never understood it.

There were longer and longer intervals between his leaving his office and his arrival at the apartment. She went through agonies of picturing him run over and bleeding, dead and covered with a sheet. Then she lost her fears for his safety and grew sullen and wounded. When a person wanted to be with a person he came as soon as possible. She desperately wanted him to want to be with her; her own hours only marked the time till he would come. It was often nearly nine o'clock before he came home to dinner. Always he had had many drinks, and their effect would die in him, leaving him loud and querulous and bristling for affronts.

He was too nervous, he said, to sit and do nothing for an evening. He boasted, probably not in all truth, that he had never read a book in his life.

"What am I expected to do—sit around this dump on my tail all night?" he would ask rhetorically. And again he would slam out.

She did not know what to do. She could not manage him. She could not meet him.

She fought him furiously. A terrific domesticity had come upon her, and she would bite and scratch to guard it. She wanted what she called "a nice home." She wanted a sober, tender husband, prompt at dinner, punctual at work. She wanted sweet, comforting evenings. The idea of intimacy with other men was terrible to her; the thought that Herbie might be seeking entertainment in other women set her frantic.

It seemed to her that almost everything she read—novels from the drugstore lending library, magazine stories, women's pages in the papers—dealt with wives who lost their husbands' love. She could bear those, at that, better than accounts of neat, companionable marriage and living happily ever after.

She was frightened. Several times when Herbie came home in the evening he found her determinedly dressed—she had had to alter those of her clothes that were not new, to make them fasten—and rouged.

"Let's go wild to-night, what do you say?" she would hail him. "A person's got lots of time to hang around and do nothing when they're dead."

So they would go out, to chop houses and the less expensive cabarets. But it turned out badly. She could no longer find amusement in watching Herbie drink. She could not laugh at his whimsicalities, she was so tensely counting his indulgences. And she was unable to keep back her remonstrances—"Ah, come on, Herb, you've had enough, haven't you? You'll feel something terrible in the morning."

He would be immediately enraged. All right, crab; crab, crab, crab, that was all she ever did. What a lousy sport *she* was! There would be scenes, and one or the other of them would rise and stalk out in fury.

She could not recall the definite day that she started drinking, herself. There was nothing separate about her days. Like drops upon a window-pane, they ran together and trickled away. She had been married six months; then a year; then three years.

She had never needed to drink, formerly. She could sit for most of a night at a table where the others were imbibing earnestly and never droop in looks or spirits, nor be bored by the doings of those about her. If she took a cocktail, it was so unusual as to cause twenty minutes or so of jocular comment. But now anguish was in her. Frequently, after a quarrel, Herbie would stay out for the night, and she could not learn from him where the time had been spent. Her heart felt tight and sore in her breast, and her mind turned like an electric fan.

She hated the taste of liquor. Gin, plain or in mixtures, made her promptly sick. After experiment, she found that Scotch whisky was best for her. She took it without water, because that was the quickest way to its effect.

Herbie pressed it on her. He was glad to see her drink. They both felt it might restore her high spirits, and their good times together might again be possible.

" 'Atta girl," he would approve her. "Let's see you get boiled, baby."

But it brought them no nearer. When she drank with him there would be a little while of gayety and then, strangely without beginning, they would be in a wild quarrel. They would wake in the morning not sure what it had all been about, foggy as to what had been said and done, but each deeply injured and bitterly resentful. There would be days of vengeful silence.

There had been a time when they had made up their quarrels, usually in bed. There would be kisses and little names and assurances of fresh starts . . . "Oh, it's going to be great now, Herb. We'll have swell times. I was a crab. I guess I might have been tired. But everything's going to be swell. You'll see."

Now there were no gentle reconciliations. They resumed friendly relations only in the brief magnanimity caused by liquor, before more liquor drew them into new battles. The scenes became more violent. There were shouted invectives and pushes, and sometimes sharp slaps. Once she had a black eye. Herbie was horrified next day at sight of it. He did not go to work; he followed her about, suggesting remedies and heaping dark blame on himself. But after they had had a few drinks—"to pull themselves together"—she made so many wistful references to her bruise that he shouted at her, and rushed out, and was gone for two days.

Each time he left the place in rage he threatened never to come back. She did not believe him, nor did she consider separation. Somewhere in her head or her heart was the lazy, nebulous hope that things would change and she and Herbie settle suddenly into soothing married life. Here were her home, her furniture, her husband, her station. She summoned no alternatives.

She could no longer bustle and potter. She had no more vicarious tears; the hot drops she shed were for herself. She walked ceaselessly about the rooms, her thoughts running mechanically round and round Herbie. In those days began the hatred of being alone that she was never to overcome. You could be by yourself when things were all right, but when you were blue you got the howling horrors.

She commenced drinking alone, little, short drinks all through the day. It was only with Herbie that alcohol made her nervous and quick in offense. Alone, it blurred sharp things for her. She lived in a haze of it. Her life took on a dream-like quality. Nothing was astonishing.

A Mrs. Martin moved into the flat across the hall. She was a great blonde woman of forty, a promise in looks of what Mrs. Morse was to be. They made acquaintance, quickly became inseparable. Mrs. Morse spent her days in the opposite apartment. They drank together, to brace themselves after the drinks of the nights before.

She never confided her troubles about Herbie to Mrs. Martin. The subject was too bewildering to her to find comfort in talk. She let it be assumed that her husband's business kept him much away. It was not regarded as important; husbands, as such, played but shadowy parts in Mrs. Martin's circle.

Mrs. Martin had no visible spouse; you were left to decide for yourself whether he was or was not dead. She had an admirer, Joe, who came to see her almost nightly. Often he brought several friends with him—"The Boys," they were called. The Boys were big, red, good-humored men, perhaps forty-five, perhaps fifty. Mrs. Morse was glad of invitations to join the parties—Herbie was scarcely ever at home at night now. If he did come home, she did not visit Mrs. Martin. An evening alone with Herbie meant inevitably a quarrel, yet she would stay with him. There was always her thin and wordless idea that, maybe, this night, things would begin to be all right.

The boys brought plenty of liquor along with them whenever they came to Mrs. Martin's. Drinking with them, Mrs. Morse became lively and good-natured and audacious. She was quickly popular. When she had drunk enough to cloud her most recent battle with Herbie, she was excited by their approbation. Crab, was she? Rotten sport, was she? Well, there were some that thought different.

Ed was one of The Boys. He lived in Utica—had "his own business" there, was the awed report—but he came to New York almost every week. He was married. He showed Mrs. Morse the then current photographs of Junior and Sister, and she praised them abundantly and sincerely. Soon it was accepted by the others that Ed was her particular friend.

He staked her when they all played poker; sat next her and occasionally rubbed his knee against hers during the game. She was rather lucky. Frequently she went home with a twenty-dollar bill or a ten-dollar bill or a handful of crumpled dollars. She was glad of them. Herbie was getting, in her words, something awful about money. To ask him for it brought an instant row.

"What the hell do you do with it?" he would say. "Shoot it all on Scotch?"

"I try to run this house halfway decent," she would retort. "Never thought of that, did you? Oh, no, his lordship couldn't be bothered with that."

Again, she could not find a definite day to fix the beginning of Ed's proprietorship. It became his custom to kiss her on the mouth when he came in, as well as for farewell, and he gave her little quick kisses of approval all through the evening. She liked this rather more than she disliked it. She never thought of his kisses when she was not with him.

He would run his hand lingeringly over her back and shoulders.

"Some dizzy blonde, eh?" he would say. "Some doll."

One afternoon she came home from Mrs. Martin's to find Herbie in the bedroom. He had been away for several nights, evidently on a prolonged drinking bout. His face was gray, his hands jerked as if they were on wires. On the bed were two old suitcases, packed high. Only her photograph remained on his bureau, and the wide doors of his closet disclosed nothing but coat hangers.

"I'm blowing," he said. "I'm through with the whole works. I got a job in Detroit."

She sat down on the edge of the bed. She had drunk much the night before, and the four Scotches she had had with Mrs. Martin had only increased her fogginess.

"Good job?" she said.

"Oh, yeah," he said. "Looks all right."

He closed a suitcase with difficulty, swearing at it in whispers.

"There's some dough in the bank," he said. "The bank book's in your top drawer. You can have the furniture and stuff."

He looked at her, and his forehead twitched.

"God damn it, I'm through, I'm telling you," he cried. "I'm through."

"All right, all right," she said. "I heard you, didn't I?"

She saw him as if he were at one end of a cañon and she at the other. Her head was beginning to ache bumpingly, and her voice had a dreary, tiresome tone. She could not have raised it.

"Like a drink before you go?" she asked.

Again he looked at her, and a corner of his mouth jerked up.

"Cockeyed again for a change, aren't you?" he said. "That's nice. Sure, get a couple of shots, will you?"

She went to the pantry, mixed him a stiff highball, poured herself a couple of inches of whisky, and drank it. Then she gave herself another portion and brought the glasses into the bedroom. He had strapped both suitcases and had put on his hat and overcoat.

He took his highball.

"Well," he said, and he gave a sudden, uncertain laugh. "Here's mud in your eye."

"Mud in your eye," she said.

They drank. He put down his glass and took up the heavy suitcase.

"Got to get a train around six," he said.

She followed him down the hall. There was a song, a song that Mrs. Martin played doggedly on the phonograph, running loudly through her mind. She had never liked the thing.

> Night and daytime,
> Always playtime.
> Ain't we got fun?

At the door he put down the bags and faced her.

"Well," he said. "Well, take care of yourself. You'll be all right, will you?"

"Oh, sure," she said.

He opened the door, then came back to her, holding out his hand.

" 'Bye, Haze," he said. "Good luck to you."

She took his hand and shook it.

"Pardon my wet glove," she said.

When the door had closed behind him she went back to the pantry.

She was flushed and lively when she went in to Mrs. Martin's that evening. The Boys were there, Ed among them. He was glad to be in town, frisky and loud and full of jokes. But she spoke quietly to him for a minute.

"Herbie blew to-day," she said. "Going to live out West."

"That so?" he said. He looked at her and played with the fountain pen clipped to his waistcoat pocket.

"Think he's gone for good, do you?" he asked.

"Yeah," she said. "I know he is. I know. Yeah."

"You going to live on across the hall just the same?" he said. "Know what you're going to do?"

"Gee, I don't know," she said. "I don't give much of a damn."

"Oh, come on, that's no way to talk," he told her. "What you need—you need a little snifter. How about it?"

"Yeah," she said. "Just straight."

She won forty-three dollars at poker. When the game broke up Ed took her back to her apartment.

"Got a little kiss for me?" he asked.

He wrapped her in his big arms and kissed her violently. She was entirely passive. He held her away and looked at her.

"Little tight, honey?" he asked anxiously. "Not going to be sick, are you?"

"Me?" she said. "I'm swell."

II

When Ed left in the morning he took her photograph with him. He said he wanted her picture to look at, up in Utica. "You can have that one on the bureau," she said.

She put Herbie's picture in a drawer, out of her sight. When she could look at it she meant to tear it up. She was fairly successful in keeping her mind from racing around him. Whisky slowed it for her. She was almost peaceful, in her mist.

She accepted her relationship with Ed without question or enthusiasm. When he was away she seldom thought definitely of him. He was good to her; he gave her frequent presents and a regular allowance. She was even able to save. She did not plan ahead of any day, but her wants were few, and you might as well put money in the bank as have it lying around.

When the lease of her apartment neared its end it was Ed who suggested moving. His friendship with Mrs. Martin and Joe had become strained over a dispute at poker; a feud was impending.

"Let's get the hell out of here," Ed said. "What I want you to have is a place near the Grand Central. Make it easier for me."

So she took a little flat in the Forties. A colored maid came in every day to clean and to make coffee for her—she was "through with that house-keeping stuff," she said, and Ed, twenty years married to a passionately domestic woman, admired this romantic uselessness and felt doubly a man of the world in abetting it.

The coffee was all she had until she went out to dinner, but alcohol kept her fat. Prohibition she regarded only as a basis for jokes. You could always get all you wanted. She was never noticeably drunk and seldom nearly sober. It required a larger daily allowance to keep her misty-minded. Too little, and she was achingly melancholy.

Ed brought her to Jimmy's. He was proud, with the pride of the transient who would be mistaken for a native, in his knowledge of small, recent restaurants occupying the lower floors of shabby brownstone houses; places where, upon mentioning the name of an habitué friend, might be obtained strange whisky and fresh gin in many of their ramifications. Jimmy's place was the favorite of his acquaintances.

There, through Ed, Mrs. Morse met many men and women, formed quick friendships. The men often took her out when Ed was in Utica. He was proud of her popularity.

She fell into the habit of going to Jimmy's alone when she had no engagement. She was certain to meet some people she knew, and join them. It was a club for her friends, both men and women.

The women at Jimmy's looked remarkably alike, and this was curious, for, through feuds, removals and opportunities of more profitable contacts, the personnel of the group changed constantly. Yet always the newcomers resembled those whom they replaced. They were all big women and stout, broad of shoulder and abundantly breasted, with faces thickly clothed in soft, high-colored flesh. They laughed loud and often, showing opaque and lusterless teeth like squares of crockery. There was about them the health of the big, yet a slight, unwholesome suggestion of stubborn preservation. They might have been thirty-six or forty-five or anywhere between.

They composed their titles of their own first names with their husband's surnames—Mrs. Florence Miller, Mrs. Vera Riley, Mrs. Lilian Block. This gave at the same time the solidity of marriage and the glamour of freedom. Yet only one or two were actually divorced. Most of them never referred to their dimmed spouses; some, a shorter time separate, described them in terms of great biological interest. Several were mothers, each of an only child—a boy at school somewhere, or a girl being cared for by a grandmother. Often, well on toward morning, there would be displays of kodak portraits and of tears.

They were comfortable women, cordial and friendly and irrepressibly matronly. Theirs was the quality of ease. Become fatalistic, especially about money matters, they were unworried. Whenever their funds dropped alarmingly, a new donor appeared; this had always happened. The aim of each was to have one man, permanently, to pay all her bills, in return for which she would have immediately given up other admirers and probably would have become exceedingly fond of him; for the affections of all of them were, by now, unexacting, tranquil, and easily arranged. This end, however, grew increasingly difficult yearly. Mrs. Morse was regarded as fortunate.

Ed had a good year, increased her allowance and gave her a sealskin coat. But she had to be careful of her moods with him. He insisted upon gayety. He would not listen to admissions of aches or weariness.

"Hey, listen," he would say, "I got worries of my own, and plenty. Nobody wants to hear other people's troubles, sweetie. What you got to do, you got to be a sport and forget it. See? Well, slip us a little smile, then. That's my girl."

She never had enough interest to quarrel with him as she had with Herbie, but she wanted the privilege of occasional admitted sadness. It was strange. The other women she saw did not have to fight their moods. There was Mrs. Florence Miller who got regular crying jags, and the men sought only to cheer and comfort her. The others spent whole evenings in grieved recitals of worries and ills; their escorts paid them deep sympathy. But she was instantly undesirable when she was low in spirits. Once, at Jimmy's, when she could not make herself lively, Ed had walked out and left her.

"Why the hell don't you stay home and not go spoiling everybody's evening?" he had roared.

Even her slightest acquaintance seemed irritated if she were not conspicuously light-hearted.

"What's the matter with you, anyway?" they would say. "Be your age, why don't you? Have a little drink and snap out of it."

When her relationship with Ed had continued nearly three years he moved to Florida to live. He hated leaving her; he gave her a large check and some shares of a sound stock, and his pale eyes were wet when he said good-bye. She did not miss him. He came to New York infrequently, perhaps two or three times a year, and hurried directly from the train to see her. She was always pleased to have him come and never sorry to see him go.

Charley, an acquaintance of Ed's that she had met at Jimmy's, had long admired her. He had always made opportunities of touching her and leaning close to talk to her. He asked repeatedly of all their friends if they had ever heard such a fine laugh as she had. After Ed left Charley became the main figure in her life. She classified him and spoke of him as "not so bad." There was nearly a year of Charley; then she divided her time between him and Sydney, another frequenter of Jimmy's; then Charley slipped away altogether.

Sydney was a little, brightly dressed, clever Jew. She was perhaps nearest contentment with him. He amused her always; her laughter was not forced.

He admired her completely. Her softness and size delighted him. And he thought she was great, he often told her, because she kept gay and lively when she was drunk.

"Once I had a gal," he said, "used to try to throw herself out of the window every time she got a can on. Jee-*zuss*," he added feelingly.

Then Sydney married a rich and watchful bride, and then there was Billy. No—after Sydney came Ferd, then Billy. In her haze she never recalled how men entered her life and left it. There were no surprises. She had no thrill at their advent nor woe at their departure. She seemed to be always able to attract men. There was never another as rich as Ed, but they were all generous to her, in their means.

Once she had news of Herbie. She met Mrs. Martin dining at Jimmy's, and the old friendship was vigorously renewed. The still admiring Joe, while on a business trip, had seen Herbie. He had settled in Chicago, he looked fine, he was living with some woman—seemed to be crazy about her. Mrs. Morse had been drinking vastly that day. She took the news with mild interest, as one hearing of the sex peccadilloes of somebody whose name is, after a moment's groping, familiar.

"Must be damn near seven years since I saw him," she commented. "Gee. Seven years."

More and more her days lost their individuality. She never knew dates, nor was sure of the day of the week.

"My God, was that a year ago!" she would exclaim, when an event was recalled in conversation.

She was tired so much of the time. Tired and blue. Almost everything could give her the blues. Those old horses she saw on Sixth Avenue—struggling and slipping along the car tracks, or standing at the curb, their heads dropped level with their worn knees. The tightly stored tears would squeeze from her eyes as she teetered past on her aching feet in the stubby, champagne-colored slippers.

The thought of death came and stayed with her and lent her a sort of drowsy cheer. It would be nice, nice and restful, to be dead.

There was no settled, shocked moment when she first thought of killing herself; it seemed to her as if the idea had always been with her. She pounced upon all the accounts of suicides in the newspapers. There was an epidemic of self-killings—or maybe it was just that she searched for the stories of them so eagerly that she found many. To read of them roused reassurance in her; she felt a cozy solidarity with the big company of the voluntary dead.

She slept, aided by whisky, till deep into the afternoons, then lay abed, a bottle and glass at her hand, until it was time to dress to go out for dinner. She was beginning to feel toward alcohol a little puzzled distrust, as toward an old friend who has refused a simple favor. Whisky could still soothe her for most of the time, but there were sudden, inexplicable moments when the cloud fell treacherously away from her, and she was sawn by the sorrow and bewilderment and nuisance of all living. She played voluptuously with the thought of cool, sleepy retreat. She had never been troubled by religious belief, and no vision of an after-life intimidated her. She dreamed by day of never again putting on tight shoes, of never having to laugh and listen and admire, of never more being a good sport. Never.

But how would you do it? It made her sick to think of jumping from heights. She could not stand a gun. At the theater, if one of the actors drew a revolver, she crammed her fingers into her ears and could not even look at the stage until after the shot had been fired. There was no gas in her flat. She looked long at the bright blue veins in her slim wrists—a cut with a razor blade, and there you'd be. But it would hurt, hurt like hell, and there would be blood to see. Poison—something tasteless and quick and painless—was the thing. But they wouldn't sell it to you in the drug stores, because of the law.

She had few other thoughts.

There was a new man now—Art. He was short and fat and exacting and hard on her patience when he was drunk. But there had been only occasionals for some time before him, and she was glad of a little stability. Too, Art must be away for weeks at a stretch, selling silks, and that was restful. She was convincingly gay with him, though the effort shook her viciously.

"The best sport in the world," he would murmur, deep in her neck. "The best sport in the world."

One night, when he had taken her to Jimmy's, she went into the dressing room with Mrs. Florence Miller. There, while designing curly mouths on their faces with lip rouge, they compared experiences of insomnia.

"Honestly," Mrs. Morse said, "I wouldn't close an eye if I didn't go to bed full of Scotch. I lie there and toss and turn and toss and turn. Blue! Does a person get blue lying awake that way!"

"Say, listen, Hazel," Mrs. Miller said impressively, "I'm telling you I'd be awake for a year if I didn't take veronal. That stuff makes you sleep like a fool."

"Isn't it poison or something?" Mrs. Morse asked.

"Oh, you take too much and you're out for the count," said Mrs. Miller. "I just take five grains—they come in tablets. I'd be scared to fool around with it. But five grains and you cork off pretty."

"Can you get it anywhere?" Mrs. Morse felt superbly Machiavellian.

"Get all you want in Jersey," said Mrs. Miller. "They won't give it to you here without you have a doctor's prescription. Finished? We'd better go back and see what the boys are doing."

That night Art left Mrs. Morse at the door of her apartment; his mother was in town. Mrs. Morse was still sober, and it happened that there was no whisky left in her cupboard. She lay in bed, looking up at the black ceiling.

She rose early, for her, and went to New Jersey. She had never taken the tube, and did not understand it. So she went to the Pennsylvania Station and bought a railroad ticket to Newark. She thought of nothing in particular on the trip out. She looked at the uninspired hats of the women about her and gazed through the smeared window at the flat, gritty scene.

In Newark, in the first drug store she came to, she asked for a tin of talcum powder, a nail brush, and a box of veronal tablets. The powder and the brush were to make the hypnotic seem also a casual need. The clerk was entirely unconcerned. "We only keep them in bottles," he said, and wrapped up for her a little glass vial containing ten white tablets, stacked one on another.

She went to another drug store and bought a face cloth, an orange-wood stick, and a bottle of veronal tablets. The clerk was also uninterested.

"Well, I guess I got enough to kill an ox," she thought, and went back to the station.

At home, she put the little vials in the drawer of her dressing table and stood looking at them with a dreamy tenderness.

"There they are, God bless them," she said, and she kissed her finger tip and touched each bottle.

The colored maid was busy in the living room.

"Hey, Nettie," Mrs. Morse called. "Be an angel, will you? Run around to Jimmy's and get me a quart of Scotch."

She hummed while she awaited the girl's return.

During the next few days, whisky ministered to her as tenderly as it had done when she first turned to its aid. Alone, she was soothed and vague, at Jimmy's she was the gayest of the groups. Art was delighted with her.

Then, one night, she had an appointment to meet Art at Jimmy's for an early dinner. He was to leave afterward on a business excursion, to be away for a week. Mrs. Morse had been drinking all the afternoon; while she dressed to go out she felt herself rising pleasurably from drowsiness to high spirits. But as she came out into the street the effects of the whisky deserted her completely, and she was filled with a slow, grinding wretchedness so horrible that she stood swaying on the pavement, unable for a moment to move forward. It was a gray night with spurts of mean, thin snow, and the streets shone with dark ice. As she slowly crossed Sixth Avenue consciously dragging one foot past the other, a big, scarred horse pulling a rickety express wagon crashed to his knees before her. The driver swore and screamed and lashed the beast insanely, bringing the whip back over his shoulder for every blow, while the horse struggled to get a footing on the slippery asphalt. A group gathered and watched with interest.

Art was waiting, when Mrs. Morse reached Jimmy's.

"What's the matter with you, for God's sake?" was his greeting to her.

"I saw a horse," she said. "Gee, I—a person feels sorry for horses. I—it isn't just horses. Everything's kind of terrible, isn't it? I can't help getting sunk."

"Ah, sunk, me eye," he said. "What's the idea of all the bellyaching? What have you got to be sunk about?"

"I can't help it," she said.

"Ah, help it, me eye," he said. "Pull yourself together, will you? Come on and sit down, and take that face off you."

She drank industriously and she tried hard, but she could not overcome her melancholy. Others joined them and commented on her gloom, and she could do no more for them than smile weakly. She made little dabs at her eyes with her handkerchief, trying to time her movements so they would be unnoticed, but several times Art caught her and scowled and shifted impatiently in his chair.

When it was time for him to go to his train she said she would leave, too, and go home.

"And not a bad idea, either," he said. "See if you can't sleep yourself out of it. I'll see you Thursday. For God's sake, try and cheer up by then, will you?"

"Yeah," she said. "I will."

In her bedroom she undressed with a tense speed wholly unlike her usual slow uncertainty. She put on her nightgown, took off her hair net, and passed the comb quickly through her dry, varicolored hair. Then she took the two little vials from the drawer and carried them into the bathroom. The splintering misery had gone from her, and she felt the quick excitement of one who is about to receive an anticipated gift.

She uncorked the vials, filled a glass with water, and stood before the mirror, a tablet between her fingers. Suddenly she bowed graciously to her reflection and raised the glass to it.

"Well, here's mud in your eye," she said.

The tablets were unpleasant to take, dry and powdery and sticking obstinately halfway down her throat. It took her a long time to swallow all twenty of them. She stood watching her reflection with deep, impersonal interest, studying the movements of the gulping throat. Once more she spoke aloud to it.

"For God's sake, try and cheer up by Thursday, will you?" she said. "Well, you know what he can do. He and the whole lot of them."

She had no idea how quickly to expect effect from the veronal. When she had taken the last tablet she stood uncertainly, wondering, still with a courteous, vicarious interest, if death would strike her down then and there. She felt in no way strange, save for a slight stirring of sickness from the effort of swallowing the tablets, nor did her reflected face look at all different. It would not be immediate, then; it might even take an hour or so.

She stretched her arms high and gave a vast yawn.

"Guess I'll go to bed," she said. "Gee, I'm nearly dead."

That struck her as comic, and she turned out the bathroom light and went in and laid herself down in her bed, chuckling softly all the time.

"Gee. I'm nearly dead," she quoted. "That's a hot one!"

III

Nettie, the colored maid, came in late the next afternoon to clean the apartment and found Mrs. Morse in her bed. But then, that was not unusual. Usually, though, the sounds of cleaning waked her, and she did not like to wake up. Nettie, an agreeable girl, had learned to move softly about her work.

But when she had done the living room and stolen in to tidy the little square bedroom, she could not avoid a tiny clatter as she arranged the objects on the dressing table. Instinctively she glanced over her shoulder at the sleeper, and without warning a sickly uneasiness crept over her. She came to the bed and stared down at the woman lying there.

Mrs. Morse lay on her back, one flabby white arm flung up, the wrist against her forehead. Her stiff hair hung untenderly along her face. The bed covers were pushed down, exposing a deep square of soft neck and a pink nightgown, its fabric worn uneven by many launderings; her great breasts, freed from their tight confiner, sagged beneath her armpits. Now and then she made knotted, snoring sounds, and from the corner of her opened mouth to the blurred turn of her jaw ran a lane of crusted spittle.

"Mis' Morse," Nettie called. "Oh, Mis' Morse! It's terrible late."

Mrs. Morse made no move.

"Mis' Morse," said Nettie. "Look, Mis' Morse. How'm I goin' get this bed made?"

Panic sprang upon the girl. She shook the woman's hot shoulder.

"Ah, wake up, will yuh?" she whined. "Ah, please wake up."

Suddenly the girl turned and ran out in the hall to the elevator door, keeping her thumb firm on the black, shiny button until the elderly car and its Negro attendant stood before her. She poured a jumble of words over the boy and led him back to the apartment. He tiptoed creakingly in to the bedside; first gingerly, then so lustily that he left marks in the soft flesh, he prodded the unconscious woman.

"Hey, there!" he cried, and listened intently, as for an echo.

"Jeez. Out like a light," he commented.

At his interest in the spectacle, Nettie's panic left her. Importance was big in both of them. They talked in quick, unfinished whispers, and it was the boy's suggestion that he fetch the young doctor who lived on the ground floor. Nettie hurried along with him. They looked forward to the limelit moment of breaking their news of something untoward, something pleasurably unpleasant. Mrs. Morse had become the medium of drama. With no ill wish to her, they hoped that her state was serious, that she would not let them down by being awake and normal on their return. A little fear of this determined them to make the most, to the doctor, of her present condition. "Matter of life and death" returned to Nettie from her thin store of reading. She considered startling the doctor with the phrase.

The doctor was in and none too pleased at interruption. He wore a yellow and blue striped dressing gown, and he was lying on his sofa, laughing, with a dark girl, her face scaly with inexpensive powder, who perched on the arm. Half-emptied highball glasses stood beside them, and her coat and hat were neatly hung up with the comfortable implication of a long stay.

Always something, the doctor grumbled. Couldn't let anybody alone after a hard day. But he put some bottles and instruments into a case, changed his dressing gown for his coat, and started out with the Negroes.

"Snap it up there, big boy," the girl called after him. "Don't be all night."

The doctor strode loudly into Mrs. Morse's flat and on to the bedroom, Nettie and the boy right behind him. Mrs. Morse had not moved; her sleep was as deep, but soundless, now. The doctor looked sharply at her, then plunged his thumbs into the lidded pits above her eyeballs and threw his weight upon them. A high, sickened cry broke from Nettie.

"Look like he tryin' to push her right on th'ough the bed," said the boy. He chuckled.

Mrs. Morse gave no sign under the pressure. Abruptly the doctor abandoned it, and with one quick movement swept the covers down to the foot of the bed. With another he flung her nightgown back and lifted the thick, white legs, cross-hatched with blocks of tiny, iris-colored veins. He pinched them repeatedly, with long, cruel nips, back of the knees. She did not awaken.

"What's she been drinking?" he asked Nettie, over his shoulder.

With the certain celerity of one who knows just where to lay hands on a thing, Nettie went into the bathroom, bound for the cupboard where Mrs. Morse kept her whisky. But she stopped at the sight of the two vials, with their red and white labels, lying before the mirror. She brought them to the doctor.

"Oh, for the Lord Almighty's sweet sake!" he said. He dropped Mrs. Morse's limp legs and pushed them impatiently across the bed. "What did she want to go taking that tripe for? Rotten yellow trick, that's what a thing like that is. Now we'll have to pump her out, and all that stuff. Nuisance, a thing like that is; that's what it amounts to. Here, George, take me down in the elevator. You wait here, maid. She won't do anything."

"She won't die on me, will she?" cried Nettie.

"No," said the doctor. "God, no. You couldn't kill her with an ax."

IV

After two days Mrs. Morse came back to consciousness, dazed at first, then with a comprehension that brought with it the slow, saturating wretchedness.

"Oh, Lord, oh, Lord," she moaned, and tears for herself and for life striped her cheeks.

Nettie came in at the sound. For two days she had done the ugly, incessant tasks in the nursing of the unconscious, for two nights she had caught broken bits of sleep on the living room couch. She looked coldly at the big, blown woman in the bed.

"What you been tryin' to do, Mis' Morse?" she said. "What kine o' work is that, takin' all that stuff?"

"Oh, Lord," moaned Mrs. Morse again, and she tried to cover her eyes with her arms. But the joints felt stiff and brittle, and she cried out at their ache.

"Tha's no way to ack, takin' them pills," said Nettie. "You can thank you' stars you heah at all. How you feel now?"

"Oh, I feel great," said Mrs. Morse. "Swell, I feel."

Her hot, painful tears fell as if they would never stop.

"Tha's no way to take on, cryin' like that," Nettie said. "After what you done. The doctor, he says he could have you arrested, doin' a thing like that. He was fit to be tied, here."

"Why couldn't he let me alone?" wailed Mrs. Morse. "Why the hell couldn't he have?"

"That's terr'ble, Mis' Morse, swearin' an' talkin' like that," said Nettie, "after what people done for you. Here I ain' had no sleep at all, an' I had to give up goin' out to my other ladies!"

"Oh, I'm sorry, Nettie," she said. "You're a peach. I'm sorry I've given you so much trouble. I couldn't help it. I just got sunk. Didn't you ever feel like doing it? When everything looks just lousy to you?"

"I wouldn't think o' no such thing," declared Nettie. "You got to cheer up. Tha's what you got to do. Everybody's got their troubles."

"Yeah," said Mrs. Morse. "I know."

"Come a pretty picture card for you," Nettie said. "Maybe that will cheer you up."

She handed Mrs. Morse a post card. Mrs. Morse had to cover one eye with her hand, in order to read the message; her eyes were not yet focusing correctly.

It was from Art. On the back of a view of the Detroit Athletic Club he had written:

Greeting and salutations. Hope you have lost that gloom. Cheer up and don't take any rubber nickels. See you on Thursday.

She dropped the card to the floor. Misery crushed her as if she were between great smooth stones. There passed before her a slow, slow pageant of days spent lying in her flat, of evenings at Jimmy's being a good sport, making herself laugh and coo at Art and other Arts; she saw a long parade of weary horses and shivering beggars and all beaten, driven, stumbling things. Her feet throbbed as if she had crammed them into the stubby champagne-colored slippers. Her heart seemed to swell and fester.

"Nettie," she cried, "for heaven's sake, pour me a drink, will you?"

The maid looked doubtful.

"Now you know, Mis' Morse," she said, "you been near daid. I don' know if the doctor he let you drink nothin' yet."

"Oh, never mind him," she said. "You get me one and bring in the bottle. Take one yourself."

"Well," said Nettie.

She poured them each a drink, deferentially leaving hers in the bathroom to be taken in solitude, and brought Mrs. Morse's glass in to her.

Mrs. Morse looked into the liquor and shuddered back from its odor. Maybe it would help. Maybe, when you had been knocked cold for a few days, your very first drink would give you a lift. Maybe whisky would be her friend again. She prayed without addressing a God, without knowing a God. Oh, please, please, let her be able to get drunk, please keep her always drunk.

She lifted the glass.

"Thanks, Nettie," she said. "Here's mud in your eye."

The maid giggled. "Tha's the way, Mis' Morse," she said. "You cheer up, now."

"Yeah," said Mrs. Morse. "Sure."

ORPHANT ANNIE

Thyra Samter Winslow

I

YESTERDAY, for the first time in perhaps, yes, at least five years, I saw Annie Robinson. Seeing her startled me just a little. It brought back so many things, mostly about Annie herself.

Strangely, Annie had not changed in the five years since I last saw her, nor, for that matter, was she in any outward way different from the Annie of five years before that, when I first met her. Somehow, when we see old friends, after a space of years, we expect to see upon them some definite signs of disintegration and decay, even while each of us says to himself, "I haven't gone down like that—why, I've hardly changed at all—in years."

Perhaps there were signs of age in Annie that I did not observe, but the usual signs were missing. There were no sagging of throat muscles, or lines around the eyes, or loosening of contour. She was, so far as I could tell, the same Orphant Annie of Rutgers & Olds, Advertising; Bingham & Son, Brokers—the others.

"How are you, Annie?" I asked. "What have you been doing?" The usual questions.

She was quite well, she told me. Yes, she was still working—had an awfully good position—confidential secretary to S. B. Hubbard of the S. B. Hubbard Company. Yes, her family was well. Did I remember Ethel, her sister? Ethel was married—an awfully nice chap—they were housekeeping—an apartment in West Seventy-eighth Street. Lester was married, too. Yes, thank you, her father was better—he always felt better when warm weather came. The family was living on Long Island now. Yes, they were buying a home in Flushing—liked it there, awfully well—the country air was good for her mother, too. Yes, it was pleasant, after all these years. . . .

Looking at Orphant Annie, and later, thinking about her, after we parted, her story came back to me, much as stories often come back to us, pieced out, a patchquilt of information and hints and intuitions. Paths cross and break, a stranger, here, offers his bit of color, an old acquaintance, two months later, fits in a missing pattern. Annie . . .

She was nicknamed Orphant Annie when I first met her, at Rutgers & Olds. I've no idea that the nickname stuck to her nor that anyone else remembers it. She was named, perhaps, because of the old jest—that she was not an orphan. At that, she had supposed orphan-like attributes. She was, as she is now, a little thing, slender, with grey eyes set wide apart. Although she is, in a way, even plump, because she is small-boned she has always given the impression of extreme fragility. She was, and is, pale, too, though her mouth is full and ripe-looking. Her face is a bit broad, her cheek-bones a trifle high for artistic perfection. Her skin is smooth and delicate-looking and her hair an unnoticeable light brown and straight. Her nose is slender and straight, with just a suspicion of a tilt to it, and, though her hips and waist are slender, her breasts are well rounded.

I wonder if I have given you a complete enough description. Perhaps her greatest characteristic is that, when you first meet her, she seems to fade completely into her background. It is only after you have seen her often, a dozen times, that she becomes complete, a person. Her clothes, of the most modest type, her soft voice, her little air of self-depreciation, all add to her neutral qualities, on first acquaintance. She is the type of whom it is so natural to say:

"Don't mind Miss Robinson, my confidential secretary, you know; say what you like in front of her—"

One, then, does ignore Annie, quite logically, at first. It is only at subsequent meetings that Annie's personality unfolds, that she becomes even

Orphant Annie—Orphant Annie of a tenement in Sixteenth Street, an apartment uptown, now, a home in Flushing, Long Island. Orphant Annie —the perfect flower of our best urban civilization.

II

ANNIE ROBINSON was born in Tenth Street. She never remembered the house in which she was born, but it is safe to say that it was much like those which became subsequently her homes. By the time she was fourteen and began to think seriously about things, the family had progressed uptown as far as West Sixteenth Street. The house she lived in, which resembled every other house in which Annie had ever lived in, except in street number, was of dingy red brick, called, by courtesy, an apartment house. The difference between it and a tenement was, perhaps, an almost imperceptible degree of cleanliness, an attempt at janitor service, an every-third-year papering and painting. The house was one of a long row of four-storied houses, which, in a previous, more prosperous era, had been "private homes," each house being occupied, unbelievable to the present tenants, by a single family. Now, each house was divided and subdivided, made over into apartments by the additions of kitchens, hall toilets and running water on each floor. Each floor was given over to one or two families, depending upon the comparative opulence of the occupants.

The first floor fronts had not been remodeled. Each house still had a neat bay window to the left of the once-white stone steps. Now, each bay window inevitably gave signs of a more commercial tenancy than the original dwellers could ever have dreamed of. Dingy hair-dyeing establishments, doubtful beauty parlors, doctors of little-known but vaguely unpleasant diseases were sandwiched between purveyors of imitation pearls and of other wares far less genuine.

Children were always tumbling out of the doors of these houses or getting under the feet of pedestrians. They were well-nourished children, their paleness due more to over- than to under-feeding. They were always dressed in rather thick, unfitting clothes with soiled neckbands. Their stockings were forever coming down, their hair rough, their noses unpleasantly moist. They were usually sucking too-red lollypops or hinting for pennies for a new supply. They were sometimes accompanied by dogs of spiritless disposition and uncertain breed which ran mostly to short grey hair, occasionally black spotted.

This, then, was the atmosphere in which Annie Robinson lived until and when she was fourteen. Her own family lived in the third floor front of one of the red houses. The family had three rooms. The front room, logically called "the front room," was the living room and served as a bedroom for the two daughters, Annie and Ethel, who slept together on the wide cot which served, day times, disguised with a rather dirty half of a pair of portieres, as a couch. There was a big red-plush rocker in the room, outlined elaborately with machine carving, three smaller chairs of lesser beauty, a big golden oak table with carved legs and, in the corner, a sort of whatnot, a bit wabbly, bought, second-hand a few years before and containing various art treasures: an enormous shell, a doll from Coney Island, a small set of dishes with handle-less cups and a book of Whittier's poems, mysteriously come by. There was a red rug in the room, violently patterned in spots but worn in other places to a softer gentility, torn, near the door, where you were apt to get your foot caught, if you happened to forget it.

The second room, opening off this, with the other half of the pair of portieres ready to provide privacy, if ever necessary, was the bedroom of Mr. and Mrs. Robinson. The furniture here was, on account of the size of the room, necessarily limited to a huge brass bed and a less elegant chest of drawers. Maud, the youngest child, also shared this room with her parents until she was about seven, when she moved into the front room with her sisters.

The third room was the kitchen, complete with stove, sink and table. The family ate in the kitchen. In the general hall were the necessary toilet facilities. The hall and the stairs were always dark, lit by a small, flickering gas flame and full of a horrible mingling of smells, each one unpleasant.

The head of the house was most inappropriately named Harold, which had shortened to Hal and which seemed to fit him poorly enough, even then. He was a big man, with a sort of pulpy quality. In his youth he had been a longshoreman and exceedingly proud of his muscle. As with many longshoremen, he had taken up boxing as a fad. He had belonged to several athletic clubs, which had combined politics and sports most advantageously to both elements. He had been a big fellow with long arms, but not especially "game" or courageous. He had never become more than a fairly interesting amateur. He had a quarrelsome nature that prevented those higher up from taking an interest in him. He was forever engaging in some long and stupid dispute. He always "had it in" for someone or was "getting ready to settle with that fellow."

After his marriage, the occupation of longshoreman became too strenuous for him. Gradually, his muscle disappeared and in its place came unhealthy-looking fat. Now, he was employed in the freight department of one of the big steamship companies whose docks extend, stretched out for blocks, along the North River. He was always getting rheumatism, complaining that he couldn't work along the river, laying off, spending a couple of weeks at home as a most quarrelsome and cursing invalid, and then, when the money disappeared, getting another job at the docks. There really was nothing else, now, that he could do. He walked with a peculiar swaying, boneless sort of gait and his skin, though tanned, had a spongy quality, too. His nose was large and red-veined. His mouth had a childish, weak-looking expression and his chin was a series of loose, pulp-like folds. His hair was light and thin—he was bald at forty—and his eyes were small and light and weak, too.

Mrs. Robinson had come from slightly better stock, though she, as well as her husband, had been born in New York's East Side. She had married Robinson when he was a husky and athletic longshoreman. She had admired him tremendously and had felt unbelievably happy and lucky when she found that he really wanted to marry her. Never very bright nor acquisitive and believing that the man, especially her man, was head of the family, she had, through years of child-bearing and motherhood and house-work, lapsed into an almost silent, rather timid wisp of a woman. She always felt lucky because she didn't have to go to work, the way so many married women did. Her husband supported her, he did! Even Robinson's gradual disintegration did not bother her. She had always been taken care of—she'd be looked out for.

She had simple beliefs. She did her buying of clothes at the end of the season and put them away for the next year, when she could. You got better material that way. She thought that a girl who had "gone wrong" was better off dead. She dismissed every new idea—and this included night school, music, books of all kinds and everything with any possible cultural trend as "nonsense." She saw that her children had one good hot meal a day—usually a stew—and she drank innumerable cups of tea and coffee. One or the other of these beverages was always simmering on her kitchen stove.

Lester was the oldest of the family. Two years older than Annie, at sixteen, he was starting to be "wild," not an entirely undesirable trait in a boy, his parents felt. He hung around the corner cigar store and poolroom, smoked cigarettes and made remarks about girls. He worked, with fair stability, in a paper box factory, but had already been in one shady deal, which required police investigation and ended in a warning.

Annie followed Lester in age, to be followed in turn by Ethel, who at twelve was still at the loose-stocking, moist-nose age. So was Frank, who was ten, and, nights, with Lester, slept in the kitchen. Maud, about seven, was the beauty of the family and had thin, pale curls. There had been a younger child who had died.

Annie, at fourteen, was pale and thin and mouse-like, no more noticeable at first glance then than later. There is no reason to start her history at fourteen, in fact, save that at that age she made to her parents her first unusual and unassisted request. Needless to say it was dismissed immediately.

Annie dared to ask that she be allowed to go to High School! High School, mind you! When the family had been waiting for her to "graduate" from the public school so she could start to work. One can start to work when one has reached the age of sixteen, no matter what one's scholastic accomplishments, or, more grandly, at whatever younger age one

may have finished the work laid out by the Board of Education for the
Grammar Schools. Annie was graduated from School Number One Hundred Something, a dingy, red-brick school with a treeless, grassless yard
when she was fourteen. Instead of great joy at this release from a formal
education she had actually asked to go on—to go to High School. Three
weeks later she had a very good job in a paper pattern house in lower Sixth
Avenue.

III

THE FAMILY WATCHED ANNIE a bit closely for a while. Something unusual,
here. Still, she seemed all right. There were no outbursts. She brought her
money home, regularly, Saturdays, and only made the usual requests for
unnecessary finery. Of course, she did take walks by herself way over to
Fifth Avenue—and to Fourteenth Street—you got to watch girls like that—
Fourteenth Street at night is no place for a young girl, alone—might go
wrong—still, outside of that. It wasn't as if Annie was one of these flashy
girls—a quiet little thing like Annie—

If it hadn't been for those walks, Annie might have settled down to
years of the factory by day, neighborhood gossip or boys from the factory
or neighborhood by night, a courtship, then, kissed in dark, unsavory
halls, amusements at places just a trifle more pleasant, marriage, another
dingy apartment, children. But Fourteenth was but two blocks to the South
—and Fifth Avenue just a little more than two long blocks away.

Funny, Annie thought, even then, why so few of the girls she knew
ever walked over to Fifth Avenue. Her own home was just West of Seventh
Avenue. The girls walked farther every day. They walked as far East as
Sixth, all the time. Somehow, something about Fifth frightened them. It
didn't frighten Annie. She liked the width of it and the quiet and the
dignified, smooth traffic—the buses. She went for bus rides, by herself,
Saturday afternoons and Sundays. The girls she knew didn't think that was
any fun. It wasn't fun, exactly. It wasn't that. It left you even unhappier
than you were when you started. Yet it drove you on. Seated on top of a
bus, Saturday afternoon, her clothes never quite warm enough except in
the warmest weather, Annie drank in what she saw—the people mostly.
Not that her thoughts about them were kind and gentle, nor even just
mildly curious. She hated them all. One after another.

"How I hate that old thing," she would mutter about a woman, fur clad,
and not necessarily old. "Nasty little child," she'd say to herself, "nasty, fat
little thing."

She would poke her nose in the air disdainfully at people in automobiles
and think, "I hate you, old fools," after they had passed.

Yet, too, she had a sharp curiosity about these very people. As the bus
jogged up Fifth Avenue or Riverside Drive she would peer into apartment-

house windows. In winter, when the days grew dark early, she was glad when folks forgot to pull down the window shades.

"Lace curtains," she'd tell herself, "big pictures there, in wide gold frames—a big blue lamp shade—rich folks," and then, "Gee, I hate them all. They don't know me, not one of them."

Sometimes she would, wistfully, put herself in the way of people, hoping to be discovered, somehow, a West Sixteenth Street Cinderella. She would be pushed aside with a careless, "look where you're going, child." No one ever discovered her.

She even tried to pretend that she was adopted, asked her mother artful questions that might lead to a disclosure of her true origin. Well she knew that the Robinsons wouldn't have adopted anyone. There were too many Robinsons as it was. She looked too much like Ethel and Frank to be an adopted child, anyhow.

Annie grew ambitious in an unformed sort of way, restless, perhaps, more than ambitious. If she had had money, a few decent pleasures, a fairly comfortable home, she might have been satisfied. Folding paper patterns in a Sixth Avenue loft by day, not especially savory food and West Sixteenth Street by night did not make life seem especially complete at fourteen.

Annie kept to the pattern of things. It's hard to break away at fourteen, at fifteen, even. She grew a bit sullen, a bit more envious of people who were more prosperous. Now, in Fifth Avenue she would issue pathetic and —she knew it, too—empty defiances to the street and the well-dressed crowds who passed her, there—"you just wait—I'll show you—I'll have nice things—"

How do you get nice things? That's it. Other folks' fathers provide them. Robinson grew more pulpy every day. His periods of being out of work grew longer. His weak, droopy mouth issued more frequent curses. No help there.

Ethel, at fourteen, went to work, too. Ethel was "fresh," a gayer, saucier type than Annie, though looking like her, in a way. Ethel worked at a milliner's and was forever bringing home rather wild and not entirely truthful stories of her adventures. Lester, who had changed jobs several times a year, now clerked in a chain cigar store and assumed a set of manners which fitted not at all with his usual behavior. At eighteen, he had already "got into trouble over a girl" and only the fact that the girl was older than he was and was wild, too, kept him from paying for his folly.

When Annie was sixteen she had passed from the loft in Sixth Avenue to a press clipping bureau and then to a Sixth Avenue department store. She didn't like the department store, really, but it was better than anything she had done. She was a cash girl for the basement aluminum ware and had a promise of being put "on the floor" when she was a year or two older.

Annie disliked the girls she worked with, much as she disliked her neighbors. They seemed stupid, dull, without any sort of an urge or inner feeling. Sometimes she would try to put out feelers, to see if the other girls felt the restless rebellion that she felt so frequently. There was never a response of any kind. They thought the store was "all right," the hours "kind-a-long." They spoke of "fellas" and "steadies" and clothes. Marriage, perhaps only a few years off, was the only thing they looked forward to. Sometimes, looking into their complacent or shallow, petulant faces, Annie wanted to stick pins into them to find out if they would squeal or scream. They laughed at her, called her a queer one, let it go at that.

Annie went to the store's school. She was not especially ambitious, now, in a scholastic way, as she had been at fourteen. Still, the more you know the faster you get ahead. She had a quick mind. She never said much about the school, at home.

When she was seventeen, Annie discovered boys—or boys discovered her. Anyhow, she found herself suddenly with masculine attention. Until then, she hadn't thought much about boys. They were all right, in a way. She hated boys of Lester's type, fresh and forward. She "couldn't stand" the slovenly youths of West Sixteenth Street. She was so quiet and mouse-like that other types never presented themselves to her. Ethel, at fifteen, already had beaux. But then, Ethel was a "fresh kid" and, besides, was satisfied with almost any kind of youthful masculine attention.

At seventeen, Annie found that the peculiar chemistry of sex brought her unconsciously with boys and men. Some young clerk or wrapper or delivery boy was always waiting at the side door of the store for her at closing time. She wasn't one of the "awfully popular" girls, and yet there was always someone.

She liked these boys, for a while. They were "good company." They were full of a sort of comfortable repartee. They took her to the movies, nights, and bought innumerable sodas. Beyond that they could not go. What could they do? Most of them lived at home and helped support a home quite similar to the one Annie came from. They certainly were not marriageable, and, if they had been, the marriage would have meant a transfer from one poor apartment to another. They were a transient pleasure. Some of them got fresh. They didn't get far with Annie. One didn't mind a kiss or two. That sort of paid for the evening's entertainment. They didn't go farther than that. Annie knew how to hold her own. You can't live in West Sixteenth Street without learning something about the world.

Roger Burson clerked in the silk department. He was a most elegant young fellow, with long white fingers. Quite unobtrusively Annie brought herself to his notice. She was clerking in the second-floor dress-notions, now. There was something different about Roger Burson. Annie watched him, when she could, at his work. He unrolled long bolts of silk, letting the material slip through his fingers. She watched him talking to feminine customers—jealous of them as she watched—and was always surprised at his smooth flow of conversation, his little deferences to his customers, his smile. He put back his head and half closed his eyes when he smiled—he seemed mysterious—deep, then. She liked his writing on his checks, a sort of large, clear, round writing. She kept a check that he had written and discarded. She was as familiar with his store number as most girls are with the telephone number of more fortunate young men.

After a seemingly long period of indifference, Burson began paying attention to Annie. He waited for her, after closing hours. She was just a bit dizzy when she saw him waiting, the first time, his sleek brown hair, his slender rather pale face. What a nice fellow he was!

Of course she couldn't ask Burson to call! He lived in an uptown apartment with a widowed mother, who had a little money. She didn't dare let him see the Sixteenth Street apartment. She did meet him, after supper, on several occasions. He took her to the theatre a couple of times. She encouraged him as much as she could. He held her hand in the theatre. He hinted at further and more violent love-making. What could come of it? He couldn't marry—had to do his share toward supporting his mother—it took all they had just to get along. His conversation was not as thrilling as Annie had hoped it would be. It was quite dull, in fact, little rather feminine gossipy things about the store and about styles, tales of his yearly two weeks' vacation, tales of his bowling club, which met once each week. She tried to get him to talk about some of the vague, restless things that were in her own mind. He never seemed to know what she was talking about.

One warm Spring evening they took a bus-ride to Central Park and then walked through the park slowly. Annie walked close to Burson, took his arm, encouraged him in every way. He kissed her. Oh, what of it? What if he did kiss her? Could anything come of it all? She'd better be careful— falling in love would be easy enough—too easy. That wouldn't get her anywhere. After that, Annie avoided Burson. It was easy enough, after all.

A few nights afterward, Annie, all alone, walked up Fourteenth Street. It was a hot night and the white lights of the street, the cheap colors from the shows and the shop windows seemed suddenly to sicken her. She was eighteen! Eighteen! She used to think, when she was a little girl, that something grand would happen to her. Nothing would. Not unless she made things happen. It was like waking up, somehow, just walking down Fourteenth Street. Her street—two blocks from her home!

In one store there was an auction. A man with a persuasive voice was begging customers to bid on an elaborately boxed tea-set of red and white Japanese china. Annie ventured inside the door. Half a dozen youths smiled invitingly, even moved toward her. She waited for a minute, hurried out again. Idly enough, she ventured into a penny arcade two doors away. The place was full of a poorly dressed, shuffling crowd, leering men, bold-eyed women. A mechanical piano blared out a popular song. A wax figure, dirty, slightly melted, held a sign which told of a fortune to be had for a penny.

There were peep-shows for pennies, too, showing partly nude women of generous proportions, music for pennies, with long and unbelievably unsanitary tubes to be fitted into your ears if you cared to receive music in this fashion. There were weighing machines and machines which told your strength or gave you a penny's worth of electricity. A fellow in a sailor's uniform grinned at Annie and pointed toward one of the peep-shows.

"Seen this?" he asked. "It's hot stuff!"

Annie gave him what she hoped was a reproving stare, hurried down the street, turned up Fifth Avenue.

IV

Yes, here she was—eighteen—and she had nothing. They were getting poorer and poorer all the time. Lester was always getting into trouble or out of work, grumbling when he had to help at home and threatening to go elsewhere to live. Ethel put her money on her back and wouldn't do a great deal to support the family. Her father's rheumatism, which usually disappeared in summer, seemed worse than ever, now. At least, he had more time at home for cursing and complaining about it. Even now, she knew he was sitting, a huge sponge which overflowed the red plush chair, cursing the weather and his rheumatism and his family. She couldn't exactly blame him. After all, he didn't get a great deal out of life.

Well, what did she get out of life? Working all day in the store wasn't fun, either. She wasn't the type who got ahead, got to be a buyer. She knew that. She might stay there forever, just behind a counter. Marriage? Whom could she get? Oh, any one of half a dozen fellows, if she tried hard enough. What would she have then? A home like she had now and babies—or no babies and a job, if she found a man who believed that a woman should keep on working after she was married. That wasn't much fun.

Men? They were easy enough—easy to get them interested, but they wouldn't do anything for you. There was old Blakeman. He had seemed interested. He had been awfully insulting, even offered her an apartment —he had pulled a lot of stuff about "making an old man happy." He hadn't helped her get ahead in the store. Of course not. Men don't help girls in that way. And women don't help other women, unless you happen to be the type—know how to get in with them and sympathize and kow-tow. Well, she wasn't the type. Men though—simple things—if there was some way—if she knew anything. Men—why of course—if she knew anything. The girl who got ahead was the girl who had a profession and knew men —how to manage things—there was Leah Fisher—a stenographer—she had married her boss, finally. There were other ways of getting ahead, too, no doubt. A stenographer. Good money, right there. Of course. Why hadn't she thought of it? All of these years wasted—and she was eighteen.

When Annie told her parents that she was going to night school they did not protest as much as she had thought they would. Going to High School, day times, was one thing. Going to a free night school, after you had already earned money during the day, that was something else. Why any big, overgrown girl of eighteen would want to keep on going to school. . . . Still, if what Annie said was true—if she really could make more money that way—well, she ought to be able to know her own mind at eighteen—time most girls were marrying and settling down. . . .

Her parents encouraged Annie, as a matter of fact. If she married, they would be deprived of her earnings. If, on the other hand, night school would mean larger earnings. . . . . .

Learning stenography, when one has been out of school four years and only went through grade school, then, isn't an easy job. Especially, it isn't easy, if one has stood up all day selling things in a noisy store, where the air isn't any too good. Still, others did it. It took Annie a year to learn to be a stenographer. It was a year of long days in the store, long hours on her feet, her head aching, frequently, a hurried and not especially good supper and then more hours in a bare schoolroom at an uncomfortable desk, an impatient teacher, impossible fellow students. That year remained a memory of never quite enough sleep or rest, trudging dully from one task to another, trying to learn word-signs between sales, during the day, and trying to keep awake sufficiently to recall those same word-signs at night. The year ended, finally. Annie was a stenographer!

Hunting for a position, then. It wasn't as easy as she had supposed. How many stenographers there were! Girls, just out of high school, not much younger than she was, but so much fresher and seemingly more eager and so full of the knowledge that high school must surely bring. There were college girls looking for jobs, even!

Annie gave up her job in the store—they wouldn't give her a trial as a stenographer there, though that didn't bother her a great deal. She had tried, at first, hunting a job in her lunch-hour. That didn't do. All good jobs were taken, by noon.

She would read the want-ads, the first thing in the morning, snatch a bite of breakfast, a roll spread with gelatinous factory-made preserves and coffee, usually, and start out looking for a job. She wore neat, colorless clothes, rather faded into the background.

Her parents were rather difficult, those weeks. She had been the steady one of the family. Her father and Lester had always been more or less out of work. Ethel couldn't be depended upon. Annie's money had come in steadily, without a question. Now, it almost seemed to her as if they thought her the whole support of the family. They made fun of her ambitions to better herself, even while they urged that she find something to do. To hear her father, melting out over the red plush rocker, you would have thought that Annie had already entered into a life of vice and crime because, for a week or two, she didn't contribute to the family's upkeep.

"Shut up about me," she said, finally. "I don't know why I'm the family goat, but if I am, I am, and that's all there is to it. I'll get something."

She did. She got a stenographic position in a small hardware company. The proprietor insulted her, finally, so she quit. She could have "called him down," kept on with her job. What was the use? There were other jobs. There weren't any possibilities there, anyhow, excepting the small salary—a salary only a degree better than she had had as a clerk in the department store. That proprietor! What a stupid, lazy, dusty fellow! If she wanted to be insulted she'd never had chosen him to do it. Certainly not. Oh, well . . . might as well get experience. . . .

She was a better stenographer now. A few weeks more of idleness and Annie was with the Cutter Rubber Company, in lower Broadway.

This was something like it—a clean office, with glass partitions, brisk girls, sleek young men, busy, pompous officials. For the first time in her life Annie felt that she fitted in. This was what she had wanted all of the time—in a way. At least she had always wanted cleanliness and order. You can't afford those when you are poor. She rather liked the work, even. She developed into rather a good stenographer, a bit uncertain, perhaps, as to punctuation, but always willing enough to consult the dictionary as to the spelling of a difficult word.

Annie began to wear the neat, unobtrusive business clothes that became almost a part of her personality later. Up to that time she had worn odds and ends of things that did not seem to belong together—a suit bought at a closing-out sale, a blouse her mother had picked up at a bargain. Annie insisted that she had to dress well now. As her salary was larger, her mother began to respect her almost enough to allow her to buy clothes without reproach for the money she was "throwing away on style."

For some time, Annie was satisfied at the office. She always arrived on time. She did her work fairly well, almost eagerly. She spent the usual amount of time gossiping with other girls in the rest room, of course, but this was more from a desire to see how the other girls lived and to find out what they knew than from any time-wasting motive. She had always had a curiosity about people.

At home things were just as bad. Lester and her father worked spasmodically, with wonderfully good excuses for their idleness. Ethel still cared for cheap finery. Frank had a job as messenger boy, but didn't make much money. Maud, the beauty of the family, wore yellow curls still, and, of course, had to have wearing apparel harmonious with her loveliness. Mrs. Robinson had dreams for Maud.

There ought to be some way to improve things. Certainly things couldn't go on that way always, that disordered apartment, never quite enough money for actual necessities, never any touch of pleasant living. Annie thought about this a lot. Her position was pleasant enough, in a way. It wasn't exciting, now that she was accustomed to the routine of the office.

Certainly, in the normal course of events, no great change would take place. She might get a slight raise once or twice a year. She might keep her position for years and years. There were several stenographers at the Cutter Rubber Company who had been there for ten years. They received only a slightly larger salary than Annie, were laughed at a bit for their faithfulness —certainly nothing to look forward to.

Occasionally a girl in the office got married. Annie would meet the "lucky man," like as not. When he was a fellow employee, his salary was just about the size of Annie's own. She couldn't afford to marry a man like that. Once in a while one of the girls managed a vacation to one of the nearby summer resorts and returned engaged and with stories of great luxuries ahead. Annie found that these summer-vacation catches were invariably old and homely and not as rich as they were supposed to be. Anyhow, Annie couldn't have managed a summer-resort vacation if it would have resulted in an engagement to the Prince of Wales.

Yes, marriage was all right—if you could afford it—if you had only yourself to look out for or if you found a rich man. Certainly no rich man was going to marry Annie. She knew that. Occasionally girls did find rich men —married their bosses, even. No such luck for her.

Then Margery Miller had an "affair." It was not the most savory sort of an affair, but Annie drank in the details eagerly. Old Man Bruntage—the last person in the world you'd suspect, unless you were familiar with business offices—took the dashing Miss Miller to Atlantic City for the weekend. Actually. Before going, he bought Miss Miller an entirely new outfit of clothes, which, rumor said, she needed badly, especially the silk underneaths. Well, Bruntage and Miss Miller returned, after the week-end, but Bruntage's wife got wind of the affair—that does happen sometimes—and, though she wasn't the sort who wanted a divorce, preferring the money and position which went with being Bruntage's wife, she did insist on "something being done about it." Something was done about it. Miss Miller was fired.

The girls talked it over in the rest room.

"What a fool she was!" Lucile Stork volunteered. "She ought to have known it would get out. Those things always do, sooner or later. And when a girl's reputation is gone, there is just nothing she can do." Lucile was holding out for matrimony.

"There's another thing, too," this from Mabel Foster, "as soon as you give in to a man he doesn't care for you any more. He's interested only as long as you keep him guessing. All Margery has got is a few clothes. You bet, if I was going to do a thing like that—though of course I wouldn't think of such a thing . . ."

The girls were right. Annie felt that. And yet, if you didn't do anything at all—excepting your work, day after day . . .

Of course if you weren't a Margery Miller—if you kept your head—well, that might be a way, too.

Annie was given the position made vacant by Miss Miller's departure. Annie was Bruntage's private secretary!

V

ANNIE was a little mouse. Of course. She dropped her eyes when Bruntage spoke to her suddenly. She said "yes, sir," and "no, sir," with unnecessary frequence. She saw that her blouses were always fresh and dainty. She pouted her lips over her pencil when she was thinking. Bruntage told her that she was "very good, indeed. Quite satisfactory in the position." Was that all? What a plain thing Margery Miller was, actually! Wasn't Annie even that nice looking? It worried her just a little—Bruntage was awfully respectful.

Perhaps men were simpler than she had imagined them to be. At least Bruntage was. Annie found that out. She began wearing rather thin stockings to the office. Bad taste? She had thought so, from things she had read in "advice to the working girl." After all, though, perhaps she and the woman who wrote the advice weren't quite in accord as to results, after all.

Annie's nice office oxfords gave way to thin slippers with buckles on them. She crossed her legs a bit. Simple? Of course. Weren't men simple? She continued wearing her plain little clothes. Occasionally her hand touched his as she was taking dictation. She would pull it away and say, "Oh, pardon me," rather dreadfully embarrassed. She kept one flower on her desk, in a glass of water.

There were a lot of questions Annie had to ask Bruntage. Men are so much wiser and more sensible than girls!

"Oh, thank you, sir—I knew you'd know. I'm sorry I had to take up your time. There was no one else around here who could have told me." And, "I don't mind working overtime, really. I know how particular you are about the reports, sir. I'd rather take a lot of time and feel that they were right."

One day she was crying. She brushed tears away, unobtrusively, as she typed a letter.

Oh, dear! Had Mr. Bruntage noticed? Annie was so sorry. It wasn't any-thing—anything he could do, really. Her—her father was ill—had been ill a long time and now there were doctors' bills. Quite a lot of them. Oh, yes, she helped pay the expenses—had the burden of things, rather . . . had worked since she was fourteen . . . went to night school to learn stenog-raphy. Oh, she had wanted to ask someone there—didn't know who to ask . . . oh, if she could . . . if there were some way to—to get some money . . . yes, it was awful to be poor . . . not a great deal—nothing to Mr. Bruntage . . . two hundred dollars . . . she'd pay it off . . . pay it every week . . . a few dollars at a time.

It was lovely of Mr. Bruntage! She could pay him—not have it go through the office at all. Oh, he was lovely to her . . . she hadn't dreamed . . .

Bruntage gave Annie the money, a little roll of bills not very new ones. Annie started a bank account the next day, at noon. Not a great deal, of course. Still! She put three one-dollar bills on Mr. Bruntage's desk every Friday, after the cashier came around with the pay-envelopes. She hadn't signed any paper, of course—this had been too personal for that—just between them. How good of Mr. Bruntage!

It was a few weeks later that Mr. Bruntage proposed a trip to Atlantic City. He'd be more discreet this time. Anyhow, what if he was found out—though he wouldn't be, of course. A nice, discreet little thing, Miss Robinson. Young, too, and innocent. There were preliminary things, of course. Then, plans.

Annie would need clothes, of course. She dropped her eyes. A tear showed in the corner of one of them.

"I've—I've never had any pretty things," she said.

That could be remedied easily enough—easily enough. After they got to Atlantic City . . .

Annie shook her head. She didn't like to say anything—she—she was ashamed of the things she had . . . wouldn't embarrass Mr. Bruntage by being seen with him. Still—she didn't know much about buying things. . . .

Mr. Bruntage was clever about buying things, it seemed. Three days later, on a Thursday, he met Annie, by appointment, in a little tea shop in East Fifty-seventh Street. He took her to some shops he knew about . . . yes, Annie had naturally good taste, it seemed—the saleswoman said so. She chose rather plain things—her style, really, but awfully expensive and well-made. Bruntage paid cash for the things. Annie had them sent to her home. Her mother wasn't clever about things like that—if clothes didn't have a lot of trimming her mother wouldn't think they were expensive.

Friday, modest and shy as ever Annie appeared at the Cutter Rubber Company. Sometimes, during the day, she caught Mr. Bruntage's eyes, dropped her own eyes, smiled. There was a delicious secret between them. They were to meet at two, on Saturday, at the Pennsylvania Station, to begin their holiday.

That evening, Annie ate the half-cold stew without protest. She didn't have anything to say when her father set forth his usual complaints—his rheumatism was worse, it seemed, and some freight that was being unloaded at the docks had gone wrong and of course he had been unjustly blamed for it.

After the evening meal, Annie wrote a letter. Letters were written seldom enough in the apartment-house in West Sixteenth Street. They were almost an event, in fact. Annie had brought home a new box of writing paper, a new bottle of ink and an office pen for the occasion. Now, she cleared off the table herself, put an old *Saturday Evening Post* on it, in lieu of a desk blotter, and sat down to write.

"Writing a letter?" asked her mother, with a nice mixture of social interest and curiosity.

"Why, yes," said Annie simply, and didn't explain. She had learned that you don't have to explain, if you don't want to.

"You needn't be so grumpy about it," her mother answered, with quite unnecessary anger, considering her question and Annie's reply. "A lot of pleasure I get from my children . . . running around at all hours . . . doing all kinds of things under my very nose. . . . It seems to me that your mother . . ."

Annie was writing her letter. She wrote it in pencil, first, on a piece of Maud's tablet paper, crossing out one sentence, substituting another. Then she copied it carefully in ink on her new paper. It was plain white paper and the ink was black. When she had copied her letter she addressed an envelope, put the letter in and sealed it. She started to tear up the first penciled draft, thought better of it, tucked it into her purse instead. After all, she had tried hard on that letter. This is what Annie had written:

My dear Mr. Bruntage:

I don't know how to tell you, after all of your kindness to me. I can't go— that's the easiest way of saying it. I just can't. I've thought it over and over. Maybe it's because of the home training I had when I was a little girl. I don't know. It just doesn't seem *RIGHT,* that's all. I never could come back to my parents and my little sister, if I did such a thing. I hope you will understand how I feel. I'm not coming back to the office, but I want you to know that I shall always remember your kindness to me—we have always been poor and never before have I ever had any pretty things—and your goodness to my father during his illness.

Sincerely,
Annie Robinson

Annie put on her hat and coat and called to her mother.

"I'm going out to mail my letter, Ma, and I may take a bus ride before I come back."

It was customary, in the Robinson household, to make some explanation of one's departure.

At the corner, Annie dropped the letter into a letter-box. She smiled as she saw, in her mind, Bruntage's expression as he read it. He'd open it himself—she had marked it "Personal" and he always opened personal mail. That stupid little Martin girl would probably be in his office, in her place. What an old fool Bruntage was! Well, he'd never show that letter to his wife, at any rate.

VI

Annie climbed onto a bus at the corner and chose a seat on top. She had always liked bus-riding. Now, as she rode uptown, she thought over things much as she had done when she was a little girl. She was a little more definite about things now. She felt a certain exaltation, a slight wave of success, such as she had never felt before. After all—she had accomplished something. Old Bruntage! What a fool he was! Yet she knew from office gossip that he had taken at least four other girls on week-end trips, besides the stupid Miss Miller, who had preceded her as private secretary. None of the other girls had rebelled. Silly little flies—they had walked into his net, perhaps even grateful to get the few things he had given them, the couple of days at a good hotel. Horrid old man! Ugh! How mad he'd be at that letter! She'd chosen expensive clothes, too, and had paid back only a trifle of that two hundred dollars. Well, he had picked her out as a poor, simple little office worm. Let him be more careful next time—the old fool.

Not that he'd see through it. He'd probably just wish she hadn't been so virtuous. That was just as well. She hoped she'd never see him again. At that, the office would have to give her good recommendations. She'd telephone in the morning—say she was ill. Bruntage wouldn't dare say anything. Not he! The old fool.

There were days ahead . . . other things. For the first time life offered a pleasant pathway, with a narrow, glittering lane of possibilities. Of course, there were limits. Annie knew she wasn't the type her employer married. Anyhow, few enough employers really married their stenographers—outside of romantic short stories. Of course offices weren't devilish holes of iniquity. Certainly not. There were thousands of business men who never noticed a pretty face during business hours. Of course. Still, there were thousands more not above a stolen kiss, awfully susceptible to flattery, easy to prey upon, no doubt because they thought that they were the stronger power. Perhaps. She would see.

As the bus jostled her uptown, Annie looked into shop windows and then into homes and apartments much as she had done when she was a little girl. She still hated these people, their comfort and their smugness. Each of these families with some man at the head earning money. Imagine her father earning enough money for the family. Cleanliness . . . nice, smooth-flowing lives . . . pretty things. Oh, well.

She could get a good salary. She was a good stenographer now, had learned about offices. Lower New York, of course. Brokers, advertising men, officials, men like that. Big offices. That was where to go. Men who dealt in abstract things—stupid men who thought they were "deep" because they knew a few seemingly important facts. Those were the men who believed silly things, who looked for a sort of pseudo-romantic relation mixed in with their dry business facts. A conference in the morning, a long luncheon with a couple of men, peppered with seemingly important business details, letters dictated during the afternoon to a sympathetic little secretary. Of course.

If she had only herself! That would be easy enough. These girls who spoke so much about being self-supporting, when all they had to do was to support themselves! Of course—she could get away—it would be physically possible just to get out—out of the whole thing, out of helping to support the family and keeping an eye on Ethel and trying to put some sort of ideas into Maud's head. The family would get along somehow. Families always did, she supposed. However, the burden of support, started when Annie was fourteen, couldn't be thus easily swept aside. After all, she was, in a way, fond of her family, even—certainly she was fond of Frank and Maud! yes, even of Lester and Ethel and her mother and father. After all, none of them had any too much, either. Maybe they liked nice things, too.

Two hundred dollars! In the bank! To do with what she wanted to! Nice clothes, too, a good coat and dress and blouses and a couple of hats. She could give Ethel a hat and a blouse and still have nicer things than she had ever had before.

Two hundred dollars! The bus lumbered past apartment-houses, blank, factory-like, solidly respectable, each with its little squares of light to indicate the families who lived, in cliff-dwelling fashion, each in its own little portion. How funny—all of these little families, each member of each family coming home each day, like little homing pigeons to a particular little nest in the cliff. Nice little nests! Why, if her family could live like this—clean and respectable—if Frank and Maud could have a chance. Why not? There was even the university up here—classes at night—you don't even have to be graduated from a high school—Annie had heard that. If Maud could come up here to live and go to school—If Frank could "get" this neighborhood—Ethel and Lester, even. Why, the only reason Ethel and Lester liked cheap things, probably, was because they hadn't ever had any better to like, if they had wanted to. After all—Annie knew she had had to fight for everything she had—stenography even. Even now—oh, well, there wasn't any better way that she could think of.

Why not? The two hundred dollars would pay for moving and for . . . Moving—that old trash? The broken-down table, the hideous brass bed— the red-plush rocker her father melted into and went to sleep in every night after dinner—the cot in the living-room. It would be great—living up here —up-town—in a new apartment, clean and new—with a bedroom for the girls and another for Lester and Frank and one for her parents—and a living-room for—why, for company even . . . and a regular dining-room and a clean—may-be even a white kitchen. It could be done! Why not? The most that could happen was that they could be put out. Even that might be more fun than Sixteenth Street.

Annie knew that her father had always been against moving, had said that the Sixteenth Street apartment was near his work. Let him complain. Why, he was out of work most of the time, anyhow. Let him take a subway to work. And he would work! She'd see to that. She'd be boss now. Lester would work, too, or he couldn't come home. Absolutely. As for the others

—well, her mother would agree, dough-like, with the strongest—and the kids would welcome anything, even if they couldn't see that it would help them.

Annie nodded abstractedly to her mother when she came in. Her father was asleep in the red rocker, a big, awkward figure, his weak mouth slightly open, a three-days' growth of hair on his face. Maud was the only young person at home. Maud was thirteen now, and finishing grade school, a round-faced girl, pretty in a dull, usual sort of way, but with good features. Her mother still considered Maud a beauty.

Annie called to Maud:

"Come out in the kitchen while I get a drink."

Wondering, Maud followed her elder sister. She rather obeyed Annie.

Drinking from the kitchen tin cup, Annie said:

"Now, don't yell about this—not one word to anyone else, understand. You're the only one I'm going to tell."

"All right," nodded Maud, importantly, eager for a confidence.

"If you lived in a swell—I mean, well, a grand apartment uptown, which had a bathroom and a big living-room where you could have company and near the park and all, would you keep on going to school—to high school, I mean?"

"Say, who's going to leave the family a fortune?" asked Maud.

"Nobody. You answer me. Give me your word of honor you'll keep on going to school—clear through high school—and—and college, maybe?"

"Sure," said Maud. She'd just as soon go to school. She never made very good grades, but, anyhow, it certainly was better than working. Then:

"But say, what's that got to do with us? Thinking of moving? A swell chance this family has got for anything. What's it all about, anyhow?"

"Nothing," said Annie, "only you go in there—and not a word out of you—understand. Only you got something to think about."

VII

ANNIE WENT TO SLEEP that night with a wonderfully warm feeling of sacrifice. She was going to do a lot of things—for her little sister—for the rest of the family. Yet even, through all this she sensed something else. Of course it wasn't all for her little sister—not quite all—it was more than that —a desire for nice things, a few comforts—and under that—a desire to try her own skill—to sort of get into a battle.

She dreamed about apartments and new furniture—kept walking up steps that tumbled down as she walked on them and woke up with a horrible picture in her mind, of herself struggling with a man who had a knife in his hand. The picture would have frightened her even more if she hadn't remembered that she had seen that same picture in front of a show on

Fourteenth Street just a day before. Oh, well, hadn't she heard some place that dreams go by contraries or that they show your disposition or something?

She didn't tell her family she had quit working. She left, dressed in her new coat and hat, at her usual hour, but took a bus uptown. Annie was apartment hunting!

At ten, as a slow-moving janitor was showing her through a far. too elaborate eight-room apartment—might as well look at all kinds and get an idea of how other folks live—Annie glanced at her cheap wristwatch and laughed. At ten was the time Bruntage got to the office and looked over his mail. What a fool the man was, anyhow.

Annie found a six-room apartment three days later. It was in One Hundred and Twelfth Street and was convenient to the One Hundred and Tenth Street Subway station, the buses, Central Park and Columbia University. To city dwellers with exacting tastes, the apartment might not have been exactly without faults. Annie dared not consider anything more expensive.

Anyhow, it was quite a step from West Sixteenth Street. The long, rather dark hall might not have been the last word in apartment buildings, but there was a nice, though not extremely large, front living-room, with three windows, three bedrooms, with a court window to each of them, a bathroom with quite modern appointments, a square dining-room with a dome, a plate rail and two court windows, and a nice kitchen, complete with gas stove, ice-box and built-in cupboards. Annie examined it carefully, spoke about decorations, gave her father's business address, explained that he was "in the shipping business" and made a deposit.

A few days later she called at the apartment again, made final arrangements for decorating—as much ivory paint as the owner would allow and tan wall-paper throughout the house—she hadn't read magazines all these years without profiting by them. The renting agent was glad enough to get the apartment rented, it seemed. He had not inquired too closely into the references. Annie paid a month's rent in advance.

Well, that was done! She'd get the money somehow. She'd always worked, when it came to that—always expected to . . . probably. Lots of men had made advances—men always did that—what had she ever got out of it? She'd see.

A few pleasant, exciting days, now, of applying for positions in the morning—or writing letters of application—and furniture hunting in the afternoon. Life was fun these days!

A job then—at a better salary than she had ever had. Nothing doing there. She found that out in a few days. Such respectable people. Still, she had to have something—expenses went on—the apartment was nearly ready.

During her lunch hour, one day, she made final arrangements about the furniture. She bought it at a large time-payment house. An instalment would be due the first of every month. If there were more than two lapses in payment—she believed it was two—the furniture would be taken away. Fair enough! She gave her father's business address—he was working, temporarily, again—Ethel's employer's name and her own. She made a first payment on the furniture. There would be just enough of the two hundred dollars left for moving the small amount of wearing apparel, the few things her mother probably wouldn't part with.

She liked the furniture she picked out. There was a davenport, covered in a cotton tapestry, though the design wasn't half bad. This opened out into, the salesman assured her, "a full-sized bed." This was for Maud. You couldn't put three people into one of those tiny bedrooms! There was a wing chair to match it, and another chair covered in blue velour. After all, her father had to have some chair in which he could sprawl—relax after his day's work or his day's idleness. There were several smaller chairs, a stylish "library table," a small, open book-shelf, though, so far, the family owned no books, a plain tan rug. For the bedrooms there were inexpensive "sets," nearly alike, in grey, white and ivory enamel. For the dining-room there was a plain round oak table, a buffet, ten chairs—three extra for possible company. The Robinsons had never had company at mealtime. The kitchen needed no furniture save a plain table and a couple of chairs. Well, that was done.

The furniture was delivered on Saturday. Saturday was a half-holiday for Annie. She went to the apartment on the Subway, sitting in a nervous tension the whole way. She reached the apartment before the furniture did. The floors had been varnished. The smell of paint was clean. The empty rooms were fresh with the cheap tan paper. Annie had a pleasant, electric feeling of adventure. What would the family say? How had she dared?

The men came with the furniture. There was much untying of string, setting of bedroom mirrors in the dressing-table frames. The furniture was in place! The papers were pushed onto the dumbwaiters. The apartment was finished!

To Annie it looked perfect. Cheap, perhaps. What of it? There was a floor lamp, with a yellow silk shade. There were bright rag rugs for each room. How well the tapestry pieces looked and the big blue chair! Empty —well, perhaps. Still, when the family got in, put a scarf on the table, get a Victrola, maybe, later, and a few books and magazines. Gee, what would the family say?

Annie had arranged for gas and electricity and—yes—a telephone. She could hardly believe her own daring. She didn't know anyone to telephone to, excepting a few girls who had worked where she had. What of that? She'd meet people. It would be nice for Maud and Ethel, too. It's awfully hard for girls to get invitations to things if they haven't a telephone.

She closed the apartment, opened it again with her own key, to see if it were really there, took a bus home. A cheap apartment—what could it mean to all of these people in cars, who passed, smug in expensive clothes.

What did they know—of—anything, those fat-faced women who never earned a cent in their lives, with their sleek husbands next to them.

She looked hate at them, as she had when she was a little girl. She'd—no —she couldn't show them—it wasn't that . . . exactly . . . she'd get things . . . her way—something, anyhow.

VIII

ANNIE WAS TREMBLING when she got home. She took off her coat, hung it carefully on a hanger in the crowded closet—she and Ethel would have a closet all of their own now. . . .

She went into the kitchen, began, mechanically, to set the table.

"Time you're getting home," her mother growled at her. "Saturday afternoon, and you and Ethel walk the streets all day . . . a lot of help you are to me. . . ."

She didn't answer. She peeled potatoes.

All of the family were home except Lester. She waited until they had finished the thin fried steak and the watery potatoes. She started, mechanically, to eat the canned peaches. Then:

"We—we move tomorrow," she said.

"What do you mean . . . ? What are you talking about?"

Annie felt triumphant, a bit dizzy. She went on:

"I don't want one word out of anyone here. I'm tired of—this dirt and— and everything. Sixteenth Street—it isn't good for Maud—or Ethel, either. I've got a place all picked out—"

"You've got a place picked out," her mother said, "you—"

"Yes, I have," said Annie. "I got the furniture, too. Everything. It's ready this minute. The family can come with me or not, as you want to. I'm going. Not one cent of mine goes into this house again. You keep that place up nice or I'm gone. I bring in the money and I'm boss. I spoke to Thompson —on the corner—he's coming for the things. You can get boxes from the grocer in the morning. Thompson will give you a price on things. I'm—I'm boss in this family."

There were squeaks, groans, curses. Annie felt as if she were living in a sort of dream. She loved it. It was the first big dramatic moment she had ever had. And to think—she had been able to create this—this scene—out of her own mind! Anything was possible!

Mrs. Robinson, Ethel and Maud were finally moved to inspect the apartment at once. Annie went with them. They got into their coats and made the trip on the Subway. Annie never found out what they thought of it —they were too incoherent for that. At least they were going to move!

At twelve that night, Hal Robinson was swearing and saying things about "an ungrateful daughter—after all the years I've spent working for this family. . . ." At one, the next day—there were so few things to move it might as well be done right away, if it was Sunday—Robinson was bawling out orders to Thompson and talking about "his new apartment" and what he was "getting ready to do, moving uptown." Annie was boss, though. The family recognized that. If her mother wailed a bit about "girls who don't confide in their mothers" and "girls who go wrong, these days," her wails were tempered a bit and became almost a gentle accompaniment to living. After all—it was rather nice, having a six-room apartment uptown . . . easier to keep clean, too, though Annie did seem to be getting an awful crank about wanting things too particular.

Annie left the new job after three months of it. Outside of borrowing one hundred dollars for an operation for her mother—she was to pay it back three dollars at a time until the sympathetic boss told her "not to mind" after the fifth pitiful payment—Annie's relations with the firm were quite businesslike. They were only too glad to give her excellent recommendations when she found a more remunerative position.

It was at Rutgers & Olds, Advertising, that Annie got it. It was a good position, secretary to Rutgers, the president, a bluff old man, though with rather a good reputation. He liked to drink a bit, but then, didn't most men of his age? He was nearly sixty, with heavy white hair and a white mustache of which he was perhaps unnecessarily proud. Mrs. Rutgers was an invalid who traveled rather constantly. Rutgers accompanied her frequently—that is, he was always able to get away for a six weeks' winter vacation at Palm Beach or Lake Placid, a two months' European trip in the summer. He seemed fairly content, so far as his friends could tell, with both his domestic and business arrangements.

The office force at Rutgers & Olds knew that Annie came in answer to an advertisement. She came in quiet, mouse-like, unobtrusive. A slender little thing, with mild grey eyes and a nice mouth, a pale little thing with a low, gentle voice. Certainly no one to make a fuss about. You could tell why the old man picked her out from among the dozens who applied for the position. She was just the sort of a private secretary a man would pick out if he wanted his work done well and quietly, without any nonsense.

It was at Rutgers & Olds that she got her nickname. It was quite probable that she knew of it right away. She learned soon enough, and, for some reason, didn't seem to resent it. It is certain that she never altered her manner nor her mode of dressing.

It was Quigley, one of the usual and always present smart alecks, who named her.

"What's the new stenog's name?" he asked, elegantly.

"Robinson—Annie Robinson, I believe," someone told him.

"I thought so—Annie . . . as I live, 'Little Orphant Annie' to the life. To think that Orphant Annie's come to our office to play! Ain't she grand?"

The office force all rather resented Quigley. We—for it was there that I first met Orphant Annie—took up for her. A nice little thing—did her work well—quiet and shy. Well, what of it—better than the usual office vamp who hung around trying to start something. Orphant Annie never tried anything with the office force, that hard-working, small-salaried contingent which did all of the work except the "conferences."

"Orphant Annie isn't an orphan at all," Miss Drucker, Olds' secretary, reported, a few weeks later. "She's got a lot of parents—two of them—and she lives up near Columbia and studies nights"—we somehow felt that she did—"and her father's awfully ill and about to have an operation."

No one knew how Miss Drucker found out about the operation. It came to several hundred dollars, it seemed. Rutgers lent her the money.

It was the furniture, next, I believe. Everyone felt sorry about that. It leaked out as such things usually do. Little Orphant Annie—who would have been better off, doubtless, if she had been an orphan, but who was supporting invalid parents, instead, was buying furniture on the instalment plan. She had paid the first instalment and perhaps even the second one. Then illness had come to the household—the illness that had necessitated the operation on her father. Now the furniture was threatened—every piece was to be taken away. Rutgers wasn't in town—Palm Beach, I believe. I think we were all ready to add our names to a subscription when someone —perhaps Olds—came to the rescue. Anyhow, the furniture was not removed. Orphant Annie, smaller and more mouse-like than ever, continued at the office. She had Rutgers' private room, all alone, now, and seated at his enormous desk, took care of all of his private correspondence while he was away.

A little thing, then—a rumor—scarcely that—concerning a certain Jacobson, one of the firm's clients—yes, the collar man—and our little Orphant Annie. Jacobson had a way of breezing in—which meant a "conference," when Rutgers or Olds was about. Now, he would go into Rutgers' office and have a chat with Orphant Annie—business, of course. If it had been anyone else except Orphant Annie, with her pale face and candid eyes, everyone in the office would have gossiped—that Miss Flint, now, who used too much rouge—or the young and quite too flip Bailey girl. Orphant Annie! We all felt that someone ought to warn Annie—Jacobson's reputation—all that. She seemed too young and untouched. No one had the indelicacy to say anything.

Someone saw them together at luncheon—it could have been a business luncheon, of course. Another time, one of the less important and perhaps quite jealous stenographers was sure she saw the two of them pass her, Saturday afternoon, in Jacobson's limousine. That was about all—excepting Jacobson's reputation and the fact that he was married.

The book-keeper, a quiet, rather lanky and certainly slow and stupid chap named Western, rather fell in love with Orphant Annie. We could see him, mooning around after her. We were a trifle surprised because she didn't encourage him more—after all, he was a nice boy—only a book-keeper and not apt to go higher, but young and pleasant . . . after all, Orphant Annie was only a stenographer, herself. He quite forced his attentions on her—little things—flowers and candy and a book, occasionally. Finally, he confessed to someone that Annie had allowed him to give her a ring—not a large diamond, you know—they really weren't engaged—but, if she had the diamond he felt that she'd be prejudiced a bit in his favor. He'd been out to call, too, awfully nice, their apartment—he'd met the mother and a younger sister or two.

IX

WE ALL FELT SORRY when Orphant Annie left Rutgers & Olds. In a way, in spite of her quiet, mouse-like personality, she had added interest to the place. Rutgers had got back by that time and he and Olds were sorry, too. We heard that they even called off the small debts she owed them—she'd been paying a couple of dollars at a time. Western took it hardest of all. He knew a lot of inside stuff, it seemed, though gradually a little of it leaked out to the rest of us. Jacobson was at the bottom of it. If we had only warned her! We were all sorry enough. We hadn't wanted to worry her. So, Jacobson, dog that he was, had led her on, tempted her with a promise of—well, of things a girl like Annie doesn't have. We remembered things she had said, little things, "I've never had anything pretty all of my life"—things like that. A sick father and a mother who wasn't strong! Worked since she was fourteen! Going to school at night! Little and quiet and grey-eyed! And Jacobson had tempted her!

She had nearly yielded to him, it seemed. Western didn't blame her for that any more than the rest of us did. Poor little Orphant Annie. Jacobson had given her presents—had planned a trip—the trip was to Paris—we heard even that—had bought her things preparatory to sailing—had helped her when her father needed a second operation. Then . . . well, she couldn't go on. . . .

We never knew how Western found out about it all—even about the note Annie had written.

"He won't forget that in a hurry," Western told us. "She was noble, that little girl. Only outside, in a most superficial way, was she tempted at all. You can see how that was. The things she said in her letter—how she couldn't go through with it. At the last minute she saw it wasn't right—told him so. She—she don't care for me—but she said she'd keep my ring—and if she ever did care . . ."

It is so easy to lose track of a mere office acquaintance in New York. I lost track of Orphant Annie for over a year, then. Then, it happened that a friend of mine, a Miss Dorset, was employed by the firm of Bingham & Sons, Brokers. Calling for her, one afternoon, I saw Orphant Annie—nice little Annie—in a big office . . . clad in a neat little frock, her smooth hair as tidy and her eyes as candid as ever. Somehow, Annie and I got to talking, a talk that was continued over a dozen teacups and Annie told me, in a most fragmentary way, the things that I have put down here . . . other things, too. Rutgers, for instance—sly old Rutgers with the white hair and white whiskers—to think that he. . . .

Miss Dorset told me, at the time, that Annie was well liked at Bingham & Sons. No—she didn't know anything about her history—hadn't heard that she was called Orphant Annie, even. I didn't tell Miss Dorset more than that. To be truthful, she didn't ask me. She was all sympathy for Annie, all full of little tales about her. Annie's oldest brother—his name was Lester, it seemed—had got into trouble over money—hadn't quite understood about it—and was threatened with arrest—a jail sentence, even. Annie had come to Mr. Bingham, the youngest Mr. Bingham, about it, and of course he had loaned Annie the money—he had an awfully good heart. Annie had started to pay the money back, a little at a time, every week—it was just pitiful the way she tried—but Miss Dorset had heard that Bingham was just going to call the debt settled. After all, a poor little thing like Miss Robinson—did I know that her mother was an invalid?

I didn't keep up with Orphant Annie, I wish, now, that I had had more time for her. She was—and is—worth cultivating, I'm sure. A year after I talked with her at Bingham & Sons, her name came up, at a business luncheon one day. A man was telling a story.

"It served the fellow right," he was saying. "Men try to get away with too much in business. If the girl had been the usual office vamp, I'd have thought it was blackmail and might even have sympathized with the fellow, but in this case the conditions were exactly the opposite. You could tell by the way the girl acted. At that, she escaped just in time—probably always will carry the memory of the thing—the nicest sort of a girl—modest—lives at home with her folks—her mother is ailing—some sort of an incurable disease. . . . Well, I'm glad she got some money out of the fellow—under the circumstances. . . ."

What was the girl's name? I wanted to know.

Ordinarily, he couldn't have told me, of course, but as long as she was so absolutely innocent, absolutely without blame—everyone who knew the details was in absolute sympathy with her—Robinson or Robertson the name was . . . girl's first name was Annie—oh, a nice, decent little thing. Did I know her?

The name sounded familiar. I admitted that. Yes—an ordinary enough name, to be sure.

The other bits that have come to me about Annie have fitted in, as such things always fit in, as we always meet just the one old friend we think we never will see again—just as we always come across old acquaintances and old names—forming more complete pictures than we had ever thought it possible to form, when we were young.

Recently, at a dinner, a woman said, "I want you to meet someone you used to know," and there was a stranger who turned out to be a former certain little Rose Smith, whom I'd gone to school with—second grade public school, St. Louis, when I was seven. Last week I had a picture post-card from India with the signature of an Irish lad I'd known fifteen years ago—he'd been a Russian dancer in vaudeville, then.

So there is nothing odd, then, in the fact that yesterday, I should have seen Orphant Annie. I shall see her again, I hope, through the years. Per-haps, too, when I do not see her I shall hear little things, like the things I have heard that complete, in a way, the picture of her that I carry with me . . . . the story of Hanson, the builder, who fell in love with her and wanted to divorce his wife—the story of Dewit, who fell at her feet and apologized —and was overheard—because he had misjudged her . . . Pinnet, who sent Annie's little sister through college.

A house in the country—Lester and Ethel married—Frank well estab-lished in business—little Maud grown up and graduated from college. I al-most shed a tear over Orphant Annie—a sentimental tear for her goodness and her gentleness—a shy little thing in quiet clothes, a dear little thing with big grey eyes and a pale eager little face. Then I thought of Hilden and the money he lent her for that always-necessary family operation, of Lewis and the letter his wife received by mistake.

But, after all, Orphant Annie doesn't need any sort of a tear, I'm sure. She did what she could, in her way.

"I wouldn't have made things the way they are," she told me, one day, "I just tried to get something out of the world, the best way I can."

I see her, jogging along up Fifth Avenue, on top of a bus, looking into windows to see how "nice folks" live, hating folks that had things without even wishing for them, wondering about things. How many of us . . . well . . . who are we to say? . . .

NUNS AT LUNCHEON

Aldous Huxley

(1894–   )

"WHAT HAVE I BEEN DOING since you saw me last?" Miss Penny repeated my question in her loud, emphatic voice. "Well, when did you see me last?"

"It must have been June," I computed.

"Was that after I'd been proposed to by the Russian General?"

"Yes; I remember hearing about the Russian General."

Miss Penny threw back her head and laughed. Her long ear-rings swung and rattled—corpses hanging in chains: an agreeably literary simile. And her laughter was like brass, but that had been said before.

"That was an uproarious incident. It's sad you should have heard of it. I love my Russian General story. '*Vos yeux me rendent fou.*'" She laughed again.

Vos yeux—she had eyes like a hare's, flush with her head and very bright with a superficial and expressionless brightness. What a formidable woman. I felt sorry for the Russian General.

"'*Sans cœur et sans entrailles,*'" she went on quoting the poor devil's words. "Such a delightful motto, don't you think? Like '*Sans peur et sans reproche.*' But let me think; what have I been doing since then?" Thoughtfully she bit into the crust of her bread with long, sharp, white teeth.

"Two mixed grills," I said parenthetically to the waiter.

"But of course," exclaimed Miss Penny suddenly. "I haven't seen you since my German trip. All sorts of adventures. My appendicitis; my nun."

"Your nun?"

"My marvellous nun. I must tell you all about her."

"Do." Miss Penny's anecdotes were always curious. I looked forward to an entertaining luncheon.

"You knew I'd been in Germany this autumn?"

"Well, I didn't, as a matter of fact. But still——"

"I was just wandering round." Miss Penny described a circle in the air with her gaudily jewelled hand. She always twinkled with massive and improbable jewellery. "Wandering round, living on three pounds a week, partly amusing myself, partly collecting material for a few little articles. 'What it Feels Like to be a Conquered Nation'—sob-stuff for the Liberal press, you know—and 'How the Hun is Trying to Wriggle out of the Indemnity,' for the other fellows. One has to make the best of all possible worlds, don't you find? But we mustn't talk shop. Well, I was wandering round, and very pleasant I found it. Berlin, Dresden, Leipzig. Then down to Munich and all over the place. One fine day I got to Grauburg. You know Grauburg? It's one of those picture-book German towns with a castle on a hill, hanging beer-gardens, a Gothic church, an old university, a river, a pretty bridge, and forests all round. Charming. But I hadn't much opportunity to appreciate the beauties of the place. The day after I arrived there —bang!—I went down with appendicitis—screaming, I may add."

"But how appalling!"

"They whisked me off to hospital, and cut me open before you could say knife. Excellent surgeon, highly efficient Sisters of Charity to nurse me—I couldn't have been in better hands. But it was a bore being tied there by the leg for four weeks—a great bore. Still, the thing had its compensations. There was my nun, for example. Ah, here's the food, thank Heaven!"

The mixed grill proved to be excellent. Miss Penny's description of the nun came to me in scraps and snatches. A round, pink, pretty face in a winged coif; blue eyes and regular features; teeth altogether too perfect —false, in fact; but the general effect extremely pleasing. A youthful Teutonic twenty-eight.

"She wasn't my nurse," Miss Penny explained. "But I used to see her quite often when she came in to have a look at the *tolle Engländerin*. Her name was Sister Agatha. During the war, they told me, she had converted any number of wounded soldiers to the true faith—which wasn't surprising, considering how pretty she was."

"Did she try and convert you?" I asked.

"She wasn't such a fool." Miss Penny laughed, and rattled the miniature gallows of her ears.

I amused myself for a moment with the thought of Miss Penny's conversion—Miss Penny confronting a vast assembly of Fathers of the Church, rattling her earrings at their discourses on the Trinity, laughing her appalling laugh at the doctrine of the Immaculate Conception, meeting the stern look of the Grand Inquisitor with a flash of her bright, emotionless hare's eyes. What was the secret of the woman's formidableness?

But I was missing the story. What had happened? Ah yes, the gist of it was that Sister Agatha had appeared one morning, after two or three days' absence, dressed, not as a nun, but in the overalls of a hospital charwoman, with a handkerchief instead of a winged coif on her shaven head.

"Dead," said Miss Penny; "she looked as though she were dead. A walking corpse, that's what she was. It was a shocking sight. I shouldn't have thought it possible for anyone to change so much in so short a time. She walked painfully, as though she had been ill for months, and she had great burnt rings round her eyes and deep lines in her face. And the general expression of unhappiness—that was something quite appalling."

She leaned out into the gangway between the two rows of tables, and caught the passing waiter by the end of one of his coat-tails. The little Italian looked round with an expression of surprise that deepened into terror on his face.

"Half a pint of Guinness," ordered Miss Penny. "And, after this, bring me some jam roll."

"No jam roll to-day, madam."

"Damn!" said Miss Penny. "Bring me what you like, then."

She let go of the waiter's tail and resumed her narrative.

"Where was I? Yes, I remember. She came into my room, I was telling you, with a bucket of water and a brush, dressed like a charwoman. Naturally I was rather surprised. 'What on earth are you doing, Sister Agatha?' I asked. No answer. She just shook her head, and began to scrub the floor. When she'd finished, she left the room without so much as looking at me again. 'What's happened to Sister Agatha?' I asked my nurse when she next came in. 'Can't say.'—'Won't say,' I said. No answer. It took nearly a week to find out what really had happened. Nobody dared tell me; it was *strengst verboten,* as they used to say in the good old days. But I wormed it out in the long run. My nurse, the doctor, the charwomen—I got something out of all of them. I always get what I want in the end." Miss Penny laughed like a horse.

"I'm sure you do," I said politely.

"Much obliged," acknowledged Miss Penny. "But to proceed. My information came to me in fragmentary whispers. 'Sister Agatha ran away with a man.'—Dear me!—'One of the patients.'—You don't say so.—'A criminal out of the jail.'—The plot thickens.—'He ran away from her.'—It seems to grow thinner again.—'They brought her back here; she's been disgraced. There's been a funeral service for her in the chapel—coffin and all. She had to be present at it—her own funeral. She isn't a nun any more. She has to do charwoman's work now, the roughest in the hospital. She's not allowed to speak to anybody, and nobody's allowed to speak to her. She's regarded as dead.'" Miss Penny paused to signal to the harassed little Italian. "My small 'Guinness,'" she called out.

"Coming, coming," and the foreign voice cried "Guinness" down the lift, and from below another voice echoed, "Guinness."

"I filled in the details bit by bit. There was our hero, to begin with; I had to bring him into the picture, which was rather difficult, as I had never seen him. But I got a photograph of him. The police circulated one when he got away; I don't suppose they ever caught him." Miss Penny opened her bag. "Here it is," she said. "I always carry it about with me; it's become a superstition. For years, I remember, I used to carry a little bit of heather tied up with string. Beautiful, isn't it? There's a sort of Renaissance look about it, don't you think? He was half-Italian, you know."

Italian. Ah, that explained it. I had been wondering how Bavaria could have produced this thin-faced creature with the big dark eyes, the finely modelled nose and chin, and the fleshy lips so royally and sensually curved.

"He's certainly very superb," I said, handing back the picture.

Miss Penny put it carefully away in her bag. "Isn't he?" she said. "Quite marvellous. But his character and his mind were even better. I see him as one of those innocent, childlike monsters of iniquity who are simply unaware of the existence of right and wrong. And he had genius—the real Italian genius for engineering, for dominating and exploiting nature. A true son of the Roman aqueduct builders he was, and a brother of the electrical engineers. Only Kuno—that was his name—didn't work in water; he worked in women. He knew how to harness the natural energy of passion; he made devotion drive his mills. The commercial exploitation of love-power, that was his specialty. I sometimes wonder," Miss Penny added in a different tone, "whether I shall ever be exploited, when I get a little more middle-aged and celibate, by one of these young engineers of the passions. It would be humiliating, particularly as I've done so little exploiting from my side."

She frowned and was silent for a moment. No, decidedly, Miss Penny was not beautiful; you could not even honestly say that she had charm or was attractive. That high Scotch colouring, those hare's eyes, the voice, the terrifying laugh, and the size of her, the general formidableness of the woman. No, no, no.

"You said he had been in prison," I said. The silence, with all its implications, was becoming embarrassing.

Miss Penny sighed, looked up, and nodded. "He was fool enough," she said, "to leave the straight and certain road of female exploitation for the dangerous courses of burglary. We all have our occasional accesses of folly. They gave him a heavy sentence, but he succeeded in getting pneumonia, I think it was, a week after entering jail. He was transferred to the hospital. Sister Agatha, with her known talent for saving souls, was given him as his particular attendant. But it was he, I'm afraid, who did the converting."

Miss Penny finished off the last mouthful of the ginger pudding which the waiter had brought in lieu of jam roll.

"I suppose you don't smoke cheroots," I said, as I opened my cigar-case.

"Well, as a matter of fact, I do," Miss Penny replied. She looked sharply round the restaurant. "I must just see if there are any of those horrible little gossip paragraphers here to-day. One doesn't want to figure in the social and personal column to-morrow morning: 'A fact which is not so generally known as it ought to be is, that Miss Penny, the well-known woman journalist, always ends her luncheon with a six-inch Burma cheroot. I saw her yesterday in a restaurant—not a hundred miles from Carmelite Street—smoking like a house on fire.' You know the touch. But the coast seems to be clear, thank goodness."

She took a cheroot from the case, lit it at my proffered match, and went on talking.

"Yes, it was young Kuno who did the converting. Sister Agatha was converted back into the worldly Melpomene Fugger she had been before she became the bride of holiness."

"Melpomene Fugger?"

"That was her name. I had her history from my old doctor. He had seen all Grauburg, living and dying and propagating, for generations. Melpomene Fugger—why, he had brought little Melpel into the world, little Melpchen. Her father was Professor Fugger, the great Professor Fugger, the *berümter Geolog*. Oh, yes, of course, I know the name. So well . . . He was the man who wrote the standard work on Lemuria—you know, the hypothetical continent where the lemurs come from. I showed due respect. Liberal-minded he was, a disciple of Herder, a world-burgher, as they beautifully call it over there. Anglophile, too, and always ate porridge for breakfast—up till August 1914. Then, on the radiant morning of the fifth, he renounced it for ever, solemnly and with tears in his eyes. The national food of a people who had betrayed culture and civilisation—how could he go on eating it? It would stick in his throat. In future he would have a lightly boiled egg. He sounded, I thought, altogether charming. And his daughter, Melpomene—she sounded charming, too; and such thick, yellow pigtails when she was young! Her mother was dead, and a sister of the great Professor's ruled the house with an iron rod. Aunt Bertha was her name. Well, Melpomene grew up, very plump and appetising. When she was seventeen, something very odious and disagreeable happened to her. Even the doctor didn't know exactly what it was; but he wouldn't have been surprised if it had had something to do with the then professor of Latin, an old friend of the family's, who combined, it seems, great erudition with a horrid fondness for very young ladies."

Miss Penny knocked half an inch of cigar ash into her empty glass.

"If I wrote short stories," she went on reflectively "(but it's too much bother), I should make this anecdote into a sort of potted life history, beginning with a scene immediately after this disagreeable event in Melpomene's life. I see the scene so clearly. Poor little Melpel is leaning over the bastions of Grauburg Castle, weeping into the June night and the mulberry trees in the garden thirty feet below. She is besieged by the memory of what happened this dreadful afternoon. Professor Engelmann, her father's old friend, with the magnificent red Assyrian beard . . . Too awful—too awful! But then, as I was saying, short stories are really too much bother; or perhaps I'm too stupid to write them. I bequeath it to you. You know how to tick these things off."

"You're generous."

"Not at all," said Miss Penny. "My terms are ten per cent commission on the American sale. Incidentally there won't be an American sale. Poor Melpchen's history is not for the chaste public of Those States. But let me hear what you propose to do with Melpomene now you've got her on the castle bastions."

"That's simple," I said. "I know all about German university towns and castles on hills. I shall make her look into the June night, as you suggest; into the violet night with its points of golden flame. There will be the black silhouette of the castle, with its sharp roofs and hooded turrets, behind her. From the hanging beer-gardens in the town below the voices of the students, singing in perfect four-part harmony, will float up through the dark-blue spaces. *'Röslein, Röslein, Röslein rot'* and *'Das Ringlein sprang in zwei'*— the heart-rendingly sweet old songs will make her cry all the more. Her tears will patter like rain among the leaves of the mulberry trees in the garden below. Does that seem to you adequate?"

"Very nice," said Miss Penny. "But how are you going to bring the sex problem and all its horrors into your landscape?"

"Well, let me think." I called to memory those distant foreign summers

when I was completing my education. "I know I shall suddenly bring
a swarm of moving candles and Chinese lanterns under the mulberry trees.
You imagine the rich lights and shadows, the jewel-bright leafage, the faces
and moving limbs of men and women, seen for an instant and gone again.
They are students and girls of the town come out to dance, this windless,
blue June night, under the mulberry trees. And now they begin, thumping
round and round in a ring, to the music of their own singing:

> "Wir können spielen
> Vio-vio-vio-lin,
> Wir können spielen
> Vi-o-lin.

Now the rhythm changes, quickens:

> "Und wir können tanzen Bumstarara,
> Bumstarara, Bumstarara,
> Und wir können tanzen Bumstarara,
> Bumstarara-rara.

The dance becomes a rush, an elephantine prancing on the dry lawn under
the mulberry trees. And from the bastion Melpomene looks down and
perceives, suddenly and apocalyptically, that everything in the world is sex,
sex, sex. Men and women, male and female—always the same, and all, in the
light of the horror of the afternoon, disgusting. That's how I should do it,
Miss Penny."

"And very nice, too. But I wish you could find a place to bring in my
conversation with the doctor. I shall never forget the way he cleared his
throat, and coughed before embarking on the delicate subject. 'You may
know, ahem, gracious Miss,' he began—'you may know that religious
phenomena are often, ahem, closely connected with sexual causes.' I replied
that I had heard rumours which might justify me in believing this to be
true among Roman Catholics, but that in the Church of England—and I
for one was a practitioner of Anglicanismus—it was very different. That
might be, said the doctor; he had had no opportunity in the course of his
long medical career of personally studying Anglicanismus. But he could
vouch for the fact that among his patients, here in Grauburg, mysticismus
was very often mixed up with the *Geschlechtsleben*. Melpomene was a case
in point. After that hateful afternoon she had become extremely religious;
the Professor of Latin had diverted her emotions out of their normal
channels. She rebelled against the placid Agnosticismus of her father, and
at night, in secret, when Aunt Bertha's dragon eyes were closed, she would
read such forbidden books as *The Life of St. Theresa, The Little Flowers of
St. Francis, The Imitation of Christ,* and the horribly enthralling *Book of
Martyrs*. Aunt Bertha confiscated these works whenever she came upon
them; she considered them more pernicious than the novels of Marcel
Prévost. The character of a good potential housewife might be completely

undermined by reading of this kind. It was rather a relief for Melpomene when Aunt Bertha shuffled off, in the summer of 1911, this mortal coil. She was one of those indispensables of whom one makes the discovery, when they are gone, that one can get on quite as well without them. Poor Aunt Bertha!"

"One can imagine Melpomene trying to believe she was sorry, and horribly ashamed to find that she was really, in secret, almost glad." The suggestion seemed to me ingenious, but Miss Penny accepted it as obvious.

"Precisely," she said; "and the emotion would only further confirm and give new force to the tendencies which her aunt's death left her free to indulge as much as she liked. Remorse, contrition—they would lead to the idea of doing penance. And for one who was now wallowing in the martyrology, penance was the mortification of the flesh. She used to kneel for hours, at night, in the cold; she ate too little, and when her teeth ached, which they often did,—for she had a set, the doctor told me, which had given trouble from the very first,—she would not go and see the dentist, but lay awake at night, savouring to the full her excruciations, and feeling triumphantly that they must, in some strange way, be pleasing to the Mysterious Powers. She went on like that for two or three years, till she was poisoned through and through. In the end she went down with gastric ulcer. It was three months before she came out of hospital, well for the first time in a long space of years, and with a brand new set of imperishable teeth, all gold and ivory. And in mind, too, she was changed—for the better, I suppose. The nuns who nursed her had made her see that in mortifying herself she had acted supererogatively and through spiritual pride; instead of doing right, she had sinned. The only road to salvation, they told her, lay in discipline, in the orderliness of established religion, in obedience to authority. Secretly, so as not to distress her poor father, whose Agnosticismus was extremely dogmatic, for all its unobtrusiveness, Melpomene became a Roman Catholic. She was twenty-two. Only a few months later came the war and Professor Fugger's eternal renunciation of porridge. He did not long survive the making of that patriotic gesture. In the autumn of 1914 he caught a fatal influenza. Melpomene was alone in the world. In the spring of 1915 there was a new and very conscientious Sister of Charity at work among the wounded in the hospital of Grauburg. Here," explained Miss Penny, jabbing the air with her forefinger, "you put a line of asterisks or dots to signify a six years' gulf in the narrative. And you begin again right in the middle of a dialogue between Sister Agatha and the newly convalescent Kuno."

"What's their dialogue to be about?" I asked.

"Oh, that's easy enough," said Miss Penny. "Almost anything would do. What about this, for example? You explain that the fever has just abated; for the first time for days the young man is fully conscious. He feels himself to be well, reborn, as it were, in a new world—a world so bright and novel and jolly that he can't help laughing at the sight of it. He looks about him; the flies on the ceiling strike him as being extremely comic. How do they manage to walk upside down? They have suckers on their feet, says Sister Agatha, and wonders if her natural history is quite sound. Suckers on their feet—ha, ha! What an uproarious notion! Suckers on their feet—that's good, that's damned good! You can say charming, pathetic, positively tender things about the irrelevant mirth of convalescents—the more so in this particular case, where the mirth is expressed by a young man who is to be taken back to jail as soon as he can stand firmly on his legs. Ha, ha! Laugh on, unhappy boy! It is the quacking of the Fates, the Parcæ, the Norns!"

Miss Penny gave an exaggerated imitation of her own brassy laughter. At the sound of it the few lunchers who still lingered at the other tables looked up, startled.

"You can write pages about Destiny and its ironic quacking. It's tremendously impressive, and there's money in every line."

"You may be sure I shall."

"Good! Then I can get on with my story. The days pass and the first hilarity of convalescence fades away. The young man remembers and grows sullen; his strength comes back to him, and with it a sense of despair. His mind broods incessantly on the hateful future. As for the consolations of religion, he won't listen to them. Sister Agatha perseveres—oh, with what anxious solicitude!—in the attempt to make him understand and believe and be comforted. It is all so tremendously important, and in this case, somehow, more important than in any other. And now you see the *Geschlechtsleben* working yeastily and obscurely, and once again the quacking of the Norns is audible. By the way," said Miss Penny, changing her tone and leaning confidentially across the table, "I wish you'd tell me something. Tell me, do you really—honestly, I mean—do you seriously believe in literature?"

"Believe in literature?"

"I was thinking," Miss Penny explained, "of Ironic Fate and the quacking of the Norns and all that."

"'M yes."

"And then there's this psychology and introspection business; and construction and good narrative and word pictures and *le mot juste* and verbal magic and striking metaphors."

I remembered that I had compared Miss Penny's tinkling ear-rings to skeletons hanging in chains.

"And then, finally, and to begin with—Alpha and Omega—there's ourselves: two professionals gloating, with an absolute lack of sympathy, over a seduced nun, and speculating on the best method of turning her misfortunes into cash. It's all very curious, isn't it?—when one begins to think about it dispassionately."

"Very curious," I agreed. "But, then, so is everything else if you look at it like that."

"No, no," said Miss Penny. "Nothing's so curious as our business. But I shall never get to the end of my story if I get started on first principles."

Miss Penny continued her narrative. I was still thinking of literature. Do you believe in it? Seriously? Ah! Luckily the question was quite meaningless. The story came to me rather vaguely, but it seemed that the young man was getting better; in a few more days, the doctor had said, he would be well—well enough to go back to jail. No, no. The question was meaningless. I would think about it no more. I concentrated my attention again.

"Sister Agatha," I heard Miss Penny saying, "prayed, exhorted, indoctrinated. Whenever she had half a minute to spare from her other duties she would come running into the young man's room. 'I wonder if you fully realise the importance of prayer?' she would ask, and, before he had time to answer, she would give him a breathless account of the uses and virtues of regular and patient supplication. Or else, it was: 'May I tell you about St. Theresa?' or 'St. Stephen, the first martyr—you know about him, don't you?' Kuno simply wouldn't listen at first. It seemed so fantastically irrelevant, such an absurd interruption to his thoughts, his serious, despairing thoughts about the future. Prison was real, imminent and this woman buzzed about him with her ridiculous fairy-tales. Then, suddenly, one day he began to listen, he showed signs of contrition and conversion. Sister Agatha announced her triumph to the other nuns, and there was rejoicing over the one lost sheep. Melpomene had never felt so happy in her life, and Kuno, looking at her radiant face, must have wondered how he could have been such a fool as not to see from the first what was now so obvious. The woman had lost her head about him. And he had only four days now —four days in which to tap the tumultuous love power, to canalise it, to set it working for his escape. Why hadn't he started a week ago? He could have made certain of it then. But now? There was no knowing. Four days was a horribly short time."

"How did he do it?" I asked, for Miss Penny had paused.

"That's for you to say," she replied, and shook her ear-rings at me. "I don't know. Nobody knows, I imagine, except the two parties concerned and perhaps Sister Agatha's confessor. But one can reconstruct the crime, as they say. How would you have done it? You're a man, you ought to be familiar with the processes of amorous engineering."

"You flatter me," I answered. "Do you seriously suppose——" I extended my arms. Miss Penny laughed like a horse. "No. But, seriously, it's a problem. The case is a very special one. The person, a nun; the place, a hospital; the opportunities, few. There could be no favourable circumstances— no moonlight, no distant music; and any form of direct attack would be sure to fail. That audacious confidence which is your amorist's best weapon would be useless here."

"Obviously," said Miss Penny. "But there are surely other methods. There is the approach through pity and the maternal instincts. And there's the approach through Higher Things, through the soul. Kuno must have worked on those lines, don't you think? One can imagine him letting himself be converted, praying with her, and at the same time appealing for her sympathy and even threatening—with a great air of seriousness—to kill himself rather than go back to jail. You can write that up easily and convincingly enough. But it's the sort of thing that bores me so frightfully to do. That's why I can never bring myself to write fiction. What is the point of it all? And the way you literary men think yourselves so important—particularly if you write tragedies. It's all very queer, very queer indeed."

I made no comment. Miss Penny changed her tone and went on with the narrative.

"Well," she said, "whatever the means employed, the engineering process was perfectly successful. Love was made to find out a way. On the afternoon before Kuno was to go back to prison, two Sisters of Charity walked out of the hospital gates, crossed the square in front of it, glided down the narrow streets towards the river, boarded a tram at the bridge, and did not descend till the car had reached its terminus in the farther suburbs. They began to walk briskly along the high road out into the country. 'Look!' said one of them, when they were clear of the houses; and with the gesture of a conjurer produced from nowhere a red leather purse. 'Where did it come from?' asked the other, opening her eyes. Memories of Elisha and the ravens, of the widow's cruse, of the loaves and fishes, must have floated through the radiant fog in poor Melpomene's mind. 'The old lady I was sitting next to in the tram left her bag open. Nothing could have been simpler.' 'Kuno! You don't mean to say you stole it?' Kuno swore horribly. He had opened the purse. 'Only sixty marks. Who'd have thought that an old camel, all dressed up in silk and furs, would only have sixty marks in her purse. And I must have a thousand at least to get away.' It's easy to reconstruct the rest of the conversation down to the inevitable, 'For God's sake, shut up,' with which Kuno put an end to Melpomene's dismayed moralising. They trudge on in silence. Kuno thinks desperately. Only sixty marks; he can do nothing with that. If only he had something to sell, a piece of jewellery, some gold or silver—anything, anything. He knows such a good place for selling things. Is he to be caught again for lack of a few marks? Melpomene is also thinking. Evil must often be done that good may follow. After all, had not she herself stolen Sister Mary of the Purification's clothes when she was asleep after night duty? Had not she run away from the convent, broken her vows? And yet how convinced she was that she was doing rightly! The mysterious Powers emphatically approved; she felt sure of it. And now there was the red purse. But what was a red purse in comparison with a saved soul—and, after all, what was she doing but saving Kuno's soul?" Miss Penny, who had adopted the voice and

gestures of a debater asking rhetorical questions, brought her hand with a
slap on to the table. "Lord, what a bore this sort of stuff is!" she exclaimed.
"Let's get to the end of this dingy anecdote as quickly as possible. By this
time, you must imagine, the shades of night were falling fast—the chill
November twilight, and so on; but I leave the natural descriptions to you.
Kuno gets into the ditch at the roadside and takes off his robes. One
imagines that he would feel himself safer in trousers, more capable of
acting with decision in a crisis. They tramp on for miles. Late in the evening they leave the high road and strike up through the fields towards
the forest. At the fringe of the wood they find one of those wheeled huts
where the shepherds sleep in the lambing season."

"The real 'Maison du Berger.'"

"Precisely," said Miss Penny, and she began to recite:

> Si ton cœur gémissant du poids de notre vie
> Se traine et se débat comme un aigle blessé. . . .

How does it go on? I used to adore it all so much when I was a girl:

> Le seuil est perfumé, l'alcôve est large et sombre,
> Et là parmi les fleurs, nous trouverons dans l'ombre,
> Pour nos cheveux unis un lit silencieux.

I could go on like this indefinitely."

"Do," I said.

"No, no. No, no. I'm determined to finish this wretched story. Kuno
broke the padlock of the door. They entered. What happened in that little
hut?" Miss Penny leaned forward at me. Her large hare's eyes glittered, the
long ear-rings swung and faintly tinkled. "Imagine the emotions of a virgin
of thirty, and a nun at that, in the terrifying presence of desire. Imagine the
easy, familiar brutalities of the young man. Oh, there's pages to be made out
of this—the absolutely impenetrable darkness, the smell of straw, the voices,
the strangled crying, the movements! And one likes to fancy that the emotions pulsing about in that confined space made palpable vibrations like a
deep sound that shakes the air. Why, it's ready-made literature, this scene.
In the morning," Miss Penny went on, after a pause, "two woodcutters
on their way to work noticed that the door of the hut was ajar. They
approached the hut cautiously, their axes raised and ready for a blow if
there should be need of it. Peeping in, they saw a woman in a black dress
lying face downward in the straw. Dead? No; she moved, she moaned.
'What's the matter?' A blubbered face, smeared with streaks of tear-clotted
grey dust, it lifted towards them. 'What's the matter?'—'He's gone!' What
a queer, indistinct utterance. The woodcutters regard one another. What
does she say? She's a foreigner, perhaps. 'What's the matter?' they repeat
once more. The woman bursts out violently crying. 'Gone, gone! He's gone,'
she sobs out in her vague, inarticulate way. 'Oh, gone.' That's what she says.

'Who's gone?'—'He's left me.'—'What?'—'Left me . . . .'—'What the devil
. . . ? Speak a little more distinctly.'—'I can't,' she wails; 'he's taken my
teeth.'—'Your what?'—'My teeth!'—and the shrill voice breaks into a
scream, and she falls back sobbing into the straw. The woodcutters look
significantly at one another. They nod. One of them applies a thick yellow-
nailed forefinger to his forehead."

Miss Penny looked at her watch.

"Good heavens!" she said, "it's nearly half-past three. I must fly. Don't
forget about the funeral service," she added, as she put on her coat. "The
tapers, the black coffin in the middle of the aisle, the nuns in their white-
winged coifs, the gloomy chanting, and the poor cowering creature without
any teeth, her face all caved in like an old woman's, wondering whether she
wasn't really and in fact dead—wondering whether she wasn't already in
hell. Good-bye."

THE RICH BOY

F. Scott Fitzgerald

(1896–   )

BEGIN WITH AN INDIVIDUAL, and before you know it you find that you have
created a type; begin with a type, and you find that you have created—
nothing. That is because we are all queer fish, queerer behind our faces
and voices than we want any one to know or than we know ourselves.
When I hear a man proclaiming himself an "average, honest, open fellow,"
I feel pretty sure that he has some definite and perhaps terrible abnormality
which he has agreed to conceal—and his protestation of being average and
honest and open is his way of reminding himself of his misprision.

There are no types, no plurals. There is a rich boy, and this is his and
not his brothers' story. All my life I have lived among his brothers but this
one has been my friend. Besides, if I wrote about his brothers I should have
to begin by attacking all the lies that the poor have told about the rich and
the rich have told about themselves—such a wild structure they have
erected that when we pick up a book about the rich, some instinct prepares
us for unreality. Even the intelligent and impassioned reporters of life have
made the country of the rich as unreal as fairy-land.

Let me tell you about the very rich. They are different from you and me.
They possess and enjoy early, and it does something to them, makes them

soft where we are hard, and cynical where we are trustful, in a way that unless you were born rich, it is very difficult to understand. They think, deep in their hearts, that they are better than we are because we had to discover the compensations and refuges of life for ourselves. Even when they enter deep into our world or sink below us, they still think that they are better than we are. They are different. The only way I can describe young Anson Hunter is to approach him as if he were a foreigner and cling stubbornly to my point of view. If I accept his for a moment I am lost—I have nothing to show but a preposterous movie.

II

Anson was the eldest of six children who would some day divide a fortune of fifteen million dollars, and he reached the age of reason—is it seven?—at the beginning of the century when daring young women were already gliding along Fifth Avenue in electric "mobiles." In those days he and his brother had an English governess who spoke the language very clearly and crisply and well, so that the two boys grew to speak as she did—their words and sentences were all crisp and clear and not run together as ours are. They didn't talk exactly like English children but acquired an accent that is peculiar to fashionable people in the city of New York.

In the summer the six children were moved from the house on 71st Street to a big estate in Northern Connecticut. It was not a fashionable locality—Anson's father wanted to delay as long as possible his children's knowledge of that side of life. He was a man somewhat superior to his class, which composed New York society, and to his period, which was the snobbish and formalized vulgarity of the Gilded Age, and he wanted his sons to learn habits of concentration and have sound constitutions and grow up into right-living and successful men. He and his wife kept an eye on them as well as they were able until the two older boys went away to school, but in huge establishments this is difficult—it was much simpler in the series of small and medium-sized houses in which my own youth was spent—I was never far out of the reach of my mother's voice, of the sense of her presence, her approval or disapproval.

Anson's first sense of his superiority came to him when he realized the half-grudging American deference that was paid to him in the Connecticut village. The parents of the boys he played with always inquired after his father and mother, and were vaguely excited when their own children were asked to the Hunters' house. He accepted this as the natural state of things, and a sort of impatience with all groups of which he was not the center—in money, in position, in authority—remained with him for the rest of his life. He disdained to struggle with other boys for precedence—he expected it to be given him freely, and when it wasn't he withdrew into his family. His family was sufficient, for in the East money is still a somewhat feudal

thing, a clan-forming thing. In the snobbish West, money separates families to form "sets."

At eighteen, when he went to New Haven, Anson was tall and thick-set,
with a clear complexion and a healthy color from the ordered life he had
led in school. His hair was yellow and grew in a funny way on his head, his
nose was beaked—these two things kept him from being handsome—but
he had a confident charm and a certain brusque style, and the upper-class
men who passed him on the street knew without being told that he was a
rich boy and had gone to one of the best schools. Nevertheless, his very
superiority kept him from being a success in college—the independence
was mistaken for egotism, and the refusal to accept Yale standards with the
proper awe seemed to belittle all those who had. So, long before he graduated, he began to shift the center of his life to New York.

He was at home in New York—there was his own house with "the kind
of servants you can't get any more"—and his own family, of which, because
of his good humor and a certain ability to make things go, he was rapidly
becoming the center, and the débutante parties, and the correct manly
world of the men's clubs, and the occasional wild spree with the gallant
girls whom New Haven only knew from the fifth row. His aspirations
were conventional enough—they included even the irreproachable shadow
he would some day marry, but they differed from the aspirations of the
majority of young men in that there was no mist over them, none of that
quality which is variously known as "idealism" or "illusion." Anson
accepted without reservation the world of high finance and high extravagance, of divorce and dissipation, of snobbery and of privilege. Most of
our lives end as a compromise—it was as a compromise that his life began.

He and I first met in the late summer of 1917 when he was just out of
Yale, and, like the rest of us, was swept up into the systematized hysteria
of the war. In the blue-green uniform of the naval aviation he came down
to Pensacola, where the hotel orchestras played "I'm Sorry, Dear," and we
young officers danced with the girls. Everyone liked him, and though he
ran with the drinkers and wasn't an especially good pilot, even the instruc-
tors treated him with a certain respect. He was always having long talks
with them in his confident, logical voice—talks which ended by his getting
himself, or, more frequently, another young officer, out of some impending
trouble. He was convivial, bawdy, robustly avid for pleasure, and we were
all surprised when he fell in love with a conservative and rather proper girl.

Her name was Paula Legendre, a dark, serious beauty from somewhere
in California. Her family kept a winter residence just outside of town, and
in spite of her primness she was enormously popular; there is a large class
of men whose egotism can't endure humor in a woman. But Anson wasn't
that sort, and I couldn't understand the attraction of her "sincerity"—that
was the thing to say about her—for his keen and somewhat sardonic mind.

Nevertheless, they fell in love—and on her terms. He no longer joined the twilight gathering at the De Sota bar, and whenever they were seen together they were engaged in a long, serious dialogue, which must have gone on several weeks. Long afterward he told me that it was not about anything in particular but was composed on both sides of immature and even meaningless statements—the emotional content that gradually came to fill it grew up not out of the words but out of its enormous seriousness. It was a sort of hypnosis. Often it was interrupted, giving way to that emasculated humor we call fun; when they were alone it was resumed again, solemn, low-keyed, and pitched so as to give each other a sense of unity in feeling and thought. They came to resent any interruptions of it, to be unresponsive to facetiousness about life, even to the mild cynicism of their contemporaries. They were only happy when the dialogue was going on, and its seriousness bathed them like the amber glow of an open fire. Toward the end there came an interruption they did not resent—it began to be interrupted by passion.

Oddly enough, Anson was as engrossed in the dialogue as she was and as profoundly affected by it, yet at the same time aware that on his side much was insincere, and on hers much was merely simple. At first, too, he despised her emotional simplicity as well, but with his love her nature deepened and blossomed, and he could despise it no longer. He felt that if he could enter into Paula's warm safe life he would be happy. The long preparation of the dialogue removed any constraint—he taught her some of what he had learned from more adventurous women, and she responded with a rapt holy intensity. One evening after a dance they agreed to marry, and he wrote a long letter about her to his mother. The next day Paula told him that she was rich, that she had a personal fortune of nearly a million dollars.

III

It was exactly as if they could say "Neither of us has anything: we shall be poor together"—just as delightful that they should be rich instead. It gave them the same communion of adventure. Yet when Anson got leave in April, and Paula and her mother accompanied him North, she was impressed with the standing of his family in New York and with the scale on which they lived. Alone with Anson for the first time in the rooms where he had played as a boy, she was filled with a comfortable emotion, as though she were pre-eminently safe and taken care of. The pictures of Anson in a skull cap at his first school, of Anson on horseback with the sweetheart of a mysterious forgotten summer, of Anson in a gay group of ushers and bridesmaids at a wedding, made her jealous of his life apart from her in the past, and so completely did his authoritative person seem to sum up and typify these possessions of his that she was inspired with the idea of being married immediately and returning to Pensacola as his wife.

But an immediate marriage wasn't discussed—even the engagement was to be secret until after the war. When she realized that only two days of his leave remained, her dissatisfaction crystallized in the intention of making him as unwilling to wait as she was. They were driving to the country for dinner and she determined to force the issue that night.

Now a cousin of Paula's was staying with them at the Ritz, a severe, bitter girl who loved Paula but was somewhat jealous of her impressive engagement, and as Paula was late in dressing, the cousin, who wasn't going to the party, received Anson in the parlor of the suite.

Anson had met friends at five o'clock and drunk freely and indiscreetly with them for an hour. He left the Yale Club at a proper time, and his mother's chauffeur drove him to the Ritz, but his usual capacity was not in evidence, and the impact of the steam-heated sitting-room made him suddenly dizzy. He knew it, and he was both amused and sorry.

Paula's cousin was twenty-five but she was exceptionally naïve, and at first failed to realize what was up. She had never met Anson before, and she was surprised when he mumbled strange information and nearly fell off his chair, but until Paula appeared it didn't occur to her that what she had taken for the odor of a dry-cleaned uniform was really whisky. But Paula understood as soon as she appeared; her only thought was to get Anson away before her mother saw him, and at the look in her eyes the cousin understood too.

When Paula and Anson descended to the limousine they found two men inside, both asleep; they were the men with whom he had been drinking at the Yale Club, and they were also going to the party. He had entirely forgotten their presence in the car. On the way to Hempstead they awoke and sang. Some of the songs were rough, and though Paula tried to reconcile herself to the fact that Anson had few verbal inhibitions, her lips tightened with shame and distaste.

Back at the hotel the cousin, confused and agitated, considered the incident, and then walked into Mrs. Legendre's bedroom, saying: "Isn't he funny?"

"Who is funny?"

"Why—Mr. Hunter. He seemed so funny."

Mrs. Legendre looked at her sharply.

"How is he funny?"

"Why, he said he was French. I didn't know he was French."

"That's absurd. You must have misunderstood." She smiled: "It was a joke."

The cousin shook her head stubbornly.

"No. He said he was brought up in France. He said he couldn't speak any English, and that's why he couldn't talk to me. And he couldn't!"

Mrs. Legendre looked away with impatience just as the cousin added thoughtfully, "Perhaps it was because he was so drunk," and walked out of the room.

This curious report was true. Anson, finding his voice thick and uncontrollable, had taken the unusual refuge of announcing that he spoke no English. Years afterwards he used to tell that part of the story, and he invariably communicated the uproarious laughter which the memory aroused in him.

Five times in the next hour Mrs. Legendre tried to get Hempstead on the phone. When she succeeded, there was a ten-minute delay before she heard Paula's voice on the wire.

"Cousin Jo told me Anson was intoxicated."

"Oh, no. . . ?"

"Oh, yes. Cousin Jo says he was intoxicated. He told her he was French, and fell off his chair and behaved as if he was very intoxicated. I don't want you to come home with him."

"Mother, he's all right! Please don't worry about——"

"But I do worry. I think it's dreadful. I want you to promise me not to come home with him."

"I'll take care of it, mother. . . ."

"I don't want you to come home with him."

"All right, mother. Good-by."

"Be sure now, Paula. Ask some one to bring you."

Deliberately Paula took the receiver from her ear and hung it up. Her face was flushed with helpless annoyance. Anson was stretched asleep out in a bedroom upstairs, while the dinner-party below was proceeding lamely toward conclusion.

The hour's drive had sobered him somewhat—his arrival was merely hilarious—and Paula hoped that the evening was not spoiled, after all, but two imprudent cocktails before dinner completed the disaster. He talked boisterously and somewhat offensively to the party at large for fifteen minutes, and then slid silently under the table; like a man in an old print —but, unlike an old print, it was rather horrible without being at all quaint. None of the young girls present remarked upon the incident—it seemed to merit only silence. His uncle and two other men carried him upstairs, and it was just after this that Paula was called to the phone.

An hour later Anson awoke in a fog of nervous agony, through which he perceived after a moment the figure of his uncle Robert standing by the door.

". . . I said are you better?"

"What?"

"Do you feel better, old man?"

"Terrible," said Anson.

"I'm going to try you on another bromo-seltzer. If you can hold it down, it'll do you good to sleep."

With an effort Anson slid his legs from the bed and stood up.

"I'm all right," he said dully.

"Take it easy."

"I thin' if you gave me a glassbrandy I could go down-stairs."

"Oh, no——"

"Yes, that's the only thin'. I'm all right now. . . . I suppose I'm in Dutch dow' there."

"They know you're a little under the weather," said his uncle deprecatingly. "But don't worry about it. Schuyler didn't even get here. He passed away in the locker-room over at the Links."

Indifferent to any opinion, except Paula's, Anson was nevertheless determined to save the débris of the evening, but when after a cold bath he made his appearance most of the party had already left. Paula got up immediately to go home.

In the limousine the old serious dialogue began. She had known that he drank, she admitted, but she had never expected anything like this—it seemed to her that perhaps they were not suited to each other, after all. Their ideas about life were too different, and so forth. When she finished speaking, Anson spoke in turn, very soberly. Then Paula said she'd have to think it over; she wouldn't decide tonight; she was not angry but she was terribly sorry. Nor would she let him come into the hotel with her, but just before she got out of the car she leaned and kissed him unhappily on the cheek.

The next afternoon Anson had a long talk with Mrs. Legendre while Paula sat listening in silence. It was agreed that Paula was to brood over the incident for a proper period and then, if mother and daughter thought it best, they would follow Anson to Pensacola. On his part he apologized with sincerity and dignity—that was all; with every card in her hand Mrs. Legendre was unable to establish any advantage over him. He made no promises, showed no humility, only delivered a few serious comments on life which brought him off with rather a moral superiority at the end. When they came South three weeks later, neither Anson in his satisfaction nor Paula in her relief at the reunion realized that the psychological moment had passed forever.

IV

He dominated and attracted her, and at the same time filled her with anxiety. Confused by his mixture of solidity and self-indulgence, of sentiment and cynicism—incongruities which her gentle mind was unable to resolve—Paula grew to think of him as two alternating personalities. When she saw him alone, or at a formal party, or with his casual inferiors, she felt a tremendous pride in his strong, attractive presence, the paternal, understanding stature of his mind. In other company she became uneasy when what had been a fine imperviousness to mere gentility showed its other face. The other face was gross, humorous, reckless of everything but pleasure. It startled her mind temporarily away from him, even led her into a short covert experiment with an old beau, but it was no use—after four months of Anson's enveloping vitality there was an anæmic pallor in all other men.

In July he was ordered abroad, and their tenderness and desire reached a crescendo. Paula considered a last-minute marriage—decided against it only because there were always cocktails on his breath now, but the parting itself made her physically ill with grief. After his departure she wrote him long letters of regret for the days of love they had missed by waiting. In August Anson's plane slipped down into the North Sea. He was pulled onto a destroyer after a night in the water and sent to hospital with pneumonia; the armistice was signed before he was finally sent home.

Then, with every opportunity given back to them, with no material obstacle to overcome, the secret weavings of their temperaments came between them, drying up their kisses and their tears, making their voices less loud to one another, muffling the intimate chatter of their hearts until the old communication was only possible by letters, from far away. One afternoon a society reporter waited for two hours in the Hunters' house for a confirmation of their engagement. Anson denied it; nevertheless an early issue carried the report as a leading paragraph—they were "constantly seen together at Southampton, Hot Springs, and Tuxedo Park." But the serious dialogue had turned a corner into a long-sustained quarrel, and the affair was almost played out. Anson got drunk flagrantly and missed an engagement with her, whereupon Paula made certain behavioristic demands. His despair was helpless before his pride and his knowledge of himself: the engagement was definitely broken.

"Dearest," said their letters now, "Dearest, Dearest, when I wake up in the middle of the night and realize that after all it was not to be, I feel that I want to die. I can't go on living any more. Perhaps when we meet this summer we may talk things over and decide differently—we were so excited and sad that day, and I don't feel that I can live all my life without you. You speak of other people. Don't you know there are no other people for me, but only you. . . ."

But as Paula drifted here and there around the East she would sometimes mention her gayeties to make him wonder. Anson was too acute to wonder. When he saw a man's name in her letters he felt more sure of her and a little disdainful—he was always superior to such things. But he still hoped that they would some day marry.

Meanwhile he plunged vigorously into all the movement and glitter of post-bellum New York, entering a brokerage house, joining half a dozen clubs, dancing late, and moving in three worlds—his own world, the world of young Yale graduates, and that section of the half-world which rests one end on Broadway. But there was always a thorough and infractible eight hours voted to his work in Wall Street, where the combination of his influential family connection, his sharp intelligence, and his abundance of sheer physical energy brought him almost immediately forward. He had one of those invaluable minds with partitions in it; sometimes he appeared at his office refreshed by less than an hour's sleep, but such occurrences were rare. So early as 1920 his income in salary and commissions exceeded twelve thousand dollars.

As the Yale tradition slipped into the past he became more and more of a popular figure among his classmates in New York, more popular than he had ever been in college. He lived in a great house, and had the means of introducing young men into other great houses. Moreover, his life already seemed secure, while theirs, for the most part, had arrived again at precarious beginnings. They commenced to turn to him for amusement and escape, and Anson responded readily, taking pleasure in helping people and arranging their affairs.

There were no men in Paula's letters now, but a note of tenderness ran through them that had not been there before. From several sources he heard that she had "a heavy beau," Lowell Thayer, a Bostonian of wealth and position, and though he was sure she still loved him, it made him uneasy to think that he might lose her, after all. Save for one unsatisfactory day she had not been in New York for almost five months, and as the rumors multiplied he became increasingly anxious to see her. In February he took his vacation and went down to Florida.

Palm Beach sprawled plump and opulent between the sparkling sapphire of Lake Worth, flawed here and there by house-boats at anchor, and the great turquoise bar of the Atlantic Ocean. The huge bulks of the Breakers and the Royal Poinciana rose as twin paunches from the bright level of the sand, and around them clustered the Dancing Glade, Bradley's House of Chance, and a dozen modistes and milliners with goods at triple prices from New York. Upon the trellised veranda of the Breakers two hundred women stepped right, stepped left, wheeled, and slid in that then celebrated calisthenic known as the double-shuffle, while in half-time to the music two thousand bracelets clicked up and down on two hundred arms.

At the Everglades Club after dark Paula and Lowell Thayer and Anson and a casual fourth played bridge with hot cards. It seemed to Anson that her kind, serious face was wan and tired—she had been around now for four, five, years. He had known her for three.

"Two spades."

"Cigarette? . . . Oh, I beg your pardon. By me."

"By."

"I'll double three spades."

There were a dozen tables of bridge in the room, which was filling up with smoke. Anson's eyes met Paula's, held them persistently even when Thayer's glance fell between them. . . .

"What was bid?" he asked abstractedly.

"Rose of Washington Square,"

sang the young people in the corners:

> "I'm withering there
> In basement air——"

The smoke banked like fog, and the opening of a door filled the room with blown swirls of ectoplasm. Little Bright Eyes streaked past the tables seeking Mr. Conan Doyle among the Englishmen who were posing as Englishmen about the lobby.

"You could cut it with a knife."

". . . cut it with a knife."

". . . a knife."

At the end of the rubber Paula suddenly got up and spoke to Anson in a tense, low voice. With scarcely a glance at Lowell Thayer, they walked out the door and descended a long flight of stone steps—in a moment they were walking hand in hand along the moonlit beach.

"Darling, darling. . . ." They embraced recklessly, passionately, in a shadow. . . . Then Paula drew back her face to let his lips say what she wanted to hear—she could feel the words forming as they kissed again. . . . Again she broke away, listening, but as he pulled her close once more she realized that he had said nothing—only "Darling! Darling!" in that deep, sad whisper that always made her cry. Humbly, obediently, her emotions yielded to him and the tears streamed down her face, but her heart kept on crying: "Ask me—oh, Anson, dearest, ask me!"

"Paula. . . . Paula!"

The words wrung her heart like hands, and Anson, feeling her tremble, knew that emotion was enough. He need say no more, commit their destinies to no practical enigma. Why should he, when he might hold her so, biding his own time, for another year—forever? He was considering them both, her more than himself. For a moment, when she said suddenly that she must go back to her hotel, he hesitated, thinking, first, "This is the moment, after all," and then: "No, let it wait—she is mine. . . ."

He had forgotten that Paula too was worn away inside with the strain of three years. Her mood passed forever in the night.

He went back to New York next morning filled with a certain restless dissatisfaction. Late in April, without warning, he received a telegram from Bar Harbor in which Paula told him that she was engaged to Lowell Thayer, and that they would be married immediately in Boston. What he never really believed could happen had happened at last.

Anson filled himself with whisky that morning, and going to the office, carried on his work without a break—rather with a fear of what would happen if he stopped. In the evening he went out as usual, saying nothing of what had occurred; he was cordial, humorous, unabstracted. But one thing he could not help—for three days, in any place, in any company, he would suddenly bend his head into his hands and cry like a child.

V

In 1922 when Anson went abroad with the junior partner to investigate some London loans, the journey intimated that he was to be taken into the firm. He was twenty-seven now, a little heavy without being definitely stout, and with a manner older than his years. Old people and young people liked him and trusted him, and mothers felt safe when their daughters were in his charge, for he had a way, when he came into a room, of putting himself on a footing with the oldest and most conservative people there. "You and I," he seemed to say, "we're solid. We understand."

He had an instinctive and rather charitable knowledge of the weaknesses of men and women, and, like a priest, it made him the more concerned for the maintenance of outward forms. It was typical of him that every Sunday morning he taught in a fashionable Episcopal Sunday-school—even though a cold shower and a quick change into a cut-away coat were all that separated him from the wild night before.

After his father's death he was the practical head of his family, and, in effect, guided the destinies of the younger children. Through a complication his authority did not extend to his father's estate, which was administered by his Uncle Robert, who was the horsy member of the family, a good-natured, hard-drinking member of that set which centers about Wheatley Hills.

Uncle Robert and his wife, Edna, had been great friends of Anson's youth, and the former was disappointed when his nephew's superiority failed to take a horsy form. He backed him for a city club which was the most difficult in America to enter—one could only join if one's family had "helped to build up New York" (or, in other words, were rich before 1880)—and when Anson, after his election, neglected it for the Yale Club, Uncle Robert gave him a little talk on the subject. But when on top of that Anson declined to enter Robert Hunter's own conservative and somewhat neglected brokerage house, his manner grew cooler. Like a primary teacher who has taught all he knew, he slipped out of Anson's life.

There were so many friends in Anson's life—scarcely one for whom he had not done some unusual kindness and scarcely one whom he did not occasionally embarrass by his bursts of rough conversation or his habit of getting drunk whenever and however he liked. It annoyed him when anyone else blundered in that regard—about his own lapses he was always humorous. Odd things happened to him and he told them with infectious laughter.

I was working in New York that spring, and I used to lunch with him at the Yale Club, which my university was sharing until the completion of our own. I had read of Paula's marriage, and one afternoon, when I asked him about her, something moved him to tell me the story. After that he frequently invited me to family dinners at his house and behaved as though there was a special relation between us, as though with his confidence a little of that consuming memory had passed into me.

I found that despite the trusting mothers, his attitude toward girls was not indiscriminately protective. It was up to the girl—if she showed an inclination toward looseness, she must take care of herself, even with him.

"Life," he would explain sometimes, "has made a cynic of me."

By life he meant Paula. Sometimes, especially when he was drinking, it became a little twisted in his mind, and he thought that she had callously thrown him over.

This "cynicism," or rather his realization that naturally fast girls were not worth sparing, led to his affair with Dolly Karger. It wasn't his only affair in those years, but it came nearest to touching him deeply, and it had a profound effect upon his attitude toward life.

Dolly was the daughter of a notorious "publicist" who had married into society. She herself grew up into the Junior League, came out at the Plaza, and went to the Assembly; and only a few old families like the Hunters could question whether or not she "belonged," for her picture was often in the papers, and she had more enviable attention than many girls who undoubtedly did. She was dark-haired, with carmine lips and a high, lovely color, which she concealed under pinkish-gray powder all through the first year out, because high color was unfashionable—Victorian-pale was the thing to be. She wore black, severe suits and stood with her hands in her pockets, leaning a little forward, with a humorous restraint on her face. She danced exquisitely—better than anything she liked to dance—better than anything except making love. Since she was ten she had always been in love, and, usually, with some boy who didn't respond to her. Those who did—and there were many—bored her after a brief encounter, but for her failures she reserved the warmest spot in her heart. When she met them she would always try once more—sometimes she succeeded, more often she failed.

It never occurred to this gypsy of the unattainable that there was a certain resemblance in those who refused to love her—they shared a hard intuition that saw through to her weakness, not a weakness of emotion but a weakness of rudder. Anson perceived this when he first met her, less than a month after Paula's marriage. He was drinking rather heavily, and he pretended for a week that he was falling in love with her. Then he dropped her abruptly and forgot—immediately he took up the commanding position in her heart.

Like so many girls of that day Dolly was slackly and indiscreetly wild. The unconventionality of a slightly older generation had been simply one facet of a post-war movement to discredit obsolete manners—Dolly's was both older and shabbier, and she saw in Anson the two extremes which the emotionally shiftless woman seeks, an abandon to indulgence alternating with a protective strength. In his character she felt both the sybarite and the solid rock, and these two satisfied every need of her nature.

She felt that it was going to be difficult, but she mistook the reason—she thought that Anson and his family expected a more spectacular marriage; but she guessed immediately that her advantage lay in his tendency to drink.

They met at the large débutante dances, but as her infatuation increased they managed to be more and more together. Like most mothers, Mrs. Karger believed that Anson was exceptionally reliable, so she allowed Dolly to go with him to distant country clubs and suburban houses without inquiring closely into their activities or questioning her explanations when they came in late. At first these explanations might have been accurate, but Dolly's worldly ideas of capturing Anson were soon engulfed in the rising sweep of her emotion. Kisses in the back of taxis and motor-cars were no longer enough; they did a curious thing:

They dropped out of their world for a while and made another world just beneath it where Anson's tippling and Dolly's irregular hours would be less noticed and commented on. It was composed, this world, of varying elements—several of Anson's Yale friends and their wives, two or three young brokers and bond salesmen and a handful of unattached men, fresh from college, with money and a propensity to dissipation. What this world lacked in spaciousness and scale it made up for by allowing them a liberty that it scarcely permitted itself. Moreover, it centered around them and permitted Dolly the pleasure of a faint condescension—a pleasure which Anson, whose whole life was a condescension from the certitudes of his childhood, was unable to share.

He was not in love with her, and in the long feverish winter of their affair he frequently told her so. In the spring he was weary—he wanted to renew his life at some other source—moreover, he saw that either he must break with her now or accept the responsibility of a definite seduction. Her family's encouraging attitude precipitated his decision—one evening when Mr. Karger knocked discreetly at the library door to announce that he had left a bottle of old brandy in the dining room, Anson felt that life was hemming him in. That night he wrote her a short letter in which he told her that he was going on his vacation, and that in view of all the circumstances they had better meet no more.

It was June. His family had closed up the house and gone to the country, so he was living temporarily at the Yale Club. I had heard about his affair with Dolly as it developed—accounts salted with humor, for he despised unstable women, and granted them no place in the social edifice in which he believed—and when he told me that night that he was definitely breaking with her I was glad. I had seen Dolly here and there, and each time with a feeling of pity at the hopelessness of her struggle, and of shame at knowing so much about her that I had no right to know. She was what is known as "a pretty little thing," but there was a certain recklessness which rather fascinated me. Her dedication to the goddess of waste would have been less obvious had she been less spirited—she would most certainly throw herself away, but I was glad when I heard that the sacrifice would not be consummated in my sight.

Anson was going to leave the letter of farewell at her house next morning. It was one of the few houses left open in the Fifth Avenue district, and he knew that the Kargers, acting upon erroneous information from Dolly, had foregone a trip abroad to give their daughter her chance. As he stepped out the door of the Yale Club into Madison Avenue the postman passed him, and he followed back inside. The first letter that caught his eye was in Dolly's hand.

He knew what it would be—a lonely and tragic monologue, full of the reproaches he knew, the invoked memories, the "I wonder if's"—all the immemorial intimacies that he had communicated to Paula Legendre in what seemed another age. Thumbing over some bills, he brought it on top again and opened it. To his surprise it was a short, somewhat formal note, which said that Dolly would be unable to go to the country with him for the week-end, because Perry Hull from Chicago had unexpectedly come to town. It added that Anson had brought this on himself: "—if I felt that you loved me as I love you I would go with you at any time, any place, but Perry is *so* nice, and he so much wants me to marry him——"

Anson smiled contemptuously—he had had experience with such decoy epistles. Moreover, he knew how Dolly had labored over this plan, probably sent for the faithful Perry and calculated the time of his arrival—even labored over the note so that it would make him jealous without driving him away. Like most compromises, it had neither force nor vitality but only a timorous despair.

Suddenly he was angry. He sat down in the lobby and read it again. Then he went to the phone, called Dolly and told her in his clear, compelling voice that he had received her note and would call for her at five o'clock as they had previously planned. Scarcely waiting for the pretended uncertainty of her "Perhaps I can see you for an hour," he hung up the receiver and went down to his office. On the way he tore his own letter into bits and dropped it in the street.

He was not jealous—she meant nothing to him—but at her pathetic ruse everything stubborn and self-indulgent in him came to the surface. It was a presumption from a mental inferior and it could not be overlooked. If she wanted to know to whom she belonged she would see.

He was on the door-step at quarter past five. Dolly was dressed for the street, and he listened in silence to the paragraph of "I can only see you for an hour," which she had begun on the phone.

"Put on your hat, Dolly," he said, "we'll take a walk."

They strolled up Madison Avenue and over to Fifth while Anson's shirt dampened upon his portly body in the deep heat. He talked little, scolding her, making no love to her, but before they had walked six blocks she was his again, apologizing for the note, offering not to see Perry at all as an atonement, offering anything. She thought that he had come because he was beginning to love her.

"I'm hot," he said when they reached 71st Street. "This is a winter suit. If I stop by the house and change, would you mind waiting for me downstairs? I'll only be a minute."

She was happy; the intimacy of his being hot, of any physical fact about him, thrilled her. When they came to the iron-grated door and Anson took out his key she experienced a sort of delight.

Down-stairs it was dark, and after he ascended in the lift Dolly raised a curtain and looked out through opaque lace at the houses over the way. She heard the lift machinery stop, and with the notion of teasing him pressed the button that brought it down. Then on what was more than an impulse she got into it and sent it up to what she guessed was his floor.

"Anson," she called, laughing a little.

"Just a minute," he answered from his bedroom . . . then after a brief delay: "Now you can come in."

He had changed and was buttoning his vest. "This is my room," he said lightly. "How do you like it?"

She caught sight of Paula's picture on the wall and stared at it in fascination, just as Paula had stared at the pictures of Anson's childish sweethearts five years before. She knew something about Paula—sometimes she tortured herself with fragments of the story.

Suddenly she came close to Anson, raising her arms. They embraced. Outside the area window a soft artificial twilight already hovered, though the sun was still bright on a back roof across the way. In half an hour the room would be quite dark. The uncalculated opportunity overwhelmed them, made them both breathless, and they clung more closely. It was eminent, inevitable. Still holding one another, they raised their heads—their eyes fell together upon Paula's picture, staring down at them from the wall.

Suddenly Anson dropped his arms, and sitting down at his desk tried the drawer with a bunch of keys.

"Like a drink?" he asked in a gruff voice.

"No, Anson."

He poured himself half a tumbler of whisky, swallowed it, and then opened the door into the hall.

"Come on," he said.

Dolly hesitated.

"Anson—I'm going to the country with you tonight, after all. You understand that, don't you?"

"Of course," he answered brusquely.

In Dolly's car they rode on to Long Island, closer in their emotions than they had ever been before. They knew what would happen—not with Paula's face to remind them that something was lacking, but when they were alone in the still, hot Long Island night they did not care.

The estate in Port Washington where they were to spend the week-end belonged to a cousin of Anson's who had married a Montana copper operator. An interminable drive began at the lodge and twisted under imported poplar saplings toward a huge, pink, Spanish house. Anson had often visited there before.

After dinner they danced at the Linx Club. About midnight Anson assured himself that his cousins would not leave before two—then he explained that Dolly was tired; he would take her home and return to the dance later. Trembling a little with excitement, they got into a borrowed car together and drove to Port Washington. As they reached the lodge he stopped and spoke to the night watchman.

"When are you making a round, Carl?"

"Right away."

"Then you'll be here till everybody's in?"

"Yes, sir."

"All right. Listen: if any automobile, no matter whose it is, turns in at this gate, I want you to phone the house immediately." He put a five-dollar bill into Carl's hand. "Is that clear?"

"Yes, Mr. Anson." Being of the Old World, he neither winked nor smiled. Yet Dolly sat with her face turned slightly away.

Anson had a key. Once inside he poured a drink for both of them—Dolly left hers untouched—then he ascertained definitely the location of the phone, and found that it was within easy hearing distance of their rooms, both of which were on the first floor.

Five minutes later he knocked at the door of Dolly's room.

"Anson?" He went in, closing the door behind him. She was in bed, leaning up anxiously with elbows on the pillow; sitting beside her he took her in his arms.

"Anson, darling."

He didn't answer.

"Anson. . . . Anson! I love you. . . . Say you love me. Say it now—can't you say it now? Even if you don't mean it?"

He did not listen. Over her head he perceived that the picture of Paula was hanging here upon this wall.

He got up and went close to it. The frame gleamed faintly with thrice-reflected moonlight—within was a blurred shadow of a face that he saw he did not know. Almost sobbing, he turned around and stared with abomination at the little figure on the bed.

"This is all foolishness," he said thickly. "I don't know what I was thinking about. I don't love you and you'd better wait for somebody that loves you. I don't love you a bit, can't you understand?"

His voice broke, and he went hurriedly out. Back in the salon he was pouring himself a drink with uneasy fingers, when the front door opened suddenly, and his cousin came in.

"Why, Anson, I hear Dolly's sick," she began solicitously. "I hear she's sick."

"It was nothing," he interrupted, raising his voice so that it would carry into Dolly's room. "She was a little tired. She went to bed."

For a long time afterward Anson believed that a protective God sometimes interfered in human affairs. But Dolly Karger, lying awake and staring at the ceiling, never again believed in anything at all.

VI

When Dolly married during the following autumn, Anson was in London on business. Like Paula's marriage, it was sudden, but it affected him in a different way. At first he felt that it was funny, and had an inclination to laugh when he thought of it. Later it depressed him—it made him feel old.

There was something repetitive about it—why, Paula and Dolly had belonged to different generations. He had a foretaste of the sensation of a man of forty who hears that the daughter of an old flame has married. He wired congratulations and, as was not the case with Paula, they were sincere—he had never really hoped that Paula would be happy.

When he returned to New York, he was made a partner in the firm, and, as his responsibilities increased, he had less time on his hands. The refusal of a life-insurance company to issue him a policy made such an impression on him that he stopped drinking for a year, and claimed that he felt better physically, though I think he missed the convivial recounting of those Celliniesque adventures which, in his early twenties, had played such a part of his life. But he never abandoned the Yale Club. He was a figure there, a personality, and the tendency of his class, who were now seven years out of college, to drift away to more sober haunts was checked by his presence.

His day was never too full nor his mind too weary to give any sort of aid to anyone who asked it. What had been done at first through pride and superiority had become a habit and a passion. And there was always something—a younger brother in trouble at New Haven, a quarrel to be patched up between a friend and his wife, a position to be found for this man, an investment for that. But his specialty was the solving of problems for young married people. Young married people fascinated him and their apartments were almost sacred to him—he knew the story of their love affair, advised them where to live and how, and remembered their babies' names.

Toward young wives his attitude was circumspect: he never abused the trust which their husbands—strangely enough in view of his unconcealed irregularities—invariably reposed in him.

He came to take a vicarious pleasure in happy marriages, and to be inspired to an almost equally pleasant melancholy by those that went astray. Not a season passed that he did not witness the collapse of an affair that perhaps he himself had fathered. When Paula was divorced and almost immediately remarried to another Bostonian, he talked about her to me all one afternoon. He would never love any one as he had loved Paula, but he insisted that he no longer cared.

"I'll never marry," he came to say; "I've seen too much of it, and I know a happy marriage is a very rare thing. Besides, I'm too old."

But he did believe in marriage. Like all men who spring from a happy and successful marriage, he believed in it passionately—nothing he had seen would change his belief, his cynicism dissolved upon it like air. But he did really believe he was too old. At twenty-eight he began to accept with equanimity the prospect of marrying without romantic love; he resolutely chose a New York girl of his own class, pretty, intelligent, congenial, above reproach—and set about falling in love with her. The things he had said to Paula with sincerity, to other girls with grace, he could no longer say at all without smiling, or with the force necessary to convince.

"When I'm forty," he told his friends, "I'll be ripe. I'll fall for some chorus girl like the rest."

Nevertheless, he persisted in his attempt. His mother wanted to see him married, and he could now well afford it—he had a seat on the Stock Exchange, and his earned income came to twenty-five thousand a year. The idea was agreeable: when his friends—he spent most of his time with the set he and Dolly had evolved—closed themselves in behind domestic doors at night, he no longer rejoiced in his freedom. He even wondered if he should have married Dolly. Not even Paula had loved him more, and he was learning the rarity, in a single life, of encountering true emotion.

Just as this mood began to creep over him a disquieting story reached his ear. His aunt Edna, a woman just this side of forty, was carrying on an open intrigue with a dissolute, hard-drinking young man named Cary Sloane. Everyone knew of it except Anson's Uncle Robert, who for fifteen years had talked long in clubs and taken his wife for granted.

Anson heard the story again and again with increasing annoyance. Something of his old feeling for his uncle came back to him, a feeling that was more than personal, a reversion toward that family solidarity on which he had based his pride. His intuition singled out the essential point of the affair, which was that his uncle shouldn't be hurt. It was his first experiment in unsolicited meddling, but with his knowledge of Edna's character he felt that he could handle the matter better than a district judge or his uncle.

His uncle was in Hot Springs. Anson traced down the sources of the scandal so that there should be no possibility of mistake and then he called Edna and asked her to lunch with him at the Plaza next day. Something in his tone must have frightened her, for she was reluctant, but he insisted, putting off the date until she had no excuse for refusing.

She met him at the appointed time in the Plaza lobby, a lovely, faded, gray-eyed blonde in a coat of Russian sable. Five great rings, cold with diamonds and emeralds, sparkled on her slender hands. It occurred to Anson that it was his father's intelligence and not his uncle's that had earned the fur and the stones, the rich brilliance that buoyed up her passing beauty.

Though Edna scented his hostility, she was unprepared for the directness of his approach.

"Edna, I'm astonished at the way you've been acting," he said in a strong, frank voice. "At first I couldn't believe it."

"Believe what?" she demanded sharply.

"You needn't pretend with me, Edna. I'm talking about Cary Sloane. Aside from any other consideration, I didn't think you could treat Uncle Robert——"

"Now look here, Anson—" she began angrily, but his peremptory voice broke through hers:

"—and your children in such a way. You've been married eighteen years, and you're old enough to know better."

"You can't talk to me like that! You——"

"Yes, I can. Uncle Robert has always been my best friend." He was tremendously moved. He felt a real distress about his uncle, about his three young cousins.

Edna stood up, leaving her crab-flake cocktail untasted.

"This is the silliest thing——"

"Very well, if you won't listen to me I'll go to Uncle Robert and tell him the whole story—he's bound to hear it sooner or later. And afterward I'll go to old Moses Sloane."

Edna faltered back into her chair.

"Don't talk so loud," she begged him. Her eyes blurred with tears. "You have no idea how your voice carries. You might have chosen a less public place to make all these crazy accusations."

He didn't answer.

"Oh, you never liked me, I know," she went on. "You're just taking advantage of some silly gossip to try and break up the only interesting friendship I've ever had. What did I ever do to make you hate me so?"

Still Anson waited. There would be the appeal to his chivalry, then to his pity, finally to his superior sophistication—when he had shouldered his way through all these there would be admissions, and he could come to grips with her. By being silent, by being impervious, by returning constantly to his main weapon, which was his own true emotion, he bullied her into frantic despair as the luncheon hour slipped away. At two o'clock she took out a mirror and a handkerchief, shined away the marks of her tears and powdered the slight hollows where they had lain. She had agreed to meet him at her own house at five.

When he arrived she was stretched on a *chaise-longue* which was covered with cretonne for the summer, and the tears he had called up at luncheon seemed still to be standing in her eyes. Then he was aware of Cary Sloane's dark anxious presence upon the cold hearth.

"What's this idea of yours?" broke out Sloane immediately. "I understand you invited Edna to lunch and then threatened her on the basis of some cheap scandal."

Anson sat down.

"I have no reason to think it's only scandal."

"I hear you're going to take it to Robert Hunter, and to my father."

Anson nodded.

"Either you break it off—or I will," he said.

"What God damned business is it of yours, Hunter?"

"Don't lose your temper, Cary," said Edna nervously. "It's only a question of showing him how absurd——"

"For one thing, it's my name that's being handed around," interrupted Anson. "That's all that concerns you, Cary."

"Edna isn't a member of your family."

"She most certainly is!" His anger mounted. "Why—she owes this house and the rings on her fingers to my father's brains. When Uncle Robert married her she didn't have a penny."

They all looked at the rings as if they had a significant bearing on the situation. Edna made a gesture to take them from her hand.

"I guess they're not the only rings in the world," said Sloane.

"Oh, this is absurd," cried Edna. "Anson, will you listen to me? I've found out how the silly story started. It was a maid I discharged who went right to the Chilicheffs—all these Russians pump things out of their servants and then put a false meaning on them." She brought down her fist angrily on the table: "And after Tom lent them the limousine for a whole month when we were South last winter——"

"Do you see?" demanded Sloane eagerly. "This maid got hold of the wrong end of the thing. She knew that Edna and I were friends, and she carried it to the Chilicheffs. In Russia they assume that if a man and a woman——"

He enlarged the theme to a disquisition upon social relations in the Caucasus.

"If that's the case it better be explained to Uncle Robert," said Anson dryly, "so that when the rumors do reach him he'll know they're not true."

Adopting the method he had followed with Edna at luncheon he let them explain it all away. He knew that they were guilty and that presently they would cross the line from explanation into justification and convict themselves more definitely than he could ever do. By seven they had taken the desperate step of telling him the truth—Robert Hunter's neglect, Edna's empty life, the casual dalliance that had flamed up into passion—but like so many true stories it had the misfortune of being old, and its enfeebled body beat helplessly against the armor of Anson's will. The threat to go to Sloane's father sealed their helplessness, for the latter, a retired cotton broker out of Alabama, was a notorious fundamentalist who controlled his son by a rigid allowance and the promise that at his next vagary the allowance would stop forever.

They dined at a small French restaurant, and the discussion continued —at one time Sloane resorted to physical threats, a little later they were both imploring him to give them time. But Anson was obdurate. He saw that Edna was breaking up, and that her spirit must not be refreshed by any renewal of their passion.

At two o'clock in a small night-club on 53rd Street, Edna's nerves suddenly collapsed, and she cried to go home. Sloane had been drinking heavily all evening, and he was faintly maudlin, leaning on the table and weeping a little with his face in his hands. Quickly Anson gave them his terms. Sloane was to leave town for six months, and he must be gone within forty-eight hours. When he returned there was to be no resumption of the affair, but at the end of a year Edna might, if she wished, tell Robert Hunter that she wanted a divorce and go about it in the usual way.

He paused, gaining confidence from their faces for his final word.

"Or there's another thing you can do," he said slowly, "if Edna wants to leave her children, there's nothing I can do to prevent your running off together."

"I want to go home!" cried Edna again. "Oh, haven't you done enough to us for one day?"

Outside it was dark, save for a blurred glow from Sixth Avenue down the street. In that light those two who had been lovers looked for the last time into each other's tragic faces, realizing that between them there was not enough youth and strength to avert their eternal parting. Sloane walked suddenly off down the street and Anson tapped a dozing taxi-driver on the arm.

It was almost four; there was a patient flow of cleaning water along the ghostly pavement of Fifth Avenue, and the shadows of two night women flitted over the dark façade of St. Thomas's church. Then the desolate shrubbery of Central Park where Anson had often played as a child, and the mounting numbers, significant as names, of the marching streets. This was his city, he thought, where his name had flourished through five generations. No change could alter the permanence of its place here, for change itself was the essential substratum by which he and those of his name identified themselves with the spirit of New York. Resourcefulness and a powerful will—for his threats in weaker hands would have been less than nothing—had beaten the gathering dust from his uncle's name, from the name of his family, from even this shivering figure that sat beside him in the car.

Cary Sloane's body was found next morning on the lower shelf of a pillar of Queensboro Bridge. In the darkness and in his excitement he had thought that it was the water flowing black beneath him, but in less than a second it made no possible difference—unless he had planned to think one last thought of Edna, and to call out her name as he struggled feebly in the water.

VII

Anson never blamed himself for his part in this affair—the situation which brought it about had not been of his making. But the just suffer with the unjust, and he found that his oldest and somehow his most precious friendship was over. He never knew what distorted story Edna told, but he was welcome in his uncle's house no longer.

Just before Christmas Mrs. Hunter retired to a select Episcopal heaven, and Anson became the responsible head of his family. An unmarried aunt who had lived with them for years ran the house, and attempted with helpless inefficiency to chaperone the younger girls. All the children were less self-reliant than Anson, more conventional both in their virtues and in their shortcomings. Mrs. Hunter's death had postponed the début of one daughter and the wedding of another. Also it had taken something deeply material from all of them, for with her passing the quiet, expensive superiority of the Hunters came to an end.

For one thing, the estate, considerably diminished by two inheritance taxes and soon to be divided among six children, was not a notable fortune any more. Anson saw a tendency in his youngest sisters to speak rather respectfully of families that hadn't "existed" twenty years ago. His own feeling of precedence was not echoed in them—sometimes they were conventionally snobbish, that was all. For another thing, this was the last summer they would spend on the Connecticut estate; the clamor against it was too loud: "Who wants to waste the best months of the year shut up in that dead old town?" Reluctantly he yielded—the house would go into the market in the fall, and the next summer they would rent a smaller place in Westchester County. It was a step down from the expensive simplicity of his father's idea, and, while he sympathized with the revolt, it also annoyed him; during his mother's lifetime he had gone up there at least every other week-end—even in the gayest summers.

Yet he himself was part of this change, and his strong instinct for life had turned him in his twenties from the hollow obsequies of that abortive leisure class. He did not see this clearly—he still felt that there was a norm, a standard of society. But there was no norm, it was doubtful if there had ever been a true norm in New York. The few who still paid and fought to enter a particular set succeeded only to find that as a society it scarcely functioned—or, what was more alarming, that the Bohemia from which they fled sat above them at table.

At twenty-nine Anson's chief concern was his own growing loneliness. He was sure now that he would never marry. The number of weddings at which he had officiated as best man or usher was past all counting—there was a drawer at home that bulged with the official neckties of this or that wedding-party, neckties standing for romances that had not endured a year, for couples who had passed completely from his life. Scarf-pins, gold pencils, cuff-buttons, presents from a generation of grooms had passed through his jewel-box and been lost—and with every ceremony he was less and less able to imagine himself in the groom's place. Under his hearty good-will toward all those marriages there was despair about his own.

And as he neared thirty he became not a little depressed at the inroads that marriage, especially lately, had made upon his friendships. Groups of people had a disconcerting tendency to dissolve and disappear. The men from his own college—and it was upon them that he had expended the most time and affection—were the most elusive of all. Most of them were drawn deep into domesticity, two were dead, one lived abroad, one was in Hollywood writing continuities for pictures that Anson went faithfully to see.

Most of them, however, were permanent commuters with an intricate family life centering around some suburban country club, and it was from these that he felt his estrangement most keenly.

In the early days of their married life they had all needed him; he gave them advice about their slim finances, he exorcised their doubts about the advisability of bringing a baby into two rooms and a bath, especially he stood for the great world outside. But now their financial troubles were in the past and the fearfully expected child had evolved into an absorbing family. They were always glad to see old Anson, but they dressed up for him and tried to impress him with their present importance, and kept their troubles to themselves. They needed him no longer.

A few weeks before his thirtieth birthday the last of his early and intimate friends was married. Anson acted in his usual role of best man, gave his usual silver tea-service, and went down to the usual *Homeric* to say good-by. It was a hot Friday afternoon in May, and as he walked from the pier he realized that Saturday closing had begun and he was free until Monday morning.

"Go where?" he asked himself.

The Yale Club, of course; bridge until dinner, then four or five raw cocktails in somebody's room and a pleasant confused evening. He regretted that this afternoon's groom wouldn't be along—they had always been able to cram so much into such nights: they knew how to attach women and how to get rid of them, how much consideration any girl

deserved from their intelligent hedonism. A party was an adjusted thing
—you took certain girls to certain places and spent just so much on their
amusement; you drank a little, not much, more than you ought to drink,
and at a certain time in the morning you stood up and said you were going
home. You avoided college boys, sponges, future engagements, fights, sentiment, and indiscretions. That was the way it was done. All the rest was
dissipation.

In the morning you were never violently sorry—you made no resolutions,
but if you had overdone it and your heart was slightly out of order, you
went on the wagon for a few days without saying anything about it, and
waited until an accumulation of nervous boredom projected you into another party.

The lobby of the Yale Club was unpopulated. In the bar three very young
alumni looked up at him, momentarily and without curiosity.

"Hello there, Oscar," he said to the bartender. "Mr. Cahill been around
this afternoon?"

"Mr. Cahill's gone to New Haven."

"Oh . . . that so?"

"Gone to the ball game. Lot of men gone up."

Anson looked once again into the lobby, considered for a moment, and
then walked out and over to Fifth Avenue. From the broad window of one
of his clubs—one that he had scarcely visited in five years—a gray man with
watery eyes stared down at him. Anson looked quickly away—that figure
sitting in vacant resignation, in supercilious solitude, depressed him. He
stopped and, retracing his steps, started over 47th Street toward Teak
Warden's apartment. Teak and his wife had once been his most familiar
friends—it was a household where he and Dolly Karger had been used to
go in the days of their affair. But Teak had taken to drink, and his wife had
remarked publicly that Anson was a bad influence on him. The remark
reached Anson in an exaggerated form—when it was finally cleared up, the
delicate spell of intimacy was broken, never to be renewed.

"Is Mr. Warden at home?" he inquired.

"They've gone to the country."

The fact unexpectedly cut at him. They were gone to the country and he
hadn't known. Two years before he would have known the date, the hour,
come up at the last moment for a final drink, and planned his first visit to
them. Now they had gone without a word.

Anson looked at his watch and considered a week-end with his family,
but the only train was a local that would jolt through the aggressive heat
for three hours. And tomorrow in the country, and Sunday—he was in no
mood for porch-bridge with polite undergraduates, and dancing after dinner
at a rural roadhouse, a diminutive of gayety which his father had estimated
too well.

"Oh, no," he said to himself. . . . "No."

He was a dignified, impressive young man, rather stout now, but otherwise unmarked by dissipation. He could have been cast for a pillar of something—at times you were sure it was not society, at others nothing else—for the law, for the church. He stood for a few minutes motionless on the sidewalk in front of a 47th Street apartment house; for almost the first time in his life he had nothing whatever to do.

Then he began to walk briskly up Fifth Avenue, as if he had just been reminded of an important engagement there. The necessity of dissimulation is one of the few characteristics that we share with dogs, and I think of Anson on that day as some well-bred specimen who had been disappointed at a familiar back door. He was going to see Nick, once a fashionable bartender in demand at all private dances, and now employed in cooling non-alcoholic champagne among the labyrinthine cellars of the Plaza Hotel.

"Nick," he said, "what's happened to everything?"

"Dead," Nick said.

"Make me a whisky sour." Anson handed a pint bottle over the counter. "Nick, the girls are different; I had a little girl in Brooklyn and she got married last week without letting me know."

"That a fact? Ha-ha-ha," responded Nick diplomatically. "Slipped it over on you."

"Absolutely," said Anson. "And I was out with her the night before."

"Ha-ha-ha," said Nick, "ha-ha-ha!"

"Do you remember the wedding, Nick, in Hot Springs where I had the waiters and the musicians singing 'God save the King'?"

"Now where was that, Mr. Hunter?" Nick concentrated doubtfully. "Seems to me that was——"

"Next time they were back for more, and I began to wonder how much I'd paid them," continued Anson.

"——seems to me that was at Mr. Trenholm's wedding."

"Don't know him," said Anson decisively. He was offended that a strange name should intrude upon his reminiscences; Nick perceived this.

"Naw—aw—" he admitted, "I ought to know that. It was one of *your* crowd—Brakins . . . . Baker——"

"Bicker Baker," said Anson responsively. "They put me in a hearse after it was over and covered me up with flowers and drove me away."

"Ha-ha-ha," said Nick. "Ha-ha-ha."

Nick's simulation of the old family servant paled presently and Anson went up-stairs to the lobby. He looked around—his eyes met the glance of an unfamiliar clerk at the desk, then fell upon a flower from the morning's marriage hesitating in the mouth of a brass cuspidor. He went out and walked slowly toward the blood-red sun over Columbus Circle. Suddenly he turned around and, retracing his steps to the Plaza, immured himself in a telephone-booth.

Later he said that he tried to get me three times that afternoon, that he tried everyone who might be in New York—men and girls he had not seen for years, an artist's model of his college days whose faded number was still in his address book—Central told him that even the exchange existed no longer. At length his quest roved into the country, and he held brief disappointing conversations with emphatic butlers and maids. So-and-so was out, riding, swimming, playing golf, sailed to Europe last week. Who shall I say phoned?

It was intolerable that he should pass the evening alone—the private reckonings which one plans for a moment of leisure lose every charm when the solitude is enforced. There were always women of a sort, but the ones he knew had temporarily vanished, and to pass a New York evening in the hired company of a stranger never occurred to him—he would have considered that that was something shameful and secret, the diversion of a traveling salesman in a strange town.

Anson paid the telephone bill—the girl tried unsuccessfully to joke with him about its size—and for the second time that afternoon started to leave the Plaza and go he knew not where. Near the revolving door the figure of a woman, obviously with child, stood sideways to the light—a sheer beige cape fluttered at her shoulders when the door turned and, each time, she looked impatiently toward it as if she were weary of waiting. At the first sight of her a strong nervous thrill of familiarity went over him, but not until he was within five feet of her did he realize that it was Paula.

"Why, Anson Hunter!"

His heart turned over.

"Why, Paula——"

"Why, this is wonderful. I can't believe it, *Anson!*"

She took both his hands, and he saw in the freedom of the gesture that the memory of him had lost poignancy to her. But not to him—he felt that old mood that she evoked in him stealing over his brain, that gentleness with which he had always met her optimism as if afraid to mar its surface.

"We're at Rye for the summer. Pete had to come East on business—you know of course I'm Mrs. Peter Hagerty now—so we brought the children and took a house. You've got to come out and see us."

"Can I?" he asked directly. "When?"

"When you like. Here's Pete." The revolving door functioned, giving up a fine tall man of thirty with a tanned face and a trim mustache. His immaculate fitness made a sharp contrast with Anson's increasing bulk, which was obvious under the faintly tight cut-away coat.

"You oughtn't to be standing," said Hagerty to his wife. "Let's sit down here." He indicated lobby chairs, but Paula hesitated.

"I've got to go right home," she said. "Anson, why don't you—why don't you come out and have dinner with us tonight? We're just getting settled, but if you can stand that——"

Hagerty confirmed the invitation cordially.

"Come out for the night."

Their car waited in front of the hotel, and Paula with a tired gesture sank back against silk cushions in the corner.

"There's so much I want to talk to you about," she said, "it seems hopeless."

"I want to hear about you."

"Well"—she smiled at Hagerty—"that would take a long time too. I have three children—by my first marriage. The oldest is five, then four, then three." She smiled again. "I didn't waste much time having them, did I?"

"Boys?"

"A boy and two girls. Then—oh, a lot of things happened, and I got a divorce in Paris a year ago and married Pete. That's all—except that I'm awfully happy."

In Rye they drove up to a large house near the Beach Club, from which there issued presently three dark, slim children who broke from an English governess and approached them with an esoteric cry. Abstractedly and with difficulty Paula took each one into her arms, a caress which they accepted stiffly, as they had evidently been told not to bump into Mummy. Even against their fresh faces Paula's skin showed scarcely any weariness— for all her physical languor she seemed younger than when he had last seen her at Palm Beach seven years ago.

At dinner she was preoccupied, and afterward, during the homage to the radio, she lay with closed eyes on the sofa, until Anson wondered if his presence at this time were not an intrusion. But at nine o'clock when Hagerty rose and said pleasantly that he was going to leave them by themselves for a while, she began to talk slowly about herself and the past.

"My first baby," she said—"the one we call Darling, the biggest little girl —I wanted to die when I knew I was going to have her, because Lowell was like a stranger to me. It didn't seem as though she could be my own. I wrote you a letter and tore it up. Oh, you were *so* bad to me, Anson."

It was the dialogue again, rising and falling. Anson felt a sudden quickening of memory.

"Weren't you engaged once?" she asked—"a girl named Dolly something?"

"I wasn't ever engaged. I tried to be engaged, but I never loved anybody but you, Paula."

"Oh," she said. Then after a moment: "This baby is the first one I ever really wanted. You see, I'm in love now—at last."

He didn't answer, shocked at the treachery of her remembrance. She must have seen that the "at last" bruised him, for she continued:

"I was infatuated with you, Anson—you could make me do anything you liked. But we wouldn't have been happy. I'm not smart enough for you. I don't like things to be complicated like you do." She paused. "You'll never settle down," she said.

The phrase struck at him from behind—it was an accusation that of all accusations he had never merited.

"I could settle down if women were different," he said. "If I didn't understand so much about them, if women didn't spoil you for other women, if they had only a little pride. If I could go to sleep for a while and wake up into a home that was really mine—why, that's what I'm made for, Paula, that's what women have seen in me and liked in me. It's only that I can't get through the preliminaries any more."

Hagerty came in a little before eleven; after a whisky Paula stood up and announced that she was going to bed. She went over and stood by her husband.

"Where did you go, dearest?" she demanded.

"I had a drink with Ed Saunders."

"I was worried. I thought maybe you'd run away."

She rested her head against his coat.

"He's sweet, isn't he, Anson?" she demanded.

"Absolutely," said Anson, laughing.

She raised her face to her husband.

"Well, I'm ready," she said. She turned to Anson: "Do you want to see our family gymnastic stunt?"

"Yes," he said in an interested voice.

"All right. Here we go!"

Hagerty picked her up easily in his arms.

"This is called the family acrobatic stunt," said Paula. "He carries me up-stairs. Isn't it sweet of him?"

"Yes," said Anson.

Hagerty bent his head slightly until his face touched Paula's.

"And I love him," she said. "I've just been telling you, haven't I, Anson?"

"Yes," he said.

"He's the dearest thing that ever lived in this world; aren't you, darling? . . . Well, good night. Here we go. Isn't he strong?"

"Yes," Anson said.

"You'll find a pair of Pete's pajamas laid out for you. Sweet dreams—see you at breakfast."

"Yes," Anson said.

VIII

The older members of the firm insisted that Anson should go abroad for the summer. He had scarcely had a vacation in seven years, they said. He was stale and needed a change. Anson resisted.

"If I go," he declared, "I won't come back any more."

"That's absurd, old man. You'll be back in three months with all this depression gone. Fit as ever."

"No." He shook his head stubbornly. "If I stop, I won't go back to work. If I stop, that means I've given up—I'm through."

"We'll take a chance on that. Stay six months if you like—we're not afraid you'll leave us. Why, you'd be miserable if you didn't work."

They arranged his passage for him. They liked Anson—everyone liked Anson—and the change that had been coming over him cast a sort of pall over the office. The enthusiasm that had invariably signaled up business, the consideration toward his equals and his inferiors, the lift of his vital presence—within the past four months his intense nervousness had melted down these qualities into the fussy pessimism of a man of forty. On every transaction in which he was involved he acted as a drag and a strain.

"If I go I'll never come back," he said.

Three days before he sailed Paula Legendre Hagerty died in childbirth. I was with him a great deal then, for we were crossing together, but for the first time in our friendship he told me not a word of how he felt, nor did I see the slightest sign of emotion. His chief preoccupation was with the fact that he was thirty years old—he would turn the conversation to the point where he could remind you of it and then fall silent, as if he assumed that the statement would start a chain of thought sufficient to itself. Like his partners, I was amazed at the change in him, and I was glad when the *Paris* moved off into the wet space between the worlds, leaving his principality behind.

"How about a drink?" he suggested.

We walked into the bar with that defiant feeling that characterizes the day of departure and ordered four Martinis. After one cocktail a change came over him—he suddenly reached across and slapped my knee with the first joviality I had seen him exhibit for months.

"Did you see that girl in the red tam?" he demanded, "the one with the high color who had the two police dogs down to bid her good-by."

"She's pretty," I agreed.

"I looked her up in the purser's office and found out that she's alone. I'm going down to see the steward in a few minutes. We'll have dinner with her tonight."

After a while he left me, and within an hour he was walking up and down the deck with her, talking to her in his strong, clear voice. Her red tam was a bright spot of color against the steel-green sea, and from time to time she looked up with a flashing bob of her head, and smiled with amusement and interest, and anticipation. At dinner we had champagne, and were very joyous—afterward Anson ran the pool with infectious gusto, and several people who had seen me with him asked me his name. He and the girl were talking and laughing together on a lounge in the bar when I went to bed.

I saw less of him on the trip than I had hoped. He wanted to arrange a foursome, but there was no one available, so I saw him only at meals. Sometimes, though, he would have a cocktail in the bar, and he told me about the girl in the red tam, and his adventures with her, making them all bizarre and amusing, as he had a way of doing, and I was glad that he was himself again, or at least the self that I knew, and with which I felt at home. I don't think he was ever happy unless someone was in love with him, responding to him like filings to a magnet, helping him to explain himself, promising him something. What it was I do not know. Perhaps they promised that there would always be women in the world who would spend their brightest, freshest, rarest hours to nurse and protect that superiority he cherished in his heart.

THE IMPOSITION

L. A. G. Strong

(1896–   )

"Six."

"Sir!"

"Very well, then. Five."

"*Sir!*"

"You know perfectly well by now, Russell, that if you are dissatisfied with my marking I'm always ready to revise it—in the downward direction."

"Oh, *sir!*"

"Are you satisfied, or do you wish me to revise still further?"

The victim sighed, rolling his eyes with every symptom of polite ill-usage.

Roger Champernown looked down at his book. He took a grip on himself, digging his nails into the palms of his hands. The moment had arrived. He glanced at the next few lines of the text. No, they were not unfairly hard. No one could say that he was deliberately choosing them because they were hard. Even supposing they contained opportunities for just the sort of mistake that the boy would be likely to make . . .

Was it fair for a man, whispered some inner voice, to use his psychological knowledge, his knowledge of a boy's character, in a guess to the boy's undoing? Nonsense, he retorted. Nonsense. It was the boy's business to know the whole piece, every word of it!

"Henderson. Translate."

A fair-haired, handsome boy looked up with an air of surprise.

"Me, sir?"

"Your name is Henderson, I believe."

"Quite right, sir."

"What did you say?"

"Yes, sir."

Champernown ventured to look up, and glared into the blue eyes that with deceptive frankness met his own.

"Translate, then—if you will be so good."

The boy smiled. He stretched out his arms, as if shooting imaginary cuffs; pulled up his trousers; settled himself erect at his desk; smiled once more obligingly; and gave the passage his attention. He looked at it for a couple of seconds, then raised his eyebrows. The man must be humoured, said his gesture. It contrived also subtly to suggest that what was being asked of him was unreasonable.

"Let me see, now," he murmured, as if to himself.

"Get on," exclaimed Champernown thickly, and stopped, saying savagely to himself, Fool, fool; don't let yourself be drawn.

"I beg your pardon, sir."

"Get on," said Champernown.

The boy looked again at the text, inclining his head first to one side and then to the other.

"*Inde*," he began. "Thence—or thenceforward."

He paused, and looked expectantly at Champernown, like a dog who has done a trick, and expects applause. Champernown kept his eyes fixed on his book.

"*Inde*," repeated Henderson. "Thenceforward, or thence. No, thenceforward, I think. Thenceforward. *Atrocius certamen*." He hesitated. "The atrocious strife . . . ."

Champernown uttered a noise between a growl and a hiss.

"Isn't that right, sir?" asked the boy, leaning forward, as one deeply disappointed by the failure of his effort to please.

"Tacitus, as you may possibly have noticed," observed the master with sarcasm, "has an occasional habit of leaving out the verb."

"Yes, sir. So thoughtless of him."

"What?"

"Yes, sir. I had noticed."

"It is a pity, then, Henderson, that you do not learn by experience."

"Mr. Bernard Shaw says that we never learn by experience, sir."

Champernown saw red. The boy was deliberately provoking him. Never mind. He would not be led into making a fool of himself again before the class. Henderson did not know his piece. He had probably concentrated upon the difficult bit near the end, the bit with the hard words in it, supposing that Champernown would give it to him out of spite. Champernown had guessed he would, and outwitted him by giving him this earlier, ap-

parently easier bit. Evidently, the guess had been sound. All that was necessary was to sit tight and let the wretched boy establish his ignorance.

Champernown sat tight, refusing every red rag, every bait, until he was
able legitimately to pass sentence.

"Since you have omitted the formality of preparing your lesson, Henderson, you will remain and repair the omission this afternoon."

"Repair what, sir?"

"Do the lesson which you have not done."

"I'm awfully sorry, sir, but I'm afraid that's impossible."

Shaking his head from side to side, the boy regarded him with sad blue
eyes.

"Impossible?"

"Quite, I'm afraid, sir. You see, I have to attend fielding practice with
Mr. Bevan."

Champernown swallowed.

"Very well, then. You will do it to-morrow afternoon."

"Impossible too, sir, I'm afraid. The Silchester match."

It was a point of principle, and Champernown was not going to let it
go. He had had Henderson on his nerves for weeks. He had been ready
to like the boy, to be friendly with him. *He* hadn't begun all this. Yet, for
no reason at all, the boy baited him, without mercy, seldom giving him a
loophole for open action. Even so, he told himself, this was not the reason
for pursuing him. It was a point of principle.

As he expected, the day after the match found Henderson equally elusive.
Apparently he had another rendezvous with the headmaster. Doggedly,
Champernown made his way after lunch to Bevan's study. He felt at a dis-
advantage before he had begun, but persisted, face and ears reddening.

"Oh, come." The bluff, prematurely bald man eyed him tolerantly. "Oh,
come. Rather ancient history, isn't it?"

Champernown swallowed. He had known before he started that he was
on a difficult errand. Henderson was the apple of the cricketing headmaster's eye, and, to make matters worse, he had made seventy-four in the
match.

"Very well," Champernown was saying in a few minutes. "As you wish,
of course. It will make matters difficult for me with my form if I have to
show preferential treatment, but . . ."

The headmaster raised his eyebrows, but refused to be ruffled.

"Hardly preferential treatment, Champernown," he said benignly. "Boys
are understanding creatures, you know. They'll understand all right."

"You are making this very difficult for me, sir."

"Oh come, Champernown, you exaggerate." The headmaster spoke
heartily. "You take these little matters too seriously. A good fault, my dear
fellow, but, nevertheless, a fault."

Champernown stood, pale, dogged.

"It has happened before, sir."

"What has?"

"Only a couple of weeks ago, when I had occasion to keep Henderson in, you—you excused him the imposition. The boy is clearly presuming on it. He defies me openly. I'm afraid he—and the others—may get the impression that you support him."

The headmaster's face crimsoned. He turned impatiently on his heel.

"Oh, very well," he snapped over his shoulder. "Have it your own way, Champernown. Have it your own way."

At twenty past three, two afternoons later, Champernown decided he must have a breath of air. Even with the windows wide open, the empty classroom was stifling. Henderson's exercise book lay open before him. He had taken twenty minutes over it, looking closely for faults, then over-marking the boy in his morbid, self-exculpatory anxiety to be fair. Henderson had not yet done his imposition. Bevan had found various reasons for keeping him on the cricket field. But he should do it. He should do it, by God he should! Champernown set his jaw. He would resign, he would pull the whole place up by the roots, sooner than allow that imposition to be evaded.

With an overwrought gesture, he put the pile of exercise books inside the desk, slammed down the lid, and made for the field. Coming out round the corner of the chapel, he ran straight into a small and white-faced procession carrying a limp figure.

"Henderson. . . . In the nets. . . . Ball came smack through . . . . I always said that net was dangerous. . . . Full on the temple. . . . Yes, one of Lacey's hardest."

The whole school, buildings, playing fields, and all, lay under a cloud till five, when it was announced that the victim was sitting up, declaring that he felt perfectly all right, and demanding to be allowed to return to ordinary life. The doctor had seen him, and could find no injury.

At about half past six, Champernown, after long debate, nerved himself to go up to the sick bay and inquire how the boy was getting on. He might even be allowed to see him. After all, why shouldn't he? It was only natural he should want to know. He was the boy's form master.

With beating heart, he went up the leaded stairs, and down the long, bare passage, decorated only with fire extinguishers. Opening the green baize door, he heard voices in the ante-room, and stopped short.

"Very well, then, Matron. Keep him where he is till bedtime, and let him go back to the dormitory."

"No thank you, Mr. Bevan. I'm going to keep him where he is all night, and sit up with him too."

"Really, Matron, I must say, I think you're making too much of this.

You've heard Dr. Slater's opinion. Fussing like this will only create a bad impression. The school is quite sufficiently upset as it is. You'd much better let him go down."

"No thank you, Mr. Bevan. This is my responsibility."

"Really, Matron——"

Stepping back, Champernown silently closed the door. It would be injudicious to go in at the moment. He could inquire again later.

He was a little late for breakfast the next morning, and made his way self-consciously up the big hall between the tables, half annoyed and half pleased at the occasional cries of "Good morning, sir," which greeted him as he passed. He never knew whether to acknowledge them or not.

When he reached the top table, he noticed with surprise that the headmaster was absent. Only three of the men were there, silent, with long faces.

"Haven't you heard?"

"Heard what?"

"About Henderson."

"Henderson? What about him?"

"Died in the night."

"No! Good God!"

"Yes. Sat up suddenly in bed, squinted, cried out, and then fell back dead."

The room began to spin around Champernown. Half conscious, he heard the hushed voices.

"By Jove, it's a feather in Matron's cap, anyway. Lucky she insisted on sitting up with him. Bevan will be thankful enough to her when it comes to the inquest."

As soon as he regained proper consciousness of his surroundings, Champernown felt himself unable to eat. He swallowed a few mouthfuls of his coffee, then made his way out. As he did so, he passed the Matron coming in, grimly justified. Two minutes later, he was knocking at the door of the headmaster's study.

"I really can't see you now, Champernown. I'm—that is, there's a great deal to do."

"I've only just come to tell you . . . to hand in my resignation."

The man was not listening. His back was turned. He was ferreting among papers. He looked pale, ill, blotchy, and old.

"Yes, yes, yes. Well, come later on, Champernown. I really can't see you now."

Suddenly Champernown stamped uncontrollably.

"I resign, I tell you," he shouted. "I resign! Do you understand? I resign!"

Then he turned round, and ran away, blundering down the passage, talking to himself and sobbing. At a corner, he charged into a colleague. The younger man's pupils contracted to pin-points. He stared after the retreating figure, then uttered a long, low whistle.

"Well," he exclaimed. "Whoever would have thought he'd take it like that!"

But Champernown was not weeping for the dead. He was weeping because, in a sudden searing flash, he had seen what his calling had made of him. He did not feel sorrow. He felt simply that Henderson had escaped him, that he had been cheated. In a mad corner of his mind, he would have wished that afternoon to go up to the sick bay, take the corpse, and set it at its desk in the empty class-room, that justice might be satisfied.

TURN ABOUT

William Faulkner

(1897–)

THE AMERICAN—the older one—wore no pink Bedfords. His breeches were of plain whipcord, like the tunic. And the tunic had no long London-cut skirts, so that below the Sam Browne the tail of it stuck straight out like the tunic of a military policeman beneath his holster belt. And he wore simple putties and the easy shoes of a man of middle age, instead of Savile Row boots, and the shoes and the putties did not match in shade, and the ordnance belt did not match either of them, and the pilot's wings on his breast were just wings. But the ribbon beneath them was a good ribbon, and the insigne on his shoulders were the twin bars of a captain. He was not tall. His face was thin, a little aquiline; the eyes intelligent and a little tired. He was past twenty-five; looking at him, one thought, not Phi Beta Kappa exactly, but Skull and Bones perhaps, or possibly a Rhodes scholarship.

One of the men who faced him probably could not see him at all. He was being held on his feet by an American military policeman. He was quite drunk, and in contrast with the heavy-jawed policeman who held him erect on his long, slim, boneless legs, he looked like a masquerading girl. He was possibly eighteen, tall, with a pink-and-white face and blue eyes, and a mouth like a girl's mouth. He wore a pea-coat, buttoned awry and stained with recent mud, and upon his blond head, at that unmistakable and rakish swagger which no other people can ever approach or imitate, the cap of a Royal Naval officer.

"What's this, Corporal?" the American captain said. "What's the trouble? He's an Englishman. You'd better let their M. P.'s take care of him."

"I know he is," the policeman said. He spoke heavily, breathing heavily, in the voice of a man under physical strain; for all his girlish delicacy of limb, the English boy was heavier—or more helpless—than he looked. "Stand up!" the policeman said. "They're officers!"

The English boy made an effort then. He pulled himself together, focusing his eyes. He swayed, throwing his arm about the policeman's neck, and with the other hand he saluted, his hand flicking, fingers curled a little, to his right ear, already swaying again and catching himself again. "Cheerio, sir," he said. "Name's not Beatty, I hope."

"No," the captain said.

"Ah," the English boy said. "Hoped not. My mistake. No offense, what?"

"No offense," the captain said quietly. But he was looking at the policeman. The second American spoke. He was a lieutenant, also a pilot. But he was not twenty-five and he wore the pink breeches, the London boots, and his tunic might have been a British tunic save for the collar.

"It's one of those navy eggs," he said. "They pick them out of the gutters here all night long. You don't come to town often enough."

"Oh," the captain said. "I've heard about them. I remember now." He also remarked now that, though the street was a busy one—it was just outside a popular café—and there were many passers, soldier, civilian, women, yet none of them so much as paused, as though it were a familiar sight. He was looking at the policeman. "Can't you take him to his ship?"

"I thought of that before the captain did," the policeman said. "He says he can't go aboard his ship after dark because he puts the ship away at sundown."

"Puts it away?"

"Stand up, sailor!" the policeman said savagely, jerking at his lax burden. "Maybe the captain can make sense out of it. Damned if I can. He says they keep the boat under the wharf. Run it under the wharf at night, and that they can't get it out again until the tide goes out tomorrow."

"Under the wharf? A boat? What is this?" He was now speaking to the lieutenant. "Do they operate some kind of aquatic motorcycles?"

"Something like that," the lieutenant said. "You've seen them—the boats. Launches, camouflaged and all. Dashing up and down the harbor. You've seen them. They do that all day and sleep in the gutters here all night."

"Oh," the captain said. "I thought those boats were ship commanders' launches. You mean to tell me they use officers just to——"

"I don't know," the lieutenant said. "Maybe they use them to fetch hot water from one ship to another. Or buns. Or maybe to go back and forth fast when they forget napkins or something."

"Nonsense," the captain said. He looked at the English boy again.

"That's what they do," the lieutenant said. "Town's lousy with them all night long. Gutters full, and their M.P.'s carting them away in batches, like nursemaids in a park. Maybe the French give them the launches to get them out of the gutters during the day."

"Oh," the captain said, "I see." But it was clear that he didn't see, wasn't listening, didn't believe what he did hear. He looked at the English boy. "Well, you can't leave him here in that shape," he said.

Again the English boy tried to pull himself together. "Quite all right, 'sure you," he said glassily, his voice pleasant, cheerful almost, quite courteous. "Used to it. Confounded rough *pavé*, though. Should force French do something about it. Visiting lads jolly well deserve decent field to play on, what?"

"And he was jolly well using all of it too," the policeman said savagely. "He must think he's a one-man team, maybe."

At that moment a fifth man came up. He was a British military policeman. "Nah then," he said. "What's this? What's this?" Then he saw the American's shoulder bars. He saluted. At the sound of his voice the English boy turned, swaying, peering.

"Oh, hullo, Albert," he said.

"Nah then, Mr. Hope," the British policeman said. He said to the American policeman, over his shoulder: "What is it this time?"

"Likely nothing," the American said. "The way you guys run a war. But I'm a stranger here. Here. Take him."

"What is this, Corporal?" the captain said. "What was he doing?"

"He won't call it nothing," the American policeman said, jerking his head at the British policeman. "He'll just call it a thrush or a robin or something. I turn into this street about three blocks back a while ago, and I find it blocked with a line of trucks going up from the docks, and the drivers all hollering ahead what the hell the trouble is. So I come on, and I find it is about three blocks of them, blocking the cross streets too; and I come on to the head of it where the trouble is, and I find about a dozen of the drivers out in front, holding a caucus or something in the middle of the street, and I come up and I say, 'What's going on here?' and they leave me through and I find this egg here laying——"

"Yer talking about one of His Majesty's officers, my man," the British policeman said.

"Watch yourself, Corporal," the captain said. "And you found this officer——"

"He had done gone to bed in the middle of the street, with an empty basket for a pillow. Laying there with his hands under his head and his knees crossed, arguing with them about whether he ought to get up and move or not. He said that the trucks could turn back and go around by another street, but that he couldn't use any other street, because this street was his."

"His street?"

The English boy had listened, interested, pleasant. "Billet, you see," he said. "Must have order, even in war emergency. Billet by lot. This street mine; no poaching, eh? Next street Jamie Wutherspoon's. But trucks can go by that street because Jamie not using it yet. Not in bed yet. Insomnia. Knew so. Told them. Trucks go that way. See now?"

"Was that it, Corporal?" the captain said.

"He told you. He wouldn't get up. He just laid there, arguing with them. He was telling one of them to go somewhere and bring back a copy of their articles of war——"

"King's Regulations; yes," the captain said.

"—and see if the book said whether he had the right of way, or the trucks. And then I got him up, and then the captain come along. And that's all. And with the captain's permission I'll now hand him over to His Majesty's wet nur——"

"That'll do, Corporal," the captain said. "You can go. I'll see to this." The policeman saluted and went on. The British policeman was now supporting the English boy. "Can't you take him home?" the captain said. "Where are their quarters?"

"I don't rightly know, sir, if they have quarters or not. We—I usually see them about the pubs until daylight. They don't seem to use quarters."

"You mean, they really aren't off of ships?"

"Well, sir, they might be ships, in a manner of speaking. But a man would have to be a bit sleepier than him to sleep in one of them."

"I see," the captain said. He looked at the policeman. "What kind of boats are they?"

This time the policeman's voice was immediate, final and completely inflectionless. It was like a closed door. "I don't rightly know, sir."

"Oh," the captain said. "Quite. Well, he's in no shape to stay about pubs until daylight this time."

"Perhaps I can find him a bit of a pub with a back table, where he can sleep," the policeman said. But the captain was not listening. He was looking across the street, where the lights of another café fell across the pavement. The English boy yawned terrifically, like a child does, his mouth pink and frankly gaped as a child's.

The captain turned to the policeman:

"Would you mind stepping across there and asking for Captain Bogard's driver? I'll take care of Mr. Hope."

The policeman departed. The captain now supported the English boy, his hand beneath the other's arm. Again the boy yawned like a weary child. "Steady," the captain said. "The car will be here in a minute."

"Right," the English boy said through the yawn.

Once in the car, he went to sleep immediately with the peaceful suddenness of babies, sitting between the two Americans. But though the aerodrome was only thirty minutes away, he was awake when they arrived, apparently quite fresh, and asking for whisky. When they entered the mess he appeared quite sober, only blinking a little in the lighted room, in his raked cap and his awry-buttoned pea-jacket and a soiled silk muffler, embroidered with a club insignia which Bogard recognized to have come from a famous preparatory school, twisted about his throat.

"Ah," he said, his voice fresh, clear now, not blurred, quite cheerful, quite loud, so that the others in the room turned and looked at him. "Jolly. Whisky, what?" He went straight as a bird dog to the bar in the corner, the lieutenant following. Bogard had turned and gone on to the other end of the room, where five men sat about a card table.

"What's he admiral of?" one said.

"Of the whole Scotch navy, when I found him," Bogard said.

Another looked up. "Oh. I thought I'd seen him in town." He looked at the guest. "Maybe it's because he was on his feet that I didn't recognize him when he came in. You usually see them lying down in the gutter."

"Oh," the first said. He, too, looked around. "Is he one of those guys?"

"Sure. You've seen them. Sitting on the curb, you know, with a couple of limey M. P.'s hauling at their arms."

"Yes. I've seen them," the other said. They all looked at the English boy. He stood at the bar, talking, his voice loud, cheerful. "They all look like him too," the speaker said. "About seventeen or eighteen. They run those little boats that are always dashing in and out."

"Is that what they do?" a third said. "You mean, there's a male marine auxiliary to the Waacs? Good Lord, I sure made a mistake when I enlisted. But this war never was advertised right."

"I don't know," Bogard said. "I guess they do more than just ride around."

But they were not listening to him. They were looking at the guest. "They run by clock," the first said. "You can see the condition of one of them after sunset and almost tell what time it is. But what I don't see, is how a man that's in that shape at one o'clock every morning can even see a battleship the next day."

"Maybe when they have a message to send out to a ship," another said, "they just make duplicates and line the launches up and point them toward the ship and give each one a duplicate of the message and let them go. And the ones that miss the ship just cruise around the harbor until they hit a dock somewhere."

"It must be more than that," Bogard said.

He was about to say something else, but at that moment the guest turned from the bar and approached, carrying a glass. He walked steadily enough, but his color was high and his eyes were bright, and he was talking, loud, cheerful, as he came up.

"I say. Won't you chaps join——" He ceased. He seemed to remark something; he was looking at their breasts. "Oh, I say. You fly, All of you. Oh, good gad! Find it jolly, eh?"

"Yes," somebody said. "Jolly."

"But dangerous, what?"

"A little faster than tennis," another said. The guest looked at him, bright, affable, intent.

Another said quickly, "Bogard says you command a vessel."

"Hardly a vessel. Thanks, though. And not command. Ronnie does that. Ranks me a bit. Age."

"Ronnie?"

"Yes. Nice. Good egg. Old, though. Stickler."

"Stickler?"

"Frightful. You'd not believe it. Whenever we sight smoke and I have the glass, he sheers away. Keeps the ship hull down all the while. No beaver then. Had me two down a fortnight yesterday."

The Americans glanced at one another. "No beaver?"

"We play it. With basket masts, you see. See a basket mast. Beaver! One up. The *Ergenstrasse* doesn't count any more, though."

The men about the table looked at one another. Bogard spoke. "I see. When you or Ronnie see a ship with basket masts, you get a beaver on the other. I see. What is the *Ergenstrasse?*"

"She's German. Interned. Tramp steamer. Foremast rigged so it looks something like a basket mast. Booms, cables, I daresay. I didn't think it looked very much like a basket mast, myself. But Ronnie said yes. Called it one day. Then one day they shifted her across the basin and I called her on Ronnie. So we decided to not count her any more. See now, eh?"

"Oh," the one who had made the tennis remark said, "I see. You and Ronnie run about in the launch, playing beaver. H'm'm. That's nice. Did you ever pl——"

"Jerry," Bogard said. The guest had not moved. He looked down at the speaker, still smiling, his eyes quite wide.

The speaker still looked at the guest. "Has yours and Ronnie's boat got a yellow stern?"

"A yellow stern?" the English boy said. He had quit smiling, but his face was still pleasant.

"I thought that maybe when the boats had two captains, they might paint the sterns yellow or something."

"Oh," the guest said. "Burt and Reeves aren't officers."

"Burt and Reeves," the other said, in a musing tone. "So they go too. Do they play beaver too?"

"Jerry," Bogard said. The other looked at him. Bogard jerked his head a little. "Come over here." The other rose. They went aside. "Lay off of him," Bogard said. "I mean it, now. He's just a kid. When you were that age, how much sense did you have? Just about enough to get to chapel on time."

"My country hadn't been at war going on four years, though," Jerry said.

"Here we are, spending our money and getting shot at by the clock, and it's not even our fight, and these limeys that would have been goose-stepping twelve months now if it hadn't been——"

"Shut it," Bogard said. "You sound like a Liberty Loan."

"——taking it like it was a fair or something. 'Jolly.'" His voice was now falsetto, lilting. "'But dangerous, what?'"

"Sh-h-h-h," Bogard said.

"I'd like to catch him and his Ronnie out in the harbor, just once. Any harbor. London's. I wouldn't want anything but a Jenny, either. Jenny? Hell, I'd take a bicycle and a pair of water wings! I'll show him some war."

"Well, you lay off him now. He'll be gone soon."

"What are you going to do with him?"

"I'm going to take him along this morning. Let him have Harper's place out front. He says he can handle a Lewis. Says they have one on the boat. Something he was telling me—about how he once shot out a channel-marker light at seven hundred yards."

"Well, that's your business. Maybe he can beat you."

"Beat me?"

"Playing beaver. And then you can take on Ronnie."

"I'll show him some war, anyway," Bogard said. He looked at the guest. "His people have been in it three years now, and he seems to take it like a sophomore in town for the big game." He looked at Jerry again. "But you lay off him now."

As they approached the table, the guest's voice was loud and cheerful: ". . . if he got the glasses first, he would go in close and look, but when I got them first, he'd sheer off where I couldn't see anything but the smoke. Frightful stickler. Frightful. But *Ergenstrasse* not counting any more. And if you make a mistake and call her, you lose two beaver from your score. If Ronnie were only to forget and call her we'd be even."

At two o'clock the English boy was still talking, his voice bright, innocent, and cheerful. He was telling them how Switzerland had been spoiled by 1914, and instead of the vacation which his father had promised him for his sixteenth birthday, when that birthday came he and his tutor had had to do with Wales. But that he and the tutor had got pretty high and that he dared to say—with all due respect to any present who might have had the advantage of Switzerland, of course—that one could see probably as far from Wales as from Switzerland. "Perspire as much and breathe as hard, anyway," he added. And about him the Americans sat, a little hard-bitten, a little sober, somewhat older, listening to him with a kind of cold astonishment. They had been getting up for some time now and going out and returning in flying clothes, carrying helmets and goggles. An orderly entered with a tray of coffee cups, and the guest realized that for some time now he had been hearing engines in the darkness outside.

At last Bogard rose. "Come along," he said. "We'll get your togs." When they emerged from the mess, the sound of the engines was quite loud—an idling thunder. In alignment along the invisible tarmac was a vague rank of short banks of flickering blue-green fire suspended apparently in mid-air. They crossed the aërodrome to Bogard's quarters, where the lieutenant, McGinnis, sat on a cot fastening his flying boots. Bogard reached down a Sidcott suit and threw it across the cot. "Put this on," he said.

"Will I need all this?" the guest said. "Shall we be gone that long?"

"Probably," Bogard said. "Better use it. Cold upstairs."

The guest picked up the suit. "I say," he said. "I say. Ronnie and I have a do ourselves, tomor—today. Do you think Ronnie won't mind if I am a bit late? Might not wait for me."

"We'll be back before teatime," McGinnis said. He seemed quite busy with his boot. "Promise you." The English boy looked at him.

"What time should you be back?" Bogard said.

"Oh, well," the English boy said, "I daresay it will be all right. They let Ronnie say when to go, anyway. He'll wait for me if I should be a bit late."

"He'll wait," Bogard said. "Get your suit on."

"Right," the other said. They helped him into the suit. "Never been up before," he said, chattily, pleasantly. "Daresay you can see farther than from mountains, eh?"

"See more, anyway," McGinnis said. "You'll like it."

"Oh, rather. If Ronnie only waits for me. Lark. But dangerous, isn't it?"

"Go on," McGinnis said. "You're kidding me."

"Shut your trap, Mac," Bogard said. "Come along. Want some more coffee?" He looked at the guest, but McGinnis answered:

"No. Got something better than coffee. Coffee makes such a confounded stain on the wings."

"On the wings?" the English boy said. "Why coffee on the wings?"

"Stow it, I said, Mac," Bogard said. "Come along."

They recrossed the aërodrome, approaching the muttering banks of flame. When they drew near, the guest began to discern the shape, the outlines, of the Handley-Page. It looked like a Pullman coach run upslanted aground into the skeleton of the first floor of an incomplete skyscraper. The guest looked at it quietly.

"It's larger than a cruiser," he said in his bright, interested voice. "I say, you know. This doesn't fly in one lump. You can't pull my leg. Seen them before. It comes in two parts: Captain Bogard and me in one; Mac and 'nother chap in other. What?"

"No," McGinnis said. Bogard had vanished. "It all goes up in one lump. Big lark, eh? Buzzard, what?"

"Buzzard?" the guest murmured. "Oh, I say. A cruiser. Flying. I say, now."

"And listen," McGinnis said. His hand came forth; something cold fumbled against the hand of the English boy—a bottle. "When you feel yourself getting sick, see? Take a pull at it."

"Oh, shall I get sick?"

"Sure. We all do. Part of flying. This will stop it. But if it doesn't. See?"

"What? Quite. What?"

"Not overside. Don't spew it overside."

"Not overside?"

"It'll blow back in Bogy's and my face. Can't see. Bingo. Finished. See?"

"Oh, quite. What shall I do with it?" Their voices were quiet, brief, grave as conspirators.

"Just duck your head and let her go."

"Oh, quite."

Bogard returned. "Show him how to get into the front pit, will you?" he said. McGinnis led the way through the trap. Forward, rising to the slant of the fuselage, the passage narrowed; a man would need to crawl.

"Crawl in there and keep going," McGinnis said.

"It looks like a dog kennel," the guest said.

"Doesn't it, though?" McGinnis agreed cheerfully. "Cut along with you." Stooping, he could hear the other scuttling forward. "You'll find a Lewis gun up there, like as not," he said into the tunnel.

The voice of the guest came back: "Found it."

"The gunnery sergeant will be along in a minute and show you if it is loaded."

"It's loaded," the guest said; almost on the heels of his words the gun fired, a brief staccato burst. There were shouts, the loudest from the ground beneath the nose of the aëroplane. "It's quite all right," the English boy's voice said. "I pointed it west before I let it off. Nothing back there but Marine office and your brigade headquarters. Ronnie and I always do this before we go anywhere. Sorry if I was too soon. Oh, by the way," he added, "my name's Claude. Don't think I mentioned it."

On the ground, Bogard and two other officers stood. They had come up running. "Fired it west," one said. "How in hell does he know which way is west?"

"He's a sailor," the other said. "You forgot that."

"He seems to be a machine gunner too," Bogard said.

"Let's hope he doesn't forget that," the first said.

Nevertheless, Bogard kept an eye on the silhouetted head rising from the round gunpit in the nose ten feet ahead of him. "He did work that gun, though," he said to McGinnis beside him. "He even put the drum on himself, didn't he?"

"Yes," McGinnis said. "If he just doesn't forget and think that that gun is him and his tutor looking around from a Welsh alp."

"Maybe I should not have brought him," Bogard said. McGinnis didn't answer. Bogard jockeyed the wheel a little. Ahead, in the gunner's pit, the guest's head moved this way and that continuously, looking. "We'll get there and unload and haul air for home," Bogard said. "Maybe in the dark —— Confound it, it would be a shame for his country to be in this mess for four years and him not even to see a gun pointed in his direction."

"He'll see one tonight if he don't keep his head in," McGinnis said.

But the boy did not do that. Not even when they had reached the objective and McGinnis had crawled down to the bomb toggles. And even when the searchlights found them and Bogard signaled to the other machines and dived, the two engines snarling full speed into and through the bursting shells, he could see the boy's face in the searchlight's glare, leaned far overside, coming sharply out as a spotlighted face on a stage, with an expression upon it of childlike interest and delight. "But he's firing that Lewis," Bogard thought. "Straight too"; nosing the machine farther down, watching the pinpoint swing into the sights, his right hand lifted, waiting to drop into McGinnis's sight. He dropped his hand; above the noise of the engines he seemed to hear the click and whistle of the released bombs as the machine, freed of the weight, shot zooming in a long upward bounce that carried it for an instant out of the light. Then he was pretty busy for a time, coming into and through the shells again, shooting athwart another beam that caught and held long enough for him to see the English boy leaning far over the side, looking back and down past the right wing, the undercarriage. "Maybe he's read about it somewhere," Bogard thought, turning, looking back to pick up the rest of the flight.

Then it was all over, the darkness cool and empty and peaceful and almost quiet, with only the steady sound of the engines. McGinnis climbed back into the office, and standing up in his seat, he fired the colored pistol this time and stood for a moment longer, looking backward toward where the searchlights still probed and sabered. He sat down again.

"O. K.," he said. "I counted all four of them. Let's haul air." Then he looked forward. "What's become of the King's Own? You didn't hang him onto a bomb release, did you?" Bogard looked. The forward pit was empty. It was in dim silhouette again now, against the stars, but there was nothing there now save the gun. "No," McGinnis said; "there he is. See? Leaning overside. Dammit, I told him not to spew it! There he comes back." The guest's head came into view again. But again it sank out of sight.

"He's coming back," Bogard said. "Stop him. Tell him we're going to have every squadron in the Hun Channel group on top of us in thirty minutes."

McGinnis swung himself down and stooped at the entrance to the passage. "Get back!" he shouted. The other was almost out; they squatted so, face to face like two dogs, shouting at one another above the noise of the still unthrottled engines on either side of the fabric walls. The English boy's voice was thin and high.

"Bomb!" he shrieked.

"Yes," McGinnis shouted, "they were bombs! We gave them hell! Get back, I tell you! Have every Hun in France on us in ten minutes! Get back to your gun!"

Again the boy's voice came, high, faint above the noise: "Bomb! All right?"

"Yes! Yes! All right. Back to your gun, damn you!"

McGinnis climbed back into the office. "He went back. Want me to take her awhile?"

"All right," Bogard said. He passed McGinnis the wheel. "Ease her back some. I'd just as soon it was daylight when they come down on us."

"Right," McGinnis said. He moved the wheel suddenly. "What's the matter with that right wing?" he said. "Watch it. . . . See? I'm flying on the right aileron and a little rudder. Feel it."

Bogard took the wheel a moment. "I didn't notice that. Wire somewhere, I guess. I didn't think any of those shells were that close. Watch her, though."

"Right," McGinnis said. "And so you are going with him on his boat tomorrow—today."

"Yes. I promised him. Confound it, you can't hurt a kid, you know."

"Why don't you take Collier along, with his mandolin? Then you could sail around and sing."

"I promised him," Bogard said. "Get that wing up a little."

"Right," McGinnis said.

Thirty minutes later it was beginning to be dawn; the sky was gray. Presently McGinnis said: "Well, here they come. Look at them! They look like mosquitoes in September. I hope he don't get worked up now and think he's playing beaver. If he does he'll just be one down to Ronnie, provided the devil has a beard. . . . Want the wheel?"

At eight o'clock the beach, the Channel, was beneath them. Throttled back, the machine drifted down as Bogard ruddered it gently into the Channel wind. His face was strained, a little tired.

McGinnis looked tired, too, and he needed a shave.

"What do you guess he is looking at now?" he said. For again the English boy was leaning over the right side of the cockpit, looking backward and downward past the right wing.

"I don't know," Bogard said. "Maybe bullet holes." He blasted the port engine. "Must have the riggers——"

"He could see some closer than that," McGinnis said. "I'll swear I saw tracer going into his back at one time. Or maybe it's the ocean he's looking at. But he must have seen that when he came over from England." Then Bogard leveled off; the nose rose sharply, the sand, the curling tide edge fled alongside. Yet still the English boy hung far overside, looking backward and downward at something beneath the right wing, his face rapt, with utter and childlike interest. Until the machine was completely stopped he continued to do so. Then he ducked down, and in the abrupt silence of the engines they could hear him crawling in the passage. He emerged just as the two pilots climbed stiffly down from the office, his face bright, eager; his voice high, excited.

"Oh, I say! Oh, good gad! What a chap! What a judge of distance! If Ronnie could only have seen! Oh, good gad! Or maybe they aren't like ours—don't load themselves as soon as the air strikes them."

The Americans looked at him. "What don't what?" McGinnis said.

"The bomb. It was magnificent; I say, I shan't forget it. Oh, I say, you know! It was splendid!"

After a while McGinnis said, "The bomb?" in a fainting voice. Then the two pilots glared at each other; they said in unison: "That right wing!" Then as one they clawed down through the trap and, with the guest at their heels, they ran around the machine and looked beneath the right wing. The bomb, suspended by its tail, hung straight down like a plumb bob beside the right wheel, its tip just touching the sand. And parallel with the wheel track was the long, delicate line in the sand where its ultimate tip had dragged. Behind them the English boy's voice was high, clear, child-like:

"Frightened, myself. Tried to tell you. But realized you knew your business better than I. Skill. Marvelous. Oh, I say, I shan't forget it."

A marine with a bayoneted rifle passed Bogard onto the wharf and directed him to the boat. The wharf was empty, and he didn't even see the boat until he approached the edge of the wharf and looked directly down into it and upon the backs of two stooping men in greasy dungarees, who rose and glanced briefly at him and stooped again.

It was about thirty feet long and about three feet wide. It was painted with gray-green camouflage. It was quarter-decked forward, with two blunt raked exhaust stacks. "Good Lord," Bogard thought, "if all that deck is engine——" Just aft the deck was the control seat; he saw a big wheel, an instrument panel. Rising to a height of about a foot above the freeboard, and running from the stern forward to where the deck began, and continuing on across the after edge of the deck and thence back down the other gunwale to the stern, was a solid screen, also camouflaged, which inclosed the boat save for the width of the stern, which was open. Facing the steersman's seat like an eye was a hole in the screen about eight inches in diameter. And looking down into the long, narrow, still, vicious shape, he saw a machine gun swiveled at the stern, and he looked at the low screen—including which the whole vessel did not sit much more than a yard above water level—with its single empty forward-staring eye, and he thought quietly: "It's steel. It's made of steel." And his face was quite sober, quite thoughtful, and he drew his trench coat about him and buttoned it, as though he were getting cold.

He heard steps behind him and turned. But it was only an orderly from the aërodrome, accompanied by the marine with the rifle. The orderly was carrying a largish bundle wrapped in paper.

"From Lieutenant McGinnis to the captain," the orderly said.

Bogard took the bundle. The orderly and the marine retreated. He opened the bundle. It contained some objects and a scrawled note. The objects were a new yellow silk sofa cushion and a Japanese parasol, obviously borrowed, and a comb and a few sheets of flimsy paper. The note said:

Couldn't find a camera anywhere and Collier wouldn't let me have his mandolin. But maybe Ronnie can play on the comb.

Mac

Bogard looked at the objects. But his face was still quite thoughtful, quite grave. He rewrapped the things and carried the bundle on up the wharf a way and dropped it quietly into the water.

As he returned toward the invisible boat he saw two men approaching. He recognized the boy at once—tall, slender, already talking, voluble, his head bent a little toward his shorter companion, who plodded along beside him, hands in pockets, smoking a pipe. The boy still wore the pea-coat beneath a flapping oilskin, but in place of the rakish and casual cap he now wore an infantryman's soiled Balaclava helmet, with, floating behind him as though upon the sound of his voice, a curtainlike piece of cloth almost as long as a burnous.

"Hullo, there!" he cried, still a hundred yards away.

But it was the second man that Bogard was watching, thinking to himself that he had never in his life seen a more curious figure. There was something stolid about the very shape of his hunched shoulders, his slightly down-looking face. He was a head shorter than the other. His face was ruddy, too, but its mold was of a profound gravity that was almost dour. It was the face of a man of twenty who has been for a year trying, even while asleep, to look twenty-one. He wore a high-necked sweater and dungaree slacks; above this a leather jacket; and above this a soiled naval officer's warmer that reached almost to his heels and which had one shoulder strap missing and not one remaining button at all. On his head was a plaid fore-and-aft deer stalker's cap, tied on by a narrow scarf brought across and down, hiding his ears, and then wrapped once about his throat and knotted with a hangman's noose beneath his left ear. It was unbelievably soiled, and with his hands elbow-deep in his pockets and his hunched shoulders and his bent head, he looked like someone's grandmother hanged, say, for a witch. Clamped upside down between his teeth was a short brier pipe.

"Here he is!" the boy cried. "This is Ronnie. Captain Bogard."

"How are you?" Bogard said. He extended his hand. The other said no word, but his hand came forth, limp. It was quite cold, but it was hard, calloused. He said no word; he just glanced briefly at Bogard and then away. But in that instant Bogard caught something in the look, something strange—a flicker; a kind of covert and curious respect, something like a boy of fifteen looking at a circus trapezist.

But he said no word. He ducked on; Bogard watched him drop from sight over the wharf edge as though he had jumped feet first into the sea. He remarked now that the engines in the invisible boat were running.

"We might get aboard too," the boy said. He started toward the boat, then he stopped. He touched Bogard's arm. "Yonder!" he hissed. "See?" His voice was thin with excitement.

"What?" Bogard also whispered; automatically he looked backward and upward, after old habit. The other was gripping his arm and pointing across the harbor.

"There! Over there. The *Ergenstrasse*. They have shifted her again." Across the harbor lay an ancient, rusting, sway-backed hulk. It was small and nondescript, and, remembering, Bogard saw that the foremast was a strange mess of cables and booms, resembling—allowing for a great deal of license or looseness of imagery—a basket mast. Beside him the boy was almost chortling. "Do you think that Ronnie noticed?" he hissed. "Do you?"

"I don't know," Bogard said.

"Oh, good gad! If he should glance up and call her before he notices, we'll be even. Oh, good gad! But come along." He went on; he was still chortling. "Careful," he said. "Frightful ladder."

He descended first, the two men in the boat rising and saluting. Ronnie had disappeared, save for his backside, which now filled a small hatch leading forward beneath the deck. Bogard descended gingerly.

"Good Lord," he said. "Do you have to climb up and down this every day?"

"Frightful, isn't it?" the other said, in his happy voice. "But you know yourself. Try to run a war with makeshifts, then wonder why it takes so long." The narrow hull slid and surged, even with Bogard's added weight. "Sits right on top, you see," the boy said. "Would float on a lawn, in a heavy dew. Goes right over them like a bit of paper."

"It does?" Bogard said.

"Oh, absolutely. That's why, you see." Bogard didn't see, but he was too busy letting himself gingerly down to a sitting posture. There were no thwarts; no seats save a long, thick, cylindrical ridge which ran along the bottom of the boat from the driver's seat to the stern. Ronnie had backed into sight. He now sat behind the wheel, bent over the instrument panel. But when he glanced back over his shoulder he did not speak. His face was merely interrogatory. Across his face there was now a long smudge of grease. The boy's face was empty, too, now.

"Right," he said. He looked forward, where one of the seamen had gone. "Ready forward?" he said.

"Aye, sir," the seaman said.

The other seaman was at the stern line. "Ready aft?"

"Aye, sir."

"Cast off." The boat sheered away, purring, a boiling of water under the stern. The boy looked down at Bogard. "Silly business. Do it shipshape, though. Can't tell when silly four-striper——" His face changed again, immediate, solicitous. "I say. Will you be warm? I never thought to fetch——"

"I'll be all right," Bogard said. But the other was already taking off his oilskin. "No, no," Bogard said. "I won't take it."

"You'll tell me if you get cold?"

"Yes. Sure." He was looking down at the cylinder on which he sat. It was a half cylinder—that is, like the hot-water tank to some Gargantuan stove, sliced down the middle and bolted, open side down, to the floor plates. It was twenty feet long and more than two feet thick. Its top rose as high as the gunwales and between it and the hull on either side was just room enough for a man to place his feet to walk.

"That's Muriel," the boy said.

"Muriel?"

"Yes. The one before that was Agatha. After my aunt. The first one Ronnie and I had was Alice in Wonderland. Ronnie and I were the White Rabbit. Jolly, eh?"

"Oh, you and Ronnie have had three, have you?"

"Oh yes," the boy said. He leaned down. "He didn't notice," he whispered. His face was again bright, gleeful. "When we come back," he said. "You watch."

"Oh," Bogard said. "The *Ergenstrasse*." He looked astern, and then he thought: "Good Lord! We must be going—traveling." He looked out now, broadside, and saw the harbor line fleeing past, and he thought to himself that the boat was well-nigh moving at the speed at which the Handley-Page flew, left the ground. They were beginning to bound now, even in the sheltered water, from one wave crest to the next with a distinct shock. His hand still rested on the cylinder on which he sat. He looked down at it again, following it from where it seemed to emerge, beneath Ronnie's seat, to where it beveled into the stern. "It's the air in here, I suppose," he said.

"The what?" the boy said.

"The air. Stored up in here. That makes the boat ride high."

"Oh, yes. I daresay. Very likely. I hadn't thought about it." He came forward, his burnous whipping in the wind, and sat down beside Bogard. Their heads were below the top of the screen.

Astern the harbor fled, diminishing, sinking into the sea. The boat had begun to lift now, swooping forward and down, shocking almost stationary for a moment, then lifting and swooping again; a gout of spray came aboard over the bows like a flung shovelful of shot. "I wish you'd take this coat," the boy said.

Bogard didn't answer. He looked around at the bright face. "We're out-side, aren't we?" he said quietly.

"Yes. . . . Do take it, won't you?"

"Thanks, no. I'll be all right. We won't be long, anyway, I guess."

"No. We'll turn soon. It won't be so bad then."

"Yes. I'll be all right when we turn." Then they did turn. The motion became easier. That is, the boat didn't bang head-on, shuddering, into the swells. They came up beneath now, and the boat fled with increased speed, with a long, sickening, yawning motion, first to one side and then the other. But it fled on, and Bogard looked astern with that same soberness with which he had first looked down into the boat. "We're going east now," he said.

"With just a spot of north," the boy said. "Makes her ride a bit better, what?"

"Yes," Bogard said. Astern there was nothing now save empty sea and the delicate needlelike cant of the machine gun against the boiling and slewing wake, and the two seamen crouching quietly in the stern. "Yes. It's easier." Then he said: "How far do we go?"

The boy leaned closer. He moved closer. His voice was happy, confi-dential, proud, though lowered a little: "It's Ronnie's show. He thought of it. Not that I wouldn't have, in time. Gratitude and all that. But he's the older, you see. Thinks fast. Courtesy, *noblesse oblige*—all that. Thought of it soon as I told him this morning. I said, 'Oh, I say. I've been there. I've seen it'; and he said, 'Not flying'; and I said, 'Strewth'; and he said 'How far? No lying now'; and I said, 'Oh, far. Tremendous. Gone all night'; and he said, 'Flying all night. That must have been to Berlin'; and I said, 'I don't know. I daresay'; and he thought. I could see him thinking. Because he is the older, you see. More experience in courtesy, right thing. And he said, 'Berlin. No fun to that chap, dashing out and back with us.' And he thought and I waited, and I said, 'But we can't take him to Berlin. Too far. Don't know the way, either'; and he said—fast, like a shot—said, 'But there's Kiel'; and I knew——"

"What?" Bogard said. Without moving, his whole body sprang. "Kiel? In this?"

"Absolutely. Ronnie thought of it. Smart, even if he is a stickler. Said at once, 'Zeebrugge no show at all for that chap. Must do best we can for him. Berlin,' Ronnie said. 'My gad! Berlin.'"

"Listen," Bogard said. He had turned now, facing the other, his face quite grave. "What is this boat for?"

"For?"

"What does it do?" Then, knowing beforehand the answer to his own question, he said, putting his hand on the cylinder: "What is this in here? A torpedo, isn't it?"

"I thought you knew," the boy said.

"No," Bogard said. "I didn't know." His voice seemed to reach him from a distance, dry, cricketlike: "How do you fire it?"

"Fire it?"

"How do you get it out of the boat? When that hatch was open a while ago I could see the engines. They were right in front of the end of this tube."

"Oh," the boy said. "You pull a gadget there and the torpedo drops out astern. As soon as the screw touches the water it begins to turn, and then the torpedo is ready, loaded. Then all you have to do is turn the boat quickly and the torpedo goes on."

"You mean——" Bogard said. After a moment his voice obeyed him again. "You mean you aim the torpedo with the boat and release it and it starts moving, and you turn the boat out of the way and the torpedo passes through the same water that the boat just vacated?"

"Knew you'd catch on," the boy said. "Told Ronnie so. Airman. Tamer than yours, though. But can't be helped. Best we can do, just on water. But knew you'd catch on."

"Listen," Bogard said. His voice sounded to him quite calm. The boat fled on, yawing over the swells. He sat quite motionless. It seemed to him that he could hear himself talking to himself: "Go on. Ask him. Ask him what? Ask him how close to the ship do you have to be before you fire. . . . Listen," he said in that calm voice. "Now, you tell Ronnie, you see. You just tell him—just say——" He could feel his voice ratting off on him again, so he stopped it. He sat quite motionless, waiting for it to come back; the boy leaning now, looking at his face. Again the boy's voice was solicitous:

"I say. You're not feeling well. These confounded shallow boats."

"It's not that," Bogard said. "I just—— Do your orders say Kiel?"

"Oh, no. They let Ronnie say. Just so we bring the boat back. This is for you. Gratitude. Ronnie's idea. Tame, after flying. But if you'd rather, eh?"

"Yes, some place closer. You see, I——"

"Quite. I see. No vacations in wartime. I'll tell Ronnie." He went forward. Bogard did not move. The boat fled in long, slewing swoops. Bogard looked quietly astern, at the scudding sea, the sky.

"My God!" he thought. "Can you beat it? Can you beat it?"

The boy came back; Bogard turned to him a face the color of dirty paper. "All right now," the boy said. "Not Kiel. Nearer place, hunting probably just as good. Ronnie says he knows you will understand." He was tugging at his pocket. He brought out a bottle. "Here. Haven't forgot last night. Do the same for you. Good for the stomach, eh?"

Bogard drank, gulping—a big one. He extended the bottle, but the boy refused. "Never touch it on duty," he said. "Not like you chaps. Tame here."

The boat fled on. The sun was already down the west. But Bogard had lost all count of time, of distance. Ahead he could see white seas through the round eye opposite Ronnie's face, and Ronnie's hand on the wheel and the granitelike jut of his profiled jaw and the dead upside-down pipe. The boat fled on.

Then the boy leaned and touched his shoulder. He half rose. The boy was pointing. The sun was reddish; against it, outside them and about two miles away, a vessel—a trawler, it looked like—at anchor swung a tall mast.

"Lightship!" the boy shouted. "Theirs." Ahead Bogard could see a low, flat mole—the entrance to a harbor. "Channel!" the boy shouted. He swept his arm in both directions. "Mines!" His voice swept back on the wind. "Place filthy with them. All sides. Beneath us too. Lark, eh?"

Against the mole a fair surf was beating. Running before the seas now, the boat seemed to leap from one roller to the next; in the intervals while the screw was in the air the engine seemed to be trying to tear itself out by the roots. But it did not slow; when it passed the end of the mole the boat seemed to be standing almost erect on its rudder, like a sailfish. The mole was a mile away. From the end of it little faint lights began to flicker like fireflies. The boy leaned. "Down," he said. "Machine guns. Might stop a stray."

"What do I do?" Bogard shouted. "What can I do?"

"Stout fellow! Give them hell, what? Knew you'd like it!"

Crouching, Bogard looked up at the boy, his face wild. "I can handle the machine gun!"

"No need," the boy shouted back. "Give them first innings. Sporting. Visitors, eh?" He was looking forward. "There she is. See?" They were in the harbor now, the basin opening before them. Anchored in the channel was a big freighter. Painted midships of the hull was a huge Argentine flag. "Must get back to stations!" the boy shouted down to him. Then at that moment Ronnie spoke for the first time. The boat was hurtling along now in smoother water. Its speed did not slacken and Ronnie did not turn his head when he spoke. He just swung his jutting jaw and the clamped cold pipe a little, and said from the side of his mouth a single word:

"Beaver."

The boy, stooped over what he had called his gadget, jerked up, his expression astonished and outraged. Bogard also looked forward and saw Ronnie's arm pointing to starboard. It was a light cruiser at anchor a mile away. She had basket masts, and as he looked a gun flashed from her after turret. "Oh, damn!" the boy cried. "Oh, you putt! Oh, confound you, Ronnie! Now I'm three down!" But he had already stooped again over his gadget, his face bright and empty and alert again; not sober; just calm, waiting. Again Bogard looked forward and felt the boat pivot on its rudder and head directly for the freighter at terrific speed, Ronnie now with one hand on the wheel and the other lifted and extended at the height of his head.

But it seemed to Bogard that the hand would never drop. He crouched, not sitting, watching with a kind of quiet horror a painted flag increase like a moving picture of a locomotive taken from between the rails. Again the gun crashed from the cruiser behind them, and the freighter fired point-blank at them from its poop. Bogard heard neither shot.

"Man, man!" he shouted. "For God's sake!"

Ronnie's hand dropped. Again the boat spun on its rudder. Bogard saw the bow rise, pivoting; he expected the hull to slam broadside on into the ship. But it didn't. It shot off on a long tangent. He was waiting for it to make a wide sweep, heading seaward, putting the freighter astern, and he thought of the cruiser again. "Get a broadside, this time, once we clear the freighter," he thought. Then he remembered the freighter, the torpedo, and he looked back toward the freighter to watch the torpedo strike, and saw to his horror that the boat was now bearing down on the freighter again, in a skidding turn. Like a man in a dream, he watched himself rush down upon the ship and shoot past under her counter, still skidding, close enough to see the faces on her decks. "They missed and they are going to run down the torpedo and catch it and shoot it again," he thought idiotically.

So the boy had to touch his shoulder before he knew he was behind him. The boy's voice was quite calm: "Under Ronnie's seat there. A bit of a crank handle. If you'll just hand it to me——"

He found the crank. He passed it back; he was thinking dreamily: "Mac would say they had a telephone on board." But he didn't look at once to see what the boy was doing with it, for in that still and peaceful horror he was watching Ronnie, the cold pipe rigid in his jaw, hurling the boat at top speed round and round the freighter, so near that he could see the rivets in the plates. Then he looked aft, his face wild, importunate, and he saw what the boy was doing with the crank. He had fitted it into what was obviously a small windlass low on one flank of the tube near the head. He glanced up and saw Bogard's face. "Didn't go that time!" he shouted cheerfully.

"Go?" Bogard shouted. "It didn't—— The torpedo——"

The boy and one of the seamen were quite busy, stooping over the windlass and the tube. "No. Clumsy. Always happening. Should think clever chaps like engineers—— Happens, though. Draw her in and try her again."

"But the nose, the cap!" Bogard shouted. "It's still in the tube, isn't it? It's all right, isn't it?"

"Absolutely. But it's working now. Loaded. Screw's started turning. Get it back and drop it clear. If we should stop or slow up it would overtake us. Drive back into the tube. Bingo! What?"

Bogard was on his feet now, turned, braced to the terrific merry-go-round of the boat. High above them the freighter seemed to be spinning on her heel like a trick picture in the movies. "Let me have that winch!" he cried.

"Steady!" the boy said. "Mustn't draw her back too fast. Jam her into the head of the tube ourselves. Same bingo! Best let us. Every cobbler to his last, what?"

"Oh, quite," Bogard said. "Oh, absolutely." It was like someone else was using his mouth. He leaned, braced, his hands on the cold tube, beside the others. He was hot inside, but his outside was cold. He could feel all his flesh jerking with cold as he watched the blunt, grained hand of the seaman turning the windlass in short, easy, inch-long arcs, while at the head of the tube the boy bent, tapping the cylinder with a spanner, lightly, his head turned with listening, delicate and deliberate as a watchmaker. The boat rushed on in those furious, slewing turns. Bogard saw a long, drooping thread loop down from somebody's mouth, between his hands, and he found that the thread came from his own mouth.

He didn't hear the boy speak, nor notice when he stood up. He just felt the boat straighten out, flinging him to his knees beside the tube. The seaman had gone back to the stern and the boy stooped again over his gadget. Bogard knelt now, quite sick. He did not feel the boat when it swung again, nor hear the gun from the cruiser which had not dared to fire and the freighter which had not been able to fire, firing again. He did not feel anything at all when he saw the huge, painted flag directly ahead and increasing with locomotive speed, and Ronnie's lifted hand drop. But this time he knew that the torpedo was gone; in pivoting and spinning this time the whole boat seemed to leave the water; he saw the bow of the boat shoot skyward like the nose of a pursuit ship going into a wing-over. Then his outraged stomach denied him. He saw neither the geyser nor heard the detonation as he sprawled over the tube. He felt only a hand grasp him by the slack of his coat, and the voice of one of the seamen: "Steady all, sir. I've got you."

A voice roused him, a hand. He was half sitting in the narrow starboard runway, half lying across the tube. He had been there for quite a while; quite a while ago he had felt someone spread a garment over him. But he had not raised his head. "I'm all right," he had said. "You keep it."

"Don't need it," the boy said. "Going home now."

"I'm sorry I——" Bogard said.

"Quite. Confounded shallow boats. Turn any stomach until you get used to them. Ronnie and I both, at first. Each time. You wouldn't believe it. Believe human stomach hold so much. Here." It was the bottle. "Good drink. Take enormous one. Good for stomach."

Bogard drank. Soon he did feel better, warmer. When the hand touched him later, he found that he had been asleep.

It was the boy again. The pea-coat was too small for him; shrunken, perhaps. Below the cuffs his long, slender, girl's wrists were blue with cold. Then Bogard realized what the garment was that had been laid over him. But before Bogard could speak, the boy leaned down, whispering; his face was gleeful: "He didn't notice!"

"What?"

"*Ergenstrasse!* He didn't notice that they had shifted her. Gad, I'd be just one down, then." He watched Bogard's face with bright, eager eyes. "Beaver, you know. I say. Feeling better, eh?"

"Yes," Bogard said, "I am."

"He didn't notice at all. Oh, gad! Oh, Jove!"

Bogard rose and sat on the tube. The entrance to the harbor was just ahead; the boat had slowed a little. It was just dusk. He said quietly: "Does this often happen?" The boy looked at him. Bogard touched the tube. "This. Failing to go out."

"Oh, yes. Why they put the windlass on them. That was later. Made first boat; whole thing blew up one day. So put on windlass."

"But it happens sometimes, even now? I mean, sometimes they blow up, even with the windlass?"

"Well, can't say, of course. Boats go out. Not come back. Possible. Not ever know, of course. Not heard of one captured yet, though. Possible. Not to us, though. Not yet."

"Yes," Bogard said. "Yes." They entered the harbor, the boat moving still fast, but throttled now and smooth, across the dusk-filled basin. Again the boy leaned down, his voice gleeful.

"Not a word, now!" he hissed. "Steady all!" He stood up; he raised his voice: "I say, Ronnie." Ronnie did not turn his head, but Bogard could tell that he was listening. "That Argentine ship was amusing, eh? In there. How do you suppose it got past us here? Might have stopped here as well. French would buy the wheat." He paused, diabolical—Machiavelli with the face of a strayed angel. "I say. How long has it been since we had a strange ship in here? Been months, eh?" Again he leaned, hissing. "Watch, now!" But Bogard could not see Ronnie's head move at all. "He's looking, though!" the boy whispered, breathed. And Ronnie was looking, though his head had not moved at all. Then there came into view, in silhouette against the dusk-filled sky, the vague, basketlike shape of the interned vessel's foremast. At once Ronnie's arm rose, pointing; again he spoke without turning his head, out of the side of his mouth, past the cold, clamped pipe, a single word:

"Beaver."

The boy moved like a released spring, like a heeled dog freed. "Oh, damn you!" he cried. "Oh, you putt! It's the *Ergenstrasse!* Oh, confound you! I'm just one down now!" He had stepped in one stride completely over Bogard, and he now leaned down over Ronnie. "What?" The boat was slowing in toward the wharf, the engine idle. "Aren't I, Ronnie? Just one down now?"

The boat drifted in; the seaman had again crawled forward onto the deck. Ronnie spoke for the third and last time. "Right," he said.

"I want," Bogard said, "a case of Scotch. The best we've got. And fix it up good. It's to go to town. And I want a responsible man to deliver it."

The responsible man came. "This is for a child," Bogard said, indicating the package. "You'll find him in the Street of the Twelve Hours, somewhere near the Café Twelve Hours. He'll be in the gutter. You'll know him. A child about six feet long. Any English M. P. will show him to you. If he is asleep, don't wake him. Just sit there and wait until he wakes up. Then give him this. Tell him it is from Captain Bogard."

About a month later a copy of the *English Gazette* which had strayed onto an American aërodrome carried the following item in the casualty lists:

Missing: Torpedo Boat XOOI. Lieutenants R. Boyce Smith and L. C. W. Hope, R. N. R., Able Seamen, Machinist's Mate Burt and Torpedoman Reeves, Channel Fleet, Light Torpedo Division. Failed to return from coast patrol duty.

Shortly after that the American Air Service headquarters also issued a bulletin:

For extraordinary valor over and beyond the routine of duty, Captain H. S. Bogard, with his crew, composed of Second Lieutenant Darrel McGinnis and Aviation Gunners Watts and Harper, on a daylight raid and without scout protection, destroyed with bombs an ammunition depot several miles behind the enemy's lines. From here, beset by enemy aircraft in superior numbers, these men proceeded with what bombs remained to the enemy's corps headquarters at ——— and partially demolished this château, and then returned safely without loss of a man.

And regarding which exploit, it might have added, had it failed and had Captain Bogard come out of it alive, he would have been immediately and thoroughly court-martialed.

Carrying his remaining two bombs, he had dived the Handley-Page at the château where the generals sat at lunch, until McGinnis, at the toggles below him, began to shout at him, before he ever signaled. He didn't signal until he could discern separately the slate tiles of the roof. Then his hand dropped and he zoomed, and he held the aëroplane so, in its wild snarl, his lips parted, his breath hissing, thinking: "God! God! If they were all there —all the generals, the admirals, the presidents and the kings—theirs, ours— all of them."

THE DOLL

J. Kessel

(1898–   )

TRANSLATED BY VYVYAN HOLLAND

LENOSHKA, who was reading the adventures of Tom Sawyer in an odd volume of Mark Twain, suddenly broke into a clear laugh. But she immediately turned round timidly, as though she had done something wrong. The austerity of the old house, the large empty study, the tall uncurtained windows through which the sun poured pitilessly down, reminded the little girl that laughter was forbidden. She could almost hear the gloomy voice of Ivan Michailovitch, her father, saying: "Don't make so much noise, Lena. These are no days for laughter."

The child's lips pursed up in a sad little pout. She shrugged her shoulders in a way that outlined their slight form beneath her linen dress and resumed her reading.

It was a sultry summer afternoon in Russian Turkestan. The town of Tashkent was dozing beneath the torrid sky. A scorching haze rose from the street in which the dust accumulated in thick muggy waves. Melancholy-eyed camels, dragged along by Sarts from the Steppes, passed slowly before the Orthodox churches, whose domes were furnaces of incandescent light, and before mosques whose minarets, like the fingers of God, seemed to be pointing out the way to Heaven to the faithful.

A large fly filled the room with its senseless buzzing in such a way that it appeared to be everywhere at the same time. Lenoshka followed its flight with her eyes. A tiny brown, glittering creature, the fly soared up to the ceiling, sped like a bullet past the child's ears, collided with the walls and rebounded in noisy spirals. It was like some strange jewel, a piece of mingled sun and earth, a mad atom of happiness in the gloomy room.

The metallic humming of the insect produced a slight feeling of numbness in the little girl's body. She shut her eyes and, limp with the heat, her short hair covering her forehead, she sat there without moving and vaguely envied the fly's existence.

"You're happy enough," she thought. "You can do what you like. You haven't got to carry buckets of water from the well to the house every morning and evening. You can find plenty to eat and you don't go to school."

And gradually Lenoshka imagined that she too was a free aerial creature, that the daily work of the house did not exist and that she had nothing to do but to fly about, to go in and out of houses and to sing in the sunlight.

The sound of dragging footsteps approaching the door and a low cough interrupted her reveries, and she rose as a tall, lean, slightly bowed figure appeared in the doorway. It was her father. A deep line on each side of his mouth imparted a look of gloomy sensuality to his lips. His expression was austere and his eyes, which were of too light a shade of blue, looked as if they were blind beneath the thick blackness of his eyebrows A short beard covered his chin. His general appearance suggested breeding, coupled at the same time with a note of instability, of lack of balance and inadaptability which could not be defined but was at the same time very strongly marked. He kissed the little girl on the forehead and she shrank away from the clamminess of her father's face.

"Are you tired, Father?" she asked.

Ivan Michailovitch showed by a gesture how unnecessary this question was and let himself drop into an arm-chair. He stretched out his long legs, placed his thin, trembling, ink-stained hands on his knees and sat there motionless, with his lips apart. He looked so weary that the little girl said to him:

"Would you like some water?"

"Yes, get me some."

She fetched a glass from the kitchen and held it out to him. Ivan Michailovitch put it eagerly to his lips but, after the first mouthful, he said, peevishly:

"It's quite hot."

"You know quite well, Father," observed the little girl seriously, "that it can't be anything else. We've sold the refrigerator and ice costs a fortune."

He smiled brokenly and murmured:

"You're twelve, aren't you, child?"

"Why, yes, Father."

"Twelve, and you already know so much!"

He was moved to sudden pity, he who usually, after his tedious work at a Government office, forgot his daughter and lost himself in vague memories in which he recalled his life as a rich aristocrat, a lazy, ridiculous life, but agreeable enough on the whole, which had been annihilated by Bolshevism.

"Come and sit on my knee, darling, and kiss me," he said.

Surprised by this unexpected show of affection, Lena timidly obeyed. But Ivan Michailovitch was already feeling embarrassed. He was always stopped from any form of demonstration by a strange fear of ridicule, a sort of diffidence with regard both to himself and to other people which surrounded him with an atmosphere of discomfort and boredom. This fear had developed along morbid lines since his wife had deserted him, leaving him with Lena, who was two years old at the time; and he suffered from it even in his daughter's presence. He never knew what to say to her, his hands were too clumsy to caress the child and it always seemed to him that everything he said to her rang false.

Lena instinctively felt this embarrassment and got off her father's knee.

Ivan Michailovitch was once more obsessed with the feeling of distress to which his daily dealings with his daughter inevitably gave rise. He would have liked to gain the child's confidence, to guide her and warm her, and yet all this longing, all his love, which was really deep and sincere, resolved itself into empty commonplace phrases.

Once again he thought: "It's no use. How unfortunate it all is!"

Yet he tried to react:

"Have you been to school to-day?"

Lenoshka replied without a moment's hesitation:

"Yes, all day."

From the way in which she dropped her eyes he knew that she was lying, but did not follow the matter up. An immense weariness overcame him.

What was the use of questioning her? What was the good of getting angry, since he had never been able to make friends with her, and now he could not even do anything for her in a material way? He gazed at his daughter, that little girl who came from himself and who was yet so far away from him. Ivan Michailovitch felt a desire to cry from sheer misery and perplexity in the presence of that little fine active body, of that full-lipped mouth which seemed modelled on his own, and beneath the gaze of those alert, eager, golden-brown eyes. He guessed that dangerous thoughts were seething behind that smooth brow and that precocious appetites plagued that mind which was such a mystery to him.

He tried to sigh but found himself unable to do so. All that issued from his lips was a queer, harsh sort of rattling sound.

In the meantime the child dragged a deal table into the centre of the room and placed on it a few cucumbers in a cracked dish. Ivan Michailovitch drew from his pocket a piece of hard brown bread bristling with bits of straw. Lenoshka raised her eyes to her father and he seemed to read a reproach in their large pupils.

"That's all I could get after waiting for an hour in the queue," he said, by way of excuse. "It's yesterday's ration."

She made no reply and they sat down to their meal. They ate rapidly and in silence. The heat was so oppressive that the effort of breaking the rough bread made them sweat. Even when the last crumb of bread and the last shred of cucumber-skin were gone, they felt the pangs of hunger just as keenly as before in their unsatisfied stomachs.

"I'll wash the plates," said Lena. "They haven't been done for three days."

She went into the kitchen and set to work. Nothing revolted her so much as this task. She had an innate love of clean, pretty, bright objects and her heart ached with misery as she recalled the days of plenty when she had been spoiled by governesses whom no one controlled, with a father whom she seldom saw and who made up for his absence by lavishing presents on her. But she was certain that her life could not always be restricted to dirty plates and unappetising meals. She knew that some miracle would occur to set her free and she awaited it with all the fibres of her being and all the ardour of her youthful enthusiasm.

She was still occupied with her task when her father, in the neighbouring room, uttered an exclamation:

"Philip Adrianovitch! What chance brings you here?"

Lenoshka carefully washed her hands and ran back into the living room. She adored Philip, her father's friend, a lean, dapper, bald-headed old man who was always jolly and well-dressed and whose pockets were always full of sweets. He was the only man she knew who had not changed during the last hateful years.

Philip Adrianovitch, even though he was of noble birth and had possessed a large fortune, had a certain Asiatic suppleness of character which enabled him to adapt himself to any circumstances without losing his air of careless dignity. As he had always been careful to make friends among the most advanced political parties, the advent of the Revolution had not succeeded in ruining him. Thanks to these friends he was able to save a small portion of his property, and he set himself to turn this to account in some mysterious way.

Ivan Michailovitch often said of him, with secret envy, mixed, however, with a certain admiration:

"He will end in the cellars of the Cheka, as a specualtor, but in the meantime he lives like a fighting-cock."

When the little girl came in, Philip Adrianovitch smiled in a way which gave an odd twist to his thin lips.

"Good evening, my pretty Lena. Have you got a kiss for me?"

He always treated the child with a sort of gallantry which embarrassed her. She put her forehead up to the old man who kissed it, playing lightly with her fine hair as he did so. Then, turning gaily to Ivan Michailovitch, he asked:

"Well, Vania, how's business?"

"I'd like to know what you call business. I go on covering paper with ink and starving to death. That's all. But one gets used to it."

"Come! Don't be so despondent. Everything will come right in the end. Do you want some money?"

"Yes, I do," replied Ivan Michailovitch, in a voice that betrayed neither eagerness nor embarrassment. "Are you in funds?"

"I've just brought off a small deal. A cigarette?"

"Give me one!" said Ivan Michailovitch, greedily stretching out his hand. "I haven't smoked for two days."

His fingers trembled as his friend handed him his cigarette case and the first puffs gave him such pleasure that it almost amounted to pain.

"And you, Lena? Would you like a cigarette too?" asked Philip Adrianovitch.

"Oh, how good of you, Uncle Philip!" cried the little girl. "You don't mind, Father?"

Ivan Michailovitch shrugged his shoulders.

"Since that's what they teach you at school now, I suppose you can. Only," he added, in his listless voice, "you're wrong to lead her astray, Philip. You are morally wrong, I mean, because your cigarette won't really do her any harm."

Exhausted by this long speech, he crossed over to the window. Darkness was beginning to descend upon the town. He shut his eyes in order to taste the smoke better.

Meanwhile, Philip Adrianovitch was talking to Lenoshka. He knew what to say to the little girl; indeed he spoke too well, his voice was too soft, his eyes too veiled, his movements too studied and restrained. This jarred on Ivan Michailovitch like a false note in music, and a baffled look came into his face. But what could he do?

And when his friend asked him: "Will you let me take Lena out for a drive?" What else could he reply but: "Of course. It will amuse her."

Then, as an after thought, he added:

"By the way, Philip Adrianovitch, can you leave me a few cigarettes?"

The little girl and the old man left the house together. Night had fallen rapidly; the sky was already full of stars. At first they walked along in silence, deeply inhaling the cool night air. Then Philip Adrianovitch hailed a passing cab and said to the driver:

"Take us where you like and don't worry about the fare."

They drove through the town. The minarets were now pale grey ghosts beneath the bright light of the stars. The moonlight coated the leaves in the orchards and in the gardens with a layer of silver and made the thin streams of water in the middle of the streets glitter faintly. The child's body was filled with the dry warmth of the oriental night. Through her flimsy dress she felt its boisterous spell which insensibly affected her so much that she could not abandon herself to the unexpected pleasure of the drive.

Philip Adrianovitch placed his hand on her shoulder in a lingering caress. Now and then his fingers would stray on to the bare flesh of her neck. Then Lena would shut her eyes and feel a strange desire to laugh and cry at the same time. Suddenly he asked her:

"Would you like to go away, dear?"

He said this with a detached, almost timid air. But the question did not startle Lena, because it followed quite naturally on her constant day-dreams.

"Oh, yes, Uncle Philip!" she replied.

She said this with such eagerness and enthusiasm that the blood rushed to the old man's head and his hand trembled on the child's shoulder, as he muttered to her:

"Listen, Lenoshka darling, I love you dearly, much more than you think. It hurts me to see you working like a scullery maid. You ought to have pretty frocks, sweets, flowers. You like that sort of thing, don't you?"

"Toys, Uncle Philip, that's what I really like. Especially dolls."

"Dolls, of course!" he cried, as though the child's wish filled him with delight. "Well, you shall have them. I'll give you plenty."

"How kind you are, Uncle darling. When will you give me them? Soon?"

"Oh, here, you know, it's impossible. There aren't any dolls here. Now, listen carefully, Lena. I'm leaving for Moscow at the end of the week. Moscow is a big town with wide streets, motor cars passing up and down the whole time and huge high houses. There I can get you everything you want. Will you come with me?"

"Yes, of course, but will Father let me go?"

"Why should you need his permission? Aren't you a big girl, free to do as you like? You need not even mention it to him."

Lenoshka made no reply. She remembered what they taught her at school where Comrade Zotof, the Communist teacher, told them that middle-class parents ought not to have any more authority over their children and that after the age of ten everyone had the right to independence and that it was absurd for a free human being to pay attention to the opinions of grown-up people. She had not been convinced by this, because she did not like Comrade Zotof, a rough working-man who was covered with red hair and had a nasty smell. But now Uncle Philip, whom she admired, was confirming the truth of this teaching. How could she hesitate?

And yet one final objection of a practical nature occurred to her, for in her pretty head an early experience mingled strangely with her childish eagerness.

"But what shall I do about a passport?" she asked.

Her solemn, matter-of-fact air pleased Philip Adrianovitch so much that he pressed her to him and kissed her. She was accustomed to the old man's kisses, but this time he put a new ardour into his lips which made her shudder secretly.

"Don't be afraid, dear child," he replied, his voice hoarse with emotion. "I'll arrange all that. It's all settled then? You'll come to Moscow with me?"

There was something in his keen, feverish voice that frightened the little girl. But, as she did not yet know how to detect passion in a man's voice, she answered:

"Whenever you like, Uncle Philip."

He kissed her and again she felt his body yield to hers and glow.

When the cab dropped her at her house she saw a scarcely distinguishable shadow and a luminous point at the window of the big study. Ivan Michailovitch was still smoking. A hard little lump came into Lena's throat, but she thought of the doll, the large doll dressed in velvet and silk which Uncle Philip had promised her and she firmly resolved not to say a word to her father.

II

When Philip Adrianovitch deserted Lenoshka in Moscow, after making her his little mistress, all that he left her was a bundle of ruble notes and a vague idea that a little girl can earn money with her body.

On the day on which he did not return she did not at first realise that she was alone. When her landlady made her understand, the room which they had occupied together suddenly seemed enormous to her and she left the house to get away from it. The delicate warmth of the late summer twilight permeated the city. Lenoshka made her way through the avenues and streets until, tired out, she leaned for support against a rickety hoarding. Her eyes were attracted by the antics of three sparrows playing in the street and it was only then that she began to weep silently. There was none of the abandonment of childhood about her crying. She wept noiselessly with the slow, heavy tears of an old woman.

Her face was hidden in her hands, so she did not notice that a stranger was studying her. The stranger was a little girl scarcely taller than herself, perched upon immensely high crooked heels and dressed in a scarlet frock, which revealed a large expanse of bony chest. Her head was topped by a mass of outrageously false red hair which seemed to cast a garish glow over her painted lips, her rouge-daubed cheeks and her solemn, wistful eyes. This strange apparition said slowly:

"Why are you crying, you little idiot?"

Lenoshka raised her head and examined the stranger through her tears. The stranger went on gravely:

"You mustn't cry. It spoils one's eyes, and you've got nice eyes. Come and walk with me. One always has better luck in pairs. My name's Aniuta. What's yours?"

"Lena."

As though this interchange of names had been enough to give them mutual confidence, Lena followed the red-haired girl.

"Why, you don't even know how to walk!" cried Aniuta, contemptuously. "You must sway from side to side like the pendulum of a clock."

"Why?" asked Lena.

"To attract men, silly. You're not an infant, you ought to know that."

Lena began to understand. Besides, her friend began to explain, with the protective air of an elder sister:

"I'll teach you everything. You must come and live with me in the *Khitrof Rynok.*[1] We've got a house there where there are about a hundred of us, without any grown-up people to worry us. We're fairly cramped for space but we'll find room for you. You'll see, there are some important people there. Mitri is the eldest. He's seventeen and sells cocaine: he's very sharp and makes a lot of money. Then there's his wife, Tania, who is only about my age but knows how to look after herself: she sells doped cigarettes. Vassia is pretty clever too, but he'll end badly; he steals too much and they say that he's even killed people. There are about thirty of my profession, but they don't know how to please men. They are too small, smaller even than you. I won't take any of them out with me. Providence sent you along so that we should work together. You've got a nice new frock, and I'll do your hair for you, because we must look like big girls and then everything will be all right."

Lena listened and a smile passed over her full lips at the prospect of the new life upon which she was about to enter.

III

Autumn had come and the rain kept the streets in a perpetual state of dampness. The wind beating furiously against the rickety house-tops already held the icy breath of winter.

It was nearly five o'clock in the afternoon and the day was dying. Aniuta and Lena had just got up and were alone in the vast dormitory. The little girls and the youths who lived there had already all left to go about their shady and mysterious occupations. The bareness of the shabby room was very depressing. A few piles of straw littering the floor and a broken bottle in one corner comprised the entire furniture of the place.

Aniuta took a piece of red paper from her blouse, unfolded it carefully and, having damped it with spittle, made up her lips and cheeks. She then handed it to Lena, who did the same. Thus adorned they looked at each other. They had to go out and the evening looked so wretched and cold through the broken panes of the windows. They could not bring themselves to make a move, even though they were ready: this disinclination had started with the first rainy days and increased in intensity as the nights drew in more and more. Suddenly Lena began to laugh.

"You've put on one brown boot and one black one!" she said.

"I know," replied her friend, solemnly, "they're all I've got left."

[1] A wretched quarter in which tramps, thieves and prostitutes have always found shelter and which the Bolsheviks have not been able to clean up any more than the Tsarist police were able to do.

"It's a bit of luck that they're different feet," decided Lena. And she laughed again.

Aniuta was angry at first, but was eventually conquered by Lena's gaiety and they went out together.

Their two little figures were immediately swallowed up in the turmoil of the great city. A vague feeling of terror came over them and forced them to quicken their pace. There was a cold mist in the air and they kept on passing their hands over their heads to keep it out of their false hair. They did not speak to each other, being too depressed by the darkness, the lowering sky, hunger and especially by that tragic air of mystery which prowls through the deserted quarters of great cities

Shadows passed them which seemed either too frightened or too unfriendly: sometimes a wild-eyed dog whose hanging jaws they could picture to themselves followed them for a short way; then they huddled close to each other, for they had heard that starving animals often attacked children.

At last they reached a dimly-lit avenue. At long intervals street lamps shone through the rain which covered them with a glistening closely-woven web. The two little girls breathed more freely now that they were away from the agony of darkness. Lena was the first to recover herself, straightened her back, held up her head and adopted a swaying gait, modelled on the contortions of professional prostitutes and which she thought constituted their most powerful attraction.

Thus they continued on their way, provocative and alert, sometimes in the middle of the pavement and sometimes hugging the wall if they thought that someone was taking too much interest in them. For the secret police were making a drive against prostitution. This walking about in the penetrating mist, this anxious hunt for a crust of bread, did not perturb their souls which disgust and weariness had not yet had time to blight. This strange game even amused them, especially Lena who was the braver of the two and had not been at it for so long. From beneath her long lashes her glance sped, with a bold smile, towards the rare passers-by who hurried along, their emaciated or unhealthily puffy faces, which hunger had ground in its terrible mill, bent low towards the ground.

These had no interest for these huntresses armed with their precocious but very definite experience. They knew that they were as surly as sick animals and gloomier than a winter's evening. They wanted to find some rich "speculator" or some Commissar in festive mood, men who were not haunted by the question of their daily bread, and who were greedy and open-handed.

They wandered about thus for about an hour. Aniuta's odd boots, soaked with water, had assumed the same neutral colour; Lena kept her arms as far apart as possible, because whenever she touched her body with them the cold of her soaking garments seemed to be accentuated. The coquetry which made them maintain their swinging gait had become mechanical and the brilliance of their eyes was gone. They were thinking of moving to some other quarter of the city when luck suddenly came their way.

A man, whose approach they had not heard because of the patter of the rain, passed by them and, turning sharply, said to them:

"Well, little girls, it's not much of an evening for a walk."

The two children started with pleased surprise, but Aniuta replied, with an affectation of innocence:

"We're looking for company, sir."

The man looked carefully round and then suggested:

"All right, come along with me. But don't make it look too obvious."

He walked quietly away and they followed him with apparent unconcern. Lena nudged her companion and whispered:

"Did you see his fur-lined coat?"

"Yes," said the other. "It's marvellous. We're in luck to-night, Lena, great luck."

She gazed gratefully at the round shoulders which preceded them, covered with thick cloth, a symbol of luxury and plenty. Every now and then the man turned round and, seeing them pattering along behind him, waved to them.

When they had left the central quarter of the city and the indiscreet light of the street lamps was no more than a silvery mist in the distance, he let the two little girls catch up with him and, placing himself between them, he put his arms round them. They shivered.

"You're cold, children," he said. "Wait, we'll soon warm you. I'll take you somewhere so nice that you'll hardly believe it."

He stumbled over a rut. Lena laughed, but Aniuta, who was less high-spirited and more cunning, said kindly:

"Forgive her, sir, she is too young, she isn't used to things."

"It doesn't matter, it doesn't matter at all," replied the man. "They're like that at her age. I love youth and gaiety. Laugh as much as you like, my pet, but be careful not to break your leg."

They were walking down a rutted alley full of holes which were so many mud traps. Pieces of broken fencing littered the ground and the air was full of the stench of household refuse and rotting wood.

The man quickened his pace and the weary children could scarcely keep up with him. At last he came to a halt before a wooden house the outline of whose two stories could be vaguely distinguished in the darkness.

"An old private house," said the man, proudly. "I live there with a noble-woman who knows which side her bread's buttered."

He took a key from his pocket, opened the door and led the children through a narrow passage to his room. Even before looking round it they were conscious of an atmosphere of comfort. An oil lamp with a violet shade shed a soft light through the room. It was warm and heavy, russet curtains hung over the windows and the door. Solid, comfortable, old-fashioned furniture seemed to invite one to rest and to a kind of dreamy intimacy. And yet, in contrast with the discreet cleanliness of the place, a dirty shaving-brush and a razor still covered with soap lay upon the table.

"Well, do you like it here?" the man asked Lena, taking her by the chin.

"Yes, sir!"

"What do you mean, 'sir'? I'm not a gentleman, I'm just a merchant. My name is Nikita Vassilitch. Just call me Uncle Nikita. Is that all right?"

He rubbed his hands together good-humouredly and, removing his fur-lined coat, appeared in a pair of check trousers, a brown jacket and a high-necked Russian blouse. He was short and plump and had broad shoulders and a high bald forehead. In spite of his rather common face, there was a certain shrewdness in his small, red-circled eyes. Without quite knowing why, their expression reminded Lena of that of Philip Adrianovitch, her first lover.

The girls' clothes were so wet that they were afraid of sitting down for fear of soiling the furniture. Nikita Vassilitch noticed this and rang the bell.

In answer to it a grey-haired woman came in who still retained a natural dignity behind a servile smile.

"Good evening, Countess," said Nikita. "Allow me to introduce two little friends of mine who are cold and hungry. We must first give them a dressing-gown each. Then bring us some sandwiches, some cakes and *my* vodka."

As he spoke the sound of rattling plates came from the next room.

"Ah! I see you've got customers this evening!" said the man.

"A few, thank Heavens, Nikita Vassilitch."

"All the better for you, Countess, but don't forget to keep the best tid-bits for us. After all, I'm your oldest and richest guest."

When the old lady had gone, Nikita Vassilitch raised a curtain which covered a freshly-made hole in the wall and called to the little girls:

"Come and look. It will amuse you."

They came over and looked, curiously, standing on tip-toe. Their host had not lied, it was a strange sight.

In the middle of a large room whose walls were covered with old tapestry which gave them an air of quiet wealth, and in which a divan, piled up with delicate silk cushions, stood sentinel beneath the gilded dream of a magnificent ikon, stood a table. From its dimensions, from the care which had been put into its installation, one knew that it was the most important object in the room. It was imposing, it ruled the room. One felt that at that table one could really eat.

Around it the guests waited in silence. In the commonness and in the shrewd vigour of their features they nearly all resembled Nikita Vas-silitch. Thick-set, short-necked, rough-bearded, dressed in stout, unstylish

clothes, they formed a strange company in that room which still bore
traces of tasteful opulence. Their thick fingers, whose nails were either
bitten or not over-clean, manipulated the finely-wrought cutlery and the
exquisite glasses with a certain hesitating respect. One guessed that those
hands were more accustomed to other activities: to dragging sacks of
produce about in country districts, to be sold eventually in towns at fabulous prices; to opening the heavy gates of carriage drives; to sweeping
courtyards; to taking horses to water at frozen troughs in which the ice
had to be broken by hatchets; and, perhaps, who knows, to strangling
travellers on moonless, starless nights.

"They're all lads after my own heart," observed Nikita Vassilitch, waving towards the guests with a satisfied smile. "They're none of them
mother's darlings. They're go-getters, pals. It's all very fine for the Commissars to squeal, those who aren't idiots know quite well that we're the
masters now."

The children gazed at them, fascinated. They had heard of the secret
restaurants where, for fabulous sums of money, white bread, cakes, cream,
meat and wine were provided. They dared not say anything, overawed as
they would have been in church, and indeed they scarcely dared to breathe.
And when a shudder passed through their soaked bodies, they did not even
realise that it was because of the cold.

Nikita Vassilitch's hostess interrupted their examination. She placed two
dressing-gowns on an arm-chair and left the room.

"Come along," said the merchant, "put these on quickly."

Aniuta began to unlace her boots; Lena had already begun to unbutton
her blouse when Nikita interrupted her hoarsely:

"Come along, dear, let me undress you!"

The child went submissively over to him. The man's hands did not
tremble but his whole face suddenly grew pale and became suffused with
little nervous wrinkles.

"It's like boiling milk," thought Lena.

He slowly removed the little girl's blouse and slipped down her skirt.
She was naked. Her half-starved little body still retained some remnant
of its former gracefulness. When she looked at its pure amber-coloured
form, Lena was sometimes seized with a foolish desire to cry. But this
evening she felt no shame at being naked and laughed at Aniuta lost in her
huge dressing-gown.

Nikita slowly stroked the smooth skin with his rough hand. His eyes
looked dead behind the mist which veiled them; large drops of moisture
stood on his forehead: the red circles round his eyes seemed to spread and
to be about to burst at any moment. Suddenly he pushed the child roughly
away from him and shouted:

"Hide your body, you spawn of the Devil! Don't tempt me any more!"

He breathed heavily to relieve his congested lungs and yelled:

"Food and drink, you miserable Countess!"

Then he stretched himself upon his bed and shut his eyes, his mouth twisted with suffering.

The old woman brought in a tray on which stood a bowl of caviare, some slices of white bread, some ham and a decanter full of vodka. Nikita Vassilitch sighed.

"I'm seeing it again, Countess."

She silently filled a large glass with vodka, which he drank at a gulp. Then his face relaxed and, standing up, he cried:

"Come, children, don't let's be sad. We must laugh this evening. I want to be gay; my ghost has gone!"

He lowered his voice.

"I've got a ghost, you know; but it's nothing. When I drink it goes away."

The two children were not listening to him. Their whole souls were concentrated in their eyes, hypnotised by the food. Aniuta asked, diffidently:

"Is that for us too?"

"But whom do you think it's for?" cried Nikita Vassilitch, suddenly excited to pity. "Of course it's for you, you poor little waifs! And if there's not enough, we'll send for more. When Nikita entertains no one ever has any cause for complaint. And what the hell does one care for the law when one has plenty of money to pay with?"

He slapped his bulging coat-pocket boastfully, drank another glass of vodka and coughed. The little girls were seated at the table but had not touched anything yet, waiting for their host to give the word.

"Go on! Help yourselves! I'm not hungry myself," he added, laying stress on the last words which expressed the height of wealth.

Lena made the first move, taking a slice of ham, at which she gazed in bewilderment, as though unable to believe that it could be eaten all at once. Then suddenly she began to devour it, Aniuta following her example. Minutes went by, punctuated only by the greedy crunching of the children's jaws. The little girls' movements were stiff and their whole bodies shivered. Even though Nikita Vassilitch was not a man to be easily moved to pity and although the misery of which he had himself been a witness had made him indifferent to the sufferings of others, a queer kind of emotion brought a lump into his throat, and he drank another glass of vodka in little sips.

The children were at last satisfied and stopped eating. A little colour had come into their cheeks and their eyes were brighter. Aniuta got up and, putting her arms round Nikita Vassilitch's neck, kissed him full on his wet mouth. Lena clapped her hands.

"I want to kiss you too, Uncle Nikita!" she cried.

He took one of them on each knee and, after caressing them for a while, he said, in a very serious voice:

"Now, children, you must have some vodka."

They consented gravely, already imbued with that Russian truth that drinking is a sacred rite. He filled his glass and handed it to Aniuta:

"You drink first. You're the elder."

The little girl took a few sips, but a violent fit of coughing seized her. Nikita Vassilitch observed contemptuously:

"It isn't as strong as all that, my pet!"

Lena took the glass from her friend's hand and emptied it at a gulp. Big tears came into her eyes and the room swam round her, but she held firm. This feat threw Nikita Vassilitch into a frenzy of enthusiasm.

"Well done! There's a brave girl for you!" he cried. "What a wench! Without drawing a breath! Here, take this for your trouble."

Fumbling in his pockets he pulled out a bundle of filthy notes and pressed it into the child's hand. She passed the money over to Aniuta.

"Oh, so she's the banker, is she?" observed Nikita Vassilitch, with another laugh. "You're not steady enough to be trusted with it, I suppose. That's why I prefer you: I don't like serious people. They're difficult to get the better of in business and in the evenings they don't know how to laugh. Wait till I've had a little more to drink and you'll see how amusing I can be."

He seized the decanter, still half full of vodka, put it to his lips and threw back his head, and the little girls saw the silvery liquid vanish. When he put the decanter down it was quite empty. His face had gone purple and for a moment or two he seemed quite stunned; then he broke into a harsh, jerky, agonised laugh.

"Why did I bring you here?" he groaned. "Do I need you here? Do you bring me any gaiety? You just sit there and gape at me instead of laughing and amusing me. You see quite well that I'm miserable, so miserable that I could howl like a dog; even though I'm rolling in money I can't forget. *They* killed my son, my big son who was an army officer. Yes, I, Nikita, the simple merchant, had a fine officer son, who was the light of my eyes! They turned him into a ghost for me."

Exhausted by this long speech he paused for a moment, then he resumed violently:

"Stop me, for God's sake! I mustn't talk like that! We must be gay this evening. Come along! Shout! Dance! Oh, hell, one can't even amuse oneself nowadays! In the old days when I felt depressed I used to go and see the gipsies. I made them drunk and then what songs they sang! Songs more beautiful than Paradise, songs that made one almost die of sadness."

With a sweeping gesture he conjured up his past orgies, the dazzling bubble of champagne, the shouts, the shrieks, the laughter of the violins, the wild dances of the women, and over his contracted features there passed for a moment the frenzy of these frantic feasts with their mixture of hysterical joy and mortal misery.

The empty decanter caught his eye. He banged his fist on the table and screamed:

"Countess! Where's that bloody Countess?"

She came in, her face ashen-pale.

"Vodka, more vodka. Do you think I'm a schoolboy to be served like this, you old bitch?"

"Nikita Vassilitch," the old woman pleaded in a broken voice, "I must implore you not to use such language and not to talk so loudly. I've got people here."

"People? What people? Oh! Your guests! Well, they prevent me from enjoying myself, your guests do. They've put the evil eye on me and made me miserable, so you've got to chuck them out at once."

"But I can't do that, Nikita Vassilitch. Just think . . ."

"I'll pay for all of them. Here's some money. There isn't to be a sign of them in this house in one minute's time. When Nikita's making merry he wants the place empty."

In spite of the fortune which the presence of the speculator in her house represented for her, she would gladly have been rid of him, but as she looked at him she grew afraid. He was capable of anything in his wild state of intoxication and of unbridled lust. He might make an appalling scene and attract the attention of the militia and that would mean the dungeons of the Cheka and torture for the Countess. So she muttered submissively:

"Very well, Nikita Vassilitch, I'll say I'm expecting a raid."

"That's better, Countess! And don't be depressed about it. Nikita will pay."

Hours passed and more decanters of vodka were drunk. Nikita never stopped talking; sometimes full of wild gaiety, sometimes shaken with sobs. A sort of delirium took possession of him. With frightful tenacity he groped for the happiness which eluded him like a bird that was too magnificent for him. Sometimes he showered brutal caresses on the children and bit them, and they, stiff with weariness and scorched by the vodka, understanding nothing of this desperate savage drunkenness, began to loathe him.

Exhausted at last, he sprawled on the divan, unbuttoned his coat and, after trying unsuccessfully to open his blouse, the collar of which was choking him, mumbled:

"Can't you help me, you little bitches?"

When Lena reached the sofa to obey him he was already snoring, his cheeks swollen, his eyelids limp and his lips black. Lena began in disgust:

"A scarecrow has . . ."

She did not finish but stood there, holding her breath and calling her friend's attention to the man's pocket. A huge pocket-book, bulging with bank-notes, was protruding from it. The covetousness in Lena's face was so intense that Aniuta understood. She nodded her head in approval and then cautiously whispered:

"Let's get dressed first."

Quietly, with swift silent movements, the children resumed their wet rags. Their hearts beat so loudly in the echoing room that it seemed as if the noise must wake Nikita. But he went on sleeping undisturbed. Only his hands kept moving like giant captive insects and one of them, obeying an unconscious instinct of caution, fumbled for the pocket-book and grasped it. The children waited a moment, but the hand did not move. Time was pressing and they had to act. Lena, looking round the room, caught sight of the open razor. She seized it and, without hesitation, slit Nikita Vassilitch's throat from ear to ear in a single sweeping stroke.

Then the rainy night swallowed up the two little shadows.

IV

Comrade Sokolnikoff, Investigator of Criminal Affairs to the Revolutionary Tribunal, entered his office in high good humour. There was little work for him to do that day and he hoped to be able to spend the whole afternoon with his children, of whom he was very fond. He passed his hands contentedly over his fat cheeks and thought how nice it was to be able to keep clean at a time when soap was so scarce. Then he told the soldier acting as orderly to have the accused in the Miassine murder brought in.

He waited, whistling between his teeth, without troubling to look at the file before him. He knew nothing about the case, preferring to rely on his instinct and to judge by appearances. He was a man who was not concerned with legal quibbles. But when the door opened and the "accused" came in, he could not restrain an exclamation.

It was Lena. Her head had been shaved and in her long grey prison dress she looked like an under-nourished boy.

Comrade Sokolnikoff drew a deep breath.

"Are you the person accused of having killed Citizen Miassine?" he asked.

"It was I who cut Nikita's throat," the child replied.

"Well! Well!" muttered the Investigator. "And why did you do it?"

"His pocket was full of rubles and I wanted them."

Her voice did not falter. There was no sign of remorse, no sign of fear in her childish eyes. Sokolnikoff, even though he was Investigator to the Revolutionary Tribunal, felt uncomfortable. He tried to blot out the picture of his daughter Masha, whom he had stupidly got into his mind and who now refused to leave it. He stroked his cheeks mechanically; their smoothness embarrassed him now. At last, with deep tenderness of which even he himself was unaware, he said to her, as though speaking to his own child:

"But my poor little girl, what you've done is horrible. Just think of it!" The kindness in his voice had a profound effect on Lena, who for months and months had forgotten what kindness was.

She lowered her eyes, which until then had gazed boldly into those of Sokolnikoff. A few moments passed in silence and then suddenly the office was filled with the sound of sobbing, of that childish sobbing which seems to stifle children's throats and burst their lungs.

"Well," said Sokolnikoff, "you see, little girl, you see how your crime . . ." But she interrupted him:

"Oh, Mister Judge, Mister Judge, you have a kind voice! Tell them to give me back the doll which I bought afterwards, the lovely doll which they took away from me in prison!"

And in the presence of that little girl standing there like a weakly boy, Comrade Sokolnikoff, hardened Communist, Investigator to the Revolutionary Tribunal, felt, for the first time in his life, as though he himself were on trial.

REDUCED

Elizabeth Bowen

(1899–)

THE CARBURYS' TWO LITTLE GIRLS, Penny and Claudia, went upstairs again with their governess, Miss Rice, as soon as lunch was over: their steps could be heard retreating along the pitch-pine gallery round the hall. The visitors were disappointed—Mrs. Laurie liked children, and Frank Peele had been hoping to see more of the governess. Rain drummed on the hall skylight; still smoking their host Godwin Carbury's rather musty cigarettes, the grown-ups allowed themselves to be driven into the library. Here no chair invited you, the uninviting books must have been bought in lots and looked gummed in the shelves. It could have been a pretty September day; the plum-tree leaves in the tilting orchards round were bright yellow, but for days the Forest of Dene had been clouded and sodden.

Mrs. Laurie, who was vivacious and had married at nineteen, and Mrs. Carbury, who was muddled and dim, had been friends years ago in India when they were both young girls. They had kept in touch, Mrs. Carbury having no other vivacious friend, life having taught Mrs. Laurie that there was no knowing when anybody devoted might not come in useful—besides, she had always been sorry for Mima.

Mima's life had been unrewarding. She returned flatly from India after her friend's wedding, and it had not been till she was twenty-seven or eight that she met Godwin Carbury, who at forty was looking round for a wife. He had the reputation of being the most unpopular man in his part of the country, and that reputation followed him up to London. He was careful, savagely careful, about money, and not careful enough about seeing this was not known. Added to this, he had a dour self-importance. It was understood that economy kept him single as long as his mother had lived to keep house at Pendlethwaite. Possibly Mima saw something in him that no one else saw; she was anxious to 'settle' suitably and not herself accustomed to being liked. At all events, they married, and had had after some years these two thin, remote little girls. They had few neighbours at Pendlethwaite, and Godwin's peculiarities cut them off more and more from anybody there was. Whatever misgivings she had, Mima pandered to him blindly. On her own account she had just a little money, so once or twice a year she came up to London, gazed into shop windows, met Mrs. Laurie (now widowed) and bought reduced coats and shoes for the little girls. She had begun lately to talk of giving up London; the girls' education would be a heavy expense, she said.

It surprised Mrs. Laurie to find herself at Pendlethwaite, but she had been at a loose end, with nowhere to go for a week. So she thought, 'Try the Carburys,' and had written to Mima. She was a shiftless woman, maintaining herself by the exercise of a good deal of charm: she could say daring things without sounding impertinent, and determined to get a little fun out of Godwin—apart from this, she did not expect very much.

Pendlethwaite was not a lovable house. Built about 1880 of unpleasing maroon brick, it creaked inside with pitch-pine: its churchlike windows peered narrowly at the smiling landscape round; its grounds darkened a valley with belts of laurel and stiff, damp-looking clumps of unindigenous firs. The house looked dedicated to a perpetual January: sunnier seasons beat back from its walls. The bloomy red plums and mellow apples bending the boughs this month were pagan company for it. Indoors, there was no electricity, panels absorbed the lamp-light; before October, no fires were lit till night. It had not even the insidious charm of decay, for Godwin had great ideas of 'keeping things up'; the laurels were kept clipped, the thrifty meals served formally. . . . Mrs. Laurie had been diverted to find that she had a fellow-guest, but this did not see her far. Frank Peele, just back on leave from Siam, was Mima's second cousin. He must have asked himself here because he had to be somewhere; she thought he was not a man you would scramble to entertain. At about thirty, he was a haggard schoolboy —shambling, facetious, huffy, forlorn, melancholic, with perhaps (she feared most of all) a romantic soul. She supposed Mima must enjoy being even sorrier for him than she need be for herself. . . . Entertaining on this scale must be a plunge for the Carburys. Mrs. Laurie could almost hear Godwin saying to Mima: 'Well then, in for a penny, in for a pound.' He went through with his duties as host with glum correctness. 'But if one stayed a day too long he'd cut off supplies.' As it was, his rigid economies hit you everywhere.

The one startling un-economy was the governess. Mrs. Laurie, though unhappily childless, knew an expensive governess when she saw one. Miss Rice's technique was perfect. Her first appearance, at lunch, took Nella's breath away with its serene unobtrusiveness. Penny and Claudia—their dark eyes set close in, tucking their long fair hair back behind their shoulders primly—clearly revolved round her. 'Those two little mice adore her,' thought Mrs. Laurie, recalling the composed retreat after lunch: three people going back to a world of their own. But the adoration was kept within nice bounds. 'How does Mima *keep* the woman in this mausoleum? She might be anywhere. Mima can't be such a fool as I thought. . . . I must find out.'

In the library, she lost no time doing this. In the bow window, Frank Peele with his hands in his pockets stood looking out unexpectingly at the rain; Mima poured out thin coffee; Godwin glumly handed the cups round. Mrs. Laurie said affably: 'So you got a governess? Last time we met, you were busy looking for one.'

'Yes, oh yes. We did,' Mima said in her flustered way.

'Miss Rice came in May,' said Godwin firmly.

'She seems a great success. . . .'

Frank Peele grunted.

'When she first came in,' went on Mrs. Laurie, 'I felt certain I'd seen her somewhere. I wonder where she was before? She's startlingly good-looking, but in such a tactful way. Hag-ridden—but that's the life, I suppose.'

'She appears content with us,' said Godwin, handing the sugar to Mrs. Laurie bitterly. 'Mima, what are your plans for this afternoon?' His wife looked blank.

'Our guests should be entertained.'

'It struck me,' said Frank, wheeling round, 'as one of the few faces I had *not* seen before.'

'Really?' said Godwin.

Mima touched the coffee-tray clumsily; everything on it skidded. Did she not want cousin Frank to fall for the governess? The nicest women like having unattached men around. 'She must be full of brains,' said Mrs. Laurie vaguely.

'She teaches wonderfully; she's got the children *on* so. They seem to be learning everything.'

'Can we have them all down after tea to play Up Jenkin or something?'

'They do preparation then,' said Godwin repressively. ('Set,' thought his guest, 'on getting his money's worth.') Mima's eyes, oddly overwrought in her pink creased face, stole to meet her husband's. 'Frank,' Godwin continued, 'I could show you those maps now.' Clearly, any discussion of Miss Rice was closed.

'Not to-day, thanks,' said Frank, 'I've got a crick in my neck.' Godwin, after one more forbidding look at Mima, left them, shutting the door reprovingly. Frank loafed along the bookshelves, pulled out *Monasteries of the Levant,* and folded himself in a chair with an air of resigned discomfort. A man with a book is practically not present. Mrs. Laurie whipped out her *petit point,* and the two women, pulling their chairs together zestfully, settled down for a talk. Rain streamed down the windows, paper rustled inside the cold grate.

Mima saw so few friends that talk went to her head like wine. Evenly sing-song, the women's voices began rising and falling. After half an hour, Frank's book slipped on to his knee; his head rolled back, jaw dropping; he let out a sharp snore. 'Really . . .' exclaimed Mima, stopping the talk to titter. 'A tropical habit,' said Mrs. Laurie. This was better than Frank with a book, they were quite alone. She hopped back to her topic.

'Mima, what's Godwin got up his sleeve about Miss Rice?'

'Miss Rice?—nothing,' Mima said, overacting.

'His one wicked extravagance?'

'No,' faltered Mima. 'That's just the point—she's not.'

'A bargain? You amaze me. Can she be at all fishy?'

'My *dear* Nella—she's good with the children, isn't she?' Mima fixed her friend with such oddly imploring eyes that Mrs. Laurie, startled, put down her work: 'She's made princesses of them,' she said extravagantly. 'How wise you have been, Mima!'

'You do really think so? Godwin and I wanted the best we could get, you see: he has such ideas for Penny and Claudia.'

'It does him credit,' said Mrs. Laurie warmly.

'I suppose so,' blurted out Mima, then, looking wretched, put her hand to her cheek. 'I've never quite liked—I mean if she—I can't help wondering—'

'Why did Godwin snap me up when I said I thought I knew her face?'

'We'd hoped no one *would* think that,' said Mima surprisingly. 'As a rule, you see, almost nobody comes here, and in every other way she seemed quite ideal: she is. In the ordinary way, we never could have afforded her. It *did* seem such an opportunity. You see, we could not offer a high salary.'

'That would narrow things down. . . .'

'It did. All the ones I had interviewed were so vulgar and pushing, besides seeming to know nothing at all. The agency woman said, "For *that,* what can you expect?" I was in despair.'

'Oh? So then—?'

'I came round more and more to Godwin's idea. As he said, it was practically a charity. It did seem unfair that the thing should count against her. When she had paid for her defence she hadn't a penny, and no other future, of course. And she *was* acquitted.'

'What on earth do you mean?'

Looking thoroughly frightened, Mima caught herself up. 'Oh dear,' she said, 'and I swore never to speak of it. Nella, will you *swear* to let this go no further? It's such a relief to tell you: it's on my mind the whole time. You see, Godwin had followed all the evidence carefully. The witnesses gave her such magnificent testimonials, almost all her former employers were called. Even the Prosecution didn't make out she wasn't a good *governess*. And after all, she *was* cleared. (If only they'd found who'd done it. . . .)'

'Begin at the beginning.'

'Well. . . . Do you ever read murder trials?'

'Hardly ever miss one.'

'Do you remember that Sir Max Rant dying suddenly?'

'Mima—she's not *Henrietta Post?*'

'Sssh—sssh,' whispered Mima, glancing Frank's way cautiously. Then she nodded at Nella with frightened important eyes.

Mrs. Laurie stared, galvanized, at her hostess. Then: 'She's lucky to be alive,' she said, 'it was touch and go.'

'He was a dreadful old man, apparently. At the very worst, they said nothing against her *morals.*'

'No wonder she's haunted-looking. That was an appalling ordeal. . . . But, after that, how on earth . . . ?'

'Godwin got me to write to her three weeks after the trial, offering her a new life and twenty-five pounds a year. . . .'

'Godwin is on the spot! Well, they're your children, not mine—*Henrietta Post!*'

Immovably, without batting a closed eyelid, Frank said, 'Who is Henrietta Post?'

II

'Miss Rice's hands are cold again,' said Penny.

Claudia went on painting a moment longer, then, balancing her brush on the glass jar of paint-water, which gave out a prussic smell and had a red sediment, looked intently across the table at Penny, who stood by Miss Rice's chair, chafing her right hand. Their governess, with her book propped on the table, her pale cheek on her left hand, read on, smiling unnoticingly. Once she withdrew her hand from Penny's to turn over a page.

'Whatever will she do in winter?' said Claudia.

'There'll be fires then.'

'This fire never burns much.' They shared the same desperate thought: 'Suppose our darling should leave us?'

This afternoon, the black chill of the grate focused your fancy as firelight might have done. The schoolroom had a faded sea-blue wallpaper cut into by pitch-pine presses and two doors: not a colour warmed it; the high windows looked into a rain-blurred hill. Miss Rice had put nothing of her own on the mantelpiece, along which marched a file of plasticine animals modelled by the little girls. About the room were products of other hobbies good governesses encourage children to have: on the window-sill a nursery-garden in pots. Pink-cheeked 'Bubbles' and 'Cherry Ripe' looked queerly down at the bleak room where these three people were living as best they could.

Miss Rice put away the book, and with it her happy, forgetful smile—the book had been *Emma*. 'Have you stopped painting?' she said.

She had given them for the subject a Greek temple. Claudia's temple had a sunset behind it, Penny had filled in the columns with Mediterranean blue. Miss Rice came round and looked. 'A sunset like that would make reflections on white stone, Claudia. Penny, on such a fine day there would be shadows.' They saw. She always thought of something they had not thought of: they wrinkled up their foreheads in ecstatic despair. 'Penny, if you are stopping, wash that blue off your paint-brush.'

'Are paints poison?'

'Sometimes. Well, are you cold, too?'

They would admit nothing that could distress her.

'Then push the table back and get the skipping-ropes out.'

The little girls were alike, though there were two years between them, as though they could not decide to part in any particular. There was not much difference in size, as though Penny had waited for Claudia. Their voices were pitched on the same persuasive note; when their vehement dark eyes met they seemed to consult. What they thought of being alive their parents would never know: their characters were like batteries storing something up. Before Miss Rice was here, the doctor's sister had come in every morning to give them lessons. They had known before how to read and write, so all they had learnt from the doctor's sister was what every one else knew: just why their house was avoided, how bitterly father was laughed at and mother pitied because of him. They learnt that it was wretched to be themselves. They marked the contempt with which every morning she bicycled up their avenue, and how insolently she ate what there was at lunch. Her raspy fingertips, the pearls screwed tight in her fleshy ears, her horsesense, all seemed part of her power to mortify them. She was the world and they prayed she might die, but she married. After that they waited, in armour. Then came Miss Rice.

'If you want to keep warm you must hurry,' said Miss Rice.

Claudia unwound the skipping-ropes and they took one each: they stood with their arms out, gripping the handles eagerly. 'One, two, three—go!' The ropes zip-zipped on the oilcloth. Penny stumbled at fifty-six, but

Claudia kept in and skipped seventy-eight: her toes bounced and bounced, her hair flopped, her eyes started out of her head. At last the rope caught her toe. 'That's the record,' said Miss Rice, 'but Penny may beat it next time.' Both breathless, they knelt on the hearthrug, life tingling up through them from their toes to their cheeks.

. 'If *you* skipped,' said Claudia, 'you might skip a hundred.'

'The rope is too short,' said Miss Rice.

'What else used you to do—dance?'

'Yes, once.'

They had never seen anyone dancing except in pictures of ballrooms: they preferred to imagine Miss Rice not on the crook of an arm, but floating alone round a floor, with her ageless, shining white face, unfrivolous as an angel. At this happy moment, near her and warm from skipping, they felt on the edge of the story she did not tell. . . . But *she* looked down at the skipping-ropes on the floor. 'Better put those away,' she said. Except when she was reading she never stayed quiet long: something they could feel creep up behind her chair would make her speaking eyes go suddenly cold and dark as the grate. Against this their love was powerless. This dreadful expectation seemed wrong in their darling—mother without her worries would not be anyone, father was there to stare and bite his moustache, but *she* seemed to them born to inherit light. . . . Feeling their enemy here now the children, helpless, got up to put the skipping-ropes back in the press.

'Someone's coming!' said Penny. They heard the baize door at the far end of their passage swing to behind somebody, then a man's step. A knuckle rapped the door once, unconfidently. Miss Rice and the children waited. 'Come in!' she said.

Frank Peele peered round the door. 'Oh?' he said. 'May I come in? Sorry. I was exploring. Looking for secret passages. Exercise before tea.' Miss Rice smiled composedly. 'So here you all are,' he went on. He looked at the table. 'Painting?'

'Yes.'

'What a day!' he said to Miss Rice humbly. 'Very cheery up here, though. You believe in fresh air?' Then he saw that both windows were bolted: what he felt were the draughts. Miss Rice had moved to the table where she had been reading; Frank dropped into the wicker chair with a creak. The children shut their paint-boxes up. 'Must be getting on tea-time,' remarked Frank.

'Are you hungry, Cousin Frank?' said Claudia gently.

Frank looked relieved at hearing someone say something. 'I don't deserve tea; I slept like a log in the library. Your mother and Mrs. Laurie complain I snored.' He looked round the schoolroom wistfully, like a dog. 'They were talking nineteen to the dozen. When I dropped off they were well away about India, when I came to it was one Henrietta Post.'

Penny laughed. 'Who's Henrietta Post?' she said.

'Don't ask *me*,' said Frank, '—Miss Rice, who's Henrietta Post?'

Miss Rice pondered while the clock ticked several seconds and a cart rattled off into silence behind the wet orchards. The children turned to see how she took Frank's joke. She looked twice at him with steady, considering, dark eyes. 'Surely you know?' she said at last.

'I don't know a soul,' said Frank, 'I've been in Siam.'

'But you get the papers there, don't you?'

'She's a celebrity, is she?'

'She was accused of murder,' said Miss Rice, as though giving a history lesson, 'tried last spring, acquitted but never properly cleared. So she disappeared, hoping to be forgotten.'

'Good God,' exclaimed Frank. 'Where would a woman go to, after a show like that?'

'She is fortunate to be anywhere.'

'—Stop: it's coming back!' Frank said, delighted to have a topic. 'Wasn't she that governess? The old swine whose house she was in had been making up to her, so when someone did him in they tried to fix it on her. I remember I thought at the time—'

Miss Rice's marked unresponse reminded Frank where he was. Chidden, he stopped awkwardly, with a glance at the children. *They* sat stone-still, clasped hands thrust down between their knees; you could not possibly tell what was going on in their heads, which were both turned intently away from their governess. Frank kicked himself. But for the life of him he couldn't stop blurting out: 'She was very good-looking, wasn't she?'

'You never saw any photographs?'

'Out where I am I only get *The Times*, you see. No pretty pictures in it.'

'I see.'

Frank went on violently: 'I know I thought at the time, what a shocking unfair thing to happen to any woman!' . . . . Miss Rice with her cold smile looked thoughtfully into the grate as though there were a fire burning there: she said nothing more. Her charges' agonized tension became startling. Frank hummed and beat a nonplussed tattoo on his knee. They were waiting to see the last of him. Whatever brick one had dropped, they were all very odd up here. . . .

III

This wet autumn evening closed in so early that the children had to stop work and wait for the lamp to come; when Mrs. Carbury looked in they were all in the dark. 'Why, whatever are you doing?' she said nervously. 'Where's Miss Rice? Why doesn't she ring for the lamp?'

'It never comes any sooner.'

'Father wouldn't like you wasting your time like this. Where *is* Miss Rice?'

'In her room,' Penny said, so indifferently that there seemed to be something foolish about the fuss. At this point a band of light appeared in the passage; the housemaid brought in the lamp and Mima saw her daughters facing each other like images across the table of lesson books, their unchildish eyes dark in the sudden lamplight. She sat down, acting calm while the housemaid was in the room; all the same, her manner made the girl so jumpy that she went away again without drawing down the blinds. Mrs. Carbury sat eyeing the other door: the children's bedroom opened off the schoolroom and Miss Rice's room was beyond, connecting with theirs. Her relief at *not* finding the governess was tremendous: all the same, she felt she was being defied.

'Does she always leave you to do preparation alone?'

'She's tired,' said Claudia. 'Cousin Frank was up here.'

'Oh? . . . Well, tell her I want to speak to her. Then you can leave your lessons, just for this evening, and go downstairs; Mrs. Laurie says she will play games with you.'

The children looked at their books without stirring, and Mima for the first time felt mutiny in the air. . . . Mima had had to brace herself to come in; twice already since tea she had started up to the schoolroom, then turned back before the baize door to that wing. Ever since her revelation to Mrs. Laurie she had been in a fearful state: the way Mrs. Laurie took it brought her own most persistent throttling fears to the top. '*Henrietta Post.* . . . *Well, they're your children, not mine.*' What Nella said was what anybody who knew would say. Mima had shrunk back from the schoolroom door, feeling: 'No, I really cannot face her.' Then she had been forced to think: 'But that is the woman my children are with the whole time. . . .' Once she had got as far as Godwin's study to tell him he must agree to send Miss Rice away to-morrow, but the way he had looked up at her settled that. 'Nothing has changed since I agreed to engage her.' Mima knew too well that her husband found her a fool. 'I will give her notice first, then tell Godwin. It won't be so bad with Nella here in the house. Nella will back me up. *But when Godwin hears I've told Nella?* . . . He said before she came to stay: "Suppose your friend is inquisitive?" . . . What are they doing up there? What does she say to them? What goes on the whole time? My own children are strangers; they don't like being downstairs now. *What was it the prosecution said about influence?*' That thought had brought Mima past the schoolroom door.

Mima raised her voice. 'Run along now at once, children: Mrs. Laurie is waiting.'

'We would much rather not, mother.'

'Then you're very ungrateful. Besides, I have got something to say to Miss Rice—Penny and Claudia, don't look at each other like that! It's rude to look at each other when mother speaks!'

'Miss Rice is tired,' repeated Claudia gently.

'If you give us the message,' said Penny, 'we'll tell her.'

'No, I want to talk to Miss Rice,' said Mima, her voice unnatural.

'Do you, mother?' said Penny. 'You don't generally.'

The wicker chair Mima sat in creaked convulsively. 'When we're alone again you may learn to make mother happy. You may understand mother then and not be unkind to her. To-morrow, Miss Rice will be going away, children.'

Penny and Claudia looked at the chair their mother now sat in, then up at *Emma* left on the edge of the mantelpiece. Claudia looked at their row of young plants in the window-sill, sharp in the lamplight against the rain-lashed dark outside, Penny at the wrinkled rug where that afternoon they had knelt at their darling's feet. Then their gentle, vehement, dark eyes, meeting, paused to consult again. They said in their quiet voices: 'Then we will go too.'

MARÍA CONCEPCIÓN

Katherine Anne Porter

(1894–   )

MARÍA CONCEPCIÓN WALKED CAREFULLY, keeping to the middle of the white dusty road, where the maguey thorns and the treacherous curved spines of organ cactus had not gathered so profusely. She would have enjoyed resting for a moment in the dark shade by the roadside, but she had no time to waste drawing cactus needles from her feet. Juan and his chief would be waiting for their food in the damp trenches of the buried city.

She carried about a dozen living fowls slung over her right shoulder, their feet fastened together. Half of them fell upon the flat of her back, the balance dangled uneasily over her breast. They wriggled their benumbed and swollen legs against her neck, they twisted their stupefied eyes and peered into her face inquiringly. She did not see them or think of them. Her left arm was tired with the weight of the food basket, and she was hungry after her long morning's work.

Her straight back outlined itself strongly under her clean bright blue cotton rebozo. Instinctive serenity softened her black eyes, shaped like almonds, set far apart, and tilted a bit endwise. She walked with the free, natural, guarded ease of the primitive woman carrying an unborn child. The shape of her body was easy, the swelling life was not a distortion, but the right inevitable proportions of a woman. She was entirely contented. Her husband was at work and she was on her way to market to sell her fowls.

Her small house sat half-way up a shallow hill, under a clump of pepper-trees, a wall of organ cactus enclosing it on the side nearest to the road. Now she came down into the valley, divided by the narrow spring, and crossed a bridge of loose stones near the hut where María Rosa the bee-keeper lived with her old godmother, Lupe the medicine woman. María Concepción had no faith in the charred owl bones, the singed rabbit fur, the cat entrails, the messes and ointments sold by Lupe to the ailing of the village. She was a good Christian, and drank simple herb teas for headache and stomachache, or bought her remedies bottled, with printed directions that she could not read, at the drugstore near the city market, where she went almost daily. But she often bought a jar of honey from young María Rosa, a pretty, shy child only fifteen years old.

María Concepción and her husband, Juan Villegas, were each a little past their eighteenth year. She had a good reputation with the neighbors as an energetic religious woman who could drive a bargain to the end. It was commonly known that if she wished to buy a new rebozo for herself or a shirt for Juan, she could bring out a sack of hard silver coins for the purpose.

She had paid for the license, nearly a year ago, the potent bit of stamped paper which permits people to be married in the church. She had given money to the priest before she and Juan walked together up to the altar the Monday after Holy Week. It had been the adventure of the villagers to go, three Sundays one after another, to hear the banns called by the priest for Juan de Dois Villegas and María Concepción Manríquez, who were actually getting married in the church, instead of behind it, which was the usual custom, less expensive, and as binding as any other ceremony. But María Concepción was always as proud as if she owned a hacienda.

She paused on the bridge and dabbled her feet in the water, her eyes resting themselves from the sun-rays in a fixed gaze to the far-off mountains, deeply blue under their hanging drift of clouds. It came to her that she would like a fresh crust of honey. The delicious aroma of bees, their slow thrilling hum, awakened a pleasant desire for a flake of sweetness in her mouth.

"If I do not eat it now, I shall mark my child," she thought, peering through the crevices in the thick hedge of cactus that sheered up nakedly, like bared knife blades set protectingly around the small clearing. The place was so silent she doubted if María Rosa and Lupe were at home.

The leaning jacal of dried rush-withes and corn sheaves, bound to tall saplings thrust into the earth, roofed with yellowed maguey leaves flattened and overlapping like shingles, hunched drowsy and fragrant in the warmth of noonday. The hives, similarly made, were scattered towards the back of the clearing, like small mounds of clean vegetable refuse. Over each mound there hung a dusty golden shimmer of bees.

A light gay scream of laughter rose from behind the hut; a man's short laugh joined in. "Ah, hahahaha!" went the voices together high and low, like a song.

"So María Rosa has a man!" María Concepción stopped short, smiling, shifted her burden slightly, and bent forward shading her eyes to see more clearly through the spaces of the hedge.

María Rosa ran, dodging between beehives, parting two stunted jasmine bushes as she came, lifting her knees in swift leaps, looking over her shoulder and laughing in a quivering, excited way. A heavy jar, swung to her wrist by the handle, knocked against her thighs as she ran. Her toes pushed up sudden spurts of dust, her half-raveled braids showered around her shoulders in long crinkled wisps.

Juan Villegas ran after her, also laughing strangely, his teeth set, both rows gleaming behind the small soft black beard growing sparsely on his lips, his chin, leaving his brown cheeks girl-smooth. When he seized her, he clenched so hard her chemise gave way and ripped from her shoulder. She stopped laughing at this, pushed him away and stood silent, trying to pull up the torn sleeve with one hand. Her pointed chin and dark red mouth moved in an uncertain way, as if she wished to laugh again; her long black lashes flickered with the quick-moving lights in her hidden eyes.

María Concepción did not stir nor breathe for some seconds. Her forehead was cold, and yet boiling water seemed to be pouring slowly along her spine. An unaccountable pain was in her knees, as if they were broken. She was afraid Juan and María Rosa would feel her eyes fixed upon them and would find her there, unable to move, spying upon them. But they did not pass beyond the enclosure, nor even glance towards the gap in the wall opening upon the road.

Juan lifted one of María Rosa's loosened braids and slapped her neck with it playfully. She smiled softly, consentingly. Together they moved back through the hives of honey-comb. María Rosa balanced her jar on one hip and swung her long full petticoats with every step. Juan flourished his wide hat back and forth, walking proudly as a game-cock.

María Concepción came out of the heavy cloud which enwrapped her head and bound her throat, and found herself walking onward, keeping the road without knowing it, feeling her way delicately, her ears strumming as if all María Rosa's bees had hived in them. Her careful sense of duty kept her moving toward the buried city where Juan's chief, the American archeologist, was taking his midday rest, waiting for his food.

Juan and María Rosa! She burned all over now, as if a layer of tiny fig-cactus bristles, as cruel as spun glass, had crawled under her skin. She wished to sit down quietly and wait for her death, but not until she had cut the throats of her man and that girl who were laughing and kissing under the cornstalks. Once when she was a young girl she had come back from market to find her jacal burned to a pile of ash and her few silver coins gone. A dark empty feeling had filled her; she kept moving about the place, not believing her eyes, expecting it all to take shape again before her. But it was gone, and though she knew an enemy had done it, she could not find out who it was, and could only curse and threaten the air. Now here was a worse thing, but she knew her enemy. María Rosa, that sinful girl, shameless! She heard herself saying a harsh, true word about María Rosa, saying it aloud as if she expected someone to agree with her: "Yes, she is a whore! She has no right to live."

At this moment the gray untidy head of Givens appeared over the edges of the newest trench he had caused to be dug in his field of excavations. The long deep crevasses, in which a man might stand without being seen, lay crisscrossed like orderly gashes of a giant scalpel. Nearly all of the men of the community worked for Givens, helping him to uncover the lost city of their ancestors. They worked all the year through and prospered, digging every day for those small clay heads and bits of pottery and fragments of painted walls for which there was no good use on earth, being all broken and encrusted with clay. They themselves could make better ones, perfectly stout and new, which they took to town and peddled to foreigners for real money. But the unearthly delight of the chief in finding these worn-out things was an endless puzzle. He would fairly roar for joy at times, waving a shattered pot or a human skull above his head, shouting for his photographer to come and make a picture of this!

Now he emerged, and his young enthusiast's eyes welcomed María Concepción from his old-man face, covered with hard wrinkles and burned to the color of red earth. "I hope you've brought me a nice fat one." He selected a fowl from the bunch dangling nearest him as María Concepción, wordless, leaned over the trench. "Dress it for me, there's a good girl. I'll broil it."

María Concepción took the fowl by the head, and silently, swiftly drew her knife across its throat, twisting the head off with the casual firmness she might use with the top of a beet.

"Good God, woman, you do have nerve," said Givens, watching her. "I can't do that. It gives me the creeps."

"My home country is Guadalajara," explained María Concepción, without bravado, as she picked and gutted the fowl.

She stood and regarded Givens condescendingly, that diverting white man who had no woman of his own to cook for him, and moreover appeared not to feel any loss of dignity in preparing his own food. He squatted now, eyes squinted, nose wrinkled to avoid the smoke, turning the roasting fowl busily on a stick. A mysterious man, undoubtedly rich, and Juan's chief, therefore to be respected, to be placated.

"The tortillas are fresh and hot, señor," she murmured gently. "With your permission I will now go to market."

"Yes, yes, run along; bring me another of these tomorrow." Givens turned his head to look at her again. Her grand manner sometimes reminded him of royalty in exile. He noticed her unnatural paleness. "The sun is too hot, eh?" he asked.

"Yes, sir. Pardon me, but Juan will be here soon?"

"He ought to be here now. Leave his food. The others will eat it."

She moved away; the blue of her rebozo became a dancing spot in the heat waves that rose from the gray-red soil. Givens liked his Indians best when he could feel a fatherly indulgence for their primitive childish ways. He told comic stories of Juan's escapades, of how often he had saved him, in the past five years, from going to jail, and even from being shot, for his varied and always unexpected misdeeds.

"I am never a minute too soon to get him out of one pickle or another," he would say. "Well, he's a good worker, and I know how to manage him."

After Juan was married, he used to twit him, with exactly the right shade of condescension, on his many infidelities to María Concepción. "She'll catch you yet, and God help you!" he was fond of saying, and Juan would laugh with immense pleasure.

It did not occur to María Concepción to tell Juan she had found him out. During the day her anger against him died, and her anger against María Rosa grew. She kept saying to herself, "When I was a young girl like María Rosa, if a man had caught hold of me so, I would have broken my jar over his head." She forgot completely that she had not resisted even so much as María Rosa, on the day that Juan had first taken hold of her. Besides she had married him afterwards in the church, and that was a very different thing.

Juan did not come home that night, but went away to war and María Rosa went with him. Juan had a rifle at his shoulder and two pistols at his belt. María Rosa wore a rifle also, slung on her back along with the blankets and the cooking pots. They joined the nearest detachment of troops in the field, and María Rosa marched ahead with the battalion of experienced women of war, which went over the crops like locusts, gathering provisions for the army. She cooked with them, and ate with them what was left after the men had eaten. After battles she went out on the field with the others to salvage clothing and ammunition and guns from the slain before they should begin to swell in the heat. Sometimes they would encounter the women from the other army, and a second battle as grim as the first would take place.

There was no particular scandal in the village. People shrugged, grinned. It was far better that they were gone. The neighbors went around saying that María Rosa was safer in the army than she would be in the same village with María Concepción.

María Concepción did not weep when Juan left her; and when the baby was born, and died within four days, she did not weep. "She is mere stone," said old Lupe, who went over and offered charms to preserve the baby.

"May you rot in hell with your charms," said María Concepción.

If she had not gone so regularly to church, lighting candles before the saints, kneeling with her arms spread in the form of a cross for hours at a time, and receiving holy communion every month, there might have been talk of her being devil-possessed, her face was so changed and blind-looking. But this was impossible when, after all, she had been married by the priest. It must be, they reasoned, that she was being punished for her pride. They decided that this was the true cause for everything: she was altogether too proud. So they pitied her.

During the year that Juan and María Rosa were gone María Concepción sold her fowls and looked after her garden and her sack of hard coins grew. Lupe had no talent for bees, and the hives did not prosper. She began to blame María Rosa for running away, and to praise María Concepción for her behavior. She used to see María Concepción at the market or at church, and she always said that no one could tell by looking at her now that she was a woman who had such a heavy grief.

"I pray God everything goes well with María Concepción from this out," she would say, "for she has had her share of trouble."

When some idle person repeated this to the deserted woman, she went down to Lupe's house and stood within the clearing and called to the medicine woman, who sat in her doorway stirring a mess of her infallible cure for sores: "Keep your prayers to yourself, Lupe, or offer them for others who need them. I will ask God for what I want in this world."

"And will you get it, you think, María Concepción?" asked Lupe, tittering cruelly and smelling the wooden mixing spoon. "Did you pray for what you have now?"

Afterward everyone noticed that María Concepción went oftener to church, and even seldomer to the village to talk with the other women as they sat along the curb, nursing their babies and eating fruit, at the end of the market-day.

"She is wrong to take us for enemies," said old Soledad, who was a thinker and a peace-maker. "All women have these troubles. Well, we should suffer together."

But María Concepción lived alone. She was gaunt, as if something were gnawing her away inside, her eyes were sunken, and she would not speak a word if she could help it. She worked harder than ever, and her butchering knife was scarcely ever out of her hand.

Juan and María Rosa, disgusted with military life, came home one day without asking permission of anyone. The field of war had unrolled itself, a long scroll of vexations, until the end had frayed out within twenty miles of Juan's village. So he and María Rosa, now lean as a wolf, burdened with a child daily expected, set out with no farewells to the regiment and walked home.

They arrived one morning about daybreak. Juan was picked up on sight by a group of military police from the small barracks on the edge of town, and taken to prison, where the officer in charge told him with impersonal cheerfulness that he would add one to a catch of ten waiting to be shot as deserters the next morning.

María Rosa, screaming and falling on her face in the road, was taken under the armpits by two guards and helped briskly to her jacal, now sadly run down. She was received with professional importance by Lupe, who helped the baby to be born at once.

Limping with foot soreness, a layer of dust concealing his fine new clothes got mysteriously from somewhere, Juan appeared before the captain at the barracks. The captain recognized him as head digger for his good friend Givens, and dispatched a note to Givens saying: "I am holding the person of Juan Villegas awaiting your further disposition."

When Givens showed up Juan was delivered to him with the urgent request that nothing be made public about so humane and sensible an operation on the part of military authority.

Juan walked out of the rather stifling atmosphere of the drumhead court, a definite air of swagger about him. His hat, of unreasonable dimensions and embroidered with silver thread, hung over one eyebrow, secured at the back by a cord of silver dripping with bright blue tassels. His shirt was of a checkerboard pattern in green and black, his white cotton trousers were bound by a belt of yellow leather tooled in red. His feet were bare, full of stone bruises, and sadly ragged as to toenails. He removed his cigarette from the corner of his full-lipped wide mouth. He removed the splendid hat. His black dusty hair, pressed moistly to his forehead, sprang up suddenly in a cloudy thatch on his crown. He bowed to the officer, who appeared to be gazing at a vacuum. He swung his arm wide in a free circle upsoaring towards the prison window, where forlorn heads poked over the window sill, hot eyes following after the lucky departing one. Two or three of the heads nodded, and a half dozen hands were flipped at him in an effort to imitate his own casual and heady manner.

Juan kept up this insufferable pantomime until they rounded the first clump of fig-cactus. Then he seized Givens' hand and burst into oratory. "Blessed be the day your servant Juan Villegas first came under your eyes. From this day my life is yours without condition, ten thousand thanks with all my heart!"

"For God's sake stop playing the fool," said Givens irritably. "Some day I'm going to be five minutes too late."

"Well, it is nothing much to be shot, my chief—certainly you know I was not afraid—but to be shot in a drove of deserters, against a cold wall, just in the moment of my home-coming, by order of that . . ."

Glittering epithets tumbled over one another like explosions of a rocket. All the scandalous analogies from the animal and vegetable worlds were applied in a vivid, unique and personal way to the life, loves, and family history of the officer who had just set him free. When he had quite cursed himself dry, and his nerves were soothed, he added: "With your permission, my chief!"

"What will María Concepción say to all this?" asked Givens. "You are very informal, Juan, for a man who was married in the church."

Juan put on his hat.

"Oh, María Concepción! That's nothing. Look, my chief, to be married in the church is a great misfortune for a man. After that he is not himself any more. How can that woman complain when I do not drink even at fiestas enough to be really drunk? I do not beat her; never, never. We were always at peace. I say to her, Come here, and she comes straight. I say, Go there, and she goes quickly. Yet sometimes I looked at her and thought, Now I am married to that woman in the church, and I felt a sinking inside, as if something were lying heavy on my stomach. With María Rosa it is all different. She is not silent; she talks. When she talks too much, I slap her and say, Silence, thou simpleton! and she weeps. She is just a girl with whom I do as I please. You know how she used to keep those clean little bees in their hives? She is like their honey to me. I swear it. I would not harm María Concepción because I am married to her in the church; but also, my chief, I will not leave María Rosa, because she pleases me more than any other woman."

"Let me tell you, Juan, things haven't been going as well as you think. You be careful. Some day María Concepción will just take your head off with that carving knife of hers. You keep that in mind."

Juan's expression was the proper blend of masculine triumph and sentimental melancholy. It was pleasant to see himself in the rôle of hero to two such desirable women. He had just escaped from the threat of a disagreeable end. His clothes were new and handsome, and they had cost him just nothing. María Rosa had collected them for him here and there after battles. He was walking in the early sunshine, smelling the good smells of ripening cactus-figs, peaches, and melons, of pungent berries dangling from the pepper-trees, and the smoke of his cigarette under his nose. He was on his way to civilian life with his patient chief. His situation was ineffably perfect, and he swallowed it whole.

"My chief," he addressed Givens handsomely, as one man of the world to another, "women are good things, but not at this moment. With your permission, I will now go to the village and eat. My God, *how* I shall eat! Tomorrow morning very early I will come to the buried city and work like seven men. Let us forget María Concepción and María Rosa. Each one in her place. I will manage them when the time comes."

News of Juan's adventure soon got abroad, and Juan found many friends about him during the morning. They frankly commended his way of leaving the army. It was in itself the act of a hero. The new hero ate a great deal and drank somewhat, the occasion being better than a feast-day. It was almost noon before he returned to visit María Rosa.

He found her sitting on a clean straw mat, rubbing fat on her three-hour-old-son. Before this felicitous vision Juan's emotions so twisted him that he returned to the village and invited every man in the "Death and Resurrection" pulque shop to drink with him.

Having thus taken leave of his balance, he started back to María Rosa, and found himself unaccountably in his own house, attempting to beat María Concepción by way of reëstablishing himself in his legal household.

María Concepción, knowing all the events of that unhappy day, was not in a yielding mood, and refused to be beaten. She did not scream nor implore; she stood her ground and resisted; she even struck at him. Juan, amazed, hardly knowing what he did, stepped back and gazed at her inquiringly through a leisurely whirling film which seemed to have lodged behind his eyes. Certainly he had not even thought of touching her. Oh, well, no harm done. He gave up, turned away, half-asleep on his feet. He dropped amiably in a shadowed corner and began to snore.

María Concepción, seeing that he was quiet, began to bind the legs of her fowls. It was market-day and she was late. She fumbled and tangled the bits of cord in her haste, and set off across the plowed fields instead of taking the accustomed road. She ran with a crazy panic in her head, her stumbling legs. Now and then she would stop and look about her, trying to place herself, then go on a few steps, until she realized that she was not going towards the market.

At once she came to her senses completely, recognized the thing that troubled her so terribly, was certain of what she wanted. She sat down quietly under a sheltering thorny bush and gave herself over to her long devouring sorrow. The thing which had for so long squeezed her whole body into a tight dumb knot of suffering suddenly broke with shocking violence. She jerked with the involuntary recoil of one who receives a blow, and the sweat poured from her skin as if the wounds of her whole life were shedding their salt ichor. Drawing her rebozo over her head, she bowed her forehead on her updrawn knees, and sat there in deadly silence and immobility. From time to time she lifted her head where the sweat formed steadily and poured down her face, drenching the front of her chemise, and her mouth had the shape of crying, but there were no tears and no sound. All her being was a dark confused memory of grief burning in her at night, of deadly baffled anger eating at her by day, until her very tongue tasted bitter, and her feet were as heavy as if she were mired in the muddy roads during the time of rains.

After a great while she stood up and threw the rebozo off her face, and set out walking again.

Juan awakened slowly, with long yawns and grumblings, alternated with short relapses into sleep full of visions and clamors. A blur of orange light seared his eyeballs when he tried to unseal his lids. There came from somewhere a low voice weeping without tears, saying meaningless phrases over and over. He began to listen. He tugged at the leash of his stupor, he strained to grasp those words which terrified him even though he could not quite hear them. Then he came awake with frightening suddenness, sitting up and staring at the long sharpened streak of light piercing the corn-husk walls from the level disappearing sun.

María Concepción stood in the doorway, looming colossally tall to his betrayed eyes. She was talking quickly, and calling his name. Then he saw her clearly.

"God's name!" said Juan, frozen to the marrow, "here I am facing my death!" for the long knife she wore habitually at her belt was in her hand. But instead, she threw it away, clear from her, and got down on her knees, crawling toward him as he had seen her crawl many times toward the shrine at Guadalupe Villa. He watched her approach with such horror that the hair of his head seemed to be lifting itself away from him. Falling forward upon her face, she huddled over him, lips moving in a ghostly whisper. Her words became clear, and Juan understood them all.

For a second he could not move nor speak. Then he took her head between both his hands, and supported her in this way, saying swiftly, anxiously reassuring, almost in a babble:

"Oh, thou poor creature! Oh, madwoman! Oh, my María Concepción, unfortunate! Listen. . . . Don't be afraid. Listen to me! I will hide thee away, I thy own man will protect thee! Quiet! Not a sound!"

Trying to collect himself, he held her and cursed under his breath for a few moments in the gathering darkness. María Concepción bent over, face almost on the ground, her feet folded under her, as if she would hide behind him. For the first time in his life Juan was aware of danger. This was danger. María Concepción would be dragged away between two gendarmes, with him following helpless and unarmed, to spend the rest of her days in Belén Prison, maybe. Danger! The night swarmed with threats. He stood up and dragged her up with him. She was silent and perfectly rigid, holding to him with resistless strength, her hands stiffened on his arms.

"Get me the knife," he told her in a whisper. She obeyed, her feet slipping along the hard earth floor, her shoulders straight, her arms close to her side. He lighted a candle. María Concepción held the knife out to him. It was stained and dark even to the handle with drying blood.

He frowned at her harshly, noting the same stains on her chemise and hands.

"Take off thy clothes and wash thy hands," he ordered. He washed the knife carefully, and threw the water wide of the doorway. She watched him and did likewise with the bowl in which she had bathed.

"Light the brasero and cook food for me," he told her in the same peremptory tone. He took her garments and went out. When he returned, she was wearing an old soiled dress, and was fanning the fire in the charcoal burner. Seating himself cross-legged near her, he stared at her as at a creature unknown to him, who bewildered him utterly, for whom there was no possible explanation. She did not turn her head, but kept silent and still, except for the movements of her strong hands fanning the blaze which cast sparks and small jets of white smoke, flaring and dying rhythmically with the motion of the fan, lighting her face and darkening it by turns.

Juan's voice barely disturbed the silence: "Listen to me carefully, and tell me the truth, and when the gendarmes come here for us, thou shalt have nothing to fear. But there will be something for us to settle between us afterward."

The light from the charcoal burner shone in her eyes; a yellow phosphorescence glimmered behind the dark iris.

"For me everything is settled now," she answered, in a tone so tender, so grave, so heavy with suffering, that Juan felt his vitals contract. He wished to repent openly, not as a man, but as a very small child. He could not fathom her, nor himself, nor the mysterious fortunes of life grown so instantly confused where all had seemed so gay and simple. He felt too that she had become invaluable, a woman without equal among a million women, and he could not tell why. He drew an enormous sigh that rattled in his chest.

"Yes, yes, it is all settled. I shall not go away again. We must stay here together."

Whispering, he questioned her and she answered whispering, and he instructed her over and over until she had her lesson by heart. The hostile darkness of the night encroached upon them, flowing over the narrow threshold, invading their hearts. It brought with it sighs and murmurs, the pad of secretive feet in the near-by road, the sharp staccato whimper of wind through the cactus leaves. All these familiar, once friendly cadences were now invested with sinister terrors; a dread, formless and uncontrollable, took hold of them both.

"Light another candle," said Juan, loudly, in too resolute, too sharp a tone. "Let us eat now."

They sat facing each other and ate from the same dish, after their old habit. Neither tasted what they ate. With food half-way to his mouth, Juan listened. The sound of voices rose, spread, widened at the turn of the road along the cactus wall. A spray of lantern light shot through the hedge, a single voice slashed the blackness, ripped the fragile layer of silence suspended above the hut.

"Juan Villegas!"

"Pass, friends!" Juan roared back cheerfully.

They stood in the doorway, simple cautious gendarmes from the village, mixed-bloods themselves with Indian sympathies, well known to all the community. They flashed their lanterns almost apologetically upon the pleasant, harmless scene of a man eating supper with his wife.

"Pardon, brother," said the leader. "Someone has killed the woman María Rosa, and we must question her neighbors and friends." He paused, and added with an attempt at severity, "Naturally!"

"Naturally," agreed Juan. "You know that I was a good friend of María Rosa. This is bad news."

They all went away together, the men walking in a group, María Concepción following a few steps in the rear, near Juan. No one spoke.

The two points of candlelight at María Rosa's head fluttered uneasily; the shadows shifted and dodged on the stained darkened walls. To María Concepción everything in the smothering enclosing room shared an evil restlessness. The watchful faces of those called as witnesses, the faces of old friends, were made alien by the look of speculation in their eyes. The ridges of the rose-colored rebozo thrown over the body varied continually, as though the thing it covered was not perfectly in repose. Her eyes swerved over the body in the open painted coffin, from the candle tips at the head to the feet, jutting up thinly, the small scarred soles protruding, freshly washed, a mass of crooked, half-healed wounds, thorn-pricks and cuts of sharp stones. Her gaze went back to the candle flame, to Juan's eyes warning her, to the gendarmes talking among themselves. Her eyes would not be controlled.

With a leap that shook her her gaze settled upon the face of María Rosa. Instantly her blood ran smoothly again: there was nothing to fear. Even the restless light could not give a look of life to that fixed countenance. She was dead. María Concepción felt her muscles give way softly; her heart began beating steadily without effort. She knew no more rancor against that pitiable thing, lying indifferently in its blue coffin under the fine silk rebozo. The mouth drooped sharply at the corners in a grimace of weeping arrested half-way. The brows were distressed; the dead flesh could not cast off the shape of its last terror. It was all finished. María Rosa had eaten too much honey and had had too much love. Now she must sit in hell, crying over her sins and her hard death forever and ever.

Old Lupe's cackling voice arose. She had spent the morning helping María Rosa, and it had been hard work. The child had spat blood the moment it was born, a bad sign. She thought then that bad luck would come to the house. Well, about sunset she was in the yard at the back of the house grinding tomatoes and peppers. She had left mother and babe asleep. She heard a strange noise in the house, a choking and smothered calling, like someone wailing in sleep. Well, such a thing is only natural. But there followed a light, quick, thudding sound—

"Like the blows of a fist?" interrupted an officer.

"No, not at all like such a thing."

"How do you know?"

"I am well acquainted with that sound, friends," retorted Lupe. "This was something else."

She was at a loss to describe it exactly. A moment later, there came the sound of pebbles rolling and slipping under feet; then she knew someone had been there and was running away.

"Why did you wait so long before going to see?"

"I am old and hard in the joints," said Lupe. "I cannot run after people. I walked as fast as I could to the cactus hedge, for it is only by this way that anyone can enter. There was no one in the road, sir, no one. Three cows, with a dog driving them; nothing else. When I got to María Rosa, she was lying all tangled up, and from her neck to her middle she was full of knife-holes. It was a sight to move the Blessed Image Himself! Her eyes were—"

"Never mind. Who came oftenest to her house before she went away? Did you know her enemies?"

Lupe's face congealed, closed. Her spongy skin drew into a network of secretive wrinkles. She turned withdrawn and expressionless eyes upon the gendarmes.

"I am an old woman. I do not see well. I cannot hurry on my feet. I know no enemy of María Rosa. I did not see anyone leave the clearing."

"You did not hear splashing in the spring near the bridge?"

"No, sir."

"Why, then, do our dogs follow a scent there and lose it?"

"God only knows, my friend. I am an old wo—"

"Yes. How did the footfalls sound?"

"Like the tread of an evil spirit!" Lupe broke forth into a swelling oracular tone that startled them. The Indians stirred uneasily, glanced at the dead, then at Lupe. They half expected her to produce the evil spirit among them at once.

The gendarme began to lose his temper.

"No, poor unfortunate; I mean, were they heavy or light? The footsteps of a man or of a woman? Was the person shod or barefoot?"

A glance at the listening circle assured Lupe of their thrilled attention. She enjoyed the dangerous importance of her situation. She could have ruined that María Concepción with a word, but it was even sweeter to make fools of these gendarmes who went about spying on honest people. She raised her voice again. What she had not seen she could not describe, thank God! No one could harm her because her knees were stiff and she could not run even to seize a murderer. As for knowing the difference between footfalls, shod or bare, man or woman, nay, between devil and human, who ever heard of such madness?

"My eyes are not ears, gentlemen," she ended grandly, "but upon my heart I swear those footsteps fell as the tread of the spirit of evil!"

"Imbecile!" yapped the leader in a shrill voice. "Take her away, one of you! Now, Juan Villegas, tell me—"

Juan told his story patiently, several times over. He had returned to his wife that day. She had gone to market as usual. He had helped her prepare her fowls. She had returned about mid-afternoon, they had talked, she had cooked, they had eaten, nothing was amiss. Then the gendarmes came with the news about María Rosa. That was all. Yes, María Rosa had run away with him, but there had been no bad blood between him and his wife on this account, nor between his wife and María Rosa. Everybody knew that his wife was a quiet woman.

María Concepción heard her own voice answering without a break. It was true at first she was troubled when her husband went away, but after that she had not worried about him. It was the way of men, she believed. She was a church-married woman and knew her place. Well, he had come home at last. She had gone to market, but had come back early, because now she had her man to cook for. That was all.

Other voices broke in. A toothless old man said: "She is a woman of good reputation among us, and María Rosa was not." A smiling young mother, Anita, baby at breast, said: "If no one thinks so, how can you accuse her? It was the loss of her child and not of her husband that changed her so." Another: "María Rosa had a strange life, apart from us. How do we know who might have come from another place to do her evil?" And old Soledad spoke up boldly: "When I saw María Concepción in the market today, I said, 'Good luck to you, María Concepción, this is a happy day for you!'" and she gave María Concepción a long easy stare, and the smile of a born wise-woman.

María Concepción suddenly felt herself guarded, surrounded, upborne by her faithful friends. They were around her, speaking for her, defending her, the forces of life were ranged invincibly with her against the beaten dead. María Rosa had thrown away her share of strength in them, she lay forfeited among them. María Concepción looked from one to the other of the circling, intent faces. Their eyes gave back reassurance, understanding, a secret and mighty sympathy.

The gendarmes were at a loss. They, too, felt that sheltering wall cast impenetrably around her. They were certain she had done it, and yet they could not accuse her. Nobody could be accused; there was not a shred of true evidence. They shrugged their shoulders and snapped their fingers and shuffled their feet. Well, then, good night to everybody. Many pardons for having intruded. Good health!

A small bundle lying against the wall at the head of the coffin squirmed like an eel. A wail, a mere sliver of sound, issued. María Concepción took the son of María Rosa in her arms.

"He is mine," she said clearly, "I will take him with me."

No one assented in words, but an approving nod, a bare breath of complete agreement, stirred among them as they made way for her.

María Concepción, carrying the child, followed Juan from the clearing. The hut was left with its lighted candles and a crowd of old women who would sit up all night, drinking coffee and smoking and telling ghost stories.

Juan's exaltation had burned out. There was not an ember of excitement left in him. He was tired. The perilous adventure was over. María Rosa had vanished, to come no more forever. Their days of marching, of eating, of quarreling and making love between battles, were all over. Tomorrow he would go back to dull and endless labor, he must descend into the trenches of the buried city as María Rosa must go into her grave. He felt his veins fill up with bitterness, with black unendurable melancholy. Oh, Jesus! what bad luck overtakes a man!

Well, there was no way out of it now. For a moment he craved only to sleep. He was so drowsy he could scarcely guide his feet. The occasional light touch of the woman at his elbow was as unreal, as ghostly as the brushing of a leaf against his face. He did not know why he had fought to save her, and now he forgot her. There was nothing in him except a vast blind hurt like a covered wound.

He entered the jacal, and without waiting to light a candle, threw off his clothing, sitting just within the door. He moved with lagging, half-awake hands, to strip his body of its heavy finery. With a long groaning sigh of relief he fell straight back on the floor, almost instantly asleep, his arms flung up and outward.

María Concepción, a small clay jar in her hand, approached the gentle little mother goat tethered to a sapling, which gave and yielded as she pulled at the rope's end after the farthest reaches of grass about her. The kid, tied up a few feet away, rose bleating, its feathery fleece shivering in the fresh wind. Sitting on her heels, holding his tether, she allowed him to suckle a few moments. Afterward—all her movements very deliberate and even—she drew a supply of milk for the child.

She sat against the wall of her house, near the doorway. The child, fed and asleep, was cradled in the hollow of her crossed legs. The silence overfilled the world, the skies flowed down evenly to the rim of the valley, the stealthy moon crept slantwise to the shelter of the mountains. She felt soft and warm all over; she dreamed that the newly born child was her own, and she was resting deliciously.

María Concepción could hear Juan's breathing. The sound vapored from the low doorway, calmly; the house seemed to be resting after a burdensome day. She breathed, too, very slowly and quietly, each inspiration saturating her with repose. The child's light, faint breath was a mere shadowy moth of sound in the silver air. The night, the earth under her, seemed to swell and recede together with a limitless, unhurried benign breathing. She drooped and closed her eyes, feeling the slow rise and fall within her own body. She did not know what it was, but it eased her all through. Even as she was falling asleep, head bowed over the child, she was still aware of a strange, wakeful happiness.

THE CHERRY FEAST

Ernst Glaeser

(1902–)

TRANSLATED BY BASIL CREIGHTON

I HAD FOUND WORK in Rheinhesse, but after eight days the job was done. With three marks in my pocket and a litre bottle of wine in my rucksack I set off for Mainz.

In a wine-shop on the quay I met up with a pipe-layer from Gladbach, who was out of a job too and on the tramp through Germany as I was. First we drank a quarter litre together and before we could look round we'd drunk four and by the time we had told each other our life-stories we'd drunk eight and my money was gone. Thereupon my pal ransacked his trouser pockets and, lo and behold, the innkeeper brought two more quarters and then we embraced and drank to our eternal friendship. Then he began telling me about all the jobs he had ever had and I, not to be outdone, started up and told him all about my travels as a fitter in Germany, Rumania and Sweden, until he chipped in with: "Man, those were the days . . ."

But all the same a lump came into my throat and I flourished my last glass of wine and sang: "What's the good of a pretty garden for others to walk in and pick my roses . . ."

Then the innkeeper came and sat down at our table and suddenly we were all talking about the War. "That time at Cambrai . . ." my pal shouted, and then the innkeeper got up and fetched a jug and we drank that empty too and our souls took flight for the open country, on the Aisne, round Bapaume and in the forest of Argonne. But I'll never forget how my pal's eyes suddenly went quite dark and he muttered as though to himself: "My lads, if we had known then what sort of a peace it was going to be . . ." At that we fell silent; only the clock ticked and the wine swayed in the glasses.

Suddenly I found myself in the street. My pal was sprawling with his arms across the table and weeping. He would not hear of parting. "Cover!" he was shouting. "Take cover where you can!" So I left him as he was drunk. The innkeeper came to the door with me. There in the forgotten light of day he said to me: "Things'll mend soon." I shook him by the hand and answered, as I did time and time again: "Pray God they may, my friend."

At first the houses looked a bit askew and the motor-cars drove as if there was no one on the road but themselves. That didn't worry me, though, and I set off along the quay-side. Then a motor-car had to pull up sharp and my poor little self was hauled over the coals by a man inside it. That amused me and I shouted back at him as he cursed: "You're nothing but a stuffed shirt," and went happily on my way. Soon, however, my eyes cleared and I saw life in its wonted clarity. My pal, the pipe-layer, our host and war comrade, the divine consolation of the wine and the cheerful belly of the jug died away behind me in the haze of the old town. I walked straight ahead and, after a few minutes, there I stood on the bridge over the Rhine. My heart laughed aloud as I saw the river. I leant over the green-painted rails, the March breeze refreshed me and, as I took a close look at the river, I saw that far and wide there was not a vessel of any kind to be seen on it; they all lay at the quays, moored and tarred —unemployed as I was.

But there was still the town before my eyes; the fronts of the houses stood up in a thin haze and above them rose the Cathedral, and over them all, over the roofs and the water and the whole width of the Rhine, lay the light. It was all one single radiance of light, and the seagulls waddled about on the piers of the bridge, and in the sky were little white clouds, sailing to Holland. At that I held my tongue and only used my eyes, and I felt that a man could never go under as long as there was so much light and so much good water and such a cosy town in his own native land. I set off light-heartedly through drab outskirts and past silent factories—but soon all that came to an end and I was on a country road lined by walnut trees.

The wind, blowing over stretches of asparagus, bowled yellow dust in front of me. Far away on the horizon I saw a range of blue hills. It was the Odenwald, and that was my destination.

It was evening by the time I reached Darmstadt. I was refused a lodging, for I still reeked of wine, but I didn't care; for on the edge of the town I found a loft and slept in the hay. It was warm and I slept soundly. I burrowed in and let the darkness enfold me.

I was wakened by the singing of birds and, as I was shivering, I called the litre bottle to my aid and the never-failing miracle of wine soon ran through my chilled limbs. I washed in a pond where a boat called

"Elfriede" was moored. Then I climbed the road up into the forest. There the birds were already busy and the dew shone on the anemones.

I had been walking for two hours when hunger assailed me, but there was no village to be seen. The air was bright and clear. The sun fell in a thousand flecks of light through the thin foliage. The wind sighed through the tree tops. Poor wretch, I thought, what good to you is the peace of nature if there is no peace in your belly?

After another half hour I began to feel weak. I sat myself down and breathed deeply. That stilled the beating of my heart. At last I lay down at full length and fell asleep. That's the best thing, I thought. If you have no bread, then sleep; for sleep is the bread of the poor.

Nevertheless I dreamt that my conscience arose and sat on my chest.

"Henry," it said so severely that I quailed before it, "you have drunk your three marks and now, Henry, you go hungry."

But my counter-conscience jumped up and said: "You silly old woman, how is the poor fellow to endure life without a few quarter litres?" At that my conscience sprang from my chest and rushed upon my counter-conscience to beat it, but my counter-conscience transformed itself into a singing tone. It leapt up into the windy tree-tops. It passed into the light of the sun. It descended again in dew. It was to be seen everywhere and nowhere and at last it hid as a chuckling echo in a distant stony brook.

But I lay stretched out at ease in the lap of nature and slept the divine sleep of a boy for whose favour the Muses are rivals . . .

I was awakened by a blow. A horse towered above me. I heard curses. "Drunken sot!" And then I observed that I was lying in the middle of the road. I must have rolled there in my sleep. The farmer jumped down from his cart and I got up. There he stood, purple in the face; he was a young man, and he gripped me by the shoulder. "Seven o'clock in the morning and sozzled already," he shouted and tried to throw me into the ditch. But I gave him such a push that he fell over. Whereupon, as was only natural, we went for each other for some time in silence. But as I knew how to box, I soon laid him out and he said no more. Whereupon I took a deep breath of the fragrant forest air and all at once my strength was renewed. I drew myself up proudly and was just going to take a drink from my litre bottle when a woman jumped down from the cart.

"Schickedanz," she screamed and running to the man she took his head in her hands and began stroking his forehead.

"It's all right, madam," I said, and going to the pair, I held the bottle under the farmer's nose—and what happened? He woke up. When he was on his feet with his wife beside him, he said: "What's up?"

"I laid you out," I answered. His wife laughed at this, for the man looked at me so stupidly. "But in case you think I'm a thief or one of those scoundrels who drive about the country in motor-cars," I went on, "I'll tell you what I am. I'm an out-of-work fitter, driven by hunger to tramp his native land, and that's why I fell asleep."

At this the woman laughed again. She had black hair under a red handkerchief and such lovely teeth as you never saw.

"Schickedanz," she said, dusting the earth from his forehead, "you could have asked the man first. You're always so hasty and that's what you get for it."

Schickedanz looked at me for a full minute nearly. "Where are you going?" he said.

And I replied that I didn't know, but to some village anyway to cadge a bite of food, a slice of bread and butter or a few potatoes.

"Jump in!" Schickedanz said, and I jumped in.

The horse went at a walk; Schickedanz sat in front and drove; I sat next the woman. The forest sighed around us. And so we went along.

I don't know to this day how it happened that I stayed on with Schickedanz. We never spoke a word on the way and when we got to the village in its green hollow, we stopped at a rambling farmhouse and we went into a sitting-room and then I came over bad. When I woke up I was in a high bed and on the window-ledge sat a cat. I looked round the room and my eyes rested with joy on a guardian angel who was leading a child over a rickety bridge in a dark wood. A picture like that hung over my bed when I was a little boy. Then a cow suddenly mooed and I thought I was at Aunt Amelia's in Mecklenburg. She was the sister of my poor father and when the cow mooed a second time I thought: "You're out on rest in Flanders and Conrad will be in in a moment and the tailor and then we'll sit down to a game of skat." However, when the cow mooed for the third time, Schickedanz came in and told me I had slept for two days and two nights. He sat down on my bed, took a look at me and then said he could give me work, for his man had died four days since.

"In this bed," he added, pointing to where I lay.

I jumped up. "Free board and lodging and I'll do all the work you want."

"Right," said Schickedanz. Then we went downstairs and drank some gin and ate some bread and cheese.

It was not very hard work on the farm. Schickedanz let me do what I liked. First I put all his implements in good repair, the reaper and binder and the chaff-cutter; then the electric lighting had its turn and the engine. I tended the animals and helped with the book-keeping, and then one evening Schickedanz confessed to me over a glass of Hollands that he wanted to have a motor bicycle, so we went to Neustadt and bought a second-hand one. I rode it home and every evening for the next fortnight Schickedanz buzzed up the hairpin bends that climbed the range of hills behind the house. So, what with working and resting, the time went on. How happy

I was when I had seen to the animals. There they stood in the stalls, their coats groomed, and as I walked down the row, I rejoiced in their contentment. Schickedanz went out of his way to praise me. Sometimes he took me pillion on his motor bicycle to an inn in the forest.

His wife was called Joan. She was young and beautiful. She spoke to me very seldom and I avoided looking at her, for I could not help thinking of Fanny whenever she was there—that was the name of the first girl I ever loved—and never won. So the days went by between working, sleeping and eating—and life was good. I had been six weeks on the farm and my cheeks had filled out and the girls in the village turned their heads to look at me. I often went for a stroll in the soft evening air and sometimes I slipped out of my room late at night and down to the meadows because I was thinking of Joan and how beautiful she was. But when my heart beat too hard, I lit a pipe or went to the inn and drank to the Fatherland with the fellows there.

Spring came with a bang. I worked like a horse and Schickedanz said he had never had a man on the farm to touch me. Soon the whole valley was in blossom and there was such a smell from the meadows at night that you couldn't sleep. Schickedanz boozed. He spoke little. Joan sat in the sitting-room and sewed.

My heart was heavy those days, but I worked on as well as I could and one day Schickedanz called me into the room and there sat Joan, and Schickedanz said: "Henry, the cherry trees are in blossom." He pointed out of the window. "That hill there covered with cherry trees in blossom belongs to me. It's worth more to me than anything else on the farm. When the cherries are ripe you must take them to Zwingenberg market with Joan and sell them. Will you stay on till then?"

At this Joan looked at me and I said: "Yes."

The cherry trees were in blossom and the fruit set well. The sun was strong. The cherries ripened.

One morning, when I had seen to the animals and Schickedanz was off on his motor-bike on some political business, Joan came out to me in the yard and said: "Henry, we'll go to the cherry orchard."

We went, taking two baskets with us. First there was a clayey sunken road, then a narrow path across a meadow, then a little brook to cross and then came the cherry orchard. There stood the trees and the fruit shone like lacquer in the spring sunshine. Joan opened a shed and I got out a ladder and then I climbed up the trees and picked the cherries. Joan collected them in the large baskets. She called to me after two hours and I sat down beside her in the moist grass. The village lay below us. The church clock was striking six and a light breeze combed the grass.

"Henry," Joan said after a while, "the cherry orchard really belongs to me. I brought it with me as a dowry. And I can gather the crop as I please."

"Indeed," said I, "but that's fine to have the crop to gather."

"Yes," Joan said, "Schickedanz only has the money, but the trees belong to me."

We drank cold coffee out of a metal can and cut slices from the loaf in the basket.

Then I set the ladder against the trees again and picked cherries. Joan gathered them into her baskets. By eight o'clock we had four large baskets full. Then Joan whistled across to the farm and it was not long before a farm girl came with a cart. We hoisted the baskets up, Joan took the reins and we drove to Zwingenberg.

It was a little town on the mountain road with a white church, and when the sun blazed down the dust in the streets glowed. We had driven through dense forest and sometimes I took the reins and the little horse trotted along—what happiness, I thought, and I looked at Joan. She had her eyes half closed and let the sun blaze on her face. Then my heart was far away and I began to whistle. The pony trotted and Joan slept.

We sold our cherries very well that day. Joan had a pocketful of money. We drank coffee at a pastrycook's. At five o'clock we set off home. The horse knew his way. I left the reins slack. Joan sat beside me. The forest towered above us and the road went uphill.

Then the devil leapt onto my shoulders and I clasped Joan round the hips. She did not mind. So I stopped the horse and wanted to kiss Joan. Then she smiled and said: "I am not your wife, Henry," and at that my cheeks burned. The horse went on again at a walk, the air was cool in the forest, and the empty baskets bumped about at the back of the cart. Joan began to talk.

"Henry," she said, "I'm Schickedanz's wife. I married him because the man I loved didn't come back from the war. But a woman's got to marry and Schickedanz at that time was a fine young fellow and he pleased me because he was so strong. So we made a match of it, Henry. But it wasn't love. It was common sense, Henry. But it's not right to behave like that. When I look at you I know that quite well. I've been looking at you for six weeks now. And now I know it. Before I didn't."

"Joan," I said—nothing else but "Joan."

"I'm only a stupid farmer's wife," she went on, "but my heart is like yours—always far away. I've looked at you for six weeks. You are sad too like I am."

"Joan," I said. Nothing else.

"But it's all up with me," Joan said. "I'm going to have a baby and Schickedanz can hardly wait to know it's a boy."

It was chill in the forest. The horse trotted along and my heart stood still.

"I do really love you, Henry," Joan said, "I do really. It came quite simply and I tell it to you the same way, but the child is Schickedanz's and you, after all, are only something that the wind has brought."

At that I held my tongue and thought: Yes, I am only something the wind has brought.

We drew slowly nearer the village. "Schickedanz is a good farmer and he wants to have a son and wants me to be the sort of wife who does as he expects. And I do. But, Henry, I often want to run away, away from the village, away from the valley; but all that is so remote and you too—you're a man who'll never settle down. But that is not for me, because after all I'm fond of Schickedanz and the child is his."

We got home and Schickedanz was standing at the door. And Joan gave him the bag of money. Schickedanz laughed at the sight of it and took us into the sitting-room and got out the gin and we drank, Schickedanz and I, for two hours and when Joan had gone to bed, Schickedanz laughed and got out currant wine and we drank that as well and Schickedanz said that in three months' time he would have a son and then there would be a feast and I mustn't go before that.

I went every morning for a fortnight with Joan to the cherry orchard. We picked the cherries and drove to Zwingenberg market. For fourteen days long I knew that Joan loved me because I was one whom the wind brought and not one of those she saw every day. For fourteen days long Joan was true to Schickedanz.

Then one day Schickedanz said to me: "It's the cherry feast the day after tomorrow."

I asked Joan what that was and she said it was a festival to give thanks for the cherry crop, and all their relations came from the farms round about, and musicians and the lads and girls from the village. That morning Joan and I drove off again with the cherries, and on the way home I kissed her and she said that the child would arrive in two months and she would call it Henry. We drove through the forest and Joan cried because we could not sin together.

"Oh, Joan," I said, "I don't know where the wind will blow me, but your love I can never forget, because it is so near and yet so far."

At this Joan stopped the horse and said: "Henry . . ." and kissed me on the eyes. That was right up on the hill where the road is swept bare by the wind and the grass flaps like a flag. The village lay below and the meadows were soft and green.

"My life," Joan said, "is not there," and she pointed to the village; "but the child belongs there, and you, Henry, will understand what a woman who was born there needs."

"Yes," I said. "Joan, I have only love for you and you shall live as you must."

At this Joan cried, but I whipped up the horse and the cart rumbled down into the valley.

What happened next dances before my eyes to this day. We had hardly reached the village when women came running to meet us; men followed and then a rabble of children and they all stared at us. Joan looked up and asked: "What is the matter?" But they said nothing, so I whipped up the horse. We reached the farm and there stood the musicians, the trees in the garden were decorated with garlands of paper, and the flag of Germany blew from the gable of the house. I jumped down and Joan got down and stood beside me. "What is the matter?" she cried out and the men who were standing in the yard made way a little and Schickedanz was lying on a bench. Blood flowed from a gash in his forehead, his coat was bloody and so was the ground beneath him. "What is the matter?" Joan cried out. Then the man who was standing beside Schickedanz, he was the doctor from Neustadt, came up and said: "He has had an accident on his motor-bicycle and there is no hope."

At this Joan uttered a cry such as I have never heard; she cried out again and again, she wept, then she laughed; the men shrank back, the women ran up, and there stood Joan with her hands to her body and then with another cry she sank to the ground. The women picked her up and carried her, still crying aloud, into the house.

But we, three men and the doctor, stood beside Schickedanz and we could hear the animals moving restlessly. Then the women cried out again from the house and the church bell began to toll for curfew, and then Schickedanz started up, with blood and white spittle at his mouth, and he asked: "Is the boy there?"

My God, at that a shudder went through me, and we lifted him up and carried him into the best sitting-room, and there he lay, and as soon as ever he got his breath he asked: "Is the boy there?" Then he fell back and muttered something.

There was silence in the yard outside. I sat beside Schickedanz. His breast bone was smashed in and the blood pulsed out over his cheeks. His wife was crying out upstairs. Sometimes he tried to say something; his lips moved, and I felt a great love for him when he could not get out what he wanted.

The doctor came back and gave him an injection. Then he grew quieter. I held his hand. "Schickedanz," I asked him, "do you know me?"

"The boy?" he muttered.

"Yes," I said. "The boy——"

Then he held out his hand and said: "Henry, the boy, that's all. I'll go gladly if only the boy is there . . ."

I laid a vinegar bandage on his forehead, but he pushed it away and sat up. His eyes were set, I have never seen such determination in any eye, he sat right up and his breast bones crunched. "Listen!" he whispered. "Listen!"

Three abrupt cries came from above and then a whimper, and while the soft June air came over the meadows and in at the window and while the cherry feast garlands rustled on the trees in the garden, the young farmer got to his feet, staggered to the door and fell down sobbing: "The boy first, then I, God the Father . . ."

I tried to lift him up, but he struggled. Then I heard steps. The doctor came in, he was laughing and rubbing his hands. "A fine boy," he shouted, "a little too early, but a strapping young Schickedanz."

At that the farmer stood up and went straight to bed and lay down and spat blood.

"Ah, yes," the doctor said, "I'd almost forgotten him . . ." But then Schickedanz sat up, his chest swelled, the white of eternity was in his eyes; he took three deep breaths and then collapsed.

"Amen," the doctor said and closed his eyelids. The child whimpered on the first floor. I went to the stable and packed my rucksack. The musicians were standing in the yard and eighteen women with them. The doctor came to the door and said: "A young Schickedanz!" At that the musicians struck up and the women rubbed their hands on their skirts for joy. And as the chorale burst forth, I walked out onto the road, into the dust from which we come and to which we return.

NO MORE TROUBLE FOR JEDWICK

Louis Paul

(1901–   )

JEDWICK SMILED at the woman drawing water from the well. "Kin I have me a drink, ma'am?" he drawled, his broad shoulders drooped shyly in a half bow.

She was tall and dark. The sun blazed down on the white-hot Virginia highway. Jedwick's clothes were saturated with sweat. Scintillant beads shone like translucent jewels against his shiny skin. The black man shook his head like a hound dog coming up out of a creek.

"I reckon," she nodded. The Negro woman, lighter than Jedwick, was not wholly at ease. Her husband was in the village getting groceries. Roamin' niggers . . .

"Yas ma'am," Jedwick said, and dipped into the barrel.

The woman dried her hands on her apron. "Y'all f'om round hyeah?"

Jedwick stared at her a moment. "I ain't f'om hyeah." he murmured between immense gulps, "ner neither I ain't gonna stay hyeah. Whereat I git to Alexandria?"

"Right smart piece yonder."

"How fur?"

She speculated. "Eight-twelve mile."

Jedwick finished his water and looked at the blue and gold cauldron over his head. "Hot, ain't it?"

"Do git hot."

"Yo' man wuk in town?"

"No. He after groceries."

Jedwick glanced down the hill toward the little village. The view was empty.

She understood his movement.

He smiled. He had fine healthy teeth. She was aware of a frightened sensation in the pit of her stomach. Jedwick bent and rubbed his ankle as though that were an habitual gesture. The flaming orb in the sky shone down remorselessly. Something about the Negro's beautiful black arms hypnotized her. She stood poised, enchanted, like a statue: made to flee, but forever motionless. The midday silence was oppressive, like the sun. She waited.

"I ain't seed no woman fo' a long time," Jedwick said, almost in apology.

"He after groceries."

Closer to hers, his face was more strikingly handsome than ever. His lips were very cool, strangely. Perspiration came off on her mouth and cheeks . . .

Later he said, "Thank you sho' nuff fo' that there water, ma'am. Ain't they some law gin doin' much wawkin' thisyere state highways?"

"Is," she looked up at the stranger, embarrassed, "if them troopers ketches you."

Jedwick nodded and suddenly disappeared down the embankment. Couldn't trust the road from here in. Stick to the tracks.

He wrapped a long red handkerchief around his shoulders to keep his neck from frying, and stepped gingerly along the single-tracked roadbed, trying to pace the ties to his long swinging gait. Oughta lay these hyeah ties out even, so's a man could wawk. Wa'n't no cinder path like usual. Say ten mile. 'Bout fo' hours in thisyere sun. Should be makin' up a string o' boxes fo' Manhattan Junction in Alex some'rs round six.

He wanted after an hour to crawl under the shade of some green leafy trees. Lay out yo' legs an' sleep. Thoughts that came like hunger or dreams, unwanted; but they were only a whip-flick to sting the flesh of his determination. Gits me out o' the sun in one o' them boxes in Alex, yassuh! There I rests. He visualized a phrase: Jedwick escapes.

Waves of hypnotic steel-gray heat shimmered up off the two metal radiators that converged in the distance. His eyes began to burn. He thought it would be nice to be rich. He would buy a boat with a motor in it, all covered with a striped canvas canopy, and sail out of sight of land. There would be a breeze off in the ocean. Nice gal, that there brown lady by the highway crossin'. Like a scared cottontail. She liked him. They all liked Jedwick. Lovin' ain't harmin' no gal, he thought.

Bugs. Chrissakes! Little gnats and fuzzy things and leg-squirming beetles popped up in front of him; some kind of a locust whanged with a flat noise on his chest, and he slapped it down. Flies and ticks smelled your sweat. A breath of wind floated lazing over the treetops, but died itself of the heat. Jedwick sighed.

Sighing wasn't natural to him. He thought he'd sing. He bugled a tentative air.

A slick-tawkin' man f'om Bumminham . . .

The plaintive lyric echoed magnificently between the banks of woods. Jedwick's cello-like bass rose through the dazzling, brain-sizzling heat to heaven, and he laughed about some dimly felt deliciousness in solitude's freedom. His voice took up the lilt.

> A slick-tawkin' man f'om Bumminham
> Come up my way, an' his name was Sam;
> I pay no attention, ner I din give a damn,
> Till he stoled my gal away.

He hummed the rest of the melody: it was too hot to think of the words A little garter snake, sunning itself under the vast ceiling of broiling light, was startled and jiggled off noisily into the brush. Maybe, he confided to the vanished reptile, maybe tomor' I gonna be in *New* York. Yassuh. Wonder how fur they is after me? Think they can ketch thisyere Jedwick? Yo' completely crazy. How fur I is to Alex, I wonder? Damn me! but it do git hot!

Three mile an hour, 'bout. 'Thout stoppin' I git me in them yards fo' sundown. Yassuh. Sundown. Don't seem like ole sun ever gone go down.

> I hates t' see
> Thet evenin' sun go down . . .

Nossuh. Man said that jes crazy's that snake.

There was a shack directly around a bend, and the white man saw him first. "Where you going to, boy?"

He had a wrinkled skin and sandy gray hair and wore gray uniform pants.

"I goin' t' ask you fo' some water, has you got any?" Jedwick smiled brightly with his thick lips.

"Where you goin'?" the man repeated.

"Well, y'see, cap'n, well, suh, I'm goin' in t' the Districk. Yassuh. Dassit."

"Washin'ton? What you traipsin' up here for?"

"Don't like to wawk on the highway, cap'n, boss. 'S y'all got a little water?"

"Alexandria's along up hyeah. You makin' for one of them boxes?"

"Nossuh, nossuh! Ain't layin' over no place, cap'n, suh. Ole friend in town gonna ride me into the Districk."

"You must be runnin' away, boy," the man in the shack said, squinting lowered eyes at the big sweating Negro.

"Me? I ain't runnin' no place, suh, cap'n," he protested. "Why fo' I gonna run any place?"

The white man fetched up an iron pail and handed him a different dipper. "Too hot," he said, shaking his head, "to hit them ties 'less yo-all runnin' away. Why ain't you takin' a sleep in some cool place?"

"Me, suh? I gotta git in D. C. Yassuh. I got me friends in the Districk, suh."

The wrinkled man glanced down at Jedwick's right ankle.

"Goin' git me a job," Jedwick stammered uncertainly, "in—like, suh, now, a 'partment house. Dassit," he said. "Yassuh."

"Take all you want," the other said about the water; "they's a crick below here. Ain't my business where-at you're runnin' to."

"Nossuh, cap'n. I ain't runnin'."

"Matter o' fact, they's some empties makin' up in Alexandria about seven to-night. You going t' New York," he stated.

Jedwick was amazed. "How you figger that there, boss?"

"If'n I don't know a chain-gang nigger," he told Jedwick calmly, "I'll go and jump in that there crick."

The big Negro's face curled into a magnificent smile. "Come f'om thataway?"

"Been around," the man said expressionlessly.

"Yassuh," murmured Jedwick. He added, "Thank y'all fo' that water."

"Not 'tall."

"Thank y'all," he repeated.

The man drew himself in out of the heat. Jedwick started off toward Alexandria, but caught a phrase which he thought was the man calling him back—until he analyzed it.

"I want Colonel Saunders, yessum," he was saying, "the police chief in——"

Jedwick sauntered back, and the man in the shack stepped away from the phone when he saw him. His hand slipped into a drawer and the Negro saw a pearl butt come out. Jedwick muttered softly as he crashed over the flimsy table, rolling the white man backward out of his chair. He twisted, and leapt again. They bowled heavily through the door, rocking the flimsy shack. The leather-faced, wiry man struggled up almost successfully, but Jedwick got his feet on him. The black kicked scientifically, as a boxer uses his hands.

In a moment the white man lay still, his head battered. His shirt was torn where his stomach had been gashed. Jedwick felt very sorry for him. How foolish the man had been. Jedwick hated to hurt anybody.

He stopped long enough to bundle the body inside the shack, take another drink and dip his face in the bucket of cold water. It seemed hotter in the sun than ever.

Now he dumped the pail empty and resumed his trek in the oily tropical sun's glare. In a few moments the water he had drunk sank through the pores of his skin and oozed out in driblets. If it's hotter down in Africa, he joked to himself, I'm glad my folks done been slaves. Yassuh. Slaves.

At least it wasn't too hot to whistle. Instead of his bit of excoriation of a slick-tawkin' man from Bumminham the great black figure chanted a whistley refrain as he trudged on tirelessly toward his destination. He loped along, picking the ties carefully. The song was a monotonous, fugitive melody about a man named Joe, who

> —Done his Susie wrong, yassuh,
> But he love her all the same.

He seemed almost to skip along the ties to that repetitious lilt.

Jedwick was, as he saw the shacks of Alexandria's outskirts loom glaringly in the terrific blaze of afternoon, neither blithe nor desperate, neither coward nor cruel. He was escaping. A criminal—or any man—would. He felt very sorry for the gray-haired man, did he not? Of course. Glimpsing the freight-yards of Alexandria, Virginia, he lapsed into the weakness of a sigh again. Like when the cap'n blowed his whistle at sundown and yo' pick drapped outn yo' fingers . . . like when the las' sack o' cotton was drug down t' the baler, an'—, yassuh. He shook these memories off. Jedwick wasn't really a sighing man.

He hadn't eaten for forty hours. You travels light and fast and lives offn yo' flesh. But yo' gits hongry. Whereat you kin promote a vittle or that in Alex? Better crawl in one of them cars. They gonna trace that phone cawl. Find that wrinkled man an' they gonna be hell poppin' round Alex.

Down in behind the fence. That was the place. He saw a bum duck between two cars and hop over the coupling, coming toward him.

"Hi," he greeted this specimen.

"Know what time d'Junction empties goin' out t'night?" The bum screwed up a weather-scarred face.

"Yassuh. Seven."

"You eat?"

"No suh!"

"Where ya come in?"

Jedwick thumbed his hand back.

"Leggin'—you out in that there sun?"

"Sho nuff, likely, brother," Jedwick answered.

"Got a coupla hours," said the bum. "They's a jungle overn 'em weeds. Some liver here, an' haffa loaf o' breard."

Jedwick thanked the man from the North.

They toasted the liver. The bum, whose name was Sully, dug some whole coffee beans out of a bag, battered them on a rock, and had a can going. They split the "breard" and the big Negro was very grateful. After the meal Sully pulled a razor from a leather bag around his neck and began to shave a light beard. Jedwick, in payment for the bum's life-giving coffee, related the incidents of his story. The man shaving exhibited a great curiosity concerning the details of Jedwick's encounter with the brown up on the hill yonder. He chuckled, vicariously amused.

Jedwick added that he had killed the trackman.

Sully squinted. "You must be one o' dese tough black boys."

"Nossuh," said Jedwick, particular not to be misunderstood. "Whut else I gonna do?"

"Coulda flattened him, or tied him up." Sully put away his razor.

"Sho'. You figger out jes' whut to do. That man had a big gun. He gonna blow off my haid ifn I don't get him."

"Every man fer himself, sonny," the bum shrugged his shoulders. "You set?"

"Les go git stowed away fo some no-count railroad bull git rampagin' round."

They idled through the yard, trained soldiers expertly taking cover back of every bump in the topography. Jedwick pried a loose door. Sully was boosted half way up. A metallic voice startled them.

"What you guys doin'?"

Sully's wits left him and he stared up at the man blankly. Jedwick grinned with silly surprise. "We's jes' gonna ride in, suh."

"Oh, yer jist gonna ride in?"

"Yassuh," he said innocently.

"Just gonna ride in." The voice was pregnant with unpleasant suggestions.

Jedwick wrinkled his brow into a puzzled expression. "Yassuh, cap'n, boss. Ain't it aw right?"

"Ain't it aw right!" he mimicked, and spat. "Where you two bums from?"

"We, suh?"

"Who the hell y' think I'm talkin' to?"

"Yassuh. I got a fren in New York, boss," he explained. "He gits me a job in a big apartment house. Sully hyeah goin' to try to get a job too, cap'n."

"Well, maybe I don't know stiffs no more," the man said. "Don't you know you can't ride on no freight train?"

"Can't ride on no freight train?" Jedwick almost believed in this innocence himself. "Nossuh, boss, nossuh. Is thisyere a freight train? Look like they is all epty. I never know they is hahm in ridin' in epty car. Never

would come in hyeah did we knows that, suh. Dassit." He was talking fast
—for his life. "Yassuh, boss, gentman, suh."

The train-bull shook himself impatiently. "Better take yourselfs outa
here big and pronto," he said with positiveness, "or you'll be gettin' about
sixty days apiece for vags."

"'Scuse us, mister cap'n, boss, suh, yassuh," Jedwick murmured with
elegant unctuousness, "we is goin'."

The Law swung himself up the side ladder and disappeared momentarily along the line of cars.

"You gettin' in?" the black man whispered to Sully coolly.

Sully backed away. "Not me!" he exclaimed hoarsely.

Jedwick shook a finger, said "Hi!" got his belly up on the platform,
clipped the door to, and disappeared into the black interior.

He heard the bull coming back, tapping on each door. "Hey, you, come
outa' there!" He got to Jedwick's door and cried, "Hey, you, come outa
there!" There was only silence inside. Footsteps crunched away along
the gravel.

Jedwick lay motionless for an unconscionable time. At last the train gave
three bone-rattling jerks that knocked him into another corner. The
couplings shrieked, another gentle bump, and the train moved slowly out
of the yards. The engineer's hoot-hoot sounded to Jedwick's ears like a wild
pæan to freedom. The car was like a furnace, but of course he didn't care.

He crawled over to the door and lay with his head to the floor crack,
afraid to push the thing ajar.

Wonder and excitement to freedom! The train rattled on, carriages
hitting track-cracks with ever-increasing crescendo. Fool, anyone who
risked life unnecessarily. That trackman. Why hadn't he let well enough
alone? Dead now, and nothing gained. Never would *he* risk the quickness
of life except in the defense of his own.

On into the night the bumping freight train sped. North. Where he
could achieve that departure from the old and sink into the blissful
anonymity of its millions, renascence, born again, with only dead memories
to remind him of the past. Yassuh, he speculated. Dassit. Goin' git free in
New York. But gotta watch out fo' that bull. Whereat I wonder is fust
division stop on thisyere line? Some'rs 'long hyeah. He pried the door
open a crack. The sun had set and blue darkness had fallen over the countryside that bobbed swiftly by his limited vision. A hot wind blew in his
face.

Yassuh. Like sho' nuff git me a leetle shet-eye, can't takin' no chances.
Bull goin' look in these hyeah cars fust crack outn the box do we make a
division stop. We git in the Junction mornin' sometime . . . then, nigger,
you is free. Yassuh. Dassit—free! The thought made his brain spin airily.
No more trouble for Jedwick!

Well, no more later; but just now the cars pulled up under brakes and came to a jerking halt. He shoved open the door and glanced out. Blackness. Tall brush alongside the cinder roadbed. Lucky. Jedwick was always lucky. He jumped down and squatted behind the weeds. Sure enough. The bull had a flash, and he peered into the recesses of every car. Another train, a passenger, thundered on past in the opposite direction. Jedwick waited until the freight train began to move, then he hopped out like a big rabbit scooting across an open space, and swung himself up into the car. That was all right. He was good for another hour.

That hour found him asleep. Fatigue fells all men. Jedwick fell asleep, woke when the train stopped again—which was too late. He was on his knees when the light flashed in.

"What the hell you doin' in there?" the bull shouted.

Jedwick, a thinking animal in danger, murmured in a much broader accent than his own, "Cain't po' man rahd in disyere train, yo' honoah?"

"Comin' outa there?"

"Sho gwine come out, passuh."

He jumped down, but squatted his great frame into a much smaller figure. The railroad bull clicked his light into Jedwick's face. "Say, ain't you the same nigger I chased in Alexandria?"

"Whut Alesandria?"

"Din I tell yer to stay outa them cars?"

"Me, yo' honah? Nossuh." Jedwick exhibited surprise.

"Hell I ain't!"

"Nossuh," Jedwick said gently but firmly.

"Where'd y' git on?"

"Bout a nour back yander, yo' honah, suh. Ah bo'd de train when de cyahs stoppin' sahd them there weeds. 'Scuse me, suh."

"Well," said the man, not exactly satisfied, "git on outa here. You can't ride in these here trains. An' I ketch y' ridin' agin," he showed Jedwick an army Colt strapped to his trousers, "I'm gonna plug ya." He meant it. "I see you agin," the white man added, "you git it."

Jedwick hunched his shoulders. "I'se so'y, yo' honah. Ah gone git away f'om hyeah jes lahk y'all say. Gone right now." He started off toward the rear of the train. "Ain't meant nary hahm, suh," he murmured.

"See you stay 'way," the bull called after him.

When the freight train pulled out again Jedwick was on it. After the next stop the bull knew he was on it. It was a game of hide and seek. At each stop the Negro ran for cover in the weeds, and thanked the night for being darker than the ace of spades. He saw the blue steel of a gun behind the flash as the detective prowled through the cars.

Jedwick wondered why the man wouldn't let well enough alone. Damn me! but people sho' huntin' trouble wid big guns. Why fo' ever body come messin' 'round me? What I wanna harm nobody fo'? They keeps messin' 'round stid leavin' me be, an' mo' trouble happen fo' you know it.

That man goin' kill me ifn he ketches me, he thought, or I goin' try to kill him. Why anybody want kill someone else?

The bull wouldn't, of course, let well enough alone. He knew there was only one way to nab the black bastard—that was on the moving train. There was some danger in that, but the bull didn't consider danger. His job was to get that pernicky nigger the hell and gone off his train.

Crawling along the tops of the cars, he swung himself down over the one he suspected. He gently wedged it open and slipped in. Jedwick sat square in front of the door, his legs spread and tensed, waiting. The bull plopped between the black man's outstretched legs, and Jedwick caught him full in the face with a large but cunning heel. The man's pistol cracked against the side of the car, and the white bull's body dropped out like a sack of potatoes and hit the cinders with a thud. Jedwick sighed as at the completion of an unpleasant duty. Trouble, he thought philosophically; why people allus huntin' 'round fo' trouble?

The sunrise got pink in the east. He sized up the land about him. Wasn't but a few minutes out of the Junction. Better slip off before that cop was missed. Shortly the freight slowed. He hopped it from the ladder.

It was a mile or so to the highway. The sun was just blazing up properly. Another boiling day. A truck was the thing.

Free. Escape was almost certain now. They couldn't pin the railroad bull's accident on him. And Alabama would never get him if he reached New York. Of course he'd reach New York. One of those wonderful red vans came chugging up the highway. By God, this was luck! A colored chauffeur was at the wheel. Going right into the city. Jedwick's luck was an enchanted affair. When the truck approached he flicked his hand and smiled teethily. The driver jammed his brakes. Didn't he say his luck was magic?

"Sho' nice of you," he said as he skipped up on the seat. He sank into the leather cushion blissfully. "Yassuh."

"Goin' into New York?"

"Yassuh."

"Where you from?"

"Been bummin' my way up from the Districk," said Jedwick. "Ole feller goin' far as the las' town in a little Fo'd brang me thus far."

"I got a samwich I ain't et," said the driver. "You're perfectly welcome to it."

"Sho' nice of you," he repeated. He took the sandwich and swallowed it whole. "My name Jedwick," he grunted past the last mouthful.

At Canal and Sixth Avenue the driver said, "Like you to drop off here, buddy. I get caught ridin' anybody in, it's jes' too bad fo' me."

"Yassuh," said Jedwick gratefully. "Sho' nice of you." He dropped down and the truck turned up Sixth Avenue.

IF YOU CAN'T BE GOOD, BE CAUTIOUS

T. O. Beachcroft

(1902–   )

AN OLD LYCETT LORRY came lumberingly into a garage near the Great West Road. This was a ramshackle place with a draughty concrete yard, corrugated iron roofs, and doors hanging by a hinge. It was much used by lorry drivers as a port of call for a chat.

'Hullo, Tom,' said the garage hand to the driver of the lorry. 'You haven't been this way lately.'

'Hullo,' said Tom. 'Cheerio, everyone. I'll have six gallons of the usual, please, and perhaps Bessie will give me a cup of tea if I promise her a kiss.'

Presently Tom, sitting in the cab of his lorry and stirring his tea with a pencil, shouted: 'Did you hear about that young fellow who works for our crowd—Bob Curtain? Curt, we all call him. He's been up before the magistrates to-day.'

'No, go on,' said the garage hand. 'What for—speeding?'

'I don't know,' said Tom. 'It wasn't anything to do with driving. He's a bit of a lad.'

At that moment a second Lycett lorry swung into the filling station, rather too fast, scattering a heap of gravel and a couple of buckets. It pulled up with a jerk, almost striking the tailboard of Tom's lorry. It was Curt.

'Hullo, young fellow,' said Tom. 'How did you get on to-day? So they didn't put you in quod?'

Curt got out of his lorry and glared at him without answering. He began to lounge round the yard with his hands in his pockets.

'No,' he said at length. 'Nor are they likely to.'

'Well,' said Tom. 'What was it all about? What was the trouble?'

'Nothing. All a lot of rot. Just those blasted bobbies trying to put me wrong.'

'But what was the charge?' said Tom. 'If it isn't a rude answer. If you don't mind my asking.'

'No, I don't mind,' said Curt. 'Why should I? It was carrying a gun without a licence, if you want to know.'

Tom pushed his cap off his forehead, and shook his head. 'Well, you're a funny one,' said the garage hand. 'What on earth do you want with a gun?'

'No harm in it,' said Curt. 'I'm just interested in fire-arms, that's all.'

'What did the magistrate say?'

'Oh, a lot of stuff. He tried to make the most of it. Anybody'd have thought I'd committed a crime. A lot of talk about getting into bad company. I didn't listen to half of it.'

'Well, it's all right, isn't it?' said Tom. 'He let you off scot free?'

'No, he didn't. I was bound over. I've got to go and report every bloody month.'

'Well, there's no great harm in that.'

'Yes, there is,' said Curt. 'That's just the swine of it. Didn't I tell you I'd got a better job?'

'I do remember something. What was it?'

'It was up in Manchester, that's what it was, driving a taxi for a chap I know. It was a good opening. Now this has mucked everything up. I can't take it.'

Curt went on mouching round the yard with his hands in his pockets. 'Damn fools,' he said. 'Damned swines. I tell you what it is, Tom. Those swines of police: once they've got their hands on you, they mean to get you. They mean to put you wrong. I'd like to get hold of that fool of a magistrate.'

'Well,' said Tom. 'I'm sorry. Still, if you can't be good, be cautious. That's what I always tell my kids. "Be good if you can, and if you can't, be cautious!"'

A silence followed this.

'Sorry,' said Tom self-consciously. 'It ain't often I go chucking these pearls of wisdom round. Where are you for to-night, Curt? Bristol?'

'Taunton,' said Curt. 'I've got a load of petrol—hundreds of gallons. Some muck the boss has got hold of cheap.'

'I'm on that game, too. I've got to go and pick my load up, then I'll be getting along.'

'Right,' said Curt. 'We're meeting at the usual place later on. That fellow Sid's coming.'

'I'll be there,' said Tom. 'Cheer up, you'll be all right.'

Curt nodded. He cranked up his lorry and moved off but, after driving for a few minutes, decided to wait on the Great West Road for Tom to catch him up. He wanted to unburden himself.

It was now the brown dusk of an October twilight. Lights began to gleam in the evening. A brooding silence fell, and was shattered, and fell again as an occasional lorry crashed by on the first stage of a long night journey.

The river's vaporous breath swirled up from Kew, from Gunnersbury, from Brentford. It coiled round the lamps and across the tattered half-made roads and dying fields. Curt shuddered. He felt the raw edge of the mist against his skin. Its looming shapes hung before him, filling his mind with vague fears of the police, of the bosses, and the power they held over his whole life.

Presently he found a man in a mackintosh was looking up into the cab of the lorry, and asking for a lift.

'Get up if you like,' said Curt, rousing himself. 'She's not exactly one of those super luxury coaches, still, she gets along somehow. Where do you want to go to?'

'Oh, west,' said the other.

Curt laughed. 'West?' he said. 'That seems a bit uncertain. I mean, do you want to go to Bath or Cardiff or Salisbury? They're all west from here. Where *are* you aiming for?'

'Where are you going?' said the stranger.

'Oh, me; I'm going down past Bristol; but I'm meeting one or two pals half-way, and we might find something to do.'

He found the stranger staring at him.

'What's the matter?' he said. 'We have to do something to amuse ourselves. A lot of chaps, who drive lorries, don't get home for a week or more together, so we arrange meeting-places on the road.'

'What for?'

'Oh, just for a bit of talk; you get to feel a bit cut off when you live and sleep on one of these barrows for days together. The married men feel it most, and this night driving, too, it works on you. Of course, the bosses try to stop our meeting, but then they do so many things against the Act all the time, what the hell can they expect?'

'Do they?' said the stranger. 'What sort of things? You mean they keep you on too long hours?'

'Yes, of course I do,' said Curt angrily. 'You aren't on their side, are you? Because if you are you can get a lift off somebody else, see? I'll pull up right away.'

He began to slow down.

'All right, mate. That's all right,' the stranger said hastily. 'It isn't my trade, you see. I was only asking.'

'Well, I'm telling you. How would you like to drive fifty-seven hours, on a stretch, with only three hours off the whole time? That's what happened to a London man last week. I knew him slightly; the chap lived round Dalston way. Then he crashed, and got killed. At the inquest it came out that he'd been driving for fifty-seven hours without sleep. He leaves a wife and kiddies. He was quite a young chap, not much older than me. How would you like that?'

The stranger made no answer.

'Bit thick isn't it?' said Curt. 'Bit bloody thick, isn't it? By God, it makes me see red. They're all the same, all these bosses. To hell with them! An extra quid's worth more to them than a man's happiness, or a man's life. And the police are simply there to back them up. That's what I say. Throat-cutting would be a damn sight too good for them.'

The stranger still made no answer.

It was now quite dark. They rushed along in that narrow and lonely world that closes round night drivers. They sped through an endless silent tunnel—a cave of darkness. The yellow light of the headlamps flashed on the ribbed walls and roofs to this side and that as deep banks and hedges streamed past. Trees, remote and still, stood for an instant before them, their leaves showing faint and dusty in the light. Then they vanished. The headlamps bored and bored through the darkness of the tunnel. Occasionally a fast-moving car slipped quietly by them.

The stranger watched Curt as his talk ran on and on. He was a young man, twenty-three, or twenty-four at the most. He was good looking, unshaved, unwashed, with black, oily smears on his forehead and face. His hair flew in the wind, and he lounged at ease behind the wheel, driving the lorry with reckless speed and skill. He talked ceaselessly, seeming to keep only half his attention on the yellow rings of light, and the wall of darkness ahead.

They scraped a corner, two wheels mounting a bank and tilting the lorry up at a sharp angle.

'All right, all right,' said Curt. 'Don't get windy. It's this blasted steering. You just ought to feel the back lash. I tighten up the ball joints after every journey. The worm-and-segment's not too good. Takes a bit of getting used to. Of course the boss got her cheap, and he's never spent a penny on repairs yet.'

'How are the brakes?' said the stranger.

'Brakes?' said Curt. 'They're comic. I oughtn't to take her out on the road like this at all, really. The hand brake acts on the back wheel, only it doesn't act. And I don't like using the foot-brake much; it puts too much strain on the rear gearbox bearing.'

'Why don't you drive slower?' said the stranger. 'Be more careful.'

'Hells bells,' said Curt. 'You couldn't drive much slower. Still, I expect you're wise. A pal of mine was telling me to be cautious only to-day. What he said to me was: "If you can't be good, be cautious." Don't you think that's a pretty good way of putting it?'

The stranger said nothing.

'Well,' said Curt, 'I think it is, especially when the police are such swine. They love to get it in for you.'

'What makes you say that?'

'Because they are,' said Curt angrily.

'I'll tell you what's been happening to me.' And he drew the lorry up at the side of the road and looked intently down the long moonlit stretch in front of him.

'Or perhaps I won't tell you,' he said. 'I'm afraid I'll have to put you off here—I've got to meet some friends of mine.'

As the stranger was getting down, another lorry lumbered by, and Tom leaned out of the cab and waved to Curt.

'Look here,' said Curt. 'We're getting near Savernake. This is all Lord Harleigh's Estate round here; if you care to wait a bit, you'll get another lift. Sorry I can't take you any further.'

'That's all right,' said the other man. 'I shall do fine.'

'So long,' said Curt. 'Good luck, old man.'

He let in his clutch, and with many jolts the transmission took up the load and the lorry started forward. In a mile or two he swung off into a side lane and nosed cautiously along. It was little more than a soft, grassy track. The trees of a thick wood bordered it on each side—their branches scraping and slapping the lorry as it passed. Then his headlights picked out a dark, bulky shape under the boughs, and he pulled up. As his eyes became accustomed to the clouded moonlight, he saw there were two other lorries waiting for him.

'Hullo,' said Curt. 'Cheerio, Tom. Hullo, Sid, how's things?'

Sid was on the road from Bristol up to London. He had brought a friend with him, a butcher's assistant from Bristol, who wanted a night out. Curt promised to take the butcher back to Bristol by the morning.

'Who was it that you were talking to when I passed?' said Tom.

'Oh, just a chap I'd given a lift to,' said Curt.

'You're a fool to go picking up with people,' said Sid. 'As long as you didn't start blabbing to him——'

'Of course not,' said Curt. 'What do you take me for? I think I shall turn round right away,' he went on. 'Might as well get it done.'

Sid nodded.

'How's she starting up nowadays?' he asked.

'Not too bad. It takes two of us most mornings. When I swing her alone, it leaves me feeling as if I hadn't the guts left to pull the skin off a rice pudding.'

Tom laughed.

'Blow the top off a glass of beer, you mean,' he said.

'When I'm too weak for that, I'll give you the beer,' said Curt. After a lot of manœuvring he backed his lorry round.

'Aren't you chaps going to turn?' he said, getting down.

'Why?' said Sid. 'Plenty of time later. Are you getting windy?'

Sid was a country chap by birth—yet he looked more of a townee than either of the others. His hair was black, and smoothed back, and he wore a bright-coloured jumper, and a ring on his signet finger.

They spoke all the time in low voices, saying as little as they could. Presently they fell silent.

'Well,' said Curt. 'Shall we start?'

'Might as well,' said Sid. 'Rouse up, Tom.'

'Not me, Sid,' said Tom, who was sitting with his feet up in the cab of his lorry. 'I'm not in this. I've got a wife and two kids at home.'

'Come on,' said Sid. 'It's only a bit of sport.'

'Not me,' said Tom. 'You'd better buck up. It'll be daylight soon.'

Curt left Tom in his lorry, and walked off with the others in the darkness. His heart was beating.

'What's the idea?' he whispered to Sid. 'Same as last time?'

'Yes,' said Sid. 'That, and a bit more. Don't talk. There's the torch; keep by me, I know this place like a book.'

Sid moved so quickly and quietly in the dense darkness under the trees it was hard to keep track of him. Curt could feel the other fellow, the butcher, somewhere close by, though he couldn't see him.

Suddenly Sid crouched down.

'Wait,' he said. He touched Curt's arm. 'Quick, you fool.'

Curt knew what to do. He shone the electric torch full on the branches of the tree about him. In the sudden glare, it seemed that the whole tree was full of roosting pheasants as a hen house. They showed up black and flustered in the sudden light.

Sid at once fired into the tree point blank with a sawn-off sporting gun. There was an immense crash of noise, which filled the whole night with repeated echoings: wings beat and branches rustled.

Curt felt a touch on his arm.

'I've got two,' said Sid. 'Quick, we'd better move away from here.'

After a little while they stopped and Sid gave Curt the dead birds.

'This is a good place,' said Sid. 'Let's try again.'

'That shooting will bring along every keeper in the place,' said Curt. 'That's enough for one night. I always said it was a damn fool way.'

'Don't get milky,' said Sid. 'Put the light on.'

Another tree was silhouetted: the gun crashed again. They got another bird.

'Christ!' said Sid. 'There's someone coming.' They lay stock still. Curt could feel his heart in the roots of his tongue. The footsteps were coming nearer.

A voice called. Sid whispered: 'They're coming this way.'

Suddenly there was a light in the trees, and the voices were right on top of them.

'Run!' said Sid.

Curt found himself at once alone, running over the broken ground in pitch darkness. There were loud shouts and lights just behind, and he hurled the two birds away as he ran. He plunged into brambles, which slashed his face and his clothes.

He fought with the clinging brambles frenziedly, as if they had been hands in the darkness holding him. He felt they nearly had him now. He'd put himself in their hands this time. What was going to happen?

Then he was clear of the brambles and running on open grass skirting the side of the wood. He saw sheep starting up in the darkness across a field. Then he found he was no longer being followed. He lay for a while in the deepest shadow, till the distant voices died right away.

After wandering in the woods for another half-hour, he found his way to the lorries. The others were still missing.

'You're a damn fool,' Tom said, when he told him what had happened. 'Why can't you keep out of this sort of thing for a bit?'

They waited, Curt only anxious now to get away as quickly as possible. Presently they heard voices.

The clouds were clearing and the moonlight grew brighter every moment. They saw Sid and the other man coming towards them dragging a heavy burden.

'What the hell——' said Tom.

It was the carcase of a newly killed last season's lamb. Tom took a look at it and went to the handle of his lorry.

'When it comes to sheep-stealing,' he said, 'I'm going.'

'Don't be in such a hurry,' said Sid. 'What d'you think I brought a butcher with me for? You stay and have a joint off it, Tom.'

'Not me,' said Tom.

'Look here,' said Sid to Curt. 'You're going to take this bloke back to Bristol, aren't you? He knows just where to sell this bit of mutton.'

'I'll get you retail prices for it,' said the butcher.

'Right,' said Sid. 'We'll just sling it on Curt's lorry.'

'All right,' said Curt, watching them, but his heart sank.

'Don't you take it,' said Tom.

'Shut your mouth,' said Sid. 'He'll take it.'

'All right,' said Curt. 'Let's move off. I've had enough for one night.'

'It's easy,' said Sid. 'We'll do it again.' He spoke with perfect assurance.

Curt started up his lorry. But as the engine fired and banged into life in the night silence, they heard the sound of another car. All listened, looking at each other without speaking. 'It's only a car passing in the distance,' Curt thought. But what if it were something else—someone who'd got wind of them? The sound was coming nearer, then he saw headlights flash. In another moment a car bumped slowly into view along the rough lane.

'Christ!' said Sid. 'That's a police car—a Morris.'

Curt leaped into the driving seat of his lorry, raced the engine, and let in the clutch. His was the only one of the three lorries which faced the way of escape: and he had the stolen sheep.

As the car approached his lorry jerked forward. In the glare of his headlights Curt saw the man who had travelled with him, and he could see now that he had plain-clothes-man written all over him.

'The swine,' he said to himself.

In another moment he was clanging up the broken lane. The lorry lurched from one side to the other as he struck deep ruts and pits. He held on to the steering-wheel with all his strength, letting the engine gather power. He could feel the dangerous give of the steering-gear as the front wheels took shock after shock.

After a few minutes of this rough work, he turned out into the main road. He was on a long, straight stretch, dipping and rising in the moon-light. With the accelerator jammed against the footboards he was soon doing fifty down the slopes. Then he saw the headlights of another car rising and dipping behind him. He was being chased. Soon he knew the car behind was coming up quickly. The headlights began to lighten the road all round him. His lorry was making noise enough for a traction en-gine. He crashed and thundered down the hills. Every bolt in the old Lycett banged and rattled. The wheel kicked violently in his hands, he could hardly hold it. He was only waiting for something to go.

The deep shadows of the trees and banks tumbled by him, writhing as they went; streaming, interlacing, barring his way. The black silhouette of his own lorry hovered beside him. He felt the car drawing nearer: he felt hands closing in on him. Dark fears of punishment, imprisonment, bubbled up from his lowest level. What would they do with him?

He clutched the wheel more firmly. The other car was right on him. A side turning rushed towards him, and he wrenched his lorry round. It struck a bank, swayed at a sickening angle, and then was on the road again. The turning was a narrow lane, climbing steeply.

He heard shouts behind him and knew that the other car had overshot the turning. He raced his engine in low gear, climbing slowly. By the time he had reached the top of the hill he saw the lights coming after him again.

Then he was rushing, thirty, forty, fifty miles an hour again, holding desperately to a narrow dropping road that overhung a deep valley. The road on his near side vanished into sheer emptiness.

The engine began to pop back in the carburetor. Curt knew there was plenty of petrol and he had cleaned the pipes and filters recently. An inlet valve must have burnt out or stuck. He muttered curses to himself.

Then he could see a flame through the floorboards, where the clutch pedal came through. As he glanced down, it was spreading. He opened the offside door in readiness. He tried the brakes, but they made no difference. 'I shall be dead before they get me,' he thought. 'I shall be dead in five minutes.'

He heard a loud metallic crash against the bottom of the crankcase. At the same instant he found the steering-wheel twisting loosely in his hands. 'The track rod's gone,' he thought. 'That's the end.'

His lorry leapt up the offside bank at fifty miles an hour; it lurched off and rushed at the other edge. Curt tried to jump clear, and saw the clouds and stars beneath his feet. Then the lorry came over on top of him—a huge black hurtling mass ....

At the same instant the Morris car with a dry skid and a scream of brakes drew up in his tracks. Two men flung the door open and began to climb out. For a second or so they watched in silence.

With crash after crash the lorry plunged down into the valley, turning over and over. It came to rest, and instantly a column of red flame rose straight in the darkness as the petrol exploded into fire. Then it turned to smoke and fitful bursts of flame thirty and forty feet high.

'Good God,' said one of the policemen. 'That's the end of him.'

'Young fool, young fool.'

They began to stumble quickly down the hill in the darkness.

Curt watched them vanish. He was lying beside the hedge where he had been thrown as the lorry overturned. He found he was quite unhurt.

As the police officers vanished in the darkness, he began to walk quickly away.

'It was bad luck on Curt,' he began thinking to himself. 'But perhaps he's better dead. I'll be in Manchester to-night. I'll be in Manchester to-night, and start on that new job.'

After a few minutes walking and running the flames were hidden by a shoulder of the hill and he slackened his pace.

'I'll get away with it all right,' he whispered. 'I shall always get away with it. Watch me!'

THE BALL

Irène Némirovsky

(1905–   )

TRANSLATED BY VYVYAN HOLLAND

Madame Kampf entered the school-room and shut the door so sharply behind her that the draught made by it caused all the glass crystals of the chandelier to knock together with a clear, bell-like tinkle. But Antoinette did not interrupt her reading, her head bowed so low over the desk that her hair swept the pages of her book. Her mother looked at her for a moment in silence; then she crossed the room and stood before her with her arms folded over her chest.

"You might at least get up when your mother comes into the room!" she shouted at her. "Or can't you? Perhaps you're glued to your chair? What manners! Where's Miss Betty?"

From the next room came the sound of a sewing-machine keeping time with a song whose words: "What shall I do, what shall I do, when you are gone away . . . ?" were being sung in an undertone by a clear but untrained voice.

"Miss Betty!" called Madame Kampf.

"Yes, Madame Kampf!"

The English girl slid in through the half-open door. She had pink cheeks, soft, rather timid eyes and long, honey-coloured hair swathed round her neat head.

"I engaged you to look after my daughter and to educate her, didn't I?" began Madame Kampf severely, "and not to spend your time making yourself frocks. Doesn't Antoinette know that she must get up when her mother comes into a room?"

"Oh, Antoinette, how *could* you?" cried the governess in a sort of wounded, bird-like twitter.

Antoinette was standing up now, balancing herself awkwardly on one foot. She was a tall, thin child of fourteen with the pale face natural to her age, which was so fleshless that to the eyes of grown-up people it looked like a round light-coloured blur, without features save a pair of heavy, dark-ringed eyes and a small, tightly shut mouth. Fourteen, with budding breasts that strained her tight school dress and seemed to hamper the weak childish body. Large feet and those long sticks, ending in red hands, which one day, who knows, might become the most lovely arms in the world. A fragile-looking neck and fine, straight, pale, short hair.

"You know, Antoinette, your manners are quite deplorable, my poor child. Sit down. I'll come in again and you will be good enough to get up at once, do you understand?"

Madame Kampf went back to the door and opened it again. Antoinette rose slowly and with such obvious reluctance that her mother pursed her lips threateningly and asked her sharply:

"You're not sulky by any chance are you, Miss?"

"No, Mother," replied Antoinette in a low voice.

"Then why do you put on that face?"

Antoinette smiled in a sort of laborious, craven effort that distorted her features painfully. Sometimes she hated grown-up people so much that she would have liked to kill them, to disfigure them or at least to stamp on the floor and scream: "Oh, how you bore me!" But she had been afraid of her parents from her very earliest childhood. Years before, when Antoinette was quite little, her mother had often taken her on her lap and hugged and kissed and caressed her. Antoinette had forgotten all that, but she retained firmly fixed in her mind the memory of outbursts in an exasperated voice, above her head: "The child's always getting under my feet! You've ruined my dress again with your dirty shoes! Go and stand in the corner, do you hear? That'll teach you! Little fool!" And one day—for the first time in her life she had wanted to die on that day—at the corner of a street, during a scene her mother had suddenly cried out in a rage, so loud that passers-by had turned round to see what was happening: "You want your face slapped, do you?" and then a stinging smack, in the open street. She was eleven at the time and tall for her age. The grown-up people in the street had not mattered so much; but at that very moment some boys were coming out of school and they had looked at her and laughed and shouted: "How's that, old girl?" And their sniggers had pursued her as she walked with her head bowed in the autumn twilight, while the street lamps danced through her tears. And her mother had gone on: "Can't you stop snivelling? What a foul temper you've got. When I punish you, it's for your own good, do you hear? That will teach you not to annoy me again!"

Horrible people. And nowadays, just in order to torture her and torment her and humiliate her, it was nothing from morning till night but: "Look how you're holding your fork!" (And in front of the footman too.) "Sit up straight! Do try not to look like a hunchback!" She was fourteen now, she was a young woman and, in her day-dreams, a beautiful and admired one. Men spoiled her and petted her, just as André Sperelli did to Hélène and Marie and Julien de Suberceaux to Maud de Rouvre in the books she had been reading. Love! She started. Madame Kampf was still talking.

"And if you think I get you an English governess for you to have manners like that, you're wrong, my beauty."

And then in a quieter voice, while she pushed back a strand of hair that had fallen across her daughter's forehead, she said:

"You always forget that we are rich now, Antoinette."

She turned to the governess:

"Miss Betty, there are a lot of things I want you to do this week. I'm giving a ball on the fifteenth."

"A ball?" echoed Antoinette, opening her eyes wide.

"Yes," said Madame Kampf with a smile, "a ball."

She looked at Antoinette with a self-satisfied look in her eyes, then she nodded stealthily in the direction of the English girl.

"You haven't told her anything?"

"No, Mother," declared Antoinette emphatically.

She was aware of this constant anxiety on her mother's part. At the start—that is, two years before—when they had left the old Rue Favart after lucky stock-exchange speculations by Alfred Kampf, first on the fall of the franc and afterwards on that of the pound sterling in 1926, speculations which had made them rich, Antoinette had been called into her parents' room every morning. Her mother would be sitting up in bed polishing her fingernails. In the dressing-room next door her father, a spare little Jew with very bright eyes, would be shaving, washing and dressing with that mad haste which characterised all his actions and which had formerly earned him the nickname of "Fire" from his German-Jewish friends on the exchange.

He had kicked his heels on the broad steps of the exchange for a great many years. Antoinette knew that before then he had been employed at the Bank of Paris, and that at an even more remote period he had been a page boy in a blue livery at the door of the Bank. Shortly before Antoinette's birth he had married his mistress, Mademoiselle Rosine, the manager's typist, and for eleven years they had lived in a gloomy little flat behind the Opéra Comique. Antoinette remembered how she used to do her home-work in the evenings on the dining-room table while the servant washed up noisily in the kitchen, and Madame Kampf read novels, her elbows on the table beneath the light, which consisted of a large ground-glass globe in which a bright gas-flame spluttered. Sometimes Madame Kampf would heave a deep sigh of irritation, so loud and so sudden that it made Antoinette jump. Kampf would then ask: "What's the matter now?" And Rosine would answer: "It makes me sick to think of all the people living happily and in comfort while I spend the best years of my life in this filthy hole, darning your socks."

Kampf would shrug his shoulders without a word. Then Rosine would usually turn towards Antoinette and say very angrily: "What are you listening for? You've no right to listen to what grown-ups say." And she would go on: "Yes, my girl, if you're going to wait until your father makes his fortune, as he's kept on promising to do ever since we were married, you've a long time to wait. A lot of water will pass under the bridge. You'll grow up and you'll have to go on waiting, as your poor mother has done." And when she uttered the word "waiting", a vaguely pathetic expression would pass over her hard, drawn, sullen features, which affected Antoinette despite herself and often made her instinctively put her lips up to her mother's face.

"My poor child," Rosine would say, stroking her forehead. But once she had cried: "Oh, leave me alone! You infuriate me. You're just as exasperating yourself!" And never again had Antoinette tried to kiss her except in the morning and in the evening, kisses which mean as little between parents and children as the hand-shakes of two strangers.

And then one day they had suddenly become rich, how she had never quite understood. They had gone to live in a large white apartment and her mother had her hair dyed a beautiful bright gold colour. Antoinette stole a timid glance at that flamboyant head which she did not recognise.

"Antoinette," ordered Madame Kampf, "tell me again. What do you say when people ask you where we lived last year?"

"Don't be silly," Kampf would say from the next room. "Who do you think is going to talk to the child? She doesn't know anyone."

"I know what I'm doing," retorted Madame Kampf, raising her voice. "What about the servants?"

"If I hear her saying one word to the servants, I'll deal with her. Do you understand, Antoinette? She knows that she's to keep her mouth shut and learn her lessons and that's all she's got to do." And turning to his wife: "She's not an idiot, you know."

But as soon as he had gone, Madame Kampf would start again:

"If anyone questions you, Antoinette, you must tell them that we lived all the year round in the South. There's no need to specify whether it was at Cannes or at Nice, just say the South . . . unless they press you, then it's better to say Cannes, it sounds better. But of course your father is right; talk as little as possible to grown-up people."

And she would dismiss her with a wave of her fine bare arm, a trifle too plump, on which shone the diamond bracelet which her husband had just given her and which she never took off except in her bath.

All this passed vaguely through Antoinette's mind while her mother was asking the governess:

"Is Antoinette's handwriting good?"

"Yes, Madame Kampf."

"Why?" asked Antoinette timidly.

"Because," explained Madame Kampf, "you can help me to address envelopes this evening. You see, I'm sending out nearly two hundred invitations. I shall never get through them all alone. Miss Betty, Antoinette may go to bed an hour later than usual this evening. Aren't you glad?" she added, turning to her daughter.

But Antoinette, once more buried in her reflections, said nothing. Madame Kampf shrugged her shoulders.

"The child's always wool-gathering," she muttered. "Doesn't it make you feel proud to think that your parents are giving a ball? You're not very affectionate I'm afraid, my poor child," she ended, with a sigh, leaving the room.

II

That evening Antoinette, who was usually taken off to bed by her governess sharp at nine o'clock, remained behind in the drawing-room with her parents. She so seldom entered that room that she gazed curiously at the white panelling and the gilt furniture, as though she were in a strange house. Her mother pointed to a little table on which were a bottle of ink, a pen, a packet of cards and some envelopes.

"Sit down there. I'll dictate the addresses to you. Are you coming, my dear?" she asked her husband in a louder voice, because the man-servant was clearing the table in the next room and for some months the Kampfs had always been very formal in their conversation before him.

When Monsieur Kampf came in Rosine whispered to him: "Send the menial away, will you, he gets on my nerves."

Then, catching Antoinette's eye, she coloured and said sharply:

"Come, George, haven't you finished yet? Clear away the rest of the things and leave us, please."

Then they three sat silently in their chairs until the man had gone. Madame Kampf sighed.

"I hate that George. I don't know why I should. When he's waiting at table and I feel that he's behind me, it takes away my appetite. What are you grinning like that for, Antoinette? Come, let's get to work. Have you got the list of guests, Alfred?"

"Yes," replied Kampf, "but wait till I get my coat off; it's hot in here."

"Yes, and above all don't forget not to leave it lying about the room as you did last time. I could see from George's and Lucie's faces what they thought of people sitting in the drawing-room in their shirt-sleeves."

"I don't care a damn what the servants think," growled Kampf.

"You're wrong then. It's they who make people's reputation by going about gossiping. I should never have known that the Baroness on the third floor . . ."

She lowered her voice and whispered something which Antoinette did not succeed in catching in spite of all her efforts.

". . . had it not been for Lucie, who was with her for three years."

Kampf took out of his pocket a piece of paper covered with names and erasures.

"Let's begin with the people I know, shall we, Rosine? Write, Antoinette: Monsieur and Madame Banyuls. I don't know their address. You've got the telephone book there. You can look the addresses out as we go along."

"They're very rich, aren't they?" muttered Rosine in an awed voice.

"Very."

"Do you think they'll come? I don't know Madame Banyuls."

"Nor do I. But I do business with the husband, and that's quite enough. They say the wife is charming; besides, she hasn't been invited out much by her own set since that business. . . . You know, the notorious orgies in the Bois de Boulogne two years ago. . . ."

"Alfred! Be careful in front of the child!"

"She doesn't understand. Write it down, Antoinette. She makes a very good start, anyway."

"Don't forget the Ostiers," said Rosine eagerly. "They're said to give lovely parties."

"Monsieur and Madame Ostier d'Arrachon, with two r's, Antoinette. But I won't guarantee their coming. They're very stuck up. The wife was once . . ."

He made a gesture.

"Not really?"

"Yes, really. I know someone who often saw her in a bawdy-house in Marseilles. Yes, really, I assure you. But that was long ago, nearly twenty years. She's been completely white-washed by her marriage and knows some of the best people; she's very difficult to get hold of. As a general rule all women who've had a gay youth get like that . . ."

"Heavens, how difficult it all is!" sighed Madame Kampf.

"One has to do things by easy stages, my dear. For your first party you want people and more people, as many as you can get hold of. For your second or third you can start weeding out. This time you must invite people wholesale."

"But if only one were sure of everyone coming. If some of them refuse to come I think I shall die of shame."

Kampf contorted his face in a silent laugh.

"If some of them refuse to come you must ask them again next time and again the following time. Shall I tell you something? The fact is, to get on in Society, one has only to follow literally the precept of the Gospels."

"Which one?"

"'Whoever smiteth thee on the right cheek, turn to him the other also.' Society is the best school in which to learn Christian humility."

"I often ask myself," observed Madame Kampf, vaguely shocked, "where you get all your nonsense from."

Kampf smiled.

"Come, come! Let's get on. Here are some addresses already written out. You can just copy them out, Antoinette."

Madame Kampf leaned over her daughter's shoulder as she wrote, bowed over the table:

"Yes, she's got a very nice handwriting, very well formed. Here, Alfred, isn't Monsieur Julien Nassan the man who went to prison over that swindle . . . ?"

"Nassan? Yes, that's right."

"Oh!" murmured Rosine, rather taken aback.

Kampf said:

"What's the matter with you? He's been cleared, he's received everywhere, he's a charming fellow and above all a very shrewd business man."

"Monsieur Julien Nassan, 23b Avenue Hoche," read Antoinette. "Next, please, Father."

"That only makes twenty-five," groaned Madame Kampf. "We'll never get two hundred people, Alfred."

"Of course we shall. Don't start fussing. Where's your own list? All the people you met at Nice, at Deauville, at Chamonix last year."

Madame Kampf took a note-book from the table.

"Count Moïssi, Monsieur, Madame and Mademoiselle Lévy de Brunelleschi and the Marquis d'Itcharra: he's Madame Lévy's gigolo and they're always asked everywhere together."

"There really is a husband I suppose?" asked Kampf, doubtfully.

"Naturally. They're very respectable people. Here are some more Marquises. Five altogether. The Marquis de Liguès y Hermosa, the Marquis . . . By the way, Alfred, does one call them by their titles in addressing them? I think it's better, don't you? Not Monsieur le Marquis, naturally, like servants, but 'dear Marquis,' 'dear Countess,' otherwise the others won't even know that we've got titled guests."

"I suppose you'd like to stick a label on their backs, eh?"

"Oh, you and your stupid jokes! Come, Antoinette, hurry up and copy them out, dear."

Antoinette wrote for a moment, then she read out loud:

"Baron and Baroness Levinstein-Lévy, the Count and Countess du Poirier. . . ."

"That's Abraham and Rebecca Birnbaum," mused her mother. "They bought the title. Silly to call themselves du Poirier. Now I myself . . ."

She fell into a deep reverie.

"Just Count and Countess Kampf," she muttered. "It doesn't sound bad at all."

"We must wait a little," advised Kampf. "In ten years time perhaps."

In the meantime Rosine was sorting out the visiting cards thrown in confusion into a malachite bowl ornamented by two gilt-bronze Chinese dragons.

"I wish I knew who all these people were, all the same," she said. "They're all cards I received at the New Year. Lots of little gigolos whom I met at Deauville. . . ."

"You want as many of those as possible. They're decorative and if they dress well . . ."

"My dear, you're joking. They're all Counts, Marquises or Viscounts at the very least. But I can't put faces to their names, they're all so exactly alike. Though it makes no difference really. You saw what they did at the Rothwan de Fiesques? One greets everyone in exactly the same words: 'I'm so delighted . . .' and if one is forced to introduce two people to each other one smothers the names. No one ever hears them anyway. Look, Antoinette, these are quite easy; all the addresses are on the cards themselves."

"But, Mother, this is the furniture man's card."

"What's that? Show me. Yes, she's right. Heavens! I'm losing my head, I really am, Alfred. How many have you got now, Antoinette?"

"A hundred and seventy-two, Mother."

"Oh, well!"

The Kampfs sighed together in relief and smiled at one another, like two actors on the stage after a third recall, with an expression composed of happy weariness and triumph.

"Not bad, eh?"

"Is . . . is Mademoiselle Isabelle Cossette my Mademoiselle Isabelle?"

"Why yes."

"Oh!" exclaimed Antoinette. "Why are you asking her?"

She immediately blushed violently, expecting a sharp: "Mind your own business" from her mother; but Madame Kampf explained awkwardly:

"She's a kind-hearted woman, and one must be pleasant to people."

"She's as sour as a lemon," protested Antoinette.

Mademoiselle Isabelle, a cousin of the Kampfs and music-teacher to several families of rich Jewish outside brokers, was a flat-chested old maid, as straight and stiff as a ramrod; she gave Antoinette piano and singing lessons. She was extremely short-sighted, but she never wore glasses, because she was vain of her fairly handsome eyes and her thick eyebrows. So she glued her long, fleshy, pointed nose, purple with powder, to the score, and whenever Antoinette made a mistake she rapped her knuckles with an ebony ruler, as flat and hard as herself. She was as malicious and inquisitive as an old magpie. The day before her lesson Antoinette would mutter furiously, in the course of her evening prayers (her father was converted at the time of his marriage, so Antoinette had been brought up in the Catholic faith): "Please God, make Mademoiselle Isabelle die tonight!"

"The child's right," observed Kampf in surprise; "why do you want to invite that old fool? You know you can't bear the sight of her."

Madame Kampf shrugged her shoulders impatiently.

"Oh, you don't understand a thing. How do you suppose the family will hear about it unless I do? Can't you see Aunt Loridon's face (you remember she quarrelled with me because I married a Jew) and Julie Lacombe's and Uncle Martial's and those of all the rest of the family who used to put on such condescending airs with us because they were richer than we were, you remember? Well, to be perfectly frank with you, if Isabelle isn't asked and if I didn't know that next day they'll all die of jealousy, I'd just as soon not give the ball at all! Send her a card, Antoinette."

"Shall we dance in both drawing-rooms?"

"Naturally, and in the corridor as well. You know our corridor is rather impressive. I'll hire masses of flowers; you'll see how well it will look, in the big corridor, all the women with ball-dresses and lovely jewelry and all the men in dress-clothes. At the Lévy de Brunelleschis' it was a marvellous sight. They turned the lights out during the tangos, leaving only two large alabaster lamps in the corner with red lights in them."

"I don't like that, it's too much like a night-club."

"Apparently everyone is doing it now; women adore being mauled to music. And of course we'll have supper at small tables."

"And why not a buffet to start with?"

"That's an idea. They'll want thawing out a bit when they arrive. We can put the buffet in Antoinette's room. She can sleep in the linen-room or in the little box-room at the end of the passage for one night."

Antoinette started violently. She went quite white and asked in a low, stifled voice:

"Mayn't I stay just for a few minutes?"

A ball! Good heavens, could it be possible that within a few yards of her there could take place that splendid thing which she pictured to herself vaguely as a confused mixture of wild music, intoxicating perfumes and brilliant clothes, of words of love whispered in dark, cool, secluded corners, and that she herself should be put to bed like a baby, at nine o'clock that evening, as on any other evening? Perhaps some of the men who knew that Kampf had a daughter would ask where she was; and her mother would reply, with her hateful little laugh: "Oh, she's been in bed a long time." And yet what harm could it do her for Antoinette, too, to have her share of happiness in this world? Oh, to dance once, only once, in a pretty frock, like a real grown-up girl, clasped in a man's arms! She closed her eyes and pleaded once more with a sort of desperate courage, as though she were pressing a loaded revolver to her bosom:

"Only a few minutes, Mother, please!"

"What?" cried Madame Kampf in amazement. "What's that? The child must be mad."

Suddenly Antoinette cried, her features convulsed:

"I implore you, Mother, I beg of you! I'm fourteen now. I'm no longer a child. I know one comes out at fifteen; I look fifteen and next year . . ."

Madame Kampf broke in:

"That's a good one, to be sure!" she cried in a voice hoarse with rage. "A brat, a chit like you, at the ball! Can you see it? You wait, I'll rid you of all your big ideas, my girl! So you think you'll be coming out next year, do you? Who has been putting ideas like that into your head? I'll have you know that I'm only just beginning to live myself, do you hear? myself, and I've no intention of saddling myself with a marriageable daughter yet. I wonder I don't box your ears to put some sense into your head," she went on in the same voice, taking a step towards Antoinette.

Antoinette shrank back and grew still paler; the wild, despairing look in her face moved Kampf to a sort of pity:

"Leave the child alone," he said, catching hold of Rosine's outstretched hand; "she's tired and nervy, poor child, and doesn't know what she's saying. Go to bed, Antoinette."

Antoinette did not move; her mother pushed her gently by the shoulders.

"Come, get along with you, and don't answer back. Be off or it will be the worse for you!"

Antoinette was trembling in every limb, but she got up and went slowly and dry-eyed out of the room.

"Charming," observed Madame Kampf when she had gone. "She promises well. However, I was just the same at her age; but I'm not like my own poor mother, who could never refuse me anything. I'll tame her, I promise you that."

"She'll be all right when she's had a sleep; she's tired; it's already eleven and she's not used to such late hours; that's what's put her on edge. Let's get on with the list, it's much more interesting," said Kampf.

III

Miss Betty was awakened in the middle of the night by the sound of sobs coming from the next room. She switched on the light and listened for a moment through the partition. It was the first time she had heard the child cry; as a rule, when Madame Kampf scolded her, Antoinette succeeded in swallowing her tears in silence.

"What's the matter with you, dear? Are you ill?" the governess asked. The sobbing stopped immediately.

"I suppose your mother has been scolding you. It's all for your own good, Antoinette. Tomorrow you'll beg her pardon and kiss her and that'll be the end of it; but you must go to sleep now; would you like a hot drink? No? You might at least answer me," she added, as Antoinette still kept silence. "Oh, dear! What an awful thing a sulky little girl can be. You're making your guardian angel very unhappy."

Antoinette made a face and whispered: "Beastly Englishwoman," beneath her breath and shook her feeble clenched fists at the wall. Selfish beasts, hypocrites! All of them. What did they care if she suffocated all by herself in the dark through crying so much, or whether she felt as miserable and lonely as a lost dog? No one loved her, not a single soul in all the world. Couldn't they see, blind fools, that she was a thousand times more intelligent, more deserving, more profound than the whole lot of them, these people who presumed to bring her up and to educate her? Vulgar, uncultured upstarts! Oh, how she had been laughing at them all the evening and they, naturally, had noticed nothing. She could laugh or cry in front of them without their ever noticing anything. . . . A child of fourteen, a brat, something as contemptible and as negligible as a dog in their eyes. What right had they to pack her off to bed, to punish her, to insult her? "Oh, how I wish they'd die!" On the other side of the partition she could hear the governess breathing softly in her sleep. Antoinette began to cry again, but more gently, tasting the tears which flowed into the corners of her mouth and between her lips; suddenly an odd feeling of pleasure came over her; for the first time in her life she was crying like this, without making a face or hiccoughing, silently, like a woman. Later she would cry other tears like these, for love. For a long time she listened to the sobs throbbing in her bosom like the deep low rumble of the sea. Her tear-wet mouth tasted of salt and water. She lit the lamp and examined herself curiously in the glass. Her eyelids were swollen and her cheeks were red and mottled. Like those of a little girl who has been whipped. She was ugly, terribly ugly. She began to cry again.

"I want to die! O God! Let me die. O God, O Blessed Virgin Mary, why was I made to be born among them? Punish them, I implore you! Punish them just once and then I shall die happily!"

She stopped and suddenly said, in a loud voice:

"And perhaps after all they're just nonsense, God and the Virgin Mary, just like kind parents and the age of happiness."

"Yes! The age of happiness, what a joke, eh? What a joke!" she kept furiously repeating over and over again, biting her hands so hard that she felt them bleed between her teeth.

"Happy . . . Happy . . . I'd rather be dead and buried."

Slavery, prison, having to go through the same routine day after day. To get up, to dress. Ugly dresses, thick boots, ribbed stockings, all done on purpose, like a livery, so that no one in the street should think for a moment of looking at that insignificant brat passing by. Idiots! You will never again see that flower-like body and those eyes, so bright, so pure, so clear and deeply ringed, those beautiful, proud, frightened eyes with their appeal, their innocence, their patience. Never, perhaps never again. To have to wait, and with all those evil desires of hers. Why did such shameful, desperate envy gnaw at her heart at the sight of a couple of lovers kissing one another as they strolled along in the twilight, swaying gently from side to side as though intoxicated? An old maid's bitterness at the age of fourteen? And yet she knew quite well that her turn would come; but it was so far ahead that it seemed as though it never would come and, in the meantime, there was her narrow, degrading life, her lessons, harsh discipline and a scream-ing mother.

"To think that woman threatened me!"

And she added, in a deliberately loud voice:

"She would never have dared . . ."

But she remembered the raised hand.

"If she had touched me I would have clawed her and bitten her and then . . . one can always escape for ever . . . the window," she thought fever-ishly. And she saw herself on the pavement, lying in a pool of blood. No ball on the fifteenth. People would say: "She might have chosen another time to kill herself." As her mother had said: "I myself want to live." Per-haps, after all, it was that which hurt her more than anything else. Never before had Antoinette seen that cold, feminine, jealous look in her mother's eyes.

"Selfish beasts! I'm the one that wants to live, I, I! I'm young. They're robbing me, stealing my birthright of happiness in this world. Oh, to be able to get into the ball by a miracle and to be the most beautiful, the most dazzling girl there, with all the men at my feet!"

She went on in a whisper:

"Don't you know her? She's Mademoiselle Kampf. She's not exactly beautiful, perhaps, but she has extraordinary charm. She is so dazzling that she puts all the others in the shade, doesn't she? As for her mother, she looks like a charwoman beside her."

She laid her head on the tear-soaked pillow and closed her eyes; her tired limbs gradually relaxed with a gentle sensual feeling. She touched her body lightly through her night-dress, with tenderness and wonder. Beautiful body meant for love! She murmured:

"Fifteen. Oh, Romeo! Just Juliet's age!"

When she was fifteen the world would be a different place.

IV

The next day Madame Kampf made no reference to the scene of the night before; but all through breakfast she made a point of letting her daughter feel her irritation by a series of those sharp rebukes in which she excelled when she was in a bad temper:

"Don't sit there dreaming with your mouth open. Keep your mouth shut and breathe through your nose. I suppose you think it amuses your parents to have a child who is always up in the clouds. Try to eat more tidily. I'm sure you've made a mess on the table-cloth. You ought to have better table-manners at your age. And don't scowl at me. You'll have to learn to listen when you're spoken to without making faces. Can't you say anything? Are you dumb? Good, now we're going to have tears!" She concluded, flinging her napkin down on the table. "I'd rather go away than watch you sitting there like the picture of misery. Silly little fool!"

She left the room, slamming the door behind her: Antoinette and the English governess were left facing each other across the remains of breakfast.

"Finish your fruit, Antoinette," whispered the governess. "You'll be late for your German lesson."

With a shaking hand Antoinette put the piece of orange she had been peeling into her mouth. She set herself to eat it slowly and calmly, so that the footman who stood motionless behind her chair might think that she was indifferent to all this scolding, and despised "that woman"; but in spite of all her efforts tears began to start from her eyes and flowed in round shining drops onto her dress.

A little later Madame Kampf came into the schoolroom, holding in her hand the packet of invitations they had written the night before.

"You're going to your piano lesson after luncheon, aren't you, Antoinette? Well, you can give Isabelle her invitation yourself and you, Miss Betty, can post the others."

"Yes, Mrs. Kampf."

.   .   .

The post-office was crowded; Miss Betty looked at the clock.

"Oh, we haven't got time, it's too late. I'll post them during your lesson, dear," she said, lowering her eyes and suddenly blushing scarlet. "That'll be all right, won't it?"

"Yes," muttered Antoinette.

Nothing further was said, but when the governess, telling her to hurry, left her at Mademoiselle Isabelle's door, Antoinette waited a moment, hidden in the embrasure, and watched the English girl hurry towards a taxi waiting at the corner of the street. The taxi passed quite close to Antoinette, who raised herself on tip-toe and looked eagerly and timidly into it. But she could see nothing. She stood there for another moment or two, following the retreating taxi with her eyes.

"I thought she had a lover. No doubt they're kissing one another now, as people do in books. I wonder if he's telling her he loves her. And she? Is she his . . . mistress?" she mused with a sudden feeling of shame and disgust, not unmixed with a certain vague distress. "Free, alone with a man! How lucky she is! They'll probably go to the Bois de Boulogne. I wish Mother could see them, oh, how I wish she could!" she muttered, clenching her fists. "But no. Lovers are so fortunate. They're happy; they're together; they can kiss each other . . . The world is full of men and women who love each other. Why not me?"

Her school satchel swung at arms' length before her and she looked at it with loathing. Then she sighed, turned on her heel and crossed the courtyard. She was late. Mademoiselle Isabelle would say: "Haven't you been taught that punctuality is the first duty of a well-brought-up child towards its teachers, Antoinette?"

"How old and stupid and ugly she is!" she thought in a wave of exasperation, and out loud she said: "Good-afternoon, Mademoiselle. Mother kept me; it's not my fault I'm late; and she asked me to give you this."

As she handed her the envelope she added, with sudden inspiration:

"And she wants you to let me go five minutes earlier than usual."

In that way she might see her governess returning with her young man. But Mademoiselle Isabelle was not listening. She was reading Madame Kampf's invitation. Antoinette saw her long, gaunt, tanned cheeks suddenly redden.

"What's this? A ball? Your mother's giving a ball?"

She turned the card over and over between her fingers, then she passed it furtively over the back of her hand to find out whether it was engraved or merely printed. It made at least forty francs difference. From the feel of it she immediately recognised that it was engraved. She shrugged her shoulders angrily. These Kampfs had always been insanely vain and extravagant. In the old days, when Rosine worked at the Banque de Paris (and it wasn't so long ago, either, Heaven knew!) she had spent her whole salary on clothes. She used to wear silk underclothing and have clean gloves every week. But no doubt she got money from men. Only women like that were really happy. The others . . . And she said bitterly:

"Your mother has always been lucky."

"She's furious," thought Antoinette, and with a sly upward glance she asked:

"You'll be sure to come, won't you?"

"Well, I'll do my best, because I really do want to see your mother very much," said Mademoiselle Isabelle; "on the other hand I don't yet know if I can. Some friends of mine, the parents of one of my pupils, named Gros, Aristide Gros, an ex-Permanent-Under-Secretary—your father must have heard me speak of them, I've known them for years—well, they've asked me to go to the theatre with them on that day, and I've definitely accepted, you see. Anyway I'll try to get out of it," she concluded, non-committally. "But in any case you can tell your mother that I shall be delighted to drop in for a short time.

"And now to work. Come and sit down."

Antoinette slowly adjusted the screw of the plush music stool before the piano. She could have drawn from memory all the stains and holes in its seat. She began her scales, staring with dreary fixedness at a yellow vase on the mantelpiece, the interior of which was black with dust. Not a single flower in the room, and those hideous little shell-covered boxes on the shelves of the overmantel. How ugly, shabby and dismal was that little dark flat to which she had been dragged for years.

While Mademoiselle Isabelle was arranging the music, she turned her head furtively toward the window and thought how lovely it must be in the Bois at dusk with its delicate leafless winter trees and the pearly whiteness of the sky overhead. Three times a week, every week for six years. Would it go on until she died?

"Really, Antoinette, look how you're holding your hands! Now start again, please. Will there be many people at your mother's party?"

"I believe Mother has asked about two hundred."

"Oh! Does she think there's enough room for them all? Doesn't she think it will be too hot or too crowded? Play harder, Antoinette; put some life into it; your left hand is too loose, dear. And learn that scale for next time and the eighteenth exercise in Czerny's third book."

Scales, exercises, month after month: *The Death of Asa*, Mendelssohn's *Songs without Words*. The Barcarolle from the *Contes d'Hoffmann*. And under the awkward childish fingers they all merged into a sort of formless noisy clamour.

Mademoiselle beat time strenuously with a rolled-up exercise book.

"Why do you press so heavily on the keys? *Staccato, staccato.* Do you think I can't see how you are holding your third and fourth fingers? Did you say two hundred people? Do you know them all?"

"No."

"Is your mother going to wear her new pink Premet dress?"

"I don't know."

"And you? I suppose you'll be at the ball? You're big enough now."

"I don't know," muttered Antoinette, quivering with misery.

"Faster, faster! This is the time it should be played in. One two, one two, one two! You're half asleep. Now the suite."

The suite, that passage bristling with sharps over which one's fingers fumbled the whole time! A baby started crying in the next flat. Mademoiselle Isabelle lit the lamp. Outside, the sky had grown dark and the daylight had almost disappeared. The clock struck four. Another hour wasted, ruined, trickled through her fingers like water, never to return. She thought: "I would like to go far, far away, or else die."

"Are you tired, Antoinette? Already? At your age I played six hours a day. Wait a moment; don't run away so quickly. Why are you in such a hurry? What time should I come on the fifteenth?"

"It's on the card. Ten o'clock."

"Good. But I'll see you before then."

"Yes, Mademoiselle."

When Antoinette got outside the street was empty. She leaned up against the wall and waited. A moment or two later Miss Betty came hurrying along, clinging to a young man's arm. Antoinette sprang forward and stumbled against them. Miss Betty uttered a faint scream.

"Oh, Miss Betty, I've been waiting for you for over a quarter of an hour."

Her governess's face suddenly seemed so changed that for a moment she scarcely recognised her. But the pitiful little half-pathetic lips, bruised like a battered flower, escaped her notice; her eyes were on "the man."

He was a very young man. A student. Perhaps even a school-boy with his tender chin inflamed from its first contact with the razor. Nice bold eyes. He was smoking. He broke into Miss Betty's halting excuses and said quickly, in a clear voice:

"Won't you introduce me?"

"This is my cousin, Antoinette," breathed the governess.

Antoinette held out her hand. The boy gave a short laugh but made no comment; then he thought a moment and finally suggested:

"Shall I see you home?"

They walked down the dark, empty street together in silence. The wind blew the clean rain-soaked air, which felt as though it were saturated with tears, into Antoinette's face. She slackened her pace and gazed at the lovers walking in front of her without speaking, pressed against each other. How quickly they walked! She stopped, but they did not even turn their heads. "If I were run over by a car I don't think they'd even notice it," she thought, with an odd feeling of bitterness. Someone bumped into her; she shrank back in an instinctive movement of fear. But it was only a lamplighter; she watched him touching the lamps one by one with his long pole and saw them suddenly flare up in the dark. They all seemed to twinkle and flicker like candles in the wind. Panic suddenly seized her and she started running as hard as she could.

She caught the lovers up by the Alexandre III bridge. They were talking rapidly with their heads close together. When he saw Antoinette, the boy made a movement of impatience. For a moment Miss Betty seemed non-plussed, then, in a sudden inspiration, she opened her bag and took out the packet of letters.

"Look, darling, here are your mother's invitations. I haven't had time to post them yet. Run along to the letter-box there in the street on the left, where the light is. Just put them in the box. We'll wait for you here."

She put the packet into Antoinette's hand and walked rapidly away. Antoinette saw her stop on the middle of the bridge and wait there for the boy. They leaned over the parapet together.

Antoinette did not move at once. It was so dark that she could only distinguish two shadowy figures and, all around, the dark river full of reflected light. Even when they kissed she guessed at, rather than saw, their faces come together in a sort of soft confusion. She twisted her fingers violently together like a jealous woman, and as she did so one of the envelopes slipped out and fell in the street. She was afraid and picked it up quickly and, at the same instant, she was ashamed of her fear. Was she always going to tremble like a small child at the slightest thing? She did not deserve to be a woman. And what about those two who were still kissing? They had not unglued their lips yet. A sort of giddiness came over her, and a savage need for bravado and wickedness. She clenched her teeth, crumpled the envelopes in her hands, tore them up and threw them all together into the Seine. For some moments, with a beating heart, she watched them fluttering against the arch of the bridge. Then the wind carried them down into the water below.

v

Antoinette returned from her walk with Miss Betty at about six o'clock. As no one seemed to answer the bell, the governess knocked. They could hear the sound of furniture being moved inside the house.

"They must be getting the cloak-room ready," said the English girl. "The ball's tonight; I keep on forgetting about it, don't you, darling?"

She gave Antoinette an affectionate smile of timid complicity. And yet she had not seen her young lover again in the child's presence. But since that last meeting Antoinette had become so taciturn that she alarmed her governess by her silence and her glances.

The footman opened the door.

Madame Kampf, who was watching the electrician in the dining-room, swept out on them.

"Can't you come in by the back way?" she screamed in a fury. "You know quite well that the cloak-room is being put in the hall. Now we've got to start all over again and nothing will ever be finished," she concluded, seizing hold of a table to help the concierge and George who were getting the place ready.

In the dining-room and in the long corridor which led out of it, six waiters in white coats were arranging the supper tables. In the centre of the room stood the buffet, profusely adorned with bright flowers.

Antoinette wanted to go in and look, but Madame Kampf began shouting again.

"Not there! Don't go in there! The bar is in your room, and we're using yours too, Miss Betty. You can sleep in the linen-room for to-night and you, Antoinette, in the box room; it's right at the end of the apartment and you'll be able to sleep all right; you won't even hear the music. What are you doing?" she went on, turning to the electrician who was humming as he went unhurriedly about his job. "You can see that bulb isn't working."

"Oh, it all takes time, lady . . ."

Rosine shrugged her shoulders angrily.

"Time, time! And he's been here nearly an hour already!" she said, half to herself.

She twisted her fingers hard together as she spoke, in a gesture which was so exactly like Antoinette's when she was angry that the child, who was still standing in the doorway, started suddenly as one does when one finds oneself unexpectedly confronted by a mirror.

Madame Kampf was wearing a dressing-gown, with her bare feet thrust into slippers; her hair was loose and writhed in serpentine coils round her scarlet face. She noticed that the florist, his arms full of roses, was trying to get past Antoinette as she stood with her back to the wall.

"Come, get out of the way!" shouted Madame Kampf, so sharply that Antoinette, in trying to obey as quickly as possible, bumped into the man and broke off one of the roses.

"You're intolerable!" said her mother in a voice so loud that the glasses on the table rang. "What do you mean by getting into people's way and annoying everyone? Go to your room, not your own room, but to the linen-room or wherever you like so long as you're neither seen nor heard!"

When Antoinette was gone, Madame Kampf strode swiftly through the dining-room and the pantry crammed with champagne-coolers full of ice and reached her husband's study. Kampf was telephoning. As soon as he replaced the receiver she exploded:

"But what's the matter with you? You're not even shaved!"

"At six o'clock? You're crazy."

"In the first place it's half-past six, and then there may be things to be fetched at the last moment; it's better to be prepared for everything."

"You're crazy," he repeated, impatiently; "if there's anything to be fetched the servants can do it."

"I like that—coming the aristocrat and the gentleman now! 'The servants can do it!'" she mimicked, shrugging her shoulders. "You can keep that sort of thing for the guests."

"Oh, don't, for God's sake, get all upset!" ground out Kampf.

"But how can you expect me not to be upset?" cried Rosine, with tears in her voice. "Nothing's going right! The filthy servants will never be ready! I have to be everywhere and supervise everything, and I haven't slept for three nights; I'm coming to the end of my strength and I feel I'm going mad."

She picked up a little silver ash-tray and threw it on the floor. This act of violence seemed to calm her down. She smiled rather shamefacedly.

"It's not my fault, Alfred."

Kampf shook his head without replying; Rosine started to move away, but he called her back.

"Tell me, I meant to ask you. Have you still had no reply from any of the people you asked to-night?"

"No, why?"

"I don't know. It seems funny to me. It's as though it was done deliberately. I meant to ask Barthélemy if he had received his invitation, but I haven't seen him at the exchange for a week. Suppose I telephone him?"

"At this time of day? It would be silly."

"All the same, it's funny," observed Kampf.

"Well," put in his wife, "it means that it's not fashionable to reply, that's all. People either come or they don't. And I'll tell you something else. I'm really rather pleased. It means that no one thought of refusing from the start, or they would have written to excuse themselves. Don't you agree?"

As her husband did not reply she asked him impatiently:

"Don't you think I'm right, Alfred, eh? What do you think?"

Kampf spread out his hands.

"I don't know. What do you want me to say? I don't know any more than you do."

They looked at each other in silence for a moment. Then Rosine dropped her eyes and sighed.

"Oh, I feel quite lost, don't you?"

"You'll get over it," said Kampf.

"I know, but in the meantime . . . If you only knew how frightened I am! I wish it was all over!"

"Don't get all upset," prompted Kampf again, weakly.

He himself was absent-mindedly turning a paper-knife over in his hands.

"Above all," he advised her, "talk as little as possible. Use only conventional phrases such as: 'I'm delighted you've been able to come . . . . Won't you take something? . . . How warm it is! . . . How cold it is! . . .'"

"What will be awful will be the introductions," said Rosine anxiously. "Just think, all those people whom I have only seen once in my life and whose faces I can hardly remember, and who won't know one another and have nothing in common."

"Heavens! You'll muddle through somehow. After all, everyone is in the same position as we are. They all had to start once."

"Do you remember our little flat in the Rue Favart?" asked Rosine suddenly. "And how we hesitated before getting a new divan for the dining-room in place of the one that was all broken? That's only four years ago and look now!" And she pointed to the heavy, ornate furniture around them.

"You mean," added Kampf, "that in four years from now we'll be entertaining Ambassadors, and then we shall remember how we trembled with fear this evening because a few dozen pimps and old tarts were coming to the house. Eh?"

She laughed and put her hand over his mouth.

"Shut up, do!"

As she left the room she ran into the butler who was coming to tell her that the mossers had not been sent with the champagne and that the barman thought there would not be enough gin for the cocktails.

Rosine seized her head in both hands.

"Good, that's the last straw!" she began to shout. "I suppose you couldn't have told me that before. Where do you think I'm going to get gin at this time of night? Everything's shut . . . and the mossers too!"

"Send the chauffeur, dear," suggested Kampf.

"The chauffeur has gone to dinner," said George.

"Naturally!" cried Rosine, beside herself. "Naturally! He doesn't care a . . ." She hesitated ". . . a blow whether we want him or not, his lordship goes away, his lordship goes to dinner. There's another who'll get the sack first thing tomorrow," she added, addressing George in such a tone of fury that he tightened his long, shaven lips.

"If Madame is referring to me . . ." he began.

"No, no, you must be mad. I hardly know what I'm saying; you see what a state of nerves I'm in," said Rosine, shrugging her shoulders; "take a taxi and go to the wine-merchants at once. Give him some money, Alfred."

And she retired to her room, putting finishing touches to the arrangement of the flowers as she went along and scolding the servants:

"That plate of cakes is in a bad place. Pull the pheasant's tail up a bit more. Where are the caviare sandwiches? Don't put them too near the front, or they'll all throw themselves on them. And the foie gras has been forgotten! Unless I do everything myself! . . ."

"We're unpacking it now, Madame," said the butler, looking at her with ill-concealed scorn.

"I must look ridiculous," suddenly thought Rosine, catching a glimpse in the glass of her scarlet face, the wild look in her eyes, and her trembling lips. But, like an overwrought child, in spite of all she could do she could not calm herself; she was exhausted and on the verge of tears.

She retired to her own room.

The maid was laying out her ball-dress on the bed: it was made of silver tissue ornamented with thick fringes of pearls. Shoes that shone like jewels and a pair of gossamer stockings completed the outfit.

"Will Madame dine now? Dinner's being served here, so as not to disturb the tables, I suppose."

"I'm not hungry," cried Rosine in a frenzy.

"As Madame wishes; but may I go and dine?" asked Lucie tartly, for Madame Kampf had kept her for four hours sewing on the pearls that were coming off the fringes. "I would like to point out to Madame that it is nearly eight o'clock and that human beings are not animals."

"Run along, my dear girl, nobody's keeping you!" exclaimed Madame Kampf.

When she was alone, she threw herself on the sofa and closed her eyes. But the room was as cold as an ice-house; all the radiators in the flat had been turned off since the morning. She got up and went over to the dressing-table.

"I look frightful . . ."

She began carefully to make up her face; first a thick layer of cream which she worked between her two hands, then liquid rouge on her cheeks, mascara on her eyelashes, a little line to lengthen the eyelids towards the temples, and powder. She made herself up with extreme deliberation, stopping every now and then to gaze at her reflection in the mirror with passionate, anxious care and an expression which was a mixture of severity, diffidence and shrewdness. Suddenly she seized a white hair on her temple and pulled it out furiously. How badly arranged life was! She thought of her face at the age of twenty, with its lovely complexion, and of her darned stockings and patched underclothing. And now she had jewelry and all the clothes she wanted, but the first wrinkles were appearing. All these things seemed to go together. How she would have to hurry up and live, to attract men and to love! What was the good of money and pretty clothes and fine motor-cars if one had not a man in one's life, a young lover? How she had waited for that lover! She had listened and given in to men who spoke to her of love when she was still a poor girl, because they were well dressed and because their hands were clean and well-kept. They were all fools. But she had never ceased waiting. And now was her last chance, the last years before old age, real, irreparable old age. She closed her eyes and imagined young lips and eager tender eyes, charged with desire.

Then hurriedly, as though she were preparing for a lover's tryst, she flung off her dressing-gown and began to array herself; she put on her stockings, her shoes and her dress with the peculiar agility of women who have had to do without maids all their lives. Jewelry; she had boxes full of it. Kampf used to say that it was the safest form of investment. She put on a big necklace consisting of a double row of pearls, all her rings and huge diamond bracelets which imprisoned her arms from wrist to elbow; then she pinned a large sapphire, ruby and emerald brooch on her bosom. She shone and glittered like a shrine. She stepped back a few paces and looked at herself with a happy smile. Life was beginning at last! That evening, perhaps, who could tell? . . . .

VI

Antoinette and her governess had finished eating their dinner from an ironing-board supported by two chairs in the linen-room. From the other side of the door came the sound of servants running about and of rattling dishes. Antoinette sat motionless, her hands clasped together between her knees. At nine o'clock Miss Betty looked at her watch.

"You must go to bed now, darling," she said. "You won't hear the music in the box-room and you'll sleep well there."

As Antoinette made no answer, the governess clapped her hands together playfully.

"Come, Antoinette, wake up; what's the matter with you?"

And she led her to the little badly-lit box-room, which had been hastily furnished with an iron bed-stead and two chairs. Opposite, across the court-yard, she could see the brilliantly lit windows of the dining-room and the drawing-room.

"There are no shutters, so you can see the people dance from here," said Miss Betty lightly.

When she was gone Antoinette pressed her forehead timidly and long-ingly against the window; a large section of the wall opposite was lit up by the warm golden brilliance of the windows. Shadows, those of the servants, kept passing rapidly to and fro behind the muslin curtains. Someone opened one of the windows, and Antoinette distinctly caught the sound of instru-ments being tuned at the far end of the drawing-room. The band was there already. Heavens! It was past nine o'clock. For a whole week she had been vaguely expecting some sort of catastrophe to occur which should swallow up the world before anything should be discovered; but the evening was passing just like any other evening. In a neighbouring flat a clock struck the half-hour. Another thirty minutes or three quarters of an hour and then. . . . Nothing would happen, of course, since, when they had come in that day, Madame Kampf had accosted Miss Betty with her usual impetuous-ness which made nervous people lose their heads at once, and had asked her: "Well? Did you post the invitations? You didn't lose any? You're sure?" And Miss Betty had replied: "Quite sure, Madame Kampf." Of course she alone was responsible. If she got the sack so much the worse for her; and so much the better too; it would teach her a lesson.

"I don't care, I don't care!" she stammered and she bit her knuckles with her sharp young teeth until they bled.

"And the other woman can do what she likes to me, I'm not afraid. I don't care!"

She gazed down into the deep, dark well the courtyard below.

"I shall kill myself and, before dying, I shall say that it is her fault, so there!" she muttered. "I'm not afraid of anything and I've already got my revenge!"

She renewed her vigil; the window became clouded by her breath; she wiped it impatiently and glued her face to it again and finally lost patience and opened the casement wide. The night air was fresh and sharp. Now, with the sharp eyes of fifteen, she could clearly distinguish the chairs ranged along the wall and the band grouped round the piano. She stood there without moving for so long that her cheeks and her bare arms grew numb with cold. For a moment she deceived herself into believing that nothing had happened and that she had dreamed of the bridge, the dark waters of the Seine and the torn invitations floating in the wind, that the guests would arrive miraculously and that the party would soon begin. She heard the three-quarters strike and then ten strokes—*the* ten strokes—at which she shuddered and slipped out through the door.

She made her way to the drawing-room like a murderer being drawn back to the scene of his first crime. She crossed the passage where two waiters with their heads tilted back were drinking champagne out of bottles. She reached the dining-room. It was empty and all ready with the large table in the centre loaded with game, fish in aspic, linen edged with Venetian lace, flowers spread between the dishes and fruit piled into two equal pyramids. All around, tables laid for four or six glittered with glass, fine china, silver and silver-gilt. Afterwards, Antoinette could never understand how she had dared to walk right through that huge room, twinkling with lights. She hesitated a moment on the threshold of the drawing-room and then she caught sight of the big silk-covered sofa in the neighbouring boudoir. She went down on her hands and knees and slid between the back of the sofa and the hanging curtains; there was just enough room for her there if she kept her arms and knees close to her body, and by craning her head forward she could see the drawing-room as though she were looking at the stage of a theatre. She was shivering a little, still frozen from her long wait before the open window. At present the room was calm and silent and half asleep. The musicians were talking together in low voices. There was a negro with dazzling teeth, a lady in a silk dress, cymbals as big as the big drum at a country fair and something like an enormous 'cello standing in one corner. The negro sighed and swept his finger-nails over the strings of a kind of guitar which gave out a dull moaning sound.

"People start and finish later and later nowadays."

The pianist said something which Antoinette could not catch and which made the others laugh. Then Monsieur and Madame Kampf came in briskly.

When Antoinette saw them she cowered back instinctively, as though trying to dig herself into the ground; she huddled against the wall with her mouth hidden in the crook of her bent arm; but she could hear their footsteps approaching. They were quite close to her now. Kampf sat down in an armchair facing Antoinette. Rosine walked about the room for a moment or two; she lit the bracket-lamps on each side of the mantelpiece and turned them out again. She was glittering with diamonds.

"Sit down," said Kampf in a low voice. "It's silly to get agitated like this."

She placed herself in such a position that Antoinette, who had opened her eyes and thrust forward her head until it touched the back of the sofa, could see her mother standing before her and she was struck by the expression on that usually arrogant face, an expression which she had never seen before: a mixture of humility, of fervour and of fear.

"Do you think it will be all right, Alfred?" she asked in the clear, uncertain accents of a little child.

Alfred had no time to reply, for the bell echoed shrilly through the flat. Rosine clasped her hands.

"Oh, heavens, it's starting!" she whispered, as though talking of an earthquake.

They hurried towards the open doors of the drawing-room.

A moment later Antoinette saw them return, one on each side of Mademoiselle Isabelle, who was talking very loudly, in a voice entirely different from her usual one, rather high and staccato, with little bursts of laughter.

"I'd forgotten all about her," thought Antoinette horrified.

Madame Kampf, now radiant, chattered unceasingly; she had recovered her arrogance; she winked maliciously at her husband, furtively calling his attention to Mademoiselle Isabelle's dress, which was made of yellow muslin, while round her long lean neck she wore a feather boa which she kept twisting coquettishly with her hands: a silver lorgnette hung from the end of an orange velvet ribbon round her wrist.

"I don't think you know this room, Isabelle?"

"No, but it's very pretty. Who furnished it for you? Oh, what lovely little vases! I see you still like the Japanese style, Rosine. I myself always defend it; I was only saying the other day to the Bloch-Lévys, you know, the Solomon Bloch-Lévys, who declared that it was in bad taste and had a suggestion of *nouveau-riche* (according to their own expression): 'You may say what you like, but it's gay and lively and the fact that it is cheaper than Louis-Quinze is not a fault but quite the opposite.'"

"But you're very much mistaken, Isabelle," protested Rosine eagerly. "Early Chinese and Japanese objects fetch fantastic prices. For instance, for that vase with the birds on it . . ."

"Not a very good period . . ."

". . . my husband paid ten thousand francs at auction. What did I say? Ten thousand? Twelve thousand, wasn't it, Alfred? I scolded him at the time, but not for long; I love rummaging about in antique shops. It's a real passion of mine."

Kampf rang the bell.

"I'm sure you'd like a glass of port, wouldn't you, ladies? Oh, George," he said as the footman came in, "bring in three glasses of Sandeman's port and some sandwiches—some caviare sandwiches."

As Mademoiselle Isabelle moved away to examine a Buddha seated on a velvet cushion through her lorgnette, Madame Kampf hissed in her husband's ear:

"Sandwiches? You must be mad. You're not going to have the whole arrangement of the table spoiled for her! George, bring the cakes in the Dresden dish; you know which the Dresden dish is?"

"Yes, Madame."

He returned in a moment with the cake-dish and a cut-glass decanter. The three of them drank in silence. Then Madame Kampf and Mademoiselle Isabelle sat down on the sofa behind which Antoinette was hidden. By stretching out her hand she could have touched her mother's silver shoes and her music teacher's yellow satin slippers. Kampf walked up and down, casting furtive glances at the clock.

"Tell me who is coming to-night," asked Mademoiselle Isabelle.

"Oh," replied Rosine, "some charming people, and some old bores too, like the Marquise de San Palacio, to whom I owe an invitation; but she does love coming here so much. I saw her yesterday and she told me that she had really meant to be away. She said to me: 'My dear, I've put off my departure for the South for a week because of your party: it's always so amusing at your house!' "

"Oh, so you've given balls before?" asked Mademoiselle Isabelle, pursing her lips.

"Oh, no!" Madame Kampf hastened to explain. "Only tea-parties; I did not ask you because I know how terribly busy you are in the day-time."

"Yes, indeed; besides, I am thinking of giving some concerts next year . . ."

"Really? That's an excellent idea."

They stopped talking. Mademoiselle Isabelle resumed her inspection of the walls.

"It's charming, quite charming, and such taste!"

Silence fell again. Both ladies cleared their throats and Isabelle carefully arranged the folds of her dress.

"What lovely weather we have been having lately, haven't we?"

Kampf suddenly interrupted:

"Come, we can't sit like this, like dummies. How late everyone is. You did say ten o'clock on the invitations, didn't you, Rosine?"

"I'm afraid I came much too early."

"Not at all, my dear; what do you mean? It's a very bad habit to arrive late; quite deplorable."

"Let's have a dance," said Kampf, playfully clapping his hands.

"That's a very good idea!" cried Madame Kampf and, turning to the orchestra: "You may begin to play: play a charleston. Do you dance the charleston, Isabelle?"

"Yes, a little, like everyone else."

"Well, you won't lack partners. The Marquis de Itcharra, for instance, who's a nephew of the Spanish Ambassador, takes all the prizes at Deauville, doesn't he, Rosine? In the meantime let's open the ball."

They went off together and the band blared out through the deserted room. Antoinette saw Madame Kampf get up, run over to the window and in her turn glue her face to the pane. The clock struck half-past ten.

"Heavens! What on earth has happened to them all?" whispered Madame Kampf distractedly. "I wish that silly old frump would go to blazes," she added, almost aloud and then she clapped her hands and cried laughingly:

"Charming, charming! I didn't know you danced so well, Isabelle!"

"Why, she dances like Josephine Baker herself," put in Kampf from the other end of the room.

At the end of the dance Kampf called out:

"Rosine, I'm taking Isabelle to the bar. Don't be jealous!"

"But won't you come too, dear?"

"Excuse me for half a moment. I've a few orders to give the servants and then I'll join you."

"I warn you, Rosine, I'm going to flirt with Isabelle the whole evening."

Madame Kampf forced herself to laugh and to wag a threatening finger at them; but she said nothing and, as soon as she was alone, she hurried back to the window. She could hear the motor-cars going up and down the Avenue; some of them slowed down before the house; then Madame Kampf craned forward and scanned the cold dark street with her eyes, but the cars passed on, the sound of their engines growing fainter in the distance and finally dying down into the shadows. Besides, as time went on even the motor-cars became scarcer and scarcer and for minutes together there was not a sound in the street, which might have been a street in a provincial town. Nothing but the rumble of the tramcars in a near-by street and the far-off sound of motor horns, softened by distance.

Rosine's teeth chattered as though she had a chill. A quarter to eleven. Ten to eleven. In the empty drawing-room a clock struck with a busy, silvery little sound, brisk and clear. The dining-room clock echoed it and from the other side of the street a large church clock boomed out slowly and solemnly, growing louder and louder with each succeeding stroke.

"Nine, ten, eleven," cried Madame Kampf, raising her diamond-studded arms up to heaven. "What on earth's the matter? But what in the name of God has happened?"

Alfred returned with Isabelle; all three looked at one another in silence. Madame Kampf laughed nervously:

"It's a little odd, isn't it? I hope nothing has happened."

"But my dear, nothing but an earthquake . . ." began Mademoiselle Isabelle, in a triumphant voice.

But Madame Kampf was not going to give in yet. Fingering her pearls she said, in a voice hoarse with anxiety:

"It doesn't mean anything. The other day, when I was with my friend the Countess de Brunelleschi, the first guests only began to come at a quarter to twelve. So that . . ."

"It's very annoying for the hostess, very exasperating," muttered Isabelle softly.

"Oh, one gets used to it, doesn't one?"

At that moment the bell rang. Alfred and Rosine hurled themselves towards the door.

"Play!" cried Rosine to the band.

They started vigorously attacking a blues. No one came. Rosine could not contain herself any longer. She called out:

"George, George! The bell! Didn't you hear it?"

"It's only the ices from Rey's."

Madame Kampf burst out:

"But I tell you something must have happened, an accident, a misunderstanding, a mistake in the date or the time, or something, I don't know what. Ten past eleven. It's ten past eleven!" she repeated despairingly.

"Ten past eleven already?" exclaimed Mademoiselle Isabelle. "Really time does fly in your house. I congratulate you. Actually it's a quarter past; I think I heard it strike."

"Well, they won't be long now!" said Kampf in a loud voice.

They all sat down again, but they no longer talked. They could hear the servants laughing uproariously in the pantry.

"Go and make them be quiet, Alfred," said Rosine at length, in a voice trembling with rage. "Go along at once."

At half past eleven the pianist came up.

"Shall we wait any longer, Madame?"

"No! Go away, all of you!" cried Rosine roughly, on the verge of hysterics. "We'll give you your money and then you can go! There won't be any ball, or anything. It's an outrage, an insult, a trick played on us by our enemies to make us a laughing-stock. If anyone comes now they're not to be let in, do you hear?" she continued with increasing violence. "Tell them that there's illness in the house, death, anything you like!"

Mademoiselle Isabelle tried to calm her.

"Come, dear, it isn't quite hopeless yet. Don't torment yourself like this. You'll make yourself ill. Naturally, I understand your feelings, my poor dear friend; but the world is so cruel, alas! You ought to say something to her, Alfred, to soothe her and console her. . . ."

"What a farce!" hissed Kampf between his clenched teeth, his face white with rage. "Are you going to be quiet?"

"Come, Alfred, don't scream at her; try to calm her."

"Why, if she wants to make a fool of herself?"

He turned sharply on his heel and addressed the band:

"Why are you still here? How much do I owe you? And clear out at once, for God's sake."

Mademoiselle Isabelle slowly picked up her feather boa, her lorgnette and her bag.

"I think I had better go, Alfred, unless I can be of any use to you, my poor friend."

As he did not answer she bent down and kissed Rosine on the forehead. Rosine did not move, she did not even cry, but sat there with dry, staring eyes.

"Good-bye, darling, and believe me when I tell you that I am deeply distressed and that I offer you my most sincere sympathy," said Mademoiselle Isabelle mechanically, as though she were at a funeral. "No, no! There's no need to see me home, Alfred. I'm going at once. Have a good cry, Rosine, it helps a lot," she called out at the top of her voice from the centre of the deserted room.

Alfred and Rosine heard her tell the servants as she passed through the dining-room:

"Take care not to make a noise. Madame is very much upset and very overwrought."

Then came the drone of the lift and the distant sound of the street door being opened and shut.

"Old bitch!" muttered Kampf. "If only . . ."

He did not finish his sentence. Rosine sprang up from the sofa, her face streaming with tears, and shook her fist at him, shouting:

"It's your fault, you old fool! It's your filthy vanity, your stupid pride! It's all your fault. His lordship wants to give balls, to hold receptions! It's too ridiculous for words! Do you think that nobody knows who you are, and where you came from? *Nouveau riche!* They've made a nice fool of you, your fine friends! Thieves! Crooks!"

"And what about yours? Your Counts and Marquises and pimps?"

They went on shouting both at once, in a torrent of violent, passionate abuse. Then Kampf lowered his voice and said, between his teeth:

"When I picked you up you had already racketed about God knows where. Did you flatter yourself that I didn't know all about it and that I never noticed anything? I thought you were pretty and intelligent and that if I became rich you would be a credit to me. And look at you now! The manners of a fish-wife, a stupid old woman with the manners of a cook."

"Other people have been perfectly satisfied with me."

"I doubt it. But don't enter into details. You'll be sorry tomorrow if you do."

"Tomorrow? Do you think I'll stop another hour with you, after what you've said to me? Beast!"

"Get out, then! Go to hell!"

He left the room, slamming the door after him.

Rosine shouted:

"Come back, Alfred!"

And she waited, her head turned towards the drawing-room, breathing hard. But he had already gone down the stairs. In the street she could hear him angrily calling for a taxi; and then his voice died away round a corner.

The servants had gone to bed, leaving all the lights on and all the doors open. Rosine collapsed into an armchair in her bright dress and her pearls.

She suddenly made a violent movement, so abrupt and so sudden that it made Antoinette start, and in doing so she struck her forehead against the wall. She cowered further back, but her mother had heard nothing and was tearing off her bracelets and throwing them one by one onto the floor. One of them, a beautiful, heavy bracelet set with enormous diamonds, rolled under the sofa to Antoinette's feet. Antoinette stared at it, unable to move hand or foot.

She looked at her mother's face, down which the tears coursed, mixing with the paint; a wrinkled, distorted, purple, childish, comic, pathetic face. But Antoinette was not touched; she felt nothing but a sort of disdain, of scornful indifference. Later she would say to some man: "Oh, you know I was a dreadful little girl. On one occasion . . ."

She suddenly felt the richness of her future and of her untried strength and of being able to think: "How can one cry like that for such a cause? And love? And death? She will die one day. Has she forgotten that?"

So grown-up people suffered so deeply for futile, passing things. And she, Antoinette, had been afraid of them, had trembled before them and their shouting and anger and their vain, absurd threats. Slowly she crept out from her hiding-place. For a moment longer, hidden in the shadow, she contemplated her mother, who was not sobbing, but was completely absorbed in herself, her tears flowing down to her mouth without her making any attempt to dry them. Then she got up and went over to her.

"Mother!"

Madame Kampf started up in her chair.

"What do you want? What are you doing here?" she cried in confusion. "Go away, go away at once and leave me alone. I can't get a moment's peace in my own house these days!"

Antoinette, rather pale, stood her ground with her head bowed. The sound of her mother's voice rang in her ears, but it sounded weak now and had lost its power over her, and reminded her of stage thunder. One day, soon, she would say to some man: "Mother will make a fuss, but never mind. . . ."

She put out her hand gently and placed it on her mother's hair, which she stroked with light, trembling fingers.

"Poor Mother! . . ." she began.

For a moment longer Rosine struggled automatically, thrust her away and shook her head convulsively:

"Leave me alone! Go away! Leave me alone, I tell you!"

And then a weak, broken, pitiful expression passed over her features.

"Oh, my poor child, my poor little Antoinette! You're very lucky; you don't yet know how unfair and wicked and cynical the world is. All those people who smiled at me and invited me to their parties, were all laughing at me behind my back and despised me because I was not of their world. A lot of brutes, of . . . But you can't understand, my poor child! And your father! I've no one but you now!" she wound up suddenly. "No one but you, my poor little child!"

She took her into her arms and, as she pressed the mute little face to her pearls, she saw that it was not smiling.

"You're a good girl, Antoinette."

It was the moment, the imperceptible moment when "on the path of life" they crossed and one was going to go on upward and the other to sink into the gloom. But they were unaware of this. And yet Antoinette repeated softly:

"Poor Mother!"

KNEEL TO THE RISING SUN

Erskine Caldwell

(1902–)

A SHIVER went through Lonnie. He drew his hand away from his sharp chin, remembering what Clem had said. It made him feel now as if he were committing a crime by standing in Arch Gunnard's presence and allowing his face to be seen.

He and Clem had been walking up the road together that afternoon on their way to the filling station when he told Clem how much he needed rations. Clem stopped a moment to kick a rock out of the road, and said that if you worked for Arch Gunnard long enough, your face would be sharp enough to split the boards for your own coffin.

As Lonnie turned away to sit down on an empty box beside the gasoline pump, he could not help wishing that he could be as unafraid of Arch Gunnard as Clem was. Even if Clem was a Negro, he never hesitated to ask for rations when he needed something to eat; and when he and his family did not get enough, Clem came right out and told Arch so. Arch stood for that, but he swore that he was going to run Clem out of the country the first chance he got.

Lonnie knew without turning around that Clem was standing at the corner of the filling station with two or three other Negroes and looking at him, but for some reason he was unable to meet Clem's eyes.

Arch Gunnard was sitting in the sun, honing his jack-knife blade on his boot top. He glanced once or twice at Lonnie's hound, Nancy, who was lying in the middle of the road waiting for Lonnie to go home.

"That your dog, Lonnie?"

Jumping with fear, Lonnie's hand went to his chin to hide the lean face that would accuse Arch of short-rationing.

Arch snapped his fingers and the hound stood up, wagging her tail. She waited to be called.

"Mr. Arch, I——"

Arch called the dog. She began crawling towards them on her belly, wagging her tail a little faster each time Arch's fingers snapped. When she was several feet away, she turned over on her back and lay on the ground with her four paws in the air.

Dudley Smith and Jim Weaver, who were lounging around the filling station, laughed. They had been leaning against the side of the building, but they straightened up to see what Arch was up to.

Arch spat some more tobacco juice on his boot top and whetted the jack-knife blade some more.

"What kind of a hound dog is that, anyway, Lonnie?" Arch said. "Looks like to me it might be a ketch hound."

Lonnie could feel Clem Henry's eyes boring into the back of his head. He wondered what Clem would do if it had been his dog Arch Gunnard was snapping his fingers at and calling like that.

"His tail's way too long for a coon hound or a bird dog, ain't it, Arch?" somebody behind Lonnie said, laughing out loud.

Everybody laughed then, including Arch. They looked at Lonnie, waiting to hear what he was going to say to Arch.

"Is he a ketch hound, Lonnie?" Arch said, snapping his finger again.

"Mr. Arch, I——"

"Don't be ashamed of him, Lonnie, if he don't show signs of turning out to be a bird dog or a fox hound. Everybody needs a hound around the house that can go out and catch pigs and rabbits when you are in a hurry for them. A ketch hound is a mightly respectable animal. I've known the time when I was mighty proud to own one."

Everybody laughed.

Arch Gunnard was getting ready to grab Nancy by the tail. Lonnie sat up, twisting his neck until he caught a glimpse of Clem Henry at the other corner of the filling station. Clem was staring at him with unmistakable meaning, with the same look in his eyes he had had that afternoon when he said that nobody who worked for Arch Gunnard ought to stand for short-rationing. Lonnie lowered his eyes. He could not figure out how a Negro could be braver than he was. There were a lot of times like that when he would have given anything he had to be able to jump into Clem's shoes and change places with him.

"The trouble with this hound of yours, Lonnie, is that he's too heavy on his feet. Don't you reckon it would be a pretty slick little trick to lighten the load some, being as how he's a ketch hound to begin with?"

Lonnie remembered then what Clem Henry had said he would do if Arch Gunnard ever tried to cut off his dog's tail. Lonnie knew, and Clem knew, and everybody else knew, that that would give Arch the chance he was waiting for. All Arch asked, he had said, was for Clem Henry to overstep his place just one little half-inch, or to talk back to him with just one little short word, and he would do the rest. Everybody knew what Arch meant by that, especially if Clem did not turn and run. And Clem had not been known to run from anybody, after fifteen years in the country.

Arch reached down and grabbed Nancy's tail while Lonnie was wondering about Clem. Nancy acted as if she thought Arch were playing some kind of a game with her. She turned her head around until she could reach Arch's hand to lick it. He cracked her on the bridge of the nose with the end of the jackknife.

"He's a mighty playful dog, Lonnie," Arch said, catching up a shorter grip on the tail, "but his wagpole is way too long for a dog his size, especially when he wants to be a ketch hound."

Lonnie swallowed hard.

"Mr. Arch, she's a mighty fine rabbit tracker. I——"

"Shucks, Lonnie," Arch said, whetting the knife blade on the dog's tail, "I aint never seen a hound in all my life that needed a tail that long to hunt rabbits with. It's way too long for just a common, ordinary, everyday ketch hound."

Lonnie looked up hopefully at Dudley Smith and the others. None of them offered any help. It was useless for him to try to stop Arch, because Arch Gunnard would let nothing stand in his way when once he had set his head on what he wished to do. Lonnie knew that if he should let himself show any anger or resentment, Arch would drive him off the farm before sundown that night. Clem Henry was the only person there who would help him, but Clem . . .

The white men and the Negroes at both corners of the filling station waited to see what Lonnie was going to do about it. All of them hoped he would put up a fight for his hound. If anyone ever had the nerve to stop

Arch Gunnard from cutting off a dog's tail, it might put an end to it. It was plain, though, that Lonnie, who was one of Arch's share-croppers, was afraid to speak up. Clem Henry might; Clem was the only one who might try to stop Arch, even if it meant trouble. All of them knew that Arch would insist on running Clem out of the country, or filling him full of lead.

"I reckon it's all right with you, aint it, Lonnie?" Arch said. "I don't seem to hear no objections."

Clem Henry stepped forward several paces, and stopped.

Arch laughed, watching Lonnie's face, and jerked Nancy to her feet. The hound cried out in pain and surprise, but Arch made her be quiet by kicking her in the belly.

Lonnie winced. He could hardly bear to see anybody kick his dog like that.

"Mr. Arch, I . . ."

A contraction in his throat almost choked him for several moments, and he had to open his mouth wide and fight for breath. The other white men around him were silent. Nobody liked to see a dog kicked in the belly like that.

Lonnie could see the other end of the filling station from the corner of his eye. He saw a couple of Negroes go up behind Clem and grasp his overalls. Clem spat on the ground, between outspread feet, but he did not try to break away from them.

"Being as how I don't hear no objections, I reckon it's all right to go ahead and cut it off," Arch said, spitting.

Lonnie's head went forward and all he could see of Nancy was her hind feet. He had come to ask for a slab of sowbelly and some molasses, or something. Now he did not know if he could ever bring himself to ask for rations, no matter how much hungrier they became at home.

"I always make it a habit of asking a man first," Arch said. "I wouldn't want to go ahead and cut off a tail if a man had any objections. That wouldn't be right. No, sir, it just wouldn't be fair and square."

Arch caught a shorter grip on the hound's tail and placed the knife blade on it two or three inches from the rump. It looked to those who were watching as if his mouth were watering, because tobacco juice began to trickle down the corners of his lips. He brought up the back of his hand and wiped his mouth.

A noisy automobile came plowing down the road through the deep red dust. Everyone looked up as it passed in order to see who was in it.

Lonnie glanced at it, but he could not keep his eyes raised. His head fell downward once more until he could feel his sharp chin cutting into his chest. He wondered then if Arch had noticed how lean his face was.

"I keep two or three ketch hounds around my place," Arch said, honing the blade on the tail of the dog as if it were a razor strop until his actions brought smiles to the faces of the men grouped around him, "but I never could see the sense of a ketch hound having a long tail. It only gets in their way when I send them out to catch a pig or a rabbit for my supper."

Pulling with his left hand and pushing with his right, Arch Gunnard docked the hound's tail as quickly and as easily as if he were cutting a willow switch in the pasture to drive the cows home with. The dog sprang forward with the release of her tail until she was far beyond Arch's reach, and began howling so loud she could be heard half a mile away. Nancy stopped once and looked back at Arch, and then she sprang to the middle of the road and began leaping and twisting in circles. All that time she was yelping and biting at the bleeding stub of her tail.

Arch leaned backward and twirled the severed tail in one hand while he wiped the jack-knife blade on his boot sole. He watched Lonnie's dog chasing herself around in circles in the red dust.

Nobody had anything to say then. Lonnie tried not to watch his dog's agony, and he forced himself to keep from looking at Clem Henry. Then, with his eyes shut, he wondered why he had remained on Arch Gunnard's plantation all those past years, share-cropping for a mere living on short-rations, and becoming leaner and leaner all the time. He knew then how true it was what Clem had said about Arch's share-croppers' faces becoming sharp enough to hew their own coffins. His hands went to his chin before he knew what he was doing. His hand dropped when he had felt the bones of jaw and the exposed tendons of his cheeks.

As hungry as he was, he knew that even if Arch did give him some rations then, there would not be nearly enough for them to eat for the following week. Hatty, his wife, was already broken down from hunger and work in the fields, and his father, Mark Newsome, stone-deaf for the past twenty years, was always asking him why there was never enough food in the house for them to have a solid meal. Lonnie's head fell forward a little more, and he could feel his eyes becoming damp.

The pressure of his sharp chin against his chest made him so uncomfortable that he had to raise his head at last in order to ease the pain of it.

The first thing he saw when he looked up was Arch Gunnard twirling Nancy's tail in his left hand. Arch Gunnard had a trunk full of dogs' tails at home. He had been cutting off tails ever since anyone could remember, and during all those years he had accumulated a collection of which he was so proud that he kept the trunk locked and the key tied around his neck on a string. On Sunday afternoons when the preacher came to visit, or when a crowd was there to loll on the front porch and swap stories, Arch showed them off, naming each tail from memory just as well as if he had had a tag on it.

Clem Henry had left the filling station and was walking alone down the road towards the plantation. Clem Henry's house was in a cluster of Negro cabins below Arch's big house, and he had to pass Lonnie's house to get there. Lonnie was on the verge of getting up and leaving when he saw Arch looking at him. He did not know whether Arch was looking at his lean face, or whether he was watching to see if he were going to get up and go down the road with Clem.

The thought of leaving reminded him of his reason for being there. He had to have some rations before suppertime that night, no matter how short they were.

"Mr. Arch, I . . ."

Arch stared at him for a moment, appearing as if he had turned to listen to some strange sound unheard of before that moment.

Lonnie bit his lips, wondering if Arch was going to say anything about how lean and hungry he looked. But Arch was thinking about something else. He slapped his hand on his leg and laughed out loud.

"I sometimes wish niggers had tails," Arch said, coiling Nancy's tail into a ball and putting it into his pocket. "I'd a heap rather cut off nigger tails than dog tails. There'd be more to cut, for one thing."

Dudley Smith and somebody else behind them laughed for a brief moment. The laughter died out almost as suddenly as it had risen.

The Negroes who had heard Arch shuffled their feet in the dust and moved backwards. It was only a few minutes until not one was left at the filling station. They went up the road behind the red wooden building until they were out of sight.

Arch got up and stretched. The sun was getting low, and it was no longer comfortable in the October air. "Well, I reckon I'll be getting on home to get me some supper," he said.

He walked slowly to the middle of the road and stopped to look at Nancy retreating along the ditch.

"Nobody going my way?" he asked. "What's wrong with you, Lonnie? Going home to supper, aint you?"

"Mr. Arch, I . . ."

Lonnie found himself jumping to his feet. His first thought was to ask for the sowbelly and molasses, and maybe some corn meal; but when he opened his mouth, the words refused to come out. He took several steps forward and shook his head. He did not know what Arch might say or do if he said "no."

"Hatty'll be looking for you," Arch said, turning his back and walking off.

He reached into his hip pocket and took out Nancy's tail. He began twirling it as he walked down the road towards the big house in the distance.

Dudley Smith went inside the filling station, and the others walked away.

After Arch had gone several hundred yards, Lonnie sat down heavily on the box beside the gas pump from which he had got up when Arch spoke to him. He sat down heavily, his shoulders drooping, his arms falling between his outspread legs.

Lonnie did not know how long his eyes had been closed, but when he opened them, he saw Nancy lying between his feet, licking the docked tail. While he watched her, he felt the sharp point of his chin cutting into his chest again. Presently the door behind him was slammed shut, and a minute later he could hear Dudley Smith walking away from the filling station on his way home.

II

Lonnie had been sleeping fitfully for several hours when he suddenly found himself wide awake. Hatty shook him again. He raised himself on his elbow and tried to see into the darkness of the room. Without knowing what time it was, he was able to determine that it was still nearly two hours until sunrise.

"Lonnie," Hatty said again, trembling in the cold night air, "Lonnie, your pa aint in the house."

Lonnie sat upright in bed.

"How do you know he aint?" he said.

"I've been lying here wide awake ever since I got in bed, and I heard him when he went out. He's been gone all that time."

"Maybe he just stepped out for a while," Lonnie said, turning and trying to see through the bedroom window.

"I know what I'm saying, Lonnie," Hatty insisted. "Your pa's been gone a heap too long."

Both of them sat without a sound for several minutes while they listened for Mark Newsome.

Lonnie got up and lit a lamp. He shivered while he was putting on his shirt, overalls, and shoes. He tied his shoelaces in hard knots because he couldn't see in the faint light. Outside the window it was almost pitch-dark, and Lonnie could feel the damp October air blowing against his face.

"I'll go help look," Hatty said, throwing the covers off and starting to get up.

Lonnie went to the bed and drew the covers back over her and pushed her back into place.

"You try to get some sleep, Hatty," he said; "you can't stay awake the whole night. I'll go bring Pa back."

He left Hatty, blowing out the lamp, and stumbled through the dark hall, feeling his way to the front porch by touching the wall with his hands. When he got to the porch, he could still barely see any distance ahead, but his eyes were becoming more accustomed to the darkness. He waited a minute, listening.

Feeling his way down the steps into the yard, he walked around the corner of the house and stopped to listen again before calling his father.

"Oh, Pa!" he said loudly. "Oh, Pa!"

He stopped under the bedroom window when he realized what he had been doing.

"Now that's a fool thing for me to be out here doing," he said, scolding himself. "Pa couldn't hear it thunder."

He heard a rustling of the bed.

"He's been gone long enough to get clear to the crossroads, or more," Hatty said, calling through the window.

"Now you lay down and try to get a little sleep, Hatty," Lonnie told her. "I'll bring him back in no time."

He could hear Nancy scratching fleas under the house, but he knew she was in no condition to help look for Mark. It would be several days before she recovered from the shock of losing her tail.

"He's been gone a long time," Hatty said, unable to keep still.

"That don't make no difference," Lonnie said. "I'll find him sooner or later. Now you go on to sleep like I told you, Hatty."

Lonnie walked towards the barn, listening for some sound. Over at the big house he could hear the hogs grunting and squealing, and he wished they would be quiet so he could hear other sounds. Arch Gunnard's dogs were howling occasionally, but they were not making any more noise than they usually did at night, and he was accustomed to their howling.

Lonnie went to the barn, looking inside and out. After walking around the barn, he went into the field as far as the cotton shed. He knew it was useless, but he could not keep from calling his father time after time.

"Oh, Pa!" he said, trying to penetrate the darkness.

He went further into the field.

"Now, what in the world could have become of Pa?" he said, stopping and wondering where to look next.

After he had gone back to the front yard, he began to feel uneasy for the first time. Mark had not acted any more strangely during the past week than he ordinarily did, but Lonnie knew he was upset over the way Arch Gunnard was giving out short-rations. Mark had even said that, at the rate they were being fed, all of them would starve to death inside another three months.

Lonnie left the yard and went down the road towards the Negro cabins. When he got to Clem's house, he turned in and walked up the path to the door. He knocked several times and waited. There was no answer, and he rapped louder.

"Who's that?" he heard Clem say from bed.

"It's me," Lonnie said. "I've got to see you a minute, Clem. I'm out in the front yard."

He sat down and waited for Clem to dress and come outside. While he waited, he strained his ears to catch any sound that might be in the air.

Over the fields towards the big house he could hear the fattening hogs grunt and squeal.

Clem came out and shut the door. He stood on the doorsill a moment speaking to his wife in bed, telling her he would be back and not to worry.

"Who's that?" Clem said, coming down into the yard.

Lonnie got up and met Clem half-way.

"What's the trouble?" Clem asked then, buttoning up his overall jumper.

"Pa's not in his bed," Lonnie said, "and Hatty says he's been gone from the house most all night. I went out in the field, and all around the barn, but I couldn't find a trace of him anywhere."

Clem then finished buttoning his jumper and began rolling a cigarette. He walked slowly down the path to the road. It was still dark, and it would be at least an hour before dawn made it any lighter.

"Maybe he was too hungry to stay in bed any longer," Clem said. "When I saw him yesterday, he said he was so shrunk up and weak he didn't know if he could last much longer. He looked like his skin and bones couldn't shrivel much more."

"I asked Arch last night after suppertime for some rations—just a little piece of sowbelly and some molasses. He said he'd get around to letting me have some the first thing this morning."

"Why don't you tell him to give you full rations or none?" Clem said. "If you knew you wasn't going to get none at all, you could move away and find a better man to share-crop for, couldn't you?"

"I've been loyal to Arch Gunnard for a long time now," Lonnie said. "I'd hate to haul off and leave him like that."

Clem looked at Lonnie, but he did not say anything more just then. They turned up the road towards the driveway that led up to the big house. The fattening hogs were still grunting and squealing in the pen, and one of Arch's hounds came down a cotton row beside the driveway to smell their shoes.

"Them fattening hogs always get enough to eat," Clem said. "There's not a one of them that don't weigh seven hundred pounds right now, and they're getting bigger every day. Besides taking all that's thrown to them, they make a lot of meals off the chickens that get in there to peck around."

Lonnie listened to the grunting of the hogs as they walked up the driveway towards the big house.

"Reckon we'd better get Arch up to help look for Pa?" Lonnie said. "I'd hate to wake him up, but I'm scared Pa might stray off into the swamp and get lost for good. He couldn't hear it thunder, even. I never could find him back there in all that tangle if he got into it."

Clem said something under his breath and went on towards the barn and hog pen. He reached the pen before Lonnie got there.

"You'd better come here quick," Clem said, turning around to see where Lonnie was.

Lonnie ran to the hog pen. He stopped and climbed half-way up the wooden-and-wire sides of the fence. At first he could see nothing, but gradually he was able to see the moving mass of black fattening hogs on the other side of the pen. They were biting and snarling at each other like a pack of hungry hounds turned loose on a dead rabbit.

Lonnie scrambled to the top of the fence, but Clem caught him and pulled him back.

"Don't go in that hog pen that way," he said. "Them hogs will tear you to pieces, they're that wild. They're fighting over something."

Both of them ran around the corner of the pen and got to the side where the hogs were. Down under their feet on the ground Lonnie caught a glimpse of a dark mass splotched with white. He was able to see it for a moment only, because one of the hogs trampled over it.

Clem opened and closed his mouth several times before he was able to say anything at all. He clutched at Lonnie's arm, shaking him.

"That looks like it might be your pa," he said. "I swear before goodness, Lonnie, it does look like it."

Lonnie still could not believe it. He climbed to the top of the fence and began kicking his feet at the hogs, trying to drive them away. They paid no attention to him.

While Lonnie was perched there, Clem had gone to the wagon shed, and he ran back with two singletrees he had somehow managed to find there in the dark. He handed one to Lonnie, poking it at him until Lonnie's attention was drawn from the hogs long enough to take it.

Clem leaped over the fence and began swinging the singletree at the hogs. Lonnie slid down beside him, yelling at them. One hog turned on Lonnie and snapped at him, and Clem struck it over the back of the neck with enough force to drive it off momentarily.

By then Lonnie was able to realize what had happened. He ran to the mass of hogs, kicking them with his heavy stiff shoes and striking them on their heads with the iron-tipped singletree. Once he felt a stinging sensation, and looked down to see one of the hogs biting the calf of his leg. He had just enough time to hit the hog and drive it away before his leg was torn. He knew most of his overall leg had been ripped away, because he could feel the night air on his bare wet calf.

Clem had gone ahead and had driven the hogs back. There was no other way to do anything. They were in a snarling circle around them, and both of them had to keep the singletrees swinging back and forth all the time to keep the hogs off. Finally Lonnie reached down and got a grip on Mark's leg. With Clem helping, Lonnie carried his father to the fence and lifted him over to the other side.

They were too much out of breath for a while to say anything, or to do anything else. The snarling fattening hogs were at the fence, biting the wood and wire, and making more noise than ever.

While Lonnie was searching in his pockets for a match, Clem struck one. He held the flame close to Mark Newsome's head.

They both stared unbelievingly, and then Clem blew out the match. There was nothing said as they stared at each other in the darkness.

Clem walked several steps away, and turned and came back beside Lonnie.

"It's him, though," Clem said, sitting down on the ground. "It's him, all right."

"I reckon so," Lonnie said. He could think of nothing else to say then.

They sat on the ground, one on each side of Mark, looking at the body. There had been no sign of life in the body beside them since they had first touched it. The face, throat, and stomach had been completely devoured.

"You'd better go wake up Arch Gunnard," Clem said after a while.

"What for?" Lonnie said. "He can't help none now. It's too late for help."

"Makes no difference," Clem insisted. "You'd better go wake him up and let him see what there is to see. If you wait till morning, he might take it into his head to say the hogs didn't do it. Right now is the time to get him up so he can see what his hogs did."

Clem turned around and looked at the big house. The dark outline against the dark sky made him hesitate.

"A man who short-rations tenants ought to have to sit and look at that till it's buried."

Lonnie looked at Clem fearfully. He knew Clem was right, but he was scared to hear a Negro say anything like that about a white man.

"You oughtn't talk like that about Arch," Lonnie said. "He's in bed asleep. He didn't have a thing to do with it. He didn't have no more to do with it than I did."

Clem laughed a little, and threw the singletree on the ground between his feet. After letting it lie there a little while, he picked it up and began beating the ground with it.

Lonnie got to his feet slowly. He had never seen Clem act like that before, and he did not know what to think about it. He left without saying anything and walked stiffly to the house in the darkness to wake up Arch Gunnard.

III

Arch was hard to wake up. And even after he was awake, he was in no hurry to get up. Lonnie was standing outside the bedroom window, and Arch was lying in bed six or eight feet away. Lonnie could hear him toss and grumble.

"Who told you to come and wake me up in the middle of the night?" Arch said.

"Well, Clem Henry's out here, and he said maybe you'd like to know about it."

Arch tossed around on the bed, flailing the pillow with his fists.

"You tell Clem Henry I said that one of these days he's going to find himself turned inside out, like a coat-sleeve."

Lonnie waited doggedly. He knew Clem was right in insisting that Arch ought to wake up and come out there to see what had happened. Lonnie was afraid to go back to the barnyard and tell Clem that Arch was not coming. He did not know, but he had a feeling that Clem might go into the bedroom and drag Arch out of bed. He did not like to think of anything like that taking place.

"Are you still out there, Lonnie?" Arch shouted.

"I'm right here, Mr. Arch. I——"

"If I wasn't so sleepy, I'd come out there and take a stick and—I don't know what I wouldn't do!"

Lonnie met Arch at the back step. On the way out to the hog pen Arch did not speak to him. Arch walked heavily ahead, not even waiting to see if Lonnie was coming. The lantern that Arch was carrying cast long flat beams of yellow light over the ground; and when they got to where Clem was waiting beside Mark's body, the Negro's face shone in the night like a highly polished plowshare.

"What was Mark doing in my hog pen at night, anyway?" Arch said, shouting at them both.

Neither Clem nor Lonnie replied. Arch glared at them for not answering. But no matter how many times he looked at them, his eyes returned each time to stare at the torn body of Mark Newsome on the ground at his feet.

"There's nothing to be done now," Arch said finally. "We'll just have to wait till daylight and send for the undertaker." He walked a few steps away. "Looks like you could have waited till morning in the first place. There wasn't no sense in getting me up."

He turned his back and looked sideways at Clem. Clem stood up and looked him straight in the eyes.

"What do you want, Clem Henry?" he said. "Who told you to be coming around my house in the middle of the night? I don't want niggers coming here except when I send for them."

"I couldn't stand to see anybody eaten up by the hogs, and not do anything about it," Clem said.

"You mind your own business," Arch told him. "And when you talk to me, take off your hat, or you'll be sorry for it. It wouldn't take much to make me do you up the way you belong."

Lonnie backed away. There was a feeling of uneasiness around them.

That was how trouble between Clem and Arch always began. He had seen it start that way dozens of times before. As long as Clem turned and went away, nothing happened, but sometimes he stayed right where he was and talked up to Arch just as if he had been a white man, too.

Lonnie hoped it would not happen this time. Arch was already mad enough about being waked up in the middle of the night, and Lonnie knew there was no limit to what Arch would do when he got good and mad at a Negro. Nobody had ever seen him kill a Negro, but he had said he had, and he told people that he was not scared to do it again.

"I reckon you know how he came to get eaten up by the hogs like that," Clem said, looking straight at Arch.

Arch whirled around.

"Are you talking to me . . . ?"

"I asked you that," Clem stated.

"God damn you, yellow-blooded . . ." Arch yelled.

He swung the lantern at Clem's head. Clem dodged, but the bottom of it hit his shoulder, and it was smashed to pieces. The oil splattered on the ground, igniting in the air from the flaming wick. Clem was lucky not to have it splash on his face and overalls.

"Now, look here . . ." Clem said.

"You yellow-blooded nigger," Arch said, rushing at him. "I'll teach you to talk back to me. You've got too big for your place for the last time. I've been taking too much from you, but I aint doing it no more."

"Mr. Arch, I . . ." Lonnie said, stepping forward partly between them. No one heard him.

Arch stood back and watched the kerosene flicker out on the ground.

"You know good and well why he got eaten up by the fattening hogs," Clem said, standing his ground. "He was so hungry he had to get up out of bed in the middle of the night and come up here in the dark trying to find something to eat. Maybe he was trying to find the smokehouse. It makes no difference, either way. He's been on short-rations like everybody else working on your place, and he was so old he didn't know where to look for food except in your smokehouse. You know good and well that's how he got lost up here in the dark and fell in the hog pen."

The kerosene had died out completely. In the last faint flare, Arch had reached down and grabbed up the singletree that had been lying on the ground where Lonnie had dropped it.

Arch raised the singletree over his head and struck with all his might at Clem. Clem dodged, but Arch drew back again quickly and landed a blow on his arm just above the elbow before Clem could dodge it. Clem's arm dropped to his side, dangling lifelessly.

"You Goddamn yellow-blooded nigger!" Arch shouted. "Now's your time, you black bastard. I've been waiting for the chance to teach you your lesson. And this's going to be one you won't never forget."

Clem felt the ground with his feet until he had located the other single-tree. He stooped down and got it. Raising it, he did not try to hit Arch, but held it in front of him so he could ward off Arch's blows at his head. He continued to stand his ground, not giving Arch an inch.

"Drop that singletree," Arch said.

"I won't stand here and let you beat me like that," Clem protested.

"By God, that's all I want to hear," Arch said, his mouth curling. "Nigger, your time has come, by God!"

He swung once more at Clem, but Clem turned and ran towards the barn. Arch went after him a few steps and stopped. He threw aside the singletree and turned and ran back to the house.

Lonnie went to the fence and tried to think what was best for him to do. He knew he could not take sides with a Negro, in the open, even if Clem had helped him, and especially after Clem had talked to Arch in the way he wished he could himself. He was a white man, and to save his life he could not stand to think of turning against Arch, no matter what happened.

Presently a light burst through one of the windows of the house, and he heard Arch shouting at his wife to wake her up.

When he saw Arch's wife go to the telephone, Lonnie realized what was going to happen. She was calling up the neighbors and Arch's friends. They would not mind getting up in the night when they found out what was going to take place.

Out behind the barn he could hear Clem calling him. Leaving the yard, Lonnie felt his way out there in the dark.

"What's the trouble, Clem?" he said.

"I reckon my time has come," Clem said. "Arch Gunnard talks that way when he's good and mad. He talked just like he did that time he carried Jim Moffin off to the swamp—and Jim never came back."

"Arch wouldn't do anything like that to you, Clem," Lonnie said excitedly, but he knew better.

Clem said nothing.

"Maybe you'd better strike out for the swamps till he changes his mind and cools off some," Lonnie said. "You might be right, Clem."

Lonnie could feel Clem's eyes burning into him.

"Wouldn't be no sense in that, if you'd help me," Clem said. "Wouldn't you stand by me?"

Lonnie trembled as the meaning of Clem's suggestion became clear to him. His back was to the side of the barn, and he leaned against it while sheets of black and white passed before his eyes.

"Wouldn't you stand by me?" Clem asked again.

"I don't know what Arch would say to that," Lonnie told him haltingly.

Clem walked away several paces. He stood with his back to Lonnie while he looked across the field towards the quarter where his home was.

"I could go in that little patch of woods out there and stay till they get tired of looking for me," Clem said, turning around to see Lonnie.

"You'd better go somewhere," Lonnie said uneasily. "I know Arch Gunnard. He's hard to handle when he makes up his mind to do something he wants to do. I couldn't stop him an inch. Maybe you'd better get clear out of the country, Clem."

"I couldn't do that, and leave my family down there across the field," Clem said.

"He's going to get you if you don't."

"If you'd only sort of help me out a little, he wouldn't. I would only have to go and hide out in that little patch of woods over there a while. Looks like you could do that for me, being as how I helped you find your pa when he was in the hog pen."

Lonnie nodded, listening for sounds from the big house. He continued to nod at Clem while Clem was waiting to be assured.

"If you're going to stand up for me," Clem said, "I can just go over there in the woods and wait till they get it off their minds. You won't be telling them where I'm at, and you could say I struck out for the swamp. They wouldn't ever find me without bloodhounds."

"That's right," Lonnie said, listening for sounds of Arch's coming out of the house. He did not wish to be found back there behind the barn where Arch could accuse him of talking to Clem.

The moment Lonnie replied, Clem turned and ran off into the night. Lonnie went after him a few steps, as if he had suddenly changed his mind about helping him, but Clem was lost in the darkness by then.

Lonnie waited for a few minutes, listening to Clem crashing through the underbrush in the patch of woods a quarter of a mile away. When he could hear Clem no longer, he went around the barn to meet Arch.

Arch came out of the house carrying his double-barreled shotgun and the lantern he had picked up in the house. His pockets were bulging with shells.

"Where is that damn nigger, Lonnie?" Arch asked him. "Where'd he go to?"

Lonnie opened his mouth, but no words came out.

"You know which way he went, don't you?"

Lonnie again tried to say something, but there were no sounds. He jumped when he found himself nodding his head to Arch.

"Mr. Arch, I——"

"That's all right, then," Arch said. "That's all I need to know now. Dudley Smith and Tom Hawkins and Frank and Dave Howard and the rest will be here in a minute, and you can stay right here so you can show us where he's hiding out."

Frantically Lonnie tried to say something. Then he reached for Arch's sleeve to stop him, but Arch had gone.

Arch ran around the house to the front yard. Soon a car came racing down the road, its headlights lighting up the whole place, hog pen and all. Lonnie knew it was probably Dudley Smith, because his was the first house in that direction, only half a mile away. While he was turning into the driveway, several other automobiles came into sight, both up the road and down it.

Lonnie trembled. He was afraid Arch was going to tell him to point out where Clem had gone to hide. Then he knew Arch would tell him. He had promised Clem he would not do that. But try as he might, he could not make himself believe that Arch Gunnard would do anything more than whip Clem.

Clem had not done anything that called for lynching. He had not raped a white woman, he had not shot at a white man; he had only talked back to Arch, with his hat on. But Arch was mad enough to do anything; he was mad enough at Clem not to stop at anything short of lynching.

The whole crowd of men was swarming around him before he realized it. And there was Arch clutching his arm and shouting into his face.

"Mr. Arch, I . . ."

Lonnie recognized every man in the feeble dawn. They were excited, and they looked like men on the last lap of an all-night foxhunting party. Their shotguns and pistols were held at their waist, ready for the kill.

"What's the matter with you, Lonnie?" Arch said, shouting into his ear. "Wake up and say where Clem Henry went to hide out. We're ready to go get him."

Lonnie remembered looking up and seeing Frank Howard dropping yellow twelve-gauge shells into the breech of his gun. Frank bent forward so he could hear Lonnie tell Arch where Clem was hiding.

"You aint going to kill Clem this time, are you, Mr. Arch?" Lonnie asked.

"Kill him?" Dudley Smith repeated. "What do you reckon I've been waiting all this time for if it wasn't for a chance to get Clem. That nigger has had it coming to him ever since he came to this county. He's a bad nigger, and it's coming to him."

"It wasn't exactly Clem's fault," Lonnie said. "If Pa hadn't come up here and fell in the hog pen, Clem wouldn't have had a thing to do with it. He was helping me, that's all."

"Shut up, Lonnie," somebody shouted at him. "You're so excited you don't know what you're saying. You're taking up for a nigger when you talk like that."

People were crowding around him so tightly he felt as if he were being squeezed to death. He had to get some air, get his breath, get out of the crowd.

"That's right," Lonnie said.

He heard himself speak, but he did not know what he was saying.

"But Clem helped me find Pa when he got lost looking around for something to eat."

"Shut up, Lonnie," somebody said again. "You damn fool, shut up!"

Arch grabbed his shoulder and shook him until his teeth rattled. Then Lonnie realized what he had been saying.

"Now, look here, Lonnie," Arch shouted. "You must be out of your head, because you know good and well you wouldn't talk like a nigger-lover in your right mind."

"That's right," Lonnie said, trembling all over. "I sure wouldn't want to talk like that."

He could still feel the grip on his shoulder where Arch's strong fingers had hurt him.

"Did Clem go to the swamp, Lonnie?" Dudley Smith said. "Is that right, Lonnie?"

Lonnie tried to shake his head; he tried to nod his head. Then Arch's fingers squeezed his thin neck. Lonnie looked at the men wild-eyed.

"Where's Clem hiding, Lonnie?" Arch demanded, squeezing.

Lonnie went three or four steps towards the barn. When he stopped, the men behind him pushed forward again. He found himself being rushed behind the barn and beyond it.

"All right, Lonnie," Arch said. "Now which way?"

Lonnie pointed towards the patch of woods where the creek was. The swamp was in the other direction.

"He said he was going to hide out in that little patch of woods along the creek over there, Mr. Arch," Lonnie said. "I reckon he's over there now."

Lonnie felt himself being swept forward, and he stumbled over the rough ground trying to keep from being knocked down and trampled upon. Nobody was talking, and everyone seemed to be walking on tip-toes. The gray light of early dawn was increasing enough both to hide them and to show the way ahead.

Just before they reached the fringe of the woods the men separated, and Lonnie found himself a part of the circle that was closing in on Clem.

Lonnie was alone, and there was nobody to stop him, but he was unable to move forward or backward. It began to be clear to him what he had done.

Clem was probably up a tree somewhere in the woods ahead, but by that time he had been surrounded on all sides. If he should attempt to break and run, he would be shot down like a rabbit.

Lonnie sat down on a log and tried to think what to do. The sun would be up in a few more minutes, and as soon as it came up, the men would close in on the creek and Clem. He would have no chance at all among all those shotguns and pistols.

Once or twice he saw the flare of a match through the underbrush where some of the men were lying in wait. A whiff of cigarette smoke struck his nostrils, and he found himself wondering if Clem could smell it wherever he was in the woods.

There was still no sound anywhere around him, and he knew that Arch Gunnard and the rest of the men were waiting for the sun, which would in a few minutes come up behind him in the east.

It was light enough by that time to see plainly the rough ground and the tangled underbrush and the curling bark on the pine trees.

The men had already begun to creep forward, guns raised as if stalking a deer. The woods were not large, and the circle of men would be able to cover it in a few minutes at the rate they were going forward. There was still a chance that Clem had slipped through the circle before dawn broke, but Lonnie felt that he was still there. He began to feel then that Clem was there because he himself had placed him there for the men to find more easily.

Lonnie found himself moving forward, drawn into the narrowing circle. Presently he could see the men all around him in dim outline. Their eyes were searching the heavy green pine tops as they went forward from tree to tree.

"Oh, Pa!" he said in a hoarse whisper. "Oh, Pa!"

He went forward a few steps, looking into the bushes and up into the tree tops. When he saw the other men again, he realized that it was not Mark Newsome being sought. He did not know what had made him forget like that.

The creeping forward began to work into the movement of Lonnie's body. He found himself springing forward on his toes, and his body was leaning in that direction. It was like creeping up on a rabbit when you did not have a gun to hunt with.

He forgot again what he was doing there. The springing motion in his legs seemed to be growing stronger with each step. He bent forward so far he could almost touch the ground with his fingertips. He could not stop now. He was keeping up with the circle of men.

The fifteen men were drawing closer and closer together. The dawn had broken enough to show the time on the face of a watch. The sun was beginning to color the sky above.

Lonnie was far in advance of anyone else by then. He could not hold himself back. The strength in his legs was more than he could hold in check.

He had for so long been unable to buy shells for his gun that he had forgotten how much he liked to hunt.

The sound of the men's steady creeping had become a rhythm in his ears.

"Here's the bastard!" somebody shouted, and there was a concerted crashing through the dry underbrush. Lonnie dashed forward, reaching the tree almost as quickly as anyone else.

He could see everybody with guns raised, and far into the sky above the sharply outlined face of Clem Henry gleamed in the rising sun. His body was hugging the slender top of the pine.

Lonnie did not know who was the first to fire, but the rest of the men did not hesitate. There was a deafening roar as the shotguns and revolvers flared and smoked around the trunk of the tree.

He closed his eyes; he was afraid to look again at the face above. The firing continued without break. Clem hugged the tree with all his might, and then, with the far-away sound of splintering wood, the top of the tree and Clem came crashing through the lower limbs to the ground. The body, sprawling and torn, landed on the ground with a thud that stopped Lonnie's heart for a moment.

He turned, clutching for the support of a tree, as the firing began once more. The crumpled body was tossed time after time, like a sackful of kittens being killed with an automatic shotgun, as charges of lead were fired into it from all sides. A cloud of dust rose from the ground and drifted overhead with the choking odor of burned powder.

Lonnie did not remember how long the shooting lasted. He found himself running from tree to tree, clutching at the rough pine bark, stumbling wildly towards the cleared ground. The sky had turned from gray to red when he emerged in the open, and as he ran, falling over the hard clods in the plowed field, he tried to keep his eyes on the house ahead.

Once he fell and found it almost impossible to rise again to his feet. He struggled to his knees, facing the round red sun. The warmth gave him the strength to rise to his feet, and he muttered unintelligibly to himself. He tried to say things he had never thought to say before.

When he got home, Hatty was waiting for him in the yard. She had heard the shots in the woods, and she had seen him stumbling over the hard clods in the field, and she had seen him kneeling there looking straight into the face of the sun. Hatty was trembling as she ran to Lonnie to find out what the matter was.

Once in his own yard, Lonnie turned and looked for a second over his shoulder. He saw the men climbing over the fence at Arch Gunnard's. Arch's wife was standing on the back porch, and she was speaking to them.

"Where's your pa, Lonnie?" Hatty said. "And what in the world was all that shooting in the woods for?" Lonnie stumbled forward until he had reached the front porch. He fell upon the steps.

"Lonnie, Lonnie!" Hatty was saying. "Wake up and tell me what in the world is the matter. I've never seen the like of all that's going on."

"Nothing," Lonnie said. "Nothing."

"Well, if there's nothing the matter, can't you go up to the big house and ask for a little piece of streak-of-lean? We ain't got a thing to cook for breakfast. Your pa's going to be hungrier than ever after being up walking around all night."

"What?" Lonnie said, his voice rising to a shout as he jumped to his feet.

"Why, I only said go up to the big house and get a little piece of streak-of-lean, Lonnie. That's all I said."

He grabbed his wife about the shoulders.

"Meat?" he yelled, shaking her roughly.

"Yes," she said, pulling away from him in surprise. "Couldn't you go ask Arch Gunnard for a little bit of streak-of-lean?"

Lonnie slumped down again on the steps, his hands falling between his outspread legs and his chin falling on his chest.

"No," he said almost inaudibly. "No. I aint hungry."

THE NOWAKS

Christopher Isherwood

(1904–)

I FOUND the Wassertorstrasse without much difficulty. The entrance to it was a big stone archway, a bit of old Berlin, daubed with hammers and sickles and Nazi crosses and plastered with tattered bills which advertised auctions or crimes. It was a deep shabby cobbled street, littered with sprawling children in tears. Youths in woollen sweaters circled waveringly across it on racing bikes and whooped at girls passing with milk-jugs. The pavement was chalk-marked for the hopping game called Heaven and Earth. At the end of it, like a tall, dangerously sharp, red instrument, stood a church.

Frau Nowak herself opened the door to me. She looked far iller than when I had seen her last, with big blue rings under her eyes. She was wearing the same hat and mangy old black coat. At first, she didn't recognize me.

'Good afternoon, Frau Nowak.'

Her face changed slowly from poking suspicion to a brilliant, timid, almost girlish smile of welcome:

'Why, if it isn't Herr Christoph! Come in, Herr Christoph! Come in and sit down.'

'I'm afraid you were just going out, weren't you?'

'No, no, Herr Christoph—I've just come in; just this minute.' She was wiping her hands hastily on her coat before shaking mine: 'This is one of my charring days. I don't get finished till half-past two and it makes the dinner so late.'

She stood aside for me to enter. I pushed open the door and, in doing so, jarred the handle of the frying-pan on the stove which stood just behind it. In the tiny kitchen there was barely room for the two of us together. A stifling smell of potatoes fried in cheap margarine filled the flat.

'Come and sit down, Herr Christoph,' she repeated, hastily doing the honours. 'I'm afraid it's terribly untidy. You must excuse that. I have to go out so early and my Grete's such a lazy great lump, though she's turned twelve. There's no getting her to do anything, if you don't stand over her all the time.'

The living-room had a sloping ceiling stained with old patches of damp. It contained a big table, six chairs, a sideboard and two large double-beds. The place was so full of furniture that you had to squeeze your way into it sideways.

'Grete!' cried Frau Nowak. 'Where are you? Come here this minute!'

'She's gone out,' came Otto's voice from the inner room.

'Otto! Come out and see who's here!'

'Can't be bothered. I'm busy mending the gramophone.'

'Busy, indeed! You! You good-for-nothing! That's a nice way to speak to your mother! Come out of that room, do you hear me?'

She had flown into a rage instantly, automatically, with astonishing violence. Her face became all nose; thin, bitter and inflamed. Her whole body trembled.

'It doesn't really matter, Frau Nowak,' I said. 'Let him come out when he wants to. He'll get all the bigger surprise.'

'A nice son I've got! Speaking to me like that . . .'

She had pulled off her hat and was unpacking greasy parcels from a string bag: 'Dear me,' she fussed, 'I wonder where that child's got to? Always down in the street, she is. If I've told her once, I've told her a hundred times. Children have no consideration.'

'How has your lung been keeping, Frau Nowak?'

She sighed: 'Sometimes it seems to me it's worse than ever. I get such a burning, just here. And when I finish work it's as if I was too tired to eat. I come over so bilious . . . I don't think the doctor's satisfied, either. He talks about sending me to a sanatorium later in the winter. I was there before, you know. But there's always so many waiting to go . . . Then, the flat's so damp at this time of year. You see those marks on the ceiling? There's days we have to put a foot-bath under them to catch the drips. Of course, they've no right to let these attics as dwellings at all, really. The Inspector's condemned them time and time again. But what are you to do?'

One must live somewhere. We applied for a transfer over a year ago and they keep promising they'll see about it. But there's a lot of others are worse off still, I daresay . . . My husband was reading out of the newspaper the other day about the English and their Pound. It keeps on falling, they say. I don't understand such things, myself. I hope you haven't lost any money, Herr Christoph?'

'As a matter of fact, Frau Nowak, that's partly why I came down to see you to-day. I've decided to go into a cheaper room and I was wondering if there was anywhere round here you could recommend me?'

'Oh dear, Herr Christoph, I *am* sorry!'

She was quite genuinely shocked: 'But you can't live in this part of the town—a gentleman like you! Oh no. I'm afraid it wouldn't suit you at all.'

'I'm not so particular as you think, perhaps. I just want a quiet clean room for about twenty marks a month. It doesn't matter how small it is. I'm out most of the day.'

She shook her head doubtfully: 'Well, Herr Christoph, I shall have to see if I can't think of something . . .'

'Isn't dinner ready yet, mother?' asked Otto, appearing in shirtsleeves at the doorway of the inner room: 'I'm nearly starving!'

'How do you expect it to be ready when I have to spend the whole morning slaving for you, you great lump of laziness!' cried Frau Nowak, shrilly, at the top of her voice. Then, transposing without the least pause into her ingratiating social tone, she added: 'Don't you see who's here?'

'Why . . . it's Christoph!' Otto, as usual, had begun acting at once. His face was slowly illuminated by a sunrise of extreme joy. His cheeks dimpled with smiles. He sprang forward, throwing one arm around my neck, wringing my hand: 'Christoph, you old soul, where have you been hiding all this time?' His voice became languishing, reproachful: 'We've missed you so much! Why have you never come to see us?'

'Herr Christoph is a very busy gentleman,' put in Frau Nowak, reprovingly: 'He's got no time to waste running after a do-nothing like you.'

Otto grinned, winked at me: then he turned reproachfully upon Frau Nowak:

'Mother, what are you thinking of? Are you going to let Christoph sit there without so much as a cup of coffee? He must be thirsty, after climbing all these stairs!'

'What you mean is, Otto, that *you're* thirsty, don't you? No, thank you, Frau Nowak, I won't have anything—really. And I won't keep you from your cooking any longer . . . Look here, Otto, will you come out with me now and help me find a room? I've just been telling your mother that I'm coming to live in this neighbourhood . . . You shall have your cup of coffee with me, outside.'

'What, Christoph—you're going to live here, in Hallesches Tor!' Otto began dancing with excitement: 'Oh, mother, won't that be grand! Oh, I am so pleased!'

'You may just as well go out and have a look round with Herr Christoph, now,' said Frau Nowak. 'Dinner won't be ready for at least an hour, yet. You're only in my way here. Not *you*, Herr Christoph, of course. You'll come back and have something to eat with us, won't you?'

'Well, Frau Nowak, it's very kind of you indeed, but I'm afraid I can't, to-day. I shall have to be getting back home.'

'Just give me a crust of bread before I go, mother,' begged Otto piteously. 'I'm so empty that my head's spinning round like a top.'

'All right,' said Frau Nowak, cutting a slice of bread and half throwing it at him in her vexation, 'but don't blame me if there's nothing in the house this evening when you want to make one of your sandwiches . . . Good-bye, Herr Christoph. It was very kind of you to come and see us. If you really decide to live near here, I hope you'll look in often . . . though I doubt if you'll find anything to your liking. It won't be what you've been accustomed to. . . .'

As Otto was about to follow me out of the flat she called him back. I heard them arguing; then the door shut. I descended slowly the five flights of stairs to the courtyard. The bottom of the court was clammy and dark, although the sun was shining on a cloud in the sky overhead. Broken buckets, wheels off prams and bits of bicycle tyre lay scattered about, like things which have fallen down a well.

It was a minute or two before Otto came clattering down the stairs to join me:

'Mother didn't like to ask you,' he told me, breathless. 'She was afraid you'd be annoyed . . . But I said that I was sure you'd far rather be with us, where you can do just what you like and you know everything's clean, than in a strange house full of bugs . . . Do say yes, Christoph, please! It'll be such fun! You and I can sleep in the back room. You can have Lothar's bed—he won't mind. He can share the double-bed with Grete . . . And in the mornings you can stay in bed as long as ever you like. If you want, I'll bring you your breakfast . . . You will come, won't you!?'

And so it was settled.

My first evening as a lodger at the Nowaks was something of a ceremony. I arrived with my two suit-cases soon after five o'clock, to find Frau Nowak already cooking the evening meal. Otto whispered to me that we were to have lung hash, as a special treat.

'I'm afraid you won't think very much of our food,' said Frau Nowak, 'after what you've been used to. But we'll do our best.' She was all smiles, bubbling over with excitement. I smiled and smiled, feeling awkward and in the way. At length, I clambered over the living-room furniture and sat down on my bed. There was no space to unpack in, and nowhere, apparently, to put my clothes. At the living-room table, Grete was playing with her cigarette-cards and transfers. She was a lumpish child of twelve years old, pretty in a sugary way, but round-shouldered and too fat. My presence made her very self-conscious. She wriggled, smirked and kept calling out, in an affected, sing-song, 'grown-up' voice:

'Mummy! Come and look at the pretty flowers!'

'I've got no time for your pretty flowers,' exclaimed Frau Nowak at length, in great exasperation: 'Here am I, with a daughter the size of an elephant, having to slave all by myself, cooking the supper!'

'Quite right, mother!' cried Otto, gleefully joining in. He turned upon Grete, righteously indignant: 'Why don't you help her, I should like to know? You're fat enough. You sit around all day doing nothing. Get off that chair this instant, do you hear! And put those filthy cards away, or I'll burn them!'

He grabbed at the cards with one hand and gave Grete a slap across the face with the other. Grete, who obviously wasn't hurt, at once set up a loud, theatrical wail: 'Oh, Otto, you've *hurt* me!' She covered her face with her hands and peeped at me between the fingers.

'*Will* you leave that child alone!' cried Frau Nowak shrilly from the kitchen. 'I should like to know who *you* are, to talk about laziness! And you, Grete, just you stop that howling—or I'll tell Otto to hit you properly, so that you'll have something to cry for. You two between you, you drive me nearly distracted.'

'But, mother!' Otto ran into the kitchen, took her round the waist and began kissing her: 'Poor little Mummy, little Mutti, little Muttchen,' he crooned, in tones of the most mawkish solicitude. 'You have to work so hard and Otto's so horrid to you. But he doesn't mean to be, you know—he's just stupid . . . Shall I fetch the coal up for you to-morrow, Mummy? Would you like that?'

'Let go of me, you great humbug!' cried Frau Nowak, laughing and struggling. 'I don't want any of your soft soap! Much *you* care for your poor old mother! Leave me to get on with my work in peace.'

'Otto's not a bad boy,' she continued to me, when he had let go of her at last, 'but he's such a scatterbrain. Quite the opposite of my Lothar—there's a model son for you! He's not too proud to do any job, whatever it is, and when he's scraped a few groschen together, instead of spending it on himself he comes straight to me and says: "Here you are, mother. Just buy yourself a pair of warm house-shoes for the winter."' Frau Nowak held out her hand to me with the gesture of giving money. Like Otto, she had the trick of acting every scene she described.

'Oh, Lothar this, Lothar that,' Otto interrupted crossly: 'It's always Lothar. But tell me this, mother, which of us was it that gave you a twenty mark note the other day? Lothar couldn't earn twenty marks in a month of Sundays. Well, if that's how you talk, you needn't expect to get any more; not if you come to me on your knees.'

'You wicked boy,' she was up in arms again in an instant, 'have you no more shame than to speak of such things in front of Herr Christoph! Why, if he knew where that twenty marks came from—and plenty more besides— he'd disdain to stay in the same house with you another minute; and quite right too! And the cheek of you—saying you *gave* me that money! You know very well that if your father hadn't seen the envelope . . .'

'That's right!' shouted Otto, screwing up his face at her like a monkey and beginning to dance with excitement: 'That's just what I wanted! Admit to Christoph that you stole it! You're a thief! You're a thief!'

'Otto, how dare you!' Quick as fury, Frau Nowak's hand grabbed up the lid of a saucepan. I jumped back a pace, to be out of range, tripped over a chair and sat down hard. Grete uttered an affected little shriek of joy and alarm. The door opened. It was Herr Nowak, come back from his work.

He was a powerful, dumpy little man, with pointed moustaches, cropped hair and bushy eyebrows. He took in the scene with a long grunt which was half a belch. He did not appear to understand what had been happening; or perhaps he merely did not care. Frau Nowak said nothing to enlighten him. She hung the saucepan-lid quietly on a hook. Grete jumped up from her chair and ran to him with outstretched arms: 'Pappi! Pappi!'

Herr Nowak smiled down at her, showing two or three nicotine-stained stumps of teeth. Bending, he picked her up, carefully and expertly, with a certain admiring curiosity, like a large valuable vase. By profession he was a furniture-remover. Then he held out his hand—taking his time about it, gracious, not fussily eager to please:

'Servus, Herr.'

'Aren't you glad that Herr Christoph's come to live with us, Pappi?' chanted Grete, perched on her father's shoulder, in her sugary sing-song tones. At this Herr Nowak, as if suddenly acquiring new energy, began shaking my hand again, much more warmly, and thumping me on the back:

'Glad? Yes, of course I'm glad!' He nodded his head in vigorous approval. 'Englisch Man? Anglais, eh? Ha, ha. That's right! Oh yes, I talk French, you see. Forgotten most of it now. Learnt in the war. I was *feldwebel*—on the West Front. Talked to lots of prisoners. Good lads. All the same as us . . .'

'You're drunk again, father!' exclaimed Frau Nowak, in disgust. 'Whatever will Herr Christoph think of you!'

'Christoph doesn't mind; do you, Christoph?' Herr Nowak patted my shoulder.

'Christoph, indeed! He's *Herr* Christoph to you! Can't you tell a gentleman when you see one?'

'I'd much rather you called me Christoph,' I said.

'That's right! Christoph's right! We're all the same flesh and blood. . . .
Argent, money—all the same! Ha, ha!'

Otto took my other arm: 'Christoph's quite one of the family, already!'

Presently we sat down to an immense meal of lung hash, black bread, malt
coffee and boiled potatoes. In the first recklessness of having so much
money to spend (I had given her ten marks in advance for the week's
board) Frau Nowak had prepared enough potatoes for a dozen people.
She kept shovelling them on to my plate from a big saucepan, until I
thought I should suffocate:

'Have some more, Herr Christoph. You're eating nothing. '

'I've never eaten so much in my whole life, Frau Nowak.'

'Christoph doesn't like our food,' said Herr Nowak. 'Never mind, Christoph, you'll get used to it. Otto was just the same when he came back
from that week-end in the country. He'd got used to all sorts of fine ways,
with his Herr Baron . . .'

'Hold your tongue, father!' said Frau Nowak warningly. 'Can't you leave
the boy alone? He's old enough to be able to decide for himself what's
right and wrong—more shame to him.'

We were still eating when Lothar came in. He threw his cap on to the
bed, shook hands with me politely but silently, with a little bow, and took
his place at the table. My presence did not appear to surprise or interest
him in the least: his glance barely met mine. He was, I knew, only twenty;
but he might well have been years older. He was a man already. Otto
seemed almost childish beside him. He had a lean, bony, peasant's face,
soured by racial memory of barren fields.

'Lothar's going to night-school,' Frau Nowak told me, with pride. 'He
had a job in a garage, you know; and now he wants to study engineering.
They won't take you in anywhere nowadays, unless you've got a diploma
of some sort. He must show you his drawings, Herr Christoph, when
you've got time to look at them. The teacher said they were very good
indeed.'

'I should like to see them.'

Lothar didn't respond. I sympathized with him and felt rather foolish.
But Frau Nowak was determined to show him off:

'Which nights are your classes, Lothar?'

'Mondays and Thursdays.' He went on eating, deliberately, obstinately,
without looking at his mother. Then, perhaps to show that he bore me no
ill-will, he added: 'From eight to ten thirty.' As soon as he had finished, he
got up without a word, shook hands with me, making the same small bow,
took his cap and went out.

Frau Nowak looked after him and sighed: 'He's going round to his
Nazis, I suppose. I often wish he'd never taken up with them at all. They
put all kinds of silly ideas into his head. It makes him so restless. Since he
joined them he's been a different boy altogether. . . . Not that I under-

stand these politics myself. What I always say is—why can't we have the Kaiser back? Those were the good times, say what you like.'

'Ach, to hell with your old Kaiser,' said Otto. 'What we want is a communist revolution.'

'A communist revolution!' Frau Nowak snorted. 'The idea! The communists are all good-for-nothing lazybones, like you, who've never done an honest day's work in their lives.'

'Christoph's a communist,' said Otto. 'Aren't you, Christoph?'

'Not a proper one, I'm afraid.'

Frau Nowak smiled: 'What nonsense will you be telling us next! How could Herr Christoph be a communist? He's a gentleman.'

'What I say is——' Herr Nowak put down his knife and fork and wiped his moustaches carefully on the back of his hand: 'we're all equal as God made us. You're as good as me. I'm as good as you. A Frenchman's as good as an Englishman. An Englishman's as good as a German. You understand what I mean?'

I nodded.

'Take the war, now——' Herr Nowak pushed back his chair from the table: 'One day I was in a wood. All alone, you understand. Just walking through the wood by myself, as I might be walking down the street . . . And suddenly—there before me, stood a Frenchman. Just as if he'd sprung out of the earth. He was no further away from me than you are now.' Herr Nowak sprang to his feet as he spoke. Snatching up the bread-knife from the table he held it before him, in a posture of defence, like a bayonet. He glared at me from beneath his bushy eyebrows, re-living the scene: 'There we stand. We look at each other. That Frenchman was as pale as death. Suddenly he cries: "Don't shoot me!" Just like that.' Herr Nowak clasped his hands in a piteous gesture of entreaty. The bread-knife was in the way now: he put it down on the table. ' "Don't shoot me! I have five children." (He spoke French, of course: but I could understand him. I could speak French perfectly in those days; but I've forgotten some of it now.) Well, I look at him and he looks at me. Then I say: "Ami." (That means Friend.) And then we shake hands.' Herr Nowak took my hand in both of his and pressed it with great emotion. 'And then we begin to walk away from each other—backwards; I didn't want him to shoot me in the back.' Still glaring in front of him, Herr Nowak began cautiously retreating backwards, step by step, until he collided violently with the sideboard. A framed photograph fell off it. The glass smashed.

'Pappi! Pappi!' cried Grete in delight. 'Just look what you've done!'

'Perhaps that'll teach you to stop your fooling, you old clown!' exclaimed Frau Nowak angrily. Grete began loudly and affectedly laughing, until Otto slapped her face and she set up her stagey whine. Meanwhile, Herr Nowak had restored his wife's good temper by kissing her and pinching her cheek.

'Get away from me, you great lout!' she protested laughing; coyly pleased that I was present: 'Let me alone, you stink of beer.'

At that time I had a great many lessons to give. I was out most of the day. My pupils were scattered about the fashionable suburbs of the west—rich, well-preserved women of Frau Nowak's age, but looking ten years younger; they liked to make a hobby of a little English conversation on dull afternoons when their husbands were away at the office. Sitting on silk cushions in front of open fireplaces, we discussed 'Point Counter-Point' and 'Lady Chatterley's Lover.' A manservant brought in tea with buttered toast. Sometimes, when they got tired of literature, I amused them by descriptions of the Nowak household. I was careful, however, not to say that I lived there: it would have been bad for my business to admit that I was really poor. The ladies paid me three marks an hour, a little reluctantly, having done their best to beat me down to two marks fifty. Most of them also tried, deliberately or subconsciously, to cheat me into staying longer than my time. I always had to keep my eye on the clock.

Fewer people wanted lessons in the morning; and so it happened that I usually got up much later than the rest of the Nowak family. Frau Nowak had her charring, Herr Nowak went off to his job at the furniture-removers', Lothar, who was out of work, was helping a friend with a paper-round, Grete went to school. Only Otto kept me company; except on the mornings when, with endless nagging, he was driven out to the labour bureau by his mother, to get his card stamped.

After fetching our breakfast, a cup of coffee and a slice of bread and dripping, Otto would strip off his pyjama jacket and do exercises, shadow-box or try to stand on his head. He flexed his muscles for my admiration. He was very proud of his figure. Squatting on my bed, he told me stories:

'Did I ever tell you, Christoph, how I saw the Hand?'

'No, I don't think so.'

'Well, listen . . . Once, when I was very small, I was lying in bed at night. It was very dark and very late. And suddenly I woke up and saw a great big black hand stretching over the bed. I was so frightened I couldn't even scream. I just drew my legs up under my chin and stared at it. Then, after a minute or two, it disappeared and I yelled out. Mother came running in and I said: "Mother, I've seen the Hand." But she only laughed. She wouldn't believe it.'

Otto's innocent face, with its two dimples, like a bun, had become very solemn. He held me with his absurdly small bright eyes, concentrating all his narrative powers:

'And then, Christoph, several years later, I had a job as apprentice to an upholsterer. Well, one day—it was in the middle of the morning, in broad daylight—I was sitting working on my stool. And suddenly it seemed to go all dark in the room and I looked up and there was the Hand, as near to me as you are now, just closing over me. I felt my arms and legs turn cold and I couldn't breathe and I couldn't cry out. The master saw how pale I was and he said: "Why, Otto, what's the matter with you? Aren't you well?" And as he spoke to me it seemed as if the Hand drew right away from me again, getting smaller and smaller, until it was just a little black speck. And when I looked up again the room was quite light, just as it always was, and where I'd seen the black speck there was a big fly crawling across the ceiling. But I was so ill the whole day that the master had to send me home.'

Otto's face had gone quite pale during this recital and, for a moment, a really frightening expression of fear had passed over his features. He was tragic now; his little eyes bright with tears:

'One day I shall see the Hand again. And then I shall die.'

'Nonsense,' I said laughing. 'We'll protect you.'

Otto shook his head very sadly:

'Let's hope so, Christoph. But I'm afraid not. The Hand will get me in the end.'

'How long did you stay with the upholsterer?' I asked.

'Oh, not long. Only a few weeks. The master was so unkind to me. He always gave me the hardest jobs to do—and I was such a little chap then. One day I got there five minutes late. He made a terrible row; called me a *verfluchter Hund*. And do you think I put up with that?' Otto leant forward, thrust his face, contracted into a dry monkey-like leer of malice, towards me. *'Nee, nee. Bei mir nicht.'* His little eyes focussed upon me for a moment with an extraordinary intensity of simian hatred; his puckered-up features became startlingly ugly. Then they relaxed. I was no longer the upholsterer. He laughed gaily and innocently, throwing back his hair, showing his teeth: 'I pretended I was going to hit him. I frightened him, all right.' He imitated the gesture of a scared middle-aged man avoiding a blow. He laughed.

'And then you had to leave?' I asked.

Otto nodded. His face slowly changed. He was turning melancholy again.

'What did your father and mother say to that?'

'Oh, they've always been against me. Ever since I was small. If there were two crusts of bread mother would always give the bigger one to Lothar. Whenever I complained they used to say: "Go and work. You're old enough. Get your own food. Why should we support you?"' Otto's eyes moistened with the most sincere self-pity: 'Nobody understands me here. Nobody's good to me. They all hate me, really. They wish I was dead.'

'How can you talk such rubbish, Otto! Your mother certainly doesn't hate you.'

'Poor mother!' agreed Otto. He had changed his tone at once, seemingly utterly unaware of what he had just said: 'It's terrible. I can't bear to think of her working like that, every day. You know, Christoph, she's very, very ill. Often, at night, she coughs for hours and hours. And sometimes she spits out blood. I lie awake wondering if she's going to die.'

I nodded. In spite of myself I began to smile. Not that I disbelieved what he had said about Frau Nowak. But Otto himself, squatting there on the bed, was so animally alive, his naked brown body so sleek with health, that his talk of death seemed ludicrous, like the description of a funeral by a painted clown. He must have understood this, for he grinned back, not in the least shocked at my apparent callousness. Straightening his legs he bent forward without effort and grasped his feet with his hands: 'Can you do that, Christoph?'

A sudden notion pleased him: 'Christoph, if I show you something, will you swear not to tell a single soul?'

'All right.'

He got up and rummaged under his bed. One of the floor-boards was loose in the corner by the window: lifting it, he fished out a tin box which had once contained biscuits. The tin was full of letters and photographs. Otto spread them out on the bed:

'Mother would burn these if she found them . . . Look, Christoph, how do you like her? Her name's Hilde. I met her at the place where I go dancing . . . And this is Marie. Hasn't she got beautiful eyes? She's wild about me—all the other boys are jealous. But she's not really my type,' Otto shook his head seriously: 'You know, it's a funny thing, but as soon as I know that a girl's keen on me, I lose interest in her. I wanted to break with her altogether; but she came round here and made such a to-do in front of mother. So I have to see her sometimes to keep her quiet . . . And here's Trude—honestly, Christoph, would you believe she was twenty-seven? It's a fact! Hasn't she a marvellous figure? She lives in the west end, in a flat of her own! She's been divorced twice. I can go there whenever I like. Here's a photo her brother took of her. He wanted to take some of us two together, but I wouldn't let him. I was afraid he'd sell them, afterwards—you can be arrested for it, you know . . .' Otto smirked, handed me a packet of letters: 'Here, read these; they'll make you laugh. This one's from an Englishman. He's got the biggest car I ever saw in my life—here's a photo of it. He writes to me sometimes. Father got wind of it, and now he watches out to see if there's any money in the envelopes—the dirty dog! But I know a trick worth two of that! I've told all my friends to address their letters to the bakery on the corner. The baker's son is a pal of mine . . . Oh, that reminds me: I must write to the Baron and warn him at once . . .'

Down in the murky pit of the courtyard where the fog, in this clammy autumn weather, never lifted, the street singers and musicians succeeded each other in a performance which was nearly continuous. There were parties of boys with mandolins, an old man who played the concertina and a father who sang with his little girls. Easily the favourite tune was: *Aus der Jugendzeit*. I often heard it a dozen times in one morning. The father of the girls was paralysed and could only make desperate throttled noises like a donkey; but the daughters sang with the energy of fiends: 'Sie *kommt, sie kommt* nicht mehr!' they screamed in unison, like demons of the air, rejoicing in the frustration of mankind. Occasionally a groschen, screwed in a corner of newspaper, was tossed down from a window high above. It hit the pavement and ricochetted like a bullet, but the little girls never flinched.

Now and then the visiting nurse called to see Frau Nowak, shook her head over the sleeping arrangements and went away again. The inspector of housing, a pale young man with an open collar (which he obviously wore on principle), came also and took copious notes. The attic, he told Frau Nowak, was absolutely insanitary and uninhabitable. He had a slightly reproachful air as he said this, as though we ourselves were partly to blame. Frau Nowak bitterly resented these visits. They were, she thought, simply attempts to spy on her. She was haunted by the fear that the nurse or the inspector would look in at a moment when the flat was untidy. So deep were her suspicions that she even told lies—pretending that the leak in the roof wasn't serious—to get them out the house as quickly as possible.

Another regular visitor was the Jewish tailor and outfitter, who sold clothes of all kinds on the instalment plan. He was small and gentle and very persuasive. All day long he made his rounds of the tenements in the districts, collecting fifty pfennigs here, a mark there, scratching up his precarious livelihood, like a hen, from this apparently barren soil. He never pressed hard for money; preferring to urge his debtors to take more of his goods and embark upon a fresh series of payments. Two years ago Frau Nowak had bought a suit and an overcoat for Otto for three hundred marks. The suit and the overcoat had been worn out long ago but the money was not nearly repaid. Shortly after my arrival Frau Nowak invested in clothes for Grete to the value of seventy-five marks. The tailor made no objection at all.

The whole neighbourhood owed him money. Yet he was not unpopular: he enjoyed the status of a public character, whom people curse without real malice. 'Perhaps Lothar's right,' Frau Nowak would sometimes say: 'when Hitler comes, he'll show these Jews a thing or two. They won't be so cheeky then.' But when I suggested that Hitler, if he got his own way, would remove the tailor altogether, then Frau Nowak would immediately change her tone: 'Oh, I shouldn't like that to happen. After all, he makes very good clothes. Besides, a Jew will always let you have time if you're in difficulties. You wouldn't catch a Christian giving credit like he does . . . You ask the people round here, Herr Christoph: they'd never turn out the Jews.'

Towards evening Otto, who had spent the day in gloomy lounging—either lolling about the flat or chatting with his friends downstairs at the courtyard entrance—would begin to brighten up. When I got back from work I generally found him changing already from his sweater and knicker-bockers into his best suit, with its shoulders padded out to points, small tight double-breasted waistcoat and bell-bottomed trousers. He had quite a large selection of ties and it took him half an hour at least to choose one of them and to knot it to his satisfaction. He stood smirking in front of the cracked triangle of looking-glass in the kitchen, his pink bun-face dimpled with conceit, getting in Frau Nowak's way and disregarding all her protests. As soon as supper was over he was going out dancing.

I generally went out in the evenings too. However tired I was, I couldn't go to sleep immediately after my evening meal: Grete and her parents were often in bed by nine o'clock. So I went to the cinema or sat in a café and read the newspapers and yawned. There was nothing else to do.

At the end of our street there was a cellar *lokal* called the Alexander Casino. Otto showed it to me one evening, when we happened to leave the house together. You went down four steps from the street level, opened the door, pushed aside the heavy leather curtain which kept out the draught and found yourself in a long, low, dingy room. It was lit by red chinese lanterns and festooned with dusty paper streamers. Round the walls stood wicker tables and big shabby settees which looked like the seats of English third-class railway-carriages. At the far end were trellis-work alcoves, arboured over with imitation cherry-blossom twined on wires. The whole place smelt damply of beer.

I had been here before: a year ago, in the days when Fritz Wendel used to take me on Saturday evening excursions round the 'queer dives' of the city. It was all just as we had left it; only less sinister, less picturesque, symbolic no longer of a tremendous truth about the meaning of existence—because, this time, I wasn't in the least drunk. The same proprietor, an ex-boxer, rested his immense stomach on the bar, the same hangdog waiter shuffled forward in his soiled white coat: two girls, the very same perhaps, were dancing together to the wailing of the loud-speaker. A group of youths in sweaters and leather jackets were playing Sheep's Head; the spectators leaning over to see the cards. A boy with tattooed arms sat by the stove, deep in a crime shocker. His shirt was open at the neck, with the sleeves rolled up to his armpits: he wore shorts and socks, as if about to take part in a race. Over in the far alcove, a man and a boy were sitting together. The boy had a round childish face and heavy reddened eyelids which looked swollen as if from lack of sleep. He was relating something to the elderly, shaven-headed, respectable-looking man, who sat rather unwillingly listening and smoking a short cigar. The boy told his story carefully and with great patience. At intervals, to emphasize a point, he laid his hand on the

elderly man's knee and looked up into his face, watching its every movement shrewdly and intently, like a doctor with a nervous patient.

Later on, I got to know this boy quite well. He was called Pieps. He was
a great traveller. He ran away from home at the age of fourteen because his
father, a woodcutter in the Thuringian Forest, used to beat him. Pieps set
out to walk to Hamburg. At Hamburg he stowed away on a ship bound for
Antwerp and from Antwerp he walked back into Germany and along the
Rhine. He had been in Austria, too, and Czechoslovakia. He was full of
songs and stories and jokes: he had an extraordinarily cheerful and happy
nature, sharing what he had with his friends and never worrying where
his next meal was coming from. He was a clever pickpocket and worked
chiefly in an amusement-hall in the Friedrichstrasse, not far from the Passage, which was full of detectives and getting too dangerous nowadays. In
this amusement-hall there were punch-balls and peepshows and try-your-
grip machines. Most of the boys from the Alexander Casino spent their
afternoons there, while their girls were out working the Friedrichstrasse and
the Linden for possible pick-ups.

Pieps lived together with his two friends, Gerhardt and Kurt, in a cellar
on the canal-bank, near the station of the overhead railway. The cellar belonged to Gerhardt's aunt, an elderly Friedrichstrasse whore, whose legs
and arms were tattooed with snakes, birds and flowers. Gerhardt was a tall
boy with a vague, silly, unhappy smile. He did not pick pockets, but stole
from the big department-stores. He had never yet been caught, perhaps
because of the lunatic brazenness of his thefts. Stupidly grinning, he would
stuff things into his pockets right under the noses of the shop-assistants. He
gave everything he stole to his aunt, who cursed him for his laziness and
kept him very short of money. One day, when we were together, he took
from his pocket a brightly-coloured lady's leather belt: 'Look, Christoph,
isn't it pretty?'

'Where did you get it from?'

'From Landauers',' Gerhardt told me. 'Why . . . what are you smiling
at?'

"You see, the Landauers are friends of mine. It seems funny—that's all.'

At once, Gerhardt's face was the picture of dismay: 'You won't tell them,
Christoph, will you?'

'No,' I promised. 'I won't.'

Kurt came to the Alexander Casino less often than the others. I could
understand him better than I could understand Pieps or Gerhardt, because
he was consciously unhappy. He had a reckless, fatal streak in his character,
a capacity for pure sudden flashes of rage against the hopelessness of his
life. The Germans call it *Wut*. He would sit silent in his corner, drinking
rapidly, drumming with his fists on the table, imperious and sullen. Then,
suddenly, he would jump to his feet, exclaim: *'Ach, Scheiss!'* and go strid-

ing out. In this mood, he picked quarrels deliberately with the other boys, fighting them three or four at a time, until he was flung out into the street, half stunned and covered with blood. On these occasions even Pieps and Gerhardt joined against him as against a public danger: they hit him as hard as anyone else and dragged him home between them afterwards without the least malice for the black eyes he often managed to give them. His behaviour did not appear to surprise them in the least. They were all good friends again next day.

By the time I arrived back Herr and Frau Nowak had probably been asleep for two or three hours. Otto generally arrived later still. Yet Herr Nowak, who resented so much else in his son's behaviour, never seemed to mind getting up and opening the door to him, whatever the time of night. For some strange reason, nothing would induce the Nowaks to let either of us have a latchkey. They couldn't sleep unless the door was bolted as well as locked.

In these tenements each lavatory served for four flats. Ours was on the floor below. If, before retiring, I wished to relieve nature, there was a second journey to be made through the living-room in the dark to the kitchen, skirting the table, avoiding the chairs, trying not to collide with the head of the Nowaks' bed or jolt the bed in which Lothar and Grete were sleeping. However cautiously I moved, Frau Nowak would wake up: she seemed to be able to see me in the dark and embarrassed me with polite directions: 'No, Herr Christoph—not there, if you please. In the bucket on the left, by the stove.'

Lying in bed, in the darkness, in my tiny corner of the enormous human warren of the tenements, I could hear, with uncanny precision, every sound which came up from the courtyard below. The shape of the court must have acted as a gramophone-horn. There was someone going downstairs: our neighbour, Herr Müller, probably: he had a night-shift on the railway. I listened to his steps getting fainter, flight by flight; then they crossed the court, clear and sticky on the wet stone. Straining my ears, I heard, or fancied I heard, the grating of the key in the lock of the big street door. A moment later, the door closed with a deep, hollow boom. And now, from the next room, Frau Nowak had an outburst of coughing. In the silence which followed it, Lothar's bed creaked as he turned over, muttering something indistinct and threatening in his sleep. Somewhere on the other side of the court a baby began to scream, a window was slammed to, something very heavy, deep in the innermost recesses of the building, thudded dully against a wall. It was alien and mysterious and uncanny, like sleeping out in the jungle, alone.

Sunday was a long day at the Nowaks. There was nowhere to go in this wretched weather. We were all of us at home. Grete and Herr Nowak were

watching a trap for sparrows which Herr Nowak had made and fixed up in
the window. They sat there, hour by hour, intent upon it. The string
which worked the trap was in Grete's hand. Occasionally, they giggled at
each other and looked at me. I was sitting on the opposite side of the table,
frowning at a piece of paper on which I had written: 'But, Edward, can't
you *see?*' I was trying to get on with a novel. It was about a family who lived
in a large country house on unearned incomes and were very unhappy. They
spent their time explaining to each other why they couldn't enjoy their
lives; and some of the reasons—though I say it myself—were most ingenious. Unfortunately I found myself taking less and less interest in my
unhappy family: the atmosphere of the Nowak household was not very
inspiring. Otto, in the inner room with the door open, was amusing himself by balancing ornaments on the turntable of an old gramophone, which
was now minus sound-box and tone-arm, to see how long it would be before
they flew off and smashed. Lothar was filing keys and mending locks for
the neighbours, his pale sullen face bent over his work in obstinate concentration. Frau Nowak, who was cooking, began a sermon about the Good
and the Worthless Brother: 'Look at Lothar. Even when he's out of a job
he keeps himself occupied. But all you're good for is to smash things. You're
no son of mine.'

Otto lolled sneering on his bed, occasionally spitting out an obscene word
or making a farting noise with his lips. Certain tones of his voice were mad-
dening: they made one want to hurt him—and he knew it. Frau Nowak's
shrill scolding rose to a scream:

'I've a good mind to turn you out of the house! What have you ever done
for us? When there's any work going you're too tired to do it; but you're
not too tired to go gallivanting about half the night—you wicked unnatural
good-for-nothing . . . !'

Otto sprang to his feet and began dancing about the room with cries of
animal triumph. Frau Nowak picked up a piece of soap and flung it at him.
He dodged, and it smashed the window. After this Frau Nowak sat down
and began to cry. Otto ran to her at once and began to soothe her with
noisy kisses. Neither Lothar nor Herr Nowak took much notice of the row.
Herr Nowak seemed even rather to have enjoyed it: he winked at me slyly.
Later, the hole in the window was stopped with a piece of cardboard. It
remained unmended; adding one more to the many draughts in the attic.

During supper, we were all jolly. Herr Nowak got up from the table to
give imitations of the different ways in which Jews and Catholics pray. He
fell down on his knees and bumped his head several times vigorously on
the ground, gabbling nonsense which was supposed to represent Hebrew
and Latin prayers: 'Koolyvotchka, koolyvotchka, koolyvotchka. Amen.'
Then he told stories of executions, to the horror and delight of Grete and
Frau Nowak: 'William the First—the old William—never signed a death-
warrant; and do you know why? Because once, quite soon after he'd come

to the throne, there was a celebrated murder-case and for a long time the judges couldn't agree whether the prisoner was guilty or innocent, but at last they condemned him to be executed. They put him on the scaffold and the executioner took his axe—so; and swung it—like this; and brought it down: Ker*nack!* (They're all trained men, of course: You or I couldn't cut a man's head off with one stroke, if they gave us a thousand marks.) And the head fell into the basket—flop!' Herr Nowak rolled up his eyes, let his tongue hang out from the corner of his mouth and gave a really most vivid and disgusting imitation of the decapitated head: 'And then the head spoke, all by itself, and said: "I am innocent!" (Of course it was only the nerves; but it spoke, just as plainly as I'm speaking now.) "I am innocent!" it said. . . . And a few months later, another man confessed on his death-bed that he'd been the real murderer. So, after that, William never signed a death-warrant again.'

In the Wassertorstrasse one week was much like another. Our leaky stuffy little attic smelt of cooking and bad drains. When the living-room stove was alight, we could hardly breathe; when it wasn't, we froze. The weather had turned very cold. Frau Nowak tramped the streets, when she wasn't at work, from the clinic to the board of health offices and back again: for hours she waited on benches in draughty corridors or puzzled over complicated application-forms. The doctors couldn't agree about her case. One was in favour of sending her to a sanatorium at once. Another thought she was too far gone to be worth sending at all—and told her so. Another assured her that there was nothing serious the matter: she merely needed a fortnight in the Alps. Frau Nowak listened to all three of them with the greatest respect and never failed to impress upon me, in describing these interviews, that each was the kindest and cleverest professor to be found in the whole of Europe.

She returned home coughing and shivering, with sodden shoes, exhausted and semi-hysterical. No sooner was she inside the flat than she began scolding at Grete or at Otto, quite automatically, like a clockwork doll unwinding its spring:

'You mark my words—you'll end in prison! I wish I'd packed you off to a reformatory when you were fourteen. It might have done you some good . . . And to think that, in my whole family, we've never had anybody before who wasn't respectable and decent!'

'*You* respectable!' Otto sneered: 'When you were a girl you went around with every pair of trousers you could find.'

'I forbid you to speak to me like that! Do you hear? I forbid you! Oh, I wish I'd died before I bore you, you wicked unnatural child!'

Otto skipped around her, dodging her blows, wild with glee at the row he had started. In his excitement he pulled hideous grimaces.

'He's mad!' exclaimed Frau Nowak: 'Just look at him now, Herr Christoph. I ask you, isn't he just a raving madman? I must take him to the hospital to be examined.'

This idea appealed to Otto's romantic imagination. Often, when we were alone together, he would tell me with tears in his eyes:

'I shan't be here much longer, Christoph. My nerves are breaking down. Very soon they'll come and take me away. They'll put me in a strait-waistcoat and feed me through a rubber tube. And when you come to visit me, I shan't know who you are.'

Frau Nowak and Otto were not the only ones with 'nerves.' Slowly but surely the Nowaks were breaking down my powers of resistance. Every day I found the smell from the kitchen sink a little nastier: every day Otto's voice when quarrelling seemed harsher and his mother's a little shriller. Grete's whine made me set my teeth. When Otto slammed a door I winced irritably. At nights I couldn't get to sleep unless I was half drunk. Also, I was secretly worrying about an unpleasant and mysterious rash: it might be due to Frau Nowak's cooking, or worse.

I now spent most of my evenings at the Alexander Casino. At a table in the corner by the stove I wrote letters, talked to Pieps and Gerhardt or simply amused myself by watching the other guests. The place was usually very quiet. We all sat round or lounged at the bar, waiting for something to happen. No sooner came the sound of the outer door than a dozen pairs of eyes were turned to see what new visitor would emerge from behind the leather curtain. Generally, it was only a biscuit-seller with his basket or a Salvation Army girl with her collecting-box and tracts. If the biscuit-seller had been doing good business or was drunk he would throw dice with us for packets of sugar-wafers. As for the Salvation Army girl, she rattled her way drably round the room, got nothing and departed, without making us feel in the least uncomfortable. Indeed, she had become so much a part of the evening's routine that Gerhardt and Pieps did not even make jokes about her when she was gone. Then an old man would shuffle in, whisper something to the barman and retire with him into the room behind the bar. He was a cocaine-addict. A moment later he reappeared, raised his hat to all of us with a vague courteous gesture, and shuffled out. The old man had a nervous tic and kept shaking his head all the time, as if saying to Life: No. No. No.

Sometimes the police came, looking for wanted criminals or escaped re-formatory boys. Their visits were usually expected and prepared for. At any rate you could always, as Pieps explained to me, make a last-minute exit through the lavatory window into the courtyard at the back of the house: 'But you must be careful, Christoph,' he added: 'Take a good big jump. Or you'll fall down the coal-shoot and into the cellar. I did, once. And Hamburg Werner, who was coming after me, laughed so much that the bulls caught him.'

On Saturday and Sunday evenings the Alexander Casino was full. Visitors from the West End arrived, like ambassadors from another country. There were a good number of foreigners—Dutchmen mostly, and Englishmen. The Englishmen talked in loud, high, excited voices. They discussed communism and van Gogh and the best restaurants. Some of them seemed a little scared: perhaps they expected to be knifed in this den of thieves. Pieps and Gerhardt sat at their tables and mimicked their accents, cadging drinks and cigarettes. A stout man in horn spectacles asked: 'Were you at that delicious party Bill gave for the negro singers?' And a young man with a monocle murmured: 'All the poetry in the world is in that face.' I knew what he was feeling at that moment: I could sympathize with, even envy him. But it was saddening to know that, two weeks hence, he would boast about his exploits here to a select party of clubmen or dons—warmed discreet smilers around a table furnished with historic silver and legendary port. It made me feel older.

At last the doctors made up their minds: Frau Nowak was to be sent to the sanatorium after all: and quite soon—shortly before Christmas. As soon as she heard this she ordered a new dress from the tailor. She was as excited and pleased as if she had been invited to a party: 'The matrons are always very particular, you know, Herr Christoph. They see to it that we keep ourselves neat and tidy. If we don't we get punished—and quite right too . . . I'm sure I shall enjoy being there,' Frau Nowak sighed, 'if only I can stop myself worrying about the family. What they'll do when I'm gone, goodness only knows. They're as helpless as a lot of sheep . . . .' In the evenings she spent hours stitching warm flannel underclothes, smiling to herself, like a woman who is expecting a child.

On the afternoon of my departure Otto was very depressed.

'Now you're going, Christoph, I don't know what'll happen to me. Perhaps, six months from now, I shan't be alive at all.'

'You got on all right before I came, didn't you?'

'Yes . . . but now mother's going too. I don't suppose father'll give me anything to eat.'

'What rubbish!'

'Take me with you, Christoph. Let me be your servant. I could be very useful, you know. I could cook for you and mend your clothes and open the door for your pupils . . . .' Otto's eyes brightened as he admired himself in this new rôle. 'I'd wear a little white jacket—or perhaps blue would be better, with silver buttons . . . .'

'I'm afraid you're a luxury I can't afford.'

'Oh, but, Christoph, I shouldn't want any wages, of course.' Otto paused, feeling that this offer had been a bit too generous. 'That is,' he added cautiously, 'only just a mark or two to go dancing, now and then.'

'I'm very sorry.'

We were interrupted by the return of Frau Nowak. She had come home early to cook me a farewell meal. Her string-bag was full of things she had bought; she had tired herself out carrying it. She shut the kitchen-door behind her with a sigh and began to bustle about at once, her nerves on edge, ready for a row.

'Why, Otto, you've let the stove go out! After I specially told you to keep an eye on it! Oh dear, can't I rely on anybody in this house to help me with a single thing?'

'Sorry, mother,' said Otto. 'I forgot.'

'Of course you forgot! Do you ever remember anything? You *forgot!*' Frau Nowak screamed at him, her features puckered into a sharp little stabbing point of fury: 'I've worked myself into my grave for you, and that's my thanks! When I'm gone, I hope your father'll turn you out into the streets. We'll see how you like that! You great, lazy, hulking lump! Get out of my sight, do you hear! Get out of my sight!'

'All right! Christoph, you hear what she says?' Otto turned to me, his face convulsed with rage; at that moment the resemblance between them was quite startling; they were like creatures demoniacally possessed. 'I'll make her sorry for it as long as she lives!'

He swung round and plunged into the inner bedroom, slamming the rickety door behind him. Frau Nowak turned at once to the stove and began shovelling out the cinders. She was trembling all over and coughing violently. I helped her, putting firewood and pieces of coal into her hands; she took them from me blindly, without a glance or a word. Feeling, as usual, that I was only getting in the way, I went into the living-room and stood stupidly by the window, wishing that I could simply disappear. I had had enough. On the window-sill lay a stump of pencil. I picked it up and drew a small circle on the wood, thinking: I have left my mark. Then I remembered how I had done exactly the same thing, years ago, before leaving a boarding-house in North Wales. In the inner room all was quiet. I decided to confront Otto's sulks. I had still got my suit-cases to pack.

When I opened the door Otto was sitting on his bed. He was staring as if hypnotized at a gash in his left wrist, from which the blood was trickling down over his open palm and spilling in big drops on the floor. In his right hand, between finger and thumb, he held a safety-razor blade. He didn't resist when I snatched it from him. The wound itself was nothing much; I bandaged it with his handkerchief. Otto seemed to turn faint for a moment and lolled against my shoulder.

'How on earth did you manage to do it?'

'I wanted to show her,' said Otto. He was very pale. He had evidently given himself a nasty scare: 'You shouldn't have stopped me, Christoph.'

'You little idiot,' I said angrily, for he had frightened me, too: 'One of these days you'll really hurt yourself—by mistake.'

Otto gave me a long, reproachful look. Slowly his eyes filled with tears.

'What does it matter, Christoph? I'm no good . . . . What'll become of
me, do you suppose, when I'm older?'

'You'll get work.'

'Work . . .' The very thought made Otto burst into tears. Sobbing violently, he smeared the back of his hand across his nose.

I pulled out the handkerchief from my pocket. 'Here. Take this.'

'Thanks, Christoph . . .' He wiped his eyes mournfully and blew his
nose. Then something about the handkerchief itself caught his attention.
He began to examine it, listlessly at first, then with extreme interest.

'Why, Christoph,' he exclaimed indignantly, 'This is one of mine!'

One afternoon, a few days after Christmas, I visited the Wassertorstrasse
again. The lamps were alight already as I turned in under the archway and
entered the long, damp street, patched here and there with dirty snow.
Weak yellow gleams shone out from the cellar shops. At a hand-cart under
a gas-flare, a cripple was selling vegetables and fruit. A crowd of youths with
raw, sullen faces stood watching two boys fighting at a doorway: a girl's
voice screamed excitedly as one of them tripped and fell. Crossing the
muddy courtyard, inhaling the moist, familiar rottenness of the tenement
buildings, I thought: Did I really ever live here? Already, with my comfortable bed-sitting room in the West End and my excellent new job, I had
become a stranger to the slums.

The lights on the Nowaks' staircase were out of order: it was pitch-
dark. I groped my way upstairs without much difficulty and banged on their
door. I made as much noise as I could because, to judge from the shouting
and singing and shrieks of laughter within, a party was in progress.

'Who's there?' bawled Herr Nowak's voice.

'Christoph.'

'Aha! Christoph! Anglais! Englisch Man! Come in! Come in!'

The door was flung open. Herr Nowak swayed unsteadily on the threshold, with arms open to embrace me. Behind him stood Grete, shaking like
a jelly, with tears of laughter pouring down her cheeks. There was nobody
else to be seen.

'Good old Christoph!' cried Herr Nowak, thumping me on the back. 'I
said to Grete: I know he'll come. Christoph won't desert us!' With a large
burlesque gesture of welcome he pushed me violently into the living-room.
The whole place was fearfully untidy. Clothing of various kinds lay in a
confused heap on one of the beds; on the other were scattered cups, saucers,
shoes, knives and forks. On the sideboard was a frying-pan full of dried
fat. The room was lighted by three candles stuck into empty beer-bottles.

'All light's been cut off,' explained Herr Nowak, with a negligent sweep
of his arm: 'The bill isn't paid . . . Must pay it sometime, of course. Never
mind—it's nicer like this, isn't it? Come on, Grete, let's light up the Christmas tree.'

The Christmas tree was the smallest I had ever seen. It was so tiny and feeble that it could only carry one candle, at the very top. A single thin strand of tinsel was draped around it. Herr Nowak dropped several lighted matches on the floor before he could get the candle to burn. If I hadn't stamped them out the table-cloth might easily have caught fire.

'Where are Lothar and Otto?' I asked.

'Don't know. Somewhere about . . . They don't show themselves much, nowadays—it doesn't suit them, here . . . Never mind, we're quite happy by ourselves, aren't we, Grete?' Herr Nowak executed a few elephantine dance-steps and began to sing:

'O Tannenbaum! O Tannenbaum! . . . Come on, Christoph, all together now! Wie treu sind Deine Blätter!'

After this was over I produced my presents: cigars for Herr Nowak, for Grete chocolates and a clockwork mouse. Herr Nowak then brought out a bottle of beer from under the bed. After a long search for his spectacles, which were finally discovered hanging on the water-tap in the kitchen, he read me a letter which Frau Nowak had written from the sanatorium. He repeated every sentence three or four times, got lost in the middle, swore, blew his nose and picked his ears. I could hardly understand a word. Then he and Grete began playing with the clockwork mouse, letting it run about the table, shrieking and roaring whenever it neared the edge. The mouse was such a success that my departure was managed briefly, without any fuss. 'Good-bye, Christoph. Come again soon,' said Herr Nowak and turned back to the table at once. He and Grete were bending over it with the eagerness of gamblers as I made my way out of the attic.

Not long after this I had a call from Otto himself. He had come to ask me if I would go with him the next Sunday to see Frau Nowak. The sanatorium had its monthly visiting-day: there would be a special bus running from Hallesches Tor.

'You needn't pay for me, you know,' Otto added grandly. He was fairly shining with self-satisfaction.

'That's very handsome of you, Otto . . . A new suit?'

'Do you like it?'

'It must have cost a good bit.'

'Three hundred and fifty marks.'

'My word! Has your ship come home?'

Otto smirked: 'I'm seeing a lot of Trude now. Her uncle's left her some money. Perhaps, in the Spring, we'll get married.'

'Congratulations . . . I suppose you're still living at home?'

'Oh, I look in there occasionally,' Otto drew down the corners of his mouth in a grimace of languid distaste, 'but father's always drunk.'

'Disgusting, isn't it?' I mimicked his tone. We both laughed.

'My goodness, Christoph, is it as late as that? I must be getting along . . . Till Sunday. Be good.'

We arrived at the sanatorium about midday.

There was a bumpy cart-track winding for several kilometres through snowy pine-woods and then, suddenly, a gothic brick gateway like the entrance to a churchyard, with big red buildings rising behind. The bus stopped. Otto and I were the last of the passengers to get out. We stood stretching ourselves and blinking at the bright snow: out here in the country everything was dazzling white. We were all very stiff, for the bus was only a covered van, with packing-cases and school-benches for seats. The seats had not shifted much during the journey, for we had been packed together as tightly as books on a shelf.

And now the patients came running out to meet us—awkward padded figures muffled in shawls and blankets, stumbling and slithering on the trampled ice of the path. They were in such a hurry that their blundering charge ended in a slide. They shot skidding into the arms of their friends and relations, who staggered under the violence of the collision. One couple, amid shrieks of laughter, had tumbled over.

'Otto!'

'Mother!'

'So you've really come! How well you're looking!'

'Of course we've come, mother! What did you expect?'

Frau Nowak disengaged herself from Otto to shake hands with me.

'How do you do, Herr Christoph?'

She looked years younger. Her plump, oval, innocent face, lively and a trifle crafty, with its small peasant eyes, was like the face of a young girl. Her cheeks were brightly dabbed with colour. She smiled as though she could never stop.

'Ah, Herr Christoph, how nice of you to come! How nice of you to bring Otto to visit me!'

She uttered a brief, queer, hysterical little laugh. We mounted some steps into the house. The smell of the warm, clean, antiseptic building entered my nostrils like a breath of fear.

'They've put me in one of the smaller wards,' Frau Nowak told us. 'There's only four of us altogether. We get up to all sorts of games.' Proudly throwing open the door, she made the introductions: 'This is Muttchen—she keeps us in order! And this is Erna. And this is Erika—our baby!'

Erika was a weedy blonde girl of eighteen, who giggled: 'So here's the famous Otto! We've been looking forward to seeing him for weeks!'

Otto smiled subtly, discreetly, very much at his ease. His brand-new brown suit was vulgar beyond words; so were his lilac spats and his pointed yellow shoes. On his finger was an enormous signet-ring with a square chocolate-coloured stone. Otto was extremely conscious of it and kept posing his hand in graceful attitudes, glancing down furtively to admire the effect. Frau Nowak simply couldn't leave him alone. She must keep hugging him and pinching his cheeks.

'Doesn't he look well!' she exclaimed. 'Doesn't he look splendid! Why, Otto, you're so big and strong I believe you could pick me up with one hand!'

Old Muttchen had a cold, they said. She wore a bandage round her throat, tight under the high collar of her old-fashioned black dress. She seemed a nice old lady, but somehow slightly obscene, like an old dog with sores. She sat on the edge of her bed with the photographs of her children and grandchildren on the table beside her, like prizes she had won. She looked slyly pleased, as though she were glad to be so ill. Frau Nowak told us that Muttchen had been three times in this sanatorium already. Each time she had been discharged as cured, but within nine months or a year she would have a relapse and have to be sent back again.

'Some of the cleverest professors in Germany have come here to examine her,' Frau Nowak added, with pride, 'but you always fool them, don't you, Muttchen dear?'

The old lady nodded, smiling like a clever child which is being praised by its elders.

'And Erna is here for the second time,' Frau Nowak continued. 'The doctors said she'd be all right; but she didn't get enough to eat. So now she's come back to us, haven't you, Erna?'

'Yes, I've come back,' Erna agreed.

She was a skinny, bobbed-haired woman of about thirty-five, who must once have been very feminine, appealing, wistful, and soft. Now, in her extreme emaciation, she seemed possessed by a kind of desperate resolution, a certain defiance. She had immense, dark, hungry eyes. The wedding-ring was loose on her bony finger. When she talked and became excited her hands flitted tirelessly about in sequences of aimless gestures, like two shrivelled moths.

'My husband beat me and then ran away. The night he went he gave me such a thrashing that I had the marks afterwards for months. He was such a great strong man. He nearly killed me.' She spoke calmly, deliberately, yet with a certain suppressed excitement, never taking her eyes from my face. Her hungry glance bored into my brain, reading eagerly what I was thinking. 'I dream about him now, sometimes,' she added, as if faintly amused.

Otto and I sat down at the table while Frau Nowak fussed around us with coffee and cakes which one of the sisters had brought. Everything which happened to me to-day was curiously without impact: my senses were muffled, insulated, functioning as if in a vivid dream. In this calm, white room, with its great windows looking out over the silent snowy pine-woods—the Christmas-tree on the table, the paper festoons above the beds,

the nailed-up photographs, the plate of heart-shaped chocolate biscuits—
these four women lived and moved. My eyes could explore every corner
of their world: the temperature-charts, the fire extinguisher, the leather
screen by the door. Dressed daily in their best clothes, their clean hands no
longer pricked by the needle or roughened from scrubbing, they lay out
on the terrace, listening to the wireless, forbidden to talk. Women being
shut up together in this room had bred an atmosphere which was faintly
nauseating, like soiled linen locked in a cupboard without air. They were
playful with each other and shrill, like overgrown schoolgirls. Frau Nowak
and Erika indulged in sudden furtive bouts of ragging. They plucked at
each other's clothes, scuffled silently, exploded into shrilly strained laughter.
They were showing off in front of us.

'You don't know how we've looked forward to to-day,' Erna told me, 'To
see a real live man!'

Frau Nowak giggled.

'Erika was such an innocent girl until she came here . . . . You didn't know
anything, did you, Erika?'

Erika sniggered.

'I've learnt enough since then . . . !'

'Yes, I should think you have! Would you believe it, Herr Christoph—
her aunt sent her this little mannikin for Christmas, and now she takes it to
bed with her every night, because she says she must have a man in her bed!'

Erika laughed boldly, 'Well, it's better than nothing, isn't it?'

She winked at Otto, who rolled his eyes, pretending to be shocked.

After lunch Frau Nowak had to put in an hour's rest. So Erna and Erika
took possession of us for a walk in the grounds.

'We'll show them the cemetery first,' Erna said.

The cemetery was for pet animals belonging to the sanatorium staff which
had died. There were about a dozen little crosses and tombstones, pen-
cilled with mock-heroic inscriptions in verse. Dead birds were buried there
and white mice and rabbits, and a bat which had been found frozen after a
storm.

'It makes you feel sad to think of them lying there, doesn't it?' said Erna.
She scooped away the snow from one of the graves. There were tears in
her eyes.

But, as we walked away down the path, both she and Erika were very
gay. We laughed and threw snowballs at each other. Otto picked up Erika
and pretended he was going to throw her into a snowdrift. A little further
on we passed close to a summer-house, standing back from the path on a
mound among the trees. A man and a woman were just coming out of it.

'That's Frau Klemke,' Erna told me. 'She's got her husband here to-day.
Just think, that old hut's the only place in the whole grounds where two
people can be alone together . . . .'

'It must be pretty cold in this weather.'

'Of course it is! To-morrow her temperature will be up again and she'll have to stay in bed for a fortnight . . . But who cares! If I were in her place I'd do the same myself.' Erna squeezed my arm: 'We've got to live while we're young, haven't we?'

'Of course we have!'

Erna looked up quickly into my face; her big dark eyes fastened on to mine like hooks; I could imagine I felt them pulling me down.

'I'm not really a consumptive, you know, Christoph . . . . You didn't think I was, did you, just because I'm here?'

'No, Erna, of course I didn't.'

'Lots of the girls here aren't. They just need looking after for a bit, like me . . . The doctor says that if I take care of myself I shall be as strong as ever I was . . . And what do you think the first thing is I shall do when they let me out of here?'

'What?'

'First I shall get my divorce, and then I shall find a husband.' Erna laughed, with bitter triumph, 'That won't take me long—I can promise you!'

After tea we sat upstairs in the ward. Frau Nowak had borrowed a gramophone so that we could dance. I danced with Erna. Erika danced with Otto. She was tomboyish and clumsy, laughing loudly whenever she slipped or trod on his toes. Otto, sleekly smiling, steered her backwards and forwards with skill, his shoulders hunched in the fashionable chimpanzee stoop of Hallesches Tor. Old Muttchen sat looking on from her bed. When I held Erna in my arms I felt her shivering all over. It was almost dark now, but nobody suggested turning on the light.

After a while we stopped dancing and sat round in a circle on the beds. Frau Nowak had begun to talk about her childhood days, when she had lived with her parents on a farm in East Prussia. 'We had a saw-mill of our own,' she told us, 'and thirty horses. My father's horses were the best in the district; he won prizes with them, many a time, at the show. . . . .' The ward was quite dark now. The windows were big pale rectangles in the darkness. Erna, sitting beside me on the bed, felt down for my hand and squeezed it; then she reached behind her and drew my arm round her body. She was trembling violently. 'Christoph . . .' she whispered in my ear.

'. . . and in the summer-time,' Frau Nowak was saying, 'we used to go dancing in the big barn down by the river . . .'

My mouth pressed against Erna's hot, dry lips. I had no particular sensation of contact: all this was part of the long, rather sinister symbolic dream which I seemed to have been dreaming throughout the day. 'I'm so happy, this evening . . .' Erna whispered.

'The postmaster's son used to play the fiddle,' said Frau Nowak. 'He played beautifully . . . it made you want to cry . . .'

From the bed on which Erika and Otto were sitting came sounds of scuffling and a loud snigger: 'Otto, you naughty boy . . . I'm surprised at you! I shall tell your mother!'

Five minutes later a sister came to tell us that the bus was ready to start.

'My word, Christoph,' Otto whispered to me, as we were putting on our overcoats, 'I could have done anything I liked with that girl! I felt her all over . . . Did you have a good time with yours? A bit skinny, wasn't she—but I bet she's hot stuff!'

Then we were clambering into the bus with the other passengers. The patients crowded round to say good-bye. Wrapped and hooded in their blankets, they might have been the members of an aboriginal forest tribe.

Frau Nowak had begun crying, though she tried hard to smile.

'Tell father I'll be back soon . . .'

'Of course you will, mother! You'll soon be well now. You'll soon be home.'

'It's only for a short time . . .' sobbed Frau Nowak; the tears running down over her hideous frog-like smile. And suddenly she started coughing —her body seemed to break in half like a hinged doll. Clasping her hands over her breast, she uttered short yelping coughs like a desperate injured animal. The blanket slipped from her head and shoulders: a wisp of hair, working loose from the knot, was getting into her eyes—she shook her head blindly to avoid it. Two sisters gently tried to lead her away, but at once she began to struggle furiously. She wouldn't go with them.

'Go in, mother,' begged Otto. He was almost in tears himself. 'Please go in! You'll catch your death of cold!'

'Write to me sometimes, won't you, Christoph?' Erna was clutching my hand as though she were drowning. Her eyes looked up at me with a terrifying intensity of unashamed despair. 'It doesn't matter if it's only a postcard . . . just sign your name . . .'

'Of course I will . . .'

They all thronged round us for a moment in the little circle of light from the panting bus, their lit faces ghastly like ghosts against the black stems of the pines. This was the climax of my dream: the instant of nightmare in which it would end. I had an absurd pang of fear that they were going to attack us—a gang of terrifyingly soft muffled shapes—clawing us from our seats, dragging us hungrily down, in dead silence. But the moment passed. They drew back—harmless, after all, as mere ghosts—into the darkness, while our bus, with a great churning of its wheels, lurched forward towards the city, through the deep unseen snow.

CONVALESCENCE

Kay Boyle

(1903–   )

ALL THE CHILDREN came into the room and looked at mother lying on the bed. The four of them stood still, just inside the doorway, and looked at her. She might have been dead, so strange she seemed to them, and her mouth never opened to bid or greet them. But father had said they should go up alone to see her, for a grown person might set her to weeping, and it was better that way.

"What is it that makes her weep?" said Bindy.

"It's something to do with her nerves," said father.

"I didn't know people could be sick all summer," Bindy said.

Up they went to her room, and they might have stood so within the door forever had not the wind suddenly sprung to life and flung it closed behind them. There they were, caught in the room with her, and no way to turn. The grass blinds were fanning the sunlight in the windows. Bindy said: "Hello."

"Hello," said mother softly. And then she called out, as though in fear: "Oh, Bindy!" He dropped the hands of the others and went running to her side. She lifted her quivering arm from the bed and put it around him. He could almost make out the green night-gown in the dim room, and her rings, and her hair brushed back behind her ears.

"Oh, Bindy," said mother in her soft fearful voice. "Look at mother's fingers! Her rings are all too big for her now!"

"You're not really his mother," said Anne. She spun around on one foot in the room, elated by the burden of disaster on the air. "Only Rolly and Midge belong to you," she said, spinning. Her braids swung out like two accusing fingers as she spun. Anne and Midge began to laugh together, the two of them covering their mouths to muffle their laughter in their hands. The wondrous sense of infliction set them to tittering and wavering in their little skirts in the darkened room. But mother had been ill too long; she had no patience left for them. The stone hearts of little girls belonged, like those of perverts, in a privy world of their own.

Rolly was gone from sight, under the bed on his hands and knees, and no one gave a thought to him. Mother held Bindy's fingers tight. And "what am I going to do, Bindy?" she whispered. "I haven't any friends left. Nobody cares any more."

"I'm your friend," said Bindy. He felt her arm pressing soft around him. "I'm a good friend of yours," he said.

"But I've got so old," said mother in complaint. "The color's all gone out of my eyes, you know, Bindy. They won't give me a looking-glass. They don't want me to see."

"Do your nerves hurt you very bad?" said Bindy.

"Oh, they hurt awfully, awfully," said mother, and her voice went suddenly blind with tears. The thought of herself so grieving, so gentle, defenseless as no other woman had ever been because of her beauty and her frailties; such thought returned like a specter to her mind and moved unseen from one fount of pity to the next. "It hurts the worst right here, Bindy," she said, and her throat was parched with anguish. "Put your hand right here where mother's heart is and maybe you'll help it to go away."

Bindy put his hand down on her night-dress. He could feel the soft quivering life of her heart in protest, as though he held it captive in his hand.

"There're an awful lot of kinds of sickness, aren't there?" said Bindy.

"This kind has made me so old," said mother, whispering in sorrow to him. "I know what my eyes are like, and my hair coming out in handfuls all over my head, Bindy."

"I bet you'd get a prize anywhere," said Bindy. He could not bear the tears to run down her face. "I'm not fooling. I bet you'd get a prize almost anywhere for being the most beautiful woman."

Mother lifted her head up, strong from the pillow.

"Bindy, honey, do you want to do something for mother?" she said. "Just get me my looking-glass over there, so I can have a little peek at myself."

But the little girls had sped across the room to be the first at the dressing-table. There they stood, touching one thing and then another, puzzled that they could not find it there.

"There isn't any looking-glass any more," said Anne.

"They've taken everything," mother cried out. "They've taken mother's little curved scissors, and even her nail-file, Bindy! They've taken everything that hurts as if they thought I'd hurt myself some more!"

It was then that father came in and took the hands of the little girls.

"You must come away now," he said, and he looked shyly and uncertainly at mother. "Long enough for the first time, children," said father. "Come, Bindy, son," he said. "Mother must have a rest."

Father leaned over to kiss mother's face, but she turned it sharply on the pillow.

"Oh, don't! Oh, don't!" she said in her weak grievous voice. "I'm so tired, so tired."

They went out the door with him, the two little girls and Bindy. Father closed it softly behind, and they all went soundlessly down the stairs. In a moment mother began to cry; she lay crying senselessly, weakly into her pillow. After a while, with the tears still wet on her face, she fell asleep.

A wonderful fresh darkness had come into every part of the room while she lay sleeping. When she opened her eyes, it was deep behind the chairs in the room, and hanging like a cloth flung over the table. The high-boy in the corner had a row of light brass smiles, and somewhere within the shadows was a presence. There was no sound, but she could feel its breath and its being.

"Who's in this room with me?" she said. A dew of terror had sprung out on her brow, but she spoke the words sharp and loud across the room. She could not move, but she watched the little man stand up beside her. He put out his hand to her on the bed.

"Rolly," he said, with his head cocked.

"Oh, Rolly, Rolly," breathed mother. "Oh, Rolly." But her bare limbs were shaking with cold in the sheets. "How ever did mother's baby . . ." she said, and her teeth were shaking together. It must be the heart of winter, and she would never be warm again. "Does little Rolly want to help mother?" she said softly. "Come here, Rolly, darling," she said, "and mother will tell you what to do."

The little man came close in the darkness and she seized his hand in her fingers. He seemed like a dwarf to her, twisted and weird, with his face unseen in the gloom. "Rolly," she whispered, "now Rolly only needs to walk over to mother's bureau. You see mother's big bureau? Now just walk sweetly over to mother's big bureau and open the drawer wide." She gave him a little push with her fingers, and he sat down suddenly on the floor. "Rolly," said mother. "Rolly, dear, get up." She could not lift herself from the pillows to see. "Rolly," she said, "you don't want to make mother sad, do you? You want to do what mother tells you to do." She felt the hand of ice on her heart, and she could not shake it from her. The little man stood up in the dark, and what time of life does sense begin to come to them, she thought wildly. Is it at two years of age or three that they run and do as they are bid? "Rolly," she said, "now you want to help mother, don't you? Now run quick, quick to mother's big bureau and do just as she tells you."

Suddenly Rolly drew away in the darkness, and set off towards the window. She reared up her head on her neck, like an adder watching, peering helpless, cold, into the room that the night was blotting away. She heard Rolly strike a chair in the dark, and his voice cry out in pain.

"Oh, Rolly," said mother. "Aren't you mother's big Rolly? It didn't hurt so very much, did it now, Rolly? You're not going to cry over a silly thing like that. You must be mother's big brave boy and pick yourself up and do what she tells you."

She heard him sniff and move on the floor.

"Rolly," she whispered, with her head raised, seeking. "Rolly, where are you now?"

His hand slapped the smooth side of a wooden body.

"Here," said Rolly's small voice out of the dark.

"Yes, yes," said mother softly. "Now, pull the drawer open, Rolly." Her breath went whistling through her teeth as they chattered. She could hear the bureau drawer slowly easing wide.

"Rolly dear," said mother, "just put your little hand right down inside it, right down inside, right there next to the window where you are."

She could hear Rolly grunt as he groped in the darkness, and suddenly the door opened and the nurse walked straight into the room. Mother lay still on the bed and watched the nurse switch on the small blue light in the corner. Her apron hung down from her waist, as blank as paper. When she turned around she saw the baby staring at the light.

"So this is where Rolly's been all the time!" she said.

"I've been asleep," said mother in her soft weary voice. "I didn't even know."

The nurse took him up in her arms and he did not speak nor turn his head towards the deep wide bed. She bore him out the door and left it standing wide. Mother could hear her going down the hall, down, down, down the three little steps to the nursery. In a moment she would hear the water spilling warm into the bath.

The children came up the front stairs, quietly, on their toes, as father had told them they must walk now: Bindy, and Midge, and Anne passing down the hall. Mother knew the sound of each footfall as though it were a separate hammer striking. Single and blind the blows fell on her flesh, summoning her anguish from repose, striking row upon row of brass-eyed nails into the lid that closed upon exhaustion.

"Bindy," she cried out from her room. "Just Bindy. Come and see mother."

She turned her head to watch his slight, muted body come in from the hallway. Midge and Anne went whispering away.

"Bindy," she said, borrowing ease from some other time and place. "Bindy, will you get mother something out of her bureau-drawer."

He stood still for a moment, slim and shy, looking at her.

"You're getting better, aren't you?" he said.

"I'm trying hard to get better," she said, curbing the wild speed of her blood. "Oh, so hard!" If he did not make haste, the nurse might come back to the room. "Bindy, dear, just put your hand down in the corner of the drawer that's open." Bindy set down his net of shining glassy marble eyes and crossed the soft dim room.

"There's a little bottle in there, Bindy darling," said mother. "Do you find it, darling, underneath the handkerchiefs and things?"

"Yes," said Bindy. He took it out of the drawer and held it up. "It's a pretty big bottle," he said.

"That's the one, Bindy, that's it," said mother. Her hand was shaking out before her. "Now give it to me, darling." He brought it across the room to her, treading soft and careful on the matting. She reached out her own stricken hand. "It's just between you and me, isn't it, Bindy? You and I will have a secret, you see, and we won't tell nurse or daddy or anyone at all."

"All right," said Bindy. He picked up his marbles. "Maybe if you're getting better I could play marbles here?" he said.

"But your bath must be ready now," said mother. "You'd better go now, Bindy. You'd better go and see."

She held up her head, listening to his fading steps and the hop and the skip at the nursery steps, going down. Then she set her teeth hard into the cork, and out it eased with a slow sucking gasp. Her arm was quaking in the shaded light, but she tilted the bottle up and the dark rich whiskey ran scalding down. At the first taste of it, the cold went off; she could feel it floating off, like veils from her limbs, as the cold had always done. A queer heathen laughter was beginning to shake within; the stuff ran thin against the bottle's glass and burned its way deeper and deeper into her swooning flesh.

When the nursery door opened, she flashed the bottle under the cover. But the nurse's step went past the open door and halted at the linen-closet in the hall. Mother heard her taking the towels out for the children's bath. Everything was soft and safe; the terror had been struck away, like shackles, from her wrists. Outside in the summery evening she could hear father pacing the walk below. Up and down went his steps, as if there were some distress in his soul. Up and down, walking his unrest to sleep, as if to ease its storming. What does he fear, what does he fear, thought mother, and she was shaken all over with laughter. What does he fear now that the winter has given over to spring?

After a while the little girls came down the hall, borne gently on an odorous warm wave from the bath. She could remember the smell of the powder on their flesh, and their hair brushed shining. She lay still in the swinging circles of the bed, seeking the high-boy's smile, or flower in curtain for anchor, and listening, whether she would or no, to the little girls' soft voices. This was the place allotted the grown, she thought: to eavesdrop, to watch, to spy.

"You're not my *real* sister," Anne's voice was saying. Spy on their actions, their hands, and the drop of their skirts; spy on their talk together. The warmth of the night was beating softly, softly now onto the dark shoals of the room.

"Who am I?" said Midge, hushed in wonder. "Who am I?"

The rising sea of warmth was lapping close to the bed now.

"Bindy's not your *real* brother," said Anne. "Father was married two times. Father's not your father. Bindy and father belong all to me."

"Who am I?" said Midge, lifting her voice in wonder to wisdom. Maybe these words were the words they spoke every day to each other, in worship of the mystery, or maybe they had never spoken them before.

"I don't know who you are," said the wise voice over the open sea of darkness. "Father's not your father."

The dark tide was full now, had risen; mother could no longer stir for the weight of it creeping warm upon her flesh. She was rocked close, cradled and quiet in it.

"Where's my father?" said Midge, stopped still for ever in wonder.

"Your father's dead," Anne's voice said. There was a wondrous murmur of sound now as though Bindy and Rolly too had set sail on the creeping waters.

"Did they kill him with a knife?" said Midge. Mother could hear the paddling of the oars come close, and the keels approaching. In a moment the prows would be on her, but still she did not stir. She lay floating, her arms out, her head back, drifting.

"Give me your hand, Rolly," said Bindy. He spoke in a hard whisper across the waters.

"I don't know," said Anne. "Maybe they cut his head off." The little girls tittered with laughter. "Or maybe he was sick and died in bed like everybody."

"Maybe mother will die," said Midge.

"You fools!" whispered Bindy. "Rolly, give me your hand going downstairs."

THE STATION

H. E. Bates

(1905–   )

For thirty seconds after the lorry had halted between the shack and the petrol pumps the summer night was absolutely silent. There was no wind; the leaves and the grass stalks were held in motionless suspense in the sultry air. And after the headlights had gone out the summer darkness was complete too. The pumps were dead white globes, like idols of porcelain; there was no light at all in the station. Then, as the driver and his mate alighted, slamming the cabin doors and grinding their feet on the gravel, the light in the station came suddenly on: a fierce electric flicker from the naked globe in the shack, the light golden in one wedge-shape shaft across the gravel pull-in. And seeing it the men stopped. They stood for a moment with the identical suspense of the grass and the trees.

The driver spoke first. He was a big fellow, quite young, with breezy blue eyes and stiff untrained hair and a comic mouth. His lips were elastic: thin bands of pink india-rubber that were for ever twisting themselves into grimaces of irony and burlesque, his eyes having that expression of comic and pained astonishment seen on the painted faces of Aunt Sallies in shooting galleries.

His lips twisted to the shape of a buttonhole, so that he whispered out of one corner. 'See her? She heard us come. What'd I tell you?'

The mate nodded. He too was young, but beside the driver he was boyish, his cheeks pink and smooth and shiny as white cherries, his hair yellow and light and constantly ruffled up like the fur of a fox-cub. And unlike the driver's his lips and eyes were quite still; so that he had a look of intense immobility.

He could see the woman in the shack. Short white casement curtains of transparent lace on brass rods cut across the window, but above and through them he could see the woman clearly. She was big-shouldered and dark, with short black hair, and her face was corn-coloured under the light. She seemed about thirty; and that astonished him.

'I thought you said she was young,' he said.

'So she is.' The driver's eyes flashed white. 'Wait'll you git close. How old d'ye think she is?'

'Thirty. More.'

'Thirty? She's been here four year. And was a kid when she was married, not nineteen. How's that up you?'

'She *looks* thirty.'

'So would you if you'd kept this bloody shack open every night for four year. Come on, let's git in.'

They began to walk across the gravel, but the driver stopped.

'And don't forgit what I said. She's bin somebody. She's had education. Mind your ups and downs.'

And when they opened the door of the shack and shuffled in, the driver first, the mate closing the door carefully behind him, the woman stood behind the rough-carpentered counter with her arms folded softly across her chest, in an attitude of unsurprised expectancy. The counter was covered with blue-squared oil-cloth, tacked down. By the blue alarm clock on the lowest of the shelves behind it, the time was four minutes past midnight. At the other end of the shelf a flat shallow kettle was boiling on an oil-stove. The room was like an oven. The woman's eyes seemed curiously drowsy, as though clouded over with the steam and the warm oil-fumes. And for half a minute nothing happened. She did not move. The men stood awkward. Then the driver spoke. His india-rubber mouth puckered comically to one side, and his eye flicked in a wink that was merely friendly and habitual.

'Well, here we are again.'

She nodded; the drowsiness of her eyes cleared a little. All the same there was something reserved about her, almost sulky.

'What would you like?' she said.

'Give me two on a raft and coffee,' the driver said.

'Two on a raft and coffee,' the woman said. She spoke beautifully, without effort, and rather softly. 'What's your friend going to have?'

The mate hesitated. His eyes were fixed on the woman, half-consciously, in admiration. And the driver had to nudge him, smiling his india-rubber smile of comic irony, before he became aware of all that was going on.

'Peck up,' the driver said.

'That'll do me,' the mate said.

'Two on a raft twice and coffee,' the woman said. 'Is that it?'

Though the mate did not know it for a moment, she was addressing him. He stood in slight bewilderment, as though he were listening to a language he did not understand. Then as he became aware of her looking at him and waiting for an answer the bewilderment became embarrassment and his fair cherry-smooth cheeks flushed very red, the skin under the short golden hairs and his neck flaming. He stood dumb. He did not know what to do with himself.

'I'm afraid I don't know your friend's name or his tastes yet,' the woman said. 'Shall I make it two poached twice and coffee?'

'Just like me. Forgot to introduce you,' the driver said. His mouth was a wrinkle of india-rubber mocking. 'Albie, this is Mrs. Harvey. This is Albert Armstrong. Now mate on Number 4, otherwise Albie.'

The woman smiled, and in complete subjection and fascination the boy smiled too.

'Are you sure that's all right?' she said. 'Poached and coffee? It sounds hot to me.'

'Does me all right,' the driver said.

'I could make you a fresh salad,' she said. And again she was speaking to the mate, with a kind of soft and indirect invitation. 'There would be eggs in that.'

'I'll have that,' the mate said.

'What?' the driver said. His eyes were wide open, his mouth wide also in half serious disgust, as though the mate had committed a sort of sacrilege. 'You don' know what's good.'

'So you'll have the salad?' the woman said.

'Yes, please.'

'I can give you the proper oil on it, and vinegar. You can have fruit afterwards if you'd like it.'

'Fruit?' the driver said. 'What fruit?'

She took the kettle from the oil-stove and poured a little hot water into the coffee-pot and then a little into each of the egg-poachers. 'Plums,' she said.

'Now you're talking,' the driver said. 'Plums. Some sense. Now you *are* talking.'

'Go and get yourself a few if you like them so much.'

'Show me. Show me a plum-tree within half a mile and I'm off.'

'Go straight down the garden and it's the tree on the left. Pick as many as you like.'

The driver opened the door, grinning. 'Coming, Albie?'

'You're not afraid of the dark, are you?' the woman said.

This time she was speaking to the driver. And suddenly as he stood there at the door, grimacing with comic irony at her, his whole head and face and neck and shoulders became bathed in crimson light, as though he had become the victim of a colossal blush. Startled, he lifted up his face and looked up at the shack from the outside. The bright electric sign with the naked letters saying simply *The Station* was like a fire of scarlet and white. At intervals it winked and darkened, on and out, scarlet to darkness, *The Station* to nothing. The driver stood with uplifted face, all scarlet, in surprised admiration.

'Blimey, that's a winner. When'd you get that?'

'It's new this week.'

'It's a treat. It makes no end of a difference. How's it you didn't have it on when we came in?'

'I keep forgetting it. I'm so used to sitting here in the dark I can't get used to it. It's a bit uncanny.'

The driver went down the shack steps, into the night. The woman, busy with the eggs, and the boy, leaning against the counter, could see him standing back, still faintly crimson, in admiration of the eternal winking light. And for a minute, as he stood there, the station was completely silent, the August darkness like velvet, the sultry night air oppressing all sound except the soft melancholy murmur of the simmering kettle. Then the woman called:

'You'd better get your plums. The eggs won't be two minutes.'

The driver answered something, only barely audible, and after the sound of his feet crunching the gravel the silence closed in again.

It was like a stoke-room in the shack. The smells of coffee and eggs and oil were fused into a single breath of sickening heat. Like the driver, the boy stood in his shirt-sleeves. He stood still, very self-conscious, watching the woman breaking the eggs and stirring the coffee and finally mixing in a glass bowl the salad for himself. He did not know what to do or say. Her thin white dress was like the silky husk of a seed-pod, just bursting open. Her ripe breasts swelled under it like two sun-swollen seeds. And he could not take his eyes away from them. He was electrified. His blood quivered with the current of excitement. And all the time, even though she was busy with the eggs on the stove, and the mixing of the salad, and very often not looking at him, she was aware of it. Looking up sometimes from the stove or the salad she would look past him, with an air of arrested dreaminess, her dark eyes lovely and sulky. The deliberation of it maddened him. He remembered things the driver had said as they came along the road. The words flashed in his mind as though lit up by the electricity of his veins. 'She's a peach, Albie. But I'll tell you what. One bloody wink out o' place and you're skedaddled. She won't have it. She's nice to the chaps because it's business, that's all. See what I mean, Albie? She'll look at you fit to melt your bleedin' heart out, but it don't mean damn all. She wants to make that station a success, that's all. That's why she runs the night shack. Her husband runs the day show and she's second house, kind of. It's her own idea. See?'

And suddenly his thoughts broke off. The lights in his brain, as it were, went out. His mind was blank. She was looking at him. He stood transfixed, his veins no longer electric but relapsed, his blood weak.

'Like it on the lorry?' she said.

'Yes.' He hardly spoke.

She had finished making the salad and she pushed the bowl across the counter towards him before speaking again.

'You're not very old for the job, are you?'

'I'm eighteen.'

'Get on with old Spike?'

'Yes.'

'Isn't it lonely at first? They all say it's lonely when they first begin.'

'I don't mind it.'

'What's your girl say to it?'

It was as though the electric sign had been suddenly turned on him as it had been turned on the driver. He stood helpless, his face scarlet.

'I ain't got a girl.'

'What? Not a nice boy like you?' She was smiling, half in mockery. 'I know you must have.'

'No.'

'Does she love you much?' She looked at him in mock seriousness, her eyes lowered.

'I ain't got one.'

'Honest?' She pushed the bottles of oil and vinegar across the counter towards him. 'I'll ask Spike when he comes in.'

'No, don't say anything to Spike,' he begged. 'Don't say nothing. He's always kidding me about her, anyway.'

'You said you hadn't got a girl.'

'Well——'

She took two plates from the rack behind the counter and then knives and forks from the drawer under the counter and then laid them out.

'Does she hate it when you're on nights?' she said.

'Yes.'

'What's she like—dark or fair?'

'Dark.'

'Like me?'

He could not answer. He only gazed straight at her in mute embarrassment and nodded. Every word she uttered fired him with passionate unrest. The current in his blood was renewed again. He felt himself tightened up. And she could see it all.

'You'd better call Spike,' she said. 'The eggs are ready.'

He moved towards the door. Then he turned and stopped. 'Don't say nothing,' he said.

'All right.'

He stood at the door, his face scarlet under the winking sign, and called out for Spike, singing the word, 'Spi-ike!' And he could hear the sound echoing over the empty land in the darkness. There was a smell of corn in the air, stronger and sweeter even than the smell of the heat and cooking in the shack. It came in sweet waves from across the invisible fields in the warm night air.

'I know how you feel,' she said.

He turned sharply. 'How?'

'Come and eat this salad and cool down a bit.'

He came from the door to the counter in obedience, pulling out a stool and sitting on it.

'Oil and vinegar?' she said. 'The coffee will be ready by the time Spike comes.'

'How do I feel?' he insisted.

'You know.'

'Yes, but how do you know?'

'I've felt like it myself.'

She stood with her arms folded and resting on the counter edge, and leaning slightly forward, so that he could see her breasts beneath the open dress. She looked at him with a kind of pity, with tenderness, but half-amused. He saw the breasts rise and fall with the same slow and almost sulky passion as she looked at him. He stared from her breasts to her face, and she stared back, her eyes never moving. And they stood like that, not moving or speaking, but only as it were burning each other up, until suddenly Spike came in.

The woman stood up at once. Spike's cupped hands were full of plums.

'They're green,' the woman said.

'By God, if I didn't think they was tart.'

'Didn't you find the right tree? On the left?'

'I couldn't see a blamed thing.'

'Eat your eggs. I'll get a torch and we'll go down and get some ripe ones before you go.'

'Eggs look good an' all,' Spike said.

The men ate in silence, the woman busy with bread and coffee. The boy put vinegar on his salad, but not oil, and once, noticing it, she unstoppered the oil bottle and pushed it across to him. It was her only sign towards him. The old manner of pity and intimacy had vanished. She was the proprietress; they were the drivers come in to eat. She stood almost aloof, busy with odd things at the far end of the counter. And the boy sat in fresh bewilderment, at a loss, and in wonder about her.

They each drank two cups of coffee and when the cups were finally empty she said:

'If you're ready we can go down and get the plums. But I don't want to hurry you.'

'I'm fit,' Spike said. 'And my God the eggs were a treat. You missed a treat, Albie, not having eggs.'

'The salad was all right.'

'I'll get the torch,' the woman said. 'You go out that door and I'll meet you round the back.'

She went out of the shack by a door behind the counter, and the boy followed Spike through the front door, under the electric sign. Outside, behind the shack, the sweet smell of ripened corn and night air seemed stronger than ever. At the side of the shack and a little behind it, the bungalow stood out darker than the darkness. And after a minute the torch appeared from the bungalow and began to travel towards the men. The boy could see it shining white along the cinder path and on the woman's feet as she came along.

'You walk down the path,' she said. 'I'll show the light.'

Spike began to walk down the path, the boy following him, and then the woman. The shadows strode like giants over the garden and were lost beyond the yellow snake fence in the dark land. The garden was short, and in a moment they all three stood under the plum-tree, the woman shining the torch up into the branches, the tree turned to an immense net of green and silver.

'I'll shine, Spike,' she said. 'You pick them. If they're soft and they lift off they're ripe.'

'This is better,' Spike said. His mouth was already full of plums. 'I struck one match to every blamed plum when I came down.'

The woman stood a little away from the tree, shining the torch steadily, making a great ring of white light across which little moths began to flutter like casual leaves. The boy stood still, not attempting to move, as though he were uninvited.

'What about you?' she said.

And again he could feel the old softness of sympathy and pity and insinuation in her voice, and again his blood leapt up.

'I'm about full up,' he said.

'Take some for the journey.'

He stood still, electrified.

'Take some to eat on the way. Look here, come round the other side. They're riper.'

She moved round the tree, shining the torch always away from her. He followed her in silence, and then in silence they stood against the plum-branches, in the darkness behind the light. He saw her stretch up her arm into the silver leaves, and then lower it again.

'Where's your hand?' she was whispering. 'Here. It's a beauty.' The soft ripe plum was between their hands. Suddenly she pressed it hard against his hands, and the ripe skin broke and the juice trickled over his fingers. 'Eat it, put it in your mouth,' she said. He put the plum into his mouth obediently, and the sweet juice trickled down over his lips and chin as it had already trickled over his hands.

'Was that nice?' she said softly.

'Lovely.'

'Sweet as your girl?'

It seemed suddenly as if his blood turned to water. She was touching him. She took his hand and laid it softly against her hip. It was firm and strong and soft. It had about it a kind of comforting maturity. He could feel all the sulky strength and passion of her whole body in it. Then all at once she covered his hand with her own, stroking it up and down with her fingers, until he stood helpless, intoxicated by the smell of corn and plums and the night warmth and her very light, constant stroking of his hand.

'Shine the light,' Spike called. 'I can't see for looking.'

'I'm shining,' she said. 'Albie wants to see too.'

'Getting many, Albie?'

'He's filling his pockets.'

She began to gather plums off the tree with her free hand as she spoke, keeping her other hand still on his, pressing it against her by an almost mechanical process of caressing. He reached up and tore off the plums too, not troubling if they were ripe, filling one pocket while she filled the other, the secrecy and passion of her movements half demoralizing him, and going on without interruption until Spike called:

'Albie! Plums or no plums, we shall have to get on th' old bus again.'

'All right.'

The boy could hardly speak. And suddenly as the woman took her hand away at last he felt as if the life in him had been cut off, the tension withdrawn, leaving his veins like dead wires.

He stumbled up the path behind Spike and the woman and the light. Spike was gabbling:

'The sweetest plums I ever tasted. When we come back I'll take a couple of pounds and the missus'll pie 'em.'

'When will you be back?'

'The night after to-morrow.'

'They'll be plenty,' she said.

She said nothing to the boy, and he was dumb.

'Let's pay you,' Spike said.

'A shilling for you, and ninepence for the salad,' she said.

'Salad's cheaper,' Spike said. 'I'll remember that. What about the plums?'

'The plums are thrown in.'

They paid her. Then she stood on the shack steps while they crunched across the pull-in and climbed up into the cab, the bright red sign flashing above her.

'That sign's a treat,' Spike called. 'You could see it miles off.'

'I'm glad you like it,' she called. 'Good night.'

'Good night!'

Spike started up, and almost before the boy could realize it the lorry was swinging out into the road, and the station was beginning to recede. He sat for some moments without moving. Then the lorry began to make speed and the smell of corn and plums and the summer land began to be driven out by the smells of the cab, the petrol and oil and the heat of the engine running. But suddenly he turned and looked back.

'The light's out,' he said.

Spike put his head out of the cab and glanced back. The sign was still flashing but the shack itself was in darkness.

'She's sitting in the dark,' he said. 'She always does. She says it saves her eyes and the light and she likes it better.'

'Why?'

'Better ask her.' Spike put a plum in his mouth. 'I don't know.'

'What's her husband doing, letting her run the place at night, and sit there in the dark?'

'It's her own idea. It's a paying game an' all, you bet your life it is.'

The boy took a plum from his pocket and bit it slowly, licking the sweet juice from his lips as it ran down. He was still trembling.

And glancing back again he could see nothing of the station but the red sign flashing everlastingly out and on, scarlet to darkness, *The Station* to nothing at all.

OKLAHOMA RACE RIOT

Frances W. Prentice

(1894--   )

IT HAPPENED because a girl was hysterical, and a newspaper item got past
the copy desk worded a little more strongly than it should have been. The
girl took it back later, and the newspaper perfectly properly said its function was to give the news of the town. But some forty people were dead by
then, and half the town burned up.

Maybe it didn't actually start at either of those sources. You heard people
say afterward that the niggers had been getting above themselves; that race
riots just naturally break loose every now and then anyway, and probably
they're good things.

This curious philosophy is not a sectional affair. It doesn't spring exclusively from the smouldering animosities of ex-slave owner and ex-slave.
Chicago and St. Louis, safely above the Mason and Dixon line, one would
think, have each produced something in the way of records for race riots.
Oklahoma hugs no bitter local traditions; they haven't had time for traditions yet. Only a few years ago the State was Indian territory; even the
Indians were mostly not natives. The citizens are from any State you care
to mention. About all they have in common is a variegated American
tongue, a spirit of adventure (generally genial), and an interest in crude oil.

Impossible to guess, then, where this spark smoulders, or what will fan it.
Perhaps it smokes always in the darkness of small minds and huge un-
control.

At any rate——

The Negro section was rumbling with it at four o'clock in the afternoon.
There are always agitators, and the sober, fearful members of the race have
a hard time hushing them up. They tried hushing them. Grave-faced black
men, ministers, church deacons, real-estate owners, doctors, went in to the
back rooms of the short-order barbecue parlors and pleaded with the hot-
heads. "Don't, boys. Don't you all go over there. You'll get us all burned
out. You can't do no good. Don't go mixing in. Wait and see, boys. Maybe
it's just talk. Maybe they ain't fixing to do nothing to Jim. The sheriff's a
good man. He won't let them take Jim. He's the law. Don't, boys. Don't
before God go over there!"

But the hot-heads were malcontents anyway. They had listened with **too** much imagination and too little common sense to orators who told them that the Negro was exploited and downtrodden; that if he didn't assert himself, and protect his race from the whites, what could he expect? The choc beer in those back parlors is strong stuff. It burned in the brains of the mutterers. Oklahoma wasn't the deep South, was it? Pshaw! They'd show the white folks you couldn't lynch no colored boy these days. Let the old men go along with their gloomy hushings. They'd see.

And they did see.

The town is divided straight across by railroad tracks. One side is nigger town; on the other side the whites live. The jail is in the heart of the business section. And the boy Jim was in the jail for insulting a white girl in an elevator that morning. She said later she thought she stumbled against him herself, and was just nervous, so she screamed. But no matter.

At seven o'clock three cars full of Negroes, with guns gleaming in their hands, drove over and began circling the square around the jail. Cars full of armed and half-drunk Negroes are not a popular sight in Southwestern towns. They meant to make a jail delivery; get the boy Jim out. But—fatally—they didn't quite know how to go about it. And—fatally—the sheriff didn't quite know how to stop the business and get rid of them. So he stood at a window in his office and watched.

White men began to drift in to the hot dusty square, singly and in groups. At the end of half an hour there was a big crowd. A muttering, angry crowd, waiting to see what those niggers thought they were pulling, anyway. The crowd didn't quite know what it wanted to do, either. But it was ready for anything. And then the inaction, and the breathless shifting and whispering, got on some one's nerves. Somebody fired a gun at one of the Negro cars. And one of its occupants fired back. No one was touched by those first nervous bullets. But they set the race riot off, and all the sheriffs in the country couldn't have stopped it then, though the sheriff in the window could probably have stopped it ten minutes before.

The crowd closed in on those three cars, and the Negroes deserted them, and began to run and scatter. The first one was shot on the main street, right in front of the biggest white picture palace. He lay writhing on the sidewalk, under a billboard from which smiled winsomely the face of Mary Pickford, America's Sweetheart.

His falling brought the crowd to a halt. They stood and looked at him. He was hit in the stomach, and bleeding a good deal. Three or four people must have telephoned for ambulances, because three or four ambulances clanged down to the place. But the crowd turned on them, and showed their guns. Get to hell back out of here. Don't touch the blankety blank. The ambulances didn't quite know what to do, either. So they turned off their engines and just stood there, blocking the street.

Then there was a whoop a block away. Some of the Negroes had tried to organize and get to their friend, flourishing those useless, foolish guns again. The crowd surged forward, trampling the man on the sidewalk, who was about dead anyway. The hunt was on for fair then, and there was no pausing for fourteen hours.

By midnight all the blacks who had come over in the three cars had been accounted for. They lay in alleys, or on sidewalks, or huddled in doorways. The sheriff had made up for his earlier lack of zeal, and sworn in as deputies every armed white man who came into the court-house. The oaths were a mere form. Every hardware store, every pawn shop in town had been broken into, and the firearms and ammunition taken without formality. Also a good many bathing-suits, coats, tools, tires, and little things like watches disappeared. Whether these were for immediate or future use no one stopped to inquire at the time. Every one was pretty excited, and trigger fingers were so limber that night that there was very little arguing with people about their whims.

The shooting was constant now. Pop! Pop! Pop-pop-pop-pop-pop! Not a pretty sound on the warm night air.

A melancholy and terrifying sound, heard in tense helplessness, where we sat on our porch, a dozen city blocks from the scene of activity. Behind us in the dark house slept a baby and an old Negress servant. Quite a number of the neighbors had gone down to see the fun. The woman next door moaned in high hysteria. Her husband, a good automatic Georgian, had taken down his bird gun and gone off to work. She felt worried about him, but really she needn't have. As it turned out the blacks were very inadequately armed, besides being hampered by their women and children, and vastly outnumbered.

Of course the women and children didn't get in the line of fire until around one in the morning. That was when the fighting got into their territory. The mob worked steadily down to the railroad tracks, and then across them. Some Negroes hid in a house just on the black side of the tracks, and tried to snipe out the windows. That was the place where the one white man was killed. It was also the place which suggested to the mob that fire would be effective and exciting. Whether that first house was set on fire, or caught by accident, was never quite clear. But the rest of the fires were set. Or perhaps thrown would be a more exact term.

The technic varied with different groups of the mob. But the general procedure was to go up to a cabin door and put a gun against the lock, and blow it off. The flimsy doors would have smashed easily enough; but this was gun night. Once inside the cabin everything breakable was broken, trunks and bureau drawers torn open, pictures and telephones wrenched off the walls and trampled on. They didn't often find any one in the houses, because by now the blacks were scurrying ahead of the horror, out into the hill country beyond the town. But sometimes they did find some one —with whom they dealt. When they had smashed enough they scattered around a little kerosene and threw some lighted matches in the mess. If this particular cabin didn't burn well it would be reset presently by the blaze of the one next door. The houses the mob set fire to without breaking in first were really the most unlucky. Because sometimes there were people in them. Panic-paralyzed people who didn't realize, with all the noise and fright, that the house was on fire. Not until it was too late to get out.

By two o'clock most of the houses in nigger town were ablaze. By dawn all of them were. The fire engines made a half-hearted attempt to get in and do something about it. It didn't hardly seem safe for the rest of the town, with the wind blowing and all. But the mob met the engines as it had met the ambulances. Get to hell out of here. Leave these blank blank double-blank niggers to us. A good deal of buckshot was fired into the radiators of the engines. They wavered around a little, and then withdrew. Nobody could do anything against that mob by then, anyhow. And the nigger houses weren't worth much.

There was never an accurate estimate of how many were killed that night. One white man, surely. One Mexican. The dozen Mexicans in the mob enjoyed themselves thoroughly. The Mexican laborer doesn't often have the privilege of shooting shoulder to shoulder with the whites, and he made the best of it.

The sound of shooting began to be as familiar in the hot interminable night as is the ripping hum of locusts in a summer noon. The watchman, stumping by, stopped to remark that they said a bunch of niggers was driving in from down the river. If they were they would come straight by our house. . . . A faint unreasoning stir of mob fear communicated itself to us. Right past our house. . . . What if . . . ?

For a few minutes we waited for the sound of approaching cars. Then the new tension relaxed into uneasy inaction again. The heavy air was soaked with the scent of honeysuckle, as extravagant and lavishly unreal as the gunfire. We had been in this prairie country a year. It proved always surprising. An acrid under-hint of burned powder began to cut through the perfume of the flowers.

Along about three o'clock the blacks had pretty well gone to earth. Hiding out, the watchman said as he passed again. He flashed his torch under bushes and porches. So the shooting was not so plentiful. Just singles, as it were, compared to the great coveys of game put up by the beaters earlier in the evening. Mostly fresh niggers who didn't have sense enough to realize that if you were black you'd better get to hell out of there that night.

If our choice of reported profanity seems monotonous we can answer that so is a mob's. Or else unprintable.

One "single" was a doctor. The best colored doctor in the Southwest, it was said. He came out on the steps of his house with a white handkerchief tied on his arm, and his hands over his head. His wife was by his side. "Don't shoot me, boys. I'm a doctor!"

Oh, yeah?

He was riddled with bullets where he fell. His wife went mad—suddenly and completely—there on the steps. The accommodations for insane Negresses are not very good in the South.

Five or six of the mob rushed into an isolated garage. "Any niggers in here?" There was a boy in the back washing a car. "Just me, boss," he said, and came out quickly. One shot through the head got him.

Just as the sky began to show faint gray in the east the shooting took on a new, barking authority. Distant. Intermittent staccato. There is a hill which overlooks low streets filled with Negro cabins. For some time that hill was pointed out as having been the position of a machine-gun which raked down into those narrow alleys. . . . But there were so many rumors. . . . And that was one which an ultimately sobered town quite understandably did not choose to believe.

At dawn, as we said, the whole of nigger town was burning. A sight you don't often witness, that. One half of a fair-sized town flaming against the pale horizon with a curiously peaceful effect, since no one was doing anything to put it out. The shooting had almost died out, for lack of anything to shoot at. The niggers were lying very low by now. But you still heard it now and then. Pop! Pop! Pop-pop-pop-pop-pop! The morning air had a strange hush, which gave the occasional shots more significance than the steady bombardment of the night had had.

Nobody knew just what to do. Nobody had known since the evening before.

Out in our kitchen, Mally, who had been a grown girl before emancipation, went about getting breakfast. Her face was an expressionless black mask. At the first news of the trouble she had said, "Lord Jesus! That's our wild young men!" Since then she had said nothing. No one talked much. And then—clamorously—the telephone rang and brought the riot straight into our living-room. The call was for Mally. The gnarled old hand with which she held the receiver trembled visibly.

"Yes. . . . Fanny? . . . Oh, Fanny! . . . Oh, *no!* . . . Oh! . . . Oh, Fanny! . . . Hello? . . . Fanny? . . . Hello? . . ."

Fanny was our laundress. She lived over in nigger town with an ancient uncle who had been messenger in a bank for twenty years. They knew there was trouble, of course. But their house was on the edge of things, and the mob had missed them so far. Uncle Zak had never been late to the bank. And he trusted white folks. He thought maybe if he put on his uniform and they saw it. . . . He put it on, and started out to work. Some one shot him at the corner. Fanny could see him lying there. She didn't dare go out to get him, the mob was so close. She called Mally. . . . But while she was talking they broke in and tore the telephone out of her hands. . . . We were as powerless to reach her as though she had called from San Francisco.

Breakfast, served by a silent Mally, was somehow an awkward meal.

We found Fanny the next day, all right. They didn't shoot many women.

Cars began to drive slowly along our street. Cars driven by the sort of men who wear their caps backward, the visors down their necks. Probably not to interfere with their rifle gaze. "Any niggers in these houses?" they would shout. The gaping children were called in hastily from the curbs. It didn't seem a very educational sight. Nor a very safe one. After the first car or so people sent their servants down in the cellar, or up in the attic. And waited.

Nobody knew just what to do.

Around eight o'clock the train came in with the militia. Riot call. They detained and marched up the street in splendid military form. They made preparations for breakfast. One citizen who had served with the Marines in Haiti got a little impatient then. He was from Maine, and had a feeling that the militia could cut their breakfast a trifle short. He searched out the commander and said as much. If they'd give him a squad of men he'd go over and stop this thing. Didn't the militia realize that shooting and loot- ing were still going on? People were being robbed and killed while they were getting ready to have their coffee.

The commandant had him jailed. Martial law. Something was said about nigger lovers. He was bailed out later in the day.

Finally, having eaten, the troops got into nigger town and stopped the shooting. It had more or less stopped itself by then. The shooters had been out all night, and were sort of tired. There was still some desultory sniping, though. One man stood on a down-town corner and got his sight on the stair windows of an office building. The colored janitor was walking up those stairs. When he appeared at the fourth-floor window a very neat shot picked him off.

For weeks you heard that So-and-so had a certain number of notches on his gun. And then that some one else had more. But it was hard to check up on the boasters. Just as it was hard to check up on the casualties.

Lots of Negroes never turned up at their homes or their jobs again. Some of them probably simply kept going, once they were out of town that night. And others . . .

There was the son of a cook in our street, for example. Around nine o'clock the man he worked for came and asked for Hatty. He was in a car, with some other men. It seemed that the boy, like Fanny's uncle, thought he ought to get to his job. Before he knew it he had been caught in the fighting around the railroad tracks, and crawled under a freight car to hide. Some one went in after him, and shot him with a pistol. Now that things were quieting down a little he was lying in the town-hall, where the militia were assembling the blacks. But his employer was afraid he wouldn't live many hours. If Hatty wanted to see the boy he would take her down, and look out for her. But she was afraid to go. You couldn't blame her, really. Some of the house Negroes who had allowed themselves to be put in those wandering cars and escorted to the safety of the town-hall had been shot at as they drove through the streets. It wasn't a ride an old woman wanted to undertake, even to see her boy alive. The boy's boss understood. He went back himself, and got a doctor, and stayed with the boy till he died.

But that night when he went to get the body for Hatty it was gone. He was an influential man, the boy's boss, and he had every coffin in the town opened, looking for that boy. He never found him. It seemed that some time in the afternoon some men came to the town-hall with a truck, saying they were from an undertaker. They took off a dozen or so corpses. And no one ever saw them again. Colored people share with whites the sentimentality of liking to know where their dead are buried.

But nobody knew what to do about it.

Either because the militia was efficient or because the game was played out after such a very active night, things were fairly peaceful by afternoon. Most of the black population was herded in the town-hall. It was easier to protect them there. But there had been difficulties in getting them concentrated. The look of the men who were escorting the blacks to the town-hall hadn't inspired confidence. Housewife after housewife refused to surrender servants to their dubious protection. Several small dramas took place in our street, when a woman with three or four terrified Negroes in her kitchen declined entrance to those amateur deputies with shotguns. Belief in the law had not been strengthened in the town during the last eighteen hours.

The Red Cross came down, and the fair-grounds were equipped with hundreds of temporary beds, to shelter the homeless. The homeless were marched five miles through the dust and heat to reach that haven. It was hard on the women and small children, because the food problem hadn't yet been met, and most of them hadn't had anything to eat. The thermometer was 102. It wouldn't have been an easy day to face, even on a full stomach.

On the second day any black whose employer would vouch for him or her was released, wearing a yellow arm-band. The arm-band was to indicate that the wearer was harmless. No attempt was made, of course, to indicate which members of the mob had now returned to sanity.

Those yellow-banded people wandered dazed and disconsolate through the still smoking ruins of nigger town, subdued to apathy. Twisted iron and cinders marked their homes. Broken trunks and bureaus, caked with sodden ashes, gaped empty as the looters had left them. With the help of the Red Cross an attempt was made to reunite scattered families. Largely, one might state, with the sole help of the Red Cross. Except for its professional services only ten white women worked at the relief station. One of them was staying at a hotel in the town, and three of them were district nurses anyway. Maybe those who didn't volunteer were wise. It was depressing at the relief station.

There was the problem of scattered families, missing children, fathers, mothers; of trying to coax the fugitives back in from their retreats. Airplanes would locate a little huddled group off in the country a mile or so. But when they sent cars after them the groups would melt away, running like rabbits. White men in cars didn't strike them as healthy contacts.

And then there was the matter of funerals. Complicated by that "undertaker's" wagon.

And there was the problem of getting those houses rebuilt. The Red Cross took voluminous depositions of losses. But wherever those depositions were filed they probably still remain. Almost no houses were insured. Blacks are bad riot risks. The whole affair drifted into comfortable oblivion surprisingly soon. At least on the white side of the tracks. What Mally's "wild young men" thought we do not know.

Eventually, of course, houses did struggle up out of the ashes, and the black people repossessed their part of the town. Most of them had jobs they could go on with. House or no house, missing family or not, you can still cook or wash, or dig, or drive mules.

But there were a few who didn't pick up the threads so easily. One gray-haired Negro doctor who worked tirelessly at the Red Cross centre said, courteously, that there was no use his taking up their time filling out a list of his losses. It was, he said, the second time he had been burned out. The first time, in another State, he had lost his house, his instruments, his horse and buggy. He was younger then, and had begun again. This time he had lost his brick house and office, his drugstore, his equipment, his operating table, his automobile, his new instruments, and his daughter's half-paid-for piano. He didn't, he said, think he would try again.

Things like that made for indignant talk for a few months, among certain people. Those same people thought that the photographs of riot victims in the more dramatic poses of violent death, enterprisingly printed on post-cards, and sold surreptitiously, in the manner of naughty postals in Paris, were not very nice. The opinion that a race riot now and then kept the niggers in their place was hotly contested.

But even that talk finally died down. No one really knew what to do about such things.